MW01156343

THE STUDENT'S
SANSKRIT-ENGLISH DICTIONARY

The Student's
Sanskrit-English Dictionary

Containing Appendices on Sanskrit Prosody and Important Literary and Geographical Names in the Ancient History of India

VAMAN SHIVRAM APTE

MOTILAL BANARSIDASS PUBLISHERS
PRIVATE LIMITED • DELHI

Second Edition: Delhi, 1970
Reprint: Delhi, 1973, 1976, 1979, 1982,
1986, 1988, 1993, 1997, 2000, 2005

ISBN: 81-208-0044-3 (Cloth)
ISBN: 81-208-0045-1 (Paper)

MOTILAL BANARSIDASS
41 U.A. Bungalow Road, Jawahar Nagar, Delhi 110 007
8 Mahalaxmi Chamber, 22 Bhulabhai Desai Road, Mumbai 400 026
236, 9th Main III Block, Jayanagar, Bangalore 560 011
120 Royapettah High Road, Mylapore, Chennai 600 004
Sanas Plaza, 1302 Baji Rao Road, Pune 411 002
8 Camac Street, Kolkata 700 017
Ashok Rajpath, Patna 800 004
Chowk, Varanasi 221 001

Printed in India
BY JAINENDRA PRAKASH JAIN AT SHRI JAINENDRA PRESS,
A-45 NARAINA, PHASE-I, NEW DELHI 110 028
AND PUBLISHED BY NARENDRA PRAKASH JAIN FOR
MOTILAL BANARSIDASS PUBLISHERS PRIVATE LIMITED,
BUNGALOW ROAD, DELHI 110 007

PREFACE

—— :o: ——

THE Dictionary that is now offered to the public has been intended to supply a want, long felt by the student, of a Sanskrit-English Dictionary such as would meet all his ordinary requirements, and be at the same time within his easy reach. Without dwelling, therefore, on the necessity of bringing out a work like this, I shall proceed to state its scope. As its name indicates, the Dictionary is designed to meet all the ordinary wants of a High-School or College student. With this object in view I have not thought it necessary to include Vedic words or Vedic senses of words, but have confined myself chiefly to what may be called the post-Vedic literature. But even this covers a very large field, as it includes Epics like the Rāmāyaṇa, Mahābhārata, the several Purāṇas, the Smṛiti literature, the several Darsanas or systems of philosophy, such as Nyāya Vedānta, Mīmāmsā &c , Grammar, Rhetoric, Poetry in all its branches, Dramatic literature, Mathematics, Medicine Botany, Astronomy, Music, and such other technical or scientific branches of learning. Very few of the existing Dictionaries have tried to deal with and explain the innumerable technical terms pertaining to all the various branches of learning above specified, except perhaps the great Vāchaspatya, which, too, however, is defective in some respects. Much less can a Dictionary like this, designed mainly for the University student, be expected to do so. It principally aims at serving as an aid to the student and the general reader, and embraces all words occurring in the general post-Vedic literature, *i. e.* Prose tales, Kāvyas, Dramas, epics &c. It includes most of ordinary and more important terms in Grammar, Nyāya, Rhetoric, Law, Medicine, Astronomy, Mathematics, &c., but gives special prominence to the explanation of all important terms in the first three departments, as they are generally studied at College for University examinations. It omits Vedic words or Vedic senses of words, the names of authors and their works—which are too many to be noticed in a Dictionary—except the most important ones, the names of plants and trees except such as are noteworthy and met with in general literature, obscure or unimportant words or senses of words not generally used in classical literature, and simple derivatives from verbs, adjectives &c. which can be very easily formed by the student for himself. But these omissions will, it is hoped, not in any way lessen the usefulness of the Dictionary, as it gives in a small compass all that a student of Sanskrit will ordinarily require—perhaps even more in some cases—during his School or College career.

Having thus explained the scope of the work, I shall say a few words with regard to its plan and arrangement. As will be seen from even a cursory glance at the contents, the chief feature of the Dictionary is that it gives quotations and references to the peculiar and noteworthy meanings of words, especially such as occur in books read by the student at School or College. It has been thought necessary to do so, because a student naturally expects that the Dictionary he uses will give appropriate equivalents for such words and expressions as have some peculiarity in use or meaning. Moreover, quotations and references often help the reader in determining any particular meaning of a word in a particular passage by enabling him to see and compare how the word is used elsewhere. In some cases these quotations might appear to be superfluous but to a student, especially a beginner, they are very useful as they supply him with illustrations of the uses of words, and firmly impress their meanings upon his mind.

Another noticeable feature of the Dictionary is that it gives explanations of the more important technical terms, particularly in Nyāya, Alankāra, Grammar, Dramaturgy, with quotations in Sanskrit wherever necessary ; *e. g.* see the words अप्रस्तुतप्रशंसा, उपनिषद्, सांख्य, मीमांसा, स्थायिभाव, प्रवेशक, रस, वार्तिक, अनैकांतिक &c. In the case of Alankāras I have chiefly drawn upon the Kāvyaprakāsa, though I have occasionally referred to the Chandrāloka, Kuvalayānanda and Rasagangādhara. In the explanation of Dramatic terms I have generally followed the Sāhityadarpaṇa. Similarly, striking phrases, some choice expressions and idioms or peculiar combinations of words, have been noticed under every word wherever necessary ; *e. g.* see the words गम्, सेतु, हस्त, मयूर, दा, कृ &c. Mythological allusions in the case of all important names have been briefly but clearly explained, so as to give the reader most of the facts connected with those personages ; see इंद्र कार्तिकेय, प्रह्लाद, &c. Etymology had not been generally given except where pecul ar; *e. g.* see the words अतिथि, पुत्र, जाया, हृषीकेश. The work also gives information about words though not of a technical nature, which it is believed, will be useful to the student ; *e. g.* see the words मंडल, मानस, वेद, हंस. Some of the Nyāyas or maxims such as are frequently used in illustrations, have been collected under the word न्याय for easy reference. To add to the usefulness of the work, I have added at the end three Appendices. The first is on Sanskrit Prosody which gives in a clear and intelligible form all the common metres, with definitions, schemes in Gaṇas, and examples. In the preparation of this Appendix I have chiefly drawn upon the two popular works on Prosody, the Vṛittaratnākara and Chhando-Manjari, but some common metres which are omitted therein have been added from the poems of Māgha, Bhāravi, Daṇḍin, Bhaṭṭi &c. The second Appendix gives the dates, writings &c. of some of the important Sanskrit writers, such as Kālidāsa, Bhavabhūti, Bāṇa &c. Here I have selected only those names about which something definite—something more than mere guesses and surmises—is known, and I have derived some hints from the Introduction of Vallabhadeva's Subhāshitāvali and Max Müller's 'India', for which my thanks are due to the authors. The third Appendix gives the most important names in the ancient Geography of India with identifications on the modern map wherever ascertained, and in this part of the work I have to cordially acknowledge the help I have derived from Cunningham. Ancient Geography, but particularly from Mr. Borooah's Essay prefixed to the third volume of his English-Sanskrit Dictionary. Thus this Dictionary aims at serving as a useful aid to the student of Sanskrit by giving him almost everything that he is likely to require for ordinary purposes, and with this view I have incorporated as much useful information as could to be given within the limits of the book.

The arrangement of the work will be best understood from the "Directions to the student" which follow. I have only to refer to one point—the use of the *anusvāra* instead of nasals throughout. This practice, whatever may be said with regard to its correctness, is very convenient for puropses of printing, and will not, it is believed, affect the usefulness of the work. The several contrivances used to effect saving in *space* will be understood by the reader with very short practice.

Before concluding I must gratefully acknowledge the help that I have derived from different sources. And in doing so I must give the first place to the great Sanskrit Encyclopaedia, the Vāchaspatya of Professor Tārānātha Tarkavāchaspati. Much of the general information given in this Dictionary has been derived from that work, though I have had to supplement it wherever defective. Several words and meanings not given in the existing Sanskrit-English Dictionaries, as also some quotations, have been borrowed from the same work. The Sanskrit-English Dictionary of Prof. Monier Williams is the next work to which I have been greatly indebted. I have constantly kept it by my side, and have freely utilized his renderings of some words, expressions &c. when I found them better than those I myself had to suggest. And though there is much in this Dictionary that is not to be found in that work, I must freely acknowledge the assistance it has often rendered me in the explanation of words and expressions. And the last, but not the least, is the great German Worterbuch of Drs. Roth and Bothlingk. This great work abounds with references and quotations, but the works belonging to Vedic literature have been comparatively more copiously drawn upon by them than those belonging to the post-Vedic literature. A glance at the contents will show that I have drawn upon works seldom or not at all referred to by those scholars; such as the works of Bhavabhūti, Jagannāth Pandit, Rājsekhara, Bāṇa, the Kāvyaprakāsa, Sisupālvadha, Kirātārjuniya, Naishadhacharita, Sānkara-Bhāshya, Veṇī-Samhāra &c. and the great majority of quotations and references is from my own collection. But I am free to acknowledge that I have availed myself of the quotations in that Dictionary where my own collection was defective. To these authors, as well as to the authors and Editors of several other works—too many to be here enumerated from which I have derived occasional help of one kind or another, my grateful thanks are due.

In conclusion I trust that "*The Student's Sanskrit-English Dictionary*" will be found useful not only by those for whom it is mainly intended, but by the general Sanskrit reader also. No work, howsoever carefully prepared, can pretend to be entirely free from defects, and my work cannot be an exception, especially as it has had to be carried through the Press in great haste. I have, therefore, to request such persons as will do me the honour to use this Dictionary, to be so good as to inform me if they discover any mistake, and also to make any suggestions for its improvement, and I shall be very glad to give them my best consideration in the second edition.

Poona, 15th Feburary, 1890. V. S. APTE.

———

Directions to the Student.

:o:

(TO BE STUDIED BEFORE USING THE DICTIONARY).

1. Words are arranged in the Nāgari alphabetical order.

2. The different parts of speech of a word are indicated by large black dashes, after which the nominative singular of the part of speech is usually given, or the letters *m f.*, *n.* or *ind.* are put after the dash, the leading word being given only once. Where a word is used as an adjective and also as a substantive, the senses of the adjective are invariably given first ; *e. g.* वीर, साधु.

3 Where two words, though identical in form, differ entirely in meaning, they are generally repeated as separate words ; *e g.* हा, हि. In a few cases they have been grouped together.

4. Some words which are used as adverbs, but derived by case-inflections from a noun or adjective, are given within brackets under the noun or adjective, and their senses given in the usual way ; *e. g.* परेण, परे under पर, or समीपतस् or समीपे under समीप.

5. The several meanings of a word, when they can be sufficiently distinguished from one another, are given separately and marked by black Arabic figures. Mere *shades* of meaning are not considered as separate senses, but in such cases several synonyms are given under the same meaning, from which the reader will have to make his choice. Where the shades of meaning are sufficiently broad, they are numbered as separate meanings.

6. The meanings of words are arranged in the order of their importance and frequency of use. It had not been possible to do so in *every* case, but the system has been generally followed.

7. (a) Compounds are grouped under the first word in the compounds in the alphabetical order of their *second* members, the small black dash before them denoting that first word ; *e. g.*—होत्र, under अग्नि means अग्निहोत्र.

N. B.—In giving compounds, the changes which the final letters undergo, *e. g* the dropping, assimilation of letters &c. are assumed ; *e. g.*—अपर under पूर्व stands for पूर्वापर ; -गतिः under अधस् for अधोगतिः &c. In some cases the compound words, where not easily intelligible are given in full within brackets

(b) Where a compound itself is used as the first member of other compounds, these latter are given immediately after, their second member being preceded by which represents the first compound ; *e. g.*—°इंद्र, °राज &c. given under द्वि stand not for द्वींद्र or द्विराज, but for द्विजेंद्र or द्विजराज.

(c) All *aluk* compounds (*e. g.* कुशेशय, मनसिज, हृदिस्पृश् &c.) are given separately in their proper places, and not under the first member.

8. All words formed by Kṛit or Tadhita affixes are given separately ; Thus कूलंकष, भयंकर, अन्नमय, प्रातस्तन, हिमवत् &c. will be found not under कूल, भय, &c. but in their own places.

9. (a) In the case of substantives the nominative singular, wherever it may at once denote the gender, is given throughout, the *visarga*, unless followed by *f.*, indicating masculine gender, and the *anusvāra* neuter gender. Where the nominatives singular is not indicative of the gender, it is specified as *m. f.* or *n.* as the case may be. All substantives ending in consonants have their genders specified as *m. f.* or *n.*

(b) The feminine forms of nouns are usually given as separate leading words, but in some cases, especially in the first three or four hundred pages, they are given under the leading word after the masculine gender.

10. In the case of adjectives the simple base only is given. The feminine of the majority of adjectives is अ ends in आ and adjectives ending in इ or उ have generally the same base for all genders. In all such cases the simple base is given, the feminine being formed according to similar substantive bases. All irregular feminines are, however, denoted within brackets. Adjectives ending in त्, न् or स् form their feminines regularly in ती, नी, or सी, where irregular, they are denoted within brackets.

11. (a) In the case of verbs, the Arabic figure before P., A. and U. denotes the conjugation to which the root belongs ; P. denoting Parasmaipada, A. Atmanepada, U. Ubhayapada (P. and A.). Den, stands for Denominative, and here the 3rd pers. sing. present tense is given throughout.

(b) Under each root the 3rd person singular present tense, and the past passive participle wherever noteworthy, are given throughout. The forms of the *Passive, Causal* and *Desiderative*, wherever noteworthy are given after them, or after the senses of the primitive base, where there is any peculiarity in their senses.

(c) Verbs formed by prefixing prepositions to roots are given *under* the roots in aplhabetical order. The small black dash (—) preceding a preposition stands for the word '*with*' (which is used only before the first preposition) and shows that the preposition must be added to the root to give the meanings specified after it.

(d) Roots sometimes change their form or *pada* (voice) or both, when used in particular senses, or when preceded by particular prepositions. Such changes are denoted within brackets.

(e) When a root belongs to different conjugations with different meanings, Roman figures are used to mark this difference (cf. अस्, गुप्, हा &c.), the root being repeated only once.

12. (a) All possible derivatives from a word are not always given when they may be easily supplied, more especially in the case of potential passive participles (formed by तव्य, अनीय and य), present participles, and abstract nouns from adjectives (formed by adding ता, त्व or य). Where there is any peculiarity either in the formation or meaning of these derivatives, they are given. But in many cases the student will have to supply the forms according to the general rules given in Grammar.

(b) Similarly all the equivalents given under the radical word are not always repeated in the derivatives; they may, if necessary, be ascertained by a reference to the radical word.

13. Mythological allusions are explained in *small* type in the body of the work between rectangular brackets [ ]. Here long vowels like ā, ī, ū, and letters of the lingual class, as also ऋ and श are, for the convenience of the press, denoted by corresponding *italic* letters; *e. g.* Pandava and Kripi stand for पांडव and कृपी.

14. A few allusions and words that were accidentally omitted in the body of the work, are given in the *Supplement*.

Grammatical and other Abbreviations, and Symbols.

:o:

A. or Atm. ... Atmanepada.
a. ... ... Adjective.
abl. ... ... Ablative.
acc. ... ... Accusative.
adv. ... ... Adverb.
alg. ... ... Algebra.
Arith. ... ... Arithmetic.
astr.... ... ... Astronomy.
Avyayī.... ... Avyayībhāva.
Bah. ... ... Bahuvrīhi.
Caus. ... ... Causal.
cf. ... ... Compare.
comp. ... ... Compound.
compar. ... ... Comparative.
dat. ... ... Dative.
Den. ... ... Denominative.
desid. ... ... Desiderative.
du. ... ... Dual.
e. g. ... ... *Exempli gratia*, for example.
f. or fem. ... Feminine.
fig. ... ... Figurative.
freq. ... ... Frequentative.
gen. ... ... Genitive.
gram. ... ... Grammar.
ibid. ... ... The same.
i. e. ... ... *id est*, that is.
ind. ... ... Indeclinable.
inf. ... ... Infinitive.
instr. ... ... Instrumental.
lit. ... ... Literal.
loc. ... ... Locative.
m. or mas. ... Masculine.
Mar. ... ... Marāṭhī.
Math. ... ... Mathematics.
Medic. ... ... Medicine.
n. ... ... Neuter.
N. ... ... Name.
Nom. ... ... Nominative.
num. a. ... ... Numeral adjective.
oft. ... ... Often times.
opp. ... ... Opposite of.
P. ... ... Parasmaipada.
pass. ... ... Passive.
phil. ... ... Philosophy
pl. ... ... Plural.
pot. p. ... ... Potential passive participle.
p.p. ... ... Past passive participle.
Pres. ... ... Present tense.
pres. p. ... ... Present participle.
pron. a. ... ... Pronominal adjective.
q. v. ... ... *quod vide*, which see.
Rhet. ... ... Rhetoric.
sing. ... ... Singular.
Subst. ... ... Substantive.
superl. ... ... Superlative.
s. v. ... ... *sub voice*, see under the word.
Tat. ... ... Tatpurusha.
U. ... ... Ubhayapada(Parasmai. and Atmane.)
Vārt. ... ... Vārtika.
Ved. ... ... Vedic.
v. l. ... ... Various reading.
Voc. ... ... Vocative.
= ... ... Equal or equivalent to, same as.
&c. ... ... Et cetera.
°... ... ... denotes that the rest of the word under consideration is to be supplied; *e.g.* °रत्नप्रभवस्य यस्य under अनन्त mean अनतरत्न &c.

A LIST OF ABBREVIATIONS USED IN THE DICTIONARY

of the names of works or authors.

———————:॥०॥:———————

N. B.—Except where otherwise specified, the Editions of works referred to are mostly those printed at Calcutta.

Ait. Br.	Aitareya Brāhmaṇa (Bombay) .
Ak.	Amarkosha ("),
A. L.	Anandalaharī.
Amaru.	Amarusataka.
A. R.	Anargharāghava (published in the Kāvyamālā) .
Aryā S.	Aryāsaptasati (published in the Kavyamālā) .
Asvad.	Asvadhāṭī (published in the Subhāshitaratnākara) .
Asval.	Asvalāyana's Sūtras.
Bg.	Bhagavadgītā (Bombay) .
Bh.	Bhrtṛihari's three Satakas (the figures 1., 2., 3, after Bh. denoting Sṛingāra, Nīti°, and Vairāgya°
Bhāg.	Bhāgavata (Bombay) .
Bhāshā P. ...	Bhāshāparichchheda.
Bk	Bhaṭṭikāvya.
B. R.	Bālarāmāyaṇa (Benares) .
Bṛi. S. / Bri. S. ...	Varāhamihira's Bṛihatsamhita.
Bṛi. Kath. ...	Bṛihatkathā.
Br. Sūt.	Brahmasūtras.
Bri. Ar. Up / Bri. Up.	Bṛihadāraṇyakopanishad.
Bv.	Bhāminīvilāsa (Bombay) .
Chand. K. ...	Chaṇḍakausika.
Chanḍ. M. ...	Chhandomanjarī.
Chandr.	Chandrāloka.
Chāṇ.	Chāṇakyasataka.
Chāt.	Chātakāshṭaka (in two parts) .
Ch. P.	Chaurapanchāsikā.
Ch. Up.	Chhandogyopanishad.
Dāy. B., Dāy ...	Dāyabhāga.
Dhan. V. ...	Dhananjayavijaya
Dharm.	Dharmaviveka.
Dk.	Dasakumāracharita (Bombay) .
D. R.	Dasarūpa (Hall's Edition) .
Dṛi. *S*.	Dṛishṭantasataka.
Gaut S. or / Gaut. Sūt. ...	Gautamasūtra.
Ghaṭ	Ghaṭakarparakāvya.
Gīt.	Gītagovinda.
G. L.	Gangālaharī.
G. M.	Gaṇaratnamahodadhi of Vardhamāna.
H.	Hitopdesa (Nirṇaya Sāgara Edition)
Halāy.	Halāyudha.
Hch.	Harshacharita.
H. D....	Hamsadūta.
J. N. V.	Jaiminīyanyāyamālāvistara. (Goldstücker's Edition) .
K.	Kādambarī. (Bombay) .
Kām.	Kāmandakinītisāra.
Kāsi.	Kāsikāvṛitti (Benares) .
Karpūr.	Karpūrmanjarī (published in the Kāvyamalā) .
Kaṭh....	Kaṭhopanishad.
Kāty.	Kātyāyana.
Kaus....	Kausikasūtra.
Kāv.	Kāvyādarsa.
Ken.	Kenopanishad.
Ki.	Kirātārjunīya.
Kīr. K.	Kirtikaumudī (Bombay) .
K. P.	Kāvyaprakāsa (Bombay) .
K. R....	Kavirahasya.
Ks.	Kathāsaritsāgara.
Ku.	Kumārsambhava (Bombay.)
Kull....	Kullūka.
Kusum.	Kusumānjali.
Kuval.	Kuvalayānanda
Līli.	Līlāvatī.
M.	Mālvikāgnimitra (Bombay) .
Mālah. N.... ...	Mādhavanidāna.
Māl.	Mālatīmādhava (Bombay) .
Malli.	Mallinātha.
Mārk. P.	Mārkaṇḍeya Purāṇa.
Mb.	Mahābhārata (Bombay) .
Mbh.	Mahābhāshya (") .
Me.	Meghadūta ("),
Med.	Medinīkosha.
Mit.	Mitāksharā (Bombay)
Mk.	Mṛichchhakaṭika.
Moha M.	Mohamudgara.
Ms.	Manusmṛiti.
Mu.	Mudrārākshasa (Bombay) .

Mugdha. ... Mugadhabodha.

Mv. ... ... Mahāvīrcharita (Borooah's Edition).

N. ... ... Naishadhacharita.

Nāg. ... ... Nāgānanda.

Nala. ... ... Nalopākhyāna (Bombay).

Nalod. ... ... Nalodaya.

Nir. ... ... Nirukta

Nīti. ... ... Nītisāra.

Nītipr. ... ... Nītipradīpa.

P. ... ... Paṇini's Ashṭādhyāyī.

Pad. D. ... ... Padānakadūta.

P. R. ... ... Prasannarāghava.

Prab. ... ... Prabodhchandrodaya (Bombay).

Pt. ... ... Panchatantra (").

R. ... ... Raghuvamsa (").

Rāj. P. ... ... Rājaprasasti.

Rāj. T. ... ... Rājataranginī.

Rām. ... ... Rāmāyaṇa (Bombay).

Ratn. ... ... Ratnāvali (").

R. G. ... ... Rasagangādhara (published in the Kāvyamālā).

Rs. ... ... Ritusamhāra (Bombay)

Rv. ... ... Rigveda (Max Muller's Edition).

S. ... ... Sakuntalā (Bombay).

Sabd. k. ... ... Sabdhakalpadruma.

Sān. K. / Sānkhya K. } Sānkhyakārikā.

Sān. S. ... ... Sānkhyasūtra.

Sānti. ... ... Sāntisataka.

Sar. K. ... ... Sarasvatikaṇṭhābharaṇa.

Sarva.S. / Sar. S. } ... Sarvadarsanasamgraha.

Sid. Mukt. or Muktā. } Siddhāntamuktāvali.

Sat. Br. ... ... Satapatha Brāhmana.

Sāy ... ... Sāyaṇa.

S. B. ... ... Sārirabhashya.

S. D. ... ... Sāhityadarpaṇa.

Si. ... ... Sisupālavadha.

Sik. ... ... Sikshā.

Siva P. ... ... Siva Purāṇa.

Sk. ... ... Siddhānta-Kaumudī (Bombay).

S. L. ... ... Sudhālaharī (published in the Kāvyamālā).

Srut. ... ... Srutabodha.

S. Til. ... ... Sṛingārtilaka.

Subh. ... ... Subhāshitaratnākara (Bombay).

Subhāsh. ... ... Subhāshita.

Subh. Ratn. ... Subhāshitaratnabhāṇḍāgāra (Bombay).

Susr. ... ... Susruta.

Svet. Up. ... Svetāsvataropanishad.

Tarka K. ... Tarkakaumudī (Bombay).

Trik. ... ... Trikāṇḍashesha.

T. S. ... ... Tarkasamgraha (Bombay).

Tv. ... ... Tārānātha's Vāchaspatyam.

U. ... ... Uttararāmacharita.

Udb. ... ... Udbhaṭa.

Ud. D. ... ... Uddhavadūta.

Ud. S. ... ... Uddhavasandesa.

Ujjval. ... ... Uj aladata.

Up / Upan. } ... Upanishad.

V. ... ... Vikramorvasīyam (Bombay).

Vais. ... ... Vaiseshika.

Vais. Sūt. ... ... Vaiseshikasūtras.

Vāj. ... ... Vājasaneyi Samhitā.

Vāk. P. ... ... Vākyapadīya.

Vās. ... ... Vāsavadattā (Hall's Edition).

Vb. ... ... Viddhasālabhanjikā (Bombay).

Ve. ... ... Veṇīsamhāra.

Vedānta P. ... Vedāntaparibhāshā.

Vet. ... ... Vetālapanchavimsati.

Vikr. ... ... Vikramānkadevacharita (Bombay)

Vīr. M. ... ... Vīramitrodaya.

V. May. ... ... Vyavahāramayūkha (Mr. Mandlik's. Edition).

V. P. ... ... Vishṇu Purāṇa.

V. Sah. ... ... Vishṇusahasranāma

Y. ... ... Yājnavalkya (Mr. Mandlik's Edition)

Yoga S. ... ... Yogasūtras.

Yv., Yaj. ... ... Yajurveda.

Note.—After the Abbreviations given above, where one Arabic figure is followed by another, the former indicates the canto, chapter, part, act &c.; and the latter, the number of the verse. A single Arabic figure indicates the page, act, &c.

THE STUDENT'S
SANSKRIT-ENGLISH DICTIONARY.

अ The first letter of the Nâgarî Alphabet.—अः 1 N. of Vishṇu, the first of the three sounds constituting the sacred syllable ओम्; अकारो विष्णुरुद्दिष्ट उकारस्तु महेश्वरः । मकारस्तु स्मृतो ब्रह्मा प्रणवस्तु त्रयात्मकः ॥ 2 N. of Śiva, Brahmâ, Vâyu, or Vaiśvânara.—*ind.* 1 A prefix corresponding to Latin *in*, Eng. *in* or *un*, Gr. *a* or *an* and joined to nouns, adjectives, indeclinables (or even to verbs) as a substitute for the negative particle **नञ्** and changed to **अन्** before vowels except in the word अऋणिन्. The senses of न usually enumerated are six:—(*a*) साद्दश्य 'likeness' or 'resemblance'; अब्राह्मणः one like a Brâhmaṇa (wearing the sacred thread &c.), but not a Brâhmaṇa, but a Kshatriya or Vaiśya. (*b*) अभाव 'absence', 'negation', 'want,' 'privation;' अज्ञानं absence of knowledge, ignorance; अक्रोधः, अनंगः, अकंटकः, अघटः &c. (*c*) भेद 'difference' or 'distinction'; अपटः not a cloth, something different from, or other than, a cloth. (*d*) अल्पता 'smallness', 'diminution', used as a diminutive particle; अनुदरा having a slender waist (कृशोदरी or तनुमध्यमा). (*e*) अप्राशस्त्य 'badness', 'unfitness', having a depreciative sense; अकालः wrong or improper time; अकार्य not fit to be done, improper, unworthy, bad act. (*f*) विरोध 'opposition', 'contrariety'; अनीतिः the opposite of morality, immorality; असित not white, black. These senses are put together in the following verse:—तत्साद्दश्यमभावश्च तदन्यत्वं तदल्पता ॥ अप्राशस्त्यं विरोधश्च नञर्थाः षट् प्रकीर्तिताः ॥ See न also. With verbal derivatives, it has usually the sense of 'not'; अदृष्ट्वा; अपश्यन् not seeing; so असकृत् not once; sometimes अ does not affect the sense of the second member; as अपश्चिम, अनुत्तम, see the words. 2 An interjection of (*a*) Pity (*ah!*) अ अवद्यं. (*b*) Reproach, censure (fie, shame); अ पचासि त्वं जाल्म, see अकरणि, अजीवनि also. (*c*) Used in addressing; अ अनंत. (*d*) It is also used as a particle of prohibition. 3 The augment prefixed to the root in the formation of the Imperfect, Aorist and Conditional Tenses.

अऋणिन् *a.* (ऋ being regarded as a consonant) Not a debtor, free from debt. The form अनृणिन् also occurs in this sense.

अंश् 10 U. (अंशयति-ते) To divide, distribute, share among; also अंशापयति in this sense. With **वि-** 1 to distribute.-2 to cheat.

अंशः 1 A share, part, portion; सकृदंशो निपतति Ms. 9. 47; R. 8. 16; अंशेन दर्शितानुकूलता K. 159 partly. 2 A share in property, inheritance; स्वतोंशतः Ms. 8. 408; 9. 201; Y. 2. 3 The number of a fraction; sometimes used for fraction itself. 4 A degree of latitude (or longitude). 5 The shoulder (more generally written अंस, q. v.). -Comp.-**अंशः** a secondary incarnation; part of a portion.-**अंशि** *adv.* share by share. -**अवतारः-तरणं** descent (on earth) of parts of deities, partial incarnation; °तार इव धर्मस्य Dk. 153; N. of Adhyâyas 64–67 of Âdiparvan of Bhârata. -**भाज्, -हर, -हारिन्** *m. f.* an heir, coheir; पिंडदोंशहरश्चैषां पूर्वाभावे परः परः Y. 2. 132, 133.-**सवर्णनं** -reduction of fractions to the same denominator. -**स्वरः** the keynote.

अंशकः 1 One having a share, a coheir; relative. 2 A share, portion, division.-**कं** A solar day.

अंशनं Act of dividing.

अंशयितृ *m.* A divider, sharer.

अंशल *a.* 1 Having, or entitled to, a share. 2=अंसल, q. v.

अंशिन् *a.* 1 Sharer, coheir; (पुनर्विभागकरणे) सर्वे वा स्युः समांशिनः Y. 2. 114. 2 Having parts.

अंशुः 1 A ray, beam of light; चंड°, घर्म° hot-rayed, the sun; सूर्यांशुभिर्भिन्नमिवारविंदं Ku. 1. 32; lustre, brilliance. 2 A point or end. 3 A small or minute particle. 4 End of a thread. 5 Garment; docoration; dress. 6 Speed.-Comp. -**जालं** a collection or rays, blaze or halo of light. -**धरः, -पतिः -भृत्, -बाणः, भर्तृ, -स्वामी, -हस्तः** the sun, (bearer of rays or lord of rays.). -**पट्टं** a kind of silken cloth. -**माला** a garland of light, halo.-**मालिन्** *m.* the sun.

अंशुमत् *a.* 1 Luminous, radiant; ज्योतिषां रविरंशुमान् Bg. 10. 21. 2 Pointed. -*m.* (**मान्**) 1 The sun; वालखिल्यैरिवांशुमान् R. 15. 10. 2 N. of the grandson of Sagara, son of Asamanjasa and father of Dilîpa.

अंशुकं 1 A cloth, garment in general; सितांशुका V. 3. 12; यत्रांशुकाक्षेपविलज्जितानां Ku. 1. 14; *S.* 1. 34. 2 A fine or white cloth; Me. 62; usually silken or muslin. 3 An upper garment; a mantle; also an under garment. 4 A leaf. 5 Mild or gentle blaze of light.

अंशुमत्फला The plantain tree.

अंशुल *a.* Radiant, luminous.-**लः** N. of the sage Châṇakya.

अंस् (अंसयति, अंसापयति) See अंश्.

अंसः 1 A part, portion, see **अंश**. 2 Shoulder, shoulderblade.—Comp. -**कूटः** a bull's hump, the protuberance between the shoulders.-**त्रं** 1 an armour to protect the shoulders. -2 a bow.-**फलकः** the upper part of the spine.-**भारः** a burden or yoke put upon the shoulder. -**भारिक, -भारिन्** *a.* (अंसे°) bearing a yoke or burden on the shoulder.-**विवर्तिन्** *a.* turned towards the shoulders; *S.* 3. 26.

अंसल *a.* Strong, lusty, powerful, having strong shoulders; युवा युगव्यायतबाहुरंसलः R. 3. 34.

अंह् 1 A. (अंहते, अंहितुं, अंहित) To go, approach; set out.-*Caus.* 1 To send. 2 To shine. 3 To speak.

अंहतिः—ती *f.* 1 A gift. 2 Anxiety; trouble, care, distress; illness. (Ved.).

अंहस् *n.* (अंहः-हसी &c.) 1 A sin; सहसा संहतिमंहसां विहंतुं...अलं Ki. 5. 17. 2 Trouble, anxiety, care.

अंहितिः—ती *f.* A gift, donation.

अंह्रिः 1 A foot. 2 The root of a tree, cf. अंघ्रि. 3 The number four. -Comp. -**पः** 'foot-drinker', a tree. -**स्कंधः** the upper part of the sole of the foot.

अक् 1 P. (अकति, अकित) To go, tortuously like a serpent.

अकं Absence of happiness; pain, misery; sin.

अकच *a.* Bald.—**चः** N. of Ketu (the descending node).

अकनिष्ठ *a.* Not the youngest (such

as eldest, middle); elder, superior. —द्धः N. of Buddha Gautama.

अकन्या No virgin, a maid that is not so any longer.

अकर *a.* 1 Handless, maimed. 2 Exempt from tax or duty. 3 Not doing or acting; not disposed to work, ceasing from work.

अकरणं Not doing, absence of action; अकरणात् मंदकरणं श्रेयः; cf. the English phrases "Something is better than nothing," "Better late than never."

अकरणिः *f.* Failure, disappointment, non-accomplishment, mostly used in imprecations; तस्याकरणिरेवास्तु Sk. may he be disappointed, or experience a failure!

अकर्ण *a.* 1 Devoid of ears; deaf. 2 Destitute of Karṇa.–र्णः A serpent.

अकर्तन *a.* Dwarfish.

अकर्मन् *a.* 1 Without work, idle; inefficient. 2 Wicked, degraded. 3 (Gram.) Intransitive, generally in this sense अकर्मक. —*n.* (–र्म) 1 Absence of work. 2 An improper act; crime, sin.–Comp. –अन्वित *a.* 1 unengaged, unoccupied, idle. –2 criminal.–कृत् *a.* free from action, or doing an improper act. –भोगः enjoyment of freedom from the fruits of action.

अकर्मक *a.* Intransitive; (*f.*) अकर्मिका.

अकल *a.* Not in parts, without parts, epithet of the Supreme Spirit.

अकल्क *a.* 1 Free from sediment, pure. 2 Sinless.—ल्का Moon-light.

अकल्प *a.* 1 Uncontrolled, unrestrained. 2 Weak, unable. 3 Incomparable.

अकस्मात् *ind.* 1 Accidentally, suddenly, unexpectedly, all of a sudden; अकस्मादागंतुना सह विश्वासो न युक्तः H. 1. 2 Without cause or ground, causelessly, in vain; नाकस्मात् शांडिलीमाता विक्रीणाति तिलैस्तिलान् Pt. 2. 65; कथं त्वां त्यजेदकस्मात्पतिरार्यवृत्तः R. 14. 55, 73.

अकांड *a.* 1 Accidental, unexpected, sudden; पुनरकांडविवर्तनदारुणः U. 4. 15; Mâl. 5. 31. 2 Destitute of stem or stock.–Comp. –जात *a.* suddenly born or produced. –पातः unexpected occurrence. –पातजात *a.* dying as soon as born. –शूलं a sudden attack of colic.

अकांडे *adv.* Unexpectedly, all of a sudden, suddenly; दर्भांकुरेण चरणः क्षत इत्यकांडे तन्वी स्थिता कतिचिदेव पदानि गत्वा *S.* 2. 12.

अकाम *a.* 1 Free from desire, affection, or love. 2 Reluctant, unwilling. 3 Uninfluenced by, not subject to, love, *S.* 1. 23. 4 Unconscious, unintentional.

अकामतः *adv.* Unwillingly, reluctantly, unintentionally, unconsciously; इतरे कृतवंतस्तु पापान्येतान्यकामतः Ms. 9. 242.

अकाय *a.* 1 Without body, incorporeal. 2 An epithet of Râhu. 3 Epithet of the Supreme Spirit.

अकारण *a.* Causeless, groundless, spontaneous.—णं Absence of a cause, motive or ground; किमकारणमेव दर्शनं विलपंत्यै रतये न दीयते Ku. 4. 7; अकारणात्–रणं–णे causelessly, in vain.

अकार्य *a.* Improper. –र्यं An unworthy or bad act, a criminal action –Comp. कारिन् *a.* an evil-doer, one who commits a misdeed; one that neglects one's duty.

अकाल *a.* Untimely, premature, R. 15. 44. –लः Wrong, inauspicious or unseasonable time, not the proper time (for any thing); अत्यारूढो हि नारीणामकालज्ञो मनोभवः R. 12. 33. –Comp. –कुसुमं, –पुष्पं a flower blossoming out of season. –कूष्मांडः a pumpkin produced out of season; (fig.) useless birth. –ज,-उत्पन्न,-जात *a.* produced out of season, premature; unseasonable. –जलदोदयः, –मेघोदयः 1 an unseasonable rise or gathering of clouds. –2 mist or fog. –वेला unseasonable or improper time. –सह *a.* 1 not enduring delay or loss of time, impatient. –2 not able to hold out as a castle.

अकिंचन *a.* Without any thing, quite poor, utterly destitute; अकिंचनः सन् प्रभवः स संपदां Ku. 5. 77.

अकिंचिज्ज्ञ *a.* Not knowing anything, quite ignorant; Bh. 2. 8.

अकिंचित्कर *a.* 1 Useless; परतंत्रमिदमकिंचित्करं च Ve. 3. 2 Innocent.

अकुंठ *a.* 1 Not blunted, unobstructed; आशस्त्रग्रहणादकुंठपरशोः Ve. 2. 2. 2 Vigorous, able to work. 3 Fixed. 4 Excessive.

अकुतः *adv.* Not from anywhere (in comp. only).–Comp. –चलः N. of Śiva. –भय *a.* secure, not threatened from any quarter, safe; मादृशानामपि °यः संचारो जातः U. 2; यानि श्रीण्यकुतोभयानि च पदान्यासन्खरायोधने *v. l.* for अपराङ्मुखाणि 5. 35.

अकुप्यं 1 Not a base metal, gold or silver. 2 Any base metal.

अकुशल *a.* 1 Inauspicious, unlucky. 2 Not clever or skilful. –लं Evil or misfortune.

अकूपारः 1 The sea. 2 The sun. 3 A tortoise in general. 4 King of tortoise sustaining the world.

अकृच्छ्र *a.* Free from difficulty. –च्छ्रं Absence of difficulty, ease, facility.

अकृत *a.* 1 Not done or prepared. 2 Wrongly or differently done. 3 Incomplete, not ready (as food). 4 Uncreated. 5. One who has done no works. 6 Unripe, immature. –ता One not legally regarded as a daughter and placed on a level with sons. –तं An unperformed act; non-performance of an act; an unheard-of deed. –Comp.–अर्थ *a.* unsucessful. –अस्त्र *a.* unpractised in arms. –आत्मन् *a.* 1 ignorant, foolish. –2 not identified with Brahmâ or the Supreme Spirit. –उद्वाह *a.* unmarried. –ज्ञ *a.* ungrateful. – धी –बुद्धि *a.* ignorant.

अकृष्ट *a.* Not tilled; not drawn. Comp. –पच्य,-रोहिन् *a.* growing or ripening in unploughed land, growing exuberant or wild; °च्या इव शस्यसंपदः Ki. 1. 17; R. 14. 77.

अक्का A Mother.

अक्त *a.* Smeared, anointed; usually in comp.; as घृत°. –क्ता Night.

अक्तं An armour (वर्मन्).

अक्रम *a.* Confused.–मः 1 Want of order, confusion, irregularity. 2 Breach of propriety or decorum.

अक्रिय *a.* Inactive, dull. –या Inactivity; neglect of duty.

अक्रूर *a.* Not cruel. –रः N. of a Yâdava, a friend and uncle of Krishṇa.

अक्रोध *a.* Free from anger. –धः Absence or suppression of anger.

अक्लिष्ट *a.* Unwearied, undisturbed indefatigable. 2 Not marred, unimpaired; *S.* 5. 19.

अक्षू 1. 5. P. (अक्षति-अक्ष्णोति, अक्षित) 1 To reach. 2 To pervade, penetrate. 3 To accumulate.

अक्षः 1 An axis, axle. 2 The pole of a cart. 3 A cart, car; also a wheel. 4 The beam of a balance. 5 Terrestrial latitude. 6 A die for playing with; cube. 7 The seed of which rosaries are made. 8 A weight equal to 16 mâshas and called कर्ष. 9 N. of the plant Terminalia Belerica (बिभीतक). 10 A serpent. 11 Garuda. 12 The soul. 13 Knowledge. 14 Legal procedure, a law-suit. 15 A person born blind. –क्षं 1 An organ of sense; an object of sense;. 2 Sochal salt, seasalt. 3 Blue vitriol. –Comp. –अग्रकीलः –लकः a linch-pin. –आवपनं a dice-board. –आवापः a gambler. –कर्णः hypotenuse. –कुशल –शौंड *a.* skilful in gambling. –कूटः the pupil of the eye. कोविद्,–ज्ञ *a.* skilled in dice. –ग्लहः gambling, playing at dice. –जं 1 direct knowledge or cognition.–2 a thunderbolt. –a diamond. –जः N. of Vishṇu. –तत्वं, –विद्या the science of gambling. –दर्शकः,–दृश 1 a judge. –2 a superintendent of gambling.–देविन् *m.* a gambler, gamester. –द्यूतं dice-play, gambling. –धूर्तः a gamester, a gambler. –धूर्तिलः a bull or ox yoked to the pole of a cart.– पटलं 1 a court of law. –2 a depository of legal documents – पाटकः one who is well-versed in law, a judge.–पातः cast of dice.–पादः N. of the sage Gautama, founder of the Nyâya system of philosophy, or a follower of that system.-भागः, अंशः a degree of latitude.-भारः a cart-load. -माला, -सूत्रं a rosary, string of beads; कृतोऽक्षसूत्रप्रणयी तया करः Ku. 5. 11. -राजः one addicted to gambling; the chief of dice, the die called *Kali* -वाटः a gambling house; the gambling table. -हृदयं perfect skill in or conversancy with gambling.-अक्षवती gaming, playing with dice, a game at dice.

अक्षणिक *a.* Steady, firm, not frail or transitory; steadfast (as a gaze or look).

अक्षत *a.* (*a*) Uninjured, unhurt; त्वमनंगः कथमक्षता रतिः Ku. 4. 9. (*b*) Unbroken, whole; undivided, -तः 1 Śiva. 2 Thrashed and winnowed rice dried in the sun; (*pl.*) whole grain, entire, unhusked and pounded rice washed with water, and used as an article of worship in all religious and sacred ceremonies; साक्षतपात्रहस्ता R. 2. 21. 3 Barley (यवाः) said to be also *n.*- तं 1 Corn, grain of any kind. 2 Eunuch (also *m.*). -ता A virgin. -Comp. -योनिः a virgin, not yet blemished by sexual intercourse; Ms. 9. 176.

अक्षम *a.* 1 Unfit, unable; non-forbearing; impatient; R. 13. 16. -मा 1 Impatience; jealousy. 2 Anger, passion.

अक्षय *a.* 1 Undecaying, imperishable, unfailing; त्रिसाधना शक्तिरिवार्थमक्षयं R. 4. 13. -Comp. -तृतीया the festival falling on the third day of the bright half of Vaiśākha.

अक्षय्य *a.* Inexhaustible; imperishable; तपः षड्भागमक्षय्यं ददत्यारण्यका हि नः S. 2. 13.

अक्षर *a.* 1 Imperishable, indestructible; Ku. 3. 50; Bg. 15. 16. 2 Fixed, firm.-रः 1 Siva. 2 Vishnu-रं 1 (*a*) A letter of the alphabet; अक्षराणामकारोऽस्मि Bg. 10. 33; त्र्यक्षर &c. (*b*) A syllable; एकाक्षरं परं ब्रह्म Ms. 2. 83. (*c*) A word or words, speech collectively; प्रतिषेध° विक्लवाभिरामं S. 3. 25. 2 A document, writing in general (in pl.) 3 The indestructible spirit, Brahma. 4 Water. 5 The sky. 6 Final beatitude.-Comp.-अर्थ meaning (of words) -च (चुं) चुः -चणः -नः a scribe, writer, copyist; so °जीवकः, -जीवी, °जीविकः a professional writer. -च्युतकं getting out a different meaning by the omission of a letter. -छंदस् *n.*,-वृत्तं a metre regulated by the number of syllables it contains. -जननी -तूलिका a reed or pen.-(वि) न्यासः 1 writing; arrangement of letters -2 the alphabet. -3 scripture. -भूमिका tablet or board; R. 18. 46.-मुखः a scholar, student. -वर्जित *a.* unlettered, illiterate. -शिक्षा the science of (mystic) syllables. -संस्थानं arrangement of letters; writing; alphabet.

अक्षरकं A vowel, a letter.

अक्षरशः *adv.* 1 Syllable by syllable. 2 To the very letter; literally.

अक्षांतिः *f.* Intolerance, envy, jealousy.

अक्षार *a.* Free from artificial salt. -रः Natural salt.

अक्षि *n.* (अक्षिणी, अक्षीणि, अक्ष्णा, अक्ष्णः &c.) 1 The eye. 2 The number two -Comp. - कंपः twinkling; R. 15. 67. -कूटः -टकः,-गोलः, -तारा the eyeball; pupil of the eye. -गत *a.* 1 visible, present; Si. 9. 81. -2 rankling in the eye, an eye-sore, hated; °तोऽहमस्य हास्यो जातः Dk. 159. -पक्ष्मन्, -लोमन् the eye-lash. -पटलं 1 a coat of the eye. 2 disease of the eye pertaining to this coat.-विकूणितं, विकूशितं a side-look, leer, a look with the eyelids partially closed.

अक्षुण्ण *a.* 1 Unbroken, uncurtailed. 2 Not conquered or defeated; successful; अक्षुण्णोनुनयः Ve. 1. 2. 3 Not trodden or beaten, unusual; Si. 1. 32.

अक्षेत्र *a.* Destitute of fields; uncultivated. -त्रं 1 A bad field. 2 (fig.) A bad pupil, unworthy recipient or receptacle (of anything). -Comp. -वाद् *a.* destitute of spiritual knowledge.

अक्षोटः A walnut (Mar. डोंगरी अक्रोड).

अक्षोभ्य *a.* Immovable, imperturbable; R. 17. 74.

अक्षौहिणी A large army consisting of 21870 choriots, as many elephants, 65610 horse, and 109350 foot.

अखंड *a.* Unbroken, whole, entire; अखंडं पुण्यानां फलमिव S. 2. 10. - डं *adv.* Uninterruptedly.

अखंडन *a.* 1 Unbroken. 2 Full, entire.-नं 1 Not breaking. 2 Non-refutation. -नः Time.

अखंडित *a.* 1 Unbroken. 2 Uninterrupted, undisturbed.-Comp. -उत्सव *a.* always festive. -ऋतुः time or season which yields its usual produce of flowers &c. (*a.*) fruitful.

अखर्व *a.* 1 Not dwarfish, short or stunted. 2 Not small, great; अखर्वेण गर्वेण विराजमानः Dk. 3.

अखात *a.* Not dug; not buried. -तः - तं 1 A natural lake. 2 A pool before a temple.

अखिल *a.* 1 Whole, entire, complete; oft., with सर्व; एतद्धि मत्तोऽधिजगे सर्वमेषोऽखिलं मुनिः Ms. 1. 59°; लेन entirely. 2 Not fallow, ploughed.

अखेटिकः 1 A tree in general. 2 A dog trained to the chase.

अख्यातिः *f.* Infamy, ill-repute; °कर *a.* disgraceful, disreputable.

अग् 1 P. (अगति, आगीत्, अगिष्यति, अगित) 1 To wind, move tortuously. 2 To go (अंगति, आंगीत् &c.).

अग *a.* 1 Unable to walk. 2 Unapproachable.—गः 1 A tree. 2 A mountain; also a stone. 3 A snake. 4 The sun. 5 The number seven.-Comp.-आत्मजा the daughter of the mountain, N. of Pârvatî.-ओकस् *m.* 1 a mountain-dweller. -2 a bird (वृक्षवासी). -3 the animal शरभ supposed to have 8 legs. -4 a lion. -ज *a.* roaming or wandering through mountains, wild (-जं) bitumen.

अगच्छ *a.* Not going. —च्छः A tree.

अगतिः *f.* 1 Want of resort or recourse, necessity. 2 Want of access (lit. & fig.)

अगति (ती) क *a.* 1 Helpless; without any resort or resource; बालमेनमगतिमादाय Dk. 9; दंडस्त्वगतिका गतिः Y. 1. 346.

अगद *a.* Healthy, sound, free from disease.—दः 1 A medicine, a medicinal drug. 2 Health. 3 The science of antidotes. -Comp. -अगदंकारः a physician. **अगम** =अग q. v.

अगम्य *a.* 1 Not fit to be walked in or approached, unapproachable, inaccessible (lit. & fig.); योगिनामप्यगम्यः &c. 2 Inconceivable, incomprehensible; याः संपदस्ता मनसोऽप्यगम्याः Si. 3. 59, see under गम्य also. -Comp.-रूप *a.* of unsurpassed or inconceivable nature, form &c.; °रूपां पदवीं प्रपित्सुना Ki. 1. 9.

अगम्या A woman not deserving to be approached, (for cohabitation), one of the low castes; °गमनं चैव जातिभ्रंशकराणि वा &c. -Comp. -गमनं illicit intercourse. -गामिन् *a.* practising illicit intercourse.

अगरु *n.* Agallochum.

अगस्तिः, अगस्त्यः 1 'Pitcher-born', N. of a celebrated *Rishi* or sage. 2 N. of the star Canopus.

अगाध *a.* Unfathomable, very deep, bottomless; अगाधसलिलात्समुद्रात् H. 1. 52; (fig.) profound, sound, very deep; °सत्त्व R. 6. 21; यस्य ज्ञानदयासिंधोरगाधस्यानघा गुणाः Ak. unfathomable, incomprehensible. —धः, -धं a deep hole or chasm. -Comp. -जलः a deep pool or pond, deep lake.

अगारं A house; शून्यानि चाप्यगाराणि Ms. 9. 265; °दाहिन् an incendiary.

अगिरः Heaven. -Comp. -ओकस् *a.* dwelling in the heaven (as a god).

अगुण *a.* 1 Destitute of attributes (referring to God). 2 Having no good qualities, worthless; अगुणोऽयमशोकः M. 3. —णः A fault, demerit.

अगुरु *a.* (रु-र्वी *f.*) 1 not heavy, light. 2 (In prosody) Short. 3 Having no teacher. —रु *n.* (*m.* also) The fragrant aloe wood and tree.

अगृहः A houseless wanderer, a hermit.

अगोचर *a.* Imperceptible by the senses, not obvious; वाचामगोचरां हर्षा-

वस्थामस्पृशत् Dk. 169. —तं 1 Anything beyond the cognizance of the senses. 2 Not being seen or observed, or known. 3 Brahma.

अग्नायी 1 The wife of Agni and Goddess of Fire, Svâhâ. 2 The Tretâ age.

अग्निः 1 Fire; कोप°, चिता° &c. 2 The God of fire. 3 Sacrificial fire of three kinds गार्हपत्य, आहवनीय & दक्षिण. 4 The fire of the stomach, digestive faculty. 5 Bile. 6 Gold. 7 The number three. In Dvandva Comp. as first member with names of deities, and with particular words अग्नि is changed to अग्ना, as °विष्णू, °मरुतौ or to अग्नी, as °पर्जन्यौ, °वरुणौ, °षोमौ. –Comp. –अ (आ) गारं-रः, –आलयः, –गृहं a fire-sanctuary; R. 5. 25. –अस्त्रं fire-missile, a rocket, so °बाणः. –आधानं consecrating the fire; so °–आहितिः.—आधेयः Brâhmaṇa who maintains the sacred fire. (–यं)= °आधानं. –आहितः one who maintains the sacred fire; see आहिताग्नि. –उत्पातः a fiery portent, meteor comet &c. –उपस्थानं worship of Agni; the mantra or hymn with which Agni is worshipped. –कणः, –स्तोकः a spark. कर्मन् n. 1 action of fire. –2 oblation to Agni, worship of Agni; so °कार्य; निर्वर्तिताग्निकार्यः K. 16. –कारिका 1 the means of consecrating the sacred fire, the *rik* called अग्नीध्र. –2=अग्निकार्य. –काष्ठं agallochum (अगुरु). –कुक्कुटः a fire-brand. –कुंडं an enclosed space for keeping the fire, a fire-vessel. –कुमारः, –तनयः, –सुतः N. of Kârtikeya said to be born from fire, see कार्त्तिकेय. –केतुः smoke. –कोणः, –दिक् the south-east corner ruled over by Agni. -क्रिया 1 obsequies, funeral ceremonies. –2 branding. –क्रीडा fire-works, illuminations. –गर्भ *a.* having fire in the interior; °र्भां शमीमिव S. 4. 3. (–र्भः) the sun-stone, supposed to contain and give out fire when touched by the rays of the sun; cf. S. 2. 7. (–र्भा) 1 N. of the Samî plant. –2 N. of the earth. –चित् *m.* one who has kept the sacred fire; यतिभिः सार्धमनाग्निमग्निचित् R. 8. 25. –चयः, –चयनं,–चित्या arranging or keeping the sacred fire. (अग्न्याधान). –ज *a.* born from fire. –जः. –जातः 1 N. of Kârttikeya. –2 Vishṇu. (–जं, –जातं) gold; so °जन्मन्. –जिह्वा 1 a tongue or flame of fire. –2 one of the 7 tongues of Agni (कराली धूमिनी श्वेता लोहिता नीललोहिता। सुवर्णा पद्मरागा च जिह्वाः सप्त विभावसोः). –तपस् *a.* growing, shining or burning. –त्रयं, त्रेता the three fires, see under अग्नि. –द *a.* 1 tonic, stomachic. –2 incendiary. –दातृ *m.* one who performs the last ceremonies of a man. –दीपन *a.* stomachic, tonic. –दीप्तिः, वृद्धिः *f.* improved digestion, good appetite. –देवा the third lunar mansion, the Pleiades (कृत्तिका). –धानं the place or receptacle for keeping the sacred fire, the house of an अग्निहोत्रिन्. –धारणं maintaining the sacred fire. –परिक्रिण्क्रि-या worship of fire. –परिच्छदः the whole sacrificial apparatus Ms. 6. 4. –परीक्षा ordeal by fire. –पर्वतः a volcano. –पुराणं one of the 18 Purâṇas ascribed to Vyâsa. –प्रतिष्ठा consecration of fire, especially the nuptial fire. –प्रवेशः, –शनं entering the fire, self-immolation of a widow on the funeral pile of her husband. –प्रस्तरः a flint, a stone producing fire. –बाहुः smoke. –भं 1 N. of कृत्तिकाः –2 gold. –भु 1 water. –2 gold. –भूः 'fire-born' N. of Kârttikeya. –मणिः the sun-stone; a flint. –मंथः, –थनं, producing fire by friction. –मांद्यं loss of appetite, dyspepsia. –मुखः 1 a deity. –2 a Brâhmaṇa in general. –3 'fire-mouthed', sharp-biting, an epithet of a bug Pt. 1. (–खी) a kitchen. –रक्षणं consecrating or preserving the sacred (domestic) fire or अग्निहोत्र. –रजः, –रजस् *m.* 1 scarlet insect by name इंद्रगोप. –2 the might or power of Agni –3 gold. –लोकः the world of Agni, which is situated below the summit of Meru. –वधूः Svâhâ, the daughter of Daksha and wife of Agni. –वर्धक *a.* tonic. –वाहः 1 smoke. –2 a goat. –वीर्यं 1 power or might of Agni. –2 gold. –शरणं-शाला-लं a fire sanctuary; a house or place for keeping the sacred fire; °रक्षणाय स्थापितोऽहं V. 3. –शिखः 1 lamp. –2 rocket, fiery arrow. –3 an arrow in general. –4 safflower plant. –5 saffron. (–खं) 1 saffron. –2 gold. –ष्टुत्,–ष्टुभ्,–ष्टोम &c. see °–स्तुत, °–स्तुभ् &c. संस्कारः 1 consecration of fire. –2 burning on the funeral pile; नास्य कार्योऽग्निसंस्कारः Ms. 5. 69, R. 12. 56. –सखः, सहायः 1 the wind. –2 wild pigeon. –3 smoke. –साक्षिक *a* or *adv.* keeping fire for a witness, in the presence of fire; पंचबाण° M. 4. 12. –स्तुत् N. of a portion of that sacrifice which extends over one day. –स्तोमः (ष्टोमः) N. of a portracted ceremony or sacrificial rite extending over several days in spring and forming an essential part of the ज्योतिष्टोम. –होत्रं 1 an oblation to Agni. –2 maintenance of the sacred fire and offering oblations to it. –होत्रिन् *a.* one who practises the Agnihotra, or consecrates and maintains the sacred fire. –अग्निसात् *ind.* To the state of fire; used in comp. with कृ 'to burn', 'to consign to flames,' न चकार शरीरमग्निसात् R. 8. 72; °भू to be burnt.

अग्र *a.* 1 First, foremost, chief, best, principal; °महिषी chief queen –2 Excessive. —ग्रं 1 (*a.*) The foremost or topmost point, tip, point (opp. मूलं, मध्यं); (fig.) sharpness, keenness; नासिका° tip of the nose; समस्ता एव विद्या जिह्वाग्रेऽभवन् K. 346 stood on the tip of the tongue. (*o*) Top, summit, surface; कैलास, °पर्वत,° &c. 2 Front. 3 The best of any kind. 4 Goal, aim. 5 Beginning. 6 Overplus, excess. In compounds as first member meaning 'the forepart,' 'front,' 'tip' &c.; *e. g.* °पादः, –चरणः. –Comp. –अनी (णी) कः (कं) van-guard; Ms. 7. 193. –आसनं chief seat, seat of honour Mu. 1. 12. –करः =अग्रहस्तः q. v.– गः a leader, a guide; taking the lead. –गण्य *a.* foremost; to be ranked first. –ज *a.* first born or produced; (–जः) 1 the first born, an elder brother; अस्त्यंव मन्युर्भरताग्रजे मे R. 14 73. –2 a Brâhamaṇa. (–जा) an elder sister; so °जात, °जातक, °जाति.–जन्मन् *m.* 1 the first born, an elder brother. –2 a Brâhmaṇa; Dk. 13. –जिह्वा the tip of tongue, –दानिन् a (degraded) Brâhamaṇa who takes presents offered in honour of the dead –दूतः a harbinger; कृष्णाक्रोधाग्रदूतः Ve. 1. 22; R. 6. 12. –नीः (णीः) a leader foremost अप्यग्रणीर्मंत्रकृतामृषीणां R. 5. 4. –पादः the forepart of the foot; toes. –पूजा the highest or first mark of reverence or respect. –पेयं precedence in drinking. –भागः 1 the first or best part. –2 remnant, remainder. –3 tip, point. –भागिन् *a.* first to take or claim (the remnant). –भूः =°ज. –भूमिः *f.* goal of ambition or object aimed at. –मांसं flesh in the heart, the heart itself; °सं चानितं Ve. 3. – यायिन् *a.* taking the lead, leading the van; पुत्रस्य ते रणशिरस्यमग्रयायी S. 7. 26. –योधिन् *m.* the principal hero, champion. –संधानी the register of human actions kept by Yama. –संध्या early dawn; कर्कंधूनामुपरि तुहिनं रंजयत्यग्रसंध्या S. 4 *v. l.* –सर =यायिन् taking the lead; R. 9. 23; 5. 71. –हस्तः (–°करः, –°पाणिः) the forepart of the hand or arm; forepart of the trunk (of an elephant); often used for a finger or fingers taken collectively; also the right hand; अथाग्रहस्ते मुकुलीकृतांगुलौ Ku. 5. 63. –हायनः (णः) the beginning of the year; N. of the month मार्गशीर्ष.–हारः a grant of land given by kings (to Brâhmaṇas) for sustenance; कस्मिंश्चिद्ग्रहारे Dk. 8, 9.

अग्रतः *adv.* (with gen.) 1 Before, in front of, at the head of; forward. 2 In the presence of. 3 First –Comp. –सरः a leader.

अग्रिम *a.* 1 First (in order, rank &c.); foremost, chief. 2 Elder, eldest.—मः An elder brother.

अग्रिय *a.* Foremost, &c.—यः An elder brother.

अग्रीय *a.* Fore-most, best &c.=अग्रिम q. v.

अग्रे *adv.* **1** In front of, before (in time or space). **2** In the presence of. **3** At the head. **4** Subsequently, in the sequel; एवमग्रे वक्ष्यते, एवमग्रेऽपि द्रष्टव्यं &c. **5** At first, first. **6** First, in preference to others.–Com. **गः** a leader.–**दिधिषुः-षूः** a man (of one of the first three castes) who marries a wife married before (पुनर्भूविवाहकारी). (–**षूः** *f.*) a married woman whose elder sister is still unmarried (ज्येष्ठायां यद्यनूढायां कन्यायामुह्यतेऽनुजा । सा चाग्रेदिधिषूर्ज्ञेया पूर्वा च दिधिषूः स्मृता); °**पतिः** the husband of such a woman.—**वनं -णं** the border or skirt of a forest.–**सर** *a.* going in front, a leader ; मानमहतामग्रेसरः केसरी Bh. **2. 29.**

अग्र्य *a.* **1** Foremost, best, choicest, highest, first; तदंगमग्र्यं मघवन् महाक्रतोः R. 3. 46; ° महिषी 10. 66; also with loc.; Ms. 3. 184.—**ग्र्यः** An elder brother.

अघ्=अंघ् q. v.—(10 U.) To wrong, sin.

अघं 1 Sin; अघौघविध्वंसविधौ पटीयसीः *S*i. **1**, 18, 26; ° मर्षण &c. **2** Misdeed, fault, crime; *S*i. 4. 37. **3** An evil, accident, calamity; क्रियादघानां मघवा विघातं Ki. 3. 52; see अनघ. **4** Impurity (अशौचं). **5** Chief, distress.—**घः** N. of a demon, brother of Baka and Pûtanâ and commander-in-chief of Kamsa.–Comp.–**असुरः** see अघ above.–**अहः**(अहन्) a day of impurity (अशौचदिनं). –**आयुस्** *a.* leading a wicked life. –**नाश,–नाशन** *a.* expiatory, destroying sin.–**मर्षण** *a.* expiatory, removing or destroying sin, usually applied to a prayer repeated by Brâhmaṇas (the 190th hymn of Rv. 10.) सर्वेनसामपध्वंसि जप्यं त्रिष्वघमर्षणं Ak.–**विषः** a serpent. –**शंसः** a wicked man, such as a thief. –**शंसिन्** *a.* reporting or telling one's sin or guilt.

अघर्म *a.* Not hot, cold; °अंशु, ° धामन् the moon, whose rays are cold.

अघोर *a.* Not terrific or fearful,—**रः 1** N. of *S*iva or of one of his forms, where अघोर=घोर.–Comp.–**पथः, मार्गः** a follower of *S*iva. –**प्रमाणं** a terrific oath or ordeal.

अघोष *a.* Hard-sounding.—**षः** The hard sound of a consonant.

अंक् 1 A. To move in a curve.—10 U. (अंकयति-ते, अंकयितुं, अंकित) **1** To mark, stamp; स्वनामधेयांकित *S*. 4. stamped with his name; नयनोदबिंदुभिः अंकितं स्तनांशुकं V. 4. 7. **2** To count. **3** To stain, stigmatize; तस्को नाम गुणो भवेत्सुगुणिनां यो दुर्जनैर्नांकितः Bh. **2.** 54. **4** To walk, stalk, go.

अंकः 1 The lap (*n.* also); अंकाययायंकमुदीरिताशीः Ku 7. 5. **2** A mark, sign; अलक्तकांकां पदवीं ततान R. 7. 9; a stain, spot, stigma, brand; इंदोः किरणेष्विवांकः Ku. 1. 3; कथ्यां कृतांको निर्वास्यः Ms. 8. 281. **3** A numerical figure; a number; the number 9. **4** A side, flank; proximity, reach; समुत्सुकेवांकमुपैति सिद्धिः Ki. 3. 40; सिंहो जंबुकमंकमागतमपि त्यक्त्वा निहंति द्विपं Bh. 2. 30. **5** An act of a drama. **6** A hook or curved instrument. **7** A species of dramatic composition, one of the ten varieties of रूपक, see S. D. 519. **8** A line, curved line; a curve or bend generally, the bend in the arm.—Comp.–**अवतारः** when an act, hinted by persons at the end of the preceding act, is brought in continuity with the latter, it is called अंकावतार (descent of an act), as the sixth act of *S*âkuntala or second of Mâlavikâgnimitra. –**तंत्रं** the science of numbers (arithmetical or algebraical). –**धारणं-णा 1** bearing or having marks. – **2** manner of holding the person, figure.–**परिवर्तः 1** turning on the other side. –**2** rolling or dallying in the lap or on the person; (an occasion for) embrace.–**पालिः-ली** *f.* **1** an embrace; तावद्गाढं वितर सकृदप्यंकपालीं प्रसीद Mâl. 8. **2.**–**2** a nurse. –**पाशः** an operation in arithmetic by which a peculiar concatenation or chain of numbers is formed by making the figures 1, 2 &c. exchange places.–**भाज्** *a.* **1** seated in the lap or carried on the hip, as an infant.–**2** being within easy reach; drawing near, soon to be obtained; Ki. 5. 52. –**मुखं** (or **आस्यं**) that part of an act, wherein the subject of all the acts is intimated, is called अंकमुख, which suggests the *germ* as well as the *end e.g.* in Mâl. 1 कामंदकी and अवलोकिता hint the parts to be played by भूरिवसु and others and give the arrangement of the plot in brief.–**विद्या** the science of numbers, arithmetic.

अंकनं 1 A mark, token. **2** Act of marking **3** Means of marking, stamping, &c.

अंकतिः 1 Wind. **2** Fire. **3** Brahmâ. **4** A Brâhmaṇa who keeps the sacred fire.

अंकुटः A key.

अंकुरः-रं 1 A sprout, shoot, blade ; दर्भांकुरेण चरणः क्षतः *S*. **2.** 10; oft. in comp. in the sense of ' pointed, ' ' sharp ' &c. ; मकरवक्त्रदंष्ट्रांकुरात् Bh. **2.** 4 pointed jaws ; (fig.) scion, offspring, progeny ; अनेन कस्यापि कुलांकुरेण *S*. 7. 19. **2** Water. **3** Blood. **4** A hair. **5** A tumour, swelling.

अंकुरित *a.* Having sprouts; arisen; ° तं मनसिजेनेव V. 1. 12 as if Love has put forth sprouts.

अंकुशः A hook, a goad ; (fig.) one who checks, a corrector, governor, director ; a restraint or check. निरंकुशाः कवयः poets have free license or are unfettered. Comp.–**ग्रहः** an elephant-driver; अन्वेतुकामोऽवमतांकुशग्रहः *S*i. 12. 16.–**दुर्धरः** a restive elephant.–**धारिन्** *m.* a keeper of an elephant.

अंकुशित *a.* Urged on by a hook, goaded.

अंकुशिन् *a.* Having a hook or goad.

अंकूरः Sprout, see अंकुर.

अंकूषः =अंकुश q. v.

अंकोटः, ठः, लः N. of a tree (Mar. पिस्ते.)

अंकोलिका An embrace.

अंक्य *a.* Fit to be branded, marked or counted.—**क्यः** A sort of drum or tabor.

अंख् 10 P. (अंखयति, अंखित) **1** To crawl. **2** To cling. **3** To check, hold back.

अंग् 1 P. (अंगति, आनंग, अंगितुं, अंगित) To go, walk.–10 P. **1** to walk, go round. **2** To mark, (cf. अंक्).

अंग *ind.* A vocative particle meaning ' well ' ' well, sir, ' ' indeed, ' ' true;' ' assent ' (as in अंगीकृ); अंग कच्चित्कुशली तातः K. 221; with किं in the sense of ' how much less, ' or ' how much more; ' तृणेन कार्यं भवतीश्वराणां किमंग वाग्हस्तवता नरेण Pt. 1. 71. Lexicographers give the following senses of अंगः–क्षिप्रे च पुनरर्थे च संगमासूययोस्तथा । हर्षे संबोधने चैव ह्यंगशब्दः प्रयुज्यते ॥ See also " The Student's Guide to Sanskrit Composition " § 243.—**गं 1** The body. **2** A limb or member of the body ; शेषांगनिर्माणविधौ विधातुः Ku. 1. 33. **3**.(*a*) A division or department (of anything), a part or portion, as of a whole; as सप्तांगं राज्यं, चतुरंगं बलं. (Hence) (*b*) A supplementary or auxiliary portion, supplement. (*c*) A constituent part, essential requisite or component; तदंगमग्र्यं मघवन् महाक्रतोः R. 3. 46. (*d*) An attributive or secondary part; secondary, auxiliary or dependent member (serving to help the principal one) (opp. प्रधान or अंगिन्); अंगी रौद्ररसस्तत्र सर्वेऽगानि रसाः पुनः S. D. 517 (*e*) An auxiliary means or expedient. **4** (Gram.) A name for the base of a word. **5** (*a*) One of the sub-divisions of the five joints or sandhis (in dramas). (*b*) The whole body of subordinate characters. **6** A symbolical expression for the six. **7** The mind.—**गः** (pl.) N. of a country and the people inhabiting it, the country about the modern Bhâgalpur in Bengal.—Comp. –**अंगि, –अंगिभावः** the relation of a limb of the body, of subordinate to the principal, or of that which is helped or fed to the helper or feeder (गौणमुख्यभावः, उपकार्योपकारकभावश्च); अविश्रांतिजुषामात्मन्यंगांगित्वं तु संकरः K. P. 10 (अनुग्राह्यानुग्राहकत्वं). **अधीपः-अधीशः** lord of the Angas, N. of Karṇa (cf. °राजः, °पतिः, °ईश्वरः, °अधीश्वरः).–**ग्रह** spasm.–**ज-जात** *a.* 1 produced from or on the body, being in or on the body, bodily. -2 beautiful, ornamental. (जः),-जनुस् 1 a son.-2 hair of the body (*n* also).-3 love; Cupid; intoxicating passion.-4 drunkenness, intoxication -5 a disease. (-जा) a daughter. (-जं) blood -द्वीपः one of the six minor Dvîpas.-न्यासः touching the limbs of the body with the hand accompanied by appropriate Mantras.-पालिः *f.* an embrace.-पालिका=अंकपालि q. v. -प्रत्यंगं every limb large and small. -भूः 1 a son. -2 Cupid. -भंगः 1 palsy or paralysis of limbs; °विकल इव भूत्वा स्थास्यामि *S.* 2. -2 twisting or stretching out of the limbs (as is done by a man just after he rises from sleep). -मंत्रः N. of a Mantra.-मर्दः 1. one who shampoos his master's body.-2 act of shampooing; so °मर्दक: or °मर्दिन्.-मर्षः rheumatism.-यज्ञः, यागः a subordinate sacrificial act. -रक्षकः a body-guard, personal attendant ; Pt. 3.-रक्षणी a coat of mail, or a garment. (-णं) protection of a person.-रागः 1 scented cosmetic, application of perfumed unguents to the body, fragrant unguent; R. 12. 27, 6. 60; Ku. 5. 11.-2 act of anointing. -विकल *a.* 1 maimed, paralysed.-2 fainting.- विकृतिः *f.* 1 change of bodily appearance ; collapse.-2 an apoplectic fit, apoplexy.-विकारः a bodily defect. -विक्षेपः movement of the limbs ; gesticulation. -विद्या 1 the science of grammar &c. contributing to knowledge. -2 the science of foretelling good or evil by the movements of limbs ; N. of chapter 51 of Bṛhat Samhitâ which gives full details of this science.-विधिः a subordinate or subsidiary act subservient to a knowledge of the principal one.-वीरः chief or principal hero. -वैकृतं 1 a sign, gesture or hint -2 a nod, wink -3 changed bodily appearance. -संस्कारः, -संस्क्रिया embellishment of person, personal decoration. -संहतिः *f.* compactness symmetry; body; strength of the body. -संगः bodily contact, union; coition. -सेवकः a personal attendant. -हारः gesticulation; a dance. -हारिः 1 gesticulation.-2 stage; dancing-hall.-हीन *a.* 1 mutilated; crippled. -2 having some defective limb.

अंगकं 1 A limb; अकृतमधुरैरंबानां मे कुतूहलमंगकैः U. 1. 20, 24. 2 The body; *Si.* 4. 66.

अंगणं=अंगनं q. v.

अंगतिः 1 A conveyance, vehicle (*f.* also). 2 Fire. 3 Brahmâ. 4 A Brâhmaṇa who maintains the sacred fire.

अंगदं An ornament, bracelet &c. worn on the upper arm, an armlet; तप्तचामीकरांगदः V. 1. 14; संघट्टयन्नंगदमंगदेन R. 6. 73.-दः 1 N. of a son of Vâli, monkey-king of Kishkindhâ. 2 N. of a son of Lakshmaṇa by Urmilâ (R. 15. 90), his capital being called Angadîyâ.

अंगनं-णं 1 A place to walk in, a courtyard, an area, yard, court; गृह°; गगन ° the wide firmament; °भुवः केसरवृक्षस्य Mâl. l. 2 A conveyance. 3. Going, walking &c.

अंगना 1 A woman or female in general; नृप °, गज °, हरिण °&c. 2 A beautiful woman. 3 (Astr.) Virgo. -Comp.- जनः 1 the female sex, woman-kind. -2 women. -प्रिय *a.* beloved of women. (-यः) N. of the tree Aśoka.

अंगस *m.* A bird.

अंगारः-रं 1 Charcoal (whether heated or not); उष्णो दहति चांगारः शीतः कृष्णायते करं H. 1. 80; त्वया स्वहस्तेनांगाराः कर्षिताः Pt. 1 you have ruined yourself with your own hands ; cf. "to dig a mine under one's feet". 2 The planet Mars. -रं Red colour. -Comp. -धानिका a portable fire-pan, brazier.-पात्री,-शकटी a portable fire-pan. -वल्लरी, -वल्ली N. of various plants, particularly गुंजा.

अंगारकः-कं 1 Charcoal. 2 Mars; °विरुद्धस्य प्रक्षीणस्य बृहस्पतेः Mk. 9. 33 ; °चारः course of Mars. 3 Tuesday (°दिनं, °वासरः). -कं a small spark. -Comp.-मणिः a coral.

अंगारी A portable fire-pan, brazier.

अंगाराकित *a.* Charred, roasted.

अंगारिका 1 A portable fire-pan. 2 The stalk of the sugar-cane. 3 The bud of the tree किंशुक.

अंगारिणी 1 A small fire-pan. 2 A creeper in general.

अंगारित *a.* Charred, roasted, half-burnt. -तः-तं An early bud of the किंशुक tree. -ता 1 = अंगारधानी q. v. 2 A bud in general. 3 A creeper.

अंगिका A bodice or jacket.

अंगिन् *a.* 1 Corporeal ; incarnate ; धर्मार्थकाममोक्षाणामवतार इवांगवान् R. 10. 84, 38. 2 Having subordinate parts; chief, principal; य रसस्यांगिनो धर्माः; एक एव भवेदंगी शृंगारो वीर एव वा, S. D.

अंगारीय *a.* To be used for preparing coal.

अंगिरः, अंगिरस् *m.* N. of a celebrated sage to whom many hymns of the Ṛgveda are ascribed. -(pl.) Descendants of Angiras.

अंगीकारः -कृतिः *f.* **करणं** 1 Acceptance. 2 Agreement, promise, undertaking &c.

अंगीय *a.* Belonging to the body.

अंगुः A hand.

अंगुरिः-री = अंगुलि q. v.

अंगुलः 1 A finger. 2 thumb (*n.* also) 3 A finger's breadth (*n.* also), equal to 8 barley-corns, 12 Angulas making a वितस्ति or span, and 24, a हस्त or cubit.

अंगुलिः-ली-रिः-री. *f.* 1 A finger (the names of the 5 fingers are अंगुष्ठ thumb, तर्जनी forefinger, मध्यमा middle finger, अनामिका ring-finger, and कनिष्ठा or कनिष्ठिका the little finger); a toe (of the foot). 2 The thumb, great toe. 3 The tip of an elephant's trunk. 4 The measure अंगुल. -Comp. तोरणं a mark on the forehead of the form of the half-moon made with sandal &c.-त्रं,- त्राणं a finger-protector (a contrivance like a thimble used by archers to protect the thumb or finger from being injured by the bow-string).-मुद्रा, मुद्रिका a seal-ring.-मोटनं-स्फोटनं snapping or cracking the fingers (Mar. चुटकी).-संज्ञा a sign made by the finger ; मुखार्पितैकांगुलिसंज्ञयैव Ku. 3. 41.-संदेशः making signs with fingers as a sign. -संभूतः a finger-nail.

अंगुलिका=अंगुलि.

अंगुली (री) यं-कं, -यकं A finger-ring ; तव सुचरितमंगुलीयं नूनं प्रतनु ममेव *S.* 6. 10. *m.* also ; काकुत्स्थस्यांगुलीयकः Bk. 8 118.

अंगुष्ठः 1 The thumb ; great toe. 2 A thumb's breadth, usually regarded as equal to अंगुल. -Comp. -मात्र *a.* of the length or size of a thumb; °त्रं पुरुषं निश्चकर्ष बलाद्यमः Mb.

अंगुष्ठ्यः The thumb-nail.

अंगूषः 1 An ichneumon. 2 An arrow.

अंघ् 1 A. (अंघते, अंघित) 1 To go. 2 To commence. 3 To hasten. 4 To scold.

अंघस् *n.* A sin; Ve. 1. 12. v. 1.

अंघ्रि (अंह्रिः) 1 A foot. 2 The root of a tree. 3 A quarter of a stanza (चतुर्थपादः).-Comp.-पः a tree ; दिक्षु व्यूढांघ्रिपांगः Ve. 2. 18. -पान *a.* sucking his foot or toes, as an infant. -स्कंधः the ankle.

अच् 1 U. (अचति-ते,-अंचति, आनंच, अंचित-अक्त) 1 To go, move; to honour; request, ask &c, &c.; connected with अंच् q. v.-च् *m.* (Gram.) A term for vowels.

अचक्षुस् *a.* Eyeless, blind; °विषय *a.* invisible.-*n.* A bad or miserable eye.

अचंड *a.* Not hot-tempered, mild, gentle. -डी A mild or tractable cow.

अचतुर *a.* 1 Destitute of four. 2 Not skilful.

अचर *a.* Immovable; चराचरं विश्वं Ku. 2. 5; चराणामन्नमचराः Ms. 5. 29.

अचल *a.* Steady, immovable ; fixed, permanent ; चित्रन्यस्तमिवाचलं चामरं V. 1. 4.-लः 1 A mountain; (rarely) a rock. 2 A bolt or pin (शंकु). 3 The number seven.-ला The earth. -लं Brahma. -Comp.-कन्यका, -सुता, -दुहिता, -तनया &c. N. of Pârvatî, daughter of the Himâlaya mountain. -कीला the earth.-ज, -जात a. mountain-born. (जा-जाता) N. of Pârvatî. -त्विष् m. a cuckoo. -द्विष् m. the enemy of mountains, epithet of Indra who clipped off their wings.-पतिः,-राज् lord of mountains, N. of Himâlaya; so °अधिपः, °श्रेष्ठः.

अचापल-ल्य a. Devoid of fickleness, steady. —लं-ल्यं Steadiness.

अचित् a. Ved. 1 Devoid of understanding. 2 Irreligious. 3 Material.

अचित a. Ved. 1 Gone. 2 Not thought of. 3 Not collected.

अचित्त a. 1 Inconceivable. 2 Destitute of intellect, senseless, stupid. 3 Unnoticed.

अचिंत्य-तनीय a. Inconcievable, incomprehensible; °यस्तु तव प्रभावः R. 5. 33. —त्यः Siva.

अचिंतित a. Unexpected, sudden; Pt. 2. 3.

अचिर a. 1 Brief, transitory, of short duration; °द्युति, °भास्, °प्रभा &c. q. v. 2 New; R. 8. 20. In compounds अचिर may be rendered by 'recently', 'just', 'not long ago'; प्रवृत्तं ग्रीष्मसमयमधिकृत्य S. 1 just set in; °प्रसूता S. 4 having recently brought forth (who died not long after delivery, said of a doe); or a cow that has recently calved. —रं adv. (also अचिरेण, अचिराय, अचिरात्, अचिरस्य in the same senses) 1 Not long since, not long ago. 2 Recently, lately. 3 Soon, quickly, not long hence. -Comp. -अंशु, -आभा, -द्युतिः, -प्रभा, -भास्, -रोचिस् f. lightning, °शुविलासचंचला लक्ष्मीः Ki. 2. 19; °भासां तेजसा चानुलिप्तैः S. 7. 7.

अचेतन a. 1 Inanimate, irrational; चेतन °नेषु Me. 5. 2 Insensible; senseless.

अच्छ a. Clear, pellucid, transparent, pure; मुक्ताच्छदंतच्छविदंतुरंयं U. 6. 27; Me. 51; किं रत्नमच्छा मतिः Bv. 1. 16. —च्छः 1 A crystal. 2 A bear; cf. also °भल्ल. -Comp. -उदन् a. (i. e. अच्छोद) having clear water. (-दं) N. of a lake on the Himâlaya (mentioned in Kâdambarî). -भल्लः a bear.

अच्छ-च्छा ind. Ved. To, towards (with acc.).

अच्छावाकः The invoker or inviter, a priest or Ṛtvij who is employed at Soma sacrifices, and is a co-adjutor of होतृ.

अच्छंदस् a. 1 Not studying the Vedas (as a boy before the मुंज ceremony), or not entitled to that study. (as a Súdra). 2 Not metrical.

अच्छिद्र a. Unbroken, uninjured, faultless, without defect; जपच्छिद्रं तपच्छिद्रं यच्छिद्रं श्राद्धकर्मणि । सर्वं भवतु मेऽच्छिद्रं ब्राह्मणानां प्रसादतः - द्रं A faultless action, or condition, absence of defect; °द्रेण uninterruptedly, from first to last.

अच्छिन्न a. 1 Uninterrupted, continuous, constant. 2 Not cut or divided, uninjured, inseparable.

अच्छोटनं Hunting.

अच्युत a. 1 Not fallen, firm; fixed; not giving way, solid. 2 Imperishable, permanent. -तः N. of Vishṇu; of the Almighty being; गच्छाम्यच्युतदर्शनेन K. P. 5 (where अ° also means 'one who is firm, does not yield to passions').-Comp. -अग्रजः N. of Balarâm or Indra. -अंगजः, पुत्रः, आत्मजः N. of Cupid, son of Kṛshṇa and Rukmiṇî.-अवासः, वासः the sacred figtree.

अज् 1 P. (optionally replaced by the root वी in non-conjugational tenses; अजति, अजितवीत) 1 To go. 2 To drive, lead. 3 To throw, cast (used with prepositions found only in Vedic literature).

अज a. Unborn, existing from all eternity; अजस्य गृह्णतो जन्म R. 10. 24. -जः 1 The 'un-born,' epithet of the Almighty Being; also N. of Vishṇu, Siva or Brahmâ. 2 The (individual) soul (जीव). 3 A ram, he-goat. 4 The sign Aries. 5 A sort of corn or grain 6 N. of the Moon or Kâmadeva. -Comp. -अदनी a kind of pricly nightshade, (Mar. धमासा). -अविकं small cattle. -अश्वं goats and horses -एडकं goats and rams. -गरः a hug serpent (boa constrictor) who is said to swallow goats. (-री) N. of a plant. -गल see अजागल below. -जीवः; -जीविकः a goat-herd; so -°पः, -°पालः. -मारः 1 a butcher. -2 N. of a country (the modern Ajmeer). -मीढः 1 N. of the place called Ajmeer. -2 Surname of Yudhishṭhira. -मोदा, मोदिका N. of a very useful medicinal plant, (Mar. ओंवा) -शृंगी N. of plant (Mar. मेढशिंगी).

अजन Moving, driving.-नः Brahmâ.

अजका, -अजिका A young shegoat.

अजकवः -वं The bow of Siva.

अजकावः-वं Siva's bow.

अजगवं,-गावः, Siva's bow, Pinaka.

अजड a. Not stupid.

अजन a. Tenantless, desert.

अजनिः f. A path, road.

अजन्मन् a. Unborn, epithet of the Unborn Being. —m Final beatitude, absolution.

अजन्य a. Not fit to be produced; not favourable to mankind. -न्यं A portentous phenomenon inauspicious to mankind, such as earth-quake.

अजपः A Brâhmaṇa who does not (properly) repeat his prayers.

अजंभ a. Toothless. -भः 1 A frog. 2 The sun. 3 Toothless state (of a child).

अजय a. invincible, unsurpassed, unconquerable. -यः A defeat.—या Hemp or भांग.

अजय्य a. Invincible S. 6. 29; R. 18. 8.

अजर a. 1 Not subject to old age or decay, ever young. 2 Undecaying, imperishable; पुराणमजरं विदुः R. 10. 19. —रः A god. —रं the Supreme Spirit.

अजर्यं (With संगतं expressed or understood) Friendship; मृगैरजर्यं जरसोपदिष्टं R. 18. 7.

अजस्र a. Not ceasing, constant, perpetual; °दीक्षाप्रयतस्य R. 3. 44. —स्रं ind. Ever, constantly, perpetually; तच्च धूनोत्यजस्रं U. 4. 26.

अजहत्स्वार्था A kind of लक्षणा, in which the primary or original sense of a word (which is used elliptically) does not disappear; as कुंताः प्रविशंति = कुंतधारिणः पुरुषाः; also called उपादानलक्षणा.

अजहल्लिंगं A noun which does not change its original gender even when used like an adjecive; e. g. वेदः or श्रुतिः प्रमाणं (not प्रमाणः or °णा).

अजा 1 (According to Sânkhya philosophy) Prakriti or Mâyâ. 2 A she-goat. -Comp. -गलस्तनः the fleshy protuberance or nipple hanging down from the neck of goats; (fig.) an emblem of anything worthless or useless; धर्मार्थकाममोक्षाणां यस्यैकोपि न विद्यते । °स्तनस्येव तस्य जन्म निरर्थकं ॥ -जीवः, -पालकः a goat-herd, see अजजीव &c.

अजाजिः-जी f. Cumin seed.

अजात a. Unborn; अजातमृतमूर्खेभ्यो मृताजातौ सुतौ वरं Pt. 1.; not yet born, produced, or fully developed; °ककुद्, °पक्ष &c.-Comp.-अरि, शत्रु a. having no enemy or adversary; not an enemy of any one. (-रिः-त्रुः) epithet of Yudhishṭhira; हंत जातमजातारेः प्रथमेन त्वयारिणा Si. 2. 102; न द्वेक्षि यज्जनमतस्त्वमजातशत्रु Ve. 3. 13; also of Siva and various other persons. -ककुत्-द् m. a young bull whose hump is not yet fully developed. -व्यंजन a. having no distinctive marks or features (as a beard) -व्यवहारः a minor (who has not attained his majority).

अजानिः Without a wife; a widower.

अजानिकः A goat-herd.

अजानेय a. Of high breed, undaunted (as a horse).

अजित a. 1 Invincible, unconquerable, irresistible; °तं पुण्यं...महः U. 5. 27. 2 Not conquered or won (as a country &c.); not restrained, curbed, controlled; °आत्मन्, °इंद्रिय one who has not subdued his mind or his senses -तः N. of Vishṇu or Siva or of Buddha.

अजिनं 1 The (hairy) skin of a tiger, lion, elephant &c., especially of a black antelope (used as a seat, garment &c.); अथाजिनाषाढधरः Ku. 5. 30, 67, Ki. 11. 15. 2 A sort of leather bag or bellows.–Comp. **–पत्रा–त्री–त्रिका** a bat.–**योनिः** a deer, an antelope.–**वासिन्** *a.* clad in an antelope-hide.–**संधः** a furrier.

अजिर *a.* Quick, swift (शीघ्र).—**रं** 1 A court-yard, an enclosed space, arena ; उटजाजिरप्रकीर्ण K. 39. 2 The body. 3 Any object of sense. 4 The wind, air. 5 A frog.—**रा** 1 N. of a river. 2 N. of Durgâ.

अजिह्म *a.* 1 Straight. 2 Upright, straight-forward, honest ; °गामिभिः Si. 1. 63 straight and honest. —**ह्मः** A frog. –Comp. –**ग** *a.* going straight on; व्रजेद्दिशमजिह्मगः Ms. 6. 31. (–**गः**) an arrow.

अजिह्वः A frog.

अजीकवं *Siva's* bow.

अजीगर्तः A serpent.

अजीर्ण *a.* Undigested ; undecomposed.—**र्णं,–र्णिः** *f.* 1 Indigestion ; केऽजीर्णभयाद्भ्रातर्भोजनं परिहीयते H. 2. 57. 2 Vigour, energy, absence of decay.

अजीव *a.* Devoid of life ; lifeless.–**–वः** Non-existence, death.

अजीवनिः *f.* Death, non-existence (used as an imprecation); अजीवनिस्ते शठ भूयात् Sk. may death seize thee, rogue ! mayest thou cease to live !

अज्झलं 1 A shield. 2 A live coal.

अज्ञ *a.* 1 Not knowing, devoid of knowledge or experience; अज्ञो भवति वै बालः Ms. 2. 153. 2 Ignorant, unwise, foolish, silly, stupid (said of men as well as animals); अज्ञः सुखमाराध्यः Bh. 2. 3. 3 Inanimate; not endowed with the power of understanding.

अज्ञात *a.* Unknown, unexpected, unaware ; °पातं सलिले ममज्ज R. 16. 72.–Comp.–**चर्याः,–वासः** remaining *incognito* (said of the Pândavas).

अज्ञान *a.* Ignorant, unwise.—**नं** 1 Ignorance. 2 Especially, spiritual ignorance (अविद्या) which makes one consider himself as distinct from the Supreme Spirit, and the material world as a reality. In compounds अज्ञान may be translated by 'unawares,' 'inadvertently,' 'unconsciously'; °आचरित, °उच्चारित &c.

अंच् 1 U. (अंचति-ते, आनंच, अंचितुं, अच्यात् or अंच्यात्, अक्त or अंचित) 1 To bend; शिरोंऽचित्वा Bk. 9. 40. 2 To go, move, tend towards; स्वतंत्रा कथमंचसि Bk. 4. 22; त्वं चेदंचसि लोभं Bv. 1. 46 art greedy. 3 To worship, honour, reverence; to adorn, grace; see अंचित below. 4 To request, desire. 5 To murmur ; speak indistinctly. —*Caus.* or 10. U. To manifest, unfold; मुदमंचय Git. 10. With **अप** to put away, drive away ; (intr.) to run away. –**आ** to bend. –**उत्** 1 to go up. –2 to rise, appear; उदंचन्मात्सर्य G. L. 6. –**उप** to draw or raise (water). –**नि** 1 to bend down; incline. –2 to diminish, pass away; न्यंचति वयसि प्रथमे Bv. 2. 47. –**परा** to turn or go back; याताश्चेन्न परांचंति द्विरदानां रदा इव Bv. 1. 65. –**परि** to cause to revolve, whirl, twist. –**वि** to draw or bend as under; to extend, stretch out. –**सं** to crowd or drive together, to bend together.

अंचलः–लं 1 The border or end (of a garment), skirt or hem (Mar. पदर); क्षीणांचलमिव पीनस्तनजघनायाः Udb. 2 Corner or outer angle (as of the eye) दृगंचलैः पश्यति केवलं मनाक् *ibid.*

अंचित *p. p.* 1 (*a*) Curved, bent; R. 18. 58. (*b*) Arched and handsome (as eyebrows); °आक्षिपक्ष्मन् R. 5. 76; crisped; curled (as hair). 2. Honoured, adorned; graced; graceful; handsome; गतेषु लीलांचितविक्रमेषु Ku. 1. 34; °ताभ्यां गताभ्यां R. 2. 18, 9. 24. 3 Sewn or woven, arranged; अर्धांचिता सत्वरमुत्थितायाः (रशना) R. 7. 10 half strung or woven. –Comp. –**भ्रूः** a woman having arched or handsome eyebrows.

अंज् 7 P. (rarely A.) (अनक्ति or अंक्ते, अक्त) 1 To anoint, smear with, bedaub. 2 To make clear, represent, characterize. 3 To go. 4 To shine. 5 To honour, celebrate. 6 To decorate. —*Caus.* 1 To smear with. 2 To speak or shine. –With **अधि** to equip, furnish. –**अभि** 1 to anoint, smear with –2 to pollute, defile. –**अभिवि** to reveal, manifest. –**आ** 1 to anoint. –2 to smooth, prepare. –3 to honour. –**वि** To reveal, manifest, show; अकिंचनत्वं मखजं व्यनक्ति R. 5. 16, Si. 1. 26.

अंजनः N. of the guardian elephant (of the west or s. w.)—**नं** 1 Anointing, smearing with; mixing. 2 Unfolding, manifesting. 3 Collyrium or black pigment used to paint the eyelashes; विलोचनं दक्षिणमंजनेन संभाव्य R. 7. 8; अमृत° U. 4. 19; Mk. 1. 34; (fig. also) अज्ञानांधस्य लोकस्य ज्ञानांजनशलाकया । चक्षुरुन्मीलितं येन तस्मै पाणिनये नमः ॥ Sik. 45; cf. दारिद्र्यं परमांजनं. 4 Paint; a cosmetic ointment. 5 Ink. 6 Fire. 7 Night. 8 (नं–ना) (Rhet.) A suggested meaning; also the process by which such meaning is suggested ; the use of a a word of several meanings in a special sense determined by the context; cf. अनेकार्थस्य शब्दस्य वाचकत्वे नियंत्रिते । संयोगाद्यैरवाच्यार्थधीकृद्व्यापृतिरंजनं ॥ K. P. 2, see व्यंजना also. –Comp.–**अंभस्** *n.* eyewater.–**शलाका** a stick or pencil for the application of collyrium.

अंजना 1 N. of the female elephant of the north. 2 N. of the mother of Mâruti or Hanûmat.

अंजलिः 1 A cavity formed by folding and joining the open hands together, the hollow of the hands ; hence, a cavity-ful of any thing; सुपूरो मूषिकांजलिः Pt. 1. 25; प्रकीर्णः पुष्पाणां हरिचरणयोरंजलिरयं Ve. 1. 1 a cavity-ful of flowers; so जलस्यांजलयो दश Y. 3. 105, 10 cavity-fuls or libations of water; श्रवणांजलिपुटपेयं Ve. 1. 4; अंजलिं रच्, बंध्, कृ or आधा fold the hands together and raise them to the head in supplication or salutation. 2 Hence, a mark of respect or salutation; R. 11. 78. 3 A measure of corn =कुडव.–Comp. –**कर्मन्** *n.* folding the hands, respectful salutation. –**कारिका** an earthen doll. –**पुटः–टं** the cavity formed by joining the hands together ; hollowed palms of the hand.

अंजलिका A small mouse.

अंजस *a.* (**सी** *f.*) Not crooked, straight; honest, upright.

अंजसा *adv.* 1 Straight on. 2 Truly, properly, rightly ; विग्रहं शठ पलायनच्छलान्यंजसा R. 19. 31. 3 Soon, quickly, instantly.

अंजिष्ठः–ष्णुः The sun.

अंजीरः–रं A species of the fig-tree and its fruit.

अट् 1 P. (rarely A.) (अटति, अटित) To wander or roam about (with loc.); roam over (sometimes with acc.); भो बटो भिक्षामट Sk. go to beg alms ; आट नैकटिकाश्रमान् Bk. 4. 12. –*freq.* अटाट्यते to wander about habitually, as a religious mendicant.

अट *a.* wandering (in comp.).

अटनं Wandering, roaming ; भिक्षा°, रात्रि° &c.

अटनिः–नी *f.* The notched extremity of a bow ; निन्यतुः स्थलनिवेशिताटनी लीलयैव धनुषी अधिज्यतां R. 11. 14.

अटा The habit of roaming about (as a religious mendicant) so अट्या, अटाट्या.

अटरूः–रूषः N. of a very useful medicinal plant (Mar. अडुळसा).

अटविः–वी *f.* A forest, wood; आहिंड्यते अटव्या अटवीं S. 2.

अटविकः A forester=आटविकः q. v.

अट्ट 1 A. 1 To kill. 2 To transgress, go beyond (fig. also).—*Caus.* 1 To lesson, diminish. 2 To despise, contemn.

अट्ट *a.* 1 High, loud. 2 Frequent, constant. 3 Dried, dry. —**ट्टं–ट्टः** An apartment on the roof or upper story. 2 A turret, buttress, tower; नरेंद्रमार्गाट्ट इव R. 6. 67. 3 A market-place, market. 4 A palace, palatial building.—**ट्टं** Food, boiled rice: अट्टशूला जनपदाः Mb. (अट्टं अन्नं शूलं विक्रेयं येषां ते Nilakantha).–Comp.–**अट्टहासः** very loud laughter.–**हासः–हसितं,–हास्यं** a loud or boisterous laughter, a horse-laugh, usually of Siva; त्र्यंबकस्य Me. 58. –**हासिन्** *m.* 1 N. of Siva. –2 one who laughs very loudly.

अट्टकः An apartment on the roof of a house; palace also.

अट्टालः–लकः An apartment on the roof, an upper story; a palace.

अट्टालिका A palace, lofty mansion. -COMP.-**कारः** a mason, a bricklayer (one who builds royal mansions.)

अड्डनं A shield.

अण् 1 P. 1 To sound. 2 (4 A.) To breathe, live (for अन्).

अण (न) क *a.* Very small, contemptible, insignificant, wretched; oft. in com. in the sense of deterioration or contempt ; °कुलालः Sk. a contemptible potter.

अणिः *m.*, **णी** 1 The point of a needle. 2 A linch-pin, the pin or bolt at the end of the pole of a carriage. 3 A limit.

अणिमन् *m.*, **अणुता-त्वं** 1 Minuteness. 2 Atomic nature. 3 The superhuman power of becoming as small as an atom, one of the 8 powers or siddhis of *S*iva.

अणु *a.* (णु-ण्वी *f.*) Minute, fine, small, little; atomic; अणोरणीयान् Bg. 8. 9. —**णुः** 1 An atom; अणुं पर्वतीकृ Bh. 2. 78 to magnify; cf. also 'To make mountains of molehills.' 2 An atom of time. 3 N. of *S*iva. -COMP.-**भा** lightning.-**रेणुः** atomic dust. -**वादः** the doctrine of atoms, atomic theory.

अणुक *a.* 1 Very small, atomic. 2 Subtle, too fine. 3 Acute.

अणीयस्, अणिष्ठ *a.* Smaller, smallest, very small; अणोरणीयांसं Bg. 8. 9.

अंडः-डं 1 The testicles. 2 The scrotum. 3 An egg; oft. used with reference to the world as having sprung from the primordial egg of Brahmâ. 4 The musk bag. 5 Semen virile. 6 N. of *S*iva. -COMP. -**आकर्षणं** castration. -**आकार, -आकृति** *a.* egg-shaped, oval, elliptical. (-**रः-तिः**) an ellipse. -**कोशः-षः-षकः** the scrotum.-**ज** *a.* born from an egg. (-**जः**) 1 a bird, oviparous being; Ku. 3. 42. -2 a fish. -3 a snake. -4 a lizard. -5 Brahmâ. (-**जा**) musk. -**धरः** N. of *S*iva. -**वर्धनं, -वृद्धिः** *f.* swelling of the scrotum. -**सू** *a.* oviparous.

अंडकः The scrotum. —**कं** A small egg ; जगदंडकैकतरखंडमिव *S*i. 9. 9.

अंडालुः A fish.

अंडीरः A full-grown or full-developed man, a strong or powerful person.

अत् 1 P. (अतति, अत्त-अतित) 1 To go, walk; wander, to go constantly. 2 To obtain (mostly Ved.). 3 To bind.

अतनं Going, wandering. —**नः** A wanderer, a passer-by.

अतट *a.* Precipitate, steep. —**टः** A precipice, a steep crag.

अतथा *ind.* Not so ; °उचित *a.* not deserving that, not used to such things.

अतदर्हं *ind.* Unjustly, undeservedly.

अतद्गुणः (Rhet.) The 'non-borrower,' N. of a figure of speech, in which the thing in question does not assume the quality of another though there is a reason for it; K. P. 10.

अतंत्र *a.* (**त्री** *f.*) 1 Having no ropes or musical strings. 2 Unrestrained. 3 Not necessarily binding ; not being the object of the rule under consideration ; ह्रस्वग्रहणमतंत्रं Sk. 4 Without formulas or empirical actions.

अतंद्र-द्रित-न्द्र-ल *a.* Alert, unwearied, careful, vigilant ; अतंद्रिता सा स्वयमेव वृक्षकान् Ku. 5. 14 ; R. 17. 39.

अतपस्-स्क One who neglects his religious austerities.

अतर्क *a.* Illogical, void of reasoning. —**र्कः** 1 Absence of argument or reasoning, bad logic. 2 An illogical reasoner.

अतर्कित *a.* Unthought of, unexpected. —**तं** *adv.* Unexpectedly. -COMP. -**आगत, -उपपन्न** *a.* occurring or befalling unexpectedly, quite accidental °उपपन्नं दर्शनं Ku. 6. 54.

अतल *a.* Bottomless. —**लं** N. of a पाताल or lower region. —**लः** N. of *S*iva. -COMP. -**स्पृश्, स्पर्श** *a.* bottomless, very deep, unfathomable.

अतस् *ind.* 1 Than this ; from this (generally having a comparative force); किमु परमतो नर्तयसि मां Bh. 3. 6. 2 From this or that cause, hence, so, therefore (corr. to यत्, यस्मात् or हि, expressed or understood); R. 2. 43, 3. 50; Ku. 2. 5. 3 Hence, from this place ; henceforth (of time or place) ; (-परं, -ऊर्ध्वं), afterwards. -COMP. -**अर्थं-निमित्तं** on this account, hence, for this reason. -**एव** for this very reason.-**ऊर्ध्वं** henceforth ; afterwards. -**परं** (*a*) further on, any longer (with abl.) ; hereafter. (*b*) beyond this, further than this ; भाग्यायत्तमतःपरं *S*. 4. 16.

अतसः 1 Wind, air. 2 The soul. 3 A garment made of the fibre of flax (°सं generally).

अतसी 1 Common flax. 2 Hemp. 3 Linseed.

अति *ind.* 1 A prefix used with adjectives and adverbs, meaning 'very,' 'too' 'exceedingly,' 'excessively,' and showing उत्कर्ष; नातिदूरे not very far from; also with verbs or verbal forms ; स्वभावो ह्यतिरिच्यते &c. 2 (With verbs) Over, beyond; अति-इ go beyond, over-step; so °क्रम्, °चर्, °वह् &c. In this case अति is regarded as a preposition (उपसर्ग). 3 (*a*) (With nouns or pronouns) beyond, surpassing, superior to, eminent, distinguished, higher, above, (used with acc. as a कर्मप्रवचनीय, or as first member of Bah. or Tat. Comp. ; in which last case it has usually the sense of eminence or higher degree ; अतिगो, °गार्ग्यः,=प्रशस्ता गौः, शोभनो गार्ग्यः ; °राजन् an excellent king; or the sense of अतिक्रांत must be understood with the latter member which will then stand in the accusative case; अतिमर्त्यः=मर्त्यमतिक्रांतः; °मालः=अतिक्रांतो मालां; so अतिकाय, °केशर, q. v.); अति देवान् कृष्णः Sk. (b) (With nouns derived from roots) Extravagant, exaggerated, excessive, *e. g.* °आदरः excessive regard; °आशा extravagent hope; so °भयं, °तृष्णा, °आनंदः &c. &c. (*c*) Unfit, improper, in the sense of असंप्रति or क्षेप 'censure' ; अतिनिद्रं=निद्रा संप्रति न युज्यते Sk.

अतिकथा 1 An exaggerated tale. 2 Idle or meaningless talk.

अतिकर्षणं Afflicting very much, excessive exertion.

अतिकश *a.* Past the whip, unmanageable as a horse.

अतिकाय *a.* Of an extraordinary size, gigantic.

अतिकृच्छ्र *a.* Very difficult.—**च्छ्रं -च्छ्रः** Extraordinary hardship; a kind of severe penance to be finished in 12 nights; Ms. 11. 213-4.

अतिक्रमः 1 Act of overstepping, going beyond &c. 2 Breach of decorum or duty; transgression, violation; trespass; disrespect, injury, opposition; ब्राह्मण° त्यागो भवतामेव भूतये Mv. 2. 10. 3 Lapse, passing away (of time); अनेकसंवत्सरातिक्रमेऽपि U. 4. 4. Overcoming, surpassing; mostly with दुर् ; स्वजातिर्दुरतिक्रमा. 5 Neglect, omission, disregard. 6 A vigorous attack. 7 Excess. 8 Misapplication. 9 Imposition.

अतिक्रमणं Overstepping, spending of time, excess; fault, offence.

अतिक्रमणीय *pot. p.* To be transgressed, violated, neglected or avoided; ° यं मे सुहृद्वाक्यं *S*. 2, 3, 6,7.

अतिक्रांत *p. p.* Exceeded, surpassed, gone beyond &c.; सोऽतिक्रांतः श्रवणाविषयं Me. 103; past, gone by; former. -**तं** A past thing, a thing of the past, the past.

अतिखट्व *a.* Without a bedstead, able to dispense with a bedstead.

अतिग *a.* (in comp.) Exceeding, transcending, excelling; सर्वलोक° Mu. 1. 2; किमौषधपथातिगैरुपहतो महाव्याधिभिः Mu. 6 by diseases defying the powers of medicine.

अतिगंध *a.* Having an excessive or overpowering smell.—**धः** Sulphur.

अतिगव *a.* 1 Very foolish, quite stupid. 2 Indescribable.

अतिगुण *a.* 1 Having excellent or superior qualities. 2 Devoid of merits, worthless.-**णः** Excellent merits.

अतिगो *f.* An excellent cow.

अतिग्रह *a.* Incomprehensible.—**हः, ग्राहः** 1 Object of an apprehensive organ, such as स्पर्श 'touch' the object of त्वच्, रस of जिह्वा &c. 2 Right knowledge. 3 Act of overtaking, surpassing &c.

अतिचमू *a.* Victorious over armies.

अतिचर *a.* Very changeable, transient.—**रा** A lotus plant (पद्मिनी, स्थलपद्मिनी or पद्मचारिणीलता).

अतिचरणं Excessive practice, over doing

अतिचारः 1 Transgression. 2 Excelling. 3 Overtaking &c. 4 Accelerated motion of planets; passage from one zodiacal sign to another.

अतिच्छत्र-त्रा,-च्छत्रका A mush-room, anise.

अतिजगत *a.* Not tenanted or inhabited.

अतिजन *a.* Superior to his parentage.

अतिडीनं Extraordinary flight (of birds.).

अतितरां,-अतितमां *ind.* 1 More, higher (abl.). 2 Exceedingly, very much; excessive, great.

अतितृष्णा Rapacity, excessive greed or desire; °ष्णा न कर्तव्या Pt. 5 one should not to be too greedy.

अतिथिः (*lit.* a 'travelier'; according to Manu एकरात्रं तु निवसन्नतिथिर्ब्राह्मणः स्मृतः । अनित्यं हि स्थितो यस्मात्तस्मादतिथिरुच्यते 3. 102) A guest (fig. also); अतिथिनेव निवेदितं *S.* 4; कुसुमलताप्रियातिथे *S.* 6; dear or welcome guest. –COMP. –**क्रिया,** –**पूजा,** –**सत्कारः,** –**सत्क्रिया,** –**सेवा** hospitable reception of guests, rite of hospitality, hospitality, attention to the guests. –**धर्मः** title or claim to hospitality; hospitality due to guests.

अतिदानं Munificence, liberality; अतिदाने बलिर्बद्धः Chân. 50.

अतिदेशः 1 Transfer, making over, assigning. 2 (Gram.) Extended application, application by analogy, transference of one attribute to another; अतिदेशो नाम इतरधर्मस्य इतरस्मिन् प्रयोगाय आदेशः (मीमांसा); or अन्यत्रैव प्रणीतायाः कृत्स्नाया धर्मसंहतेः । अन्यत्र कार्यतः प्राप्तिरतिदेशः स उच्यते ॥ गोसदृशो गवयः is an instance of रूपातिदेश or analogy.

अतिद्वय *a.* Surpassing the two (बृहत्कथा and वासवदत्ता), or having no second or equal, incomparable, matchless; धिया निबद्धेयमतिद्वयी कथा K. 5.

अतिधन्वन् *m.* An unrivalled archer or warrior.

अतिनिद्रा Excessive sleeping. —**द्र** *a.* 1 Given to excessive sleep. 2 Without sleep, sleepless. —**द्रं** *ind.* Past sleeping time.

अतिनौ-नु *a.* Disembarked, landed.

अतिपंचा A girl past five.

अतिपतनं Flying past or beyond; omission, neglect, transgressing; exceeding, going beyond due bounds.

अतिपत्तिः *f.* 1 Going beyond, passing, lapse. 2 Non-performance, failure.

अतिपत्रः The teak tree.

अतिपथिन् *m.* A better road than common, a good road.

अतिपर *a.* One who has vanquished his enemies. —**रः** A great or superior enemy.

अतिपरिचयः Excessive familiarity or intimacy; Prov. अतिपरिचयादवज्ञा 'Familiarity breeds contempt.'

अतिपातः 1 Passing away, lapse (of time). 2 Neglect, omission; transgression; न चेदन्यकार्यातिपातः *S.* 1 if no other duty be neglected thereby; deviation from established laws or customs. 3 Befalling, occurrence. 4 Ill-treatment, or usage. 5 Opposition, contrariety.

अतिपातक A very heinous sin, incest.

अतिपातिन् *a.* Surpassing in speed, swifter than (in comp.); R. 3. 30.

अतिपात्य *pot. p.* To be delayed or put off; काममनतिपात्यं धर्मकार्यं देवस्य *S.* 5.

अतिप्रबंधः Great continuity; °प्रहिताम्रवृष्टिभिः R. 3. 58.

अतिप्रगे *ind.* Very early in the morning, in the early dawn Ms. 4. 62.

अतिप्रश्नः A question about transcendental truths; a vexatious or extravagant question *e. g.* Vâlâki's question to Yâjñavalkya about Brahma in बृहदारण्यकोपनिषद्.

अतिप्रसंगः-, ऽसक्तिः *f.* 1 Excessive attachment. 2 Over-rudeness. 3 Extraordinary or unwarrantable stretch of a (grammatical) rule or principle; =अतिव्याप्तिः q. v. 4 A very close contact. 5 Prolixity; अलमतिप्रसंगेन Mu. 1.

अतिप्रौढा A girl who has attained a marriageable age, a grown-up girl.

अतिबल *a.* Very strong or powerful. —**लः** An eminent or matchless warrior.—**लं** Great strength or power. —**ला** N. of a powerful charm or lore taught by Visvâmitra to Râma.

अतिबाला A cow two years old.

अतिभ (भा) रः Excessive burden, great load; सा मुक्तकंठं व्यसनातिभारात् चक्रंद R. 14. 68 through excessive grief.—COMP.—**गः** mule.

अतिभवः Surpassing, defeating, conquering.

अतिभावः Superiority.

अतिभीः *f.* Lightning; flash of Indra's thunderbolt.

अतिभूमिः *f.* 1. Excess, culmination, highest pitch; •मिं गम्, या to go to excess, to reach the climax; तत्र सर्वलोकस्य•मिं गतः प्रवादः Mâl. 7 noised abroad; *Si.* 9. 78, 10. 80. 2 Boldness, impropriety, violation of due limits (अमर्यादा); *Si.* 8. 20. 3 Eminence, superiority.

अतिमतिः *f.*-**मानः** Haughtiness, very great pride; अतिमाने च कौरवाः Chân. 50.

अतिमर्त्य-मानुष *a.* Superhuman.

अतिमात्र *a.* Exceeding the proper measure, inordinate, excessive; •दुःसहानि *S.* 4. 3 quite insupportable; मुनिव्रतैस्त्वामतिमात्रकर्शितां Ku. 5. 48.—**त्रं-मात्रशः** *ind.* Beyond measure, inordinately, excessively.

अतिमाय *a.* Finally liberated, emancipated from the Mâyâ or illusion of the world.

अतिमुक्त *a.* 1 Finally emancipated. 2 Barren. 3 Surpassing (a necklace of) pearls.—**क्तः-क्तकः** A kind of creeper (माधवी Mar. कुसरी or कस्तुरमोगरा) represented as twisting itself round the mango-tree and as the beloved of that tree.

अतिमुक्तिः *f.*-**मोक्षः** Final liberation (from death).

अतिरंहस् *a.* Very fleet or swift; सारंगेणातिरंहसा *S.* 1. 5.

अतिरथः An unrivalled warrior fighting from his car (अमितान् योधयेद्यस्तु संप्रोक्तोऽतिरथस्तु सः).

अतिरभसः Great speed, precipitateness, rashness.

अतिराजन् *m.* 1 An extraordinary or excellent king. 2 One who surpasses a king.

अतिरात्रः 1 An optional part of the Jyotishṭoma sacrifice. 2 Dead of night.

अतिरिक्त *a.* 1 Surpassed. 2 Redundant. 3 Excessive. 4 Unequalled; elevated.

अति (ती) रेकः 1 Excess, exuberance, excellence, eminence. 2 Redundancy, surplus, superfluity. 3 Difference.

अतिरुच् *m.* The knee.—**क्** *f.* A very beautiful woman.

अति- रो-लो-मश *a.* Very hairy, shaggy.-**शः** 1 A wild goat. 2 A large monkey.

अतिलंघनं 1 Excessive fasting. 2 Transgression.

अतिलंघिन् *a.* Erring, committing mistakes.

अतिवयस् *a.* Very old, aged, advanced in years.

अतिवर्णाश्रमिन् *m.* One who is beyond castes and orders.

अतिवर्तनं A pardonable offence or misdemeanour; exemption from punishment; ten cases are mentioned in Ms. 8. 290.

अतिवर्तिन् *a.* Crossing; surpassing, excelling; transgressing, violating.

अतिवादः *a.* Very harsh, abusive or insulting language, reproof; अतिवादांस्तितिक्षेत Ms. 6. 47.

अतिवादिन् *a.* Talkative; very eloquent.

अतिवाहनं 1 Passing, spending. 2 Excessive toiling or enduring; too heavy burden. 3 Despatching, sending away, ridding oneself of.

अतिविकट *a.* Very fierce.—**टः** A vicious elephant.

अतिविषा N. of a poisonous yet highly medicinal plant (Mar. अतिविष or अतिविख.)

अतिविस्तरः Prolixity, diffuseness.

अतिवृत्तिः *f.* Surpassing; violation, hyperbole.

अतिवृष्टिः *f.* Excessive or heavy rain, one of the six calamities of the season. See ईति.

अतिवेल *a.* Excessive, extravagant; boundless.—**लं** *adv.* 1 Excessively. 2 Out of season, unseasonably.

अतिव्याप्तिः *f.* 1 An unwarrantable stretch of a rule or principle. 2 Including what is not intended to be included in a proposition; (in Nyâya) unwarranted extension of a definition to things not intended to be defined by it, so that it includes such things as ought not to fall under it; one of the three faults to which a definition is open.

अतिशयः 1 Excess, pre-eminence, excellence ; वीर्य° R. 3. 62 ; तस्मिन् विधानातिशये विधातुः R. 6. 11. 2 Superiority (in quality, rank, quantity &c.); oft. in comp. with adjectives in the sense of 'excessively'; आसीदातिशयप्रेक्ष्यः R. 17. 25. —*a.* Superior, pre-eminent ; excessive, very great, abundant. -Comp. -**उक्तिः** *f.* 1 exaggerated or hyperbolical language, extreme assertion. -2 a figure of speech, (corr. to hyperbole) said to be of 5 kinds in S. D., but of 4 in K. P.

अतिशयन *a.* Surpassing (in comp.); great, eminent; abundant. —**नं** Excess; abundance, superfluity.

अतिशयालु *a.* Tending to excel or surpass.

अतिशयिन् *a.* 1. Superior, excellent; pre-eminent ; इदमुत्तममतिशयिनि व्यंग्ये वाच्याद् ध्वनिर्बुधैः कथितः K. P. 1 ; V. 5. 21. 2 Excessive, abundant.

अतिशायनं Excellence, superiority.

अतिशायिन् *a.* 1 Excelling, surpassing. 2 Excessive.

अतिशेषः Remainder ; remnant (as of time); a small remainder.

अतिश्रेयसिः A man superior to the most excellent woman.

अतिश्व *a.* 1 Surpassing in strength a dog (such as a boar &c.). 2 Worse than a dog.—**श्वा** Service.

अतिश्वन् *m.* An excellent dog.

अतिसक्तिः *f.* Close contact or proximity; great attachment.

अतिसंधानं Cheating, deception; परातिसंधान° S. 5. 25; trick, fraud.

अतिसरः *a.* 1 One who goes beyond or exceeds. 2 Leader.

अतिसर्गः 1 granting, giving; R. 10. 42. 2 Granting permission (to do what one likes कामचारानुज्ञा). 3 Dismissal, discharge.

अतिसर्जनं 1 Giving, granting; consigning; Ku. 4. 32. 2 Liberality, munificence. 3 Killing. 4 Separation.

अतिसर्व *a.* Transcending or superior to all, above all. —**र्वः** The Supreme Being; अतिसर्वाय शर्वाय Mugdha.

अति (ती) सारः Dysentery, violent straining at stool.

अति (ती) सारिन् *m.* The disease called अतिसार. —*a.*, **-अतिसारकिन्** Affected by, afflicted with, dysentery.

अतिस्नेहः Over-affection; °हः पापशंकी S. 4 is apt to suspect evil.

अतिस्पर्शः A term for semivowels and vowels.

अतीत *p. p.* 1 Gone beyond, crossed. 2 (Used actively) Exceeding, going beyond; past, gone by &c.; dead; संख्यामतीत or संख्यातीत innumerable.

अतींद्रिय *a.* Beyond the cognizance (reach) of the senses.—**यः** The Soul or Purusha (in Sânkhya phil.); the Supreme Soul. —**यं** 1 Pradhâna or Nature (in Sânkhya phil.). 2 The mind (in Vedânta).

अतीव *ind.* Exceedingly, excessively, very much, quite, too; °पीडित, °हृष्ट &c.

अतुल *a.* Unequalled, matchless, peerless, incomparable. —**लः** The sesamum seed and plant (तिलकवृक्ष).

अतुल्य *a.* Unequalled &c.

अतुषार *a.* Not cold. -Comp. -**करः** the Sun ; so °अतुहिनकर, °रश्मि, °धामन्, °रुचि &c.

अतृण्या A small quantity of grass.

अतेजस् *a.* 1 Not bright, dim. 2 Weak, feeble. 3 Insignificant ; so **अतेजस्क, अतेजस्विन्.** —**स्** *m.* Dimness, shadow, darkness.

अत्ता 1 A mother. 2 An elder sister. 3 A mother-in-law.

अत्तिः *f.*, **अत्तिका** An elder sister &c.

अत्नः -त्नुः 1 Wind. 2 The sun.

अत्यग्निः Morbidly rapid digestion.

अत्यग्निष्टोमः The optional second part of the Jyotishṭoma sacrifice.

अत्यंकुश *a.* Past the goad, uncontrollable, unmanageable, as an elephant.

अत्यंत *a.* 1 Excessive, much, very great or strong ; °वैरं great enmity ; so °मैत्री. 2 Complete, perfect, absolute. 3 Endless, perpetual, everlasting ; किं वा तवात्यंतवियोगमोघे हतजीविते R. 14. 65 ; कस्यात्यंतं सुखमुपनतं Me. 109. —**तं** *ind.* 1 Excessively, very much. 2 For ever, to the end (of life), through life. -Comp. -**अभावः** absolute or complete non-existence, absolute non-entity. -**गत** *a.* gone or departed for ever, gone never to return ; कथमत्यंतगता न मां दहेः R. 8. 56. -**गामिन्** *a.* 1 going or walking very much, going too fast or quickly. -2 excessive, much. -**वासिन्** *m.* one who constantly stays with his preceptor, as a student. -**संयोगः** 1 close proximity, uninterrupted continuity; कालाध्वनोरत्यंतसंयोगे. -2 inseparable co-existence.

अत्यंतिक *a.* 1 Going too much or too fast. 2 Very near. 3 Not near, distant. —**कं** Close proximity, immediate neighbourhood or being in close proximity.

अत्यंतीन *a.* Going or walking too much, going too fast ; लक्ष्मीं परंपरीणां त्वमत्यंतीनत्वमुन्नय Bk.

अत्ययः 1 Passing away, lapse; काल°. 2 End, conclusion, termination ; absence, disappearance. 3 Death, destruction. 4 Danger, injury, evil ; प्राणात्यये च संप्राप्ते Y. 1. 179. 5 Distress 6 Guilt, offence; transgression. 7 Attack, assault.

अत्ययिक=आत्ययिक q. v.

अत्ययित *a.* 1 Exceeded, surpassed. 2 Violated, outraged.

अत्ययिन् *a.* Exceeding, surpassing.

अत्यर्थ *a.* Excessive ; very great, exorbitant. —**र्थं** *adv.* Very much, exceedingly, excessively.

अत्यह्न *a.* Exceeding a day in duration.

अत्याकारः 1 Contempt, blame, censure ; श्लाघात्याकारतदंवेतेषु P. V. 1. 134. 2 Bigness of person, a very large body.

अत्याचार *a.* Deviating from established usages or customs, negligent. —**रः** Performance of works not sanctioned by usage ; irreligious conduct.

अत्यादित्य *a.* Surpassing the (lustre of the) sun; अत्यादित्यं हुतवहमुखे संभृतं तद्धि तेजः Me. 43.

अत्यानंदा Morbid indifference to the pleasures of sexual union.

अत्यायः 1 Transgression, violation. 2 Excess.

अत्यारूढ *a.* Grown to excess.—**ढं,-ढिः** *f.* A very high position, great elevation or rise.

अत्याश्रमः 1 The highest order of life, संन्यास. 2 An ascetic of this order संन्यासिन्.

अत्याहितं 1 A great calamity, danger, misfortune, mishap, accident; न किमप्यत्याहितं S. 1; oft. as an exclamation, 'Ah, me !' 'alas ! alas ! '. 2 A rash or daring deed; पांडुपुत्रैर्न किमप्यत्याहितमाचेष्टितं भवेत् Ve. 2.

अत्युक्तिः *f.* Exaggeration, hyperbole, over-drawn or coloured description ; अत्युक्तौ न यदि प्रकुप्यसि मृषावादं च नो मन्यसे Vdb. See अतिशयोक्ति also.

अत्युपध *a.* Trustworthy, tried.

अत्यूहः 1 Close or deep meditation or thinking; earnest reasoning. 2 A gallinule.

अत्र *ind.* 1 In this place, here ; अपि सन्निहितोऽत्र कुलपतिः S. 1. 2 In this respect, matter, or case; as to this.—COMP.-अंतरे *adv.* in the meanwhile, meantime *S.* 3. 11. -भवत् (*m.* भवान्) an honorific epithet meaning 'worthy', 'revered', 'honourable', 'your or his honour', and referring to a person that is present or near the speaker. (opp. तत्रभवत्); °भवती *f.* 'your or her lady-ship' (पूज्य तत्रभवानत्रभवांश्च भगवानपि); अत्रभवान् प्रकृतिमापन्नः *S.* 2; वृक्षसेचनादेव परिश्रांतामत्रभवतीं लक्षये *S.* 1.

अत्रत्य *a.* 1 Belonging to, or connected with, this place. 2 Produced or found here, of this place; local.

अत्रप *a.* Shameless, impudent, immodest.

अत्रिः (properly अत्त्रि) N. of a celebrated sage and author of many Vedic hymns.-COMP.—जः, -जातः, -दृग्जः, -नेत्रप्रसूतः -प्रभवः,-भवः the moon; cf. अथ नयनसमुत्थं ज्योतिरत्रेरिव द्यौः R. 2. 75.

अथ *ind.* 1 A particle used at the beginning (of works) mostly as a sign of auspiciousness, and translated by 'here', 'now' (begins) (मंगल, आरंभ, अधिकार). (Properly speaking), 'auspiciousness' or मंगल is not the sense of अथ, but the very utterance or hearing of the word is considered to be indicative of auspiciousness, as the word is supposed to have emanated from the throat of Brahmâ: ओंकारश्चाथशब्दश्च द्वावेतौ ब्रह्मणः पुरा । कंठं भित्त्वा विनिर्यातौ तेन मांगलिकावुभौ ॥ and therefore we find in Sankara Bhâshya अर्थांतरप्र युक्तः अथशब्दः श्रुत्या मंगलमारचयति ; अथ निर्वचनं ; अथ योगानुशासनं (usually followed by इति at the end, इति प्रथमोंऽकः here ends &c.). 2 Then, afterwards ; अथ प्रजानामधिपः प्रभाते वनाय धेनुं मुमोच R. 2. 1 ; often as a correlative of यदि or चेत्. 3 If, supposing, now if, in case, but if; अथ कौतुकमावेदयामि K. 144 ; अथ मरणमवश्यमेव जंतोः किमिति मुधा मलिनं यशः कुरुध्वे Ve. 3. 4. 4 And, so also, as also, likewise ; भीमोऽथार्जुनः G. M. 5 Used in asking or introducing questions (प्रश्न), oft. with the interrogative word itself ; अथ सा तत्रभवती किमाख्यस्य राजर्षेः पत्नी *S.* 7. 6 Totality, entirety; अथ धर्मं व्याख्यास्यामः G. M. we shall explain the whole धर्म (धर्म in all its details). 7 Doubt, uncertainty ; शब्दो नित्योऽथानित्यः G. M. -COMP. -अपि moreover, and again &c. (=अथ in most cases). -किं what else, yes, exactly so, quite so, certainly. -च moreover, and likewise. -वा 1 or. -2 or rather, or why, or perhaps, modifying a previous statement; गमिष्याम्युपहास्यतां ... अथवा कृतवाग्द्वारे वंशेऽस्मिन् R. 1. 3-4 ; अथवा मृदु वस्तु हिंसितुं S. 45 ; दीर्घे किं न सहस्रधाहमथवा रामेण किं दुष्करं U. 6. 40.

अथर्वन् *m.* 1 A priest who has to worship fire and Soma. 2 A Brâhmana. -(pl.) Descendants of Atharvan; hymns of this Veda.—र्वः-र्वं *m. n.*, °वेदः The Atharvaveda, regarded as the fourth Veda, containing many forms of imprecations for the destruction of enemies, and also a great number of prayers for safety and averting mishaps, evils, sins or calamities, and a number of hymns, as in the other Vedas, addressed to the gods with prayers to be used at religious and solemn rites.-COMP.-निधिः, विद् *m.* receptacle of the (knowledge of) Atharvaveda, or conversant with it; गुरुणाऽथर्वविदा कृतक्रियः R. 8. 4, 1. 59.

अथर्वणिः A Brâhmana versed in this Veda; or skilled in the performance of the rites enjoined by it.

अथर्वाणं Ritual of the Atharvaveda.

अथवा See under अथ.

अथो=अथ q. v.

अद् 2 P. (अत्ति, अन्न-जग्ध) 1 To eat, devour. 2 To destroy. 3= अंद् q. v. —*Caus.* To feed with. —*Desid.* जिघत्सति To wish to eat.

अद्-द *a.* (at the end of comp.) Eating, devouring.

अदंष्ट्र *a.* Toothless. —ष्ट्रः A serpent without teeth; one whose fangs have been taken out.

अदक्षिण *a.* 1 Not right, left. 2 Not bringing in Dakshinâ to the priests; without any gifts (as a sacrifice). 3 Simple, weak-minded, silly. 4 Not handy, skilful or clever; awkward. 5 Unfavourable.

अदंड्य *a.* 1 Not deserving punishment. 2 Exempt or free from punishment.

अदत् *a.* Toothless.

अदत्त *a.* 1 Not given. 2 Unjustly or improperly given. 3 Not given in marriage.—त्ता An unmarried girl. —त्तं A gift which is null and void. -COMP.-आदायिन् *a.* the receiver of such a gift; one who takes what has not been given away, such as a thief. -पूर्वा not affianced or betrothed before; अदत्तपूर्वेत्याशंक्यते Mâl. 4.

अदंत *a.* 1 Toothless. 2 Ending in अत् or अ.—तः A leech.

अदंत्य *a.* 1 Not dental. 2 Not fit for the teeth; injurious to them.

अदभ्र *a.* Not scanty, plentiful, copious.

अदर्शनं 1 Not seeing, non-vision; absence, not being seen. 2 (Gram.) Disappearance, elision, omission; अदर्शनं लोपः P. I. 1. 60.

अदस् *pron. a.* (असौ *m. f.*, अदः *n.*) That (referring to a person or thing, not present or near the speaker)' इदमस्तु सन्निकृष्टं समीपतरवर्ति चैतदो रूपम् । अदसस्तु विप्रकृष्टं तदिति परोक्षे विजानीयात् ॥ used also in the sense of 'this here, 'yonder.' It is often used in the sense of तत् as a correlative of यत्. But when it immediately follows the relative pronoun (योऽसौ, ये अमी &c.) it conveys the sense of प्रसिद्ध 'well-known,' 'celebrated,' see तद् also.

अदातृ *a.* 1 Not giving, miserly. 2 Not giving (a daughter) in marriage.

अदादि *a.* Having अद् at the head, a term used to mark roots of the second conjugation.

अदाय *a.* Not entitled to a share.

अदायाद *a.* 1 Not entitled to be an heir. 2 Destitute of heirs.

अदायिक *a.* (की *f.*) 1 That which is not claimed by an heir ; destitute of heirs ; अदायिकं धनं राजगामि Kâty. 2 Not relating to inheritance.

अदितिः *f.* 1 The earth. 2 The goddess Aditi, mother of the Adityas ; in mythology represented as the mother of gods. 3 Speech. 4 A cow. -COMP. -जः, -नंदनः a god, divine being.

अदुर्ग *a.* 1 Not inaccessible, not difficult of access. 2 Destitute of forts ; °विषयः an unfortified country.

अदूर *a.* Not distant, near (in time or space). —रं Proximity, vicinity ; वसन्नदूरे किल चंद्रमौलेः R. 6. 34 ; त्रिंशतोऽदूरे वर्तते इति अदूरत्रिंशाः Sk.; अदूरं,-रं,-रेण,-रतः, -रात् (with gen. or abl.) not far from, at no great distance from.

अदृश् *a.* Sightless, blind.

अदृष्ट *a.* 1 Invisible, not seen ; °पूर्व not seen before. 2 Not felt. 3 Unforeseen, not observed or thought of; unknown, unobserved. 4 Not permitted or sanctioned, illegal. —ष्टं 1 The invisible one. 2 Destiny, fate, luck (good or bad). 3 Virtue or vice as the eventual cause of pleasure or pain. 4 An unforeseen calamity or danger. (such as from fire, water &c.) -COMP. -अर्थ *a.* having a metaphysical or occult meaning, metaphysical. -कर्मन् *a.* not practical, inexperienced. -फल *a.* that of which the consequences are not yet visible. (-लं) the (future) result of good or bad actions.

अदृष्टिः *f.* 1 An evil or malicious eye, evil look. —*a.* Blind.

अदेय *a.* Not to be given ; what can not or ought not to be given away. —यं That which it is not right or necessary to give. Wife, sons, deposits, and a few other things belong to this class.

अदेव *a.* 1 Not god-like or divine. 2 Godless, impious, irreligious.—वः One who is not a god. -COMP. -मातृक *a.* not rained upon; (lit.) not having the god of rain as mother to suckle or water; वितन्वति क्षेममदेवमातृकाश्चिराय तस्मिन्कुरवश्चकासते Ki. 1. 17.

अदेशः 1 A wrong place. 2 A bad

country. –COMP. –कालः wrong place and time.–स्थ *a.* in the wrong place, out of place.

अदोष *a.* **1** Free from faults, vices, or defects &c.; innocent. **2** Free from the faults of composition, such as अश्लीलता, ग्राम्यता &c., see दोष ; अदोषौ शब्दार्थौ K. P. 1. अदोषं गुणवत् काव्यं Sar. K. 1.

अदोहः 1 The time when milking is not practicable. **2** Not milking.

अद्धा *ind.* **1** Truly, surely, certainly, indeed; R. 13. 65. **2** Manifestly, clearly ; व्यालाविधं च यतते परिरब्धुमद्धा Bv. 1. 95.

अद्भुत *a.* Wonderful, marvellous ; °कर्मन्, °गंध, °दर्शन, °रूप ; transcendental, supernatural.—तं **1** A wonder; a wonderful thing or occurence, a prodigy, miracle. **2** Surprise, astonishment, wonder (*m.*) also.—तः One of the 8 or 9 *Rasas*, the marvellous sentiment; see रस.–COMP.–सारः the wonderful resin (of the खदिर or Catechu plant).–स्वनः N. of *S*iva.

अद्मनिः Fire.

अद्मर *a.* Voracious, gluttonous.

अद्य *a.* Eatable.—द्यं Food, anything eatable.—*ind.* To-day, this day; अद्य त्वां त्वरयति दारुणः कृतांतः Mâl. 5. 25; °रात्रौ to-night, this night. –COMP.–अपि still, yet, even now, to this day; न° not yet ; गुरुः खेदं खिन्ने मयि भजति नाद्यापि कुरुषु Ve. 1. 11; (every one of the 50 stanzas of Ch. P. begins with अद्यापि). –अवधि 1 from to-day.–2 till to-day.–पूर्वं before, now.–प्रभृति *ind.* from today, this day forward; अद्यप्रभृत्यवनतांगि तवास्मि दासः Ku. 5. 86.–श्वीना *a.* a female near delivery. (आसन्नप्रसवा); अद्यश्वीनावष्टब्धे P.

अद्यतन *a.* (नी *f.*) **1** Pertaining or referring to, extending over, to-day. **2** Modern.—नः The current or this day; period of the current day; see अनद्यतन also. —नी (*scil.* वृत्तिः) A name given to the Aorist tense (=°भूतः).

अद्यतनीय=अद्यतन 1 Of to-day. **2** Modern.

अद्रव्यं A worthless thing, an object which is good for nothing ; नाद्रव्ये विहिता काचित्क्रिया फलवती भवेत् H. Pr. 43; a worthless or bad pupil or recipient of instruction.

अद्रिः 1 A mountain. **2** A stone. **3** A thunder-bolt. **4** A tree. **5** The sun. **6** A mass of clouds; a cloud. **7** A kind of measure. **8** The number 7.–COMP.–ईशः, –पतिः, –नाथः &c. 1 the lord of mountains, the Himâlaya.–2 N. of *S*iva (Lord of Kailâsa).–कीला the earth.–कन्या, –तनया, –सुता &c. Pârvatî.–जं red chalk.–तनया, –नंदिनी N. of Pârvatî. –द्विष्, –भिद्, *m.* the enemy or splitter of mountains, epithet of Indra.–द्रोणि–णी *f.* 1 a mountain valley.–2 a river taking its rise in a mountain. –पतिः –राजः &c. see °ईश.–शय्यः N. of *S*iva. –शृंगं, –सानु, mountain peak.–सारः ' the essence of mountains', iron.

अद्रोहः Absence of malice or ill-feeling ; moderation, mildness; Ms. 4. 2.

अद्वय *a.* **1** Not two. **2** Without a second, unique ; sole. —यः N. of Buddha. —यं Non-duality, unity, identity ; especially, the identity of Brahma and the universe, or of spirit and matter; the highest truth. –COMP. –वादिन्(=अद्वैत°), 1 one who propounds the identity of spirit and matter or of Brahma and the universe. –2 Buddha.

अद्वारं Not a door, any passage or entrance, which is not intended to serve as a regular door ; अद्वारेण न चातीयाद् ग्रामं वा वेश्म वा पुरं Ms. 4. 73.

अद्वितीय *a.* **1** Without a second, matchless, peerless ; न केवलं रूपे शिल्पेप्यद्वितिया मालविका M. 2. 2. Without a companion, alone. —यं Brahma.

अद्वैत *a.* **1** Not dual ; of one or uniform nature, equable, unchanging ; °तं सुखदुःखयोः U. 1. 39. **2** Matchless, peerless; sole, unique. –तं **1** Non-duality, identity ; especially that of Brahma with the universe or with the soul, or of soul and matter ; see अद्वय also. **2** The supreme or highest truth or Brahma itself. –COMP. –वादिन्= अद्वयवादिन् q. v. above ; a Vedântin.

अधम *a.* The lowest, vilest, meanest; very bad, or low, or vile (in quality, worth, position &c.) (opp. उत्तम). —म : An unblushing sensualist; वापीं स्नातुमितो गतासि न पुनस्तस्याधमस्यान्तिकं K. P. 1. —मा A bad mistress.–COMP. –अंगं the foot. –अर्धं lower half of the body (below the navel). –ऋणः, –ऋणिकः a debtor (opp. उत्तमर्णः).—भृतः, –भृतकः a porter, groom.

अधर *a.* **1** Lower, under, nether. **2** Low, mean, vile; lower in quality, inferior. **3** Silenced, worsted. —रः The nether (or sometimes the upper) lip; a lip in general; पक्वबिंबाधरोष्ठी Me. 82; पिबसि रतिसर्वस्वमधरं *S*. 1. 24. —रं **1** The lower part (of the body). **2** Address, speech (opp. उत्तर); sometimes used for reply also. –COMP. –उत्तर *a.* 1 higher and lower, worse and better; राज्ञः समक्षमेवावयोः °व्यक्तिर्भविष्यति M. 1.–2 sooner and later.–3 in a contrary way, topsy-turvy.–4 nearer and further. –ओष्ठः the lower lip. –कंठः the lower part of the neck. –पानं kissing, lit. drinking the lower lip. –मधु,–अमृतं the nectar of the lips. –स्वस्तिकं the nadir.

अधरस्मात्,-रतः,-स्तात्, -रात्,- तात्, -रेण *ind.* Below, beneath, in the lower regions.

अधरीकृ 8 U. To surpass, beat down, worst.

अधरीण *a.* **1** Lower. **2** Traduced, vilified, reproached.

अधरेद्युः *ind.* **1** On a previous day. **2** The day before yesterday.

अधर्मः 1 Unrighteousness, wickedness, injustice; अधर्मेण unjustly. **2** An unjust act; a guilty or wicked deed; sin; (धर्म and अधर्म are two of the twenty-four qualities mentioned in Nyâya, and they pertain only to the soul. They are the peculiar causes of pleasure and pain respectively. They are imperceptible, but inferred from reasoning and from transmigration). **3** N. of a Prajâpati or of an attendant of the sun. —र्मा Unrighteousness personified. —र्मं Devoid of attributes, an epithet of ब्रह्मन्. –COMP.–आत्मन्, –चारिन् *a.* wicked, sinful.

अधवा A widow.

अधस्, अधः *ind.* **1** Below, down; पतत्यधो धाम विसारि सर्वतः *S*i. 1. 2; in the lower region, to the infernal regions or hell; (according to the context अधः may have the sense of the nominative, °अंशुकं &c.; ablative, अधो वृक्षात् पतति; or locative, अधो गृहे शेते). **2** Beneath, under, used like a preposition with gen.; तरूणां° *S*. 1. 14; (when repeated) lower and lower, down and down; अधोऽधो गंगेयं पदमुपगता स्तोकं Bh. 2. 10; from under, just below (with acc.); नवानधोऽधो बृहतः पयोधरान् *S*i. 1. 4. –COMP.–अंशुकं the lower garment. –अक्षजः N. of Vishnu. –अधस् See above.–उपासनं sexual intercourse. –करः the lower part of the hand (करभ)–करणं excelling, defeating, degradation.–खननं undermining.–गतिः *f.*, गमनं, –पातः 1 a downward fall or motion, descent. –2 degradation, downfall. –गंतृ *m.* a mouse.–चरः a thief. –जिह्विका the uvula (Mar. पडजीभ). –दिश् *f.* the nadir; the southern direction. –दृष्टिः *f.* a downward look. –पातः=°गतिः q. v. above.–प्रस्तरः a seat of grass for persons in mourning to sit upon.–भागः 1 the lower part (of the body). –2 the lower part of anything.–भुवनं, लोकः the nether world, lower regions. –मुख, –वदन *a.* having the face downwards. –लंबः 1 a plummet. –2 a perpendicular. –वायुः breaking wind, flatulency. –स्वस्तिकं the nadir.

अधस्तन *a.* (नी *f.*) Lower, situated beneath.

अधस्तात् *adv.* or *prep.* Down, below, under, beneath, underneath &c. (with gen.), see अधः; धर्मेण गमनमूर्ध्वं गमनमधस्ताद्भवत्यधर्मेण Sânkhya K.

अधामार्गवः =अपामार्ग q. v.

अधारणक *a.* Not profitable; °कं

ममैतस्थानं Pt. 2.

अधि *ind*. 1 (As a prefix to verbs) Over, above; °रुह् to grow over or above; besides in addition (आधिक्य). 2 (As a separable adverb) Over, above. 3 (As a preposition) (with acc.) (*a*) Above, over, upon, in. (*b*) With reference to, concerning, on the subject of. (*c*) (With loc.) Over, above (showing lordship or sovereignty over something); अधि भुवि रामः 4 (as first member of Tatpurusha compounds) (*a*) Chief, supreme, principal; °देवता presiding deity. (*b*) Redundant, superfluous; °दन्तः=अध्यारूढः दन्तः; excessive; °अधिक्षेपः high censure.

अधिक *a*. 1 More, additional, greater. (In comp. with numerals), plus, greater by; अष्टाधिकं शतं 100 plus 8=108. 2 (*a*) Surpassing in quantity, more numerous, copious, excessive, abundant; in comp. or with instr. (*b*) Inordinate, grown, abounding in, full of; strong in; शिशुराधिकवयाः Ve. 3. 30 old, advanced in years; भवनेषु रसाधिकेषु पूर्वं *S*. 7. 20. 3 More, greater, stronger; ऊनं न सत्त्वेष्वधिको बबाधे R. 2. 14 the stronger animal did not prey on the weaker. 4 Eminent, uncommon, special, peculiar; ईज्याध्ययनदानानि वैशस्य क्षत्रियस्य च । प्रतिग्रहोऽधिको विप्रे याजनाध्यापने तथा ॥ Y. 1. 118; *S*. 7. 5 Redundant, superfluous; °अङ्ग having a redundant limb; नोद्वहेत्कपिलां कन्यां नाधिकांगीं न रोगिणीं Ms. 3. 8. —कं 1 Surplus, excess, more; लाभोऽधिकं फलं Ak. 2 Redundancy, superfluity. 3 A figure of speech equivalent to hyperbole.—*adv*. 1 More, in a greater degree; R. 4. 1; in comp.; इयमधिकमनोज्ञा *S*. 1. 20; °सुरभि Me. 21. 2 Exceedingly, too much. —COMP. —अंग *a*. (गी *f*.) having a redundant limb. -अर्थ *a*. exaggerated; °वचनं exaggeration, an exaggerated statement or assertion (whether of praise or of censure). -ऋद्धि *a*. abundant, prosperous; R. 19. 5. -तिथिः *f*., -दिनं-दिवसः an intercalated lunar day. -वाक्योक्तिः *f*. exaggeration, hyperbole.

अधिकरणं 1 Placing at the head of, appointing &c. 2 Relation, reference, connection. 3 (in gram.) Agreement, concord, goverment or grammatical relation. 4 A receptacle or subject, technically substratum. 5 Location, place, the sense of the locative case; आधारोऽधिकरणं P. 1. 4. 45. 6 A topic, subject; a complete argument treating of one subject; (according to the Mîmâmsakas a complete Adhikaraṇa consists of five members; विषयो विशयश्चैव पूर्वपक्षस्तथोत्तरं । निर्णयश्चेति सिद्धांतः शास्त्रेऽधिकरणं स्मृतम् ॥). 7 Court of justice, court, tribunal; स्वान्दोषान् कथयंति नाधिकरणे Mk. 9. 3. 8 A claim. 9 Supremacy. -COMP. -भोजकः a judge. -मंडपः court or hall of justice. -सिद्धांतः a conclusion which involves others.

अधिकरणिकः 1 A judge, magistrate; Mk. 9. 2 A government official.

अधिकर्मन् *n*. 1 A higher or superior act. 2 Superintendence. —*m*. One who is charged with superintendence. -COMP. -करः, कृत् a sort of servant, overseer of workmen.

अधिकर्मिकः The overseer of a market whose duty it is to recover toll or duties from the traders.

अधिकाम *a*. Of vehement desires, impassioned, lustful. —मः Strong desire.

अधिकारः 1 Superintendence, watching over. 2 duty, charge; power, post of authority; authority; द्वीपिनस्तांबूलाधिकारी दत्तः Pt. 1; स्वाधिकारात् प्रमत्तः Me. 1; अधिकारे मम पुत्रको नियुक्तः M. 5. 3 Sovereignty, government or administration, jurisdiction, rule. 4 Right, privilege, claim, title (as to wealth, property &c.); right of ownership or possession; आधिकारः फले स्वाम्यमधिकारी च तत्प्रभुः S. D. 296. 5 Prerogative (of a king). 6 A topic, paragraph or section; प्रायश्चित्त° Mit.; see अधिकरण. 7 (In gram.) A head or governing rule. -COMP. -विधिः determination or statement of qualifications to do particular acts. -स्थ,-आढ्य *a*. invested with office.

अधिकारिन्, अधिकारवत् *a*. 1 Possessed of authority, having power. 2 Entitled to, having a right to, सर्वे स्युरधिकारिणः. 3 Belonging to, owned by. 4 Fit for. —*m*. (री-वान्) 1 An official, officer; a functionary, superintendent, head, director, governor. 2 A rightful claimant, master, owner.

अधिकृत *a*. Authorised, appointed &c. —तः An officer, official, one in charge of any thing.

अधिकृतिः *f*. Right, privilege, ownership. See अधिकार.

अधिकृत्य *ind*. With reference to, regarding, concerning; ग्रीष्मसमयमधिकृत्य गीयतां *S*. 1.; शकुंतलामधिकृत्य ब्रवीमि *S*. 2.

अधिक्रमः,-क्रमणं An attack, invasion.

अधिक्षेपः 1 Abuse, insulting, insult; भवत्यधिक्षेप इवानुशासनं Ki. 1. 28. 2 Dismissal.

अधिगत *p. p.* 1 Acquired, obtained &c.; Bh. 2. 17. 2 Studied, learnt; किमित्येवं पृच्छस्यनधिगतरामायण इव U. 6. 30.

अधिगमः -मनं 1 Aquisition, obtaining. 2 Mastery, study, knowledge. 3 Mercantile return, profit; acquiring property; निध्यादेः प्राप्तिः Mit. or धनप्राप्तिः. 4 Acceptance. 5 Intercourse.

अधिगुण *a*. 1 Possessing superior qualities, worthy, meritorious; याच्ञा मोघा वरमधिगुणे नाधमे लब्धकामा Me. 6. 2 Well strung (as a bow).

अधिचरणं Act of walking over something.

अधिजननं Birth.

अधिजिह्वः A serpent. -ह्वा-जिह्विका 1 The uvula. 2 A sort of swelling of the tongue.

अधिज्य *a*. Having the bowstring stretched, well strung (as a bow). -COMP. -धन्वन्, -कार्मुक *a*. having the bow strung; त्वयि चाधिज्यकार्मुके *S*. 1. 6.

अधित्यका A table-land, high-land: स्थाणुं तपस्यंतमधित्यकायां Ku. 3. 17; अधित्यकायामिव धातुमय्यां R. 2. 29.

अधिदंतः A (redundant) tooth growing over another.

अधिदेव ः-वता A presiding or tutelary deity; ययाचे पादुके पश्चात्कर्तुं राज्याधिदेवते R. 12. 17; 16. 9; Bv. 3. 3.

अधिदैवं-दैवतं The presiding god or deity.

अधिनाथः The supreme lord.

अधिनायः Fragrance, odour.

अधिपः-पतिः A lord, ruler, king, sovereign, head; अथ प्रजानामधिपः प्रभाते R. 2. 1; mostly in comp.

अधिपत्नी Ved. A female ruler, mistress (स्वामिनी).

अधिपु (पू) रुषः The Supreme Being.

अधिप्रज *a*. Having many children (as a man, woman &c.).

अधिभूः A master, superior; foremost.

अधिभूतं The highest being; the Supreme Spirit or its all pervading influence.

अधिमात्र *a*. Beyond measure, excessive, inordinate.

अधिमासः An intercalary (lunar) month.

अधियज्ञः 1 Principal sacrifice. 2 The agency effecting or causing such sacrifice.

अधिरथ *a*. Being on or over a car. —थः 1 A charioteer, driver. 2 N. of a charioteer who was king of Anga and foster-father of Karṇa.

अधिराज् *m*.,-जः A sovereign or supreme ruler, an emperor; अयास्तमेतु भुवनेष्वधिराजशब्दः U. 6. 16; king, head, lord (of men, animals &c.); हिमालयो नाम नगाधिराजः Ku. 1. 1; so मृग°, नाग° &c.

अधिराज्यं-ज्यं 1 Imperial or sovereign sway, supremacy; imperial dignity. 2 An empire. 3 N. of a country.

अधिरूढ *p. p.* 1 Mounted, ascended &c. 2 Increased.

अधिरोहः 1 An elephant rider. 2 Mounting; ascent.

अधिरोहणं Ascending, mounting; चिता° R. 8.57.—णी A ladder, flight of steps (of wood &c.) (Mar. शिडी).

अधिरोहिन् *a*. Ascending, mounting, rising above &c.—णी A ladder, flight of steps.

अधिलोकं *ind.* 1 Concerning the universe. 2 In the universe.

अधिवचनं 1 Advocacy, speaking in favour of. 2 A name, epithet, appellation.

अधिवासः 1 Abode, residence; dwelling; तस्यापि स एव गिरिराधिवासः K. 137; settlement, habitation. 2 Obstinate pertinacity in making a demand. 3 Consecration of an image especially before the commencement of a sacrificial rite; see अधिवासनं also. 4 A garment, mantle. 5 Application of perfumes or fragrant cosmetics; scenting, perfuming; fragrance, scent, fragrant odour itself; अधिवासस्पृहयेव मारुतः R. 8. 34; Si. 2. 20.

अधिवासनं 1 Scenting with perfumes or odorous substances. 2 Preliminary consecration (प्रतिष्ठा) of an image, making a divinity assume its abode in an image.

अधिविन्ना A superseded wife, one whose husband has married again; Y. 1. 73, 74; Ms. 9. 80–83.

अधिवेत्तृ *m.* A husband who supersedes his first wife.

अधिवेदः-वेदनं Marrying an additional wife.

अधिश्रयः 1 A receptacle. 2 Boiling, making hot (by putting on fire).

अधिश्रयणं-पणं Warming, boiling. **—णी** An oven, a fire-place.

अधिश्री *a.* Of exalted dignity, supreme; very rich, sovereign lord; इयं महेंद्रप्रभृतीनधिश्रियश्चतुर्दिगीशानवमत्य मानिनी Ku. 5. 53.

अधिष्ठानं 1 Standing or being near, approach. 2 A position, site, basis; seat, place, town 3 Residence, abode. 4 Authority, power, power of control. 5 Government; dominion. 6 A wheel (of a car &c.). 7 A precedent, prescribed rule. 8 A benediction.

अधिष्ठित *p. p.* 1 (Used actively) (*a*) Standing, being. (*b*) Possessed of. (*c*) Directing, presiding over. 2 (Passively) (*a*) Occupied, possessed by. (*b*) Full of, affected, overpowered. (*c*) Watched over, guarded, superintended. (*d*) Led, conducted, commanded by, presided over.

अधीकारः =अधिकार q. v.; स्वागतं स्वानधीकारानवलंब्य Ku. 2. 18.

अधीतिन् *a.* Well-read, proficient in (with loc.); अधीती चतुर्ष्वाम्नायेषु Dk. 120; वेदे, व्याकरणे &c.

अधीतिः *f.* 1 Study, perusal °बोधाचरणप्रचारणैः N. 1. 4. 2 Remembrance, recollection.

अधीन *a.* Subject to, subservient, dependent on; usually in comp.; स्थाने प्राणाः कामिनां दूत्यधीनाः M. 3. 14; त्वदधीनं खलु देहिनां सुखं Ku. 4. 10; इक्ष्वाकूणां दुरापेऽर्थे त्वदधीना हि सिद्धयः R. 1. 72.

अधीयानः *pres. p.* A student, one who goes over the Vedas.

अधीर *a.* 1 Not bold, timid. 2 Confused; excited, excitable. 3 Fitful. 4 Unsteady, rolling (of eyes). **—रा** 1 Lightning. 2 A capricious or quarrelsome mistress.

अधीवासः A long coat or mantle covering the whole person; see अधिवास also.

अधीशः Lord, supreme lord or master, sovereign ruler; अंग°, मृग°, मनुज° &c.

अधीश्वरः A supreme lord or an employer.

अधीष्ट *a.* Honorary, solicited. **—ष्टः** Honorary office or duty; one of the cases in which the Potential may be used; (अधीष्टः =सत्कारपूर्वको व्यापारः Sk.).

अधुना *ind.* Now, at this time; प्रमदानामधुना विडंबना Ku. 4. 11.

अधुनातन *a.* (**नी** *f.*) Belonging to the present times, modern.

अधूमकः Burning or blazing fire.

अधृतिः *f.* 1 Want of firmness or control, looseness. 2 Incontinence. 3 Unhappiness.

अधृष्य *a.* 1 Invincible, unassailable; unapproachable (opp. अभिगम्य); अधृष्यश्चाभिगम्यश्च यादोरत्नैरिवार्णवः R. 1. 16. 2 Modest, shy. 3 Proud.

अधोऽक्ष, अधोंऽशुक, अधोऽक्षज See under अधस्.

अध्यक्ष *a.* 1 Perceptible to the senses, visible; धैर्यध्यक्षैरथ निजसखं नीरदं स्मारयाद्रिः Bv. 4. 17. 2 One who exercises supervision, presiding over. **—क्षः** A superintendent, president, head; मयाऽध्यक्षेण प्रकृतिः सूयते सचराचरं Bg. 9. 10; oft. in comp.; गज°, सेना°, ग्राम°, द्वार°.

अध्यक्षरं The mystic syllable ओम्.

अध्यग्नि *ind.* Over, by or near the nuptial fire.—*n.* (**ग्नि**) A gift made to a woman at the time of marriage: विवाहकाले यत्स्त्रीभ्यो दीयते ह्यग्निसन्निधौ । तदध्यग्निकृतं सद्भिः स्त्रीधनं परिकीर्तितम् ॥

अध्यधि *ind.* On high (acc.); लोकं Sk.

अध्यधिक्षेपः Excessive abuse or censure, gross abuse; Y. 3. 228.

अध्यधीन *a.* Completely subject or dependent, as a slave.

अध्ययः 1 Learning, study; remembrance. 2=अध्याय, q. v.

अध्ययनं Learning, study, reading (especially the Vedas); one of the six duties of a Brâhmaṇa. The study of the Vedas is allowed to the first three classes, but not to Sûdra Ms. 1. 81–21.

अध्यर्ध *a.* Having an additional half; शतमध्यर्धमायता Mb., *i. e.* 150; °योजनशतात् Pt. 2. 18.

अध्यवसानं 1 Effort, determination &c. See अध्यवसाय. 2 (In Rhet.) Identification of two things (प्रकृत and अप्रकृत) in such a manner that the one is completely absorbed into the other निगीर्याध्यवसानं तु प्रकृतस्य परेण यत् K. P. 10; on such identification is founded the figure called अतिशयोक्ति and the लक्षणा called साध्यवसाना. See K. P. 2.

अध्यवसायः 1 An attempt, effort, exertion. 2 Determination, resolution; mental effort or apprehension. 3 Perseverance, diligence, energy, constancy.

अध्यवसायिन् *a.* Attempting; resolute, persevering, energetic.

अध्यशनं Excessive eating, eating again before the last meal is digested.

अध्यात्म *a.* Belonging to self or person.—**त्मं** *ind.* Concerning self. —**त्मं** The supreme spirit (manifested as the individual self) or the relation between the supreme and the individual soul. —COMP. **—ज्ञानं, -विद्या** knowledge of the supreme spirit or आत्मन् theosophical or metaphysical knowledge (the doctrines taught by the Upanishads &c.). **—रति** *a.* one who delights in the contemplation of the supreme spirit.

अध्यात्मिक *a.* (**की** *f.*) Relating to अध्यात्म.

अध्यापकः A teacher, preceptor, instructor; especially of the Vedas; व्याकरण°; न्याय°; भृतक° mercenary teacher. According to Vishṇu-Smṛiti an *adhyápaka* is of two kinds: he is either an *Achárya i. e.* one who invests a boy with the sacred thread and initiates him into the Vedas, or he is an *Upádhyáya i. e.* one who teaches for livelihood (वृत्त्यर्थं). See M. 2. 140–141 and the two words.

अध्यापनं Teaching, instrucing, lecturing, one of the six duties of a Brâhmaṇa. According to Indian law-givers अध्यापन is of three kinds: (1) undertaken for charity, (2 for wages, and (3) in consideration of services rendered.

अध्यापयितृ *m.* A teacher, instructor.

अध्यायः 1 Reading, study, especially of the Vedas. 2 Proper time for reading or for a lesson. 3 A lesson, lecture. 4 A chapter, a large division of a work. The following are some of the names used by Sanskrit writers to denote chapters or divisions of works: सर्गो वर्गः परिच्छेदोद्घाताध्यायांकसंग्रहाः । उच्छ्वासः परिवर्तश्च पटलःकांडमाननं । स्थानं प्रकरणं चैव पर्वोल्लासाह्निकानि च । स्कंधांशौ तु पुराणादौ प्रायशः परिकीर्तितौ ॥

अध्यायिन् *a.* Studying, studious.

अध्यारूढ *a.* 1 Mounted, ascended. 2 Raised above, elevated. 3 Above, superior to; below, inferior.

अध्यारोपः 1 Raising, elevating &c.

2 (In Vedânta phil.) Act of attributing falsely or through mistake ; erroneously attributing the properties of one thing to another ; considering through mistake a rope (which is not really a serpent) to be a serpent, आर्पभूतरज्जौ सर्पारोपवत्, अजगद्रूपे ब्रह्मणि जगद्रूपारोपवत्, वस्तुनि अवस्त्वारोपोऽध्यारोपः Vedântasâra. 3 Erroneous knowledge.

अध्यारोपणं 1 Raising &c. 2 Sowing (seed).

अध्यावापः 1 Act of sowing or scattering (seed &c.). 2 A field wherein seed &c. is sown.

अध्यावाहनिकं One of the six kinds of स्त्रीधन, the property which a woman gets when leaving her father's house for her husband's ; यत् पुनर्लभते नारी नीयमान तु पैतृकात् (गृहात्) । अध्यावाहनिकं नाम स्त्रीधनं परिकीर्तितम् ॥

अध्यासः-सनं 1 Sitting down upon, occupying, presiding over. 2 A seat, place.

अध्यासः 1 False attribution, wrong supposition; see अध्यारोप also. 2 An appendage. 3 Putting down upon ; पादाध्यासे शतं दमः Y. 2. 217.

अध्याहार :-हरणं 1 Supplying an ellipsis 2 Arguing ; inferring; new supposition ; inference or conjecture.

अध्युष्ट्रः A carriage drawn or borne by camels.

अध्यूढ *a.* Raised, elevated, **—ढः** *Siva.* **—ढा** A wife whose husband has married another wife and thus superseded her (=अधिविन्ना q. v.).

अध्येषणं Causing one to do a thing, especially a preceptor &c. as an honorific duty. **—णा** Solicitation, entreaty.

अध्रुव *a.* 1 Uncertain, doubtful. 2 Unstable, unsteady, separable. **—वं** An uncertainty; यो ध्रुवाणि परित्यज्य अध्रुवाणि निषेवते । ध्रुवाणि तस्य नश्यंति अध्रुवं नष्टमेव च॥

अध्वन् *m.* 1 A way, road, passage, orbit(of planets &c). 2 (*a*) Distance, space (traversed or to be traversed); अपि लंघितमध्वानं बुबुधे न बुधोपमः R. 1. 47; उल्लंघिताध्वा Me. 45. (*b*) Journey, travel, course, march; नैकः प्रपद्येताध्वानं Ms. 4. 60. 3 Time (Kâla), time personified. 4 Sky, atmosphere. 5 Means, resource;method. 6 Attack.-Comp.**—गः** 1 one who travels; a traveller, wayfarer संतानकतरुच्छायासुप्तविद्याधराध्वगं Ku. 6. 46(°गामिन्). -2 a camel. -3 a mule. -4 the sun. **-गा** the Ganges.**-पतिः** the sun.**-रथः** 1 a travelling coach. -2 a messenger skilled in travelling.

अध्वनीन, अध्वन्य *a.* Able to undertake a journey, speeding on a journey; क्षिप्रं ततोऽध्वन्यतुरंगयायी Bk. 2. 44. **—नः, न्यः** A traveller going fast, way-farer.

अध्वरः A sacrifice, a religious ceremony; also a Soma sacrifice; तमध्वरे विश्वजिति R. 5. 1. **—रः-रं** Sky or air. -Comp.**-दीक्षणीया** consecration connected with an Adhvara; so °प्रायश्चित्तिः an expiation &c.**-मीमांसा** N. of Jaimini's Pûrvamîmâmsâ.

अध्वर्युः 1 Any officiating priest; technically distinguished from होतृ, उद्गातृ and ब्रह्मन्. 2 The Yajurveda itself. -Comp.**-वेदः** Yajurveda.

अध्वाति=**अध्वग.**

अध्वांतं Twilight; gloom.

अन् 2 P. (अनिति, अनित) 1 To breathe. 2 To move, live.-*Caus.* आनयति; *Desid.* अनिनिषति. -(4 A.) To live. With प्र to be alive; यदहं पुनरेव प्राणिमि K. 35; प्राणिमस्तव मानार्थे Bv. 4. 38.

अनः Breath, respiration.

अनंश *a.* Not entitled to a share in the inheritance.

अनकदुंदुभिः=आनकदुंदुभि q. v.

अनक्ष *a.* Sightless, blind.

अनक्षर *a.* 1 Unable to speak, mute, dumb. 2 Unlettered. 3 Unfit to be uttered. **—रं** Foul or abusive words, censure or abusive words, censure. —*adv.* Without the use of words; °व्यंजितदौर्हृदेन R. 14. 26.

अनग्निः 1 Non-fire, substance other than fire; यदधीतमविज्ञातं निगदेनैव शब्द्यते । अनग्नाविव शुष्केधो न तज्ज्वलति कर्हिचित् Nir. 2 Absence of fire; —*a.* 1 Without the use of fire; विदधे विधिमस्य नैष्ठिकं यतिभिः सार्धमनग्निमग्निचित् R. 8. 25. 2 Not maintaining the sacred fire. 3 Irreligious, impious. 4 Dyspeptic. 5 Unmarried.

अनघ *a.* 1 Sinless, innocent; अवैमि चैनामनघेति R. 14. 40. 2 Faultless, handsome; रूपमनघं *S.* 2. 13; यस्य ज्ञानदयासिंधोरगाधस्यानघा गुणाः Ak. 3 Safe, unhurt, without injury, secure; कच्चिन्मृगीणामनघा प्रसूतिः R. 5. 7; मृगवधूर्यदा अनघप्रसवा भवति *S.* 4 safely delivered or brought to bed. 4 Pure, spotless. **—घः** 1 White mustard. 2 N. of Vishṇu; also of *Siva.*

अनंकुश *a.* 1 Ungovernable, unruly. 2 Taking license (as a poet).

अनंग *a.* Bodiless, without a body; incorporeal; त्वमनंगः कथमक्षता रतिः Ku. 4. 9. **—गः** Cupid (the bodiless one). **—गं** 1 Sky, air, ether. 2 The mind. -Comp.**-क्रीडा** amorous sports. **-लेखः** (=मदनलेखः) a love letter; °लेखक्रिययोपयोगं (व्रजंति) Ku. 1. 7. °**शत्रुः**, °**असुहृत** &c. N. of *Siva.*

अनंजन *a.* Without collyrium, pigment, or paint; **नेत्रे दूरमनंजने** S. D. **—नं** 1 The sky; atmosphere. 2 The supreme spirit (परब्रह्म); Vishṇu or Nârâyaṇa (*m.* also).

अनडुह् *m.* (अनड्वान् °ड्वाहो, °डुद्भ्यां &c.) 1 An ox, bull. 2 The sign Taurus.**— ही** or **अनड्वाही** A cow.

अनति *ind.* Not very much; compounds beginning with अनति may be analysed by referring to अति.

अनतिविलंबिता Absence of delay; fluency as a speaker's qualification, one of the 35 Vâggunas, q. v.

अनद्यतन *a.* (**नी** *f.*) Not pertaining to this or the current day; a term used by Pâṇini to denote the sense of the Imperfect and the Periphrastic future.**—नः** Not the current day ; अतीताया रात्रेः पश्चार्धेन आगामिन्या रात्रेः पूर्वार्धेन सहितो दिवसोऽद्यतनः Sk., तद्भिन्नः कालः.

अनधिक *a.* 1 Not more or excessive. 2 Boundless; perfect.

अनधीनः An independent carpenter working on his own accout.

अनध्यक्ष *a.* 1 Not perceptible or observable, invisible. 2 Without controller or ruler &c.

अनध्यायः, अनध्ययनं Not studying, intermission of study; the time when there is or ought to be such intermission, a holiday (°दिवसः); अद्य शिष्टानध्यायः U. 4 a holiday (given) in honor of distinguished guests.

अननं Breathing, living.

अननुभावुक *a.* Unable to comprehend.

अनंत *a.* Endless, infinite, boundless, inexhaustible; °रत्नप्रभवस्य यस्य Ku. 1. 3. **—तः** 1 N. of Vishṇu also of Vishṇu's couch,the serpent *S*hesha; of Krishṇa and his brother; of *S*hiva; Vâsuki, the lord of serpents. 2 A cloud. 3 Talc. 4 A silken cord with fourteen knots tied round the right arm on the अनंतचतुर्दशी day. **—ता** 1 the earth (the endless). 2 The number one. 3 N. of Pârvatî. 4 N. of various plants; शारिवा, अनंतमूल, दूर्वा &c. **—तं** 1 The sky, atmosphere. 2 Infinity. 3 Absolution. 4 The supreme spirit, Brahma (परब्रह्म). -Comp. **-तृतीया** the third day of the bright half of भाद्रपद, मार्गशीर्ष or वैशाख. **-दृष्टि :** N. of *S*iva, or of Indra. **-देव :** 1 the serpent *S*esha. -2. N. of Nârâyaṇa who sleeps on *S*esha. **-पार** *a.* of endless width, boundless; °रं किल शब्दशास्त्रं Pt. 1. **-रूप** *a.* of innumerable forms or shapes; epithet of Vishṇu. **-विजय :** N. of Yudhisṭhira's conch-shell; Bg. 1. 16.

अनंतर *a.* 1 Having no interior or interior space, limitless. 2 Having no interval or interstice or pause (of space or time); compact, close. 3 Contiguous, neighbouring, immediately adjoining; not distant from (with abl.); ब्रह्मावर्तादनंतरः Ms. 2. 19. 4 Following, coming close upon (in comp.). 5 Belonging to the caste immediately following. **—रं** 1 Contiguity, proximity. 2 Brahma, the Supreme Soul. **—रं** *ind.* 1 Immediately after, afterwards. 2 (with a prepositional force) After (with abl.); पुराणपत्रापगमादनन्तरं R. 3. 7. गोदानविधेरनन्तरं R. 3. 33, 36.; 2. 71.–Comp. –जः or जा 1 the child of a Kshatriyâ or Vaisyâ mother, by a father belonging to the caste immediately above the mother's, Ms. 10, 4.–2 born immediately before or after; a younger or elder brother. (–जा) a younger or elder sister; अनुष्ठितानंतरजाविवाहः R. 7. 32.; so °जात.

अनंतरीय *a.* Next in succession.

अनन्य *a.* 1 Not different, identical, same, not other than. 2 Sole, unique, without a second. 3 Undivided, undistracted (mind &c.); having no object or person to think of &c.; अनन्याश्चिंतयंतो मां ये जनाः पर्युपासते Bg. 9. 22. In comp. अनन्य may be translated by 'not by another,' 'directed or devoted to no one else,' 'having no other object,' –Comp. –गतिः *f.* sole resort or resource left; अनन्यगतिके जने विगतपातकं चातकं Udb. –चित्त, –चिंत, –चेतस्, –मनस्, –मानस, –हृदय *a.* giving one's undivided thought or attention to, with undivided mind –जः, –जन्मन् *m.* Cupid, the god of love; मा मूमुहन्खलु भवंतमनन्यजन्मा Mâl. 1. 32. –पूर्वः having no other wife. (–र्वा) a virgin, a woman having no other husband; R. 4. 7. –भाज् *a.* not devoted to any other person; अनन्यभाजं पतिमाप्नुहि Ku. 3. 63. –विषय *a.* not applicable or belonging to any one else.–वृत्ति *a.* 1 of the same nature. –2 having no other means of livelihood. –3 closely attentive. –सामान्य, –साधारण *a.* not common to any one else, uncommon, exclusively devoted, applicable or belonging to one; अनन्यनारीसामान्यो दासस्त्वस्याः पुरूरवाः V. 3. 18 ; °राजशब्दः R. 6. 38. –सदृश *a.* (शी *f.*) matchless, peerless.

अनन्वयः 1 Want of connection. 2 (Rhet.) A figure of speech in which a thing is compared to itself, the object being to show that it is matchless and can have no other उपमान; *e. g.* गगनं गगनाकारं सागरः सागरोपमः । रामरावणयोर्युद्धं रामरावणयोरिव ॥.

अनप *a.* Destitute of much water (as a puddle).

अनपकारणं-कर्मन्, –क्रिया 1 Not injuring. 2 Non-delivery. 3 (In law) Non-payment.

अनपकारः Harmlessness.–कारिन् *a.* Harmless, innocent.

अनपत्य *a.* 1 Without issue, childless, without heir.

अनपत्रप *a.* Impudent, shameless.

अनपभ्रंशः Not a corrupt word; a properly formed word.

अनपसर *a.* Having no egress or passage to creep out of, unjustifiable, inexcusable.–रः An usurper.

अनपाय *a.* 1 Free from loss or decay. 2 Imperishable, undiminished, undecaying: प्रणमंत्यनपायमुत्थितं (चंद्रं) Ki. 2. 11.–यः 1 Freedom from decay or wear and tear; permanence. 2 N. of Siva.

अनपायिन् *a.* Imperishable, firm, steady, unfailing, constant, durable, not transient; प्रसादाभिमुखे तस्मिन् श्रीरासीदनपायिनी R. 17. 46; 8. 17; अनपायिनि संश्रयद्रुमे गजभग्ने पतनाय वल्लरी. Ku. 4. 31.

अनपेक्ष-क्षिन् *a.* 1 Regardless. 2 Careless, not minding or heeding, indifferent. 3 Independent or irrespective (of another), not requiring any other thing. 4 Impartial. 5 Irrelevant.–क्षा Disregard, indifference. –क्षं *adv.* Without regard to, independently or irrespectively of; carelessly.

अनपेत *a.* 1 Not gone off, not past. 2 Not deviating from (with abl.); अर्थादनपेतं अर्थ्यं Sk. 3 Not devoid of, possessed of; ऐश्वर्यादनपेतमीश्वरमयं लोकोऽर्थतः सेवते Mu. 1. 14.

अनभिज्ञ *a.* Ignorant of, unacquainted with, unused to, (usually with gen.), °ज्ञः कैतवस्य *S.* 5 ; °ज्ञः परमेश्वरगृहाचारस्य Mv.2.

अनभ्यावृत्तिः *f.* Non-repetition; मनागनभ्यावृत्त्या वा कामं क्षाम्यतु यः क्षमी Si. 2 43.

अनभ्याश,–स *a.* Not near, distant &c. °समित्य *a.* to be shunned from afar Sk.

अनभ्र *a.* Cloudless ; इयमनभ्रा वृष्टिः this is (like) a shower from a cloudless sky, *i. e.* something quite unexpected or sudden.

अनमः A Brâhmaṇa (one who does not bow down to others and returns salutations made to him by others with a blessing)

अनमितंपच (= मितंपच) *a.* Miserly, niggardly.

अनंबर *a.* Wearing not garment, naked.–रः A Buddhist mendicant.

अनयः 1 Bad management or conduct; injustice; unfairness. 2 Bad policy or course of conduct, evil course. 3 Adversity, distress, Ms. 10. 95. 4 Misfortune, ill-luck. 5 Gambling.

अनर्गल *a.* 1 Free to move, unrestrained ; तुरंगमुत्सृष्टमनर्गलं R. 3. 39. 2 Unlocked.

अनर्घ *a.* Invaluable, priceless, inestimable. –र्घः Wrong or improper value

अनर्घ्य *a.* Invaluable; highly respected.

अनर्थ *a.* 1 Useless, worthless. 2 Unfortunate, unhappy. 3 Harmful. 4 Nonsensical, meaningless.–र्थः 1 Non-use or value. 2 Worthless or useless object. 3 A calamity, misfortune; रंध्रोपनिपातिनोऽनर्थाः *S.* 6; छिद्रेष्वनर्था बहुलीभवंति. 4 Nonsense, want of sense. –Comp. –कर *a.* (री *f.*) mischievous, harmful.

अनर्थ्य, अनर्थक *a.* 1 Useless; meaningless. 2 Not significant, as a particle used expletively. 3 Nonsensical. 4 Unprofitable. 5 Unfortunate. –कं Nonsensical or incoherent talk.

अनर्ह *a.* 1 Not deserving, not fit. 2 Not worthy of (with gen. or in comp.)

अनलः 1 Fire. 2 Agni or the god of fire. 3 Digestive power. 4 Bile. –Comp. –द *a.* 1 removing or destroying heat or fire. –2 =अग्निद q. v. –दीपन *a.* promoting digestion, stomachic. –प्रिया N. of Agni's wife स्वाहा. –सादः loss of appetite, dyspepsia.

अनलस *a.* 1 Not lazy, active, diligent. 2 Unable, incompetent.

अनल्प *a.* 1 Numerous. 2 Not a little; liberal, noble (as mind &c.); much ; जल्पंत्यनल्पाक्षरं Pt. 1. 136 ; विकसितवदनामनल्पजल्पेपि Bv. 1. 100 ; 2. 138.

अनवकाश *a.* 1 Uncalled for. 2 Inapplicable. 3 Having no opportunity or space. –शः Absence of room or scope.

अनवग्रह *a.* Irresistible ; सुकुमारकायमनवग्रहः स्मरः (अभिहंति) Mâl. 1. 39.

अनवच्छिन्न *a.* 1 Not bounded or marked off, not separated or cut. 2 Unlimited ; excessive. 3 Undefined ; undiscriminated ; unmodified. 4 Uninterrupted.

अनवद्य *a.* Faultless, blameless, irreproachable ; R. 7. 70. –Comp. –अंग, –रूप *a.* having faultless limbs or form exquisitely handsome. (–गी) a woman with a faultless form.

अनवधान *a.* Careless, inattentive. –नं Inadvertence, inattention ; °ता carelessness

अनवधि *a.* Unlimited, infinite.

अनवम *a.* Not low or inferior ; high exalted; सुधर्मानवमां सभां R. 17. 27, 9. 14.

अनवरत *a.* Incessant, uninterrupted, °धनुर्ज्यास्फालनक्रूरपूर्वं *S.* 2. 4. –तं *adv.* Incessantly, continuously.

अनवराध्य *a.* Chief, best, excellent.

अनवलंब –बन *a.* Not dependent. –बः –बनं Independence.

अनवलोभनं A sort of purificatory ceremony to be performed in the case of a pregnant woman in the third month after conception.

अनवसर *a.* 1 Busy. 2 Inopportune. –रः 1 Absence of leisure. 2 Ill-timedness, unseasonableness ; कं याचे यत्र तत्र ध्रुवमनवसरग्रस्त एवार्थिभावः Mâl. 9. 30.

अनवस्कर *a.* Free from dirt, pure, clear.

अनवस्थ *a.* Unsteady. –स्था 1 Instability, unsettled condition. 2 Loose conduct, incontinence. 3 (In phil.) Absence of finality or conclusion, an endless series of statements or causes and effects, one of the faults of reasoning; एवमप्यनवस्था स्याद्या मूलक्षतिकारिणी K. P. 2; एवं च °प्रसंगः S. B.

अनवस्थान *a.* Unstable, unsteady, fickle. —**नः** Wind. —**नं 1** instability. **2** Looseness of conduct, incontinence.

अनवस्थित *a.* **1** Unsteady, unsettled. **2** Changed. **3** Dissolute.

अनवेक्षक *a.* Regardless of; careless, indifferent.

अनवेक्ष-क्षा = अनपेक्ष—क्षा q. v.

अनवेक्षणं Carelessness, inattention.

अनशनं Fasting, fasting oneself to death.

अनश्वर *a.* (**री** *f.*) Imperishable.

अनस् *n.* **1** A cart. **2** Food; boiled rice. **3** Birth. **4** A living being. **5** A kitchen.

अनसूय-यक *a.* Free from malice, not envious. —**या 1** Absence of envy. **2** N. of Atri's wife, the highest type of chastity and wifely devotion.

अनहन् *n.* A bad or unlucky day.

अनाकालः 1 Inopportune time. **2** Famine (perhaps an irregular form for अन्नाकाल).-COMP. -**भृतः** one who, to save himself from starvation in a famine, voluntarily becomes a slave of another.

अनाकुल *a.* **1** Calm, collected, self-possessed. **2** Consistent.

अनागत *a.* **1** Not come or arrived; तावद्भयस्य भेतव्यं यावद्भयमनागतं H. 1. 57. **2** Not got or obtained. **3** Future, to come; see compounds below. **4** Unknown.—**तं** The future time, future. -COMP. -**अवेक्षणं** looking to the future, foresight.-**आबाध** : future (physical) trouble or calamities. -**आर्तवा** a maiden who has not yet arrived at puberty. —**विधातृ** *m.* one who provides for the future, provident, prudent, (used as the name of a fish in Pt. 1. 318; H. **4.** 5).

अनागमः 1 Non-arrival. **2** Non-attainment.

अनागस् *a.* Innocent, blameless; आर्तत्राणाय वः शस्त्रं न प्रहर्तुमनागसि S. 1. 11.

अनाचारः Improper conduct, departure from established usage or principle.

अनातप *a.* Free from heat, not exposed to heat, cool.

अनातुर *a.* **1** Not eager, indifferent. **2** Not fatigued, unwearied; भेजे धर्ममनातुर : R. 1. 21. **3** Well, healthy.

अनात्मन् *a.* **1** Destitute of spirit or mind. **2** Not spiritual. **3** One who has not restrained his self.—*m.* Not self, another, something different from आत्मन् (spirit or soul) *i. e.* the perishable body. -COMP.-**ज्ञ, वेदिन्** *a.* not knowing oneself, foolish, silly; मीं तावदनात्मज्ञे S. 6. -**संपन्न** *a.* foolish.

अनात्मनीन *a.* Not adapted to, or for the benefit of, self; disinterested.

अनात्मवत् *a.* Not self-possessed; having no control over the senses.

अनाथ *a.* Helpless, poor, forlorn; parentless, orphan (as a child); widowed (as a wife); without a protector in general; नाथवंतस्त्वया लोकास्त्वमनाथा विपत्स्यसे U. 1. 43. -COMP. -सभा a poor-house.

अनादर *a.* Indifferent, regardless. —**रः 1** Disregard, disrespect, disdain; षष्ठी चानादरे P. II. 3. 38.

अनादि *a.* Having no beginning, external, existing from eternity; जगदादिरनादिस्त्वं Ku. 2. 6.-COMP. -**अनंत, -अंत** *a.* without beginning and end; eternal. (-**तः**) N. of Siva. -**निधन** *a.* having neither beginning nor end, eternal. —**मध्यान्त** *a.* having no beginning, middle or end; eternal.

अनादीनव *a.* Faultless; यद्रासुदेवेनादीनमनादीनवमीरितं Si. 2. 22.

अनाद्य *a.* **1**=अनादि q. v. **2** Not eatable; what ought not to be eaten.

अनानुपूर्व्यं 1 Separation of the different members of compounds by the intervention of others. **2** Not coming in regular order.

अनाप्त *a.* **1** Not obtained. **2** Unfit, unskilful. —**प्तः** A stranger.

अनामक *a.* Nameless, infamous. —**कः -कं**=अनामन् below.

अनामन् *a.* **1** Nameless. **2** Infamous. -*m.* **1** 'The nameless' month, an intercalary month. **2** The ring-finger; see अनामिका below. —*n.* Piles.

अनामा, अनामिका The ring-finger, so called because it has no name like the other fingers; पुरा कवीनां गणनाप्रसंगे कनिष्ठिकाधिष्ठितकालिदासा । अद्यापि तत्तुल्यकवेरभावादनामिका सार्थवती बभूव ॥ Subhâsh.

अनामय *a.* Healthy, sound. —**यः** —**यं** Health, well-being; महाश्वेता कादंबरीमनामयं पप्रच्छ K. 192 inquired about her health. —**यः** N. of Vishṇu (or Siva according to some).

अनायत्त *a.* Not dependent; °त्तो रोषस्य K. 45 not swayed by anger; independent; एतावज्जन्मसाफल्यं यदनायत्तवृत्तिता H. 2. 22. independent livelihood.

अनायास *a* Not troublesome or difficult, easy; ममाप्यकस्मिन् °से कर्मणि त्वया सहायेन भवितव्यं S. 2. —**सः 1** Ease, absence of difficulty or exertion; °सेन easily, without difficulty.

अनारत *a.* **1** Incessant, continuous, uninterrupted. **2** Eternal. —**तं** *ind.* Continuously, eternally; अनारतं तेन पदेषु लंभिताः Ki. 1. 15, 40.

अनारंभः Non-commencement; विकारं खलु परमार्थतोऽज्ञात्वा °भः प्रतीकारस्य S. 3.

अनार्जव *a.* Crooked; dishonest —**वं 1** Crookedness (moral also), fraud. **2** Disease.

अनार्तव *a.* (**वी** *f.*) Unseasonable. —**वा** A girl who has not attained to puberty (the menstruation period).

अनार्य *a.* Not respectable, base, mean. —**र्यः 1** One who is not an Arya. **2** A country not inhabited by the Aryas. **3** A Sûdra. **4** A Mlechchha. **5** An ignoble person.

अनार्यकं Agallochum or aloe wood.

अनार्ष 1 Not belonging to the Rishis, not Vedic; संबुद्धौ शाकल्यस्येतावनार्षे P. I. 1. 16 (=अवैदिके Sk.). **2** Not added to a Rishi's name (as an affix).

अनालंब *a.* Without support or stay. —**बः** Want of support; despondency. —**बी** Siva's lute.

अनालंबु (भु) का A woman during menstruation (रजस्वला).

अनावर्तिन् *a.* Not recurring or returning.

अनाविद्ध *a.* Not pierced or perforated.

अनावृत्तिः *f.* **1** Non-return. **2** Non-return (to birth), final emancipation.

अनावृष्टिः *f.* Drought, one of the kinds of ईति q. v.

अनाश्रमिन् *m.* One who does not belong to or follow any of the 4 orders of life; अनाश्रमी न तिष्ठेत्तु क्षणमेकमपि द्विजः.

अनाश्रव *a.* Not listening to, obstinate, turning a deaf ear to; भिषजामनाश्रवः R. 19. 49.

अनाश्वस् *a.* Not having eaten or enjoyed, fasting.

अनास्था 1 Indifference, unconcern, want of consideration; अनास्था बाह्यवस्तुषु Ku. 6. 63; पिंडेष्वनास्था खलु भौतिकेषु R. 2. 57; स्त्री पुमानित्यनास्थैषा वृत्तं हि महितं सतां Ku. 6. 12. **2** Want of faith or confidence; disrespect.

अनाहत *a.* **1** Unbeaten. **2** New and unbleached (as cloth) (Mar. कोरें).

अनाहार *a.* Abstaining from food, fasting —**रः** Abstinence from food, fasting.

अनाहुतिः *f.* **1** Not sacrificing; a sacrifice not worthy of that name. **2** An improper oblation.

अनाहूत *a.* Not called, uninvited.-COMP.—**उपजल्पिन्** an uncalled-for speaker or boaster.-**उपविष्ट** *a.* seated as an uninvited guest.

अनिकेत *a.* Houseless, vagrant; having no fixed abode (as a recluse).

अनिगीर्ण *a.* **1** Not swallowed. **2** (In Rhet.) Not hidden or concealed, present. not to be supplied.

अनिच्छ, -च्छक, -च्छु, -च्छुक, -च्छत् *a.* Not desirous, unwilling, reluctant.

अनित्य *a.* **1** Not eternal or everlasting, transient, non-eternal, perishable. **2** Occasional, casual ; not peremptory or obligatory as a rule &c.; special. **3** Unusual, irregular. **4**

Unsteady, fickle. **5** Uncertain, doubtful ; विजयस्य ह्यनित्यत्वात् Pt. 3. 22. **—त्यं** *adv.* Occasionally, casually. -COMP. **-कर्मन् -क्रिया** an occasional act, such as a sacrifice for a special purpose, a voluntary and occasional act. **-दत्तः, -दत्तकः, -दत्रिमः** a son given by his parents to another temporarily. **-भावः** transitoriness, transient state. **-समासः** a compound which it is not obligatory to form in every case (the sense of which may be equally expressed by resolving it into its constituent members).

अनिद्र *a.* Sleepless, awake ; (fig.) vigilant.

अनिन्द्रियं **1** Reason. **2** Not an organ of sense, the mind.

अनिभृत *a.* **1** Public, open, not hidden. **2** Immodest, bold. **3** Unsteady, not firm. See निभृत also.

अनिमकः **1** A frog. **2** A cuckoo. **3** A bee.

अनिमित्त *a.* Causeless, groundless ; casual ; आलक्ष्यदंतमुकुलाननिमित्तहासैः *S.* 7. 17. **—त्तं** **1** Absence of an adequate cause or occasion. **2** A bad omen, ill-omen ; ममानिमित्तानि हि खेदयंति Mk. 10. —*adv.*-°**तः** groundlessly, causelessly. -COMP. **-निराक्रिया** averting ill-omens.

अनिमि (मे) ष *a.* Steadfastly or intently fixed ; without twinkling ; शतैस्तमक्ष्णामनिमेषवृत्तिभिः R. 3. 43. **—षः** **1** A god. **2** A fish. **3** Vishṇu. -COMP. **-दृष्टि, -लोचन** *a.* looking steadfastly or with a fixed gaze.

अनियत *a.* **1** Uncontrolled. **2** Indefinite, uncertain, irregular (forms also); °वेलं आहारोऽस्यते *S.* 2. **3** Causeless, casual. **4**. Perishable. -COMP.- **अंकः** an indeterminate digit (in Math).**-आत्मन्** *a.* not self-possessed. **-पुंस्का** a woman loose in conduct, unchaste **-वृत्ति** *a.* 1 having no regular or fixed employment or application (as a word). -2 having no regular income.

अनियंत्रण *a.* Unrestrained, uncontrolled, free; °अनुयोगो नाम तपस्विजनः *S.* 1.

अनियमः **1** Absence of rule, control, regulation, or fixed order; no settled rule or direction; पंचमं लघु सर्वत्र सप्तमं द्विचतुर्थयोः । षष्ठे पादे गुरु ज्ञेयं शेषेष्वनियमो मतः ॥ Ch. M. **2** Uncertainty, indefiniteness, doubt. **3** Improper conduct.

अनिरुक्त *a.* **1** Not clearly spoken. **2** Not clearly stated or explained, not plain or well-defined.

अनिरुद्ध *a.* Unobstructed, free, uncontrolled, self-willed, unruly, ungovernable.**—द्धः** **1** A spy **2** N. of a son of Pradyumna. -COMP. **-पथं** 1 unobstructed path.-2 the sky, atmosphere.**-भाविनी** Anirudha's wife Ushâ.

अनिर्णयः Uncertainty, indecision.

अनिर्देश, अनिर्दशाह *a.* Within the 10 days of impurity caused either by child-birth or death.

अनिर्देशः Absence of positive rule or direction.

अनिर्देश्य *a.* Undefinable, indescribable.**—श्यं** An epithet of the Supreme Being.

अनिर्धारित *a.* Not determined or ascertained.

अनिर्वचनीय *a.* **1** Unutterable, indescribable. **2** Improper to be mentioned. **—यं** (In Vedânta) **1** Mâyâ or illusion, ignorance. **2** The world.

अनिर्वाण *a.* Unwashed; unbathed.

अनिर्वेदः Non-depression, absence of dejection or despondency; self-reliance, plucking up courage.

अनिर्वृत *a.* Ill at ease, uneasy, unhappy.

अनिर्वृतिः-त्तिः *f.* **1** Uneasiness, anxiety. **2** Poverty; अनिर्वृतिनिशाचरी मम गृहांतरालं गता Udb.

अनिलः **1** Wind. **2** The god of wind. **3** One of the subordinate deities, 49 of whom form the class of winds. **4** The wind in the body, one of the humours. **5** Rheumatism or any disease referred to disorder of the wind.—COMP.**—अयनं** way or course of the wind. **-अशन,-आशिन्** *a.* feeding on the wind, fasting. **(-न्)** *m.* a serpent.**—आत्मजः** son of the wind, epithet of Bhîma and Hanûmat. **—आमयः** 1 flatulence. -2 rheumatism. **-सखः** fire (the friend of wind); so °**बंधुः**.

अनिर्लोडित *a.* Not well considered, ill-judged; °कार्यस्य वाग्जालं वाग्मिनो वृथा; *Si.* **2. 27**.

अनिशं *ind.* Incessantly, ceaselessly; अनिशमपि मकरकेतुर्मनसो रुजमावहन्नभिमतो मे *S.* 3. 4; Bv. **2**. 162.

अनिष्ट *a.* **1** Unwished, undesirable; unfavourable. **2** Evil.**3** Bad, unlucky, ominous. **4** Not honoured with a sacrifice.**—ष्टं** **1** An evil, misfortune, calamity. **2** Disadvantage; unwelcome thing.-COMP.**-आपत्तिः** *f.*, **-आपादनं** getting what is not desired, an undesired occurrence.**—ग्रहः** an evil or malignant planet. **-प्रसंगः** 1 an undesired occurrence. -2 connection with a wrong object, argument or rule. **-फलं** an evil result. **-शंका** fear of evil. **-हेतुः** an evil omen.

अनिष्पत्रं *ind.* So that the arrow (the feathery portion of it) does not come out on the other side; *i. e.* not with great force.

अनिस्तीर्ण *a.* **1** Not crossed or got rid of. **2** Unanswered, unrefuted (as a charge).

अनीकः-कं **1** Army, forces; troop, host; दृष्ट्वा तु पांडवानीकं Bg. **1.2. 2** A collection, group. **3** Battle, fight, combat. **4** A row, line, marching column. **5** Front, head; chief.-COMP **-स्थः** 1 a warrior.-2 a sentinel, (armed) watch.-3 an elephant driver or its trainer.-4 a war-drum or trumpet. -5 a signal, mark, sign.

अनीकिनी **1** An army, host, forces. **2** Three chamûs or one tenth of a complete army (अक्षौहिणी), q. v.

अनील *a.* Not blue, white &c.; वाजिन् *m.* 'white-horsed' N. of Arjuna.

अनीश *a.* **1** Paramount, supreme. **2** Having no mastery or control over, not master of (with gen.); गात्राणामनीशोऽस्मि संवृत्तः *S.* **2. —शः** N. of Vishṇu.

अनीश्वर *a.* **1** Having no superior, uncontrolled. **2** Unable; शयिता सविधेप्यनीश्वरा सफलीकर्तुमहो मनोरथान् Bv. **2. 182. 3** Not relating to God. **4** Atheistical. -COMP.**-वादः** Atheism, not acknowledging God as the Supreme ruler, an atheist.

अनीह *a.* Indifferent, listless. **—हा** Disregard, indifference.

अनु *ind.* (Either used with nouns to form adverbial compounds, or as a prefix to verbs and verbal derivatives, or as a separable preposition with acc. and regarded as a कर्मप्रवचनीय) **1** After, behind; सर्वे नारदमनु उपविशांति V. 5; क्रमेण सुप्तामनु संविवेश सुप्तोत्थितां प्रातरनूदतिष्ठत् R. 2. 24; अनुविष्णु=विष्णोः पश्चात् Sk. **2** Along, along-side; जलानि सा तीरनिखातयूपा वहत्ययोध्यामनु राजधानीं R. **13. 61**; अनुगंगं वाराणसी situated along the Ganges. **3** After, in consequence of, being indicated by; जपमनु प्रावर्षत्. **4** With, along with, connected with; नदीमनु अवसिता सेना Sk. **5** Inferior or subordinate to ; अनु हरिं सुराः=हरेर्हीनाः. **6** In a particular relation or state ; भक्तो विष्णुमनु Sk. **7** Having a part or share, participation; लक्ष्मीर्हरिमनु. **8** Repetition; अनुदिवसं day by day, every day. **9** Towards, in the direction of; near to, at; अनुवनमशानिर्गतः Sk.; °नदि *Si.* 7. 24 near the river. **10** In orderly succession, according to; अनुक्रमं in regular order; अनुज्येष्ठं in order of seniority. **11** Like, in imitation of; सर्वं मामनु ते प्रियाविरहजां त्वं तु व्यथां मानुभूः V. 4. 25; so अनुगर्ज् to roar after or in imitation of. **12** Conformable to; तथैव सोऽभूदन्वर्थो राजा प्रकृतिरंजनात् R. 4. 12 (अनुगतोऽर्थस्य).

अनुक *a.* **1** Greedy; desirous. **2** Libidinous, lustful.

अनुकथनं **1** Subsequent mention. **2** Relation, discourse, conversation.

अनुकनीयस् *a.* The next youngest.

अनुकंपक *a.* Pitying, taking compassion on.

अनुकंपनं Compassion, pity, tenderness, sympathy.

अनुकंपा Compassion, pity.

अनुकंप्य *pot. p.* Pitiable, worthy of sympathy; किं तन्न येनासि ममानुकंप्या R. 14.

74; Ku. 3. 76. **–च्यः** A courier, express messenger.

अनुकरणं, –कृतिः *f.* 1 Imitation. 2 Copy, resemblance, similarity; शब्दानुकरणं onomatopœia.

अनुकर्षः –कर्षणं 1 Dragging after, attraction in general. 2 Grammatical attraction. 3 The axle-tree or bottom of a carriage. 4 Delayed performance of a duty; also अनुकर्षन्.

अनुकल्पः A secondary direction or precept, a substitute or alternative to be used in times of necessity when the primary one (प्रथमकल्प) is not possible; प्रभुः प्रथमकल्पस्य योऽनुकल्पेन वर्तते Ms. 11. 30. 3. 147.

अनुकामीन *a.* Going at will or pleasure; one who acts as he pleases; अनुकामीनतां त्यज Bk.

अनुकार=अनुकरणं q. v.

अनुकाल *a.* Opportune, timely.

अनुकीर्तनं Act of proclaiming or publishing.

अनुकूल *a.* 1 Favourable, agreeable, as wind, fate &c. 2 Friendly, kind. 3 Conformable to **—लः** 1 A faithful or kind husband (एकरतिः S. D. or एकनिरतः एकस्यामेव नायिकायां आसक्तः), a variety of नायक. **—लं** Favour, kindness; नारीणामनुकूलमाचरसि चेत् K. P. 9.

अनुकूलयति Den. P. To conciliate, propitiate.

अनुक्रकच *a.* Serrated, dentated like a saw.

अनुक्रमः 1 Succession, order, sequence, arrangement, method, due order; प्रचक्रमे वक्तुमनुक्रमज्ञा R. 6. 70. श्वश्रूजनं सर्वमनुक्रमेण 14. 60. 2 A table of contents, index.

अनुक्रमणं 1 Proceeding in order. 2 Following. **—णी, –णिका** A table of contents, an index showing the successive contents of a work.

अनुक्रिया=अनुकरणं q. v.

अनुक्रोशः Pity; compassion, tenderness (with loc.); भगवन्कामदेव न ते मय्यनुक्रोशः *S.* 3; Me. 115.

अनुक्षणं *ind.* Every instant, constantly, frequently.

अनुक्षत्तृ *m.* (त्ता) The attendant of a door-keeper or charioteer.

अनुक्षेत्रं Stipend given to certain temple-worshippers in Orissa (?)

अनुख्यातिः *f.* 1 Descrying. 2 Reporting, revealing.

अनुग *a.* (In comp.) Following; tallying with **—गः** A follower, obedient servant, companion; तद्भूतनाथानुग R. 2. 58; 9. 12.

अनुगतिः *f.* Following; गतानुगतिको लोकः following, imitating; see under गत.

अनुगमः–मनं 1 Following. 2 Following in death, self-immolation of a widow on her husband's funeral pile. 3 Imitating; approaching. 4 Conformity, accordance.

अनुगर्जित *p. p.* Roared. **—तं** A roaring echo.

अनुगवीनः A cowherd.

अनुगामिन् *m.* A follower, companion.

अनुगुण *a* Having similar qualities, of the same nature; favourable or agreeable to, suitable, according to, congenial with; (वीणा) उत्कंठितस्य हृदयानुगुणा वयस्या Mk. 3. 3 agreeable or pleasing to the heart, exactly after the heart (Tv. here takes °णा to mean तंत्रीयुक्तवीणा itself). **—णं** *adv.* 1 Favourably, conformably to one's desires. 2 Agreeably or conformably to (in comp.). 3 Naturally.

अनुग्रहः–हणं 1 A favour, kindness, obligation; obliging; निग्रहानुग्रहकर्ता Pt. 1; पादार्पणानुग्रहपूतपृष्ठं R. 2. 35. 2 Acceptance. 3 Rear-guard.

अनुग्रासकः A mouthful.

अनुचरः 1 A companion, follower, attendant, servant; तेनानुचरेण धेनोः R. 2. 4; 26, 52. **–री,–रा** A female attendant.

अनुचारकः A follower, servant &c. **—रिका** A female servant.

अनुचित *a.* 1 Wrong, improper. 2 Unusual; unfit.

अनुचिंता, चिंतनं 1 Calling to mind, thinking of, meditating upon. 2 Recalling, recollecting. 3 Constant thinking, anxiety.

अनुच्छादः The part of a man's under garment which is allowed to hang down in front from the waist to the feet (Mar. नि-या).

अनुच्छित्तिः *f.* **अनुच्छेदः** Non-extirpation; non-destruction; indestructibility.

अनुज–जात *a.* Born after, later, younger; असौ कुमारस्तमजोऽनुजातः R. 6. 78. **—जः, –जातः** 1 A younger brother. **—जा, –जाता** A younger sister.

अनुजन्मन् *m.* A younger brother; जननाथ तवानुजन्मनां Ki. 2. 17.

अनुजीविन् *a.* Dependent, living on or upon. —*m.* A dependent, servant, follower; अवंचनीयाः प्रभवोऽनुजीविभिः Ki. 1. 4, 10.

अनुज्ञा,–ज्ञानं 1 Permission, consent, sanction. 2 Permission or leave to depart. 3 Excusing. 4 An order, command.

अनुज्ञापकः one who commands or orders.

अनुज्ञापनं,–ज्ञप्तिः *f.* 1 Authorising. 2 Issuing an order or command.

अनुज्येष्ठं *ind.* According to seniority.

अनुतर्षः 1 Thirst; सोपचारमुपशांतविचारं सानुतर्षमनुतर्षपदेन Si. 10. 2 (thirst and liquor). 2 Wish, desire. 3 A drinking vessel. 4 Liquor itself.

अनुतापः Repentance, remorse; जातानुतापेव सा V. 4. 38 stung with remorse.

अनुतर्षणं=अनुतर्ष 3 and 4.

अनुतिलं *ind.* Grain after grain, *i. e.* by grains, or very minutely.

अनुत्क *a.* Not over-anxious, not repentant or regretful.

अनुत्तम *a.* 1 Having no superior or better, unsurpassed, the very best or highest, pre-eminently the best; सर्वद्रव्येषु विद्यैव द्रव्यमाहुरनुत्तमं H. Pr. 4; कांक्षन् गतिमनुत्तमां Ms. 2. 242. 2 (In gram.) Not used in the उत्तम or first person.

अनुत्तर *a.* 1 Principal, chief. 2 Best, excellent. 3 Without a reply, silent, unable to answer; भवत्यवज्ञा च भवत्यनुत्तरात् Naishadha. 4 Fixed, firm. 5 Low, inferior, base, mean. 6 Southern.**—रं** No reply, a reply which, being evasive, is considered to be no reply.**—रा** The south.

अनुत्तरंग *a.* Steady, not ruffled (by waves); अपामिवाधारमनुत्तरंगं Ku. 3. 48.

अनुत्थानं Absence of exertion.

अनुत्सूत्र *a.* Not deviating from the Sûtra (of Pâṇini or of morality); not anomalous or irregular; ° पदन्यासा सद्वृत्तिः सन्निबंधना *Si.* 2 112.

अनुत्सेकः Absence of haughtiness or pride; °को लक्ष्म्यां Bh. 2. 63; modesty.

अनुत्सेकिन् *a.* Not puffed up; भाग्येषु °नी भव *S.* 4. 17.

अनुदर *a.* 1 Having a slender waist; thin, lank; (see अ).

अनुदर्शनं Inspection.

अनुदात्त *a.* Grave (accent); not elevated or raised (not pronounced with the Uda'tta accent); accentless.**—त्तः** The grave accent.

अनुदार *a.* 1 Not liberal, niggardly; not high or noble. 2 Adhering to or followed by a wife: यस्मिन्प्रसीदसि पुनः स भवत्युदारोऽनुदारश्च K. P. 4 (used in sense 1 also). 3 Having a suitable worthy wife.

अनुदिनं-दिवसं *ind.* Daily, day after day.

अनुदेशः 1 Pointing back; a rule or direction which refers or points back to a previous rule; यथासंख्यमनुदेशः समानां P. I. 3. 10. 2 Direction, order.

अनुद्धत *a.* Not raised or puffed up; °ताः सत्पुरुषाः समृद्धिभिः *S.* 5. 12.

अनुद्भट *a.* 1 Not bold; soft, mild. 2 Not exalted or lofty.

अनुद्रुत *p. p.* 1 Followed, pursued; (sometimes used actively). 2 Sent or brought back (as sound).**—तं** A measure of time in music=half *druta*.

अनुद्वाहः Non-marriage, celibacy.

अनुधावनं 1 Going or running after, following, pursuing; तुरग° कंडितसंधेः *S.* 2. 2 Close pursuit of an object; research, investigation. 3 Seeking a mistress, though unattainable. 4 Cleansing, purification.

अनुध्यानं 1 Thought, meditation, religious contemplation. 2 Thinking of, remembrance; या नः प्रीतिर्विरूपाक्ष त्वदनुध्यानसंभवा Ku. 6. 21. 3 Wishing well of, affectionate solicitude for.

अनुनयः 1 Conciliation, propitiation; प्रकृतिवक्रः स कस्यानुनयं प्रतिगृह्णाति S. 4. 2 Courtesy, civility, conciliatory act. 3 An humble supplication or entreaty, a request in general ; ° आमंत्रणं conciliatory address. 4 Discipline, training, regulation of conduct.

अनुनादः Sound, noise, reverberation, echo.

अनुनायक *a.* Submissive, humble, supplicating.

अनुनायिक *a.* Conciliating.—**का** A female character, subordinate to the Nâyikâ or leading character, such as a friend, nurse, maid-servant &c.; सखी प्रव्रजिता दासी प्रेष्या धात्रेयिका तथा । अन्याश्च शिल्पकारिण्यो विज्ञेया ह्यनुनायिकाः ॥.

अनुनासिक *a.* 1 Nasal, pronounced through the nose. -**कं** The nasal twang. —COMP.--**आदिः** a conjunct consonant beginning with a nasal.

अनुनिर्देशः Description or relation following the previous order or sequence ; भूयसामुपदिष्टानां क्रियाणामथ कर्मणाम् । क्रमशो योऽनुनिर्देशो यथासंख्यं तदुच्यते ॥ S. D.

अनुनीतिः=अनुनय q. v.

अनुपघातः Absence of damage or detriment ; °**अर्जित** obtained without any detriment (to the paternal estate).

अनुपतनं,-पातः 1 Falling upon, alighting upon in succession. 2 Following, pursuit. 3 Proportion. 4 Rule of three. —**तं** *ind.* (regarded as a ṇamul from पत्) Following in succession, going after ; लतानुपातं कुसुमान्यगृह्णात् Bk. 2. 11 (लतामनुपात्य going to creeper after creeper, or, after bending the creepers.

अनुपथ *a.* Following the road. —**थं** *adv.* Along the road.

अनुपद *a.* Following the feet closely. —**दं** A chorus, burden of a song. —*ind.* 1 Along the feet, near the feet. 2 Step by step, at every step. 3 Word for word. 4 On the heels of, close behind or after, immediately after (of time or space) ; गच्छतां पुरो भवंतौ । अहमप्यनुपदमागत एव *S.* 3 ; oft. with gen. or in comp. in this sense ; (तौ) आशिषामनुपदं समस्पृशत् पाणिना R. 11. 31 ; अमोघाः प्रतिगृह्णंतावर्घ्यानुपदमाशिषः 1. 44.

अनुपदवी A way, road.

अनुपदिन् *a.* Following, seeking after or for, a searcher, inquirer ; अनुपदमन्वेष्टा गवामनुपदी Sk.

अनुपदीना A shoe (boot, buskin, or slippers) of the length of the foot.

अनुपधः 'Having no उपधा or penultimate', a letter or syllable not preceded by another.

अनुपधि *a.* Guileless, without fraud रहस्यं साधूनामनुपधि विशुद्धं विजयते U. 2. 2.

अनुपन्यासः 1 Not mentioning; non-statement. 2 Uncertainty, doubt, failure of proof.

अनुपपत्तिः *f.* 1 Failure, failing to be; लक्षणा शक्यसंबंधस्तात्पर्यानुपपत्तितः Bhâshâ. P. 82 (तात्पर्य° being the failure of the meaning aimed at, or of any connected meaning) 2 Inapplicability, not being applicable. 3 Inconclusive reasoning: absence of reasonable grounds.

अनुपम *a.* Incomparable, matchless, best, most excellent. —**मा** The female elephant of the south-west (mate of कुमुद.).

अनुपमेय-मित *a.* Matchless, incomparable.

अनुपलब्धिः *f.* Non-recognition, non-perception, one of the instruments of knowledge according to the Mimâmsakas, but not according to the Naiyâyikas.

अनुपलंभः Want of apprehension, non-perception.

अनुपवीतिन् *m.* One who does not wear the sacred thread (belonging to his caste).

अनुपशयः Any thing or circumstance that aggravates a malady.

अनुपसंहारिन् *m.* A kind of हेत्वाभास or fallacy in Nyâya, which includes every known thing in the पक्ष and thus prevents the corroboration of a general rule of causation by illustrations, positive, or negative; as सर्वं नित्यं प्रमेयत्वात्.

अनुपसर्गः 1 A word (particle &c.) that is not, or has not the force of an *Upasarga*. 2 That which has no Upasarga.

अनुपस्थानं Absence, not being at hand.

अनुपस्थित *a.* Not present, absent.

अनुपस्थितिः *f.* 1 absence. 2 Inability to remember.

अनुपहत *a.* 1 Not injured. 2 Not used, unbleached, new (as cloth).

अनुपाख्य *a.* Not clearly visible or discernible.

अनुपात=अनुपतनं q. v.

अनुपातकं A heinous crime such as theft, murder, adultery &c. 35 such sins are enumerated in Vishṇusmṛiti; Manu mentions 30 kinds.

अनुपानं A drink taken with or after medicine; a fluid vehicle in medicine.

अनुपालनं Preserving, keeping up, obeying.

अनुपुरुषः A follower.

अनुपूर्व *a.* 1 Regular, having a suitable measure, symmetrical; वृत्तानुपूर्वे च न चातिदीर्घे Ku. 1. 35. °केश who has regular hair; °गात्र having regularly-shaped limbs; so ° दंष्ट्र, °नाभि, °पाणि . 2 Orderly successive.-COMP. -**ज** *a.* descended in a regular line.-**वत्सा** a cow that calves regularly.

अनुपूर्वशः,-पूर्वेण *adv.* In regular order, successively.

अनुपेत *a.* 1 Not endowed with. 2 Not invested with the sacred thread (अनुपनीत).

अनुप्रज्ञानं Tracing, tracking.

अनुप्रपातं-दं *ind.* Going in succession ; गेह° तं-दं आस्ते, गेहं अनुप्रपातं-दं Sk.

अनुप्रयोगः Additional use, repetition.

अनुप्रवेशः 1 Entrance into; R. 3. 22; 10. 51. 2 Adapting oneself to the will of.

अनुप्रश्नः A subsequent question (having reference to what the teacher has previously said).

अनुप्रसक्तिः *f.* 1 Very close attachment. 2 Very close logical connection (of words).

अनुप्रसादनं Propitiation, conciliation.

अनुप्राप्तिः *f.* Getting to, reaching.

अनुप्लवः A follower, servant; सानुप्लवः प्रभुरपि क्षणदाचराणा R. 13. 75.

अनुप्रासः Alliteration, repetition of similar letters, syllables or sounds ; वर्णसाम्यमनुप्रासः K. P. For definitions and examples see S. D. 633-38 and K. P. 9th Ullâsa.

अनुबद्ध *p. p.* 1 Bound, tied to. 2 Following in the train, coming as a consequence. 3 Connected with. 4 Constantly sticking to, continuous

अनुबंधः 1 Binding or fastening on, connection, attachment, tie (lit. & fig.) 2 Uninterrupted succession, continuity; series, chain; बाष्पं कुरु स्थिरतया विरतानुबंधं *S.* 4. 14; वैर°, मत्सर°; सानुबंधाः कथं न स्युः संपदो मे निरापदः R. 1. 64. 3 Consequence, result (good or bad). 4 Intention, design, motive, cause; अनुबंधं परिज्ञाय देशकालौ च तत्त्वतः । सारापराधौ चालोक्य दंडं दंड्येषु पातयत् Ms. 8. 126. 5 An adjunct of a thing, a secondary member. 6 Introductory reasons (an indispensable element of the Vedânta). 7 (Gram) An indicatory syllable or letter intended to denote some peculiarity in the inflection, accent &c. of the word to which it is attached ; as ऌ in गम्ऌ. 8 An obstacle, impediment. 9 Beginning, commencement. 10 Course, pursuit.

अनुबंधनं Connection, succession, series &c.

अनुबंधिन् *a.* (oft. at the end of comp.) 1 Connected with, attached or related to. 2 Having in its train, resulting in, having as a consequence; दुःखं दुःखानुबंधि V. 4 one misfortune closely follows another, or misfortunes never come single. **3** Thriving, prosperous, uninterrupted; ऊर्ध्वं गतं यस्य न चानुबंधि R. 6. 77 uninterrupted or allpervading.

अनुबंध्य *a.* **1** Principal, chief. **2** To be killed (as a bull).

अनुबलं A rear-guard, an auxiliary army following another.

अनुबोधः **1** An after-thought, recollection. **2** Reviving the scent of faded perfumes.

अनुबोधनं Recollection, reminding.

अनुभवः **1** Direct perception or cognition, knowledge derived from personal observation or experiment, the impression on the mind not derived from memory, one of the kinds of knowledge, See T. S. 34. (The Naiyâyikas recognize प्रत्यक्ष, अनुमान, उपमान and शाब्द as the four sources of knowledge ; the Vedântins and Mîmâmsakas add two more अर्थापत्ति and अनुपलब्धि). **2** Experience ; अनुभवं वचसा सखि लुंपसि N.4. 105. **3** Understanding. **4** Result, consequence. –Comp. **–सिद्ध** *a.* established by experience.

अनुभावः **1** Dignity, consequence or dignity of person, majestic lustre, splendour, might, power, authority ; (परिमेयपुरःसरौ) अनुभावविशेषात्तु सेनापरिवृताविव R. 1. 37 ; संभावनीयानुभावा अस्याकृतिः *S.* 7. **2** (In Rhet.) An external manifestation or indication of a feeling (भाव) by appropriate symptoms, such as by look, gesture &c.; भावं मनोगतं साक्षात् स्वगतं व्यंजयंति ये तेऽनुभावा इति ख्याताः; यथा भ्रूभंगः कोपस्य व्यंजकः; see S. D. 162 &c. **3** Determination, belief.

अनुभावक *a.* Causing to understand, indicative.

अनुभावनं Indication of feelings by signs, gestures &c.

अनुभाषणं **1** Repetition of an assertion to refute it. **2** Repeating what has been said.

अनुभूतिः *f.* =अनुभव q. v.

अनुभोगः **1** Enjoyment. **2** A grant of land in perpetuity for service done.

अनुभ्रातृ *m.* A younger brother.

अनुमत *p.p.* **1** Approved, permitted, allowed, granted ; °गमना *S.* 4. 9 allowed to depart. **2** Liked, beloved, dear to. **—तः** A lover. **—तं** Consent, approval, permission.

अनुमतिः *f.* **1** Permission, consent, approval. **2** The 15th day of the moon's age on which she rises one digit less than full. –Comp. **–पत्रं** a deed expressing assent.

अनुमननं **1** Assent ; sufferance. **2** Independence.

अनुमंत्रणं Consecration by hymns and prayers.

अनुमरणं Following in death ; तन्मरणे चानुमरणं करिष्यामीति मे निश्चयः H. 3 ; post-cremation of a widow.

अनुमा Inference, conclusion from given premises ; see अनुमिति.

अनुमानं **1** Inferring as the instrument of an अनुमिति, conclusion from given premises ; an inference, conclusion ; one of the four means of obtaining knowledge according to the Nyâya system. **2** A guess, conjecture. **3** Analogy. **4** (In Rhet.) A figure which consists in a notion, expressed in a peculiarly striking manner, of a thing established by proof; S. D 711 ; यत्र पतत्यबलानां दृष्टिर्निशिताः पतंति तत्र शराः । तच्चापरोपितशरो धावत्यासां पुरः स्मरो मन्ये ॥ See K. P. 10. –Comp. **–उक्ति** *f.* reasoning, logical inference.

अनुमापक *a.* (**पिका** *f.*) causing an inference as an effect, being the ground of an inference.

अनुमासः The following month. **—सं** *ind.* Every month.

अनुमितिः *f.* Inference from given premises ; the knowledge that arises from deduction or syllogistic reasoning.

अनुमेय *pot. p.* Inferable, to be inferred ; फलानुमेयाः प्रारंभाः R. 1. 20.

अनुमोदनं Approval, seconding, acceptance, compliance.

अनुयाजः A part of a sacrificial ceremony (यज्ञांगं) ; secondary or supplementary sacrificial rite ; usually written अनूयाज ; also **अनुयागः**.

अनुयातृ *m.* A follower.

अनुयात्रं-त्रा Retinue, train ; attendance upon ; following.

अनुयात्रिकः A follower, attendant ; S. 1, 2.

अनुयानं Following.

अनुयायिन् *a.* Following ; attending, consequent. —*m.* A follower (lit. & fig.); रामानुजानुयायिनः; a dependant or attendant ; न्यषेधि शेषोऽप्यनुयायिवर्गः R. 2. 4, 19.

अनुयोक्तृ *m.* An examiner, inquirer ; a teacher.

अनुयोगः **1** A question, inquiry, examination. **2** Censure, reproof. **3** Solicitation. **4** Exertion. **5** Religious meditation. **6** Comment. –Comp. **–कृत** *m.* 1 an interrogator. –2 a teacher ; spiritual preceptor.

अनुयोजनं A question, inquiry,

अनुयोज्यः A servant.

अनुरक्त *p. p.* **1** Reddened, coloured. **2** Pleased, contented ; loyally devoted.

अनुरक्तिः *f.* Love, attachment, devotion, affection.

अनुरंजक *a.* Gratifying, pleasing.

अनुरंजनं Conciliating, satisfying, gratifying, pleasing, keeping contented.

अनुरणनं **1** Sounding conformably to ; a continuous tinkling echo produced by the sounds of bells, anklets &c. **2** The power of words called व्यंजना q. v.; the meaning suggested by what is actually stated ; क्रमलक्ष्यत्वादेवानुरणनरूपो यो व्यंग्यः. S. D. 4.

अनुरतिः *f.* Love, attachment.

अनुरथ्या A foot-path, a by-road.

अनुरसः, **–रसितं** Echo. reverberation.

अनुरहस *a.* Secret, solitary, private. **—सं** *adv.* In secret.

अनुरागः **1** Redness. **2** Devotion, attachment, loyalty (opp. अपरागः) ; love, affection (with loc. or in comp.); कंटकितेन प्रथयति मय्यनुरागं कपोलेन *S.* 3. 15 ; R. 3. 10 ; °इंगित a gesture or external sign expressive of love.

अनुरागिन्, **अनुरागवत्** *a.* Attached, inspired with love.

अनुरात्रं *adv.* In the night ; every night, night after night.

अनुराधा N. of the 17th of the 27 lunar mansions or asterism. It consists of four stars.

अनुरूप *a.* **1** Like, resembling, corresponding to ; worthy of ; अनुरूपं वरं *S.* 1. **2** Suitable or fit, according to ; with gen. or in comp.; भव पितुरनुरूपस्त्वं गुणैर्लोककांतैः V. 5. 21.

अनुरूपं, **–पतः**, **–पेण**, **–पशः** *adv.* Conformably or agreeably to.

अनुरोधः **–धनं** **1** Compliance, gratification, fulfilling one's wishes &c. **2** Conformity, obedience, regard, consideration ; धर्मानुरोधात् K. 160, 180, 192. **3** Pressing entreaty, solicitation, request. **4** Bearing of a rule.

अनुरोधिन्, **–धक** *a.* Compliant.

अनुलापः Repetition, tautology.

अनुलासः-स्यः A peacock.

अनुलेपः **–लेपनं** **1** Unction, anointing. **2** Ointment, unguent; सुरभिकुसुमधूपानुलेपनानि K. 324.

अनुलोम *a.* **1** 'With the hair,' regular, in natural order (opp. प्रतिलोम); (hence), favourable; °कृष्टं क्षेत्रं प्रतिलोमं कर्षति Sk. ploughed in the regular direction. **2** Mixed (as a tribe).—**मं** *adv.* In regular or natural order.—**माः** (pl.) Mixed castes.–Comp. **–अर्थ** *a.* speaking in favour of ; जडानप्यनुलोमार्थान् प्रवाचः कृतिनां गिरः *Si.* 2.25.**–ज**,**–जन्मन्** *a.* born in due gradation, offspring of a mother inferior in caste to the father; said of the mixed tribes.

अनुल्बण *a.* **1** Not excessive, neither more nor less **2** Not clear or manifest.

अनुवंशः A genealogical table.

अनुवक्र *a.* Very crooked; somewhat crooked or oblique (said of planets.)

अनुवचनं Repetition, recitation ; teaching.

अनुवत्सरः A year.

अनुवर्तनं 1 Following (fig. also); compliance, obedience, conformity. 2 Gratifying, obliging. 3 Approval. 4 Result, consequence. 5 Supplying from a preceding Sûtra.

अनुवर्तिन् *a.* 1 Following, obeying, conforming to, with acc. or in com.

अनुवश *a.* Subject to the will of another, obedient. **—शः** Subjection, obedience.

अनुवाकः 1 Repeating. 2 subdivision of the Vedas, section, chapter.

अनुवाचनं 1 Causing to recite, teaching, instructing. 2 Reading to oneself; see वच् with अनु.

अनुवातः The windward direction.

अनुवादः 1 Repetition (in general). 2 Repetition by way of explanation, illustration or corroboration. 3 Explanatory repetition or reference to what is already mentioned; particularly, any portion of the Brâhmaṇas which comments on, illustrates, or explains a *Vidhi* or direction previously laid down and which does not itself lay down any directions. 4 Corroboration. 5 Report, rumour.

अनुवादक,-वादिन् *a.* 1 Explanatory. 2 Conformable to, in harmony with.

अनुवाद्य *pot. p.* 1 To be explained or illustrated 2 (In gram.) To be made the subject of an assertion (in a sentence), opposed to विधेय which affirms or denies something about the subject. In a sentence the अनुवाद्य or subject which is supposed to be already known is repeated to mark its connection with the विधेय or predicate, and should be placed first; अनुवाद्यमनुक्त्वैव न विधेयमुदीरयेत्.

अनुवारं *ind.* Time after time, repeatedly, frequently.

अनुवासः-सनं 1 Perfuming or scenting (in general,) with incense &c. 2 Perfuming clothes by dipping the ends. 3 (°नः also) A syringe, clyster-pipe (Mar. पिचकारी); an oily enema or the operation itself.

अनुवासित *a.* Fumigated, perfumed.

अनुवित्तिः *f.* Finding, obtaining.

अनुविद्ध *p. p.* 1 Pierced, bored; कीटानुविद्धरत्नादिसाधारण्येन काव्यता S. D. 2 Overspread, intertwined; full of, pervaded by, mixed or blended with, intermixed; सरसिजमनुविद्धं शैवलेनापि रम्यं *S.* 1 20. 3 Connected with, relating to. 4 Set, inlaid; variegated; रत्नानुविद्धार्णवमेखलाया दिशः सपत्नी भव दक्षिणस्याः R. 6. 63.

अनुविधानं 1 Obedience. 2 Acting in conformity to (orders &c.).

अनुविधायिन् *a.* Obedient, submissive.

अनुविनाशः Perishing after.

अनुविष्टंभः Being obstructed in consequence of.

अनुवृत्त *p. p.* 1 Obeying, following &c. 2 Uninterrupted, continued.

अनुवृत्तिः *f.* 1 Approval. 2 Obedience, conformity, following, continuity. 3 Acting according or suitably to, compliance, acquiescence; gratifying, pleasing; कांता ° चातुर्यमपि शिक्षितं वत्सेन U. 3, Mal. 9. 4 (Gram.) Being supplied or repeated in a following rule; continued influence of a preceding on a following rule. 5 Repetition; वर्णानामनुवृत्तिरनुप्रासः.

अनुवेधः=अनुव्याध q. v.

अनुवेलं *ind.* Ever and anon, constantly; इति स्म पृच्छत्यनुवेलमादृतः R. 3. 5.

अनुवेशः-शनं 1 Following, entering after. 2 Marriage of a younger brother before the elder is married.

अनुव्यंजनं A secondary token.

अनुव्यवसायः (In Nyâya) Consciousness of the perception; (in Vedânta phil.) perception of a sentiment or judgment.

अनुव्याधः-वेधः 1 Hurting, piercing, perforating; न हि कीटानुवेधादयो रत्नस्य रत्नत्वं व्याहंतुमीशाः S. D. 1. 2 Contact, union; मुखामोदं मदिरया कृतानुव्याधमुद्वमन् *Si.* 2. 20. 3 Blending. 4 Obstructing.

अनुव्याहरणं, -व्याहारः 1 Repetition, repeated utterance. 2 A curse, imprecation.

अनुव्रजनं-व्रज्या Following, going after, especially a departing guest.

अनुव्रत *a.* Devoted or faithful to, attached to (with acc. or gen.).

अनुशतिक *a.* Accompanied with or bought for a hundred.

अनुशयः 1 Repentance, remorse; regret, sorrow; नन्वनुशयस्थानमेतत् Mâl. 8; इतो गतस्यानुशयो मा भूदिति V. 4; *Si.* 2. 14. 2 Intense enmity or anger, शिशुपालोऽनुशयं परं गतः *Si.* 16. 2; यस्मिन्नमुक्तानुशया सदैव जागर्ति भुजंगी Mâl. 6. 1. 3 Hatred. 4 Close connection, as with a consequence; close attachment (to any object). 5 (In Vedânta phil.) The result or consequence of bad deeds which very closely clings to them and makes the soul enter other bodies after enjoying temporary freedom from recurring births. 6 Regret in the case of purchases, technically called rescission; see क्रीतानुशय.

अनुशयान *a.* Regretting &c. **—ना** A variety of heroine; one who is sad and dejected, being apprehensive of the loss of her lover.

अनुशयिन् *a.* 1 Devotedly attached to, faithful. 2 Repentant, penitent. 3 Hating intensely. 4 Connected as with a consequence.

अनुशरः A sort of evil spirit, Râkshasa.

अनुशासक,-शासिन्,-शास्तृ, or **शासितृ** *a.* One who directs, instructs, governs or punishes; कविं पुराणमनुशासितारं Bg. 8. 9. ruler; एष चोरानुशासी राजेति भयादुत्पतितः V. 4.

अनुशासनं Advice, persuasion, instruction, laying down rules or precepts; a law, rule, or precept; भवत्यधिक्षेप इवानुशासनं Ki. 1. 28. words of advice; तन्मनोरनुशासनं Ms. 8. 139; नामलिंग° laying down rules on the gender of nouns, explanation of gender &c.; शब्दानुशासनं Sk.

अनुशिक्षिन् *a.* Practising, learing.

अनुशिष्टिः *f.* Instruction, teaching; order, command.

अनुशीलनं Intent or assiduous application, constant pursuit or exercise, constant or repeated practice or study.

अनुशोकः,-शोचनं Sorrow, repentance regret; अनुशु (शो) चितं in the same sense.

अनुश्रवः Vedic or sacred tradition.

अनुषक्त *p. p.* 1 Connected with. 2 Clinging or adhering to.

अनुषंगः 1 Close adherence or attendance; connection, conjunction, association. 2 Coalition. 3 Connection of word with word. 4 Necessary consequence. 5 Compassion, pity, tenderness.

अनुषंगिक *a.* Following as a necessary result; concomitant.

अनुषंगिन् *a.* 1 Connected with, adhering or sticking to. 2 Following as a necessary consequence. 3 Related or applicable to, common, prevailing; विभुतानुषंगि भयमेति जनः Ki. 6. 35.

अनुषंजनीय *pot. p.* To be supplied from a preceding sentence (as a word).

अनुषेकः, -सेचनं Rewatering, sprinkling over again.

अनुष्टुतिः *f.* Praise (in due order).

अनुष्टुभ् *f.* 1 Following in praise; speech. 2 Sarasvatî. 3 N. of a class of metres consisting of four Pâdas of 8 syllables each, the whole stanza consisting of 32 syllables.

अनुष्ठातृ, -ष्ठायिन् *a.* Doing, performing.

अनुष्ठानं 1 Doing, performance, execution, accomplishment &c.; obeying; उपरुध्यते तपोऽनुष्ठानं *S.* 4 practice of religious austerities. 2 Commencing, undertaking, engaging in. 3 Commencement or course of conduct, procedure, course of action. 4 practice of religious rites or ceremonies, any religious rite or ceremony.

अनुष्ठापनं Causing to do an act.

अनुष्ण *a.* 1 Not hot, cold. 2 Apathetic; lazy, sluggish. **—ष्णः** Cold touch or sensation. **—ष्णं** A water-lily, blue lotus (उत्पल).

अनुष्यंदः A hind wheel.

अनुसंधानं 1 Inquiry, investigation; close inspection or scrutiny, examination. 2 Aiming at. 3 Planning, arranging, getting ready &c. 4 Suitable connection.

अनुसंहित *p. p.* Inquired into, investigated. —**तं** *adv.* In the Samhitâ text; according to this text.

अनुसमयः Regular or proper connection, as of words.

अनुसमापनं Regular completion.

अनुसंबद्ध *a.* Connected with.

अनुसरः Follower, companion, attendant.

अनुसरणं 1 Following, pursuing, going after. 2 Conformity to.

अनुसर्पः A reptile (in general).

अनुसवनं *ind.* 1 After a sacrifice. 2 At every sacrifice. 3 Every moment.

अनुसाम *a.* Conciliated, friendly, favourable.

अनुसायं *ind.* Every evening.

अनुसूचनं Indication, pointing out.

अनुसारः 1 Going after, following (fig. also); pursuit ; शब्दानुसारेण अवलोक्य *S.* 7 looking in the direction of the sound. 2 Conformity to, accordance with; conformity to usage. 3 Custom, usage, established practice. 4 Received or established authority.

अनुसारक,-सारिन् *a.* 1 Following, pursuing, going after, attendant on; मृगानुसारिणं पिनाकिनं *S.* 1. 6; कृपणानुसारि च धनं Pt. 1. 278. 2 According or conformable to, following यथाशास्त्र° Ms. 7. 31. 3 Seeking, looking out for, investigating, scrutinizing.

अनुसारणा Going after, pursuit; तस्मात्पलायमानानां कुर्यान्नात्यनुसारणां Mb.

अनुसूचक Indicating, pointing out to.

अनुसृतिः *f.* Going after, following, conforming to, in accordance with.

अनुसैन्यं The rear of an army, rearguard.

अनुस्कंदं *ind.* Having entered or gone into in succession; गेहं गेहमनुस्कंदं Sk.

अनुस्तरणं Strewing or spreading round.-**णी** A cow; especially the cow sacrificed at the funeral ceremony.

अनुस्मरणं 1 Recollection, remembering. 2 Repeated recollection.

अनुस्मृतिः *f.* 1 Cherished recollection. 2 Thinking of one thing to the exclusion of others.

अनुस्यूत *a.* 1 Woven together, regularly and uninterruptedly. 2 Sewn on, fastened to. 3 Closely attached or linked to.

अनुस्वानः 1 Sounding conformably to. 2 An after sound; echo; see अनुरणन.

अनुस्वारः The nasal sound which is marked by a dot above the line (.) and which always belongs to a preceding vowel.

अनुहरणं,-हारः Imitation, resemblance, similarity.

अनूकः -कं 1 Family, race. 2 Disposition, temperament; character, peculiarity of race.

अनूचान *a.* or **—नः** 1 One devoted to study, learned; especially one well versed in the Vedas with their Angas so as to be able to repeat, and teach them; इदमूचुरनूचानाः Ku. 6. 15. 2 Modest.

अनूढ *a.* 1 Not borne or carried. 2 Unmarried. **—ढा** An unmarried woman. –Comp. **–मान** *a.* bashful. **–गमनं** (°ढा°) Fornication. **–भ्रातृ** *m.* (°ढा°) 1. the brother of an unmarried woman. —2 the brother of the concubine of a king.

अनूदकं Want of water; drought.

अनूद्देशः 'Relative order,' N. of a figure of speech in which a reference is made in successive order to what precedes; यथासंख्यमनुद्देश उद्दिष्टानां क्रमेण यत् S. D. 732.

अनून *a.* 1 Not inferior, not less; not wanting or lacking in; वृंदावने चैत्ररथादनूने R. 6. 50; गुणैरनूनां R. 6. 37. 2 Full, whole, entire; large, great; *Si.* 4. 11.

अनूप *a.* Watery, rich or abounding in water, marshy. **–पः –पं** 1 A watery place or country. 2. N. of a particular country (**–पाः** pl.); R. 6. 37. 3. A marsh, bog. 4 A pond or tank of water. 5 Bank or side (of a river, mountain). 6 A buffalo. 7 A frog. 8 A kind of partridge. 9 An elephant.–Comp.–**जं** moist, ginger. **–प्राय** *a.* marshy, boggy.

अनूयाज, अनूराधा=अनुयाज, अनुराधा.

अनूरु *a.* Thighless.—**रुः** Aruṇa, the charioteer of the sun (who is represented as having no thighs); the dawn; see अरुण. –Comp.–**सारथिः** the sun (having अनूरु for his charioteer); गतं तिरश्चीनमनूरुसारथेः *Si.* 1. 2.

अनूर्जित *a.* 1 Not strong, weak, powerless. 2 Free from pride.

अनूषर *a.* 1 Saline, the same as ऊषर; cf. उत्तम and अनुत्तम. 2 Not saline.

अनृच् –च *a.* 1 Without a hymn, 2 Not conversant with, or not studying, the *Rig*veda; one not invested with the sacred thread and hence not yet entitled to study the Vedas (as a boy;) अनृचो माणवकः Mugdha.

अनृजु *a.* Not straight, crooked; (fig.) unfair, wicked, dishonest.

अनृण *a.* Free from debt, with gen. of person or thing एनामनृणां करोमि *S.* 1; प्राणैर्दशरथप्रीतेरनृणं (गृध्रं) R. 12. 54. Every one that is born has three debts to pay off:—to Sages, Gods, and the Manes; and he who learns the Vedas offers sacrifices to Gods, and begets a son, becomes अनृण (free from debt); see R. 8. 30.

अनृणिन् *a.*=अनृण.

अनृत *a.* 1 Not true, false (words) प्रियं च नानृतं ब्रूयात् Ms. 4. 138.—**तं** Falsehood, lying, deception, fraud. 2 Agriculture (opp. सत्य); Ms. 4. 5. –Comp. **–वदनं, भाषणं आख्यानं** lying, falsehood.–**वादिन्–वाच्** *a.* a liar. **–व्रत** *a.* false to one's vows or premises.

अनृतुः Unfit season, improper or premature time. –Comp. **–कन्या** a girl before menstruation.

अनेक *a.* 1 Not one; more than one, many; अनेकपितृकाणां तु पितृतो भागकल्पना Y. 2. 120, Ki. 1. 16; several, various. 2 Separated; divided.—Comp. **–अक्षर, अच्** *a.* having more than one vowel or syllable; polysyllabic. **—अंत** *a.* 1 uncertain, doubtful, variable ; स्यादिस्त्यव्ययमनेकांतयाचकं –2=अनैकांतिक q. v. (**–तः**) 1 unsettled condition, absence of permanence. –2 uncertainty, an unessential part, as the several *anubandhas*. °**वादः** scepticism; °वादिन् *m.* a sceptic, an Arhat of the Jainas. **–अर्थ** *a.* 1 having many (more than one) meanings, homonymous; as the words गो, अमृत, अक्ष &c. अनेकार्थस्य शब्दस्य K. P. 2. –2 having the sense of the word अनेक. –3 having many objects or purposes. (**–र्थः**) multiplicity of objects, topics &c.-**आश्रय, –आश्रित** *a.* (in Vais. phil.) dwelling or abiding in more than one (such as संयोग, सामान्य).–**गुण** *a.* of many kinds, manifold, diverse.-**गोत्र** *a.* belonging to two families (such as a boy when adopted), *i. e.* that of his own, and that of his adoptive father. **–चित्त** *a.* fickle-minded. **–ज** *a.* born more than once. (**–जः**) a bird. **–पः** an elephant cf. द्विप; वन्येतरानेकपदर्शनेन R. 5. 47; *Si.* 5. 35, 12. 75. **–मुख** *a.* (**खी** *f.*) *a.* 1 many-faced. –2 dispersed, going in various directions; (बलानि) जगाहिरेऽनेकमुखानि मार्गान् Bk. 2. 54.—**युद्धविजयिन्, विजयिन्** *a.* victorious in many battles. **–रूप** *a.* 1 of various forms, multiform. –2 of various kinds or sorts.–3 fickle, changeable, of a varying nature; वेश्यांगनेव नृपनीतिरनेकरूपा Pt. 1. 425. **–लोचनः** N. of Siva; also of Indra. **–वचनं** the plural number ; dual also. **–वर्ण** *a.* involving more than one (unknown) quantity.-**विध** *a.* various, different. **–शफ** *a.* cloven-hoofed. **–साधारण** *a.* common to many.

अनेकधा *ind.* in various ways, variously; जगत्कृत्स्नं प्रविभक्तमनेकधा Bg. 11. 13.

अनेकशः *ind.* 1 Several or many times, frequently; अनेकशो निर्जितराजकस्त्वं Bk. 2. 52. 2 In various ways or manners. 3 In large numbers or quantities; पुत्रा अनेकशो मृता दाराश्च H. 1.

अनेडः A foolish or stupid person, fool. –COMP. **–मूक** *a.* 1 deaf and dumb; °मूकतायैश्च यतु दोषैरसंमतान् K. P. 7. –2. blind.–3 dishonest, wicked, perverse.

अनेनस् *a.* Sinless, blameless.

अनेहस् *m.* (हा-हसौ &c.) Time.

अनेकांत Variable, uncertain, unsteady; occasional.

अनेकांतिक *a.*(की *f.*) 1 Unsteady, not very important. 2 (in Logic) Name of one of the five main divisions of हेत्वाभास (fallacies,) otherwise called सव्यभिचार. It is of three kinds:— (*a*) साधारण, where the हेतु is found both in the सपक्ष and विपक्ष, the argument being therefore too general. (*b*) असाधारण where the *hetuis* in the पक्ष alone, the argument being not general enough. (*c*) अनुपसंहारी which embraces every known thing in the पक्ष, the argument being non-conclusive.

अनैक्यं 1 Absence of one, plurality. 2 Want of union, confusion. 3 Disorder, anarchy.

अनैतिह्यं Absence of traditional sanction or authority, or that which is without such sanction.

अनो *ind.* No, not.

अनोकशायिन् *m.* (यी) Not sleeping in a house, a beggar.

अनोकहः A tree; अनोकहाकंपितपुष्पगंधी R. 2. 13; 5. 69.

अनौचित्यं Unfitness, impropriety; अनौचित्यादृते नान्यद्रसभंगस्य कारणं K. P. 7.

अनौजस्यं Want of vigour, energy or strength; S. D. thus defines it; दौर्गत्याद्यैरनौजस्यं दैन्यं मलिनतादिकृत्.

अनौद्धत्यं 1 Freedom from pride, modesty, humility. 2 Tranquility, नदीरनौद्धत्यमपंकता महीं Ki. 4. 22.

अनौरस *a.* Not legitimate, not one's own, adopted (as a son).

अंत *a.* 1 Near. 2 Last. 3 Handsome, lovely; Me. 23; *Si.* 4. 40 (where, however, the ordinary sense of 'border' or 'skirt' may do as well, though Malli. renders अंत by रम्य, quoting the authority of शब्दार्णव). 4 Lowest, worst. 5 Youngest.—**तः** (*n.* in some senses) 1 (*a*) End, limit, boundary (in time or space); final limit, last or extreme point; स सागरांतां पृथिवीं प्रशास्ति H. 4. 50; दिगंते श्रूयंते Bv. 1. 2. 2 Skirt, border, edge, precinct; a place or ground in general; यत्र रम्यो वनांतः U. 2. 25; ओदकांतात् स्निग्धो जनोऽनुगंतव्यः *S.* 4; R. 2. 58. 3 End of a texture edge, skirt, वस्त्र°, पट°. 4 Vicinity, proximity, neighbourhood, presence; गंगाप्रपातांतविरूढशष्पं (गह्वरं) R. 2. 26.; पुंसां यमांतं व्रजतः Pt. 2. 115. 5 End, conclusion, termination, सेकांते R. 1. 51; दिनांते निहितं R. 4. 1. 6 Death, destruction; end or close of life; एका भवेत्स्वस्तिमती त्वदंते R. 2. 48; अद्य कांतः कृतांतो वा दुःखस्यांतं करिष्यति Udb. 7 (In gram.) A final syllable or letter of a word. 8 The last word in a compound. 9 Ascertainment or settlement (of a question); definite or final settlement; उभयोरपि दृष्टोऽतस्त्वनयोस्तत्त्वदर्शिभिः Bg. 2. 16. 10 The last portion or remainder; as निशांत, वेदांत. 11 Nature, condition; sort, species. 12 Disposition; essence; शुद्धांतः– COMP.**–अवशायिन्** *m.* a chân̄dâla.**–अवसायिन्** 1 a barber. –2 a chân̄dâla, low-caste. **–कर, करण कारिन्** *a.* fatal, mortal, destructive.**–कर्मन्** *n.* death.**–कालः, –वेला** time or hour of death. **–कृत्** *m.* death. **–ग** *a.* going to the end of, thoroughly conversant or familiar with, (in comp.) **गति, –गामिन्** *a.* perishing.**–गमनं** finishing, completing.–2 death.**–दीपकं** a figure of speech (in Rhetoric).**–पालः** 1 frontier-guard.–2 a door-keeper (rare).–**लीन** *a.* hidden, concealed.**–लोपः** dropping of the final of a word. **–वासिन्** (°ते°) *a.* dwelling near the frontiers; dwelling close by. (–*m.*) a pupil (who always dwells near his master to receive instruction); a chân̄dâla (who dwells at the extremity of a village). **–वेला**=°कालः q. v. **–शय्या** 1 a bed on the ground.–2 the last bed, death-bed.–3 a place for burial or burning.**–सत्क्रिया** funeral ceremonies. **–सद्** *m.* a pupil; तमुपासते गुरुमिवांतसदः Ki. 6. 34.

अंतक *a.* Causing death, destroying; fatal; R. 11. 21. **–कः** 1 Death. 2 Death personified, the destroyer; Yama, the god of death; ऋषिप्रभावान्मयि नांतकोऽपि प्रभुः प्रहर्तुं R. 2. 62.

अंततः *ind.* 1 From the end. 2 At last, finally; at length, lastly. 3 In part, partly. 4 inside, within. 5 In the lowest way (अंततः may have all the senses of अंत).

अंते *ind.* (loc. of अंत; oft. used adverbially) 1 In the end, at last. 2 Inside. 3 In the presence of, near, close by.–COMP.**–वासः** 1 a neighbour; companion.–2 a pupil; *Si.* 3. 55; Ve. 3. 7.**–वासिन्**=अंतवासिन् q. v. above.

अंतर् *ind.* 1 (Used as a prefix to verbs and regarded as a preposition or गति) (*a*) In the middle, between; in, into, inside; °हन्, °धा, °गम्, °भू, °इ, °ली &c. (*b*) Under 2 (Used adverbially) (*a*) Between, betwixt, amongst, within, in the middle or interior, inside (opp. बहिः) अवहितांतः R. 2. 32; अंतर्यश्च मृग्यते V. 1. 1 internally, in the mind. (*b*) By way of seizing or holding; अंतर्हत्या गतः (हतं परिगृह्य). 3 (As a separable preposition) (*a*) In, into, between, in the middle, within, (with loc.); निवसन्नंतर्दारुणि लंघ्यो वह्निः Pt. 1. 31; अप्स्वंतरमृतमप्सु Rv. 1. 23. 19. (*b*) Between (with acc.) Ved.; हिरण्मय्योर्ह कुश्योरंतरवहित आस *S*at. Br. (*c*) In, into, inside, in the interior, in the midst (with gen); प्रतिबलजलधेरंतरौर्वायमाणे Ve. 3. 5; अंतःकंचुकिकंचुकस्य Ratn. 2. 3; लघुवृत्तितया भिदां गतं बहिरंतश्च नृपस्य मंडलं Ki. 2. 53. 4 It is frequently used as the first member of compounds in the sense of 'internally' 'within,' 'in the interior,' 'having in the interior,' 'filled with,' or in the sense of 'inward,' 'internal' 'secret' forming Adverbial' Bahuvrîhi or Tatpurusha compounds. (*Note.* In comp. the र् of अंतर् is changed to a visarga before hard consonants, as अंतःकरणं, अंतःस्थ &c.). –COMP.**–अग्निः** inward fire, the fire which stimulates digestion. **–अंग** *a.* 1 inward, internal, comprehended, (with abl.); त्रयमंतरंगं पूर्वेभ्यः Pat. Sûtra. –2 related to, essential to or referring to the essential part of the अंग or base of a word. –3 dear, most beloved. **(–गं)** 1 the inmost limb or organ, the heart, mind. –2 an intimate friend, near or confidential person. **–आकाशः** the ether or Brahma that resides in the heart of man (a term often occurring in the Upanishads). **–आकूतं** secret or hidden intention.**–आत्मन्** *m.* (त्मा) 1 the inmost spirit or soul, the soul or mind; also the internal feelings, the heart; जीवसंज्ञोंतरात्मान्यः Ms. 12. 13, Bg. 6. 47. –2 (In phil.) the inherent supreme spirit or soul (residing in the interior of man); अंतरात्मासि देहिनां Ku. 6. 21. **–आराम** *a.* rejoicing in oneself, finding pleasure in his soul or heart; योंतः सुखोंतरारामस्तथांतर्ज्योतिरेव सः Bg. 5. 24.**–इंद्रियं** an internal organ or sense. **–करणं** the heart, soul; the seat of thought and feeling, thinking faculty, mind, conscience; प्रमाणं °प्रवृत्तयः *S.* 1. 22. **कुटिल** *a.* inwardly crooked (fig. also). (**–लः**) a conch-shell. **–कोणः** the inner corner. **–कोपः** secret anger, inward wrath. **–गडु** *a.* useless, unnecessary, unavailing; किमिनेनांतर्गडुना Sar. S. **–गम्-गत** &c. See under अंतर्गम्. **–गर्भ** *a.* bearing young, pregnant. **–गिर-रि** *ind.* in mountains. **–गुडवलयः** the sphincter muscle. **–गूढ** *a.* concealed inside; °**विषः** with poison concealed in the heart. **–गृहं,-गेहं,-भवनं** the inner apartment of a house.**–घणः –णं** the open space before the house between the entrance-door and the house (= porch or court). **–चर** *a.* pervading the body. **–जठरं** the stomach. **–ज्वलनं** inflammation. **–ताप** *a.* burning inwardly. (**–पः**) internal fever or heat *S*. 3. 13. **–दहनं-दाहः** 1 inward heat. –2 inflammation. **–देशः** an intermediate region of the compass. **–द्वारं** a private or secret door within the house. **–धि, हित** &c. see s. v.**–पटः –टं** a screen of cloth held between two persons who are to be united until the actual time union arrives. **–पदं** *ind*. in the interior of an inflected word. **–परिधानं** the innermost garment. **–पातः, पात्यः** 1 insertion of a letter (in gram.) –2 a post fixed in the middle of the sacrificial ground (used in ritual works). **–पतित, –पातिन्** *a*. 1 inserted. –2 included or comprised in; falling within. **–पुरं** 1 inner apartments of a palace (set apart for women); female or women's apartments, harem; कन्यांतःपुरे काश्चित्प्रविशति Pt. 1. –2 inmates of the female apartments, a queen or queens, the ladies taken collectively; °विरहपर्युत्सुकस्य राजर्षेः *S*. 3. °**प्रचारः** gossip of the harem; कदाचिदस्मत्प्रार्थनामंतःपुरेभ्यः कथयेत् *S*. 2. °**जन** women of the palace, inmates of the female apartments; °**चर,-अध्यक्षः-रक्षकः,-वर्ती** guardian or superintendent of the harem, chamberlain; °**सहायः** one belonginng to the harem. **–पुरिकः** a chamberlain = °चर. **–प्रकृतिः** *f*. 1 the internal nature or constitution of man. –2 the ministry or body of ministers of a king. –3 heart or soul **–प्रकोपनं** sowing internal dissensions. **–प्रतिष्ठानं** residence in the interior. **–बाष्प** *a*. 1 with suppressed tears; अंतर्बाष्पश्चिरमनुचरो राजराजस्य दध्यौ Me. 3.—2 with tears gushing up inside. **–भावः, भावना** see under अंतर्भू separately. **–भूमिः**. *f*. interior of the earth.**—भेदः** discord, internal dissensions. **–भौम** *a*. subterranean. **–मनस्** *a*. sad, distracted.**–मृत** *a*. still-born. **–यामः** a suppression of the breath and voice. **–लीन** *a*. 1 latent, hidden, concealed inside; °नस्य दुःखाग्नेः U. 3. 9 –2 inherent. **-वंशः**=°पुरं q. v. **वंशिकः,-वासिकः** a superintendent of the women's apartments.**–वत्नी** a pregnant woman. **–वस्त्रं –वासस्** *n*. an undergarment**–वाणि** *a*. very learned. **–वेगः** inward uneasiness or anxiety, inward fever. **–वेदिः –दी** the tract of land between the rivers Gangâ and Yamunâ. **–वेश्मन्** *n*. the inner apartments, interior of a house. **–वेश्मिकः** a chamberlain.**–शरीरं** internal and spiritual part of man; the interior of the body. **–शिला** N. of a river rising from the Vindhya mountain. **–संज्ञ** *a*. inwardly conscious. **–सत्त्वा** a pregnant woman. **–संतापः** internal pain, sorrow, regret. **–सलिल** *a*. with water (flowing) underground; नदीमिवांतःसलिलां सरस्वतीं R. 3. 9. **–सार** *a*. full or strong inside powerful, strong ; heavy or ponderous; °रं घन तुलयितुं नानिलः शक्ष्यति त्वां Me. 20. (**–रः**) internal treasure or store, inner store or contents. **–सेनं** *ind*. into the midst of armies. **–स्थः** (also written अंतस्थ) a term applied to the semivowels, as standing between vowels and consonants and being formed by a slight contact of the vocal organs.**–स्वेदः** an elephant (in rut.). **–हासः** a secret or suppressed laugh. **–हृदयं** the interior of the heart.

अंतर *a*. 1 Being in the inside, interior, (opp. बाह्य). 2 Near, proximate. 3 Related, intimate, dear; अयमत्यंतरो मम Bharata. 4 Similar (also अंतरतम) (of sounds and words); स्थानेऽन्तरतमः P. I. 1. 50. 5 Different from; other than (with abl.). 6 Exterior, situated outside, or to be worn outside. (In this sense it is declined optionally like सर्व in nom. pl. and abl and loc. sing); so अंतरायां पुरि, अंतरायै नगर्यै.**–रं 1** (*a*.) The interior, inside; लीयंते मुकुलांतरेषु Ratn. 1 26. (*b*) A hole, an opening. 2 Soul, heart; mind; सदृशं पुरुषांतरविदो महेंद्रस्य V. 3. 3 The supreme Soul. 4 Interval, intermediate time or space; अल्पकुचांतरा V. 4. 26; बृहद्भुजांतरं R. 3. 54; अंतरे oft. translated by between, betwixt; न मृणालसूत्रं रचितं स्तनांतरे *S*. 6. 17. 5 Room, place, space in general; मृणालसूत्रांतरमप्यलभ्यं Ku. 1. 40; पौरुषं श्रय शोकस्य नांतरं दातुमर्हसि Râm. do not give way to sorrow. अंतरं अंतरं Mk. 2 make way. 6 Access, entrance, admission, footing; लेभेंतरं चेतसि नोपदेशः R. 6. 66; लब्धांतरा सावरणेऽपि गेहे 16. 7. 7 Period (of time), term; मासांतरे देयं Ak.; इति तौ विरहांतरक्षमौ R. 8. 56. 8 Opportunity, occasion, time; यावत्त्वामिंद्रगुरवे निवेदयितुं अंतरान्वेषी भवामि *S*. 7. 9 Difference (between two things), (with gen. or in comp.); तव मम च समुद्रपल्वलयोरिवांतरं M. 1; यदंतरं सर्षपशैलराजयोर्यदंतरं वायसवैनतेययोः Râm.; द्रुमसानुमतां किमंतरं R. 8. 90. 10 (Math.) Difference, remainder. 11 (*a*) Difference, another, other, changed, altered (manner, kind, way &c.). (Note that in this sense अंतर always forms the latter part of a compound and its gender remains unaffected i. e. neuter, whatever be the gender of the noun forming the first part; कन्यांतरं (अन्या कन्या), राजांतरं (अन्यो राजा) गृहांतरं (अन्यद्गृहं); in most cases it may be rendered by the English word 'another'); इदमवस्थांतरमारोपिता *S*. 3 changed condition. (*b*) Various, different (used in pl.); लोको नियम्यत इवात्मदशांतरेषु *S*. 4. 2. 12 Peculiarity, a (peculiar) sort, variety, or kind; व्रीह्यंतरेऽप्यणुः Trik.; मीनो राश्यंतरे, *ibid*. 13 Weakness, weak or vulnerable point; a failing, defect, or defective point; प्रहरेदंतरे रिपुं Sabdak.; सुजयः खलु तादृगंतरे Ki. 2. 52. 14 Surety, gaurantee, security. 15 Excellence, as in गुणांतरं व्रजति शिल्पमाधातुः M. 1. 6 (this meaning may be deduced from 11) 16 A garment (परिधान). 17 Purpose, object, (Malli. on R. 16. 82). 18 Representative, substitution. 19 Being without. –Comp. **–अपत्या** a pregnant woman. **–ज्ञ** *a*. knowing the interior, prudent, fore-seeing; नांतरज्ञाः श्रियो जातु प्रियैरासां न भूयते Ki. 11. 24. **–दिशा, अंतरा दिक्** intermediate region or quarter of the compass.**–पु (पू) रुषः** the internal man, soul (the deity that resides in man, and witnesses all his deeds).**–प्रभवः** one of a mixed origin or caste.**–स्थ,-स्थायिन्,-स्थित** *a*. 1 inward, internal, inherent. –2 interposed, intervening.

अंतरतः *ind*. 1 In the interior ; internally, between or betwixt. 2 within (with gen.).

अंतरतम *a*. Nearest, internal, most immediate, most intimate, or related like, analogous. **—मः** A letter of the same class.

अंतरयः –रायः An impediment, obstacle, hindrance ; स चेत् त्वमंतरायो भवसि च्युतो विधिः R. 3. 45, 14. 65 ; अस्य ते बाणपथवर्तिनः कृष्णसारस्य अंतरायौ तपस्विनो संवृत्तौ *S*. 1vl.

अंतरयति Den. P. 1 To cause to intervene, divert, put off; भवतु तावदंतरयामि U. 6. 2 To oppose. 3 To remove (to a distance), push after.

अंतरयण=अंतरय.

अंतरा *ind*. 1 (Used adverbially) (*a*) In the interior, inside, inwardly. (*b*) In the middle, between; त्रिशंकुरिवांतरातिष्ठ *S*. 2. R. 15. 20. (*c*) On the way, midway; विलंबेथां च मांतरा Mv. 7. 28. (*d*) In neighbourhood, near at hand; almost. (*e*) In the meantime. (*f*) At intervals, here and there; now and then, for some time, now-now (when repeated); अंतरा पितृसक्तमतरा मातृसंबद्धमंतरा शुकनासमयं कुर्वन्नालापं K. 118. 2 (used as a preposition with acc.) (*a*) Between ; अंतरा त्वां च मां च कमंडलुः Mbh. (*b*) Without, except ; न च प्रयोजनमंतरा चाणक्यः स्वप्नेपि चेष्टते Mu. 3. –Comp.**–अंसः** breast.**—भवदेहः –भवसत्त्वं** the soul or embodied soul existing between the two stages of death and birth. **–दिश्** see **अंतरादिश्**. **–वेदिः–दी** *f*. 1 a veranda resting on columns, porch, portico. –2 a kind of wall R. 12. 93. **–शृंगं** *ind*. between the horns.

अंतराय=अंतरय q. v.

अंतरालं, अंतरालकं 1 Intermediate space or region or time, interval ; दक्षिणस्याः पूर्वस्याश्च दिशोरंतरालं दक्षिणपूर्वा Sk.; अंतराले in midway, in the middle or midst; in the interval; बाष्पांभः परिपतनोद्गमांतराले U. 1. 31. 2 Interior, inside, inner or middle part. **3** Mixed tribe or caste.

अंतरि (री) क्षं The intermediate region between heaven and earth; the air, atmosphere, sky. -COMP. **-उदरं** the interior of the atmosphere. **-गः, -चरः** a bird. **-जलं** dew. **-लोकः** the intermediate region, regarded as a distinct world.

अंतरित *p. p.* **1** Gone between, intervening. **2** Gone within, hidden, covered, screened, protected (from view) by something ; पादपांतरित एव विश्वस्तामेनां पश्यामि *S.* 1 hid behind a creeper; सारसेन स्वदेहांतरितो राजा H. 3 screened. **3** Gone in, reflected; स्फटिकभित्त्यंतरितान् मृगशावकान् (*a*) Impeded; hindered, prevented त्वद्वांछांतरितानि साध्यानि Mu. 4. 15; नोपालभ्यः पुमांस्तत्र दैवांतरितपौरुषः Pt. 2. 133. (*b*) Separated, lost to view, made invisible by interposition ; सुहृत्तीतरितमाधवा दुर्मनायमाना Mâl. 8; मेघैरंतरितः प्रिये तव मुखच्छायानुकारी शशी S. D. (*c*) Drowned obscured. **4** Disappeared, vanished, departed, withdrawn ; अंतरिते तस्मिञ्शबरसेनापतौ K. 33. **5** Passed over, omitted.

अंतरीपः A portion of land stretching out into the sea, promontory; an island.

अंतरीयं An undergarment.

अंतरेण *ind.* **1** (Used as a preposition with acc.) (*a*) Except, without; क्रियांतरांतरायमंतरेण आर्य द्रष्टुमिच्छामि Mu. **3**; न राजापराधमंतरेण प्रजास्वकालमृत्युश्चरति U. 2; मार्मिकः को मरंदानामंतरेण मधुव्रतं Bv. 1. 117. (*b*) With regard or reference to, with respect to; अथ भवंतमंतरेण कीदृशोऽस्या दृष्टिरागः *S.* 2; तदस्या देवीं वसुमतीमंतरेण महदुपालंभनं गतोऽस्मि *S.* 5. (*c*) Between, त्वां मां चांतरेण कमंडलुः Mbh. **2** (Used as an adverb) (*a*) Between, amidst. (*b*) At heart.

अंतर्गत *p. p.* **-गामिन्** *a.* **1** Gone into or between, crept into (as a bad word &c.). **2** Being or seated in, included in or by, existing in, belonging to. **3** Hidden, internal, inward, secret ; अंतर्गतमपास्तं मे रजसोपि परं तमः Ku. 6. 60 ; सोमित्रिरंतर्गतबाष्पकंठः R. 14. 53 ; नेत्रवक्त्रविकारैश्च लक्ष्यतेऽन्तर्गतं मनः Pt. 1. 44. **4** Slipped out of memory, forgotten. **5** Vanished, disapeared. **6** Destroyed. -COMP. **-उपमा** a concealed simile. **-मनस्**=अंतर्मनस् q. v.

अंतर्धा Covering &c.; concealment; अंतर्धामुपययुरुत्पलावलीषु *Si.* 8. 12.

अंतर्धानं Being invisible, disappearance, passing out of sight; °व्यसनरासिका रात्रिकापालिकीयं K. P. 10; °गम् or इ to become invisible, disappear.

अंतर्धिः *f.* Disappearance, concealment.

अंतर्भव *a.* Inward, internal.

अंतर्भावः **1** The being included or comprised in, inclusion: तेषां गुणानामोजस्यंतर्भावः K. P. 8. **2** Inherent disposition.

अंतर्भावना **1** Inclusion. **2** Inward meditation or anxiety.

अंतर्य *a.* Internal, in the middle.

अंतर्हित **1** Placed between, separated, rendered invisible by interposition, hidden, concealed ; अंतर्हिता शकुंतला वनराज्या *S.* 4. **2** Disappeared, vanished, become invisible; अंतर्हिते शशिनि *S.* 4.2. -COMP. **-आत्मन्** *m.* N. of *S*iva.

अंति *ind.* To, in the vicinity of (with gen.). **—तिः** *f.* An elder sister (in dramas).

अंतिका **1** An elder sister. **2** An oven, fire-place. **3** N. of a plant (सातशा-तलाख्योषधिः).

अंतिक *a.* **1** Near, proximate (with gen. or able.) **2** Reaching to. **3** Lasting, up to. **—कं** Nearness, proximity, vicinity, presence ; न त्यजंति ममांतिकं H. 1. 46. °न्यस्त R. 2. 24. कर्ण-°चर *S.* 1.24. *—adv.* (with abl. gen. or as last member of comp.) Near (to), in the vicinity; अंतिकं ग्रामात्-ग्रामस्य वा Sk.; into the presence or proximity of; अंतिकेन near (with gen.); अंतिकात् near, from near, from (abl. or gen.); कादागतः; अंतिके near ; दमयंत्यास्तदांतिके निपेतुः Nala. 1. 22.-COMP. **-आश्रयः** resorting to what is near, contiguous support (that given by a tree to a creeper).

अंतिम *a.* **1** Immediately following. **2** Last, final, ultimate ; अजातमृतमूर्खाणां वरमाद्यौ न चांतिमः H. 1. -COMP. **-अंकः** the last digit, the number nine. **-अंगुलिः** the little figure (कनिष्ठिका).

अंती An oven, fire-place.

अंते See below अंततः.

अंत्य *a.* **1** Last, final (as a letter, word &c.); last (in time, order or place); as ह of letters, Revatî of asterisms; अंत्ये वयसि in old age R. 9. 79; अंत्यं ऋणं R. 1: 71 last debt; °मंडनं 8. 71, Ku. 4. 22. **2** Immediately following (in comp.). **3** Lowest, worst, inferior, vile.**—त्यः** **1** A man of the lowest caste. **2** The last syllable of a word. **3** The last lunar month *i. e.* Phâlguna. **4** Mlechchha. **—त्या** A woman of the lowest tribe. **—त्यं** **1** A measure of number, 1000 billions. **2** The 12th sign of the zodiac. **3** The last member or term of a progression. -COMP. **-अवसायिन्** *m. f.* (°यी, °यिनी) a man or woman of the lowest caste, the following 7 are regarded as belonging to this class ; चांडालः श्वपचः क्षत्ता सूतो वैदेहकस्तथा । मागधायोगवौ चैव सप्तैतेंऽत्यावसायिनः ॥. **-आहुतिः -इष्टिः** *f.* **-कर्मन्-क्रिया** last or funeral oblations, sacrifices or rites. **-ऋणं** the last of the three debts which every one has to pay, *i. e.* begetting children; see अनृण. **-जः -जन्मन्** *m.* 1 a Sûdra. -2 one of the 7 inferior tribes; Chândâla &c. **-जन्मन्, -जाति, -जातीय** *a.* 1 one belonging to lowest caste. -2 a Sûdra. -3 a Chândàla. **-भं** the last lunar mansion रेवती. **-युगं** the last or Kali age. **-योनि** *a.* of the lowest origin ; Ms. 8. 68. **-लोपः** dropping of the last letter or syllable of a word. **-वर्णः, -वर्णा** a man or woman of the lowest caste, a Sûdra male or female.

अंत्यकः A man of the lowest tribe.

अंत्रं An entrail, intestine ; अंत्रभेदनं क्रियते प्रश्रयश्च Mv. 3. -COMP.**-कूजः, -कूजनं, -विकूजनं** the rumbling noise in the bowels. **-वृद्धिः** *f.* inguinal hernia, rupture, swelling of the scrotum. **-शिला** N. of a river rising from the Vindhya mountain. **-स्रज्** *f.* a garland of intestines (worn by नृसिंह). **-अंत्रंधमिः** *f.* Indigestion, flatulence.

अंदुः-दूः *f.* also **अंदुकः, अंदूकः** **1** A chain or fetter. **2** A chain for the elephant's feet. **3** A sort of ornament worn round the ankles ; cf. नुपुर.

अंदोलनं Swinging, oscillating, waving; द्राक्चामरांदोलनात् Udb.

अंध् 10 U. **1** To make blind, blind; अंधयन् भृंगमालाः Si. 11. 19. **2** To be or become blind.

अंध *a.* **1** Blind (lit. and fig.); devoid of sight, unable to see (at particular times): blinded ; स्रजमपि शिरस्यंधः क्षिप्तां धुनोत्यहिशंकया *S.* **7. 24** ; मदांधः blinded by intoxication ; so दर्पांधः, क्रोधांधः. **2** Making blind, preventing the sight, utter, complete; सीदन्नंधे तमसि U. 3. 38. **—धं** Darkness. **2** Water; also, turbid water. -COMP. **-कारः** darkness. (lit. and fig.); काम°, मदन°; अंधकारतामुपयाति चक्षुः K. 36 grows dim. **-कूपः** 1 a well the mouth of which is hidden; a well overgrown with plants &c. -2 N. of a hell. **-तमसं, -तामसं, अंधातमसं** deep or complete darkness; R. 11.24. **-तामिस्रः -श्रः** (°तामिस्र also) complete or deep darkness. **-धी** *a.* mentally blind. **-पूतना** a demoness supposed to cause diseases in children.

अंधंकरण *a.* Making blind.

अंधंभविष्णु, -भावुक *a.* Becoming blind.

अंधक *a.* Blind. **—कः** N. of an Asura, son of Kasyapa and Diti and killed by *S*iva.-COMP. **-अरिः, -रिपुः, शत्रुः, -घाती, -असुहृद्** &c. slayer of Andhaka, epithets of *S*iva. **-वर्तः** N. of a mountain. **-वृष्णि** *m. pl.* descendants of अंधक and वृष्णि.

अंधस् *n.* Food; द्विजातिशेषेण यदेतदंधसा Ki. 1. 39.

अंधिका **1** Night. **2** A kind of game or sport, probably blindman's-buff; gambling. **3** A disease of the eye.

अंधुः A well.

अंध्रः (*pl.*) **1** N. of a people and the country inhabited by them. **2**

N. of a dynasty of kings. **3** A man of a mixed (low) caste.

अन्नं 1 Food (in general). **2** Food as representing the lowest form in which the Supreme Soul is manifested. **3** Boiled rice. **—न्नः** The sun. –COMP. **–अद्यं** proper food; food in general. **–आच्छादनं, –वस्त्रं** food and clothing, the bare necessaries of life. **–कालः** hour of dinner; meal-time. **–किट्टः**=°मल q. v. **–कूटः** a large heap of boiled rice. **–कोष्ठकः** 1 a cupboard; granary. –2 Vishṇu. –3 the sun. **–गंधिः** dysentary, diarrhœa. **–जलं** food and water, bare subsistence. **–दासः** a servant who works for food only, one who becomes a servant or slave by getting food only. **–देवता** the deity supposed to preside over articles of food. **–दोषः** sin arising from the eating of prohibited food. **–द्वेषः** dislike of food, loss of appetite. **–पूर्णा** a form of Durgâ (the goddess of plenty). **प्राशः—प्राशनं** the ceremony of giving a new-born child food to eat for the first time, one of the 16 *Saṃskâras* performed between the 5th and 8th month (usually in the sixth, Ms. 2. 34) with preliminary oblations to fire (Mar. उष्टावण). **–ब्रह्मन्, –आत्मन्** *m.* Brahma as represented by food. **–भुज्** *a.* eating food, epithet of Siva. **–मय** *a.* see below. **मलं** 1 excrement. –2 spirituous liquor. **–रक्षा** precautions as to eating food. **रसः** essence of food, chyle. **–वस्त्रं**=°आच्छादनं q. v. **व्यवहारः** the law or custom relating to food, *i. e.* the custom of eating together or not with other persons. **–शेषः** leavings of food, offal. **संस्कारः** consecration of food.

अन्नमय *a.* (**यी** *f.*) Consisting or made of food; °**कोशः –षः** the gross material body, the स्थूलशरीर, which is sustained by food and which is the fifth or last vesture or wrapper of the soul; hence, also the material world, the coarsest or lowest form in which Brahma is considered as manifesting itself in the wordly existence. **–यं** Plenty of food.

अन्य *a.* [*n.* अन्यत् &c.] **1** Another different, other (भिन्न); another, other (generally); स एव त्वन्यः क्षणेन भवतीति विचित्रमेतत् Bh. **2.** 40. **2** Other than, different from, else than (with abl. or as last member of comp.); नास्ति जीवितादन्यदभिमततरमिह सर्वजंतूनां K. 35. उत्थितं ददृशेऽन्यच्च कबंधेभ्यो न किंचन R. 12. 49. **3** Strange, unusual, extraordinary; अन्या जगद्धितमयी मनसः प्रवृत्तिः Bv. 1. 69; धन्या मृदन्यैव सा S. D. **4** Ordinary, any one. **5** Additional, new, more; अन्यच्च moreover, besides, and again (used to connect sentences together); एक-अन्य the one the other; Me. 78; see under एक also; अन्य-अन्य one-another अम्यन्मुखे अन्यन्निर्वहणे Mu. 5; अन्यदुच्छृंखलं सत्त्वमन्यच्छास्त्रनियंत्रितं Si. 2. 62; अन्य-अन्य-अन्य &c. one, another, third, fourth, &c.-COMP.**—असाधारण** *a.* not common to others, peculiar. **–उदर्य** *a.* born from another. (**–र्यः**) a step-mother's son, a half-brother. (**–र्या**) a half-sister. **–ऊढा** *a.* married to another; another's wife. **—क्षेत्रं** 1 another field. –2 another or foreign territory. –3 another's wife. **—ग-गामिन्** *a.* 1 going to another. –2 adulterous, unchaste. **–गोत्र** *a.* of a different family or lineage. **–चित्त** *a.* having the mind fixed on something or some one else; see °**मनस्** . **–ज-जात** *a.* of a different origin. **–जन्मन्** *n.* another life or existence, regeneration, metempsychosis. **–दुर्वह** *a.* difficult to be borne by others. **–देवत, –त्य, –दैवत्य** *a.* addressed or referring to another deity (as a Vedic Mantra). **–नाभि** *a.* belonging to another family. **–पदार्थः** 1 another substance. –2 the sense of another word; °प्रधानो बहुव्रीहिः the Bahuvrîhi compound essentially depends on the sense of another word. **पर** *a.* 1 devoted to another or something else. –2 expressing or referring to something else. **–पुष्टः-ष्टा-भृतः-ता** 'reared by another', epithet of the cuckoo which is supposed to be reared by the crow (called अन्यभृत्); अप्यन्यपुष्टा प्रतिकूलशब्दा Ku. 1. 45; कलमन्यभृतासु भाषितं R. 8. 59. **–पूर्वा** 1 a woman already promised or betrothed to another. –2 a remarried widow. **–बीजः, –बीज-समुद्भवः, –समुत्पन्नः** an adopted son (born from other parents), one who may be adopted as a son for want of legitimate issue. **–भृत्** *m.* a crow (rearing another). **–मनस्, मनस्क, –मानस** *a.* 1 inattentive. –2 fickle, unsteady. **–मातृजः** a half-brother (born of another mother). **–रूप** changed, altered.**–लिंग –गक** *a.* following the gender of another word (*i e.* the substantive), an adjective. **–वापः** the cuckoo. **–विवर्धित** *a.*=पुष्ट a cuckoo.**—संगमः** intercourse with another; illicit intercourse. **–साधारण** *a.* c mmon to many others. **–स्त्री** another's wife, a woman not one's own. [In Rhetoric she is considered as one of three chief female characters in a poetical composition, the other two being स्वीया and साधारणी स्त्री. अन्या may be either a damsel or another's wife. The 'damsel' is one not yet married, who is bashful and arrived at the age of puberty. As 'another's wife' she is fond of festivals and similar occasions of amusement, who is a disgrace to her family and utterly destitute of modesty, see S. D. 108-110]. °**गः** an adulterer.

अन्यक=अन्य.

अन्यतम *a.* (declined like a noun) One of many, any one out of a large number.

अन्यतर *a.* (declined like a pronoun) One of two (persons or things), either of the two (with gen.); संतः परीक्ष्याम्यतरद्भजंते M. 1. 2; अन्यतरस्यां (loc. of °रा) either way, in both ways, optionally.

अन्यततः *adv*. On one of two sides.

अन्यतेद्युः *adv*. On either of two days, on one day or on another.

अन्यतः *adv*. **1** From another. **2** On one side; अन्यतः-अन्यतः एकतः-अन्यतः on the one side, on the other side; तपनमंडलदीपितमेकतः सततनैशतमोवृतमन्यतः Ki. 5. 2. **3** From another ground or motive.

अन्यत्र *adv*. (oft.=अन्यस्मिन् with a subst. or adj. force) **1** Elsewhere, in another place. **2** On another occasion. **3** Except, without. **4** Otherwise, in the other case or sense.

अन्यथा *ind*. **1** Otherwise, in another way or manner, in a different manner; यदभावि न तद्भावि भावि चेन्न तदन्यथा H. 1; अन्यथा-अन्यथा in one way-in another (different) way; अन्यथा कृ to do otherwise, change or alter, undo, falsify; त्वया कदाचिदपि मम वचनं नान्यथा कृतं Pt. 4. **2** Otherwise, or else, in the contrary case; व्यक्तं नास्ति कथमन्यथा वासंस्यपि तां न पश्येत् U. 3. **3** On the other hand. **4** Falsely, untruly; किमन्यथा भट्टिनी मया विज्ञापितपूर्वा V. **2. 5** Wrongly, erroneously, badly, as in अन्यथासिद्ध q. v. below. –COMP. **–अनुपपत्तिः** *f.* see अर्थापत्ति. **कारः** changing, altering. (**–रं**) *adv*. in a different manner, differently P. III. 4. 27. **ख्यातिः** *f.* erroneous conception of the spirit, wrong conception in general (in phil.) **–भावः** alteration, change, difference. **–वादिन्** *a.* speaking differently or falsely; (in law) a prevaricating witness. **–वृत्ति** *a.* 1 changed, altered. –2 affected, disturbed by strong emotions; Me. 3. **–सिद्ध** *a.* proved or demonstrated wrongly; (in Nyâya) said of a cause (कारण) which is not the true one, but only refers to accidental and remote circumstances. **–सिद्धं, –सिद्धिः** *f.* wrong demonstration; an unessential cause, an accidental or concomitant circumstance; Bhâshâ P. 16. **–स्तोत्रं** satire, irony; Y. 2. 204.

अन्यदा *ind*. **1** At another time, on another occasion, in any other case; अन्यदा भूषणं पुंसां क्षमा लज्जेव योषिताम् Si. 2

44, R. 11. 73. 2 Once, at one time, once upon a time. 3 Sometimes.

अन्यदीय *a.* 1 Belonging to another. 2 Being or existing in another.

अन्यार्हि *ind.* At another time (=अन्यदा).

अन्यादृक्ष्-श्-श *a.* Changed, unusual, strange.

अन्याय *a.* Unjust, improper. -यः 1 Any unjust, or unlawful action; see न्याय; अन्यायेन unjustly, improperly. 2 Injustice, impropriety. 3 Irregularity.

अन्यायिन् *a.* Unjust, improper.

अन्याय्य *a.* 1 Uujust, unlawful. 2 Improper, unbecoming. 3 Not authoritative.

अन्यून *a.* Not defective or deficient, complete, whole, entire; °अधिक neither deficient nor superfluous.-COMP. -अंग *a.* not having a defective limb.

अन्येद्युः *ind.* 1 On the other or following day; अन्येद्युरात्मानुचरस्य भाव जिज्ञासमाना R. 2. 26. 2 One day, once.

अन्योन्य *ind.* One another, each other, mutual (treated like a pronoun); oft. in comp.; °कलहः mutual quarrel; so °घातः. -न्यं *ind.* Mutually. -COMP. -अभावः mutual non-existence or negation; one of the two main kinds of अभाव; (equivalent to difference) (भेद). -आश्रय *a.* mutually dependent. (-यः) mutual or reciprocal dependence, reciprocal relation of cause and effect (a term in Nyâya). -उक्तिः *f.* conversation. -भेदः mutual dissension or enmity.-विभागः mutual partition of an inheritance made by the sharers (without the presence of any other party).-वृत्तिः *f.* mutual effect of one thing upon another. व्यतिकरः-संश्रयः reciprocal action or influence; mutual relation of cause and effect.

अन्वक्ष *a.* 1 Visible. 2 Immediately following. -क्षं *ind.* 1 Afterwards, after. 2 Immediately after, forthwith, directly; Y. 3. 21.

अन्वक् *ind.* 1 Afterwards. 2 From behind. 3 Friendly disposed, favourably; अन्वग्भूत्वा-भावं-आस्ते becoming friendly disposed. 4 (with acc.) After; तां...अन्वगयौ मध्यमलोकपालः R. 2. 16.

अन्वंच् *a.* Going after, following; अनूचि in the rear or behind, from behind.

अन्वयः 1 Going after, following; also follower, retinue, attendants; का त्वमेकाकिनी भीरु निरन्वयजने वने Bk. 5. 66. 2 Association, connection, relation. 3 The natural order or connection of words in a sentence, grammatical order or relation; तात्पर्याख्यां वृत्तिमाहुः पदार्थान्वयबोधने S. D.; logical connection of words. 4 Drift, tenor, purport. 5 Race, family, lineage; रघूणामन्वयं वक्ष्ये R. 1. 9, 12. 6 Descendants, posterity; ताभ्य ऋते अन्वयः Y. 2. 117. 7 Logical connection of cause and effect, logical continuance; जन्माद्यस्य यतोऽन्वयादितरतः Bhâg. 8 (In Nyâya) Statement of the constant and invariable concomitance of the हेतु (middle term) and the साध्य (major term) of an Indian syllogism (हेतुसाध्ययोर्व्याप्तिरन्वयः). -COMP.-आगत *a.* hereditary. -ज्ञः a genealogist; R. 6. 8. -व्यतिरेक (°कौ or °कं) 1 positive and negative assertion, agreement and contrariety or difference. -2 rule and exception. - व्याप्तिः *f.* affirmative assertion or agreement, affirmative universal.

अन्वर्थ *a.* Having a meaning easily deducible from the etymology of the word; true to the sense, significant; तथैव सोऽभूदन्वर्थो राजा प्रकृतिरंजनात् R. 4. 12; अन्वर्था तैर्वसुंधरा Ki. 11. 64.-COMP. -ग्रहणं literal acceptation of the meaning of a word (opp. to रूढ).-संज्ञा 1 an appropriate name, a technical term which directly conveys its own meaning. -2 a proper name the meaning of which is obvious.

अन्ववकिरणं Scattering about successively.

अन्ववसर्गः 1 Slackening. 2 Permission to do as one likes (कामचारानुज्ञा). 3 Following one's own will.

अन्ववसित *a.* Connected with, bound or fastened to.

अन्ववायः A race, family, lineage.

अन्ववेक्षा Regard, consideration.

अन्वष्टका The 9th day of the dark half of the three months following the full moon in मार्गशीर्ष, *i. e.* पौष, माघ and फाल्गुन.

अन्वष्टक्यं A Srâddha or any such ceremony performed on the अन्वष्टका days.

अन्वष्टमदिशं *ind.* Towards the north-west direction.

अन्वहं *ind.* Day after day, every day.

अन्वाख्यानं Subsequent mention or enumeration; an explanation referring to what is mentioned before.

अन्वाचयः 1 Statement of a secondary (गौण) rite or action after the mention of a primary (प्रधान) one; adding an object of secondary importance to the main object, one of the senses of the particle च; as भो भिक्षामट गां चानय where going out to beg is enjoined to the beggar as his principal object, and the bringing of a cow (if he can see any) is tacked on to it as a secondary object. 2 Such an object itself.

अन्वाजे *ind.* (Used like उपाजे only with कृ) So as to assist or support the weak, optionally regarded as a preposition; °कृत्य or °कृत्वा.

अन्वादिष्ट *p. p.* 1 Mentioned after or according to; employed again. 2 (Hence) Inferior, of secondary importance.

अन्वादेशः Subsequent or repeated mention, referring to what has been previously mentioned.

अन्वाधानं Putting on or depositing fuel on the sacred fires.

अन्वाधिः (In civil law) 1 A bail, deposit or security delivered to a third person to be handed over ultimately to the right owner. 2 A second deposit. 3 Constant anxiety, remorse repentance.

अन्वाधेयं-यकं A sort of स्त्रीधन or woman's property, presented to her after marriage by her husband's or father's family, or by her own relatives; विवाहात्परतो यच्च लब्धं भर्तृकुलास्त्रिया। अन्वाधेयं तु तद्द्रव्यं पितृ (v. l. बंधु-) कुलात्तथा॥.

अन्वारंभः, -भणं Touching, contact, especially touching the यजमान (the performer of a sacrifice) to make him entitled to the fruits and merits of the holy rite.

अन्वारोहणं A woman's ascending the funeral pile after or with the body of her husband.

अन्वासनं 1 Service, attendance, worship. 2 Taking a seat after another. 3 Regret, sorrow.

अन्वाहार्यः (also-र्यं), -र्यकं The monthly Srâddha performed in honor of the manes on the day of new moon.

अन्वाहिक *a.* (की) *f.* Daily, diurnal.

अन्वाहित=अन्वाधेय q. v.

अन्वित *p. p.* 1 Followed or attended by, in company with, joined by. 2 Possessed of, having; struck with, overpowered by; with instr. or in compound. 3 Connected with, linked to, following (as a consequence.). 4 Connected grammatically. -COMP. -अर्थ *a.* having a meaning which is easily understood from the context. -अर्थवादः-अभिधानवादः a doctrine of the Mimâmsakas that words in a sentence convey meanings not independently or generally, but as connected with one another in that particular sentence; see K. P. 2, and अभिहितान्वयवाद also.

अन्वीक्षणं-,क्षा 1 Search, seeking for, investigation. 2 Reflection.

अन्वीत=अन्वित q. v.

अन्वृचं *ind.* Verse after verse.

अन्वेषः-षणं-णा 1 Search after, seeking for, watching; वयं तत्त्वान्वेषान्मधुकर हताः *S.* 1. 24; रंध्रान्वेषणदक्षाणां द्विषां R. 12. 11

अन्वेषक, अन्वेषिन्, अन्वेष्टृ *a.* Searching after, seeking for, inquiring &c.

अप् *f.* (Declined in classical language only in pl.; आपः, अपः, अद्भिः, अद्भ्यः, अपां and अप्सु, but in singular and pl. in Veda) Water; खानि चैव स्पृशेदद्भिः Ms. 2. 60. Water is generally considered to be the first of the 5 elements of creation, as in अप एव ससर्जादौ तासु बीजमवासृजत् Ms. 1. 8, *S.* 1. 1; but in Ms. 1. 78. it is said to have been created from ज्योतिस् or तेजस् after मनस्, आकाश, वायु and ज्योतिस् or अग्नि. –COMP. **–चरः** an aquatic animal. **–पतिः** 1 'lord of waters', N. of Varuṇa –2 the ocean. For other comps. see s. v.

अप *ind.* 1 (As a prefix to verbs it means) (*a*) Away from; अपयाति, अपनयति; (*b*) deterioration, अपकरोति does wrongly or badly; (*c*) opposition, negation, contradiction, अपकर्षति, अपचिनोति; (*d*) exclusion, (वर्जन); अपवह्, अपस् *caus.* 2 As first member of Tat. or Bahuvrîhi comp. it has all the above senses; अपयानं, अपशब्दः a bad or corrupt word; °भी fearless; अपरागः discontent (opp. to अनुराग). In most cases अप may be translated by 'bad', 'inferior,' 'corrupt', 'wrong' 'unworthy,' &c. 3 As a separable preposition (with a noun in the abl.) (*a*) away from; यत्संप्रत्यपलोकेभ्यो लंकायां वसतिर्भयात् Bk. 8. 87; (*b*) without, on the outside of; अपहरेः संसारः Sk.; (*c*) with the exception of, excepting; अप त्रिगर्तेभ्यो वृष्टो देवः Sk. on the outside of, with the exception of. In these senses अप may form adverbial compounds also; °विष्णु संसारः Sk. without Vishṇu; °त्रिगर्तं वृष्टो देवः excepting T. &c. अप also implies negation, contradiction &c.; °कामं, °शंकं.

अपकरणं 1 Acting improperly. 2 Doing wrong, injuring; illtreating, offending.

अपकर्तृ *a.* Injurious, offensive. –*m.* An enemy.

अपकर्मन् 1 Discharge, paying off (of a debt); दत्तस्यानपकर्म च Ms. 8. 4. 2 An improper or unworthy act; any degrading or impure act. 3 Wickedness, violence, oppression.

अपकर्षः 1 (*a*) Drawing off or down; diminution, reduction; loss, destruction; तेजोपकर्षः Ve. 1; deterioration. (*b*) dishonour, degradation; (opp. उत्कर्ष in all senses). 2 Anticipation of a word occurring later on (in gram., poetry or mîma'msa' &c.).

अपकर्षक *a.* Lessening, diminishing, detracting from; दोषास्तस्य (काव्यस्य) अपकर्षकाः S. D. 1.

अपकर्षणं 1 Removing, drawing away or down, depriving (one) of; extracting. 2 Lessening, detraction. 3 Superseding.

अपकारः 1 Harm, injury, hurt, offence, (opp. उपकार); उपकर्त्रारिणा संधिर्न मित्रेणापकारिणा । उपकारापकारौ हि लक्ष्यं लक्षणमेतयोः *Si.* 2. 37; अपकारोऽप्युपकारायैव संवृत्तः, &c. 2 Thinking ill of, desire to offend or hurt. 3 Wickedness, violence, oppression. 4 A mean or degraded action. –COMP. **–अर्थिन्** *a.* malevolent, malicious. **–गिर्** *f*, (**–गीः**), **–शब्दः** abusive words, menacing or insulting speech.

अपकारक, –कारिन् *a.* Injuring, mischievous, harmful, injurious; Pt. 1. 95, *Si.* 2. 37. **—कः, –री** An evil-doer.

अपकृति =अपकार q. v.; so also **अपक्रिया** Hurt, injury, disservice; fault, misdeed; paying or clearing off (debts).

अपकृष्ट *p. p.* 1 Drawn or taken away, removed. 2 Low, vile, mean (opp. उत्कृष्ट); न कश्चिद्वर्णानामपथमपकृष्टोपि भजते *S.* 5. 10. **–ष्टः** A crow.

अपकौशली News, information.

अपक्तिः *f.* 1 Unripeness, immaturity. 2 Indigestion.

अपक्रमः 1 Going away, escape, retreat. 2 Gliding or passing away (of time). —*a.* 1 Without order. 2 Irregular, in wrong order.

अपक्रमणं, –क्रामः Retreat, retiring, flight, escape &c.

अपक्रोशः Abuse, reviling.

अपक्ष *a.* 1 Without wings or the power of flight. 2 Not belonging to the same side or party. 3 Having no adherents of friends. 4 Opposed to, adverse. –COMP. **–पातः** impartiality. **–पातिन्** *a.* Impartial.

अपक्षयः Decline, decay, wane.

अपक्षेपः, –क्षेपणं 1 Casting away or throwing down. 2 Throwing or putting down, one of the 5 kinds of कर्मन् in the Vaiseshika phil., see कर्मन्.

अपगंडः One who has attained his majority ; see अपोगंड.

अपगमः,–मनं 1 Going away or departure, separation; समागमाः सापगमाः H. 4. 65. 2 Falling off; removal, disappearance ; पुराणपत्रापगमादनंतरं R. 3. 7. 3 Death; decease.

अपगतिः *f.* A bad fate.

अपगरः 1 Censure, reviling. 2 One who reviles or says what is disagreeable, reviler.

अपगर्जित *a.* Thunderless, (as a cloud).

अपगुणः A demerit, fault.

अपगोपुर *a.* Deprived of its gateways (as a town).

अपघनः A limb or member of the body, as a hand or foot (अपघनोऽंगम् P. III. 3. 81. अंगं शरीरावयवः स च न सर्वं किंतु पाणिः पादश्चेत्याहुः Sk. and Kâsikâ); but it is also used in the sense of 'the body'; लौहोद्घनघनस्कंधा ललितापघना स्त्रियं Bk. 7. 92 (where the commentators take अपघन to mean the body itself).

अपघातः 1 Striking or cutting off, warding off, preventing. 2 Killing. 3 A violent death, any evil accident proving fatal.

अपघातिन् *a.* Killing, murdering.

अपचः 1 Unable to cook, or one who does not cook for himself. 2 A bad cook, a term of abuse.

अपचयः 1 Diminution, decrease, decay, decline, fall (fig. also); कफापचयः Dk. 160. 2 Loss, failure, defect.

अपचरितं A fault, wrong or wicked deed, misdeed; आहोस्वित्प्रसवो ममापचरितैर्विष्टंभितो वीरुधां *S.* 5. 9.

अपचारः 1 Departure ; death ; सिंहघोषश्च कांतकापचारं निर्भिद्य Dk. 72. 2 Want, absence. 3 A fault; offence, misdeed, improper conduct, crime; राजन्प्रजासु ते कश्चिदपचारः प्रवर्तते R. 15. 47. 4 Injurious or hurtful conduct, injury. 5 A defect or deficiency ; नापचारमगमन् क्वचित्क्रियाः *Si.* 14. 32. 6 Unwholesome or improper regimen (अपथ्य); कृतापचारोपि परैरनाविष्कृतविक्रियः । असाध्यः कुरुते कोपं प्राप्ते काले गदो यथा ॥ *Si.* 2. 84 (where अ° also means hurt or injury).

अपचारिन् *a.* Offending, doing wrong; wicked, bad.

अपचितिः *f.* 1 Loss, decline, destruction. 2 Expense. 3 Atonement, compensation, expiation of sin. 4 Honouring, worshipping, showing reverence, worship; विहितापचितिर्महीभृता *Si.* 16. 9. (where it also means loss, destruction).

अपच्छत्र *a.* Without a parasol or umbrella.

अपच्छाय *a.* 1 Shadowless. 2 Devoid of brightness, dim. **—यः** One that has no shadow, i. e. a god; cf. N. 14. 21 ; श्रियं भजतां कियदस्य देवाश्छाया नलस्यास्ति तथापि नैषाम् । इतीरयंतीव तया निरैक्षि सा (छाया) नैषधे न त्रिदशेषु तेषु ॥

अपच्छेदः=दनं 1 Cutting off or away. 2 Loss. 3 Interruption.

अपजयः Defeat, overthrow.

अपजातः A bad son who has turned out ill; one inferior to his parents in qualities; मातृतुल्यगुणो जातस्त्वनुजातः पितुः समः । अतिजातोधिकस्तस्मादपजातोऽधमाधमः ॥ Subhâsh.

अपज्ञानं Denying, concealing.

अपंचीकृतं A simple elementary substance not made of the five (पंच) gross elements; the five subtle elements.

अपटी 1 A screen or wall of cloth, particularly the screen or *kanât* surrounding tent. 2 A curtain.–COMP. **–क्षेपः** (अपटक्षेपः) tossing aside the curtain; °क्षेपेण (=अकस्मात्) 'with a (hurried) toss of the curtain', frequently occurring as a stage-direction and denoting precipitate entrance on the stage which arises from fear, hurry, agitation &c., as when a character tossing up the curtain suddenly enters without the usual introduction ततः प्रविशति &c.

अपटु *a.* 1 Not clever or skilful: dull, awkward. 2 Ineloquent (as a speaker). 3 Sick.

अपठ *a* Unable to read; not reading; a bad reader; cf. अपच.

अपंडित *a.* 1 Not learned or wise, foolish, ignorant; विभूषणं मौनमपंडितानाम् Bh. 2. 7. 2 Wanting in skill, taste, appreciation &c.

अपण्य *a.* Not saleable; जीविकार्थे चापण्ये P. V. 3. 99.

अपतर्पणं 1 Fasting (in sickness). 2 Absence of satisfaction.

अपतानकः Spasmodic contraction with occasional convulsive fits.

अपति,-तिक *a.* Without a master; without a husband, unmarried.

अपत्नीक *a.* Without a wife.

अपतीर्थं A bad Tîrtha or place of pilgrimage.

अपत्यं 1 Offspring, child, progeny, issue (of animals and men): offspring in general (male or female); sons or grandsons and other later generations of a Gotra; अपत्यं पौत्रप्रभृति गोत्रं P. IV. 1. 62; अपत्यैरिव नीवारभागधेयोचितैर्मृगैः R. 1. 50. 2 A patronymic affix.–Comp. **–काम** *a.* desirous of progeny.**–पथः** the vulva. **–प्रत्ययः** a patronymic affix.**–विक्रयिन्** *m.* a seller of his children, a father who sells his girl for money to a bridegroom. **–शत्रुः** 1 a crab. –2 a serpent.

अपत्रप *a.* Shameless, impudent. **–पा –पणं** Shame, bashfulness.

अपत्रपिष्णु *a.* Bashful.

अपत्रस्त *p. p.* Afraid of, deterred from; तरंगापत्रस्तः (slightly) afraid of waves.

अपथ *a.* Pathless, roadless. **-थं**, (also अपंथाः Not a way, absence of a way or road, a bad or wrong road (lit.); (fig.) a moral irregularity or deviation, bad or evil course; अपंथे पदमर्पयंति हि श्रुतवंतोपि रजोनिमीलिताः R. 9. 74.–Comp. **–गामिन्** *a.* pursuing evil courses; heretical.

अपथ्य *a.* 1 Unfit, improper, inconsistent, obnoxious; अकार्यं कार्यसंकाशमपथ्यं पथ्यसंमितं Râm. 2 (In medicine) Unwholesome, unsalutary (as food, regimen &c.); संतापयंति कमपथ्यभुजं नरोगाः H. 3. 117. 3 Bad, unlucky.–Comp. **–कारिन्** *a.* an offender.

अपदः A reptile. **–दं** 1 No place or abode. 2 A wrong or bad place or abode. 3 A word which is not a *pada* or an inflected word. 4 Ether. –Comp. **–अंतर** *a.* adjoining, contiguous, very near. (**–रं**) proximity, contiguity.

अपदक्षिणं *ind.* To the left side.

अपदम *a.* Without self-restraint.

अपदश *a.* Far from ten.

अपदानं –दानकं 1 Pure conduct, approved course of life. 2 A great or noble work, excellent work (perhaps for अवदानं q. v.). 3 A work well or completely done, an accomplished work.

अपदार्थः 1 Nothing, non-entity. 2 Not the meaning of words actually used in a sentence ; अपदार्थोपि वाक्यार्थः समुल्लसति K. P. 2.

अपदिशं *ind.* Half a point between two regions of the compass, in an intermediate region.

अपदेशः 1 Statement, adducing (उपदेश) ; pointing out, mentioning the name of ; नैष न्यायो यद्यातुरपदेशः Dk. 60; हेत्वपदेशात् प्रतिज्ञायाः पुनर्वचनं निगमनं Nyâya S. 2 A pretext, pretence, plea, excuse; केनापदेशेन पुनराश्रमं गच्छामः *S.* 2; रक्षापदेशान्मुनिहोमधेनोः ; R. 2. 8. 3 Statement of the reason, adducing a cause, the second (हेतु)of the five members of an Indian syllogism (according to the Vaiseshikas). 4 A butt, mark. 5 A place, quarter. 6 Refusal. 7 Fame, reputation. 8 Deceit.

अपदेवता A goblin, evil spirit.

अपद्रव्यं A bad thing.

अपद्वारं A side-door or entrance, an entrance other than the proper door.

अपधूम *a.* Free from smoke.

अपध्यानं Evil thoughts, thinking ill of, cursing mentally.

अपध्वंसः Degradation, falling off or from, disgrace. –Comp. **–जः, –जा** a person of a mixed, degraded and impure caste ; Ms. 10. 41, 46.

अपध्वस्त *p. p.* 1 Reviled, cursed; accursed, to be disdained. 2 Pounded badly or imperfectly. 3 Abandoned. **—स्तः** A vile wretch, lost to all sense of right and virtue.

अपनयः 1 Taking away, removing; refuting (as an assertion). 2 A bad policy or conduct. 3 Injury, offence (अपकार); ततःसपत्नापनयस्मरणानुशयस्फुरा Si 2. 14.

अपनयनं 1 Taking away, removing; नातिश्रमापनयनाय *S.* 5. 6. 2 Healing, curing. 3 Discharge or acquittance of a debt or obligation.

अपनस *a.* without a nose, असिंकौक्षेयमुद्यम्य चकारापनसं मुखं Bk. 4. 31.

अपनुत्तिः *f.* **–नोदः –नोदनं** Removing, taking away, destroying, expiation, atonement (as of a sin); पापानामपनुत्त्यै Ms. 11. 215.

अपपाठः A wrong or bad reading (in a text); mistake in reading; द्वादशापपाठा अस्य जाताः.

अपपात्र *a.* Deprived of the use of common vessels, of low caste.

अपपात्रितः One who has lost his caste through some great sin or offence, and who is, therefore, not allowed by his relatives to eat or drink from a common vessel.

अपपानं A bad drink.

अपपूत *a.* Having badly formed hips. **—तौ** Badly formed hips.

अपप्रजाता A female that has suffered a miscarriage.

अपप्रदानं A bribe.

अपभय –भी *a.* Free from fear, fearless, undaunted; R. 3. 51.

अपभरणी The last asterism.

अपभाषणं Reviling, defamation.

अपभ्रंशः *a.* 1 Falling down or away, a fall; अत्यारूढिर्भवति महतामप्यपभ्रंशनिष्ठा *S.* 4 v. 1. 2 A corrupted word, corruption; (hence) an incorrect word whether formed against the rules of grammar or used in a sense not strictly Sanskrit; see अपशब्द. 3 A corrupt language, one of the lowest forms of the Prâkrita dialect used by cow-herds &c. (in kâvyas); (in *S*âstras) any language other than Sanskrit; आभीरादिगिरः काव्येष्वपभ्रंश इति स्मृताः । शास्त्रेषु संस्कृतादन्यदपभ्रंशतयोदितम् ॥ Kav. 1.

अपमः (In astr.) Declination; the ecliptic.

अपमर्दः What is swept away, dust, dirt.

अपमर्शः Touching, grazing.

अपमानः Disrespect, dishonour, disgrace; लभते बुद्ध्यवज्ञानमपमानं च पुष्कलं Pt. 1. 63.

अपमार्गः A by-path, side way; a bad way.

अपमुख *a.* 1 Having the face averted. 2 Ill-favoured, ill-looking.

अपमूर्धन् *a.* Headless; °कलेवरं Ak.

अपमार्जनं 1 Wiping away, cleansing, purifying. 2 Shaving, paring.

अपमृत्युः 1 Sudden or untimely death, accidental death. 2 Any great danger, illness &c. from which a person, hopelessly given up for lost, recovers, quite contrary to expectation.

अपमृषित *a.* 1 Unintelligible, obscure, as a वाक्य or speech. 2 Unbearable, not borne or liked; विहितं मयाद्य सदसीदमपमृषितमच्युतार्चनं । यस्य &c.*Si*.15.46.

अपयशस् *n.* (**शः**) Infamy, disgrace, ill-repute; अपयशो यद्यस्ति किं मृत्युना Bh. 2. 55.

अपयानं Going away, retreat, flight.

अपर *a.* (treated as a pronoun in some senses) 1 Unrivalled, matchless; cf. अनुत्तम, अनुत्तर. 2 (*a*) Another other (used as adj. or subst.). (*b*)

More, additional. (*c*) Second, another. (*d*) Different, other Ms. 1. 85. (*e*) Ordinary, of the middle sort (मध्यम). **3** Belonging to another, not one's own (opp. स्व). **4** Hinder, posterior, latter, later, (in time or space) (opp. पूर्व); the last; रात्रेरपरः कालः Nir.; oft. used as first member of a genitive Tatpurusha comp. meaning 'the hind part', 'latter part or half'; °पक्षः the latter half of a month; °हेमंतः latter half of winter; °कायः hind part of the body &c.; °वर्षा, °शरद् latter part of the rains, autumn &c. **5** Following, the next. **6** Western; *Si*. 9. 1. Ku. 1. 1. **7** Inferior, lower. **8** (In Nyâya) Nonextensive, not covering too much. When अपर is used in the singular as a correlative to एक the one, former, it means the other, the latter; एको ययौ चैत्ररथप्रदेशान् सौराज्यरम्यानपरो विदर्भान् R. 5. 60; when used in pl. it means 'others', 'and others,' and the words generally used as its correlatives are एके, केचित्–काश्चित् &c. अपरे अन्ये; एके समूहुर्बलरेणुसंहतिं शिरोभिराज्ञामपरे महीभृतः *Si*. 12. 45 some–others; शिखानः कचिदध्यष्ठुर्न्यमांश्चुरपरेंबुधौ । अन्ये स्थलंविवुः शैलान् गुहास्वन्ये न्यलेषत ॥ केचिदासिषत स्तब्धा भयात्केचिद्घूर्णिषुः । उदतारिषुरंभोधिं वानराः संतुनापरं Bk. 15. 31.—33.—**रः** 1 The hind foot of an elephant. **2** An enemy. —**रा 1** Western direction. **2** The hind part of an elephant. **3** The womb; the outer skin of the embryo. **4** Suppressed menstruation in pregnancy. –**रं** 1 The future. **2** The hind quarter of an elephant.—**रं** *adv*. Again, in future; अपरंच moreover; अपरेण behind, west of, to the west of (with gen. or acc.)–Comp. –**अग्नि** (अग्नी dual) the southern and western fires (दक्षिण and गार्हपत्य). –**अंगं** one of the 8 divisions of गुणीभूतव्यंग्य (the second kind of काव्य) mentioned in K. P. 5. In this the व्यंग्य or suggested sense is subordinate to something else; *e. g.* अयं स रसनोत्कर्षी पीनस्तनविमर्दनः । नाभ्यूरुजघनस्पर्शी नीविविस्रंसनः करः, where शृंगार is subordinate to करुण. –**अंत** *a*. living at the western borders. (–**तः**) 1 the western border or extremity, the extreme end or term; the western shore–2 (pl.) the country or inhabitants of the western borders near the Sahya mountain; अपरांतजयोद्यतैः (अनीकैः) R. 4. 53. western people.–3 the kings of this country.–4 death. —**अंतकः** =°**अंतः** pl. –**अपराः,—रे, –राणि** another and another, several, various –**अर्धं** the latter or second half. –**अह्नः** the afternoon, closing or last watch of the day. –**इतरा** the east. –**कालः** later period. –**जनः** an inhabitant of the west, the western people. –**दक्षिणं** *ind*. in the south-west. –**पक्षः** 1 the second or dark half of the month. –2 the other or opposite side; a defendant (in law). –**पर** *a*. one and the other, several, various; अपरपराः सार्थाः गच्छंति P. VI. 1. 144 Sk. several caravans go. –**पाणिनीयाः** the pupils of Pâṇini living in the west. –**प्रणेय** *a*. easily led or influenced by others, tractable. –**रात्रः** the latter or closing part of night, the last watch of night. –**लोकः** the other world, the next world, Paradise. –**स्वस्तिकं** the western point in the horizon. –**हैमन** *a*. belonging to the latter half of winter.

अपरता–त्वं Being another or different (one of the 24 guṇa); difference, contrariety, relativeness.

अपरत्र *adv*. In another place, elsewhere; एकत्र or क्वचित्–अपरत्र in one place-in another place.

अपरक्त *a*. 1 Colourless, bloodless, pale; श्वासापरक्ताधरः *S*. 6. 5. **2** Discontented, dissatisfied.

अपरतिः *f*. 1 Cessation (=अवरति q. v.). **2** Dissatisfaction.

अपरवः 1 Contest, dispute (about the enjoyment of property); °उज्झित uncontested, undisputed (as possession of anything). **2** Ill-repute.

अपरस्पर *a*. One after another, uninterrupted, continued; °राः सार्था गच्छंति सततमविच्छेदेन गच्छंतीत्यर्थः Sk.

अपराग *a* Colourless. –**गः** 1 Discontent, dissatisfaction, disaffection; अपरागसमीरणेरितः Ki. 2. 50. **2** Apathy, enmity.

अपरांच् *a*. [°राङ्, °राची, °राक्] Not averted, fronting, facing, in front —*ind*. (–**राक्**) In front of. –Comp. –**मुख** *a*. (खी *f*.) 1 not turning away the face, with unaverted face –2 presenting a bold front.

अपराजित *a*. Unconquered, invincible. —**तः** 1 A sort of poisonous insect **2** N. of Vishṇu, *Siva*. —**ता 1** N. of Durgâ, to be worshipped on the Vijayâdasamî or *Dasarâ* day. **2** A kind of plant (or ओषधि) fastened round wrist and serving as a charm or amulet. **3** The nort-east quarter.

अपराद्ध *p. p*. 1 Sinned, offended, having committed an offence, an offender, (used in an active sense); कस्मिन्नपि पूजार्हेऽपराद्धा शकुंतला *S*. 4. **2** Missed, not hitting the mark (as an arrow); निमित्तादपराद्धेषोर्धानुष्कस्येव वल्गितं *Si*. 2. 27. **3** Violated, transgressed.—**द्धं** An offence.

अपराद्धिः *f*. 1 Fault, offence. **2** Sin.

अपराधः An offence, a fault, crime, sin; कमपराधलवं मयि पश्यसि V. 4. 29; यथापराधदंडानां R. 1. 6.

अपराधिन् *a*. Offending, guilty.

अपरिग्रह *a*. Without possessions or belongings, attendants &c.; quite destitute, as in निराशीरपरिग्रहः. —**हः** 1 Non-acceptance, rejection **2** Destitution, poverty.

अपरिच्छद *a*. Poor, destitute.

अपरिच्छिन्न *a*. 1 Undiscerned. **2** Continuous.

अपरिणयः Celibacy.

अपरिणीता An unmarried girl.

अपरिसंख्यानं Infinity, innumerableness.

अपरीक्षित *a*. 1 Unexamined; untested, unproved. **2** Ill-considered, foolish, thoughtless (of person or thing); °कारकं नाम पंचमं तंत्रं Pt. 5 'the inconsiderate doer.' **3** Not clearly proved or established.

अपरुष् *a*. Free from anger अपरुषापरुषाक्षरमीरिता R. 9. 8.

अपरूप *a*. (–**पा**,– **पी** *f*.) Ugly, deformed, odd-shaped.—**पं** Deformity.

अपरेद्युः *ind*. On the following day.

अपरोक्ष *a*. 1 Not invisible, perceptible to the senses. **2** Not distant or remote. –**क्षं** *adv*. In the presence of (with gen.) अपरोक्षात् perceptibly, visibly.

अपरोधः Exclusion, prohibition.

अपर्ण *a*. Leafless. –**र्णा** N. of Durgâ or Pârvatî; Kâlidâsa thus accounts for the name:–स्वयंविशीर्णद्रुमपर्णवृत्तिता परा हि काष्ठा तपसस्तया पुनः । तदप्यपाकीर्णमिति प्रियंवदां वदंत्यपर्णेति च तां पुराविदः Ku. 5. 28.

अपर्याप्त *a*. 1 Not sufficient or enough, incomplete, insufficient. **2** Unlimited. **3** Unable (to do its work), incompetent; अपर्याप्तं तदस्माकं बलं भीष्माभिरक्षितं Bg. 1. 30.

अपर्याप्तिः *f*. Insufficiency.

अपर्याय *a*. Without order. –**यः** Want of order or method.

अपर्युषित *a*. Not standing overnight, fresh, new (as a flower).

अपर्वन् *a*. Without a joint. –*n*. 1 No joint or point of conjunction. **2** A day which is not a पर्वन् *i. e*. not the proper time or season.

अपल *a*. Without flesh. –**लं** A pin or bolt.

अपलपनं, अपलापः 1 Concealing, hiding. **2** Concealment or denial of knowledge, evasion; न हि प्रत्यक्षसिद्धस्यापलापः कर्तुं शक्यते S. B. **3** Detraction, concealment of truth, thoughts, feelings &c. –Comp. –**दंडः** (in law) a fine laid on one who denies the charge on which he is convicted.

अपलापिन् *a*. One who denies, disowns, hides &c.

अपलाषिका Excessive thirst or desire, or thirst in general; (अपलासिका is sometimes used in the same sense, but regarded as an incorrect word).

अपलाषिन्, -लाषुक *a.* 1 Thirsty. 2 Free from thirst or desire; प्रलापिनो भविष्यंति कदा न्वेतेऽपलाषुकाः Mb.

अपवन *a.* Without wind or air, sheltered from wind.—**नं** A grove, a garden or park planted near a town.

अपवरकः-का 1 An inner apartment; the lying-in chamber. 2 An air-hole, aperture; ततश्चैकस्मादपवरकात् Mu. 1.

अपवरणं 1 Covering, screening. 2 A garment, cloth.

अपवर्गः 1 Completion, end, fulfilment or accomplishment of an action; अपवर्गे तृतीया P. II. 3. 6; क्रियापवर्गेष्वनुजीविसात्कृताः Ki. 1. 14 अपवर्गे तृतीयेति भणतः पाणिनेरपि N. 17. 68; Ki. 16. 49. 2 An exception, special rule; अभिव्याप्यापकर्षणमपवर्गः Susr. 3 Absolution, final beatitude; अपवर्गमहोदयार्थयोर्भुवमंशाविव धर्मयोर्गतौ R. 8. 16. 4 A gift, donation. 5 Abandonment. 6 Throwing, discharge (as of arrows).

अपवर्जनं 1 Leaving, fulfilling (a promise); discharging (debt &c.). 2 A gift or donation. 3 Final beatitude.

अपवर्तः 1 Taking away, removing. 2 (Math.) The (common) divisor which is applied to both or either of the quantities of an equation.

अपवर्तनं 1 Removal, transferring from one place to another; स्थान°. 2 Taking away, depriving one of; न त्यागोऽस्ति द्विषंत्याश्च न च दायापवर्तनं Ms. 9. 79.

अपवादः 1 Censuring, reproach, blame; लोकापवादो बलवान्मतो मे. R. 14. 40; scandal, evil report. देव्यामपि हि वैदेह्यां सापवादो यतो जनः U. 1. 6. 2 An exception (opp. उत्सर्ग); अपवादैरिवोत्सर्गाः कृतव्यावृत्तयः परैः Ku. 2. 27; R. 15. 7. 3 An order, command ततोऽपवादेन पताकिनीपतेश्चचाल निन्हादवती महाचमूः Ki. 14. 27. 4 Refutation; (Vedânta phil.) refutation as of a wrong imputation or belief; रज्जुविवर्तस्य सर्पस्य रज्जुमात्रत्ववत्, वस्तुभूतब्रह्मणो विवर्तस्य प्रपंचादेः वस्तुभूतरूपतापदेशः अपवादः Tv. 5 Confidence. 6 Love; familiarity.

अपवादक, अपवादिन् *a.* 1 Blaming, censuring, defaming; मृगयापवादिना माढव्येन *S.* 2. 2 Opposing, setting aside, excluding.

अपवारणं 1 Covering, concealment. 2 Disappearance.

अपवारित *p. p.* Covered, concealed. —**तं, अपवारितकं** Concealed or secret manner.—**तं, अपवारितकेन, अपवार्य** *ind.* Frequently occurring in dramas in the sense of 'apart' 'aside to another' (opp. प्रकाशं); it is speaking in such a way that only the person addressed may hear it; तद्भवेदपवारितं रहस्यं तु यदन्यस्य परावृत्य प्रकाश्यते । त्रिपताककरेणान्यमपवार्यांतरा कथां S. D. 6.

अपवाहः, -हनं 1 Taking or carrying away, removal. 2 Deduction, subtraction (as of fractions).

अपविघ्न *a.* Unobstructed, uninterrupted; R. 3. 38.

अपविद्ध *p. p.* 1 Cast or thrown off, dismissed, rejected, neglected, removed; oft. used in the sense of 'freed from,' 'devoid of.' 2 Abject, mean. **—द्धः**, °पुत्रः A son that is abandoned by the father or mother or by both, and adopted by a stranger; one of the 12 kinds of sons among Hindus; Ms. 9. 171; Y. 2. 132.

अपविद्या Ignorance, spiritual ignorance, Mâyâ or illusion (अविद्या); तत्त्वस्य संवित्तिरिवापविद्यां Ki. 16. 32.

अपवीण *a.* Having no lute, or having a bad lute. **—णा** A bad lute.

अपवृक्तिः *f.* Fulfilment, accomplishment, completion.

अपवृतिः *f.* Opening, uncovering.

अपवृत्तिः *f.* End.

अपवेधः Piercing through (a pearl, ruby &c.) wrongly, or in the wrong direction.

अपव्ययः Extravagant expenditure, prodigality.

अपशकुनं A bad omen.

अपशंक *a.* Fearless. **—कं** *adv.* Fearlessly.

अपशदः =अपसद q. v.

अपशब्दः 1 A bad or ungrammatical word, a corrupted word (in form or meaning); त एव शक्तिवैकल्यप्रमादालसतादिभिः । अन्यथोच्चारिताः शब्दा अपशब्दा इतीरिताः ॥; अपशब्दशतं माघे Subha'sh. 2 Vulgar speech. 3 Ungrammatical language. 4 A reproachful word, offensive expression, censure.

अपशिरस्-शीर्ष-र्षन् *a.* Headless.

अपशुच् *a.* Without sorrow.—*m.* The soul.

अपशोक *a.* Without sorrow or grief. **—कः** The *Asoka* tree.

अपश्चिम *a.* 1 Having no other in the rear, last (used much in the same sense as पश्चिम; cf. उत्तम and अनुत्तम, उत्तर and अनुत्तर); अयमपश्चिमस्ते रामस्य शिरसि पादपंकजस्पर्शः U. 1; प्रसीदतु महाराजो ममानेनापश्चिमेन प्रणयेन Ve. 6. 2 Not last, first, foremost. 3 Extreme; अपश्चिमामिमां कष्टामापदं प्राप्तवत्यहं Râm.

अपश्रयः A bolster, pillow.

अपश्री *a.* Deprived of beauty; *Si.* 11. 64.

अपश्वासः = अपान q. v.

अपष्ठ The point of the goad of an elephant.

अपष्ठु *a.* 1 Contrary, opposite. 2 Unfavourable, adverse. 3 Left. **-ष्ठु** *adv.* 1 Contrary. 2 Falsely. 3 Faultlessly. 4 Well, properly.

अपष्ठुर-ल *a.* Contrary, opposite.

अपसदः 1 An outcast, a low man; usually at the end of comp. in the sense of 'vile,' 'wretched,' 'accursed'; कापालिक° Mâl. 5; रेरे क्षत्रियापसदाः Ve. 3. 2 N. for the children of six degrading connections, *i. e.* of men of the first three castes with women of the castes inferior to their own; विप्रस्य त्रिषु वर्णेषु नृपतेर्वर्णयोर्द्वयोः । वैश्यस्य वर्णे चैकस्मिन् षडेतेऽपसदाः स्मृताः ॥ Ms. 10. 10.

अपसरः 1 Departure, retreat. 2 A proper excuse or apology, valid reason.

अपसरणं Going away, retreating, escape.

अपसर्जनं 1 Leaving, abandonment. 2 A gift or donation. 3 Final beatitude.

अपसर्पः,-र्पकः A secret agent or emissary, spy; सोपसर्पैर्जजागार यथाकालं स्वपन्नपि R. 17. 51, 14. 31.

अपसर्पणं Going back, retreating; observing as a spy.

अपसव्य, -सव्यक *a.* 1 Not left, right; अपसव्येन हस्तेन Ms. 3. 214. 2. Contrary, opposite. **—व्यं** *ind.* To the right, making the sacred thread hang down towards the left part of the body over the right shoulder (opp. सव्यं when it hangs over the left); °व्यं कृ to go round one so as to keep the right side towards him; to ake the sacred thread hang over the right shoulder.

अपसव्यवत् *a.* Wearing the sacred thread over the right shoulder.

अपसारः 1 Going out, retreating. 2 An outlet, egress.

अपसारणं-णा Removing to a distance, driving, expelling; किमर्थमपसारणा क्रियते Mu. 4; making room (cf. Mar. बाजू, बाजू).

अपसिद्धांतः A wrong or erroneous conclusion.

अपसृतिः *f.* going away or forth.

अपस्करः 1 Any part of a carriage except the wheel (**-रं** also) 2 Excrement. 3 Vulva. 4 Anus.

अपस्नानं 1 Bathing, as after mourning or upon the death of a relative. 2 Impure bathing, bathing in water in which a person has previously washed himself.

अपस्पश *a.* Devoid of spies; शब्दविद्येव नो भाति राजनीतिरपस्पशा *Si.* 2. 112.

अपस्पर्श *a.* Insensible.

अपस्मारः,-स्मृतिः *f.* 1 Forgetfulness. 2 Epilepsy, falling sickness.

अपस्मारिन् *a.* Epileptic.

अपस्मृति *a.* Forgetful.

अपह *a.* (At the end of comp.) Warding or keeping off, removing, destroying; स्रगियं यदि जीवितापहा R. 8. 46.

अपहतिः *f.* Removing, destroying.

अपहननं Warding off, repelling.

अपहरणं 1 Taking or carrying away, removing. 2 Stealing.

अपहसितं, -हासः Silly or causless laughter; often laughter with tearful eyes (नीचानामपहसितं).

अपहस्तित *p. p.* Thrown away, discarded, given up; °सकलसखीजनं त्वयि विश्वसिति मे हृदयं K. 233, 202.

अपहानिः *f.* 1 Leaving, abandonment. 2 Ceasing, vanishing. 3 Exception, exclusion.

अपहारः 1 Taking or carrying away, stealing, destroying; निद्रापहार, विष°. 2 Concealing, dessembling; कथमात्मापहारं करोमि *S*. 1 how shall I dissemble myself, conceal my real name and character.

अपह्नवः 1 Concealment, hiding, concealment of one's knowledge, feelings &c. 2 Denial or disowning of the truth, dissimulation; °वे ज्ञः P. I. 3. 44. 3 Love, affection.

अपह्नुतिः *f.* 1 Concealment of knwoledge, denial. 2 (In rhet.) A figure of speech, in which the real charactor of the thing in question is denied and that of another (alien or imaginary) object is ascribed to, or superimposed upon, it; *e. g.* नेदं नभोमंडलमंबुराशिर्नैताश्च तारा नवफेनभंगाः ॥ see also K. P. 10 and S. D. 683-84.

अपह्रासः Reduction, diminution.

अपाक् *ind.* See अपाच्.

अपाकः 1 Indigestion (of food &c.). 2 Immaturity.

अपाकरणं 1 Driving away, removal. 2 Rejection, refutation. 3 Payment, liquidation.

अपाकर्मन् *n.* (°र्म) Payment, liquidation.

अपाकृतिः *f.* 1 Rejection, removal &c. 2 Emotion resulting from anger, fear &c.; Ki. 1. 27.

अपाक्ष *a.* 1 Present, perceptible. 2 Eyeless; having bad eyes.

अपांक्त,-पांक्तेय,-पांक्त्य *a.* 'Not in the same row or in line'; especially one who is not allowed by his castemen to sit in the same row with them at meals, an outcast.

अपांगः-गकः *a.* 1 The outer corner or angle of the eye; चलापांगां दृष्टिं *S*. 1. 24. 2 A sectarial mark on the forehead. 3 Cupid, the god of love. -Comp. **-दर्शनं, -दृष्टिः** *f.*, **-विलोकितं, -वीक्षणं** &c. a side-glance; side-long look, wink. **-देशः** the corner itself. **-नेत्र** *a.* (said of a lady) having eyes with beautiful (or long) outer corners; यदियं पुनरप्यपांगनेत्रा परिवृत्तार्धमुखी मयाद्य दृष्टा V. 1. 17. (a better interpretation would, hewever, be 'with the eyes turned towards the corner').

अपाच्,-अपांच् 1 Going or situated backwards, behind. 2 Not open or clear. 3 Western. 4 Southern. **—क्** *ind.* 1 Behind, backwards. 2 Westward or southward.

अपाची The south or west, °इतरा the north.

अपाचीन *a.* 1 Situated backwards or behind, turned backwards. 2 Not visible, imperceptible; Rv. 7. 6. 4. 3 Southern. 4 Western. 5 Opposite.

अपाच्य *a* western or southern.

अपाणिनीय *a.* 1 Not taught by Pâṇini in his works (as a rule &c.). 2 One who does not (properly) study Pâṇini's grammar; *i. e.*, a superficial scholar, smatterer of Sanskrit.

अपात्रं 1 A worthless vessel or utensil. 2 (fig.) An unworthy or undeserving person, unfit receptacle or recipient. 3 One unfit or disqualified to receive gifts, -Comp. **-कृत्या, अपात्रीकरणं** doing degrading or unworthy acts; disqualification, see Ms. 11. 70. **-दायिन्** *a.* giving to unworthy persons **-भृत्** *a.* supporting the unworthy or worthless; प्रायेणापात्रभृद्भवति राजा Pt. 1.

अपादानं 1 Taking away, removal, ablation. 2 (In gram.) The sense of the ablative case; ध्रुवमपायेऽपादानं P. I. 4. 24.

अपाध्वन् *m.* A bad way.

अपानः Breathing out, respiration, one of the five lifewinds in the body which goes downwards and out at the anus.—**नः -नं** The anus. -Comp. **-द्वारं** the anus. **-पवनः, -वायुः** the lifewind called अपान.

अपानृत *a.* Free from falsehood; true.

अपाप-पिन् *a.* Sinless, pure, virtuous.

अपां gen. pl. of अप् water; first member of some compounds:— **-ज्योतिस्** *n.* lightning. **-नपात्** an epithet of fire and Savitri. **-नाथः, -पतिः** 1 the ocean. -2 N. Varuna. **निधिः** 1 the ocean. 2- N. of of Vishṇu. **-पाथस्** *n.* food. **-पित्तं** fire. **-योनिः** the ocean.

अपामार्गः N. of a plant (Mar. आघाडा).

अपामार्जनं Cleansing, purifying, removing (diseases, evils &c.).

अपायः 1 Going away, departure. 2 Separation; ध्रुवमपायेऽपादानं P. 1. 4. 24; येन जातं प्रियापाये कद्वदं हंसकोकिलं Bk. 6. 75. 3 Disappearance, vanishing, absence. 4 Destruction, loss, annihilation; करणापायविभिन्नवर्णया R. 8. 42. 5. An evil, misfortune, calamity, danger (oft. opp. उपाय); कायः संनिहितापायः H. 4. 65. 6. Loss, injury.

अपार *a.* 1. Shoreless. 2 Boundless, unlimited. 3 Inexhaustible, immense. 4 Out of reach. 5 Difficult to be crossed; difficult to be surmounted or overcome. **—रं** The opposite bank of a river.

अपार्ण *a.* 1 Distant, remote. 2 Near.

अपार्थ, अपार्थक *a.* 1 Useless, unprofitable, worthless. 2 Meaningless, senseless. **—र्थं** Senseless or incoherent talk or argument (regarded as one of the faults of composition in rhetoric); cf. also Kâv. 3. 28; समुदायार्थशून्यं यत्तदपार्थमितीष्यते ।.

अपावरणं, अपावृतिः *f.* 1 Opening. 2 Covering, enclosing, surrounding. 3 Concealing, hiding.

अपावर्तनं,-वृत्तिः *f.* 1 Turning away or from, retreating, repulse. 2 Revolution.

अपाश्रय *a.* Without support or refuge, helpless.—**यः** 1 Refuge, recourse, that to which recourse is had for refuge. 2 As awning or canopy spread over a court-yard. 3 Head.

अपासंगः A quiver.

अपासनं 1 Throwing away, discarding. 2 Quitting. 3 Killing.

अपासरणं Departure, retreat, removal; see अपसरण.

अपासु *a.* Lifeless, dead.

अपि *ind.* (Sometimes with the अ dropped according to the opinion of Bhâguri; वष्टि भागुरिरल्लोपमवाप्योरुपसर्गयोः; पिधा, पिधान &c.) 1 (Used with roots and nouns in the sense of) Placing near or over, taking towards, reaching or going up to, proximity, nearness &c. 2 (As a separable adverb or conjunction) And, also, too, moreover, besides, in addition अस्ति मे सोदरस्नेहोऽप्येतेषु *S*. 1; on one's part, in one's turn; विष्णुशर्मणापि राजपुत्राः पाठिताः Pt. 1; अपिअपि or अपिच as well as, and also; अपि स्तुहि, अपि सिंच Sk. न नापिन चैव, न वापि, नापि वा, न चापि neither-nor. 3 It is often used to express emphasis in the sense of 'too', 'even,' very'; अद्यापि still even now इदानीमपि even now; यद्यपि though, although, even if; तथापि still, nevertheless; sometimes यद्यपि is understood तथापि only being used; as in Ki. 1 28. 4 Though (oft. translatable by 'even', 'even if'); सरसिजमनुविद्धं शैवलेनापि रम्यं *S*. 1. 20 though overspread &c.; इयमधिकमनोज्ञा वल्कलेनापि तन्वी *ibid.* though in her bark dress. 5 Used at the beginning of sentences अपि introduces a question; अपि सन्निहितोऽत्र कुलपतिः *S*. 1; अपि क्रियार्थसुलभं समित्कुशं...अपि स्वशक्त्या तपसि प्रवर्तसे Ku. 5. 33, 34, 35. 6 Hope, expectation (usually with the potential mood); कृतं रामसदृशं कर्म । अपि जीवेत्स ब्राह्मणशिशुः U. 2 I hope the Brâhmaṇa boy comes to life. Note—In this sense अपि is frequently used with नाम and has the sense of (*a*) 'is it likely', 'may it be'; (*b*) 'perhaps', 'in all probability;' or (*c*) 'would that', I wish or hope that'; अपि नाम कुलपतेरियमसवर्णक्षेत्रसंभवा स्यात् *S*. 1; *S*. 7; तदपि नाम मनागवतीर्णोऽसि रतिरमणबाणगोचरं Mâl. 1 perhaps, in all probability; अपिनामाहं पुरूरवा भवेयं V. 2 I wish I were P. 7 Affixed to interrogative words अपि makes the sense indefinite, 'any', 'some'; कोपि some one; किमपि something; कुत्रापि

somewhere. It may often be translated by 'unknown', 'indescribable', 'inexpressible;' व्यतिषजति पदार्थानांतरः कोपि हेतुः U. 6. 12. 8 After words expressing number अपि has the sense of 'totality', 'all'; चतुर्णामपि वर्णानां of all the 4 castes. 9 It sometimes expresses 'doubt' or 'uncertainty', 'fear' (शंका); अपि चोरो भवेत् G. M. there is perhaps a thief. 10 (With pot. mood) It has the sense of संभावना 'possibility', 'supposition'; अपि स्तुयाद्विष्णुं. 11 Contempt, censure; अपि जायां त्यजासि जातु गणिकामाधत्से गर्हितमेतत् Sk. shame to, or fie upon, you &c; धिग्जाल्मं देवदत्तमपि सिंचेत्पलांडुं. 12 It is also used with the Imperative mood to mark 'indifference on the part of the speaker', where he permits another to do as he likes; अपि स्तुहि Sk. you may praise (if you like); अपि स्तुह्यपि सेधास्मांस्तथ्यमुक्तं नराशन Bk. 8. 92. 13 अपि is sometimes used as a particle of exclamation. 14 Rarely in the sense of 'therefore,' 'hence' (अत एव). 15 Used as a separable preposition with gen. it is said to express the sense of a word understood; the example usually given is सर्पिषोपि स्यात् where some word like बिंदुरपि 'a drop,' 'a little' &c. has to be understood, there may perhaps be a drop of ghee'.

अपिगीर्ण *a.* 1 Praised, celebrated. 2 Told, described.

अपिच्छिल *a.* 1 Not muddy, clear, free from sediment. 2 Deep.

अपितृक *a.* 1 Fatherless. 2 Not ancestral or paternal, not inherited; (अपैतृक also in this sense).

अपित्र्य *a.* Not ancestral.

अपिधानं,-पिधानं 1 Covering, concealing. 2 A cover, lid, covering (fig. also).

अपिधिः *f.* Concealment.

अपिव्रत *a.* Sharing in the same religious acts or other works; connected by blood.

अपिहित-पिहित *p. p.* 1 Shut, closed, covered, concealed (fig. also); बाष्पापिहित covered, with tears. 2 Not concealed, plain, clear; अर्थो गिरामपिहितः पिहितश्च किंचित् सत्यं चकास्ति मरहट्टवधूस्तनाभः Subhâsh.

अपीतिः *f.* 1 Entering into, approaching. 2 Dissolution, destruction, loss. 3 Destruction of the world (प्रलय); अपीतौ तद्वत् प्रसंगादसमंजसं Br. Sutra.

अपीनसः Dryness of the nose, cold (in the head).

अपुंस्का *f.* A woman without a husband; नापुंस्कासीति मे मतिः Bk. 5. 70.

अपुत्रः Not a son. —*a.*, -**पुत्रक** *a.* (°त्रिका *f.*) Having no son or heir.

अपुत्रिका The daughter of a sonless father, who herself has no male child; one who is not appointed by her father to beget male issue for him on failure of a son; cf. अकृता.

अपुनर् *ind.* Not again, once for all, for ever. -Comp. -**अन्वय** *a.* not returning; dead. -**आदानं** not taking back or again. -**आवृत्तिः** *f.* 'non-return', final beatitude. -**प्राप्य** *a.* irrecoverable. -**भवः** 1 not being born again (of diseases also).-2 final beatitude.

अपुष्ट *a.* 1 Not nourished or fed, lean, not fat. 2 Not loud or violent, soft, low (as sound). 3 (In Rhet.) Not feeding or assisting (the meaning), irrelevant (मुख्यानुपकारिन्), regarded as one of the *arthadoshas* (faults of the sense or meaning); as in the instance given under S. D. 576 विलोक्य वितते व्योम्नि विधुं मुंच रुषं प्रिये, the adjective वितत 'expanded,' as applied to the sky, does not in any way help the cessation of anger, and is, therefore, irrelevant.

अपूपः A small round cake of flour, meal &c. (Mar. वडा, घारगा, अनरसा &c.), thicker than ordinary cakes and mixed with sugar and spices.

अपूपीय, अपूप्य *a.* Belonging to, intended for, अपूप.—**प्यं** Flour, meal.

अपूरणी The silk-cotton tree (शाल्मली) (Mar. सांवरी).

अपूर्ण *a.* Not full or completed, incomplete, imperfect; अपूर्णमेकेन शतं क्रतूनां R. 3 88; अपूर्ण एव पंचरात्रे दोहदस्य M. 3.

अपूर्व *a.* 1 Not preceded, not having existed before, quite new; °र्वं नाटकं S. 1. 2. Strange, extraordinary, wonderful; अपूर्वो दृश्यते वह्निः कामिन्याः स्तनमंडले। दूरतो दहतीवांगं हृदि लग्नस्तु शीतलः॥ S. Til. 17; singular, unexampled, unprecedented; अपूर्वकर्मचांडालमयि मुग्धे विमुंच मां U. 1. 46 committing an unparalleled atrocity. 3 Unknown. 4 Not first. —**र्वं** 1 The remote consequence of an act (as the acquisition of heaven which is the result of good deeds). 2 Virtue and vice as the eventual cause of future happiness or misery. —**र्वः** The supreme soul. -Comp. -**पतिः** *f.* one who has had no husband before, a virgin. -**विधिः** an authoritative direction or injunction which is quite new.

अपृथक् *ind.* Not separately, together with, collectively.

अपेक्षा-क्षणं 1 Expectation, hope, desire. 2 Need, requirement, necessity; oft. in comp.; स्फुलिंगावस्थया वह्निरेधापेक्ष इव स्थितः S. 7. 15 awaiting kindling. 3 Consideration, reference, regard, with the obj. in loc. case; more usually in comp.; the instr. and sometimes loc. of this word (अपेक्षया, अपेक्षायां) frequently occur in comp. meaning 'with reference to', 'out of regard for,' 'for the sake of;' नियमापेक्षया R. 1. 94. प्रथमसुकृतापेक्षया Me. 17; अत्र व्यंग्यं गुणीभूतं तदपेक्षया वाच्यस्यैव चमत्कारित्वात् K. P. 1 as compared with it. 4 Connection, relation. 5 Care, attention, heed; देशापेक्षास्तथा यूयं यातादायांगुलीयकं Bk. 7. 49. 6 Respect, deference. 7 (In gram.)=आकांक्षा q. v.

अपेक्ष्य,-क्षितव्य,-क्षणीय *pot. p.* To be desired, wanted, hoped for, expected, considered &c.; desirable.

अपेक्षित *p. p.* Looked for, expected; wanted, required; considered &c. —**तं** Desire, wish; regard, reference.

अपेत *p. p.* 1 Gone away, disappeared; अपेतयुद्धाभिनिवेशसौम्यः Si. 3. 1. 2 Departing or deviating from, contrary (with abl.); अर्थादनपेतं अर्थ्यं Sk. 3 Free from, deprived of (with abl. or in comp.); सुखादपेतः Sk.; उदवहदनवद्यां तामवद्यादपेतः R. 7. 70. faultless.

अपेहि (Imper. 2nd sing.) Used as the first member of some compounds (belonging to the class मयूरव्यंसकादि); °करा, °द्वितीया, °स्वागता &c. where it has the sense of 'excluding,' 'expelling,' 'refusing admission to'; *e. g.* °वाणिजा a ceremony where merchants are excluded; so °द्वितीया &c.

अपोगंडः *a.* 1 Having a limb too many or too few (redundant or deficient) 2 Not under 16 years of age; Ms. 8. 148. 3 A child or infant. 4 Very timid 5 Wrinkled.

अपोढ *a.* Removed from (with abl.); कल्पनापोढः=कल्पनायाः अपोढः; see वह् with अप.

अपोहः 1 Removing, driving away, healing &c. 2 Removal of doubt by the exercise of the reasoning faculty. 3 Reasoning, arguing. 4 Negative reasoning (opp. ऊह) (अपरतर्कनिरासाय कृतो विपरीतस्तर्कः), स्वयमूहापोहासमर्थः Mbh.; ऊहापोहमिमं सरोजनयना यावद्विधत्तेतरां Bv. 2. 74; hence ऊहापोह=complete discussion of a question. 5 Excluding all things not coming under the category in point; तद्वानपोहो वा शब्दार्थः (where Mahesvara paraphrases अपोह by अतद्व्यावृत्ति *i. e.* तद्भिन्नत्यागः)

अपोहनं 1 Removal &c.=अपोह above. 2 Reasoning faculty; मत्तः स्मृतिर्ज्ञानमपोहनं च Bg. 15. 15.

अपोह्य, अपोहनीय *pot. p.* To be removed, taken away, expiated (as sin); to be established by reason.

अपौरुष-पौरुषेयं *a.* 1 Unmanly, cowardly, timid. 2 Superhuman, not of the authorship of man, of divine origin; अपौरुषेया वेदाः; अपौरुषेयप्रतिष्ठः सुवर्णबिंदुरित्याख्यायते Mâl. 9 not set up by (the hand of) man. —**षं, -षेयं** 1 Cowardice. 2 Superhuman power.

अप्तोर्यामः, -मन् *m.* N. of a sacrifice and of a verse of the Sâma Veda closing that rite; the last or 7th part of the Jyotishṭoma sacrifice.

अप्ययः 1 Approaching, meeting. 2 Pouring out (of rivers). 3 Entrance into, vanishing, disappearance: absorption, dissolution into oneself. 4 Destruction.

अप्रकरणं Not the main or principal topic, incidental or irrelevant matter.

अप्रकाश *a.* 1 Not shining or bright, dark, wanting in brightness (fig. also) प्रकाशश्चाप्रकाशश्च लोकालोक इवाचलः R. 1. 68. 2 Self-illuminated. 3 Hidden, secret. —**शं,-शे** *ind.* In secret, secretly.

अप्रकृत *a.* 1 Not principal or chief, incidental. 2 Not to the point, irrelevant; see प्रकृत, प्रस्तुत; अप्रकृतं अनुसंधा to beat about the bush, not to come to the point. —**तं** (In Rhet.) उपमान *i. e.* the standard of comparison (opp. प्रकृतं of उपमेय).

अप्रगम *a.* Going too fast to be followed by others.

अप्रगल्भ *a.* Not bold, bashful, modest (opp. धृष्ट); धृष्टः पार्श्वे वसति नियतं दूरतश्चाप्रगल्भः H. 2. 26.

अप्रगुण *a.* Perplexed, confounded.

अप्रज *a.* 1 Without progeny, childless. 2 Unborn. 3 Unpeopled.

अप्रजस्, अप्रजात *a.* Childless, having no issue or progeny; अतीतायामप्रजासि बांधवास्तदवाप्नुयुः Y. 2. 144.—**ता** A woman who has borne no child, a barren woman.

अप्रतिकर्मन् *a.* 1 Of unequalled deeds or achievements. 2 Irresistible.

अप्रति (ती) कार *a.* Irremediable, helpless.

अप्रतिघ *a.* 1 Not to be vanquished, invincible. 2 Not to be warded or kept off. 3 Not angry.

अप्रतिद्वंद्व *a.* 1 Having no adversary in battle, irresistible. 2 Unsurpassed, unrivalled.

अप्रतिपक्ष *a.* 1 Without a rival or opponent. 2 Unlike.

अप्रतिपत्ति *f.* 1 Non-performance, non-acceptance. 2 Neglect, disregard. 3 Want of understanding. 4 Absence of determination, confusion, perplexity; °विह्वल &c. K. 159; (अप्रतिपत्तिर्जडता स्यादिष्टानिष्टदर्शनश्रुतिभिः); °त्तिसाध्वसजडा K. 240. 5 (Hence) absence of mind or ready wit (स्फूर्त्यभाव); उत्तरस्याप्रतिपत्तिरप्रतिभा Gaut. S.

अप्रतिबंध *a.* 1 Unimpeded, unobstructed. 2 Undisputed; (in law) got by birth without any obstruction, not collateral (as inheritance).

अप्रतिबल *a.* Of irresistible might, of unequalled power.

अप्रतिभ *a.* 1 Modest, bashful. 2 Not ready-witted, dull.

अप्रतिभट *a.* Unrivalled.—**टः** An unrivalled warrior.

अप्रतिम *a.* Incomparable, matchless, unrivalled; so अप्रतिमान.

अप्रतिरथ *a.* or—**थः** (A hero) who has no प्रतिरथ or rival warrior, a matchless or unrivalled warrior; दौष्यंतिमप्रतिरथं तनयं निवेश्य S. 4. 19, S. 7, 7. 33.

अप्रतिरव *a.* Uncontested, undisputed; वर्षशताधिकभोगः संततोऽप्रतिरवः स्वत्वं गमयति Mit.

अप्रतिरूप *a.* 1 Not corresponding with, unfit. 2 Of unequalled form. 3 Incomparable.

अप्रतिवीर्य *a.* Of incomparable prowess.

अप्रतिशासन *a.* Having no rival ruler, subject to one rule; R. 8. 27.

अप्रतिष्ठ *a.* 1 Not stable or firmly fixed, not made permanent. 2 Unprofitable, useless. 3 Disreputable.

अप्रतिष्ठानं Instability, want of solidity or firmness (fig. also); तर्काप्रतिष्ठानादप्यन्यथानुमेयं S. B.

अप्रतिहत *a.* 1 Not obstructed or impeded, irresistible; अस्मद्गृहे °गतिः Pt. 1; जृंभतामप्रतिहतप्रसरमार्यस्य क्रोधज्योतिः Ve. 1; °शक्ति of irresistible power. 2 Unimpaired, unmarred, unaffected; सा बुद्धिरप्रतिहता Bh. 2. 40; Pt. 5. 26; so °चित °मनस्. 3. Not disappointed. –Comp. –**नेत्र** *a.* of unimpaired eyes.

अप्रतीत *a.* 1 Not pleased or delighted. 2 (In rhet.) Not understood or clearly intelligible (as a word), one of the defects of a word (शब्ददोष); a word is said to be अप्रतीत if it be used in a sense which it has in particular classes of works only (and not general or popular use). See K. P. 7.

अप्रत्ता A girl, one not given away in marriage.

अप्रत्यक्ष *a.* 1 Invisible, imperceptible. 2 Unknown. 3 Absent.

अप्रत्यय *a.* 1 Diffident, distrustful (with loc.); बलवदपि शिक्षितानामात्मन्यप्रत्ययं चेतः S. 1. 2. 2 Having no knowledge. 3 (In gram.) Having no affix. —**यः** 1 Diffidence, distrust, disbelief; क्षेत्रमप्रत्ययानां Pt. 1. 191. 2 Not being understood. 3 Not an affix; अर्थवदधातुरप्रत्ययः प्रातिपदिकं P. I. 2. 45.

अप्रदक्षिणं *ind.* From the left to the right.

अप्रधान *a.* Subordinate, secondary, inferior; आवां तावदप्रधानौ H. 2.—**नं** (°ता °त्वं) 1 Subordinate or secondary state, inferiority. 2 A secondary or subordinate act. (The word अप्रधान usually occurs in the neuter gender either by itself or as last member of comp.).

अप्रधृष्य *a.* Unconquerable, invincible; यदाश्रौषं भीष्ममत्यंतशूरं हतं पार्थेनाहवेष्वप्रधृष्यं Mb.; M. 5. 17.

अप्रभु *a.* 1 Wanting power, not powerful. 2 Having no power or control over, unable, incompetent; with gen. or loc.

अप्रमत्त *a.* Not careless, careful, attentive, vigilant.

अप्रमद *a.* Devoid of festivities, sad, joyless; Bk. 10. 9.

अप्रमा Incorrect knowledge (opp. प्रमा q. v.).

अप्रमाण *a.* 1 Unlimited, immeasurable. 2 Unauthorized. 3 Not regarded as an authority, not trustworthy; S. 5. 25. —**णं** 1 That which cannot be taken as authority in actions; *i. e.* a rule, direction &c. which cannot be accepted as obligatory. 2 Irrelevancy.

अप्रमाद *a.* Careful, vigilant. —**दः** Care, attention, vigilance.

अप्रमेय *a.* 1 Immeasurable, unbounded, boundless. 2 That which cannot be properly ascertained, understood &c.; inscrutable; अचिंत्यस्याप्रमेयस्य कार्यतत्त्वार्थवित्प्रभुः Ms. 1. 3. —**यं** Brahma.

अप्रयाणिः *f.* Not going or progressing (used only in uttering imprecations); अप्रयाणिस्ते शठ भूयात् Sk. mayest thou not move onward or progress. See अजीवनि.

अप्रयुक्त *a.* 1 Not used or employed, not applied. 2 Wrongly used, as a word. 3 (In Rhet.) Rare, unusual (as a word when used in a particular sense or gender though that sense or gender be sanctioned by lexicographers); *e. g.* तथा मन्ये दैवतोऽस्य पिशाचो राक्षसोऽथवा। K. P. 7 where mas. gender of दैवत, though sanctioned (by Amara), is not used by poets, and is, therefore, अप्रयुक्त.

अप्रवृत्तिः *f.* 1 Not engaging in action or proceeding, not taking place. 2 Inertia, inactivity, absence of incentive or stimulus.

अप्रसंगः 1 Want of attachment. 2 Want of connection. 3 Inopportune time or occasion; अप्रसंगाभिधाने च श्रोतुः श्रद्धा न जायते।

अप्रसिद्ध *a.* 1. Unknown, insignificant, Ku. 3. 19. 2 Unusual, uncommon.

अप्रस्ताविक *a.* (**की** *f.*) Not belonging to the subject-matter, irrelevant (=अप्रास्ताविक q. v.)

अप्रस्तुत *a.* 1 Unsuitable to the time or subject, not to the point, irrelevant. 2 Absurd, nonsensical. 3 Accidental or extraneous.-Comp.-**प्रशंसा** a figure of speech which, by describing the अप्रस्तुत (what is not the subject-matter) conveys a reference to the प्रस्तुत or subject-matter; अप्रस्तुतप्रशंसा सा या सैव प्रस्तुताश्रया K. P. 10. It is of 5 kinds :—कार्ये निमित्ते सामान्ये विशेषे प्रस्तुते सति। तदन्यस्य वचस्तुल्ये तुल्यस्येति च पंचधा॥ *i. e.* when the subject-matter is viewed (*a*) as an effect, information of which is conveyed by stating the cause ; (*b*) when viewed as a cause by stating the effect ; (*c*) when viewed as a general assertion by stating a particular instance ; (*d*) when viewed as a particular instance by stating a general assertion; and (*e*) when viewed as similar by stating what is similar to it, see K. P. 10 ; and S. D. 706 for examples.

अप्रहत *a.* 1 Unhurt. 2 Waste, unploughed. 3 New and unbleached (as cloth).

अप्राकरणिक *a.* (**की** *f.*) 1 Not belonging to the subject-matter ; अप्राकरणिकस्याभिधानेन प्राकरणिकस्याक्षेपोऽप्रस्तुतप्रशंसा K. P. 10.

अप्राकृत *a.* 1 Not vulgar. 2 Not original. 3 Not ordinary, extraordinary. 4 Special.

अप्राग्र्य *a.* Secondary, subordinate ; inferior.

अप्राप्त *a.* 1 Not obtained or got ; अप्राप्तयोस्तु या प्राप्तिः सैव संयोग ईरितः । Bhâshâ P. 2 Not arrived or come. 3 Not authorised or following, as a rule. 4 Not come to or reached.–Comp.–**अवसर**. -**काल** *a.* inopportune, ill-timed, unseasonable; °लं वचनं बृहस्पतिरपि ब्रुवन् । लभते बुद्ध्यवज्ञानमपमानं च पुष्कलं Pt. 1. 63. -**यौवन** *a.* not arrived at puberty. -**व्यवहार, वयस्** *a.* (in law) under age, not old enough to engage in public business on one's own responsibility, a minor (a boy before he reaches his 16th year); अप्राप्तव्यवहारोऽसौ यावत् षोडशवार्षिकः Daksha.

अप्राप्तिः *f.* 1 Non-acquisition ; तदप्राप्तिमहादुःखविलीनाशेषपातका K. P. 4. 2 Not being proved or established by a rule before ; विधिरत्यंतमप्राप्तौ नियमः पाक्षिके सति Mîm. 3 Not taking place or occurring.

अप्रामाणिक *a.* (**की** *f.*) 1 Unauthoritative, unwarranted ; इदं वचनमप्रामाणिकं. 2 Untrustworthy, unreliable.

अप्रिय *a.* 1 Disliked, disagreeable, offensive; अप्रियस्य च पथ्यस्य वक्ता श्रोता च दुर्लभः Râm.; Ms. 4. 138. 2 Unkind, unfriendly.—**यः** A foe, an enemy.—**यं** An unfriendly or offensive act ; पाणिग्राहस्य साध्वी स्त्री नाचरेत्किंचिदप्रियं Ms. 5. 156 -Comp. -**कर, -कारिन्, -कारक** *a.* unfriendly, ill-disposed. -**वद्**, (°**यं**°) -**वादिन्** *a.* speaking unkind or harsh words ; वंध्यार्थघ्न्यप्रियंवदा Y. 1. 73 ; माता यस्य गृहे नास्ति भार्या चाप्रियवादिनी Chân. 44.

अप्रीतिः *f.* 1 Dislike, aversion. 2 Enmity.

अप्रौढ *a.* 1 Not arrogant. 2 Timid, gentle, not bold. 3 Not full-grown. —**ढा** 1 An unmarried girl. 2 A girl very recently married and not arrived at puberty or womanhood.

अप्लुत *a.* Not protracted (as a vowel).

अप्सरस् *f.* (**-राः-रा**) (for etym. cf. Râm. अप्सु निर्मथनादेव रसात्तस्माद्वरस्त्रियः । उत्पेतुर्मनुजश्रेष्ठ तस्मादप्सरसोऽभवन्) A class of female divinities or celestial damsels who reside in the sky and are regarded as the wives of the Gandharvas. They are very fond of bathing, can change their shapes, and are endowed with superhuman power (प्रभाव). They are called स्वर्वेश्याः, and are usually described as the servants of Indra. Bâṇa mentions 14 different families of these nymphs (see K. 136). The word is usually said to be in pl. (स्त्रियां बहुष्वप्सरसः); but the singular, as also the form अप्सरा, sometimes occur; नियमविघ्नकारिणी मेनका नाम अप्सराः प्रेषिता *S.* 1; एकाप्सरः &c. R. 7. 53. -Comp. -**तीर्थं** N. of a sacred pool in which the Apsarasas bathe; probably it is the name of a place; see *S.* 6. -**पतिः** lord of the Apsarasas, epithet of Indra.

अफल *a.* 1 Unfruitful, fruitless, barren (lit. & fig.); °ला ओषधयः; °लं कार्यं &c. 2 Unproductive, useless, vain; यथा षंढोऽफलः स्त्रीषु यथा गौर्गवि चाफला । यथा यज्ञेऽफलं दानं तथा विप्रोऽनृचोऽफलः Ms. 2–18. 3 Deprived of virility, emasculated; अफलोऽहं कृतस्तेन क्रोधात्सा च निराकृता Râm. -Comp. -**आकांक्षिन्, -प्रेप्सु** *a.* one who desires no reward (for his labours), disinterested; अफलाकांक्षिभिर्यज्ञः क्रियते ब्रह्मवादिभिः Mb.

अफेन *a.* Frothless, without scum or foam. -**नं** Opium.

अबद्ध-द्धक *a.* 1 At liberty, not bound or restrained. 2 Unmeaning, nonsensical, absurd, contradictory; *e. g.* यावज्जीवमहं मौनी ब्रह्मचारी च मे पिता । माता तु मम वंध्यासीदपुत्रश्च पितामहः ॥ (contradictory); जरद्गवः कंबलपादुकाभ्यां द्वारि स्थितो गायति मंगलानि । Râyamukuta on Ak. -Comp. -**मुख** *a.* foul-mouthed, abusive, scurrilous.

अबंधु,-बांधव *a.* Friendless, lonely.

अबल *a.* 1 Weak, feeble. 2 Unprotected.—**ला** A woman (as belonging to the weaker sex); नूनं हि ते कविवरा विपरीतबोधा ये नित्यमाहुरबला इति कामिनीनाम् । याभिर्विलोलतरतारकदृष्टिपातैः शक्रादयोपि विजितास्त्वबलाः कथं ताः ॥ Bh. 1. 11; °जनः a woman.—**लं** Weakness, want of strength; see बलाबलं also.

अबाध *a.* 1 Unrestrained, unobstructed. 2 Free from pain. —**धः** 1 Non-obstruction. 2 Non-refutation.

अबाल *a.* 1 Not childish, youthful. 2 Not young, full (as the moon.)

अबाह्य *a.* 1 Not exterior, internal. 2 (fig.) Familiar or conversant with.

अबिंधनः The submarine fire (that feeds on the waters of the ocean); अबिंधनं वह्निमसौ बिभर्ति R. 13. 4.

अबुद्ध *a.* Foolish, unwise; अपवादमात्रमबुद्धानां Sân. S.

अबुद्धिः *f.* 1 Want of understanding. 2 Ignorance, stupidity. -Comp. -**पूर्व-पूर्वक** *a.* not wanton or intentional. (**-र्वं, -र्वकं**) *adv.* unconsciously or ignorantly.

अबुध्-बुध *a.* Foolish, stupid.—*m.* A fool —*f.* (अभुत्) Ignorance, want of intellect.

अबोध *a.* Ignorant, foolish, stupid. —**धः** 1 Ignorance, stupidity, want of understanding: °धोपहताश्चान्ये Bh. 3. 2; निसर्गदुर्बोधमबोधविक्लवाः क्व भूपतीनां चरितं क्व जंतवः Ki. 1. 6. 2 Not knowing or being aware of. -Comp. -**गम्य** *a.* incomprehensible, inconceivable.

अब्ज *a.* Born in or produced from water. -**ब्जं** 1 A lotus. 2 One thousand millions -Comp. -**कर्णिका** the seedvessel of a lotus. -**जः,-भवः, -भूः,-योनिः** epithets of Brahmâ.-**बांधवः** 'a friend of lotuses,' the sun. -**वाहनः** epithet of *S*iva.

अब्जा A pearl-oyster.

अब्जिनी 1 A collection of lotuses. 2 A place full of lotuses. 3 A lotus plant. -Comp. -**पतिः** the sun.

अब्दः 1 A cloud. 2 A year (in this sense *n.* also). 3 N. of a mountain. -Comp.-**अर्धं** half a year.-**वाहनः** N. of *S*iva.-**शतं** a century.-**सारः** a kind of camphor.

अब्धिः 1 The ocean, receptacle of water; (fig. also), दुःख, कार्य, ज्ञान &c.; store or reservoir of anything. 2 A pond, lake. 3 (In Math.) A symbolical expression for the number 7; sometimes for 4. -Comp.-**अग्निः** the submarine fire. -**कफः,-फेनः** froth, foam. -**जः** 1 the moon. -2 conch. (-**जा**) 1 spirituous liquor (produced from the ocean). -2 the Goddess Lakshmî. -**द्वीपा** the earth. -**नगरी** N. of Dwârakâ, the capital of Krishṇa. -**नवनीतकः** the moon. -**मंडूकी** the pearl-oyster. -**शयनः** N. of Vishṇu. -**सारः** a gem.

अब्रह्मचर्य *a.* Unchaste. —**र्यं-र्यकं** 1 Unchastity. 2 Sexual union.

अब्रह्मण्य *a.* 1 Not fit for a Brâhmaṇa; अब्रह्मण्यमवर्णं स्यात् ब्रह्मण्यं ब्रह्मणो हितम् Halây. 2 Inimical to Brâhmaṇas.—**ण्यं** An act not befitting a Brâhmaṇa ; an unbrahmanical act. In dramas usually found as an exclamation uttered by a Brâhmaṇa in the sense of 'to the rescue', 'help', 'help', 'a horrible or disgraceful deed has been committed' ; अथैत्य योगनंदस्य व्याडिना क्रंदितं पुरः । अब्रह्मण्यमनुत्क्रांतजीवो योगस्थितो द्विजः Bri. Kath.

अब्रह्मन् *a.* Separated from or devoid of Brâhmaṇas ; नाब्रह्म क्षत्रमृध्नोति Ms. 9. 322.

अभक्तिः *f.* 1 Want of devotion or attachment. 2 Unbelief, incredulity.

अभक्ष्य *a.* 1 Not to be eaten. 2 Prohibited from eating. —क्ष्यं A prohibited article of food.

अभग *a.* Unfortunate, ill-fated.

अभद्र *a.* Inauspicious, bad, wicked. —द्रं 1 Evil, sin, wickedness. 2 Sorrow.

अभय *a.* Free from fear, secure, safe; वैराग्यमेवाभयं Bh. 3. 35. —यं 1 Absence or removal of fear. 2 Security safety, protection from fear or danger ; मया तस्याभयं दत्तं Pt. 1. –Comp.–**कृत्** *a.* 1 not terrific, mild. –2 giving safety. **-डिंडिमः** 1 proclamation of assurance or safety. –2 a military or war-drum. **-द, -दायिन्, -प्रद** *a.* giving a guaranttee or promise of safety.–**दक्षिणा, -दानं,-प्रदानं** giving a promise, assurance, or guarantee of safety or protection (from danger); सर्वप्रदानेष्व-भयप्रदानं (प्रधानं) Pt. 1. 290. **-पत्रं** a written document or paper granting assurance of safety ; cf. the modern 'safe-conduct '. **-याचना** asking for protection. **-वचनं, -वाच्** *f.* an assurance or promise of safety.

अभयंकर-कृत् *a.* 1 Not dreadful. 2 Causing security.

अभवः 1 Non-existence; मत्त एव भवा-भवौ Mb. 2 Absolution, final beatitude ; प्राप्तमभवमभिवांछति वा Ki. 12. 30, 18. 27. 3 End or destruction ; भवाय सर्वभूतानामभवाय च रक्षसां Râm.

अभव्य *a.* 1 Not to be. 2 Improper, inauspicious. 3 Unfortunate, luckless; उपनतमवधीरयंत्यभव्याः Ki. 10. 51.

अभाग *a.* 1 Without a share (of inheritance). 2 Undivided.

अभावः 1 Not being or existing, non-existence ; गतो भावोऽभावं Mk. 1 has disappeared. 2 Absence, want, failure ; सर्वेषामप्यभावे तु ब्राह्मणा रिक्थभागिनः Ms. 9. 188 ; mostly in comp.; सर्वाभावे हरेन्नृपः 189 failing all. 3 Annihilation death, destruction, non-entity ; नाभाव उपलब्धेः S. B. 4 (In phil.) Privation, non-existence, nullity or negation, supposed to be the seventh category or पदार्थ in the system of Kaṇâda. It is of two principal kinds संसर्गाभाव and अन्योन्याभाव ; the first comprising three varieties प्रागभाव, प्रध्वंसाभाव and अत्यंताभाव.

अभावना 1 Absence of judjment or right discernment.. 2 Absence of religious meditation.

अभाषित *a.* Not told. –Comp. **-पुंस्कः** a word which cannot become mas. or neuter, *i. e.* always feminine.

अभि *ind.* 1 (as a prefix to verbs and nouns) It means (*a*) 'to,' 'towards', 'in the direction of'; अभिगम् go towards, अभिया, °गमनं, °यानं &c. (*b*) 'for', 'against', °लष् °पत् &c.; (*c*) 'on','upon,' °सिंच् to sprinkle on &c.; (*d*) 'over', 'above' 'across'; °भू to overpower, °तन्; (*e*) 'greatly,' 'excessively', °कंप्. 2 (As a prefix to nouns not derived from verbs,and to adjectives). It expresses (*a*) intensity or superiority ; °धर्मः 'supreme duty'; °ताम्र 'very red'; °नव 'very new'; (*b*) 'towards', 'in the direction of,' forming adv. compounds ; °चैद्यं, °मुखं, °दूति &c. 3 (As a preposition with acc.) (*a*) To, towards, in the direction of, against; (with acc. or in comp. in this sense; अभ्यग्नि or अग्निमभि शलभाः पतंति; वृक्षमभि द्योतते विद्युत् Sk. (*b*) Near, before, in front or presence of (*c*) On, upon, with regard or reference to ; साधुर्देवदत्तो मातरमभि Sk. (*d*) Severally, one after another (in a distributive sense) ; वृक्षं वृक्षमभिसिंचति Sk.

अभि (भी) क *a.* Lustful, libidinous, voluptuous; सोधिकारमभिकः कुलोचितं काश्चन स्वयमवर्तयत्समाः R. 19. 4; अपि सिंचेः कृशानौ त्वं दर्पं मय्यपि योऽभिकः Bk. 8. 92.

अभिकांक्षा Wish, desire, longing.

अभिकांक्षिन् *a.* Longing, wishing.

अभिकाम *a.* Affectionate, loving, desirous, wishing for, lustful, with the object of love in acc. or in comp.; याचे त्वामभिकामाहं Mb. —मः 1 Affection, love. 2 Wish, desire.

अभिक्रमः 1 Beginning, attempting, an undertaking; नेहाभिक्रमनाशोऽस्ति प्रत्यवायो न विद्यते Bg.2.4. 2 A determined attack or onset, assault, onslaught. 3 Ascending, mounting.

अभिक्रमणं, -क्रांतिः *f.* Approaching, attacking &c. =अभिक्रम above.

अभिक्रोशः 1 Calling out, crying. 2 Reviling, censure.

अभिक्रोशकः One who calls out; a reviler, calumniator.

अभिख्या 1 Splendour, beauty, lustre ; काप्यभिख्या तयोरासीद् व्रजतोः शुद्धवेषयोः R. 1. 46. सूर्यापाये न खलु कमलं पुष्यति स्वामभिख्यां Me. 80; Ku. 1. 43; 7. 18. 2 Telling, declaring. 3 Calling, addressing. 4 A name, appellation. 5 A word, synonym. 6 Fame, glory; notoriety (in a bad sense) greatness (माहात्म्यं).

अभिख्यानं Fame, glory.

अभिगमः, -गमनं 1 (*a*) Approaching, going or coming to, visit, arrival; तवार्हतो नाभिगमेन तृप्तं R. 5. 11, 17. 72; ज्येष्ठाभिगमनात्पूर्वं तेनाप्यनभिनंदिता 12. 35. 2 Sexual intercourse (with a man or woman); परदाराभिगमनं K. 147; प्रसह्य दास्यभिगमे Y. 2. 291.

अभिगम्य *pot. p.* 1 To be approached, visited or sought ; Ku. 6. 56. 2 Accessible, inviting ; भीमकांतैर्नृपगुणैः... अधृष्यश्चाभिगम्यश्च R. 1. 16.

अभिगर्जनं, अभिगर्जितं A wild, or ferocious roar; up-roar.

अभिगामिन् *a.* Approaching, having intercourse with.

अभिगुप्तिः *f.* Guarding, protecting.

अभिगोप्तृ *m.* Protector, guardian.

अभिग्रहः 1 Seizing, robbing, plundering. 2 Attack, assault. 3 Challenge. 4 Complaint. 5 Authority ; weight.

अभिग्रहणं Robbing, siezing.

अभिघर्षणं 1 Rubbing, friction. 2 Possession by an evil spirit.

अभिघातः 1 Striking, beating, smiting ; attack ; तटाभिघातादिव लग्नपंके Ku. 7. 49. 2 Extirpation, complete destruction or removal ; दुःखत्रयाभिघाताज्जिज्ञासा तदभिघातके हेतौ Sân. K. 1. —तं A harsh pronunciation caused by the neglect of *Sandhi* rules.

अभिघातक *a.* (**तिका** *f.*) Repelling, warding off.

अभिघातिन *m.* An enemy.

अभिघारः 1 Ghee or clarified butter. 2 Dropping down ghee upon offerings at sacrifices ; प्रणीतपृषदाज्याभिघारघोरस्तनूनपात् Mv. 3.

अभिघारणं Act of sprinkling (with ghee).

अभिचरः A follower, servant.

अभिचरणं Enchanting, exorcising, employment of spells for malevolent purposes (such as श्येनयाग).

अभिचारः 1 Exorcising, enchanting, employment of magical spells for malevolent purposes, magic itself. 2 Killing. –Comp. **-ज्वरः** a fever caused by magical spells. **-मंत्रः** a magical formula, an incantation or formula for working a charm; Si. 7. 58. **-यज्ञः, -होमः** a sacrifice made for magical purposes.

अभिचारक,-चारिन् (°रिकी, रिणी *f.*) *a.* Conjuring, enchanting, —कः, -रि A conjurer, magician.

अभिजनः 1 (*a*) A family, race ; lineage. (*b*) Birth, extraction, descent. 2 High or noble descent, noble birth or family ; स्तुतं तन्माहात्म्यं यदभिजनतो यच्च गुणतः Mâl. 2. 13 ; शीलं शैलतटात्पतत्वभिजनः संदह्यतां वह्निना Bh. 2. 39. 3 Native country, mother land, ancestral abode (opp. निवास) ; यत्र पूर्वैरुषितं सोऽभिजनः Sk. 4 Fame, celebrity. 5 The head or ornament of family. 6 Attendants, retinue (=परिजन q. v.)

अभिजनवत् *a.* Of noble descent, nobly born ; °वतो भर्तुः श्लाघ्ये स्थिता गृहिणीपदे S. 4. 18.

अभिजयः Conquest ; complete victory.

अभिजात *p. p.* 1 (*a*) Born to or for; Bg. 16. 3, 5. (*b*) Produced all around. (*c*) Born in consequence of. 2 Born, produced. 3 Noble, nobly or well born, of noble descent; जात्यस्तेनाभिजातेन शूरः शौर्यवता कुशः R. 17. 4 ; courteous, polite ; अभिजातं खल्वस्य वचनं V. 1. 4 Fit, proper, worthy. 5 Sweet, agreeable; प्रजल्पितायामभिजातवाचि Ku. 1. 45. 6. Handsome, beautiful. 7 Learned, wise ; distinguished ; संकीर्णे नाभिजातेषु नाप्रबुद्धेषु संस्कृतं (वदेत्).

अभिजातिः *f.* Noble birth.

अभिजिघ्रणं Touching the head with the nose (as a sign of affection &c.)

अभिजित् *m.* **1** N. of Vishṇu. **2** N. of one of the lunar mansions.

अभिज्ञ *a.* **1** Knowing, aware of, one who understands or is acquainted with experiencing or having had experienc of (with gen. or loc. or in comp.); यद्वा कौशलमिद्रसूनुदमने तत्राप्यभिज्ञो जनः U. 5. 35; अभिज्ञाश्छेदपातानां क्रियंते नंदनद्रुमाः Ku. 2. 41, Me. 16; R. 7. 64; अनभिज्ञे भवान्सेवाधर्मस्य 1. **2**. Skilled in, skilful, clever. **—ज्ञा 1** Recognition. **2** Remembrance, recognition.

अभिज्ञानं 1 Recognition; तदभिज्ञानहेतोर्हि दत्तं तेन महात्मना Râm. **2** Remembrance, recollection. **3** (*a*) A sign or token of recognition (person or thing); वत्स योगिन्यस्मि मालत्यभिज्ञानं च धारयामि Mâl. 9; Bk. 8. 118, 124; so °शकुंतलं. **4** The dark portion in the disc of the moon. -Comp.—**आभरणं** a recognition-ornament, a token-ring *S.* 4.

अभितस् *ind.* (Used as an adverb or preposition with acc.) **1** Near to, to, towards; अभितस्तं पृथासूनुः स्नेहेन परितस्तरे Ki. 11. 8. **2** (*a*) Near, hard by, in the proximity of; ततो राजाब्रवीद्वाक्यं सुमंत्रमभितः स्थितं Râm. (*b*) Before, in the presence of; तन्वंतमिद्धमभितो गुरुमंशुजालं Ki. 2. 59. **3** Opposite to, facing, in front of; Ki. 6. 1, 5. 14. **4** On both sides ; चूडाचुंबितकंकपत्रमभितस्तूणीद्वयं पृष्ठतः U. 4. 20; Bk. 9. 137. **5** Before and after. **6** On all sides, round, round about (with acc. or gen.); परिजनो यथाव्यापारं राजानमभितः स्थितः M. 1. **7** Entirely, completely, throughout. **8** Quickly.

अभितापः Extreme heat, whether of body or mind; agitation, affliction, great distress or pain; *S*i. 9. 1; Ki. 9. 4; बलवान्पुनर्मे मनसोऽभितापः V. 3.

अभिताम्र *a.* Very red, dark-red; R. 15. 49.

अभिदक्षिणं *ind.* To or towards the right (=प्रदक्षिणं q. v.).

अभिद्रवः,-वणं An attack.

अभिद्रोहः 1 Injuring, plotting against, harm, cruelty. **2** Abuse; censure.

अभिधर्षणं 1 Possession by evil spirits, demons &c. **2** Oppressing.

अभिधा 1 A name, an appellation; oft. in comp.; कुसुमवसंताद्यभिधः S. D. **2** A word, sound. **3** The literal power or sense of a word, *denotation*. one of the three powers of a word; वाच्योर्थोऽभिधया बोध्यः S. D. 2 (अभिधा conveys to the understanding the meaning which belongs to the word by common consent or convention (संकेत) (which primarily made it a word at all); स मुख्योऽर्थस्तत्रमुख्यो यो व्यापारोऽस्याभिधोच्यते K. P. 2. -Comp. **-ध्वंसिन्** *a.* losing one's name. **-मूल** *a.* founded on a word's denotation or literal meaning.

अभिधानं 1 Telling, speaking, naming, denotation; एतावतामर्थानामिदमभिधानं Nir. **2** Predication, assertion; See P. II. 3. 2. Sk. **3** A name, appellation, designation; अभिधानं तु पश्चात्तस्याहमश्रौषं K. 32; तवाभिधानाद्व्यथते नताननः Ki. 1. 24; (at the end of comp.) called, named; ऋणाभिधानाद् बंधनात् R. 3. 20. **4** Speech, discourse. **5** A dictionary, vocabulary (of words), lexicon (in these last 2 senses said to be also *m.*). -Comp.-**कोशः,-माला** a dictionary.

अभिधायक (यिका *f.*), अभिधायिन् *a.* **1** Naming, expressing, denoting; कर्पूरः कुल्याभिधायिनी Ak. denotes, means, has the sense of. **2** Saying, speaking, telling; लक्ष्मीमित्याभिधायिनि प्रियतमे Amaru. 23; वाच्याभिधायी पुरुषः पृष्ठमांसाद उच्यते Trik.

अभिधावनं Assault, pursuit.

अभिधेय *pot. p.* **1** To be named, mentioned, expressed &c. **2** Nameable, (in logic); अभिधेयाः पदार्थाः. **—यं 1** Signification, meaning, sense, import; Ki. 14. 5. **2** A substance. **3** The subject-matter ; इहाभिधेयं सप्रयोजनं K. P. 1 ; इति प्रयोजनाभिधेयसंबंधाः Mugdha. **4** The primary or literal sense of a word (=अभिधा); अभिधेयाविनाभूतप्रतीतिर्लक्षणोच्यते K. P. 2.

अभिध्या 1 Coveting another's property. **2** Longing, wish ; desire in general ; अभिध्योपदेशात् Br. Sût. **3** Desire of taking (in general).

अभिध्यानं 1 Desiring or longing for, coveting ; a wish or desire. **2** Meditation, profound thought.

अभिनंदः 1 Rejoicing, joy, delight. **2** Praising, applauding, congratulating. **3** Wish, desire. **4** Encouraging, inciting to action.

अभिनंदनं 1 Rejoicing at, greeting, welcoming. **2** Praising, approving. **3** Wish, desire.

अभिनंदनीय-नंद्य *pot. p.* To be rejoiced at, praised, or applauded ; काममंतदभिनंदनीयं *S.* **5**; R. 5. 31.

अभिनम्र *a.* Bent, deeply bowed or bent ; स्तनाभिरामस्तबकाभिनम्रां R. 13. 32.

अभिनयः 1 Acting, gesticulation, any theatrical action (expressive of some sentiment, passion &c. by look, gesture, posture &c.); नृत्याभिनयक्रियाच्युतं Ku. 5. 79 ; अभिनयान् परिचेतुमिवोद्यता R. 9. 33 ; नर्तकीरभिनयातिलंघिनीः 19. 14. **2** Dramatic representation, exhibition on the stage ; ललिताभिनयं तमद्य भर्ता मरुतां द्रष्टुमनाः सलोकपालः V. 2. 18. S. D. thus defines and classifies अभिनयः-भवेदभिनयोऽवस्थानुकारः स चतुर्विधः। आंगिको वाचिकश्चैवमाहार्यः सात्विकस्तथा ॥ 274, 'acting is the imitation of condition'; it is of four kinds:- (1) *gestural*, conveyed by bodily actions; (2) *vocal*, conveyed by works; (3) *extraneous*, conveyed by dress, ornaments, decoration &c.; (4) *internal*, conveyed by the manifestation of the internal feelings such as perspiration, thrilling &c.

अभिनव *a.* **1** Quite new or fresh (in all senses); पदपंक्तिर्दृश्यतेऽभिनवा *S.* **3. 8** ; 5. 1; °वा वधूः K. 2. newly married. **2** Very young, not having experience. -Comp. **-यौवन, -वयस्क** youthful, very young.

अभिनहनं A bandage (over the eyes), a blind.

अभिनियुक्त *a.* Occupied in, busy.

अभिनिर्मुक्त *a.* **1** Left or quitted (by the sun when it sets). **2** One asleep at sunset.

अभिनिर्याणं 1 A march. **2** Invasion, marching against an enemy.

अभिनिविष्ट *p. p.* **1** Intent on, engrossed in, applying oneself to. **2** Firmly or steadily fixed, attentive, intent. **3** Endowed with, possessed of ; गुरुभिरभिनिविष्टं (गर्भं) लोकपालानुभावैः R. 2. 75. **4** Determined, resolute. **5** (In a bad sense) Obstinate, perverse.

अभिनिविष्टता Resoluteness, determination of purpose ; निंदाक्षेपापमाणादेरमर्षोऽभिनिविष्टता S. D. *i. e* adhering to one's purpose, not minding censure, abuse, dishonoured &c.

अभिनिवृत्तिः *f.* Accomplishment, completion.

अभिनिवेशः 1 Devotion, attachment, intentness, close application, with loc. or in comp. ; कतमस्मिंस्ते भावाभिनिवेशः V. 3.; अहो निरर्थकव्यापारेष्वभिनिवेशः K. 120; बलीयान्खलु मेऽभिनिवेशः *S.* **3**; असत्यभूते वस्तुन्यभिनिवेशः Mit. **2** Earnest desire, ardent longing or expectation. **3** Resolution, determination of purpose, perseverence: जनकात्मजायां नितांतरूक्षाभिनिवेशमीशं R. 14. 43; अनुरूप° शतोषिणा Ku. 5. 7. **4** (In Yoga phil.) A sort of ignorance causing fear of death; instinctive clinging to worldly life and bodily enjoyments and the fear that one might be cut off from all of them by death.

अभिनिवेशिन् *a.* **1** Devoted to, adhering or clinging to. **2** Fixing on, directing or turning (the mind) to. **3** Determined, resolute.

अभिनिष्क्रमणं Going out or forth.

अभिनिष्टानः A letter of the alphabet.

अभिनिष्पतनं Sallying, issuing.

अभिनिष्पत्तिः *f.* Completion, end, accomplishment, fulfilment.

अभिनिह्नवः Denial, concealment.

अभिनीत *p. p.* **1** Brought near, conveyed. **2** Performed, represented dramatically. **3** Highly finished or polished, most excellent. **4** Highly ornamented or decorated. **5** Fit, proper, suitable (योग्य); **अभिनीततर**

वाक्यमित्युवाच युधिष्ठिरः Mb. 6 Patient, forgiving, even-minded. 7 Angry. 8 Kind, friendly,

अभिनीतिः *f.* 1 Gesture, expressive gesticulation. 2 Kindness, friendship, patience; सांत्वपूर्वमभिनीतिहेतुकं Ki. 13. 36.

अभिनेतृ *m.* An actor.—त्री An actress.

अभिनेय,-नेतव्य *pot. p.* To be acted or dramatically represented &c.; इयं तत्राभिनेयं तद्रूपारोपात्तु रूपकं S. D. 273. तस्य (प्रबंधस्य) एकदेशः अभिनेयार्थः कृतः U. 4. a part of it has been adapted to the stage.

अभिन्न *a.* 1 Not broken or cut. 2. Unaffected. 3 Not changed or altered. 4 Not different from, the same, identical (with abl.); जयन्निर्थाभिन्नमभिन्नमीश्वरात् Prab.

अभिपतनं 1 Approaching. 2 Falling upon, assault, attack. 3 Going forth, departure.

अभिपत्तिः *f.* 1 Approaching, drawing near. 2 Completion.

अभिपन्न *p. p.* 1 Gone or come near, approached, run towards, gone to (a state &c.) 2 Fled, fugitive, seeking refuge with. 3 Subdued, overpowered, afflicted, seized &c. कालाभिपन्नाः सीदंति सिकतासेतवो यथा Râm.; दोष°, कश्मल°, व्याघ्र° &c. 4 Unfortunate, fallen into difficulties &c. 5 Accepted. 6 Guilty.

अभिपरिप्लुत *a.* Overflowed, filled with, inundated; shaken; शोकेन, मन्युना &c.

अभिपूरण Filling, overpowering.

अभिपूर्वं *ind.* Successively.

अभिप्रणयनं Consecrating by sacred hymns.

अभिप्रणयः Affection, favour, propitiation.

अभिप्रणीत *p. p.* 1 Consecrated: जज्वाल लोकस्थितये स राजा यथाध्वरे वह्निरभिप्रणीतः Bk. 1. 4. 2 Brought.

अभिप्रथनं Spreading or extending over, throwing over.

अभिप्रदक्षिणं *ind.* Towards the right.

अभिप्रवर्तनं 1 Advancing up to. 2 Proceeding, acting. 3 Flowing, coming forth, as of sweat.

अभिप्रातिः=प्राति. q. v.

अभिप्रायः 1 Aim, purpose, object, intention, wish, desire; अभिप्राया न सिध्यंति तेनेदं वर्तते जगत् Pt. 1. 158; साभिप्रायाणि वचांसि Pt. 2 earnest words; भावः कंवरभिप्रायः 2 meaning, sense, import, implied sense, of a word, passage &c.; तेषामयमभिप्रायः such is the meaning intended, import (of the passage &c.) 3 Opinion, belief. 4 Relation, reference.

अभिप्रेत *p. p.* 1 Meant, aimed at, intended; designed; अत्रायमर्थोऽभिप्रेतः; निवेदयाभिप्रेतं Pt. 1. 2 Wished, desired; यथाभिप्रेतमनुष्ठीयतां H. 1. 3 Approved, accepted. 4 Dear or agreeable to.

अभिप्रोक्षणं Sprinkling upon.

अभिप्लवः 1 Affliction, disturbance. 2 Inundation, overflowing.

अभिप्लुत *p. p.* Overpowered, overwhelmed (lit. and fig.).

अभिबुद्धिः *f.* An organ of apprehension a बुद्धींद्रिय or ज्ञानेंद्रिय (opp. कर्मेंद्रिय); these are the eye, tongue, ear, nose and skin.

अभिभवः 1 Defeat, subjugation, subjection; स्पर्शानुकूला इव सूर्यकांतास्तदन्यतेजोभिभवाद्वमंति *S.* 2. 7 when assailed, opposed, overpowered by another energy; अभिभवः कुत एव सपत्नजः R. 9. 4. 2 Being overpowered; जराभिभवविच्छायं K. 346; being attacked or affected, stupefied (by fever &c.) 3 Contempt, disrespect; निराभिभवसाराः परकथाः Bh. 2. 64. 4 Humiliation, mortification (of pride); अलभ्यशोकाभिभवेयमाकृतिः Ku. 5. 43. 5 Predominance, rise, spread; अधर्माभिभवात्कृष्ण प्रदुष्यंति कुलस्त्रियः Bg. 1. 41; Ki. 2. 37.

अभिभवनं Overpowering, overcoming, being overpowered by &c.

अभिभावनं Making victorious, overpowering.

अभिभविन्, -भाव (वु) क *a.* 1 Overpowering, defeating, conquering. 2 Surpassing, excelling; सर्वतेजोभिभाविना R. 1. 14; Ki. 11. 6.

अभिभाषणं Addressing; speaking to.

अभिभूतिः *f.* 1 Predominance, prevalence. 2 Conquering, defeat, subjugation; अभिभूतिभयादसूनतः सुखमुज्झंति न धाम मानिनः Ki. 2. 20. 3 Disrespect, humiliation.

अभिमत *p. p.* 1 Desired, wished, deer, beloved; agreeable, desirable; नास्ति जीवितादन्यदभिमततरमिह जगति सर्वजंतूनां K. 35, 58; अभिमतफलशंसी चारु पुस्फोर बाहुः Bk. 1. 27. 2 Approved, accepted, admitted; न किल भवतां स्थानं देव्या गृहेऽभिमतं ततः U. 3. 32; प्रसिद्धमाहात्म्याभिमतानामपि कपिलकणभुक्प्रभृतीनां S. B. honoured, respected. —तं Wish, desire. —तः A beloved person, lover.

अभिमनस् *a.* Intent on, desirous of, anxious, longing for; भवतोभिमनाः समीहते सरुषः कर्तुमुपेत्य माननां *Si.* 16. 2 (where अ° also means undaunted).

अभिमंत्रणं 1 Consecrating, making sacred by repetition of special formulas or Mantras; Y. 1. 237. 2 Charming, enchanting. 3 Addressing, inviting; advising.

अभिमरः 1 Killing, destruction, slaughter. 2 War, combat. 3 Treachery in one's own camp, danger from one's own men or party. 4 Binding, confinement; a tie or fetter.

अभिमर्दः 1 Rubbing, friction. 2 Crushing down, ravage, devastation of a country (by an enemy). 3 War, battle. 4 Spirituous liquor.

अभिमर्दन *a.* Crushing down, oppressing. —नं Crushing, oppression.

अभिमर्शः,-र्शनं, -मर्षः, -र्षणं 1 Touch, contact. 2 Assault, violence, outrage; sexual intercourse; कृताभिमर्शामनुमन्यमानः *S.* 5. 20 carnally touched or embraced, seduced, outraged; पराभिमर्शो न तवास्ति Ku. 5. 43 (Malli.=परधर्षणं); Ms. 8. 352, Y. 2. 284.

अभिमर्शक -र्षक, -मर्शिन् -र्षिन् *a.* 1 Touching, coming in contact with. 2 Outraging; त्वत्कलत्राभिमर्षी वैरास्पदं धनमित्रः Dk. 63.

अभिमादः Intoxication.

अभिमानः 1 Pride (in a good sense) self-respect, honourable or worthy feeling; सदाभिमानैकधना हि मानिनः Si. 1. 67. 2. Self-conceit, pride, arrogance, high opinion of oneself; °वत् proud, conceited. 3 Referring all objects to self, the act of अहंकार, personality. 4 Conceit, conception; supposition, belief, opinion. 5 Affection, love. 6 Desire, wishing for. 7 Injury, killing, seeking to injure. –COMP. –शालिन् *a.* proud. –शून्य *a.* void of pride or arrogance, humble.

अभिमानिन् *a.* 1 Possessed of self-respect. 2 Having a high opinion of oneself, proud, arrogant, conceited. 3 Regarding all objects as referring to one's own self.

अभिमुख *a.* (खी *f.*) 1 With the face turned or directed towards, towards, turned towards, facing; अभिमुखे मयि संहृतमीक्षितं *S.* 2. 11. 2 Coming or going near, approaching near. V. 2. 9. 3 Disposed or intending to, inclined to; ready for, about (to do something), in comp.; अस्ताभिमुखे सूर्ये Mu. 4. 19; प्रसादाभिमुखो वेधाः प्रत्युवाच दिवौकसः Ku. 2. 16; 5. 60; U. 7. 4, Mâl. 10. 13. 4 Favourable, friendly or favourably disposed. 5 With the face turned upwards. —खं, खे *ind.* Towards, in the direction of, facing, in front or presence of, facing, in front or presence of, near to; with acc., gen. or in comp., or by itself; आसीताभिमुखं गुरोः Ms. 2. 193; तिष्ठन्मुनेरभिमुखं स विकीर्णधाम्नः Ki. 2. 59; नेपथ्याभिमुखमवलोक्य *S.* 1; कर्णं ददात्यभिमुखं मयि भाषमाणे *S.* 1. 31.

अभियाचनं, -याच्ञा Asking for, request, an entreaty, solicitation.

अभियातृ, -यातिन्- *a.* Approaching, assailing.

अभियातिः, -यायिन्-तृ *m.* (-यी, -ता) Approaching with hostile intentions, enemy, a foe; R. 12. 43.

अभियानं 1 Approaching. 2 Marching against, attack, assault; रणाभियानेन Dk. 10 marching out for battle.

अभियुक्त *p. p.* 1 (*a*) Engaged or occupied or absorbed in, intent on. (*b*) Diligent, persevering, resolute, intent, attentive, careful; इदं विश्वं पाल्यं निधिवदभियुक्तेन मनसा U. 3. 30. 2 Well-versed or proficient in; शास्त्रार्थेष्वभियुक्तानां पुरुषाणां Kumârila. 3 (Hence) Learned, of acknowledged position; a competent judge, a learned person (*m.* also in this sense); न हि शक्यते दैवमन्यथा कर्तुमभियुक्तेनापि K. 62. 4 Attacked, assailed; अभियुक्तं त्वयैनं ते गंतारस्त्वामतः परे *Si.* 2. 101; Mu. 3. 25. 5 Accused, charged, indicted Mk. 9. 9; prosecuted; a defendant; अभियुक्तोऽभियोगस्य यदि कुर्यात्पह्नवं Nârada. 6 Appointed.

अभियोक्तृ *a.* Assailing, attacking, accusing –*m.* (क्ता) 1 An enemy, assailant, invader. 2 (In law) A complainant, plaintiff, accuser, prosecutor; Ms. 8. 52, 58; Y. 2. 95. 3 A pretender.

अभियोगः 1 Application or devotion; connection; गुरुचर्यातपस्तंत्रमंत्रयोगाभियोगजां Mâl. 9. 51; Ch. P. 11. 2 Close application, perseverance, energetic effort, exertion; संतः स्वयं परहितेषु कृताभियोगाः Bh. 2. 73. 3 (*a*) Application or devotion to learn something; कस्यां कलायामभियोगो भवत्योः M. 5. (*b*) Learning, scholarship; अनभियोगश्च शब्दादेरशिष्टानां अभियोगश्चेतरेषां S'abarasvâmin. 4 (*a*) Attack, assault; invasion (of a town or country); क्षुभितं वनगोचराभियोगात् Ki. 13. 10, 2. 46. 5 (In law) A charge, accusation, plaint; अभियोगमनिस्तीर्य नैनं प्रत्यभियोजयेत् Y. 2. 9.

अभियोगिन् *a.* 1 Devoted to, intent on. 2 Attacking, assaulting. 3 Accusing. —*m.* A plaintiff, complainant.

अभिरक्षा, -रक्षणं Universal or complete protection; protection in every quarter; प्रशांतबाधं दिशतोऽभिरक्षया Ki. 1. 18.

अभिरतिः *f.* Pleasure, delight, satisfaction; attachment or devotion to; न मृगयाभिरतिर्न दुरोदरं (तमपाहरत्) R. 9. 7; Ki. 6. 44.

अभिराम *a.* 1 Pleasing, delightful, sweet, agreeable; मनोभिरामाः (केकाः) R. 1. 39; 2. 72. 2 Beautiful, lovely, graceful, charming; स्यादस्थानोपगतयमुनासंगमेवाभिरामा Me. 51. राम इत्यभिरामेण वपुषा तस्य चोदितः R. 10. 67. -मं *ind.* Gracefully; ग्रीवाभंगाभिरामं *S.* 1. 7.

अभिरुचिः *f.* 1 Desire, taste, liking, relish, delight, pleasure; यशसि चाभिरुचिः Bh. 2. 63; परस्पराभिरुचिनिष्पन्नो विवाहः K. 367. 2 Desire of fame, Ambition.

अभिरुचितः A lover; *Si.* 10. 68.

अभिरुतं A sound, cry, noise.

अभिरूप *a.* 1 Corresponding with, conformable or suitable to; अभिरूपमस्या वयसो वल्कलं *S.* 1. v. l. 2 Pleasing, delightful; उत्कृष्टायाभिरूपाय वराय सदृशाय च (कन्यां दद्यात्) Ms. 9. 88. 3 Dear to, beloved or liked by, favourite. 4 Learned, wise, enlightened; अभिरूपभूयिष्ठा परिषदियं *S.* 1. —पः 1 The moon. 2 Siva. 3 Vishṇu. 4 Cupid, –COMP. –पतिः 'having an agreeable husband,' N. of a fast or rite performed to secure a good husband in the next world; Mk. 1.

अभिलंघनं Jumping across or over, flying at.

अभिलषणं Desiring, longing.

अभिलषित *p. p.* Desired, wished, longed for. —तं Desire, wish, will.

अभिलापः 1 Expression, word, speech. 2 Declaration, mention, specification. 3 Declaration of the object of a vow or religious obligation.

अभिलावः Cutting, reaping, mowing.

अभिलाषः (°सः sometimes) A desire, wish, longing for, affection, longing of a lover, love, (usually with loc. of the object of desire); अतोऽभिलाषे प्रथमं तथाविधे मनो बबंध R. 3. 4; न खलु सत्यमेव शकुंतलायां ममाभिलाषः *S.* 2, Pt. 5. 67.

अभिलाषक, -लाषि (सि) न्, -लाषुक *a.* Wishing or desiring for (with acc., loc. or in comp.); desirous, covetous, greedy of; यदार्यमस्यामभिलाषि मे मनः *S.* 1. 22. जयमत्रभवान्नूनमरातिष्वभिलाषकः Ki. 11. 18; *Si.* 15. 59.

अभिलिखित *a.* Written, inscribed. —तं, **अभिलेखनं** 1 Writing, inscribing. 2 A writing.

अभिलीन *a.* 1 Adhering or clinging to, attached to; R. 3. 8. 2 Embracing, shrouding; Me. 36.

अभिलुलित *a.* 1 Agitated, disturbed. 2 Playful, unsteady.

अभिलूता A sort of spider.

अभिवदनं 1 Addressing. 2 Salutation.

अभिवंदनं Respectful salutation; पाद° holding the feet (of another) as an humble obeisance; see अभिवादनं below.

अभिवर्षणं Raining upon, rain; watering.

अभिवादः, -वादनं Reverential salutation, salutation of a superior or elder by an inferior or junior, or of a teacher by his disciple. It consists in (1) rising from one's seat (प्रत्युत्थान), (2) seizing the feet (पादोपसंग्रह), and (3) repeating the form of salutation (अभिवाद) which includes the name or title of the person addressed, followed by the mention of the person's own name.

अभिवादक *a.* (दिका *f.*) 1 Saluting. 2 Polite, respectful, humble.

अभिविधिः 1 Complete comprehension or inclusion; one of the senses of the particle आ; आङ् मर्यादाभिविध्योः P. II. 1. 13, the limit *inceptive* as opposed to the limit *conclusive*, and translated by 'from,' 'commencing with,', 'including'; as in आबालं-आबालेभ्यः-हरिभक्तिः. 2 Complete pervasion.

अभिविश्रुत *a.* Widely celebrated, renowned.

अभिवृद्धिः *f.* Increase, growth, addition; success, prosperity.

अभिव्यक्तः *p. p.* 1 Manifested, revealed, declared. 2 Distinct, plain, clear.

अभिव्यक्तिः *f.* Manifestation (of a cause as an effect); distinction, display, exhibition; सर्वांगसौष्ठवाभिव्यक्तये M. 1; दूतीसंप्रेषणैर्नार्या भावाभिव्यक्तिरिष्यते S. D. 6.

अभिव्यंजनं Manifesting, revealing.

अभिव्यापक-, व्यापिन् *a.* Including, comprehending, pervading.

अभिव्याप्तिः *f.* Inclusion, comprehension, universal pervasion.

अभिव्याहरणं,- व्याहारः 1 Uttering, pronunciation, speaking. 2 An articulate and significant word, a name, appellation.

अभिशंसक,-शंसिन् *a.* Accusing, calumniating, insulting.

अभिशंसनं Accusation, charge, (whether true or false); मिथ्या° Y. 2. 289; abuse, insult, affront; पंचाशद् ब्राह्मणो दंड्यः क्षत्रियस्याभिशंसने Ms. 8. 268.

अभिशंका Doubt, suspicion, alarm, anxiety.

अभिशपनं-शापः 1 A curse, imprecation. 2 A serious charge, accusation; Y. 2. 99; अभिशापः पातकाभियोगः Mit. 3 Slander, calumny- –COMP. –ज्वरः fever caused by the pronunciation of a curse.

अभिशब्दित *a.* Declared, or announced; said, named.

अभिशस्त *p. p.* 1 Calumniated, abused, insulted; Ms. 8. 116, 373; Y. 1. 161. 2 Hurt, injured, attacked (supposed to be from अभिशस्) देवि केनाभिशस्तासि केन वासि विमानिता Râm. 3 Cursed (for अभिशप्त). 4 Wicked, sinful.

अभिशस्तक *a.* Falsely accused, defamed.

अभिशस्तिः *f.* 1 A curse. 2 Misfortune, evil, calamity. 3 Censure, calumny, defamation, insult. 4 Asking, begging.

अभिशापनं Pronouncing a curse.

अभिशीत *a.* Cold, chilly, as wind.

अभिशोचनं Intense grief or pain, torment.

अभिश्रवणं Repeating Vedic texts, while Brâhmaṇas are sitting down to a Srâddha.

अभिषंगः (also **अभिसंगः**) 1 Complete contact or union; attachment, connection. 2 Defeat, mortification, discomfiture; जाताभिषंगो नृपतिः R. 2. 30. 3 A sudden blow, shock or grief, sudden calamity or misfortune; ततोऽभिषंगानिलविप्रविद्धा R. 14. 54, 77; °जडं विजज्ञिवान् R. 8. 75. **4** Possession by devils or evil spirits; अभिधाताभिषंगाभ्यामभिचाराभिशापतः Mâdh. N. **5** An oath. **6** Embracing; copulation. **7** A curse or imprecation, abuse. **8** A false accusation, calumny or defamation. **9** Contempt, disrespect.

अभिषंजनं=अभिषंग q. v.

अभिषवः **1** Extracting or pressing out the Soma juice. **2** Distillation or extraction (of liquors &c.) **3** Religious bathing, ablution preparatory to religious rites. **4** Bathing or ablution (in general). **5** A sacrifice in general.—**वं** Sour gruel.

अभिषवणं Bathing.

अभिषिक्त *p. p.* **1** Sprinkled over, wetted; संगे पुनर्बहुतराममृताभिषिक्तां Ch. P. 29. **2** Crowned, inaugurated, installed.

अभिषेकः **1** Sprinkling, watering. **2** Anointing, inaugurating or consecrating by sprinkling water (a king, idol &c.) **3** (Particularly) Coronation, inauguration, installation (of kings); royal unction; अथाभिषेकं रघुवंशकेतोः R. 14. 7. **4** The (holy) water required at inauguration, coronation water; R. 17. 14. **5** Bathing; ablution, holy or religious bathing; अभिषेकोत्तीर्णाय काश्यपाय *S.* 4; अत्राभिषेकाय तपोधनानां R. 13. 51. **6** Bathing or sprinkling with water (of a divinity to whom worship is offered). –Comp. –**अहः** the day of coronation. –**शाला** coronation-hall.

अभिषेचनं **1** Sprinkling. **2** Coronation, inauguration.

अभिषेणनं Marching against an enemy, encountering a foe.

अभिषेणयति Den. P. To march against (with an army), to attack, to face or encounter (another) with an army; कः सिंधुराजमभिषेणयितुं समर्थः Ve. 2. 25; *Si.* 6. 64.

अभिष्टवः Praise, eulogy.

अभिष्यं (स्यं) दः **1** Oozing, flowing, trickling. **2** Weakness of, or running at, the eyes. **3** Great increase or enlargement, surplus, excess, superfluous portion; स्वर्गाभिष्यंदवमनं कृत्वेवोपनिवेशितं (ओषधिप्रस्थं) Ku. 6. 37 by drawing off the surplus population *i. e.* by emigration; cf. also R. 15. 29.

अभिष्वंगः **1** Contact. **2** Intense attachment, love, affection; विद्यास्वभिष्वंगः Dk. 155; अहो अभिष्वंगः Mâl. 1.

अभिसंश्रयः Refuge, shelter.

अभिसंस्तवः High praise.

अभिसंतापः War, battle, contest; अन्यं स्यादभिसंतापः Halây.

अभिसंदेहः **1** Exchange. **2** Organ of generation.

अभिसंधः, –धकः **1** A deceiver, cheat. **2** Traducer, calumniator.

अभिसंधा **1** Speech, declaration, word, assertion, promise; तेन सत्याभिसंधेन त्रिवर्गमनुतिष्ठता Râm. true to his word. **2** Deceit.

अभिसंधानं **1** Speech, word, deliberate declaration, promise; सा हि सत्याभिसंधाना Râm. **2** Cheating, deception; पराभिसंधानपरं यद्यप्यस्य विचेष्टितं R. 17. 76. **3** Aim, intention, purpose; अन्याभिसंधानेनान्यवादित्वमन्यकर्तृत्वं च Mit. **4** Making peace.

अभिसंधायः=अभिसंधि.

अभिसंधिः **1** Speech; deliberate declaration, promise. **2** Intention, object, purpose, aim. **3** Implied sense, the meaning intended, as in अयमभिसंधिः (frequently occurring in explanatory glosses). **4** Opinion, belief. **5** Special agreement, terms of an agreement, condition, stipulation.

अभिसमवायः Union.

अभिसंपत्तिः *f.* Becoming or being effected completely; going over, transition.

अभिसंपरायः Futurity.

अभिसंपातः **1** Meeting together, concourse, confluence. **2** War, battle, contest. **3** A curse.

अभिसंबंधः Connection, relation; conjunction, contact; sexual connection; Ms. 5. 63.

अभिसंमुख *a.* Facing, fronting; looking respectfully towards.

अभिसरः **1** A follower, an attendant. **2** A companion.

अभिसरणं **1** Approaching, going to meet (also with hostile intentions). **2** Meeting, rendezvous, assignation or appointment of lovers; त्वदभिसरणरभसेन वलंती पतति पदानि कियंति चलंती Gît. 6.

अभिसर्गः Creation.

अभिसर्जनं **1** A gift, donation. **2** Killing.

अभिसर्पणं Approaching, drawing near (with hostile intentions).

अभिसां (शां) त्वः, –त्वनं Conciliation consolation.

अभिसायं *ind.* At sunset, about evening; श्रितोदयाद्रेरभिसायमुच्चकै *Si.* 1. 16; Ki. 11. 51.

अभिसारः **1** Going to meet (as a lover), appointment, assignation; रतिसुखसारे गतमभिसारे मदनमनोहरवेषं Gît. 5. **2** The place where lovers meet by appointment, rendezvous; त्वरितमुपैति न कथमभिसारं Gît. **6. 3** An attack, assault; श्वोऽभिसारः पुरस्य नः Râm. –Comp. –**स्थानं** a place fit for making appointments; see under अभिसारिका below.

अभिसारिका A woman who either goes to meet her lover or keeps an appointment made by him; Ku. 7. 43; R. 16. 12; कांतार्थिनी तु या याति संकेतं साभिसारिका Ak. The S. D. recommends the following 8 places as eligible spots for lovers to meet:—(1) a field; (2) a garden; (3) a ruined temple; (4) the house of a female messenger; (5) forest; (6) caravansary (a place for pilgrims &c.) (7) a cemetery; and (8) the bank of a river; क्षेत्रं वाटी भग्नदेवालयो दूतीगृहं वनं । मालयं च श्मशानं च नद्यादीनां तटी तथा ॥

अभिसारिन् *a.* Going to meet, visiting; attacking, rushing out, going forth; युद्धाभिसारिणः U. 5. –**णी**=अभिसारिका see above.

अभिस्नेहः Attachment, affection; love, desire; यः सर्वत्रानभिस्नेहः Bg. 2. 57.

अभिस्फुरित *a.* Expanded to the full, full-grown (as a blossom).

अभिहत *p. p.* **1** Struck (fig. also), beaten, smitten, injured; धाराभिरातप इवाभिहतं सरोजं M. 5. 3, Amaru. 2. **2** Struck, affected, overcome; शोक°, काम°, दुःख°. **3** Obstructed. **4** (In Math.) Multiplied.

अभिहतिः *f.* **1** Striking, beating, hurting &c. **2** (In Math.) Multiplication.

अभिहरणं **1** Bringing near, fetching; R. 11. 43. **2** Robbing.

अभिहवः **1** Invocation, calling. **2** Sacrificing fully or completely. **3** Sacrificing.

अभिहारः **1** Carrying away, robbing, stealing. **2** An attack, assault. **3** Arming oneself, taking up arms.

अभिहासः Jest, joke, mirth.

अभिहित *p. p.* **1** Said, spoken, declared, mentioned. **2** Addressed, called. –Comp. –**अन्वयवादः**, –**वादिन्** *m.* a particular doctrine (or the follower of that doctrine) on the import of words. The followers of this doctrine (the Naiyâyikas) hold that words by themselves can express their own independent meanings, which are afterwards combined into a sentence expressing one connected idea; that, in other words, it is the logical connection between the words of a sentence, and not the sense of the words themselves, that suggests the import or purport of a sentence; they thus believe in a *tâtparyârtha* as distinguished from *vâchyârtha*. See K. P. 2.

अभिहोमः Offering an oblation of clarified butter.

अभी *a.* Without fear; R. 9. 63; 15. 8.

अभीक *a* **1** Longing after; anxious. **2** Lustful, libidinous, voluptuous; मेदस्विनः सरभसोपगतानभीकान् *Si.* 5. 64. **3** Fearless.

अभीक्ष्ण *a.* **1** Repeated, frequent. **2** Constant, perpetual. **3** Excessive. –**क्ष्णं** *ind.* **1** Frequently, repeatedly. **2** Constantly. **3** Very much, exceedingly.

अभीघात = अभिघात q. v.

अभीप्सित *a*. Desired, wished. **-तं** A wish, desire.

अभीप्सिन्, अभीप्सु *a*. Wishing for, desirous of obtaining.

अभीरः 1 A cowherd. 2 N. of a pastoral people; more usually written आभीर q. v. -COMP.-**पल्ली** a hamlet of cowherds.

अभीशापः A curse; see अभिशाप.

अभीशुः-षुः 1 A rein, bridle; तेन हि मुच्यंतामभीशवः *S* 1. 2 A ray of light; प्रफुल्लतापिच्छनिभैरभीषुभिः *Si*. 1. 22; °मत् resplendent, splendid. 3 Desire. 4 Attachment.

अभीष्ट *p. p*. 1 Wished, desired. 2 Dear, favourite, darling. **—ष्टः** A darling. **—ष्टा** A mistress, beloved woman. **—ष्टं** 1 An object of desire. 2 A desirable object (अभिमत): अन्यस्मै हृदयं देहि नानभीष्टे घटामहे Bk. 20. 24.

अभीषंग=अभिषंग q. v.

अभुग्न *a*. 1 Not bent or crooked, straight. 2 Well, free from disease.

अभुज *a*. Armless, maimed.

अभुजिष्या Not a slave or servant, an independent woman.

अभूः 'Unborn,' N. of Vishṇu.

अभूत *a*. Non-existent, what is not or has not been; not true or real, false.-COMP. **-आहरणं** 'utterance of an unreality,' a covert expression, a speech founded on fraud. **-तद्भावः** the becoming or being changed into, or making, that which it is not before; अभूततद्भावेच्वि; अकृष्णः कृष्णः संपद्यते तं करोति कृष्णीकरोति Sk.; cf. पयोधरीभूतचतुःसमुद्रां R. 2, 3. **—पूर्व** *a*. unprecedented, unsurpassed; अभूत °र्वो राजा चिंतामणिर्नाम Vâs. 1, Ve. 3. 2. **-प्रादुर्भावः** becoming manifest of what has not been before. **-शत्रु** *a*. having no enemy.

अभूतिः *f*. 1 Non-existence, nonentity. 2 Poverty.

अभूमिः *f*. 1 Non-earth, any thing but earth. 2 An unfit place or object, no proper object for; अभूमिरियमविनयस्य *S*. 7. स खलु मनोरथानामप्यभूमिर्विसर्जनावसरसत्कारः *ibid*. far exceeded or transcended my (highest) expectations; Si. 1. 42.

अभृत, अभृत्रिम *a*. 1 Not hired or paid. 2 Not supported.

अभेद *a*. 1 Undivided. 2 Identical, same. **—दः** 1 Absence of difference or distinction, identity, sameness; तद्रूपकमभेदो य उपमानोपमेययोः K. P. 10. 2 Close union; इच्छतां सह वधूभिरभेदं Ki. 9. 13; H. 3. 79; आशास्महे विग्रहयोरभेदं Bh. 1. 24.

अभेद्य, अभैदिक *a*. 1 Impenetrable. 2 Indivisible. **-द्यं** A diamond.

अभोज्य *a*. 1 Not to be eaten, prohibited as food, unholy; °अन्न *a*. one whose food is prohibited from being eaten by others.

अभ्यग्र *a*. 1 Near, proximate. 2 Fresh, new; इदं शोणितमभ्यग्रे संप्रहारेऽच्युतत्तयोः Mb. **-ग्रं** Proximity, vicinity.

अभ्यंक *a*. Recently marked.

अभ्यंगः 1 Smearing the body with unctuous or oily substances, smearing with oil; अभ्यंगनेपथ्यमलंचकार. Ku. 7. 7. 2 Smearing in general, inunction. 3 An unguent.

अभ्यंजनं 1 Smearing the body with oily substances. 2 Smearing or anointing in general. 3 Applying collyrium to the eyelashes. 4 An oily substance; oil, unguent.

अभ्यधिक *a*. 1 More than, exceeding. 2 Surpassing, more than in quality or quantity, higher, greater; एष चाभ्यधिकोऽस्माकं गुणः Râm.; न त्वत्समोस्त्यभ्यधिकः कुतोन्यः Bg. 11. 43; sometimes with abl. or instr.; धान्यं दशभ्यः कुंभेभ्यो हरतोऽभ्यधिकं वधः Ms. 8. 320. 3 More, extraordinary, pre-eminent; भव पंचाभ्यधिकः *S*. 6. 2.

अभ्यनुज्ञा,-ज्ञानं 1 Consent, approval, permission; कृताभ्यनुज्ञा गुरुणा गरीयसा Ku. 5. 7, R. 2. 69. 2 Order, command. 3 Granting leave of absence, dismissing. 4 Admission of an argument.

अभ्यंतर *a*. 1 Interior, internal, inner (opp. बाह्य); R. 17. 45; K. 66; Y. 3. 293. 2 Being included in, one of a group or body; देवीपरिजनाभ्यंतरः M. 5. Initiated in, familiar or conversant with; with loc., or in comp.; संगीतकेऽभ्यंतरे स्वः M. 5; अहो प्रयोगाभ्यंतरः प्राश्निकः M. 2. 4 Nearest, intimate, closely or intimately related; त्यक्ताश्चाभ्यंतरा येन Pt. 1. 259. **-रं** 1 The inside or interior, inner or interior part (of anything), space within; शमीमिवाभ्यंतरलीनपावकां R. 3. 9; Bg. 5. 27. 2 Included space, interval (of time or place); षण्मासाभ्यंतरे Pt. 4. 3 The mind. -COMP. **-करण** *a*. having the organs (concealed) inside, internally possessed of the powers of perception; V. 4. **-कला** the secret art, the art of coquetry or flirtation.

अभ्यंतरकः An intimate friend.

अभ्यंतरीकृ 8 U. 1 To initiate, familiarize with; प्रागल्भ्याद्वक्तुमिच्छंति मंत्रेष्वभ्यंतरीकृताः R'am. 2 To admit or introduce to; सर्वविश्रंभेषु अभ्यंतरीकरणीया K. 101; Dk. 159, 162. 3 To make a near friend of (a person); बाह्याश्चाभ्यंतरीकृताः Pt. 1. 259.

अभ्यंतरीकरणं Initiating, introducing &c.; सजीवनिर्जीवासु च द्यूतकलास्वभ्यंतरीकरणं Dk. 39.

अभ्यमनं 1 Attack, injury. 2 Disease.

अभ्यमित, अभ्यांत *p. p*. 1 Diseased, sick. 2 Injured.

अभ्यमित्रं An attack on an enemy. *-adv*. Towards or against the enemy.

अभ्यमित्रीणः-यः, -मित्र्यः A warrior who valiantly encounters his enemy; उद्योगमभ्यमित्रीणो यथेष्टं त्वं च संतनु Bk. 5. 47; मारीचाऽऽनुनयंस्त्रास दभ्यमित्र्यो भवामि ते 46.

अभ्ययः 1 Coming, arrival. 2 Setting (of the sun).

अभ्यर्चनं, -र्चा Worship, adoration, reverence.

अभ्यर्ण *a*. Near, proximate, being close or near (of space); approaching, drawing near (of time); अभ्यर्णमागस्कृतमस्पृशद्भिः R. 2. 32. **-र्णं** Proximity, vicinity; अंधकारिणि वनाभ्यर्णे किमद्भ्राम्यति Gît. 7; अभ्यर्णे परिरभ्य निर्भरभरः प्रेमांधया राधया Gît. 1, *Si*. 3. 21.

अभ्यर्थनं -ना A request, an entreaty, petition, suit; °नाभंगभयेन Ku. 1. 52.

अभ्यर्थिन् *a*. One who begs, asks, &c.

अभ्यर्हणा 1 Worship. 2 Respect, honour, reverence.

अभ्यर्हित *a*. 1 Honoured, revered, greatly respectable or venerable. 2 Fit, becoming, suitable; अभ्यर्हिता बंधुषु तुल्यरूपा वृत्तिर्विशेषेण तपोधनानां Ki. 3. 11.

अभ्यवकर्षणं Extraction, drawing out.

अभ्यवकाशः An open space.

अभ्यवस्कंदः-दनं 1 Vigorously encountering an enemy, marching against an enemy. 2 Striking so as to disable an enemy. 3 A blow in general.

अभ्यवहरणं 1 Throwing away or down. 2 Eating, taking food; throwing down the throat (कंठाद्धोनयनं Mit).

अभ्यवहारः 1 Eating, taking food, eating, drinking &c. 2 Food; जंभशब्दोऽभ्यवहारार्थवाची K'asi.; °संवादापेक्षी M. 4.

अभ्यवहार्य *pot. p*. Fit to eat, eatable. **-र्यं** Food; सर्वत्रौदरिकस्य अभ्यवहार्यमेव विषयः V. 3.

अभ्यसनं 1 Repetition, repeated practice or exercise. 2 Constant study, close application (to anything); (तां) विद्यामभ्यसनेनेव प्रसादयितुमर्हसि R. 1. 88.

अभ्यसूयक *a*. (यिका *f*.) Jealous, envious; a detractor, calumniator; मामात्मपरदेहेषु प्रद्विषंतोऽभ्यसूयकाः Bg. 16. 18.

अभ्यसूया Envy, jealousy, disfavour, anger; शक्राभ्यसूयाविनिवृत्तये यः R. 6. 74; रूपेषु वेशेषु च साभ्यसूयाः 7. 2, 9. 64.

अभ्यस्त *p. p*. 1 Repeated, frequently practised, exercised; नयनयोरभ्यस्तमामीलनं Amaru. 92; used or accustomed to; अनभ्यस्तरथचर्याः U. 5. 2 Learnt, studied; शैशवेऽभ्यस्तविद्यानां R. 1. 8; Bh. 3. 89. 3 (In Math.) Multiplied. 4 (In gram). Reduplicated.

अभ्याकर्षः Striking the breast with the flat of the hand as a sign of defiance (as by wrestlers &c.).

अभ्याकांक्षितं 1 A false charge, groundless complaint. 2 A desire.

अभ्याख्यानं A false charge; calumny, detraction.

अभ्यागत *p. p.* 1 Come near, arrived. 2 Come as a guest; सर्वत्राभ्यागतो गुरुः H. 1. 108. -तः A guest, visitor.

अभ्यागमः 1 Coming or going near, arrival; a visit; तपोधनाभ्यागमसंभवा मुदः Si. 1. 23; किं वा मदभ्यागमकारणं ते R. 16. 8. Mv. 2. 22. 2 Vicinity, neighbourhood. 3 Encountering, attacking. 4 War, battle. 5 Enmity, hostility.

अभ्यागमनं Approach, arrival, visit; हेतुं तदभ्यागमने परीप्सुः Ki. 3. 4.

अभ्यागारिकः One who is diligent in supporting a family.

अभ्याघातः An attack, assault.

अभ्यादानं Beginning, commencement, first beginning.

अभ्याधानं Laying on, adding (as fuel).

अभ्यांत *a.* Ill, diseased.

अभ्यापातः A calamity, misfortune.

अभ्यामर्दः,-मर्दनं War, battle, conflict, attack.

अभ्यारोहः -रोहणं Ascending, mounting, going up to.

अभ्यावृत्तिः *f.* Repetition, recurrence (so many times); see अनभ्यावृत्ति also.

अभ्याश *a.* Near, proximate. -शः 1 Reaching to, pervading. 2 Proximate neighbourhood, vicinity (also written as अभ्यास q. v.); वायसाभ्याशे समुपविष्टः Pt. 2; सहसाभ्यागतां भैमीमभ्याशपरिवर्तिनीं Mb., Dk. 62. 3 Result, consequence. 4 Prospect, hope of gaining; hence oft. used in the sense of 'quickly'.

अभ्यासः 1 Repetition in general; व्याख्याता व्याख्याता इति पदाभ्यासोऽध्यायपरिसमाप्तिं द्योतयति S. B.; नाभ्यासक्रममीक्षिते Pt. 1. 151. 2 Repeated practice or exercise, continued practice or use; अविरतश्रमाभ्यासात् K. 30. अभ्यासेन तु कौंतेय वैराग्येण च गृह्यते Bg. 6. 35, 44 by constant practice (to remain pure and unmodified); 12. 12; °निगृहीतेन मनसा R. 10. 23; so शर°, अस्त्र° &c. 3 Habit, custom, practice; अमंगलाभ्यासरतिं Ku. 5. 65; Y. 3. 68. 4 Discipline in arms, exercise, military discipline. 5 Reciting, study काव्यज्ञशिक्षयाभ्यासः K. P. 1. 6 Vicinity, proximity, neighbourhood (for अभ्याश); चूतयष्टिरिवाभ्यासे (शे) मधौ परभृतोन्मुखी Ku. 6. 2; (अभ्यासे-शे मधौ must mean here speaking to 'Madhu who was *near* her,' *scil.* by having manifested himself before her, which fully preserves the simile of Pârvatî, herself silent, speaking to her lover who was near her through her friend); अर्पितेयं तवाभ्यासे सीता पुण्यव्रता वधूः U. 7. 17 given in your charge; अभ्यासा-शा-दागतः Sk. (regarded as an Aluk compound). 7 (In gram.) Reduplication. 8 The first syllable of a reduplicated base, reduplicative syllable. 9 (in Math.) Multiplication. 10 Chorus, burden of a song. -COMP. -गत *a.* approached, gone near. योगः abstraction of mind resulting from continuous deep meditation; अभ्यासयोगेन ततो मामिच्छाप्तुं धनंजय Bg. 12. 9. -लोपः dropping of the reduplicative syllable. व्यवायः interval caused by the reduplicative syllable.

अभ्यासादनं Attacking or facing an enemy.

अभ्याहननं 1 Striking, hurting, killing. 2 Impeding, obstructing.

अभ्याहारः 1 Bringing near or towards, conveying. 2 Robbing.

अभ्युक्षणं 1 Sprinkling over, wetting; परस्पराभ्युक्षणतत्पराणां (तासां) R. 16. 57. 2 Consecration by sprinkling.

अभ्युचित *a.* Usual, customary.

अभ्युच्चयः 1 Increase, augmentation. 2 Prosperity.

अभ्युत्क्रोशनं Loud acclamation.

अभ्युत्थानं 1 Rising (from a seat) to do honour, rising in honour of. 2 Starting, departure, setting out. 3 Rise (lit. and fig.), elevation, prosperity, dignity; (तस्य) नवाभ्युत्थानदर्शिन्यो ननंदुः सप्रजाः प्रजाः R 4. 3. यदा यदा हि धर्मस्य ग्लानिर्भवति भारत । अभ्युत्थानमधर्मस्य तदात्मानं सृजाम्यहं Bg. 4. 7.

अभ्युत्पतनं Springing or leaping against, sudden spring or leap, assault; अलक्षिताभ्युत्पतनो नृपेण R. 2. 27.

अभ्युदयः 1 Rise (of heavenly bodies); sunrise. 2 Rise, prosperity, good fortune, elevation, success; सृशंति नः स्वामिनमभ्युदयाः Ratn. 1; भवो हि लोकाभ्युदयाय तादृशां R. 3. 14. 3 A festival; festive occasion. 4 Beginning, commencement.

अभ्युदाहरणं An example or illustration of a thing by its reverse.

अभ्युदित *p. p.* 1 Risen. 2 Elevated. 3 Asleep at sunrise.

अभ्युद्गमः, -मनं, -गतिः *f.* 1 Going forth to meet or to do honour (to a guest or to a venerable person). 2 Rising, occurring, originating.

अभ्युद्यत *p. p.* 1 Raised, lifted up; as °आयुध, °शस्त्र. 2 Prepared or ready, exerting oneself for (with inf., dat., loc. or in comp.). 3 Gone forth, risen, appearing forth, or approaching; कुलमभ्युद्यतनूतनेश्वरं R. 8. 15. 4 Given or brought unsolicited.

अभ्युन्नत *a.* 1 Raised, elevated; S. 3. 8. 2 Projecting upwards; very high; Ku. 1. 33.

अभ्युन्नतिः *f.* Great elevation or prosperity.

अभ्युपगमः 1 Approach, arrival. 2 Granting, admitting, accepting to be true; confession (as of guilt). 3 Undertaking, promising; निर्णय° M. 1; a contract, agreement, promise. -COMP. -सिद्धांतः an admitted proposition or axiom.

अभ्युपपत्तिः *f.* 1 Approaching to assist, taking pity or compassion on, favouring; a favour, kindness; अनयाभ्युपपत्त्या S. 4. 2 Consolation. 3 Protection, defence; ब्राह्मणाभ्युपपत्तौ च शपथे नास्ति पातकं Ms. 8. 112. 4 An agreement, assent, promise. 5 Impregnation of a woman (especially of a brother's widow as an act of duty).

अभ्युपायः 1 A promise, an engagement, agreement. 2 A means, an expedient, remedy; अस्मिन्नुराणां विजयाभ्युपाये Ku. 3. 19.

अभ्युपायनं A complimentary present; inducement, bribe.

अभ्युपेत *ind.* Having approached; having agreed or promised. -COMP. -अशुश्रूषा one of the 18 titles of Hindu law, breach of contract or engagement between master and servant.

अभ्युपेत्य *p. p.* 1 Come near, approached. 2 Promised, accepted, undertaken; Me. 38.

अभ्युषः, अभ्यूषः, अभ्योषः A sort of cake or bread.

अभ्यूहः 1 Arguing, reasoning, discussion. 2 Deduction, inference, guess, conjecture; पराभ्यूहस्थानान्यपि तनुतराणि स्थगयति Mal. 1. 14. 3 Supplying an ellipsis. 4 Understanding.

अभ्र् 1 P. [अभ्रति, आनभ्र, अभ्रित] To go, wander about; वनेष्वानभ्र निर्भयः Bk. 4. 11; 14. 110.

अभ्रं 1 A cloud. 2 Atmosphere, sky; परितो विपांडु दधदभ्रशिरः Si. 9. 3, see अभ्रंलिह &c. 3 Talc, mica. 4 (In arith.) A zero or cypher. -COMP. -अवकाशः clouds as the only shelter; fall of rain. -अवकाशिक, -काशिन् *a.* exposed to the rain (and so practising penance), not seeking shelter from the rain. -उत्थः 'sky-born' the thunder bolt of Indra. -नागः one of the elephants supporting the globe; N. of Airavata. -पथः 1 atmosphere. -2 balloon. -पिशाचः,-चकः 'sky-demon', epithet of Râhu.-पुष्पः N. of a cane (Mar. वेत) Calamus Rotang. (-ष्पं) 1. water. -2 'a sky flower', anything impossible, a castle in the air. -मातंगः Indra's elephant, Airâvata -माला, वृंदं a line, succession, or mass of clouds.

अभ्रंलिह *a.* 'Cloud-licking', touching or scraping the clouds (very high); अभ्रंलिहाग्राः प्रासादाः Me. 64; प्रासादमभ्रंलिहमारुरोह R 14. 29. -हः Wind.

अभ्रकं Talc, mica. -COMP -भस्मन् *n.* calx of talc. -सत्त्वं steel.

अभ्रंकष *a.* Touching or scraping the clouds, very high; आदायाभ्रंकषं प्रायाम्लयं फलशालिनं Bk. —षः 1 Wind, air. 2 A mountain.

अभ्रमुः *f.* The female elephant of the east, the mate of Airâvata, Indra's elephant. -COMP. -**प्रियः**, -**वल्लभः** Airâvata.

अभ्रिः-भ्री *f.* 1 A wooden scraper or sharp-pointed stick (for cleaning a boat). 2 A spade, hoe in general.

अभ्रित *a.* Overcast with clouds, clouded; R 3. 12.

अभ्रिय *a* Belonging to or produced from clouds, sky or mustaka. -**यः** Lightning. -**यं** A mass of thunder-clouds.

अभ्रेषः Non-deviation, fitness, propriety.

अम् *ind.* 1 Quickly. 2 A little.

अम् 1 P. [अमति, अमितुं, अमित] 1 To go; to go to or towards. 2 To serve, honour. 3 To sound. 4 To eat. —10 P. or *Caus.* (आमयति) 1 To come upon, attack, afflict with sickness or pain from disease. 2 To be ill or be afflicted or diseased.

अम *a.* Unripe (as fruit). —**मः** 1 Going. 2 Sickness, disease. 3 A servant, follower. 4 This, self.

अमंगल-ल्य *a.* 1 Inauspicious, evil, ill; R. 12. 43; °अभ्यासरतिं Ku. 5. 65; अमंगल्यं शीलं तव भवतु नामैवमखिलं Pushpadanta. 2 Unlucky, unfortunate.—**लः** The castor-oil tree (एरंड). —**लं** Inauspiciousness, ill-luck; evil; oft. used in dramatic literature; शांतं पापं प्रतिहतममंगलं; cf.; God forbid.

अमंड *a.* 1 Without decoration or ornaments. 2 Without froth or scum (as boiled rice). -**डः** The castor oil tree (एरंड).

अमत *a.* 1 not felt, not perceptible by the mind, unknown. 2 Disliked, not agreed to -**तः** 1 Time. 2 Sickness, disease. 3 Death.

अमति *a.* Evil-minded, wicked, depraved. —**तिः** 1 A rogue, cheat. 2 The moon. 3 Time. —**तिः** *f.* 1 Ignorance, unconsciousness, absence of knowledge, intention, or forethought; अमत्यैतानि षड् जग्ध्वा; Ms. 5. 20; 4. 222. -COMP. -**पूर्व** *a.* unconscious, unintentional.

अमत्त *a.* Sober, sane.

अमत्रं 1 A pot, vessel, utensil. 2 Strength, power.

अमत्सर *a.* Not jealous or envious, charitable.

अमनस्,-अमनस्क *a.* 1 Without the organ of desire, thought &c. 2 Devoid of intellect (as a child). 3 Inattentive. 4 Having no control over the mind. 5 Devoid of affection. —*n.* (-**नः**) 1 Not the organ of desire, non-perception. 2 Inattentive. —*m.* The Supreme Being. -COMP. -**गत** *a.* unknown, unthought of.-**नीत** -**ज्ञ** *a.* disapproved, condemned; reprobate.—**योगः** inattention. -**हर** *a.* displeasing, disagreeable.

अमनाक् *ind.* Not a little, greatly, very much.

अमनुष्य *a.* 1 Not human, not manly. 2 Not frequented by man. —**ष्यः** 1 Not a man. 2 A demon.

अमंत्र, त्रक *a.* 1 Not accompanied by Vedic verses, not requiring the repetition of Vedic texts, as a ceremony &c. 2 Not entitled to Vedic verses, such as a Sûdra, a female &c. 3 Not knowing Vedic text, अव्रतानाममंत्राणां Ms. 12 114. 4 not accompanied by the use of spells or incantations, as a cure &c.; अनया कथमन्यथावलीढा न हि जीवंति जना मनागमंत्राः Bv. 1. 111.

अमंद *a.* 1 Not slow or dull, active, intelligent. 2 Sharp, strong, violent (wind &c.). 3 Not little, much, excessive, great, violent; अमंदमद्दुर्दिन U. 5. 5; अमंदमिलदिंदिरे निखिलमाधुरीमंदिरे Bv. 4. 1.

अमम *a.* Without egotism, without any selfish or worldly attachment शरणेष्वममश्चैव वृक्षमूलनिकेतनः Ms. 6. 26.

अममता, -त्वं Indifference, disinterestedness.

अमर *a.* Undying, immortal, imperishable; अजरामरवत् प्राज्ञो विद्यामर्थं च साधयेत् H. Pr. 3, Ms. 2. 148. —**रः** 1 A god, deity. 2 Quicksilver. 3 Gold. 4 The number 33 (that being the number of Gods). 5 N. of Amarasimha. 6 A heap of bones. -**रा** 1 The residence of Indra (cf. अमरावती). 2 The navel string. 3 The womb. 4 A house-post. -**री** 1 A female of gods. 2 Indra's capital. -COMP.-**अंगना, -स्त्री** a celestial nymph, heavenly damsel; मुषाण रत्नानि हरामरांगनाः Si. 1. 51. -**अद्रिः**, 'mountain of the gods,' N. of the mountain Sumeru. -**अधिपः, इंद्रः, ईशः, ईश्वरः, पतिः, भर्ता, राजः** &c. 'the lord of the gods', epithets of Indra; sometimes of Siva and Vishṇu also. -**आचार्यः, -गुरु,-इज्यः** 'preceptor of the gods,' epithets of Brihaspati.-**आपगा -तटिनी,-सरित्** *f* the heavenly river, epithets of the Ganges; °तटिनीरोधसि वसन् Bh. 3. 123.-**आलयः** the abode of the gods, heaven.-**कंटकं** N. of that part of the Vindhya range which is near the source of the river Narmadâ -**कोशः,-षः** N. of the most popular Sanskrit lexicon called after the author अमरसिंह. -**तरुः-दारुः** 1 a celestial tree, a tree in the paradise of Indra; अमरतरुकुसुमसौरभसेवनसंपूर्णसकलकामस्य Bv. 1. 28.-2 = देवदारु. -3 the wish-yielding tree -**द्विजः** a Brâhmaṇa who lives by attending a temple or idol; or one who superintends a temple. -**पुरं** the residence of the gods, celestial paradise. -**पुष्पः,-ष्पकः** the wish-yielding tree (कल्पवृक्ष). -**प्रख्य-प्रभ** *a.* like an immortal. -**रत्नं** a crystal. -**लोकः** the world of the gods, heaven; °**ता** heavenly bliss; तेषु सम्यग्वर्तमानो गच्छत्यमरलोकतां Ms. 2. 5. -**सिंहः** N. of the author of *Amarakosha*; he was a Jaina and is said to have been one of the 9 gems that adorned the court of king Vikramâditya.

अमरता,-त्वं Immortality.

अमरावती Abode of the gods, residence of Indra.; ससंभ्रमेंद्रद्रुतपातितार्गला निमीलिताक्षीव भियाऽमरावती K. P. 1.

अमर्त्य *a.* Immortal, divine, imperishable; °भावेपि R. 7. 53; °भुवनं heaven; °ता immortality. —**र्त्यः** A god -COMP. -**आपगा** the celestial river, epithet of the Ganges; Vikr. 18. 104.

अमर्मन् *n.* Not a vital organ or part of the body.-COMP. -**वेधिन्** *a.* not injuring the vital parts; mild, soft.

अमर्याद *a.* 1 Exceeding due limits or bounds, transgressing every bound, disrespectful, improper; मर्यादायाममर्यादाः स्त्रियस्तिष्ठंति सर्वदा Pt. 1. 142. तादृशं स्वभमर्यादं कर्म कर्तुं चिकीर्षसि Râm. 2 Boundless, infinite. -**दा** Transgression of due limits or bounds, impropriety of conduct, disrespect, violation of due respect.

अमर्ष *a.* Not enduring or bearing. -**र्षः** 1 Non-endurance, intolerance, impatience; अमर्षशून्येन जनस्य जंतुना न जातहार्देन न विद्विषादरः Ki. 1. 33; jealousy, jealous anger; किं नु भवतस्तातप्रतापोत्कर्षेप्यमर्षः U. 5. In Rhet. अमर्ष is one of the 33 minor feelings or व्यभिचारिभाव See S. D.; R. G. thus defines it: परकृतावज्ञादिनानापराधजन्यो मौनवाक्पारुष्यादिकारणभूतश्चित्तवृत्तिविशेषोऽमर्षः. 2 Anger, passion, wrath; पुत्रवधामर्षोद्दीपितेन गांडीविना Ve. 4; सामर्ष angry, indignant; सामर्षं angrily. 3 Impetuosity, violence. -COMP. -**ज** *a.* arising from anger or impatience. -**हासः** an angry laugh, sarcastic sneer.

अमर्षण,-र्षित,-र्षिन्,-र्षवत् *a.* 1 Impatient, intolerant, unforgiving Pt. 1. 326. 2 Angry, indignant, passionate; हृदि क्षतो गोत्रभिदप्यमर्षणः R. 3. 53; अभिमन्युवधामर्षितैः पांडुपुत्रैः Ve. 4. 3 Impetuous, determined.

अमल *a.* 1 Free from dirt or impurities, pure, stainless, spotless; अमलाः सुहृदः Pt. 2. 171 pure, sincere. 2 White, shining; कर्णावसक्तामलदंतपत्र Ku. 7. 23; R. 6. 80. -**ला** 1 N. of the goddess Lakshmî. 2 The navel cord. 3 N. of a tree (Mar. आंवळा). -**लं** 1 Purity. 2 Talc. 3 The Supreme Spirit. -COMP. -**पतत्रिन्** *m.* (त्री) the wild goose.-**रत्नं,-मणिः** a crystal.

अमलिन *a.* Clean, spotless, pure (morally also); कुलममलिनं न त्वेवायं जनो न च जीवितं M'al. 2. 2.

अमसः 1 Disease. 2 Stupidity. 3 A fool. 4 Time.

अमा *a.* Measureless. *-ind.* 1 With, near, close to. 2 Together with, in conjunction or company with, as in अमात्य, अमावास्या q. v. *-f* 1 The day of the new moon, the day of the conjunction of the sun and moon; अमायां तु सदा सोम ओषधीः प्रतिपद्यते Vyâsa. 2 The sixteenth digit of the moon. *-m.* The soul.–COMP. **-अंतः** the end of the the day of new moon.–**पर्वन्** *n.* the sacred time of अमा, day of new moon.

अमांस *a.* 1 Without flesh, not containing flesh. 2 Lean, thin, weak-**सं** Not flesh, anything but flesh.–COMP. **-ओदनिक** *a.* (**की** *f.*) not relating to a preparation of rice with meat.

अमात्यः A companion or follower of a king, minister; अमात्यपुत्रैः सवयोभिरन्वितः R. 3. 28

अमात्र *a.* 1 Boundless, immeasurable. 2 Not whole or entire. 3 Not elementary. **-त्रः** The Supreme Spirit.

अमाननं,-ना Disrespect insult; disobedience.

अमानस्यं Pain.

अमानिन् *a.* Modest, humble.

अमानुष *a.* (**षी** *f.*) 1 Not human, not belonging to man, supernatural, unearthly, superhuman; आकृतिरेवानुमापयत्यमानुषतां K. 132.

अमानुष्य *a.* Not human, superhuman &c.

अमाम (मा) सी=अमावसी or अमावास्या q. v.

अमाय *a.* 1 Not cunning or sagacious, guileless, sincere. 2 Immeasurable. **—या** 1 Absence of fraud or deceit, honesty, sincerity. 2 (In Vedânta phil.) Absence of delusion or error, knowledge of the supreme truth.—**यं** The Supreme Spirit (ब्रह्म).

अमायिक,-मायिन् *a.* Guileless, honest.

अमावस्या,-वास्या,-वसी,-वासी (also written अमामसी-मासी) The day of new moon, when the sun and moon dwell together or are in conjunction; the 15th day of the dark half of every lunar month; सूर्याचंद्रमसोः यः परः सन्निकर्षः साऽमावस्या Gobhila.

अमित *a.* 1 Unmeasured, boundless, unlimited, immense; मितं ददाति हि पिता मितं भ्राता मितं सुतः । अमितस्य हि दातारं भर्तारं का न पूजयेत् Râm. 2 Neglected, disregarded. 3 Unknown. 4 Unpolished. –COMP. **-अक्षर** *a.* prosaic. **-आभ** *a.* of great lustre, of unbounded splendour. **-ओजस्** *a.* of unbounded energy, all-powerful, Almighty. **तेजस्, -द्युति** *a.* of unbounded lustre or glory. **-विक्रमः** 1 of unbounded valour. -2 a name of Vishnu.

अमित्रः Not a friend, an enemy, adversary, foe, rival, opponent; स्यातामामित्रौ मित्रे च सहजप्राकृतावपि *Si.* 2. 36; तस्य मित्राण्यमित्रास्ते 101; प्रकृत्यमित्रा हि सतामसाधवः Ki 14. 21.–COMP.-**घात,-घातिन्, -घ्न,-हन्** killing enemies.-**जित्** *a.* conquering one's enemies; अमित्राजिन्मित्रजिदोजसा यत् N. 1. 13.

अमिथ्या *adv.* Not falsely, truly; ताम्रचतुस्ते प्रियमप्यमिथ्या R. 14. 6.

अमिन् *a.* Sick, diseased.

अमिषं 1 An object of worldly enjoyment, luxury. 2 Honesty, absence of fraud or deceit. 3 Flesh.

अमीवा 1 Affliction, sickness, disease. 2 Distress, terror.—**वं** Affliction, distress, pain, injury.

अमुक *pron. a.* A certain person or thing, so and so (to be used when a person or thing is referred to without a name); मतं मेऽमुकपुत्रस्य यदत्रोपरिलेखितम् Y. 2 86–87; उभयाभ्यर्थितेनैतन्मया ह्यमुकसूनुना। लिखितं ह्यमुकेनेति लेखकोंते ततो लिखेत् 88.

अमुक्त *a.* 1 Not loosened, not let go. 2 Not liberated from recurring birth and death, not having got final beatitude. **—क्तं** A weapon (a knife, sword &c.) that is always grasped and not thrown. -COMP. **-हस्त** *a.* sparing, stingy (in a bad sense), frugal, economical; सदा प्रहृष्टया भाव्यं व्यये चामुक्तहस्तया Ms. 5. 150.

अमुक्तिः *f.* 1 Non-liberation. 2 Want of freedom or liberty.

अमुतः *ind.* 1 From there, there. 2 From that place, from above, *i. e.* from the other world or heaven. 3 Upon this, thereupon; henceforth.

अमुत्र *ind.* (opp. इह) 1 There, in that place, therein; अमुत्रासन् यवनाः Dk. 127. 2 There (in what precedes or has been said), in that case. 3 There above, in the next world, in the life to come; यावज्जीवं च तत्कुर्याद्येनामुत्र सुखं वसेत्. 4 There; अनेनैवार्भकाः सर्वे नगरेऽमुत्र भक्षिताः Ks.

अमुथा *ind.* Thus, in that manner.

अमुष्य (gen. of अदस्) Of such a one (in comp. only). -COMP. **-कुल** *a.* belong to the family of such a one. (**-लं**) a wellknown family. **-पुत्रः,-त्री** the son or daughter of such a one or of a good or well-known family or origin; see आमुष्यायण.

अमूदृश्, -श, -क्ष, *a.* (**-शी, -क्षी** *f.*) Such-like, such a one, of such a form or kind.

अमूर्त *a.* Formless, incorporeal, unembodied (opp. मूर्त where Muktâ. says मूर्तत्वं=अवच्छिन्नपरिमाणवत्त्वं). **—र्तः** N. of *Siva.* -COMP.-**गुणः** (In Vais. phil.) a quality considered to be अमूर्त or incorporeal such as धर्म, अधर्म &c.

अमूर्ति *a.* Formless, shapeless. **—र्तिः** N. of Vishnu. **—र्तिः** *f.* Shapelessness.

अमूल,-लक *a.* 1 Rootless (lit.); (fig.) without basis or support, baseless, groundless. 2 Without authority; not being in the original; न.मूलं लिख्यते किंचित् Malli. 3 Without material cause, as the *Pradhâna* of the Sânkhyas.

अमूल्य *a.* Priceless, invaluable.

अमृणालं The root of a fragrant grass (वरिण, Mar. काळा वाळा) used for screens &c.

अमृत *a.* 1 Not dead. 2 Immortal. 3 Imperishable, indestructible. **—तः** 1 A God, an immortal, a deity. 2 N. of Dhanvantari, physician of the gods. **—ता** 1 Spirituous liquor. 2 N. of various plants.**—तं** 1 (*a*) Immortality. (*b*) Final beatitude, absolution; Ms. 12. 104; स श्रियै चामृताय च Ak. 2 The collective body of immortals. 3 The world of immortality, Paradise, Heaven. 4 Nectar of immortality, ambrosia, beverage of the gods (opp. विष) supposed to be churned out of the ocean; देवासुरैरमृतमंबुनिधिर्ममंथे Ki. 5. 30; विषादप्यमृतं ग्राह्यं Ms. 2. 239; विषमप्यमृतं क्वचिद्भवेदमृतं वा विषमीश्वरेच्छया R. 8. 46; oft. used in combination with words like वाच्, वचनं, वाणी &c. कुमारजन्मामृतसंमिताक्षरं R. 3. 16. 5 The Soma juice. 6 Antidote against poison. 7 The residue or leavings of a sacrifice (यज्ञशेष); Ms. 3. 285. 8 Unsolicited alms, alms got without solicitation; मृतं स्यायाचितं भैक्ष्यममृतं स्यादयाचितं Ms. 4. 4–5. 9 Water; अमृताध्मातजीमूत U. 6. 21; cf. also the formulas अमृतोपस्तरणमसि स्वाहा and अमृतापिधानमसि स्वाहा repeated by Brâhmanas at the time of sipping water before the commencement and at the end of meals. 10 A drug. 11 Clarified butter; अमृतं नाम यत् संतो मंत्रजिह्वेषु जुह्वति *Si.* 2. 107. 12 Milk. 13 Food in general. 14 Boiled rice. 15 Anything sweet, anything lovely or charming. 16 Gold. 17 Quicksilver. 18 Poison. 19 The Supreme Spirit (ब्रह्म). -COMP. **-अंशुः -करः,-दीधितिः, -द्युतिः, -रश्मिः** &c. epithets of the moon; अमृतदीधितिरेष विदर्भजे N. 4. 104. **-अंधस्, -अशनः, -आशिन्** *m.* 'one whose food is nectar'; a god, an immortal. **—आहरणः** N. of Garuda who once stole Amrita.-**उत्पन्ना** a fly. (**-न्नं**), **उद्भवं** a kind of collyrium. **-कुंडं** a vessel containing nectar. **-क्षारं** sal ammoniac. **-गर्भ** *a.* filled with water or nectar; ambrosial. (**-र्भः**) 1 the individual soul. -2 the supreme soul. **-तरंगिणी** moonlight. **-द्रव** *a.* shedding nectar. (**-वः**) flow of nectar.–**धारा** 1 N. of a metre. -2 flow of nectar. **-पः** 1 a drinker of nectar, a god or deity. -2 N. of Vishnu. -3 one who drinks wine; भ्रवममृतपनामवांछयासावधरमहुं मधुपस्तषाजिहीते Si 7. 42 (where अ° has sense 1 also). –फला a bunch of grapes, vine plant, a grape (द्राक्षा). –बंधुः 1 a god or deity in general –2 a horse or the moon. –भुज् *m.* an immortal, a god, deity; one who tastes the sacrificial residues.—भू *a.* free from birth and death. —मंथनं churning (of the ocean) for nectar. –रसः 1 nectar, ambrosia; काव्यामृतरसास्वादः H. 1; विविधकाव्यामृतरसान् पिबामः Bh. 3. 40. –2 the Supreme Spirit. –लता,–लतिका a nectar-giving creeping plant.–वाक् *a.* producing nectar-like sweet words –सार *a.* ambrosial. (–रः) 1 clarified butter. –सूः, –सूतिः 1 the moon (distilling nectar). –2 mother of the gods. –सोदरः 'brother or nectar', the horse called उच्चैःश्रवस्. –स्रवः flow of nectar. –स्रुत् *a.* shedding or distilling nectar; Ku. 1. 45.

अमृतकं The nectar of immortality.

अमृतता,–त्वं Immortality.

अमृतेशयः N. of Vishnu (sleeping in waters).

अमृषा *ind.* Not falsely, truly.

अमृष्ट *a.* Unrubbed.—Comp. –मृज *a.* of unimpaired purity.

अमेदस्क *a.* Fatless, lean

अमेधस् *a.* Foolish, stupid, an idiot.

अमेध्य *a.* 1 Not able or allowed to sacrifice. 2 Unfit for a sacrifice; नामेध्यं प्रक्षिपेदग्नौ Ms. 4. 53, 56; 5. 5, 132. 3 Unholy, filthy, foul, dirty, impure, Bg. 17. 10; Bh. 3. 106.—ध्यं 1 Excrement, ordure; समुत्सृजेद्राजमार्गे यस्त्वमेध्यमनापदि Ms. 9. 282; 5. 126. 2 An unlucky or inauspicious omen; अमेध्यं दृष्ट्वा सूर्यमुपतिष्ठेत Kâty.–Comp. –कुणपाशिन् *a.* feeding on carrion. –युक्त,–लिप्त *a.* smeared with ordure, foul, defiled, dirty.

अमेय *a.* 1 Immeasurable, boundless; अमेयो मितलोकस्त्वं R. 10. 18. 2 Unknowable. –Comp. –आत्मन् *a.* possessing an immeasurable soul, magnanimous. (–*m.*) N. of Vishṇu.

अमोघ *a.* 1 Unfailing, reaching the mark; धनुष्यमोघं समधत्त बाणं Ku. 3. 66; R. 3. 53; 12. 97; कामिलक्ष्येष्वमोघैः Me. 73. 2 Unerring, infallible (words, boon &c.); अमोघाः प्रतिगृह्णंतावर्घ्यानुपद्माशिषः R. 1. 44. 3 Not vain or useless, fruitful, productive; यदमोघमपामंतरुप्तं बीजमज त्वया Ku. 2. 5; so °बलं, °शक्ति, °वीर्य, °क्रोधः &c. –घः 1 Not failing or erring. 2 N. of Vishṇu.–Comp. –दंडः unerring in punishment, N. of Siva. –दर्शिन्,–दृष्टि *a.* of unerring mind or view. –बल *a.* of never-failing strength or vigour.–वाच् *f.* words not vain or idle, that are sure to be fulfilled. (*-a.*) one whose words are not vain. –वांछित *a.* never disappointed. –विक्रमः of never failing valour, N. of Siva.

अंब् 1 P. 1 To go. 2 (A.) To sound.

अंबः A father. –बं 1 The eye. 2 Water.—ब *ind.* A particle of affirmation; 'well,' 'well now.'

अंबकं 1 An eye (in त्र्यंबक). 2 A father.

अंबरं 1 Sky, atmosphere, ether; तावतर्जयदंबरे R. 12. 41. 2 Cloth, garment, clothing, dress; दिव्यमाल्यांबरधर Bg. 11. 11; R. 3. 9; दिगंबर; सागरांबरा मही the sea-girt earth. 3 Saffron. 4 Talc. 5 A kind of perfume (Ambergris). –Comp. –अंतः 1 the end of a garment. –2 the horizon. –ओकस् *m.* dwelling in heaven, a god; (भस्मरजः) विलिप्यते मौलिभिरंबरौकसां Ku. 5. 79.–दं cotton. –मणिः the sun.–लेखिन् *a.* skytouching; R. 13. 26.

अंबरीषं (In some senses अंबरीषः also) 1 A frying-pan. 2 Regret, remorse. 3 War, battle. 4 One of the hells. 5 A young animal, colt. 6 The sun. 7 N. of Vishṇu. 8 N. of Siva.

अंबष्ठः 1 The offspring of a man of the Brâhmaṇa and a woman of the Vaisya tribe; ब्राह्मणाद्वैश्यकन्यायामंबष्ठो नाम जायते Ms. 10. 8, Y. 1. 91. 2 An elephant-driver. 3 (pl.) N. of a country and its inhabitants. –ष्ठा N. of several plants:—(*a*) गणिका, यूथिका (Mar. जुई) (*b*) पाठा (Mar. पहाडमूळ); (*c*) चुक्रिका (Mar. चुका); (*d*) another plant (Mar. अंबाडा)—ष्ठा,–ष्ठी An Ambashṭha woman.

अंबा (Voc. अंबे Ved ; अंब in later Sanskrit) 1 A mother; also used as an affectionate or respectful mode of address;'good woman,' 'good mother'; किमंबाभिः प्रेषितः, अंबानां कार्यं निर्वर्तय S. 2; कृतांजलिस्तत्र यदंब सत्यात् R. 14. 16. 2 N. of Durgâ, wife of S'iva. 3 N. of Pâṇḍu's mother, a daughter of Kâsirâja. [She and her two sisters were carried off by Bhishma to be the wives of Vichitra-Virya who had no issue. Amba, however, had been previously betrothed to a king of Sala and Bhishma sent her to him; but the latter rejected her because she had been in another man's house. So she came back to Bhishma and prayed him to accept her; but he could not break his vow of life-long celibacy, and being enraged she returned to the forest and practised austere penance to revenge herself on Bhishma. Siva favoured her and promised her the desired vengeance in another birth. Afterwards she was born as Sikhandini, daughter of Drupada, who came to be called Sikhandin and became the cause of Bhishma's death.]

अंबाडा–ला A mother.

अंबालिका 1 A mother; good woman (as a term of respect or endearment). 2 N. of a plant (Mar. अंबाडा). 3 N. of the youngest daughter of Kâsirâja wife of Vichitra-Vîrya. She became the mother of Pâṇḍu by Vyâsa who was invoked by Satyavatî to beget a son to Vichitra-Vîrya who had died without issue.

अंबिका 1 A mother, good woman, also used like अंबा as a term of respect or endearment; अत्तिके अंबिके शृणु मम विज्ञाप्तिं Mk. 1. 2 N. of Pârvatî, wife of Siva; अशीर्भिरेधयामासुः पुरःपाकाभिरंबिकां Ku. 6. 90. 3 N. of the middle daughter of Kâsirâja and the eldest wife of Vichitra-Vîrya. Like her youngest sister she had no progeny, and Vyâsa begot on her a son named धृतराष्ट्र; see अंबा above –Comp.–पतिः,–भर्ता N. of Siva. –पुत्रः,–सुतः N. of धृतराष्ट्र.

अंबिकेयः,–यकः N. of Ganesa, Kârttikeya or Dhṛitarâshṭra; more correctly written आंबिकेय q. v.

अंबु *n.* 1 Water; गांगमंबु सितमंबु यामुनं K. P. 10. 2 The watery element of the blood (cf. *imber*). –Comp. –कणः a drop of water. –कंटकः (short-nosed) alligator.–किरातः alligator. –कीशः, –कूर्मः a porpoise. –केशरः lemon-tree (छालंगवृक्ष). –क्रिया libation of water; presentation of water to the Manes of the deceased. –ग, –चर, –चारिन् *a.* moving or living in water, aquatic. –घनः hail. –चत्वरं a lake. –ज *a.* produced in water, aquatic (opp. स्थलज); सुगंधीनि च माल्यानि स्थलजान्यंबुजानि च Râm. (–जः) 1 the moon. –2 camphor. –3 the Sârasa bird. –4 the conch. (–जं) 1 a lotus; इंदीवरेण नयनं मुखमंबुजेन S. Til 3. –2 the thunderbolt of Indra. °भूः, °आसनः 'the lotus-born god', Brahmâ; °आसना the goddess Lakshmî. –जन्मन् *n.* a lotus. (–*m.*) 1 the moon. –2 the conch. –3 Sârasa. –तस्करः 'water-thief', the sun. –द *a.* giving or yielding water. (–दः) a cloud; नवांबुदानीकमुहूर्तलांछने R. 3. 53. –धरः 1 a cloud; बशिनश्चांबुधराश्च योनयः Ku. 4. 43; शरत्प्रमृष्टांबुधरोपरोधः R. 6 44. –2 talc. –धिः 1 any receptacle of waters; such as a jar; अंबुधिर्घटः Sk. –2 the ocean; क्षार° Bh. 2. 6. –3 the number four (in Math.). –निधिः 'treasure of waters', the ocean; देवासुरैरमृतमंबुनिधिर्ममंथे Ki. 5. 30. –प *a.* drinking water. (–पः) 1 the ocean. –2 Varuṇa, the regent of waters. –पातः current, flow or stream of water, cascade; गंगांबुपातप्रतिमा गृहेभ्यः Bk. 1. 8. –प्रसादः, –प्रसादनं the clearing nut tree (कतक) q. v.; फलं कतकवृक्षस्य यद्यप्यंबुप्रसादकं । न नामग्रहणादेव तस्य वारि प्रसीदति. –भवं a lotus. –भृत् *m.* 1 water-bearer, a cloud. –2 the ocean. –3 talc. –मात्रज *a.* produced only in water. (–जः) a conchshell. –मुच् *m.*

a cloud; ध्वनितसूचितमंबुमुचां चयं Ki. 5. 12.–राजः 1 the ocean. -2 Varuṇa. –राशिः receptacle or store of water, the ocean; त्वयि ज्वलत्यौर्व इवांबुराशौ S. 3.3; चंद्रोदयारंभ इवांबुराशिः Ku. 3. 67. R. 6. 57; 9.82. –रुह् n. 1 a lotus. -2 Sârasa. –रुहः, –हं, a lotus; विपुलिनांबुरुहा न सरिद्वधूः Ki. 5. 10. –रोहिणी a lotus. –वाहः 1 a cloud; तडिल्वंतमिवांबुवाहं Ki. 3. 1; भर्तुर्मित्रं प्रियमविधवे विद्धि मामम्बुवाहं Me. 99.–2 a lake. –3 water-bearer. –वाहिन् a. carrying or conveying water. (–m.) a cloud.–वाहिनी a wooden vessel, a sort of bucket. –विहारः sporting in water. –वेतसः a kind of cane or reed growing in water. –सरणं flow or current of water. –सर्पिणी a leech –सेचनी a wooden baling vessel.

अंबुमत् a. Watery, containing water. – ती N. of a river.

अंबूकृत a. Sputtered, pronounced indistinctly in shutting the lips, the sound thus remaining as it were in the mouth; uttered while emitting saliva from the mouth. –तं A sputtering noise, the growling of a bear; दधति कुहरभाजामत्र भल्लूकयूनामनुरसितगुरूणि स्त्यानमंबूकृतानि U. 2. 21; Mâl. 9. 6; Mv. 5. 41.

अंभ् 1 A. [अंभते, अंभित] To sound.

अंभस् n. 1 Water; कथमप्यंभ सामंतरानिष्पत्तेः प्रतीक्षते Ku. 2. 37; स्वेद्यमानज्वरं प्राज्ञः कोंभसा परिषिंचति Si. 2. 54; अंभसाकृतं done by water P. VI. 3. 3. 2 The sky. 3 The fourth sign of the zodiac. –COMP. –ज a. aquatic. (–जः) 1 the moon. –2 the (Indian) crane of Sârasa. (–जं) a lotus; बाले तव मुखांभोजे कथमिंदीवरद्वयं S. Til. 17; so पाद°, नेत्र°. °खंडः–डं a group of lotus flowers; कुमुदवनमपाश्रि श्रीमदंभोजखंडं Si. 1. 64. °जन्मन् m., °जनिः, °योनिः the lotus born God, epithet of Brahmâ. –जन्मन् n. a lotus. दः,–धरः a cloud. –धिः, –निधिः, –राशिः 'receptacle of waters', the ocean; संभूयांभोधिमभ्येति महानद्या नगापगा Si. 2. 100; यादवांभोनिधीन्रुंद्धे वेलेव भवतः क्षमा 58; so अंभसां निधिः; शिखाभिराश्लिष्ट इवांभसां निधिः Si. 1. 20; °वल्लभः a coral. –रुह् n. (ट्), –रुहं a lotus; हेमांभोरुहसस्यानां तद्वाप्यो धाम सांप्रतं Ku. 2. 44. (m.) the (Indian) crane.–सारं a pearl.–सूः smoke; cloudiness.

अंभोजिनी 1 A lotus-plant or its flowers; °वननिवासविलासं Bh. 2. 18. 2 A group of lotus flowers. 3 A place abounding in lotuses.

अम्मय a. (यी f.) Watery, formed from water.

अम्र=आम्र q. v.

अम्ल a. Sour, acid; कट्वम्ललवणात्युष्णतीक्ष्णरूक्षविदाहिनः (आहाराः) Bg. 17. 9. –म्लः 1 Sourness, acidity, one of the six kinds of tastes or *rasas* q. v. 2 Vinegar. 3 Wood-sorrel. 4 The common citron tree. 5 Belch. –COMP. –अक्त a. acidulated. –उद्गारः sour eructation. –केशरः the citron tree. –गंधि a. having a sour smell. –गोरसः sour butter-milk. –जंबीरः, –निंबकः the lime-tree.–पित्तं acidity of stomach, sour bile. –फलः the tamarind tree. (–लं) tamarind fruit.–रस a. having an acid taste. (–सः) sourness, acidity. –वृक्षः the tamarind tree. –सारः the lime tree. –हरिद्रा N. of a plant.

अम्लकः N. of a plant (लकुच), a sort of bread-fruit tree.

अम्लान a. 1 Not withered or faded (flowers &c.). 2 Clean, clear, bright (face): pure, unclouded; परार्थन्यायवादेषु काणोऽप्यम्लानदर्शनः. —नः Globe-amaranth (Mar. आबोली).

अम्लानि a. Vigorous, not fading. —निः f. 1 Vigour. 2 Freshness; verdure.

अम्लानिन् a. Clear, clean.—नी A collection of globe-amaranths.

अम्लि (म्ली) का 1 Sour taste in the mouth, sour eructation. 2 The tamarind tree.

अम्लिमन् m. Sourness.

अय् 1 A. (sometimes P. also, especially with उद्) (अयते, अयांचक्रे, अयितुं, अयित) To go. –WITH अंतर् to interpose, intervene; दर्दुरक उपसृत्यांतरयति Mk. 2. –अभ्युद् 1 to rise (as the sun, moon &c.). –2 to thrive, prosper. –उद् 1 to rise (as the sun &c.); उदयति हि शशांकः कामिनीगंडपांडुः Mk. 1. 57. –2 to appear, come in sight; मुहूर्तो यज्ञियः प्रातश्चोदयंतीह याजकाः Mb. –3 to spring, arise, originate, proceed from; तदोदयेदन्यवधूनिषेधः N. 3. 92; यथाग्नेर्धूम उदयते Sat. Br. –परा (रा being changed to ला) to run away, retreat, fly away.

अयः 1 Going, moving (mostly in comp., as in अस्तमय.). 2 Good actions of former birth. 3 Good fortune, good luck; शुद्धपार्ष्णिरयान्वितः R. 4. 26. 4 A die or cube (to play with). –COMP. –अन्वित, अयवत् a. fortunate, lucky; सुलभैः सदा नयवताऽयवता Ki. 5. 20.

अयक्ष्मं Healthiness, freedom from disease.

अयज्ञ a. Not offering sacrifice. –ज्ञः No sacrifice, a bad sacrifice.

अयज्ञिय a. 1 Not fit for sacrifice (as माष). 2 Not fit to perform a sacrifice (as a boy not invested with the sacred thread). 3 Profane, vulgar.

अयत्न a. Not requiring any effort; °पटवासतां R. 4. 55. —त्नः Absence of effort or exertion; –अयत्नेन, –त्नात्, –त्नतः without effort or exertion, easily, readily.

अयथा ind. Not as it should be or is intended to be, unfitly, improperly, wrongly. –COMP. – अर्थ a. 1 not true to the sense, unmeaning, nonsensical. –2 incongruous, unfit, false, S. 3. 2; incorrect, wrong; अनुभवो द्विविधो यथार्थोऽयथार्थश्च T. S.; °अनुभवः incorrect or untrue knowledge, wrong notion. –इष्ट a. 1 not as wished or desired, disliked. –2 not enough or sufficient. –उचित a. unfit, unworthy. –तथ a. 1 not as it should be, unfit, unsuitable, unworthy; इदमयथातथं स्वामिनश्चेष्टितं Ve. 2. –2 vain, useless, profitless. (–थं) ind. 1 unfitly, unsuitably. –2 in vain, uselessly; तद्गच्छति अ° Ms. 3. 240.–तथ्यं unsuitableness, incongruity; uselessness. –द्योतनं intimation or occurrence of some thing or act which is not expected –पुर,–पूर्व a. unprecedented, unparalleled.–वृत्त a. acting wrongly. –शास्त्रकारिन् a. not acting according to the Sastras, irreligious; अयथाशास्त्रकारी च न विभागे पिता प्रभुः Na′rada.

अयथावत् ind. Wrongly; improperly.

अयनं a. 1 Going, moving, walking, as in रामायणं. 2 A walk, path, way, road; अगस्त्यचिह्नादयनात् R. 16. 44. 3 A place, site, abode. 4 A way of entrance, an entrance (to an array of troops or व्यूह); अयनेषु च सर्वेषु यथाभागमवस्थिताः Bg. 1. 11. 5 The sun's passage, north and south of the equator. 6 (Hence) The period of duration of this passage, half year, the time from one solstice to another; see उत्तरायण and दक्षिणायन. 7 The equinoctial and solstitial points; दक्षिणं अयनं winter solstice; उत्तरं अयनं summer solstice. 8 Final emancipation; नान्यः पंथा विद्यतेऽयनाय Svet. Up. –COMP. –कालः the interval between the solstices. –वृत्तं the ecliptic.

अयंत्रित a. Unrestrained, unchecked, self-willed.

अयमित a. 1 Unrestrained, unchecked. 2 Untrimmed, undecorated (as nails &c.) Me. 92.

अयशस् a. Disreputable, infamous, disgraceful; also अयशस्क in this sense. –n. (शः) Infamy, disgrace, ill-repute, dishonour, scandal; अयशो महदाप्नोति Ms. 8. 128; किमयशो ननु घोरमतः परं U. 3. 27; स्वाभावलोलेत्ययशः प्रमृष्टं R. 6. 41. –COMP. –कर a. (री f.) disgraceful, ignominious.

अयशस्य a. Infamous, ignominious.

अयस् n. 1 Iron; अभितप्तमयोऽपि मार्दवं भजते कैव कथा शरीरिषु R. 8. 43. 2 Steel. 3 Gold. 4 A metal in general. 5 Aloe wood. —m. Fire. –COMP. –अग्रं, –अग्रकं a hammer; a pestle (for cleaning grain).–कांडः 1 an iron-arrow. –2 excellent iron. –3 a large quantity of iron. –कांतः (अयस्कांतः) 1 a magnet, load-stone; शंभोर्यतध्वमाक्रष्टुमयस्कांतेन लोहवत् Ku. 2. 59; स चकर्ष परस्मात्तदयस्कांत इवायसं R. 17. 63; U. 4. 21. –2 a precious stone; °मणिः a loadstone; अयस्कांतमणिशलाकेव लोहधातुमंतःकरणमाकृष्टवती M'al. 1. -कारः an iron-smith, black-smith. -कीटं rust of iron.-कुंभः an iron vessel, boiler &c.; so °पात्रं. -घनः an iron hammer; अयोघनेनाय इवाभितप्तं R. 14. 33. -चूर्णं iron filings. -जालं an iron net-work. -दंडः an iron club. -धातुः iron metal; U. 4. 21. -प्रतिमा an iron image. -मलं rust of iron; so °रजः, °रसः. -मुखः an arrow (iron-pointed); भेत्स्यत्यजः कुंभमयोमुखेन R. 5. 55. -शंकुः 1 an iron spear. 2 an iron nail, pointed iron spike, R. 12. 95. -शूलं 1 an iron lance. -2 a forcible means, a violent proceeding (तीक्ष्णः उपायः Sk.); (cf. आयः शूलिकः also K. P. 10; अयःशूलेन अन्विच्छतीत्यायःशूलिकः). -हृदय a. ironhearted, stern, unrelenting; सुहृदयोहृदयः प्रतिगर्जताम् R. 9. 9.

अयस्मय or **अयोमय** n. (यी f.) made of iron or of any metal.

अयाचित a. Unasked, unsolicited (as alms, food &c.); अमृतं स्यादयाचितं Ms. 4. 5. -तं Unsolicited alms.-Comp. -उपनत, उपस्थित a. got unasked or without solicitation; अयाचितोपस्थितमंबु केवलं Ku. 5. 22. -वृतिः,-व्रतं susbsisting on alms got without begging or solicitation.

अयाज्य a. 1 (A person) for whom one must not perform sacrifices, not competent to offer sacrifices (as a Sûdra &c.) 2 (Hence), Out-cast; degraded. 3 Not fit for sacrificial offerings.—Comp. याजनं, संयाज्यं sacrificing for a person for whom one must not perform sacrifices; Ms. 3. 65; 11. 60.

अयात a. Not gone &c. -Comp.-याम a. not stale, fresh, not worn out by use; °मं च यौवनं Dk. 123 fresh, blooming.

अयाथार्थिक a. (की f.) 1 Not true, unjust, improper. 2 Not real or genuine, incongruous, absurd.

अयाथार्थ्यं 1 Unfitness, incorrectness. 2 Absurdity, incongruity.

अयानं 1 Not going or moving; stopping, halt. 2 Natural disposition.

अयि ind. 1 As a gentle address in the sense of 'friend', 'Oh', 'ah', or simply as a vocative particle; अयि विवेकविश्रांतमभिहितं M. 1; अयि भो महार्षिपुत्र S. 7; आयि विद्युत्प्रमदानां त्वमपि च दुःखं न जानासि Mk. 5. 32; see also Ev. 1. 5, 11, 44. 2 As a particle of entreaty or solicitation, 'I pray', 'prythee'; अयि संप्रति देहि दर्शनं Ku. 4. 28; also of encouragement or persuasion; अयि मंदस्मितमधुरं वदनं तन्वंगि यदि मनाकुरुषे Bv. 2. 150. 3 As a particle of gentle or kind inquiry (प्रश्न); अयि जीवितनाथ जीवसि Ku. 4. 3. अयीदमेवं परिहासः 5. 62.

अयुक्त a. 1 not yoked or harnessed. 2. Not joined, united or connected. 3 Not devout or pious, inattentive, negligent. 4 Unpractised, unused, unemployed; °बुद्धि, °चार. 5 Unfit, improper, unsuitable; अयुक्तोयं निर्देशः P. IV. 2. 64, Mbh. 6 Untrue, wrong. -Comp. -कृत् a. doing improper or wrong acts. -पदार्थः the sense of a word to be supplied, as the sense of अपि q. v. -रूप a. incongruous, unsuitable; अयुक्तरूपं किमतः परं वद Ku. 5. 69.

अयुग,-गल a. 1 Separate, single. 2 Odd, uneven.-Comp. अर्चिस् m. fire. -नेत्रः, -नयनः, -शरः see under अयुग्म. -सप्तिः having seven horses, the sun.

अयुगपद् ind. Not all together, gradually, *seriatim*. -Comp. -ग्रहणं apprehending gradually. -भावः successive order, successiveness.

अयुग्म a. 1 Single, separate. 2 Odd, uneven (as a number).-Comp.-छदः, -पत्रः having an odd (i. e. 7) number of leaves; the सप्तपर्ण tree. -नयनः,-नेत्रः, -लोचनः having odd (3) eyes, N. of Siva; Ku. 3. 51, 69. -बाणः, शरः &c. having odd (5) arrows; N. of Cupid. -वाहः, -सप्तिः having seven horses, the sun.

अयुज् a. Odd, uneven (opp. युज् even).-Comp. -इषुः, -बाणः, -शरः N. of Cupid (having 5 arrows). छदः =सप्तपर्ण; ववुरयुक्छदगुच्छसुगंधयः Si. 6. 50. -पलाशः=सप्तपलाश. -पाद् -यमकं a kind of alliteration having the same syllables (in a different sense) in the first and third pâdas. -नेत्र,-लोचन, -अक्ष, शक्ति N. of Siva.

अयुत a. Disjoined, detached, not connected. -तं Ten thousand, a myriad.-Comp.-अध्यापकः a good teacher. -सिद्ध a. (in Vais. phil.) proved to be inseparable and inherent. -सिद्धिः f. proof that certain things or notions are inseparable and inherent.

अये ind. 1 As a vocative particle, or as a kind of gentle address (=आयि); अये गौरीनाथ त्रिपुरहर शंभो त्रिनयन Bh. 3 123. 2 An interjection showing (a) 'surprise' or 'wonder' and translated by 'oh', 'ah', अये मातलिः S. 6; (b) 'grief', 'dejection'; अये देवपादपद्मोपजीविनोऽवस्थेयं Mu. 2 (alas!); (c) 'anger'; (d) 'flurry,' 'agitation;' (e) 'recollection'; (f) 'fear'; (g) 'fatigue'.

अयोगः 1 Separation, disjunction; interval. 2 Unfitness, impropriety, incongruity. 3 An improper conjunction. 4 A widower; absent lover or husband (विधुर). 5 A hammer (for अयोग्र, अयोघन). 6 Dislike.

अयोगवः (वा or वी f.) The son of a Sûdra man and Vaisya woman; see आयोगव.

अयोग्य a. 1 Unfit, unsuitable; useless.

अयोध्य a. Unassailable; irresistible; अद्यायोध्या महाबाहो अयोध्या प्रतिभाति नः R'am. -ध्या The capital of solar kings, born of the line of Raghu, (the modern Oudh) situated on the river Sarayû.

अयोनि a. 1 Without origin or source, eternal; जगद्योनिरयोनिस्त्वं Ku. 2. 9. 2 Not born from the womb; born in a manner not approved by law or religion. -निः f. Not the womb. -निः N. of Brahm'a and Siva. -Comp. -ज, -जन्मन् a. not born from the womb, not produced in the ordinary course of generation; तनयां अयोनिजां R. 11. 47, 48; कन्यारत्नमयोनिजन्म भवतामास्ते Mv. 1. 30. °ईशः, ईश्वरः N. of Siva. (-जा), -संभवा N. of Sîtâ, daughter of Janaka, who was born from a furrow in a field.

अयौगपद्यं Absence of simultaneity.

अयौगिक (की f.) Not etymologically derived (as a word).

अरः The spoke or radius of a wheel. (°रं also); अरैः संधार्यते नाभिर्नाभौ चाराः प्रतिष्ठिताः Pt. 1. 81. -Comp. -अंतर (pl.). the intervals of the spokes; V. 1. 4. -घट्टः, -घट्टकः, 1 a wheel or machine for raising water from a well (Mar. राहाट); °घटी a bucket so used; कूपमासाद्य °टीमार्गेण सर्पस्तेनानीतः Pt. 4. -2 a deep well.

अरजस्, अरज, अरजस्क a. 1 Dustless, clean, pure (fig. also). 2 Free from passion (रजस्). 3 Not having the monthly courses. -f. (जाः) A girl before menstruation.

अरज्जु a. Not consisting of, or furnished with, cords. -n. A prison house.

अरणिः m. f., -णी f. A piece of wood (of the Samî tree) used for kindling the sacred fire by attrition, the fire producing wooder stick; cf. Pt. 1. 216. -णी (dual) The two pieces of wood used in kindling the sacred fire.-णिः 1 The sun. 2 Fire. 3 Flint.

अरण्यं (sometimes m. also,) wilderness, forest, desert; प्रियानाशे कृत्स्नं किल जगदरण्यं हि भवति U. 6. 30; माता यस्य गृहे नास्ति भार्या चाप्रियवादिनी । अरण्यं तेन गंतव्यं यथारण्यं तथा गृहं । Chân. 44; as first member of comp. in the sense of 'wild', 'grown or produced in forest;' °बीजं wild seed; so °मार्जारः, °मूषकः. -Comp.-अध्यक्षः forest keeper or ranger. -अयनं,-यानं going into the forest, becoming a hermit -ओकस्-सद् a. 1 dwelling in woods, being in a forest; वैक्लव्यं मम तावदीदृशमपि स्नेहादरण्यौकसः S. 4. 5. -2 (especially) one who has left his family and become an anchorite, forest-dweller. -कदली wild plantain. -गजः a wild elephant (not tamed). -चटकः a wild sparrow. -चंद्रिका (lit.) moonlight in a forest; (fig.)

an ornament or decoration which is useless, or does not serve its purpose; just as moonlight in a forest is useless there being no human beings to view, enjoy, and appreciate it, so is decoration when not viewed and appreciated by those for whom it is intended; thus Malli. on स्त्रीणां प्रियालोकफलो हि वेषः Ku. 7. 22 remarks: अन्यथाऽरण्यचंद्रिका स्यादिति भावः. –चर (°ण्येचर also) –जीव *a.* wild. –ज *a.* wild. –धर्मः wild state or usage, wild nature; तथारण्यधर्माद्वियोज्य ग्राम्यधर्मे नियोजितः Pt. 1. –नृपतिः, –राज् (ट्), –राजः 'lord of the woods', epithet of a lion or a tiger; so अरण्यानां पतिः. –पंडितः 'wise in a forest'; (fig.) a foolish person (who can display his learning only in a forest where no one will hear him and correct his errors). –भव *a.* growing in a forest, wild. –मक्षिका a gadfly. –यानं retiring to the woods. –रक्षकः forest-keeper. –रुदितं (°ण्ये°) 'weeping in a forest', a cry in the wilderness; (fig.) a vain or useless speech, or a cry with no one to heed it; hence anything done to no purpose; अरण्ये मया रुदितं *S.* 2; प्रोक्तं श्रद्धाविहीनस्य अरण्यरुदितोपमं Pt. 1. 393; तदलमधुनारण्यरुदितैः Amaru. 76. –वायसः a wild crow, raven. –वासः, –समाश्रयः retiring into woods, residence in a forest. –वासिन् *a.* living in a forest, wild. (–*m.*) a forest-dweller, an anchorite. –विलपितं, –विलापः (°ण्ये°) =रुदितं above. –श्वन् *m.* 'a wild hound', wolf. –सभा a forest-court.

अरण्यकं A forest.

अरण्यानिः –नी *f.* A large forest or desert, vast wilderness.

अरत *a.* 1 Dull, languid, apathetic. 2 Dissatisfied, discontented, averse to. –तं Noncopulation. –COMP. –त्रप *a.* not ashamed of copulation (–पः) a dog (as copulating even in the streets without shame).

अरति *a.* 1 Dissatisfied. 2 Dull, languid. –तिः *f.* 1 Absence of pleasure or amusement, regarded as arising from the longings of love; स्वाभीष्टवस्त्वलाभेन चेतसो याऽनवस्थितिः। अरतिः सा S. D. 2 Pain, distress. 3 Anxiety, regret, uneasiness, agitation; संधत्ते भृशमरतिं हि सद्वियोगः Ki. 5. 51. 4 Dissatisfaction, discontent. 5 Languor, dulness. 6 A bilious disease.

अरत्निः (*m.* or *f.*) 1 The elbow sometimes the fist itself. 2 A cubit of the middle length, from the elbow to the tip of the little finger, an ell; अरत्निस्तु निष्कनिष्ठेन मुष्टिना Ak.; मध्यांगुलीकूर्परयोर्मध्ये प्रामाणिकः करः । बद्धमुष्टिकरो रत्निररत्निः सकनिष्ठिकः ॥ Hal'ay.; Ki. 18. 6.

अरत्निकः The elbow.

अरं *ind.* 1 Swiftly, near, at hand, present. 2 Readily.

अरमण, अरममाण *a.* 1 Not pleasing or gratifying, disagreeable. 2 Unceasing, incessant.

अररं 1 The leaf or panel of a door (कपाटं); सरभसमरराणि द्रागपावृत्य Mv. 6. 27 (–रः, –री also); चंचूकोटिविपाटितारपुटो यास्याम्यहं पंजरात् Bv. 1. 58. 2 covering or sheath in general.–रः An awl.

अररे *ind.* A vocative particle expressive of (1) great haste; (2) contempt or disdain; अररे महाराजं प्रति कुतः क्षत्रियाः G. M.

अरविंदं 1 A lotus (it is one of the 5 arrows of Cupid; see under पंचबाण); शक्यमरविंदसुरभिः *S.* 3. 7. It is a sun-lotus; cf. सूर्यांशुभिर्भिन्नमिवारविंदं Ku. 1. 32; स्थल°, चरण°, मुख° &c. 2 Also, a red or blue lotus.–दः 1 The (Indian) crane. 2 Copper.–COMP. –अक्ष *a.* lotus-eyed, an epithet of Vishṇu. –दलप्रभं copper. –नाभिः, –भः N. of Vishṇu; हृदये मदीये देवश्चिरायास्तु भगवानरविंदनाभः Bv. 4. 8. –सद् *m.* N. of Brahm'a.

अरविंदिनी 1 A lotus plant; प्रपीतमधुका भृंगैः सुदिवेवारविंदिनी Bk. 5. 70. 2 An assemblage of lotus flowers. 3 A place abounding in lotus flowers.

अरस *a.* 1 Sapless, tasteless, insipid. 2 Dull, flat. 3 Weak, having no strength, inefficacious.

अरसिक *a.* 1 Devoid of taste, sapless, insipid, flavourless (of a thing). 2 Void of feeling or taste, dull, inappreciative, insensible to the charms (of poetry &c.); अरसिकेषु कवित्वनिवेदनं शिरसि मा लिख मा लिख मा लिख Udb.

अराग, अरागिन् *a.* Cool, dispassionate; तमहमरागमकृष्णं कृष्णद्वैपायनं वंदे Ve. 1. 4.

अराजक *a.* Having no king, anarchical; नाराजके जनपदे Râm.; Ms. 7. 3. अराजके जीवलोके दुर्बला बलवत्तरैः । पीड्यंते न हि वित्तेषु प्रभुत्वं कस्यचित्तदा ॥ Mb.; शोच्यं राज्यमराजकं Châṇ. 57.

अराजन् *m.* Not a king. –COMP. –भोगीन *a.* not fit for the use of a king. –स्थापित *a.* not established by a king, illegal.

अरातिः 1 An enemy, foe; देशः सोयमरातिशोणितजलैर्यस्मिन्ह्रदाः पूरिताः Ve. 3. 31. 2 The number six. –COMP. –भंगः destruction of enemies.

अराल *a.* Curved, crooked; पादावरालांगुली M. 2. 3. –लः 1 A bent or crooked arm. 2 An elephant in rut. –ला An unchaste woman, harlot, courtezan. –COMP. –केशी a woman with curled hair; भित्त्वा निराक्रामदरालकेश्याः R. 6. 81. –पक्ष्मन् *a.* having curved eyelashes; Ku. 5. 49.

अरिः 1 An enemy, foe; विजितारिपुरःसरः R. 1. 59, 61; 4. 4. 2 An enemy of mankind (said of the six feelings which disturb man's mind); कामः क्रोधस्तथा लोभो मदमोहौ च मत्सरः; कृतारिषड्वर्गजयेन Ki. 1. 9. 3 N. of the number six (from the six enemies) 4 Any part of a carriage. 5 A wheel. –COMP. –कर्षण *a.* tamer or subduer of enemies. –कुलं 1 a host of enemies. –2 an enemy. –घ्नः destroyer of enemies. –चिंतनं, –चिंता schemes directed against enemies; administration of foreign affairs. –नंदन *a.* 'an enemy's joy', affording triumph to an enemy. –भद्रः the foremost or most powerful enemy; R. 14. 31. –सूदनः, –हन्, –हिंसकः destroyer of enemies; R. 9. 18.

अरिंदम *a.* Subduer of enemies, victorious, conquering.

अरिक्थभाज्, अरिक्थीय *a.* Not entitled to a share in the ancestral property (as an heir incapacitated by impotence &c.).

अरित्रं 1 An oar; लोलैररित्रैश्चरणैरिवाभितः Si. 12. 71. 2 A rudder, helm.

अरिपं A continuous down-pour of rain. –षः A sort of disease in the anus.

अरिष्ट *a.* Unhurt; perfect, imperishable, safe. –ष्टः 1 A heron. 2 A raven, crow. 3 An enemy. 4 N. of various plants: (*a*) the soap-berry tree (Mar. रिठा); (*b*) another plant (Mar. निंब). 5 Garlic. –ष्टं 1 Bad or ill luck, evil, misfortune. 2 A portentous phenomenon foreboding misfortune, unlucky omen. 3 Unfavourable symptom, especially of approaching death; रोगिणो मरणं यस्मादवश्यं भावि लक्ष्यते । तल्लक्षणमरिष्टं स्यादिष्टमप्यभिधीयते ॥ 4 Good fortune or luck, happiness. 5 The lying-in-chamber. 6 Buttermilk. 7 Spirituous liquor; Si. 18. 77. –COMP. –गृहं the lying-in-chamber. –ताति *a.* making fortunate or happy, auspicious. (–तिः *f.*) security, succession of good fortune, continuous happiness; तदत्रभवता निष्पन्नाशिषं काममरिष्टतातिमाशास्महे Mv. 1. –मथनः N. of Siva or Vishṇu. –शय्या a lying-in-couch; अरिष्टशय्यां परितो विसारिणा R. 3. 15. –सूदनः, –हन् *m.* killer of Arishṭa, epithet of Vishṇu.

अरुचिः *f.* 1 Aversion, dislike in general; क्व सा भोगानामुपर्यरुचिः K. 146. 2 Want of appetite, disrelish, disgust; सन्निपातक्षयश्वासकासहिक्कारुचिप्रणुत् Susr. 3 Absence of a satisfactory explanation.

अरुचिर, अरुच्य *a.* Disagreeable, disgusting.

अरुज् *a.* Free from disease, sound, healthy.

अरुज *a.* Sound, healthy.

अरुण *a.* (णा,–णी *f.*) 1 Reddish brown, tawny, red, ruddy (of the colour of the morning as opposed to the darkness of night); नयनान्यरुणानि घूर्णयन् Ku. 4. 12. 2 Perplexed, embarrassed. 3 Dumb. -णः 1 Red colour, the colour of the dawn or morning twilight. 2 The dawn personified as the charioteer of the sun; आविष्कृतारुणपुरःसर एकतोऽर्कः S. 4. 1, 7. 4; विभावरी यद्यरुणाय कल्पते Ku. 5. 44; R. 5. 71. 3 The sun; रागेण बालारुणकोमलेन Ku. 3. 30; संसृज्यते सरसिजैररुणांशुभिन्नैः R. 5. 69. -णं 1 Red colour. 2 Gold. 3 Saffron.-COMP. -अग्रजः N. of Garuḍu.-अनुजः, अवरजः N. of Garuḍa, younger brother of Aruṇa. —अर्चिस् m. the sun. -आत्मजः 1. son of Aruṇa, N. of Jaṭâyu.- 2 N. of Saturn, Sâvarṇi Manu, Karna, Sugrîva, Yama and the two Asvins. (-जा) N. of Yamunâ and Tâpti. -ईक्षण a. red-eyed. -उदयः break of day, dawn; चतस्रो घटिकाः प्रातररुणोदय उच्यते. -उपलः a ruby. -कमलं a red lotus. -ज्योतिस् m. N. of Siva.-प्रिय 'beloved of red flowers and lotuses', N. of the sun. (-या) 1 the sun's wife.-2 shadow. -लोचन a. red-eyed. (-नः) a pigeon. -सारथिः 'having Aruṇa for his charioteer,' the sun.

अरुणित, अरुणीकृत a. Reddened, dyed red, impurpled; स्तनांगरागारुणिताच्च कंदुकात् Ku. 5. 11.

अरुंतुद a. 1 Cutting or wounding the vital parts, inflicting wounds, painful, sharp (fig. also); caustic; अरुंतुदमिवालानमनिर्वाणस्य दंतिनः R. 1. 71; Ki. 14. 55. 2 Acrimonious, sour (disposition).

अरुंधती 1 N. of the wife of Vasishṭha; अन्वासितमरुंधत्या स्वाहयेव हविर्भुजं R. 1. 56. 2 The morning star personified as the wife of Vasishṭha; one of the Pleiades. [In mythology Arundhatî is represented as the wife of the sage Vasishtha one of the 7 sages. She was one of the 9 daughters of Kardama Prajâpati by Devahûti. She is regarded as the highest pattern of conjugal excellence and wifely devotion and is so invoked by the bridegroom at nuptial ceremonies. Though a woman she was regarded with the same-even more-veneration as the Saptarshis; cf. Ku. 6. 12. She, like her husband, was the guide and controller of Raghu's line in her own department, and acted as guardian angel to Sîtà after she had been abandoned by Ràma. It is said that Arundhatì (the star) is not seen by persons whose end has approached: see H. 1. 76.] -COMP. जानिः,-नाथः,-पतिः N. of Vasishṭha, one of the seven Rishis or stars in the Ursa Major. —दर्शनन्यायः see under न्याय.

अरुष्-ष्ट a. Not angry, calm.

अरुष a. 1 Not angry. 2 Shining, bright.

अरुस् a. Wounded, sore. —m. (रुः) 1 The Arka tree. 2 Red *Khadira*. —n. 1 A vital part. 2 A wound, sore (—m. also).—COMP. -कर a. causing or inflicting wounds, wounding.

अरूप a. 1 Formless, shapeless. 2 Ugly, deformed. 3 Dissimilar, unlike.—पं 1 A bad or ugly figure. 2 The Pradhâna of the Sânkhyas and Brahma of the Vedântins. -COMP. —हार्य a. not to be attracted or won over by beauty; अरूपहार्यं मदनस्य निग्रहात् Ku. 5. 53.

अरूपक a. Without any figure or metaphor, not figurative, literal.

अरे ind. An interjection of (a) calling to inferiors; आत्मा वा अरे द्रष्टव्यः श्रोतव्यः; न वा अरे पत्युः कामायास्याः पतिः प्रियो भवति Sat. Br. (said by Yâjnavalkya to his wife Maitreyî); (b) of anger; अरे महाराजं प्रति कुतः क्षत्रियाः U. 4; (c) of envy.

अरेपस् a. 1 Sinless, spotless. 2 Clear, pure.

अरेरे ind. An interjection of (a) calling out angrily; अरेरे दुर्योधनप्रमुखाः कुरुबलसेनाप्रभवः Ve. 3; अरेरे वाचाट *ibid*; or of (b) addressing inferiors or by way of contempt; अरेरे राधागर्भभारभूत सूतापसद *ibid*.

अरोक a. Without splendour, obscured, dim.

अरोग a. Free from disease, healthy, sound, well; अरोगाः सर्वसिद्धार्थाश्चतुर्वर्षशतायुषः Susr. —गः Sound health; न नाममात्रेण करोत्यरोगं H. 1. 167.

अरोगिन्,-अरोग्य a. Healthy.

अरोचक a. (चिका f.) 1 Not shining or bright. 2 Causing loss of appetite. —कः Loss of appetite; disgust, loathing.

अर्क् 10 P. 1 To heat or warm. 2 To praise.

अर्कः 1 A ray of light, a flash of lightning. 2 The sun; आविष्कृतारुणपुरःसर एकतोऽर्कः S. 4. 1. 3 Fire. 4 A crystal. 5 Copper. 6 Sunday. 7 The sun-plant, (Mar. रुई), a small tree with medicinal sap and rind; अर्कस्योपरि शिथिलं च्युतमिव नवमल्लिकाकुसुमं S. 2. 8; यमाश्रित्य न विश्रामं क्षुधार्ता यांति सेवकाः । सोऽर्कवन्नृपतिस्त्याज्यः सदापुष्पफलोऽपि सन् Pt. 1. 51. 8 N. of Indra. 9 Food. (अर्क also). 10 The number 12. —COMP. —अश्मन् m. -उपलः the sun-stone. -आह्वः the swallow wort. -इंदुसंगमः the time of conjunction of the sun and moon (दर्श or अमावास्या).—कांता sun's wife. -चंदनः a kind of red sandal (रक्तचंदन). —जः epithet of Karṇa, Yama, and Sugrîva. (-जौ) the two Asvins regarded as the physicians of Heaven. -तनयः 'a son of the sun', an epithet of Karṇa, Yama and Saturn; see अरुणात्मज. (-या) N. of the rivers Yamunâ and Tâpti.—त्विष् f. light of the sun. -दिनं,-वासरः Sunday. -नंदनः, -पुत्रः-सुतः, -सूनुः N. of Saturn, Karṇa or Yama. -बंधुः,-बांधवः a lotus (the sun-lotus). —मंडलं the disc of the sun. -विवाहः marriage with the *arka* plant (enjoined to be performed before a man marries a *third* wife, who thus becomes his fourth); चतुर्थादिविवाहार्थं तृतीयेऽर्कं समुद्वहेत् Kâsyapa.

अर्गलः-ला-ली-लं 1 A wooden belt, pin, bar &c. (for fastening a door or the cover of a vessel), a bolt, latch, bar; पुरार्गलादीर्घभुजो बुभोज R. 18. 4; 16. 6; अनायतार्गलं Mk. 2; ससंभ्रमेंद्रद्रुतपातितार्गला निमीलिताक्षीव भियाऽमरावती K. P. 1; oft. used figuratively in the sense of a bar, impediment, something intervening as an obstruction; ईप्सितं तदवज्ञानाद्विद्धि सार्गलमात्मनः R. 1. 79 obstructed; वार्यर्गलाभंग इव प्रवृत्तः 5. 45. कंठे केवलमर्गलेव निहिता जीवस्य निर्गच्छतः K. P. 8; see अनर्गल also. 2 A wave or billow.

अर्गलिका A small door-pin, small bolt.

अर्घ् 1 P. [अर्घति, अर्घित] To be worth, have value, to cost; परीक्षका यत्र न संति देशे नार्घति रत्नानि समुद्रजानि Subâsh.

अर्घः 1 Price, value; कुर्युरर्घं यथापण्यं Ms. 8. 398; Y. 2. 251; कुत्स्याः स्युः कुपरीक्षकाहि मणयो यैरर्घतः पातिताः Bh. 2. 15 reduced in their true value, depreciated, so अनर्घ priceless; महार्घ very costly. 2 A material of worship, respectful offering or oblation to gods or venerable men; कुटजकुसुमैः कल्पितार्घाय तस्मै Me. 4; (the ingredients of this offering are:—आपः क्षीरं कुशाग्रं च दधि सर्पिः सतंडुलम्। यवः सिद्धार्थकश्चैव अष्टांगोऽर्घः प्रकीर्तितः ॥ see अर्घ्य below).- -COMP.-अर्ह a. worthy of a respectful offering.-बलाबलं rate of price, proper price, fall or rise in prices; Ms. 9. 329.-संख्यानं,-संस्थापनं appraising, assizes of goods; कुर्वीत चैषां (वणिजां) प्रत्यक्षमर्घसंस्थापनं नृपः Ms. 8. 402.

अर्घीशः N. of Siva.

अर्घ्य a. 1 Valuable; अनर्घ्य invaluable; see s. v. 2 Venerable; तानर्घ्यानर्घ्यमादाय दूरात्प्रत्युद्ययौ गिरिः Ku. 6. 50; Si. 1. 14. —र्घ्यं A respectful offering or oblation to a god or venerable person; अर्घ्यमस्मै V. 5; ददतु तरवः पुष्पैरर्घ्यं फलैश्च मधुश्च्युतः U. 3. 24; अर्घ्यमर्घ्यमिव वादिनं नृपं R. 11. 69; Ku. 1. 58, 6. 50.

अर्च् 1 U. (अर्चति-ते, अर्चित) 1 (a) To adore or worship; salute, welcome with respect; R. 2. 21, 1. 6, 90; 4. 84, 12. 89; Ms. 3. 93; आर्चीद् द्विजातीन् परमार्थविंदान् Bk. 1. 15, 14. 63; 17. 5. (b) To honour, *i. e.* decorate, adorn; U. 2. 9. 2 To praise (Ved.). -10 P. or *Caus.* To honour, adore, worship; स्वगौकसामर्चितमर्चयित्वा Ku. 15. 9.—WITH अभि, समभि to worship, adore, honour; आशीर्भिरभ्यर्च्य ततः क्षितींद्रं Bk. 1. 24, Bg. 18. 46. —प्र 1 to praise, sing praises of. -2 to honour, worship; प्रानर्चुरर्च्या जगद्वन्द्यं Bk. 2. 20.

अर्चक *a.* Worshipping, adoring. —कः Worshipper; गुरुदेवद्विजार्चकः Ms. 11. 225.

अर्चन *a.* Worshipping, praising —नं-ना Worship, reverence or respect paid to deities and superiors.

अर्चनीय, अर्च्य *pot. p.* To be adored or worshipped, venerable, respectable; R. 2. 10; Bk. 6. 70.

अर्चा 1 Worship, adoration. 2 An idol or image intended to be worshipped; मौर्यैर्हिरण्यार्थिभिरर्चाः प्रकल्पिताः Mbh.

अर्चिः *f.* Ray, flame (of fire or of the morning twilight); आसीदासन्ननिर्वाणप्रदीपार्चिरिवोषसि R. 12. 1; नैशस्यार्चिर्हुतभुज इव छिन्नभूयिष्ठधूमा V. 1. 8.

अर्चिस् *n.* (-र्चिः) 1 A ray of light, flame; प्रदक्षिणार्चिर्हविरग्निराददे R. 3. 14. 2 Light, lustre; प्रशमादर्चिषां Ku. 2. 20, Ratn. 4. 16. (said to be also *f.*). —*m.* 1 A ray of light. 2 Fire.

अर्चिसत् *a.* Flaming, brilliant, bright; V. 3. 2. —*m.* 1 Fire. 2 The sun.

अर्ज् 1 P. (अर्जति, अर्जित) 1 To procure, secure, gain, earn, usually in the *caus.* in this sense; पितृद्रव्याविरोधेन यदन्यत्स्वयमर्जितं Y. 2. 118. 2 To take up; आनर्जुर्नृभुजोऽस्त्राणि Bk. 14. 74.—10 P. or *caus.* To procure, acquire, obtain; स्वयमर्जित, स्वार्जित self-acquired. With उप to obtain or procure.

अर्जक *a.* (-र्जिका *f.*) Procuring, acquiring; one who acquires or gets.

अर्जनं Getting, acquisition; अर्थानामर्जने दुःखं Pt. 1. 163; अर्जयितृव्यापारोऽर्जनं Dây. B.

अर्जुन *a.* (ना-नी *f.*) 1 White, clear, bright, of the colour of day; पिशंगमौञ्जीयुजमर्जुनच्छविं Si. 1. 6. 2 Silvery. —नः 1 The white colour. 2 A peacock. 3 A tree (Mar. अर्जुनसादडा), with useful rind. 4 N. of the third Pândava who was a son of Kuntî by Indra and hence called ऐन्द्रि also. [Arjuna was so called because he was 'white' or 'pure in actions'. He was taught the use of arms by Dro*n*a and was his favourite pupil. By his skill in arms he won Draupad*i* at her Svayamvara (see Draupad*i*). For an involuntary transgression he went into temporary exile and during that time he learnt the science of arms from Parasu*rama*. He married Ulu*pi*, a Naga Princess, by whom he had a son named Ir*a*vat, and also Chitrangad*a*, daughter of the king of Ma*n*ipura, who bore him a son named Babhruv*a*hana. During this exile he visited Dwara*k*a, and with the help and advice of Krish*n*a succeeded in marrying Subhadr*a*. By her he had a son named Abhimanyu. Afterwards he obtained the bow G*a*nd*i*va from the god Agni whom he assisted in burning the Kh*and*ava forest. When Dharma, his eldest brother, lost the kingdom by gambling, and the five brothers went into exile, he went to the Him*a*layas to propitiate the gods and to obtain from them celestial weapons for use in the contemplated war against the K*au*ravas. There he fought with Siva who appeared in the disguise of a Kir*a*ta; but when he discovered the true character of his adversary he worshipped him and Siva gave him the P*a*supat*a*stra. Indra, Varu*n*a, Yama and Kubera also presented him with their own weapons. In the 13th year of their exile, the P*and*avas entered the service of the king of Vir*a*ta and he had to act the part of a eunuch, and music and dancing master. In the great war with the Kauravas Arjuna took a very distinguished part. He secured the assistance of Krish*n*a who acted as his charioteer and related to him the Bhagavadg*i*t*a* when on the first day of the battle he hesitated to bend his bow against his own kinsmen. In the course of the great struggle he slew or vanquished several redoubtable warriors on the side af the Kauravas, such as Jayadratha Bh*i*shma, Kar*n*a &c. After Yudhish*th*ira had been installed sovereign of Hastinapura, he resolved to perform the A*s*vamedha sacrifice, and a horse was let loose with Arjuna as its guardian. Arjuna followed it through many cities and countries and fought with many kings. At the city of Ma*n*ipura he had to fight with his own son Babhruv*a*hana and was killed; but he was restored to life by a charm supplied by his wife Ul*u*pî. He traversed, the whole of Bharatakha*n*d*a* and returned to Hastin*a*pura, loaded with spoils and tributes, and the great horse-sacrifice was then duly performed. He was afterwards called by Krish*n*a to Dvarak*a* amid the intestine struggles of Y*a*davas and there he performed the funeral ceremonies of Vasudeva and Krish*n*a. Soon after this the five P*and*avas repaired to heaven having installed Par*i*kshit—the only surviving son of Abhimanyu-on the throne of Hastin*a*pura. Arjuna was the bravest of the P*and*avas, highminded, generous, upright, handsome and the most prominent figure of all his brothers.] 5 N. of K'artavîrya, slain by Parasura'ma. See कार्तवीर्य. 6 The only son of his mother. —नी 1 A procuress, bawd. 2 A cow. 3 N. of a river commonly called करतोया. —नं Grass. -Comp. -उपमः the teak tree. -छवि *a.* white, of a white colour. -ध्वजः 'white-bannered', N. of Hanumat.

अर्णः 1 The teak tree. 2 A letter (of the alphabet).

अर्णवः The (foaming) sea, ocean (fig. also); शोक° ocean of grief; so चिंता°; जन° ocean of men; संसारार्णवलंघन Bh. 3. 10 -Comp. -अंतः the extremity of the ocean. -उद्भवः the moon. (-वा) Lakshmî. (-वं) nectar. -पोतः -यानं a boat or ship. -मंदिरः 1 'inhabiting the ocean', N. of Varu*n*a, regent of the waters. -2 N. of Vishnu.

अर्णस् *n.* Water. -Comp. -दः a cloud. -भवः conch-shell.

अर्णस्वत् *a.* Having much water. -*m.* The ocean.

अर्तनं Censure, reproach, abuse.

अर्तिः *f.* 1 Pain, sorrow, grief; शिरोऽर्ति head-ache. 2 The end of a bow.

अर्तिका An elder sister (in dramas).

अर्थ् 10 A. [अर्थयते, अर्थित] 1 To request, beg, supplicate, ask, entreat, solicit (with two acc.); त्वामिममर्थमर्थयते Dk. 71; तमभिक्रम्य सर्वेऽद्य वयं चार्थामहे वसु Mb.; प्रहस्तमर्थयांचक्रे योद्धुं Bk. 14. 99. 2 To strive to obtain, desire, wish. -With अभि to beg, supplicate, request; इमं सारंगं प्रियाप्रवृत्तिनिमित्तमभ्यर्थये V. 4; अवकाशं किलोदन्वान् रामायाभ्यर्थितो ददौ R. 4. 58. -अभिप्र 1 to ask, request. -2 to desire. -प्र 1 to ask or pray for, beg, request; तेन भवंतं प्रार्थयंते S. 2. -2 to desire, want, wish or long for; अहो विघ्नवत्यः प्रार्थितार्थसिद्धयः S. 3; स्वर्गतिं प्रार्थयंते Bg. 9. 20; Bk. 7. 48. R. 7. 50, 64. -3 to look for, search, be in search of; प्रार्थयध्वं तथा सीतां Bk. 7. 48. -4 To attack, seize or fall upon; असौ अश्वानीकेन यवनानां प्रार्थितः M. 5; दुर्जयो लवणः शूली विशूलः प्रार्थ्यतामिति R. 15. 5, 956. -प्रति to challenge (to combat), encounter, seek as an opponent; एत सीताद्रुहः संख्ये प्रत्यर्थयत राघवं Bk. 6. 25. -2 to make an enemy of. -सं 1 to believe, consider, regard, think; समर्थये यत्प्रथमं प्रियां प्रति V. 4. 39; मया न साधु समार्थितं V. 2; अनुपयुक्तमिवात्मानं समर्थये S. 7. -2 to corroborate, support, substantiate by proof; उक्तमेवार्थमुदाहरणेन समर्थयति. -समभि or संप्र to beg, request &c.

अर्थः 1 Object, purpose, end and aim; wish, desire; ज्ञातार्थो ज्ञातसंबंधः श्रोतुं श्रोता प्रवर्तते; सिद्ध° °परिपंथी Mu. 5; oft. used in this sense as the last member of compounds and translated by 'for,' intended for,' 'for the sake of,' 'on account of,' 'on behalf of', and used like an adj. to qualify nouns; संतानार्थाय विधये R. 1. 34; तां देवतापित्रतिथिक्रियार्थां (धेनुं) 2. 16; द्विजार्था यवागूः Sk.; यज्ञार्थात्कर्मणोऽन्यत्र Bg. 3. 9. It mostly occurs in this sense as अर्थं, अर्थे or अर्थाय and has an adverbial force; किमर्थं for what purpose, why; वेलोपलक्षणार्थं S. 4; तद्दर्शनादभूच्छंभोर्भूयान्दारार्थमादरः Ku. 6. 13; गवार्थे ब्राह्मणार्थे च Pt. 1. 420; मदर्थे त्यक्तजीविताः Bg. 1. 9; प्रत्याख्याता मया तत्र नलस्यार्थाय देवताः Nala. 13. 19; ऋतुपर्णस्य चार्थाय 23. 9. 2 Cause, motive, reason, ground, means; अलुप्तश्च मुनेः

क्रियार्थः R. 2. 55 means or cause. **3** Meaning, sense, signification, import; अर्थ is of 3 kinds:—वाच्य or expressed, लक्ष्य or indicated (secondary), and व्यंग्य or suggested; तद्दोषौ शब्दार्थौ K. P. 1. अर्थो वाच्यश्च लक्ष्यश्च व्यंग्यश्चेति त्रिधा मतः ॥ S. D. 2. **4** A thing, object, substance; अर्थो हि कन्या परकीय एव *S.* 4. 21; that which can be perceived by the senses, an object of sense; इंद्रिय° H. 1. 146; Ku. 7. 71; इंद्रियेभ्यः परा ह्यर्था अर्थेभ्यश्च परं मनः Kaṭh. (the objects of sense are five रूप, रस, गंध, स्पर्श and शब्द). **5** (*a*) An affair, business, matter, work; प्राक् प्रतिपन्नोऽयमर्थोऽगराजाय Ve. 3; अर्थोऽयमर्थांतरभाव्य एव Ku. 3. 18; अर्थोऽयर्थानुबंधी Dk. 67; संगीतार्थः Me. 56 business of singing, *i. e.* musical concert (apparatus of singing); संदेशार्थाः Me. 5 matters of message, *i. e.* messages. (*b*) Interest, object; स्वार्थसाधनतत्परः Ms. 4. 196; द्वयमेवार्थसाधनं R. 1. 19; दूरापेऽर्थे 1. 72; सर्वार्थचिंतकः **Ms. 7. 121**; मालविकायां न मे कश्चिदर्थः M. 3 I have no interest in M. (*c*) Subject matter, contents (as of letters &c.); त्वामवगतार्थं करिष्यति Mu. I will acquaint you with the matter; तेन हि अस्य गृहीतार्थो भवामि V. 2 if so I should know its contents. **6** Wealth, riches, property, money; त्यागाय संभृतार्थानां R. 1. 7; धिगर्थाः कष्टसंश्रयाः Pt. 1. 163. **7** Attainment of riches or worldly prosperity, regarded as one of the four ends of human existence, the other three being धर्म काम and मोक्ष; with अर्थ and काम, धर्म forms the well-known triad; cf. Ku. 5. 38; अप्यर्थकामौ तस्यास्तां धर्म एव मनीषिणः R. 1. 25. **8** (*a*) Use, advantage, profit, good; तथाहि सर्वे तस्यासन् परार्थैकफला गुणाः R. 1. 29; यावानर्थ उदपाने सर्वतः संप्लुतोदके Bg. 2. 46; also व्यर्थ, निरर्थक q. v. (*b*) Use, want, need, concern, with instr.; कोऽर्थः पुत्रेण जातेन Pt. 1 what is the use of a son being born; कश्च तेनार्थः Dk. 59; कोर्थस्तिरश्चां गुणैः Pt. 2. 33 what do brutes care for merits; Bh. 2. 48; योग्येनार्थः कस्य न स्याज्जनेन *Si.* 18. 66; नैव तस्य कृतेनार्थो नाकृतेनेह कश्चन Bg. **3. 18.** **9** Asking, begging; request, suit, petition. **10** Action, plaint (in law). **11** The actual state, fact of the matter; as in यथार्थ, अर्थतः, °तत्वविद्. **12** Manner, kind, sort. **13** Prevention, warding off; मशकार्थो धूमः; prohibition, abolition (this meaning may also be derived from 1 above). **14** N. of Vishṇu. –COMP. **–अधिकारः** charge of money, office of treasurer; °रे न नियोक्तव्यौ H. 2. **–अधिकारिन्** *m.* a treasurer. **–अंतरं** 1 another or different meaning. –2 another cause or motive; अर्थोयमर्थांतरभाव्य एव Ku. **3.** 18. –3 a new matter or circumstance, new affair. –4 opposite or antithetical meaning, difference of meaning. °**न्यासः** a figure of speech in which a general proposition is adduced to support a particular instance, or a particular instance, to support a general proposition; it is an inference from particular to general and *vice versa* उक्तिरर्थांतरन्यासः स्यात् सामान्यविशेषयोः । (१) हनुमानब्धिमतरद् दुष्करं किं महात्मनां ॥ (२) गुणवद्वस्तुसंसर्गाद्याति नीचोपि गौरवं । पुष्पमालानुषंगेण सूत्रं शिरसि धार्यते Kuval.; cf. also K. P. 10 and S. D. 709. **–अन्वित** *a.* 1 rich, wealthy. –2 significant. **–अर्थिन्** *a.* one who longs for or strives to get wealth or gain any object. **–अलंकारः** a figure of speech determined by and dependent on the sense, and not on sound (opp. शब्दालंकार). **–आगमः** 1 acquisition of wealth, income. –2 conveying of a sense. **–आपत्तिः** *f.* 1 an inference from circumstances, presumption, implication, one of the five sources of knowledge or modes of proof, according to the Mîmâ'msakas. It is an inference used to account for an apparent inconsistency; as in the familiar instance पीनो देवदत्तो दिवा न भुंक्ते the apparent inconsistency between 'fatness' and 'not eating by day' is accounted for by the inference of his 'eating by night'. –2 a figure of speech (according to some rhetoricians) in which a relevant assertion suggests an inference not actually connected with the subject in hand, or *vice versa*; it corresponds to what is popularly called कैमुतिकन्याय or दंडापूपन्याय; *e. g.* हारोयं हरिणाक्षीणां लुठति स्तनमंडले । मुक्तानामप्यवस्थेयं के वयं स्मरकिंकराः Amaru. 100; अभितप्तमयोपि मार्दवं भजते कैव कथा शरीरिषु R. 8. 43. **–उत्पत्तिः** *f.* acquisition of wealth; so °उपार्जनं. **–उपक्षेपकः** an introductory scene (in dramas); अर्थोपक्षेपकाः पंच S. D. 308. **–उपमा** a simile dependent on sense and not on sound; see under उपमा. **–उष्मन्** *m.* the glow or warmth of wealth; अर्थोष्मणा विरहितः पुरुषः स एव Bh. 2. 40. **–ओघः, –राशिः** treasure, hoard of money. **–कर** (**री** *f.*), **–कृत्** *a.* **1** enriching. –2 useful, advantageous. **–काम** *a.* desirous of wealth. (**–मौ** dual), wealth and (sensual) desire or pleasure; R. 1. 25. **–कृच्छ्रं** 1 a difficult matter. –2 pecuniary difficulty; न मुह्येदर्थकृच्छ्रेषु Nîti. **–कृत्य** doing or execution of a business; अभ्युपेतार्थकृत्याः Me. 38. **–गौरवं** depth of meaning; भारवेरर्थगौरवं Udb., Ki. 2. 27. **–घ्न** *a.* (**–घ्नी** *f.*) extravagant, wasteful, prodigal. **–जात** *a.* full of meaning. (**–तं**) 1 a collection of things. –2 a large amount of wealth, considerable property. **–तत्त्वं** 1 the real truth, the fact of the matter. –2 the real nature or cause of anything. **–द** *a.* 1 yielding wealth. –2 advantageous, useful. –3 liberal. **–दूषणं** 1 extravagance, waste. –2 unjust seizure of property or withholding what is due. –3 finding fault with the meaning. **–दोषः** a literary fault or blemish with regard to the sense, one of the four *doshas* or blemishes of literary composition, the other three being पददोष, पदांशदोष and वाक्यदोष; for definitions &c. see K. P. 7. **–निबंधन** *a.* dependent on wealth. **–निश्चयः** determination, decision. **–पतिः** 1 'the lord of riches'; a king; किंचिद्विहस्यार्थपतिं बभाषे R. 2. 46; 1. 59; 9. 3; 18. 1; Pt. 1. 74. –2 an epithet of Kubera. **–पर, –लुब्ध** *a.* 1 intent on gaining wealth, covetous. –2 niggardly. **–प्रकृतिः** *f.* the leading source or occasion of the grand object in a drama; (the number of these 'sources' is five:—बिजं बिंदुः पताका च प्रकरी कार्यमेव च । अर्थप्रकृतयः पंच ज्ञात्वा योज्या यथाविधि S. D. 317). **–प्रयोगः** usury. **–बंधः** arrangement of words, composition, text; stanza, verse; *S.* 7. 5; ललितार्थबंधं V. 2. 14. **–बुद्धि** *a.* selfish. **–बोधः** indication of the (real) import. **–भेदः** distinction or difference of meaning; अर्थभेदेन शब्दभेदः. **–मात्रं, –त्रा** 1 property, wealth. **–युक्त** *a.* significant. **–लाभः** acquisition of wealth. **–लोभः** avarice. **–वादः** 1 declaration of any purpose. –2 affirmation, declaratory assertion, an explanatory remark; speech or assertion having a certain object; a sentence. (It usually recommends a विधि or precept by stating the good arising from its proper observance, and the evils arising from its omission, and also by adducing historical instances in its support.) –3 praise, eulogy; अर्थवाद एषः । दोषं तु मे कंचित्कथय U. 1. **–विकल्पः** 1 deviation from truth, perversion of fact, –2 prevarication; also °वैकल्यं. **–वृद्धिः** *f.* accumulation of wealth. **–व्ययः** expenditure; °ज्ञ *a.* conversant with money-matters. **–शास्त्रं** 1 the science of wealth (political economy). –2 science of polity, political science, politics; Dk. 120. इह खलु अर्थशास्त्रकारास्त्रिविधां सिद्धिमुपवर्णयंति Mu. 3; °**व्यवहारिन्** a politician. –3 the science of practical life. **–शौचं** purity or honesty in money-matters; सर्वेषां चैव शौचानामर्थशौचं परं स्मृतं Ms. 5. 106. **–संस्थानं** 1 accumulation of wealth. –2 treasury. **–संबंधः** connection of the sense with the word or sentence. **–सारः** considerable wealth; Pt. 2. 42. **–सिद्धिः** *f.* fulfilment of a desired object, success.

अर्थतः *ind.* **1** With reference to the meaning or a particular object;

यच्चार्थतो गौरवं Mâl. 1. 7 depth of meaning. **2** In fact, really, truly; न नामतः केवलमर्थतोऽपि *Si.* 3. 56. **3** For the sake of money, gain or profit; ऐश्वर्यादनपेतमीश्वरमयं लोकोऽर्थतः सेवते Mu. 1. 14. **4** By reason of.

अर्थना Request, entreaty, suit, petition; N. 5. 112.

अर्थवत् *a.* **1** Wealthy. **2** Significant, full of sense or meaning; अर्थवान् खलु मे राजशब्दः *S.* 5. **3** Having meaning; अर्थवदधातुरप्रत्ययः प्रातिपदिकं P. I. 2. 45. **4** Serving some purpose; successful, useful.

अर्थवत्ता Wealth, property.

अर्थात् *ind.* (abl. of अर्थ) **1** As a matter of course, of course, in fact; मूषिकेण दंडो भक्षित इत्यनेन तत्सहचरितमपूपभक्षणमर्थादायातं भवति S. D. 10 **2** According to the circumstances or state of the case; as a matter of fact. **3** That is to say, namely.

अर्थिकः **1** a crier, watchman. **2** Especially, a minstrel whose duty it is to announce (by song &c.) the different fixed periods of the day, such as the hours of rising, sleeping, eating &c.

अर्थित *p. p.* Requested, asked, desired. **–तं** Wish, desire; petition.

अर्थिता, –त्वं **1** Begging, request. **2** Wish, desire.

अर्थिन् *a.* **1** Seeking to gain or obtain, wishing for, desirous of, with instr. or in Comp.; कोषदंडाभ्यां Mu. 5; को वधेन ममार्थी स्यात् Mb.; अर्थार्थी Pt. 1. 4, 9. **2** Entreating or begging any one (with gen.); अर्थी वररुचिर्मेऽस्तु Ks. **3** Possessed of desires. **—***m.* **1** One who asks, begs or solicits; a beggar, suppliant, suitor; यथाकामार्चितार्थिनां R. 1. 6; 2. 64; 5. 31; 9. 27; कोऽर्थी गतो गौरवं Pt. 1. 146; कन्यारत्नमयोनिजन्म भवतामास्ते वयं चार्थिनः Mv. 1. 30. **2** (In law) A plaintiff, complainant, prosecutor; स धर्मस्थसखः शश्वदर्थिप्रत्यर्थिनां स्वयं। ददर्श संशयच्छेद्यान् व्यवहारानतंद्रितः ॥ R. 17. 39. **3** A servant, follower. –Comp. **–भावः** state of a suppliant, begging, request; Mâl. 9. 30. **–सात्** *adv.* at the disposal of beggars; विभज्य मेरुर्न यदर्थिसात्कृतः N. 1. 16.

अर्थीय *a.* (In comp.) **1** Destined or intended for, doomed to suffer; शरीरं यातनार्थीयं Ms. 12. 16. **2** Belonging or relating to; कर्म चैव तदर्थीयं Bg. 17. 27.

अर्थ्य *a.* **1** first to be asked or sought for. **2** Fit, proper. **3** Appropriate, not deviating from the sense, significant; स्तुत्यं स्तुतिभिरर्थ्याभिरुपतस्थे सरस्वती R. 4. 6; Ku. 2. 3. **4** Rich, wealthy. **5** Wise, intelligent. **–र्थ्यं** Red chalk.

अर्द् 1 P. [अर्दति, अर्दित] **1** to afflict, torment; strike, hurt, kill; रक्षःसहस्राणि चतुर्दशार्दीत् Bk. 12. 56, see *caus.* below. **2** To beg, request, ask; निर्गलितांबुगर्भं शरद्घनं नार्दति चातकोपि R. 5. 17. —*Caus.* (or 10 P.) **1** (*a*) To afflict, torment, distress; कामार्दित, कोप°, भय° &c. (*b*) To strike, hurt, injure, kill; येनार्दिदत् दैत्यपुरं पिनाकी Bk. 2. 46. –With **अति** to torment excessively, fall upon or attack; अत्यार्दीत् वालिनः पुत्रं Bk. 15. 115. **–अभि** to distress, afflict, pain.

अर्दन *a.* **1** Distressing, afflicting. **–नं** Pain, trouble, anxiety, excitement, agitation. **–नं, –ना** **1** Going, moving. **2** Asking, begging. **3** Killing, hurting; giving pain.

अर्ध *a.* Half, forming a half. **–र्धं, –र्धः** **1** A half, half portion; सर्वनाशे समुत्पन्ने अर्धं त्यजति पंडितः; गतमर्धं दिवसस्य V. 2; यदर्धे विच्छिन्नं *S.* 1. 9. divided in half, (अर्ध may be compounded with almost every noun and adjective; as first member of compound with nouns it means 'a half of', °कायः = अर्धं कायस्य; with adjectives, it has an adverbial force; °श्याम half dark; with ordinal numerals 'with a half of that number'; °तृतीयं containing two and the third only half; *i. e.* two and a half. –Comp. **–अक्षि** *n.* side-look, wink; Mk. 8. 42. **–अंगं** half the body. **–अंशः** a half, the half; **–अंशिन्** *a.* sharing a half. **–अर्धः, –र्धं** **1** half of a half, quarter; चरोरर्धार्धभागाभ्यां तामयोजयतामुभे R. 10 56. –2 half and half. **–अवभेदकः** hemicrania (Mar. अर्धशिशि). **–अवशेष** *a.* having only a half left. **–आसनं** **1** half a seat; अर्धासनं गोत्रभिदोऽधितष्ठौ R. 6. 73; मम हि त्रिदिवौकसां समक्षमर्धासनोपवेशितस्य *S.* 7. (it being considered a mark of very great respect to make room for a guest &c. on the same seat with oneself); –2 greeting kindly or with great respect. –3 exemption from censure. **–इंदुः** 1 the half or crescent moon. –2 semicircular impression of a finger-nail, crescent shaped nail-print; N. 6. 25 –3 an arrow with a crescent-shaped head (= अर्धचंद्र below). °**मौलि** N. of *S*iva Me. 56. **–उक्त** *a.* half said or uttered; राभभद्र इति अर्धोक्ते महाराज U. 1 **–उक्तिः** *f.* a broken speech; an interrupted speech. **–उदय.** 1 the rising of the half moon. –2 partial rise. °**आसनं** a sort of posture in meditation. **—ऊरुकं** a short petticoat (Mar. परकर). **–कृत** *a.* half done, incomplete. **–खारं, –री** a kind of measure, half a Khâri. **गंगा** N. of the river Kâverî so °**जाह्नवी.** **–गुच्छः** a necklace of 24 strings. **–गोलः** a hemisphere. **–चंद्र** *a.* crescent-shaped, (**–द्रः**) 1 the half moon, crescent moon; सार्धचंद्रं बिभर्ति यः Ku. 6. 75.—2 the semicircular marks on a peacock's tail. –3 an arrow with a crescent-shaped head; अर्धचंद्रमुखैर्बाणैश्चिच्छेद कदलीसुखम् R. 12. 96. —4 a crescent-shaped nailprint. –5 the hand bent into a semicircle, as for the purpose of seizing or clutching anything; °**र्ढं दा** to seize by the neck and turn out; दीयतामेतस्यार्धचंद्रः Pt. 1. **—चंद्राकार, —चंद्राकृति** *a.* half-moon-shaped. **–चोलकः** a short bodice. **–दिनं, –दिवसः** 1 half a day, mid-day. —2 a day of 12 hours. **–नाराचः** a crescent-shaped iron-pointed arrow. **–नारीशः, –नारीश्वरः** a form of *S*iva, (half male and half female). **–नावं** half a boat. **–निशा** midnight. **–पंचाशत्** *f.* twenty-five. **–पणः** a measure containing half a paṇa.**– पथं** half way. (**–थे**) midway.**—प्रहरः** half a watch, one hour and a half. **–भागः** a half, half a share or part; तदर्धभागेन लभस्व कांक्षितं Ku. 5. 50; R. 7. 45.**–भागिक** *a.* sharing a half. **–भाज्** *a.* 1 sharing a half, entitled to a half. —2 a companion, sharer. **–भास्करः** mid-day. **–माणवकः –माणवः** a necklace of 12 strings (माणवक consisting of 24). **–मात्रा** 1 half a (short) syllable. –2 a term for a consonant. **–मार्गे** *ind.* midway; V. 1. 3. **–मासः** half a month, a fortnight. **मासिक** *a.* happening every fortnight –2 lasting for a fortnight. **–मुष्टिः** *f.* a half-clenched hand. **–यामः** half a watch. **–रथः** a warrior who fights on a car with another (who is not so skilled as a रथी); रणे रणेऽभिमानी च विमुखश्चापि दृश्यते। घृणी कर्णः प्रमादी च तेन मेऽर्धरथो मतः Mb. **–रात्रः** mid-night; अथार्धरात्रे स्तिमितप्रदीपे R. 16. 4. **–विसर्गः, –विसर्जनीयः** the Visarga sound before क्, ख्, प्, and फ्. **–वीक्षणं** a side-look, glance. **–वृद्ध** *a.* middle-aged. **–वैनाशिकः** N. of the followers of Kaṇâda (arguing half perishableness). **–वैशसं** half or incomplete murder; Ku. 4. 31. **–व्यासः** the radius of a circle. **–शतं** fifty. **–शेष** *a.* having only a half left. **–श्लोकः** half a sloka or verse. **–सीरिन्** *m.* 1 a cultivator, ploughman who takes half the crop for his labour; Y. 1. 166. –2 = अर्धिक p. v. **–हारः** a necklace of 64 strings. **–ह्रस्वः** half a (short) syllable.

अर्धक *a.* Half; see अर्ध.

अर्धिक *a.* (की *f.*) **1** Measuring a half. **2** Entitled to half a share. **–कः** A half-caste man; वैश्यकन्यासमुत्पन्नो ब्राह्मणेन तु संस्कृतः। अर्धिकः स तु विज्ञेयो भोज्यो विप्रैर्न संशयः Parâsara.

अर्धिन् *a.* Sharing or entitled to a half.

अर्पणं **1** Placing or putting upon, setting upon; पादार्पणानुग्रहपूतपृष्ठं R. 2. 35. **2** Inserting, placing or putting in. **3** Giving, offering, resigning;

स्वदेहार्पणनिष्क्रयेण R. 2. 55. मुखार्पणेषु प्रकृतिप्रगल्भाः 13. 9; तस्कुरुष्व मदर्पणं Bg. 9. 27. **4** Restoration, delivery, giving back; न्यास° Ak. **5** Piercing, perforating; तीक्ष्णतुंडार्पणैर्ग्रीवां नखैः सर्वा व्यदारयत् Râm.

अर्पिसः The heart; flesh in the heart.

अर्ब् 1 P. (अर्बति, आनर्ब, अर्बितुं) **1** To go towards. **2** To kill, hurt.

अर्बु (र्बु) दः-दं **1** A swelling, tumour, (various kinds). **2** One hundred millions. **3** N. of a mountain in the west of India (Abu). **4** A serpent. **5** A cloud. **6** A long round mass, lump of flesh. **7** A serpent-like demon killed by Indra.

अर्भक *a.* **1** Small, minute, short. **2** Weak, lean. **3** Foolish. **4** Young, childish. **—कः** **1** A boy, child; श्रुतस्य यायादयमंतमर्भकः R. 3. 21, 25, 7. 67. **2** The young of an animal. **3** A fool, idiot.

अर्य **1** *a.* Excellent, best. **2** Respectable. **—र्यः** **1** A master, lord. **2** A man of the third tribe, Vaisya. **—र्या** **1** A mistress. **2** A woman of the Vaisya tribe. **—र्यी** The wife of a Vaisya. -Comp. **-वर्यः** A Vaisya of rank.

अर्यमन् *m.* **1** The sun. **2** The head of the Manes; पितॄणामर्यमा चास्मि Bg. 10. 29. **3** N. of the *arka* plant.

अर्याणी A woman of the Vaisya tribe.

अर्वन् *m.* **1** A horse; श्लथीकृतप्रग्रहमर्वतां व्रजाः *Si.* 12. 31. **2** One of the ten horses of the moon. **3** Indra. **4** A short span (गोकर्णपरिमाण). **—ती** **1** A mare. **2** A bawd, procuress.

अर्वाच् *a.* **1** Coming hitherward (opp. परांच्). **2** Turned towards, coming to meet any one. **3** Being on this side. **4** Being below or behind (in time or place). **5** Following, subsequent. **—क्** *ind.* **1** Hitherward, on this side. **2** From a certain point. **3** Before (in time or place); यत्स्रष्टेरर्वाक् सलिलमयं ब्रह्मांडमभूत् K. 125; अर्वाक् संवत्सरात्स्वामी हरेत परतो नृपः Y. 2. 173, 113; 1. 254. **4** On the lower side, behind, downwards (opp. ऊर्ध्वं). **5** Afterwards, subsequently. **6** (With loc.) Within, near; एते चार्वाग्उपवनभुवि छिन्नदर्भांकुरायां। *S.* 1. 15. -Comp.-**कालः** posterior time.-**कालिक** *a.* belonging to proximate time, modern; °**ता** modernness, posteriority of time.**—कूलं** the near bank of a river.

अर्वाचीन *a.* **1** Modern, recent. **2** Reverse, contrary.**—नं** *ind.* (With abl.) **1** On this side of. **2** Later than; यदूर्ध्वं पृथिव्या अर्वाचीनमंतरिक्षात् Sat. Br.

अर्शस् *n.* Piles.—Comp. **-घ्न** *a.* destroying piles. (**-घ्नः**) **1** N. of the plant शुरण, so called because it is said to cure piles.

अर्शस *a.* Afflicted with piles.

अर्ह् 1 P. [अर्हति, अर्हितुं, आनर्ह, अर्हित] (epic A. as रावणो नार्हते पूजां Râm.) **1** To deserve, merit, be worthy of with acc. or inf.); किमिव नायुष्मानमरेश्वरान्नार्हति *S.* 7. **2** To have a right to, be entitled to; ननु गर्भः पित्र्यं रिक्थमर्हति *S.* 6. न स्त्री स्वातंत्र्यमर्हति Ms. 9. 3. **3** To be fit or deserve to be done; अर्थना मयि भवद्भिः कर्तुमर्हति N. 5. 112; Dk. 137. **4** To be equal to; be worth; न ते गात्राण्युपचारमर्हति *S.* 3. 18; सर्वे ते जपयज्ञस्य कलां नार्हंति षोडशीं Ms. 2. 86. **5** To be able, translateable by 'can'; न मे वचनमन्यथा भवितुमर्हति *S.* 4. **6** To worship, honour; see *caus.* below. **7** (Used with inf. in the second pers. and sometimes in the third) **अर्ह्** represents a mild form of command, advice or courteous request, and may be translated by 'pray,' 'deign,' 'be pleased to,' will be pleased to'; द्वित्राण्यहान्यर्हसि सोढुमर्हन् R. 5. 25 pray wait &c; नार्हसि मे प्रणयं विहंतुं 2. 58. —*Caus.* or 10 P. To honour, worship; राजार्जिहत्तं मधुपर्कपाणिः Bk. 1. 17; Ms. 3. 3, 119.

अर्ह *a.* **1** Respectable, worthy of respect, deserving; अर्हाविभोजयन् विप्रो दंडमर्हति माषकं Ms. 8. 392. **2** Worthy of, having a claim to, entitled to, with acc., inf., or in comp.; नैवार्हः पैतृकं रिक्थं पतितोत्पादितो हि सः Ms. 9. 144; संस्कारमर्हस्त्वं न च लप्स्यसे Râm.; तस्मान्नार्हा वयं हंतुं धार्तराष्ट्रान् स्वबांधवान् Bg. 1. 37; so मान°, वध°, दंड° &c. **3** Becoming, proper, fit; केवलं यानमर्हं स्यात् Pt. 3; with gen. also, स भृत्योर्हो महीभुजां Pt. 1. 87-92. **4** Worth (in money), costing; see below. **—र्हः** **1** N. of Indra. **2** N. of Vishṇu. **3** Price (as in महार्ह); महार्हशय्यापरिवर्तनच्युतैः Ku. 5. 12 (महान्नर्हो यस्याः Malli.). **—र्हा** Worship, adoration.

अर्हण-णा Worship, adoration, honour, treating with respect or veneration; अर्हणामर्हते चक्रुर्मुनयो नयचक्षुषे R. 1. 55; *Si.* 15. 22.

अर्हत् *a.* Worthy, deserving, adorable. **—m.** **1** A Buddha; the highest rank in Buddhist hierarchy. **2** A superior divinity with the Jainas; सर्वज्ञो जितरागादिदोषस्त्रैलोक्यपूजितः। यथास्थितार्थवादी च देवोर्हन् परमेश्वरः॥

अर्हंत *a.* Worthy, deserving. **—तः** **1** A Buddha. **2** A Buddhist mendicant.

अर्हंती The quality of being fit to be worshipped, veneration, adoration श्रौत्राऽर्हंतीचणैर्गुण्यैः Sk.

अर्ह्य *pot. p.* **1** Worthy, respectable. **2** Fit to be praised.

अल् 1 U (अलति-ते, अलितुं, अलित) **1** To adorn. **2** To be competent or able. **3** To prevent, ward off; see अलम्.

अलं **1** The sting in the tail of a scorpion. **2** Yellow orpiment; cf. आल.

अलकः **1** A curl, lock of hair, hair in general; ललाटिकाचंदनधूसरालका Ku. 5. 55; अलके बालकुंदानुविद्धं Me. 65 (the word is *n.* also, as appears from a quotation of Malli.: स्वभाववक्राण्यलकानि तासां). **2** Curls on the fore-head. **3** Saffron besmeared on the body. **—का** **1** A girl from eight to ten years of age. **2** N. of the capital of Kubera, and of the lord of the Yakshas; विभाति यस्यां ललितालकायां मनोहरा वैश्रवणस्य लक्ष्मीः Bv. 2. 10; गंतव्या ते बसतिरलका नाम यक्षेश्वराणां Me. 7.- Comp. **-अधिपः,-पतिः, -ईश्वरः** 'lord of Alakâ', N. of Kubera; अल्पजीवदमरालकेश्वरौ R. 19. 15.**—अंतः** the end of a curl or ringlet. **—नंदा** **1** N. of the Ganges, or a river falling into it.**-2** a girl from eight to ten years of age. **—प्रभा** N. of the capital of Kubera. **-संहतिः** *f.* rows of curls; *Si.* 6. 3.

अलक्तः-क्तकः The red resin of certain trees, red lac or sap (formerly used by women to dye certain parts of their body, particularly the soles of the feet and lip); (दंतवाससा) चिरोज्झितालक्तकपाटलेन Ku. 5. 34, M. 3. 5; अलक्तकांकां पदवीं ततान R. 7. 7; स्त्रियो हृतार्थाः पुरुषं निरर्थं निष्पीडितालक्तकवत्त्यजंति Mk. 4. 15. -Comp. **—रसः** red lac, juice; अलक्तरसरक्ताभावलक्तरसवर्जितौ। अद्यापि चरणौ तस्याः पद्मकोशसमप्रभौ Râm. **-रागः** the red colour of *alakta*.

अलक्षण *a.* **1** Having no signs or marks. **2** Undefined, undistinguished. **3** Having no good marks, inauspicious, illomened; क्लेशावहा भर्तुरलक्षणाहम् R. 14. 5. **—णं** **1** A bad or inauspicious sign. **2** That which is no definition, a bad definition.

अलक्षित *a.* Unseen, unobserved; अलक्षिताभ्युत्पतनो नृपेण R. 2. 27.

अलक्ष्मीः *f.* Evil fortune, bad luck, poverty.

अलक्ष्य *a.* **1** Invisible, unknown, unobserved. **2** Unmarked. **3** Having no particular marks. **4** Insignificant in appearance. **5** Having no pretence, free from fraud. **6** Not लक्ष्य or secondary (as meaning). -Comp. **-गति** *a.* moving invisibly. **-जन्मता** unknown birth, obscure origin; वपुर्विरूपाक्षमलक्ष्यजन्मता Ku. 5. 72. **-लिंग** *a.* disguised, *incognito* **-वाच्** *a.* addressing words to no visible object; Ku. 5. 57.

अलगर्दः A water-serpent.

अलघु *a.* (**घु-घ्वी** *f.*) **1** Not light, heavy, big. **2** Not short, long (in prosody). **3** Serious, solemn. **4** Intense, violent, very great. **-Comp.**

–उपलः a rock. –प्रतिज्ञ *a.* solemnly pledged or promised.

अलंकरणं 1 Decoration, ornamenting. 2 An ornament (lit. and fig.); सृजति तावदशेषगुणाकरं पुरुषरत्नमलंकरणं भुवः Bh. 2. 92.

अलंकरिष्णु *a.* 1 Fond of ornaments. 2 Decorating, skilled in decorating.

अलंकारः 1 Decoration, act of decorating or ornamenting. 2 An ornament (fig. also); अलंकारः स्वर्गस्य V. 1. 3 A figure of speech, of which there are three kinds:–शब्द°, अर्थ°, and शब्दार्थ°. 4 The whole science of Rhetoric.–Comp. –शास्त्रं the science and art of rhetoric, poetics.—सुवर्णं gold used for ornaments.

अलंकारकः Ornament, decoration; Ms. 7. 220.

अलंकृतिः *f.* 1 Decoration. 2 An ornament; कर्णालंकृति Amaru. 13. 3 A rhetorical ornament, a figure of speech; तददोषौ शब्दार्थौ सगुणावनलंकृती पुनः क्वापि K. P. 1; यो विद्वान् मन्यते काव्यं शब्दार्थावनलंकृती । असौ न मन्यते कस्मादनुष्णमनलं कृती ॥ Chandr. 1; सालंकृतिः श्रवणकोमलवर्णराजिः Bv. 3. 6 (where अ° has senses 2 and 3).

अलंक्रिया Adorning, ornamenting, decoration (fig. also).

अलंघनीय *a.* Insurmountable, inaccessible, beyond the reach of.

अलजः A kind of bird.

अलंजरः, –जुरः An earthen jar.

अलम् *ind.* 1 (*a*) Enough, sufficient for, adequate to (with dative or inf.); तस्यालमेषा क्षुधितस्य तृप्त्यै R. 2. 39; अन्यथा प्रातराशाय कुर्याम त्वामलं वयम् Bk. 8. 98. (*b*) A match for, equal to (with dat.); दैत्येभ्यो हरिरलं Sk.; अलं मल्लो मल्लाय Mbh. 2 Able, competent (with inf.); अलं भोक्तुं Sk.; वरेण शमितं लोकानलं दग्धुं हि तत्तपः Ku. 2. 56; with loc. also; त्रयाणामपि लोकानामलमस्मि निवारणे Ram. 3 A way with, enough of, no need of, no use of (having a prohibitive force), with instr. or gerund; अलमन्यथा गृहीत्वा M. 1. 20; आलप्यालमिदं बभ्रोर्यत्स दारानपाहरत् *Si.* 2. 40; अलं महीपाल तव श्रमेण R. 2. 34; Ku. 5. 82; अलमियद्भिः कुसुमैः *S.* 4 so many flowers will do. 4 (*a*) Completely, thoroughly; अर्हस्येनं शमयितुमलं वारिधारासहस्रैः Me. 53; त्वमपि विततयज्ञः स्वर्गिणः प्रीणयालम् *S.* 7. 34. (*b*) Greatly, excessively, to a high degree; तुदंति अलम् K. 2; यो गच्छत्यलं विद्विषतः प्रति Ak. –Comp. –कर्मीण *a.* competent to do any act; skilful, clever. –कृ see under कृ. –जीविक *a.* sufficient for livelihood. –धन *a.* possessing sufficient wealth, rich; निरादिष्टधनश्चेत्तु प्रतिभूः स्यादलंधनः Ms. 8. 162. –धूमः thick smoke, volume of smoke. –पुरुषीण *a.* fit for a man or sufficient for a man. –बल *a.* strong enough, having sufficient power. –बुद्धिः sufficient sense. –भूष्णु *a.* able, competent; विनाप्यस्मदलंभूष्णुरिज्यायै तपसः सुतः Si. 2. 9.

अलंपट *a.* Not libidinous, chaste. –टः Women's apartments.

अलंबुषः 1 Vomiting. 2 The palm of the hand with the fingers extended.

अलय *a.* 1 Houseless, moving about. 2 Without destruction or loss, imperishable. –यः 1 Non-destruction; permanence. 2 Birth, production.

अलर्कः 1 A mad dog or one rendered furious. 2 N. of a plant (श्वेतार्क).

अलले *ind.* A word of no import, occurring in the dialect of the pis'achas (mostly used in dramas).

अलवालं A basin for water at the root of a tree; see आलवाल.

अलस् *a.* Not shining.

अलस *a.* 1 Inactive, without energy, lazy, indolent. 2 Tired, fatigued, languid; मार्गश्रमादलसशरीरे दारिके M. 5; Amaru. 4, 90; V. 3. 2; गमनमलसं Mâl. 1. 17. 3 Soft, gentle. 4 Slow, dull (as in gait or motion); श्रोणीभारादलसगमना Me. 82. –Comp. –ईक्षणा a woman with languishing looks.

अलसक *a.* Indolent, idle. –कः Flatulence.

अलातः–तं A fire-brand, half-burnt wood; निर्वाणालातलाघवं Ku. 2. 23.

अलाबुः–बूः *f.* The bottle-gourd. –बु (*n.*) 1 A vessel made of gourd. 2 A fruit of the gourd which is very light and floats in water; किं हि नामैतत् अंबुनि मज्जंत्यलाबूनि ग्रावाणः प्लवंत इति Mv. 1; Ms. 6. 54. –Comp. –कटं the dust or down (रजः) of the bottle-gourd. –पात्रं a jar made of the bottle-gourd.

अलारं A door.

अलिः 1 A black bee. 2 A scorpion. 3 A crow. 4 The (Indian) cuckoo. 5 Spirituous liquor. –Comp. –कुलं a flight or number of bees. °संकुल full of a swarm of bees; अलिकुलसंकुलकुसुमनिराकुलनवदलमालतमाले Git. 1. °संकुलः the *kubja* plant. –जिह्वा,–ह्विका the uvula, soft palate. –प्रिय *a.* pleasing to the bees. (–यः) the red lotus. (–या) the trumpet flower. –माला a flight of bees. –विरावः,–रुतं song or hum of a bee. –वल्लभः=°प्रिय q. v.

अलिकं The forehead; अलिकेन च हेमकांतिना Bv. 2. 171; Vb. 3. 6.

अलिन् *m.* 1 A scorpion. 2 A bee; मलिनिमाऽलिनि माधवयोषिताम् *Si.* 6. 4. –नी 1 A swarm of bees; अरमतालिनी शिलींध्रे *Si.* 6. 72; अलिनीजिष्णुः कचानां चयः Bh. 1. 5.

अलिगर्दः A kind of snake.

अलिंग *a.* 1 Having no characteristic marks, having no marks. 2 Having bad marks. 3 (In gram.) Having no gender.

अलिंजरः A water-jar; see अलंजर.

अलिंदः 1 A terrace before a house-door; मुखालिंदतोरणं M. 5. 2 A place (like a square) at the door.

अलिपकः 1 A cuckoo. 2 A bee. 3 A dog.

अलिमकः =अनिमक q. v.

अलिंपक–बक see अनिमक.

अलीक *a.* 1 Unpleasing, disagreeable. 2 Untrue, false, pretended; अलीककोपकतिन K. 147; °वचन Amaru. 23, 33, 43. –कं 1 The forehead. 2 Falsehood, untruth.

अलीकिन् *a.* 1 Disagreeable, unpleasant. 2 False, deceiving.

अलुः A small water-pot.

अलुक्, °**समासः** A compound in which the case terminations are not dropped, but retained; *e. g.* सरसिज, आत्मनेपद.

अले } *ind.* Unmeaning words in
अलेले } the dialect of the Pis'achas chiefly introduced in plays.

अलेपक *a.* Stainless. –कः An epithet of the Supreme Spirit.

अलोक *a.* 1 That which cannot be seen, as in लोकालोक इवाचलः R. 1. 68 (न लोक्यत इत्यलोकः Malli.). 2 Having no people. 3 One who does not go to any other world after death (not having performed meritorious deeds). –कः,–कं 1 Not the world. 2 End or destruction of the world; absence of people; रक्ष सर्वानिमाँल्लोकान् नालोकं कर्तुमर्हसि Râm. –Comp. –सामान्य *a.* extraordinary, uncommon.

अलोकनं Invisibility, disappearance.

अलोल *a.* 1 Tranquil, unagitated. 2 Firm, steady. 3 Not fickle. 4 Not thirsty, free from desire.

अलोलुप *a.* 1 Free from desire. 2 Not greedy or covetous, indifferent to sensual objects.

अलौकिक *a.* (–की *f.*) 1 Not current in the world, uncommon, supernatural. 2 Unusual, rare. 3 Not current in the usual language, peculiar to the sacred writings, not used in classics, Vedic. 4 Theoretical; °त्वं rare occurrence of a word; अलौकिकत्वादमरः स्वकोषे न यानि नामानि समुल्लिलेख । विलोक्य तैरप्यधुना प्रचारमयं प्रयत्नः पुरुषोत्तमस्य Trik.

अल्प *a.* 1 Trifling, unimportant, insignificant (opp. महत् or गुरु); Ms. 11. 36. 2 Small, little, minute, scanty (opp. बहु); अल्पस्य हेतोर्बहु हातुमिच्छन् R. 2. 47; 1. 2. 3 Mortal, of short existence. 4 Seldom, rare. –ल्पं,–ल्पेन, –ल्पात् *adv.* 1 A little. 2 For a slight reason; प्रीतिरल्पेन भिद्यते Ram. 3 Easily, without much trouble or difficulty. –Comp. –अल्प *a.* very little or minute, little by little. –असु °=प्राण q. v. –आकांक्षिन् *a.* desiring little, contented or satisfied with little. –आयुस् *a.* shortlived; Ms. 4. 157. (–युः *m.*) 1 a young one, cub. –2 a goat. –आहार,

आहारिन् *a.* eating little, moderate in diet. (-रः) moderation, abstinence in food. -इतर *a.* 1 other than small, large. -2 other than few, many; as °राः कल्पनाः many or various ideas. -ऊन *a.* slightly defective, not quite complete. -उपायः small means. -गंध *a* having little scent or odour. (-धं) a red lotus.-चेष्टित *a.* inert.-छद्,-छाद *a.* scantily clad; Mk. 1. 37. -ज्ञ *a.* knowing little, shallow, superficial. -तनु *a.* 1 dwarfish, short. -2 weak, thin. -दृष्टि *a.* narrow-minded, short-sighted. -धन *a.* not affluent or rich, poor; Ms. 3. 66; 11. 40. -धी *a.* weak-minded, foolish. -प्रजस् *a.* having few descendants or subjects. -प्रमाण, -प्रमाणक *a.* 1 of little weight or measure 2 of little authority, resting on little evidence. -प्रयोग *a.* of rare application or use, rarely used. -प्राण-असु *a.* having short breath, asthmatic. (-णः) 1 slight breathing or weak aspiration. -2 (in gram.) a name given to the unaspirated letters of the alphabet, *i. e.* the vowels, semivowels, nasals and the letters क् च् ट् त् प् ग् ज् ड् द् ब्. -बल *a.* weak, feeble, having little strength. -बुद्धि -मति *a.* weak-minded silly, ignorant; Ms. 12. 74.-भाषिन् *a.* taciturn. -मध्यम *a.* slender waisted. -मात्रं a little, a little merely. -मूर्ति *a.* small-bodied, dwarfish. (-र्तिः *f.*) a small figure or object. -मूल्य *a.* of small value, cheap. -मेधस् *a.* of little understanding, ignorant, silly. -वयस् *a.* young in age, youthful. -वादिन् *a.* taciturn. -विद्य *a.* ignorant, uneducated. -विषय *a.* of limited range or capacity; क्व चाल्पविषया मतिः R. 1. 2. -शक्ति *a.* weak, feeble. -सरस् *n.* a basin, a small pond (one which is shallow or dry in hot season).

अल्पक *a.* (ल्पिका *f.*) 1 Small, little. 2 Contemptible, mean.

अल्पंपच *a.* Cooking little, stingy, niggardly. -चः A miser.

अल्पशः *ind.* 1 In a low degree, slightly, a little; बहुशो ददाति अभ्युदयिकेषु, अल्पशः श्राद्धेषु P. V. 4. 42 Com. 2 Seldom, now and then.

अल्पित *a.* 1 Diminished. 2. Lowered in estimation, disparaged; मृषा न चक्रेऽल्पितकल्पपादपः N. 1. 15.

अल्पिष्ठ *a.* Least, smallest, very small.

अल्पीकृ 8 U. To make small, diminish, reduce in number.

अल्पीयस् *a.* Smaller, less; very small.

अल्ला A mother (Voc. अल्ल).

अव् 1 P. [अवति, अवित or ऊत] 1 To protect, defend; यमवतामवतां च धुरि स्थितः R. 9. 1; प्रत्यक्षाभिः प्रपन्नस्तनुभिरवतु वस्ताभिरष्टाभिरीशः *S.* 1 1. 2 To please, satisfy, give pleasure to; विक्रमस्तेन मामवति माजिते त्वयि R. 11. 75; न मामवति सद्वीपा रत्नसूरपि मेदिनी 1. 65. 3 To like, wish, desire. 4 To favour, promote. (In the Dhâtupâṭha several other meanings are assigned to this root, but they are very rarely used in classical literature).

अव *ind.* (the initial अ is sometimes dropped, as in पूर्वापरौतोयनिधी वगाह्य Ku. 1. 1) 1 (As a preposition) Away, off, away from, down. 2 (As a prefix to verbs) It expresses (*a*) determination; अवधृ; (*b*) diffusion, pervasion; अवकॄ; (*c*) disrespect; अवज्ञा; (*d*) littleness; व्रीहीनवहंति; (*e*) support, resting upon; अवलम्ब्; (*f*) purification, अवदात; (*g*) depreciation, discomfiture; अवहंति शत्रून् (पराभवति); (*h*) commanding; अवक्लृप्; (*i*) depression, bending down; अवतॄ, अवगाह्; (*j*) knowledge; अवगम्, अवइ. 3 As the first member of Tat. compounds it means अवकुष्ट; अवकोकिलः=अवकुष्टः कोकिलया Sk.

अवकट *a.* 1 Downwards; backwards. 2 Opposite, contrary. —टं Contrariety, opposition.

अवकरः Dust, sweepings.

अवकर्तः A part cut off, a strip.

अवकर्तनं Cutting off, stripping &c.

अवकर्षणं 1 Putting out, extraction. 2 Expulsion.

अवकलित *a.* 1 Seen, observed. 2 Known. 3 Taken, received.

अवकाशः 1 Occasion, opportunity; ताते चापद्वितीये वहति रणधुरां को भयस्यावकाशः Ve. 3. 5; oft. used with लभ् in the sense of 'to get an opportunity or scope for action'; लब्धावकाशोऽविध्यन्मां तत्र दग्धो मनोभवः Ks. 1. 41. 2 (*a*) Place, space, room; अवकाशं किलोदन्वाचामायाभ्यर्थितो ददौ R. 4. 58; so अन्यमवकाशमवगाहे V. 4; यथावकाशं नी to take to its proper place, R. 6. 14; अस्माकमस्ति न कथंचिदिहावकाशः Pt. 4. 8; अवकाशो विविक्तोयं महानद्योः समागमे Râm. (*b*) Footing; admission, access, entrance; (छाया) शुद्धे तु दर्पणतले सुलभावकाशा *S.* 7. 32; oft. used in these senses with लभ्; लब्धावकाशो मे मनोरथः *S.* 1; शोकावेगदूषिते मे मनसि विवेक एव नावकाशं लभते Prab.; also with कृ or दा 'to make room for', 'admit', 'give way to'; असौ हि दत्वा तिमिरावकाशं Mk. 3. 6; तस्माद्वेयो विपुलमतिभिर्नावकाशोऽधमानां Pt. 1. 366; अवकाशं रुध् to obstruct, hinder or impede; नयनसलिलोत्पीडरुद्धावकाशां (निद्रां) Me. 91. 3 Interval, intermediate space or time. 4 An aperture, opening.

अवकीर्णिन् *a.* Violating the vow or engagements of continence. —*m.* (—र्णी) A religious student who has committed an act of incontinence (such as sexual intercourse) against his vow of celibacy; अवकीर्णी भवेद्गत्वा ब्रम्हचारी तु योषितम्। गर्दभं पशुम लभ्य नैर्ऋतं स विशुध्यति॥ Y. 3. 280; Ms. 3 155.

अवकुंचनं Bending, curving, contraction.

अवकुंठनं 1 Investing, surrounding. 2 Attracting, engaging.

अवकुंठित *a.* 1 Invested, surrounded, 2 Attracted.

अवकृष्ट *p. p.* 1 Pulled down. 2 Removed. 3 Expelled, turned out or away. 4 Inferior, low, degraded, outcast (opp. उत्कृष्ट or प्रकृष्ट). —ष्टः A servant who performs the lowest menial duties (such as sweeping &c.) (संमार्जनशोधनविनियुक्त); पणो देयोऽवकृष्टस्य षडुत्कृष्टस्य वेतनं Ms. 7. 126.

अवक्लृप्तिः *f.* 1 Considering as possible, possibility, probability; क्वेव भोक्ष्यसे अनवक्लृप्तावेव Sk. (अनवक्लृप्तिरसंभावना). 2 Suitableness.

अवकेशिन् *a.* Unfruitful, barren (as a tree).

अवकोकिल *a.* Drawn or called down to by a cuckoo.

अवक्र *a.* Not crooked; (fig.) honest, upright.

अवक्रंद *a.* Crying slowly; roaring, neighing —दः A cry.

अवक्रंदनं Crying out, weeping aloud.

अवक्रमः Descending, descent.

अवक्रयः 1 Price. 2 Wages, hire, farm, rent. 3 Letting out to hire, leasing. 4 A tax or tribute (to be paid to the king), duty (राजग्राह्यं द्रव्यं Sk.)

अवक्रांतिः *f.* 1 Descent. 2 Approach.

अवक्रिया Omission, neglect.

अवक्रोशः 1 Discordant noise. 2 A curse. 3 Abuse, censure.

अवक्लेशः 1 Trickling, descent of moisture. 2 Ichor.

अवक्लेदनं Trickling, falling (as of dew or moisture).

अवक्वणः A discordant note.

अवक्वाथः Imperfect digestion or decoction.

अवक्षयः Destruction, decay, waste, loss.

अवक्षयणं Means of extinguishing (fire &c.)

अवक्षेपः 1 Blaming, reviling. 2 Objection.

अवक्षेपणं 1 Throwing down, considered as one of the five kinds of *karman*, q. v. 2 Contempt, despising. 3 Censure, blame. 4 Overcoming, subduing. —णी Rein, bridle.

अवखंडनं Dividing, destroying.

अवखातं A deep ditch.

अवगणनं 1 Disobedience, contempt, disregard. 2 Censure, blame. 3 Insult, mortification.

अवगंडः A boil or pimple upon the face or cheeks.

अवगतिः *f.* 1 Knowledge, perception, comprehension. 2 True or determinate knowledge; ब्रह्मावगतिर्हि पुरुषार्थः; ब्रह्मावगतिस्त्वप्रतिज्ञाता S. B.

अवगमः-गमनं 1 Going near; descending. 2 Understanding, perception, knowledge.

आवगाढ *p. p.* 1 Plunged into, entered into, immersed; अमृतहृदमिवावगाढोऽस्मि *S.* 7. 2 Depressed, low, deep (lit. and fig.); अभ्युन्नता पुरस्तादवगाढा जघनगौरवात्पश्चात् *S.* 3. 8. 3 Congealed, curdling (as blood).

अवगाहः,-हनं 1 Bathing; सुभगसलिलावगाहाः *S.* 1. 3; सदावगाहक्षमवारिसंचयः Rs. 1. 1. 2. Plunging, immersing (in general) entering into; परदेशावगाहनात् H. 3. 95; जलावगाहक्षणमातशांता R. 5. 47; दग्धानामवगाहनाय विधिना रम्यं सरो निर्मितं *S.* Til. 1. 3 (fig) Mastering, learning. 4 A place of bathing.

अवगीत *p. p.* 1 Sung in a discordant tone, sung badly. 2 Reproached, abused, censured. 3 Wicked, vile. 4 Satirized in song. **—तं** 1 Satire in song, derision. 2 Reproach, blame.

अवगुणः A fault, defect, demerit; अन्यदोषं परावगुणं Malli. on Ki. 13. 48.

अवगुंठनं 1 The act of covering the head of women; hiding, veiling. 2 A veil (for the face); (fig. also); अवगुंठनसवीता कुलजाभिसरेय्यदि S. D.; कृत शीर्षावगुंठनः Mu. 6. 3 A covering, mantle (in general).

अवगुंठनवत् *a.* Covered with a veil, veiled; °वती नारी *S.* 5.

अवगुंठिका 1 Veiling, covering. 2 A veil. 3 A curtain.

अवगुंठित *p. p.* Veiled, covered, concealed; रजनीतिमिरावगुंठिते Ku. 4. 11.

अवगुरणं-गोरणं Menacing, assaulting with intent to kill, assailing with weapons.

अवगूहनं 1 Hiding, concealing. 2 Embracing.

अवग्रहः 1 Separation of the component parts of a compound, or of other grammatical forms. 2 The mark or interval of such a separation. 3 A hiatus, absence of sandhi (as in धिक् तां च तं च मदनं च इमां च मां च instead of चेमां च) Bh. 2. 2. 4 The mark (ऽ) used to mark the elision of अ after ए and ओ. 5 Withholding of rain, drought, failure of rain; वृष्टिर्भवति शस्यानामवग्रहविशोषिणां R. 1. 62; 10. 48; नभोनभस्ययोर्वृष्टिमवग्रह इवांतरे 12. 29; वृषेव सीतां तदवग्रहक्षतां Ku. 5. 61. 6 An obstacle, impediment. 7 A herd of elephants. 8 The forehead of an elephant. 9 Nature, original temperament 10 Punishment (opp. अनुग्रह). 11 An imprecation, a term of abuse.

अवग्रहणं 1 An obstacle, impediment 2 Disrespect, disregard.

अवग्राहः 1 Breaking, separation. 2 Impediment. 3 A curse; see अवग्रह.

अवघट्टः 1 A hole in the ground, a cave, a cavern. 2 A grind-stone, stone-mill for grinding corn. 3 Stirring up, shaking.

अवघर्षणं 1 Rubbing into. 2 Rubbing off. 3 Grinding.

अवघातः 1 Striking. 2 Hurting, killing. 3 A violent or sharp blow, a stroke or blow in general; कर्णावघातनिपुणेन च ताड्यमाना दूरीकृताः करितरेण...भंगाः Nîtipr. 2. 4 Threshing corn by bruising it with a pestle in a mortar.

अवघूर्णनं Rolling or whirling round.

अवघोषणं-णा 1 Proclaiming 2 A proclamation.

अवघ्राणं The act of smelling at.

अवचन *a.* Not speaking, silent, speechless; शकुंतला साध्वसादवचना तिष्ठति *S.* 1. **—नं** 1 Absence of assertion, silence, taciturnity. 2 Censure, blame, reproof; °**कर** *a.* disobedient.

अवचनीय *a.* 1 Not to be spoken or uttered, obscene or indecent (language); वादेष्ववचनीयेषु तदेव द्विगुणं भवेत् Ms. 8. 269. 2 Not censurable, not blamable, free from censure; लोकैरवचनीया भवति Mk. 2; °**ता** impropriety of speech, freedom from censure; सर्वथा व्यवहर्तव्ये कुतो ह्यवचनीयता U. 1. 5.

अवच(चा)यः Gathering (such as flowers, fruits &c.); ततः प्रविशत कुसुमावचयमभिनयंत्यौ सख्यौ *S.* 4; अविरतकुसुमावचायखेदात् *Si.* 7. 71.

अवचारणं Employing, application, mode of proceeding.

अवचूडः-लः The pendent cloth on a chariot, an ornament (like a *chowri*) hanging from the top of a banner; पिच्छावचूडमनुमाधवधाम जग्मुः *Si.* 5. 13; दिवसकरवारणरयावचूलचामरकलापः K. 26.

अवचूर्णनं 1 Pounding, grinding, reducing to powder. 2 Sprinkling with powder; especially, throwing absorbent powders on wounds.

अवचूल=अवचूड q. v.

अवचूलकः,-कं A *chowri* or brush for fanning off flies.

अवच्छ (च्छा) दः A cover, covering; कांचनावच्छदान् (खरान्) Râm.

अवच्छिन्न *p. p.* 1 Cut off. 2 Separated, divided, detached. 3 (In Logic) Separated or excluded from all other things by the properties predicated of a thing as peculiar to itself. 4 Bounded; modified, determined; दिक्कालाद्यनवच्छिन्न Bh. 2. 1. 5 Particularized, distinguished, characterized, as by an attributive word.

अवच्छुरित *a.* Mixed. **— तं** A horse-laugh.

अवच्छेदः 1 A part, portion. 2 Boundary, limit. 3 Separation. 4 Distinction, distinguishing, particularization, (as by attributes). 5 Determination, decision, settlement, शब्दार्थस्यानवच्छेदे विशेषस्मृतिहेतवः Vâk. P. 6 That property of a thing which distinguishes it from every thing else, a characteristic property. 7 Bounding, defining.

अवच्छेदक *a.* 1 Separating. 2 Determining, deciding. 3 Bounding. 4 Distinguishing, particularizing. 5 Peculiar, characteristic. **—कः** 1 That which distinguishes. 2 A predicate, characteristic, property.

अवजयः Defeat; victory over; येनेंद्रलोकावजयाय दृतः R 6 62. **अवजितिः** *f.* Conquest, defeat. **अवज्ञा** Disrespect, contempt; low opinion; disregard (with the obj. in loc. or gen.); आत्मन्यवज्ञां शिथिलीचकार R. 2. 41; ये नाम केचिदिह नः प्रथयंत्यवज्ञां Mâl. 1. 6.–Comp. **—उपहत** *a.* treated with contempt, humiliated. **—दुःखं** the agonies of humiliation; मा जीवन् यः परावज्ञादुःखदग्धोपि जीवति *Si.* 2 45.

अवज्ञानं Disrespect, contempt.

अवटः 1 A hole, cavity. 2 A pit; अवटे चापि मे राम प्रक्षिपेमं कलेवरं, अवटे ये निधीयंते Râm. 3 A well. 4 Any low or depressed part of the body, sinus; अवटश्चैवमेतानि स्थानान्यत्र शरीरके Y. 3. 98. 5 A juggler. –Comp. **–कच्छपः** a tortoise in a hole; (fig.) one who has had no experience, who has seen nothing of the world.

अवटिः, – टी *f.* 1 A hole. 2 A well.

अवटीट *a.* Having a flat nose, flat-nosed.

अवटुः 1 A hole in the ground. 2 A well. 3 The back or nape of the neck. 4 The depressed part of the body. **–टुः** *f.* The raised portion of the neck. **–टु** *n.* A hole, a rent.

अवडीनं The flight of a bird, flying down-wards.

अवतंसः-सं 1 A garland. 2 An earing, a ring-shaped ornament, an ear-ornament (fig. also); गणा नमेरुप्रसवावतंसाः Ku. 1. 55; स्ववाहनक्षोभचलावतंसाः 7. 38; R. 13. 49. 3 An ornament worn on the head, crest; (fig.) any thing that serves as an ornament; तामरसावतंसा जलसंनिवेशाः Chât. 2. 3; पुंडरीकावतंसाभिः परिखाभिः Râm. पुष्पावतंसं सलिलं Susr.

अवतंसक: An ear-ornament; an ornament in general.

अवतंसयति Den. P. To use as earring, make ear-rings of; अवतंसयंति दयमानाः प्रमदाः शिरीषकुसुमानि *S.* 1. 4.

अवततिः *f.* Stretching, extending.

अवतप्त *p. p.* Heated, irradiated; अवतप्तेनकुलस्थितं an ichneumon's standing on hot ground (metaphorically said of the inconstancy of man) अवतप्तेनकुलस्थितं त एतत् Sk.

अवतमसं 1 Slight or dim darkness क्षीणेऽवतमसं तमः Ak. 2 Darkness (ii.

general); अवतमसभिदायै भास्वताभ्युद्गतेन *Si.* 11. 57 (where Malli. says यद्यपि क्षीणेऽवतमसं तमः इत्युक्तं तथापि इह विरोधाद्विशेषतादरेण सामान्यमेव ग्राह्यं).

अवतरः Descent; N. 3. 53; *Si*. 1. 43.

अवतरणं 1 Descending for bathing in water &c., descending (in general), coming down. 2 An incarnation; see अवतार. 3 Crossing. 4 A holy bathing place. 5 Translating from one language into another. 6 Introduction. 7 An extract, a quotation.

अवतरणिका 1 A short prayer at the beginning of a work which, it is supposed, causes the divinity so addressed to descend from heaven. 2 Introduction, preface.

अवतरणी Preface

अवतर्पणं A soothing remedy.

अवताडनं 1 Crushing, trampling or treading under; नैसर्गिकी सुरभिणः कुसुमस्य सिद्धा मूर्ध्नि स्थितिर्न चरणैरवताडनानि U. 1. 14. 2 Striking.

अवतानः 1 Stretching. 2 The unbending of a bow. 3 A cover (in general.)

अवतारः 1 Descent; advent, setting in वसंतावतारसमये *S*. 1. 2 Form, manifestation; मत्स्यादिभिरवतारैरवतारवतावताऽवता-सुधां *S*ankara. 3 Descent of a deity upon earth, incarnation in general; कोप्येष संप्रति नवः पुरुषावतारः U. 5. 34; धर्मार्थकाममोक्षाणामवतार इवांगवान् R. 10. 84. 4 An incarnation of Vishnu; विष्णुर्येन दशावतारगहने क्षिप्तो महासंकटे Bh. 3. 95. (There are ten incarnations of Vishnu; the following verse from Git. describes them; वेदानुद्धरते जगन्निवहते भूगोलमुद्बिभ्रते दैत्यं दारयते बलिं छलयते क्षत्रक्षयं कुर्वते । पौलस्त्यं जयते हलं कलयते कारुण्यमातन्वते म्लेच्छान्मूर्च्छयते दशाकृतिकृते कृष्णाय तुभ्यं नमः ॥ मत्स्यः कूर्मो वराहश्च नरसिंहोथ वामनः । रामो रामश्च कृष्णश्च बुद्धः कल्की च ते दश ॥. 5 Any new appearance, growth, rise; नवावतारं कमलादिवोत्पलम् R. 3. 36; 5. 24. 6 A landing-place. 7 A sacred bathing-place. 8 Translation. 9 A pond, tank. 10 Introduction, preface.

अवतारक *a*. (**-रिका** *f*.) 1 Making one's appearance. 2 Making a descent.

अवतारणं 1 Causing to descend. 2 Translation. 3 Possession by an evil spirit. 4 Worship, adoration. 5 Preface or introduction (to a work).

अवतीर्ण *p p*. 1 Descended, alighted. 2 Bathed in. 3 Crossed, passed over; अपि नामावतीर्णोसि बाणगोचरं Mal. 1.

अवतोका A woman or a cow miscarrying from accident.

अवत्क्विन् *a*. One who divides or cuts off; पंच° dividing into five parts.

अवदंशः Any pungent food which excites thirst, stimulant.

अवदाघः 1 Heat. 2 The hot season.

अवदात *a*. 1 Beautiful; अवदातकांतिः Dk. 107. 2 Clean, pure, spotless, polished; सर्वविद्यावदातचेताः K. 36. 3 Bright, white; रजनिकरकलावदातं कुलं K. 233; कुंदावदाताः कलहंसमालाः Bk. 2. 18. 4 Virtuous, meritorious; अन्यस्मिन्न् जन्मनि न कृतमवदातं कर्म K. 62. 5 Yellow. **—तः** White or yellow colour.

अवदानं 1 A pure or approved occupation. 2 An accomplished act. 3 A valorous or glorious act, heroic act, heroism, glorious achievement-संगीयमानत्रिपुरावदानः Ku. 7. 48; प्रापदस्त्रम्; वदानतोषितात् R. 11. 21. 4 Object of a legend. 5 Cutting into pieces.

अवदारणं 1 Tearing, dividing, digging down, cutting into pieces. 2 A spade, hoe.

अवदाहः Heat; burning down.

अवदीर्ण *p p*. 1 Divided, broken. 2 Melted, fused. 3 Bewildered.

अवदोहः 1 Milking. 2 Milk.

अवद्य *a*. 1 Fit to be condemned, censurable, not to be praised; न चापि काव्यं नवमित्यवद्यं M. 1. 2. 2 Defective, faulty, blamable, disagreeble, disliked; उदवहदनवद्यां तामवद्यादपेतः R. 7. 70; see अनवद्य also. 3 Unfit to be told. 4 Low, inferior. **—द्यं** 1 A fault, defect, imperfection. 2 Sin, vice. 3 Blame, censure, reproach; उदवहदनवद्यां तामवद्याद-पेतः R. 7. 70.

अवद्योतनं Light.

अवधानं 1 Attention; अवधानपरे चकार सा प्रलयांतोन्मिषिते विलोचने Ku. 4. 2; intentness, attentiveness; दत्तावधानः शृणोति hears attentively. 2 Devotion, care, carefulness; अवधानात् carefully or attentively; शृणुत जना अवधानात् क्रियामिमां कालिदासस्य V. 1. 2. v. 1.

अवधारः Accurate determination, limitation.

अवधारक *a*. Determining accurately.

अवधारण *a*. Restrictive, limiting. **—णं, -णा** 1 Ascertainment, determination. 2 Affirmation, emphasis. 3 Limitation (of the sense of words); यावदवधारणे, एवावधारणे; मात्रं कार्त्स्न्येऽवधारणे Ak. 4 Restriction to a certain instance or instances to the exclusion of all others

अवधिः Application, attention. 2 Boundary; limit exclusive or inclusive, (in time or space); end, termination; स्मरशापावधिदां सरस्वतीं Ku. 4. 43; conclusion; oft. at the end of comp., in the sense of 'ending with,' 'as far as', 'till'; एष ते जीविताविधिः प्रवादः U. 1. 3 Period of time, time; R. 16. 52; शेषान् मासान् विरहदिवसस्थापितस्यावधेर्वा Mc. 87. यदवधि-तवधि from or ever since-till. 4 An engagement. 5 appointment. 6 A division, district, department. 7 A hole, pit.

अवधीर् 10 P. To disregard, disrespect, slight; अवधीरितसुहृद्वचनस्य H. 1; to despise, repulse.

अवधीरणं Treating with disrespect.

अवधीरणा Disrespect, repulse; कृतवत्यसि नावधीरणामपराद्धेऽपि यदा चिरं मयि R. 8. 48; M. 3. 19; अयं स ते तिष्ठति संगमोत्सुको विशंकसे भीरु यतोवधीरणां *S*. 3. 14.

अवधूत *p p*. 1 Shaken, waved. 2 Discarded, rejected, despised; R. 19. 43. 3 Insulted, humiliated. **—तः** An ascetic who has renounced all worldly attachments and connections; यो विलंघ्याश्रमान्वर्णानात्मन्येव स्थितः पुमान् । अतिवर्णाश्रमी योगी अवधूतः स उच्यते ॥ or अक्षरत्वात् वरेण्यत्वात् धुतसंसारबंधनात् । तत्त्वमस्यर्थसिद्धत्वाद-वधूतोऽभिधीयते ॥.

अवधूननं 1 Shaking, waving. 2 Agitation, trembling. 3 Disregarding.

अवध्य *a*. Inviolable, sacred, exempt from death.

अवध्वंसः 1 Abandoning, quitting. 2 Powder, dust. 3 Disrespect, censure, blame. 4 Falling off or form. 5 Sprinkling.

अवनं 1 Protection, defence; Nalod. 1. 4. 2 Gratifying, pleasing. 3 Wish, desire. 4 Delight, satisfaction.

अवनत *p*. *p*. 1 Bent down, downcast; विनय°, प्रश्रय°. 2 Setting. 3 Bending, stooping.

अवनति *f*. 1 Bending, bowing down, stooping; अवनातिमवनेः Mu. 1. 2; *Si*. 9. 8. 2 Declining in the west, setting. 3 A bow, prostration. 4 Bending (as a bow); धनुषामवनतिः K. (where अ° also means 'stooping'). 5 Modesty, humility.

अवनद्ध *p*. *p*. 1 Formed, made. 2 Fixed, seated; bound on, tied; fastened, put together. **—द्धं** A drum.

अवनम्र *a*. Bowed, bent; पर्याप्तपुष्पस्तबकावनम्रा Ku. 3. 54; पाद° fallen at the feet.

अवन (ना) यः 1 Throwing down. 2 Causing to descend.

अवनाट *a*. Flat-nosed.

अवनामः 1 Bending or bowing, falling at the feet. 2 Causing to bend down.

अवनाहः Binding, girding, putting on.

अवनिः-नी *f*. 1 The earth. 2 A figure. 3 A river. —Comp. **-ईशः, ईश्वरः, -नाथः, -पतिः, -पालः** lord of the earth, king ; पतिरवनिपतीनां तैश्चकाशे चतुर्भिः R. 10. 86, 11. 93. **-चर** *a*. roving over the earth, vagabond. **-ध्रः** a mountain. **-तलं** the surface of the earth. **-मंडलं** the globe. **-रुहः, -द्** a tree.

अवनेजनं 1 Washing, ablution ; न कुर्याद्गुरुपुत्रस्य पादयोश्चावनेजनम् Ms. 2. 209. 2 Water for washing, foot-bath. 3

Sprinkling water on the *darbha* grass at a Srâddha ceremony.

अवंतिः -ती *f.* 1 N. of a city, the modern उज्जयिनी, one of the seven sacred cities of the Hindus, to die at which is said to secure eternal happiness; cf. अयोध्या मथुरा माया काशी कांचिरवंतिका । पुरी द्वारावती चैव सप्तैता मोक्षदायिकाः ॥. The women of Avanti are said to be very skilful in all erotic arts; cf. आवंत्य एव निपुणाः सुदृशो रतकर्मणि B. R. 10. 82. 2 N. of a river.—*m.* (pl.) N. of a country identified with the modern Ma'lva', and its inhabitants; its capital being उज्जयिनी on the river सिप्रा; and there is also the temple of महाकाल in the suburbs; अवंतिनाथोऽयमुदग्रबाहुः R. 6. 32; असौ महाकालनिकेतनस्य वसन्नदूरे किल चंद्रमौलेः 6. 34, 35; प्राप्यावंतीनुदयनकथाकोविदग्रामवृद्धान् Me. 30; अवंतीष्वुज्जयिनी नाम नगरी K. 52. -COMP.-**पुरं** the city of Avanti, उज्जयिनी.

अवंध्य *a.* Not barren, fruitful, productive.

अवपतनं Alighting, descending.

अवपाक *a.* Badly or ill cooked. -**कः** Bad cooking.

अवपातः 1 Falling down; अधश्चरणावपातं Bh. 2. 31 falling down at the feet; (fig.) cringing. 2 Descent descending. 3 A hole, pit. 4 Particularly, a hole or pit for catching elephants; अवपातस्तु हस्त्यर्थे गर्ते छन्ने तृणादिना Yadava; रोधासि निघ्नन्नवपातमग्नः करीव वन्यः परुषं ररास R. 16. 78.

अवपातनं Felling, knocking down, throwing down.

अवपात्रित *a.* One who has lost his caste, a person not allowed by his kindred to eat in a common vessel; see अपपात्रित.

अवपीडः 1 Pressing down, pressure. 2 A kind of medicinal drug used to cause sneezing, sternutatory.

अवपीडनं 1 The act of pressing down. 2 A sternutatory. -**ना** Damage, violation.

अवबोधः 1 Waking, becoming awake (opp. स्वप्न); यौ तु स्वप्नावबोधौ तौ भूतानां प्रलयोदयौ Ku. 2. 8; Bg. 6. 17. 2. Knowledge, perception; स्वभर्तृनामग्रहणाद्बभूव सांद्रे रजस्यात्मपरावबोधः R. 7. 41; 5. 64; प्रतिकूलेषु तैक्ष्ण्यस्यावबोधः क्रोध इष्यते S. D. 3 Discrimination, judgment. 4 Teaching, informing.

अवबोधक *a.* Indicating, showing; -**कः** 1 The sun. 2 A bard. 3 A teacher.

अवबोधनं Knowledge, perception.

अवभंगः Humbling, overcoming, defeating.

अवभासः 1 Splendour, lustre, light. 2 Knowledge, perception. 3 Appearance, manifestation, inspiration. 4 Space, reach, compass. 5 False knowledge.

अवभासक *a.* Luminous. -**कं** The Supreme spirit.

अवभुग्न *p. p.* Contracted, bent, crooked.

अवभृथः 1 Bathing at the end of a principal sacrifice for purification; भुवं कोष्णेन कुंडोध्नी मेध्येनावभृथादपि R. 1. 84; 9. 22; 11. 31; 13. 61. 2 The water of purification. 3 A supplementary sacrifice to atone for defects in a principal and preceding one; a sacrifice in general; स्नातवत्यवभृथे ततस्त्वयि Si. 14. 10.-COMP. -**स्नानं** ablution after a sacrificial ceremony.

अवभ्रः Abduction, carrying off.

अवभ्रट *a.* Flat-nosed.

अवम *a.* 1 Sinful. 2 Contemptible, mean. 3 Base, low, inferior (opp. परम); अनलकानलकानवमां पुरीं R. 9. 14, see अनवम. 4 Next, intimate. 5 Last, youngest.

अवमत *p. p.* Despised, contemned &c. -COMP.-**अंकुशः** a restive elephant (that disdains the hook), one in rut; अन्वेतुकामोऽवमतांकुशग्रहः Si. 12. 16.

अवमतिः *f.* 1 Disregard, disrespect. 2 Aversion, dislike.

अवमर्दः 1 Trampling upon. 2 Devastation, oppression.

अवमर्शः Touch, contact.

अवमर्षः 1 Consideration investigation. 2 One of the five principal parts or *sandhis* of a play; यत्र मुख्यफलोपाय उद्भिन्नो गर्भतोऽधिकः । शापाद्यैः सांतरायश्च सोऽवमर्ष इति स्मृतः S. D. 366; also written विमर्ष. 3 Attacking.

अवमर्षणं 1 Intolerance, impatience. 2 Effacing, obliterating, banishing from recollection.

अवमानः Disrespect, contempt, disregard.

अवमाननं,-ना Disrespect, contempt.

अवमानिन् *a.* Contemning, despising, slighting; धिङ्मामुपस्थितश्रेयोवमानिनं S. 6; अयि आत्मगुणावमानिनि S. 3.

अवमूर्धन् *a.* With one's head hanging down. -COMP. -**शय** *a.* lying with the head hanging down, such as man (opp. देव); उत्तानशया देवा अवमूर्धशया मनुष्याः

अवमोचनं Setting at liberty, letting go, loosening.

अवयवः 1 A limb (of the body); मुखावयवलूनां तां R. 12. 43, Amaru. 40, 46; a member (in general); कस्मिंश्चिदपि जीवति नंदान्वयावयवे Mu. 1. 2 A part, portion (as of a whole). 3 A member or a component part of a logical argument or syllogism. (These are five:—प्रतिज्ञा, हेतु, उदाहरण, उपनय and निगमन). 4 The body. 5 A component, constituent, ingredient (in general), as of a compound &c. -COMP. -**अर्थः** the meaning of the component parts of a word.

अवयवशः *a. ind.* Part by part, severally, piece-meal.

अवयविन् *a.* Having limbs, having portions or subdivisions (as a whole). -*m.* (**वी**) 1 A whole. 2 A syllogism, or any logical agreement.

अवर *a.* 1 (*a*) Younger in years); मासेनावरः=मासावरः Sk. (*b*) Later; posterior, hinder (in time or space); यदवरं कौशांब्याः, यदवरमाग्रहायण्याः Sk. 2 Following, succeeding. 3 Below, lower, inferior, less. 4 Mean, unimportant, worst, lowest (opp. उत्तम); अध्यंग्यमवरं स्मृतं K. P. 1; दूरेण ह्यवरं कर्म बुद्धियोगाद्धनंजय Bg. 2. 49; श्रद्दधानः शुभां विद्यामाददीतावरादपि Ms. 2. 238. 5 Last (opp. प्रथम); सामान्यमेषां प्रथमावरत्वं Ku. 7. 44. 6. Least; usually as the last member of comp. with numerals; त्र्यवरैः साक्षिभिर्भाव्यः Ms. 8. 60. त्र्यवरा परिषद् ज्ञेया 12. 112; Y. 2. 69. 7 Western. —**रं** The hind thigh of an elephant (also °रा). -COMP. -**अर्धः** 1 the least part, the minimum.-2 the last half. -3 the hinder part of the body. -**अवर** *a.* lowest, most inferior of all; न हि प्रकृष्टान् प्रेष्यांस्तु प्रेषयंत्यवरावरान् Râm. -**उक्त** *a.* named last. —**ज** *a.* younger, junior. (-**जः**) 1 a younger brother. -2 a Sûdra. (-**जा**) a younger sister; विदर्भराजावरजा R. 6. 58, 84; 12. 32. -**वर्ण** *a.* belonging to a low caste or tribe. (-**र्णः**) 1 a Súdra -2 the last or fourth tribe. —**वर्णकः**, -**वर्णजः** a Súdra. -**व्रतः** the sun. -**शैलः** the western mountain (behind which the sun is supposed to set).

अवरतः *ind.* Behind, afterwards, hinder, posterior.

अवरतिः *f.* 1 Stopping; cessation. 2 Repose, relaxation, rest.

अवरीण *a.* Degraded, debased, despised.

अवरुग्ण 1 Broken, torn. 2 Diseased.

अवरुद्धिः *f.* 1 Obstruction, restraint. 2 Besieging. 3 Gaining.

अवरूप *a.* Ugly, deformed.

अवरोचकः Loss of appetite.

अवरोधः 1 Hindrance, obstruction. 2 Restraint; अंतः प्राणावरोध Mk. 1. 1. 3 Inner apartments or women's apartments, harem, seraglio; निन्येविनीतैरवरोधदक्षैः Ku. 7. 73; °गृहेषु राज्ञः S. 5. 3, 6. 11. 4 The wives of a king taken collectively (oft. pl.); अवरोधे महत्यपि R. 1. 32, 4. 68, 87, 6. 48, 16. 58. 5 An enclosure, confinement. 6 Siege, blockade. 7 A covering. 8 A fence, a pen. 9 A watchman. 10 Depression, hollow.

अवरोधक *a.* 1 Impeding. 2 Besieging. **—कः** A guard. **—कं** A barrier, fence.

अवरोधः 1 A siege, blockade. 2 Hindering. 3 An obstacle, impediment. 4 The inner or women's apartments in a royal palace; राजावरोधनवधूरवतारयंतः *Si.* 5. 18.

अवरोधिक *a.* Obstructive, impeding. **—कः** A guard of the queen's apartments. **—का** A female of the inner apartments; ययुस्तुरंगाधिरुहोऽवरोधिकाः *Si.* 12. 20.

अवरोधिन् *a.* 1 Obstructing, hindering. 2 Besieging.

अवरोपणं 1 Uprooting. 2 Causing to descend. 3 Taking away, depriving; diminishing.

अवरोहः 1 Descent. 2 A creeping plant winding itself round a tree from the bottom to the top. 3 Heaven. 4 A pendent branch, as of the fig-tree (वट); अवरोहशताकीर्णं वटमासाद्य तस्थतुः Râm. 5 (In music) The descending scale of notes.

अवरोहणं 1 Alighting, descending. 2 Ascending

अवर्ण *a.* 1 Colourless. 2 Bad, low. **—र्णः** 1 Scandal, ill-repute, stigma, spot; सोढुं नतत्पूर्वमवर्णमीशे R. 14. 38. 2 Blame, censure; न चावदद्भर्तुरवर्णमार्या 57 spoke no ill words.

अवलक्ष *a.* (also written वलक्ष) White. **—क्षः** The white colour.

अवलग्न *a.* Clinging or adhering to, touching. **—ग्नः** The waist.

अवलंब 1 Hanging down. 2 Hanging on, dependence on (fig. also); तंतुजालावलंबाः Me. 70; कुनृपतिभवनद्वारसेवा° Bh. 1. 67. 3 A prop, stay, support (lit. and fig.); सावलंबगमना R. 19. 50 walking supported by others; संततिविच्छेदनिरवलंबानां *S.* 6; दैवेनेत्थं दत्तहस्तावलंबे Ratn. 1. 8. 4 Hence, a crutch or stick for support.

अवलंबनं 1 A prop, support, stay; अवलंबनाय दिनभर्तुरभून्न पतिष्यतः करसहस्रमपि *Si.* 9. 6; प्रस्थानविक्लवगतेरवलंबनार्थं *S.* 5. 3; मम पुच्छे करावलंबनं कृत्वोत्तिष्ठ H. 1. 2 Help, assistance.

अवलिप्त *p. p.* 1 Proud, arrogant, haughty. 2 Anointed, smeared.

अवलीढ *p. p.* 1 Eaten, chewed; दर्भैरर्धावलीढैः *S.* 1. 7. 2 Licked, lapped; touched (fig. also); नवयौवनावलीढावयवा Dk. 17 pervaded by youth; अस्त्रज्वालावलीढप्रतिबलजलधेरंतरौर्वायमाणे Ve. 3. 5 surrounded (on all sides). 3 Devoured, destroyed.

अवलीला 1 Sport, play, mirth. 2 Disrespect, contempt.

अवलुंचनं 1 Cutting off, tearing or pulling out; केश°. 2 Uprooting.

अवलुंठनं 1 Rolling or wallowing on the ground. 2 Robbing.

अवलेखः 1 Breaking, scraping or scratching off. 2 Anything scraped off.

अवलेखा 1 Rubbing. 2 Adorning the person.

अवलेपः 1 Pride, haughtiness; प्रियसंगमेष्वनवलेपमदः Si. 9. 51 (where अ° also means ointment); व्यक्तमानावलेपाः Mu. 3. 22. 2 Violence, attack, insult, outrage; किं भवतीनामसुरावलेपेनापराद्धं V. 1; ददृशे पवनावलेपजं सृजती बाष्पमिवांजनाविलं R. 8. 35. 3 Smearing, anointing. 4 Ornament (भूषा). 5 Union, association (संग)

अवलेपनं 1 Anointing. 2 Oil, any unctuous substance. 3 Union. 4 Pride.

अवलेहः 1 Licking, lapping. 2 An extract (as of Soma). 3 An electuary.

अवलेहिका=अवलेह (3).

अवलोकः 2 Seeing, beholding. 2 Sight.

अवलोकनं 1 Looking at, beholding, seeing; नो बभ्रुवुरवलोकनक्षमाः R. 11. 60. 2 Looking over, commanding a view of; दीर्घिकावलोकनगवाक्षगता M. 1. 2 Sight, eye. 4 A look, glance; योगनिद्रांतविशदैः पावनैरवलोकनैः R. 10. 14. 5 Looking out for, inquiry.

अवलोकित *p. p.* Seen &c. **—तं** A look, glance.

अववरकः 1 An aperture. 2 Window; see अपवरक.

अववादः 1 Censure. 2 Trust, confidence. 3 Disregard, disrespect. 4 Support, defendence on. 5 Evil report. 6 A command.

अवव्रश्चः A splinter, chip.

अवश *a.* 1 Independent, free. 2 Not compliant or docile, disobedient, self-willed. 3 Not subject to or swayed by; अवशो विषयाणां K. 45. 4 Not master of oneself, subject to the senses; Ku. 6. 95. 5 Dependent, helpless, powerless; कार्यते ह्यवशः Bg. 3. 5; कथमवशो ह्ययशोविषं पिबामि Mk. 10. 13.—Comp.—**इंद्रियचित्त** *a.* whose mind and senses are not held in subjection.

अवशंगमः Not submitting to another's will.

अवशातनं 1 Destroying, cutting or lopping off. 2 Withering, drying up.

अवशेषः Remnant, rest, remainder; वृत्तांत° M. 5 the rest of the story; in this sense usually in comp.; अर्ध° having only one half left, कथा° or नाम° one who survives only in narration or name, having only the name left behind; used figuratively for dead; see the words s. v.; सावशेषमिव भट्टिन्या वचनं M. 4 unfinished; शृणु मे सावशेषं वचः *S.* 2 hear me out, let me finish my speech.

अवश्य *a.* 1 Untameable, ungovernable. 2 Inevitable; अथमरणमवश्यमेव जंतोः Ve. 4. 4. 3 Indispensable, necessary.—Comp. **—पुत्रः** a son whom it is impossible to govern or teach.

अवश्यं *ind.* 1 Necessarily, inevitably; त्वामप्यस्रं नवजलमयं मोचयिष्यत्यवश्यं Me. 93. 2 Certainly, at all events, by all means, surely, of course; अवश्यं यातार श्चिरतरमुषित्वापि विषयाः Bh. 3. 16; तां चावश्यं दिवसगणनातत्परामेकपत्नीं (द्रक्ष्यसि) Me. 10, 61; अवश्यमेव most surely; if compounded with pot. pass. the final nasal is dropped; अवश्यपाच्य to be necessarily cooked; अवश्यकार्य to be necessarily done.

अवश्यंभाविन् *a.* Destined to take place, inevitable; अवश्यंभाविनो भावा भवंति महातापमि H. Pr. 28.

अवश्यक *a.* Necessary, inevitable, indispensable.

अवश्या Hoar-frost, a fog or mist.

अवश्यायः 1 Frost, dew. 2 Hoar-frost, white dew; अवश्यायावसिक्तस्य पुंडरीकस्य चारुतां U. 6. 29. 3 Pride.

अवश्रयणं Taking anything from off the fire (opp. अधिश्रयण); अधिश्रयणावश्रयणांतादिपूर्वापरीभूतो व्यापारकलापः पाकादिशब्दवाच्यः S. D. 2.

अवष्टब्ध *p. p.* 1 Supported; held, seized. 2 Hanging from or upon. 3 Near, contiguous. 4 Obstructed, stooped. 5 Bound, tied.

अवष्टंभः 1 Leaning, resting upon. 2 Support, prop; पक्षाभ्यामीषत्कृतावष्टंभः K. 34; खड्गलतावष्टंभनिश्चलः Mâl. 3; तत्कथमहं धैर्यावष्टंभं करोमि Pt. 1. 3 Haughtiness, pride. 4 A post, pillar. 5 Gold. 6 Commencement, beginning. 7 Stopping, staying. 8 Courage, resolute determination. 9 Paralysis, stupefaction.

अवष्टंभनं 1 Resting upon. 2 Supporting. 3 A post, pillar.

अवष्टंभमय *a.* (**यी** *f.*) Golden, made of gold, or as large as a post; रघोरवष्टंभमयेन पत्रिणा R. 3. 53 (अ° is usually rendered in the above manner, but from the immediate context, it should more properly mean 'full of dignified boldness', 'breathing defiance').

अवसक्त *p. p.* 1 Suspended from, placed. 2 In contact with, touching.

अवसक्थिका 1 A cloth girt round the legs and knees (by a person), when sitting on his hams; also, the act of girding round this cloth, or the posture itself; शयानः प्रौढपादश्च कृत्वा चैवावसक्थिकाम् Ms. 4 112. 2 (Hence) A wrapper, a girth or band in general.

अवसंडीनं The downward flight of birds in a body.

अवसथः 1 A dwelling place, habitation. 2 A village. 3 A school, college; see आवसथ.

अवसथ्यः A college, school.

अवसन्न *p. p.* 1 Sunk down (fig. also), drooping. 2 Ended, terminated, gone off; अवसन्नायां रात्रौ H. 1. 3 Lost, deprived of; R. 9. 77.

अवसरः 1 Occasion, opportunity, time; नास्यावसरं दास्यामि S. 2; भवद्गिरामवसरप्रदानाय वचांसि नः Si. 2. 8; विसर्जन° सत्कारः S. 7; °प्राप्त suited to the occasion M. 1. 2 (Hence) A fit or proper opportunity; शशंस सेवावसरं सुरेभ्यः Ku. 7. 40; अवसरोऽयमात्मानं प्रकाशयितुं S. 1; see अनवसर also. 3 Space, room, scope. 4 Leisure, advantageous position. 5 A year. 6 Raining. 7 Descent. 8 A consultatiou in private.

अवसर्गः 1 Letting off, relaxation. 2 Allowing one to follow one's inclinations. 3 Independence.

अवसर्पः A spy, a secret emissary.

अवसर्पणं Stepping or going down.

अवसादः 1 Sinking, fainting, sitting down. 2 Ruin, loss; विपदेति तावदवसादकरी Ki. 18. 23, 6. 41. 3 End, termination. 4 Want of energy, exhaustion, fatigue. 5 (In law) Badness of a cause, defeat, losing (a cause).

अवसादक *a.* 1 Causing to sink, faint, or fail. 2 Causing dejection or fatigue.

अवसादनं 1 Decline, loss. 2 Oppression. 3 Finishing.

अवसानं 1 Stopping. 2 Conclusion, termination, end; दोहावसाने पुनरेव दोग्ध्रीं R. 2. 23; तच्छिष्याध्ययननिवेदितावसानां 1. 95. 3 Death, decease; Ve. 5. 38; मूलपुरुषावसाने संपदः परमुपतिष्ठंति S. 6. 4 Boundary, limit 5 (In gram.) The last part of a world or period (opp. आदि). 6 A pause. 7 A place (स्थान); resting place, residence.

अवसायः 1 Conclusion, end, termination. 2 Remainder. 3 Completion. 4 Determination, resolution, decision.

अवसित *p. p.* 1 Finished, ended, completed; यूपवत्यवसिते क्रियाविधौ R. 11. 37; अवसितश्च पशुरसौ Dk. 91 it is all over with the brute; वचस्यवसिते तस्मिन्ससर्ज गिरमात्मभूः Ku. 2. 53 2 Known, understood 3 Resolved, determined, ascertained. 4 Stored, gathered (as grain) 5 Tied, fastened, bound.

अवसेकः Sprinkling, bedewing; देशः को नु जलावसेकशिथिलः Mk. 3. 12.

अवसेचनं 1 Sprinkling. 2 Water used for sprinkling; पाद° Ms. 4. 151. 3 Bleeding.

अवस्कंदः, -दनं 1 Attacking, attack, assault. 2 Descending. 3 A camp.

अवस्कंदिन् *a.* Attacking, assaulting; outraging.

अवस्करः 1 Ordure, excrement. 2 The privities (गुह्यदेश). 3 Dirt, sweepings (in general).

अवस्तरणं Spreading out.

अवस्तात् *ind.* 1 Below, from below, downwards. 2 Under.

अवस्तारः 1 A curtain. 2 A covering; a screen or wall of cloth round a tent. 3 A mat.

अवस्तु *n.* 1 A worthless thing or matter; अवस्तुनिर्बंधपरे कथं नु ते Ku. 5. 66. 2 Unreality (of matter), insubstantiality; वस्तुन्यवस्त्वारोपोऽज्ञानं.

अवस्था 1 State, condition, situation; स्वामिनो महत्यवस्था वर्तते Pt. 1 a critical state; तुल्यावस्थः स्वसुः कृतः R. 12. 80; तां तामवस्थां प्रतिपद्यमानं 13. 5; ईदृशीमवस्थां प्रपन्नोऽस्मि S. 5; Ku. 2. 6; oft. in comp.; **तदवस्थः** Pt. 5 reduced to that state. 2 Position, circumstance. 3 Period, stage (of life &c.); यौवन°; वयोवस्थां तस्याः शृणुत N'al. 9. 29. 4 Form, appearance. 5 Degree, proportion. 6 Stability, fixity, as in अनवस्थ q. v. 7 Appearance in a court of law. –COMP. **-अंतरं** another or altered state. **-चतुष्टयं** the four periods or states of human life; *i. e.* बाल्यं (childhood); कौमारं (youth); यौवनं (manhood); and वार्धकं (old age). **-त्रयं** the three states; *i. e.* जागृति (waking), स्वप्न (dreaming), and सुषुप्ति (sound sleep). **-द्वयं** the two states of life, *i. e.* सुखं and दुःखं (happiness and misery).

अवस्थानं 1 Standing, residing, dwelling. 2 Situation, position. 3 Residence, abode, place. 4 Period of staying.

अवस्थायिन् *a.* Staying, residing.

अवस्थित *p. p.* 1 Remained, stayed; &c. **एवमवस्थिते** K. 158 under these circumstances. 2 Firm of purpose, steady. 3 Resting with, dependent on.

अवस्थितिः *f.* 1 Abiding, dwelling. 2 Residence, abode.

अवस्यदनं Trickling, oozing.

अवस्रंसनं Dropping or falling down; a fall.

अवहतिः *f.* Beating, threshing.

अवहननं 1 Threshing, beating off rice; अवहननायोलूखलं Mbh. 2 The lungs; वपा वसावहननं Y. 3. 94 (अवहननं=फुप्फुसः Mit.).

अवहरणं 1 Taking away, removing. 2 Throwing away. 3 Stealing, plundering. 4 Re-delivery. 5 Temporary suspension of hostilities, truce.

अवहस्तः The back of the hand.

अवहानिः *f.* Loss.

अवहारः 1 A thief. 2 A shark. 3 Temporary cessation of hostilities, truce. 4 Summoning, inviting. 5 Apostacy. 6 Re-delivery, redeeming.

अवहारकः A shark.

अवहार्य *pot. p.* 1 To be taken away or removed. 2 Finable, punishable 3 Recoverable, redeemable.

अवहालिका A wall.

अवहासः 1 Smiling, a smile. 2 A jest, joke, ridicule; यच्चावहासार्थमसत्कृतोऽसि Bg. 11. 42.

अव (व) हित्था-त्थं 1 Dissimulation in general. 2 Dissimulation or concealment of an internal feeling, regarded as one of the 33 subordinate feelings (व्यभिचारिभाव); भयगौरवलज्जादेर्हर्षाद्याकारगुप्तिरवहित्था S. D.; or according to R. G. व्रीडादिना निमित्तेन हर्षाद्यनुभावानां गोपनाय जनितो भावविशेषोऽवहित्थं; for ex. see Ku. 6. 84, or Bv. 2. 80.

अवहेलः -ला Disrespect, contempt, disregard; अवहेलां कुटज मधुकरे मा गाः Bv. 1. 6.

अवहेलनं-ना Disregard.

अवाक् *ind.* 1 Downwards. 2 Southern, southward. –COMP. **-ज्ञानं** disrespect. **-भव** *a.* southern. **-मुख** *a.* (**खी** *f.*) 1 looking downwards; अवाङ्मुखस्योपरि पुष्पवृष्टिः R. 2. 60; 15. 78. -2 headlong. **-शिरस्** *a.* having the head hung downwards; स मूढो नरकं याति कालसूत्रमवाक्शिराः Ms. 3. 249, 8. 94.

अवाक्ष *a.* A gurdian, keeper.

अवाग्र *a.* Stooping; bowed.

अवाच् *a.* Speechless, dumb. —*n.* Brahma.

अवाच् or **अवांच्** *a.* 1 Turned downwards, stooping; कुर्वंतमित्यतिभरेण नगानवाचः Si. 6. 79. 2 Being or situated below, lower than (with abl.). 3 Headlong. 4 Southern. —*m*, *n.* Brahma.—**ची** 1 The south. 2 The lower region.

अवाचीन *a.* 1 Downward, headlong. 2 Southern. 3 Descended.

अवाच्य *a.* 1 Not proper to be addressed; अवाच्यो दीक्षितो नाम्ना यवीयानपि यो भवेत् Ms. 2. 128. 2 Improper to be uttered; vile, bad; अवाच्यं वदतो जिह्वा कथं न पतिता तव Ram; Bg. 2. 36. 3 Not distinctly expressed, not expressible in words. –COMP. **-देशः** 'the unspeakable place,' the vulva.

अवांचित *a.* Bent, low.

अवानः Breathing, inhaling.

अवांतर *a.* 1 Situated or standing between; see compounds. 2 Included, involved. 3 Subordinate, secondary. 4 Not closely connected, extraneous, extra. –COMP. **-दिश्, -दिशा** an intermediate quarter (such as the आग्नेयी, ऐशानी, नैर्ऋती and वायवी). **-देशः** a place situated between (two others), an intermediate region,

अवाप्तिः *f.* Obtaining, getting; तपः किलेदं तदवाप्तिसाधनं Ku. 5. 64.

अवाप्य *pot. p.* Attainable.

अवारः -रं 1 The near bank of a river. 2 This side. –COMP. **-पारः** the ocean. **-पारीण** *a.* 1 belonging to the ocean. -2 crossing a river.

अवारीण *a.* Crossing a river.

अवावटः The son of a woman by any man (of the same caste) other than her first husband; द्वितीयेन तु यः

पित्रा सवर्णायां प्रजायते । अवावट इति ख्यातः शूद्रधर्मा स जातितः ॥.

अवावन् *m.* A thief; stealing away.

अवासस *a.* Unclothed, naked. *-m.* N. of Buddha.

अवास्तव *a.* (वी *f.*) 1 Unreal. 2 Unfounded, irrational.

अविः 1 A sheep; (*f.* also in this sense); जीनकार्मुकवस्ताविन् Ms. 11. 139, 3. 6. 2 The sun. 3 A mountain. 4 Air, wind. 5 A woollen blanket, (of the skin of mice). 6 A blanket, shawl in general. 7 A wall, enclosure. 8 A rat. **—विः** *f.* 1 An ewe. 2 A woman in her courses. -Comp. **-कटः** a flock of sheep. **-कटोरणः** a kind of tribute (consisting of sheep).**-दुग्धं, दूसं, -मरीसं,-सोढं** the milk of an ewe. **-पटः** sheep's skin, a woollen cloth. **-पाद्ः** a shepherd **-स्थलं** sheep-place; N. of a town; अविस्थलं वृकस्थलं माकंदी वारणावतं Mb.

अविकः A sheep. **—का** An ewe. **-कं** A diamond.

अविता An ewe, a sheep.

अविकत्थ *a.* Not boasting or vaunting.

अविकत्थनं *a.* One who does not boast, not vaunting; विद्वांसोऽविकत्थना भवंति Mu. 3.

अविकल *a.* 1 Unimpaired, entire, perfect, whole, all; तानींद्रियाण्यविकलानि Bh. 2. 40; °लं फलं Me. 24, 34; °शरच्चंद्रमधुरः Mâl. 2. 11 full, full-orbed. 2 Regular, orderly; consistent, not discordant; कलमविकलतालं गायकैर्बोधहेतोः *Si.* 11. 10.

अविकल्प *a.* Unchangeable. **—ल्पः** 1 Absence of doubt. 2 Absence of option or alternative. 3 Positive act or precept. **-ल्पं** *ind.* Without doubt, unhesitatingly.

अविकार *a.* Immutable. **—रः** Immutability.

अविकृतिः *f.* 1 Absence of change. 2 (In Sân. phil.) The inanimate principle called प्रकृति, regarded as the material cause of the universe; मूलप्रकृतिरविकृतिः Sân. K.

अविक्रम *a.* Powerless, feeble. **—मः** Cowardice.

अविक्रिय *a.* Unchangeable, immutable. **—यं** Brahma.

अविक्षत *a.* Unimpaired, whole, entire; विक्रेतुः प्रतिदेयं तत्तस्मिन्नेवाह्न्यविक्षतम् Smriti.

अविग्रह *a.* Bodiless, incorporeal; epithet of the Supreme Being. **—हः** (In gram.) A compound the sense of which cannot be expressed by its constituent parts separately (नित्यसमास).

अविघात *a.* Unimpeded, unobstructed; °**गति** *a* unobstructed in one's course.

अविघ्न *a.* Unobstructed. **-घ्नं** Freedom from obstacle or impediment, welfare (this word is usually neuter, though विघ्न is *m.*); साधयाम्यहमविघ्नमस्तु ते R 11 19; अविघ्नमस्तु ते स्थेयाः पितेव धुरि पुत्रिणां 1. 91.

अविचार *a.* Void of judgment, ill-judging. **—रः** Absence of judgment, indiscretion.

अविचारित *a.* Ill-judged, not well thought out or considered. —Comp. **-निर्णयः** a prejudice, prejudiced opinion.

अविचारिन् *a.* 1 Inconsiderate, indiscreet. 2 Prompt.

अविज्ञातृ *a.* Not knowing.—*m.* (**ता**) The Supreme Being (परमेश्वर).

अविडीनं *a.* A direct flight of birds.

अवितथ *a.* 1 Not false, true; तदवितथमवादीर्यन्मम त्वं प्रियेति *Si.* 11. 33; अवितथा वितथा सखि मा गिरः 6. 18. 2 Realised, not fruitless. **—थं** Truth; अवितथमाह प्रियंवदा *S.* 3, P. is right, what P. says is right. **—थं** *ind.* Not falsely, according to truth; Ms. 2. 144.

अवित्यजः-जं Quicksilver.

अविदूर *a.* Not distant, near, contiguous. **—रं** Proximity. **—रं** *ind.* Near to, not far from; so अविदूरेण, आविदूरात्, -दूरतः,-दूरे.

अविद्य *a.* Not educated, foolish, unwise. **-द्या** 1 Ignorance, folly, want of learning. 2 Spiritual ignorance. 3 Illusion, illusion personified or Mâyâ (a term frequently occurring in Vedânta; by means of this illusion one perceives the universe, which does not really exist, as inherent in Brahma which alone really exists).

अविद्यामय *a.* Caused by ignorance or illusion.

अविधवा Not a widow, a married woman whose husband is still living; भर्तुर्मित्रं प्रियमविधवे विद्धि भामंबुवाहं Me. 99.

अविधा *ind.* An interjection meaning 'help, help' used in calling for help in danger.

अविधेय *a.* Unmanageable, adverse; विधेराविधेयतां Mu 4. 2.

अविनय *a.* Immodest, ill-behaved, ill-mannered. **—यः** 1 Want of good manners or modesty. 2 Rude behaviour, rudeness, immodest or rude act; अयमाचरत्यविनयं मुग्धासु तपस्विकन्यासु *S.* 1. 25; indecorum, impropriety of conduct. 3 Incivility, disrespect. 4 Offence, crime, fault. 5 Pride, arrogance, insolence; अविनयमपनय विष्णो Sankara.

अविनाभावः 1 Non-separation. 2 Inherent or essential character, inseparable connection. 3 Connection (in general); अविनाभावोऽत्र संबंधमात्रं न तु नांतरीयकत्वं K. P. 2.

अविनीत *a.* 1 Immodest, illbred. 2 Insolent, rude.

अविभक्त *a.* 1 Undivided, unpartitioned, joint, (as property of a family, or co-heirs). 2 Not broken, entire.

अविभाग *a.* Unpartitioned, undivided. **-गः** 1 Not dividing. 2 Undivided inheritance.

अविभाज्य *a.* Indivisible. **-ज्यं** 1 Indivisibility. 2 Not being liable to be partitioned; (said of certain articles which are not to be divided at the time of partition); *e. g.* वस्त्रं पात्रमलंकारं कृतान्नमुदकं स्त्रियः । योगक्षेमं प्रचारं च न विभाज्यं प्रचक्षते Ms. 9. 219. °ता indivisibility, unfitness for partition.

अविरत *a.* Not desisting or ceasing from (with abl); uninterrupted, continual, perpetual; आविरतोत्कंठमुत्कंठितेन Me. 102; Prov. मंदोप्यविरतोद्योगः सदैव विजयी भवेत् 'slow and steady wins the race.' **-तं** *ind.* Eternally, continually; अविरतं परकार्यकृतां सतां Bv. 1. 113.

अविरति *a.* Incessant. **-तिः** *f.* 1 Continuity, uninterruptedness. 2 Incontinence.

अविरल *a.* 1 Thick, dense; °वारिधारा U. 6. sharp-driving shower. 2 Contiguous. 3 Coarse; gross, substantial. 4 Uninterrupted, continuous. **-लं** *ind.* 1 Closely; अविरलमालिंगितुं पवनः *S.* 3. 7. 2 Uninterruptedly, constantly.

अविरोधः Consistency, compatibility; सामान्यास्तु परार्थमुद्यमभृतः स्वार्थाविरोधेन ये Bh. 2. 74 consistently with their own interest.

अविलंब *a.* Prompt. **-बः** Absence of delay, promptitude. **-बं, अविलंबेन** *ind.* Without delay, quickly.

अविलंबित *a.* Without delay, quick, expeditious, prompt.**-तं** *ind.* Quickly, without delay.

अविला An ewe.

अविवक्षित *a.* 1 Not intended or aimed at; भ्रातरः इत्यत्र एकशेषग्रहणमविवक्षितं. 2 Not to be said or spoken.

अविविक्त *a.* 1 Uninvestigated, not properly thought out. 2 Indiscriminate, confounded. 3 Public.

अविवेक *a.* Wanting in judgment, thoughtless.**—कः** 1 Want of discrimination or judgment, imprudence; अविवेकः परमापदां पदं Ki. 2. 30. 2 Hastiness, rashness.

अविशंक *a.* Having no fear or doubt, fearless. **—का** Absence of doubt or fear, confidence. **—कं, -अविशंकेन** *ind.* Without doubt, or hesitation.

अविशंकित *a.* 1 Unapprehensive, fearless. 2 Without doubt, confiding; गृध्रवाक्यात्कथं मूढास्त्यजध्वमविशंकिताः K. P.

अविशेष *a.* Without any difference, alike, similar **—षः, -षं** 1 Absence of difference, similarity. 2 Identity, sameness. -Comp. **-ज्ञ** *a.* not knowing the difference (in things), undiscriminating.

अविष *a.* Not poisonous. **—षः** 1 An ocean. 2 A king. **—षी** 1 A river. 2 The earth. 3 Heaven.

अविषय *a.* Unperceived, invisible. **—यः** 1 Absence, disappearance; रवेरविषये किं न प्रदीपस्य प्रकाशनं H. 2. 79. 2 Not an object of (anything), not within the reach of, beyond, transcending; न कश्चिद्धीमतामविषयो नाम *S.* 4; सकलवचनानामविषयः Mâl. 1. 30 beyond the reach (power) of words. 3 Disregard of the objects of sense.

अवी A woman in her courses.

अवीचि *a.* Waveless. **—चिः** N. of a particular hell.

अवीर *a.* 1 Unmanly, cowardly. 2 Having no son (as a woman). **—रा** A woman who has neither sons nor husband; अजातपुत्रा विधवा साऽवीरा परिकीर्तिता (opp. वीरा which is thus defined; पतिपुत्रवती नारी वीरा प्रोक्ता मनीषिभिः); अनार्चितं वृथा मांसमवीरायाश्च योषितः Ms. 4. 213.

अवृत्ति *a.* 1 Not existing, not being in. 2 Having no livelihood. **—त्तिः** *f.* 1 Absence of subsistence or means of livelihood, inadequate support; अवृत्तिकर्षिता हि स्त्री प्रदुष्येत् स्थितिमत्यपि Ms. 9. 74; 10. 101; आददीतामेवास्मादवृत्ताविकरात्रिकं 4. 223. 2 Absence of wages; °त्वं nonexistence.

अवृथा *ind.* Not in vain, successfully. -Comp. **-अर्थ** *a.* successful.

अवृष्टि *a.* Not pouring down rain (as a cloud). **—ष्टिः** *f.* Want of rain, drought.

अवेक्षक *a.* Inspecting, supervising; a superintendent.

अवेक्षणं 1 Looking towards or at, seeing. 2 Guarding, taking care of, attending to, supervision, inspection; वर्णाश्रमावेक्षणजागरूकः R. 14. 85. 3 Attention, care, observation. 4 Regarding, considering; see अनवेक्षणं.

अवेक्षणीय *pot. p.* To be looked to or respected, to be looked upon or considered; तपस्विसामान्यमवेक्षणीया R. 14. 67.

अवेक्षा 1 Seeing, looking at. 2 Attention, care, regard.

अवेद्य *a.* 1 Unknowable, secret. 2 Unattainable. **—द्यः** A calf.

अवेल *a.* 1 Having no boundary or limit, unlimited. 2 Untimely. **—लः** Concealment of knowledge. **—ला** Unfavourable time.

अवैध *a.* (**धी** *f.*) 1 Irregular not conformable to law or rule; अवैधं पंचमं कुर्वन् राज्ञो दंडेन शुध्यति. 2 Not sanctioned by the Sâstras.

अवैमत्यं Unanimity.

अवोक्षणं Sprinkling with the hand slightly bent; उत्तानेनैव हस्तेन प्रोक्षणं परिकीर्तितं । न्यंचताभ्युक्षणं प्रोक्तं तिरश्चावोक्षणं स्मृतं ॥.

अवोदः Sprinkling, moistening.

अव्यक्त *a.* 1 Indistinct, not manifest or apparent, inarticulate; °वर्ण indistinct accents *S.* 7. 17. 2 Invisible, imperceptible. 3 Undetermined; अव्यक्तोयमचिंत्योयं Bg. 2. 25; 8. 20. 4 Undeveloped, uncreated. 5 (In alg.) Unknown (as a quantity or number) **—क्तः** 1 N. of Vishṇu. 2 N. of *S*iva. 3 Cupid. 4 Primary matter which has not yet entered into real existence. 5 A fool. **-क्तं** (In Vedânta phil.) 1 Brahma. 2 Spiritual ignorance. 3 (In S'an. phil.) The primary germ of nature (सर्वकारण), the primordial element or productive principle from which all the phenomena of the material world are developed; बुद्धेरिवाव्यक्तमुदाहरंति R. 13. 60; महतः परमव्यक्तमव्यक्तात्पुरुषः परः Kath. 4 The soul. **—क्तं** *ind.* Imperceptibly, indistinctly. -Comp. **—अनुकरणं** imitating inarticulate or unmeaning sounds. **—आदि** *a.* whose beginning is inscrutable. **—क्रिया** an algebraic calculation. **-पद** *a.* inarticulate. **—मूलप्रभवः** the tree of mundane existence (in Sân. phil.). **—राग** *a.* dark-red, ruddy. (**-गः**) the colour of the dawn; **अव्यक्तरागस्त्वरुणः** Ak. **—राशिः** an unknown number or quantity (in algebra). **—लक्षणः**, **—व्यक्तः** epithets of *S*iva.**—वर्त्मन्**, **—मार्ग** *a.* whose ways are mysterious or inscrutable. **—वाच्** *a.* speaking indistincctly. **—साम्यं** an equation of unknown quantities.

अव्यग्र *a.* 1 Not agitated or ruffled, steady, cool. 2 Not engaged or occupied (in business).

अव्यंग *a.* Not mutilated or defective, well made, sound, perfect.

अव्यंजन *a.* 1 Having no distinctive or characteristic marks or signs (as of the sex); °ना कन्या. 2 Indistinct. **—नः** An animal without horns, though of an age to have them.

अव्यथ *a.* Free from pain. **—थः** A snake.

अव्यथिषः 1 The Sun. 2 The ocean. **—षी** 1 The earth. 2 Midnight; night.

अव्यभि (भी) चारः 1 Non-separation; अन्योन्यस्याव्यभीचारो भवेदामरणांतिकः Ms. 9 101. 2 Constancy, fidelity.

अव्यभिचारिन् *a.* 1 Not opposed or adverse, favourable; Ku. 6. 86. 2 Not subject to exceptions, true in all cases, without any instance to the contrary; यदुच्यते पार्वति पापवृत्तये न रूपमित्यव्यभिचारि तद्वचः Ku. 5. 39; रंध्रोपनिपातिनोऽनर्था इति यदुच्यते तदव्यभिचारि वचः *S.* 6, 3 Virtuous, moral, chaste. 4 Steady, permanent, faithful.

अव्यय *a.* 1 (*a*) Not liable to change, imperishable, immutable; वेदाविनाशिनं नित्यं य एनमजमव्ययं Bg. 2. 21; विनाशमव्ययस्यास्य न कश्चित्कर्तुमर्हति 17. (*b*) Eternal, everlasting; अश्वत्थं प्राहुरव्ययं Bg. 15. 1; अकीर्तिं कथयिष्यंति तेऽव्ययां 2. 34. 2 Unexpended, unwasted. 3 Economical. 4 Giving imperishable fruit. **—यः** 1 N. of Vishṇu. 2 N. of *S*iva. **—यं** 1 Brahma. 2 (In gram) An indeclinable particle &c.; सदृशं त्रिषु लिंगेषु सर्वासु च विभक्तिषु । वचनेषु च सर्वेषु यन्न व्येति तदव्ययम् ॥. -Comp. **-आत्मन्** *a.* of an imperishable or eternal nature. (**-त्मा**) the soul or spirit. **—वर्गः** the class of indeclinable words.

अव्ययीभावः 1 N. of one of the four principal kinds of compounds in Sanskrit, an adverbial or indeclinable compound (formed of an indeclinable, *i. e.* a preposition or an adverb, and a noun); अधिहरि, सतृणं &c. 2 Absence of expenditure (owing to poverty); द्वंद्वो द्विगुरपि चाहं मद्गहे नित्यमव्ययीभावः । तत्पुरुष कर्मधारय येनाहं स्यां बहुव्रिहिः ॥ Udb. (which, by the bye, gives the names of compounds in Sanskrit). 3 Imperishableness.

अव्यलीक *a.* 1 Not false, true. 2 Agreeable, having no disagreeable feelings (प्रिय); इत्थं गिरः प्रियतमा इव सोव्यलीकाः शुश्राव सूततनयश्च तदा व्यलीकाः *Si.* 5. 1.

अव्यवधान *a.* 1 Close, immediate; direct. 2 Open. 3 Not covered, bare. 4 Careless, inattentive. **—नं** Carelessness.

अव्यवस्थ *a* 1 Not fixed, moving, unstable; स्थलारविंदश्रियमव्यवस्थां Ku. 1 33. 2 Unsettled, indiscriminate, irregular.**—स्था** 1 Irregularity, deviation from established rule. 2 An incorrect opinion given on a point of religious or civil law.

अव्यवस्थित *a.* 1 Not conformable to law or practice. 2 Illregulated, fickle, unstable; अव्यवस्थितचित्तस्य प्रसादोपि भयंकरः Nîti 9. 3 Not in due order, unmethodical.

अव्यवहार्य *a.* 1 Not entitled to eat, drink, or commune in general with people of the same caste, excommunicated. 2 Not to be made the subject of litigation.

अव्यवहित *a.* Immediate, direct.

अव्याकृत *a.* 1 Not developed, not manifest; तद्धेदं तर्ह्यव्याकृतमासित्, इदं नामरूपाभ्यामव्याकृतं S. B. 2 Elementary. **—तं** (In Vedânta phil.) 1 An elementary substance from which all things were created (considered identical with Brahma). 2 (In Sân. phil.) The prime germ of nature (प्रधान).

अव्याजः-जं 1 Absence of guile or fraud, honesty. 2 Simplicity, artlessness; oft. in comp. with सुंदर, मनोहर &c. in the sense of 'artlessly', 'naturally'; इदं किलाव्याजमनोहरं वपुः *S.* 1. 18.

अव्यापक *a.* 1 Not comprehensive. 2 Not spread over or pervading the whole; special.

अव्यापार *a* Having no work, unemployed. **-रः** 1 Cessation from work. 2 A business not practised or understood. 3 Not one's own business; अव्यापारेषु व्यापारं कृ to meddle with affairs not one's own (which do not concern one).

अव्याप्ति *f.* 1 Inadequate extent or pervasion of a proposition. 2 Non-inclusion or exclusion of a part of the thing defined, one of the three faults of a definition; लक्ष्यैकदेशे लक्षणस्यावर्तनमव्याप्तिः.

अव्याप्य *a.* Not extending to the whole circumstances, not pervading the whole extent; वह्निर्धूमस्याव्याप्यः.-Comp. -**वृत्तिः** *f.* (In Vais. phil.) a category of limited application, partial inherence with regard to time or space, as pleasure, pain &c.; अव्याप्यवृत्तिः क्षणिको विशेषगुण इष्यते Bhâshâ P. 27.

अव्याहत *a.* Not broken or interrupted, unobstructed; obeyed; भर्तुरव्याहताज्ञा R. 19. 57.

अव्युत्पन्न *a.* 1 Not proficient, inexperienced, not practised, ignorant; अव्युत्पन्नो बालभावः K. 196. 2 Having no proper or regular derivation (as a word). -**न्नः** A person not versed in the grammar, idiom &c. of a language, a smattering or superficial linguist.

अव्रत *a.* Not observing (the prescribed) religious rites or obligations; अव्रतानाममंत्राणां जातिमात्रोपजीविनाम्। सहस्रशः समेतानां परिषत्त्वं न विद्यते ॥ Ms. 12. 114; 3. 170.

अश् I. 5 A. [अश्नुते, अशित-अष्ट] 1 To pervade, fill completely, penetrate; खं प्रावृषेण्यैरिव चानशेऽब्दैः Bk. 2. 30; Ki. 12. 21. 2 To reach, go or come to, arrive at, attain to; सर्वमानंत्यमश्नुते Y. 1. 260. 3 To get, obtain, enjoy, experience; अत्युत्कटैः पापपुण्यैरिहैव फलमश्नुते H. 1. 83; R. 9. 9; न वेदफलमश्नुते Ms. 1. 109 फलं दशोरानशिरे महिष्यः N. 6. 43. -With उप to obtain, enjoy, acquire; न च लोकानुपाश्नुते Mb.; क्रियाफलमुपाश्नुते Ms. 6. 82 -वि to fill completely, pervade, occupy; प्रतापस्तस्य भानोश्च युगपद् व्यानशे दिशः R. 4. 15; Bk. 9. 4, 14. 96. II. 9 P. (अश्नाति, अशित) 1 To eat, to consume; निवेद्य गुरवेऽश्नीयात् Ms. 2. 51; अश्नीमहि वयं भिक्षां Bh. 3. 117. 2 To taste, enjoy; यद्ददाति यदश्नाति तदेव धनिनो धनं H. 1. 164–65; अश्नंति दिव्यान् दिवि देवभोगान् Bg. 9. 20; प्रत्यक्षं फलमश्नंति कर्मणां Mb. -*Caus.* (आशयति) To feed, give to eat, cause to eat or drink (with acc. of person); आशयच्चामृतं देवान् Sk. -With प्र 1 to drink; न प्राश्नीतोदकमपि Mb -2 to eat, devour; प्राश्नन्नथ सुरामिषं Bk. 17. 3, 1. 13, 15. 29. -सं 1 to eat; नक्तं चान्नं समश्नीयात् Ms. 6. 19, 11 219. -2 taste, experience, enjoy; यथा फलं समश्नाति Mb.

अशकुनः-नं An inauspicious or bad omen.

अशक्तिः *f.* 1 Weakness, power-lessness. 2 Inability, incapacity; श्रमेण तदशक्त्या वा न गुणानामियत्तया R. 10. 32.

अशक्य *a.* Impossible, impracticable.

अशंक, अशंकित *a.* 1 Fearless, undaunted; प्रविशत्यशंकः H. 1. 81. 2 Secure, having no doubt.

अशनं 1 Pervasion, penetration. 2 The act of eating, feeding. 3 Tasting, enjoying. 4 Food; अशनं धात्रा मरुत्कल्पितं व्यालानां Bh. 3. 10; oft. at the end of adjective comp. in the sense of 'eating', 'one whose food is' &c.; फलमूलाशन, हुताशन, पवनाशन &c.

अशना Desire to eat, hunger.

अशनाया Hunger; च्युताशनायः फलवद्विभूत्या Bk 3. 40; अन्नाद्वाऽशनाया निवर्तते पानात्पिपासा Sat. Br.

अशनायित, अशनायुक *a* Hungry.

अशनिः *m.f.* 1 Indra's thunderbolt; शक्रस्य महाशनिध्वजं R. 3. 56. 2 Flash of lightning; अनुवनमशनिर्गतः Sk.; अशनिः कल्पित एष वेधसा R. 8. 47; अशनेरमृतस्य चोभयोर्वशिनश्चांबुधराश्च योनयः Ku. 4. 43 3 A missile. 4 The tip of a missile. -**निः** *m.* 1 Indra. 2 Fire. 3 Fire produced from lightning.

अशब्द *a.* Not expressed in words; किमर्थमशब्दं रुद्यते K. 60 inaudibly. -**ब्दं** 1 The 'inexpressible,' *i. e.* Brahm. 2 (In Sân. phil.) प्रधान or primary germ of nature; ईक्षतेर्नाशब्दं S. B.

अशरण *a.* Helpless, forlorn, destitute of refuge; बलवदशरणोस्मि *S.* 6; so अशरण्य.

अशरीर *a.* Bodiless, incorporeal. -**रः** 1 The Supreme Being, Brahma. 2 Cupid, the god of love. 3 An ascetic who has renounced all worldly connections.

अशरीरिन् *a.* Incorporeal, unearthly, heavenly; usually with words like वाणी, वाच् &c.

अशास्त्र *a.* Not conformable to sacred authority, heterodox. -Comp. -**विहित,-सिद्ध** *a.* not sanctioned or enjoined by scriptures.

अशास्त्रीय *a.* Unscriptural; illegal, immoral.

अशित *p. p.* 1 Eaten, satisfied. 2 Enjoyed.

अशितंगवीन Formerly grazed by cattle; see आशितंगवीन.

अशित्रः 1 A thief. 2 An oblation of rice.

अशिरः 1 The fire. 2 The sun. 3 Wind. 4 A demon. -**रं** A diamond.

अशिरस् *a.* Headless. -*m.* A body without head; a trunk.

अशिव *a.* 1 Inauspicious, causing or threatening mischief; अशिवा दिशि दीप्तायां शिवास्तत्र भयावहाः (रुरुवुः) Râm 2 Unlucky, unfortunate. -**वं** 1 Ill-luck, misfortune. 2 Mischief. —Comp. —**आचारः** 1 improper behaviour, rudeness of conduct. —2 conduct opposed to every (sacred) authority.

अशिष्ट *a.* 1 Ill-bred, rude. 2 Unrefined, barbarous, unworthy. 3 Atheistical, profane. 4 Not sanctioned by any recognized authority. 5 Not prescribed in any work of authority.

अशीत *a.* Not cold, hot. —Comp. —**करः, —रश्मिः** &c. the sun.

अशीतिः *f.* Eighty (used in the singular and fem. gender whatever be the noun it qualifies).

अशीर्षक *a.* =अशिरस् q. v.

अशुचि *a.* 1 Not clean, dirty, foul, impure; सोऽशुचिः सर्वकर्मसु; in mourning. 2 Black. —**चिः** *f.* 1 Impurity. 2 Degradation.

अशुद्ध *a.* 1 Impure. 2 Incorrect, wrong.

अशुद्धि *a.* 1 Impure, foul. 2 Wicked. -**द्धिः** *f.* Impurity, foulness.

अशुभ *a.* 1 Inauspicious. 2 Impure, foul (opp शुभ) 3 Unlucky, unfortunate. -**भं** 1 Inauspiciousness. 2 Sin. 3 Misfortune, calamity; नाथे कुतस्त्वय्यशुभं प्रजानां R. 5. 13. -Comp. -**उदयः** an inauspicious omen.

अशून्य *a.* 1 Not empty or vacant. 2 Not unattended to, fulfilled, executed; स्वनियोगमशून्यं कुरु (occurring frequently in dramas) execute or go about your business.

अशृत *a.* Uncooked, raw, unripe.

अशेष *a.* Without remainder, whole, entire, complete, perfect; अशेषशेमुषीमोषं माषमश्नामि केवलं Udb.; क्रतोरशेषेण फलेन युज्यता R. 3 65, 48. —**षः** Non-remainder. -**षं, अशेषेण, अशेषतः** *ind.* Wholly, entirely, completely; तथाविधस्तावदशेषमस्तु सः Ku. 5. 82; येन भूतान्यशेषेण द्रक्ष्यस्यात्मन्यथो मयि Bg. 4. 35, 10. 16; Ms. 1. 59.

अशोक *a.* Without sorrow; not feeling or causing sorrow. —**कः** N. of a tree having red flowers; (said, according to the convention of poets, to put forth flowers when struck by ladies with the foot decked with jingling anklets; cf. असूत सद्यः कुसुमान्यशोकः...पादेन नापेक्षत सुंदरीणां संपर्कमाशिंजितनूपुरेण Ku. 3 26; Me. 78; R. 8. 62; M. 3. 12, 16 2 N. of Vishṇu. 3 N. of a celebrated king of the Maurya dynasty.—**कं** 1 The blossom of the Asoka tree (forming one of the five arrows of Cupid). 2 Quicksilver. -Comp. -**अरिः** the कदंब tree. -**अष्टमी** the eighth day in the first half of *Chaitra*. -**तरुः,-नगः,-वृक्षः** the Asoka tree. -**त्रिरात्रः, -त्रं** N. of a festival or व्रत which lasts for three nights. -**वनिका** a grove of Asoka trees; °**न्याय** see under न्याय.

अशोच्य *a.* Not to be lamented or deplored; अशोच्यानन्वशोचस्त्वं प्रज्ञावादांश्च भाषसे Bg. 2. 11.

अशौचं 1 Impurity, dirtiness, foulness; Pt. 1. 195. 2 Defilement caused either by child-birth (called जनना

शौच) or by the death of some relation (called मृताशौच): अहोरात्रमुपासीरन्नशौचं बांधवैः सह Ms. 11. 184.

अश्नया Hunger.

अश्नीतपिबता Invitation to eat and drink, a feast where people are called to eat and drink; अश्नीतपिबतीयंती प्रस्तुता स्मरकर्मणि Bk. 5. 92.

अश्मकः (pl.) **1** N. of a country in the south. **2** The inhabitants of the country.

अश्मन् *m.* **1** A stone; नाराचक्षेपणीयाश्मनिष्पेषोत्पतितानलं R. 4. 77. **2** Flint. **3** A cloud. **4** A thunderbolt. –Comp.–**उत्थं** bitumen. **–कुट्ट, –कुट्टक** *a.* breaking anything on stones. (**–ट्टः,–ट्टकः**) a class of devotees; a वानप्रस्थ; Y. 3. 49; Ms. 6. 17. **–गर्भः,–र्भं,–गर्भजः,–जं, योनिः** an emerald. **–जः,–जं** 1 red-chalk. –2 iron **–जतु** *n.*, **–जतुकं** bitumen. **–जातिः** an emerald named पान्ना. **–दारणः** an axe or crow for breaking stones. **–पुष्पं** bitumen. **–भालं** a mortar of stone or iron. **–सार** *a* like iron or stone. (**–रः,–रं**) 1 iron. –2 sapphire.

अश्मंतं 1 A fire-place. **2** A field, plain. **3** Death.

अश्मंतकः-कं A fire-place.—**कः** N. of a plant from the fibres of which a Brâhmaṇa's girdle may be made.

अश्मरी (In medicine) A disease called *stone* (in the bladder), gravel.

अश्रः A corner, mostly at the end of comp. **–श्रं 1** A tear. **2** Blood (usually written अस्र q. v.). —Comp. **–पः** a blood-drinker, a fiend, cannibal.

अश्रवण *a.* Deaf, having no ears. **—णः** A snake.

अश्राद्ध *a.* Not performing the Srâddha- ceremony. —**द्धः** Non-performance of a Srâddha q. v. —Comp. **—भोजिन्** *a.* one who has vowed not to eat during the performance of a Srâddha ceremony.

आश्रांत *a.* **1** Unwearied, untired. **2** Incessant, continual. —**तं** *ind.* Incessantly, continually.

अश्रिः-श्री *f.* **1** A corner, angle (of a room, house &c.) (changed to अस्र at the end of comp with चतुर्, त्रि, षट् and a few other words; see चतुरस्र). **2** The sharp side or edge (of a weapon &c.); वृत्रस्य हंतुः कुलिशं कुंठिताश्रीव लक्ष्यते Ku. 2. 30. **3** The sharp side of anything.

अश्रीक-ल *a.* **1** Having no splendour, without beauty, pale; Si. 15. 96. **2** Unlucky, not prosperous.

अश्रु *n.* **A** tear; पपात भूमौ सह सैनिकाश्रुभिः R. 3. 61. —Comp. —**उपहत** *a.* affected by tears, covered with tears. **–कला** a tear-drop. **–परिपूर्ण** *a.* filled with tears. °**अक्ष** having eyes filled with tears.—**परिप्लुत** *a.* suffused with tears, bathed in tears. —**पातः** flow of tears, shedding tears. **—पूर्ण** *a.* filled with tears; °**आकुल** troubled and filled with tears; Rg. **2**. 1. **—मुख** *a.* suffused with tears, (suddenly) bursting into tears. **—लोचन, —नेत्र** *a.* with tears in the eyes, with tearful eyes.

अश्रुत *a.* **1** Unheard, inaudible. **2** Foolish, uneducated.

अश्रौत *a.* Not sanctioned by the Vedas.

अश्रेयस् *a.* **1** Not better, inferior. *–n.* (स्) Mischief, unhappiness.

अश्लील *a.* **1** Unpleasant, ugly. **2** Vulgar, obscene, coarse; अश्लीलप्रायान् कलकलान् Dk. 49; °परिवाद Y. 1. 33. **3** Abusive. **–लं 1** Rustic or coarse language, low abuse. **2** (In Rhet.) A fault of composition; using such words as produce in the mind of the hearer a feeling of shame, disgust, or inauspiciousness; *e. g.* in साधनं सुमहद्यस्य, मुग्धा कुड्मलिताननेन दधती वायुं स्थिता तत्र सा and मृदुपवनविभिन्नो मत्प्रियाया विनाशात् the words साधन, वायु, and विनाश are अश्लील, and produce respectively a sense of shame, disgust, and inauspiciousness, साधन suggesting the sense of लिंग (male organ of generation), वायु, of the अपान wind (that escaping at the anus), and विनाश, of मृत्यु (death).

अश्लेषा 1 The 9th Nakshatra or luner mansion containing five stars. **2** Disunion, disjunction. –Comp. **–जः, –भवः, –भूः** N. of Ketu, *i. e.* the descending node.

अश्वः 1 A horse. **2** A symbolical expression for the number 'seven'. **3** A race of men (horse-like in strength); काष्ठतुल्यवपुर्धृष्टो मिथ्याचारश्च निर्भयः । द्वादशांगुलमेढ्रश्च दरिद्रस्तु हयो मतः ॥. **–श्वौ** (du.) A horse and a mare. –Comp. **–अजनी** a whip, **–अधिक** *a.* strong in cavalry, superior in horses **–अध्यक्षः** commander of cavalry. **–अनीकं** cavalry. **–अरिः** a buffalo. **–आयुर्वेदः** veterinary science. **–आरोह** *a.* riding or mounted on a horse. (**–हः**) 1 a horseman, rider. –2 a ride. **–उरस** *a.* broad-chested like a horse. **–कर्णः, –कर्णकः** 1 a kind of tree. –2 the ear of a horse. **–कुटी** a stable for horses. **–कुशल,–कोविद** *a.* skilled in managing houses. **–खरजः** mule. **–खुरः** a horse's hoof. **–गोष्ठं** a stable. **–घासः** a pasture for horses **–चलनशाला** a riding-house. **–चिकित्सकः, –वैद्यः** a farrier, a veterinary surgeon. **–चिकित्सा** farriery, veterinary science. **–जघनः** a kind of centaur. **–दूतः** a riding messenger. **–नायः** one who has the charge of a drove of grazing horses; a horse-herd. **–निबंधिकः** a groom, a horse-fastener. **–पः** a groom. **–पालः, –पालकः, –रक्षः** a horse-groom **–बंधः** a groom. **–भा** lightning. **–महिषिका** the natural enmity between a horse and a buffalo. **–मुख** *a.* having the head or face of a horse. (**–खः**) a horse-faced creature; a Kinnara or celestial chorister. (**–खी**) a Kinnara woman; भिंदंति मंदां गतिमश्वमुख्यः Ku. 1. 11. **–मेधः** horse-sacrifice; यथाश्वमेधः क्रतुराट् सर्वपापापनोदनः **Ms. 11. 261. –मेधिक, –मेधीय** *a.* fit for a horse-sacrifice, or relating to it. (**–कः, –यः**) a horse fit for the *Asvamedha* sacrifice. **–युज्** *a.* having horses yoked to it (as a carriage). (*–f.*) 1 N. of a constellation, the head of Aries. –2 the first lunar mansion. –3 the month of Asvina. **–रक्षः** the keeper or rider of a horse, a groom. **–रथः** a carriage drawn by horses. (**–था**) N. of a river near गंधमादन. **–रत्नं, –राजः** the best or lord of horses; *i. e.* उच्चैःश्रवस्. **–लाला** a kind of snake. **–वक्त्र=** अश्वमुख q. v.; a Kinnara or Gandharva. **–वडवं** a stud of horses and mares. **–वहः** a horseman **–वारः, –वारकः** a horseman, groom. **–वाहः, –वाहकः** a horseman. **–विद्** *a.* 1 skilled in taming or managing horses. –2. procuring horses. (*–m.*) 1 a jockey. –2 an epithet of Nala. **–वृषः** a stallion. **–वैद्यः** a farrier. **–शाला** a stable. **–शावः** a colt, foal. **–शास्त्रं** a manual or text-book of veterinary science. **–शृगालिका** the natural enmity between a horse and a jackal. **–सादः –सादिन्** *m.* a horseman, a rider, a horse-soldier; R. **7**. **47**. **–सारथ्यं** coachmanship, charioteership, management of horses and chariots; सूतानामश्वसारथ्यं Ms. 10. 47. **–स्थान** *a.* born in a stable. (**–नं**) a stable or stall for horses. **–हारकः** a horse-stealer. **–हृदयं** 1 the desire or intention of a horse. –2 horsemanship.

अश्वक *a.* Horselike. **–कः 1** A small horse; horse. **2** A hack, a bad horse. **3** A horse (in general).

अश्वकिनी The first Nakshatra or lunar mansion (अश्विनी).

अश्वतरः (री *f.*) A mule.

अश्वत्थः The holy fig-tree; उर्ध्वमूलोऽवाक्शाख एषोऽश्वत्थः सनातनः Kath., Bg. 15. 1.

अश्वत्थामन् *m.* [cf. Mb. अश्वस्येवास्य यत्स्थाम नदतः प्रदिशो गतम् ॥ अश्वत्थामैव बालोयं तस्मान्नाम्ना भविष्यति ॥] N. of a celebrated Brâhmaṇa warrior and general on the side of the Kaurava kings, son of Droṇa and Kripî. [He is represented as a very brave, fiery-tempered, young warrior, the embodiment of Brâhma*n*ic and saintly lustre, and his altercation with Kar*n*a about the nomination of a general to succeed Dro*n*a clearly brings out the chief features of his character; see Ve. 3rd act. He is one of the 7 *Chirajivins* 'ever-living persons'].

अश्वस्तन, -स्तनिक *a.* 1 Not of to-morrow, of to-day 2 One makes no provision for the morrow; Ms. 4. 7.

अश्विक *a.* Drawn or carried by horses.

अश्विन् *m.* A cavalier, a horsetamer. **-नौ** (du.) The two physicians of the gods who are represented as the twin sons of the sun by a nymph in the form of a mare.

अश्विनी 1 The first of the 27 Nakshatras or luner mansions (consisting of three stars). 2 A nymph considered in later times as the mother of the Asvins, the wife of the sun, who concealed herself in the form of a mare. -Comp. **-कुमारौ, -पुत्रौ, -सुतौ** the twin sons of Asvinî, the sun's wife.

अश्वीय *a.* Belonging or relating to a horse, agreeable to horses. **-यं** A number of horses, cavalry: *Si.* 18. 5.

अषडक्षीण *a.* Not seen by six eyes, known or determined by two persons only. **-णं** A secret.

अषाढः The month Ashâḍha (usually written आषाढ q. v.)

अष्टक *a.* Consisting of 8 parts, eight-fold. **-कः** 1 One who studies or is acquainted with the eight books of Pâṇini's grammar. **-का** 1 A collection of three days (7th, 8th, 9th) beginning from the seventh day after the full moon. 2 The 8th day of three months on which the Manes are to be propitiated. 3 A *S*râddha ceremony to be performed on the above days. **-कं** 1 A whole consisting of 8 parts. 2 The 8 chapters of Pâṇini's Sûtras. 3 A division of the Ṛigveda (it being divided into 8 Ashṭakas or 10 Maṇḍalas). 4 Any group of eight; as वानराष्टकं, ताराष्टकं, गंगाष्टकं &c. 5 The number eight. -Comp. **-अंगः, -गं** a kind of board or cloth for playing with dice on (having eight divisions).

अष्टन् *num. a.* (nom. acc. अष्ट-ष्टौ) Eight. It often occurs in comp. as अष्टा with numerals and some other nouns; as अष्टादशन्, अष्टाविंशतिः, अष्टापद &c. -Comp **-अंग** *a.* consisting of eight parts or members. (**-गं**) 1 the eight parts of the body with which a very low obeisance is performed; °**पातः, -प्रमाणः, साष्टांगनमस्कारः** a respectful obeisance made by the prostration of the eight limbs of the body; (जानुभ्यां च तथा पद्भ्यां पाणिभ्यामुरसा धिया । शिरसा वचसा दृष्ट्या प्रणामोऽष्टांग ईरितः ।।). -2 the 8 parts of Yoga or concentraction. -3 materials of worship taken collectively. °**अर्घ्यं** an offering of eight articles. °**धूपः** a sort of medical incense removing fever. °**मैथुनं** 'sexual enjoyment of 8 kinds'; the eight stages in the progress of a love-suit; स्मरणं कीर्तनं केलिः प्रेक्षणं गुह्यभाषणं । संकल्पोऽध्यवसायश्च क्रियानिष्पत्तिरेव च ॥. **-अध्यायी** N. of Pâṇini's grammatical work consisting of 8 Adhyáyas or chapters. **-अस्रं** an octagon. **-अस्रिय** *a.* octangular. **-अह (न्)** *a.* lasting for 8 days. **-कर्णः** *a.* eight-eared, an epithet of Brahmâ. **-कर्मन्** *m.*, **गतिकः** a king who has 8 duties to perform; (they are:—आदाने च विसर्गे च तथा प्रैषनिषेधयोः । पंचमे चार्थवचने व्यवहारस्य चेक्षणे ॥ दंडशुद्ध्योः सदा रक्तस्तेनाष्टगतिको नृपः ।. **-कृत्वस्** *ind.* eight times. **-कोणः** an octagon. **-गव** a flock of 8 cows **-गुण** *a.* eight-fold; दाप्योऽष्टगुणमत्ययं Ms. 8. 400. (**-णं**) the eight qualities which a Brâhmaṇ should possess; दया सर्वभूतेषु, क्षांतिः, अनसूया, शौचं, अनायासः, मंगलं, अकार्पण्यं, अस्पृहा चेति ॥ Gautama. °**आश्रय** *a.* endowed with these eight qualities. **-ष (ष्टा) चत्वारिंशत्** *a.* forty-eight. **-तय** *a.* eight-fold. **-त्रिंशत् (-ष्टा)** *a.* thirty-eight. **-त्रिकं** the number 24. **-दलं** 1 a lotus having eight petals. -2. an octagon. **-दशन् (°ष्टा°)** see below. **-दिश्** *f.* the eight cardinal points; पूर्वाग्नेयी दक्षिणा च नैर्ऋत्ती पश्चिमा तथा । वायवी चोत्तरैशानी दिशा अष्टाविमाः स्मृताः ॥. °**करिण्यः** the eight female elephants living in the eight points. °**पालाः** the eight regents of the cardinal points; इंद्रो वह्निः पितृपतिः (यमः) नैर्ऋतो वरुणो मरुत् (वायुः) कुबेर ईशः पतयः पूर्वादिनां दिशां क्रमात् ॥ Ak. °**गजाः** the eight elephants guarding the 8 quarters; ऐरावतः पुंडरीको वामनः कुमुदोंऽजनः । पुष्पदंतः सार्वभौमः सुप्रतीकश्च दिग्गजाः ॥ Ak. **-धातुः** the eight metals taken collectively; स्वर्णं रूप्यं च ताम्रं च रंगं यशदमेव च । शीसं लौहं रसश्चेति धातवोऽष्टौ प्रकीर्तिताः ॥. **-पद, -द् (°ष्ट or °ष्टा°)** *a.* eight-footed. **पदः (°ष्टा°)** 1 a spider. -2 a fabulous animal called *S*arabha. -3 a pin or bolt. -4 the mountain Kailas (**-दः, -दं**) 1 gold; आवर्जिताष्टापदकुंभतोयैः Ku. 7. 10; *Si*. 3. 28. -2 a kind of chequered cloth or a board for drafts, dice-board (Mar पट). °**पत्रं** a sheet of gold. **-मंगलः** a horse with a white face, tail, mane, breast and hoofs. (**-लं**) a collection of eight lucky things; according to some they are:—मृगराजो वृषो नागः कलशो व्यजनं तथा । वैजयंती तथा भेरी दीप इत्यष्टमंगलम् ॥; according to others लोकेऽस्मिन्मंगलान्यष्टौ ब्राह्मणो गौर्हुताशनः । हिरण्यं सर्पिरादित्य आपो राजा तथाष्टमः॥. **-मानं** one kuḍava. **-मासिक** *a.* occurring once in 8 months. **—मूर्तिः** the 'eight-formed', an epithet of *S*iva; the 8 forms being the 5 elements (earth, water, fire, air and ether), the sun and moon, and the sacrificing priest; cf. *S*. 1. 1—या सृष्टिः स्रष्टुराद्या वहति विधिहुतं या हविर्या च होत्री । ये द्वे कालं विधत्तः श्रुतिविषयगुणा या स्थिता व्याप्य विश्वं । यामाहुः सर्वभूतप्रकृतिरिति यया प्राणिनः प्राणवंतः । प्रत्यक्षाभिः प्रपन्नस्तनुभिरवतु वस्ताभिरष्टाभिरीशः ॥; or, briefly expressed, the names in Sanskrit (in the above order) are:— जलं वह्निस्तथा यष्टा सूर्याचंद्रमसौ तथा । आकाशं वायुरवनी मूर्तयोऽष्टौ पिनाकिनः ॥. °**धरः** 'having 8 forms', *S*iva. **—रत्नं** the eight jewels taken collectively. **—रसाः** the 8 sentiments in dramas &c.; शृंगारहास्यकरुणरौद्रवीरभयानकाः । बीभत्साद्भुतसंज्ञौ चेत्यष्टौ नाट्ये रसाः स्मृताः ॥ K. P. 4 (to which is sometimes added a 9th Rasa called शांत; निर्वेदस्थायिभावोस्ति शांतोपि नवमो रसः *ibid*); °**आश्रय** *a.* embodying or representing the eight sentiments; V. 2. 18. **—विध** *a.* eight-fold, of eight kinds. **—विंशतिः** *f.* (°ष्टा°) the number twently-eight. **-श्रवणः, —श्रवस्** N. of Brahma (having 8 ears or four heads).

अष्टतय *a.* Having eight parts or limbs. **—यं** An aggregate of eight.

अष्टधा *ind.* 1 Eight-fold, eight times. 2 In 8 parts or sections; भिन्ना प्राकृतिरष्टधा Bg. 7. 4; भिन्नोऽष्टधा विप्रससार वंशः R. 16. 3.

अष्टम *a.* (**मी** *f.*) Eighth. **—मः** The eighth part. **—मी** The eighth day in a lunar half month. —Comp. **—अंशः** an 8th part. **—कालिक** *a.* one who omits seven meal times (*i. e.* full three days and the morning of the fourth) and partakes only of the 8th; Ms. 6. 19.

अष्टमक *a.* The eighth; योंशमष्टमकं हरेत् Y. 2. 244.

अष्टमिका A weight of four Tolas.

अष्टादशन् *a.* Eighteen. —Comp. **—उपपुराणं** a secondary or minor Pur'aṇa; अष्टान्युपपुराणानि मुनिभिः कथितानि तु । आद्यं सनत्कुमारोक्तं नारसिंहमतः परं । तृतीयं नारदं प्रोक्तं कुमारेण तु भाषितं । चतुर्थं शिवधर्माख्यं साक्षान्नंदीशभाषितं । दुर्वाससोक्तमाश्चर्यं नारदोक्तमतः परं । कापिलं मानवं चैव तथैवोशनसेरितं । ब्रह्मांडं वारुणं चाथ कालिकाह्वयमेव च । माहेश्वरं तथा शांबं सौरं सर्वार्थसंचयं । पराशरोक्तं प्रवरं तथा भागवतद्वयं । इदमष्टादशं प्रोक्तं पुराणं कौर्मसंज्ञितं । चतुर्धा संस्थितं पुण्यं संहितानां प्रभेदतः ॥ Hemâdri. **—पुराणं** the eighteen Purâṇas: ब्राह्मं पाद्मं वैष्णवं च शैवं भागवतं तथा । तथान्यन्नारदीयं च मार्कंडेयं च सप्तमं ॥ आग्नेयमष्टकं प्रोक्तं भविष्यन्नवमं तथा । दशमं ब्रह्मवैवर्तं लिंगमेकादशं तथा ॥ वाराहं द्वादशं प्रोक्तं स्कांदं चात्र त्रयोदशं । चतुर्दशं वामनं च कौर्मं पंचदशं तथा ॥ मात्स्यं च गारुडं चैव ब्राह्मांडाष्टादशं तथा ॥. **—विद्या** the eighteen kinds of learning or lores; अंगानि वेदाश्चत्वारो मीमांसा न्यायविस्तरः । धर्मशास्त्रं पुराणं च विद्या ह्येताश्चतुर्दश ॥ आयुर्वेदो धनुर्वेदो गांधर्वश्चेति ते त्रयः । अर्थशास्त्रं चतुर्थं तु विद्या ह्यष्टादशैव तु ॥. **-विवादपदं** the eighteen subjects of litigation (causes of dispute); see Ms. 8. 4-7.

अष्टिः *f.* 1 A die for playing. 2 The number sixteen. 3 Seed. 4 Kernel.

अष्ठीला 1 A globular or round body. 2 A round pebble or stone. 3 Kernal. 4 Seed-corn.

अस् I. 2 P. [अस्ति, आसीत्, अस्तु, स्यात्; defective in non-conjugational tenses, its forms being made up from the root भू] **1** To be, live, exist (showing mere existence); नासदासीनो सदासीत् Rv. 10. 129. 1; न त्वेवाहं जातु नासं Bg. **2.** 12; आसीद्राजा नलो नाम Nala. 1. 1. **2** To be (used as a copula or verb of incomplete predication, being followed by a noun or adjective or adverb, or some other equivalent); धार्मिके सति राजनि Ms. 11. 11; आचार्ये संस्थिते सति 5. 80. **3** To belong to, be in the possession of (expressed in English by *have*), with gen. of possessor; यन्ममास्ति हरस्व तत् Pt. 4. 76; यस्य नास्ति स्वयं प्रज्ञा 5. 70 **4** To fall to the share of; तस्य प्रेत्य फलं नास्ति Ms. 3. 139. **5** To arise, occur; आसीच्च मम मनसि K. 142. **6** To become. **7** To lead or tend to, turn out or prove to be (with dat.); स स्थाणुः स्थिरभक्तियोगसुलभो निःश्रेयसायास्तु वः V. 1. 1. **8** To suffice (with dat.); सा तेषां पावनाय स्यात् Ms. 11. 86; अन्यैर्नृपालैः परिदीयमान शाकाय वा स्याल्लवणाय वा स्यात् Jagannâtha. **9** To stay, reside, dwell, live; हा पितः क्वासि हे सुभ्रु Bk. 6. 11. **10** To be in a particular relation, to be affected (with loc.); किं नु खलु यथा वयमस्यामेवमियमप्यस्मान् प्रति स्यात् *S*. 1. अस्तु well, let it be; एवमस्तु, तथास्तु so be it, amen. The form आस joined to roots in forming their periphrastic perfect is sometimes separated from the root and used by itself; तं पातयां प्रथममास पपात पश्चात् R. 9. 61, 16. 86. —With **अति** to be over, excel, surpass. **-अभि** to belong to, to fall to one's share; यन्ममाभिष्यात् Sk. **—आविस्** to arise, spring up, be visible; आचार्यकं विजयि मान्मथमाविरासीत् M'al. 1. 26. **—प्रादुस्** to appear, spring up; प्रादुरासीत्तमोनुदः Ms. 1. 6; R. 11. 15. **—व्यति** (Atm. व्यतिहे, व्यतिसे व्यतिस्ते) to excel, surpass, be above or superior to, outweigh; अन्यो व्यतिस्ते तु ममापि धर्मः Bk. 2 35. **-II** 4 P. (अस्यति, अस्त) **1** To throw, cast, hurl, discharge, shoot (with loc. of the mark); तस्मिन्नास्थदिषीकास्त्रं R. 12. **23**; Bk. 15. 91. **2** To throw or take away, let go, leave, give up; as in अस्तमान, अस्तशोक, अस्तकोप; see अस्त. —With **अति** to shoot beyond or at, overpower (with arrows); अत्यस्त having shot beyond, having surpassed or excelled; joined in acc. Tat. comp. **-अधि** 1 to place upon another, add to. -2 to attribute the nature of one thing to another; बाह्यधर्मानात्मन्यध्यस्यति S. B. **—अप** 1 to fling or throw away, cast off, leave, abandon, discard, reject; किमित्यपास्याभरणानि यौवने Ku. **5. 44**; सारं ततो ग्राह्यमपास्य फल्गु Pt. 1; *Si*. 1. **55**; समरमपास्य Ve. 3. 4; इत्यादीनां काव्यलक्षणत्वमपास्तं S. D. rejected, refuted, -2 to drive away, disperse. **—अभि** 1 to practise, exercise; अभ्यस्यतीव व्रतमासिधारं R. 13. 67; M'al. 9. 32. **-2** to perform repeatedly, repeat; मृगकुलं रोमंथमभ्यस्यतु *S* 2. 6; Ku. 2. 50 -3 to study, recite, read; वेदमेव सदाऽभ्यस्येत् Ms 2. 166, 4. 147. **—उद्** 1 to raise or throw up, erect; पुच्छमुदस्यति Sk. -2 to turn away from. -3 to expel, turn out. **—उपनि** 1 to place or put near, deposit. -2 to state, hint, suggest. propose: किमिदमुपन्यस्तं *S*. 5. सदुपन्यस्यति कृत्यवर्त्म यः Ki. **2**. 3 -3 to prove. -4 to entrust or commit to the care of. -5 to describe in detail. **—नि** 1 to set or put down, place, throw down; शिखरिषु पदं न्यस्य Me. 13; दृष्टिपूतं न्यसेत्पादं Ms. 6. 46. -2 to lay or throw aside, abandon, give up, resign, relinquish; स न्यस्तचिह्नामपि राजलक्ष्मीं R. 2. 7; न्यस्तशस्त्रस्य Ve. **3**. 18; so प्राणान् न्यस्यति. -3 to put in, place within, place or put down upon anything (with loc.); शिरस्याज्ञा न्यस्ता Amaru 82. चित्रन्यस्त committed to a picture V. 1. 4. स्तनन्यस्तोशीरं *S*. 3 9 applied; अयोग्ये न माद्विधो न्यस्यति भारमग्र्यं Bk. . 22: Me. 59.-4 To entrust, consign, commit to the care of; अहमपि तव सूनौ न्यस्तराज्यः V. 5. 17; भ्रातरि न्यस्य मां Bk. 5. 82. -5 to give to, confer or bestow upon; रामे श्रीर्न्यस्तामिति R. **12**. 2.-6 to state, bring forward, adduce; अर्थांतरं न्यस्यति Malli. on *Si*. 1. 17. **—निस्** 1 to cast out, throw or drive away, give up, quit, drive or send back; निरस्तगांभीर्यमपास्तपुष्पकं *Si*. 1. 55, 9 63. -2 to destroy, ward off, defeat, annihilate, dispel; अह्नाय तावदरुणेन तमो निरस्तं R. 5. 71; रक्षांसि वेदीं परितो निरास्थत् Bk. 1. 12, 2. 36. -3 to turn out, expel, banish; गृहान्निरस्ता न तेन वैदेहसुता मनस्तः R. **14** 84. -4 to throw out, discharge (as arrows). -5 to reject, repudiate (as opinions) -6 to eclipse, obscure, throw into the back-ground; Bk. 1. 3. **—परा** 1 to leave, give up, quit, abandon; परास्तवसुधा सुधाधिवसति Ki. 5. 27. -2 to expel. -3 to reject, repudiate, refute; इति यदुक्तं तदपि परास्तं S. D. 1. **—परि** 1 to throw or cast round, spread round, diffuse. -2 to spread over, surround; ताम्रौष्ठपर्यस्तरुचः स्मितस्य Ku. 1. 44. -3 to turn round; पर्यस्तविलोचनेन Ku. 3. 68. -4 to shed, to throw down (as tears); R. 10. 76; Ms. 11. 183. -5 to overturn, upset. -6 to throw about; R. 13. 13, 5. 49. **—परिनि** to spread, stretch. **—पर्युद्** 1 to reject, exclude. -2 to prohibit, object to. **—प्र** to throw, hurl or fling forth. **—वि** 1 to toss about, scatter, cast or throw asunder; dispel, destroy; Bk. 8. 116, 9. 31. -2 to divide into parts, separate, arrange; स्वयं वेदान् व्यस्यन् Pt. 4 50; विव्यास वेदान् यस्मात्स तस्माद् व्यास इति स्मृतः Mb.; R. 10. 85. -3 to take separately or singly; तदस्ति किं व्यस्तमपि त्रिलोचने Ku. 5. 72 even one. -4 to throw over, upset. -5 to expel, remove. **-विनि** 1 to put down, deposit, place; विन्यस्यंती भुवि गणनया देहलीदत्तपुष्पैः Me. 88; Bk. 3. 3. -2 to fix in or on, direct towards; रामे विन्यस्तमानसाः Ram. -3 to deliver or make over, commit to the care of, entrust; सुतविन्यस्तपत्नीकः Y. 3. 45. -4 to arrange, dispose. **—विपरि** 1 to overturn, reverse, invert. -2 to change, alter; U. 1. -3 to take wrongly, misunderstand; प्रतीकारो व्याधेः सुखमिति विपर्यस्यति जनः Bh. **3**. 92.-4 to undergo change (intrans.). **—सं** 1 to join or bring together, unite, combine; Ms. 3. 85, 7. 57. -2 to join in a compound, compound. -3 to take collectively or jointly; समस्तैरथवा पृथक् Ms. 7. 198 jointly or severally. **—संनि** 1 to place or put down, deposit. -2 to lay down or aside, give up, abandon, quit; संन्यस्तशस्त्रः R. **2**. 59; संन्यस्ताभरणं गात्रं Me. 93; Ku. 7. 67. -3 to make or deliver over, entrust, commit to the care of; Bg. 3. 30. **4** (used intrans.) to resign the world, to discard all worldly ties and attachments and become an anchorite; संदृश्य क्षणभंगुरं तदखिलं धन्यस्तु संन्यस्यति Bh. **3**. **132**.—III 1 U. (असति-ते, असित) **1** To go. **2** To take or receive, seize. **3** To shine. (The examples usually cited to illustrate this sense are निष्प्रभश्च प्रभुरास भूभृतां R. 11. 81; तेनास लोकः पितृमान् विनेत्रा 14. 23; लावण्य उत्पाद्य इवास यत्नः Ku. 1. 35. But the sense of दिदीपे or 'shone' is far-fetched, though Vâmana is disposed to take it. It seems preferable to regard आस in these instances as equivalent to बभूव, either taking it as *S*âkaṭâyana does, as an indeclinable तिङंतप्रतिरूपकमव्ययं, or considering it, as Vallabha does, as an ungrammatical form used against the rules of grammar, प्रामादिकः प्रयोगः; see Malli. on Ku. 1. 35).

असंयत *a.* **1** Unrestrained, not under control. **2** Not tied, as in असंयतोऽपि मोक्षार्थी.

असंयमः Absence of control or restraint, especially of the senses.

असंव्यवहित *a.* Immediate, without any interval (of time or space)

असंशय *a.* Free from doubt, certain. -**यं** *ind.* Without doubt, undoubtedly, certainly; असंशयं क्षत्रपरिग्रहक्षमा *S*. 1. 22.

असंश्रव *a.* Out of hearing, inaudible; असंश्रवे out of the hearing of; Ms. 2 203.

असंसृष्ट *a.* **1** Not mixed with, not connected. **2** Not living in common, not reunited after partition of property (as an heir).

असंस्कृत *a.* 1 Unpolished, not refined or cleansed &c. 2 Not decorated or adorned. 3 One over whom no purificatory rite (any one of the samskâras) has been performed.—**तः** An ungrammatical form (अपशब्द).

असंस्तुत *a.* 1 Unknown, unacquainted, not familiar; असंस्तुत इव परित्यक्तो बांधवो जनः K. 173; Ki. 3. 2. 2 Unusual, strange. 3 Not in harmony or agreement with; धावति पश्चादसंस्तुतं चेतः *S.* 1. 34.

असंस्थानं 1 Absence of cohesion. 2 Disorder, confusion. 3 Want, destitution.

असंस्थित *a.* 1 Not arranged, irregular. 2 Not collected.

असंस्थितिः *f.* Disorder, confusion.

असंहत *a.* Not joined or united, scattered. **-तः** The *Purush* or soul (in Sân. phil.).

असकृत् *ind.* Not once, repeatedly, often and often; असकृदेकरथेन तरस्विना R. 9. 23; Me. 92, 93. –Comp.**-समाधिः** repeated meditation. **-गर्भवासः** repeated birth.

असक्त *a.* 1 Not excessively attached, not feeling interested in, indifferent (to); असक्तः सुखमन्वभूत् R. 1. 21. 2 Not entangled; *S.* 2. 12. 3 Not attached to worldly feelings and connections. **—क्तं** *ind.* 1 Without being excessively attached or addicted to. 2 Incessantly, ceaselessly.

असक्थ *a.* Thighless.

असखिः An enemy, adversary.

असगोत्र *a.* Not belonging to the same *Gotra* or family.

असंकुल *a.* Not crowded, open, clear, broad (as a road &c.). **-लः** A broad road.

असंख्य *a.* Beyond calculation, countless, innumerable; Ms. 1. 80; 12. 15; °ता-त्वं infinity.

असंख्यात *a.* Countless, innumerable.

असंख्येय *a.* Innumerable. **—यः** An epithet of *S*iva.

असंग *a.* 1 Not attached, free from worldly ties. 2 Not hindered or obstructed, not blunted. 3 Not united, solitary, unassailed. **-गः** 1 Non-attachment; Ms. 6. 75. 2 *Purusha* or soul (in Sân. phil.).

असंगत *a.* 1 Ununited, unaccompanied with. 2 Improbable, inconsistent. 3 Rude, ill-mannered, unpolished.

असंगतिः *f.* 1 Not associating with. 2 Incongruity, improbability. 3 (In Rhet.) A figure of speech in which a cause and the effect are represented as locally different or separated (in which there is an apparent violation of the relation between cause and effect).

असंगम *a.* Not united. **-मः** 1 Separation, disunion. 2 Incongruity.

असंगिन् *a.* 1 Not united or associated. 2 Not attached to the world.

असंज्ञ *a.* Insensible. **-ज्ञा** Disunion, disagreement, discord.

असत् *a.* 1 Not being or existing; असति त्वयि Ku. 4. 12; Ms. 9. 154. 2 Non-existent, unreal; आत्मनो ब्रह्मणाऽभेदमसंतं कः करिष्यति. 3 Bad (opp. सत्); सदसद्व्यक्तिहेतवः R. 1. 10. 4 Wicked, vile, evil; as °विचार. 5 Not manifest. 6 Wrong, improper, false, untrue; इति यदुक्तं तदसत् (oft. occurring in controversial works). **—***m.* (**न्**) Indra. **—***n.* (**त्**) 1 Non-existence, non-entity. 2 Untruth, falsehood. **—ती** An unchaste woman; असती भवति सलज्जा Pt. 1. 418. –Comp. **-अध्येतृ** *m.* a Brâhmaṇa who reads heterodox works, one who neglects his own *S*âkhâ and studies another; also called शाखारंडः; स्वशाखां यः परित्यज्य अन्यत्र कुरुते श्रमं । शाखारंडः स विज्ञेयो वर्जयेत्तं क्रियासु च ॥. **-आगमः** 1 a heterodox *S*âstra or doctrine. -2 acquisition (of wealth) by unfair or foul means. —3 a foul means itself. **-आचार** *a.* following evil practices, wicked. (**-रः**) an evil practice. **-कर्मन्**, **-क्रिया** 1 a bad deed. -2 bad treatment. **-कल्पना** 1 an untrue action. -2 fabrication of falsehood. **-ग्र (ग्रा) हः** 1 a bad trick. -2 a bad opinion, prejudice. -3 childish desire. **-चेष्टितं** harm, injury; प्राणिष्वसच्चेष्टितं *S.* 5. 6. **-दृश्** *a.* evil-eyed. **-पथः** 1 a bad road (lit.). -2 evil practices or doctrines; नाशो हंत सतामसत्पथजुषामायुः समानां शतं Bv. 4. 36. **-परिग्रहः** acceptance of a bad road. **प्रतिग्रहः** 1 present of bad things. -2 receiving unfit presents (such as तिल) or from improper persons. **-भावः** 1 non-existence, absence. -2 a bad or wicked opinion. -3 an evil disposition. **-वृत्ति**,**-व्यवहार** *a.* following evil practices, wicked. (**-त्तिः** *f.*) 1 a low or degrading occupation. -2 wickedness. **-शास्त्रं** 1 wrong doctrine. -2 a heterodox doctrine. **-संसर्गः** bad company. **-हेतुः** a bad or fallacious *hetu*: see हेत्वाभास.

असतायी Wickedness.

असत्ता 1 Non-existence. 2 Untruth. 3 Wickedness, badness.

असत्त्व *a.* 1 Without energy or strength. 2 Having no animal. **—त्त्वं** 1 Non-existence. 2 Unreality, untruth.

असत्य *a.* 1 Untrue, false. 2 Imaginary, unreal. **-त्यः** A liar. **-त्यं** Falsehood, lying, untruth. –Comp. **-वादिन्** *a.* speaking falsely, liar. **-संध** *a.* not true to one's promise, false, perfidious, treacherous; °धे जने सखी पदं कारिता *S.* 4.

असदृश *a.* (**शी** *f.*) 1 Dissimilar, unlike. 2 Unfit, improper, incongruous; °संयोगकारिन् K. 12 unworthy; मातः किमप्यसदृशं विकृतं वचस्ते Ve. 5. 3.

असद्यस् *ind.* Not immediately, after delay.

असन् *n.* Blood (used only in the declension of असृज् after acc. pl.).

असनं Throwing, discharging, casting; as in इष्वसन a bow. **-नः** N of a tree (पीतसाल); निरसनैरसनैरवृथार्थता *Si.* 6. 47.

असंदिग्ध *a.* 1 Not doubtful, distinct, clear. 2 Confident, unsuspected. **—ग्धं** *ind.* Certainly, undoubtedly.

असंधि *a.* 1 Not joined together (as words). 2 Not bound or restrained, at liberty. **-धिः** Absence of *Sandhi* or euphony.

असंनद्ध 1 *a.* Unarmed 2 Pretending to knowledge, conceited (पंडितंमन्य).

असंनिकर्षः 1 Non-perception of objects, not bringing them to the mind. 2 Remoteness.

असंनिवृत्तिः *f.* Non-return; असंनिवृत्त्यै तदतीतमेव *S.* 6. 9 gone never to return; R. 8. 49.

असपिंड *a.* Not connected by offerings of rice-balls; or, not connected by blood-relationship.

असभ्य *a.* Unfit for an assembly, vulgar, low, obscene, indecent (words &c.).

असम *a.* 1 Uneven, odd (as a number). 2 Unequal (in space, number or dignity); असमैः समीयमानः Pt. 1. 74. 3 Unequalled, matchless, unsurpassed .—Comp. **—इषुः**, **-बाणः**, **-सायकः** 'having an odd number of arrows', epithets of Cupid who has five arrows. **-नयन**, **-नेत्र**, **-लोचन** *a.* 'having an odd number of eyes,' epithets of *S*iva, who has three eyes.

असमंजस *a.* 1 Indistinct, unintelligible; स्खलदसमंजसमुग्धजल्पितं ते U. 4. 4; Mâl. 10. 2. 2 Unbecoming, improper; यद्यपि न कापि हानिर्द्राक्षामन्यस्य रासभे चरति । असमंजसमिति मत्वा तथापि तरलायते चेतः ॥ Udb. 3 Absurd, nonsensical, foolish.

असमवायिन् *a.* Not intimate or inherent, accidental, separable. –Comp. **-कारणं** (In logic) an accidental cause, not inherent and intimate relation; गुणकर्ममात्रवृत्तिज्ञेयमथाप्यसमवायिहेतुत्वं Bhâshâ. P.; यथा तंतुयोगः पटस्य.

असमस्त *a.* 1 Incomplete; partial, not whole. 2 (In gram.) Not joined in a compound, not compounded. 3 Separate, detached, unconnected (opp. व्यस्त). **-स्तं** An uncompounded word (the sentence showing the dissolution of a compound).

असमाप्त *a.* 1 Not completed or finished, left incomplete; R. 8. 76; Ku. 4. 19. 2 Not fully acquired.

असमीक्ष्य *ind.* Not having (properly) considered. –Comp. **–कारिन्** *a.* acting inconsiderately, imprudent, not circumspect.

असंपत्ति *a.* Poor, miserable. **–त्तिः** *f.* **1** Ill-luck. **2** Non-accomplishment, failure.

असंपूर्ण *a.* **1** Not complete, unfinished. **2** Not whole or entire. **3** Not full, partial, as the moon; चंद्रमसंपूर्णमंडलमिदानीं Mu. 1. 6.

असंबद्ध *a.* **1** Unconnectod, incoherent. **2** Nonsensical, absurd, unmeaning; °आ (प्र) लापिन् talking nonsense; असंबद्धः खल्वसि Mk. 9 absurd fellow. **3** Improper, wrong; Ms. 12. 6. **–द्धं** An absurd sentence, unmeaning or non-sensical speech; *e. g.* यावज्जीवमहं मौनी when uttered by some one. see अबद्ध also.

असंबंध *a.* Unconnected, not relating or belonging to. **–धः** Non-connection, absence of any relation or connection; यद्वा साध्यवदन्यस्मिन्नसंबंध उदाहृतः Bhâshâ P. 68.

असंबाध *a.* **1** Not narrow, spacious. **2** Not crowded with people, lonely, solitary. **3** Open, accessible.

असंभव *a.* Improbable, unlikely. **—वः 1** Non-existence. **2** Improbability, impossibility.

असंभव्य, असंभाविन् *a.* **1** Impossible. **2** Incomprehensible.

असंभावना 1 Difficulty or impossibility of comprehending. **2** Improbability.

असंभृत *a.* **1** Not brought about by artificial means, not artificial, natural; असंभृतं मंडनमंगयष्टेः Ku. 1. 31. **2** Not properly nourished.

असंमत *a.* **1** Disapproved, not allowed or permitted, not consented to. **2** Disliked; averse. **3** Dissentient, differing from. **—तः** An enemy; यतु दोषैरसंमतान् K. P. 7. –Comp. **—आदायिन्** *a.* taking without the consent of the possessor, such as a thief.

असंमतिः *f.* **1** Dissent, disagreement. **2** Disapproval; dislike.

असंमोहः 1 Absence of infatuation. **2** Steadiness, composure, coolness. **3** Real knowledge, true insight (into a thing).

असम्यच् *a.* (**मीची** *f.*) **1** Bad, improper, incorrect. **2** Imperfect, incomplete.

असलं 1 Iron. **2** A Mantra used in discharging a missile. **3** Arms.

असवर्ण *a.* Of a different caste or tribe; अपि नाम कुलपतेरियमसवर्णक्षेत्रसंभवा स्यात् *S.* 1.

असह *a.* **1** Not enduring; intolerant, impatient. **2** Unable to bear, support, or endure; oft. with gen. of object; सा स्त्रीस्वभावादसहा भरस्य Mu. 4. 13.

असहन *a.* Not enduring, intolerant, envious. **—नः** An enemy. **—नं** Intolerance, impatience; परगुणासहनं=असूया.

असहनीय, असहितव्य, असह्य *a.* Unbearable, insufferable, intolerable; असह्यपीडं भगवन्नृणमंत्यमवेहि मे R. 1. 71; 18. 25; Ku. 4. 1.

असहाय *a.* **1** Friendless, lonely, solitary. **2** Without companions or assistants; Ms. 7. 30, 55; °ता, **—त्वं** loneliness, solitude.

असाक्षात् *ind.* **1** Not before the eyes, invisibly, imperceptibly **2** Indirectly.

असाक्षिक *a.* (**की** *f.*) Having no witness, unattested, unwitnessed; असाक्षिकेषु त्वर्थेषु मिथो विवदमानयोः Ms. 8. 109.

असाक्षिन् *a.* **1** Not an eye-witness. **2** One whose evidence is not admissible (in law). **3** One who is disqualified to attest a legal document.

असाधनीय, असाध्य *a.* **1** Not to be accomplished or completed. **2** Not capable of being proved. **3** Incurable, (as a disease or patient); असाध्यः कुरुते कोपं प्राते काले गदो यथा *Si.* 2. 84.

असाधारण *a.* **1** Not common, peculiar, special, specific. **2** (In logic) Existing neither in सपक्ष or विपक्ष as a *hetu*; यस्तूभयस्माद् व्यावृत्तः स त्वसाधारणो मतः **3** Not to be claimed by any one else, exclusively belonging to one (as wealth &c.). **—णः** A fallacy or हेत्वाभास in Logic; one of the three kinds of अनैकांतिक q. v.

असाधु *a.* **1** Not good, bad, distasteful, unpleasant; अतोर्हसि क्षंतुमसाधु साधु वा Ki. 1. 4. **2** Wicked. **3** Ill-behaved (with loc.); असाधुर्मातरि Sk. **4** Corrupt, not properly formed or *Sanskrit* (as a word).

असामयिक *a.* (**की** *f.*) Inopportune, unseasonable; Ki. 2. 40.

असामान्य *a.* **1** Not common, peculiar; R. 15. 39. **2** Extra-ordinary. **—न्यं** A peculiar or special property.

असांप्रत *a.* Unfit, unbecoming, improper. **—तं** *ind.* Improperly, unfitly; oft. used with an adjectival force =असांप्रत; विषवृक्षोऽपि संवर्ध्य स्वयं छेत्तुमसांप्रतं Ku. 2. 55; संप्रत्यसांप्रतं वक्तुमुक्ते मुसलपाणिना *Si.* 2. 71; R. 8. 60.

असार *a.* **1** Sapless, insipid. **2** (*a*) Without essence, useless; (*b*) worthless, without strength, stuff or value, deprived of its essence; असारं संसारं परिमुषितरत्नं त्रिभुवनं Mâl. 5. 30; U. 1; असारे खलु संसारे सारमेतच्चतुष्टयं Dharm. 12, 13. **3** Vain, unprofitable. **4** Weak, feeble, infirm; बहूनामप्यसाराणां संहतिः कार्यसाधिका (समवायो हि दुर्जयः) Pt. 1. 331; *Si.* 2. 50. **—रः,–रं 1** Unessential or unimportant portion. **2** N. of a tree (एरंड). **3** Aloe wood.

असारता 1 Saplessness. **2** Worthlessness. **3** Unsubstantial nature; transitory state; धिगिमां देहभृतामसारतां R. 8. 51.

असाहसं Absence of violence, gentleness.

असिः 1 A sword. **2** A knife used for killing animals. **—सि** *ind.* Thou; cf. अस्मि. –Comp. **—गंडः** a small pillow for the cheeks. **—जीविन्** *a.* one who earns his livelihood by means of swords, a soldier fighting for wages **—दंष्ट्रः,–दंष्ट्रकः** the marine monster *makara* or crocodile. **–दंतः** a crocodile.**—धारा** the edge of a sword; सुरगज इव दंतैर्भग्नदैत्यासिधारैः R. 10. 86, 41. **—धाराव्रतं 1** (according to some) the vow of standing on the edge of a sword; (according to others) the vow of keeping constant company with a young wife and yet steadily resisting the temptation of sexual intercourse with her; यत्रैकशयनस्थापि प्रमदा नोपभुज्यते । असिधाराव्रतं नाम वदंति मुनिपुंगवाः ॥; or युवा युवत्या सार्धं यन्मुग्धभर्तृवदाचरेत् । अंतर्निवृत्तसंगः स्यादसिधाराव्रतं हि तत् Y'adava. –2 (hence fig.) any hopelessly difficult task; सतां केनोद्दिष्टं विषममसिधाराव्रतमिदं Bh. 2. 28, 64. **—धावः —धावकः** an armourer, furbisher. **—धेनुः, —धेनुका** a knife; Vikr. 4. 69. **—पत्र** *a.* having sword-shaped leaves; R. 14. 48. **(–त्रः)** 1 the sugar-cane. –2 a kind of tree which grows in the lower world. **(–त्रं)** 1 the blade of a sword. –2 a sheath. °**वनं** a hell where the trees have leaves as sharp as swords.**—पत्रकः** a sugar-cane.**–पुच्छः,–पुच्छकः** the Gangetic porpoise. **—पुत्रिका, —पुत्री** a knife. **—मेदः** the fetid *Khadira*. **–हत्यं** fighting with knives or swords. **—हेतिः** a swordsman

असिकं The part of the face be tween the underlip and the chin.

असिक्नी 1 A young maid-servant of the harem. **2** N. of a river in the Punjab.

असिक्निका A young womanservant.

असित *a.* Not white, black, dark-blue, dark-coloured; असिता मोहरजनी Sânti. 3. 4; Y. 3. 166; °लोचना, °नयना &c. **—तः 1** The dark or blue colour. **2** The dark fortnight of a lunar month. **3** N. of the planet Saturn. **4** A black snake. **—ता 1** The Indigo plant. **2** A girl attending upon the harem (whose hair is not whitened by age); see असिक्नी. **3** The river Yamunâ. –Comp. **—अंबुजं, —उत्पलं** the blue lotus. **—अर्चिस्** *m.* fire. **—अश्मन्,** *m.* **—उपलः** a dark-blue stone.**—केशा** a woman having black hair. **–केशांत** *a.* having black locks of hair. **–गिरिः, —नगः** 'the blue mountain'; N. of a mountain. **—ग्रीव** *a.* having a black neck. **(–वः)** fire. **—नयन** *a.* black-eyed Me. 112. **—पक्षः** the dark fortnight. -फलं the sweet cocoanut. -मृगः the black antelope.

असिद्ध *a.* 1 Not accomplished. 2 Imperfect incomplete. 3 Unproved. 4 Unripe, raw. 5 Not derivable by inference.—द्धः A fallacious *hetu*; one of the five principal divisions of हेत्वाभास or fallacies. It is of three kinds:- (1) आश्रयासिद्ध where the existence of any such locality (आश्रय) as that where the property is said to reside, is not established; (2) स्वरूपासिद्ध where the nature (स्वरूप) alleged does not really reside in the subject (पक्ष); and (3) व्याप्यतासिद्ध where the alleged invariableness of concomitancy is not real.

असिद्धिः *f.* 1 Imperfect accomplishment, failure. 2 Want of ripeness. 3 Non-accomplishment (in Yoga phil.). 4 (In logic) Conclusion not warranted by the premises.

असिरः 1 A beam, a ray. 2 An arrow, a bolt.

असुः 1 Breath, life, spiritual life. 2 Life of departed spirits. 3 (pl.) The five vital breaths or life-winds in the body; असुभिः स्थास्तु यशश्चिचीषतः Ki. 2. 19. *-n.* (सु) Grief. -COMP. **-धारणं-णा** sustenance of life, life, existence. **-भंगः** 1 destruction or loss of life; मालिनमसुभंगेप्यसुकरं Bh. 2. 28. -2 danger or fear about life. **-भृत्** *m.* a living being, a creature. **-सम** *a.* as dear as life. (**-मः**) a husband, lover.

असुमत् *a.* Living, breathing. —*m.* 1 A living being; *S*i. 4. 29. 2 Life.

असुख *a.* 1 Unhappy, sorrowful. 2 Not easy (to obtain), difficult. —**खं** Sorrow, pain. -COMP. **-आवह** *a.* pained with grief. **-आविष्ट** *a.* causing great pain. **-उदय** *a.* causing or ending in unhappiness; Ms. 11. 10. —**जीविका** an unhappy life.

असुखिन् *a.* Unhappy, sorrowful.

असुत *a.* Childless.

असुरः 1 An evil spirit, a demon; the Râm. thus accounts for the name:—सुराप्रतिग्रहाद्देवाः सुरा इत्यभिविश्रुताः। अप्रतिग्रहणात्तस्या दैतेयाश्चासुरास्तथा ॥. 2 A general name for the enemies of gods, Daityas and Dânavas. 3 A ghost. 4 The sun. 5 An elephant. 6 An epithet of Râhu. 7 A cloud. —**रा** 1 Night. 2 A zodiacal sign. 3 A prostitute.—**री** A female demon, wife of an Asura. -COMP. **-अधिपः,-राज्,-जः** 1 the lord of the Asuras. -2 an epithet of Bali, grandson of Pralhâda. **-आचार्यः, -गुरुः** 1 N. of the preceptor of the Asuras, *S*ukrâchârya. -2 the planet Venus.**-आह्वं** bell-metal.**-क्षयण, -क्षिति** *a.* destroying the Asuras. **-द्विष्** *m.* an enemy of the Asuras, *i. e*, a god. **-माया** demoniacal magic.**-रिपुः -सूदनः** 'destroyer of Asuras', an epithet of Vishṇu.**-हन्** *m.* 1 one who destroys the Asuras, an epithet of Agni, Indra &c. -2 N. of Vishṇu.

असुर्य *a.* Demoniacal.

असुरसा N. of a plant; a variety of तुलसी.

असुलभ *a.* Not easily attainable, difficult to secure; V. 2. 9.

असुसुः An arrow; स सासिः सासुसूः सासो येयायेयाययाययः Ki. 15. 5.

असुहृद् *m.* An enemy; *S*i. 2. 117.

असूक्षणं Disrespect.

असूत, असूतिक *a.* One who has not brought forth, barren.

असूतिः *f.* 1 Non-production, barrenness. 2 Obstruction, removal.

असूयति Den. P. 1 To envy, to be jealous of; कथं चित्रगतो भर्ता मयाऽसूयितः M. 4. 2 To detract from; be displeased with, scorn, be discontented with or angry with (with dat. of person or thing); असूयंति सचिवोपदेशाय K. 108; असूयंति मह्यं प्रकृतयः V. 4; Bg. 3. 31.

असूयक *a.* 1 Envious, detracting, calumnious. 2 Discontented, displeased. **-कः** A detractor, an envious man; Ms. 2. 114; *S*ânti. 3. 7; Y. 1. 28.

असूयनं 1 Detraction, calumny. 2 Envy, jealousy.

असूया 1 Envy, intolerance, jealousy; क्रुधद्रुहेर्ष्यासूयार्थानां यं प्रति कोपः P. I. 4. 37; सासूयं enviously. 2 Calumny, detraction; असूया परगुणेषु दोषाविष्करणं Sk.; R. 4. 23. 3 Anger, indignation; वधूरसूयाकुटिलं ददर्श R. 6. 82.

असूयुः 1 Envious, jealous. 2 Displeased.

असूर्य *a.*Sunless.

असूर्यंपश्य *a.* Not seeing even the sun; said of the wives of a king who, being shut up in the harem, have no opportunity of seeing the sun; असूर्यंपश्या राजदाराः Sk. —**श्या** A chaste and loyal wife.

असृज् *n.* 1 Blood. 2 The planet Mars. 3 Saffron. -COMP. **-करः** lymph. **-धरा** the skin. **-धारा** 1 a stream of blood. -2 the skin. **-पः, पाः** 'a blood-drinker', a Râkshasa. **-पातः** the falling of blood. **-वहा** a blood-vessel; pulse **-विमोक्षणं** bleeding. **-श्रा (स्रा) -वः** bleeding.

असेचन,-नक *a.* That on which one cannot look enough, charming, lovely.

असौष्ठव *a.* 1 Devoid of beauty, or loveliness, not in good trim; शरीरमसौष्ठवं Mâl. 1. 17. 2 Ugly, deformed —**वं** Worthlessness, absence of merit. 2 Deformity, ugliness.

अस्खलित *a.* 1 Unshaken, firm, permanent. 2 Unhurt. 3 Undeviating, careful; R. 5. 20.

अस्त *p. p.* 1 Thrown, cast, given up, left; असमये यत्त्वयास्तोऽभिमानः Ve. 6. 2 Finished. 3 Despatched. -COMP. **-करुण** *a.* merciless. **-धी** *a.* foolish. **-व्यस्त** *a.* scattered here and there, confused, disordered. **-संख्य** *a.* innumerable.

अस्तः 1 Setting or western mountain (behind which the sun is supposed to set); अधिरोढुमस्तगिरिमभ्यपतत् *S*i. 9. 1; विडंबयत्यस्तनिमग्नसूर्यं R. 16. 11; *S*. 4. 1. 2 Sunset. 3 Setting in general; (fig.) fall, decline; see below. **-अस्तं गम्, -या, -इ, प्राप्** (*a*) To set, decline in the western horizon; गतोऽस्तमर्कः the sun has set. (*b*) To cease, vanish, be removod, disappear, be at an end; विषयिणः कस्यापदोऽस्तं गताः Pt. 1. 146; धृतिरस्तमिता R. 8. 66. (*c*) To die; अथ चास्तमिता त्वमात्मना R. 8. 51, 12. 11. -COMP. **-अचलः -अद्रिः -गिरिः, -पर्वतः** the setting or western mountain. **-अवलंबनं** the resting of a heavenly body on the western part of the horizon, being about to set **-उदयौ** (dual) rising and setting, rise and fall; अस्तोदयावदिशदप्रविभिन्नकालं Mu. 3. 17. **-ग** *a.* set, become invisible (as a planet of star). **-गमनं** 1 setting, disappearance. -2 death, sunset of life; Mâl. 9.

अस्तमनं Setting (of the sun).

अस्तमयः 1 Setting (of the sun); करोत्यकालास्तमयं विवस्वतः Ki 5. 35; (opp. उदय). 2 Destruction, end, decline, loss. 3 Fall, subjugation; उदयमस्तमयं च रघूद्वहात R. 9. 9. 4 Obscuring, eclipsing; प्रभाप्ररोहास्तमयं रजांसि R. 6. 33. 5 Conjunction (of a planet) with the sun.

अस्ति *ind.* 1 Being, existent, present; as in अस्तिक्षीरा, °काय. 2 Often used at the commencement of a tale or narrative in the sense of 'so it is,' 'there,' or merely as an expletive; अस्ति सिंहः प्रतिवसति स्म Pt. 4. -COMP. **-कायः** a category or predicament (with the Jainas). **-क्षीर** *a.* having milk. **-नास्ति** *ind.* doubtful, partly true and partly not.

अस्तित्वं Existence.

अस्तेयं Not stealing.

अस्त्यानं Reproach, blame.

अस्त्रं 1 A missile; a weapon in general; प्रयुक्तमप्यस्त्रमितो वृथा स्यात् R. 2. 34; प्रत्याहतास्त्रो गिरिशप्रभावात् 2. 41, 3. 58; अशिक्षतास्त्रं पितुरेव R. 3. 31 the science of missiles. 2 An arrow; sword. 3 A bow. -COMP.**-अ (आ) गारं** an arsenal, armoury. **-आघातः** a wound, a cut.**-कंटकः** an arrow. **-कारः, -कारकः, कारिन्** a maker of weapons. **-चिकित्सकः** a surgeon. **-चिकित्सा** surgery. **-जीवः जीविन्** *m.*-**धारिन्** *m.* a soldier, pro-warrior. **-निवारणं** the warding of a weapon. -मंत्रः a Mantra to be repeated in discharging or withdrawing a missile.-मार्जः-र्जकः a furbisher. -युद्धं fighting with weapons. -लाघवं dexterity in wielding or throwing missiles. -विद् a. skilled in the science of arms. -विद्या, -शास्त्रं, -वेदः the art or science of throwing missiles, science of arms.-वृष्टिः f. a shower of missiles. -शिक्षा military exercise.

अस्त्रिन् a. Fighting with a missile weapon, an archer.

अस्त्री 1 Not a woman. 2 (In gram.) The masculine and neuter genders.

अस्थान a. Very deep. —नं 1 A bad or wrong place. 2 An improper place or object or occasion

अस्थाने ind. Unseasonably, out of place, inopportunely, in a wrong place, on an unworthy object; उभयोरप्यस्थाने प्रयत्नः Mu. 2; अस्थाने महानर्थोत्सर्गः क्रियते Mu. 3.

अस्थावर a. 1 Movable, moving, not fixed, 2 (In law) Personal, as property, money, catte &c. (=जंगम).

अस्थि n. 1 A bone (changed to अस्थ at the end of certain compounds; cf. अनाथ, पुरुषास्थ). 2 The kernel or stone of a fruit; न कार्पासास्थि न तुषान् Ms. 4. 78. -COMP.-कृत्, -तेजस्, m. -संभवः, -सारः, -स्नेहः marrow. -जः 1 marrow.-2 thunderbolt. -तुंडः a bird.-धन्वन् m. N. Siva. -पंजरः 'a cage of bones', a skeleton. -प्रक्षेपः throwing the bones of the dead into the Ganges or any holy waters.-भक्षः, -'भुक् an eater of bones,' a dog.-भंगः fracture of the bones. -माला 1 a string or wreath of bones. 2 a row of bones. -मालिन् m. N. of Siva. -शेष a. reduced to a skeleton. -संचयः 1 collecting the bones or their ashes after burning a corpse.-2 a heap of bones. -संधिः a joint, an articulation. -समर्पणं throwing the bones of the dead body into the Ganges or holy waters. -स्थूणः 'having the bones for its pillars', the body.

अस्थितिः f. 1 Want of firmness or fixity (fig. also.). 2 Want of good manners or decorum.

अस्थिर a. Not stable or firm, unsteady, fickle.

अस्पर्शनं Non-contact, avoiding the contact (of anything); प्रक्षालनाद्धि पंकस्य दूरादस्पर्शनं वरं; cf. 'Prevention is better than cure'.

अस्पष्ट a. 1 Not clear, not clearly visible. 2 Indistinct, not clearly understood, doubtful; अस्पष्टब्रह्मलिंगानि वेदांतवाक्यानि S. B.

अस्पृश a. 1 Not to be touched. 2 Impure, unholy.

अस्फुट a. Indistinct, obscure. -टं An indistinct speech. -COMP. -फलं indistinct fruit or result. -वाच् a. lisping, speaking indistinctly.

अस्मद् pron. A pronominal base from which several cases of the 1st personal pronoun are derived; it is also abl. pl. of the word.—m. The individual soul, the embodied soul. -COMP. -विध, -अस्मादृश a. similar or like us.

अस्मदीय a. Our, ours; यदस्मदीयं न हि तत्परेषां Pt. 2. 105; Bg. 12. 26.

अस्मार्त a. 1 Not within memory, immemorial. 2 Illegal, not according to the Aryan institutes of Law. 3 Not belonging to the Smarta sect.

अस्मृतिः f. Want of memory, forgetfulness.

अस्मि ind. (Strictly 1st. pers. sing. Pres. of अस् to be) Used in the sense of 'I', अहं; आसंसृतेरस्मि जगत्सु जातः Ki. 3. 6; अन्यत्र यूयं कुसुमावचायं कुरुध्वमत्रास्मि करोमि सख्यः K. P. 3.

अस्मिता Egotism.

अस्रः 1 A corner, an angle. 2 Hair of the head. —स्रं 1 Tear. 2 Blood. -COMP. -कंठः an arrow.-जं flesh. -पः 1 'a blood-drinker', a Râkshasa or goblin. -पा a leech. -मातृका chyle, chyme.

अस्व a. 1 Indigent, poor. 2 Not one's own.

अस्वतंत्र a. 1 Dependent, subject, not one's own master; अस्वतंत्रा स्त्री पुरुषप्रधाना Vasishṭha. 2 Docile.

अस्वप्न a. Sleepless, wakeful. —प्नः A god, deity.

अस्वरः 1 A low tone. 2 A consonant. —रं ind. Not aloud, in a low tone.

अस्वर्ग्य a. Not securing or leading to heaven; अस्वर्ग्यं लोकविद्विष्टं धर्ममप्याचरेन्न तु Y. 1. 156.

अस्वाध्यायः 1 One who has not yet commenced his studies, not being invested with the sacred thread. 2 Interruption of studies (as on अष्टमी, eclipses &c.).

अस्वस्थ a. 1 Not well, indisposed; बलवत् अस्वस्था S. 3 seriously indisposed.

अस्वामिन् a. Having no right to anything, not being master of it. —COMP. -विक्रयः a sale without ownership.

अह् 1 A. or 10 U.=अंह् q. v.

अह ind. A particle implying. (a) praise; (b) separation; (c) resolution; (d) rejecting; (e) sending; (f) deviation from custom.

अहंयु a. Proud, haughty, selfish; Bk. 1. 20.

अहत a. 1 Not hurt or struck. 2 Unwashed, new. -तं An unwashed or new cloth; cf. अप्रहत.

अहन् n. (Nom. अहः, अह्नी-अहनी, अहानि, अह्ना, अहोभ्यां &c.) 1 A day (including day and night; अघाहानि Ms. 5. 84. 2 Day-time; सव्यापारामहनि न तथा पीडयेन्मद्वियोगः Me. 88; यदह्ना कुरुते पापं by day. (At the end of comp. अहन् is changed to अहः,-हं or to अह्न. Note. At the beginning of comp. it assumes the forms अहम् or अहर्; अहःपतिः or अहर्पतिः &c. &c.). -COMP. -आगमः (अहरा° the approach of day. -आदिः dawn. -करः the sun. -गणः (°हर्ग°) 1 a series of sacrificial days.-2 a month. -दिवं ind. daily, every day, day by day. -निशं ind. day and night. -पतिः the sun. -बांधवः the sun. -मणिः the sun. -मुखं commencement of the day, morning, dawn. -रात्रः -त्रं a day and night; त्रिंशत्कला मुहूर्तः स्यादहोरात्रं तु तावतः Ms. 1. 64, 65. -शेषः, -षं evening.

अहम् pron. (Nom. Sing. of अस्मद्) I. -COMP. -अग्रिका a contest for superiority, rivalry. —अहमहमिका 1 emulation, competition, assertion of superiority; अहमहमिकया प्रणामलालसानां K. 14.-2 egotism. -3 military vaunting. -कारः 1 egotism, sense of self, self-love considered as an अविद्या or spiritual ignorance in Vedânta phil.; Bg. 2. 71, 7. 4; Ms. 1. 14. -2 pride, self-conceit, haughtiness. -3 (in Sân. phil.) the third of the eight producers or elements of creation, i. e. the conceit or conception of individuality. -कारिन् a proud, self-conceited. -कृतिः f. egotism, pride, -पूर्व a. desirous of being first -पूर्विका-प्रथमिका 1 the running forward of soldiers with emulation; (hence) emulation, competition, जवादहंपूर्विकया यियासुभिः Ki. 14. 32. -2 bragging, vaunting. -भद्रं self-conceit, high opinion of one's own superiority. -भावः 1 pride, egotism; Bv. 4. 10. -2 =°मति q. v. मतिः f. 1 self love or self-illusion regarded as spiritual ignorance (in Vedânta phil.). -2 conceit, pride, egotism.

अहरणीय, अहार्य a. 1 Not to be stolen, removed, or taken away; अहार्यं ब्राह्मणद्रव्यं राज्ञां नित्यमिति स्थितिः Ms. 9. 189. 2 Devoted, loyal. 3 Firm, unflinching, inexorable; Ku. 5. 8. -र्यः A mountain.

अहल्य a. Unploughed. —ल्या N. of the wife of Gautama. [According to the Ramayana she was the first woman created by Brahma, who gave her to Gautama. She was seduced by Indra who assumed the form of her husband and so deceived her, or, according to another version, she knew the god and was flattered by the great God's condescension. There is another story which states that Indra secured the assistance of the moon who, assuming the form of a cock, crowed at midnight. This roused Gautama to his morning devotions, and Indra went in and took his place. Gautama, when he knew of her seduction, expelled her from his hermitage and cursed her to be a stone and become invisible till she should be touched by the feet of Dasarathi Rama which would restore her to her former shape. Rama afterwards delivered her from her wretched state, and she was reconciled to her husband. Ahalya is one of the five very chaste and pure women whose names every one is recommended to repeat in the morning; अहल्या द्रौपदी सीता तारा मंदोदरी तथा। पंचकन्याः स्मरेन्नित्यं महापातकनाशिनीः ॥ –COMP. –जारः Indra. –नंदनः the sage Satânanda, son of Ahalyâ.

अहह *ind.* A particle or interjection implying (*a*) sorrow or regret ('alas,' 'ah'); अहह कष्टमपंडितताविधेः Bh. 2. 92, 3. 21; अहह ज्ञानराशिर्विनष्टः Mu. 2. (*b*) Wonder or surprise; अहह महतां निस्सीमानश्चरित्रविभूतयः Bh. 2. 35, 36. (*c*) Pity; Bv. 4. 39. (*d*) Calling. (*e*) Fatigue.

अहिः 1 A serpent, snake; अहयः सविषाः सर्वे निर्विषा डुंडुभाः स्मृताः Ks. 14. 84. 2 The sun. 3 The planet Râhu. 4 The demon Vritra. 5 A cheat, rogue. 6 A cloud. –COMP. –कांतः air, wind. –कोषः the slough of a snake. –छत्रकं a mushroom. –जित् *m.* 1. N. of Krishṇa (the slayer of the serpent Kâliyâ). –2 N. of Indra. –तुंडिकः a snake-catcher, conjurer, juggler. –द्विष, –द्रुह्, –मार, –रिपु, विद्विष्, *m.* 1. N. of Garuḍa. –2 an ichneumon. –3 a peacock. –4 Indra. –5 Krishṇa; Ki. 4. 27; Si. 1. 41. –नकुलं snakes and ichneumons. –नकुलिका the natural antipathy between a serpent and an ichneumon. –निर्मोकः, slough of a snake.–पतिः 1. 'the lord of snakes,' Vâsuki. –2 any large serpent. –पुत्रकः a kind of boat (serpent-shaped). –फेनः, नं opium. –भयं 1 the fear of a lurking snake. –2 apprehension of treachery, of danger arising from one's own allies. –भुज् *m.* 1. N. of Garuḍa. –2 a peacock. –3 an ichneumon—भृत् *m.* Siva.

अहिंसा 1 Harmlessness, abstaining from killing or giving pain to others in thought, word, or deed; as अहिंसा परमो धर्मः; Bg. 10. 5; Ms. 10. 63, 5. 44; 6. 75. 2 Security.

अहिंस्र *a.* Harmless, innocent; Ms. 4. 246.

अहिकः A blind snake.

अहित *a.* 1 Not placed, put, or fixed. 2 Unfit, improper; Ms. 3. 20. 3 Hurtful, injurious. 4 Disadvantageous. 5 Inimical, hostile. –तः An enemy; अहिताननिलोद्धूतैस्तर्जयन्निव केतुभिः R. 4. 28, 9. 17, 11. 68. –तं Damage.

अहिम *a.* Not cold, hot.–COMP. –अंशुः, –करः, –तेजस्, –द्युतिः, –रुचिः the sun.

अहीन *a.* 1 Unimpaired, whole, entire. 2 Not inferior, great; अहीनबाहुद्रविणः शशास R. 18. 14. 3 Not deprived of, possessed of; Ms. 2. 183. 4 Not outcast or vile. –नः A sacrifice lasting for several days (–नं also). –COMP. –वादिन् *m.* a witness unfit for or incapable of giving evidence.

अहीरः A cowherd.

अहुत *a.* Not sacrificed or offered (as an oblation); Ms. 12. 68. –तः Religious meditation, prayer, and the study of the Vedas (considered as one of the five great Yajnas and necessary duties); Ms. 3. 73, 74.

अहे *ind.* A particle implying (*a*) Reproach. (*b*) Regret. (*c*) Separation.

अहेतु *a.* Causeless, spontaneous; अहेतुः पक्षपातो यः U. 5. 17.

अहे (है) तुक *a.* Groundless, causeless, without any motive; Bg. 18. 22.

अहो *ind.* 1 A particle showing (*a*) Surprise or wonder often agreeable (ah, how great or wonderful); अहो कामी स्वतां पश्यति S. 2. 2; अहो मधुरमासां दर्शनं S. 1. अहो बकुलावलिका M. 1 Oh, it is B.; अहो रूपमहो वीर्यमहो सत्त्वमहो द्युतिः Râm. (how wonderful his form &c.). (*b*) Painful surprise; अहो ते विगतचेतनत्वं K. 146. 2 Sorrow or regret in general; ('alas,' 'ah'); अहो दुष्यंतस्य संशयमारूढाः पिंडभाजः S. 6; विधिरहो बलवानिति मे मतिः Bh. 2. 91. 3 Praise ('bravo,' 'well done'); अहो देवदत्तः पचति शोभनं Sk. 4 Reproach ('fie,' 'shame'). 5 Calling out or addressing. 6 Envy or jealousy. 7 Enjoyment, satisfaction. 8 Fatigue. 9 Sometimes merely as an expletive; अहो नु खलु (भोः) generally indicates surprise, often agreeable (आश्चर्य); अहो नु खल्वीदृशीमवस्थां प्रपन्नोऽस्मि S. 5; अहो नु खलु भोस्तदेतत्काकतालीयं नाम Mâl. 5. अहो बत shows (*a*) compassion, pity, regret; अहो बत महत्पापं कर्तुं व्यवसिता वयं Bg. 1. 44; (*b*) satisfaction or admiration (संतोष); अहो बतासि स्पृहणीयवीर्यः Ku. 3. 20 (Malli. here takes अहो बत in the sense of संबोधन); (*c*) addressing, calling; (*d*) fatigue.–COMP. –पुरुषिका =आहोपुरुषिका q. v.

अह्नाय *ind.* Instantly, speedily, at once; अह्नाय सा नियमजं क्लममुत्ससर्ज Ku. 5. 86; अह्नाय तावदरुणेन तमो निरस्तं R. 5. 71; Ki. 16. 16.

अ-ह्रीक *a.* Shameless, impudent.–कः A Buddhist mendicant.

आ.

आ The second letter of the Alphabet.

आ 1 Used as a particle, or interjection showing (*a*) assent; 'yes'. (*b*) Compassion 'Ah'. (*c*) Pain or regret (usually written आस् or आः q. v.), 'alas'. (*d*) Recollection 'Ah', 'Oh'; आ एवं किलासीत् U. 6. (*e*) Sometimes used as an expletive; आ एवं मन्यसे. 2 (As a prefix to verbs and nouns) (*a*) it expresses the senses of near, near to, towards, from all sides, all around (see the several verbs). (*b*) With verbs of motion, taking, carrying &c. it shows the reverse of the action; as गम् to go, आगम् to come; दा to give, आदा to take. 3 (As a separable preposition with abl.) it shows either (*a*) the limit inceptive (अभिविधि), from, ever since, away from, out of, off, from among; आमूलात् श्रोतुमिच्छामि S. 1; आ जन्मनः S. 5. 25. (*b*) Or, it expresses the limit exclusive or conclusive (मर्यादा), till, until, upto, as far as, unto; आ परितोषाद्विदुषां S. 1. 2; कैलासात् Me. 11 upto or as far as Kailâsa. (*c*) In both these senses आ frequenly enters into compound, forming either Avyayîbhâva comp. or compound adjectives; आबालं (or आबालेभ्यः) हरिभक्तिः. Sometimes the compound so formed stands as the first member of other compounds; सोऽहमाजन्मशुद्धानामाफलोदयकर्मणां । आसमुद्रक्षितीशानामानाकरथवर्त्मनां R. 1. 5; आगंडविलंबि S. 6. 17. 4 With adjectives (or sometimes with nouns) आ has a diminutive force; आपांडुर little white, whitish; आलक्ष्य S. 7. 17 आकंपः gentle shaking; so आनील, आरक्त;

आं=आम् q. v.

आः 1 =आस् q. v. 2 N. of Lakshmî (आ).

आकत्थनं Boasting, swaggering.

आकंपः 1 Shaking a little. 2 Shaking, trembling.

आकंपनं Trembling motion, shaking.

आकंपित, आकंप्र *a.* Shaking, trembling; moved, agitated.

आकरः 1 A mine; मणिराकरोद्भवः R. 3. 18; आकरे पद्मरागाणां जन्म काचमणेः कुतः H. Pr. 44; (fig.) a mine or rich source of anything; मासो नु पुष्पाकरः V. 1. 9; अशेषगुणाकरं Bh. 2. 92. 2 A collection, group; पद्माकरं दिनकरो विकचीकरोति Bh. 2. 65; Ku. 2. 29. 3 Best, excellent.

आकरिक A person appointed (by the king) to superintend a mine.

आकरिन् *a.* 1 Produced in a mine, mineral. 2 Of good breed; दधतमाकरिभिः करिभिः क्षतैः Ki. 5. 7.

आकर्णनं Hearing, listening.

आकर्षः 1 Attracting or drawing towards oneself. 2 Drawing away from, withdrawing. 3 Drawing (a bow). 4 Attraction, fascination. 5 Playing with dice. 6 A die or dice. 7 A board for a game with dice. 8 An organ of sense. 9 A touch-stone.

आकर्षक *a.* Attracting, attractive. **—कः** A magnet, a loadstone.

आकर्षणं 1 Pullling, drawing, attracting. 2 Seduction. **—णी** A curved stick for pulling down fruits, flowers &c. (Standing on elevated places).

आकर्षिक *a.* (**की** *f.*) Magnetic, Attractive.

आकर्षिन् *a.* Attractive (as a smell at a distance).

आकलनं 1 Laying hold of, seizing; मेखलाकलन K. 183; confinement. 2 Counting, reckoning. 3 Wish, desire. 4 Inquiry. 5 Comprehending, understanding.

आकल्पः 1 An ornament, decoration; आकल्पसारो रूपाजीवाजनः Dk. 63; R. 17. 22, 18. 52. 2 Dress (in general). 3 Sickness, disease.

आकल्पकः 1 Remembering with regret, missing. 2 Fainting. 3 Joy or delight. 4 Darkness. 5 A knot or joint.

आकषः A touch-stone.

आकषिक *a.* Testing, touching.

आकस्मिक *a.* (**की** *f.*) 1 Accidental, unforeseen, unexpected, sudden. 2 Causeless, groundless; नन्वदृष्टानिष्टौ जगद्वैचित्र्यमाकस्मिकं स्यात् S. B.

आकांक्षा 1 Desire, wish; भक्त° Susr., Amaru. 41. 2 (In gram. &c.) The presence of a word necessary to complete the sense, one of the three elements necessary to convey a complete sense or thought (the other two being योग्यता and आसत्ति); आकांक्षा प्रतीतिपर्यवसानाविरहः S. D. 2 the absence of the completion of a sense. 3 Looking at or towards. 4 Purpose, intention. 5 Inquiry. 6 The significancy of a word.

आकायः 1 The fire on the funeral pile. 2 A funeral pile.

आकारः 1 Form, shape, figure; द्विधा° of two forms or sorts. 2 Aspect, appearance, mien, countenance; आकारसदृशप्रज्ञः R. 1. 15, 16. 7. 3 (Particularly) expression of the face, as giving a clue to one's inward thoughts or mental disposition; तस्य संवृतमंत्रस्य गूढाकारेंगितस्य च R. 1. 20; भयानपि संवृताकारमास्ता V. 2. 4 Hint, sign, token. –COMP. **-गुप्तिः** *f.*, **-गोपनं**, **-गूहनं** dissimulation, suppressing all outward manifestation of the internal feelings.

आका (क) रण,—णा 1 Invitation, calling भवदाकारणाय Dk. 175. 2 A challenge.

आकालः The right time.

आकालिक *a.* (**की** *f.*) 1 Momentary, transitory; Ms. 4. 103. 2 Unseasonable, premature, untimely; आकालिकीं वीक्ष्य मधुप्रवृत्तिम् Ku. 3. 34; Mk. 5. 1. **—की** Lightning.

आकाशः—शं 1 The sky; आकाशभवा सरस्वती Ku. 4. 39; °ग, °चारिन् &c. 2 Ether (considered as the fifth element). 3 The subtle and ethereal fluid pervading the whole universe; one of the 9 *dravyas* or substances recognized by the Vaiseshikas. It is the substratum of the quality 'sound;' शब्दगुणमाकाशं cf. also श्रुतिविषयगुणा या स्थिता व्याप्य विश्वं S. 1. 1; अथात्मनः शब्दगुणं गुणज्ञः पदं (scil. आकाशं) विमानेन विगाहमानः R. 13. 1. 4 Free space or vacuity. 5 Space, place in general; सपर्वतवनाकाशां पृथिवीं Mb. भवनाकाशमजायतांबुराशिः Bv. 2 165. 6 Brahma (as identical with ether); आकाशस्तल्लिंगात् Br. Sút.; यावानयमाकाशस्तावानयमंतर्हृदयाकाशः Ch. Up. 7 Light, clearness. आकाशे in the sense of 'in the air' is used in dramas as a stage direction when a character on the stage asks questions to some one not on the stage, and listens to an imaginary speech supposed to be a reply, which is usually introduced by the words किं ब्रवीषि, किं कथयसि &c.; दूरस्थाभाषणं यत्स्यादशरीरनिवेदनं । परोक्षांतरितं वाक्यं तदाकाशे निगद्यते ॥ Bharata; cf. आकाशभाषितं below; (आकाशे) प्रियंवदे कस्येदमुशीरानुलेपनं मृणालवंति च नलिनीपत्राणि नीयंते। (श्रुतिमभिनीय) किं ब्रवीषि &c. S. 3.–COMP. **-ईशः** 1. an epithet of Indra.-2 (in law) any helpless person (such as a child, a woman, a pauper) who has no other possession than the air. **-कक्षा** horizon. **-कल्पः** Brahma. **-गः** a bird. (**-गा**) the heavenly Ganges. **-गंगा** the celestial Ganges; नद्याकाशगंगायाः स्रोतस्युद्दामदिग्गजे R. 1. 78. **-चमसः** the moon. **-जननिन्** *m.* a casement, an embrasure. **-दीपः**, **-प्रदीपः** 1 a lamp lighted in honour of Lakshmî or Vishṇu and raised on a pole in the air at the Divâli festival in the month of Kârtika. -2 a beacon-light, a lantern on a pole. **-भाषितं** 1 speaking off the stage, a supposed speech to which a reply is made as if it had been actually spoken and heard; किं ब्रवीषीति यन्नाट्ये विना पात्रं प्रयुज्यते। श्रुत्वेवानुक्तमप्यर्थं तत्स्यादाकाशभाषितं S. D. 425. -2 a sound or voice in the air **-मंडलं** the celestial sphere. **-यानं** 1 a heavenly car, a balloon. -2 moving or travelling through the sky. **-रक्षिन्** *m.* a watchman on the outer battlements of a castle. **-वचनं** =°भाषितं q. v. **-वर्त्मन्** *n.* 1 the firmament. -2 the atmosphere, air. **वाणी**–a voice from heaven, an incorporeal speech (अशरीरिणी वाणी) **-सलीलं** rain; dew. **-स्फटिकः** hail (करका).

आकिंचनं, आकिंचन्यं Poverty, want of any possession.

आकीर्ण *p. p.* 1 Scattered or spread over. 2 Filled or overspread with, crowded, full of, abounding in; जनाकीर्णं मन्ये हुतवहपरीतं गृहमिव S. 5. 10; आकीर्णमृषिपत्नीनामुटजद्वाररोधिभिः R. 1. 50.

आकुंचनं 1 Bending, contraction, compression. 2 Contraction regarded as one of the 5 *karmans* q. v. 3 Collecting, heaping. 4 Curving.

आकुल *a.* 1 Full of, filled with (in general); प्रचलदूर्मिमालाकुलं (समुद्रं) Bh. 2 4; बाष्पाकुलां वाचं Nala. 4. 18; आलापकुतूहलाकुलतरे श्रोत्रे Amaru. 81. 2 Overcome, affected or afflicted, smit; हर्ष°, शोक°, विस्मय°, स्नेह° &c. 3 Busily or intently engaged or absorbed in. 4 Confounded, agitated, distracted; अभिचैद्यं प्रतिष्ठासुरासीत्कार्यद्वयाकुलः Si. 2. 1; perplexed, at a loss what to do, undetermined; °आकुल very much agitated. 5 Dishevelled, disordered (as hair). 6 Incoherent, contradictory. **—लं** An inhabited place.

आकुलित *a.* 1 Distressed, confounded, agitated; मार्गाचलव्यतिकराकुलितेव सिंधुः Ku. 5 85. 2 Entangled. 3 Obscured, blinded; धूम° दृष्टेः S. 4. 4 Overcome or affected; शोक°, पिपासा° &c.

आकूणित *a.* Contracted a little; मदनशरशल्यवेदनाकूणितत्रिभागेन K. 166. 81.

आकूतं 1 Meaning, intention, purpose; इतीरिताकूतमनीलवाजिनं Ki. 14. 26. 2 A feeling, state of heart, emotion; चूडामंडलबंधनं तरलयत्याकूतजो वेपथुः U. 5. 36; भावाकूत Amaru. 4; Mâl. 9. 11; साकूतं feelingly, meaningly (oft. occurring in plays as a stage-direction). 3 Wonder or curiosity. 4 Wish, desire.

आकृतिः *f.* 1 Form, figure, shape (of anything); गोवर्धनस्याकृतिरन्वकारि Si. 3. 4. 2 Bodily form, body; किमिव हि मधुराणां मंडनं नाकृतीनां S. 1. 20; विकृताकृति Ms. 11. 53; so घोर°. 3 Appearance; oft. a good or noble appearance, good form; न ह्याकृतिः सुसदृशं विजहाति वृत्तं Mk. 9. 16; यत्राकृतिस्तत्र गुणा वसंति Subbâsh. 4 Specimen, character. 5 Tribe, species. —COMP. **-गणः** a list of words belonging to a certain grammatical rule which does not give every word belonging to that rule, but only specimens, a list of specimens (frequently occurring in the Gaṇapâtha); *c. g.* अर्श आदिगण,

स्वरादिगण, चादिगण &c. -छन्ना the plant Achyranthes Aspera.

आकृष्टिः *f.* 1 Attraction (in general). 2 Attraction, gravitation (in astr.); आकृष्टिशक्तिश्च मही तया यत् खस्थं गुरु स्वाभिमुखं स्वशक्त्या । आकृष्यते तत्पततीव भाति समे समंतात् क्व पतत्वियं खे ॥ Golâdh. 1. 3 Drawing or bending of a bow; ज्या° Amaru. 1.

आकेकर *a.* Half-shut, half-closed (eyes); निमीलदाकेकरलोलचक्षुषा Ki. 8. 53; Mu. 3. 21; दृष्टिराकेकरा किंचित्स्फुटापांगे प्रसारिता । मीलितार्धपुटालोके ताराव्यावर्तनोत्तरा ॥.

आकोकेरः The sign Capricornus; (a word of Greek origin).

आक्रंदः 1 Weeping, crying out. 2 Calling out to, invoking. 3 Sound, a cry. 4 A friend, defender. 5 A brother. 6 A fierce or violent combat, battle. 7 A place of crying. 8 A king who prevents an ally from aiding another; a king whose kingdom lies next but one; Ms. 7. 207 (see Kull. thereon).

आक्रंदनं 1 Lamentation, cry of lamentation. 2 Calling out.

आक्रंदिक *a.* One who runs to a place where cries (of distress) are heard.

आक्रंदित *p. p.* 1 Roaring, crying or weeping bitterly. 2 Invoked. -तं A cry, roar.

आक्रमः,-मणं 1 Coming near, approaching. 2 Falling upon, attacking; an attack. 3 Seizing, covering, occupying. 4 Overcoming; obtaining. 5 Spreading or going over, surpassing. 6 Overloading.

आक्रांत *p. p.* 1 Seized, taken possession of, defeated, overcome; आक्रांतविमानमार्गं R. 13. 37 reaching upto; full of, occupied, covered; शुशुभे तेन चाक्रांतं मंगलायतनं महत् R. 17. 29; वलिभिर्मुखमाक्रांतं Bh. 3. 14; so मदन,° भय,° शोक,° &c. B. T. Loaded (as with a burden). 3 Surpassed, eclipsed, superseded; R. 10. 38; M. 3. 5. 4 Obtained, possessed.

आक्रांतिः *f.* 1 Placing upon, occupying; stepping or treading upon; आक्रांतिसंभावितपादपीठं Ku. 2. 11. 2 Overcoming; pressing upon, loading. 3 Ascending; surpassing. 4 Might, valour, force.

आक्रामकः An invader.

आक्रीडः-डं 1 Play, sport, pleasure. 2 A pleasure-grove, pleasure-garden आक्रीडपर्वतास्तेन कल्पिताः स्वेषु वेश्मसु Ku. 2. 43; कमप्याक्रीडमासाद्य तत्र विशिश्रमिषुः Dk. 12.

आक्रुष्ट *p. p.* 1 Scolded, censured, abused, calumniated &c.; *Si.* 12. 27. 2 Sounded, vociferated. 3 Cursed. -ष्टं 1 Calling out. 2 A harsh cry or sound, an abusive speech; मार्जारमूषिकास्पर्शे आक्रुष्टे क्रोधसंभवे Kâty.

आक्रोशः,-शनं 1 Calling or crying out, loud cry or sound. 2 Censure, blame, reviling; abuse Y. 2. 302. 3 A curse, imprecation. 4 An oath.

आक्लेदः Moistening, wetting, sprinkling.

आक्षद्यूतिक *a.* (की *f.*) Effected or completed by gambling.

आक्षपणं 1 Fasting, purifying by fasting, abstinence.

आक्षपाटिकः 1 A judge at playing with dice, superintendent of a gambling house. 2 A judge.

आक्षपाद *a.* (दी *f.*) Taught by Akshapâda or Gautam. -दः A follower of the Nyâya system of philosophy, a logician.

आक्षारः A charge or calumny, accusation (of adultery).

आक्षारणं,-णा Calumny, accusation (especially of adultery).

आक्षारित *p. p.* 1 Calumniated. 2 Guilty, criminal.

आक्षिक *a.* (की *f.*) 1 One who plays at dice. 2 Won by gambling. 3 Relating to dice or gambling; आक्षिकं ऋणं Ms. 8. 159 incurred in gambling. -कं 1 Money gained by gambling. 2 Gambling debt.

आक्षिप्तिका A particular air or song sung by a character while approaching the stage; V. 4.

आक्षीव *a.* 1 Some-what drunk. 2 Drunk, intoxicated.

आक्षेपः 1 Throwing off, tossing, pulling off, snatching away; अंशुकाक्षेपविलज्जितानां Ku. 1. 14; withdrawing. 2 Reviling, censure, blame, abuse, defiant censure; °प्रचंडतया U. 5. 29; विरुद्धमाक्षेपवचस्तितिक्षितं Ki. 14. 25. 3 Distraction, allurement; विषयाक्षेपपर्यस्तबुद्धेः Bh. 3. 47, 23. 4 Applying, laying on, putting in or into (as a colour); गोरोचनाक्षेपनितांतगौरैः Ku. 7. 17. 5 Hinting at, taking to oneself or assuming (as the meaning of another word); स्वसिद्धये पराक्षेपः K. P. 2. 6 An inference. 7 A deposit. 8 An objection or doubt. 9 (In Rhet.) A figure of speech in which something really intended to be said is apparently suppressed or denied to convey a particular meaning; see K. P. 10, S. D. 714. and *Akshepaprakarana* in R. G.

आक्षेपकः 1 A thrower. 2 A detractor, calumniator, accuser. 3 A hunter.

आक्षेपणं Throwing, tossing.

आक्षोटः-ड A walnut; see अक्षोट.

आक्षोदनं Hunting (for आच्छोदनं).

आखः, आखनः A spade, hoe.

आखंडलः Indra; आखंडलः काममिदं बभाषे Ku. 3. 11; तमीशः कामरूपाणामत्याखंडलविक्रमम् R. 4. 83; Me. 15.

आखनिकः 1 A digger, miner. 2 A mouse or rat. 3 A hog. 4 A thief. 5 A spade.

आखरः 1 A spade. 2 A digger, miner.

आखातः तं A natural pond or pool of water, bay.

आखानः-1 Digging all around. 2 spade. 3 A digger.

आखुः 1 A mouse, rat, mole; अन्नं वांछति शांभवो गणपतेराखुं क्षुधार्तः फणी Pt. 1. 159. 2 A thief. 3 A hog. 4 spade. 5 A miser; विभवे सति नैवात्ति न ददाति जुहोति न तमाहुराखु. -Comp. -उत्करः a mole-hill -उत्थ *a.* produced from a mouse. (-त्थं) the rising or appearance of rats, a swarm of rats.-गः,-पत्रः,-रथः, -वाहनः epithets of Ganesa (whose vehicle is a rat). -घातः a Súdra or a man of low caste and profession; (lit.) rat-catcher or killer. -पाषाणः a loadstone. -भुज्,-भुजः a cat.

आखेटकः Hunting, chase. -Comp.- शीर्षकं 1 a smooth floor or ground. -2 a mine, cavern.

आखेटक *a.* Hunting. -कः A hunter -कं Hunting.

आखेटिकः 1 A hunter. 2 A hound.

आखोटः The walnut tree.

आख्या 1 A name, appellation; किं वा शकुंतलेत्यस्य मातुराख्या S. 7, 7. 33; पश्चादुमाख्यां सुमुखी जगाम Ku. 1. 26; तदाख्यया भुवि पप्रथे R 15. 101; often at the end of compounds meaning 'named' or 'called'; अथ किमाख्यस्य राजर्षेः सा धर्मपत्नी *S.* 7; रघुवंशाख्यं काव्यं &c.

आख्यात *p. p.* 1 Said, told, declared 2 Counted, recited. 3 Made known. 4 Inflected or conjugated. -तं A verb; भावप्रधानमाख्यातं Nir.; धात्वर्थेन विशिष्टस्य विधेयत्वेन बोधने । समर्थः स्वार्थयत्नस्य शब्दो वाख्यातमुच्यते ॥.

आख्यातिः *f.* 1 Telling, communication, publication. 2 Fame. 3 A name.

आख्यानं 1 Speaking, declaration, making known, communication. 2 Allusion to some old tale; आख्यानं पूर्ववृत्तोक्तिः S. D.; (*e. g.* देशः सोऽयमरातिशोणितजलैर्यस्मिन्ह्रदाः पूरिताः Ve. 3. 31). 3 A tale, story; especially, a legendary story, legend; अप्सराः पुरूरवसं चकम इत्याख्यानविद आचक्षते Mâl. 2; Ms. 3. 232. 4 A reply, प्रश्नाख्यानयोः P. VIII. 2. 105. 5 A differentiating property.

आख्यानकं A tale, a short legendary narrative, an episode; आख्यानकाख्यायिकेतिहासपुराणाकर्णनेन K. 7.

आख्यायक *a.* Telling, informing. —कः 1 A messenger, courier; आख्यायकेभ्यः श्रुतसूनुवृत्तिः Bk. 2. 44. 2 A herald.

आख्यायिका A species of prose composition, a connected story or narrative; आख्यायिका कथावत् स्यात् कवेर्वंशादिकीर्तनं । अस्यामन्यकवीनां च वृत्तं गद्यं क्वचित् क्वचित् । कथांशानां व्यवच्छेद आश्वास इति बध्यते । आर्यावक्त्रापवक्त्राणां छंदसा येन केनचित् । अन्यापदेशेनाश्वासमुखे भाव्यर्थसूचनं । S. D. 568.

Writers on Rhetoric usually divide prose composition into कथा and आख्यायिका, and make a distinction between them; thus they regard Bâṇa's हर्षचरित as an आख्यायिका and कादंबरी as a कथा; according to Daṇḍin, however, (Kâv. 1. 28) there is no distinction between the two; तत्कथाख्यायिकेत्येका जातिः संज्ञाद्वयांकिता ।.

आख्यायिन् *a.* One who tells, informs, or communicates; रहस्याख्यायीव स्वनसि मृदु कर्णांतिकचरः *S.* 1. 24.

आख्येय *pot. p.* Fit to be communicated or told; शब्द° fit to be told in words, a verbal message; Me. 103

आगतिः *f.* 1 Arrival, coming; लोकस्यास्यगतागतिं Râm.; इति निश्चितप्रियतमागतयः *S*i. 9. 43. 2 Acquisition. 3 Return. 4 Origin.

आगंतु *a.* 1 Coming, arriving. 2 Stray. 3 Coming from the outside; external (as a cause &c.). 4 Adventitious, incidental, casual. **-तुः** A newcomer, stranger, guest. -COMP. **-ज** *a.* arising accidentally or casually.

आगंतुक *a.* (**का, की** *f.*) 1 Coming of one's own accord, arriving uninvited; आगंतुका वयं Dhúrtas. 2 Stray (as an animal); Y. 2. 163. 3 Incidental, accidental; adventitious; इत्यागंतुका विकाराः *A*sval. 4 Interpolated, spurious (as a reading); अत्र गंधवद्वंधमादनामित्यागतुंकः पाठः Malli. on Ku. 6. 46. **—कः** 1 An intruder, interloper. 2 A stranger, guest, new-comer.

आगमः 1 Coming, arrival, appearance; लतायां पूर्वलूनायां प्रसूनस्यागमः कुतः U. 5. 20; अव्यक्ताद् व्यक्तयः सर्वाः प्रभावंत्यहरागमे रात्र्यागमे प्रलीयंते Bg. 8. 18; R. 14. 80; Pt. 3. 48. 2 Acquisition; एषोऽस्या मुद्राया आगमः Mu. 1; *S*. 6; विद्यागमनिमित्तं V. 5. 3 Birth, origin, source; आगमापायिनोऽनित्यास्तांस्तितिक्षस्व भारत Bg. 2. 14. 4 Addition, acquisition (of wealth); अर्थ°, धन° &c. 5. Flow, course, current (of water); रक्त°, फेण°. 6 A voucher or written testimony; see अनागम. 7 Knowledge; शिष्यप्रदेयागमाः Bh. 2. 15; प्रज्ञया सदृशागमः आगमैः सदृशारंभः R. 1 15. 8 Income, revenue. 9 Lawful acquisition of anything; आगमेपि बलं नैव भुक्तिः स्तोकापि यत्र नो Y. 2. 27. 10 Increase of property. 11 A traditional doctrine or precept, a sacred writing or scripture, *S*âstra; अनुमानेन न चागमः क्षतः Ki. 2. 28; परिशुद्ध आगमः 33. 12 The study of *S*âstras, sacred knowledge or learning. 13 Science, a system of philosophy; बहुधाप्यागमैर्भिन्नाः पंथानः सिद्धिहेतवः R. 10. 26. 14 The Vedas, the sacred scripture; न्यायनिर्णीतसारत्वान्निरपेक्षमिवागमे Ki. 11. 39. 15 The last of the four kinds of proof, recognized by the Naiyâyikas (also called शब्द or आप्तवाक्य, the Vedas being so regarded.) 16 An affix or suffix. 17 The addition or insertion of a letter. 18 An augment; इडागमः. 19 Theory (opp. प्रयोग). -COMP. **-नीत** *a.* studied, read, examined. **-वृद्ध** *a.* advanced in knowledge, a very learned man; प्रतीप इत्यागमवृद्धसेवी R. 6. 41. **-वेदिन्** *a.* 1 knowing the Vedas. -2 learned in *S*âstras. **-सापेक्ष** *a.* supported by a voucher.

आगमनं 1 Coming, approaching, arrival; R. 12. 24. 2 Return. 3 Acquisition. 4 Approaching a woman for sexual inter-course.

आगमिन्, आगामिन् *a.* 1 Coming, future. 2 Impending, arriving.

आगस् *n.* 1 Fault, offence, transgression; सहिष्ये शतमागांसि सूनोस्त इति यत्त्वया *S*i. 2. 108; द्वौ रिपू मम मतौ समागसौ R. 11. 74; कृतागाः Mu. 3. 11. 2 Sin. -COMP. **-कृत्** *a.* committing an offence, offender, criminal; अभ्यर्णभागस्कृतमस्पृशद्भिः R. 2. 32.

आगस्ती The south.

आगस्त्य *a.* Southern.

आगाध Very deep or unfathomable (fig. also).

आगामिक *a. f.* (**की**) 1 Relating to the future time; मतिरागामिका ज्ञेया बुद्धिस्तत्कालदर्शिनी Haima. 2 Impending, arriving.

आगामुक *a.* 1 Coming, arriving. 2 Future.

आगारं A house, dwelling. -COMP. **-दाहः** setting a house on fire. **-दाहिन्** *a.* an incendiary. **-धूमः** smoke coming out from a house.

आगुर् *f.* Assent, agreement, promise.

आगु (गू) रणं A secret suggestion.

आगूः (*f.*) An agreement, promise.

आग्निक *a.* (**की** *f.*) Belonging to fire, belonging to the sacrificial fire.

आग्नीध्रं 1 The place where the sacrificial or sacred fire is kindled. **—ध्रः** The priest who kindles the sacred fire.

आग्नेय *a.* (**यी** *f.*) 1 Belonging to Agni; fiery. 2 Offered or consecrated to Agni. **—यः** 1 An epithet of Skanda or Kârtikeya. **—यी** 1 N. of अग्नायी the wife of Agni. 2 The south-east quarter (presided over by Agni). **—यं** The lunar mansion called Krittikâ. 2 Gold. 3 Blood. 4 Ghee. 5 A missile presided over by Agni.

आग्रभोजनिकः A Brâhmaṇa always entitled to occupy the foremost seat at a dinner.

आग्रयणः The first Soma libation at the Agnishṭoma sacrifice. **—णं** An oblation consisting of first fruits at the end of the rainy season.

आग्रहः 1 Seizing, taking. 2 Attack. 3 Determination, strong attachment, persistence; चलेपि काकस्य पदार्पणाग्रहः Naishadha; also Malli. on Ku. 5. 7. 4 Favour, patronage.

आग्रहायणः N. of the month of मार्गशीर्ष. **-णी** 1 The full moon day of मार्गशीर्ष. 2 N. of a constellation called मृगशिरस्.

आग्रहायण (णि) कः The month of मार्गशीर्ष.

आग्रहारिक *a.* (**की** *f.*) One who appropriates to himself an अग्रहार (endowments of land conferred upon Brâhmaṇas).

आघट्टना 1 Moving, shaking, striking against; रणद्भिराघट्टनया नभस्वतः *S*i. 1. 10. 2 Friction, contact.

आघर्षः, -र्षणं Rubbing, friction, striking against; गंडस्थलाघर्षगलन्मदोदकद्रवद्रुमस्कंधानिलायिनोऽलयः *S*i. 12. 64.

आघाटः Boundary, limit.

आघातः 1 Striking, killing. 2 A blow, stroke, wound; तीव्राघातप्रतिहततरुस्कंधलग्नैकदंतः *S*. 1 33; अभ्यस्यंति तटाघातं Ku. 2. 50. 3 Misfortune, calamity. 4 Slaughter-house; आघातं नीयमानस्य H. 4. 67.

आघारः 1 Sprinkling (in general). 2 Especially, sprinkling clarified butter upon the fire at certain sacrifices. 3 Ghee, clarified butter.

आघूर्णनं 1 Rolling. 2 Tossing about, whirling round, swimming.

आघोषः Calling out, invocation.

आघोषणं-णा A proclamation, public announcement; एवमाघोषणायां कृतायां Pt. 5.

आघ्राणं 1 Smelling. 2 Satisfaction, satiety.

आंगारं A multitude of firebrands.

आंगिक *a.* (**की** *f.*) 1 Bodily, corporeal. 2 Gesticulated, expressed by bodily actions; आंगिकोऽभिनयः, see अभिनय. **—कः** A player on a tabor or drum.

आंगिरसः N. of Brihaspati, son of Angiras.

आचक्षुस् *m.* A learned man.

आचमः Rinsing the mouth, sipping.

आचमनं Rinsing the mouth, sipping water before religious ceremonies, before and after meals &c. from the palm of the hand; दद्यादाचमनं ततः Y. 1. 242.

आचमनकं A spitting pot (Mar. पिकदाणी).

आचयः 1 Collecting, gathering. 2 A collection.

आचरणं 1 Practising, doing, following, observing; धर्म°, मंगल° &c. 2 Conduct, behaviour; अधीतिबोधाचरणप्रचारणैः N. 1. 4 example (opp precept). 3 Usage, practice. 4 An institute.

आचांत *a.* 1 One who has rinsed his mouth, or sipped water. 2 Fit for sipping.

आचामः 1 Sipping water, rinsing the mouth. 2 The water or foam of boiled water (Mar. पेज.)

आचारः 1 Conduct, behaviour, manner of action or of conducting oneself. 2 A custom, usage, practice, तस्मिन्देशे य आचारः पारंपर्यक्रमागतः Ms. 2. 18. 3 An established usage, customary law, (opp. व्यवहार in law); oft. as the first member of comp. in the sense of 'customary', 'usual', 'according to form,' 'as a formality'; see °धूम, °लाज below. 4 A form, formality; आचार इत्यवहितेन मया गृहीता S. 5. 3; Mv. 3. 26. 5 Usual formality; आचारं प्रतिपद्यस्व S. 4. –Comp. **–दीपः** a lamp waved about a person as a formality and token of auspiciousness. **–धूमग्रहणं** inhaling smoke as a customary rite (as of the sacrificial ceremony); R. 7. 27; Ku. 7. 82. **–पूत** *a.* purified by customary observances, R. 2. 13. **–भेदः** difference in the customary law. **–भ्रष्ट,–पतित** *a.* apostate, fallen from established usages or rules of conduct. **–लाज** (*m.* pl.) fried grain customarily showered upon a king or other important personage as a mark of respect; R. 2. 10. **–वेदी** 'altar of religious customs,' N. of *A*ryâvarta, the sacred region of the *A*ryas.

आचारिक *a.* Conformable to rule or practice, authorized.

आचार्यः 1 A teacher or preceptor (in general). 2 A spiritual guide or preceptor, holy teacher (one who invests a boy with the sacred thread, instructs him in the Vedas &c.); उपनीय तु यः शिष्यं वेदमध्यापयेत् द्विजः। सकल्पं सरहस्यं च तमाचार्यं प्रचक्षते Ms. 2. 140; see अध्यापक also. 3 One who propounds a particular doctrine. 4 (When affixed to proper names) Learned, venerable (somewhat like the English Dr.). **–र्या** A female preceptor, a spiritual preceptress. –Comp. **–उपासनं** waiting upon or serving the spiritual preceptor. **–मिश्र** *a.* venerable, honourable.

आचार्यकं 1 Instruction, tuition, teaching (lessons &c.); लंकास्त्रीणां पुनश्चक्रे विलापाचार्यकं शरैः R. 12. 78; आचार्यकं विजयि मान्मथमाविरासीत् Mâl. 1. 26. 2 The proficiency of a spiritual teacher.

आचार्यानी The wife of an आचार्य or holy preceptor: शत्रुमूलमनुत्खाय न पुनर्द्रष्टुमुत्सहे। त्र्यंबकं देवमाचार्यमाचार्यानीं च पार्वतीं Mv. 3. 6.

आचित *p. p.* 1 Filled, loaded with, covered with; कचाचितौ विष्वगिवागजौ गजौ Ki. 1. 36; आचितनक्षत्रा द्यौः &c. 2 Tied, strung, woven; अर्धाचिता सत्वरमुत्थितायाः R. 7. 10 (v. 1. for; अर्धाचिता); Ku. 7. 61 3 Collected, accumulated, heaped. **–तः** 1 A cart-load. 2 (*n.* also) A measure of 10 Bhâras or cart-loads (80,000 Tolas).

आचूषणं 1 Suction, sucking up. 2 Sucking out. (In medic.) Application of cupping-glasses to the skin.

आच्छादः Cloth, clothes.

आच्छादनं 1 Covering, concealing. 2 A covering, sheath. 3 Cloth, clothes; भूषणाच्छादनाशनैः Y. 1. 82. 4 The wooden frame of a roof.

आच्छुरित *a.* 1 Mixed, blended with. 2 Scratched; irritated. **–तं** 1 Making a noise with the finger-nails by rubbing them on one another (नखवाद्यं). 2 A horse-laugh.

आच्छुरितकं 1 A scratch with a finger-nail. 2 A horse-laugh.

आच्छेदः,–दनं 1 Cutting off, excision. 2 Cutting a little.

आच्छोटनं Cracking the fingers.

आच्छोदनं Hunting, chase.

आजकं A flock of goats.

आजगवं The bow of *S*iva.

आजननं High birth or origin, famous or well-known origin.

आजानः Birth, origin. **—नं** Birthplace.

आजानेय *a.* (**यी** *f.*) 1 Of good breed (as a horse). 2 Fearless, undaunted. **—यः** A well-bred horse; शक्तिभिर्भिन्नहृदयाः स्खलंतोपि पदे पदे। आजानंति यतः संज्ञामाजानेयास्ततः स्मृताः ॥ *S*abdak.

आजिः 1 A battle, fight, combat; ते तु यावंत एवाजौ तावान् स ददृशे परैः R. 12. 45. 2 A fighting or running match. 3 Battle-field; शस्त्राण्याजौ नयनसलिलं चापि तुल्यं मुमोच V. 3. 9.

आजीवः वनं 1 Livelihood, subsistence, maintenance; भवस्थाजीवनं तस्मात् Pt. 1. 48; cf. words like रूपाजीव, अजाजीव, शस्त्राजीव &c. 2 Profession, the means of maintaining oneself. **–वः** A Jaina beggar.

आजीविका Profession, means of subsistence.

आजुर् *f*.,**–आजू** *f.* 1 Working without wages. 2 A servant working without wages. 3 Doomed residence in hell.

आज्ञप्तिः *f.* An order, command.

आज्ञा 1 An order, command; तथेति शेषामिव भर्तुराज्ञां Ku. 3. 22. 2 Permission, allowance. -Comp. **–अनुग,–अनुगामिन्, अनुयायिन्, –अनुवर्तिन्, –अनुसारिन्, –संपादक,** **–वह** *a.* obedient, submissive. **–कर,–कारिन्** *a.* obeying or executing orders, obedient. (**–रः**) a servant. **–करणं, -पालनं** obedience, execution of commands. **–पत्रं** an edict, written order. **–प्रतिघातः, –भंगः** disobedience, insubordination; नाज्ञाभंगं सहंते नृवर नृपतयस्त्वादृशाः सार्वभौमाः Mu. 3. 22.

आज्ञापनं 1 Ordering, commanding. 2 Making known.

आज्यं 1 Clarified butter, ghee; आज्यधूमोद्गमेन S. 1 (it is often distinguished from घृत; सर्पिर्विलीनमाज्यं स्याद् घनीभूतं घृतं भवेत्). –Comp. **–पात्रं, स्थाली** a vessel or dish to hold clarified butter. **–भुज्** *m.* 1 an epithet of Agni –2 a god, deity.

आंचनं Partial extraction of thorns, arrows, and the like from the body.

आंछ् 1. P. (आंछति, आंछित) 1 To lengthen, extend. 2 To regulate, set (as a bone or leg.).

आंछनं Setting (a bone or leg).

आंजनं 1 Ointment especially for the eyes 2 Fat. **–नः** N. of Mâruti or Hanûmat; दाशरथिबलैरिवांजननीलनलपरिगतप्रांतैः K. 58.

आंजनी Ointment especially for the eyes. –Comp. **–कारी** a woman who anoints or prepares ointments.

आंजनेयः N. of Mâruti.

आटविकः 1 A forester; a woodman. 2 A pioneer.

आटिः 1 A kind of bird (शरारि) (also written आटि).

आटीकनं The leaping motion of a calf.

आटीकरः A bull.

आटोपः 1 Pride, self-conceit, arrogance; साटोपं proudly, in a stately or majestic manner, frequently used as a stage direction. 2 Swelling, spreading, expanding, puffing; Prov. फटाटोपो भयंकरः; *S*i. 3. 74.

आडंबरः 1 Pride, arrogance. 2 Show; means, external appendage; विरचितनारसिंहरूपाडंबरं K. 5; निर्गुणः शोभते नैव विपुलाडंबरोपि ना Bv. 1. 115. 3 The sounding of a trumpet as a sign of attack. 4 Commencement. 5 Fury, anger, passion. 6 Happiness, pleasure. 7 The roaring of clouds and of elephants. 8 A drum used in a battle. 9 The din or uproar of the battle.

आडंबरिन् *a.* Arrogant, proud.

आढकः, कं A measure of grain, the 4th of a Droṇa; अष्टमुष्टिर्भवेत् कुंचिः कुंचयोऽष्टौ तु पुष्कलं। पुष्कलानि च चत्वारि आढकः परिकीर्तितः ॥

आढ्य *a.* 1 Rich, wealthy; आढ्योऽभिजनवानस्मि कोन्योस्ति सदृशो मया Bg. 16. 15; Pt. 5. 8. 2 (*a*) Rich in, abounding in, possessing abundantly, with instr. or as the last member of comp.; सत्य° Pt. 3. 9 very truthful; वंशसंपल्लावण्याढ्याय Dk. 18 (*b*) Mixed with, watered with; गंधाढ्य; स्रजः उत्तमगंधाढ्याः Mb. 3 Abundant, copious. –Comp. **–चर** *a.* (**री** *f.*) once opulent.

आढ्यंकरण *a.* (**णी** *f.*) Enriching. **–णं** The means of enriching, wealth.

आढ्यंभविष्णु,–भावुक *a.* Becoming rich or eminent.

आणक *a* Low, inferior, vile. **–कं** Sexual enjoyment in a particular position; आणकं सुरतं नाम दंपत्योः पार्श्वसंस्थयोः।

आणव *a.* (**वी** *f.*) Exceedingly small. **-वं** Exceeding smallness or minuteness.

आणिः *m. f.* **1** The pin of the axle of a cart, the linch-pin. **2** The part of the leg just above the knee. **3** A boundary, limit. **4** The edge of a sword.

आंड *a.* Born from an egg (as a bird). **-डः** An epithet of Hiranya-garbha or Brahmâ. **-डं 1** A multitude of eggs, brood. **2** Scrotum.

आंडीर *a.* **1** Having many eggs. **2** Grown up, full-grown (as a bull).

आतंकः 1 Disease, sickness of the body; दीर्घतीव्रामयग्रस्तं ब्राह्मणं गामथापि वा। दृष्टा पथि निरातंकं कृत्वा वा ब्रह्महा शुचिः । Y. 3. 245. **2** Pain, affiiction (of the mind), anguish. agony; किन्निमित्तोयमातंकः; *S.* 3; आतंकस्फुरितकठोरगर्भगुर्वी U. 1. 49; V. 3. 3 Fear, apprehension; पुरुषायुषजीविन्यो निरातंका निरीतयः R. 1. 63; fright terror. **4** The sound of a drum or tabor.

आतंचनं 1 Causing to coagulate or curdle. **2** Curdled milk. **3** A sort of whey. **4** Gratifying, satisfying. **5** Danger, calamity. **6** Speed, velocity.

आतत *a.* **1** Spread, extended. **2** Stretched (as a bow-string).

आततायिन् *a.* or *s.* **1** Endeavouring to kill some one; a desperado; गुरुं वा बालवध्वौ वा ब्राह्मणं वा बहुश्रुतं । आततायिनमायांतं हन्यादेवाविचारयन् ॥ Ms. 8. 350-1; Bg. 1. 36. **2** Any one who commits a heinous crime, such as a thief, ravisher, murderer, incendiary, a felon &c.; अग्निदो गरदश्चैव शस्त्रोन्मत्तो धनापहः। क्षेत्रदारहरश्चैतान् षड् विद्यादाततायिनः॥ Sukra N.

आतपः 1 Heat (of the sun, fire &c.), sunshine; आतपायोज्झितं धान्यं Mb. exposed to the sun; प्रचंड° Rs. 1. 11. **2** Light.-Comp. **-अत्ययः** passing of the sun's heat, sunset आतपात्ययसंक्षिप्तनीवारासु R. 1. 52. **-अभावः** shadow or shade. **-उदकं** mirage. **-त्रं, -त्रकं** an umbrella; तमातपक्लांतमनातपत्रं R. 2. 13, 47; पद्म° **4. 5**; राज्यं स्वहस्तधृतदंडमिवातपत्रं *S.* 5. 6. **-लंघनं** being exposed to heat, catching the sun-stroke; आतपलंघनाद्बलवदस्वस्थशरीरा शकुंतला *S.* 3. **-वारणं** an umbrella, parasol; नृपतिककुदं दत्वा यूने सितातपवारणं R. 3. 70, 9 15. **-शुष्क** *a.* dried in the sun-shine.

आतपनः N. of *Siva*.

आतरः, **-आतारः** Fare for being ferried over a river, passegemoney, freight.

आतर्पणं 1 Satisfaction. **2** Pleasing, satisfying. **3** Whitewashing the wall, floor or seat (on festive occasions).

आतापि (यि) न् N. of a bird, a kite.

आतिथेय *a.* (**यी** *f.*) **1** Attentive to guests, hospitable (as a man); प्रत्युज्जगामातिथिमातिथेयः R. 5. 2, 12. 25; तमातिथेयी बहुमानपूर्वया Ku. 5. 31. **2** Proper for, or suited to, a guest; आतिथेयः सत्कारः *S.* 1. **-यं** Hospitality; आतिथेयमनिवारितातिथिः *Si.* 14. 38; सज्जातिथेया वयं Mv. 2. 50. **-यी** Hospitality; Bv. 1 85.

आतिथ्य *a.* Hospitable, proper for a guest &c. **-थ्यः** A guest. **-थ्यं** Hospitable reception, hospitality; तमातिथ्यक्रियाशांतरथक्षोभपरिश्रमं R. 1. 58.

आतिदेशिक *a.* (**की** *f.*) (In gram.) Connected with अतिदेश q. v.

आतिरे (रै) क्यं Superfluity excess, abundance.

आतिशय्यं Excess, abundance, large quantity.

आतुः A raft, float.

आतुर *a.* **1** Hurt, injured. **2** Suffering from, influenced or affected by, afflicted; रावणावरजा तत्र राघवं मदनातुरा R. 12. 32; काम°, भय° &c. **3** Sick (in body or mind); आकाशेशास्तु विज्ञेया बालवृद्धकृशातुराः Ms. 4. 184. **4** Eager, over-anxious **5** Weak, feeble. **-रः** A patient. -Comp. **-शाला** an hospital.

आतोद्यं-द्यकं A musical instrument आतोद्यविन्यासादिका विधयः Ve. 1; स्रजमातोद्यशिरोनिवेशितां R. 8. 34, 15. 88; U. 7.

आत्त *p. p.* (fr. आ-दा) **1** Taken, received, assumed, accepted; एवमात्तरतिः R. 11. 57; M. 5. 1. **2** Agreed to; undertaken. **3** Attracted. **4** Drawn out, extracted; गामात्तसारां रघुरप्यवेक्ष्य R. 5. 26; so आत्तबलं 11. 76. taken away -Comp. **-गंध** *a.* **1** having one's pride humbled, attacked, defeated; केनात्तगंधो माणवकः *S* 6. **2** already smelt (as flower); आत्तगंधमवधूय शत्रुभिः *Si.* 14. 84. (where आ° has sense 1 also). **-गर्व** *a.* humiliated, insulted; degraded. **-दंड** *a.* assuming the royal sceptre. **-मनस्क** *a.* one whose mind is transported (with joy &c.).

आत्मक *a.* (At the end of comp.) Made up or composed of, of the nature or character of &c.; पंच° five-fold; संशय° of a doubtful nature; so दुःख°, दहन°.

आत्मकीय, आत्मीय *a.* Belonging to oneself, one's own; सर्वः कांतमात्मीयं पश्यति *S.* 2; स्वामिनमात्मीयं करिष्यामि H. 2. win over; प्रसादमात्मीयमिवात्मदर्शः R. 7. 68; Ku. 2. 19; kindred, related, of kin.

आत्मन् *m.* **1** The soul; the individual soul; किमात्मना यो न जितेंद्रियो भवेत् H. 1; आत्मानं रथिनं विद्धि शरीरं रथमेव तु Kath. **2** Self, oneself; in this sense mostly used reflexively for all three persons and in the singular number masculine gender, whatever be the gender or number of the noun to which it refers; आश्रमदर्शनेन आत्मानं पुनीमहे *S.* 1; गुप्तं ददृशुरात्मानं सर्वाः स्वप्नेषु वामनैः R. 10. 60; देवी...प्राप्तप्रसवमात्मानं गंगादेव्यां विमुंचति U. 7. 2; गोपायंति कुलस्त्रिय आत्मानमात्मना Mb. **3** Supreme Soul, Brahman तस्माद्वा एतस्मादात्मन आकाशः संभूतः Upan., U. 1. 1. **4** Essence, nature; see आत्मक above. **5** Character, peculiarity. **6** The natural temperament or disposition. **7** The person or whole body; स्थितः सर्वोन्नतेनोर्वीं क्रांत्वा मेरुरिवात्मना R. 1. 14; Ms. 12. 12. **8** Mind, intellect; मंदात्मन्, महात्मन् &c. **9** The understanding; cf. आत्मसंपन्न, आत्मवत् &c. **10** Thinking faculty, faculty of thought or reason. **11** Spirit, vitality, courage. **12** Form, image. **13** A son; आत्मा वै पुत्रनामासि. **14** Care, efforts. **15** The sun. **16** Fire. **17** Wind. आत्मन् is used as the last member of comp. in the sense of 'made or consisting of'; see आत्मक. -Comp. **—अधीन** *a.* dependent on oneself, independent. (**-नः**) **1** a son. **2** a wife's brother. **3** the jester or विदूषक (in dramatic literature). **—अनुगमनं** personal attendance. **-अपहारः** concealing oneself; कथं वा आत्मापहारं करोमि *S.* 1. **-अपहारकः** an impostor, a pretender. **-आराम** *a.* **1** striving to get knowledge (as an ascetic or योगिन्) seeking spiritual knowledge; आत्मारामा विहितरतयो निर्विकल्पे समाधौ Ve. 1. 23. **2** delighted in self.**—आशिन्** *m.* a fish supposed to feed on its young, or on the weakest of its species; cf. मत्स्या इव जना नित्यं भक्षयंति परस्परं। Râm. **-आश्रयः** self-dependence. **-ईश्वर** *a.* self-possessed, master of self; आत्मेश्वराणां न हि जातु विघ्नाः समाधिभेदप्रभवो भवंति Ku. 3. 40. **-उद्भवः 1** a son. **2** Cupid. (**-वा**) a daughter. **—उपजीविन्** *m.* **1** one who lives by his own labour. **2** a daylabourer. **3** one who lives by his wife (Kull on Ms. 8. 362). **4** an actor, public performer. **—काम** *a.* **1** loving oneself, possessed of self-conceit, proud. **2** loving Brahma or the Supreme spirit only. **—गत** *a.* produced in one's mind; °तो मनोरथः *S.* 1. (**-तं**) *ind.* aside (to oneself) being considered to be spoken privately (opp. प्रकाशं aloud); frequently used as a stage-direction in dramas; it is the same as स्वगतं which is thus defined; अश्राव्यं खलु यद्वस्तु तदिह स्वगतं मतं S. D. 6. **-गुप्तिः** *f.* a cave, the hiding-place of an animal. **-ग्राहिन्** *a.* selfish, greedy. **—घातः 1** suicide. **2** heresy. **-घातकः -घातिन्** *m.* **1** a suicide, self-destroyer; व्यापादयेत् वृथात्मानं स्वयं योऽग्न्युदकादिभिः। अवैधेनैव मार्गेण आत्मघाती स उच्यते॥. **2** a heretic. **-घोषः 1** a cock. **2** a crow. **-जः**, **-जन्मन्** *m.*, **-जातः**, **-प्रभवः**,**-संभवः 1** a son; तमात्मजन्मानमजं चकार R. 5. 36; तस्यामात्मानुरूपायामात्मजन्मसमुत्सुकः R. 1. 33; Mâl. 1; Ku. 6. 28. 2 Cupid. **-जा 1** a daughter; वंद्यं युगं चरणयोर्जनकात्मजायाः R,

12. 78; cf. नगात्मजा &c. 2 the reasoning faculty, understanding.—जयः victory over oneself, self-denial or abnegation. —ज्ञः, -विद् m. a sage, one who knows himself. —ज्ञानं 1 self-knowledge of the soul or the supreme spirit. 3 true wisdom.-तत्त्वं the true nature of the soul or the supreme spirit. —त्यागः 1 self-sacrifice. 2 self-destruction, suicide. —त्यागिन् m. 1 a suicide; आत्मत्यागिन्यो नाशौचोदकभाजनाः Y. 3. 6. 2 a heretic. —त्राणं 1 self preservation. 2 a bodyguard. —दर्शः a mirror; प्रसादमात्मीयमिवात्मदर्शः R. 7. 69. —दर्शनं 1 seeing oneself. 2 spiritual knowledge, true wisdom -द्रोहिन् a. 1 self-tormenting 2 a suicide. -नित्य a. being constantly in the heart, greatly endeared to oneself. -निंदा self-reproach. -निवेदनं offering oneself (as a living sacrifice to the deity). -निष्ठ a. one who constantly seeks for spiritual knowledge. -प्रभ a. self-illuminated. -प्रभवः=°जः q. v. प्रशंसा self-praise. -बंधुः, -बांधवः one's own kinsman; आत्ममातुः स्वसुः पुत्रा आत्मपितुः स्वसुः सुताः। आत्ममातुलपुत्राश्च विज्ञेया ह्यात्मबांधवाः Sabdak., i. e. mother's sister's son, father's sister's son, and mother's brother's son. -बोधः 1 spiritual knowledge. 2 knowledge of self. -भूः, -योनिः 1 N. of Brahmâ; बचस्यवसिते तस्मिन् ससर्ज गिरमात्मभूः Ku. 2. 53. 2 N. of Vishṇu. 3 N. of Siva; S. 7. 35. 4 Cupid, god of love. 5 a son. (-भूः f.) 1 a daughter. 2 talent, understanding. -मात्रा a portion of the Supreme spirit. -मानिन् a. 1 self-respecting, respectable. 2 proud. -याजिन् a. sacrificing for oneself or himself. (-m.) a learned man who studies his own nature and that of the soul (of others) to secure eternal felicity, one who looks upon all beings as self; सर्वभूतेषु चात्मानं सर्वभूतानि चात्मनि। समं पश्यन्नात्मयाजी स्वाराज्यमधिगच्छति Ms. 12. 91. योनिः=-भू (m.) q. v.; Ku. 3. 70. रक्षा self-protection. -लाभः birth, production, origin; यैरात्मलाभस्त्वया लब्धः Mu. 3. 1, 5. 23; Ki. 3. 32, 17. 19. -वंचक a. self-deceiver. -वंचना self-delusion; self-deception. -वधः, -वध्या, -हत्या suicide. -वश a. depending on one's own will. (-शः) 1 self-control, self-government. 2 one's control, subjection; °शं नी, °वशीकृ to reduce to subjection, win over. -वश्य a. having control over self, self-possessed, self-restrained. -विद् m. a wise man, sage; as in तरति शोकमात्मवित्. -विद्या knowledge of the soul, spiritual knowledge. -वीरः 1 a son. 2 a wife's brother. 3 a jester (in dramas). -वृत्ति a. dwelling in Atman or soul. (-त्तिः f.) 1 state of the heart. 2 action as regards oneself, one's own state or circumstances; विस्मापयन् विस्मितमात्मवृत्तौ R. 2. 33. -शक्तिः f. one's own power or ability, inherent power or effort; दैवं निहत्य कुरु पौरुषमात्मशक्त्या Pt. 1. 361 to the best of one's power. -श्लाघा, -स्तुतिः f. self praise, boasting, bragging. -संयमः self-restraint. -संभवः, -समुद्भवः 1 a son; चकार नाम्ना रघुमात्मसंभवं R. 3. 21, 11. 57, 17. 8. 2 Cupid, the god of love. 3 epithet of Brahmâ, Vishṇu, or Siva. (-वा) 1 a daughter. 2 understanding. -संपन्न a. 1 self-possessed. 2 talented, intelligent. -हन्= °घातिन् q. v. -हननं, -हत्या suicide. -हित a. beneficial to oneself. (-तं) one's own good or welfare.

आत्मना ind. (instr. of आत्मन्) Used reflexively; अथ चास्तमिता त्वमात्मना R. 8. 51. thou thyself. It is oft. compounded with ordinal numerals; e. g. °द्वितीयः second including himself, i. e. himself and one more.

आत्मनीन a. 1 Belonging to oneself, one's own; कस्यैष आत्मनीनः M. 4. 2 Beneficial to oneself; आत्मनीनमुपतिष्ठते Ki. 13. 69. -नः 1 A son. 2 A wife's brother. 3 A jester (in dramas).

आत्मनेपदं 1 A voice for oneself, one of the two voices in which roots are conjugated in Sanskrit. 2 The terminations of this voice.

आत्मंभरि a. Selfish, greedy (one who feeds his own self); आत्मंभरिस्त्वं पिशितैर्नराणां Bk. 2. 33; H. 3. 128.

आत्मवत् a. 1 Self-possessed. 2 Composed, prudent, wise; किमिवावसादकरमात्मवतां Ki. 6. 19.

आत्मवत्ता Self-possession, self-control, wisdom; प्रकृतिष्वात्मजमात्मवत्तया R. 8. 10, 84.

आत्मसात् ind. In one's own possession, one's own; mostly in combination with कृ or भू; दुरितैरपि कर्तुमात्मसात् R. 8. 2.

आत्यंतिक a. (की f.) 1 Continual, uninterrupted, endless, permanent, everlasting; स आत्यंतिको भविष्यति Mu. 4; विष्णुगुप्तहतकस्यात्यंतिकश्रेयसे 2. 15: Bg 6. 21. 2 Excessive, abundant, superlative. 3 Supreme, absolute; आत्यंतिकी स्वस्वनिवृत्तिः Mit.

आत्ययिक a. (की f.) 1 Destructive, disastrous. 2 Painful, unpropitious, ill-omened. 3 Pressing, urgent, emergent.

आत्रेय a. (यी f.) Belonging to, descended or sprung from, Atri. -यः A descendant of Atri. —यी 1 A female descendant of Atri. 2 The wife of Atri. 3 A woman in her courses (रजस्वला).

आत्रेयिका A woman in her courses.

आथर्वण a. (णी f.) Originating from, relating or belonging to, the Atharvaveda or the Atharvans. -णः 1 A Brâhmaṇa knowing or studying the Atharvaveda. 2 A priest whose ritual is comprised in the Atharvaveda. 3 The Atharvaveda itself. 4 A house-priest.

आथर्वणिकः A Brâhmaṇa who has studied the Atharvaveda.

आदंशः 1 A bite, a wound caused by biting. 2 A tooth.

आदरः 1 Respect, reverence, honour; निर्माणमेव हि तदादरलालनीयं Mâl 9. 49; न जातहार्देन न विद्विषादरः Ki. 1. 33; Ku. 6. 20. 2 Attention, care, close application; Ku. 6. 91. 3 Eagerness, desire, regard; भूयान्दारार्थमादरः Ku. 6. 13; यत्किंचनकारितायामादरः K. 120. 4 Effort, endeavour; गृहयंत्रपताकाश्रीरपौरादरनिर्मिता Ku. 6. 41. 5 Commencement, beginning. 6 Love, attachment.

आदरणं Notice, respect.

आदर्शः 1 A mirror, a looking-grass; आत्मानमालोक्य च शोभमानमादर्शबिंबे स्तिमितायताक्षी Ku. 7. 22. 2 The original manuscript from which a copy is taken; (fig.) a pattern, model, type; आदर्शः शिक्षितानां Mk. 1. 48; आदर्शः सर्वशास्त्राणां K. 5; so गुणानां &c. 3 A copy of a work. 4 A commentary, gloss.

आदर्शकः A mirror.

आदर्शनं 1 Showing, displaying. 2 A mirror.

आदहनं 1 Burning. 2 Injuring, killing. 3 Reviling; despising. 4 A cemetery.

आदानं 1 Taking, accepting, seizing; कुशांकुरादानपरिक्षतांगुलिः Ku. 5. 11; आदानं हि विसर्गाय सतां वारिमुचामिव R. 4. 86. 2 Earning, getting. 3 A symptom (of a disease).

आदायिन् a. Taking, receiving &c.

आदि a. 1 First, primary, primitive; निदानं त्वादिकारणं; Ak. 2 Chief, first, principal, pre-eminent; oft. at the end of comp. in this sense; see below. 3 First in time. —दिः 1 Beginning, commencement (opp. अंत); अप एव ससर्जादौ तासु बीजमवासृजत् Ms. 1. 8; Bg. 3. 41; जगदादिरनादिस्त्वं Ku. 2. 9; oft. at the end of comp. and translated by 'beginning with,' 'et cætera' 'and others,' 'and so on' (of the same nature or kind), 'such like'; इंद्रादयो देवाः the gods Indra and others (इंद्रः आदिर्येषां ते); भ्वादयो धावंतः, भू and others, or words beginning with भू, are called roots; oft. used by Pâṇini to denote classes or groups of grammatical words; अदादि, दिवादि, स्वादि &c. 2 First part or portion. 3 Prime cause. -COMP. -अंत a. having beginning and end. (-तं) beginning and end. °वत् finite. -उदात्त a. having the acute accent on the first syllable. -करः, -कर्तृ, -कृत् m. the creator, an epithet of Brahmâ; Bg. 11. 37. -कविः

'the first poet', an epithet of Brahmâ; and of Vâlmîki; the former is so called because he first produced and promulgated the Vedas; and the latter, because he was the first to show to others 'the path of poets'; when he beheld one of a pair of Kraunch birds being killed by a fowler, he cursed the wretch, and his grief unconsciously took the form of a verse (श्लोकत्वमापद्यत यस्य शोकः); he was subsequently told by Brahmâ to compose the life of Râma, and he thus gave to the world the first poem in Sanskrit, the Râmâyaṇa. **–कांडं** the first book of the Râmâyaṇa. **–कारणं** the first or primary cause (of the universe), which, according to the Vedântins, is Brahma; while, according to the Naiyâyikas and particularly the Vaiseshikas, atoms are the first or material cause of the universe, and not God. **–काव्यं** the first poem, *i. e.* the Râmâyaṇa; see आदिकवि. **–देवः** 1 the first or Supreme God; पुरुषं शाश्वतं दिव्यं आदिदेवमजं विभुं Bg. 10. 12, 18. 38. 2 Nârâyaṇa or Vishṇu. 3 *S*iva. 4 the sun. **–दैत्यः** an epithet of Hiraṇyakasipu. **–पर्वन्** *n.* N. of the first book of the Mahâbhârata **–पु(पू)रुषः** 1 the first or primeval being, the lord of the creation. 2 Vishṇu, Krishṇa, or Nârâyaṇa; ते च प्रापुरुदन्वंतं बुबुधे चादिपूरुषः R. 10. 6; तमर्घ्यमर्घ्यादिकयादिपूरुषः Si. 1. 14. **–बलं** generative power; first vigour. **–भव, –भूत** *a.* produced at first. **–वः, –तः)** 1 'the first-born', primeval being, an epithet of Brahmâ. 2 also N. of Vishṇu; रसातलादादिभवेन पुंसा R. 13. 8. 3 an elder brother. **–मूलं** first foundation, primeval cause. **–वराहः** 'the first boar', an epithet of Vishṇu, alluding to his third or boar incarnation. **–शक्तिः** *f.* 1 the power of माया or illusion. 2 an epithet of Durgâ. **–सर्गः** the first creation.

आदितः, आदौ *ind.* From the first or beginning, at first; तद्दैवेनादितो हतं U. 5. 20.

आदितेयः 1 A son of Aditi. 2 A god, divinity in general.

आदित्यः 1 A son of Aditi; a god, divinity in general. 2 N. of 12 divinities (suns) taken collectively; आदित्यानामहं विष्णुः Bg. 10. 21; Ku. 2. 24. (These 12 suns are supposed to shine only at the destruction of the universe; cf. Ve. 3. 6; दग्धुं विश्वं दहनकिरणैर्नोदिता द्वादशार्काः). 3 The sun. 4 A name of Vishṇu in his fifth or dwarf-incarnation. COMP **–मंडलं** the disc or orb of the sun. **–सूनुः** 'the son of the sun', N. of Sugrîva, Yama, Saturn and Karṇa.

आदि(दी)नवः, –वं 1 Misfortune, distress. 2 Fault; see अनादीनव.

आदिम *a.* First, primitive, original.

आदीनव See आदिनव.

आदीपनं 1 Setting on fire. 2 Exciting; embellishing. 3 Whitening the walls, floor &c. on festive occasions.

आदृत *p. p.* 1 Honoured, respected. 2 (Used actively) (*a*) Zealous, diligent; attentive, careful. (*b*) Respectful.

आदेवनं 1 Gambling. 2 A die used in gambling 3. A board for gambling; place for playing.

आदेशः 1 An order, command; भ्रातुरादेशमादाय Râm.; आदेशं देशकालज्ञः प्रतिजग्राह R. 1. 92; राजद्विष्टादेशकृतः Y. 2.304 doing acts forbidden by the king. 2 Advice, instruction, precept, rule. 3 Account, information, indication. 4. A prediction; विप्रश्निकादेशवचनानि K. 64. 5 (In gram.) A substitute; धातोः स्थान इवादेशं सुग्रीवं संन्यवेशयत् R. 12. 58.

आदेशिन् *a* 1 Ordering, commanding. 2 Exciting, instigating; R. 4. 68. —*m.* 1 A commander. 2 An astrologer.

आद्य *a* 1 First, primitive. 2 Being at the head, pre-eminent, foremost; आसीन्महीक्षितामाद्यः प्रणवश्छंदसामिव R. 1. 11. 3 (At the end of comp.) Beginning with, and so on; see आदि. **—द्या** 1 An epithet of Durgâ. 2 The first day (तिथि) of a month. **—द्यं** 1 The beginning. 2 Grain, food.—COMP.**–कविः** 'the first poet,' an epithet of Brahmâ or Vâlmîki.; see आदिकवि. **–बीजं** the primary or material cause of the universe, which, according to the Sânkhyas, is प्रधान or the inanimate principle.

आद्यून *a.* Shamelessly voracious, gluttonous, hungry; Ki. 11. 5.

आद्योतः Light, brilliance.

आधमनं 1 A deposit, pledge; एको ह्यनीशः सर्वत्र दानाधमनविक्रये Kâty.; योगाधमनविक्रीतं योगदानप्रतिग्रहं Ms. 8 165. 2 Fraudulent puffing of goods at a sale.

आधमर्ण्यं The state of being indebted.

आधार्मिक *a.* Unjust, unrighteous.

आधर्षः 1 Contempt. 2 Injuring forcibly.

आधर्षणं 1 Conviction of crime or error; sentence. 2 Refutation. 3 Injuring, annoying.

आधर्षित *p. p.* 1 Injured. 2 Refuted in argument. 3 sentenced; convicted.

आधानं 1 Placing, putting upon. 2 Taking, assuming, receiving, recovering. 3 Keeping the sacred fire (अग्न्याधान); पुनर्दारक्रियां कुर्यात् पुनराधानमेव च Ms. 5. 168. 4 Doing, executing, performing. 5 Infusing, putting in, imparting, गुणो विशेषाधानहेतुः सिद्धो वस्तुधर्मः S. D. 2; प्रजानां विनयाधानाद्रक्षणाद्भरणादपि R. 1. 24. 6 Engendering, producing; कौतुकाधानहेतोः Me. 3; गर्भाधानक्षणपरिचयात् 9. 7 A pledge, deposit; Y. 2. 238, 247.

आधानिकः A ceremony performed after cohabitation to cause or favour conception.

आधारः 1 Support, prop, stay. 2 (Hence) Power of sustaining, aid, patronage, assistance; त्वमेव चातकाधारः Bh. 2. 50. 3 A receptacle, reservoir; तिष्ठत्याप इवाधारे Pt. 1. 67; चराचराणां भूतानां कुक्षिराधारतां गतः Ku. 6. 67; Ku. 3. 48; *S.* 1. 14. 4 A basin round the foot of a tree; आधारबंधप्रमुखैः प्रयत्नैः R. 5. 6. 5 A dike, dam, embankment. 6 A canal. 7 The sense of the locative case, location; आधारोऽधिकरणं.

आधिः 1 Mental pain or anguish, agony, anxiety, (opp. व्याधि which is bodily pain); न तेषामापदः संति नाधयो व्याधयस्तथा Mb.; मनोगतमाधिहेतुं *S.* 3. 11; R. 8. 27, 9. 54; Bh. 3. 105; Bv. 4. 11. 2 A bane, curse, misery; यांत्येवं गृहिणीपदं युवतयो वामाः कुलस्याधयः *S.* 4. 17; Mv. 6. 28 3 A pledge, deposit, pawn, mortgage; Y. 2. 23; Ms. 8. 143. 4 A place, residence. 5 Location, site. 6 A man solicitous for the maintenance of his family. COMP. **–ज्ञ** *a.* suffering pain. **–भोगः** the use or enjoyment of a deposit (as of a horse, cow &c. when pledged). **–स्तेनः** one who uses a deposit without the owner's consent.

आधिकरणिकः A judge; Mk. 9.

आधिकारिक *a.* (**की** *f.*) 1 Supreme, superior. 2 Official.

आधिक्यं 1 Excess, abundance, preponderance. 2 Superiority, supremacy.

आधिदैविक *a.* (**की** *f.*) 1 Relating to अधिदेव or tutelary deity (as a Mantra); Ms 6. 83. 2 Caused by fate (as pain &c.); according to Susruta pain is of three kinds; आध्यात्मिक, आधिभौतिक or आधिदैविक.

आधिपत्यं 1 Supremacy, power, sovereignty; राज्यं सुराणामपि चाधिपत्यं (अवाप्य) Bg. 2. 8. 2 The duties of a king; पांडोः पुत्र प्रकुरुष्वाधिपत्ये Mb.

आधिभौतिक *a.* (**की** *f.*) 1 Caused by animals (as pain). 2 Relating to beings. 3 Elementary, material.

आधिराज्यं Royalty, sovereignty, supreme sway; बभौ भूयः कुमारत्वादाधिराज्यमवाप्य सः R. 17. 30.

आधिवेदनिकं Property, gifts &c. made to a first wife upon marrying a second; यच्च द्वितीयविवाहार्थिना पूर्वस्त्रियै पारितोषिकं धनं दत्तं तदाधिवेदनिकं Vishṇu.; cf. Y. 2. 143, 148 also.

आधुनिक *a.* (**की** *f.*) New, modern, of recent origin.

आधोरणः The rider or driver of an elephant; आधोरणानां गजसंनिपाते R. 7 46, 5. 48, 18. 39.

आध्मानं 1 Blowing, inflation; (fig.) growth. 2 Boasting. 3 A bellows. 4 Swelling of the belly, body &c., dropsy.

आध्यात्मिक *a.* (**की** *f.*) 1 Relating to the Supreme Spirit. 2 Spiritual, holy. 3 Relating to self. 4 Caused by the mind (pain, sorrow &c.); see आधिदैविक.

आध्यानं 1 Anxiety. 2 Pensive or sorrowful recollection. 3 Meditating.

आध्यापकः A teacher, a spiritual preceptor.

आध्यासिक *a.* (**की** *f.*) Caused by *adhyása, i. e.* by attributing the nature and properties of one thing to another (in Vedânta phil.).

आध्वनिक *a.* (**की** *f.*) Being on a journey, wayfaring; कांतारेष्वपि विश्रामो जनस्याध्वनिकस्य वै Mb.

आध्वर्यव *a.* (**वी** *f.*) Belonging to the *adhvaryu* (q. v.), or to the Yajurveda. **—वं** 1 Service at a sacrifice. 2 Particularly, the office of an Adhvaryu priest.

आनः 1 Inhalation. 2 Breathing, blowing.

आनकः 1 A large military drum (beaten at one end); पणवानकगोमुखाः सहसैवाभ्यहन्यंत Bg. 1. 13. 2 The thunder-cloud. -Comp. **-दुंदुभिः** epithet of Vasudeva, father of Krishṇa. (**-भिः,-भी** *f.*) a large drum or *dhol*, kettle-drum (beaten at one end).

आनतिः *f.* 1 Bending, bowing, stooping (fig. also); गुणवन्निरमिवानतिं प्रपेदे Ki. 13. 15; चरणानतिव्यतिकरे Amaru. 44, 22. 2 A bow or salutation. 3 Homage, reverence.

आनद्ध *a.* 1 Bound, tied. 2 Costive (as stomach). **—द्धः** 1 A drum in general. 2 Dressing, putting on clothes &c.

आननं 1 The mouth, face; R. 3. 3; नृपस्य कांतं पिबतः सुताननं 17. 2 A large division of a work, chapter, book &c. (*e. g.* the two *ânanas* of Rasa-gangâdhara).

आनंतर्यं 1 Immediate succession. 2 Immediate proximity.

आनंत्यं 1 Infinity, endlessness (in time, space or number); आनंत्याद् व्यभिचाराच्च K. P. 2. 2 Boundlessness. 3 Immortality, eternity. 4 An upper world, heaven, future happiness; यस्तु नित्यं कृतमतिर्धर्ममेवाभिपद्यते । अशंकमानः कल्याणि सोऽमुत्रानंत्यमश्नुते Mb.

आनंदः 1 Happiness, joy, delight, pleasure; आनंदं ब्रह्मणो विद्वान्न बिभेति कदाचन 2 God, Supreme spirit (ब्रह्म) (said to be *n.* also in this sense). 3 N. of Siva. -Comp. **-काननं,-वनं** N. of Kâśî. **-पटः** a bridal garment. **-पूर्ण** *a.* full of bliss. (**-र्णः**) the Supreme spirit. **-प्रभवः** semen.

आनंदथु *a.* Happy, joyful. **—थुः** Happiness, joy, pleasure.

आनंदन *a.* Pleasing, delighting. **-नं** 1 Delighting, making happy. 2 Paying respects to. 3 Courteous treatment of a friend or a guest at meeting and parting, courtesy, civility.

आनंदमय *a.* Blissful, made up or consisting of happiness. **-यः** The Supreme spirit. °**कोषः** the innermost wrapper or vesture of the body.

आनंदिः 1 Joy, happiness. 2 Curiosity.

आनंदिन् *a.* 1 Happy, delighted. 2 Pleasing.

आनर्तः 1 A stage, theatre, a dancing-hall. 2 War, battle. 3 N. of a country (also called Saurâshṭra).

आनर्थक्यं 1 Uselessness, unprofitableness; श्रुत्यानर्थक्यमितिचेत् Kâty ; आम्नायस्य क्रियार्थत्वादानर्थक्यमतदर्थानां Jaimini S. 2 Unfitness.

आनायः A net.

आनायिन् *m.* A fisherman, fisher; आनायिभिस्तामपकृष्टनक्रां R. 16. 55, 75.

आनाय्य *a.* To be brought near. **-य्यः** Consecrated fire taken from गार्हपत्य (also called दक्षिणाग्नि).

आनाहः 1 Binding. 2 Constipation. 3 Length (especially of cloth).

आनिल *a.* (**ली** *f.*) Proceeding from or produced by wind. **—लः**, **-आनिलिः** N. of Hanúmat or Bhîma.

आनील *a.* Darkish, slightly blue. **—लः** A black horse.

आनुकूलिक *a.* (**की** *f.*) Favourable, conformable.

आनुकूल्यं 1 Favourableness, suitableness; यत्रानुकूल्यं दंपत्योस्त्रिवर्गस्तत्र वर्धते Y. 1. 74. 2 Kindness; favour.

आनुगत्यं Acquaintance, familiarity.

आनुगुण्यं Favourableness, suitableness, congruity.

आनुग्रामिक *a.* (**की** *f.*) Rural, rustic.

आनुनासिक्यं Nasality.

आनुपदिक *a.* (**की** *f.*) Following, pursuing, tracking; studying.

आनुपूर्वं,-र्व्यं-र्वी 1 Order, succession, series; Ms. 2. 41. 2 (In law). The regular order of the castes; षडानुपूर्व्या विप्रस्य क्षत्रस्य चतुरोऽवरान् Ms. 3. 23.

आनुपूर्वे-र्व्ये-ण *ind.* One after another, in due order.

आनुमानिक *a.* (**की** *f.*) 1 Relating to a conclusion. 2 Derived from an inferential. **—कं** The Pradhâna of the Sânkhyas; आनुमानिकमप्येकेषामिति चेन्न Br. Sût.

आनुयात्रिकः A follower, attendant.

आनुरक्तिः *f.* Passion, affection.

आनुलोमिक *a.* (**की** *f.*) 1 Regular, orderly. 2 Favourable.

आनुलोम्यं 1 Natural or direct order, proper arrangement; आनुलोम्येन संभूता जात्या ज्ञेयास्त एव ते Ms. 10. 5, 13. 2 Regular series or succession. 3 Favourableness.

आनुवेश्यः A neighbour who lives next to the next-door neighbour; प्रातिवेश्यानुवेश्यौ च कल्याणे विंशतिद्विजे Ms. 8. 392; (on which Kull. says :—निरंतरगृहवासी प्रातिवेश्यः, तदनंतरगृहवास्यानुवेश्यः). The word is also found to be written as अनुवेश्य.

आनुषंगिक *a.* (**की** *f.*) 1 Connected with, concomitant. 2 Implied. 3 Inevitable, necessary. 4 Of secondary importance, secondary; अणुभिः स्थास्तु यशश्चिचीषतः ननु लक्ष्मीः फलमानुषंगिकं Ki. 2. 19; अन्यतरस्यानुषंगिकत्वेऽन्वाचयः Sk. see अन्वाचय. 5 Attached to, fond of. 6 Relative, proportionate. 7 (In gram.) Elliptical.

आनूप *a.* (**पी** *f.*) 1 Watery, marshy, wet. 2 Produced in a marshy place. **-पः** Any animal frequenting marshy or watery places (as a buffalo).

आनृण्यं Aquittance of debt or obligation; see अनृणता.

आनृशंस-स्य *a.* Mild, kind; merciful. **-सं,-स्यं** 1 Mildness. 2 Kindness; Ms. 1. 101, 8. 411. 3 Compassion, pity, mercy.

आनैपुणं,-ण्यं Clumsiness, stupidity.

आंत *a.* (**ती** *f.*) Final, terminal. **-ते** *ind.* Completely, to the end.

आंतर *a.* 1 Internal, secret, hidden; U. 6. 12; Mâl. 1. 24. 2 Inmost inward. **—रं** Inmost nature.

आंतरि (री) क्ष *a.* (**क्षी** *f.*) 1 Atmospherical, heavenly, celestial. 2 Produced in the atmosphere. **—क्षं** The firmament, the intermediate region between the earth and sky.

आंतर्गणिक *a.* (**की** *f.*) Included (as in a class, troop &c).

आंतर्गेहिक *a.* (**की.** *f.*) Being or produced inside a house.

आंतिका An elder sister.

आंदोल् 10 P. [-दोलयति, दोलित] 1 To swing, rock or move to and fro. 2 To shake, tremble.

आंदोलः 1 Swinging, a swing. 2 Trembling.

आंदोलनं 1 Swinging. 2 Moving to and fro, shaking; rocking; किंत्वासामरविंदसुंदरदृशां द्राक्चामरांदोलनात् Udb. 3 Trembling.

आंधसः The scum of boiled rice.

आंधसिकः A cook.

आंध्यं Blindness.

आंध्र *a.* Belonging to Andhra (as language). **—ध्राः** (pl.) The Telagu country, modern Telangaṇa; see अंध्र.

आन्वयिक *a.* (की *f.*) 1 Of a good family, well-born, of noble birth. 2 Orderly.

आन्वाहिक *a.* (की *f.*) Daily, occurring or to be performed every day; पङ्क्तिं चान्वाहिकीं Ms. 3 67.

आन्वीक्षिकी 1 Logic, logical philosophy. 2 Metaphysics (आत्मविद्या q. v.) आन्वीक्षिक्यात्मविद्या स्यादीक्षणात्सुखदुःखयोः । ईक्षमाणस्तया तत्वं हर्षशोकौ व्युदस्यति ॥ Kâm. 2. 11; आन्वीक्षिकिश्रवणाय Mâl. 1; Ms. 7. 43.

आप् 5. P. (आप्नोति, आप्त) 1 To obtain, attain, get; पुत्रमेवंगुणोपेतं चक्रवर्तिनमाप्नुहि *S*. 1 12; अनुद्योगेन तैलानि तिलेभ्यो नाप्तुमर्हति H. Pr. 30; शतं क्रतूनामपविघ्नमाप सः R. 3. 38; so फलं, कीर्तिं, सुखं &c. 2 To reach, go to; overtake, meet; Bk. 6. 59. 3 To pervade, occupy. 4 To under-go; suffer, meet with; द्विष्टांतमाप्स्यति भवान् R. 9. 69. –WITH –अनुप्र 1 to get, obtain. 2 to reach, go to, overtake; गंगानदीमनुप्राप्ताः Mb. 3 to arrive, come to. –अव 1 to get, obtain, secure; पुत्रं त्वमपि सम्राजं सेव पुरुमवाप्नुहि *S*. 4. 6; R. 3. 33; अवाप्तोत्कंठानां Mâl. 2. 12. 2 to reach, overtake. –परि (used generally in *p. p.*) 1 to be competent; पर्याप्तं त्विदमेतेषां बलं भीष्माभिरक्षितं Bg. 1. 10; Ms. 11. 7. 2 to be able. 3 to be full; as in पर्याप्तकलः, or पर्याप्तदक्षिणः. 4 to save, defend, preserve; इमां परीप्सुर्दुर्जातेः M. 5. 11. 5 to make an end of, finish. –प्र 1 to get, obtain. 2 to go to, reach; यथा महाह्रदं प्राप्य क्षिप्तं लोष्टं विनश्यति Ms. 11. 264; R. 1. 48, Bk. 15. 106; so आश्रमं, नदीं, वनं &c. 3 to meet, overtake; Bk. 5. 96; see प्राप्त. –वि to fill completely, pervade; श्रुतिविषयगुणा या स्थिता व्याप्य विश्वं *S*. 1. 1; so V. 1. 1; Bg. 10. 16; R. 18. 40; Bk. 7. 56. –सं 1 to get, obtain. 2 to finish, complete (in *caus.* also); यावदेतां समाप्येरन् यज्ञाः पर्याप्तदक्षिणः R. 17. 17, 24; समाप्य सांध्यं च विधिं 2. 23.

आपकर *a.* (री *f.*) Offensive, unfriendly, mischievous.

आपक्व *a.* Crude, half-baked. –क्वं A cake, bread.

आपगा A river, stream; फेनायमानं पतिमापगानां *Si*. 3. 72.

आपगेयः A son of the river, an epithet of Bhîshma or Krishṇa.

आपणः A market, a shop.

आपणिक *a.* (की *f.*) 1 Relating to traffic, market &c.; mercantile. 2 Got from the market. –कः A shopkeeper, merchant, dealer.

आपतनं 1 Approaching, coming, assailing &c. 2 happening, occurrence. 3 Obtaining. 4 Knowledge; क्वचित् प्राकरणिकादर्थादप्राकरणिकस्यार्थस्यापतनं S. D. 10. 5 Natural sequence, necessarily following.

आपतिक *a.* (की *f.*) Accidental, unforeseen, sent from heaven. –कः A hawk, falcon.

आपत्तिः *f.* 1 Turning or changing into. 2 Obtaining, procuring, getting. 3 Misfortune, calamity. 4 (In phil.) An undesirable conclusion or occurrence (अनिष्टप्रसंग).

आपद् *f.* A calamity, misfortune, danger; दैवीनां मानुषीणां च प्रतिहर्ता त्वमापदां R. 1. 60; अविवेकः परमापदां पदम् Ki. 2. 30, 14; प्रायो गच्छति यत्र भाग्यरहितस्तत्रैव यात्यापदः Bh. 2. 90.–COMP. –कालः days of adversity, time of distress, –गत,-ग्रस्त-प्राप्त *a.* 1 fallen into misfortune. 2 unfortunate, distressed. –धर्मः a practice, profession, or course of procedure, not usually proper for a caste, but allowable in times of extreme distress or calamity.

आपदा *f.* Misfortune, calamity.

आपनिकः 1 An emerald, sapphire, 2 A *Kirata* or barbarian.

आपन्न *p. p.* 1 Gained, obtained, जीविकापन्नः. 2 Gone or reduced to, fallen into; कष्टां दशामापन्नोपि Bh. 2. 29; so दुःख°. Afflicted, distressed, being in difficulty; आपन्नाभयसत्रेषु दीक्षिताः खलु पौरवाः *S*. 2. 16; Me. 53. –COMP. –सत्त्वा pregnant, quick or big with child; a pregnant woman; सममापन्नसत्त्वास्ता रेजुरापांडुरत्विषः R. 10. 59.

आपमित्यक *a.* Received by barter or exchange. –कं Property or anything obtained by barter or for a consideration.

आपराह्णिक *a.* (की *f.*) Being in the afternoon.

आपस् *n.* 1 Water; आपोभिर्मार्जनं कृत्वा. 2 Sin.

आपातः 1 Rushing or falling upon, attack, descending, alighting; तदापातभयात्पथि Ku. 2. 45; गरुडापातविश्लिष्टमेघनादास्त्रबंधनः R. 12. 76. 2 Causing to descend or fall; falling down. 3 (*a*) The present or current moment, the instant; आपातरम्या विषयाः पर्यंतपरितापिनः Ki. 11. 12; आपातसुरसे भोगे निमग्नाः किं न कुर्वते S. D.; Bv. 1. 115; Mâl. 5. (*b*) (Hence) First sight or appearance; see आपाततः. 4 Happening; appearance.

आपाततः *ind.* At the first sight or attack, instantly.

आपादः 1 Attainment, obtaining. 2 Reward, remuneration.

आपादनं 1 Causing to arrive at, bringing about; tending to; द्रव्यस्य संख्यांतरापादने Sk.

आपानं,-नकं 1 A drinking party, banquet; Mk. 8; आपाने पानकलिता दैवेनाभिप्रणोदिताः Mb. 2 A tavern, liquorshop; तांबूलीनां दलैस्तत्र रचितापानभूमयः R. 4. 42; Ku. 6. 42; आपानकमुत्सवः K. 32.

आपालिः A louse.

आपीडः 1 Giving pain, hurting. 2 Squeezing, compressing. 3 A chaplet, garland in general; चूडापीडकपालसंकुलगलन्मंदाकिनीवारयः Mâl. 1. 2. 4 (Hence fig.) A crest-jewel; तस्मिन्कुलापीडनिभे विपीडं R. 18. 29; Mâl. 1, 6, 7.

आपीन *p. p.* Stout, fat, strong. –नः A well; आपीनोंऽधः Sk. –नं An udder, teat; आपीनभारोद्वहनप्रयत्नात् R. 2. 18.

आपूपिक *a.* (की *f.*) 1 A good maker of अपूप (cakes). 2 Accustomed to eat cakes. –कः A baker; confectioner. –कं A multitude of cakes.

आपूप्यः Flour.

आपूरः 1 Flow, current, quantity; स्वेदापूरोयुवतिसरितां व्याप गंडस्थलानि *Si*. 7. 74. 2 Filling, making full.

आपूरणं Filling, making full; गर्त° कृतं Pt. 1.

आपूषं A kind of metal (perhaps tin.)

आपृच्छा 1 Conversation. 2 Bidding farewell. 3 Curiosity.

आपोशानः N. of a kind of prayer or formula repeated before and after eating (the formulas being respectively अमृतोपस्तरणमसि स्वाहा and अमृतापिधानमसि स्वाहा); Y. 1. 31, 106. –नं The act of making an उपस्तरण (seat) and अपिधान (covering) for the food eaten.

आप्त *p. p.* 1 Got, obtained, gained; °कामः, °शापः &c. 2 Reached, overtaken. 3 Trustworthy, reliable, credible (as news &c.). 4 Trusty, confidential, faithful (person); R. 3. 12; 5. 39. 5 Intimate, acquainted. 6 Reasonable, sensible –प्तः 1 A trustworthy, reliable, or fit person; credible person or source; आप्तः यथार्थवक्ता T. S. 2 A relative, friend; निग्राहस्त्वसुराप्तानां वधाच्च धनदानुजः R. 12. 52; कथमाप्तवर्गोयं भवत्याः M. 5. –प्तं 1 A quotient. 2 (In Math.) Equation of a degree. –COMP. –काम *a.* 1 one who has obtained his desire. 2 one who has renounced all worldly desires and attachments. (–मः) supreme soul. –गर्भा a pregnant woman. –वचनं the words of a credible or trustworthy person; R. 11. 42, 15. 48. –वाच् *a.* worthy of belief, one whose words are credible and authoritative; परातिसंधानमधीयते यैर्विधेति ते संतु किलाप्तवाचः *S*. 5 25. (*–f.*) 1 the advice of a friend or credible person. 2 the Vedas or *Sruti*; a word of authority (said to apply to Smritis, Itihâsas and Purâṇas also, which are considered as authoritative evidence); आप्तवागनुमानाभ्यां साध्यं त्वां प्रति का कथा R. 10. 28. –श्रुतिः *f.* 1 the Vedas. 2 Smritis &c.

आप्तिः *f.* 1 Getting, obtaining, gain, acquisition. 2 Reaching, meeting with. 3 Fitness, aptitude, propriety. 4 Completion, fulfilment.

आप्य *a.* 1 Watery. 2 Obtainable.

आप्यान *p. p.* 1 Fat, stout, robust, strong. 2 Pleased, satisfied. **—नं** 1 Love. 2 Growth, increase.

आप्यायनं -ना 1 The act of making full or fat. 2 Satisfaction, satiety; देवस्याप्यायना भवति Pt. 1. 3 Advancing, promoting. 4 Corpulency. 5 A strengthening medicine.

आप्रच्छनं 1 Bidding adieu, taking leave at the time of departure. 2 Welcoming, hailing.

आप्रपदीन *a.* Reaching to the feet (as dress).

आप्लवः,-प्लवनं 1 Bathing, immersing. 2 Sprinkling with water (on all sides).-Comp.**—व्रतिन्** or **आप्लुतव्रतिन्** *m.* a householder who has passed through the first order (ब्रह्मचर्य) and is admitted into the second (गार्हस्थ्य), an initiated house-holder; cf. स्नातक.

आप्लावः 1 Bathing. 2 Sprinkling 3 A flood, an inundation.

आफूकं Opium.

आबद्ध *p. p.* 1 Bound, tied. 2 Fixed; R. 1. 40. 3 Formed, made; आबद्धमंडला तापसपरिषद् K. 49 sitting in a circle. 4 Obtained. 5 Hindered. **-द्धं** (द्धः also). 1 Binding, joining. 2 A yoke. 3 Ornament. 4 Affection.

आबंधः,—धनं 1 A tie or bond (fig. also); प्रेमाबंधविवर्धित Ratn. 3. 18; Amaru. 38. 2 The tie of a yoke. 3 Ornament, decoration. 4 Affection.

आबर्हः 1 Tearing or pulling out. 2 Killing.

आबाधः 1 Affliction, injury, trouble, molestation, damage; न प्राणाबाधमाचरेत् Ms. 4. 54, 51. **—धा** 1 Pain, distress. 2 Mental agony or anguish.

आबुत्त=आवुत्त q. v.

आबोधनं 1 Knowledge, understanding. 2 Instructing, informing.

आब्द *a.* (**ब्दी** *f.*) Belonging to, or produced from, a cloud.

आब्दिक *a.* (**की** *f.*) Annual, yearly, आब्दिकः करः Ms. 7. 129, 3. 1.

आभरणं 1 An ornament, decoration (fig. also); किमित्यपास्याभरणानि यौवने धृतं त्वया वार्द्धकशोभि वल्कलं Ku. 5. 44; प्रशमाभरणं पराक्रमः Ki. 2. 32. 2 The act of nourishing.

आभा 1 Light, splendour, lustre; दीपाभां शलभा यथा Pt. 4. 2 Colour, appearance, beauty; प्रशांतमिव शुद्धाभं Ms. 12. 27. 3 Likeness, resemblance; oft. at the end of comp. in these two senses; यमदूताभं Pt. 1. 58; मरुत्सखाभं R. 2. 10. 4 A reflected image; shadow, reflection.

आभाणकः A popular saying, proverb.

आभाषः 1 Addressing. 2 An introduction, preface.

आभाषणं 1 Addressing, speaking to (संबोधन). 2 Conversation; संबंधमाभाषणपूर्वमाहुः R. 2. 58.

आभासः 1 Splendour, light, lustre. 2 A reflection; तत्राज्ञानं धिया नश्येदाभासात्तु घटः स्फुरेत् Vedânta. 3 (*a*) Resemblance, likeness; oft. at the end of comp.; नभश्च रुधिराभासं Râm. &c. (*b*) Semblance, phantom; तत्साहसाभासं Mâl. 2 looks like wantonness. 4 Any unreal or fallacious appearance (as in हेत्वाभास). 5 A fallacy, semblance of a reason; see हेत्वाभास. 6 An intention, purpose.

आभासु (स्व) रः *a.* Splendid, bright. **—र** A collective name of 64 demigods.

आभिचारिक *a* (**की** *f.*) 1 Magical. 2 Imprecatory, maledictory. **-कं** A spell or incantation, magic.

आभिजन *a.* (**नी** *f.*) Relating to birth (अभिजन), patronymic (as a name); तां पार्वतीत्याभिजनेन नाम्ना Ku. 1. 26. **—नं** Nobility or loftiness of birth.

आभिजात्यं 1 Nobility of birth; Ratn. 3. 18. 2 Rank. 3 Learning. 4 Beauty.

आभिधा 1 A sound, word. 2 A name; mentioning; see अभिधा.

आभिधानिक *a.* (**की** *f.*) Contained in a dictionary. **-कः** A lexicographer.

आभिमुख्यं 1 Direction towards; °ख्यं याति goes to meet or encounter. 2 Being in front of; or face to face; निताभिमुख्यं पुनः Ratn. 1. 2. 3 Favourableness.

आभिरूपक, आभिरूप्यं Beauty.

आभिषेचनिक *a.* (**की** *f.*) Relating to the inauguration of a king आभिषेचनिकं यत्त रामार्थमुपकल्पितं Râm.; Mv. 4.

आभिहारिक *a.* (**की** *f.*) To be offered as a present. **—कं** A present.

आभीक्ष्ण्यं Continued repetition; बहुलमाभीक्ष्ण्ये P. III. 2. 81.

आभीरः 1 A cowherd; आभीरवामनयनाहृतमानसाय दत्तं मनो यदुपते तदिदं गृहाण Udb. 2 (pl.) N. of a country or its inhabitants. **—री** 1 A cowherd's wife. 2 A woman of the *A*bhîra tribe. -Comp. **-पल्लिः,-ल्ली** *f.*, **-पल्लिका** a station or abode of herds-men, a village inhabited by cowherds.

आभील *a.* Fearful, terrible **—लं** Injury, physical pain.

आभुग्न *a.* A little curved or bent.

आभोगः 1 Circuit, circumference, expanse, extension, precincts; environs; अकाथितोऽपि ज्ञायत एव यथायमाभोगस्तपोवनस्येति *S.* 1; गगनाभोगः the expanse of heaven. 2 Magnitude, fulness, extent; गंडाभोगात् Me. 92 from the broad cheek. 3 Effort. 4 The expanded hood of a cobra (used by Varuṇa as his umbrella). 5 Enjoyment, satiety; विषयाभोगेषु नैवादरः Sântilakshaṇa.

आभ्यंतर *a.* (**री** *f.*) Interior, inner, inward.

आभ्यवहारिक *a.* (**की** *f.*) Eatable (as food &c).

आभ्यासिक *a.* (**की** *f.*) 1 Resulting from practice. 2 Practising, repeating. 3 Being near, neighbouring, adjoining (आभ्याशिक)

आभ्युदयिक *a.* (**की** *f.*) 1 Tending to good, granting prosperity; अनाभ्युदयिकं श्रमणकदर्शनं Mk. 8. 2 High, exalted, important. **-कं** A *S*râddha or offering to ancestors; an occasion of rejoicing.

आम् *ind.* An interjection of (*a*) assent, acceptance, 'oh', 'yes'; आं कुर्मः M. 1; (*b*) recollection; आं ज्ञातम् *S.* 3, Oh, I see it now; (*c*) determination, 'surely,' 'verily'; आं चिरस्य खलु प्रतिबुद्धोस्मि; (*d*) reply.

आम *a.* 1 Raw, uncooked, undressed (opp. पक्व); आमान्नं Ms. 4. 223. 2 Unripe, immature. 3 Unbaked (as jar). 4 Undigested **—मः** 1 Disease; sickness. 2 Indigestion; constipation. 3 Grain freed from chaff (आम also). -Comp. **-आशयः** 'receptacle of undigested food,' the upper part of the belly, stomach. **-कुंभः** a jar of unbaked clay; H. 4. 66. **-गंधि** *n.* smelling of raw meat or of a burning corpse **-ज्वरः** a kind of fever; cf. स्वेद्यमानज्वरं प्राज्ञः कोंऽभसा परिषिंचति *Si.* 2. 54. **-त्वच्** *a.* of tender skin. **-पात्रं** an unannealed vessel; विनाशं व्रजति क्षिप्रमामपात्रमिवांभसि Ms. 3. 179. **-रक्तं** dysentery. **-रसः** imperfect chyme. **-वातः** constipation. **-शूलः** pain of indigestion, colic.

आमंजु *a.* Lovely, charming.

आमंडः The castor-oil plant.

आम (मा) नस्यं Pain, sorrow.

आमंत्रणं णा 1 Addressing, calling, calling out to. 2 Bidding adieu, taking leave of. 3 Greeting. 4 Invitation; अनिंद्यामंत्रणादृते Y 1. 112. 5 Permission. 6 Conversation, अन्योन्यामंत्रणं यत्स्याज्जनांते तज्जनांतिकं S. D. 6. 7 The vocative case.

आमंद्र *a.* Having a slightly deep tone, rumbling: आमंद्राणां फलमविकलं लप्स्यसे गर्जितानां Me. 34. **-न्द्रः** A slightly deep tone, rumbling.

आमयः 1 Disease, sickness, distemper; दर्पामयः Mv. 4. 22; आमयस्तु रतिरागसंभवः R. 19. 48; *Si.* 2. 10. 2 Damage, hurt.

आमयाविन् *a.* Sick, dyspeptic, affected with indigestion.

आमरणांत,-न्तिक *a*. (**की** *f*.) Lasting till death, lasting for life; आमरणांताः प्रणयाः कोपास्तत्क्षणभंगुराः H. 1. 118; अन्योन्यस्याव्यभीचारो भवेदामरणांतिकः Ms. 9. 101.

आमर्दः 1 Crushing. 2 Rough handling.

आमर्शः 1 Touching, rubbing. 2 Counsel, advice.

आमर्षः-र्षणं Anger, wrath, impatience; see अमर्ष.

आमलकः -की The tree, Emblic Myrobalan (Mar. आंवळा). **—कं** Fruit of the Emblic Myrobalan; बदरामलकाम्रदाडिमानां Bv. 2. 8.

आमात्यः A minister, counsellor; see अमात्य.

आमानस्यं Pain, sorrow.

आमिक्षा Curd of milk and whey, a mixture of boiled and coagulated milk.

आमिषं 1 Flesh; उपानयत् पिंडमिवामिषस्य R. 2. 59. 2 (Hence fig.) A prey, victim, object of enjoyment; (राज्यं) रंध्रान्वेषणदक्षाणां द्विषामामिषतां ययौ R. 12. 11 fell a prey &c.; Dk. 164. 3 Food, bait. 4 A bribe. 5 Desire, lust. 6 Enjoyment; pleasing or lovely object.

आमीलनं Shutting or closing of the eyes.

आमुक्तिः *f*. Wearing, putting on (clothes, armour &c.).

आमुखं 1 Commencement. 2 (In dramas) A prologue, prelude (प्रस्तावना); (every Sanskrit play is introduced by आमुख). It is thus defined in S. D. नटी विदूषको वापि पारिपार्श्वक एव वा। सूत्रधारेण सहिताः संलापं यत्र कुर्वते ॥ चित्रैर्वाक्यैः स्वकार्योत्थैः प्रस्तुताक्षेपिभिर्मिथः। आमुखं तत्तु विज्ञेयं नाम्ना प्रस्तावनापि सा ॥ 287. **-खं** *ind*. To the face.

आमुष्मिक *a*. (**की** *f*.) Belonging to the next or other world; आमुष्मिकं श्रेयः Susr.; नैवालोच्य गरीयसीरपि चिरादामुष्मिकीर्यातनाः S. D.

आमुष्यायण *a*. or **-णः** (**णी** *f*.) Well-born, a son or descendant of such a one; *i. e*. of an illustrious person or family; आमुष्यायणो वै त्वमसि Sat. Br.; तदामुष्यायणस्य तत्रभवतः सुगृहीतनाम्नो भट्टगोपालस्य पौत्रः Mâl. 1; Mv. 1.

आमोचनं 1 Loosing, liberating. 2 Emitting, shedding, discharging. 3 Putting or tying on.

आमोटनं Crushing; Mâl. 3.

आमोदः 1 Joy, pleasure, delight. 2 Fragrance (diffusive), perfume; आमोदमुपजिघ्रंतौ स्वनिःश्वासानुकारिणं R. 1. 43; आमोदं कुसुमभवं मृदेव धत्ते मृद्गंधं न हि कुसुमानि धारयंति Subhâsh.; Si. 2. 20; Me. 31.

आमोदन *a*. Delighting, pleasing. **-नं** 1 Delighting, rejoicing. 2 Making fragrant.

आमोदिन् *a*. 1 Happy. 2 Fragrant Bh. 1. 35.

आमोषः Theft, robbing.

आमोषिन् *m*. A thief.

आम्नात *p. p*. 1 Considered, regarded, said to be; समौ हि शिष्टैराम्नातौ वर्त्स्यंतावामयः स (शत्रुः) च Si. 2. 10. 2 Studied, repeated. 3 Remembered. 4 Handed down traditionally. **-तं** Study.

आम्नानं 1 Recitation or study of the sacred texts or Vedas. 2 Mention; repetition in general.

आम्नायः 1 (*a*) Sacred tradition. (*b*) Hence, the Veda, Vedas taken collectively (including Brâhmaṇas, Upanishads and *A*raṇyakas also); अधीती चतुर्ष्वाम्नायेषु Dk. 120; आम्नायवचनं सत्यमित्ययं लोकसंग्रहः । आम्नायेभ्यः पुनर्वेदाः प्रसृताः सर्वतोमुखाः ॥ Mb. 2 Traditional usage, family or national customs. 3 Received doctrine. 4 Advice or instruction.

आंबिकेयः An epithet of (*a*) Dhṛitarâshṭra; (*b*) Kârtikeya.

आंभसिक *a*. (**की** *f*.) Aquatic. **-कः** A fish.

आम्रः The mango-tree. **-म्रं** The fruit of the mango-tree. -Comp. **-कूटः** the name of a mountain. सानुमानाम्रकूटः Me. 17. **-पेशी** a portion of dried mango-fruit. **-वणं** a grove of mango-trees; सोहमाम्रवणं छित्त्वा Râm.

आम्रातः The hog-plum. **-तं** The fruit of this tree.

आम्रातकः 1 The hog-plum. 2 Inspissated mango juice (Mar. साट)

आम्रेडनं Tautology; repetition of words or sounds.

आम्रेडितं 1 Repetition of sound or word. 2 (In gram.) Reduplication; the second word in reduplication.

आम्लः, -म्ला The tamarind tree. **-म्लं** Sourness, acidity.

आम्लि (म्ली) का 1 The tamarind tree. 2 Acidity of stomach.

आयः 1 Arrival, approach. 2 Gaining or acquisition of money, acquiring (opp. व्यय). 3 Income, revenue, receipt; ग्रामेषु स्वामिग्राह्यो भाग आयः Sk.; Y. 1. 322, 326; Mk. 2. 6; Ms. 8. 419; आयाधिकं व्ययं करोति he lives beyond his means. 4 Gain, profit. 5 The guard of the women's apartments. -Comp. **-व्ययौ** (dual) income and expenditure.

आयःशूलिक *a*. (**की** *f*.) Active, diligent, indefatigable. **-कः** A man who, in order to gain an object, uses forcible instead of gentle means (तीक्ष्णोपायेन योऽन्विच्छेत्स आयःशूलिको जनः); cf. K. P. 10; अयःशूलेन अन्विच्छति (scil. अर्थान्) इत्यायःशूलिकः.

आयत *p. p*. 1 Long; शतमध्यर्धं (योजनं) आयता Mb. 2 Diffuse, prolix. 3 Big, large, great. 4 Drawn, attracted. 5 Curbed, restrained.**—तः** An oblong (in geometry). -Comp. **अक्ष** *a*. (**क्षी** *f*.), **-ईक्षण, -नेत्र, -लोचन** *a*. (a woman) with large eyes. **-अपांग** *a*. having long-cornered eyes. **-आयतिः** *f*. long continuance, remote futurity; Si. 14. 5. **-छदा** a plantain tree. **-लेख** *a*. long-curved; Ku. 1. 47. **-स्तुः** *m*. a panegyrist, bard.

आयतनं 1 Place, abode, house, resting-place; (fig. also); शूलायतनाः Mu. 7 hangmen; स्नेहस्तदेकायतनं जगाम Ku. 7. 5 was centred in her; R. 3. 36; सर्वाविनयानामेकैकमप्येषामायतनं K. 103; (hence) a receptacle, home. 2 The place of the sacred fire, altar. 3 A sanctuary, sacred place; as in देवायतनं मठायतनं &c. 4 The site of a house.

आयतिः *f*. 1 Length, extension. 2 Future time, the future; °भंग K. 44 (length also); भूयसी तव यदायतायतिः Si. 14. 5; रहयत्यापदुपेतमायतिः Ki. 2. 14. 3 Future consequence or result; आयतिं सर्वकार्याणां तदात्वं च विचारयेत् Ms. 7. 178. Ki. 1. 15, 2. 43. 4 Majesty, dignity. 5 Stretching the hand, accepting, obtaining. 6 Work (कर्मन् ;) यथा मित्रं ध्रुवं लब्ध्वा कृशमप्यायतिक्षमं Ms. 7; 208 (कर्मक्षमं Kull.). 7 Restraint (of mind).

आयत्त *p. p*. 1 Dependent on, resting with (with loc. or in comp.), दैवायत्तं कुले जन्म मदायत्तं तु पौरुषं Ve. 3. 33; भाग्यायत्तमतःपरं S. 4. 16. 2 Docile; tractable.

आयत्तिः *f*. 1 Dependence, subjection. 2 Affection. 3 Strength, power. 4 Boundary, limit. 5 An expedient, remedy. 6 Majesty, dignity. 7 Steadiness of conduct.

आयथातथ्यं Unfitness, unsuitableness, impropriety; Si 2. 56.

आयमनं 1 Length, extension. 2 Restraint, curbing. 3 Stretching (as a bow).

आयल्लकः Impatience, longing,

आयस *a*. (**सी** *f*.) Made of iron, iron, metallic; आयसं दंडमेव वा Ms. 8. 315; सखि मा जल्प तवायसी रसज्ञा Bv. 2. 59. **—सी** A coat of mail, an armour for the body. **-सं** 1 Iron; मूढं बुद्धमिवात्मानं हैमीभूतमिवायसं Ku. 6. 55; स चकर्ष परस्मात्तदयस्कांत इवायसं R. 17. 63. 2 Anything made of iron. 3 A weapon.

आयस्त *p. p*. 1 Pained, distressed. 2 Hurt. 3 Vexed; angry. 4 Sharpened.

आयानं 1 Coming, arrival. 2 Natural temperament, disposition.

आयामः 1 Length; तिर्यगायामशोभी Me. 57. 2 Expansion, extension; Ki. 7. 6. 3 Stretching, extending. 4 Restraint, control, stopping; प्राणायामपरायणाः Rg. 4. 26; प्राणायामः परं तपः Ms. 2. 83.

आयामवत् Extended, long; V. 1. 4; Si. 12. 65.

आयासः 1 Effort, exertion, trouble, difficulty, labour; बहुलायास Bg. 18. 24; cf. अनायास also. 2 Fatigue, weariness; स्नेहमूलानि दुःखानि देहजानि भयानि च। शोकहर्षौ तथायासः सर्वं स्नेहात् प्रवर्तते ॥ Mb.

आयासिन् *a*. 1 Exhausted, fatigued. 2 Making exertion, striving; मनस्तु तद्भावदर्शनायासि *S*. 2. 1. v. l.

आयुक्त *p. p.* 1 Appointed, charged with (with gen. or loc.); Bk. 8. 115. 2 United; obtained. **-क्तः** A minister, an agent or deputy.

आयुधः -धं A weapon, shield &c.; it is of three kinds (1) प्रहरण *e. g.* a Sword; (2) हस्तमुक्त *e. g.* a disc; (3) यंत्रमुक्त *e. g.* an arrow; न मे त्वदन्येन विसोढमायुधं R. 3. 63. -Comp. **-(अ) आगारं** an armoury, arsenal; अहमप्यायुधागारं प्रविश्यायुधसहायो भवामि Ve. 1; Ms. 9. 280. **-जीविन्** *a*. living by one's weapon. (*-m.*) a warrior, soldier.

आयुधिक *a*. Relating to arms. **-कः** A soldier, warrior.

आयुधिन्, आयुधीय *a*. Bearing or using weapons. —*m*. (**धी**), **-धीयः** A warrior.

आयुष्मत् *a* 1 Alive, living. 2 Long lived. (Generally used in dramas by elderly persons in addressing a nobly-born person; *e. g.* a charioteer addresses a prince as आयुष्मन्. A Brâhmaṇa is also so addressed in saluting; cf. Ms. 4. 125; आयुष्मन् भव सौम्येति वाच्यो विप्रोऽभिवादने.

आयुष्य *a*. Promoting long life, vital, preservative of life; इदं यशस्यमायुष्यमिदं निःश्रेयसं परं Ms. 1. 106, 3. 106. **-ष्यं** Vital power.

आयुस् *n*. 1 Life, duration of life; दीर्घमायुः R. 9. 62; तक्षकेणापि दष्टस्य आयुर्मर्माणि रक्षति H. 2. 16; शतायुर्वै पुरुषः Ait. Br. 2 Vital power. 3 Food. (In comp. the final स् of this word is changed to ष् before hard consonants, and to र् before soft ones). -Comp. **-कर** *a*. (**री** *f*.) promoting long life. **-काम** *a*. wishing for long life or health. **-द्रव्यं** 1 a medicament. 2 ghee. **-वृद्धिः** *f*. long life, longevity. **-वेदः** the science of health or medicine. **-वेददृश्** **-वेदिक, -वेदिन्** *a*. belonging to medicine. (*-m.*) a physician. **-शेषः** 1 remainder of life; °शेषतया Pt. 1. 2 end or decline of life. **-स्तोमः** (आयुष्टोमः) a sacrifice performed to obtain long life.

आये *ind*. An interjection of calling, expressive of affection.

आयोगः 1 Appointment. 2 Action, performance of an act. 3 Offering flowers, perfumes &c. 4 A shore or bank.

आयोगवः The son of a *S*údra by a Vaisya wife (his business being carpentry; cf. Ms 10. 48). **-वी** A woman of this tribe.

आयोजनं 1 Joining. 2 Seizing, taking. 3 Effort, exertion.

आयोधनं 1 A battle, fight, war; आयोधने कृष्णगतिं सहायं R. 6. 42; आयोधनाग्रसरतां त्वयि वीर याते 5. 71. 2 Battle-field.

आर., -रं 1 Brass. 2 Oxide of iron. 3 An angle, corner. **-रः** 1 The planet Mars. 2 The planet Saturn. **-रा** 1 A shoemaker's awl. 2 A knife, probe. -Comp. **-कूटः, -टं** brass; U. 5. 14.

आरक्ष *a*. Preserved. **-क्षः, -क्षा** 1 Protection, preservation, guard; आरक्षे मध्यमे स्थितान् Râm.; Sânti. 3. 5.; Ms. 3. 204. 2 The junction of the frontal sinuses of an elephant (कुंभसंधि) 3 An army.

आरक्ष (क्षि) कः 1 A watchman, sentinel. 2 A village or police magistrate.

आरटः An actor.

आरणिः An eddy, whirlpool.

आरण्य *a*. (**ण्या,-ण्यी** *f*.) Wild, forest-born.

आरण्यक *a*. Relating to or produced in a forest, wild, forest-born. **—कः** A forester, an inhabitant of the woods; तपः षड्भागमक्षय्यं ददत्यारण्यका हि नः *S*. 2. 13. **—कं** An *Araṇyaka*; it is one of a class of religious and philosophical writings (connected with the Brâhmaṇas) which are either composed in a forest, or must be studied there; अरण्येऽनूच्यमानत्वात् आरण्यकं Bri. Art. Up.; अरण्येऽध्ययनादेव आरण्यकमुदाहृतं.

आरति; *f*. 1 Cessation. 2 Waving lights before an image (Mar. आरती).

आरनालं Gruel made from the fermentation of boiled rice.

आराब्धिः *f*. Beginning, commencement.

आरभटः An enterprising or courageous man. **—टः, —टी** Boldness, confidence **—टी** 1 A branch of the dramatic art, see S. D. 420 *et. seq*. 2 A kind of literary style (वृत्ति). 3 A particular style of dancing.

आरंभः 1 Beginning, commencement; °**उपायः** plan of commencement; नृत्यारंभे हर पशुपतेरार्द्रनागाजिनेच्छां Me. 99. 2 An introduction. 3 An act, undertaking, deed, work; आगमैः सदृशारंभः R. 1. 15; R. 7. 31; Bg 12. 16 4 Haste; speed. 5 Effort, exertion; Bg. 14. 12. 6 Scene, action, चित्रार्पितारंभ इवावतस्थे R. 2. 31. 7 Killing, slaughter.

आरभणं 1 Taking hold of, seizing. 2 The place of, seizing, a handle.

आर (रा) वः 1 Sound. 2 A cry, howling.

आरस्यं Insipidity, tastelessness.

आरा See under आर.

आरात् *ind*. 1 Near, in the vicinity of; (with abl. or by itself); तमर्च्यमारादभिवर्तमानं R. 2. 10; 5. 3. 2 Far from; with acc. also in both these senses; *S*i. 3. 31; to a distant place, distant. 3 Far, from a distance; U. 2. 24.

आरातिः An enemy.

आरातीय *a*. 1 Near, proximate. 2 Remote.

आरात्रिकं 1 Waving a light (or the vessel containing it) at night before an idol (Mar. आरती ओंवाळणें); सर्वेषु चांगेषु च सप्तवारान् आरात्रिकं भक्तजनस्तु कुर्यात्. 2 The light so waved; शिरसि निहितभारं पात्रमारात्रिकस्य भ्रमयति मयि भूयस्ते कृपार्द्रः कटाक्षः *S*ankara.

आराधनं 1 Pleasing, satisfaction, enterainment; येषामाराधनाय U. 1; यदि वा जानकीमपि आराधनाय लोकानां मुंचतो नास्ति मे व्यथा 1. 12. 2 Serving, worshipping, adoration, propitiation (as of a deity); आराधनायास्य सखीसमेताम् Ku. 1 58; Bg. 7. 22 3 A means of pleasing; इदं तु ते भक्तिनम्रं सतामाराधनं वपुः Ku. 6. 73. 4 Honouring, respecting; U. 4. 17. 5 Cooking. 6 Accomplishment, undertaking, attainment. **—ना** Service. **—नी** Worship, adoration, propitiation (of a deity).

आराधयितृ *a*. An adorer, humble servant, worshipper.

आरामः 1 Delight, pleasure; इंद्रियारामः Bg. 3. 16; आत्मारामाः Ve. 1. 31; एकाराम Y. 3. 58. 2 A garden, grove; प्रियारामा हि वैदेह्यासीत् U. 2; आरामाधिपतिर्विवेकविकलः Bv. 1. 31.

आरामिकः A gardener.

आरालिकः A cook.

आरुः 1 A hog. 2 A crab.

आरू *a*. Of a tawny colour.

आरूढ *p. p.* Mounted, ascended; seated on; आरूढो वृक्षो भवता Sk.; oft. used actively; आरूढमद्रीन् R. 6. 77.

आरूढिः *f*. Ascent, rise, elevation (lit. and fig.); अत्यारूढिर्भवति महतामप्यपभ्रंशनिष्ठा *S*. 4 v. 1.

आरेकः 1 Emptying. 2 Contraction.

आरेचित *a*. Contracted (eyebrows &c.).

आरोग्यं Good health.

आरोपः 1 Attributing the nature or properties of one thing to another; वस्तुन्यवस्त्वारोपोऽध्यारोपः Vedânta S.; imputation; दोषारोपो गुणेष्वपि Ak. 2 Considering (as in सारोपा लक्षणा). 3 Superimposition. 4 Imposing (as a burden), burdening or charging with.

आरोपणं 1 Placing or fixing in or upon, putting; आर्द्राक्षतारोपणमन्वभूतां R 7. 28; Ku. 7. 88; (fig.) establishing, installing; अधिकारारोपणं Nu. 3. 2 Planting. 3 The stringing of a bow.

आरोहः 1 One who mounts, a rider, as in अश्वारोह, स्यंदनारोह. 2 Ascent, rising; riding. 3 An elevated place, elevation, height. 4 Haughtiness, pride. 5 A mountain; a heap. **6** A woman's waist; the buttocks; सा रामा न वरारोहा Udb.; आरोहैर्निबिडबृहन्नितंबबिंबैः Si. 8. 8. **7** Length. **8** A kind of measure. **9** A mine.

आरोहकः A rider, driver.

आरोहणं 1 the act of rising, ascending, mounting, आरोहणार्थं नवयौवनेन कामस्य सोपानमिव प्रयुक्तं Ku 1. 39. **2** Riding (on a horse &c.). **3** A staircase, ladder.

आर्किः A son of **अर्क**, epithet of (1) Yama, (2) the planet Saturn, (3) Karṇa, (4) Sugrîva, (5) वैवस्वतमनु.

आर्क्ष *a.* (**र्क्षी** *f.*) Stellar, regulated by stars or pertaining to them.

आर्घा A kind of yellow bee.

आर्घ्यं Wild honey.

आर्च *a.* (**र्ची** *f.*) Devout, worshipping, pious.

आर्चिक *a.* (**की** *f.*) Relating to the *R*igveda, or explaining it **—कं** An epithet of the Sâma-Veda.

आर्जवं 1 Straightness. **2** Straightforwardness, rectitude of conduct, uprightness, honesty, sincerity, open heartedness; अहिंसा क्षांतिरार्जवं Bg. 13. 7; क्षेत्रमार्जवस्य K. 45. **3** Simplicity, humility.

आर्जुनिः The son of Arjuna, अभिमन्यु.

आर्त *a.* **1** Afflicted with, struck by, suffering from, usually in comp., कामार्त, क्षुधार्त, तृषार्त &c. **2** Sick, diseased; आर्तस्य यथौषधं R. 1. 28; Ms. 4. 236. **3** Distressed, afflicted, struck by calamity, oppressed, unhappy; आर्तत्राणाय वः शस्त्रं न प्रहर्तुमनागसि *S*. 1. 11; R. 2. 28, 8. 31, 12. 10, 32.–Comp. **–नादः,–ध्वनिः, –स्वरः** a cry of distress. **बंधुः, –साधुः** a friend of the distressed.

आर्तव *a.* (**वा-वी** *f.*) **1** Conforming or relating to the season; seasonal: अभिभूय विभूतिमार्तवीं R. 8. 36; Ku. 4. 68; vernal; R. 9. 28. **2** Menstrual. **—वः** A section or the year. **—वी** A mare. **—वं 1** The menstrual discharge (of women); नोपगच्छेत्प्रमत्तोऽपि स्त्रियमार्तवदर्शने Ms. 4. 40, 3. 48. **2** Certain days after menstrual discharge favourable to conception. **3** A flower.

आर्तवेयी A woman during her courses

आर्तिः *f.* **1** Distress, affliction, suffering, pain, injury (bodily or mental); आर्तिं न पश्यसि पुरूरवसस्तदर्थे V. 2. 16; आपन्नार्तिप्रशमनफलाः संपदो ह्युत्तमानां Me. 53. **2** Mental agony, anguich: उत्कंठार्ति Amaru. 39. **3** Sickness, disease. **4** the end of a bow. **5** Ruin, destruction.

आर्त्विजीन *a.* (**नी** *f.*) Fit for the office of a sacrficial priest (ऋत्विज्).

आर्त्विज्यं The office of a priest, his rank.

आर्थ *a.* (**र्थी** *f.*) **1** Relating to a thing or object. **2** Relating to, dependent on, sense (opp. **शब्द**); आर्थी उपमा &c.

आर्थिक *a.* (**की** *f.*) **1** Significant. **2** Wise. **3** Rich. **4** Substantial, real.

आर्द्र *a.* **1** Wet, moist, damp: तंत्रीमार्द्रां नयनसलिलैः Me. 86, 43. **2** Not dry, green, juicy. **3** Fresh, new; कामीवार्द्रापराधः Amaru. 2; कांतमार्द्रापराधं M. 3. 12. **4** Soft, tender, oft. used with words like स्नेह, दया, करुणा in the sense of 'flowing with,' 'moved,' 'melted'; स्नेहार्द्रं हृदयं a heart wet or melted with pity. **—र्द्रा** N. of a constellation or the sixth lunar mansion so called (consisting of one star)–Comp. **—काष्ठं** green wood. **—पृष्ठ** *a.* watered, refreshed; आर्द्रपृष्ठाः क्रियंतां वाजिनः *S*. 1. **—शाक** fresh ginger.

आर्द्रकं Ginger in its undried state, wet ginger.

आर्द्रयति Den. P. To wet, moisten; Bh. 2. 51.

आर्ध *a.* (Only used at the beginning of comp.) Half. —Comp. **—धातुक** *a.* (**की** *f.*) (In gram.) applicable to half the root or to the shorter form of the verbal base. (**-कं**) a name given to those terminations and affixes which belong to the six non-conjugational or general tenses (opp. सार्वधातुक). **—मासिक** *a.* (**की** *f.*) lasting for half a month.

आर्धिक *a.* (**की** *f.*) Sharing a half, relating to a half. **—कः** One who ploughs the land for half the crop; one born of a Vaisya woman, and brought up by a Brâhmaṇa; see the quotation under अर्धिक.

आर्य *a.* **1** *A*ryan; or worthy of an *A*rya. **2** Worthy, respectable, honourable, noble, high; यदार्यमस्यामभिलाषि मे मनः *S*. 1. 22; oft. used in theatrical language as an honorific adjective and a respectful mode of address; आर्य revered or honoured Sir; आर्ये revered or honoured lady. The following rules are laid down for the use of आर्य in addressing persons:— (1) वाच्यौ नटीसूत्रधारावार्यनाम्ना परस्परं। (2) वयस्येत्युत्तमैर्वाच्यो मध्यैरार्येति चाग्रजः। (3) (वक्तव्यो) अमात्य आर्येति चेतरैः। (4) स्वेच्छया नामभिर्विप्रैर्विप्र आर्येति चेतरैः। S. D. 431. **3** Noble, fine, excellent. **–र्यः 1** N. of the Hindu and Iranian people, as distinguished from अनार्य, दस्यु and दास. **2** A man who is faithful to the religion and laws of his country; कर्तव्यमाचरन् कार्यमकर्तव्यमनाचरन्। तिष्ठति प्रकृताचारे स वा आर्य इति स्मृतः॥. **3** N. of the fiirst three castes (as opp. to शूद्र). **4** A respectable or honourable man, esteemed person. **5** A man of noble birth. **6** A man of noble character. **7** A master, owner. **8** A preceptor, teacher. **9** A friend. **10** A Vaisya. **11** A father-in-law (as in आर्यपुत्र). **12** A Buddha. **—र्या 1** N. of pârvatî. **2** A mother-in-law. **3** A respectable woman. **4** N. of a metre, see Appendix. —Comp. **—आवर्तः** 'abode of the noble or excellent (*A*ryas)'; particularly, N. of the tract extending from the eastern to the western ocean, and bounded on the north and south by the Himâlaya and Vindhya respectively; cf. Ms. 2. 22; आसमुद्रात्तु वै पूर्वादासमुद्राच्च पश्चिमात्। तयोरेवांतरं गिर्योः (हिमवद्विंध्ययोः) आर्यावर्तं विदुर्बुधाः; also 10. 34. **—गृह्य** *a.* **1** to be respected by the noble. **2** a friend of the noble, readily accessible to honourable men; तमार्यगृह्यं निगृहीतधेनुः R. 2. 33. **3** respectable, right. **–देशः** a country inhabited by the *A*ryas. **–पुत्रः 1** son of an honourable man **2** the son of a spiritual preceptor. **3** honorific designation of the son of the elder brother; of a husband by his wife; or of a prince by his general &c. **4** the son of the father-in-law, *i. e* a husband (occurring in every drama; mostly in the vocative case in the last two senses). **–प्राय** *a.* **1** inhabited by the *A*ryas **2** abounding with respectable people. **–मिश्र** *a.* respectable, worthy, distinguished. (**-श्रः**) a gentleman, a man of consequence; (pl.) worthy or respectable men; an assembly of honourable men; आर्यमिश्रान् विज्ञापयामि V. 1. **2** your reverence or honour (a respectful address); नन्वार्यमिश्रैः प्रथममेव आज्ञप्तं *S*. 1. **–लिंगिन्** *m.* an impostor. **–वृत्त** *a.* virtuous, good; R. 14. 55. **–वेश** *a.* well-clothed, having a respectable dress. **–सत्यं** a noble or sublime truth. **–हृद्य** *a.* liked by the noble.

आर्यकः 1 An honourable or respectable man. **2** A grandfather.

आर्यका, आर्यिका A respectable woman.

आर्ष *a.* (**र्षी** *f.*) **1** Used by a *R*ishi only, relating or belonging to sages, archaic, Vedic (opp. लौकिक or classical); आर्षः प्रयोगः; संबुद्धौ शाकल्यस्येतावनार्षे Sk. **2** Sacred, holy; superhuman. **–र्षः** A form of marriage derived from the *R*ishis; one of the eight forms of marriage in which the father of the bride receives one or two pairs of cows from the bride–groom; आदायार्षस्तु गोद्वयम् Y. 1. 59; Ms. 9. 196; for the names of the 8 forms see उद्वाह. **–र्षं** The holy text, the Vedas.

आर्षभ्यः A steer sufficiently grown to be used or let loose.

आर्षेय *a.* (**यी** *f.*) **1** Relating to a *R*ishi. **2** Worthy, venerable, respectable.

आर्हत *a.* (**ती** *f.*) Belonging to the Jaina doctrines. **-तः** A Jaina, a follower of Jaina doctrines. **-तं** The doctrines of the Jainas.

आर्हंती -त्यं Fitness.

आलः-लं 1 Spawn. 2 Yellow arsenic.

आलगर्दः A water cobra.

आलभनं 1 Taking hold of, seizing. 2 Touching 3 Killing.

आलंबः 1 Depending on or from. 2 That on which one rests or leans, prop, stay, इह हि पततां नास्त्यालंबो न चापि निवर्तनं *S*ânti. 3. 2. 3 Support, protection; तवालंबादंब स्फुरदलघुगर्वेण सहसा Jag. 4 Receptacle.

आलंबनं 1 Depending on or from. 2 Support, prop, stay; Ki. 2. 13; supporting; Me. 4. 3 Receptacle, abode. 4 Reason, cause. 5 (In Rhet.) That on which a रस or sentiment, as it were, hangs, a person or thing with reference to which a sentiment arises, the natural and necessary connection of a sentiment with the cause which excites it. The causes (विभाव) giving rise to a *Rasa* are classified as two:- आलंबन and उद्दीपन; *e. g.* in the Bîbhatsa sentiment stinking flesh &c. is the आलंबन of the *Rasa*, and the attendant circumstances which enhance the feeling of loathing the worms &c. in the flesh are its उद्दीपनानि (exciters); for the other *Rasas* see S. D. 210. 238.

आलंबिन् *a.* 1 Hanging from, resting or leaning upon. 2 Supporting, maintaining, upholding. 3 Wearing.

आलंभः,-भनं 1 Taking hold of, seizing, touching. 2 Tearing off. 3 Killing (especially an animal at a sacrifice); अश्वालंभ, गवालंभ.

आलयः,-यं 1 An abode, a house, a dwelling; न हि दुष्टात्मनामार्या निवसंत्यालये चिरं Râm.; सर्वाञ्जनस्थानकृतालयान् Râm. who lived or dwelt in Janasthâna. 2 A receptacle; seat, or place; हिमालयो नाम नगाधिराजः Ku. 1.; so देवालयं, विद्यालयं &c.

आलर्क *a.* Relating to or caused by a mad dog; आलर्कं विषमिव सर्वतः प्रसृतं U. 1. 40.

आलवण्यं 1 Insipidity, tastelessness. 2 Ugliness.

आलवालं A basin or trench for water (round the root of a tree); °पूरणे नियुक्ता *S.* 1; विश्वासाय विहगानामालवालांबुपायिनां R. 1. 51.

आलस *a.* (**सी** *f.*) Idle, lazy, slothful.

आलस्य *a.* Idle, slothful, apathetic. **—स्यं** Idleness, sloth, want of energy; शक्तस्य चाप्यनुत्साहः कर्मस्वालस्यमुच्यते Susr.; आलस्य 'want of energy' is regarded as one of the 33 subordinate feelings (व्यभिचारिभाव); for example:- न तथा भूषयत्यंगं न तथा भाषते सखीं । जृंभते मुहुरासीना बाला गर्भभरालसा S. D. 183.

आलातं A fire-brand.

आलानं 1 The post to which an elephant is tied; tying post, also the rope that ties him; अरुंतुदमिवालानमनिर्वाणस्य दंतिनः R. 1. 71, 4. 69, 81; आलाने गृह्यते हस्ती Mk. 1. 50. 2 A fetter, tie. 3 A chain, rope. 4 Tying, binding.

आलानिक *a.* (**की** *f.*) Serving as a post to which an elephant is tied; आलानिकं स्थाणुमिव द्विपेंद्रः R. 14. 38.

आलापः 1 Talking, speech, conversation; अये दक्षिणेन वृक्षवाटिकामालाप इव श्रूयते *S.* 1. 2 Narration, mention.

आलापनं Speaking to, conversation.

आलाबुः (**बूः**) *f.* A pumpkin gourd; see अलाबु.

आलावर्तं A fan made of cloth.

आलि *a.* 1 Useless, idle. 2 Honest. **-लिः** 1 A scorpion. 2 A bee. **-लिः,-ली** *f.* 1 A female companion or friend (of a woman); निवार्यतामालि किमप्ययं बटुः Ku. 5. 83, 7. 68. Amaru. 23. 2 A row, range, continuous line; (cf. आवलि); तोयांतर्भास्करालीव रेजे मुनिपरंपरा Ku. 6. 49; रथ्यालि Amaru. 82. 3 A line, streak. 4 A bridge. 5 A dike.

आलिंगनं Embracing, clasping, an embrace; (स प्राप) आलिंगनानिर्वृतिं R. 12. 65.

आलिंगिन् *a.* Embracing &. —*m.* (**-गी**), **आलिंग्यः** A small drum shaped like a barley-corn (यव).

आलिंजरः A large earthen water jar.

आलिंदः,—दकः 1 A terrace before a house. 2 A raised place for sleeping upon; see अलिंद.

आलिंपनं Whitening the walls, floor &c. on festive occasions; cf. आदीपन.

आलीढं A particular attitude in shooting, the right knee being advanced and the left leg retracted अतिष्ठदालीढविशेषशोभिना R. 3. 52; see Malli. on Ku. 3. 70.

आलुः 1 An owl. 2 Ebony; black ebony. **—लुः** *f.* A pitcher. **—लु** (*n.*) A raft, float.

आलुंचनं Rending, tearing to pieces.

आलेखनं 1 Writing. 2 Painting. 3 Scratching. **—नी** A brush, pencil.

आलेख्यं A painting, picture; इति संरंभिणो वाणीर्बलस्यालेख्यदेवताः *S*i. 2. 67; R. 3. 15. 2 A writing. -Comp. **-लेखा** outline, a painting. **-शेष** *a.* having nothing left but a painting, *i. e.* deceased, dead; आलेख्यशेषस्य पितुः R. 14. 15.

आलेपः-पनं 1 Anointing, smearing 2 Liniment.

आलोकः, —कनं 1 Seeing, beholding 2 Sight, aspect, appearance; यदालोके सूक्ष्मं *S.* 1. 9; Ku. 7. 22, 46; सुख° V. 4. 24. 3 Range of sight; आलोके ते निपतति पुरा सा बलिव्याकुला वा Me. 85; R. 7. 5; Ku. 2. 45. 4 Light, lustre, splendour; निरालोकं लोकं Mâl. 5. 30; 9. 37. 5 Panegyric; especially, a word of praise uttered by a bard (such as जय, आलोकय); ययावुदीरितालोकः R. 17. 27, 2. 9; K. 14.

आलोचक *a.* Seeing, beholding. **—कं** The faculty of vision; the cause of sight.

आलोचनं -ना 1 Seeing, perceiving, survey, view. 2 Considering, reflecting.

आलोडनं -ना 1 Stirring, shaking, agitating 2 Mixing.

आलोल *a.* 1 Slightly trembling, rolling (as eyes). 2 Shaken, agitated; Amaru. 3; Me. 61.

आवनेयः 'Son of the earth', an epithet of the planet Mars.

आवंत्य *a.* Coming from or belonging to Avantî. **—त्यः** 1 A prince or an inhabitant of Avantî. 2 The offspring of a degraded Brâhmaṇa; see Ms. 10. 21.

आवपनं 1 The act of sowing, throwing, scattering. 2 Sowing seed. 3 Shaving. 4 A vessel, jar, ewer.

आवरकं A cover, veil.

आवरणं 1 Covering, concealing, obscuring; सूर्ये तपत्यावरणाय दृष्टेः कल्पेत लोकस्य कथं तमिस्रा R. 5. 13, 10. 46, 19. 16. 2 Shutting, enclosing. 3 A covering. 4 Obstruction. 5 An enclosure, fence, surrounding wall; R. 16. 7; Ki. 5. 25. 6 A cloth or garment. 7 A shield. —Comp. **-शक्तिः** mental ignorance (which veils the real nature of things.)

आवर्तः 1 Turning round, revolving. 2 A whirlpool, an eddy; नृपं तमावर्तमनोज्ञनाभिः R. 6. 52; दर्शितावर्तनाभेः Me. 28; आवर्तः संशयानां Pt. 1. 191; 3 Deliberation, revolving (in the mind). 4 A lock of hair curling backwards, especially on a horse. 5 A crowded place (where many men live closely together). 6 A kind of jewel.

आवर्तकः 1 N. of a form of cloud personified; जातं वंशे भुवनविदिते पुष्करावर्तकानां Me. 6; Ku. 2. 50. 2 A whirlpool. 3 Revolution. 4 A curl of hair.

आवर्तनं 1 Turning round, revolution. 2 Circular motion, gyration. 3 Melting together, fusion, (said of metals). 4 Repeating. **—नः** Vishṇu. **—नी** A crucible.

आवलिः, —ली *f.* 1 A line, row, range; अरावलीं V. 1. 4; so अलक°, दंत°, हार°, रत्न° &c. 2 A series, continuous line.

आवलित *a.* Slightly turned.

आवश्यक *a.* (**की** *f.*) Inevitable, necessary; एतेष्वावश्यकस्त्वसौ Bhâshâ P.

22. —कं 1 Necessity, inevitable act or duty. 2 An inevitable conclusion.

आवसतिः *f.* Night (the time during which one rests); midnight.

आवसथः 1 A dwelling, dwelling-place, house, habitation ; निवसन्नावसथे पुराद्बहिः R. 8. 14. 2 A resting place, asylum. 3 A dwelling for pupils and ascetics.

आवसथ्य *a.* Being in a house. —थ्यः The sacred fire kept in the house, one of the five fires used in sacrifices ; see पंचाग्नि. —थ्यः, —थ्यं A dwelling for pupils and ascetics. —थ्यं A house.

आवसित *a.* 1 Finished, or completed. 2 Decided, determined, settled. —तं Ripe corn (when thrashed).

आवह *a.* (As last member of comp.) Producing, leading or tending to, bringing on ; क्लेशावहा भर्तुरलक्षणाऽहं R. 14. 5 ; so दुःख°, भय°.

आवापः 1 Sowing seed. 2 Scattering, throwing in general. 3 A basin for water round the root of a tree (आलवाल). 4 A vessel, jar for corn. 5 A kind of drink. 6 A bracelet (आवापक) 7 Uneven ground.

आवापकः A bracelet.

आवापनं A loom.

आवालं A basin for water round the root of a tree ; cf. आलवालं.

आवासः 1 A house, habitation. 2 A place of refuge, abode ; आवासवृक्षोन्मुखबर्हिणानि R. 2. 17.

आवाहनं 1 Sending for, inviting, calling. 2 Invoking a deity (to be present) (opp. विसर्जन). 3 Offering oblations to fire ; Y. 1. 251.

आविक *a.* (की *f.*) 1 Relating to a sheep ; आविकं क्षीरं Ms. 5. 8, 2. 41. 2 Woollen. —कं A woollen cloth.

आविग्न *a.* Distressed, troubled.

आविद्ध *p. p.* 1 Pierced, bored. 2 Curved, crooked. 3 Thrown with force; put in motion.

आविर्भावः 1 Manifestation, presence, appearance. 2 An incarnation.

आविल *a.* 1 Turbid, foul, dirty ; पंकाच्छिदः फलस्येव निकषेणाविलं पयः M. 2. 8; तस्याविलांभः परिशुद्धिहेतोः R. 13. 36. 2 Impure, spoiled: (fig. also) ; त्वदीयैश्चरितैरनाविलैः Ku. 5. 37. 3 Darkcoloured, darkish. 4 Dim, obscure ; आविलां मृगलेखां R. 8. 42.

आविलयति Den. P. To stain, blot.

आविष्करणं, आविष्कारः Manifestation, making apparent or visible ; असूया गुणेषु दोषाविष्करणं Ak.

आविष्ट *p. p.* 1 Entered. 2 Possessed (by an evil spirit). 3 Possessed of, full of, overpowered or overcome ; भय° क्रोध°. 4 Engrossed or occupied in, intent on.

आविस् *ind.* A particle meaning 'before the eyes', 'openly', 'evidently' (usually prefixed to the roots अस्, भू and कृ,) ; आचार्यकं विजयि मान्मथमाविरासित् Mâl . 1. 26 ; (याति) आविष्कृतारुणपुरस्सर एकतोर्कः S. 4. 1; तेषामाविरभूद् ब्रह्मा Ku. 2. 2; R. 9. 55.

आवीतं The sacrificial cord worn in any particular position.

आवुकः A father (in theatrical language).

आवुत्तः A sister's husband ; brother-in-law ; U. 1 ; S. 6.

आवृत् *f.* 1 Turning towards or round ; entering. 2 Order, succession ; method, manner. अनयैवावृता कार्यं पिंडनिर्वपणं सुतैः Ms. 3. 248 ; Y. 3. 2. 3 Turn of a path, course, direction. 4 A purificatory rite ; Ms 2. 66.

आवृत्त *p. p.* 1 Turned round, whirled ; returned. 2 Repeated ; द्विरावृत्ता दश द्विदशाः Sk. 3 Learnt (by heart) studied.

आवृत्तिः *f.* 1 Turning towards ; return, coming back ; तपोवनावृत्तिपथं R. 2. 18 ; Bg. 1. 23. 2 Reversion ; retreat. 3 Revolving, going round. 4 Recurrence to the same point or place (of the sun) ; उदगावृत्तिपथेन नारदः R. 8. 33. 5 Repetition of birth and death, worldly existence ; अनावृत्तिभयं Ku. 6. 77. 6 Repetition in general ; an edition (modern use). 7 Repeated reading, study ; आवृत्तिः सर्वशास्त्राणां बोधादपि गरीयसी Udb.

आवृष्टिः *f.* Raining, a shower of rain.

आवेगः Uneasiness ; anxiety, excitement, agitation, flurry ; अलमावेगेन S. 3 ; Amaru. 83. 2 Hurry, haste ; S. 4. 3 Agitation, regarded as one of the 33 subordinate feelings.

आवेदनं 1 Communicating, reporting. 2 Representation. 3 Stating a complaint (in law). 4 A plaint.

आवेशः 1 Entering into, entrance. 2 Taking possession of, influence, exercise ; स्मय° influence of pride R. 5. 19. 3 Intentness, devotedness to an object 4 Pride, arrogance. 5 Flurry, agitation ; anger, passion. 6 Demoniacal possession. 7 Apoplectic or epileptic giddiness.

आवेशनं 1 Entering, entrance. 2 Demoniacal possession. 3 Passion, anger, fury. 4 A manufactory, workshop ; Ms. 9. 265. 5 A house.

आवेशिक *a.* (की *f.*) 1 Peculiar, one's own. 2 Inherent.—कः A guest, visitor.

आवेष्टकः A wall, fence, an enclosure.

आवेष्टनं 1 Wrapping round, tying, binding. 2 A wrapper, an envelope. 3 A wall, fence, enclosure.

आश *a.* One who eats, eater (mostly as the last member of comp.) ; *e. g.* हुताश, आश्रयाश &c. &c. —शः Eating (as in प्रातराश).

आशंसनं 1 Expecting, wishing ; इष्टाशंसनमाशीः Sk. 2 Telling, declaring.

आशंसा 1 Desire, wish, hope ; निदधे विजयाशंसां चापे सीतां च लक्ष्मणे R. 12. 44 ; Bk. 19. 5. 2 Speech, declaration. 3 Imagination ; आशंसापरिकल्पितास्वपि भवत्यानंदसांद्रो लयः Mâl. 5. 7.

आशंसु *a.* Desirous, hopeful.

आशंका 1 Fear, apprehension ; नष्टाशंका हरिणशिशवो मंदमंदं चरंति S. 1. 16 ; आशंकया मुक्तं Bh. 3. 5. 2 Doubt, uncertainty ; इत्याशंक्याऽऽमाह Gadâdhara. 3 Distrust, suspicion.

आशंकित *p. p.* 1 Feared, dreaded &c. —तं 1 Fear. 2 Doubt, uncertainty.

आशयः 1 A bed-chamber, resting-place, asylum. 2 A place of residence, abode, seat, retreat ; वायुर्गंधानिवाशयात् Bg. 15. 8 ; अपृथक्° U. 1. 45. 3 Receptacle, reservoir; विषमेपि विगाह्यते नयः कृततीर्थः पयसामिवाशयः Ki. 2. 3 ; cf. also words like जलाशय, आमाशय, रक्ताशय &c. 4 The stomach. 5 Meaning, intention, purport, gist ; इत्याशयः ; एवं कवेराशयः (oft. used by commentators; see अभिप्राय). 6 The seat of feelings, mind, heart ; अहमात्मा गुडाकेश सर्वभूताशयस्थितः Bg. 10. 20 ; Mv. 2. 37. 7 Prosperity. 8 A barn. 9 Will or pleasure. 10 Fate, fortune. 11 A kind of pit (made for catching animals); आस्ते परमसंतप्तो नूनं सिंह इवाशये Mb.—Comp. —आशः fire.

आशरः 1 Fire. 2 A demon, goblin (रक्षस्). 3 Wind.

आशवं 1 Speed, quickness. 2 Distilled spirit more usually written आसव, q. v.

आशा 1 (*a*) Hope, expectation, prospect ; तामाशां च सुरद्विषां R. 12. 96 ; आशा हि परमं दुःखं नैराश्यं परमं सुखं Subhâsh. ; त्वमाशे मोघाशे Bh. 3. 6 ; so भग्न,° हत°. (*b*) Wish, desire. 2 False hope or expectation. 3 Space, region, quarter of the compass, direction ; अगस्त्याचरितामाशामनाशास्यजयो ययौ R. 4. 44 ; Ki 7. 9. —Comp. —अन्वित, —जनन *a.* hopeful, inspiring hope. —गजः a guardian elephant of a quarter of the compass ; see अष्टदिग्गज. —तंतुः a thread of hope, slender hope ; Mâl. 4. 3, 9. 26.—पालः a guardian or regent of the regions or quarters; see अष्टदिक्पाल. —पिशाचिका phantom of hope. —बंधः 1 the tie or bond of hope, confidence, trust, expectation ; गुर्वपि विरहदुःखमाशाबंधः साहयति S. 4. 15 ; Me. 10. 2 consolation. 3 a spider's web —भंगः disappointment. —हीन *a.* despairing, despondent.

आशाढः See अ (आ) षाढ.

आशास्य *pot. p.* **1** To be obtained by a boon. **2** To be wished for, desirable; R. 4. 44. **—स्यं 1** A thing to be wished for, wish, desire; M. 5. 20. **2** A blessing, benediction; आशास्यमन्यत् पुनरुक्तभूतं R. 5. 34.

आशिंजित *a.* Tinkling; Ku 3. 26.

आशित *a.* **1** Eaten, given to eat. **2** Satisfied by eating. **—तं** Eating.

आशितंगवीन *a.* Formerly grazed by cattle.

आशितंभव *a.* Satiating, satisfying (as food). **—वं 1** Food, victuals. **2** Satisfaction, satiety (*m.* also); फलैर्यैष्वाशितंभवं Bk. 4. 11.

आशिर *a.* Voracious. **—रः** 1 Fire. **2** The sun. 3 A demon.

आशिस् *f.* (°शीः, °शीर्ष्यौ &c) 1 A blessing, benediction. (It is thus defined:—वात्सल्यायत्र मान्येन कनिष्ठस्याभिधीयते । इष्टावधारकं वाक्यमाशीः सा परिकीर्तिता ॥) आशिस् is sometimes distinguished from वर, the former being taken to be merely an expression of one's good wishes which may or may not be realized; while a वर is a boon which is more permanent in character and surer of fulfilment; cf. वरः खल्वेष नाशीः *S.* 4; आशिषो गुरुजनवितीर्णा वरतामापद्यंते K. 291; आमोधाः प्रतिगृह्णंतावर्ध्यानुपदमाशिषः R. 1. 44; जयाशीः Ku. 7. 47. **2** A prayer, wish, desire; Ku. 5. 76; Bg. 4. 21. **3** A serpent's fang (cf. आशीर्विष). Comp **—वादः**, **—वचनं** (आशीर्वादः &c.) a blessing, benediction, expression of a prayer or wish; आशीर्वचनसंयुक्तां नित्यं यस्मात् प्रकुर्वते S. D. **6**; Ms. **2.** 33. **—विषः** (आशीर्विषः) a snake.

आशी 1 A serpent's fang. **2** A kind of venom. **3** A blessing, benediction. —Comp. **—विष 1** a snake; गरुत्मदाशीविषभीमदर्शनैः R. 3. 57. **2** a particular kind of snake; कर्णाशीविषभोगिनि प्रशमिते Ve. 6. 1.

आशु *a.* Fast, quick. **—शुः—शु** *n.* Rice (ripening quickly in the rainy season). **—शु** *ind.* Fast, quickly, immediately, directly; वर्त्म भानोस्त्यजाशु Me. 39, 22. —Comp. **—कारिन्**, **—कृत्** *a.* doing anything quickly, smart, active. **—कोपिन्** *a.* irascible, irritable **—ग** *a.* swift, quick. (**—गः**) **1** the wind. **2** the sun. **3** an arrow; पपावनास्वादितपूर्वमाशुगः R. 3. 54, 11. 82, 12. 91. **—तोष** *a.* easily appeased or pleased. (**—षः**) an epithet of *S*iva. **—व्रीहिः** rice ripening in the rainy season.

आशुशुक्षणिः 1 Wind, air. **2** Fire; मंत्रपूतानि हवींषि प्रतिगृह्णात्येतत्प्रीत्याशुशुक्षणिः **K.** 44.

आशेकुटिन् *m.* A mountain.

आशोषणं The act of drying.

आशौचं Impurity, see अशौचं; दशाहं शावमाशौचं ब्राह्मणस्य विधीयते Ms. **5.** 59, 61, 62, Y. 3. 18.

आश्चर्य *a.* Marvellous, wonderful, extraordinary, astonishing, strange; आश्चर्यो गवां दोहोऽगोपेन Sk.; तदनु ववृषुः पुष्पमाश्चर्यमेघाः R. 16 87; आश्चर्यदर्शनो मनुष्यलोकः *S.* 7. **—र्यं 1** A wonder, miracle, marvel; किमाश्चर्यं क्षारदेशे प्राणदा यमदूतिका Udb.; कर्माश्चर्याणि U. 1 wonderful deeds; Bg. 11. 6, 2. 29. **2** Surprise, wonder, astonishment. **3** (Used as an exclamation) A wonder, (how strange or curious); आश्चर्यं परिपीडितोऽभिरमते यच्चातकस्तृष्णया Chât. 2. 4.

आश्चो-श्च्यो-तनं 1 Aspersion, sprinkling. **2** Applying ghee &c. to the eyelids.

आश्म *a.* (**श्मी** *f.*) Made of stone, stony.

आश्मन (**नी** *f.*) Stony; made of stones. **—नः 1** Anything made of stone. **2** N. of Aruṇa, the charioteer of the sun.

आश्मिक *a.* (**की** *f.*) **1** Made of stone. **2** Carrying or bearing stones.

आश्यान *p. p.* **1** Congealed, consolidated; Ki. 16. 10. **2** Partially dried; पथश्चाश्यानकर्दमान् R. 4. 24 Ku. 7. 9; dried by fumigation (as hair): R. 17. 22.

आश्रं Tear.

आश्रपणं The act of cooking or boiling.

आश्रमः, **-मं 1** A hermitage, hut, cell, dwelling or abode of ascetics. **2** A stage, order, or period of the (religious) life of a Brâhmaṇa. (These are four:-ब्रह्मचर्य, गार्हस्थ्य, वानप्रस्थ, and संन्यास; Kshatriyas (and Vaisyas also) can enter upon the first three *A*s*ramas*; cf. *S.* **7.** 20; V. 5; according to some authorities they can enter the fourth also; (cf. स किलाश्रममंत्यमाश्रितः R. 8. 14); पूर्वाश्रमः Ku. 5. 50. 3 A college, school. **4** A wood or thicket (where ascetics practise penance). -Comp. **-गुरुः** the head of a religious order, a preceptor, principal. **-धर्मः 1** the special duties of each order or life. **2** the duties of one leading a hermit's life; य इमामाश्रमधर्मे नियुंक्ते *S.* 1. **-पदं**, **-मंडलं**, **-स्थानं** a hermitage (Including the surrounding grounds), a penance forest or grove (तपोवनं); शांतमिदमाश्रमपदं S. 1. 16. **-भ्रष्ट** *a.* fallen from any religious order, apostate. **-वासिन्**, **-आलयः**, **-सद्** *m.* an ascetic, hermit.

आश्रमिक, **आश्रमिन्** *a.* Belonging to one of the four orders or periods of religious life.

आश्रयः 1 A resting place, seat substratum; सौहृदादपृथगाश्रयामिमां U. I. 45 v. 1. **2** That on which anything depends or rests. **3** Recipient, receptacle; तमाश्रयं दुष्प्रसहस्य तेजसः R. 3. 58. **4** (*a*) A place of refuge, asylum; भर्ता वै ह्याश्रयः स्त्रीणां Vet.; तदहमाश्रयोन्मूलनेनैव त्वामकामां करोमि Mu. 2. (*b*) A dwelling, house. **5** Having recourse or resort to, resort; oft. in comp. **6** Dependence on; oft. in comp. **7** Patron, supporter; विनाश्रयं न तिष्ठंति पंडिता वनिता लताः Udb. **8** A prop, support; R. 9. 60. **9** A quiver; बाणमाश्रयमुखात् समुद्धरन् R. 11. 26. **10** Authority, sanction, warrant. **11** Connection, relation, association. **12** Seeking shelter or protection with another (= संश्रय), one of the six *gunas*, q. v. -Comp. **-असिद्धः**, **-द्धिः** *f.* a kind of fallacy, one of the three sub-divisions of असिद्ध. **-आशः**, **-भुज्** *a.* consuming every thing with which it comes in contact (**-शः**, **-क्**) fire; दुर्वृत्तः क्रियते धूर्तैः श्रीमानात्मविवृद्धये । किं नाम खलसंसर्गः कुरुते नाश्रयाशवत् ॥ Udb. **-लिंगं** an adjective (a word which must agree in gender with the word which it qualifies or refers to).

आश्रयणं 1 Betaking oneself to, taking refuge with. **2** Accepting, choosing. **3** Refuge, asylum.

आश्रयिन् *a.* **1** Resting with, dependent on. **2** Related to, concerning; V. 3. 10.

आश्रव *a.* Obedient, compliant; भिषजामनाश्रवः R. 19. 49, N. **3.** 84. **-वः 1** A stream, river. **2** A promise, engagement. **3** A fault, transgression; see आस्रव also.

आश्रिः *f* The edge of a sword.

आश्रित *p. p.* (Used actively) (with an acc.) **1** Resorting to; कृष्णाश्रितः=कृष्णमाश्रितः Sk. **2** Dwelling in, inhabiting, stationing oneself at or on. **3** Using, employing. **4** Following, practising, observing; Ku. 6. 6; Bk. 7. 42. **5** Dependent on **6** (Passively used) Resorted to, inhabited &c. **—तः** A dependent, servant, follower; अस्मदाश्रितानां H. I; प्रभुणां प्रायश्चलं गौरवमाश्रितेषु Ku. 3. 1.

आश्रुत *p. p.* **1** Heard. **2** Promised; agreed; accepted. **—तं** Calling so as to make one listen.

आश्रुतिः *f.* **1** Hearing **2** Accepting.

आश्लेषः 1 Embracing, clasping, an embrace; आश्लेषलोलुपवधूस्तनकार्कश्यसाक्षिणीं *S*i 2. 17; Amaru. 15, 72, 94; कंठाश्लेषप्रणयिनि जने Me. 3, 106. **2** Contact, intimate connection; relation. **—षा** N. of the 9th asterism.

आश्व *a.* (**श्वी** *f.*) Belonging to or coming from a horse. **—श्वं** A number of horses.

आश्वत्थ *a.* (**त्थी** *f.*) Relating to or made of the holy fig-tree. **—त्थं** The fruit of the holy fig-tree.

आश्वयुज *a.* (**जी** *f.*) Belonging to the month *A*s*vina*. **—जः** The month आश्विन; Ms. 6. 15. **—जी** The day of the full moon in *A*s*vina*.

आश्वलक्षणिकः A farrier, groom.

आश्वासः 1 Taking or recovering breath, breathing freely, recovery. 2 Consolation, cheering up. 3 An assurance of safety or protection. 4 Cessation 5 A chapter or section of a book.

आश्वासनं Encouraging, cheering up, consolation; तादिदं द्वितीयं हृदयाश्वासनं *S.* 7.

आश्विकः A cavalier.

आश्विनः N. of a month (in which the moon is near the constellation Asvinî).

आश्विनेयौ (du.) 1 The two Asvins (physicians of gods). 2 N. of Nakula and Sahadeva, the last two of the five Pâṇḍava princes.

आश्विन *a.* (**नी** *f.*) Made or traversed by a horse (as a journey &c.); °नीऽध्वा Sk.

आषाढः 1 N. of a Hindu month (corresponding to June and July); आषाढस्य प्रथमदिवसे **Me.** 2; शेते विष्णुः सदाषाढे कार्तिके प्रतिबोध्यते V. P. 2 A staff of the Palâsa wood carried by an ascetic; अथाजिनाषाढधरः प्रगल्भवाक् Ku. 6. 30. **—ढा** The 20th and the 21st lunar mansions, usually called पूर्वाषाढा and उत्तराषाढा **—ढी** The day of full moon in the month of *A*shâḍha.

आष्टमः The 8th part.

1 **आस्**, **आः** *ind.* An interjection implying (*a*) Recollection; आः उपनयतु भवान् भूर्जपत्रं V. 2. (*b*) Anger; आः कथमद्यापि राक्षसत्रासः U. 1; आः पापे तिष्ठ तिष्ठ Mâl. 8. (c) Pain; आः शीतं K. P. 10. (*d*) Angry contradiction (अपाकरण); आः क एष मयि स्थिते Mu. 1; आः वृथामंगलपाठक Ve. 1. (*e*) Sorrow, regret; विद्यामातरमाः प्रदर्श्य नृपसून् भिक्षामहे निस्त्रपाः Udb.

2 **आस्** 2 A. (आस्ते, आसित) 1 To sit, lie, rest; एतदासनमास्यतां V. 5; आस्यतामिति चोक्तः सन्नासीताभिमुखं गुरोः Ms. 2. 193. 2 To live, dwell; तावद्वर्षाण्यासते देवलोके Mb.; यत्रास्मै रोचते तत्रायमास्तां K. 196; कुरूनास्ते Sk. 3 To sit quietly, take no hostile measures, remain idle; आसीनं त्वामुत्थापयति द्वयम् *Si.* 2. 57. 4 To be, exist. 5 To be contained in; जगंति यस्यां सविकाशमासत *Si.* 1. 23. 6 To abide, remain, continue or be in any state; oft. used with present participles to denote a continuous or uninterrupted action; विदारयन्प्रगर्जंश्चास्ते Pt. 1 kept on tearing up and bellowing. 7 To lead to, result in (with dat.) आस्तां मानसतुष्टये सुकृतिनां नीतिर्नवोढेव वः H. 1. 212. 8 To let go, lay or put aside; आस्तां तावत let it aside, let it go. —*Caus.* To cause to sit, seat, fix; आसयत्सलिलं पृथ्वीं Sk. WITH **अधि** to lie down; settle upon, occupy, enter into (with acc. of place); निर्दिष्टां कुलपतिना स पर्णशालामध्यास्य R. 1. 95, 2. 17, 4. 74, 6. 10; भगवत्या प्राश्निकपदमध्यासितव्यं M 1. —**अनु** 1 to be seated near or round. 2 to serve, wait upon; सखीभ्यामन्वास्यते *S.* 3; अन्वासितमरुंधत्या R. 1. 56. 3 to sit down after one; तां अन्वास्य R. 2. 24. —**उद्** to be indifferent or unconcerned, be careless or apathetic, be passive or inactive; तत्किमित्युदासते भरताः Mâl. 1; विधाय वैरं सामर्षे नरोऽरौ य उदासते *Si.* 2. 72; Bg. 9. 9; Mu. 1. —**उप** 1 to wait upon, serve, worship; अंबामुपास्स्व सदयां Asvad. 13; उद्यानपालसामान्यमृतवस्तमुपासते Ku. 2 36. 2 to approach, go to or towards; उपासांचक्रिरे द्रष्टुं देवगंधर्वकिन्नराः Bk. 5. 107, 7. 89. 3 to take part in, perform (as a sacred rite). 4 to pass (as time); उपास्य रात्रिशेषं तु Râm 5 to undergo, suffer; अलं ते पांडुपुत्राणां भक्त्या क्लेशमुपासितुं Mb.; Ms. 11. 184. 6 to resort to; employ, use; लक्षणोपास्यंते यस्य कृते S. D. 2. 7. to practise archery. 8 to expect, wait for.—**पर्युप** 1 to attend upon, worship, attend respectfully; पर्युपास्यंत लक्ष्म्या R. 10. 62; Ku. 2. 38; Ms. 7. 37. 2 to go to (for protection), seek shelter or patronage with; अशक्ता एव सर्वत्र नरेंद्रं पर्युपासते Pt. 1. 241. 3 to enclose, surround. 4 to share in, partake of. 5 to resort to, frequent. —**सं** 1 to sit down; प्रत्युवाच समासीनं वसिष्ठं Râm. 2 to sit round or together. —**समुप** 1 to wait or attend upon, worship, serve; समुपास्यत पुत्रभोग्यया स्नुषयेवाविकृतेंद्रियः श्रिया R. 8. 14. 2 to perform; ते त्रयः संध्यां समुपासत Râm.

आसः 1 A seat. 2 A bow (**—सं** also) स सासिः सासुसूः सासः Ki. 15. 5.

आसक्त *p. p.* 1 Strongly attached to, intent on, devoted or addicted to, (usually with loc. or in comp.) 2 Fixed on, resting on; शिखरासक्तमेघाः Ku. 6. 40. 3 Continuous, perpetual, eternal.—COMP.—**चित्त**, **—चेतस्**, **—मनस्** *a.* having the mind fixed on any object.

आसक्तिः *f.* 1 Attachment, devotion, fondness; बालिशचारितेष्वासक्तिः K. 120. 2 intentness, application.

आसंगः 1 Attachment, devotion (to any object) सुखासंगलब्धः K. 173. 2 Contact, adherence, clinging; (पंकजं) सशैवलासंगमपि प्रकाशते Ku. 5 9; 3. 46. 3 Association, connection, union; त्यक्त्वा कर्मफलासंगं Bg. 4. 20; so कांतासंग &c. 4 Fixing, fastening to.

आसंगिनी A whirlwind.

आसंजनं 1 Fastening to, fixing, putting on the body. 2 Getting entangled, clinging; व्रततिवलयासंजनात् *S.* 1. 33 v. l. 3 Attachment, devotion 4 Contact proximity.

आसत्तिः *f.* 1 Meeting, junction. 2 Intimate union, close contact; किमपि किमपि मंदं मंदमासत्तियोगात् U. 1. 27. 3 Gain, profit, acquirement. 4 (In Logic) Proximity, relation between two or more proximate terms and the sense conveyed by them, कारणं सन्निधानं तु पदस्यासत्तिरुच्यते Bhâshâ P. 83.

आसन् *n.* Mouth (a word optionally substituted for आस्य in all cases after acc. dual).

आसनं 1 Sitting down. 2 A seat, place, stool; स वासवेनासनसंनिकृष्टं Ku. 3. 2; आसनं मुच् to leave one's seat, rise; R. 3. 11. 3 A particular posture or mode of sitting; cf. पद्म, °वीर. ° 4 Sitting down or halting. 5 Any peculiar mode of sexual enjoyment. 6 Maintaining a post against an enemy (opp. यानं), one of the six modes of foreign policy; which are:-संधिर्नो विग्रहो यानमासनं द्वैधमाश्रयः Ak.; Ms. 7. 160 Y. 1. 346. 7. The front part of an elephant's body, withers. **—ना** A seat, stool, stay. **—नी** 1 Stay, sitting. 2 A small seat or stool. 3 A shop, stall. —COMP. **—बंधधीर** *a.* resolute to sit down, firm in one's seat; निषेदुषीमासनबंधधीरः R. 2. 6.

आसंदी A small couch or oblong chair.

आसन्न *p. p.* 1 Approached, near (in time, place or number); आसन्नविंशाः nearly or about 20. 2 Impending, imminent; आसन्नपतने कूले S. B. —COMP—**कालः** 1 the hour of death. 2 one whose death is near. **—परिचारकः**, **—चारिका** personal attendant, bodyguard.

आसंबाध *a.* Blocked up, obstructed, confined (on all sides); आसंबाधा भविष्यंति पंथानः शरवृष्टिभिः Râm.

आसवः 1 Distillation. 2 Decoction. 3 Any spirituous liquor; अनासवाख्यं करणं मदस्य Ku. 1. 31; द्राक्षा° &c.

आसादनं 1 Obtaining, attaining. 2 Attacking.

आसारः 1 A hard or sharp-driving shower (of anything); आसारसिक्तक्षितिबाष्पयोगात् R. 13. 29; Me. 17; पुष्पासारैः 43; so तुहिन °, रुधिर ° &c.; धारासारैर्वृष्टिर्बभूव H. 3 it rained in torrents. 2 Surrounding an enemy. 3 Attack, incursion. 4 The army of an ally or king. 5 Provision, food: Pt. 3. 41.

आसिकः A swordsman.

आसिधारं N. of a particular vow; अभ्यस्यतीव व्रतमासिधारं R. 13. 67; for explanation see असिधारा under असि.

आसुतिः *f.* 1 Distillation. 2 Decoction.

आसुर *a.* (**री** *f.*) (opp. दैव) 1 Belonging to *Asuras.* 2 Belonging to evil spirits; आसुरी माया, आसुरी रात्रिः &c 3 Infernal, demoniacal; आसुरं भावमाश्रितः Bg. 7. 15 (for a full exposition of what constitutes आसुर conduct see Bg. 16. 7-24). **—रः** 1 A demon. 2 One of the eight forms of marriage, in which the bridegroom purchases the bride from her father or other paternal kinsmen ; (see उद्वाह) ; आसुरो द्रविणादानात् Y. 1. 61 ; Ms. 3. 31. -री 1 Surgery. 2 A female demon ; संभ्रमादासुरीभिः Ve. 1. 3.

आसूत्रित *a.* 1 Forming or wearing a garland. 2 Interwoven.

आसेकः Wetting, watering, pouring in.

आसेचनं Pouring into, wetting, sprinkling.

आसेधः Arrest, custody, legal restraint ; it is of four kinds:-स्थानासेधः कालकृतः प्रवासात् कर्मणस्तथा Nârada.

आसेवा,-वनं 1 Zealous practice, assiduous performance of any action. 2 Frequency, repetition ; P. VIII. 3. 102 ; आसेवनं पौनःपुन्यं Sk.

आस्कंदः, -दनं 1 attack, assault ; outraging ; परवनिता ° प्रगल्भस्य Ve. 2. 2 Ascending, mounting ; stepping over. 3 Reproach, abuse. 4 The walk of a horse. 5 Battle, war.

आस्कंदितं,-तकं The walk of a horse, galloping at full speed.

आस्कंदिन् *a.* Jumping upon, assailing, attacking ; R. 17. 52.

आस्तरः 1 A covering, coverlet. 2 A carpet, bed, mat ; *S*ânti. 2. 20. 3 Spreading (clothes &c.).

आस्तरणं 1 Spreading, strewing. 2 A bed, layer ; कुसुम° a bed of flowers; Ku. 4. 35 ; तमालपत्रास्तरणासु रंतुं R. 6. 64. 3 A cushion, quilt, bedclothes. 4 A carpet. 5 An elephant's housings, painted cloth (thrown on his back).

आस्तारः Spreading, strewing, scattering. -COMP. -पंक्तिः N. of a metre; see. App.

आस्तिक *a.* (की *f.*) 1 One who believes in God and another world. 2 A believer in sacred tradition. 3 Pious, faithful, believing ; आस्तिकः श्रद्दधानश्च Y. 1. 268.

आस्तिकता,-त्वं, आस्तिक्यं 1 Belief in God and another world. 2 Piety, faith, belief ; Bg. 18. 42 ; आस्तिक्यं श्रद्दधानता परमार्थेष्वागमार्थेषु *S*ankara.

आस्तीकः N. of an old saint, son of Jaratkâru ; (at whose intercession King Janamejaya spared the Nâga Takshaka from the destruction to which he had doomed the serpent race).

आस्था 1 Regard, care, respect, consideration, care for (with loc.); मर्त्येष्वास्थापराङ्मुखः R. 10. 43 ; मय्यप्यास्था न ते चेत् Bh. 3. 30 ; see अनास्था also. 2 Assent, promise. 3 Prop, support, stay. 4 Hope, confidence. 5 An effort. 6 State, condition. 7 An assembly.

आस्थानं 1 A place, site. 2 Ground, base. 3 An assembly. 4 Care, regard; see आस्था. 5 A hall of audience. 6 Recreation-ground (विश्रामस्थानं) -नी An assembly-room. -COMP. -गृहं,-निकेतनं, -मंडपः an assembly-room.

आस्थित *p. p.* (Used actively) Dwelling, abiding ; resorting to, using, practising, betaking oneself to &c.

आस्पदं 1 A place, site, seat, room ; तस्यास्पदं श्रीर्युवराजसंज्ञितं R. 3. 36 ; ध्यानास्पदं भूतपतेर्विवेश Ku. 3. 43. 5. 10, 48, 69. 2 (Fig.) An abode, subject, receptacle करिण्यः कारुण्यास्पदं Bv. 1. 2. 3 Rank, position, station. 4 Dignity, authority, office. 5 Business, affair. 6 Prop, support.

आस्पंदनं Throbbing, trembling.

आस्पर्धा Emulation, rivalry.

आस्फालः 1 Striking, rubbing, causing to move gently. 2 Flapping. 3 Particularly, the flapping motion of an elephant's ears.

आस्फालनं 1 Rubbing, striking or pressing against, stirring (as water &c.) ; flapping ; अनवरतधनुर्ज्यास्फालनक्रूरपूर्वं *S*. 2. 4 ; आसां जलास्फालनतत्पराणां R. 16. 62, 3. 55, 6. 73 ; Amaru. 54; ऐरावत° कर्कशेन हस्तेन Ku. 3. 22. 2 Pride, arrogance.

आस्फोटः 1 The Arka plant. 2 The sound made by striking on the arms (Mar. छड्डु ठोकणें). -टा The नवमल्लिका plant, wild variety of jasmin.

आस्फोटनं 1 Flapping. 2 Trembling. 3 Blowing, expanding. 4 Contracting, closing. 5 Slapping or clapping the arms, or the sound produced by it.

आस्माक *a.* (की *f.*), **आस्माकीन** *a.* Our, ours ; आस्माकदंतिसान्निध्यात् *S*i. 2. 63, 8. 50.

आस्यं 1 The mouth, jaws ; आस्यकुहरे, विवृतास्यः. 2 Face ; आस्यकमलं. 3 A part of the mouth used in pronouncing letters. 4 Mouth, opening ; व्रणास्यं, अंकास्यं &c. -COMP.-आसवः spittle, saliva. -पत्रं a lotus. -लांगलः 1 a dog. 2 boar. -लोमन् *n.* beard.

आस्यंदनं Flowing, oozing.

आस्यंधय *a.* Kissing.

आस्या—आसना q. v.

आस्रं Blood. -COMP. -पः 'blood-drinker', a demon.

आस्रवः 1 Pain, affliction, distress. 2 Flowing, running. 3 Discharge, emission. 4 Fault, transgression. 5 The foam on boiling rice.

आस्रावः 1 A wound. 2 Flow, discharge. 3 Spittle. 4 Pain, affliction.

आस्वादः 1 Tasting, eating ; चूतांकुरास्वादकषायकंठः Ku. 3. 32 ; H. 1. 152. 2 Relish ; ज्ञातास्वादो विवृतजघनां को विहातुं समर्थः Me. 41 ; सुखास्वादपरः H. 4. 76. 3 Enjoying, experiencing. °वत् *a.* delicious in flavour, palatable; आस्वादवद्भिः कवलैस्तृणानां R. 2. 5.

आस्वादनं Tasting, eating.

आह *ind.* 1 An interjection showing (*a*) reproof ; (*b*) severity ; (*c*) command ; (*d*) casting, sending. 2 An irregular verbal form of the 3rd pers. sing Pres. of a defective verb meaning 'to say,' or 'to speak' (supposed by Indian grammarians to be derived from ब्रू and by European scholars from अह् ; the only forms of the root existing in the language are:—आत्थ, आहथुः, आह, आहतुः and आहुः).

आहत *p. p.* 1 Struck, beaten (as a drum &c.). 2 Trodden ; पादाहतं यदुत्थाय मूर्धानमधिरोहति *S*i. 2. 46. 3 Injured ; killed. 4 Multiplied (in Math.). 5 Rolled (as dice). 6 Uttered falsely. —तः A drum. —तं 1 A new cloth or garment. 2 A nonsensical or meaningless speech, an assertion of impossibility ; *e. g.* एष वंध्यासुतो याति Subhâsh. -COMP. —लक्षण *a.*= आहितलक्षण q. v.

आहतिः *f.* 1 Killing. 2 A blow, hit ; striking, beating. 2 A stick.

आहर *a.* (At the end of comp.) Bringing, fetching, taking, समित्कुशफलाहरैः R. 1. 49. —रः 1 Taking, seizing. 2 Accomplishing, performing. 3 Offering a sacrifice.

आहरणं 1 Fetching, bringing (near) समिदाहरणाय प्रस्थिता वयं *S*. 1. 2 Seizing, taking. 3 Removing, extracting. 4 Performing, accomplishing (as a sacrifice). 5 A dowry or present given to a bride (at the time of her marraige) ; सत्त्वानुरूपाहरणी कृतश्रीः R. 7. 32.

आहवः 1 Battle, war, fight ; एवंविधेनाहवचेष्टितेन R. 7. 67; हत्वा स्वजनमाहवे Bg. 1. 31. 2 Challenge, provoking, calling; °काम्या desire of fighting. 3 A sacrifice ; तत्र नाभवदसौ महाहवे *S*i. 14. 44.

आहवनं 1 A sacrifice; द्रष्टुमाहवनमग्रजन्मनाम् *S*i 14. 38. 2 An oblation.

आहवनीय *pot. p.* To be offered as an oblation. —यः A consecrated fire taken from the house-holder's perpetual fire, one of the three fires (*i. e.* the eastern) burning at a sacrifice see अग्नित्रेता under अग्नि.

आहारः 1 taking, fetching, or bringing near. 2 Taking food. 3 Food ; °वृत्तिमकरोत् Pt. 1. took his dinner.—COMP. —पाकः digestion (of food). —विरहः want of food, starvation. —संभवः the juice of the body, chyle.

आहार्य *pot. p.* 1 To be taken or seized. 2 To be fetched or brought near. 3 Artificial, adventitious, external ; आहार्यशोभारहितैरमायैः Bk. 2. 14 ; न रम्यमाहार्यमपेक्षते गुणं Ki. 4. 23 ; also Malli. on Ku. 7. 20. 4 Purposed, intended; as, for instance, the identification or आरोप of उपमान or उपमेय in रूपक of which the speaker is fully cognisant. **5** Conveyed or effected by decoration or ornamentation, one of the 4 kinds of अभिनय q. v.

आहावः **1** A trough near a well for watering cattle. **2** War, battle. **3** Invoking, calling. **4** Fire.

आहिंडिकः A man of mixed origin, the son of a Nishâda father and Vaidehî mother; आहिंडिको निषादेन वैदेह्यामेव जायते Ms. 10. 37.

आहित *p. p.* **1** Placed, set, deposited. **2** Felt, entertained. **3** Performed, done,-COMP.—**अग्निः** a Brâhmaṇa who consecrates the sacred fire. -**अंक** *a.* marked, spotted. -**लक्षण** *a.* bearing a characteristic epithet; ककुत्स्थइत्याहितलक्षणोऽभूत् R. 6. 71 (according to Malli. = noted for good qualities).

आहितुंडिकः A juggler, a snake-catcher, conjurer; अहं खल्वाहितुंडिको जीर्णविषो नाम Mu. 2.

आहुतिः *f.* **1** Offering an oblation to a deity, any solemn rite accompanied with oblations; होतुराहुतिसाधनं R. 1. 82. **2** An oblation offered to a deity.

आहूतिः *f.* Calling, invoking.

आहेय *a.* Pertaining to a serpent; Pt. 1. 111.

आहो *ind.* An interjection expressing (*a*) Doubt or alternative (or), and usually standing as a correlative of किं; किं वैखानसं व्रतं निषेवितव्यं... आहो निवत्स्यति समं हरिणांगनाभिः *S.* 1. 27; दारत्यागी भवाम्याहो परस्त्रीस्पर्शपांसुलः *S.* 5. 26. (*b*) Interrogation.—COMP. -**पुरुषिका** **1** great self-conceit or pride; आहोपुरुषिका दर्पाद्या स्यात्संभावनात्मनि Ak.; आहोपुरुषिकां पश्य मम सद्रत्नकांतिभिः Bk. 5. 27. **2** military vaunting, boasting. **3** vaunting of one's own prowess; निजभुजबलाहोपुरुषिकां Bv. 1. 84. -**स्वित्** *ind.* a particle implying doubt, 'or perhaps,' or 'may it be' &c., (corr. of **किं**); आहोस्वित्प्रसवो ममापचरितैर्विष्टंभितो वीरुधाम् *S.* 5. 9; किं द्विजः पचति आहोस्विद् गच्छति Sk.

आह्न A series of days, many days.

आह्निक *a.* (**की** *f.*) Daily, diurnal, performed every day or on a day; आह्निकः स्वाध्यायः daily course of study. —**कं** **1** Any religious rite or duty which is to be performed every day at a fixed hour; anything to be performed daily, such as taking meals, bathing &c.; कृताह्निकः संवृत्तः V. 4. **2** Daily food. **3** Daily work or occupation.

आह्लादः Delight, joy; साल्हादं वचनं Pt. 4.

आह्लादनं Gladdening, delighting.

आह्व *a.* Who or what calls, a crier. —**ह्वा** **1** Calling, calling out. **2** A name, appellation, oft. at the end of comp; अमृताह्वः, शताह्वः &c.

आह्वयः **1** A name, appellation (as last member of comp.); काव्यं रामायणाह्वयं Râm. **2** A law-suit arising from a dispute about games with animals, as cock-fighting &c.; (one of the 18 titles of law); पणपूर्वकपक्षिमेषादियोधनं आह्वयः Râghavânanda on Ms. 8. 7.

आह्वयनं Name, appellation.

आह्वानं **1** Calling, inviting. **2** A call, invitation, summons, (in general); सुहृदाह्वानं प्रकुर्वीत Pt. 3. 47. **3** A legal summons (from court or govt. to appear before a tribunal). **4** Invocation of a deity; Ms. 9. 126. **5** A challenge. **6** A name, appellation.

आह्वायः **1** A summons. **2** A name.

आह्वायकः A messenger, courier; आह्वायकान् भूमिपतेरयोध्यां Bk. 2. 43.

इ.

इः N. of Kâmadeva. —*ind.* An interjection of (1) anger; (2) calling; (3) compassion; (4) reproach; (5) wonder.

इ I. 2 P. (एति, इत) **1** To go, go to or towards, come to or near; शशिनं पुनरेति शर्वरी R. 8. 56. **2** To arrive at, reach, attain to, go to; निर्बुद्धिः क्षयमेति Mk. 1. 14 goes to ruin, is ruined. so वशं,शत्रुत्वं, शूद्रतां &c. —II. 1 U. =अयै q. v. —III. 4. A. **1** To come, appear, **2** To run, wander. **3** To go quickly or repeatedly. WITH **अति** **1** to go over or beyond, cross; pass over; जवादतीये हिमवानधोमुखैः Ki. 14. 54; स्थातव्यं ते नयनविषयं यावदत्येति भानुः Me. 34 passes out of sight. **2** to excel, surpass, outstrip; सत्यमतीत्य हरितो हरींश्च वर्तंते वाजिनः *S.* 1; त्रिस्रोतसः कांतिमतीत्य तस्थौ Ku. 7. 15; Si; 2. 23. **3** to pass by, leave behind; omit, neglect; *S.* 6. 16; R. 15. 37. **4** to pass, elapse (as time); अत्येति रजनी या तु Râm.; अतीते दशरात्रे; see अतीत. —**अधि** **1** (P.) to remember, think of, remember with regret (with gen.); रामस्य दयमानोसावध्येति तव लक्ष्मणः Bk. 8. 119, 18. 38; Ki 11. 74. **2** (अधीते, always Atm. in this sense) to learn, study, read through; उपाध्यायादधीते Sk; सोऽध्यैष्ट वेदान् Bk. 1. 2. (-*Caus.* अध्यापयति; *desid.* अधिजिगांसते). —**अनु** **1** to follow, go after; प्रयतं प्रातरन्वेतु R. 1 90. **2** to succeed. **3** to follow, (in grammar or construction). **4** to obey, conform to; imitate. —**अन्वा** to go after, follow —**अंतर्** **1** to go between, intervene. **2** to hinder, obstruct. **3** to hide, conceal, screen; see अंतरित. —**अप** **1** to go away, depart, withdraw, retire; अपेहि begone, avaunt. **2** to be deprived of, be free from; see अपेत. **3** to die, perish. —**अभि** **1** to go to, approach; draw near; अस्मानत्तुमितोऽभ्येति Bk. 7. 84. **2** to follow, serve. **3** to get, meet with, undergo (said of good or bad things). —**अभिप्र** to go to; intend, mean, aim at; कर्मणा यमभिप्रैति स संप्रदानं P. 1. 4. 32. —**अभ्या** to approach, —**अभ्युद्** **1** to rise, go up. **2** (fig.) to thrive, prosper. —**अभ्युप** **1** to go near, approach, arrive; व्यतीतकालस्त्वहमभ्युपेतः R. 5. 14, 16. 22. **2** to go to a particular state, attain to; सत्यं न तद्यच्छलमभ्युपैति H. 3. 61. **3** to undertake, to agree, accept, promise (to do a thing); मंदायंते न खलुसुहृदामभ्युपेतार्थकृत्याः Me. 38. **4** to admit, own, grant. **5** to obey, submit to. —**अव** to know, learn, be aware of; अवेहि मां किंकरमष्टमूर्तेः R. 2. 35; Ku. 3. 13, 4. 9. —**आ** to come, draw near. —**उद्** **1** to rise; (as a star &c.); (fig. also); come or go up; उदेति पूर्वं कुसुमं ततः फलं *S.* 7. 30; उदेति सविता ताम्रः &c. **2** to arise, spring, be produced. **3** to thrive, prosper. —**उप** **1** to approach, draw near; go to; योगी परं स्थानमुपैति चाद्यं Bg. 8. 28. **2** to go to or pass into, attain to, reach (a state); उपैति सस्यं परिणामरम्यतां Ki. 4. 22. **3** to befall. —**निर्** to depart, go or set out. —**परा** **1** to go or run away, flee, retreat; यः परैति स जीवति Pt. 5. 88. 'he who runs away saves his life'; cf. 'to run for one's life'. **2** to reach, attain to; Ki. 1. 39. **3** to depart from this world, die; see परेत. —**परि** **1** to go round, circumambulate; चरणन्यासं भक्तिनम्रः परीयाः Me. 55, Ms. 2. 48. **2** to surround, encompass; हुतवहपरीतं गृहमिव *S.* 5. 10; विषवल्लिभिः परीतामिर्महौषधिः R. 12. 61; so कोपपरीत. **3** to go to, think of (objects &c.). **4** to change, transform oneself. —**प्र** **1** to go out of, depart from; धीराः प्रेत्यास्माल्लोकादमृता भवंति Ken. **2** (hence) to depart life, die; प्रेत्य after death; नच तत्प्रेत्य नो इह Bg. 17. 28; Ms. 2. 9, 26. —**प्रति** **1** to go back to, return; प्रतीयाय गुरोः सकाशं R. 5. 35, Bk. 3. 19. **2** to believe, trust; कः प्रत्येति सैवेयमिति U. 4.

3 to learn, understand, know ; प्रतीयते धातुरिवेहितं फलैः Ki. 1. 20 ; Si. 1. 69. 4 to be well-known or celebrated ; सोयं वटः श्याम इति प्रतीतः R. 13. 53. 5 to be pleased or satisfied ; R. 3. 12, 16. 21. (—*Caus.* प्रत्याययति) to convince, inspire confidence बलवत्तु दूयमानं प्रत्याययतीव मे हृदयं S. 5. 31 ; ताः स्वचारित्र्यमुद्दिश्य प्रत्याययतु मैथिली R. 15. 73. **—प्रत्युद्** to go forth to meet or receive ; सपर्यया प्रत्युदियाय पार्वती Ku. 5. 31. **—वि 1** to go away, depart ; तस्यामहं त्वयि च संप्रति वीतचिंतः S. 4. 12 ; so वीतभय, वीतक्रोध. 2 to undergo change : सदृशं त्रिषु लिंगेषु सर्वासु च विभक्तिषु । वचनेषु च सर्वेषु यन्न व्येति तदव्ययं Sk. 3 to spend; see व्यय. **—विपरि** to change (usually for the worse) ; see विपरीत. **—व्यति 1** to go out of, swerve from, transgress ; रेखामात्रमपि क्षुण्णादा मनोर्वर्त्मनः परम् । न व्यतीयुः प्रजास्तस्य नियंतुर्नेमिवृत्तयः ॥ R. 1. 17. 2 to pass, elapse (as time) ; सप्त व्यतीयुस्त्रिगुणानि तस्य दिनानि R. 2. 25 ; व्यतीते काले &c. 3 to pass beyond, leave behind ; R. 6. 67. **—व्यप 1** to depart or deviate from, be free from ; व्यपेतमदमत्सरः Y. 1. 267 ; स्मृत्याचारव्यपेतेन मार्गेण 2. 5. 2 to go away, separate, part asunder ; समेत्य च व्यपेयातां H. 4. 69 ; Ms. 9. 142, 11. 97. **—सं** to come together or meet. **—समनु** to accompany, follow. **—समव 1** to assemble, come together ; समवेता युयुत्सवः Bg. 1. 1. 2 to be related or connected, see समवाय **—समा** to come together or meet ; समेत्य च व्यपेयातां H. 4. 69. **—समुद्** to be heaped together or collected ; अयं समुदितः सर्वो गुणानां गणः Ratn. 1. 6.**—समुप** to get, obtain. **—संप्रति** to decide, settle, determine, judge ; किं तत्कथं वेत्युपलब्धसंज्ञा विकल्पयंतोपि न संप्रतीयुः Bk. 11. 10.

इक्षवः Sugar-cane.

इक्षुः Sugar-cane. —Comp. **—कांडः —डं** N. of two different species of sugar-cane (काश and मुंजतृण). **—कुट्टकः** a gatherer of sugar-cane. **—दा** N. of a river. **—पाकः** molasses. **—भक्षिका** a meal of sugar and molasses. **—मती, —मालिनी, —मालवी** N. of a river. **—मेहः** diabetes. **—यंत्रं** a sugar-mill. **—रसः 1** the juice of sugar-cane. 2 molasses. **—वणं** a sugarcane wood. **—वाटिका,—वाटी** a garden of sugar-canes. **—विकारः** sugar ; molasses. **—सारः** molasses.

इक्षुकः Sugar-cane ; see इक्षु.

इक्षुकीया A place abounding in sugar-cane.

इक्षुरः Sugar-cane.

इक्ष्वाकुः 1 N. of the celebrated ancestor of the solar kings who ruled in Ayodhyâ; (he was the first of the the Solar kings, and was a son of Manu Vaivaswata) ; इक्ष्वाकुवंशोऽभिमतः प्रजानां U. 1. 44. 2 A descendant of Ikshvâku ; गलितवयसामिक्ष्वाकूणामिदं हि कुलव्रतं R. 3. 70.

इख्, इंख् 1. P. (एखति, इंखति) To go, move ; usually with प्र, to move, shake ; Mâl 6.

इंग् 1 U. (इंगति-ते, इंगित) 1 To move shake, be agitated ; यथा दीपो निवातस्थो नेंगते Bg. 6. 19, 14. 23. 2 To go, move.

इंग *a.* 1 Movable. 2 Wonderful, surprising. **—गः 1** A hint or sign. 2 An indication of a sentiment by gesture.

इंगनं 1 Moving, shaking 2 Knowledge; see इंग .

इंगितं 1 Palpitation, shaking. 2 Internal thought, intention, purpose ; °आकारवेदिभिः K. 7; Pt. 1. 43; अगूढसद्भावमितींगितज्ञया Ku. 5. 62 ; R 1. 20 ; Si. 9. 69. 3 A hint, sign, gesture ; Pt. 1. 44. 4 Particularly, the gesture or motion of the various limbs of the body indicating one's intentions; gesture suited to betray internal feelings ; आकारैरिंगितैर्गत्या ... गृह्यतेऽंतर्गतं मनः Ms. 8. 26. —Comp. **—कोविद्, —ज्ञ** *a.* skilled in the interpretation of internal sentiments by external gestures, understanding signs.

इंगुदः,—दी N. of a medicinal tree (Mar. हिंगणबेट); इंगुदीपादपः सोऽयं U. 1. 14. **—दं** The nut of the tree.

इच्छा 1 Wish, desire, will; इच्छया at will. 2 (In Math.) A question or problem. 3 (In gram.) The form of the desiderative. –Comp. **–दानं** fulfilment of a wish. **—निवृत्तिः** *f.* suppression of desires ; indifference to worldly desires. **—फलं** the solution of a question or problem. **–रतं** desired sports ; Me. 89. **–वसुः** N. of Kubera. **–संपद्** *f.* fulfilment of one's wishes.

इज्यः 1 A teacher. 2 An epithet of बृहस्पति, the teacher of the gods.

इज्या 1 A sacrifice; जगत्प्रकाशं तदशेषमिज्यया R. 3. 48, 1. 68, 15. 2. 2 A gift, donation. 3 An image. 4 A bawd or procuress. 5 A cow. –Comp. **–शीलः** a constant sacrificer.

इट्चरः A bull or steer allowed to go at liberty.

इडा-ला 1 The earth. 2 Speech. 3 Food. 4 A Cow. 5 N. of a goddess, daughter of Manu. (She was the wife of Budha and mother of Purûravas).

इडिका The earth.

इतर *pron. a.* (**–रा** *f.*,**–रत्** *n.*) 1 Another, the other (of two), the remaining one of the two ; इतरो दहने स्वकर्मणां R. 8. 20 v. l. 2 The rest or others (pl.) 3 Other than, different from (with abl.) ; इतरतापशतानि यथेच्छया वितर तानि सहे चतुरानन Udb. ; इतरो रावणादेष राघवानुचरो यदि Bk. 8. 106. 4 Opposite of, either used by itself as an adj., or at the end of comp. ; जंगमानीतराणि च Râm. ; विजयायेतराय वा Mb. ; so दक्षिण° left ; वाम° right &c. 5 Low, mean, vulgar, ordinary ; इतर इव परिभूय ज्ञानं मन्मथेन जडीकृतः K. 154. –Comp **–इतर** *pron. a.* mutual, respective, reciprocal; °**आश्रयः** mutual dependence, inter-connection. ° **योगः 1** mutual connection or union ; Si. 10. 24. 2 a variety of the Dvandva compound (opp. समाहारद्वंद्व) where each member of the compound is viewed separately.

इतरतः, इतरत्र *ind.* Otherwise than, different from, elsewhere ; see अन्यतः, अन्यत्र.

इतरथा *ind.* 1 In another manner, in a contrary manner. 2 Perversely. 3 On the other hand.

इतरेद्युः *ind.* On another day ; the other day.

इतस् *ind.* 1 Hence, from here or hence. 2 From this person, from me; इतः स दैत्यः प्राप्तश्रीर्नेत एवार्हति क्षयं Ku. 2. 55. 3 In this direction, towards me, here; इतो निषीदेति विसृष्टभूमिः Ku. 3. 2 ; प्रयुक्तमप्यस्त्रमितो वृथा स्यात् R. 2. 34 ; इत इतो देवः this way, this way, my lord .(in dramas). 4 From this world. 5 From this time ; इतः–इतः on the one hand-on the other hand ; or, in one place-in another place, here-there.

इति *ind.* 1 This particle is most generally used to report the very words spoken or supposed to be spoken by some one, as represented by the quotation marks in English. The speech reported may be (1) a single word used merely to express what the form of the word is, when it is used as it is (शब्दस्वरूपद्योतक); राम रामेति रामेति कूजंतं मधुराक्षरं Râm. ; अत एव गविरयाह Bhartri. ; (2) or a substantive, which must be put in the nominative case when its meaning is to be indicated (प्रातिपदिकार्थद्योतक) ; चयस्त्विषामित्यवधारितं पुरा... क्रमादमुं नारद इत्यबोधि सः Si. 1. 3 ; अवैमि चैनामनघेति R. 14. 40 ; दिलीप इति राजेंदुः R. 1. 12 ; (3) or a whole sentence when इति is merely used at the end of that sentence; (वाक्यार्थद्योतक) ; ज्ञास्यसि कियद्भुजो मे रक्षति मौर्वीकिणांक इति S. 1. 13. 2 Besides this general sense इति has the following senses:— (a) Cause, as expressed by ' because ', ' since', ' on the ground that', in English ; वैदेशिकोस्मीति पृच्छामि U. 1; पुराणमित्येव न साधु सर्वं M. 1. 2 ; oft. with किं q. v. (*b*) Motive or purpose ; R. 1. 37. (*c*) Thus, to mark the conclusion (opp. अथ) ; इति प्रथमोंऽकः thus (or here ends) the first Act. (*d*) So, thus, in this manner ; इत्युक्तवंतं परिरभ्य दोर्भ्यां Ki. 11. 80. (*e*) Of this nature or description ; गौरश्वः पुरुषो हस्तीति जातिः. (*f*) As follows, to the following effect ; रामाभि-

धानो हरिरित्युवाच R. 13. 1. (*g*) As for, in the capacity of, as regards (showing capacity or relation) ; पितेति स पूज्यः, अध्यापक इति निंद्यः, शीघ्रमिति सुकरं निभृतमिति चिंतनीयं भवेत् *S*. 3. (*h*) Illustration (usually with आदि) ; इंदुरिंदुरिव श्रीमानित्यादौ तदनन्वयः Chandr.; गौः शुक्लश्चलो डित्थ इत्यादौ K. P. 2. (*i*) A quotation or an opinion accepted; इति पाणिनिः, इत्यापिशलिः, इत्यमरः, विश्वः &c. (*j*) Manifestation. -COMP. **-अर्थः** sum and substance, meaning in short. **-अर्थं** *ind*. for this purpose, hence. **-कथा** a meaningless or nonsensical talk. **-कर्तव्य -करणीय** *a*. proper or necessary to be done according to certain rules. (**-व्यं, -यं**) duty, obligation ; °**ता, -कार्यता, कृत्यता** any proper or necessary duty, obligation ; इतिकर्तव्यतामूढः wholly at a loss what to do, embarrassed, perplexed. **-मात्र** *a*. of such extent or quality.**-वृत्तं 1** occurrence, event. **2** a tale, story.

इतिह *ind*. Thus indeed, quite in conformity to tradition.

इतिहासः 1 History (legendary or traditional) ; धर्मार्थकाममोक्षाणामुपदेश समन्वितं । पूर्ववृत्तं कथायुक्तमितिहासं प्रचक्षते ॥. **2** Heroic history (such as the Mahâbhârata). **3** Historical evidence, tradition (which is recognized as a proof by the Paurâṇikas). —COMP. **-निबंधनं** legendary composition or narrative.

इत्थं *ind*. Thus, so, in this manner ; इत्थं रतेः किमपि भूतमदृश्यरूपं Ku. 4. 45 ; इत्थं गते under these circumstances.-COMP. **—कारं** *ind*. in this manner. **—भूत** *a*. **1** so circumstanced, being in this state; Ku. 6. 26 ; कथमित्थंभूता M. 5; K. 146. **2** true or faithful (as a story).**-विध** *a*. 1 of such kind. **2** endowed with such qualities.

इत्य *a*. To be gone towards or approached ; इत्यः शिष्येण गुरुवत्. **—त्या 1** Going ; way **2** A litter, palanquin.

इत्वर *a*. (**री** *f*.) **1** Going, travelling, a traveller. **2** Cruel, harsh **3** Low, vile. **4** Despised, contemned. **5** Poor. **—रः** A eunuch. **—री 1** A disloyal or unchaste woman. **2** An Abhisârikâ q. v.

इदं *pron. a*. [अयं *m*.; इयं *f*., इदं *n*.] **1** This here, (referring to something near the speaker ; इदमस्तु संनिकृष्टं रूपं); इदं तत् ...इति यदुच्यते *S*. 5 here is the truth of the saying. **2** Present, seen; the nominative forms are used with verbs in the sense of ' here '; इयमास्मि here am I; so इमे स्मः; अयमागच्छामि here I come. **3** It often refers to something immediately following, while एतद् refers to what precedes; अनुकलस्त्वयं ज्ञेयः सदा सद्भिरनुष्ठितः । Ms. 3. 147 (अयं=वक्ष्यमाणः Kull.) ; श्रत्वैतादिदमूचुः. **4** It occurs connected with यत्, तत्, एतद्, अदस्, किं or a personal pronoun, either to point out anything more distinctly, and emphatically, or sometimes pleonastically; कोयमाचरत्यविनयं *S*. 1. 25 ; सेयं, सोयं, this here ; अयमहं भोः *S*. 4 ho, here am I.

इदानीं *ind*. Now, at this moment, in this case, just now, even now ; वत्से प्रतिष्ठस्वेदानीं *S*. 4 ; आर्यपुत्र इदानीमसि U. 3 ; इदानीमेव just now ; इदानीमपि now also, in this case also.

इदानींतन *a*. (**नी** *f*.) Present, momentary, of the present moment.

इद्ध *p. p*. (fr. इंध्) Kindled &c. **—द्धं 1** Sunshine, heat. **2** Refulgence, splendour. **3** Wonder.

इध्मः-ध्मं Fuel, especially that used for the sacred fire; R. 14. 70. -COMP. **-जिह्वः** fire.**-प्रव्रश्चनः** hatchet, an axe.

इध्या Kindling, lighting.

इन *a*. **1** Able, powerful, mighty. **2** Bold. **—नः 1** A lord. **2** The sun ; *Si*. 2. 65. **3** A king ; न न महीनमहीनपराक्रमं R. 9. 5.

इंदिंदिरः A large bee; लोभादिंदिंदिरेषु निपतत्सु Bv. 2. 183.

इंदिरा N. of Lakshmî, wife of Vishṇu. -COMP. **-आलयं** ' abode of Indirâ', the blue lotus. **-मंदिरः** an epithet of Vishṇu. (**-रं**) the blue lotus.

इंदीवरिणी A group of blue lotuses.

इंदीवारः A blue lotus.

इंदुः 1 The moon ; दिलीप इति राजेंदुरिंदुः क्षीरनिधाविव R. 1. 12. **2** (In Math.) The number ' one. ' **3** Camphor. -COMP. **-कमलं** the white lotus. **-कला** a digit of the moon. (These are 16, each of which is mythologically said to be devoured by 16 deities in succession). **-कलिका 1** N. of a plant (केतकी). **2** a digit of the moon.**-कांतः** the moon-stone. (**-ता**) night. **-क्षयः 1** waning of the moon. **2** the new-moon day. **-जः, -पुत्रः** the planet Mercury. (**-जा**) N. of the river Revâ or Narmadâ. **-जनकः** the ocean.**-दलः** a digit, crescent.**-भा** a kind of water lily. **-भृत्,-शेखरः-मौलिः** ' the moon-crested god, ' epithets of Siva. **-मणिः** the moonstone. **-मंडलं** the orb or disc of the moon. **-रत्नं** a pearl. **-ले (रे) खा** a digit of the moon. **-लोहकं, -लौहं** silver. **-वदना** N. of a metre ; see Appendix. **-वासरः** Monday.

इंदुमती 1 A day of full moon. **2** The wife of अज and sister of भोज.

इंदूरः A rat, mouse.

इंद्रः 1 The lord of gods. **2** The god of rain; rain **3** A lord or ruler (as of men &c.) ; first or best (of any class of objects), always as the last member of comp. ; नरेंद्रः a lord of men, *i. e*. a king; so मृगेंद्रः a lion; गजेंद्रः, योगींद्रः, कपींद्रः.**—द्रा** The wife of Indra, Indrânî. [Indra, the god of the firmament, is the Jupiter Pluvius of the Indian *A*ryans. In the Vedas he is placed in the first rank among the gods. But in later mythology he falls in the second rank. He is said to be one of the sons or Kasyapa and Dakshayani or Aditi. He is inferior to the triad Brahma, Vishnu and Mahesa, but he is the chief of all the other gods, and is commonly styled Suresa, Devendra &c. As in the Vedas so in later mythology, he is the regent of the atmosphere, and of the east quarter, and his world is called Svarga. He sends the lightning, uses the thunderbolt, and sends down rain. He is frequently at war with Asuras, whom he constantly dreads and by whom he is sometimes defeated. The Indra of mythology is famous for his incontinence and adultery, one prominent instance of which is his seduction of Ahalya, the wife of Gautama (seo Ahalya), and for which he is often spoken of as **Ahalya-jara**. The curse of the sage impressed upon him a thousand marks resembling the female organ, and he was therefore called Sayoni ; but these marks were afterwards changed into eyes, and he is hence called Netra-yoni and Sahasraksha. In the Ramayana Indra is represented as having been defeated and carried off to Lanka by Ravana's son called Meghanada, who for this exploit received the title of ' Indrajit. ' It was only at the intercession of Brahma and the gods that Indra was released. Indra is often represented as trying to prevent kings from completing one hundred sacrifices, it being believed that he who completed the 100th would obtain the seat of Indra ; and hence it was that he carried off the sacrificial horses of Sagara and Raghu ; see R. 3rd canto. He is represented as being in constant dread of sages practising potent penances, and as sending down nymphs to beguile their minds (see *Apsaras*). He is also said to have cut off the wings of mountains when they grew troublesome, and to have killed the demons Bala and Vritra. His wife is Indrani, the daughter of the demon Puloman, and his son is named Jayanta. He is also said to be the father of Arjuna.] -COMP. **-अनुजः, -अवरजः** an epithet of Vishṅu and of Nârâyaṇa. **-अरिः** an Asura or demon. **-आयुधं** Indra's weapon, the rainbow ; R. 7. 4. **-कीलः 1** N. of the mountain मंदर. **2** a rock. (**-लं**) the banner of Indra. **-कुंजरः** Indra's elephant, Airâvata. **-कूटः** N. of a mountain. **-कोशः-षः, -षकः 1** a couch, sofa. **2** a plat-form. **3** a pin or bracket projecting from the wall (नागदंत). **-गिरिः** the महेंद्र mountain. **-गुरुः, -आचार्यः** the teacher of Indra, *i. e*. बृहस्पति. **-गोपः,-गोपकः** a kind of insect, of red or white colour. **-चापं,**

-धनुस् *n.* **1** a rainbow. **2** the bow of Indra. -जालं **1** a weapon used by Arjuna ; a stratagem or trick in war. **2** conjuring, jugglery ; स्वमेंद्रजालसदृशः खलु जीवलोकः Sânti. 2. 2. -जालिक *a.* deceptive unreal, delusive. (-कः) a juggler, conjurer. -जित् *m.*'conqueror of Indra', N. of a son of Râvaṇa. who was killed by Lakshmaṇa. [Indrajit is another name of Meghanada a son of Ravana. When Ravana warred against Indra in his own heaven, his son Meghanada was with him, and fought most valiantly. During the combat, Meghanada, by virtue of the magical power of becoming invisible which he had obtained from Siva, bound Indra, and bore him off in triumph to Lanka. Brahma and the other gods hurried thither to obtain his release, and gave to Meghanada the title of Indrajit, 'conqueror of Indra'; but the victor refused to release his prisoner unless he were promised immortality. Brahma refused to grant this extravagant demand, but he strenuously persisted, and achieved his object. In the Ramayana he is represented to have been decapitated by Lakshmana while he was engaged in a sacrifice]. ° हंतृ or विजयिन् *m.* N. of Lakshmaṇa. -तूलं, -तूलकं a flock of cotton. -दारुः the tree Pinus Devadâru. -नीलः a sapphire. -नीलकः an emerald. -पत्नी Indra's wife, शची. -पुरोहितः N. of बृहस्पति. -प्रस्थं N. of a city on the Yamunâ, the residence of the Pâṇḍavas (identified with the modern Delhi); इंद्रप्रस्थगमस्तावत्कारि मा संतु चेदयः Si. 2. 63. -प्रहरणं Indra's weapon, the thunderbolt. -भेषजं dried ginger. -महः **1** a festival in honour of Indra. **2** the rainy season. -लोकः Indra's world, Svarga or Paradise. -वंशा,-वज्रा N. of two metres, see Appendix. -शत्रुः **1** an enemy or destroyer of Indra (when the accent is on the last syllable), an epithet of प्रह्लाद; R. 7. 35. **2** one whose enemy is Indra, an epithet of वृत्र (when the accent is on the first syllable). (This refers to a legend in the Sat. Br., where it is said that Vritra's father intended his son to become the destroyer of Indra, and asked him to say इंद्रशत्रुर्वर्धस्व &., but, through mistake, he accented the word on the first syllable, and was killed by Indra ; cf. Sik. 52: मंत्रो हीनः स्वरतो वर्णतो वा मिथ्याप्रयुक्तो न तमर्थमाह । स वाग्वज्रो यजमानं हिनस्ति यथेंद्रशत्रुः स्वरतोपराधात् ॥. -शलभः a kind of insect. -सुतः, -सूनुः N. of (*a*) Jayanta ; (*b*) Arjuna ; (*c*) Vâli, the king of monkeys. -सेनानीः the leader of Indra's armies, epithet of Kârtikeya.

इंद्रकं An assembly room, a hall.

इंद्राणी The wife of Indra.

इंद्रियं **1** Power, force, (the quality which belongs to Indra). **2** An organ of sense. There are two kinds of Indriyas: (*a*) ज्ञानेंद्रियाणि or बुद्धींद्रियाणिः–श्रोत्रं त्वक्चक्षुषी जिह्वा नासिका चैव पंचमी (also मनः according to some); and (*b*) कर्मेंद्रियाणिः—पायूपस्थं हस्तपादं वाक् चैव दशमी स्मृता Ms. 2. 99. **3** Bodily or virile power, power of the senses. **4** Semen. **5** Symbolical expression for the number '5.' -Comp. -अगोचर *a.* imperceptible. -अर्थः **1** an object of sense ; these objects are:—रूपं शब्दो गंधरसस्पर्शाश्च विषया अमी Ak. ; Bg. 3. 34 ; R. 14. 25. -आयतनं the abode of the senses, *i. e.* the body. -गोचर *a.* Perceptible to the senses. (-रः) an object of sense. -ग्रामः, -वर्गः the assemblage or collection of organs, the five organs of sense taken collectively ; बलवानिंद्रियग्रामो विद्वांसमपि कर्षति Ms. 2. 215 ; निर्ववार मधुनींद्रियवर्गः Si. 10. 3. -ज्ञानं consciousness, the faculty of perception. -निग्रहः restraint of senses. -वधः insensibility. -विप्रतिपत्तिः *f.* perversion of the organs. -सन्निकर्षः the contact of an organ of sense (either with its object or with the mind). -स्वापः insensibility, unconsciousness, stupor.

इंध् 7. A. (इंद्धे or इंधे, इद्ध) To kindle, light, set on fire.—*pass.* (इध्यते) To be lighted, blaze, flame. -With सं to kindle.

इंधः Fuel.

इंधनं **1** Kindling, lighting. **2** Fuel, wood &c.

इभः An elephant. —भी A female elephant. -Comp. -अरिः a lion. -आननः N. of Gaṇesa ; cf. गजानन. निमीलिका shrewdness, sagacity, sharpness. -पालकः the driver or keeper of an elephant. -पोटा a young female elephant. -पोतः a young elephant, a cub. -युवतिः *f.* a female elephant.

इभ्य *a.* Wealthy, rich. —भ्यः **1** A king. **2** An elephant-driver. -भ्या A female elephant.

इभ्यक *a.* Wealthy, rich.

इयत् *a.* **1** So much, so large, of this extent ; इयत्तवायुः Dk. 93 ; इयंति वर्षाणि तया सहोग्रं R. 13. 67 so many years ; इयं नीतिरितीयती Si. 2. 30 this much.

इयत्ता, इयत्त्वं **1** (*a*) So much, fixed measure or quantity ; ईदृक्तया रूपमियत्तया वा R. 13. 5 ; न...यशः परिच्छेत्तुमियत्तयालं 6. 77. (*b*) Limited number, limitation ; न गुणानामियत्तया R. 10. 32. **2** Limit, standard.

इरणं **1** A desert. **2** Salt or barren ground; cf. इरिण.

इरंमदः **1** A flash of lightning, the fire attending the fall of a thunderbolt. **2** The submarine fire.

इरा **1** The earth. **2** Speech. **3** The goddess of speech, Sarasvatî. **4** Water. **5** Food. **6** Spirituous liquor. -Comp. -ईशः N. of Varuṇa, of Vishṇu and of Gaṇesa. -चरं hail ; so इरांबरं.

इरावत् *m.* The ocean.

इरिणं A salt ground, saline soil.

इर्वारु-लु *a.* Destructive, carnivorous (हिंसक).—रुः *m. f.* A cucumber.

इल् 6 P. (इलति, इलित) or 10 U. **1** To go, to move. **2** To sleep. **3** To throw, send, cast.

इला **1** The earth. **2** A cow. **3** Speech &c. ; see इडा. -Comp. -गोलः, -लं the earth, the globe. -धरः a mountain.

इलिका The earth.

इल्वकाः,-लाः (pl.) N. of the five stars in the head of Orion (मृगशिरस्)

इव *ind.* **1** Like, as (showing उपमा or comparison); वागर्थाविवसंपृक्तौ R. 1. 1. **2** As if, as it were (denoting उत्प्रेक्षा); पश्यामीव पिनाकिनं S. 1. 6 ; लिंपतीव तमोंगानि वर्षतीवांजनं नभः Mk. 1. 34. **3** A little, somewhat, perhaps ; कडार इवायं G. M. **4** (Added to interrogative words), 'possibly', 'I should like to know', 'indeed'; विना सीतादेव्या किमिव हि न दुःखं रघुपतेः U. 6. 30 ; क इव of what sort, what-like मुहूर्तमिव but for a moment ; किंचिदिव just a little bit; so ईषदिव, नाचिरादिव &c.

इशीका—इषीका q. v.

इष् I. 6 P. (इच्छति, इष्ट) **1** To wish, desire, long for ; इच्छामि संवर्धितमाज्ञया ते Ku. 3. 3. **2** To choose. **3** To endeavour to obtain, strive or seek for. **4** To be favourable. **5** To assent or consent. —*pass.* **1** To be wished or liked. **2** To be prescribed or laid down ; हस्तच्छेदनामिष्यते Ms. 8. 322.–With अनु to search, try, endeavour. -अभि to long for, desire. -परि to search. -प्रति to receive, accept ; देवस्य शासनं प्रतीष्य S. 6.–II. 4 P. (इष्यति, इषित) **1** To go, move. **2** To spread. **3** To cast, throw.–With अनु to search, go in search of ; न रत्नमन्विष्यति मृग्यते हि तत् Ku. 5. 45. -प्र (usually in *caus.*) **1** to send forth, cast, hurl; Bk. **15. 77. 2** to send, despatch; किमर्थमृषयः प्रेषिताः स्युः S. 5.–III. 1 U. (एषित) To go, move.–With अनु to follow.

इषः **1** One possessed of sap or strength. **2** The month आश्विन; ध्वानिमिषेऽनिमिषेक्षणमग्रतः Si. 6. 49.

इषि (षी) का **1** Reed, rush; °अस्त्रं R. 12. 23. **2** An arrow.

इषिरः Fire.

इषुः **1** An arrow. **2** The number five. -Comp. -अग्रं,-अनीकं the point of an arrow.-असनं, अस्त्रं the bow ; R. 11. 37. -आसः 1 a bow. 2 an archer, a warrior; Bg. 1. 4, 17. -कारः,-कृत् *m.* an arrow-maker. -धरः, -भृत् *m.* an archer. -पथः, -विक्षेपः an arrow-shot, the range of an arrow. -प्रयोगः discharging an arrow; R. 2. 42.

इषुधिः A quiver.

इष्ट *p. p.* 1 Wished, desired, longed for, wished for. 2 Beloved, liked, favourite, dear 3 Worshipped, reverenced. 4 Respected, honoured. 5 Sacrificed, worshipped with sacrifices. -ष्टः A lover, husband. -ष्टं 1 Wish, desire. 2 A holy ceremony or संस्कार. 3 A sacrifice. *-ind.* Voluntarily. -COMP.-अर्थः desired object. -आपत्तिः *f.* occurrence of what is desired ; a statement by a debater which is favourable to his opponent also ; इष्टापत्तौ दोषांतरमाह Jag. -गंध *a.* fragrant. (-धः) any fragrant substance. (-धं) sand. -देवः, -देवता a favourite god, one's tutelary deity.

इष्टका A brick; Mk. 3. -COMP. -गृहं a brick-house. -चित *a.* made of bricks; also इष्टकचित. -न्यासः laying the foundation of a house -पथः a road made of bricks.

इष्टापूर्त Performing sacrifices, and digging wells and doing other acts of charity ; इष्टापूर्तविधेः सपत्नशमनात् Mv. 3. 1.

इष्टिः *f.* 1 Wish, request, desire. 2 Seeking. 3 Any desired object. 4 A desired rule or desideratum ; (a term used with reference to Patanjali's additions to Kâtyâyana's Vârtikas; इष्टयो भाष्यकारस्य); cf. उपसंख्यान. 5 Impulse, hurry. 6 Invitation, order. 7 A sacrifice. -COMP. -पचः a miser; so °मुष. -पशु an animal to be killed at a sacrifice.

इष्टिका A brick &c. ; see इष्टका.

इष्मः 1 Cupid. 2 The spring.

इष्यः, -ष्यं The Spring.

इस् *ind.* An interjection of anger, pain, or sorrow.

इह *ind.* 1 Here (referring to time, place or direction); in this place or case. 2 In this world (opp. परत्र or अमुत्र). -Comp. -अमुत्र *ind* in this world and the next world, here and there. -लोकः this world or life. -स्थ *a.* standing here.

इहत्य *a.* Being here, of this place or world.

ई.

ईः (*m*) N. of Kâmadeva, Cupid. *—ind.* An interjection of (1) dejection ; (2) pain ; (3) sorrow ; (4) anger ; (5) compassion ; (6) perception or consciousness ; (7) calling.

ई I. 4 A. (ईयते) To go. -II. 2 P. 1 To go. 2 To shine. 3 To pervade. 4 To desire, wish. 5 To throw. 6 To eat. 7 To beg (A.) 8 To become pregnant.

ईक्ष् 1 A. (ईक्षते, ईक्षित) 1 To see, behold, perceive, observe, look or gaze at. 2 To regard, consider, look upon ; सर्वभूतस्थमात्मानं...ईक्षते योगयुक्तात्मा Bg. 6. 29. 3 To take into account, care for ; नाभिजनमीक्षते K. 104 ; न कामवृत्तिर्वचनीयमीक्षते Ku. 5. 82. 4 To think, reflect ; तत्तेज ऐक्षत बहुस्यां प्रजायेय Ch. Up. 5 To look to, or to investigate, the good or bad luck of any one (with dat. of the person) ; कृष्णाय ईक्षते गर्गः Sk. (शुभाशुभं पर्यालोचयति इत्यर्थः). -WITH अधि to suspect ; कुहकचकितो लोकः सत्येप्यपायमधीक्षते H. 4. 102 v. l. -अनु to keep in view; to search, seek after, inquire into. -अप 1 to await, wait for; न कालमपेक्षते स्नेहः Mk. 7 ; Ku. 3.26. 2 to require; need; want; शब्दार्थौ सत्कविरिव द्वयं विद्वानपेक्षते Si. 2. 86; V. 4. 12; Ku. 3. 18. 3 to look to, have regard to, have in view ; किमपेक्ष्य फलं Ki. 2. 21 ; यतः शब्दोयं व्यंजकत्वेऽर्थांतरमपेक्षते S. D. 4 to take into account, think of, consider, respect; oft. with न; तदानपेक्ष्य स्वशरीरमार्दवं Ku. 5. 18. -अभिवि to look at or towards. -अव 1 to look at, perceive, observe. 2 to aim at, have in view ; योत्स्यमानानवेक्षेहं Bg. 1. 23; have regard to; R. 3. 21 ; त्रिदिवोत्सुकयाप्यवेक्ष्य मां 8. 60 out of regard for me. 3 to watch over, protect ; श्लाघ्यां दुहितरमवेक्षस्व U. 1. 4 to think, consider; यदवोचदवेक्ष्य मानिनी Ki. 2. 3. -उद् 1 to look up to, behold, see ; सप्रणाममुदीक्षिताः Ku. 6. 7, 7. 67. 2 to wait; त्रीणि वर्षाण्युदीक्षेत कुमार्यृतुमती सती Ms. 9. 90. -उत्प्र 1 to anticipate, see in prospect; उत्प्रेक्षमाणा जघनाभिघातं Mu. 2. 2 to guess, conjecture ; किमुत्प्रेक्षसे कुतस्त्योयमिति U. 4. 3 to believe, fancy ; उत्प्रेक्षामो (Par. epic) वयं तावन्मतिमंतं बिभीषणं Râm. -उद्वि to look up to.-उप 1 to neglect, overlook, disregard ; उपेक्षते यः श्लथलंबिनीर्जटाः Ku 5. 47 ; R. 14. 34. 2 to let escape, let go, connive at ; नोपेक्षेत क्षणमपि राजा साहसिकं नरं Ms. 8. 344. 3 to look at, consider. -निर् 1 to gaze at steadfastly, mark or view completely ; धेन्वा...निरीक्ष्यमाणः सुतरां दयालुः R. 2. 52; Bg. 1. 22; Ms. 4. 38. 2 to look for, search after ; निरीक्षते केलिवनं प्रविश्य क्रमेलकः कंटकजालमेव Vikr, 1. 29. -परि 1 to examine, look at or scrutinize carefully ; अतः परीक्ष्य कर्तव्यं विशेषात्संगतं रहः S. 5. 24 ; M. 1. ; Ms. 9. 14. 2 to test, try, put to the test ; मायां मयोद्भाव्य परीक्षितोसि R. 2. 62 ; यत्नात्परीक्षितः पुंस्त्वे Y. 1. 55 carefully tested as to potency. -प्र to see, behold, perceive ; तमायांतं प्रेक्ष्य Pt. 1 ; R. 12. 44 ; Ku. 6. 47 ; Ms. 8. 147. -प्रति to wait for ; संपत्स्यते वः कामोयं कालः कश्चित्प्रतीक्ष्यतां Ku. 2. 54 ; Ms. 9. 77. -प्रतिवि to look at in return. -वि to see, behold; तं वीक्ष्य वेपथुमती Ku. 5. 85.- व्यप to mind, care for, respect (oft. with न) ; न व्यपैक्षत समुत्सुकाः प्रजाः R. 19. 6. -सं 1 to see, behold 2 to think of, consider, take into account तेजसां हि न वयः समीक्ष्यते R. 11. 1 ; Ku. 5. 16. 3 to examine carefully ; as in असमीक्ष्यकारिन्. -समव 1 to see, inspect. 2 to consider. -समुप to neglect, disregard ; see -उप above.

ईक्षकः A spectator.

ईक्षणं 1 Seeing, beholding &c. 2 A look, sight. 3 An eye ; इत्यग्निशोभाप्रहितेक्षणेन R. 2. 27 ; so अलसेक्षणा.

ईक्षणिकः A fortune-teller.

ईक्षतिः Looking, sight ; ईक्षतेर्नाशब्दं Br. Sút.

ईक्षा 1 Sight. 2 Viewing, considering.

ईक्षिका 1 An eye. 2 A glance.

ईक्षित *p. p.* Seen, beheld, regarded &c. —तं 1 Look, sight. 2 An eye ; अभिमुखे मयि संहृतमीक्षितं S. 2. 11.

ईख्, ईंख् 1 P. (ईखति, ईखित) 1 To go, move, vacillate. *—Caus.* To swing, oscillate. 2 To shake. —WITH प्र to shake, tremble; प्रेंखच्च क्षुभिता क्षितिः Bk. 17. 108 ; प्रेंखद्भूरिमयूख Mâl. 6. 5; Amaru. 1.

ईज्—ईंज् 1 A. 1 To go. 2 To censure, blame.

ईड् 2 A. (ईट्टे, ईडित) To praise; अग्निमीडे पुरोहितं Rv. 1. 1. 1 ; शालीनतामव्रजदीड्यमानः R. 18. 17; Bk. 9. 57, 18 15.

ईडा Praise, commendation.

ईड्य *pot. p.* Praiseworthy, laudable ; भवंतमीड्यं भवतः पितेव R. 5. 34.

ईतिः *f.* 1 Plague, distress, a calamity of the season. The *ítis* are usually said to be six:- 1 excessive rain; 2 drought ; 3 locusts ; 4 rats ; 5 parrots ; and 6 foreign invasions ; अतिवृष्टिरनावृष्टिः शलभा मूषकाः शुकाः । प्रत्यासन्नाश्च राजानः षडेता ईतयः स्मृताः ॥ निरातंका निरीतयः R. 1. 63. 2 An infectious disease. 3

Travelling (in a foreign country), sojourning. 4 An affray

ईदृक्ता Quality (opp. इयत्ता); विष्णोरिवास्यानवधारणीयं ईदृक्तया रूपमियत्तया वा R. 13. 5.

ईदृक्ष -श *a.* (क्षी-शी *f.*), also **ईदृश्** Such, of this kind, of this aspect, endowed with such qualities.

ईप्सा 1 Desire to obtain 2 A wish, desire.

ईप्सित *a.* Desired, wished for, dear to. —**तं** Desire, wish.

ईप्सु *a.* Striving to obtain, wishing or desiring to get (with acc. or inf., but usually in comp.); सौरभ्यमीप्सुरिव ते मुखमारुतस्य R. 5. 63.

ईर् 2 A. (ईर्ते, ईर्ण); also 1 P. (*p. p.* ईरित) 1 To go, move, shake (trans. also) 2 To rise, arise or spring from. —10 U. or *Caus.* (ईरयति, ईरित) 1 To throw, cast; disharge, dart; ऐरिरच्च महाद्रुमं Bk. 15. 52. 2 To utter, pronounce, repeat; इतीरयंतीव तया निरैक्षि N. 14. 21; Si. 9. 69; Ki 1 26; R 9 8, Mâl. 1. 25. 3 To set in motion, move, shake; वातेरितपल्लवांगुलिभिः *S.* 1. 4 To employ, use. —WITH **उद्** to rise. (—*Caus.*) 1 to utter, pronounce, tell, speak; उदीरितोर्थः पशुनापि गृह्यते Pt. 1. 43; R. 2. 9. 2 to put forth; यद्शोकोयमुदीरयिष्यति R. 8. 62. 3 to throw, roll down (as dice); R. 6. 18. 4 to raise (as dust). 5 to display; bring about. —**प्र** 1 to cast. throw; *S.* 2. 2. 2 to propel, send forth; R. 4. 24. 3 to incite, instigate, set on. **-सं** 1 to utter. 2 to shake, move. **-समुद्** to utter, pronounce.

ईरणः The wind —**णं** 1 Agitating, moving, driving. 2 Going. 3 =इरण q. v.

ईरिण *a.* Desert, barren. —**णं** A desert, barren soil; मुहूर्तमिव निःशब्दमासीदीरिणसंनिभं Râm.

ईर्क्ष्य् See ईर्ष्य्.

ईर्मं A wound.

ईर्या Wandering about (as a religious mendicant).

ईर्वारुः *m. f.* A cucumber.

ईर्षा=ईर्ष्या q. v.

ईर्ष्य्, ईर्क्ष्य् 1 P. (ईर्ष्यति, ईर्ष्यित) To envy, be jealous of, be impatient of the success of (with dat. of person) हरये ईर्ष्यति Sk.; *Si.* 8. 36.

ईर्ष्य, ईर्ष्यु, ईर्ष्यक *a.* Envious, jealous.

ईर्ष्या -र्षा Envy, jealousy, envy of another's success.

ईर्ष्या (र्षा) लु, ईर्ष्यु (र्षु) *a.* Envious, impatient.

ईलिः (ली *f.*) A weapon, a cudgel or a short sword.

ईश् 2 A. (ईष्टे, ईशित) 1 To rule, be master of. govern, command (with gen.); अर्थानामीशिषे त्वं वयमपि च गिरामीश्महे यावदर्थं Bh. 3. 30. 2 To be able, have power; expressed by 'can'; माधुर्यमीष्टे हरिणान् ग्रहीतुं R. 18. 13. 3 To own, possess.

ईश *a.* 1 Owning, master or lord of; see below. 2 Powerful, supreme. —**शः** 1 A lord, master; with gen. or in comp; कथंचिदीशा मनसां बभूवुः Ku. 3. 34; so वागीश, सुरेश &c. 2 A husdand. 3 The number 11. 4 N. of *S*iva. **-शा** 1 N. of Durgâ. 2 A woman having supremacy; a rich lady. —COMP. —**कोणः** the north-east quarter. **-पुरी,** —**नगरी** N. of Benares. —**सखः** an epithet of Kubera.

ईशानः 1 A ruler, master, lord. 2 N. of *S*iva; Ku. 7. 56. 3 The sun (as a form of *S*iva). 4 N. of Vishṇu. —**नी** N. of Durgâ.

ईशिता, -त्वं Superiority, greatness, one of the eight *siddhis* or attributes of *S*iva. See अणिमन् or सिद्धि.

ईश्वर *a.* (**रा-री** *f.*) 1 Powerful, able, capable of (with inf.); Ku. 4. 11. 2 Rich. wealthy. —**रः** 1 A lord, master; ईश्वरं लोकोर्थतः सेवते Mu. 1. 14. 2 A king, prince, ruler 3 A rich or great man, मा प्रयच्छेश्वरे धनं H 1. 15; cf. "To carry coals to Newcastle." 4 A husband; Ki 9 39. 5 The Supreme God (परमेश्वर). 6 N. of *S*iva; V. 1. 1. 7 The God of love, Cupid. **-रा, -री** N. of Durgâ. —COMP. **-निषेधः** denial of the existence of god, athe sm. —**पूजक** *a.* pious, devout. **-सद्मन्** *n.* a temple. —**सभं** a royal court or assembly.

ईष् 1 U. (ईषति-ते, ईषित) 1 To fly away. 2 To look, see. 3 To give. 4 To kill.

ईषः The month *A*svina; cf. इष.

ईषत् *ind.* Slightly, to some extent, a little; ईषत् चुंबितानि *S.* 1. 3. —COMP. **-उष्ण** *a.* tepid. **-कर** *a.* 1 doing little. 2 easy to be accomplished. **-जलं** shallow water. **-पांडु** *a.* a little white or pale, whitish. **-पुरुषः** a mean or contemptible person. **-रक्त** *a.* pale red **-लभ, -प्रलंभ** *a.* to be got for little. —**हासः** slight laughter, a smile.

ईषा The pole or shafts of a carriage or a plough.

ईषिका 1 An elephant's eyeball. 2 A painter's brush. 3 A weapon, arrow, dart.

ईषिरः Fire.

ईषीका 1 A painter's brush. 2 An ingot-mould. 3=इषीका q. v.

ईष्मः-ष्वः See इष्मः, इष्वः.

ईह् 1 A. (ईहते, ईहित) 1 To wish, desire, think of (with acc. or inf.); Bg. 16. 12; Bk. 1. 11. 2 To endeavour to obtain. 3 To aim at or attempt, endeavour, strive; माधुर्यं मधुबिंदुना रचयितुं क्षारांबुधेरीहते Bh. 2. 6; Y. 2. 116. —WITH **सं** 1 to wise, desire. 2 to strive to do or perform, strive for; प्रियाणि वांछत्यसुभिः समीहितुं Ki. 1. 19.

ईहा 1 Wish, desire. 2 Effort, exertion, activity; Ms. 9. 205. -COMP. **-मृगः** 1 a wolf. 2 a division of the drama consisting of four acts; for definition &c. see S. D. 518. —**वृकः** a wolf.

ईहित *p. p* Wished; sought, striven for &c. —**तं** 1 A wish, desire. 2 Effort, exertion. 3 An undertaking, deed, act; Ki. 1. 20.

उ.

उः N. of *S*iva, the second of the three syllables in ओम्; see अ. —*ind.* 1 As a particle used expletively; उ उमेशः Sk. 2 An interjection of:— (*a*) calling; उ मेति मात्रा तपसो निषिद्धा पश्चादुमाख्यां सुमुखी जगाम Ku. 1. 26; (*b*) anger; (*c*) compassion; (*d*) command; (*e*) acceptance; (*f*) interrogation; or (*g*) used merely as an expletive. In classical literature used chiefly with अथ (अथो), न (नो) and किम् (किमु); see these words.

उक्त *p. p.* (fr. **वच्**) 1 Said, spoken. 2 Utterd, spoken (opp अनुमित or संभावित). 3 Told, addressed; असावनुक्तोपि सहाय एव Ku. 3. 26. 4 Describeb, related. —**क्तं** A speech, words collectively; a sentence. —COMP. —**अनुक्त** *a.* spoken and not spoken —**उपसंहारः** a brief description, résumé, peroration. —**निर्वाहः** maintaining an assertion. —**पुंस्कः** a word (feminine or neuter) of which also a masculine exists, and the meaning of which differs from that of the masculine only by the notion of gender. —**प्रत्युक्तं** speech and reply, discourse.

उक्तिः *f.* 1 Speech, expression, statement; उक्तिरर्थांतरन्यासः स्यात्सामान्यविशे-

षयोः Chandr. 5. 120; Ms. 8. 104. 2 A sentence. 3 Power of expression, the expressive power of a word; as in एकयोक्त्या पुष्पवंतौ दिवाकरनिशाकरौ Ak.

उक्थं 1 A saying, sentence, verse, (स्तोत्रं). 2 Eulogy, praise. 3 N of the Sâmaveda.

उक्ष् 1. 6. U. (उक्षति, उक्षित) 1 To sprinkle, wet, moisten, pour down upon; औक्षन् शोणितमंभोदाः Bk. 17. 9, 3. 5; Si. 5. 30: R. 11. 5, 20; Ku. 1. 54. 2 To emit, send forth. —WITH अभि to sprinkle, with holy or consecrated water; शिरसि शकुंतलामभ्युक्ष्य S 4. —परि to sprinkle round about. -प्र to consecrate by sprinkling holy water; प्राणात्यये तथा श्राद्धे प्रोक्षितं द्विजकाम्यया Y. 1. 179 Ms. 5 27. -संप्र to consecrate by sprinkling; Y. 1. 24.

उक्षणं 1 Sprinkling. 2 Consecrating as by sprinkling; वासिष्ठमंत्रोक्षणजात् प्रभावात् R. 5. 27.

उक्षन् *m.* An ox or bull; Ku. 7. 70; (changed to उक्ष in some comp महोक्षः, वृद्धोक्षः &c) —Comp. —तरः a small bull or ox, cf. वत्सतर.

उख्, उंख् 1 P. (ओखति, उंखति, ओखित, उंखित) To go, move.

उखा A boiling vessel, a boiler or cooking pot (such as a sauce-pan).

उख्य *a.* Dressed or boiled in a pot (as flesh &c.); शुल्यमुख्यं च होमवान् Bk. 4. 9.

उग्र *a.* 1 Fierce, cruel, ferocious, savage (as a look &c.); °दर्शनः. 2 Formidable, terrific, frightful, fearful; सिंहनिपातमुग्रं R. 3. 60; Ms. 6. 75, 12. 75. 3 Powerful, strong, violent. intense; उग्रातपां वेलां S. 3. intensely hot उग्रशोकां Me. 113 v. l. 4 Sharp, Pungent, hot. 5 High, noble —ग्रः 1 N. of Siva or Rudra. 2 N. of a mixed tribe, descendant of a Kshatriya father and Súdra mother. 3 N. of a country called Kerala (modern Malabar). 4 The sentiment called रौद्र. -COMP. -गंध *a.* strong-smelling. (-धः) 1 the Champaka tree. 2 garlic. —चारिणी, —चंडा N. of Durgâ. —जाति *a.* base-born. -दर्शन -रूप *a.* frightful in appearance, fierce-looking. —धन्वन् *a.* having a powerful bow. (*-m.*) N. of Siva and Indra. —शेखरा 'crest of Siva', N. of the Ganges. —सेनः N. of a king of mathurâ and father of Kamsa. He was deposed by his son; but Krishṇa, after having slain Kamsa, restored him to the throne.

उग्रंपश्य *a.* Fierce-looking, frightful, hideous.

उच् 4 P. (उच्यति, उचित or उग्र, mostly used in *p. p.*) 1 To collect, to gather together. 2 To be fond of, delight in. 3 To be proper or fit. 4 To be accustomed or used to.

उचित *p. p.* 1 Fit, proper, right, suitable; उचितस्तदुपालंभः U. 3; usually with inf.; उचितं न ते मंगलकाले रोदितुं S. 4. 2 Usual, customary; उचितेषु करणीयेषु S. 4. 3 Accustomed or used to, in comp.; नीवारभागधेयोचितैः R. 1. 50, 2. 25; 3. 54, 60; 11. 9; Ki. 1. 34. 4 Praiseworthy.

उच्च *a.* 1 High (in all senses); tall; क्षितिधारणोच्चं Ku. 7. 68; elevated, exalted (family &c.). 2 Loud, high-sounding; उच्चाः पक्षिगणाः Si. 4. 18. 3 Intense, violent, strong. —COMP. —तरुः the cocoa-nut tree. —तालः (heightened) music, dancing &c. at a tavern. -नीच *a.* 1 high and low. 2 various. —ललाटा टिका a woman with a high or projecting forehead. -संश्रय *a.* occupying a high station (said of a planet); R. 3. 13; see Malli. thereon.

उच्चकैः *ind.* 1 High, above, lofty (fig. also); श्रितोदयाद्रिरभिसायमुच्चकैः Si. 1. 16, 16. 46. 2 Loud.

उच्चक्षुस् *a.* 1 With the eyes directed upwards, looking upwards. 2 With the eyes taken out, blind.

उच्चंड *a.* 1 Fierce, terrible, formidable. 2 Quick. 3 Loud. 4 Angry, irascible.

उच्चंद्रः The last watch of the night.

उच्चयः 1 A collection, heap, multitude; रूपोच्चयेन S. 2. 9; cf. शिलोच्चय also. 2 Gathering, collecting (flowers &c.) पुष्पोच्चयं नाटयति S. 4; Ku. 3. 61. 3 The knot of a woman's (wearing) garment. 4 Prosperity, rise.

उच्चरणं 1 Going up or out. 2 Utterance.

उच्चल *a.* Moving. -लं Mind.

उच्चलनं Moving away, setting out.

उच्चलित *p. p.* On the point of going, setting out; R. 2. 6.

उच्चाटनं 1 Driving away, expulsion. 2 Separation. 3 Eradication, extirpation (of a plant). 4 A kind of charm or magical incantation. 5 Working this charm; ruining one's enemy.

उच्चारः 1 Utterance, pronunciation, declaration. 2 Excrement, dung; मातुरुच्चार एव सः H. Pr. 16; Ms. 4. 50. 3 Discharge (in general).

उच्चारणं 1 Pronuciation, utterance; वाचः Sik. 2; वेद°. 2 Declaration, enunciation.

उच्चावच *a.* 1 High and low, irregular; Ms. 6. 73. 2 Various, diverse; Ms. 1. 38; Si. 4. 46.

उच्चूडः-लः The flag of a banner or the banner itself.

उच्चैः *ind.* 1 Aloft, high, above, upwards (opp. नीचं-चैः); विपद्युच्चैः स्थेयं Bh. 2. 28; उच्चैरुदात्तः P. I. 2. 29. 2 Loudly, with a loud noise. 3 Powerfully; very much, greatly; विद्धति भयमुच्चैर्वीक्ष्यमाणा वनांताः Rs. 1. 22. 4 (Used as an adj. in comp. or by itself) (*a*) high, noble; जनोयमुच्चैः पदलंघनोत्सुकः Ku. 5. 64; S. 4. 15; Ratn. 4. 19. (*b*) distinguished, pre-eminent, famous; उच्चैरुच्चैःश्रवास्तेन Ku. 2. 47. -COMP. -घुष्टं 1 clamour, uproar. 2 loud proclamation. -वादः high praise. -शिरस् *a.* high-minded, magnanimous; Ku. 1. 12. -श्रवस्,-स *a.* 1 long eared. 2 deaf. (*-m.*) N. of the horse of Indra (said to be churned out of the ocean).

उच्चैस्तमां *ind.* 1 Exceedingly high. 2 Very loudly.

उच्चैस्तरं-रां *ind.* 1 Very loud. 2 Exceedingly high; Ku. 7. 68.

उच्छन्न *a.* 1 Destroyed, cut down (perhaps for उत्सन्न); see उच्छिन्न. 2 Extinct (as a work).

उच्छलत् *pres. a.* 1 Shining, moving about. 2 Moving, going on. 3 Flying up or away, going up high.

उच्छलनं Going or moving upwards.

उच्छादनं 1 Covering. 2 Rubbing the body with perfumes.

उच्छासन *a.* Not amenable to rule or command, unruly.

उच्छास्त्र, °वर्तिन् *a.* 1 Contrary or opposed to शास्त्र (civil or religious law-books). 2 Deviating from or transgressing the law books.

उच्छिख *a.* 1 Crested. 2 Flaming, blazing up; R. 16. 87.

उच्छित्तिः *f.* Extirpation, destruction; कोसल° Ratn 4.

उच्छिन्न *p. p.* 1 Extirpated destroyed; cut down or off; उच्छिन्नाश्रयकातरेव कुलटा गोत्रांतरं श्रीर्गता Mu. 6. 5. 2 Abject, vile.

उच्छिरस् *a.* 1 With the neck raised (lit). 2 High. 3 (Hence) Noble, great, exalted; शैलात्मजापि पितुरुच्छिरसोऽभिलाषं Ku. 3. 75, 6. 70.

उच्छिलींध्र *a.* Full of mushrooms (shot up); कर्तुं यच्च प्रभवति महीमुच्छिलींध्रामवंध्याम् Me. 11. -ध्रं A mushroom.

उच्छिष्ट *p. p.* 1 Left as a remainder. 2 Rejected, abandoned; R. 12. 15. 3 Stale; °कल्पना stale idea or invention. -ष्टं 1 Leavings, fragments, remainder (especially of food or sacrifice); नोच्छिष्टं कस्यचिद् दद्यात् Ms 2. 56. -COMP. -अन्नं leavings, offal. -मोदनं wax.

उच्छीर्षक 1 A pillow. 2 The head.

उच्छुष्क *a.* Dried up, withered.

उच्छून *a.* 1 Swollen; प्रबलरुदितोच्छूननेत्रं प्रियायाः Me. 84; उत्तानोच्छूनमंडूकपाटितोदरसंनिभे K. P. 7; अनवरतरुदितोच्छूनताम्रदृष्टिं Dk. 95. 2 Fat. 3 High, lofty.

उच्छृंखल *a.* 1 Unbridled, unrestrained, uncurbed; °वाचा Pt. 3; अन्यदुच्छृंखलं सत्त्वमन्यच्छास्त्रनियंत्रितं Si. 2. 62. 2

Self willed. **3** Irregular, desultory.

उच्छेदः, -दनं **1** Cutting off. **2** Extirpation, eradication, putting an end to; सतां भवोच्छेदकरः पिता ते R. 14. 74. **3** Excision.

उच्छेष -षणं Remainder.

उच्छोषण *a*. **1** Making dry, withering up; यच्छोकमुच्छोषणमिंद्रियाणां Bg. 2. 8. **2** Burning. **-णं** Drying up; parching, withering.

उच्छ्र (च्छ्रा) यः **1** Rising (of a planet &c.). **2** Raising, erecting. **3** Height, elevation (physical and moral); शृंगोच्छ्रायैः कुमुदविशदैर्यो वितत्य स्थितः खं Me. 58; Ki. 7. 27, 8. 23. **4** Growth, increase, intensity; गुण° Ki. 8. 21; नीतोच्छ्रायं 5. 31. **5** Pride.

उच्छ्रयणं Raising, elevation.

उच्छ्रित *p. p.* **1** Raised, lifted up. **2** Gone up, risen. **3** High, tall, lofty exalted. **4** Produced, born. **5** Increasing, prosperous, increased, grown. **6** Proud.

उच्छ्रितिः =उच्छ्रय q. v.

उच्छ्वसनं **1** Breathing, sighing. **2** Heaving.

उच्छ्वसित *p. p.* (Used actively). **1** Heaving, breathing. **2** Emitting or sending out vapour (refreshed). **3** Full-blown, opened. **4** Refreshed; Me. 42. **5** Consoled; उत्कंठोच्छ्वसितहृदया Me. 100. **-तं** **1** Breath, the (very) life; सा कुलपतेरुच्छ्वसितमिव S. 3. **2** Blooming, blowing. **3** Exhalation; R. 8. 3. **4** Heaving, upheaval, throbbing. **5** The vital airs of the body.

उच्छ्वासः **1** Breath, exhalation, breathing out; मुखोच्छ्वासगंधं V. 4. 22; Rs. 1. 3; Me. 102. **2** Support of life. **3** A sigh. **4** Consolation, encouragement; Amaru. 11. **5** An airhole. **6** A division or chapter of a book, as of the Harshâ-charita; cf. अध्याय.

उच्छ्वासिन् *a*. **1** Breathing. **2** Heaving; sighing. **3** Vanishing, fading away.

उछ् 6 P. **1** To bind. **2** To finish. **3** To give up, abandon.

उज्जय (यि) नी N. of a city, the modern Oujein in Mâlvâ, and one of the seven sacred cities of the Hindus (cf. अवंति); सौधोत्संगप्रणयविमुखो मा स्म भूरुज्जयिन्याः Me. 27.

उज्जासनं Killing; चौरस्योज्जासनं Sk.

उज्जिहान *a*. Going up, rising (as sun); उज्जिहानस्य भानोः Mu. 4. 21. **2** Departing, going out; °जीवितां वराकीं Mâl 10

उज्जृंभ *a*. **1** Blown, expanded; उज्जृंभवदनांभोजा भिनत्त्यंगानि सांगना S. D. **2** Gaping, open. **-भः** **1** Opening, expansion, blowing. **2** Breaking asunder, parting.

उज्जृंभा, -भणं **1** Yawning. **2** Opening. **3** Spreading, increase.

उज्ज्य *a*. Having the bow-string loosened.

उज्ज्वल *a*. Bright, shining, splendid; उज्ज्वलकपोलं मुखं Si. 9. 48. **2** Lovely, beautiful; सर्गो निसर्गोज्ज्वलः N. 3. 136. **3** Blown, expanded. **4** Unrestrained. **—लः** Love, passion. **—लं** Gold.

उज्ज्वलनं **1** Burning; shining. **2** Splendour, brilliance.

उज्झ् 6 P. (उज्झति, उज्झित) **1** To abandon, leave, quit; सपदि विगतनिद्रस्तल्पमुज्झांचकार R. 5. 75; 1. 40, 51; आतपायोज्झितं धान्यं Mb. exposed to the sun. **2** To avoid, escape from; उदये मदवाच्यमुज्झता R. 8. 84. **3** To emit, give out; अविरतोज्झितवारिविपांडुभिः Ki. 5. 6; Si. 4. 63.

उज्झकः **1** A cloud. **2** A devotee.

उज्झनं Abandoning, removing, leaving.

उंछ् 6 P. (उंछति, उंछित) To glean, gather (bit by bit); शिलानप्युंछतः Ms. 3. 100.

उंछः Gleaning or gathering grains; तान्युंछषष्ठांकितसैकतानि R. 5. 8; Ms. 10. 112. **—छं** Gleaning. —Comp. **—वृत्ति, -शील** *a*. one who lives by gleaning grains, a gleaner.

उंछनं Gleaning grains of corn in market-places &c.

उटं **1** A leaf. **2** Grass. –Comp. **-जः -जं** a hut, cottage, hermitage (being mostly made of grass or leaves); उटजद्वारविरूढं नीवारबलिं विलाकयतः S. 4. 20; R. 1. 52, 50.

उडुः *f.*, **उडु** *n* **1** A lunar mansion; a star; इंदुप्रकाशांतरितोडुतुल्याः R. 16. 65. **2** Water (said to be *n.* only). –Comp. **-चक्रं** zodiacal circle. **-पः, -पं** a raft; तितीर्षुर्दुस्तरं मोहादुडुपेनास्मि सागरं R. 1. 2; केनोडुपेन परलोकनदीं तरिष्ये Mk. 8. 23. (-पः) the moon; Mk. 4. 23. **-पतिः, -राज्** the moon; जितमुडुपतिना Ratn. 1. 5; रसात्मकस्योडुपतेश्च रश्मयः Ku. 5. 22. **-पथः** the sky, the firmament.

उडुंबरः **1** N. of a tree (Mar. औदुंबर) **2** The threshold of a house. **3** A eunuch. **4** A kind of leprosy (**—रं** also). **—रं** **1** The fruit of the उडुंबर tree. **2** Copper.

उडूपः =उडुपः q. v.

उड्डयनं Flying up, soaring; गतो विरुत्योड्डयने निराशतां N. 1. 125.

उड्डामर *a* **1** Agreeable, excellent. **2** Formidable, terrific; उड्डामरव्यस्तविस्तारिदोःखंडपर्यासितक्ष्माधरम् Mâl. 5. 23.

उड्डीन *p. p.* Flown up, flying up. **—नं** **1** Flying up, soaring. **2** A particular flight of birds.

उड्डीयनं Flying up.

उड्डीशः N. of Siva.

उड्र : N of a country; the modern Orissa; see ओड्र.

उंडेरकः A ball of flour, roll, loaf; तथैवोंडेरकस्रजः Y. 1. 288.

उत् *ind.* A particle of (*a*) doubt; (*b*) interrogation; (*c*) deliberation; (*d*) intensity.

उत *ind.* **1** A particle expressing (*a*) doubt, uncertainty, guess (*or*); तत्किमयमातपदोषः स्यादुत यथा मे मनसि वर्तते S. 3; स्थाणुरयमुत पुरुषः G. M. (*b*) alternative; usually a correlative of किं (whether-or); किमिदं गुरुभिरुपदिष्टमुत धर्मशास्त्रेषु पठितमुत मोक्षप्राप्तियुक्तिरियं K. 155; Ku. 6. 23; the place of उत is also taken by आहो or आहोस्वित्; sometimes आहो, आहोस्वित् or स्वित् are joined to उत. (*c*) association, connection, (having a cumulative force, 'and', 'also'); उत बलवानुताबलः; (*d*) interrogation; उत दंडः पतिष्यति. **2** With a preceding प्रति=on the contrary, on the other hand, but; सामवादाः सकोपस्य तस्य प्रत्युत दीपकाः Si. 2. 55. **3** With a preceding किं=how much more or how much less; see किम्. उत, -उत either-or; एकमेव वरं पुंसामुत राज्यमुताश्रमः G. M.

उतथ्यः N of a son of Angiras and elder brother of Brihaspati.–Comp – **अनुजः, —अनुजन्मन्** *m.* Brihaspati, teacher of the gods; तथ्यामुतथ्यानुजवज्जगादाग्रे गदाग्रजं Si. 2. 69.

उत्क *a*. **1** Desirous of, longing for, anxiously wishing for (in comp.); अद्रिसुतासमागमोत्कः Ku. 6. 95; मानसोत्काः Me. 11; sometimes with an inf.; Si. 4. 18. **2** Regretting, sad, sorrowful. **3** Absent-minded.

उत्कंचुक *a*. Without a bodice or coat of mail.

उत्कट *a*. **1** Large, spacious; U. 4. 29. **2** Powerful, mighty; fierce. **3** Excessive, much; अत्युत्कटैः पापपुण्यैरिहैव फलमश्नुते H. 1. 83. **4** Abounding in, richly endowed with. **5** Drunk, mad, furious; मदोत्कटः. **6** Superior, high. **7** Uneven. **—टः** **1** A fluid (ichor) dropping from the temples of an elephant in rut. **2** An elephant in rut.

उत्कंठ *a*. **1** Having the neck uplifted; (hence) prepared, ready, on the point of (doing anything), in comp.; आज्ञापनोत्कंठः S. 2; रथस्वनोत्कंठमृगे वाल्मीकीये तपोवने R. 15. 11. **2** (Hence) Anxious, eager. **—ठः, -ठा** A mode of sexual enjoyment.

उत्कंठा **1** Anxiety, uneasiness (in general); यास्यत्यद्य शकुंतलेति हृदयं संस्पृष्टमुत्कंठया S. 4. 5. **2** Longing for a beloved person or thing; दृष्टिरधिकं सोत्कंठमुद्वीक्षते Amaru. 24. **3** Regret, sorrow, missing anything or person; गाढोत्कंठा Mâl. 1. 15; Me. 83.

उत्कंठित *p. p.* **1** Anxious, grieving for, sorrowful. **2** Longing for a beloved person or things —ता A mistress longing for her absent lover or husband, one of the eight heroines; she is thus defined:—आगंतुं कृतचित्तोऽपि दैवान्नायाति यत्प्रियः । तदनागमदुःखार्ता विरहोत्कंठिता तु सा ॥ S. D. 121.

उत्कंधर *a*. Having the neck uplifted; उत्कंधरं दारुकमित्युवाच *Si*. 4. 18.

उत्कंप *a*. Trembling –पः; –पनं Trembling, tremor, agitation : किमधिकत्रासोत्कंपं दिशः समुदीक्षसे Amaru 28 ; Me 72.

उत्करः 1 A heap, multitude. 2 A pile, stack. 3 Rubbish, (मूषिकोत्कर) Mk. 3.

उत्ककरः A kind of musical instrument

उत्कर्तनं 1 Cutting off. tearing out. 2 Rooting out. eradication.

उत्कर्षः 1 Pulling off or upwards. 2 Elevation, eminence, rise, prosperity; निनीषुः कुलमुत्कर्ष Ms. 4. 244, 9. 24. 3 Increase, abundance, excess ; पंचानामपि भूतानामुत्कर्ष पुपुषुर्गुणाः R. 4 11. 4 Excellence, highest merit, glory ; उत्कर्षः स च धन्विनां यदिषवः सिध्यंति लक्ष्ये चले *S*. 2. 5. 5 Self-conceit, boasting. 6 Joy.

उत्कर्षणं 1 Drawing upwards. 2 Taking or pulling off.

उत्कलः 1 N. of a country, the modern Orissa, or the inhabitants of that country (pl.); जगन्नाथप्रांतदश उत्कलः परिकीर्तितः see ओड्र; उत्कलादाशतपथः R. 4. 38. 2 A fowler, bird catcher. 3 A porter.

उत्कलाप *a*. Having the tail erect and expanded ; R. 16. 64.

उत्कलिका 1 Anxiety in general ; uneasiness ; जाता नोत्कलिका Amaru. 78. Longing for, regretting, missing anything or person. 3 Wanton sport, dalliance (हेला). 4 A bud. 5 A wave; क्षुभितमुत्कलिकातरलं मनः ruffled by waves Mâl. 3 10 (where उत्कलिका also means anxiety); *Si*. 3. 70. –COMP. –प्रायं a variety of prose composition abounding in compound words and hard letters; भवेदुत्कलिकाप्रायं समासाढ्यं दृढाक्षरं Chand. M. 6.

उत्कषणं 1 Tearing, pulling up. 2 Ploughing, drawing through (as a plough); सद्यः सीरोत्कषणसुरभि क्षेत्रमारुह्य मालं Me. 16. 3 Rubbing; Bv. 1 73.

उत्कारः 1 Winnowing corn. 2 Piling up corn. 3 One who sows corn.

उत्कासः, –सनं, उत्कासिका Hemming, clearing the throat of mucus.

उत्किर *a*. Wafting, scattering upwards; bearing ; Ku. 5. 26, 6. 5 ; R. 1. 38.

उत्कीर्तनं 1 Praising, celebrating. 2 Proclaiming.

उत्कुटं Lying down or sleeping with the face (or head) upwards.

उत्कुणः 1 A bug. 2 A louse.

उत्कुल *a*. Fallen from the family, disgracing or dishonouring one's family ; यदि यथा वदति क्षितिपस्तथा । त्वमसि किं पितुरुत्कुलया त्वया ॥ *S*. 5. 27.

उत्कूजः The singing (of the cuckoo).

उत्कूटः A parasol or umbrella.

उत्कूदनं Jumping up, sprining upwards.

उत्कूल *a*. Overflowing the bank.

उत्कूलित *a*. Reaching the bank ; *Si*. 3. 70.

उत्कृष्ट *p. p*. 1 Drawn up or out, raised, elevated. 2 Excellent, eminent, best, highest ; Ms. 5. 163, 8. 281 : बल° Pt 3. 36 superior in strength 3 Tilled ; ploughed.

उत्कोचः A bribe ; उत्कोचमिव ददती K. 232 : Y. 1. 338.

उत्कोचकः 1 A bribe. 2 The receiver of a bribe ; Ms. 9. 258.

उत्क्रमः 1 Going up or out, departure. 2 Progressive increase. 3 Deviation, transgression, violation.

उत्क्रमणं 1 Going up or out, departure. 2 Ascent. 3 Surpassing, exceeding. 4 The flight or passage of the soul (out of the body) *i. e*. death ; Ms. 6. 63.

उत्क्रांतिः *f*. 1 Going up or out, departure. 2 The fight or passage of the soul (out of the body), death.

उत्क्रामः 1 Going out or up, departure 2 Surpassing. 3 Violation, transgression.

उत्क्रोशः 1 Clamour, outcry. 2 Proclamation. 3 An osprey (कुररी).

उत्क्लेदः Becoming wet or moist.

उत्क्लेशः 1 Excitement, disquietude 2 Disorder of the humours. 3 Sickness; particularly, sea-sickness.

उत्क्षिप्त *p. p*. 1 Thrown upwards, tossed, raised. 2 Held up, supported. 3 Seized or overcome with, struck with; विस्मय° Ratn. 1. 4 Demolished, destroyed. —प्तः The thorn apple, the Dhattûra plant.

उत्क्षिप्तिका A crescent-shaped ornament worn in the upper part of the ear.

उत्क्षेपः 1 Throwing or tossing up ; पक्ष्मोत्क्षेप Me. 47. 2 That which is thrown or tossed up ; बिंदूत्क्षेपान् पिपासुः M. 2 13. 3 Sending, despatching. 4 Vomiting.

उत्क्षेपक *a*. One who throws or tosses up, who or what elevates or raises; Y. 2. 274.–कः 1 A stealer of clothes &c. ; वस्त्राद्युत्क्षिप्यपहरतीत्युत्क्षेपकः Mit. 2 One who sends or orders.

उत्क्षेपणं 1 Throwing upwards, lifting or tossing up ; अतिमात्रलोहिततलौ बाहू घटोत्क्षेपणात् *S*. 1. 30. 2 Throwing upwards, regarded by the Vaiseshikas as one of the five *karmans* q. v. 3 Vomiting. 4 Sending away, despatching. 5 A kind of basket for cleaning corn. 6 A fan.

उत्खचित *a*. Intermixed, interwoven, set or inlaid with; कुसुमोत्खचितान् वलीभृतः R. 8. 53. 13. 54.

उत्खला A kind of perfume.

उत्खात *p. p* 1 Excavated, dug up. 2 Extracted, drawn out ; U. 3. 3 Uprooted, plucked up by the roots (lit.); लीला° U 3. 16. 4 (fig.) (*a*) Eradicated, totally destroyed, annihilated ; किमुत्खातं नंदवंशस्य Mu. 1 ; °लवणो मधुरेश्वरः प्राप्तः U. 7. (*b*) Deposed, deprived of power or authority ; फलैः संवर्धयामासुरुत्खातप्रतिरोपिताः R 4. 37 (where उत्खात means 'uprooted' also). –तं A hole, cavity, uneven ground. –COMP –केलिः *f*. digging out earth in sport (by means of horns, tusks &c); उत्खातकेलिः शृंगाद्यैर्वप्रक्रीडा निगद्यते.

उत्खातिन् *a*. Uneven, having ups and downs, rugged (opp सम); उत्खातिनी भूमिरिति मया रश्मिसंयमनाद्रथस्य मंदीकृतो वेगः *S*. 1.

उत्त *a*. Wet, moist.

उत्तंसः 1 A crest, chaplet, an ornament worn on the crown of the head; उत्तंसानहरत वारि मूर्धजेभ्यः *Si*. 8. 57 ; cf. कर्णोत्तंसः. 2 An ear-ring; Mâl 5. 18, Bv. 2. 55.

उत्तंसित *a*. 1 Having ear-rings. 2 Put or worn on the crest; Bh. 3. 129.

उत्तट *a* Overflowing the bank; R. 11. 58.

उत्तप्त *p. p*. Burnt, heated, seared ; °कनक K. 43. –प्तं Dried flesh.

उत्तम *a*. 1 Best, excellent (oft. in comp.) ; द्विजोत्तम, so सुर° &c. ; प्रायेणाधममध्यमोत्तमगुणः संसर्गतो जायते Bh. 2. 67 2 Foremost, uppermost, highest. 3 Most elevated chief, principal. 4 Greatest, first ; Ms 2. 249. —मः 1 N. of Vishnu. 2 The last person (=first person according to English phraseology). —मा An excellent woman. –COMP. –अंगं 'the best limb of the body', the head ; कश्चिद् द्विषत्खड्गहृतोत्तमांगः R. 7. 51 ; Ms. 1. 93, 8. 300 ; Ku. 7. 41 ; Bg 11 27. –अधम *a*. high and low ; °मध्यम good, middling, and bad. –अर्धः 1 the best half. 2 the last half or part. –अहः the last or latest day ; a fine or lucky day.–ऋणः, –ऋणिकः (उत्तमर्णः) a creditor (opp. अधमर्णः) –पदं a high office. –पु (पू) रुषः 1 the last person in verbal conjugation ; (= first person according to English phraseology). 2 the Supreme Spirit. 3 an excellent man. –श्लोक *a*. of excellent fame, illustrious, glorious, well-known. –संग्रहः (°स्त्री°) intriguing with another man's wife, *i. e*. speaking amorously at her &c. –साहसः, -सं 1 the highest (of the fixed) pecuniary punishments ; a fine of 1000 (or according to some 80,000) paṇas.

उत्तमीय *a.* Uppermost, highest, best, principal.

उत्तंभः,-भनं 1 Upholding, propping, supporting ; भुवनोत्तंभनस्तंभान् K. 260. 2 A prop, stay, support. 3 Stopping, arresting.

उत्तर *a.* 1 Being or produced in the north, northern (declined like a pronoun). 2 Upper, higher (opp. अधर.); अवनतोत्तरकायं R. 9. 60. 3 (*a*) Later, latter, following, subsequent (opp. पूर्व); पूर्वमेघः-उत्तरमेघः, °मीमांसा ; उत्तरार्धः &c.; °रामचरितं. (*b*) Future, concluding. 4 Left (opp. दक्षिण). 5 Superior, chief, excellent. 6 More, more than (generally as the last member of a comp. with numerals); षड्त्तरा विंशतिः 26 ; अष्टोत्तरं शतं 108. 7 Accompanied or attended with, full of, consisting chiefly of, followed by (at the end of comp.); राज्ञां तु चरितार्थता दुःखोत्तरेव *S.* 5 ; अस्रोत्तरमीक्षिता Ku. 5. 61. 8 To be crossed over. **—रः** 1 Future time, futurity. 2 N. of Vishṇu. 3 N. of *Siva.* 4 N. of a son of Virâṭa. **—रा** 1 The north ; अस्त्युत्तरस्यां दिशि देवतात्मा Ku 1. 1. 2 A lunar mansion. 3 N. of the daughter of Virâṭa and wife of Abhimanyu. **—रं** 1 An answer, reply ; प्रचक्रमे च प्रतिवक्तुमुत्तरं R. 8. 47 ; उत्तरादुत्तरं वाक्यं वदतां संप्रजायते Pt 1. 60 2 (In law) Defence, a rejoinder. 3 The last part or following member of a compound. 4 (In Mîm.) The fourth member of an अधिकरण q. v. ; the answer. 5 The upper surface or cover. 6 Conclusion. 7 Remainder, rest. 8 Excess, over and above ; see above (उत्तर *a.* 8). 9 Remainder, difference (in arith.). **—रं** *ind.* 1 Above. 2 Afterwards ; तत उत्तरं, इत उत्तरं &c. –Comp. **अधर** *a.* higher and lower (fig also) **-अधिकारः, -रिता, -त्वं** right to property, heirship, inheritance. **-अधिकारिन्** *m.* an heir. **-अयनं** (°यणं. न being changed to ण) 1 the progress of the sun to the north (of the equator) ; Bg. 8. 24. 2 the period or time of the summer solstice. **-अर्धं** 1 the upper part of the body 2 the northern part. 3 the latter half (opp. पूर्वार्ध). **-अहः** the following day. **-आभासः** a false reply. **-आशा** the northern direction. °अधिपतिः,-पतिः an epithet of Kubera. **-आषाढा** the 21st lunar mansion consisting of three stars. **-आसंगः** an upper garment ; कृतोत्तरासंगं K. 43 ; *Si.* 2. 19. ; Ku 5. 16. **-इतर** *a.* other than उत्तर *i. e* southern. **(-रा)** the southern direction. **-उत्तर** *a.* 1 more and more, higher and higher. 2 successive, ever increasing ; °स्नेहेन दृष्टः Pt. 1 ; Y. 2. 136. **(-रं)** a reply to an answer, reply on reply अलमुत्तरोत्तरेण Mu. 3. **-ओष्ठः** the upper lip. (उतरोष्ठः). **-कांडं** the seventh book of the Râmâyaṇa. **-कायः** the upper part of the body ; R. 9. 60. **-कालः** future time. **-कुरु** (*m.* pl.) one of the nine divisions of the world, the country of the northern Kurus. **-कोसलाः** (*m.* pl.) the northern Kosalas ; पितुरनंतरमुत्तरकोसलान् R. 9. 1. **-क्रिया** funeral rites, obsequies. **-छदः** a bed-covering, covering (in general) ; R. 5. 65, 17. 21. **-ज** *a.* born subsequently or afterwards. **-ज्योतिषाः** (*m.* pl.) the northern Jyotishas. **-दायक** *a.* disobedient, impertinent. **-दिश्** *f* the north °ईशः,-पालः Kubera the regent of the north. **-पक्षः** 1 the northern wing or side. 2 the dark half of a lunar month. 3 the second part of an argument, *i e.* a reply, the reason *pro.* (opp. पूर्वपक्ष); प्रापयन् पवनव्याधेर्गिरमुत्तरपक्षताम् *Si.* 2. 15. 4 a demonstrated truth or conclusion. 5 the minor proposition in a syllogism. 6 (in Mîm.) the fifth member of an *Adhikarana* q. v. **-पटः** 1 an upper garment. 2 a bed-covering (उत्तरच्छदः) **-पथः** the northern way, way leading to the north. **-पदं** 1 the last member of a compound. 2 a word that can be compounded with another. **-पश्चिमा** the north-west. **-पादः** the second division of a legal plaint **-पुरुषः** =उत्तमपुरुषः q. v **-पूर्वा** the north-east. **-प्रच्छदः** a coverlid, quilt. **-प्रत्युत्तरं** 1 a dispute, debate ; retort. 2 the pleadings in a law-suit. **-फ (फा) ल्गुनी** the twelfth lunar mansion consisting of two stars **-भाद्रपद्-दा** the 26th lunar mansion consisting of two stars. **—मीमांसा** the l ter Mîmâmsâ, the Vedânta philosophy, (distinguished from मीमांसा proper, which is usually called पूर्वमीमांसा). **-लक्षणं** the indication of an (actual) reply. **-वयसं,-स्** *n.* old age, the declining period of life. **-वस्त्रं-वासस्** *n.* an upper garment, mantle, cloak. **-वादिन्** *m.* a defendant, respondent. **-साधकः** an assistant, helper.

उत्तरंग *a* 1 Ruffled or washed by waves, inundated ; tremulous ; Mu. 6. 3 2 With surging waves ; R. 7. 36 ; Ku. 3 48.

उत्तरतः,-रात् *ind.* 1 From the north: to the north. 2 To the left (opp. दक्षिणतः). 3 Behind. 4 Afterwards.

उत्तरत्र *ind* Subsequently, later or further on, below (in a work), in the sequel.

उत्तराहि *ind.* Northerly, to the north of (with abl); Bk 8 107.

उत्तरीयं -यकं An upper garment.

उत्तरेण *ind.* (With gen., acc. or at the end of a comp.) Northward, on the north side of; तत्रागारं धनपतिगृहानुत्तरेणास्मदीयं Me. 75 v. l.; Mâl. 9. 24.

उत्तरेद्युः *ind.* On a subsequent day, on the day following, to-morrow.

उत्तर्जनं Violent threatening.

उत्तान *a.* 1 Stretched or spread out, expanded, dilated; U. 3-23. 2 (*a*) Lying on the back, with the face upwards; Mâl. 3; उत्तानोच्छूनमंडूकपाटितोदरसंनिभे K. P. 7. (*b*) Upright, erect. 3 Open. 4 Open, unreserved, candid; स्वभावोत्तानहृदयं *S.* 5 frank-minded. 5 Concave 6 Shallow. –Comp. **-पादः** N. of a king, father of Dhruva. °**जः** N. of Dhruva, the polar star. **-शय** *a.* sleeping supinely or on the back, lying with the face upwards; कदा उत्तानशयः पुत्रकः जनयिष्यति मे हृदयाह्लादं K 62. (**-यः, या**) a little child, suckling, infant.

उत्तापः 1 Great heat, inflammation. 2 Affliction, torment. 3 Excitement, passion.

उत्तारः 1 Transporting over, conveying. 2 Fording. 3 Landing, disembarking. 4 Getting rid of. 6 Vomiting.

उत्तारकः 1 A deliverer, saviour. 2 N. of *Siva*

उत्तारणं The act of landing, delivering or rescuing. **-णः** N. of Vishṇu.

उत्ताल *a.* 1 Great, strong. 2 Violent, loud (as sound); *Si.* 12. 31. 3 Formidable, terrific, fierce; उत्तालास्त इमे गभीरपयसः पुण्याः सरित्संगमाः U. 2. 30; *Si.* 20. 8; Mâl 5 11, 23. 4 Arduous, difficult. 5 Elevated, lofty, tall; *Si.* 3. 8 **—लः** An ape.

उत्तुंग *a.* Lofty, high, tall ; करप्रचेयामुत्तुंगः प्रभुशक्तिं प्रथीयसीं *Si.* 2. 89 ; °हेमपीठानि 2. 5.

उत्तुषः 'Freed from husks,' fried grain.

उत्तेजक *a.* 1 Instigating, stirring up. 2 Exciting, stimulating ; क्षुध्,° काम° &c.

उत्तेजनं,-ना 1 Excitement, instigation, stirring up ; °समर्थैः श्लोकैः Mu. 4; Mv. 2. 2 Urging on, driving. 3 Sending, despatching. 4 Whetting, sharpening, polishing (weapons &c.) 5 An exciting speech. 6 An inducement, incentive

उत्तोरण *a.* Adorned with raised or upright arches; उत्तारणं राजपथं प्रपेदे Ku. 7. 63 ; R. 14. 10.

उत्तोलनं Lifting up, raising.

उत्त्यागः 1 Abandonment, leaving. 2 Throwing, tossing. 3 Renunciation of all worldly attachments.

उत्त्रासः Extreme fear, terror.

उत्थ *a* (Used only at the end of comp) 1 Born or produced from, arising, or originating from; दरीमुखो-

स्थेन समरिणेन Ku. 1. 8; 6. 59; R. 12. 82. 2 Standing up, coming up or forth.

उत्थानं 1 The act of rising or standing up, getting up; शनैर्यष्ट्युत्थानं Bh. 3.9. 2 Rising (as of luminaries); R. 6. 31. 3 Rise, origin. 4 Resurrection. 5 Effort, exertion, activity; मेदश्छेदकृशोदरं लघु भवत्युत्थानयोग्यं वपुः S. 2.5; यद्युत्थानं भवेत्सह Ms. 9. 215, effort (for money), acquisition of property. 6 Energy 7 Joy, pleasure. 8 War, battle. 9 An army 10 A courtyard; a shed where sacrifices are offered. 11 A term, limit, boundary. 12 Awakening. –COMP. –एकादशी the eleventh day in the light fortnight of Kârtika when Vishṇu rises from his four months' sleep (also called प्रबोधिनी).

उत्थापनं 1 Causing to rise, come up, or get up. 2 Raising, elevating. 3 Exciting, instigating. 4 Awakening, rousing (fig. also). 5 Vomiting.

उत्थित *p.p.* 1 Risen or rising (as from a seat); वचो निशम्योत्थितमुत्थितः सन् R. 2. 61, 7. 10, 3. 61; Ku. 7. 61. 2 Raised, gone up; पांशुः Si. 11. 3 Born, produced, sprung up, arisen; वचः R. 2. 61; broken out (as fire). 4 Increasing, growing (in strength), advancing. 5 Bounded. 6 Extended, stretched; S. 4. 4. –COMP. –अंगुलिः the palm of the hand with the fingers extended.

उत्थितिः *f.* Elevation, rising up.

उत्पक्ष्मन् *a.* With up-turned eyelashes; उत्पक्ष्मणोर्नयनयोरुपरुद्धवृत्तिं S. 4. 15; V. 2.

उत्पतः A bird.

उत्पतनं 1 Flying up, a spring. 2 Rising or going up, ascending.

उत्पताक *a.* With uplifted banners, where flags are hoisted; पुरंदरश्रीः पुरमुत्पताकं R. 2. 74.

उत्पतिष्णु *a.* Flying, going up.

उत्पत्तिः *f.* 1 Birth; विपदुत्पत्तिमतामुपस्थिता R. 8. 83. 2 Production; कुसुमे कुसुमोत्पत्तिः श्रूयते न तु दृश्यते S. Til. 17. 3 Source, origin; उत्पत्तिः साधुतायाः K. 45. 4 Rising, going up, becoming visible. 5 Profit, productiveness, produce.–COMP. –व्यंजकः a type of birth (as investiture with the sacred thread); a mark of twice-born; Ms. 2. 68.

उत्पथः A wrong road (fig. also); गुरोरप्यवलिप्तस्य कार्याकार्यमजानतः । उत्पथप्रतिपन्नस्य न्याय्यं भवति शासनं ॥ Mb. (परित्यागो विधीयते Pt. 1. 306); Si. 12. 24. –थं *ind.* Astray, on the wrong road.

उत्पन्न *p. p.* 1 Born, produced, arisen. 2 Risen, gone up. 3 Acquired.

उत्पल *a.* Fleshless, emaciated, lean. —लं 1 A blue lotus, any lotus or water-lily; नवावतारं कमलादिवोत्पलं R. 3. 36, 12. 86; Me. 26; नीलोत्पलपत्रधारया S. 1. 18; so रक्त° 2 A plant in general. –COMP. –अक्ष, –चक्षुस् *a.* lotus-eyed –पत्रं 1 a lotus-leaf. 2 a wound caused by a female's finger-nail, nail-print.

उत्पलिन् *a.* Abounding in lotus-flowers. —नी 1 An assemblage of lotus-flowers. 2 A lotus plant having lotuses.

उत्पवनं Cleaning, purifying; Ms. 5. 115.

उत्पाटः 1 Eradication, destroying root and branch. 2 A disease of the external ear.

उत्पाटनं Uprooting, eradicating, destroying root and branch.

उत्पाटिका The external bark of a tree.

उत्पाटिन् *a.* (oft. at the end of comp.) Eradicating, tearing out; कीलोत्पाटीव वानरः Pt. 1. 21.

उत्पातः 1 Flying up, a spring, jump; एकोत्पातेन at one jump. 2 Rebounding, rising up (fig also); करनिहतकंदुकसमाः पातोत्पाता मनुष्याणां H. 1. v. l. 3 A portent, any portentous or unusual phenomenon boding calamity; उत्पातेन ज्ञापिते च Vârt.; Ve. 1. 22; सापि सुकुमारसुभगेत्युत्पातपरंपरा केयं K. P. 10. 4 Any public calamity (as an eclipse, earthquake &c.); °केतु K. 5; °धूमलेखा Ketu; Mâl. 9. 48. –COMP. –पवनः, –वातः, –वातालिः portentous or violent wind, whirlwind a hurricane; R. 15. 23.

उत्पाद *a.* With the feet up-lifted. –दः Birth, production, appearance; दुःखे च शोणितोत्पादे शाखांगच्छेदने तथा Y. 2. 225; °भंगुरं Pt. 2. 177. –COMP. –शयः, –यनः 1 a child. 2 a kind of partridge.

उत्पादक *a.* (दिका *f.*) Productive, effective, bringing about. —कः A producer, generator, a father. —कं Origin, cause.

उत्पादनं Giving birth, production, generating; उत्पादनमपत्यस्य जातस्य परिपालनं Ms. 9. 27.

उत्पादिन् *a.* Produced, born; सर्वमुत्पादि भंगुरं H. 1. 208.

उत्पादिका 1 N. of a certain insect, the white ant. 2 A mother.

उत्पाली Health.

उत्पिंजर-ल *a.* 1 Unconfined, uncaged. 2 Out of order, excessively confused.

उत्पीडः 1 Pressing out. 2 (*a*) Gush, gushing flow; बाष्पोत्पीडः K. 296; उत्पीड इव धूमस्य मोहः प्रागावृणोति मां U. 3 9; नयनसलिलोत्पीडरुद्धावकाशा Me. 91. (*b*) Overflow, excess; पूरोत्पीडे तडागस्य परीवाहः प्रतिक्रिया U. 3. 29. 3 Froth, foam.

उत्पीडनं 1 Pressing out 2 Pressing or striking against; K. 82.

उत्पुच्छ *a.* With the tail erect.

उत्पुलक *a.* 1 Thrilled, bristling. 2 Joyful, delighted.

उत्प्रभ *a.* Flashing forth or diffusing light, bright. —भः Blazing fire.

उत्प्रसवः Abortion.

उत्प्रासः,-सनं 1 Hurling, flinging away. 2 Jest, joke. 3 Violent burst of laughter. 4 Ridicule, derision, satire.

उत्प्रेक्षणं 1 Looking into, perceiving. 2 Looking upwards. 3 Guess, conjecture. 4 Comparing.

उत्प्रेक्षा 1 Conjecture, guess. 2 Carelessness, indifference. 3 (In Rhet.) A figure of speech, which consists in supposing उपमेय and उपमान as similar to each other in some respects and in indicating, expressly or by implication, a probability of their identity based on such similarity; *e. g.* लिंपतीव तमोंगानि वर्षतीवांजनं नभः Mk. 1. 34; स्थितः पृथिव्या इव मानदंडः Ku. 1. 1; cf. S. D. 686-692 and R. G. under उत्प्रेक्षा also.

उत्प्लवः A jump, leap, bound. –वा A boat.

उत्प्लवनं Jumping or leaping up, springing upon.

उत्फल An excellent fruit.

उत्फालः 1 A jump, spring, rapid motion; Mk. 6. 2 The jumping attitude.

उत्फुल्ल *p. p.* 1 Opened, full blown (as flowers). 2 Widely opened, expanded, dilated (eyes). 3 Swollen, increased in bulk. 4 Sleeping supinely or on the back; cf. उत्तान. –ल्लं The female organ of generation.

उत्सः 1 A spring, fountain. 2 A watery place.

उत्संगः 1 The lap; पुत्रपूर्णोत्संगा U. 1; V. 5. 10; न केवलमुत्संगश्चिरान्मनोरथोपि मे पूर्णः U. 4; Me. 87. 2 Embrace, contact, union; Mâl. 8. 6. 3 Interior, vicinity; दरीगृहोत्संगनिषक्तभासः Ku. 1. 10; शय्योत्संगे Me. 93. 4 Surface, side, slope; दृषदो वासितोत्संगाः R. 4. 74, 14. 76. 5 The haunch or part above the hip (नितंब) 6 The upper part, top. 7 The acclivity or edge of a hill; तुंगं नगोत्संगमिवारुरोह R. 6. 3. 8 The roof of a house.

उत्संगित *a.* 1 Associated, joined, brought in contact with; Si. 3. 79. 2 Taken in the lap.

उत्संजनं Throwing upwards, lifting up.

उत्सन्न *p. p.* 1 Decayed. 2 Destroyed, ruined, uprooted, left off; उत्सन्नोस्मि K. 164 undone; मकरध्वज इवोत्सन्नविग्रहः K. 54; Rg. 1. 44; °निद्रा K. 171 3 Cursed, wretched. 4 Fallen into disuse, extinct (as a book)

उत्सर्गः 1 Laying or leaving aside, abandoning, suspension; Ku. 7. 45. 2 Pouring out, dropping down, emission; तोयोत्सर्गद्रुततरगतिः Me. 19, 37. 3 A gift, donation, giving away;

Ms. 11. 194. 4 Spending. 5 Loosening, letting loose; as in वृषोत्सर्गः. 6 An oblation, libation. 7 Excretion, voiding by stool &c.; पुरीष°, मलमूत्र°. 8 Completion (as of study or a vow); cf. उत्सृष्टा वै वेदाः 9 A general rule or precept (opp. अपवाद a particular rule or exception); अपवादैरिवोत्सर्गाः कृतव्यावृत्तयः परैः Ku. 2. 27; अपवाद इवोत्सर्गं व्यावर्तयितुमीश्वरः R. 15. 7. 10 The anus.

उत्सर्जनं 1 Leaving, abandoning, letting loose, quitting &c. 2 A gift, donation. 3 Suspension of a Vedic study. 4 A ceremony connected with this suspension (to be performed half yearly); वेदोत्सर्जनाख्यं कर्म करिष्ये Srâvaṇî Mantra ; Ms. 4. 96.

उत्सर्पः,-र्पणं 1 Going or gliding upwards. 2 Swelling, heaving.

उत्सर्पिन् *a.* 1 Moving or gliding upwards, rising; R. 16. 62. 2 Soaring, towering; उत्सर्पिणी खलु महतां प्रार्थना S. 7.

उत्सवः 1 A festival, joyous or festive occasion, jubilee; रत° S. 6. 19; तांडव° festive or joyous dance; U. 3. 18; Ms. 3. 59. 2 Joy, merriment, pleasure; स कृत्वा विरतोत्सवान् R. 4. 17, 16. 10; पराभवोप्युत्सव एव मानिनां Ki. 1. 41. 3 Height, elevation. 4. Wrath. 5 Wish, rising of a wish. –COMP. –संकेताः (*m.* pl) N. of a people, a wild tribe of the Himâlaya; शरैरुत्सवसंकेतान् स कृत्वा विरतोत्सवान् R. 4. 78.

उत्सादः 1 Destruction, decay, ruin, loss; गीतमुत्सादकारि मृगाणां K. 32.

उत्सादनं 1 Destroying, overturning; उत्सादनार्थं लोकानां Mb.; Bg. 17. 19. 2 Suspending, interrupting. 3 Cleaning the person with perfumes; Ms. 2. 209, 211. 4 Healing a sore. 5 Going up, ascending, rising. 6 Elevating, raising. 7 Ploughing a field twice (thoroughly)

उत्सारकः 1 A policeman. 2 A guard. 3 A porter, door-keeper.

उत्सारणं 1 Removing, keeping at a distance, driving out of the way. 2 Reception of a guest.

उत्साहः 1 Effort, exertion; धृत्युत्साहसमन्वितः Bg. 18. 26. 2 Energy, inclination, desire ; मंदोत्साहः कृतोस्मि मृगयापवादिना माठव्येन S. 2; ममोत्साहभंगं मा कृथाः H. 3. do not damp my energy. 3 Perseverance, energy, one of the three Saktis or powers of a ruler (the other two being मंत्र and प्रभाव); Ku. 1. 22. 4 Determination, resolution; हसितेन भाविमरणोत्साहस्तया सूचितः Amaru. 10. 5 Power, ability; Ms. 5. 86. 6 Firmness, fortitude, strength. 7 (In Rhet.) Firmness or fortitude regarded as the feeling which gives rise to the वीर or heroic sentiment ; कार्यारंभेषु संरंभः स्थेयानुत्साह उच्यते S. D. 3; or परपराक्रमदानादिस्मृतिजन्मा औन्नत्याख्यः उत्साहः R. G. 8 Happiness. –COMP. –वर्धनः the heroic sentiment (वीररस) (–नं) increase of energy, heroism. –शक्तिः *f.* firmness, energy ; see (3) above. –हेतुक *a.* one who encourages or excites to exertion; S. 2.

उत्साहनं 1 Effort, perseverance. 2 Encouraging, exciting.

उत्सिक्त *p. p.* 1 Sprinkled. 2 Proud, haughty, puffed up. 3 Flooded, overflowing, excessive; see सिच् with उत्. 4 Fickle, disturbed (in mind) ; जानीयादस्थिरां वाचमुत्सिक्तमनसां तथा Ms. 8. 71.

उत्सुक *a.* 1 Anxiously desirous, eagerly expecting, striving for (any object) (with instr. or loc. or comp.); निद्रया निद्रायां वोत्सुकः Sk.; मनो नियोगक्रिययोत्सुकं मे R. 5. 11; R. 2. 45; Me. 99; संगम° S. 3. 14. 2 Restless uneasy, anxious; R. 12. 24. 3 Fond of, attached to; वत्सोत्सुकापि R. 2. 22. 4 Regretting, repining, sorrowing for.

उत्सूत्र *a.* 1 Unstrung, loose, detached (from the string) ; Si. 8. 53. 2 Irregular. 3 Deviating from the rule (सूत्र) of Pâṇini ; Si. 2. 112.

उत्सूरः Evening, twilight.

उत्सेकः 1 Sprinkling, pouring. 2 Spouting out or over, showering. 3 Overflow, increase, excess ; रुधिरोत्सेकाः Mv. 5. 33; दर्प°, बल° &c. 4 Pride, haughtiness, insolence ; उपदा विविशुः शश्वन्नोत्सेकाः कोसलेश्वरं R. 4. 70; अनुत्सेको लक्ष्म्यां Bh. 2. 64.

उत्सेकिन् *a.* 1 Overflowing, excessive. 2 Proud, haughty, puffed up; भाग्येष्वनुत्सेकिनी S. 4. 17.

उत्सेचनं The act of showering or spouting upwards.

उत्सेधः 1 A height, elevation; (fig. also); पयोधरोत्सेधविशीर्णसंहति (वल्कलं)Ku. 5. 8, 24 high or projecting breasts. 2 Thickness, fatness. 3 The body. –धं Killing, slaughter.

उत्स्मयः Smile.

उत्स्वन *a.* High-sounding. –नः A loud sound.

उत्स्वप्नायते Den. A. To talk in one's sleep dream through uneasiness.

उद् *ind.* A prefix to verbs and nouns. G. M. gives the following senses with illustrations:– 1 Superiority in place, rank or power; up, upwards, upon, on, over, above; (उद्गल). 2 Separation ; disjunction ; out, out of, from, apart &c.; (उद्गच्छति) 3 Motion upwards (उत्तिष्ठति). 4 Acquisition, gain ; (उपार्जति). 5 Publicity ; उच्चरति. 6 Wonder; anxiety ; उत्सुक. 7 Liberation ; उद्गत. 8 Absence; उत्पथ. 9 Blowing, expanding, opening ; उत्फुल. 10 Pre-eminence ; उद्दिष्ट. 11 Power ; उत्साहः. With nouns it forms adj. and adv. compounds , उदर्चिस, उच्छिख, उद्बाहु, उन्निद्रं, उत्पथं, उद्दामं &c

उदक् *ind.* Northward, to the north of, above (with abl),

उदकं Water ; अनीत्वा पंकतां धूलिमुदकं नावतिष्ठते Si 2. 34. –COMP. –अंतः margin of water, bank, shore; ओदकांतात्स्निग्धो जनोऽनुगंतव्य इति श्रूयते S. 4. –अर्थिन् *a.* thirsty. –आधारः a reservoir, a cistern, well. –उदंजनः a water-jar. –उदरं dropsy. –कर्मन्, –कार्यं, –क्रिया, –दानं presentation of (a libation of) water to dead ancestors or the Manes वृकोदरस्योदकक्रियां कुरु Ve. 6 ; Y. 3. 4. –कुंभः a water-jar. –गाहः entering water, bathing. –ग्रहणं drinking water. –द, –दातृ, –दायिन्, –दानिक *a.* giver of water, (–दः) 1 a giver of water to the Manes. 2 an heir, kinsman. –दानं =°कर्मन् q. v. –धरः a cloud. –भारः, –वीवधः a yoke for carrying water. –वज्रः a thunder-shower. –शाकं any aquatic herb. –शांतिः *f.* sprinkling holy or consecrated water over a sick person to allay fever; cf. शांत्युदकं. –स्पर्शः touching different parts of the body with water. –हारः a water-carrier.

उदक (कि) ल *a.* watery, containing water.

उदकेचरः An aquatic animal.

उदक्त *a.* Raised or lifted up ; उदक्तमुदकं कूपात् Sk.

उदक्य *a.* Requiring water. –क्या A woman in her courses.

उदग्र *a.* 1 With elevated top, projecting, pointing upwards ; as in °दंत. 2 Tall, lofty, high, elevated, exalted (fig. also); उदग्रदशनांशुभिः Si. 2. 21, 4. 19 ; उदग्रः क्षत्रस्य शब्दः R. 2. 53 ; उदग्रप्लुतत्वात् S. 1. 7 high leaps. 3 Large, broad, vast, big ; अवंतिनाथोयमुदग्रबाहुः R. 6. 32. 4 Advanced in age. 5 Conspicuous, distinguished, exalted, magnified, increased ; स मंगलोदग्रतरप्रभावः R. 2. 71, 9. 64, 13. 50. 6 Intense, unbearable (as heat). 7 Fierce, fearful; संदधे दृशमुदग्रतारकां R. 11. 69. 8 Excited, furious, enraptured ; मदोदग्राः ककुद्मंतः R. 4. 22.

उदंकः A leathern vessel (for oil &c.).

उदच्, उदंच् *a.* (*m.* उदङ्, *n.* उदक्, *f.* उदीची) 1 Turned or going upwards. 2 Upper, higher. 3 Northern, turned towards the north. 4 Subsequent. –COMP –अद्रिः the northern mountain, Himâlaya. –अयनं the sun's progress north of the equator (=उत्तरायणं q. v.). –आवृत्तिः *f.* return from the north; उदगावृत्तिपथेन नारदः R. 8. 33. –पथः a northern country. –प्रवण *a.* inclining or sloping towards the north. –मुख *a.* facing the north ; उत्पतोदङ्मुखः खं Me. 14.

उदंचनं 1 A bucket, a pail for drawing water out of a well; उदंचनं

सरज्जुं पुरः चिक्षेप Dk. 130. **2** Rising, ascending. **3** A cover or lid.

उदंजलि *a.* One who hollows the palms and then raises them.

उदंडपालः **1** A fish. **2** A kind of snake.

उदधिः See under उदन्.

उदन् *n.* Water (usually occurring in compounds either at the beginning or at the end, and as an optional substitute for उदक after the acc. dual. It has no forms for the first five inflections. In comp. drops its न्); *e. g.* उदधि, अच्छोद, क्षीरोद &c –COMP. –**कुंभः** a water-jar; Ms. 2. 182, 3. 68. –**ज** *a.* aquatic, watery. –**धानः** **1** a water-jar. **2** a cloud. –**धिः** **1** the receptacle of waters, ocean; उदधेरिव निम्नगाशतेष्वभवन्नास्य विमानना क्वचित् R. 8. 8. **2** a cloud. **3** a lake, any large reservoir of water. **4** a water-jar. °**कन्या, तनया, सुता** Lakshmî, the daughter of the ocean. °**मेखला** the earth. °**राजः** the king of waters, *i. e.* the chief ocean. –**सुता** N. of Lakshmî, and of Dvârakâ, the capital of Kṛishṇa. –**पात्रं,-त्री** a water-jug, vessel. –**पानः-नं** a small pool or pond near a well, or the well itself. °**मंडूकः** (lit) a frog in a well ; (fig.) one who has had no experience of the world at large, a man of limited ideas who knows only his own neighbourhood; cf. कूपमंडूक. –**पेषं** a paste. –**बिंदुः** a d op of water ; Ku. 5. 24. –**भारः** a water-carrier, *i. e.* a cloud. –**मंथः** barley-water. –**मानः,-नं** a fiftieth part of an आढक q. v. –**मेघः** a watery cloud. –**लावणिक** *a.* salted, briny. –**वज्रः** a thunder-shower; water-spout. –**वासः** standing or residence in water; सहस्यरात्रीरुदवासतत्परा Ku. 5. 26. –**वाह** *a* bringing water. (–**हः**) a cloud. –**वाहनं** a water-vessel. –**शरावः** a jar filled with water –**श्वित्** *n.* butter-milk containing fifty per cent water (*i. e.* 2 parts of butter-milk and 1 part of water). –**हरणः** a vessel for drawing water.

उदंतः **1** News, intelligence, full tidings, account, history; श्रुत्वा रामः प्रियोदंतं R. 12. 66 ; कांतोदंतः सुहृदुपगतः संगमात्किंचिदूनः Me. 100. **2** A pure and virtuous man (साधु).

उदंतकः News, intelligence.

उदंतिका Satisfaction, satiety.

उदन्य *a.* Thirsty. –**न्या** Thirst; निर्वर्त्यंतामुदन्याप्रतीकारः Ve. 3; Bk. 3. 40.

उदन्वत् *m.* The ocean ; उदन्वच्छन्नाभूः B. R. 1. 8; R. 4. 52, 58; 10. 6; Ku. 7. 73.

उदयः **1** Rise (fig. also); चंद्रोदय इवोदधेः R. 12. 36, 2. 73; going upwards. **2** Appearance, production ; घनोदयः प्राक् S. 7. 30 ; फलोदय R. 1. 5 rising or accomplishment of the fruit ; Ku. 3. 18. **3** Creation (opp. प्रलय) ; Ku 2. 8. **4** The eastern mountain (behind which the sun is supposed to rise उयदगूढशशाकमरीचिभिः V. 3. 6. **5** Advancement, prosperity, rise (opp. व्यसन); तेजोद्वयस्य युगपद्व्यसनोदयाभ्यां *S*. 4 1 ; R. 8. 84, 11. 73. **6** Elevation, exaltation, rise, growth ; उदयमस्तमयं च रघूद्वहात् R. 9. 9, 7. **7** Result, consequence. **8** Accomplishment, fulfilment ; उपस्थितोदयं R. 3. 1 ; प्रारंभसदृशोदयः 1. 15. **9** Profit, advantage. **10** Income, revenue. **11** Interest. **12** Light, splendour. –COMP. –**अचलः** –**अद्रिः**, –**गिरिः**, –**पर्वतः**, –**शैलः** the eastern mountain behind which the sun, moon &c. are supposed to rise ; उदयगिरिवनालीबालमंदारपुष्पं Udb ; श्रितोदयाद्रेरभिसायमुच्चकैः *S*i. 1. 16 ; तत उदयगिरेरिवैक एव Mâl. 2. 10. –**प्रस्थः** the plateau of the mountain behind which the sun is supposed to rise.

उदयनं **1** Rising, ascending, going up. **2** Result. –**नः** **1** N. of Agastya. **2** N of the king Vatsa ; प्राप्यावंतीनुदयनकथाकोविदग्रामवृद्धान् Me. 30 [A celebrated Prince of the lunar race, who is usually styled Vatsar*a*ja. He reigned at Kaus*a*mbi. V*a*savadatt*a*, Princess of Ujjayini, saw him in a dream and fell in love with him. He was decoyed to that city and there kept in prison by Cha*n*d*amaha*sena, the king. But on being released by the minister he carried off V*a*savadatt*a* from her father and a rival suitor. Udayana is the hero of the play called Ratn*a*vali and his life has been made the subject of several other minor compositions. See Vatsa also].

उदरं **1** The belly ; दुष्पूरोदरपूरणाय Bh. 2. 119 ; cf. कृशोदरी, उदरंभरि &c. **2** The interior or inside of anything, cavity; तडाग° Pt. 2. 150 ; R. 5. 70; त्वां कारयामि कमलोदरबंधनस्थं *S*. 6. 19; 1. 19 ; Amaru. 88. **3** Enlargement of the abdomen from dropsy or flatulence ; तस्य होदरं जज्ञे Ait. Br. **4** Slaughter. —COMP. —**आध्मानः** flatulence of the belly. –**आमयः** dysentery, diarrhœa. –**आवर्तः** the navel. –**आवेष्टः** the tape-worm. –**त्राणं** **1** a cuirass, armour covering the front of the body **2** a belly-band —**पिशाच** *a.* gluttonous, voracious (having a devilish appetite). (–**चः**) a glutton. –**पूरं** *ind.* till the belly is full; उदरपूरं भुंक्ते Sk. eats his fill. –**पोषणं, -भरणं** feeding the belly, support of life –**शय** *a.* sleeping on the face or on the belly. (–**यः**) fœtus. –**सर्वस्वः** a glutton, an epicure (one to whom the belly is all in-all).

उदरथिः **1** The ocean. **2** The sun.

उदरंभरि *a.* **1** Nourishing one's own belly, selfish. **2** Gluttonous.

उदरवत्, उदरिक-ल *a.* Having a large belly, corpulent, fat.

उदरिन् *a.* Having a large belly, fat, corpulent. —**णी** A pregnant woman.

उदर्कः **1** (*a*) End, conclusion ; सुखोदर्क K. 328 (*b*) Result, consequence, future result of an action ; किंतु कल्याणोदर्कं भविष्यति U. 4 ; प्रयत्नः सफलोदर्क एव Mâl. 8 ; Ms. 4. 176, 11. 10. **2** Future time, futurity.

उदर्चिस् *a.* Shining or blazing upwards, radiant, glowing ; स्फुरदुदर्चिः सहसा तृतीयादक्ष्णः कृशानुः किल निष्पपात Ku. 3. 71, 7. 79; R. 7. 24, 15. 76. –*m.* **1** Fire ; प्रक्षिप्योदर्चिषं कक्षे शेरते तेऽभिमारुतं *S*i. 2. 42, 20. 75. **2** The god of love. **3** N. of *S*iva.

उदवसितं A house, dwelling.

उदश्रु *a.* Bursting into tears, one whose tears gush forth, weeping; R. 12. 14; Amaru. 11.

उदसनं **1** Throwing, raising, erecting. **2** Expelling.

उदात्त *a.* **1** High, elevated; °अन्वयैः K. 92; Ve. 1. **2** Noble, dignified. **3** Generous, bountiful. **4** Famous, illustrious, great; ललितोदात्तमहिमा Bv. 1. 79. **5** Dear, beloved. **6** Highly or acutely accented (as a Svara), see below. —**त्तः** **1** The acute accent; उच्चैरुदात्तः P. I. 2. 29, ताल्वादिषु सभागेषु स्थानेषूर्ध्वभागेनिष्पन्नोऽजुदात्तः Sk ; see under अनुदात्त also ; निहत्यरीनेकपदे य उदात्त; स्वरानिव *S*i. 2. 95. **2** Gift, donation. **3** A kind of musical instrument, a large drum. —**त्तं** (In Rhet.) A figure of speech; S. D. 752; cf. also K. P. 10; उदात्तं वस्तुनः संपन्महतां चोपलक्षणं.

उदानः **1** Breathing upwards. **2** Breathing, breath in general **3** One of the five vital airs or life-winds which rises up the throat and enters into the head; the other four being प्राण, अपान, समान and व्यान ; स्पंदयत्यधरं वक्त्रं गात्रनेत्रप्रकोपनः । उद्वेजयति मर्माणि उदानो नाम मारुतः ॥ **4** The navel.

उदायुध *a.* With uplifted weapons, upraising weapons; मनुजपशुभिर्निर्मर्यादैर्भवद्भिरुदायुधैः Ve. 3. 22; उदायुधानापततस्तान्दृप्तान्प्रेक्ष्य राघवः R. 12. 44.

उदार *a.* **1** Generous, liberal, munificent. **2** (*a*) Noble, exalted ; स तथेति विनेतुरुदारमतेः R. 8. 91, 5. 12; Bg. 7. 18. (*b*) High, illustrious, distinguished ; °कीर्तेः Ki. 1. 18. **3** Honest, sincere, upright **4** Good, nice, fine ; उदारः कल्पः *S*. 5. **5** Eloquent. **6** Large, extensive, grand, splendid; R. 13. 79; उदारनेपथ्यभृतां 6. 6 richly dressed. **7** Beautiful, charming, lovely ; Ku. 7. 14 ; *S*i. 5. 21. —**रं** *ind.* Loudly; *S*i 4. 33. –COMP. —**आत्मन्, -चेतस्, -चरित, -मनस्, -सत्व** *a.* noble-minded, magnanimous ; उदारचरितानां तु वसुधैव कुटुंबकं H. 1. –**धी** *a.* of sublime genius, highly intelligent ; R. 3. 30. –**दर्शन** *a.* good-looking (having large eyes); Ku. 5. 36.

उदारता 1 Liberality. 2 Richness (as of expression); वचसां Mâl. 1. 7.

उदास *a.* Indifferent, apathetic, unconcerned. –सः,–सिन् *m.* 1 A stoic, philosopher. 2 Indifference, apathy.

उदासीन *pres. p.* 1 indifferent, unconcerned, passive; तद्दर्शिनमुदासीनं त्वामेव पुरुषं विदुः Ku. 2. 13 (taking no part in the creation of the material universe); see सांख्य. 2 (In law) Not involved in any dispute. 3 Neutral (as a king or nation). —नः 1 A stranger. 2 A neutral, an indifferent person; Bg. 6. 9. 3 A common acquaintance.

उदास्थितः 1 A superintendent. 2 A door-keeper. 3 A spy, an emissary. 4 An ascetic who has given up his vow.

उदाहरणं 1 Relating, declaration, saying. 2 Narration, recital, opening a conversation; अथांगिरसमग्रण्यमुदाहरणवस्तुषु Ku. 6. 65. 3 A declaratory song or poem, a sort of panegyric beginning with words like जयति and full of alliteration चरणेभ्यस्त्वदीयं जयोदाहरणं श्रुत्वा V. 1; जयोदाहरणं बाह्वोर्गापयामास किन्नरान् R. 4. 78; V. 2. 14; (येन केनापि तालेन गद्यपद्यसमन्वितं । जयत्युपक्रमं मालिन्यादिप्रासविचित्रितम् ॥ तदुदाहरणं नाम विभक्त्यष्टांगसंयुतं। Prataparudra) 4 An instance, example, illustration; समूलघातमघ्नंतः परान्नोद्यंति मानिनः । प्रध्वंसितांधतमसस्तत्रोदाहरणं रविः ॥ Si. 2. 33. 5 (In Nyâya) The third member of an Indian syllogism (which has five members). 6 (In Rhet.) An illustration reckoned as a figure of speech by some rhetoricians. It resembles अर्थांतरन्यास; *e. g.* अमितगुणोपि पदार्थो दोषेणैकेन निंदितो भवति । निखिलरसायनराजो गंधेनोग्रेण लशुन इव ॥ R. G. (For a clear distinction between the two figures see R. G., under उदाहरण).

उदाहारः 1 An example or illustration. 2 The beginning of a speech.

उदित *p. p.* 1 Risen, ascended; उदितभूयिष्ठः Mâl. 1; Bv. 2. 85. 2 High, tall, lofty. 3 Grown, augmented. 4 Born, produced. 5 Spoken, uttered (fr. वद्), –Comp. –उदित *a.* well grounded in the Sâstras.

उदीक्षणं 1 Looking up to. 2 Seeing, beholding.

उदीची The north; तेनोदीचीं दिशमनुसरेः Me. 57.

उदीचीन *a.* 1 Turned towards the north. 2 Northern.

उदीच्य *a.* Living or being in the north. —च्यः The country to the north and west of the river Sarasvatî. 2 (Pl.) The inhabitants of this country; R. 4. 66. —च्यं A kind of perfume.

उदीपः High water, inundation, flood.

उदीरणं 1 Utterance, pronunciation, expression; उद्घातः प्रणवो यासां न्यायैस्त्रिभिरुदीरणं Ku. 2. 12. 2 Speaking, saying. 3 Throwing, discharging (as a missile).

उदीर्ण *p. p.* 1 Grown, risen, produced. 2 Puffed up, elated. 3 Increased, intense.

उदुंबरः See उडुंबर.

उदूखल = उलूखल q. v.

उदूढा A married woman.

उदेजय *a.* Shaking, causing to tremble, terrifying; उदेजयान् भूतगणान् न्यषेधीत् Bk. 1. 15.

उद्गतिः *f.* 1 Going up, rising, ascent. 2 Appearance; rise, origin. 3 Vomiting.

उद्गंधि *a.* 1 Fragrant; विजृंभणोद्गंधिषु कुड्मलेषु R. 16. 47. 2 Having a strong smell (good or bad).

उद्गमः 1 Going up, rising (of stars); ascent; आज्यधूमोद्गमेन S. 1. 15. 2 Standing erect (of hair); रोमोद्गमः प्रादुरभूदुमायाः Ku. 7. 77; M. 4. 1; Amaru. 36. 3 Going out, departure. 4 Birth, production, creation, पारिजातस्योद्गमः Mâl. 2; appearance; फलेन सहकारस्य पुष्पोद्गम इव प्रजाः R. 4. 9; कतिपयकुसुमोद्गमः कदंबः U. 3. 20; Amaru. 81. 5 Projection, elevation. 6 A shoot (of a plant); हरिततृणोद्गमशंकया मृगीभिः Ki. 5. 38. 7 Vomiting, casting up.

उद्गमनं Rising, becoming visible.

उद्गमनीय *pot. p.* To be gone up or ascended. —यं A pair of bleached or washed clothes (तत्स्यादुद्गमनीयं यद्धौतयोर्वस्त्रयोर्युगं); धौतोद्गमनीयवासिनी Dk. 42; गृहीतपत्युद्गमनीयवस्त्रा Ku. 7. 11 (where Malli. renders उ० by धौतवस्त्रं, and says युगग्रहणं तु प्रायिकाभिप्रायं &c.; see *ad loc.*).

उद्गाढ *a.* Deep, intense, excessive, much; उद्गाढरागोदया Mâl. 5. 7, 6. 6. –ढं Excess. —*ind.* Excessively, extremely.

उद्गातृ *m.* One of the four principal priests at a sacrifice, one who chants the hymns of the Sâmaveda.

उद्गारः 1 (*a*) Ejection, spitting out, vomiting, giving out, emitting; खर्जूरीस्कंधनद्धानां मदोद्गारसुगंधिषु R. 4. 57; Bh. 2. 36; Me. 63, 69; Si. 12. 9. (*b*) Oozing, stream, issuing out; R. 6. 60; Mv. 6. 33. 2 Repeating, narration; Mâl. 2. 13. 3 Spittle, saliva 4 Eructation, belching.

उद्गारिन् *a.* 1 Going up, rising. 2 Emitting, sending forth; R. 13. 47.

उद्गिरणं 1 Vomiting. 2 Slavering. 3 Eructation. 4 Extermination

उद्गीतिः *f.* 1 Singing aloud. 2 Chanting of the Sâmaveda. 3 A variety of the *Aryâ* metre; see Appendix.

उद्गीथः 1 Chanting of the Sâmaveda (the office of an udgâtṛi). 2 The second part of the Sâmaveda; भूयांस उद्गीथविदो वसंति U. 2. 3. 3 Designation of ओम् the three syllabled name of God.

उद्गीर्ण *a.* 1 Vomited. 2 Emitted, poured out.

उद्गूर्ण *a.* Raised, uplifted; Ve. 6. 12.

उद्ग्रंथः A section, chapter.

उद्ग्रंथि *a.* Untied (fig. also).

उद्ग्रहः,–हणं 1 Taking up, raising. 2 An object that can be accomplished by religious or other acts. 3 Eructation.

उद्ग्राहः 1 Lifting or taking up. 2 Replying in argument; rejoinder.

उद्ग्राहणिका Replying in argument.

उद्ग्राहित *p. p.* 1 Lifted or taken up. 2 Taken away. 3 Excellent; exalted. 4 Deposited, delivered. 5 Bound, tied. 6 Recalled, remembered.

उद्ग्रीव, उद्ग्रीविन् *a.* With the neck uplifted; उद्ग्रीवैर्मयूरैः M. 1. 21; Amaru. 63.

उद्धः 1 Excellence, eminence; (at the end of comp.); ब्राह्मणोद्धः = an excellent or superior Brâhmaṇa; उद्बाद्यश्च नियतलिंगा न तु विशेष्यलिंगाः Sk.; cf. मतल्लिकामचर्चिका प्रकांडमुद्घतल्लजौ प्रशस्तवाचकान्यमूनि Ak. 2 Happiness. 3 The hollow hand. 4 Fire. 5 A model. 6 Organic air in the body.

उद्घनः A carpenter's bench (the plank on which he works); लौहोद्घनघनस्कंधां ललितापघनां स्त्रियं Bk. 7. 62.

उद्घट्टनं, —ना Friction, striking against; Me. 61.

उद्घर्षणं 1 Rubbing, rubbing up; यस्योद्घर्षणलोष्टकैरपि सदा पृष्ठे न जातः किणः Mk. 2. 11. 2 A cudgel.

उद्घाटः A watch or guard-house.

उद्घाटकः 1 A key. 2 The rope and bucket of a well (—कं also).

उद्घाटन *a.* (नी *f.*) Opening, unlocking; धर्मं यो न करोति निंदितमतिः स्वर्गार्गलोद्घाटनं H. 1. 153. —नं 1 Opening; Ve. 1. 2 Raising, lifting up. 3 A key. 4 The rope and bucket of a well; a water-wheel.

उद्घातः 1 Beginning, commencement; उद्घातः प्रणवो यासां Ku. 2. 12; आकुमारकथोद्घातं शालिगोप्यो जगुर्यशः R. 4. 20. 2 Allusion, reference. 3 Striking, wounding. 4 A stroke, blow, wound. 5 Jolting, shaking (as of a carriage); Si. 12. 2; R. 2. 72; Ve. 2. 28. 6 Rising, elevation. 7 A club, mallet. 8 A weapon (in general). 9 A division of a book, chapter; section.

उद्घोषः 1 Announcing aloud, proclaiming. 2 Popular talk, general report.

उद्दंशः 1 A bug. 2 A louse. 3 A mosquito.

उद्दंड *a.* 1 With the stalk, stem, or staff raised or rising up; उद्दंडपद्मं गृहदीर्घिकाणां R. 16. 46; °धवलातपत्राः Mâl. 6. 2 Formidable, terrific. –COMP.–पालः 1 a punisher. 2 a kind of fish. 3 a kind of serpent; (cf. उद्दंडपाल)

उद्दंतुर *a.* 1 Large-toothed or having projecting teeth. 2 High, tall. 3 Terrific, formidable.

उद्दांत *a.* 1 Energetic. 2 Humble.

उद्दानं 1 Binding, confinement; उद्दाने क्रियमाणे तु मत्स्यानां तत्र रज्जुभिः Mb. 2 Taming, subduing. 3 The middle, the waist. 4 A fire-place. 5 The submarine fire.

उद्दाम *a.* 1 Unbound, unrestrained, unchecked, free; *Si.* 4. 10. 2 (*a*) Strong, powerful; Pt. 3. 148. (*b*) Furious, intoxicated; स्रोतस्युद्दामादिग्गजे R. 1. 78; *Si.* 11. 19. 3 Dreadful. 4 Self-willed. 5 Luxuriant; large, great, excessive; Me. 25; Ratn. 2. 4.—मः 1 N. of Yama. 2 N. of Varuna. —मं *ind.* Violently, fiercely, strongly; अयोद्दामं ज्वलिष्यतः U. 3. 9.

उद्दालकं A kind of honey.

उद्दित *a.* Tied, bound.

उद्दिष्ट *p. p.* 1 Mentioned, particularized, specially told. 2 Desired, wished for. 3 Explained, taught &c.

उद्दीपः 1 Inflaming, lighting. 2 An inflamer.

उद्दीपक *a.* 1 Exciting. 2 Lighting, inflaming.

उद्दीपनं 1 Inflaming, exciting. 2 (In Rhet.) That which excites or feeds (a sentiment or *rasa*), see आलंबनं. 3 Illuminating, lighting. 4 Burning of a body.

उद्दीप्त *a.* Shining, blazing.—प्रः,-प्रं Bdellium.

उद्दृप्त *a.* Proud, haughty.

उद्देशः 1 Pointing to or at, directing. 2 Mention, specification. 3 Illustration, explanation, exemplification. 4 Ascertainment, inquiry, investigation, search. 5 A brief statement or account; एष तूद्देशतः प्रोक्तो विभूतेर्विस्तरो मया Bg. 10. 40. 6 Assignment. 7 Stipulation. 8 Object, motive. 9 A spot, region, place; अहो प्रवातसुभगोयमुद्देशः *S.* 3; M. 3.

उद्देशकः 1 An illustration, example. 2 (In Math.) A question, problem.

उद्देश्य *pot. p.* 1 To be illustrated or explained. 2 To be intended or aimed at.—श्यं 1 The object in view, an incentive. 2 The subject of an assertion (opp. विधेय); see the word अनुवाद्य also.

उद्द्योतः Light, lustre (lit. and fig.); त्रिभिर्नेत्रैः कृतोद्द्योतं Mb.; कुलोद्द्योतकरी तव Râm. adorning or gracing. 2 A division of a book, chapter, section.

उद्द्रावः Flight, retreat.

उद्धत *p. p.* 1 Raised up, elevated, lifted up; लांगूलमुद्धतं धुन्वन् Bk. 9. 7, आत्मोद्धतैरपि रजोभिः *S.* 1. 8 raised; R. 9. 50; heaved; Ki. 8. 53. 2 Excessive, very much, exceeding. 3 Haughty, vain, puffed up; अक्षवधोद्धतः R. 12. 63. 4 Harsh. 5 Excited, inflamed, intensified; °मनोभवरागा Ki. 9. 68, 69; मदोद्धताः प्रत्यनिलं विचेरुः Ku. 3. 31. 6 Majestic, stately; धीरोद्धता नमयतीव गतिर्धरित्रीं U. 6. 19 Rude; ill-mannered. —तः A king's wrestler. –COMP. –मनस्,-मनस्क *a.* high-minded, haughty, proud.

उद्धतिः *f.* 1 Elevation. 2 Pride, haughtiness; *Si.* 3. 28. 3 Rudeness, insolence. 4 A stroke.

उद्धमः 1 sounding, blowing. 2 Breathing hard, panting.

उद्धरणं 1 Drawing or taking out, taking off (clothes &c.). 2 Extraction, pulling or tearing out; कंटक° Ms. 9. 252; चक्षुषोरुद्धरणं Mit. 3 Extricating, deliverance, rescuing (from danger); दीनोद्धरणोचितस्य R. 2. 25; स बंधुर्यो विपन्नानामापदुद्धरणक्षमः H. 1. 3. 4 Eradication, extermination, deposition. 5 Lifting, raising. 6 Vomiting. 7 Final emancipation. 8 Acquittance of debt.

उद्धर्तृ, उद्धारक *a.* 1 One who raises or lifts up. 2 A sharer, co-heir.

उद्धर्ष *a.* Delighted, glad. -र्षः 1 Great joy or delight. 2 Courage to undertake a thing. 3 A festival (especially a religious one).

उद्धर्षणं 1 Animating. 2 Erection of the hair (on the body), thrill.

उद्धवः 1 A sacrificial fire. 2 A festival, holiday. 3 N. of a Yâdava, uncle and friend of Krishṇa. [When Kris*hn*a was taken by Akr*u*ra to Mathur*a*, Uddhava was implored by the citizens of Gokula to go and fetch him. He was very much attached to Kris*hn*a. On seeing the destruction of the Y*a*davas to be inevitable, he went to Kris*hn*a and asked him what to do; whereupon he was told to go to Badarik*as*rama to practise penance and to secure heaven. He is the subject of two short poems, उद्धवदूत and उद्धवसंदेश.]

उद्धस्त *a.* Extending or raising the hands.

उद्धानं 1 A fire-place. 2 Ejecting, vomiting.

उद्धांत *a.* Ejected, vomited. -तः An elephant out of rut.

उद्धारः 1 Drawing out, extraction. 2 Deliverance, redemption, saving, rescuing, extrication. 3 Raising, lifting up. 4 (In law) A part to be set aside from the paternal property for the benefits of the eldest son; the surplus allowed by Law to the eldest beyond the shares of the younger brothers; Ms. 9. 112. 5 The sixth part of booty taken in war which belongs to the king; Ms. 7. 97. 6 Debt. 7 Recovering property. 8 Final beatitude.

उद्धारणं 1 Raising, elevating. 2 Rescuing, drawing out of (danger), delivering.

उद्धुर *a.* Unrestrained, unchecked, free. 2 Firm, intrepid. 3 Heavy, full of; *Si.* 5. 64. 4 Thick, gross. 5 Able, competent; Bv. 4. 40.

उद्धूत *p. p.* 1 Shaken off, fallen from; raised or thrown up; मारुतभरोद्धूतोपि धूलिव्रजः Dhan. V. 2 Exalted, high.

उद्धूननं 1 Throwing upwards, raising. 2 Shaking.

उद्धूपनं Fumigating.

उद्धूलनं Powdering, sprinkling with dust or powder; भस्मोद्धूलन K. P. 10.

उद्धूषणं Erection of the hair (on the body), thrill, horripilation.

उद्धृत *p. p.* 1 Drawn up or out, extracted &c. 2 Raised, elevated, lifted up. 3 Uprooted, eradicated; उद्धृतारिः R. 2. 30.

उद्धृतिः *f.* 1 Drawing or pulling out, extracting. 2 An extract, passage selected. 3 Delivering, rescuing. 4 Especially, delivering or purifying from sin, final liberation; त्रपते तीर्थानि त्वरितमिह यस्योद्धृतिविधौ G. L. 28.

उद्ध्मानं A fire-place, stove.

उद्ध्यः (उज्झत्युदकमितिउद्ध्यः Malli.) N. of a river; तोयदागम इवोद्ध्यभिद्ययोः; R. 11. 8.

उद्बंध *a.* Loosened. —धः, —धनं 1 Tying up, hanging. 2 Hanging oneself.

उद्बंधकः N. of a mixed tribe (doing the duty of washermen); cf. Usanas:—आवेागवेन विप्रायां जातास्ताम्रोपजीविनः। तस्यैव नृपकन्यायां जातः सूनिक उच्यते॥ सूनिकस्य नृपायां तु जाता उद्बंधकाः स्मृताः। निर्णेजयेयुर्वस्त्राणि अपृशाश्च भवंत्यतः॥.

उद्बल *a.* Strong, powerful.

उद्बाष्प *a.* Filled or suffused with tears; Ki. 3. 59.

उद्बाहु *a.* Having the arms raised, stretching or extending the arms; प्रांशुलभ्ये फले लोभादुद्बाहुरिव वामनः R. 1. 3.

उद्बुद्ध *p. p.* 1 Awakened, aroused, excited. 2 Opened, expanded, full-blown; Mâl. 1. 40. 3 Reminded. 4 Recalled to memory (as an object seen before).

उद्बोधः, -धनं 1 Awakening, reminding. 2 Recalling to memory, rousing up; ननु कथं रामादिरत्याद्युद्बोधकारणैः सीतादिभिः सामाजिकानां रत्युद्बोधः S. D. 3; so रस°.

उद्बोधक *a.* 1 Reminding, that which reminds or calls to remembrance. 2 Exciting. —कः N. of the sun.

उद्भट *a*. 1 Excellent, pre-eminent; पदे पदे संति भटा रणोद्भटाः N. 1. 132. 2 Exalted, magnanimous. —टः 1 A fan for winnowing corn. 2 A tortoise.

उद्भवः 1 Production, creation, birth, generation (lit. and fig.); इति हेतुस्तदुद्भवे K. P. 1; Y. 3. 80; oft at the end of comp. in the sense of 'springing or arising from,' 'produced from'; ऊरूद्भवा V. 1. 3; मणिराकरोद्भवः R. 3. 18. 2 Source, origin. 3 N. of Vishṇu.

उद्भावः 1 Production, generation. 2 Magnanimity.

उद्भावनं 1 Thinking, thinking over. 2 Production, generation, creation. 3 Inattention, neglect, disregard.

उद्भावयितृ *a*. Raising upwards, exalting (fig. also).

उद्भासः Radiance, splendour.

उद्भासिन्, उद्भासुर *a*. Shining, radiant, splendid; विभूषणाद्भासि पिनद्धभोगि वा Ku. 5. 78; Mk. 8. 38; Amaru. 81.

उद्भिद् *a*. Sprouting shooting forth. *-m*. 1 A sprout or shoot (of a plant); अंकुरोऽभिनवोद्भिदि Ak. 2 A plant. 3 A spring, fountain. –Comp. –ज *a*. (उद्भिज्ज) sprouting, germinating (as a plant). (–जः) a plant. –विद्या the science of botany.

उद्भिद *a*. Sprouting, germinating.

उद्भूत *p. p*. 1 Born, produced, generated. 2 Lofty (lit. and fig.). 3 Perceptible, capable of being perceived by the senses; as a गुण.

उद्भूतिः *f*. 1 Generation, production, 2 Elevation, exaltation, prosperity; वरः शंभुरलं ह्येष त्वत्कुलोद्भूतये विधिः Ku. 6. 82.

उद्भेदः, –दनं 1 Breaking through or out, becoming visible; appearance, manifestation, or growth; उमास्तनोद्भेदमनु प्रवृद्धः Ku. 7. 24; तं यौवनोद्भेदविशेषकांतं R. 5. 38; Si. 18. 36. 3 A spring, fountain. 4 Horripilation; as in पुलकोद्भेद.

उद्भ्रमः 1 Whirling turning round, flourishing. (as of a sword). 2 Wandering. 3 Regret.

उद्भ्रमणं 1 Moving or wandering about. 2 Rising.

उद्यत *p. p*. 1 Raised, lifted up; °असिः, °पाणिः &c. 2 Persevering, diligent, active. 3 Bent, drawn (as a bow); Ki. 1. 21. 4 Ready, prepared, on the point of, eager, bent or intent on, engaged in; with dat., loc., inf. or usually in comp.; उद्यतः स्वेषु कर्मसु R. 17. 61; हंतुं स्वजनमुद्यताः Bg. 1. 45; जय°, वध° &c.

उद्यमः 1 Raising, elevation. 2 Strenuous or assiduous effort, exertion, diligence, perseverance; निशम्य चैनां तपसे कृतोद्यमां Ku. 5. 3; शशाक मेना न नियंतुमुद्यमात् 5 firm resolve; उद्यमेन हि सिध्यंति कार्याणि न मनोरथैः Pt. 2. 131. 3 Readiness, preparation. –Comp. –भृत् *a*. striving hard; Bh. 2. 74.

उद्यमनं Raising, elevation.

उद्यमिन् *a*. Diligent, persevering.

उद्यानं 1 Going or walking out. 2 A garden, park, pleasure-garden; बाह्योद्यानस्थितहरशिरश्चंद्रिकाधौतहर्म्या Me. 7, 26, 33. 3 Purpose, motive. –Comp. –पालः, –पालकः, –रक्षकः a gardener, superintendent or keeper of a garden; Ku. 2. 36.

उद्यानकं A garden, park.

उद्यापनं Bringing to a conclusion, completing finishing (as व्रतोद्यापन).

उद्योगः 1 Effort, exertion, industry; तदेवमिति सचिंत्य त्यजेन्नोद्योगमात्मनः Pt 2. 140. 2 Work, duty, office; तुल्योद्योगस्तव दिनकृतश्चाधिकारो मतो नः V. 2. 1. 3 Perseverance, diligence.

उद्योगिन् *a*. Active, persevering, industrious.

उद्रः A king of aquatic animal.

उद्रथः 1 The pin of the axle of a carriage. 2 A cock.

उद्रावः A loud noise, uproar.

उद्रिक्त *p. p*. 1 Increased, excessive, abundant. 2 Distinct, evident.

उद्रुज *a*. Destroying, undermining (as a bank); as in कूलमुद्रुज q. v.

उद्रेकः Increase, excess, preponderance, abundance; ज्ञानोद्रेकाद्विघटिततमोग्रंथयः सत्त्वनिष्ठाः Ve. 1. 23; गत्वोद्रेकं जघनपुलिने Si. 7. 74.

उद्वत्सरः A year.

उद्वपनं 1 A gift, donation. 2 Pouring or shaking out.

उद्वमनं, उद्वांतिः *f*. Vomiting, ejecting.

उद्वर्तः 1 A remainder, surplus. 2 Excess, preponderance. 3 Rubbing or smearing the body with perfumes.

उद्वर्तनं 1 Going up, rising. 2 Springing up, growth. 3 Prosperity, elevation. 4 Turning from side to side; springing up; चटुलशफरोद्वर्तनप्रेक्षितानि Me. 40. 5 Grinding, pounding. 6 Rubbing and cleaning the body with perfumes or fragrant unguents, or the unguents used for this purpose or to relieve pain.

उद्वर्धनं 1 Increase. 2 Sly or suppressed laughter.

उद्वह *a*. 1 Carrying, leading up. 2 Continuing, perpetuating (as a family); कुल° U. 4; so रघूद्वह° 4. 22; R. 9 9. 11. 54. —हः 1 A son. 2 One (*i. e*. the 4th) of the seven courses of air. 3 Marriage. —हा A daughter.

उद्वहनं 1 Marrying. 2 Supporting, holding or lifting up, carrying; भुवः प्रयुक्तोद्वहनक्रियायाः R. 13. 1, 14. 20; R. 2. 18; Ku. 3. 13. 3 Being carried on, riding; Ms. 8. 370.

उद्वान *a*. Vomited, ejected. —नं 1 Ejecting, vomiting. 2 A stove.

उद्वांत *a*. 1 Vomited. 2 Out of rut (as an elephant).

उद्वापः 1 Ejection, throwing out. 2 Shaving. 3 (In logic) Non-existence of a subsequent consequent on the absence of an antecedent (Wilson).

उद्वासः 1 Banishment. 2 Abandonment. 3 Killing.

उद्वासन 1 Expelling, banishing. 2 Abandoning. 3 Taking out of or away (from the fire) 4 Killing.

उद्वाहः 1 Bearing up, supporting. 2 Marriage, wedding; असवर्णास्वयं ज्ञेयो विधिरुद्वाहकर्मणि Ms. 3. 43. (The Smṛitis mention 8 forms of marriage:— ब्राह्मो दैवस्तथा चार्षः प्राजापत्यस्तथासुरः। गांधर्वो राक्षसश्चैव पैशाचश्चाष्टमःस्मृतः) ॥.

उद्वाहनं 1 Lifting up. 2 Marriage. —नी 1 A cord. 2 A small shell, *cowarie* (वराटिका).

उद्वाहिक *a*. Relating to marriage, matrimonial (as a Mantra); Ms. 9. 95.

उद्वाहिन् *a*. 1 Raising, drawing up. 2 Marrying. —नी A rope, cord.

उद्विग्न *p. p*. Grieved, afflicted, sorrowful, anxious (as for any absent lover).

उद्वीक्षणं 1 Looking up or upwards. 2 Sight, an eye, seeing, looking at; सखीजनोद्वीक्षणकौमुदीमुखं R. 3. 1.

उद्वीजनं Fanning.

उद्वृंहणं Increase, growth.

उद्वृत्त *p. p*. 1 Raised, elevated. 2 Flowing out, overflowing; उद्वृत्तः क इव सुखावहः परेषां Si. 8. 18. (where उ० means also 'gone astray, ill behaved'.

उद्वेगः 1 Trembling, shaking, waving. 2 Agitation, excitement; Bg. 12. 15. 3 Alarm, fear; शांतोद्वेगस्तिमितनयनं दृष्टभक्तिर्भवान्या Me. 36; R. 8. 7. 4 Anxiety, regret, sorrow. 5 Admiration, astonishment. —गं A betelnut (fruit).

उद्वेजनं 1 Agitation, anxiety. 2 Infliction of pain, torture; उद्वेजनकरैर्दंडैश्चिह्नयित्वा प्रवासयेत् Ms. 8. 352. 3 Regret.

उद्वेदि *a*. Having a raised seat or throne in it; विमानं नवमुद्वेदि R. 17. 9.

उद्वेपः Shaking, trembling, excessive tremor.

उद्वेल *a*. 1 Overflowing its banks (as a river); R. 10. 34; K. 333. 2 Transgressing the proper limits.

उद्वेल्लित *p. p*. Shaken, tossed up. —तं Shaking.

उद्वेष्टन *a*. 1 Loosened; कयाचिदुद्वेष्टनवांतमाल्यः R. 7. 6; Ku. 7. 57. 2 Freed from bonds, unbound. —नं 1 The act of surrounding or enclosing. 2 An enclosure, fence. 3 A pain in the buttocks or back of the body.

उद्वोढृ *m*. A husband.

उधस् *n.* An udder; see ऊधस्.

उंद् 7. P. (उनत्ति, उत्त-उन्न) To wet, moisten, bathe ; याः पृथिवीं पयसोंदति.

उंदनं Moistening, wetting.

उंदरुः, उंदुरः, उंदुरुः, उंदूरः A mouse, rat.

उन्नत *p. p* 1 Raised, elevated, uplifted (fig. also); Bh. 3. 24; *Si.* 9. 79 ; नतोन्नतभूमिभागे *S.* 4. 14. 2 High (fig. also), tall, lofty; great, eminent R. 1. 14; V. 5. 22; Ki. 5. 15; 14. 23. 3 Plump, full (as breasts). --तः A boa (अजगर). —तं 1 Elevation. 2 Ascension, altitude.–Comp.–आनत *a.* elevated and depressed, uneven ; बंधुरं तून्नतानतं Ak. –चरण *a.* rampant. –शिरस् *a.* carrying the head, high proud.

उन्नतिः *f.* 1 Elevation, height (fig. also) ; see उन्नतिमत् below. 2 Exaltation, dignity , rise, prosperity ; स्तोकेनोन्नतिमायाति स्तोकेनायात्यधोगतिं Pt. 1. 150; *Si.* 16. 22; Bv. 1. 40 ; महाजनस्य संपर्कः कस्य नोन्नतिकारकः H. 3. 3 Raising.–Comp. °ईशः N. of Garuda (lord of उन्नति).

उन्नतिमत् *a.* Elevated, projecting, plump (as breasts); सा पीनोन्नतिमत्पयोधरयुगं धत्ते Amaru. 30; *Si.* 9. 72.

उन्नमनं 1 Raising,lifting up. 2 Height.

उन्नम्र *a.* Erect, upright, lofty, high (fig. also); उन्नम्रताम्रपटमंडपमंडितं तत् *Si.* 5. 61.

उन्नयः, उन्नायः 1 Raising, elevating. 2 Height, elevation. 3 Analogy, resemblance. 4 Inference.

उन्नयनं 1 Raising, elevating, lifting up. 2 Drawing up water. 3 Deliberation, discussion. 4 Inference.

उन्नस *a.* Having a prominent nose; उन्नसं दधती वक्त्रं Bk. 4. 18.

उन्नादः Crying out, roar; humming, chirping &c.

उन्नाभ *a.* 1 Having a projecting navel, corpulent.

उन्नाहः 1 Projection, protuberance. 2 Tying up, binding. —हं Sour gruel made from the fermentation of rice.

उन्निद्र *a.* 1 Sleepless, awake ; तामुन्निद्रामवनिशयनां सौधवातायनस्थः Me. 88. विगमयत्युन्निद्र एव क्षपाः *S.* 6. 4; Mu. 4. 2 Expanded, full-blown, budded (as lotuses); उन्निद्रपुष्पाक्षिसहस्रभाजा *Si.* 4. 13, 8. 28.

उन्नेतृ *a* Raising. —*m.* One of the 16 priests at a sacrifice.

उन्मज्जनं Emerging, coming out of water.

उन्मत्त *p. p.* 1 Drunk, intoxicated. 2 Insane, frantic, mad ; द्वावत्रोन्मत्तौ V. 2; Ms. 9. 79. 3 Puffed, elevated; wild; Pt. 1. 161; *Si.* 6. 31. 4 Possessed by a ghost or an evil spirit, Y. 2. 32; Ms, 3. 161. (वातपित्तश्लेष्मसंनिपातग्रहसंभवेनोपसृष्टः Mit.) —त्तः The thorn apple (धत्तूर) –Comp. –कीर्तिः, –वेशः N. of *Siva.* °गंगं N. of a country (where the Gangâ roars furiously along). –दर्शन, –रूप *a.* mad in appearance. –प्रलपित *a.* spoken in drunkenness or madness. (–तं) the words of a madman.

उन्मथनं 1 Shaking off, throwing off or down. 2 Killing, slaughter ; अन्योन्यसूतोन्मथनात् R. 7. 52.

उन्मद *a.* 1 Intoxicated, drunk ; R. 2. 9, 16. 54. 2 Mad, furious, extravagant ; *Si.* 10. 4, 16. 69. 3 Causing intoxication, intoxicating ; मधुकरांगनया मुहुरुन्मदध्वनिभृता निभृताक्षरमुज्जगे *Si.* 6. 20. –दः 1 Insanity. 2 Intoxication.

उन्मदन *a.* Affected or inflamed with love ; तत्राप्रभृत्युन्मदना बभूव Ku. 5. 55.

उन्मदिष्णु *a.* 1 Mad. 2 Intoxicated, drunk. 3 In rut (as an elephant).

उन्मनस्,–नस्क *a.* 1 Excited or disturbed in mind, agitated, uneasy; R. 11. 22; Ki. 14. 45. 2 Regretting, repining for a lost or departed friend. 3 Anxious, eager, impatient.

उन्मनायते Den. A., **उन्मनीभू** To be uneasy ; to be disturbed in mind.

उन्मंथः 1 Agitation. 2 Killing, slaughter.

उन्मंथनं 1 Shaking off, agitating. 2 Killing, slaughter, hurting. 3 Beating (with a stick).

उन्मयूख *a.* Shining, radiant ; R. 16. 69.

उन्मर्दनं 1 Rubbing, kneading. 2 A fragrant essence used for the purpose of rubbing.

उन्माथः 1 Torment, deep pain. 2 Shaking, agitation. 3 Killing, slaughter. 4 A snare or trap.

उन्माद *a.* 1 Mad, insane. 2 Extravagant.—दः 1 Madness, insanity ; अहो उन्मादः U. 3. 2 Intense passion. 3 Lunacy, mania (considered as a disease of the mind). 4 (In Rhet.) Madness considered as one of the 33 subordinate feelings ; चित्तसंमोह उन्मादः कामशोकभयादिभिः S. D. 3; or according to R. G. विप्रलंभमहापत्तिपरमानंदादिजन्माऽन्यस्मिन्नन्यावभास उन्मादः 5 Bloom ; उन्मादं वीक्ष्य पद्मानां S. D. 2.

उन्मादन *a.* Maddening, intoxicating —नः One of the five arrows of Cupid.

उन्मानं 1 Weighing, measuring upwards. 2 A measure of size or quantity. 3 Price.

उन्मार्ग *a.* Going to a wrong path. —र्गः 1 A wrong road, deviation from the right road (fig. also). 2 An improper conduct, evil course ; उन्मार्गप्रस्थितानि इंद्रियाणि K. 155 ; °प्रवर्तकः 103. —र्गं *ind.* Astray ; Pt. 1. 161.

उन्मार्जनं Rubbing, wiping off, removing.

उन्मितिः *f.* Measure; price.

उन्मिश्र *a.* Mixed with ; variegated.

उन्मिषित *p.p.* Opened (as eyes), blown, expanded &c. —तं A look, glance; Ku. 5. 25.

उन्मीलः,–लनं 1 Opening (of the eyes), awaking. 2 Unfolding, opening; U. 6. 34. 3 Expanding, blowing.

उन्मुख *a.* (खी *f.*) 1 Raising the face, looking up; अद्रेः शृंगं हरति पवनः किंस्विदित्युन्मुखीभिः Me. 14, 100; R. 1. 39, 11. 26 ; आश्रम° 1. 53. 2 Ready, intent on, on the point of, prepared for ; तमरण्यसमाश्रयोन्मुखं R. 8. 12 about to retire to the woods ; 16 9, 3. 12. 3 Eager, waiting for, expecting ; तस्मिन् संयमिनामाद्ये जाते परिणयोन्मुखे Ku. 6. 34 ; R. 12. 26, 6. 21, 11. 23. 4 Sounding, speaking or making a sound ; Ku. 6. 2.

उन्मुखर *a.* Loud sounding, noisy.

उन्मुद्र *a.* 1 Unsealed 2 Opened, blown, expanded. (as a flower).

उन्मूलनं Plucking up by the roots, eradication, uprooting; न पादपोन्मूलनशक्ति रंहः R. 2. 34.

उन्मेदा Corpulence, fatness.

उन्मेषः, –षणं 1 Opening (of the eyes), winking; Mu. 3. 21. 2 Blowing, opening, expansion ; उन्मेषं यो मम न सहते जातिवैरी निशायां K. P. 10 ; दीर्घिकाकमलोन्मेषः Ku. 2. 33. 3 Light, flash, brilliancy ; सतां प्रज्ञोन्मेषः Bh. 2. 114 ; विद्युदुन्मेषदृष्टिं Me. 81. 4 Awakening, rising, becoming visible, manifestation; ज्ञान° *Sânti* 3. 13.

उन्मोचनं Unfastening, loosening.

उप *ind.* 1 As a prefix to verbs and nouns it expresses (1) nearness, contiguity ; उपविशति, उपगच्छति ; (2) power, ability; उपकरोति : (3) pervasion; उपकीर्ण ; (4) advice, instructing as by a teacher ; उपदिशति, उपदेश ; (5) death, extinction, उपरत ; (6) defect, fault ; उपघात ; (7) giving ; उपनयति, उपहरति ; (8) action, effort ; उपत्वा नेष्यं ; (9) beginning, commencement; उपक्रमते, उपक्रम ; (10) study ; उपाध्यायः ; (11) reverence, worship ; उपस्थानं, उपचरति पितरं पुत्रः. 2 As unconnected with verbs and prefixed to nouns, it expresses nearness, resemblance, contiguity in space, number, time, degree &c., but generally involving the idea of subordination or inferiority ; उपकनिष्ठिका the finger next to the little finger ; उपपुराणं a secondary Purâna ; उपगुरुः an assistant master ; उपाध्यक्षः a vicepresident. It usually, however, forms Avyayî. comp. in these senses; उपगंगं–गंगायाः समीपे ; उपकूलं, °वनं &c. 3 With numerals it forms संख्याबहुव्रीहि and means 'nearly,' 'almost'; उपत्रिंशाः

nearly thirty. **4** As a separable preposition (*a*) with acc. when it means inferiority; उप हरिं सुराः Sk. the gods are inferior to Hari. (*b*) With loc. it expresses (1) over, above, superior to; उपनिष्के कार्षापणं, उप परार्धे हरेर्गुणाः ; (2) addition.

उपकंठः-ठं **1** Proximity, vicinity, neighbourhood; प्राप तालीवनश्याममुपकंठं महोदधेः R. 4. 34, 13. 48; Ku. 7. 51; Mâl. 9. 2. **2** Space near a village or its boundary. *-ind* **1** Upon the neck, near the throat. **2** In the vicinity of, near.

उपकथा A short story or tale.

उपकनिष्ठिका The finger next to the little finger.

उपकरणं **1** Doing service or favour, helping. **2** Material, implement, instrument, means; उपकरणीभावमायाति U. 3. 3; परोपकारोपकरणं शरीरं K. 207; Y. 2. 276; Ms. 9. 270. **3** Means of subsistence, anything supporting life. **4** The insignia of royalty.

उपकर्णनं Hearing.

उपकर्णिका Rumour, report.

उपकर्तृ *a.* One who does a service or favour, useful, friendly; हीनान्यनुपकर्तृणि प्रवृद्धानि विकुर्वते R. 17. 58; उपकर्त्री रसादीनां S. D. 624; Si. 2. 37.

उपकल्पनं, -ना **1** Preparation. **2** Fabricating, making.

उपकारः **1** Service, help, assistance, favour, obligation (opp. अपकार); उपकारापकारौ हि लक्ष्यं लक्षणमेतयोः Si. 2. 37; शाम्येत्प्रत्यपकारेण नोपकारेण दुर्जनः Ku. 2. 40, 3. 73; Y. 3. 284. **2** Preparation. **3** Ornament, decoration. **—री** **1** A royal tent, palace. **2** Caravansera.

उपकार्य *a.* To be assisted. **—र्या** A royal house, palace; रम्यां रघुप्रतिनिधिः स नवोपकार्यां बाल्यात्परामिव दशां मदनोध्युवास R. 5 63; a royal tent; 5. 41, 11. 93, 13. 79, 16. 55, 73.

उपकुंचिः,—चिका Small cardamoms.

उपकुंभ *a.* **1** Near, proximate. **2** Solitary, retired, secluded.

उपकुर्वाणः A Brâhmaṇa in a state of pupilage (ब्रह्मचारिन्) who wishes to pass on to the state of a householder (गृहस्थ).

उपकुल्या A canal, trench.

उपकूपं-पे *ind.* Near a well; °जलाशयः a trough near a well for watering cattle.

उपकृतिः *f.*, **उपक्रिया** Favour, obligation.

उपक्रमः **1** Beginning, commencement; रामोपक्रममाचख्यौ रक्षःपरिभवं नवं R. 12. 42 begun by Râma. **2** Approach, advance; साहस° forcible advance Mâl. 7; so योषितः सुकुमारोपक्रमाः *ibid.* **3** An undertaking, work, enterprize. **4** A plan, means, expedient, stratagem, remedy; सामादिभिरुपक्रमैः Ms. 7. 107, 159; R. 18. 15; Y. 1. 345; Si. 20. 76. **5** Attendance on a patient, practice of medicine. **6** A test of honesty; see उपधा.

उपक्रमणं **1** Approaching. **2** Undertaking. **3** Commencement. **4** (Medic.) Treatment, physicking.

उपक्रमणिका A preface, introduction.

उपक्रीडा A play-ground, a place for playing.

उपक्रोशः, -शनं Censure, reproach, ignominy; प्राणैरुपक्रोशमलीमसैर्वा R. 2. 53.

उपक्रोष्टृ *m.* An ass (braying aloud).

उपक्क (क्का) णं The sound of a lute.

उपक्षयः **1** Waste, decay, loss. **2** Expenditure.

उपक्षेपः **1** Throwing at hurling. **2** Mention, allusion, hint, suggestion; कार्योपक्षेपमादौ तनुमपि रचयन् Mu. 4. 3; दारुणः खलूपक्षेपः पापस्य Ve. 5. **-3** A threat, specific mention or charge.

उपक्षेपणं **1** Throwing or casting down. **2** Accusing, charging.

उपग *a.* (At the end of comp. only) **1** Approaching, following, joining. **2** Receiving; Ms. 1. 46; Si. 16. 68.

उपगणः A small or subordinate class.

उपगत *p. p.* **1** Gone to, approached. **2** Occurred. **3** Got. **4** Experienced. **5** Promised, agreed.

उपगतिः *f.* **1** Approach, going near. **2** Knowledge, acquaintance. **3** Acceptance. **4** Attainment, acquirement.

उपगमः,-मनं **1** Going to, drawing towards, approach; सीमंते च त्वदुपगमजं यत्र नीपं वधूनां Me. 65 your advent; व्यावर्ततान्योपगमात्कुमारी R. 6. 69, 9. 50. **2** Knowledge, acquaitance. **3** Attainment, acquiring; विश्वासोपगमादभिन्नगतयः S. 1. 14. **4** Intercourse (as of the sexes). **5** Society, company; न पुनरधमानामुपगमः H. 1. 136. **6** Undergoing, suffering, feeling. **7** Acceptance. **8** An agreement, promise.

उपगिरि-रं *ind.* Near a mountain.**-रिः** N. of a country situated near a mountain in the north.

उपगु *ind.* Near a cow. **—गुः** A cowherd.

उपगुरुः An assistant teacher.

उपगूढ *p. p.* Hidden; clasped. **-ढं** An embrace; उपगूढानि सवेपथूनि च Ku 4. 17; Si. 10. 88; कंठाश्लेषोपगूढं Bh. 3. 82; Me. 97.

उपगूहनं **1** Hiding, concealing. **2** An embrace. **3** Astonishment, surprise.

उपग्रहः **1** Confinement, seizure. **2** Defeat, frustration; Mu. 4. 2. **3** A prisoner. **4** Joining, addition. **5** Favour, encouragement. **6** A minor planet (राहु, केतु &c.).

उपग्रहणं **1** Seizing (from below); taking hold of; as in पादोपग्रहणं. **2** Seizure, capture. **3** Supporting, promoting. **4** Holy study; वेदोपग्रहणार्थाय तावग्राहयत प्रभुः Râm.

उपग्राहः **1** Making a present. **2** A present.

उपग्राह्यः **1** An offering or present. **2** Particularly, a present or offering to a great man or king; the modern *Nazarana*.

उपघातः **1** A stroke, injury; insult; Ms. 2. 179; Y. 2. 256. **2** Destruction, ruin. **3** Touch, contact. **4** Assault, violence. **5** Disease. **6** Sin.

उपघोषणं Proclaiming, publication, making known.

उपघ्नः **1** Contiguous support; छेद्रादिवोपघ्नतरोर्व्रतत्यौ R. 14. 1. **2** Shelter, support, protection.

उपचक्रः A variety of the ruddy goose.

उपचक्षुस् *n.* An eye-glass, spectacles.

उपचयः **1** Accumulation, addition, accession. **2** Increase, growth, excess; बल° K. 105; स्वशक्त्युपचये Si. 2. 57, 9. 32. **3** Quantity, heap. **4** Prosperity, elevation, rise.

उपचरः **1** Cure, treatment. **2 -उपचरणं** Approach.

उपचाय्यः A kind of sacred fire.

उपचारः **1** Service, attendance; honouring, worshipping, entertaining; अस्खलितोपचारां R. 5. 20. **2** Civility, politeness, courtesy, polite behaviour, (external display of courtesy); °परिभ्रष्टः H. 1. 133; °विधिर्मनस्विनीनां M. 3. 3; °पदं न चेदिदं Ku. 4. 9 a merely complimentary saying, a flattering compliment. **3** Salutation, usual or customary obeisance, homage; नोपचारमर्हति S. 3. 18; °यंत्रणया M. 4; °अंजलिः R. 3. 11 folding the hands in salutation. **4** A form or mode of address or salutation; रामभद्र इत्येव मां प्रत्युपचारः शोभते तातपरिजनस्य U. 1; यथा गुरुस्तस्थोपचारेण 6. **5** External show or form, ceremony; प्रावृषेण्यैरेव लिंगैर्मम राजोपचारः V. 4. **6** A remedy, physicking, application of cure or remedy; शिशिर° Dk. 15. **7** Practice, performance, conduct, management; व्रतचर्या° Ms. 1. 111, 10. 32; कामोपचारेषु. Dk. 81 in the conduct of love-affairs. **8** Means of doing homage or showing respect; प्रकीर्णाभिनवोपचारं (राजमार्गं) R. 7. 4; 5. 41. **9** Hence, any necessary or requisite article, (of worship, ceremony, furniture &c.); सन्मंगलोपचाराणां R. 10. 77; Ku. 7. 88; R. 6. 1 (the Upachâras or articles of worship are variously numbered, being 5, 10, 16, 18 or 64). **10** Behaviour, conduct, demeanour; वैश्यशूद्रोपचारं च Ms. 1. 116. **11** Employment, use. **12** Any religious performance, a ceremony;

प्रयुक्तपाणिग्रहणोपचारौ Ku. 7. 86; Mv. 1. 24. 13 (*a*) Figurative or metaphorical use, secondary application (opp. मुख्य or primary sense); अचेतनेपि चेतनवदुपचारदर्शनात् S. B.; न चास्य करधृतत्वं तत्त्वतोस्तीति मुख्येपि उपचार एव शरणं स्यात् K. P. 10. (*b*) Supposed or fancied indentification founded on resemblance; उभयरूपा चेयं शुद्धा उपचारेणामिश्रितत्वात् K. P. 2. 14 A bribe. 15 A pretext; *Si.* 10-2. 16 A request, solicitation. 17 Occurrence of स् and ष् in the place of Visarga,

उपचितिः *f.* Accumulation, collection; growth, increase.

उपचूलनं Heating, burning.

उपच्छदः A coverlet.

उपच्छंदनं 1 Coaxing, persuading; उपच्छदनैरेव स्वं ते दापयितुं प्रयतिष्यते Dk. 65. 2 Inviting.

उपजनः 1 Addition, increase. 2 Appendage. 3 Rise, origin.

उपजल्पनं-ल्पितं Talk.

उपजापः 1 Secretly whispering into the ear or communicating; परकृत्य° Mu. 2. 2 Secret overtures or negotiations (with the enemy's friends), sowing the seeds of dissension instigating to rebellion; उपजापः कृतस्तेन तानाकोपवतस्त्वयि *Si.* 2. 99; उपजापसहान् विलंघयन् स विधाता नृपतीन्मदोद्धतः Ki. 2. 47, 16. 42. 3 Disunion, separation.

उपजीवक, -विन् *a.* Living upon, subsisting by (instr. or in comp.); जातिमात्रोपजीविनां Ms. 12. 114, 8. 20; नानापण्योपजीविनां 9. 257; यतोपजीव्यस्मि Mk. 2. —*m.* A dependant, servant; भीमकांतैर्नृपगुणैः स बभूवोपजीविनाम् R. 1. 16.

उपजीवनं, -जीविका 1 Living. 2 Subsistence, livlihood; निंदितार्थोपजीवनं Y. 3. 236. 3 A means of living, such as property; किंचिद्दत्वोपजीवनं Ms. 9. 207.

उपजीव्य *pot. p.* 1 Affording a livelihood; Y. 2. 227. 2 Giving patronage, patronizing. 3 (fig.) Supplying materials for writing, that from which one derives materials; सर्वेषां कविमुख्यानामुपजीव्यो भविष्यति Mb. **—व्यः** 1 A patron. 2 A source or authority (from which one derives his materials); इत्यलमुपजीव्यानां मान्यानां व्याख्यानेषु कटाक्षनिक्षेपेण S. D. 2.

उपजोषः-षणं 1 Affection. 2 Enjoy ment. 3 Frequenting.

उपज्ञा 1 Knowledge acquired by oneself and not handed down by tradition, invention, usually in comp. which is treated as a neuter noun; पाणिनेरुपज्ञा पाणिन्युपज्ञं ग्रंथः Sk.; प्राचेतसोपज्ञं रामायणं R. 15. 63. 2 Undertaking or commencing a thing not done before; लोकेऽभूयदुपज्ञमेव विदुषां सौजन्यजन्यं यशः Malli. on Raghuvamsa.

उपढौकनं A respectful offering or present, *Nazarânâ.*

उपतापः 1 Heat, warmth. 2 Trouble, distress, pain, sorrow; सर्वथा न कंचन न स्पृशंत्युपतापाः K. 135. 3 Calamity, misfortune. 4 Sickness. 5 Haste, hurry.

उपतापनं 1 Heating. 2 Distressing, tormenting.

उपतापिन् *a.* 1 Heating, inflaming. 2 Suffering heat or pain, being sick.

उपतिष्यं 1 N. of the lunar mansion or asterism called अश्लेषा. 2 N. of another asterism called पुनर्वसु.

उपत्यका A land at the foot of a mountain, low land; मलयाद्रेरुपत्यकाः R. 4. 46; एते खलु हिमवतो गिरेरुपत्यकारण्यवासिनः संप्राप्ताः *S.* 5.

उपदंशः 1 Anything which excites thirst or appetite, a relish, condiment &c.; द्वित्रानुपदंशानुपपाद्य Dk. 133; अग्रमांसोपदंशं पिब नवशोणितासवं Ve. 3. 2 Biting, stinging. 3 The venereal disease.

उपदश *a.* (pl.) About or nearly ten.

उपदर्शकः 1 One who shows the way, a guide. 2 A door-keeper. 3 A witness.

उपदा 1 A present, an offering to a king or a great man a *Nazarânâ*; उपदा विविशुः शश्वन्नोत्सेकाः कोशलेश्वरं R. 4. 70, 5. 41, 7. 30. 2 A bribe.

उपदानं,—नकं 1 An oblation, a present (in genearal). 2 A gift made for procuring favour or protection, such as a bribe.

उपदिश् *f.*, **उपदिशा** 1 An intermediate quarter, such as ऐशानी, आग्नेयी नैर्ऋती and वायवी.

उपदेवः —देवता A minor or inferior god.

उपदेशः 1 Instruction, teaching, advice, prescription; सुशीशिक्षितापि सर्व उपदेशेन निपुणो भवति M. 1; स्थिरोपदेशामुपदेशकाले प्रपेदिरे प्राक्तनजन्मविद्याः Ku. 1. 30; M. 2. 10; S. 2. 3; Ms. 8. 272; Amaru. 26; R. 12. 57; परोपदेशे पांडित्यं H. 1. 103. 2 Specification, mentioning. 3 A plea, pretext. 4 Initiation, communication of an initiatory Mantra or formula; चंद्रसूर्यग्रहे तीर्थे सिद्धक्षेत्रे शिवालये । मंत्रमात्रप्रकथनमुपदेशः स उच्यते ॥.

उपदेशक *a.* Giving instruction, teaching. **-कः** An instructor, a guide, preceptor.

उपदेशनं Advising, instructing.

उपदेशिन् *a.* Advising, instructing.

उपदेष्टृ *a.* Giving instruction or advice. —*m.* (**ष्टा**) A teacher, preceptor; especially a spiritual preceptor; चत्वारो वयमृत्विजः स भगवान्कर्मोपदेष्टा हरिः Ve. 1. 23.

उपदेहः 1 An ointment. 2 A cover.

उपदोहः 1 A nipple of the udder of a cow. 2 A milking vessel.

उपद्रवः 1 An unhappy accident, misfortune, calamity. 2 Injury, trouble, harm; पुंसामसमर्थानामुपद्रवायात्मनो भवेत्कोपः Pt. 1. 324; निरुपद्रवं स्थानं Pt. 1. 3 Outrage, violence. 4 A national distress (whether caused by the king or famine, seasons &c.). 5 A national disturbance, rebellion. 6 A symptom, a supervenient disease.

उपधर्मः A by-law, a secondary or minor religious precept (opp. पर); Ms. 2. 237, 4. 147.

उपधा 1 Imposition, forgery, fraud, deceit; Ms. 8. 193. 2 Trial or test of honesty, (धर्माद्यैर्यत्परीक्षणं); (said to be of 4 kinds: 1 loyalty, 2 disinterestedness, 3 continence, 4 courage); (शोधयेत्) धर्मोपधाभिर्विप्रांश्च सर्वाभिः सचिवान् पुनः Kâlikâ P. 3 A means or expedient; अयशोभिदुरा लोके कोपधा मरणादृते *Si.* 19. 58. 4 (In gram.) A penultimate letter. –Comp. **-भृतः** a servant who has been guilty of dishonesty. **–शुचि** *a.* tried, of approved loyalty.

उपधातुः 1 An inferior metal, semimetal. They are seven; सप्तोपधातवः स्वर्णं माक्षिकं तारमाक्षिकं । तुत्थं कांस्यं च रीतिश्च सिंदूरं च शिलाजतु ॥. 2 A secondary secretion of the body (six in number); स्तन्यं रजो वसा स्वेदो दंताः केशास्तथैव च । औज्यस्यं सप्तधातूनां क्रमात्सप्तोपधातवः ॥.

उपधानं 1 Placing or resting upon. 2 A Pillow, cushion; विपुलमुपधानं भुजलता Bh. 3. 79. 3 Puculiarity, individuality. 4 Affection, kindness. 5 A religious observance. 6 Excellence or excellent quality; सोपाधानां धियं धीराः स्थेयसीं खट्वांति ये *Si.* 2. 77 (where उ. also means a pillow). 7 Poison.

उपधानीयं A pillow.

उपधारणं 1 Consideration, reflection. 2 Drawing, pulling (as by a hook).

उपधिः 1 Fraud, dishonesty; अरिषु हि विजयार्थिनः क्षितीशा विदधति सोपधि संधिदूषणानि Ki. 1. 45, see अनुपधि also. 2 (In law) Suppression of the truth, a false suggestion; Ms. 8. 165. 3 Terror, threat, compulsion, false inducement; बलोपधिविनिर्वृत्तान् व्यवहारान्निवर्तयेत् Y. 2. 31, 89. 4 The part of a wheel between the nave and the circumference, or the wheel itself.

उपधिकः A cheat, knave; see औपधिक the more correct form.

उपधूपित *a.* 1 Fumigated. 2 Being at the point of death. 3 Suffering extreme pain. **—तः** Death.

उपधृतिः *f.* A ray of light.

उपध्मानः A lip. **—नं** Blowing upon, breathing.

उपध्मानीयः The aspirate Visarga before the letters प and फ्; उपूपध्मानीयानामोष्ठौ Sk.

उपनक्षत्रं A subordinate constellation, secondary star (their number is said to be 729).

उपनगरं A suburb

उपनत *p.p.* Come, arrived, got, befallen &c. ; नम् with उप.

उपनतिः *f.* 1 Approach. 2 Bending, bow, salutation.

उपनयः 1 Bringing near, fetching. 2 Gaining, attaining, procuring. 3 Employing. 4 Investiture with the sacred thread, initiation into sacred study ; गृह्योक्तकर्मणा येन समीपं नीयते गुरोः । बालो वेदाय तद्योगात् बालस्योपनयं विदुः ॥. 5 The fourth member of the five-membered Indian syllogism (in logic), the application to the special case in question ; व्याप्तिविशिष्टस्य हेतोः पक्षधर्मताप्रतिपादकं वचनमुपनयः Tarka K.

उपनयनं 1 Leading to or near. 2 Presenting, offering. 3 Investiture with the sacred thread ; आसमावर्तनात्कुर्यात् कृतोपनयनो द्विजः Ms. 2. 108, 173.

उपनागरिका A variety of वृत्त्यनुप्रास. It is formed by sweetsounding letters (माधुर्यव्यंजकवर्ण); *e.g.* cf. the example cited in K. P. 9; अपसारय घनसारं कुरु हारं दूर एव किं कमलैः । अलमलमालि मृणालैरिति वदति दिवानिशं बाला ॥

उपनायः,नायनं =उपनय q. v.

उपनायकः 1 A character in a dramatic or any other work of art next in importance to the hero; *e. g.* Lakshmaṇa in Râm.; Makaranda in Mâl. &c. &c. 2 A paramonr.

उपनायिका A character in a dramatic or any other work of art next in importance to the heroine; *e. g.* Madayantikâ in Mâl.

उपनाहः 1 A bundle. 2 An unguent applied to a wound or sore. 3 The tie of a lute, a peg to which the strings of a lyre are attached and by which they are tightened .

उपनाहनं 1 Applying an unguent. 2 Anointing, plastering.

उपनिक्षेपः 1 The act of depositing or placing down. 2 An open deposit, any article given in another's charge by letting him know its form, quantity &c.; Y. 2. 25; (on which Mit. says:—उपनिक्षेपो नाम रूपसंख्याप्रदर्शनेन रक्षणार्थं परस्य हस्ते निहितं द्रव्यं).

उपनिधानं 1 Placing near. 2 Depositing, entrusting to one's care. 3 A deposit.

उपनिधिः 1 A deposit, pledge. 2 (In law) A sealed deposit; Y. 2. 25; Ms. 8. 145, 149; cf. Medhâtithi:—यद्प्रदर्शितरूपं सचिह्नवस्त्रादिना पिहितं निक्षिप्यते; also cf. Y. 2. 65 and Nârada quoted in Mit.

उपनिपातः 1 Approaching, coming near. 2 A sudden and unexpected attack or occurrence.

उपनिपातिन् *a.* Coming (unexpectedly); रंध्रोपनिपातिनोऽनर्थाः *S.* 6.

उपनिबंधनं 1 A means of accomplishment. 2 Binding.

उपनिमंत्रणं Invitation, inauguration.

उपनिवेशित *a.* Placed, established, colonized ; Ku. 6. 37 ; R. 15. 29.

उपनिषद् *f.* 1 N. of certain mystical writings attached to the Brâhmaṇas, the chief aim of which is to ascertain the secret meaning of the Vedas ; Bv. 2. 40 ; Mâl. 1. 7 ; (the following etymologies are given to explain the name :— (1) उपनीय तमात्मानं ब्रह्मापास्तद्वयं यतः । निहंत्यविद्यां तज्जं च तस्मादुपनिषद्भवेत् ॥ or (2) निहत्यानर्थमूलं स्वाविद्यां प्रत्यक्तया परं । नयत्यपास्तसंभेदमतो वोपनिषद्भवेत् ॥ or (3) प्रवृत्तिहेतून्निःशेषांस्तन्मूलोच्छेदकत्वतः । यतोवसादयेद्विद्यां तस्मादुपनिषद्भवेत् ॥. In the मुक्तकोपनिषद् 108 Upanishads are mentioned, but some more have been added to this number. 2 (*a*) An esoteric or secret doctrine. (*b*) Mystical knowledge or instruction ; Mv. 2. 2. 3 True knowledge regarding the Supreme Spirit. 4 Sacred or religious lore. 5 Secrecy, seclusion. 6 A neighbouring mansion.

उपनिष्करः A street, a principal road, high way.

उपनिष्क्रमणं 1 Going out, issuing. 2 One of the Samskâras or religious rites, *i. e.* taking out a child for the first time into the open air (which is usually performed in the fourth month of its age) ; cf. Ms. 2. 34. 3 A main or royal road.

उपनृत्यं A place for dancing.

उपनेतृ *a.* One who leads or brings near, fetching; Ku. 1. 60; मालत्यभिज्ञानस्योपनेत्री Mâl. 9. —*m.* (ता) A preceptor who performs the उपनयन ceremony.

उपन्यासः 1 Placing near to, jaxtaposition. 2 A deposit, pledge. 3 (*a*) Statement, suggestion, proposal; पावकः खलु एष वचनोपन्यासः *S.* 5. (*b*) Preface, introduction; निर्यातः शनकैरलीकवचनोपन्यासमालीजनः Amaru. 23; (*c*) Allusion, reference; आत्मन उपन्यासपूर्व *S.* 3. 4 A precept, law.

उपपतिः A paramour; उपपतिरिव नीचैः पश्चिमांतेन चंद्रः *Si.* 11. 65, 15. 63; Ms. 3. 155; 4. 216, 217.

उपपत्तिः *f.* 1 Happening, occurring, appearance, production, birth; *Si.* 1, 69 ; Bg. 13. 9. 2 Cause, reason, ground ; Ki. 3. 52. 3 Reasoning, argument ; उपपत्तिमदूर्जितं वचः Ki. 2. 1 argumentative. 4 Fitness, propriety. 5 Ascertainment, demonstration, demonstrated conclusion; उपपत्तिरुदाहृता बलात् Ki. 2. 28. 6 (In Arith. or Geom.) Proof, demonstration. 7 A means, an expedient. 8 Doing, effecting, gaining, accomplishment ; स्वार्थोपपत्ति दुर्बलाशः R. 5. 12; तात्पर्यानुपपत्तितः Bhâshâ P.; see अनुपपत्ति. 9 Attainment getting ; असंशयं प्राक् तनयोपपत्तेः R. 14. 78; Ki. 3. 1.

उपपदं 1 A word prefixed or previously uttered ; धनुरुपपदं वेदं Ki. 18. 44. (धनुर्वेदं); तस्याः स राजोपपदं निशांतं R. 16. 40. 2 A title, a degree ; epithet of respect, such as आर्य, शर्मन् ; कथं निरुपपदमेव चाणक्यमिति न आर्यचाणक्यमिति Mu. 3. 3 A secondary word of a sentence, a preposition, particle &c. prefixed to a verb or a noun derived from a verb which determines or qualifies the sense of the verb.

उपपन्न *p. p.* 1 Obtained ; attended by, in company with, endowed with. 2 Right, fit, proper, suitable (with gen. or loc.); उपपन्नमिदं विशेषणं वायोः V. 2; उपपन्नमेतदस्मिन् राजनि *S.* 2.

उपपरीक्षा-क्षणं Investigation, examination.

उपपातः 1 An unexpected occurrence. 2 A calamity, misfortune, accident.

उपपातकं A minor sin, crime or sin of the second degree ; महापातकतुल्यानि पापान्युक्तानि यानि तु । तानि पातकसंज्ञानि तन्न्यूनमुपपातकम् ॥ ; Y. 2. 210.

उपपादनं 1 Effecting, accomplishing, doing. 2 Giving, delivering, presenting. 3 Proving, demonstration, establishing by arguments. 4 Examination, ascertainment.

उपपापं=उपपातकं q. v.

उपपार्श्वः-र्श्वं 1 A shoulder. 2 A flank, side. 3 The opposite side.

उपपीडनं 1 Pressting down, devastating, laying waste. 2 Inflicting pain, injuring ; व्याधिभिश्चोपपीडनं Ms. 6. 62, 12. 80. 3 Pain, agony.

उपपुरं A suburb.

उपपुराणं A secondary or minor Purâṇa (for an enumeration of their names, see under अष्टादशन्).

उपपुष्पिका Yawning, gaping.

उपप्रदर्शनं Pointing out, indication.

उपप्रदानं 1 Delivering over, entrusting. 2 A bribe, present ; उपप्रदानैर्मार्जारो हितकृत्प्रार्थ्यते जनैः Pt. 1. 95. 3 A tribute.

उपप्रलोभनं 1 Seducing, alluring. 2 A bribe, an inducement, allurement; उच्चावचान्युपप्रलोभनानि Dk. 48.

उपप्रेक्षणं Overlooking, disregarding.

उपप्रैषः Invitation, summons.

उपप्लवः 1 Misfortune, evil, calamity, distress, adversity; अथ मदनवधूरुपप्लवांतं... परिपालयांबभूव Ku. 4. 46 ; जीवन्पुनः शश्वदुपप्लवेभ्यः प्रजाः पासि R. 2. 48. 2 (*a*) An unlucky accident, injury, trouble ; कच्चिन्न वाय्वादिरुपप्लवो वः R. 5. 6 ; Me. 17. (*b*) An obstacle, impediment. 3 Oppression, harassing, troubling ; उपप्लवाय लोकानां धूमकेतुरिवोत्थितः Ku. 2. 32. 4 Danger, fear ; see उपप्लविन् below. 5

A portent or natural phenomenon forboding evil. 6 Particularly, an eclipse of the sun or moon. 7 N. of Râhu, the ascending node. 8 Anarchy.

उपप्लविन् *a.* 1 Distressed, troubled. 2 Suffering oppression ; नृपा इवोपप्लविनः परेभ्यः R. 13. 7.

उपबंधः 1 Connection. 2 An affix. 3 A particular mode of sexual enjoyment.

उपबर्हः-र्हणं A pillow.

उपबहु *a.* A few, a tolerable number.

उपबाहुः The lower arm.

उपभंगः 1 Fleeing away, retreat. 2 A division (of a verse).

उपभाषा A secondary dialect.

उपभृत् *f.* A round cup used in sacrifices.

उपभोगः 1 (*a.*) Enjoyment, eating, tasting; न जातु कामः कामानामुपभोगेन शाम्यति Ms. 2. 94, Y. 2. 171; काम° Bg. 16. 11. (*b*) Use, application ; *S*. 4. 4. 2 Enjoyment (of a woman), cohabitation ; R. 14. 24. 3 Usufruct. 4 Pleasure, satisfaction.

उपमंत्रणं 1 The act of addressing, inviting, calling. 2 Persuading (उपच्छंदनं).

उपमंथनी A staff for stirring (fire).

उपमर्दः 1 Friction, rubbing or pressing down, crushing under one's weight ; अन्यासु तावदुपमर्दसहासु भृंग लोलं विनोदय मनः सुमनोलतासु S. D. (where उ० also means rough handling or enjoyment). 2 Destruction, injury, killing. 3 Reproach, abuse, insult. 4 Unhusking. 5 Refutation of a charge.

उपमा 1 Resemblance, similarity, equality; स्फुटोपमं भूतिसितेन शंभुना *Si*. 1. 4, 17. 69. 2 (In Rhet.) Comparison of two objects different from each other, simile, comparison ; साधर्म्यमुपमा भेदे K. P. 10; or सादृश्यं सुंदरं वाक्यार्थोपस्कारकमुपमालंकृतिः R. G.; or उपमा यत्र सादृश्यलक्ष्मीरुल्लसति द्वयोः । हंसीव कृष्ण ते कीर्तिः स्वर्गीगानवगाहते ॥ Chandr. 5. 3; उपमा कालिदासस्य Subhâsh. 3 The standard of comparison (उपमान); यथा दीपो निवातस्थो नेंगते सोपमा स्मृता Bg. 6. 19 ; see °द्रव्य below; mostly at the end of comp., 'like,' 'resembling'; बुबुधे न बुधोपमः R. 1. 47; so अमरोपम, अनुपम &c. 4 A likeness (as a picture, portrait &c.). –Comp. –द्रव्यं any object used for a comparison ; सर्वोपमाद्रव्यसमुच्चयेन Ku. 1. 49.

उपमातृ *f.* 1 'A second mother,' wet nurse. 2 A near female relative; मातृष्वसा मातुलानी पितृव्यस्त्री पितृष्वसा । श्वश्रूः पूर्वजपत्नी च मातृतुल्याः प्रकीर्तिताः *S*abdak.

उपमानं 1 Comparison, resemblance; जातास्तदूर्वोरुपमानबाह्याः Ku. 1. 36. 2 The standard of comparison, that with which anything is compared (opp. उपमेय); one of the four requisites of an उपमा; उपमानमभूद्विलासिनां Ku. 4. 5 ; उपमानस्यापि सखे प्रत्युपमानं वपुस्तस्याः V. 2. 3; *S*i. 20. 49. 3 (In Nyâya phil.) Analogy, recognition of likeness, considered as one of the four kinds of pramanas or means of arriving at correct knowledge. It is defined as प्रसिद्धसाधर्म्यात् साध्यसाधनं ; or उपमितिकरणमुपमानं तच्च सादृश्यज्ञानात्मकं Tarka K.

उपमितिः *f.* 1 Resemblance, comparison, similarity ; पल्लवोपमितिसाम्यसपक्षं S. D.; तदाननस्योपमितौ दरिद्रता N. 1. 24. 2 (In Nyâya phil.) Analogy, deduction, knowledge of things derived from analogy, a conclusion deduced by means of an उपमानः प्रत्यक्षमप्यनुमितिस्तथोपमितिशब्दजे Bhâshâ P. 52. 3 A figure of speech=उपमा q. v.

उपमेय *pot. p.* Fit to be likened or compared, comparable with ; (with instr. or in comp.); भूयिष्ठमासीदुपमेयकांतिः गुहेन R. 6. 4 ; 18. 34, 37; Ku. 7. 2. –यं The subject of comparison, that which is compared (opp. उपमान); उपमानोपमेयत्वं यदेकस्यैव वस्तुनः Chandr. 5. 7. 9. –Comp. –उपमा a figure of speech in which the उपमान and उपमेय are compared to each other with a view to imply that the like of them does not exist ; विपर्यास उपमेयोपमानयोः K. P. 10.

उपयंतृ *m.* A husband; अथोपयंतारमलं समाधिना Ku. 5. 45; R. 7. 1. *S*i. 10. 45.

उपयंत्रं A minor surgical instrument.

उपयमः 1 Marriage, marrying ; कन्या त्वजातोपयमा सलज्जा नवयौवना S. D. 2 Restraint.

उपयमनं 1 Marrying. 2 Restraining 3 Placing down the fire.

उपयष्टृ *m.* One who repeats उपयज्, one of the 16 priests at a sacrifice.

उपयाचक *a.* One who asks or solicits, suitor, beggar.

उपयाचनं Soliciting, begging, approaching with a request or prayer.

उपयाचित *p.p.* Begged, requested. –तं 1 A request or prayer in general. 2 A present promised to a deity for the fulfilment of a desired object and generally to propitiate her, (the present may be an animal or even a human being); निक्षेपी म्रियते तुभ्यं प्रदास्याम्युपयाचितं Pt. 1. 14 ; अद्य मया भगवत्याः करालायाः प्रागुपयाचितं स्त्रीरत्नमुपहर्तव्यं Mâl. 5. 3 A request or prayer to a deity for the accomplishment of a desired object.

उपयाचितकं=उपयाचित above ; सिद्धायतनानि कृतविविधदेवतोपयाचितकानि K. 64.

उपयाजः Additional formulæ at a sacrifice.

उपयानं Approaching, coming near; हरोपयाने त्वरिता बभूव Ku. 7. 22.

उपयुक्त *p. p.* 1 Attached &c. 2 Fit, right, proper. 3 Serviceable, useful.

उपयोगः 1 Employment, use, application, service ; व्यंजितं...अनंगलेखक्रियोपयोगं Ku. 1. 7. 2 Administration of medicine or preparation of them. 3 Fitness, suitableness, propriety. 4 Contact, proximity.

उपयोगिन् *a.* 1 Employing, using. 2 Serviceable, useful. 3 Fit, proper.

उपरक्त *p. p.* 1 Afflicted, overtaken by calamity, distressed. 2 Eclipsed. 3 Tinged, coloured; *S*i. 2. 18. –क्तः The sun or moon in eclipse.

उपरक्षः A body-guard.

उपरक्षणं A guard, an out-post.

उपरत *p. p.* 1 Stopped, ceased ; रजस्युपरते Ms. 5. 66. 2 Dead ; अद्य दशमो मासस्तातस्योपरतस्य Mu. 4. –Comp. –कर्मन् *a.* not relying on worldly acts. –स्पृह *a.* void of desire, indifferent to worldly attachments or possessions.

उपरतिः *f.* 1 Ceasing, stopping, 2 Death. 3 Abstaining from sexual enjoyment. 4 Indifference. 5 Abstaining from prescribed acts; the conviction that ceremonial acts are futile and ceasing to rely on them.

उपरत्नं A secondary or inferior gem; उपरत्नानि काचश्च कर्पूरोऽश्मा तथैव च । मुक्ता शुक्तिस्तथा शंख इत्यादीनि बहून्यपि ॥ गुणा यथैव रत्नानामुपरत्नेषु ते तथा । किंतु किंचित्ततो हीना विशेषोऽयमुदाहृतः ॥.

उपर (रा) मः 1 Ceasing, stopping. 2 Abstaining from, giving up. 3 Death.

उपरमणं 1 Abstaining from sexual pleasures. 2 Refraining from ceremonial acts. 3 Ceasing, stopping.

उपरसः 1 A secondary mineral. 2 A secondary passion or feeling. 3 A subordinate flavour.

उपरागः 1 An eclipse of the sun or moon: उपरागांते शशिनः समुपगता रोहिणी योगं *S*. 7. 22 ; *S*i. 20. 45. 2 Hence, Râhu or the ascending node. 3 Redness, red colour; colour. 4 A calamity, affliction, injury ; मृणालिनी हैममिवोपरागं R. 16. 7. 5 Reproach, blame, abuse.

उपराजः A viceroy, one inferior to the ruling authority.

उपरि *ind.* 1 As a separable preposition (usually with gen., rarely with acc. or loc.) it means (*a*) Above, over, upon, on, towards ; (opp. अधः) (with gen. ; गतमुपरि घनानां *S*. 7. 7 ; अवाङ्मुखस्योपरि वृष्टिः पपात R. 2. 60 ; अर्कस्योपरि *S*. 2. 8; oft. at the end of comp.; रथ°, तरुवर°. (*b*) At the end of, at the head of ; सर्वानंदानामुपरि वर्तमाना K. 158. (*c*) Beyond, in addition, to Y. 2. 253. (*d*) In connection with, with regard to, towards, upon; परस्परस्योपरि पर्यचीयत R. 3. 24 ; Sânti. 3. 23 ; तवोपरी प्रायोपवेशनं करिष्यामि

on your account. (*e*) After; मुहूर्तादुपरि उपाध्यायश्चेदागच्छेत् P. III. 3. 9 Sk. उपरि joined to उपरि (with acc. or gen. or by itself) means (*a*) Just above; लोकानुपर्युपर्यास्ते माधवः Vop. (*b*) higher and higher, far high, high above, उपर्युपरि सर्वेषामादित्य इव तेजसा Mb. **2** (As a separable adverb) It means (*a*) high above, upon, towards the upper side of (opp. अधः); उपर्युपरि पश्यंतः सर्व एव दरिद्रति H. 2. 2; oft. in comp.; स्वमुद्रोपरिचिह्नितं Y. 1. 319. (*b*) Besides, in addition, further, more; शतान्युपरि चैवाष्टौ तथा भूयश्च सप्ततिः Mb. (*c*) Afterwards; यदा पूर्वं नासीदुपरि च तथा नैव भविता Sânti. 2. 7; सर्पिः पीत्वोपरि पयः पिबेत् Susr.–Comp. **–चर** *a.* moving above (as a bird). **–तन, –स्थ** *a.* upper, higher. **–भागः** the upper, portion or side. **–भावः** being above or higher. **–भूमिः** *f.* the ground above.

उपरिष्टात् *ind.* [cf. P. V. 3. 31] **1** As an adverb it means (*a*) Over, above, on high; Bh. 3. 131; Y. 1. 106. (*b*) Further or later on, afterwards; कल्याणावतंसा हि कल्याणसंपदुपरिष्टाद्भवति Mâl. 6; इदमुपरिष्टात् व्याख्यातं in the sequel. (*c*) Behind (opp. पुरस्तात्). **2** (As a preposition) it means (*a*) Over, upon (with gen., rarely acc.); Si. 11. 3. (*b*) Down upon. (*c*) Behind (with gen.).

उपरीतकः A particular mode or posture of sexual enjoyment; (also called विपरीतक); ऊरावेकपदं कृत्वा द्वितीयं स्कंधसंस्थितं। नारीं कामयते कामी बंधः स्यादुपरीतकः ॥ Sabdak.

उपरूपकं A drama of an inferior class, of which 18 kinds are enumerated; नाटिका त्रोटकं गोष्ठी सट्टकं नाट्यरासकं। प्रस्थानोल्लाप्यकाव्यानि प्रेंखणं रासकं तथा ॥ संलापकं श्रीगदितं शिल्पकं च विलासिका। दुर्मल्लिका प्रकरणी हल्लीशो भाणिकेति च ॥ S. D. 276.

उपरोधः **1** Obstruction, impediment, obstacle; R. 6. 44; Si. 20. 74. **2** Disturbance, trouble; तपोवननिवासिनामुपरोधो मा भूत् S. 1; अनुग्रहः खल्वेष नोपरोधः V. 3. **3** Covering, surrounding, blocking up. **4** Protection, favour.

उपरोधक *a.* **1** Obstructing. **2** Covering, surrounding. **–कं** An inner room, a private apartment.

उपरोधनं Obstruction, impediment &c.; see उपरोध.

उपलः **1** A stone, rock; उपलशकलमेतद्भेदकं गोमयानां Mu. 3. 15; कांते कथं घटितवानुपलेन चेतः S. Til. 3; Me. 19; S. 1. 14. **2** A precious stone, jewel.

उपलकः A stone. **–ला** **1** Sand. **2** Refined sugar.

उपलक्षणं **1** Looking at, beholding, marking; वेलांपलक्षणार्थं S. 4. **2** A mark, characteristic or distinctive feature; V. 4. 33. **3** Designation. **4** Implying something that has not been actually expressed, implication of something in addition or any similar object where only one is mentioned; synecdoche of a part for the whole, of an individual for the species, &c. (स्वप्रतिपादकत्वे सति स्वेतरप्रतिपादकत्वं); मंत्रग्रहणं ब्राह्मणस्याप्युपलक्षणं P. II. 4. 80 Sk.

उपलब्धिः *f.* **1** Getting, obtaining, acquisition; वृथा हि मे स्यात्स्वपदोपलब्धिः R. 5. 56, 8. 17. **2** Observation, perception, knowledge (ज्ञान); नाभाव उपलब्धेः cf. Nyâya S. 2. 28. **3** Understanding, mind (मति). **4** A conjecture or guess. **5** Perceptibility, appearance (recognized as a kind of proof by the Mîmâmsakas); see अनुपलब्धि.

उपलंभः **1** Acquisition; अस्मादंगुलीयोपलंभात्स्मृतिरुपलब्धा S. 7. **2** Direct perception or recognition, comprehension otherwise than from memory (same as अनुभव q. v.) प्राक्तनोपलंभ Mâl. 5; ज्ञातौ सुतस्पर्शसुखोपलंभात् R. 14. 2. **3** Ascertaining, knowing; अविघ्नक्रियोपलंभाय S. 1.

उपलालनं Fondling.

उपलालिका Thirst.

उपलिंगं A portent, natural phenomenon, considered as boding evil.

उपलिप्सा A desire to obtain.

उपलेपः **1** Anointiug, smearing. **2** Cleaniug, white-washing. **3** Obstruction; becoming deadened or dull (said of senses).

उपलेपनं **1** Smearing, anointing, plastering. **2** An ointment, unguent.

उपवनं A garden, grove, a planted forest; पांडुच्छायोपवनवृतय; केतकैः सूचिभिन्नैः Me. 23; R. 8. 73, 13. 79; °लता a garden creeper.

उपवर्णः Minute or detailed description.

उपवर्णनं Minute description, delineation in detail; अतिशयोपवर्णनं व्याख्यानं Susr.; Y. 1320.

उपवर्तनं **1** A place for exercise. **2** A district or *Parganâ.* **3** A kingdom (राज्य) **4** A bog, marshy place.

उपवसथः A village.

उपवस्तं A fast.

उपवासः **1** A fast; सोपवासस्त्र्यहम् वसेत् Y. 1. 175, 3. 190; Ms. 11. 196. **2** Kindling a sacred fire.

उपवाहनं Carrying to, bringing near.

उपवाह्यः,–ह्या **1** A king's riding elephant (male or female); चंद्रगुप्तोपवाह्यां गजवशां Mu. 2. **2** A royal vehicle (in general).

उपविद्या Profane science, inferior kind of knowledge.

उपविषः–षं **1** An artificial poison. **2** A narcotic, any poisonous drug; अर्कक्षीरं स्नुहीक्षीरं तथैव कालिहारिका। धत्तूरः करवीरश्च पंच चोपविषाः स्मृताः ॥

उपवीणयति Den. P. To play on the Vînâ or lute (before a deity &c.); उपवीणयितुं ययौ रवेरुदयावृत्तिपथेन नारदः R. 8. 33; N. 6. 65; Ki. 10. 38.

उपवीतं **1** Investiture with the sacred thread. **2** The sacred thread worn by the first three classes of Hindus; पित्र्यमंशमुपवीतलक्षणं मातृकं च धनुरूर्जितं दधत् R. 11. 64; Ku. 6. 6; Si. 1. 7; Ms. 2. 44, 64, 4. 36.

उपबृंहणं Increase, collection.

उपवेदः 'Inferior knowledge', a class of writings subordinate to the Vedas. There are four such *Upavedas*, one being attached to each of the four Vedas:—thus आयुर्वेद or Medicine to ऋग्वेद; (according to some authorities such as Susruta it is a part of the Atharvaveda); धनुर्वेद or military science to यजुर्वेद; गांधर्ववेद or Music to सामवेद, and स्थापत्यशास्त्र-वेद or Mechanics to अथर्ववेद.

उपवेशः–शनं **1** Sitting, sitting down; as in प्रायोपवेशन. **2** Being attached to. **3** Voiding by stool.

उपवैणवं The three periods of the day; *i. e.* morning, midday, and evening (त्रिसंध्यं).

उपव्याख्यानं A supplementary explanation or interpretation.

उपव्याघ्रः A small hunting leopard.

उपशमः **1** Becoming quiet, assuagement, pacification; कुतोऽस्या उपशमः Ve. 3; मन्युर्दुःसह एष यात्युपशमं नो सांत्ववादैः स्फुटं Amaru. 5; cessation, stopping, extinction. **2** Relaxation, intermission. **3** Tranquility, calmness, patience. **4** Control or restraint of the senses.

उपशमनं **1** Quieting, calming, appeasing. **2** Mitigation. **3** Extinction, cessation.

उपशयः **1** Lying by the side of. **2** A lair, ambush; Si. 2. 80.

उपशल्यं An open place in the vicinity of a town or village, suburb; अथोपशल्ये रिपुमग्नशल्यः R. 16. 37, 15. 50; Si. 5. 8.

उपशाखा A secondary branch.

उपशांतिः *f.* **1** Cessation, allaying, alleviation; R. 8. 31; Amaru. 65. **2** Appeasing, assuaging.

उपशायः Sleeping in turn, rotation for sleeping with (another who keeps watch at night.)

उपशालं A place near a house, a court before a house. **—लं** *ind.* Near a house.

उपशास्त्रं A minor science or treatise.

उपशिक्षा–क्षणं Learning, training.

उपशिष्यः The pupil of a pupil; शिष्योपशिष्यैरुपगीयमानमवेहि तन्मंडनमिश्रधाम Udb.

उपशोभनं,–शोभा Adorning, ornamenting.

उपशोषणं Drying up, withering.

उपश्रुतिः *f.* 1 Hearing, listening. 2 Range of hearing. 3 A supernatural voice heard at night and personified as a nocturnal deity revealing the future; नक्तं निर्गत्य यत्किंचिच्छुभाशुभकरं वचः । श्रूयते तद्विदुर्धीरा देवप्रश्नमुपश्रुतिं ॥ Hârâvali; परिजनोऽपि चास्याः सततमुपश्रुत्यै निर्जगाम K. 65. 4 Promise, assent.

उपश्लेषः,-षणं 1 Juxta-position, contact 2 An embrace.

उपश्लोकयति Den. P. To extol or praise in verses.

उपसंयमः 1 Curbing, restraining, binding. 2 The end of the world, universal destruction.

उपसंयोगः A secondary connection, modification.

उपसंरोहः Growing together or over, cicatrizing.

उपसंवादः An agreement, a contract.

उपसंव्यानं An under-garment; अंतरं बहिर्योगोपसंव्यानयोः P. I. 1. 36.

उपसंहरणं 1 Withdrawing, taking away or back. 2 Withholding. 3 Excluding. 4 Attacking, invading.

उपसंहारः 1 Drawing in or together, contracting. 2 Withdrawing, withholding. 3 A collection, assemblage. 4 Summing up, winding up, conclusion. 5 A peroration (of a speech &c.). 6 A compendium, *re'sume'*. 7 Brevity, conciseness. 8 Perfection. 9 Destruction, death. 10 Attacking, invading.

उपसंहारिन् *a.* 1 Comprehending. 2 Exclusive.

उपसंक्षेपः An abstract, summary, re'sume'.

उपसंख्यानं 1 Addition. 2 Supplementary addition, further or additional enumeration (a term technically applied to the *Vârtikas* of Kâtyâyana which are intended to supply omissions in Pâṇini's Sûtras and generally to supplement them.); *e. g.* जुगुप्साविरामप्रमादार्थानामुपसंख्यानं ; cf. इष्टि. 3 (In gram.) A substitute in form or sense.

उपसंग्रहः,-हणं 1 Keeping pleasant, supporting, maintaining 2 Respectful salutation (as by touching the feet of the person saluted); स्फुरति रभसात्पाणिः पादोपसंग्रहणाय च Mv. 2. 30. 3 Accepting, adopting. 4 Polite address, obeisance. 5 Collecting, joining. 6 Taking, accepting (as a wife) दारोपसंग्रहः Y. 1. 56. 7 (An external) appendage, any necessary article either for use or decoration (उपकरण).

उपसत्तिः *f.* 1 Connection, union. 2 Service, worship, attendance upon. 3 Gift, donation.

उपसदः 1 Approach. 2 A gift, donation.

उपसदनं 1 Going near to, approaching. 2 Sitting at the feet of a teacher, becoming a pupil; तत्रोपसदनं चक्रे द्रोणस्येष्वस्त्रकर्मणि Mb. 3 Neighbourhood. 4 Service.

उपसंतानः 1 Immediate connection. 2 A descendant.

उपसंधानं Adding, joining.

उपसंन्यासः Laying down, giving up, resignation.

उपसमाधानं Gathering together, heaping; उपसमाधानं राशीकरणं Sk.

उपसंपत्तिः *f.* 1 Approaching, arriving at. 2 Entering into any condition.

उपसंपन्न *p. p.* 1 Gained. 2 Arrived at. 3 Furnished with, possessing. 4 Killed at a sacrifice (as an animal), immolated; Ms. 5. 81. —**न्नं** Condiment.

उपसंभाषः -षा 1 Conversation; Ki. 3. 3. 2 Friendly persuasion; उपसंभाषा उपसांत्वनं P. I. 3. 47 Sk.

उपसरः 1 Approaching (as a cow). 2 The first pregnancy of a cow; गवामुपसरः Sk.

उपसरणं 1 Going towards. 2 That which is approached as a refuge

उपसर्गः 1 Sickness, disease, change occasioned by a disease; क्षीणं हन्युश्चोपसर्गाः प्रभूताः Susr. 2 Misfortune, trouble, calamity, injury, harm; Ratn. 1. 10. 3 Portent, natural phenomenon foreboding evil. 4 An eclipse. 5 An indication or symptom of death. 6 A preposition prefixed to roots; निपाताश्चादयो ज्ञेयाः प्रादयस्तूपसर्गकाः । द्योतकत्वात् क्रियायोगे लोकादवगता इमे ॥ *Upasargas* are 20 in number:—प्र, परा, अप, सम्, अनु, अव, निस् or निर्, दुस् or दुर्, वि, आ (ङ्), नि, अधि, अपि, अति, सु, उद्, अभि, प्रति, परि, उप; or 22 if निस्-निर् and दुस्-दुर् be taken as separate words. There are two theories as to the character of these prepositions. According to one theory roots have various meanings in themselves (अनेकार्था हि धातवः) when prepositions are prefixed to them they simply bring to light those meanings already existent but hidden in them, but they do not *express* them, being meaningless themselves. According to the other theory prepositions *express* their own independent meanings; they modify, intensify; and sometimes entirely alter, the senses of roots; cf. Sk.:—उपसर्गेण धात्वर्थो बलादन्यत्र नीयते । प्रहाराहारसंहारविहारपरिहारवत् ॥ cf. also धात्वर्थं बाधते कश्चित्कश्चित्तमनुवर्तते । तमेव विशिनष्टयन्य उपसर्गगतिस्त्रिधा ॥.

उपसर्जनं 1 Pouring on. 2 A misfortune, calamity (as an eclipse), portent. 3 Leaving. 4 Eclipsing. 5 Any person or thing subordinate to another, a substitute. 6 (In gram.) A word which either by composition or derivation loses its original independent character, while it also determines the sense of another word (opp प्रधान).

उपसर्पः Approach, access.

उपसर्पणं Going near, approaching, advancing towards.

उपसर्या A cow fit for a bull.

उपसुंदः N. of an Asura, son of Nikumbha and younger brother of Sunda.

उपसूर्यकं The disc of the sun or its halo.

उपसृष्ट *p. p.* 1 Joined, connected with, accompanied by. 2 Seized or possessed by (a demon or evil spirit); उपसृष्टा इव क्षुद्राधिष्ठितभवनाः K. 107. 3 Troubled, affected, injured; रोगोपसृष्टतनुदुर्वसतिं मुमुक्षुः R. 8. 94. 4 Eclipsed. 5 Furnished with an उपसर्ग (as a root); क्रुधद्रुहोरुपसृष्टयोः कर्म P. I. 4. 38. **-ष्टः** The sun or moon when eclipsed. **—ष्टं** Sexual union.

उपसेचनं, उपसेकः 1 Pouring or sprinkling upon, watering. 2 Infusion; juice. **—नी** A ladle or cup for pouring.

उपसेवनं,-सेवा 1 Worshipping, honouring, adoring. 2 Service; राज° Ms. 3. 64. 3 Addiction to; विषय°. 4 Using, enjoying (carnally also); परदार° Ms 4. 134.

उपस्करः 1 Any article which serves to make anything complete, an ingredient. 2 (Hence) Condiment or seasoning for food (as mustard, pepper &c.). 3 Furniture, appurtenance, apparatus, instrument (उपकरणं); Si. 18. 72. 4 Any article or implement of household use (such as a broomstick); Y. 1. 83, 2. 193; Ms. 3. 68, 12. 66, 5. 150. 5 An ornament. 6 Censure, blame.

उपस्करणं 1 Killing, injuring. 2 A collection. 3 A change, modification. 4 An ellipsis. 5 Blame, censure.

उपस्कारः 1 Anything additional, supplement. 2 (Supplying) an ellipsis; साकांक्षमनुपस्कारं विष्वग्गति निराकुलं Ki. 11. 38. 3 Beautifying, ornamenting by way of adding grace; उक्तमेवार्थं सोपस्कारमाह Malli. on R. 11. 47. 4 An ornament. 5 A stroke. 6 A collection.

उपस्कृत *p. p.* 1 Prepared. 2 Collected. 3 Beautified, ornamented. 4 Supplied (as an ellipsis) 5 Modified.

उपस्कृतिः *f.* Supplement.

उपस्तंभः,-भनं 1 Stay, support. 2 Encouragement, incitement, aid. 3 Basis, ground, occasion.

उपस्तरणं 1 Spreading out, scattering. 2 A covering. 3 A bed. 4 Anything spread out (as a covering); अमृतोपस्तरणमसि स्वाहा.

उपस्त्री *f.* A concubine.

उपस्थः 1 the lap. 2 The middle part in general. —**स्थः -स्थं** 1 The organ of generation (of men and women, particularly of the latter); स्नानं मौनोपवासिज्यास्वाध्यायोपस्थनिग्रहाः Y. 3. 314. (male); स्थूलोपस्थस्थलीषु Bh. 1. 20 (female); हस्तौ पायुरुपस्थश्च Y. 3. 92 (where the word is used in both senses). 2 The anus. 3 The haunch or hip. -COMP. -**निग्रहः** restraint of sensual passions, continence; Y. 3. 314. -**पत्रः**, -**दलः** the Indian fig-tree (so called because its leaves resemble in shape the female organ of generation).

उपस्थानं 1 Presence, proximity. 2 Approaching, coming, appearance, coming into the presence of. 3 (*a*) Worshipping, waiting upon (with prayers); attendance, service; सूर्योपस्थानात्प्रतिनिवृत्तं पुरूरवसं मामुपेत्य V. 1; सूर्यस्योपस्थानं कुर्वः V. 4; Y. 1. 22. (*b*) Obeisance; greeting. 4 An abode. 5 The sanctuary, any sacred place (approached with respect). 6 Remembrance, recollection, memory; Y. 3. 160.

उपस्थापनं 1 Placing near, getting ready. 2 The awakening of memory. 3 Attendance, service.

उपस्थायकः A servant.

उपस्थितिः *f.* 1 Approach. 2 Proximity, presence. 3 Obtaining, getting. 4 Accomplishing, effecting. 5 Remembrance, recollection. 6 Service, attendance.

उपस्नेहः Moistening.

उपस्पर्शः-र्शनं 1 Touching, contact. 2 Bathing, ablution, washing oneself. 3 Rinsing the mouth, sipping and ejecting water as a religious act.

उपस्मृतिः *f.* A minor law-book (They are 18 in all.).

उपस्रवणं 1 The periodical flow of a woman, menses. 2 Flow (in general).

उपस्वत्वं Revenue, profit (derived from land or capital).

उपस्वेदः Moisture; sweat.

उपहत *p. p.* 1 Injured, struck, impaired; pained, hurt; Ku. 5. 76. 2 Affected, smit, struck with, overpowered; दारिद्र्य°, लोभ°, दर्प°, काम°, शोक°, &c. 3 Doomed (to destruction); कथमत्रापि दैवेनोपहता वयं Mu. 2; दैवेनोपहतस्य बुद्धिरथवा पूर्वं विपर्यस्यति Mu. 6. 8. 4 Censured, rebuked, disregarded. 5 Vitiated, polluted, made impure; शारीरैर्मलैः सुराभिर्मद्यैर्वा यदुपहतं तदत्यंतोपहतं Vishnu. —COMP. -**आत्मन्** *a.* agitated in mind, mentally affected. -**दृश्** *a.* dazzled, blinded; Ki. 12. 18.-**धी** *a.* infatuated.

उपहतक *a.* Ill-fated, unfortunate.

उपहतिः *f.* 1 Stroke. 2 Killing.

उपहत्या Dazzling of the eyes.

उपहरणं 1 Bringing near, fetching. 2 Taking, seizing 3 Offering gifts to superiors, deities &c. 4 Offering victims. 5 Serving out food or distributing it.

उपहसित *p. p.* Ridiculed, derided —**तं** Satirical laughter, ridicule.

उपहस्तिका A small purse (or box) containing the ingredients necessary for betel-chewing (*e. g.* leaves, chunam, catechu, betel &c.) (Mar. चंची, बटवा, झोळणा); उपहस्तिकायास्तांबूलं कर्पूरसहितमुद्धृत्य Dk. 116.

उपहारः 1 An oblation. 2 A gift, present (in general) R. 4. 84. 3 A victim, sacrifice, an offering to a deity; R. 16. 39. 4 A complimentary gift, present to a superior &c. 5 Honour. 6 Indemnity presents given as the price of peace; H. 4. 110. 7 Food distributed to guests.

उपहारिन् *a.* Giving, presenting, bringing on.

उपहालकः N. of the Kuntala country, q. v.

उपहासः 1 Ridicule, derision R. 12. 37. 2 Satirical laughter. 3 Fun, play. —COMP. —**आस्पदं**, —**पात्रं** laughing-stock, butt of ridicule.

उपहासक *a.* Ridiculing others. -**कः** A jester.

उपहास्य *pot. p.* Ridiculous; °**तां गम्** or **या** become an object of ridicule, be exposed to derision; गमिष्याम्युपहास्यतां R. 1. 3.

उपहित *a.* Placed, put &c. see **धा** with उप.

उपहूतिः *f.* Calling, calling out, inviting; *Si.* 14. 30.

उपह्वरः 1 A solitary or lonely place, privacy; उपह्वरे पुनरित्यशिक्षयं धनमित्रं Dk. 54. 2 Proximity.

उपह्वानं 1 Calling, inviting. 2 Invoking with prayers.

उपांशु *ind.* 1 In a low voice or whisper. 2 Secretly, in secret or private; परिचेतुमुपांशु धारणां R. 8. 18. —**शुः** A prayer uttered in a low voice, muttering of prayers; cf. Ms. 2. 85.

उपाकरणं 1 An invitation to begin, bringing near. 2 Preparation, beginning, commencement. 3 Commencement of reading the Veda after the performance of the preparatory rite; cf. उपाकर्मन्; वेदोपाकरणाख्यं कर्म करिष्ये *S*rāvaṇī mantra.

उपाकर्मन् *n.* 1 Preparation, beginning, commencement. 2 A ceremony performed before commencing to read the veda after the monsoons (cf. श्रावणी); Y. 1. 142; Ms. 4. 119.

उपाकृत *p. p.* 1 Brought near. 2 Killed at a sacrifice (an animal). 3 Begun, commenced.

उपाक्षं *ind.* Before the eyes, in the presence of.

उपाख्यानं, -**नकं** A short tale or narrative, an episode; उपाख्यानैर्विना तावत् भारतं प्रोच्यते बुधैः Mb.

उपागमः 1 Approach, arrival. 2 Occurrence. 3 A promise, agreement. 4 Acceptance.

उपाग्रं 1 The part next to the end or top. 2 A secondary member.

उपाग्रहणं Reading the Vedas after being initiated to them.

उपांगं 1 A subdivision, subhead. 2 Any minor limb or member (of anything.) 3 A supplement of a supplement. 4 A supplementary work (of inferior value). 5 A secondary portion of science; a class of writings supplementary to the Vedângas; (these are four:– पुराणन्यायमीमांसाधर्मशास्त्राणि).

उपचारः 1 Position (of a word in a sentence). 2 Procedure.

उपाजे *ind.* (Used only with the root कृ) Supporting; उपाजेकृत्य or कृत्वा having supported; P. I. 4. 73 Sk.

उपांजनं Anointing, plastering the ground with cow-dung, chunam &c.; Ms. 5. 105, 122, 124; मठादेः (सुधागोमयादिना संमार्जनानुलेपनं Medhâtithi).

उपात्ययः Transgression, deviation from (estblished customs).

उपादानं 1 Taking, receiving, acquisition, obtaining; विश्रब्धं ब्राह्मणः शूद्रात् द्रव्योपादानमाचरेत् Ms. 8. 417; विद्या° K. 75. 2 Mention, enumeration. 3 Including, containing. 4 Withdrawing the organs of sense and perception from the external world and its objects. 5 A cause, motive, natural or immediate cause; पाटवोपादानो भ्रमः U. 3 v. l. 6 The material out of which anythiug is made, the material cause; निमित्तमेव ब्रह्म स्यादुपादानं च वेक्षणात् Adhikaraṇamâlâ. 7 A mode of expression in which a word used elliptically, besides retaining its own primary sense, conveys another (in additon to that which is actually expressed); स्वसिद्धये पराक्षेपः ...उपादानं K. P. 2. -COMP. -**कारणं** a material cause; प्रकृतिश्चोपादानकारणं च ब्रह्माभ्युपगंतव्यं S. B. -**लक्षणा**= अजहत्स्वार्था q. v.; see K. P. 2; S. D. 14 also.

उपाधिः 1 Fraud, deceit, trick. 2 Deception, disguise (in Vedânta). 3 Discriminative or distinguishing property, attribute, peculiarity; तदुपधावेव संकेतः K. P. 2. It is of four kinds:—जाति, गुण, क्रिया, संज्ञा. 4 A title, nick-name; (भट्टाचार्य, महामहोपाध्याय, पंडित &c.). 5 Limitation, condition (as of time, space &c.); (oft. occurring in Vedânta phil.). 6 A purpose, occasion, object. 7 (In logic) A special cause for a general effect. 8 A man who is careful to support his family

उपाधिक *a.* Exceeding, supernumerary, additional.

उपाध्यायः 1 A teacher or preceptor in general. 2 Particularly, a spiritual teacher, religious preceptor ; (a subteacher who instructs for wages only in a part of the Veda and is inferior to an आचार्य); cf. Ms 2. 141;—एकदेशं तु वेदस्य वेदांगान्यपि वा पुनः । योऽध्यापयति वृत्त्यर्थमुपाध्यायः स उच्यते ॥ see अध्यापक, and under आचार्य also.—**या** A female preceptor. —**यी** 1 A female preceptor. 2 The wife of a preceptor.

उपाध्यायानी The wife of a preceptor.

उपानह् *f.* A sandal, shoe ; उपानद्गूढपादस्य सर्वा चर्मवृतेव भूः H. 1. 142 ; Ms. 2. 246 ; श्वा यदि क्रियते राजा स किं नाश्नात्युपानहं H. 3. 58.

उपांतः 1 Border, edge, margin, skirt, point (of anything); उपांतयोर्निष्कुषितं विहंगैः R. 7. 50; Ku. 3. 69, 7. 32; Amaru. 23 ; U. 1. 26 ; वल्कल° K. 136. 2 The corner or angle of the eye ; R. 3. 26. 3. Immediate proximity, vicinity ; तयोरुपांतस्थितसिद्धसैनिकं R. 3. 57, 7. 24, 16. 21 ; Me. 24. 4 Side or slope (नितंब); Me. 18.

उपांतिक *a.* Near, proximate, neighbouring. —**कं** Vicinity, proximity.

उपांत्य *a.* Last but one ; उत्तमपदमुपांत्यस्योपलक्षणार्थम् Sk. —**त्यः** The corner of the eye. —**त्यं** Vicinity.

उपायः 1. (*a*) Means, an expedient, remedy; उपायं चिंतयेत्प्राज्ञस्तथापायं च चिंतयेत् Pt. 1. 406. Amaru. 21; Ms. 8. 48, 7. 177. (*b*) A mode, way, stratagem. 2 Beginning ; commencement. 3 Effort, exertion; Bg. 6. 36 ; Ms. 9. 248, 10. 2. 4 A means of success against an enemy ; (these are four :— सामन् conciliation or negotiation ; दानं bribery ; भेदः sowing dissensions ; and दंडः punishment (open attack); some authorities add three more :—माया deceit; उपेक्षा trick, deceit or neglect ; इंद्रजाल conjuring; thus making the total number 7) ; चतुर्थोपायसाध्ये तु रिपौ सांत्वमपक्रिया Si. 2. 54; सामादीनामुपायानां चतुर्णामपि पंडिताः Ms. 7. 109. 5 Joining (as in singing). 6 Approach. –COMP. –**चतुष्टयं** the four expedients against an enemy ; see above (4). –**ज्ञ** *a.* fertile in expedients. –**तुरीयः** the 4th expedient, *i. e.* दंड or punishment. –**योगः** application of means or remedy; Ms. 9. 10.

उपायनं 1 Going near, approach. 2 Becoming a pupil of. 3 Engaging in any religious rite. 4 A present, gift ; मालविकोपायनं प्रेषिता M. 1 ; तस्योपायनयोग्यानि वस्तूनि सरितां पतिः Ku. 2. 37; R. 4. 79.

उपारंभः Beginning, commencement.

उपार्जनं,–ना Acquiring, gaining.

उपार्थ *a.* Of little worth.

उपालंभः,–भनं 1 Abuse, taunt, censure ; अस्या महदुपालंभनं गतोस्मि *S.* 5; तवोपालंभे पतितास्मि M. 1 laid myself open to your censure. 2 Delaying, putting off.

उपावर्तनं 1 Coming or turning back, return ; त्वदुपावर्तनशंकि मे मनः (करोति) R. 8. 53. 2 Revolving, turning round. 3 Approaching.

उपाश्रयः 1 Recourse (for aid), asylum, support; Bh. 2. 48. 2 Receptacle, recipient. 3 Reliance, dependence upon.

उपासकः 1 One who waits upon, a worshipper. 2 A servant, follower. 3 A *S*údra, a low fellow.

उपासनं, –ना 1 Service, attendance, waiting upon; शीलं खलोपासनात् (विनश्यति), Pt. 1. 169 ; उपासनामेत्य पितुः स्म सृज्यते N. 1. 34; Ms. 3. 107 ; Bg. 13. 7; Y. 3. 156. 2 Engaging in, being intent on, performing ; संगीत° Mk. 6 ; Ms. 2. 69. 3 Worship, respect, adoration. 4 Practice of archery. 5 Religious meditation. 6 The sacred fire.

उपासा 1 Service, attendance. 2 Worship, adoration. 3 Religious meditation.

उपास्तमनं Sunset.

उपास्तिः *f.* 1 Service, attendance upon (especially a deity). 2 Worship, adoration.

उपास्त्रं A secondary or minor weapon.

उपहारः Slight refreshment (fruits, sweetmeats &c).

उपाहित *p. p.* 1 Placed, deposited, put on &c. 2 Connected, joined.—**तः** Danger or destruction from fire.

उपेक्षणं=उपेक्षा

उपेक्षा 1 Overlooking, disregard, neglect. 2 Indifference, contempt, disdain ; कुर्यामुपेक्षां हतजीवितेऽस्मिन् R. 14. 65. 3 Leaving, quitting. 4 Neglect, trick or deceit (one of the 7 expedients in war).

उपेत *p. p.* 1 Come near, approached. 2 Present. 3 Endowed with, possessed of ; with, instr. or in comp. ; पुत्रमेवंगुणोपेतं चक्रवर्तिनमाप्नुहि *S.* 1. 12.

उपेंद्रः N. of Vishṇu or Krishṇa as the younger brother of Indra in his 5th or dwarf incarnation; see इंद्र; उपेंद्र वज्रादपि दारुणोऽसि Gît. 5; यदुपेंद्रस्त्वमतींद्र एव सः Si. 11. 70.

उपेय *pot p.* 1 To be approached. 2 To be got. 3 To be effected by any means.

उपोढ *p. p.* 1 Collected, accumulated, stored up. 2 Brought near, near. 3 Arrayed for battle. 4 Begun. 5 Married.

उपोत्तम *a.* Last but one. —**मं**(अक्षरं) The last letter but one.

उपोद्घातः 1 A beginning. 2 An introduction, a preface. 3 An example, an apposite argument or illustration. 4 An occasion, medium, means ; तत्प्रतिच्छंदकमुपोद्घातेन माधवांतिकमुपेयात् Mâl. 1. 5 Analysis, ascertaining the elements of anything.

उपोद्बलक *a.* Confirming.

उपोद्बलनं Confirmation, corroboration.

उपोषणं, उपोषितं A fast.

उप्तिः *f.* Sowing seed.

उब्ज् 6 P. (उब्जति, उब्जित) 1 To press down, subdue. 2 To make straight.

उभ्, उंभ् 6. 9. P. (उभति or उंभति, उभ्नाति, उंभित) 1 To confine. 2 To compact together. 3 To fill with; जलकुंभमुंभितरसं सपदि सरस्याः समानयंत्यास्ते Bv. 2. 144. 4 To cover or overspread with ; सर्वमर्मसु काकुत्स्थमौंभत्तीक्ष्णैः शिलीमुखैः Bk. 17. 88.

उभ *pron. a.* (Used only in the dual) Both ; उभौ तौ न विजानीतः Bg. 2. 19 ; Ku. 4. 43; Ms. 2. 14; *Si.* 3. 8.

उभय *pron. a.* (**यी** *f.*) (Though dual in sense, it is used in the singular and plural only ; according to some grammarians in the dual also) Both (of persons or things); उभयमप्यपरितोषं समर्थये *S.* 7; उभयमानशिरे वसुधाधिपाः R. 9. 9; उभयीं सिद्धिमुभाववापतुः 8. 23, 17. 38 ; Amaru. 60 ; Ku. 7. 78; Ms. 2. 55, 4. 224, 9. 34. –COMP. –**चर** *a.* living in water and on land or in the air, amphibious. –**विद्या** two-fold sciences *i. e.* religious knowledge and knowledge about worldly affairs. –**विध** *a.* of both kinds. –**वेतन** *a.* receiving wages from both (parties), serving two masters, treacherous. –**व्यंजन** *a.* having the marks of both sexes. –**संभवः** a dilemma.

उभयतः *ind.* 1 from both sides ; on both sides, to both sides (with acc.); उभयतः कृष्णं गोपाः Sk. ; Y. 1. 58 ; Ms. 8. 315. 2 in both cases. 3 In both ways; Ms. 1. 47. –COMP. –**दत्,–दंत** *a.* having a double row of teeth ; Ms. 1. 43. –**मुख** *a.* 1. looking either way. 2 two-faced (as a house &c.). (–**खी**) a cow ; Y. 1-206-7.

उभयत्र *ind.* 1 In both places. 2 on both sides. 3 In both cases ; Ms. 3. 125, 167

उभयथा *ind.* 1 In both ways ; उभयथापि घटते V. 3 2 In both cases.

उभये (**य**) **द्युस्** *ind.* 1 On both days. 2 On two subsequent days.

उम् *ind.* An interjection of (1) anger; (2) interrogation; (3) promise or assent ; (4) cordiality or pacification.

उमा 1 N. of the daughter of Himavat and Menâ and wife of *S*iva; Kâlidâsa thus derives the name:— उमेति (oh do not, *scil.* practise penance) मात्रा तपसो निषिद्धा पश्चादुमाख्यां सुमुखी जगाम Ku. 1. 26; उमावृषांकौ R. 3. 23. **2** Light, splendour. **3** Fame, reputation. **4** Tranquility, calmness. **5** Night. **6** Turmeric. **7** Flax —Comp —**गुरुः**, **-जनकः** N. of the Himâlaya (as the father of उमा). **-पतिः** N. of *S*iva; मुहुरनुस्मरयंतमनुक्षपं त्रिपुरदाहमुमापतिसेविनः Ki. 5. 14; so °ईशः, °वल्लभः, °सहायः &c. **-सुतः** N. of Kârtikeya or of Ganesa.

उंब (बु) रः The upper timber of a door-frame.

उरः A sheep.

उरगः (**गी** *f.*) **1** A serpent, snake; अंगुलीवोरगक्षता R. 1. 28, 12. 5, 91. **2** A Nâga or semidivine serpent usually represented in mythology with a human face; देवगंधर्वमानुषोरगराक्षसान् Nala. 1. 28; Ms. 3. 196. **3** Lead. —**गा** N. of a city; R. 6. 59. -Comp. **-अरिः**, **-अशनः**, **-शत्रुः 1** N. of Garuda (enemy of snakes) **2** a pea-cock. **-इंद्रः**, **-राजः** N. of Vâsuki or *S*esha. **-प्रतिसर** *a.* having a serpent for a wedding-ring. —**भूषणः** N. of *S*iva (decked with serpents) **-सारचंदनः**, **-नं** a kind of sandal wood. **-स्थानं** the abode of the Nâgas, *i. e.* Pâtâla

उरंगः, **-गमः** A snake.

उरणः (**णी** *f.*) **1** A ram, sheep; वृकीवोरणमासाद्य मृत्युरावाय गच्छति Mb. **2** A certain demon killed by Indra. —**णी** A ewe.

उरणकः 1 A ram. **2** A cloud.

उरभ्रः A ram.

उररी *ind.* A particle implying (1) assent admission or acceptance. (In this sense it is usually used with the roots कृ, भू, or अस्, and it has the force of a **गति** or preposition उररीकृत्य not उररीकृत्वा. Other forms of the word are उरी, उररि, ऊरी and ऊररी); (2) extension. (**उररीकृ** 8 U. To consent, allow, accept; गिरं न कां कामुररीचकार Bv. 2. 13; *Si*. 10. 14).

उरस् *n.* (उरः) The breast, bosom; व्यूढोरस्को वृषस्कंधः R. 1. 13, Ku. 6. 51; उरसि कृ to clasp to the bosom. -Comp. **-क्षतं** injury to the chest. **-ग्रहः**, **-घातः** a disease of the chest, pleurisy. **-छदः**, **-त्राणं** a cuirass, breastplate; *Si*. 15. 80. **-जः**, **-भूः**, **उरसिजः**, **उरसिरुहः** the female breast; रेजाते रुचिरदृशामुरोजकुंभौ *Si*. 8. 53, 25, 59. **-भूषणं** an ornament of the breast. **-सूत्रिका** a necklace of pearls hanging over the breast. **-स्थलं** the breast, bosom.

उरस्य *a.* **1** Being in the breast. **2** Legitimate (as a son or daughter); born from a married couple of the same tribe or caste. **3** Excellent. —**स्यः** A son.

उरस्वत्, **उरसिल** *a.* Broad-chested, full-breasted.

उरी A particle of assent; see उररी. (**उरीकृ 1** To allow, admit, accept; दक्षिणेरीकृतं त्वया Bk. 8, 11; R. 15. 70. **2** To follow, have recourse to; अयि रोषमुरीकरोषि नो चेत् Bv. 1. 44).

उरु *a.* (**रु-र्वी** *f.*; compar. वरीयस्; superl. वरिष्ठ) **1** Wide, spacious. **2** Great, large; R. 6. 74. **3** Excessive, much, abundant. **4** Excellent, precious, valuable. -Comp. **-कीर्ति** *a.* renowned, well-known; R. 14. 74. **-क्रमः** an epithet of Vishṇu in the dwarf incarnation. **-गाय** *a.* sung or praised by the great; Asvad. 61. **-मार्गः** a long road. **-विक्रम** *a.* valiant, mighty. **-स्वन** *a.* having a loud voice, stentorian. **-हारः** a valuable necklace.

उरुरी=उररी q. v.

उरूकः=उलूक q. v.

उर्णनाभः A spider; cf. ऊर्णनाभ.

उर्णा 1 Wool, felt. **2** A circle of hair between the eye-brows; see ऊर्णा.

उर्वटः 1 A calf. **2** A year.

उर्वरा 1 Fertile soil; *Si*. 15. 66. **2** Land in general.

उर्वशी N. of a famous Apsaras or nymph of Indra's heaven who became the wife of Purúravas. [Urva*s*i is frequently mentioned in the *R*igveda; at her sight the seed of Mitra and Varu*n*a fell down, from which arose Agastya and Vasish*th*a; (see Agastya). Being cursed by Mitra and Varu*n*a she came down to the world of mortals and became the wife of Pur*u*ravas, whom she chanced to see while descending, and who made a very favourable impression upon her mind. She lived with him for some time, and went up to heaven at the expiration of her curse. Pur*u*ravas was sorely grieved at her loss, but succeeded in securing her company once more. She bore him a son named *A*yus, and then left him for ever The account given in the Vikramorva*s*iyam differs in many respects. Mythologically she is said to have sprung from the thigh of the sage N*a*ray*an*a, q. v.]. **-रमणः**, **-सहायः**, **-वल्लभः** N. of Purúravas.

उर्वारुः A kind of cucumber; see इर्वारु.

उर्वी 1 'Wide region' the earth; स्तोकमुर्व्यां प्रयाति *S*. 1. 7; जुगोप गोरूपधरामिवोर्वी R. 2. 3, 1. 14, 30, 75, 2. 66. **2** Land, soil. **3** The open space or expanse. -Comp. **-ईशः**, **-ईश्वरः**, **-पतिः**, **-धवः** a king. **-धरः 1** a mountain. **2** the serpent *S*esha. **-भृत्** *m.* **1** a king. **2** a mountain. **-रुहः** a tree; *Si*. 4. 7.

उलपः 1 A creeping plant, a spreading creeper. **2** Soft grass (कोमलं तृणं); गोगर्भिणीप्रियनवोलपमालभारिसेव्योपकंठविपिनावलयो भवंति Mâl. 9. 2; *Si*. 4. 8.

उलूपः=उलप q. v.

उलूकः 1 An owl; नोलूकोप्यवलोकते यदि दिवा सूर्यस्य किं दूषणं Bh., **2**. 93; त्यजति मुदमुलूकः प्रीतिमांश्चक्रवाकः *Si*. 11. 64. **2** N. of Indra.

उलूखलं A wooden mortar used for cleansing rice (from the husk &c); अवहननायोलूखलं Mbh.; Ms. 3. 88, 5. 117.

उलूखलकं A mortar.

उलूखलिक *a.* Pounded in a mortar.

उलूतः A large snake, the Boa.

उलूपी A Nâga princess. [**She was the daughter of the serpent Kauravya. While one day she was bathing in the Ganges, she happened to see Arjuna, and being enamoured of his handsome form, she managed to have him conveyed to her home, the P*a*tala, and there induced him to take her as his wife, which he, after considerable hesitation, consented to do. She bore him a son named Ir*a*vat. When Arjuna's head was cut off by Babhruv*a*hana's arrow, it was with her assistance that he was restored to life; see Arjuna**].

उल्का 1 A fiery phenomenon in the sky, a meteor; *Si*. 15. 92; Ms. 1. 38, Y. 1. 145. **2** A fire-brand, torch. **3** Fire, flame; Me. 53. -Comp. **-धारिन्** *a.* a torch-bearer. **-पातः** the fall of a meteor. **-मुखः** a demon or goblin (having a mouth of fire); Ms. 12 71; Mâl. 5. 13.

उल्कुषी 1 A meteor. **2** A fire-brand.

उल्बं, **-ल्वं 1** Fœtus. **2** The vulva. **3** The womb.

उल्ब (ल्व) ण *a.* **1** Thick, clotted, copious, abundant (blood &c.). **2** Much, excessive, intense; *Si*. 10. 54; Ku. 7. 84. **3** Strong, powerful, great; *Si*. 20. 41. **4** Manifest, clear; तस्यासीदुल्बणो मार्गः R. 4. 33.

उल्मुकः A fire-brand, torch.

उल्लंघनं 1 Leaping or passing over. **2** Transgression, violation.

उल्लल *a.* **1** Shaking, tremulous. **2** Covered with thick hair, shaggy.

उल्लसनं 1 Happiness, joy. **2** Horripilation.

उल्लसित *p. p.* **1** Shining, brilliant, splendid. **2** Happy, delighted.

उल्लाघ *a.* **1** Recovered from sickness, convalescent. **2** Dexterous, clever, skilful. **3** Pure. **4** Happy, delighted

उल्लापः 1 Speech, words; श्रुता मयार्यपुत्रस्योल्लापाः U. 3. **2** Insulting words, taunting speech, taunt; खलोल्लापाः सोढाः Bh. 3. 6. **3** Calling out in a loud voice. **4** Change of voice by emotion, sickness &c. **5** A hint, suggestion.

उल्लाप्यं A kind of drama; see S. D. 545.

उल्लासः 1 Joy, delight ; सोल्लासं U. 6 ; सकौतुकोल्लासं U. 2 ; उल्लासः फुल्लपंकेरुहपटलपतन्मत्तपुष्पंधयानां S. D. 2 Light, splendour. 3 (In Rhet.) A figure of speech thus defined:— अन्यदीयगुणदोषप्रयुक्तमन्यस्य गुणदोषयोराधानमुल्लासः R. G. ; for examples, see R. G. *ad. loc.*; or Chandr. 5. 131, 133. 4 A division of a book, such as chapter, section &c.; as the ten Ullâsas of the Kâvyaprakâsa.

उल्लासनं Splendour,

उल्लिंगित *a.* Famous, known.

उल्लीढ *a.* Rubbed, polished ; मणिः शाणोल्लीढः Bh. 2. 44.

उल्लुंचनं 1 Plucking out, cutting; पादकेशांशुककरोल्लुंचनेषु पणान् दश (दमः) Y. 2. 217. 2 Plucking or pulling out the hair.

उल्लुंठनं, उल्लुंठा Irony ; धीराधीरा तु सोल्लुंठभाषणैः खेदयेदमुं S. D. 105 ; सोल्लुंठं ironically, often occurring as a stage-direction in plays.

उल्लेखः 1 Allusion, mention. 2 Description, utterance. 3 Boring or digging out. 4 (In Rhetoric) A figure of speech:–बहुभिर्बहुधोल्लेखादेकस्योल्लेख इष्यते । स्त्रीभिः कामोऽर्थिभिः स्वर्द्रुः कालः शत्रुभिरैक्षि सः Chandr. 5. 19; cf. S. D. 682. 5 Rubbing, scratching, tearing up ; खुरमुखोल्लेख K. 191 ; कुट्टिम° 232.

उल्लेखनं 1 Rubbing, scratching, scraping &c. 2 Digging up ; Y. 1. 188 ; Ms. 5. 124. 3 Vomiting. 4 Mention, allusion. 5 Writing, painting.

उल्लोचः A canopy, an awning.

उल्लोल *a.* Violently moving, excessively tremulous ; Mâl. 5. 3. —लः A large wave or surge.

उल्व, उल्वण see उल्ब, उल्बण.

उशनस् *m.* (nom. sing. उशना ; voc. sing. उशनन्, उशन, उशनः) N. of *S*ukra, regent of the planet Venus, son of Bhrigu and preceptor of the Asuras. In the Vedas he has the epithet *Kâvya* given to him, probably because he was noted for his wisdom; cf. Bg. 10. 37 ; कवीनामुशना कविः. He is also known as a writer on civil and religious law (Y. 1. 4), and as an anthority on civil polity ; शास्त्रमुशनसा प्रणीतं Pt. 5 ; अध्यापितस्योशनसापि नीतिं Ku. 3. 6.

उशी Wish, desire.

उशी (षी) रः, –रं, उशी (षी) रकं The fragrant root of a plant (वीरणमूल, Mar. काळावाळा); स्तनन्यस्तोशीरं *S*. 3. 9.

उष् 1 P. (ओषति, ओषित-उषित-उष्ट) 1 To burn, consume ; ओषांचकार कामाग्निर्दशवक्त्रमहर्निशं Bk. 6. 1, 14 62 ; Ms. 4. 186. 2 To punish, chastise ; दंडेनैव तमप्योषेत् Ms. 6. 273. 3 To kill, injure.

उषः 1 Early morning, dawn. 2 A libidinous man. 3 Saline earth.

उषणं 1 Black pepper. 2 Ginger.

उषपः 1 Fire. 2 The sun.

उषस् *f.* 1 Dawn, morning ; प्रदीपार्चिरिवोषसि R. 12. 1 ; उषसि उत्थाय rising at day-break. 2 Morning light. 3 The deity that presides over the morning and evening twilights (used in dual). —सी The end of the day, evening twilight. –Comp. –बुधः fire; U. 6.

उषा 1 Early morning, dawn. 2 Morning light. 3 Twilight. 4 Saline earth. 5 A boiler, cooking-pot (उखा). 6 N. of the daughter of the demon Bâna and wife of Aniruddha. [She beheld Aniruddha in a dream and became passionately enamoured of him. She sought the assistance of her friend Chitralekha, who advised her to have with her the portraits of all young princes living round about her. When this was done, she recognized Aniruddha and had him carried to her city, where she was married to him ; see अनिरुद्ध also]. –Comp. –कालः a cock. –पतिः, –रमणः, –ईशः N. of Aniruddha, husband of Ushâ.

उषित *a.* 1 Dwelt. 2 Burnt.

उषीर—उशीर q. v.

उष्ट्रः 1 A camel; अथोष्ट्रवामीशतवाहितार्थं R. 5. 32; Ms. 3. 162, 4. 120, 11. 202. 2 A buffalo. 3 A bull with a hump. —ष्ट्री A she-camel.

उष्ट्रिका 1 A she-camel. 2 An earthen wine-vessel of the shape of a camel; *S*i. 12. 26.

उष्ण *a.* Hot, warm, °अंशुः, °करः &c. 2 Sharp, strict, active ; आददे नातिशीतोष्णो नभस्वानिव दक्षिणः R. 4. 8 (where उष्ण has sense 1 also). 3 Pungent, acrid (as a रस). 4 Clever, sharp. 5 Choleric. –ष्णः, –ष्णं 1 Heat, warmth. 2 The hot season (ग्रीष्म). 3 sunshine. —ष्णः An onion. –Comp. –अंशुः, –करः, –गुः, –दीधितिः, –रश्मिः, –रुचिः 'hot-rayed', the sun ; R. 5. 4, 8. 30 ; Ku. 3. 25. –अभिगमः, –आगमः, –उपगमः approach of heat, hot season. –उदकं warm or hot water. –कालः, –गः the hot season. —बाष्पः 1 tears. 2 hot vapour. —वारणः-णं an umbrella, parasol ; यदर्थमंभोजमिवोष्णवारणं Ku. 5. 52.

उष्णक *a.* 1 Sharp, smart, active. 2 Sick with fever, suffering pain. 3 Warming, heating. —कः 1 Fever. 2 The hot season, summer.

उष्णालु *a.* Not being able to bear heat; scorched by, suffering from, heat ; उष्णालुः शिशिरे निषीदति तरोर्मूलालवाले शिखी V. 2. 23.

उष्णिका Rice-gruel.

उष्णिमन् *m.* Heat.

उष्णीषः, –षं 1 Anything wound round the head. 2 Hence, a turban, diadem, crownet; बलाकापांडुरोष्णीषं Mk. 5. 19. 3 A distinguishing mark.

उष्णीषिन् *a.* Wearing a diadem ; K. 229. —*m.* N. of *S*iva.

उष्मः, उष्मकः 1 Heat. 2 The hot season. 3 Anger, warmth of temper. 4 Ardour, eagerness, zeal. –Comp. –अन्वित *a.* enraged. –भास् *m.* the sun. –स्वेदः a vapour bath.

उष्मन् *m.* 1 Heat, warmth ; अर्थोष्मन् Bh. 2. 40 ; Ms. 9. 231, 2. 23 ; Ku. 5. 46, 7. 14. 2 Steam, vapour ; Ku. 5. 23. 3 The hot season. 4 Ardour, eagerness. 5 The letters श्, ष्, स् and ह्, (in gram.); see ऊष्मन्.

उस्रः 1 A ray (of light), beam; सर्वैरुस्रैः समग्रैस्त्वमिव नृपगुणैर्दीप्यते सप्तसप्तिः M. 2. 13 ; R. 4. 66 ; Ki. 5. 31. 2 A bull. 3 A god. —स्रा 1 Morning, dawn. 2 Light. 3 A cow.

उह् 1 P. (ओहति, उहित) 1 To hurt or give pain. 2 To kill, destroy. With अप or व्यप see ऊह्.

उह, उहह *ind.* An interjection of calling.

उह्नः A bull.

ऊ.

ऊः 1 N. of *S*iva. 2 The moon.–*ind.* 1 A particle used to introduce a subject. 2 An interjection of (*a*) calling ; (*b*) of compassion ; (*c*) protection.

ऊढ *a.* (fr. वह्) 1 Borne, carried, as a load or burden. 2 Taken. 3 Married —ढः A married man. —ढा A girl who is married. —Comp. –कंकट *a.* mailed. –भार्य *a.* one who haa married a wife. –वयसः a young man.

ऊढिः *f.* Marriage.

ऊतिः *f.* 1 Weaving, sewing. 2 Protection. 3 Enjoyment. 4 Sport, play.

ऊधस् *n.* An udder (changed to ऊधन् in Bah . comp.).

ऊधन्यं or **ऊधस्यं** Milk (produced from the udder) ; ऊधस्यमिच्छामि तवोपभोक्तुं R. 2. 66.

ऊन *a.* 1 Wanting, deficient, defective ; किंचिदूनमनूनर्धेः शरदामयुतं ययौ R. 10

1; incomplete, insufficient. 2 Less than (in number, size or degree); ऊनद्विवर्षं निखनेत् Y. 3. 1 less than two years old. 3 Weaker, inferior; ऊनं न सत्त्वेष्वधिको बबाधे R. 2. 14. 4 Minus (in this sense used with numerals); एकोन less by one; °विंशतिः 20 minus 1 = 19.

ऊम् *ind.* An interjection of (*a*) interrogation; (*b*) anger; (*c*) reproach, abuse (*d*) arrogance; (*e*) envy.

ऊय् 1 A. [ऊयते, ऊत] To weave, sew.

ऊररी = उररी q. v.

ऊरव्यः (व्या *f.*) A Vaisya, a man of the third tribe (as born from the thighs of Brahmâ or Purusha); cf. Ms. 1. 31, 87.

ऊरुः (*m.*) 1 The thigh; ऊरू तदस्य यद्वैश्यः Rv. 10. 90. 12. —COMP. -अष्ठीवं thigh and knee. -उद्भव *a.* born or sprung from the thigh; V. 1. 3. -ज, -जन्मन्, -संभव *a.* sprung from the thigh. (-*m.*) a Vaisya. -दघ्न, -द्वयस, -मात्र *a.* as high as or reaching the thighs, knee-deep. -पर्वन् *m. n.* the knee. -फलकं the thigh-bone, hip-bone.

ऊरुरी = उररी q. v.

ऊर्ज् *f.* 1 Strength, vigour. 2 Sap. 3 Food.

ऊर्जः 1 N. of the month Kârtika; *S*i. 6. 50. 2 Energy. 3 Power, strength. 4 Procreative power. 5 Life, breath. —र्जा 1 Food. 2 Energy. 3 Strength, sap. 4 Growth.

ऊर्जस् *n.* 1 Vigour, energy. 2 Food.

उर्जस्वत् *a.* 1 Rich in food; juicy. 2 Powerful.

ऊर्जस्वल *a.* Great, powerful, strong, mighty; R. 2. 50; Bk. 3. 55.

ऊर्जास्विन् *a.* Mighty, strong, great.

ऊर्जित *a.* 1 Powerful, strong, mighty; मातृकं च धनुरूर्जितं दधत् R. 11. 64; vigorous, strong (speech); *S*i. 16. 38. 2 Distinguished, superior; excellent, beautiful; °श्रीः *S*i. 16. 85; मकरोर्जितकेतनं R. 9. 39. 3 High, noble, spirited; °आश्रयं वचः Ki. 2. 1 spirited or noble. —तं 1 Strength, might. 2 Energy.

ऊर्णं 1 Wool. 2 A woollen cloth. -COMP. -नाभः, -पटः, -नाभिः a spider. -म्रद, -द्स् *a.* soft as wool.

ऊर्णा 1 Wool; R. 16. 87. 2 A circle of hair between the eyebrows.-COMP. -पिंडः a ball of wool.

ऊर्णायु *a.* Woollen. -युः 1 A ram. 2 A spider; Bv. 1. 90. 3 A woollen blanket.

ऊर्णु 2 U. [ऊर्णो (र्णौ) ति, ऊर्णित] To cover, surround, hide; Bk. 14. 103; *S*i. 20. 14. -*Caus.* ऊर्णावयति. -*Desid.* ऊर्णुनूषति, ऊर्णन-नु-विषति. WITH प्र to cover, hide &c.

ऊर्ध्व *a.* 1 Erect, upright, above; ° केश &c.; rising or tending upwards. 2 Raised, elevated, erected; °हस्तः, ° पादः, &c. 3 High, superior, upper. 4 Not sitting (opp. आसीन). 5 Torn (as hair). —र्ध्वं Elevation, height. —र्ध्वं *ind.* 1 Upwards, aloft, above. 2 In the sequel (= उपरिष्टात्). 3 In a high tone, aloud. 4 Afterwards, subsequent to (with abl.); ते त्र्यहादूर्ध्वमाख्याय Ku. 6. 93; R. 14. 66. -COMP. -कच, -केश *a.* 1 having the hair erect. 2 one whose hair is torn. (-चः) N. of Ketu. -कर्मन् *n.* -क्रिया 1 motion upwards. 2. action for attaining a high place. (-*m.*) N. of Vishnu. —कायः, -यं the upper part of the body. -ग, -गामिन् *a.* going upwards ascended, rising. -गति *a.* going upwards. (-तिः *f.*), -गमः, -गमनं 1 ascent, elevation. 2 going to heaven. -चरण, -पाद् *a.* having the feet upwards. (-णः) a fabulous animal called *S*arabha. -जानु, -ज्ञ, -ज्ञु *a.* 1 raising the knees, sitting on the hams; *S*i. 11. 11. 2 longshanked. -दृष्टि, -नेत्र *a.* 1 looking upwards. 2 (fig.) aspiring, ambitious. (-ष्टिः *f.*) concentrating the sight on the spot between the eyebrows (in Yoga phil.). -देहः a funeral ceremony. -पातनं causing to ascend, sublimation (as of mercury). -पात्रं a sacrificial vessel; Y. 1. 182. -मुख *a.* having the mouth or opening upwards; cast or directed upwards; Ku. 1. 16; R. 3. 57. -मौहूर्तिक *a.* happening after a short time. -रेतस् *a.* one who lives in perpetual celibacy or abstains from sexual intercourse. (-*m.*) 1 N. of *S*iva. 2 Bhîshma. -लोकः the upper world, heaven. -वर्त्मन् *m.* the atmosphere. -वातः, -वायुः the wind in the upper part of the body. -शायिन् *a.* sleeping with the face upwards (as a child). (-*m.*) N. of *S*iva. -शोधनं vomiting. -श्वासः expiration. -स्थितिः *f.* 1 the rearing of a horse. 2 a horse's back. 3 elevation, superiority.

ऊर्मिः *m. f.* 1. A wave, billow; पयो वेत्रवत्याश्चलोर्मि Me. 24. 2 Current, flow. 3 Light. 4 Speed, velocity. 5 A fold or plait in a garment. 6 A row, line. 7 Distress, uneasiness, anxiety. -COMP. -मालिन् *a.* wreathed or adorned with waves. (-*m.*) the ocean.

ऊर्मिका 1 A wave. 2 A fingering (shining like a wave). 3 Regret, sorrow for anything lost. 4 The humming of a bee. 5 A plait or fold in a garment.

ऊर्व *a.* Extensive, great. -र्वः Submarine fire.

ऊर्वरा Fertile soil.

ऊलुपिन् A porpoise; see उलुपिन्.

ऊलूक=उलूक q. v.

ऊष् 1. P. (ऊषति, ऊषित) To be diseased or disordered; be ill.

ऊषः 1 Salt ground. 2 An acid. 3 A cleft, fissure. 4 The cavity of the ear. 5 The Malaya. mountain. 6 Dawn, daybreak (-षं according to some).

ऊषकं Dawn, day-break.

ऊषणं -णा 1 Black pepper. 2 Ginger.

ऊषर *a.* Impregnated with salt or saline particles. -रः, -रं A barren spot with saline soil; *S*i. 14. 46.

ऊषवत्=ऊषर *a.* q. v.

ऊष्मः 1 Heat. 2 Summer.

ऊष्मण,-ण्य *a.* Hot, steaming.

ऊष्मन् *m.* 1 Heat, warmth. 2 The hot season, summer. 3 Steam, vapour, exhalation. 4 Ardour, passion. violence. 5 (In gram.) The sounds श्, ष्, स् and ह्. -COMP. -उपगमः approach of summer. -पः 1 fire. 2 a class of Manes (pl.).

ऊह् I. 1 U. (ऊहति-ते, ऊहित) 1 To note, mark, observe. 2 To guess, conjecture, infer; अनुक्तमप्यूहति पंडितो जनः Pt. 1. 43. 3 To comprehend, conceive, perceive, expect; ऊहांचक्रे जयं न च Bk. 14. 72. 4 To reason, deliberate about. -*Caus.* To cause to reason, think, infer or conjecture; Ki. 16. 19. WITH अप 1 to remove, drive away; स हि विघ्नानपोहति *S*. 3. 1. 2 to follow immediately. -अपवि to prevent, ward off. -अभि 1 to guess, conjecture. 2 to cover. -उप to bring near or down. -निर्वि to accomplish, bring about (see निर्व्यूढ). -परिसं to sprinkle round about. -प्रति 1 to oppose, interrupt, impede. 2 to deny; see प्रत्यूह. -प्रतिवि to array troops against. -वि 1 to arrange troops in battle array; सूच्या वज्रेण चैवैतान् व्यूहेन व्यूह्य योधयेत् Ms. 7. 191. -सं to gather, assemble.

ऊहः 1 A guess, conjecture. 2 Examination and determination. 3 Understanding. 4 Reasoning, arguing. 5 Supplying an ellipsis. -COMP. -अपोहः full discussion, consideration of the *pros* and *cons*; Bv. 2. 74; see अपोह.

ऊहनं Inferring, guessing.

ऊहनी A broom.

ऊहिन् *a.* Who or what reasons; inferring. -नी 1 An assemblage, collection. 2 Arrangement, a multitude reduced to order (cf. अक्षौहिणी).

ऋ.

ऋ *ind.* An interjection of (1) calling; (2) ridicule; (3) censure or abuse.

ऋ I. 1 P. (ऋच्छति, ऋत; *caus.* अर्पयति; *desid.* अरिरिषति) 1 To go, move ; अंभश्छायामच्छामृच्छति *Si.* 4. 44. 2 To raise, tend towards.- II. 3 P. (इयर्ति, ऋत) (Mostly used in the Veda) 1 To go. 2 To move, shake. 3 To obtain, acquire, reach, meet with 4 To move, excite. -III. 5 P. (ऋणोति, ऋण) 1 To injure, hurt. 2 To attack. —*Caus.* (अर्पयति, अर्पित) 1 To throw, cast, fix or implant in; R. 8. 87. 2 To put or place on, fix upon, direct or cast towards (as the eye &c.). 3 To place in, insert, give, set or place. 4 To hand or make over, give to, consign, deliver; इति सुतस्याभरणान्यर्पयति *S.* 1, 4. 19.

ऋक्ण *a.* Wounded, injured, hurt.

ऋक्थं 1 Wealth. 2 Especially property, possessions, effects (left at death); see रिक्थ. 3 Gold. -Comp. -ग्रहणं receiving or inheriting property. -ग्राहः an inheritor or receiver of property. -भागः 1 division of property, partition. 2 a share, inheritance. -भागिन्, -हर, -हारिन् *m.* 1 an heir. 2 a co-heir.

ऋक्षः 1 A bear ; Ms. 12. 67. 2 N. of a mountain. —क्षः, -क्षं 1 A star, constellation, lunar mansion ; Ms. 2. 101. 2 A sign of the zodiac. —क्षाः (*m.* pl.) The seven stars called Pleiades ; afterwards the seven *R*ishis; R. 12. 25. -क्षा The north. -क्षी A female bear. -Comp. -चक्रं the circle of stars. -नाथः,-ईशः 'lord of stars', the moon.-नेमिः N. of Vishnu. -राज्,-राजः 1 the moon. 2 Jâmbuvat, the king of bears. -हरीश्वरः the lord of bears and apes; R. 13. 72.

ऋक्षरः 1 A priest (ऋत्विज्). 2 A thorn.

ऋक्षवत् *m.* N. of a mountain near the Narmadâ; वप्रक्रियामृक्षवतस्तटेषु R. 5. 44; ऋक्षवंतं गिरिश्रेष्ठमध्यास्ते नर्मदां पिबन् Râm.

ऋच् 6 P. (ऋचति,) 1 To praise, extol. 2 To cover, screen. 3 To shine.

ऋच् *f.* 1 A hymn (in general) 2 A verse of the *R*igveda (opp. यजुस् and सामन्). 3 The collective body of the *R*igveda (pl.). 4 Splendour (for. रुच्). 5 Praise. 6 Worship. -Comp. -विधानं the performance of certain rites by reciting verses of the *R*igveda.-वेदः the oldest of the four Vedas, and the most ancient sacred book of the Hindus. -संहिता the arranged collection of the hymns of *R*igveda.

ऋचीषः A hell. —षं A frying pan.

ऋच्छ् 6 P. (ऋच्छति) 1 To become hard or stiff. 2 To go. 3 To fail in faculties.

ऋच्छका Wish, desire.

ऋज् I. 1 A. (अर्जते, ऋजित) 1 To go. 2 To obtain, acquire. 3 To stand or be firm. 4 To be healthy or strong. -II. 1 P. To acquire, earn ; cf. अर्ज्.

ऋजीष see ऋचीष.

ऋजु, ऋजुक *a.* (जु or ज्वी *f.*) (compar. ऋजीयस् superl. ऋजिष्ठ) 1 Straight (fig. also) ; उमां स पश्यन् ऋजुनैव चक्षुषा Ku. 5. 32. 2 Upright, honest, straightforward; Pt. 1. 415. 3 Favourable, good. -Comp.-गः 1 one who is honest in his dealings. 2 an arrow. -रोहितं the straight red bow of Indra.

ऋज्वी 1 A straight-forward or plain woman. 2 A particular gait (of the planets).

ऋणं 1 Debt ; (as to the three kinds of debt, see अनृण); अंत्यं ऋणं (पितृणं) the last debt to be paid to the Manes, *i. e.* creation of a son. 2 An obligation in general. 3 (In alg.) The negative sign or quantity, minus (opp. धन). 4 A fort, stronghold. 5 Water. 6 Land. -Comp. -अंतकः the planet Mars. -अपनयनं,-अपनोदनं, -अपाकरणं, -दानं, -मुक्तिः, -मोक्षः, -शोधनं paying off debt, discharge or liquidation of debt. -आदानं 'recovery of a debt,' receipt of money lent &c. -ऋणं (ऋणार्णं) debt for a debt, debt incurred to liquidate another debt. -ग्रहः 1 borrowing (money) 2 a borrower. -दातृ,-दायिन् *a.* one who pays a debt.-दासः one who is bought as a slave by paying off his debts ; ऋणमोचनेन दास्यत्वमभ्युपगतः ऋणदासः Mit. -मत्कुणः, -मार्गणः a security, bail. -मुक्त *a.* released from debt. -मुक्तिः &c. see ऋणापनयनं. -लेख्यं ' debt-bond,' a bond acknowledging a debt (in law); (Mar. कर्जरोखा).

ऋणिकः A debtor; Y. 2. 56, 93.

ऋणिन् *a.* A debtor, one indebted to another (on any account).

ऋत *a.* 1 Proper, right. 2 Honest, true; Bg. 10. 14. 3 Worshipped, respected. -तं *ind.* Rightly, properly. -तं (Not usually found used in classical literature) 1 A fixed or settled rule, law (religious). 2 Sacred custom. 3 Divine law, divine truth. 4 Water. 5 Truth (in general), right. 6 Livelihood by picking or gleaning grains in a field (as opposed to the cultivation of ground); ऋतमुंच्छशिलं वृत्तं Ms. 4. 4. -Comp. -धामन् *a.* of a true or pure nature (-*m.*) N. of Vishnu.

ऋतीया Censure, reproach.

ऋतुः 1 A season, period of the year, commonly reckoned to be six; शिशिरश्च वसंतश्च ग्रीष्मो वर्षाः शरद्धिमः; sometimes only five; शिशिर and हिम or हेमंत being counted together. 2 An epoch, a period, any fixed or appointed time. 3 Menstruation, courses, menstrual discharge. 4 A period favourable for conception ; वरमृतुषु नैवाभिगमनं Pt. 1 ; Ms. 3. 46; Y. 1. 11. 5 Any fit season or right time. 6 Light, splendour. 7 A symbolical expression for the number 'six.' -Comp. -कालः,-समयः,-वेला 1 the time favourable for conception, *i. e.* 16 nights from menstrual discharge ; see ऋतु above. 2 the duration of a season. -गणः the seasons taken collectively. -गामिन् *a.* having intercourse with a wife (at the time fit for conception, *i. e.* after the period of menstruation) -पर्णः N. of a king of Ayodhyâ, son of Ayutâyu, a descendant of Ikshvâku. [Nala, king of Nishadha, entered into his service after he had lost his kingdom and suffered very great adversity. He was 'profoundly skilled in dice'; and he exchanged with Nala this skill for his skill in horsemanship; and by virtue of it the king succeeded in taking Nala to Ku*n*dinapura before Damayanti had put into execution her resolve of taking a second husband] -पर्यायः, -वृत्तिः the revolution of the seasons. -मुखं the beginning or first day of a season. -राजः the spring. -लिंगं 1 a characteristic or sign of the season (as the blossom of the mango tree in spring). 2 a symptom of menstruation. -संधिः the junction of two seasons. -स्नाता a woman who has bathed after menstruation and who is, therefore, fit for sexual intercourse; धर्मलोपभयाद्राज्ञीमृतुस्नातामिमां स्मरन् R. 1. 76. -स्नानं bathing after menstruation.

ऋतुमती A woman during her courses.

ऋते *ind.* Except, with the exception of without, (with abl.); ऋते क्रौर्यात्समायातः Bk. 8. 105 ; अवेहि मां प्रीतमृते तुरंगमात् R. 3. 63; पापादृते *S.* 6. 22; Ku. 1. 51; 2. 57; sometimes with acc. ऋतेऽपि त्वां न भविष्यंति सर्वे Bg. 11. 32; rarely with instr.

ऋत्विज् *m.* A priest who officiates at a sacrifice; the four chief *R*itvijas are होतृ, उद्गातृ, अध्वर्यु and ब्रह्मन् ; at grand ceremonies 16 are enumerated.

ऋद्ध *p. p.* 1 Prosperous, thriving, rich; R. 14. 30, 2. 50, 5. 40. 2 Increased, growing. 3 Stored (as grain). -द्धः N. of Vishṇu. -द्धं 1 Increase, growth. 2 A demonstrated conclusion; distinct result.

ऋद्धिः *f*. 1 Growth, increase. 2 Success, prosperity; affluence. 3 Extent or magnitude; magnificence. 4 Supernatural power or supremacy. 5 Accomplishment.

ऋध् 4. 5. P. (ऋध्यति, ऋध्नोति, ऋद्ध) 1 To prosper, flourish, thrive, succeed. 2 To grow, increase (fig. also). 3 To satisfy, gratify, please, propitiate; Mâl. 5. 29. WITH सं to thrive.

ऋभुः A deity, divinity; a god.

ऋभुक्षः 1 N. of Indra. 2 Heaven (of Indra) or paradise.

ऋभुक्षिन् *m*. (Nom. ऋभुक्षाः, acc. pl. ऋभुक्षः) N. of Indra.

ऋल्लकः A player on a kind of musical instrument.

ऋश्यः A white-footed antelope. -श्यं Killing. -COMP. -केतुः, -केतनः 1 N. of Aniruddha, son of Pradyumna. 2 N. of the god of love.

ऋष् I. 6 P. (ऋषति, ऋष्ट) 1 To go, approach. 2 To kill, injure. -II. 1 P. (अर्षति) 1 To flow. 2 To glide.

ऋषभः 1 A bull. 2 Tho best or most excellent (as the last member of a comp.); as पुरुषर्षभः, भरतर्षभः &c. 3 The second of the seven notes of the gamut; ऋषभोऽत्र गीयत इति *Aryâ S*. 141. 4 A boar's tail. 5 A crocodile's tail —भी 1 A woman with masculine features (as a beard &c.). 2 A cow. 3 A widow. -COMP. -कूटः N. of a mountain. -ध्वजः N. of *S*iva.

ऋषिः 1 An inspired poet or sage. 2 A sanctified sage, an ascetic, anchorite. 3 A ray of light. -COMP. -कुल्या a sacred river. -तर्पणं libation offered to the *R*ishis. -पंचमी N. of a festival or ceremony on the fifth day in the first half of Bhâdrapada (observed by women). -लोकः the world of the *R*ishis. -स्तोमः 1 praise of the *R*ishis. 2 a particular sacrifice completed in one day.

ऋष्टिः *m. f*. 1 A double-edged sword. 2 A sword (in general). 3 Any weapon (as a spear or lance &c.).

ऋष्यः A white-footed antelope. -COMP. -अंकः, -केतनः, -केतुः N. of Aniruddha. -मूकः a mountain near the lake Pampâ which formed the temporary abode of Râma with the monkey-chief Sugrîva; ऋष्यमूकस्तु पायाः पुरस्तात् पुष्पितद्रुमः. —शृंगः N. of a sage. [He was the son of Vibh*and*aka. He was brought up in the forest by his father, and he saw no other human being till he nearly reached his manhood. When a great drought well nigh devastated the country of Anga, its king Lomap*a*da, at the advice of Br*a*hma*n*as, caused *R*ishyas*r*inga to be brought to him by means of a number of damsels, and gave his daughter *Santa* (adopted by him, her real father being Das*a*ratha) in marriage to him, who being greatly pleased caused copious showers of rain to fall in his kingdom. It was this sage that performed for king Das*a*ratha the sacrifice which brought about the birth of R*a*ma and his three brothers].

ऋष्यकः A painted or white-footed antelope.

ॠ.

ॠ *ind*. An interjection of (1) terror; (2) warding off; (3) reproach or censure; (4) compassion ; (5) remembrance. -*m*. (ॠः) 1 N. of Bhairava. 2 A Dânava or demon.

ॠ 9 P. (ॠणाति, ईर्ण) To go, move.

ए.

एः *m*. N. of Vishṇu. -*ind*. An interjection of (1) remembering ; (2) envy ; (3) compassion; (4) calling ; (5) contempt or censure.

एक *pron. a*. 1 One, single, alone, only. 2 Not accompanied by any one. 3 The same, one and the same, identical ; मनस्येकं वचस्येकं कर्मण्येकं महात्मनां H. 1. 101. 4 Firm, unchanged. 5 Single of its kind, unique, singular. 6 Chief, supreme, prominent, sole ; एको रागिषु राजते Bh. 3. 121. 7 Peerless, matchless. 8 One of two or many ; Me. 30, 78. 9 Oft. used like the English indefinite article 'a' or 'an' ; ज्योतिरेकं *S*. 5. 30 ; एकः -अन्यः, or अपरः the one-the other ; एक is used in the plural in the sense of some, its correlative being अन्ये or अपरे (others) see अन्य, अपर also. -COMP. -अक्ष *a*. 1 having only one axle. 2 having one eye. (-क्षः) 1 a crow. 2 N. of *S*iva. -अक्षर *a*. monosyllabic. (-रं) 1 a monosyllable. 2 the sacred syllable ओम्. -अग्र *a*. 1 fixed on one object or point only. 2 closely attentive, concentrated, intent ; R. 15. 66 ; मनुमेकाग्रमासीनं Ms. 1. 1. 3 unperplexed. -अग्र्य -°अग्र. (-ग्र्यं) concentration. -अंगः 1 a body-guard 2 the planet Mercury or Mars. -अनुदिष्टं a funeral ceremony performed for only one ancestor (recently dead). -अंत *a*. 1 solitary. 2 aside, apart, 3 directed towards one point or object only. 4 excessive, great ; Ku. 1. 36. 5 absolute, invariable, perpetual ; स्वायत्तमेकांतगुणं Bh. 2. 7 ; Me. 109. (-तः) 1 a lonely or retired place, solitude. 2 exclusive aim or boundary. (-तं) an exclusive recourse, a settled rule or principle ; तेजः क्षमा वा नैकांतं कालज्ञस्य महीपतेः *Si*. 2. 83. (-तं,-तेन, -ततः, ते) *ind*. 1 solely, invariably, always, absolutely. 2 exceedingly, quite, wholly ; वयमप्येकांततो निःस्पृहाः Bh. 3. 24 ; दुःखमेकांततो वा Me. 109. -अंतर *a*. next but one, separated by one remove ; *S*. 7. 27. -अंतिक *a*. final, conclusive. -अयन *a*. 1 passable for only one (as a foot-path). 2 closely attentive, intent ; see एकाग्र. (-नं) 1 a lonely or retired place. 2 a meeting-place, rendezvous. 3 monotheism. 4 the sole object ; सा स्नेहस्य एकायनभूता M. 2. 15. -अर्थः 1 the same thing, object, or intention. 2 the same meaning. -अहन् (हः) 1 the period of one day. 2 a sacrifice lasting for one day. —आतपत्र *a*. characterized by only one umbrella (showing universal sovereignty); एकातपत्रं जगतः प्रभुत्वं R. 2. 47, *Si*. 12. 33 ; V. 3. 19. -आदेशः one substitute for two or more letters (got by either dropping one vowel, or by the blending of both); as the आ in एकायन. -आवलिः, -ली *f*. 1 a single string of pearls, beads &c. ; एकावली कंठविभूषणं वः Vikr. 1. 30. लताविटपे एकावली लग्ना V. 1. 2 (in Rhetoric) a series of statements in which there is a regular transition from a predicate to a subject, or from a subject to a predicate ; स्थाप्यतेऽपोह्यते वापि यथापूर्वं परस्परं । विशेषणतया यत्र वस्तु सैकावली द्विधा ॥ K. P. 10. -उदकः (a relative) connected by the offering of funeral libations of water to the same deceased ancestor. -उदरः, -रा uterine, (brother or sister). -उद्दिष्टं a Srâddha or funeral rite performed for one definite individual deceased, not including other ancestors. -ऊन a. less by one, minus one. -एक a. one by one, one taken singly, a single one; R. 17. 43. (-कं) -एकैकशः, *ind.* one by one, singly, severally. -ओघः a continuous current. -कर a. (-री *f.*) 1 doing only one thing. 2 (-रा) one-handed. 3 one-rayed. -कार्य a. acting in concert with, co-operating, co-worker. (-र्यं) sole or same business. -कालः 1 one time. 2 the same time. -कालिक, -कालीन a. 1 happening once only. 2 contemporary, coeval, -कुंडलः N. of Kubera; of Balabhadra; and of *S*esha. -गुरु, -गुरुक a. having the same preceptor. (-रुः, -रुकः) a spiritual brother.-चक्र a. 1 having only one wheel. 5 governed by one king only. (-क्रः) the chariot of the sun. -चत्वारिंशत् *f.* forty-one. -चर a. 1 wandering or living alone; Ki. 13. 3. 2 having one attendant. 3 living unassisted. -चारिन् a. solitary. (-णी) a loyal wife. -चित्त a. thinking of one thing only. (-त्तं) 1 fixedness of thought upon one object. 2 unanimity; एकचित्तीभूय H. 1 unanimously. -चेतस्, -मनस् a. unanimous; see °चित्त. -जन्मन् *m.* 1 a king. 2 a *S*údra; see °जाति below. —जात a born of the same parents. —जातिः a *S*ûdra (opp. द्विजन्मन्); ब्राह्मणः क्षत्रियो वैश्यस्त्रयो वर्णा द्विजातयः। चतुर्थ एकजातिस्तु शूद्रो नास्ति तु पंचमः Ms. 10. 4; 8. 270. -जातीय a. of the same kind or family. -ज्योतिस् *m.* N. of *S*iva. -तान a. concentrated or fiixed on one object only, closely attentive; ब्रह्मैकतानमनसो हि वसिष्ठमिश्राः Mv. 3. 11. -तालः harmony, accurate adjustment of song, dance, and instrumental music (cf. तौर्यत्रिकं). -तीर्थिन् a. 1 bathing in the same holy water. 2 belonging to the same religious order; Y. 2. 137. (*-m*) a fellow-student, spiritual brother. -त्रिंशत् *f.* thirty-one. -दंष्ट्रः,-दंतः " one-tusked," epithets of Gaṇesa -दंडिन् *m.* N. of a class of Sannyâsins or beggars (otherwise called हंस). They are divided into four orders:—कुटीचको बहूदको हंसश्चैव तृतीयकः। चतुर्थः परहंसश्च यो यः पश्चात्स उत्तमः॥ Hârîta. -दृश्, दृष्टि a. one-eyed. (*-m.*) 1 a crow. 2 N. of *S*iva. 3 a philosopher. -देवः the supreme god. -देशः 1 one spot or place. 2 a part or portion (of the whole), one side; तस्यैकदेशः U. 4; विभाबितैकदेशेन देयं यदभियुज्यते V. 4. 17 'what is claimed should be given by one who is proved to have got a part of it'; (this is sometimes called एकदेशविभावितन्याय).

-धर्मन्-धर्मिन् a. 1 possessing the same properties, of the same kind. 2 professing the same religion. —धुर, -धुरावह, -धुरीण a. 4 fit for but one kind of labour. 2 fit for but one yoke (as cattle for special burden; P. IV. 4. 79). -नटः the principal actor in a drama, the manager (सूत्रधार) who recites the prologue. -नवतिः *f.* ninety-one. -पक्षः one side or party; °आश्रयविक्लवत्वात् R. 14. 34. -पत्नी 1 a faithful wife (perfectly chaste); तां चावश्यं दिवसगणनातत्परामेकपत्नीं Me. 10 2 a co-wife सर्वासामेकपत्नीनामेका चेत्पुत्रिणी भवेत् Ms. 9. 183. —पदी a foot-path. -पदे *ind.* suddenly, all at once, abruptly; निहंत्यरीनेकपदे य उदात्तः स्वरानिव *S*i. 2. 95; R. 8. 48. -पादः 1 one or single foot. 2 one and the same Pâda. 3 N. of Vishṇu and *S*iva. -पिंगः, -पिंगलः N. of Kubera. -पिंड a. united by the offering of the funeral rice-ball. -भार्या a faithful or chaste wife. (-र्यः) one having one wife only. -भाव a. sincerely devoted; honest, -यष्टिः, यष्टिका a single string of pearls. -योनि a. 1 uterine. 2 of the same family of caste; Ms. 9. 148. -रसः 1 oneness of aim or feeling. 2 the only flavour or pleasure. —राज्, —राजः *m.* an absolute king. -रात्रः a ceremony lasting one night. -रिक्थिन् *m.* a co-heir. -रूप a. 1 like, similar. 2 uniform. -लिंगः 1 a word having one gender only. 2 N. of Kubera. -वचनं the singular number. -वर्णः one caste. -वार्षिका a heifer one year old. -वाक्यता consistency in meaning, unanimity, reconciling different statements. -वारं, -वारे *ind.* 1 only once. 2 at once, suddenly. 3 at one. time. -विंशतिः *f.* twenty-one -विलोचन a. one-eyed; see एकदृष्टि. -विषयिन् *m.* a rival. -वीरः a pre-eminent warrior or hero; Mv. 5. 48. -वेणिः-णी *f.* a single braid of hair (worn by a woman as a mark of her separation from her husband &c.); गंडाभोगात्कठिनविषमामेकवेणीं करेण Me. 92; *S.* 7. 21. -शफ a. whole-hoofed. (-फः) an animal whose hoof is not cloven (as a horse, ass &c.). -शरीर a. consanguineous. °अन्वयः consanguineous descent. °अवयवः blood-kinsman. —शाखः a Brâhmaṇa of the same branch or school. —शृंग a. having only one horn. (-गः) 1 a unicorn; rhinoceros. 2 N. of Vishṇu. —शेषः 'the remainder of one', a species of Dvandva compound in which one of two or more words only is retained; *e. g.* पितरौ father and mother parents, (=मातापितरौ); so श्वशुरौ, भ्रातरः &c. -श्रुत a. once heard. °धर a. keeping in mind what one has heard once.-श्रुतिः *f.* monotony. -सप्ततिः *f.* seventy-one -सर्ग a. closely attentive. -साक्षिक a. witnessed by one. -हायन a. one year old; Mâl. 4. 8; U. 3. 28. (-नी) a heifer one year old.

एकक a. 1 Single, alone, solitary, without a co-adjutor; U. 5. 5. 2 Same, identical.

एकतम a. (*n.* °मत् *f.* °मा) 1 One of many. 2 One (used as an indefinite article).

एकतर (*n.* °तरं) 1 One of two, either. 2 Other, different. 3 One of many.

एकतस् *ind.* 1 From one side, on one side. 2 Singly, one by one; एकतः-अन्यतः on one side on the other side; R. 6. 85; Ki. 5. 2.

एकत्र *ind.* 1 In one place. 2 Together, all taken together.

एकदा *ind.* 1 Once, once upon a time, at one time. 2 At the same time, all at once, simultaneously; H. 4. 93.

एकधा *ind.* 1 In one way. 2 Singly. 3 At once, at the same time. 4 Together.

एकल a. Alone, solitary; U. 4.

एकशस् *ind.* One by one, singly.

एकाकिन् a. Alone, solitary.

एकादशन् *num. a.* Eleven.

एकादश a. (शी *f.*) Eleventh. —शी The eleventh day of every fortnight of a lunar month, sacred to Vishṇu -COMP. -द्वारं the eleven holes of the body see ख. -रुद्राः (pl.) the eleven Rudras; see रुद्र.

एकीभावः 1 Combination, association. 2 Common nature or property.

एकीय a. Belonging to, or proceeding from, one. —यः A partisan, an associate.

एज् I. 1 A. (epic P.) (एजते, एजित) 1 To tremble. 2 To move, stir. 3 To shine (P.).-WITH अप to drive away. -उद् to rise, go upwards.

एजक a. Shaking.

एजनं Trembling, shaking.

एट् 1 A. (एटते, एटित) To annoy, resist, oppose.

एड a. Deaf. -डः A kind of sheep. -COMP. -मूक a. 1 deaf and dumb; cf. अनेडमूक. 2 wicked, perverse.

एडकः 1 A ram. 2 A wild goat. —का A ewe.

एणः, एणकः A kind of black antelope; the several kinds of deer are given in this verse:—अनूचो माणवो ज्ञेय एणः कृष्णमृगः स्मृतः। रुरुर्गौरमुखः प्रोक्तः शंबरः शोण उच्यते॥. -COMP. -अजिनं deer-skin. -तिलकः, -भृत् the moon; so °अंकः, °लांछनः &c. -दृश् a. one having eyes like those of a deer. (*-m.*) Capricorn.

एणी A female black deer.

एत a. (एता, एनी *f.*) Of a variegated colour; shining. —तः A deer or antelope.

एतद् *pron. a.* (*m.* एषः, *f.* एषा, *n.* एतद्) 1 This, this here, yonder (referring to what is nearest to the speaker समीपतरवर्ति चैतदो रूपं). In this sense एतद् is sometimes used to give emphasis to the personal pronouns; एषोहं कार्यवशादायोध्यिकस्तदानींतनश्च संवृत्तः U. 1. 2 It often refers to what precedes, especially when it is joined with इदं or any other pronoun; एष वै प्रथमः कल्पः Ms. 3. 147; इति यदुक्तं तदेतच्चिंत्यं. 3 It is used in connection with a relative clause, in which case the relative generally follows; Ms. 257. *-ind.* In this manner, thus, so. *Note.* एतद् appears as the first member of compounds which are mostly self-explaining; *e. g.* °अनंतर immediately after this; °अंत ending thus. -Comp. -द्वितीय *a.* one who does anything for the second time. -प्रथम *a.* one who does anything for the first time.

एतदीय *a.* Belonging to this.

एतनः Breath, expiration.

एतर्हि *ind.* Now, at this time, at present.

एतादृश्, -दृक्ष, -दृश (-शी, -क्षी *f.*) *a.* 1 Such, such like; सर्वेपि नैतादृशाः Bh. 2. 51. 2 Of this kind.

एतावत् *a.* So much, so great, so many, of such extent, so far, of such quality or kind; एतावदुक्त्वा विरते मृगेंद्रे R. 2. 51; Ku. 6. 89; एतावान्मे विभवो भवंतं सेवितुं M. 2. *-ind.* So far, so much, in such a degree, thus.

एध् 1 A. (एधते, एधित) 1 To grow, increase; Pt. 2. 164. 2 To prosper, live in comfort; द्वावेतौ सुखमेधेते Pt. 1. 318. *-Caus.* To cause to grow or increase; to greet, honour; Ku. 6. 90.

एधः Fuel; स्फुलिंगावस्थया वह्निरेधापेक्ष इव स्थितः *S.* 7. 15; *Si.* 2. 99.

एधतुः 1 A man. 2 Fire.

एधस् *n.* Fuel; यथैधांसि समिद्धोग्निर्भस्मसात् कुरुतेऽर्जुन Bg. 4. 37; अनलायागुरुचंदनैधसे R. 8. 71.

एधा Prosperity, happiness.

एधित *p. p.* 1 Grown, increased. 2 Brought up; मृगशावैः सममेधितो जनः *S.* 2. 18.

एनस् *n.* 1 Sin, offence, fault; *Si.* 14. 35. 2 Mischief, crime. 3 Unhappiness. 4 Censure, blame.

एनस्वत् or एनस्विन् *a.* Wicked, sinful.

एरंडः The castor-oil plant (a small tree with a scanty number of leaves); and hence the proverb: निरस्तपादपे देशे एरंडोपि द्रुमायते.

एलकः A ram; see एडक.

एलवालु *n.*, एलवालुकं 1 The fragrant bark of कपित्थ. 2 A granular substance (used as a drug and perfume).

एलविलः N. of Kubera; see ऐलविल.

एला 1 Cardamom plant; एलानां फलरेणवः R. 4. 47, 6. 64. 2 Cardamoms (the seed of the plant). -Comp.-पर्णी the plant Mimosa Octandra.

एलीका Small cardamoms.

एव *ind.* 1 This particle is most frequently used to strengthen and emphasize the idea expressed by a word:—(1) Just, quite, exactly; एवमेव quite so, just so; (2) same, very, identical; अर्थोष्मणा विरहितः पुरुषः स एव Bh. 2. 40; (3) only, alone, merely, (implying exclusion); सा तथ्यमेवाभिहिता भवेन Ku. 3. 63 only the truth, nothing but the truth; (4) already; (5) scarcely, the moment, as soon as; chiefly with participles; उपस्थितेयं कल्याणी नाम्नि कीर्तित एव यत् R. 1. 87; (6) like, as (showing similarity); श्रीस्त एव मेस्तु G. M. (=तव इव); and (7) generally to emphasize a statement; भवितव्यमेव तेन U. 4 it *will* (surely) take place. It is also said to imply the senses of (8) detraction; (9) diminution; (10) command; (11) restraint; or (12) used merely as an expletive.

एवं *ind.* 1 Thus, so, in this manner or way; अस्त्येवं Pt. 1 it is so; एवंवादिनि देवर्षौ Ku. 6. 84; श्रया एवं Me. 101 (what follows); एवमस्तु be it so, amen; यद्येवं if so. 2 Quite so (implying assent); एवं यदात्थ भगवन् Ku. 2. 31. -Comp. -अवस्थ *a.* so situated or circumstanced. -आदि, -आद्य *a.* such and the like. -कारं *ind.* in this manner. -गुण *a.* possessing such virtues; *S.* 1. 12. -प्रकार,-प्राय *a.* of such a kind; U. 5. 29; *S.* 7. 24. -भूत *a.* of such quality or description, so, such. -रूप *a.* of such a kind or form. -विध *a.* of such a kind, such.

एष् 1 U. (एषति-ते, एषित) 1 To go or approach. 2 To hasten towards, fly at. With परि to seek.

एषणः An iron-arrow. -णं 1 Seeking. 2 Wish. —णा Wish, desire.

एषणिका A goldsmith's balance.

एषा Desire, wish.

एषिन् *a.* Desiring, wishing (at the end of comp.); यौवने विषयैषिणाम् R. 1. 8.

ऐ.

ऐः *m.* N. of Siva. —*ind.* An interjection of (1) calling (=Halo, ho); (2) remembrance; (3) inviting.

ऐकध्यं *ind.* At once.

ऐकध्यं Singleness of time or occurrence.

ऐकपत्यं Sole sovereignty, supreme power.

ऐकपदिक *a.* (की *f.*) Belonging to a simple word.

ऐकपद्यं 1 Unity of words. 2 Being formed into one word.

ऐकमत्यं Unanimity, agreement; R. 18. 36.

ऐकागारिकः A thief; केनचित्त हस्तवतैकागारिकेण Dk. 67; *Si.* 19. 111. 2 The owner of a single house.

ऐकाग्र्यं Intentness on one object.

ऐकांगः A soldier of the bodyguard; Râj. T. 5. 249.

ऐकात्म्यं 1 Unity, unity of soul. 2 Identity, sameness. 3 Oneness with the Supreme Soul.

ऐकाधिकरण्यं 1 Oneness of relation. 2 Existence in the same subject; co-extension (in Logic); साध्येन हेतोरैकाधिकरण्यं व्याप्तिरुच्यते Bhâshâ P. 69.

ऐकांतिक *a.* (की *f.*) 1 Absolute, complete, perfect. 2 Assured, certain. 3 Exclusive.

ऐकान्यिकः A pupil who commits one error in reading or reciting (the Vedas).

ऐकार्थ्यं 1 Sameness of aim or purpose. 2 Consistency in meaning.

ऐकाहिक *a.* (की *f.*) 1 Ephemeral. 2 Of one or the same day, quotidian.

ऐक्यं 1 Oneness, unity. 2 Unanimity. 3 Identity, sameness. 4 Especially, the identity of the human soul or of the universe with the Deity. 5 An aggregate.

ऐक्षव *a.* (वी *f.*) Made of, or produced from, sugar-cane, -वं 1 Sugar. 2 A kind of spirituous liquor.

ऐक्षव्य *a.* Made of sugar-cane.

ऐक्षुक *a.* 1 Suitable for sugar-cane. 2 Bearing sugar-cane. -कः A carrier of sugar-cane.

ऐक्षुभारिक *a.* Carrying a load of sugar-canes.

ऐक्ष्वाक *a.* Belonging to Ikshvâku. —कः,-कुः 1 A descendant of Ikshvâku; सत्यमैक्ष्वाकः खल्वसि U. 5. 2 The country ruled by the Aikshvâkus.

ऐंगुद *a.* (दी *f.*) Produced from the इंगुदी tree. —दं The nut of the इंगुदी tree.

ऐच्छिक *a.* (की *f.*) 1 Optional, voluntary. 2 Arbitrary.

ऐडक *a.* (की *f.*) Belonging to a sheep. —कः A species of sheep.

ऐड (ल) विडः (लः) N. of Kubera.

ऐण *a* (णी *f.*) Of or belonging to an antelope (as skin, wool &c.); Y. 1. 259.

ऐणेय *a.* (यी *f.*) Produced from the black doe or from anything connected with her.—यः A black antelope. —यं A kind of coitus (रतिबंध).

ऐतद्दात्म्यं The state of having this property or peculiarity.

ऐतरेयिन् *m.* A reader of the Aitareya Brâhmaṇa.

ऐतिहासिक *a.* (की *f.*) 1 Traditional. 2 Historical. —कः 1 An historian. 2 One who knows or studies ancient legends,

ऐतिह्यं Traditional instruction, legendary account; ऐतिह्यमनुमानं च प्रत्यक्षमपि चागमम् Râm.; किलेत्यैतिह्ये. (ऐतिह्य is regarded as one of the Pramâṇas or proofs by the Paurâṇikas and reckoned along with प्रत्यक्ष, अनुमान &c.; see अनुभव).

ऐदंपर्यं Substance, scope, bearing (lit. state of being इदंपर, *i. e.* having this meaning, purport or scope); इदं त्वैदंपर्यं Mâl. 2. 7.

ऐनसं Sin.

ऐंदव *a.* (वी *f.*) Lunar. —वः A lunar month.

ऐंद्र *a.* (द्री *f.*) Belonging or sacred to Indra; R. 2. 50. —द्रः N. of Arjuna and of Vâli. —द्री 1 N. of a *Rik* addressed to Indra; इत्यादिका काचिदैंद्री समाम्नाता J. N. V. 1 The east, (presided over by Indra); Ki. 9. 18. 3 Misfortune, misery. 4 An epithet of Durgâ. 5 Small cardamoms.

ऐंद्रजालिक *a.* (की *f.*) 1 Deceptive, magical, illusive. 2 Familiar with magic. —कः A juggler; Si. 15. 25.

ऐंद्रलुप्तिक *a* (की *f.*) Affected with morbid baldness of the head

ऐंद्राशिरः A species of elephant.

ऐंद्रिः 1 N. of Jayanta, Arjuna, or Vâli, the monkey chief. 2 A crow; ऐंद्रिः किल नखैस्तस्या विददार स्तनौ द्विजः R. 12. 22.

ऐंद्रिय,-यक *a.* 1 Belonging to the senses, sensual. 2 Present, perceptible to the senses. —यं The world of the senses.

ऐंधन *a.* (नी *f.*) Consisting of fuel. —नः N. of the sun.

ऐयत्यं Quantity, number.

ऐरावणः Indra's elephant.

ऐरावतः 1 N. of the elephant of Indra. 2 An excellent elephant. 3 One of the chiefs of the Nâgas or serpent-race (inhabiting Pâtâlâ.) 4 The elephant presiding over the east. 5 A kind of rainbow. —ती 1 The female of Indra's elephant. 2 Lightning. 3 N. of the river Râvî in the Panjâba (=इरावती).

ऐरेयं Spirituous liquor (prepared from food).

ऐलः 1 N. of Purûravas (son of Ilâ and Budha). 2 The planet Mars.

ऐलवालुकः N. of a perfume.

ऐलविलः 1 N. of Kubera; Si. 13. 18. 2 The planet Mars.

ऐलेयः 1 A kind of perfume. 2 Mars.

ऐश *a.* (शी *f.*) 1 Belonging to Siva; R. 2. 75. 2 Supreme; regal.

ऐशान *a.* Belonging to Siva. —नी 1 The north-eastern direction. 2 N. of Durgâ.

ऐश्वर *a.* (री *f.*) 1 Majestic. 2 Powerful, mighty. 3 Belonging to Siva; R. 11. 76. 4 Supreme, royal. 5 Divine. —री N. of Durgâ.

ऐश्वर्यं 1 Supremacy, sovereignty; एकैश्वर्यस्थितोपि M. 1. 1. 2 Might, power, sway. 3 Dominion. 4 Affluence, wealth, greatness. 5 The divine faculties of omnipotence, omnipresence &c.

ऐषमस् *ind.* During this year, in the present year.

ऐषमस्तन-मस्त्य *a.* Belonging to the present year.

ऐष्टिक *a.* (की *f.*) Sacrificial, ceremonial. -Comp. -पूर्तिक *a.* belonging to इष्टापूर्त (belonging to sacrifices or charitable works).

ऐहलौकिक *a.* (की *f.*) Happening in or belonging to this world, temporal, sublunary (opp. पारलौकिक).

ऐहिक *a.* (की *f.*) 1 Of this world or place, temporal, secular, worldly. 2 Local. —कं Business (of this world).

ओ.

ओ *m.* (औः) N. of Brahmâ. *-ind.* 1 A vocative particle (oh). 2 An interjection of (1) calling; (2) remembrance; (3) compassion (ah!).

ओकः 1 A house. 2 A refuge, shelter. 3 A bird. 4 A Súdra.

ओकणः (णिः) A bug; so ओकोदनी.

ओकस् *n.* 1 A house, residence; as in दिवौकस् or स्वर्गौकस् a god. 2 An asylum, refuge.

ओख 1 P. (ओखति, ओखित) 1 To be dry. 2 To be able; be sufficient. 3 To adorn or grace. 4 To refuse. 5 To ward off.

ओघः 1 A flood, stream, current; पुनरोघेन हि युज्यते नदी Ku. 4. 44. 2 An inundation. 3 A heap, quantity, multitude 4 The whole. 5 Continuity. 6 Tradition, traditional instruction. 7 A king of dance.

ओंकारः See under ओम्.

ओज् 4. 10. U. (ओजाति, ओजयति, ओजित) To be strong or able.

ओज *a.* Odd, uneven. —जं =ओजस् q. v.

ओजस् *n.* 1 Bodily strength, vigour; energy. 2 Virility, the generative faculty. 3 Splendour, light. 4 (In Rhet.) An elaborate form of style, abundance of compounds (considered by Daṇḍin to be the 'soul of prose'); ओजः समासभूयस्त्वमेतद्गद्यस्य जीवितम् Kâv. 1. 80; said to be of 5 kinds in R. G. 5 Water. 6 Metallic lustre.

ओजसीन, ओजस्य *a.* Strong, powerful.

ओजस्वत्, ओजस्विन् *a.* Strong, vigorous, energetic, powerful.

ओड्रः (*m.* pl.) N. of a people and their country (the modern Orissa); Ms. 10. 44. —ड्रं The *Javâ*-flower.

ओत *a.* Woven, sewn with threads across. -Comp. प्रोत *a.* 1 sewn crosswise and length-wise. 2 extending in all directions.

ओतुः A cat (*f.* also); as in स्थूलो (लौ) तुः.

ओदनः,-नं 1 Food, boiled rice; *e. g.* दध्योदनः, घृत°. 2 Grain mashed and cooked with milk.

ओम् *ind.* 1 The sacred syllable *om*, uttered as a holy exclamation at the beginning and end of a reading of the Vedas, or previous to the commencement of a prayer or sacred work. 2 As a particle it implies (*a*) solemn affirmation and respectful assent (so be it, amen!); (*b*) assent or acceptance (yes, all right); ओमित्युच्यतताममात्यः Mâl. 6; ओमित्युक्तवतोथ शार्ङ्गिण इति Si. 1. 75; द्वितीयश्चेदोमिति ब्रूमः S. D. 1. (*c*) command. (*d*) auspiciousness; (*e*) removal or warding off. 3 Brahman. -Comp. -कारः 1 the sacred syllable ओम्. 2 the exclamation ओम्.

ओरंफः A hard scratch; Mal. 7.

ओल *a.* Wet, damp.

ओलंड् 1 P., 10 U. (ओलंडति, ओलंडयति, ओलंडित) To cast or throw upwards, throw up.

ओल्ल *a.* Wet, damp.-ल्लः A hostage; °आगतः come or received as a hostage; (this word occurs once or twice in Viddhaśâlabhanjikâ).

ओषः Burning, combustion.

ओषणः Pungency, sharp flavour.

ओषधिः,-धी *f.* 1 A herb, plant (in general). 2 A medicinal plant or drug. 3 An annual plant or herb which dies after becoming ripe. -Comp. -ईशः, -गर्भः, -नाथः the moon (as presiding over and feeding plants). -ज *a.* produced from plants. -धरः,-पतिः 1 a dealer in medicinal drugs. 2 a physician. 3 the moon. -प्रस्थः the capital of Himâlaya; तत्प्रयातौषधिप्रस्थं स्थितये हिमवत्पुरं. Ku. 6. 33, 36.

ओष्ठः A lip (lower or upper). -Comp. -अधरौ-रं the upper and lower lip. -ज *a.* labial. -जाहः the root of the lip. -पल्लवः-वं a sprout-like or tender lip. -पुटं the cavity made by opening the lips.

ओष्ठ्य *a.* 1 Being at the lips. 2 Labial (as the sounds).

ओष्ण *a.* A little warm, tepid.

औ.

औ *ind.* An interjection of (1) calling; (2) addressing; (3) opposition; (4) asseveration or determination.

औक्थिक्यं The text of the Ukthas.

औक्थ्यं A peculiar mode of recitation.

औक्षकं, औक्षं A multitude of oxen; *Si.* 5. 62.

औग्र्यं Formidableness, fierceness, dreadfulness, cruelty &c.

औघः Flood.

औचित्यं, औचिती 1 Aptness, fitness, propriety. 2 Congruity or fitness, as one of the several circumstances which determine the exact meaning of a word in a sentence; सामर्थ्यमौचिती देशः कालो व्यक्तिः स्वरादयः S. D. 2.

औच्चैःश्रवसः N. of Indra's horse.

औजसिक *a.* (की *f.*) Energetic, vigorous. —कः A hero.

औजस्य *a.* Conducive to vigour or energy. -स्यं Strength, vigour of life, energy.

औज्ज्वल्यं Brightness, brilliancy.

औडुपिक *a.* (की *f.*) Crossing in a boat. -कः A passenger in a boat or raft.

औडुंबर=औदुंबर q. v.

औड्रः An inhabitant, or the king, of the Odra country, q. v.

औत्कंठ्यं 1 Desire, longing for. 2 Anxiety.

औत्कर्ष्यं Excellence; superiority.

औत्तमिः N. of the third of the fourteen Manus.

औत्तर *a.* (री, -रा *f.*) Morthern. -Comp. -पथिक *a.* going in the northern direction.

औत्तरेयः N. of Parikshit, son of Abhimanyu and Uttarâ

औत्तानपादः, -दिः 1 N. of Dhruva. 2 The polar star.

औत्पत्तिक *a.* (की *f.*) 1 Inborn, innate. 2 Produced at the same time.

औत्पात *a.* Treating of portents.

औत्पातिक *a.* (की *f.*) Portentous, prodigious, calamitous; R. 14. 53. -कं A portent.

औत्संगिक *a.* (की *f.*) Borne or placed upon the hip.

औत्सर्गिक *a.* (की *f.*) 1 That which is liable to be abolished in exceptional cases, though generally valid (as a rule of grammar). 2 General (opp. to particular), not restricted. 3 Leaving, quitting. 4 Natural, inherent. 5 Derivative.

औत्सुक्यं 1 Anxiety, uneasiness. 2 Ardent desire, eagerness, zeal; औत्सुक्यमात्रमवसादयति प्रतिष्ठा *S.* 5. 6; औत्सुक्येन कृतत्वरा सहभुवा व्यावर्तमाना ह्रिया Ratn. 1. 2.

औदक *a.* (की *f.*) Aquatic, watery, referring to water.

औदंचन *a.* (नी *f.*) Contained in a bucket or pitcher.

औदनिकः A cook.

औदरिक *a.* (की *f.*) Voracious, gluttonous; a glutton; सर्वत्रौदरिकस्याभ्यवहार्यमेव विषयः V. 3; M. 4.

औदर्य *a.* 1 Being in the womb. 2 Entered into the womb.

औदश्वितं Butter-milk with an equal proportion of water.

औदार्यं 1 Generosity, nobility, magnanimity. 2 Greatness, excellence. 3 Depth of meaning (अर्थसंपत्ति); स सौष्ठवौदार्यविशेषशालिनीं विनिश्चितार्थामिति वाचमाददे Ki. 1. 3; see Malli. on Ki. 11. 40; and उदारता also under उदार.

औदासीन्यं, औदास्यं 1 Indifference, apathy; पर्याप्तोसि प्रजाः पातुमौदासीन्येन वर्तितुं R. 10. 25; इदानीमौदास्यं यदि भजसि भागीरथि G. L. 4. 2 Solitariness, loneliness. 3 perfect indifference (to worldly affairs), stoicism.

औदुंबर *a.* (री *f.*) Made of, or coming from, the Udumbara tree. -रः N. of a region abounding in Udumbara trees. -री A branch of उदुंबर tree. -रं 1 The wood of the Udumbara tree. 2 The Udumbara fruit. 3 Copper.

औद्गात्रं The office of the Udgatṛi priest.

औद्दालकं A bitter and acrid substance like honey.

औद्देशिक *a.* (की *f.*) Showing, indicative of.

औद्धत्यं 1 Arrogance, insolence. 2 Boldness, bold or adventurous deeds, औद्धत्यमायोजितकामसूत्रं Mâl. 1. 4.

औद्धारिक *a.* (की *f.*) Deducted from patrimony, portionable, heritable. -कं A portion or inheritance (deducted from patrimony).

औद्भिदं 1 Spring water. 2 Fossil salt, rock salt.

औद्वाहिक *a.* (की *f.*) 1 Relating to marriage. 2 Obtained in marriage; Y. 2. 118; Ms. 9. 206. -कं A gift made to a woman at her marriage.

औधस्यं Milk (produced from the udder); R. 2. 66 v. 1.

औन्नत्यं Height, elevation (moral also).

औपकर्णिक *a.* (की *f.*) Being near the ears.

औपकार्यं, -र्या A residence, a tent.

औपग्रस्तिकः -ग्रहिकः 1 An eclipse. 2 The sun or moon in eclipse.

औपचारिक *a.* (की *f.*) Metaphorical, figurative; secondary (opp. मुख्य). —कं Figurative application.

औपजानुक *a.* (की *f.*) Being near the knees.

औपदेशिक *a.* (की *f.*) 1 Living by उपदेश or teaching. 2 Got by instruction (as wealth).

औपधर्म्यं 1 A false doctrine, heresy. 2 Inferior virtue, or a degraded principle of virtue.

औपधिक *a.* (की *f.*) Deceitful, deceptive.

औपधेयं The wheel of a carriage (रथांगं).

औपनायनिक *a.* (की *f.*) Relating to, or serving for, उपनयन (the rite of investiture with the sacred thread); Ms. 2. 68.

औपनिधिक *a.* (की *f.*) Forming, or relating to, a deposit. -कं A deposit or pledge; anything pledged or deposited; Y. 2. 65.

औपनिषद *a.* (दी *f.*) 1 Contained or taught in an Upanishad; scriptural, theological. 2 Based or founded on, derived from, the Upanishads; औपनिषदं दर्शनं (another name for Vedânta phil.). -दः 1 The supreme soul, Brahman. **2** A follower of the doctrines of the Upanishads.

औपनीविक *a.* (की *f.*) Being or placed near नीवि (the knot of the wearing garment) (of males or females); औपनीविकमरुंद्ध किल स्त्री (करं) *Si.* 10. 60; Bk. 4. 26.

औपपत्तिक *a.* (की *f.*) **1** Ready at hand, within reach. **2** Fit, proper. **3** Theoretical.

औपमिक *a.* (की *f.*) **1** Serving for a simile or comparison. **2** Shown by a simile.

औपम्यं Comparison, resemblance, analogy; आत्मौपम्येन भूतेषु दयां कुर्वंति साधवः H. 1. 12.

औपयिक *a.* (की *f.*) **1** Proper, fit, right. **2** Obtained by efforts. **–कः –कं** A means, an expedient, a remedy; शिवमौपयिकं गरीयसीं Ki. 2. 35.

औपरिष्ट *a.* (ष्टी *f.*) Being or produced above.

औपरो (रौ) धिक *a.* (की *f.*) **1** Proceeding from, or relating to, favour or kindness. **2** Opposing, impeding. **–कः** A staff of the wood of the Pîlu tree.

औपल *a.* (ली *f.*) Stony, of stone.

औपवस्तं Fasting, a fast.

औपवस्त्रं **1** Food suitable for a fast. **2** Fasting.

औपवास्यं Fasting.

औपवाह्य *a.* **1** Serving for riding on. **–ह्यः** **1** A king's elephant. **2** Any royal vehicle.

औपवेशिक *a.* (की *f.*) Getting livelihood by entire devotion to any employment.

औपसंख्यानिक *a.* (की *f.*) **1** Mentioned in a supplementary addition. **2** Supplementary.

औपसर्गिक *a.* (की *f.*) **1** Able to cope with adversity. **2** Portentous.

औपस्थिक *a.* Living by fornication.

औपस्थ्यं Cohabitation, sexual intercourse.

औपहारिक *a.* (की *f.*) Serving as an oblation or offering. **—कं** An offering or oblation.

औपाधिक *a.* (की *f.*) **1** Conditional. **2** Pertaining to attributes or properties; an effect produced.

औपाध्यायक *a.* (की *f.*) Coming or obtained from a teacher.

औपासन *a.* (नी *f.*) Relating to गृह्याग्नि or household fire. **—नः** A fire used for domestic worship.

औम् *ind.* The sacred syllable of the *Sûdras* (for ओम् which is forbidden to be uttered by them).

औरभ्र *a.* (भ्री *f.*) Belonging to or produced from a ram. **– भ्रं** **1** Mutton. **2** Woollen cloth, coarse woollen blanket (°भ्रः also).

औरभ्रकं A flock of sheep.

औरभ्रिकः A shepherd.

औरस *a.* (सी *f.*) Produced from the breast, born of oneself, legitimate; R. 16. 88. **—सः, –सी** A legitimate son or daughter; Y. 2. 128.

औरस्य=औरस q. v.

और्ण, और्णक, और्णिक *a.* (र्णी, -की *f.*) Woollen.

और्ध्वकालिक *a.* (की *f.*) Relating to subsequent or later time.

और्ध्वदेहं A funeral ceremony.

और्ध्वदे (दै) हिक *a.* (की *f.*) Relating to a deceased person, funeral; °क्रिया obsequies, funeral rites. **—कं** Funeral rites, obsequies.

और्व *a.* (र्वी *f.*) **1** Relating to Aurva. **2** Produced from the thigh. **—र्वः** **1** N. of a celebrated *Rishi*. [He was a descendant of Bh*r*igu. The Mah*a*bh*a*rata relates that the sons of K*a*rtav*i*rya, with the desire of destroying the descendants of Bh*r*igu, killed even the children in the womb. One of the women of the family in order to preserve her embryo secreted it in her thigh (*úru*), whence the child at its birth was called Aurva. Beholding him the sons of K*a*rtav*i*rya were struck with blindness, and his wrath gave rise to a flame which threatened to consume the whole world, had he not, at the desire of his Pitris, the Bh*a*rgavas, cast it into the ocean, where it remained concealed with the face of a horse; cf. Vadav*a*gni. Aurva was afterwards preceptor to king Sagara of Ayodhy*a*]. **2** Submarine fire; त्वयि ज्वलत्यौर्व इवांबुराशौ *S.* 3. 3; so °अनलः.

औलूकं A collection of owls.

औलुक्यः N. of Kaṇâda, the propounder of the Vaiseshika philosophy (see औलूक्यदर्शन in Sarva. S.).

औल्बण्यं Excess, superabundance, virulence.

औशन, औशनस *a.* (नी, –सी *f.*) Belonging or peculiar to Usanas; originating from Usanas, or taught by him. **—सं** The law-book of उशनस् (a treatise on civil polity).

औशीनरः The son of Usînara. **— री** N. of the wife of king Purûravas.

औशीरं **1** The handle of a fan or chowri. **2** A bed; औशीरे कामचारः कृतोऽमुत् Dk. 72. **3** A seat (chair, stool &c.). **4** An unguent made of Usîra. **5** The root of the fragrant grass उशीर q. v. **6** A fan.

औषणं **1** Pungency. **2** Black pepper.

औषधं **1** A herb; herbs taken collectively. **2** A medicament, medicine in general. **3** A mineral.

औषधिः, –धी *f.* **1** A herb, plant (in general); see ओषधि. **2** A medicinal herb; अचिंत्यो हि मणिमंत्रौषधीनां प्रभावः Ratn. 2. **3** An herb which emits fire; विरमंति न ज्वलितुमौषधयः Ki. 5. 24 (तृणज्योतींषि Malli.); cf. Ku. 1. 10. **4** An annual or deciduous plant; °पतिः N. of Soma, the lord of plants.

औषधीय *a.* Medicinal, consisting of herbs.

औषरं,–रकं Rock-salt.

औषस *a.* (सी *f.*) Relating to dawn, early. **—सी** Day-break, morning.

औषसिक, औषिक *a.* (की *f.*) Early born or produced at dawn.

औष्ट्र *a.* (ष्ट्री *f.*) **1** Relating to, or produced from, a camel. **2** Abounding in camels. **— ष्ट्रं** The milk of a camel.

औष्ट्रकं A multitude of camels *Si.* 5. 65.

औष्ठ्य *a.* Relating to the lip, labial. -COMP. **–वर्णः** a labial letter; *i. e.* उ, ऊ, प्, फ्, ब्, भ्, म् and व्. **–स्थान** *a.* pronounced with the lips. **–स्वरः** a labial vowel.

औष्णं Heat, warmth.

औष्ण्यं, औष्म्यं Heat; R. 17. 33.

क.

कः **1** Brahman. **2** Vishṇu. **3** Kâmadeva. **4** Fire. **5** Wind or air. **6** Yama. **7** The sun. **8** The soul. **9** A king or prince. **10** A knot or joint. **11** A peacock. **12** The king of birds. **13** A bird. **14** The mind. **15** Body. **16** Time. **17** A cloud. **18** A word, sound. **19** Hair. **–कं** **1** Happiness, joy, pleasure (as in नाक). **2** Water; सत्येन माभिरक्ष त्वं वरुणेत्यभिशाप्य कं Y. 2. 108; के शवं पतितं दृष्ट्वा पांडवा हर्षनिर्भराः Subhâsh. (where a pun is intended on केशव). **3** The head; as in कंधरा (=कं शिरो धारयतीति)

कंसः –सं **1** A drinking-vessel, cup, goblet. **2** Bell-metal, white copper. **3** A particular measure known as आढक, q. v. **—सः** N. of a king of Mathurâ, son of Ugrasena and enemy of Krishṇa. [He is identified with the Asura K*a*lanemi, and acted inimically towards Krish*n*a and became his implacable foe. The circumstance which made him so was the following. While, after the marriage of Devakî with Vasudeva, he was driving the happy pair home, a heavenly voice warned Kamsa that the eighth child of Devakî would kill him. Thereupon he threw both of them into prison, loaded them with strong fetters, and kept the strictest watch over them. He took from Devakî every child as soon as it was born and slew it, and in this way he disposed of her first six children. But the 7th and 8th, Balarama and Krishna, were safely conveyed to Nanda's house in spite of his vigilance, and Krishna grew up to be his slayer according to the prophecy. When Kamsa heard this, he was very much enraged and sent several demons to kill Krishna, but he killed them all with ease. At last he sent Akrura to bring the boys to Mathura. A severe duel was fought between Kamsa and Krishna, in which the former was slain by the latter]. –Comp. –अरिः, अरातिः, जित्, कृष्, द्विष्, हन् *m.* 'slayer of Kamsa', *i. e.* Krishna; स्वयं संधिकारिणा कंसारिणा दूतेन Ve. 1; निषेद्धिवान् कंसकृषः स विष्टरे Si. 1. 16. –अस्थि *n.* bell-metal. –कारः (री *f.*) 1 a mixed tribe; कंसकारशंखकारौ ब्राह्मणात्संबभूवतुः Sabdak. 2 a worker in pewter or white-brass, a bell-founder.

कंसकं Bell-metal.

कक् 1 A. (ककते, ककित) 1 To wish. 2 To be proud. 3 To be unsteady; see कंक्.

ककुंजलः The Châtaka bird.

ककुद् *f.* 1 A summit, peak. 2 Chief, head; see ककुद below. 3 The hump on the shoulders of the Indian bull. 4 A horn. 5 An ensign or symbol of royalty (as the छत्र, चामर &c.) (According to Pânini V. 4. 146–147 ककुद् is the form to be substituted for ककुद in adj. or Bah. comps.; *e. g.* त्रिककुद्). –Comp. –स्थः an epithet of Puranjaya, son of Sasâda, a king of the solar race, and a descendant of Ikshvâku; इक्ष्वाकुवंश्यः ककुदं नृपाणां ककुत्स्थ इत्याहितलक्षणोऽभूत् R. 6. 71. Mythology relates that, when in their war with the demons, the gods were often worsted, they, headed by Indra, went to the powerful king Puranjaya, and requested him to be their friend in battle. The latter consented to do so, provided Indra carried him on his shoulders. Indra accordingly assumed the form of a bull, and Puranjaya, seated on its hump, completely vanquished the demons. Puranjaya is, therefore called *Kakutstha* 'standing on a hump'].

ककुदः–दं 1 The peak or summit of a mountain. 2 A hump (on the shoulders of an Indian bull). 3 Chief, fore-most, pre-eminent; ककुदं वेदविदां तपोधनश्च Mk. 1. 5; इक्ष्वाकुवंश्यः ककुदं नृपाणां R. 6. 71. 4 A sign or symbol of royalty; नृपतिककुदं R. 3. 70, 17. 27.

ककुद्मत् *a.* Furnished with a hump. —*m.* 1 A mountain (having peaks). 2 A buffalo; मदोदग्राः ककुद्मंतः R. 4. 22; a humped bull; 13. 47; Ku. 1. 56. —ती The hip and the loins.

ककुद्मिन् *a.* 1 Peaked; furnished with a hump &c. —*m.* 1 A bull with a hump on his shoulders. 2 A mountain. 3 N. of king रैवतक. °कन्या-सुता N. of Revatî and wife of Balarâma; Si. 2. 20.

ककुद्वत् *m.* A buffalo with a hump on his shoulders.

ककुंदरं The cavities of the loins; Y. 3. 96 (जघनकूप).

ककुभ् *f.* 1 A direction, quarter of the compass; वियुक्ताः कांतेन स्त्रिय इव न राजंति ककुभः Mk. 5. 26; Si. 9. 25. 2 Splendour, beauty. 3 A wreath of Champaka flowers. 4 A sacred treatise or Sâstra. 5 A peak, summit.

ककुभः 1 A crooked piece of wood at the end of the lute. 2 The tree Arjuna; ककुभसुरभिः शैलः U. 1. 33. —भं A flower of the Kutaja tree; Me. 22.

ककुलः The Bakula tree.

कक्कोलः–ली N. of a plant bearing a berry; कक्कोलीफलजग्धि Mâl. 6. 19. v. l. —लं, –लकं 1 A berry of this plant. 2 A perfume prepared from its berries.

कक्खट *a.* 1 Hard, solid. 2 Laughing.

कक्खटी Chalk.

कक्षः 1 A lurking or hidingplace. 2 The end of the lower garment; see कक्षा. 3 A climbing plant, creeper. 4 Grass, dry grass; यतस्तु कक्षस्तत एव वह्निः R. 7. 55, 11. 75; Ms. 7. 110. 5 A forest of dead trees, dry wood. 6 The arm-pit; प्रक्षिप्योदर्चिषं कक्षे शेरते तेऽभिमारुतं Si. 2. 42. 7 The harem of a king. 8 The interior of a forest; आशु निर्गत्य कक्षात् Rs. 1. 27; कक्षांतरगतो वायुः Râm. 9 The side or flank (of anything). 10 A buffalo. 11 A gate. 12 A marshy ground. —क्षा 1 Painful boils in the arm-pit. 2 An elephant's rope; also his girth. 3 A woman's girdle or zone; a girdle, waist-band (in general); Si. 17. 24. 4 A surrounding wall; a wall. 5 The waist, middle part. 6 A courtyard; area. 7 An enclosure. 8 An inner apartment, a private chamber; a room in general; Ku. 7. 70; Ms. 7. 224; गृहकलहंसकाननुसरन् कक्षांतरप्रधावितः K. 63, 182. 9 A harem. 10 Similarity. 11 An upper garment. 12 Objection or reply in argument (in Logic &c.). 13 Emulation or rivalry. 14 The end of the lower garment which, after the cloth is girt round the lower part of the body, is brought up behind and tucked into the waist-band (Mar. कासोटा). 15 Tying up the waist. 16 The wrist. —क्षं 1 A star. 2 Sin. –Comp. –अग्निः wild fire, conflagration; R. 11. 92. –अंतरं inner or private apartment. –अवेक्षकः 1 a superintendent of the harem. 2 a keeper of a royal garden. 3 a door-keeper. 4 a poet. 5 a debauchee. 6 a player; painter. 7 an actor. 8 a paramour. 9 strength of feeling or sentiment (Wilson). –धरं the shoulder-joint. –पः a tortoise. –(क्षा) पटः a cloth passed between the legs to cover the privities. –पुटः the arm-pit. –शायः –युः a dog.

कक्ष्या 1 The girth of an elephant or horse. 2 A woman's girdle or zone; Si. 10. 62. 3 The upper garment. 4 The border of a garment. 5 The inner apartment of a palace. 6 A wall, enclosure. 7 Similarity.

कख्या An enclosure; division of a large building.

कंकः 1 A heron. 2 A variety of mango. 3 N. of Yama. 4 A Kshatriya 5 A false or pretended Brâhmana. 6 Name assumed by Yudhishthira in the palace of Virâta. –Comp. –पत्र *a.* furnished with the feathers of a heron. (–त्रः) an arrow furnished with a heron's feathers; R. 2. 31; U. 4. 20; Mv. 1. 18. –पत्रिन् *m.*= कंकपत्रः. –मुखः a pair of tongs; Ve. 5. 1. –शायः a dog (sleeping like a heron).

कंकटः, कंकटकः 1 Mail; defensive armour; military accoutrements; Ve. 2. 26, 5. 1; R. 7. 59. 2 An iron hook to goad an elephant (अंकुश).

कंकणः,–णं 1 A bracelet; दानेन पाणिर्न तु कंकणेन विभाति Bh. 2. 71; इदं सुवर्णकंकणं गृह्यतां H. 1. 2 The marriage-string (fastened round the wrist); U. 1. 18; Mâl. 9. 9; देव्यः कंकणमोक्षणाय मिलिता राजन् वरः प्रेष्यतां Mv. 2. 50. 3 An ornament in general. 4 A crest. –णः Water-spray; नितंबे हाराली नयनयुगले कंकणभरम् Udb. —णी, **कंकणिका** 1 A small bell or tinkling ornament. 2 An ornament furnished with bells.

कंकतः,-तं, कंकती,-तिका A comb, hair-comb; Si. 15. 33.

कंकरं Buttermilk (mixed with water).

कंकालः–लं A skeleton; Mâl. 5. 14. –Comp. –पालिन् *m.* N. of Siva. –शेष *a.* reduced to a skeleton; U. 3. 43.

कंकालयः Body.

कंकेल्लः–ल्लिः The Asoka tree.

कंकोली = कक्कोली q. v.

कंगुलः The hand.

कच् I. 1 P. (कचति, कचित) To

sound, cry. -II. 1 U. 1 To bind, fasten (with आ); त्वक्त्रं चाचकचे वरं Bk. 14. 94. 2 To shine.

कचः 1 Hair (especially of the head); कचेषु च निगृह्यैतान् Mb.; see °ग्रह below; अलिनीजिष्णुः कचानां चयः Bh. 1. 5. 2 A dry or healed sore, scar. 3 A binding, band. 4 The hem of a garment. 5 A cloud. 6 N. of a son of Brihaspati. [In their long warfare with the demons, the gods were often times defeated, and rendered quite helpless. But such of the demons as would be slain in battle were restored to life by *S*ukra*ch*arya their preceptor, by means of a mystic charm which he alone possessed. The gods resolved to secure, if possible, this charm for themselves, and induced Kacha to go to *S*ukra*ch*arya and learn it from him by becoming his disciple. So Kacha went to the preceptor but the demons killed him twice lest he should succeed in mastering the lore; but on both occasions he was restored to life by the sage at the intercession of Devay*ani*, his daughter, who had fallen in love with the youth. Thus discomfited the Asuras killed him a third time, burnt his body, and mixed his ashes with *S*ukra's wine; but Devay*ani* again begged her father to restore to life the youth, which the kind father did. Devay*ani* thenceforward began to make stronger advances of love to him, but he steadily resisted her proposals, telling her that she was to him as a younger sister. She thereupon cursed him that the great charm he had learnt would be powerless; he, in return, cursed her that she should be sought by no br*a*hmana, but would become a Kshatriya's wife]. —**चा** A female elephant. –Comp. -**अग्रं** curls, end of hair. -**आचित** *a*. having dishevelled hair; Ki. 1. 36. -**ग्रहः** seizing the hair, seizing (one) by the hair; R. 10. 47, 19. 31. -**पक्षः**, -**पाशः**, -**हस्तः** thick or ornamented hair; (according to Ak. these three words denote a collection; पाशः पक्षश्च हस्तश्च कलापार्थाः कचात्परे). -**मालः** smoke.

कचंगनं A free market (where no duty or custom has to be paid).

कचाकाचि *ind*. 'Hair against hair', (fighting by) pulling each other's hair.

कचंगलः The ocean.

कचाटुरः A gallinule.

कच्चर *a*. 1 Bad, dirty. 2 Wicked, vile, debased.

कच्चित् *ind*. A particle of (*a*) interrogation (often translateable by 'I hope'); काच्चित् अहमिव विस्मृतवानसि त्वं *S*. 6; कच्चिन्मृगीणामनघा प्रसूतिः R. 5. 7; also 5, 6. 8, 9; (*b*) joy; (*c*) auspiciousness.

कच्छः-**च्छं** 1 Bank, margin, skirt, bordering region (whether near water or not); यमुनाकच्छमवतीर्णः Pt. 1; गंधमादनकच्छोऽध्यासितः V. 5; *S*i. 3. 80. 2 A marsh, morass, fen. 3 The hem of the lower garment tucked into the waistband; see कक्षा. 4 A part of a boat. 5 A particular part of a tortoise (as in कच्छप). —**च्छा** A cricket. –Comp. -**अंतः** the border of a lake or stream. -**पः** (पी *f*.) 1 a turtle, tortoise; केशव धृतकच्छपरूप जय जगदीश हरे Gît. 1; Ms. 1. 44, 12-42. 2 An attitude in wrestling. 3 One of the nine treasures of Kubera. (-**पी**) 1 a female tortoise. 2 A kind of lute; also the lute of Sarasvantî. -**भूः** *f*. marshy ground, morass.

कच्छ (च्छा) टिका, कच्छाटी The end or hem of a lower garment which, after being carried round the body, is gathered up behind and tucked into the waist-band.

कच्छुः-**कच्छू** *f*. Itch, scab.

कच्छुर *a*. 1 Scabby, itchy. 2 Unchaste, libidinous.

कज्जलं 1 Lamp-black or soot, considered as a collyrium and applied to the eyelashes or eyelids medicinally, or sometimes as an ornament; यथा यथा चेयं चपला दीप्यते तथा तथा दीपशिखेव कज्जलमलिनमेव कर्मकेवलमुद्वमति K. 105; अद्यापि तां विधृतकज्जललोलनेत्रां Ch. P. 15; °कालिमा Amaru. 88. 2 Sulphuret of lead or antimony (used as a collyrium). 3 Ink. —Comp. -**ध्वजः** a lamp. -**रोचकः** -**कं** the wooden stand on which a lamp is placed.

कंच् 1 A. 1 To bind. 2 To shine.

कंचारः The sun. 2 The Arka plant.

कंचुकः 1 An armour, mail. 2 The skin of a snake, slough; Pt. 1. 65. 3 A dress, garb, cloth (in general); धर्म ° प्रवेशिनः *S*. 5. 4 A dress fitting close to the upper part of the body. robe; अंतःकंचुकिकंचुकस्य विशति त्रासादयं वामनः Ratn. 2. 3; Pt. 2. 64. 5 A bodice, jacket; क्वचिदिर्वेद्रगजाजिनकंचुकः *S*i. 6. 51, 12. 20; Amaru. 81; (Phrase:-निंदति कंचुककारं प्रायः शुष्कस्तनकि नारी; cf. "a bad workman quarrels with his tools").

कंचुकालुः A snake.

कंचुकित *a*. 1 Furnished with armour, mailed. 2 Having a garment; कंथा ° Bh. 3. 130.

कंचुकिन् *a*. Furnished with armour or mail. -*m*. 1 An attendant on the women's apartments, a chamberlain; (an important character in dramas अंतःपुरचरो वृद्धो विप्रो गुणगणान्वितः। सर्वकार्यार्थकुशलः कंचुकीत्यभिधीयते॥). 2 A libidinous man, debauchee. 3 A serpent. 4 A door-keeper. 5 Barley.

कंचुलिका, कंचुली A bodice; त्वं मुग्धाक्षि विनैव कंचुकिलया धत्से मनोहारिणीं लक्ष्मीं Amaru. 23.

कंजः 1 The hair. 2 N. of Brahmâ. —**जं** 1 A lotus. 2 Ambrosia, nectar. —Comp. —**जः** N. of Brahmâ. —**नाभः** N. of Vishṇu.

कंजकः -**की** A kind of bird.

कंजनः 1 The god of love. 2 A kind of bird (the bird of Kandarpa).

कंजरः, **कंजारः** 1 The sun. 2 An elephant. 3 The belly. 4 An epithet of Brahmâ.

कंजलः A kind of bird.

कट् 1P. (कटति, कटित) 1 To go. 2 To cover. With प्र 1 to appear. 2 to shine. (*Caus*. -कटयति) to show, display, exhibit, manifest; औज्ज्वल्यं परमागतः प्रकटयत्याभोगभीमं तमः Mâl. 5. 11; सुहृदिव प्रकटय्य सुखप्रदां प्रथममेकरसामनुकूलतां U. 4. 15; Ratn. 4. 16.

कटः 1 A straw-mat; Ms. 2. 204. 2 The hip. 3 The hip and loins; the hollow above the hips. 4 The temples of an elephant; कंडूयमानेन कटं कदाचित् R. 2. 37. 3. 37, 4. 47. 5 A kind of grass 6 A corpse. 7 A hearse, bier. 8 A particular throw of the dice in hazard; नर्दितदर्शितमार्गः कटेन विनिपातितो यामि Mk. 2. 8. 9 Excess (as in उत्कट). 10 An arrow. 11 A custom. 12 A cemetery, burial-ground. –Comp. —**अक्षः** a glance, a side-long look, leer; गाढं निखात इव मे हृदये कटाक्षः Mâl. 1. 29; also 25, 28; Me. 35. -**उदकं** 1 water for a funeral libation. 2 rut, ichor (issuing from an elephant's temples). -**कारः** 1 a mixed tribe (of low social position); (शूद्रायां वैश्यतश्चौर्यात् कटकार इति स्मृतः Usanas). 2 a weaver of mats. -**कोलः** a spitting pot. -**खादकः** 1 a jackal. 2 a crow. 3 glass-vessel. -**घोषः** a hamlet inhabited by herdsmen. -**पूतनः**, -**ना** a kind of departed spirits; अमेध्यकुणपाशी च क्षत्रियः कटपूतनः Ms. 12. 71; उत्तालाः कटपूतनाप्रभृतयः सांराविणं कुर्वते Mâl. 5. 12:; (°पूतन v. l.); also 23. -**प्रूः** 1 *S*iva. 2 an imp or goblin. 3 a worm. -**प्रोथः**,-**थं** the buttocks. -**भंगः** 1 gleaning corn with the hands. 2 any royal calamity or misfortune. -**मालिनी** wine.

कटकः,-**कं** 1 A bracelet; आबद्धहेमकटकां रहसि स्मरामि Ch. P. 15. 2 A zone or girdle. 3 A string. 4 The link of a chain. 5 A mat. 6 Sea-salt 7 The side or ridge of a mountain; प्रफुल्लवृक्षैः कटकैरिव स्वैः Ku. 7. 52; R. 16. 31. 8 Table-land; *S*i. 4. 65. 9 An army, a camp; Mu. 5. 10 A royal capital or metropolis (राजधानी). 11 A house or dwelling. 12 A circle, wheel.

कटकिन् *m*. A mountain.

कटंकटः 1 Fire. 2 Gold. 3 N. of Gaṇesa; Y. 1. 285.

कटनं The roof (or thatch) of a house.

कटाहः 1 A frying pan, a shallow boiler for oil or butter (of a semispheriodal shape and furnished with handles ; Mar. कढई). 2 A turtle's shell. 3 A well. 4 A hill or mound of earth. 5 fragment of a broken jar ; *Si.* 5. 37 ; N. 22. 32.

कटिः, -टी *f.* 1 The hip. 2 The buttocks (considered by rhetoricians as vulgar and colloquial in these senses ; the word कटि in कटिस्ते हरते मनः in S. D. 574 is said to be ग्राम्य). 3 An elephant's cheek. -COMP. **-तटं** the loins ; कटीतटनिवेशितं Mk. 1. 27. **-त्रं** 1 a cloth girt round the loins. 2 a zone, girdle. **-प्रोथः** the buttocks. **-मालिका** a woman's girdle or zone. **-रोहकः** the rider of an elephant. **-शीर्षकः** the loins. **-शृंखला** a girdle furnished with small bells. **-सूत्रं** a woman's girdle or zone.

कटिका The hip.

कटीरः -रं 1 A cave, hollow. 2 The cavity of the loins. **-रं** A hip.

कटीरकं The posteriors.

कटु *a.* (टु or ट्वी *f.*) 1 Pungent, acrid ; (said of a *rasa* or flavour; the *rasas* are six ; मधुर, कटु, अम्ल, तिक्त, कषाय, & लवण) Bg. 18. 9. 2 Fragrant, exhaling strong odour ; R. 5. 43. 3 Ill-smelling, having a bad smell. 4 (*a*) Bitter, caustic (words); Y. 3. 142. (*b*) Disagreeable, unpleasant ; श्रवणकटु नृपाणामेकवाक्यं विवव्रुः R. 6. 85. 5 Envious. 6 Hot, impetuous. **—टुः** Pungency, acerbity (one of the six flavours). **—टु** *n.* 1 An improper act. 2 Scandal, reproach, censure. -COMP. **-कीटः, -कीटकः** a gnat, mosquito **-क्काणः** the टिट्टिभ bird. **-ग्रंथि** *n.* dried ginger ; so °भंगः, °भद्रं dried ginger or ginger. **-निष्प्लावः** grain not inundated. **-मोदं** a certain perfume. **-रवः** a frog.

कटुक *a.* 1 Sharp, pungent. 2 Impetuous, hot. 3 Unpleasant, disagreeable. **-कः** Pungency, acerbity (as one of the six flavours); see कटु above.

कटुकता Rough manners, rudeness.

कटुरं Buttermilk mixed with water.

कटोरं An earthen vessel.

कटोलः 1 A pungent taste or flavour. 2 A man of an inferior and degraded caste, such as a Chândâla.

कट् 1 P. To live in distress ; see **कंद्**.

कठः N. of a sage, pupil of Vaisampâyana, teacher of that branch of the Yajurveda which is called after him.**—ठाः** The followers of that sage. -COMP. **-धूर्तः** a Brâhmaṇa well-versed in the कठ branch of the Yajurveda.**-श्रोत्रियः** a Brâhmaṇa who has mastered the कठ branch of the Yajurveda.

कठमर्दः An epithet of *S*iva.

कठर *a.* Hard, stiff.

कठिका Chalk.

कठिन *a.* 1 Hard, stiff ; कठिनविषमामेकवेणीं सारयंतीं Me. 92 ; Amaru. 72; so °स्तनौ. 2 Hard-hearted, cruel, ruthless; न विदीर्ये कठिनाः खलु स्त्रियः Ku. 4. 5; Pt. 1. 64; Amaru. 6; so °हृदय. 3 Inexorable, inflexible. 4 Sharp, violent, intense (as pain &c.); नितांतकठिनां रुजं मम न वेद सा मानसीम् V. 2. 11. 5 Giving pain. **—नः** A thicket. **-ना** 1 A sweetmeat made with refined sugar. 2 An earthen vessel for cooking ; (*n.* also in this sense).

कठिनिका, कठिनी 1 Chalk. 2 The little finger.

कठोर *a.* 1 Hard, solid; कठोरास्थिग्रंथि Mâl. 5. 34. 2 Cruel, hard-hearted, ruthless ; अयि कठोर यशः किल ते प्रियं U. 3. 27; so °हृदय, °चित्त. 3 Sharp, piercing; °अंकुश *S*ânti. 1. 22. 4 Full developed, complete, full-grown ; कठोरगर्भा जानकीं विमुच्य U. 1, 1. 49 ; so कठोरताराधिपलांछनछविः *Si.* 1. 20. 5 (*Fig.*) Matured, refined ; कलाकलापालोचनकठोरमतिभिः K. 7.

कड्=कड्‌ q. v.

कड *a.* 1 Dumb. 2 Hoarse. 3 Ignorant, foolish.

कडंग (क) रः Straw.

कडंग (क) रीय *a.* To be fed with straw. **—यः** An animal fed with straw, such as a cow or buffalo ; R. 5. 9.

कडत्रं A kind of vessel.

कडंदिका Science (कलंडिका).

कडं (लं) बः Stem or stalk (of a pot-herb).

कडार *a.* 1 Tawny. 2 Proud, haughty, impudent. **-रः** 1 The tawny colour. 2 A servant.

कड्डितुलः A sword, scimitar.

कण् I. 1 P. (कणति, कणित) 1 To sound or cry (as in distress); moan. 2 To become small. 3 To go:-II. 10 P. or *Caus.* To wink, to close the eye with the lashes.

कणः 1 A grain; तंडुलकणान् H. 1 ; Ms. 11. 92. 2 An atom or particle (of anything). 3 A very small quantity; द्रविण° *S*ânti. 1. 19 ; 3. 5. 4 A grain of dust ; R. 1. 85 ; or of pollen; V. 2. 7. 5 A drop (of water) or spray ; कणवाही मालिनीतरंगाणाम् *S*. 3. 5; अंबु°, अश्रु° ; Me. 26, 45, 69 ; Amaru. 54. 6 An ear of corn. 7 Spark (as of fire). -COMP. **-अदः, -भक्षः, -भुज्** *m.* a nickname given to the philosopher who propounded the Vaiseshika system of philosophy (which may be said to be a 'doctrine of atoms'). **-जीरकं** small cumin seed. **-भक्षकः** a kind of bird. **-लाभः** a whirlpool.

कणपः A kind of iron lance or bar; लोहस्तंभस्तु कणपः Vaijayantî ; चापचक्रकणपकर्षण &c. Dk.

कणशः *ind.* In small parts or minute particles, grain by grain, little by little, drop by drop &c. ; तद्वित कणशो विकीर्यते (भस्म) Ku. 4. 27.

कणिकः 1 A grain. 2 A small particle. 3 An ear of corn. 4 A meal of parched wheat.

कणिका 1 An atom, a small or minute particle. 2 A drop (of water); Me. 98. 3 A kind of corn or rice.

कणिशः,-शं An ear of corn.

कणीक *a.* Small, diminutive.

कणे *ind.* A particle expressing the satisfaction of a desire (श्रद्धाप्रतीघात); कणेहत्य पयः पिबति Sk. 'he drinks milk to his heart's content or till he is satisfied'.

कणेरा-रुः *f.* 1 A she-elephant. 2 A courtezan, a harlot.

कंटकः,-कं 1 A thorn ; पादलग्नं करस्थेन कंटकेनैव कंटकं (उद्धरेत्) Chân. 22. 2 A prickle, sting; Y. 3. 53. 3 (*Fig.*) Any troublesome fellow who is, as it were, a thorn to the state and an enemy of order and good government ; उत्खातलोकत्रयकंटकेऽपि R. 14. 73 ; त्रिदिवमुद्धृतदानवकंटकं *S*. 7. 3 ; Ms 9. 260. 4 (Hence) Any source of vexation or annoyance, nuisance ; Ms. 9. 253. 5 Horripilation, erection of hair. 6 A finger-nail. 7 A vexing speech. **—कः** 1 A bamboo. 2 A workshop, manufactory. -COMP. **-अशनः,-भक्षकः, -भुज्** *m.* a camel. **-उद्धरणं** 1 (lit.) extracting thorns, weeding. 2 (fig.) removing annoyances ; extirpating thieves and all such sources of public annoyance; कंटकोद्धरणे नित्यमातिष्ठेद्यत्नमुत्तमम् Ms. 9. 252. **-द्रुमः** 1 a thorn, bush ; भवंति नितरां स्फीताः सुक्षेत्रे कंटकद्रुमाः Mk. 9. 7. 2 the *S*âlmali tree (Mar. सावरी) **-फलः** the bread-fruit tree. **-मर्दनं** suppressing disturbances. **-विशोधनं** extirpating every source of trouble ; राज्यकंटकविशोधनोद्यतः Vikr. 5. 1.

कंटकित *a.* 1 Thorny. 2 Covered with erect hair; thrilled, horripilated; प्रीतिकंटकितत्वचः Ku. 6. 15; R. 7. 22.

कंटकिन् *a.* (नी *f.*) 1 Thorny, prickly ; कंटकिनो वनांताः Vikr. 1. 116. 2 Vexatious, troublesome. -COMP. **-फलः** the breadfruit tree (पनस).

कंटकिलः Any thorny kind of bamboo.

कंठ् 1. 10. U. (कंठति-ते, कंठयति-ते, कंठित) 1 To mourn, grieve for. 2 To miss, be anxious or long for, remember with regret ; (in this sense generally used with the preposition उद् and a noun in the gen. or loc. or dat. case); परिष्वंगस्य वात्सल्यादयमुत्कंठते जनः U. 6. 21 ; यथा स्वर्गाय नोत्कंठते V. 3 ; सुरतव्यापारलीलाविधौ चेतः समुत्कंठते K. P. 1.

कंठः-ठं 1 The throat ; कंठे निपीडयन् मारयति Mk. 8 ; कंठः स्तंभितबाष्पवृत्तिकलुषः

S. 4. 5 ; कंठेषु स्खलितं गतेपि शिशिरे पुंस्कोकिलानां रुतम् 6. 3. 2 The neck ; कंठाश्लेषपरिग्रहे शिथिलता Pt. 4. 6 ; कंठाश्लेषप्रणयिनि जने किं पुनर्दूरसंस्थे Me. 3, 97, 112; Amaru. 19, 57 ; Ku. 5. 57. 3 The voice ; सा मुक्तकंठं चक्रंद R. 14. 65 ; किन्नरकंठि 8. 63 ; आर्यपुत्रोपि प्रमुक्तकंठं रोदिति U. 3. 4 The neck or brim of a vessel. 5 Vicinity, immediate proximity (as in उपकंठ). –COMP. –आभरणं a neck-ornament ; परीक्षितं काव्यसुवर्णमेतल्लोकस्य कंठाभरणत्वमेतु Vikr. 1. 24; cf. names like सरस्वतीकंठाभरण. –कूणिका Indian lute. –गत *a.* being at or in the throat, coming to the throat, *i. e.* on the point of departing ; न वदेद्यावनीं भाषां प्राणैः कंठगतैरपि Subhâsh. –तटः,-टं-टी the side of the neck. –दघ्न *a.* reaching to the neck. –नीडकः a kite. –नीलकः a large lamp or torch (Mar. मशाल). –पाशकः 1 a rope tied round an elephant's neck. 2 a halter in general. –भूषा a short necklace ; विदुषां कंठभूषात्वमेतु Vikr. 18. 102. –मणिः 1 a jewel worn on the neck. (fig.). 2 a dear or beloved object. –लता 1 a collar. 2 a horse's halter. –वर्तिन् *a.* being at or in the throat ; *i. e.* on the point of departing ; प्राणैः R. 12. 54. –शोषः (lit.) 1 drying up or parching of the throat. 2 (fig.) fruitless expostulation. –सज्जनं hanging on, by, or round the neck. –सूत्रं a kind of embrace ; यत्कुर्वते वक्षसि वल्लभस्य स्तनाभिघातं निबिडोपगूहात् । परिश्रमार्थं शनकैर्विदग्धास्तत्कंठसूत्रं प्रवदंति संतः; कंठसूत्रमपदिश्य योषितः R. 19. 22 ; (also called स्तनालिंगन). –स्थ *a.* 1 being in the throat. 2 guttural.

कंठतः *ind.* 1 From the throat. 2 Distinctly, explicitly.

कंठालः 1 A boat. 2 A spade, hoe. 3 War. 4 A camel. —ला A churning vessel.

कंठिका A necklace of a single string or row.

कंठी *f.* 1 Neck, throat. 2 A necklace, a collar. 3 A rope round the neck of a horse. –COMP. –रवः 1 a lion. 2 an elephant in rut ; कंठीरवमहाग्रहेण न्यपतत् Dk. 7. 3 a pigeon. 4 explicit declaration or mention ; (इति कंठीरवेणोक्तम्).

कंठीलः A camel.

कंठेकालः N. of Siva.

कंठ्य *a.* 1 Relating or suitable to, or being at, the throat. 2 Guttural. –COMP. –वर्णः a guttural letter ; namely अ, आ, क्, ख्, ग्, घ्, ङ्, and ह्. –स्वरः a guttural vowel (अ & आ).

कंड् 1 U. 1 To be glad or satisfied. 2 To be proud. 3 To unhusk. —10 U. (कंडयति-ते, कंडित) 1 To thresh (corn, grain &c.), unhusk. 2 To defend, protect.

कंडनं 1 Threshing, separating the chaff from the grain ; अजानतार्थं तत्सर्वं (अध्ययनं) तुषाणां कंडनं यथा. 2 Chaff. –नी 1 A wooden mortar in which the threshing of corn or grain is performed. 2 A pestle.

कंडरा Sinew.

कंडिका A short section, shortest subdivision ; (as in the शुक्ल यजुर्वेद).

कंडुः *m.f.* **कंडूः** *f.* 1 Scratching. 2 Itching ; कपोलकंडूः करिभिर्विनेतुं Ku. 1. 9 ; Sânti. 4. 17.

कंडूतिः *f.* 1 Scratching. 2 Itching, itch.

कंडूयति-ते Den. U. (*p. p.* कंडूयित) 1 To scratch, rub gently ; कंडूयमानेन कटं कदाचित् R. 2. 37 ; मृगीमकंडूयत कृष्णसारः Ku. 3. 36 ; शृंगे कृष्णमृगस्य वामनयनं कंडूयमानां मृगीं S. 6. 16 ; Ms. 4. 42.

कंडूयनं Scratching, rubbing ; कंडूयनैर्दंशनिवारणैश्च R. 2. 5. –नी A brush for rubbing.

कंडूयनकः A tickler ; Pt. 1. 71.

कंडूया 1 Scratching. 2 Itching.

कंडूल *a.* Having an itchy sensation, feeling the itch, itchy कंडूलद्विपगंडपिंडकषणोत्कंपेन संपातिभिः U. 2. 9.

कंडोलः 1 A basket for holding grain (of cane or bamboo). 2 A safe, store-room. 3 A camel. –ली The lute of a Chandala.

कंडोषः A caterpillar.

कण्वः N. of a sage, foster-father of Sakuntalâ and progenitor of the line of काण्व Brâhmaṇas –COMP. –दुहितृ, –सुता Sakuntalâ, Kaṇva's daughter.

कतः, कतकः The clearing nutplant (the nut of which is said to clear muddy water) ; फलं कतकवृक्षस्य यद्यप्यंबुप्रसादनम् । न नामग्रहणादेव तस्य वारि प्रसीदति Ms. 6. 67. –तं, –तकं The nut of this tree : see अंबुप्रसादन also.

कतम *pron. a.* (–मत् *n.*) Who or which of many ; अपि ज्ञायते कतमेन दिग्भागेन गतः स जाल्म इति V. 1. अथ कतमं पुनर्ऋतुमधिकृत्य गास्यामि S. 1 ; कतमे ते गुणास्तत्र यानुदाहरंत्यार्यमिश्राः Mâl. 1; (sometimes used merely as a strengthened substitute for किम्).

कतर *pron. a.* (°रत् *n.*) Who or which of two ; नैतद्विद्मः कतरन्नो गरीयो यद्वा जयेम यदि वा नो जयेयुः Bg. 2. 6.

कतमालः Fire ; cf. खतमाल.

कति *pron. a.* (always declined in the plural only ; कति कतिभिः &c.) 1 How many ; कत्यग्नयः कति सूर्यासः Rv. 10. 88. 18. 2 Some. When followed by चिद्, चन or अपि कति loses its interrogative force and becomes indefinite in sense, meaning 'some,' 'several,' 'a few'; तन्वी स्थिता कतिचिदेव पदानि गत्वा S. 2. 12 ; कत्यपि वासराणि Amaru. 25 ; तस्मिन्नद्रौ कतिचिदबलाविप्रयुक्तः स कामी नीत्वा मासान् Me. 2.

कतिकृत्वस् *ind.* How many times.

कतिधा *ind.* 1 How often. 2 In how many places or parts.

कतिपय *a.* 1 Some, several, a certain number ; कतिपयकुसुमोद्गमः कदंबः U. 3. 20; Me 23 ; कतिपयदिवसापगमे some days having elapsed ; वर्णैः कतिपयैरेव ग्रथितस्य स्वरैरिव Si. 2. 72.

कतिविध *a.* Of how many kinds.

कतिशस् *ind.* How many at a time.

कत्थ् 1 A. (कत्थते, कत्थित) 1 To boast, swagger ; कृत्वा कात्थिष्यते न कः Bk. 16. 4; कृत्वैतत्कर्मणा सर्वं कत्थेथाः Mb. 2 To praise, to celebrate. 3 To abuse, revile. –WITH वि 1 to boast; का खल्वनेन प्रार्थ्यमाना विकत्थते V. 2. 2 to depreciate, disparage ; सदा भवान् फाल्गुनस्य गुणैरस्मान् विकत्थते Mb.

कत्थनं, –ना Bragging, boasting.

कत्सवरं The shoulder.

कथ् 10 U. (कथयति, कथित) 1 To tell, communicate (usually with dat. of person) : राममिष्वसनदर्शनोत्सुकं मैथिलाय कथयांबभूव सः R. 11. 37. 2 To declare, mention ; Bg. 2. 34 ; R. 11. 15. 3 To converse; talk with, hold conversation with ; कथयित्वा सुमंत्रेण सह Râm. 4 To indicate, betray, show ; V. 1. 7 ; आकारसदृशं चेष्टितमेवास्य कथयति S. 7. 5 To describe, relate ; किं कथ्यते श्रीरुभयस्य तस्य Ku. 7. 78 ; कथाच्छलेन बालानां नीतिस्तदिह कथ्यते H. 1. 1. 6 To inform, give information about, complain against ; Mk. 3.

कथक *a.* A narrator, a relator. –कः 1 A chief actor. 2 A disputant. 3 A story-teller.

कथनं Narration, relation, description.

कथम् *ind.* 1 How, in what way, in what manner, whence ; कथं मारात्मके त्वयि विश्वासः H. 1 ; सानुबंधाः कथं न स्युः संपदो मे निरापदः R. 1. 64, 3. 44 ; कथमात्मानं निवेदयामि कथं वात्मापहारं करोमि S. 1 (where the speaker is doubtful as to the propriety of what he says). 2 It often denotes surprise (Oh ! indeed !); कथं मामेवोद्दिशति S. 6. 3 It is often connected with the particles इव, नाम, नु, वा or स्विद् in the sense of 'how indeed,' 'how possibly', 'I should like to know' (where the question is generalized) ; कथं वा गम्यते U. 3 ; कथं नामैतत् U. 6. 4 When connected with the particles चिद्, चन or अपि it means 'in every way,' 'on any account,' somehow,' 'with great difficulty', 'with great efforts;' तस्य स्थित्वा कथमपि पुरः Me. 3; कथमप्युन्नमितं न चुंबितं तु S. 3. 25 ; न लोकवृत्तं वर्तेत वृत्तिहेतोः कथंचन Ms. 4. 11, 5. 143; कथंचिदीशा मनसां बभूवुः 3. 34; कथं कथमपि उत्थितः Pt. 1; विसृज्य कथमप्युमाम् Ku. 6. 3 ; Me. 22; Amaru. 12, 39, 50, 73. –COMP. –कथिकः an inquisitive person. –कारं *ind.* in what manner, how ; कथंकारमनालंबा कीर्तिर्द्यामधिरोहति Si. 2. 52;

कथंकारं भुंक्ते Sk.; N. 17. 126. **-प्रमाण** *a.* of what measure. **-भूत** *a.* of what nature or kind (oft. used by commentators). **-रूप** *a.* of what form.

कथंता What sort or manner.

कथा **1** A tale, story. **2** A fable, feigned story; कथाच्छलेन बालानां नीतिस्तदिह कथ्यते H. 1. 1. **3** An account, allusion, mention; कथापि खलु पापानामलमश्रेयसे यतः *Si*. 2. 40. **4** Talk, conversation, speech. **5** A variety of prose composition often distinguished from आख्यायिका; (प्रबंधकल्पनां स्तोकसत्यां प्राज्ञाः कथां विदुः । परंपराश्रया या स्यात् सा मताख्यायिका बुधैः ॥); see under आख्यायिका also. का कथा, or कथा with प्रति (what mention) is often used in the sense of 'what need one say of', 'not to mention', 'to say nothing of', how much more', or 'how much less'; का कथा बाणसंधाने ज्याशब्देनैव दूरतः । हुंकारेणेव धनुषः स हि विघ्नानपोहति *S*. 3. 1; अभितप्तमयोपि मार्दवं भजते कैव कथा शरीरिषु R. 8. 43; आत्तवागनुमानाभ्यां साध्यं त्वां प्रति का कथा 10. 28; Ve. 2. 25. -COMP. **-अनुरागः** taking pleasure in conversation. **-अंतरं** **1** the course of conversation; स्मर्तव्योस्मि कथांतरेषु भवता Mk. 7. 7. **2** another tale. **-आरंभः** commencement of a tale. **-उदयः** the beginning of a tale.**-उद्घातः** **1** the second of the five kinds of प्रस्तावना; where the first character enters the stage after over-hearing and repeating either the words of the manager (सूत्रधार) or their sense; see S. D. 260; *e. g.* in Ratn.; Ve. or Mudrârâkshasa. **2** commencement of a tale or narration; आकुमारकथोद्घातं शालिगोप्यो जगुर्यशः R. 4. 20. **-उपाख्यानं** narration, relation. **-छलं** **1** the guise of a fable. **2** giving a false account. **-नायकः**, **-पुरुषः** the hero (of a story). **-पीठं** the introductory part of a tale or story. **-प्रबंधः** a tale, fiction, fable. **-प्रसंगः** **1** conversation, talk or course of conversation; नानाकथाप्रसंगावस्थितः H. 1. मिथः कथाप्रसंगेन विवादं किल चक्रतुः Ks. 22. 181; N. 1. 35. **2** a curer of poisons (विषवैद्य); कथाप्रसंगेन जनैरुदाहृतात् Ki. 1. 24 (where the word is used in sense 1 also). **-प्राणः** an actor. **-मुखं** the idtroductory portion of a story. **-योगः** course of conversation. **-विपर्यासः** changing the course of a story. **-शेष**, **-अवशेष** *a.* one of whom only the narrative remains, *i. e.* dead, deceased; (कथाशेषतां गतः 'dead,' 'deceased'). (**-षः**) the remaining part of a story.

कथानकं A small tale; *e. g.* Vetâlapanchavimsati.

कथित *p. p.* **1** Told, described, narrated. **2** Expressed (वाच्य). -COMP. **-पदं** tautology, repetition, considered as a fault of composition, relaing to a sentence, where a word is used without any specific purpose; see K. P. 7; S. D. 575 *ad loc.*

कद् I. 4. A. (कद्यते) To be confounded or confused, to suffer mentally.-II. 1 A. (कदते) also 1 P. **1** To cry, to weep or shed tears. **2** To grieve. **3** To call. **4** To kill or hurt; see कंद्.

कद् *ind.* This particle, which is a substitute for the word कु, is often used as first member of comp., and expresses the senses of badness, littleness, deterioration, uselessness, defectiveness &c. of anything. -COMP. **-अक्षरं** **1** a bad letter. **2** bad writing. **-अग्निः** a little fire. **-अध्वन्** *m.* a bad road. **-अन्नं** bad food. **-अपत्यं** a bad child. **-अभ्यासः** a bad habit or custom. **-अर्थ** *a.* useless, unmeaning. **-अर्थनं**, **-ना** troubling, tormenting, torture. **-अर्थयति** Den. P. **1** to despise, slight. **2** to trouble, torment; Bh. 3. 100; N. 8. 75. **-अर्थित** *a.* **1** despised, disdained, slighted; कदर्थितस्यापि हि धैर्यवृत्तेर्न शक्यते धैर्यगुणः प्रमार्ष्टुम् Bh. 2. 106. **2** tormented, teased; आः कदर्थितोऽहमेभिर्वारंवारं वरिसंवादविघ्नकारिभिः U. 5. **3** insignificant, mean. **4** bad, vile.**-अर्यः** a miser; Ms. 4. 210, 224; Y. 1. 161. °भावः avarice, stinginess. **-अश्वः** a bad horse. **-आकार** *a.* deformed, ugly. **-आचार** *a.* following evil practices, wicked, depraved, (**-रः**) bad conduct. **-उष्ट्रः** a bad camel.**-उष्ण** *a.* tepid, lukewarm. (**-ष्णं**) lukewarmness. **-रथः** a bad chariot or carriage; युधि कद्रथवद्भीमं बभंज ध्वजशालिनं Bk. 5. 103. **-वद** *a.* **1** speaking ill or inaccurately or indistinctly; येन जातं प्रियापाये कद्वदं हंसकोकिलम् Bk. 6. 75; वाग्विदां वरमकद्वदो नृपः *Si*. 14. 1. **2** vile, contemptible.

कदकं A canopy, awning.

कदनं **1** Destruction, slaughter, havoc. **2** War. **3** Sin.

कदंबः, **कदंबकः** **1** A kind of tree (said to put forth buds at the roaring of thunder-clouds); कतिपयकुसुमोद्गमः कदंबः U. 3. 20; Mâl. 3. 7; U. 3. 41; Me. 25; R. 12. 99. **2** A kind of grass. **3** Turmeric. **-कं** **1** A multitude; छायाबद्धकदंबकं मृगकुलं रोमंथमभ्यस्यतु *S*. 2. 6. **2** The flower of the Kadamba tree; पृथुकदंबकदंबकराजितम् Ki. 5. 9. -COMP. **-अनिलः** **1** a fragrant breeze (charged with the odour of Kadamba flowers); ते चोन्मीलितमालतीसुरभयः प्रौढाः कदंबानिलाः K. P. 1. **2** spring.**-कोरकन्यायः** see under न्याय. **-वायुः** a fragrant breeze; =°अनिल.

कदरः **1** A saw. **2** An iron goad for an elephant. **-रं** Coagulated milk.

कदलः, **कदलकः** The plantain tree; ऊरुद्वयं मृगदृशः कदलस्य कांडौ Amaru. 95. **-ली** **1** The plantain tree; किं यासि बालकदलीव विकंपमाना Mk. 1. 20; यास्यत्यूरुः सरसकदलीस्तंभगौरश्चलत्वं Me. 96, 77; Ku 1. 36; R. 12. 96; Y. 3. 8. **2** A kind of deer. **3** A flag carried by an elephant. **4** A flag or banner.

कदा *ind.* When, at what time; कदा गमिष्यसि-एष गच्छामि; कदा कथयिष्यसि &c. when connected with a following अपि it means 'now and then', 'at times', 'sometimes', 'at some time'; न कदापि never; with a following चन it means 'at some time', one day', 'at one time or another', 'once'; आनंदं ब्रह्मणो विद्वान्न बिभेति कदाचन Ms. 2. 54, 144; 3. 25, 101; with a following चित् it means 'at one time,' 'once upon a time,' 'at some time or other'; अथ कदाचित् once upon a time; R. 2. 37, 12. 21; नाक्षैः क्रीडेत्कदाचित्तु Ms. 4 74, 65, 169; कदाचित्-कदाचित् 'now-now'; कदाचित् काननं जगाहे कदाचित् कमलवनेषु रेमे K. 58 *et seq.*).

कद्रु *a.* (**द्रु** or **द्रू** *f.*) Tawny **-द्रुः**,**-द्रूः** *f.* Wife of Kasyapa and the mother of the Nâgas. -COMP. **पुत्रः**, **-सुतः** a serpent.

कनकं Gold; कनकवलयं स्रस्तं स्रस्तं मया प्रतिसार्यते *S*. 3. 13; Me 2, 37, 67. **-कः** **1** The Palâsa tree. **2** The Dhattúra tree. **3** Mountain ebony. -COMP. **-अंगदं** a gold bracelet. **-अचलः**, **-अद्रिः**, **-गिरिः**, **-शैलः** epithets of the mountain Sumeru; अधुना कुचौ ते स्पर्धेते किल कनकाचलेन सार्धम् Bv. 2. 9. **-आलुका** a golden jar or vase.**-आह्वयः** the Dhattura tree. **-टंकः** a golden hatchet **-दंडं**, **-दंडकं** (golden-sticked) the royal parasol. **-पत्रं** an earornament made of gold; जीवेति मंगलवचः परिहृत्य कोपात् कर्णे कृतं कनकपत्रमनालपंत्या Ch. P. 10. **-परागः** gold-dust. **-रसः** **1** a yellow orpiment. **2** fluid gold. **-सूत्रं** a gold necklace; काकया कनकसूत्रेण कृष्णसर्पो विनाशितः Pt. 1. 207. **-स्थली** 'a land gold,' gold-mine.

कनकमय *a.* Made of gold, golden.

कनखलं N. of a Tîrtha or sacred place and the hills adjoining it; (तीर्थं कनखलं नाम गंगाद्वारेऽस्ति पावनं); तस्माद्गच्छेरनुकनखलं शैलराजावतीर्णां जह्नोः कन्याम् Me. 50.

कनन *a.* One-eyed; cf. काण.

कनयति Den. P. To lessen, reduce in size, make small, diminish; कीर्तिं नः कनयंति च Bk. 18. 25.

कनिष्ठ *a.* (Seperl. of अल्प or युवन्) **1** The smallest, least **2** The youngest.

कनिष्ठिका The little finger. कनिष्ठिकाऽधिष्ठितकालिदासा Subhâsh.

कनीनिका, कनीनी **1** The little finger. **2** The pupil of the eye.

कनीयस् *a.* (**सी** *f.*) (Compar. of अल्प or युवन्) **1** Smaller, less. **2** Younger; कनीयान् भ्राता, कनीयसी भगिनी &c.

कनेरा **1** A harlot. **2** A female elephant; (cf. कणेरा).

कंतुः 1 Cupid, the god of love. 2 Heart (seat of thought and feeling). 3 Granary.

कंथा A patched garment, wallet (worn by ascetics); जीर्णा कंथा ततः किं Bh. 3. 74, 19, 86; *Sânti.* 4. 5, 19. —Comp.—**धारणं** wearing a patched garment, as practised by some Yogins. -**धारिन्** *m.* a religious mendicant, Yogin.

कंदः,-दं 1 A bulbous root. 2 A bulb ; Bh. 3. 69 ; (fig. also); ज्ञानकंदः. 3 Garlic. 4 A knot. —**दः** 1 Cloud. 2 Camphor. -Comp. -**मूलं** a radish. -**सारं** the garden of Indra.

कंदट्ट The white water-lily ; cf. कंदोट्ट.

कंदरः-रं A cave, a valley ; किं कंदाः कंदरेभ्यः प्रलयमुपगताः Bh. 3. 69 ; वसुधाधरकंदराभिसर्पी V. 1. 16; Me. 56. —**रः** A hook for driving an elephant. —**रा**-**री** A cave, valley, hollow. -Comp. -**आकारः** a mountain.

कंदर्पः 1 N. of Cupid, the god of love ; प्रजनश्चास्मि कंदर्पः Bg. 10. 28 ; कंदर्प इव रूपेण Mb. 2 Love.-Comp. -**कूपः** Pudenda Muliebre. -**ज्वरः** fever of love, passion, vehement, desire.-**दहनः** N. of *Siva* -**मुषलः**-**मुसलः** the male organ of generation. -**शृंखलः** 1 membrum virile. 2 a particular mode of sexual enjoyment or coitus (रतिबंध).

कंदलः-लं 1 A new shoot or sprout ; U. 3. 40. 2 Reproach, censure. 3 The cheek, or the cheek and temple. 4 A portent. 5 Sweet sound. 6 The plantain tree ; कंदलदलोल्लासाः पयोबिंदवः Amaru 48.—**लः** 1 Gold. 2 War, battle 3 (Hence) War of words, controversy. —**लं** A Kandala flower ; विद्दलकंदलकंपनलालितः *Si.* 6. 30; R. 13. 29.

कंदली 1 The plantain (or the Banana) tree ; आरक्तराजिभिरियं कुसुमैर्नवकंदली सलिलगर्भैः । कोपादंतर्बाष्पे स्मरयति मां लोचने तस्याः V. 4. 5; Me. 21; Rs. 2. 5. 2 A kind of deer. 3 A flag. 4 Lotus-seed. -Comp -**कुसुमं** a mushroom.

कंदुः *m. f.* A boiler; oven.

कंदुकः,-कं A ball for playing with; पातितोऽपि कराघातैरुत्पतत्येव कंदुकः Bh. 2. 85; Ku. 1. 29, 5. 11, 19; R. 16. 93. -Comp. -**लीला** any game with a ball

कंदोटः (-**ट्टः**) 1 The white lotus. 2 The blue lotus ; (a provincial form for नीलोत्पल); मोहमुकुलायमाननेत्रकंदोट्टयुगलः Mâl. 7.

कंधरः 1 The neck. 2 'The holder of water', a cloud. —**रा** The neck ; कंधरां समपहाय कंधरां प्राप्य संयति जहास कस्यचित् ; Y. 2. 220; Amaru. 16 ; see उत्कंधर also.

कंधिः The ocean. —*f.* The neck.

कन्नं 1 Sin. 2 A swoon, fainting fit.

कन्यका 1 A girl; संवद्धवैखानसकन्यकानि R. 14. 28; 11. 53. 2 An unmarried girl; virgin, maiden ; गृहे गृहे पुरुषाः कुलकन्यकाः समुद्वहंति Mâl. 7; Y. 1. 105. 3 A technical name for a girl ten years old ; (अष्टवर्षाभवेद्गौरी नववर्षा च रोहिणी । दशमे कन्यका प्रोक्ता अत उर्ध्वं रजस्वला *Sabdak.*). 4 (In Rhet.) One of the several kinds of heroines ; an unmarried girl serving as a chief character in a poetical composition ; see under अन्यस्त्री. 5 The sign *Virgo*. -Comp.-**छलः** seduction; पैशाचः कन्याच्छलात् Y. 1. 61. -**जनः** maiden; विशुद्धमुग्धः कुलकन्याकाजनः Mâl. 7. 1. -**जातः** the son of an unmarried girl; Y. 2. 129 (=कानीन).

कन्यसः The youngest brother. —**सा** The little finger. -**सी** The youngest sister.

कन्या 1 An unmarried girl or daughter ; R. 1. 51, 2. 10, 3. 33 ; Ms. 10. 8. 2 A girl ten years old. 3 A virgin, maiden ; Ms. 8. 367, 3. 33. 4 A woman in general. 5 The sixth sign of the zodiac, *i. e.* Virgo. 6 N. of Durgâ. 7 Large cardamoms.-Comp. --**अंतःपुरं** the women's apartments ; सुरक्षितेपि कन्यांतःपुरं कश्चित्प्रविशति Pt. 1 ; Mv 2. 50. -**आट** *a.* following after or hunting young girls. (-**टः**) 1 the inner apartments of a house. 2 a man who hunts or goes after young girls. -**कुब्जः** N. of a country. (-**ब्जं**) N. of an ancient city in the north of India, situated on a tributary of the Ganges, now called Kanoja. -**गतं** the position of a planet in the sign Virgo. -**ग्रहणं** taking a girl in marriage. -**दानं** giving away a girl in marriage. -**दूषणं** defilement of a virgin. -**दोषः** a defect or blemish in a girl, bad repute (such as a disease &c.). -**धनं** dowry. -**पतिः** 'daughter's husband', a son-in-law. -**पुत्रः** the son of an unmarried daughter (called कानीन).-**पुरं** the women's apartments. —**भर्तृ** *m.* 1 son-in-law. 2 N. of Kârtikeya.—**रत्नं** a very beautiful girl ; कन्यारत्नमयोनिजन्म भवतामास्ते Mv. 1. 30. -**राशिः** the sign *Virgo*.-**वेदिन्** *m.* a son-in-law (marrying one's girl); Y. 1. 262 -**शुल्कं** money given to the bride's father as her price, purchase-money of a girl.-**स्वयंवरः** the choice of a husband by a maiden. -**हरणं** ravishment or seduction of a maiden ; Ms. 3. 33.

कन्यका, कन्यिका 1 A young girl. 2 A virgin.

कन्यामय *a.* Consisting of, or in the form of, a young girl ; R. 6. 11, 16. 86.- **यं** The harem (consisting mostly of girls).

कपटः-टं Fraud, deceit, trick, cheating ; कपटशतमयं क्षेत्रमप्रत्ययानां Pt. 1. 191 ; कपटानुसारकुशला Mk. 9. 5. -Comp.-**तापसः** one who pretends to be an ascetic, pseudo ascetic.-**पटु** *a.* adopt in deceit, deceitful ; छलयन् प्रजास्त्वमनृतेन कपटपटुरैंद्रजालिकः *Si.* 15. 35. -**प्रबंधः** a fraudulent contrivance; H. 1. -**लेख्यं** a forged document. -**वचनं** deceitful talk. -**वेश** *a.* disguised, masked. (-**शः**) disguise.

कपटिकः A rogue, cheat.

कपर्दः, कपर्दकः 1 A small shell or cowrie (used as a coin). 2 Braided and matted hair, especially of *Siva* ; G. L. 22.

कपर्दिका A small shell or *cowrie* (used as a coin); मित्राण्यमित्रतां यांति यस्य न स्युः कपर्दि (दं) काः Pt. 2. 98.

कपर्दिन् *m.* An epithet of *Siva*.

कपाटः,-टं 1 Leaf or panel of a door ; कपाटवक्षाः परिणद्धकंधरः R. 3. 34; स्वर्गद्वारकपाटपाटनपटुर्धर्मोपि नोपार्जितः Bh. 3. 11. 2 A door; *Si.* 11. 60. -Comp. -**उद्घाटनं** the opening of a door. -**घ्नः** a house-breaker, thief. -**संधिः** the junction of the leaves of a door.

कपालः,-लं 1 The skull, skull-bone; चूडापीडकपालसंकुलगलन्मंदाकिनीवारयः Mâl. 1. 2; रुद्रो येन कपालपाणिपुटके भिक्षाटनं कारितः Bh. 2. 95. 2 A piece of a broken jar, potsherd; कपालेन भिक्षार्थी Ms. 8. 93. 3 A multitude, collection. 4 A beggar's bowl, Ms. 6. 44. 5 A cup, jar in general; पंचकपालः. 6 A cover or lid. -Comp. -**पाणिः**, -**भृत्**,-**मालिन्**, -**शिरस्** *m.* epithets of *Siva*. -**मालिनी** N. of Durgâ.

कपालिका A potsherd; Ms. 4. 78, 8. 250.

कपालिन् *a.* Furnished with or having a skull; Y 3. 243. 2 Wearing skulls; कपालि वा स्यादथवेंदुशेखरं (वपुः) Ku. 5. 78. -*m.* 1 An epithet of *Siva* ; करं कर्णे कुर्वत्यपि किल कपालिप्रभृतयः G. L. 28. 2 A man of low caste (offspring of a Brâhmana mother and fisherman father).

कपिः 1 An ape, a monkey; कपेरत्रासिषुर्नादात् Bk. 9. 11. 2 An elephant. -Comp. -**आख्यः** incense. -**इज्यः** an epithet of (1) Râma; (2) of Sugrîva. -**इंद्रः** (the chief of monkeys) an epithet of (1) Hanúmat; नश्यंति ददर्श वृंदानि कपींद्रः Bk. 10. 12 ; (2) of Sugrîva; व्यर्थं यत्र कपींद्रसख्यमपि मे U. 3. 45 ; (3) of Jâmbavat. -**कच्छुः** *f.* N. of a plant. -**केतनः**,-**ध्वजः** N. of Arjuna; Bg. 1. 20. -**जः**, -**तैलं**,-**नामन्** *n.* storax or benzoin. -**प्रभुः** an epithet of Râma. -**लोहं** brass.

कपिंजलः 1 The Châtaka bird. 2 The Tittiri bird.

कपित्थः The wood-apple tree. -**त्थं** The fruit of the above tree. -Comp. -**आस्यः** a kind of monkey.

कपिल *a.* 1 Tawny; reddish; वाताय कपिला विद्युत् Mbh. 2 Having tawny hair; Ms. 3. 8; (Kull.=कपिलकेशा). **-लः** 1 N. of a great sage. [He reduced to ashes the 60,000 sons of Sagara who, while searching for the sacrificial horse of their father taken away by Indra, fell in with him and accused him of having stolen it; (see U. 1. 23.). He is also said to have been the founder of the Sankhya system of philosophy]. 2 A dog. 3 Benzoin. 4 Incense. 5 A form of fire. 6 The tawny colour. **-ला** 1 A brown cow. 2 A kind of perfume. 3 A kind of timber. 4 The common leech. -COMP. **-अश्वः** an epithet of Indra. **-द्युतिः** the sun. **-धारा** an epithet of the Ganges. **स्मृति** *f.* the Sânkhya Sûtras of Kapila.

कपिश *a* 1 Brown, reddish-brown. 2 Reddish; (छायाः) संध्यापयोदकपिशाः पिशिताशनानां *S.* 3. 27; तोये कांचनपद्मरेणुकपिशे 7. 12; V. 2. 7; Me. 21; R. 12. 28. **-शः** 1 The brown colour. 2 Storax or coarse benzoin. **-शा** 1 The Mâdhavi creeper. 2 N. of a river.

कपिशित *a.* Embrowned; *Si* 6. 5.

कपुच्छलं, कपुष्टिका 1 The ceremony of tonsure. 2 A patch of hair on each side of the head.

कपूय *a.* Mean, worthless, abject, low.

कपोतः 1 A dove, pigeon. 2 A bird in general. -COMP. **-अंघ्रिः** *f.* a sort of perfume. **-अंजनं** antimony. **-आरिः** a hawk, falcon. **-चरणा** a sort of perfume. **-पालिका, -पाली** *f.* an aviary, a pigeon-house, dove-cot. **-राजः** the king of pigeons. **-सारं** antimony. **-हस्तः** a mode of folding the hands in supplication, fear &c.

कपोतकः A small pigeon. **-कं** Antimony.

कपोलः A cheek; शामक्षामकपोलमाननं *S.* 3. 10, 6. 14; R. 4. 68. -COMP. **-काषः** any object against which anything (especially the cheeks) is rubbed; Ki. 5. 36. **-फलकः** the (broad) cheeks. **-भित्ति** *f.* the temples and cheeks; or excellent (*i. e.* broad) cheeks; cf. गंडभित्ति. **-रागः** the flush in the cheek.

कफः 1 Phlegm, one of the three humours of the body (the other two being वात and पित्त); कफापचयादारोग्यैकमूलमाशयाग्निदीप्तिः Dk. 160; प्राणप्रयाणसमये कफवातपित्तैः कंठावरोधनविधौ स्मरणं कुतस्ते Udb. 2 A watery foam or froth in general. -COMP. **-अरिः** dry ginger. **-कूर्चिका** saliva, spittle. **-क्षयः** pulmonary consumption. **-घ्न, -नाशन, -हर** *a.* removing phlegm; antiphlegmatic. **-ज्वरः** fever caused by excess of phlegm.

कफल *a.* Phlegmatic.

कफिन् *a.* (**नी** *f.*) Affected with excess of phlegm, phlegmatic.

कफणिः, कफोणिः, (**णी** *f.*) The elbow.

कबंधः, -धं A headless trunk (especially when it retains life); (स्वं) नृत्यत्कबंधं समरे ददर्श R. 7. 51, 12. 49. **-धः** 1 The belly. 2 A cloud. 3 A comet 4 N. of Râhu. 5 Water (said to be *n.* also in this sense); *Si.* 16. 67. 6 N. of a mighty demon mentioned in the Râmâyaṇa. [While Ràma and Lakshma*n*a lived in the Da*n*dak*a* forest, Kabandha attacked them and was slain by them. It is said that, though at first a heavenly being, he was cursed by Indra to assume the form of a demon and to be in that state till killed by Rama and Lakshmana],

कबर, -री Usually written कवर, -री q. v.

काबित्थः The wood-apple tree.

कम् 1. 10. A (कामयते, कामित, कांत) 1 To love, be enamoured of, be in love with; कन्ये कामयमानं मां न त्वं कामयसे कथं Kâv. 1. 63 (an instance of ग्राम्यता); कलहंसको मंदारिकां कामयते Mâl. 1. 2 To long for, wish; desire; न वीरसूशब्दमकामयतां R. 14. 4; निष्क्रष्टुमर्थं चकमे कुबेरात् 5. 26; 4. 48; 10. 53; Bk. 14. 82. WITH **अभि** 1 to love. 2 to desire; **-नि** or **-प्र** to desire excessively, long vehemently.

कमठः 1 A tortoise; संप्रातः कमठः स चापि नियतं नष्टस्तवादेशतः Pt. 2. 184. 2 A bamboo. 3 A water jar. **-ठी** A female tortoise or a small tortoise. -COMP. **-पतिः** a king of tortoises.

कमंडलुः,-लु A water-pot (earthen or wooden) used by ascetics; कमंडलूपमोऽमात्यस्तनुत्यागो बहुग्रहः H. 2. 91; कमंडलुनोदकं सिक्त्वा; Ms. 2. 64; Y. 1. 133. -COMP. **-तरुः** the tree of which Kamaṇḍalus are made. **-धरः** an epithet of *S*iva.

कमन *a.* 1 Lustful, libidinous. 2 Lovely, beautiful. **-नः** 1 Cupid, the God of love. 2 The Asoka tree. 3 N. of Brahmâ.

कमनीय *a.* 1 To be desired, desirable; अनन्यनारीकमनीयमंकं Ku. 1. 37. 2 Lovely, charming, beautiful; शाखावसक्तकमनीयपरिच्छदानां Ki. 7. 40; तदपि कमनीयं वपुरिदं *S.* 3. 9 v. l.

कमर *a.* Lustful, desirous.

कमलं 1 A lotus; कमलमनंभसि कमले च कुवलये तानि कनकलतिकायां K. P. 10; so हस्त°, नेत्र°, चरण°, &c. 2 Water. 3 Copper. 4 A medicament, drug. 5 The Sárasa bird. 6 The bladder. **-लः** 1 The Sárasa bird. 2 A kind of deer. -COMP. **-अक्षी** *f.* a lotus-eyed lady. **-आकरः** 1 an assemblage of lotuses. 2 a lake full of lotuses. **-आलया** an epithet of Lakshmî; Mu. 2. **-आसनः** 'lotus seated' N. of Brahmâ; क्रांतानि पूर्वं कमलासनेन Ku. 7. 70, **-ईक्षणा** a lotus-eyed lady. **-उत्तरं** safflower. **-खंडं** an assemblage of lotuses. **-जः** 1 an epithet of Brahmâ. 2 the lunar asterism called Rohinî. **-जन्मन्** *m.*, **-भवः, -योनिः, -संभवः** 'lotus-born', epithets of Brahmâ.

कमलकं A small lotus.

कमला 1 an epithet of Lakshmî. 2 An excellent woman. -COMP. **-पतिः, -सखः** an epithet of Vishṇu.

कमलिनी 1 A lotus-plant; साभ्रेऽह्नीव स्थलकमलिनीं न प्रबुद्धां न सुप्तां Me. 90; रम्यांतरः कमलिनीहरितैः सरोभिः *S.* 4. 10; R. 9. 30, 19. 11. 2 An assemblage of lotuses. 3 A place abounding with lotuses.

कमा Beauty, loveliness.

कमितृ *a.* (**त्री** *f.*) Lustful, libidinous.

कंप् 1 A. (कंपते, कंपित) To shake, tremble, move about; (fig. also); चकंपे तीर्णलौहित्ये तस्मिन् प्राग्ज्योतिषेश्वरः R. 4. 81; Mk. 4. 8; Bk. 14. 31, 15. 70.- WITH **अनु** to pity, take compassion on; नीयमाना भुजिष्यात्वं कंपसे नानुकंपसे Mk. 4. 8; किं वराकीं नानुकंपसे Mâl. 10. (*Caus.*) to pity; Ku. 4. 39. **-आ** to shake, tremble. (*-Caus.*) to shake, put in motion; अनोकहाकंपितपुष्पगंधी R. 2. 13; Rs. 6. 22. **-प्र** to shake, tremble; प्राकंपत भुजः सव्यः Râm.; प्राकंपत महाशैलः Mb. (*-Caus.*) to shake, put in motion; Bk. 15. 23. **-वि** to shake, tremble; किं यासि बालकदलीव विकंपमाना Mk. 1 20; स्फुरति नयनं वामो बाहुर्मुहुश्च विकंपते 9. 13; Bg. 2. 31. (*-Caus.*) to shake; R. 11. 19; Rs. 2. 17. **-समनु** to pity, feel pity for; R. 9. 14.

कंपः 1 Shaking, tremor; कंपेन किंचित्प्रतिगृह्य मूर्ध्नः R. 13. 44 with a gentle nod or bend of the head; 13. 28; Ku. 7. 46; भयकंपः, विद्युत्कंपः &c. 2 A modification of the Svarita accent. **-पा** Shaking, moving, tremor. -COMP. **-अन्वित** *a.* tremulous, agitated. **-लक्ष्मन्** *m.* wind.

कंपन *a.* Trembling, shaking. **-नः** The *S*isira season, (November-December). **-नं** 1 Shaking, tremor. 2 Quivering pronunciation.

कंपाकः Wind.

कांपिल्ल=कांपिल्ल q. v.

कंप्र *a.* Shaking, tremulous, moving, agitating; विधाय कंप्राणि मुखानि कं प्रति N. 1. 142; कंप्रा शाखा Sk.

कंब् 1. P. (कंबति, कंबित) To go, move.

कंबर *a.* Variegated. **-रः** Variegated colour.

कंबलः 1 A blanket (of wool); कंबलवंतं न बाधते शीतं Subhâsh.; कंबलावृतेन तेन H. 3. 2 A dewlap. 3 A sort of deer. 4 An upper garment of wool. 5 A wall. **-लं** Water. -COMP. **-वाह्यकं** a kind of carriage covered with a coarse blanket, and drawn by oxen.

कंबलिका 1 A small blanket. 2 A kind of female deer.

कंबलिन् *a.* Covered with a blanket. —*m.* A bullock, ox. –COMP. **–वाह्यकं** a carriage covered with blankets and drawn by oxen, a bullock-cart.

कंबी (वी) *f.* A ladle or spoon.

कंबु *a.* (**बु** or **बू** *f.*) Spotted, variegated. —**बुः** –**बु** (*m. n.*) A conch, shell ; स्मरस्य कंबुः किमयं चकास्ति दिवि त्रिलोकीजयवादनीयः N. 22. 22. —**बुः** 1 An elephant 2 The neck. 3 The variegated colour. 4 A vein of the body. 5 A bracelet. 6 A tube-shaped bone. –COMP. –**कंठी** a lady having a neck like a conch-shell. **–ग्रीवा** 1 a conch-shaped neck, (*i. e.* a neck marked with three lines like a shell and considered as a sign of great fortune). 2 a lady having a neck like a conch-shell.

कंबोजः 1 A shell. 2 A kind of elephant. 3 (pl.) N. of a country and its inhabitants; कंबोजाः समरे सोढुं तस्य वीर्यमनीश्वराः R. 4. 69 v. l.

कम्र *a.* Lovely beautiful.

कर *a.* (**रा** or **री** *f.*) (Mostly at the end of comp.) Who or what does, makes or causes &c; दुःख°, सुख°, भयं° &c. **–रः** 1 A hand; करं व्याधुन्वत्याः पिबसि रतिसर्वस्वमधरं *S.* 1. 24. 2 A ray of light, beam ; यमुद्धर्तुं पूषा व्यवसित इवालंबितकरः V. 4. 34; also प्रतिकूलतामुपगते हि विधौ विफलत्वमेति बहुसाधनता । अवलंबनाय दिनभर्तुरभून्न पतिष्यतः करसहस्रमपि *Si.* 9. 6 (where the word is used in sense 1 also). 3 The trunk of an elephant ; सेकः सीकरिणा करेण विहितः U. 3. 16 ; Bh. 3. 20. 4 A tax, toll, tribute ; युवा कराक्रांतमहीभृदुच्चैरसंशयं संप्रति तेजसा रविः *Si.* 1. 70 ; (where कर means 'ray' also); (ददौ) अपरांतमहीपालव्याजेन रघवे करं R. 4. 58; Ms. 7. 128. 5 Hail. 6 A particular measure of length equal to 24 thumbs. 7 The asterism called हस्त. COMP. **–अग्रं** 1 the forepart of the hand. 2 the tip of an elephant's trunk. **–आघातः** a stroke or blow with the hand. **–आरोटः** a finger-ring. **–आलंबः** supporting with the hand, giving a helping hand.—**आस्फोटः** 1 the chest. 2 a blow with the hand. **–कंटकः –कं** a finger-nail. **–कमलं –पंकजं –पद्मं** a lotus-like hand, a beautiful hand; करकमलवितीर्णैरंबुनीवारशष्पैः U. 3. 25. **–कलशः, –शं** the hollow of the hand (to receive water). **–किसलयः, –यं** 1 'sprout-like hand,' a tender hand; कराकिसलयतालैर्मुग्धया नर्त्यमानं U. 3. 19 ; Rs. 6. 30. 2 a finger. **–कोषः** the cavity of the palms, hands hollowed to receive water ; °पेयमंबु Ghaṭ. 22.–**ग्रहः; –ग्रहणं** 1 levying a tax. 2 taking the hand in marriage. 3 marriage.—**ग्राहः** 1 a husband. 2 a tax-collector. **–जः** a finger-nail ; तीक्ष्णकरजक्षुण्णात् Ve. 4. 1; so Amaru. 85. (**जं**) a kind of perfume. **–जालं** a stream of light. **–तलः** the palm of the hand ; वनदेवताकरतलैः *S.* 4. 4; करतलगतमपि नश्यति यस्य तु भवितव्यता नास्ति Pt. 2. 124. °**आमलकं** (lit.) an *âmalaka* fruit (fruit of the Myrobalan) placed on the palm of the hand; (fig.) ease and clearness of perception, such as is natural in the case of a fruit placed on the palm of the hand ; cf. करतलामलकफलवदखिलं जगदालोकयता K. 43. °**स्थ** *a.* resting on the palm of the hand. **–तालः, –तालकं** 1 clapping the hands ; स जहास दत्तकरतालमुच्चकैः *Si.* 15. 39. 2 a kind of musical instrument, perhaps a cymbal. **–तालिका,–ताली** 1 clapping the hands; उच्चाटनीयः करतालिकानां दानादिदानीं भवतीभिरेषः N. 3. 7. 2 beating time by clapping the hands. **–तोया** N. of a river. **–द** *a.* 1 paying taxes. 2 tributary ; करदीकृताखिलनृपां मेदिनीं Ve. 6. 18. **–पत्रं** a saw. **–पत्रिका** splashing water about while bathing or sporting in it. **–पल्लवः** 1 a tender hand. 2 a finger ; cf. °**किसलय**. **–पालः, –पालिका** 1 a sword. 2 a cudgel. **–पीडनं** marriage ; cf. पाणिपीडन. **–पुटः** the hands joined and hollowed to receive anything **–पृष्ठं** the back of the hand. **–बालः, –वालः** 1 a sword ; अधोरघंटः करवालपाणिर्व्यापादितः Mâl 9 ; म्लेच्छानिवहनिधने कलयसि करवालम् Gît. 1. 2 a finger-nail. **–भारः** a large amount of tribute. **–भूः** a finger-nail. **–भूषणं** an ornament worn round the wrist such as a bracelet. **–मालः** smoke. **–मुक्तं** a king of weapon ; see आयुध. **–रुहः** 1 a finger-nail ; अनाघ्रातं पुष्पं किसलयमलूनं कररुहैः *S.* 2. 10 ; Me. 96. 2 a sword. **–वीरः, –वीरकः** 1 a sword or scimitar. 2 a cemetery. 3 N. of a town in the S. M. country. 4 a kind of tree. **–शाखा** a finger.**–शीकरः** water thrown out by an elephant's trunk. **–शूकः** a finger-nail. **–सारः** fading away of rays. —**सूत्रं** a marriage string worn round the wrist. **–स्थालिन्** *m.* an epithet of *Siva*. **–स्वनः** clapping the hands.

करकः, –कं The water-pot (of an ascetic) ; K. 41. —**कः** The pomegranate tree. **–कः, –का, –कं** Hail ; तान्कुर्वीथास्तुमुलकरकावृष्टिपातावकीर्णान् Me. 54; Bv. 1. 35. –COMP. **–अंभस्** *m.* the cocoa-nut tree. **–आसारः** a shower of hail. **–जं** water. **–पात्रिका** a water-pot used by ascetics.

करंकः 1 A skeleton. 2 The skull; प्रेतरंकः करंकादंकस्थादस्थिसंस्थं स्थपुटगतमपि क्रव्यमव्यग्रमत्ति Mâl. 5. 16 ; also 5. 19. 3 A small pot (of cocoa nut) ; a small box, as in तांबूलकरंकवाहिनी (used in Kâdambarî).

करंजः N. of a tree (used in medicinal preparations).

करटः 1 An elephant's cheek. 2 Safflower. 3 A crow ; *S*ânti. 4. 19. 4 An atheist, unbeliever. 5 A degraded Brâhmaṇa.

करटकः 1 A crow ; Mk. 7. 2 N. of कर्णीरथ the propounder of the science and art of theft. 3 N. of a jackal in H. and Pt.

करटिन् *m.* An elephant ; दिगंते श्रूयंते मदमलिनगंडाः करटिनः Bv. 1. 2.

कर (रे) टुः A kind of bird (crane).

करणं 1 Doing, performing, accomplishing, effecting; परहित,° संध्या°, प्रिय° &c. 2 Act, action. 3 A religious action. 4 Business, trade. 5 An organ of sense ; वपुषा करणोज्झितेन सा निपतंती पतिमप्यपातयत् R. 8. 38, 42 ; पटुकरणैः प्राणिभिः Me. 5; R. 14. 50. 6 The body; उपमानमभूद्विलासिनां करणं यत्तव कांतिमत्तया Ku. 4. 5. 7 An instrument or means of an action ; उपमितिकरणमुपमानं T. S. 8 (In Logic) The instrumental cause which is thus defined :—व्यापारवदसाधारणं कारणं करणं. 9 A cause or motive (in general). 10 The sense expressed by the instrumental case (in gram.;) साधकतमं करणं P. I. 4. 42 ; or क्रियायाः परिनिष्पत्तिर्यद्व्यापारादनंतरम् । विवक्ष्यते यदा यत्र करणं तत्तदा स्मृतम् ॥ 11 (In law) A document, a bond, documentary proof; Ms. 8. 51, 52, 154. 12 A kind of rhythmical pause, beat of the hand to keep time ; Ku. 6. 40. 13 (In astrol.) A division of the day ; (these Karaṇas are eleven). –COMP. **–अधिपः** the soul. **–ग्रामः** the organs of sense taken collectively. **–त्राणं** the head.

करंडः 1 A small box or basket (of bamboo); करंडपीडिततनोः भोगिनः Bh. 2. 84 ; सर्वमायाकरंडं 1. 77. 2 A bee-hive. 3 A sword. 4 A sort of duck (कारंडव).

करंडिका, करंडी *f.* A small box made of bamboo.

करंधय *a.* Kissing the hand.

करभः 1 The back of the hand from the wrist to the root of the fingers ; metacarpus ; as in करभोरूः R. 6. 83 ; see करभोरू below. 2 The trunk of an elephant. 3 A young elephant. 4 A young camel. 5 A camel in general. 6 A kind of perfume. –COMP. **–ऊरूः** *f.* a lady whose thighs resemble the back of the forearm ; अंके निधाय करभोरु यथासुखं ते *S.* 3. 21 ; *Si.* 10. 69 ; Amaru. 69; or (according to another explanation), whose thighs resemble the trunk of an elephant.

करभकः A camel.

करभिन् *m.* An elephant.

करंब, करंबित *a.* Mixed, intermingled, variegated ; प्रकाममादित्यमवाप्य कंटकैः करंबितामोदभरं विवृण्वती N. 1. 115 ; स्फुटतरफेनकदंबकरंबितमिव यमुनाजलपूरं Gît. 11. 2 Set, inlaid.

करंभः (बः) 1 Flour or meal mixed with curds. 2 Mud ; करंभवालुकातापान् Ms. 12. 76. (where the word is variously interpreted ; but Medhâtithi takes it to mean 'mud').

करहाटः N. of a country ; (perhaps the modern Karhâda in Satâra district) ; करहाटपतेः पुत्री त्रिजगन्नेत्रकार्मणम् Vikr. 8. 2. 2 The fibrous root or stem of a lotus.

कराल *a.* 1 Dreadful, formidable, frightful, terrible ; U. 5. 5, 6. 1; Mâl. 3; Bg. 11. 23, 25, 27; R. 12. 98; Mv. 3. 48. 2 Gaping, opening wide; U. 5. 6. 3 Great, large, high, lofty. 4 Uneven, jogged ; pointed ; Ve. 1. 6; Mâl. 1. 38. **–ला** A terrific form of Durgâ ; °आयतनं; न करालोपहाराच्च फलमन्यद्विभाव्यते Mâl. 4. 33. –Comp. **–दंष्ट्र** *a.* having terrific teeth. **–वदना** an epithet of Durgâ.

करालिकः 1 A tree. 2 A sword.

करिका Scratching, wound caused by a finger-nail.

करिणी *f.* A female elephant ; कथमेत्य मतिर्विपर्ययं करिणी पंकमिवावसीदति Ki. 2. 6; Bv. 1. 2.

करिन् *m.* 1 An elephant. 2 The number '8' (in Math.). –Comp. **–इंद्रः, –ईश्वरः, –वरः** a large elephant, lordly elephant; सदादानः परिक्षीणः शस्त एव करीश्वरः Pt. 2. 70 ; दूरीकृताः करिवरेण मदांधबुद्ध्या Nîtipr. 2. **–कुंभः** the frontal globe of an elephant ; Bv. 2. 177. **–गर्जितं** the roaring of an elephant (बृंहितं करिगर्जितम् Ak.). **–दंतः** ivory. **–पः** an elephant-driver. **–पोतः, –शावः, –शावकः** a cub, young elephant. **–बंधः** a column to which an elephant is tied. **–माचलः** a lion. **–मुखः** an epithet of Gaṇesa. **–वरः**=°इंद्र q. v. **–वैजयंती** *m.* a flag carried by an elephant. **–स्कंधः** a herd or group of elephants.

करीरः 1 The shoot of a bamboo. 2 A shoot in general ; आनिन्यिरे वंशकरीरनीलैः Si. 4. 14. 3 A thorny plant growing in deserts and eaten by camels ; पत्रं नैव यदा करीरविटपे दोषो वसंतस्य किं Bh. 2. 93; cf. also किं पुष्पैः किं फलैस्तस्य करीरस्य दुरात्मनः । येन वृद्धिं समासाद्य न कृतः पत्रसंग्रहः Subhâsh. 4 A water-jar.

करीषः,–षं Dry cow-dung. –Comp. **–अग्निः** fire of dry cow-dung.

करीषंकषा A strong wind or gale.

करीषिणी The goddess of wealth.

करुण *a.* Tender, pathetic, pitiable, exciting pity, mournful ; करुणध्वनिः U. 1 ; Si. 9. 67; विकलकरुणैरार्यचरितैः U. 1. 28. **—णः** 1 Pity, compassion, tenderness. 2 Pathetic sentiment, grief, sorrow (as one of the 8 or 9 sentiments); पुटपाकप्रतीकाशो रामस्य करुणो रसः U. 3. 1, 13 ; विलपन्...करुणार्थग्रथितं प्रियां प्रति R. 8. 70. –Comp. **–मल्ली** the Mallikâ plant. **–विप्रलंभः** (in Rhet.) the feeling of love in separation.

करुणा Compassion, pity, tenderness प्रायः सर्वो भवति करुणावृत्तिरार्द्रांतरात्मा Me. 93 ; so सकरुण kind ; अकरुण unkind. –Comp. **–आर्द्र** *a.* tender-hearted, moved with pity, sensitive. **–निधिः** store of mercy. **–पर,–मय** *a.* very kind. **–विमुख** *a.* merciless, cruel; करुणाविमुखेन मृत्युना R. 8. 67.

करेटः A finger-nail.

करेणुः An elephant in general ; करेणुरारोहयते निषादिनम् Si. 12. 5, 5. 48. 2 The Karnikâra tree. **—णुः** *f.* 1 A female elephant ; ददौ रसात्पंकजरेणुगंधि Ku. 3. 37 ; R. 16. 16. 2 N. of the mother of Pâlakâpya. –Comp. **–भूः, –सुतः** N. of Pâlakâpya the founder of the science of elephants.

करोटं, –करोटिः *f.* 1 The skull; Mv. 5. 19. 2 A cup or basin.

कर्कः 1 A crab. 2 Cancer, the fourth sign of the zodiac. 3 Fire. 4 A water-jar. 5 A mirror. 6 A white horse.

कर्कटः,–टकः 1 A crab. 2 Cancer, the fourth sign of the zodiac. 3 Compass, circuit.

कर्कटिः,–टी *f.* A sort of cucumber.

कर्कंधुः, –धूः *f.* The jujube tree ; कर्कंधुफलपाकमिश्रपचनामोदः परिस्तीर्यते U. 4. 1; कर्कंधूनामुपरि तुहिनं रंजयत्यग्रसंध्या S. 4. v. l. 2 Fruit of this tree; Y. 1. 250.

कर्कर *a.* 1 Hard, solid. 2 Firm. **—रः** 1 A hammer. 2 A mirror. 3 A bone, broken-piece (of skull); fragment; Mâl. 5. 19. 4 A strap or rope of leather. –Comp. **–अक्षः** a wagtail. **–अंगः** the Khanjuna bird. **–अंधुकः** a blind well ; cf. अंधकूप.

कर्कराटुः A side-long look, a glance, leer.

कर्कराला A curl of hair, ringlet.

कर्करी A water-jar with small holes at the bottom as in a sieve.

कर्कशः *a* 1 Hard, rough (opp. कोमल or मृदु) ; सुरद्विपास्फालनकर्कशांगुली R. 3. 55, 12. 41, 13. 73; ऐरावतास्फालनकर्कशेन हस्तेन पस्पर्श तदंगमिंद्रः Ku. 3. 22, 1. 36; Si. 15. 10. 2 Harsh, cruel, merciless (words, conduct &c.) 3 Violent, strong, excessive ; तस्य कर्कशविहारसंभवं R. 9. 68. 4 Desperate. 5 Illconducted, unchaste, unfaithful (as a woman). 6 Incomprehensible, difficult to comprehend ; तर्के वा भृशकर्कशे मम समं लीलायते भारती P. R. 4. **—शः** A sword.

कर्कशिका, कर्कशी Wild jujube.

कर्किः Cancer, the fourth sign of the zodiac.

कर्कोटः, –टकः N. of the eight principal cobras. [When king Nala, being persecuted by Kali, was made to undergo many hardships, Karkoṭa, who was once saved by him from fire, so deformed him that none might recognise him during his days of adversity].

कर्चूरः A kind of fragrant tree. **–रं** 1 Gold. 2 Orpiment.

कर्ण् 10 U. (कर्णयति, कर्णित) 1 To pierce, to bore. 2 To hear; usually with the preposition आ. With **आ** or **समा** to hear, to listen to ; सर्वे सविस्मयमाकर्णयंति S. 1 ; आकर्णयन्नुत्सुकहंसनादान् Bk. 11. 7.

कर्णः 1 The ear ; अहो खलभुजंगस्य विपरीतवधक्रमः । कर्णे लगति चान्यस्य प्राणैरन्यो वियुज्यते ॥ Pt. 1. 305, 304 also ; कर्णं दा to listen; कर्णमागम् to come to the ear, become known ; R. 1. 9 ; कर्णे कृ to put round the ear ; Ch. P. 10 ; कर्णे कथयति whispers into the ear ; see षट्कर्ण, चतुष्कर्ण &c. 2 The handle or ear of a vessel. 3 The helm or rudder of a ship. 4 The hypotenuse of a triangle. 5 N. of a celebrated warrior on the side of the Kauravas mentioned in the Mahâbhârata. [He was the son of Kunti begotten on her by the god Sun while she was yet a virgin residing at her father's house (see Kunti). When the child was born, Kunti afraid of the censure of her relatives and also of public scandal, threw the boy into the river, where he was found by Adhiratha, charioteer of Dhritarashtra and given over to his wife Radha who brought him up like her own child ; whence Karna is often called *Sûtaputra*, *Rādheya* &c. Karna, when grown up, was made king of Anga by Duryodhana, and became by virtue of his many generous acts a type of charity. On one occasion Indra (whose care it was to favour his son Arjuna) disguised himself as a Brahmana and cajoled him out of his divine arms and ear-rings, and gave him in return a charmed javelin. With a desire to make himself proficient in the science of war he, calling himself a Brahmana went to Parasurama and learnt that art from him. But his secret did not remain long concealed. On one occasion when Parasurama had fallen asleep with his head resting on Karna's lap, a worm (supposed by some to be the form assumed by Indra himself to defeat Karna's object) began to eat into his lap and made a deep rent in it ; but as Karna showed not the least sign of pain his real character was discovered by his preceptor who cursed him that the art he had learnt would avail him not in times of need. On another occasion he was cursed by a Brahmana (whose cow he had unwittingly slain in chase) that the earth would eat up the wheel of his chariot in the hour of trial. Even with such disadvantages as these, he acquitted himself most valiantly in the great war between the P*and*avas and Kauravas while acting as generalissimo of the Kaurava forces after Bhishma and Dro*n*a had fallen. He maintained the field against the P*and*avas for three days, but on the last day he was slain by Arjuna while the wheel of his chariot had sunk down into the earth. Kar*n*a was the most intimate friend of Duryodhan, and with *S*akuni joined him in all the various schemes and plots that were devised from time to time for the destruction of the P*and*avas.] –Comp. –अंजलिः the auditory passage of the outer ear. —अनुजः Yudhishthira. –अंतिक *a.* close to the ear; स्वनसि मृदु कर्णांतिकचरः *S*. 1. 24. –अंदुः-दू *f.* an ornament for the ear, ear-ring. –अर्पणं giving ear, listening. –आस्फालः the flapping of the elephant's ears.–उत्तंसः an ear-ornament or merely an ornament (according to some authorities). (Mammaṭa says that here कर्ण means कर्णस्थितत्व ; cf. also his remark *ad loc.* कर्णावतंसादिपदे कर्णादिध्वनिनिर्मितिः । संनिधानार्थबोधार्थं स्थितेष्वेतत्समर्थनं ॥ K. P. 7).–उपकर्णिका rumour; (lit. 'from ear to ear'). –क्ष्वेडः (in medic.) a constant noise in the ear. –गोचर *a.* audible. –ग्राहः a helmsman. –जप *a.* (also कर्णेजप) a secret traducer, talebearer, informer.–जपः,–जापः slandering, tale-bearing, calumniating.–जाहः the root of the ear; अपि कर्णजाहविनिवेशिताननः Mâl. 5. 8. –जित् *m.* 'conqueror of Karṇa' epithet of Arjuna, the third Pâṇḍava prince. –तालः the flapping of the elephant's ears, the noise made by it; विस्तारितः कुंजरकर्णतालैः R. 7. 39, 9. 71 ; *S*i. 17. 37. –धारः a helmsman, a pilot; अकर्णधारा जलधौ विप्लवेतेह नौरिव H. 3. 2 ; अविनयनदीकर्णधार कर्ण Ve. 4. –धारिणी a female elephant. –पथः the range of hearing. –परंपरा from ear to ear, hearsay ; इति कर्णपरंपरया श्रुतं Ratn. 1. –पालिः *f.* the lobe of the ear. –पाशः a beautiful ear. –पूरः 1 an ornament (of flowers &c.) worn round the ear, an ear-ring; इदं च करतलं किमिति कर्णपूरतामारोपितं K. 60. 2 the Asoka tree. –पूरकः 1 an ear-ring. 2 the Kadamba tree. 3 the Asoka tree. 4 the blue lotus. –प्रांतः the lobe of the ear. –भूषणं,-भूषा an ear-ornament. –मूलं the root of the ear; R. 12. 2. –पोटी *f.* a form of Durgâ. –वंशः a raised platform or *dais* of bamboo. –वर्जित *a.* earless. (–तः) a snake. –विवरं the auditory passage of the ear. –विष् *f.* ear-wax. –वेधः piercing the ears to put ear-rings on. –वेष्टः,-वेष्टनं an ear-ring.–शष्कुली *f.* the outer part of the ear (leading to the auditory passage) ; N. 2. 8. –शूलः,–लं ear-ache. –श्रव *a.* audible, loud ; कर्णश्रवेऽनिले Ms. 4. 102. –स्रावः,–संस्रवः 'running of the ear', discharge of pus or ichorous matter from the ear. –सूः *f.* Kuntî, mother of Karṇa. –हीन *a.* earless. (–नः) a snake.

कर्णाकर्णि *a.* From ear to ear.

कर्णाटः (pl.) N. of a country in the south of the Indian Peninsula ; (काव्यं) कर्णाटदेशोर्जगति विदुषां कंठभूषात्वमेतु Vikr. 18. 102. –टी *f.* A woman of the above country ; कर्णाटीचिकुराणां तांडवकरः Vb. 1. 29.

कर्णिक *a.* 1 Having ears. 2 Having a helm. –कः A steersman. –का 1 An ear-ring. 2 A knot, round protuberance. 3 Pericarp of a lotus. 4 A small brush or pen. 5 The middle finger. 6 A fruit-stalk. 7 The tip of an elephant's trunk. 8 Chalk.

कर्णिकारः 1 N. of a tree ; निर्भिद्योपरि कर्णिकारमुकुलान्यालीयते षट्पदः V. 2. 23 ; Rs. 6. 6, 20. 2 The pericarp of a lotus. —रं A flower of the Karṇikâra tree. (This flower, though it has an excellent colour, has no smell and hence is not liked ; cf. Ku. 3. 28 :— वर्णप्रकर्षे सति कर्णिकारं दुनोति निर्गंधतया स्म चेतः । प्रायेण सामग्र्यविधौ गुणानां पराङ्मुखी विश्वसृजः प्रवृत्तिः ॥).

कर्णिन् *a.* 1 Having ears. 2 Long-eared. 3 Barbed (as an arrow). –*m.* 1 An ass. 2 A helmsman. 3 An arrow furnished with knots &c.

कर्णी *f.* 1 An arrow of a particular shape (barbed arrow). 2 N. of the mother of Múladeva, the father of the science and art of thieving. –Comp.–रथः a covered litter, a lady's vehicle, palanquin; कर्णीरथस्थां रघुवीरपत्नीं R. 14. 13. –सुतः Múladeva, father of the science and art of thieving; कर्णीसुतकथेव संनिहितविपुलाचला K. 19 ; कर्णीसुतप्रहिते च पथि मतिमकरवम् Dk.

कर्तनं 1 Cutting, lopping off ; Y. 2. 229, 286. 2 Spinning cotton or thread (तर्कुः कर्तनसाधनं).

कर्तनी *f.* Scissors.

कर्तरिका, कर्तरी 1 Scissors. 2 A knife. 3 Cutlass, small sword.

कर्तव्य *pot. p.* 1 What is fit or ought to be done; हीनसेवा न कर्तव्या कर्तव्यो महदाश्रयः H. 3. 11 ; मया प्रातर्निःसत्त्वं वनं कर्तव्यं Pt. 1. 2 What ought to be cut or lopped, fit to be destroyed or put down ; पुत्रः सखा वा भ्राता वा पिता वा यदि वा गुरुः । रिपुस्थानेषु वर्तंतः कर्तव्या भूतिमिच्छता ॥ Mb. –व्यं, कर्तव्यता What ought to be done, a duty, obligation; कर्तव्यं वो न पश्यामि Ku. 6. 61, 2. 62; Y. 1. 330.

कर्तृ *a.* or *s.* 1 A doer, one who does, makes, performs &c.; व्याकरणस्य कर्ता author; ऋणस्य कर्ता one who incurs debt; हितकर्ता a benefactor; सुवर्णकर्ता a goldsmith &c. 2 (In gram.) An agent (the meaning of the instrumental case). 3 The Supreme spirit. 4 An epithet of Brahmâ. 5 N. of Vishṇu and *S*iva also.

कर्त्री 1 A knife. 2 Scissors.

कर्दः, कर्दटः Mud.

कर्दमः 1 Mud, slime, mire ; पादौ नूपुरलग्नकर्दमधरौ प्रक्षालयंती स्थिता Mk. 5. 35; पथश्चाश्यानकर्दमान् R. 4. 24. 2 Dirt, filth. 3 (Fig.) Sin. –मं Flesh. —Comp. –आटकः a receptacle for filth, sewer &c.

कर्पटः,–टं 1 Old, ragged or patched garment. 2 A piece of cloth, strip. 3 A soiled garment or a red-coloured garment.

कर्पटिक,–न् *a.* Covered with ragged garments.

कर्पणः A kind of weapon; चापचक्रकणपकर्पणप्रासपट्टिश &c. Dk. 35.

कर्परः 1 An iron sauce-pan; a frying-pan. 2 A pot or vessel in general (as of a potter). 3 A potsherd, piece of a broken jar; as in घटकर्पर; जीयेय येन कविना यमकैः परेण तस्मै वहेयमुदकं घटकर्परेण Ghaṭ. 22. 4 The skull. 5 A kind of weapon.

कर्पासः, –सं, –सी The cotton tree.

कर्पूरः,–रं Camphor. –Comp. –खंडः 1 a field of camphor. 2 a piece of camphor. –तैलं camphor liniment.

कर्फरः A mirror.

कर्बुः *a.* Variegated, spotted ; Y. 3. 166.

कर्बुर *a.* 1 Variegated, spotted ; क्वचिल्लसद्घनघनिकुरंबकर्बुरः *S*i. 17. 56. 2 Of the colour of pigeons, whitish, gray; पवनैर्भस्म कपोतकर्बुरं Ku. 4. 27. –रः 1 The variegated colour. 2 Sin. 3 An evil-spirit, demon. 4 The Dhattûra plant. –रं 1 Gold. 2 Water.

कर्बुरित *a.* Variegated ; U. 6. 4.

कर्मठ *a.* 1 Proficient in any work, clever. 2 Working diligently. 3 Exclusively devoted to the performance of religious rites. –ठः The director of a sacrifice.

कर्मण्य *a.* Skilful, clever. –ण्या Wages. –ण्यं Activity.

कर्मन् *n.* 1 Action, work, deed. 2 Execution, performance. 3 Business, office, duty; संप्रति विषवैद्यानां कर्म M. 4. 4 A religious rite (it may be either नित्य, नैमित्तिक or काम्य). 5 A specific action, moral duty. 6 Performance of religious rites as opposed to speculative religion or knowledge of Brahma (opp. ज्ञान); R. 8. 20. 7 Product, result. 8 A natural or active property (as support of earth). 9 Fate, the certain consequence of acts done in a former life ; Bh. 2. 94. 10 (In gram.) The object of an action; कर्तुरीप्सिततमं कर्म P. I. 4. 79.

11 (In Vais. phil.) Motion considered as one of the seven categories of things ; (thus defined:—एकद्रव्यमगुणं संयोगविभागेष्वनपेक्षकारणं कर्म Vais. Sûtra. It is five-fold:—उत्क्षेपणं ततोऽवक्षेपणमाकुंचनं तथा । प्रसारणं च गमनं कर्माण्येतानि पंच च ॥ Bh'asha' P. 6. –COMP. **अक्षम** *a.* incapable of doing anything. **अंगं** part of any act ; part of a sacrificial rite (as प्रयाज of the Darsa sacrifice) —**अधिकारः** the right of performing religious rites. –**अनुरूप** *a.* 1 according to action or any particular office. 2 according to actions done in a previous existence. –**अंतः** 1 the end of any business or task. 2 a work, business ; execution of a business. 3 a barn, a store of grain &c. Ms. 7. 62 (कर्मांतः इक्षुधान्यादि संग्रहस्थानं Kull.). 4 cultivated ground. –**अंतरं** 1 difference or contrariety of action. 2 penance, expiation. 3 suspension of a religious action. –**अंतिक** *a.* final. (–**कः**) a servant, workman. –**आजीवः** one who maintains himself by some profession (as that of an artisan &c.). —**आत्मन्** *a.* endowed with principles of action, active; Ms. 1. 22, 23. (–*m.*) the soul. –**इंद्रियं** an organ of action, as distinguished from ज्ञानेंद्रिय ; (they are:—वाक्पाणिपादपायूपस्थानि Ms. 11. 91; see under इंद्रिय also). –**उदारं** any valiant or noble act, magnanimity, prowess. –**उद्युक्त** *a.* busy, engaged, active, zealous. –**करः** 1 a hired labourer (a servant who is not a slave); कर्मकराः स्थपत्यादयः Pt. 1; Si. 14. 16. 2 Yama. –**कर्तृ** *m.* (in gram.) an agent who is at the same time object of the action ; *e. g.* पच्यते ओदनः; it is thus defined:—क्रियमाणं तु यत्कर्म स्वयमेव प्रसिध्यति । सुकरैः स्वैर्गुणैः कर्तुः कर्मकर्तेति तद्विदुः ॥ –**कांडः**, –**डं** that department of the Veda which relates to ceremonial acts and sacrificial rites and the merit arising from a due performance thereof. –**कारः** 1 one who does any business, a mechanic, artisan (technically a worker not hired). 2 any labourer in general (whether hired or not). 3 a black-smith ; हरिणाक्षि कटाक्षेण आत्मानमवलोकय । न हि खड्गो विजानाति कर्मकारं स्वकारणम् ॥ Udb. 4 a bull. –**कारिन्** *m.* a labourer, a workman. –**कार्मुकः**, –**कं** a strong bow. –**कीलकः** a washerman. –**क्षम** *a.* able to perform any work or duty ; आत्मकर्मक्षमं देहं क्षात्रो धर्म इवाश्रितः R. 1. 13. –**क्षेत्रं** the land of religious acts, that is, भरतवर्ष ; cf. कर्मभूमि. –**गृहीत** *a.* caught in the very act (as a thief). —**घातः** leaving off or suspending work. –**चं (चां) डालः** 1 'base in deed', a man of very low acts or deeds ; Vasistha mentions these kinds:—असूयकः पिशुनश्च कृतघ्नो दीर्घरोषकः । चत्वारः कर्मचांडाला जन्मतश्चापि पंचमः ॥. 2 one who commits an atrocious deed; U. 1. 46. 3 N. of R'ahu.–**चोदना** 1 the motive impelling one to ritual acts. 2 any positive rule enjoining a religious act. –**ज्ञः** one acquainted with religious rites. –**त्यागः** renunciation of worldly duties or ceremonial acts. –**दुष्ट** *a.* currupt in action, wicked, immoral, disrespectable. –**दोषः** 1 sin, vice; Ms. 6. 61, 95. 2 an error, defect, or blunder (in doing an act); Ms. 1. 104. 3 evil consequence of human acts. 4 discreditable conduct. –**धारयः** N. of a compound, a subdivision of Tatpurusha; (in which the members of the compound are in apposition); तत्पुरुष कर्मधारय येनाहं स्यां बहुव्रीहिः Udb. –**ध्वंसः** 1 loss of fruit arising from religious acts. 2 disappointment. –**नामन्** (in gram.) a participial noun. –**नाशा** N. of a river between Kâsî and Vihâra. –**निष्ठ** *a.* devoted to the performance of religious acts. –**पथः** 1 the direction or source of an action. 2 the path of religious rites (opp. ज्ञानमार्ग). —**पाकः** ripening of actions, reward of actions done in a former life. –**प्रवचनीयः** a term for certain prepositions, particles, or adverbs when they are not connected with verbs and govern a noun in some case; *e. g.* आ in आ मुक्तेः संसारः is a कर्मप्रवचनीय; so अनु in जपमनु प्रावर्षत् &c.; cf. उपसर्ग, गति and निपात also. –**न्यासः** renunciation of the result of religious acts. –**फलं** fruit or reward of actions done in a former life ; (pain, pleasure). –**बंधः** –**बंधनं** confinement to repeated birth, as the consequence of religious acts, good or bad (by which the soul is attached to worldly pleasures &c.). –**भूः** –**भूमिः** *f.* 1 the land of religious rites, *i. e.* भरतवर्ष. 2 ploughed ground. –**मीमांसा** the Mîmâmsâ of ceremonial acts ; see मीमांसा. –**मूलं** a kind of sacred grass called कुश. –**युगं** the fourth (the present) age of the world, *i. e.* the Kaliyuga). –**योगः** 1 performance of actions, worldly and religious rites. 2 active exertion, industry. –**वशः** fate considered as the inevitable result of actions done in a former life. –**विपाकः**=कर्मपाक. –**शाला** a workshop. –**शील**, –**शूर** *a.* assiduous, active, laborious. –**संगः** attachment to worldly duties and their results. –**सचिवः** a minister.–**संन्यासिकः**,–**संन्यासिन्** *m.* 1 a religious person who has withdrawn from every kind of worldly act. 2 an ascetic who performs religious deeds without looking to their rewards. –**साक्षिन्** *m.* 1 an eye-witness; Ku. 7. 83. 2 one who witnesses the good or bad actions of man; (there are nine divinities which are said to witness and watch over all human actions ; सूर्यः सोमो यमः कालो महाभूतानि पंच च । एते शुभाशुभस्येह कर्मणो नव साक्षिणः ॥) –**सिद्धिः** *f.* accomplishment of any business or desired object; success; Ku 3. 57. –**स्थानं** a public office, a place of business.

कर्मंदिन् *m.* An ascetic, a religious mendicant.

कर्मारः A blacksmith; Y. 1. 163; Ms. 4. 215.

कर्मिन् *a.* 1 Working, active, busy. 2 Engaged in any work or business. 3 One who performs religious deeds with the expectation of reward or recompense; कर्मिभ्यश्चाधिको योगी तस्माद्योगी भवार्जुन Bg. 6. 46 –*m.* A mechanic, artisan; Y. 2. 265.

कर्मिष्ठ *a.* Skilled in business, clever, diligent.

कर्वटः The market-town or capital of a district (of two hundred or four hundred villages).

कर्षः 1 Drawing, dragging, pulling; Y. 2. 217. 2 Attracting. 3 Ploughing. 4 A furrow, a trench. 5 A scratch. —**र्षः** –**र्षं** A weight of gold or silver equal to 16 Mâshas –COMP. –**आपणः**=कार्षापण q. v.

कर्षक *a.* Who or what draws, attracts &c. —**कः** A cultivator, husbandman ; Y. 2. 265.

कर्षणं 1 Drawing, dragging, pulling; bending (as of a bow); भज्यमानमतिमात्रकर्षणात् R. 11. 46, 7. 62. 2 Attracting. 3 Ploughing, tilling. 4 Injuring, tormenting; emaciation; Ms. 7. 112.

कर्षिणी The bit of a bridle.

कर्षूः *f.* 1 A furrow, trench. 2 A river. 3 Canal. –*m.* 1 A fire of dried cow-dung. 2 Agriculture, cultivation. 3 Livelihood.

कर्हिचित् *ind.* At any time, usually with न; Ms. 2 4, 40, 97; 4. 77; 6. 50

कल् I. 1 A. (कलते, कलित) 1 To count. 2 To sound. –II. 10 U. (कलयति-ते, कलित) 1 To hold, bear, carry, wield, have, put on ; करालकरकदलीकलितशस्त्रजालैर्बलैः U. 5. 5; म्लेंछनिवहनिधने कलयसि करवालं Gît. 1; कलितललितवनमालः ; हलं कलयते *ibid*; कलय वलयश्रेणीं पाणौ पदे कुरु नूपुरौ 12; Sânti 4. 18. 2 To count, reckon; कालः कलयतामहं Bg. 10 30. 3 To assume, take, have, possess; कलयति हि हिमांशोर्निष्कलंकस्य लक्ष्मीं Mâl 1. 22; Si. 4. 36, 9. 59 4 To know, understand, observe, take notice of, think of; कलयन्नपि सव्यथोऽवतस्थे Si. 9. 83; कोपितं विरहखेदितचित्ता कांतमेव कलयंत्यनुनिन्ये 10. 29; N. 2. 65, 3. 12, Mâl. 2 9. 5 To think, regard, consider; कलयेदमतमनसं

सखि मां Si. 9 58, 6. 54; Śânti. 4. 15; व्यालनिलयमिलनेन गरलमिव कलयति मलयसमीरं Git. 4, 7. 6 To undergo, be influenced by; मदनीलाकलितकामपाल M'al. 8; धन्यः कोपि न विक्रियां कलयति प्राप्ते नवे यौवने Bh. 1. 72. 7 To do, perform. 8 To go. 9 To attach to, lie on; furnish with.–WITH आ 1 to take hold of, seize; Si. 7. 21; कुतूहलाकलितहृदया K. 49. 2 to consider, regard know, take notice of; स्पर्शमपि पावनमाकलयंति K. 168; खिन्नमसूयया हृदय तवाकलयामि Git. 3. 3 to bind, fasten, tie up, restrain or hold together; Si. 1 6, 9. 45, K. 84, 99. 4 To cast, throw; Si. 3. 73. 5 To shake. –परि 1 to know, understand, consider, regard 2 to be aware of, remember. –वि to maim, cripple, to make defective. –सं 1 to add or sum up; cf. संकलन. 2 to consider, regard. –III. 10 U. (कालयति-ते, कलित). To urge on, drive, impel.

कल *a.* 1 Sweet and indistinct (अस्पष्टमधुर); कर्णे कलं किमपि रौति H. 1. 81; सारसैः कलनिर्ह्रादैः R. 1. 41, 8. 59; M. 5. 1. 2 Making noise, jingling, tinkling &c.; भास्वत्कलनूपुराणां R. 16. 12; कलकिंकिणीरवं Si 9. 74, 82; कलमेखलाकलकलः 6. 14, 4. 57. 4 Weak. 5 Crude, undigested —लः A low or soft and inarticulate tone. —लं Semen. –COMP. –अंकुरः the Sârasa bird. –अनुनादिन् *m.* 1 a sparrow. 2 a bee. 3 the Châtaka bird. –अविकलः a sparrow. –आलापः 1 a sweet humming sound. 2 sweet and agreeable discourse; स्फुरत्कलालापविलासकोमला करोति रागं हृदि कौतिकाधिकम् K. 2. 3 a bee. –उत्ताल *a.* high, sharp. –कंठ *a* having a sweet voice (–ठः) (ठी *f.*) 1 the (Indian) cuckoo. 2 a goose, swan. 3 a pigeon. –कलः 1 murmuring or hum of a crowd. 2 indistinct or confused noise; चालितया विदधे कलमेखलाकलकलोऽलकलोलदृशान्यया Si. 6. 14; नेपथ्ये कलकलः (in dramas); Bh. 1. 27, 37; Amaru. 28 3 N. of Siva. –कूजिका,–कूणिका a wanton woman. –घोषः the (Indian) cuckoo. –तूलिका a wanton or lascivious woman. –धौतं 1 silver; Si. 13. 51, 4. 41. 2 gold; विमलकलधौतत्सरुणा खड्गेन Ve. 3. °लिपिः *f.* 1 illumination of a manuscript with gold 2 characters written in gold मरकतशकलकलितकलधौतलिपेरिव रतिजयलेखं Git 8. –ध्वनिः 1 a low sweet tone. 2 a pigeon 3 a peacock. 4 the (Indian) cuckoo. –नादः a low sweet tone –भाषणं lisping, the prattle of childhood. –रवः 1 a low sweet tone. 2 a dove. 3 the (Indian) cuckoo. –हंसः 1 a gander, a swan; वधूदुकूलं कलहंसलक्षणं Ku. 5. 67. 2 a duck, drake; Bk. 2. 18; R. 8. 59. 3 the Supreme soul.

कलंकः 1 A spot, a mark, a dark spot (lit.); R. 13. 15. 2 (Fig.) A stain, stigma, obloquy, disrepute; व्यपनयतु कलंकं स्वस्वभावेन सैव Mk. 10. 34; R. 14. 37; so कुल°. 3 A fault, defect; Bh. 3. 48. 4 Rust of iron.

कलंकषः (षी *f.*) A lion.

कलंकित *a.* Spotted, stained, defamed.

कलंकुरः A whirlpool, eddy.

कलंजः 1 A bird 2 A deer or any other animal struck with a poisoned weapon. —जं Flesh of such an animal.

कलत्रं 1 A wife; वसुमत्या हि नृपाः कलत्रिणः R. 8. 83; 1 32; 12. 34; यद्भर्तुरेव हितमिच्छति तत्कलत्रं Bh. 2. 68. 2 The hip or loins; इंदुमूर्तिमिवोद्दाममन्मथविलासगृहीतगुरुकलत्रां K. 189 (where क° has both senses); Ki. 8. 9, 17. 3 Any royal citadel.

कलनं 1 A spot, a mark. 2 A defect, an offence, fault. 3 Taking, seizing, grasping; कलनात्सर्वभूतानां स कालः परिकीर्तितः 4 Knowing, understanding, apprehension. 5 Sounding. —ना 1 Taking, seizing, grasping; कालकलना A. L. 29. 2 Doing, effecting. 3 Subjection. 4 Understanding, comprehension. 5 Putting on, wearing.

कलंदिका Wisdom, intelligence.

कलभः (भी *f.*) 1 A young elephant, cub; ननु कलभेन यूथपतेरनुकृतं M. 5; द्विपेंद्रभावं कलभः श्रयन्निव R 3. 32; 11. 39; 18. 37. 2 An elephant 30 years old. 3 A young camel; the young of any other animal.

कलमः 1 Rice which is sown in May-June and ripens in December-January; सुतेन पांडोः कलमस्य गोपिकां Ki. 4. 9, 34; Ku. 5. 47; R. 4. 37. 2 A pen, a reed for writing with. 3 A thief. 4 A rogue, rascal.

कलंबः 1 An arrow. 2 The Kadamba tree.

कलंबुटं (Fresh) Butter.

कललः,–लं The fœtus, uterus.

कलविंकः –गः 1 A sparrow; Ms. 5. 12; Y. 1. 174. 2 A spot, stain.

कलशः, –सः (शं, –सं) A pitcher, water-pot, a jar, dish; स्तनौ मांसग्रंथी कनककलशावित्युपमितौ Bh 3. 20, 1. 97; स्तनकलस Amaru. 54. °जन्मन्, °उद्भवः N. of Agastya.

कलशी (सी *f.*) A pitcher, a jar. –COMP. —सुतः N. of Agastya.

कलहः,–हं 1 Strife, quarrel; ईर्ष्याकलहः Bh. 1. 2; लीला° S. Til. 8; so शुष्ककलहः, प्रणयकलहः &c. 2 War, battle. 3 Trick, deceit, falsehood. 4 Violence, kicking, beating &c.; Ms. 4. 121; (where Medhâtithi and Kullûka explain कलह by दंडादिनेतरेतरताडनं and दंडादंड्यादि respectively). –COMP. –अंतरिता a woman separated from her lover in consequence of a quarrel with him (one who is angry and yet sorry for it); she is thus defined in S. D.:— चाटुकारमपि प्राणनाथं रोषादपास्य या । पश्चात्तापमवाप्नोति कलहांतरिता तु सा ॥ 117. –अपहृत *a.* taken by main force or violence. –प्रिय *a.* fond of (promoting) quarrels; ननु कलहप्रियोसि M. 1. (–यः) an epithet of Nârada.

कला 1 A small part of anything; a bit, jot; कलामप्यकृतपरिलंबः K. 304; सर्वे ते मित्रगात्रस्य कलां नार्हंति षोडशीं Pt. 2. 55; Ms. 2. 86, 8 36. 2 A digit of the moon (these are sixteen); जगति जयिनस्ते ते भावा नवेंदुकलादयः Mal. 1. 36; Ku. 5. 72; Me. 89. 3 Interest on capital (consideration paid for the use of money); धनवीथिवीथिमवतीर्णवतो निधिरंभसामुपचयाय कलाः Si. 9. 32; (where कला means 'digits' also). 4 A division of time variously computed; one minute, 48 seconds, or 8 seconds. 5 The 60th part of one thirtieth part of a zodiacal sign, a minute of a degree. 6 Any practical art (mechanical or fine); there are 64 such arts, as music, dancing &c. 7 Skill, ingenuity. 8 Fraud, deceit. 9 (In Prosody) A syllabic instant. 10 A boat. 11 The menstrual discharge. –COMP. –अंतरं 1 another digit. 2 interest, profit; मासे शतस्य यदि पंच कलांतरं स्यात् Lîlâ. –अयनः a tumbler, a dancer (as on the sharp edge of a sword). –आकुलं deadly poison. –केलि *a.* gay, wanton. (–लिः) an epithet of Kâma. –क्षयः waning (of the moon); R. 5. 16. –धरः, –निधिः, –पूर्णः the moon; अहो महत्त्वं महतामपूर्वं विपत्तिकालेपि परोपकारः । यथास्यमध्ये पतितोपि राहोः कलानिधिः पुण्यचयं ददाति ॥ Udb. –भृत् *m.* the moon; so कलावत् *m.*; Ku. 5. 72.

कलादः, –दकः A gold-smith.

कलापः 1 A band, bundle; मुक्ताकलापस्य च निस्तलस्य Ku. 1. 43 a necklace of pearls; रशनाकलापः a zone of several strings. 2 A group or whole collection of things: अखिलकलाकलापालोचन K. 7. 3 A peacock's tail; तं मे जातकलापं प्रेषय मणिकंठकं शिखिनं V. 5. 13; Pt 2. 80; Rs. 1. 16, 2. 14. 4 A woman's zone or girdle; (oft. with काञ्ची or रशना &c.); Bh. 1. 57, 67; Rs. 3. 20; Mk. 1. 27. 5 An ornament in general. 6 The rope round an elephant's neck. 7 A quiver. 8 An arrow. 9 The moon. 10 A shrewd and intelligent man. 11 A poem written in one metre. —पी A bundle of grass.

कलापकं 1 A series of four stanzas on the same subject and forming one grammatical sentence (चतुर्भिस्तु कलापकं); for an illustration see Ki. 3. 41, 42, 43, 44. 2 A debt to be paid when the peacocks spread their tails. —कः 1 A band or bundle in general. 2 A string of pearls. 3 The rope round an elephant's neck. 4 A zone or girdle (=कलाप); Si. 9. 45. 5 A sectarian mark on the fore-head (विशेषक).

कलापिन् *m*. 1 A peacock; कलविलापि कलापिकदंबकं Si. 6. 31; Pt 2. 80; R. 6. 9. 2 The (Indian) cuckoo. 3 The Indian fig-tree (प्लक्ष).

कलापिनी 1 The night. 2 The moon.

कलायः N. of a leguminous seed (Mar. वाटाणा); Si 13. 21.

कलाविकः A cock.

कलाहकः A kind of musical instrument (काहल).

कलिः 1 Strife, quarrel, dissension, contention; Si. 7. 55; कलिकामजित् R. 9. 33; Amaru. 19. 2 War, battle. 3 The fourth age of the world, the iron age (consisting of 432,000 years of men and beginning from the 8th of February 3102 B. C.); Ms 1. 86, 9. 301; कलिवर्ज्यानि इमानि &c. 4 Kali age personified (this Kali persecuted Nala). 5 The worst of any class. 6 The Bibhítaka tree. 7 The side of a die which is marked with one point. 8 A hero. 9 An arrow. —*f*. A bud. -COMP. -कारः, -कारकः, -क्रियः an epithet of Nârada. —द्रुमः,-वृक्षः the Bibhîtaka tree. -युगं the Kali age, iron age; Ms 1. 85.

कलिका, कलिः *f*. 1 An unblown flower, a bud; चूतानां चिरानिर्गतापि कलिका बध्नाति न स्वं रजः S. 6. 6; किमाम्रकलिकाभंगमारभसे S. 6; Rs. 6. 17; R. 9. 33. 2 A digit streak.

कलिंगाः (pl.) N. of a country and its inhabitants (a district on the Coromandel coast); उत्कलादर्शितपथः कलिंगाभिमुखो ययौ R 4 38; (its position is thus described in Tantras:— जगन्नाथात्समारभ्य कृष्णातीरांतगः प्रिये । कालगदेशः संप्राक्तो वाममार्गपरायणः ॥

कलिंजः A mat, a screen.

कलित *a*. Hold, seized, taken; see कल्.

कलिंदः 1 N. of the mountain on which the Yamunâ rises 2 The sun. -COMP —कन्या, -जा, -तनया -नंदिनी epithets of the river Yamunâ; कलिंदकन्या मथुरां गतापि R. 6. 48; कलिंदजानीर Bv. 2 120, Gît 3. -गिरिः the Kalinda mountain. °जा, °तनया, °नंदिनी epithets of the river Yamunâ; Bv. 4. 3, 4.

कलिल *a*. 1 Covered with, full of. 2 Mixed, blended with; दृढ पवाकंदककलिलः कलकलः Mv. 1. 3 Affected by, subject to; अकल्ककलिलः Si. 19. 98. 4 Impervious, impenetrable. —लं A large heap, confused mass; विशासे हृदयंक्लेशकलिलं Bh. 3. 34; confusion; यदा ते मोहकलिलं बुद्धिर्व्यतितरिष्यति Bg 2. 52.

कलुष *a*. 1 Turbid, dirty, muddy, foul; गंगा रोधःपतनकलुषा गृह्णतीव प्रसादं V. 1. 8; Ki. 8. 32; Ghaṭ. 13 2 Choked, hoarse, husky; कंठः स्तंभितबाष्पवृत्तिकलुषः S. 4. 6. 3 Bedimmed, full of; S. 6. 4 4 Angry, displeased, excited; भावावबोधकलुषा दयितेव रात्रौ R. 5. 64. (Malli. takes कलुष to mean 'unable', 'incompetent'). 5 Wicked, sinful, bad. 6 Cruel, censurable; R. 14. 73. 7 Dark, opaque. 8 Idle, lazy. —षः A buffalo. —षं 1 Dirt, filth, mud; विगतकलुषमंभः Rs. 3. 22. 2 Sin. 3 Wrath.-COMP.-योनिज *a*. illegitimate, of impure origin; Ms. 10. 57, 58.

कलेवरः, -रं The body; यावत्स्वस्थमिदं कलेवरगृहं Bh. 3. 88; H. 1. 47; Bg. 8. 5; Bv. 1. 103, 2. 43.

कल्कः, -ल्कं 1 A viscous sediment deposited by oily substances when ground. 2 A kind of tenacious paste; Y. 1. 277. 3 (Hence) Dirt, filth (in general) 4 Ordure, fæces. 5 Meanness, deceit, hypocrisy; Si 19. 98. 6 Sin. 7 Levigated powder; तां लोध्रकल्केन हृतांगतैलां Ku. 7. 9. -COMP. -फलः the pomegranate plant.

कल्कनं Deceiving, overreaching, falsehood.

कल्किः, -कल्किन् *m*. The tenth and last incarnation of Vishṇu in his capacity of the destroyer of the wicked and liberator of the world from its enemies; (Jayadeva, while referring to the several *avatâras* of Vishṇu, thus refers to the last or *Kalki* avatâra:—म्लेच्छनिवहनिधने कलयसि करवालम् धूमकेतुमिव किमपि करालम् । केशव धृतकल्किशरीर जय जगदीश हरे ॥ Gît. 1 10)

कल्प *a*. 1 Practicable, feasible, possible 2 Proper, fit, right 3 Able, competent (with a gen., loc; inf. or at the end of comp.); धर्मस्य, यशसः, कल्पः, Bhâg. able to do his duty &c.: स्वक्रियायामकल्पः *ibid* not competent to do one's duty: अकल्प एषामधिरोढुमंजसा पद *ibid*., so स्वभरणाकल्प &c. -ल्पः 1 A sacred precept or rule, law, ordinance. 2 A prescribed rule, a prescribed alternative, optional rule; प्रभुः प्रथमकल्पस्य योऽनुकल्पेन वर्तते Ms 11. 30 'able to follow the prescribed rule to be observed in preference to all others'; प्रथमः कल्पः M. 1 a very good (or best) alternative; एष वै प्रथमः कल्पः प्रदाने हव्यकव्ययोः Ms. 3. 147. 3 (Hence) A proposal, suggestion, resolve, determination; उदारः कल्पः S 7. 4 Manner of acting, procedure, form, way, method (in religious rites); क्षात्रेण कल्पेनोपनीय U. 2; कल्पविकल्पयामास वन्यामिवास्य संविधां R. 1. 94; Ms. 7. 185. 5 End of the world, universal destruction. 6 A day of Brahmâ or 1,000 Yugas being a period of 432 million years of mortals and measuring the duration of the world; श्वेतवाराहकल्पे (the one in which we now live); कल्पं स्थितं तनुभृतां तनुभिस्ततः किम् Sânti. 4. 2. 7 Medical treatment of the sick. 8 One of the six Ved'angas; viz:—that which lays down the ritual and prescribes rules for ceremonial and sacrificial acts; see under वेदांग. 9 A termination added to nouns and adjectives in the sense of 'a little less than,' 'almost like,' 'nearly equal to,' (denoting similarity with a degree of inferiority); कुमारकल्पं सुषुवे कुमारं R. 5. 36; उपपन्नमेतदस्मिन्नृषिकल्पे राजनि S. 2; प्रभातकल्पा शशिनेव शर्वरी R. 3. 2; so मृतकल्पः, प्रतिपन्नकल्पः &c. -COMP.-अंतः end of the world, universal destruction; Bh. 2. 16. °स्थायिन् *a*. lasting to the end of a कल्प. -आदिः renovation of all things in the creation. -कारः author of a Kalpasûtra, q. v. —क्षयः end of the world, universal destruction: *e. g*. पुरा कल्पक्षये वृत्ते जातं जलमयं जगत् Ks 2. 10. -तरुः, -द्रुमः, -पादपः, -वृक्षः one of the trees of heaven or Indra's paradise; R. 1 75; 17. 26; Ku. 2 39; 6 41. 2 a tree supposed to grant all desires, 'wish-yielding tree'; नाबुद्ध कल्पद्रुमतां विहाय जात तमात्मन्यसिपत्रवृक्षं R. 14. 48; N. 1. 15. 3 (fig.) a very generous person; सकलार्थिसार्थकल्पद्रुमः Pt. 1. -पालः seller of spirituous liquors. -लता, -लतिका 1 a creeper of Indra's paradise; Bh 1. 90. 2 A creeper supposed to grant all desires; नानाफलैः फलति कल्पलतेव भूमिः Bh. 2. 46; cf. कल्पतरु above -सूत्रं a manual of ritual in the form of Sûtras.

कल्पकः 1 A rite 2 A barber

कल्पनं 1 Forming, fashioning, arranging. 2 performing, doing, effecting. 3 Clipping, cutting. 4 Fixing. 5 Anything placed upon another for decoration. -ना 1 Fixing, settlement; अनेकपितृकाणां तु पितृतो भागकल्पना Y. 2. 120, 247; Ms. 9. 16 2 Making, performing, doing. 3 Forming, arranging; Mk. 3. 14. 4 Decorating, ornamenting 5 omposition 6 Invention 7 Imagination, thought; कल्पनापोढः Sk =कल्पनाया अपोढः. 8 An idea, fancy or image (conceived in the mind); Sânti. 2. 7. 9 Fabrication. 10 Forgery. 11 A contrivance, device. 12 (In Mîm. phil.) = अर्थापत्ति q v.

कल्पनी Scissors.

कल्पित *a* Arranged, made, fashioned, formed; see क्लृप् caus.

कल्मष *a*. 1 Sinful, wicked. 2 Foul, dirty. —षः -षं 1 Stain, dirt, dregs. 2 Sin; स हि गगनविहारी कल्मषध्वंसकारी H. 1. 21; Bg. 4. 30; 5. 16; Ms. 4. 260, 12. 18, 22.

कल्माष *a* (**षी** *f.*) **1** Variegated, spotted. **2** Black and white. **–षः 1** The variegated colour. **2** A mixture of black and white. **3** A demon, goblin **–षी** N. of the river Yamunâ. –COMP. **–कंठः** an epithet of *S*iva.

कल्य *a* **1** Sound, free from sickness, healthy ; सर्वः कल्ये वयसि यतते लब्धुमर्थान्कुटुंबी V. 3., Y. 1. 28 ; यावदेव भवेत्कल्यस्तावच्छ्रेयः समाचरेत् Mb. **2** Ready, prepared ; कथयस्व कथामेतां कल्याः स्मः श्रवणे तव Mb. **3** Clever. **4** Agreeable, auspicious (as a discourse). **5** Deaf and dumb. **6** Instructive. **–ल्यं 1** Dawn, day-break. **2** To-morrow. **3** Spirituous liquor. **4** Congratulation, good wishes **5** Good news. –COMP. **–आशः,–जग्धिः** *f.* the morning meal, break-fast. **–पालः, –पालकः** a distiller. **–वर्तः** morning meal. break-fast. (**–र्तं**) (hence) anything light, trivial or unimportant ; a trifle; ननु कल्यवर्तमेतत् Mk. 2 but a trifle ; स्त्रीकल्यवर्तस्य कारणेन 4; स इदानीमर्थकल्यवर्तस्य कारणादिदमकार्यं करोति 9.

कल्या 1 Spirituous liquor. **2** Congratulation. –COMP. **–पालः, –पालकः** a distiller.

कल्याण *a.* (**–णा** or**–णी** *f.*) **1** Blessed, happy, lucky, fortunate ; त्वमेव कल्याणि तयोस्तृतीया R. 6. 29 ; Me. 109. **2** Beautiful, agreeable, lovely. **3** Excellent, illustrious. **4** Auspicious, salu tary propitious, good; कल्याणानां त्वमसि महसां भाजनं विश्वमूर्ते: M'al. 1. 3. **–णं 1** Good fortune, happiness, good, prosperity ; कल्याणं कुरुतां जनस्य भगवांश्चंद्रार्धचूडामणिः H. 1. 212 ; तद्रक्ष कल्याणपरंपराणां भोक्तारमूर्जस्वलमात्मदेहं R. 2. 50; 17. 1; Ms. 3. 60 ; so °आभिनिवेशी K. 104. **2** Virtue. **3** Festival. **4** Gold. **5** Heaven. –COMP. **–कृत्** *a.* **1** doing good, beneficial, good ; Bg. 6. 40. **2** propitious, lucky. **3** virtuous. **–धर्मन्** *a.* virtuous. **–वचनं** friendly speech, good wishes.

कल्याणक *a.* (**णिका** *f.*) Auspicious, prosperous, blessed.

कल्याणिन् *a.* (**नी** *f.*) **1** Happy, prosperous. **2** Lucky, fortunate, blessed. **3** Propitious, auspicious

कल्याणी A cow ; R. 1. 87.

कल्ल *a.* Deaf.

कल्लोलः 1 a large wave, a billow ; आयुः कल्लोललोलं Bh. 3 82 ; कल्लोलमालाकुलं Bv 1. 59. **2** An enemy. **3** Joy, happiness.

कल्लोलिनी A river; स्वर्लोककल्लोलिनि त्वं पापं तिरयाधुना मम भवव्यालावलीढात्मनः G. L. 50; so विपुलपुलिनाः कल्लोलिन्यः

कव् I A. (कवते, कवित) **1** To praise. **2** To describe, compose (as a poem) **3** To paint, picture.

कवकः A mouthful. **–कं** A mushroom ; विड्जानि कवकानि च Y. 1. 171 ; Ms. 5. 5, 6. 14.

कवचः –चं 1 An armour, coat of mail, a mail. **2** An amulet, a charm, a mystical syllable (हुं-हूं) considered as a preservative like armour. **3** A kettle-drum. –COMP. **–पत्रः** the birch tree. **–हर** *a.* **1** wearing armour. **2** old enough to wear an armour; कवचहरः कुमारः Ku. ; cf. वर्महर in R. 8. 94.

कवटी The leaf or panel of a door.

कव (ब) र *a.* (**–रा, –री** *f.*) **1** Mixed, intermingled; *S*i. 5. 19. **2** Set, inlaid. **3** Variegated. **—रः,–रं 1** Salt. **2** Sourness or acidity. **—रः** A braid or fillet of hair.

कव (ब) री A braid or fillet of hair; दधती विलोलकवरीकमाननं U. 3. 4; *S*i. 9. 28; Amaru. 59. –Comp. **–भरः-भारः** a fine head of hair ; घटय जघने कांचीमंच स्रजा कवरीभरं Gît. 12.

कवलः, –लं 1 A mouthful; आस्वादवद्भिः कवलैस्तृणानां R. 2. 5 ; 9. 59; कवलच्छेदेषु संपादिताः U. 3. 16.

कवलित *a.* **1** Eaten, swallowed up (as a mouthful). **2** Chewed. **3** (Hence) Taken, seized; as in मृत्युना कवलितः.

कवाट see **कपाट**.

कवि *a.* **1** Omniscient; Bg. 8. 9 ; Ms. 4 24. **2** Intelligent, clever, wise. **3** Thinking, thoughtful. **4** Praiseworthy.**—विः 1** A wise man, a thinker, a sage ; कवीनामुशना कविः Bg. 10. 37; Ms. 7. 49, 2. 151. **2** A poet ; तद् ब्रूहि रामचरित आद्यः कविरसि U. 2 ; मंदः कवियशःप्रार्थी R. 1. 3 ; इदं कविभ्यः पूर्वेभ्यो नमोवाकं प्रशास्महे U. 1. 1 ; *S*i. 2. 83. **3** An epithet of *S*ukra, the preceptor of the Asuras. **4** Vâlmiki, the first poet. **5** Brahmâ. **6** The sun **—***f.* The bit of a bridle ; see कविका. –COMP. **–ज्येष्ठः** an epithet of Vâlmîki the first poet. **–पुत्रः** an epithet of *S*ukra. **–राजः 1** a great poet ; श्रीहर्ष कविराजराजिमुकुटालंकारहीरः सुतं occurring in the last verse of every canto of Naishadha Charita. **2** N. of a poet, author of a poem called राघवपांडवीय. **–रामायणः** an epithet of Vâlmîki.

कविकः, का The bit of a bridle.

कविता Poetry ; सुकविता यद्यस्ति राज्येन किं Bh. 2. 21.

कवि (वी) यं The bit of a bridle.

कवोष्ण *a.* Slightly warm, tepid; R. 1. 67, 84.

कव्यं (opp हव्य) An oblation of food to deceased ancestors ; एष वै प्रथमः कल्पः प्रदाने हव्यकव्ययोः Ms. 3. 147 ; 97, 128. **–व्यः** A class of manes.– COMP.**–वाह्** *m.*, **–वाहः,–वाहनः** fire.

कशः A whip (usually in pl.). **–शा** A whip ; इदानीं सुकुमारेऽस्मिन् निःशंकं कर्कशाः कशाः। तव गात्रे पतिष्यंति सहास्माकं मनोरथैः ॥ Mk. 9. 35 (where the word may be *m.* or *f.*) **2** Flogging. **3** A string, rope.

कशिपु *m.* or *n.* **1** A mat. **2** A pillow. **3** A bed.—**पुः 1** Food. **2** Clothing. **3** Food and clothing (according to विश्व).

कशे (से) रु *m. n.* **1** The back-bone. **2** A kind of grass.

कश्मल *a.* Foul, dirty, disgraceful, ignominious ; मत्संबंधात्कश्मला किंवदंती स्याच्चेदस्मिन्हंत धिङ्मामधन्यं U. 1. 42.**—लं 1** Dejection of mind, lowness or depression of spirits; कश्मलं महदाविशत् Mb. ; कुतस्त्वा कश्मलमिदं विषमे समुपस्थितं Bg. 2. 2. **2** Sin. **3** Swoon.

कश्मीरः (pl.) N. of a country, the modern Kâshmira. (Its position is thus described in Tantras:—शारदामठमारभ्य कुंकुमाद्रितटांतकः । तावत्कश्मीरदेशः स्यात् पंचाशद्योजनात्मकः). –COMP. **–जः –जं –जन्मन्** *m. n.* saffron; कश्मीरजस्य कटुताऽपि नितांतरम्या Bv. 1. 71.

कश्य *a.* Fit to be whipped or flogged. **- श्यं** Spirituous liquor.

कश्यपः 1 A tortoise. **2** N. of a *R*ishi, the husband of Aditi and Diti and thus the father both of gods and demons. [He was the son of Mar*i*chi, the son of Brahm*a*. He bears a very important share in the work of creation. According to Mah*a*bh*a*rata and other accounts, he married Aditi and 12 other daughters of Daksha, and begot on Aditi the twelve *A*dityas. By his other twelve wives he had a numerous and very diversified progeny: serpents, reptiles, birds, demons, nymphs of the lunar constellation. He was thus the father of gods, demons, men, beasts, birds and reptiles—in fact of all living beings. He is therefore often called Praj*a*pati].

कष् I. U. (कषति-ते, काषित) **1** To rub, scratch, scrape ; समूलकाषं कषति Sk. ; Bk. 3. 49. **2** To test, try, rub on a touch-stone (as gold) ; छदहेम कषन्निवालसत्कषपाषाणनिभे नभस्तले N. 2. 69. **3** To injure, destroy. **4** To itch.

कष *a.* Rubbing, scraping. **—षः 1** Rubbing. **2** A touch-stone ; छदहेम कषन्निवालसत् कषपाषाणनिभे नभस्तले N. 2. 69 ; Mk. 3. 17

कषणं 1 Rubbing, marking, scratching ; कंडूलद्विपगंडपिंडकषणोत्कंपेन संपातिभिः U. 2. 9; कषणकंपनिरस्तमहाहिभिः Ki. 5. 47. **2** Test of gold by the touch-stone.

कषा—कशा q. v.

कषाय *a.* **1** Astringent; *S*. 2. **2** Fragrant; स्फुटितकमलामोदमैत्रीकषायः Me. 31 ; U. 2. 21 ; Mv. 5. 41. **3** Red, dark-red ; चूतांकुरास्वादकषायकंठः Ku. 3. 32. **4** (Hence) Sweet-sounding ; Mâl. 7. **5** Brown. **6** Improper, dirty. **–यः, –यं 1** Astringent flavour or taste (one of the six *rasas*) : see कटु. **2** The red colour. **3** A decoction with one part of a drug mixed with four, eight, or sixteen parts of water (the whole being boiled down until one quarter is left); Ms. 11. 154. 4 Plastering, smearing; Ku. 7. 17; anointing. 5 Perfuming the body with unguents; Rs. 1. 4. 6 Gum, resin, extract or exudation from a tree. 7 Dirt, uncleanness. 8 Dulness, stupidity. 9 Attachment to worldly objects. —यः 1 Passion, emotion. 2 Kaliyuga.

कषायित *a.* 1 Tinged, reddened, coloured; अमुनैव कषायितस्तनी Ku. 4. 34; *Si.* 7. 11. 2 Affected.

कषि *a.* Injurious, mischievous, hurtful.

कषे (से) रुका The backbone, the spine.

कष्ट *a.* 1 Bad, evil, ill, wrong; रामहस्तमनुप्राप्य कष्टात् कष्टतरं गता R. 15. 43 'gone from bad to worse', (reduced to a wretched condition). 2 Painful, grievous; मोहाद्भूस्कष्टतरः प्रबोधः R. 14. 56; कष्टोऽयं खलु भृत्यभावः Ratn. 1 full of cares; Ms. 7. 50; Y. 3. 29; कष्टा वृत्तिः पराधीना कष्टो वासो निराश्रयः। निर्धनो व्यवसायश्च सर्वकष्टा दरिद्रता ॥ Chāṇ. 59. 3 Difficult; स्त्रीषु कष्टोऽधिकारः V. 3. 1. 4 Hard to subdue (as an enemy); Ms. 7. 186, 210. 5 Mischievous, hurtful, injurious. 6 Boding evil. —ष्टं 1 Evil, difficulty, misery, suffering, hardship, pain; कष्टं खल्वनपत्यता *S.* 6; धिगर्थाः कष्टसंश्रयाः Pt. 1. 163. 2 Sin, wickedness. 3 Difficulty, effort; कष्टेन somehow or other. —ष्टं *ind.* Alas! Ah! हा धिक् कष्टं; हा कष्टं जरयाभिभूतपुरुषः पुत्रैरवज्ञायते Pt. 4. 78. –COMP. —आगत *a.* arrived or got with difficulty. —कर *a.* giving pain, troublesome. —तपस् *a.* one who practises hard penance; *S.* 7. —साध्य *a.* to be accomplished with difficulty. —स्थानं a bad station, a difficult or disagreeable place.

कष्टि *f.* 1 Test, trial. 2 Pain, trouble.

कस् I. 1. P. (कसति, कसित) To move, go, approach. With निस् (*Caus.*) 1 to take or draw out. 2 to turn or drive out, banish, expel; निरकासयद्रविमपेतवसुं वियदालयादपरदिग्गणिका *Si.* 9. 10; येनाहं जीवलोकान्निष्कासयिष्ये Mu. 6. —प्र to open, cause to expand; घनमुक्तांबुलवप्रकाशितैः (कुसुमैः) Ghaṭ. 19. —वि to open, expand (fig. also); विकसति हि पतंगस्योदये पुंडरीकं Māl. 1. 28; *Si.* 9. 47, 82; Ku. 7. 55; निजहृदि विकसंतः Bh. 2. 78. (*Caus.*) to open, cause to expand; चंद्रो विकासयति कैरवचक्रवालं Bh. 2. 73; *Si.* 15. 12; Amaru. 84.-II. 2 A. (कस्ते or कंस्ते) To go. 2 To destroy.

कस्तु (स्तू) रिका, कस्तूरी Musk; कस्तुरिकातिलकमालि विधाय सायं Bv. 2. 4; 1. 121; Ch. P. 7. –COMP. —मृगः the musk-deer.

कह्लारं The white lotus, कह्लारपद्मकुसुमानि मुहुर्विधुन्वन् Rs. 3. 15.

कह्वः A kind of cane.

कांसीयं White copper.

कांस्य *a.* Made of white copper or bell-metal; Ms. 4. 55. —स्यं 1 Bell-metal or white copper; Ms. 5. 114; Y. 1. 190. 2 A gong of bell-metal. —स्यः, —स्यं A drinking vessel (of brass), a goblet; *Si.* 15. 81. –COMP. —कारः (री *f.*) a brazier, a worker in bell-metal. —तालः a cymbal. —भाजनं a brass-vessel. —मलं verdigris.

काकः 1 A crow; काकोपि जीवति चिराय बलिं च भुंक्ते Pt. 1. 24. 2 (Fig.) A contemptible fellow, base or impudent person. 3 A lame man. 4 Bathing by dipping the head only into water (as crows do). —की A female crow. —कं A multitude of crows. –COMP. —अक्षिगोलकन्याय see under न्याय. —अरिः an owl. —उदरः a snake; काकोदरो येन विनीतदर्पः Kavirāja. —उलूकिका, —उलूकीयं the natural enmity of the owl and the crow; (काकोलूकीयं is the name of the third Tantra in the Panchatantra). —चिंचा the gunjâ plant. —छदः, —छदिः 1 a wagtail. 2 a side-lock of hair; see काकपक्ष below. —जातः the (Indian) cuckoo. —तालीय *a.* (any thing) taking place quite unexpectedly and accidentally, an accident; अहो नु खलु भोः तदेतत् काकतालीयं नाम Māl. 5; काकतालीयवत्प्राप्तं दृष्ट्वापि निधिमग्रतः H. Pr. 35; sometimes used adverbially in the sense of 'accidentally'; फलंति काकतालीयं तेभ्यः प्राज्ञा न बिभ्यति Ve. 2. 14. °न्याय see under न्याय. —तालुकिन् *a.* contemptible, vile. —दंतः (lit.) the tooth of a crow; (fig.) anything impossible or not existing; °गवेषणं searching after impossibilities, (said of any useless and unprofitable task). —ध्वजः the submarine fire. —निद्रा a light slumber (easily broken). —पक्षः, —पक्षकः side-locks of hair on the temples of boys and young men (especially of the Kshatriya caste); काकपक्षधरमेत्य याचितः R. 11. 1, 31, 42; 3. 28; U. 3. —पदं the sign (∧) in Mss. denoting that something has been left out. —दः a particular mode of sexual intercourse. —पुच्छः, -पुष्टः the (Indian) cuckoo. —पेय *a.* shallow; काकपेया नदी Sk. —भीरुः an owl. —मद्गुः a gallinule. —यवः barren corn (the ear of which has no grain); यथा काकयवाः प्रोक्ता यथारण्यभवास्तिलाः। नाममात्रा न सिद्धौ हि धनहीनास्तथा नराः ॥ Pt. 2. 86; तथैव पांडवाः सर्वे यथा काकयवा इव Mb.; (काकयवाः =निष्फलतृणधान्यं). —रुतं the shrill sound of a crow (considered as a sign of future good or evil under different circumstances); *Si.* 6. 76. —वंध्या a woman that bears only one child. —स्वरः a shrill tone (as that of a crow).

काकरु (रू) क *a.* 1 Timid, cowardly. 2 Naked. 3 Poor, indigent. —कः 1 A hen-pecked husband. 2 (की *f.*) An owl. 3 Fraud, deceit, trick.

काक (का) लः A raven. —लं A jewel worn upon the neck.

काकलिः, —ली *f.* 1 A low and sweet tone; अनुबद्धमुग्धकाकलीसहितं U. 3; Rs. 1. 8. 2 A musical instrument with a low tone used by thieves to ascertain whether a person is asleep or not; फणिमुखकाकलीसंदंशक...प्रभृत्यनेकोपकरणयुक्तः Dk. 49. 3 Scissors. 4 The Gunjâ plant. —COMP. —रवः the (Indian) cuckoo.

काकिणी, काकिणिका 1 A shell or *cowrie* used as a coin. 2 A sum of money equal to 20 *cowries* or to a quarter of a Paṇa. 3 A weight equal to a quarter of a Mâsha. 4 A part of a measure. 5 The beam of a balance. 6 A cubit.

काकिनी *f.* 1 A quarter of a Paṇa q. v. 2 A quarter of a measure. 3 A cowrie; H. 3. 123.

काकुः *f.* 1 Change of the voice under different emotions such as fear, grief, anger; भिन्नकंठध्वनिर्धीरैः काकुरित्यभिधीयते S. D.; अलीककाकुकरणकुशलतां K. 222. (Hence). 2 A word of negation used in such a manner that it implies the contrary (affirmative) as in questions of appeal; (in such cases the intended meaning is suggested by a change of the voice). 3 Muttering, murmuring. 4 Tongue.

काकुत्स्थः A descendant of ककुत्स्थ, an epithet of kings of the solar dynasty; काकुत्स्थमालोकयतां नृपाणां R. 6. 2; 12. 30, 46; see ककुत्स्थ.

काकुदं The palate.

काकोलः 1 A raven; Y. 1. 174. 2 A snake. 3 A boar. 4 A potter. 5 A division of the infernal regions or hell; Y. 3. 223.

काक्षः A sidelong look, a glance. —क्षं Frown, look of displeasure, malicious look; काक्षेणानादरोक्षितः Bk. 5. 28.

कागः A crow; cf. काक.

कांक्ष् 1 P. (epic Atm. also). (कांक्षति, कांक्षित) 1 To wish, desire, long for; यत्कांक्षति तपोभिरन्यमुनयस्तस्मिंस्तपस्यंत्यमी *S.* 7. 12; न शोचति न कांक्षति Bg. 12. 7; न कांक्षे विजयं कृष्ण 1. 32; R. 12. 58; Ms. 2. 242. 2 To expect, wait for. With अभि to long for, wish. —आ 1 to desire, long or wish for; प्रत्याश्वसंतं रिपुराचकांक्ष R. 7. 47, 5. 38; Ms. 2. 162; Me. 91; Y. 1. 153. 2 to require, need. —प्रत्या to lie in, wait for. —वि to wish, desire or long for. —समा to wish or desire.

कांक्षा 1 Wish, desire. 2 Inclination, appetite; as in भक्तकांक्षा.

कांक्षिन् *a.* (णी *f.*) Wishing for, desirous; °दर्शन, जल °&c.; Bg. 11. 52.

काचः 1 Glass, crystal; आकरे पद्मरागाणां जन्म काचमणेः कुतः H. Pr. 44; काचमूल्येन विक्रीतो हंत चिंतामणिर्मया Sânti. 1. 12. 2 A loop, a swinging shelf, a string so fastened to the yoke as to support burdens. **3** An eye-disease, an affection of the optic nerve, producing dimness of sight. -COMP. -घटी a glass ewer. -भाजनं a glass vessel. -मणिः crystal, quartz. -मलं, -लवणं, -संभवं black salt or soda.

काचनं, काचनकं A string or tape which ties a parcel or bundle of papers or the leaves of a Manuscript; cf. कचेल.

काचनकिन् *m.* A manuscript, writing

काचूकः **1** A cock. **2** The Chakravâka bird.

काजलं **1** A little water. **2** Bad water.

कांचन *a.* (नी *f.*) Golden, made of gold; तन्मध्ये च स्फटिकफलका कांचनी वासयष्टिः Me. 79 ; कांचनं वलयं *S.* 6. 5 ; Ms. 5. 112. -नं **1** Gold ; (ग्राह्यं) अमेध्यादपि कांचनं Ms. 2. 239. **2** Lustre, brilliancy. **3** Property, wealth. **4** The filament of a lotus. —नः **1** The Dhattûra plant. **2** The Champaka tree. -COMP. —अंगी a woman with a golden (*i. e.* yellow) complexion ; Bv. 2. 72. -कंदरः a gold-mine. -गिरिः N. of the mountain Meru. -भूः *f.* **1** golden (yellow) soil. **2** gold-dust. -संधिः a treaty of alliance between two parties on terms of equality ; cf. H 4. 113.

कांचनारः (-लः) The Kovidâra tree.

कांचिः, -ची *f.* **1** A woman's girdle or zone furnished with small tinkling bells or other ornaments; एतावता नन्वनुमेयशोभि कांचीगुणस्थानमनिंदितायाः Ku. 1. 37, 3. 55 ; Me. 28 ; *Si.* 9. 82 ; R. 6. 43 **2** N. of an ancient city in the south of India, regarded as one of the sacred cities of the Hindus ; (for the names of the seven cities, see अवंति). -COMP. -पुरी, -नगरी the same as कांची (2). -पदं the hips and loins.

कांजिकं, कांजिका Sour gruel.

काटुकं Acidity.

काठः A rock, stone.

काठिनं, -न्यं **1** Hardness, tightness; काठिन्यमुक्तस्तनं *S.* 3. 11. **2** Sternness, hard-heartedness, cruelty.

काण *a.* **1** One-eyed; अक्ष्णा काणः Sk.; काणेन चक्षुषा किं वा H. Pr. 12; Ms. 3. 155. **2** Perforated, broken (as a cowrie), प्रातः काणवराटकोपि न मया तृष्णेऽधुना मुंच माम् Bh. **3.** 4; (Mar. फुटकी कवडी).

काणेयः, -रः Son of a one-eyed woman.

काणेली **1** An unchaste or faithless woman. **2** An unmarried woman. -COMP. -मातृ *m.* one whose mother is an unmarried woman; son of an unmarried woman; (a term of reproach occurring usually in the voc. case only); काणेलीमातः अस्ति किंचिचिह्नं यदुपलक्षयसि Mk. 1.

कांडः,-डं **1** A section, a part in general. **2** The portion of a plant from one knot to another. **3** A stem, stock, branch; लीलोत्खातमृणालकांडकवलच्छेदेषु U. 3. 16 ; Amaru 95; Ms. 1. 46, 48. **4** Any division of a work; such as a chapter of a book; as the seven Kândas of the Râm. **5** A separate department or subject; *e. g.* ज्ञान° कर्म° &c. **6** A cluster, bundle, multitude. **7** An arrow. **8** A long bone, a bone of the arms or legs. **9** A cane, reed. **10** A stick, staff. **11** Water. **12** Opportunity, occasion. **13** Private place. **14** Vile, bad, sinful, (at the end of comp. only). -COMP. -कारः a maker of arrows. -गोचरः an iron arrow. -पटः,-पटकः a screen surrounding a tent, curtain; *Si.* 5. 22. -पातः an arrow's flight, range of an arrow. -पृष्ठः **1** one of the military profession, a soldier. **2** the husband of a Vaisya woman. **3** an adopted son, any other than one's own son. **4** (as a term of reproach) a base-born fellow, one who is faithless to his family, caste, religion, profession &c. In Mv. **3** Jâmadagnya is styled by शतानंद as कांडपृष्ठ; (स्वकुलं पृष्ठतः कृत्वा यो वै परकुलं व्रजेत् । तेन दुश्चरितेनासौ कांडपृष्ठ इति स्मृतः). -भंगः a fracture of bones or limbs. -वाणी the lute of a Chândâla. -संधिः a knot, joint (as of a plant). -स्पृष्टः one who lives by arms, warrior, soldier.

कांडवत् *m.* An archer.

कांडीरः An archer ; (this word also is sometimes used like कांडपृष्ठ as a term of reproach; cf. Mv. 3).

कांडोलः A basket of reed ; see कंडोल

कात् *ind.* An exclamation of abuse or insult, usually in combination with कृ ; कात्कृ to insult, dishonour ; यन्मयैश्वर्यमत्तेन गुरुः सदसि कात्कृतः Bhâg.

कातर *a.* **1** Cowardly, timid, discouraged ; वर्जयंति च कातरान् Pt. 4. 42; Amaru. 7, 30, 75 ; R. 11. 78 ; Me. 77. **2** Distressed, grieved, afraid; किमेवं कातरासि *S.* 4. **3** Agitated, perplexed, confused ; Bh. 1. 60. **4** Tremulous through fear (as eyes) ; R. 2. 52 ; Amaru. 79.

कातर्यं Cowardice ; कातर्यं केवला नीतिः शौर्यं श्वापदचेष्टितम् R. 17. 47

कात्यायनः **1** N. of a celebrated writer on grammar who wrote Vârtikas to supplement the Sútras of Pânini **2** N. of a sage who is a writer on civil and religious law ; Y. 1. 4.

कात्यायनी **1** An elderly or middle-aged widow ; (dressed in red clothes). **2** N. of Pârvatî. -COMP. -पुत्रः, -सुतः N. of Kârtikeya.

कार्थंचित्क *a.* (त्की *f.*) Accomplished with difficulty.

काथिकः A narrator of stories ; also a writer of stories.

कादंबः **1** A kind of goose (कलहंस) ; R. 13. 55; Rs. 4. 9. **2** An arrow ; *Si.* 18. 29. **3** A sugarcane. **4** The Kadamba tree —बं Flower of the Kadamba tree; R. 13. 27.

कादंबरं A spirituous liquor distilled from the flowers of the Kadamba tree. निषेव्य मधु माधवाः सरसमत्र कादंबरं *Si.* 4. 66. —री **1** A spirituous liquor distilled from the flowers of the कदंब tree. **2** Spirituous liquor or wine in general ; कादंबरीसाक्षिकं प्रथमसौहृदमिष्यते *S.* 6 ; or कादंबरीमदविघूर्णितलोचनस्य युक्तं हि लांगलभृतः पतनं पृथिव्याम् Udb. **3** The fluid issuing from the temples of a rutting elephant **4** An epithet of Sarasvatî, the goddess of learning. **5** A female cuckoo.

कादंबिनी *f.* A row of clouds ; मदीयमतिचुंबिनी भवतु कापि कादंबिनी R. G. ; Bv. 4. 9.

कादाचित्क *a.* (त्की *f.*) Incidental, occasional.

काद्रवेयः A kind of snake.

काननं **1** A forest, a grove; R. 12. 27, 13. 18; Me. 18, 42 ; काननावनि forest-ground. **2** A home, house. -COMP.-अग्निः wild fire, conflagration. -ओकस् *m.* **1** an inhabitant of a forest. **2** a monkey.

कानिष्ठिकं The little finger.

कानिष्ठिनेयः, -यी The offspring of the youngest child.

कानीनः **1** The son of an unmarried woman; कानीनः कन्यकाजातो मातामहसुतो मतः Y. 2. 129 ; see also the definition given in Ms 9. 172. **2** N. of व्यास. **3** N. of Karna.

कांत *a.* **1** Desired, favourite, loved, dear; कांतं क्रतुं चाक्षुषं M 1. 4. **2** Pleasing, agreeable; भूमिकांतैर्नृपगुणैः R. 1. 16. **3** Lovely, beautiful; सर्वः कांतमात्मीयं पश्यति *S.* 2. —तः **1** A lover. **2** A husband ; कांतोदंतः सुहृदुपगतः संगमात् किंचिदूनः Me. 100; *Si.* 10. 3, 29. **3** Any beloved person. **4** The moon. **5** The spring **6** A kind of iron. **7** A precious stone (in comp. with सूर्य, चंद्र and अयस्). **8** An epithet of Kârtikeya —तं Saffron. -COMP. —आयसं the loadstone -पक्षिन् *m.* a peacock. -लोहं the loadstone.

कांता **1** A beloved or lovely woman. **2** A mistress, wife in general ; कांतासखस्य शयनीयशिलातलं ते U. 3. 21 ; Me. 19 ; *Si.* 10. 73. **3** The Priyangu creeper. **4** Large cardamoms. **5** The earth. -COMP. अंघ्रिदोहदः the Asoka tree ; see अशोक.

कांतारः,ः -रं **1** A large or dreary forest; गृहं तु गृहिणीहीनं कांतारादतिरिच्यते Pt. 4. 81; Bh. 1. 86; Y. 2. 38. **2** A bad road. **3** A hole, cavity. —रः

1 A red variety of the sugarcane. 2 Mountain ebony.

कांतिः *f* 1 Loveliness, beauty; Me. 15; आक्लिष्टकांति *S*. 5. 19. 2 Brightness, lustre, brilliance; Me. 84. 3 Personal decoration or embellishment. 4 Wish, desire. 5 (In Rhet) Beauty enhanced by love; (*S*. D. thus distinguishes कांति from शोभा and दीप्तिः—रूपयौवनलालित्यं भोगाद्यैरंगभूषणं । शोभा प्रोक्ता सैव कांतिर्मन्मथाप्यायिता द्युतिः । कांतिरेवातिविस्तीर्णा दीप्तिरित्यभिधीयते, 130, 131). 6 A lovely or desirable woman. 7 An epithet of Durgâ. –COMP. –कर *a*. beautifying, illuminating. –द *a*. beautifying, adorning. (–दं) 1 bile. 2 clarified butter. –द, –दायक, –दायिन् *a*. adorning. –भृत् *m*. the moon.

कांतिमत् *a*. Lovely, beautiful, splendid; Ku. 4. 5, 5. 71; Me. 30. —*m*. The moon.

कांदवं Anything roasted or baked in an iron pan or oven.

कांदविकः A baker, a confectioner.

कांदिशीक *a*. 1 Put to flight, running away, fugitive; मृगजनः कांदिशीकः संवृत्तः Pt. 1. 2 (Hence) Terrified, afraid; Bv. 2. 178.

कान्यकुब्जः N. of a country ; see कन्याकुब्ज.

कापटिक *a*. (की *f*.) 1 Fraudulent, dishonest. 2 Wicked, perverse. —कः A flatterer, parasite.

कापट्यं Wickedness, fraud, deceit.

कापथः A bad road ; (lit. and fig.).

कापालः, कापालिकः A follower of a certain *S*aiva sect (the left-hand order) characterized by carrying skulls of men in the form of garlands and eating and drinking from them); Pt. 1. 212.

कापालिन् *m*. N. of *S*iva.

कापिक *a*. (की *f*.) Shaped or behaving like a monkey.

कापिल *a*. (ली *f*.) 1 Peculiar or belonging to Kapila. 2 Taught by, or derived from, Kapila. –लः 1 A follower of the Sânkhya system of philosophy propounded by Kapila. 2 Tawny colour.

कापुरुषः A mean contemptible fellow, coward, wretch ; सुसंतुष्टः कापुरुषः स्वल्पकेनापि तुष्यति Pt. 1. 25, 361.

कापेयं 1 The monkey species. 2 Monkey-like behaviour, monkey-tricks.

कापोत *a*. (ती *f*.) Grey, of a dirty white colour. —तं 1 A flock of pigeons. 2 Antimony. —तः The grey colour. –COMP. –अंजनं antimony applied to the eyes as collyrium.

काम् *ind*. An interjection used in calling out to another.

कामः 1 Wish, desire ; संतानकामाय R. 2. 65, 3. 67 ; oft. used with the inf. form ; गंतुकामः desirous to go ; Bg. 2. 62 ; Ms. 2. 94. 2 Object of desire ; सर्वान् कामान् समश्नुते Ms. 2. 5. 3 Affection, love. 4 Love or desire of sensual enjoyments considered as one of the four ends of life (पुरुषार्थ); cf. अर्थ 8 and अर्थकाम. 5 Desire of carnal gratification, lust ; Ms. 2. 214. 6 The god of love. 7 N. of Pradyumna. 8 N. of Balarâma. 9 A kind of mango tree. —मं 1 Object of desire. 2 Semen virile. [Kama is the Cupid of the Hindu mythology—the son of Kr*ishn*a and Rukmi*n*i. His wife is Rati. When the gods wanted a commander for their forces in their war with Taraka, they sought the aid of Kama in drawing the mind of *S*iva towards Parvati, whose issue alone could vanquish the demon. Kama undertook the mission; but *S*iva, being offended at the disturbance of his penance, burnt him down with the fire of his third eye. Subsequently he was allowed by *S*iva to be born again in the form of Pradyumna at the request of Rati. His intimate friend is Vasanta or the spring ; and his son is Aniruddha. He is armed with a bow and arrows—the bow-string being a line of bees, and arrows flowers of five different plants]. –COMP.–अग्निः 1 a fire of love, violent or ardent love. 2 violent desire, fire of passion. °संदीपनं 1 inflaming the fire of love. 2 an aphrodisiac. –अंकुशः 1 a finger-nail. 2 the male organ of generation. –अंगः the mango tree. –अधिकारः the influence of love or desire. –अधिष्ठित *a*. overcome by love. –अनलः see कामाग्नि. अंध *a*. blinded by love or passion. (–धः) the (Indian) cuckoo. –अंधा musk. —अशिन् *a*. getting food at will. –अभिकाम *a*. libidinous, lustful. –अरण्यं a pleasant grove. –अरिः an epithet of *S*iva. –अर्थिन् *a*. amorous, lustful, lascivious. –अवतारः N. of Pradyumna. –अवसायः suppression of passion or desire, stoicism. –अशनं 1 eating at will. 2 unrestrained enjoyment. –आतुर *a*. love-sick, affected by love; कामातुराणां न भयं न लज्जा Subhâsh. –आत्मजः an epithet of Aniruddha, son of Pradyumna. –आत्मन् *a*. lustful, libidinous, enamoured; Ms. 7. 27. –आयुधं 1 arrow of the god of love. 2 membrum virile. (–धः) the mango tree. –आयुस् *m*. 1 a vulture. 2 Garuda. –आर्त *a*. love-striken, affected by love ; कामार्ता हि प्रकृतिकृपणाश्चेतनाचेतनेषु Me. 5. –आसक्त *a*. overcome with love or desire, impassioned, lustful. –ईप्सु *a*. striving to obtain a desired object. –ईश्वरः 1 an epithet of Kubera. 2 the supreme soul. –उदकं 1 voluntary libation of water. 2 a voluntary libation of water to deceased friends exclusive of those who are entitled to it by law ; Y. 3. 4. –उपहत *a*. affected by or overcome with passion. –कला N. of Rati, the wife of Kâma. –काम, –कामिन् *a*. following the dictates of love or passion. –कार *a*. acting at will, indulging one's desires. (–रः) 1 voluntary action, spontaneous deed ; Ms. 11. 41, 45. 2 desire, influence of desire ; Bg. 5. 11. –कूटः 1 the paramour of a harlot. 2 harlotry. –कृत् *a*. 1 acting at will, acting as one likes. 2 granting or fulfilling a desire. (–*m*.) the Supreme soul. –केलि *a*. lustful. (–लिः) 1 a paramour. 2 copulation. –क्रीडा 1 dalliance of love, amorous sport. 2 copulation. –ग *a*. going of one's own accord, able to act or move as one likes. (–गा) an unchaste or libidinous woman ; Y. 3. 6. –गति *a*. able to go to any desired place ; R. 13. 76. गुणः 1 the quality of passion, affection. 2 satiety, perfect enjoyment. 3 an object of sense. –चर, –चार *a*. moving freely or unrestrained, wandering at will; Ku. 1. 50. –चार *a*. unchecked, unrestrained. (–रः) 1 unrestrained motion. 2 independent or wilful action, wantonness; न कामचारो मयि शंकनीयः R. 14. 62. 3 one's will or pleasure, free will, कामचारानुज्ञा Sk. Ms. 2. 220. 4 sensuality. 5 selfishness. –चारिन् *a*. moving unrestrained; Me. 63. 2 libidinous, lustful. 3 self-willed. (–*m*.) 1 Garuda. 2 a sparrow. –ज *a*. produced by passion or desire ; Ms. 7. 46, 47, 50. –जित् *a*. conquering love or passion; R. 9. 33. (–*m*.) 1 an epithet of Skanda. 2 of *S*iva. –तालः the (Indian) cuckoo.–द *a*. fulfilling a desire, granting a request or desire. –दा = कामधेनु q. v. –दर्शन *a*. looking lovely. –दुध *a*. 'milking one's desires', granting every desired object; प्रीता कामदुघा हि सा R. 1. 80, 2. 63; Mâl. 3. 11. –दुघा, –दुह् *f*. a fabulous cow yielding all desires; Bg. 10. 28. –दूती the female cuckoo. –देवः the god of love. –धेनुः *f*. the cow of plenty, a heavenly cow yielding all desires. –ध्वंसिन् *m*. an epithet of *S*iva. –पति, –पत्नी *f*. Rati, wife of Cupid. –पालः N. of Balarâm. –प्रवेदनं expressing one's desire, wish or hope. काच्चित् कामप्रवेदने Ak. –प्रश्नः an unrestrained or free question. –फलः a species of the mango tree. –भोगाः (pl.) sensual gratification. –महः a festival of the god of love celebrated on the full-moon day in the month of Chaitra.–मूढ, –मोहित *a*. influenced or infatuated by love; U.

2. 5. **-रसः** seminal discharge. **-रसिक** *a.* lustful, libidinous ; क्षणमपि युवा कामरसिकः Bh. 3. 112. **-रूप** *a.* **1** taking any form at will ; जानामि त्वां प्रकृतिपुरुषं कामरूपं मघोनः Me. 6. **2** beautiful, pleasing. (**-पाः**) (pl.) a district lying in the east of Bengal (the western portion of Assam); R. 4. 83, 84. **-रेखा -लेखा** a harlot, courtezan. **-लता** membrum virile. **-लोल** *a.* overcome with passion, love-striken. **-वरः** a gift chosen at will. **-वल्लभः 1** the spring. **2** the mango tree. (**-भा**) moon-light. **-वश** *a.* influenced by love. (**-शः**) subjection to love. **-वश्य** *a.* subject to love. **-वाद्** *a.* saying anything at will **-विहंतृ** *a.* disappointing desires. **-वृत्त** *a.* addicted to sensual gratification, licentious, dissipated ; Ms. 5. 154. **-वृत्ति** *a.* acting according to will, self-willed, independent; न कामवृत्तिर्वचनीयमीक्षते Ku. 5. 82. (**-त्तिः**) *f.* **1** free and unrestrained action. **2** freedom of will. **-वृद्धिः** *f.* increase of passion. **-वृंतं** the trumpet flower **-शरः 1** a love-shaft. **2** the mango tree. **-शास्त्र** the science of love, erotic science. **-संयोगः** attainment of desired objects. **-सखः** the spring. **-सू** *a.* fulfilling any desire ; R. 5. 33. **-सूत्रं** N. of an erotic work by Vâtsyâyana. **-हैतुक** *a.* produced by mere desire without any real cause ; Bg. 16. 8.

कामतः *ind.* **1** Of one's own accord, willingly. **2** Voluntarily, knowingly, Intentionally, wilfully ; Ms. 4. 130 ; पदा स्पृष्टं च कामतः Y. 1. 168. **3** From passion or feeling, lustfully; Ms. 3. 173. **4** At will, freely, unrestrained.

कामन *a.* Lustful, libidinous **-नं** Desire, wish. **-ना** Wish, desire.

कामनीयं Beauty, attractiveness.

कामंधमिन् *m.* A brazier.

कामम् *ind.* **1** According to wish or inclination, at will ; कामंगामी. **2** Agreeably to desire ; Mu. 1. 25; **3** To the heart's content ; U. 3. 16. **4** Willingly, joyfully ; *S*ânti. 4. 4. **5** Well, very well (a particle of assent) ; it may be that ; मनागनभ्यावृत्त्या वा कामं क्षाम्यतु यः क्षमी *S*i. 2, 43. **6** Granted or admitted (that); true that, no doubt ; (generally followed by तु, तथापि, yet, still) ; कामं न तिष्ठति मदाननसंमुखी सा भूयिष्ठमन्यविषया न तु दृष्टिरस्याः *S*. 1. 31 ; **2. 1** ; R. 4. 13, 6. 22 ; 13. 75 ; M'al. 9. 34. **7** Indeed, forsooth, really ; R. 2. 43 ; (often implying unwillingness or contradiction). **8** Better, rather (usually with न) कामामा मरणात्तिष्ठेद् गृहे कन्यर्तुमत्यपि । न चैवैनां प्रयच्छेत्तु गुणहीनाय कर्हिचित् Ms. 7. 89.

कामयमान
कामयान
कामयितृ } *a.* Lustful, libidinous; R. 19. 50 ; *S*. 3.

कामल *a.* Lustful, libidinous. **-लः 1** The spring. **2** A desert.

कामलिका Spirituous liquor.

कामवत् *a.* **1** Desirous, wishing **2** Lustful.

कामिन् *a.* (**-नी** *f.*) Lustful. **2** Desirous. **3** Loving, fond. *-m.* **1** A lover, a lustful person (paying particular attention to ladies) ; त्वया चंद्रमसा चातिसंधीयते कामिजनसार्थः *S*. 3 ; त्वां कामिनो मदनदूतिमुदाहरंति V. 4. 11 ; Amaru. 2 ; M. 3. 14. **2** A uxorious husband. The ruddy goose or चक्रवाक bird. **4** A sparrow. **5** An epithet of *S*iva. **6** The moon. **7** A pigeon. **-नी 1** A loving, affectionate or fond woman; Ms. 8. 112. **2** A lovely or beautiful woman ; उदयति हि शशांकः कामिनीगंडपांडुः Mk. 1. 57 ; केषां नैषा कथय कविताकामिनी कौतुकाय P. R. 1. 22. **3** A woman (in general) ; मृगया जहार चतुरेव कामिनी R. 9. 69 ; Me. 63, 67 ; Rs. 1 28. **4** A timid woman. **5** Spirituous liquor.

कामुक *a.* (**का** or **की** *f.*) **1** Wishing, desirous. **2** Lustful, libidinous **-कः 1** A lover, a libidinous man ; कामुकैः कुंभीलकैश्च परिहर्तव्या चंद्रिका M. 4 ; R. 19. 33 ; Rs. 6. 9. **2** A sparrow. **3** The Asoka tree **—का** A woman desirous of wealth. **—की** A libidinous or lustful woman.

कांपिल्लः, कांपिलः N. of a tree ; Mâl. 9. 31.

कांबलः A carriage covered with a woollen cloth or blanket.

कांबविकः A vendor of shell-ornaments, dealer in shells.

कांबोजः 1 A native of the Kambojas; Ms. 10. 44. **2** A king of the Kambojas. **3** The Punnâga tree. **4** A species of horse from the Kamboja country.

काम्य *a.* **1** To be desired, desirable ; सुधा विष्ठा च काम्याशनं *S*ânti. 2. 8. **2** Optional, performed for some particular object (opp. नित्य); अंते काम्यस्य कर्मणः R. 10. 50; Ms. 2. 2 ; 12. 89 ; Bg. 18. 2. **3** beautiful, lovely, charming, handsome ; नासौ न काम्यः R. 6. 30; U. 5. 12. **—म्या** A wish, desire, intention, request ; ब्राह्मणकाम्या Mk. 3; R. 1. 35 ; Bg. 10. 1. -COMP. **-अभिप्रायः** a self-interested motive or purpose. **-कर्मन्** *n.* a rite performed for some particular object and with a view to future fruition. **-गिर्** *f.* agreeable speech. **-दानं 1** an acceptable gift. **2** a free-will-offering ; voluntary gift. **-मरणं** voluntary death, suicide. **-व्रतं** a voluntary vow.

काम्ल *a.* Slightly acid, acidulous.

कायः, यं 1 The body ; विभाति कायः करुणापराणां परोपकारैर्न तु चंदनेन Bh. 2. 71 ; कायेन मनसा बुद्ध्या Bg. 5. 11 ; so कायेन, वाचा, मनसा &c. **2** The trunk of a tree. **3** The body of a lute (the whole lute except the wires). **4** A multitude, assemblage, collection. **5** Principal, capital. **6** Home, residence, habitation. **7** A butt, a mark. **8** Natural temperament. **-यं** (with or without तीर्थ) The part of the hand just below the fingers, especially the little finger, (this part being considered sacred to Prajâpati is called प्रजापतितीर्थ ; cf. Ms. 2. 58-59). **—यः** One of the eight forms of marriage, generally known as प्राजापत्य q. v. ; Y. 1. 60 ; Ms. 3. 38, -COMP. **-अग्निः** the digestive faculty. **-क्लेशः** bodily suffering or pain. **-चिकित्सा** the third of the eight departments of medical science, treatment of diseases affecting the whole body. **-मानं** measurement of the body. **-वलनं** an armour. **-स्थः 1** the writer-caste (proceeding from a क्षत्रिय father and a शूद्र mother). **2** a man of that caste ; कायस्थ इति लघ्वी मात्रा Mu. 1; Y. 1. 336 ; Mk. 9. (**-स्था** *f.*) **1** a woman of that caste. **2** the myrobalan tree. (**-स्थी** *f.*) the wife of a कायस्थ. **-स्थित** *a.* corporeal, bodily.

कायक (**-यिका** *f.*), **कायिक** (**की** *f.*) *a.* Relating to the body, bodily, corporeal ; कायिकतपः Ms. 12. 8. **-का** Interest (whatever is given for the use of money). -COMP.**—वृद्धिः** *f.* **1** interest consisting in the use of any animal or capital stock pawned. **2** interest of which the payment does not affect the principal, or the use of the body of an animal pledged by the person to whom it is pledged.

कार *a.* (**री** *f.*) At the end of comp.) Making, doing, performing, working, maker, doer, author ; ग्रंथकारः author ; कुंभकारः, सुवर्णकार &c. &c. **-रः 1** Act, action; as in पुरुषकार. **2** A term denoting a sound or a word which is not inflected; as अकार Ms. 2. 76, 126; ककार, फूत्कार &c. **3** Effort, exertion ; *S*i. 19. 27. **4** Religious austerity. **5** A husband, lord ; a master. **6** Determination. **7** Power, strength. **8** A tax or toll. **9** A heap of snow. **10** The Himâlaya mountain. -COMP. **—अवरः** a man of a mixed and low caste, born from a Nishâda father and Vaidehî mother ; cf. Ms. 10. 36. **-कर** *a.* working, acting as agent. **-भूः** a toll-station.

कारक *a.* (**रिका** *f.*) (Usually at the end of comp.). **1** Making, acting, doing, performing, creating, doer &c ; स्वप्नस्य कारकः Y. 3. 150 ; 2. 156 ; वर्णसंकरकारकैः Bg. 1. 42 ; Ms. 7. 204 ; Pt. 5. 36. **2** An agent. **—कं 1** (In gram.) **1** The relation subsisting between a noun and a verb in a sentence ; (or between a noun and other words governing it) ; there are six such Kârakas, belonging to the first seven cases, except the genitive: (1) कर्तृ ; (2) कर्मन् ; (3) करण ; (4) संप्रदान ; (5) अपादान ; (6) आधिकरण. **2** That part of grammar which treats of these relations; *i. e.* syntax –COMP. **–दीपकं** (in Rhet.) a figure of speech in which the same Kâraka is connected with several verbs in succession ; *e. g.* खियति कूणति वेल्लति विचलति निमिषति विलोकयति तिर्यक् । अंतर्नंदति चुंबितुमिच्छति नवपरिणया वधूः शयने K. P. 10. **–हेतुः** the active or efficient cause ; (opp. ज्ञापकहेतु).

कारणं **1** A cause, reason ; कारणकोपाः कुटुंबिन्यः M. 1. 18; R. 1. 74 ; Bg. 13. 21. **2** Ground, motive, object ; किं पुनः कारणं Mbh. ; Y. 2. 203 ; Ms. 8. 347 ; कारणमानुषीं तनुं R. 16. 22. **3** An instrument, means; Y. 3. 20, 65. **4** (In Nyâya phil.) A cause, that which is invariably antecedent to some product and is not otherwise constituted ; or according to Mill, 'the antecedent or concurrence of antecedents on which the effect is invariably and unconditionally consequent'; according to Naiyâyikas it is of three kinds ; (1) समवायि (intimate or inherent); as threads in the case of cloth ; (2) असमवायि (non-intimate or non-inherent); as the conjunction of the threads in the case of cloth ; (3) निमित्त (instrumental) as the weaver's loom. **5** The generative cause, creator, father ; Ku. 5. 81. **6** An element, elementary matter ; Y. 3. 148 ; Bg. 18. 13. **7** The origin or plot of a play, poem, &c. **8** An organ of sense. **9** The body. **10** A sign, document, proof or authority ; Ms. 11. 84. **11** That on which any opinion or judgment is based. –COMP. **–उत्तरं** special plea, denial of the cause of complaint ; admission of the charge generally but denial of the actual issue (in law). **–कारणं** an elementary or primary cause ; an atom. **–गुणः** a quality of the cause. **–भूत** *a.* **1** caused. **2** forming the cause. **–माला** a figure of speech, 'a chain of causes'; यथोत्तरं चेत् पूर्वस्य पूर्वस्यार्थस्य हेतुता । तदा कारणमाला स्यात् K. P. 10 ; *e. g.* Bg. 2. 62, 63 ; also S. D. 728. **–वादिन्** *m.* a complainant, plaintiff. **–वारि** *n.* the original water produced at the beginning of the creation. **–विहीन** *a.* without a cause. **–शरीरं** (in Vedânta phil.) the inner rudiment of the body, causal frame.

कारणा **1** Pain, agony. **2** Casting into hell.

कारणिक *a.* **1** An examiner, a judge. **2** Causal.

कारंडवः A sort of duck ; ततं वारि विहाय तीरनलिनीं कारंडवः सेवते V. 2. 23.

कारंधमिन् *m.* **1** Brazier. **2** A mineralogist.

कारवः A crow.

कारस्करः N. of a tree (किंपाक).

कारा **1** Imprisonment, confinement. **2** A prison-house, a jail. **3** Part of a lute below the neck. **4** Pain, affliction. **5** A female messenger. **6** A female worker in gold. –COMP. **–अगारं, –गृहं, –वेश्मन्** *n.* a prison-house, a jail ; कारागृहे निर्जितवासवेन लंकेश्वरेणोषितमाप्रसादात् R. 6 40 ; Sânti. 4. 10 ; Bh 3. 21. **–गुप्तः** a prisoner. **–पालः** a guard of a prison, jailor.

कारिः *f.* Action, act. *–m.* or *f.* An artist, mechanic

कारिका **1** A female dancer. **2** A business, trade. **3** A memorial verse, or a collection of such verses on grammatical, philosophical or scientific subjects ; *e. g.* Bhartrihari's Kàrikâs on grammar ; सांख्यकारिका. **4** Torment, torture. **5** Interest.

कारीषं A heap of dried cowdung.

कारु *a.* (रू *f.*) **1** A maker, doer, an agent, servant. **2** An artisan, mechanic, artist ; कारुभिः कारितं तेन कृत्रिमं स्वप्नहेतवे Vb. **1.** 13 ; इति स्म सा कारुतरेण लेखितं नलस्य च स्वस्य च सख्यमीक्षते N. 1. 38 ; Y. 2. 249, 1. 187 ; Ms. 5. 128 ; 10. 12. (They are:—तक्षा च तंत्रवायश्च नापितो रजकस्तथा । पंचमश्चर्मकारश्च कारवः शिल्पिनो मताः ॥). **—रुः** **1** An epithet of विश्वकर्मन् the architect of the gods. **2** An art, a science. COMP. **–चौरः** one who commits burglary, a dacoit. **–जः** **1** a piece of mechanism, any product of manufacture. **2** a young elephant. **3** a hillock, an ant-hill **4** froth.

कारुणिक *a.* (की *f.*) Compassionate, kind, tender; Nâg. 1. 1.

कारुण्यं Compassion, kindness, pity; कारुण्यमातन्वते Gît. 1 ; करिण्यः कारुण्यास्पदं Bv. 1. 1.

कार्कश्यं **1** Hardness, roughness. **2** Firmness. **3** Solidity; Si. 2. 17 ; Pt. 1. 190. **4** Hard-heartedness, sternness, cruelty ; कार्कश्यं गमितेऽपि चेतसि Amaru. 24.

कार्तवीर्यः The son of Kritavîrya and king of the Haibayas, who ruled at Mâhishmatî. [Having worshipped Dattatreya, he obtained from him several boons, such as a thousand arms, a golden chariot that went wheresoever he willed it to go, the power of restraining wrong by justice, conquest of earth, invincibility by enemies &c ; (cf. R. 6. 39.) According to the Vayu Purana he ruled justly and righteously for 85000 years and offered 10000 sacrifices. He was a contemporary of Ravana whom he once captured and confined like a beast in a corner of his city ; cf. R. 6. 40. Kartavirya was slain by Parasurama for having carried off by violence the Kamadhenu of his revered father Jamadagni. Kartavirya is also known by the name Sahasrarjuna.]

कार्तस्वरं Gold ; स तप्तकार्तस्वरभासुरांबरः Si. 1. 20 ; °दंडेन K. 82.

कार्तांतिकः An astrologer, fortune-teller ; कार्तांतिको नाम भूत्वा भुवं बभ्राम Dk. 130.

कार्तिक *a.* (की *f.*) Belonging to the month of Kârtika ; R. 19 39. **—कः** **1** N. of the month in which the full moon is near the कृत्तिका or Pleiades (corresponding to October-November). **2** An epithet of Skanda. **—की** *f.* The full moon day in the month of Kârtika.

कार्तिकेयः N. of Skanda (so called because he was reared by the six Krittikâs). [Kartikeya is the Mars or god of war of the Indian mythology. He is the son of Siva (but born without the direct intervention of a woman). Most of his epithets have reference to the circumstances of his birth. Siva cast his seed into Agni (who had gone to the god in the form of a dove while he was enjoying Parvati's company), who being unable to bear it cast it into the Ganges; (hence Skanda is called Agnibhu, Gangaputra). It was then transferred to the six Krittikas (when they went to bathe in the Ganges), each of whom therefore conceived and brought forth a son. But these six sons were afterwards mysteriously combined into one of extraordinary form with six heads and twelve hands and eyes, (hence he is called Kartikeya, Shadanana, Shanmukha &c.). According to another account the seed of S'iva was cast by the Ganges into a thicket of reeds (Sara) ; whence the boy was called Saravanabhava, or Sarajanman. He is said to have pierced the mountain Krauncha, whence his name Kraunchadarana. He was the commander of the army of the gods in their war with Taraka, a powerful demon q. v., whom he vanquished and slew ; and hence his names Senani and Tarakajit. He is represented as riding a peacock.]–COMP. **–प्रसूः** *f.* Pârvatî mother of Kârtikeya.

कात्स्न्यं Totality, entirety ; तान्निबोधत कार्त्स्न्येन द्विजाग्र्यान् पंक्तिपावनान् Ms. 3. 183.

कार्दम *a.* (मी *f.*) Muddy, soiled or covered with mud.

कार्पटः **1** A petitioner, a suitor, a candidate. **2** A rag. **3** Lac.

कार्पटिकः **1** A pilgrim. **2** One who maintains himself by carrying water from holy rivers. **3** A caravan of pilgrims. **4** An experienced man. **5** A parasite.

कार्पण्यं **1** Poverty, indigence, wretchedness ; व्यक्तकार्पण्या **2** Compassion, pity. **3** Niggardliness; imbecility; Bg. 2. 7. **4** Levity, lightness of spirit.

कार्पास *a*. (सी *f*.) Made of cotton. **–सः –सं** 1 Anything made of cotton; Ms. 8. 326 ; 12. 64. 2 Paper. **–सी** The cotton plant. COMP. **–अस्थि** *n*. the seed of the cotton plant. **–नासिका** spindle. **–सौत्रिक** *a*. made of cotton thread; Y. 2. 179.

कार्पासिक *a*. (की *f*.) Made of or from cotton.

कार्पासिका, कार्पासी *f*. The cotton plant.

कार्मण *a*. (णी *f*.) 1 Finishing a work. 2 Doing any work well or completely. **—णं** Magic, witchcraft ; निखिलमयनाकर्षणे कार्मणज्ञा Bv. 2. 79 ; Vikr. 2. 14, 8. 2.

कार्मिक *a*. (की *f*.) 1 Manufactured, made. 2 Embroidered, intermixed with coloured thread (as cloth). 3 Any variegated texture.

कार्मुक *a*. (की *f*.) Fit for or able to do a work, doing it well and completely. **—कं** 1 A bow ; त्वयि चाधिज्यकार्मुके *S*. 1. 6. 2 A Bamboo.

कार्य *pot. p*. What ought to be done, made, performed, effected &c ; कार्या सैकतलीनहंसमिथुना स्रोतोवहा मालिनी *S*. 6. 16 ; साक्षिणः कार्याः Ms. 8. 61 ; so दंडः, विचारः &c. **—र्यं** 1 Work, affair, business ; कार्यं त्वया नः प्रतिपन्नकल्पं Ku. 3. 14 ; Ms. 5. 150. 2 Duty ; *Si*. 2. 1. 3 Occupation, enterprize, emergent business. 4 A religious rite or performance. 5 A motive, object, purpose; *Si*. 2. 36; H. 4. 61. 6 Want, need, occasion, business (with instr.) ; किं कार्यं भवतो हृतेन दयितास्नेहस्वहस्तेन मे V. 2. 20 ; तृणेन कार्यं भवतीश्वराणां Pt. 1. 71 ; Amaru. 71. 7 Conduct, department. 8 A law-suit, legal business, dispute &c; बहिर्निष्क्रम्य ज्ञायतां कः कः कार्यार्थीति Mk. 9; Ms. 8. 43. 9 An effect, the necessary result of a cause (opp. कारण). 10 (In gram.) Operation, विभक्तिकार्यं declension. 11 The denouement of a drama; कार्योपक्षेपमादौ तनुमपि रचयन् Mu. 4. 3. 12 healthiness (in medicine). 13 Origin. –COMP. **–अक्षम** *a*. unable to do one's duty, incompetent. **–अकार्यविचारः** discussion as to the propriety or otherwise of anything, deliberation on the arguments for and against any proceeding. **–अधिपः** 1 the superintendent of a work or affair. 2 the planet that decides any question in astrology. **–अर्थः** 1 the object of any undertaking, a purpose; Ms. 7. 167. 2 an application for employment. 3 any object or purpose. **–अर्थिन्** *a*. 1 making a request. 2 seeking to gain one's object or purpose. 3 seeking an employment. 4 pleading a cause in court, going to law; Mk. 9. **–आसनं** seat of transacting business. **–ईक्षणं** superintendence of public affairs ; Ms. 7. 141. **–उद्धारः** discharge of a duty. **–कर** *a*. efficacious **–कारणे** (*dual*) cause and effect; object and motive. °**भावः** the relation of cause and effect. **–कालः** time for action, season, fit time or opportunity. **–गौरवं** importance of an affair. **–चिंतक** *a*. 1 prudent, cautious, considerate. (**–कः**) manager of a business, executive officer; Y. 2. 191. **–च्युत** *a*. out of work, out of employ, dismissed from an office. **–दर्शनं** 1 inspection of a work. 2 inquiry into public affairs. **–निर्णयः** settlement of an affair. **–पुटः** 1 a man who does any useless thing. 2 a mad, eccentric or crazy man. 3 an idler. **–प्रद्वेषः** dislike to work, idleness, laziness. **–प्रेष्यः** an agent, a messenger. **–वस्तु** *n*. an aim or object. **–विपत्ति** *f*. a failure, reverse, misfortune. **–शेषः** 1 the remainder of a business ; Ms. 7. 153. 2 completion of an affair. 3 part of a business. **–सिद्धिः** *f*. success. **–स्थानं** place of business, office. **–हंतृ** 1 obstructing or marrying another's work ; H. 1. 77. 2 opposed to another's interests.

कार्यतः *ind*. 1 Through some object or motive. 2 Consequently, necessarily.

कार्श्यं 1 Thinness, emaciation, leanness; Me. 29. 2 Smallness, littleness, scantiness ; R. 5. 21.

कार्षः A husbandman, a cultivator.

कार्षापणः, –णं (or **–णकः**) A coin or weight of different values ; Ms. 8. 136, 336 ; 9. 282 (=कर्ष). **—णं** Money.

कार्षापणिक *a*. (की *f*.) Worth one कार्षापण.

कार्षिक=कार्षापण q. v.

कार्ष्ण *a*. (र्ष्णी *f*.) 1 Belonging to Krishṇa or Vishṇu; R. 15. 24. 2 Belonging to Vyâsa. 3 Belonging to the black antelope ; Ms. 2. 41. 4 black.

कार्ष्णायस *a*. (सी *f*.) Made of black iron. **–सं** Iron.

कार्ष्णिः An epithet of the god of love ; *Si*. 19. 10.

काल *a*. (ली *f*.) Black, of a dark or dark-blue colour.**—लः** 1 The black or dark-blue colour. 2 Time (in general); विलंबितफलैः कालं निनाय स मनोरथैः R. 1. 33 ; तास्मिन्काले at that time ; काव्यशास्त्रविनोदेन कालो गच्छति धीमतां H. 1. 1 the wise pass their time &c. 3 Fit or opportune time (to do a thing), proper time or occasion ; (with gen. loc., dat. or inf); R. 3. 12, 4. 6, 12. 69; पर्जन्यः कालवर्षी Mk. 10. 60. 4 A period or portion of time (as the hours or watches of a day) ; षष्ठे काले दिवसस्य V. 2. 1 ; Ms. 5. 153. 5 The weather. 6 Time considered as one of the nine *dravyas* by the Vaiseshikas. 7 The supreme spirit regarded as the destroyer of the universe, being a personification of the destructive principle ; कालः काल्या भुवनफलके क्रीडति प्राणिशारैः Bh. 3. 39. 8 Yama, the God of death ; कः कालस्य न गोचरांतरगतः Pt. 1. 146. 9 Fate, destiny. 10 The black part of the eye. 11 The (Indian) cuckoo. 12 The planet Saturn. 13 N. of *S*iva. 14 A measure of time (in music or prosody). 15 A person who distils and sells spirituous liquor. 16 A section, part. **—लं** 1 Iron. 2 A kind of perfume. –COMP. **–अयस** iron. **–अक्षरिकः** a scholar, one who can read and decipher. **–अगरुः** a kind of sandal tree, black kind of aloe ; Bv. 1. 70 ; R. 4. 81. (*–n*.) the wood of that tree ; Rs. 4. 5 ; 5. 5. **–अग्निः, –अनलः** the destructive fire at the end of the world. **–अंग** *a*. having a dark blue body (as a sword with a dark-blue edge). **–अजिनं** hide of a black antelope. **–अंजनं** a sort of collyrium ; Ku. 7. 20, 82. **–अंडजः** the (Indian) cuckoo. **–आतिपातः, –अतिरेकः** loss of time, delay. **–अत्ययः** 1 delay lapse of time. 2 loss by lapse of time. **–अध्यक्षः** 1 'presiding over time,' epithet of the sun. 2 the Supreme soul. **–अनुनादिन्** *m*. 1 a bee. 2 a sparrow. 3 the Chataka bird **–अंतकः** time, regarded as the god of death, and the destroyer of everything. **– अंतरं** 1 an interval. 2 a period of time. 3 another time or opportunity. °**आवृत्त** *a*. hidden or concealed in the womb of time. °**क्षम** *a*. able to bear delay ; अकालक्षमा देव्याः शरीरावस्था K. 263 ; *S*. 4. °**विषः** an animal venomous only when enraged as a rat. **–अभ्रः** a dark, watery cloud **–अवधिः** appointed time. **–अशुद्धि** *f*. period of mourning, ceremonial impurity caused by the birth of a child or death of a relation in the family see अशौच. **–आयसं** iron. **–उप्त** *a*. sown in due season. **–कंज** a blue lotus **–कटंकटः** an epithet of *S*iva. **–कंठः** a peacock. 2 a sparrow. 3 an epithet of *S*iva ; U. 6. **–करणं** appointing or fixing time. **–कणिका, –कर्णी** *f*. misfortune. **–कर्मन्** *n*. death. **–कील** noise. **–कुंठः** Yama. **–कूटः, -टं** (*a*) deadly poison. (*b*) the poison churned out of the ocean and drunk by *S*iva ; अद्यापि नोज्झति हरः किल कालकूटं Ch P. 50. **–कृत** *m*. 1 the sun. 2 a peacock 3 supreme spirit. **–क्रमः** lapse of time course of time ; कालक्रमेण in course of process of time ; Ku. 1. 19. **–क्रिया** fixing a time. 2 death. **–क्षेपः** 1 delay loss of time. Me. 22 ; मरणे कालक्षेपं कुरु Pt. 1. 2 passing the time. **–खंज**

-खंडं the liver. -गंगा the river Yamunâ. -गंथिः a year. -चक्रं 1 the wheel of time (time being represented as a wheel always moving). 2 cycle. 3 (hence fig.) the wheel of fortune, the vicissitudes of life. -चिह्नं a symptom of approaching death. - चोदित *a*. summoned by the angel of death.—ज्ञ *a*. knowing the proper time or occasion (of any action); अत्यारूढो हि नारीणामकालज्ञो मनोभवः R. 12. 33; *Si*. 2. 83. -ज्ञः 1 an astrologer. 2 a cock. -त्रयं the three times; the past, the present and the future; °दर्शी K. 46. -दंडः death. -धर्मः, -धर्मन् *m*. 1 the line of conduct suitable to any particular time. 2 fated time, death; न पुनर्जीवितः कश्चित्कालधर्ममुपागतः Mb.; परीताः कालधर्मणा &c. -धारणा prolongation of time. -नियोगः decree of fate or destiny; Ki. 9. 13. -निरूपणं determination of time, chronology. -नेमिः the rim of the wheel of time. 2 N. of a demon, uncle of Râvaṇa, deputed by him to kill Hanûmat. 3 N. of a demon with 100 hands killed by Vishṇu. -पक्व *a*. ripened by time; *i. e.* spontaneously; Ms. 6. 17, 21; Y. 3. 49. -परिवासः standing for a time so as to become stale. -पाशः the noose of Yama or death. -पाशिकः a hangman. -पृष्ठं 1 a species of antelope. 2 a heron. (-ष्ठं) 1 N. of the bow of Karṇa; Ve. 4. 2 a bow in general. -प्रभातं autumn or *S*arad; (the two months following the rainy season considered as the best time). -भक्षः as epithet of *S*iva. -मानं measure of time. -मुखः a species of ape. -मेषी *f*. the Manjishṭha plant. -यवनः a king of Yavanas and enemy of Krishṇa and an invincible foe of the Yadavas. Kṛishṇa, finding it impossible to vanquish him on the field of battle, cunningly decoyed him to the cave where Muchukunda was sleeping who burnt him down. -यापः, -यापनं procrastination, putting off. -योगः fate, destiny. -योगिन् *m*. an epithet of *S*iva. -रात्रिः, -रात्री *f*. 1 a dark night. 2 the night of destruction at the end of the world (identified with Durgâ). -लोहं steel. -विप्रकर्षः prolongation of time. -वृद्धिः *f*. periodical interest (payable monthly, quarterly or at stated times); Ms. 8. 153. -वेला the time of Saturn, *i e*. a particular time of the day (half a watch every day) at which any religious act is improper. -संरोधः 1 keeping back for a long time; Ms. 8. 143. 2 lapse of a long period of time. -सदृश *a*. opportune, timely. -सर्पः the black and most poisonous variety of the snake. -सारः the black antelope. -सूत्रं, -सूत्रकं 1 thread of time or death. 2 N. of a particular hell; Y. 2. 222; Ms. 4. 88. -स्कंधः the tamâla tree. -स्वरूप *a*. terrible as death, (death-like in form). -हरः an epithet of *S*iva. -हरणं loss of time, delay; *S*. 3; U. 5. -हानिः *f*. delay; R. 13 16.

कालकं Liver. —कः 1 A mole, freckle. 2 A water-snake. 3 The black part of the eye.

कालंजरः 1 N. of a mountain and adjacent country (modern Kallinjar). 2 An assembly of religious mendicants. 3 An epithet of *S*iva.

कालशेयं Buttermilk (produced in a jar by churning).

काला An epithet of Durgâ.

कालापः 1 The hair of the head. 2 A serpent's hood. 3 A demon, an imp, a goblin. 4 A student of the Kalâpa grammar. 5 One who knows this grammar.

कालापकं 1 An assemblage of the pupils of Kalâpa. 2 The doctrines or teachings of Kalâpa.

कालिक *a*. (की *f*.) 1 Relating to time. 2 Depending on time; विशेषः कालिकोऽवस्था Ak. 3 Seasonable, timely. —कः 1 A crane. 2 A heron. —का 1 Blackness, black colour. 2 Ink, black ink. 3 Price of a commodity to be paid by instalments. 4 Periodical interest paid at stated times. 5 A multitude of clouds, a dark cloud threatening rain; कालिकेव निबिडा बलाकिनी R. 11. 15. 6 Flaw (alloy &c.) in gold. 7 The liver. 8 A female crow. 9 A scorpion. 10 Spirituous liquor. 11 N. of Durgâ. —कं Black sandalwood.

कालिंग *a*. (गी *f*.) Produced in or belonging to the Kalinga country. —गः 1 A king of that country; प्रतिजग्राह कालिंगस्तमस्त्रैर्गजसाधनः R. 4. 40. 2 A snake of that country. 3 An elephant. 4 A species of cucumber. —गाः (pl.) N. of a country; see कलिंग. —गं A water-melon.

कालिंद *a*. (दी *f*.) Connected with or coming from the mountain Kalinda or the river Yamunâ; कालिंद्याः पुलिनेषु केलिकुपिताम् Ve. 1. 1; R. 15. 28; *S*ânti. 4. 13. -COMP. —कर्षणः, -भेदनः an epithet of Balarâma q. v. —सूः *f*. Sanjnâ (संज्ञा), a wife of the sun. -सोदरः Yama, the god of death.

कालिमन् *m*. Blackness; Amaru. 88; *Si*. 4. 57.

कालियः N. of a tremendously large serpent who dwelt at the bottom of the Yamunâ (which was a ground forbidden to Garuḍa, the enemy of serpents, owing to the curse of the sage Saubhari). He was crushed to death by Krishna when he was but a boy; R. 6. 49. -COMP. -दमनः, -मर्दनः epithets of Krishna.

काली 1 Blackness. 2 Ink, black ink. 3 An epithet of Pârvatî, *S*iva's wife. 4 A row of black clouds. 5 A woman with a dark complexion. 6 N. of Satyavatî, mother of Vyâsa. 7 Night. -COMP.-तनयः a buffalo.

कालीकः A heron.

कालीन *a*. 1 Belonging to a particular time. 2 Seasonable.

कालीयं A kind of sandal wood; also कालीयक.

कालुष्यं 1 Foulness, dirtiness, turbidness, muddiness (fig. also); कालुष्यमुपयाति बुद्धिः K. 103 becomes muddy or defiled. 2 Opacity. 3 Disagreement.

कालेय *a*. Belonging to the Kali age. -यं 1 The liver. 2 Black sandalwood; Ku. 7. 9. 3 Saffron.

कालेयकः 1 A dog. 2 A species of sandal.

काल्पनिक *a*. (की *f*.) 1 Existing only in fancy, fictitious; काल्पनिकी व्युत्पत्तिः. 2 Counter-feit, fabricated.

काल्य *a*. 1 Timely, seasonable. 2 Agreeable, pleasant, auspicious. -ल्यं Day-break.

काल्याणकं Auspiciousness.

कावचिक *a*. (की *f*.) Armorial. -कं A multitude of men in armour.

कावृकः 1 A cock. 2 The chakravâka bird.

कावेरं Saffron.

कावेरी 1 N. of a river in the south of India; कावेरीं सरितां पत्युः शंकनीयामिवाकरोत् R. 4. 45. 2 A harlot, courtezan.

काव्य *a*. 1 possessed of the qualities of a sage or a poet. 2 Prophetic, inspired, poetical. -व्यः N. of Sukra, preceptor of the Asuras. -व्या 1 Intelligence. 2 A female friend. -व्यं 1 A poem; महाकाव्यं; मेघदूतं नाम काव्यं &c. 2 Poetics, poetry, poetical composition. (काव्य is defined by writers on Poetics in different ways; तद्दोषौ शब्दार्थौ सगुणावनलंकृती पुनः क्वापि K. P. 1.; वाक्यं रसात्मकं काव्यं S. D. 1.; रमणीयार्थप्रतिपादकः शब्दः काव्यं R. G; शरीरं तावदिष्टार्थव्यवच्छिन्ना पदावली K'av. 1.10; see (Chandr. 1. 7 also). 3 Happiness, welfare. 4 Wisdom. 5 Inspiration. -COMP. -अर्थः a poetical thought or idea. °चौरः a robber of the ideas of another poet, a plagiarist; यदस्य दैत्या इव लुंठनाय काव्यार्थचौराः प्रगुणीभवंति Vikr. 1. 11. -चौरः a stealer of other men's poems. -मीमांसकः a rhetorician, critic. -रसिक *a*. one who has a taste for and can appreciate the beauties of poetry. -लिंगं a figure of speech; thus defined:—काव्यलिंगं हेतोर्वाक्यपदार्थता K. P. 10. *e. g*. जितोसि मंद कंदर्प मच्चित्तेऽस्ति त्रिलोचनः Chandr. 5. 119.

काश् 1. 4. A. (काश-श्य-ते, काशित) 1 To shine, look brilliant or beautiful; R. 10. 86, 7. 24; Ku. 1. 24; Bk. 2. 25; *Si* 6. 74. 2 To appear, be visible; नैव भूमिर्न च दिशः प्रदिशो वा चकाशिरे Mb. 3 To appear or look like. With **निस्** (*caus.*) 1 to turn out, expel, drive, banish ; see कस् with निस्. 2 to open. 3 to take or bring out, present to the view. **–प्र** 1 to shine, look brilliant. 2 to be visible, appear ; एषु सर्वेषु भूतेषु गूढोऽऽत्मा न प्रकाशते Kath. 3 to look or appear like. (*–Caus.*) 1 to show, display, discover, disclose, reveal; अवसरोयमात्मानं प्रकाशयितुं *S*. 1 ; S'an. K. 59. 2 to bring to light, make public, proclaim ; कदाचित्कुपितं मित्रं सर्वदोषं प्रकाशयेत् Ch'aṇ 20. 3 to publish, bring out (as a work); प्रणीतः न तु प्रकाशितः U. 4. 4 to illuminate, lighten; यथा प्रकाशयत्येकः कृत्स्नं लोकमिमं रविः Bg. 13. 33 ; 5. 16. **–प्रति** 1 to appear like. 2 to shine in opposition or by contrast. **–वि** 1 to bloom, open (as a flower) . 2 to shine **–सं** to appear like.

काशः, –शं A kind of grass used for mats, roofs, &c.; Rs. 3. 1, 2. **–शं** A flower of that grass; Ku. 7· 11 ; R. 4. 17; Rs. 3. 28. **–शः=कासः** q. v.

काशि *m. pl.* N. of a country.

काशिः, –शी *f.* N. of a celebrated city on the Ganges, the modern Benares and one of the seven sacred cities ; see कांची· –Comp. **–पः** an epithet of *S*iva. **–राजः** N. of a king, father of अंबा, अंबिका and अंबालिका *q. v.*

काशिन् *a.* (नी *f.*) (Usually at the end of comp.) Shining, appearing or looking like, having the semblance of; *e. g.* जितकाशिन् one who behaves like a conqueror ; see the word.

काशी See काशि –Comp. **–नाथः** an epithet of *S*iva. **–यात्रा** pilgrimage to Benares.

काश्मरी A plant commonly called गांभारी; काश्मर्याः कृतमालमुद्गतदलं कोयष्टिकष्टीकते Mal. 9. 7.

काश्मीर *a* (री *f.*) Born in, belonging to or coming from Kâshmîra. **–राः** *pl.* N. of a country or its inhabitants ; see कश्मीर also. **–रं** 1 Saffron ; काश्मीरगंधमृगनाभिकृतांगरागां Ch. P. 8 ; Bh. 1. 48; काश्मीरगौरवपुषामभिसारिकाणां Gît. 11 ; also 1. 2 Root of a tree. –Comp. **–जं, जन्मन्** *n.* saffron ; Bv. 1. 71 ; *Si* 11. 53.

काश्यं Spirituous liquor. –Comp. **पं** flesh.

काश्यपः 1 N. of a celebrated sage. 2 N. of Kaṇâda.–Comp. **–नंदनः** 1 an epithet of Garuda. 2 N. of Aruṇa.

काश्यपिः An epithet of Garuḍa and of Aruna.

काश्यपी The earth ; तावपि दधासि मातः काश्यपि यातस्तवापि च विवेकः Bv. 1. 68.

काषः 1 Rubbing, scratching ; पथिषु विटपिनां स्कंधकाषैः सधूमः Ve. 2. 18. 2 That against which anything is rubbed (as the stock of a tree) ; लीनालिः सुरकरिणां कपोलकाषः Ki. 5. 26 ; see कपोलकाष.

काषाय *a.* (यी *f.*) Red, dyed of a Reddish colour ; काषायवसनाथवा Ak. **–यं** A red cloth or garment ; इमे काषाये गृहीते M. 5 ; R. 15. 77.

काष्ठं 1 A piece of wood, especially one used as fuel; Ms. 4. 49, 241 ; 5. 69. 2 Wood or timber, piece or log of wood in general ; यथा काष्ठं च काष्ठं च समेयातां महोदधौ H. 4. 69 ; Ms. 4. 49. 3 A stick ; Y. 2. 218. 4 An instrument for measuring length. –Comp. **–अगारः –रं** a wooden house or enclosure. **–अंबुवाहिनी** a wooden bucket. **–कदली** the wild plantain. **-कीटः** a small insect found in decayed wood. **–कुट्टः, –कूटः** a woodpecker ; Pt. 1. 332 ; (a worm generally found in wood). **–कुद्दालः** a kind of wooden shovel used for baling water out of a boat or for scraping and cleaning its bottom. **–तक्ष्** *m.*, **–तक्षकः** a carpenter. **–तंतुः** a small worm found in timber. **–दारुः** the Indian pine tree; also called देवदारु. **–द्रुः** the Palâsa tree. **–पुत्तलिका** a wooden statue or image. **–भारिकः** a wood-carrier. **—मठी** *f.* a funeral pile. **–मल्लः** a bier, a wooden frame on which dead bodies are carried. **–लेखकः** a small worm found in wood (=काष्ठकूट). **–लोहिन्** *m.* a cudgel armed with iron. **–वाटः, –टं** a wall made of wood.

काष्ठकं Aloe-wood.

काष्ठा 1 A quarter or region of the world, direction, region (दिश्) ; Ki. 3. 55. 2 A limit, boundary, स्वयं विशीर्णद्रुमपर्णवृत्तिता परा हि काष्ठा तपसः Ku. 5. 28. 3 The last limit, extremity, excess; काष्ठागतस्नेहरसानुविद्धं Ku. 3. 35. 4 Race-ground, course. 5 A mark, goal. 6 The path of the wind and cloud in the atmosphere. 7 A measure of time=$\frac{1}{30}$ Kalâ.

काष्ठिकः A bearer of wood.

काष्ठिका A small piece of wood.

काष्ठीला *f.* The plantain tree.

कास् 1 A. (कासते, कासित) 1 To shine; see **काश्**. 2 To cough, make a sound indicating any disease.

कासः,–सा 1 Cough, catarrh. 2 Sneezing. –Comp. **–कुंठ** *a.* affected with cough. **–घ्न, –हृत्** *a.* removing cough, pectoral.

कासरः (री *f.*) A buffalo.

कासारः,–रं A pond, pool, lake ; Bv. 1. 43 ; Bh. 1. 39, Gît. 2.

कासू (सू *f.*) 1 A sort of lance. 2 Indistinct speech. 3 Light, lustre. 4 Disease. 5 Devotion.

कासृति *f.* A bye-way, a secret path.

काहल *a.* 1 Dry, withered. 2 Mischievous. 3 Excessive, spacious, large. **–लः** 1 A cat. 2 A cock. 3 A crow. 4 A sound in general. **-लं** Indistinct speech. **–ला** A large drum (military). **–ली** *f.* A young woman.

किंवत् *a.* Poor, mean, insignificant.

किंशारुः 1 The beard of corn. 2 A heron. 3 An arrow.

किंशुकः A kind of tree having beautiful red blossoms but without any odour ; विद्याहीना न शोभंते निर्गंधा इव किंशुकाः Chāṇ 7; Rs. 6. 20 ; R 9. 31. **–कं** The blossom of this tree ; किं किंशुकैः शुकमुखच्छाविभिर्न दग्धम् Rs. 6. 21.

किंशुलुकः The pala'sa tree; see किंशुक.

किकिः 1 The cocoa-nut tree. 2 The blue jay. 3 The Châtaka bird ; (the bird is also named as किकिन्, किकिदिवि, किकीदिवि).

किंकणी, किंकिणिका, किंकिणी, किंकणीका A small bell or tinkling ornament ; क्वणत्कनककिंकिणीझणझणायितस्यंदनैः U. 5. 5 ; 6. 1 ; *Si*. 9. 74 ; Ku. 7. 49.

किंकिरः 1 A horse. 2 The (Indian) cuckoo. 3 A large black bee. 4 N. of Cupid, the god of love. 5 The red colour. **–रं** The frontal sinus of an elephant. **–रा** Blood.

किंकिरातः 1 A parrot. 2 The (Indian) cuckoo. 3 Cupid. 4 The Asoka tree.

किंजलः-किंजल्कः The filament or blossom of a lotus or any other plant ; आकर्षद्भिः पद्मकिंजल्कगंधान् U. 3. 2 ; R. 15. 52.

किटिः A hog.

किटिभः 1 A louse. 2 A bug.

किट्टं, किट्टकं Secretion, excrement, sediment, dirt ; अन्न°.

किट्टालः 1 A copper vessel. 2 Rust of iron.

किणः A corn, callosity, a scar; ज्ञास्यसि कियद्भुजो मे रक्षति मौर्वीकिणांक इति *S*. 1. 13 ; Mk. 2. 11 ; R. 16. 84 ; 18. 47 ; Gît 1. 2 A wart, a mole. 3 An insect found in wood.

किण्वं Sin. **—ण्वः, –ण्वं** A drug or seed used to cause fermentation in the manufacture of spirits ; Ms. 8. 326.

कित् 1 P. (केतति) 1 To desire. 2 To live. 3 (चिकित्सति). To heal, cure.

कितवः (वी *f.*) 1 A rogue, liar, cheat ; अर्हति किल कितव उपद्रवं M. 4 ; Amaru. 17, 41 ; Me. 111. 2 The Dhattûra plant. 3 A kind of perfume.

किंधिन *m.* A horse.

किन्नर See under किम्.

किम् *ind.* Used for कु only at the beginning of comp. to convey the senses of 'badness,' 'deterioration', 'defect,' 'blame' or 'censure'; *e. g.* किंसखा a bad friend; किन्नरः a bad or deformed man &c.; see comp. below:—COMP. **-दासः** a bad slave, or servant. **-नरः** a bad or deformed man; a mythical being with a human figure and the head of a horse (अश्वमुख); जयोदाहरणं बाह्वोर्गापयामास किन्नरान् R. 4. 78; Ku. 1. 8. °**ईशः**, °**ईश्वरः**. an epithet of Kubera. (**-री** *f.*) 1 a female Kinnara; Me. 56. 2 a kind of lute. **-पुरुषः** 'a low or despicable man,' a mythical being with a human head and the form of a horse; Ku. 1. 14. °**ईश्वरः** an epithet of Kubera. **-प्रभुः** a bad master or king; हितान्न यः संश्रृणुते स किंप्रभुः Ki. 1. 5. **-राजन्** *a.* having a bad king. (*-m.*) a bad king. **-सखि** *m.* (nom. sing. किंसखा) a bad friend; स किंसखा साधु न शास्ति योऽधिपं Ki. 1. 5.

किम् *pron. a.* (nom. sing. कः *m.*, का *f.*, किम् *n.*) 1 Who, what, which (used interrogatively); प्रजासु कः केन पथा प्रयातीत्यशेषतो वेदितुमस्ति शक्तिः *S.* 6. 25; करुणाविमुखेन मृत्युना हरता त्वां वद किं न मे हृतं R. 8. 67; का खल्वनेन प्रार्थ्यमानात्मना विकत्थते V. 2; कः कोऽत्र भोः. The pronoun is often used to imply 'power or authority to do a thing'; *e. g.* के आवां परित्रातुं दुष्यंतमाक्रंद *S.* 1 'who are we &c.,' *i. e.* what power have we &c. 2 The neuter (किं) is frequently used with instr. of nouns in the sense of 'what is the use of'; किं स्वामिचेष्टानिरूपणेन H. 1; लोभश्चेद्‌गुणेन किं &c. Bh. 2 55; किं तया दृष्टया *S.* 3; किं कुलेनोपदिष्टेन शीलमेवात्र कारणम् Mk. 9. 7. **अपि, चित्, चन, चिदपि** or **स्वित्** are often added to **किं** to give it an indefinite sense; विवेश कश्चिज्जटिलस्तपोवनं Ku. 5. 30 a certain ascetic &c.; कापि तत एवागतवती Mâl. 1 a certain lady; कस्यापि कोपीति निवेदितं च 1. 33; किमपि किमपि...जल्पतोरक्रमेण U. 1. 27; कस्मिंश्चिदपि महाभागधेयजन्मनि मन्मथविकारमुपलक्षितवानस्मि Mâl. 1. **किमपि, किंचित्** 'a little', 'somewhat'; Y. 2. 116; U. 6. 35. **किमपि** also means indescribable; see **अपि. इव** is sometimes added to **किम्** in the sense of 'possibly,' 'I should like to know'; (mostly adding force and elegance to the period); विना सीतादेव्या किमिव हि न दुःखं रघुपतेः U. 6. 30; किमिव हि मधुराणां मंडनं नाकृतीनां *S.* 1. 20; see **इव** also *-ind.* 1 A particle of interrogation; जातिमात्रेण किं कश्चिद्धन्यते पूज्यते क्वचित् H. 1. 58 'is any one killed or worshipped' &c.; ततः किं what then. 2 A particle meaning 'why', 'wherefore'; किमकारणमेव दर्शनं विलपंत्यै रतये न दीयते Ku. 4. 7. 3 Whether (its correlatives in the sense of 'or' being किं, उत, उताहो, आहोस्वित्, वा, किंवा, अथवा; see these words) -COMP. **-अपि** *ind.* 1 to some extent, somewhat, to a considerable extent. 2 inexpressibly, indescribably (as to quality, quantity, nature &c.). 3 very much, by far; किमपि कमनीयं वपुरिदं *S.* 3; किमपि भीषणं, किमपि करालं &c. **-अर्थ** *a.* having what motive or aim; किमर्थोऽयं यत्नः.-**अर्थं** *ind.* why, wherefore. **-आख्य** *a.* having what name; किमाख्यस्य राजर्षेः सा पत्नी. *S.* 7. **-इति** *ind.* why indeed, why to be sure, for what purpose (emphasizing the question); तत्किमित्युदासते भरताः Mâl. 1; किमित्युपास्याभरणानि यौवने धृतं त्वया वार्धकशोभि वल्कलं Ku. 5. 44. **-उ -उत** 1 whether-or (showing doubt or uncertainty); किमु विषविसर्पः किमु मदः U. 1. 35, Amaru. 9. 2 why (indeed); प्रियसुहृत्सार्थः किमु त्यज्यते. 3 how much more, how much less; यौवनं धनसंपत्तिः प्रभुत्वमविवेकिता। एकैकमप्यनर्थाय किमु यत्र चतुष्टयं ॥ H. Pr. 11; सर्वाविनयानामेकैकमप्येषामायतनं किमुत समवायः K. 103; R. 14. 35; Ku. 7. 65. **-करः** a servant, slave; अवेहि मां किंकरमष्टमूर्तेः R. 2. 35. (**-रा**) a female servant. (**-री**) the wife of a servant. **-कर्तव्यता, -कार्यता** any situation in which one asks oneself what should be done; किंकर्तव्यतामूढः 'being at a loss or perplexed what to do.' **-कारण** *a.* having what reason or cause. **-किल** *ind.* what a pity (expressing displeasure or dissatisfaction, (P. III. 3 151); न संभावयामि न मर्षयामि तत्रभवान् किंकिल वृषलं याजयिष्यति Sk. **-क्षण** *a.* one who says 'what is a moment,' a lazy fellow who does not value moments; H. 2. 91. **-गोत्र** *a.* belonging to what family. **-च** *ind.* moreover, and again, further. **-चन** *ind.* to a certain degree, a little. **-चित्** *ind.* to a certain degree, some what, a little; किंचिदुत्क्रांतशैशवौ R. 15. 33; 2. 46, 12. 21. °**ज्ञ** *a.* 'knowing little', a smatterer. °**कर** *a.* doing something, useful. °**कालः** some time, a little time. °**प्राण** *a.* having a little life. °**मात्र** *a.* only a little. **-छंदस्** *a.* conversant with which Veda. **-तर्हि** *ind.* how then, but, however. **-तु** *ind.* but, yet, however, nevertheless; अवैमि चैनामनघेति किंतु लोकापवादो बलवान्मतो मे R. 14. 40, 1. 65. **-दैवत** *a.* having what deity. **-नामधेय, -नामन्** *a.* having what name. **-निमित्त** *a.* having what cause or reason, for what purpose. **-निमित्तम्** *ind.* why, wherefore. **-नु** *ind.* 1 whether; किं नु मे मरणं श्रेयो परित्यागो जनस्य वा Nala. 10. 10. 2 much more, much less; अपि त्रैलोक्यराज्यस्य हेतोः किन्नु महीकृते Bg. 1. 35. 3 what indeed; किन्नु मे राज्येनार्थः **-नु खलु** *ind.* 1 how possibly, how is it that, why indeed, why, to be sure; किं नु खलु गीतार्थमाकर्ण्य इष्टजनविरहादृतेपि बलवदुत्कंठितोऽस्मि *S.* 5. 2 may it be that; किं नु खलु यथा वयमस्यामेवमियमप्यस्मान् प्रति स्यात् *S.* 1. **-पच, -पचान** *a.* miserly, niggardly. **-पराक्रम** *a.* of what power or energy. **-पुनर्** *ind.* how much more, or how much less; स्वयं रोपितेषु तरुषूत्पद्यते स्नेहः किं पुनरंगसंभवेष्वपत्येषु K. 291; Me. 3, 17; Ve. 3. **-प्रकारं** *ind.* in what manner. **-प्रभाव** *a.* possessing what power. **-भूत** *a.* of what sort or nature. **-रूप** *a.* of what form or shape. **-वदंती**. **-ती** *f.* rumour, report; मत्संबंधात्कश्मला किंवदंती U. 1. 42; U. 1, 4. **-वराटकः** an extravagant man. **-वा** *ind.* 1 a particle of interrogation; किं वा शकुंतलेत्यस्य मातुराख्या *S.* 7. 2 or (corr. of किं 'whether'); राजपुत्रि सुप्ता किंवा जागर्षि Pt. 1; तत्किं मारयामि किंवा विषं प्रयच्छामि किंवा पशुधर्मेण व्यापादयामि *ibid.*; *S.* Til. 7. **-विद्** *a.* knowing what. **-व्यापार** *a.* following what occupation. **-शील** *a.* of what habits. **-स्वित्** *ind.* whether, how; अद्रेः शृंगं हरति पवनः किंस्विदित्युन्मुखीभिः Me. 14.

कियत् *a.* (Nom. sing. कियान् *m.*, कियती *f.*, कियत् *n.*) 1 How great, how far, how much, how many, of what extent or qualities (having an interrogative force); कियान्कालस्तवैवं स्थितस्य संजातः Pt. 5; N. 1. 130; अयं भूतावासो विमृश कियतीं याति न दशां Sânti. 1. 25; ज्ञास्यसि कियद्भुजो मे रक्षति *S.* 1. 13; कियदवशिष्टं रजन्याः *S.* 4. 2 Of what consideration, *i. e.* of no account, worthless; राजेति कियती मात्रा Pt. 1. 40; मातः कियंतोऽरयः Ve. 5. 9. 3 Some, a little; a small number, a few (having an indefinite force); निजहृदि विकसंतः संति संतः कियंतः Bh. 2. 78; त्वदभिसरणरभसेन वलंती पतति पदानि कियंति चलंती Gît. 6. -COMP. **-एतिका** effort, vigorous and persevering exertion. **-कालम्** *ind.* 1 how long. 2 some little time. **-चिरं** *ind.* how long; कियच्चिरं श्राम्यसि गौरि Ku. 5. 50. **-दूरं** *ind.* 1 how far, how distant, how long; कियद्दूरे स जलाशयः Pt. 1; N. 1. 137. 2 for a short time, a little way.

किरः A hog.

किरकः 1 A scribe. 2 A pig.

किरणः 1 A ray or beam of light, a ray (of the sun, moon or any shining substance); रविकिरणसहिष्णु *S.* 2. 4; एको हि दोषो गुणसंनिपाते निमज्जतीन्दोः किरणेष्विवांकः Ku. 1. 3; Sânti. 4. 6; R. 5. 74; Si. 4. 58; °**मय** radiant, brilliant. 2 A small particle of dust. -COMP. **-मालिन्** *m.* the sun.

किरातः 1 N. of a degraded mountain tribe who live by hunting, a mountaineer; वैयाकरणकिरातादपशब्दमृगाः क्व यांतु संत्रस्ताः। यदि नटगणकचिकित्सकवैतालिकवदनकंदरा न स्युः ॥ Subhâsh. Ku. 1. 6, 15; Ratn. 2. 3. 2 A savage, barbarian. 3 A dwarf. 4 A groom, a horseman.

5 N. of Siva in the disguise of a Kirâta. -ताः (pl.) N. of a country. -COMP. -आशिन् *m.* an epithet of Garuda.

किराती *f.* 1 A female Kirâta, a woman of Kirâta tribe. 2 A woman who carries a fly-flap or chowri; R. 16. 57. 3 A bawd, a procuress. 4 Pârvatî in the disguise of a Kirâtî. 5 The celestial Gangâ.

किरिः 1 A hog, boar. 2 A cloud.

किरीटः, -टं 1 A diadem, crown, crest, tiara; किरीटबद्धांजलयः Ku. 7. 92. 2 A trader.-COMP. -धारिन् *m.* a king. -मालिन् *m.* an epithet of Arjuna.

किरीटिन् *a.* Wearing a crown or diadem; Bg. 11. 17, 46; Pt. 3. -*m.* N. of Arjuna; Bg. 11. 35. (Mb. thus accounts for the name:—पुरा शक्रेण मे बद्धं युध्यतो दानवर्षभैः। किरीटं मूर्ध्नि सूर्याभं तेनाहुर्मां किरीटिनं ॥).

किर्मीर *a.* Variegated, spotted. -रः 1 N. of a Râkshasa slain by Bhîma; Ve. 6. 2 The variegated colour. -COMP. -जित्, -निषूदनः, -सूदनः epithets of Bhîma.

किलः 1 Play, trifling. -COMP. -किंचितं amorous agitation, weeping, laughing, being angry &c. in the society of a lover.

किल *ind.* 1 Verily, indeed, assuredly, certainly; अर्हति किल कितव उपद्रवं M. 4; इदं किलाव्याजमनोहरं वपुः *S.* 1. 18. 2 As they say, as is reported (showiug report or tradition ऐतिह्य); भभूव योगी किल कार्तवीर्यः R. 6. 38; जघान कंसं किल वासुदेवः Mbh. 3 A feigned action (अलीक); प्रसह्य सिंहः किल तां चकर्ष R. 2. 27; Ki. 11. 2. 4 Hope, expectation or probability; पार्थः किल विजेष्यते कुरून् G. M. 5 Dissatisfaction, dislike; एवं किल केचिद्वदंति G. M. 6 Contempt; त्वं किल योत्स्यसे G. M. 7 Cause, reason (हेतु); (very rare); स किलैवमुक्तवान् G. M. 'for he said so'.

किलकिलः,-ला A sound, a cry expressing joy or pleasure.

किलकिलायते Den. A. To make a noise; Bk. 7. 102.

किलिंजं 1 A mat. 2 A thin plank of green wood, board.

किल्वित् *m.* A horse.

किल्बिषं 1 Sin; Ms. 4. 243; 10. 118; Bg. 3. 13, 6. 45. 2 A fault, offence, injury, guilt; Ms. 8. 235. 3 A disease, sickness.

किशलयः -यं A sprout, a young shoot; see किसलय.

किशोरः 1 A colt, cub, the young of any animal; केसरिकिशोरः &c. 2 A youth, lad, a boy below fifteen, a minor in law (अप्राप्तव्यवहार). 3 The sun. —री A maiden, a young woman.

किष्किंधः, -ध्यः 1 N. of a country. 2 N. of a mountain situated in that country. —धा, —ध्या N. of a city, the capital of Kishkindha.

किष्कु *a.* Vile, contemptible, bad. -ष्कुः *m.* or *f.* 1 The forearm. 2 A cubit, span.

किसलः -लं, **किसलयः** -यं A sprout, a young and tender shoot or foliage; अधरः किसलयरागः *S.* 1. 21; किसलयमलूनं कररुहैः 2. 10; किसलयैः सलयैरिव पाणिभिः R. 9. 35.

कीकट *a.* (टी *f.*) 1 Poor, indigent. 2 Miserly. —टाः (pl.) N. of a country (Behar). —टः A horse.

कीकस *a.* Hard, firm. —सं A bone.

कीचकः 1 A hollow bamboo. 2 A bamboo rattling or whistling in the wind; शब्दायंते मधुरमनिलैः कीचकाः पूर्यमाणाः Me. 56; R. 2. 12; 4. 73; Ku. 1. 8. 3 N. of a people. 4 N. of the commander-in-chief of king Virâta. [While Draupad*i* in the guise of Sairandhr*i* was residing at the court of king Vir*ata* with her five husbands also disguised, K*i*chaka once happened to see her, and her beauty stirred up wicked passion in his heart. He thenceforward kept a sinister eye on her, and endeavoured through the help of his sister, the king's wife, to violate her chastity. Draupad*i* complained of his unmannerly conduct towards herself to the king; but when he declined to interfere, she sought the assistance of Bh*i*ma, and at his suggestion showed herself favourable to his advances. It was then agreed that they should meet at mid-night in the dancing hall of the palace. Pursuant to appointment K*i*chaka went there and attempted to embrace Draupad*i* (as he fancied Bh*i*ma to be owing to the darkness of night). But the wretch was at once seized and crushed to death by the powerful Bh*i*ma]. -COMP. -जित् *m.* an epithet of Bhîma, the second Pândava prince.

कीटः 1 A worm, an insect; कीटोऽपि सुमनःसंगादारोहति सतां शिरः H. Pr. 45. 2 A term expressive of contempt (generally at the end of comp.); द्विपकीटः a wretched elephant; so पक्षिकीटः &c. -COMP. -घ्नः sulphur. -जं silk. -जा lac. -मणिः a firefly.

कीटकः 1 A worm. 2 A bard of the Mâgadha tribe.

कीदृश्, **कीदृश** (शी *f.*), **कीदृक्ष** (क्षी *f.*) Of what kind or sort, of what nature; तद्धोः कीदृगसौ विवेकविभवः कीदृक् प्रबोधोदयः Prab. 1; N. 1. 137.

कीनाश *a.* 1 Cultivating the soil. 2 Poor, indigent. 3 Niggardly. 4 Small, little. —शः 1 An epithet of Yama, the god of death. 2 A kind of monkey.

कीरः 1 A parrot; एवं कीरवरे मनोरथमयं पीयूषमास्वादयति Bv. 1. 58. —राः (pl.) The country and the people of Kâshmîra. —रं Flesh. -COMP. —इष्टः the mango tree (liked by parrots). -वर्णकं a king of perfume.

कीर्ण *a.* 1 Strewn, spread, cast, scattered. 2 Covered, filled. 3 Placed, put. 4 Injured, hurt; see कॄ.

कीर्णिः *f.* 1 Scattering. 2 Covering, hiding, concealing. 3 Injuring.

कीर्तनं 1 Telling, narrating. 2 A temple. —ना 1 Narration, recital. 2 Fame, glory.

कीर्तय्—कॄत् q. v.

कीर्तिः *f.* 1 Fame, renown, glory; इह कीर्तिमवाप्नोति Ms. 2. 9; वंशस्य कर्तारमनंतकीर्तिं R. 2. 64; Me. 45. 2 Favour, approbation. 3 Dirt, mud. 4 Extension, expansion. 5 Light, lustre. 6 Sound. -COMP. -भाज् *a.* famous, celebrated, renowned. (*-m.*) an epithet of Droṇa, the military preceptor of the Kauravas and Pândavas. -शेषः survival or remaining behind only in fame, leaving nothing behind but fame; *i. e.* death; cf. नामशेष, आलेख्यशेष.

कील् 1 P. 1 To bind. 2 To pin. 3 To stake.

कीलः 1 A wedge, a pin; कीलोत्पाटीव वानरः Pt. 1. 21. 2 A lance. 3 A post, pillar. 4 A weapon. 5 The elbow. 6 A blow with the elbow. 7 A flame. 8 A minute particle. 9 N. of Siva.

कीलकः 1 A wedge or pin. 2 A pillar, column; see कील.

कीलालः 1 A heavenly drink similar to Amrita, beverage of the gods. 2 Honey. 3 A beast. —लं 1 Blood. 2 Water. -COMP. -धिः the ocean. —पः a demon, goblin.

कीलिका The pin of an axle.

कीलित *a.* 1 Tied, bound. 2 Fixed, nailed, pinned down; तेन मम हृदयमिदमसमशरकीलितं Gît. 7; सा नश्चेतासि कीलितेव Mâl. 5. 10.

कीश *a.* Naked. —शः 1 An ape, monkey. 2 The sun. 3 A bird.

कुः *f.* 1 The earth. 2 The base of a triangle or any plane figure. -COMP. -पुत्रः Mars.

कु *ind.* A prefix implying 'badness', 'deterioration', 'depreciation', 'sin', 'reproach,' 'littleness,' 'want,' 'deficieney' &c. Its various substitutes are कद् (कदश्व), कव (कवोष्ण), का (कोष्ण), किं (किंप्रभुः); cf. Pt. 5. 17. -COMP. -कर्मन् *n.* a bad deed, a mean act. -ग्रहः an unpropitious planet. -ग्रामः a petty village or hamlet (without a king's officer, as *agnihotrin*, a physician or a river). -चेल *a.* wearing bad or ragged garments. -चर्या wickedness, evil conduct, impropriety. -जन्मन् *a.* low-born. -तनु *a.* deformed, ugly. (-नुः) an epithet of Kubera. -तंत्री a bad lute. -तर्कः 1 sophistical or fallacious argument. 2 a heterodox doctrine, free-thinking ; कुतर्केष्वभ्यासः सततपरपैशुन्यमननम् G. L. 31. °पथः a sophistical mode of arguing. -तीर्थं a bad teacher -दिनं an evil or unpropitious day. -दृष्टिः *f.* 1 weak sight. 2 an evil eye, sinister eye (fig.). 3 an opinion or doctrine opposed to the Vedas, heterodox doctrines ; Ms. 12. 95. -देशः 1 a bad place or country. 2 a country where the necessaries of life are not available or which is subject to oppression. -देह *a.* ugly, deformed. (-हः) an epithet of Kubera. -धी *a.* 1. foolish, silly, stupid. 2 wicked. -नटः a bad actor. -नदिका a small river, rill ; सुपूरा स्यात्कुनदिका Pt. 1. 25. -नाथः a bad master. -नामन् *m.* a miser. -पथः 1 a wrong road, bad way (fig. also). 2 a heterodox doctrine. -पुत्रः a bad or wicked son. -पुरुषः a low, or wicked man. -पूय *a.* low, vile, contemptible -प्रिय *a.* disagreeable, contemptible, low, mean. -प्लवः a bad boat ; कुप्लवैः संतरन् जलम् Ms. 9. 161. -ब्रह्मः, -ब्रह्मन् *m.* a bad or degraded Brâhmaṇa. -मंत्रः 1 bad advice. 2 a charm used to secure success in a bad cause. -योगः an inauspicious conjunction (of planets). -रस *a.* having bad juice or flavour. (-सः) a kind of spirituous liquor. -रूप *a.* ugly, deformed; Pt. 5.19. -रूप्यं tin. -वंगः lead. -वचस्, -वाक्य *a.* abusive, scurrilous, using abusive or foul language. (*-n.*) abuse, bad language. -वर्षः a sudden or violent shower. -विवाहः a degraded or improper form of marriage ; Ms. 3. 63. -वृत्तिः *f.* bad behaviour. -वैद्यः a bad physician, quack. -शील *a.* rude, wicked, unmannerly, ill-tempered. -स्थलं a bad place. -सरित् *f.* a small river, rill ; उच्छिद्यंते क्रियाः सर्वाः ग्रीष्मे कुसरितो यथा Pt. 2. 85. -सृतिः *f.* 1 evil conduct, wickedness. 2 conjuring magic. 3 roguery. -स्त्री a bad woman.

कु I. 1 A. (कवते) To sound. -II. 6 A. (कुवते) 1 To moan, groan. 2 To cry. -III. 2 P. (कौति) To hum, coo (as a bee).

कुकभं A kind of spirituous liquor.

कुकीलः A mountain.

कुकु (कू) दः One who gives away a girl in marriage with suitable decorations and in accordance with prescribed ceremonies.

कुकुंद (दु) रः The cavity of the loins just above the hips (जघनकूप) ; see ककुंदर.

कुकुराः (pl.) N. of a country; also called दशार्ह.

कुकूलः, -लं 1 Chaff ; कुकूलानां राशौ तदनु हृदयं पच्यत इव U. 6. 40. 2 A fire made of chaff.—लं 1 A hole, ditch (filled with stakes). 2 An armour, mail.

कुक्कुटः 1 A cock, a wild cock. 2 A whisp of lighted straw, a fire brand. 3 A spark of fire.—टी A hen

कुक्कुटिः, -टी *f.* Hypocrisy, interested observance of religious rites.

कुक्कुभः 1 A wild cock. 2 A cock in general. 3 Varnish.

कुक्कुरः (री *f.*) A dog ; यस्यैतच्च न कुक्कुरैरहरहर्जंघांतरं चर्व्यते Mk. 2. 11. -COMP. -वाच् *m.* a species of deer.

कुक्षः The belly.

कुक्षिः 1 The belly (in general); जिह्मिताध्मातकुक्षिः (भुजगपतिः) Mk. 9. 12. 2 The womb, the part of the belly containing fœtus ; कुंभीनस्याश्च कुक्षिजः R. 15. 15 ; Si. 13. 40. 3 The interior of anything ; R. 10. 65 (where the word is used in sense 2 also). 4 A cavity in general. 5 A Cavern, cave; R. 2. 38, 67. 6 The sheath of a sword. 7 A bay, gulf. -COMP. -शूलः belly-ache, colic.

कुक्षिंभरि *a.* 'Caring to feed his own belly,' selfish, gluttonous, voracious.

कुंकुमं Saffron ; लग्नकुंकुमकेसरान् (स्कंधान्) ; R. 4. 67 ; Rs. 4. 2 ; 5. 9 ; Bh. 1. 10, 25. -COMP. -अद्रिः N. of a mountain.

कुच् I. 6. P. (कुचति, कुचित) 1 To utter a shrill cry (as a bird). 2 To go. 3 To polish. 4 To contract, bend. 5 To be contracted. 6 to impede. 7 To write or delineate. WITH सम् 1 to be crooked or curved. 2 to contract oneself, to be contracted ; as in गात्रं संकुचितं ; मृगपतिरपि कोपात् संकुचत्युत्पतिष्णुः Pt. 3. 43. 3 to close, fade ; कमलवनानि समकुचन् Dk. (*-Caus.*) to close, contract, lessen. -II. 1 P. कुंच् also (कोचति, कुंचति, कुंचित) 1 to make crooked, bend or curve. 2 To move or go crookedly. 3 To make small, lessen. 4 To shrink, contract. 5 To go to or towards. With आ to contract, curve, bend (in *caus.* also) ; Ku. 3. 70 ; R. 6 15; Bh. 1. 3. -वि to contract, curve.

कुचः The female breast, a teat, nipple ; अपि वनांतरमल्पकुचांतरा V. 4. 26. -COMP. -अग्रं, -मुखं a nipple. -तटं, -तटी 1 the slope of the female breast (तट being स्वार्थे or meaningless).-फलः the pomegranate tree.

कुचर *a.* (रा,-री *f.*) 1 Going slowly, creeping. 2 Wicked low, vile. 3 Detracting, censorious.-रः A fixed star.

कुच्छं A species of lotus.

कुजः 1 A tree. 2 The planet Mars. 3 N. of a demon killed by Krishṇa (also called नरक). -जा N. of Sîtâ.

कुजंभनः, कुजंभिलः A thief who breaks into a house.

कुज्झटिः, कुज्झटिका, कुज्झटी A fog or mist.

कुंच् See कुच II.

कुंचनं Curving, bending, contraction.

कुंचिः A measure of capacity equal to eight handfuls ; अष्टमुष्टिर्भवेत्कुंचिः.

कुंचिका 1 A key ; Bh. 1. 63. 2 The shoot of a bamboo.

कुंचित *a.* Contracted, curved, bent &c.

कुंजः, -जं 1 A place overgrown with plants or creepers, a bower, an arbour ; चल सखि कुंजं सतिमिरपुंजं शीलय नीलनिचोलं Gît. 5 ; वंजुललताकुंजे 12 ; Me. 19, R. 9. 64. 2 The tusk of an elephant. -COMP. -कुटीरः a bower, a place overgrown with plants and creepers; गुंजत्कुंजकुटीरकौशिकघटा U. 2. 29 ; Mâl. 5. 19 ; कोकिलकूजितकुंजकुटीरे Gît. 1.

कुंजरः 1 An elephant. 2 Any thing pre-eminent or excellent of its class (at the end of comp. only). Amara gives the following words used similarly:—स्युरुत्तरपदे व्याघ्रपुंगवर्षभकुंजराः । सिंहशार्दूलनागाद्याः पुंसि श्रेष्ठार्थवाचकाः 3 The Asvattha tree. 4 The lunar asterism called हस्त. -COMP. -अनीकं the division of an army consisting of elephants, an elephant-corps. -अशनः the Asvattha-tree. -अरातिः 1 a lion. 2 Sarabha (a fabulous animal with 8 feet). -ग्रहः an elephant-catcher.

कुट् I. 6 P. (कुटति, कुटित) 1 To be crooked or curved. 2 To curve or bend. 3 To act dishonestly, cheat, deceive. -II. 4 P. (कुट्यति) To break to pieces, break asunder, divide, split.

कुटः -टं A water-pot, a jar, pitcher —टः 1 A fort, strong-hold. 2 A hammer. 3 A tree. 4 A house. 5 A mountain. -COMP. -जः 1 N. of a tree; Me. 4 ; R. 19. 37 ; Rs. 3. 13 ; Bh. 1. 42. 2 N. of Agastya. 3 N. of Droṇa -हारिका a female servant.

कुटकं A plough without a pole.

कुटंकः A roof, thatch.

कुटंगकः 1 An arbour formed by creeping plants overrunning a tree. 2 A small house, hut or cottage.

कुटपः 1 A measure of grain (=कुडव). 2 A garden near a house. 3 A sage, an ascetic. -पं A lotus.

कुटरः The post round which the rope of the churning stick passes.

कुटलं A roof, thatch.

कुटिः 1 The body. 2 A tree. —*f.* 1 A cottage, hut. 2 A curve, bend. -COMP. -चरः a porpoise.

कुटिरं A cottage, hut.

कुटिल *a.* 1 Crooked, bent, curved, curled; भेदात् भ्रुवोः कुटिलयोः S. 5. 23 ; R. 6. 82 ; 19. 17. 2 Tortuous, winding ; क्रोशं कुटिला नदी Sk. 3 (Fig.) Insincere, fraudulent, dishonest. -COMP. -आशय *a.* evil-minded, male-volent.

पक्ष्मन् *a.* having curved eye-lashes. –स्वभाव *a.* crooked by nature, dishonest, malevolent.

कुटिलिका 1 Coming stealthily as a hunter on his prey, crouching. 2 A blacksmith's forge.

कुटी 1 A curve. 2 A cottage, hut; प्रासादीयति कुट्यां Sk.; Ms. 11. 72; पर्ण°, अश्व° &c. 3 A bawd, procuress. –COMP. –चकः a religious mendicant of a particular order; चतुर्विधा भिक्षवस्ते कुटीचकबहूदकौ । हंसः परमहंसश्च यो यः पश्चात् स उत्तमः ॥ Mb. –चरः a kind of ascetic who entrusts the care of his family to his son and devotes himself solely to religious penance and austerities.

कुटीरः –रं, कुटीरकः A hut, cottage; U. 2, 29; Amaru. 48.

कुट्टनी A bawd, procuress; see कुट्टनी.

कुटुंबं, कुटुंबकं A household, a family; उदारचरितानां तु वसुधैव कुटुंबकं H. 1. 70; Y. 2. 45; Ms. 11. 12, 22; 8. 166. 2 The duties and cares of a family; तदुपहितकुटुंबः R. 7. 71. –बः –बं 1 kinsman, a relation by descent or marriage. 2 offspring, progeny. 3 A name. 4 Race. COMP.– कलहः, –हं domestic quarrels. –भरः the burden of the family; भर्त्रा तदर्पितकुटुंबभरेण सार्धम् *S.* 4. 19. –व्यापृत *a.* (a father) w o is provident and attentive to the good of the family.

कुटुंबिकः, कुटुंबिन् *m.* A house-holder, a *pater familias*, one who has a family to support or take care of; प्रायेण गृहिणीनेत्राः कन्यार्थेषु कुटुंबिनः Ku. 6. 85; V. 3. 1; Ms. 3. 80; Y. 2. 45. 2 A member of a family. –नी 1 The wife of a house-holder, a housewife (in charge of the house); भवतु कुटुंबिनीमाहूय पृच्छामि Mu. 1; प्रभवंत्योऽपि हि भर्तृषु कारणकोपाः कुटुंबिन्यः M. 1. 17; R. 8. 86; Amaru. 48. 3 A woman in general.

कुट्ट 10 U. (कुट्टयति, कुट्टित) 1 To cut, divide. 2 To grind, pound. 3 To blame, censure. 4 To multiply.

कुट्टकः A grinder.

कुट्टनं 1 Cutting. 2 Pounding. 3 Abusing, censuring.

कुट्ट (ट्टि) नी A bawd, procuress, a go-between.

कुट्टमितं The affected repulse of a lover's endearments or caresses (one of the 28 graces or blandishments of the heroine). The S. D. thus defines it:–केशस्तनाधरादीनां ग्रहे हर्षेऽपि संभ्रमात् । प्राहुः कुट्टमितं नाम शिरःकरविधूननम् 142.

कुट्टाक *a.* (की *f.*) Who or what divides or cuts; सारंगसंगरविधाविभकुंभकूटकुट्टाकपाणिकुलिशस्य हरेः प्रमादः Mâl. 5. 32.

कुट्टारः A mountain. –रं 1 Sexual intercourse. 2 A woollen blanket. 3 Exclusion.

कुट्टिमः–मं 1 An inlaid or paved floor, ground paved with small stones, pavement; कांतेंदुकांतोपलकुट्टिमेषु *Si.* 3. 44; R. 11. 9. 2 Ground prepared for the site of a mansion. 3 A jewel-mine. 4 The pomegranate. 5 A hut, cottage, small house.

कुट्टिहारिका A maid-servant, slave.

कुड्मल=कुडमल q. v.

कुठः A tree.

कुठर See कुटर.

कुठारः (री *f.*) An axe, a hatchet; मातुः केवलमेव यौवनवनच्छेदे कुठारा वयं Bh. 3. 11.

कुठारिकः A wood-cutter.

कुठारिका A small axe.

कुठारुः 1 A tree. 2 An ape, a monkey.

कुठिः 1 A tree. 2 A mountain.

कुडंगः A bower, an arbour.

कुडवः (–पः) A measure of grain equal to ¼ of a Prashtha and containing 12 handfuls.

कुड्मल *a.* Opening, full-blown, expanding, (as the blossom of a flower); R. 18. 37: –लः An opening, bud; विजृंभणोद्गंधिषु कुडमलेषु R. 16. 47; U. 6. 17; *Si.* 2. 7. –लं A particular hell; Ms. 4. 89; Y. 3. 222.

कुड्मलित *a.* 1 Budded, blossomed. 2 Cheerful, smiling.

कुड्यं 1 A wall; भेदे कुड्यावपातने Y. 2. 223; *Si.* 3. 45. 2 Plastering (a wall). 3 Eagerness, curiosity. –COMP. –छेदिन् *m.* a house-breaker, a thief. –छेद्यः a digger. (–द्यं) a ditch, pit, breach or opening (in a wall).

कुण् 6 P. (कुणति, कुणित) 1 To support, aid. 2 To sound.

कुणकः A young animal just born.

कुणप *a.* (पी *f.*) Smelling like a dead body, stinking. —पः,–पं A dead body, corpse; शासनीयः कुणपभोजनः V. 5. (a vulture); अमेध्यः कुणपाशी च Ms. 12. 71; often used as a term of contempt with living beings. –पः 1 A spear. 2 A foul smell, stench.

कुणिः A cripple with a withered arm.

कुंटक *a.* (की *f.*) Fat, corpulent.

कुंठ् 1 P. (कुंठति, कुंठित) 1 To be blunted or dulled. 2 To be lame or mutilated. 3 To be dull or stupid, be idle. 4 To loosen. –*Caus.* or 10 P. To hide.

कुंठ *a.* 1 Blunt, dulled; वज्रं तपोवीर्यमहत्सु कुंठं Ku. 3. 12 has no effect on &c; कुंठीभवंत्युपलादिषु क्षुराः S. B. 2 Dull, foolish, stupid. 3 Indolent, lazy. 4 Weak.

कुंठकः A fool.

कुंठित *p. p.* 1 Blunted, dulled; (fig. also); बिभ्रतोऽस्त्रमचलेऽप्यकुंठितं R. 11. 74; Bv. 2. 78; Ku. 2. 20; शास्त्रेष्वकुंठिता बुद्धिः R. 1. 19 not hampered or impeded. 2 Stupid. 3 Mutilated

कुंडः, –डं 1 A bowl-shaped vessel, a basin, bowl. 2 A round hole in the ground for receiving and preserving water. 3 A whole in general; अग्निकुंड. 4 A pool, well; especially one consecrated to some deity or holy purpose. 5 The bowl of a mendicant —डः (डी *f.*) A son born in adultery, the son of a woman by a man other than her husband while the husband is alive; पत्यौ जीवति कुंडः स्यात् Ms. 3. 174; Y. 1. 222. –COMP. –आशिन् *m.* a pander, pimp, one who depends for his livelihood on a कुंड *i. e.* a bastard, or adulterine; Ms. 3. 158; Y. 1. 224. –ऊधस् (कुंडोघ्नी) 1 a cow with a full udder. 2 a woman with a full bosom.–कीटः 1 a keeper of concubines. 2 a follower of the Chârvâka doctrine, an atheist. 3 a Brâhmaṇa born in adultery. –कीलः a low or vile man. –गोलं,–गोलकं 1 gruel. 2 a group of कुंड and गोलक (taken together).

कुंडलः–लं 1 An ear-ring, ring; श्रोत्रं श्रुतेनैव न कुंडलेन Bh. 2 71; Ch. P. 11; Rs. 2. 20, 3. 19; R. 11. 15. 2 A bracelet. 3 The coil of a rope.

कुंडलना Encircling (as a word) to denote that it is to be left out or not considered; तदोजसस्तद्यशसः स्थिताविमौ वृथेति चित्ते कुरुते यदा यदा । तनोति भानोः परिवेषकैतवात्तदा विधिः कुंडलनां विधोरपि ॥ N. 1. 14; cf. 2. 95 also.

कुंडलिन् (नी *f.*) 1 Decorated with ear-rings. 2 Circular, spiral. 3 Winding, coiling (as a serpent). –*m.* 1 A snake. 2 A peacock. 3 An epithet of Varuṇa.

कुंडिका 1 A pitcher. 2 A student's water-pot (कमंडलु).

कुंडिन् *m.* An epithet of *Siva.*

कुंडिनं N. of a city, the capital of the Vidarbhas.

कुंडि (डी) र *a.* Strong. –रः A man.

कुतपः 1 A Brâhmaṇa. 2 A twice-born man (द्विजन्मन्). 3 The sun. 4 Fire. 5 A guest. 6 An ox, a bull. 7 A daughter's son. 8 A sister's son. 9 Grain. 10 The eighth Muhúrta of the day; अह्नो मुहूर्ता विख्याता दश पंच च सर्वदा । तत्राष्टमो मुहूर्तो यः स कालः कुतपः स्मृतः ॥ –पं 1 The Kusa grass. 2 A sort of blanket.

कुतस् *ind.* 1 From where, whence; कस्य त्वं वा कुत आयातः Moha M. 3. 2 Where, where else, in what (other) place &c; ईदृग्विनोदः कुतः *S.* 2. 5. 3 Why, wherefore, from what cause or motive; कुत इदमुच्यते *S.* 5. 4 How, in what manner; स्फुरति च बाहुः कुतः फलमिहास्य S. 1. 15. 5 Much more, much less; न त्वत्समोऽस्त्यभ्यधिकः कुतोऽन्यः Bg. 11. 43, 4. 31; न मे स्तेनो जनपदे न कदर्यो...न स्वैरी स्वैरिणी कुतः Ch. Up. 6 Because, for. कुतस् is sometimes used merely for the abl. of किम्; कुतः कालात्समुत्पन्नं V. P. (=कस्मात् कालात् &c.); कुतः becomes indefinite when connected with the particles चिद्, चन or अपि.

कुतस्त्य *a.* **1** Whence come. **2** How happened.

कुतुकं **1** Desire, inclination. **2** Curiosity (=कौतुकं). **3** Eagerness, ardour, vehemence; केलिकलाकुतुकेन च काचिदमुं यमुनाजलकूले। मंजुलवंजुलकुंजगतं विचकर्ष करेण दुकूले Gît. 1.

कुतुपः, कुतूः *f.* A small leathern bottle for oil.

कुतूहल *a.* **1** Wonderful. **2** Excellent, best. **3** Praised, celebrated. **—लं 1** Desire, curiosity; उज्झितशब्देन जनितं नः कुतूहलं S. 1; यदि विलासकलासु कुतूहलं Gît. 1; (पपौ) कुतूहलेनेव मनुष्यशाणितम् R. 3. 54; 13. 2; 15. 65. **2** Eagerness. **3** What excites curiosity, anything pleasing or interesting, a curiosity.

कुत्र *ind.* **1** Where, in which case; कुत्र मे शिशुः Pt. 1; प्रवृत्तिः कुत्र कर्तव्या H. 1. **2** In which case; तेजसा सह जातानां वयः कुत्रोपयुज्यते Pt. 1. 328. (कुत्र is sometimes used for the loc. sing. of किम्) When connected with the particles चिद्, चन or अपि कुत्र becomes, indefinite in sense. कुत्रापि,-कुत्रचित् somewhere, anywhere; न कुत्रापि nowhere; कुत्रचित्-कुत्रचित् in one place-in another place, here-here; Ms. 9. 34.

कुत्रत्य *a.* Where living or residing.

कुत्स् 10 A. (कुत्सयते, कुत्सित) To abuse, revile, censure, condemn; Ms. 2. 54; Y. 1. 31; *Santi.* 2. 28.

कुत्सनं, कुत्सा Abuse, contempt, reproach, abusive language; देवतानां च कुत्सनं Ms. 4. 163.

कुत्सित *a.* **1** Despised, contemptible. **2** Low, mean, vile.

कुथः The Kusa grass.

कुथः,-थं,-था **1** A painted cloth serving as an elephant's housings. **2** A carpet (in general).

कुद्दारः,-लः,-लकः **1** A spade, hoe. **2** The Kânchana tree.

कुद्मलं—कुड्मल q. v.

कुद्रंकः, -गः **1** A watch-house. **2** A dwelling raised on a scaffold.

कुनकः A crow.

कुंतः **1** A lance, a barbed dart, spear; कुंताः प्रविशंति K. P. 2 (*i. e.* कुंतधारिणः पुरुषाः); विरहिनिकृंतनकुंतमुखाकृतिकेतकिदंतुरिताशे Gît. 1. **2** A small animal, an insect.

कुंतलः **1** The hair of the head, a lock of hair; प्रतनुविरलैः प्रांतोन्मीलन्मनोहरकुंतलैः U. 1. 20; Ch. P. 4, 6; Gît. **2. 2** A drinking cup. **3** A plough. **—लाः** (pl.) N. of a country and its inhabitants.

कुंतयः (pl. of कुंति *m.*) N. of a country and its people.

कुंतिः N. of a king, son of क्रथ. -Comp. **-भोजः** N. of a Yâdava prince, king of the Kunties, who being childless, adopted Kuntî.

कुंती N. of पृथा, daughter of a Yâdava named शूर, adopted by कुंतिभोज, [She was the first wife of P*andu*. As he was prevented by a curse from having progeny, he allowed his wife to make use of a charm she had acquired from the sage Durv*a*sas, by means of which she was to have a son by any god she liked to invoke. She invoked Dharma, V*a*yu and Indra, and had from them Yudhish*th*ira, Bh*i*ma and Arjuna respectively. She was also mother of Kar*n*a by the deity Sun whom she invoked in her virginhood to test her charm.].

कुंथ् 1. 9. P. (कुंथति, कुथ्नाति, कुंथित) **1** To suffer pain. **2** To cling to. **3** To embrace. **4** To hurt.

कुंदः,-दं A kind of jasmine (white and delicate); कुंदावदाताः कलहंसमालाः Bk. 2. 18; प्रातः कुंदप्रसवशिथिलं जीवितं धारयेथाः Me. 113. **—दं** The flower of this plant; अलके बालकुंदानुविद्धं Me. 65, 47. **—दः 1** An epithet of Vishṇu. **2** A turner's lathe. -Comp. **-करः** a turner.

कुंदमः A cat.

कुंदिनी A multitude of lotuses.

कुंदुः A rat, mouse.

कुप् 4 P. (कुप्यति, कुपित) **1** To be angry, (generally with the dat. of the person who is the object of anger, but sometimes with the acc. or gen. also); कुप्यंति हितवादिने K. 108; M. 3. 21; U. 7; चुकोप तस्मै स भृशं R. 3. 56. **2** To be excited, gather strength, be virulent; as in दोषाः प्रकुप्यंति Susr. With **अति** to be angry; Bk. 15. 55. **-परि** to be angry. **-प्र 1** to be angry; निमित्तमुद्दिश्य हि यः प्रकुप्यति ध्रुवं स तस्यापगमे प्रसीदति. Pt. 1. 283. **2** to be excited, gather strength, increase. (*-Caus.*) to provoke, irritate, exasperate.

कुपिंद See कुविंद.

कुपिनिन् *m.* A fisherman.

कुपिनी A kind of net for catching small fish.

कुपूय *a.* Despised, low, mean, contemptible.

कुप्यं **1** A base metal. **2** Any metal but silver and gold; Ki. 1. 35; Ms. 7. 96; 10. 113.

कुबे (वे) रः The god of riches and treasure and the regent of the northern quarter; कुबेरगुप्तां दिशमुष्णरश्मौ गंतुं प्रवृत्ते समयं विलंध्य Ku. 3. 25 (*vide* Malli. thereon.) [Kubera is the son of Visravas by I*d*avi*d*a, and thus the half-brother of R*a*va*n*a. Besides being the lord of riches and regent of the north, he is the king of the Yakshas and Kinnaras, and a friend of Rudra. His abode is Kail*a*s. He is represented as being deformed in body-having three legs, only eight teeth, and a yellow mark in place of one eye]. -Comp. **-अद्रिः,-अचलः** an epithet of mountain Kailâsa. **-दिश्** *f.* the north.

कुब्ज *a.* Hump-backed, crooked. **—ब्जः 1** A curved sword. **2** A hump on the back. **—ब्जा** A young female servant of Kamsa, said to be deformed in three parts of her body. [Krish*n*a and Balar*a*ma, while proceeding to Mathur*a*, saw her on the high road carrying unguent to Kamsa. They asked her if she would give them some portion of it, and she gave as much as they wanted. Krish*n*a, being very much pleased with her kindness, made her perfectly straight, and she began to appear a most beautiful woman].

कुब्जकः N. of a tree; Ms. 8. 247, 5. 2.

कुब्जिका An unmarried girl eight years old.

कुभृत् *m.* A mountain.

कुमारः **1** A son, boy: a youth; R. 3. 48. **2** A boy below five. **3** A prince, an heir-apparent; (especially in dramas); विप्रोषितकुमारं तद्राज्यमस्तमितेश्वरं R. 12. 11; कुमारस्यायुषो बाणः V. 5; उपवेष्टुमर्हति कुमारः Mu. 4 (said by Râkshasa to Malayaketu). **4** N. of Kârtikeya, the god of war; कुमारकल्पं सुषुवे कुमारं R. 5. 36; कुमारोपि कुमारविक्रमः 3. 55. **5** N. of Agni. **6** A parrot. **7** The river सिंधु -Comp. **-पालनः 1** one who takes care of children. **2** N. of king *Sâli*vâhana. **-भृत्या 1** care of young children. **2** care of a woman in pregnancy or confinement, midwifery; R. 3. 12. **-वाहिन्, -वाहनः** a peacock. **-सूः** *f.* **1** an epithet of Pârvatî. **2** or of the Ganges.

कुमारकः **1** A child, a youth. **2** The pupil of the eye.

कुमारयति Den. P. To play, sport (like a child).

कुमारिक *a.* (की *f.*) **कुमारिन्** (णी *f.*) *a.* Furnished with girls, abounding in girls.

कुमारिका, कुमारी **1** A young girl, one from 10 to 12 years old. **2** A maiden, virgin; त्रीणि वर्षाण्युदीक्षेत कुमार्यृतुमती सती Ms. 9. 90; 11. 58; व्यावर्तितान्योपगमात्कुमारी R. 6. 69. **3** A girl or daughter in general. **4** N. of Durgâ. **5** N. of several plants. -Comp. **-पुत्रः** the son of an unmarried woman **-श्वशुरः** the father in-law of a girl defiled before marriage.

कुमुद् *a.* **1** Unkind, unfriendly. **2** Avaricious. –*n.* **1** The white water-lily. **2** The red lotus.

कुमुदः,–दं **1** The white water-lily said to open at moon-rise ; नोच्छ्वसिति तपनकिरणैश्चंद्रस्येवांशुभिः कुमुदं V. 3. 16 ; so *S.* 5. 28 ; Rs. 3. 2, 21, 23; Me. 40. **1** A red lotus. **—दं** Silver. **—दः** **1** An epithet of Vishṇu. **2** N. of the elephant supposed to guard the south. **3** Camphor. **4** A species of monkey. **5** N. of a Nâga who gave his younger sister कुमुद्वती to Kusa, son of Râma ; see R. 16. 75-86: –COMP. **–अभिख्यं** silver **–आकरः,–आवास.** a pond full of lotuses. **–ईशः** the moon. **–खंडं** an assemblage of lotuses. **–नाथः,–पतिः,–बंधुः, –बांधवः; –सुहृद्** *m.* the moon.

कुमुद्वती The lotus plant.

कुमुदिनी **1** A water-lily with white lotus flowers ; यथेंद्रावानंदं व्रजति समुपोढे कुमुदिनी U. 5. 26; *Si.* 9. 34. **2** A collection of lotuses. **3** A place abounding in lotuses. –COMP. **–नायकः –पतिः** the moon.

कुमुद्वत् *a.* Abounding in lotuses ; कुमुद्वत्सु च वारिषु R. 4. 19. **—ती** **1** A water-lily with white flowers (opening at moonrise) ; अंतर्हिते शशिनि सैव कुमुद्वती मे दृष्टिं न नंदयति संस्मरणीयशोभा *S.* 4. 2 ; कुमुद्वती भानुमतीव भावं (न बबंध) R. 6. 36. **2** A collection of lotuses. **3** A place abounding in lotuses. °**ईशः** the moon.

कुमोदकः An epithet of Vishṇu.

कुंबा An enclosure round the sacrificial ground.

कुंभः **1** A pitcher, water-pot, jar; इयं सुस्तनी मस्तकन्यस्तकुंभा Jag. ; वर्जयेत्तादृशं मित्रं विषकुंभं पयोमुखं H. 1. 77 ; R. 2. 36 ; so कुच°, स्तन°. **2** The frontal globe on the forehead of an elephant ; इभकुंभ Mâl. 5. 32 ; मत्तेभकुंभदलने भुवि संति शूराः Bh. 1. 59. **3** Aquarius, the eleventh sign of the zodiac. **4** A measure of grain equal to 20 *dronas*; Ms. 8. 320. **5** (In Yoga phil.) Closing the nostrils and mouth so as to suspend breathing. **6** The paramour of a harlot. –COMP. **–कर्णः** 'pitcher-eared' N. of a gigantic Râkshasa, brother of Râvaṇa and slain by Râma. [He is said to have devoured thousands of beings including sages and heavenly nymphs, and the gods were anxiously waiting for an opportunity to retaliate upon the powerful demon. After Brahm*a* had inflicted on him a curse for the humiliation to which he subjected Indra and his elephant Airavata, Kumbhakar*n*a began to practise the most rigid austerities. Brahm*a* was pleased and was about to grant him a boon, when the gods requested Sarasvat*i* to sit on his tongue and to pervert it. Accordingly when he went to the god, instead of asking *indrapada* he asked *nidrâpada* which was readily granted. It is said that he slept for six months at a time, and, when roused, was awake for only one day. When Lank*a* was besieged by the monkey-troops of R*a*ma, R*a*va*n*a with great difficulty roused Kumbhakar*n*a, desirous of availing himself of his gigantic strength. After having drunk 2000 jars of liquor, he took Sugr*i*va prisoner, besides devouring thousands of monkeys. He was ultimately slain by R*a*ma]. **–कारः** **1** a potter; Y. 3. 146. **2** a mixed tribe (वेश्यायां विप्रतश्चौर्यात् कुंभकारः स उच्यते Usanas ; or मालाकारात्कर्मकर्यां कुंभकारो व्यजायत Parâsara). **–घोणः** N. of a town. **–जः, –जन्मन्** *m.* **–योनिः, –संभवः** **1** an epithet of Agastya ; प्रससादोदयादंभः कुंभयोनेर्महौजसः R. 4. 22 ; 15. 55. **2** an epithet of Droṇa, the military preceptor of the Kauravas and Pâṇḍavas. **3** an epithet of Vasishṭha. **–दासी** a bawd, procuress; sometimes used as a term of reproach or abuse. **–लग्नं** that time of the day in which Aquarius rises above the horizon. **–मंडूकः** **1** (lit.) a frog in a pitcher. **2** (fig.) an inexperienced man ; cf कूपमंडूक. **–संधिः** the hollow on the top of an elephant's head between the frontal globes.

कुंभकः **1** The base of a column. **2** A religious exercise (in Yoga phil.), stopping the breath by closing the mouth and both the nostrils with the fingers of the right hand.

कुंभा A harlot, whore.

कुंभिका **1** A small pot. **2** A harlot.

कुंभिन् **1** An elephant ; Bv. 1. 52. **2** A crocodile. –COMP. **–नरकः** a particular hell. **–मदः** rut, ichor.

कुंभिलः **1** A thief who breaks into a house. **2** A plagiarist. **3** A wife's brother. **4** A child of an imperfect impregnation or born at undue seasons.

कुंभी A small water-jar. –COMP. **–नसः** a kind of venomous serpent ; U. 2. 29. **–पाकः** (sing. or pl.) a particular hell in which the wicked are baked like potter's vessels ; Y. 3. 224 ; Ms. 12. 76.

कुंभीकः The Punnâga tree –COMP. **–मक्षिका** a sort of fly.

कुंभीरः A shark.

कुंभीरकः, कुंभीलः, कुंभीलकः A thief; लोप्त्रेण गृहीतस्य कुंभीरकस्यास्ति वा प्रतिवचनं V. 2 ; कुंभीलकैः कामुकैश्च परिहर्तव्या चांद्रिका M. 4.

कुर् 6. P. (कुरति, कुरित) To sound.

कुरकरः, कुरंकुरः The (Indian) crane.

कुरंगः (**गी** *f.*) **1** A deer in general; तन्मे ब्रूहि कुरंग कुत्र भवता किं नाम तप्तं तपः *S*ânti. 1. 14, 4. 6 ; लवंगी कुरंगीदृगंगीकरोतु Jag. **2** A species of deer (कुरंग ईषत्ताम्रः स्याद्धरिणाकृतिको महान्). –COMP. **–अक्षी –नयना, –नेत्रा** a deer-eyed woman. **–नाभिः** musk.

कुरंगमः The same as कुरंग q. v.

कुरचिल्लः A crab.

कुरटः A shoemaker.

कुरंटः, कुरंटकः, कुरंटिका The yellow amaranth.

कुरंडः Enlargement of the testicles or of the scrotum, hydrocele.

कुररः (**लः**) An osprey ; Y. 1. 174.

कुररी **1** A female osprey ; चक्रंद विग्ना कुररीव भूयः R. 14. 68. **2** An ewe. COMP. **–गणः** a flight of ospreys.

कुरवः (**बः**), **कुरव** (**ब**) **कं** A species of amaranth; कुरवका रवकारणतां ययुः R. 9. 29 ; Me. 78; Rs. 6. 18. **–वं** (**बं**), **–व** (**ब**) **कं** The flower of this tree; चूडापाशे नवकुरवकं Me. 65 ; प्रत्याख्यातविशेषकं कुरवकं श्यामावदातारुणं M. 3. 5.

कुरीरं A kind of head-dress for women.

कुरुः (pl.) N. of a country situated in the north of India about the site of the modern Delhi; श्रियः कुरूणामधिपस्य पालनीं Ki. 1. 1; चिराय तस्मिन् कुरवश्चकासते 1. 17. **2** The kings of this country. **–रुः** **1** A priest. **2** Boiled rice. –COMP. **–क्षेत्रं** N. of an extensive plain near Delhi, the scene of the great war between the Kauravas and Pâṇ*d*avas; धर्मक्षेत्रे कुरुक्षेत्रे समवेता युयुत्सवः Bg. 1. 1; Ms. 2. 19. **–जांगलं** = कुरुक्षेत्र q. v. **–राज्** *m.*, **–राजः** an epithet of Duryodhana. **–विस्तः** a weight of gold equal to about 700 Troy grains. **–वृद्धः** an epithet of Bhîshma.

कुरंटः A red species of amaranth. **–टी** A wooden doll or puppet.

कुरुलः A lock of hair, especially on the forehead.

कुरुवकः=कुरवक q. v.

कुरुविंदः—दं A ruby. **—दं** **1** Black salt. **2** A mirror.

कुर्कुटः **1** A cock. **2** Rubbish.

कुर्कुरः A dog; उपकर्तुमपि प्राप्तं निःस्वं मन्यंति कुर्कुरं Pt. 2. 90. v. l.

कुर्चिका=कूर्चिका q. v.

कुर्द्, कुर्दन See कूर्द्, कूर्दन.

कु (**कू**) **र्परः** **1** The knee. **2** The elbow.

कु (**कू**) **र्पासः, कु** (**कू**) **र्पासकः** A sort of bodice worn by women ; मनोज्ञकूर्पासकपीडितस्तनाः Rs 5. 8, 4. 16. v. l.

कुर्वत् *pres. p.* Doing &c. –*m.* **1** A servant. **2** A shoemaker.

कुलं **1** A race, family; निदानमिक्ष्वाकुकुलस्य संततेः R. 3. 1. **2** The residence of a family, a seat, house, an abode; वसन्नाषिकुलेषु सः R. 12. 25. **3** A high or noble family, noble descent; कुले जन्म Pt. 5. 2; कुलशीलसमन्वितः Ms. 7. 54, 62; so कुलजा, कुलकन्यका &c. **4** A herd, troops, flock, collection, multitude;

मृगकुलं रोमंथमभ्यस्यतु S. 2. 5; अलिकुलसंकुल Gît. 1; Si. 9. 71; so गो°, कृमि°, महिषी° &c. 5 A lot, gang, band (in a bad sense). 6 A country. 7 The body. 8 The front or fore part. –लः The head of a guild or corporation. –Comp. –अकुल *a.* 1 of a mixed character or origin. 2 middling. °तिथिः *m. f.* the second, sixth and the tenth lunar days of a fortnight in a month. °वारः Wednesday. –अंगना a respectable or high-born (chaste) woman. –अंगारः a man who ruins his family. –अचलः, –अद्रिः, –पर्वतः, –शैलः a principal mountain, one of a class of seven mountains which are supposed to exist in each division of the continent; their names are:—महेंद्रो मलयः सह्यः शुक्तिमान् ऋक्षपर्वतः । विंध्यश्च पारियात्रश्च सप्तैते कुलपर्वताः ॥ –अन्वित *a.* born in a noble family. –अभिमानः family pride. –आचारः a duty or custom peculiar to a family or caste. –आचार्यः 1 a family-priest or teacher. 2 a geneologist. –आलंबिन् *a.* maintaining a family. –ईश्वरः 1 the chief of a family. 2 N. of Siva. –उत्कट *a.* high-born. (–टः) a horse of a good breed. –उत्पन्न, –उद्गत, –उद्भव *a.* sprung from a noble family, high-born. –उद्वहः the head or perpetuator of a family; see उद्वह. –उपदेशः a family name. –कज्जलः one who is disgrace to his family. –कंटकः one who is a thorn or trouble to his family. –कन्यका, –कन्या a girl of high birth; विशुद्धमुग्धः कुलकन्यकाजनः Mâl. 7. 1; गृहे गृहे पुरुषाः कुलकन्यकाः समुद्वहंति Mâl. 7. –करः the founder of a family. –कर्मन् *n.* a custom peculiar to a family. –कलंकः one who is a disgrace to his family. –क्षयः 1 ruin of a family. 2 extinction of a family. –गिरिः, –भूभृत् *m.*, –पर्वतः, –शैलः see कुलाचल above. –घ्न *a.* ruining a family; दोषैरेतैः कुलघ्नानां Bg. 1. 42. –ज, –जात *a.* 1 well-born, of high birth. 2 ancestral, hereditary; Ki. 1. 31 (used in both senses.) –जनः a high-born or distinguished person. –तंतुः one who continues or perpetuates a family. –तिथिः *m. f.* an important lunar day, viz:—the 4th, 8th, 12th or 14th of a lunar fort-night. –तिलकः the glory of a family, one who does honour to his family. –दीपः –दीपकः the glory of a family. –दुहितृ *f* see कुलकन्या. –देवता a tutelary deity; the guardian deity of a family; Ku. 7. 27. –धर्मः a family custom, a duty or custom peculiar to a family; उत्सन्नकुलधर्माणां मनुष्याणां जनार्दन Bg. 1. 43; Ms. 1. 118; 8. 14 –धारकः a son. –धुर्यः (a son) able to support a family, a grown up son; न हि सति कुलधुर्ये सूर्यवंश्या गृहाय R. 7. 71. –नंदन *a.* gladdening or doing honour to a family. –नायिका a girl worshipped at the celebration of the orgies of left hand Sâktas. –नारी a high bred and virtuous woman. –नाशः 1 ruin or extinction of a family. 2 an apostate, reprobate, out-cast. 3 a camel. –परंपरा the series of generations comprising a race. –पतिः 1 the head or chief of a family. 2 a sage who feeds and teaches 10,000 pupils; thus defined:–मुनीनां दशसाहस्रं योऽन्नदानादिपोषणात् । अध्यापयति विप्रर्षिरसौ कुलपतिः स्मृतः ॥ अपि नाम कुलपतेरियमसवर्णक्षेत्रसंभवा स्यात् S. 1; R. 1. 95; U. 3. 48. –पांसुका a woman disgracing her family, an unchaste woman –पालिः, –पालिका, –पाली *f.* a chaste, high-born woman. –पुत्रः a nobly-born youth; इह सर्वस्वफलिनः कुलपुत्रमहाद्रुमाः Mk. 4. 10. –पुरुषः 1 a respectable or high-born man; कथं वति कुलपुरुषो वेश्याधरपल्लवं मनोज्ञमपि Bh. 1. 92. 2 an ancestor. –पूर्वगः an ancestor. –भार्या a virtuous wife. –भृत्या the nursing of a pregnant woman. –मर्यादा family honour or respectability. –मार्गः a family custom, the best way or the way of honesty. –योषित् –वधू *f.* a woman of good family and character. –वारः a principal day, (*i. e.* Tuesday and Friday). –विद्या knowledge handed down in a family, traditional knowledge. –विप्रः a family-priest. –वृद्धः an old and experienced member of a family. –व्रतः, –तं a family vow; गलितवयसामिक्ष्वाकूणामिदं हि कुलव्रतं R. 3. 70; विश्वसिन्नधुनाऽन्यः कुलव्रतं पालयिष्यति कः Bv. 1. 13. –श्रेष्ठिन् *m.* 1 the chief of a family or a guild. 2 an artisan of noble birth. –संख्या 1 family-respectability. 2 inclusion among respectable families; Ms. 3. 66. –संततिः *f.* posterity, descendants, continuation of a lineage; Ms. 5. 159. –संभव *a.* of respectable family. –सेवकः an excellent servant. –स्त्री a woman of good family, a noble woman; अधर्माभिभवात् कृष्ण प्रदुष्यंति कुलस्त्रियः Bg. 1. 41. –स्थितिः *f.* antiquity or prosperity of a family.

कुलक *a.* Of good family, of good birth. –कः 1 The chief of a guild. 2 Any artisan of eminent birth. 3 An ant-hill. —कं 1 A collection, multitude. 2 A number of verses in grammatical connection; (the number of verses ranging from 5 to 15 and the whole forming one sentence); *e. g.* see Si. 1. 1–10, R. 1. 5–9; so Ku. 1. 1–16.

कुलटा An unchaste woman; Mu. 6. 5; Y. 1. 215. –Comp. –पतिः a cuckold.

कुलतः *ind.* By birth.

कुलत्थः A kind of pulse.

कुलंधर *a.* One who continues or perpetuates a family.

कुलंभरः,–लः A thief.

कुलवत् *a.* Of respectable birth or origin; nobly born.

कुलायः, –यं 1 The nest of a bird; कूजत्क्लांतकपोतकुक्कुटकुलाः कूले कुलायद्रुमाः U. 2. 9, N. 1. 141. 2 The body. 3 A place or spot in general. 4 A woven texture, a web. 5 A case or receptacle. –Comp. –निलायः the act of sitting in a nest, hatching, brooding. –स्थः a bird.

कुलायिका A bird-cage, an aviary, dove-cot.

कुलालः 1 A potter; ब्रह्मा येन कुलालवन्नियमितो ब्रह्मांडभांडोदरे Bh. 2. 95. 2 A wild cock.

कुलिः A hand.

कुलिक *a.* Of a good family, well-born. —कः 1 A kinsman; Y. 2. 233. 2 The chief or head of a guild. 3 An artist of high birth. –Comp. –वेला certain portions of time on each day on which it is improper to begin any good business.

कुलिंगः 1 A bird (in general). 2 A sparrow.

कुलिन् *a.* (नी *f.*) Of good family, high-born. —*m.* A mountain.

कुलिंदः (pl.) N. of a country and its rulers.

कुलिरः, -रं 1 A crab. 2 The 4th sign of the zodiac, Cancer.

कुलि (ली) शः, –शं 1 The thunder-bolt of Indra: वृत्रस्य हंतुः कुलिशं कुंठिता श्रीव लक्ष्यते Ku. 2. 20; अवेदनाज्ञं कुलिशक्षतानां 1. 20; R. 3. 68; 4. 88; Amaru. 66. 2 The point or end of a thing; Me. 61. –Comp. –धरः, –पाणिः an epithet of Indra. –नायकः a particular mode of sexual enjoyment.

कुली A wife's elder sister.

कुलीन *a.* Of high descent, of a good family, well-born; दिव्ययोषितामिवाकुलीनां K. 11. —नः A horse of good breed.

कुलीनसं Water.

कुलीरः, –रकः 1 A crab. 2 The fourth sign of the zodiac, Cancer.

कुलुकगुंजा A fire brand.

कुलूतः (pl.) N. of a country and its rulers.

कुल्माषं Gruel. —षः A kind of grain. –Comp. –अभिषुतं gruel.

कुल्य *a.* 1 Relating to a family, race, or corporation. 2 Well-born. —ल्यः A respectable man. —ल्यं 1 Friendly inquiry after family affairs, (condolence, congratulation &c.). 2 A bone; Mv. 2. 16. 3 Flesh. 4 A winnowing basket. —ल्या 1 A virtuous woman. 2 A small river, canal, stream; कुल्यांभोभिः पवनचपलैः शाखिनो धौतमूलाः S. 1. 15; कुल्याभिरुद्यानपादपान् R. 12. 3, 7. 49. 3 A dike, trench. 4 A measure of grain equal to 8 dronas.

कुवं 1 A flower. 2 A lotus.

कुवर See तुवर.

कुवलं 1 The water-lily. 2 A pearl. 3 Water.

कुवलयं 1 The blue water-lily कुवलयदलस्निग्धैरंगैर्ददौ नयनोत्सवं U. 3. 22. 2 A water-lily in general. 3 The earth (-*m.* also).

कुवलयिनी 1 The blue water-lily plant. 2 An assemblage of lotuses. 3 A place abounding in lotuses. 4 The lotus-plant.

कुवाद *a.* 1 Detracting, undervaluing, censorious. 2 Low, vile, mean.

कुविकः (pl.) N. of a country.

कुविं (विं) दः 1 A weaver; कुविंदस्त्वं तावत्पटयसि गुणग्राममभितः K. P. 7. 2 N. of the weaver caste.

कुवेणी 1 A basket to hold fish (when caught), fish-basket 2 A badly arranged tress of hair.

कुवेलं A lotus.

कुशः 1 A kind of grass considered holy and forming an essential requisite of several religious ceremonies; पवित्रार्थे इमे कुशाः Srâddha Mantra कुशापूतं प्रवयास्तु विष्टरं R. 8. 18. 1. 49. 95. 2 N. of the elder son of Râma. [He was one of the twin sons of Rama, born after Sita had been ruthlessly abandoned in the forest; yet he was the elder of the two in point of first seeing the light of this world. He, with Lava, was brought up by the sage Valmiki, and the two boys were taught to repeat the Ramayana, the epic of the poet Kusa was made by Rama king of Kusavati and he lived there for some time after his father's death. But the presiding deity of the old capital Ayoddhya presented herself to him in his dream and besought him not to slight her. Kusa then returned to Ayoddhya; see R. 16. 3-42] —शं Water; as in कुशेशय q. v. -COMP. -अग्रं the sharp point of a blade of the Kusa grass hence often used in comp. in the sense of 'sharp', 'shrewd' 'penetrating' as intellect °बुद्धि *a.* having a penetrating intellect, sharp, shrewd; (अपि) कुशाग्रबुद्धे कुशली गुरुस्ते R. 5. 4. -अग्रीय *a.* penetrating, sharp. -अंगुरीयं a ring of Kusa grass worn at religious ceremonies. -आसनं a seat or mat of Kusa grass. -स्थलं N. of a place in the north of India; Ve. 1.

कुशल *a.* 1 Right. proper, good, auspicious; Si. 16. 41; Bg. 18. 10. 2 Happy, prosperous. 3 Able, skilful, clever, proficient, well-versed; with loc. or in comp.; दंडनीत्यां च कुशलं Y. 1. 313, 2. 181; Ms. 7. 190; R. 3. 12. —लं 1 Welfare, a happy or prosperous condition, happiness; पप्रच्छ कुशलं राज्ये राज्याश्रममुनिं मुनिः R. 1. 58; अव्यापन्नः कुशलमबले पृच्छति त्वां Me. 101; अपि कुशलं भवतः 'are you doing well' (how do you do?) 2 Virtue. 3 Cleverness, ability. -COMP. -काम *a.* desirous of happiness -प्रश्नः friendly inquiry after a person's health or welfare. -बुद्धि *a.* wise, intelligent, shrewd, sharp.

कुशलिन् *a.* (नी *f.*) Happy, doing well, prosperous; अथ भगवाँल्लोकानुग्रहाय कुशली काश्यपः S. 5; R. 5. 4; Me. 112.

कुशा 1 A rope. 2 A bridle.

कुशावती N. of a city, the capital of Kusa, Râma's son; see कुश.

कुशिक *a.* Squint-eyed. —कः N. of the grand-father of Visvâmitra (or according to some accounts, of the father of विश्वामित्र). 2 A plough-share. 3 Sediment of oil.

कुशी A plough-share.

कुशीलवः 1 A bard, singer; Ms. 8. 65, 102. 2 An actor, a dancer; तत्सर्वे कुशीलवाः संगीतप्रयोगेण मत्समीहितसंपादनाय प्रवर्तंतां Mâl. 1; तत्किमिति नारंभयासि कुशीलवैः सह संगीतकं Ve. 1 3 A news-monger. 4 An epithet of Vâlmîki.

कुशुंभः The water-pot of an ascetic.

कुशूलः 1 Granary, cupboard, store-room; को धन्यो बहुभिः पुत्रैः कुशूलापूरणाढकैः H. Pr. 20. 2 A fire made of chaff.

कुशेशयं A water-lily, a lotus in general, भूयात्कुशेशयरजोमृदुरेणुरस्याः (पंथाः) S. 4. 10; R. 6. 18. —यः The Indian crane or Sârasa bird.

कुष् 9 P. (कुष्णाति, कुषित) 1 To tear, extract, pull or draw out; शिवाः कुष्णंति मांसानि Bk. 18 12; 17. 10, 7. 95 2 To test, examine. 3 To shine. -WITH निस् to extract, tear, draw out; उपांतयोर्निष्कुषितं विहंगैः R. 7. 50; Bk. 9. 30.; 5. 42; so काकैर्निष्कुषितं श्वभिः कवलितं गोमायुभिर्लुंठितं Gangâshṭaka.

कुषाकुः 1 The son. 2 Fire. 3 An ape, a monkey.

कुष्ठः,-ष्ठं Leprosy (of which there are 18 varieties); गलत्कुष्ठाभिभूताय च Bh. 1. 90. -COMP. -अरिः 1 sulphur. 2 N. of several plants.

कुष्ठिन् *a.* (नी *f.*) -कुष्ठित *a.* Affected with leprosy.

कुष्मांडः 1 A kind of pumpkin gourd. 2 A false conception.

कुष्मांडकः A kind of pumpkin gourd.

कुस् 4 P. (कुस्यति, कुसित) 1 To embrace. 2 To surround.

कुसितः 1 An inhabited country. 2 One who lives on usury; see कुसीद below.

कुसी (सि) दः (Also written as कुशी-षी-द) A money-lender, a usurer. —दं 1 Any loan or thing lent to be repaid with interest. 2 Lending money, usury, the profession of usury; कुसीदाद् दारिद्र्यं परकरगतग्रंथिशमनात् Pt. 1. 11; -Ms. 1. 90; 8. 410; Y. 1. 119. -COMP. -पथः usury, usurious interest; any interest exceeding 5 per cent. -वृद्धिः *f.* interest on money; कुसीदवृद्धिर्द्वैगुण्यं नात्येति सकृदाहृता Ms. 8. 151.

कुसीदा A female usurer.

कुसीदायी The wife of a usurer.

कुसीदिकः, कुसीदिन् *m.* A usurer.

कुसुमं 1 A flower; उदेति पूर्वं कुसुमं ततः फलं S. 7. 30. 2 Menstrual discharge. 3 A fruit. -COMP. -अंजनं the calx of brass used as collyrium. -अंजलिः a handful of flowers. -अधिपः,-अधिराज् *m.* the Champaka tree (bearing yellow fragrant flowers); -अवचायः gathering flowers; अन्यत्र यूयं कुसुमावचायं कुरुध्वमत्रास्मि करोमि सख्यः K. P. 3. -अवतंसकं a chaplet. -अस्त्रः, -आयुधः, -इषुः, -बाणः, -शरः 1 a flowery arrow. 2 N. of the god of love; अभिनवः कुसुमेषुव्यापारः Mâl. 1 (where the word may also be read as कुसुमेषु व्यापारः); तस्मै नमो भगवते कुसुमायुधाय Bh. 1. 1; Rs. 6. 33. Ch. P. 20, 23; R. 7. 61; Si. 8. 70, 3. 2; कुसुमशरबाणभावेन Gît. 10. -आकरः 1 a garden. 2 a nosegay. 3 vernal season; ऋतूनां कुसुमाकरः Bg. 10. 35; so Bv. 1. 48 -आत्मकं saffron. -आसवं 1 honey. 2 a kind of spirituous liquor (prepared from flowers). -उज्ज्वल *a.* brilliant with blossoms. -कार्मुकः, -चापः,- धन्वन् *m.* epithets of the god of love; कुसुमचापमतेजयदंशुभिः R. 9. 39; Rs. 6. 27. -चित *a.* heaped with flowers. -पुरं N. of the town of Pâtaliputra; कुसुमपुराभियोगं प्रत्यनुदासीनो राक्षसः Mu. 2. -लता a creeper in blossom. -शयनं a bed of flowers; V. 3. 10. -स्तबकः a nosegay, bouquet; कुसुमस्तबकस्येव द्वे गती स्तो मनस्विनां Bh. 2 33.

कुसुमवती A woman in her courses.

कुसुमित *a.* Flowered, furnished with flowers.

कुसुमालः A thief.

कुसुंभः -भं 1 Safflower; कुसुंभारुणं चारु चेलं वसाना Jag.; R. 6. 6. 2 Saffron. 3 The water-pot of an ascetic. —भं Gold. -भः Outward affection (compared with the colour of safflower).

कुसूलः A granary, store-house (for corn &c.).

कुसृतिः *f.* Fraud, cheating, deceit.

कुस्तुभः 1 An epithet of Vishṇu. 2 The ocean.

कुहः Kubera, the god of riches.

कुहकः A cheat, rogue, juggler. —कं,-का Jugglery, deception. -COMP. -कार *a.* conjuring, cheating. -चकित *a.* afraid of a trick, suspicious, cautious, wary; H 4. 102. -स्वनः, -स्वरः a cock.

कुहनः 1 A mouse. 2 A snake. —नं 1 A small earthen vessel. 2 A glass vessel.

कुहना, कुहनिका Interested performance of religious austerities, hypocrisy (दंभ).

कुहरं 1 A cavity, hollow; as in नाभिकुहर, आस्य° &c. 2 The ear. 3 The throat. 4 Proximity. 5 Copulation.

कुहरितं 1 Sound in general. 2 The cry of the (Indian) cuckoo. 3 A sound uttered in copulation.

कुहुः, कुहूः *f.* 1 New moon day, *i. e.* the last day of a lunar month when the moon is invisible ; करगतैव गता यदियं कुहूः N. 4. 57. 2 The deity that presides over this day; Ms. 3. 86. 3 The cry of the (Indian) cuckoo पिकेन रोषारुणचक्षुषा मुहुः कुहूरुताहूयत चंद्रवैरिणी N. 1. 100 ; उन्मिलिंति कुहूः कुहूरिति कलोत्तालाः पिकानां गिरः Git. 1. –COMP. **–कुंठः,–मुखः, –रवः, –शब्दः** the (Indian) cuckoo.

कू 1 6. A. (कवते, कुवते) ; 9. U. (कु-कू-नाति, कु-कू-नीते) 1 To sound, make noise, cry out in distress ; खगाश्रुकुविरेऽशुभं Bk. 14. 20; 1. 20 ; 14. 5 ; 15. 26 ; 16. 29.

कूः *f.* A female imp.

कूचः The female breast, especially that of a young or unmarried woman ; see कुच.

कूचिका, कूची 1 A small brush of hair, a pencil. 2 A key.

कूज् 1 P. (कूजति, कूजित) To make any inarticulate sound, hum, coo, warble; कूजंतं राम रामेति मधुरं मधुराक्षरं Râm: पुंस्कोकिलो यन्मधुरं चुकूज Ku. 3. 32; Rs. 6. 22; R. 2. 12 ; N. 1. 127. WITH नि, परि or वि to coo, to make an indistinct noise.

कूजः, कूजनं, कूजितं 1 Cooing, warbling. 2 The rattling of wheels.

कूट *a.* 1 False; as in कूटाः स्युः पूर्वसाक्षिणः Y. 1. 80. 2 Immovable, steady. **—टः, –टं** 1 Fraud, illusion, deception. 2 A trick, fraudulent or roguish scheme. 3 A puzzling question, knotty or intricate point, as in कूटश्लोक, कूटान्योक्ति. 4 Falsehood, untruth; oft. used in comp. with the force of an adjective ; °वचनं false or deceitful words; °तुला, °मानं &c. 5 A summit or peak of a mountain ; वर्धयन्निव तत्कूटानुद्धतैर्धातुरेणुभिः R. 4. 71, Me. 113 6 Any projection or prominence. 7 The bone of the forehead with its projections, the crown of the head. 8 A horn. 9 End, corner ; Y. 3. 96. 10 Head, chief. 11 A heap, mass, multitude ; अभ्रकूटं 'a heap of clouds' ; so अन्नकूटं 'a heap of food'. 12 A hammer, an iron mallet. 13 A plough-share, the body of a plough. 14 A trap for catching deer. 15 A concealed weapon, as a dagger in a woollen case or a sword in a stick. 16 A water-jar. **—टः** 1 A house, dwelling. 2 An epithet of Agastya. –COMP. **–अक्षः** a false or loaded die ; कूटाक्षोपधिदेविनः Y. 2. 202. **–अगारं** an apartment on the top of a house. **–अर्थः** ambiguity of meaning. °**भाषिता** a tale, fiction. **–उपायः** a fraudulent plan, trick, strategem. **–कारः** a rogue, a false witness. **–कृत्** *a.* 1 cheating, deceiving. 2 forging a document ; Y. 2. 70. 3 bribing. (*–m.*) 1 a man of the writer caste (कायस्थ). 2 an epithet of Siva. **–कार्षापणः** a false कार्षापण q. v. **–खड्गः** a swordstick. **–छद्मन्** *m.* a cheat. **–तुला** a false pair of scales. **–धर्म** *a.* where falsehood is considered a duty (as a place, house, country &c.). **–पाकलः** bilious fever to which elephants are subject (हस्तिवातज्वर) ; अचिरेण वैकृतविवर्तदारुणः कलभं कठोर इव कूटपाकलः (अभिहंति) Mâl. 1. 39; (also sometimes written as कूटपालकः). **–पालकः** a potter, a potter's kiln. **–पाशः,–बंधः** a trap, snare; R. 13. 39. **–मानं** a false measure or weight. **–मोहनः** an epithet of Skanda. **–यंत्रं** a trap, a snare for deer, birds &c. **–युद्धं** treacherous or unfair warfare; R. 17. 69. **–शाल्मलिः** *f. m.* 1 a species of the Sâlmali tree. 2 a kind of tree with sharp thorns (regarded as one of the several instruments–perhaps a club–with which the wicked are tortured in the world of Yama); see R. 12. 95 and Malli. thereon. **–शासनं** a forged grant or decree. **–साक्षिन्** *m.* a false witness. **–स्थ** *a.* standing at the top, occupying the highest place (said of a person who stands at the head in a geneological table). (**स्थः**) the supreme soul (immovable, unchangeable, and perpetually the same); Bg. 6. 8; 12. 3. **–स्वर्णं** counterfeit gold.

कूटकं 1 Fraud, deceit, trick. 2 Elevation, prominence. 3 The body of a plough, a plough-share. –COMP. **–आख्यानं** an invented tale.

कूटशः *ind.* In heaps or multitudes.

कूड्यं—कुड्य q. v.

कूण् 10 U. (कूणयति-ते, कूणित) 1 To speak, converse 2 To contract, close (said to be Atm. in this sense).

कूणिका 1 The horn of any animal. 2 The peg of a lute.

कूणित *a.* Shut, closed.

कूद्दालः Mountain ebony.

कूपः 1 A well ; कूपे पश्य पयोनिधावपि घटो गृह्णाति तुल्यं जलं Bh. 2. 49 ; so नितरां नीचोस्मीति त्वं खेदं कूप मा कदापि कृथाः । अत्यंतसरसहृदयो यतः परेषां गुणग्रहीतासि Bv. 1. 9. 2 A hole, cave, hollow, cavity ; as in जघनकूप. 3 A leather oil-vessel. 4 A mast ; क्षोणीनौकूपदंडः Dk. 1. –COMP.–**अंकः, –अंगः** horripilation. **–कच्छपः, –मंडूकः –की** (lit.) a tortoise or frog in a well. (fig.) an inexperienced person, one who has had no experience of the world at large, a man of limited ideas who knows only his own neighbourhood; oft. used as a term of reproach. **–यंत्रं** a water-wheel, a contrivance for raising water from a well °**यंत्रघटी–घटिका** a bucket or pot attached to the water-wheel to draw up water. °**यंत्रघटिकान्याय** see under न्याय.

कूपकः 1 A well (temporary). 2 A hole, cave, cavity. 3 The hollow below the loins. 4 A stake to which a boat is moored. 5 The mast of a ship. 6 A funeral pile. 7 A hole under a funeral pile. 8 A leather oil-vessel. 9 A rock or tree in the midst of a river.

कूपा (वा) रः The ocean.

कूपी 1 A small well. 2 A flask, bottle. 3 The navel.

कूब (व) र *a.* (**री** *f.*) 1 Beautiful, agreeable. 2 Hump-backed. **—रः,–रं** The pole of a carriage to which the yoke is fixed. **–रः** A hump-backed man. **– री** 1 A carriage covered with a cloth or blanket. 2 The pole of a carriage to which the yoke is fixed; Ve. 4.

कूरः,–रं Food, boiled rice; इतश्च कूरच्युततैलमिश्रं पिंडं हस्ती प्रतिग्राह्यते मात्रपुरुषैः Mk. 4.

कूर्चः, –र्चं 1 A bunch of any thing, a bundle. 2 A handful of Kusa grass. 3 A Peacock's feather. 4 The beard; आगतमनध्यायकारणं सविशेषभूतमद्य जीर्णकूर्चानां U. 4 ; or पूरयितव्यमनेन चित्रफलकं लंबकूर्चानां तापसानां कदंबैः S. 6. 5 The tip of the thumb and the middle finger brought in contact so as to pinch &c. 6 The upper part of the nose, the part (or hair) between the eyebrows. 7 A brush. 8 Deceit, fraud. 9 Boasting, bragging. 10 Hypocrisy. **–र्चः** 1 The head. 2 A store-room. –COMP. **–शीर्षः, –शेखरः** the cocoa-nut tree.

कूर्चिका 1 A painting brush or pencil. 2 A key. 3 A bud, blossom. 4 Inspissated milk. 5 A needle.

कूर्द् 1 U. (कूर्दति-ते, कूर्दित) 1 To leap, jump. 2 To frolic; वत्रश्चराजुघूर्णश्च स्येमुश्चकूर्दिरे तथा Bk. 14. 77, 9; 15. 45. WITH उद् to jump up, leap up.

कूर्दनं 1 Leaping. 2 Playing, sporting. **–नी** 1 A festival in honour of Kâmadeva, held on the fifteenth day of Chaitra. 2 The full moon day in Chaitra.

कूर्पः The part between the eyebrows.

कूर्परः 1 The elbow ; *Si.* 20. 19. 2 The knee.

कूर्मः 1 A tortoise; गृहेत्कूर्म इवांगानि रक्षेद्विवरमात्मनः Ms. 7. 105; Bg. 2. 58.

2 Vishṇu in his second or Kúrma incarnation. –COMP. —अवतारः the Kûrma incarnation of Vishṇu; cf. Gît. 1:–क्षितिरतिविपुलतरे तव तिष्ठति पृष्ठे धरणिधरणकिणचक्रगरिष्ठे केशव धृतकच्छपरूप जय जगदीश हरे ॥ –पृष्ठं, –पृष्ठकं 1 the back or shell of a tortoise. 2 a lid or cover of a dish. –राजः Vishṇu in his shape of a tortoise in his second incarnation.

कूलं 1 A shore, bank; राधामाधवयोर्जयंति यमुनाकूले रहःकेलयः Gît. 1; नदी वोभयकूलभाक् R. 12. 35, 68. 2 A slope, declivity. 3 Skirt, edge, border, proximity; कुलायकूलेषु विलुठ्य तेषु ते N. 1. 141. 4 A pond. 5 The rear of an army. 6 A heap, mound. –COMP. –चर *a.* frequenting or grazing on the banks of a river. –भूः *f.* the land on a bank. –हंडकः, –हुंडकः an eddy.

कूलंकष *a.* Tearing away or undermining the bank; कूलंकषेव सिंधुः प्रसन्नमंभस्तटतरुं च *S.* 5. 21. –षः The current or stream of a river. –षा A river.

कूलंधय *a.* Kissing, *i. e.* bordering on the bank of a river.

कूलमुद्रुज *a.* Breaking down banks, (as rivers, elephants &c.); R. 4. 22.

कूलमुद्वह *a.* Tearing up or carrying away the bank; Mâl. 5. 19.

कूष्मांडः A kind of pumpkin gourd.

कूहा A fog, mist.

कृ I. 5 U. (कृणोति-कृणुते) To hurt, injure, kill. –II. 8 U. (करोति, कुरुते, कृत) 1 To do (in general); तात किं करवाण्यहं. 2 To make; गणिकामवरोधमकरोत् Dk; नृपेण चक्रे युवराजशब्दभाक् R. 3. 45; युवराजः कृतः &c. 3 To manufacture, shape, prepare; कुंभकारो घटं करोति; कटं करोति &c. 4 To build, create; गृहं कुरु; सभां कुरु मदर्थे भोः. 5 To produce, cause, engender; रतिमुभयप्रार्थना कुरुते *S.* 2. 1. 6 To form, arrange; अंजलिं करोति; कपोतहस्तकं कृत्वा. 7 To write, compose; चकार सुमनोहरं शास्त्रं Pt. 1. 8 To perform, be engaged in; पूजां करोति. 9 To tell, narrate; इति बहुविधाः कथाः कुर्वन् &c. 10 To carry out, execute, obey; एवं क्रियते युष्मदादेशः Mâl. 1; or करिष्यामि वचस्तव or शासनं मे कुरुष्व &c. 11 To bring about, accomplish, effect; सत्संगतिः कथय किं न करोति पुंसां Bh. 2. 23. 12 To throw or let out, discharge, emit; मूत्रं कृ to discharge urine, make water; so पुरीषं कृ to void excrement. 13 To assume, put on, take; स्त्रीरूपं कृत्वा; नानारूपाणि कुर्वाणः Y. 3. 162. 14 To send forth, utter; मानुषीं गिरं कृत्वा, कलरवं कृत्वा &c. 15 To place or put on (with loc.) कंठे हारमकरोत् K. 212; पाणिमुरसि कृत्वा &c. 16 To entrust (with some duty), appoint; अध्यक्षान् विविधान्कुर्यात्तत्र तत्र विपश्चितः Ms. 7. 81. 17 To cook (as food) as in कृतान्नं. 18 To think, regard, consider; दृष्टिस्तृणीकृतजगत्त्रयसत्त्वसारा U. 6. 19. 19 To take (as in the hand); कुरु करे गुरुमेकमयोघनं N. 4. 59. 20 To make a sound, as in खात्कृत्य, फूत्कृत्य भुंक्ते; so वषट्कृ, स्वाहाकृ &c. 21 To pass, spend (time); वर्षाणि दश चक्रुः spent; क्षणं कुरु wait a moment. 22 To direct towards, turn the attention to, resolve on; (with loc. or dat.); नाधर्मे कुरुते मनः Ms. 12. 118; नगरगमनाय मतिं न करोति *S.* 2. 23 To do a thing for another (either for his advantage or injury); यद्नेन कृतं मयि, असौ किं मे करिष्यति &c. 24 To use, employ, make use of; किं तया क्रियते धेन्वा Pt. 1. 25 To divide, break into parts (with adverbs ending in धा); द्विधा कृ to divide into two parts; शतधा कृ, सहस्रधा कृ &c. 26 To cause to become subject to, reduce completely to (a particular condition, with adverbs ending in सात्); आत्मसात् कृ to subject or appropriate to oneself; R. 8. 2; भस्मसात् कृ to reduce to ashes. This root is often used with nouns, adjectives and indeclinables to form verbs from them, somewhat like the English affixes 'en' or '(i) fy', in the sense of 'making a person or thing to be what it previously is not'; *e. g.* कृष्णीकृ to make that which is not already black, black, *i. e.* blacken; so श्वेतीकृ to whiten; घनीकृ to solidify; विरलीकृ to rarefy &c. &c. Sometimes these formations take place in other senses also; *e. g.* क्रोडीकृ 'to clasp to the bosom', embrace; भस्मकृ to reduce to ashes; प्रवणीकृ to incline, bend; तृणीकृ to value as little as straw; मंदीकृ to slacken, make slow; so शूलाकृ to roast on the end of pointed lances; सुखाकृ to please; समयाकृ to spend time &c. *N. B.* This root by itself admits of either Pada; but it is Atm. generally with prepositions in the following senses:— (1) doing injury to; (2) censure, blame; (3) serving; (4) outraging, acting violently or rashly; (5) preparing, changing the condition of, turning into; (6) reciting. (7) employing, using; see P. 1. 3. 32 and "Student's guide to Sanskrit composition" § 338. *Note.* The root कृ is of the most frequent application in Sanskrit literature, and its senses are variously modified, or almost infinitely extended according to the noun with which the root is connected; *e. g.* पदं कृ to set foot (fig. also); आश्रमे पदं करिष्यसि *S.* 4. 19; क्रमेण कृतं मम वपुषि नवयौवनेन पदं K. 141; मनसा कृ to think of, meditate; मनसि कृ to think; दृष्ट्वा मनस्येवमकरोत् K. 136; or to resolve or determine; सख्यं, मैत्रीं कृ to form friendship with; अस्त्राणि कृ to practise the use of weapons; दंडं कृ to inflict punishment; हृदये कृ to pay heed to; कालं कृ to die; मतिं–बुद्धिं कृ to think of, intend, mean; उदकं कृ to offer libations of water to the Manes; चिरं कृ to delay; दर्दुरं कृ to p'ay on the lute; नखानि कृ to clean the nails; कन्यां कृ to outrage or violate a maiden; विनाकृ to separate from, to be abandoned by; as in मदनेन विनाकृता रतिः Ku. 4 21; मध्ये कृ to place in the middle, to have reference to; मध्येकृत्य स्थितं क्रथकैशिकान् M. 5. 2; वशे कृ to win over, place in subjection, subdue; चमत्कृ to cause surprise; make an exhibition or a show; सत्कृ to honour, treat with respect; तिर्यक्कृ to place aside. —*Caus.* (कारयति-ते) To cause to do, perform, make, execute &c; आज्ञां कारय रक्षोभिः Bk. 8. 84; भृत्यं भृत्येन वा कटं कारयति Sk. —*Desid.* (चिकीर्षति-ते) to wish to do &c. With **अंगी** 1 to accept, betake oneself to; लवंगीकुरंगीदृगंगीकरोतु Jag.; दक्षिणामाशामंगीकृत्य K. 121. 2 to confess, acknowledge, own, admit. 3 to promise to do, undertake; किं त्वंगीकृतमुत्सृजन्कृपणवच्छ्लाघ्यो जनो लज्जते Mu. 2. 18. 4 to subdue, make one's own, favour; Amaru. 52 –अति to exceed, surpass. –अधि 1 to be entitled to, have a right; to authorise, to qualify for the discharge of some duty; नैवाध्यकारिष्महि वेदवृत्ते Bk. 2. 34; Ki. 4. 25. 2 to aim at, have reference to; (अधिकृत्य is often used in the sense of 'with reference to,' 'referring to', 'regarding', 'concerning', 'on the subject of'; ग्रीष्मसमयमधिकृत्यगीयताम् *S.* 1; शकुंतलामधिकृत्य ब्रवीमि *S.* 2; R. 11. 62.) 3 (A.) to bear; अधिचक्रे न यं हरिः Bk. 8. 20. 4 to overpower or subdue, be superior to. 5 to refrain or desist from. –अनु to do after, follow; especially to imitate (with acc. or gen.); शैलाधिपस्यानुचकार लक्ष्मीं Bk. 2. 8; Ms. 2. 199; श्यामतया हरेरिवानुकुर्वतीं K. 10; अनुकरोति भगवतो नारायणस्य 6. –अप 1 to drag away, remove, insult by dragging away; योपचक्रे वनात्सीतां Bk. 8. 20. 2 to hurt, injure, wrong, harm, do harm or injury to (with gen. of person); न किंचिन्मया तस्यापकर्तुं शक्यं Pt. 1. –अपा 1 to drive away, discard, remove, dispel; तन्नैशं तिमिरमपाकरोति चंद्रः *S.* 6. 29; न पुत्रवात्सल्यमपाकरिष्यति Ku. 5. 14. 2 to cast off, reject, put aside, give up; शिवा भुजच्छेदमपाचकार R. 7. 50. –अभ्यंतरी 1 to initiate in. 2 to make a friend of; (see under अभ्यंतर). –अलं to adorn, decorate, grace; उभावलंचक्रतुरंचिताभ्यां तपोवनावृत्तिपथं गताभ्याम् R. 11. 18; कतमो वंशोऽलंकृतो जन्मना *S.* 1. –आ (*Caus.*) 1 to call, cause to come, invite; आकारयैनमत्र. 2 to bring near. –आविस् to manifest or make visible, show, display; (see under आविस्.) –उप (Pres. उपकरोति) 1 (*a*) to befriend, serve, assist, favour, help, oblige; (oft. with gen. sometimes loc. of the person obliged); सा लक्ष्मीरुपकुरुते यया परेषां Bk. 8. 18; आत्मनश्चोपकर्तुं Me. 101; Si. 20. 74; Ms. 8. 394. (*b*) to attend or wait upon, serve. **2** (Pres. उपस्करोति). (*a*) to adorn, grace, decorate. (*b*) to make efforts (with gen. of a thing); Bk. 8. 19, 119. (*c*) to prepare, elaborate, perfect, refine. **–उपा 1** to deliver, give. **2** to perform a (preparatory) rite; Ms. 4. 95; see उपाकर्मन्. **3** to fetch, bring. **4** to begin. **–उरी, उररी, उरूरी, ऊरी** or **ऊररी** to accept, see अंगीकृ above; R. 15. 70; see उरी also. **–तिरस् 1** to abuse, revile, contemn, despise. **2** to surpass, excel, conquer; see under तिरस्. **–त्वं** to thou anybody (as an insult). **–दक्षिणी** or **–प्रदक्षिणी** to walk round something keeping the right side towards it; प्रदक्षिणीकुरुष्व सद्योहुताग्नीन् S. 4.; प्रदक्षिणीकृत्य हुतं हुताशनमनंतरं भर्तुररुंधती च । R. 2. 71. **–दुस्** to act wrongly. **–धिक्** to reproach, revile, contemn; see under धिक्. **–नमस्** to salute, adore; मुनित्रयं नमस्कृत्य Sk.; see under नमस्. **–नि** to injure, wrong. **–निस् 1** to remove, drive away; Ms. 11. 53. **2** to break, frustrate; Bk. 15. 54. **–निरा 1** to expel, drive away, repudiate; Bk. 6. 100; R. 14. 57. **2** to refute (as an opinion.) **3** to give up, abandon. **4** to destroy completely, annihilate. **5** to revile, contemn, slight. **–न्यक्** to insult, contemn. **–परा** (P.) to reject, disregard, slight, take no notice of; तां हनूमान् पराकुर्वन्नगमत् पुष्पकं प्रति Bk. 8. 50. **–परि** (परिकरोति) **1** to surround. **2** (परिष्करोति) to adorn, decorate; रथो हेमपरिष्कृतः Mb. (fig.) to refine, polish (as words) **–पुरस् 1** to place in front; राजा शकुंतलां पुरस्कृत्य वक्तव्यः S. 4; हते जरति गांगेये पुरस्कृत्य शिखंडिनं Ve. **2.** 18; see under पुरस्. **–प्र 1** to do, perform, commence (used much in the same sense as कृ); जानन्नपि नरो दैवात्प्रकरोति विगर्हितं Pt. 4. 35; Bk. 2. 36; Rs. 1. 6; Ms. 8. 54, 60; 8, 239, Amaru. 13. **2** to assault, outrage, insult; Bk. 8. 19. **3** to honour, worship. **–प्रति 1** to requite, pay back, repay; पूर्वं कृतार्थो मित्राणां नार्थं प्रतिकरोति यः । Râm. **2** to remedy; व्याधिमिच्छामि ते ज्ञातुं प्रतिकुर्यां हि तत्र वै Mb. **3** to give back, restore, replace; Ms. 9. 285. **4** to retaliate; R. 12. 94. **–प्रमाणी 1** to confide, believe. **2** to regard as authority, obey; शासनं तरुभिरपि प्रमाणीकृतं S. 6. **3** to fix upon, dispense, deal or mete out; दैवेन प्रभुणा स्वयं जगति यद्यस्य प्रमाणीकृतं Bh 2. 121. **–प्रादुस्** to make manifest, display, make visible, show; see under प्रादुस्. **–प्रत्युप** to requite, return (an obligation). **–वि** to alter, change, affect; विकारहेतौ सति विक्रियंते येषां न चेतांसि त एव धीराः Ku. 1. 59; R. 13. 42. **2** to disfigure, deform; विकृताकृति Ms. 9. 52. **3** to create, produce, effect Ms. 1. 75; नास्य विघ्नं विकुर्वंति दानवाः Mb. **4** to disturb, harm, injure (Atm.); हिनान्यनुपकर्तॄणि प्रवृद्धानि विकुर्वते R. 17. 58. **5** to utter (sound) विकुर्वाणः स्वरानद्य Bk. **8.** 20. **6** to be faithless (as a wife). **–विनि** to hurt, injure. **–विप्र 1** to tease, trouble, harass, harm; किं सत्त्वानि विप्रकरोषि S. 7; Ku. **2.** 1. **2** to wrong, ill-treat; S. 4. 17. **3** to affect, cause a change in; कमपरमवशं न विप्रकुर्युः Ku. 6. 95. **–व्या 1** to make manifest, clear up; नामरूपे व्याकरवाणि Ch Up. **2** to propound, explain. **3** to tell, narrate; तन्मे सर्वं भगवान् व्याकरोतु Mb. **–सं 1** (संकुरुते) (*a*) to commit; ये पक्षापरपक्षदोषसहिताः पापानि संकुर्वते Mk. 9. 4. (b) to manufacture, prepare. (*c*) to do, perform. **2** (संस्कुरुते) (*a*) to adorn, grace; ककुभं समस्कुरुत माघवनीं Si. 9. 25. (*b*) to refine, polish; वाण्येका समलंकरोति पुरुषं या संस्कृता धार्यते । Bh. 2. 19; Si. 14. 50. (*c*) to consecrate by repeating sacred Mantras; Ms. 5. 36. (*d*) to purify (a person) by scriptural ceremonies, perform purificatory ceremonies over (a person); संचस्कारोभयप्रीत्या मैथिलेयौ यथाविधि R. **15.** 31; Y. 2. 124. **–साची** to turn aside or askance; साचीकृता चारुतरेण तस्थौ Ku. 3. 68; R. 6. 14.

कृकः The throat.

कृकणः (रः) A kind of partridge.

कृक (कु) लासः A lizard, chameleon.

कृकवाकुः 1 A cock. **2** A peacock. **3** A lizard. –Comp. **–ध्वजः** an epithet of Kârtikeya.

कृकाटिका 1 The raised and straight part of the neck. **2** The back of the neck.

कृच्छ्र *a*. **1** Causing trouble, painful. Ms. 6. 78. **2** Bad, miserable, evil; **3** Wicked, sinful. **4** Being in a difficult or painful situation. **–च्छ्रः, -च्छ्रं 1** Difficulty, trouble, hardship, misery, calamity, danger; कृच्छ्रं महत्तीर्णः R. **14.** 6; 13. **77. 2** Bodily mortification, penance, expiation; Ms. 4. 222; 5. 21; 11. 105. **–च्छ्रं, कृच्छ्रेण, कृच्छ्रात्** With great difficulty, painfully, miserably; लब्धं कृच्छ्रेण रक्ष्यते H. 1. 185. –Comp. **–प्राण** *a*. **1** one whose life is in danger. **2** breathing with difficulty. **3** hardly supporting life. **–साध्य** *a*. **1** curable with difficulty (as a patient or disease). **2** accomplished with difficulty.

कृत् I. 6 P. (कृंतति-कृत्त) **1** To cut, cut off, divide, tear, asunder, cut in pieces, destroy; प्रहरति विधिर्मर्मच्छेदी न कृंतति जीवितं U. 3. **31, 35**; Bk. 9. 42; 15. 97; 16. 15; Ms. 8. 12. With **अव** to cut off, divide, tear asunder. **–उद् 1** to cut off or out, tear out; R. 12. 49; Ms. 11. 105. **2** to hack, cut up; उत्कृत्योत्कृत्य कृत्तिं Mâl. 5. 16. **–वि 1** to cut or tear off, tear up; विश्वासाद्भयमुत्पन्नं मूलान्यपि निकृंतति Pt. 2. 39; निकृंतन्निव मानसं Bk. 7. 11; भल्लनिकृत्तकंठैः R 7. 58. –II 7 P. (कृणत्ति, कृत्त) **1** To spin. 2 To surround.

कृत् *a*. (Generally at the end of comp.). Accomplisher, doer, maker, performer, manufacturer, composer &c.; पाप°, पुण्य°, प्रतिमा° &c. *–m*. **1** A class of affixes used to form derivatives (nouns, adjectives &c.) from roots. **2** A word so formed.

कृत *a*. Done, performed, made, effected, accomplished, manufactured &c. &c.; (*p. p.* of कृ 8 U.). **—तं 1** Work, deed, action; Ms. 7. 197. **2** Service, benefit. **3** Consequence, result. **4** Aim, object. **5** N. of that side of a die which is marked with four points. **6** N. of the first of the four Yugas of the world extending over 1728000 years of men; see Ms. 1. 69 and Kull. thereon; but, according to Mb., over 4800 years of men. **7** The number '4'. –Comp. **–अकृत** *a*. done and not done; *i. e.* done in part but not completed. **–अंक 1** marked, branded; Ms. 8. 281. **2** numbered. (**–कः**) that side of a die which is marked with four points. **–अंजलि** *a*. folding the hands in supplication; Bg. 11. 14; Ms. 4. 154. **–अनुकर** *a*. following another's example, subservient. **–अनुसारः** custom, usage. **–अंत** *a*. bringing to an end, terminating. (**–तः**) **1** Yama, the god of death; द्वितीयं कृतांतमिवाटंतं व्याधमपश्यत् H. 1. **2** fate destiny; क्रूरस्तस्मिन्नपि न सहते संगमं नौ कृतांतः Me. 105. **3** a demonstrated conclusion, dogma, a proved doctrine. **4** a sinful or inauspicious action. **5** an epithet of Saturn. **6** Saturday. **°जनकः** the sun. **–अन्नं 1** cooked food, कृतान्नमुदकं स्त्रियः Ms. 4. 219; 11. 3. **2** digested food. **3** excrement. **–अपराध** *a*. guilty, offender, criminal. **–अभय** *a*. saved from fear or danger. **–अभिषेक** *a*. crowned, inaugurated. **—अभ्यास** *a*. practised. **–अर्थ** *a*. **1** having gained one's object, successful. **2** satisfied, happy, contented; कृतः कृतार्थोऽस्मि निवर्हितांहसा Si. **1.** 29; R. 8. 3; Ki. **4.** 9. **3** clever. (**कृतार्थी** **1** to render fruitful or successful. **2** to make good; कांतं प्रत्युपचारतश्चतुरया कोपः कृतार्थीकृतः Amaru. 15). **–अवधान** *a*. careful, attentive. **–अवधि** *a*. **1** fixed, appointed. **2** bounded, limited. **–अवस्थ** *a*. **1** summoned, caused to be present. **2** fixed, settled. **–अस्त्र** *a*. **1** armed. **2** trained in the science of arms or missiles; R. 17. 62. —आगम a. advanced, proficient. (-m.) the supreme soul. -आगस् a. guilty, offending, criminal, sinful. -आत्मन् a. 1 having control over oneself, self-possessed, of a self-governed spirit. 2 purified in mind. -आभरण a. adorned. -आयास a. labouring, suffering. -आह्वान a. challenged. -उत्साह a. diligent, making effort, striving. -उद्वाह a. 1 married. 2 making penance by standing with uplifted hands. -उपकार a. 1 favoured, befriended, assisted; Ku. 3. 73. 2 friendly. -उपभोग a. used, enjoyed -कर्मन् a. 1 one who has done his work; R. 9. 3. 2 skilful, clever. (-m.) 1 the supreme spirit.. 2 a *Sannyâsin*. -काम a. one whose desires are fulfilled. -काल a. 1 fixed or settled as to time. 2 who has waited a certain time. (-लः) appointed time; Y. 2. 184. -कृत्य a. 1 who has accomplished his object; Bg. 15. 20. 2 satisfied, contented; Sânti. 3. 19. 3 having done his duty. -क्रयः a purchaser. -क्षण a. 1 waiting impatiently for the exact moment; वयं सर्वे सोत्सुकाः कृतक्षणास्तिष्ठामः Pt. 1. 2 one who has got an opportunity. -घ्न a. 1 ungrateful; Ms. 4. 214; 8. 19. 2 defeating all previous measures. -चूडः a boy on whom the ceremony of tonsure has been performed; Ms. 5. 58, 67. -ज्ञ a. 1 grateful; Ms 7. 209, 210; Y. 1. 308. 2 correct in conduct. (-ज्ञः) a dog. -तीर्थ a. 1 one who has visited or frequents holy places. 2 one who studies with a professional teacher. 3 fertile in expedients. 4 a guide. -दासः a servant hired for a stated period, a hired servant. -धी a. 1 prudent, considerate. 2 learned, educated, wise; Mu. 5. 20. -निर्णेजनः a penitent. -निश्चय a. resolute, resolved. -पुंख a. skilled in archery. -पूर्व a. done formerly. -प्रतिकृतं assault and counter-assault, attack and resistance; R. 12. 94. -प्रतिज्ञ a. 1 one who has made an agreement or engagement. 2 one who has fulfilled his promise. -बुद्धि a. learned, educated, wise; Ms. 1. 97; 7. 30. -मुख a. learned, wise. -लक्षण a. 1 stamped, marked. 2 branded; Ms. 9. 239. 3 excellent, amiable. 4 defined, discriminated. -वर्मन् m. a warrior on the side of the Kauravas who with Kripa and Asvatthâman survived the great havoc of the great Bhâratî war. He was afterwards slain by Sâtyaki. -विद्य a. learned, educated; शूरोसि कृतविद्योसि Pt. 4. 43; सुवर्णपुष्पितां पृथ्वीं विचिन्वंति त्रयो जनाः। शूरश्च कृतविद्यश्च यश्च जानाति सेवितुं ॥ Pt. 1. 45. -वेतन a. hired, paid (as a servant); Y. 2. 164. -वेदिन् a. grateful; see कृतज्ञ. -वेश a. attired, decorated; गतवति कृतवेशे केशवे कुंजशय्यां Gît. 11 -शोभ a. 1 splendid. 2 beautiful. 3 handy, dexterous. -शौच a. purified -श्रमः, -परिश्रमः one who has studied; कृतपरिश्रमोस्मि ज्योतिःशास्त्रे Mu. 1. I have devoted my time to (spent my labours on) the science of astronomy. -संकल्प a. resolved, determined.-संकेत a. making an appointment; नामसमेतं कृतसंकेतं वादयते मृदु वेणुं Gît. 5. -संज्ञ a. 1 restored to consciousness or animation. 2 aroused. -संनाह a. clad in armour. -सापत्निका a woman whose husband has married another wife, a married woman having a co-wife or a superseded wife. -हस्त,-हस्तक a. 1 dexterous, clever, skilful, handy. 2 skilled in archery. -हस्तता 1 skill, dexterity. 2 skill in archery or generally in handling arms; कौरव्ये कृतहस्तता पुनरियं देवे यथा सीरिणि Ve. 6. 12; Mv. 6. 41.

कृतक a. 1 Done, made, prepared; (opp. नैसर्गिक); यद्यत्कृतकं तत्तदनित्यं Nyâya-Sûtra. 2 Artificial, done or prepared artificially; अकृतकविधि सर्वांगीणमाकल्पजातं R. 18. 52. 3 Feigned, pretended, false, sham, assumed; कृतककलहं कृत्वा Mu. 3; Ki. 8. 46. 4 Adopted (as a son &c.); oft. at the end of comp. also; यस्योपांते कृतकतनयः कांतया वर्धितो मे (बालमंदारवृक्षः) Me. 75; सोयं न पुत्रकृतकः पदवीं मृगस्ते (जहाति) S. 4. 13.

कृतं ind. Enough, no more of; away; (with instr.); अथवा कृतं संदेहेन S. 1; अथवा गिरा कृतं R. 11. 41; कृतमश्वेन U. 4.

कृतिः f. 1 Doing, manufacturing, making, performing. 2 Action, deed. 3 Creation, work, composition; (तौ) स्वकृतिं गापयामास कविप्रथमपद्धतिं R. 15. 33, 64, 69; N. 22. 155. 4 Magic, enchantment. 5 Injuring, killing. 6 The number '20'. -Comp. -करः an epithet of Ravaṇa.

कृतिन् a. 1 One who has done his work or gained his end, satisfied, contented, happy, successful; यस्य वीर्येण कृतिनो वयं च भुवनानि च U. 1. 32; न खल्वनिर्जित्य रघुं कृती भवान् R. 3. 51; 12. 64. 2 (Hence) Lucky, fortunate, blessed; S. 1. 24; S. 7. 19. 3 Clever, competent, able, expert, skilful, wise, learned; तं क्षुरप्रशकलीकृतं कृती R. 11. 29; Ku. 2. 10; Ki. 2. 9. 4 Good, virtuous, pure, pious; तावदेव कृतिनामपि स्फुरत्येष निर्मलविवेकदीपकः Bh. 1. 56. 5 Following, obeying, doing what is enjoined.

कृते,-कृतेन ind. (with gen. or in comp.) For, for the sake of, on account of; अमीषां प्राणानां...कृते Bh. 3. 36; काव्यं यशसेऽर्थकृते K. P. 1; Bg. 1. 35; Y. 1. 216; S. 6.

कृत्तिः f. 1 Skin, hide (in general). 2 Especially, the hide of an antelope on which a religious student sits. 3 The bark of the birch-tree used for writing upon &c. 4 The birch-tree. 5 One of the lunar mansions, Pleiades. -Comp. -वासः, -वासस् m. an epithet of Siva; स कृत्तिवासास्तपसे यतात्मा Ku. 1. 54; M. 1. 1.

कृत्तिका (pl.) 1 The third of the 27 lunar mansions or asterisms, (consisting of 6 stars, the Pleiades). 2 The six stars represented as nymphs acting as nurses to Kârtikeya, the god of war. -Comp. -तनयः, -पुत्रः, -सुतः epithets of Kârtikeya. -भवः the moon.

कृत्नु a. 1 Working well, able to work, powerful. 2 Clever, skilful. —त्नुः A mechanic, an artist.

कृत्य a. 1 What should or ought to be done, right, proper, fit. 2 Feasible, practicable. 3 Who may be seduced from allegiance, treacherous; Râj. T. 5. 247. —त्यं 1 What ought to be done, duty, function; Ms. 2. 237; 7. 67. 2 Work, business, deed, commission; बंधुकृत्यं Me. 114; अन्योन्यकृत्यैः S. 7. 34. 3 Purpose, object, end; कुजन्द्रिरापादितवंशकृत्यं R. 2. 12; Ku. 4. 15. 4 Motive, cause. —त्यः A class of affixes used to form potential (future) passive participles; these are तव्य, अनीय, य and एलिम. —त्या 1 Action, deed. 2 Magic. 3 A female deity to whom sacrifices are offered for destructive and magical purposes.

कृत्रिम a. 1 Artificial, fictitious, not spontaneous, acquired; °मित्रं, °शत्रुः &c.; R. 13. 75; 14. 37. 2 Adopted (as a child); see below. —मः, °पुत्रः an artificial or adopted son; one of the 12 kinds of sons recognised by the Hindu law; he is a grown up son adopted without the consent of his natural parents; cf. कृत्रिमः स्यात्स्वयं दत्तः Y. 2. 131; cf. also Ms. 9. 169. —मं 1 A kind of salt. 2 A kind of perfume. -Comp. -धूपः-धूपकः incense, a kind of perfume. -पुत्रः see कृत्रिमः. -पुत्रकः a doll, puppet; Ku. 1. 29. -भूमि f. an artificial floor. -वनं a park, garden.

कृत्वस् ind. An affix added to numerals to denote 'fold' or 'times'; e. g. अष्टकृत्वः eight times, eight-fold; so दश,° पंच° &c.

कृत्सं 1 Water. 2 A multitude. —त्सः Sin.

कृत्स्न a. All, whole, entire; एकः कृत्स्नां नगरपरिघप्रांशुबाहुर्भुनक्ति S. 2. 15; Bg. 3. 29; Ms. 1. 105; 5. 42.

कृंतत्रं A plough.

कृंतनं Cutting, cutting off, dividing, tearing asunder.

कृपः The maternal uncle of अश्वत्थामन्. [He was born of the sage *S*aradvat by a nymph called Janapad*i*, but along with his sister Krip*i*, also born from the nymph, he was brought up by *S*antanu. He was proficient in the science of archery. In the great war he sided with the Kauravas, and after all had been slain, he was given an asylum by the Pa*n*davas. He is one of the seven Chiraj*i*vins].

कृपण *a*. 1 Poor, pitiable, wretched, helpless; राजन्नपत्यं रामस्ते पाल्याश्च कृपणाः प्रजाः U. 4. 25. 2 Void of judgment, unable or unwilling to discriminate or to do a thing; कामार्ता हि प्रकृतिकृपणाश्चेतनाचेतनेषु Me. 5; so जराजीर्णैश्वर्यग्रसनगहनाक्षेपकृपणः Bh. 3. 17. 3 Low, mean, vile; Bg. 2. 49; Mu. 2. 18; Bh. 2. 49. 4 Miserly, stingy. —णं Wretchedness. —णः A miser; कृपणेन समो दाता भुवि कोऽपि न विद्यते । अनश्नन्नेव वित्तानि यः परेभ्यः प्रयच्छति Vyâsa. -Comp. -धी, -बुद्धि *a*. little or low minded. -वत्सल *a*. kind to the poor.

कृपा Pity, tenderness, compassion; चक्रवाकयोः पुरो वियुक्ते मिथुने कृपावती Ku. 5. 26; Sânti. 4. 19; सकृपं kindly.

कृपाणः 1 A sword; स पातु वः कंसरिपोः कृपाणः Vikr. 1. 1; कृपणस्य कृपाणस्य च केवलमाकारतो भेदः Subhâsh. 2 A knife.

कृपाणिका A dagger, knife.

कृपाणी 1 A pair of scissors. 2 A dagger.

कृपालु *a*. Merciful, compassionate, kind.

कृपी The sister of कृप and wife of Dro*n*a. -Comp. -पतिः an epithet of Dro*n*a. -सुतः an epithet of अश्वत्थामन्.

कृपीटं 1 Underwood, forest wood. 2 Wood, firewood. 3 Water. 4 The belly. -Comp. -पालः 1 a rudder. 2 the ocean. 3 air, wind. -योनिः fire.

कृमि *a*. Full of worms, wormy. -मिः 1 A worm, an insect in general; कृमिकुलचितं Bh. 2. 9. 2 Worms (disease). 3 An ass. 4 A spider. 5 The lac (dye). -Comp. -कोशः, -कोषः the cocoon of a silk-worm. °उत्थं silken cloth. —जं, -जग्धं agallochum, aloe wood. —जा lac, the red dye produced by insects. —जलजः, —वारिरुहः a shell-fish, an animal (fish, &c.) living in a shell. -पर्वतः, -शैलः an ant-hill. -फलः the Udumbara tree. -शंखः the fish living in the conch. -शुक्तिः *f*. 1 a bivalve shell. 2 the animal living in it. 3 an oyster.

कृमिण or **कृमिल** *a*. Having worms, wormy.

कृमिला A fruitful woman.

कृश् 4 P. (कृश्यति, कृश). 1 To become lean or emaciated. 2 To wane (as the moon). -*Caus.* To emaciate.

कृश *a*. (Compar. क्रशीयस्; superl. क्रशिष्ठ). 1 Lean, weak, feeble, emaciated; कृशतनुः कृशोदरी &c. 2 Small, little, minute (in size or quantity); सुहृदपि न याच्यः कृशधनः Bh. 2. 28 3 Poor, insignificant; Ms. 7. 208. -Comp. -अक्षः a spider. -अंग *a*. lean, thin. (-गी) 1 a woman with a slender frame. 2 the Priyangu creeper. -उदर *a*. thin-waisted; V. 5. 16.

कृशला Hair (of the head).

कृशानुः Fire; गुरोः कृशानुप्रतिमाद्बिभेषि R. 2. 49; 7. 24; 10. 74; Ku. 1. 51; Bh. 2. 107. -Comp. -रेतस् *m*. an epithet of Siva.

कृशाश्विन् *m*. An actor.

कृष् I. 6. U. (कृषति-ते, कृष्ट) To plough, make furrows.-II. 1 P. (कर्षति, कृष्ट) To draw, drag, pull, drag away, tear; प्रसह्य सिंहः किल तां चकर्ष R. 2. 27; V. 1. 19. 2 To draw towards oneself, attract; Bk. 15. 47; Bg. 15. 7. 3 To lead or conduct as an army; स सेनां महतीं कर्षन् R. 14. 32. 4 To bend (as a bow); नात्यायतकृष्टशार्ङ्गः R. 5. 50. 5 To become master of, subdue, vanquish, overpower; बलवानिंद्रियग्रामो विद्वांसमपि कर्षति Ms. 2. 215; नक्रः स्वस्थानमासाद्य गजेंद्रमपि कर्षति Pt. 3. 46. 6 To plough, till; अनुलोमकृष्टं क्षेत्रं प्रतिलोमं कर्षति Sk. 7 To obtain, get; कुलसंख्यां च गच्छंति कर्षंति च महद्यशः Mb. 8 To take away from, deprive one of (with two acc.). -With अप 1 to draw back or away, pull off, take or drag away or off, drag out, extract; दंताग्रभिन्नमपकृष्य निरीक्षते च Rs. 4. 14; R. 16. 55. 2 To remove; U. 1. 8. 3 To lessen, diminish. -अव to draw, draw away from. -आ 1 to draw, draw towards, drag, pull, extract (fig. also); केशेष्वाकृष्य चुंबति H. 1. 109; S. 1. 33; दूरमनुना सारंगेण वयमाकृष्टाः S. 1.; Amaru. 2. 72; Ku. 2. 59; R. 1. 23. 2 to bend (as a bow); S. 3. 5; Si. 9. 40. 3 to extract, borrow; H. Pr. 9. 4 to snatch, take by force; Bk. 16. 30. 5 to supply a word or words from another rule or sentence. -उद् 1 to draw or pull up, extricate; अंगदकोटिलग्नं प्रालंबमुत्कृष्य R. 6. 14; Si. 13. 60. 2 to enhance, increase. -नि to sink down, lessen, diminish. -निस् 1 to draw or pull out. 2 to extort, exact, snatch or take by force; निष्क्रष्टुमर्थं चकमे कुबेरात् R. 5. 26. -परि to draw, pull, drag. -प्र 1 to draw away, pull, attract. 2 to lead (as an army). 3 to bend (as a bow). 4 to increase. -वि 1 to draw, pull. 2 to bend (as a bow); शरासनं तेषु विकृष्यतामिदं S. 6. 28. -विप्र to remove. -संनि to bring near.

कृषकः 1 A ploughman, husbandman. 2 A plough-share. 3 An ox.

कृषाणः, कृषिकः A ploughman, husbandman.

कृषिः *f*. 1 Ploughing. 2 Agriculture, husbandry; चीयते बालिशस्यापि सत्क्षेत्रपतिता कृषिः Mu. 1. 3; कृषिः क्लिष्टाऽवृष्ट्या Pt. 1. 11; Ms. 1. 90, 3. 64, 10. 79; Bg. 18. 44.-Comp. -कर्मन् *n*. agriculture. -जीविन् *a*. living by husbandry. -फलं agricultural produce or profit; Me. 16. -सेवा agriculture, husbandry.

कृषीवलः One who lives by husbandry, a farmer; क्राषें चापि कृषीवलः Y. 1. 276; Ms. 9. 38.

कृष्कर: An epithet of Siva.

कृष्ट *a*. 1 Drawn, pulled, dragged, attracted. 2 Ploughed.

कृष्टिः A learned man. -*f*. 1 Drawing, attracting. 2 Ploughing, cultivating the soil.

कृष्ण *a*. 1 Black, dark, dark-blue. 2 Wicked, evil. -ष्णः 1 The black colour. 2 The black antelope. 3 A crow. 4 The (Indian) cuckoo. 5 The dark half of a lunar month, (from full to new moon). 6 The Kali age. 7 Vish*n*u in his eighth incarnation, both as the son of Vasudeva and Devaki [Krish*n*a is the most celebrated hero of Indian mythology and the most popular of all the deities. Though the real son of Vasudeva and Devak*i* and thus a cousin of Kamsa, he was, for all practical purposes, the son of Nanda and Yasod*a*, by whom he was brought up and in whose house he spent his childhood. It was here that his divine character began to be gradually discovered, when he easily crushed the most redoubtable demons, such as Baka, P*u*tan*a* &c., that were sent to kill him by Kamsa, and performed many other feats of surprising strength. The chief companions of his youth were the *Gop*i*s* or wives of the cowherds of Gokula, among whom R*a*dh*a* was his special favourite; (cf. Jayadeva's *Gita-govinda*). He killed Kamsa, Naraka, Kes*i*n, Arish*t*a and a host of other powerful demons. He was a particular friend of Arjuna, to whom he acted as charioteer in the great war, and his staunch support of the cause of the P*a*ndavas was the main cause of the overthrow of the Kauravas. On several critical occasions, it was Krish*n*'as assistance and inventive mind that stood the P*a*ndavas in good stead. After the general destruction of the Y*a*dav*a*s at Prabh*a*sa, he was killed unintentionally by a hunter named Jaras who shot him with an arrow mistaking him at a distance for a deer. He had more than 16000 wives, but Rukmi*n*i and Satyabh*a*m*a*, (as also R*a*dha) were his favourites. He is said to have been of a dark-blue or cloud-like colour; cf.

बहिरिव मालिनतरं तव कृष्ण मनोपि भविष्यति नूनं Gît. 8. His son was Pradyumna.] 8 N. of Vyâsa, the reputed author of the Mahâbhârata. 9 N. of Arjuna. 10 Aloe wood. -ष्णं 1 Blackness, darkness (moral also). 2 Iron. 3 Antimony. 4 The black part of the eye. 5 Black pepper. 6 Lead. –COMP. –अगुरु *n.* a kind of sandal-wood. –अचलः an epithet of the mountain Raivataka. –अजिनं the skin of the black antelope. –अयस् *n.* –अयसं, –आमिषं iron, crude or black iron. –अध्वन्, –अर्चिस् *m.* fire. –अष्टमी the 8th day of the dark half of *S*râvaṇa when Krshṇa was born ; also called गोकुलाष्टमी. –आवासः the holy fig-tree. –उदरः a kind of snake. –कंदं a red lotus. –कर्मन् *a.* of black deeds, criminal, wicked, depraved, guilty. –काकः a raven. –कायः a buffalo. –काष्ठं a kind of sandal-wood, agallochum. –कोहलः a gambler. –गतिः fire ; आयोधने कृष्णगतिं सहायं R. 6. 42. –ग्रीवः N. of *S*iva. –तारः 1 a species of antelope (in general). –देहः a bee. –धनं money got by foul means. –द्वैपायनः N. of Vyâsa ; तमहमरागमकृष्णं कृष्णद्वैपायनं वंदे Ve. 1. 3. –पक्षः the dark half of a lunar month. –मृगः the black antelope ; शृंगे कृष्णमृगस्य वामनयनं कंडूयमानां मृगीं *S*. 6. 16. –मुखः, –वक्त्रः, –वदनः the black-faced monkey. –यजुर्वेदः the Taittirîya or black Yajurveda. –लोहः the load-stone. –वर्णः 1 black colour. 2 N. of Râhu 3 a *S*údra. –वर्त्मन् *m.* 1 fire ; R. 11. 42 ; Ms. 2. 94. 2 N. of Râhu. 3 a low man, profligate, blackguard. –वेणा N. of river. –शकुनिः a crow. –शारः, –सारः the spotted antelope ; कृष्णसारे ददच्चक्षुस्त्वयि चाधिज्यकार्मुके *S*. 1. 6 –शृंगः a buffalo. –सखः –सारथिः an epithet of Arjuna.

कृष्णकं The hide of the black antelope.

कृष्णलः The Gunjâ plant. –लं Its berry.

कृष्णा 1 N. of द्रौपदी, wife of the Pandavas ; Ki. 1. 26. 2 N. of a river in the Deccan that joins the sea at Masulipattam.

कृष्णिका Black mustard.

कृष्णिमन् *m.* Blackness.

कृष्णी A dark night.

कॄ I. 6 P. (किरति, कीर्ण) 1 To scatter, throw about, pour out, cast, disperse; समरशिरसि चंचत्पंचचूडश्चमूनामुपरि शरतुषारं कोप्यय वीरपोतः किरति U. 5. 2 ; 6. 1; दिशि दिशि किरति सजलकणजालं Gît. 4 ; *S*. 1. 7 ; Amaru. 11. 2 To strew, cover or fill with ; Bk. 3. 5, 17. 42. –WITH –अप 1 to scatter, cast about ; अपकिरति कुसुमं Sk. 2 to scrape with the feet (for food, abode &c.), through joy (said of quadrupeds and birds), (the form in this sense is अपस्किरते): अपस्किरते वृषो हृष्टः कुक्कुटो भक्षार्थी श्वा आश्रयार्थी च Sk. –अपा to cast off, reject, repudiate. –अव to scatter, throw; अवाकिरन्बाललताः प्रसूनैः R. 2. 10. –आ 1 to spread round. 2 to dig up. –उद् 1 to scatter upwards, throw up ; R. 1 42. 2 to dig up, excavate. 3 to engrave, carve, sculpture ; उत्कीर्णा इव वासयष्टिषु निशानिद्रालसा बर्हिणः V. 3. 2 ; R. 4. 59. –उप (उपस्किरति) to cut, hurt or injure. –परि 1 to surround ; परिकीर्णा परिवादिनी मुनेः R. 8. 35. 2 to hand or give over, deliver ; महीं महेच्छः परिकीर्य सूनौ R. 18. 33. –प्र 1 to scatter, throw, pour out ; प्रकीर्णः पुष्पाणां हरिचरणयोरंजलिरयं Ve. 1. 2. 2 to sow, as seed. –प्रति (प्रतिस्किरति) to hurt, injure, tear ; उरोविदारं प्रतिचस्करे नखैः *S*i. 1. 47. –वि to scatter, throw about, strew or spread about ; Ku. 3. 61 ; Ki. 2. 59 ; Bk. 13 ; 14. 25. –विनि to throw, abandon, cast off ; Ku. 4. 6. –सम् to mix, commingle or mix together. –समुद् to perforate, bore, pierce ; R. 1. 4. –II 9 U. (कृणाति, कृणीते) To injure, hurt, kill.

कॄत् 10 U. (कीर्तयति-ते, कीर्तित) 1 To mention, repeat, utter ; नाम्नि कीर्तित एव R. 1. 87 ; Ms. 7. 167, 2. 124. 2 To tell, recite, declare, communicate ; Ms. 3. 36, 9. 42. 3 To name, call. 4 To praise, glorify, commemorate; अपप्रथद्गुणान् भ्रातुरचिकीर्तच्च विक्रमं Bk. 15. 72 ; Pt. 1. 4.

कॢप् 1. A. (कल्पते, कॢप्त) 1 To be fit or adequate for, result in, bring about, accomplish, produce, tend to; (with dat.); कल्पसे रक्षणाय *S*. 5. 5; पश्चात्पुत्रैरपहृतभरः कल्पते विश्रमाय V. 3. 1 ; विभावरी यद्यरुणाय कल्पते Ku. 5. 44, 6. 29 ; 5. 79 ; Me. 55. R. 5. 13, 8. 40 ; *S*. 6. 23 ; Bk. 22. 21. 2 To be well managed or regulated, to succeed. 3 To become, happen, occur ; कल्पिष्यते हरेः प्रीतिः Bk 16. 12 ; 9. 44, 45. 4 To be prepared, be ready ; चक्लृपे चाश्वकुंजरं Bk. 14. 89. 5 To be favourable to, subserve. 6 To partake of. —*Caus.* 1 To prepare, arrange, fit out. 2 To settle, fix. 3 To divide. 4 To provide or furnish with. 5 To consider. –WITH अव to result in, tend to, accomplish; (with dat.). –आ (*Caus.*) to adorn, decorate. –उप 1 to result in, lead to, (with dat.); Ms. 3. 202. 2 to be prepared or ready at hand; Ms. 3. 208; 8. 333. –परि (*Caus.*) 1 to decide, determine, fix upon. 2 to prepare, get ready. 3 to endow with; *S*. 2 9. –प्र 1 to happen, occur. 2 to be successful. (–*Caus.*) 1 to invent, devise; plan (schemes &c.) 2 to prepare, make ready. –वि to doubt, be doubtful. (*Caus.*) to doubt. –सं (*Caus.*) 1 to resolve, determine, settle. 2 to intend, propose. –समुप to get ready.

कॢप्त *p. p.* 1 Prepared, done, got ready, equipped; कॢप्तविवाहवेषा R 6. 10 decked in her nuptial attire. 2 Cut, pared ; कॢप्तकेशनखश्मश्रु Ms. 4. 35. 3 Caused, produced. 4 Fixed, settled. 5 Thought of, invented. –COMP. –कीला a title-deed. –धूपः frank-incense.

कॢप्तिः *f.* 1 Accomplishment; success. 2 Invention, contrivance. 3 Arranging.

कॢप्तिक *a.* Bought, purchased.

केकयः (pl.) N. of a country and its people ; मगधकोसलकेकयशासिनां दुहितरः R. 9. 17.

केकर *a.* (री *f.*) Squint-eyed. —रं A squint eye ; cf. आकेकर. –COMP. –अक्ष *a.* squint-eyed.

केका The cry of a peacock ; केकाभिर्नीलकंठस्तिरयति वचनं तांडवादुच्छिखंडः Mâl. 9. 30; षड्जसंवादिनीः केकाः R. 1. 39, 7. 69, 13. 27, 16. 64; Me. 22; Bh. 1. 35.

केकावलः, –केकिकः, –केकिन् *m.* A peacock; इतः केकिक्रीडाकलकलरवः पक्ष्मलदृशां Bh. 1. 37.

केणिका A tent.

केतः 1 A house, abode. 2 Living, habitation. 3 A banner. 4 Will, intention, desire.

केतकः 1 N. of a plant ; प्रतिभांत्यद्य वनानि केतकानां Ghat. 15. 2 A banner. —कं A flower of the Ketaka plant ; केतकैः सूचिभिन्नैः Me. 24, 23; R. 6. 17, 13. 16. —की 1 N. of a plant (=केतक); हसितमिव विधत्ते सूचिभिः केतकीनां Rs. 2. 23. 2 A flower of that plant; Rs. 2. 20, 24.

केतनं 1 A house, an abode; अकलितमहिमानः केतनं मंगलानां Mâl. 2. 9; मम मरणमेव वरमातिवितथकेतना Gît. 7. 2 An invitation, summons. 3 Place, site. 4 A flag, banner ; भग्नं भीमेन मरुता भवतो रथकेतनं Ve. 2. 23; *S*i. 14. 28; R. 9. 39. 5 A sign, symbol ; as in मकरकेतन. 6 An indispensable act (also religious); निवापांजलिदानेन केतनैः श्राद्धकर्मभिः । तस्योपकारे शक्तस्त्वं किं जीवन् किमुतान्यथा Ve. 3. 16.

केतित *a.* 1 Called, summoned. 2 Dwelt, inhabited.

केतुः 1 A flag, banner ; चीनांशुकमिव केतोः प्रतिवातं नीयमानस्य *S*. 1. 34. 2 A chief, head, leader, foremost, any eminent person (oft. at the end of comp.); मनुप्रभवचसा मनुवंशकेतुं R. 2. 33; कुलस्य केतुः स्फीतस्य (राघवः) Râm. 3 A comet, meteor; Ms. 1. 38. 4 A sign, mark. 5 Brightness, clearness. 6 A ray of light. 7 The descending node considered as the ninth planet, and the body or trunk of the demon सैंहिकेय (the head being regarded as Râhu); क्रूरग्रहः स केतुश्चंद्रमसं पूर्णमंडलमिदानीं Mu. 1. 6. –COMP. –ग्रहः the descending node. –भः a cloud. –यष्टिः *f.* a flagstaff; R. 12. 103. –रत्नं lapis lazuli, (also called वैदूर्य). —वसनं a flag.

केदारः 1 A field under water; meadow. 2 A basin for water round the root of a tree. 3 A mountain. 4 A particular mountain forming part of the Himâlayas (modern Kedâr). 5 A form of *S*iva. –COMP. –खंडं a small dyke, earth raised to keep out water. –नाथः a particular form of *S*iva.

केनारः 1 The head. 2 The skull. 3 A cheek. 4 A joint.

केनिपातः A rudder, helm, a large oar used as a rudder.

केंद्रं 1 The centre of a circle. 2 The argument of a circle. 3 Distance of a planet from the first point of its orbit in the 4th, 7th or 10th degree.

केयूरः –रं A bracelet worn on the upper arm, an armlet; केयूरा न विभूषयंति पुरुषं हारा न चंद्रोज्ज्वलाः Bh. 2. 19; R. 6. 68; Ku. 7. 69. —रः A kind of coitus.

केरलः (pl.) N. of a country (in the south of India, the modern Malabar) and its inhabitants; Mâl. 6. 19; R. 4. 54. —ली *f.* 1 A woman of the Kerala country. 2 Astronomical science.

केल् 1 P. (केलति, केलित) 1 To shake. 2 To sport, be frolicsome.

केलकः A dancer, tumbler.

केलासः Crystal.

केलिः *m. f.* 1 Play, sport. 2 Amorous sport, pastime; केलिचलन्मणिकुंडल &c. Gît. 1; हरिरिह मुग्धवधूनिकरे विलासिनि विलसति केलिपरे *ibid*; राधामाधवयोर्जयंति यमुनाकूले रहःकेलयः *ibid*.; Amaru. 7, Ms. 8. 357; Rs. 4. 17. 3 Joke, jest, mirth. —लिः *f.* The earth. –COMP. –कला 1 sportive skill, wantonness, amorous address. 2 the lute of Sarasvatî. –किलः the confidential companion of the hero of a drama (a kind of विदूषक or buffoon). –किलावती Rati, wife of the god of love. –कीर्णः a camel. –कुंचिका a wife's younger sister. –कुपित *a.* angry in sport; Ve. 1. 2. –कोषः an actor, a dancer. –गृहं, –निकेतनं, –मंदिरं, –सदनं a pleasure-house, a private apartment; Amaru. 8. –नागरः a sensualist. –पर *a.* sportive, wanton, amorous. –सुखः joke, sport, pastime. –वृक्षः a species of Kadamba tree. –शयनं a pleasure-couch, sofa; केलिशयनमनुयातं Gît. 11. –शुषिः *f.* the earth. –सचिवः a boon companion, confidential friend.

केलिकः The Asoka tree.

केली 1 Play, sport. 2 Amorous sport. –COMP. –पिकः a cuckoo kept for pleasure. –वनी a pleasure-park, pleasure-grove. –शुकः a parrot kept for pleasure.

केवल *a.* 1 Peculiar, exclusive, uncommon. 2 Alone, mere, sole, only, isolated; स हि तस्य न केवलां श्रियं प्रतिपेदे सकलान् गुणानपि R. 8. 5; न केवलानां पयसां प्रसूतिमवेहि मां कामदुघां प्रसन्नां 2. 63; 15. 1; Ku. 2. 34. 3 Whole, entire, absolute, perfect. 4 Bare, uncovered (as ground); Ku. 5. 12. 5 Pure, simple, unmingled, unattended (by anything else); कातर्यं केवला नीतिः R. 17. 47. –लं *ind.* Only, merely, solely, entirely, absolutely, wholly; केवलमिदमेव पृच्छामि K. 155; न केवलं-अपि not only-but; वसु तस्य विभोर्न केवलं गुणवत्तापि परप्रयोजना R. 8. 31; cf. also 3. 19, 20, 31. –COMP. –आत्मन् *a.* one whose essence is absolute unity; Ku. 2. 4. –नैयायिकः a mere logician (not proficient in any other branch of learning); so °वैयाकरण.

केवलतस् *ind.* Simply, solely, wholly, purely, merely.

केवलिन् *a.* (नी *f.*) 1 Alone, only. 2 Devoted to the doctrine of absolute unity of the spirit.

केशः 1 Hair in general; विकीर्णकेशासु परेतभूमिषु Ku. 5. 68. 2 Especially, the hair of the head; केशेषु गृहीत्वा or केशग्राहं युध्यंते Sk.; मुक्तकेशा Ms. 7. 91; केशव्यपरोपणादिव R. 3. 56; 2. 8. 3 The mane of a horse or lion. 4 A ray of light. 5 An epithet of Varuṇa. 6 A kind of perfume. –COMP. –अंतः 1 the tip of the hair. 2 long hair hanging down, a lock or tuft of hair. 3 cutting of the hair as a religious ceremony; Ms. 2. 65. –उच्चयः much or handsome hair. –कर्मन् *n.* dressing or arranging the hair (of the head). –कलापः a mass or quantity of hair. –कीटः a louse. –गर्भः a braid of hair. –गृहीत *a.* seized by the hair. –ग्रहः –ग्रहणं pulling the hair, seizing (one) by the hair (both in amorous sports and in fighting); केशग्रहः खलु तदा द्रुपदात्मजायाः Ve. 3. 11, 29; Me. 50; so यत्र रतेषु केशग्रहः K. 8 (that is, not in battles). –घ्नं morbid baldness. –च्छिद् *m.* a hair-dresser, barber. –जाहः the root of the hair. –पक्षः, –पाशः, –हस्तः much (or ornamented) hair; तं केशपाशं प्रसमीक्ष्य कुर्युर्बालप्रियत्वं शिथिलं चमर्यः Ku. 1. 48; 7. 57; cf. कचपक्ष, कचहस्त &c. –बंधः a hair-band. –भूः, –भूमिः *f.* the head or any other part of the body on which hair grows. –प्रसाधनी, –मार्जकं, –मार्जनं a comb. –रचना dressing the hair. –वेशः a tress or fillet of hair.

केशटः 1 A goat. 2 N. of Vishṇu. 3 A bug. 4 A brother.

केशव *a.* Having much, fine or luxuriant hair. —वः An epithet of Vishṇu; केशव जय जगदीश हरे Gît. 1; केशवं पतितं दृष्ट्वा पांडवा हर्षनिर्भराः Subhâsh. –COMP. –आयुधः the mango tree. (–धं) a weapon of Vishṇu. –आलयः, –आवासः the Asvattha tree.

केशाकेशि *ind.* 'Hair to hair', (fighting) by pulling each other's hair; केशाकेश्यभवद्युद्धं रक्षसां वानरैः सह Mb; Y. 2. 283.

केशिक *a.* (की *f.*) Having fine or luxuriant hair.

केशिन् *m.* 1 A lion. 2 N. of a Râkshasa slain by Kṛishṇa. 3 N. of another Râkshasa who carried Devasenâ and who was slain by Indra. 4 An epithet of Kṛishṇa. 5 One having fine hair. –COMP. –निषूदनः, –मथनः epithets of Kṛishṇa; Bg. 18. 1.

केशिनी 1 A woman with a beautiful braid of hair. 2 N. of the wife of Visravas and mother of Râvaṇa and Kumbhakarṇa.

केस (श) रः, –रं 1 The mane (as of a lion); न हंत्यदूरेऽपि गजान्मृगेश्वरो विलोलजिह्वश्चलिताग्रकेसरः Rs. 1. 14; *S*. 7. 14. 2 The filament of a flower; नीपं दृष्ट्वा हरितकपिशं केसरैरर्धरूढैः Me. 21; *S*. 6. 17; M. 2. 11; R. 4. 67; *S*i. 9. 47. 3 The Bakula tree; रक्ताशोकश्चलकिसलयः केसरश्चात्र कांतः Me. 78; Ku. 2. 55. 4 The Punnâga tree. 5 The fibre (as of a mango fruit). —रं A flower of the Bakula tree; R. 9. 36. –COMP. –अचलः an epithet of the mountain Meru. —वरं saffron.

केस (श) रिन् *m* 1 A lion; अनुहुंकुरुते घनध्वनिं न हि गोमायुरुतानि केसरी *S*i. 16. 25; धनुर्धरः केसरिणं ददर्श R 2. 29; *S*. 7. 3. 2 The best, excellent, or most prominent of a class (at the end of comp.; *cf.* कुंजर, सिंह &c.). 3 A horse. 4 The citron plant. 5 The Punnâga tree. 6 N. of the father of Hanumat. –COMP. –सुतः an epithet of Hanumat.

कै 1 P. (कायति) To sound.

कैंशुकं A flower of the किंशुक tree.

कैकयः The king of the Kekayas; see केकय.

कैकसः A demon, goblin.

कैकेयः A prince or ruler of the Kekayas. —यी A daughter of the prince of the Kekayas and one (the youngest) of the three wives of king Dasaratha and mother of Bharata. [When Rama was about to be installed as heir-apparent, she was not less rejoiced than Kausalya. But she had a very wicked nurse called Manthara who long owed Rama a grudge. Finding this to be an excellent opportunity for her revenge, Manthara so completely perverted the mind of Kaikeyi that she became ready to ask the king, as suggested by her nurse, to grant her the two boons which he had formerly promised to her. By one of these boons she asked for the installation of her son Bharata, and by the other for the banishment of Rama for fourteen years. Dasaratha, blinded by passion as he was, severely scolded her of her wicked demands, but was at last obliged to yield. On account of this wicked act her name has become proverbial for 'a shrew', or 'Xanthippe'].

कैटभः N. of a demon killed by Vishṇu. [He was a very powerful demon. He and Madhu are said to have sprung from the ears of Vishnu while he was asleep; and when they were about to devour Brahma they were slain by Vishnu].–COMP. **–अरिः**; **–जित्** *m.*, **–रिपुः**, **–हन्** epithets of Vishṇu.

कैतकं A flower of the Ketaka plant.

कैतवं 1 The stake in a game. 2 Gambling. 3 Falsehood, deceit, fraud, roguery, trick; हृदये वससीति मत्प्रियं यदवोचस्तदवैमि कैतवं Ku. 4. 9. **—वः** 1 A cheat, rogue. 2 A gambler. 3 The Dhattûra plant. –COMP. **–प्रयोगः** a trick, device. **–वादः** falsehood, roguery.

कदारः Rice, corn. **—रं** A multitude of fields; also केदार्य.

कैमुतिकः (*scil.* न्याय) A maxim of 'how much more', an argument *a fortiori* (derived from किमुत 'how much more').

कैरवः 1 A gambler, cheat, rogue. 1 An enemy. **—वं** The white lotus opening at moon-rise; चंद्रो विकासयति कैरवचक्रवालं Bh. 2. 73. –COMP. **–बंधुः** an epithet of the moon.

कैरविन् *m.* The moon.

कैरविणी 1 A lotus plant bearing white lotuses. 2 A place (pond &c.) abounding in white lotuses. 3 An assemblage of white lotuses.

कैरवी Moonlight.

कैलासः N. of a mountain, a peak of the Himâlayas and residence of Siva and Kubera; Me. 11, 58; R. 2. 35. -COMP. **–नाथः** an epithet 1 of Siva. 2 of Kubera; कैलासनाथं तरसा जिगीषुः R. 5. 28; कैलासनाथमुपस्थाय निवर्तमाना V. 1. 2.

कैवर्तः A fisherman; मनोभूः कैवर्तः क्षिपति परितस्त्वां प्रति मुहुः (तनूजालीजालं, Sânti. 3. 16; Ms. 8. 260; (as to his descent see Ms. 10. 34).

कैवल्यं 1 Perfect isolation, soleness, exclusiveness. 2 Individuality. 3 Detachment of the soul from matter, indentification with the supreme spirit. 4 Final emancipation or beatitude.

कैशिक *a.* (की *f.*) Hair-like, fine as hair. **—कः** The sentiment of love, lust. **—कं** A quantity of hair. **—की** One of the four varieties of dramatic style, more usually and correctly written कौशिकी q. v.

कैशोरं Youth, childhood, tender age (below fifteen); कैशोरमापंचदशात्.

कैश्यं The whole mass of hair, quantity of hair.

कोकः 1 A wolf; वनयूथपरिभ्रष्टा मृगी कोकैरिवार्दिता Râm. 2 The ruddy goose (चक्रवाक); कोकानां करुणस्वरेण सदृशी दीर्घा मदभ्यर्थना Gît. 5. 3 A cuckoo. 4 A frog. 5 N. of Vishṇu. –COMP. **–देवः** a pigeon. **–बुधः** an epithet of the sun.

कोकनदं The red lotus; किंचित्कोकनदच्छदस्य सदृशे नेत्रे स्वयं रज्यतः U. 5. 36; नीलनलिनाभमपि तन्वि तव लोचनं धारयति कोकनदरूपं Gît 10; Si. 4. 46.

कोकाहः A white horse.

कोकिलः 1 The (Indian) cuckoo; पुंस्कोकिलो यन्मधुरं चुकूज Ku. 3. 32; 4. 16; R. 12. 39. 2 A firebrand. –COMP. **–आवासः**, **–उत्सवः** the mango tree.

कोंकः, **कोंकणः** (pl.) N. of a country, the strip of land between the Sahyâdri and the ocean.

कोंकणा N. of Reṇukâ, wife of Jamadagni. –COMP. **–सुतः** an epithet of Parasurâma.

कोजागरः N. of a festival held on the full moon night in the month of Asvina and celebrated with several games.

कोटः 1 A fort. 2 A hut, shed. 3 Crookedness (moral also). 4 A beard.

कोटरः-**रं** The hollow of a tree; नीवाराः शुकगर्भकोटरमुखभ्रष्टास्तरूणामधः S. 1. 14; कोटरमकालवृष्ट्या प्रबलपुरोवातया गमिते M. 4. 2; Rs. 1. 26.

कोटरी, **कोटवी** 1 A naked woman. 2 A epithet of the goddess Durgâ (represented as naked).

कोटिः **-टी** *f.* 1 The curved end of a bow; भूमिनिहितैककोटि कार्मुकं R. 11. 81; U. 4. 29. 2 The end or extremity, edge or point in general; सहचरीं दंतस्य कोट्या लिखन् Mâl. 9. 32; अंगदकोटिलग्नं R. 6. 14, 7. 46; 8. 36. 3 The edge or point of a weapon. 4 The highest point, excess, pitch, climax, excellence; परां कोटिमानंदस्याध्यगच्छन् K. 369; so कोपकोटिमापन्ना Pt. 4 excessively angry. 5 The horns or digits of the moon; Ku. 2. 26. 6 Ten millions, a crore; R. 5. 21; 12. 82; Ms. 6. 63. 7 The complement of an arc to 90° (in math.). 8 The side of a rightangled triangle (in math). 9 A class, department, kingdom; मनुष्य° प्राणि° &c. 10 One side of a question in dispute, an alternative. –COMP. **–ईश्वरः** a millionaire. **–जित्** *m.* an epithet of Kâlidâsa. **–ज्या** the co-sine of an angle in a rightangled triangle (in math.). **–द्वयं** two alternatives. **–पात्रं** a rudder. **–पालः** the guard of a stronghold. **–वेधिन्** *a.* (lit.) striking a point; (fig.) performing the most difficult things.

कोटिक *a.* Forming the highest point of anything.

कोटिरः 1 The hair collected on the forehead by ascetics in the shape of a horn. 2 An ichneumon. 3 An epithet of Indra.

कोटि (टी) शः A harrow.

कोटिशः *ind.* By crores, by tens of millions, in innumerable numbers.

कोटीरः 1 A diadem, crown. 2 A crest. 3 The hair collected (by ascetics) on the forehead in the shape of a horn, matted hair in general; कोटीरबंधनधनुर्गुणयोगपट्टव्यापारपारगमगुं भज भूतभर्तुः N. 11. 18.

कोट्टः A fort, castle.

कोट्टवी 1 A naked woman with dishevelled hair. 2 N. of the goddess Durgâ. 3 N. of the mother of Bâṇa.

कोट्टारः 1 A fortified town, stronghold. 2 The stairs of a pond. 3 A well, pond. 4 A libertine, a dissolute person.

कोणः 1 A corner, an angle (of anything); भयेन कोणे क्वचन स्थितस्य Vikr. 1. 99; शुक्रमेतत्त्व तु पुनः कोणं नयनपद्मयोः Bv. 2. 173. 2 An intermediate point of the compass. 3 The bow of a lute; a fiddle-stick. 4 The sharp edge of a sword or weapon. 5 A stick, staff, club. 6 A drum-stick 7 N. of the planet Mars. 8 N. of the planet Saturn. –COMP. **–आघातः** striking of drums, tabors &c., used in the sense of 'a mingled sound of various musical instruments'; कोणाघातेषु गर्जत्प्रलयघनघटान्योन्यसंघट्टचंडः Ve. 1. 22. (It is thus defined by Bharata :—ढक्काशतसहस्राणि भेरीशतशतानि च । एकदा यत्र हन्यंते कोणाघातः स उच्यते). **–कुणः** a bug.

कोणपः see कौणप.

कोणाकोणि *ind.* From angle to angle, corner-wise, diagonally.

कोदंडः-**डं** A bow; रे कंदर्प करं कदर्थयसि किं कोदंडटंकारवैः Bh. 3. 100; कोदंडपाणिनिनदत्प्रतिरोधकानां M. 5. 10. **—डः** An eyebrow.

कोद्रवः A species of grain eaten by the poor; छित्त्वा कर्पूरखंडान् वृतिमिह कुरुते कोद्रवाणां समंतात् Bh. 2. 100.

कोपः 1 Anger, wrath, passion; कोपं न गच्छति नितांतबलोपि नागः Pt. 1. 123; न त्वया कोपः कार्यः do not be angry. 2 (In medicine) morbid irritation or disorder of the humours of the body; *i. e.* पित्तकोप, वातकोप. –COMP. **–आकुल**, **–आविष्ट** *a.* enraged, furious. **–क्रमः** 1 an angry or passionate man. 2

the course of anger. -पदं 1 cause of anger. 2 pretended anger. -वशः subjection to anger. -वेगः violence, fury of anger.

कोपन *a.* 1 Passionate, irascible, angry. 2 Causing anger. 3 Irritating, causing morbid disorder of the humours of the body. -नं Becoming angry. —ना A passionate or angry woman; कयासि कामिन् सुरतापराधात् पादानतः कोपनयाऽवधूतः Ku. 3. 8; Amaru 65.

कोपिन् *a.* 1 Angry, irritated; सत्यमेवासि यदि सुदति मयि कोपिनी Gît. 10. 2 Causing anger. 3 Irritating, causing disorder of the humours of the body.

कोमल *a.* 1 Tender, soft, delicate (fig. also); बंधुरकोमलांगुलिं (करं) *S*. 6. 12; कोमलविटपानुकारिणौ बाहू 1. 21; संपत्सु महतां चित्तं भवत्युत्पलकोमलं Bh. 2. 66. 2 (*a*) Soft, low; कोमलं गीतं. (*b*) Agreeable, pleasing, sweet; रे रे कोकिल कोमलैः कलरवैः किं त्वं वृथा जल्पसि Bh. 3. 100. 3 Handsome, beautiful.

कोमलकं The fibres of the stalk of a lotus.

कोयष्टिः, कोयष्टिकः The lapwing; काश्मर्याः कृतमालमुद्गतदलं कोयष्टिकष्टीकते Mâl. 9. 7; Ms. 5. 13; Y. 1. 173.

कोरकः-कं 1 A bud, an unblown flower; संनद्धं यद्यपि स्थितं कुरबकं तत्कोरकावस्थया *S*. 6. 3. 2 (fig.) Any thing resembling a bud, *i. e.* partially opened but not fully developed; राधायाः स्तनकोरकोपरि चलन्नेत्रो हरिः पातु वः Gît. 12. 3 The fibres of the stalk of a lotus. 4 A kind of perfume.

कोरदूषः =कोद्रवः q. v.

कोरित *a.* 1 Budded, sprouted. 2 Ground, pounded, reduced to small particles.

कोलः 1 A hog, boar; *Si*. 14. 43. 2 A raft, boat. 3 The breast. 4 The haunch, hip, lap. 5 An embrace. 6 The planet Saturn. 7 An out-cast, one of a degraded tribe. 8 A barbarian. —लं 1 The weight of one Tola. 2 Black pepper. 3 A kind of berry. -Comp. -अंचः N. of the country of the Kalingas. -पुच्छः a heron.

कोलंबकः The body of a lute.

कोला (लिः, ली) *f*. See बदरी.

कोलाहलः,-लं A loud and confused noise, an uproar.

कोविद *a.* Experienced, learned, skilled, wise, proficient (with gen. or loc., but usually in comp.); गुणदोषकोविदः *Si*. 14. 53, 69; प्राप्यावंतीनुदयनकथाकोविदग्रामवृद्धान् Me. 30; Ms. 7. 26.

कोविदारः, रं N. of a tree; चित्तं विदारयति कस्य न कोविदारः Rs. 3. 6.

कोशः -शं (षः-षं) 1 A vessel for holding liquids, a pail. 2 A bucket, cup. 3 A vessel in general. 4 A box, cupboard, drawer, trunk. 5 A sheath, scabbard. 6 A case, cover, covering. 7 A store, mass; Ms. 1. 99. 8 A store-room. 9 A treasury, an apartment where money is kept; Ms. 8. 419. 10 Treasure, money, wealth; निःशेषविश्राणितकोषजातं R. 5. 1; (fig. also); कोशास्तपसः K. 45. 11 Gold or silver wrought or unwrought. 12 A dictionary, lexicon, vocabulary. 13 A closed flower, bud; सुजातयोः पंकजकोशयोः श्रियं R. 3. 8, 13. 29; इत्थं विचिंतयति कोशगते द्विरेफे हा हंत हंत नलिनीं गज उज्जहार Subhâsh. 14 The stone of a fruit. 15 A pod. 16 A nutmeg, nut-shell. 17 The cocoon of a silk-worm; Y. 3. 147. 18 Vulva, the womb. 19 An egg. 20 A testicle or the scrotum. 21 The penis. 22 A ball, globe. 23 (In Vedânta phil.) A term for the five vestures (sheaths or cases) which successively make the body, enshrining the soul. 24 (In law) A kind of ordeal; cf. Y. 2. 114. -Comp. -अधिपतिः, -अध्यक्षः 1 a treasurer, pay-master; (cf. the modern 'minister of finance'). 2 an epithet of Kubera. -अगारः a treasury, store-room. -कारः 1 one who makes scabbards. 2 a lexicographer. 3 the silk-worm while in the cocoon. 4 a chrysalis. -कारकः a silkworm. -कृत् *m.* a kind of sugarcane. -गृहं a treasury, store-room; R. 5. 29. -चंचुः the (Indian) crane. -नायकः, -पालः a treasurer. -पेटकः, -कं a chest in which treasure is kept, coffer. -वासिन् *m.* an animal living in a shell, a chrysalis. -वृद्धि *f.* 1 increase of treasure. 2 enlargement of the scrotum. -शायिका a clasped knife, a knife lying in a sheath. -स्थ *a.* incased, sheathed. (-स्थः) an animal living in a shell (as a snail). -हीन *a.* deprived of riches, poor.

कोशलिकं A bribe (=कौशलिक q. v. which is the more correct form).

कोशातकिन् *m.* 1 Trade, business. 2 A trader, merchant. 3 Submarine fire.

कोशि (षि) न् *m.* The mango tree.

कोष्ठः 1 Any one of the viscera of the body, such as the heart, lungs &c. 2 The belly, abdomen. 3 An inner apartment. 4 A granary, store-room. —ष्ठं 1 A surrounding wall. 2 The shell of anything. -Comp. -अगारं a store-house, store-room; पर्याप्तभारितकोष्ठागारं मांसशोणितैर्मे गृहं भविष्यति Ve. 3; Ms. 9. 280. -अग्निः the digestive faculty, gastric juice. -पालः 1 a treasurer, store-keeper. 2 a guard, watch. 3 a constable (resembling the modern municipal officer). -शुद्धिः *f.* evacuation of the bowels.

कोष्ठकः 1 A granary. 2 A surrounding wall. —कं A brick trough for watering cattle.

कोष्ण *a.* Lukewarm, tepid; R. 1. 84. —ष्णं Warmth.

कोस (श) लः (pl.) N. of a country and its people; पितुरनंतरमुत्तरकोसलान् R. 9. 9; 3. 5; 6. 71; मगधकोसलकेकयशासिनां दुहितरः 9. 17.

कोस (श) ला The city of Ayodhyâ.

कोहलः 1 A kind of musical instrument. 2 A sort of spirituous liquor.

कौक्कुटिकः 1 A poulterer. 2 A mendicant who walks always fixing his eyes on the ground for fear of treading upon worms, insects &c. 3 (Hence) A hypocrite.

कौक्ष *a.* (क्षी *f.*) 1 Tied to, or being on, the sides. 2 Abdominal.

कौक्षेय (यी *f.*) 1 Being in the belly. 2 Being in a sheath; असिं कौक्षेयमुद्यम्य चकारापनसं मुखं Bk. 4. 31.

कौक्षेयकः A sword, scimitar; वामपार्श्वावलंबिना कौक्षेयकेण K. 8; Vikr. 1. 90.

कौंकः,कौंकणः (pl.) N. of a country and its people or rulers; (see कोंकण).

कौट *a.* (टी *f.*) 1 Living in one's own house; hence, independent, free. 2 Domestic, homely, homebred. 3 Fraudulent, dishonest. 4 Snared. —टः 1 Fraud, falsehood. 2 Giving false evidence. -Comp. -जः the Kutaja tree. -तक्षः (opp. ग्रामतक्षः) an independent carpenter, one who works at home on his own account and not for the village. -साक्षिन् *m.* a false witness. -साक्ष्यं false evidence, perjury.

कौटकिकः, -कौटिकः 1 One whose business is to catch birds &c. in traps. 2 One who sells the flesh of birds, animals &c; a butcher, poacher.

कौटिलिकः 1 A hunter. 2 A blacksmith.

कौटिल्यं 1 Crookedness (lit. and fig.). 2 Wickedness 3 Dishonesty, fraud. -ल्यः 'The crooked', N. of Châṇakya, a celebrated writer on civil polity, (the work being known as चाणक्यनीति), the friend and adviser of Chandragupta and a very important character in the Mudrârâkshasa; कौटिल्यः कुटिलमतिः स एष येन क्रोधाग्नौ प्रसभमदाहि नंदवंशः Mu. 1. 7, स्पृशति मां भृत्यभावेन कौटिल्यशिष्यः Mu. 7.

कौटुंब *a.* (बीं *f.*) Necessary for the family or household. -बं Family relationship.

कौटुंबिक *a.* (की *f.*) Constituting a family. —कः The father or master of a family; *paterfamilias*.

कौणपः A goblin, demon. -Comp. -दंतः an epithet of Bhîshma.

कौतुकं 1 Desire, curiosity, wish. 2 Eagerness, vehemence, impatience. 3 Anything creating curiosity or wonder. 4 The marriage thread (worn on the wrist); R. 8. 1. 5 The ceremony with the marriage thread preceding a marriage. 6 Festivity, gaiety. 7 Particularly, auspicious festivity, solemnity or solemn occasion (such as marriage); Ku. 7. 25. 8 Delight, joy, pleasure, happiness; Bh. 3. 140. 9 Sport, pastime. 10 A song, dance, show, or spectacle. 11 Joke, mirth. 12 Friendly greeting, salutation. –COMP. –अगारः-रं,-गृहं a pleasure-house ; कौतुकागारमागात् Ku. 7. 94. –क्रिया,-मंगलं 1 a solemn ceremony. 2 particularly marriage ceremony ; R. 11. 53. –तोरणः-णं a triumphal arch erected on festive occasions.

कौतूहलं (ल्यं) 1 Desire, curiosity, interest; विषयव्यावृत्तकौतूहलः V. 1. 9; *S*. 1. 2 Eagerness, vehement or eager desire. 3 Anything exciting curiosity, a wonder, curiosity.

कांतिकः A spearman, lancer.

कौंतेयः 'Son of Kuntî', an epithet of Yudhishṭhira, Bhima or Arjuna.

कौप *a*. (पी *f*.) Relating to or coming from a well (as water).

कौपीनं 1 The pudenda. 2 A privity, privy part. 3 A small piece of cloth (usually a small strip) worn over the privities; कौपीनं शतखंडजर्जरतरं कंथा पुनस्तादृशी Bh. 3. 101. 4 (Hence sometimes) A ragged or tattered garment. 5 A sin, improper or wrong act.

कौब्ज्यं 1 Crookedness. 2 Hump-backedness.

कौमार *a*. (री *f*.) 1 Juvenile, youthful, virgin, maidenly (of men and women); कौमारः पतिः, कौमारी भार्या. 2 Soft, tender. —रं 1 Childhood (to the age of five). 2 Maidenhood (to the age of sixteen), virginity ; पिता रक्षति कौमारे भर्ता रक्षति यौवने Ms. 9. 3 ; देहिनोऽस्मिन् यथा देहे कौमारं यौवनं जरा Bg. 2. 13. –COMP. –भृत्यं the rearing and general treatment of children. –हर *a*. marrying or gaining a woman as a girl ; यः कौमारहरः स एव हि वरः K. P. 1.

कौमारकं Boyhood, juvenile or tender age ; कौमारकेऽपि गिरिवद्गुरुतां दधानः U. 6. 19.

कौमारिकः A father of girls.

कौमारिकेयः The son of an unmarried woman.

कौमुदः The month Kârtika.

कौमुदी 1 Moonlight ; शशिना सह याति कौमुदी Ku. 4. 33 ; शशिनमुपगतेयं कौमुदी मेघमुक्तं R. 6. 85; (the word is thus derived :—कौ मोदंते जना यस्यां तेनासौ कौमुदी मता). 2 Anything serving as moonlight, *i e*. causing delight and balmy coolness ; त्वमस्य लोकस्य च नेत्रकौमुदी Ku. 5. 71 ; या कौमुदी नयनयोर्भवतः सुजन्मा Mâl. 1. 34; cf. चंद्रिका. 3 The full moon day in Kârtika. 4 The full moon day in Asvina. 5 Festivity (in general). 6 Particularly, a festive day on which temples, houses &c. are illuminated. 7 (At the end of titles of works &c.) Elucidation, throwing light on the subject treated; *e. g*. तर्ककौमुदी, सांख्यतत्त्वकौमुदी, सिद्धांतकौमुदी &c. –COMP. –पतिः the moon. –वृक्षः the stick or stand of a lamp.

कौमोदकी, कौमोदी N. of the mace of Vishṇu.

कौरव *a*. (वी *f*.) Relating to the Kurus ; क्षेत्रं क्षत्रप्रधनपिशुनं कौरवं तद्भजेथाः Me. 48. –वः 1 A descendant of Kuru; मथ्नामि कौरवशतं समरे न कोपात् Ve. 1. 15. 2 A ruler of the Kurus.

कौरव्यः 1 A descendant of Kuru ; कौरव्यवंशदावेऽस्मिन् क एष शलभायते Ve. 1. 19, 25 ; कौरव्ये कृतहस्तता पुनरियं देवे यथा सीरिणि 6. 12. 2 A ruler of the Kurus.

कौर्प्यः The zodiacal sign Scorpio (a word derived from Greek).

कौल *a*. (ली *f*.) 1 Relating to a family, ancestral, hereditary. 2 Of a noble family, well-born. –लः A worshipper of शक्ति according to the left hand ritual. –लं The doctrine and practices of lefthand *S*âktas.

कौलकेयः The son of an unchaste woman, a bastard.

कौलटिनेयः 1 The son of a (chaste) female beggar. 2 A bastard.

कौलटेयः The son of a female beggar (chaste or unchaste). 2 A bastard.

कौलिक *a*. (की *f*.) 1 Belonging to a family. 2 Customary in a family, ancestral. —कः A weaver ; कौलिको विष्णुरूपेण राजकन्यां निषेवते Pt. 1. 202. 2 A heretic. 3 A follower of the left hand *S*âkta ritual.

कौलीन *a*. Belonging to a noble family. —नः 1 The son of a female beggar. 2 A follower of the left hand *S*âkta ritual. —नं 1 An evil report, a scandal ; मालविकागतं किमपि कौलीनं श्रूयते M. 3 ; तदेव कौलीनमिव प्रतिभाति V. 2 ; Me. 112 ; कौलीनमात्माश्रयमाचचक्षे R. 14. 36, 84. 2 An improper act, bad or scandalous conduct ; ख्याते तस्मिन् वितमसि कुले जन्म कौलीनमेतत् Ve. 2. 10. 3 A combat of animals. 4 Cock-fighting. 5 War, battle (in general). 6 High birth. 7 A privity, the pudenda.

कौलीन्यं 1 High birth. 2 Family scandal.

कौलूतः A king of the Kulûtas ; कौलूतश्चित्रवर्मा Mu. 1. 20.

कौलेयकः A dog, hound.

कौल्य *a*. Noble-born, of a high birth.

कौबे (वे) र *a*. (री *f*.) Belonging to or coming from Kubera ; यानं सस्मार कौबेरं R. 15. 45. —री The north (the direction presided over by Kubera); ततः प्रतस्थे कौबेरीं भास्वानिव रघुर्दिशं R. 4. 66.

कौश *a*. (शी *f*.) 1 Silken. 2 Made of Kusa grass.

कौशलं (ल्यं) 1 Well-being, happiness, prosperity. 2 Skill, skilfulness, cleverness ; किमकौशलादुत प्रयोजनापेक्षितया Mu. 3 ; हावहारि हसितं वचनानां कौशलं दृशि विकारविशेषाः *S*i. 10. 13.

कौशलिकं A bribe.

कौशलिका, कौशली 1 A present, an offering. 2 Friendly inquiry after one's health &c., greeting.

कौशलेयः An epithet of Râma, son of Kausalyâ.

कौशल्या The eldest wife of Dasaratha and mother of Râma.

कौशल्यायनिः Râma, son of Kausalyâ; Bk. 7. 90.

कौशांबी N. of an ancient city on the Ganges in the lower part of the Doab.

कौशिक *a*. (की *f*.) 1 Incased, sheathed. 2 Silken. —कः 1 An epithet of विश्वामित्र q. v. 2 An owl ; U. 2. 29. 3 A lexicographer. 4 Marrow. 5 Bdellium. 6 An ichneumon. 7 A snake-catcher. 8 The sentiment of love (शृंगार). 9 One who knows hidden treasures. 10 An epithet of Indra. –का A cup, drinking vessel. —की 1 N. of a river in Behâr. 2 N. of the goddess Durgâ. 3 N. of one of the four varieties of dramatic style ; सुकुमारार्थसंदर्भा कौशिकी तासु कथ्यते; See S. D. 411 *et. seq*. also. –COMP. –अरातिः,-अरिः a crow. –फलः the cocoa-nut tree. –प्रियः an epithet of Râma.

कौशे (षे) यं 1 Silk ; Pt. 1. 94. 2 A silken cloth in general Ms. 5. 120. 3 A woman's lower garment of silk ; निर्नाभि कौशेयमुपात्तबाणमभ्यंगनेपथ्यमलंचकार Ku. 7. 9 ; विद्रुमकौशेयः Mk. 5. 3 ; Rs. 5. 9.

कौसीद्यं 1 The practice of usury. 2 Sloth, indolence.

कौसृतिकः 1 A cheat, knave. 2 A juggler.

कौस्तुभः N. of a celebrated gem obtained with 13 other jewels at the churning of the ocean and worn by Vishṇu on his breast ; सकौस्तुभं ह्रेपयतीव कृष्णं R. 6. 49 ; 10. 10. –COMP –लक्षणः, –वक्षस् *m*., –हृदयः an epithet of Vishṇu.

क्नूय् 1 A. (क्नूयते) 1 To make a creaking sound 2 To sink. 3 To be wet.

क्रकचः A saw. –COMP. –च्छदः the Ketaka tree. –पत्रः the teak tree. –पाद् *m*., –पादः a lizard.

क्रकरः A kind of partridge. 2 A saw. 3 A poor man. 4 A disease.

क्रतुः 1 A sacrifice ; क्रतोरशेषेण फलेन युज्यतां R. 3. 65; शतं क्रतूनामपविघ्नमाप सः 3. 38; M. 1. 4, Ms. 7. 79. 2 An epithet of Vishṇu. 3 One of the ten Prajâpatis; M. 1. 35. 3 Intelligence talent. 5 Power, ability. –COMP

-उत्तमः the राजसूय sacrifice. -द्रुह्,-द्विष् *m*. a demon, goblin. -ध्वंसिन् *m*. an epithet of *S*iva (who destroyed Daksha's sacrifice.) -पतिः performer of a sacrifice. -पशुः a sacrificial horse. -पुरुषः an epithet of Vishnu. -भुज् *m*. a god, deity. -राज् *m*. 1 the lord of sacrifices; यथाश्वमेधः क्रतुराट् Ms. 9. 260. 2 the राजसूय sacrifice.

क्रथ् 1 P. (क्रथति, क्रथित) To injure, hurt, kill.

क्रथकैशिकः (pl.) N. of a country; अथेश्वरेण क्रथकैशिकानां R. 5. 39; Ms. 5. 2.

क्रथनं A slaughter.

क्रथनकः A camel.

क्रंद् 1 P. (क्रंदति, क्रंदित) 1 To cry, weep, shed tears; किं क्रंदसि दुराक्रंद स्वपक्षक्षयकारक Pt. 4. 29; क्रंदत्यतः करुणमप्सरसां गणोऽयं V. 1. 2; चक्रंद विग्ना कुररीव भूयः R. 14. 68; 15. 42; Bk. 3. 28, 5. 5. 2 To call out to, call out piteously to any one, (with acc.); क्रंदत्यविरतं सोऽथ भ्रातृमातृसुतानथ Mârk. P. —10 P. or *Caus*. 1 To cry out continuously. 2 To cause to weep. -WITH आ 1 to cry out, cry, creak, scream; तृणाग्रलग्नैस्तुहिनैः पतद्भिराक्रंदतीवोषसि शीतकालः Rs. 4. 7; Bk. 15. 50. 2 to call out to (*caus*.); पहोहीति शिखंडिनां पटुतरैः केकाभिराक्रंदितः Mk. 5. 23.

क्रंदनं, क्रंदितं 1 Cry of distress or weeping, lamentation; हा तातेति क्रंदितमाकर्ण्य विषण्णः R. 9. 75. 2 Mutual defiance, challenge.

क्रम् 1 U., 4 P. (क्रामति, क्रमते, क्राम्यति, क्रांत) 1 To walk, step, go; क्रामत्यनुदिते सूर्ये वाली व्यपगतक्लमः Râm.; गम्यमानं न तेनासीदगतं क्रामता पुरः Bk. 8. 2, 25. 2 To go to, approach (with acc.); देवा इमान् लोकानक्रमंत Sat. Br. 3 To pass or go over, go across; सुखं योजनपंचाशाक्रमेयं Râm. 4 To leap, jump; क्रमं बबंध क्रमितुं सकोपः (हरिः) Bk. 2. 9; 5. 51. 5 To go up, ascend. 6 To cover, occupy, take possession of, fill; क्रांता यथा चेतसि विस्मयेन R. 14. 17. 7 To surpass, excel; स्थितः सर्वोन्नतेनोर्वीं क्रांत्वा मेरुरिवात्मना R. 1. 14. 8 To undertake, strive after, be able or competent for, show energy for (with dat. or inf.); व्याकरणाध्ययनाय क्रमते Sk.; धर्माय क्रमते साधुः Vop.; व्युत्पत्तिरावर्जितकोविदापि न रंजनाय क्रमते जडानां Vikr. 1. 16; हत्वा रक्षांसि लविंतुमक्रमीन्मारुतिः पुनः। अशोकवनिकामेव Bk. 9. 23. 9 To be developed or increased, to have full scope, be at home (with loc.); कृत्येषु क्रमते Dk. 170; क्रमतेऽस्मिञ्शास्त्राणि, or ऋक्षु क्रमते बुद्धिः Sk.; क्रममाणोऽरिसंसदि Bk. 8. 22. 10 To fulfil, accomplish. 11 To have sexual intercourse with. (By P. I. 3. 38 क्रम् by itself is used in the Atm. in the sense of 'continuity' or 'want of interruption', 'energy or application', and 'development or increase', and also 'conquering or getting over'). -WITH अति 1 to cross, go over; सप्तकक्षांतराण्यतिक्रम्य K. 92. 2 to go beyond, pass over or by; Me. 57, 40. 3 to excel, surpass; Ms. 8. 151. 4 to transgress, violate, overstep; अतिक्रम्य सदाचारं K. 160. 5 to disregard, exclude, neglect; प्रथितयशसां प्रबंधानतिक्रम्य M. 1; किं वा परिजनमतिक्रम्य भवान्संदिष्टः M. 4; or कथं ज्येष्ठानतिक्रम्य यवीयान् राज्यमर्हति Mb. 6 to pass, elapse (as time); अतिक्रांते दशाहे Ms. 5. 76; यथा यथा यौवनमतिचक्राम K. 59. -अधि to ascend. -अध्या to occupy, fill, take; अध्याक्रांता वसतिरमुनाप्याश्रमे सर्वभोग्ये *S*. 2. 14. -अनु 1 to follow. 2 to begin. 3 to give the contents of -अन्वा to visit one after another. -अप to leave, go away from. -अभि 1 to go to, approach, enter; अभिचक्राम काकुत्स्थः शरभंगाश्रमं प्रति Râm. 2 to wander, roam over. 3 to attack. -अव to withdraw. —आ 1 to approach, go towards. 2 to attack, subdue, conquer, vanquish; पक्षिशावकानाक्रम्य H. 1; पौरस्त्यानेवमाक्रामन् R. 4. 34; Bh. 1. 70. 3 to fill, enter, take possession of; खं केशवोऽपर इवाक्रमितुं प्रवृत्तः Mk. 5. 2, 9. 12. 4 to begin, commence. 5 to come up, rise (Atm.); यावत्प्रतापनिधिराक्रमते न भानुः R. 5. 71. 6 to ascend, mount, occupy. -उद् 1 to go up, out or beyond; ऊर्ध्वं प्राणा ह्युत्क्रामंति Ms. 2. 120. 2 to neglect, disregard; आर्षं प्रमाणमुत्क्रम्य धर्मं न प्रतिपालयन् Mb.; धर्ममुत्क्रम्य. 3 to step beyond; R. 15. 33. -उप 1 to go towards, approach. 2 to assail, attack. 3 to treat, attend upon, physic (as a physician); to cure or heal. 4 to make advances of love to, win over; सर्वैरुपायैरुपक्रम्य सीतां Râm. 5 to perform, set about. 6 (Atm.) to begin, commence प्रसभं वक्तुमुपक्रमेत कः Ki. 2. 28; R. 17. 33. -निस् 1 to go away, or from, leave. 2 to issue from, come out of; Bk. 7. 71. -परा (Atm.) 1 to display courage, strength, or heroism, act bravely; बकवच्चिंतयेदर्थान् सिंहवच्च पराक्रमेत् Ms. 7. 106; Bk. 8. 22, 93. 2 to turn back. 3 to march against, attack. -परि 1 to walk about, walk round; परिक्रम्यावलोक्य च (in dramas). 2 to overtake. -प्र (Atm.) 1 to begin, commence; प्रचक्रमे च प्रतिवक्तुमुत्तरं R. 3. 47, 2. 15; Ku. 3. 2. 2 to tread on, walk on; Bk. 15. 23. 3 to go, set out. -प्रति to return. -वि (Atm.) 1 to walk along or through; विष्णुस्त्रेधा विचक्रमे took 3 steps; Bk. 8. 24. 2 to assail, overcome, conquer. 3 to cleave; open (Paras.). -व्यति 1 to transgress. 2 to pass (time). -व्युद् see -उत. -सम् 1 to come or meet together. 2 to traverse, cross, go or pass through. 3 to approach, to go. 4 to go over or be transferred (to another). 5 to enter on or in; कालो ह्ययं संक्रमितुं द्वितीयं सर्वोपकारक्षममाश्रमं ते R. 5. 10. -समा 1 to occupy, take possession of, fill; सममेव समाक्रांतं द्वयं द्विरदगामिना। तेन सिंहासनं पित्र्यमखिलं चारिमंडलं R. 4. 4. 2 to assail, conquer, subdue.

क्रमः 1 A step, pace; त्रिविक्रमः; सागरः प्लवगेंद्रेण क्रमेणैकेन लंघितः Mb. 2 A foot. 3 Going, proceeding, course; क्रमात् or क्रमेण in course of, gradually; कालक्रमेण gradually, in course of time; भाग्यक्रमः course or turn of fate; R. 3. 7, 30, 32. 4 Performance, commencement; इत्थमत्र विततक्रमे क्रतौ Si. 14. 53. 5 Regular course, order, series, succession; निमित्तनैमित्तकयोरयं क्रमः *S*. 7. 30; Ms. 7. 24, 9. 85, 2. 173, 3. 69. 6 Method, manner; नेत्रक्रमेणोपरुरोध सूर्यं R. 7. 39. 7 Grasp, hold; क्रमगता पशोः कन्यका Mâl. 3. 18. 8 A position of attack (assumed by an animal before making a spring) 9 Preparation, readiness; Bk. 2. 9. 10 An undertaking, enterprize. 11 An act or deed, manner of proceeding; कोप्येष कांतः क्रमः Amaru. 43, 33. 12 Particular manner of reciting Vedic texts. 13 Power, strength. -मं Mud. -COMP. -अनुसारः, -अन्वयः regular order, due arrangement. -आगत, -आयात *a*. descended or inherited lineally, hereditary. -ज्या the sine of a planet, declination. -भंगः irregularity.

क्रमक *a*. Orderly, methodical. -कः A student who goes through a regular course of study.

क्रमणः 1 The foot. 2 A horse. -णं 1 A step. 2 Walking. 3 Proceeding. 4 Transgressing.

क्रमतः *ind*. Gradually, successively.

क्रमशः *ind*. 1 In due order, regularly, successively, seriatim. 2 Gradually, by degrees; R. 12. 57; Ms. 1. 68, 3. 12.

क्रमिक *a*. 1 Successive, serial. 2 Descended lineally, ancestral, hereditary.

क्रमुः, क्रमुकः The betel-nut tree; आस्वादितार्द्रक्रमुकः समुद्रात् *Si*. 3. 81; Vikr. 18. 98.

क्रमेलः, क्रमेलकः A camel; निरीक्षते केलिवनं प्रविश्य क्रमेलकः कंटकजालमेव Vikr. 1. 29; *Si*. 12. 18; N. 6. 104.

क्रयः Buying, purchasing. -COMP. —आरोहः a market, fair. -क्रीत *a*. bought. —लेख्यं a deed of sale, conveyance &c.; (गृहं क्षेत्रादिकं क्रीत्वा तुल्यमूल्याक्षरान्वितं। पत्रं कारयते यत्तु क्रयलेख्यं तदुच्यते Brihaspati). -विक्रयौ (du.) trade, traffic, buying and selling; Ms. 8. 5; 7. 127. -विक्रयिकः a trader, merchant.

क्रयणं Buying, purchasing.

क्रयिकः 1 A trader, dealer. 2 A purchaser.

क्रव्य *a.* A thing exhibited for sale in the market; (opp. क्रेय which only means 'fit to be purchased').

क्रव्यं Raw flesh, carrion, स्थपुटगतमपि क्रव्यमव्यग्रमात्ति Mâl. 5. 16. –COMP. **–अद्, -अद, –भुज्** *a.* eating raw flesh; Ms. 5. 131. (*–m.*) 1 a carnivorous animal, such as a tiger &c.; U. 1. 49. 2 a demon, goblin ; R. 15. 16.

क्रशिमन् *m.* Thinness, emaciation, leanness.

क्राकचिकः A sawyer.

क्रांत *a.* Gone, passed over, traversed &c.; (*p.p.* of **क्रम्** q. v.). **–तः** 1 A horse. 2 A foot, step. –COMP. **–दर्शिन्** *a.* omniscient.

क्रांतिः *f.* 1 Going, proceeding. 2 A step, pace. 3 Surpassing. 4 Attacking, overcoming. 5 Declination of a planet. 6 The ecliptic. –COMP. **–कक्षः, –मंडलं, –वृत्तं** the ecliptic. **–पातः** the equinoctial points or nodes of the cliptic. **–वलयः** 1 the ecliptic. 2 the tropical zone, space within the tropics.

क्राय (यि) कः 1 A purchaser. 2 A trader, merchant.

क्रिमिः 1 A worm. 2 An insect; see कृमि. –COMP. **–जं** aloewood. **–शैलः** an ant-hill.

क्रिया 1 Doing, execution, performance, accomplishment ; उपचार°, धर्म°; प्रत्युक्तं हि प्रणयिषु सतामीप्सितार्थक्रियैव Me. 114. 2 An action, act, business, undertaking ; प्रणयिक्रिया V. 4. 15; Ms. 2. 4. 3 Activity, bodily action, labour. 4 Teaching, instruction; क्रिया हि वस्तूपहिता प्रसीदति R. 3. 29. 5 Possession of some art (as of singing, dancing &c.), knowledge; शिष्टा क्रिया कस्यचिदात्मसंस्था M. 1. 16. 6 Practice (opp. शास्त्र theory). 7 A literary work ; शृणुत मनोभिरवहितैः क्रियामिमां कालिदासस्य V. 1. 2 ; कालिदासस्य क्रियायां कथं परिषदो बहुमानः M. 1. 8 A purificatory rite, a religious rite or ceremony. 9 An expiatory rite, expiation. 10 (*a*) Ceremony of offering oblations to the deceased ancestors (श्राद्ध). (*b*) Obsequies. 11 Worship. 12 Medical treatment, application of remedies, cure; शीतक्रिया M. 4 cold remedies. 13 (In gram.) Action, the general idea expressed by a verb. 14 Motion. 15 Especially, motion as one of the seven categories of the Vaiseshikas; see कर्मन्. 16 (In law) Judicial investigation by human means (witnesses &c.) or by ordeals. 17 Burden of proof.–COMP. **–अन्वित** *a.* practising ritual observances. **–अपवर्गः** 1 completion or termination of an affair, execution of a task, क्रियापवर्गेष्वनुजीविसात् कृताः Ki. 1. 44. 2 liberation from ceremonial acts, absolution. **–अभ्युपगमः** a special agreement ; क्रियाभ्युपगमात्त्वेतत् बीजार्थं यत्प्रदीयते Ms. 9. 53. **–अवसन्न** *a.* one who loses a law-suit through the statements of the witnesses &c. **–इंद्रियं** see कर्मेंद्रिय. **–कलापः** 1 the whole body of ceremonies enjoined in the Hindu religious law. 2 all the particulars or points of any business. **–कारः** 1 an agent, worker. 2 a beginner, tyro, a fresh student. 3 an agreement. **–द्वेषिन्** *m.* a witness whose testimony is prejudicial to the cause (one of the five kinds of witnesses). **–निर्देशः** evidence. **–पटु** *a.* dexterous. **–पथः** mode of medical treatment. **–पदं** a verb. **–पर** *a.* diligent in the performance of one's duty. **–पादः** the third division of a legal plaint; that is, witnesses, documents and other proofs adduced by the plaintiff or complainant. **–योगः** 1 connection with the verb. 2 the employment of expedients or means. **–लोपः** omission or discontinuance of any of the essential ceremonies of the Hindu religion ; क्रियालोपात् वृषलत्वं गताः Ms. 10. 43. **–वशः** necessity, necessary influence of acts done or to be done. **–वाचक, –वाचिन्** *a.* expressing any action, as a verbal noun. **–वादिन्** *m.* a plaintiff, complainant. **–विधिः** a rule of action, manner of performing any rite ; Ms. 9. 220. **–विशेषणं** 1 an adverb. 2 a predicative adjective. **–संक्रांतिः** *f.* imparting (to others) one's knowledge ; teaching; M. 1. 19. **समभिहारः** the repetition of any act.

क्रियावत् *a.* Engaged in any actual work, versed in the practice of a thing; यस्तु क्रियावान्पुरुषः स विद्वान् H. 1. 67.

क्री 9 U. (क्रीणाति, क्रीणीते, क्रीत) 1 To buy, purchase ; महता पुण्यपण्येन क्रीतेयं कायनौस्त्वया Sânti 3. 1 ; क्रीणीष्व मज्जीवितमेव पण्यमन्यन्न चेदस्ति तदस्तु पुण्यं N. 3. 87, 88 ; Pt. 1. 13 ; Ms. 9. 174. 2 To barter, exchange ; कच्चित्सहस्रैर्मूर्खाणामेकं क्रीणासि पंडितं Mb.–WITH **आ** to buy. **–निस्** to buy off, redeem, ransom. **–परि** (in the Atm.) 1 to buy ; संभोगाय परिक्रीतः कर्तास्मि तव नाप्रियं Bk. 8. 72. 2 to hire, purchase for a time (with instr. or dat. of the price at which one is employed on stipulated wages) ; शतेन शताय वा परिक्रीतः Sk. 3 to return, requite, repay ; कृतेनोपकृतं वायोः परिक्रीणानमुत्थितं Bk. 8. 8. **–वि** 1 to sell (Atm. in this sense); गवां शतसहस्रेण विक्रीणीषे सुतं यदि Râm. ; विक्रीणीत तिलाञ्शुद्धान् Ms. 10. 90, 8. 197, 222 ; Sânti. 1. 12. 2 to barter, exchange ; नाकस्माच्छांडिलीमाता विक्रीणाति तिलैस्तिलान् Pt. 2. 65.

क्रीड् 1 P. (क्रीडति, क्रीडित) 1 To play, amuse oneself ; वानराः क्रीडितुमारब्धाः Pt. 1 ; एष क्रीडति कूपयंत्रघटिकान्यायप्रसक्तो विधिः Mk. 10. 59. 2 To gamble, play at dice ; बहुविधं द्यूतं क्रीडतः Mk. 2 ; नाक्षैः क्रीडेत्कदाचिद्धि Ms. 4. 74 ; Y. 1. 138. 3 To jest, joke or trifle with ; सद्वृत्तस्तनमंडलस्तवकथं प्राणैर्मम क्रीडति Gît. 3 ; क्रीडिष्यामि तावदेनया V. 3 ; एवमाशाग्रहग्रस्तैः क्रीडंति धनिनार्थिभिः H. 2. 23 ; Pt. 1. 187; Mk. 3. –WITH **अनु** (Atm.) to play, sport, amuse oneself ; साध्वनुक्रीडमानानि पश्य वृंदानि पक्षिणां Bk. 8. 10. **–आ, –परि, –सं** (Atm.) to play &c ; संक्रीडंते मणिभिर्यत्र कन्याः Me. 70; but **क्रीड्** with **सं** is Paras. in the sense of 'making a noise;' संक्रीडंति शकटानि Mbh. 'the carts creak.'

क्रीडः 1 Sport, pastime, play, pleasure. 2 Jest, joke.

क्रीडनं 1 Playing, sporting. 2 A play-thing, toy.

क्रीडनकः –कं, क्रीडनीयं, –यकं A plaything, toy.

क्रीडा 1 Sport, pastime, play, pleasure; तोयक्रीडानिरतयुवतिस्नानतिक्तैर्मरुद्भिः Me. 33, 61. 2 Jest, joke. –COMP. **–गृहं** a pleasure-house. **–शैलः** an artificial hill serving as a pleasure-abode, a pleasure-mountain ; क्रीडाशैलः कनककदलीवेष्टनप्रेक्षणीयः Me. 77. **–नारी** a prostitute. **–कोपः** feigned anger ; Amaru. 12. **–मयूरः** a peacock kept for pleasure; R. 16. 14. **–रत्नं** 'the gem of sports', copulation.

क्रीत *a.* Bought; see क्री. **–तः** One of the twelve kinds of sons recognised in Hindu Law ; a son purchased from his natural parents; क्रीतश्च ताभ्यां विक्रीतः Y. 2. 131 ; Ms. 9. 174. –COMP. **–अनुशयः** 'repenting a purchase', rescission, returning a thing purchased to the seller (admissible in some cases by law).

क्रुंच् *m.* **क्रुंचः** A curlew, heron.

क्रुध् 4. P. (क्रुध्यति, क्रुद्ध) To be angry (with the dat. of the person who is the object of anger) ; हरये क्रुध्यति ; but sometimes with words like उपरि, प्रति &c. also ; ममोपरि स क्रुद्धः, न मां प्रति क्रुद्धो गुरुः &c. –WITH **प्रति** to be angry in return ; क्रुध्यंतं न प्रतिक्रुध्येत् Ms. 6. 48. **–सम्** to get angry with ; संक्रुध्यसि मृषा किं त्वं दिदृक्षुं मां मृगेक्षणे Bk. 8. 76.

क्रुध् *f.* Anger.

क्रुश् 1 P. (क्रोशति, क्रुष्ट) 1 To cry, weep, lament, mourn (for); क्रोशंत्यस्तं कपिस्त्रियः Bk. 6. 124. 2 To cry out, yell, scream, bawl, call out ; अतीव चुक्रोश जीवनाशं ननाश च Bk. 14. 31. –WITH **अनु** to pity, take compassion on. **–अभि** to bewail. **–आ** 1 to cry, cry out loudly ; अये गौरीनाथ त्रिपुरहर शंभो त्रिनयन प्रसीदेत्याक्रोशन् Bh. 3. 123. 2 to revile, abuse ; शतं ब्राह्मणमाक्रुश्य क्षत्रियो

दंडमर्हति Ms. 8. 267; Bk. 5. 39. -परि to lament. -प्रत्या to revile in return. -वि 1 to call aloud, cry out loudly; आक्रोश विक्रोश लपाचिचंडं Mk. 1. 41; Bk. 14. 42; 16. 32. 2 to utter (with acc.). 3 to call out to (with acc.). 4 to resound. -व्या to lament, bewail.

क्रुष्ट *a.* 1 Cried out. 2 Called out to. —**ष्टं** Crying, a cry, yell.

क्रूर *a.* 1 Cruel, wicked, hard-hearted, pitiless; तस्याभिषेकसंभारं कल्पितं क्रूरनिश्चया R. 12. 4; Me. 105; Ms. 10. 9. 2 Hard, rough. 3 Formidable, terrible, fierce. 4 Destructive, mischievous. 5 Wounded, hurt. 6 Bloody. 7 Raw. 8 Strong. 9 Hot, sharp, disagreeable; Ms. 2. 33. —**रः** A hawk; heron. —**रं** 1 A wound. 2 Slaughter, cruelty. 3 Any horrible deed. -COMP. -**आकृति** *a.* terrible in form. (**तिः**) epithet of Râvaṇa. -**आचार** *a.* following cruel or savage practices. -**आशय** *a.* 1 containing fierce animals (as a river). 2 of a cruel disposition. -**कर्मन्** *n.* 1 a bloody act. 2 any hard labour. -**कृत्** *a.* fierce, cruel, unrelenting. -**कोष्ठ** *a.* having costive bowels unaffected by strong purgatives. -**गंधः** sulphur. -**दृश्** *a.* 1 evil-eyed, having a malignant look. 2 mischievous, villainous. -**राविन्** *m.* a raven. -**लोचनः** an epithet of the planet Saturn.

क्रेतृ *m.* A purchaser; Y. 2. 168.

क्रौंचः N. of a mountain; see क्रौंच.

क्रोडः 1 A hog. 2 The hollow of a tree, cavity; हा हा हंत तथापि जन्मविटपिक्रोडे मनो धावति Udb. 3 The chest, bosom, breast; क्रोडीकृ to clasp to the bosom; Bh. 2. 35. 4 The middle part of anything; Vikr. 11. 75; see क्रोड *n.* 5 An epithet of the planet Saturn. —**डं**, -**डा** 1 The breast, chest, the part between the shoulders. 2 The interior of anything, a cavity, hollow. -COMP. -**अंकः**, -**अंघ्रिः**, -**पादः** a tortoise. -**पत्रं** 1 marginal writing. 2 a post-script to a letter. 3 a supplement. 4 a codicil to a will.

क्रोडीकरणं Embracing, clasping to the bosom.

क्रोडीमुख A rhinoceros.

क्रोधः 1 Anger, wrath, कामात्क्रोधोऽभिजायते Bg. 2. 62; so क्रोधांधः, क्रोधानलः &c. 2 (In Rhet.) Anger considered as the feeling which gives rise to the *raudra* sentiment. -COMP -**उज्झित** *a.* free from anger, cool, composed. -**मूर्च्छित** *a.* overcome or infatuated with anger.

क्रोधन *a.* Wrathful, passionate, angry, irascible; यद्रामेण कृतं तदेव कुरुते द्रौणायनिः क्रोधनः Ve. 3. 31. —**नं** Being angry, anger.

क्रोधालु *a.* Passionate, irascible, angry.

क्रोशः 1 A cry, yell, shout, scream, noise. 2 A measure of distance equal to ¼th of a Yojana, a *Koss*; क्रोशार्धं प्रकृतिपुरःसरेण गत्वा R. 13. 79; समुद्रात्पुरी क्रोशौ or क्रोशयोः. -COMP. -**तालः** -**ध्वनिः** a large drum.

क्रोशन *a.* Crying. —**नं** A cry.

क्रोष्टु *m.* (**ष्टी** *f.*) A jackal (the strong cases of this word are necessarily formed from क्रोष्टृ and the weak ones optionally).

क्रौंचः 1 A curlew, heron; मनोहरक्रौंचनिनादितानि सीमांतराण्युत्सुकयंति चेतः Rs. 4. 8; Ms. 12. 64. 2 N. of a mountain (said to be the grandson of Himâlaya and said to have been pierced by Kârtikeya and Parasurâma); हंसद्वारं भृगुपतियशो वर्त्म यत् क्रौंचरंध्रं Me. 57. -COMP. -**अदनं** the fibres of the stalk of a lotus -**अरातिः**, -**अरिः**, -**रिपुः** 1 an epithet of Kârtikeya. 2 of Parasurâma -**दारणः** -**सूदनः** an epithet (1) of Kârtikeya (2) of Parasurâma.

क्रौर्यं Cruelty, hard-heartedness.

क्लंद् I. 1 P. (क्लंदति, क्लंदित) 1 To call, call out. 2 To cry, lament. -II. 1 A. (क्लंदते or क्लदते) To be confused.

क्लम् 1. 4. P. (क्लामति, क्लाम्यति, क्लांत) To be fatigued or tired, be exhausted or depressed; न चक्लाम न विव्यथे Bk. 5. 102; 14. 101. -WITH वि to be fatigued.

क्लमः, **क्लमथः** Fatigue, languor, exhaustion; विनोदितदिनक्लमाः कृतरुचश्च जांबूनदैः Si. 4. 66; Ms. 7. 151; S. 3. 21.

क्लांत *a.* 1 Fatigued, tired out; तमातपक्लांतं R. 2. 13, Me. 18, 36; V. 2. 22. 2 Withered, faded; क्लांतो मन्मथलेख एष नलिनीपत्रे नखैरर्पितः S. 3. 26; R. 10. 48. 3 Lean.

क्लांतिः *f.* Fatigue. -COMP. -**छिद्** *a.* refreshing, invigorating.

क्लिद् 4 P. (क्लिद्यति, क्लिन्न) To become wet, be damp, be moist. —*Caus.* To moisten, wet; न चैनं क्लेदयंत्याप Bg. 2. 23; Bk. 18. 11.

क्लिन्न *a.* Wet, moistened. -COMP. -**अक्ष** *a.* blear-eyed.

क्लिश् 4 A. (also P. according to some authorities) (क्लिश्यते, क्लिष्ट or क्लिशित) 1 To be tormented, be afflicted, suffer; अभ्युपदेशग्रहणे नातिक्लिश्यते वः शिष्या M. 1; त्रयः परार्थे क्लिश्यंति साक्षिणः प्रतिभूः कुलं Ms. 8. 169. 2 To torment, molest. -II. 9 P. (क्लिश्नाति, क्लिष्ट, क्लिशित) To torment, afflict, molest, distress; क्लिश्नाति लब्धपरिपालनवृत्तिरेव S. 5. 6; एवमाराध्यमानोपि क्लिश्नाति भुवनत्रयं Ku. 2. 40; R. 11. 58.

क्लिशित, -**क्लिष्ट** *a.* 1 Distressed, suffering pain or misery. 2 Afflicted, tormented. 3 Faded. 4 Inconsistent, contradictory; *e. g.* माता मे वंध्या. 5 Elaborate, artificial, (as a composition.) 6 Put to shame.

क्लिष्टिः *f.* 1 Affliction, anguish, distress, pain. 2 Service.

क्लीब (व) *a.* 1 Impotent, neuter, emasculated; Ms. 3. 150, 4. 205; Y. 1. 223. 2 Unmanly, timid, weak, weak-minded; R. 8. 84; क्लीबान् पालयिता Mk. 9. 5. 3 Cowardly. 4 Mean, base. 5 Idle. 6 Of the neuter gender. —**बः**, -**बं** (-**वः** -**वं**) 1 An impotent man, a eunuch; न मूत्रं फेनिलं यस्य विष्ठा चाप्सु निमज्जति । मेढ्रं चोन्मादशुक्राभ्यां हीनं क्लीबः स उच्यते ॥ Kâtyâyana quoted in Dâyabhâga. 2 The neuter gender.

क्लेदः 1 Wetness, moisture, dampness; Sânti. 1. 29; R. 7. 21. 2 Running, discharge from a sore. 3 Distress, suffering; R. 15. 32 (=उपद्रव Malli.).

क्लेशः 1 Pain, anguish, suffering, distress, trouble; किमात्मा क्लेशस्य पदमुपनीतः S. 1; क्लेशः फलेन हि पुनर्नवतां विधत्ते Ku. 5. 86; Bg. 12. 5. 2 Wrath, anger. 3 Worldly occupation. -COMP. -**क्षम** *a.* capable of enduring trouble.

क्लैब्यं (**व्यं**) 1 Impotence (lit.); वरं क्लैब्यं पुंसां न च परकलत्राभिगमनं Pt. 1. 2 Unmanliness; timidity, cowardice; क्लैव्यं मा स्म गमः पार्थ Bg. 2. 3. 3 Uselessness; impotence, powerlessness; R. 12. 86.

क्लोमं The lungs.

क्व *ind.* 1 Whither, where; क्व तेऽन्योन्यं यत्नाः क्व च नु गहनाः कौतुकरसाः U. 6. 33; क्व-क्व when repeated in co-ordinate sentences imply 'great difference,' or 'incongruity'; क्व रुजा हृदयप्रमाथिनी क्व च ते विश्वसनीयमायुधं M. 3. 2; क्व सूर्यप्रभवो वंशः क्व चाल्पविषया मतिः R. 1. 2; Ki. 1. 6; S. 2. 18. 2 Sometimes क्व is used in the sense of the loc. of किम्; क्व प्रदेशे *i. e.* कस्मिन्प्रदेशे. (*a*) With a following अपि it means (1) somewhere, anywhere. (2) sometimes. (*b*) With a following चित् it means (1) in some places; प्रस्निग्धाः क्वचिदिंगुदीफलभिदः सूच्यंत एवोपलाः S. 1. 14; Rs. 1. 2; R. 1. 41. (2) in some cases; क्वचिद् गोचरः क्वचिन्न गोचरोऽर्थः. **क्वचित्-क्वचित्** (*a*) in one place-in another place, here-here, क्वचिद्वीणावाद्यं क्वचिदपि च हाहेति रुदितं Bh. 3. 125, 1. 4. (*b*) now-now (referring to time); क्वचित् पथा संचरते सुराणां क्वचित् घनानां पततां क्वचिच्च R. 13. 19.

क्वण् 1 P. (क्वणति, क्वणित) 1 To sound (indistinctly), jingle, tinkle; इति घोषयतीव डिंडिमः करिणो हस्तिपकाहतः क्वणन् H. 2. 86; क्वणन्मणिनूपुरौ Amaru. 28; Rs. 3. 36; Me. 36. 2 To hum, warble (as bees &c.); sing indistinctly; Ku. 1. 54; U. 3. 24; Bk. 6. 84.

क्वणः, **क्वणनं**, **क्वणितं**, **क्वाणः** 1 A sound in general. 2 The sound of any musical instrument.

क्रत्य *a*. Belonging to what place, being where.

क्रथ् 1 P. (क्रथति, क्रथित) 1 To boil, decoct. 2 To digest.

क्रथः, क्राथः A decoction, solution prepared with a continued or gentle heat.

क्राचित्क *a*. (त्की) *f*. Met with occasionally, rare, unusual; इति क्राचित्कः पाठः.

क्षः 1 Destruction. 2 Disappearance, loss. 3 Lightning. 4 A field. 5 A farmer. 6 Vishṇu in his 4th or Narasimha incarnation. 7 A demon.

क्षण् (न्) 8 U. (क्षणोति, क्षणुते, क्षत्त) 1 To hurt, injure; इमां हृदि व्यायतपातमक्षणोत् Ku. 5. 54. 2 To break (to pieces); (धनुः) त्वं किलानमितपूर्वमक्षणोः R. 11. 72; (with **-उप, -परि -वि** used in the same senses as क्षण्.)

क्षणः, -णं 1 An instant, moment, measure of time equal to $\frac{4}{5}$ of a second; क्षणमात्रमृषिस्तस्थौ सुप्तमीन इव हृदः R 1. 73; 2 60; Me. 26; क्षणमवतिष्ठस्व wait a moment. 2 Leisure; अहमपि लब्धक्षणः स्वगेहं गच्छामि M. 1; गृहीतः क्षणः S. 2 'my leisure is at your disposal'; *i.e.* I pledge my word to do your work. 3 A fit moment or opportunity; रहो नास्ति क्षणो नास्ति नास्ति प्रार्थयिता नरः Pt. 1. 138; Me. 62; अधिगतक्षणः Dk. 147. 4 An auspicious or lucky moment. 5 A festival, joy, delight. 6 Dependence, servitude. 7 The centre, the middle. -COMP. **-अंतरे** *ind*. the next moment, after a little while. **-क्षेपः** a momentary delay. **-दः** an astrologer. (**-दं**) water. (**-दा**) 1 night; क्षणादथैष क्षणदापतिप्रभः N. 1. 67; R. 8. 74; 16. 45; Si. 3. 53. 2 turmeric. °**करः -पतिः** the moon; Si. 9. 70. °**चरः** a night-walker, a demon; सानुप्लवः प्रभुरपि क्षणदाचराणां R. 13. 75. °**आंध्यं** night-blindness, nyctalopsis. **-द्युतिः** *f*. **-प्रकाशा, -प्रभा** lightning. **-निःश्वासः** the porpoise. **-भंगुर** *a*. transient, frail, perishable; H. 4. 130. **-मात्रं** *ind*. for a moment. **-रामिन्** *m*. a pigeon. **-विध्वंसिन्** *a*. perishable in a moment. (*-m.*) a class of atheistic philosophers who deny the continued identity of any part of nature, and maintain that the universe perishes and undergoes a new creation every instant.

क्षणतुः A wound, sore.

क्षणनं Injuring, killing, wounding.

क्षणिक *a*. Momentary, transient; स्वप्नेषु क्षणिकसमागमोत्सवैश्च R. 8. 92; एकस्य क्षणिका प्रीतिः H. 1. 66. **-का** Lightning.

क्षणिन् *a*. (नी *f*.) 1 Having leisure. 2 Momentary. **-नी** Night.

क्षत *a*. Wounded, hurt, injured, bitten, torn, rent, broken down &c.; see क्षण्; रक्तप्रसाधितभुवः क्षतविग्रहाश्च Ve. 1. 7; R. 1. 28; 2. 56; 3. 53. **-तं** 1 Scratching. 2 A wound, hurt, injury; क्षते क्षारमिवासह्यं जातं तस्यैव दर्शनं U. 4. 7; क्षारं क्षते प्रक्षिपन् Mk. 5. 18. 3 Danger, destruction, peril; क्षतात् किल त्रायत इत्युदग्रः R. 2. 53. -COMP. **-अरि** *a*. victorious. **-उदरं** dysentery. **-कासः** a cough produced by injury. **-जं** 1 blood; स छिन्नमूलः क्षतजेन रेणुः R. 7. 43; Ve. 2. 27. 2 puss, matter. **-योनिः** *f*. a violated woman, a woman who is no longer a virgin. **-विक्षत** *a*. mangled, covered with cuts and wounds. **-वृत्तिः** *f*. destitution, being deprived of any means of support. **-व्रतः** a student who has violated his vow or religious engagements.

क्षतिः *f*. 1 Injury, wound. 2 Destruction, cutting, tearing down; विस्रब्धं क्रियतां वराहततिभिर्मुस्ताक्षतिः पल्वले S. 2. 6. 3 (Fig.) Ruin, loss, disadvantage; सुखं संजायते तेभ्यः सर्वेभ्योपीति का क्षतिः S. D. 17. 4 Decline, decay, diminution; प्रतापक्षतिशीतलाः Ku. 2. 24; H. 1. 114.

क्षत्तृ *m*. 1 One who cuts or carves anything. 2 An attendant, a doorkeeper. 3 A coachman, charioteer. 4 A man born of a Sûdra man and Kshatriya woman; cf. Ms. 10. 9. 5 The son of a female slave; (*e. g.* विदुर). 6 Brahmâ. 7 A fish.

क्षत्रः-त्रं 1 Dominion, power, supremacy, might. 2 A man of the Kshatriya caste or the Kshatriya tribe taken collectively; क्षतात्किल त्रायत इत्युदग्रः क्षत्रस्य शब्दो भुवनेषु रूढः R. 2. 53; 11. 69, 71; असंशयं क्षत्रपरिग्रहक्षमा S. 1. 21; Ms. 9. 322. -COMP. **-अंतकः** an epithet of Parasurâma. **-धर्मः** 1 bravery, military heroism. 2 the duties of a Kshatriya. **-पः** a governor, satrap. **-बंधुः** 1 a Kshatriya by caste; Ms. 2. 38. 2 a mere Kshatriya, a vile or wretched Kshatriya; (as a term of abuse); cf. ब्रह्मबंधु.

क्षत्रियः A member of the military or second caste; ब्राह्मणः क्षत्रियो वैश्यस्त्रयो वर्णा द्विजातयः Ms. 10. 4. -COMP. **-हणः** an epithet of Parasurâma.

क्षत्रियका, क्षत्रिया, क्षत्रियिका A woman of the Kshatriya caste.

क्षत्रियाणी 1 A woman of the Kshatriya caste. 2 The wife of a Kshatriya.

क्षत्रियी The wife of a Kshatriya.

क्षंतृ *a*. (त्री *f*.) Patient, forbearing, submissive.

क्षप् 1 U. (क्षपति-ते, क्षपित) To fast, to be abstinent; Ms. 5. 69. *-Caus.* or 10 U. (क्षपयति-ते, क्षपित) 1 To throw, send, cast. 2 To miss.

क्षपणः A Bauddha mendicant. **-णं** 1 Defilement, impurity (अशौचं). 2 Destroying, suppressing, expelling.

क्षपणकः A Bauddha or Jaina mendicant; नग्नक्षपणके देशे रजकः किं करिष्यति Chân. 110; कथं प्रथममेव क्षपणकः Mu. 4.

क्षपणी 1 An oar. 2 A net.

क्षपण्युः An offence.

क्षपा 1 A night; विगमयन्नुन्निद्र एव क्षपाः S. 6. 4; R. 2. 20; Me. 110. 2 Turmeric. COMP. **-अटः** 1 night-stalker. 2 a demon, goblin; ततः क्षपाटैः पृथुपिंगलाक्षैः Bk. 2. 30. **-करः, -नाथः** 1 the moon. 2 camphor. **-घनः** a dark cloud. **-चरः** a demon, goblin.

क्षम् 1 A., 4 P. (क्षमते, क्षाम्यति, क्षांत or क्षमित) 1 To permit, allow, suffer; अतो नृपाश्चक्षमिरे समेताः स्त्रीरत्नलाभं न तदात्मजस्य R. 7. 34; 12. 46. 2 To pardon, forgive (as an offence); क्षांतं न क्षमया Bh. 3. 13; क्षमस्व परमेश्वर; निग्रस्य मे भर्तृनिदेशरौक्ष्यं देवि क्षमस्वेति बभूव नम्रः R. 14. 58. 3 To be patient or quiet, wait; R. 15. 45. 4 To endure, put up with, suffer; अपि क्षमंतेऽस्मदुपजापं प्रकृतयः Mu. 2; नाज्ञाभंगकरान् राजा क्षमेत स्वसुतानपि H. 2. 107. 5 To oppose, resist. 6 To be competent or able (to do anything); ऋते रवेः क्षालयितुं क्षमेत कः क्षमातमस्कांडमलीमसं नभः Si. 1. 38, 9. 65.

क्षम *a*. 1 Patient. 2 Enduring, submissive. 3 Adequate, competent, able (with gen., loc., inf. or in comp.); मलिनो हि यथादर्शो रूपालोकस्य न क्षमः Y. 3. 141; सा हि रक्षणविधौ तयोः क्षमा R. 11. 5; हृदयं न त्ववलंबितुं क्षमाः R. 8. 59; गमनक्षम, निर्मूलनक्षम. &c. 4 Appropriate, fit, proper, suitable; तन्नो यदुक्तमशिवं न हि तत्क्षमं ते U. 1. 14; आत्मकर्मक्षमं देहं क्षात्रो धर्म इवाश्रितः R. 1. 13; S. 5. 26. 5 Fit for, capable of, suited to; उपभोगक्षमे देशे V. 2; तपःक्षमं साधयितुं य इच्छति S. 1. 18. 6 Bearable, endurable. 7 Favourable, friendly.

क्षमा 1 Patience, forbearance, forgiveness; क्षमा शत्रौ च मित्रे च यतीनामेव भूषणं H. 2; R. 1. 22; 18. 9; तेजः क्षमा वा नैकांतं कालज्ञस्य महीपतेः Si. 2. 83. 2 The earth. 3 An epithet of Durgâ. -COMP. **-जः** the planet Mars. **-भुज्, भुजः** a king.

क्षमितृ *a*. (त्री *f*.), **क्षमिन्** *a*. (नी *f*.) Patient, forbearing, of a forgiving nature; कामं क्षाम्यतु यः क्षमी Si. 2. 43; Y. 2. 200, 1. 133.

क्षयः 1 A house, residence, abode; यातनाश्च यमक्षये Ms. 6. 61; निर्जगाम पुनस्तस्मात्क्षयान्नारायणस्य ह Mb. 2 Loss, decline, waste, wane, decay, diminution; आयुःक्षयः R. 3. 69; धनक्षये वर्धति जाठराग्निः Pt. 2. 178; so चंद्रक्षयः, क्षयपक्षः &c. 3 Destruction, end, termination; निशाक्षये याति ह्रियेव पांडुतां Rs. 1. 9; Amaru. 60. 4 Pecuniary loss; Ms. 8. 401. 5 Fall (as of prices.) 6 Removal. 7 Universal destruction (प्रलय). 8 Consumption. 9 A disease in general. 10 A negative quality, minus (in algebra). -COMP. **-कर** (also **क्षयंकर**) *a*. causing decay or destruction, ruinous. –कालः 1 time of universal destruction. 2 the period of decline. –कासः consumptive cough. –पक्षः the dark fortnight. –युक्तिः *f.*, –योगः an opportunity of destroying. –रोगः consumption. –वायुः the wind that is to blow at the destruction of the world. –संपद् *f.* total loss, ruin.

क्षयथुः Consumptive cough, consumption.

क्षयिन् *a.* (णी *f.*) 1 Diminishing, decaying; आरंभगुर्वी क्षयिणी क्रमेण Bh. 2. 60; waning, wasting; न चाभूत्ताविव क्षयी R. 17. 71, Ms. 9. 314. 2 Consumptive. 3 Perishable, fragile.–*m.* The moon.

क्षयिष्णु *a.* 1 Wasting, decaying. 2 Perishable, fragile.

क्षर् 1 P. (क्षरति, क्षरित) (Used transitively or intransitively) 1 To flow, glide. 2 To send or stream forth, pour out, emit; R. 13. 74; Bk. 9. 8. **3** To drop, trickle, ooze. **4** To waste away, wane, perish. **5** To become useless, have no effect; यज्ञोऽनृतेन क्षरति तपः क्षरति विस्मयात् Ms. 4. 237. **6** To slip from, be deprived of (with abl.). –*Caus.* (क्षारयति) To accuse, traduce (usually with आ). –With वि to melt away, dissolve.

क्षर *a.* 1 Melting away. 2 Movable. 3 Perishable; क्षरः सर्वाणि भूतानि कूटस्थोऽक्षर उच्यते Bg. 15. 16. —रः A cloud. —रं 1 Water. 2 The body.

क्षरणं 1 The act of flowing, trickling, dropping, oozing. 2 The act of perspiring; अंगुलिक्षरणसन्नवर्तिकः R. 19. 18.

क्षरिन् *m.* The rainy season.

क्षल् 10 U. (क्षालयति-ते, क्षालित) 1 To wash, wash off, purify, cleanse: ऋते रवेः क्षालयितुं क्षमेत कः क्षपातमस्कांडमलीमसं नभः Si. 1. 38, H. 4. 60. 2 To wipe away. –With प्र 1 to wash, purify, cleanse; पादौ, मुखं, हस्तं &c. प्रक्षालयति. 2 to wipe away; (अयशः) तेषामनुग्रहेणाद्य राजन् प्रक्षालयात्मनः Mb. –वि to wash off; R. 5. 44.

क्षवः, क्षवथुः 1 Sneezing. 2 Cough.

क्षात्र *a.* (त्री *f.*) Relating or peculiar to the military tribe; क्षात्रो धर्मः श्रित इव तनुं ब्रह्मघोषस्य गुप्त्यै U. 6. 9; R. 1. 13. –त्रं 1 The Kshatriya tribe. 2 The qualifications of a Kshatriya; the Gîtâ thus describes them:–शौर्यं तेजो धृतिर्दाक्ष्यं युद्धे चाप्यपलायनं । दानमीश्वरभावश्च क्षात्रं कर्म स्वभावजं Bg. 18. 43.

क्षांत *p. p.* 1 Patient, forbearing, enduring. 2 Forgiven. —ता The earth.

क्षांतिः *f.* 1 Patience, forbearance, forgiveness; क्षांतिश्चेद्वचनेन किं Bh. 2. 21; Bg. 18. 42.

क्षांतु *a.* Patient, forbearing. –तुः A father.

क्षाम *a.* 1 Scorched, singed. 2 Diminished, thin, wasted, emaciated, lean; क्षामक्षामकपोलमाननं S. 3. 10; मध्ये क्षामा Me. 82; क्षामच्छायं भवनमधुना मद्वियोगेन नूनं 80, 89. 3 Slight, little, small. 4 Weak, infirm.

क्षार *a.* Corrosive, caustic, acid, pungent, saline. –रः 1 Juice, essence. 2 Treacle, molasses. 3 Any corrosive or acid substance; क्षते क्षारमिवासह्यं जातं तस्यैव दर्शनं U. 4. 7; क्षारं क्षते प्रक्षिपन् Mk. 5. 18; (क्षारं क्षते क्षिप् &c. has become proverbial and means 'to aggravate the pain which is already unbearable,' 'to make bad worse', 'to add insult to injury'). 4 Glass. 5 A rogue, cheat. —रं 1 Black salt. 2 Water. –Comp. –अच्छं sea-salt. –अंजनं an alkaline unguent. –अंबु *n.* an alkaline fluid. –उदः, –उदकः, –उदधिः, –समुद्रः the salt ocean. –त्रयं,–त्रितयं natron, salt-petre and borax. –नदी a river of alkaline water in hell. –भूमिः *f.*, –मृत्तिका saline soil; किमाश्चर्यं क्षारभूमौ प्राणदा यमदूतिका Ud. 6. –मेलकः an alkaline substance. –रसः a saline flavour.

क्षारकः 1 Alkali. 2 Juice, essence. 3 A cage, basket or net for birds. 4 A washerman. 5 A blossom; a bud or newblown flower (कलिका).

क्षारणं, –णा Accusing; especially of adultery.

क्षारिका Hunger.

क्षारित *a.* 1 Distilled from saline matter. 2 Falsely accused (especially of adultery).

क्षालनं 1 Washing, cleansing (with water). 2 Sprinkling.

क्षालित *a.* 1 Washed, cleansed, purified. 2 Wiped away, requited; तथा वृत्तं पापैर्व्यथयति यथा क्षालितमपि U. 1. 28.

क्षि I. 1 P. (क्षयति, क्षित or क्षीण) 1 To decay or waste. 2 To rule, govern, be master of. –II 1. 5. 9. P. (क्षयति, क्षिणोति, क्षिणाति) 1 To destroy, affect, ruin, corrupt; न तद्यशः शस्त्रभृतां क्षिणोति R. 2. 40. 2 To diminish, cause to waste away; R. 19. 48. 3 To kill, injure. –*Pass.* (क्षीयते) 1 To waste, wane, decay, be diminished (fig. also); प्रतिक्षणमयं कायः क्षीयमाणो न लक्ष्यते H. 4. 66; प्रत्यासन्नविपत्तिमूढमनसां प्रायो मतिः क्षीयते Pt. 2. 4; Amaru 93; Bh. 2. 19. –*Caus.* (क्षययति or क्षपयति) 1 To destroy, remove, put an end to; ममापि च क्षपयतु नीललोहितः पुनर्भवं परिगतशक्तिरात्मभूः S. 7. 35; R. 8. 47; Me. 53. 2 To spend or pass (as time). –With अप to decay, decline, be diminished. –परि, –प्र-सं 1 to decay, wane. 2 to be emaciated or lean.

क्षितिः *f.* 1 The earth. 2 A dwelling, an abode, a house. 3 Loss, destruction. 4 The end of the world. –Comp. –ईशः, –ईश्वरः a king; R. 1. 5; 3. 3; 11. 1. –कणः dust. –कंपः an earthquake. –क्षित् *m.* a king, prince. –जः 1 a tree. 2 an earth-worm. 3 the planet Mars. 4 N. of the demon Naraka killed by Vishṇu. (–जं) the horizon. (–जा) an epithet of Sîtâ. –तलं the surface of the earth. –देवः a Brâhmaṇa. –धरः a mountain; Ku. 7. 94. –नाथः, –पः, –पतिः, –पालः, –भुज् *m.* रक्षिन् *m.* a king, sovereign; R 2. 51, 5. 76, 6. 86, 7. 3, 9. 75. –पुत्रः the planet Mars. –प्रतिष्ठ *a.* dwelling on the earth. –भृत् *m.* 1 a mountain; सर्वक्षितिभृतां नाथ V. 4. 27; (where it means 'a king' also); Ki. 5. 20; Rs. 6. 26 2 a king. –मंडलं the globe. –रंध्रं a ditch, hollow. –रुह् *m.* a tree. –वर्धनः *m.* a corpse, dead body. –वृत्तिः *f.* 'the course of the earth', patient behaviour. –व्युदासः a cave within the earth, an underground hole.

क्षिद्रः 1 A disease 2 The sun. 3 A horn.

क्षिप् 6 U. (but only P. when preceded by अभि, प्रति and अति), 4 P. (क्षिपति-ते, क्षिप्यति, क्षिप्त) 1 To throw, cast, send, dispatch, discharge, let go (with loc. or sometimes dat.); मरुद्भ्य इति तु द्वारि क्षिपेदप्स्वद्भ्य इत्यपि Ms. 3. 88; शिलां वा क्षेप्स्यते मयि Mb; K. 12. 95; with प्रति also; Bh 3. 67. 2 To place, put on or upon, throw into; स्रजमपि शिरस्यंधः क्षिप्तां धुनोत्यहिशंकया S 7. 24; Y. 1. 230; Bg. 16 19. 3 To fix on, attach to (as a blame); भृत्ये दोषान् क्षिपति H. 2. 4 To cast or throw off, cast away, rid oneself of; किं कूर्मस्य भरव्यथा न वपुषि क्ष्मां न क्षिपत्येष यत् Mu. 2. 18. 5 To take away, destroy; Mâl. 1. 17. 6 To reject, disdain. 7 To insult, revile, abuse, scold; Ms. 8. 312, 270; Sânti. 3. 10. –With अधि –1 to censure, blame. 2 to offend, abuse. 3 to surpass. –अव 1 to cast down, leave, abandon 2 to slander, revile. –आ 1 to throw or cast down, hit. 2 to contract. 3 to draw back, snatch or draw away, pull or take off; अग्रपादमाक्षिप्य R. 7. 7; Bh. 1. 43; Me. 68. 4 to hint at, indicate. 5 to infer (from circumstances); जात्या व्यक्तिराक्षिप्यते. 6 to object to (as an argument). 7 to neglect, disregard. 8 to insult. –उद् to throw up; Rs 1. 22. –उप 1 to cast on, throw at; वपुषि वधाय तत्र तव शस्त्रमुपक्षिपतः Mâl. 5. 31. 2 to hint, indicate; adduce; छलं कार्यमुपक्षिपंति Mk. 9. 3. 3 to begin, commence. 4 to insult, upbraid. –नि 1 to put, place or throw down; Y. 1. 103; Amaru. 80. 2 to entrust, consign to the care of; Ms. 6. 3, 8. 179, 180. 3 to encamp. 4 to cast off, reject. 5 to bestow on. –परि 1 to surround; गंगास्रोतः परिक्षिप्तं Ku. 6. 38. 2 to embrace. –पर्या to bind or tie up, collect (as hair); (केशांतं) पर्याक्षिपत् काचिदुदारबंधं Ku. 7. 14. –प्र 1 to put into, throw at or in ; नामेध्यं प्रक्षिपेदग्नौ Ms. 4. 53 ; क्षारं क्षते प्रक्षिपन् Mk. 5. 18. 2 to insert, interpolate; इति सूत्रे कैश्चित्प्रक्षिप्तं Kaiyaṭa. –वि 1 to throw or cast. 2 to divert. 3 to distract. –सं 1 to collect, heap together ; आतपात्ययसंक्षिप्तनीवारासु निषादिभिः R. 1. 52; Bk. 5. 86. 2 to withdraw, destroy. 3 to shorten, curtail, abridge ; संक्षिप्येत क्षण इव कथं दीर्घयामा त्रियामा Me. 108 ; Ms. 7. 34.

क्षिपणं 1 Sending, throwing, casting. 2 Reviling, abusing.

क्षिपणी (**णि**) *f*. 1 An oar. 2 A net. 3 A weapon. —**णिः** A stroke.

क्षिपण्युः 1 The body. 2 The spring season.

क्षिपा 1 Sending, throwing, casting. 2 Night.

क्षिप्त *p. p.* 1 Thrown, scattered, hurled, cast. 2 Abandoned. 3 Disregarded, neglected, disrespected. 4 Placed. 5 Distracted, mad (see क्षिप्). –**तं** A wound caused by shooting. –Comp. –**कुक्कुरः** a mad dog. –**चित्त** *a*. distracted in mind, absent-minded. –**देह** *a*. prostrating the body, lying down.

क्षिप्तिः *f*. 1 Throwing, sending forth. 2 Explaining a hidden meaning (such as solving riddles).

क्षिप्र *a*. (compar. क्षेपीयस्; superl. क्षेपिष्ठ) Quick, speedy. —**प्रं** *ind*. Quickly, speedily, immediately; विनाशं व्रजति क्षिप्रमामपात्रमिवांभसि Ms. 3. 179; Sânti. 3. 6; Bk. 2. 44. –Comp. –**कारिन्** *a*. acting quickly, prompt.

क्षिया 1 Loss, destruction, waste, decay. 2 An impropriety, offence against established customs (आचारभेद); the following is an instance; स्वयमह रथेन याति उपाध्यायं पदातिं गमयति Sk.

क्षीजनं The whistling of hollow reeds.

क्षीण *a*. 1 Thin, emaciated, waned, become lean, diminished, worn away, expended; भार्यां क्षीणेषु वित्तेषु (जानीयात्) H. 1. 72; so क्षीणः शशी; क्षीणे पुण्ये मर्त्यलोके विशंति. 2 Slender, delicate. 3 Small, little. 4 Poor, miserable. 5 Powerless, weak. –Comp. –**चंद्रः** the moon on the wane. –**धन** *a*. reduced to poverty, impoverished. –**पाप** *a*. one who is purified after having suffered the consequences of sin. –**पुण्य** *a*. one who has enjoyed all his stock of merit, and must work to acquire more in another birth –**मध्य** *a*. slender-waisted. –**वासिन्** *a*. inhabiting a dilapidated house. –**विक्रांत** *a*. destitute of courage or prowess. –**वृत्ति** *a*. deprived of the means of support, out of employ.

क्षीब्, **क्षीब** See **क्षीव्**, **क्षीव**.

क्षीरः –रं 1 **Milk; हंसो हि क्षीरमादत्ते** तन्मिश्रा वर्जयत्यपः *S*. 6. 27. 2 The milky juice or sap of trees ; ये तत्क्षीरस्रुतिसुरभयो दक्षिणेन प्रवृत्ताः Me. 107; Ku. 1. 9. 3 Water –Comp. –**अदः** an infant, a sucking child. –**अब्धिः** the sea of milk. °**जः** 1 the moon. 2 a pearl. °**जं** sea-salt. °**जा** °**तनया** an epithet of Lakshmî. –**आह्वः** the pine tree. –**उदः** the sea of milk ; क्षीरोदवेलेव सफेनपुंजा Ku. 7. 26. °**तनयः** the moon. °**तनया**, °**सुता** an epithet of Lakshmî. –**उदधि**= क्षीरोद q. v. above. –**ऊर्मिः** a wave of the sea of milk; R. 4. 27. –**ओदनः** rice boiled with milk. –**कंठः** a young child (having milk in the throat); त्वया तत्क्षीरकंठेन प्राप्तमारण्यकं व्रतं Mv. 4. 52, 5. 11. –**जं** coagulated milk. –**द्रुमः** the Asvattha tree. –**धात्री** a wet-nurse. –**धिः**, –**निधिः** the sea of milk ; इंदुः क्षीरनिधाविव R. 1. 12. –**धेनुः** *f*. a milch cow. –**नीरं** 1 water and milk. 2 milk-like water. 3 a fast embrace. –**पः** a child. –**वारिः**, –**वारिधिः** the sea of milk. –**विकृतिः** inspissated milk. –**वृक्षः** 1 N. of the four trees न्यग्रोध, उदुंबर, अश्वत्थ and मधूक. 2 the glomerous fig-tree. –**शरः** cream, the skim of milk. –**समुद्रः** the sea of milk. –**सारः** butter. –**हिंडीरः** the foam of milk.

क्षीरिका A dish prepared with milk.

क्षीरिन् *a*. Milky, yielding milk.

क्षीव् 1. 4. P. (क्षीवति, क्षीव्यति) 1 To be drunk or intoxicated. 2 To spit, eject from the mouth.

क्षीव *a*. Excited, drunk, intoxicated; ध्रुवं जये यस्य जयामृतेन क्षीवः क्षमाभर्तुरभूत्कृपाणः Vikr. 1. 96 ; क्षीवो दुःशासनासृजा Ve. 5. 27.

क्षु 2 P. (क्षौति, क्षुत) 1 To sneeze ; अपयाति सरोषया निरस्ते कृतकं कामिनि चुक्षुवे मृगाक्ष्या Si. 9. 83; Ch. P. 10; Bk. 14. 75. 2 To cough.

क्षुण्ण *p. p.* 1 Beaten, trodden ; R. 1. 17. 2 (Fig.) Practised, followed; क्षुद्रजनक्षुण्ण एष मार्गः K. 146. 3 Pounded; see क्षुद्. –Comp. –**मनस्** *a*. penitent, repentant.

क्षुत् *f*, **क्षुतं –ता** Sneezing, a sneeze.

क्षुद् 7 U. (क्षुणत्ति, क्षुंते, क्षुण्ण) 1 To tread or trample upon, strike against, crush (under the foot), bruise, pound down; क्षुणत्ति सर्पान् पाताले Bk. 6. 36; ते तं व्याशिषताक्षौत्सुः पादैर्दैतैस्तथाच्छिदन् 15. 43; 17. 66. 2 To move, be agitated (A.). –With प्र to crush, bruise, pound; मित्रघ्नस्य प्रचुक्षोद गदयां बिभीषणः Bk. 14. 33.

क्षुद्र *a*. (comp. क्षोदीयस् superl. क्षोदिष्ठ) 1 Minute, small, tiny, little, trifling. 2 Mean, low, vile, base ; क्षुद्रेऽपि नूनं शरणं प्रपन्ने Ku. 1. 12. 3 Wicked. 4 Cruel. 5 Poor, indigent. 6 Miserly, niggardly; Me. 17. —**द्रा** 1 A bee. 2 A quarrelsome woman. 3 A woman maimed or crippled. 4 A prostitute; उपसृष्टा इव क्षुद्राधिष्ठितभवनाः K. 107. –Comp. –**अंजनं** a kind of unguent applied to the eyes in certain diseases. –**अंत्रः** the small cavity of the heart. –**उलूकः** an owl. –**कंबुः** small shell. –**कुष्ठ** a mild form of leprosy. –**घंटिका** 1 small bell. 2 a girdle of small bells. –**चंदनं** red sandal-wood. –**जंतुः** any small animal. –**दंशिका** a small gadfly. –**बुद्धि** *a*. low-minded, mean. –**रसः** honey. –**रोगः** a minor disease; (44 are enumerated by Susruta). –**शंखः** a small conch-shell. –**सुवर्णं** low or bad gold, *i. e.* brass.

क्षुद्रल *a*. Minute, small (applied especially to diseases and animals).

क्षुध् 4 P. (क्षुध्यति, क्षुधित) To be hungry; Bk. 5. 66, 6. 44, 9. 39.

क्षुध् *f*. **क्षुधा** Hunger ; सीदति क्षुधा Ms. 7. 134, 4. 187. –Comp. –**आर्त**, –**आविष्ट** *a*. afflicted by hunger. –**क्षाम** *a*. emaciated by hunger ; Bk. 2. 29. –**पिपासित** *a*. hungry and thirsty. –**निवृत्तिः** *f*. cessation of hunger, appeasing of appetite (in general).

क्षुधालु *a*. Hungry.

क्षुधित *a*. Hungry ; R. 2. 39.

क्षुपः A tree with small roots and branches, a shrub.

क्षुभ् 1 A., 4. 9. P. (क्षोभते, क्षुभ्यति, क्षुभ्नाति, क्षुभित–क्षुब्ध) 1 To shake, tremble, to be agitated or disturbed; महाह्रद इव क्षुभ्यन् Bk. 9. 118 ; R. 4. 21 ; Si. 8. 24. 2 To be unsteady. 3 To stumble (fig. also). –With **प्र**, **–वि** or **सम्** to tremble, be agitated or disturbed.

क्षुभित *a*. 1 Shaken, agitated &c. ; महाप्रलयमारुतक्षुभितपुष्करावर्तक &c. Ve. 3. 2. 2 Afraid. 3 Enraged.

क्षुब्ध *a*. 1 Agitated, shaken, unsteady. 2 Disturbed. 3 Afraid. –**ब्धः** A churning stick; शोभैव मंदरक्षुब्धक्षुभितांभोधिवर्णना Si. 2. 107. 2 A particular mode of sexual enjoyment.

क्षुमा Linseed, a kind of flax.

क्षुर् 6. P. (क्षुरति, क्षुरित) 1 To cut, scratch. 2 To make lines or furrows.

क्षुरः 1 A razor; R. 7. 46; Ms. 9. 262. 2 A razor-like barb attached to an arrow. 3 The hoof of a cow or horse. 4 An arrow. –Comp. –**कर्मन्** *n*. –**क्रिया** act of shaving. –**चतुष्टयं** the four things necessary for shaving. –**धानं**, –**भांडं** a razorcase. –**धार** *a*. as sharp as a razor. –**प्रः** 1 an arrow with a sharp horse-shoe-shaped head; तं क्षुरप्रशकलीकृतं कृती R. 11. 29; 9. 62. 2 a sort of hoe, a weeding-spade. –**मर्दिन्**, –**मुंडिन्** *m*. a barber.

क्षुरिका, **क्षुरी** 1 A knife, dagger. 2 A small razor.

क्षुरिणी The wife of a barber.

क्षुरिन् *m*. A barber.

क्षुल्ल *a*. Small, little. –COMP. **–तातः** the younger brother of a father; cf. खुल्ल.

क्षुल्लक *a*. 1 Little, minute. 2 Low, vile. 3 Insignificant. 4 Poor. 5 Wicked, malicious. 6 Young.

क्षेत्रं 1 A field, ground, soil; चीयते बालिशस्यापि सत्क्षेत्रपतिता कृषिः Mu. 1. 3. 2 Landed property, land. 3 Place, abode, region, repository; कपटशतमयं क्षेत्रमप्रत्ययानां Pt. 1. 191; Bh. 1. 77; Me. 16. 4 A sacred spot, a place of pilgrimage; क्षेत्रं क्षत्रप्रधनपिशुनं कौरवं तद्भजेथाः Me. 46; Bg. 1. 1. 5 An enclosed sport of ground. 6 Fertile soil. 7 Place of origin. 8 A wife; अपि नाम कुलपतेरियमसवर्णक्षेत्रसंभवा स्यात् *S*. 1; Ms. 3. 175. 9 The sphere of action, the body (regarded as the field of the working of the soul); योगिनो यं विचिन्वंति क्षेत्राभ्यंतरवर्तिनं Ku. 6. 77; Bg. 13. 1, 2, 3. 10 The mind. 11 A house; a town. 12 A plane figure, as a triangle. 13 A diagram. –COMP. **–अधिदेवता** the tutelary deity of any sacred piece of ground. **–आजीवः, –करः** a cultivator, peasant. **–गणितं** geometry. **–गत** *a*. geometrical. °**उपपत्तिः** *f*. geometrical proof. **–ज** *a*. 1 produced in a field. 2 born from the body. (**–जः**) one of the 12 kinds of sons allowed by the old Hindu Law, the offspring of a wife by a kinsman duly appointed to raise up issue to the husband; Ms. 9. 167, 180; Y. 1. 68–69, 2. 128. **–जात** *a*. begotten on the wife of another. **–ज्ञ** *a*. 1 knowing localities. 2 clever, dexterous. (**–ज्ञः**) 1 the soul; cf. Bg. 13. 1-3; Ms. 12. 12. 2 the supreme soul. 3 a libertine. 4 a husbandman. **–पतिः** a land-owner, a landlord. **–पदं** a place sacred to a deity. **–पालः** 1 a man employed to guard a field. 2 a deity protecting fields. 3 an epithet of *Siva*. **–फलं** the area or superficial contents of a figure (in math.). **–भक्तिः** *f*. the division of a field. **–भूमिः** *f*. cultivated land. **–राशिः** quantity represented by geometrical figures. **–विद्** *a*. =क्षेत्रज्ञ q. v. (*–m*.) 1 husbandman. 2 a sage, one who has spiritual knowledge; Ku. 3. 50. 3 the soul. **–स्थ** *a*. residing at a sacred place.

क्षैत्रिक *a*. (**की**) *f*. Relating to a field. **—कः** 1 A farmer; Ms. 8. 241, 9. 53. 2 A husband; Ms. 9. 145.

क्षेत्रिन् *m*. 1 An agriculturist, a cultivator; Y. 2 161. 2 A (nominal) husband; *S*. 5. 3 The soul. 4 The supreme soul; Bg. 13. 33.

क्षेत्रिय *a*. 1 Relating to a field. 2 Curable in a future body, or incurable in the present life, irremediable; दंडोयं क्षेत्रियो येन मय्यपातीति साऽब्रवीत् Bk. 4. 32. **–यं** 1 An organic disease. 2 Meadow grass, pasturage. **–यः** An adulterer.

क्षेपः 1 Throwing, tossing, casting, moving about, movement (of limbs); कंदक्षेपानुगम Me. 47; भ्रक्षेपमात्रानुमतप्रवेशां Ku. 3. 60. 2 A throw, cast. 3 Sending, dispatching. 4 Striking down. 5 Transgressing. 6 Passing away (time); कालक्षेपः. 7 Delay, dilatoriness. 8 Insult, abuse; क्षेपं करोति चेद्दंड्यः Y. 2. 204; किं क्षेपे. 9 Disrespect, contempt. 10 Pride, haughtiness. 11 A nosegay.

क्षेपक *a*. 1 A thrower, sender. 2 Interpolated, inserted (as a passage). 3 Abusive, disrespectful. **—कः** A spurious or interpolated passage.

क्षेपणं 1 Throwing, casting, sending, directing &c. 2 Spending (as time). 3 Omitting. 4 Abusing. 5 A sling. **–णिः,–णी** *f*. 1 An oar. 2 A net for fishing. 3 A sling or any instrument with which missiles are thrown.

क्षेम *a*. 1 Conferring happiness; ease or comfort; good, beneficial, well; धार्तराष्ट्रा रणे हन्युस्तन्मे क्षेमतरं भवेत् Bg. 1. 45. 2 Prosperous, at ease, comfortable. 3 Secure, happy. **–मः, –मं** 1 Peace, happiness, ease, welfare, well-being; वितन्वति क्षेममदेवमातृकाश्चिराय तस्मिन् कुरवश्चकासते Ki. 1. 17; वैश्यं क्षेमं समागम्य (पृच्छेत्) Ms. 2. 127; अधुना सर्वजलचराणां क्षेमं भविष्यति Pt. 1. 2. Safety, security; क्षेमेण व्रज बांधवान् Mk. 7. 7 safely; Pt. 1. 146. 3 Preserving, protecting; R. 15. 6. 4 Keeping what is acquired; cf. योगक्षेम. 5 Final beatitude, eternal happiness. **—मः** A kind of perfume. –COMP. **—कर** (also **क्षेमंकर**) *a*. propitious, causing peace or security.

क्षेमिन् *a*. (**णी** *f*.) Safe, secure, happy.

क्षै 1 P. (क्षायति, क्षाम) To wane, waste away, become emaciated, decline, decay.

क्षैण्यं 1 Destruction. 2 Leanness, slenderness.

क्षैत्रं 1 A multitude of fields. 2 A field.

क्षैरेय *a*. (**यी** *f*.) Milky.

क्षोडः The post to which an elephant is fastened.

क्षोणिः, क्षोणी *f*. 1 The earth. 2 The number 'one' (in math).

क्षोत्तृ *m*. A pestle.

क्षोदः 1 Pounding, grinding. 2 The stone on which anything is ground or powdered. 3 Dust, particle, any small or minute particle; U 3 2. –COMP. **–क्षम** *a*. capable of standing a test, scrutiny, or investigation.

क्षोदिमन् *m*. Minuteness.

क्षोभः 1 Shaking, moving, tossing; Me. 28, 95; so काननक्षोभः &c. 2 Jolting; R. 1. 58; V. 3. 11. 3 (*a*) Agitation, disturbance, excitement, emotion; स्वयंवरक्षोभकृतामभावः R. 7. 3; अर्थेंद्रियक्षोभमयुग्मनेत्रः पुनर्वशित्वाद्बलवन्निगृह्य Ku. 3. 69. (*b*) Provocation, irritation; प्रायः स्वं महिमानं क्षोभात्प्रतिपद्यते जंतुः *S*. 6. 31.

क्षोभणं Agitating, disturbing. **—णः** One of the five arrows of Kâmadeva.

क्षोमः –मं A room on the top of a house.

क्षौणिः –णी *f*. see क्षोणि. –COMP. **–प्राचीरः** the ocean. **–भुज्** *m*. a king. **–भृत्** *m*. a mountain.

क्षौद्रः The Champaka tree. **–द्रं** 1 Smallness. 2 Meanness, lowness. 3 Honey; सक्षौद्रपटलैरिव R. 4. 63. 4 Water. 5 A particle of dust. –COMP. **–जं** wax.

क्षौद्रेयं Wax.

क्षौमः –मं 1 Silken cloth, woven silk; क्षौमं केनचिदिंदुपांडुतरुणा मांगल्यमाविष्कृतं *S*. 4. 5; क्षौमांतरितमेखले (अंके) R. 10. 8. 2 An airy room on the top of a house. 3 The back of an edifice. **–मं** Linen cloth. 4 Linseed. **–मी** Flax.

क्षौरं Shaving.

क्षौरिकः A barber.

क्ष्णु 2 P. (क्ष्णौति, क्ष्णुत) To whet, sharpen. –WITH **सं** (Atm.) to sharpen (fig. also) Bk. 8. 40.

क्ष्मा 1 The earth; (पुत्रं) क्ष्मां लंभयित्वा क्षमयोपपन्नं R. 18. 9; किं शेषस्य भरव्यथा न वपुषि क्ष्मां न क्षिपत्येष यत् Mu. 2. 18. 2 (In math.) The number 'one'. –COMP. **–जः** the planet Mars. **–पः, –पतिः, –भुज् –m**. a king; कविक्ष्मापतिः Gît. 1; देशानामुपरि क्ष्मापाः Pt. 1. 155. **–भृत्** *m*. a king or mountain.

क्ष्माय् 1 A. (क्ष्मायते, क्ष्मायित) To shake, tremble; चक्ष्माये च मही Bk. 14. 21; 17. 73.

क्ष्विड् 1 U. (क्ष्वेडति-ते, क्ष्वेट्ट or क्ष्वेडित) To hum, roar, whistle, growl, murmur, sound indistinctly; Ms. 4. 64.

क्ष्विड् 1 A., **क्ष्विद्** 4 P. (क्ष्विद्यति, क्ष्वेदित, क्ष्विण्ण) 1 To be wet or unctuous. 2 To emit sap or discharge juice, ichor &c., exude. –WITH **प्र** to murmur, hum; Bk. 7. 103.

क्ष्वेडः 1 Sound, noise. 2 Venom, poison; गुणदोषौ बुधो गृह्णन्निंदुक्ष्वेडाविवेश्वरः। शिरसा श्लाघते पूर्वं परं कंठे नियच्छति Subhâsh. 3 Moistening. 4 Abandonment. **–डा** 1 The roaring of a lion. 2 A war-cry, war-whoop. 3 A bamboo.

क्ष्वेडितं The roaring of a lion

क्ष्वेला Play, jest, joke.

ख.

खः The sun. —खं 1 The sky; खं केशवोऽपर इवाक्रमितुं प्रवृत्तः Mk. 5. 2; यावद्गिरः खे मरुतां चरंति Ku. 3. 72; Me. 9. 2 Heaven. 3 Organ of sense. 4 A city. 5 A field. 6 A cypher. 7 A dot, an anusvâra. 8 A cavity, an aperture, hollow, hole; Ms. 9. 43. 9 An aperture of the human body; (of which there are 9, *i.e.* the mouth, the two ears, the two eyes, the two nostrils, and the organs of excretion and generation); खानि चैव स्पृशेदद्भिः Ms. 2. 60, 53; 4. 144; Y. 1. 20; cf. Ku. 3. 50. 10 A wound. 11 Happiness, pleasure. 12 Talc. 13 Action. 14 Knowledge. 15 Brahman. –COMP. –अटः (खेट्टः) 1 a planet. 2 Râhu, the ascending node. –आपगा an epithet of the Ganges. –उल्कः 1 a meteor. 2 a planet. –उल्मुकः the planet Mars. –कामिनी N. of Durgâ. –कुंतलः N. of *S*iva. –गः 1 a bird; अधुनीत खगः स नैकधा तनुं N. 2. 2; Ms. 12. 63. 2 air, wind; तमांसीव यथा सूर्यो वृक्षानग्निर्वनान्खगः Mb. 3 the sun. 4 a planet; *e. g.* आपोक्लिमे यदि खगाः स किलेंदुवारः Tv. 5 a grass-hopper. 6 a deity. 7 an arrow. °अधिपः an epithet of Garuḍa. °अंतकः a hawk, falcon. °अभिरामः an epithet of *S*iva. °आसनः 1 the eastern mountain on which the sun rises. 2 an epithet of Vishṇu. °इंद्रः, °ईश्वरः, °पतिः epithets of Garuḍa. °वती *f.* the earth. °स्थानं 1 the hollow of a tree. 2 a bird's nest. –गंगा celestial Gangâ. –गतिः *f.* flight in the air. –गमः a bird. –(खे) गमनः a kind of gallinule. –गोलः the celestial sphere. °विद्या astronomy. –चमसः the moon. –चरः (खेचरः also) 1 a bird. 2 a cloud. 3 the sun. 4 the wind. 5 a demon. (–री *i. e.* खेचरी) 1 a semi-divine female able to fly. 2 an epithet of Durgâ. –जलं 'sky-water,' dew, rain, frost &c. –ज्योतिस् *m.* a fire-fly. –तमालः 1 a cloud. 2 smoke. –द्योतः 1 a fire-fly; खद्योताली-विलसितनिभां विद्युदुन्मेषदृष्टिं Me. 81. 2 the sun –द्योतनः the sun. –धूपः a rocket; मुमुचुः खधूपान् Bk. 3. 5. –परागः darkness. –पुष्पं 'sky-flower,' used figuratively to denote anything impossible, an impossibility; cf. the four impossibilities in this verse:—मृगतृष्णांभसि स्नातः शशशृंगधनुर्धरः । एष वंध्यासुतो याति खपुष्पकृतशेखरः Subhâsh. –भं a planet. –भ्रांतिः a falcon. –मणिः 'the jewel of the sky,' the sun. –मीलनं sleepiness, weariness. –मूर्तिः an epithet of *S*iva. —वारि *n.* rain-water, dew &c. –बाष्पः snow, hoar-frost. –शय (also खेशय) *a* resting or dwelling in the air. –शरीरं a celestial body. –श्वासः wind, air. –समुत्थ, –संभव *a.* produced in the sky. –सिंधुः the moon. –स्तनी the earth. –स्फटिकं the sun or moon gem. –हर *a.* having a cypher for its denominator.

खक्खट *a.* Hard, solid. –टः Chalk.

खंकरः A curl, a lock of hair.

खच् 1. 9. P. (खचति, खच्नाति, खाचित) 1 To come forth, appear. 2 To be born again. 3 To purify. –II. 10 U. (खचयति, खाचित) To fasten, bind, set. –With उद् to intermix, intermingle, set or inlay with; R. 8. 53, 13. 54; Mu. 4. 12.

खचित *a.* 1 Fastened, joined, full of, intermixed with; शकुंतनीडखचितं बिभ्रज्जटामंडलं S. 7. 11. 2 Fixed, blended. 3 Inlaid, set, studded, in comp.; °मणि, °रत्न.

खज् 1 P. (खजति, खाजित) To churn, agitate.

खजः, –जकः A churning stick.

खजपं Clarified butter.

खजाकः A bird.

खजाजिका A ladle or spoon.

खंज् 1 P. (खंजति) To limp, halt, walk lame; खंजन् प्रभंजनजनः पथिकः पिपासुः N. 11. 107.

खंज *a.* Lame, crippled, halt; पादेन खंजः Sk.; Ms. 8. 242; Bh. 1. 64. –COMP. –खेटः, –खेलः the wag-tail.

खंजनः A species of the wag-tail; स्फुटकमलोदरखेलितखंजनयुगमिव शरदि तडागं Gît. 11; नेत्रे खंजनगंजने S. D. एको हि खंजनवरो नलिनीदलस्थः S. Til. 4, 7. —नं Going lamely. –COMP. –रतं the cohabitation of saints.

खंजना, खंजनिका A species of wag-tail.

खंजरीटः, –टकः, खंजलेखः The wag-tail; Bv. 2. 78; Ch. P. 8; Ms. 5. 14; Y. 1. 174; Amaru. 99.

खटः 1 Phlegm. 2 A blind well. 3 A hatchet. 4 A plough. 5 Grass. –COMP. –कटाहकः a spitting-box. –खादकः 1 a jackal. 2 a crow. 3 an animal. 4 a glass vessel.

खटकः 1 A man whose business is to negotiate marriages; cf. घटक. 2 The half-closed hand.

खटकामुखं A particular position of the hand in shooting.

खटिका 1 Chalk. 2 The external opening of the ear.

खड (ड) क्किका 1 A side-door, window.

खटिनी, खटी Chalk.

खट्टन *a.* Dwarfish. —नः A dwarf.

खट्टा 1 A bed-stead. 2 A kind of grass.

खट्टिः *m. f.* A bier.

खट्टिकः 1 A butcher. 2 A hunter, fowler.

खट्टेरक *a.* Dwarfish.

खट्वा 1 A bed-stead, couch, cot. 2 A swing, hammock. –COMP. –अंगः 1 a club or staff with a skull at the top considered as the weapon of *S*iva and carried by ascetics and Yogins; Mâl. 5. 4, 23. 2 N. of Dilîpa. °धर, भृत् *m.* epithets of *S*iva. –अंगिन् *m.* an epithet of *S*iva. –आप्लुत, –आरूढ *a.* 1 low, vile. 2 abandoned, wicked. 3 Silly, stupid.

खट्वाका, खट्विका A small bed-stead.

खड्ड् see खंड्.

खडः Breaking, dividing.

खडिका, खडी Chalk.

खड्गः 1 A sword; न हि खड्गो विजानाति कर्मकारं स्वकारणं Udb.; खड्गं परामृश्य &c. 2 The horn of a rhinoceros. 3 A rhinoceros; R. 9. 62; Ms. 3. 272, 5. 18. —ड्गं Iron. –COMP. –आघातः a sword-cut. –आधारः a sheath, scabbard. –आमिषं a buffalo's flesh. –आह्वः a rhinoceros. –कोशः a scabbard. –धरः a swordsman. –धेनुः, –धेनुका 1 a small sword. 2 a female rhinoceros. –पत्रं the blade of a sword. –पाणि *a.* sword in hand. —पात्रं a vessel made of buffalo's horns. –पिधानं, –पिधानकं a scabbard. –पुत्रिका a knife, small sword. –प्रहारः a swordcut. –फलं a sword-blade.

खड्गवत् *a.* Armed with a sword.

खड्गिकः 1 A swordsman. 2 A butcher.

खड्गिन् *a.* (नी *f.*) Armed with a sword. —*m.* A rhinoceros.

खड्गीकं A sickle.

खंड् 10 P. (खंडयति, खंडित) 1 To break, cut, tear, break to pieces, crush; Bk. 15. 54. 2 To defeat completely, destroy, dispel; रजनीचरनाथेन खंडिते तिमिरे निशि H. 3. 111. 3 To disappoint; frustrate, cross in love; स्त्रीभिः कस्य न खंडितं भुवि मनः Pt. 1. 146. 4 To distrub. 5 To cheat.

खंडः, –डं 1 A break, chasm, gap, fissure, fracture. 2 A piece, part, fragment, portion; दिवः कांतिमत्खंडमेकं Me. 30; काष्ठ°, मांस° &c. 3 section of a work, chapter. 4 A multitude, an assemblage, group; तरुखंडस्य K. 23. —डः 1 Candied sugar. 2 A flaw in a jewel. —डं 1 A kind of salt. 2 A sort of sugar-cane. –COMP. –अभ्रं 1 scattered clouds. 2 the impression of the teeth in amorous sports. –आलिः *f.* 1 a measure of oil. 2 a pond or lake. 3 a woman whose husband has been guilty of infidelity. -कथा a short tale. -काव्यं a small poem, such as the मेघदूत; it is thus defined :— खंडकाव्यं भवेत् काव्यस्यैकदेशानुसारि च S. D. 564. -जः a kind of sugar. -धारा scissors. -परशुः 1 an epithet of *S*iva; महेश्वर्यं लीलाजनितजगतः खंडपरशोः G. L. 1; येनानेन जगत्सु खंडपरशुर्देवो हरः ख्याप्यते Mv. 2. 33. 2 an epithet of Parasurâma, son of Jamadagni. -पर्शुः 1 N. of *S*iva. 2 of Parasurâma. 3 of Râhu. 4 an elephant with a broken tusk. -पालः a confectioner. -प्रलयः a partial destruction of the universe in which all the spheres beneath Svarga are dissolved in one common ruin. -मंडलं a segment of a circle. -मोदकः a kind of sugar. -लवणं a kind of salt. -विकारः sugar. -शर्करा candied sugar. -शीला a loose woman, an unchaste wife.

खंडकः -कं A fragment, part or piece. —कः 1 Candied sugar. 2 One who has no nails.

खंडन *a.* 1 Breaking, cutting, dividing. 2 Destroying, annihilating; स्मरगरलखंडनं मम शिरसि मंडनं Gît. 10; भवज्वरखंडन 12. —नं 1 Breaking or cutting. 2 Biting, injuring, hurting; अधरोष्ठखंडनं Pt. 1; घटय भुजबंधनं जनय रदखंडनं Gît. 10; Ch. P. 13. 3 Disappointing, frustrating (as in love). 4 Interrupting; रसखंडनवर्जितं R. 9. 36. 5 Cheating, deceiving. 6 Refuting (in argument); N. 6. 130. 7 Rebellion; opposition. 8 Dismissal.

खंडलः,-लं A piece.

खंडशस् *ind.* 1 To pieces, into fragment; °कृ to cut into pieces. 2 Bit by bit, piece by piece, piecemeal.

खंडित *p. p.* 1 Cut, broken in pieces. 2 Destroyed, annihilated. 3 Refuted (in argument), controverted. 4 Rebelled. 5 Disappointed, betrayed, abandoned; खंडितयुवतिविलापं Gît. 8. —ता A woman whose husband or lover has been guilty of infidelity and who is therefore angry with him; one of the 8 principal Nâyikâs in Sanskrit; R. 5. 67; Me. 39. She is thus described :—पार्श्वमेति प्रियो यस्या अन्यसंभोगचिह्नितः। सा खंडितेति कथिता धीरैरीर्ष्याकषायिता S. D. 114. -COMP. -विग्रह *a.* maimed, mutilated. -वृत्त *a.* immoral, dissolute, abandoned.

खंडिनी The earth.

खंडिकाः (pl.) Fried or parched grain.

खदिरः 1 N. of a tree; Y. 1. 302. 2 An epithet of Indra. 3 The moon.

खन् 1 U. (खनति-ते, खात; *pass*; खन्यते or खायते) To dig up, delve, excavate; खनन्नाखुबिलं सिंहः Pt. 3. 17, Ms. 2. 218; Bk. 1. 17. -WITH अभि to dig. -उद् to dig out, root out, uproot, eradicate (fig. also); वेगादुत्खाय तरसा R. 4. 36, 33, 14. 73; Me. 52; Bk. 12. 5; 15. 55; Mâl. 9. 34. -नि 1 to dig, dig up. 2 to bury, inter; ऊनद्विवर्षं निखनेत् Y. 3. 1; वसुधायां निचख्नतुः R. 12. 30; Bk. 4. 3; 16. 22. 3 to erect (as a column); निचखान जयस्तंभान् R. 4. 36. 4 to implant, infix, pierce into; निचखान शरं भुजे R. 3. 55, 12. 90; Bk. 3. 8; H. 4. 72. -परि to dig round (as a ditch).

खनकः 1 A miner. 2 A house-breaker. 3 A rat. 4 A mine.

खननं 1 Digging, excavating. 2 Burying.

खनिः -नी *f.* 1 A mine; R. 17. 66; 18. 22; Mu. 7. 31. 2 A cave.

खनित्रं A spade, hoe, a pick-axe.

खपुरः The betel-nut tree.

खर *a.* (opp. मृदु, श्लक्ष्ण, द्रव) 1 Hard, rough, solid. 2 Severe, sharp, strict; R. 8. 9; स्मरः खरः खलः कांतः Kâv. 1. 59. 3 Pungent, acid. 4 Dense, thick. 5 Hurtful, injurious, cutting (words). 6 Sharp-edged; देहि खरनयनशरघातं Gît. 10. 7 Hot; खरांशुः &c. 8 Cruel. —रः 1 An ass; Ms. 2. 201; 4. 115, 120, 8. 370; Y. 2. 160. 2 A mule. 3 A heron. 4 A crow. 5 N. of a demon, half-brother of Râvaṇa, and slain by Râma; R. 12. 42. -COMP. -अंशुः, -करः, -रश्मिः the sun. -कुटी 1 a stable for asses. 2 a barber's shop. -कोणः -क्वाणः the francoline partridge. -कोमलः the month Jyeshṭha. -गृहं,-गेहं a stable for asses. -णस्,-णस *a.* sharp-nosed. -दंडं a lotus. -ध्वंसिन् *m.* an epithet of Râma, who killed the demon खर. -नादः the braying of an ass. -नालः a lotus. -पात्रं an iron vessel. -पालः a wooden vessel. -प्रियः a pigeon. -यानं a donkey-cart. -शब्दः 1 the braying of an ass. 2 an osprey. -शाला a stable for asses. -स्वरा wild jasmine.

खरिका Powdered musk.

खरिंधम-य *a.* Drinking ass's milk.

खरी A she-ass. -COMP. -जंघः an epithet of *S*iva. -वृषः a jackass.

खरु *a.* 1 White. 2 Foolish, stupid. 3 Cruel. 4 Desirous of prohibited things. —रुः 1 horse. 2 A tooth. 3 Pride. 4 Cupid, the god of love. 5 *S*iva. -रुः *f.* A girl who chooses her own husband.

खर्ज् 1 P. (खर्जति, खर्जित) 1 To pain, make uneasy. 2 To creak.

खर्जनं Scratching.

खर्जिका 1 A venereal disease. 2 A relish.

खर्जुः *f.* 1 Scratching. 2 The date-tree. 3 The Dhattûra tree.

खर्जुरं Silver.

खर्जूः *f.* Itching, itch.

खर्जूरः 1 Date-tree. 2 A scorpion. —रं 1 Silver. 2 Yellow orpiment. -री The date-tree; R. 4. 57.

खर्परः 1 A thief. 2 A rogue, cheat. 3 A beggar's bowl. 4 The skull. 5 A piece of a broken jar, pot-sherd. 6 An umbrella.

खर्परिका, खर्परी A kind of collyrium.

खर्व् (खर्वति, खर्वित) 1 To go, move, go towards. 2 To be proud.

खर्व (र्ब) *a.* 1 Mutilated, crippled, imperfect. 2 Dwarfish, low, short in stature. —र्वः,-र्वं a large number (10,000,000,000). -COMP. -शाख *a.* dwarfish, small, short.

खर्वटः,-टं 1 A market-town. 2 A village at the foot of a mountain.

खल् 1 P. (खलति, खलित) 1 To move, shake. 2 To gather, collect.

खलः -लं 1 A threshing floor; Ms. 11. 17, 114; Y. 2. 282. 2 Earth, soil. 3 Place, site. 4 A heap of dust. 5 Sediment, dregs, deposit of oil &c. -लः A wicked or mischievous person; सर्पः क्रूरः खलः क्रूरः सर्पात् क्रूरतरं खलः। मंत्रौषधिवशः सर्पः खलः केन निवार्यते॥ Châṇ. 26; विषधरतोऽप्यतिविषमः खल इति न मृषा वदंति विद्वांसः। यदयं नकुलद्वेषी सकुलद्वेषी पुनः पिशुनः॥ Vâs. [खलीकृ means (1) 'to crush' (2) 'to hurt or injure'. (3) 'to ill-treat, scorn'; परोक्षे खलीकृतोऽयं यतकारः Mk. 2.] -COMP. -उक्तिः *f.* abuse, wicked language. -धान्यं a threshing floor -पूः *m. f.* a sweeper, cleaner. -मूर्तिः quick-silver. —संसर्गः keeping company with a wicked man.

खलकः A pitcher.

खलति *a.* Bald-headed, bald; युवखलतिः.

खलतिकः A mountain.

खलिः,-ली *f.* Sediment of oil or oil-cake, स्थाल्यां वैदूर्यमय्यां पचति तिलखलीमिंधनैश्चंदनाद्यैः Bh. 2. 100.

खलि (ली) नः-नं The bit of a bridle.

खलिनी A multitude of threshing floors.

खलीकारः, -कृतिः *f.* 1 Hurting, injuring. 2 Ill-treating; *S*ânti. 1. 25. 3 Evil, mischief.

खलु *ind.* A particle implying :— 1 Certainly, surely, verily, indeed; मार्गे पदानि खलु ते विषमीभवंति *S*. 4. 14; अनुत्सेकः खलु विक्रमालंकारः V. 1; न खल्वनिर्जित्य रघुं कृती भवान् R. 3. 51. 2 Entreaty, conciliation ('pray'); न खलु न खलु बाणः सन्निपात्योऽयमस्मिन् *S*. 1. 10; न खलु न खलु मुग्धे साहसं कार्यमेतत् Nâg. 3. 3 Inquiry; न खलु तामभिक्रुद्धो गुरुः V. 3 (=किं अभिक्रुद्धो गुरुः); न खलु विदितास्ते तत्र निवसंतश्चाणक्यहतकेन Mu. 2; न खल्वरुषा पिनाकिना गमितः सोऽपि सुहृद्गतां गतिं Ku. 4. 24. 4 Prohibition (with gerunds); निर्धारितेऽर्थे लेखेन खलूक्त्वा खलु वाचिकं *Si*. 2. 70. 5 Reason (for); न विदीर्ये कठिनाः खलु स्त्रियः Ku. 4. 5 (G. M. cites this as an illustration of विषाद or dejection); विधिना जन एष वंचितस्त्वदधीनं खलु

देहिनां सुखं 4. 10. 6 खलु is sometimes used as an expletive. 7 Sometimes only to add grace to the sentence (वाक्यालंकार).

खलुज् *m.* Darkness.

खलूरिका A place for military exercise.

खल्या A multitude of threshing floors.

खल्लः 1 A stone or vessel for grinding drugs, a mill. 2 A pit. 3 Leather. 4 The Châtaka bird. 5 A leather water-bag.

खल्लिका A frying-pan.

खल्लि (ल्ली) ट *a.* Bald-headed.

खल्वाट *a.* Bald, bald-headed; खल्वाटो दिवसेश्वरस्य किरणैः संतापितो मस्तके Bh. 2. 90; Vikr. 18. 99.

खशः (pl.) A mountainous country in the north of India and its inhabitants; Ms. 10. 44; (also written खस).

खशीरः (pl.) N. of a country and its people.

खष्पः 1 Anger. 2 Violence, cruelty.

खसः 1 Itch, scab. 2 N. of a country; see खश.

खसूचिः *m. f.* 1 An expression of reproach (at the end of a compound); वैयाकरणखसूचिः 'a bad grammarian', 'one who has forgotten it.'

खस्खसः Poppy. -COMP. -रसः opium.

खाजिकः Fried grain.

खाट् (त्) *ind.* The sound made in clearing the throat; **खात्कृ** to clear the throat.

खाटः-टा, -टिका-टी *f.* A bier, a bedstead on which dead bodies are carried to the pile.

खांडवः Sugar-candy. -वं N. of a forest in Kurukshetra, sacred to Indra, and burnt by Agni with the assistance of Arjuna and Krishna. -COMP. -प्रस्थः N. of a town.

खांडविकः, खांडिकः A confectioner.

खात *a.* 1 Dug up, excavated. 2 Torn, rent. -तं 1 An excavation. 2 A hole. 3 A ditch, moat. 4 An oblong pond. -COMP. -भूः *f.* a moat, ditch.

खातकः 1 A digger. 2 A debtor. -कं A moat, ditch.

खाता An artificial pond.

खातिः *f.* Digging, excavating.

खात्रं 1 A spade. 2 An oblong pond. 3 A thread. 4 A wood, forest. 5 Horror.

खाद् 1 P. (खादति, खादित) To eat, devour, feed; to prey upon, bite; प्राक्पादयोः पतति खादति पृष्ठमांसं H. 1. 81; खादन्मांसं न दुष्यति Ms. 5. 32, 53; Bk. 6. 6; 9. 78, 14. 87, 101; 15. 35.

खादक *a.* (दिका *f.*) Eating, consuming. -कः A debtor.

खादनः A tooth. -नं 1 Eating, chewing. 2 Food.

खादुक *a.* (की *f.*) Mischievous, injurious, malicious.

खाद्यं Food, victuals.

खादिर *a.* (री *f.*) Made of or coming from the Khadira tree; खादिरं यूपं कुर्वीत; Ms. 2. 45.

खानं 1 Digging. 2 Injury. -COMP. -उदकः the cocoa-nut tree.

खानक *a.* (निका *f.*) One who digs, a miner.

खानिः *f.* A mine.

खानिकः-कं A hole in a wall; breach.

खानिलः A house-breaker.

खार,-रिः-री *f.* A measure of grain equal to 16 *dronas*.

खारिंपच *a.* Cooking a Khârî by measure.

खार्वा The Tretâ age or second Yuga of the world.

खिंखिरः 1 A fox (री *f.*) 2 The foot of a bedstead.

खिद् I. 6 P. (खिदति, खिन्न) To strike, press down, afflict. -II. 4. 7. A. (खिद्यते, खिंत्ते, खिन्न) 1 To suffer pain or misery, to be afflicted or wearied, feel tired, depressed or exhausted; *S.* 5. 7; किं नाम मयि खिद्यते गुरुः Ve. 1; स पुरुषो यः खिद्यते नेंद्रियैः H. 2. 141 overpowered; *S*ânti. 3. 7; Bk. 14. 108, 17 10. 2 To frighten, terrify (in *caus.*) -With परि to suffer pain or misery, be distressed or wearied.

खिदिरः 1 An ascetic. 2 A pauper. 3 The moon.

खिन्न *p. p.* 1 Depressed, afflicted, dejected, distressed, suffering pain; गुरुः खेदं खिन्ने मयि भजति नाद्यापि कुरुषु Ve. 1. 11; अनंगबाणव्रणखिन्नमानसः Gît. 3. 2 Fatigued, tired, exhausted; खिन्नः खिन्नः शिखरिषु पदं न्यस्य गंतासि यत्र Me. 13, 38; तयोपचारांजलिखिन्नहस्तया R. 3. 11; Ch. P. 3, 20; *S*i. 9. 11.

खिलः-लं 1 A piece of waste or uncultivated land, desert, bare soil. 2 An additional hymn appended to the regular collection; Ms. 3. 232. 3 A supplement in general. 4 A compendium, compilation. 5 Vacuity. (खिल is often used in combination with भू and कृः-खिलीभू to become impassable, to be blocked up, be left unfrequented; खिलीभूते विमानानां तदापातभयात्पथि Ku. 2. 45. खिलीकृ means (*a*) to obstruct, impede, make impassable, block up; R. 11. 14, 87. (*b*) to lay waste, devastate, put down or vanquish completely; विपक्षमखिलीकृत्य प्रतिष्ठा खलु दुर्लभा *S*i. 2. 34.

खुंगाहः A tawny (or black) horse.

खुरः 1 A hoof; R. 1. 85, 2. 2; Ms. 4. 67. 2 A kind of perfume. 3 A razor. 4 The foot of a bedstead. -COMP. -आघातः -क्षेपः a kick. -नस्, -णस *a.* flatnosed. -पदवी a horse's footmarks. -प्रः an arrow with a semicircular head; see क्षुरप्र.

खुरली Military exercise or practice (as of arms, archery &c.); अस्त्रप्रयोगखुरलीकलहे गणानां Mv. 2. 34; दूरोत्पतनखुरलीकेलिजनितान् 5. 5.

खुरालकः An iron arrow.

खुरालिकः 1 A razor-case. 2 An iron arrow. 3 A pillow.

खुल्ल *a.* Small, little, mean, low; see क्षुद्र. -COMP. -तातः a father's younger brother.

खेचर see खचर.

खेटः 1 A village, small town or hamlet. 2 Phlegm. 3 The club of Balarâma. 4 A horse. (*N. B.* At the end of comp. खेट expresses defectiveness or deterioration, and may be rendered by 'miserable', 'wretched' &c.; नगरखेटं a miserable town). For खेट्ट see under ख.

खेटितानः-लः A minstrel, whose business is to awaken the master of the house with music and singing; (वैतालिक.)

खेटिन् *m.* A libertine.

खेदः 1 Depression, lassitude, dejection (of spirits). 2 Fatigue, exhaustion; अलसलुलितमुग्धान्यध्वसंजातखेदात् U. 1. 24; अध्वखेदं नयेथाः Me. 32; R. 18. 45. 3 Pain, torment; Amaru. 33. 4 Distress, sorrow; गुरुः खेदं खिन्ने मयि भजति नाद्यापि कुरुषु Ve. 1. 11; Amaru. 53.

खेयं A ditch, moat. -यः A bridge.

खेल् 1 P. (खेलति, खेलित) 1 To shake, move to and fro. 2 To tremble. 3 To play.

खेल *a.* Sportive, amorous, playful; R. 4. 22. V. 4. 16, 43.

खेलनं 1 Shaking. 2 Play, pastime. 3 A performance.

खेला Sport, play.

खेलिः *f.* 1 Sport, play. 2 An arrow.

खोटिः *f.* Cunning or shrewd woman.

खोड *a.* Crippled, lame, limping.

खोर (ल) *a.* Limping, lame.

खोलकः 1 A helmet. 2 An anthill. 3 The shell of a betelnut. 4 Sauce-pan.

खोलिः A quiver.

ख्या 2 P. (A. also in non-conjugational tenses) (ख्याति, ख्यात) To tell, declare, communicate (with dat. of person). —*Pass.* (ख्यायते) 1 To be named or called; Bk. 6. 97. 2 To be known or famous. -*Caus.* (ख्यापयति-ते) 1 To make known, proclaim; Ms. 7. 201. 2 To tell, declare, relate; Bh. 2. 59; Ms. 11. 99. 3 To extol, make renowned, praise. -WITH अभि (*pass.*) to be known. (-*caus.*) to declare, proclaim. -आ 1 to tell, declare, communicate; (usually with dat. of person); ते रामाय वधोपायमाचख्युर्विबुधद्विषः R. 15. 5; 41, 71, 93; 12. 42, 91; Bg. 11. 31; 18. 63; sometimes with gen.; आख्याहि भद्रे प्रियदर्शनस्य Pt. 4. 15. **2** to announce, signify. **3** to call, name; R. 10. 21; Ms. 4. 6. **-परि** to be well-known. **-परिसं** to enumerate. **-प्र** to be well-known. **-प्रत्या 1** to deny. **2** to decline, refuse, reject. **3** to forbid, prohibit. **4** to interdict. **5** to surpass, excel; M. 3. 5. **-वि** to be well-known or famous. **-व्या 1** to tell, communicate, declare, Bk. 14. 113. **2** to explain, relate; रावणस्यापि ते जन्म व्याख्यास्यामि Mb. **3** to name, call; विद्रुद्रुदैर्वीणावाणी व्याख्याता सा विद्युन्माला Srut. 15. **-सं** to count, enumerate, calculate, sum up; तावंत्येव च तत्त्वानि सांख्यैः संख्यायंते S. B.

ख्यात *p. p.* **1** Known: R. 18. 6. **2** Named, called. **3** Told. **4** Celebrated, famous; notorious. –COMP. **-गर्हण** *a.* notoriously vile, infamous.

ख्यातिः *f.* **1** Renown, fame, reputation, glory, celebrity; Ms. 12. 36; Pt. 1. 371. **2** A name, title, appellation. **3** Narration. **4** Praise. **5** (In phil.) Knowledge, the faculty of discriminating objects by appropriate designation; Si. 4. 55.

ख्यापनं 1 Declaring, divulging. **2** Confessing, avowing, publicly declaring; Ms. 11. 227. **3** Making renowned, celebrating.

ग.

ग *a.* (Used only at the end of comp.) Who or what goes, going, moving, being, staying, remaining, having sexual intercourse with &c. **—गः 1** A Gandharva. **2** An epithet of Gaṇesa. **3** A long syllable (used as an abbreviation of गुरु), (in prosody). **—गं** A song.

गगनं (णं) (Some suppose गगण to be an incorrect form, as is observed by a writer :—फाल्गुने गगने फेने णत्वमिच्छंति बर्बराः) **1** The sky, atmosphere; अवोचदेनं गगनस्पृशा रघुः स्वरेण R. 3. 43; गगनमिव नष्टतारं Pt. 5. 6; सोयं चंद्रः पतति गगणात् S. 4 v. l.; Si. 9. 27. **2** (In math.) A cypher. **3** Heaven. –COMP. **-अग्रं** the highest heavens. **-अंगना** a heavenly nymph, an Apsaras. **-अध्वगः 1** the sun. **2** a planet. **3** a celestial being. **-अंबु** *n.* rain-water. **-उल्मुकः** the planet Mars. **-कुसुमं-पुष्पं** 'sky-flower'; *i. e.* any unreal thing, an impossibility; see खपुष्प. **-गतिः 1** a deity. **2** a celestial being; Me. 46. **3** a planet. **-चर** (also **गगनेचर**) *a.* moving in the air. (**-रः**) **1** a bird. **2** a planet. **3** a heavenly spirit **-ध्वजः 1** the sun. **2** a cloud. **-सद्** *a.* dwelling in the air. (*-m.*) a celestial being; Si. 4. 53. **-सिंधु** *f.* an epithet of the Ganges **-स्थ, -स्थित** *a.* situated in the sky. **-स्पर्शनः 1** air, wind. **2** N. of one of the eight Maruts.

गंगा 1 The river Ganges, the most sacred river in India; अधोधो गंगेयं पदमुपगता स्तोकमथवा Bh. 3. 10; R. 2. 26; 13. 57; (mentioned in Rv. 10. 75. 5 along with other rivers); (also occasionally applied to several other rivers considered sacred in India). **2** The Ganges personified as a goddess. [Gangâ is the eldest daughter of Himavat. It is said that a curse of Brahma made her come down upon earth, where she became the first wife of King Santanu. She bore him eight sons, of whom Bhishma, the youngest, became a well-known personage, renowned for his valour and lifelong celibacy. According to another account she came down on earth being propitiated by Bhagîratha; see भगीरथ and जह्नु also; and cf. Bh. 3. 10.] –COMP. **-अंबु, -अंभस्** *n.* **1** water of the Ganges. **2** pure rain-water (such as falls in the month of आश्विन). **-अवतारः** the descent of the Ganges on the earth; भगीरथ इव दृष्टगंगावतारः K. 32 (where गं° also means 'descent into the Ganges' for ablution.) **2** N. of a sacred place. **-उद्भेदः** the source of the Ganges. **—क्षेत्रं** the river Ganges and the district two Koss on either of its banks. **-चिल्ली** Gangetic kite. **-जः 1** N. of Bhîshma. **2** of Kârtikeya. **—दत्तः** an epithet of Bhîshma. **-द्वारं** the place where the Ganges enters the plains (also called हरिद्वार). **-धरः 1** an epithet of Siva. **2** the ocean. °पुरं N. of a town. **-पुत्रः 1** N. of Bhîshma. **2** of Kârtikeya. **3** a man of a mixed and vile caste whose business is to remove dead bodies. **4** a Brâhmaṇa who conducts pilgrims to the Ganges. **-भृत्** *m.* **1** N. of Siva. **2** the ocean. **-मध्यं** the bed of the Ganges. **-यात्रा 1** a pilgrimage to the Ganges. **2** carrying a sick person to the river-side to die there. **-सागरः** the place where the Ganges enters the ocean. **-सुतः 1** an epithet of Bhîshma. **2** of Kârtikeya. **-ह्रदः** N. of a तीर्थ.

गंगाका, गंगका, गंगिका The Ganges.

गंगोलः A precious stone also called गोमेद.

गच्छः 1 A tree. **2** The period (*i. e.* number of terms) of a progression (in math.).

गज् 1 P. (गजति, गजित) **1** To sound, roar; जगजुर्गजाः Bk. 14. 5. **2** To be drunk; to be confused or inebriated.

गजः 1 An elephant; कचाचितौ विष्वगिवागजौ गजौ Ki. 1. 36. **2** The number 'eight'. **3** A measure of length; a *Gaja* or yard, (thus defined:—साधारणनरांगुल्या त्रिंशदंगुलको गजः). **4** A demon killed by Siva. –COMP. **-अग्रणी** *m.* **1** the most excellent among elephants. **2** an epithet of ऐरावत, the elephant of Indra. **-अधिपतिः** lord of elephants, a noble elephant. **-अध्यक्षः** a superintendent of elephants. **-अपसदः** a vile or wretched elephant, a common or low-born elephant. **-अशनः** the religious fig-tree (अश्वत्थ). (**-नं**) the root of a lotus. **-अरिः 1** a lion. **2** N. of Siva who killed the demon गज. **-आजीवः** 'one who gets his livelihood by elephants', an elephant-driver. **-आननः, -आस्यः** epithets of Gaṇesa. **-आयुर्वेदः** science of the treatment of elephants. **-आरोहः** an elephant-driver. **-आह्वं, -आह्वयं** N. of Hastinâpura. **-इंद्रः 1** an excellent elephant, a lordly elephant; किं रुद्धासि गजेंद्रमंदगमने S. Til. 7. **2** Airâvata, Indra's elephant. °कर्णः an epithet of Siva. **-कंदः** a large esculent root. **-कूर्माशिन्** *m.* N. of caruda. **-गतिः** *f.* **1** a stately, majestic gait like that of an elephant. **2** a woman with such a gait. **-गामिनी** a woman having a stately elephant-like gait. **-दघ्न, द्वयस** *a.* as high or tall as an elephant. **-दंतः 1** an elephant's tusk. **2** an epithet of Gaṇesa. **3** ivory. **4** a peg, pin, or bracket projecting from a wall. °मय *a.* made of ivory. **-दानं 1** the fluid (ichor) exuding from the temples of an elephant. **2** the gift of an elephant. **-नासा** the temples of an elephant. **-पतिः 1** the lord or keeper of elephants. **2** a very tall and stately elephant; Si. 6. 55. **3** an excellent elephant. **-पुंगवः** a large and excellent elephant; गजपुंगवस्तु । धीरं विलोकयति चाटुशतैश्च भुंक्ते Bh. 2. 31. **-पुरं** N. of Hastinâpura. **-बंधनी, -बंधिनी** a stable for elephants. **-भक्षकः** the sacred fig-tree. **-मंडनं** the ornaments with which elephant is decorated, particularly the coloured lines on his head. **-मंडलिका -मंडली** a ring or circle of elephants. **-माचलः**

a lion. -मुक्ता -मौक्तिकं a pearl supposed to be found in the *kumbhas* or projections on the forehead of an elephant. -मुखः,-वक्त्रः,-वदनः epithets of Gaṇesa -मोटनः a lion. -यूथं a herd of elephants; R. 9. 71. -योधिन् *a.* fighting on an elephant. -राजः a lordly or noble elephant. -व्रजः a troop of elephants. -शिक्षा the science of elephants. -साह्वयं N. of Hastinâpura. -स्नानं (lit.) bathing of an elephant; (fig.) useless or unproductive efforts resembling the ablution of elephants which, after pouring water over their bodies, and by throwing dirt, rubbish, and other foul matter; cf. अवशेंद्रियचित्तानां हस्तिस्नानमिव क्रिया H 1. 18.

गजता A multitude of elephants.

गजवत् *a.* Having elephants; R.9.10.

गंज् 1. P. (गंजति) To sound in a particular way.

गंजः 1 A mine. 2 A treasury. 3 A cow-house. 4 A mart, a place where grain is stored for sale. 5 Disrespect, contempt. -जा 1 A hut, hovel. 2 A tavern. 3 A drinking vessel.

गंजन *a.* 1 Contemning, putting to shame, surpassing, excelling; स्थलकमलगंजनं मम हृदयरंजनं (चरणद्वयं) Gît. 10; अलिकुलगंजनमंजनकं 12; नेत्रे खंजनगंजने S. D. 2 Defeating, conquering; कालियविषधरगंजन Gît. 1.

गंजिका A tavern, liquor-shop.

गड् 1 P. (गडति, गडित) 1 To distil, draw out. 2 To run (as a liquid).

गडः 1 A screen. 2 A fence. 3 A ditch, moat. 4 An impediment. 5 A kind of gold-fish. -COMP. -उत्थं, -देशजं, -लवणं rock or fossil salt, especially that found in the district called गड.

गडयंतः, गडयित्नुः A cloud.

गडिः 1 A young steer. 2 A lazy ox; गुणानामेव दौरात्म्याद्धुरि धुर्यो नियुज्यते। असंजातकिणस्कंधः सुखं स्वपिति गौर्गडिः K. P.10

गडु *a* Crooked, hump-backed.-डुः 1 A hump on the back. 2 A javelin. 3 A water-pot. 4 An earthworm. 5 Any superfluous excrescence or addition, a useless object; see अंतर्गडु

गडुकः 1 A water-pot. 2 A finger ring.

गडुर-ल *a.* Hump-backed, crooked, bent

गडेरः A cloud.

गडोलः 1 A mouthful. 2 Raw sugar.

गड्डुरः-लः A sheep.

गड्डुरिका 1 A line of sheep. 2 A continuous line, stream, current; °प्रवाहः 'a stream of sheep,' used to signify 'blindly following other people like a flock of sheep;' cf. इति गड्डुरिकाप्रवाहेणैषां भेदः K. P. 8.

गड्डुकः A golden vase.

गण् 10 U. (गणयति-ते, गणित) 1 To count, number; enumerate; लीलाकमलपत्राणि गणयामास पार्वती Ku. 6. 84; नामाक्षरं गणय गच्छसि यावदंतं S. 6. 11. 2 To calculate, compute. 3. To sum or add up, reckon. 4 To estimate, value at (with instr.); न तं तृणेनापि गणयामि. 5 To class with or among, reckom among अगण्यतामरेषु Dk.154. 6 To take into account, give consideration to; वार्णीं काणभुजीमजीगणत् Malli. 7 To regard, consider, think or take to be; त्वया विना सुखमेतावदजस्य गण्यतां R. 8. 69, 5. 20, 11. 75; जातस्तु गण्यते सोऽत्र यः स्फुरत्यन्वयाधिकं Pt. 1. 27; किसलयतल्पं गणयति विहितहुताशविकल्पं Gît. 4. 8 To ascribe or impute to, attribute to (with loc.); जाड्यं ह्रीमति गण्यते Bh. 2. 54. 9. To attend to, take notice of, mind; प्रणयमगणयित्वा यन्ममापद्गतस्य V. 4. 13. 10. (With a negative particle) not to care for, not to mind; न महातमपि क्लेशमजीगणत् K. 64; मनस्वी कार्यार्थी न गणयति दुःखं न च सुखं Bh. 2. 81, 9; Sânti. 1. 10; Bk. 2. 53; 15. 5, 45; H. 2. 142. -With अधि 1 to praise. 2. to enumerate, count. -अव to disregard. -परि 1 to enumerate, count. 2 to consider, regard, think; अपरिगणयन् Me. 5. -प्र to calculate. -वि 1 to number; Y. 3. 104. 2 to regard, consider; Me. 109; R. 1. 87. 3 to disregard, not to mind. 4 to reflect, think; Pt. 3. 43.

गणः 1 A flock, multitude, group, troop, collection; गुणिगणगणना, भगणः &c. 2 A series, a class. 3 A body of followers or attendants. 4 Particularly, a troop of demigods considered as Siva's attendants and under the special superintendence of Gaṇesa; a demigod of this troop; गणानां त्वा गणपतिं हवामहे कविं कवीनां &c.; गणा नमेरुप्रसवावतंसाः Ku. 1. 55, 7. 40, 71; Me. 33, 55; Ki. 5. 13. 5 Any assemblage or society of men formed for the attainment of the same objects. 6 A sect (in philosophy or religion). 7 A small body of troops (a sub-division of अक्षौहिणी), consisting of 27 chariots, as many elephants, 81 horses and 135 foot. 8 A number (in math.) 9 A foot (in prosody). 10 (In gram.) A series of roots or words belonging to the same rule and called after the first word of that series; *e. g.* भ्वादिगण *i. e.* the class of roots which begin with भू. 11 An epithet of Gaṇesa. -COMP. -अग्रणी *m.* N. of Gaṇesa. -अचलः N. of the mountain Kailâsa, as the residence of the Gaṇas of Siva. -अधिपः -अधिपतिः 1 N. of Siva; Si. 9. 27. 2 N. of Gaṇesa. 3 the chief of a troop of soldiers or of a class of disciples, of a body of men or animals. -अन्नं a mess, food prepared for a number of persons in common; Ms. 4. 209, 219. -अभ्यंतर *a.* one of a troop or number (-रः) the leader or member of any religious association; Ms. 3. 154. -ईशः N. of Gaṇapati, Siva's son (see गणपति below). °जननी an epithet of Pârvati. °भूषणं red-lead -ईशानः, -ईश्वरः 1 an epithet of Gaṇesa. 2 of Siva. -उत्साहः the rhinoceros. -कारः 1 a classifier. 2 an epithet of Bhîmasena. -कृत्वस् *ind.* for a whole series of times, for a number of times. -गतिः a particular high number. -चक्रकं a dinner eaten in common by a party of virtuous men. -छंदस् *n.* a metre regulated and measured by feet. -तिथ *a.* forming a troop or collection. -दीक्षा 1 initiation of a number or a class. 2 performance of rites for a number of persons. -देवताः (Pl.) groups of deities who generally appear in classes or troops; Ak. thus classifies them —आदित्यविश्वसवस्तुषिता भास्वरानिलाः। महाराजिकसाध्याश्च रुद्राश्च गणदेवताः॥ -द्रव्यं public property, common stock. -धरः 1 the head of a class or number. 2 the teacher of a school. -नाथः, -नायकः 1 an epithet of Siva. 2 of Gaṇesa. -नायिका an epithet of Durgâ. -पः, -पतिः 1 N. of Siva. 2 N. of Gaṇesa. [He is the son of Siva and Parvati, or of Parvati only, for, according to one legend, he sprang from the scurf of her body. He is the god of wisdom and remover of obstacles; hence he is invoked and worshipped at the commencement of every important undertaking. He is usually represented in a sitting posture-short and fat, with a protuberant belly, and four hands; riding a mouse, and with the head of an elephant. This head has only one tusk, the other having been lost in a scuffle between him and Parasurâma when he opposed the latter's entrance to Siva's inner apartments; (whence he is called Ekadanta, Ekadanshtra &c.) There are several legends accounting for his elephant head. It is said that he wrote the Mahâbhârata at the dictation of Vyâsa who secured his services as a scribe from the god Brahmâ]. -पर्वत see गणाचल. -पटिकं the breast, bosom. -पुंगवः the head of a tribe or class. (pl.) N. of a country and its people. -पूर्वः the leader of a tribe or class. -भर्तृ *m.* 1 an epithet of Siva; गणभर्तुरुक्षा Ki. 5. 42. 2 of

Gaṇesa. **3** the leader of a class. **–भोजनं** mess, eating in common. **–यज्ञः** a rite common to all. **–राज्यं** N. of an empire in the Dekkan. **–रात्रं** a series of nights. **–वृत्तं** see गणछंदस्. **–हासः**; **–हासकः** a species of perfume.

–गणक *a.* (**णिका** *f.*) Bought for a large sum. **–कः** **1** An arithmetician. **2** An astrologer; रे पांथ पुस्तकधर क्षणमत्र तिष्ठ वैद्योसि किं गणकशास्त्रविशारदोसि। केनौषधेन मम पश्यति भर्तुरंबा किंवा गमिष्यति पतिः सुचिरप्रवासी Subha'sh. **–की** The wife of an astrologer.

–गणनं **1** Counting, calculation. **2** Adding, enumerating. **3** Considering, supposing, regarding. **4** Believing, thinking.

–गणना Calculation, consideration, regard, account; का वा गणना सचेतनेषु अपगतचेतनान्यपि संघट्टयितुमलं (मदनः) K. 157 (what need we say of &c.; cf. कथा); Me. 10, 87; R. 11. 64; Si. 16. 59; Amaru. 64. –COMP. **–गतिः** *f.* =गणगति q. v. **–पतिः** an arithmetician. **–महामात्रः** a minister of finance.

–गणशस् *ind.* In troops or flocks, by classes.

गणिः *f.* Counting.

गणिका **1** A harlot, courtezan; गुणानुरक्ता गणिका च यस्य वसंतशोभेव वसंतसेना Mk. 1. 6; गणिका नाम पादुकांतरप्रविष्टेव लेष्टुका दुःखेन पुनर्निराक्रियते Mk. 5; निरकाशयद्रविमपेतवसुं वियदालयादपरदिग्गणिका Si. 9. 10. **2** A female elephant. **3** A kind of flower.

–गणित *a.* **1** Counted, numbered, calculated. **2** Regarded, cared for &c.; see –गण्. **–तं** **1** Reckoning, calculating. **2** The science of computation, mathematics; (it comprises पाटीगणित or व्यक्तगणित, arithmetic, बीजगणित, algebra and रेखागणित geometry) गणितमथ कलां वैशिकीं हस्तिशिक्षां ज्ञात्वा Mk. 1. 4. **3** The sum of a progression. **4** A sum (in general).

गणितिन् *m.* **1** One who has made a calculation. **2** A mathematician.

गणिन् *a.* (**नी** *f.*) Having a flock or troop (of anything); श्वगणिन् 'having a pack of hounds'; R. 9 53. *–m.* A teacher (having a class of pupils).

गणेय *a.* Numerable, what may be counted.

गणेरुः The Karnikâra tree. *–f.* **1** A harlot. **2** A female elephant.

गणेरुका **1** A bawd, procuress. **2** A female servant.

गंडः **1** The cheek, the whole side of the face including the temple; गंडाभोगे पुलकपटलं Mal. 2. 5; तदीयमार्द्रारुणगंडलेखं Ku. 7. 82. Me. 26. 92; Amaru. 81; Rs. 4. 6; 6. 10. S. 6. 17; Si. 72. 54. **2** An elephant's temple; Mâl. 1. 1. **3** A bubble. **4** A boil, tumour, swelling; pimple; अयमपरो गंडस्योपरि विस्फोटः Mu 5; तदा गंडस्योपरि पिटिका संवृत्ता S. 2. **5** Goitre and other excrescences of the neck. **6** A joint, knot. **7** A mark, spot. **8** A rhinoceros. **9** The bladder. **10** A hero, warrior. **11** Part of a horse's trappings, a stud or button fixed as an ornament upon the harness. –COMP. **–अंग** a rhinoceros. **–उपधानं** a pillow; मृदुगंडोपधानानि शयनानि सुखानि च Susr. **–कुसुमं** the juice that exudes from the elephant's temples during rut, ichor. **–कूपः** a well on the peak or summit of a mountain. **–ग्रामः** any large or considerable village. **–देशः**,**–प्रदेशः** the cheek. **–फलकं** a broad cheek; धृतमुग्धगंडफलकैर्विबभुर्विकसद्भिरास्यकमलैः प्रमदाः Si. 9. 47. **–भित्तिः** *f.* **1** the opening in the temples of an elephant from which ichor exudes during rut. **2** 'a wall-like cheek', an excellent *i. e.* broad and expansive cheek; निर्धौतदानामलगंडभित्तिः (गजः) R. 5. 43. (where Malli. says प्रशस्तौ गंडौ गंडभित्ती see *et seq.*) 12. 102. **–मालः**, **–माला** inflammation of the glands of the neck; **–मूर्ख** *a.* exceedingly foolish, very stupid. **–शिला** any large rock. **–शैलः** **1** a huge rock thrown down by an earthquake or storm; Ki. 7. 37. **2** the forehead. **–साह्वया** N. of a river, also called गंडकी. **–स्थलं**, **–स्थली** the cheek; गंडस्थलेषु मदवारिषु Pt. 1. 123; S. Til. 7; गंडस्थलीः प्रोषितपत्रलेखाः R. 6. 72; Amaru. 77. **2** the temples of an elephant.

गंडकः **1** A rhinoceros. **2** An impediment, obstacle. **3** A joint, knot. **4** A mark, spot. **5** A boil, tumour, pimple. **6** Disjunction, separation. **7** A coin of the value of four cowries. –COMP. **–वती** see गंडकी q. v.

गंडका A lump, a ball.

गंडकी **1** N. of a river flowing into the Ganges. **2** A female rhinoceros. –COMP. **–पुत्रः** **–शिला** the Sâligrâma stone.

गंडलिन् *m.* N. of Siva.

गंडिः The trunk of a tree from the root to the beginning of the branches.

गंडिका **1** A sort of pebble. **2** A kind of beverage.

गंडीरः A hero, champion.

गंडुः *m. f.* **1** A pillow. **2** A joint, knot.

गंडू *f.* **1** A joint, knot. **2** A bone. **3** A pillow. **4** Oil. –COMP. **–पदः** a kind of worm °भवं lead. **–पदी** a small गंडूपद.

गंडूषः-षा A mouthful, handful (of water); गजया गंडूषजलं करेणुः (ददौ) Ku. 3. 37; U. 3. 16; Mâl. 9. 34; गंडूषजलमात्रेण शफरी फर्फरायते Udb. **2** The tip of an elephant's trunk

गंडोलः **1** Raw sugar. **2** A mouthful

गत *p. p.* (of गम्) **1** Gone, departed, gone for ever; Mu 1. 25. **2** Passed away, elapsed, past; गतायां रात्रौ **3** Dead, deceased, departed to the next world; Ku. 4. 30. **4** Gone to, arrived at, reaching to. **5** Being in, situated in, seated in, resting on, contained in; usually in comp.; प्रासादप्रांतगतः Pt. 1 seated on &c.; सदोगतः R. 3. 66 seated in the assembly; so आद्य°; सर्वगत exisiting everywhere. **6** Fallen into, reduced to; *e. g.* आपद्गतः **7** Referring or relating to, with regard to, about, concerning, connected with (usually in comp.); राजा शकुंतलागतमेव चिंतयति S. 5; भर्तृगतया चिंतया S. 4. वयमपि भवत्यौ सखीगतं किमपि पृच्छामः S. 7; so पुत्रगतः स्नेहः &c. **—तं** **1** Motion, going; गतमुपरि घनानां वारिगर्भोदराणां S 7. 7; Si. 1 2. **2** Gait, manner of going; Ku. 1. 34; V. 4. 16. **3** An event. As first member of comp translated by 'free from', 'bereft of', 'deprived of', 'without.' –COMP. **–अक्ष** *a.* sightless, blind. **–अध्वम्** *a.* **1** one who has accomplished or finished a journey. **2** conversant, familiar (with anything). (*–f.*) the time immediately preceding new moon when a small streak of the moon is still visible; (चतुर्दशीयुक्ताऽमावास्या). **–अनुगतं** following custom or precedent. **–अनुगतिक** *a.* doing as others do, a blind follower; गतानुगतिको लोको न लोकः पारमार्थिकः Pt. 1. 342 people are blind followers or servile imitators; Mu. 6. 5. **–अंतः** *a.* one whose end has arrived. **–अर्थ** *a.* **1** poor. **2** meaningless (the meaning being already expressed). **–असु**, **–जीवित**, **–प्राण** *a.* expired, dead; Bg. 2. 11. **–आगतं** **1** going and coming; frequent visits, Bh. 3. 7; Bg. 9. 21; Mu. 4. 1. **2** irregular course of the stars (in astronomy). **–आधि** *a.* free from anxiety, happy. **–आयुस्** *a.* decrepit, infirm, very old. **–आर्तवा** a woman past her child-bearing. **–उत्साह** *a.* dispirited, dejected. **–ओजस्** *a.* bereft of strength or energy. **–कल्मष** *a.* freed from crime or sin, purified. **–क्लम** *a.* refreshed. **–चेतन** *a.* deprived of sense or consciousness, insensible, senseless. **–दिनं** *ind.* yesterday. **–प्रत्यागत** *a.* returned after having gone away; Ms. 7. 146. **–प्रभ** *a.* bereft of splendour, dim, obscured, faded. **–प्राण** *a.* lifeless, dead. **–प्राय** *a.*

almost gone, nearly passed away; गतप्रायारजनी. –भर्तृका 1 a widow. 2 (rarely) a woman whose husband has gone abroad (=प्रोषितभर्तृका). –लक्ष्मीक a. 1 bereft of lustre or splendour, faded. 2 deprived of wealth, impoverished; suffering losses. –वयस्क a. advanced in years, aged, old. –वर्षः,–र्ष the past year. –वैर a. at peace (with), reconciled. –व्यथ a. free from pain. –शैशव a. past child-hood. –सत्व a. 1 dead, annihilated, lifeless. 2 base. –सन्नक: an elephant out of rut. –स्पृह a. indifferent to worldly attachments.

गतिः f. 1 Motion, going, moving, gait; गतिर्विगलिता Pt. 4. 78; अभिन्नगतयः S. 1. 14; (न) भिंदंति मंदां गतिमश्वमुख्यः Ku. 1. 11 do not mend their slow gait (do not mend their pace); so गगनगतिः Pt. 1; लघुगतिः Me. 16, 10, 46; U. 6. 23· 2 Access, entrance; मणौ वज्रसमुत्कीर्णे सूत्रस्येवास्ति मे गतिः R. 1. 4. 3 Scope, room; अस्त्रगतिः Ku. 3. 19; मनोरथानामगतिर्न विद्यते Ku. 5. 64; नास्त्यगतिर्मनोरथानां V. 2. 4 Turn, course; दैवगतिर्हि चित्रा. 5 Going to, reaching, obtaining; वैकुंठीया गतिः Pt. 1 obtaining Heaven. 6 Fate, issue; भर्तुर्गतिर्गतव्या Dk. 103. 7 State, condition; दानं भोगो नाशस्तिस्रो गतयो भवंति वित्तस्य Bh. 2. 43; Pt. 1. 106. 8 Position, station, situation, mode of existence; पराघ्यंगतेः पितुः R. 8. 27; कुसुमस्तबकस्येव द्वे गती स्तो मनस्विनां Bh. 2. 104; Pt. 1. 41, 420. 9 A means, expedient, course, alternative अनुपेक्षणे द्वयी गतिः Mu. 3; का गतिः what help is there, can't help (often used in dramas) Pt. 1. 319; अन्या गतिर्नास्ति K. 158. 10 Recourse, shelter, refuge, asylum, resort; विद्यमाना गतिर्येषां Pt. 1. 320, 322, आसयत् सलिले पृथ्वीं यः स मे श्रीहरिर्गतिः Sk; 11 Source, origin, acquisition; Bg. 2. 43; Ms. 1. 10. 12 A way, path. 13 A march, procession. 14 An event, issue, result. 15 The course of events, fate, fortune. 16 Course of asterisms. 17 The diurnal motion of a planet in its orbit. 18 A running wound or sore, fistula. 19 Knowledge, wisdom. 20 Transmigration, metempsychosis; Ms. 6. 73. 21 A stage or period of life (as शैशव, यौवन, वार्धक). 22 (In gram.) A term for prepositions and some other adverbial prefixes (such as अलं, तिरस् &c.) when immediately connected with the tenses of a verb or verbal derivatives. –COMP. –अनुसरः following the course of another. –भंगः stoppage. –हीन a. without refuge, helpless, forlorn.

गत्वर a. (री f.) 1 Going, movable locomotive. 2 Transcient, perishable; गत्वरैरसुभिः Ki. 2. 19; गत्वर्यो यौवनश्रियः 11. 12.

गद् 1 P. (गदति, गदित) 1 To speak articulately, speak, say, relate; जगादाग्रे गदाग्रजं Si. 2. 69; बहु जगद पुरस्तात्तस्य मत्ता किलाहं 11 39; शुद्धांतरक्ष्या जगदे कुमारी R. 6. 45. 2 To enumerate. –WITH नि to declare, say, speak; R. 2. 33.

गदः 1 Speaking, speech. 2 A sentence. 3 Disease, sickness; असाध्यः कुरुते कोपं प्राप्ते काले गदो यथा Si. 2. 84; जनपदे न गदः पदमादधौ R. 9. 4; 17. 81. 4 Thunder. –दं A kind of poison. –COMP. –अगदौ (du.) the two Asvins, physicians of gods. –अग्रणी; the chief of all diseases; i. e. consumption. –अंबरः a cloud अरातिः a drug, medicament.

गदयित्नु a. 1 Loquacious, garrulous, talkative. 2 Libidinous, lustful. –त्नुः N. of Kâma, the god of love.

गदा A mace, club; संचूर्णयामि गदया न सुयोधनोरू Ve. 1. 15. –COMP. –अग्रजः N. of Krishṇa; Si. 2. 84. –अग्रपाणि a. having a mace in the right hand. –धरः an epithet of Vishṇu. –भृत् a. a club-bearer, one who fights with a mace. (-m) an epithet of vishuṇ –युद्धं a fight with clubs. –हस्त a. armed with a club.

गदिन् a. (नी f.) 1 Armed with a club; Bg. 11. 17. 2 Affected with sickness, diseaesd. –m. An epithet of Vishṇu.

गद्गद a. Stammering, stuttering; तत्किं रोदिषि गद्गदेन वचसा Amaru. 53; गद्गदगलत्त्रुट्यद्विलीनाक्षरं को देहीति वदेत् Bh. 3 8; सानंदगद्गदपदं हरिरित्युवाच Gît. 10. –दं ind. In a faltering or stammering tone; विललाप स बाष्पगद्गदं R. 8. 43. –दः, –दं Stammering, indistinct or convulsive speech. –COMP. –ध्वनिः low inarticulate sound expressive of joy or grief. –वाच् f. inarticulate or convulsive speech, interrupted by sobbing &c. –स्वर a. uttering stammering sounds. (–रः) 1 indistinct or stammering utterance. 2 a buffalo.

गद्य pot. p. To be spoken or uttered; गद्यमेतत्त्वया मम Bk. 6. 47. –द्यं Prose, elaborate prose composition, composition not metrical yet framed with due regard to harmony; one of the three classes into which all compositions may be divided; See Kâv. 1. 11.

गद्याण (न-ल) कः A weight equal to 41 Gunjâs.

गंतृ a. (त्री f.) 1 One that goes or moves. 2 Having sexual intercourse with a woman.

गंत्री A car drawn by oxen; गंत्रीरथ in the same sense.

गंध् 10 A (गंधयते) 1 To injure, hurt. 2 To ask, beg. 3 To move, go.

गंधः 1 Smell, odour; गंधमाघ्राय चोर्व्याः Me. 21; अपघ्नंतो दुरितं हव्यगंधैः S. 4. 7; R. 12. 27. (गंध is changed to गंधि when as the last member of a Bah. comp. it is preceded by उद्, पूति, सु, सुरभि, or when the compound implies comparison; सुगंध, सुरभिगंधि, कमलगंधि मुखं; also when गंध is used in the sense of 'a little') 2 Smell considered as one of the 24 properties or guṇas of the Vaiseshikas; it is a property characteristic of पृथिवी or earth which is defined as गंधवती पृथ्वी T. S. 3. The mere smell of anything, a little, a very small quantity; घृतगंधि भोजनं Sk. 4 A perfume, any fragrant substance; एषा मया सेविता गंधयुक्तिः Mk. 8; Y. 1. 231. 5 Sulphur. 6 Pounded sandal wood. 7 Connection, relationship. A neighbour. 9 Pride, arrogance; as in आत्तगंध q. v. –धं 1 Smell. 2 Black aloewood. –COMP. –अधिकं a kind of perfume. –अपकर्षणं removing smells. –अंबु n. fragrant water. –अम्ला the wild lemon tree. –अश्मन् m. sulphur. –अष्टकं a mixture of 8 fragrant substances offered to deities, varying in kind according to the nature of the deity to whom they are offered. –आखुः the musk-rat –आजीवः a vendor of perfumes. –आढ्य a. rich in odour, very fragrant स्रजश्चोत्तमगंधाढ्याः Mb. (–ढ्यः) the orange tree. (–ढ्यं) sandal-wood. –इंद्रियं the organ of smell. –इभः, –गजः, –द्विपः –हस्तिन् m. 'the scent-elephant' an elephant of the best kind; शमयति गजानन्यान्गंधद्विपः कलभोऽपि सन् V. 5. 18; R. 6. 7; 17. 70; Ki. 17. 17. –उत्तमा spirituous liquor. –उदं scented water. –उपजीविन् m. one who lives by perfumes, a perfumer. –ओतुः (forming गंधोतु or गंधौतु) the civet-cat. –कारिका 1 a female servant whose business is to prepare perfumes. 2 a female artisan living in the house of another, but not altogether subject to another's control. –कालिका, –काली f. N. of Satyavatî, mother of Vyâsa. –काष्ठं aloewood. –कुटी a kind of perfume. –केलिका, –चेलिका musk. –गुण a. having the property of odour. –घ्राणं the smelling of any odour. –जलं fragrant water. –ज्ञा the nose. –तूर्यं a musical instrument of a loud sound used in battle (as a drum or trumpet). –तैलं a fragrant oil, a kind of oil prepared with fragrant substances.–दारु n. aloe-wood. –द्रव्यं a fragrant substance. –धूलिः f. musk. –नकुलः the musk-rat. –नालिका, –नाली the nose. -निलया a kind of jasmine. -पं: N. of a class of manes. -पत्रा, -पलाशी a species of zedoary. -पलाशिका turmeric. -पाषाणः sulphur. -पिशाचिका the smoke of burnt fragrant resin (so called from its dark colour or cloudy nature, or perhaps from its attracting demons by its fragrance). -पुष्पः 1 the Vetasa plant. 2 the Ketaka plant (-ष्पं) a fragrant flower. -पुष्पा an indigo plant. -पूतना a kind of imp or goblin. -फली 1 the Priyangu creeper. 2 a bud of the Champaka tree. -बंधुः the mango tree. -मातृ *f.* the earth. -मादनः 1 a large black bee. 2 sulphur. (-नः -नं). N. of a particular mountain to the east of Meru renowned for its fragrant forests. -मादनी spirituous liquor. -मादिनी lac. -मार्जारः the civet-cat. -मुखा, -मूषिकः -मूषी *f.* the musk-rat. -मृगः 1 the civet cat. 2 the musk-deer. -मैथुनः a bull. -मोदनः sulphur. -मोहिनी a bud of the Champaka tree. -युक्तिः *f.* preparation of perfumes. -राजः a kind of jasmine (-जं) 1 a sort of perfume. 2 sandal-wood. -लता the Priyangu creeper. -लोलुपा a bee. -वहः the wind; रात्रिंदिवं गंधवहः प्रयाति *S.* 5. 4; दिग्दक्षिणा गंधवहं मुखेन Ku. 3. 25. -वहा the nose. -वाहकः 1 the wind. 2 the musk-deer. -वाही the nose. -विह्वलः wheat. -वृक्षः the *S*âla tree. -व्याकुलं a kind of fragrant berry (कक्कोल). -शुंडिनी the musk-rat. -शेखरः musk. -सारः sandal. -सोमं the white water-lily. -हारिका a female servant whose business is to prepare perfumes; cf. गंधकारिका.

गंधकः Sulphur.

गंधनं 1 Continued effort, perseverance. 2 Hurting, injury, killing. 3 Manifestation. 4 Intimation, information, hint.

गंधवती 1 The earth. 2 Wine. 3 N. of Satyavatî, mother of Vyâsa. 4 A variety of jasmine.

गंधर्वः A celestial musician, a class of demi-gods regarded as the singers or musicians of gods and said to give good and agreeable voice to girls; सोमं शौचं ददावासां गंधर्वश्च शुभां गिरं Y. 1. 71. 2 A singer in general. 3 A horse. 4 The musk-deer. 5 The soul after death and previous to its being born again. 6 The black cuckoo. -Comp. -नगरं, -पुरं the city of Gandharvas, an imaginary city in the sky, probably the result of some natural phenomenon, such as mirage. -राजः Chitraratha, the chief of the Gandharvas. -विद्या the science of music. -विवाहः one of the eight forms of marriage described in Ms. 3. 27. &c.; in this form marriage proceeds entirely from love or the mutual inclination of a youth and maiden without ceremonies and without consulting relatives; it is, as Kâlidâsa observes, कथमन्यबांधवकृता स्नेहप्रवृत्तिः *S.* 4. 16. -वेदः one of the four subordinate Vedas or *Upavedas*, which treats of music; see उपवेद. -हस्तः, -हस्तकः the castor-oil-plant.

गंधारः (pl.) N. of a country and its rulers.

गंधाली 1 A wasp. 2 Continued fragrance. —Comp. -गर्भः small cardamoms.

गंधालु *a*. Fragrant, perfumed, scented.

गंधिक *a*. (Used only at the end of comp.) 1 Having the smell of; as उत्पलगंधिक. 2 Having a very small quantity of; भ्रातृगंधिकः a brother only in name. -कः 1 A seller of perfumes. 2 Sulphur.

गभस्ति *m. f.* A ray of light, a sunbeam or moonbeam. -स्तिः *m.* The sun. -*f.* An epithet of Svâhâ, the wife of Agni. -Comp. -करः, -पाणिः, -हस्तः the sun.

गभस्तिमत् *m.* The sun; घनव्यपायेन गभस्तिमानिव R. 3. 37. -*n.* One of the seven divisions of Pâtâla.

गभीर *a.* 1 Deep (in all senses) उत्तालास्त इमे गभीरपयसः पुण्याः सरित्संगमाः U. 2. 30; Bv. 2. 105. 2 Deep sounding (as a drum). 3 Thick, dense, impervious (as a forest.) 4 Profound, sagacious. 5 Grave, serious, solemn, earnest. 6 Secret, mysterious. 7 Inscrutable, difficult to be perceived or understood.-Comp. -आत्मन् the supreme soul. -वेध *a.* very penetrating.

गभीरिका A large drum with a deep sound.

गभोलिकः A small round pillow.

गम् 1 P. (गच्छति, गत; *caus.* गमयति, *desid.* जिगमिषति, जिगांसते Atm.) 1 To go, move in general; गच्छत्वार्या पुनर्दर्शनाय V. 5; गच्छति पुरः शरीरं धावति पश्चादसंस्तुतं चेतः *S.* 1 34; क्वाधुना गम्यते 'where art thou going'. 2 To depart, go forth, go away, set forth or out; उत्क्षिप्यैनां ज्योतिरेकं जगाम *S.* 5. 30. 3 To go to, reach, resort to, arrive at, approach; यद्गम्योपि गम्यते Pt. 1. 7; एनो गच्छति कर्तारं Ms. 8. 19 the sin goes to (recoils on) the doer; 4. 19; so धरणिं मूर्ध्ना गम् &c. 4 To pass, pass away, elapse (as time); दिनेषु गच्छत्सु R. 3. 8 as days rolled on, in course of time; काव्यशास्त्रविनोदेन कालो गच्छति धीमतां H. 1. 1; गच्छता कालेन in the long run. 5 To go to the state or condition of, become, undergo, suffer, partake of &c. (usually joined with nouns ending in ता,-त्व &c. or any noun in the acc.); गमिष्याम्युपहास्यतां R. 1. 3; पश्चादुमाख्यां सुमुखी जगाम Ku. 1, 29 went by or received the name of Umâ; so तृप्तिं गच्छति becomes satisfied; विषादं गतः became dejected; कोपं न गच्छति does not become angry; आनृण्यं गतः released from debt. 6 To cohabit, have sexual intercourse with; गरोः सुतां...यो गच्छति पुमान् Pt. 2 107; Y. 1. 80. —*Caus.* 1 To cause to go, lead to, reduce to (as a state). 2 To spend, pass (as time). 3 To make clear, explain, expound. 4 To signify, denote, convey an idea or sense of; द्वौ नञौ प्रकृतार्थं गमयतः 'two negatives make one affirmative.' -With अति to go or pass away. -अधि 1 to acquire, obtain, get; अधिगच्छति महिमानं चंद्रोऽपि निशापरिगृहीतः M. 1. 13.; खनन्वायेधिगच्छति Ms. 2. 218; 7. 33; Bg. 2. 64; R. 2. 66, 5. 34. 2 to accomplish, secure, fulfill; अर्थं सप्रतिबंधं प्रभुरधिगंतुं सहायवानेव M. 1. 9. 3 to approach, go towards, reach, have access to; गुणालयोऽप्यसन्मंत्री नृपतिर्नाधिगम्यते Pt. 1. 384. 4 to know, learn, study, understand, तेभ्योऽधिगंतुं निगमांतविद्यां U. 2. 3; Ki. 2. 41; Ms. 7. 39; Y. 1. 99. 5 to marry or take (as a husband); Ms. 9. 91. -अध्या to find, get, meet with. -अनु 1 to go after, follow, accompany; ओदकांतात् स्निग्धो जनोऽनुगंतव्यः *S.* 4; मार्गं मनुष्येश्वरधर्मपत्नी श्रुतेरिवार्थं स्मृतिरन्वगच्छत् R. 2. 2, 6; Ki. 5. 2; Ms. 12. 115; Pt. 1. 73. 2 to approach, arrive at, go to. 3 to imitate, resemble, respond to; आस्फालितं यत्प्रमदाकराग्रैर्मृदंगधीरध्वनिमन्वगच्छत् R. 16. 13; Ki. 4. 36. -अंतर् to go between, be included or comprised; see अंतर्गत. -अप 1 to go away, depart, pass away, (as time &c.); Pt. 3. 8. 2 to vanish, disappear, go away from. -अभि to go near, approach, visit; एनमभिजग्मुर्महर्षयः R. 15. 59; Ki. 10. 21; मनुमेकाग्रमासीनमभिगम्य महर्षयः Ms. 1. 1. 2 to find, meet with (casually or by chance). 3 to cohabit, have sexual intercourse with; Y. 2. 205. -अभ्या 1 to approach, arrive, come or draw near; सर्वत्राभ्यागतो गुरुः H. 1. 108. 2 to come to, obtain. -अभ्युद् 1 to rise, go up. 2 to go towards, go forth to meet. -अभ्युप to agree to, accept, undertake, admit, grant, own. -अव 1 to know, learn, think, understand, believe, परस्तादवगम्यत एव *S.* 1. कथं शांतामित्यभिहिते श्रांत इत्यवगच्छति मूर्खः Mk. 1; Bg. 10. 41, R. 8. 88; Bk. 5. 81. 2

to consider, take for, regard as. (-*Caus.*) to convey, denote, signify, show, tell; Bk. 10. 62. **-आ** 1 to come, approach. 2 to arrive at, attain, reach (a particular state) (-*Caus.*) 1 to lead towards, bring, convey; आगमितापि विदूरं Gît. 12. 2 to learn, study; R. 10. 71. 3 to wait (Atm.) **-उद्** 1 to rise or go up; असह्यवातोद्गतरेणुमंडला Rs. 1. 10. v.l. 2 to shoot up, appear; V. 4. 23. 3 to rise or spring from, proceed, originate; इत्युद्गताः पौरवधूमुखेभ्यः शृण्वन् कथाः R. 7. 16; Amaru. 91. 4 to be famous or well-known; R. 18. 20. **-उप** 1 to go, to approach, attain reach to; R. 6. 85. 2 to penetrate, enter into; Si. 9. 39. 3 to undergo, suffer; तपो घोरमुपागमत् Râm. 4 to go to the state of, attain, acquire; प्रतिकूलतामुपगते हि विधौ Si 9. 6; तानप्रदायित्वमिवोपगंतुं Ku. 1 8. 5 to admit, consent or agree to. 6 to approach a woman for sexual intercourse; सुप्तां मत्तां प्रमत्तां वा रहो यत्रोपगच्छति Ms. 3. 34; 4. 40. **-उपा** 1 to come to, approach (a person or place). 2 to go to, go to the state of, attain; तृप्तिमुपागतः, पंचत्वमुपागतः &c. 3 to get, obtain; Y. 2. 143. **-नि** 1 to go to, attain, acquire, obtain; यत्र दुःखांतं च निगच्छति Bg. 18. 36, 9. 31. 2 to get knowledge, learn **-निस्** (**निर्**) 1 to go out, depart; प्रकाशं निर्गतः S. 4. हुतवहपरिखेदादाशु निर्गत्य कक्षात् Rs. 1. 27; Ms. 9. 83; S. 6. 3; Amaru. 61. 2 to remove; as in निर्गतविशंकः. 3 to be cured (of a disease). **-परा** 1 to return; तदयं परागत एवास्मि U. 5. 2 to surround, encompass, pervade; स्फुटपरागपरागतपंकजं Si. 6. 2. **-परि** 1 to go or walk round; तं हयं तत्र परिगम्य Râm.; यथा हि मेरुः सूर्येण नित्यशः परिगम्यते Mb. 2 to surround; Si. 9. 26; Bk. 10. 1; सेनापरिगत &c. 3 to spread everywhere, pervade all directions. 4 to obtain; वृषलतां &c. 5 to know, understand, learn; R. 7. 71. 6 to die, go forth (from this world); वयं येभ्यो जाताश्चिरपरिगता एव खलु ते Bh. 3. 38. 7 to overpower, affect; as in क्षुधया परिगतः **-पर्या** 1 to approach, go towards. 2 to complete, finish. 3 to conquer, subdue. **-प्रति** 1 to return. 2 to advance or go towards. **-प्रत्या** to return, come back. **-प्रत्युद्** to go forth or advance towards to meet (as a mark of respect); प्रत्युज्जगामातिथिमातिथेयः R. 5. 2; प्रत्युद्गच्छति मूर्च्छति स्थिरतमःपुंजे निकुंजे प्रियः Gît. 11; Bv. 3. 3. **-वि** 1 to pass away (as time &c.); संध्यापि सपदि व्यगमि Si. 9. 17. 2 to vanish, disappear; सलज्जाया लज्जापि व्यगमदिव दूरं मृगदृशः Gît. 11; Bg. 11. 1; Ms. 3. 2, 59. (-*Caus.*) to spend, pass; विगमयत्युन्निद्र एव क्षपाः S. 6. 4. **-विनस्** 1 to go out. 2 to disappear, vanish. **-विप्र** to separate. **-सं** (Used, in Atm.) to come or join together, meet, encounter; अक्षधूर्तैः समगंसि Dk.; एते भगवत्यौ कलिंदकन्यामंदाकिन्यौ संगच्छेते A. R. 7. 2 to cohabit, have sexual intercourse with; भार्या च परसंगता Pt. 1. 208; Ms. 8. 378. (-*Caus.*) to bring together, join or unite; R. 7. 17. **-समधि** 1 to approach. 2 to study. 3 to get, acquire; यत्ते समधिगच्छंति यस्यैते तस्य तद्धनं Ms. 8. 416. **-समव** to know fully. **-समुपा** 1 to approach. 2 to befall.

गम *a.* (At the end of comp.) Going, moving, going to, reaching, attaining, getting &c.; खगम, पुरोगम, हृदयंगम &c. **—मः** 1 Going, moving. 2 March; अश्वस्यैकाहगमः 3 The march of an assailant. 4 A road. 5 Inconsiderateness, thoughtlessness. 6 Superficiality, careless perusal. 7 (Sexual) intercourse with a woman, cohabitation; गुर्वंगनागमः Ms. 11. 55; Y. 2. 293. 8 A game played with dice and men. -Comp. **—आगमः** going and coming.

गमक *a.* (**मिका** *f.*) 1 Indicative or suggestive, a proof or index of; तदेव गमकं पांडित्यवैदग्ध्ययोः Mal. 1. 7. 2 Convincing.

गमनं 1 Going, motion, gait; श्रोणीभारादलसगमना Me. 82; so गजेंद्रगमने S. Til. 7. 2 Going, motion considered as one of the five *karmans* by the Vaiseshikas. 3 Approaching, going to. 4 March of an assailant. 5 Undergoing, suffering. 6 Obtaining, attaining. 7 Cohabitation.

गमिन् *a.* Intending to go; as in ग्रामंगमी. **—m** A passenger.

गमनीय, गम्य *pot. p.* 1 Accessible, approachable; विकारस्य गमनीयास्मि संवृत्ता S. 1. 2 Intelligible, easy to be comprehended. 3 Intended, implied, meant. 4 Suitable, desirable, fit; Y. 1. 64. 5 Fit for cohabitation; दुर्जनगम्या नार्यः Pt. 1. 278; अभिकामां स्त्रियं यश्च गम्यां रहसि याचितः। नैपैति Mb. 6 Curable (by a drug &c.); न गम्यो मंत्राणां Bh. 1. 89.

गंभारिका, गंभारी N. of a tree.

गंभीर *a.* =गभीर q. v.; R. 1. 36; Me. 64, 66. **—रः** 1 A lotus. 2 A citron. -Comp. **-वेदिन्** *a.* restive (as an elephant).

गंभीरा, गंभीरिका N. of a river; गंभीरायाः पयसि Me. 40.

गयः 1 N. of the people living round Gayâ and the district inhabited by them. 2 N. of an Asura. **-या** N. of a city in Behar which is a place of pilgrimage.

गर *a.* (**री** *f.*) Swallowing.**—रः** 1 Any drink or fluid, beverage. 2 Sickness, disease. 3 Swallowing (गरा also in this sense) **-रः -रं** 1 Poison. 2 An antidote. **-रं** Sprinkling, wetting. -Comp. **-अधिका** 1 the insect called Lâkshâ. 2 the red dye obtained from it. **-घ्नी** a kind of fish. **-द** *a.* poisoning, giving poison. (**-दं**) poison. **-व्रतः** a peacock.

गरणं 1 The act of swallowing. 2 Sprinkling. 3 Poison.

गरभः Fœtus, embryo; see गर्भ.

गरलः-लं 1 Poison or venom in general; कुवलयदलश्रेणी कंठे न सा गरलद्युतिः Gît. 3; गरलमिव कलयति मलयसमीरं 4; स्मरगरलखंडनं मम शिरसि मंडनं 10. 2 The venom of a snake. **-लं** A bundle of grass. —Comp. **-अरिः** an emerald.

गरित *a.* Poisoned.

गरिमन् *m.* 1 Weight, heaviness; Si. 9. 49. 2 Importance, greatness; dignity; Pt. 1. 30. 3 Worth, excellence. 4 One of the eight *Siddhis* or faculties of Siva, by which he can make himself heavy or great at will; see सिद्धि.

गरिष्ठ *a.* 1 Heaviest. 2 Most important; (superl. of गुरु *a.* q. v.)

गरीयस् *a.* Heavier, weightier, more important (compar. of गुरु *a.* q. v.); मतिरेव बलाद्गरीयसी H. 2. 86; वृद्धस्य तरुणी भार्या प्राणेभ्योऽपि गरीयसी H. 1 112. Si. 2. 24, 37.

गरुडः 1 N. of the king of birds. [He is a son of Kasyapa by his wife Vinatâ. He is the chief of the feathered race, an implacable enemy of serpents and elder brother of Aruna. In a dispute between his mother and Kadrû, her rival, about the colour of उच्चैःश्रवस् Kadrû defeated Vinatâ, and, in accordance with the conditions of the wager, made her her slave. Garuḍa brought down the heavenly beverage (Amrita) to purchase her freedom, not however without a hard struggle with Indra for the same. Vinatâ, was then released; but the Amrita was taken away by Indra from the serpents. Garuḍa is represented as the vehicle of Vishṇu and as having a white face, an aquiline nose, red wings and a golden body]. 2 A building shaped like Garuḍa. 3 N. of a particular military array. -Comp. **-अग्रजः** an epithet of Aruṇa, the charioteer of the sun. **-अंकः** an epithet of Vishṇu. **-अंकितं, -अश्मन्** *m.*, **-उत्तीर्णं** an emerald. **-ध्वजः**

an epithet of Vishṇu. -व्यूहः a particular military array; see (3) above.

गरुत् *m.* 1 The wing of a bird. 2 Eating, swallowing. -COMP. -योधिन् *m.* a quail.

गरुत्मत् *a.* Winged; गरुत्मदाशीविषभीमदर्शनैः R. 3. 57. -*m.* 1 Garuḍa, 2 A bird in general.

गरुलः Garuḍa, the chief of birds.

गर्गः 1 N. of an old sage, one of the sons of Brahmâ. 2 A bull. 3 An earth-worm. —(pl.) The descendants of Garga. -COMP. -स्रोतस् *n.* N. of a Tîrtha.

गर्गरः 1 A whirlpool, an eddy. 2 A kind of musical instrument. 3 A kind of fish. 4 A churn. -री A churn; a vessel for holding water.

गर्गाटः A kind of fish.

गर्ज् 1 P., 10 U. (गर्जति, गर्जयति-ते, गर्जित) 1 To roar, growl; गर्जन् हरिः सांभसि शैलकुंजे Bk. 2. 9; 15. 21. रणे न गर्जंति वृथा हि शूराः Râm. हृष्टो गर्जति चातिदर्पितबलो दुर्योधनो वा शिखी Mk. 5. 6. 2 To emit a deep or thundering sound, thunder; यदि गर्जति वारिधरो गर्जतु तन्नाम निष्ठुराः पुरुषाः Mk. 5. 32 (and in several other verses of the same Act); गर्जति शरदि न वर्षति वर्षति वर्षासु निःस्वनो मेघः Udb. -WITH अनु to thunder in return, echo; Ku. 6 40. -प्रति 1 to roar at, to roar against; (fig.) 2 to resist, oppose; अयोहृदयः प्रतिगर्जतां R. 9. 9.

गर्जः 1 The roaring of elephants. 2 The rumbling or thundering of clouds.

गर्जनं 1 Roaring, a roar, growl, thunder. 2 (Hence) sound, noise in general. 3 Passion, wrath. 4 War, battle. 5 Reproach.

गर्जा, गर्जिः The thundering of clouds.

गर्जित *a.* Sounded, roared. —तं The thunder of clouds. -तः A roaring elephant in rut.

गर्तः -र्तं A hollow, hole, cave; ससत्त्वेषु गर्तेषु Ms. 4. 47, 203. (गर्ता also in this sense.) -र्तः 1 The hollow of the loins. 2 A kind of disease. 3 N. of a country, a part of the *Trigartas* q. v. —COMP. -आश्रयः an animal living in holes or under ground; as a mouse or rat.

गर्तिका A weaver's work-shop; (so called because the weaver sits at his loom with his feet in a hole below the level of the floor.)

गर्द् 1 P., 10 U. (गर्दति, गर्दयति-ते) To sound, roar.

गर्दभः (भी *f.*) 1 An ass; न गर्दभा वाजिधुरं वहंति Mk. 4. 17; प्राप्ते तु षोडशे वर्षे गर्दभी ह्यप्सरायते Subhâsh. The ass is noted for three remarkable qualities:-अविश्रांतं वहेद्भारं शीतोष्णं च न विंदति। ससंतोषस्तथा नित्यं त्रीणि शिक्षेत गर्दभात्॥ Châṇ 70. 2 Smell, odour. —भं The white water-lily. -COMP. -अंडः -ण्डकः 1 N. of a particular tree. 2 a tree in general. -आह्वयं a white lotus. -गदः a particular disease of the skin.

गर्धः 1 Desire, eagerness. 2 Greediness.

गर्धन, गर्धित *a.* Covetous, greedy.

गर्धिन् *a.* (नी *f.*) 1 Desirous, greedy, covetous; नवान्नामिषगर्धिनः Ms. 4. 28. 2 Following or pursuing (anything) with eagerness.

गर्भः 1 The womb, the belly; गर्भेषु वसतिः Pt. 1; पुनर्गर्भे च संभवं Ms. 6. 63. 2 A fœtus, embryo; act of conception; नरपतिकुलभूत्यै गर्भमाधत्त राज्ञी R. 2. 75; गर्भोऽभवद्भूधरराजपत्न्याः Ku. 1. 19. 3 The time of conception; गर्भाष्टमेऽब्दे कुर्वीत ब्राह्मणस्योपनायनं Ms. 2. 36. 4 The child (in the womb;) *S.* 6. 5 A child, brood or offspring of birds. 6 The inside, middle, or interior of anything (in comp. in this sense); हिमगर्भैर्मयूखैः S. 3. 3; अग्निगर्भां शमीमिव 4. 1; R. 3. 9, 5. 17, 9. 55; Si. 9. 62; Mâl. 3. 12; Mu. 1. 12. 7 The offspring of the sky, *i. e.* the vapours and fogs drawn upwards by the rays of the sun during 8 months and sent down again in the rainy season; cf. Ms. 9. 305. 8 An inner apartment, a lying-in-chamber. 9 Any interior chamber. 10 A hole. 11 Fire. 12 Food. 13 The rough coat of the jackfruit (पनसकंटक). 14 The bed of a river, especially of the Ganges on the fourteenth day of the dark half of Bhâdrapada or in the very height of the rains when the river is fullest. -COMP. -अंक (also गर्भांकः) an interlude during an act, as the scene of the birth of Kusa and Lava in U. 7, or the सीतास्वयंवर in Bâlarâmayaṇa. The S. D. thus defines it:-अंकोदरप्रविष्टो यो रंगद्वारामुखादिमान्। अंकोऽपरः स गर्भांकः सबीजः फलवानपि॥ 279. -अवक्रांतिः *f.* descent of the soul into the womb. -अंगारं 1 uterus. 2 an inner and private room, the female apartments. 3 a lying-in-chamber. 4 the body or sanctuary of a temple, the chamber where the image of a deity is placed. -आधानं 1 impregnation; गर्भाधानक्षणपरिचयान्नूनमाबद्धमालाः (बलाकाः) Me. 9. 2 one of the Samskâras or purificatory ceremonies performed after menstruation to ensure or facilitate conception; (this ceremony legalizes in a religious sense the *consummation* of marriage); Y. 1. 11. -आशयः the uterus, the womb. -आस्रावः mis-carriage, abortion. -ईश्वरः one born rich (cf. 'born in the purple') a sovereign or rich man by birth. -उत्पत्तिः the formation of the embryo. -उपघातः miscarriage. -उपघातिनी a cow or female miscarrying from unseasonable gestation. -कर *a.* procreative. -कालः time of impregnation -कोशः -षः uterus. -क्लेशः pains caused by the embryo, the throes of parturition or child-birth. -क्षयः miscarriage. -गृहं, -भवनं, -वेश्मन् *n.* 1 an inner apartment, the body of a house. 2 a lying-in-chamber. 3 the sanctuary or body of a temple; निर्गत्य गर्भभवनात् Mâl. 1 -ग्रहणं impregnation, conception. -घातिन् *a.* causing abortion. -चलनं quickening, motion of the fœtus in the uterus. -च्युतिः *f.* 1 birth, delivery. 2 miscarriage. -दासः -सी a slave by birth; (often used as a term of abuse or reproach.) -द्रुह् *a.* (nom. sing. °ध्रुक्) causing abortion. -धरा pregnant. -धारणं, -धारणा gestation, impregnation. -ध्वंसः abortion. -पाकिन् *m.* rice ripening in sixty days. -पातः miscarriage after the fourth month of pregnancy. -पोषणं -भर्मन् *n.* nourishment of the fœtus, gestation; अनुष्ठिते भिषग्भिराप्तैरथ गर्भभर्मणि R. 3. 42. -मंडपः an inner apartment, a bed-chamber. -मासः month of pregnancy. -मोचनं delivery, birth. -योषा a pregnant woman; (fig.) the Ganges overflowing its banks. -रक्षणं protecting the fœtus. -रूपः -रूपकः a child, an infant, a youth. -लक्षणं a symptom of pregnancy. -लंभनं a ceremony performed for the sake of facilitating and developing pregnancy. -वसतिः *f.*, -वासः 1 the womb; Ms. 12. 78. 2 being in the womb. -विच्युतिः *f.* abortion in the beginning of pregnancy. -वेदना throes of childbirth. -व्याकरणं the formation of the embryo. -शंकुः a kind of instrument for extracting the dead fœtus. -शय्या the abode of the fœtus or uterus. -संभवः, -संभूतिः *f.* becoming pregnant -स्थ *a.* 1 situated in the womb. 2 interior, internal. -स्रावः abortion, miscarriage; कं गर्भस्रावः Pt. 1; Y. 3. 2; Ms. 5. 66.

-**गर्भकः** A chaplet of flowers worn in the hair. -कं A period of two nights with the intermediate day.

गर्भंडः Enlargement of the navel.

गर्भवती A pregnant woman.

गर्भिणी A pregnant female (whether of men or animals); गोगर्भिणीप्रियनवोलपमालभारिसेव्योपकंठविपिनावलयो भवंति Mâl. 9. 2; Y. 1. 105; Ms. 3. 114. —COMP. –अवेक्षणं mid-wifery, care and attendance of pregnant women and new-born infants. –दौहदं the longings of a pregnant woman –व्याकरणं, –व्याकृतिः *f.* 'science of the progress of pregnancy', (a particular head in medical works).

गर्भित *a.* Pregnant, filled with.

गर्भेतृप्त *a.* 1 'Contented in the womb' as a child. 2 Contented as to food or issue. 3 Indolent.

गर्मुत् *f.* 1 A kind of grass. 2 A kind of reed. 3 Gold.

गर्व् 1 P. (गर्वति, गर्वित) To be proud or haughty; (used only in *p. p.* which is also supposed to be an adjective derived from गर्व); कोर्थान्प्राप्य न गर्वितः Pt. 1. 146.

गर्वः 1 Pride, arrogance; मा कुरु धनजनयौवनगर्वं हरति निमेषात्कालः सर्वं Moha M. 4; सुधेदानीं यौवनगर्वं वहसि M. 4. 2 Pride considered as one of the 33 subordinate feelings in rhetoric; रूपधनाविद्यादिप्रयुक्तात्मोत्कर्षज्ञानाधीनपरावहेलनं गर्वः R. G.; or, according to S. D. गर्वो मदः प्रभावश्रीविद्यासत्कुलतादिजः । अवज्ञा सविलासांगदर्शनाविनयादिकृत् ॥

गर्वाटः A watchman, door-keeper.

गर्ह् 1. 10. A. (sometimes P. also) (गर्हते, गर्हयते, गर्हित) 1 To blame, censure, reproach; विषमां हि दशां प्राप्य दैवं गर्हयते नरः H. 4. 3; Ms. 4. 199. 2 To accuse, charge with. 3 To be sorry for. –WITH वि to blame, censure, reproach; तं विगर्हति साधवः Ms. 9. 68, 3. 46, 11. 52.

गर्हणं,–णा Censure, blame, reproach, abuse.

गर्हा Abuse, censure.

गर्ह्य *a.* Deserving censure, censurable, blamable; गर्ह्यं कुर्यादिमे कुले Ms. 5. 149. –COMP. –वादिन् *a.* speaking ill, speaking vilely.

गल् 1. P. (गलति, गलित) 1 To drop, drip, ooze, trickle: जलमिव गलत्युपदिष्टं K. 103; अच्छकपोलमूलगलितैः (अश्रुभिः) Amaru. 26, 91, Bv. 2. 21; R. 19. 22. 2 To drop or fall down; शरदमच्छगलद्वसनोपमा Si. 6. 42; 9. 75. प्रतोदा जगलुः Bk. 14. 99; 17. 87; गलद्भ्रमिल्ल Gît. 2; R. 7. 10; Me. 44. 3 To vanish, disappear, pass away, be removed; शैशवेन सह गलति गुरुजनस्नेहः K. 289; विद्यां प्रमादगलितामिव चिंतयामि Ch. P. 1; Bh. 2; 44. Bk. 5. 43; R. 3. 70. 4 To eat, swallow (connected with गृ). *-Caus.* or 10 U. (*p. p.* गालित) 1 To pour out. 2 To filter, strain. 3 To flow (A) –WITH निस् to ooze or flow out, trickle down, R. 5. 17. –पर्या to drop down; Bk. 2. 4. –वि 1 to drop down; V. 4. 10. 2 to ooze, or trickle. 3 to vanish, disappear.

गलः 1 The throat, neck; न गरलं गले कस्तूरियं; cf. अजागलस्तन; Bh. 1. 64; Amaru. 88. 2 The resin of the Sâla tree. 3 A kind of musical instrument. –COMP. –अंकुरः a particular disease of the throat (inflammation). –उद्भवः the tuft of hair on the neck of a horse. –ओघः tumor in the throat. –कंबलः a bull's dewlap –गंडः goitre. –ग्रहः, –ग्रहणं 1 seizing by the throat, throttling, smothering. 2 a kind of disease. 3 N. of certain days in the dark fortnight of a month:—*i. e.* the 4th, 7th 8th, 9th, 13th and the three following days. –चर्मन् *n.* the gullet, throat –द्वारं the mouth. –मेखला a necklace –वार्त *a.* 1 safe in the work of the throat, able to eat much and digest it, healthy, sound; दृश्यंते चैव तीर्थेषु गलवार्तास्तपस्विनः Pt. 3. v. l. 2 a parasite. –व्रतः a peacock. –शुंडिका the uvula. –शुंडी swelling of the glands of the neck. –स्तनी (also गलेस्तनी) a she-goat. –हस्तः 1 seizing by the throat, throttling, collaring. 2 an arrow with a crescent-shaped head; cf. अर्धचंद्र. –हस्तित *a.* seized by the throat, throttled, strangled.

गलकः 1 The throat, the neck. 2 A kind of fish.

गलनं 1 Oozing, trickling, dripping. 2 Leaking, melting away.

गलंतिका, गलंती 1 A small pitcher. 2 A small water-jar with a hole in the bottom from which the water drops upon the object of worship (an image, Linga, Tulasî &c.) placed below.

गलिः A strong but lazy bull; see गडि.

गलित *p. p.* 1 Dropped or fallen down. 2 Melted. 3 Oozed, flowing. 4 Lost, vanished, deprived. 5 United, got loose. 6 Emptied, leaked away. 7 Filtered. 8 Decayed, impaired. –COMP. –कुष्ठं advanced or incurable leprosy when the fingers and toes fall off. –दंत *a.* toothless. –नयन *a.* one who has lost his eyes, blind.

गलितकः A kind of dance.

गलेगंडः A kind of bird, so called from the pendulous fleshy purse hanging from its throat.

गल्भ् 1 A. (गल्भते, गल्भित) To be bold or confident. –WITH प्र to be bold or confident; या कथंचन सखीवचनेन प्रागभिप्रियतमं प्रजगल्भे Si. 10. 18. न मौक्तिकच्छिद्रकरी शलाका प्रगल्भते कर्मणि टंकिकायाः Vikr. 1. 16 cannot be bold (competent) enough to do the work of a hatchet.

गल्भ *a.* Bold, confident, audacious.

गल्या A multitude of throats.

गल्लः The cheek; especially, the part of the cheek near the corners of the mouth. (Rhetoricians consider this word to be ग्राम्य or vulgar;) cf. the instance given in K. P. 7:—तांबूलभृतगल्लोयं मल्लं जल्पति मानुषः but cf. Bhavabhûti's use:—पातालप्रतिमल्लगल्लविवरप्रक्षिप्तसप्तार्णवं Mâl. 5. 22. –COMP. –चातुरी a small round pillow to put underneath the cheek.

गल्लकः A wine-glass. 2 Sapphire; गल्वर्क below.

गल्लर्कः 1 A vessel for drinking spirituous liquor; एवं बृहत्तरे गल्लर्कप्रमाणे कुले जातः Mk. 8; गल्लर्कशतपरिवृतः.

गल्वर्कः 1 Crystal. 2 Lapis lazuli. 3 A goblet, a vessel for drinking spirituous liquor.

गल्ह् 1 A. (गल्हते, गल्हित) To blame, censure.

गव (A substitute for गो at the beginning of certain compounds, especially with words beginning with vowels). –COMP. –अक्षः 1 an air-hole, a round window; विलोलनेत्रभ्रमरैर्गवाक्षाः सहस्रपत्राभरणा बभूवुः R. 7. 11; कुवलयितगवाक्षां लोचनैरंगनानां 7. 93; Ku. 7. 58; Me. 98. °जालं a lattice. –अक्षित *a.* furnished with windows. –अग्रं a multitude of cows (written as गोऽग्रं, गोअग्रं and गवाग्रं) –अदनं pasture or meadow grass. –अदनी 1 a pasture. 2 a manger, a trough for holding grass &c. for feeding cattle. –अधिका lac. –अर्ह *a.* of the value of a cow. –अविकं cattle and sheep. –अशनः 1 a shoemaker. 2 an out-cast. –अश्वं bulls and horses. –आकृति *a.* cow-shaped. –आह्निकं the daily measure of food given to a cow. –इंद्रः 1 an owner of kine. 2 an excellent bull. –ईशः, –ईश्वरः an owner of cows. –उद्वः an excellent cow or bull.

गवयः A species of ox; गोसदृशो गवयः T. S.; दृष्टः कथंचिद्गवयैर्विविग्नैः Ku. I. 56; Rs. 1. 23.

गवलः The wild buffalo. –लं Buffalo's horn; Si. 20. 12.

गवालूकः=गवय q. v.

गविनी A herd of cows.

गव्य *a.* 1 Consisting of cattle or cows. 2 Coming or got from a cow (as milk, curds &c.). 3 Proper or fit for cattle.—व्यं 1 Cattle, herd of cows. 2 Pasture-land. 3 The milk of a cow. 4 A bow-string. 5 A colouring substance, yellow pigment. —व्या 1 A herd of cows. 2 A measure of distance equal to two Krosas. 3 A bow-string. 4 A colouring substance, yellow pigment.

गव्यूतं--तिः *f.* 1 A measure of length nearly equal to two miles, or one Krosa. 2 A measure of distance equal to two Krosas.

गवेडुः,-धुः,-धुका kind of grass eaten by cattle.

गवेरुकं Red chalk.

गवेष् 1 A., 10 P. (गवेषते, गवेषयति, गवेषित) 1 To seek, hunt for, search or inquire for; तस्मादिष यतः प्रातस्तत्रिवान्यो गवेष्यतां Ks. 55. 176. 2 To strive after, desire ardently or fervently, make efforts for; गवेषमाणं महिषीकुलं जलं Rs. 1. 21.

गवेष *a.* Searching for. —षः Search, inquiry.

गवेषणं,-णा Search or inquiry after anything.

गांवेषेत *a.* Searched, sought, inquired or looked for.

गह्व 10 U. (गहयति-ते) 1 To be thick or impervious (as a forest) 2 To enter deeply into.

गहन *a.* 1 Deep, dense, thick. 2 Impervious, impenetrable, impassable, inaccessible. 3 Hard to be understood, inexplicable, mysterious; सेवाधर्मः परमगहनो योगिनामप्यगम्यः Pt 1. 285; Bh. 2. 58; गहना कर्मणो गतिः Bg. 4. 17; Sânti. 1. 8. 4 Hard, difficult, causing pain of trouble; गहनः संसारः Sânti. 3. 15. 5 Deepened, intensified; Mal. 1. 30 —नं 1 An abyss, depth. 2 A wood, thicket, deep or impenetrable forest; यदनुगमनाय निशिगहनमपि शीलितं Gît. 7; Bv. 1. 25. 3 A hiding-place. 4 A cave. 5 Pain, distress.

गह्वर *a.* (रा or रीf.) Deep, impervious.—रं 1 An abyss, a depth. 2 A thicket, forest. 3 A cave, cavern; गौरीगुरोर्गह्वरमाविवेश R. 2. 26, 46; Rs. 1. 21. 4 An inaccessible place. 5 A hiding-place. 6 A riddle. 7 Hypocrisy. 8 Weeping, crying. —रः An arbour, bower. —री 1 A cave, cavern, recess in a rock or mountain.

गा A song, verse.

गांग *a.* (गीf.) Being in or on the Ganges. 2 Coming from or relating to the Ganges; गांगमंबु सितमंबु यामुनं कज्जलाभमुभयत्र मज्जतः K. P. 14; Ku. 5. 37 —गः 1 An epithet of Bhîshma. 2 Of Kârtikeya. —गं 1 Rainwater of a peculiar kind (supposed to fall down from the heavenly Ganges.) 2 Gold.

गांगटः-टेयः A kind of prawn or shrimp.

गांगायनिः N. of Bhîshma or Kârtikeya.

गांगेय *a.* (यीf.) Being in or on the Ganges. —यः N. of Bhishma or Kârtikeya.—यं Gold.

गाजरं A carrot.

गिजांकायः A quail.

गाढ *p. p.* 1 Dived or plunged into, bathed in, deeply entered. 2 Frequently plunged into, resorted to, thickly crowded or inhabited; तपस्विगाढां तमसां प्राप नदीं तुरंगमेण R. 9. 72. 3 Closely pressed together, tightly drawn, fast, close, tight; गाढांगदैर्बाहुभिः R. 16. 60; गाढालिंगन Amaru. 36, a close embrace; Ch. P. 6. 4 Thick, dense. 5 Deep, impervious. 6 Strong, vehement, excessive, intense; गाढोत्कंठाललितलुलितैरंगकैस्ताम्यतीति Mâl. 1. 15.; Me. 83; प्राणमाढप्रकंपां *S.* Til. 12; Amaru. 72; गाढतप्तेन तप्तं Me. 102. -ढं *ind.* Closely, fast, much excessively, heavily, vehemently, powerfully. -Comp. -मुष्टि *a.* close-fisted, avaricious, miserly. (-ष्टिः) a sword.

गाणपत *a.* (ती *f*) 1 Relating to the leader of a troop. 2 Relating to Ganesa.

गाणपत्यः A worshipper of Ganesa. -त्यं 1 Worship of Ganesa. 2 The leadership of a troop, chieftainship.

गाणिक्यं A group of harlots.

गाणेशः A worshipper of Ganesa.

गांडि (डी) वः -वं 1 The bow of Arjuna, presented by Soma to Varuna, by Varuna to Agni, and by Agni to Arjuna, when the latter assisted him in consuming the खांडववन; गांडिवं स्रंसते हस्तात् Bg. 1. 29. 2 A bow in general. -Comp. -धन्वन् *m.* an epithet of Arjuna; Me. 48.

गांडीविन् *m.* An epithet of Arjuna, the third Pândava prince; Ve. 4.

गातागतिक *a.* (कीf.) Caused by going or coming.

गतानुगतिक *a.* (कीf.) Caused by blindly following or imitating custom or example.

गातुः 1 A song. 2 A singer. 3 A celestial chorister. 4 The male (Indian) cuckoo. 5 The large black bee.

गातृ *m.* (त्रीf.) 1 A singer. 2 A Gandharva.

गात्रं 1 The body; अपचितमपि गात्रं व्यावतत्वादलक्ष्यं *S.* 2. 4; तपति तनुगात्रि मदन. 3. 17 2 A limb or member of the body; गुरुपरितापानि न ते गात्राण्युपचारमर्हंति *S.* 3. 18; Ms. 2. 209; 5. 109. 3 The fore-quarter of an elephant. -Comp. -अनुलेपनी a fragrant unguent applied to the body. --आवरणं a shield. -उत्सादनं cleaning the body with perfumes.-कर्षण *a.* emaciating or weakening the body. -मार्जनी a towel. -यष्टिः a thin or slender body; R. 6. 81. -रुहं the hair on the body. -लता a thin or tender body, slim figure. -संकोचिन् *m.* the polecat; (so called because it contracts its body in order to spring). -संप्लवः a small bird, the diver.

गाथः A song, singing.

गाथकः -थिकः 1 A musician, singer. 2 A chanter of sacred poems or Purânas.

गाथा 1 verse. 2 A religious verse, but not belonging to any one of the Vedas. 3 A stanza, song. 4 A Prâkrita dialect. -Comp. -कारः a writer of Prâkrita verses.

गाथिका A song, verse; Y. 1.45.

गाधृ 1 A. (गाधते, गाधित) 1 To stand, stay, remain. 2 To set out for; dive or plunge into; गाधितासे नभो भूयः Bk 22. 2; 8. 1. 3 To seek, search or inquire for. 4 To compile, string or weave together.

गाध *a.* Fordable, not very deep, shallow; सरितः कुर्वती गाधाः पथश्चाश्यानकर्दमान् R. 4. 24; cf. अगाध. -धं 1 A shallow place, ford. 2 A place, site. 3 Desire of gain, cupidity. 4 Bottom.

गाधिः, गाधिन् *m.* N. of the father of Visvâmitra (he is supposed to have been an incarnation of Indra and born as the son of king Kausâmba). -Comp. -जः -नंदनः, -पुत्रः an epithet of Visvâmitra. -नगरं, -पुरं an epithet of Kânyakubja, the modern Kanoja.

गाधेयः An epithet of Visvamitra.

गानं Singing, a song.

गांत्री A carriage drawn by oxen.

गांदिनी 1 An epithet of the Ganges. 2 N. of a princess of Kasi, wife of Svaphalka and mother of Akrûra. -Comp. -सुतः an epithet (1) of Bhîshma. (2) of Kârtikeya. (3) of Akrûra.

गांधर्व *a.* (र्वी *f.*) Relating to the Gandharvas. — र्वः 1 A singer, celestial chorister. 2 One of the eight forms of marriage; गांधर्वः समयान्मिथः Y. 1. 161; (for explanation, see गंधर्वविवाह). 3 A subordinate Veda treating of music attached to the Sâmaveda; see उपवेद. 4 A horse. —र्वं The art of the Gandharvas; *i. e.* music, singing; कापि वेला चारुदत्तस्य गांधर्वं श्रोतुं गतस्य Mk. 3. -Comp. -चित्त *a.* one whose mind is possessed by a Gandharva. -शाला a music saloon, a concert-hall.

गांधर्व (र्वि) कः A singer.

गांधारः 1 The third of the seven primary notes of the Indian Gamut; (commonly denoted by ग in musical notation). 2 Red lead. 3 N. of a country between India and Persia, the modern Kandâhâra 4 A native or a ruler of that country.

गांधारिः An epithet of Sakuni, Duryodhana's maternal uncle.

गांधारी N. of the daughter of Subala, King of the Gândhâras and wife of Dhritarâshtra. (She bore to her husband 100 sons—Duryodhana and his 99 brothers. As her husband was blind she always wore a scarf over her face (probably to reduce herself to his state). After the destruction of all the Kauravas, she and her husband lived with their nephew Yudhish*th*ira).

गांधारेयः An epithet of Duryodhana.

गांधिकः 1 A vendor of perfumes, a perfumer. 2 A scribe, clerk. –कं Fragrant wares, perfumes; पण्यानां गांधिकं पण्यं किमन्यैः कांचनादिकैः Pt. 1. 13.

गामिन् *a*. (Only at the end of comp.) 1 Going, moving, walking वैदिशगामी M. 5; मृगेंद्रगामी R. 2. 30 having the gait of a lion; कुब्ज° Pt. 2. 5; अलस° Amaru. 51. 2 Riding; द्विरद° R. 4. 4. 3 Going or reaching to, extending or applying to, relating to; ननु सखीगामी दोषः S. 4; द्वितीयगामी न हि शब्द एष नः R. 3. 49. 4 Leading or going to, accruing to; चित्रकूटगामी मार्गः; कर्तृगामि क्रियाफलं. 5 United with; सदृशभर्तृगामिनी M. 5. 6 Passing over to, devolving on; *S*. 6; Y. 2 145.

गांभीर्यं 1 Deepness, depth (of water, sound &c.) 2 Depth, profundity (of meaning, character &c.); समुद्र इव गांभीर्ये Ram. ; *Si*. 1. 55; R. 3. 32.

गायः Singing, a song; Y. 3. 112.

गायकः A singer, musician; न नटा न विटा न गायकाः Bh. 3. 27.

गायत्रः – त्रं A song or hymn.

गायत्री 1 A Vedic metre of 24 syllables; गायत्री छंदसामहं Bg. 10. 35. 2 N. of a very sacred verse repeated by every Brâhmana at his Sandhyâ (morning and evening devotions) and on other occasions also. Great sins even are said to be expiated by a pious repetition of this verse, which is as follows:- तत्सवितुर्वरेण्यं भर्गो देवस्य धीमहि धियो यो नः प्रचोदयात् Rv. 3. 62. 10. –त्रं A hymn composed and recited in the Gâyatrî metre.

गायत्रिन् *a*. (णी *f*.) One who sings hymns, especially of the Sâmaveda.

गायनः (नी *f*.) A singer; तथैव तत्पौरुषगायनीकृताः N. 1. 103; Bh. 3. 27. v. l. –नं Singing, a song. 2 Practising singing as a means of subsistence.

गारुड *a*. (डी *f*.) 1 Shaped like Garuḍa 2 Coming from or relating to Garuḍa. –डः, –डं 1 An emerald; R. 13. 53 2 A charm against (snake) poison; संगृहीतगारुडेन K. 51 (where it has sense 1 also). 3 A missile presided over by Garuḍa. 4 Gold.

गारुडिकः A charmer, dealer in antidotes.

गारुत्मत *a*. (ती *f*.) 1 Shaped like Garuḍa. 2 Sacred or presided over by Garuḍa (as a missile); R. 16. 77. –तं An emerald.

गार्दभ *a*. (भी *f*.) Belonging to or coming from an ass, asinine.

गार्द्ध्यं Greediness; *Si*. 3. 73.

गार्ध्र *a*. (र्ध्री *f*.) Derived from a vulture. –र्ध्रः 1 Greediness (probably for गार्ध्यं). 2 An arrow. —Comp. –पक्षः, –वासस् *m*. an arrow furnished with a vulture's feathers.

गार्भ *a*. (र्भी *f*.) गार्भिक (की *f*.) *a*, 1 Uterine, fetal. 2 Relating to gestation; Ms. 2. 27.

गार्भिणं, –ण्यं A number of pregnant women.

गार्हपतं The position and dignity of a householder (गृहपति).

गार्हपत्यः 1 One of the three sacred fires perpetually maintained by a householder, which he receives from his father and transmits to his descendants, and from which fires for sacrificial purposes are lighted; cf. Ms. 2. 231. 2 The place where this sacred fire is kept. –त्यं The government of a family; position and dignity of a householder.

गार्हमेध *a*. (धी *f*.) Fit or proper for a householder. –धः The five Yajñas to be performed by a householder.

गार्हस्थ्यं 1 The order or stage of life of a householder (गृहस्थ), domestic affairs, household. 2 The five Yajñas to be daily performed by a householder.

गालनं 1 Straining (fluids). 2 Fusing, liquefying, melting.

गालवः 1 The Lodhara tree. 2 A kind of ebony. 3 N. of a sage, a pupil of Viswâmitra (said in Hariv. to be his son).

गालिः *f*. 1 Abuse, abusive or foul language; ददतु ददतु गालीर्गालिमंतो भवंतो वयमपि तदभावाद्गालिदानेऽसमर्थाः Bh. 3. 133.

गालित *a*. 1 Strained. 2 Distilled 3 Melted, fused.

गालोड्यं The seed of a lotus.

गावल्गणिः An epithet of Sanjaya, son of Gavalgaṇa.

गाह् 1 A. (गाहते, गाढ or गाहित) 1 To dive or plunge into, bathe, immerse oneself into (as water); गाहंतां महिषा निपानसलिलं श्रृंगैर्मुहुस्ताडितं *S*. 2 6. गाहितासेऽथ पुण्यस्य गंगामूर्तिमिव द्रुतां Bk. 22. 11, 14. 67; (fig. also); मनस्तु मे संशयमेव गाहते Ku. 5. 46 is plunged into or entertains doubts. 2 To enter deeply into, penetrate, roam or range over; कदाचित्कानन जगाहे K. 58; ऊनं न सत्वेष्वधिको बबाधे तस्मिन्वनं गोप्तरि गाहमाने R. 2. 14; Me. 48; H. 1. 171; Ki. 13. 24. 3 To stir up, agitate, shake, churn. 4 To be absorbed in (with loc.) 5 To hide oneself in. 6 To destroy. –With –अव (with the अ often dropped) 1 to plunge into, bathe or dive into; तमोपहंत्रीं तमसां वगाह्य R. 14. 76; स्यंमेऽवगाहतेऽत्यर्थं जलं Y. 1. 272. 2 to enter, penetrate, pervade fully; पूर्वापरौ तोयनिधी वगाह्य स्थितः पृथिव्या इव मानदंडः Ku. 1. 1, 7. 40. –उप to break in, enter into. –वि 1 to plunge or dive into, bathe; (दीर्घिकाः) स व्यगाहत विगाढमन्मथः R. 19. 9. 2 to enter, penetrate into, pervade (fig. also); विषमोऽपि विगाह्यते नयः कृततीर्थः पयसामिवाशयः Ki. 2. 3; R. 13. 1. 3 to stir about, agitate; विगाह्यमानां सरयूं च नौभिः R. 14. 30. –सं to enter, go to or into, penetrate into; समगाहिष्ट चांबरं Bk. 15. 59.

गाहः 1 Diving into, plunging, bathing. 2 Depth, interior.

गाहनं The act of diving into, plunging, bathing &c.

गाहित *a*. 1 Bathed in, plunged into. 2 penetrated, entered into; see गाह्.

गिंदुकः 1 A ball for playing with, 2 N. of a tree; see गेंदुक.

गिर् *f*. (nom. sing. गीः; instr. dual गीर्भ्यां &c.) 1 Speech, words, language ; वचस्यवसिते तस्मिन् ससर्ज गिरमात्मभूः Ku. 2. 53 ; भवतीनां सूनृतयैव गिरा कृतमातिथ्यं S. I. प्रवृत्तिसाराः खलु मादृशां गिरः Ki. I; 25 ; *Si*. 2. 15 ; Y. 1. 71. 2 Invocation, praise, song. 3 N. of Sarasvati, the goddess of speech and learning. —Comp. –देवी (गीर्देवी) Sarasvati, the goddess of speech. –पतिः (written गीःपतिः, गीष्पतिः and गीर्पतिः) 1. N. of Brihaspati, the preceptor of the gods. 2 a learned man. –रथः (गीरथः) N. of Brihaspati. –वा (बा) णः (गीर्वाण) a god, deity; परिमलो गीर्वाणचेतोहरः Bv. 1. 63 84.

गिरा Speech, speaking, language, voice.

गिरि *a*. Venerable, respectable worshipful. –रिः 1 A hill-mountain, an elevation; पश्याधःखनने मूढ गिरयो न पतंति किं *S*. Til. 19; ननु प्रवातेऽपि

निष्कंपा गिरयः S. 6. 2 A huge rock. 3 A disease of the eyes. 4 An honorific title given to Sannyâsins; *e.g.* आनंदगिरिः 5 (In math.) The number 'eight'. 6 A ball with which children play (गेंदुक). —रिः *f.* 1 Swallowing. 2 A rat, mouse (written also गिरी in this sense). —COMP. —इन्द्रः 1 a high mountain. 2 An epithet of *S*iva. 3 the Himâlaya mountain. —ईशः 1 an epithet of the Himâlaya mountain. 2 an epithet of *S*iva; सुतां गिरीशप्रतिसक्तमानसां Ku. 5. 3. —कच्छपः a species of tortoise living in mountains. —कंटकः Indra's thunderbolt. —कदंबः, —बकः a species of the Kadamba tree. —कंदरः a cave, cavern. —कर्णिका the earth. —काणः a blind or one-eyed man. —काननं a mountain grove. —कूटं the summit of a mountain. —गंगा N. of a river. —गुडः a ball for playing with. —गुहा a mountain cave. —चर *a.* roaming or wandering on a mountain; गिरिचर इव नागः प्राणसारं बिभर्ति *S*. 2. 4. (—रः) a thief. —ज *a.* mountain-born. (—जं) 1 talc. 2 red chalk. 3 benzoin. 4 bitumen. 5 iron. (—जा) 1 N. of Pârvati (the daughter of Himâlaya). 2 the hill-plantain (पर्वतकदली). 3 the Mallikâ creeper. 4. an epithet of the Ganges. °तनयः —नंदनः, —सुतः 1 an epithet of Kârtikeya. 2 of Ganesa. °पतिः an epithet of *S*iva. °मलं talc. —जालं a range of mountains. —ज्वरः Indra's thunderbolt. —दुर्गं a hill-fort, any stronghold among mountains; नृदुर्गं गिरिदुर्गं वा समाश्रित्य वसेत्पुरं Ms. 7. 70, 71. —द्वारं a mountain-pass. —धातुः red chalk. —ध्वजः Indra's thunderbolt. —नगरं N. of a district in Dakshinâpatha. —णदी (नदी) a mountain-torrent, rill. —णद्ध (नद्ध) *a.* inclosed by a mountain. —नंदिनी 1 N. of Pârvati. 2 of the Ganges 3 a river in general (flowing from a mountain); कलिंदगिरिनंदिनीतटसुरद्रुमालंबिनी Bv. 4. 3. —णितंबः (नितंबः) the declivity of a mountain —पीलुः N. of a fruit-tree. —पुष्पकं bitumen. —पृष्ठः the top of a hill. —प्रपातः the declivity or slope of a mountain —प्रस्थः the table-land of a mountain. —प्रिया a female of the Bos Grunniens. —भिद् *m.* an epithet of Indra. —भू *a.* mountain-born. (—भूः *f.*) 1 an epithet of the Ganges. 2 of Pârvati. —मल्लिका the Kutaja tree. —मानः an elephant, especially a large and powerful one. —मृद्, —मृद्भवं red chalk. —राज् *m.* 1 a high mountain. 2 an epithet of the Himâlaya. —राजः the Himâlaya mountain. —व्रजं N. of a city in Magadha. —शालः a kind of bird. —शृंगः an epithet of Ganesa. (—गं) the peak of a mountain —षद् (सद्) *m.* an epithet of *S*iva —सानु *n.* tableland. —सारः 1 iron. 2 tin. 3 an epithet of the Malaya mountain. —सुतः the Mainâka mountain. —सुता an epithet of Pârvati —स्रवा a mountain torrent.

गिरिकः, गिरियकः, गिरियाकः A ball for playing with.

गिरिका A small mouse.

गिरिशः An epithet of *S*iva; प्रत्याहतास्त्रो गिरिशप्रभावात् R. 2. 41; गिरिशमुपचचार प्रत्यहं सा सुकेशी Ku. 1. 60, 37.

गिल् 6 P. (गिलति, गिलित) To swallow; (properly speaking: this is not a separate root, but is connected with गॄ.)

गिल *a.* Who or what swallows or devours; *e. g.* तिमिंगिलगिलोऽप्यस्ति तद्गिलोऽप्यस्ति राघवः; see तिमिंगिल. —लः The citron tree. COMP. —गिलः; —ग्राहः a crocodile, shark.

गिलनं गिलिः *f.* Swallowing, eating up.

गिलायुः A hard tumour in the throat.

गिलि (रि) त *a.* Eaten, swallowed.

गि (गे) ष्णुः 1 A singer. 2 Especially, a Brâhmana versed in the hymns of the Sâmaveda and who chants them.

गीत *p. p.* 1 Sung, chanted (lit); आर्ये साधु गीतं *S*. 1. चारणद्वंद्वगीतः शब्दः *S*. 2. 14. 2. Declared, told, said; गीतश्चायमर्थोऽङ्गिरसा Mâl. 2; (see under गै also). —तं Singing, a song; तवास्मि गीतरागेण हारिणा प्रसभं हृतः S. 1. 5; गीतमुरसादकारि मृगाणां K. 32. —COMP. —अयनं a means or instrument of singing, *i. e.* a lute, flute &c. —क्रमः the arrangement of a song. —ज्ञ *a.* versed in the art of singing. —प्रिय *a.* fond of songs or music. (—यः) an epithet of *S*iva. —मोदिन् *m.* a Kinnara. —शास्त्रं the science of music.

गीतकं A song.

गीता A name given to certain sacred writings in verse (often in the form of a dialogue) which are devoted to the exposition of particular religious and theosophical doctrines; *e.g.* शिवगीता, रामगीता, भगवद्गीता. But the name appears to be especially confined to the last, the Bhagavadgitâ; गीता सुगीता कर्तव्या किमन्यैः शास्त्रविस्तरैः। या स्वयं पद्मनाभस्य मुखपद्माद्विनिःसृता॥ quoted by Sridharasvâmin.

गीतिः *f.* 1 A song, singing; अहो रागपरिवाहिणी गीतिः *S*. 5; श्रुताप्सरोगीतिरपि क्षणेऽस्मिन् हरः प्रसंख्यानपरो बभूव Ku. 3. 40. 2 N. of a metre; see App.

गीतिका 1 A short song. 2 Singing.

गीतिन् *a* (नी *f.*). One who recites in a singing manner; गीति शीघ्री शिरःकंपी तथा लिखितपाठकः *S*ik. 32.

गीर्ण *a.* 1 Swallowed, eaten up. 2 Described, praised; (see गॄ).

गीर्णिः *f.* 1 Praise. 2 Fame. 3 Eating up, swallowing.

गु 6 P. (गुवति, गून) To void by stool, void excrement, discharge fæces.

गुग्गुलः—लुः A particular fragrant gum resin.

गुच्छः 1 A bundle, bunch (in general). 2 A bunch of flowers a cluster of blossoms, a clump (of trees &c.). अक्ष्णोर्निक्षिपदंजनं श्रवणयोस्तापिच्छगुच्छावलिं Git. 11, Ms. 1. 48; *S*i. 6. 50. 3 The plumage of a peacock. 4 A necklace of pearls (in general). 5 A pearl-necklace of 32 (or, according to some, of 70) strings —COMP. —अर्धः a pearl necklace of 24 strings. (—र्धः-र्धः) half of a cluster. —कणिशः a kind of corn. —पत्रः the palm tree. —फलः 1 the vine. 2 plantain tree.

गुच्छकः see गुच्छ.

गुज् I. P. (गोजति), often I P. गुंज् (गुंजति, गुंजित of गुजित) To sound inarticulately or indistinctly, hum, buzz; न षट्पदोऽसौ न जुगुंज यः कलं Bk. 2. 19; 6. 143; 14. 2; U. 2. 29. अयि दलदरविंद स्यंदमानं मरंदं तव किमपि लिहंतो मंजु गुंजंतु भृंगाः Bv. 1. 5.

गुंजः 1 Humming. 2 A cluster of blossoms, bunch of flowers, a nosegay; cf. गुच्छ. —COMP. —कृत् a large black bee.

गुंजनं Sounding low, humming, buzzing.

गुंजा 1 A small shrub of that name, bearing a red black berry; अंतर्विषमया (for °य्यः) ह्येता बहिश्चैव मनोरमाः। गुंजाफलसमाकारा योषितः केन निर्मिताः। Pt. 1. 169; किं जातु गुंजाफलभूषणानां सुवर्णकारेण वनेचराणां Vikr. 1. 25. 2 A berry of this shrub used as a weight, measuring on an average $1\frac{5}{16}$ grains Troy, or an artificial weight called *Gunja* measuring $2\frac{3}{16}$ grains. 3 Humming, a low murmuring sound. 4 A kettle-drum; Bk. 14. 2. 5 A tavern. 6 Reflection, meditation.

गुंजिका A berry of the Gunjâ plant.

गुंजितं Humming, murmuring; स्वच्छंदं दलदरविंद ते मरंदं विंदंतो विदधतु गुंजितं मिलिंदाः Bv. I. 15. न गुंजितं तन्न जहार यन्मनः Bk. 2. 29.

गुटिका 1 A pill. 2 A round pebble, any small globe or ball; लोष्टगुटिकाः क्षिपति Mk. 5. 3 The cocoon of the silkworm. 4 A pearl; निर्धौतहारगुटिकाविशदं हिमांभः R. 5. 70. —COMP. —अंजनं a kind of collyrium.

गुटी-गुटिका q. v.

गुडः 1 Treacle, molasses ; गुडधानाः Sk. ; गुडौदनः Y. 1. 303 ; गुडद्वितीयां हरीतकीं भक्षयेत् Susr. 2 A globe, ball. 3 A ball for playing with. 4 A mouthful. 2 An elephant's armour. -COMP. -**उदकं** water mixed with molasses. -**उद्भवा** sugar. -**ओदनं** rice boiled with coarse sugar. -**तृणं**; -**दारुः** -**रु** *n.* sugar-cane. -**धेनुः** *f.* a milchcow symbolically represented by molasses and offered as a present to Brâhmaṇas. -**पिष्टं** a sort of sweatmeat, flour and molasses ground and boiled together. -**फलः** The Pîlu tree. -**शर्करा** refined sugar. -**शृंगं** a cupola. -**हरीतकी** myrobalan preserved in molasses ; (Mar. मुरांवळा).

गुडकः 1 A ball. 2 A mouthful. 3 A kind of drug prepared with molasses.

गुडलं Spirituous liquor distilled from molasses.

गुडा 1 The cotton plant. 2 A pill.

गुडाका 1 Sloth. 2 Sleep.

गुडाकेशः 1 An epithet of Arjuna; मम देहे गुडाकेश यच्चान्यद् द्रष्टुमर्हसि Bg. 11. 7 (and in several other places of the Gitâ). 2 An epithet of Siva.

गुडगुडायनं A rattling in the throat (as breath) caused by cough.

गुडेरः 1 A ball, globe. 2 A mouthful, bit.

गुण 10 U. (गुणयति-ते, गुणित) 1 To multiply. 2 To advise. 3 To invite.

गुणः 1 A quality (good or bad); सुगुण, दुर्गुण. 2 (*a*) A good quality, merit, virtue, excellence ; कतमे ते गुणाः Mal. 1 ; R. 1. 9, 22 ; साधुत्वे तस्य को गुणः Pt. 4. 108. (*b*) Eminence 3 Use, advantage, good (with instr. usually) ; Mu. 1. 15. 4 Effect, result, efficacy, good result. 5 A thread, string, rope, cord ; मेखलागुणैः Ku. 4. 8; 5. 10 ; यतः परेषां गुणग्रहीतासि Bv. 1. 9. (where गुण also means 'a merit'). 6 The bow-string ; तणकृत्ये धनुषो नियोजिता Ku 4. 15, 29 ; कनकपिंगतडिद्गुणसंयुतं R. 9. 54. 7 The string of a musical instrument; Si. 4. 57. 8 A sinew. 9 A quality, attribute, property in general; Ms. 9. 22. 10 A quality, characteristic or property of all substances, one of the seven categories or *padarthas* of the Vaiseshikas, (the number of these properties is 24.). 11 An ingredient or constituent of nature, any one of the three properties belonging to all created things ; (these are सत्त्व, रजस्, and तमस्); गुणत्रयविभागाय Ku. 2. 4; Bg. 14. 5; R. 3. 27. 12 A wick, cotton thread. 13 An object of sense; (these are five रूप, रस, गन्ध, स्पर्श and शब्द). 14 Repetition, multiplication, denoting 'folds' or 'times' usually at the end of comp. after numerals; आहारो द्विगुणः स्त्रीणां बुद्धिस्तासां चतुर्गुणा। षड्गुणो व्यवसायश्च कामश्चाष्टगुणः स्मृतः ॥ Chân. 78; so त्रिगुण, शतगुणीभवति becomes a hundred-fold. 15 A secondary element, a subordinate part (opp. मुख्य.) 16 Excess, abundance, superfluity. 17 An adjective, a word subordinate to another in a sentence. 18 The substitution of ए, ओ, अर्, and अल् for इ, उ, ऋ (short or long) and ऌ, or the vowels अ, ए, ओ, अर् and अल्. 19 (In Rhet.) Quality considered as an inherent property of a *Rasa* or sentiment; *m*ammaṭa thus defines गुणः- ये रसस्यांगिनो धर्माः शौर्यादय इवात्मनः । उत्कर्षहेतवस्ते स्युरचलस्थितयो गुणाः ॥ K. P. 8. (Some writers on rhetoric such as Vamana, Jagannâtha Pandita, Daṇḍin and others consider *Gunas* to be properties both of शब्द and अर्थ and mention ten varieties under each head. Mammaṭa, however, recognises only three, and, after discussing and criticizing the views of others, says:-माधुर्यौजः प्रसादाख्यास्त्रयस्ते न पुनर्दश K. P. 8.) 20 (In gram. and Mîm.) Property considered as the meaning of a class of words; *e. g.* grammarians recognise four kinds of the meaning of words; जाति, गुण, क्रिया and द्रव्य, and give गौः, शुक्लः, चलः and डित्थः as instances to illustrate these meanings. 21 (In politics) A proper course of action, an expedient. (The expedients to be used by a king in foreign politics are six:—1 संधि peace or alliance 2 विग्रह war ; 3 यान march or expedition ; 4 स्थान or आसन halt ; 5 संश्रय seeking shelter ; 6 द्वैध or द्वैधीभाव duplicity ; संधिर्ना विग्रहो यानमासनं द्वैधमाश्रयः Ak. ; see Y. 1. 346 ; Ms. 7. 160 ; Si. 2. 26; R. 8. 21 22 The number 'three' (derived from the three qualities). 23 The chord of an arc (in geom.). 24 An organ of sense. 25 A subordinate dish; Ms. 3. 224, 233. 26 A cook. 27 An epithet of Bhima. 28 Leaving, abandoning. -COMP. -**अतीत** *a.* freed from all properties, being beyond them. -**अधिष्ठानकं** the region of the breast where the girdle is fastened. -**अनुरागः** love or appreciation of the good qualities of others ; Ki. 1. 11. -**अनुरोधः** conformity or suitableness to good qualities. -**अन्वित** *a.* endowed with good qualities, meritorious, worthy, good, excellent. -**अपवादः** disparagement, detraction. -**आकरः** 'a mine of merits', one endowed with all virtues. -**आढ्य** *a.* rich in virtues. -**आत्मन्** *a.* having qualities. -**आधारः** 'a receptacle of virtues', a virtuous or meritorious person. -**आश्रय** *a.* virtuous, excellent. -**उत्कर्षः** excellence of merit, possession of superior qualities. -**उत्कीर्तनं** panegyric, eulogium. -**उत्कृष्ट** *a.* superior in merit. -**कर्मन्** *n.* 1 an unessential or secondary action. 2 (In gram.) the secondary or less immediate (*i. e.* indirect) object of an action; *e. g.* in the example नेताऽश्वस्य स्रुघ्नं स्रुघ्नस्य वा स्रुघ्नं is a गुणकर्मन्. -**कार** *a.* productive of good qualities, profitable, salutary. (-**रः**) 1 a cook who prepares side-dishes or any secondary articles of food. 2 an epithet of Bhîma. -**गान** singing of merits, panegyric, praise. -**गृध्नु** *a.* 1 desiring good qualities. 2 possessing good qualities -**गृह्य** *a.* appreciating or admiring merits (wherever they may be), attached to merits, appreciative; ननु वक्तृविशेषनिःस्पृहा गुणगृह्या वचने विपश्चितः Ki. 2. 5. -**ग्रहीतृ**, -**ग्राहक**, -**ग्राहिन्** *a.* appreciating the merits (of others); Ratn. 1. 6; Bv. 1, 9. -**ग्रामः** a collection of virtues or merits; गुरुतरगणग्रामांभोजस्फुटोज्ज्वलचंद्रिका Bh. 3. 116; गणयति गुणग्रामं Git. 2; Bv. 1. 103. -**ज्ञ** *a.* knowing how to admire or appreciate merits, appreciative ; भगवति कमलालये-भृशमगुणज्ञासि Mu. 2 ; गुणागुणज्ञेषु गुणा भवंति H. Pr. 47. -**त्रयं**, -**त्रितयं** the three constituent properties of nature ; *i. e.* सत्त्व, रजस् and तमस्. -**धर्मः** the virtue or duty incidental to the possession of certain qualities. -**निधिः** a store of virtues. -**प्रकर्षः** excellence of merits, great merit. -**लक्षणं** mark of indication of an internal property. -**लयनिका**, -**लयनी** a tent. -**वचनं**, -**वाचकः** a word which connotes an attribute or quality, an adjective, or substantive used attributively ; as श्वेत in श्वेतोऽश्वः. -**विवेचना** discrimination in appreciating the merits of others, a just sense of merit. -**वृक्षः**, -**वृक्षकः** a mast or a post to which a ship or boat is fastened. -**वृत्तिः** *f.* a secondary or unessential condition or relation (opp. मुख्यवृत्ति). -**वैशेष्यं** pre-eminence of merit. -**शब्दः** an adjective. -**संख्यानं** 'enumeration of the three essential qualities', a term applied to the Sânkhya (including the Yoga) system of philosophy. -**संगः** 1 association with qualities or merits. 2 attachment to objects of sense or worldly pleasures. **-संपद्** *f.* excellence or richness of merits, great merit, perfection. **-सागरः** 1 an ocean of merit, a very meritorious man. 2 an epithet of Brahmâ.

गुणकः 1 A calculator. 2 A multiplier (in math.)

गुणनं 1 Multiplication. 2 Enumeration. 3 Describing merits or qualities, pointing out or enumerating qualities ; इह रसभणने कृतहरिगुणने मधुरिपुपदसेवके Git. 7. **—नी** Examining books, studying, collating and correcting copies to determine the value of variants.

गुणनिका 1 Study, repeated reading, repetition ; विशेषविदुषः शास्त्रं यत्तवोद्ग्राह्यते पुरः । हेतुः परिचयस्थैर्ये वक्तुर्गुणनिकैव सा ॥ *Si.* 2. 75. (आम्रेडितं Malli.) 2 Dancing, the science or profession of dancing. 3 The prologue or introduction to a drama. 4 A garland, necklace ; दरिद्राणां चिंतामणिगुणनिका A. L. 3. 5. A cypher, the character in arithmetic which expresses nothing.

गुणनीय *a.* 1 To be multiplied. 2 To be enumerated. 3 To be advised. **—यः** Study, practice.

गुणवत् *a.* Endowed with virtues, good, meritorious, excellent.

गुणिका A tumour, a swelling.

गुणित 1 *p. p.* Multiplied. 2 Heaped together, collected. 3 Enumerated.

गुणिन् *a.* 1 Possessed of or endowed with merits, meritorious ; गुणी गुणं वेत्ति न वेत्ति निर्गुणः ; Ms. 8. 73 ; Y. 2. 78. 2 Good, auspicious; गुणिन्यहनि Dk. 61. 3 Familiar with the merits of anything. 4 Possessing qualities (as an object), 5 Having (subordinate) parts, principal (opp. गुण); गुणगुणिनोरेव संबंधः.

गुणीभूत *a.* 1 Deprived of the original meaning of importance. 2 Made secondary or subordinate. 3 Invested with attributes. -Comp. **-व्यंग्यं** (in Rhet.) the second of the three divisions of Kâvya (poetry), in which the charm of the suggested sense is not more striking than that of the expressed one. S. D. thus defines it:—अपरं तु गुणीभूतव्यंग्यं वाच्यादनुत्तमे व्यंग्ये 265. This division of Kâvya is further subdivided into 8 classes; see S. D. 266 and K. P. 5.

गुंठ् 10 U. (गुंठयति-ते, गुंठित) 1 To encircle, surround, envelope, enclose. 2 To hide, conceal. -With **अव** to cover, screen, hide, envelope; रजनीतिमिरावगुंठिते पुरमार्गे Ku. 4. 11.

गुंठनं 1 Concealing, covering, hiding. 2 Smearing, as in भस्मगुंठनं.

गुंठित *a.* 1 Surrounded, covered. 2 Pounded, ground, reduced to dust.

गुड् 10 P. (गुंडयति, गुंडित) 1 To cover, hide. 2 To pound, reduce to powder.

गुंडकः 1 Dust, powder. 2 An oil-vessel. 3 A low pleasing tone.

गुंडिकः Flour, meal, powder.

गुंडित *a.* 1 Pounded; ground. 2 Covered with dust.

गुण्य *a.* 1 Endowed with merits or virtues. 2 To be enumerated. 3 To be described or praised. 4 To be multiplied, the multiplicand.

गुत्सः-गुच्छ q. v.

गुत्सकः 1 A bundle, bunch. 2 A nosegay. 3 A cow-tail, chowrie. 4 The section or chapter of a book.

गुद् 1 A. (गोदते, गुदित) To play sport.

गुदं The anus; Y. 93. 9; Ms. 5. 136; 8. 282. -Comp. **-अंकुरः** piles. **-आवर्तः** obstruction of the bowels. **-उद्भवः** piles. **-ओष्ठः** the opening of the anus. **-कीलः,-कीलकः** piles. **-ग्रहः** constipation, flatulence. **-पाकः** inflammation of the anus. **-भ्रंशः** *prolapsus ani.* **-वर्त्मन्** *n.* the anus. **-स्तंभः** constipation

गुध् I. 4 P. (गुध्यति, गुधित) To wrap up, cover, envelope, clothe.-II. 9 P. (गुध्नाति) To be angry.-III. 1 A. (गोधते) To play, sport.

गुंदलः The sound of a small oblong drum.

गुंदा (द्रा) लः The Châtaka bird.

गुप् I. 1 P. (गोपायति, गोपायित or गुप्त) 1 To guard, protect, defend, watch over; गोपायंति कुलस्त्रिय आत्मानं Mb.; जुगोपात्मानमत्रस्तः R. 1. 21; जुगोप गोरूपधरामिवोर्वी 2. 3; Bk. 17. 80. 2 To hide, conceal; किं वक्षश्चरणानतिव्यतिकरव्याजेन गोपाय्यते Amaru. 22; see गुप्त.-II. 1 A. (जुगुप्सते strictly desid. of गुप्) 1 To despise, shun, abhor, detest, censure; (with abl., sometimes acc. also); पापाज्जुगुप्से Sk.; किं त्वं मामजुगुप्सिष्ठाः Bk. 15. 19; Y. 3. 296. 2 To hide, conceal (गोपते in this sense). -III. 4 P. (गुप्यति) To be confused or disturbed. -IV. 10 U. (गोपयति-ते) 1 To shine. 2 To speak. 3 To conceal; (the following stanza from कविरहस्य illustrates the root in its different conjugations:—गोपायति क्षितिमिमां चतुरब्धिसीमां पापाज्जुगुप्सत उदारमतिः सदैव । वित्तं न गोपयति यस्तु वणीयकेभ्यो धीरो न गुप्यति महत्यपि कार्यजाते ॥).

गुपिलः 1 A king. 2 A protector.

गुप्त *p. p.* 1 Protected, preserved, guarded; R. 10. 60. 2 Hidden, concealed, secret; Ms 2. 160, 7. 76, 8. 374 3 Invisible, withdrawn from sight. 4 Joined.—**प्तः** An appellation usually (though not necessarily) added to the name of a Vaisya; as चंद्रगुप्तः, समुद्रगुप्तः &c. (Usually शर्मन् or देव is added to the name of a Brâhmaṇa, वर्मन् or त्रातृ to that of a Kshatriya, गुप्त, भूति or दत्त to that of a Vaisya, and दास to that of a Sûdra; cf. शर्मा देवश्च विप्रस्य वर्मा त्राता च भूभुजः। भूतिर्दत्तश्च वैश्यस्य दासः शूद्रस्य कारयेत्) **—प्तं** *ind.* Secretly, privately. apart.**—प्ता** One of the principal female characters in a poetical composition, a lady married to another (परकीया) who conceals her lover's caresses and endearments past, present or future; वृत्तसुरतगोपना वर्तिष्यमाणसुरतगोपना and वर्तमानसुरतगोपना; see Rasamanjarî 24. -Comp. **-कथा** a secret or confidential communication, a secret. **-गतिः** a spy, an emissary. **-चर** *a.* going secretly. (**-रः**) 1 an epithet of Balarâma. 2 a spy, an emissary. **-दानं** a secret gift or present. **-वेशः** a disguise.

गुप्तकः A preserver.

गुप्तिः *f.* 1 Preserving, protection; सर्वस्यास्य तु सर्गस्य गुप्त्यर्थं Ms. 1. 87, 94, 99; Y. 1. 198. 2 Concealing, hiding. 3 Covering, sheathing; असिधारासु कोषगुप्तिः K. 11. 4. A hole in the ground, a cavern, sink, cellar. 5 Digging a hole in the ground. 6 A means of protection, fortification, rampart. 7 Confinement, prison; सरभस इव गुप्तिस्फोटमर्कः करोति Si 11. 60. 8 The lower deck of a boat. 9 Check, stoppage.

गुफ् or **गुंफ्** 6 P. (गु-गुं-फति, गुफित) 1 To string or weave together, tie, wind round; Bk. 7. 105. 2 (fig.) To write, compose.

गु (गुं) फित *p. p.* Strung together, tied, woven.

गुंफः 1 Tying, stringing together; गुंफो वाणीनां B. R. 1. 1. 2 Putting together, composing, arrangement. 3 A bracelet. 4 A whisker, a mustachio.

गुंफना 1 Stringing together. 2 Arranging, composing. 3 Good adjustment, (of words and their senses), good composition; वाक्ये शब्दार्थयोः सम्यग्रचना गुंफना मता.

गुर् I. 6 A. (गुरते, गूर्त, गूर्ण) To make an effort or exertion. -II. 4 A. (*p. p.* गूर्ण) 1 To hurt, kill, injure. 2 To go.

गुरणं Effort, perseverance.

गुरु *a.* (**रु-र्वी**) (*f.*, compar. गरीयस्; superl. गरिष्ठ) 1 Heavy, weighty (opp. लघु); (fig. also); तेन धूर्जगतो गुर्वी सचिवेषु निचिक्षिपे R. 1. 34; 3 35; 12. 102; Rs. 1. 7. 2 Great, large, long, extended. 3 Long (in duration or length); आरंभगुर्वी Bh. 2. 60; गुरुषु दिवसेष्वेषु गच्छत्सु Me. 83. 4 Important, momentous, great; विभवगुरुभिः कृत्यैः *S.* 4. 18; स्वार्थात्सतां गुरुतरा प्रणयिक्रियैव V. 4. 15. 5. Arduous, difficult (to bear);

कांताविरहगुरुणा शापेन Me. 1. 6 Great, excessive, violent, intense; गुरुः प्रहर्षः प्रबभूव नात्मनि R. 3. 17; गुर्वपि विरहदुःखं S. 4. 15; Bg. 6. 22. 7 Venerable, respectable 8 Heavy, hard of digestion (as food) 9 Best, excellent. 10 Dear, beloved. 11 Haughty, proud (as a speech). 12 (In prosody) Long, as a syllable, either in itself, or being short, followed by a conjunct consonant &c.; *e. g.* ई in ईड् or त in तस्कर. (It is usually represented by ग in works on prosody; मात्तौ गौ चेच्छालिनी वेदलोकैः &c.) —रुः 1 A father; न केवलं तद्गुरुरेकपार्थिवः क्षितावभूदेकधनुर्धरोऽपि सः R. 3. 31, 48; 4. 1; 8. 29. 2 Any venerable or respectable person, an elderly personage or relative, the elders (pl.) शुश्रूषस्व गुरून् S. 4. 14; Bg. 2. 5; Bv. 2. 7, 18, 19, 49; आज्ञा गुरूणां ह्यविचारणीया R. 14. 46. 3 A teacher, preceptor; गुरुशिष्यौ. 4 Particularly a religious teacher, spiritual preceptor; तौ गुरुर्गुरुपत्नी च प्रीत्या प्रतिननंदतुः R. 1. 57; (technically a *Guru* is one who performs the purificatory ceremonies over a boy and instructs him in the Vedas; स गुरुर्यः क्रियाः कृत्वा वेदमस्मै प्रयच्छति Y. 1. 34). 5 A lord, head, superintendent, ruler; वर्णाश्रमाणां गुरवे स वर्णी R. 5. 19 head of the castes or orders; गुरुर्नृपाणां गुरवे निवेद्य 2. 68. 6 N. of Brihaspati, the preceptor of the gods; गुरुं नेत्रसहस्रेण चोदयामास वासवः Ku. 2. 29. 7 The planet Jupiter; गुरुकाव्यानुगां बिभ्रच्चांद्रीमभिनभः श्रियं Si. 2. 2 8 The propounder of a new doctrine. 9 The lunar asterism called पुष्य. 10 N. of Droṇa, teacher of the Kauravas and Pâṇḍavas. 11 N. of Prabhâkara, the leader of a school of the Mîmâmsakas as (called after him Prâbhâkarîya). –COMP. –अर्थः a preceptor's fee for instructing a pupil; गुर्वर्थमाहर्तुमहं यतिष्ये R. 5 7. –उत्तम *a.* highly revered. –मः) the Supreme soul. –कारः worhip, adoration. –क्रमः instruction handed down through a series of teachers, traditional instruction –जन any venerable person, an elderly relative, the elders collectively; नापेक्षितो गुरुजनः K. 158; Bv. 2 7. –तल्पः 1 the bed of a teacher. 2 violation or violator of a teacher's bed. –तल्पगः, –तल्पिन् *m.* 1 one who violates his teacher's bed (wife), (ranked in Hindu law as a sinner of the worst kind, committer of an अतिपातक; cf. Ms. 11. 103) 2 one who defiles his stepmother. –दक्षिणा fee given to a spiritual preceptor; R. 5. 1. –दैवतः the constellation पुष्य. –पाक *a.* difficult of digestion. –भं 1 the constellation पुष्य. 2 a bow. –मर्दलः a kind of drum or tabor. –रत्नं a topaz. –लाघवं relative importance or value. –वर्तिन्, –वासिन् *m.* a student (ब्रह्मचारिन्) who resides at his preceptor's house. –वासरः Thursday. –वृत्तिः *f.* the conduct of a pupil towards his preceptor.

गुरुक *a.* (की *f.*) 1 A little heavy. 2 Long (in Prosody.)

गु (गू) र्जरः 1 The district of Gujarâth; तेषां मार्गे परिचयवशादर्जितं गुर्जराणां यः संतापं शिथिलमकरोत् सोमनाथं विलोक्य Vikr. 18. 97.

गुर्विणी, गुर्वी A pregnant woman; *e. g.* गुर्विणीं नानुगच्छति न स्पृशंति रजस्वलां.

गुलः Molasses; cf. गुड.

गुलुच्छः, गुलुंछः A bunch or cluster; see गुच्छ.

गुल्फः The ankle; आगुल्फकीर्णापणमार्गपुष्पं Ku. 7. 55; गुल्फावलंबिना K. 10.

गुल्मः, –ल्मं 1 A clump or cluster of trees, a thicket, wood, bush; Ms. 1. 48; 7. 192; 12. 58; Y. 2. 229. 2 A troop of soldiers, a division of an army, consisting of 45 foot, 27 horse, 9 chariots and 9 elephants. 3 A fort. 4 The spleen. 5 A chronic enlargement of the spleen. 6 A village police-station. 7 A wharf of stairs (Mar. घांट).

गुल्मिन् *a.* (नी *f.*) 1 Growing in a clump or cluster, clustered. 2 Having a diseased spleen, or a spleen affected by गुल्म.

गुल्मी A tent.

गु (गू) वाकः The betel-nut tree.

गुह् 1 U. (गूहति-ते, गूढ) To cover, hide, conceal, keep secret; गुह्यं च गूहति गुणान् प्रकटीकरोति Bh. 2. 72; गूहेत्कूर्म इवांगानि Ms. 7. 105; R. 14. 49; Bk. 16. 49. –WITH उप to embrace; तरंगहस्तैरुपगूहतीव R. 13. 63; 18. 47; Bk. 14. 52; Si. 9. 38. –नि to hide, conceal.

गुहः 1 An epithet of Kârtikeya; गुह इवाप्रतिहतशक्तिः K. 8; Ku. 5. 14. 2 A horse. 3 N. of a Chânḍâla or *Nishâda*, King of Sṛingavera and a friend of Rama.

गुहा 1 A cave, cavern, hiding place; गुहानिबद्धप्रतिशब्ददीर्घं R 2. 28, 51; धर्मस्य तत्त्वं निहितं गुहायां Mb. 2 Hiding, concealing. 3 A pit, hole in the ground. 4 The heart. –COMP. –आहित *a.* placed in the heart. –चरं Brahman –मुख *a.* 'cave-mouthed,' wide mouthed, open-mouthed. –शयः 1 a mouse. 2 a tiger or lion. 3 the supreme soul.

गुहिनं A wood, thicket.

गुहेरः 1 A guardian, protector. 2 A blacksmith.

गुह्य *pot. p.* 1 To be concealed' covered or kept secret, private; गुह्यं च गूहति Bh. 2. 72. 2 secret, solitary, retired. 3 Mysterious; Bg. 18. 63. —ह्यः 1 Hypocrisy. 2 A tortoise. —ह्यं 1 A secret, mystery; मौनं चैवास्मि गुह्यानां Bg. 10. 38; 9. 2; Ms. 12. 117. 2 A privity, the male or female organ of generation. –COMP. –गुरुः an epithet of Siva. –दीपकः the fire-fly. –निष्यंदः urine. –भाषितं 1 secret speech or conversation. 2 a secret. –मयः an epithet of Kârtikeya.

गुह्यकः N. of a class of demigods who, like the Yakshas, are attendants of Kubera and guardians of his treasures; गुह्यकस्तं ययाचे Me. 5. Ms. 12. 47.

गूः *f.* 1 Dirt. 2 Ordure, excrement.

गूढ *p. p.* 1 Hidden, concealed, kept secret. 2 Covered. –COMP. –अंगः a tortoise. –अंघ्रिः a snake. –आत्मन् (the compound word being गूढोत्मन् thus accounted for in Sk.; भवेद् वर्णागमाद् हंसः सिंहो वर्णाविपर्ययात् गूढोत्मा वर्णविकृतेर्वर्णलोपात्पृषोदरः) the Supreme soul. –उत्पन्नः, –जः one of the 12 kinds of sons in Hindu law; he is a son born secretly of a woman, when her husband is absent, the real father being unknown; गृहे प्रच्छन्न उत्पन्नो गूढजस्तु सुतः स्मृतः Y. 2. 129; Ms. 9. 159, 170. –नीडः the wag-tail. –पथः 1 a hidden path. 2 a bypath. 3 the mind, intellect. –पाद्, पादः a snake. –पुरुषः a spy, secret emissary, disguised agent. –पुष्पकः the Bakula tree. –मार्गः a passage underground. –मैथुनः a crow. –वर्चस् *m.* a frog. –साक्षिन् *m.* 'a concealed witness', one placed to overhear secretly what has been said by the defendant.

गूथः—थं Feces, ordure.

गून *a.* Voided by stool (as ordure).

गूरणं see गुरण.

गूषणा The eye in a peacock's tail.

गृ 1 P. (गरति) To sprinkle, moisten, wet.

गृज्, गृंज् 1 P. (गर्जति or गृंजति) To sound, roar, grumble &c.

गृंजनः 1 A small red variety of garlic. 2 A turnip. 3 The tops of hemp chewed to produce intoxication, the *Gânjâ* —नं The meat of an animal destroyed by poisoned arrows.

गृडि (डी) वः A species of jackal.

गृध् 4 P. (गृध्यति, गृद्ध) To covet, desire, strive after greedily; to long for, be desirous of.

गृधु *a.* Lustful, libidinous. –धुः The God of love.

गृध्नु *a.* 1 Greedy, covetous; अगृध्नुराददे सोऽर्थं R. 1: 21. 2 Eager, desirous.

गृध्यं-ध्या Desire, greediness.

गृध्र *a.* Greedy, covetous. –ध्रः, ध्रं A vulture; मार्जारस्य हि दोषेण हतो गृध्रो जरद्गवः H. 1. 59; R. 12. 50, 54. –COMP. –कूटः N. of a mountain near Râjagriha. –पतिः, –राजः the lord of the vultures, an epithet of Jatâyu; अस्यैवासीन्महति शिखरे गृध्रराजस्य वासः U. 2.25. -वाज, -वाजित *a.* furnished with vulture feathers (as an arrow).

गृष्टिः *f.* 1 A cow which has had only one calf, a young cow; (एकप्रसूता गौः); आपीनभारोद्वहनप्रयत्नाद् गृष्टिः R. 2. 18; स्त्री तावत्संस्कृतं पठंती दत्तनवनास्या इव गृष्टिः सूसूशद्वं करोति Mk. 3. 2 (In comp. with the names of other animals) Any young female animal ; वासितागृष्टिः 'a young she-elephant'.

गृहं 1 A house, dwelling, habitation, mansion; न गृहं गृहमित्याहुर्गृहिणी गृहमुच्यते Pt. 4. 81; पश्य वानरमूर्खेण सुगृही निर्गृहीकृता Pt. 1. 390. 2 A wife; (the first quotation in 1 is sometimes cited as an illustration). 3 The life of a householder. 4 A sign of the zodiac. 5 A name or appellation. —हाः (*m.* pl.) 1 A house, dwelling: इमे नो गृहाः Mu. 1; स्फटिकोपलविग्रहा गृहाः शशभृद्वित्तनिरंकभित्तयः N. 2. 74; तत्रागारं धनपतिगृहानुत्तरेणास्मदीयं Me. 75. 2 A wife. 3 The inhabitants of a house, family. -COMP- -अक्षः a loop-hole, eyelet-hole, a round or oblong window. —अधिपः, -ईशः,-ईश्वरः 1 a householder. 2 a regent of a sign of the zodiac. -अयनिकः a house-holder. -अर्थः domestic affairs, any household matter; गृहार्थोऽग्निपरिष्क्रिया Ms. 2. 67. -अम्लं a kind of sourgruel. -अवग्रहणी the threshold. -अश्मन् *m.* a flat oblong stone upon which condiments are ground; (Mar. पाटा). -आरामः a garden attached to a house. -आश्रमः the order of a householder, the second stage in the religious life of a Brâhmaṇa; see आश्रम. -आश्रमिन् *m.* a householder. -उत्पातः any domestic nuisance. -उपकरणं a domestic utensil, anything required for household use. —कच्छपः =गृहाश्मन् q. v. -कपोतः-तकः a tame or domestic pigeon. -करणं 1 household affairs. 2 house-building. -कर्मन् *n.* household affairs °दासः a menial, domestic servant; शंभुस्वयंभुहरयो हरिणेक्षणानां येनाक्रियंत सततं गृहकर्मदासाः Bh. 1. 1 -कलहः domestic feuds, intestine broils. -कारकः a house-builder, mason; Y. 3. 146. -कुक्कुटः a domestic cock. -कार्यं household affairs; Ms. 5. 150. -चूल्ली a house with two rooms contiguous to each other, but one facing west, the other, east. -छिद्रं 1 a family secret or scandal. 2 family dissensions. -जः, -जातः a slave born in the house. -जालिका deceit, disguise. -ज्ञानिन् (also गृहेज्ञानिन्) 'wise only in the inside of the house,' inexperienced, stupid, foolish. -तटी a terrace in front of the house. -दासः a domestic slave. -देवता the goddess of a house; (pl.) a class of household deities. -देहली the threshold of a house, यासां बलिः सपदि मद्गृहदेहलीनां Mk. 1. 9 -नमनं wind. -नाशनः a wild pigeon. -नीडः a sparrow. -पतिः 1 a householder, a man who has entered on the second stage of life, one who after having completed his studies is married and settled. 2 a sacrificer. 3 the virtue of a house-holder; *i. e.* hospitality. -पालः 1 the guardian of a house. 2 a house-dog. -पोतकः the site of a house, the ground on which it stands and which surrounds it. -प्रवेशः a solemn entrance into a house according to prescribed rites. -बभ्रुः a domestic ichneumon. -बलिः a domestic oblation, offering of the remnants of a meal to all creatures, such as animals, supernatural beings, and particularly household deities; Ms. 3. 265. °भुज् *m.* 1 a crow. 2 a sparrow; नीडारंभैर्गृहबलिभुजामाकुलग्रामचैत्याः Me. 23. °देवता a deity to whom a domestic oblation is offered. -भंगः 1 one who is driven from his house, an exile. 2 destroying a house, 3 breaking into a house. 4 failure, ruin or destruction of a house, firm &c. -भूमिः *f.* the site of a house. -भेदिन् *a.* 1 prying into domestic affairs. 2 causing domestic quarrels. -मणिः a lamp. -माचिका a bat. -मृगः a dog. -मेधः 1 a householder. 2 a domestic sacrifice. -मेधिन् *m.* a householder (गृहैर्दारैर्मेधंते संगच्छंते Malli.); प्रजायै गृहमेधिनां R. 1 7; see गृहपति above. -यंत्रं a stick or other instrument to which, on solemn occasions, flags are fastened; गृहयंत्रपताकाश्रीरपौरादरनिर्मिता Ku. 4. 41. -वाटिका-वाटी a garden attached to a house. -वित्तः the owner of a house. -शुकः a domestic parrot, one kept for pleasure; Amaru. 13. -संवेशकः a house-builder by profession. -स्थः a householder, one who has entered on the stage of a householder; संकटा ह्याहिताग्नीनां प्रत्यवायैर्गृहस्थता U. 1. 9. see गृहपति above and Ms. 3. 68; 6. 90. आश्रमः the life of a householder; see गृहाश्रम. धर्मः the duty of a householder.

गृहयाय्यः A householder; (according to Tv. the form गृहयाप्य given in शब्दकल्पद्रुम is not correct).

गृहयालु *a.* Disposed to catch hold of or seize.

गृहिणी 'The mistress of a house', a wife, house-wife, (the lady in charge of the house); न गृहं गृहमित्याहुर्गृहिणी गृहमुच्यते । गृहं तु गृहिणीहीनं कांतारादतिरिच्यते Pt. 4. 81. -COMP. -पदं the position or dignity of the mistress of the house ; यांत्येवं गृहिणीपदं युवतयो वामाः कुलस्याधयः S. 4. 17; स्थितागृहिणीपदे 18.

गृहिन् The master of a house, a householder; पीड्यंते गृहिणः कथं नु तनयाविश्लेषदुःखैर्नवैः S. 4. 5. U 2. 22; Santi 2. 24.

गृहीत *p. p.* 1 Taken, seized; केशेषु गृहीतः. 2 Accepted. 3 Obtained, attained. 4 Worn. 5 Robbed. 6 Learnt, understood (see ग्रह्). -COMP. —गर्भा a pregnant woman. दिश् *a.* 1 run away, fugitive, dispersed. 2 disappeared.

गृहीतिन् *a.* (नी *f.*) Who has grasped or comprehended (with loc.); गृहीती षट्स्वंगेषु Dk. 120.

गृह्य *a.* 1 To be attracted or pleased ; as in गुणगृह्य q. v. 2 Domestic. 3. Not master of oneself, dependent. 4 Tame, domesticated. 5 Situated outside of; ग्रामगृह्या सेना 'an army out-side a village '. —ह्यः 1 The inmate of a house. 2 A tame animal.—ह्य The anus. -COMP. -अग्निः a sacred fire which every Brâhmaṇa is enjoined to maintain.

गृह्या A village adjoining to a city.

गॄ I. 9. P. (गृणाति, गूर्ण) 1 To utter a sound, call out, invoke. 2 To announce, speak, utter, proclaim; R. 10. 13. 3 To relate, promulgate. 4 To praise, extol; केचिद्भीताः प्रांजलयो गृणंति Bg. II. 21; Bk. 8. 77. -WITH अनु to encourage; Bk. 8 77. —11. 6. P. (गिरति or गिलति) 1. To swallow, devour, eat up. 2 To send forth, pour out, spit out, or eject, from the mouth. —WITH. अव (Atm,) to eat, devour ; तथावगिरमाणैश्च पिशाचैर्मांसशोणितं Bk. 8 30. -उद् to eject, spit out, vomit; उद्गिरतो यद्गरलं फणिनः पुष्णासि परिमलोद्गारैः Bv. 1. 11 ; Si. 14. 1. 2 to emit, discharge, send forth (words also); Ku. 1. 33; R. 14. 53; Ve. 5. 14; Pt. 5. 67. -नि to swallow, eat up; Bv. 1. 38. -सम् 1 to swallow. 2 to promise, make a vow (Atm.) समुद् 1 to throw out, eject. 2 to cry aloud.—III 10 A (गारयते) 1 To make known, relate. 2 To teach

गेंदु (दु) कः A ball for playing with (also गेंडूक).

गेय *a.* 1 A singer, one who sings; गेयो माणवकः साम्नां P. III. 4. 68 Sk. 2 To be sung. -यं 1 A song singing, also the art of singing; गेये केन विनीतौ वां R. 15. 69. Me. 86. अनंता वाङ्मयस्याहो गेयस्येव विचित्रता Si. 2. 72.

गेष् 1 A. (गेषते, गेष्ण). To seek, search, investigate; cf. गवेष्.

गेहं A house, habitation; सा नारी

विधवा जाता गेहे रोदिति तत्पतिः Subhâsh. *N. B.* The loc. of this word is used with several words to form *aluk* Tat. compounds; *e. g.* **गेहेक्ष्वेडिन्** *a.* 'bellowing at home only' *i. e.* a coward, poltroon. **गेहेदाहिन्** *a.* 'sharp at home only', *i. e.* a coward. **गेहेनर्दिन्** *a.* 'shouting defiance at home only'; *i. e.* a coward, dunghill-cock. **गेहेमेहिन्** *a.* 'making water at home;' *i. e.* indolent. **गेहेव्याडः** a braggadocio, braggart, boaster. **गेहेशूरः** 'a house-hero'. a carpet-knight, boasting coward.

गेहिन् *a.* (**नी** *f.*) –गृहिन् q. v.

गेहिनी A wife, the mistress of the house; धैर्यं यस्य पिता क्षमा च जननी शांतिश्चिरं गेहिनी *Sânti.* 4. 9; मद्गेहिन्याः प्रिय इति सखे चेतसा कातरेण Me. 77.

गै I. P. (गायति, गीत) **1** To sing, sing a song; अहो साधु रेभिलेन गीतं Mk. 3; ग्रीष्मसमयमधिकृत्य गीयतां *S.* 1; Ms. 4 64; 9. 42. **2** To speak or recite in a singing tone. **3** To relate declare, tell (especially in metrical language); गीतश्चायमर्थोंगिरसा Mâl. 2. **4** To describe, relate or celebrate in song; चारणद्वंद्वगीतः *S.* **2.** 14; प्रभवस्तस्य गीयते Ku. 2. 5. –WITH **–अनु** to follow in singing; अनुगायति काचिदुदंचितपंचमरागं Git. I.; Ki. 3. 60. **–अव** to censure, blame. **–उद्** to sing aloud, sing in a high tone; उद्गास्यतामिच्छति किन्नराणां Ku. 1. 8. गेयमुद्गातुकामा Me. 86. उद्गीयमानं वनदेवताभिः R. 2. 12. **–उप** to sing. sing near; शिष्यप्रशिष्यैरुपगीयमानमवेहि तन्मंडनमिश्रधाम Udb; Ki. 18. 47. **–परि** to sing, relate, describe. **–वि** **1** to censure, reproach, blame; विगीयसे मन्मथदेहदाहिना. N. 1. 79. **2** to sing in a discordant tone.

गैर *a.* (**री** *f.*) Coming from a mountain, mountain-born.

गैरिक *a.* (**की** *f.*) Mountainborn. **–कः, –कं** Red chalk. **–कं** Gold.

गैरेयं Bitumen.

गो *m. f.* (*Nom.* **गौः**) **1** Cattle, kine (pl.). **2** Anything coming from a cow; such as milk, flesh, leather &c. **3.** The stars. **4** The sky. **5** The thunderbolt of Indra. **6** A ray of light. **7** A diamond. **8** Heaven. **9** An arrow. **—***f.* **1** A cow; जुगोप गोरूपधरामिवोर्वीं R.; **2.** 3. क्षीरिण्यः सन्तु गावः Mk. 10. 60. **2** The earth; दुदोह गां स यज्ञाय R. 1. 26. गामात्तसारां रघुरप्यवेक्ष्य 5. 26; 11. 36; Bg. 15. 13; Me. 30, **3** Speech, words; रघोरुदारामपि गां निशम्य R. 5. 12. 2. 59, Ki. 4. 20. **4** The goddess of speech, Sarasvati. **5** A mother. **6** A quarter of the compass. **7** Water (Pl.) **8** The eye. **—***m.* **1** A bull an ox; असंजातकिरणस्कंधः सुखं स्वपिति गौर्गडिः K. P. 10: Ms. 4. 72; cf. जरद्गव. **2** The hair of the body. **3** An organ of sense. **4** The sign Taurus of the zodiac. **5** The sun. **6** The number 'nine' (in math.). **7** The moon. **8** A horse. –COMP. **–कंटकः, –कं** **1** a road or spot trodden down by oxen and thus made impassable. **2** the cow's hoof. **3** the point of a cow's hoof. **–कर्णः** **1** a cow's ear. **2** a mule. **3** a snake. **4** a span (from the tip of the thumb to that of the ring-finger) **5** N. of a. place of pilgrimage in the south, sacred to *Siva*; श्रितगोकर्णनिकेतमीश्वरं R. 8. 33. **6** a kind of arrow. **–किराटा–किराटिका** the *Sârika* bird. **–किलः, –कीलः** **1** a plough. **2** a pestle. **–कुलं** **1** a herd of kine; वृष्टिव्याकुलगोकुलावनरसादुद्धृत्य गोवर्धनं Git. 4;, गोकुलस्य तृषार्तस्य Mb. **2** a cow-house. **3** N. of a village (where Krishna was brought up). **–कुलिक** *a.* **1** one who does not help a cow in the mud. **2.** squint-eyed. **–कृतं** cow-dung. **—क्षीरं** cow's milk. **—खा** a nail. **—गृष्टिः** a young cow which has had only one calf. **–गोयुगं** a pair of oxen. **गोष्ठं** a cow-pen, cattle shed. **ग्रंथिः** **1** dried cowdung. **2** a cow-house. **–ग्रहः** capture of cattle. **–ग्रासः** the ceremony of offering a morsel (of grass) to a cow when performing an expiatory rite. **–घृतं** **1** rain-water. **2** clarified butter coming from a cow. **–चंदनं** a kind of sandalwood. **–चर.** *a.* **1** grazed over by cattle. **2** frequenting, resorting to, haunting; पितृसद्मगोचरः Ku. 5. 77. **3** within the scope, power, or range of; अवाङ्मनसगोचरं R. 10. 15; so बुद्धि°, दृष्टि°, श्रवण° &c. **4** moving on earth. **(–रः)** **1** the range of cattle, pasturage; उपारताः पश्चिमरात्रिगोचरात् Ki. 4. 10. **2** a district department, province, sphere. **3** range of the organs of sense, an object of sense; श्रवणगोचरे तिष्ठ be within ear-shot; नयनगोचरं या to become visible. **4** scope, range, reach in general हर्तुर्याति न गोचरं Bh. 2. 16 **5** (fig.) grip, hold; power, influence, control; कः कालस्य न गोचरांतरगतः Pt. 1. 146.; अपि नाम मनागवतीर्णोऽसि रतिरमणबाणगोचरं Mal. 1. **6** horizon. **–चर्मन्** *n.* **1** a cow's hide. **2** a particular measure of surface thus defined by Vasishtha:—दशहस्तेन वंशेन दशवंशान् समंततः। पंच चाभ्यधिकान् दद्यादेतद्गोचर्म चोच्यते॥ **°वसनः** an epithet of *Siva*. **चारकः** a cowherd. **–जरः** an old ox or bull **–जलं** the urine of a bull or cow. **–जागरिकं** auspiciousness, happiness. **–तल्लजः** an excellent bull or cow. **–तीर्थं** a cowhouse. **–त्रं** **1** a cowpen. **2** a stable in general. **3** a family, race, lineage; गोत्रेण माटरोऽस्मि Sk.; so कौशिकगोत्राः, वसिष्ठगोत्राः &c.; Ms. 3. 109, 9. 141. **4** a name, appellation; जगाद गोत्रस्खलिते च का न तं N. 1. 30; see °स्खलित below; मद्गोत्रांकं विरचितपदं गेयमुद्गातुकामा Me. 86. **5** a multitude. **6** increase. **7** a forest. **8** a field. **9** a road. **10** possessions, wealth. **11.** an umbrella, a parasol. **–12.** knowledge of futurity. **13.** a genus, class, species (**–त्रः**) a mountain. **°कीला** the earth. **°ज** *a.* born in the same family, gentile, a relation; Y. **2.** 135. **°पटः** a genealogical table, pedigree. **°भिद्** *m.* an epithet of Indra; हृदि क्षतो गोत्रभिदप्यमर्षणः R. 3. 53, 4. 73; Ku. **2.** 52. **°स्खलनं, °स्खलितं** blundering or mistaking in calling (one) by his name, calling by a wrong name; स्मरसि स्मर मेखलागुणैरुत गोत्रस्खलितेषु बंधनं Ku. 4. 8. **(–त्रा) 1** a multitude of cows. **2** the earth **–दंतं** a yellow orpiment. **–दा** the river Godâvarî. **–दानं 1.** the gift of cutting the hair; अथास्य गोदानविधेरनंतरं R. 3 33; (see **Mallinâtha's** explanation of the word); कृतगोदानमंगलाः U. 1. (Râm. explains the word diffierently). **–दारणं 1.** a plough. **2.** a spade, hoe. **–दावरी** N. of a river in the south. **–दुह्** *m.* **दुहः** a cowherd. **–दोहः 1.** the milking of cows. **2** the milk of cows. **3.** the time of milking cows. **–दोहनं** **1** the time of milking cows. **2** the milking of cows. **–दोहनी** a milk-pail. **–द्रवः** the urine of a bull or cow. **–धनं** a herd or multitude of cows, cattle. **–धरः** a moutain. **–धुमः, –धूमः** **1** wheat. **2** the orange, **–धूलिः** 'dust of the earth, the time of sunset or evening twilight (so called because cows, which generally return home at about sunset, raise up clouds of dust by their treading on the earth). **–धेनुः** a milchcow with a calf. **–ध्रः** a mountain. **–नंदी** the female of the Sârasa bird. **–नर्दः** the (Indian) crane. **2** N. of a country. **–नर्दीयः** an epithet of Patanjali, author of the Mahâbhâshya. **–नसः, –नासः** **1** a Kind of snake. **2** a kind of gem. **–नाथः** **1** a bull. **2** an owner of land. **3** a herdsman. **4** an owner of kine. **–नायः** a cowherd. **–निष्यंदः** cow's urine. **–पः** **1** a cowherd (considered as belonging to a mixed tribe); गोपवेशस्य विष्णोः Me. 15. **2** the chief of a cowpen. **–3** the superintendent of a village. **–4** a king. **–5** a protector, guardian. **(–पी) 1** a cowherd's wife; गोपीपीनपयोधरमर्दनचंचलकरयुगशाली Git. 5 **°अध्य-**

क्षः, °इन्द्रः, °ईशः the chief of herdsmen, an epithet of Krishna. °दलः the betel-nut tree °वधूः *f.* a cowherd's wife. °वधूटी a young cowherdess, a young wife of a cowherd; गोपवधूटीदुकूलचौराय Bhâshâ P. 1. -पतिः 1 an owner of cows. 2 a bull. 3 a leader, chief. 4 The sun. 5 Indra. 6 N. of Krishna. 7 N. of *S*iva. 8 N. of Varuṇa. 9 a king. -पशुः a sacrificial cow. -पानसी a curved beam which supports a thatch. -पालः 1 a cowherd. 2 a king. 3 an epithet of Krishṇa. °धानी a cow-pen, cowshed. -पालकः 1 a cowherd. 2 an epithet of *S*iva. -पालिका, -पाली the wife of a cowherd. -पीतः a species of wagtail. पुच्छं a cow's tail (-च्छः) 1 a sort of monkey. 2 a sort of necklace consisting of two or four or thirtyfour strings. -पुटिकं the head of *S*iva's bull. -पुत्रः a young bull. -पुरं 1 a town-gate. 2 a principal gate; Ki. 5. 5. 3 the ornamental gate-way of a temple. -पुरीषं cowdung. -प्रकांडं an excellent cow or bull. प्रचारः pasture-ground, pasturage for cattle; Y. 2. 166. -प्रवेशः the time when cows return home, Sunset or evening-twilight. -भृत् *m.* a mountain. -मक्षिक a gadfly. -मंडलं 1 the globe. 2. multitude of cows. -मतं=गव्यूति q. v. -मतल्लिका a tractable cow, an excellent cow. -मथः a cowherd.-मांसं beef. -मायुः 1 a kind of frog. 2 a jackal; अनुहुंकुरुते घनध्वनिं न हि गोमायुरुतानि केसरी *S*i. 16. 25. 3 bile of a cow. 4 N. of a Gandharva. -मुखः, -मुखं a kind of musical instrument; Bg. 1. 13. (-खः) 1 a crocodile, shark. 2 a hole of a particular shape in a wall made by thieves. (-खं) a house built unevenly. (-खं, -खी) a cloth-bag of the shape of a gnomon containing a rosary, the beads of which are counted by the hand thrust inside. -मूढ *a.* stupid as a bull. -मूत्रं cow's urine. -मृगः a kind of ox (गवय). -मेदः a gem brought from the Himâlaya and Indus, described as of four different colours:—white, pale, yellow, red, and dark-blue. -यानं a carriage drawn by oxen. -रक्षः 1 a cowherd. 2 keeping or tending cattle. 3 the orange. -रंकुः. 1 a water-fowl. 2 a prisoner. 3 a naked man, a mendicant wandering about without clothes. -रसः 1 cow's milk. 2 curds. 3 buttermilk. °जं buttermilk. -राजः an excellent bull. -रुतं a measure of distance equal to two Krosas. -राटिका, -राटी the Sârikâ bird.-रोचना a bright yellow pigment prepared from the urine or bile of a cow, or found in the head of a cow. -लवणं a measure of salt given to a cow. -लांगु (गू) लः a kind of monkey with a dark body, red cheeks, and a tail like that of a cow; Mâl. 9. 30. -लोमी a prostitute. -वत्सः a calf. °आदिन् *m.* a wolf. -वर्धनः a celebrated hill in वृंदावन the country about Mathurâ. °धरः, °धारिन् *m.* an epithet of Krishṇa. -वशा a barren cow. -वाटं, -वासः a cowpen. -विंदः 1 a cowkeeper, a chief herdsman. 2 N. of Krishṇa. 3 Brihaspati -विष् *f.*, -विष्ठा cowdung. -विसर्गः daybreak (when cows are let loose to graze in forests) -वीर्यं the price received for milk. -वृंदं a drove of cattle. -वृंदारकः an excellent bull or cow. -वृषः an excellent bull. °ध्वजः an epithet of *S*iva. -व्रजः 1 a cowpen. 2 a herd of cows. 3 a place where cattle graze. -शकृत् *n.* cowdung. -शालं,-ला a cowstall. -षड्गवं three pairs of kine. -ष्ठः of गोष्ठः See s. v. -संख्यः a cow-herd -सदृक्षः a species of ox (गवय). -सर्गः the time at which cows are usually let loose, day-break; see गोविसर्ग. -सूत्रिका a rope fastened at both ends having separate halters for each ox or cow. -स्तनः 1 the udder of a cow. 2 a cluster of blossoms, nosegay &c. 3 a pearl necklace of four strings. -स्तना, -नी a bunch of grapes. स्थानं a cow pen. -स्वामिन् *m.* 1 an owner of cows. 2 a religious mendicant. 3 an honorary title affixed to proper names; (*e. g.* बोपदेवगोस्वामिन्). -हत्या cow-slaughter. -हनं (sometimes written हनं) cowdung. -हित *a.* cherishing or protecting kine.

गोडुंबः The water-melon.

गोणी 1 A sack. 2 A measure of capacity equal to a Droṇa. 3 Ragged garment, torn clothes.

गोंडः 1 A fleshy navel. 2 A man of a low tribe, mountaineer, especially one inhabiting the eastern portion of the Vindhya range between Narmada and Krishnâ.

गोतमः N. of a sage belonging to the family of Angiras, father of *S*atânanda and husband of Ahalyâ.

गोतमी Ahalyâ, wife of गोतम. -Comp. -पुत्रः an epithet of *S*atânanda.

गोधा 1 A leathern fence fastened round the left arm to prevent injury from the bow-string. 2 The alligator. 3 A sinew, chord.

गोधिः *m.* 1 The forehead. 2 The Gangetic alligator.

गोधिका A kind of lizard.

गोपः (पी *f.*) 1 One who guards or protects; शालिगोप्यो जगुर्यशः R. 4. 20. 2 Hiding, concealment. 3 Reviling, abuse 4 Flurry, agitation. 5 Light, lustre, splendour.

गोपायनं Protecting, guarding, defending.

गोपायित *a.* Protected, defended.

गोप्तृ (त्री *f.*) A Protector, preserver, guardian; तस्मिन्वनं गोप्तरि गाहमाने R. 2. 14; 1. 55; M. 5. 20; Bg. 11. 11. 2 One who hides or conceals. -*m.* An epithet of Vishṇu.

गोमत् *a.* 1 Rich in cows. —ती N. of a river.

गोमयः -यं Cowdung. °छत्रं, -प्रियं a mushroom, a fungus.

गोमिन् *m.* 1 An owner of cattle. 2 A jackal. 3 A worshipper. 4 An attendant on a Buddha.

गोरणं Energy, continued effort, perseverance.

गोर्द Brain; (also गोद).

गोलः 1 A ball, globe. 2 The celestial or terrestrial globe. 3 A sphere. 4 A widow's bastard; cf. कुंड. 5 The conjunction of several planets or the presence of several in one sign. —ला 1 A wooden ball with which children play. 2 A large globular water-jar. 3 Read arsenic. 4 Ink. 5 A woman's female friend. 6 N. of Durgâ. 7 N. of the river Godâvarî.

गोलकः 1 A ball, globe. 2 A wooden ball for playing with. 3 A globular water-jar. 4 A widow's bastard. 5 A conjunction of six or more planets. 6 Molasses. 7 Gum myrrh.

गोष्ट् 1 A. (गोष्टते) To assemble, collect, heap together.

गोष्ठः-ष्ठं (Usually गोष्ठं only) 1 A cowpen, cowhouse, cow-station. 2 A station of cowherds. —ष्ठः 1 An assembly or meeting. °श्वः a dog in a cowpen which barks at every one; applied figuratively to a slanderous person, one who stays idly at home and slanders his neighbours. गोष्ठेपंडितः 'wise in a cowpen,' a braggart, vain boaster.

गोष्ठि ष्ठी *f.* 1 An assembly, meeting. 2 Society, association. 3 Conversation, chitchat, discourse; गोष्ठी सत्कविभिः समं Bh. 1. 28; Mâl. 10. 25; तेनैव सह सर्वदा गोष्ठिमनुभवति Pt. 2. 4 A multitude or collection. 5 Family connections, relatives, especially such as require to be maintained. 6 A kind of dramatic composition in one act. °पतिः 1. the chief of an assembly, president.

गोष्पदं 1 A cow's foot. 2 The mark or impression of a cow's foot in the soil. 3 The quantity of water sufficient to fill such an impression;

i. e. a very small puddle. **4** As much as a cow's footstep will hold. **5** A spot frequented by cows.

गोह्य What ought to be concealed, secret.

गौंजिकः A goldsmith.

गौडः **1** N. of a country ; the स्कंदपुराण thus describes its position:—वंगदेशं समारभ्य भुवनेशांतगः शिवे । गौडदेशः समाख्यातः सर्वविद्याविशारदः ॥ **2** A particular subdivision of Brâhmanas **—डाः** (pl.) The inhabitants of Gauda. **–डी 1** Spirit distilled from molasses; गौडी पैष्टी च माध्वी च विज्ञेया त्रिविधा सुरा Ms. 11. 94. **2** One of the Râgiṇîs. **3** (In rhet.) One of the *Rîtis* or *Vrittis* or styles of poetic composition ; S. D. mentions four *Ritis*; while K. P. only three, गौडी being another name for परुषा वृत्ति; औजः प्रकाशकैस्तैः (वर्णैः) तु परुषा (*i. e.* गौडी) K. P. 7 ; ओजः प्रकाशकैर्वर्णैर्बंध आडंबरः पुनः समासबहुला गौडी S. D. 627.

गौडिकः Sugar-cane.

गौण *a.* (**णी** *f.*) **1** Subordinate, secondary, unessential. **2** (In gram.) Indirect or less immediate (opp. मुख्य or प्रधान.) ; गौणे कर्मणि दुह्यादेः प्रधाने नीहृकृष्वहां Sk. **3** Figurative, metaphorical, used in a secondary sense (as a word or sense). **4** Founded on some resemblance between the primary and secondary sense of a word ; as in गौणीलक्षणा. **5** Relating to enumeration of multiplication. **6** Attributive.

गौण्यं Subordination, inferior position.

गौतमः N. of (1) the sage Bhâradvâja ; (2) of Satânanda, Gotama's son ; (3) N. of Kripa, Droṇa's brother-in-law ; (4) of Buddha ; (5) of the propounder of the Nyâya system of philosophy. –Comp. **–संभवा** the river Godâvarî

गौतमी 1 N. of Kripî, wife of Droṇa. **2** An epithet of the Godâvarî. **3** The teaching of Buddha. **4** The Nyâya system of philosophy propounded by Gautama. **5** Turmeric. **6** A kind of yellow pigment.

गौधूमीनं A field where wheat is grown.

गौनर्दः An epithet of Patanjali, the author of the Mahâbhâshya.

गौपिकः The son of a Gopî or herdsman's wife.

गौसेयः The son of a Vaisya Woman.

गौरः *a.* (**रा** or **री** *f.*) **1** White ; कैलासगौरं वृषमारुरुक्षोः R. 2. 35; द्विरददशनच्छेदगौरस्य तस्य Me. 59. 52; Rs. 1. 6. **2** Yellowish, pale-red ; गोरोचनाक्षेपनितांतगौरे Ku. 7. 17; R. 6. 65 ; गौरांगि गर्वं न कदापि कुर्याः R. G. **3** Reddish. **4** Shining, brilliant. **5** Pure, clean, beautiful. **—रः 1** The white colour. **2** The yellowish colour. **3** The reddish colour. **4** White mustard. **5** The moon. **6** A kind of buffalo. **7** A kind of deer. **—रं 1** The filament of a lotus. **2** Saffron. **3** Gold. –Comp. **–आस्यः** a kind of black monkey; with a white face. **–सर्षपः** white mustard.

गौरक्ष्यं The office of a herdsman.

गौरवं 1 Weight, heaviness (lit.); सुरेंद्रमात्राश्रितगर्भगौरवात् R. 3. 11. **2** Importance, high value or estimation; स्वविक्रमे गौरवमादधानं R. 14. 18; 18. 19; कार्यगौरवेण Mu. 5 importance or urgent nature. **3** Respect, regard, consideration ; तथापि यन्मय्यपि ते गुरुरित्यस्ति गौरवं Si. 2. 71. प्रयोजनापेक्षितया प्रभूणां प्रायश्चलं गौरवमाश्रितेषु Ku. 3. 1 ; Amaru. 19. **4.** Respectability, dignity, venerableness; कोऽर्थी गतो गौरवं Pt. 1 146 ; Ms. 2. 145. **5** Cumbrousness. **6** (In prosody) Length (as of a syllable), **7** Depth (as of meaning); यच्चार्थतो गौरवं Mâl. 1. 7. –Comp. **–आसनं** a seat of honour. **–ईरित** *a.* praised, famed, celebrated.

गौरवित *a.* Highly esteemed or honoured.

गौरिका A virgin, a young girl.

गौरिलः 1 White mustard. **2** Dust of iron or steel.

गौरी 1 N. of Pârvatî ; as in गौरीनाथ. **2** A young girl eight years old ; अष्टवर्षा भवेद्गौरी. **3** A young girl prior to menstruation, virgin, maid. **4** A woman with a white or yellowish complexion. **5** The earth. **6** Turmeric. **7** A yellow pigment or dye ; (called गोरोचना) **8** The wife of Varuna. **9** The Mallikâ creeper. **10** The Tulasî plant. **11** The Manjishṭhâ plant. –Comp. **–कांतः, –नाथः** an epithet of *Siva.* **–गुरुः** the Himâlaya mountain ; गौरीगुरोर्गह्वरमाविवेश R. 2. 26 ; Ki 5. 21. **–जः** N. of Kârtikeya. (**–जं**) talc. **–पट्टः** the horizontal plate of the Linga or Phallus of Siva, symbolizing the female organ. **–पुत्रः** N. of Kârtikeya. **–ललितं** a yellow orpiment. **–सुतः 1** N. of कार्तिकेय. **2** the son of a girl married when 8 years old.

गौरुतल्पिकः The violator of the preceptor's bed.

गौलक्षणिकः One who knows the good or bad marks of a cow.

गौल्मिकः A single soldier of a troop.

गौशतिक *a.* (**की** *f.*) Possessing a hundred cows.

ग्मा The earth.

ग्रथ् or **ग्रंथ्** 1. A. (ग्रथते, ग्रंथते) **1** To be crooked. **2** To be wicked. **3** To bend.

ग्रथनं 1 Coagulation, thickening; becoming obstructed or clogged with knotty lumps. **2** Stringing together. **3** Composing, writing ; (ना also in these two senses).

ग्रथ्नः A cluster, bunch, tuft.

ग्रथित *p. p.* **1** Strung or tied together. **2** Composed ; वर्णैः कतिपयैरेव ग्रथितस्य स्वरैरिव *Si*. 2. 72. **3** Arranged, classed. **4** Thickened, coagulated. **5** Knotty.

ग्रंथ् 1. 9. P., 10 U., 1 A. (ग्रंथति, ग्रथ्नाति, ग्रंथयति-ते, also ग्रथति, ग्रथते) **1** To fasten, tie or string together; Bk. 7. 105; स्रजो ग्रथयते &c. **2** To arrange, class together, connect in a regular series. **3** To wind round. **4** To write, compose; ग्रथ्नामि काव्यशशिनं विततार्थरश्मि K. P. 10. **5** To form, make, produce; ग्रथ्नंति बाष्पबिंदुनिकरं पक्ष्मपंक्तयः K. 60; Bk. 17. 69.–With **उद् 1** to tie up, tie or sew together; Mu. 1. 4; to intertwine, लताप्रतानोद्ग्रथितैः स केशैः R. 2. 8. **2** to unbind, loosen.

ग्रंथः 1 Binding, stringing together (fig. also) **2.** A work, treatise, composition, literary production, book; ग्रंथारंभे, ग्रंथकृत्, ग्रंथसमाप्ति &c. **3** Wealth, property. **4** A verse consisting of 32 syllables, written in the Anushṭubh metre. –Comp. **–कारः, –कृत्** *m.* a writer, an author ; ग्रंथारंभे समुचितेष्टदेवतां ग्रंथकृत्परामृशति K. P. 1. **–कुटी, –कूटी 1** a library. **2** a studio. **–विस्तरः, –विस्तारः** voluminousness, diffuse style. **–संधिः** a section or chapter of a work ; (for the several names by which sections, or chapters of works in Sanskrit, are called, see under अध्याय).

ग्रंथनं, –ना See ग्रथन.

ग्रंथिः 1 A knot, bunch, protuberance in general ; स्तनौ मांसग्रंथी कनककलशावित्युपमितौ Bh. 3. 20 ; so मेदोग्रंथि. **2** A tie or knot of a cord, garment &c ; इदमुपहितसूक्ष्मग्रंथिना स्कंधदेशे *S*. 1. 18 ; Mk. 1. 1 ; Ms. 2. 43 ; Bh. 1. 57. **3** A knot tied in the end of a garment for keeping money ; hence, purse, money, property ; कुसीदाद् दारिद्र्यं परकरगतग्रंथिशमनात् Pt. 1. 11. **4** The joint or knot of a reed, cane &c. **5** A joint of the body. **6** Crookedness, distortion, falsehood, perversion of truth. **7** Swelling and hardening of the vessels of the body. –Comp. **–छेदकः, भेदः, मोचकः** a cut-purse, a pickpocket ; अंगुलीग्रंथिभेदस्य छेदयेत् प्रथमे ग्रहे Ms. 9. 277 ; Y. 2. 274 **–पर्णः–र्णं 1** N. of a fragrant tree ; न ग्रंथिपर्णप्रणयाश्चरंति कस्तूरिकागंधमृगास्तृणेषु Vikr. 1. 17. **2** a kind of perfume. **–बंधनं 1** tying together the garments of the bride and the bridegroom at the marriage ceremony. **2** a ligament. **-हरः** a minister.

ग्रंथिकः **1** An astrologer, a fortune-teller. **2** The name assumed by Nakula when at the palace of Virâṭa.

ग्रंथित see ग्रथित.

ग्रंथिन् *m.* **1** One who reads books, bookish; अज्ञेभ्यो ग्रंथिनः श्रेष्ठा ग्रंथिभ्यो धारिणो वराः Ms. **12.** 103. **2** Learned, well-read.

ग्रंथिल *a.* Knotted, knotty.

ग्रस् I. 1 A. (ग्रसते, ग्रस्त) **1** To swallow, devour, eat up, consume; स इमां पृथिवीं कृत्स्नां संक्षिप्य ग्रसते पुनः Mb.; Bg. 11. 30. **2** To seize. **3** To eclipse; द्राविव ग्रसते दिनेश्वरनिशाप्राणेश्वरौ भासुरौ Bh. **2.** 34; हिमांशुमाशु ग्रसते तन्म्रदिम्नः स्फुटं फलं Si. 2. 49. **4** To slur over words. **5** To destroy. -WITH **सं** to destroy; Bk. 12. 4.-II. 1. P., 10 U. (ग्रसति, ग्रासयति-ते) To eat, devour.

ग्रसनं **1** Swallowing, eating. **2** Seizing. **3** A partial eclipse of the sun or moon.

ग्रस्त *p. p.* **1** Eaten, devoured. **2** Seized, stricken, affected, possessed; ग्रह°, विपद्° &c. **3** Eclipsed. **-स्तं** A word or sentence half-uttered or slurred over. -COMP. **-अस्तं** the setting of the sun or moon while eclipsed. **-उदयः** rising of the sun or moon while eclipsed.

ग्रह् 9 U. (In Vedic literature **ग्रभ्**; गृह्णाति, गृहीत; *caus.* ग्राहयति; *desid.* जिघृक्षति) **1** To seize, take, take or catch hold of, lay hold of, catch, grasp; तयोर्जगृहतुः पादान् राजा राज्ञी च मागधी R. 1. 57; आलाने गृह्यते हस्ती वाजी वल्गासु गृह्यते; Mk. 1. 50; तं कंठे जग्राह K. 363 पाणिं गृहीत्वा, चरणं गृहीत्वा &c. **2** To receive, take, accept, exact; प्रजानामेव भूत्यर्थं स ताभ्यो बलिमग्रहीत् R. 1. 18; Ms. 7. 124; 9. 162. **3** To apprehend, capture, take prisoner; बंदिग्राहं गृहीता V. 1; यांस्तत्र चारान् गृह्णीयात् Ms. 8. 34 **4** To arrest, stop, catch, Bg. 6. 35, **5** To captivate, attract; महाराजगृहीतहृदयया मया V. 4; हृदये गृह्यते नारी Mk. 1. 50; माधुर्यमीष्टे हरिणान् ग्रहीतुं R. 18. 13. **6** To win over, persuade, induce to one's side; लुब्धमर्थेन गृह्णीयात् Chân. 33. **7** (Hence) To please, gratify, satisfy, propitiate; ग्रहीतुमार्यान् परिचर्यया मुहुर्महानुभावा हि नितांतमर्थिनः Si. 1. 17. 33. **8** To affect, seize or possess (as a demon, spirit &c.); as in पिशाचगृहीत, वेतालगृहीत. **9** To assume, take द्युतिमग्रहीद् ग्रहगणः Si. 9. 23; Bk. 19. 29. **10** To learn, know, recognize, understand; Ki. 10. 8. **11** To regard, consider, believe, take for; मयापि मृत्पिंडबुद्धिना तथैव गृहीतं S. 6; परिहासविजल्पितं सखे परमार्थेन न गृह्यतां वचः S. 2. 18; एवं जनो गृह्णाति M. 1; Mu. 3. **12** To catch or perceive (as by an organ of sense); ज्यानिनादमथ गृह्णती तयोः R. 11. 15. **13** To master, grasp, comprehend, R. 18, 46. **14** To guess, conjecture, infer; नेत्रवक्त्रविकारैश्च गृह्यतेऽतर्गतं मनः Ms. 8. 26. **15** To utter, mention (as a name); यदि मयान्यस्य नामापि न गृहीतं K. 305; न तु नामापि गृह्णीयात् पत्यौ प्रेते परस्य तु Ms. 5. 157. **16** To buy, purchase; कियता मूल्येनैतत्पुस्तकं गृहीतं Pt. 2; Y. 2. 169; Ms. 8. 201. **17** To deprive (one) of, take away from, rob or seize away; Bk. 9. 9; 15. 63. **18** To wear, put on (as clothes &c.); वासांसि जीर्णानि यथा विहाय नवानि गृह्णाति नरोऽपराणि Bg. 2. 22. **19** To conceive. **20** To observe (as a fast). **21** To eclipse. **22** To undertake. [The senses of this root may be variously modified according to the noun with which it is joined.]-*Caus* **1** To cause to take, catch, seize or accept. **2** To give away in marriage. **3** To teach, make one aquainted with. -WITH **अनु** to favour, oblige, show kindness to; अनुगृहीतोऽहमनया मघवतः संभावनया S. 7; अनुगृहीताः स्मः 'many thanks', 'we are much obliged' **-अनुसं** to salute humbly. **-अप** to take away, tear off. **-अभि** to seize forcibly. **-अव** **1** to oppose or resist. **2** to punish. **3** to capture, overpower. **-आ** to persist in. **-उद्** **1** to raise, lift up, erect; उद्गृहीतालकांताः Me 8; Bk. 15. 52. **2** to deposit. **3** to draw out. **-उप** **1** to provide. **2** to seize, take possession of; Ms. 7. 184. **3** to accept, approve. **4** to support, favour. **-नि** **1** to keep or hold down, keep in check. **2** to curb, restrain, suppress, control; Bg. 2. 68. **3** to stop, obstruct; निगृहीतो बलाद् द्वारि Mb. **4** to punish, chastise; Ms. 8. 310; 9 308. **5** to seize, catch, lay hold of; तमार्यगृह्यं निगृहीतधेनुः R. 2. 33. **6** to close or contract (as eyes); माथुरोऽक्षिणी निगृह्य Mk. 2. **-परि** **1** to clasp round, embrace. **2** to surround. **3** to lay hold of, seize. **4** to take, assume. **5** to accept. **6** to support, patronize. **-प्र** **1** to take, hold. **2** curb, restrain **3** to stretch forth, extend. **-प्रति** **1** to hold, seize, take, support; वर्षधरप्रतिगृहीतमेनं M. 4; Ms. 2. 48. **2** to take, accept, receive; ददाति प्रतिगृह्णाति Pt. 2; अमोघाः प्रतिगृह्णंतावर्घ्यानुपदमाशिषः R. 1. 44, 2. 22. **3** to receive or accept as a present. **4** to receive inimically, oppose, encounter, resist; प्रतिजग्राह काकुत्स्थस्तमस्त्रैर्गजसाधनः R. 4. 40, 12. 47. **5** to take in marriage; Ms. 9. 72. **6** to obey, conform to, listen to. **7** to resort to, betake oneself to. **-वि** **1** to hold or seize. **2** to quarrel, fight, contend; विगृह्य चक्रे नमुचिद्विषा बली य इत्थमस्वास्थ्यमहर्दिवं दिवः Si. 1. 51; Bk. 6. 86. 17. 23. **-सं** **1** to collect, gather, accumulate, hoard; संगृह्य धनं, पाशान्, &c. **2** receive kindly. **3** to curb, restrain, rein in (as horses). **4** to unstring (as a bow.)-II. 1. P., 10 U. (ग्रहति, ग्राहयति-ते) To take, receive, &c.

ग्रहः **1** Seizing, grasping, laying hold of, seizure; रुरुधुः कचग्रहैः R. 19. 31. **2** A grip, grasp, hold; कर्कटकग्रहात् Pt. 1. 260. **3** Taking, receiving, accepting; receipt. **4** Stealing, robbing अंगुलीग्रंथिभेदस्य छेदयेत्प्रथमे ग्रहे Ms. 9. 277; so गोग्रहः **5** Booty, spoil. **6** Eclipse; see ग्रहण. **7** A planet. (The planets are nine:—सूर्यश्चंद्रो मंगलश्च बुधश्चापि बृहस्पतिः। शुक्रः शनैश्चरो राहुः केतुश्चेति ग्रहा नव ॥); नक्षत्रताराग्रहसंकुलापि (रात्रिः) R. 6. 22, 3. 13; **12.** 28; गुरुणा स्तनभारेण मुखचंद्रेण भास्वता। शनैश्चराभ्यां पादाभ्यां रेजे ग्रहमयीव सा ॥ Bh. 1. 17. **8** Mentioning, utterance, repeating (as of a name); नामजातिग्रहं त्वेषामभिद्रोहेण कुर्वतः Ms. 8. 271; Amaru. 83. **9** A shark, crocodile. **10** An imp. in general. **11** A particular class of evil demons supposed to seize upon children and produce convulsions &c **12** Apprehension, perception. **13** An organ or instrument of apprehension. **14** Tenacity, perseverance, persistence. **15** Purpose, design. **16** Favour, patronage. -COMP. **-अधीन** *a.* subject to planetary influence **-अवमर्दनः** an epithet of Râhu. (**-नं**) friction of the planets. **-अधीशः** the sun. **-आधारः**; **-आश्रयः** polar star (as the fixed centre of the planets). **-आमयः** **1** epilepsy. **2** demoniacal possession. **-आलुंचनं** pouncing on one's prey, tearing it to pieces; श्येनो ग्रहालुंचने Mk. 3. 20. **-ईशः** the sun. **-कल्लोलः** an epithet of Râhu. **-गतिः** the motion of the planets. **-चिंतकः** an astrologer. **-दशा** the aspect of a planet, the time during which it continues to exercise its influence. **-देवता** the deity that presides over a planet. **-नायकः** **1** the sun. **2** an epithet of Saturn. **-विग्रहौ** (du.) reward and punishment. **-नेमि** the moon. **-पतिः** **1** the sun. **2** the moon. **-पीडनं**, **-पीडा** **1** oppression caused by a planet. **2** an eclipse; शशिदिवाकरयोर्ग्रहपीडनं Bh. 2. 91. **-युद्धं** opposition of planets. **-राजः** **1** the sun. **2** the moon. **3** Jupiter. **-मंडलं -ली** the circle of the planets. **-युतिः** *f.* conjunction of planets. **-वर्षः** the planetary year. **-विप्रः** an astrologer. **-शांतिः** *f.* propitiation of planets by sacrifices &c. **संगमं** conjunction of planets.

ग्रहणं 1 Seizing, catching, seizure; श्वा मृगग्रहणेऽशुचिः Ms. 5. 130. 2 Receiving, accepting, taking; आचारधूमग्रहणात् R. 7. 27. 3 Mentioning, uttering; नामग्रहणं. 4 Wearing, putting on; सोत्तरच्छदमध्यास्त नेपथ्यग्रहणाय सः R. 19. 21. 5 An eclipse; Y. 1. 218. 6 Understanding, comprehension, knowledge; न परेषां ग्रहणस्य गोचरां N. 2. 95 7 Learning, acquiring, grasping mentally, mastering; लिपेर्यथावद्ग्रहणेन वाङ्मयं नदीमुखेनेव समुद्रमाविशत् R. 3. 28 8 Taking up of sound, echo; अद्रिग्रहणगुरुभिर्गर्जितैर्नर्तयेथाः Me. 44. 9 The hand. 10 An organ of sense.

ग्रहणिः,-णी *f.* Diarrhœa, dysentery.

ग्रहिल *a.* 1 Taking, accepting. 2 Unyielding, relentless, obstinate; न निशाखिलयापि वापिका प्रससाद ग्रहिलेव मानिनी N. 2. 77.

ग्रहीतृ *a.* (त्री *f.*) 1 A taker, an acceptor; as in गुणग्रहीतृ q. v. 2 Perceiver, observant. 3 Debtor.

ग्रामः 1 A village, hamlet; पत्तने विद्यमानेऽपि ग्रामे रत्नपरीक्षा M. 1; त्यजेदेकं कुलस्यार्थे ग्रामस्यार्थे कुलं त्यजेत्। ग्रामं जनपदस्यार्थे स्वात्मार्थे पृथिवीं त्यजेत्॥ H. 1. 149; R. 1. 44; Me. 30. 2 A race, community. 3 A multitude, collection (of anything); *e. g.* गुणग्राम, इंद्रियग्राम; Bg. 8. 19, 9. 8. 4 A gamut, scale in music. –COMP. –अधिकृतः, –अध्यक्षः, –ईशः; –ईश्वरः Superintendent, head, chief of a village. –अंतः the border of a village, space near a village; Ms. 4. 116; 11. 78. –अंतरं another village. –अंतिकं the neighbourhood of a village. –आचारः a village-custom. आधानं hunting. –उपाध्यायः the village-priest.–कंटकः 1 'the village-pest,' one who is a source of trouble to the village. 2 a tale-bearer. कुक्कुटः a domestic cock –कुमारः 1 one beautiful in a village. 2 a village-boy. –कूटः 1 the noblest man in a village. 2 a Śúdra. –गृह्य *a.* being outside a village. –गोदुहः the herdsman of a village. –घातः plundering a village. –घोषिन् *m.* an epithet of Indra. –चर्या sexual intercourse; (स्त्रीसंभोग). –चैत्यः a sacred fig-tree of a village; Me. 23 –जालं a number of villages, a destrict. –णीः 1 the leader or chief of a village, or communuty. 2 a leader or chief in general. 3 barber. 4 a libidinous man. (*-f.*) 1 a whore, harlot. 2 the indigo plant. –तक्षः a village-carpenter. –देवता the tutelary deity of a village. –धर्मः sexual intercourse. –प्रेष्यः the messenger or servant of a community or village –मद्गुरिका a riot, fray, village tumult. –मुखः a market. –मृगः a dog. –याजकः –याजिन् *m.* 1 'the village priest', a priest who conducts the religious ceremonies for all classes and is consequently considered as a degraded Brâhmaṇa. 2 the attendant of an idol. –लुंठनं plundering a village –वासः (ग्रामिवासः also) residence in a village. –षंढः an impotent man (क्लीब). –संघः a village-corporation. –सिंहः a dog. –स्थ *a.* 1 a villager. 2 a co-villager. –हासकः a sister's husband.

ग्रामटिका A wretched or miserable village; कतिपयग्रामटिकापर्यटनदुर्विदग्ध P. R. 1.

ग्रामिक *a.* (की *f.*) 1 Rural, rustic. 2 Rude. –कः The headman of a village; Ms. 7. 116, 118.

ग्रामीणः 1 A villager; ग्रामीणवध्वस्तमलक्षिता जनैश्चिरं वृतीनामुपरि व्यलोकयन् Si. 12. 37; Amaru. 11. 2 A dog. 3 A crow. 4 A hog.

ग्रामेय *a.* (यी *f.*) Village-born, rustic.

ग्रामेयी A prostitute, harlot.

ग्राम्य *a.* 1 Relating to or used in a village; Ms. 6. 3; 7. 120. 2 Living in a village, rural, rustic; अल्पव्ययेन सुंदरि ग्राम्यजनो मिष्टमश्नाति Chand. M. 1. 3 Domesticated, tame (as an animal). 4 Cultivated (opp. वन्य 'growing wild'). 5 Low, vulgar, used only by low people (as a word); चुंबनं देहि मे भार्ये कामचांडालतृप्तये R. G.; or कटिस्ते हरते मनः S. D. 574 are instances of ग्राम्य expressions. 6 Indecent, obscene. –म्यः A tame hog. –म्यं 1 A rustic speech. 2 Food prepared in a village. 3 Sexual intercourse. –COMP. –अश्वः an ass. –कर्मन् *n.* the occupation of a villager. –कुंकुमं safflower. –धर्मः 1 the duty of a villager. 2 sexual intercourse, copulation. –पशुः a domestic animal. –बुद्धि *a.* boorish, clownish, ignorant. –वल्लभा a harlot, prostitute. –सुखं sexual intercourse, copulation.

ग्रावन् *m.* 1 A stone or rock; किं हि नामैतदंबुनि मज्जंत्यलाबूनि ग्रावाणः संप्लवंत इति Mv. 1.; अपि ग्रावा रोदित्यपि दलति वज्रस्य हृदयं U. 1. 28; Si. 4. 23. 2 A mountain. 2 A. cloud.

ग्रासः 1 A mouthful, a quantity of anything equal to a mouthful; Ms. 3. 133; 6. 28; Y. 3. 55. 2 Food, nourishment. 3 The part of the sun or moon eclipsed. –COMP. –आच्छादनं food and clothing; *i. e.* bare subsistence. –शल्यं any extraneous substance lodged in the throat.

ग्राह *a.* (ही *f.*) Seizing, clutching; taking, holding, receiving &c. –हः 1 Seizing, grasping. 2 A crocodile, shark; रागग्राहवती Bh. 3. 45. 3 A prisoner. 4 Accepting. 5 Understanding, knowledge. 6 Persistence, importunity. 7 Determination, resolve; Bg. 17. 19. 8 A disease.

ग्राहक *a.* (हिका *f.*) One who receives, takes. –कः 1 A hawk, falcon. 2 A curer of poison. 3 A purchaser. 4 A police-officer.

ग्रीवा The neck, the back part of the neck; ग्रीवाभंगाभिरामं मुहुरनुपतति स्यंदने दत्तदृष्टिः S. 1. 7. –COMP. –घंटा a bell hanging down from the neck of a horse.

ग्रीवालिका See ग्रीवा.

ग्रीविन् *m.* A camel.

ग्रीष्म *a.* Hot, warm. –ष्मः 1 The summer, the hot season, corresponding to the months of Jyeshṭha and Asâḍha, ग्रीष्मसमयमधिकृत्य गीयतां S. 1; R. 16. 54; Bv. 1. 35. 2 Heat, warmth. –COMP. –कालीन *a.* pertaining to summer. –उद्भवा, –जा, –भवा the Navamallikâ creeper, (double jasmine).

ग्रैव (वी *f.*), **ग्रैवेय** (यी *f.*) *a.* Being on or belonging to the neck. –वं, –यं 1 A collar or necklace. 2 A chain worn round the neck of an elephant; नास्त्रसत् करिणां ग्रैवं त्रिपदीच्छेदिनामपि R. 4. 48, 75.

ग्रैवेयकं 1 A neck-ornament; *e. g.* अस्माकं सखि वाससी न रुचिरे ग्रैवेयकं नोज्ज्वलं S. D. 3. 2 A chain worn round the neck of an elephant.

ग्रैष्मक *a.* (ष्मिका *f.*) 1 Sown in summer. 2 To be paid in summer (as a debt).

ग्लपनं 1 Withering, drying up. 2 Exhaustion.

ग्लस् 1 A. (ग्लसते, ग्लस्त) To eat, devour.

ग्लह् 1 U., 13 A. (ग्लहति-ते, ग्लाहयति-ते) 1 To gamble, to win by gambling. 2 To take, receive.

ग्लहः 1 A dice-player. 2 A stake, wager, bet. 3 A die. 4 Gambling, playing. 5 A dice-box.

ग्लान *p. p.* 1 Weary, languid, tired, fatigued, exhausted. 2 Sick, ill.

ग्लानि *f.* 1 Exhaustion, languor, fatigue; मनश्च ग्लानिमृच्छति Ms. 1. 53; अंगग्लानिं सुरतजनितां Me. 70, 31; Sânti. 4. 4. 2 Decay, decline; आत्मोदय; परग्लानिर्द्वयं; नीतिरितीयती Si. 2. ३; यदा यदा हि धर्मस्य ग्लानिर्भवति भारत Bg. 4. 7. 3 Debility, weakness. 4 Sickness.

ग्लास्नु *a.* Languid, wearied.

ग्लुच् 1 P. (ग्लोचति, ग्लुक्त) 1 To go, move. 2 To steal, rob. 3 To take away, deprive of बहूनामग्लुचत् प्राणानग्लोचीच्च रणे यशः Bk. 15. 30.

ग्लै 1 P. (ग्लायति, ग्लान) 1 To feel aversion or dislike, be unwilling or disinclined to do anything (with inf.). 2 To be fatigued or wearied, feel tired or exhausted. 3 To despond, sink in spirit, be dejected; Bk. 19. 17, 6. 12. 4 To wane, faint away. –*Caus.* (ग्ल-ग्ला-पयति). 1 To cause to fade away, wither up, hurt, injure. 2 To tire out.

ग्लौ *m.* 1 The moon. 2 Camphor.

घ.

घ *a.* (Used only as the last member of comp.) Striking, killing, destroying ; as in पाणिघ, राजघ &c. -घः 1 A bell. 2 Rattling, gurgling or tinkling noise.

घट् I 1 A. (घटते, घटित). 1 To be busy with, strive after, exert oneself for, be intently occupied with anything (with inf., loc. or dat.); दयितां त्रातुमलंघटस्व Bk. 10. 40 ; अंगदेन समं योद्धुमघटिष्ट 15. 77, 12. 26, 16. 23; 20. 24 ; 22. 31. 2 To happen, take place, be possible ; प्राणैस्तपोभिरथवाऽभिमतं मदीयैः कृत्यं घटेत सुहृदो यदि तत्कृतं स्यात् Mâl. 1. 9 if it can be effected ; कस्यापरस्यो द्रुमयैः प्रसूनैर्वादिभ्रसृष्टिर्घटेत भटस्य N. 22. 22. 3 To come to, reach. *-Caus.* (घटयति) 1 To unite, join, bring together ; इत्थं नारीर्घटयितुमलं कामिभिः *Si*. 9. 87 ; अनेन भैमीं घटयिष्यतस्तथा N. 1. 46 ; कृथा सार्धं भीमां विघटयति यूयं घटयत Ve. 1. 10; Bk. 11. 11. 2 To bring or place near to, bring in contact with, put on ; घटयति धनं कंठाश्लेषे रसान्न पयोधरौ Ratn. 3. 9 ; घटय जघने कांचीं Gît. 12. 3 To accomplish, bring about, effect ; तटस्थः स्वानर्थान् घटयति च मौनं च भजते Mâl. 1. 14 ; (अभिमतं) आनीय झटिति घटयति Ratn. 1. 6. 4 To form, fashion, shape, work out, make ; एवमभिधाय वैनतेयं...अघटयत् Pt. 1 ; कांते कथं घटितवानुपलेन चेतः *S*. Til. 3 ; घटयभुजबंधनं Gît. 10. 5 To prompt, impel ; स्नेहोघो घटयति मां तथापि वक्तुं Bk. 10 73. 6 To rub, touch. -WITH प्र 1 to be busy with, be occupied in Bk. 21. 17. 2 to begin, commence ; Bk. 14. 77. -वि 1 to be disunited or separated. 2 to be spoiled or ruined, come to a standstill, be stopped, break down. (*-Caus.*) to separate, break. -सं to be united.-II. 10 U (घाटयति, घाटित) 1 To hurt, injure, kill. 2 To unite, join, bring or collect together. -WITH -उद् to open, break open ; कपाटमुद्घाटयति Mk. 3 ; निरयनगरद्वारमुद्घाटयंती Bh. 1. 63.

घटः 1 A large earthen waterjar, pitcher, jar, watering-pot ; कूपे पश्य पयोनिधावपि घटो गृह्णाति तुल्यं जलं Bh. 2. 49. 2 The sign Aquarius of the zodiac (also called कुंभ) 3 An elephant's frontal sinus. 4 Suspending the breath as a religious exercise. 5 A measure equal to 20 droṇas. 6 A part of a column. -COMP., —आटोपः covering for a carriage or any article of furniture. -उद्भवः,-जः,-योनिः, -संभवः epithets of the sage Agastya. -ऊधस् *f.* (forming घटोध्नी) a cow with a full udder ; गावः कोटिशः स्पर्शयता घटोध्नीः R. 2. 49. -कर्परः 1 N. of a poet. 2 a piece of a broken jar, potsherd ; जीयेय येन कविना यमकैः परेण तस्मै वहेयमुदकं घटकर्परेण Ghat 22. -कारः, -कृत् *m.* a potter. -ग्रहः a water-bearer. -दासी a procuress ; *cf.* कुंभदासी -पर्यसनं the ceremony of performing the funeral rites of a *patita* or apostate (who is unwilling to go back to his caste &c.) during his very life-time. -भेदनकं an instrument used in making pots. राजः a water-jar of baked clay. -स्थापनं placing a water-pot as a type of Durgâ.

घटक *a.* 1 Exerting oneself, striving for ; एते सत्पुरुषाः परार्थघटकाः स्वार्थं परित्यज्य ये Bh. 2. 74. 2 Bringing about, accomplishing. 3 Forming a constituent part, constituent, component. -कः 1 A tree that produces fruit without apparent flowers. 2 A match-maker, an agent who ascertains genealogies and negotiates matrimonial alliances. 3 A genealogist.

घटनं-ना 1 Effort, exertion. 2 Happening, occuring. 3 Accomplishment, bringing about, effecting ; as in अघटितघटना. 4 Joining, union, mixing or bringing together, combination ; ततेन तनमयसा घटनाय योग्यं V. 2. 16 ; देहद्वयार्धघटनारचितं K. 239. 5 Making, forming, shaping.

घटा 1 An endeavour, effort, exertion. 2 A number, troop, assemblage; प्रलयघनघटा K. 111 ; कौशिकघटा U. 2. 29 ; 5. 6 ; मातंगघटा *Si*. 1. 64 3 A troop of elephants assembled for martial purposes. 4 An assembly.

घटिकः A waterman. -कं The hip, the posteriors.

घटिका 1 A small water-jar, bucket, a small earthen vessel ; नार्यः श्मशानघटिका इव वर्जनीयाः Pt. 1. 192 ; एष क्रीडति कूपयंत्रघटिकान्यायप्रसक्तो विधिः Mk. 10 59. 2 A measure of time equal to 24 minutes. 3 A water-pot used in calculating the ghaṭikâs of the day. 4 The ankle.

घटिन् *m.* The sign Aquarius of the zodiac (also called कुंभ).

घटिंधम *a.* One who drinks a pitchful (of water &c.).

घटी 1 A small jar. 2 A measure of time equal to 24 minutes. 3 A small water-pot used in calculating the Ghaṭikâs or time of the day.- COMP -कारः a potter. -ग्रह, -ग्राह *a.* See घटग्रह. -यंत्रं a machine for raising water (largely used in India), the rope and bucket of a well ; see अरघट्ट. 2 a contrivance (like a clepsydra) to ascertain the ghaṭikâs or time of the day

घटोत्कचः N. of a son of Bhîma by a female demon named हिडिंबा. [He was a very powerful person and fought valiantly in the great war between the Pandavas and Kauravas on the side of the former, but was slain by Karna with the Sakti or missile he had received from Indra; cf. Mu. 2. 15.]

घट्ट् 1 A. (घट्टते), usually 10 U. (घट्टयति-ते, घट्टित) 1 To shake, stir about; as in वायुघट्टिता लताः. 2 To touch, rub, rub the hands over ; विटजननखघट्टितेव वीणा Mk. 1. 24 ; Bk. 14. 2. 3 To smooth, stroke. 4 To speak spitefully or malignantly. 5 To disturb.- WITH अव to open. -परि to strike; *Si*- 9. 64. -वि 1 to strike down, disperse, scatter, scare away; *Si*. 1. 64; Bh. 3. 54. 2 to rub, strike, rub against; कारंडवाननविघट्टितवीचिमालाः Rs. 3. 8, 4. 9; Ku. 1. 9; Ki. 8. 45; Si. 8. 24. 13. 41. -सं 1 to strike. 2 to bring together, unite. 3 to gather, collect. 4 to rub, rub against or press against ; R. 6. 73.

घट्टः 1 A landing place, steps on the side of a river leading to the waters (Mar. घाट). 2 Stirring, agitating. 3 A toll-station. -COMP. -कुटी a toll-station. प्रभातन्याय see under न्याय. जीविन् *m.* 1 a ferryman. 2 a man of a mixed tribe; (वैश्यायां रजकाज्जातः).

घट्टना 1 Shaking, moving, stirring round, agitating. 2 Rubbing. 3 A means of livelihood, practice, business, profession.

घंटः A kind of dish, a sort of sauce.

घंटा 1 A bell. 2 A plate of iron or mixed metal struck as a clock. COMP. -अगारं a belfry. -फलकः -कं a shield furnished with small bells. -ताडः a bellman. -नादः the sound of a bell. -पथः the chief road through a village, a highway, main road; (दशधन्वंतरो राजमार्गो घंटापथः स्मृतः Kauṭilya).-शब्दः 1 bellmetal. 2 the sound of a bell.

घंटिका A small bell.

घंटुः 1 A string of bells tied on an elephant's chest by way of ornament. 2 Heat, light.

घंडः A bee.

घन *a.* 1 Compact, firm, hard, solid; संजातश्च घनाघनः Mâl. 9. 39; नासा घनास्थिका Y. 3. 89; R. 11. 18. 2 Thick, close, dense; घनविरलभावः U. 2. 27; R. 8. 81; Amaru. 57. 3 Thick-set, full, fully developed (as breasts); घटयति सुघने कुचयुगगगने मृगमदरुचिरूषिते Gît. 7; अगुरुचतुष्कं भवति गुरू द्वौ घनकुचयुगमे शशिवदनाऽसौ Srut. 8; Bh. 1. 8; Amaru. 28. 4

Deep (as sound); Mâl. 2. 12. 5 Uninterrupted, permanent. 6 Impenetrable 7 Great, excessive, violent. 8 Complete. 9 Auspicious, fortunate. –नः A cloud; घनोदयः प्राक् तदनंतरं पयः *S*. 7. 30; घनरुचिरकलापो निःसपत्नोऽस्य जातः V. 4. 10. 2 An iron club, a mace. 3 The body. 4 The cube of a number (in math.). 5 Extension, diffusion. 6 A collection, multitude, quantity, mass, assemblage. 7 Talc. –नं 1 A cymbal, a bell, a gong. 2 Iron. 3 Tin. 4 Skin; rind, bark. –COMP.–अत्ययः, अंतः 'disappearance of the clouds,' the season succeeding the rains, autumn; (शरद्). अंबु *n*. rain. आकरः the rainy season.–आगमः 'the approach of clouds', the rainy season; घनागमः कामिजनप्रियः प्रिये Rs. 2. 1. –आमयः the date tree.–आश्रयः the atmosphere, firmament –उपलः hail. –ओघः gathering of clouds. –कफः hail. –कालः the rainy season. –गर्जितं 1 thunder, peal or thundering noise of clouds, roar of thunder. 2 a deep loud roar. –गोलकः alloy of gold and silver. –जंबालः thick mire.–तालः a kind of bird. (सारंग).–तोलः the Châtaka bird. –नाभिः smoke (being supposed to be a principal ingredient in clouds; Me. 5). –नीहारः thick hoar-frost or mist. –पदवी 'the path of clouds', firmament, sky; क्रामद्भिर्घनपदवीमनेकसंख्यैः Ki. 5. 34 –पाषंडः a peacock –फलं (in geom.). the solid or cubical contents of a body or of an excavation. –मूलं cube root (in math.). रसः 1 a thick juice. 2 extract, decoction. 3 camphor. 4 water.–वर्गः the square of a cube, the sixth power (in math.). वर्त्मन् *n* the sky; घनवर्त्म सहस्रधेव कुर्वन् Ki. 5. 17.–वल्लिका, –वल्ली lightning.–वासः a kind of pumpkin-gourd. –वाहनः 1 *S*iva. 2 Indra.–श्याम *a*. 'dark like a cloud', deep-black, dark. (–मः) an epithet (1) of Râma, (2) of Krishṇa.–समयः the rainy season. –सारः 1 camphor; घनसारनीहारहार &c. Dk. 1 (mentioned among white substances). 2 mercury. 3 water. –स्वनः the roaring of clouds –हस्तसंख्या the contents of an excavation or of a solid (in math).

घनाघनः 1 Indra. 2 A vicious elephant or one in rut or intoxicated. 3 A thick or raining cloud.

घरट्टः A grinding stone.

घर्घर *a*. 1 Indistinct, purring, gurgling (as a sound); घर्घररवा परिश्मशानं सरित् Mâl. 5. 19 2 Murmuring, muttering (as clouds).–रः 1 An indistinct murmur, a low, murmuring or gurgling sound. 2 Noise in general. 3 A door, gate. 4 Mirth, laughter. 5 An owl. 6 A fire of chaff.

घर्घरा-री 1 A bell used as an ornament. 2 A gurgle of small bells. 3 The Ganges. 4 A kind of lute.

घर्घरिका 1 A bell used as an ornament. 2 A kind of musical instrument.

घर्घरितं The grunting of a hog.

घर्मः 1 Heat, warmth; H. 1. 97. 2 The hot season, summer, निःश्वासहार्यांशुकमाजगाम घर्मः प्रियावेशमिवोपदेष्टुं R. 16. 43. 3 Sweat, perspiration; *S*i. 1. 58. 4 A cauldron, boiler. –COMP. –अंशुः the sun; *S*. 5. 14. –अंतः the rainy season. –अंबु, अंभस् *n*. sweat, perspiration; *S*. 1. 30; Mâl. 1. 37. –चर्चिका eruptions caused by heat and suppressed perspiration. –दीधितिः the sun; R. 11. 64.–द्युतिः the sun; Ki. 5. 41.–पयस् *n*. sweat, perspiration; *S*i. 9. 35.

घर्षः,–घर्षणं 1 Rubbing, friction. 2 Grinding, pounding.

घस् 1. 2. P. (घसति, घस्ति, घस्त) To eat, devour (a defective root used only to form certain tenses of अद्).

घस्मर *a*. 1 Voracious; gluttonous; दावानलो घस्मरः Bv. 1. 34. 2 Devourer, destroyer; द्रुपदसुतचमूघस्मरो द्रौणिरस्मि Ve. 5. 36.

घस्र *a*. Hurtful, injurious.–स्रः 1 A day; घस्रो गमिष्यति भविष्यति सुप्रदोषं Subhâsh. 2. The sun; Mv. 6. 8.–स्रं Saffron.

घाटः–टा The back of the neck.

घांटिकः 1 A bell-ringer. 2 A bard who sings in chorus, especially in honour of gods or kings. 3 The Dhattûra plant.

घातः 1 A blow, stroke, bruise, hit; ज्याघात *S*. 3. 13; नयनशरघात Gît. 10; so पार्ष्णिघात; शिरोघात &c. 2 Killing, hurting, destruction, slaughter; वियोगो मुग्धाक्ष्याः स खलु रिपुघातावधिरभूत् U. 3. 44; पशुघातः Gît. 1; Y. 2. 159; 3. 252. 3 An arrow. 4 The product (of a sum in multiplication). –COMP. –चंद्रः the moon when in an inauspicious mansion. –तिथिः an inauspicious lunar day. –नक्षत्रं an inauspicious constellation. –वारः an inauspicious day of the week. –स्थानं a slaughter-house, place for execution.

घातक *a*. Killing, destroying, a killer, destroyer, murderer &c.

घातन *a*. A killer, murderer. –नं 1 Striking, killing, slaughter. 2 Killing (as an animal at a sacrifice), immolating.

घातिन् *a*. (नी *f*.) 1 Striking, killing. 2 Catching or killing (birds &c.). 3 Destructive. –COMP. –पक्षिन्, –विहगः a hawk, falcon.

घातुक *a*. (की *f*.) 1 Killing, destructive, mischievous, hurting. 2 Cruel, savage, ferocious.

घात्य *a*. Proper or fit to be killed.

घारः Sprinkling, wetting.

घार्तिकः A kind of dish or cake prepared with clarified butter which is full of small holes; and hence one of the learned fools in the Panchatantra says on seeing the cake served to him; "छिद्रेष्वनर्था बहुलीभवंति".

घासः 1 Food. 2 Meadow or pasture grass; घासाभावात् Pt. 5; घासमुष्टिं परगवे दद्यात् संवत्सरं तु यः Mb. –COMP. –कुंदं, –स्थानं a pasture.

घु 1 A. (घवते, घुत) To sound, make an indistinct noise.

घुः The indistinct sound of a pigeon.

घुट् I. 6 P. (घुटति, घुटित) 1 To strike again, retaliate, resist. 2 To protest. –II. 1. A. (घोटते) 1 To come back, return. 2 To barter, exchange.

घुटः; घुटिः–टी *f*., घुटिकः–का The ankle.

घुण् I. 1 A. 6 P. (घोणते, घुणति, घुणित) To roll, whirl, stagger, reel –II. 1 A. To take, receive.

घुणः A particular kind of insect found in timber. –COMP.–अक्षरं,–लिपिः *f*. an incision in wood or in the leaf of a book made by an insect or worm and resembling somewhat the form of a letter. °न्यायः see under न्याय.

घुंटः,–घुंटकः, घुंटिका The ankle.

घुंडः A large black bee.

घुर् 6 P. (घुरति, घुरित) 1 To sound, make a noise, snore, snort, grunt (as a pig, dog &c.); कः कः कुत्र न घुर्घुरायितघुरीघोरो घुरेच्छूकरः K P. 7. 2 To be frightful or terrible. 3 To cry in distress.

घुरी The nostrils, especially of a hog; घुर्घुरायितघुरीघोरो घुरेच्छूकरः K. P. 7.

घुर्घुरः 1 Guinea-worm. 2 Snorting, growling, grumbling.

घुर्घुरी The grunting of a hog.

घुलघुलारवः A sort of pigeon.

घुष् I. 1 P., 10 U. (घोषति, घोषयति-ते, घुषित, घुष्ट or घोषित) 1 To sound, make any sound or noise. 2 To cry or proclaim aloud, announce or declare publicly; स स पापादृते तासां दुष्यंत इति घुष्यतां *S*. 6. 22; घोषयतु मन्मथनिदेशं Gît. 10; इति घोषयतीव डिंडिमः करिणो हस्तिपकाहतः क्वणन् H. 2. 86; R. 9. 10. –WITH आ 1 to proclaim aloud, announce publicly; Bk. 3. 2. 2 to weep aloud, announce publicly; Bk. 3. 2. 2 to weep aloud. –उद् to proclaim aloud, announce publicly. –II. 1 A. (घुषते) To be beautiful or brilliant.

घुसृणं Saffron; यत्र स्त्रीणां मसृणघुसृणालेपनोष्णा कुचश्रीः Vikr. 18. 31.

घूकः An owl. –COMP. –अरिः a crow.

घूर्ण् 1 A., 6 P. (घूर्णते, घूर्णति, घूर्णित) To roll about, move to and fro, whirl, turn round, shake, reel, stagger; योषितामतिमंदेन जुघूर्णविभ्रमातिशयपुंषि वपूंषि Si. 10. 32; भयात्केचिद्घूर्णिषुः Bk. 15. 32, 118; Si. 11. 18; अद्यापि तां सुरतजागरघूर्णमानां Ch. P. 5. -*Caus.* (घूर्णयति-ते) To cause to skake, reel or roll about; नयनान्यरुणानि घूर्णयन् Ku. 4. 12; Si. 2. 16; Bh. 1. 89; (with prepositions like **आ, वि** the root retains the same meaning).

घूर्ण *a* Shaking, moving to and fro. -Comp.-**वायुः** a whirl wind.

घूर्णनं,-ना Shaking, reeling, whirling or turning round, revolving; मौलिघूर्णनचलत् Git. 9; घूर्णनामात्रपतनभ्रमणादर्शनादिकृत् S. D.

घृ I. 1 P. (घरति, घृत) To sprinkle. -II. 10 U. (घारयति-ते, घारित), To sprinkle over, wet, moisten. -With. **अभि** to sprinkle.-**आ** to sprinkle.

घृण् 8 P. (घृणोति, घृण्ण) To shine, burn.

घृणा 1 Compassion, pity, tenderness; तां विलोक्य वनितावधे घृणां पत्रिणा सह मुमोच राघवः R. 11. 17; 9. 81; Ki. 15. 13. 2 Disgust, aversion, contempt; तत्याज तोषं परपुष्टघुष्टे घृणां च वीणाक्कणिते वितेने N. 3. 60; 1. 20; R. 11. 65. 3 Reproach, censure.

घृणालु *a*. Compassionate, merciful, tender-hearted.

घृणिः 1 Heat, sunshine. 2 A ray of light. 3 The sun. 4 A wave. -*n.* Water.-Comp. -**निधिः** the sun.

घृतं 1 Ghee, clarified butter; (सर्पिर्विलीनमाज्यं स्याद् घनीभूतं घृतं भवेत् Sây.). 2 Butter. 3 Water. -Comp. -**अन्नः, -अर्चिस्** *m.* blazing fire. -**आहुतिः** *f.* an oblation of ghee. -**आह्वः** the Sarala tree. -**उदः** 'ocean of ghee', one of the seven oceans. -**ओदनः** boiled rice mixed with ghee. -**कुल्या** a stream of ghee. -**दीधितिः** fire -**धारा** a continuous stream of ghee. -**पूरः, -वरः** a kind of sweetmeat. -**लेखनी** a ladle for ghee.

घृताची 1 Night. 2 N. of Sarasvatī 3 N. of an *apsaras*; (the following are the principal nymphs of Indra's heaven; घृताची मेनका रंभा उर्वशी च तिलोत्तमा । सुकेशी मंजुघोषाद्याः कथ्यंतेऽप्सरसो बुधैः). -Comp. -**गर्भसंभवा** large cardamoms.

घृष् 1 P. (घर्षति, घृष्ट) 1 To rub, strike against; अद्यापि तत्कनककुंडलघृष्टमास्यं Ch. P. 11; Pt 1. 144. 2 To brush, furbish, polish. 3 To crush, grind, pound; द्रौपद्या ननु मत्स्यराजभवने घृष्टं न किं चंदनं Pt. 3. 175. 4 To compete, rival (as in संघृष् q. v.). -With **उद्** to scratch; चूडामणिभिरुद्घृष्टपादपीठं महीक्षितां R. 17. 28. **सं** 1 to rival, emulate compete or vie with; स प्रयोगनिपुणैः प्रयोक्तृभिः संजघर्ष सह मित्रसंनिधौ R. 19. 36. 2 to rub, scratch.

घृष्टिः A hog. -*f.* 1 Grinding, pounding, rubbing. 2 Emulation, rivalry, competition.

घोटः, घोटकः A horse.-Comp. -**अरिः** a buffalo.

घोटी, घोटिका A mare, horse in general; आटीकसेऽग करिघोटिपदातिजुषि बाटिभुवि क्षितिभुजां Asvad. 5.

घोण (न) सः A sort of reptile.

घोणा 1 The nose; घोणोन्नतं मुखं Mk. 9. 16. 2 The nose of a horse, snout (of a hog); घुर्घुरायमाणघोरघोणेन K. 78.

घोणिन् *m.* A hog.

घोंटा The jujube tree.

घोर *a.* 1 Terrific, frightful, horrible, awful; शिवाघोरस्वनां पश्चाद्बुबुधे विकृतेति तां R. 12. 39; or तत्किं कर्मणि घोरे मां नियोजयसि केशव Mb.; घोरं लोके विततमयशः U. 7. 6; Ms. 1. 50; 12. 54. 2 Violent, vehement. -**रः** N. of Siva. -**रा** Night. -**रं** 1 Horror, awfulness. 2 Poison. -Comp. **आकृति, -दर्शन** *a.* frightful in appearance, terrific, hideous. -**घुष्यं** bellmetal. -**रासनः रासिन्, -वाशनः, वाशिन्** *m.* a jackal. -**रूपः** an epithet of Siva.

घोलः -लं Butter-milk having no water in it; (तत्तु सस्नेहमजलं मथितं घोलमुच्यते Susr.)

घोषः 1 Noise, tumult, cry or sound in general; स घोषो धार्तराष्ट्राणां हृदयानि व्यदारयत् Bg. 1. 19; so रथ°, तुर्य°, शंख° &c. 2 The thundering of clouds; स्निग्धगंभीरघोषं Me. 64. 3 Proclamation. 4 Rumour, report. 5 A herdsman; हैयंगवीनमादाय घोषवृद्धानुपस्थितान् R. 1. 45. 6 A hamlet, station of cowherds; गंगायां घोषः K. P. 2; घोषादानीय Mk. 7. 7. (In gram). The soft sound heard in the articulation of the soft consonant. 8 A Kâyastha. -**षं** Bellmetal.

घोषणं, -णा Proclamation, declaring, or speaking aloud, public announcement; व्याघातो जयघोषणादिषु बलादस्मद्बलानां कृतः Mu. 3. 26; R. 12. 72.

घोषयित्नुः 1 A crier, bard, herald. 2 A Brâhmaṇa. 3 A cuckoo.

घ्न *a.* (घ्नी *f*) (Used only at the end of comp.) Killing, destroying, removing, curing; ब्राम्हणघ्नः, बालघ्नः, वातघ्नः, पित्तघ्नः; depriving one of, taking away; पुण्यघ्न, धर्मघ्न &c.

घ्रा 1 P. (जिघ्रति, घ्रात-घ्राण) 1 To smell, smell at, perceive by smell; स्पृशन्नपि गजो हंति जिघ्रन्नपि भुजंगमः H. 3. 14; Bv. 1. 99. 2. To kiss. -*Caus.* (घ्रापयति) To cause to smell; Bk. 15. 109. (Prepositions like **अव, आ, उप, वि, सं** &c. are added to this root without any material change of meaning; गंधमाघ्राय चोर्व्याः Me. 21; आमोदमुपजिघ्रंतौ R. 1. 43; see Bk. 2. 10; 14. 12; R. 3. 3; 13. 70; Ms. 4. 209 also).

घ्राण *p. p.* Smelt. -**णं** 1 The act of smelling; घ्राणेन सूकरो हंति Ms. 3. 241. 2 Odour, scent. 3 The nose; बुद्धींद्रियाणि चक्षुः श्रोत्रघ्राणरसनात्वगाख्यानि Sân. K. 26; Rs. 6. 27; Ms. 5. 135. -Comp.-**इंद्रियं** the organ or sense of smell; नासाग्रवर्ति घ्राणं T. S. -**चक्षुस्** *a.* 'having nose for the eyes', blind (who smells out his way). -**तर्पण** *a.* grateful or pleasant to the nose, fragrant, odorous. (-**णं**) fragrance, odour.

घ्रातिः *f.* 1 the act of smelling; घ्रातिरगेयमद्ययोः Ms. 11. 68. 2 The nose.

च.

चः 1 The moon. 2 A tortoise. 3 A thief. —*ind.* A particle expressing 1 Copulation (and, also, as well as, moreover) used to join words or assertions together; (in this sense it is used with each of the words or assertions which it joins together, or it is used after the last of the words or assertions so joined, but it never stands first in a sentence); मनो निष्ठाशून्यं भ्रमति च किमप्यालिखति च Mâl. 1. 31; तौ गुरुर्गुरुपत्नी च प्रीत्या प्रतिननंदतुः R. 1. 57; Ms. 1. 64; 3. 5; कुलेन कांत्या वयसा नवेन गुणैश्च तैस्तैर्विनयप्रधानैः R. 6. 79; Ms. 1. 105; 3. 115. 2 Disjunction (but, still, yet); शांतमिदमाश्रमपदं स्फुरति च बाहुः S. 1. 16. 3 Certainty, determination (indeed, certainly, exactly, quite, having the force of एव); अतीतः पंथानं तव च महिमा वाङ्मनसयोः G. M.; ते तु यावंत एवाजौ तावांश्च ददृशे स तैः R. 12. 45. 4 Condition (if=चेत्); जीवितुं चेच्छसे (=इच्छसे चेद्) मूढ हेतुं मे गदतः शृणु Mb.; लोभश्चास्ति (अस्ति चेद्) गुणेन किं Bh. 2. 45. v. l. 5 It is often used expletively (पादपूरणार्थे); भीमः पार्थस्तथैव च G. M. (Lexicographers give, besides the above, the following senses of च which are included in the general idea of *copulation*; 1 अन्वाचय joining a subordinate fact with a principal one; भो भिक्षामट गां चानय; see अन्वाचय. 2 समाहार collective combination; as पाणी च पादौ च पाणिपादं. 3 इतरेतरयोग or mutual connection; as प्लक्षश्च न्यग्रोधश्च प्लक्षन्यग्रोधौ. 4 समुच्चय aggregation; as पचति च पठति

च). च is frequently repeated with two assertions (1) in the sense of 'on the one hand– on the other hand,' 'though–yet,' to denote antithesis; न सुलभा सकलेंदुमुखी च सा किमपि चेदमनंगविचेष्टितं V. 2. 9; 4. 3; R. 16. 7; or (2 to express simultaneous or undelayed occurrence of two events (no sooner than, as soon as); ते च प्रापुरुदन्वंतं बुबुधे चादिपूरुषः R. 10. 6; 3. 40; Ku. 3. 58, 66; S. 6. 7; Mâl 9. 39.

चक् 1 U (चकति–ते, चकित) 1 To be satiated, be contented or satisfied 2 To repel, resist.

चकास् 2 P. (rarely A.) (चकास्ति-स्ते, चकासित) 1 To shine, be bright; गंडश्रीडि चकास्ति नीलनलिनश्रीमोचनं लोचनं Git. 10; चकासतं चारुचमूरुचर्मणा Si. 1. 8; Bk. 3. 37. 2 (Fig.) To be happy or prosperous; वितन्वतिक्षेममदेवमातृकाश्चिराय तस्मिन् कुरवश्चकासते Ki. 1. 17. –*Caus.* To cause to shine, illuminate; Si. 3. 6. –With वि to shine, be bright.

चकित *a.* 1 Shaking, trembling (through fear); भय°, साध्वस°; Ve. 27. 2 Frightened, made to tremble, startled; व्याधानुसारचकिता हरिणीव यासि Mk. 1. 17; Amaru. 46; Me. 13. 3 Afraid, timid, apprehensive; चकितविलोकितसकलदिशा Git. 2; पौलस्त्यचकितेश्वराः (दिशः) R. 10. 73. –तं *ind.* With fear, in a startled manner, alarmingly, with awe; चकितमुपैमि तथापि पार्थमस्य M. 1. 11; समयचकितं Git. 5; Sânti. 4. 4.

चकोरः A kind of bird, the Greek partridge (said to feed on moonbeams); ज्योत्स्नापानमदालसेन वपुषा मत्ताश्चकोरांगनाः Vb. 1. 11; इतश्चकोराक्षि विलोकयेति R. 6. 59; 7. 25; स्फुरदधरसीधवे तव वदनचंद्रमा रोचयति लोचनचकोरं Git. 10.

चक्रं 1 The wheel of a carriage; चक्रवत्परिवर्तंते दुःखानि च सुखानि च H. 1. 173. 2 A potter's wheel. 3 A sharp circular missile weapon, a disc (especially applied to the weapon of Vishṇu). 4 An oil-mill. 5 A circle, ring; कलापचक्रेषु निवेशिताननं Rs. 2. 14. 6 A troop, multitude, collection, Si. 20. 16. 7 A realm, sovereignty. 8 A province, district, a group of villages. 9 A form of military array in a circle. 10 A circle or depression of the body. 11 A cycle, cycle of years. 12 The horizon. 13 An army, a host. 14 Section of a book. 15 A whirlpool. 16 The winding of a river.–क्रः 1 The ruddy goose (also called चक्रवाक). 2 A multitude, troop, group. –Comp. –अंगः 1 a gander having a curved neck. 2 a carriage. 3 the ruddy goose (चक्रवाक).–अटः 1 a juggler, snake-catcher. 2 a rogue, knave, cheat. 3 a particular coin, a *dinâra.* आकार, –आकृति *a.* circular, round. –आयुधः an epithet of Vishṇu. –आवर्तः whirling or rotatory motion. –आह्वः, –आह्वयः the ruddy goose; चक्राह्वं ग्रामकुक्कुटं Ms. 5. 12.–ईश्वरः 1 'lord of the discus,' N. of Vishṇu. 2 the officer in charge of a district. –उपजीविन् *m.* an oil-man. –कारकं 1 a nail. 2 a kind of perfume –गंडुः a round pillow. –गतिः *f.* rotation, revolution. –गुच्छः the Asoka tree. –ग्रहणं,–णी *f.* a rampart, an entrenchment. –चर *a.* moving in a circle. –चूडामणिः a round jewel in a crownet or diadem.–जीवकः –जीविन् *m.* a potter. तीर्थं N. of a holy place. दंष्ट्रः a hog.–धरः 1 an epithet of Vishṇu; चक्रधरप्रभावः R. 16. 55. 2 a sovereign, governor or ruler of a province. 3 a village tumbler or juggler. –धारा the periphery of a wheel. –नाभिः the nave of a wheel. –नामन् *m.* 1 the ruddy goose (चक्रवाक). 2 a pyritic ore of iron. –नायकः 1 the leader of a troop 2 a kind of perfume. –नेमिः *f.* the periphery or circumference of a wheel; नीचैर्गच्छत्युपरि च दशा चक्रनेमिक्रमेण Me. 109. –पाणिः an epithet of Vishṇu. –पादः, –पादकः 1 a carriage. 2 an elephant. –पालः 1 the governor of a province. 2 an officer in charge of a division of an army. 3 horizon. –बंधुः, –बांधवः the sun. –बालः–डः वालः–लं, –डं 1 a ring, circle. 2 a collection, group, multitude, mass; कैरवचक्रवालं Bh. 2. 74. 3 horizon. (–लः) 1 a mythical range of mountains supposed to encircle the orb of the earth like a wall and to be the limit of light and darkness. 2 the ruddy goose. –भृत् *m.* 1 one who holds a disc. 2 N. of Vishṇu. –भेदिनी night. –भ्रमः, –भ्रमिः *f.* a lathe or grindstone; आरोप्य चक्रभ्रमिमुष्णतेजास्त्वष्ट्रेव यत्नोल्लिखितो विभाति R. 6. 32. –मंडलिन् *m.* a species of cobra. –मुखः a hog. –यानं a wheel-carriage –रदः a hog. –वर्तिन् *m.* 1 an emperor, universal monarch, sovereign of the world, a ruler whose dominions extend as far as the ocean (आसमुद्रक्षितीश Ak.); पुत्रमेवंगुणोपेतं चक्रवर्तिनमाप्नुहि S. 1. 12; तव तन्वि कुचावेतौ नियतं चक्रवर्तिनौ । आसमुद्रक्षितीशोऽपि भवान् यत्र करप्रदः ॥ Udb; (where there is a pun on the word चक्रवर्तिन्, the other meaning being 'resembling in shape the ruddy goose', 'round'). –वाकः (की *f.*) the ruddy goose; दूरीभूते मयि सहचरे चक्रवाकीमिवैकां Me. 83. –वाटः 1 a limit, boundary. 2 a lampstand. 3 engaging in an action. –वातः a whirlwind, hurricane. –वृद्धिः interest upon interest, compound interest; Ms. 8. 153, 156. –व्यूहः a circular array of troops. –संज्ञं tin. (–ज्ञः) the ruddy goose. –साह्वयः the ruddy goose. –हस्तः an epithet of Vishṇu.

चक्रक *a.* Wheel-shaped, circular. –कः Arguing in a circle (in logic).

चक्रवत् *a.* 1 Wheeled. 2 Circular. –*m.* 1 An oilman. 2 A sovereign, emperor. 3 N. of Vishṇu.

चक्राकी, चक्रांकी A goose.

चक्रिका 1 A heap, troop. 2 A fraudulent device. 3 The knee.

चक्रिन् *m.* 1 An epithet of Vishṇu; Si. 13. 22. 2 A potter. 3 An oilman. 4 An emperor, a universal monarch, absolute ruler. 5 The governor of a province. 6 An ass. 7 The ruddy goose. 8 An informer. 9 A snake. 10 A crow. 11 A kind of tumbler or juggler.

चक्रिय *a.* Going in a carriage, being on a journey.

चक्रीवत् *m.* An ass; Si. 5. 8.

चक्ष् 2 A. (चष्टे) (Defective in non-conjugational tenses) 1 To see, observe, perceive. 2 To speak, say, tell (with dat. of the person). With आ to speak, declare, relate, narrate, tell, teach, communicate; (with dat. of the person); R. 5. 19; 12. 55; Ms. 4. 59, 80; इत्याख्यानविद् आचक्षते Mâl. 2. 2. to say or address oneself to; Bv. 1. 63. 3 to name, call. –परि 1 to declare, relate. 2 to enumerate. 3 to mention. 4 to name, call; वेदप्रदानादाचार्यं पितरं परिचक्षते Ms 2. 171; Bg. 17. 13, 17. –प्र 1 to say, speak, lay down; स्वजनाश्रु किलातिसंततं दहति प्रेतमिति प्रचक्षते R. 8. 86. 2 to name, call; यौऽस्यात्मनः कारयिता तं क्षेत्रज्ञं प्रचक्षते Ms. 12. 12, 2. 17, 3, 28, 10. 14. –प्रत्या to repudiate, cast off, repulse. –व्या to explain, comment upon.

चक्षुस् *m.* 1 A teacher, an instructor in sacred science, a spiritual teacher. 2 An epithet of Brihaspati.

चक्षुष्य *a.* 1 Good-looking, agreeable to the sight, pleasing, beautiful. 2 Good for the eyes. –ष्या A pleasing or agreeable woman.

चक्षुस् *n.* 1 The eye; दृश्यं तमसि न पश्यति दीपेन विना सचक्षुरपि M. 1. 9; कृष्णसारे ददच्चक्षुः S. 1. 6; cf. words like घ्राणचक्षुस्, ज्ञानचक्षुस्, नयचक्षुस्, चारचक्षुस् &c. 2 Sight, look, vision, the faculty of sight; चक्षुरायुश्चैव प्रहीयते Ms 4. 41, 42. –Comp. –गोचर *a.* Visible, being within the range of the eye. –दानं the ceremony of anointing the eyes of an image at the time of consecrating it. –पथः the range of sight, the horizon. –मलं the excretion of the eyes –रागः (चक्षूरागः) 1 redness in the eyes. 2 'eye-love', love or liking as expressed by an exchange of glances; पुरश्चक्षूरागस्तदनु मनसोऽनन्यपरता Mâl. 6. 15; चक्षूरागः कोकिलेषु न परकलत्रेषु K. 41 (where the word has sense 1 also). –रोगः (चक्षूरोगः): a disease of the eye.

-विषयः 1 the range of sight, ken, presence, visibility; चक्षुर्विषयातिक्रांतेषु कपोतेषु H. 1; Ms. 2. 198. 2 an object of sight, any visible object. 3 the horizon. -श्रवस् m. a serpent; Ki. 16. 42; N. 1. 28.

चक्षुष्मत् *a.* 1 Seeing, furnished with eyes, endowed with the faculty of sight; तदा चक्षुष्मतां प्रीतिरासीत्समरसा द्वयोः R. 4. 18; °ता 4. 13. 2 Having a clear sight or good eyes.

चंक्रुणः, -रः 1 A tree. 2 A carriage. 3 A vehicle in general (*n.* also).

चंक्रमणं 1 Moving or going about, walking; विषं चंक्रमणं रात्रौ Chân. 97. चक्रे स चक्रनिभचंक्रमणच्छलेन N. 1. 144. 2 Going slowly or tortuously.

चंच् 1. P. (चंचति, चंचित) 1 To move, wave, shake; समरशिरसि चंचत्पंचचूडश्चमूनां U. 5. 2. Mâl. 5. 23; चंचच्चंचू Nâg. 4; चंचत्पराग Gît. 1. 2 To dangle about; विलपति हसति विषीदति रोदिति चंचति मुंचति तापं Gît. 4.

चंचः 1 A basket. 2 A measure of length equal to 5 fingers (पंचांगुलं मानं).

चंचरिन् *m.* The large black bee; करी बरीभरीति चेद् दिशं सरीसरीति कां । स्थिरी चरीकरीति चेन्न चंचरीति चंचरी Udb.

चंचरीकः A largo black bee; चुलुकयति मदीयां चेतनां चंचरीकः R. G. कुंदलताया विमुक्तमकरंदरसाया अपि चंचरीकः । प्रणयप्ररूढप्रेमभर-भंजनकातरभावभीतः ॥ Vb. 1. 4; Vikr. 1. 2; Bv. 1. 48.

चंचल *a.* 1 Moving, shaking, trembling, tremulous; श्रुत्वैव भीतहरिणीशिशुचंचलाक्षीं Ch. P. 27; चंचलकुंडल Gît. 7; Amaru. 79. 2 (Fig.) Inconstant, fickle, unsteady; भोगा मेघवितानमध्यविलसत्सौदामिनीचंचलाः Bh. 3. 54; Ki. 2. 19; मनश्चंचलमस्थिरं Bg. 6. 26. -लः 1 The wind. 2 A lover. 3 A libertine. -ला 1 Lightening. 2 Lakshmi, the goddess of wealth.

चंचा 1 Anything made of cane. 2 A straw-man, doll.

चंचु *a.* 1 Celebrated, renowned, known. 2 Clever (as अक्षरचंचु) see चुंचु. -चुः A deer. -चुः, -चू *f.* A beak, bill. -Comp. -पुटः, -टं the bill of a bird when shut; चंचूपुटं चपलयंति चकोरपोताः R. G.; Bv. 2. 99; अमोचि चंचूपुटमौनमुद्रा विहायसा तेन विहस्य भूयः N. 3. 99; व्यालिखच्चंचुपुटेन पक्षती 2. 2, 4; Amaru. 13. -प्रहारः a peck with the beak. -भृत्, -मत्, *m.* a bird. -सूचिः the tailor-bird.

चंचुर *a.* Clever, expert.

चट् I. 1 P. (चटति, चटित) To break, fall off, separate. -II. 10 U. (चाटयति-ते) 1 To kill, injure. 2 To pierce, break. -With उद् 1 to scare away, terrify, frighten. 2 to root out, remove, destroy; N. 3. 7. 3 to kill, injure.

चटकः A sparrow.

चटका, चटिका A hen-sparrow.

चटु -टु *n.* Kind or flattering words; see चाटु. -टुः The belly.

चटुल *a.* 1 Trembling, tremulous, unsteady, moving about, shaking; आयस्तमैक्षत जनश्चटुलाग्रपादं Si. 5, 6; त्रासातिमात्रचटुलैः स्मरतः सुनेत्रैः R. 9. 58; चटुलशफरोद्वर्तनप्रेक्षितानि Me. 40. 2 Fickle, inconstant (as love &c.); किं लब्धं चटुल त्वयेह नयता सौभाग्यमेतां दशां Amaru. 14; चटुलप्रेम्णा दयितेन 71. 3 Fine, beautiful, agreeable; इति चटुलचाटुपटुचारु मुरवैरिणो राधिकामधि वचनजातं Gît. 10. -ला Lightening.

चटुलोल, चट्टलोल *a.* 1 Tremulous. 2 Lovely, beautiful. 3 Talking sweet words.

चण *a.* (At the end of comp.) Renowned, celebrated, skilled in, famous for; अक्षरचणः. -णः The chick-pea.

चणकः Chick-pea; उत्पतितोपि हि चणकः शक्तः किं भ्राष्ट्रकं भंक्तुं Pt. 1 132.

चंड *a.* 1 (*a*) Fierce, violent, impetuous, passionate, angry, wrathful; अथैकधेनोरपराधचंडात् गुरोः कृशानुप्रतिमाद् बिभेषि R. 2. 49; M. 3. 20; see चंडी below. 2 Hot, warm; as in चंडांशु. 3 Active, quick. 4 Pungent, acrid. -डं 1 Heat, warmth. 2 Passion, wrath. -Comp. -अंशुः, -दीधितिः, -भानुः the sun. -ईश्वरः a form of Siva. -मुंडा a form of Durgâ; (=चामुंडा q. v.). -मृगः a wild animal. -विक्रम *a.* of impetuous valour, fierce in prowess.

चंडा, -डी *f.* 1 An epithet of Durgâ. 2 A passionate or angry woman; चंडी चंडं हंतुमभ्युद्यता मां M. 3. 21; चंडी मामवधूय पादपतितं जातानुतापेव सा V. 4. 28; R. 12. 5; Me. 105. -Comp. -ईश्वरः, -पतिः an epithet of Siva; पुण्यं यायास्त्रिभुवनगुरोर्धाम चंडीश्वरस्य Me. 33.

चंडातः The fragrant oleander.

चंडातकः, -कं A short petticoat.

चंडाल *a.* Wicked or cruel in deeds, of black deeds (क्रूरकर्मन्); *cf.* कर्मचांडाल. -लः A general name for the lowest and most despised of the mixed castes originating from a Sudra father and a Brâhmanna mother. 2 A man of this caste, an outcast; चंडालः किमयं द्विजातिरथवा Bh. 3. 56; Ms. 5. 131; 10. 12, 16; 11. 175. -Comp. -वल्लकी the lute of a Chânḍala, a common or vulgar lute.

चंडालिका The lute of a Chânḍâla.

चंडिका N. of Durgâ.

चंडिमन् *m.* 1 Passion, violence, impetuosity, wrath, 2 Heat, warmth.

चंडिलः A barber.

चतुर् *num. a.* (always in pl.; चत्वार *m.* चतस्रः *f.*; चत्वारि *n.*) Four; चत्वारो वयमृत्विजः Ve. 1. 22; चतस्रोऽवस्था बाल्यं कौमारं यौवनं वार्धकं चेति; चत्वारि श्रृंगा त्रयोऽस्य पादाः &c.; शेषान् मासान् गमय चतुरो लोचने मीलयित्वा Me. 110. [In comp. the र् of चतुर् is changed to a visarga (which in some cases becames स्, ष् or remains unchanged) before words beginning with hard consonants]. Comp. -अंशः a fourth part. -अंग *a.* having 4 members, quadripartite. (-गं) 1 a complete army consisting of elephants, chariots, cavalry, and infantry; एको हि खंजनवरो नलिनीदलस्थो दृष्टः करोति चतुरंगबलाधिपत्यं Si. Til. 4; चतुरंगबलो राजा जगतीं वशमानयेत् । अहं पंचांगबलवानाकाशं वशमानये Subhâsh. 2 a sort of chess. -अंत *a.* bordered on all sides; भूत्वा चिराय चतुरंतमहीसपत्नी S. 4. 19. -अंता the earth. अशीत *a.* eighty-fourth. अशीति- *a.* or *f.* eighty-four.-अश्र,-अस्र *a.*(for अश्रि-स्रि) 1 four-cornered, quadrangular; R. 6. 10. 2 symmetrical, regular or handsome in all parts; बभूव तस्याश्चतुरस्र शोभि वपुः Ku. 1. 32. (श्रः,-स्रः) a square. -अहं period of four days. -आननः an epithet of Brahmâ; इतरतापशतानि यथेच्छया वितर तानि सहे चतुरानन Udb. -आश्रमं the four orders or stages of the religious life of a Brâhmaṇa. -उत्तर *a.* increasing by four. -कर्ण (चतुष्कर्ण) *a.* heard by two persons only. -कोण (चतुष्कोण) *a.* square, quadrangular. (-णः) a square, tetragon, any quadrilateral figure. -गतिः 1 the supreme soul. 2 a tortoise -गुण *a.* four-times, four-fold, quadruple. -चत्वारिंशत् (चतुश्चत्वारिंशत्) *a.* forty-four; °िंश forty-fourth. -णवत (चतुर्णवत) *a.* ninety-fourth, or with ninety-four added; चतुर्णवतं शतं 'one hundred and ninety-four'. -दंतः an epithet of Airâvata, the elephant of Indra. -दश *a.* fourteenth. -दशन् *a.* fourteen. °रत्नानि (pl.) the fourteen 'jewels' churned out of the ocean; (their names are contained in the following popular Mangalâshṭaka:—लक्ष्मीः कौस्तुभपारिजातकसुरा धन्वंतरिश्चंद्रमा गावो कामदुघाः सुरेश्वरगजो रंभादिदेवांगनाः । अश्वः सप्तमुखो विषं हरिधनुः शंखोऽमृतं चांबुधे रत्नानीह चतुर्दश प्रतिदिनं कुर्युः सदा मंगलं). ॥ -°विद्याः (pl.) the fourteen lores; (they are :-षडंगमिश्रिता वेदा धर्मशास्त्रं पुराणकं । मीमांसा तर्कमपि च एता विद्याश्चतुर्दश ॥). -दशी the fourteenth day of a lunar fortnight. -दिशं the four quarters taken collectively. -दिशं *ind.* towards the four quarters, on all sides.-दोलः, -लं a royal litter.-द्वारं 1 a house with four entrances on four sides. 2 four doors taken collectively. -नवति *a.* or *f.* ninety-four. -पंच *a.* (चतुः पंच or चतुष्पंच) four or five. पंचाशत् *f.* (चतुः पंचाशत् or चतुष्पंचाशत्) fifty four.-पथः (चतुः पथः or चतुष्पथः) (-थं also) a place where four roads meet, a crossway; Ms. 4. 39, 9. 264. (-थः) a Brâhmaṇa. -पद *a.* (चतुष्पद) 1

having four feet. 2 consisting of four limbs. (**-दः**) a quadruped. (**-दी**) a stanza of four lines; पद्यं चतुष्पदी तच्च वृत्तं जातिरिति द्विधा Chand. M. 1. **पाठी** (चतुष्पाठी) a school for Brâhmaṇas in which the four Vedas are taught and repealed. **-पाणिः** (चतुष्पाणिः) an epithet of Vishṇu. **-पाद्-द** (चतुष्पाद् द) *a.* 1 quadruped. 2 consisting of four members or parts. (*-m.*) 1 a quadruped. 2 (in law) a judicial procedure (trial of suits) consisting of four processes; *i. e.* plea, defence rejoinder and judgment. **-बाहुः** an epithet of Vishṇu. (**-हु** *n.*) a square. **-भद्रं** the aggregate of the four ends of human life (पुरुषार्थ); *i. e.* धर्म, अर्थ, काम and मोक्ष. **-भागः** the fourth part, a quarter. **-भुज्** *a.* 1 quadrangular. 2 having four arms; Bg. 11. 46. (*-m.*) an epithet of Vishṇu; R. 16. 3. (*-n.*) a square. **-मासं** a period of four months; (reckoned from the 11th day in the bright half of आषाढ to the 11th day in the bright half of कार्तिक). **-मुख** having four faces. (**-खः**) an epithet of Brahmâ; त्वत्तः सर्वं चतुर्मुखात् R. 10. 22. (**-खं**) 1 four faces; Ku. 2. 17. 2 a house with four entrances. **-युगं** the aggregate of the four *Yugas* or ages of the world. **-रात्रं** (चतूरात्रं) an aggregate of four nights. **-वक्त्रः** an epithet of Brahmâ. **-वर्गः** the four ends of human life taken collectively (पुरुषार्थ); *i. e.* धर्म अर्थ, काम and मोक्ष; R. 10. 22. **-वर्णः** the four classes or castes of the Hindus; *i. e.* ब्राम्हण, क्षत्रिय, वैश्य and शूद्र; चतुर्वर्णमयो लोकः R. 10. 22. **-वर्षिका** a cow four years old. **-विंश** *a.* 1 twenty-four. 2 having twenty-four added; as चतुर्विंशशतं (124). **विंशति** *a.* or *f.* twenty-four. **-विंशतिक** *a.* consisting of twenty-four. **-विद्य** *a.* one who has studied the four Vedas. **-विद्या** the four Vedas. **-विध** *a.* of four sorts or kinds, fourfold. **-वेद** *a.* familiar with the four Vedas. (**-दः**) the supreme soul. **-व्यूहः** N. of Vishṇu. (**-हं**) medical science. **-शालं** (चतुः शालं, चतुश्शालं, चतुःशाली, चतुश्शाली) a square of four buildings, a quadrangle enclosed by four buildings. **-षष्टि** *a.* or *f.* sixty-four. °**कलाः** (pl.) the sixty-four arts. **-सप्तति** *a.* or *f.* seventy-four. **-हायन-ण** *a.* four years old; (the *f.* of this word ends in आ if it refers to an inanimate object, and in ई if it refers to an animal). **-होत्रकं** the four priests taken collectively.

चतुर *a.* 1 Clever, skilful, ingenious, sharp-witted; सर्वात्मना रतिकथाचतुरेव दूती Mu. 3. 9; Amaru. 15, 44; मृगया जहार चतुरेव कामिनी R. 9. 69; 18. 15. 2 Quick, swift. 3 Charming, beautiful, lovely, agreeable; न पुनरेति गतं चतुरं वयः R. 9. 47; Ku. 1. 47; 3. 5; 5 49. **—रं** 1 Cleverness, ingenuity. 2 An elephant's stable.

चतुर्थ *a.* (**र्थी** *f.*) The fourth. **-र्थं** A quarter, a fourth part. –Comp. **-आश्रमः** the fourth stage of a Brâhmaṇa's religious life, *Sannyâsa*. **-भाज्** *a.* receiving a fourth part of every source of income from the subjects, as a king; (this is allowed only in times of financial embarrassments, the usual share being a sixth.).

चतुर्थक *a.* The fourth. **-कः** A fever that returns or is repeated every four days, a quartan.

चतुर्थी 1 The fourth day of a lunar fortnight. 2 The dative case (in gram.).– Comp. **-कर्मन्** *n.* the ceremonies to be performed on the fourth day of the marriage.

चतुर्धा *ind.* In four ways, fourfold.

चतुष्क *a.* 1 Consisting of four. 2 Increased by four; द्विकं त्रिकं चतुष्कं च पंचकं च शतं समं Ms. 8. 142 (*i. e.* 102, 103, 104, or 105, or interest at the rate of 2 to 5 per cent). **-ष्कं** 1 A collection of four. 2 A crossway. 3 A quadrangular courtyard. 4 A hall resting on (four) pillars, a hall or saloon in general; Ku. 5. 69, 7. 9. **-ष्की** 1 A large four-sided pond. 2 A mosquito curtain.

चतुष्टय *a.* (**यी** *f.*) Four-fold, consisting of four; पुराणस्य कवेस्तस्य चतुर्मुखसमीरिता । प्रवृत्तिरासीच्छब्दानां चरितार्था चतुष्टयी ॥ Ku. 2. 17. **-यं** A group or collection of four; एकैकमप्यनर्थाय किमु यत्र चतुष्टयं H. Pr. 11; Ku. 7. 62; मासचतुष्टयस्य भोजनं H. 1. 2 A square.

चत्वरं 1 A quadrangular place or courtyard. 2 A place where many roads meet; सखलु श्रेष्ठिचत्वरं निवसति Mk. 2. 3 A levelled spot of ground prepared for a sacrifice.

चत्वारिंशत् *f.* Forty.

चत्वालः 1 A hole in the ground prepared for an oblation or for the sacrificial fire. 2 Kuṡa grass. 3 Womb.

चद् 1 U. (चदति-ते) To ask, beg.

चदिरः 1 The moon. 2 Camphor. 3 An elephant. 4 A snake.

चन *ind.* Not, not also, even not (not used by itself but used in combination with the pronoun किम् or its derivatives, such as कद्, कथं, क, कदा, कुतः to which it imparts an indefinite sense; see under किम्). *Note*–Some regard चन to be not a separate word, but a combination of च and न.

चंद् 1 P. (चंदति, चंदित) 1 To shine, to be glad or rejoiced.

चंदः 1 The moon. 2 Camphor.

चंदनः-नं Sandal, (the tree, the wood, or any unctuous preparation of the wood, held in high estimation as a perfume and refrigerant application); अनलाया गुरुचंदनैधसे R. 8. 71; मणिप्रकाराः सरसं च चंदनं शुचौ प्रिये यांति जनस्य सेव्यतां Rs. 1. 2; एवं च भाषते लोकश्चंदनं किल शीतलं । पुत्रगात्रस्य संस्पर्शश्चंदनादातिरिच्यते Pt. 5. 20; विना मलयमन्यत्र चंदनं न प्ररोहति 1. 41. –Comp. **-अचलः**, **-गिरिः**, **-अद्रिः** the Malaya mountain. **-उदकं** sandal-water. **-पुष्पं** cloves. **-सारः** the most excellent sandal-wood.

चंदिरः 1 An elephant. 2 The moon; अपि च मानसमंबुनिधिर्यशो विमलशारदचंदिरचंद्रिका Bv. 1. 113; मुकुंदमुखचंदिरे चिरमिदं चकोरायतां 4. 1.

चंद्रः 1 The moon; यथा प्रल्हादनाच्चंद्रः R. 4. 12; हृतचंद्रा तमसेव कौमुदी 8. 37; न हि संहरते ज्योत्स्नां चंद्रश्चांडालवेश्मनि H. 1. 61; मुख°, वदन° &c.; पर्याप्तचंद्रेव शरत्त्रियामा Ku. 7. 26 (for mythological account see सोम). 2 The moon, as a planet. 3 Camphor; विलेपनस्याधिकचंद्रभागताविभावनाच्चापललाप पांडुता N. 1. 51. 4 The eye in a peacock's tail. 5 Water. 6 Gold. (Used at the end of comp. चंद्र means 'excellent', 'eminent', or 'illustrious'; as पुरुषचंद्रः 'a moon of men', an excellent or illustrious man). **—द्रा** 1 The cardamoms. 2 An open hall only furnished with a roof. –Comp. **-अंशुः** a moonbeam. **-अर्धः** the half moon. °**चूडामणिः, मौलिः,** °**शेखरः** epithets of *Siva*. **-आतपः** 1 moon-light. 2 awning. 3 an open hall only furnished with a roof. **-आत्मजः**, **औरसः**, **-जः**, **-जातः**, **-तनयः**, **नंदनः**, **-पुत्रः** the planet Mercury. **-आनन** *a.* moon-faced. (**-नः**) an epithet of Kârtikeya. **आपीडः** an epithet of *Siva*. **-आभासः** 'false moon', an appearance in the sky resembling the real moon. **-आह्वयः** camphor. **-इष्टा** a lotus plant, or a collection of lotuses, blossoming during the night. **-उदयः** moon-rise. **-उपलः** the moon-stone. **-कांतः** the moon-stone (supposed to ooze away under the influence of the moon); द्रवति च हिमरश्मावुद्गते चंद्रकांतः U. 6. 12; *Si.* 4. 58; Amaru. 57; Bh. 1. 21; Mâl. 1. 24. (**-तः -तं**) the white water-lily blossoming during the night. (**-तं**) sandal-wood **-कला** a digit of the moon; राहोश्चंद्रकलामिवाननचरीं दैवात्समासाद्य मे Mâl. 5. 28. **कांता** 1 a night. 2 moon-light. **-कांतिः** moon-light. (*-n.*) silver. **-क्षयः** the new-moon-day or the last day of a lunar month (अमा) when the moon is not visible. **-गृहं** the fourth sign of the zodiac, *Cancer*. **-गोलः** the world of the moon, lunar sphere. **गोलिका** moon-light. **-ग्रहणं**

an eclipse of the moon. -चंचला a small fish. -चूडः, -मौलिः, -शेखरः, चूडामणिः epithets of *S*iva; रहस्युपालम्यत चंद्रशेखरः Ku. 5. 58, 86; R. 6. 34. -दाराः (*m. pl.*) 'the wives of the moon', the 27 lunar mansions mythologically regarded as so many daughters of Daksha and married to the moon. -द्युतिः sandalwood (*-f.*) moonlight. -नामन्. *m.* comphor. -पादः a moonbeam; Me. 70; Mâl. 3. 12. -प्रभा moonlight. -बाला 1 large cardamoms. 2 moonlight. -बिंदुः the sign for the nasal (ँ). -भस्मन् *n.* camphor. -भागा N. of a river in the south. -भासः a sword; see चंद्रहास. -भूति *n.* silver. मणिः the moon-stone रेखा,-लेखा the digit or streak of the moon. -रेणुः a plagiarist. -लोकः the world of the moon. -लोहकं, -लौहं, -लौहकं Silver. -वंशः the lunar race of kings, the second great line of royal dynasties in India. -वदन *a.* moon faced. -व्रतं a kind of vow or penance =चांद्रायण q. v. -शाला 1 a room on the top (of a house &c.); R. 13.40. 2 moonlight. -शालिका a room on the top of a house. -शिला the moonstone; Bk 11. 15. -संज्ञः camphor -संभवः N. of Budha or Mercury. (-वा) small cardamoms. -सालोक्यं attainment of the lunar heaven. -हन् *n.* an epithet of Râhu. -हासः 1 a glittering sword. 2 the sword of Râvaṇa; हे पाणयः किमिति वांछथ चंद्रहासं B. R. 1. 56, 61. 3 N of a king of Kerala, son of Sudhârmika. [He was born under the Mûla asterism and his left foot had a redundant toe; for this his father was killed by his enemies, and the boy was left an orphan in a state of destitution. After much exertion he was restored to his kingdom. He became a friend of Krish*n*a and Arjuna when they came to the South in the course of their wanderings with the sacrificial horse].

चंद्रकः 1 moon. 2 The eye in a peacock's stail. 3 A fingernail. 4 A circle of the moon's shape (formed by a drop of oil thrown into water).

चंद्रकिन् *m.* A peacock; *S*i. 3. 49.

चंद्रमस् *m.* The moon; नक्षत्रताराग्रहसंकुलापि ज्योतिष्मती चंद्रमसैव रात्रिः R. 6. 22.

चंद्रिका 1 Moonlight; इतः स्तुतिः का खलु चंद्रिकाया यदब्धिमप्युत्तरलीकरोति N. 3. 116; R. 19. 39; कामुकैः कुंभीलकैश्च परिहर्तव्या चंद्रिका M. 4. 2 (At the end of comp.) Elucidation, throwing light on the subject treated; अलंकारचंद्रिका, काव्यचंद्रिका; cf. कौमुदि. 3 Illumination. 4 A large cardamom. 5 The river Chandrabhâgâ. 6 The Mallikâ creeper. —Comp. —अंबुजं the white lotus opening at moonrise. -द्रावः the moon-stone. पायिन् *m.* the Chakora bird.

चंद्रिलः 1 A barber. 2 An epithet of *S*iva.

चप् I 1 P. (चपति) To console, soothe —II. 10 U. (चपयति ते) To grind, pound, knead.

चपटः=चपेट q. v.

चपल *a.* 1 Shaking, trembling, tremulous; कुल्याम्भोभिः पवनचपलैः शाखिनो धौतमूलाः *S*. 1. 15; चपलायताक्षी Ch. P. 8. 2 Unsteady, fickle, inconstant, wavering; Sânti. 2. 11; चपलमति &c. 3 Frail, transient, momentary; नलिनीदलगतजलमतितरलं तद्वज्जीवितमतिशयचपलं Moha M. 5. 4 Quick, nimble, agile; (गतं) शैशवाच्चपलमप्यशोभत K. 11. 8. 5 Inconsiderate, rash; cf. चापल. -लः 1 A fish. 2 Quicksilver. 3 The Châtaka bird. 4 Consumption. 5 A sort of perfume.

चपला 1 Lightning; कुरवककुसुमं चपलासुषमं रतिपतिमृगकानने Gît. 7. 2 An unchaste or disloyal wife. 3 Spirituous liquor. 4 Lakshmî, the goddess of wealth. 5 The tongue. -Comp. जनः a fickle or unsteady woman; *S*i. 9. 16.

चपेटः 1 The palm of the hand with the fingers extended. 2 A blow with the open hand.

चपेटा, चपेटिका A blow with open hand; खंडिकोपाध्यायः शिष्याय चपेटिकां ददाति Mbh.

चम् 1 P. (चमति, चांत) 1 To drink sip, drink off; चचाम मधु माध्वीकं Bk. 14. 94. 2 To eat. -With आ (आचामति) 1 To sip, drink off, lick; नाचेमे हिममपि वारि वारणेन Ki. 7. 34; Bv. 4. 38; U. 4. 1. 2 To lick up, dry or drink up, absorb; आचामति स्वेदलवान्मुखे ते R. 13. 20, 9. 68. **चमत्करणं, चमत्कारः, चमत्कृतिः** *f.* 1 Admiration, surprise. 2 Show, spectacle. 3 Poetical charm, that which constitutes the essence of poetry; चेतश्चमत्कृतिपदं कवितेवरम्या Bv. 3.1. तदपेक्षया वाच्यस्यैव चमत्कारित्वात् K. P. 1.

चमरः A kind of deer. **रः -रं** A chowrie most usually made of the tail of Chamara. -री The female Chamara; यस्यार्थयुक्तं गिरिराजशब्दं कुर्वंति बालव्यजनैश्चमर्यः Ku. 1. 1', 48; *S*i. 4. 60. Me. 53, -Comp. -पुच्छं the tail of a Chamara used as a fan. (-च्छः) a squirrel.

चमरिकः The Kovidâra tree.

चमसः -सं A vessel (can, ladle &c). used at sacrifices for drinking the Soma juice; Y. 1. 183 (also चमसी).

चमूः *f.* 1 An army (in general). पश्यैतां पांडुपुत्राणामाचार्य महतीं चमूं Bg. 1. 3; बासवीनां चमूनां Me 43; गजवती जवतीव्रहया चमूः R. 9. 10. 2 A division of an army consisting of 729 elephants, as many cars, 2187 horse, and 3645 foot. -Comp. -चरः a soldier, warrior. -नाथः-पः, -पतिः the leader of an army, a general, commander R. 13. 74. -हरः an epithet of *S*iva.

चमूरः A kind of deer; चकासतं चारुचमूरुचर्मणा *S*i. 1. 8.

चंप् 10 U. (चंपयति-ते) To go, move.

चंपकः 1 A tree bearing yellow, fragrant flowers. 2 A kind of perfume. कं-A flower of this tree; अद्यापि तां कनकचंपकदामगौरीं Ch. P. 1. —Comp. -माला 1 N. of a neck-ornament worn by women. 2 a garland of Champaka flowers. 3 kind of metre (see App.). -रंभा a species of plantain.

चंपकालुः The jack or breadfruit tree.

चंपकावती, चंपा, चंपावती N. of an ancient city on the Ganges, capital of the Angas and identified with the modern Bhagalpura.

चंपालुः=चंपकालु q. v.

चंपूः *f.* A kind of elaborate and highly artificial composition in which the same subject is continued through alterations in prose and verse; गद्यपद्यमयं काव्यं चंपूरित्यभिधीयते S. D. 569; for instance भोजचंपू, नलचंपू, भारतचंपू &c.

चय् 1 A. (चयते) To go to or towards, move.

चयः 1 An assemblage, collection, multitude, heap, mass, चयस्त्विषामित्यवधारितं पुरा *S*i. 1. 3; मृदां चयः U. 2. 9 a lump of clay; कचानां चयः Bh. 1. 5 a braid of hair; so चमरीचयः *S*i. 4. 60 कुसुमचय, तुषारचय. &c. 2 A mound of earth raised to form the foundation of a building. 3 A mound of earth raised from the ditch of a fort. 4 A rampart. 5 The gate of a fort. 6 A seat, stool. 7 A pile of buildings, any edifice. 8 Stacked wood.

चयनं 1 The act of collecting (especially flowers &c). 2 Pilling, heaping.

चर् 1 P. (चरति, चरित) 1 To walk, move, go about, roam, wander; नष्टाशंका हरिणशिशवो मंदमंदं चरंति *S*. 1. 15 (चर may mean here 'to graze' also); इंद्रियाणां हि चरतां Bg. 2. 67; कपयश्चेरुरार्तस्य रामस्येव मनोरथाः R. 12. 59; Ms. 2. 23, 6. 68; 8. 236; 9. 306; 10. 55. 2 To practise, perform, observe; चरतः किल दुश्चरं तपः R. 8 79; Y. 1. 60; Ms. 3. 30. 3 To act, behave towards, conduct oneself (oft. with loc. of the person) चरंतीनां च कामतः Ms. 5. 90; 9. 287; आत्मवत्सर्वभूतेषु यश्चरेत् Mb.; तस्यां त्वं साधु नाचरः R. 1. 76 (where the root may be also आचर्). 4 To graze; सुचिरं हि चरन् शस्यं H. 3. 9. 5 To eat, consume. 6 To be engaged in, be busy with. 7 to live, continue to be, continue in any state.—*Caus.* (चारयति) 1 To cause to move or go. **2** To send, direct, move. **3** To drive away. **4** To cause to perform or practice. **5** To cause to copulate. WITH **अति** **1** to transgress, violate, disobey. **2** To offend. **–अनु** to follow. **–अन्वा** to imitate, follow. **–अप 1** to transgress, offend. **2.** to disgregard. **–अभि 1** to offend, trespass. **2** to be faithless to (as a husband), betray ; Ms. 5. 162 ; 9. 102. **3** to conjure, charm ; तथैवाभिचरन्नपि Y. 1. 295; 3.289. **–आ 1** to act, practise, do, perform ; तपस्विकन्यास्वविनयमाचरति *S*. 1. 25; त्वं च तस्येष्टमाचरेः V. 5. 20; R. 1. 89; Ms. 5. 156 ; न चाप्याचरितः पूर्वैरयं धर्मः Mb. **2** to act or behave towards, treat ; पुत्रमिवाचरेत् शिष्यं Sk.; पुत्रं मित्रवदाचरेत् Chan. 11. **3** to wander, roam over or about. **4** to resort to, follow; R. 4. 44. **–उद् 1** to go upwards; rise, issue or go forth; *Si*. 17. 52. **2** to rise, appear forth, rise (as a voice); उच्चचार निनदोंऽभसि तस्याः R. 9. 73; 15. 46; 16. 87; कोलाहलध्वनिरुदचरत् K. 27. **3** to utter, pronounce; शब्द उच्चरित एव मामगात् R. 11. 73. **4** to empty the body by evacuations, void one's excrement; तिरस्कृत्योच्चरेत्काष्ठलोष्ठपत्रतृणादिना Ms. 4. 49. **5** (Used in the Atm). (*a*) to transgress; stray or deviate from; Bk. 8. 31. (*b*) to rise upto, ascend; N. 5. 48. (*–Caus*). to cause to utter, pronounce. **–उप 1** to serve, attend, wait upon; गिरिशमुपचचार प्रत्यहं सा सुकेशी Ku. 1. 60; समसुपचर भद्रे सुप्रियं चाप्रियं च Mk. 1. 31; R. 5. 62; Ms. 3. 193. **2** to attend on (as a patient), treat (medically), nurse. **3** to act or deal towards. **4** to approach. **–दुस्** to cheat, deceive. **–परि 1** to go or walk about. **2** to serve, wait or attend upon; Ms. 2. 243; Bh 3. 40. **3** to take care of, nurse, tend. **–प्र 1** to walk about, [stalk forth. **2** to spread, be prevalent or current. **3** to prevail (as a custom). **4** to set about (anything), proceed to work; Ms. 9. 284. (*-Caus*). to cause to wander about. **–वि 1** to wander about, roam over; R. 2. 8; Me. 115. **2** to do, perform, practise. **3** to act, deal, behave. (*–Caus.*) **1** to think, reflect for meditate upon. **2** to discuss, debate; R. 14. 46. **3** to calculate, estimate, take into account consider; परेषामात्मनश्चैव यो विचार्य बलाबलं Pt. 3; सुविचार्य यत्कृतं H. 1. 22. **व्यभि 1** to go astray, deviate from. **2** to transgress against, be faithless to. **3** to act crookedly. **–सं** (Atm. when used with the instrumental of a conveyance) **1** to move, walk, go, pass, walk about ; यानैः समचरंतान्ये Bk. 8. 32 ; क्वचित्पथा संचरते सुराणां R. 13. 19 ; N. 6. 57 ; संचरतां घनानां Ku. 1. 6. **2** to practise, perform. **3** to pass over, be transferred to. (*–Caus.*) **1** to cause to go about, lead, conduct ; *S*. 5. 5. **2** to cause to spread, circulate. **3** to transmit, communicate, pass over, deliver over to (as a disease &c.). **4** to turn out to graze.

चर *a*. (**री** *f*.) **1** Moving, going, walking (at the end of comp.). **2** Trembling, shaking. **2** Moveable ; see चराचर below Ms. 3. 201 ; Bg. 13. 15. **4** Animate ; Ms. 5. 29 ; 7. 15. **5** (Used as an affix) formerly, late; आढ्यचर 'one who was formerly rich' ; so देवदत्तचर, अध्यापकचर late teacher &c. **–रः 1** A spy. **2** A wagtail. **3** A game played with dice and men. **4** A cowrie. **5** The planet Mars. **6** (Hence) Tuesday. –COMP. **–अचर** *a*. moveable and immoveable; चराचराणां भूतानां कुक्षिराधारतां गतः Ku. 6. 67 ; 2. 5; Bg. 11. 43. (**–रं**) **1** the aggregate of all created things, the world ; Ms. 1. 57, 63 ; 3. 75 ; Bg 11. 7 ; 9. 10. **2** the sky, the atmosphere. **–द्रव्यं** a moveable thing. **–मूर्तिः** an idol which is carried about in procession.

–चरकः 1 A spy. **2 A** wandering mendicant, a vagrant.

चरटः The wag-tail.

चरणः –णं 1 A foot ; शिरसि चरण एष न्यस्यते वारयैनं Ve. 3. 38 ; जात्या काममवध्योसि चरणं त्विदमुद्धृतं 39. **2** A support, pillar, prop. **3** The root of a tree. **4** The single line of a stanza. **5** A quarter. **6** A school or branch of any of the Vedas. **7** A race. **–णं 1** Moving, roaming, wandering. **2** Performance, practising ; Ms. 6. 75. **3** Conduct of life, behaviour (moral). **4** Accomplishment. **5** Eating, consuming. –COMP. **–अमृतं –उदकं** water in which the feet of a (revered) Brâhmaṇa or spiritual guide have been washed. **–अरविंदं, –कमलं –पद्मं** a lotus-like foot. **–आयुधः** a cock. **–आस्कंदनं** trampling, treading under foot. **–ग्रंथिः** *m*. **–पर्वन्** *n*. the ankle. **–न्यासः** a footstep. **–पः** a tree. **–पतनं** falling down or prostration (at the feet of another); Amaru. 17. **–पतित** *a*. prostrate at the feet : Me. 105. **–शुश्रूषा, –सेवा 1** prostration. **2** service, devotion.

चरम *a*. **1** Last, ultimate, final ; चरमा क्रिया 'the final or funeral ceremony'. **2** Posterior, back ; पृष्ठं तु चरमं तनोः Ak. **3** Old (as age). **4** Outermost. **5** Western, west. **6** Lowest, least. **–मं** *ind*. At last ; at the end. –COMP. **–अचलः –अद्रिः, –क्ष्माभृत्** *m*. the western mountain behind which the sun and moon are supposed to set. **–अवस्था** the last state (old age). **–कालः** the hour of death.

चरिः An animal.

चरित *pp*. **1** Wandered or roamed over, gone. **2** Performed, practised. **3** Attained. **4** Known. **5** Offered. **–तं 1** Going, moving, course. Acting, doing, practice, behaviour, acts, deeds ; उदारचरितानां H. 1. 70 ; सर्वं खलस्य चरितं मशकः करोति 1. 81 **3** Life, biography, adventures, history, story ; उत्तरं रामचरितं तत्प्रणीतं प्रयुज्यते U. 1 2 ; so दशकुमारचरितं &c. –COMP. **–अर्थ** *a*. **1** that has accomplished its end or desired object, successful ; रामरावणयोर्युद्धं चरितार्थमिवाभवत् R. 12. 87; 10. 36 ; 2. 17. Ki. 13. 62. **2** satisfied, contented. **3** effected, accomplished.

चरित्रं 1 Behaviour, habit, conduct, practice, acts, deeds, **2** performance, observance. **3** History, life, biography, account, adventure. **4** Nature, disposition. **5** Duty, established or instituted observance ; Ms. 2. 20. 9. 7.

चरिष्णु *a*. Moveable, active, wandering about ; Ms. 1. 56.

चरुः An oblation of rice, barley and pulse boiled for presentation to the gods and the manes ; R. 10 52, 54, 56. –COMP. **–स्थाली** a vessel for boiling rice &c. for presentation to the gods and the manes.

चर्च् I. 10 U. (चर्चयति-ते, चर्चित). To read, read carefully, peruse, study. –II. 6 P. (चर्चति, चर्चित) **1** To abuse, condemn, censure, menace. **2** To discuss, consider.

चर्चनं 1 Studying, repetition, reading repeatedly. **2** Smearing the body with unguents.

चर्चरिका, चर्चरी 1 A kind of song. **2** Striking the hands to beat time (in music). **3** The recitation of scholars. **4** Festive sport, festive cries or merriment. **5** A festival. **6** Flattery. **7** Curled hair.

चर्चा, चर्चिका 1 Repetition, recitation, study, repeated reading. **2** Discussion, inquiry, investigation. **3** Reflection. **4** Smearing the body with unguents ; अंगचर्चामरचयं K. 157 ; श्रीखंडचर्चा विषं Gît. 9.

चर्चिक्यं 1 Anointing the body. **2** An unguent.

चर्चित *p.p*. **1** Anointed, smeared perfumed, scented &c. ; चंदनचर्चितनीलकलेवरपीतवसनवनमाली Gît. 1; Rs. 2. 21. **2** Discussed, considered, investigated.

चर्पटः The open palm of the hand with the fingers extended, cf. चपेट.

चर्पटी A thin cake or biscuit of flour (पिष्टकभेद).

चर्भटः A kind of cucumber.

चर्भटी 1 Noise of merriment. 2 Cucumber.

चर्म A shield.

चर्मण्वती N. of a river flowing into the Ganges, the modern Chambal.

चर्मन् *n.* 1 Skin (of the body). 2 Leather, hide; Ms. 2. 41, 174. 3 The sense of touch. 4 A shield; *Si.* 18. 21. –COMP. **–अंभस्** *n.* lymph. **–अवकर्तनं** working in leather. **–अवकर्तिन्, अवकर्तृ** *m.* a shoe-maker. **–कारः, कारिन्** *m.* a shoe-maker, currier. **–कीलः –लं** a wart. **–चित्रकं** white leprosy. **–जं** 1 hair. 2 blood. **–तरंगः** a wrinkle. **–दंडः, नालिका** a whip. **–द्रुमः, –वृक्षः** the Bhûrja tree. **–पट्टिका** a flat piece of leather for playing upon with dice. **–पत्रा** a bat, the small house-bat. **–पादुका** a leather shoe. **–प्रभेदिका** a shoe-maker's awl. **–प्रसेवकः, प्रसेविका** a bellows. **–बंधः** a leather band or strap. **–मुंडा** an epithet of Durgâ. **–यष्टिः** *f.* a whip. **–वसनः** 'clad in skin,' N. of *Siva.* **–वाद्यं** a drum, tabor &c. **–संभवा** large cardamoms. **–सारः** lymph, serum.

चर्ममय *a.* Leathern.

चर्मरुः, –चर्मारः A shoe-maker, a worker in leather, currier.

चर्मिक *a.* Armed with a shield.

चर्मिन् *a.* (**णी** *f.*) 1 Armed with a shield. 2 Leathern. –*m.* 1 A soldier armed with a shield. 2 Plantain. 3 The Bhûja tree.

चर्या 1 Going about, moving, walking about. 2 Course, motion; as in राहुचर्या. 3 Behaviour, conduct, deportment. 4 Practice, performance, observance; Ms. 1. 111; व्रतचर्या, तपश्चर्या 5 Regular performance of all rites or customs. 6 Eating. 7 A custom, usage; Ms. 6. 32.

चर्व् 1. P., 10 U. (चर्वति, चर्वयति-ते, चर्वित) 1 To chew, chop, eat, browse, bite; लांगूलं गाढतरं चर्वितुमारब्धवान् Pt. 4; यस्यैतच्च न कुक्कुरैरहरहर्जंघांतरं चर्व्यते Mk. 2. 11. 2 To suck up. 3 To relish, taste.

चर्वणं, –णा 1 Chewing, eating. 2 Sipping. 3 (Fig.) Tasting, relishing, enjoying; प्रमाणं चर्वणैवात्र स्वाभिन्ने विदुषां मतं S. D. 57; (com.=चर्वणा आस्वादनं तच्च स्वादः काव्यार्थसंभेदादात्मानंदसमुद्भव इत्युक्तप्रकारं); so also; निष्पत्त्या चर्वणस्यास्य निष्पत्तिरुपचारतः 58.

चर्वा A blow with the flat of the hand (said to be also **चर्वन्** *m.*)

चर्वित् *p p.* 1 Chewed, bitten, eaten. 2 Tasted. –COMP. **–चर्वणं** (lit.) chewing the chewed; (fig.) tautology, useless repetition. **–पात्रं** a spitting pot.

चल् I. P. (चलति, rarely चलते, चलित) 1 To shake, tremble, throb, palpitate, stir; छिन्नाश्चेलुः क्षणं भुजाः Bk. 14. 40; सपक्षोद्रिरिवाचालीत् 15. 24; 6. 84. 2 (*a*) To go, move on, walk, stir or move (from one's place); पदात्पदमपि चलितुं न शक्नोति Pt. 4; चलत्येकेन पादेन तिष्ठत्येकेन बुद्धिमान् Chân. 32; चचाल बाला स्तनभिन्नवल्कला Ku. 5. 84; Mk. 1. 56. (*b*) To proceed (on one's way), depart, set out, start off; चेलुश्चीरपरिग्रहाः Ku. 6. 93. 3 To be affected, to be disturbed, confused or disordered (as mind), be agitated or perturbed; मुनेरपि यतस्तस्य दर्शनाच्चलते मनः Pt. 1. 400; लोभेन बुद्धिश्चलति H. 1. 140. 4 To deviate or swerve (with abl.); चलति नयान्न जिगीषतां हि चेतः Ki. 10. 29; to fall off, leave; Ms. 7. 15; Y. 1. 360. –*Caus.* (च-चा-लयति, चलित, चालित 1 To cause to move, shake, stir 2 To drive away, remove or expel from. 3 To lead away from. 4 To cherish, foster (चालयति only). –WITH **उद्** 1 to start, set out; स्थितः स्थितामुच्चलितः प्रयातां R. 2. 6; उच्चचाल बलभित्सखो वशी 11. 51; नगरायोदचलं Dk. 2 to go away, move from, or leave one's place; स्थानादनुच्चलन्नपि *S.* 1. 29; पुष्पोच्चलितषट्पदं R. 12. 27. **–प्र** 1 to shake, move, tremble; Bh. 2. 4. 2 to go; walk, move on, set out, start off. 3 to be affected, disturbed or agitated. 4 to swerve, deviate. **–वि** 1 to shake, move; पतति पतत्रे विचलति पत्रे शंकितभवदुपयानं Gît. 5. 2 to go, proceed, set out. 3 to be agitated or disturbed, be rough (as the sea); व्यचालीदंभसां पतिः Bk. 15. 70. 4 to deviate, swerve; Y. 1. 358.– II. 6 P. (चलति, चलित) To sport, play, frolic about.

चल *a* 1 (*a*) Moving, trembling, shaking, tremulous, rolling (as eyes &c.); चलापांगां दृष्टिं स्पृशसि *S.* 1. 24; चलकाकपक्षकैरमात्यपुत्रैः R. 3. 28. waving; Bh. 1. 6. (*b*) Moveable; (opp. स्थिर), moving; चले लक्ष्ये *S.* 2. 5. 2 Unsteady, fickle, inconstant, loose, unfixed; दयितास्वनवस्थितं नृणां न खलु प्रेम चलं सुहृज्जने Ku. 4. 28; प्रायश्चलं गौरवमाश्रितेषु 3. 1; 3 Frail, transitory, perishable; चला लक्ष्मीश्चलाः प्राणाश्चलं जीवितयौवनं. 4 Confused. **–लः** 1 Trembling, shaking, agitation. 2 Wind. 3 Quicksilver. **–ला** 1 Lakshmî, the goddess of wealth. 2 A kind of perfume. –COMP. **–अचल** *a.* 1 moveable and immoveable. 2 fickle, unsteady, very transitory (=अतिचल); चलाचले च संसारे धर्म एको हि निश्चलः Bh. 3. 128; लक्ष्मीमिव चलाचलां Ki. 11. 30. (चलाचला=चंचला Malli.) N. 1. 60. (–लः) a crow. **–अंतकः** rheumatism. **–आत्मन्** *a.* inconstant, fickle-minded. **–इंद्रिय** *a.* 1 sensitive. 2 sensual. **–इषुः** one whose arrow flies unsteadily or misses the mark, a bad archer. **–कर्णः** the true distance of a planet from the earth. **–चंचुः** the Chakora bird. **–चित्त** *a.* fickle-minded. **–दलः, –पत्रः** the Asvattha tree.

चलन *a.* Moving, tremulous, trembling, shaking. **–नः** 1 A foot. 2 A deer. **–नं** 1 Trembling, shaking or shaking motion; चलनात्मकं कर्म T. S.; हस्त°, जानु° &c. तरलदृगंचलचलनमनोहरवदनजनितरतिरागं Gît. 11. 2 Roaming, wandering. **–नी** 1 A short petticoat worn by common women. 2 The rope for tying an elephant.

चलनकं A short petticoat worn by low women.

चलिः A cover, wrapper.

चलित *p. p.* 1 Shaken, moved, stirred, agitated. 2 Gone, departed; एवमुक्त्वा स चलितः. 3 Attained. 4 Known, understood; (see चल्). **–तं** 1 Shaking, moving. 2 Going, walking. 3 A kind of dance; चलितं नाम नाट्यमंतरेण M. 1.

चलुः A mouthful (of water).

चलुकः 1 Water taken up in the hollowed palm for rinsing the mouth. 2 A handful or mouthful (of water); cf. चुलुक.

चष् I. 1. U. (चषति-ते) To eat. II. 1. P. (चषति) To kill, injure, hurt.

चषकः –कं A vessel used for drinking spirits, a goblet, a wine-glass; च्युतैः शिरस्त्रैश्चषकोत्तरेव R. 7. 49; मुखं लालाक्लिन्नं पिबति चषकं सासवमिव *Sânti.* 1. 29; Ki. 9. 56, 57. **–कं** 1 A kind of spirituous liquor. 2 Honey.

चषतिः 1 Eating. 2 Killing. 3 Decay, infirmity, decline.

चषालः A wooden ring on the top of a sacrificial post. 2 A hive.

चह् 1 P., 10 U. (चहति चहयति ते) 1 To be wicked. 2 To cheat, deceive. 3 To be proud or haughty.

चाकचक्यं Brilliancy, lustre.

चाक्र *a.* (**क्री** *f.*) 1 Carried on with the discus (as a battle). 2 Circular. 3 Relating to a wheel.

चाक्रिक *a.* (**की** *f.*) see चाक्र above. **–कः** 1 A potter. 2 An oil-maker; Y. 1. 165. (=तैलिक according to Mit.; शाकटिक or cartman according to others). 3 A coachman, driver.

चाक्रिण The son of a potter or oil-maker.

चाक्षुष *a.* (**षी** *f.*) 1 Depending on, or produced from, sight. 2 Belonging to the eye, visual, optical. 3 Visible, to be seen. **–षं** Knowledge dependent on vision. –COMP. **–ज्ञानं** ocular evidence or proof.

चांगः 1 Wood sorrel. 2 Whiteness or beauty of the teeth.

चांचल्यं 1 Unsteadiness, quick motion, rolling, tremour (as of the eyes &c.); Bv. 2. 60. 2 Fickleness. 3 Transitoriness.

चाटः A rogue or cheat, one who wins the confidence of the person he wishes to deceive; Y. 1. 336; (चाटाः =प्रतारकाः विश्वास्य ये परधनमपहरंति Mit.).

चाटु: -टु *n.* 1 Pleasing or agreeable words, sweet or coaxing speech, flattery (especially of a lover to his sweetheart); प्रियः प्रियायाः प्रकरोति चाटुं Rs. 6. 14; विरचितचाटुवचनरचनं चरणरचितप्रणिपातं Gît. 11; Amaru. 83; Pt. 1. Sânti. 8. 14; Ch. P. 20; (the greater part of the 10th canto of गीतगोविंद consists of such coaxing). 2 Distinct or clear speech. -Comp. **-उक्तिः** *f.* flattering or coaxing language. **-उल्लोल, -कार** *a.* speaking agreeably or sweetly, flatterer; शिप्रावातः प्रियतम इव प्रार्थनाचाटुकारः Me. 31. **-पटु** *a.* skilful in using flattering or coaxing language, an accomplished flatterer. **-बटु:** a jester, buffoon. **-लोल** *a.* elegantly tremulous. **-शतं** a hundred entreaties, repeated coaxing; पटुचाटुशतैरनुकूलं Gît. 2; गजपुंगवस्तु धीरं विलोकयति चाटुशतैश्च भुंक्ते Bh. 2. 31.

चाणक्यः N. of a celebrated writer on civil polity; also known as विष्णुगुप्त, कौटिल्य; see कौटिल्य.

चाणूरः A celebrated wrestler in the service of Kamsa. When Krishṇa was taken by Akrûra to Mathurâ, Kamsa sent this redoubtable wrestler to fight with him; but in the duel which ensued, Krishṇa whirled him round and round several times and smashed his head.

चांडालः (ली *f.*) An out-cast; see चंडाल; चांडालः किमयं द्विजातिरथवा Bh. 3. 56; Ms 3. 239; 4. 29; Y. 1. 93.

चांडालिका=चंडालिका q. v.

चातकः (की *f.*) N. of a bird which is supposed to live only on rain-drops; सूक्ष्मा एव पतंति चातकमुखे द्वित्राः पयोबिंदवः Bh. 2. 121; see 2. 51 and R. 5. 17. -Comp. **-आनंदनः** 1 the rainy season. 2 a cloud.

चातनं 1 Removing. 2 Injuring.

चातुर *a.* (री *f.*) 1 Relating to four. 2 Clever, able, shrewd. 3 Speaking well, flattering. 4 Visible, perceptible. **-रं** A fourwheeled carriage. **-री** Skill, dexterity, ability; तद्भटचातुरीतुरी N. 1. 12.

चातुरक्षं Four casts in playing at dice. **-क्षः** A small round pillow.

चातुरर्थिकः (In gram.) A suffix added to words in four different senses.

चातुराश्रमिक *a.* (की *f*), **चातुराश्रमिन्** *a.* (णी *f.*) Being in one of the four periods of the religious life of a Brâhmaṇa; see आश्रम.

चातुराश्रम्यं The four periods of the religious life of a Brâhmana; see आश्रम.

चातुरिक-चातुर्थक,-चातुर्थिक *a.* (की *f.*) 1 Quartan, occurring every fourth day. **-कः** A quartan ague.

चातुर्थाह्निक *a.* (की *f.*) Belonging to the fourth day.

चातुर्दशं A demon (Sk.)

चातुर्दशिकः One who studies on the fourteenth day of a lunar fortnight (that being a day of अनध्याय q. v.)

चातुर्मासक *a.* (सिका *f.*) One who performs the Châturmâsya sacrifice.

चातुर्मास्यं N. of a sacrifice performed every four months; *i. e.* at the beginning of कार्तिक, फाल्गुन and आषाढ.

चातुर्यं 1 Skill, cleverness, dexterity, shrewdness. 2 Loveliness, amiableness, beauty; भ्रूचातुर्यं Bh. 1. 3.

चातुर्वर्ण्यं 1 The aggregate of the four original castes of the Hindus; एवं सामासिकं धर्मं चातुर्वर्ण्येऽब्रवीन्मनुः Ms. 10. 63; Rg. 6. 13. 2 The duties of these four castes.

चातुर्विध्यं Four kinds (collectively), a four-fold division.

चात्वालः 1 A hole in the ground to receive an oblation or the sacred fire. 2 Kusa grass (दर्भ).

चांदनिक *a.* (की *f.*) 1 Made of or derived from sandal. 2 Perfumed with sandal juice &c.

चांद्र *a.* (द्री *f.*) Relating to the moon, lunar; गुरुकाव्यानुगां बिभ्रच्चांद्रीमभिनभः श्रियं Si. 2. 2. **-द्रः** 1 A lunar month. 2 The bright fortnight (शुक्लपक्ष). 3 The moon-stone. **-द्रं** 1 The vow called चांद्रायण q. v. 2 Fresh ginger. The lunar mansion called मृगशीर्ष. **-द्री** Moonlight. -Comp. **-भागा** the river Chandrabhâgâ. **-मासः** a lunar month. **-व्रतिकः** one who observes the चांद्रायण vow.

चांद्रकं Dried ginger.

चांद्रमस *a.* (सी *f.*) Relating to the moon, lunar; लब्धोदया चांद्रमसीव लेखा Ku. 1. 25. चंद्रं गता पद्मगुणान्न भुंक्ते पद्माश्रिता चांद्रमसीमभिख्यां 1. 43; R. 2. 39; Bg. 8. 25. **-सं** The constellation मृगशिरस.

चांद्रमसायनः, —निः The planet Mercury.

चांद्रायणं A religious observance or expiatory penance regulated by the moon's age (the period of its waxing and waning); (in it the daily quantity of food, which consists of fifteen mouthfuls at the full moon, is diminished by one mouthful every day during the dark fortnight till it is reduced to zero at the new moon, and is increased in like manner during the bright fortnight); cf Y. 3. 324 *et seq.*, and Ms. 11. 217.

चांद्रायणिक *a.* (की *f.*) 1 One who performs the चांद्रायण vow.

चापं 1 A bow; ताते चापद्वितीये वहति रणधुरां को भयस्यावकाशः Ve. 3. 5; so चापपाणिः 'with a bow in hand' 2 The rain-bow. 3 (In geom.) An arc of a circle. 4 The sign of the zodiac called *Sagittarius*.

चापलं, -ल्यं 1 Quick motion, swiftness. 2 Fickleness, unsteadiness, transitoriness; Ki. 2. 41. 3 Inconsiderate or rash conduct, rashness, rash act; धिक् चापलं U. 4; तद्गुणैः कर्णमागत्य चापलाय प्रचोदितः R. 1. 9; स्वचित्तवृत्तिरिव चापलेभ्यो निवारणीया K. 101. 4 Restiveness (as of a horse); पुनः पुनः सूतनिषिद्धचापलं R. 3. 42.

चामरः, -रं (also **-रा -री** sometimes) 1 A *chowrie* or bushy tail of the Chamara (Bos Grunniens) used as a fly-flap or fan, and reckoned as one of the insignia of royalty (and sometimes used as a sort of streamer on the heads of horses); व्याधुन्वंते निचुलतरुभिर्मंजरीचामराणि V 4. 4. अदेयमासीत् त्रयमेव भूपतेः शशिप्रभं छत्रमुभे च चामरे R. 3. 16; Ku. 7. 42; H 2. 29; Me. 35; चित्रन्यस्तमिवाचलं हयशिरस्यायामवच्चामरं V. 1. 4; S. 1. 8. -Comp. **-ग्राहः -ग्राहिन्** *m.* a person who carries a *chowrie*. **-ग्राहिणी** a waiting girl who carries in her hand a *chowrie* and waves it over the head of a king &c.; पृष्ठे लीलावलयरणितं चामरग्राहिणीनां Bh. 3. 61. **-पुष्पः, -पुष्पकः** 1 the betel-nut tree. 2 the Ketaka plant. 3 the mango tree.

चामरिन् *m.* A horse.

चामीकरं 1 Gold; ततचामीकराङ्गः V. 1. 14; R. 7. 5; Si. 4. 24; Ku. 7. 49. 2 The Dhattûra plant. -Comp. **-प्रख्य** *a.* like gold.

चामुंडा A terrific form of Durgâ; Mâl. 5. 25.

चांपिला The river Champâ; (perhaps the modern Chambal).

चांपेयः 1 The Champaka tree. 2 The Nâgakesara tree. **-यं** 1 Filament, especially of a lotus flower. 2 Gold. 3 The Dhattûra plant; (*m.* also in the last two senses).

चाय् 1. U. (चायति-ते) 1 To observe, discern, see; Si. 12. 51. 2 To worship.

चारः 1 Going, walking, gait, wandering about; मंडलचारशीघ्रः V. 5. 2; क्रीडाशैले यदि च विचरेत् पादचारेण गौरी Me. 60. walk on foot. 2 Motion, course, progression; मंगलचार; शनिचार &c. 3 A spy, scout, secret, emissary; Ms. 7. 184; 9. 261; see चारचक्षुस् below. 4 Performing, practising. 5 A prison. 6 A bond, fetter. **-रं** An artificial poison. -Comp **-अंतरितः** a spy. **ईक्षणः, -चक्षुस्** *m.* 'using spies as eyes', a king (or a statesman) who employs spies and sees through their medium; चारचक्षुर्महीपतिः Ms. 9. 256 cf. Kâmandaka: गावः पश्यंति गंधेन वेदैः पश्यंति च द्विजाः। चारैः पश्यंति राजान-

अक्षुभ्यामितरे जनाः ॥. also Râm.—यस्मात्पश्यंति दूरस्थाः सर्वानर्थान्नराधिपाः । चारेण तस्मादुच्यंते राजानश्चारचक्षुषः -चण, -चंचु *a.* graceful in gait, of graceful carriage. -पथः a place where two roads meet. -भटः a valorous warrior. -वायुः summer-air, zephyr.

चारकः 1 A spy. 2 A herdsman. 3 A leader, driver. 4 An associate. 5 A groom, cavalier. 6 A prison; निगडितचरणा चारके निरोद्धव्या Dk. 32.

चारणः 1 A wanderer, a pilgrim. 2 A wandering actor, or singer, a dancer, mimic, bard; Ms. 12. 44. 3 A celestical singer, heavenly chorister; S 2. 14. 4 A reader of scripture. 5 A spy.

चारिका A female attendant.

चारितार्थ्यं Attainment of an object, successfulness.

चारित्रं (also written चारित्र्यं) 1 Conduct, behaviour, manner of acting. 2 Good name or character, reputation, probity, uprightness, good conduct; अनृतं नाभिधास्यामि चारित्रभ्रंशकारणं Mk. 3. 26, 25; चारित्र्यविहीन आढ्योऽपि च दुर्गतो भवति 1. 43. 3 Chastity, purity of life (of women). 4 Disposition, temperament. 5 Peculiar observance or practice. 6 Hereditary observance. -COMP. कवच *a.* cased in the armour of chastity.

चारु *a.* (रु or र्वी *f.*) 1 Agreeable, welcome, beloved, esteemed, dear (with dat. or loc.); वरुणाय or वरुणे चारुः 2 Pleasing, lovely, beautiful, elegant, pretty; प्रिये चारुशीले मुंच मयि मानमनिदानं Gît. 10; सर्वं प्रिये चारुतरं वसंते Rs. 6. 2; चकासतं चारुचमूरुचर्मणा Si. 1. 8; 4. 49. -रुः An epithet of Brihaspati. -रु *n.* Saffron. -COMP. -अंगी a beautifully formed woman. -घोण *a.* handsome-nosed. -दर्शन *a.* good-looking, lovely. -धारा Sachi, Indra's wife. -नेत्र, लोचन *a.* having beautiful eyes. (-त्रः, -नः) a deer. -फला a vine, grape. -लोचना a woman with lovely eyes. -वक्त्र *a.* having a beautiful face. -वर्धना a woman. -व्रता a female who fasts for a whole month. -शिला 1 a jewel, gem. 2 a beautiful slab of stone. -शील *a.* of a lovely disposition or character. -हासिन् *a.* sweet-smiling.

चार्चिक्यं 1 Perfuming the person, smearing with sandal &c. 2 An unguent.

चार्म *a.* (र्मी *f.*) 1 Leathern. 2 Covered with leather (as a car). 3 Shielded, provided with a shield.

चार्मण (णी *f.*) Covered with skin or leather. -णं A multitude of hides or shields.

चार्मिक *a.* (की *f.*) Made of leather; Ms. 289.

-चार्मिणं A number of men armed with shields.

चार्वाकः 1 N. of a sophistical philosopher (said to have been a pupil of Brihaspati), who propounded the grossest form of atheism or materialism (for a summary of the doctrines of Chârvâka, see Sarva. S. 1.). 2 N. of Râkshasa described in the Mahâbhârata, as a friend of Duryodhana and an enemy of the Pândavas. [When Yudhishthira entered Hastinapura in triumph, he assumed the form of a Brahmana and reviled him and the assembled Brahmanas, but he was soon detected, and the real Brahmanas, filled with fury, are said to have killed him on the spot. He also tried to deceive Yudhishthira at the end of the great war by telling him that Bhima was slain by Duryodhana; see Ve. 6.]

चार्वी 1 A beautiful woman. 2 Moonlight. 3 Intelligence. 4 Splendour, lustre, brilliancy. 5 Wife of Kubera.

चालः 1 The thatch or roof of a house. The blue jay. 3 Shaking, moving. 4 Being moveable.

चालकः A restive elephant.

चालनं 1 Causing to move, shaking, wagging (as a tail). 2 Causing to pass through a sieve, sifting, sieve. -नी A sieve, strainer.

चाषः -सः The blue jay; Mâl. 6. 5; Y. 1. 175.

चि 5 U. (चिनोति, चिनुते, चित; *caus.* चाययति, चापयति, also चययति, चपयति *desid.* चिचीषति-चिकीषति) 1 To collect, gather, accumulate (said to govern two accusatives being a द्विकर्मक root, but this use is very rare in classical literature); वृक्षं पुष्पाणि चिन्वती. 2 To pile or heap up, place in a line; पर्वतानिव ते भूमावचैषुर्वानरोत्तमान् Bk. 15. 76. 3 To set, inlay, cover or fill with; see चित. *-pass.* To bear fruit, grow, increase, thrive, prosper; सिच्यते चीयते चैव लता पुष्पफलप्रदा Pt. 1. 222 bears fruit; चीयते बालिशस्यापि सत्क्षेत्रपतिता कृषिः Mu. 1. 3; राजहंस तव सैव शुभ्रता चीयते न च न चापचीयते K. P. 10. -WITH अप to diminish, loss, be deprived of; chiefly in pass. (*-pass.*) 1 to decrease, diminish, become less; राजहंस तव सैव शुभ्रता चीयते न च न चापचीयते K. P. 10. 2 to be reduced in bulk, waste away. -आ 1 to accumulate, heap up. 2 to fill or cover with, cover over; Bk. 17. 69; 14. 46-47.-उद् to gather, collect; Bk. 3. 38. -उप to add to, increase; उपाचिचन्वन्प्रभां तन्वीं प्रत्याह परमेश्वरः Ku. 6. 25. (*-pass.*) to grow, increase; अवेक्षध्वं पश्यतः कस्य महिमा नोपचीयते H. 2. 2; Bk. 6. 33; Si. 4. 10. -नि to cover or fill with, strew, overspread (chiefly in *p. p.*); निचितं खमुपेत्य नीरदैः Ghat. 1; शकुंतनीडनिचितं बिभ्रज्जटामंडलं S. 7. 11; Bk. 10. 4. -निस् to determine, resolve, ascertain. -परि 1 to practice. 2 to get, acquire. (*-pass.*) to increase; R. 3. 24. -प्र 1 to gather, collect. 2 to add to, increase, develop. (*-pass.*) to grow, be developed; प्रचीयमानावयवा रराज सा R. 3. 7. -वि 1 to gather, collect. 2 to search for, look out for; विचितश्चैष समंतात् श्मशानवाटः Mâl. 5. -विनिस् to determine, resolve, ascertain; विनिश्चेतुं शक्यो न सुखमिति वा दुःखमिति वा U. 1. 35. -सं 1 to gather, collect, hoard; रक्षायोगादयमपि तपः प्रत्यहं संचिनोति S. 2. 14; R. 19. 2; Ms 6. 15. 2 to arrange, put in order, put or place; Bk. 3. 35. -समुद् to collect, heap up.

चिकित्सकः A physician, doctor; उचितवेलातिक्रमे चिकित्सका दोषमुदाहरंति M. 2; Bh. 1. 87; Y. 1. 162.

चिकित्सा Administering remedies or medicine, medical treatment, curing, healing.

चिकिलः Mud, a slough, bog, mire.

चिकीर्षा Desire of doing (anything), will, wish, desire.

चिकीर्षित *a.* Wished, desired, purposed. -तं Design, intention, purpose.

चिकीर्षु *a.* Desirous of doing anything, desirous for; Bg. 1. 23; 3. 25.

चिकुर *a.* 1 Moving, tremulous, fickle, unsteady. 2 Inconsiderate, rash. -रः 1 The hair of the head; मम रुचिरे चिकुरे कुरु मानद....कुसुमानि Gît. 12; so घनचयरुचिरे रचयति चिकुरे तरलिततरुणानने 7. 2 A mountain. 3 A reptile, snake. -COMP. -उच्चयः, -कलापः -निकरः, -पक्षः, -पाशः, भारः, हस्तः a mass or tuft of hair; यस्याश्चोरश्चिकुरनिकरः कर्णपूरो मयूरः P. R. 1. 22.

चिकूरः The hair.

चिक्कः The musk-rat.

चिक्कण *a.* (णा or णी *f.*) 1 Smooth, glossy. 2 Slippery. 3 Bland. 4 Unctuous, greasy; लघु परित्रायतामेनां भावन् मा कस्यापि तपस्विन इंगुदीतैलचिक्कणशीर्षस्य हस्ते पतिष्यति S. 2. -णः The betel-nut tree. -णं A fruit of that tree, a betel-nut.

चिक्कणा-णी 1 The betel-nut tree. 2 A betel-nut.

चिक्कसः Barley-meal.

चिक्का=चिक्कणा q. v.

चिक्किरः A mouse.

चिक्लिदं Moisture, freshness.

चिचिंडः A sort of gourd.

चिच्छिलाः (*m.* pl.) N. of a country and its people.

चिंचा 1 The tamarind tree, or its fruit. 2 The Gunjâ plant.

चिट् 1 P., 10 U. (चेटति, चेटयति-ते) To send forth or out (as a servant.)

चित् 1 P. 10, A. (चेतति, चेतयते, चेतित) 1 To perceive, see, notice, observe;

नेघूनचेतन्नस्यंत Bk. 17. 16; चिचेत रामस्तत्कृच्छ्रं 14. 62; 15. 38; 2. 29. 2 To know, understand, be aware or conscious of; पैरध्यारुह्यमाणमात्मानं न चेतयते Dk. 154 3 To regain consciousness. 4 To appear, shine.

चित् *f.* 1 Thought, perception. 2 Intelligence, intellect, understanding; Bh. 2 1; 3. 1. 3 The heart, mind. 4 The soul, spirit, the animating principle of life. 5 Brahman. –COMP. –आत्मन् *m.* 1 the thinking principle or faculty 2 pure intelligence, the supreme spirit. –आत्मकं consciousness. –आभास: the individual soul (जीव) (which still sticks to worldly defilements). –उल्लास: gladdening the heart of spirit. –घन: the supreme spirit or Brahman. –प्रवृत्ति: *f.* reflection, thinking. –शक्ति: *f.* mental power, intellectual capacity. –स्वरूपं the supreme spirit. –*ind.* 1 A particle added to किं and its derivatives (such as कद्, कथं, क, कदा, कुत्र, कुतः &c.) to impart to them an indefinite sense; कुत्रचित् somewhere; केचित् some &c. 2 The sound चित्.

चित *p. p.* 1 Collected, piled up, heaped, gathered. 2 Hoarded, accumulated. 3 Got, acquired. 4 Covered with, full of; कृमिकुलचितं Bh. 2. 11. 5 Set or inlaid with. –तं A building.

चिता A funeral pile, pyre; कुरु संप्रति तावदाशु मे प्रणिपातांजलियाचितश्चितां Ku. 4. 35; चिताधिरोहणं R. 8. 57; चिताभस्मन् Ku. 5. 69. –COMP. –अग्नि: the funeral fire. –चूडकं a pyre.

चिति: *f.* 1 Collecting, gathering. 2 A heap, multitude, quantity. 3 A layer, pile, stack. 4 A funeral pile. 5 An oblong with quadrangular sides. 6 The understanding.

चितिका 1 A pile, stack. 2 A funeral pile. 3 A small chain (or girdle) worn as an ornament round the loins.

चित्त *a.* 1 Observed, perceived. 2 Considered, reflected or meditated upon. 3 Resolved. 4 Intended, wished, desired.—त्तं 1 Observing, attending. 2 Thought, thinking, attention, desire, intention, aim; मच्चित्तः सततं भव Bg. 18. 57; अनेकचित्तविभ्रांत 16. 16. 3 The mind; यदासौ दुर्वारः प्रसरति मदश्चित्तकरिणः Sânti. 1. 22; so चलचित्त and comps. below. 4 The heart (considered as the seat of intellect). 5 Reason, intellect, reasoning faculty, –COMP. –अनुवर्तिन् *a.* acting according to one's will, humouring. –अपहारक, –अपहारिन् *a.* heart-stealing', attractive, captivating. –आभोग: attention of the mind to its own feelings, exclusive attachment to one thing. –आसंग: attachment, love. –उद्रेक: pride, arrogance. –ऐक्य agreement, unanimity. –उन्नति:, समुन्नति: *f.* 1 noble-mindedness. 2 pride, arrogance. –चारिन् *a.* acting according to the will of another. –ज:, –जन्मन् *m.*, –भू: –योनि: 1 love, passion. 2 Cupid, the god of love; चित्तयोनिरभवत्पुनर्नवः R. 19. 46; सोयं प्रसिद्धविभवः खलु चित्तजन्मा Mâl. 1. 20. –ज्ञ *a.* knowing the mind of another. –नाश: loss of conscience. –निर्वृति: *f.* contentment, happiness. –प्रशम *a.* composed, tranquil. (–म:) tranquility of heart. –प्रसन्नता joy, pleasure. –भेद: 1 difference of view. 2 inconsistency, inconstancy. –मोह: infatuation of the mind. –विकार: change of thought or feeling. –विक्षेप: distraction of the mind. –विप्लव:, विभ्रम: aberration, disturbance or derangement of mind, madness, insanity –विश्लेष: breach of friendship. –वृत्ति: *f.* 1 disposition or state of the mind, inclination, feeling; एवमात्माभिप्रायसंभावितेष्टजनचित्तवृत्तिः प्रार्थयिता विडंब्यते *S.* 2. 2 inward purpose, emotion. 3 (in Yoga phil.) inward working of the mind, mental vision; योगश्चित्तवृत्तिनिरोधः Yoga. S. –वेदना affliction, anxiety. –वैकल्यं bewilderment of the mind, distraction. –हारिन् *a.* fascinating, attractive, agreeable.

चित्तवत् *a.* 1 Reasonable, endowed with reason. 2 Kindhearted, amiable.

चित्यं The place at which a corpse is burnt. –त्या 1 A funeral pile. 2 Piling up, building (as an altar).

चित्र *a.* 1 Bright, clear. 2 Variegated, spotted, diversified. 3 Interesting, agreeable; Mâl. 1. 4. 4 Various, different, manifold; Pt. 1. 136; Ms. 9. 248; Y. 1. 288. 5 Surprising, wonderful, strange. –त्र: 1 The variegated colour. 2 The Asoka tree. –त्रं 1 A picture, painting, delineation; चित्रे निवेश्य परिकल्पितसत्त्वयोगा *S.* 2. 9; पुनरपि चित्रीकृता कांता *S.* 6. 20, 13, 21 &c. 2 A brilliant ornament or ornament. 3 An extraordinary appearance, wonder. 4 A sectarial mark on the forehead. 5 Heaven, sky. 6 A spot. 7 The white or spotted leprosy. 8 (In Rhet.) The last of the three main divisions of *Kâvya* (poetry.) (It is of two kinds शब्दचित्र and अर्थ-वाच्य-चित्र, and the poetical charm lies mainly in the use of figures of speech, dependent on the sound or sense of words. Mammaṭa thus defines it:—शब्दचित्रं वाच्यचित्रमव्यंग्यं त्ववरं स्मृतं K. P. 1). As an instance of शब्दचित्र may be cited the following verse from R. G.:—मित्रात्रिपुत्रनेत्राय त्रयीशात्रवशत्रवे । गोत्रारिगोत्रजैत्राय गोत्रात्रे ते नमो नमः ॥—त्रं *ind.* Oh!, how strange!, what a wonder! चित्रं बाधिरी नाम व्याकरणमध्येष्यते Sk. –COMP. –अक्षी, –नेत्रा, –लोचना a kind of bird commonly called Sârika.–अंग *a.* striped, having a spotted body. (–गं) vermilion.–अन्नं rice dressed with coloured condiments; Y. 1. 304. –अपूप: a kind of cake. अर्पित *a.* committed to a picture, painted °आरंभ *a.* painted; R. 2. 31; Ku. 3. 42. –आकृति: *f.* a painted resemblance, portrait.–आयसं steel –आरंभ: a painted scene, outline of a picture; V. 1. 4 उक्ति: *f.* 1 agreeable or eloquent discourse; जयंति ते पंचमनादमित्रचित्रोक्तिसंदर्भविभूषणेषु Vikr. 1. 10. 2 a voice from heaven. 3 a surprising tale. –ओदन: boiled rice coloured with turmeric &c. –कंठ: a pigeon. –कथालाप: telling agreeable or charming stories.–कंबल: 1 painted cloth used as an elephant's housing. 2 a variegated carpet. –कर: 1 a painter. 2 an actor. –कर्मन् *n.* 1 an extraordinary act. 2 ornamenting, decorating. 3 a picture. 4 magic. (–*m.*) 1 magician who works wonders. 2 a painter. विद् *m.* 1 a painter. 2 a magician. –काय: a tiger in general. 2 a leopard or panther. –कार: 1 a painter. 2 N. of a mixed tribe; (स्थपतेरपि गांधिक्यां चित्रकारो व्यजायत Parâsara). –कूट: N. of a hill and district near Prayâga; R. 12. 15, 13. 47; U. 1. –कृत *m.* a painter. –क्रिया painting. –ग, –गत् *a.* painted. –गंधं yellow orpiment. –गुप्त: one of the beings in Yama's world recording the vices and virtues of mankind; Mu. 1. 20. –गृहं a painted room. –जल्प: a random or incoherent talk, talk on various subjects. –त्वच् *m.* the Bhúrja tree. –दंडक: the cotton-plant. –न्यस्त *a.* painted, drawn in a picture; Ku. 2. 24. –पक्ष: the francoline partridge. –पट:,-ट्ट: 1 a painting, a picture. 2 a coloured or chequered cloth.–पद *a.* 1 divided into various parts. 2 full of graceful expressions. –पादा the bird called Sârikâ. –पिच्छक: a peacock. –पंख: a kind of arrow. –पृष्ठ: a sparrow. –फलकं a tablet for painting, a picture-board. –बर्ह: a peacock. –भानु: 1 fire. 2 the sun; (चित्रभानुर्विभातीति दिने रवौ रात्रौ वह्नौ K. P. 2. given as an instance of one of the modes of अंजन). 3 N. of Bhairava. 4 the Arka plant. –मंडल: a kind of snake. –मृग: the spotted antelope. –मेखल: a peacock. –योधिन् *m.* an epithet of Arjuna. –रथ: 1 the sun. 2 N. of a king of the Gandharvas, one of the sixteen sons of Kasyapa by his wife Muni; अत्र मुनेस्तनयाश्चित्रसेनादीनां पंचदशानां भ्रातॄणामधिको गुणैः षोडशश्चित्ररथो नाम समुत्पन्नः K. 136; V. 1. –लेख *a.* of beautiful outlines, highly arched; रुचिरस्त्र कलावती

रुचिरचित्रलेखे भ्रुवौ Gît. 10. (-खा) N. of a friend and companion of Ushâ, daughter of Bâṇa. [When Ushâ, related to her her dream, she suggested the idea of taking the portraits of all young princes in the neighbourhood; and on Ushâ's recognising Aniruddha, Chitralekha, by means of her magical power, conveyed him to her palace]. -लेखकः a painter. -लेखनिका a painter's brush. -विचित्र *a.* 1 variously coloured, variegated. 2 multiform. -विद्या the art of painting. -शाला a painter's studio. शिखंडिन् *m.* an epithet of the seven sages:—मरीचि, अंगिरस्, अत्रि, पुलस्त्य, पुलह, क्रतु and वसिष्ठ. °जः an epithet of Brihaspati. -संस्थ *a.* painted. -हस्तः a particular position of the hands in fighting.

चित्रकः 1 A painter. 2 A tiger in general. 3 A small hunting leopard. 4 N. of a tree -कं A sectarial mark on the forehead.

चित्रल *a.* Variegated, spotted. -लः The variegated colour.

चित्रा N. of the fourteenth lunar mansion consisting of one star; हिमनिर्मुक्तयोर्योगे चित्राचंद्रमसोरिव R. 1. 46. -COMP -अटीरः, -ईशः the moon.

चित्रिकः The month called Chaitra.

चित्रिणी N. for a woman 'endowed with various talents and excellences', one of the four divisions into which writers on erotical science class women :—पद्मिनी, चित्रिणी, शंखिनी and हस्तिनी or करिणी. The Ratimanjarî thus defines चित्रिणीः—भवति रतिरसज्ञा नाति खर्वा न दीर्घा तिलकुसुमसुनासा स्निग्धनीलोत्पलाक्षी । घनकठिनकुचाढ्या सुंदरी बद्धशीला सकलगुणविचित्रा चित्रिणी चित्रवक्त्रा ॥ 5.

चित्रित *a.* 1 Variegated, spotted. 2 Painted.

चित्रिन् *a.* (णी *f.*) 1 Wonderful. 2 Variegated.

चित्रीयते *Den.* A. 1 To cause wonder, to be an object of wonder; एवमुत्तरोत्तरभावश्चित्रीयते जीवलोकः Mv. 5; Bk. 17. 64; 18. 23. 2 To wonder.

चित् 10 U. (चिंतयति-ते, चिंतित) 1 To think, consider, reflect, ponder over; तच्छ्रुत्वा पिंगलकश्चिंतयामास Pt. 1; चिंतय तावत्केनापदेशेन पुनराश्रमपदं गच्छामः S. 2. 2 To think of, have an idea of, bring before the mind; तस्मादेतत् (वित्तं) न चिंतयेत् H. 1; तस्मादस्य वधं राजा मनसापि न चिंतयेत् Ms. 8. 381, 4, 258 ; Pt. 1. 135; Ch. P. 1. 3 To mind, take care of, look to; R. 1. 64. 4 To call to mind, remember. 5 To find out, devise, discover, think out; कोप्युपायश्चिंत्यतां H. 1. 6 To regard as, esteem. 7 To weigh, discriminate. 8 To discuss, treat of, consider. -WITH अनु to think over or about, call to mind, ponder over; *S.* 2. 9; Bg. 8. 8. -परि 1 to think, consider, judge; त्वमेव तावत्परिचिंतय स्वयं कदाचिदेते यदि योगमर्हतः Ku. 5. 67; Bg. 10. 17. 2 to think of, remember, bring before the mind. 3 to devise, find out. -वि 1 to think, consider. 2 to think of, ponder over, call to mind; *S.* 4. 1. 3 to take into consideration, have regard to, regard; अस्मान्साधु विचिंत्य संयमधनानुच्चैः कुलं चात्मनः *S.* 4. 16. 4 to intend, fix upon, determine. 5 to devise, find out, discover. -सं 1 to think, consider, reflect, think over; Y. 1. 359; Ch. P. 32. 2 to weigh (in the mind), discriminate.

चिंतनं,-ना 1 Thinking, thinking of, having an idea of; मनसाऽनिष्टचिंतनं Ms. 12. 5. 2 Anxious thought.

चिंता 1 Thinking, thought. 2 Sad or sorrowful thought, care, anxiety; चिंताजडं दर्शनं *S* 4. 5; so वीतचिंतः 12. 3 Reflection, consideration. 4 (In Rhet.) Anxiety, considered as one of the 33 subordinate feelings; ध्यानं चिंता हितानाप्तेः शून्यताश्वासतापकृत् S. D. 201. -COMP. -आकुल *a.* full of care, disturbed in mind, anxious. -कर्मन् *n.* anxiety. —पर *a* thoughtful, anxious. —मणिः a fabulous gem supposed to yield to its possessor all desires, the philosopher's stone; काचमूल्येन विक्रीतो हंत चिंतामणिर्मया Sânti. 1. 12; तदेकलुब्धे हृदि मेऽस्ति लब्धुं चिंता न चिंतामणिमप्यनर्घ्यं N. 3. 81, 1. 145. -वेश्मन् *n.* a council-hall.

चिंतिडी The tamarind tree.

चिंतित *a.* 1 Thought, reflected. 2 Devised, found out.

चिंतितिः *f.* चिंतिया Consideration, reflection, thought.

चिंत्य *pot. p.* 1 To be considered or thought over. 2 To be discovered, to be devised or found out. 3 Requiring consideration, doubtful, questionable; यच्च क्वचिदस्फुटालंकारत्वे उदाहृतं (यः कौमारहरः &c.) एतच्चिंत्यं S. D. 1.

चिन्मय *a.* Consisting of pure intelligence, spiritual (as the supreme spirit). —यं 1 Pure intelligence. 2 The Supreme spirit.

चिपट *a.* Flat-nosed. -टः Rice or grain flattened.

चिपिटः *a.* See चिपट. -COMP. -ग्रीव *a.* short-necked. -नास, -नासिक *a.* flat-nosed.

चिपिटकः, चिपुटः Flattened rice.

चिबु (बु) कं The chin; चिबुकं सुदशः स्पृशामि यावत् Bv. 2. 34; Y. 3. 98.

चिमिः A parrot.

चिर *a.* Long, lasting a long time, existing from a long time, old; चिरविरह; चिरकाल; चिरमित्रं &c. -रं A long time. *Note.*—The singular of any of the oblique cases of चिर may be used adverbially in the sence of 'long', 'for a long time', 'after a long time', 'long since', 'at last', 'finally', न चिरं पर्वते वसेत् Ms. 4. 60; ततः प्रजानां चिरमात्मना धृतां R. 3. 35, 62; Amaru. 79; क्रियाच्चिरेणार्यपुत्रः प्रतिपत्तिं दास्यति *S.* 6; R. 5. 64; प्रीतास्मि ते सौम्य चिराय जीव R. 14. 59; Ku. 5. 47; Amaru. 3; चिरात्सुतस्पर्शरसज्ञतां ययौ R. 3. 26; 11. 63, 12. 67; चिरस्य वाच्यं न गतः प्रजापतिः *S.* 5. 15; चिरे कुर्यात् Sat. Br. -COMP. -आयुस् *a.* long-lived. (*-m.*) a god. -आरोधः a protracted siege, blockade. -उत्थ *a.* existing for a long time. -कार, -कारिक, -कारिन्, -क्रिय *a.* acting slowly, delaying, tarrying, dilatory. -कालः a long time. -कालिक, -कालीन *a.* of long standing, old, long-continued, chronic (as a disease). -जात *a.* born long ago, old.-जीविन् *a.* long-lived. (*-m.*) an epithet of seven persons who are considered to be 'deathless'; अश्वत्थामा बलिर्व्यासो हनुमांश्च बिभीषणः । कृपः परशुरामश्च सप्तैते चिरजीविनः ॥ -पाकिन् *a* ripening late. -पुष्पः the Bakula tree. -मित्रं an old friend. -मेहिन् *m.* an ass. -रात्रं a period of many nights, a long time. °उषित *a.* having lodged for a long time. -विप्रोषित *a.* long banished, a long sojourner. -सूता, -सूतिका a cow that has borne many calves. —सेवकः an old servant. -स्थ, -स्थायिन्, -स्थित *a.* lasting, long-enduring, continuing, durable.

चिरंजीव *a.* Long-lived. -वः An epithet of Kâma.

चिरटी, चिरिंटी 1 A woman married or single who continues to reside after maturity in her father's house. 2 A young woman (in general).

चिरत्न *a.* (त्नी *f.*) Of long standing, old, ancient.

चिरंतन *a.* (नी *f.*) Of long standing, old, ancient; स्वहस्तदत्ते मुनिमासनं मुनिश्चिरंतनस्तावदभिन्यवीविशत् *Si.* 1. 15; चिरंतनः सुहृद् &c.

चिरयति Den. P.; also चिरायते To delay, tarry: कथं चिरयति पांचाली Ve. 1; किं चिरायितं भवता; संकेतके चिरयति प्रवरो विनोदः Mk. 3. 3.

चिरिः A parrot.

चिरुः The shoulder-joint.

चिर्भटी A sort of cucumber.

चिल् 6. P. (चिलति) To put on clothes.

चिलमी (मि) लिका 1 A kind of necklace. 2 A fire-fly. 3 Lightning.

चिल्ल् 1. P. (चिल्लति, चिल्लित) 1 To become loose, be slack or flacid. 2 To act wantonly, sport.

चिल्लः-ल्ला The (Bengal) kite. COMP. -आभः a petty thief, a pickpocket.

चिल्लिका; चिल्ली A cricket; cf झिल्लिका.

चिविः The chin.

चिह्नं 1 mark, spot, stamp, symbol, emblem, badge, symptom; ग्रामेषु यूपचिह्नेषु R. 1. 44; 3. 55; संनिपातस्य चिह्नानि Pt. 1. 177. 2 A sign, indication; प्रसादचिह्नानि पुरः फलानि R. 2. 22; प्रहर्षचिह्न 2. 68. 3 A sign of the zodiac. 4 Aim, direction. –COMP. –**कारिन्** *a.* 1 marking, spotting. 2 striking, wounding, killing. 3 frightful, hideous.

चिह्नित *a.* 1 marked, signed, stamped, bearing the badges of an office; Y. 2. 86; 1. 318; दिवा चरेयुः कार्यार्थं चिह्निता राजशासनैः Ms. 10. 55., 2. 170. 2 Branded. 3 Known, designated.

चीत्कारः An onomatopoetic word, the cry of certain animals, particularly of the ass or elephant; स विषीदति चीत्काराद्गर्दभस्ताडितो यथा H. 2. 31; वैनायक्याश्चिरं वो वदनविधुतयः पांतु चीत्कारवत्यः Mâl. 1. 1.

चीनः 1 N. of a country, the modern China. 2 A kind of deer. 3 A sort of cloth. –**नाः** (*m.* pl.) The rulers or people of China. –**नं** 1 A banner. 2 A kind of bandage for the corners of the eyes. 3 Lead. –COMP. –**अंशुकं**, –**वासस्** *n.* China-cloth, silk, silken cloth; चीनांशुकमिवं केतोः प्रतिवातं नीयमानस्य S. 1. 34; Ku. 7. 3; Amaru. 75. –**कर्पूरः** a kind of camphor. –**जं** steel. –**पिष्टं** 1 red lead. 2 lead. –**वंगं** lead.

चीनाकः A kind of camphor.

चीरं 1 A rag, a tattered cloth, a long strip of garment; Ms. 6. 6. 2 A bark. 3 Clothes or garment in general. 4 A necklace of pearls consisting of four strings. 5 A stripe, stroke, line. 6 A manner of writting with strokes. 7 Lead. –COMP. –**परिग्रह**, –**वासन्** *a.* 1 clothed in bark; Ku. 6. 92; Ms. 11. 101. 2 dressed in rags or tatters.

चीरिः *f.* 1 A veil for covering the the eyes. 2 A cricket. 3 The hem of an under-garment.

चिरि (रु) का A cricket.

चीर्ण *a.* 1 Done, performed, observed. 2 Studied, repeated. 3 Split, divided. –COMP. –**पर्णः** the Kharjura tree.

चीलिका A cricket.

चीव् 1 U. (चीवति-ते) 1 To wear, cover. 2 To take or receive. 3 To seize.

चीवरं 1 A garment (in general). a tatter, rag; प्रेतचीवरवसा स्वनोग्रया R. 11. 16. 2 The dress of any mendicant, particularly of a Buddhist mendicant; चविराणि परिधत्ते Sk.; चीरचीवरपरिच्छदां Mâl. 1; प्रक्षालितमेतन्मया चीवरखंडं Mk. 8.

चीवरिन् *m.* 1 A Buddhist or Jaina mendicant. 2 A mendicant (in general).

चुकारः The roaring of a lion.

चुक्रः 1 A kind of cane or sorrel. 2 Sourness. –**क्रं** Sourness; acidity. –COMP. –**फलं** the tamarind fruit. –**वास्तूकं** wood sorrel.

चुक्रा The temarind tree.

चुक्रिमन् *m.* Sourness.

चुचुकः-कं, चुचूकं The nipple of the breast.

चुंचु *a.* (At the end of certain comp.) Celebrated, famous, renowned, skilled in; अक्षर°, चार° &c.

चुंटा-डा A small well or reservoir.

चुत् 1. P. (चोतति) To ooze, trickle; see च्युत्.

चुतः The anus.

चुद् 10 U. (चोदयति-ते, चोदित) 1 To send, direct, throw forward, urge or drive on, push on; चोदयाश्वान् S. 1. 2 To prompt, inspire, impel, animate, excite; R. 4. 24; to lead, induce; R. 10. 67. 3 To hasten, accelerate. 4 To question, ask. 5 To press with a request. 6 To put forward, adduce, as an argument or objection. –WITH **परि** 1 to push on, direct, send. 2 to incite, prompt. –**प्र** 1 to impel, prompt, urge, incite; चापलाय प्रचोदितः R. 1. 9. 2 to drive or urge on, push on. 3 to direct. –**सं** 1 to direct, incite, impel. 2 to throw, send forth.

चुंदी A procuress, bawd.

चुप् 1 P. (चोपति) To move slowly, creep or steal along.

चुबुकः The chin.

चुंब् 1. 10. U. (चुंबति-ते, चुंबयति-ते, चुंबित) 1 To kiss (fig. also); श्लिष्यति चुंबति जलधरकल्पं हरिरुपगत इति तिमिरमनल्पं Gît 6; प्रियामुखं किंपुरुषश्चुचुंबे Ku. 3. 38; Amaru. 16; H. 4. 132. 2 To touch softly, graze; U. 4. 19. –WITH **परि** to kiss; Rs. 6. 17; Amaru. 77.

चुंबः-बा A kiss.

चुंबकः 1 A kisser. 2 A lecher, a lustful man, libertine. 3 A rogue, cheat. 4 One who has kissed or dipped in a variety of subjects, a superficial scholar. 5 A loadstone.

चुंबनं Kissing, a kiss; चुंबनं देहि मे भार्ये कामचांडालतृप्तये R. G.

चुर् 10. U. (चोरयति-ते, चोरित) 1 To rob, steal; Ms. 8. 333; V. 3. 17. 2 (Fig.) To bear, have, possess, take, assume; अचूचुरच्चंद्रमसोभिरामतां Si. 1. 16

चुरा Theft.

चुरिः-री *f.* A small well.

चुलुकः 1 Deep mud. 2 A mouthful of water or the hand hollowed to hold water or anything; ममौ स भद्रं चुलुके समुद्रः N. 8. 45; ज्ञात्वा विधातुश्चुलुकात् प्रसूतिं Vikr. 1. 37. 3 A small vessel.

चुलुकिन् *m.* A porpoise.

चुलुंप् 1 P. (चुलुंपति) 1 To swing, rock, move to and fro, agitate. –WITH **उद्** 1 to swing. 2 to agitate; अंबोधेर्नालिकेलीरसमिव चुलुकैरुच्चुलुंपत्यपोये Mv. 5. 8.

चुलुंपः Fondling children.

चुलुंपा A she-goat.

चुल्ल् 1 P. (चुल्लति) To play, sport, to make amorous gestures.

चुल्लिः A fire-place.

चुल्ली 1 A fire-place. 2 A funeral pile.

चूचुकं, चूचूकं The nipple of a breast; Si. 7. 19.

चूडकः A well.

चूडा 1 The hair on the top of the head, a single lock on the crown of the head (left after the ceremony of tonsure); R. 18. 51. 2 The ceremony of tonsure. 3 The crest of a cock or peacock. 4 Any crest, plume or diadem. 5 The head. 6 Top, summit. 7 A room on the top of a house. 8 A well. 9 An ornament (like bracelet worn on the wrist). –COMP. –**करणं**, –**कर्मन्** *n.* the ceremony of tonsure; Ms. 2. 35. –**पाशः** a mass of hair; चूडापाशे नवकुरबकं Me. 65. –**मणिः**, –**रत्नं** 1 a jewel worn on the top of the head, a crest-jewel (fig. also). 2 best, excellent (usually at the end of comp.).

चूडार-ल *a.* 1 Having a single lock of hair on the crown of the head. 2 Crested.

चूतः 1 The mango tree. ईषद्बद्धरजःकणाग्रकपिशा चूते नवा मंजरी V. 2. 7; चूतांकुरास्वादकषायकंठः Ku. 3. 32; one of the 5 arrows of Cupid; see पंचबाण. –**तं** The anus.

चूर्ण् 10 U. (चूर्णयति-ते, चूर्णित) 1 To reduce to powder, pulverize, pound. 2 To bruise, crush. –WITH. –**सं** to bruise, crush; संचूर्णयामि गदया न सुयोधनोरू Ve. 1. 15.

चूर्णः-र्णं 1 Powder. 2 Flour. 3 Dust. 4 Aromatic powder, pounded sandal, camphor &c; भवति विफलप्रेरणा चूर्णमुष्टिः Me. 68. –**र्णः** 1 Chalk. 2 Lime. –COMP. –**कारः** a lime-burner. –**कुंतलः** a curl, curly hair; समं केरलकांतानां चूर्णकुंतलवल्लिभिः Vikr. 4. 2. –**खंडं** gravel, pebble. –**पारदः** vermilion. –**योगः** perfumed powder.

चूर्णकः Grain fried and pounded. –**कं** 1 A fragrant powder. 2 A style of prose-composition which is easy, does not contain hard letters, and has very few compounds; अकठोराक्षरं स्वल्पसमासं चूर्णकं विदुः Chand. M. 6.

चूर्णनं Crushing, pounding.

चूर्णिः -र्णी *f.* 1 Pounding, powder. 2 A sum of hundred cowries.

चूर्णिका 1 Grain fried and powdered. 2 A style of prose composition.

चूर्णित *a.* **1** Pounded, pulverized. **2** Crushed, bruised, smashed, shattered to pieces; Ku. 5. 24.

चूलः Hair. **–ला 1** An upper room. **2** A crest. **3** The crest of a comet.

चूलिका 1 The crest or comb of a cock. **2** The root of an elephant's ear. 3 (In dramas). The hinting or indication of the occurrence of any event by characters behind the stage. अंतर्जवनिकासंस्थैः सूचनार्थस्य चूलिका S. D. 310. *e. g.* in the beginning of the 4th act of Mv.

चूष् 1 P. (चूषति, चूषित) To drink, suck up or out.

चूषा 1 A leathern girth (for an elephant). **2** Sucking. **3** A girdle.

चूष्यं Any article of food to be sucked.

चृत् 1. 6. P. (चृतति) **1** To hurt, kill. **2** To tie, bind or connect together –II. 1. P., 10. U. (चर्तति चर्तयति-ते) To light, kindle.

चेकितानः 1 An epithet of *S*iva. **2** N. of a Yâdava prince, who fought on the side of the Pâṇḍavas in the great war.

चेटः (–डः) 1 A servant. **2** A paramour.

चेटि (डि) का, चेटि (डी) *f.* A female slave or servant.

चेतन *a.* (नी *f.*) **1** Animate, alive, living, sentient, feeling; चेतनाचेतनेषु Me. 5. animate and inanimate. **2** Visible. **–नः 1** A sentient being, a man. **2** Soul, mind. **3** The supreme soul. **–ना 1** Sense, consciousness; चुलुकयति मदीयां चेतनां चंचरीकः R. G.; R. 12 14; चेतनां प्रतिपद्यते regains one's consciousness. **2** Understanding. intelligence; पश्चिमाद्यामिनीयामात्प्रसादमिव चेतना R. 17. 1. **3** Life, vitality, animation; Bg. 13 6. **4** Wisdom, reflection.

चेतस् *n.* **1** Consciousness, sense. **2** Thinking soul, reasoning faculty. **3** The mind; heart, soul; चेतः प्रसादयति Bh. 2. 21; गच्छति पुरः शरीरं धावति पश्चाद्संस्तुतं चेतः *S.* 1. 34.–Comp. **जन्मन्,–भवः, –भूः** *m.* **1** love, passion. **2** the god of love. **–विकारः** disturbance of the mind, emotion, agitation.

चेतोमत् *a.* Living, sentient.

चेद् *ind.* If, provided that, although (never used at the beginning of a sentence); अयि रोषिमुरीकरोषि नो चेत्किमपि त्वां प्रतिबारिधे वदामः Bv. 1. 44; Ku. 4. 9; इति चेद् **–न** 'if it be urged that...(we reply) not so' (frequently used in controversial works); सन्निधानमात्रेण राजप्रभृतीनां दृष्ट कर्तृत्वमिति चेन्न S. B.; अथ चेद् but if.

चेदिः (*m. pl.*) N. of a country; तदीशितारं चेदीनां भवांस्तमवमंस्त मा *Si.* 2. 95, 63. –Comp. **–पतिः, –भूभृत** *m.*, **–राज्** *m.*, **–राजः** N. of *S*isupâla, son of Damaghosha and king of the Chedis; *Si.* 2. 96; see शिशुपाल.

चेय *a.* **1** To be piled up. **2** To be gathered or collected.

चेल् 1. P. (चेलति) **1** To go, move. **2** To shake, be disturbed, tremble.

चेलं 1 A garment; कुसुंभारुणं चारु चेलं वसाना Jag. **2** (At the end of comp.) Bad, wicked, vile; भार्याचेलं 'a bad wife' –Comp. **–प्रक्षालकः** a washerman.

चेलिका A bodice.

चेष्ट् 1 A. (चेष्टते, चेष्टित) **1** To move about, stir, be active, show signs of life; यदा स देवो जागर्ति तदेदं चेष्टते जगत् Ms. 1. 52. **2** To make effort, endeavour, exert oneself, struggle. **3** To perform, do (anything). **4** To behave, act. –With **–वि 1** to stir, move, be in motion, move about. **2** to act, behave.

चेष्टकः A particular mode of sexual enjoyment or coitus.

चेष्टनं 1 Motion. **2** Effort, exertion.

चेष्टा 1 Motion, movement; किमस्माकं स्वामिचेष्टानिरूपणेन H. 3. **2** Gesture, action; चेष्टया भाषणेन च नेत्रवक्त्रविकारैश्च लक्ष्यतेंऽतर्गतं मनः Ms 8. 26. **3** Effort, exertion. **4** Behaviour. –Comp. **–नाशः** loss or destruction of the world. **–निरूपणं** observing a person's movement.

चेष्टित *p. p.* Moved, stirred &c. **–तं 1** Motion, gesture, act. **2** Doing, action, behaviour; कपोलपाटलादेशि बभूव रघुचेष्टितं R. 4. 68; तत्तत्कामस्य चेष्टितं Ms. 2. 4. doing or work.

चैतन्यं 1 Spirit, life, intelligence, vitality, sensation. **2** (In Vedânta phil.) The suppreme spirit considered as the essence of all being and source of all sensation.

चैत्तिक *a.* Mental, intellectual.

चैत्यः-त्यं 1 A pile of stones forming a land-mark. **2** A monument, tombstone. **3** A sacrificial shed. **4** A place of religious worship, altar, sanctuary. **5** A temple. **6** A Bauddha or Jaina temple. **7** A religious fig-tree or any tree growing by the side of streets; Me. 23 (रथ्यावृक्ष Malli.) -Comp. **–तरुः, –द्रुमः, –वृक्षः** a fig-tree standing on a sacred spot. **–पालः** the guardian of a sanctuary. **–मुखः** a hermit's water-pot.

चैत्रः 1 N. of a lunar month in which the full moon stands in the constellation Chitrâ (corresponding to March–April). **2** A Buddhist mendicant. **–त्रं** A temple, monument for the dead. –Comp. **–आवलिः** *f.* the full-moon day of Chaitra. **–सखः** an epithet of the god of love.

चैत्ररथं (थ्यं) N. of the garden of Kubera; एको ययौ चैत्ररथप्रदेशान् सौराज्यरम्यानपरो विदर्भान् R. 5. 60. 50.

चैत्रिः, चैत्रिकः, चैत्रिन् *m.* The month called Chaitra.

चैत्री The day of full-moon in the month of Chaitra.

चैद्यः N. of *S*isupâla; अभिचैद्यं प्रतिष्ठासु Si. 2. 1.

चैलं A piece of cloth, garment. –Comp. **–धावः** a washerman.

चोक्ष *a.* **1** Pure, clean. **2** Honest. **3** Clever, dexterous, skilful. **4** Pleasing, agreeable, delightful.

चोचं 1 A bark, rind. **2** Skin, hide. **3** The cocoa-nut.

चोटी A petticoat.

चोडः A bodice.

चोदना 1 Sending, directing, throwing. **2** Urging or driving onward. **3** Prompting, inciting, encouraging, inspiration. **4** A precept, sacred commandment, scriptural injunction. –Comp. **–गुडः** a ball for playing with.

चोदित *p. p.* **1** Sent, directed. **2** Urged on, driven. **3** Incited, Prompted, inspired. **4** Put forward as an argument.

चोद्यं 1 Objecting, asking a question. **2** An objection. **3** Wonder.

चो (चौ) रः A thief, robber; सकलं चोर गतं त्वया गृहीतं V. 4. 16; इंदीवरदलप्रभाचोरं चक्षुः Bh. 3. 67.

चो (चौ) रिका Theft, robbery.

चोरित *a.* Stolen, robbed.

चोरितकं 1 Petty theft, larceny. **2** Anything stolen.

चोलः (*m. pl.*) N. of a country in southern India, the modern Tanjore. **–लः ली–** A short jacket, a bodice.

चोलकः 1 breast-plate. **2** A barkdress. **3** A bodice.

चोलकिन् *m.* **1** A soldier armed with a breast-plate. **2** The orange tree. **3** The wrist.

चोलं (लों) डुकः A fillet for the head, a turban, tiara or diadem.

चोषः 1 Sucking. **2** Inflammation (in medicine).

चोष्यं=चूष्य q. v.

चौड (डी *f.*) चौल (ली *f.*) *a.* **1** Crested. **2** Relating to tonsure. **–डं–लं** The ceremony of tonsure.

चौर्यं 1 Theft, robbery. **2** Secrecy, concealment. –Comp. **–रतं** secret sexual enjoyment. **–वृत्तिः** *f.* the habit of robbery.

च्यवनं 1 Moving, motion. **2** Being deprived of, loss; deprivation. **3** Dying, perishing. **4** Flowing, trickling.

च्यु 1 A. (च्यवते, च्युत) **1** To fall or drop down, slip, sink (fig. also); *S.* 2. 8. **2** To come out of, flow or issue from, drop, trickle or stream forth from; स्वतश्च्युतं वह्निमिवाद्रिरंबुदः R. 3. 58; Bk. 9. 74. **3** To deviate or swerve from, fall off or away from, leave

(duty &c.); (with abl.); अस्माद्धर्मान्न च्यवेत Ms. 7. 98, 12. 71-72. 4 To lose, be deprived of; अच्योष्ट सत्त्वान्नृपतिः Bk. 3. 20, 7. 92. 5 To vanish, disappear, perish, be an end; R. 8. 65; Ms. 12. 96. 6 To decrease. -WITH -परि 1 to go away or fly off from, to escape. 2 to proceed from. 3 to swerve, fall off from, leave. 4 to lose, be deprived of. 5 to drop or fall down &c. -प्र to fall off from, drop down &c. (nearly the same as च्यु with परि).

च्युत् 1 P. (च्योतति) 1 To drop, flow; ooze, trickle, stream forth; इदं शोणितमभ्यगं संप्रहारेऽच्युतत्तयोः Bk. 6. 28. 2 To drop or fall down, slip; इदं कवचमच्योतीत् Bk. 6. 29. 3 To cause to drop or stream forth.

च्युत *p. p.* 1 Fallen down, slipped, fallen. 2 Removed, expelled. 3 Strayed, erred. 4 Lost. —COMP. -अधिकार *a.* dismissed from office. -आत्मन् *a.* of a depraved soul, evil-minded; Ku. 5. 81.

च्युतिः *f.* 1 Falling down, a fall. 2 Deviation from. 3 Dropping, oozing. 4 Losing, deprivation; धैर्यच्युतिं कुर्या Ku. 3. 10. 5 Vanishing, perishing. 6 The vulva. 7 The anus.

च्यूतः The mango-tree.

छ.

छः A part, fragment.

छगः (गी *f.*) A goat.

छगलः (ली *f.*) A goat. -लं A blue cloth.

छगलकः A goat.

छटा 1 Mass, lump, number, assemblage; सटाच्छटाभिन्नघनेन *Si.* 1. 47. 2 A collection of rays of light, lusture, splendour, light; *Si.* 8. 38. 3 A continuous line, streak; छातेतरांबुच्छटा K. P. -COMP. -आभा lightening. फलः the betel-nut tree.

छत्रः A mushroom. -त्रं A parasol, an umbrella; अदेयमासीत्त्रयमेव भूपतेः शशिप्रभं छत्रमुभे च चामरे R. 3. 16; Ms. 7. 96. -COMP. -धरः, -धारः the bearer of an umbrella. धारणं 1 carrying or bearing an umbrella; Ms. 2. 178. 2 carrying an umbrella as a type of royal authority. -पतिः 1 a king over whom an umbrella is carried as a mark of dignity, a sovereign, emperor. 2 N. of an ancient king in जंबुद्वीप. -भंगः 1 'destruction of the royal parasol', loss of dominion, deposition. 2 dependence. 3 wilfulness. 4 a forlorn condition, widowhood.

छत्रकः A temple in honour of *Siva*. -कं A mushroom.

छत्रा छत्राकः A mushroom; Ms. 5. 19; Y. 1. 176.

छत्रिकः The bearer of an umbrella.

छत्रिन् *a.* (णी *f.*) Having or bearing an umbrella. -*m.* A barber.

छत्वरः 1 A house. 2 A bower, arbour.

छद् 1. 10. U. (छदति-ते, छादयति-ते, छन्न, छादित) 1 to cover, cover over, veil; हैमैश्छन्ना Me. 76; चक्षुः खेदात्सलिलगुरुभिः पक्ष्मभिश्छादयंतीं Me. 90; छन्नोपांत....काननाम्रैः 18. 2 To spread anything (as a cover.), cover oneself. 3 To hide, conceal, eclipse; (fig.); keep secret; ज्ञानपूर्वं कृतं कर्म छादयंते ह्यसाधवः Mb.; छन्नं दोषमुदाहरंति Mk. 9. 4. -WITH अव to hide, conceal, cover. -आ 1 to cover (in general); नाच्छादयति कौपीनं Pt. 3. 97. 2 to hide, conceal; भानोराच्छादयत्प्रभां Mb. 3 to clothe, put on clothes; Ms. 3. 27; वस्त्रमाच्छादयति &c. उद् to uncover, undress. -उप 1 to cover, 2 to hide, conceal. -परि 1 to cover, clothe; दर्भैस्तं परिच्छाद्य Pt. 2; द्विपिचर्मपरिच्छन्नः (गर्दभः) H. 3. 9. 2 to hide, conceal. -प्र 1 to cover, wrap up, veil, envelope; (वनं) प्राच्छादयदमेयात्मा नीहारेणेव चंद्रमाः Mb. 2 to hide, conceal, disguise; प्रच्छाद्य स्वान् गुणान् Bh. 2. 77; प्रदानं प्रच्छन्नं 2. 64; Ms 4. 198; 10. 40; Ch. P. 4. 3 to clothe oneself, put on clothes. 4 to stand in the way, become an obstacle. -प्रति 1 to hide, conceal. 2 to cover, wrap up. -सं 1 to hide. 2 to envelope, wrap up.

छदः छदनं 1 A covering, cover; अल्पच्छद, उत्तरच्छद &c. 2 A wing; छदहेम कषन्निवालसत् N. 2. 69. 3 A leaf. 4 A sheath, case.

छदिः *f.*, **छदिस्** *n.* 1 The roof of a carriage. 2 The roof or thatch of a house.

छद्मन् *n.* 1 A deceptive dress, a disguise. 2 A plea, pretext, guise; ब्रह्मछद्मा सामर्थ्यसारः Mv. 2. 25; पलितछद्मना जरा R. 12. 2; *Si.* 2. 21. 8 Fraud, dishonesty, trick; छद्मना परिददामि मृत्यवे U. 1. 45; Ms. 4. 199; 9. 72. -COMP. तापसः a religious hypocrite, -रूपेण *ind.* incognito, in disguise. -वेशिन् *m.* a player, a cheat, dressed in disguise.

छद्मिन् *a.* (नी *f.*) 1 Fraudulent, deceitful. 2 Disguised (at the end of comp.); *e. g.* ब्राह्मणच्छद्मिन् disguised as a Brâhmaṇa.

छनच्छन् *ind.* An imitative sound, expressive of the noise of falling drops &c.; छनच्छनिति बाष्पकणाः पतंति Amaru. 89.

छंद् 10 U. (छंदयति-ते, छंदित) 1 To please, gratify. 2 To persuade, coax. 3 To cover. 4 To be delighted in.— WITH उप 1 to flatter, coax, invite; त्वयोपच्छंदित उदकेन *S.* 5. coaxed to drink water. 2 to request, beseech. 3 to persuade one to do a thing. 4 to give one something.

छंदः 1 Wish, desire, fancy, liking, will; विज्ञप्यतां देवि यस्ते छंद इति V. 3 just as you like. 2 Free will, one's own choic, whim, free or wilful conduct; षष्ठे काले त्वमपि दिवसस्यात्मनश्छंदवर्ती V. 2. 1; Gît. 1; Y. 2. 195; स्वछंदं according to one's own free will, independently. 3 (Hence) subjection, control. 4 Meaning intention, purport. 5 Poison.

छंदस् *n.* 1 Wish, desire, fancy, will, pleasure; (गृह्णीयात्) मूर्खं छंदोऽनुवृत्तेन याथातथ्येन पंडितं Châṇ. 33. 2 Free will, free or wilful conduct. 3 Meaning, intention. 4 Fraud, trick, deceit. 5 The Vedas, the sacred text of the Vedic hymns; स च कुलपतिराद्यश्छंदसां यः प्रयोक्ता U. 3. 48; बहुलं छंदसि frequently used by Pâṇini; प्रणवश्छंदसामिव R. 1. 11; Y. 1. 143; Ms. 4. 95. 6 A metre; ऋक्छंदसा आशास्ते *S.* 4; गायत्री छंदसामहं Bg. 10. 35; 13. 14. 7 Metrical science, prosody; (regarded as one of the six Vedângas or auxiliaries to the Vedas, the other five being शिक्षा, व्याकरण, कल्प, निरुक्त and ज्योतिष). -COMP. -कृतं any metrical part of the Vedas or other sacred compositions यथोदितेन विधिना नित्यं छंदस्कृतं पठेत् Ms. 4. 100; -गः (छंदोगः) 1 a reciter in Metre. 2 a student or chanter of the Sâmaveda; Ms. 3. 145; (छंदोगः सामवेदाध्यायी) -भंगः a violation of the laws of metre -विचितिः *f.* 'examination of metres', N. of a work on metres, sometimes ascribed to Daṇḍin; छंदोविचित्यां सकलस्तत्प्रपंचो निदर्शितः Kâv. 1. 12.

छन्न *a.* 1 Covered. 2 Hidden, concealed, secret &c; see छद्.

छमंडः An orphan.

छर्द् 10 U. (छर्दयति, छर्दित) To vomit.

छर्दः, **छर्दनं**, **छर्दिः** *f.*, **छर्दिका**, **छर्दिस्** *f.* Vomiting, sickness.

छलः -लं 1 Fraud, trick, deceit, deception; विद्यहे शठ पलायनच्छलानि R. 19. 31; छलमत्र न गृह्यते Mk. 9. 18; Y. 1. 61; Ms. 8. 49, 187; Amaru. 16; *Si.* 13. 11. 2 Roguery, knavery 3 A plea, pretext, guise, semblance (often used in this sense to denote an उत्प्रेक्षा); परिखावलयच्छलेन या न परेषां ग्रहणस्य

गोचरा N. 2. 95; प्रत्यर्प्य पूजामुपदाच्छलेन R. 7. 30. 54, 16. 28; Bk. 1. 1; Amaru 15; Mâl. 9. 1 **4** Intention. **5** Wickedness. **6** A fallacy. **7** Design, device.

छलयति Den. P. To outwit, deceive, cheat; बलिं छलयते Gît. 1; शैवाललोलांश्छलयंति मीनान् R. 16. 61; Bg. 10. 36; Amaru, 41.

छलिकं A kind of drama or dancing, छलिकं दुष्प्रयोज्यमुदाहरंति M. 2.

छलनं, –ना Deceiving, cheating, outwitting.

छलिन् *m*. A cheat, swindler, rogue.

छल्लि, –ल्ली *f*. **1** Bark, rind. **2** A spreading creeper. **3** offspring, progeny, posterity.

छविः *f*. **1** Hue, colour of the skin, complexion; हिमकरोदयपांडुमुखच्छविः R. 9. 38; छविः पांडुरा *S*. 3. 10; Me. 33. **2** Colour in general. **3** Beauty, splendour, brilliance; छविकरं मुखचूर्णमृतुश्रियः R. 9. 45. **4** Light, lustre. **5** Skin, hide.

छाग *a* (**गी** *f.*) Relating to a goat or she-goat; Y. 1. 258. **–गः** (**गी** *f.*) **1** A goat; ब्राम्हणश्छागतो यथा (वंचितः) H. 4. 53; Ms. 3. 269. **2** The sign Aries of the zodiac. **–गं** The milk of a she-goat. –COMP. **–भोजन** *m*. a wolf. **–मुखः** an epithet of Kârtikeya. **–रथः, वाहनः** an epithet of Agni, the god of fire.

छागणः A fire of dried cowdung.

छागल *a*. (**–ली** *f*.) Coming from or relating to a goat. **–ल** A goat.

छात *a*. **1** Cut, divided, **2** Feeble, thin, emaciated (*p. p.* of छो q. v.).

छात्रः A pupil, disciple. **–त्रं** A kind of honey. –COMP. **–गंडः** an indifferent poetical scholar, knowing only the beginings of stanzas. **–दर्शनं** fresh butter prepared from milk one day old. **–व्यसंकः** a roguish or dull-witted pupil.

छादं A thatch, roof.

छादनं **1** A cover, screen (fig. also); विनिर्मितं छादनमज्ञतायाः Bh. 2. 7. **2** Concealing. **3** A leaf. **4** Clothing.

छादिन *a*. see छन्न.

छाद्मिकः A rogue; Ms. 4. 195.

छांदस *a*. (**सी** *f*.) **1** Vedic, peculiar to the Vedas; as छांदसः प्रयोगः. **2** Studying or familiar with the Vedas. **3** Metrical. **–सः** A Brâhmaṇa versed in the Vedas.

छाया **1** Shade, shadow (changed at the end of Tat. comp. into छायं when बाहुल्य or thickness of shade is meant; *e. g*. इक्षुच्छायनिषादिन्यः R. 4. 20; so 7. 4. 12. 50; Mu. 4. 21); छायामधःसानुगतां निषेव्य Ku. 1. 5; 6. 46, अनुभवति हि मूर्ध्ना पादपस्तीव्रमुष्णं शमयति परितापं छायया संश्रितानां *S*. 5. 7; R. 1. 75, 2. 6, 3. 70; Me. 67. **2** A reflected image, a reflection; छाया न मूर्छति मलोपहतप्रसादे शुद्धे तु दर्पणतले सुलभावकाशा *S*. 7. 32. **3** Resemblance, likeness. **4** A shadowy fancy, hallucination. **5** Blending of colours. **6** Lustre, light; छायामंडललक्ष्येण R. 4. 5; रत्नच्छायाव्यतिकरः Me. 15, 35. **7** Colour; Mâl. 6. 5. **8** Colour of the face, complexion; केवलं लावण्यमयी छाया त्वां न मुंचति *S*. 3; मेघैरंतरितः प्रिये तव मुखच्छायानुकारी शशी S. D. **9** Beauty; क्षामच्छायं भवनं Me. 80. 104. **10** Protection. **11** A row, line. **12** Darkness. **13** A bribe. **14** N. of Durgâ. **15** N. of a wife of the sun (she was but a shadow or likeness of संज्ञा the wife of the sun; consequently when संज्ञा went to her father's house, without the knowledge of her husband, she put छाया in her own place. छाया bore to the sun three children:—two sons Sâvarṇi and *S*ani, and one daughter Tapanî). –COMP. **–अंकः** the moon. **–करः** the bearer of an umbrella **–ग्रहः** a mirror. **–तनयः, –सुतः** Saturn, son of छाया. **–तरुः** a large umbrageous tree; Me. 1. **–द्वितीय** *a* 'accompanied only by one's shadow', alone **–पथः** the atmosphere, R. 13. 2. **–भृत्** *m*. the moon **–मानः** the moon. **–नं** measure of a shadow. **–मित्रं** a parasol. **–मृगधरः** the moon. **–यंत्रं** a sun-dial.

छायामय *a*. Reflected, shadowy.

छिः *f*. Abuse, reproach.

छिक्का Sneezing.

छित *a*. see छात.

छित्तिः *f*. Cutting, dividing.

छित्वर *a* (**री** *f*.) **1** Fit for cutting. **2** Hostile, fraudulent, roguish.

छिद् 7. U. (छिनत्ति छिंते, छिन्न) **1** To cut, cut or lop off, hew, mow, tear, pierce, break asunder, rend, split, divide; नैनं छिंदंति शस्त्राणि Bg. **2** 23; R. 12. 80; Ms. 4. 61, 70; Y. 2. 302. **2** To disturb, interrupt (as sleep) **3** To remove, drive off, destroy, quell, annihilate; तृष्णां छिंद्धि Bh. 2. 77; एतन्मे संशयं छिंद्धि मतिर्मे संप्रमुह्यति Mb.; राघवो रथमप्राप्तां तामाशां च सुरद्विषां । अर्धचंद्रमुखैर्बाणैश्चिच्छेद कदलीसुखं ॥ R. 12. 96; Ku. 7. 16. -WITH. **–अव** to cut off, tear to pieces, separate, divide. **2** to distinguish, discriminate. **3** to modify, define, limit (frequently used in Nyâya in this sense), see अवच्छिन्न. **–आ** **1** to cut off or away, tear, cut in pieces **2** to snatch away, tear from, take away; Ku. 2. 46; Mâl. 5. 28. **3** to cut off, exclude; Ms. 4. 219. **4** to remove, pull off. **5** to draw or pull off, extract, draw out. **6** to disregard, take no notice of. **–उद्** **1** to cut off, destroy, extirpate, eradicate; नोच्छिंद्यात्आत्मनो मूलं परेषां चातितृष्णया Mb.; किं वा रिपूंस्तव गुरुः स्वयमुच्छिनत्ति R. 5. 71, 2. 23; Pt. 1 47. **2** to interfere with, interrupt, stop; अर्थेन तु विहीनस्य पुरुषस्याल्पमेधसः । उच्छिद्यंते क्रियाः सर्वा ग्रीष्मे कुसरितो यथा ॥ Pt. 2. 84; Ms. 3. 101. **–परि** **1** to tear, cut off, tear to pieces. **2** to wound, mutilate. **3** to separate, divide, part; शतेन परिच्छिद्य Sk. **4** to fix accurately, set limits to, define, decide, distinguish or discriminate; मध्यस्था भगवती नौ गुणदोषतः परिच्छेत्तुमर्हति M. 1; (न) यशः परिच्छेत्तुमियत्तयालं R. 6. 77; 17. 59; Ku. 2. 58. **–प्र** **1** to cut off, cut to pieces. **2** to take away, withdraw. **–वि** **1** to cut off, break, tear asunder, divide; यदर्धे विच्छिन्नं भवति कृतसंधानमिव तत् *S*. 1. 9; R. 16. 20; Bh. 1. 96. **2** to interrupt, break off, terminate, end, destroy, make extinct (as a family); विच्छिद्यमानेऽपि कुले परस्य Bk. 3. 52; Amaru. 74. **–सं** **1** to cut, cut off, divide **2** to drive off, clear, solve, remove (as a doubt &c).

छिद् *a*. (At the end of comp.) Cutting, dividing, destroying, removing, splitting &c; श्रमच्छिदामाश्रमपादपानां R. 5. 6; पंकच्छिदः फलस्य M. 2. 8.

छिदकं **1** Indra's thunderbolt. **2** A diamond.

छिदा Cutting, dividing.

छिदिः *f*. **1** An axe. **2** Indra's thunderbolt.

छिदिरः **1** An axe. **2** A word. **3** Fire. **4** A rope, cord.

छिदुर *a*. **1** Cutting, dividing. **2** Easily breaking. **3** Broken, disordered, deranged, संलक्ष्यते न च्छिदुरोऽपि हारः R. 16. 62. **4** Hostile. **5** Roguish, knavish.

छिद्र *a*. Pierced, containing holes. **–द्रं** **1** A hole, slit, cleft, fissure, rent, pit, opening, crack; नवच्छिद्राणि तान्येव प्राणस्यायतनानि तु Y. 3. 99; Ms. 8. 239; अयं पटश्छिद्रशतैरलंकृतः Mk 2. 9. so काष्ठ°, भूमि° &c. **2** A defect, flaw, blemish; त्वं हि सर्षपमात्राणि परच्छिद्राणि पश्यसि । आत्मनो बिल्वमात्राणि पश्यन्नपि न पश्यसि ॥ Mb. **3** A vulnerable or weak point, weak side, imperfection, foible; नास्य छिद्रं परो विद्याद्विद्याच्छिद्रं परस्य तु । गूहेत् कूर्म इवांगानि रक्षेद्विवरमात्मनः ॥ Ms 7. 105, 102; छिद्रं निरूप्य सहसा प्रविशत्यशंकः H. 1. 81 (where छिद्र means a hole also); Pt. 3 39. –COMP. **–अनुजीविन्, –अनुसंधानिन्, –अनुसारिन्, अन्वेषिन्** *a*. **1** looking out for faults or flaws. **2** seeking the weak points of another, picking holes, censorious; सर्पाणां दुर्जनानां च परिच्छिद्रानुजीविनां Pt. 1. **–अंतरः** a cane, reed. **–आत्मन्** *a*. one who exposes his weak points to the attack of others. **–कर्ण** *a*. having the ear pierced. **–दर्शन** *a*. **1** exhibiting faults. **2** seeking the weak points.

छिद्रित *a*. **1** Having holes. **2** Bored, perforated.

छिन्न *p. p.* 1 Cut, divided, rent, chopped, riven, torn, broken. 2 Destroyed, removed; see छिद्. **-न्ना** A whore, harlot. –COMP. **-केश** *a.* shorn, shaven. **-द्रुमः** a riven tree. **-द्वैध** *a.* whose doubt is dispelled. **-नासिक** *a.* noseless. **-भिन्न** *a.* cut up through and through, mutilated, mangled, cut up. **-मस्त, -मस्तक** *a.* decapitated. **-मूल** *a.* cut up by the roots; R. 7. 43. **-श्वासः** a kind of asthma. **-संशय** *a.* 'one whose doubt is dispelled', free from doubt, confirmed.

छुछुंदरः (**री** *f.*) The musk-rat; Y. 3. 213; Ms. 12. 65.

छुप् 6. P. (छुपति) To touch.

छुपः 1 Touch. 2 A shrub, bush. 3 Combat, war,

छुर् I. 1 P. (छोरति, छुरित) 1 To cut, divide. 2 engrave. –II. 6. P. (छुरति छुरित) 1 To cover, smear, daub, inlay, coat, envelop. 2 To intermix. –WITH **-वि** to smear, anoint, cover, coat; मनः शिलाविच्छुरिता निषेदुः Ku. 1. 55; Ch. P. 11; V. 4. 45.

छुरणं Smearing, anointing; ज्योत्स्नाभस्मच्छुरणधवला रात्रिकापालिकीयं K. P. 10.

छुरा Lime.

छुरिका A knife.

छुरित *p. p.* 1 Set, inlaid. 2 Overspread, coaled, covered over with; अनेकधातुच्छुरिताश्मराशेः *Si.* 3. 4. 7; इंदुकिरणच्छुरितमुखीं K. 10. 3 Blended, intermixed; परस्परेण छुरितामलच्छवी *Si.* 1. 22.

छुरी, छूरिका, छूरी A knife.

छृद् I. 1 P., 10. U. (छर्दति, छर्दयति-ते) To kindle. –II. 7. U. (छृणत्ति, छृन्न) 1 To play. 2 To shine. 3 To vomit.

छेक *a.* 1 Tame, domesticated (as a beast). 2 Citizen, townbred. 3 Shrewd, trained in the acuteness and vice of towns.-COMP. **-अनुप्रासः** one of the five kinds of अनुप्रास, 'the single alliteration,' which is a similarity occurring *once* (or singly) and in more than one way among a collection of consonants; *e. g.* आदाय बकुलगंधानंधीकुर्वन्पदे पदे भ्रमरान्। अयमेति मंदमंदं कावेरीवारिपावनः पवनः॥ S. D. 634. **-अपन्हुतिः** *f.* a figure of speech; one of the varieties of अपन्हुति. The Chandrâloka thus defines and illustrates it:— छेकापन्हुतिरन्यस्य शंकातस्तस्य निह्नवे। प्रजल्पन्मत्पदे लग्नः कांतः किं न हि नूपुरः 5. 27. **उक्तिः** *f.* insinuatory, insinuating, *double entendre.*

छेदः 1 Cutting, felling down, breaking down, dividing; अभिज्ञाश्छेदपातानां क्रियंते नंदनद्रुमाः Ku. 2. 41; छेदो दंशस्य दाहो वा M. 4. 4; R. 14. 1; Ms. 8. 270, 370; Y. 2. 223, 240. 2 Solving, removing, dissipating, clearing; as in संशयच्छेद. 3 Destruction, interruption; निद्राच्छेदाभिताम्रा Mu. 3. 21. 4 Cessation, end, termination, disappearance as in धर्मच्छेद. 5 A piece, bit, cut, fragment, section; बिसकिसलयच्छेदपाथेयवंतः Me. 11. 59; अभिनवकरिदंतच्छेदपांडुः कपोलः Mâl. 1. 22; Ku. 1. 4; *S.* 3. 7; R. 12. 100. 6 (In math.) A divisor, the denominator of a fraction.

छेदनं 1 Cutting, tearing, cutting off, splitting, dividing; Ms. 8. 280, 292, 322. 2 A section, portion, bit, part. 3 Destruction, removel.

छेदिः A carpenter.

छेमंडः An orphan.

छेलकः A goat.

छैदिकः A cane.

छो 4. P. (छयति, छात, or छित, *caus.* छापयति) To cut, cut asunder, mow, reap; Bk. 14. 101; 15. 40.

छोटिका Snapping the thumb and fore-finger together (Mar. चुटकी).

छोरणं Abandoning, leaving.

ज.

ज *a.* (At the end of comp.) Born from or in, produced or caused by, descended from, growing in, living or being at or in &c.; अविनेत्रज, कुलज, जलज, क्षत्रियज, अंडज, उद्भिज्ज &c. **-जः** 1 A father. 2 Production., birth. 3 Poison. 4 An imp or पिशाच. 5 A conqueror. 6 Lustre. 7 N. of Vishṇu.

जकुटः 1 The Malaya mountain. 2 A dog.

जक्ष् 2 P. (जक्षिति, जक्षित or जग्ध) To eat, eat up, destroy, consume; Bk. 4. 39; 13. 28; 15. 46, 18. 19.

जक्षणं, जक्षिः Eating, consuming.

जगत् *a.* (**ती** *f.*) Moving, moveable; सूर्य आत्मा जगतस्तस्थुषश्च Rv. 1. 115. 1; इदं विश्वं जगत्सर्वमजगच्चापि यद्भवेत् Mb. —*m.* Wind, air. -*n.* The world; जगतः पितरौ वंदे पार्वतीपरमेश्वरौ R. 1. 1. –COMP. **-अंबा, -अंबिका** N. of Durgâ. **-आत्मन्** *m.* the supreme spirit. **-आदिजः** an epithet of Siva. **-आधारः** 1 time. 2 air, wind. **-आयुः, -आयुस्** *m.* wind. **-ईशः, -पतिः** 'the lord of the universe', the supreme deity. **-उद्धारः** salvation of the world. **-कर्तृ, -धातृ** *m.* the creator of the world. **-चक्षुस्** *m.* the sun. **-नाथः** the lord of the universe. **-निवासः** 1 the Supreme Being. 2 an epithet of Vishṇu; जगन्निवासो वसुदेवसद्मनि *Si.* 1. 1. 3 worldly existence. **-प्राणः** **-बलः** wind. **-योनिः** 1 the Supreme Being. 2 an epithet of Vishṇu. 3 of *Siva.* 4 of Brahmâ. (**-निः** *f.*) the earth. **-वहा** the earth. **-साक्षिन्** *m.* 1 the supreme spirit. 2 the sun.

जगती 1 The earth; (समीहते) नयेन जेतुं जगतीं सुयोधनः Ki. 1. 7; समतीत्य भाति जगती जगती 5. 20. 2 People, mankind. 3 A cow. 4 A kind of metre; (See App.).–COMP. **अधीश्वरः,-ईश्वरः** a king; N. 2. 1. **-रुह्** *m.* a tree.

जगनुः (**नुः**) 1 Fire. 2 An insect. 3 An animal.

जगरः An armour.

जगल *a.* Roguish, tricky, knavish. **-लं** 1 Cowdung. 2 An armour 3 A kind of liquor (*m.* also in the last two senses).

जग्ध *a.* Eaten.

जग्धिः *f.* 1 Eating. 2 Food.

जग्मिः Wind.

जघनं 1 The hip and the loins, the buttocks; घटय जघने कांचीमंच स्रजा कबरीभरं Gît. 12. 2 The pudenda. 3 Rear-guard, the reserve of an army.–COMP. **-कूपकौ** (dual) the hollows of the loins of a handsome woman. **-चपला** an unchaste or libidinous woman; पत्युर्विदेशगमने परमसुखं जघनचपलायाः Pt. 1. 173.

जघन्य *a.* 1 Hind-most, last; Bg. 14. 18; Ms. 8. 270. 2 Worst, vilest, base, lowest, censurable. 3 Of low origin or rank. **-न्यः** A *S*ûdra.–COMP. **-जः** 1 a younger brother. 2 a *S*udra.

जघ्निः A weapon (offensive).

जघ्नु *a.* Striking, killing.

जंगम *a* Moving, living, moveable; चिताग्निरिव जंगमः R. 15. 16; शोकाग्निरिव जंगमः Mv. 5. 20; Ms. 1. 41. **-मं** A moveable thing; R. 2. 44. –COMP. **-इतर** *a.* immoveable. **-कुटी** an umbrella.

जंगलं 1 A desert, dreary ground, waste land. 2 A thicket, forest. 3 A secluded or unfrequented place.

जंगालः A ridge of earth running along the edge of a field to collect water and to form a passage over it, landmark.

जंगुलं Poison, venom.

जंघा Leg from the ankle to the knee; the shank. –COMP. **-आरः, -कारिकः** a runner, courier, an express. **-त्राणं** an armour for the legs.

जंघाल *a.* Running swiftly, rapid. **-लः** 1 A courier. 2 A deer, an antelope.

जंघिल *a.* Running swiftly, rapid, quick.

जज्, जंज् 1 P. (जजति or जंजति) To fight.

जट् 1 P. (जटति) To clot, become twisted or matted together (as hair).

जटा 1 The hair matted and twisted together, matted or clotted hair; अंसव्यापि शकुंतनीडनिचितं बिभ्रज्जटामंडलं S. 7. 11; जटाश्च बिभृयान्नित्यं Ms. 6. 6; Mâl. 1. 2. 2 A fibrous root. 3 A root in general. 4 A branch. 5 The शतावरी plant. –COMP. –चीरः,टंकः,–टीरः,–धरः epithets of *Siva*. –जूटः 1 a mass of twisted hair (in general). 2 the twisted hair of *Siva*; जटाजूटग्रंथौ यदसि विनिबद्धा पुरभिदा G. L. 14. –ज्वालः a lamp. –धर *a.* wearing matted hair.

जटायुः A son of *Syenî* and *Aruṇa*, a semi-divine bird. [He was a great friend of Dasaratha. While Râya*n*a was carrying away Sîtâ, Jatâyu heard her cries in the chariot, and fought most desperately with the formidable giant to rescue her from his grasp. But he was mortally wounded, and remained in that state till Râma passed by that place in the course of his search after Sîtà. The kind-hearted bird told Ràma that his wife had been carried away by Râva*n*a and then breathed his last. His funeral rites were duly performed by Râma and Lakshma*n*a.]

जटाल *a.* 1 Wearing a coil of twisted hair. 2 Collected together (like matted hair); Bv. 1. 36. –लः The (Indian) fig-tree.

जटिः (टी) *f.* 1 The (Indian) fig-tree. 2 Clotted hair. 3 An assemblage, multitude.

जटिन् *a.* (नी *f.*) Having twisted hair. –*m.* 1 An epithet of *Siva*. 2 The waved-leaf fig-tree (प्लक्ष).

जटिल *a.* 1 Wearing matted or twisted hair (as an ascetic); विवेश कश्चिज्जटिलस्तपोवनं Ku. 5. 30; (जटिल may be here a noun meaning 'an ascetic'). 2 Complicated, confused, intermixed, intermingled; विजानंतोऽप्येते वयमिह विपज्जालजटिलान् न मुंचामः कामानहह गहनो मोहमहिमा Bh. 3. 21. 3 Dense, impervious. –लः 1 A lion. 2 A goat.

जठर *a.* Hard, stiff, firm. –रः,–रं 1 The stomach, belly; जठरं को न बिभर्ति केवलं Pt. 1. 22. 2 The womb. 3 The interior of anything. –COMP. –अग्निः the digestive fire of the stomach, the gastric fluid. –आमयः dropsy.–ज्वाला, –व्यथा belly-ache, colic, यंत्रणा,–यातना pain endured by the child in the womb.

जड *a.* 1 Cold, frigid, chilly. 2 Dull, paralysed, motionless, benumbed; चिंताजडं दर्शनं S. 4. 5; परामृशन् हर्षजडेन पाणिना R. 3. 68, 2. 42. 3 Dull, senseless, stupid, irrational, dull-witted; जडानंधान् पंगून्...त्रातुं G. L. 15, so जडधी, जडमति &c.; Y. 2. 25; Ms. 2. 110. 4 Dulled, made senseless or apathetic, devoid of appreciation or taste; वेदाभ्यासजडः कथं नु विषयव्यावृत्तकौतूहलः V. 1. 9. 5 Stunning, benumbing, stupefying. 6 Dumb, 7 Unable to learn the Vedas (Dâyabhâga). –डं 1 Water. 2 Lead. –COMP. –क्रिय *a.* slow, dilatory. –भरतः an idiot.

जडता,-त्वं 1 Dulness, aversion to work, slothfulness. 2 Ignorance, stupidity. 3 (In Rhet.) Dulness, regarded as one of the 33 subordinate feelings; S. D. 175.

जडिमन् *m.* 1 Frigidity. 2 Stupidity. 3 Dulness, apathy. 4 Stupor, stupefaction.

जतु *n.* Lac. –COMP. –अश्मकं red arsenic. –पुत्रकः a man at chess. –रसः lac.

जतुकं Lac.

जतुका 1 Lac. 2 A bat.

जतुकी, जतूका A bat.

जत्रु *n.* The collar bone, the clavicle.

जन् 4 A. (जायते, जात; *pass.* जन्यते or जायते) 1 To be born or produced (with abl. of source of birth); अजनि ते वै पुत्रः Ait. Br.; Ms. 1. 9; 3. 39, 41; प्राणाद्वायुरजायत Rv. 10. 90. 12; Ms. 10. 8; 3. 76; 1. 75. 2 To rise, spring up, grow (as a plant &c). 3 To be, become, happen, take place, occur; अनिष्टादिष्टलाभेऽपि न गतिर्जायते शुभा H. 1. 6; रक्तनेत्रोऽजनि क्षणात् Bk. 6. 32; Y. 3. 226; Ms. 1. 99. –*Caus.* (जनयति) To give birth, beget, cause to produce. –WITH अनु 1 to be born after; पुत्रिकायां कृतायां तु यदि पुत्रोऽनुजायते Ms. 9. 134. 2 to be born similar to; असौ कुमारस्तमजोऽनुजातः R. 6. 78 (तस्माज्जातः Malli.). –अभि 1 to be born or produced, arise, spring from; कामात्क्रोधोऽभिजायते Bg. 2. 62; H. 1. 205. 2 to be, become. 3 to be turned into. 4 to be born of a high family. 5 to be born to or for; Bg. 16. 3. –उप 1 to be born or produced, arise, grow; ऊष्मणश्चोपजायंते Ms. 1. 45; संगस्तेषूपजायते Bg. 2. 62, 14. 11. 2 to be born again; Y. 3. 256; Bg. 14. 2. 3 to be, become. –प्र, -वि, –सं 1 to grow, arise, spring. 2 to be born or produced.

जनः 1 A creature, living being, man. 2 An individual or person (whether male or female); क्व वयं क्व परोक्षमन्मथो मृगशावैः सममेधितो जनः S. 2. 18; तत्तस्य किमपि द्रव्यं यो हि यस्य प्रियो जनः U. 2. 19; so सखीजनः a female friend; दासजनः a slave, अबलाजनः &c. (In this sense जनः or अयं जनः is often used by the speaker-whether male or female-in the sing. or pl.- instead of the first personal pronoun to speak of himself in the third person); अयं जनः प्रष्टुमनास्तपोधने Ku. 5. 40. (male); भगवन्परवानयं जनः प्रतिकूलाचरितं क्षमस्व मे R. 8. 81 (female); पश्यानंगशरातुरं जनमिमं त्रातापि नो रक्षसि Nâg. 1. 1 (female and pl.). 2 Men collectively, the people, the world (in sing. or pl.); एवं जनो गृह्णाति M. 1; सतीमपि ज्ञातिकुलैकसंश्रयां जनोऽन्यथा भर्तृमतीं विशंकते S. 5. 17. 3 Race, nation, tribe. 4 The world beyond Maharloka, the heaven of deified mortals. –COMP. –अतिग *a.* extraordinary, uncommon, superhuman. अधिपः,–अधिनाथः a king. –अंतः 1 a place removed from men, an uninhabited place. 2 a region. 3 an epithet of Yama.–अंतिकं secret communication, whispering or speaking aside (to another) (–*ind.*) aside (to another) (in dramas); the S. D. thus defines this stage-direction:— त्रिपताककरेणान्यानपवार्यांतरा कथां । अन्योन्यामंत्रणं यत् स्याज्जनांते तज्जनांतिकं ॥ 425. –अर्दनः an epithet of Vishṇu or Krishṇa. –अशनः a wolf. =आकीर्ण *a.* thronged or crowded with people. –आचारः a popular usage or custom.–आश्रयः an asylum for people, an inn, caravansary. –आश्रयः a pavilion. –इंद्रः, –ईशः, –ईश्वरः a king. इष्ट *a.* desired or liked by the people. (–ष्टः) a kind of jasmine. –उदाहरणं glory, fame. –ओघः a concourse of people, crowd, mob. –कारिन् *m.* lac. –चक्षुस् *n.* 'the people's eye', the sun. –त्रा an umbrella, a parasol. –देवः a king. –पदः 1 a community, race, nation; Y. 1. 360. 2 a kingdom, an empire, an inhabited country; जनपदे न गदः पदमादधौ R. 9. 4; दाक्षिणात्ये जनपदे Pt. 1; Me. 48. 3 the country (opp. the town पुर, नगर); जनपदवधूलोचनैः पीयमानः Me 16. 4 the people, subjects (opp. the sovereign). 5 mankind. –पदिन् *m.* the ruler of a country or community. –प्रवादः 1 rumour, report. 2 scandal, calumny. –प्रिय *a.* 1 philanthropic. 2 liked by the people, popular. –मर्यादा established custom. –रंजनं gratifying the people, courting popular favour. –रवः 1 rumour. 2 calumny, scandal. –लोकः one, *i. e.* the fifth, of the seven divisions of the universe situated above Maharloka.–वादः (also जनेवादः) 1 news, rumour. 2 a scandal. –व्यवहारः popular usage. –श्रुत *a.* well-known (among people, famous.) –श्रुतिः *f.* rumour, report. –संबाध *a.* densely crowded with people. –स्थानं N. of a part of the Daṇḍakâ forest; R. 12. 42; 13. 22. U. 1. 28, 2. 17.

जनक *a.* (निका *f.*) Generating, producing, causing; क्लेशजनक, दुःखजनक &c. –कः 1 A father, progenitor. 2 N. of a famous king Videha or Mithilâ, foster-father of Sîtâ. He was remarkable, for his great knowledge, good works, and holiness. After the abandonment of Sîtâ, by Râma he became anchorite—indifferent to pleasure or pain—and spent his time in philosophical discussions. The sage याज्ञवल्क्य was his priest and adviser.–COMP. आत्मजा, –तनया, –नंदिनी, –सुता epithets of Sîtâ, daughter of King Janaka.

जनंगमः A Chândâla.

जनता 1 Birth. 2 A number or assemblage of people, mankind, community; पश्यति स्म जनता दिनात्यये पार्वणौ शशिदिवाकराविव R. 11. 82; 15. 67; *Si.* 9. 14.

जनन a. Producing, causing, &c. –नं 1 Birth, being born; यावज्जननं तावन्मरणं Moha M. 13. 2 Causing, production, creation; शोभाजननात् Ku. 1. 42. 3 Appearance, manifestation, rise. 4 Life, existence; यदैव पूर्वे जनने शरीरं सा दक्षरोषात्सुदती ससर्ज Ku. 1. 53; *S.* 5. 2. 5 Race, family, lineage.

जननिः *f.* 1 A mother. 2 Birth.

जननी 1 A mother. 2 Mercy, tenderness, compassion. 3 A bat. 4. Lac.

जनमेजयः N. of a celebrated king of Hastinâpura, son of Parîkshit, the grandson of Arjuna. [His father died, being bitten by a serpent; and Janamejaya, determined to avenge the injury, resolved to exterminate the whole serpent-race. He accordingly instituted a serpent sacrifice. and burnt down all serpents except Takshaka, who was saved only by the intercession of the sage *A*stika, at whose request the sacrifice was closed. It was to this king that Vais'ampa'yana related the Maha-bha'rata, and the king is said to have listened to it to expiate the sin of killing a Bra'hman'a].

जनयितृ *a.* (त्री *f.*) Producing, begetting, creator, —*m.* A father.

जनयित्री A mother.

जनस् *n.* See जन 3.

जनिः, –जनिका, –जनी *f.* 1 Birth, creation, production. 2 A woman. 3 A mother. 4 A wife. 5 A daughter-in-law.

जनित *a.* 1 Given birth to. 2 Produced, created, caused.

जनितृ *m.* A father.

जनित्रि A mother.

जनु (नू) *f.* Birth, production.

जनुस् *n.* 1 Birth; धिग्वारिधीनां जनुः Bv. 1. 16. 2 Creation, production. 3 Life, existence; जनुः सर्वश्लाघ्यं जयति ललितोत्तंस भवतः Bv. 2. 55. –COMP. –जनुषांधः blind from birth, born blind.

जंतुः 1 A creature, a living being, man; *S.* 5. 2; Ms. 3. 71. 2 The (individual) soul. 3 An animal of the lowest organization. COMP. –कंबुः 1 a snail's shell. 2 a snail. –फलः the Udumbara tree.

जंतुका Lac.

जंतुमती The earth.

जन्मं Birth.

जन्मन् *n.* 1 Birth; तां जन्मने शैलवधूं प्रपेदे Ku. 1. 21 2 Origin, arise, production, creation; आकारे पद्मरागाणां जन्म काचमणेः कुतः H. Pr. 44; Ku. 5: 60; (at the end of comp). arising or born from; सरलस्कंधसंघट्टजन्मा दवाग्निः Me. 53. 3 Life, existence; पूर्वेष्वपि हि जन्मसु Ms. 9. 100; 5. 38; Bg. 4. 5. 4 Birth place. 5 Nativity. –COMP. –अधिपः 1 an epithet of *S*iva 2 the regent of a constellation under which a person is born (in astrology). –अंतरं another life. अंतरीय *a.* belonging to or done in another life. –अंध *a.* born blind. –अष्टमी the eighth day of the dark fortnight of *S*râvaṇa, the birthday of Krishṇa. –कीलः an epithet of Vishṇu. –कुंडली a diagram in a horoscope in which the positions of different planets at the time of one's birth are marked. –कृत् *m.* a father. –क्षेत्रं birth-place. –तिथिः *m. f.* –दिनं, –दिवसः birth-day. –दः a father. –नक्षत्रं-भं the natal star. –नामन् *n.* the name received on the 12th day after birth. –पत्रं, –पत्रिका a horoscope. –प्रतिष्ठा 1 a birth-place. 2 a mother; *S.* 6. –भाज् *m.* a creature, living being; मोदंतां जन्मभाजः सततं Mk. 10. 60. –भाषा a mother-tongue; यत्र स्त्रीणामपि किमपरं जन्मभाषावदेव प्रत्यावासं विलसति वचः संस्कृतं प्राकृतं च Vikr. 18. 6. –भूमि *f.* birth-place, native country. –योगः a horoscope. –रोगिन् *a.* sickly from birth. –लग्नं the sign of the zodiac under which a person is born. –वर्त्मन् *n.* the vulva. –शोधनं discharging the obligations derived from birth. –साफल्यं attainment of the ends of existence, –स्थानं 1 birth-place, native country, home. 2 the womb.

जन्मिन् *m.* A creature, a living being

जन्य *a.* 1 To be born or produced. 2 Born, produced. 3 (At the end of comp.) Born from, occasioned by. 4 Belonging to a race or family. 5 Vulgar, common. 6 Nationl. –न्यः 1 A father. 2 A friend, attendant or relative of a bride-groom. 3 A common man. 4 A report, rumour. –न्यः 1 Birth, production, creation. 2 That which is born or created, a created thing, an effect (opp. जनक) जन्यानां जनकः कालः Bhâshâ P. 45; जनकस्य स्वभावो हि जन्ये तिष्ठति निश्चितं *S*abdak. 3 The body. 4 A portent occurring at birth. 5 A market, a fair. 6 War, battle; तत्र जन्यं रघोर्घोरं पार्वतीयैर्गणैरभूत् R. 4. 77. 7 Censure, abuse. –न्या 1 The friend of a mother. 2 The relation of a bride, a bride's maid; याहाति जन्यामवदत्कुमारी R. 6. 30. 3 Pleasure; happiness. 4 Affection.

जन्युः 1 Birth. 2 A creature, living being 3 Fire. 4 The creator or Brahmâ.

जप् 1 P. (जपति, जपित or जप्त) 1 To utter in a low voice, repeat internally, mutter; जपन्नपि तवैवालापमंत्राविं Git. 5; हरिरिति हरिरिति जपति सकामं 4; N. 11. 26. 2 To mutter prayers or spells; Ms. 11. 194, 251, 259. –WITH उप to whisper into the ears of, to win over to one's party by secretly suggesting anything in the ear, to instigate or rouse to rebellion; उपजप्यानुपजपेत् Ms. 7 197.

जपः 1 Muttering prayers, repeating prayers &c. in an under-tone. 2 Repeating passages of the Veda or names of deities &c.; Ms 3. 74; Y. 1. 22. 3 A muttered prayers. –COMP. –परायणः *a.* engaged in muttering prayers –माला a rosary of beads.

जपा The China rose (the plant or its flower); (सांध्यं तेजः प्रतिनवजपापुष्परक्तं दधानः Me. 36.

जप्यः –प्यं A muttered prayer.

जभ्, जंभ् I. 1. P, (जभति, जंभति) To copulate; cf. यभ्. –II. 1. A (जभते, जंभते) To yawn, gape.

जम् 1. P. (जमति) To eat.

जमदग्निः A Brâhmaṇa and a descendant of Bhrigu and father of Parasurâma. [Jamadagni was the son of *R*ichika and Satyavati. He was a pious sage, deeply engaged in study and said to have obtained entire possession of the Vedas. His wife was Re*n*uka who bore him five sons. One day when she had gone out to bathe, she beheld a loving pair of Gandharvas (according to some Chitraratha and his queen) sporting and dallying in the water. The lovely sight made her feel envious of their pleasure, and she returned defiled by unworthy thoughts, 'wetted but not purified by the stream'. Her husband, who was anger incarnate, seeing her shorn of the lustre of her sanctity, furiously scolded her, and ordered his sons as they came in to cut off her head. But the first four sons shrank from that cruel deed. It was only Parasurama, the youngest, that with characteristic obedience to his father's command struck off her head with his axe. The deed pacified the father's anger and he desired Parasurama to ask a boon. The kind-hearted son begged that his mother might be restored to life which the father readily granted].

जमनं–जेमन q. v.

जपंती *m.* du. Hasband and wife; cf. दंपती and जायापती.

जंबालः 1 Mud. 2 Moss. 3 The Ketaka plant.

जंबालिनी A river.

जंबीरः The citron tree. -रं A citron.

जंबु-बू *f.* The rose apple and its fruit. -COMP. -खंडः -द्वीपः N. of one of the seven continents surrounding the mountain Meru.

जंबु (बू) कः (की *f.*) 1 A jackal. 2 A low man.

जंबूलः A kind of tree. (जंबू). -लं Jest or jesting compliments addressed to the bride and the bridegroom by the friends and female relatives of the bridegroom (or of the bride).

जंभः 1 The jaws (usually in pl.) 2 A tooth. 3 Eating. 4 Biting asunder. 5 A part, portion. 6 A quiver. 7 The chin. 8 Yawning, gaping. 9 N. of a demon killed by Indra. 10 The citron tree. -COMP. -अरातिः, -द्विष्, -भेदिन्, -रिपुः epithet of Indra. -अरिः 1 fire. 2 Indra's thunderbolt. 3 Indra.

जंभका, जंभा, जंभिका A yawn, gaping.

जंभ (भी) रः The lime or citron tree.

जयः 1 Conquest, triumph, victory; success, winning (in battle, game or a law-suit). 2 Restraint, curbing, conquest; as in इंद्रियजय. 3 N. of the sun. 4 N. of Jayanta, son of Indra. 5 N. of Yudhishthira, the first Pâṇḍava prince. 6 N. of an attendant of Vishṇu. 7 An epithet of Arjuna. —या 1 N. of Durgâ. 2 N. of an attendant of the goddess Durgâ. 3 A kind of banner. -COMP. -आवह *a.* conferring victory. -उद्धुर *a.* exulting in victory. -कोलाहलः 1 a shout of victory. 2 a kind of game with dice. -घोषः, -घोषणं -णा a proclamation of victory. -ढक्का a kind of drum beaten as a sign of victory. -पत्रं a record of victory. -पालः 1 a king. 2 an epithet of Brahmâ. 3 an epithet of Vishṇu. -पुत्रकः a kind of dice. -मंगलः a royal elephant. 2 a remedy for fever. -वाहिनी an epithet of *Sachi*. -शब्दः 1 a shout of victory. 2 the exclamation '*jaya*' (hail! glory!) uttered by bards &c. -स्तंभः a trophy, a column erected to commemorate a victory, a triumphal column; निचखान जयस्तंभान् गंगास्रोतोंऽतरेषु सः R. 4. 36, 69.

जयनं 1 Conquering, subduing. 2 Armour for cavalry, elephants &c. -COMP. -युज् *a.* caparisoned. 2 victorious.

जयंतः 1 N. of the son of Indra; पौलोमीसंभवेनेव जयंतेन पुरंदरः V. 5. 14; *S.* 7. 2, R. 3. 23, 6. 78. 2 N. of *S*iva. 3 The moon. -ती 1 A flag or banner. N. of daughter of Indra. 3 N. of Durgâ. COMP. -पत्रं (in law) 1 the written award of the judge in favour of either party. 2 the label on the forehead of a horse turned loose for the Asvamedha sacrifice.

जयद्रथः A king of Sindhu district and brother-in-law of Duryodhana, having married Duhsalâ, daughter of Dhritarâshtra. [Once while out on hunting, he chanced to see Draupad*i* in the forest, and asked of her food for himself and his retinue. Draupad*i*, by virtue of her magical *stha'li*, was able to supply him with materials sufficient for their break-fast. Jayadratha was so much struck with this act, as well as her personal charms, that he asked her to elope with him. She of course, indignantly refused but he succeeded in carrying her off, as her husbands were out on hunting. When they returned they pursued and captured the ravisher and released Draupad*i*; and he himself was allowed to go after having been subjected to many humiliations. He took a leading part in compassing the death of Abhimanyu, and met his doom at the hands of Arjuna in the great war.].

जयिन् *a.* 1 Conquering, vanquishing; विरूपाक्षस्य जयिनीस्ताः स्तुवे वामलोचनाः Vb. 1. 2. 2 Successful, winning a law-suit; Y. 2. 79. 3 Fascinating, captivating, subduing the heart; जगति जयिनस्ते ते भावा नवेंदुकलादयः Mâl. 1. 36. -*m.* A victor, a conqueror; पौरस्त्यानेवमाक्रामंस्तांस्ताञ्जनपदाञ्जयी R. 4. 34.

जय्य *a.* Conquerable, vulnerable, that can be conquered (opp. जेय).

जरठ *a.* 1 Hard, solid. 2 Old, aged; अयमतिजरठाः प्रकामगुर्वीः परिणतदिक्करिकास्तटीर्बिभर्ति *Si.* 4. 29. (where जरठ means 'hard' also). 3 Decayed, decrepit, infirm. 4 Full-grown, ripe, matured; जरठकमल *Si.* 11. 14. 5 Hard-hearted, cruel. -ठः N. of Paṇḍu, father of the five Pâṇḍavas.

जरण *a.* Old, decayed, Infirm.

जरत् *a.* 1 Old, aged. 2 Infirm, decrepit. COMP. -कारुः N. of a great sage who married a sister of the serpent Vâsuki. [One day as he was fallen asleep on the lap of his wife, the sun was about to set. His wife, perceiving that the time of offering his evening prayers was passing away, gently roused him. But he became angry with her for having disturbed his sleep, and left her never to return. He however, told her, as he went, that she was pregnant and would give birth to a son who would be her support, and at the same time the saviour of the serpant-race. This son was *Astika*] -गवः an old ox; दारिद्र्यस्य परा मूर्तिर्यन्मानद्रविणाल्पता। जरद्गवधनः शर्वस्तथापि परमेश्वरः॥ Pt. 2. 159.

जरती An old woman.

जरंतः 1 An old man. 2 A buffalo.

जरा (The word जरस् is optionally substituted for जरा before vowel terminations after acc. dual) 1 Old age; कैकेयीशंकयेवाह पलितच्छद्मना जरा R 12. 2; तस्य धर्मरतेरासीद् वृद्धत्वं जरया (जरसा) विना 1. 23. 2 Decrepitude, infirmity, general debility consequent on old age. 3 Digestion. 4 N. of a female demon; see जरासंध below. -COMP. -अवस्था decrepitude. -जीर्ण *a.* old through age, debilitated, infirm; Bh. 3. 17. संधः N. of a celebrated king and warrior, son of Brihadratha. [According to a legend, he was born divided in two halves which were put together by a R*a*kshas*i* called Jar*a*, whence the boy was called Jar*a*sandha. He became king of Magadha and Chedi after his father's death. When he heard that Krish*n*a, had slain his son-in-law Kamsa, he gathered a large army and besieged Mathur*a* eighteen times, but was as often repulsed. When Yudhish*t*hira performed the great Raja*su*ya sacrifice, Krish*n*a, Arjuna and Bh*i*ma went to the capital of Jar*a*sandha disguised as Brahma*n*as, chiefly with the object of slaying their enemy and liberating the kings imprisoned by him. He, however, refused to release the kings whereupon Bh*i*ma challenged him to a single combat. The challenge was accepted; a hard fight ensued, but Jara-sandha was at last overpowered and slain by Bhima.].

जरायणिः N. of Jarasandha.

जरायु *n.* The slough or cast-off skin of a serpent. 2 The outer skin of the embryo. 3 The uterus, womb. -COMP. -ज *a.* born from the womb, viviparous; Ms. 1. 43 and Malli. on Ku. 3. 42.

जरित *a.* 1 Old, aged. 2 Decayed, infirm.

जरिन् *a.* (णी *f.*) Old, aged.

जरूथं Flesh.

जर्जर *a.* 1 Old, infirm, decayed. 2 Worn out, torn, shattered, broken to pieces, divided in parts, split up into thin particles: जराजर्जरितविषाणकोटयो मृगाः K. 21; गात्रं जराजर्जरितं विहाय Mv. 7. 18; विसर्पन् धाराभिर्लुठति धरणीं जर्जरकणः U. 1. 29; *Si* 4. 23. 3 Wounded, hurt. 4 Dull, hollow (as the sound of a broken vessel). -रं The banner of Indra.

जर्जरित *a.* 1 Old, decayed, infirm. 2 Worn out, torn to pieces, shattered, splintered &c. 3 Completely overpowered, disabled; स्मरशरजर्जरितापि सा प्रभाते Gît. 8.

जर्जरीक *a.* 1 Old, decayed. 2 Ragged, full of holes, perforated.

जर्तुः 1 The vulva. 2 An elephant.

जल *a.* Dull, cold, frigid =जड q. v. -लं 1 Water; तातस्य कूपोयमिति ब्रुवाणाः क्षारं जलं कापुरुषाः पिबंति। Pt. 1. 322. 2

A kind of fragrant medicinal plant or perfume (ह्रीवेर). 3 Frigidity. 4 The constellation called पूर्वाषाढा —COMP. —अंचलं 1 A spring. 2 a natural water course. 3 moss. —अंजलिः 1 a handful of water. 2 a libation of water presented to the manes of a deceased person ; कुपुत्रमासाद्य कुतो जलांजलिः Chāṇ. 95 ; मानस्यापि जलांजलिः सरभसं लोके न दत्तो यथा Amaru. 97 (where जलांजलिं दा means 'to leave or give up'). अटनः a heron. —अटनी a leech —अंटकः a shark. —अत्ययः autumn (शरद्). —अधिदैवतः —तं an epithet of Varuṇa. (तं) the constellation called पूर्वाषाढा. —अधिपः an epithet of Varuṇa. —अंबिका a well. —अर्कः the image of the sun reflected in water. अर्णवः 1 the rainy season. 2 the ocean of sweet water. अर्थिन् *a.* thirsty. अवतारः a landing-place at a river side. —अष्ठीला a large square pond. —असुका a leech. —आकरः a spring, fountain, well. —आकांक्षः, —कांक्षः, —कांक्षिन् *m.* an elephant. आखुः an otter. आत्मिका a leech. आधारः a pond, lake, reservior of water. —आयुका a leech. —आर्द्र *a.* wet. (—र्द्रं) wet garment or clothes (द्रा) a fan wetted with water. —आलोका a leech. —आवर्तः eddy, whirlpool. —आशयः 1 a pond, lake, reservoir. 2 a fish. 3 the ocean. —आश्रयः 1 a pond. 2 a water-house. आह्वयं a lotus. —इंद्रः 1 an epithet of Varuṇa. 2 the ocean. —इंधनः the submarine fire. —इभः a water-elephant. —ईशः, —ईश्वरः 1 an epithet of Varuṇa 2 the ocean. उच्छ्वासः 1 a channel made for carrying off excess of water, drain (cf. परीवाह). 2 overflow of a river. —उदरं dropsy. —उद्भव *a.* aquatic. उरगा, —ओकस् *m.* ओकसः a leech. —कंटकः a crocodile. कपिः the Gangetic porpoise. —कपोतः a water-pigeon —करंकः 1 a shell. 2 cocoa-nut. 3 a cloud. 4 a wave. 5 a lotus. —कल्कः mud. —काकः the diverbird. —कांतः the wind. —कांतारः an epithet of Varuṇa. किराटः a shark. —कुक्कुटः a water-fowl. कुंतलः, कोशः moss. —कूपी 1 a spring, well. 2 a pond. 3 a whirlpool. कूर्मः the porpoise. —केलिः, *m.*, or *f.* —क्रीडा playing in water, splashing one another with water. क्रिया presenting libations of water to the manes of the deceased. —गुल्मः 1 a turtle. 2 a quadrangular tank. 3 a whirpool. —चर *a.* (also जलेचर) aquatic. °आजीवः, °जीवः a fisherman. —चारिन् *m.* 1 an aquatic animal. 2 a fish —ज *a.* born or produced in water. (—जः) 1 an aquatic animal. 2 a fish. 3 moss. 4 the moon. (—जः, —जं) 1 a shell. 2 the conch-shell ; अधरोष्ठे निवेश्य दध्मौ जलजं कुमारः R. 7. 63, 11. 60. (—जं) a lotus. °आजीवः a fisherman. °आसनः an epithet of Brahmâ ; वाचस्पतिरुवाचेदं प्रांजलिर्जलजासनं Ku. 2. 30. —जंतुः 1 a fish. 2 any aquatic animal. —जंतुका a leech. —जन्मन् a lotus. —जिह्वः a crocodile. —जीविन् *m.* a fisherman. —तरंगः 1 a wave. 2 a metal cup filled with water producing harmonic notes like a musical glass. —ताडनं (lit.) 'beating water'; (fig.) any useless occupation. —त्रा an umbrella.— त्रासः hydrophobia. —दः 1 a cloud ; जायंते विरला लोके जलदा इव सज्जनाः Pt. 1. 29. 2 camphor. —अशनः the Sâla tree. —आगमः the rainy season. °कालः the rainy season. °क्षयः autumn. —दर्दुरः a kind of musical instrument. —देवता a naiad, water-nymph. —द्रोणी a bucket. —धरः 1 a cloud. 2 the ocean. —धारा a stream of water. —धि 1 the ocean. 2 a hundred billions. 3 the number 'four.' °गा a river. °जः the moon. °जा Lakshmi, the goddess of wealth. °रशना the earth. —नकुलः an otter. —नरः a merman. —निधिः 1 the ocean. 2 the number 'four'. —निर्गमः 1 a drain, water-course. 2 a water-fall, descent of a spring &c. into a river below. —नीलिः moss. —पटलं a cloud. —पतिः 1 the ocean. 2 an epithet of Varuṇa. —पथः a sea-voyage ; R. 17. 81. —पारावतः a water-pigeon. —पित्तं fire. —पुष्पं an aquatic flower. —पूरः 1 a flood of water. 2 a full stream of water. —पृष्ठजा moss. —प्रदानं presenting libations of water to the manes of the deceased. —प्रलयः destruction by water. —प्रांतः the bank of a river. —प्रायं a country abounding with water जलप्रायमनूपं स्यात् Ak. —प्रियः 1 the Châtaka bird. 2 a fish. —प्लवः an otter. —प्लावनं a deluge, an inundation. —बंधुः a fish. —बालकः, —वालकः the Vindhya mountain. —बालिका lightning. —बिडालः an otter. —बिंबः, —बं a bubble. —बिल्वः 1 a (quadrangular) pond, lake. 2 a tortoise. 3 a crab. —भू *a.* produced in water.—भूः *m.* 1 a cloud. 2 a place for holding water. 3 a kind of camphor. —भृत् *m.* 1 a cloud. 2 a jar. 3 camphor. —मक्षिका a water-insect. —मंडूकं a kind of musical instrument; (=जलदर्दुर). —मार्गः a drain, canal. —मुच् *m.* 1 a cloud ; Me. 69. 2 a kind of camphor. —मूर्तिः an epithet of Siva. —मूर्तिका hail. —यंत्रं 1 a machine for raising water. 2 a fountain. °गृहं, °निकेतनं, °मंदिरं, a house erected in the midst of water (a summerhouse) or one supplied with artificial fountains ; क्वचिद्विचित्रं जलयंत्रमंदिरं Rs. 1. 2. —यात्रा a voyage. —यानं a ship. —रंकुः a kind of gallinule. —रंडः, —रुंडः 1 a whirl-pool. 2 drop of water, drizzle, thin sprinkling. 3 a snake. —रसः sea-salt. —राशिः the ocean. —रुह, —हं a lotus. —रूपः a crocodile. —लता a wave, billow. —वायसः a diverbird. —वासः residence in water. —वाहः a cloud. —वाहनी an aqueduct. —विषुवं the autumnal equinox. —वृश्चिकः a prawn. —व्यालः a water-snake. —शयः,—शयनः,—शायिन् *m.* an epithet of Vishṇu. —शूकं moss. —शूकरः a crocodile. —शोषः drought. —सर्पिणी a leech. —सूचिः *f.* 1 the Gangetic porpoise. 2 a kind of fish. 3 a crow. 4 a leech. —स्थानं, —स्थायः a pond, lake, reservoir. —हं a small water-house (rather summerhouse) furnished with artificial fountains. —हस्तिन् *m.* a water-elephant. —हारिणी a drain. —हासः 1 foam. 2 cuttlefish-bone considered as the foam of the sea.

जलंगमः A chândâla.

जलमसिः 1 A cloud. 2 Camphor (a variety of it).

जलाका, जलालुका, जलिका, जलुका, जलूका A leech.

जलेजं, जलेजातं A lotus.

जलेशयः 1 A fish. 2 N. of Vishṇu.

जल्प् 1. P. (जल्पति, जल्पित) 1 To speak, talk, speak or converse (with another) : अविरलितकपोलं जल्पतोरक्रमेण U. 1. 21; बकेन जल्पंत्यनल्पाक्षरं Pt. 1. 116; Bh. 1. 82. 2 To murmur, speak inarticulately. 3 To chatter, prattle, babble. —WITH —अभि to talk, talk with. —प्र 1 to speak, say, talk; Ku. 1. 45. 2 to call. —सं to talk, converse.

जल्पः 1 Talk, speech. 2 Discourse, conversation. 3 Babble, prattling, gossip. 4 Debate, wrangling discussion.

जल्पक *a.* (ल्पिका *f.*) जल्पाक *a.* Talkative, garrulous.

जव *a.* Swift, expeditious.—वः 1 (*a*) speed, swiftness, quickness, rapidity; जवो हि सप्तेः परमं विभूषणं Bh. 3. 121 ; S. 1. 8. (*b*) Haste, hurry ; जवेन पीठादुदतिष्ठदच्युतः Si. 1. 12. 2 Velocity. —COMP. —अधिकः a fleet horse, a courser. —अनिलः a strong wind, hurricane.

जवन *a.*(नी *f.*) Quick, swift, fleet; R. 9. 56. —नः A courser, a swift horse. —नं Speed, quickness, velocity.

जवनिका, जवनी 1 A screen of cloth surrounding a tent. 2 A curtain, screen in general ; नरः संसारांते विशति यमधानीजवनिकां Bh. 3. 112.

जवसः Pasture-grass.

जवा The China rose; see जपा.

जष् 1. U. (जषति-ते) To injure, hurt, kill.

जस् 1. 4. P. (जस्यति) To set free, release. —II. 1. 10. P. (जसति, जासयति) 1 To hurt, injure, strike. 2 To disregard, slight. —WITH. —उद्

to kill; निजौजसोज्जासियतुं जगद्द्रुहां Si 1. 37; Bk. 8. 120.

जहकः 1 Time. 2 A child. 3 The slough of a snake.

जहत् *a.* (ती *f.*) Leaving, abandoning. –Comp.–**लक्षणा, –स्वार्था** a kind of लक्षणा (also called लक्षणलक्षणा) in which a word loses its primary sense, but is used in one which is in some way connected with the primary sense; *e g.* in the familiar instance गंगायां घोषः 'a hamlet on the Ganges,' गंगा loses its primary sense and means गंगातट; cf. अजहत्स्वार्था also.

जहानकः Total destruction of the world.

जहुः A young animal.

जन्हुः N. of an ancient king, son of Suhotra, who adopted the river Gangâ as his daughter. [The river Ganges when brought down from heaven by the austerities of Bhag*i*ratha, was forced to flow over earth to follow him to the lower regions. In its course it inundated the sacrificial ground of king Jahnu, who being angry drank up its waters. But the gods and sages, and particularly Bhag*i*ratha, appeased his anger, and he consented to discharge those waters from his ears. The river is therefore regarded as his daughter, and is styled जाह्नवी, जन्हुतनया, –कन्या, –सुता, नंदिनी &c; cf. R. 6. 85, 8. 95].

जागरः 1 Wakefulness, waking, keeping awake; रात्रिजागरपरो दिवाशयः R. 9. 34. 2 A vision in a waking state. 3 An armour, mail.

जागरणं 1 Waking, wakefulness. 2 Watchfulness, vigilance.

जागरा See जागरण.

जागरित *a.* One who has been long awake –**तं** Waking.

जागरितृ *a.* (त्री *f.*), **जागरूक** *a.* 1 Wakeful, waking, sleepless; स्वपतो जागरूकस्य याथार्थ्यं वेद कस्तव R. 10. 24. 2 Watchful, vigilant; वर्णाश्रमावेक्षणजागरूकः R. 14. 15; Si. 20. 36.

जागर्तिः, जागर्या, जाग्रिया Wakefulness, keeping awake.

जागुडं Saffron.

जागृ 2. P. (जागर्ति, जागरित) 1 To be awake, be watchful or attentive (fig. also); सौऽपसर्पैर्जजागार यथाकालं स्वपन्नपि R. 17. 51; गुरौ षाड्गुण्यचिंतायामार्ये चार्ये च जाग्रति Mu. 7. 13; to sit up during the night; या निशा सर्वभूतानां तस्यां जागर्ति संयमी Bg. 2. 69. 2 To be roused from sleep, awake. To foresee, be provident.

जाघनी 1 A tail. 2 The thigh.

जांगल *a.* (ली *f.*) 1 Rural, picturesque. 2 Wild. 3 Savage, barbarous. 4 Arid, desert. –**लः** The francoline partridge. –**लं** Flesh, flesh of deer &c.

जांगुलं Poison, venom.

जांगुलिः, जांगुलिकः A snake-doctor, a dealer in antidotes (विषवैद्य).

जांघिकः 1 A courier, an express. 2 A camel

जाजिन् *m.* A warrior, combatant; जजौजोजाजिजिज्जाजी Si. 19. 3.

जाठर *a.* (री *f.*) Belonging to or being in the stomach, stomachic, abdominal.–**रः** The digestive faculty, gastric fluid.

जाड्यं 1 Coldness, frigidity. 2 Apathy, sluggishness, inactivity. 3 Dulness of intellect, folly, stupidity; तज्जाड्यं वसुधाधिपस्य Bh. 2. 15; जाड्यं धियो हरति 2. 23; जाड्यं ह्रीमति गण्यते 54. 4 Tastelessness of the tongue.

जात *p. p.* 1 Brought into existence, engendered, produced. 2 Grown, arisen. 3 Caused, occasioned. 5 Felt, affected by; oft. in comp; see जन्. –**तः** A son, male offspring (in dramas often used as a term of endearment; अयि जात कथयितव्यं कथय U. 4. 'dear boy' 'oh my darling &c.'). –**तं** 1 A creature, living being. 2 Production, origin. 3 Kind, sort, class, species. 4 A collection of things forming a class; निःशेषविश्राणितकोशजातं R. 5. 1. all that goes to form wealth *i. e.* every kind of property; so कर्मजातं the whole aggregate of actions; सुख° everything included under the name of सुख or pleasure. 5 A child, a young one. –Comp. –**अपत्या** a mother. –**अमर्ष** *a.* vexed, enraged. –**अश्रु** *a.* shedding tears. –**इष्टिः** *f.* a sacrifice performed at the birth of a child. –**उक्षः** a young bullock. –**कर्मन्** *n.* a ceremony performed at the birth of a child; R. 3. 18. –**कलाप** *a.* having a tail (as a peacock). –**काम** *a.* enamoured. –**पक्ष** *a.* having wings; अजातपक्ष unfledged. –**पाश** *a.* fettered. –**प्रत्यय** *a.* inspired with confidence. –**मन्मथ** *a.* fallen in love. –**मात्र** *a.* just born. –**रूप** *a.* beautiful, brilliant. (–**पं**) gold; अप्याकरसमुत्पन्ना मणिजातिरसंस्कृता। जातरूपेण कल्याणि न हि संयोगमर्हति M. 5. 18; N. 1. 129. –**वेदस्** *m.* an epithet of fire; Ku 2. 46, Si. 2. 51; R. 12. 104, 15. 72.

जातक *a.* Born, produced. –**कः** 1 A new born infant. 2 A mendicant. –**कं** 1 ceremony performed after the birth of a child (जातकर्मन्). 2 Astrological calculation of a nativity. 3 An aggregate of similar things.

जातिः *f.* 1 Birth, production; Ms. 2. 148. 2 The form of existence fixed by birth. 3 Race, family, lineage. 4 A caste, tribe or class (of men); अरे मूढ जात्या चेदवध्योऽहं एषा सा जातिः परित्यक्ता Ve. 3; (the primary castes of the Hindus are only four:–ब्राह्मण, क्षत्रिय, वैश्य and शूद्र). 5 A class, genus, kind, species; पशुजातिः, पुष्पजातिः &c. 6 The properties which are peculiar to a class and distinguish it from all others, the essential characteristics of a species; as गोत्व अश्वत्व of cows, horses &c.; see गुण, क्रिया and द्रव्य; Si. 2. 47 and cf. K. P. 2. 7 A fire-place. 8 Nutmeg. 9 The Jasmine plant or its flower; पुष्पाणां प्रकरः स्मितेन रचितो नो कुंदजात्यादिभिः Amaru. 40. (written also as जाती in these two senses). 10 (In Nyâya) Futile answer. 11 (In music) The seven primary notes of the Indian gamut. 12 A class of metres; see App. –Comp. –**अंध** *a.* born blind; Bh. 1. 90. –**कोशः, –षः –षं** nutmeg. –**कोशी, –षी** the outer skin of the nutmeg. –**धर्मः** 1 the duties of a caste. 2 a generic property. –**ध्वंसः** loss of caste or its privileges. –**पत्री** the outer skin of the nutmeg. –**ब्राह्मणः** a Brâhmaṇa only by birth, but not by knowledge or religious austerities, an ignorant Brâhmaṇa; (तपः श्रुतं च योनिश्च त्रयं ब्राह्मण्यकारणं। तपः श्रुताभ्यां यो हीनो जातिब्राह्मण एव सः॥ शब्दार्थचिंतामणि). –**भ्रंशः** loss of caste; Ms. 9. 67. –**भ्रष्ट** *a.* outcast. –**मात्रं** 1 'mere birth', position in life obtained by mere birth. 2 caste only (but not the performance of duties pertaining to it); Ms. 8. 20; 12. 114. –**लक्षणं** generic distinction, a characteristic of a class. –**वाचक** *a.* expressing a genus, generic (as a word); गौरश्वः पुरुषो हस्ती. –**वैरं** instinctive hostility. –**वैरिन्** *m.* a born enemy. –**शब्दः** a name conveying the idea of a genus, a generic word, common noun; गौः, अश्वः, पुरुषः, हस्ती &c. –**संकरः** admixture of caste, mixed blood. –**संपन्न** *a.* belonging to a noble family. –**सारं** nutmeg. –**स्मर** *a.* remembering one's condition in a former life; जातिस्मरो मुनिरस्मि जात्या K. 355. –**स्वभावः** generic character or nature. –**हीन** *a.* of low birth, outcast.

जातिमत् *a.* Nobly born, of high rank.

जातु *ind.* A particle meaning:—1 At all, over, at any time, possibly; किं तेन जातु जातेन मातुर्यौवनहारिणा Pt. 1. 26; न जातु कामः कामानामुपभोगेन शाम्यति Ms. 2. 94; Ku. 5 55. 2 Perhaps, sometimes; R. 19. 7. 3 Once, once upon a time, sometime, at some day. 4 Used with the potential mood जातु has the sense of 'not allowing or putting up with;' जातु तत्रभवान्वृषलं याजयेन्नावकल्पयामि (न मर्षयामि) Sk. 5 Used with a present indicative it denotes censure (गर्हा); जातु तत्रभवान् वृषलं याजयति *ibid*.

जातुधानः A demon, imp.

जातुष *a.* (षी *f.*) 1 Made of, or covered with, lac. 2 Sticky, adhesive.

जात्य *a.* 1 Of the same family, related. 2 Noble, well-born, sprung from a noble family; जात्यस्तेनाभिजातेन शूरः शौर्यवता कुशः R. 17. 4. 3 Lovely, beautiful, pleasing.

जानकी N. of Sîtâ, wife of Râma.

जानपदः 1 An inhabitant of the country, a rustic, boor, peasant (opp. पौर). 2 A country. 3 A subject. **-दा** A popular expression.

जानि A substitute for जाया at the end of Bah. comp.

जानु *n.* The knee; जानुभ्यामवनिं गत्वा kneeling (or falling on one's knees) on the ground. -COMP. **-दघ्न** *a* reaching to, as high as, the knees, knee-deep. **-फलकं, -मंडलं** the knee pan. **-संधिः** the knee-joint.

जापः 1 Muttering prayers, whispering, murmuring. 2 A muttered prayer.

जाबालः A goat-herd.

जामदग्न्यः N. of Parasurâma q. v.

जामा 1 A daughter. 2 A daughter-in-law.

जामातृ *m.* 1 A son-in-law; जामातृयज्ञेन वयं निरुद्धाः U. 1. 11; जामाता दशमो ग्रहः Subhâsh. 2 A lord, master. 3 The sun flower.

जामिः *f.* 1 A sister. 2 A daughter. 3 A daughter-in-law. 4 A near female relative (सन्निहितसपिंडस्त्री Kull.); Ms. 3. 57-58. 5 A virtuous and respectable woman.

जामित्रं The seventh zodiacal sign from the natal sign (लग्न); तिथौ च जामित्रगुणान्वितायां Ku. 7. 1 (जामित्रं लग्नात्सप्तमं स्थानं Malli.). *Note*—Some derive the word from जाया, because in astrology, the **जामित्र** sign indicates the future good-luck of one's wife (जायामित्रं ?); but the word is obviously connected with the Greek *diametron*.

जामेयः A sister's son.

जांबवं 1 Gold. 2 The fruit of the Jambu tree.

जांबवत् *m.* N. of a king of bears who was of signal service to Râma at the siege of Lankâ. He was also noted for his medical skill. [This same Jâmbavat appears to have lived up to the time of Krishna, or perhaps he was another being of that time; for there was a fight between Krishna and Jâmbavat for the *Syamantaka* jewel which the latter had got from Prasena, brother of Satrâjit. Krishna vanquished Jâmbavat, who placed the jewel, along with his daughter Jâmbavatî, at his entire disposal.].

जांबीरं (लं) A citron.

जांबूनदं 1 Gold; R. 18. 44. 2 A golden ornament; कृतरुचश्च जांबूनदैः Si. 4. 66. 3 The Dhattûra plant.

जाया A wife. (The word is thus derived:-पतिर्भार्यां संप्रविश्य गर्भो भूत्वेह जायते। जायायास्तद्धि जायात्वं यदस्यां जायते पुनः Ms. 9. 8; see also Malli. on R. 2. 1). As last member of Bah. comp. जाया is changed to जानि; सीताजानिः 'one who has Sîtâ for his wife'; so युवजानिः, वामार्धजानिः -COMP. **-अनुजीविन्** *m.*, **-आजीवः** 1 an actor, a dancer. 2 the husband of a harlot. 3 a needy man, pauper. **-पती** (dual) husband and wife. (The other forms of the comp. are दंपती and जंपती q. v.).

जायिन् *a.* (**नी** *f.*) Conquering, subduing. -*m.* The burden of a song (in music.)

जायुः 1 Medicine. 2 A physician.

जारः 1 A paramour, gallant, lover; रथकारः स्वकां भार्यां सजारां शिरसावहत् Pt. 4. 54. -COMP **-जः, जन्मन्, -जातः** a bastard. **-भरा** an aduteress.

जारिणी An adulteress.

जालं 1 A net, snare. 2 A web, cob-web. 3 A coat of mail, a helmet made of wire. 4 An eye-hole, lattice, window; जालांतरप्रेषितदृष्टिरन्या R. 7. 9; धूपैर्जालविनिःसृतैर्वलभयः संदिग्धपारावताः V. 3. 2; Ku. 7. 60. 5 A collection, an assemblage, number, mass; चिंतासंततितंतुजालनिबिडस्यूतेव Mâl. 5. 10; Ku. 7 89; *Si.* 4. 56; Amaru. 58. 6 Magic. 7 Illusion, deception 8 An unblown flower. -COMP. **-अक्षः** a loop—hole, window. **-कर्मन्** *n* the occupation of catching fish, fishing. **कारकः** 1 a net-maker. 2 a spider. **-गोणिका** a kind of churning vessel. **-पाद्, -पादः** a goose. **-प्राया** mail, armour.

जालकं 1 A net. 2 A multitude, collection बद्धं कर्णशिरीषरोधि वदने घर्माम्भसां जालकं *S.* 1. 30; R. 9. 68. 3 A lattice, window. 4 A bud, an unblown flower; अभिनवैर्जालकैर्मालतीनां Me; 98; so यूथिकाजालकानि 26. 5 A kind of ornament (worn in the hair); तिलकजालकजालकमौक्तिकैः R. 9. 44 (आभरणविशेषः) 6 A nest. 7 Illusion, deception. -COMP. **-मालिन्** *a.* veiled.

जालकिन् *m.* A cloud.

जालकिनी A ewe.

जालिकः 1 A fisherman. 2 A fowler, bird-catcher. 3 A spider. 4 The governor or chief ruler of a province 5 A rogue, cheat. **-का** 1 A net. 2 A chain-armour. 3 A spider. 4 A leech. 5 A widow. 6 Iron. 7 A veil, woollen cloth.

जालिनी A room ornamented with pictures.

जाल्म *a.* (**ल्मी** *f.*) 1 Cruel, severe, harsh. 2 Rash, inconsiderate. **-ल्मः** (**ल्मी** *f.*) 1 A rogue, rascal, villain, wretch, miscreant; अपि ज्ञायते कतमेन दिग्भागेन गतः स जाल्म इति V. 1. 2 A poor man, a low or degraded man.

जाल्मक *a.* (**ल्मिका** *f.*) Despised, low, mean, contemptible.

जावन्यं 1. Speed, swiftness. 2 Haste, hurry.

जाहं A termination added to nouns expressive of the parts of the body in the sense of 'the root of;' कर्णजाहं the root of the ear; so अक्षि°. ओष्ठ° &c.

जाह्नवी An epithet of the river Ganges.

जि 1 P. (Atm. when preceded by परा and वि) (जयति, जित) 1 To conquer, defeat, overcome, vanquish, subjugate; जयति तुलामधिरूढो भास्वानपि जलदपटलानि Pt. 1. 330; Bk. 15. 76, 16. 2. 2 To surpass, excel; गर्जितानंतरां वृष्टिं सौभाग्येन जिगाय सा Ku. 2. 53; R. 3. 34; Ghaṭ. 22; *Si.* 1. 19. 3 To win (by conquest or in gambling), acquire by conquest; प्रागजीयत घृणा ततो मही R. 11. 65 (where जि means 'to conquer' also); Ms. 7. 96 4 To curb, restrain, control, conquer (as passions.). 5 To be victorious, be supreme or pre-eminent (generally used in benedictory stanzas or salutations); जयतु जयतु महाराजः (in dramas); स जयति परिणद्धः शक्तिभिः शक्तिनाथः Mâl. 5. 1; जितमुडुपतिना नमः सुरेभ्यः Ratn. 1. 4; Bh. 2. 2; Gît. 1. 1. -*Caus* (जापयति) To cause to win or conquer. -*Desid.* (जिगीषति) To wish to win, acquire or excel, to vie with, emulate.-WITH **अधि** to conquer, defeat, vanquish; Bh. 19. 2. **-निस्** 1 to conquer, defeat; R 3. 51; Bk. 2. 52; 7. 94; Y 3. 292. 2 to win, acquire by conquest; Ms. 8. 154. **-परा** (Atm.) 1 to defeat, conquer, overcome, subdue; यं पराजयसे मृषा Y. 2. 75; Bk. 8. 9. 2 to lose, be deprived of. 3 to be conquered or overcome by, find (something) unbearable; अध्ययनात्पराजयते Sk. finds it unbearable or difficult to study; Bk. 8. 71. **-वि** (Atm). 1 to conquer, defeat, overcome, subdue; व्यजेष्ट षड्वर्गं Bk. 1. 2; प्रायस्त्वन्मुखसेवया विजयते विश्वं स पुष्पायुधः Gît. 10; Bk. 2. 39; 15. 39 2 to surpass, excel; चक्षुर्भेचकमंबुजं विजयते Vb. 1. 33 3 to win, acquire by conquest; भुजविजितविमान R. 12. 104; 1. 59; *S*ânti. 2. 13. 4 to be victorious, be supreme or pre-eminent; विजयतां देवः *S.* 5.

जिः A demon (पिशाच).

जिगत्नुः Breath, life.

जिगीषा 1 Desire of conquering, subduing or overcoming; यानं सस्मार कौबेरं वैवस्वतजिगीषया R. 15. 45. 2 Emulation, rivalry. 3 Eminence. 4 Exertion, profession, habit of life.

जिगीषु *a.* Desirous of conquering.

जिघत्सा 1 Desire of eating, hunger. 2 striving for. 3 Contending with.

जिघत्सु *a.* Hungry.

जिघांसा Desire of killing; R. 15 19.

जिघांसु *a.* Desirous of killing, murderous.**—सुः** An enemy.

जिघृक्षा Desire of taking or seizing.

जिघ्र *a.* **1** Smelling. **2** Conjecturing, guessing, observing; *e. g.* मनोजिघ्रः सपत्नीजनः S. D.

जिज्ञासा Desire of knowing, curiosity, inquisitiveness.

जिज्ञासु *a.* **1** Desirous of knowing, inquisitive, curious; Bg. 6. 44. **2** Desirous of getting absolution (मुमुक्षु).

जित् *a.* (At the end of comp.) Conquering, defeating, winning &c.; तारकाजित्, कंसाजित्, सहस्रजित् &c.

जित *p. p.* **1** Conquered, subdued, curbed, restrained (as enemies, passions &c.). **2** Won, got, obtained (by conquest). **3** Surpassed, excelled. **4** Subject to, enslaved or influenced by; कामजित; स्त्रीजित &c. –COMP-**अक्षर** *a.* reading well or readily. **–अमित्र** *a.* one who has conquered his foes, triumphant, victorious. **–अरि** *a.* one who has conquered his enemies. (**–रिः**) an epithet of Buddha. **–आत्मन्** *a.* self subdued, void of passion. **–आहव** *a.* victorious. **–इंद्रिय** *a.* one who has conquered his passions or subdued the senses (रूप, रस, गंध, स्पर्श & शब्द); श्रुत्वा स्पृष्ट्वाथ दृष्ट्वा च भुक्त्वा घ्रात्वा च यो नरः । न हृष्यति ग्लायति वा स विज्ञेयो जितेंद्रियः Ms. 2. 98. **–काशिन्** *a.* appearing victorious, proud of victory, assuming the airs of a victor; चाणक्योऽपि जितकाशितया Mu. 2; जितकाशी राजसेवकः *ibid*. **–कोप, –क्रोध** *a.* imperturbable, not excitable.**–नेमिः** a staff made of the Asvatha tree. **–श्रम** *a.* inured to fatigue, hardy. **–स्वर्गः**one who has won heaven.

जितिः *f.* Victory, conquest.

जितुमः, जित्तमः Gemini, the **3**rd sign of the zodiac (a word of Greek origin).

जित्वर *a.* (**री** *f.*) Victorious, conquering, triumphant; शस्त्राण्युपायंसत जित्वराणि Bk. 1. 16; कदलीकृतभूपालो भ्रातृभिर्जित्वरैर्दिशां Si. 2. 9.

जिन *a.* **1** Victorious, triumphant. **2** Very old. **–नः 1** A generic term applied to a chief, Bauddha or Jaina saint. **2** N. applied to the Arhats of the Jainas. **3** An epithet of Vishṇu –COMP. **–इंद्रः, –ईश्वरः 1** a chief Bauddha saint. **2** an Arhat of the Jainas. **–सद्मन्** *n.* a Jaina temple or monastery.

जिवाजिवः The Chakora bird.

जिष्णु *a.* **1** Victorious, triumphant; R. 4. 85; 10. 18. **2** Winning, gaining. **3** (At the end of comp). Conquering, excelling; अलिनीजिष्णुः कचानां चयः Bk. 1. 6; Si. 13. 21. **–ष्णुः 1** The sun. **2** N. of Indra. **3** N. of Vishṇu. **4** N. of Arjuna.

जिह्म *a.* **1** Sloping, athwart, oblique. **2** Crooked, awry, squint; Rs. 1. **12. 3** Tortuous, curved, going irregularly. **4** Morally crooked, deceitful, dishonest, wicked, unfair; धृतहेतिरप्यधृतजिह्ममतिः Ki. 6. 24; सुहृदर्थमीहितमजिह्मधियां Si. 9. 62. **5** Dim, dark, pale-coloured; विधिसमयनियोगाद्दीप्तिसंहारजिह्मं Ki. 1. 46. **6** Slow, lazy. **–ह्मं** Dishonesty, falsehood. –COMP. **–अक्ष** *a.* crooked-eyed, squinting. **–गः** a snake. **–गति** *a.* meandering, going tortuously; Rs. 1. 13. **–मेहनः** a frog. **–योधिन्** *a.* fighting unfairly. **–शल्यः** the Khadira tree.

जिह्नः The tongue.

जिह्वल *a.* Voracious, greedy.

जिह्वा 1 The tongue. **2** The tongue of fire; *i. e.* a flame –COMP.-**आस्वादः** licking, lapping. **–उल्लेखनी, –उल्लेखनिका, –निर्लेखनं** a tongue-scraper. **–पः 1** a dog. **2** a cat. **3** a tiger. **4** a leopard. **5** a bear. **–मूलं** the root of the tongue. **–मूलीय** *a.* a term particularly applied to the Visarga before क् and ख् and also to ऋ, ऌ and the guttural class of consonants (in gram). **–रदः** a bird. **–लिह्** *m.* a dog. **–लौल्यं** greediness. **–शल्यः** the Khadira tree.

जीन *a.* Old, aged, decayed. **–नः** A leather bag; जीनकार्मुकबस्तावीन् पृथग् दद्याद्विशुद्धये Ms. 11. 139.

जीमूतः 1 A cloud; जीमूतेन स्वकुशलमयीं हारयिष्यन् प्रवृत्तिं Me. 4. **2** An epithet of Indra. –COMP. **–कूटः** a mountain. **–वाहनः 1** N. of Indra. **2** N. of a king of Vidyâdharas, hero of the play called Nâgânanda; (mentioned also in कथासरित्सागर) [He was the son of Jimutaketu and renowned for his benevolent and charitable disposition. When his father's kingdom was invaded by his kinsmen, he scorned the idea of fighting with them and induced his father to leave it to those who sought for it and to repair with him to the Malaya mountain to lead a holy life. It is related that there he one day took the place of a young serpent who was by virtue of an agreement, to be offered to Garuda as his daily meal, and induced, by his generous and touching behaviour, the enemy of serpents to give up his practice of devouring them. The story is very pathetically told in the play]. **–वाहिन्** *m.* smoke.

जीरः 1 A sword. **2** Cumin-seed.

जीरकः, जीरणः Cumin-seed.

जीर्ण *a.* **1** Old, ancient. **2** Worn out, ruined, wasted, decayed, tattered (as clothes); वासांसि जीर्णानि यथा विहाय Bg. 2. 22. **3** Digested; सुजीर्णमन्नं सुविचक्षणः सुतः H. 1. 22. **–र्णः 1** An old man. **2** A tree. **–र्णं 1** Benzoin, **2** Old age, decrepitude. –COMP **–उद्धारः** 'renewing the old', repairs, especially of a temple or any charitable or religious institution. **–उद्यानं** ruined or neglected garden. **–ज्वरः** a lingering fever. **–पर्णः** the Kadamba tree. **–वाटिका** a ruined house. **–वज्रं** a particular gem.

जीर्णक *a.* Almost dried up or withered.

जीर्णिः *f.* **1** Old age, decrepitude, decay, infirmity. **2** Digestion.

जीव् 1 P. (जीवति, जीवित) **1** To live, be alive; यस्मिञ्जीवति जीवंति बहवः सोऽत्र जीवति Pt. 1. 23 ; मा जीवन् यः परावज्ञादुःखदग्धोपि जीवति Si. 2. 45; Ms. 2, 235. **2** To revive, come to life. **3** To live by, subsist on, make a livelihood by (with instr.); सत्यानृतं तु वाणिज्यं तेन चैवापि जीव्यते Ms. 4. 6; विपणेन च जीवंतः 3. 152, 162; 11. 26; sometimes used with a cognate accusative in this sense; अजिह्मामशठां शुद्धां जीवेद् ब्राम्हणजीविकां Ms. 4. 11. **4** (Fig). To live or prey upon, depend upon as one's source of existence (with loc.); चौराः प्रमत्ते जीवंति व्याधितेषु चिकित्सकाः । प्रमदाः कामयानेषु यजमानेषु याचकाः ॥ राजा विवदमानेषु नित्यं मूर्खेषु पंडिताः ॥ Mb. –*Caus*. **1** To restore to life. **2** To nourish, nurture, bring up. –WITH **अति 1** to survive. **2** to surpass in the mode of living (live more splendidly &c); अत्यजीवदमरालकेश्वरौ R. 19. 15. **–अनु 1** to hang on, live by or upon, serve; स तु तस्याः पाणिग्राहकमनुजीविष्यति Dk. 122. **2** to see without envy; यां तां श्रियमसूयामः पुरा दृष्ट्वा युधिष्ठिरे । अद्य तामनुजीवामः Mb. **3** to live for any one. **4** to follow in living; R. 19. 15. vl., (अन्वजीवत् or अत्यजीवत्). **5** to survive. **–उद्** to revive, return to life; उदजीवत् सुमित्राभूः Bk. 17. 95. **–उप 1** to live upon, subsist, derive livelihood from; का वृत्तिमुपजीवत्यार्यः; संवाहकवृत्तिमुपजीवामि Mk. 2; शेषास्तमुपजीवेयुर्यथैव पितरं तथा Ms. 9. 105; Y. 2. 301. **2** to serve, depend on; Si. 9. 32.

जीव *a.* Living, existing. **–वः 1** The principle of life, the vital breath, life, soul; गतजीव, जीवत्याग, जीवाशा &c.; **2** The individual or personal soul enshrined in the human body and imparting to it life, motion and sensation (called जीवात्मन् as opposed to परमात्मन् the Supreme soul); Y. 3 131; Ms. 12. 22-23. **3** Life, existence. **4** A creature, living being. **5** Livelihood, profession. **6.** N. of Karṇa. **7** N. of one of the Maruts. **8** The constellation पुष्य. –COMP. **–अंतकः 1** a birdcatcher, fowler. **2** a murderer, slayer. **–आत्मन्** *m.* the individual soul enshrined in the human body. (as oppossed to परमात्मन् 'the Supreme soul'). **–आदानं** abstracting healthy blood, bleeding (in medic.). **–आधानं** preservation of life. **–आधारः** the heart. **–इंधनं** glowing fire-wood, burning wood. –उत्सर्गः 'casting off life', voluntary death, suicide –ऊर्णा the wool of a living animal. –गृहं, –मंदिरं 'the abode of the soul'; the body. –ग्राहः a prisoner taken alive –जीवः (also जीवंजीवः) the Chakora bird. –दः 1 a physician. 2 an enemy –दशा mortal existence. –धनं 'living wealth', property in the shape of living creature, livestock. –धानी the earth. –पतिः *f.* –पत्नी a woman whose husband is alive. –पुत्रा, –वत्सा a woman whose son is living –मातृका the seven mothers or female divinities; (कुमारी धनदा नंदा विमला मंगला बला। पद्मा चेति च विख्याताः सप्तैता जीवमातृकाः). –रक्तं menstrual blood. लोकः 1 the world of living beings, the world of mortals, the world or worldly existence; त्वत्प्रयाणे शांतालोकः सर्वतो जीवलोकः Mâl. 9 37; जीवलोकतिलकः प्रलीयते 21. 80 स्वप्नेंद्रजालसदृशः खलु जीवलोकः Sânti. 2. 2; Bg. 11 7; U. 4. 17. 2 living beings, mankind; दिवस इवाभ्रश्यामस्तपात्यये जीवलोकस्य S. 3. 12; or आलोकमर्कादिव जीवलोकः R. 5. 55. –वृत्तिः *f.* breeding or keeping cattle. –शेष *a.* one to whom only life is left, escaping only with life and nothing more. –संक्रमणं transmigration of soul. –साधनं grain, corn. –साफल्यं realization or attainment of the chief end of human existence. –सूः 'the mother of living beings', a woman whose children are living. –स्थानं a joint, an articulation.

जीविकः 1 A living being. 2 A servant. 3 A Buddhist mendicant, any mendicant who lives by begging. 4 A usurer. 5 A snake-catcher. 6 A tree.

जीवत् *a.* (न्ती *f.*) Living, alive. –Comp. तोका a woman whose children are living. –पतिः *f.* –पत्नी *f.* a woman whose husband is living –मुक्त *a.* 'liberated while living', a man who being purified by a true knowledge of the Supreme spirit is freed from the future birth and all ceremonial rites while yet living. –मुक्तिः *f.* final liberation in the present state of life. मृत *a.* 'dead while alive'; one who, though alive, is as good as dead and useless to the world (said of a mad man or one whose character is lost).

जीवथः 1 Life, existence. 2 A tortoise. 3 A peacock. 4 A cloud.

जीवन *a.* (नी *f.*) Enlivening, animating, giving life. –नः 1 A living being. 2 Wind. 3 A son. –नं 1 Life, existence; (fig. also); त्वमसि मम भूषणं त्वमसि मम जीवनं Gît. 10. 2 The principle of life, vital energy; Bg. 7. 9. 3 Water; बीजा[illegible] नमोऽस्तु जीवनाम Ki. 18. 39; or जीवनं जीवनं (life) हंति प्राणान् हंति समीरणः Udb. 4 Livelihood, profession, means of existence. (fig. also); Ms. 11. 76; H. 3. 33. 5 Butter made from milk one day old. 6 Marrow. –Comp. –अंतः death. –आघातं poison. –आवासः 1 'residing in water', epithet of Varuṇa, the regent of water. 2 the body. –उपायः livelihood. –ओषधं 1 elixir vitæ. 2 a life-giving medicine.

जीवनकं Food.

जीवनीयं 1 Water. 2 Fresh milk.

जीवंतः 1 Life, existence. 2 A drug, medicament.

जीवंतिकः A fowler.

जीवा 1 Water. 2 The earth. 3 A bow-string; मुहुर्जीवाघोषैर्बधिरयति Mv. 6. 30. 4 The chord of an arc. 5 Means of living. 6 The tinkling of metallic ornaments. 7 N. of a plant (वचा).

जीवातु *m.*, *n.* 1 Food. 2 Life, existence. 3 Restoration to life, revival; रे हस्त दक्षिण मृतस्य शिशोर्द्विजस्य जीवातवे विसृज शूद्रमुनौ कृपाणं U. 2. 10. 4 A medicine for restoring life.

जीविका Means of living, livelihood.

जीवित *a.* 1 Living, existent, alive; R. 12. 75. 2 Returned to life. 3 Animated, enlivened. 4 Lived through (as a period). –तं 1 Life, existence; त्वं जीवितं त्वमसि मे हृदयं द्वितीयं U. 3. 26; कन्येयं कुलजीवितं Ku. 6. 63; Me. 83; नाभिनंदेत मरणं नाभिनंदेत जीवितं Ms. 6 45; 7. 111. 2 Duration of life. 3 Livelihood. 4 A living being. –Comp. अंतकः an epithet of Siva. –आशा hope of life, love of life. –ईशः 1 a lover, husband. 2 an epithet of Yama; जीवितेशवसतिं जगाम सा R. 11. 20 (where the word is used in sense 1 also). 3 the sun. 4 the moon –कालः duration of life. –ज्ञा an artery. –व्ययः sacrifice of life. –संशयः risk of life; jeopardy, danger to life; स आतुरो जीवितसंशये वर्तते 'he is dangerously ill'; Bv. 2. 20.

जीविन् *a.* (नी *f.*) (generally at the end of comp.) 1 Living, alive, existing; R. 1. 63. 2 Living upon or by; शस्त्रजीविन्, आयुधजीविन् &c. *m.* A living being.

जीव्या Means of livelihood.

जुगुप्सनं, जुगुप्सा 1 Censure, reproach. 2 Dislike, aversion, disgust, abhorrence. 3 (In Rhet.) Disgust considered as the feeling which gives rise to the Bîbhatsa sentiment, thus defined.—दोषेक्षणादिभिर्गर्हा जुगुप्सा विषयोद्भवा S. D. 207.

जुष् I. 6. A. (जुषते-जुष्ट) 1 To be pleased or satisfied. 2 To be favourable or propitious. 3 To like, be fond of, take pleasure or delight in, enjoy; सत्त्वं जुषाणस्य भवाय देहिनां Bhâg. 4 To devote or attach oneself to, practise, undergo, suffer; पौलस्त्योऽजुषत शुचं विपन्नबंधुः Bk. 17. 112. 3 To frequent, visit, inhabit; जुषंते पर्वतश्रेष्ठमृषयः पर्वसंधिषु Mb. 6 To enter, seat oneself, resort to; रथं च जुजुषे शुभं Bk. 14. 95. 7 To choose.–II. 1 P., 10 U. (जोषति, जोषयति-ते) 1 To reason, think. 2 To investigate, examine. 3 To hurt. 4 To be satisfied.

जुष् *a.* (At the end of comp.) 1 Liking, enjoying, taking delight in; Bh. 3. 103. 2 Visiting, approaching, going to, taking, assuming, resorting to &c.; परलोकजुषां R. 8. 85; रजोजुषे जन्मनि K. 1.

जुष्ट *p. p.* 1 Pleased, gratified. 2 Practised, resorted to, visited, suffered &c; Bg. 2. 2. 3 Furnished or endowed with, possessed of.

जुहूः *f.* A crescent-shaped wooden ladle used for pouring the sacrificial butter into the fire.

जुहोतिः A technical name for those sacrificial ceremonies to which the verb जुहोति is applied as distinguished from those to which यजति is applied; क्षरंति सर्वा वैदिक्यो जुहोतियजतिक्रियाः Ms. 2. 84 (See Medhâtithi and other commentators; सर्वज्ञनारायण shortly renders जुहोति by उपविष्टहोम and यजति by तिष्ठद्धोम. See: Asvalâyana I. 2. 5 also).

जूः *f.* 1 Speed. 2 Atmosphere. 3 A female demon. 4 An epithet of Sarasvatî.

जूकः The sign Libra of the zodiac (a word of Greek origin).

जूटः The mass of twisted or matted hair; भूतेशस्य भुजंगवल्लिवलयस्रङ्नद्धजूटा जटाः Mâl. 1. 2.

जूटकं Matted hair.

जूतिः *f.* Speed, velocity.

जूर् 4 A. (जूर्यते, जूर्ण) 1 To hurt, injure, kill. 2 To be angry with (with dat.); भर्त्रे नखेभ्यश्च चिरं जुजूरे Bk. 11. 8. 3 To grow old.

जूर्तिः *f.* Fever.

जॄ 1 P. (जरति) 1 To make low or humiliate. 2 To excel.

जृभ्, जृंभ् 1 A. (जृभते, जृंभते जृंभित, जृब्ध) 1 To gape, yawn; Ms. 4. 43. 2 to open, expand, burst open (as a flower &c.); परयुवतिमुखाभं पंकजं जृंभतेऽद्य Rs. 3. 22. 3 To increase, spread or extend everywhere; जृभतां जृंभतामप्रतिहतप्रसरं क्रोधज्योतिः Ve. 1; तृष्णे जृंभसि (Paras. is irregular) Bh. 3 5; भोगः कोपि स एक एव परमो नित्योदितो जृंभते 3. 80. 4 To appear, rise, show oneself, become visible or manifest; संकल्पयोनेरभिमानभूतमात्मानमाधाय मधुर्जजृंभे Ku. 3. 24. 5 To be at ease. 6 To recoil or fly back (as a bow). –*Caus.* To cause to yawn or expand. –With उद् to appear, rise, spring up; N. 2. 105. –वि 1 to yawn, gape, open the mouth; व्यजृंभिषत चापरे Bk. 15. 108; विजृंभितमिवांतरिक्षेण Mk. 5. **2** to open, expand (as a flower). **3** to spread everywhere, pervade, fill; सुखश्रवा मंगलतूर्यनिःस्वनाः...न केवलं सद्मनि मागधीपतेः पथि व्यजृंभंत दिवौकसामपि R. 3. 18. 12. 72; रजोंधकारस्य विजृंभितस्य 7. 42. **4** to rise, appear. **-समुद्** to attempt, strive, endeavour; व्यालं बालमृणालतंतुभिरसौ रोद्धुं समुज्जृंभते Bh. 2. 6.

जृंभः, -भं, जृभणं, जृंभा, जृंभिका 1 Yawning, gaping. **2** Opening, blossoming, expanding; कलिकाश्रयी जृंभा प्रभवति K. 257; जृंभारंभप्रविततदलोपांतजालप्रविष्टैः Ve. 2. 7; मालती शिरसिजृंभणोन्मुखी Bh. 1 25. **3** Stretching (the limbs); (अंगानि) मुहुर्मुहुर्जृंभणतत्पराणि Rs. 6. 10.

जॄ 1. 4. 9. P., 10. U. (जरति, जीर्यति, जृणाति, जारयति-ते, जीर्ण or जीरित) **1** To grow old, wear out, wither, decay; जीर्यंते जीर्यतः केशा दंता जीर्यंति जीर्यतः। जीर्यतश्चक्षुषी श्रोत्रे तृष्णैका तरुणायते Pt 5. 83; Bk. 9. 41. **2** To perish, be consumed (fig. also); अजारीदिव च प्रज्ञा बलं शोकात्तथाऽजरत् Bk. 6. 30.; जेरुराशा दशास्यस्य 14. 112. **3** To be dissolved or digested; जीर्णमन्नं प्रशंसीयात् Châṇ: 79; उदरे चाजरन्नन्ये Bk. 15. 50.

जेतृ *m.* **1** A conqueror, victor. **2** An epithet of Vishnu.

जेंताकः A heated chamber for inducing perspiration, a dry hot bath.

जेमनं 1 Eating. **2** Food.

जैत्र *a.* (**त्री** *f.*) **1** Victorious, successful, leading to victory; इदमिह मदनस्य जैत्रमस्त्रं विफलगुणातिशयं भविष्यतीति Mâl. 2. 5; धनुर्जैत्रं रघुर्दधौ R. 4. 66, 16. 72. **2** Superior. **-त्रः 1** A victor, conqueror. **2** Quick-silver. **-त्रं 1** Victory, triumph. **2** Superiority.

जैनः A Jaina, a follower of Jaina doctrines.

जैमिनिः N. of a celebrated sage and philosopher, founder of the Mîmâmsâ school of philosophy (properly पूर्वमीमांसा); मीमांसाकृतमुन्ममाथ सहसा हस्ती मुनिं जैमिनिं Pt. 2. 33.

जैवातृक *a.* (**की** *f.*) **1** Long-lived, one for whom long life is desired; जैवातृक ननु श्रूयते पतिरस्याः Dk. **2** Thin, lean. **-कः 1** The moon; राजानं जनयांबभूव सहसा जैवातृक त्वां तु यः Bv. 2. 78. **2** Camphor. **3** A son. **4** A drug, medicament. **5** A peasant.

जैवेयः An epithet of Kacha, son of Brihaspati.

जैह्म्यं Crookedness, deceit, falsehood.

जोंगटः The longings of a pregnant woman (दोहद).

जोटिंगः An epithet of Siva.

जोषः 1 Satisfaction, enjoyment, happiness, pleasure. **2** Silence. **-षं** *ind.* **1** According to one's wish, with ease. **2** Silently; किमिति जोषमास्यते *S.* 5; Bv. 2. 17.

जोषा, जोषित् *f.* A woman; cf. योषा, योषित्.

जोषिका 1 A cluster of young buds. **2** A woman.

ज्ञ *a.* (At the end of comp.) **1** knowing, familiar with; कार्यज्ञ, निमित्तज्ञ, शास्त्रज्ञ, सर्वज्ञ &c. **2** Wise; as in ज्ञंमन्य thinking oneself to be wise. **-ज्ञः 1** A wise and learned man. **2** The sentient soul. **3** The planet Mercury. **4** The planet Mars. **5** An epithet of Brahmâ.

ज्ञपित, ज्ञप्त *a.* Made known, informed, expounded, taught.

ज्ञप्तिः *f.* **1** Understanding **2** Intellect. **3** Promulgating.

ज्ञा 9 U. (जानाति, जानीते, ज्ञात) **1** To know (in all senses), to learn, become acquainted with; महा ज्ञासीस्त्वं सुखी रामो यदकार्षीत्स रक्षसां Bk. 15. 9. **2** To know, be aware of, be familiar or conversant with; जाने तपसो वीर्यं *S.* 3. 1; जानन्नपि हि मेधावी जडवल्लोक आचरेत् Ms. 2. 110, 123; 7. 148. **3** To find out, ascertain, investigate; ज्ञायतां कः कः कार्यार्थीति Mk. 9. 4. To comprehend, apprehend, understand, feel, experience; as in दुःखज्ञ, सुखज्ञ &c. **5** To test, try, know the true character of; आपत्सु मित्रं जानीयात् H. 1. 72; Châṇ. 21. **6** To recognise; न त्वं दृष्ट्वा न पुनरलकां ज्ञास्यसे कामचारिन् Me. 63. **7** To regard, consider, know to be; जानामि त्वां प्रकृतिपुरुषं कामरूपं मघोनः Me. 6. **8** To act, engage in (with gen. of the instrument), सर्पिषो जानीते Sk. 'he engages in sacrifice with clarified butter (सर्पिषा = सर्पिषः), *-Caus.* (ज्ञापयति, ज्ञपयति) **1** To announce, inform, make acquainted with, make known, notify. **2** To request, ask (Atm). *-Desid.* (जिज्ञासते) To desire to know, investigate, ascertain; R. 2. 26; Bk. 8. 33; 4 91. -WITH **अनु 1** to permit, allow, assent, or consent to, agree to, sanction; अनुजानीहि मां गमनाय U. 3. **2** to betroth, affiance, promise (in marriage; मां जातमात्रां धनमित्रनाम्नेऽन्वजानाद्भार्यां मे पिता Dk. 50. **3** to excuse, forgive. **4** To request. **5** to own **-अप** to conceal, hide, disown, deny (Atm.); शतमपजानीते Sk.; आत्मानमपजानानः शशमात्रोऽनयद्दिनं Bk. 8. 26. **-अभि 1** to recognise; नाभ्यजानान्नलं नृपं Mb. **2** to know, understand, be acquainted with, be aware of; Bg. 4. 14, 7. 13, 18. 55. **3** to regard, consider, know to be. **4** to admit, acknowledge. **-अव** to slight, despise, disregard, neglect; अवजानासि मां यस्मात् R. 1. 77; Bk. 3. 8; Bg. 9. 11, **-आ** to know, understand, find out, ascertain. (*-Caus.*) **1** to order, command, direct. **2** to assure. **3** to dismiss, give leave to go. **-परि 1** to be aware of, know, be acquainted with; वृषभोऽयमिति परिज्ञाय Pt. 1; Ms. 8. 126. **2** to find out, ascertain; सम्यक् परिज्ञाय Pt. 1. **3** to recognise; तपस्विभिः कैश्चित्परिज्ञातोऽस्मि *S.* 2. **-प्रति** (Atm.) **1** to promise हरचापारोपणेन कन्यादानं प्रतिजानीते P. R. 4; Bk. 8. 26, 64; Ms. 9. 99. **2** to confirm. **3** to state, affirm, assert. **-वि 1** to know, be aware of; Bh. 3. 21. **2** to learn, comprehend, understand. **3** to ascertain, find out. **4** to regard, know to be, consider (*-Caus.*) **1** to request, beg (opp. आज्ञापयति); आर्यपुत्र अस्ति मे विज्ञाप्यं; (रामः) नन्वाज्ञापय U. 1; R. 5. 20. **2** to communicate, inform. **3** to say, speak in general. **-सं** (Atm.) **1** to know, understand, be aware of. **2** to recognise. **3** to live in harmony, agree together (with acc. or instr.); पित्रा पितरं वा संजानीते Sk. **4** to watch, be on the alert; Bk. 8. 27. **5** to accede to, agree with. **6** (Paras.) to remember, think of; मातुः मातरं वा संजानाति Sk. (*-Caus.*) to inform.

ज्ञात *a.* Known, ascertained, understood, learnt, comprehended &c; see ज्ञा above. COMP. **-सिद्धांतः** a man completely versed in any *S*âstra

ज्ञातिः 1 A Paternal relation, a father, brother &c.; agnate relatives collectively. **2** A kinsman or kindred in general. **3** A father. -COMP. **-भावः** kin, relationship. **-भेदः** dissension among relatives. **-विद्** *a.* one who makes near relatives.

ज्ञातेयं Relationship.

ज्ञातृ *m.* **1** A wise man. **2** An acquaintance. **3** A bail, surety.

ज्ञानं 1 Knowing, understanding, becoming acquainted with, proficiency; सांख्यस्य योगस्य च ज्ञानं Mâl. 1. 7. **2** Knowledge, learning; बुद्धिर्ज्ञानेन शुध्यति Ms. 5. 109; ज्ञाने मौनं क्षमा शक्तौ R. 1. 22. **3** Consciousness, cognizance; knowledge; ज्ञानतोऽज्ञानतो वापि Ms. 8. 288 knowingly or unknowingly, consciously or unconsciously. **4** Sacred knowledge; especially, knowledge derived from meditation on the higher truths of religion and philosophy which teaches man how to understand his own nature and how he may be reunited to the Supreme spirit (opp. कर्मन्); cf. ज्ञानयोग and कर्मयोग in Bg. 3. 3. **5** The organ of intelligence, sense, intellect. -COMP. **-अनुत्पादः** ignorance, folly. **-आत्मन्** *a.* all-wise. **-इंद्रियं** an organ of perception; (these are five त्वच्, रसना, चक्षुस्, कर्ण and घ्राण the skin, tongue, eyes, ear and nose; see बुद्धींद्रिय under इंद्रिय). **-कांडं** that inner or esoteric portion of the Veda which refers to true spiritual knowledge, or knowledge of the Supreme spirit, as distinguished from the knowledge of ceremonial rites (opp. कर्मकांड). **-कृत** *a.* done knowingly or intentionally. **-गम्य** *a.* attainable by the understanding. **-चक्षुस्** *n.* the eye of intelligence, the mind's eye, intellectual vision (opp चर्मचक्षुस्); सर्वं तु समवेक्ष्येदं निखिलं ज्ञानचक्षुषा Ms. 2. 8 ; 4. 24. (*-m.*) a wise and learned man. **-तत्त्वं** true knowledge, knowledge of god. **-तपस्** *n.* penance consisting in the acquisition of true knowledge. **-दः** a preceptor. **-दा** an epithet of Sarasvatî. **-दुर्बल** *a.* wanting in knowledge. **-निश्चयः** certainty, ascertainment. **-निष्ठ** *a.* intent on acquiring true (spiritnal) knowledge. **-यज्ञः** a man possessed of true or spiritual knowledge, philosopher. **-योगः** contemplation is the principal means of attaining the Supreme spirit or acquiring true or spiritual knowledge. **-शास्त्रं** the science of fortune-telling. **-साधनं** **1** a means of acquiring true or spiritual knowledge. **2** an organ of perception.

ज्ञानतः *ind.* Consciously, knowingly, intentionally.

ज्ञानमय *a.* **1** Consisting of knowledge, spiritual; इतरो दहने स्वकर्मणां ववृते ज्ञानमयेन वह्निना R. 8. 20. **2** Containing knowledge. **-यः** **1** The Supreme spirit. **2** An epithet of *S*iva.

ज्ञानिन् *a.* (**नी** *f.*) Intelligent, wise. *-m.* **1** An astrologer, a fortune-teller. **2** A sage, one possessing true or spiritual knowledge.

ज्ञापक *a.* Making known, teaching, informing, indicating &c. **-कः** **1** A teacher. **2** A commander, a master. **-कं** (In phil.) A significant expression, a suggestive rule or precept, said of such rules as imply something more than what is actually expressed by the words of those rules themselves.

ज्ञापनं Making known, informing, teaching, announcing, indicating.

ज्ञापित *a.* Made known, informed, announced, declared.

ज्ञीप्सा The desire of knowing.

ज्या **1** A bow-string ; विश्रामं लभतामिदं च शिथिलज्याबंधमस्मद्धनुः *S*. 2. 6 ; R. 3. 59, 11. 15 : 12. 104. **2** The chord of an arc. **3** The earth. **4** A mother.

ज्यानिः *f.* **1** Old age, decay. **2** Quitting, abandoning. **3** A river, stream.

ज्यायस् *a.* (**सी** *f.* ; compar. of प्रशस्य, वृद्ध) **1** Elder, senior ; प्रसवक्रमेण स किल ज्यायान् U. 6. **2** Superior, more excellent or worthy ; Ms. 4. 8, 3. 137 ; Bg 3. 1, 8. **3** Larger, greater. **4** (In law) One not a minor ; *i. e.* come of age and responsible for his own actions.

ज्येष्ठ *a.* (Superl. of प्रशस्य or वृद्ध). **1** Eldest, most senior. **2** Most excellent, best. **3** Pre-eminent, first, chief, highest. **-ष्ठः** **1** An elder brother ; R. 12. 19, 35. **2** N. of a lunar month (=ज्यैष्ठ q. v.). **-ष्ठा** **1** An eldest sister. **2** N. of the eighteenth lunar mansion (consisting of three stars). **3** The middle finger. **4** A small house-lizard. **5** An epithet of the Ganges. -COMP. **-अंशः** **1** the eldest brother's share. **2** the right of the eldest brother to a larger share of the patrimonial property. **3** the best share. **-अंबु** *n* **1** water in which grain has been washed. **2** the scum of boild rice. **-आश्रम** **1** the highest or most excellent order in the religious life of a Brâhmaṇa; *i. e.* that of a householder **2** a householder. **-तातः** a father's eldest brother. **-वर्णः** **1** the highest caste (that of Brâhmaṇas **-वृत्तिः** the duties of seniority. **-श्वश्रूः** *f.* a wife's eldest sister.

ज्यैष्ठः N. of a lunar month in which the full moon stands in the constellation ज्येष्ठा (corresponding to May-June). **-ष्ठी** **1** The full-moon day in the month of ज्यैष्ठ. **2** A small house-lizard.

ज्यैष्ठ्यं **1** Precedence, priority of birth, primogeniture, seniority. **2** Pre-eminence, sovereignty.

ज्यो 1 A. (ज्यवते) **1** To advise, instruct. **2** To observe any religious obligation (such as a vow).

ज्योतिर्मय *a.* Consisting of stars, starry; R. 15. 59; Ku. 6. 3.

ज्योतिष. *a.* (**षी** *f.*) **1** Astronomical or astrological. **-षः** **1** An astronomer or astrologer. **2** One of the six Vedângas (being a short tract on astronomy). -COMP. **-विद्या** astronomical or astrological science.

ज्योतिषी, ज्योतिष्कः A planet, star, luminary.

ज्योतिष्मत् *a.* **1** Luminous, bright, shining, possessed of luminous bodies; नक्षत्रताराग्रहसंकुलापि ज्योतिष्मती चंद्रमसैव रात्रिः R. 6. 22. **2** Celestial. *-m.* The sun. **-ती** **1** The night (as illminated by the stars). **2** (In phil.) A state of mind pervaded by सत्त्वगुण *i. e.* a tranquil state of mind.

ज्योतिस् *n.* **1** Light, lustre, brightness, flash; ज्योतिरेकं जगाम *S*. 5. 30; R. 2. 75; Me 5. **2** Light of Brahman, light regarded as the Supreme spirit; Bg 5. 24, 13. 17. **3** Lightning. **4** A heavenly body, a luminary (planet, star &c.); ज्योतिर्भिरुद्यद्भिरिव त्रियामा Ku. 7 21. Bg. 10. 21; H. 1. 21. **5** The faculty of seeing. **6** The celestial world. *-m.* **1** The sun. **2** Fire.-COMP. **-इंगः,-इंगणः** the fire-fly. **-कणः** a spark of fire. **-गणः** the heavenly bodies collectively. **-चक्रं** the zodiac. **-ज्ञः** an astronomer or astrologer. **-मंडलं** the stellar sphere. **-रथः** (ज्योतीरथः) the polar star. **-विद्** *m.* an astronomer or astrologer. **-विद्या,-शास्त्रं** (ज्योतिश्शास्त्रं) astronomy or astrology. **-स्तोमः** (ज्योतिष्टोमः) a Soma sacrifice considered as the type of a whole class of sacrificial ceremonies.

ज्योत्स्ना **1** Moonlight ; स्फुरत्स्फारज्योत्स्नाधवलितत े क्वापि पुलिने Bh. 3. 42; ज्योत्स्नावतो निर्विशति प्रदोषान् R. 6. 34. **2** Light (in general). -COMP. **-ईशः** the moon. **-प्रियः** the Chakora bird. **-वृक्षः** a lamp-stand, a candle-stick.

ज्योत्स्नी A moonlight-night.

ज्यौः The planet Jupiter, (a word connected with Greek Zeus).

ज्यौतिषिकः An astronomer or astrologer.

ज्यौत्स्नः The bright half of a month.

ज्वर् 1 P (ज्वराति, जूर्ण) **1** To be hot with fever or passion, be feverish **2** To be diseased.

ज्वरः **1** Fever, feverish heat (in medicine); स्विद्यमानज्वरं प्राज्ञः कोंऽभसा परिषिंचति *S*i. 2. 54 ; also used fig.; दर्पज्वरः, मदनज्वरः, मद्ज्वरः &c. **2** Fever of the soul, mental pain, affliction, distress, grief, sorrow ; व्येतु ते मनसो ज्वरः Râm.; मनसस्तदुपस्थिते ज्वरे R. 8. 84 ; Bg. 3. 30. -COMP. **-अग्निः** the paroxysm of fever. **-अंकुशः** a febrifuge. **-प्रतीकारः** cure of fever, febrifuge.

ज्वरित्, ज्वरिन् *a.* (**णी** *f.*) Attacked with fever.

ज्वल् 1 P. (ज्वलति, ज्वलित) **1** To burn brightly, blaze, glow, shine ; ज्वलति चलितेंधनोऽग्निः *S*. 6. 30 ; Ku. 5 30. **2** To be burnt up, be consumed or afflicted (as by fire); अमृतमधुरमृदुतरवचनेन ज्वलति न सा मलयजपवनेन Gît. 7. **3** To be ardent ; जज्वाल लोकस्थितये स राजा Bh. 1. 4.-*Caus.* (ज्वलयति-ते, ज्वालयति-ते) **1** To set on fire, light kindle. **2** To irradiate, illuminate, brighten. -WITH **उद्** (*Caus.*) **1** to kindle, light; **2** to irradiate, illumine, light up ; ककुभां मुखानि सहसोज्ज्वलयन् *S*i. 9. 42 ; त्वदधरचुंबनलंबितकज्जलमुज्ज्वलय प्रियलोचने Gît 12. **-प्र** to burn brightly, blaze up ; रणागानि प्रजज्वलुः Bk. 14. 98. (-*Caus*) **1** to kindle, light. **2** to brighten, illumine.

ज्वलन *a.* **1** Flaming, shining, **2** Combustible. **-नः** **1** Fire ; तदनु ज्वलनं मदर्पितं त्वरयेर्दक्षिणवातवीजनैः Ku. 4. 36, 32 ; Bg 11. 29. **2** The number three. **-नं** Burning, blazing, shining. -COMP. **-अश्मन्** *m.* the sunstone.

ज्वलित *a.* **1** Burnt, kindled, illuminated. **2** Flaming, blazing.

ज्वालः **1** Light, flame. **2** A torch.

ज्वाला A blaze, flame, illumination ; R. 15. 16 ; Bh. 1. 95. -COMP. **जिह्वः, ध्वजः** fire. **-मुखी** a volcano. **-वक्त्रः** an epithet of *S*iva.

ज्वालिन् *m.* An epithet of *S*iva.

झ.

झः 1 Beating time. 2 Jingling, clanking or any similar sound. 3 Wind accompanied by rain. 4 N. of Bṛihaspati.

झगझगायति Den. P. To flash, sparkle.

झग (गि) ति *ind*. Quickly, at once; साप्यप्सरा झगित्यासीच्चद्रूपाकृष्टलोचना Mb.

झंकारः, झंकृतं A low murmuring sound, as the buzzing of bees; (अयं) दिगंतानातिने मधुपकुलझंकारभरितान् Bv. 1. 33, 4. 29; Bh. 1. 9; Amaru. 48; Pt. 5. 53.

झंकारिणी The river Ganges.

झंकृतिः *f*. A clanking or jingling sound as of metal ornaments.

झंझनं 1 Jingling and clanking of metal ornaments. 2 A rattling or ringing sound.

झंझा 1 The noise of the wind or of falling rain. 2 Wind and rain, hurricane, gale. 3 A clanking sound, jingling. –Comp. –अनिलः –मरुत्, –वातः wind with rain, a storm, squall, stormy gale; झंझावातः सवृष्टिकः Ak. हिमांशुझंझानिलविह्वलस्य (पद्मस्य) Bv. 2. 69; Amaru. 48; Mâl. 9. 17.

झटिति *ind*. Quickly, at once; मुक्ताजालमिव प्रयाति झटिति भ्रश्यद्दृशोऽदृश्यतां Bh. 1. 96, 70.

झणझणं, –णा Jingling sound.

झणझणायित *a*. Tinkling, jingling, making a tinkling sound; U. 5. 5.

झण (न) त्कारः Jingling, tinkling or clinking, as of metallic ornaments झणत्कारक्रूरक्वणितगुणगुंजद्गुरुधनुर्धृतप्रेमा बाहुः U. 5. 26; उद्वेजयति दरिद्रं परमुद्रागणनझणत्कारः Udb.

झंपः, झंपा A spring, jump, leap; Mv. 5. 63.

झंपाकः, झंपारुः, झंपिन् *m*. A monkey, an ape.

झरः, झरा, झरी A cascade, spring, fountain, stream; प्रत्यग्रक्षतजझरीनिवृत्तपाद्यः Mv. 6. 14; Bv. 4. 37.

झर्झरः 1 A sort of drum. 2 The Kali age. 3 A cane staff. 4 A cymbal. –रा A whore, harlot.

झर्झरिन् *m*. An epithet of Śiva.

झलज्झला The noise of falling drops or of the flapping of an elephant's ears.

झला 1 A girl, daughter. 2 Sunshine, glittering light, splendour.

झल्लः 1 A prize fighter. 2 N. of one of the degraded classes; Ms. 10. 22, 12. 45. –ल्ली A kind of drum.

झल्लकं –की Cymbal.

झल्लकंठः A pigeon.

झल्लरी A cymbal.

झल्लिका 1 Dirt rubbed off the body by the application of perfumes. 2 Light, lustre, splendour.

झषः 1 I fish in general; झषाणां मकरश्चास्मि Bg. 10. 31; cf. words like झषकेतन below. 2 A large fish. 3 The sign Pisces of the zodiac. 4 Heat, warmth. –षं A desert, dreary forest. –Comp. –अंकः, –केतनः, –केतुः, –ध्वजः N. of the god of love; स्त्रीमुद्रां झषकेतनस्य Pt. 4. 34. –अशनः a porpoise. –उदरी an epithet of Satyavatī, mother of Vyâsa.

झांकृतं 1 A tinkling ornament worn round the feet. 2 A splashing sound (as of falling cascades); स्थाने स्थाने मुखरककुभो झांकृतैर्निर्झराणां U. 2. 14.

झाटः 1 An arbour, bower. 2 A wood, thicket.

झिंटिः *f*. A kind of shrub.

झिरिका A cricket.

झिल्लीः *f*. 1 cricket. 2 A kind of musical instrument.

झिल्लिका 1 Cricret. 2 The light of sunshine; splendour.

झिल्लिः *f*. 1 A cricket. 2 The wick of a lamp. 3 Light, lustre. –Comp. –कंठः a domestic pigeon.

झीरुका A cricket.

झुंटः 1 A tree. 2 A shrub, bush.

झोडः The betel-nut tree.

ट.

टंक् 10 U. (टंकयति-ते, टंकित) 1 To bind, tie, fasten. 2 To cover.–With उद् 1 to scrape, scratch. 2 to bore out, pierce through.

टंकः, –कं 1 A hatchet, an axe: a stone-cutter's chisel; टंकैर्मनःशिलगुहेव विदार्यमाणा Mk. 1. 20; R. 12. 80. 2 A sword. 3 The sheath of sword. 4 A peak shaped like the edge of a hatchet; the slope or declivity of a hill; Bk. 1. 8. 5 Anger. 6 Pride. 7 The leg. –का The leg.

टंककः A stamped coin, especially of silver. –Comp. पतिः a mint-master –शाला a mint.

टंकणं (नं) Borax. –णः (नः) 1 A species of horse. 2 N. of a people. –Comp. –क्षारः borax. टंकारः 1 The twang of a bowstring. 2 A howl, cry, shout.

टंकारिन् *a*. (णी *f*.) Twanging, making a hissing or twanging sound; टंकारिचापमतुलंकाशरक्षतजपंकावरूषितशरं Asvad 1

टंकिका. A hatchet; Vikr. 1. 15.

टंगः, –गं A spade, hoe, hatchet.

टंगणः –णं Borax.

टंगा The leg.

टट्टरी 1 A kind of musical instrument. 2 A joke, jest.

टांकारः A clang, twang.

टिक् 1 A. (टेकते) To go, move.

टिटि (ट्टि) भः (भी *f*.) A kind of bird; उत्क्षिप्य टिट्टिभः पादावास्ते भंगभयादिवः Pt. 1 314; Ms. 5. 11; Y. 1. 172; also टिट्टिभक.

टिप्पणी (नी) A gloss, a comment; sometimes used in the sense of 'a gloss on a gloss;' as Kaiyaṭa's commentary on the Mahâbhâshya, or Nâgojibhaṭṭa's gloss on Kaiyaṭa's gloss.

टीक् 1 A. (टीकते) To move, go, resort to; काश्मर्याः कृतमालमुद्गतदलं कोयष्टिकष्टीकते Mâl. 9. 7. –With आ to go, move, go about; आटीकसेऽग करिघोटीपदातिजुषि वाटीभुवि क्षितिभुजां Asvad. 5.

टीका A commentary, gloss; काव्यप्रकाशस्य कृता गृहे गृहे टीका तथाप्येष तथैव दुर्गमः

टुंडुक *a*. 1 Small, little. 2 Vile, cruel. 3 Harsh.

ठ.

ठः An imitative sound, as of a metallic jar rolling down steps; रामाभिषेके मद्विह्वलायाः कक्षाच्च्युतो हेमघटस्तरुण्याः । सोपानमार्गे प्रकरोति शब्दं ठठं ठठं ठं ठठठं ठठं ठः Subhâsh.

ठक्कुरः 1 An idol, a deity. 2 An honorific title added to the name of a distinguished person; (*e. g.* गोविंदठक्कुर the author of the Kâvyapradîpa).

ठालिनी A girdle.

ड.

डमः A despised and mixed caste. (Dom).

डमरः 1 Riot, tumult, affray. 2 Terrifying an enemy by shouts and gestures. **-रं** Running away through fear, rout.

डमरुः A sort of small drum, shaped like an hour-glass and generally used by Kâpâlikas; (sometimes regarded as *n.* also).

डंब् 10 U. (डंबयति-ते) 1 To throw, send. 2 To order. 3 To behold. -WITH **वि** 1 to imitate, copy, resemble; (तं) ऋतुर्विडंबयामास न पुनः प्राप तच्छ्रियं R. 4. 17; वपुप्रकर्षेण विडंबितेश्वरः 3. 12, 13. 29, 16. 11; Ki. 5· 46, 12. 38; *Si.* 1. 6; 12. 5. 2 to ridicule, deride, mock; संमोहयंति मदयंति विडंबयंति निर्भर्त्सयंति रमयंति विषादयंति Bh. 1. 22; यथा न विडंब्यसे जनैः K. 109. 3 to cheat, deceive; एवमात्माभिप्रायसंभावितेष्टजनचित्तवृत्तिः प्रार्थयिता विडंब्यते *S.* 2. 4 to afflict, pain.

डंबर *a.* Famous, renowned. **-रः** 1 An assemblage, collection, mass; Mâl. 9. 16. 2 Show, pomp. 3 Resemblance, likeness, appearance. 4 Pride, arrogance.

डंभ् 10 U. (डंभयति-ते) To collect.

डयनं 1 Flight. 2 A litter carried upon men's shoulders, palanquin.

डवित्थः A wooden antelope.

डाकिनी A kind of female imp, a female goblin.

डांकृतिः *f* The clang of a bell, ding-dong &c.

डामर *a.* 1 Terrific, dreadful, awful; पर्याप्तं मयि रमणीयडामरत्वं संधत्ते गगनतलप्रयाणवेगः Mâl. 5. 3. 2 Riotous, tumultous. 3 Resembling, having the appearance (*i. e.* lovely, beautiful). रतिगलिते ललिते कुसुमानि शिखंडकडामरे (चिकुरे) Gît. 12. **-रः** 1 An uproar, rout, affray, riot. 2 The bustle and confusion of festivity or strife.

डालिमः=दाडिम q. v.

डाहलः (pl.) N. of a people and their country; कीर्तिः समाश्लिष्यति डाहलोर्वीं Vikr. 1. 103.

डिंगरः 1 A servant. 2 A knave, cheat, rogue. 3 A depraved or low man.

डिंडिमः A kind of small drum (fig. also); इति घोषयतीव डिंडिमः H. 2. 86; मुखरयस्व यशोनवडिंडिमं N. 4. 53; Amaru. 28; चंडि रणितरसनारवडिंडिममभिसर सरसमलज्जं Gît. 11; आर्यबालचरितप्रस्तावनाडिंडिमः Mv. 1. 54.

डिंडी (डि) रः 1 Cuttle-fish-bone considered as the foam of the sea. 2 Foam (in general); उद्दंडातेन डिंडीरे पिंडपंक्तिरदृश्यत Vikr. 4. 64, 2. 4.

डिमः One of the ten kinds of dramas; मायेंद्रजालसंग्रामक्रोधाद्भ्रांतादिचेष्टितैः । उपरागैश्च भूयिष्ठो डिमः ख्यातोऽतिवृत्तकः ॥ S. D. 517.

डिंबः 1 Affray, riot 2 Sound or noise occasioned by terror. 3 A young child or animal. 4 An egg. 5 A globe or ball. -COMP. **-आहवः, -युद्धं** petty warfare, an affray without weapons, skirmish, sham-fight; Ms. 5. 95.

डिंबिका 1 A libidinous woman. 2 A bubble.

डिंभः 1 A young child. 2 Any young animal such as a cub; जृंभस्व रे डिंभ दंतांस्ते गणयिष्यामि *S.* 7. 3 A fool, a block-head.

डिंभकः (**भिका** *f*) 1 A young child. 2 Any young animal.

डी 1. 4. A. (डयते, डीयते, डीन) 1 To fly, pass through the air. 2 To go. -WITH **उद्** to fly in the air, fly up; सर्वैरुड्डीयतां H 1 (हंसैः) उदडीयत वैकृतात्करग्रहजादस्य विकस्वरस्वरैः N. 2. 5. **-प्र** to fly up; हंसैः प्रडीनैरिव Mk. 5. 5. **-प्रोद्** to fly up;प्रोड्डीयेव बलाकया सरभसं सोत्कंठमालिंगितः 23.

डीन *p. p.* Flown up. **-नं** The flight of a bird. The varieties of the flight of birds are said to be 101, the word prefixed to डीन showing the particular mode of flight; *e. g.* अवडीनं, उड्डीनं, प्रडीनं, अभिडीनं, विडीनं, परिडीनं, पराडीनं, &c.

डुंडुभः A kind of snakes, not poisonous (निर्विषाः डुंडुभाः स्मृताः).

डुलिः *f.* A small turtle.

डोमः A man of a very low caste.

ढ.

ढक्का A large or double drum; न त हुड्डुक्कंन न सोपि ढक्कया न मर्दलैः सापि न तेऽपि ढक्कया ॥ N. 15. 17.

ढामरा A goose.

ढालं A shield.

ढालिन् *m.* A warrior armed with a shield.

ढुंढिः An epithet of Gaṇesa.

ढौलः A large drum or tabor.

ढौक् 1 A. (ढौकते, ढौकित) To go, approach; यांतं वने रात्रिचरी डुढौके Bk. 2. 23; 14. 71, 15. 79.-*Caus.* (ढौकयति-ते) 1 To bring near, cause to approach; तम्मांसं चैव गोमायोस्तैः क्षणादाशु ढौकितं Mb.; Bk. 17. 103. 2 To present, offer. -WITH **उप** to present, offer.

ढौकनं 1 Offering. 2 A present, bribe.

ण.

[There are hardly any words in Sanskrit beginning with ण. Many roots which, in the Dhâtupâṭha are written with an initial ण really begin with न. They are so written to show that the न is liable to be changed to ण when preceded by prepositions, like प्र, परि, अंतर् &c.]

त.

तकिल *a.* Fraudulent, crafty, rogue.

तक्रं Buttermilk. –COMP. **–अटः** a churning stick. **–सारं** fresh butter.

तक्ष् 1. 5. P. (तक्षति, तक्ष्णोति, तष्ट) **1** To chop, cut off, pare, chisel, slice, split; आत्मानं तक्षति ह्येष वनं परशुना यथा Mb; निधाय तक्ष्यते यत्र काष्ठे काष्ठं स उद्धनः Ak. **2** To fashion, shape, form (out of wood &c.). **3** To make, create in general. **4** To wound, hurt. **5** To invent, form in the mind. –WITH **निस्** to slice out of. **–सं 1** to pare off, chisel, chop. **2** to wound, hurt, strike; निस्त्रिंशाभ्यां सुतीक्ष्णाभ्यामन्योन्यं संततक्षतुः **Mb.**; Bri S. 42. 29.

तक्षकः 1 A carpenter, woodcutter (whether by caste or profession). **2** The chief actor in the prelude of a drama (*i. e.* the सूत्रधार). **3** N. of the architect of the gods. **4** N. of one of the principal Nâgas or serpents of the Pâtâla, son of Kasyapa and Kadru; (saved at the intercession of the sage *Astîka* from being burnt down in the serpent-sacrifice performed by king Janamejaya, in which many others of his race were burnt down to ashes).

तक्षणं Paring, cutting; दारवाणां च तक्षणं Ms. 5. 115; Y. 1. 185.

तक्षन् *m* **1** A carpenter, woodcutter (whether by caste or profession); अतक्षा तक्षा K. P. 'one not a तक्षन् by caste is called तक्षन् when he acts like or follows the profession of a **तक्षन्** (carpenter)'; *Si.* 12 25. **2** N. of the architect of the gods.

तगरः A kind of plant.

तंक् 1 P. (तंकति, तंकित) **1** To endure, bear. **2** To laugh. **3** To live in distress.

तंकः 1 Living in distress, a miserable life. **2** Grief produced by separation from a beloved object. **3** Fear, terror. **4** A stone-cutter's chisel.

तंकनं Living in distress, miserable living.

तंग् 1 P. (तंगति, तंगित) **1** To go, move. **2** To shake, tremble. **3** To stumble.

तंच् 7 P. (तनक्ति, तंचित) To contract, shrink; तनच्मि व्योम विस्तृतं Bk 6. 38.

तटः 1 A slope, declivity, precipice. **2** The sky or horizon. **–टः-टा,-टी,-टं 1** The shore or bank, declivity, slope; शीलं शैलतटात्पततु Bh. 2. 39; प्रोत्तुंगचिंतातटी Bh. 3. 45; सिंधोस्तटावोघ इव प्रवृद्धः Ku. 3. 6; उच्चारणात्पक्षिगणास्तटीस्तं *Si.* 4. 18. **2** A term applied to certain parts of the body which have, as it were, sloping sides; पद्मापयोधरतटीपरिरंभलग्न Gît. 1; नो लुप्तं सखि चंदनं स्तनतटे *S.* Tit. 7; so जघनतट, कटितट, श्रोणीतट, कुचतट, कंठतट, ललाटतट &c. **-टं** A field.–COMP.**–आघातः** butting, striking against a bank or declivity; अभ्यस्यंति तटाघातं निर्जितैरावता गजाः Ku. 2. 50. **-स्थ** *a.* (lit.) **1** situated on a bank or declivity. **2** (fig.) standing aloof, neutral, indifferent, alien, passive; तटस्थः स्वानर्थान् घटयति च मौनं च भजते Mâl. 1. 14; तटस्थं नैराश्यात् U. 3. 13; मया तटस्थस्त्वमुपद्रुतोसि N. 3. 55 (where तटस्थ has sense 1 also).

तटाकः –कं A pond (deep enough for the lotus and other aquatic plants); see तडाग.

तटिनी A river; कदा वाराणस्याममरतटिनीरोधसि वसन् Bh. 3. 123; Bv. 1. 23.

तड् 10 U. (ताडयति-ते, ताडित) **1** To beat, strike (in general), dash against; गाहंतां महिषा निपानसलिलं शृंगैर्मुहुस्ताडितं *S.* 2. 5; (नौः) ताडिता मारुतैर्यथा Râm.; R. **3**. 61; Ku. 5. 24; Bh. 1. 50. **2** To beat, strike, punish by beating, hit; लालयेत्पंचवर्षाणि दशवर्षाणि ताडयेत् Châṇ 11, 12; न ताडयेत्तृणेनापि Ms. 4. 169; पादेन यस्ताड्यते Amaru. 52. **3** To strike, beat (as a drum); ताड्यमानासु भेरिषु Mb.; अताडयन् मृदंगांश्च Bk. 17. 7; Ve. 1. 22. **4** To play on, strike the wires of (a musical instrument); श्रोतुर्वितंत्रीरिव ताड्यमाना Ku. 1. 45. **5** To shine. **6** To speak.

तडगः See तडाग.

तडागः A pond, a deep pool, tank; स्फुटकमलोदरखेलितखंजनयुगमिव शरदि तडागं Gît. 11; Ms. 4 203; Y. 3. 237.

तडाघातः See तटाघात; (उच्चैः करिकराक्षेपे तडाघातं विदुर्बुधाः *S*abdak.)

तडित् *f.* Lightning; घनं घनांते तडितां गुणैरिव *Si.* 1. 7; Me. 76; R. 6. 65. –COMP. **–गर्भः** a cloud. **–लता** forked lightning.**–लेखा** a streak of lightning.

तडित्वत् *a.* Containing or having lightning; अवरोहति शैलाग्रं तडित्वानिव तोयदः V. 1. 14; Ki. 5. 4.–*m.* A cloud; *Si.* 1. 12.

तडिन्मय *a.* Consisting of lightning; Ku. 5. 25.

तंड् 1 A. (तंडते, तंडित) To strike.

तंडकः The खंजन bird.

तंडुलः Grain after threshing, unhusking, and winnowing; (especially rice); (शस्य, धान्य, तंडुल and अन्न are thus distinguished from one another :—शस्यं क्षेत्रगतं प्रोक्तं सतुषं धान्यमुच्यते। निस्तुषः तंडुलः प्रोक्तः स्विन्नमन्नमुदाहृतं ॥).

तत *p. p.* Spread, extended, covered over &c.; (see तन्); स तमीं तमोभिरभिगम्य ततां *Si.* 9. 23, 6. 50; Ki. 5 11. **—तं** Any stringed musical instrument.

ततस् (**ततः**) *ind.* **1** From that (person or place &c.), thence; न च निम्नादिव हृदयं निवर्तते मे ततो हृदयं *S.* 3. 1; Mâl. 2. 10; Ms. 6. 7; 12. 85. **2** There, thither. **3** Then, thereupon, afterwards; ततः कतिपयदिवसापगमे K. 110. Amaru. 66; Ki. 1. 27; Ms. 2. 93, 7. 59. **4** Therefore, consequently, for that reason. **5** Then, in that case (as a corr. of **यदि**); यदि गृहीतमिदं ततः किं K. 120; अमोच्यमश्वं यदि मन्यसे प्रभो ततः समाप्ते &c. R. 3. 65. **6** Beyond that (in place), further, further more, moreover; ततः परतो निर्मानुषमरण्यं K. 121. **7**. Than that, other than that; यं लब्ध्वा चापरं लाभं मन्यते नाधिकं ततः Bg. 6. 22, 2. 36. **8** Sometimes used for the ablative forms of तद् such as तस्माद्, तस्याः; ततोऽन्यत्रापि दृश्यते Sk. **यतः ततः** means (*a*) where-there; यतः कृष्णस्ततः सर्वे यतः कृष्णस्ततो जयः Mb.; **Ms.** 7. 188. (*b*) since-therefore **यतो यतः –ततस्ततः** wherever there; यतोयतः षट्चरणोभिवर्तते ततस्ततः प्रेरितवामलोचना *S.* 1. 23. **ततः किं** 'what then,' 'of what use is it,' 'what avails it'; प्राप्ताः श्रियः सकलकामदुधास्ततः किं Bh. 3 73, 74; *S*ânti. 4. 2; **ततस्ततः** (*a*) 'here and there', 'to and fro'; ततो दिव्यानि माल्यानि प्रादुरासंस्ततस्ततः Mb. (*b*) 'what next,' 'what further,' 'well proceed' (occurring in dramas); **ततः प्रभृति** thence-forward, (corr. of

यतः प्रभृति); तृष्णा ततः प्रभृति मे द्विगुणत्वमेति Amaru 68; Ms. 9. 68.

ततस्त्य *a* Coming or proceeding from thence; Ki. 1. 27.

तति *pron. a.* (Declined only in plural, nom. and acc. तति) So many; *e. g.* तति पुरुषाः संति &c. **-तिः** *f.* **1** A series, row, line; विस्रब्धं क्रियतां वराहततिभिर्मुस्ताक्षतिः पल्वले *S.* 2. 5. बलाहकततीं *Si.* 4. 54; 1. 5 **2** A number, troop, group. **3** A sacrificial act.

तत्त्वं (Sometimes written as तत्वं) **1** True state or condition, fact; वयं तत्त्वान्वेषान्मधुकर हतास्त्वं खलु कृती *S.* 1. 24. **3** True or essential nature; संन्यासस्य महाबाहो तत्त्वमिच्छामि वेदितुं Bg. 18. 1, 3. 28; Ms. 1. 3, 3. 96, 5. 42. **4** The real nature of the human soul or the material world as being identical with the Supreme spirit pervading the universe. **5** A true or first principle. **6** An element, a primary substance. **7** The mind. **8** Sum and substance. **9** Slow time in music. **10** A kind of dance. -Comp. **-अभियोगः** a positive charge or declaration. **-अर्थः** truth, reality. the exact truth, real nature. **-ज्ञ, -विद्** *a.* **1** a philosopher. **2** knowing the true nature of Brahman. **-न्यासः** N. of a ceremony performed in honour of Vishṇu consisting in the application of mystical letters or other marks to different parts of the body while certain prayers are repeated.

तत्त्वतः *ind.* Truly, really, accurately; तत्त्वत एनामुपलप्स्ये *S.* 1; Ms. 7. 10.

तत्र *ind.* **1** In that place, there, yonder, thither. **2** On that occasion, under those circumstances, then, in that case. **3** For that, in that; निरीतयः यन्मदीयाः प्रजास्तत्र हेतुस्त्वद्ब्रह्मवर्चसं R. 1. 63. **4**. Oft. used for the loc. case of तद्; Ms. 2. 112, 3. 60; 4. 186; Y. 1. 263. **तत्रापि** 'even then' 'nevertheless'; (corr. cf. यद्यपि). **तत्रतत्र** 'in various places or cases, 'here and there,' 'to every place;' अध्यक्षान्विविधान्कुर्यात् तत्रतत्र विपश्चितः Ms. 7. 81. -Comp. **-भवत्** *a.* (**ती** *f.*) his honour, his reverence, revered, respectable, worthy, a respectful title given in dramas to persons not near the speaker; (पूज्ये तत्रभवानत्रभवांश्च भगवानपि); आदिष्टोऽस्मि तत्रभवता काश्यपेन *S.* 4; तत्रभवान् काश्यपः *S.* 1 &c. **-स्थ** *a.* standing or being there, belonging to that place.

तत्रत्य *a.* Born or produced there, belonging to that place.

तथा *ind.* **1** So, thus, in that manner; तथा मां वंचयित्वा *S.* 5; सूतस्तथा करोति V. 1. **2** And also, so also, as well as; अनागतविधाता च प्रत्युत्पन्नमतिस्तथा Pt. 1. 315; R. 3. 21. **3** True, just so, exactly so; यद्रात्थ राजन्यकुमार तत्तथा R. 3. 48; Ms. 1. 42 **4** (In forms of adjuration) As surely as (preceded by यथा); see यथा. (For some of the meanings of तथा as a correlative of यथा; see under यथा). **तथापि** (oft. corr. of यद्यपि) 'even then,' 'still', 'yet', 'never-the-less'; प्रथितं दुष्यंतस्य चरितं तथापीदं न लक्षये *S.* 5; वरं महत्याम्रियते पिपासया तथापि नान्यस्य करोम्युपासनां Chât. 2. 6; वपुःप्रकर्षादजयद्गुरुं रघुस्तथापि नीचैर्विनयाद्दृश्यत R. 3. 34, 62 **तथेति** shows 'assent' or 'promise'; तथेति शेषामिव भर्तुराज्ञामादाय मूर्ध्ना मदनः प्रतस्थे Ku. 3. 22: R. 1. 92, 3. 67; तथेति निष्क्रांतः (in dramas) **तथैव** 'even so', 'just so'; 'exactly so' **तथैव च** 'in like manner'; **तथा च** 'and also,' 'and like wise', 'in like manner' 'so it has been said'; **तथाहि** 'for so' 'as for instance', for this (it has been said)'; तं वेधा विदधे नूनं महाभूतसमाधिना। तथाहि सर्वे तस्यासन् परार्थैकफला गुणाः॥ R. 1. 29; *S.* 1. 31. -Comp. **-कृत** *a.* thus done. **-गत** *a.* 1 being in such a state or condition; तथागततायां परिहासपूर्वं R. 6. 82. **2** of such quality. (**-तः**) **1** Buddha; कालि मितं वाक्यमुदर्कपथ्यं तथागतस्येव जनः सुचेताः *Si.* 20. 81. **2** a Jina. **-गुण** *a.* endowed with such qualities or nature. **2** so circumstanced, in that condition; तथाभूतां दृष्टा नृपसदसि पांचलतनयां Ve. 1. 11. **-राजः** an epithet of Buddha. **-रूप, -रूपिन्** *a.* thus shaped, looking thus. **-विध** *a.* of such a sort, of such qualities or nature; तथाविधस्तावदशेषमस्तु सः Ku. 5. 82, R. 3. 4, **-विधं** *ind.* **1** thus, in this manner. **2** likewise, equally.

तथात्वं **1** Such a state, being so. **2** True state or nature, truth.

तथ्य *a.* True, real, genuine; प्रियमपि तथ्यमाह प्रियंवदा *S.* 1. **-थ्यं** Truth, reality; सा तथ्यमेवाभिहिता भवेन Ku. 3. 63; Ms. 8. 274.

तद् *pron. a.* (Nom. sing. सः *m.*, सा *f.*, तत् *n.*) **1** That, reffering to something not present; (तदिति परोक्षे विजानीयात्). **2** He, she, it; (oft as corr. of यद्); यस्य बुद्धिर्बलं तस्य Pt. **1**. **3** That, *i. e.* well-known; सा रम्या नगरी महान्स नृपतिः सामंतचक्रं च तत् Bh. 3. 37; Ku. 5. 71. **4** That (referring to something seen or experienced before, अनुभूतार्थे); उत्कंपिनी भयपरिस्खलितांशुकांता ते लोचने प्रतिदिशं विधुरे क्षिपंती K. P. 7; Bv. 2. 5. **5** The same, identical, that, very; usually with एव; तानींद्रियाणि सकलानि तदेव नाम Bh. 2. 40. Sometimes the forms of तद् are used with the first and second personal pronouns, as well as with demonstratives and relatives, for the sake of emphasis; (often translateable by 'therefore'; 'then'); सोऽहमिज्याविशुद्धात्मा R. 1. 68; 'I that very person,' 'I therefore'; (I who am so and so); स त्वं निवर्तस्व विहाय लज्जां 2. 40 'thou, therefore, shouldst return,' &c. When repeated **तद्** has the sense of 'several' 'various'; तेषु तेषु स्थानेषु K 369; Bg. 7. 20; Mâl. 1. 35. **तेन** the instr. of तद् is often used with an adverbial force in the sence of 'therefore' 'on that account' 'in that case', 'for that reason'. **तेन हि** if so, well then *-ind* **1** there, thither. **2** Then, in that case, at that time. **3** For that reason, therefore, consequently; तदेहि विमर्दक्षमां भूमिमवतराव: U. 5; Me. 7, 110; R. 3. 46. **4** Then (corr. of यदि); तथापि यदि महत्कुतूहलं तत्कथयामि K. 136; Bg. 1. 45. -Comp. **-अनंतरं** *ind.* immediately after that, thereupon. **-अनु** *ind.* after that, afterwards; संदेशं मे तदनु जलद श्रोष्यसि श्रोत्रपेयं Me. 13; R. 16. 87; Mâl. 9. 26. **-अंत** *a.* perishing in that, ending thus. **-अर्थ, -अर्थीय** *a.* **1** intended for that. **2** having that meaning. **-अर्ह** *a.* meriting that. **-अवधि** *ind.* **1** so far, upto that period, till then; तदवधि कुशली पुराणशास्त्रस्मृतिशतचारुविचारजो विवेकः Bv. 2. 14. **2** from that time, since then; श्वासो दीर्घस्तदवधि मुखे पांडिमा Bv. 2. 69. **-एकचित्त** *a.* having the mind solely fixed on that. **-कालः** the current moment, present time. **धी** *a.* having presence of mind. **-काले** *ind.* instantly, immediately. **-क्षणः** **1** time present, time being, present or current moment; R. 1. 51. **-क्षणं, -क्षणात्** *ind.* immediately, directly, instantly; R. 3. 14; *Si.* 9. 5; Y. 2. 14; Amaru 83. **-क्रिय** *a.* working without wages. **-गत** *a.* gone or directed to that, intent on, devoted to that, belonging to that. **-गुणः** a figure of speech (in Rhetoric); स्वमुत्सृज्य गुणं योगादत्युज्ज्वलगुणस्य यत्। वस्तु तद्गुणतामेति भण्यते स तु तद्गुणः K. P. 10; see Chandr. 5. 141. **-ज** *a.* immediate, instantaneous. **-ज्ञः** a knowing or intelligent man, wise man, philosopher. **-तृतीय** *a.* doing that for the third time. **-धन** *a.* miserly, niggardly. **-पर** *a.* **1** following that, coming after that, inferior. **7** having that as the highest object, closely intent on, exclusively devoted to, eagerly engaged in (usually in comp.); सम्राट् समाराधनतत्परोऽभूत R. 2. 5, 1. 66; Me. 10; Y. 1. 83; Ms. 3. 262. **-परायण** *a.* solely devoted or attached to anything. **-पुरुषः** **1** the original or Supreme spirit. **2** N. of a class of compounds in which the first member determines the sense of the other member, or in which the last member is defined or qualified by the first without losing its original independence; as तत्पुरुषः; तत्पुरुष कर्मधारय येनाहं स्यां बहुव्रीहिः Udb. -पूर्व *a.* happening or occurring for the first time; अकारि तत्पूर्वनिबद्धया तया Ku. 5. 10. **7.** 30; R. 2. 42, 14. 38. **2** prior, former. -प्रथम *a.* doing that for the first time. -बलः a kind of arrow. -भावः becoming that. -मात्रं **1** merely that, only a trifle, a very small quantity. **2** (in phil.) a subtle and primary element (such as शब्द, रस, स्पर्श, रूप and गंध). -वाचक *a.* denoting or signifying that. -विद् *a.* **1** knowing that. **2** knowing the truth. -विध *a.* of the kind or sort; R. 2. 22. Ku. 5. 73; Ms. 2. 112. -हित *a.* good for that. (-तः) an affix added to primary bases to form derivative or secondary bases from them.

तदा *ind.* **1** Then, at the time. **2** Then, in that case; (corr. of यदा); Bg. 2. 52-53; Ms. 1. 52, 54-56; **यदा यदा-तदा तदा** 'when-ever'; **तदाप्रभृति** 'since then', 'thenceforward'; Ku. 1. 53. -Comp. -मुख *a.* begun, commenced. (-खं) beginning.

तदात्वं The time being, present time.

तदानीं *ind.* Then, at that time.

तदानींतन *a.* Belonging to that time, contemporary of that time; एषोस्मि कार्यवशादायोध्यिकस्तदानींतनश्च संवृत्तः U. 1.

तदीय *a.* Belonging to that, his, hers, its, theirs; R. 1 81, 2. 28; 3 8, 25.

तद्वत् *a.* Containing or possessed of that; as in तद्वानपोहः K. P. **2.** -*ind.* **1** Like that, in that manner. **2** Equally, in like manner, so also.

तन् I. 8 U. (तनोति, तनुते, तत; *pass.* तन्यते, तायते; *deside*; तितंसति, तितांसति, तितनिषति) **1** To stretch, extend, lengthen, lengthen out; बाह्वोः सकरयोस्ततयोः Ak. **2** To spread, shed, diffuse; Bk. 2. 3, 10 32, 15 91. **3** To cover, fill; स तमीं तमोभिरभिगम्य ततां Si. 9. 23; Ki. 5. 11. **4** To cause, produce, form, give, grant, bestow; त्वयि विमुखे मयि सपदि सुधानिधिरपि तनुते तनुदाहं Git. 4; पितुर्मुदं तेन ततान सोऽर्भकः R. 3. 25; 7. 7; यो दुर्जनं वशयितुं तनुते मनीषां Bv. 1. 95, 10. **5** To perform, do, accomplish (as a sacrifice); इति क्षितिशो नवतिं नवाधिकां महाक्रतूनां महनीयशासनः । समारुरुक्षुर्दिवमायुषःक्षये ततान सोपानपरंपरामिव ॥ R. 3. 69; Ms. 4. 205. **6** To compose, write (as a work, &c); as in नाम्नां मालां तनोम्यहं or तनुते टीकां **7** To stretch or bend (as a bow). **8.** To spin out, weave. **9.** To propagate, or be propagated. **10** To continue, last.—With अव **1** to cover, spread. **2** to descend.-आ **1** to extend, stretch over, cover, overspread; Ki. 16. 15. **2** to spread, diffuse. **3** to cause, produce, create, make; Ki. 6. 18. **4** to stretch (as a bow or bowstring); मौर्वीं धनुषि चातता R. 1 19; 11. 45.—उद् to stretch up. -प्र **1** to spread, diffuse; ख्यातस्त्वं विभवैर्यशांसि कवयो दिक्षु प्रतन्वंति नः Bh. 3. 24. **2** to cover. **3** to cause, produce, create. **4** to show, display, exhibit; तदूरीकृत्य कृतिभिर्वाचस्पत्यं प्रतायते Si. 2. 30. **5** to perform, do (as a sacrifice). -वि **1** to spread, stretch; स्फुरितविततजिह्वः Mk. 9. 12. **2** to cover, fill; प्रस्वेदबिंदुविततं वदनं प्रियायाः Ch. P. 9; यो वितत्य स्थितः खं Me. 58 **3** to form, make; श्रेणीबंधाद्वितन्वद्भिरस्तंभां तोरणस्रजं R. 1. 41. **4** to stretch (as a bow); धनुर्वितत्य किरतोः शरान् U. 6. 1; Bk. 3. 47. **5** to cause, produce, create, give, bestow. **6** to write or compose (as a work); विराटपर्वप्रयोती भावदीपो वितन्यते. **7** to do, perform (as a sacrifice or any other rite); Ku. 2. 46 **8** to show, exhibit. -सं to continue.—II. 1 P., 10 U. (तनति, तानयति-ते) **1** To confide, trust, place confidence in **2** To help, assist, aid. **3** To pain or afflict with disease. **4** To be harmless.

तनयः **1** A son. **2** A male decendant. —या A daughter; गिरि°, कलिंग° &c.

तनिमन् *m.* Thinness, slenderness, minuteness.

तनु *a.* (**नु, न्वी** *f.*) **1** Thin, lean, emaciated. **2** Delicate, slender, slim (as limbs, as a mark of beauty); R. 6. 32; cf. तन्वंगी **3** Fine, delicate (as cloth); Rs. 1. 7. **4** Small, little, tiny, scanty, few, limited; तनुवाग्विभवोऽपि सन् R. 1. 9. 3. 2; तनुत्यागोबहुग्रहः H. 2. 91. giving little. **5** Trifling, unimportant, little; Amaru. 27. **6** Shallow (as a river). —*f.* **1** The body, the person **2** (Outward) form, manifestation; प्रत्यक्षाभिः प्रपन्नस्तनुभिरवतु वस्ताभिरष्टाभिरीशः S. 1. 1; M. 1. 1; Me. 19. **3** Nature, form or character of anything. **4** Skin.—Comp. —अंग *a.* having slender limbs, delicate. (—गी) a delicate woman. —कूपः a pore of the skin. —छदः an armour; R. 9. 51; 12. 86. -जः a son. -जा a daughter. -त्यज *a.* **1** risking one's life. **2** giving up one's person, dying. -त्याग *a.* spending little, sparing, niggardly. -त्रं, -त्राणं an armour. -भवः a son. (-वा) a daughter. -भस्त्रा the nose. -भृत् *m.* any being furnished with a body, a living being; particularly a human being; कल्पं स्थितं तनुभृतां तनुभिस्ततः किं Bh. 3. 73. -मध्य *a.* having a slender waist. -रसः perspiration. -रुह्, -रुहं the hair of the body. -वारं an armour. -व्रणः a pimple. -संचारिणी a young woman, a girl ten years old. -सरः perspiration. -ह्रदः the anus.

तनुल *a.* Spread, expanded.

तनुस् *n.* The body.

तनू *f.* The body.—Comp. -उद्भवः -जः a son. -उद्भवा, -जा a daughter. -नपं clarified butter, ghee. **नपात्** *m.* fire; तनूनपाद्धूमवितानमाधिजैः Si. 1. 62; अधःकृतस्यापि तनूनपातो नाधः शिखा याति कदाचिदेव ॥ H. 2. 67. -रुहं **1** the hair of the body (*m.* also) **2** the wing of a bird, a feather. (-हः) a son.

तंतिः *f.* **1.** A cord, line, string. **2** A row, series. —Comp. -पालः **1** a guardian of (the rows of) cows. **2** N. assumed by Sahadeva when living at the house of Virâta.

तंतुः **1** A thread, cord, wire, string, line; चिंतासंततितंतु Mâl. 5. 10; Me. 70. **2** A cob-web; R. 16. 20. **3** A filament; बिसतंतुगुणस्य कारितं Ku. 4. 29. **4** Offspring, issue, race. **5** A shark. **6** The Supreme Being. —Comp. काष्ठं a piece of wood or brush used by weavers for cleaning threads. -कीटः a silk-worm. -नागः a (large) shark. -निर्यासः the palmyra tree. -नाभः a spider. -भः **1** the mustard seed. **2** a calf. वाद्यं any stringed musical instrument. -वानं weaving. -वापः **1** a weaver. **2** a loom. **3** weaving. -विग्रहा a plaintain. -शाला a weaver's workshop. -संतत *a.* women, sewn. —सारः the betel-nut tree.

तंतुकः The mustard seed.

तंतुनः-णः A shark.

तंतुरं-लं The fibrous root of a lotus.

तंत्र् 10 U. (तंत्रयति-ते, तंत्रित) **1** To rule, control, govern; प्रजाः प्रजाः स्वा इव तंत्रयित्वा S. 5. 5. **2** (A) To support, maintain (as a family).

तंत्रं **1** A loom. **2** A thread. **3** The warp or threads extended lengthwise in a loom. **4** Posterity. **5** An uninterrupted series. **6** The regular order of ceremonies and rites, system, framework, ritual; कर्मणां युगपद्भावस्तंत्रं Kâty. **7** Main point. **8** Principal doctrine, rule, theory, science; जितमनसिजतंत्रविचारं Git. 2. **9** Subservience, dependence; as in स्वतंत्र, परतंत्र; दैवतंत्रं दुःखं Dk. **5.** **10** A scientific work. **11** A chapter, section, as of a work; तंत्रैः पंचभिरेतच्चकार शास्त्रं Pt. 1. **12** A religious treatise teaching magical and mystical formularies for the worship of the deities or the attainment of superhuman power. **13** The cause of more than one effect. **14** A spell. **15** A chief remedy or charm. **16** A drug, medicament. **17** An oath, ordeal. **18** Raiment. **19** The right way of doing anything. **20** Royal retinue, train, court. **21** A realm, country, authority. **22** Government, ruling, administration ; लोकतंत्राधिकारः *S*. 5. **23** An army. **24** A heap, multitude. **25** A house. **26** Decoration. **27** Wealth. **28** Happiness. —COMP. —**काष्ठं**=तंतुकाष्ठ q. v. **वापः-पं** 1 weaving. **2** a loom. **-वायः** 1 a spider. **2** a weaver.

तंत्रकः A new garment (unbleached cloth).

तंत्रणं Maintenance of order, dicipline, Government.

तंत्रिः -त्री *f*. 1 A string, cord ; Ms. 4. 38. **2** A bow-string. **3** The wire of a lute ; तंत्रीमार्द्रां नयनसलिलैः सारयित्वा कथंचित् Me. 86. **4** A sinew. **5** A tail.

तंद्रा 1 Lassitude, wearinsss, fatigue, exhaustion. **2** Sleepiness, sluggishness ; तंद्रालस्यविवर्जनं Y. 3. 158; Mv. 7. 42 ; H. 1. 34.

तंद्रालु *a*. 1 Tired, exhausted. **2** Sleepy, slothful.

तंद्रीः, -द्री *f*. Sleepiness, drowsiness.

तन्मय *a*. (**यी** *f*.) Made up of that. **2** Wholly absorbed in that ; Mâl. 1. 41 ; *S*. 6. 21. **3** Identical with that, become one with that.

तन्वी A delicate or slender woman; इयमधिकमनोज्ञा वल्कलेनापि तन्वी *S*. 1. 20 ; तव तन्वि कुचावेतौ नियतं चक्रवर्तिनौ Udb.

तप् 1 P. rarely A. (तपति, तप्त). **1** (Intransitively used) (*a*) To shine, blaze (as fire or sun) ; तमस्तपति घर्मांशौ कथमाविर्भविष्यति *S*. 5. 14 ; R. 5. 13 ; U. 6. 14 ; Bg. 9. 19. (*b*) To be hot or warm, give out heat. (*c*) To suffer pain ; तपति न सा किसलयशयनेन Git. 7. (*d*) To mortify the body, undergo penance (with तपस्) ; अगणिततनूतापं तप्त्वा तपांसि भगीरथः U. 1. 23. **2** (Transitively used) (*a*) To make hot, heat, warm ; Bk. 9. 2 ; Bg. 11. 19. (*b*) To inflame, burn, consume by heat ; तपति तनुगात्रि मदनस्त्वामनिशं मां पुनर्दहत्येव *S*. 3. 17 ; अंगैरनंगतप्तैः 3. 7. (*c*) To hurt, injure, damage, spoil ; यास्यन् सुतस्तप्स्यति मां समन्युं Bk. 1. 23 ; Ms. 7. 6. (*d*) To pain, distress. *-Pass*. तप्यते (regarded by some as a root of the 4th conjugation). **1** To be heated, suffer pain. **2** To undergo severe penance (oft. with तपस्). *-Caus*. (तापयति-ते, तापित) 1 To heat, make warm ; गगनं तापितपायितासिलक्ष्मी *Si*. 20. 75 ; न हि तापयितुं शक्यं सागराम्भस्तृणोल्कया H. 1. 86. **2** To torment, pain, disease ; भृशं तापितः कंदर्पेण Git. 11 ; Bk. 8. 13.—WITH **अनु** 1 to rue, be sorry, grieve. **2** To repent. —**उद्** 1 To warm, make hot, scorch, melt (as gold) (Atm. when used intransitively in the sense of 'to shine', or when it has a limb of the body for its object) ; उत्तपति सुवर्णं सुवर्णकारः Mbh. ; but उत्तपमान आतपः Bk. 8. 1. ; *Si*. 20. 40; उत्तपते पाणी Mbh. **2** To consume, torment; pain, torture by heat ; *Si*. 9. 67. **-उप** 1 to heat warm. **2** to pain, distress ; *Si*. 9. 65. **-निस्** 1 to heat. **2** to purify. **3** to burnish. **-परि** 1 to heat, burn, consume. **2** to inflame, set on fire. **-पश्चात्** to repent, be sorry for. **-वि** 1 to shine (Atm. like उद् q. v.) ; रविर्वितपतेऽत्यर्थं Bh. 8. 14. **2** to warm, heat. **-सं** 1 to heat, warm ; संतप्तचामीकर Bk. 3. **3** ; संतप्तायसि संस्थितस्य पयसो नामापि न ज्ञायते Bh. 2. 67. **2** to be distressed, suffer pain, be sorry ; संतप्तानां त्वमसि शरणं Me. 7 of the afflicted ; दिवापि मयि निष्क्रांते संतप्येते गुरू मम Mb. Bh. **2**. **87**. **3** to repent.

तप *a*. 1 Burning, warming, consuming by heat. **2** Causing pain or trouble, destressing. —**पः** 1 Heat, fire, warmth. **2** The sun. **3** The hot season ; *Si*. 1. 66- **4** Penance, religious austerities. -COMP. **-अत्ययः, -अंतः** the end of the hot season and the beginning of the rainy season ; रविपीतजला तपात्यये पुनरोघेन हि युज्यते नदी Ku. 4. 44 ; 5, 23.

तपती The river Tâptî.

तपनः 1 The sun ; प्रतापात्तपनो यथा R. 4. 12 ; ललाटंतपस्तपति तपनः U. 6 ; Mâl. 1. **2** The hot season. **3** The sunstone. **4** N. of a hell. **5** An epithet of Siva **6** The Arka plant. —COMP. **आत्मजः -तनयः** an epithet (1) of Yama (2) of Karṇa. (3) of Sugriva. **-आत्मजा, -तनया** an epithet of the Yamunâ and of the Godâvari. **-इष्टं** copper. **-उपलः, -मणिः** the sunstone. **-छदः** the sun-flower.

तपनी The river Godâvarî or the river Tâptî

तपनीयं Gold ; especially gold purified with fire ; तपनीयाशोकः M. 3 ; तपनीयोपानद्युगलमार्यः प्रसादीकरोतु Mv. 4 ; असंस्पृशंतौ तपनीयपीठं R. 18. 41.

तपस् *n*. 1 Warmth, heart, fire. **2** Pain, suffering. **3** Penance, religious austerity, mortification ; तपः किलेदं तदवाप्तिसाधनं Ku. 5. 64. **4** Meditation connected with the practice of personal self-denial or bodily mortification. **5** Moral virtue, merit. **6** Special duty or observance of any particular caste. **7** One of the seven worlds ; *i*. *e*. the region above the world called **जनस्**.—*m*. The month of Mâgha ; तपसि मंदगभस्तिरभीषुमान् *Si*. 6. 63.—*m*.,—*n*. **1** The cold season ; (शिशिर). **2** The winter (हेमंत). **3** The hot season (ग्रीष्म). COMP —**अनुभावः** the influence of religious penance. **-अवटः** the Brahmâvarta country. **-क्लेशः** the pain of religious austerity. **-चरणं, -चर्या** the practice of penance. **-तक्षः** an epithet of Indra. **-धनः** 'rich in penance,' an ascetic, devotee ; रम्यस्तपोधनानां क्रिया : *S*. 1. 13 ; शमप्रधानेषु तपोधनेषु 2. 6 ; 4. 1 ; *Si*. 1. 23 ; R. 14. 19 ; Ms. 11. 242. **-निधिः** an eminently pious man, an ascetic ; R. **1**. 56. **-प्रभावः, -बलं** the power acquired by religious austerities ; efficacy or potency of devotion. **-राशिः** an ascetic. **-लोकः** the region above the world called जनस्. **-वनं** a penance-grove, a sacred grove in which ascetics practice penance ; कृतं त्वयोपवनं तपोवनमिति प्रेक्षे *S*. 1 ; R **1** ; 90, 2. 18 ; 3. 8. **-वृद्ध** *a*. very ascetic **-विशेषः** excellence of devotion, preeminent religious austerities. **-स्थली** 1 a seat of religious austerity. **2** N. of Benares.

तपसः 1 The sun. **2** The moon. **3** A bird.

तपस्यः 1 The month of Phâlguna. **2** An epithet of Arjuna. **-स्या** Religious austerity, penance.

तपस्यति Den. P. To practise penance ; सुरासुरगुरुः सोऽत्र सपत्नीकस्तपस्यति *S*. 7. 9, 12 ; R. 13. 41 ; I5 49 ; Bk. 18 21.

तपस्विन् *a*. 1 Practising penance, devout. **2** Poor, miserable, helpless, pitiable ; सा तपस्विनी निर्वृता भवतु *S*. 4 ; Mâl **3** ; N. 1. 135. —*m*. An ascetic ; तपस्विसामान्यमवेक्षणीया R. 14. 67. -COMP. **-पत्रं** the sun flower.

तप्त *p*. *p*. **1** Heated, burnt. **2** Redhot, hot. 3 Melted, fused. 4 Distressed, pained, afflicted. **5** Practised (as penance). -COMP. **-कांचनं** gold purified with fire. **-कृच्छ्रं** a kind of penance. **-रूपकं** purified silver.

तम् 4 P. (ताम्यति, तांत) **1** To choke, be suffocated. **2** To be exhausted or fatigued ; ललितशिरीषपुष्पहननैरपि ताम्यति यत् Mâl. 5. 31. **3** To be distressed (in body or mind), be uneasy or pained, pain, waste away ; प्रविशति मुहुः कुंजं गुंजन्मुहुर्बहु ताम्यति Git. 5 ; गाढोत्कंठा ललितलुलितैरंगकैस्ताम्यतीति Mâl. 1. 15, 9. 33 ; Amaru. 7. - WITH **उद्** to be impatient ; हृदय किमेवमुत्ताम्यसि *S*. 1.

तमं 1 Darkness. **2** The tip of the foot. —**मः** 1 An epithet of Râhu. **2** The Tamâla tree.

तमस् *n*. Darkness ; किं वाऽभविष्यदरुणस्तमसा विभेत्ता तं चेत्सहस्रकिरणो धुरि नाकरिष्यत् *S*. 7. 4 ; V. 1. 7 ; Me. 37. **2** The gloom or darkness of hell ; Ms. 4. 242. **3** Mental darkness, illusion, error ; मुनिसुताप्रणयस्मृतिरोधिना मम च मुक्तमिदं तमसा मनः *S*. 6. **6**. **4** (In Sân. phil.) Darkness or ignorance, as one of the three qualities or constituents of every thing in nature (the other two being सत्त्व and रजस्); Ku. 6. 61 ; Ms. 12. 24. **5** Grief, sorrow. **6** Sin.

-*m. n.* An epithet of Râhu. -COMP. -अपह *a.* removing darkness or ignorance, illumining, enlightening; Ki. 5. 22. (-हः) 1 the sun. 2 the moon. 3 fire. -कांडः -डं great or spreading darkness. -गुणः see तमस् above (4). -घ्नः 1 the sun. 2 the moon. 3 fire. 4 Vishṇu. 5 Siva. 6 knowledge. 7 a Buddha. -ज्योतिस् *m.* a fire-fly. -ततिः spreading darkness. -नुद् : *m.* 1 a shining body. 2 the sun. 3 the moon. 4 fire. 5 a lamp, light. -नुदः 1 the sun 2 moon.-भिद्, -मणिः a fire-fly. -विकारः sickness, disease. -हन्, -हर *a.* dispersing darkness. (-*m.*) 1 the sun. 2 the moon.

तमसः 1 Darkness. 2 A well.

तमस्विनी, तमा A night.

तमालः 1 N. of a tree with a very dark bark; तरुणतमालनीलबहलोन्नमदंबुधराः Mâl. 9. 19; R. 13. 15, 49; Git. 11. 2 A sectarial mark of sandal upon the forehead. 3 A sword, scimitar. -COMP. -पत्रं a sectarial mark upon the forehead. 2 a Tamâla leaf.

तमिः, -मी *f.* 1 Night, especially a dark night; स तमीं तमोभिरभिगम्य ततां Si. 9. 23. 2 A swoon, faint. 3 Turmeric.

तमिस्र *a.* Dark. -स्रं 1 Darkness; एतत्तमालदलनीलतमं तमिस्रं Gît. 11; करचरणोरासि मणिगणभूषणकिरणविभिन्नतमिस्रं 2; Ki. 5. 2. 2 Mental darkness, illusion. 3 Anger, wrath. -COMP. पक्षः the dark fort-night (of a lunar month); R. 6 34.

तमिस्रा 1 A (dark) night; सूर्ये तपत्यावरणाय दृष्टेः कल्पेत लोकस्य कथं तमिस्रा R. 5. 13; Si. 6. 43. 2 Extensive darkness.

तमोमयः N. of Râhu.

तंबा, तंबिका A cow.

तय् 1 A. (तयते) 1 To go, move; अध्युवास रथं तेये पुरात् Bk. 14. 75, 908. 2 To guard, protect.

तरः 1 Passing over, crossing, passage; Bk. 7 55. 2. Freight; दीर्घाध्वनि यथादेशं यथाकालं तरो भवेत् Ms. 8. 406. 3 A road. 4 A ferry-boat. -COMP. -पण्यं freight. -स्थानं a landing-place, wharf.

तरक्षः, -क्षुः A hyena.

तरंगः 1 A wave; U 3. 47; Bh. 1. 81; R. 13. 63; S. 3. 7. 2 A section or part of a work (as of the कथासरित्सागर). 3 A leap, jump, gallop, jumping motion (as of a horse). 4 Cloth or clothes.

तरंगिणी A river.

तरंगित *n.* 1 Wavy, tossing with waves. 2 Overflowing. 3 Tremulous. -तं Waving; अपांगतरंगितानि बाणाः Gît. 3.

तरणः 1 A boat, raft. 2 Svarga or heaven. -णं 1 Crossing over. 2 Conquering, overcoming. 3 An oar.

तरणिः 1 The sun. 2 A ray of light. -णिः, -णी *f.* A raft, float, boat. -COMP. -रत्नं a ruby.

तरंडः, -डं 1 A boat in general. 2 A raft or flot made of bamboos tied together and floated on jars or inverted hollow gourds. 3 An oar. -COMP. -पादा a kind of boat.

तरंडी, तरद् *f.*, तरंती A boat, raft, float.

तरंतः 1 The ocean. 2 A hard shower. 3 A frog. 4 A demon or Râkshasa.

तरल *a.* 1 Trembling, waving, shaking, tremulous; तारापतिस्तरलविद्युदिवाभ्रवृंदं R. 13. 76; घन इव तरलबलाके Git. 5; Si. 10. 40; S. 1. 26. 2 Fickle, unsteady, transient; वैरायितारस्तरलाः स्वयं मत्सरिणः परे Si. 2. 115; Amara. 27. 3 Splendid, sparkling, glittering. 4 Liquid. 5 Libidinous, wanton. —लः 1 The central gem of a neckless; मुक्तामयोऽप्यतरलमध्यः Vâs. 35; or हारांस्तारांस्तरलगुटिकान् (Malli. considers this as an interpolation in Meghadûta). 2 A necklace. 3 A level surface. 4 Bottom, depth. 5 A diamond. 6 Iron. —ला Gruel.

तरलयति Den. P To, cause to shake, to wave, move to and fro; Amaru. 87.

तरलायते Den. A. To tremble, shake, move to and fro.

तरलयित A large wave, surf.

तरलित *a.* Shaking, tremulous, undulating; °तुंगतरंग Git. 11; °हारा 7.

तरवारिः A sword.

तरस् *n.* 1 Speed, velocity. 2 Vigour, strength, energy; कैलासनाथं तरसा जिगीषुः R. 5. 28, 11. 77; Si. 9. 72. 3 A bank, a place of crossing. 4 A float, raft.

तरसं Meat, flesh.

तरसानः A boat.

तरस्विन् *a* (नी *f.*) 1 Swift, quick. 2 Strong, powerful, courageous; mighty; R. 9. 23, 11. 89; 16. 77. -*m.* 1 A courier, an express. 2 A hero. 3 Air, wind. 4 An epithet of Garuḍa.

तरांधुः, -तरालुः A large flat-botomed boat.

तरिः -री *f.* 1 A boat; जीर्णा तरिः सरिदतीव गभीरनीरा Udb.; Si. 3 76. 2 A box for clothes. 3 The end or hem of a garment. -COMP. -रथः an oar.

तरिकः, -तरिकिन् *m.* A ferry-man.

तरिका, -तरित्रं, -तरित्री, -तरिणी A boat, ship.

तरीषः 1 A raft, boat. 2 The ocean. 3 A fit or competent person. 4 Heaven. 5 Work, business, practice, profession.

तरुः A tree; नवसंरोहणशिथिलस्तरुरिव सुकरः समुद्धर्तुं M. 1. 8. -COMP. -खंडः डं, -षंडः -डं an assemblage or clump of trees. -जीवनं the root of a tree. -तलं the ground about the foot of a tree, foot of tree. -नखः a thorn. -मृगः a monkey. -रागः 1 a bud or blossom. 2 a young shoot, sprout. -राजः the Tâla tree. -रुहा a parasitical plant. -विलासिनी the Navamallikâ creeper. -शायिन् *m.* a bird.

तरुण *a.* 1 Young, youthful, juvenile, (as a man). 2 (*a*) Young, newly born or produced, tender, soft; Bh 3. 49. (*b*) Newly risen, not high in the sky (as the sun); Ku. 3. 54. 3 New, fresh; तरुणं दधि Châṇa. 64; तरुणं सर्षपशाकं नवौदनं पिच्छिलानि च दधीनि। अल्पव्ययेन सुंदरि ग्राम्यजनो मिष्टमश्नाति॥ Chand. M. 1. 4 Lively, vivid. -णः A young man, youth; Pt. 1. 11; Bv. 2. 62. -णी A young or youthful woman; वृद्धस्य तरुणी विषं Châṇ. 98. -COMP. -ज्वरः fever lasting for a week. -दधि *n.* coagulated milk five days old. -पीतिका red arsenic.

तरुश *a.* Full of or abounding in trees.

तर्क् 10 U. (तर्कयति-ते, तर्कित) 1 To suppose, guess, suspect, believe, conjecture, infer; त्वं तावत्कतमां तर्कयसि S. 6; Me. 96. 2 To reason, speculate about, reflect. 3 To consider or regard as (with two acc.) 4 To think of, intend, mean, have in view (पातुं) त्वं चेदच्छस्फटिकविशदं तर्कयेस्तिर्यगंभः Me. 51. 5 To ascertain. 6 To shine. 7 To speak. -WITH प्र 1 to reason, reflect. 2 to think, believe, consider, suppose; Bk. 2. 9. -वि 1 to guess, conjecture. 2 To think, suppose, believe. 3 to reflect, reason.

तर्कः 1 Supposition, conjecture, guess प्रसन्नस्ते तर्कः V. 2. 2 Reasoning, speculation, discussion, abstract reasoning; कुतः पुनरस्मिन्नवधारिते आगमार्थे तर्कनिमित्तस्याक्षेपस्यावकाशः; इदानीं तर्कनिमित्त आक्षेपः परिह्रियते S. B.; तर्कोऽप्रतिष्ठः स्मृतयो विभिन्नाः Mb.; Ms. 12. 106. 3 Doubt. 4 Logic, the science of logic; यस्याक्ष्यं मधुवर्षि धर्षितपरास्तर्केषु यस्योक्तयः N. 22. 155; तर्कशास्त्रं, तर्कदीपिका. 5 (In logic) Reduction to absurdity, a conclusion opposed to the premises, a *reductio ad absurdum*. 6 Wish, desire. 7 Cause, motive. -COMP.-विद्या logic.

तर्ककः 1 A suitor, an inquirer, a petitioner. 2 A logician.

तर्कुः *m. f.* A spindle, an iron pin upon which cotton is first drawn out; तर्कुः कर्तनसाधनं. -COMP. -पिंडः,-पीठी a ball at the lower end of a spindle.

तर्क्षुः A hyena.

तर्क्ष्यः Nitre, saltpetre.

तर्ज् 1 P., 10 A. (often P. also) (तर्जति, तर्जयति-ते, तर्जित) 1 To threaten, menace, terrify; सखीमंगुल्या तर्जयति *S*. 1; अहिताननिलोद्धूतैस्तर्जयन्निव केतुभिः R. 4. 28, 11. 78, 12. 41; Bk. 14. 80. 2 To scold, revile, censure, blame; Bk. 6. 3, 8. 101, 17. 103. 3 To mock, deride.

तर्जनं,-ना 1 Threatening, frightening. 2 Censuring; R. 19. 17; Ku. 6. 45.

तर्जनी The fore-finger.

तर्णः, तर्णकः A calf; *Si*. 12. 41.

तर्णिः 1 A raft. 2 The sun.

तर्द् 1 P. (तर्दति) 1 To injure, hurt. 2 To kill, cut through; Bk. 14. 108; see तृद् also.

तर्पणं 1 Pleasing, satisfying. 2 Satisfaction, pleasure. 3 One of the five daily Yajnas (performed by men), presenting libations of water to the manes of the deceased ancestors (पितृयज्ञ). 4 Fuel for the secred fire. –Comp. –इच्छुः an epithet of Bhîshma.

तर्मन् *n*. The top of the sacrificial post.

तर्षः 1 Thirst. 2 Wish, desire. 3 The ocean. 4 A boat. 5 The sun.

तर्षणं Thirst.

तर्षित, तर्षुल *a*. 1 Thirsty. 2 Wishing, desiring.

तर्हि *ind*. 1 At that time, then. 2 In that case; यदा-तर्हि 'when then'; यदि तर्हि 'if-then'; कथं-तर्हि 'how then.'

तलः-लं 1 A surface; भुवस्तलमिव व्योम कुर्वन् व्योमेव भूतलं R. 4. 29; sometimes used at the end of comp. without much alteration of meaning; महीतलं 'surface of the earth; *i. e.* earth itself; शुद्धे तु दर्पणतले सुलभावकाशा *S*. 7. 32; नभस्तलं &c. 2 The palm of the hand; R. 6. 18. 3 The sole of the foot. 4 The fore-arm. 5 A slap with the hand. 6 Lowness, inferiority of position. 7 A lower part, part underneath, base, foot, bottom; रेवारोधसि वेतसीतरुतले चेतः समुत्कंठते K. P. 1. 8 (Hence) The ground under a tree or any other object, shelter afforded by anything; फणी मयूरस्य तले निषीदति Rs. 1. 13. 9 A hole, pit –लः 1 The hilt of a sword. 2 The palmyra tree. –लं 1 A pond. 2 A forest, wood. 3 Cause, origin, motive 4 A leathern fence worn round the left arm (तला also in this sense). –Comp. –अंगुलिः *f*. a toe. –अतलं the fourth of the seven divisions of hell. –ईक्षणः a hog. –उदा a river. –घातः a slap with the palm of the hand. –तालः a kind of musical instrument. –त्रं, -त्राणं, -वारणं a leathern glove of an archer. –प्रहारः a slap with the hand. –सारकं a martingale.

तलकं A large pond.

तलतः *ind*. From the bottom.

तलाची A mat.

तलिका A martingale.

तलितं Fried meat.

तलिन *a*. 1 Thin, meagre, spare. 2 Small, little. 3 Clear, clean. 4 Situated under or beneath. 5 Separate. –नं A bed, couch.

तलिमं 1 Paved ground, a pavement. 2 A bed, cot, couch. 3 An awning. 4 A large sword or knife.

तलुनः Wind.

तल्कं A forest.

तल्पः-ल्पं 1 A couch, bed, sofa; सपदि विगतनिद्रस्तल्पमुज्झांचकार R. 5. 751 'left the bed', rose. 2 (Fig.) A wife (as in गुरुतल्पग q. v.) 3 The seat of a carriage. 4 An upper story, a turret, tower.

तल्पकः One whose business it is to make or prepare beds (as a servant)

तल्लजः 1 Excellence, superiority, happiness. 2 (At the end of comp.) Excellent (in this sense the word is always masculine whatever be the gender of the first member of the compound); गोतल्लजः 'an excellent cow'; so कुमारीतल्लजः 'an excellent maiden'.

तल्लिका A key.

तल्ली A youthful woman.

तष्ट *a*. 1 Hewn, cut, chiseled, split. 2 Fashioned; see तक्ष्.

तष्टृ *m*. 1 A carpenter in general. 2 The architect of gods (विश्वकर्मन्).

तस्करः 1 A thief, robber, मा संचर मनः पांथ तत्रास्ते स्मरतस्करः Bh. 1. 86; Ms. 4. 135, 8. 67. 2 (At the end of comp.) Anything bad or contemptible.–री A passionate woman.

तस्थु *a*. Stationary, immoveable, stable.

ताक्षण्यः, ताक्ष्णः The son of a carpenter.

ताच्छीलिकः N. of an affix used to denote a particular inclination, tendency, or habit.

ताटंकः An ornament for the ear, a large ear-ring.

ताटस्थ्यं 1 Proximity. 2 Indifference, disregard, neutrality; see तटस्थ.

ताडः 1 A blow, knock, thump. 2 Noise. 3 A sheaf. 4 A mountain.

ताडका N. of a female fiend, daughter of Suketu, wife of Sunda and mother of Mârîcha. [She was changed into a fiend by the sage Agastya whose devotions she had disturbed. She was killed by Rama when she began to disturb the sacrificial rites of Visvamitra. Rama was first unwilling to bend his bow against a *woman*, but the sage overcame his scruples; see R. 11. 14–20].

ताडकेयः An epithet of the demon Mârîcha, son of Tâdakâ.

ताडंकः, ताडपत्रं see ताटंक.

ताडनं Beating, whipping, flogging; लालने बहवो दोषास्ताडने बहवो गुणाः Chân. 12; अवतंसोत्पलताडनानि वा Ku. 4. 8; *S*. Til. 9. –नी A whip.

ताडिः -डी *f*. 1 A kind of palm. 2 A kind of ornament.

ताड्यमान *a*. Being beaten or struck. –नः A musical instrument struck with a stick &c. (as a drum).

तांडवः-वं 1 Dancing in general; मदतांडवोत्सवांते U. 3. 18. 2 Particularly the frantic or violent dance of *S*iva; त्र्यंबकानंदि वस्तांडवं देवि भूयादभीष्टयै च हृष्टयै च नः Mâl. 5. 23, 1. 1. 3 The art of dancing. 4 A sort of grass. –Comp. –प्रियः N. of *S*iva.

तातः 1 A father; मृष्यंतु लवस्य बालिशतां तातपादाः U. 6; हा ताततेति क्रंदितमाकर्ण्य विषण्णः R. 9. 75. 2 A term of affection, endearment, or pity, applied to any person, but usually to inferiors or juniors, pupils, children &c.; तात चंद्रापीड K. 106; रक्षसा भक्षितस्तात तव तातो वनांतरे Mb. 3 A term of respect applied to elders or other venerable personages; न्हपिता हि बहवो नरेश्वरास्तेन तात धनुषा धनुर्भृतः R. 11. 40; तस्मान्मुच्ये यथा तात संविधातुं तथार्हसि 1. 72.–Comp. –गु *a*. agreeable to a father. (–गुः) a paternal uncle.

ताततः The Khanjana or wagtail.

तातलः 1 A disease. 2 An iron club or spike. 3 Cooking, maturing. 4 Heat.

तातिः Offspring. –तिः *f*. Continuity, succession, as in अरिष्टताति or शिवताति q. v.

तात्कालिक *a*. (की *f*.) 1 Simultaneous. 2 Immediate.

तात्पर्य 1 Purport, meaning, scope, अत्रेदं तात्पर्यं &c. 2 Purport of propositions; K. P. 2. 3 Aim, object intended, reference to any object, purpose, intention (with loc.); इह यथार्थकथने तात्पर्यं P. II 3. 43 Com. 4 The object or intention of the speaker (in using particular words in a sentence); वक्तुरिच्छा तु तात्पर्यं परिकीर्तितं Bhâshâ P. 84; तात्पर्यानुपपत्तितः 82.

तात्त्विक *a*. True, real, essential; किं चासीदमृतस्य भेदविगमः साचिस्मिते तात्त्विकः Bv. 2. 81; तात्त्विकः संबंधः &c.

तादात्म्यं Sameness of nature, identity, unity; नयनयोस्तादात्म्यमंभोरुहां Bv. 2. 81; भगवत्यात्मनस्तादात्म्यं &c.

तादृक्ष *a*. (क्षी *f*.) तादृश *a*. तादृश् *a*. (शी *f*.) Such-like, like him, her or it, like that; तादृग्गुणा Ms. 9. 22. 32; Amaru. 46; यादृशस्तादृशः any body, whoever, common or ordinary man; उपदेशो न दातव्यो यादृशे तादृशे जने Pt. 1. 390.

तानः 1 A thread, fibre. 2 (In music) A protracted tone, a keynote ; यथा तानं विना रागः Bv. 1. 119; तानप्रदायित्वमिवोपगंतुं Ku. 1. 8. -नं 1 Expanse, extension. 2 An object of sense.

तानवं Thinness, smallness; हास्यप्रभा तानवमाससाद Vikr. 1. 106.

तानूरः A whirlpool.

तांत *a.* 1 Wearied, languid, fatigued. 2 Troubled, afflicted. 3 Faded, withered; see तम्.

तांतवं 1 Spinning, weaving. 2 A web. 3 A woven cloth.

तांत्रिक *a.* (की *f.*) 1 Well-versed in any science or doctrine. 2 Relating to the Tantras. 3 Taught or contained in them. -कः A follower of Tantra doctrines.

तापः 1 Heat, glow; अर्कमयूखतापः *S.* 4 10; Mâl. 1. 13; Ms. 12. 76; Ku. 7. 84. 2 Torment, pain, affliction, misery, agony; इतरतापशतानि तवेच्छया वितर तानि सहे चतुरानन Udb.; समस्तापः कामं मनसिजनिदाघप्रसरयोः *S.* 3. 9; Bh. 1. 16. 3 Sorrow, distress. —Comp. -त्रयं the three kinds of miseries which human beings have to suffer in this world; *i.e.*, आध्यात्मिक, आधिदैविक and आधिभौतिक. -हर *a.* cooling.

तापनः 1 The sun. 2 The hot season. 3 The sun-stone. 4 N. of one of the arrows of Cupid. -नं 1 Burning. 2 Distressing. 3 Chastising.

तापस *a.* (सी *f.*) 1 Relating to religious penance or to an ascetic. 2 Devout. —सः (सी *f.*) A hermit, devotee, an ascetic.—Comp. -इष्टा a grape. -तरुः, -द्रुमः the tree of ascetics, also called इंगुदी.

तापस्यं Asceticism.

तापिच्छः The Tamâla tree or its flower (*n*) प्रफुल्लतापिच्छनिभैरभीषुभिः *Si.* 1. 22; व्योम्नस्तापिच्छगुच्छावलिभिरिव तमोवल्लरीभिर्व्रियंते Mâl. 5. 6 (तापिंज used in the same sense).

तापी 1 N. of the river Tâptî which joins the sea near Surat. 2 The river Yamunâ.

तामः 1 An object of terror. 2 A fault, defect. 3 Anxiety, distress. 4 Desire.

तामरं 1 Water. 2 Clarified butter.

तामरसं 1 The red lotus; Pt. 1. 94; R. 6. 37, 9. 12, 37; Amaru. 70, 88. 2 Gold. Copper. -सी A lotus-pond.

तामस *a.* (सी *f.*) 1 Dark. 2 Affected by or relating to तमस् or the quality of darkness (the third of the three qualities of nature); Bg. 7. 12, 17. 2; M. 1. 1; Ms. 12. 33-34. 3 Ignorant. 4 Vicious. -सः 1 A malignant person, an incendiary, villain. 2 A snake. 3 An owl. -सं Darkness, -सी 1 Night, a dark night. 2 Sleep. 3 An epithet of Durgâ.

तामसिक *a.* (की *f.*) 1 Dark. 2 Belonging to, derived from, or connected with, तमस्.

तामिस्रः A division of hell.

तांबूलं 1 The areca-nut. 2 The leaf of piper-betel, which together with the areca-nut, catechu, chewed after meals; तांबूलभृतगल्लोऽयं भल्लं जल्पति मानुषः K P. 7; रागो न स्खलितस्तवाधरपुटे तांबूलसंवर्धितः *S.* Til. 7. -Comp. -करंकः, -पेटिका a betel-box; (Mar. पानदान, पानपुडा). -दः -धरः -वाहकः a servant attached to men of rank to carry the betel-box and to provide them with तांबूल whenever necessary. -वल्ली the betel-plant; R. 6. 64.

तांबूलिकः A seller of betel.

तांबूली The batel-plant; तांबूलीनां दलैस्तत्र रचितापानभूमयः R. 4. 42.

ताम्र *a.* Of a coppery red colour, red; उदेति सविता ताम्रस्ताम्र एवास्तमेति च. -स्रं Copper. -Comp. -अक्षः 1 a crow. 2 the (Indian) cuckoo. -अर्धः bell-metal. -अश्मन् *m.* a kind of jewel (पद्मराग). -उपजीविन् *m.* a copper-smith. -ओष्ठः (forming ताम्रोष्ठ or ताम्रौष्ठ) a red or cherry lip; Ku. 1. 44. -कारः -कुट्टः a brazier, copper-smith. -कृमिः a kind of red insect (इंद्रगोप). -गर्भं sulphate of copper. -चूडः a cock, -त्रपुजं brass. -द्रुः the red sandal-wood. -पट्टः, -पत्रं a copper-plate on which grants of land were frequently inscribed; Y. 1. 319. -पर्णी N. of a river rising in Malaya celebrated for its pearls; R. 4. 52. -पल्लवः the As'oka tree. -लिप्तः N. of a country. (-प्ताः pl.) its people or rulers. -वृक्षः a species of sandal.

ताम्रिक *a.* (की *f.*) Made of copper, coppery. —कः A brazier, copper-smith.

ताय् 1 A. (तायते, तायित) 1 To spead, extend, proceed in a continuous line. 2 To protect, preserve. -With वि to spread, create; Bk. 16. 105.

तार *a* 1 High (as a note). 2 Loud, shrill (as a sound); Mâl. 5. 20. 3 Shining, radiant, clear; हारांस्तारांस्तरलगुटिकान् (regarded as an interpolation in Me. by Malli.); उरसि निहितस्तारो हारः Amaru. 28. 4 Good, excellent, well-flavoured. -रः 1 The bank of a river. 2 The clearness of a pearl. 3 A beautiful or big pearl; हारममलतरतारमुरसि दधतं Gît. 11. 4 A high tone or note. -रः,-रं 1 A star or planet. 2 Camphor. -रं 1 Silver. 2 The pupil of the eye; (said to be *m.* also). 3 A pearl (said to be *f.* also). -Comp.-अभ्रः camphor.-अरिः a pyritic ore of iron. -पतनं the falling of a star or meteor. -पुष्पः the Kunda or Jasmine creeper. -वायुः loud-sounding wind, a whistling breeze. -शुद्धिकरं lead. -स्वर *a.* having a loud or shrill sound. -हारः 1 a necklace of big or beautiful pearls. 2 a shining necklace.

तारक *a.* (रिका *f.*) 1 Carrying over. 2 Protecting, preserving, rescuing. -कः 1 A pilot, helmsman. 2 A deliverer, saviour. 3 N. of a demon killed by Kârtikeya. [He was the son of Vajranga and Varangi. He propitiated the god Brahmadeva by means of his penance on the Pariyatra mountain, and asked as a boon that he should not be killed by any one except a child seven days old. On the strength of this boon he began to oppress the gods who were obliged to go to Brahma and ask his assistance in the destruction of the demon; (see Ku. 2). But they were told that the offspring of *Siva* could alone vanquish him. Afterwards Kartikeya was born and he slew the demon on the seventh day of his birth]. -कः,-कं A float, raft. -कं 1 The pupil of the eye. 2 The eye. -Comp. -अरिः,-जित् *m.* an epithet of Kârtikeya.

तारका 1 A star. 2 A meteor, falling star. 3 The pupil of the eye; संदधे दृशमुदग्रतारकां R. 11. 69; Ch. P. 5; Bh. 1. 11.

तारकिणी A starry night, night during which stars are visible.

तारकित *a.* Starry, star-spangled, studded with stars.

तारणः A boat, float. -णं 1 Crossing. 2 Rescuing, delivering, liberating.

तारणिः,-णी *f.* A float, raft.

तारतम्यं 1 Gradation, proportion, relative importance, comparative value. 2 Difference, distinction; निर्धनं निधनमेतयोर्द्वयोस्तारतम्यविविमुक्तचेतसां । बोधनाय विधिना विनिर्मिता रेफ एव जयवैजयंतिका ॥ Udb.

तारलः A libidinous man, a lecher, libertine.

तारा 1 A star or planet in general; हंसश्रेणीषु तारासु R. 4. 19; Bh. 1. 15. 2 A fixed star; R. 6. 22. 3 The pupil of the eye, the eye-ball; कांतामंतःप्रमोदादभिसरति मदभ्रांततारश्चकोरः Mâl. 9. 30; विस्मयस्मेरतारैः 1. 28, Ku. 3. 47. 4 A pearl. 5 N. of (*a*) the wife of Vâli, king of the monkeys and mother of Angada. She in vain tried to dissuade her husband Vâli from fighting with Râma and Sugrîva, and married Sugrîva after Vâli had been killed by Râma. (*b*) N. of the wife of Brihaspati, the preceptor of the gods. She was on one occasion carried off by Soma (the moon) who refused to deliver her up to her husband when demanded. A fierce contest then ensued and Brahmâ had at last to compel Soma to restore her to her husband. Târâ gave birth to a son named Budha who became the ancestor of the Lunar race of kings. (*c*) N. of the wife of Harischandra and mother of Rohidâsa (also called Târâmatî). –COMP. –अधिपः,–आपीडः, –पतिः the moon: R. 13. 76; Ku. 7. 48; Bh. 1. 71. –पथः the atmosphere, firmament. –प्रमाणं sidereal measure, sidereal time. –भूषा the night. –मंडलं 1 the starry region, the zodiac. 2 the pupil of the eye. –मृगः the constellation मृगशिरस्.

तारिकं Fare, freight.

तारुण्यं 1 Youth, youthfulness. 2 Freshness (fig.).

तारेयः 1 The planet Mercury. 2 An epithet of Angada, son of Vâli.

तार्किकः 1 A dialectician, a logician. 2 A philosopher.

तार्क्ष्यः 1 An epithet of Garuḍa; त्रस्तेन तार्क्ष्यात् किल कालियेन R. 6. 49. 2 N. of Garuḍa's elder brother Aruṇa. 3 A car. 4 A horse. 5 A snake. 6 A bird in general. –COMP. –ध्वजः an epithet of Vishṇu. –नायकः an epithet of Garuḍa.

तार्तीय *a.* The third.

तार्तीयीक *a.* The third; तार्तीयीकतया मितोऽयमगमत्तस्य प्रबंधे N. 3. 136; तार्तीयीकं पुरारेस्तद्वतु मदनप्लोषणं लोचनं वः Mâl. 1 v. l.

तालः 1 the palmyra tree; Bh. 2. 90; R 15. 23. 2 A banner formed of the palm. 3 Slapping or clapping the hands together. 4 Flapping in general. 5 Flapping of the ears of an elephant. 6 Beating time (in music); करकिसलयतालैर्मुग्धया नर्त्यमानं U. 3. 19; Me. 79. 7 A musical instrument made of bell-metal; R. 9. 71. 8 The palm of the hand. 9 A lock, bolt. 10 The hilt of a sword. –लं 1 The nut of the palmyra tree. 2 Yellow orpiment. –COMP. –अंकः 1 N. of Balarâma. 2 the palmleaf used for writing. 3 a book. 4 a saw. –अवचरः a dancer, an actor. –केतुः an epithet of Bhîshma. –क्षीरकं, –गर्भः the exudation of the palm. –ध्वजः, –भृत् *m.* an epithet of Balarâma. –पत्रं 1 the palm-leaf used for writing. 2 a kind of ear-ornament (hollow cylinder of gold thrust through the *lobe* of the ear). –बद्ध, –शुद्ध *a.* measured, rhythmical, regulated by musical time. –मर्दलः a kind of musical instrument, a cymbal. –यंत्रं a kind of surgical instrument. –रेचनकः a dancer, an actor. –लक्षणः an epithet of Balarâma. –वनं a grove of trees. –वृंतं a fan; S. 3. 21, Ku. 2. 35.

तालकं 1 Yellow orpiment. 2 A bolt, latch. –COMP. –आभ *a.* green. (–भः) the green colour.

तालकः A kind of ear-ornament (=ताडंक q. v.).

तालव्य *a.* Relating to the palate, palatal. –COMP. –वर्णः a palatal letter; *i. e.* इ, ई, च् छ् ज् झ् ञ् and य्. –स्वरः a palatal vowel; *i. e.*, इ and ई.

तालिकः 1 The open palm of the hand. 2 Clapping the hands (तालिका also); यथैकेन न हस्तेन तालिका संप्रपद्यते Pt. 2. 128; उच्चाटनीयः करतालिकानां दानादिदानीं भवतीभिरेषः N. 3. 7.

तालितं 1 Coloured cloth. 2 A string; tie.

ताली 1 A species of the mountain-palm, palm-tree. 2 The common Toddy (*tâḍî*). 3 Fragrant earth. 4 A sort of key. –COMP. –वनं a grove of palm trees; R. 4. 34, 6. 57.

तालु *n.* The palate; तृषा महत्या परिशुष्कतालवः Rs. 1. 11. –COMP. –जिह्वः a crocodile. –स्थान *a.* palatal. (–नं) the palate.

तालूरः A whirlpool, an eddy.

तालूषकं The palate.

तावक *a.* (की *f.*), **तावकीन** *a.* Thy, thine; तपः क वत्से क च तावकं वपुः Ku. 5. 4; Ki. 3 12; Bv. 1. 36. 96.

तावत् *a.* (Correlative of यावत् q. v.) 1 So much, that much, so many; ते तु यावंत एवाजौ तावांश्च ददृशे स तैः R. 12, 45; H. 4. 72; Ku. 2. 33. 2 So great, so large, of this extent; यावती संभवेद् वृत्तिस्तावतीं दातुमर्हसि Ms. 8. 155, 9. 249; Bg. 2. 46. 3 All (expressing totality); यावद्दत्तं तावद्भुक्तं G. M.—*ind.* 1 First (before doing anything else); आर्ये इतस्तावदागम्यतां *S.* 1; आल्हादयस्व तावच्चंद्रकरश्चंद्रकांतमिव V. 5. 11; Me. 13. 2 On one's part, in the meanwhile; सखे स्थिरप्रतिबंधो भव । अहं तावत् स्वामिनाश्चित्तवृत्तिमनुवर्तिष्ये *S.* 2; R. 7. 32. 3 Just now; गच्छ तावत्. 4 Indeed, (to emphasize an expression); त्वमेव तावत्प्रथमो राजद्रोही Mu. 1 thou thyself; त्वमेव तावत्परिचिंतय स्वयं Ku. 5. 67. 5 Truly, really (to express assent); दृढस्तावद्बंधः H. 1. 6 As for, with respect to; वियद्गस्तावदुपस्थितः H. 3; एवं कृते तव तावत्क्लेशं विना प्राणयात्रा भविष्यति Pt. 1. 7 Completely; तावत्प्रकीर्णाभिनवोपचारां R. 7. 4 (तावत्प्रकीर्णा=साकल्येन प्रसारित Malli.). 8 Surprise (oh !, what a wonder). (For the senses of तावत् as a correlative of यावत्, see यावत्). —COMP. –कृत्वस् *ind.* so many times. –मात्रं just so much. –वर्ष *a.* so many years old.

तावतिक *a.*, **तावत्क** *a.*, Bought for so much, worth so much, of so much value.

तावुरिः The sign Taurus of the zodiac, (a word borrowed from the Greek *Tauros*).

तिक्त *a.* 1 Bitter, pungent (as one of the six flavours or *Rasas*); Me. 20. 2 Fragrant; Me. 33. –क्तः 1 A bitter taste; (see under कटु). 2 The Kutaja tree. 3 Pungency. 4 Fragrance. –COMP. –गंधा mustard. –धातुः bile. –फलः, –मरिचः the clearing-nut plant. –सारः the Khadira tree.

तिग्म *a.* 1 Sharp, pointed (as a weapon). 2 Violent. 3 Hot, scorching. 4 Pungent, acrid. 5 Fiery, passionate. –ग्मं 1 Heat. 2 Pungency. –COMP. –अंशुः 1 the sun; तिग्मांशुरस्तं गतः Git. 5. 2 fire. 3 N. of Siva. –करः, –दीधितिः –रश्मिः the sun.

तिज् I. 1 A. (Strictly *desid.* of तिज्) (तितिक्षते, तितिक्षित) 1 To endure, bear; to put up with, suffer patiently or with courage; तितिक्षमाणस्य परेण निंदां M. 1. 17; तांस्तितिक्षस्व भारत Bg. 2. 14; Mv. 2. 12; Ki. 13. 68; Ms. 6. 47; –II. 10 U. or *Caus.* (तेजयति–ते, तेजित) 1 To sharpen, whet; कुसुमचापमतेजयदंशुभिः R. 9. 39. 2 To stir up, excite, instigate.

तितउः A sieve. –*n.* A parasol.

तितिक्षा Endurance, patience, resignation, forbearance.

तितिक्षु *a.* Patient, forbearing, enduring.

तितिभः 1 A fire fly. 2 A kind of insect (इंद्रगोप).

तितिरः, तित्तिरः The francoline patridge.

तित्तिरिः 1 The francoline partridge. 2 N. of a sage said to be the first teacher of the Krishṇa Yajurveda.

तिथः 1 Fire. 2 Love. 3 Time. 4 The rainy season or autumn.

तिथिः *m.* or *f.* 1 A lunar day; तिथिरेव तावन्न शुद्ध्यति Mu. 5; Ku. 6. 93, 7. 1. 2 The number '15'. –COMP. –क्षयः 1 the day of new moon. 2 the day which a *tithi* begins and ends without one sunrising or between two sunrises. –पत्री an almanac. –प्रणीः the moon. –वृद्धिः the day in which a *tithi* is completed under two suns (one which comprises two sunrises).

तिनिशः A particular tree; दात्यूहैस्तिनिशस्य कोटरवति स्कंधे निलीय स्थितं Mâl. 9. 7.

तिंतिडः, –डी, तिंतिडिका, तिंतिडीकः The tamarind tree.

तिंदुः, तिंदुकः, तिंदुलः N. of a tree.

तिम् 1 P. (तेमति, तिमित) To make wet or damp, moisten.

तिमिः 1 The ocean. 2 A kind of whale or fish of an enormous size; R. 13. 10. –COMP. –कोषः the ocean. –ध्वजः N. of a demon killed by Indra with the assistance of Dasaratha. (It was in the fight with this demon that Kaikeyî saved the life of Dasaratha while in a swooning fit, and got from him two boons which she afterwards used to send Râma into exile.

तिमिंगिलः A kind of fish which swallows a *timi*; Bv. 1. 55. °अशनः, °गिलः a large fish swallows even a *timingila*; तिमिंगिलगिलोऽप्यस्ति तद्गिलोऽप्यस्ति राघवः।

तिमित *a.* Motionless, steady, unshaken. **2** Wet, moist, damp.

तिमिर *a.* Dark; विन्यस्यंतीं दृशौ तिमिरे पथि Gît. 5; बभूवुस्तिमिरा दिशः Mb. **-रः -रं** Darkness; तन्वेशं तिमिरमपाकरोति चंद्रः *S*. 6. 29; Ku. 4. 11; *Si*. 4. 57. **2** Blindness. **3** Iron-rust. —COMP. **अरिः, -नुद्** *m*., **-रिपुः** the sun.

तिरश्ची The female of any animal, beast or bird.

तिरश्चीन *a*. **1** Oblique, sideways, awry; गतं तिरश्चीनमनूरुसारथेः *Si*. 1. 2; यथा तिरश्चीनमलातशल्यं U. 3. 35. **2** Irregular.

तिरस् *ind*. **1** Croockedly, obliquely, awry; स तिर्यङ् यस्तिरोंऽचति Ak. **2** Without; apart from. **3** Secretly, covertly, invisibly. [In classical literature तिरस् is rarely used by itself, but chiefly occurs in composition with (*a*) **कृ** to cover, despise, excel; (R. 3. 8, **16**. 20; Ms. **4**. 49; Amaru. 81; Bk. 9. 62; H. 3. 8). (*b*) **धा** to cover, conceal, overpower, disappear; (R. 10. 48. 11. 91), and (*c*) **भू** to disappear; (R. 16. 20; Bk. 6. 71, 14. 44]. —COMP. **-करिणी, -कारिणी 1** a curtain, veil; तिरस्करिण्यो जलदा भवंति Ku. 1 14; M. 2. 1. **2** an outer tent, screen of cloth. **-कारः, -क्रिया 1** concealment, disappearance. **2** abuse, censure, reproach. **3** contempt, disdain. **-कृतः** *a*. **1** disregarded, dispised, abused. **2** condemned. **3** concealed, covered. **-धानं 1** disappearance, removal; अथ खलु तिरोधानमधियां G. L. 18. **2** a covering, veil, sheath. **-भावः** disappearsnce. **-हित** *a*. **1** vanished, disappeared. **2** covered, concealed, hidden.

तिरयति Den. P. **1** To conceal, keep concealed or secret. **2** To hinder, stop, obstruct, obscure; तिरयति करणानां ग्राहकत्वं प्रमोहः Mâl. 1. 40; वारंवारं तिरयति दृशोरुद्गमं बाष्पपूरः 35. **3** To conquer.

तिर्यक् *ind*. Obliquely, crookedly, in a shanting or oblique direction; विलोकयति तिर्यक् K. P. 10; Me. 51; Ku. 5. 74.

तिर्यच् *a*. (**तिरश्ची** *f*., rarely **तिर्यची**) **1** Oblique, transverse, horizontal, awry. **2** Crooked, curved. —*m*.-*n*. An animal (going horizontally, as distinguished from man who walks erect), a lower or irrational animal; विधाय दिव्ये न तिरश्चि कश्चित् पाशादिरासादितपौरुषः स्यात् N. 3. 20; Ku. 1. 48. —COMP. **-अंतरं** intermidiate space measured across, breadth. **-अयनं** the annual revolution of the sun. **-ईक्ष** *a*. looking obliquely. **-जातिः** *f*. the brute kind (opp. man). **—प्रमाणं** breadth. **-प्रेक्षणं** a side-look. **-योनिः** *f*. animal creation or race; तिर्यग्योनौ च जायते Ms. 4. 200. **-स्रोतस्** *m*. the animal world.

तिलः 1 The sesamum plant; नासाभ्येति तिलप्रसूनपदवीं Gît. 10. **2** The seed of this plant; नाकस्माच्छांडिलीमाता विक्रीणाति तिलैस्तिलान्। लुंचितानितरैर्येन कार्यमत्र भविष्यति ॥ Pt. 2. 55. **3** A mole, spot. **4** A small particle, as much as a sesamum seed. —COMP. **—अंबु, —उदकं** water with sesamum seed offered to the dead as a libation; *S*. 3; Ms. 3. 223. **-उत्तमा** N. of an Apsaras. **-ओदनः, नं** a dish of milk, rice and sesamum. **-कल्कः** dough made of ground sesamum. °**जः** oil-cake made of the sediment of ground sesamum. **-कालकः** a mole, a dark spot under the skin. **-किट्टं, -खलिः** *f*., **-खली,** or **-चूर्णं** the caky sediment of sesamum after the oil is extracted. **-तंडुलकं** an embrace (so called because in it the two bodies are united together like rice mixed up with sesamum-seed). **-तैलं** sesamum oil. **-पर्णः** turpentine. (**-र्णं**) sandal-wood. **-पर्णी 1** the sandal tree. **2** frank-incense. **3** turpentine. **—रसः** sesamum oil. **—स्नेहः** sesamum oil. **-होमः** a burnt offering of sesamum.

तिलंतुदः An oil-man.

तिलशः *ind*. In pieces as small as sesamum seed, in very small quantities.

तिलवः The Lodhra tree.

तिलकः 1 A species of tree with beautiful flowers; आक्रांता तिलकक्रियापि तिलकैर्लीनद्विरेफांजनैः M. 3. 5; न खलु शोभयति स्म वनस्थलीं न तिलकास्तिलकः प्रमदामिव R. 9. 41. **2** A freckle or natural mark under the skin. **-कः -कं 1** A mark made with sandal wood or unguents &c.; मुखे मधुश्रीस्तिलकं प्रकाश्य Ku. 3. 30; कस्तूरिकातिलकमालि विधाय सायं Bv. 2. 4; 1. 121. **2** The ornament of anything (used at the end of comp. in the sense of 'best', 'chief' or 'distinguished'). **-का** A kind of necklace. **-कं 1** The bladder. **2** The lungs. **3** A kind of salt. —COMP. **-आश्रयः** the forehead.

तिलित्सः A large snake.

तिष्ठद्गु *ind*. At the time when cows stand to be milked (*i.e.*, after an hour or an hour and a half after evening; आतिष्ठद्गु जपन् संध्यां Bk. 4. 14 (तिष्ठद्गु=रात्रेः प्रथमनाडिका).

तिष्यः 1 The eighth of the 27 constellations, also called पुष्य. **2** The lunar month Pausha. **-ष्यं** The Kali yuga.

तीक् 1 A. (तीकते) To go, move; cf. टीक्.

तीक्ष्ण *a*. **1** Sharp (in all senses), pungent; *Si* 2. 109. **2** Hot, warm (as rays); Rs 1. 18. **3** Fiery, passionate. **4** Hard, forcible, strong (as उपाय). **5** Rude, cross. **6** Severe, harsh, rough, strict; Ms. 7. 140. **7** Injurious, noxious, inauspicious. **8** Keen. **9** Intelligent, clever. **10** Zealous, vehement, energetic. **11** Devoted, self-abandoning. **-क्ष्णः 1** Nitre. **2** Long pepper. **3** Black pepper. **4** Black mustard. **—क्ष्णं 1** Iron. **2** Steel. **3** Heat, pungency. **4** War, battle. **5** Poison. **6** Death. **7** A weapon. **8** Sea-salt. **9** Haste. —COMP. **—अंशुः 1** the sun. **2** fire. **—आयसं** steel. **—उपायः** a forcible means, strong measure. **—कंदः** the onion. **—कर्मन्** *a*. active, zealous, energetic. **-दंष्ट्रः** a tiger. **-धारः** a sword. **-पुष्पं** cloves. **-पुष्पा 1** the clove tree. **2** the Ketaka plant. **-बुद्धि** *a*. sharp-witted, acute, clever, shrewd. **-रश्मिः** the sun. **-रसः 1** salt-petre. **2** any poisonous liquid, a poison; शत्रुप्रयुक्तानां तीक्ष्णरसदायिनां Mu. 1. 2. **-लौहं** steel. **-शूकः** barley.

तीम् 4 P. (तीम्यति) To be wet or moist.

तीरं 1 A shore, bank; नदीतीर, सागरतीर, &c. **2** Margin, brim, edge. **—रः 1** A sort of an arrow. **2** Lead. **3** Tin.

तीरित *a*. Settled, adjusted, decided according to evidence. **-तं** Completion of any affair.

तीर्ण *a*. **1** Crossed, passed over. **2** Spread, expanded. **3** Surpassed, excelled.

तीर्थं 1 A passage, road, way, ford. **2** A descent into a river, the stairs of a landing place; (Mar. घाट); विषमोपि विगाह्यते नयः कृततीर्थः पयसामिवाशयः Ki. 2. 3. (where तीर्थ means 'a remedy or means' also); तीर्थं सर्वविद्यावताराणां K. 44. **3** A place of water. **4** A holy place, place of pilgrimage, a shrine &c. dedicated to some holy object (especially on or near the bank of a sacred river &c.); शुचि मनो यद्यस्ति तीर्थेन किं Bh. 2. 55; R. 1. 85. **5** A channel, medium, means; तदनेन तीर्थेन घटेत &c. Mâl. 1. **6** A remedy, expedient. **7** A sacred or holy personage, worthy person, object of veneration, fit recipient; क्व पुनस्तादृशस्य तीर्थस्य साधोः संभवः U. 1; Ms. 3. 103.

8 A sacred preceptor, a teacher; मया तीर्थादभिनयविद्या शिक्षिता M. 1. 9 Source, origin. 10 A sacrifice. 11 A minister. 12 Advice, instruction. 13 Right place or moment. 14 The Right or usual manner. 15 Certain parts of the hand sacred to deities, manes &c. 16 A school of philosophy. 17 Pudendum muliebre. 18 Menstrual courses of a woman. 19 A Brâhmaṇa. 20 Fire. **-र्थः** An honorary affix added to the names of ascetics, saints &c.; *e. g.* आनंदतीर्थ. -COMP. **-उदकं** holy water; तीर्थोदकं च वह्निश्च नान्यतः शुद्धिमर्हतः U. 1. 13. **-करः** 1 a Jaina *Arhat*, sanctified teacher or saint of the Jainas; (also तीर्थंकर in this sense). 2 an ascetic. 3 the founder of a new religious or philosophical school. 4 N. of Vishṇu. **-काकः, -ध्वांक्षः, -वायसः** 'a crow at a sacred bathing-place', *i. e.* a very greedy person; (लोलुप). **-भूत** *a.* sacred, holy. **-यात्रा** a visit to a holy place, a pilgrimage. **-राजः** N. of Prayâga. **-राजिः, -जी** *f.* an epithet of Benares. **-वाकः** the hair of the head. **-विधिः** rites observed at a place of pilgrimage, such as क्षौर). **-सेविन्** *a.* a pilgrim. (*-m*). a crane.

तीर्थिकः A pilgrim, an ascetic Brâhmaṇa (visiting holy places).

तीवरः 1 The ocean. 2 A hunter. 3 The adulterine offspring of a Râjaputrî by a Kshatriya (one of the mixed tribes).

तीव्र *a.* 1 Severe, intense, sharp, acute, violent, poignant, pungent, impetuous; विलंबिताधोरणतीव्रयत्नाः R. 5. 48. strong or violent efforts; U. 3. 35. 2 Hot, warm. 3 Flashing. 4 Pervading. 5 Endless, unlimited. 6 Horrible, dreadful. **-व्रं** 1 Heat, pungency. 2 A shore. 3 Iron, steel. 4 Tin. **-व्रं** *ind.* Violently, sharply, excessively. -COMP. **-आनंदः** an epithet of Śiva. **-गति** *a.* quick, swift. **-पौरुषं** 1 daring heroism. 2 heroism. (in general). **-संवेग** *a.* 1 of strong impulse, resolute. 2 very poignant or sharp.

तु *ind.* (Never used at the beginning of a sentence, but usually after the first word). 1 An adversative particle meaning 'but', 'on the contrary', 'on the otherhand', 'nevertheless'; स सर्वेषां सुखानामंतं ययौ । एकं तु सुतमुखदर्शनसुखं न लेभे K. 59; विपर्यये तु पितुरस्याः समीपनयनमवस्थितमेव *S.* 5; (in this sense तु is often added to किं, and परं, and किंतु and परंतु are, unlike तु, always used at the beginning of a sentence). 2 And now, on one's part, and; एकदा तु प्रतीहारी समुपसृत्याब्रवीत् K. 8; राजा तु तामार्यां श्रुत्वाब्रवीत् 12. 3 As to, as regards, as for; प्रवर्त्यतां ब्राम्हणानुद्दिश्य पाकः । चंद्रोपरागं प्रति तु केनापि विप्रलब्धासि Mu. 1. 4 It sometimes marks a difference (भेद) or superior quality; मृष्टं पयो मृष्टतरं तु दुग्धं G. M. 6 Sometimes it is used as an emphatic particle; भीमस्तु पांडवानां रौद्रः G. M. 6 And sometimes it is used as a mere expletive; निरर्थकं तुहीत्यादि पूरणैकप्रयोजनं Chandr. 2. 6.

तुक्खारः, तुखारः, तुषारः N. of a people inhabiting the Vindhya mountain; cf. Vikr. 18. 93.

तुंग *a.* 1 High, elevated, tall, lofty, prominent; जलनिधिमिव विधुमंडलदर्शनतरलिततुंगतरंगं Gît. 11; तुंगं नगोत्संगमिवारुरोह R. 6. 3, 4. 70; *Si.* 2. 48; Me. 12, 64. 2 Long. 3 Vaulted. 4 Chief, principal. 5 Strong, passionate. **-गः** 1 A height, elevation. 2 A mountain. 3 Top, summit. 4 The planet Mercury. 5 A rhinoceros. 6 The cocoanut tree. -COMP. **-बीजः** quicksilver. **-भद्रः** a restive elephant, an elephant in rut. **-भद्रा** N. of a river flowing into the Krishṇâ. **-वेणा** N. of a river. **-शेखरः** a mountain.

तुंगी 1 Night. 2 Turmeric. -COMP. **-ईशः** 1 the moon. 2 the sun. 3 an epithet of Śiva. 4 an epithet of Krishṇa. **-पतिः** the moon.

तुच्छ *a.* 1 Empty, void, vain, light. 2 Small, little, trifling. 3 Abandoned, deserted. 4 Low, mean, insignificant, contemptible, worthless. 5 Poor, miserable, wretched. **-च्छं** Chaff. -COMP. **-द्रुः** the castor-oil tree. **-धान्यः, -धान्यकः** straw, chaff.

तुंजः Indra's thunderbolt.

तुटुमः A mouse or rat.

तुण् 6. P. (तुणति) 1 To curve, make crooked, bend. 2 To act fraudulently, deceive.

तुंडं 1 Mouth, face, beak, snout (of a hog); तुंडैराताम्रकुटिलैः (शुकाः) Kâv. 2. 9. 2 The trunk of an elephant. 3 The point of an instrument.

तुंडिः 1 Face, mouth. 2 A beak. **-डिः** *f.* The navel.

तुंडिन् *m.* N. of the bull of Śiva.

तुंडिभ see तुंदिभ.

तुंडिल *a.* 1 Talkative, loquacious. 2 Having a prominet navel. 3 Talking severely; cf. तुंदिल.

तुत्थः 1 Fire. 2 A stone. **-त्थं** Sulphate of copper usually applied to the eyes as a sort of collyrium or medical ointment. **-त्था** 1 Small cardamoms. 2 The indigo plant. -COMP **-अंजनं** blue vitriol applied to the eyes as medical ointment.

तुद् 6. P. (तुदति, तुन्न) 1 To strike, wound, hit; तुतोद गदया चारिं Bk. 14. 81; 15. 37; *Si.* 20. 77. 2 To prick, goad. 3 To bruise, hurt. 4 To pain, vex, torment, afflict; सुतीक्ष्णधारापतनोग्रसायकैस्तुदंति चेतः प्रसभं प्रवासिना Rs. 2. 4, 6. 28. -WITH आ to strike, beat; Ms. 4. 68. -प्र to strike, hurt, wound. (*-Caus*). to urge on, drive forward; (fig.) to press, urge repeatedly (to do a thing); प्रविश गृहमिति प्रतोद्यमाना न चलति भाग्यकृतां दशामवेक्ष्य Mk. 1. 56.

तुंदं The belly, a corpulent or protuberant belly. -COMP. **-कूपिका, -कूपी** the cavity of the navel. **-परिमार्ज, -परिमृज, -मृज** *a.* lazy, sluggish.

तुंदवत् *a.* Corpulent, fat.

तुंदिक, तुंदिन्, तुंदिभ, तुंदिल *a.* 1 Having a protuberant belly. 2 Corpulent. 3 Filled or laden with; मकरंदतुंदिलानामरविंदानामयं महामान्यः Bv. 1. 6.

तुन्न *a.* 1 Struck, hurt, wounded. 2 Toormented. -COMP. **-वायः** a tailor; Ms. 4. 214.

तुभ् 4. 9. P. (तुभ्यति, तुभ्नाति) To hurt, injure, strike, Bk. 17. 79, 90.

तुमुल *a.* Tumultuous, noisy, Bg. 1. 13, 19. 2 Fierce, raging; R. 3. 57. 3 Excited. 4 Perplexed, confused; R. 5. 49. **—*m.*, *-n.*** 1 An uproar, tumult. 2 A confused combat, melêe.

तुंबः A kind of gourd.

तुंबरः N. of a Gandharva; see तुंबरु. **-रं** A kind of musical instrument.

तुंबा 1 A kind of long gourd. 2 A milch cow.

तुंबिः, बी *f.* A sort of gourd; न हि तुंबीफलविकलो वीणादंडः प्रयाति महिमानं Bv. 1. 80.

तुंब (बु) रुः N. of a Gandharva.

तुरगः 1 A horse; तुरगखुरहतस्तथा हि रेणुः *S.* 1. 31; R. 1. 42, 3. 51. 2 The mind, thought. **—गी** A mare. -COMP. **आरोहः** a horseman. **-उपचारकः** a groom. **-प्रियः -यं** barley. **—ब्रह्मचर्यं** forced or compulsory celibacy, leading a life of celibacy simply in consequence of the absence of the female society.

तुरगिन् *m.* A horseman.

तुरंगः A horse; भानुःसकृद्युक्ततुरंग एव *S.* 5. 5; R. 3. 38, 13. 3. **—गं** The mind, thought. **—गी** A mare. —COMP. **-अरिः** A buffalo. **-द्विषणी** a she-buffalo. **—प्रियः —यं** barley. **-मेधः** a horse-sacrifice; R. 13. 61. **—यायिन्, —सादिन्** *m.* a horseman. **-वक्त्रः, -वदनः** a Kinnara. **-शाला, —स्थानं** a horse-stable **—स्कंधः** a troops of horses.

तुरंगमः A horse; R. 3. 63, 9. 72.

तुरायणं 1 Non-attachment to any object or pursuit (असंग). 2 A kind of sacrifice.

तुरासाह् *m.* (Nom. sing. तुराषाट् ड्) N. of Indra; Ku. 2. 1; R. 15. 40.

तुरी 1 The fibrous stick used by weavers to clear and separate the threads of the woof. **2** A shuttle: तद्भटचातुरीतुरी N. 1. 12. **3** A painter's brush.

तुरीय *a*. The fourth. —यं **1** A quarter, a fourth part, fourth. (In Vedânta phil.). **2** The fourth state of the soul in which it becomes one with Brahman or the Supreme spirit. —COMP. —**वर्णः** a man of the fourth caste, a Súdra.

तुरुष्कः (pl.) N. of the Turks.

तुर्य *a*. Fourth; N. 4. 123. -**र्यं 1** A quarter, a fourth part. **2** (In Vedânta phil.) The fourth state of the soul in which it becomes one with Brahman.

तुल् 1 P., 10 U. (तोलति, तोलयति-ते, also तुलयति-ते which some suppose to be a denominative from तुला). **1** To weigh, measure. **2** To weigh in the mind, ponder, consider. **3** To raise, lift up; केलासे तुलिते Mv 5. 37; पौलस्त्यतिलस्याद्रेरादधान इव ह्रियं R. 4. 80, 12. 89; Si. 15. 30. **4** To bear up, hold up, support; पृथिवीतले तुलितभूभृदुच्यसे Si. 15. 30, 61. **5** To compare, liken (with instr.); मुखं श्लेष्मागारं तदपि च शशांकेन तुलितं Bh. 3. 20; Si. 8. 12. **6** To match, be equal to (with acc.); प्रासादास्त्वां तुलयितुमलं यत्र तैस्तैर्विशेषैः Me. 64. **7** To make light of, condemn, despise; अंतःसारं घन तुलयितुं नानिलः शक्ष्यति त्वां Me. 20 (where तु° also means 'to bear up or carry away'); Si. 15. 30. **8** To suspect, examine with distrust; कः श्रद्धास्यति भूतार्थं सर्वो मां तुलयिष्यति Mk. 3. 24, 5. 43 (where some editions read तूलयिष्यति for तुलयिष्यति). **9** To try, put to the test, reduce to a wreched state; हा अवस्थे तुलयसि Mk. 1 (तुलयासे). —With **उद्** to bear up, support, poise.

तुलनं 1 Weight. **2** Lifting. **3** Comparing, likening, &c. -**ना 1** Comparison. **2** Weighing. **3** Lifting, raising. **4.** Rating, assessing, estimating. **5** Examining.

तुलसी The holy basil held in veneration by the Hindus, especially by the worshippers of Vishṇu. -COMP. -**पत्रं** (lit.) a Tulasî leaf; (fig.) a very small gift. -**विवाहः** the marriage of an image of Bâlakrishṇa with the holy basil performed on the 12th day of the bright half of Kârtika.

तुला 1 A balance or the beam of a balance; तुलया धृ to hold in a balance, to weigh. **2** A measure, weight. **3** Weighing. **4** Resemblance, likeness, equality, similarity (with gen., instr. or in comp.); किं धूर्जटेरिव तुलामुपयाति संख्ये Ve. 3. 8; तुलां यदारोहति दंतवाससा Ku. 5. 34; R. 8. 15 सद्यः परस्परतुलामधिरोहतां द्वे R. 5. 68, 19. 8, 50. **5** Libra, the seventh sign of the zodiac; जयति तुलामधिरूढो भास्वानपि जलदपटलानि Pt. 1. 330. **6** A sloping beam or timber in the roof of a house. **7** A measure of gold or silver equal to 100 *palas*. -COMP. -**कूटः** a false weight. -**कोटिः,-टी** an ornament (an anklet or नूपुर) worn on the feet by women; लीलाचलस्त्रीचरणारुणोत्पलस्खलत्तुलाकोटिनिनादकोमलः Si. 12. 44. -**कोशः,-षः** ordeal by weighing. -**दानं** the gift to a Brâhmaṇa of as much gold or silver as equals the weight of one's body. -**धटः** the scale of a balance. -**धरः 1** a trader, merchant. **2** the sign Libra of the zodiac.-**धारः** a dealer, trader or merchant. -**परीक्षा** ordeal by the balance. -**पुरुषः** gold, jewels or other valuable things equal to a man's weight (given to a Brâhmaṇa as a gift); cf. तुलादान. -**प्रग्रहः,-प्रग्राहः** the string or beam of a balance. **यानं,-यष्टिः** the beam of a balance. **वीजं** the berry of the Gunjâ plant. -**सूत्रं** the string of a balance.

तुलित *p. p.* **1** Weighed, counterpoised. **2** Compared, likened, equalled; Bh. 3. 36; see तुल्.

तुल्य *a*. **1** Of the same kind or class, well-matched, similar, like, resembling (with gen. or instr. or in comp.); Ms. 4. 86; Y. 2. 77; R. 2. 35, 12. 80, 18, 38. **2** Fit for. **3** Identical, same. **4** Indifferent.-COMP. -**दर्शन** *a*. regarding with the same or indifferent eyes. —**पानं** drinking together, compotation. -**योगिता** (in Rhet.) a figure of speech, a combination of several objects having the same attribute, the objects being either all relevant or all irrelevant; नियतानां सकृद्धर्मः सा पुनस्तुल्ययोगिता K. P. 10 cf. Chandr. 5. 41. -**रूप** *a*. like, similar, analogous.

तुवर *a*. **1** Astringent. **2** Beardless; also तूवर.

तुष् 4 P. (तुष्यति, तुष्ट) To be pleased or satisfied, be contented or delighted with anything (usually with instr.) रत्नैर्महार्हैस्तुतुषुर्न देवाः Bh. **2.** 80, Ms. 3. 207; Bg. 2. 55; Bk. 2. 13, 15. 8; R. 3. 62. —*Caus.* (तोषयति-ते) To please, gratify, satisfy. —With **परि** to be satisfied, be delighted or contented; वयमिह परितुष्टा वल्कलैस्त्वं च लक्ष्म्या Bh. 3. 50; अस्मत्कृते च परितुष्यति काचिदन्या 2. 2. —**सं** to be pleased, satisfied or contented; संतुष्टो भार्यया भर्ता भर्त्रा भार्या तथैव च Ms. 3. 60; Bh. 3. **5**; Bg. 3. 17

तुषः The husk or chaff of grain; अजानतार्थं तत्सर्वं (अध्ययनं) तुषाणां कंडनं यथा; Ms. 4 78. -COMP. -**अग्निः, -अनलः** fire of the chaff or husk of corn. -**अंबु** *n*., -**उदकं** sour rice-gruel or barley-gruel. -**ग्रहः, -मारः** fire.

तुषार *a*. Cold, frigid, frosty or dewy; Si. 9. 7; अपां हि तृप्ताय न वारिधारा स्वादुः सुगंधिः स्वदते तुषारा N. 3. 93. -**रः 1** Frost, cold. **2** Ice, snow; Ku. 1. 6; Rs. 4. 1. **3** Dew; R. 14. 84; S. 5. 19. **4** Mist, thin rain, spray, especially of cold water; पृक्तस्तुषारैर्गिरिनिर्झराणां R. **2.** 13; 9. 68. **5** A kind of camphor. —COMP. —**अद्रिः, -गिरिः, -पर्वतः** the Himâlaya mountain; तुषाराद्रिवाताः Me. 107. -**कणः** a dew-drop, an icicle, hoar-frost. -**कालः** winter. -**किरणः, -रश्मिः** the moon; Amaru. 49; Si. 9. 27. -**गौरः** *a*. **1** white as snow. **2** white with snow. (-**रः**) camphor.

तुषिताः (pl.) A class of subordinate deities, said to be 12 or 36 in number.

तुष्ट *p. p.* **1** Pleased, satisfied, delighted, gratified, contented. **2** Contented with what one possesses and indifferent to everything else.

तुष्टिः *f*. **1** Satisfaction, gratification, pleasure, contentment. **2** (In Sân. phil.) Acquiescence, indifference to everything except that which is possessed.

तुष्टुः A jewel worn in the ear.

तुस्=तुष् q. v.

तुहिन *a*. Cold, frigid. -**नं 1** Snow, ice. **2** Dew or frost; तृणाग्रलग्नैस्तुहिनैः पतद्भिः Rs. 4. 7, 3. 15. **3** Moonlight. **4** Camphor. -COMP. -**अंशुः, -करः, -किरणः, -द्युतिः, -रश्मिः 1** the moon; Si. 9. 30. **2** Camphor. —**अचलः,** —**अद्रिः,** —**शैलः** the Himâlaya mountain; R. 8. 54. -**कणः** a dew-drop; Amaru. 54. -**शर्करा** ice.

तूण् I. 10 U. (तूणयति-ते) To contract. —II. 10 A. (तूणयते) To fill, fill up.

तूणः A quiver; मिलितशिलीमुखपाटलिपटलकृतस्मरतूणविलासे Git. 1; R. 7. 57. -COMP. -**धारः** an archer.

तूणी, तूणीर, A quiver; R. 9. 56.

तूबरः 1 A beardless man. **2** A bull without horns. **3** Astringent flavour. **4** A eunuch.

तूर् 4 A (तूर्यते, तूर्ण) **1** To go quickly, make haste. **2** To hurt, kill.

तूरं A kind of musical instrument.

तूर्ण *a*. Quick, rapid, expeditious. **2** Fleet. -**र्णः** Rapidity, quickness. -**र्णं** *ind*. Quickly, speedily; चूर्णमानीयतां तूर्णं पूर्णचंद्रनिभानने Subhâsh.

तूर्यः -र्यं A kind of musical instrument; Ms. 7. 225; Ku. 7. 10. -COMP. -**ओघः** a band of instrument.

तूलः —लं Cotton. —**लं 1** The atmosphere, sky, air. **2** A tuft of grass. **3** The mulberry. -**ला 1** The cotton tree. **2** The wick of a lamp. -**ली 1** Cotton **2** The wick of a lamp. **3** A weaver's fibrous stick or brush. **4** A painter's brush. **5** The indigo plant. –COMP. **–कार्मुकं, –धनुस्** *n.* a cotton-bow; *i.e*, a bow used for cleaning cotton. **—पिचुः** cotton. **–शर्करा** a seed of the cotton plant.

तूलकं Cotton.

तूलिः *f.* A painter's brush.

तूलिका 1 A painter's brush, a pencil; उन्मीलितं तूलिकयेव चित्रं Ku. 1. 32. **2** A wick of cotton either for a lamp or for applying unguents. **3** A matress filled with cotton, a down or cotton-bed. **4** A boaring instrument, probing-rod.

तूष्णीक *a.* Silent, taciturn.

तूष्णीं *ind.* In silence, silently, quietly, without speaking or noise; किं भवांस्तूष्णीमास्ते V. 2; न योत्स्य इति गोविंदमुक्त्वा तूष्णीं बभूव ह Bg. **2.** 9. –COMP. **–भावः** silence, taciturnity. **–शील:** *a.* silent, taciturn.

तूस्तं 1 Matted hair. **2** Dust. **3** Sin. **4** An atom, any minute particle.

तृंह 6 P. (तृंहति) To kill, hurt; see तृह्.

तृणं 1 Grass in general; किं जीर्णं तृणमत्ति मानमहतामग्रेसरः केसरी Bh. 2. 29. **2** A blade of grass, reed, straw. **3** Anything made of straw (as a mat for sitting); often used as a symbol of worthlessness; तृणमिव लघुलक्ष्मीर्नैव तान्संरुणद्धि Bh. **2.** 17; see तृणीकृ also. —COMP. **–अग्निः 1** a fire of chaff or straw; Ms. 3. 168. **2** fire quickly extinguished. **–अंजनः** a chameleon. **–अटवी** a forest abounding in grass. **—आवर्तः** a whirlwind. **—असृज्** *n.*, **–कुंकुमं, –गौरं** a variety of perfume. **–इन्द्रः** the palmyra tree. **–उल्का** a torch of hay, a fire brand made of straw. **–ओकस्** *n.* a hut of straw. **–कांडः, –डं** a heap of grass, **–कुटी, –कुटीरकं** a hut of straw. **–केतुः** the palmyra tree. **—गोधा** a kind of chameleon. **—ग्राहिन्** *m.* sapphire. **—चरः** a kind of gem (गोमेद). **–जलायुका, –जलूका** a caterpillar. **–द्रुमः 1** the palm tree. **2** Cocoanut tree. **3** the bebelnut tree. **4** the Ketaka tree. **5** the date-tree. **–धान्यं** grain growing wild or without cultivation. **—ध्वजः 1** the palmyra tree. **2** a bamboo. **–पीडं** hand-to-hand fighting. **—पूली** a mat, seat made of reeds. **–प्राय** *a.* worth a straw, worthless, insignificant. **–बिंदुः** N. of a sage; R. 8. 79. **–मणिः** a sort of gem (amber). **–मत्कुणः** a bail or surety (perhaps wrong reading for ऋणमत्कुण). **–राजः 1** the cocoa-nut tree. **2** the bamboo. **3** the sugarcane. **4** the palmyra tree. **–वृक्षः 1** the palm tree. **2** the date-tree. **3** the cocoa-nut tree. **4** the areca-nut tree. **–शीतं** a kind of fragrant grass. **–सारा** the plantain tree. **–सिंहः** an axe. **–हर्म्यः** a house of straw.

तृण्या A heap of grass or straw.

तृतीय *a.* The third. **–यं** A third part. –COMP. **–प्रकृतिः** *m.* or *f.* a eunuch.

तृतीयक *a.* Recurring every third day, tertian (as a fever).

तृतीया 1 The third day of a lunar fort-night. **2** (In gram.) The instrumental case or its terminations. –COMP. **–कृत** *a.* thrice ploughed (as a field). **—तत्पुरुषः** the instrumental Tatpurusha. **—प्रकृतिः** *m. f.* a eunuch.

तृतीयिन् *a.* Entitled to a third portion (of inheritance. &c.).

तृद् 1 P., 7 U. (तर्दति, तृणत्ति, तृंते, तृण्ण) **1** To cleave, split, pierce. **2** To kill, destroy, annihilate; Bk. 6. 38, 14. 33, 108; 15. 36, 44. **3** To set free. **4** To disregard.

तृप् 1. 4. 5. 6. P. तृप्यति, तृप्नोति, तृपति, तृप्त) **1** To become satisfied, be pleased or contented; अद्य तर्प्स्यति मांसादाः Bk. 16. 29; प्राशीन्न चातृपत् क्रूरः 15. 29; (usually with instr.; but sometimes with gen. or loc. also); को न तृप्यति वित्तेन H. 2. 174; तृप्तस्तत्पिशितेन Bh. 2. 34; नाग्निस्तृप्यति काष्ठानां नापगानां महोदधिः। नांतकः सर्वभूतानां न पुंसां वामलोचनाः॥ Pt. 1. 137; तस्मिन्हि तत्पुर्देवास्तते यज्ञे Mb. **2** To please, gratify,—*Caus.* To gratify, please.–*Desid.* तितृप्सति, तितर्पिषति. –II. 1 P., 10 U., (तर्पति, तर्पयति-ते) **1** To light up, kindle. **2** (Atm.) To be satisfied.

तृप्त *a.* Satiated, satisfied, contented.

तृप्ति *f.* Satisfaction, contentment; R. 2. 39, 73; 3. 3; Ms. 3. 271; Bg. 10. 18. **2** Satiety, disgust. **3** Pleasure, gratification.

तृष् 4. P (तृष्यति, तृषित) **1** To be thirsty; Bk. 7. 106, 14. 30; 15. 51. **2** To wish, wish excessively, be eager or greedy.

तृष् *f.* (nom. sing. तृट्-ड्) **1** thirst; तृषा शुष्यत्यास्ये पिबति सलिलं स्वादु सुरभि Bh. 3. 92; Rs. 1. 11. **2** strong desire, eagerness.

तृषा See तृष् –COMP. **–आर्त** *a.* suffering from thirst, thirsty. **–हं** water.

तृषित *p. p.* **1** Thisty; Ghaṭ. 9; Rs. 1. 18. **2** Greedy, thirsting for, desirous of gain.

तृष्णज् *a.* Covetous, greedy, thirsting.

तृष्णा 1 Thirst (lit. and fig.); तृष्णां छिनत्त्यात्मनः H. 1. 171; Rs. 1. 15. **2** Desire, strong desire, greed, avidity, desire of gain; तृष्णां छिंद्धि Bh. **2.** 77, 3. 5; R. **8.** 2. –COMP. **–क्षयः** cessation of desire, tranquility of mind, contentment.

तृष्णालु *a.* Very thirsty.

तृह् 7. P., 10 U. (तृणेढि, तर्हयति-ते, तृढ *desid.* तितृक्षति, तितृंहिषति) To injure. hurt, kill; strike; न तृणेह्मीति लोकोऽयं बिंत्ते मां निष्पराक्रमं Bk. 6. 39; (तानि) तृणेढु रामः सह लक्ष्मणेन 1. 19.

तॄ 1 P. (तरति, तीर्ण) **1** To cross over, cross; केनोडुपेन परलोकनदीं तरिष्ये Mk. 8. 23; स तीर्त्वा कपिशां R. 4. 38; **Ms.** 4. 77. **2** To cross over, traverse (as a way); Ku. 7. 48; Me. 18. **3** To float, swim; शिला तरिष्यत्युदके न पर्णं Bk. 12. 77. **4** To get over, surmount, overcome, overpower; धीरा हि तरंत्यापदं K. 175; कृच्छ्रं महत्तीर्णः R. 14. 6; Bg. 18. 58; **Ms. 11.** 34. **5** To go to the end of, master completely; R. **3.** 30. **6** To fulfil, accomplish, perform (as a promise); दैवात्तीर्णप्रतिज्ञः Mu. 4. 12. **7** To be saved or rescued, escape from; गावो वर्षभयात्तीर्णा वयं तीर्णा महाभयात् Hariv. *–Pass.* (तीर्यते) To be crossed &c. *–Caus.* (तारयति-ते) **1** To carry or lead over. **2** To cause to arrive at. **3** To save, rescue, liberate. *–Desid.* (तितीर्षति तितरिषति, तितरीषति) To wish to cross &c.; दोर्भ्यां तितीर्षति तरंगवतीभुजंगं K. P. 10. –WITH **अति 1** to cross over. **2** to surmount, overcome; Bg. 13. 25; H. **4.** **–अव 1** to descend, alight; रथादवततार च R. 1. 54, 13. 68; Me. 50. **2** to flow or run into; सागरं वर्जयित्वा कुत्र वा महानद्यवतरति *S.* 3. **3** to enter, enter into, come to; M. 1. 22; *Si.* 9. 32. **4** to get over, subdue, overcome. **5** to descend (as a deity) into the world of mortals in the form of a mortal; cf. अवतार (*–Caus*). to bring or fetch down, set down, R. 1. 34. **–उद् 1** to pass out of (water), disembark, to rise from; R. **2.** 17; *Si.* **8.** 63 **2** to pass or cross over; उदतारिषुरंभोधिं Bk. 15. 33; 10; R. 12. 71. 16. 33; Me. 47. **3** to subdue, overcome, get over; व्यसनमहार्णवादुत्तीर्णं Mk. 10. 49; so रोगोत्तीर्ण. **–निस् 1** to cross over; Bh. 3. 4. **2** to fulfil, accomplish, attain. **3** to pass or get over, surmount, overcome; R 3. 7. **4** to complete, go to the end; R. 14. 21. **–प्र** to cross over. (*–Cause*). to cheat, deceive; मां तथा प्रतार्य *S.* 5; किंत्वेवं कविभिः प्रतारितमनास्तत्त्वं विजानन्नपि Bh. 1 78. **–वि 1** to cross or pass over, go beyond; R. 6. 77. **2** to give, grant, impart, confer or bestow on, vouchsafe, favour with; भगवान् मारीचस्ते दर्शनं वितरति *S.* 7; वितरति गुरुः प्राज्ञे विद्यां यथैव तथा जडे U. 2. 4; निवासहेतोरुटजं वितेरुः R. 14. 81; Mâl. 1. 3. **3** to cause, produce; ज्योत्स्नाशंकामिह वितरति हंसश्रेणी Ki. 5. 31;

Gît. 1. **4** to carry over. **–व्यति** to cross, get over, overcome. **–सं 1** to cross over. **2** to swim, float. **3** to get over, overcome, go to the end of.

तेजनं 1 A bamboo. **2** Sharpening, whetting. **3** Kindling. **4** Rendering bright. **5** Polishing. **6** A reed. **7** The point of an arrow, the edge of a weapon.

तेजलः The francoline partridge.

तेजस् *n.* **1** sharpness. **2** The sharp edge (of a knife &c.) **3** The point or top of a flame. **4** Heat, glow, glare. **5** Lustre, light, brilliance, splendour; R. 4. 1; Bg. **7.** 9, 10. 30, **6** Heat or light considered as the third of the five elements of creation (the other four being; पृथिवी, अप्, वायु and आकाश). **7** The bright appearance of the hnman body, beauty; R. **3.** 15. **8** Fire of energy; *S.* 2. 14, U. **6.** 14. **9** Might, prowess, strength, courage, valour, martial or heroic lustre; तेजस्तेजसि शाम्यतु U. 5. **10** One possessed of heroic lustre; तेजसां हि न वयः समीक्ष्यते R. 11. 1. **11** Spirit, energy. **12** Strength of character, not bearing insult or ill-treatment with impunity. **13** Majestic lustre, majesty, dignity, authority, consequence; तेजोविशेषानुमितां (राजलक्ष्मीं) दधानः R. 2. 7. **14** Semen, seed, semen virile; स्याद्रक्षणीयं यदि मे न तेजः R. 14. 65; R. 2. 75; दुष्यंतेनाहितं तेजो दधानां भूतये भुवः *S.* 4. 1. **15** The essential nature of anything. **16** Essence, quintessence. **17** Spiritual, moral, or magical power. **18** Fire. **19** Marrow. **20** Bile. **21** The speed of a horse. **22** Fresh butter. **23** Gold. –Comp. **–कर** *a.* **1** illuminating. **2** granting vital power or strength. **–भंगः 1** disgrace, destruction of dignity. **2** depression, discouragement. **–मंडलं** a halo of light. **–मूर्तिः** the sun. **–रूपः** the Supreme Spirit, Brahman.

तेजस्वत्, तेजोवत् *a.* **1** Bright, brilliant, splendid. **2** Sharp, pungent. **3** Brave, heroic. **4** Energetic.

तेजस्विन् *a.* (**नी** *f.*) **1** Brilliant, bright. **2** Powerful, heroic, strong; Ki. 16. 16. **3** Dignified, noble. **4** Famous, illustrious. **5** Violent. **6** Haughty. **7** Lawful.

तेजित् *a.* **1** Sharpened, whetted. **2** Excited, stimulated, prompted.

तेजोमय *a.* **1** Glorious. **2** Bright, brilliant, luminous; Bg. 11. 47.

तेमः Becoming wet or moist, moisture.

तेमनं 1 Wetting, moistening, **2** Moisture. **3** Sauce, condiment.

तेवनं 1 Play, pastime. **2** A pleasure-garden, play-ground.

तैजस *a.* (**सी** *f.*) **1** Bright, splendid, luminous. **2** Made up or consisting of light; तैजसस्य धनुषः प्रवृत्तये R. **11. 43.** **3** Metallic. **4** Passionate **5** Vigorous, energetic. **6** Powerful, intense. **–सं** Ghee. Comp. **–आवर्तनी** a crucible.

तैतिक्ष *a.* (**क्षी** *f.*) Patient, enduring.

तैतिरः A partridge.

तैतिलः 1 A rhinoceros. **2** A god.

तैत्तिरः 1 A partridge. **2** A rhinoceros. **–रं** A flock of partridge. **5.**

तैत्तिरीय *m.* pl. The followers of the Taittirîya school of the Yajurveda. **–यः** the Taittirîya branch of the Yajurveda (कृष्णयुजर्वेद).

तैमिरः A disease of the eyes (dimness).

तैर्थिकः *a.* Sacred, holy. **–कः 1** An ascetic. **2** One who propounds a new religious or philosophical doctrine. **–कं** Holy water (such as that brought from a sacred bathing place).

तैलं 1 Oil; लभेत सिकतासु तैलमपि यत्नतः पीडयन् Bh. 2. 5; Y. 1. 283; R. 8. 38. **2** Benzoin. –Comp. **–अटी** a wasp. **–अभ्यंगः** amointing the body with oil. **–कल्कजः** oil-cake. **–पर्णिका, –पर्णी 1** sandal. **2** insense. **3** turpentine. **–पिंजः** the white sesamum. **–पिपीलिका** the small red ant. **–फलः** the Ingudî tree. **–भाविनी** Jasmine. **–माली** the wick of a lamp. **–यंत्रं** an oil-mill. **–स्फटिकः** a kind of gem.

तैलंगः N. of a country, the modern Carnatic. **–गाः** (*pl.*) The people of this country.

तैलिकः, तैलिन् *m.* An oilman, an oil-grinder or manufacturer.

तैलिनी The wick of a lamp.

तैलीनं A field of sesamum.

तैषः N. of the lunar month Pausha.

तोकं An offspring, a child.

तोककः The Châtaka bird.

तोडनं 1 Splitting, dividing. **2** Tearing. **3** Hurting, injuring.

तोत्त्रं A goad for driving cattle or elephants.

तोदः Pain, anguish, torture.

तोदनं 1 Pain, anguish. **2** A goad. **3** Face, mouth (तुंड).

तोमरः, –रं 1 An iron club. **2** A javelin. –Comp. **–धरः** fire (considered as a deity).

तोयं Water; *S.* 7. 12. –Comp. **–अधिवासिनी** trumpet-flower. **–आधारः –आशयः** a lake, well, any reservoir of water; तोयाधारपथाश्च वल्कलशिखानिष्यंदरेखांकिताः *S.* 1. 14. **–आलयः** the ocean, sea. **–ईशः** an epithet of Varuṇa. (**–शं**) the constellation called पूर्वाषाढा. **–उत्सर्गः** discharge of water, raining; Me. **37.** **–कर्मन्** *n.* **1** ablutions of various parts of the body performed with water. **2** libations of water to the deceased. **–कृच्छ्रः, –च्छ्रं** a kind of penance, drinking nothing but water for a fixed period. **–क्रीडा** sporting in water; Me. 33. **–गर्भः** the cocoa-nut. **–चरः** an aquatic animal. **–डिंबः, –भः** hail. **–दः** a cloud; R. 6. 65; V. 1. 14. °**अत्ययः** the autumn. **–धरः** a cloud. **–धिः, –निधिः** the ocean. **–नीवी** the earth. **–प्रसादनं** the clearing-nut tree, or its nut; see अंबुप्रसादन, कतक. **–मलं** seafoam. **–मुच्** *m.* a cloud. **–यंत्रं 1** a water-clock. **2** an artificial jet or fountain of water. **–राज्, –राशिः** the ocean. **–वेला** the edge of water, shore. **–व्यतिकरः** confluence (as of rivers); R. 8. 95. **–शुक्तिका** an oyster. **–सर्पिका, –सूचकः** a frog.

तोरणः, –णं 1 An arched doorway, a portal. **2** An outer door or gateway; गणो नृपाणामथ तोरणाद् बहिः *Si.* 12. 1. दूराल्लक्ष्यं सुरपतिधनुश्चारुणा तोरणेन **Me. 75. 3** Any temporary and ornamental arch; Ku. 7. 3; R. 1. 41, 7. 4, 11. 5. **4** An elevated place near a bathing-place **–णं** The neck, throat.

तोलः, –लं 1 Weight or quantity measured by the balance. **2** A weight of gold or silver equal to 12 *Máshas* or a tolâ.

तोषः Satisfaction, contentment, pleasure, delight.

तोषणं Satisfaction, contentment. **2** Anything that gives satisfaction, gratification.

तोषलं A club (मुसल).

तौक्षिकः The sign Sagittarius of the zodiac (a word borrowed from Greek).

तौतिकः The pearl-oyster. **–कं** A pearl.

तौर्यं The sound of musical instruments. –Comp. **–त्रिकं** the union of song, dance, or instrumental music, triple symphony; तौर्यत्रिकं बुधाष्टचा च कामजो दशको गणः **Ms.** 7. 47; U. 4.

तौलं A balance.

तौलिकः, तौलिकिकः A painter.

त्यक्त *p.p.* **1** Abandoned, forsaken, left, quitted. **2** Resigned, surrenderd. **3** Shunned, avoided; see त्यज्. —Comp. **—अग्निः** a Brâhmaṇa who has given up household fire. **–जीवित, –प्राण** *a.* ready to abandon life, willing to run any risk; मदर्थे त्यक्तजीविताः Bg. 1. 9. **—लज्ज** *a.* shameless.

त्यज् 1. P. (त्यजति, त्यक्त) **1** To leave (in all senses); abandon, quit, go away from; वर्त्म भानोस्त्यजाशु Me. 39; Ms. 6. 77, 9. 177; *S.* 5. 26. **2** To let go, dismiss, discharge; Bk. 6. 122. **3** To give up, renounce, resign, surrender; Bh. 3. 16; Ms. 2. 95, 6. 33; Bg. 6. **24,** 16. 21. **4** To shun, avoid. **5** To get rid of, free oneself from; Bg. 2. 3. **6** To set aside, disregard; त इमेऽवस्थिता युद्धे प्राणांस्त्यक्त्वा धनानि च Bg. 1. 33. **7** To except. **8** To distribute, give away ; कृतं (संचयं) आश्वयुजे त्यजत् Y. 3. 47 ; Ms. 6. 15. –*Caus.* To cause to give up, &c. –*Desid.* (तित्यक्षति) To wish to leave, &c. –WITH परि 1 to leave, quit, abandon. 2 to resign, give up, discard, renounce ; प्रारब्धमुत्तमगुणा न परित्यजंति Mu. 2 17. 3 to except ; तृणमप्यपरित्यज्य सतृणं. –सं 1 to abandon ; जायामदोषामुत संत्यजामि R. 14. 34. 2 to avoid, shun ; Bh. 1. 81. 3 to give up, renounce ; Ms. 4. 181. 4 to except ; *e. g* , संत्यज्य विक्रमादित्यं धैर्यमन्यत्र दुर्लभं Râj. T. 3. 343.

त्यागः 1 Leaving, forsaking, abandoning, deserting, separation ; न माता न पिता न स्त्री न पुत्रस्त्यागमर्हति Ms. 8. 319, 9. 78. 2 Giving up, resigning, renouncing ; Ms. 11. 112 ; Bg. 12. 41. 3 Gift, donation, giving away as charity ; करे श्लाघ्यस्त्यागः Bh. 2. 65 ; H. 1. 154 ; त्यागाय संभृतार्थानां R. 1. 17. 4 Liberality, generosity ; R. 1. 22. 5 Secretion, excretion. –COMP. –युत, –शील *a.* liberal, generous, munificant.

त्यागिन् *a.* 1 Leaving, abandoning, giving up, &c. 2 Giving away, donor. 3 Heroic, brave. 4 One who does not look to any reward or result from the performance of ceremonial rites ; यस्तु कर्मफलत्यागी सत्यागीत्यभिधीयते Bg. 18. 11.

त्रप् 1 A (त्रपते, त्रपित) To be ashamed or abashed, be embarrassed; त्रपंते तीर्थानि त्वरितमिह यस्योद्धृतिविधौ G. L. 28. –WITH अप to turn away or retire through shame ; तस्माद्वलैरपत्रेपे Bk. 14. 84 ; येनापत्रपते साधुरसाधुस्तेन तुष्यति Mb.

त्रपा 1 Bashfulness, modesty ; मंदत्रपाभर Git. 12. 2 Shame (in a good or bad sense). 3 A libidinous or unchaste woman. 4 Fame, celebrity. –COMP. निरस्त, हीन *a.* shameless, impudent. –रंडा a harlot.

त्रपिष्ठ *a.* (Superl. of तृप्र) Highly satisfied.

त्रपीयस् *a.* (सी *f.*) (Compar. of तृप्र) More satisfied.

त्रपु *n.* Tin ; यदि मणिस्त्रपुणि प्रतिबध्यते Pt. 1. 75.

त्रपुलं, –ष, –त्रपुस् *n.*, –सं Tin.

त्रप्स्यं Diluted curds.

त्रय *a.* (यी *f.*) Triple, three-fold, divided into three parts of three kinds ; त्रयी वै विद्या ऋचो यजूंषि सामानि *S*at. Br. ; Ms. 1. 23. –यं A triad, a group or collection of three ; अदेयमासीत्त्रयमेव भूपते शशिप्रभं छत्रमुभे च चामरे R. 3. 16 ; लोकत्रयं Bg. 11. 20, 43 ; Ms. 2. 76.

त्रयस् (Nom. pl. *m.* of त्रि, entering into comp. with some numerals) Three. –COMP. –त्त्वारिंश *a.* forty-third. –त्त्वारिंशत् *a.* or *f.* forty-three. –त्रिंश *a.* thirty-third. –त्रिंशत् *a.* or *f.* thirty-three. –दश *a.* 1 thirteenth. 2 having thirteen added; त्रयोदशं शतं 'one hundred and thirteen'. –दशन् *a. pl.* thirteen. –दशम *a.* thirteenth. –दशी the thirteenth day of a lunar fortnight. –नवतिः *f.* ninety-three. –पंचाशत् *f.* fifty-three. –विंश *a.* 1 twenty-third. 2 consisting of twenty-three. –विंशतिः *f.* twenty-three. –षष्टिः *f.* sixty-three. –सप्ततिः *f.* seventy-three.

त्रयी 1 The three Vedas taken collectively (ऋग्यजुः सामानि); त्रयीमयाय त्रिगुणात्मने नमः K. 1. तौ त्रयीवर्जमितरा विद्याः परिपाठितौ U. 2; Ms. 4. 125. 2 A triad, triplet; व्यद्योतिष्ट सभावेद्यामसौ नरशिखित्रयी *S*i. 2. 3. 3 A matron or married woman whose husband and children are living. 4 Intellect, understanding. –COMP. –तनुः 1 an epithet of the sun; so त्रयीमयः. 2 an epithet of *S*iva. –धर्मः the duty enjoined by the three Vedas; Bg. 9. 21. –मुखः a Brâhmaṇa.

त्रस् I. 1. 4. P. (त्रसति, त्रस्यति, त्रस्त) 1 To quake, tremble, shake, start with fear. 2 To fear, dread, be afraid of (with abl., sometimes with gen. or instr.); प्रमदवनात्त्रस्यति K. 255; कपेस्त्रासिषुर्नादात् Bk. 9. 11. 5. 75, 14. 48, 15. 58; *S*i. 8. 24; Ki. 8. 7. –*Caus.* To frighten, terrify. –WITH. वि to be frightened or terrified; वित्रस्तमुग्धहरिणीसदृशैः कटाक्षैः Bh. 1. 9. –सं to fear, be afraid or terrified; Bk. 14. 39. II. 10 U. (त्रासयति-ते) 1 To go, move. 2 To hold. 3 To take, seize. 4 To oppose, prevent.

त्रस *a.* Moveable, locomotive. –सः The heart. –सं 1 A wood, forest. 2 Animals. –COMP. –रेणुः an atom, the mote or atom of dust which is seen moving in a sunbeam; cf. जालांतरगते भानौ सूक्ष्मं यद्दृश्यते रजः । प्रथमं तत्प्रमाणानां त्रसरेणुं प्रचक्षते ॥ Ms. 8. 132; also Y. 1. 361.

त्रसरः A shuttle.

त्रसुर, त्रस्नु *a.* Fearful, trembling, timid; अत्रस्नुभिर्युक्तधुरं तुरंगैः R. 14. 47; सीतां सौमित्रिणा त्यक्तां सध्रीचीं त्रस्नुमेकिकां Bk. 6. 7.

त्रस्त *p. p.* 1 Frightened, terrified, alarmed; त्रस्तैकहायनकुरंगविलोलदृष्टेः Mâl. 4. 8. 2 Timid, fearful. 3 Quick, rolling.

त्राण *p. p.* Protected, guarded, preserved, saved. –णं 1 Protection, defence, preservation; आर्तत्राणाय वः शस्त्रं न प्रहर्तुमनागसि *S*. 1. 11. R. 15. 3. 2 Shelter, help, refuge; Bk. 3. 70.

त्रात *p. p.* 1 Preserved, saved, protected (*p. p.* of त्रै q. v.).

त्रापुष *a.* (षी *f.*) Made of tin.

त्रास *a.* 1 Moveable, moving. 2 Frightening. –सः 1 Fear, terror, alarm; अंतः कंचुकिकंचुकस्य विशति त्रासादयं वामनः Ratn. 2. 3; R. 2. 38, 9. 58. 2 Alarming, frightening. 3 A flaw or defect in a jewel.

त्रासन *a.* Terrifying, frightening, alarming. –नं The act of frightening or causing alarm.

त्रासित *a.* Frightened, alarmed, terrified.

त्रि *num. a.* (declined in pl. only; nom. त्रयः *m.*, तिस्रः *f.*, त्रीणि *n.*) Three; त एव हि त्रयो लोकास्त एव त्रय आश्रमाः &c. Ms. 2. 299; प्रियतमाभिरसौ तिसृभिर्बभौ R. 9. 18; त्रीणि वर्षाण्युदीक्षेत कुमार्यृतुमती सती Ms. 9. 90. –COMP. –अंशः 1 a three-fold share. 2 a thrid part. –अक्षः –अक्षकः an epithet of *S*iva. –अक्षरः 1 the mystic syllable ओम् consisting of three letters ; see under अ. 2 a match-maker or घटक (that word consisting of three syllables). –अंकटं, –अंगटं 1 three strings suspended to either end of a pole for carrying burdens. 2 a sort of collyrium. –अंजलं, –लि three handfuls taken collectively. अधिष्ठानः the soul. –अध्वगा, –मार्गणा, –वर्त्मगा epithets of the river Ganges (flowing through the three worlds). –अंबकः (also त्रियंबक in the same sense, though rarely used in classical literature) 'having three eyes', N. of *S*iva ; त्रियंबकं संयमिनं ददर्श Ku. 3. 44 ; जडीकृतस्त्र्यंबकवीक्षणेन R. 2. 42, 3. 49. °सखः an epithet of Kubera. –अंबका an epithet of Pârvati. –अब्द *a.* three years old. (–ब्दं) three years taken collectively. –अशीत *a.* eighty-third. –अशीतिः *f.* eighty-three. –अष्टन् *a.* twenty-four. –अश्र, –अस्र triangular. (–सं) a triangle. –अहः a period of three days. –आहितः *a.* 1 performed or produced in three days. 2 recurring after the third day, tertian (as fever). –ऋचं (तृचं also) three *Riks* taken collectively ; Ms. 8. 106. –ककुद् *m.* 1 N. of the mountain Trikûṭa. 2 N. of Vishṇu or Krishṇa. –कर्मन् *m.* the chief three duties of a Brâhmaṇa, *i.e.*, —sacrifice, study of the Vedas, and making gifts or charity. (–*m.*) one who engages in these three duties (as a Brâhmaṇa). –कायः N. of Buddha. –कालं 1 the three times, *i.e.*, the past, present, and future, or morning, noon and evening. 2 the three tenses (the past, present and future) of a verb. °ज्ञ, °दर्शिन् *a.* omniscient. –कूटः N. of a mountain in Ceylon on the top of which was situated Lankâ, the capital of Râvaṇa ; *S*i. 2. 5. –कूर्चकं a knife with three edges. –कोण *a.* triangular, forming a triangle. (–णः) 1 a triangle. 2 the vulva. –खट्वं, –खट्वी three bed-steads taken collectively. –गणः an aggregate of the three objects of worldly existence ; *i.e.*, धर्म, अर्थ and काम ; न

बाधतेऽस्य त्रिगणः परस्परं Ki. 1. 11; see त्रिवर्ग below. —गत *a.* 1 tripled. 2 done in three days. —गर्ताः (pl.) 1 N. of a country, also called जलंधर in the north-west of India. 2 the people or rulers of that country. –गर्ता a lascivious woman, a wanton. –गुण *a.* 1 consisting of threads; प्रताय मौंजीं त्रिगुणां बभार यां Ku. 5. 10. 2 three-times repeated, thrice, treble, three-fold, triple; सत्त व्यतीयुस्त्रिगुणानि तस्य (दिनानि) R. 2. 25. 3 containing the three Guṇas सत्व, रजस् and तमस्. (–णं) the Pradhâna (in Sân. phil.). (–णा) 1 Mâyâ or illusion (in Vedânta phil.). 2 an epithet of Durgâ. –चक्षुस् *m.* an epithet of *S*iva. –चतुर *a.* (pl.) three or four; गत्वा जवात्त्रिचतुराणि पदानि सीता B. R. 6. 34. –चत्वारिंश *a.* forty-third. –चत्वारिंशत् *f.* forty-three. –जगत् *n.* –जगती the three worlds, (1) the heaven, atmosphere, and the earth; or (2) the heaven, the earth, and the lower world. –जटः an epithet of *S*iva. –जटा N. of a female demon, one of the Râkshasa attendants kept by Râvaṇa to watch over Sîtâ, when she was retained as a captive in the Asokâ-vanikâ. She acted very kindly towards Sîtâ and induced her companions to do the same. —जीवा, —ज्या the sine of three signs or 90°, a radius. —णता a bow. –णव, –णवन् *a.* pl. three times nine, *i. e.* 27. –तक्षं, –तक्षी three carpenters taken collectively. –दंडं 1 the three staves of a *S*annyâsin (who has resigned the world) tied together so as to form one. 2 the triple subjection of thought, word, and deed. (–डः) the state of a religious ascetic. –दंडिन् *m.* a religious mendicant or *Sannyâsin* who has renounced all worldly attachments and who carries three long staves tied together so as to form one in his right hand. 2 one who has obtained command over his mind, speech, and body (or thought, word, and deed); cf. वाग्दंडोऽथ मनोदंडः कायदंडस्तथैव च। यस्यैते निहिता बुद्धौ त्रिदंडीति स उच्यते ॥ Ms. 12. 10. –दशाः (pl.) 1 thirty 2 the thirty-three gods. (–शः) a god, an immortal; Ku. 3. 1. °अंकुशः, °आयुधं Indra's thunderbolt, R. 9. 54. °अधिपः, °ईश्वरः, °पतिः epithets of Indra. °अध्यक्षः an epithet of Vishṇu. °अरिः a demon. °आचार्यः an epithet of Brihaspati. °आलयः, °आवासः 1 heaven. 2 the Mountain Meru. °आहारः 'the food of Gods'. °गुरुः an epithet of Brihaspati. °गोपः a kind of insect; (cf. इंद्रगोप); अङ्गे त्रिदशगोपमात्रके दाहशक्तिमिव कृष्णवर्त्मनि R. 11. 42. °मंजरी the holy basil. °वधू, °वनिता An Apsaras or heavenly damsel; कैलासस्य त्रिदशवनितादर्पणस्यातिथिः स्याः Me. 58. °वर्त्मन् the sky. –दिनं three days collectively. –दिवं 1 the heaven; त्रिमार्गेयेव त्रिदिवस्य मार्गः Ku. 1. 28; *S*. 7.3. 2 sky, atmosphere. 3 happiness. °अधीशः; °ईशः 1 an epithet of Indra. 2 a god. °उद्भवा the Ganges. °ओकस् *m.* a god. –दृश् *m.* an epithet of *S*iva –दोषं vitiation or derangement of the three humours of the body; *i. e.* वात, पित्त and कफ. –धारा the Ganges. –नयनः (नयनः), –नेत्रः, –लोचनः epithets of *S*iva; R. 3. 66; Ku. 3. 66, 5. 72. –नवत *a.* ninety-third. –नवतिः *f.* ninety-three. –पंच *a.* three-fold five, *i. e.* fifteen. –पंचाश *a.* fifty-third. –पंचाशत् *f.* fifty-three. –पटुः glass (काच). –पताकः 1 the hand with three fingers stretched out or erect. 2 the forehead marked naturally with three horizontal lines. –पत्रकं the Palâsa tree. –पथं 1 the three paths taken collectively; *i. e.* the sky, atmosphere, and the earth, or the sky, earth and the lower world. 2 a place where three roads meet. °गा an epithet of the Ganges; धृतसत्पथस्त्रिपथगामभितः स तमारुरोह पुरुहूतसुतः Ki. 6. 1; Amaru. 99. –पदं, –पदिका a tripod. –पदी 1 the girth of an elephant; नास्त्रसत्करिणां ग्रैवं त्रिपदीच्छेदिनामपि R. 4. 48. 2 the Gâyatrî metre. 3 a tripod. 4 the plant गोधापधी. –पर्णः the Kimsuka tree. –पाद् *a.* 1 having three feet. 2 consisting of three parts, having three-fourths; R. 15. 96. 3 trinomial. (–*m.*) an epithet of Vishṇu in his dwarf incarnation. –पुट *a.* triangular (–टः) 1 an arrow. 2 the palm of the hand. 3 a cubit. 4 a bank or shore. –पुटकः a triangle. पुटा an epithet of Durgâ. –पुंड्रं, पुंड्रकं a mark on the forehead consisting of three lines made with cowdung, ashes, sandal &c. –पुरं 1 a collection of three cities. 2 the three cities of gold, silver, and iron in the sky, air and earth built for demons by Maya; (these cities were burnt down, along with the demons inhabiting them, by *S*iva at the request of the gods); Ku. 7. 48; Amaru. 2; Me. 56; Bh. 2. 123; (–रः) N. of a demon or demons presiding over these cities. °अंतकः, अरिः, घ्नः, दहनः, द्विष् *m* हरः &c. epithets of *S*iva; Bh. 2. 123; R. 17. 14. °दाहः burning of the three cities; Ki. 5. 14 (–री) 1 N. of a place near Jabbalpura formerly capital of the kings of Chedi. 2 N. of a country. –पौरुष *a.* belonging to, or extending over, three generations of men. –प्रसुतः an elephant in rut. –फला the three myrobalans taken collectively (Mar. हिरडा, बेहडा and आंवळकटी). –बलिः, –बली, –वलिः, –वली *f.* the three folds of skin above the navel of a woman (regarded as a mark of beauty); क्षामोदरोपरिलसात्त्रिवलिलतानां Bh. 1. 93, 81; cf. Ku. 1. 39. –भद्रं copulation, sexual union, cohabitation. –भुजं a triangle. –भुवनं the three worlds; पुण्यं यायास्त्रिभुवनगुरोर्धाम चंडीश्वरस्य Me. 33; Bh. 1. 99. –भूमः a palace with three floors. –मार्गा the Ganges; Ku. 1. 28. –मुकुटः the Trikûta mountain. –मुखः an epithet of Buddha. –मूर्तिः the united form of Brahma, Vishnu, and Mahesa, the Hindu triad; Ku. 2. 4. –यष्टिः a necklace of three strings. –यामा night (consisting of 3 watches or *praharas*, the first and last half *prahara* being excluded); संक्षिप्येत क्षण इव कथं दीर्घयामा त्रियामा Me. 108. Ku. 7. 21, 26; R. 9. 70 V. 3. 22. –योनिः a law-suit (in which a person engages from anger, covetousness, or infatuation). रात्रं a period of three nights. –रेखः a conch-shell. –लिंग *a.* having three genders, *i. e.* an adjective. (–गः) the country called Telanga. (–गी) the three genders taken collectively. –लोकं the three worlds. °ईशः the sun. °नाथः 'lord of the three worlds', an epithet of 1 Indra; R. 3. 45. 2 of *S*iva; Ku. 5. 77. (–की) the three worlds taken collectively, the universe; सत्यामेव त्रिलोकीसरिति हरशिरश्चुंबिनीविच्छटायां Bh. 3. 95; *S*ânti. 4. 22. –वर्गः 1 the three objects of worldly existence; *i. e.* धर्म, अर्थ, and काम; Ku. 5. 38. 2 the three states of loss, stability, and increase; क्षयः स्थानं च वृद्धिश्च त्रिवर्गो नीतिवेदिनां Ak. –वर्णकं the first three of the four castes of Hindus taken collectively. –वारं *ind.* three times, thrice. –विक्रमः Vishnu in his fifth or dwarf incarnation. –विद्यः a Brâhmana versed in the three Vedas. –विध *a.* of three kinds, three-fold. –विष्टपं, –पिष्टपं the world of Indra, heaven; त्रिविष्टपस्येव पतिं जयंतः R. 6. 78. °सद् *m.* a god. –वेणिः –णी *f.* the place near Prayâga where the Ganges joins the Yamunâ and receives under ground the Sarasvati. –वेदः a Brâhmana versed in the three Vedas. –शंकुः 1 N. of a celebrated king of the Solar race, king of Ayodhyâ and father of Harischandra. [He was a wise, pious and just king, but his chief fault was that he loved his person to an inordinate degree. Desiring to celebrate a sacrifice by virtue of which he could go up to heaven in his mortal body, he requested his family-priest Vasishtha to officiate for him; but being refused he next requested his hundred sons who also rejected his absurd pro-

posal. He, therefore, called them cowardly **and** impotent, and was in return for these insults cursed and degraded by **them** to be a Ch*a*nd*a*la. While he was **in this** wretched condition, Vis*v*amitra, **whose** family Tris*a*nku had in times of **famine** laid under deep obligations, **undertook** to celebrate the sacrifice, and **invited** all the gods to be present. They, however, declined; whereupon the enraged Vis*v*amitra by his own power lifted up Tris*a*nku to the skies with his cherished mortal body. He began to soar higher till his head struck against the vault of of the heaven, when he was hurled down headforemost by Indra and the other gods. The mighty Vis*v*amitra, however arrested him in his downward course, saying 'Stay Tris*a*nku,' and the unfortunate monarch remained suspended with his head towards the earth as a constellation in the southern hemisphere. Hence the well known proverb; त्रिशंकुरिवांतरा तिष्ठ *S*. 2]. **2** the Châtaka bird. **3** a cat. **4** a grass-hopper. **5** a fire-fly °जः an epithet of Harischandra. °याजिन् *m*. an epithet of Visvâmitra. **-शत** *a.* three hundred. (**-तं**) one hundred and three. **2** three hundred **-शिखं** **1** a trident. **2** a crown or crest (with three points). **-शिरस्** *m*. N. of a demon killed by Râma. **-शूलं** a trident. °अंकः, °धारिन् *m*. an epithet of *S*iva. **-शूलिन्** *m*. an epithet of *S*iva. **-शृंगः** the Trikuta mountain. **-षष्टिः** *f*. sixty-three. **-संध्यं, -संध्यी** the three periods of the day; *i. e.* dawn, noon, and sunset. **-संध्यं** *ind.* at the time of the three Sandhyâs. **-सप्त** *a.* seventy third. **-सप्ततिः** seventy-three. **सप्तन्,-सप्त** *a. pl.* three times 7, *i. e.* 27. **-साम्यं** equilibrium of the three (qualities). **-स्थली** the three sacred places, काशी, प्रयाग and गया. **-स्रोतस्** *f*. an epithet of the Ganges; त्रिस्रोतसं वहति यो गगनप्रतिष्ठां *S*. 7. 6; R. 10. 63; Ku. 7. 15. **-सीत्य, -हल्य** *a.* ploughed thrice (as a field). **-हायण** *a.* three years old.

त्रिंश *a*. (**शी**) Thirtieth. **2** Joined with thirty; *e. g.* त्रिंशं शतं one hundred and thirty. **3** Consisting of thirty.

त्रिंशक *a*. **1** Consisting of thirty. **2** Bought for or worth thirty.

त्रिंशत् *f*. Thirty. -Comp. **-पत्रं** a lotus opening at moonrise.

त्रिंशत्कं An aggregate of thirty.

त्रिंशतिः *f*. Thirty.

त्रिक *a*. **1** Triple, three-fold. **2** Forming a triad. **3** Three per cent. **-कं** **1** A triad. **2** A place where three roads meet. **3** The lower part of the spine, the part about the hips; त्रिके स्थूलता Pt. 1. 190. कश्चिद्विवृत्तत्रिकभिन्नहारः R. 6. 16. **4** The part between the shoulderblades. **5** The three spices. **-का** A contrivance for raising water (like a wheel) over which passes the rope of the bucket.

त्रितय *a*. (**यी** *f.*) Consisting of three parts, three-fold. **-यं** A triad, a group of three; श्रद्धावित्तं विधिश्चेति त्रितयं तत्समागतं *S*. 7. 29; R. 8. 78; Y. 3 266.

त्रिधा *ind.* In three ways or in three parts; Ku. 7. 44; Bg. 18. 19.

त्रिस् *ind.* Thrice, three times.

त्रुट् 4. 6. P. (त्रुटयति, त्रुटति, त्रुटित) To tear, break, fall asunder, snap, be slipt (fig. also); गद्गदगलत्त्रुट्यद्विलीनाक्षरं Bh. 3. 8, 1. 96; अयं ते बाष्पौघस्त्रुटित इव मुक्तामणिसरः U. 1. 29.

त्रुटिः, -टी *f*. **1** Cutting, breaking, tearing. **2** A small part, an atom. **3** A very minute space of time equal to ¼ of a *Kshana* or ½ of a *Lava*. **4** Doubt, uncertainty. **5** Loss, destruction. **6** Small cardamoms (the plant).

त्रेता **1** A traid, triplet. **2** The three sacred fires taken collectively; Ms. 2. 231; R. 13. 37. **3** A particular throw at dice, a cast of three or trey; त्रेताहृतसर्वस्वः Mk. 2. 8. **4** The second of the four Yugas of the Hindus; see युग.

त्रेधा *ind.* Trebly, in three ways or parts; तदेकं सत्त्रेधाख्यायते Sat. Br ; (नमः) तुभ्यं त्रेधा स्थितात्मने R. 10. 16.

त्रै 1 A. (त्रायते, त्रात or त्राण) To protect, preserve, rescue or save from, defend from (usually with abl.); क्षतात्किल त्रायत इत्युदग्रः क्षत्रस्य शब्दो भुवनेषु रूढः R. 2. 53; Bg. 2. 40; Ms. 9. 138; Bk. 5. 54; 15. 120. -With **परि** to save &c.; परित्रायस्व, परित्रायस्व (in dramas).

त्रैकालिक *a*. (**की** *f.*) Relating to the three times; *i. e.* past, present, and future.

त्रैकाल्यं The three times-past, present and future.

त्रैगुणिक *a*. Triple, three-fold.

त्रैगुण्यं **1** The state of consistiug of three theads, qualities &c. **2** Triplicity. **3** The three Gunas or properties (सत्त्व, रजस् and तमस्) taken collectively; त्रैगुण्योद्भवमत्र लोकचरितं नानारसं दृश्यते M. 1. 4.

त्रैपुरः **1** The Tripura country. **2** A ruler or inhabitant of that country.

त्रैमातुरः An epithet of Lakshmana.

त्रैमासिक *a*. (**की** *f.*) **1** Three months old. **2** Lasting for or occurring every three months. **3** Quarterly.

त्रैराशिकं The rule of three (in math.).

त्रैलोक्यं The three worlds taken collectively; R. 10. 53.

त्रैवर्णिक *a*. (**की** *f.*) Relating to the first three castes.

त्रैविक्रम *a*. Belonging to Trivikrama or Vishnu; R. 7. 35.

त्रैविद्यं **1** The three Vedas. **2** The study of the three Vedas. **3** The three sciences. **-द्यः** A Brâhmana versed in the three Vedas; Rg. 9. 20,

त्रैविष्टपः, त्रैविष्टपेयः A god.

त्रैशंकवः An epithet of Harischandra, son of Trisanku.

त्रोटकं A species of drama:—सप्ताष्टनवपंचांकं दिव्यमानुषसंश्रयं । त्रोटकं नाम तत्प्राहुः प्रत्यंकं सविदूषकं ॥ S. D. 540; *e. g.* Kâlidâsa's Vikramorvasîyam.

त्रोटिः *f*. A bill, beak. -Comp. **-हस्तः** a bird.

त्रोत्रं A goad.

त्वक्ष् 1. P. (त्वक्षति, त्वष्ट) To pare, hew, peel.

त्वंकारः Addressing disrespectfully with a 'thou', theeing and thouing.

त्वंग् 1. P. (त्वंगति) **1** To go, move. **2** To jump, gallop. **3** To tremble.

त्वच् *f*. **1** Skin (of men, serpents &c.) **2** Hide (as of a cow, deer &c.) R. 3. 31. **3** Bark, rind; Ku. 1. 7; R. 2. 37, 17. 12. **4** Any cover or coating. **5** The sense of touch. -Comp. **-अंकुरः** horripilation. **-इंद्रियं** the organ of touch. **-कंडुरः** a sore. **-गंधः** the orange. **-छेदः** a skin-wound, scratch, bruise. **-जं** **1** blood. **2** hair (on the body). **-तरंगकः** a wrinkle. **-त्रं** an armour; त्वक्त्रं चाचकचे वरं Bk. 14. 94. **-दोषः** disease of the skin, leprosy. **-पारुष्यं** roughness of the skin. **-पुष्पः** horripilation. **-सारः** (**त्वचिसारः**) a bamboo; त्वक्सारंरंध्रपरिपूरणलब्धगीतिः Si. 4. 61. **-सुगंधः** an orange.

त्वचा see त्वच्.

त्वदीय *a*. Thy, thine, your, yours; R. 3. 50.

त्वद् A form of the second personal pronoun occuring as the first member of some compounds; *e. g.* त्वदधीन, त्वत्सादृश्यं &c.

त्वद्विध *a*. Like thee or you.

त्वर् 1 A. (त्वरते, त्वरित) To hurry, make haste, move with speed, do anything quickly ; भवान्सुहृदर्थे त्वरतां M. 2; नानुनेतुमबलाः स तत्वरे R. 19. 38. -*Caus.* (त्वरयति) To cause to hasten, expediate, urge forward.

त्वरा, त्वरिः *f*. Haste, hurry, speed; औत्सुक्येन कृतत्वरा सहभुवा व्यावर्तमाना ह्रिया Ratn. 1. 2.

त्वरित *a*. quick, swift, speedy. **-तं** Despatch, haste. —*ind.* Quickly, fast, speedily, hastily.

त्वष्टृ *m*. **1** A carpenter, builder, workman. **2** Visvakarman, the architect of the gods. [Twash*t*ri is the Vulcan of the Hindu mythology. He had a son named Trisiras and a daughter called संज्ञा, who was given in marriage to the sun. But she was unable to bear the severe light of her husband, and therefore Tvash*t*ri mounted the sun upon his lathe and carefully trimmed off a part of his bright disc; (cf. R. 6. 32; आरोप्य चक्रभ्रमिमुष्णतेजास्त्वष्ट्रेव यत्नोल्लिखितो

विभाति). The part trimmed off is said to have been used by him in forming the discus of Vishṇu, the Triśula of Śiva, and some other weapons of the gods].

त्वादृश्, त्वादृश (शी *f.*) *a.* Similar to thee or you, of thy kind; Me. 69.

त्विष् 1 U. (त्वेषति-ते) To shine, glitter, sparkle, blaze.

त्विष् *f.* 1 Light, lustre, splendour, brilliance; चयत्विषामित्यवधारितं पुरा Si. 1. 3, 9. 13; R. 4. 75; Ratn. 1. 18 2 Beauty. 3 Authority, weight. 4 Wish, desire. 5 Custom, practice. 6 Violence. 7 Speech. COMP. -ईशः, also त्विषांपतिः the sun.

त्विषिः A ray of light.

त्सरुः 1 Any creeping animal. 2 The hilt or handle of a sword or any other weapon; सुप्रग्रहविमलकलधौतत्सरुणा खड्गेन Ve. 3; त्सरुप्रदेशादपवार्जितांगः Ki. 17. 58; R. 18. 48.

थ.

थः A mountain. -थं 1 Protection, preservation. 2 Terror, fear. 3 Auspiciousness.

थुड् 6. P. (थुडति) 1 To cover, screen. 2 To hide or conceal.

थुडनं Covering, wrapping up.

थुत्कारः The sound थुत् made in spitting.

थुर्व् 1 P. (थुर्वति) To hurt, injure.

थूत्कारः, थूत्कृतं The sound थूत् made in spitting

थै थै *ind.* The imitative sound of a musical instrument.

द.

द *a.* (At the end of comp.), Giving, granting, producing, causing, cutting off, destroying, removing; as धनद, अन्नद, गरद, तोयद, अनलद &c. —दः 1 A gift, donation. 2 A mountain. —दं A wife.—दा 1 Heat. 2 Repentance.

दंश् 1 P. (दशति, दष्ट; *Desid.* दिदङ्क्षति) To bite, sting; Bk. 15. 4, 16. 19; मृणालिका अदशत् K. 32 ate, browsed. -WITH उप to eat anything as a condiment; मूलकेनोपदश्य भुंक्ते Sk. -सं 1 to bite, sting; संदष्टाधरपल्लवा Amaru. 32. 2 to stick or adhere closely, cling; उरसा संदष्टसर्पत्वचा S. 7. 11, 3. 18; संदष्टवस्त्रेष्वबलानितंबेषु R. 16. 65, 48.

दंशः 1 Biting, stinging; मुग्धे विदेहि मयि निर्दयदंतदंशं Gît. 10. 2 The sting of a snake. 3 A bite, the spot bitten; छेदो दंशस्य दाहो वा M. 4. 4. 4 Cutting, tearing 5 A gad-fly; R. 2. 5; Ms. 1. 40; Y. 3. 215. 6 A flaw, fault, defect (in a jewel). 7 A tooth. 8 Pungency. 9 An armour. 10 A joint, limb. -COMP. -भीरुः a buffalo.

दंशकः 1 A dog. 2 A gadfly. 3 A fly.

दंशनं 1 The act of biting or stinging; *e. g.* दष्टाश्च दंशनैः कांतं दासीकुर्वंति योषितः S. D. 2 An armour, mail; Si. 17. 21.

दंशित *a.* 1 Bitten. 2 Mailed, furnished with an armour.

दंशिन् *m.* See दंशक.

दंशी A small gadfly.

दंष्ट्रा A large tooth, tusk, fang; प्रसह्य मणिमुद्धरेन्मकरवक्त्रदंष्ट्रांकुरात् Bk. 2. 4; R. 2. 46; दंष्ट्राभंगं मृगाणामधिपतय इव व्यक्तमानावलेपा । नाज्ञाभंगं सहंते नृवर नृपतयस्त्वादृशाः सार्वभौमाः ॥ Mu. 3. 22. —COMP. -अस्त्रः, -आयुधः a wild boar. -कराल *a.* having terrible tusks. -विषः a kind of snake.

दंष्ट्राल *a.* Having large tusks.

दंष्ट्रिका—दंष्ट्रा q. v.

दंष्ट्रिन् *m.* 1 A wild boar. 2 A snake. 3 A hyena.

दक्ष *a.* 1 Able, competent, expert, clever, skilful; नाट्ये च दक्षा वयं Ratn. 1. 6; मेरौ स्थिते दोग्धरि दोहदक्षे Ku. 1. 2; R. 12. 11. 2 Fit, suitable. 3 Ready, careful, attentive, prompt; Y. 1. 76. 4 Upright, honest. —क्षः 1 N. of a celebrated Prajâpati. [He was one of the ten sons of Brahma, being born from his right thumb, and was the chief of the patriarchs of mankind. He is said to have had many daughters, 27 of whom became the wives of the moon, thus forming the 27 lunar mansions, and 13 the wives of Kaśyapa. At one time Daksha celebrated a great sacrifice, but did not invite his daughter Sati nor husband Śiva—the chief of the gods. Sati, however, went to the sacrifice, but being greatly insulted threw herself into fire and perished; cf. Ku. 1. 21. When Śiva heard this he was very much provoked, and, according to one account, himself went to the sacrifice, completely destroyed it and pursued Daksha, who assumed the form of a deer, and at last decapitated him. But Śiva is said to have afterwards restored him to life, and he thenceforward acknowledged the god's supremacy. According to another account, Śiva, when provoked, tore off a hair from his matted hair and dashed it with great force against the ground, when lo! a powerful demon started up and awaited his orders. He was told to go and destroy Daksha's sacrifice; whereupon the mighty demon attended by several demigods went to the sacrifice, routed the gods and priests, and, according to one account, beheaded Daksha himself.] 2 A cock. 3 Fire. 4 The bull of Śiva. 5 A lover attached to many mistresses. 6 An epithet of Śiva. 7 Mental power, ability, capacity. -COMP. -अध्वरध्वंसकः, -क्रतुध्वंसिन् *m.* epithets of Śiva. -कन्या, -जा, -तनया 1 an epithet of Durgâ. 2 a lunar mansion. -सुतः a god.

दक्षाय्यः 1 A vulture. 2 An epithet of Garuḍa.

दक्षिण *a.* 1 Able, skilful, dexterous, competent, clever. 2 Right (opp. वाम). 3 Situated on the right side. 4 South, southern; as in दक्षिणवायु, दक्षिणदिक्. 5 Situated to the south. 6 Sincere, straight-forward, honest, impartial. 7 Pleasing, amiable. 8 Courteous, civil. 9 Compliant, submissive. 10 Dependent. -णः 1 The right hand or arm. 2 A civil or courteous person, applied in poetic composition to a lover who professes attachment to one mistress, while his heart has been entirely taken up by another. 2 An epithet of Śiva or Vishṇu. -COMP. -अग्निः the southern fire, the sacred fire placed southwards; also called अन्वाहार्यपचन q. v. -अग्र *a.* pointing to the south.-अचलः the southern mountain; *i. e.* Malaya. -अभिमुख *a.* facing the south, directed towards the south. -अयनं the sun's progress south of the equator, the half year in which the sun moves from the north to the south, the winter solstice. -अर्धः 1 the right hand. 2 the right or southern side. -आचार *a.* 1 honest, well behaved. 2 a worshipper of Śakti according to the right hand (or purer) ritual. -आशा the south. °पतिः an epithet of Yama. -इतर *a*. 1 left (as hand or foot); Ku. 4. 19. 2 northern. (-रा) the north. -उत्तर *a*. turned or lying to the south and the north. °वृत्तं the meridian line. -पश्चात् *ind*. to the south-west. -पश्चिम *a*. south-western. (-मा) the south-west. -पूर्व-प्राच् *a*. south-east. —पूर्वा, -प्राची the south-eastern quarter. -समुद्रः the southern ocean. -स्थः a charioteer.

दक्षिणतः *ind*. 1 From the right or south. 2 To the right hand. 3 To the south or southward (with gen.).

दक्षिणा *ind*. 1 On the right or south of. 2 In the southern direction (with abl.). —णा 1 A present or gift to Brâhmanas (at the completion of a religious rite, such as a secrifice). 2 Dakshinâ regarded as a daughter of Prajâpati and as the wife of Sacrifice personified; पत्नी सुदक्षिणेत्यासीदध्वरस्येव दक्षिणा R. 1. 31. 3 A gift, offering or donation in general, fee, remuneration; प्राणदक्षिणा, गुरुदक्षिणा &c. 4 A good milchcow, prolific cow. 5 The south. 6 The southern country, the *Deccan*. -COMP. -अर्ह *a*. deserving or worthy of a gift. -आवर्त *a*. 1 curved to the right. 2 turned towards the south. -कालः the time of receiving *Daksihnâ*. -पथः the southern part of India, the south or Deccan; अस्ति दक्षिणापथे विदर्भेषु पद्मपुरं नाम नगरं Mâl. 1. -प्रवण *a*. inclining to the south.

दक्षिणाहि *ind*. 1 Far on the right. 2 Far in the south, to the south of (with abl.); दक्षिणाहि ग्रामात् Sk.

दक्षिणीय, दक्षिण्य *a*. Worthy of or deserving a sacrificial gift, such as a Brâhmaṇa.

दक्षिणेन *ind*. On the right side of (with acc. or gen.); दक्षिणेन वृक्षवाटिकामालाप इव श्रूयते *S*. 1 दक्षिणेन ग्रामस्य &c.

दग्ध *p. p*. 1 Burnt, consumed by fire. 2 (Fig.) Consumed by grief, tormented, distressed. 3 Famished. 4 Inauspicious. 5 Dry, tasteless, insipid. 6 Wretched, accursed, vile (used as a term of abuse before a word); नाद्यापि मे दग्धदेहः पतति U. 4; अस्य दग्धोदरस्यार्थे कः कुर्यात्पातकं महत् H. 1. 68; so दग्धजठरस्यार्थे Bh. 3. 8.

दग्धिका Scorched rice.

दघ्न *a*. (घ्नी *f*.) A termination added to nouns in the sense of 'reaching to', 'as high or deep as'; ऊरुदघ्नेन पयसोत्तीर्य K. 310; कीलालव्यतिकरगुल्फदघ्नपंकः (मार्गः) Mâl. 3. 17, 5. 14, Y. 2. 108.

दंड् 10 U. (दंडयति-ते, दंडित) To punish, fine, chastise; (this is one of the 16 roots that govern two accusatives); तान् सहस्रं च दंडयेत् Ms. 9. 234, 8. 123; Y. 2. 269; स्थित्यै दंडयतो दंड्यान् R. 1. 25.

दंडः-डं 1 A stick, staff, rod, mace, club, cudgel; पततु शिरस्यकांड यमदंड इवैष भुजः Mâl. 5. 31; काष्ठदंडः 2 The sceptre of a king, the rod as a symbol of authority and punishment; आत्तदंड *S*. 5. 8. 3 The staff given to a twice-born man at the time of investiture with the sacred thread; cf. Ms. 2. 45-47. 4 The staff of a संन्यासिन् or ascetic. 5 The trunk of an elephant. 6 The stem or stalk; as of a lotus; tree &c.; the handle as of an umbrella; ब्रम्हांडछत्रदंडः &c. Dk. 1 (opening verse); राज्यं स्वहस्तधृतदंडमिवातपत्रं *S*. 5. 6; Ku. 7. 89; so कमलदंड &c. 7 The oar of a boat. 8 A churning stick. 9 Fine; Ms. 8. 341, 9. 229; Y. 2. 237. 10 Chastisement, corporal punishment, punishment in general; यथापराधदंडानां R. 1. 6; एवं राजापथ्यकारिषु तीक्ष्णदंडो राजा Mu. 1; दंडं दंड्येषु पातयेत् Ms. 8. 126; कृतदंडः स्वयं राज्ञा लेभे शूद्रः सतां गतिं R. 15. 53. 11 Imprisonment. 12 Attack, assault, violence, punishment, the last of the four expedients; see उपाय; Ms. 7. 109; *Si*. 2. 54. 13 An army; तस्य दंडवतो दंडः स्वदेहान्न व्यशिष्यत R. 17. 62; Ms. 7. 65, 9. 294; Ki 2. 12. 14 A form of military array. 15 Subjection, control, restraint; वाग्दंडोऽथ मनोदंडः कायदंडस्तथैव च । यस्यैते निहिता बुद्धौ त्रिदंडीति स उच्यते ॥ Ms. 12. 10. 16 A measure of length equal to 4 Hastas. 17 The penis. 18 Pride. 19 The body. 20 An epithet of Yama. 21 N. of Vishṇu. 22 N. of *Siva*. 23 An attendant on the sun. 24 A horse; (said to be *m*. only in the last five senses). -COMP. -अजिनं 1 staff and hide (as outer badges of devotion), 2 (fig.) hypocrisy, deceit. -अधिपः a chief magistrate. -अनीकं a detachment or division of an army; तव हृतवतो दंडानीकैर्विदर्भपतेः श्रियं M. 5. 2. -अपूपन्याय see under न्याय. -अर्ह *a*. fit to be chastised, deserving punishment. -अलसिका cholera. -आज्ञा judicial sentence. -आहातं buttermilk. -कर्मन् *n*. infliction of punishment, chastisement. -काकः a raven. -काष्ठं a wooden club or staff. -ग्रहणं assumption of the staff of an ascetic or pilgrim, becoming a mendicant. -छदनं a room in which utensils of various kinds are kept. -ढक्का a kind of drum. -दासः one who has become a slave from non-payment of a debt. -देवकुलं a court of justice. -धर, -धार *a*. 1 carrying a staff, staff-bearer. 2 punishing, chastising; U. 2. 10 (-रः) 1 a king; श्रमनुदं मनुदंडधरान्वयं R. 9. 3. 2 N. of Yama. 3 the judge, supreme magistrate. -नायकः a judge, a head police officer, a magistrate. 2 the leader of an army, a general. -नीतिः *f*. 1 administration of justice, judicature. 2 the system of civil and military administration, the science of politics, polity; R. 18. 46. -नेतृ *m*. a king. -पातः 1 falling of a stick. 2 infliction of punishment. -पः a king. -पांशुलः a porter, door-keeper. -पाणिः an epithet of Yama. -पातनं infliction of punishment, chastisement. -पारुष्यं 1 assault, violence. 2 hard or cruel infliction of punishment. -पालः, -पालकः 1 a head magistrate. 2 a door-keeper, porter. -पोणः a strainer furnished with a handle. -प्रणामः 1 bowing without bending the body, (keeping it erect like a stick). 2 falling flat or prostrate on the ground. -बालधिः an elephant. -भंगः non-execution of a sentence. -भृत् *m*. 1 a potter. 2 an epithet of Yama. -माण (न) वः 1 a staff-bearer. 2 an ascetic bearing a staff. -माथः a principal road, highway, -यात्रा 1 a solemn procession (particularly bridal). 2 warlike expedition, conquest (of a region). -यामः 1 an epithet of Yama. 2 of Agastya. 3 a day. -वादिन्, -वासिन् a door-keeper, warder. -वाहिन् *m*. a police officer. -विधिः 1 rule of punishment. 2 criminal law. -विष्कंभः the post to which the string of a churning stick is fastened. -व्यूहः a particular form of arranging troops, arranging them in columns. -शास्त्रं the science of inflicting punishment; criminal law. -हस्तः 1 a door-keeper, warder, porter. 2 an epithet of Yama.

दंडकः 1 A stick, staff &c. 2 A line, row. 3 N. of a metre; see App. -कः, -का, -कं N. of a celebrated district in the Deccan situated between the rivers Narmadâ and Godâvarî, (it was a vast region, said to be tenantless in the time of Râma); प्रातानि दुःखान्यपि दंडकेषु R. 14. 25; किं नाम दंडकेयं U. 2; क्रायोध्यायाः पुनरुपगमो दंडकायां वने वः U. 2. 13, 14, 15.

दंडनं Punishing, chastising, fining.

दंडादंडि *ind*. 'Stick against stick', fighting with sticks and staves, cudgelling.

दंडारः 1 A carriage. 2 A potter's wheel. 3 A raft, boat. 4 An elephant in rut.

दंडिकः A staff-bearer, a mace-bearer.

दंडिका 1 A stick. 2 A row, line, series. 3 A string of pearls, a necklace. 4 A rope.

दंडिन् *m*. 1 A Brâhmaṇa of the fourth order, a Sannyâsin. 2 A doorkeeper, porter. 3 An oarsman. 4 A Jaina ascetic. 5 An epithet of Yama. 6 A king. 7 N. of a poet, author of Kâvyâdarsa, and Dasakumâracharita; जाते जगति वाल्मीके कविरित्यभिधाऽभवत् । कवी इति ततो व्यासे कवयस्त्वयि दंडिनि ॥ Udb.

दत् *m.* A tooth (A word optionally substituted for दंत in all the case-forms after the acc. dual. It has no forms for the first five inflections). -COMP. -छदः (दच्छदः) a lip.

दत्त *p. p.* 1 Given, given away, presented. 2 Made over, delivered, assigned. 3 Placed, stretched forth; see दा.-त्तः 1 One of the twelve kinds of sons in Hindu law; (also called दत्त्रिम); माता पिता वा दद्यातां यमद्भिः पुत्रमापदि। सदृशं प्रीतिसंयुक्तं स ज्ञेयो दत्त्रिमः सुतः ॥ Ms. 9. 168. 2 A title added to the names of Vaisyas; cf. the quotation under गुप्त. 3 N. of a son of Atri and Anasûyâ; see दत्तात्रेय below. -त्तं Gift, donation. -COMP. -अनपकर्मन्, अप्रदानिकं non-delivery or resumption of gifts, one of the 18 titles of Hindu law. -अवधान *a.* attentive. -आत्रेयः N. of a sage, son of Atri and Anasûyâ, considered as an incarnation of Brahmâ, Vishnu and Mahesa. आदर *a.* 1 showing respect, respectful, 2 treated with respect.-शुल्का a bride for whom a dowry has been paid. -हस्त *a.* having a hand given for support, supported by the hand of; शंभुना दत्तहस्ता Me. 60. leaning on Sambhus arm; स कामरूपेश्वरदत्तहस्तः R. 7. 17; (fig.) being given a helping hand, supported, aided, assisted; दैवेनेत्थं दत्तहस्तावलंबे Ratn. 1. 8.; वात्या खेदं कृशांग्याः सुचिरमवयवैर्दत्तहस्ता करोति Ve. 2. 21.

दत्तकः An adopted son; Y. 2. 130; see दत्त above.

दद् 1 A (ददते) To give, offer.

दद *a.* Giving, offering.

ददनं Gift, donation.

दध् 1 A (दधते) 1 To hold. 2 To retain, possess. 3 To give, present.

दधि *n.* 1 Coagulated milk, thick sour milk; क्षीरं दधिभावेन परिणमते S. B; दध्योदनः &c. 2 Turpentine. 3 A garment. -COMP.-अन्नं,-ओदनं boiled rice mixed with दधि. -उत्तरं, -उत्तरकं-गं the skim of curdled milk, whey. -उदः, -उदकः the ocean of coagulated milk. -कूचिका mixture of boiled and coagulated milk. -चारः a churning stick. -जं fresh butter. -फलः the wood-apple (कपित्थ). -मंडः,-वारि *n.* whey. -मंथनं churning coagulated milk. -शोणः a monkey. -सक्तु *m. pl.* barley-meal mixed with coagulated milk. -सारः, -स्नेहः fresh butter. -स्वेदः butter-milk.

दधित्थः The wood-apple (कपित्थ).

दधीचः N. of a celebrated sage, who became ready to die and offered his bones to the gods; with these bones the architect of the gods made a thunderbolt with which Indra defeated Vritra and other demons. -COMP. अस्थि *n.* 1 the thunderbolt of Indra. 2 a diamond.

दनुः *f.* N. of one of the daughters of Daksha given in marriage to Kasyapa and mother of the *Dânavas.* -COMP. -जः, -पुत्रः, -संभवः, -सूनुः a demon. °अरिः, -द्विष् *m.* a god.

दंतः 1 A tooth, tusk, fang (as of serpents, beasts &c.); वदसि यदि किंचिदपि दंतरुचिकौमुदी हरति दरतिमिरमतिघोरं Git. 10; सर्पदंत, वराह° &c. 2 An elephant's tusk, ivory; °पांचालिका Mâl. 10. 5. 3 The point of an arrow. 4 The peak of a mountain. 5 A bower, an arbour (कुंज). -COMP. -अग्रं the point of a tooth. -अंतरं the space between the teeth. -उद्भेदः dentition. -उलूखलिकः, -खलिन् *m.* one who uses his teeth for a mortar, (grinding grain to be eaten between his teeth), an anchorite; cf. Ms. 6. 17. -कर्षणः a lime or citron tree. -कारः an artist who works in ivory. -काष्ठं a piece of stick or twig used as a toothbrush. -क्रूरः fight. -ग्राहिन् *a.* injuring the teeth, causing them to decay. -घर्षः chattering or grinding the teeth. -चालः looseness of the teeth. -छदः a lip; वारंवारमुदारशीत्कृतकृतो दंतच्छदान् पीडयन् Bh. 1. 43; Rs. 4. 12. -जात *a.* (a child) that is teething. -जाहं the root of a tooth. -धावनं 1 cleaning or washing the teeth. 2 a tooth-brush. (-नः) 1 the Bakula tree. 2 the Khadira tree. -पत्रं a sort of ear-ornament; R. 6. 17; Ku. 7 23 (often used in Kâdambari). -पत्रकं 1 an ear-ornament. 2 a Kunda flower. -पत्रिका 1 an ear-ornament; Si. 1. 60. 2 Kunda. -पवन 1 a tooth-brush. 2 cleaning or washing the teeth. -पातः falling out of the teeth. -पाली 1 the point of tooth. 2 gum. -पुष्पं 1 the Kunda flower. 2 fruit of the clearingnut plant (कतकफल). प्रक्षालनं washing the teeth. -भागः the fore part of an elephant's head (where the tusks appear). -मलं the tartar of the teeth. -मांसं, -मूलं, -वल्कं gums. -मूलीयाः pl the dental letters viz: ऌ, त्, थ्, द्, ध्, न्, ल् and स्. रोगः tooth-ache. -वक्त्रं, -वासस् *n.* the lip; तुलां यदारोहति दंतवाससा Ku. 5. 34; Si. 10. 86. -बीजः, -वीजः, -बीजकः, -वीजकः the pomegranate tree -वीणा 1 a kind of musical instrument or harp. 2 chattering of the teeth; दंतवीणां वादयन् Pt. 1. -वैदर्भः loosening of the teeth through external injury. -व्यसनं fracture of the teeth. -शठ *a.* sour, acid. (-ठः) the citron tree. -शर्करा tartar of the teeth. -शाणः a kind of tooth-powder, dentifrice. शूलः. -लं tooth-ache. -शोधनिः *f.* a tooth-pick. -शोफः swelling of the gums. -संघर्षः gnashing or rubbing together the teeth. -हर्षः morbid sensitiveness of the teeth (as when they are set on edge). -हर्षकः the citron tree.

दंतकः 1 A peak, summit. 2 A pin or shelf projecting from a wall, bracket.

दंतादंति *ind.* 'Tooth against tooth', biting one another.

दंतावलः, दंतिन् *m.* An elephant; Bv. 1. 60; तृणैर्गुणत्वमापन्नैर्बध्यंते मत्तदंतिनः H. 1. 35; R. 1. 71; Ku. 16. 2.

दंतुर *a.* 1 Having long or projecting teeth; शूकरे निहते चैव दंतुरो जायते नरः Tv.; Si. 6. 54. 2 Jagged, dentated, notched, serrated, uneven (fig. also); अखर्वगर्वस्मितदंतुरेण Vikr. 1. 50. 3 Undulatory. 4 Rising, bristling (as hair) -COMP. -छदः the lime-tree.

दंतुरित *a.* 1 Having long or projecting teeth. 2 Notched, serrated, bristling; केतकिदंतुरिताशे Git. 1; पुलकभर° 11; K. 286.

दंत्य *a.* Dental.-त्यः (*i. e.* वर्णः) A letter of the dental class; see दंतमूलीय above.

दंदशः A tooth.

दंदशूक *a.* 1 Biting, venomous. 2 Mischievous. -कः 1 A serpent, snake. 2 A reptile in general. 3 A demon, Râkshasa; इषुमति रघुसिंहे दंदशूकाञ्जिघांसौ Bk. 1. 26.

दभ्, दंभ्, I. 1. 5. P. (दभति or दभ्नोति, दब्ध; *desid.* धिप्सति, धीप्सति, दिदंभिषति) 1 To injure, hurt. 2 To deceive, cheat. 3 To go. -II. 10 U. (दंभयति-ते) To impel, propel, drive on-ward.

दभ्र *a.* Little, small; अदभ्रदर्भामधिशय्य स स्थलीं Ki. 1. 38; see अदभ्र. -भ्रः The ocean. -भ्रं *ind.* A little, slightly, to some extent.

दम् 4 P. (दाम्यति, दमित, दांत; *Caus.* दमयति) 1 To be tamed. 2 To be calm or tranquil; Ms. 4. 35, 6. 8, 7. 141. 3 To tame, subdue, conquer, restrain; यमो दाम्यति राक्षसान् Bk. 18. 20; दमित्वाप्यरिसंघातान् 9. 42, 19; 15. 37. 4 To pacify.

दमः 1 Taming subduing. 2 Self-command, subduing or curbing the passions, self-restraint; Bg. 10. 4; (निग्रहो बाह्यवृत्तीनां दम इत्यभिधीयते). 3 Drawing the mind away from evil deeds or curbing its evil propensities; (कुत्सितात्कर्मणो विप्र यच्च चित्तनिवारणं स कीर्तितो दमः) 4 Firmness of mind. 5 Punishment, fine; Ms. 9. 284, 290; Y. 2. 4. 6 Mire, mud.

दमथः,-थुः 1 Subduing or curbing the passions, self-restraint. 2 Punishment.

दमन *a.* (नी *f.*) Taming, subduing, overpowering, conquering, defeating, जामदग्न्यस्य दमने नैव निर्वक्तुमर्हसि U. 5. 32; Bh. 3. 89; so सर्वदमन, अरिंदमन &c. **2** Tranquil, passionless. **–नं 1** Taming, subjugation, curbing, restraint. **2** Punishing, chastising; दुर्दांतानां दमनविधयः क्षत्रियेष्वायतंते Mv. 3. 34. **3** Self-restraint.

दमयंती N. of the daughter of Bhîma, king of the Vidarbhas. [She was so called because by her matchless beauty she subdued the pride of all lovely women;cf. N. 2. 18:—भुवनत्रयसुभ्रुवामसौ दमयंती कमनीयतामदं । उदियाय यतस्तनुश्रिया दमयंतीति ततोऽभिधां दधौ ॥. A golden swan first described to her the beauty and virtues of king Nala, and through him she communicated her love to Nala. Afterwards at a Svayamvara she chose Nala for her husband from out of a host of competitors among whom were the four gods Indra, Agni, Yama and Varuna themselves, and the lovely pair spent some years very happily. But their happiness was not destined to last long. Kali envious of the good fortune of Nala entered his body and induced him to play at dice with his brother Pushkara. In the heat of the play the infatuated monarch staked and lost everything expect himself and his wife. Nala and Damayati were therefore driven out of the kingdom, 'clad in a single garment.' While wandering through the wilderness, Damayanti had to pass through several trying adventures, but her devotion to her husband remained entirely unshaken. One day while she was asleep, Nala in the frenzy of despair abandoned her, and she was obliged to go to her father's house. After some time she was united with her husband, and they passed the rest of their lives in the undisturbed enjoyment of happiness. See Nala and *R*ituparna also].

दमयितृ *a.* **1** Taming, subduing. **2** A punisher, chastiser. **3** An epithet of Vishnu.

दमित *a.* **1** Tamed, calmed, tranquilised. **2** Conquered, curbed, subdued, defeated.

दमु (मू) नस् *m.* Fire.

दंपती *m.* du. (comp. of जाया पति) Husband and wife; R. 1. 35, 2. 70; Ms. 3.116.

दंभः 1 Deceit, fraud, trickery. **2** Religious hypocrisy; Bg. 16 4. **3** Arrogance, pride, ostentation. **4** Sin, wickedness. **5** The thunderbolt of Indra.

दंभनं Cheating, deceiving, deceit.

दंभिन् *m.* A hypocrite, an impostor; Y. 1. 130 ; Bg. 13. 7.

दंभोलिः Indra's thuderbolt.

दम्य *a.* **1** To be tamed or traided. **2** Punishable.**-म्यः 1** A young bullock (requiring training and experience); नार्हति तातः पुंगवधारितायां धुरि दम्यं नियोजयितुं V. 5; गुर्वीं धुरं यो भुवनस्य पित्रा धुर्येण दम्यः सदृशं बिभर्ति R. 6. 78; Mu. 3. 3. **2** A steer that has to be tamed.

दय् 1 A. (दयते, दयित) **1** To feel pity or compassion for, pity, sympathise with (with gen.); रामस्य दयमानोऽसावध्येति तव लक्ष्मणः Bk. 8 119; तेषां दयसे न कस्मात् 1. 33, 15. 63. **2** To love, like, be fond of; दयमानाः प्रमदाः *S*. 1. 3. ; Bk. 10. 9. **3** To protect ; नगजा न गजा दयिता दयिताः Bk. 10 9. **4** To go, move **5** To grant, give, divide or allot. **6** To hurt.

दया Pity, tenderness, compassion, mercy, sympathy ; निर्गुणेष्वपि सत्वेषु दयां कुर्वंति साधवः H. 1 60 R. **2.** 11; so भूतदया. –Comp. **-कूटः, कूर्चः** epithets of Buddha. **-वीरः** (in Rhet.) the sentiment of heroic compassion ; the sentiment of heroism arising out of compassion. *e. g.* **Jîmûtavâhana's** remark to Garuḍa in Nâg:—शिरामुखैः स्यंदत एव रक्तमद्यापि देहे मम मांसमस्ति । तृप्तिं न पश्यामि तवापि तावत् किं भक्षणात्त्वं विरतो गरुत्मन्॥ cf. also R. G. under दयावीर.

दयालु *a.* Kind, tender, merciful, compassionate; यशःशरीरे भव मे दयालुः R. 2. 52, 3.

दयित *p. p.* Beloved, desired, liked; Bk. 10. 9.**–तः** A husband, lover, a beloved person; V. 3- 5; Bv. **2. 182. –ता** A wife, one's beloved woman ; दयिताजीवितालंबनार्थी Me, 4; R. **2.** 3 ; Bv. 2. 182; Ki 6. 13 ; दयिताजितः a henpecked husband.

दर *a.* Tearing, rending &c. (at the end of comp).**—रः,-रं 1** A cave, cavity, hole. **2** A conchshell.**–रः 1** Fear, terror, dread ; सा दरं पृतना निन्ये हीयमाना रसादरं *Si*. **19. 23**; न जातहार्देन न विद्विषादरः Ki. **1. 33.–रं** *ind.* A little, slightly (in comp.); दरमीलन्नयना निरीक्षते Bv. **2**. 182, 7 ; दरविगलितमल्लीवल्लिचंचत्पराग &c. Gît **1** ; so दरदलित–विकसित U. 4; Mâl. 3. -Comp. **–तिमिरं** the darkness of fear; हरति दरतिमिरमतिघोरं Gît. 10.

दरणं Breaking, splitting.

दरणिः *m. f.*, **दरणी 1** An eddy. **2** A current. **3** Surf.

दरद् *f.* **1** The heart. **2** Terror, fear. **3** A mountain. **4** A precipice. **5** A bank or mound.

दरदाः *m. pl.* A country bordering on Kâshmîra. **—दः** Fear, terror. **—दं** Red lead.

दरिः –री *f.* A cave, cavern, valley; दरीगृह Ku. 1. 10; एका भार्या सुंदरी वा दरी वा Bh. **3.** 120.

दरिद्रा 2 P. (दरिद्राति, दरिद्रित; *Caus.* दरिद्रयति; *Desid.* दिदरिद्रासति, दिदरिद्रिषति) **1** To be poor or needy; अधोऽधः पश्यतः कस्य महिमा नोपजायते । उपर्युपरि पश्यंतः सर्व एव दरिद्रति ॥ H. 2. 2: Bk. 18. 31. **2** To be in distress; युक्तं ममैव किं वक्तुं दरिद्राति यथा हरिः Bk. **5. 86. 3** To become thin or sparse; दरिद्रति वियद्द्रुमे कुसुमकोतयस्तारकाः Vikr 11. 74.

दरिद्र *a.* Poor, needy, indigent, in distressed circumstances; स तु भवतु दरिद्रो यस्य तृष्णा विशाला । मनसि च परितुष्टे कोऽर्थवान् को दरिद्रः Bh. **2.** 50. **°ता** Poverty; शंकनीया हि लोकेऽस्मिन्निष्प्रतापा दरिद्रता Mk. 3 24.

दरोदरः 1 A gamester. **2** A stake at play. **—रं 1** Gambling. **2** A die, dice; see दुरोदर.

दर्दरः 1 A mountain. **2** A jar slightly broken.

दर्दरीकः 1 A frog **2** A cloud. **3** A kind of musical instrument. **-कं** A musical instrument in general.

दर्दुरः 1 A frog; पंकक्लिन्नमुखाः पिबंति सलिलं धाराहता दर्दुराः Mk. 5 14. **2** A cloud. **3** A kind of musical instrument such as a flute **4** A mountain. **5** N. of a mountain in the south (associated with Malaya); स्तनाविव दिशस्तस्याः शैलौ मलयदर्दुरौ R. 4. 51.

दर्द्रुः (द्रू) A kind of leprosy.

दर्पः 1 Pride, arrogance, insolence, haughtiness; Ms 8 213; Bg, 16. 4. **2** Rashness., **3** Vanity, conceit. **4** Sullenness, sulkiness. **5** Heat. **6** Musk. –Comp. **आध्मात** *a.* inflated or puffed up with pride. **–छिद्, –हर** *a.* humbling, humiliating.

दर्पकः N. of Kâmadeva, the god of love.

दर्पणः A looking-glass, mirror; लोचनाभ्यां विहीनस्य दर्पणः किं करिष्यति Châṇ. 109; Ku. 7. 26; R. 10. 10; 16. 37. **–णं 1** The eye. **2** Kindling, inflaming.

दर्पित, दर्पिन् *a.* (णी *f.*) Proud, arrogant, haughty.

दर्भः A kind of sacred grass (Kusa grass) used at sacrificial ceremonies &c.; *S*. 1. 7; R. 11. 31; Ms. 2. 43; 3. 208, **4.** 36. —Comp. **—अंकुरः** a pointed blade of *darbha* grass; *S*. **2. 12. –अनूपः** a watery place full of *darbha* grass. **–आह्वयः** the Munja grass.

दर्भटं A private apartment, a retired room.

दर्वः 1 A mischievous or harmful person (हिंस्र). **2** A demon, goblin. **3** A ladle.

दर्वटः 1 A village-constable, a police-officer. **2** A door-keeper.

दर्वरिकः 1 An epithet of Indra. **2** A kind of musical instrument. **3** Air, wind.

दर्विका A ladle, spoon.

दर्वी (र्विः) *f.* A ladle, spoon. **2** The expanded hood of a snake; *Si*. 20 42. —Comp. **–करः** a snake, serpent.

दर्शः 1 Sight, view, appearance (usually in comp); दुर्दर्शः, प्रियदर्शः. 2 The day of the new moon (अमावास्या) 3 The half monthly sacrifice, a sacrificial rite performed on the day of the new moon. –COMP. –पः a god. —यामिनी the night of the new moon. विपद् *m.* the moon.

दर्शक *a.* 1 Seeing, observing; &c. 2 Showing, pointing out; Ku. 6 52. —कः 1 One who shows or exhibits. 2 A doorkeeper, warder. 3 A skilful man, one proficient in any art or science.

दर्शनं Looking at, seeing, observing; R. 3. 4. 2 Knowing, understanding, perceiving, foreseeing; R. 8. 72. 3 Sight, vision, चिंताजडं दर्शनं *S.* 4. 5. 4 The eye. 5 Inspection, examination. 6 Showing, displaying, exhibition. 7 Becoming visible. 8 Visiting, paying a visit, a visit; देवदर्शनं. 9 (hence) Going into the presence of, audience; मारीचस्ते दर्शनं वितरति *S.* 7; राजदर्शनं मे कारय &c. 10 Colour, aspect, appearance; Bg. 11. 10; R. 3. 57. 11 Appearance, producing; (in court); Ms. 8. 158, 160. 12 A vision, dream. 13 Discernment, understanding, intellect. 14 Judgment, apprehension. 15 Religious knowledge. 16 A doctrine or theory prescribed in a system. 17 A system of philosophy; as in सर्वदर्शनसंग्रह. 18 A mirror. 19 Virtue, moral merit. 20 A sacrifice. –COMP. ईप्सु *a.* anxious to see. –पथ the range of sight or vision, horizon. –प्रतिभूः a bail or surety for appearance.

दर्शनीय *a.* 1 Visible, observable, perceptible. 2 Fit to be seen, good-looking, handsome, beautiful. 3 To be produced in a court of justice.

दर्शयितृ *m.* 1 Warder, an usher, door-keeper. 2 A guide (in general).

दर्शित *a.* 1 Shown, displayed, manifested, exhibited. 2 Seen, understood. 3 Explained, proved. 4 Apparent.

दर्शिन् *a.* (नी *f.*) (At the end of comp.) Seeing, perceiving, observing, knowing, understanding, showing, exhibiting &c.

दल् 1 P. (दलति, दलित) 1 To burst open, split, cleave, crack; दलति हृदयं गाढोद्वेगं द्विधा तु न भिद्यते U. 3. 31; अपि ग्रावा रोदित्यपि दलति वज्रस्य हृदयं 1. 28; Mâl. 9. 12. 20; दलति न सा हृदि विरहभरेण Git. 7; Amaru. 38. 2 To expand, bloom, open (as a flower). दलन्नवनीलोत्पल U. 1; स्वच्छंदं दलदरविंद ते मरंदं विंदंतो विदधतु गुंजितं मिलिंदाः Bv. 1. 15; *Si.* 6. 23; Ki. 10. 39.—*Caus.* (द-दा-लयति) 1 To cause to burst, tear asunder. 2 To cut, divide, split. WITH उद् *caus.* to tear up. –वि 1 to break, split, crack; स्वदिशुमिर्व्यदलिष्यदसावपि N. 4. 88. 2 to dig up.

दलः–लं 1 A piece, portion, part. fragment; *Si.* 4, 44. 2 A degree. 3 A half, the half. 4 A sheath, scabbard. 5 A small shoot or blade, a petal, leaf; R. 4. 42; *S.* 3. 21, 22. 6 The blade of any weapon. 7 A clump, heap, quantity. 8 A detachment, a body of troops –COMP. आढकः 1 foam. 2 a cuttle-fish bone. 3 a ditch, moat. 4 a hurricane, high wind. 5 red chalk. –कोषः the Kunda creeper. –निर्मोकः the Bhúrja tree. –पुष्पा the Ketaka plant. –सूचिः, –ची *f.* a thorn. –स्नसा the fibre or vein of a leaf.

दलनं Bursting, breaking, cutting, dividing, crushing, grinding, splitting मत्तेभकुंभदलने भुवि संति शूराः Bh. 1. 59.

दलनी, दलिः *m. f.* A clod of earth.

दलपः 1 A weapon. 2 Gold. 3 *S*âstra.

दलशः *ind.* By pieces, in fragments.

दलित *p. p.* 1 Broken, torn, rent, burst, split. 2 Opened, expanded.

दल्भः 1 A wheel. 2 Fraud, dishonesty. 3 Sin.

दवः 1 A wood, forest. 2 Wild fire, forest-conflagration; वितर वारिद वारि दवातुरे Subhâsh. 3 Fire, heat. 5 Fever, pain. –COMP. –अग्निः, –दहनः a forest-conflagration; यस्य न सविधे दयिता दवदहनस्तुहिनदीधितिस्तस्य। यस्य च सविधे दयिता दवदहनस्तुहिनदीधितिस्तस्य ॥ K. P. 9; Bv. 1. 36; Me. 53; शशाम वृष्ट्यापि विना दवाग्निः R. 2. 14.

दवथुः 1 Fire, heat. 2 Pain, anxiety, distress. 3 Inflammation of the eye.

दविष्ठ *a.* (Superl. of दूर) 1 Most distant &c.

दवीयस् *a.* (Compar. of दूर) 1 More distant or remote. 2 Far beyond or removed from; विद्यावतां सकलमेव गिरां दवीयः Bv. 1. 69.

दशक *a.* Consisting of ten, tenfold; कामजो दशमो गणः Ms. 7. 47. —कं A group of ten.

दशत् *f.*, **दशतिः** *f.* A group of ten, decad.

दशन् *num. a.* (pl.) Ten; स भूमिं विश्वतो वृत्वाऽत्यतिष्ठद्दशांगुलं Rv. 10. 90. 1. –COMP. –अंगुल *a.* ten fingers long. –अर्ध *a.* five. (–र्धः) an epithet of Buddha. –अवताराः *m. pl.* the ten incarnations of Vishnu; see under अवतार. –अश्वः the moon. –आननः, -आस्यः epithets of Râvaṇa; R. 10. 75. –आमयः an epithet of Rudra. –ईशः a superintendent of 10 villages. –एकादशिक *a.* who lends 10 and receives 11 in return; *i. e.* who lends money at ten per cent. –कंठः, –कंधरः epithets of Râvaṇa; सत्तलोकैकवीरस्य दशकंठकुलद्विषः U. 4. 27. °जरिः, °जित् *m.* रिपुः epithets of Râma; R. 8. 29. –गुण *a.* ten-fold, ten times larger. –ग्रामिन् *m.*, –पः a superintendent of ten villages. –ग्रीवः=दशकंठ q. v. –पारमिताध्वरः 'possessing the ten perfections,' an epithet of Buddha. –पुरः N. of an ancient city, capital of king Rantideva; Me. 47. –बलः, –भूमिगः epithets of Buddha. –मालिकाः pl. 1 N. of a country. 2 the people or rulers of this country. –मास्य *a.* 1 ten months old. 2 ten months in the womb (as a child before birth). –मुखः an epithet of Râvaṇa. °रिपुः an epithet of Râma; R. 14. 87. –रथः N. of a celebrated king of Ayodhyâ, son of Aja, and father of Râma and his three brothers. [He had three wives Kausalya, Sumitra, and Kaikeyi, but was for several years without issue. He was therefore recommended by Vasis*th*a to perform a sacrifice which he successfully did with the assistance of *R*ishyasringa. On the completion of this sacrifice, Kausalya bore to him Rama, Sumitra Laksamana and Satrughna, and Kaikeyi Bharata. Dasaratha was extremely fond of his sons, but Rama was his greatest favourite—'his life,—his very soul'. Thus when Kaikeyi at the instigation of Manthara demanded the fulfilment of the two boons he had previously promised to her, the king tried to dissuade her mind from her wicked resolve by threats, and, failing these, by the most servile supplications. But Kaikeyi remained inexorable, and the poor monarch was obliged to send his beloved son into exile. He soon afterwards died of a broken heart.]. –रश्मिशतः the sun; R. 8. 29. –रात्रं a period of ten nights. (–त्रः) a particular sacrifice lasting for ten days. –रूपभृत् *m.* an epithet of Vishṇu. –वक्त्रः,– वदनः see दशमुख. –वाजिन् *m.* the moon. –वार्षिक *a.* happening after or lasting for ten years. –विध *a.* of ten kinds. –शतं 1 a thousand. 2 one hundred and ten. °रश्मिः the sun. –शती a thousand. –साहस्रं ten thousands. –हरा 1 an epithet of the Ganges. 2 a festival in honour of the Ganges held on the 10th day of Jyeshṭha. 3 a festival in honour of Durgâ held on the tenth of Asvina.

दशतय *a.* (यी *f.*) Consisting of ten parts, ten-fold.

दशधा *ind.* 1 In ten ways. 2 In ten parts.

दशनः –नं 1 A tooth; मुहुर्मुहुर्दशनविखंडितोष्ठया *Si.* 17. 2; शिखरिदशना Me. 90; Bg. 10. 27. 2 Biting. –नः The peak of a mountain. –नं An armour.–COMP. –अंशुः brightness of the teeth; Ku. 6. 25. –अंकः a tooth-mark, bite. –उच्छिष्टः 1 a lip. 2 a kiss. 3 a sigh. छदः,–वासस् *n.* 1 a lip. 2 a kiss. –पदं

a bite, tooth-mark; दशनपदं भवदधरगतं मम जनयति चेतसि खेदं Gît. 8. -बीजः the pomegranate tree.

दशम *a.* (मी *f.*) Tenth.

दशमिन् *a.* (नी *f.*) Very old.

दशमी 1 The tenth day of a lunar fort-night. 2 The tenth decad of the human life. 3 The last ten years of a century. -COMP. -स्थ, दशमींगत above ninety years old.

दष्ट *a.* Bitten, stung; see दंश्.

दशा 1 The threads at the end of a piece of woven cloth, the fringe of a garment, the skirt, edge or hem of a garment; रक्तांशुकं पवनलोलदशं वहंती Mk. 1. 20; छिन्ना इवांबरपटस्य दशाः पतंति 5. 4. 2 The wick of a lamp; Bh. 3. 129; Ku. 4. 30. 3 Age or condition of life; see दशांत below. 4 A period or stage of life; as बाल्य, यौवन &c.; R. 5. 40. 5 A period in general. 6 State, condition, circumstances; नीचैर्गच्छत्युपरि च दशा चक्रनेमिक्रमेण Me. 109; विषमां हि दशां प्राप्य दैवं गर्हयते नरः H. 4. 3. 7 State or condition of mind. 8 The result of actions, fate. 9 The aspect or position of planets (at birth). 10 The mind, understanding. COMP. -अंतः 1 the end of a wick. 2 the end of life; निर्विष्टविषयस्नेहः स दशांतमुपेयिवान् R. 12. 1 (where the word is used in both senses). -इंधनः a lamp. -कर्षः 1 the end of a garment. 2 a lamp. -पाकः, -विपाकः 1 the fulfilment of fate. 2 a changed condition of life.

दशार्णः pl. 1 N. of a country; संपत्स्यंते कतिपयदिनस्थायिहंसा दशार्णाः Me. 23. 2 The people of this country.

दशिन् *a.* (नी *f.*) Having ten. *-m.* A superintendent of ten villages.

दशेर *a.* Biting, mischievous, injurious, hurtful. -रः A mischievous or venomous animal.

दशे (से) रकः A young camel.

दस्युः 1 N. of a class of evil-beings or demons, enemies of gods and men and slain by Indra, (mostly Vedic in this sense). 2 An outcast, a Hindu who has become an outcast by neglect of the essential rites; cf. Ms. 5. 131, 10. 45. 3 A thief, robber, bandit; पात्रीकृतो दस्युरिवासि येन *S.* 5. 20; R. 9. 53; Ms. 7. 143. 4 A villain, miscreant; Mâl. 5. 28. 5 A desperado, violator, oppressor.

दस्र *a.* Savage, fierce, destructive. —स्रौ (*m.* du.) The two Asvins, the physicians of the gods.—स्रः 1 An ass. 2 The lunar mansion Asvinî.–स्रूः *f.* wife of the sun and mother of the Asvins, संज्ञा q. v.

दह् 1 P. (दहति, दग्ध; *desid.* दिधक्षति) 1 To burn, scorch (fig. also); दग्धुं विश्वं दहनकिरणैर्नोदिता द्वादशार्काः Ve. 3. 6, 5. 20; सपदि मदनानलो दहति मम मानसं देहि मुखकमलमधुपानं Gît. 10; *S.* 3. 17. 2 To consume, destroy completely. 3 To pain, torment, afflict, distress; इत्यमात्मकृतमप्रतिहतं चापलं दहति *S.* 5. तत्सविषमिव शल्यं दहति मां 6. 8; एतत्तु मां दहति यद् गृहमस्मदीयं क्षीणार्थमित्यतिथयः परिवर्जयंति Mk. 1. 12; R. 8. 86. 4 To cauterize (in medicine). -WITH निस् 1 to burn, consume. 2 to torment, distress, pain. -परि to burn, scorch; दिशि दिशि परिदग्धा भूमयः पावकेन Rs. 1. 24; Bg. 1. 30. -प्र 1 to burn. 2 to burn completely. 3 to pain, torment. 4 to trouble, tease. -सं to burn; अभिजनः संदह्यतां वह्निना Bh. 2. 39.

दहन् *a.* (नी *f.*) 1 Burning, consuming by fire; Bh. 1. 71. 2 Destructive, injurious. -नः 1 Fire. 2 A pigeon. 3 The number 'three'. 4 A bad man. 5 The भल्लातक plant. -नं 1 Burning, consuming by fire (fig. also); R. 8. 20. 2 Cauterizing. -COMP. -अरातिः water. -उपलः the sun-stone. -उल्का a fire-brand.-केतनः smoke. -प्रिया Svâhâ, wife of Agni. -सारथिः wind.

दहर *a.* 1 Small, subtle, fine, thin. 2 Young in age. -रः 1 A child, an infant. 2 Any young animal. 3 A younger brother. 4 The cavity of the heart or the heart itself. 5 A mouse or rat.

दहः 1 Fire. 2 A forest-conflagration.

दा I. 1 P. (यच्छति, दत्त) To give, grant.-WITH प्रति to exchange; तिलेभ्यः प्रतियच्छति माषान् Sk. -II. 2 P. (दाति) To cut; ददाति द्रविणं भूरि हाति दारिद्र्यमर्थिनां K. R. -III. 3 U. (ददाति, दत्ते, दत्त; but with आ the *p. p.* is आत्त; with उप, उपात्त; with नि, निदत्त or नीत्त and with प्र, प्रदत्त or प्रत्त) 1 To give, grant, bestow, offer, yield, impart, present (usually with acc. of the thing and dat., sometimes gen. or loc. also, of the person); अवकाशं किलोदन्वान् रामायाभ्यर्थितो ददौ *R.* 4. 58; सेचनघटैः बालपादपेभ्यः पयो दातुमित एवाभिवर्तते *S.* 1; Ms. 3. 31, 9. 271; कथमस्य स्तनं दास्ये Hariv. 2 To pay (as debt, fine &c) 3 To hand or deliver over. 4 To restore, return. 5 To give up, sacrifice, surrender; प्राणान् दा to sacrifice one's life; so आत्मानं दा to sacrifice oneself. 6 To put, place, apply, plant; कर्णे करं ददाति &c. 7 To give in marriage, यस्मै दद्यात् पिता त्वेनां Ms. 5. 151; Y. 2. 146, 3. 24. 8 To allow, permit (usually with inf.); बाष्पस्तु न ददात्येनां द्रष्टुं चित्रगतामपि *S.* 6. 21. (The meanings of this root may be variously modified or extended according to the noun with which it is connected; *c. g.* अवकाशं दा to give place to, make room; see अवकाश; कर्णं दा to give ear to or listen; दर्शनं दा to show oneself to, grant audience to; शब्दं दा to make a noise; तालं दा to clap the hands; आत्मानं खेदाय दा to expose oneself to trouble; आतपे दा to expose to the sun's heat; आज्ञां, निदेशं दा to issue orders, command; आशिषं दा to pronounce a blessing; चक्षुः, -दृष्टिं दा to cast a glance. see; मनो दा to direct the mind to a thing; वाचं दा to address a speech to; प्रतिवच-वचनं or प्रत्युत्तरं दा to give a reply; शोकं दा to cause grief; श्राद्धं दा to perform a Srâddha; मार्गं दा to make way for, allow to pass, stand out of the way; वरं दा to grant a boon; संग्रामं दा to fight; अर्गलं दा to bolt, fasten or secure with a latch; निगडं दा to put in chains, fetter; संकेतं दा to make an appointment; शापं दा to curse; वृत्तिं दा to enclose, fence in; अग्नि-पावकं दा to set on fire &c. &c. —*Caus.* (दापयति-ते); To cause to give grant &c. *-desid* (दित्सति-ते) To wish to give &c. With आ (Atm.) 1 to receive, take, accept, resort to; व्यवहारासनमाददे युवा R. 8. 18; 10. 40; 3. 46; प्रदक्षिणार्चिर्हविरग्निराददे 3. 14, 1. 45. 2 to utter as words; Ki. 1. 3; Si. 2. 13. 3 to seize, take hold of; Ku. 7. 94. 4 to exact, take in (as taxes); अगृध्नुराददे सोऽर्थं R. 1. 21; Ms. 8. 341. 5 to carry, take, bear; तोयमादाय गच्छेः Me. 20. 46; कुशानादाय *S.* 3. 6 to perceive, comprehend; घ्राणेन रूपमादत्स्व रसानादत्स्व चक्षुषा &c. Mb. 7 to imprison, make captive -उपा (Atm.) 1 to receive, accept. 2 to acquire, obtain; उपात्तविद्यो गुरुदक्षिणार्थी R. 5. 1; भूर्या पितामहोपात्ता Y. 2. 121. 3 to take, assume, carry 4 to feel, perceive. 5 to seize, attack. -परि to hand over, deliver over, consign; छद्मना परिददामि मृत्यवे U. 1. 45; Ms. 9. 327. -प्र 1 to grant, give, offer; स्वं प्रागहं प्रादिषि नामराय किं नाम तस्मै मनसा नराय N. 6. 95; Ms. 3. 99, 108, 273; Y. 2. 90. 2 to impart, teach (as learning); Bh. 1. 15.-प्रति 1 to exchange, barter. 2 to give back, return; Cb. P. 35. 3 to recompense.-व्या (P. and A.) to open, break open; न व्याददात्याननमत्र मृत्युः Ki. 16. 16; नदी कूलं व्याददाति or व्याददते पिपीलिकाः पतंगस्य मुखं Mb.-संप्र 1 to give, grant, bestow or confer upon; तं तेऽहं संप्रदास्यामि. 2 to hand down by tradition; see संप्रदाय 3 to bequeath.

दाक्षायणी 1 Any one of the 27 lunar mansions (they being mythologically regarded as so many daughters of Daksha). 2 N. of Diti, wife of Kasyapa and mother of the gods. 3 N. of Pârvatî. 4 The lunar constellation called Revatî. 5 N. of Kadru or Vinatâ. 6 The Dantî plant. -COMP.-पतिः 1 an epithet of Siva. 2 the moon.-पुत्रः a god.

दाक्षाय्यः A vulture.

दाक्षिण *a.* (णी *f.*) 1 Relating to a sacrificial gift or to a gift in general. 2 Relating to the south. -**णं** A collection of sacrificial gifts.

दाक्षिणात्य *a.* Belonging to or living in the south, southern ; आस्ति दाक्षिणात्ये जनपदे महिलारोप्यं नाम नगरं Pt. 1.-**त्यः** A southerner, a native of the Deccan; आरंभशूराः खलु दाक्षिणात्याः 2 The cocoa-nut.

दाक्षिणिक *a.* (की *f.*) Connected with a sacrificial gift.

दाक्षिण्यं 1 (*a*) Politeness, civility, courtesy; तस्य दाक्षिण्यरूढेन नाम्ना मगधवंशजा R. 1. 31. (*b*) Kindness; V. 1. 2; Bh. 2. 23; Mâl. 1. 8. 2 Insincere or overcourteous conduct of a lover (towards his beloved); *S.* 6. 5. 3 The state of relating to or coming from the south; स्नेहदाक्षिण्ययोर्योगात् कामीव प्रतिभाति मे V. 2. 4. (where the word has sense 1 or 2 also). 4 Concord, harmony, agreement. 5 Talent, cleverness.

दाक्षी 1 A daughter of दक्ष. 2 N. of the mother of Pâṇini.—Comp. -**पुत्रः** N. of Pâṇini.

दाक्षेयः A metronymic of Pâṇini.

दाक्ष्यं 1 Cleverness, skill, fitness, dexterity, ability; Bg. 18. 43. 2 Probity, integrity, honesty.

दाघः Burning.

दाडकः A tooth, tusk.

दाडि (लि) मः, -मा 1 The pomegranate tree; पाकारुणस्फुटितदाडिमकांति वक्त्रं Mâl. 9. 31, Amaru. 13. 3 Small cardamoms. -**मं** The fruit of the pomegranate tree. -Comp. -**प्रियः, -भक्षणः** a parrot.

दाडिंबः The pomegranate tree.

दाढा 1 A large tooth or tusk. 2 A multitude. 3 Wish, desire.

दाढिका The beard; Ms. 8. 283 (Kull. श्मश्रु).

दांडाजिनिक *a.* (की *f.*) Carrying a staff and hide (as mere outward signs of religious devotion). -**कः** A cheat, hypocrite, impostor.

दांडिकः A chastiser, punisher.

दात *a.* Divided, cut. 2 Washed, purified. 3 Reaped.

दातिः *f.* 1 Giving. 2 Cutting, destroying. 3 Distribution.

दातृ *a.* (त्री *f.*) 1 Giving, granting. 2 Liberal. -*m.* (ता) 1 A giver (in general); Ku. 6. 1. 2 A donor; Bv. 1. 66. 3 A lender, creditor. 4 A teacher.

दात्यूहः 1 The gallinule; दात्यूहेस्तिनिशस्य कोटरवति स्कंधे निलीय स्थितं Mâl. 9. 7. 2 The Châtaka bird. 3 A cloud. 4 A watercrow (written also दात्यौह).

दात्रं An instrument of cutting, a sort of sickle or knife.

दादः A gift, donation. -Comp. -**दः** a donor.

दान् *a.* 1 U. (दानति-ते) To cut, divide. —*Desid.* (दीदांसति-ते) To make straight (*desid.* inform, but not in sense).

दानं 1 Giving, granting, teaching &c. (in general). 2 Delivering, handing over. 3 A gift, donation, present; Ms. 2. 158; Bg. 17. 20; Y. 3. 274. 4 Liberality, charity, giving away as charity, munificence; R. 1. 69; Bh. 9. 43. 5 Ichor or the juice that exudes from the temples of an elephant in rut; सदानतोयेन विषाणि नागः *Si.* 4. 63; Ki. 5. 9; v. 4. 25; Pt. 2. 70 (where the word has sense 4 also); R. 2. 7, 4. 45. 5. 43. 6 Bribery, as one of the four Upâyas or expedients of overcoming one's enemy; see उपाय. 7 Cutting, dividing. 8 Purification, cleaning. 9 Protection. 10 Posture. -Comp. -**कुल्या** the flow of rut from an elephant's temples. -**धर्मः** alms-giving, charity. -**पतिः** 1 an exceedingly liberal man. 2 Akrûra, a friend of Krishṇa. -**पत्रं** a deed of gifts. -**पात्रं** 'a worthy recipient,' a Brâhmaṇa fit to recieve gifts. -**प्रातिभाव्यं** security for payment of a debt. **भिन्न** *a.* made hostile by bribes. —**वीरः** 1 a very liberal man. 2 (In Rhet.) the sentiment of heroism arising out of liberality, the sentiment of chivalrous liberality; *e. g.* Parasurâma who gave away the earth with its seven continents: cf. the instance given in R. G. under दानवीरः—कियदिदमधिकं मे यद्द्विजायार्थयित्रे कवचमरमणीयं कुंडले चार्पयामि । अकरुणमवकृत्य द्राक्कृपाणेन निर्यद्बहलरुधिरधारं मौलिमावेदयामि ॥. -**शील, -शूर -शौंड** *a.* exceedingly liberal or munificent.

दानकं A mean gift.

दानवः A demon, Râkshasa; त्रिदिवमुद्धृतदानवकंटकं *S.* 7. 3. -Comp. -**अरिः** 1 a god. 2 an epithet of Vishṇu.-**गुरुः** an epithet of Sukra.

दानवेयः=दानव q. v.

दांत *p. p.* 1 Tamed, subdued, curbed, restrained, bridled; see दम्. 2 Tame, mild. 3 Resigned. 4 Liberal. -**तः** 1 A tamed ox. 2 A donor. 3 N. of a tree (दमनक).

दांतिः *f.* Self-restraint, subjection, control.

दांतिक *a.* Made of ivory.

दापित *a.* 1 Caused to be given. 2 Condemned to pay fine, fined. 3 Adjudged. 4 Assigned, awarded.

दामन् *n.* 1 A string, thread, fillet, rope. 2 A chaplet, a garland in general; आद्ये बद्धा विरहदिवसे या शिखा दाम हित्वा Me. 92; कनकचंपकदामगौरीं Ch. P. 1; Si. 4. 50. 2 A line, streak (as of lightning); विद्युद्दाम्ना हेमराजीव विंध्यं M. 3. 20; Me. 27. 4 A large bandage. -Comp. -**अंचलं,-अंजनं** a foot-rope for horses, &c; Si. 5. 61. -**उदरः** an epithet of Krishṇa.

दामनी A foot-rope.

दामिनी Lightning.

दांपत्यं Matrimony, the matrimonial relation.

दांभिक *a.* (की *f.*) 1 Deceitful, hypocritical. 2 Proud, imperious. 3 Ostentatious, sanctimonious.

दायः 1 A gift, present, donation; रहसि रमते प्रीत्या दायं ददात्यनुवर्तते Mâl. 3. 2; प्रीतिदायः Mâl. 4; M. 8. 199. 2 A nuptial present (given to the bride or the bride-groom). 3 Share, portion, inheritance, patrimony; अनपत्यस्य पुत्रस्य माता दायमवाप्नुयात् Ms. 9. 217, 77, 164, 203. 4 A part or share in general. 5 Delivering, handing over. 6 Dividing, distributing. 7 Loss, destruction. 8 Irony. 9 Site, place. -Comp. -**अपवर्तनं** forfeiture of inheritance; Ms. 9. 79. -**अर्ह** *a.* claiming inheritance. -**आदः** 1 one entitled to a share of patrimony, an heir; पुमान्दायादोऽदायादा स्त्री Nir.; Y. 2. 118; Ms. 8. 160. 2 a son. 3 a relative, kinsman, near or remote, a distant descendant. 4 a claimant or pretender in general; गयां गोष्ठ वा दायादः Sk. -**आदा,-दी** 1 an heiress. 2 a daughter. -**आद्यं** 1 inheritance. 2 the state of being an inheritor. -**कालः** the time of the partition of an inheritance. -**बंधुः** 1 a partner in the inheritance. 2 a brother. -**भागः** division of property among heirs, partition (of inheritance).

दायक *a.* (यिका *f.*) Giving, granting, bestowing &c. (at the end of comp.); उत्तर°, पिंड° &c.

दारः 1 A rent, gap, cleft, hole. 2 A ploughed field. -**राः** (pl.) A wife; एते वयममी दाराः कन्येयं कुलजीवितं Ku. 6 63; दशरथदारानधिष्ठाय वसिष्ठः प्राप्तः U. 4; Pt. 1. 100; Ms. 1. 112, 2. 217; *S.* 4. 16, 5. 29. -Comp. -**अधीन** *a.* dependent on a wife. -**उपसंग्रहः, -ग्रहः, -परिग्रहः, -ग्रहणं** marriage; नवे दारपरिग्रहे U. 1. 19. -**कर्मन्** *n.*, -**क्रिया** marriage; R. 5. 40.

दारक *a.* (रिका *f.*) Breaking, tearing, splitting; दारिका हृदयदारिका पितुः -**कः** 1 A boy, a son. 2 A child, infant. 3 Any young animal. 4 A village.

दारणं Splitting, tearing, rending, opening, cleaving.

दारदः 1 Quicksilver. 2 The ocean. -**दः, -दं** Vermilion.

दारिका 1 A daughter. 2 A harlot.

दारित *a.* Torn, divided, split, rent.

दारिद्र्यं Poverty, indigence; दारिद्र्यदोषो गुणराशिनाशी Subhâsh.

दारी 1 A cleft. 2 A kind of disease.

दारु *a*. Tearing, rending. **-रुः** **1** A liberal or munificent man. **2** An artist. **-रु** *n*. (said to be *m*. also) **1** Wood, piece of wood, timber. **2** A block. **3** A lever. **4** A bolt. **5** The pine or Devadâru tree. **6** Ore. **7** Brass. -Comp. **-अंडः** the peacock. **-आघाटः** the woodpecker. **-गर्भा** a wooden puppet. **-जः** a kind of drum. **-पात्रं** a wooden vessel, such as a trough. **-पुत्रिका,-पुत्री** a wooden doll. **-मुख्याह्वया, -मुख्याह्वा** a lizard. **-यंत्रं 1** a wooden-puppet moved by strings. **2** any machinery of wood. **-वधूः** a wooden doll. **-सारः** sandal. **-हस्तकः** a wooden spoon.

दारुकः 1 The Devadâru tree. **2** N. of Krishṇa's charioteer; उत्कंधरं दारुक इत्युवाच *Si*. 4. 18. **-का 1** A puppet. **2** A wooden figure.

दारुण *a*. Hard, rough; U. 3. 34. **2** Harsh, cruel, ruthless, pitiless; मय्येव विस्मरणदारुणचित्तवृत्तौ *S*. 5. 23; पशुमारणकर्मदारुणः 6. 1; Ms. 8. 270. **3** Fierce, terrible, frightful; *S*. 6. 29. **4** Heavy, violent, intense, poignant, agonizing (grief, pain &c); हृदयकुसुमशोषी दारुणो दीर्घशोकः U. 5. **5** Sharp, severe (as words). **6** Atrocious, shocking.—**णः** The sentiment of horror (भयानक).-**णं** Severity, cruelty, horror &c.

दार्ढ्यं 1 Hardness, tightness, firmness **2** Confirmation, corroboration.

दार्दुरः-रं 1 A conch-shell, the valve of which opens to the right. **2** Water.

दार्भ *a*. (**र्भी** *f* .) Made of *darbha* grass; दार्भं मुंचत्त्युटजपटलं वीतनिद्रो मयूरः *S*. 4. v. 1.

दार्व *a*. (**र्वी** *f*.) Wooden.

दार्वटं A council-house, court (a word derived from the Persian).

दार्शनिकः One familiar with the Darsanas or systems of philosophy.

दार्षद *a*. (**दी** *f*.) **1** Stony, mineral. **2** Ground on a flat stone (as सक्तु &c.).

दार्ष्टांत *a*. (**ती** *f*.) Explained or illustrated by a दृष्टांत q. v., that which is the subject of an illustration (उपमेय); स्वापस्य दार्ष्टांतिकत्वेन विवक्षितं Sankara.

दाल्भिः N. of Indra.

दावः=दाव q. v.-Comp.-**अग्निः,-अनलः, दहनः** a forest-conflagration; आनंदमृगदावाग्निः शीलशाखिमदद्विपः । ज्ञानदीपमहावायुरयं खलसमागमः ॥ Bv. 1. 190, 34.

दाशः A fisherman; Ms. 8. 408, 409, 10. 34. -Comp. **-ग्रामः** a village mostly inhabited by fishermen. **-नंदिनी** an epithet of Satyavatî, mother of Vyâsa.

दाशरथः, दाशरथि 1 A son of Dasaratha in general; R. 10. 44. **2**. N. of Râma and his three borthers, but especially of Râma; R. 12. 45.

दाशार्हाः (pl.) The descendants of Dasârha, the Yâdavas; *Si*. 2. 64.

दाशेरः 1 The son of a fisherman. **2** A fisherman. **3** A camel.

दाशेरकः The Mâlava country. **—काः** (pl.). The rulers or inhabitants of that country; see दाशेर also.

दासः 1 A slave, servant in general; गृहकर्मदासाः Bh. 1. 1; गृह° कर्म° &c. **2** A fisherman. **3.** A Sûdra, a man of the fourth caste. **4** A word added to the name of a Sûdra; cf गुप्त. -Comp. **-अनुदासाः** 'a slave of a slave,' (the humblest of the servants); (sometimes used by the speaker as a mark of humility). **-जनः** a servant or slave; कमपराधलवं मयि पश्यसि त्यजसि मानिनि दासजनं यतः V. 4. 29; (**दासस्य कुलं** is used as a compound in the sense of 'the mob or the common people').

दासी 1 A female servant or slave. **2** The wife of a fisherman. **3** The wife of a Sûdra. **4** A harlot. -Comp. **-पुत्रः, -सुतः** the son of a female slave. **-सभं** a collection of female slaves. (The gen. sing. **दास्याः** enters into some compounds, but loses it literal sense; *e. g*. **दास्याः पुत्रः-सुतः** 'a whoreson', used as a term of abuse; दास्याः पुत्रैः शकुनिलुब्धकैः *S*. 2; but **दास्याः** सदृशी like a female slave).

दासेरः,-रकः 1 The son of a female slave. **2** A Sûdra. **3** A fisherman. **4** A camel; *Si*. 12. 32, 5. 66; (also दासेय in this sense).

दास्यं Servitude, slavery, service, bondage; पतिकुले तव दास्यमपि क्षमं *S*. 5. 27; Ms. 8. 410.

दाहः 1 Burning, conflagration; दाहशक्तिमिव कृष्णवर्त्मनि R. 11. 42; छेदो दंशस्य दाहो वा M. 4. 4; Ki. 5. 12. **2** Glowing redness (as of the sky). **3** The sensation of burning. **4** Feverish or morbid heat. -Comp. **-अगुरु** *n*., **-काष्ठं** a kind of agallochum. **-आत्मक** *a*. combustible. **-ज्वरः** inflammatory fever. **-सरः, -सरस्** *n*., **-स्थलं** a place where dead bodies are burnt, cemetery. **-हर** *a*. allaying heat. (**-रं**) the Usira plant.

दाहक *a*. (**हिका** *f*.) **1** Burning, kindling. **2** Incendiary, inflammatory **3** Cauterizing. **-कः** Fire.

दाहनं 1 Burning, reducing to ashes. **2** Cauterizing.

दाह्य *a*. **1** To be burnt. **2** Combustible.

दिक्कः A young elephant (**करभ**) twenty years old.

दिग्ध *a*. **1** Smeared, anointed, daubed; हस्ताबस्रदिग्धौ Ms. 3. 132; R. 16 15; दिग्धोऽमृतेन च विषेण च पक्ष्मलाक्ष्या गाढं निखात इव मे हृदये कटाक्षः Mâl. 1. 29. **2** Soiled, defiled. **3** Poisoned; Ku. 4. 25. **—ग्धः 1** Oil, ointment. **2** Any oily substance or unguent. **3** Fire. **4** A poisoned arrow. **5** A story (true or fictitious).

दिंडिः, दिंडिरः A kind of musical instrument.

दित *a*. Cut, torn, rent, divided.

दितिः *f*. **1** Cutting, splitting, dividing. **2** Liberality. **3** N. of a daughter of Daksha, wife of Kasyapa and mother of the demons or *daityas*. -Comp. **-जः, -तनयः** a demon, a Râkshasa.

दित्यः A demon.

दित्सा Desire of giving; Bv. 1. 125.

दिदृक्षा Desire of seeing एकस्थसौंदर्यदिदृक्षयेव Ku. 1. 49.

दिदृक्षु *a*. Desirous of seeing, curious.

दिधिषुः The second husband of a woman, married again or twice. *-f*. A virgin widow remarried.

दिधि (धी) षूः *f*. **1** A woman twice married. **2** An unmarried elder sister whose younger sister is married; ज्येष्ठायां यद्यनूढायां कन्यायामुह्यतेऽनुजा । सा चाग्रेदिधिषूर्ज्ञेया पूर्वा च दिधिषूः स्मृता ॥. Comp. **-पतिः** a man who has a sexual intercourse with the widow of his brother (not as a sacred duty but for carnal gratification); भ्रातुर्मृतस्य भार्यायां योऽनुरज्येत कामतः । धर्मेणापि नियुक्तायां स ज्ञेयो दिधिषूपतिः Ms. 3. 173.

दिधीर्षा Desire to sustain or support. दिक्कुंजराः कुरुत तत्त्रितये दिधीर्षा B. R. 1. 48

दिनं 1 Day (opp. रात्रि); दिनांते निहित तेजः सवित्रेव हुताशनः R. 4. 1; यामिनयंति दिनानि च सुखदुःखवशीकृते मनसि K. P. 10 दिनांते निलयाय गंतुं 2. 15. **2** A day (including the night, a period of 24 hours); दिने दिने सा परिवर्धमाना Ku 1. 25 सत व्यतीयुस्त्रिगुणानि तस्य दिनानि R. 2. 25 -Comp. **-अंडं** darkness. **-अत्ययः,-अंतः -अवसानं** evening, sunset; R. 2. 15, 45 **अधीशः** the sun. **-अर्धः** midday, noon **-आगमः, -आदिः, -आरंभः** daybreak morning. **-ईशः, -ईश्वरः** the sun **°आत्मजः 1** an epithet of Saturn. **2** of Karna. **3** of Sugriva. **-करः,-कर्तृ,-कृत्** *m*. the sun; तुल्योद्योगस्तव दिनकृतश्चाधिकारो मतो नः V. 2. 1; दिनकरकुलचंद्रचंद्रकेतो U. 6. 8. R. 9. 23. **-केशरः, -वः** darkness. **-क्षयः** evening.**-चर्या** daily occupation, daily routine of business. **-ज्योतिस्** *n*. sunshine. **-दुःखितः** the Chakravâka bird. **-पः, -पतिः, -बंधुः, -मणिः, -मयूखः, -रत्नं** the sun.**-मुखं** morning; R. 9. 25. **-मूर्द्धन्** *m*. the eastern mountain behind which the sun is supposed to rise. **-यौवनं** mid-day, noon (the youth of day).

दिनिका A day's wages.

दिरिपकः A ball for playing with.

दिलीपः A king of the Solar race, son of अंशुमत् and father of भगीरथ, but according to Kâlidâsa, of Raghu. [He is described by Kalidasa as a grand ideal of what a king should be. His wife was Sudakshi*na*, a woman in every respect worthy of her husband, but they had no issue. For this he went to his family priest Vasis*th*a who told him and his wife to serve the celestial cow Nandi*ni*. They accordingly served her for 21 days and were on the 22nd day favoured by the cow. A glorious boy was then born who conquered the whole world and became the founder of the line of the Raghus].

दिव् I. 4 P. (दीव्यति, द्यूत, or द्यून; *desid*. दुद्यूषति, दिदेविषति) 1 To shine, be bright. 2 To throw, cast (as a missile); Bk. 17. 87, 5. 81. 3 To gamble, play with dice (with acc. or instr. of the 'dice'); अक्षैरक्षान्वा दीव्यति Sk.; Ve. 1. 13. 4 To play, sport. 5 To joke, trifle with, make sport of, rally; (with acc.). 6 To stake, make a bet. 7 To sell, deal in (with gen.); अदेवीद्बंधुभोगानां Bk. 8. 122 (but with acc. or gen. when the root is preceded by a preposition; शतं शतस्य वा परिदीव्यति Sk.). 8 To squander, make light of. 9 To praise. 10 To be glad, rejoice. 11 To be mad or drunk. 12 To be sleepy. 13 To wish for. -II. 1 P., 10. U. (देवति, देवयति-ते) To cause to lament, pain, vex, torment. -III. 10 A. (देवयते) To suffer pain, lament, moan. -WITH **परि** to lament, moan, suffer pain; Bk. 4. 34.

दिव् *f*. (Nom. sin. द्यौः) 1 The heaven; R. 3. 4, 12; Me. 30. 2 The sky. 3 A day. 4 Light, brilliance. *N. B.* The compounds with दिव् as first member are mostly irregular; *e. g.* **दिवस्पतिः** an epithet of Indra; अनतिक्रमणीया दिवस्पतेराज्ञा *S*. 6. **दिवस्पृथिव्यौ** heaven and earth. **दिविजः, दिविष्ठः, दिविस्थः, दिविस (ष) द् *m*., दिवोकस् *m*., दिवौकस्-सः** 'inhabitant of the heaven', a god; *S*. 7; R. 3. 19, 47; दिविषद्वृंदैः Git. 7.

दिवं 1 Heaven. 2 The sky. 3 A day. 4 A forest, wood, thicket.

दिवसः,-सं A day; दिवस इवाभ्रश्यामस्तपात्यये जीवलोकस्य *S*. 3. 12. -COMP. **-ईश्वरः, करः** the sun; Rs 3. 22. **-मुखं** morning, day-break. **-विगमः** evening, sunset; Me. 99.

दिवा *ind*. By day, in the day time; **दिवा भू** 'to become day.'-COMP.**-अटनः** a crow.**-अंधः** an owl.**-अंधकी, अंधिका** a musk-rat**-करः** 1 the sun; Ku. 1. 12, 4. 48 2 a crow. 3 the sun-flower.**-कीर्तिः** 1 a Chândâla, a man of low caste. 2 a barber 3 an owl. **-निशं** *ind*. day and night. **-प्रदीपः** a lamp by day, an obscure man. **-भीतः -भीतिः** 1 an owl; दिवाकराद्रक्षति यो गुहासु लीनं दिवाभीतमिवांधकारं Ku. 1. 12. 2 a thief, house-breaker. **-मध्यं** midday. **-रात्रं** *ind*. day and night. **-वसुः** the son. **-शय** *a*. sleeping by day; R. 19. 34. **-स्वप्नः, -स्वापः** sleep during day-time.

दिवातन *a*. (**नी** *f*.) Of or belonging to the day; Ku. 4. 46; Bk. 5. 65.

दिविः The Châsha bird (also दिवः).

दिव्य *a*. 1 Divine, heavenly, celestial. 2 Supernatural, wonderful; परदेशेक्षणदिव्यचक्षुषः Si. 16. 29; Bg. 11. 8. 3 Brilliant, splendid. 4 Charming, beautiful. **-व्यः** 1 A superhuman or celestial being; दिव्यानामपि कृतविस्मयां पुरस्तात् Si. 8. 64. 2 Barley. 3 An epithet of Yama. 4 A philospher. **-व्यं** 1 Celestial nature, divinity. 2 The sky. 3 An ordeal (of which 10 kinds are enumerated); cf. Y. 2. 22, 95. 4 An oath, a solemn declaration. 5 Cloves. 6 A kind of sandal. -COMP. **-अंशुः** the sun. **-अंगना, -नारी,-स्त्री** a heavenly nymph, celestial damsel, an *apsaras*. **-अदिव्य** *a*. partly human and partly divine (as a hero, such as Arjuna). **-उदकं** rain-water. **-कारिन्** *a*. 1 taking an oath. 2 undergoing an ordeal. **-गायनः** a Gandharva. **-चक्षुस्** *a*. 1 having divine vision, heavenly-eyed; R. 3. 45. 2 blind. (*-m.*) a monkey. (*-m.*) divine or prophetic eye, supernatural vision, the power of seeing what is invisible by the human eye. **-ज्ञानं** supernatural knowledge. **दृश्** *m*. an astrologer. **-प्रश्नः** inquiry into celestial phenomena or future course of events, augury. **-मानुषः** a demi-god. **-रत्नं** a fabulous gem said to grant all desires of its possessor, the philosopher's stone; cf. चिंतामणि. **-रथः** a celestial car moving through the air. **-रसः** quicksilver. **-वस्त्र** *a*. divinely dressed. (**-स्त्रः**) 1 sunshine. 2 a kind of sun-flower. **—सरित्** *f*. the celestial Ganges. **-सारः** the Sâla tree.

दिश् 6. U. (दिशति-ते, दिष्ट; *Caus*. देशयति-ते; *desid*. दिदिक्षति-ते) 1 To point out, show, exhibit, produce (as a witness); साक्षिणः संति मेत्युक्त्वा दिशेत्युक्तो दिशेन्न यः Ms. 8. 57, 53. 2 To assign, allot इष्टां गतिं तस्य सुरा दिशंति Mb. 3 To give, grant, bestow upon, deliver or make over to; बाणमत्रभवते निजं दिशन् Ki. 13. 68; R. 5. 30, 11. 2, 16. 72. 4 To pay (as tribute). 5 To consent to; R. 11. 49. 6 To direct, order, command. 7 To allow, permit; स्मर्तुं दिशंति न दिवः सुरसुंदरीभ्यः Ki. 5. 28. -WITH **अति** 1 to assign, make over. 2 to extend the application of, extend by analogy; इति ये प्रत्यया उक्तास्तेऽत्रातिदिश्यंते Sk. or प्रधानमलुनिर्बहणन्यायेनातिदिशति S. B. **-अप** 1 to point out, indicate, show. 2 to declare, put forward, say, announce, tell, inform against; Ms. 8. 54. 3 to feign, pretend; मित्रकृत्यमपदिश्य R. 19. 31, 32, 54; शिरःशूलस्पर्शनमपदिशन् Dk. 50. pleading head-ache as an excuse. 4 to refer to, have reference to; रहसि भर्त्रा मद्गोत्रापदिष्टा Dk. 102. **-आ** 1 to point out, show (as way). 2 to order, command, direct; पुनरभ्यादिश तावदुत्थितः Ku. 4. 16; आदिक्षदस्याभिगमं वनाय Bk. 3. 9, 7. 28; R. 1. 54, 2. 65; Ms. 11. 193. 3 to aim at, single out, assign; Bk. 3. 3. 4 to teach, advise, instruct, lay down, prescribe; R. 12. 68. 5 to specify. 6 to foretell. **-उद्** 1 to point out, denote, signify, mention; प्रथमोद्दिष्टमासनं Ku. 6. 35; यथोद्दिष्टव्यापारा *S*. 3; अनेडमूक उद्दिष्टः शठे Med. 2 to refer or allude to, have reference to स्मरमुद्दिश्य Ku. 4. 38. 3 to mean, aim at, direct towards, assign or dedicate to; फलमुद्दिश्य Bg. 17. 21; उद्दिष्टामुपनिहितां भजस्व पूजां Mâl. 5. 25; वध्यशिलामुद्दिश्य प्रस्थितः Pt. 1. 4 to teach, advise; सतां केनोद्दिष्टं विषममसिधाराव्रतमिदं Bk. 2. 28. **-उप** 1 to teach, advise, instruct; सुखमुपदिश्यते परस्य K. 156; M. 1. 5; R. 16. 43; Bg. 4. 34. 2 to point out, indicate, refer to; गुणशेषामुपदिश्य R. 8. 73. 3 to mention, tell, announce; किं कुलेनोपदिष्टेन शीलमेवात्र कारणं Mk. 9. 7. 4 to prescribe, lay down, sanction, settle; न द्वितीयश्च साध्वीनां क्वचिद्भर्तोपदिश्यते Ms. 5. 162, 2. 190. 5 to name, call **-निस्** 1 to point out, indicate, show; एकैकं निर्दिशन् *S*. 7; अंगुल्या निर्दिशति &c. 2 to assign to, give; निर्दिष्टां कुलपतिना स पर्णशालामध्यास्य R. 1. 95. 3 to allude to, mention, make a reference to. 4 to prediet. 5 to advice. 6 to tell, communicate. **-प्र** 1 to point out, indicate, show, assign; तस्याधिकारपुरुषैः प्रणतैः प्रदिष्टां R. 5. 63, 2. 39. 2 to tell, mention; Bg. 8. 28; Bk. 4. 5. 3 to give, grant, offer, bestow or confer upon; वियोयोः पथि मुनिप्रदिष्टयोः R. 11. 9, 7. 35; निःशब्दोऽपि प्रदिशसि जलं याचितश्चातकेभ्यः Me. 114; Ms. 8. 265. **-प्रत्या** 1 (*a*) to reject, discard, shun; प्रत्यादिष्टविशेषमंडनविधिः *S*. 6. 5; (*b*) to repulse; R. 6. 25. 2 to cast off, repudiate (as a person); कामं प्रत्यादिष्टां स्मरामि न परिग्रहं मुनेस्तनयां *S* 5. 31. 3 to obscure, eclipse, defeat, throw into the shade or back-ground; R. 1. 61, 10. 68. 4 to order back, countermand. **-व्यप** 1 to name, call; व्यपदिश्यसे जगति विक्रमीत्यतः Si. 15. 28. 2 to name or call falsely; मित्रं च मां व्यपदिशस्यपरं च यासि Mk. 4. 9. 3 to speak of, profess; जन्मेदोर्विमले कुले व्यपदिशसि Ve. 6. 7. 4 to pretend, feign; Mv. 2. 11. **-सं** 1 to give, grant, assign, make over; Bk. 6. 141; Y. 2. 232. 2 to order, direct, instruct, advise, send as a message; किं नु खलु दुष्यंतस्य युक्तरूपमस्माभिः संदेष्टव्यं *S*. 4; Si. 9. 56, 61. 3 to send as a message, entrust with a message; अथ विश्वात्मने गौरी संदिदेश मिथः सखीं Ku. 6. 1,

दिश् *f.* (Nom. sing. दिक्-ग्) 1 A direction, cardinal point, point of compass, quarter of the sky; दिशः प्रसेदुर्मरुतो ववुः सुखाः R. 3. 14; दिशि दिशि किरति सजलकणजालं Gît. 4. 2 (*a*) The mere direction of a thing, hint, indication (of the general lines); इति दिक् (often used by commentators &c.) (*b*) (Hence) Mode, manner, method; मुनेः पाठोक्तदिशा S. D.; दिगियं सूत्रकृता प्रदर्शिता; दासीसमं नृपसभं रक्षःसममिमा दिशः Ak. 3 Region, space, place in general. 4 A foreign or distant region. 5 A point of view, manner of considering a subject. 6 A precept, order. 7 The number 'ten'. 8 A side or party. 9 The mark of a bite. (*N. B.* In comp. दिश् becomes दिग् before words beginning with vowels and soft consonants, and दिक् before words begining with hard consonants; *e. g.* दिगंबर, दिग्गज, दिक्पथ, दिक्करिन् &c). –Comp. **–अंतः** end of the directions or horizon, remote distance, remote place; Bv. 1. 2; R. 3. 4, 5. 67, 16, 87; नानादिगंतागता राजानः &c. **–अंतरं** 1 another direction. 2 the intermediate space, atmosphere, space. 3 a distant quarter, another or foreign country. **–अंबर** *a.* having only the directions for his clothing, stark naked, unclothed; दिगंबरत्वेन निवेदितं वसु Ku. 5. 72. (**–रः**) 1 a naked mendicant (of the Jain or Buddha sect). 2 a mendicant, an ascetic.) 3 an epithet of Siva. 4 darkness. **—ईशः, –ईश्वरः**; the regent of a quarter; Ku. 5. 53; see अष्टदिक्पाल. **–करः** 1 a youth, youthful man. 2 an epithet of Siva. **–कारिका, –करी** a young girl or woman. **–करिन्, –गजः, –दंतिन्, –वारणः** *m.* one of the eight elephants said to guard and preside over the eight cardinal points; (see अष्टदिग्गज); दिग्दंतिशेषाः ककुभश्चक्रार Vikr. 7. 1. **–ग्रहणं** observation of the quarters of the compass. **–चक्रं** 1 the horizon. 2 the whole world. **–जयः, –विजयः** 'conquest of the direction', the conquest of various countries in all directions, conquest of the world; स दिग्विजयमव्याजवीरः स्मरः इवाकरोत् Vikr. 4. 1. **–दर्शनं** showing merely the direction, pointing out only the general mode or manner. **–नागः** 1 an elephant of the quarter of the compass; see दिग्गज. 2 N. of a poet said to be a contemporary of Kâlidâsa. (This interpretation is based on Mallinâtha's gloss on Me. 14 which is however very doubtful). **मंडलं**=दिक्चक्रं. q. v. **–मात्रं** the mere direction or indication. **–मुखं** any quarter or part of the sky; हरति मे हरिवाहनदिङ्मुखं V. 3. 6; Amaru. 5. **–मोहः** mistaking the way or direction. **–वस्त्र** *a.* stark naked, unclothed. (**–स्त्रः**) 1 a Jaina or Buddha mendicant of the दिगंबर class. 2 an epithet of Siva. **–विभावित** *a.* renowned or celebrated in all quarters.

दिशा Direction, quarter of the compass, region &c. –Comp. **–गजः, –पालः** see दिग्गज, दिक्पाल.

दिश्य *a.* Belonging to or situated towards any quarter of the compass.

दिष्ट *a.* 1 Shown, indicated, assigned, pointed out. 2 Discribed, referred to. 3 Fixed, settled. 4 Directed, ordered &c. **–ष्टं** 1 Assignment, allotment. 2 Fate, destiny, good or ill luck; मा दिष्टं *S.* 2. 3 Order, direction, command. 4 Aim, object. —Comp. **–अंतः** 'the end of one's appointed time', death; दिष्टांतमाप्स्यति भवानपि पुत्रशोकात् R. 9. 79.

दिष्टिः *f.* 1 Assignment, allotment. 2 Direction, command, instruction, rule, precept. 3 Fate, fortune, destiny. 4 Good fortune, happiness, any auspicious event (such as the birth of a son); दिष्टिवृद्धिमिव शुश्राव K. 55; दिष्टिवृद्धिसंभ्रमो महानभूत् K. 73.

दिष्ट्या *ind.* (Strictly the instr. sing. of दिष्टि) Fortunately, luckily, thank God, how glad I am, how fortunate, bravo; (an exclamation of joy or gratulation); दिष्ट्या प्रतिहतं दुर्जातं Mâl. 4; दिष्ट्या सेयं महाबाहुरंजनानंदवर्धनः U. 1. 37; Ve. 2. 12. **दिष्ट्या वृध्** means 'to congratulate one upon'; दिष्ट्या धर्मपत्नीसमागमेन पुत्रमुखदर्शनेन चायुष्मान्वर्धते *S.* 7.

दिह् 2 U. (देग्धि, दिग्धे, दिग्ध; *desid.* दिधिक्षति) 1 To anoint, smear, plaster, spread over; Bk. 3. 21, 7. 54. 2 To soil, defile, pollute; R. 16. 15. —With **सं** 1 to doubt, be uncertain about; Y. 2. 16; संदिग्धो विजयो युधि Pt. 3. 12. 2 to mistake for, confound with (in pass); पांतु श्यामकठोरकेतकशिखासंदिग्धमुग्धेंदवः (जटाः) Mâl. 1. 2; or धूपैर्जालविनिःसृतैर्वलभयः संदिग्धपारावताः V. 3. 2. Ku. 6. 40. 3 to start an objection.

दी 4 A. (दीयते, दीन) To perish, die.

दीक्ष् 1 A. (दीक्षते, दीक्षित) 1 To consecrate or prepare oneself for the performance of a sacred rite; see दीक्षित below. 2 To dedicate oneself to. 3 To initiate or introduce a pupil. 4 To invest with the sacred thread. 5 To sacrifice. 6 To practice self-restraint.

दीक्षकः A spiritual guide.

दीक्षणं Initiation, consecration.

दीक्षा 1 Consecration for a religious ceremony, initiation in general; R. 3. 44, 65. 2 A ceremony preliminary to a sacrifice. 3 A ceremony or religious rite in general; विवाहदीक्षा R. 3. 33; Ku. 7. 1, 8, 24. 4 Investiture with the sacred thread. 5 Dedicating oneself to a particular object. –Comp. **–अंतः** a supplementary sacrifice made to atone for the defects in a preceding one.

दीक्षित *p. p.* 1 Consecrated, initiated (as for a religious ceremony ; एते विवाहदीक्षिता यूयं U. 1 ; आपन्नाभयसत्रेषु दीक्षिताः खलु पौरवाः *S*- 2. 16; R. 8. 75, 11. 24; Ve. 12. 5. 2 Prepared for a sacrifice. 3 Prepared for, having taken a vow of; R. 11. 67. 4 Crowned ; R. 4. 5.—**तः** 1 A priest engaged in a Dîkshâ. 2 A pupil. 3 A person who or whose ancestors may have performed a grand sacrificil ceremony, such as ज्योतिष्टोम.

दीदिविः 1 Boiled rice. 2 Heaven.

दीधितिः *f.* 1 A ray of light; R. 3. 22, 17. 48; N. 2. 69. 2 Splendour. brightness. 3 Bodily lustre, energy; Bh. 2. 29.

दीधितिमत् *a.* Brilliant.—*m.* The sun ; Ku. 2. 2, 7. 70.

दीधी 2 A. (दीधीते) 1 To shine. 2 To seem, appear.

दीन *a.* 1 Poor, indigent. 2 Distressed, ruined, afflicted, miserable, wretched. 3 Sorry, dejected, melancholy, sad ; सा विरहे तव दीना Gît. 4. 4 Timid, frightened. 5 Mean, piteous ; Bh. 2 51. —**नः** A poor person, one in distress or misery ; दीनानां कल्पवृक्षः Mk. 1. 48 ; दिनानि दीनोद्धरणोचितस्य R. 2. 25. –Comp. **–दयालु, –वत्सल** *a.* kind to the poor. **–बंधुः** a friend of the poor.

दीनारः 1 A particular gold coin ; जितश्चासौ मया षोडशसहस्राणि दीनाराणां Dk. 2 A coin in general. 3 A gold ornament.

दीप् 4 A. (दीप्यते, दीप्त, *freq.* देदीप्यते) 1 To shine, blaze (fig. also); सर्वैरुस्त्रैः समग्रैस्त्वमिवनृपगुणैर्दीप्यते सप्तसप्तिः M. 2. 13; तरुणीस्तन एव दीप्यते मणिहारावलिरामणीयकं N. 2. 44 ; Bk. 2. 2, R. 14. 64 ; H. Pr. 46. 2 To burn, be lighted ; यथा यथा चेयं चपला दीप्यते K. 105. 3 To glow, be inflamed or excited, increase (fig. also); R. 5. 47: Bk. 14. 88; Si. 20. 71. 4 To be fired with anger; Ki. 3. 55. 5 To be illustrious. –*Caus.* (दीपयति-ते) To kindle, inflame, illuminate, light; वृंदावनांतरमदीपयदंशुजालैः (इंदुः) Gît. –7. With. **उद्** *Caus.* 1 to kindle. 2 to rouse, excite, light up. **–प्र, –सं** to shine, blaze &c.

दीपः 1 A lamp, light; नृपदीपो धनस्नेहं प्रजाभ्यः संहरन्नपि । अंतरस्थैर्गुणैः शुभ्रैर्लक्ष्यते नैव केनचित् ॥ Pt. 1. 221; न हि दीपौ परस्परस्योपकुरुतः S. B.; so ज्ञानदीप &c. –Comp. **–अन्विता** 1 the day of new moon (अमा). 2=दीपाली q. v. **–आराधनं** worshipping an idol by waving a light before it. **–आलिः, -ली, -आवली, –उत्सवः** 1 a row of lights, nocturnal illumination. 2 particularly, the festival called *Diwali* held on the night of new moon in आश्विन. -कलिका the flame of a lamp. -किट्टं lampblack, soot. -कूपी, -खरी the wick of a lamp. -ध्वजः lampblack. -पादपः, -वृक्षः a lampstick, lamp-stand. —पुष्पः the Champaka tree. -भाजनं a lamp; R. 19. 51. -माला lighting, illumination. -शत्रुः a moth. -शिखा the flame of a lamp. -शृंखला a row of lights, illumination.

दीपक *a.* (पिका *f.*) 1 Kindling, inflaming. 2 Illuminating, making bright. 3 Illustrating, beautifying, making illustrious. 4 Exciting, making intense ; *Si.* 2. 55. 5 Tonic, stimulating digestion, digestive.—कः 1 A light, lamp ; तावदेव कृतिनामपि स्फुरत्येष निर्मलविवेकदीपकः Bh. 1. 56. 2 A falcon. 3 An epithet of Kâmadeva (also दीप्यक).—कं 1 Saffron. 2 (In Rhet.) A figure of speech in which two or more objects (some प्रकृत relevant and some अप्रकृत irrelevant) having the same attribute are associated together or in which several attributes (some relevant and some irrelevant) are predicated of the same object (सकृद्वृत्तिस्तु धर्मस्य प्रकृताप्रकृतात्मनां । सैव क्रियासु बह्वीषु कारकस्येति दीपकं ॥ K. P. 10; cf; Chandr:—वदंति वर्ण्यावर्ण्यानां धर्मैक्यं दीपकं बुधाः । मदेन भाति कलभः प्रतापेन महीपतिः ॥ 5. 45. दीपनं 1 Kindling, illuminating. 2 A tonic, stimulating digestion. 3 Exciting, stimulating. 4 Saffron.

दीपिका 1 A light, torch ; R. 4. 45. 9. 70. 2. (At the end of comp.) Illustrator, elucidator ; तर्कदीपिका.

दीपित *a.* 1 Set on fire. 2 Inflamed. 3 Illuminated. 4 Manifested.

दीप्त *p. p.* 1 Lighted; inflamed, kindled. 2 Glowing, hot, flashing, radiant. 3 Illuminated. 4 Excited, stimulated.—प्तः 1 A lion. 2 The citron tree.—प्तं Gold.-Comp.-अंशुः the sun.-अक्षः a cat.-अग्नि *a.* kindled (as fire). (-ग्निः) 1 blazing fire, 2 N. of अगस्त्य. -अंगः a peacock.-आत्मन् *a.* having a fiery nature.-उपलः the sunstone.-किरणः the sun. -कीर्तिः an epithet of Kârtikeya. -जिह्वा a fox or vixen; (used figuratively for an ill-tempered quarrelsome woman). -तपस् *a.* of glowing piety, fervent in devotion. -पिंगलः a lion. -रसः an earth-worm. -लोचनः a cat. -लोहं brass; bell-metal.

दीप्तिः *f.* 1 Brightness, splendour, brilliance, lustre. 2 Brilliancy of beauty, extreme loveliness; (for the difference between दीप्ति and कांति see under कांति). 3 Lac. 4 Brass.

दीप्र *a.* Shining, brilliant, radiant. —प्रः Fire.

दीर्घ *a.* (compar. द्राघीयस्, superl. द्राघिष्ट) 1 Long (in time or space), reaching far; दीर्घाक्षं शरदिंदुकांति वदनं M. 2. 3; दीर्घान् कटाक्षान् Me. 35; दीर्घापांग &c. 2 Of long duration, lasting long, tedious; दीर्घयामा त्रियामा Me. 108; V. 3. 4; *S.* 4. 15. 3 Deep (as a sigh); Amaru. 11; दीर्घमुष्णं च निश्वस्य. 4 Long (as a vowel), as the आ in काम. 5 Lofty, high, tall. -र्घं *ind.* 1 Long, for a long time. 2 Deeply. 3 Far. -र्घः 1 A camel. 2 A long vowel. -Comp. -अध्वगः a messenger, an express. -अहन् *m.* summer, (ग्रीष्म). -आकार *a.* oblong. -आयु, -आयुस् *a.* long-lived. -आयुधः 1 a spear. 2 any long weapon. 3 a hog. -आस्यः an elephant. -कंठः, -कंठकः, -कंधरः the (Indian) crane. -काय *a.* tall (in stature). -केशः a bear. -गतिः-ग्रीवः, -घाटिकः.-जंघ a camel.-जिह्वः a snake, serpent. -तपस् *m.* an epithet of Gautama, husband of Ahalyâ; R. 11. 34. -तरुः, -दंड:, -द्रुः the palm tree. -तुंडी musk-rat. -दर्शिन् *a.* 1 provident, prudent, far-seeing, long-sighted; Pt. 3. 167. 2 sagacious, wise. (-*m.*) 1 a bear. 2 an owl. -नाद *a.* making a long continued noise. (-दः) 1 a dog. 2 a cock. 3 a conch-shell. -निद्रा 1 long sleep. 2 the long sleep, sleep of death; R. 12. 11. -पत्रः the palm tree. -पादः a heron. -पादपः 1 the cocoa-nut tree. 2 the areca-nut tree. 3 the palm tree. -पृष्ठः a snake. -बाला a kind of deer (चमरी) of whose tails chowries are made. -मारुतः an elephant. -रतः a dog. -रदः a hog. -रसनः a snake. -रोमन् *m.* a bear. -वक्त्रः an elephant. -सक्थ *a.* having long thighs. -सत्रं a long-continued Soma sacrifice. (-त्रः) one who performs such a sacrifice; R. 1. 80. -सूत्र, -सूत्रिन् *a.* working slowly, slow, dilatory, procrastinating; दीर्घसूत्री विनश्यति Pt. 4.

दीर्घिका 1 A long or oblong lake; M. 2. 13, R. 16. 13. 2 A well or lake in general.

दीर्ण *a.* 1 Torn, rent, split &c. 2 Frightened, afraid.

दु 5 P. (दुनोति, दूत or दून) 1 To burn, consume with fire; Bk. 14. 85. 2 To torment, afflict, distress; उद्भासीनि जलेजानि दुन्वंत्यदयितं जनं Bk. 6. 74, 5. 98. 17. 99; (मुखं) तव विश्रांतकथं दुनोति मां R. 8. 55. 3 To pain, produce sorrow; वर्णप्रकर्षे सति कर्णिकारं दुनोति निर्गंधतया स्म चेतः Ku. 3. 28. 4 (Intrans.) To be afflicted or pained; देहि सुंदरि दर्शनं मम मन्मथेन दुनोमि Gît. 3. -*Pass.* (or 4 A. according to some) To be afflicted or pained &c.; नायातः सखि निर्दयो यदि शठस्त्वं दूति किं दूयसे Gît. 7; Ku. 5. 12, 48; R. 1. 70, 10. 21.

दुःख *a.* 1 Painful, disagreeable, unpleasant; सिंहानां निनदा दुःखाः श्रोतुं दुःखमतो वनं Râm. 2 Difficult, uneasy. -खं 1 Sorrow, grief, unhappiness, distress, pain, agony; सुखं हि दुःखान्यनुभूय शोभते Mk. 1. 10; यदेवोपनतं दुःखात्सुखं तद्रसवत्तरं V. 3. 21; so दुःखसुख, समदुःखसुख &c. 2 Trouble, difficulty, *S.* Til. 12. (दुःखं and दुःखेन are used as adverbs in the sense of 'hardly', 'with great difficulty or trouble': *S.* 7. 13; Bg. 12. 5, R. 19. 49; H. 1. 158). -Comp. -अतीत *a.* freed from pain. -अंतः final emancipation. -कर *a.* painful, troublesome. -ग्रामः 'the scene of suffering', worldly existence. -छिन्न *a.* 1 tough, hard. 2 pained, distressed. -प्राय, बहुल *a.* full of trouble or grief. -भाज् *a.* unhappy. -लोकः worldly life, the world as a scene of constant suffering. -शील *a.* hard to please or manage, bad-tempered, irritable; R. 3. 6.

दुःखित, -दुःखिन् *a.* (नी *f.*) 1 Distressed, afflicted, pained. 2 Poor, unhappy, miserable.

दुकूलं Woven silk, a silk-garment, a very fine garment in general; श्यामलमृदुलकलेवरमंडनमधिगतगौरदुकूलं Gît. 11; Ku. 5. 67, 78; Bk. 3. 34, 10. 1; R. 17. 25.

दुग्ध *a.* 1 Milked. 2 Milked out, extracted, drawn out &c. see दुह्. -ग्धं 1 Milk. 2 Milky juice of plants. -Comp. -अग्रं, -तालीयं the skim of milk, cream. -पाचनं a vessel for boiling milk. -पोष्य *a.* living on its mother's milk (as a child), a suckling. -समुद्रः the ocean of milk, one of the seven oceans.

दुघ *a.* (Mostly at the end of comp.) 1 Milking. 2 Yielding, granting; as in कामदुघा q. v.

दुघा A milch cow.

दुंडुक *a.* Dishonest, bad-hearted, fraudulent.

दुंडुभः=डुंडुभ q. v.

दुद्रुमः A green onion.

दुंदमः A kind of drum; see दुंदुभि.

दुंदुः 1 A kind of drum. 2 N. of Vasudeva, Krishṇa's father.

दुंदुभः 1 A sort of large kettledrum. 2 A kind of water-snake.

दुंदुभिः *m. f.* 1 A sort of large kettle-drum, drum; विजयदुंदुभितां ययुरर्णवाः R. 9. 11. -*m.* 1 An epithet of Vishṇu. 2 Of Krishṇa. 3 A kind of poison. 4 N. of a demon slain by Valî. When Sugrîva showed to Râma the skeleton of this demon to show him how powerful Vâli was, Râma kicked it with but a gentle force and threw it many miles away.

दुर् *ind.* (A prefix substituted for दुस् before words beginning with vowels or soft consonants in the sense of 'bad,' 'hard or difficult to do a certain thing'; for compounds with दुस् as first member see दुस् s. v.). –COMP.–अक्ष *a.* 1 weak-eyed. 2 evil-eyed. (–क्षः) a loaded or false die.–अतिक्रम *a.* 1 difficult to be overcome or conquered, unconquerable; स्वजातिर्दुरतिक्रमा Pt. 1. 2. insurmountable. 3 inevitable.–अत्यय *a.* 1 difficult to be overcome; R. 11. 88. 2 hard to be attained or fathomed.–अदृष्टं ill luck, misfortune.–अधिग, –अधिगम *a.* 1 hard to reach or attain, unattainable; Pt. 1. 330. 2 insurmountable. 3 hard to be studied or understood; Ki. 5. 18. –अधिष्ठित *a.* badly performed, managed, or executed. –अध्यय *a.* 1 difficult of attainment. 2 hard to be studied. –अध्यवसायः a foolish undertaking. –अध्वः a bad road. –अंत *a.* 1 whose end is difficult to be reached, endless, infinite; संकर्षणाय सूक्ष्माय दुरंतायांतकाय च Bhâg. 2 ending ill or in misery, unhappy; अहो दुरंता बलवद्विरोधिता Ki. 1. 23; नृत्यति युवतिजनेन समं सखि विरहिजनस्य दुरंते (वसंते) Gît. 1. –अन्वय *a.* 1 difficult to be passed along. 2 hard to be carried out or followed. 3 difficult to be attained or understood. (–यः) 1 a wrong conclusion, one wrongly inferred from given premises. –अभिमानिन् *a.* vain-glorious, disagreeably proud. –अवगम *a.* incomprehensible. –अवग्रह *a.* difficult to be restrained or subjugated. –अवस्थ *a.* ill off, badly or poorly circumstanced. –अवस्था a wretched or miserable state. –आकृति *a.* ugly, misshaped. –आक्रम *a.* 1 invincible, unconquerable. 2 difficult to be passed. –आक्रमणं 1 unfair attack. 2 difficult approach. –आगमः improper or illegal acquisition.-आग्रहः foolish obstinacy, head-strongness, pertinacity. –आचर *a.* hard to be performed.–आचार *a.* 1 ill-conducted, badly behaved. 2 following bad practices, wicked, depraved; Bg. 9. 30. (–रः) bad practice, ill-conduct, wickedness. –आत्मन् *m.* a rascal, villain, scoundrel. –आधर्ष *a.* 1 hard to be approached or assailed, unassailable. 2 not to be attacked with impunity. 3 haughty.–आनम *a.* difficult to bend or draw; R. 11. 38. –आप *a.* difficult to be obtained; श्रिया दुरापः कथमीप्सितो भवेत् *S.* 3. 14; R. 1, 72; 6. 62. –आराध्य *a.* difficult to be propitiated, hard to be won over or conciliated. –आरोह *a.* difficult of ascent. (–हः) 1 the cocoa-nut tree. 2 the palm tree. 3 the date tree. –आलापः 1 curse, imprecation. 2 foul or abusive language. –आलोक *a.* 1 difficult to be seen or perceived. 2 pain-fully bright, dazzling; दुरालोकः स समरे निदाघांबररत्नवत् K. P. 10. (–कः) (–कः) dazzling splendour. –आवार *a.* 1 difficult to be covered. 2 difficult to be restrained, shut in, kept back or stopped.-आशय *a.* evilminded, wicked, malicious.–आशा 1 a bad or wicked desire. 2 hoping against hope. –आसद *a.* 1 difficult to be approched or overtaken, unassailable, unconquerable; R. 3. 66, 8. 4; Mv. 2. 5, 4. 15. 2 difficult to be found or met with. 3 unequalled, unparalleled. –इत *a.* 1 difficult. 2 sinful. (–तं) 1 a bad course, evil, sin; दरिद्राणां दैन्यं दुरितमथ दुर्वासनहृदां द्रुतं दूरीकुर्वन् G. L. 2; R. 8. 2; Amaru. 2; Mv. 3. 43. 2 difficulty, danger. 3 a calamity. –इष्टं 1 a curse, imprecation. 2 a spell or sacrificial rite performed to injure another person. –ईशः a bad lord or master. –ईषणा, –एषणा a curse, an imprecation. –उक्तं, –उक्तिः offensive speech, reproach, abuse, censure. –उत्तर *a.* unanswerable. –उदाहर *a.* difficult to be pronounced, or composed; अनुज्झितार्थसंबंधः प्रबंधो दुरुदाहरः *Si.* 2. 73· –उद्वह *a.* burdensome, unbearable. –ऊह *a.* abstruse. –ग *a.* 1 difficult of access, inaccessible, impassable. 2 unattainable. 3 incomprehensible. (–गः, –गं) 1 difficult or narrow passage through a wood or over a stream, mountain &c., a defile, narrow pass. 2 a citadel, fortress, castle. 3 rough ground. 4 difficulty, adversity, calamity, distress, danger; निस्तारयति दुर्गाच्च Ms. 3. 98, 11. 43; Bg. 18. 58. °अध्यक्षः, °पतिः, पालः the commandant or governor of a castle. °कर्मन् *n.* fortification. °मार्गः a defile, gorge. °लंघनं surmounting difficulties. (–नः) a camel. °संचरः 1 a difficult passage as to a fort &c., a bridge &c. over a defile., (–र्गा) an epithet of Pârvatî, wife of *S*iva. –गत *a.* 1 unfortunate, in bad circumstances; Bk. 18. 10, 2 indigent, poor. 3 distressed, in trouble. –गतिः *f.* 1 misfortune, poverty, want, trouble, indigence; Bg. 6. 40. 2 a difficult situation or path. 3 hell. –गंध *a.* ill-smelling. (–धः) bad odour, stink. 2 any ill-smelling substance. 3 an onion. 4 the mango tree. –गंधि, –गंधिन् *a.* ill-smelling. –गम *a.* 1 impassable, inaccessible, impervious; कामिनीकायकांतारे कुचपर्वतदुर्गमे Bh. 1. 86; *Si.* 12. 49. 2 unattainable, difficult of attainment. 3 hard to be understood. –गाढ, –गाध, –गाह्य *a.* difficult to be fathomed or investigated, unfathomable. –ग्रह *a.* 1 difficult to be gained or accomplished 2 difficult to be conquered or subjugated; R. 17. 52. 3 hard to be understood. (–हः) a cramp, spasm. –घट *a.* 1 difficult. 2 impossible. –घोषः 1 a harsh cry. 2 a bear. –जन *a.* 1 wicked, bad, vile. 2 slanderous, malicious, mischievons. (–नः) a bad or wicked person, a malicious or mischievous man, villain; दुर्जनः प्रियवादी च नैतद्विश्वासकारणं Châṇ. 24, 25; शाम्येत्प्रत्यपकारेण नोपकारेण दुर्जनः Ku. 2. 40. –जय *a,* invincible. –जर *a.* 1 ever youthful. 2 hard (as food), indigestible. 3 difficult to be enjoyed. –जात *a.* 1 unhappy, wretched. 2 bad-tempered, bad, wicked. 3 false, not genuine. (–तं) misfortune, calamity, difficulty, R. 13. 72; –जाति *a.* 1 bad-natured, vile, wicked; Amaru. 96. 2 outcast. (–तिः *f.*) misfortune, ill-condition. –ज्ञान, –ज्ञेय *a.* difficult to be known, incomprehensible. –णयः, –नयः 1 bad conduct. 2 impropriety. 3 injustice. –णामन्, –नामन् *a.* having a bad name. –दम, –दमन, –दम्य *a.* difficult to be subdued, untamable, indomitable. –दर्श *a.* 1 difficult to be seen. 2 dazzling; Bg. 11. 52. –दांत *a.* 1 hard to be tamed or subdued; untamable; *Si.* 12. 22. 2 intractable, proud, insolent; दुर्दांतानां दमनविधयः क्षत्रियेष्वायतंते Mv. 3. 34. (–तः) 1 a calf. 2 a strife, quarrel. –दिनं 1 a bad day in general. 2 a rainy or cloudy day, stormy or rainy weather; उन्नमत्यकालदुर्दिनं Mk. 5; Ku. 6. 43; Mv. 4. 57. 3 a shower (of anything), R. 4. 41, 82; 5. 47; U. 5. 5. 4 thick darkness. –दृष्ट *a.* ill-judged or seen, wrongly decided. –दैवं ill-luck, misfortune.–द्यूतं an unfair game. –द्रुमः onion. –धर *a.* 1 irresistible, difficult to be stopped. 2 difficult to be borne or suffered; दुर्धरेण मदनेन साद्यते Ghaṭ. 11; Ms. 7. 28. (–रः) quicksilver. –धर्ष *a.* 1 inviolable, unassailable. 2 inaccessible; H. Pr. 5 3 fearful, dreadful. 4 haughty. –धी *a.* stupid, silly. –नामकः piles.–निग्रह *a.* irrepressible, ungovernable, irresistible, unruly; मनो दुर्निग्रहं चलं Bg. 6. 35.–निमित *a.* carelessly put to or placed on the ground; पदे दुर्निमिते गलंती R. 7. 10. –निमित्तं a bad omen; R. 14. 50. 2 a bad pretext.–निवार, निवार्य *a.* difficult to be checked or warded off, irresistible, invincible. –नीतं misconduct, bad policy, misbehaviour. –नीतिः *f.* maladministration; Bv. 4. 36. –बल *a.* 1 weak, feeble. 2 enfeebled, spiritless; U. 1. 24. 3 small, scanty, little; R. 5. 12. –बाल *a.* bald-headed, –बुद्धि *a.* 1 silly, foolish, stupid. 2 perverse, evil-minded, wicked; Bg. 1. 23. –बोध *a.* unintelligible, unfathomable, inscrutable; निसर्गदुर्बोधमबोधविक्लवाः क्व भूपतीनां चरितं क्व जंतवः Ki. 1. 6. –भग *a.* unfortunate, unlucky –भगा

1 a wife disliked by her husband. 2 an ill-tempered woman, a shrew. -भर *a.* insupportable, burdensome. -भाग्य *a.* unfortunate, unlucky. (-ग्यं) ill luck.-भिक्षं 1 scarcity of provisions, dearth, famine; Y. 2. 147; Ms. 8. 22; H. 1. 73. 2 want in general. -भृत्यः a bad servant. -भ्रातृ *m.* a bad brother. -मति *a.* 1 silly, stupid, foolish, ignorant. 2 wicked, evil-minded; Ms. 11. 30.-मद *a.* drunken, ferocious, maddened, infatuated. -मनस् *a.* troubled in mind, discouraged dispirited, sad, melancholy. -मनुष्यः a bad or wicked man. -मंत्रः, -मंत्रितं evil advice, bad counsel. -मरणं violent or unnatural death. -मर्याद *a.* immodest, wicked. -मल्लिका, -मल्ली: a minor drama, comedy, farce; S. D. 553. -मित्रः 1 a bad friend. 2 an enemy. -मुख *a.* 1 having a bad face, hideous, ugly; Bh. 1. 90. 2 foul-mouthed, abusive, scurrilous; Bh. 2. 69. -मूल्य *a.* highly priced, dear. -मेधस् *a.* silly, foolish, dull-headed, dull. (*-m.*) a dunce, dull-headed man, block-head; ग्रंथानधीत्य व्याकर्तुमिति दुर्मेधसोऽप्यलं *Si.* 2. 26. -योध, -योधन *a.* invincible, unconquerable. (-नः) the eldest of the hundred sons of Dhṛitarâshṭra and Gândhârî. [From his early years he conceived a deep hatred for his cousins the P*a*ndavas, but particularly Bh*i*ma, and made every effort he could to compass their destruction. When his father proposed to make Yudhish*th*ira heir-apparent, Duryodhana did not like the idea, as his father was the reigning sovereign, and prevailed upon his blind father to send the P*a*nd*a*vas away into exile. *Varana*vata was fixed upon as their abode, and under pretext of constructing a palatial building for their residence, Duryodhana caused a palace to be built mostly of lac, resin and other combustible materials, thereby hoping to see them all destroyed when they should enter it. But the Pàndavas were forewarned and they safely escaped. They then lived at Indraprastha, and Yudhish*th*ira performed the Ràjasûya sacrifice with great pomp and splendour. This event further excited the anger and jealousy of Duryodhana who was already vexed to find that his plot for burning them up had signally failed, and he induced his father to invite the P*a*nd*a*vas to Hastin*a*pura to play with dice (of which Yudhish*th*ira was particularly fond). In that gambling match Duryodhana, who was ably assisted by his maternal uncle *S*akuni, won from Yudhish*th*ira everything that he staked, till the infatuated gambler staked himself, his brothers, and Drupadi herself, all of whom shared the same fate. Yudhish*th*ira, as a condition of the wager, was forced to go to the forest with his wife and brothers, and to remain there for twelve years and to pass one additional year *incognito*. But even this period, long as it was, expired, and after their return from exile, both the P*a*ndavas and Kauravas made great preparations for the inevitable struggle and the great Bh*a*r*a*ti war commenced. It lasted for eighteen days during which all the Kauravas, with most of their allies, were slain. It was on the last day of the war that Bhîma fought a duel with Duryodhana and smashed his thigh with his club]. —योनि *a.* of a low birth. -लक्ष्य *a.* difficult to be seen or perceived, hardly visible. -लभ *a.* 1 difficult to be attained, or accomplished; R. 1. 67, 17. 70; Ku. 4. 40, 5. 46, 61. 2 difficult to be found or met with, scarce, rare; शुद्धांतदुर्लभं *S.* 1. 16. 3 best, excellent, eminent. 4 dear, beloved. 5 costly. -ललित *a.* spoilt by fondling, fondled too much, hard to please; हा मदंकदुर्ललित Ve. 4; V. 2. 8; Mâl. 9. 2 (hence) wayward, naughty, ill-bred, unruly; स्पृहयामि खलु दुर्ललितायास्मै *S.* 7. (-तं) waywardness, rudeness. -लेख्यं a forged document. -वच *a.* 1 difficult to be described, indescribable. 2 not to be talked about. 3 speaking improperly, abusing. (-चं) abuse, censure, foul language. -वचस् *n.* abuse, censure. वर्ण *a.* bad-coloured. (-र्णं) silver. -वसतिः *f.* painful residence; R. 8. 94. -वह *a.* heavy, difficult to be born; U. 2. 10; Ku. 1. 10. -वाच्य *a.* 1 difficult to be spoken or uttered. 2 abusive, scurrilous. 2 3 harsh, cruel (as words). (-च्यं) 1 censure, abuse. 2 scandal, ill repute. -वाद: slander, defamation, calumny. -वार, -वारण *a.* irresistible, unbearable; R. 14. 87; Ku. 2. 21. -वासना 1 evil propensity, wicked desire; Bv. 1. 86. 2 a chimera. -वासस् *a.* 1 ill-dressed. 2 naked. (*-m*) N. of a very irascible saint or Ṛishi, son of Atri and Anasûyâ. He was very hard to please, and he cursed many a male and female to suffer misery and degradation. His anger, like that of Jamadagni, has become almost proverbial. -विगाह, -विगाह्य *a.* difficult to be penetrated or fathomed, unfathomable. -विचिंत्य inconceivable, inscrutable. -विदग्ध 1 unskilled, raw, foolish, stupid, silly. 2 wholly ignorant. 3 foolishly puffed up, elated, vainly proud; वृथाशास्त्रग्रहणदुर्विदग्ध Ve. 3; ज्ञानलवदुर्विदग्धं ब्रह्मापि नरं न रंजयति Bh. 2. 3. -विध *a.* 1 mean, base, low. 2 wicked, vile. 3 poor, indigent; विदधाते रुचिमर्वदुर्विधं N. 2. 23. 4 stupid, foolish, silly. विनयः misconduct, imprudence. -विनीत *a.* 1 (*a*) badly educated, ill-mannered, ill-behaved, wicked; शासितरि दुर्विनीतानां *S.* 1. 25. (*b*) rude, naughty, mischievous. 2 stubborn, obstinate. -विपाकः 1 bad result or consequence U. 1 40, Mv. 6. 7. 2 evil consequence of acts done either in this or in a former birth. -विलसितं a wayward act, rudeness, naughtiness. -वृत्त *a.* 1 vile, wicked, ill-behaved. 2 roguish. (-त्तं) misconduct, ill-behaviour. -वृष्टिः *f.* insufficient rain, drought. -व्यवहारः a wrong judgment (in law). -व्रत *a.* not conforming to rules, disobedient. -हुतं a badly offered sacrifice. -हृद् *a.* wicked-hearted, ill-disposed, inimical. (*-m.*) any enemy. -हृदय *a.* evil-minded, evil-intentioned, wicked.

दुरोदरः 1 A gamester. 2 A dice-box. 3 A stake. -रं Gambling, playing at dice; दुरोदरछद्मजितां समीहते नयेन जेतुं जगतीं सुयोधनः Ki. 1. 7; R. 9. 7.

दुल् 10 U. (दोलयति-ते, दोलित) 1 To swing, shake to and fro, cause to oscillate or move about; कटिं चेद्दोलयेदाशु Ratimanjarî; दोलयन्द्राविवाक्षौ Bh. 3. 39. 2 To move or shake upwards, throw up; दोलयति धुलिं वायुः *S*abdak.

दुलिः *f.* A small or female tortoise.

दुष् 4 P. (दुष्यति, दुष्ट) 1 To be bad or corrupted, be spoiled or suffer damage. 2 To be defiled or violated (as a woman &c.), be stained, be or become impure, or contaminated; Pt. 1. 66; Ms. 7. 24, 9. 318, 10. 102. 3 To sin, commit a mistake, be wrong. 4 To be unchaste or faithless. —*Caus.* (दूषयति, but दूषयति or दोषयति in the sense of 'making depraved, or ' corrupting ') 1 To corrupt, spoil, cause to perish, hurt, destroy, defile, taint, contaminate, vitiate, pollute (lit. and fig.); न भीतो मरणादस्मि केवलं दूषितं यशः Mk. 10. 27; पुरा दूषयति स्थलीं R. 12. 30, 8. 68, 10. 47, 12. 4; Ms. 5. 1, 104; 7. 195; Y. 1. 189; Amaru. 70; न त्वेवं दूषयिष्यामि शस्त्रग्रहमहाव्रतं Mv. 3. 8 shall not sully, violate or break &c. 2 To corrupt the morals, demoralize. 3 To violate or dishonour (as a girl or another's wife); Ms. 8. 364, 368. 4 To abrogate, rescind, annul. 5 To blame, censure, find fault with, speak ill of, accuse; दूषितः सर्वलोकेषु निषादत्वं गमिष्यति Râm; Y. 1. 66. 6 To adulterate. 7 To falsify. 8 To refute, disprove. —WITH प्र 1 to be corrupted or spoiled, be vitiated; Y. 3. 19. 2 to sin, err, be faithless or unchaste; Bg. 1. 40; Ms. 9. 74. (—*Caus.*) 1 to spoil, corrupt, soil, taint. 2 to blame, censure, find fault with. -सं to be defiled or stained &c. (*-Caus*). 1 to defile, corrupt, soil, taint. 2 to violate. 3 to accuse, censure, find fault with.

दुष्ट *p. p.* 1 Spoiled, damaged, injured, ruined. 2 Defiled, tainted, violated, sullied. 3 Depraved, corrupted. 4 Vicious, wicked; as दुष्टवृषः 5 Guilty, culpable. 6 Low, vile. 7 Faulty or defective, as a हेतु in logic. 8. Painful. 9 Worthless. -COMP. -आत्मन्, -आशय *a.* evil-minded, wicked. —गजः a vicious elephant. चेतस्, -धी, -बुद्धि *a.* evil-minded, malevolent, wicked. -वृषः a strong but stubborn ox which refuses to draw, a vicious ox.

दुष्टिः *f.* Corruption, depravity.

दुष्टु *ind.* 1 Ill, bad. 2 Improperly, incorrectly, wrongly.

दुष्यंतः N. of a king of the lunar race, descendant of Puru, husband of Sakuntalâ and father of Bharata. [Once upon a time Dushyanta, while hunting in the forest, went to the hermitage of the sage Kanva, while pursuing a deer. There he was hospitably received by S'akuntalâ, the adopted daughter of the Sage, and her transcendent beauty made so great an impression on his mind that he prevailed on her to become his Queen, and married her according to the *Gandharva* from of marriage. Having passed some time in her company the king returned to his capital. After some months S'akuntalâ. was delivered of a son, and her father thought it advisable to send her with the boy to her husband. But when they went and stood before Dushyanta, he (for fear of public scandal) denied all knowledge of having ever before seen or married her. But a heavenly voice told him that she was his lawful wife, and he thereupon admitted her, along with the boy, into his harem and made her first Queen. The happy pair lived to a good old age, and committing the realm to the care of Bharata, retired to the woods. Such is the account of Dushyanta and S'akuntalâ given in the Mahâbhârata; the story told by Kàlidàsa differs in several important respects; see "S'akuntalà."].

दुस् A prefix to nouns and sometimes to verbs meaning 'bad, evil, wicked, inferior, hard or difficult &c.' (*N. B.* The स् of दुस् is changed to र् before vowels and consonants, see दुर्; to a Visarga before sibiliant, to श् before च् and छ् and to ष् before क् and प्). -COMP. -कर *a.* 1 wicked, acting badly. 2 hard to be done or accomplished, arduous, difficult; वक्तुं सुकरं कर्तुं दुष्करं 'sooner said than done'; Amaru. 41; Mk. 3. 1; Ms. 7. 55. (-रं) 1 a difficult or painful task or act, a difficulty. 2 atmosphere, ether. कर्मन् *m.* any bad act, sin, crime. -कालः 1 bad times; Mu. 7. 5. 2 the time of universal destruction. 3 an epithet of *S*iva. -कुलं a bad or low family; (आददीत) स्त्रीरत्नं दुष्कुलादपि Ms. 2. 238. -कुलीन *a.* low-born. कृत् *m.* a wicked person. -कृतं, -कृतिः *f.* a sin, misdeed; उभे सुकृतदुष्कृते Bg. 2. 50. -क्रम *a.* ill-arranged, unmethodical, unsystematic. -चर *a.* 1 hard to be performed or accomplished, arduous, difficult; R. 8. 79, Ku. 7. 65. 2 inaccessible, unapproachable. 3 acting ill; behaving wickedly. (-रः) 1 a bear. 2 a bi-valve shell. °चारिन् *a.* practising very austere penance. -चरित *a.* wicked, ill-behaved, abandoned. (-तं) misbehaviour, ill conduct. -चिकित्स्य *a.* difficult to be cured, incurable. -च्यवनः an epithet of Indra. -च्यावः an epithet of *S*iva. -तर *a.* (दुष्टर or दुस्तर) 1 difficult to be crossed; R. 1. 2; Ms. 4. 242; Pt. 1. 111. 2 difficult to be subdued, insuperable, invincible. -तर्कः false reasoning. -पच (दुष्पच) *a.* difficult to be digested. -पतनं 1 falling badly. 2 a word of abuse, abusive epithet (अपशब्द). -परिग्रह *a.* difficult to be seized, taken or kept. (-हः) bad wife. -पूर *a.* difficult to be filled or satisfied. -प्रकाश *a.* obscure, dark, dim. -प्रकृति *a.* ill-tempered, evil-natured.-प्रजस् *a.* having bad progeny. -प्रज्ञ *a.* (दुष्प्रज्ञ) week-minded, stupid.-प्रधर्ष, -प्रधृष्य unassailable; see दुर्धर्ष; R. 2. 27. -प्रवादः slander, calumnious report, scandal. -प्रवृत्तिः *f.* bad news, evil report; R. 12. 51.-प्रसह (-दुष्प्रसह) *a.* 1 irresistible, terrible. 2 hard to bear or endure; M. 5. 10.-प्राप, -प्रापण *a.* unattainable, hard to get; K. 1. 48; Bg. 6. 36. -शकुनं a bad omen. -शला N. of the only daughter of धृतराष्ट्र given in marriage to Jayadratha. -शासन *a.* difficult to be managed or governed, intractable. (-नः) N. of one of the 100 sons of धृतराष्ट्र. [He was brave and warlike, but wicked and intractable. When Yudhishthira staked and lost even Draupadi, Duh*s*asana dragged her into the assembly by her hair and began to strip her of every clothing; but Krish*n*a, ever ready to help the distressed, covered her from shame and ignominy. Bhima was so much exasperated at this dastardly act of Duh*s*asana that he vowed in the assembly that he would not rest till he had drunk the villain's blood. On the 16th day of the great war Bhima encountered Duh*s*asana in a single combat, killed him with ease, and drunk, according to his resolution his blood to his heart's content.]. -शील (दुश्शील) *a.* ill-mannered or behaved, reprobate. -सम (दुःसम or दुस्सम) *a.* 1 uneven, unlike, unequal. 2 adverse, unfortunate, 3 evil, improper, bad.-समं *ind.* ill, wickedly. -सत्वं an evil being-संधान. -संधेय *a.* difficult to be united or reconciled.-सह (दुस्सह) *a.* unbearable, irresistible, insupportable.-साक्षिन् *m.* a false witness. -साध, -साध्य *a.* 1 difficult to be accomplished or managed. 2 difficult to be cured. 3 difficult to be conquered. -स्थ, -स्थित *a.* (written also दुस्थ and दुस्थित) 1 ill. conditioned, poor, miserable. 2 suffering pain, unhappy, distressed. 3 unwell, ill. 4 unsteady, disquieted. 5 foolish, unwise, ignorant. (-स्थं *ind.*) badly, ill, unwell. -स्थितिः *f.* 1 bad condition or situation, unhappiness, misery. 2 instability. स्पृष्टं (दुस्पृष्टं) 1 slight touch or contact. 2 slight touch or action of the tongue which produces the sounds य्, र्, ल् and व्. -स्मर *a.* hard or painful to remember; U. 6. 34. -स्वप्नः a bad dream.

दुह् 2 U. (दोग्धि, दुग्धे, दुग्ध) 1 To milk or squeeze out, extract (with two acc.); भास्वंति रत्नानि महौषधीश्च पृथूपदिष्टां दुदुहुर्धरित्रीं Ku. 1. 2; यः पयो दोग्धि पाषाणं स रामाद्भूतिमाप्नुयात् Bk. 8. 82; पयो घटोध्नीरपि गां दुहंति 12 73; R. 5. 33. 2 To draw anything out of another (with two acc.); प्राणान्दुदुहविवात्मानं शोकं चित्तमवारुधत् Bk. 8. 9. 3 To drain a thing of its contents, to make profit out of; दुदोह गां स यज्ञाय शस्याय मघवा दिवं R. 1. 26. 4 To yield or grant (any desired object); कामान्दुग्धे विप्रकर्षत्यलक्ष्मीं U. 5. 31. 5 To enjoy. *-Caus.* (दोहयति) To cause to milk. *-Desid.* (दुधुक्षति) To wish to milk; राजन् दुधुक्षसि यदि क्षितिधेनुमेनां Bh. 2. 56.

दुहितृ *f.* A daughter. -COMP. -पतिः, also दुहितुः पतिः a son-in-law.

दू 4 A. (दूयते, दून) 1 To be afflicted, suffer pain, be sorry; न दूये सात्वतीसूनुर्यन्मह्यमपराध्यति *Si.* 2. 11; कथमथ वंचयसे जनमनुगतमसमशरज्वरदूनं Gît. 8. afflicted or distressed; see दु pass. 2 To give or cause pain.

दूतः, दूतकः A messenger, an envoy, an ambassador; Châṇ 106.-COMP. -मुख *a.* speaking by an ambassador.

दूतिका,-दूती 1 A female messenger, a confidante. 2 A go-between, or mischief-making woman. (*N. B.* The ती of दूती is sometimes shortened; see R. 18. 53, 19. 18; Ku. 4. 16 and Malli. thereon.).

दूत्यं 1 Employment of a messenger. 2 An embassy. 3 A message.

दून *a.* Pained, afflicted &c.; see under दु and दू.

दूर *a*. (*Compar*. दवीयस्, *superl*. दविष्ठ) Distant, remote, far off, a long way off, long; किं दूरं व्यवसायिनां Chân. 73; न योजनशतं दूरं बाह्यमानस्य तृष्णया H. 1. 146, 49. **–रं** Distance, remoteness. [*N. B*. Some of the oblique cases of **दूर** are used adverbially as follows :—(*a*) **दूरं 1** to a distance, far away, far or distant from (with abl. or gen.); ग्रामात् or ग्रामस्य दूरे Sk. **2** high above. **3** deeply, far below. **4** highly, in a high degree, very much; नेत्रे दूरमनंजने S. D. **5** entirely, completely; निमग्नां दूरमंभसि Ks. 10. 29; दूरमुद्धृतपापाः Me. 55. (*b*) **दूरेण 1** far, from a distant place, from afar; खलः कापट्यदोषेण दूरेणैव विसृज्यते Bv. 1. 78. **2** by far, in a high degree; दूरेण ह्यवरं कर्म बुद्धियोगाद्धनंजय Bg. 2. 49; R. 10. 30 vl. (*c*) **दूरात् 1** from distance, from afar; प्रक्षालनाद्धि पंकस्य दूरादस्पर्शनं वरं; दूरादागतः come from afar (regarded as comp.); नदीयमभितो........दूरात्परित्यज्यतां Bh. 1. 81; R. 1. 61. **2** in a remote degree. **3** from a remote period. (*d*) **दूरे** far, far away, in a distant place; न मे दूरे किंचित्क्षणमपि न पार्श्वे रथजवात् S. 1. 9; भोः श्रेष्ठिन् शिरसि भयमतिदूरे तत्प्रतीकारः Mu. 1; Bh. 3. 88. **दूरीकृ** means **1** to remove to a distance, remove, take away; आश्रमे दूरीकृतश्रमे Dk. 5; Bv. 1. 122. **2** to deprive (one) of, separate; Mk. 9. 4. **3** to prevent, ward off. **4** to surpass, excel, distance; S. 1. 17; so **दूरीभू** to be away or removed, be separated from, be at a distance; दूरीभूते मयि सहचरे चक्रवाकीमिवैकां]. –Comp. **–अंतरित** *a*. separated by a long distance. **–आपातः** shooting from afar. **–आप्लाव** *a*. jumping or leaping far. **–आरूढ** *a*. **1** mounted high. **2** far-advanced, intense, vehement; दूरारूढः खलु प्रणयोऽसहनः V. 4. **–ईरितेक्षण** *a*. squinteyed. **–गत** *a*. **1** far removed, distant, gone far, far advanced; grown intense; दूरगतमन्मथाक्षमेयं कालहरणस्य S. 3. **–ग्रहणं** the supernatural faculty of seeing objects though situated at a distance. **–दर्शनः 1** a vulture. **2** a learned man, a Pandit. **–दर्शिन्** *a*. far-seeing, foresighted, prudent. (*–m*.) **1** a vulture. **2** learned man. **3** a seer, prophet, sage. **–दृष्टिः 1** long-sightedness. **2** prudence, foresight. **–पातः 1** a long fall. **2** a long flight. **3** falling from a great height. **–पात्र** *a*. having a wide channel, or bed (as a river). **–पार** *a*. **1** very broad (as a river). **2** difficult to be crossed. **–बंधु** *a*. banished from wife and kinsmen; Me. 6. **–भाज्** *a*. distant, remote. **–वर्तिन्** *a*. being in the distance, far removed, remote, distant. **–वस्त्रक** *a*. naked. **–विलंबिन्** *a*. hanging far down. **–वेधिन्** *a*. piercing from afar. **–संस्थ** *a*. being at a distance, remote, far away; कंठाश्लेषप्रणयिनि जने किं पुनर्दूरसंस्थे Me. 3.

दूरतः *ind*. **1** From afar, from a distance; तद्राज्यं दूरतस्त्यजेत् Pt. 5. 69; वहति च परीतापं दोषं विमुंचति दूरतः Git. 2. 2 Far away, to a distance; Pt. 1. 9.

दूरेत्य *a*. Being far, come from afar.

दूर्यं Feces, ordure.

दूर्वा Bent grass, panic grass (considered as a sacred article of worship and offered to deities &c.). –Comp. **–अंकुरः** a soft blade of Durvâ grass; Vi. 3. 12.

दूलिका, दूली The Indigo plant.

दूष *a*. (At the end of comp.) Defiling, polluting; *e. g*. पंक्तिदूष.

दूषक *a*. (**षिका** *f*.) **1** Corrupting, polluting, vitiating, defiling, spoiling. **2** Violating, dishonouring, seducing. **3** Offending, trespassing, guilty. **4** Disfiguring. **5** Sinful, wicked (as an action). **–कः 1** A seducer, a corrupter. **2** Any infamous or wicked person.

दूषणं 1 Spoiling, corrupting, vitiating, ruining, polluting &c. **2** Violating, breaking (as an agreement). **3** Seducing, violating, dishonouring (as a woman) **4** Abuse, censure, blame; R. 12. 46. **5** Detraction, disparagement. **6** Adverse agreement or criticism, objection. **7** Refutation. **8** A fault, offence, defect, sin crime; नोलूकोप्यवलोकते यदि दिवा सूर्यस्य किं दूषणं Bh. 2. 93; हाहा धिक् परगृहवासदूषणं U. 1. 40; Ms. 2. 213; H. 1. 98, 115; 2. 180. **–णः** N. of a demon, one of the generals of Râvana, slain by Râma. –Comp. **–अरिः** an epithet of Râma. **–आवह** *a* involving (one) in blame.

दूषिः–षी *f*. The rheum of the eyes.

दूषिका 1 A pencil, paint-brush. **2** A kind of rice. **3** Rheum of the eyes.

दूषित *a*. **1** Corrupted, defiled, spoiled. **2** Hurt, injured. **3** Damaged, demoralized. **4** Blamed, censured. **5** Falsely accused, traduced, vilified.

दूष्य *a*. **1** Corruptible. **2** Condemnable, culpable, blamable. **—ष्यं 1** Matter, pus. **2** Poison. **3** Cotton. **4** A garment, clothes. **5** A tent; Si. 12. 65. **—ष्या** Leathern girth of an elephant.

दृ 6 A. (द्रियते, दृत; *desid*. दिदरिषते) (rarely used by itself usually found in combination with आ) **1** To respect, honor, worship, reverence; द्वितीयाद्रियते सदा H. Pr. 7; Mu. 7. 3, Bk. 6. 55. **2** To care for, mind; usually with न. **3** To apply or devote oneself closely to, have regard for; भूरि श्रुतं शाश्वतमाद्रियते Mâl. 1. 5. **4** To desire.

दृंह I, 1 P. (दृंहति, दृंहित) To make firm, strengthen. II. 1 A. **1** To be firm. **2** To grow or increase.

दृंहित *p. p*. **1** Made firm, strengthened. **2** Grown, increased.

दृकं A hole, an opening.

दृढ *a*. **1** Fixed, firm, strong, unswerving, untiring; Bg. 15. 3, H. 3. 65; R. 13. 78. **2** Solid, massive. **3** Confirmed, established. **4** Steady, presevering; Bg. 7. 28. **5** Firmly fastened, shut fast. **6** Compact. **7** Tight, close, dense. **8** Strong, intense, great, excessive, mighty, severe, powerful; तस्याः करिष्यामि दृढानुतापं Ku. 3. 8; R. 11. 46. **9** Tough. **10** Difficult to be drawn or bent (as a bow). **11** Durable. **12** Reliable. **13** Certain, sure. **–ढं 1** Iron. **2** A stronghold, fortress. **3** Excess, abundance, high degree. **—ढं** *ind*. **1** Firmly, fast. **2** Very much, excessively, vehemently. **3** Thoroughly. —Comp. **–अंग** *a* strong-limbed, stout. (**–गं**) diamond. **–इषुधि** *a*. having a strong quiver. **–कांडः, –ग्रंथिः** a bamboo. **–ग्राहिन्** *a*. seizing firmly; *i. e*. pursuing an object with untiring energy. **–दंशकः** a shark. **–द्वार** *a*. having the gates well-secured. **–धनः** an epithet of Buddha. **–धन्वन्–धन्विन्** *m*. a good archer. **–निश्चय** *a*. **1** of firm resolve, resolute, firm. **2** confirmed. **–नीरः, –फलः** the cocoanut tree. **–प्रतिज्ञ** *n*. firm to a promise, true to one's word, faithful to an agreement. **–प्ररोहः** the holy fig-tree. **–प्रहारिन्** *a*. **1** striking hard. **2** hitting firmly, shooting surely. **–भक्ति** *a*. faithful, devoted. **–मति** *a*. resolute, strongwilled, firm. **–मुष्टि** *a*. close-fisted, miserly, niggardly. (**–ष्टिः**) a sword. **–मूलः** the cocoa nut tree. **–लोमन्** *m*. a wild hog. **–वैरिन्** *m*. a relentless foe, an inveterate enemy. **–व्रत** *a*. **1** firm in religious austerity. **2** firm, faithful. **3** Persevering, persistent. **–संधि** *a*. **1** firmly united, closely joined. **2** close, compact. **3** thick-set. **–सौहृद** *a*. firm in friendship.

दृतिः *m. f*. **1** A leathern bag for holding water &c.; Ms 2. 99; Y. 3. 268. **2** A fish. **3** A skin, hide. **4** A pair of bellows. –Comp. **–हरिः** a dog.

दृन्फूः *f*. **1** A snake. **2** Thunderbolt.

दृन्भूः 1 The thunderbolt (of Indra). **2** The sun. **3** A king. **4** Yama, god of death (अंतक).

दृप् I. **1** P., 10 U. (दर्पति, दर्पयति-ते) To light, inflame, kindle.–II. **4** P. (दृप्यति, दृप्त) **1** To be proud, be arrogant or insolent; स किलनात्मना दृप्यति U. 5; दृप्यद्दानवदूयमानदिविषद्दुर्वारदुःखापदां Git. 9. 2 To be greatly delighted. 3 To be wild or extravagant.

दृप्त *a.* Proud, arrogant. 2 Mad, wild, frantic.

दृप्र *a.* 1 Proud, arrogant, Strong, powerful.

दृश् 1 P. (पश्यति, दृष्ट) 1 To see, look at, observe, view, behold, perceive; द्रक्ष्यसि भ्रातृजायां Me. 10, 19; R. 3. 42. 2 To look upon, regard, consider; आत्मवत्सर्वभूतेषु यः पश्यति स पंडितः Chân. 5. 3 To visit, wait or call upon; प्रत्युद्ययौ मुनिं द्रष्टुं ब्रम्हाणमिव वासवः Râm. 4 To perceive with the mind, learn, know, understand; Ms. 1. 110, 12. 23. 5 To inspect, discover. 6 To search, investigate, examine, decide; Y. 1. 327, 2. 305. 7 To see by divine intuition; ऋषिर्दर्शनात्स्तोमान् ददर्श Nir. 8 To look helplessly on (without power to prevent what is taking place). —*Pass.* (दृश्यते) 1 To be seen or perceived, become visible or manifested, तव तच्चारु वपुर्न दृश्यते Ku. 4. 11, 3; R. 3. 40; Bk. 3. 19; Me. 112. 2 To appear or look like, seem, look; R 3. 34. To be found or seen, occur (as in a book &c.); द्वितीयाम्रेडितातेषु ततोऽन्यत्रापि दृश्यते Sk.; इति प्रयोगो भाष्ये दृश्यते. 4 To be considered or regarded; सामान्यप्रतिपत्तिपूर्वकमियं दारेषु दृश्या त्वया S. 4. 16. —*Caus.* (दर्शयति-ते) 1 To cause any one (acc., dat. or gen.) to see anything (acc.), to show, point out; दर्शय तं चौरसिंहं Pt. 1; दर्शयति भक्तान् हरिं Sk; प्रत्यभिज्ञानरत्नं च रामायादर्शयत्कृती R. 12. 64; 1. 47, 13. 24; Ms. 4. 57. 2 To prove, demonstrate; Bk. 15. 12. 3 To exhibit, display, make visible; तदेव मे दर्शय देव रूपं Bg. 11. 45. 4 To produce (as in a court of justice) Ms. 8. 158. 5 To adduce (as evidence); अत्र श्रुतिं दर्शयति. 6 (Atm.) To show oneself, appear, show oneself or anything belonging to oneself; भवो भक्तान् दर्शयते Sk. (*i. e.* स्वयमेव); स्वां गृहेऽपि वनितां कथमास्यं न्हीनिमीलि खलु दर्शयिताहे N. 5. 71; स संततं दर्शयते गतस्मयः कृताधिपत्यामिव साधु बंधुतां Ki. 1. 10. —*desid.* (दिदृक्षते) To wish or desire to see. —WITH अनु to see in prospect. (*-Caus*). 1 to show, exhibit. 2 to make clear or explain. –आ *Caus.* to show or point out; उत्कूलादर्शितपथः कलिंगाभिमुखो ययौ R. 4. 38. –उद् to expect, look up to, foresee, see in prospect; उत्पश्यतः सिंहनिपातमुग्रं R. 2. 60; उत्पश्यामि द्रुतमपि सखे मत्प्रियार्थं यियासोः कालक्षेपं ककुभसुरभौ पर्वते पर्वते ते Me. 22. –उप to see, behold. (*-Caus*). to place before, communicate, make one acquainted with; राज्ञः पुरो मामुपदर्श्य H. 3; नयविद्भिर्नवे राज्ञि सदसच्चोपदर्शितं R. 4. 10. –नि *Caus.* 1 to show, point out; R. 6. 31. 2 to prove, demonstrate. 3 to consider, treat of, discuss (as in a book &c.) 4 to teach. 5 to illustrate by an example; see निदर्शना. –प्र *Caus* 1 to show, point out, discover, exhibit. 2 to prove, demonstrate. –सं 1 to see, behold; Bk. 16. 9. 2 to see well. (*-Caus*). to show, exhibit, discover; आत्मानं मृतवत्संदर्श्य H. 1; Bk. 4. 33; M. 4. 9.

दृश् *a.* (At the end of comp.) 1 Seeing, superintending, surveying, viewing. 2 Discerning, knowing. 3 Looking like, appearing. *-f.* 1 Seeing, viewing, perceiving 2 The eye, sight; संदधे दृशमुदग्रतारकां R. 11. 69. 3 Knowledge. 4 The number 'two'. 5 The aspect of a planet. –COMP. –अध्यक्षः the sun. –कर्णः a snake. –क्षयः decay or loss of sight, becoming dim-sighted. –गोचरः the range of sight. –जलं tears. –क्षेपः, –ज्या the sine of the zenith-distance. –पथः the range of sight. –पातः a look, glance. –प्रिया beauty, splendour. –भक्तिः *f.* a look of love, an amorous glance. –लंबनं vertical parallax. –विषः a snake. –वृत्तं a vertical circle. –श्रुतिः a snake, serpent.

दृशद् *f.* A stone; see दृषद्.

दृशा The eye. –COMP. –आकांक्ष्यं a lotus. –उपमं a white lotus.

दृशानः 1 A spiritual teacher. 2 A Brâhmaṇa. 3 A guardian of the world (लोकपाल). –नं Light, brightness.

दृशिः, –शी *f.* 1 The eye. 2 A Sâstra.

दृश्य *pot. p.* 1 To be seen, visible. 2 To be looked at. 3 Beautiful, pleasing to the sight, lovely; R. 6. 31; Ku. 7. 64. –श्यं A visible object; M. 1. 9.

दृश्वन् *a.* (At the end of comp.) 1 Seeing, perceiving. 2 (Fig.) Familiar or conversant with; as in श्रुतिपारदृश्वा R. 5. 24; विद्यानां पारदृश्वनः 1. 23.

दृषद् *f.* 1 A rock, large stone or stone in general; Me. 55; R. 4. 74; Bh. 1. 38. 2 A mill-stone, a flat stone for grinding condiments upon –COMP. –उपलः a grind-stone for grindidg condiments upon. (दृषदिमाषकः a tax raised from mill-stones).

दृषद्वत् *a.* Stony, rocky. –ती N. of a river flowing into the Saraswatî and forming the eastern boundary of the *A*ryâvarta; cf. Ms. 2. 17.

दृष्ट *p. p.* 1 Seen, looked, perceived, observed, beheld. 2 Visible, observable. 3 Regarded, considered. 4 Occuring, found. 5 Appearing, manifested. 6 Known, learned, understood. 7 Determined, decided, fixed. 8 Valid. 9 Allotted; see दृश्. –ष्टं Danger from dacoits &c. –COMP. –अंतः –तं 1 an example, illustration, parable; पूर्णेन्दुोदयाकांक्षी दृष्टांतोऽत्र महार्णवः *S*i. 2. 31. 2 (in Rhet.) a figure of speech in which an assertion or statement is illustrated by an example, (distinguished from उपमा and प्रतिवस्तूपमा; See K. P. 10. and R. G. *ad loc.*) 3 a *S*âstra or science. 4 death (cf. दिष्टांत). –अर्थ *a.* 1 having the object or meaning obvious or quite apparent. 2 practical. –कष्ट, –दुःख &c. one who has experienced or suffered misery, inured to hardships. –कूटं a riddle, an enigma. –दोष *a.* 1 found fault with, considered to be faulty. 2 vicious. 3 exposed, detected. –प्रत्यय *a.* 1 having confidence manifested. 2 Convinced. –रजस् *f.* a girl arrived at puberty. –व्यतिकर *a.* one who has experienced a misfortune. 2 one who foresees evil.

दृष्टिः *f.* 1 Seeing, viewing. 2 Seeing with the mental eye. 3 Knowing, knowledge. 4 The eye, the faculty of seeing, sight; केनेदानीं दृष्टिं विलोभयामि V. 2; चलापांगां दृष्टिं स्पृशसि *S*. 1. 24; दृष्टिस्तृणीकृतजगत्त्रयसत्त्वसारा U. 6. 19; R. 2. 8; *S*. 4. 2; देव दृष्टिप्रसादं कुरु H. 1. 5 A look, glance. 6 View, notion; क्षुद्रदृष्टिरेषा K. 173; एतां दृष्टिमवष्टभ्य Bg. 16. 9. 7 Consideration, regard. 8 Intellect, wisdom, knowledge. –COMP. –कृत, –कृतं a kind of lily (स्थलपद्मं). –क्षेपः a glance, look. –गुणः a mark for archers, abutt, target. –गोचर *a.* within the range of sight, in sight, visible. –पातः 1 a look, glance; मार्गे मृगप्रेक्षिणि दृष्टिपातं कुरुष्व R. 13. 18; Bh. 1. 11, 94; 3. 66. 2 act of seeing, function of the eye; रजःकणैर्विघ्नितदृष्टिपाताः Ku. 3. 31 (Malli. interprets—unnecessarily in our opinion—पात by प्रभा). –पथः the range of sight. –पूत *a.* 'kept pure by the sight', watched that no impurity is contracted; दृष्टिपूतं न्यसेत्पादं Ms. 6. 46. –बंधुः a fire-fly. –विक्षेपः a side-glance, leer, oblique look. –विद्या optics. –विभ्रमः an amorous glance, a coquettish look. –विषः a serpent.

दृह्, दृंह्, 1. P. (दृंहति, दंहति) 1 To be fixed or firm. 3 To grow, increase. 3 To prosper. 4 To fasten.

दॄ 4. 9. P. (दीर्यति, दृणाति, दीर्ण) 1 To burst or break asunder, split open. 2 To cause to burst, tear, divide, rend, sunder, pull to pieces. –*Pass.* (दीर्यते) 1 To burst, break open, be sundered; कथमेवं प्रलपतां वः सहस्रधा न दीर्णमनया जिह्वया Ve. 3. 2 To separate. –*Caus* (द-दा-रयति-ते) 1 To split, tear asunder, divide by digging. **2** To disperse, scatter. —WITH **वि** **1** to split, tear asunder, divide, cut to pieces, दंद्रिः किल नखैस्तस्या विददार स्तनौ द्विजः R. 12. 22; न विदीर्ये कठिनाः खलु स्त्रियः Ku. 4. 5, R. 14. 33. **2** to rend (fig.) चित्तं विदारयति कस्य न कोविदारः Rs. 3. 6; Bg. 1. 19. (With prepositions like **अव, आ, प्र,** &c. the root does not change its meaning).

दे 1 A. (दयते, दात; *Desid.* दित्सते) To protect, cherish.

देदीप्यमान *a.* Shining intensely, blazing, resplendent.

देय *a.* **1** To be given, offered or presented; R. 3. 16. **2** Fit to be given, proper for a gift. **3** To be returned or restored; विभावितैकदेशेन देयं यदभियुज्यते Vikr. 4. 17; Ms. 8. 139, 185.

देव् 1 A. (देवते) **1** To sport, play, gamble. **2** To lament. **3** To shine. —WITH **परि** to lament, mourn.

देव *a.* (वी *f.*) Divine, celestial; Bg. 9. 11; Ms. 12. 117. —वः **1** A god, deity; एको देवः केशवो वा शिवो वा Bh. 3. 120. **2** The god of rain, an epithet of Indra; as in द्वादशवर्षाणि देवो न ववर्ष. **3** A divine man, a Brâhmaṇa. **4** A king, ruler, as in मनुष्यदेव. **5** A title affixed to the names of Brâhmaṇas; as in गोविंददेव, पुरुषोत्तमदेव &c. **6** (In dramas) A title of honour used in addressing a king ('My lord', 'Your Majesty'); ततश्च देव Ve. 4; यथाज्ञापयति देवः &c. **7** (At the end of comp.) Having as one's deity; as in °मातृ, पितृ° &c. —COMP. —अंशः a partial incarnation of god. —अगारः, -रं a temple. —अंगना a celestial damsel, an *apsaras*.—अतिदेवः,—अधिदेवः **1** the highest god. **2** an epithet of *S*iva. —अधिपः an epithet of Indra. —अंधस् *n.*,—अन्नं **1** the food of gods, divine food, ambrosia. **2** food that has been first offered to an idol: see Ms. 5. 7 and Kull. thereon. —अभीष्ट *a.* **1** liked by or dear to gods. **2** sacred or dedicated to a deity. (—ष्टा) piper betel. —अरण्यं the garden; R. 10. 80. —अरिः a demon. अर्चनं,-ना the worship of gods. —अवसथः a temple. —अश्वः an epithet of उच्चैःश्रवस्, the horse of Indra. —आक्रीडः 'the garden of the gods,' Nandana garden. —आजीवः, आजीविन् *m.* **1** an attendant upon an idol. **2** a low Brâhmaṇa subsisting by attendance upon an idol and upon the offerings made to it. आत्मन् *m.* the holy fig-tree. —आयतनं a temple; Ms. 4. 46. —आयुधं **1** a divine weapon. **2** rain-bow. —आलयः **1** heaven. **2** a temple. —आवासः **1** heaven. **2** the holy fig-tree (अश्वत्थ). **3** a temple. **4** the Sumeru mountain. —आहारः nectar, ambrosia. —इज् *a.* (nom. sing. देवेट्-ड्) worshipping the gods. —इज्यः an epithet of Brihaspati, preceptor of the gods. —इंद्रः, —ईशः **1** an epithet of Indra. **2** of *S*iva. —उद्यानं **1** divine garden. **2** the Nandana garden. **3** a garden near a temple. —ऋषिः (देवर्षिः) **1** a deified saint, divine sage, such as अत्रि, भृगु, पुलस्त्य, अंगिरस् &c.; एवं वादिनि देवर्षौ Ku. 6. 84 (*i. e.* अंगिरस्). **2** an epithet of Nârada; Bg. 10. 13, 26. —ओकस् *n.* the mountain Sumeru.—कन्या a celestial damsel, a nymph. —कर्मन् *n.*, —कार्यं **1** a religious act or rite. **2** the worship of gods. —काष्ठं the Devadâru tree. —कुंडं a natural spring. —कुलं **1** a temple. **2** a race of gods. **3** a group of gods. —कुल्या the celestial Ganges. —कुसुमं cloves. —खातं, -खातकं **1** a natural hollow among mountains. **2** a natural pond or reservoir; Ms. 4. 203 **3** a pond near a temple. —°बिलं a cavern, chasm. —गणः a class of gods —गणिका an *apsaras*; q. v. —गर्जनं thunder. —गायनः a celestial chorister, a Gandharva. —गिरिः N. of a mountain; Me. 42.—गुरुः an epithet of **1** Kasyapa (the father of gods); **2** Brihaspati (the preceptor of gods). —गुही an epithet of Sarasvatî or of a place situated on it. —गृहं **1** a temple. **2** the palace of a king. —चर्या the worship or service of gods. —चिकित्सकौ (du.) Asvins, the twin physicians of gods. —छंदः a pearl-necklace of hundred strings. —तरुः **1** the holy fig-tree. **2** one of the trees of paradise (*i. e.* मंदार, पारिजात, संतान, कल्प and हरिचंदन). —ताडः **1** fire. **2** an epithet of Râhu. —दत्तः **1** N. of the conch-shell of Arjuna; Bg. 1. 15. **2** a certain person (used in speaking of men indefinitely); देवदत्तः पचति, पीनो देवदत्तो दिवा न भुंक्ते &c. —दारु *m. n.* a species of pine; Ku. 1. 54; R. 2. 36. —दासः a servant or attendant upon a temple. (—सी) **1** a female in the service of gods or temple. **2** a courtezan (employed as a dancer in a temple). —दीपः the eye. —दूतः a divine envoy, an angel. —दुंदुभिः **1** a divine drum. **2** the holy basil with red flowers. —देवः an epithet of Brahmâ. **2** *S*iva; Ku. 1. 52. **3** Vishṇu. —द्रोणी a procession with idols. —धर्मः a religious duty or office. —नदी **1** the Ganges. **2** any holy river; Ms. 2. 17. —नंदिन् *m.* N. of the door-keeper of Indra. —नागरी N. of the character in which Sanskrit is usually written. —निकायः 'residence of gods', paradise, heaven. —निंदकः a blasphemer, an unbeliever, heretic, an atheist. —निर्मित *a.* 'god-created', natural. —पतिः an epithet of Indra. —पथः **1** 'heavenly passage', heaven, firmament. **2** the milky way. —पशुः any animal consecrated to a deity. —पुर, —पुरी *f.* an epithet of Amarâvatî, the city of Indra. —पूज्यः an epithet of Brihaspati. —प्रतिकृतिः *f.*, —प्रतिमा an idol, the image of a deity. —प्रश्नः 'consulting deities', astrology, fortune-telling. —प्रियः 'dear to the gods', an epithet of *S*iva; (देवानांप्रियः an irreg. comp. meaning **1** a goat. **2** a fool, idiot like a brute beast, as in तेप्यतात्पर्यज्ञा देवानांप्रियाः K. P.). —बलिः an oblation to the gods. —ब्रह्मन् *m.* an epithet of Nârada. —ब्राह्मणः **1** a Brâhmaṇa who lives on the proceeds of a temple. **2** a venerable Brâhmaṇa. —भवनं **1** the heaven. **2** a temple. **3** the holy fig-tree. —भूमिः *f.* heaven. —भूतिः *f.* an epithet of the Ganges. —भूयं divinity, godhead. —भृत् *m.* an epithet **1** of Vishṇu. **2** of Indra. —मणिः **1** the jewel of Vishṇu called कौस्तुभ. **2** the sun. —मातृक *a.* 'having the god of rain or clouds as foster-mother, watered only by the clouds, depending on rain-water and not on irrigation, deprived of every other kind of water (as a country); देशो नद्यंबुवृष्ट्यंबुसंपन्नव्रीहिपालितः । स्यान्नदीमातृको देवमातृकश्च यथाक्रमं ॥ Ak.; cf. also वितन्वति क्षेममदेवमातृकाः (*i. e.* नदीमातृकाः) चिराय तस्मिन् कुरवश्चकासते Ki. 1. 17. —मानकः the jewel of Vishṇu called कौस्तुभ. —मुनिः a divine sage. —यजनं a sacrificial place, a place where a sacrifice is performed; देवयजनसंभवे सीते U. 4. —यजि *a.* making oblations to gods. —यज्ञः a sacrifice to the superior gods made by oblations to fire or through fire to the gods (one of the five daily sacrifices of a Brâhmaṇa; see Ms. 3. 81, 85; and पंचयज्ञ also). —यात्रा 'an idol procession', any sacred festival when the idols are carried in procession. —यानं, —रथः a celestial car. युगं the first of the four ages of the world also called कृतयुग. —योनिः **1** a superhuman being, a demigod. **2** a being of divine origin. —योषा an *apsaras*. —रहस्यं a divine mystery. राज्, —राजः an epithet of Indra. —लता the Navamallikâ or double jasmine plant. —लिंगं the image or statue of a deity. —लोकः heaven, paradise; Ms. 4. 182. —वक्त्रं an epithet of fire. —वर्त्मन् *n.* the sky. —वर्धकिः, —शिल्पिन् *m.* Visvakarman, the architect of gods. —वाणी 'a divine voice', a voice from heaven. —वाहनः an epithet of Agni. —व्रतं a religious observance, any religious observance, any religious vow. (—तः) an epithet of **1** Bhîshma. **2** Kârtikeya. —शत्रुः a demon. —शुनी an epithet of Saramâ, the bitch of the gods. —शेषं the remnants of a sacrifice offered to gods. —श्रुतः an epithet of **1** Vishṇu. **2** Nârada. **3** a sacred treatise. **4** a god in general.

-सभा 1 an assembly of the gods (सुधर्मन्). 2 a gambling house. -सभ्यः 1 a gambler. 2 a frequenter of gaming houses. 3 an attendant on a deity. सायुज्यं identification or unification with a deity, conjunction with the gods, deification. -सेना 1 the army of gods. 2 N. of the wife of Skanda; स्कंदेन साक्षादिव देवसेनां R. 7. 1 (Malli.:—देवसेना=स्कंदपत्नी; perhaps it merely means 'the army of the gods' personified as Skanda's wife) °पतिः an epithet of Kârtikeya. -स्वं 'property of gods,' property applicable to religious purposes or endowments; यद्धनं यज्ञशीलानां देवस्वं तद्विदुर्बुधाः Ms. 11. 20, 26. -हविस् n. an animal offered to gods at a sacrifice.

देवकी N. of a daughter of Devaka and wife of Vasudeva and mother of Krishṇa. -Comp. -नंदनः, -पुत्रः, -मातृ m. -सूनुः epithets of Krishṇa.

देवटः An artisan, a mechanic.

देवता 1 Divine dignity or power, divinity. 2 A deity, god; Ku. 1. 1. 3 The image of a deity. 4 An idol. 5 An organ of sense. -Comp. -अगारः, -रं, -आगारः, -रं, -गृहं a temple. -अधिपः an epithet of Indra. -अभ्यर्चनं worshipping a deity. -आयतनं, -आलयः, -वेश्मन् n. a temple or chapel. -प्रतिमा the image of a god, an idol. -स्नानं the ablution of an idol.

देवद्र्यंच् a. Adoring a deity.

देवन् m. The younger brother of a husband.

देवनः A die. -नं 1 Beauty. splendour, lustre. 2 Gaming, gambling, a game at dice. 3 Play, sport, pastime. 4 A pleasure ground, a garden. 5 A lotus. 6 Emulation, desire to excel. 7 Affair, business. 8 Praise. -ना Gambling, a game at dice.

देवयानी N. of the daughter of *S*ukra, preceptor of the *Asuras*. [She fell in love with Kacha, her father's pupil, but he rejected her advances. On this she cursed the youth, who in return cursed her that she should become the wife of a Kshatriya; (see कच) Once upon a time Devay*ani* and her companion *S*armish*tha*—the daughter of *V*rishaparvan, the king of the Daityas, went to bathe, keeping their clothes on the shore. But the god Wind changed their clothes, and when they were dressed they began to quarrel about the change until *S*armish*tha* so far lost her temper that she slapped Devay*ani*'s face and threw her into a well. There she remained until she was seen and rescued by Yay*ati*, who with the consent of her father, married her, and *S*armish*tha* became her servant as a recompense for her insulting conduct towards her. Devay*ani* lived happily with Y*ayati* for some years and bore him two sons, Yadu and Turvasu. Subsequently her husband became enamoured of *S*armish*tha*, and Devay*ani*, feeling herself aggrieved, abruptly left her husband and went home to her father, who at her request condemned Yây*ati* with the infirmity of old age; see Yay*ati* also].

देवरः, देवृ m. A husband's brother (elder or younger); Ms. 3. 55; 9. 59; Y. 1. 68.

देवलः An attendant upon an idol, a low Brâhmaṇa who subsists upon the offerings made to an idol.

देवसात् *ind.* To the nature of a god or gods;° भू to be changed into a god.

देविक a. (की f-), देविल a. 1 Divine, godly. 2 Derived from a god.

देवी 1 A female deity, a goddess. 2 N. of Durgâ. 3 N. of Sarasvatî. 5 A queen, especially a crowned queen (अग्रमहिषी who has undergone the consecration along with her husband); प्रेष्यभावेन नामेयं देवीशब्दक्षमा सती। स्नानीयवस्त्रक्रियया पत्रोर्णं वोपयुज्यते ॥ M. 5. 12; देवीभावं गमिता परिवारपदं कथं भजत्येषा K. P. 10. 6 A respectful title applied to a lady of the first rank.

देशः 1 A place or spot in general; देशः को नु जलावसेकशिथिलः Mk. 3. 12; so स्कंधदेशे *S*. 1. 19, द्वारदेश, कंठदेश &c. 2 A region, country, province; यं देशं श्रयते तमेव कुरुते बाहुप्रतापार्जितं H. 1. 171. 3 A department, part, side, portion (as of a whole); as in एकदेश, एकदेशीय q. v. 4 An institute, an ordinance. -Comp. -अतिथिः a foreigner. -अंतरं another country, foreign parts; Ms. 5. 78. -अंतरिन् m. a foreigner. -आचारः, -धर्मः a local law or custom, the usage or custom of any country; Ms. 1. 188. -कालज्ञ a. knowing the proper place and time. -ज, -जात a. 1 native, indigenous. 2 produced in the right country. 3 genuine, of genuine descent. -भाषा the dialect of a country. -रूपं propriety, fitness. -व्यवहारः a local usage, custom of the country.

देशकः 1 A ruler, governor. 2 An instructor, preceptor. 3 A guide in general.

देशना Direction, instruction.

देशिक a. Local, pertaining to a particular place, native. -कः 1 A spiritual teacher (गुरु). 2 A traveller. 3 A guide. 4 One familiar with places.

देशिनी The fore-finger.

देशी The dialect of a country, one of the varieties of the Prâkṛita dialect; see Kâv. 1. 33.

देशीय a. 1 Belonging to a province, provincial. 2 Native, local. 3 Inhabiting any country (at the end of comp.); as in मगधदेशीय, तद्देशीय, वंगदेशीय &c. 4 Not far or distant from, almost, bordering on (used as an affix at the end of words); अष्टादशवर्षदेशीयां कन्यां ददर्श K. 131 a girl about 18 years old (whose age bordered on 18); R. 18. 39; so पटुदेशीय &c.

देश्य a. 1 To be pointed out or proved. 2 Local, provincial. 3 Born in a country, native. 4 Genuine, of genuine descent. 5 Not far from, almost; see देशीय above. -श्यः 1 An eyewitness of anything; अभियोक्ता दिशेद्देश्यं Ms. 8. 52.-53. 2 The inhabitant of a country. -श्यं The statement of a question or argument, the thing to be proved or substantiated (पूर्वपक्ष).

देहः,-हं The body; देहं दहंति दहना इव गंधवाहाः Bv. 1. 104; see compounds below. -Comp. -अंतरं another body. °प्राप्तिः f. transmigration. -आत्मवादः materialism, the doctrines of Chârvâka. आत्मवादिन् m. a materialist, a Chârvâka. -आवरणं armour, dress. -ईश्वरः the soul. उद्भव,-उद्भूत a. born in the body, inborn, innate. -कर्तृ m. 1 the sun. 2 the Supreme soul. 3 father. -कोषः 1 the covering of the body. 2 a feather, wing &c. 3 skin. -क्षयः 1 decay of the body. 2 sickness, disease. -गत a. incarnate, embodied. -जः a son. -जा a daughter. -त्यागः 1 death (in general). 2 voluntary death; resigning the body; तीर्थे तोयव्यतिकरभवे जह्नुकन्यासरय्वोर्देहत्यागात् R. 8. 95. -दः quicksilver. -दीपः the eye. -धर्मः the function of the body. -धारकं a bone. -धारणं living, life. -धिः a wing. -धृष् m. air, wind. -बद्ध a. embodied, incarnate; R. 11. 35. -भाज् m. any being possessed of a body or life; especially a man. -भुज् m. 1 the soul. 2 the sun. -भृत् m. 1 a living being especially a man; धिगिमां देहभृतामसारतां R. 8. 51; Bg. 8. 4; 14. 14. 2 an epithet of *S*iva. 3 life, vitality. -यात्रा 1 dying, death. 2 nourishment, food. -लक्षणं a mole, a black or dark spot upon the skin. -वायुः one of five vital airs or life-winds; see प्राण. -सारः marrow. -स्वभावः bodily temperament.

देहंभर a. Gluttonous.

देहवत् a. Embodied. -m. 1 A man. 2 The soul.

देहला Spirituous liquor.

देहलिः-ली f. The threshold of a door, the sill or lower part of the wooden frame of a door; विन्यस्यंती भुवि गणनया देहलीदत्तपुष्पैः Me. 87; Mk. 1. 9. -Comp. -दीपः a lamp suspended over the threshold; °न्याय see under न्याय.

देहिन् *a.* (**नी** *f.*) Incarnate, embodied. –*m.* **1** A living being, especially a man; त्वदधीनं खलु देहिनां सुखं Ku. 4. 10; *Si.* **2**. 46; Bg. 2. 13, 17. 2; Ms. 1. 30, 5. 49. **2** The soul, spirit (enshrined in the body); तथा शरीराणि विहाय जीर्णान्यन्यानि संयाति नवानि देही Bg. 2. 22, 13; 5. 14. **–नी** The earth.

दै (दायति, दात) **1** To purify, cleanse. **2** To be purified. **3** To protect. –WITH **अव 1** to whiten, brighten. **3** to purify.

दैतेयः 'A son of Diti,' a Râkshasa, demon. –COMP. **–इज्यः**, **–गुरुः**, **–पुरोधस्** *m.* **–पूज्यः** epithets of *S*ukra, the preceptor of the Asuras. **–निषूदनः** an epithet of Vishṇu. **–मातृ** *f.* Diti, mother of the demons. **–मेदजा** the earth.

दैत्यः See दैतेय. –COMP. **–अरिः 1** a god **2** an epithet of Vishṇu. **–देवः 1** an epithet of Vishṇu. **2** wind. **–पतिः** an epithet of Hiraṇyakasipu; q. v.

दैत्या 1 A drug. **2** Spirituous liquor.

दैन (**नी** *f.*), **दैनंदिन** (**नी** *f.*), **दैनिक** (**की** *f.*), *a.* Diurnal, daily; Bv. 1. 103.

दैनिकी Daily wages, day's hire.

दैर्ध्य (**र्घ**) Length, longness.

दैनं,–न्यं 1 Poverty, poor and pitiable condition, miserable state; दरिद्राणां दैन्यं G. L. 2; इंदोर्दैन्यं त्वदनुसरणक्लिष्टकांतेर्बिभर्ति Me. 74. **2** Affliction, sorrow, dejection, grief, low-spiritedness. **3** Feebleness. **4** Meanness.

दैव *a.* (**वी** *f.*) **1** Relating to gods, divine, celestial; संस्कृतं नाम दैवी वागन्वाख्याता महर्षिभिः Kâv. 1. 33; R. 1. 60; Y. **2**. 235; Bg. **4**. 25, 9. 13, 16. 3; Ms. 3. 75. **2** Royal. **—वः** (*i. e.* विवाहः) One of the eight forms of marriage, that in which the daughter is given away at a sacrifice to the officiating priest; यज्ञस्य ऋत्विजे दैवः Y. 1. 59; (for the eight forms of marriage see उद्वाह or Ms. 3. 21). **—वं 1** Fate, destiny, luck, fortune; दैवमविद्वांसः प्रमाणयंति Mu. 3; विना पुरुषकारेण दैवमत्र न सिध्यति 'God helps those who help themselves'; दैवं निहत्य कुरु पौरुषमात्मशक्त्या Pt. 1. 361; **दैवात्** by chance, luckily, accidentally. **2** A god, deity. **3** A religious rite or offering, an oblation to gods. –COMP. **–अत्ययः** evil resulting from unusual natural phenomena. **–अधीन,–आयत्त** *a.* dependent on fate; दैवायत्तं कुले जन्म मदायत्तं तु पौरुषं Ve. 3. 33. **–अहोरात्रः** a day of the gods; *i. e.* the human year. **–उपहत** *a.* ill-fated, unfortunate; Mu. 6. 8. **–कर्मन्** *n.* offering oblations to gods. **–कोविद्**, **–चिंतकः**, **–ज्ञः** an astrologer, a fortune-teller; Y. 1. 313; Kâm. 9. 25. **–गतिः** *f.* turn or course of fate; मुक्ताजालं चिरपरिचितं त्याजितो दैवगत्या Me. 96. **–तंत्र** *a.* dependent on fate. **–दीपः** the eye. **–दुर्विपाकः** hardness of fortune, adverseness or unpropitiousness of fate; U. 1. 40. **–दोषः** badness of fate. **–पर** *a.* **1** trusting to fate, a fatalist. **2** fated, predestined. **–प्रश्नः** fortune-telling, astrology. **–युगं** 'a Yuga of the gods', said to consist of 12000 divine years but see Kull. on Ms. 1. 71. **–योगः** a lucky coincidence, fortuitous combination, fortune, chance; दैवयोगेन, दैवयोगात् fortunately, accidentally. **–लेखकः** a fortune-teller, an astrologer. **–वशः,–शं** the power of destiny, subjection to fate. **—वाणी 1** a voice from heaven. **2** the Sanskrit language; cf. Kâv. 1. 33 quoted above. **–हीन** *a.* ill-fated, unfortunate, unlucky.

दैवकः A god, deity.

दैवत *a.* (**ती** *f.*) Divine. **—तं 1** A god, deity, divinity; मृदं गा दैवतं विप्रं घृतं मधु चतुष्पदं प्रदक्षिणानि कुर्वीत Ms. 4. 39; 1. 53; Amaru. 3. **2** A number of gods, the whole class of gods. **3** An idol. (The word is said to be *m.* also, but is rarely used in that gender. Mammaṭa notices it as a fault of a word called अप्रयुक्तत्व; see अप्रयुक्त.

दैवतस् *ind.* By chance, fortunately, luckily.

दैवत्य *a.* Addressed or sacred to a deity; Y. 1. 99; Ms. 2. 189; 4. 124

दैवलः, **–लकः** The servant of an evil spirit.

दैवारिपः A conch-shell (शंख).

दैवासुरं The natural enmity subsisting between the gods and the demons.

दैविक *a.* (**की** *f.*) Relating to the gods, divine; Ms. 1 65, **8**. 409. **—कं** An inevitable accident.

दैविन् *m.* An astrologer.

दैव्य *a* (**व्या** or **व्यी** *f.*) Divine. **—व्यं** Fortune, fate. **2** Divine power.

दैशिकः *a.* (**की** *f.*) **1** Local, provincial. **2** National, belonging to the whole country. **3** Belonging or having reference to space. **4** Acquainted with any place. **5** Teaching, pointing, directing, showing. **—कः 1** A teacher, preceptor. **2** A guide.

दैष्टिक *a.* (**की** *f.*) Fated, predestined. **–कः** A fatalist.

दैहिक *a.* (**की** *f.*) Bodily, corporal.

दैह्य *a.* Bodily. **—ह्यः** The soul (enshrined in the body).

दो 4 P (द्यति, दित; *Caus.* दापयति; *Desid.* (दित्सति) **1** To cut, divide. **2** To mow, reap. –WITH **अव** to cut or lop off; यदन्यास्मिन्यज्ञे स्रुच्यवद्यति Sat Br.

दोग्धृ *m.* **1** A cowherd, milkman; मेरौ स्थिते दोग्धरि दोहदक्षे Ku. 1. **2**. **2**. A calf. **3** A panegyrist, one who writes verses for hire or reward. **4** One who performs anything out of interested motives (with a view to profit himself).

दोग्ध्री 1 A cow which yields milk. **2** A wet nurse (having much milk).

दोधः A calf.

दोरः A rope (रज्जु).

दोलः 1 Swinging, rocking, oscillating. **2** A swing, litter. **3** A festival held on the fourteenth or full-moon day of the month of Phâlguna when figures of 'young Krishṇa' (बालकृष्ण) are swung in a swing.

दोला, दोलिका 1 A litter, palanquin. **2** A swing, hammock fig. also);. आसीत्स दोलाचलचित्तवृत्तिः R. 14. 34; 9. 46; 19. 44; संदेहदोलामारोप्यते K 207, 246. **3** Swinging, fluctuation. **4** Doubt, uncertainty. –COMP. **–अधिरूढ,–आरूढ** *a.* (lit.) mounted on a swing; (fig.) uncertain, irresolute, disquieted. **—युद्धं** uncertainty of success, a fight with varying success; *S*i. 18. 80.

दोलायते Den. A. **1** To swing. rock to and fro, oscillate. fluctuate, vacillate (fig. also). **2** To be restless or uneasy.

दोषः 1 (*a*) A fault, blame, censure, defect, blemish, weak point; पत्रं नैव यदा करीरविटपे दोषो वसंतस्य किं Bh. 2. 93; नात्रकुलपतिर्दोषं ग्रहीष्यति *S.* **3** will not find fault or take exception; so पुनरुक्तदोषा R. 14. 9. (*b*) An error, mistake. **2** A crime, sin, guilt, offence; जायामदोषामुत संत्यजामि R. 14. 34; Ms. **8**. 245; Y. 3. 79. **3** Noxious quality, badness, injurious nature or quality; as in आहारदोष. **4** Harm, evil, danger, injury; बहुदोषा हि शर्वरी Mk. 1. 58; को दोषः what harm is there. **5** Bad or injurious consequence. detrimental effect; तत्किमयमातपदोषः स्यात् *S.* 3. अदाता वंशदोषेण कर्मदोषाद् दरिद्रता Chāṇ. 48; Ms. 10. 14. **6** Morbid affection, disease. **7** Disorder of the three humours of the body, or the three humours when in a disordered state. **8** (In Nyâya &c.) A fault of a definition; (अव्याप्ति, अतिव्याप्ति and असंभव). **9** (In Rhet.) A fault or defect of composition (such as पददोष, पदांशदोष, वाक्यदोष, रसदोष and अर्थदोष which are defined and illustrated in the 7th Ullâsa of K. P.). **10** A calf. **11** Refutation. –COMP.**– आरोपः** charge, accusation. **–एकदृश्** *a.* fault-finding, censorious, picking holes. **–कर**, **–कृत्** *a.* causing evil, hurtful.**–ग्रस्त** *a.* **1** convicted, guilty. **2** full of faults or defects. **ग्राहिन्** *a.* **1** malicious, malignant. **2** censorious. **–ज्ञ** *a.* knowing faults &c. (**–ज्ञः**) **1** a wise or learned man; R 1. 93- **2** a physician.**–त्रयं** disorder or vitiation of the three humours of the body; (*i. e.* वात, पित्त and कफ).

–दृष्टि *a.* censorious. –प्रसंगः attaching blame, condemnation, censure. –भाज् *a.* faulty, guilty, wrong.

दोषणं Accusation, charge.

दोषन् *m., n.* (This word has no forms for the first five inflection, *i. e* before acc. pl.) An arm.

दोषल *a.* Faulty, defective, corrupt.

दोषस् *f.* Night. –*n.* Darkness.

दोषा *ind.* At night; दोषाऽपि नूनमहिमांशुरसौ किलेति *Si.* 4. 46 62. –*f.* 1 The arm. 2 The darkness of night, night; घर्मकालदिवस इव क्षपितदोषः K. 37 (where the word means a 'fault or sin' also). –COMP. –आस्यः, –तिलकः a lamp. –करः the moon.

दोषातन *a.* (नी *f.*) Nightly, nocturnal: R. 13. 76.

दोषिक *a.* (की *f.*) Faulty, bad, defective. –कः Sickness, disease.

दोषिन् *a.* (णी *f.*) 1 Impure, defiled, contaminated. 2 Faulty, defective. Criminal, wicked, bad.

दोस् *m. n.* (दोषन् is optionally substituted for this word after acc dual) 1 The forearm, the arm तमुपाद्रवदुद्यम्य दक्षिणं दोर्निशाचरः R 15. 23; हेमपात्रगतं दोर्भ्यामादधानं पयश्चरु 10. 51; Ku. 3. 76. 2 The part of an arc defining its sine. –COMP. –गडु (दोर्गडु) *a.* crooked armed, –ग्रह (दोर्ग्रह) *a.* strong, powerful. (–हः) pain in the arm. –ज्या (दोर्ज्या) the sine of the base. –दंडः (दोर्दंड.) a stick-like arm, strong arm; Mv. 7. 8; Bv. 1. 128. –मूलं (दोर्मूलं) the arm-pit. –युद्धं (दोर्युद्धं) a duel; Mv. 5. 37. –शालिन् *a.* (दोःशालिन्) possessed of strong arms, warlike, brave; Ve. 3. 32. –शिखरं (दोःशिखरं) the shoulder. –सहस्रभृत् (दोःसहस्रभृत्) *m.* 1 an epithet of the demon Bâṇa. 2 an epithet of Sahasrârjuna. –स्थः (दोस्थः) 1 a servant. 2 service. 3 a player. 4 play, sport.

दोहः 1 Milking; आश्चर्यो गवां दोहोऽगोपेन Sk.; Ku. 1. 2; R. 2. 22; 17. 19. 2 Milk. 3 A milkpail. COMP. –अपनयः –जं milk.

दोहदः, –दं The longing of a pregnant woman; प्रजावती दोहदशंसिनी ते R. 14. 45; उपेत्य सा दोहददुःखशीलतां यदेव वव्रे तदपश्यदाहृतं 3. 6, 7. 2 Pregnancy. 3 The desire of plants at budding time (as for instance of the Asoka to be kicked by young ladies, of the Bakula to be sprinkled by mouthfuls of liquor &c.); महीरुहा दोहदसेकशक्तेराकालिकं कोरकमुद्गिरंति N. 3. 21; R. 8. 62; Me. 78; see प्रियंगु. 4 Vehement desire; प्रवर्तितमहासमरदोहदा नरपतयः Ve. 4. 5 Wish or desire in general. –COMP. –लक्षणं 1 the fœtus, the embryo (=दौहृदलक्षण q. v.). 2 the period of passing one stage of life to another.

दोहदवती A pregnant woman longing for anything.

दोहन *a.* 1 Milking. 2 Yielding or granting (desirable objects). –नं 1 Milking. 2 A milkpail –नी A milk-pail.

दोहलः see दोहद; वृथा वहसि दोहलं (v. l.) ललितकामिसाधारणं M. 3. 16.

दोहली The Asoka tree.

दोह्य *a.* To be milked, milkable. –ह्यं Milk

दौःशील्यं Bad temper, wickedness, wicked disposition.

दौःसाधिकः 1 A door-keeper, porter. 2 The superintendent of a village.

दौकू (गू) लः A car covered with silk cloth. –लं Fine silk cloth.

दौत्यं Message, mission.

दौरात्म्यं 1 Wickedness, evil or wicked temper, depravity; R 15. 72. 2 Mischievousness; गुणानामेव दौरात्म्याद् धुरि धुर्यो नियुज्यते K. P. 10.

दौर्गत्यं 1 Poverty, want, destitution; Pt. 2. 92. 2 Wretchedness, distress.

दौर्गंध्यं Bad or disagreeable smell.

दौर्जन्यं Wickedness, depravity.

दौर्जीवित्यं A wretched or miserable life.

दौर्बल्यं Impotency, debility, weakness, feebleness; Ms. 8 171; Bg. 2. 3.

दौर्भागिनेयः The son of a woman disliked by her husband.

दौर्भाग्यं Ill-luck, misfortune; Y. 1. 283.

दौर्भ्रात्रं A quarrel or disagreement between brothers.

दौर्मनस्यं 1 Evil disposition. 2 Mental pain, affliction, dejection, sorrow. 3 Despair.

दौर्मंत्र्यं Evil advice, bad counsel; दौर्मंत्र्यान्नृपतिर्विनश्यति Bh. 2. 42.

दौर्वचस्यं Evil speech, bad language.

दौर्हदं, दौहृदं 1 Evil disposition of the mind, enmity; (also दौर्हार्द in this sense). 2 Pregnancy; सुदक्षिणा दौर्हृदलक्षणं दधौ R. 3. 1. 3 The longing of apregnant woman. 4 Desire in genaral.

दौर्हृदयं Evil disposition of mind, enmity.

दौलिमः An epithet of Indra.

दौवारिकः (की *f.*) A door-keeper, warder; R. 6. 59.

दौश्चर्यं 1 Evil conduct, wickedness. A bad deed.

दौष्कुल *a.* (ली *f.*), **दौष्कुलेय** *a.* (यी *f.*) Sprung from a low family born in a contemptible family.

दौष्ठवं Badness, wickedness.

दौष्यं (ष्मं) तिः A son of Dushyanta; दौष्यंतिमप्रतिरथं तनयं निवेश्य S. 4. 20.

दौहित्रः A daughter's son; Ms. 3. 148, 9. 131. –त्रं Sesamum seed.

दौहित्रायणः The son of a daughter's son.

दौहित्री A daughter's daughter.

दौहृदिनी A pregnant woman.

द्यु 2 P. (द्यौति) To advance towards, encounter, attack, assail; Bk. 6. 118, 14. 104.

द्यु *n.* 1 A day. 2 The sky. 3 Brightness 4 Heaven. –*m.* Fire. (द्यु is a substitute for दिव् *f.* before terminations beginning with consonants and in compounds). –COMP. –गः a bird. –चरः 1 a planet. 2 a bird. –जयः attainment or gaining of heaven. –धुनिः *f.*, –नदी the heavenly Ganges –निवासः a deity, god; शोकाग्निनाऽगाद् द्युनिवासभूयं Bk. 3. 21. –पतिः 1 the sun 2 an epithet of Indra. –मणिः the sun. –लोकः heaven. –षद्, –सद् *m.* 1 a god, deity; *Si.* 1. 43. 2 a planet. –सरित् *f.* the Ganges.

द्युकः An owl. –COMP. –अरिः a crow.

द्युत् 1 A. (द्योतते, द्युतित or द्योतित; *desid.* (दिद्युतिषते, दिद्योतिषते) To shine, be bright or brilliant; दिद्युते च यथा रविः Bk. 14. 104. 6. 26, 7 107; 8. 89. –*Caus* (द्योतयति) 1 To illuminate, irradiate; Bk. 8. 46; Ku. 6. 4 2 To make clear, explain, elucidate. 3 To express, mean. –WITH अभि (*caus.*) to illuminate; R. 6 34. –उद् to illuminate, light up, adorn, grace; R. 10. 80. –वि to shine, be bright; व्यद्योतिष्ट सभावेद्यामसौ नरशिखित्रयी *Si.* 2 3; 1. 20

द्युतिः *f.* 1 Splendour, brightness, lustre, beauty; काचः कांचनसंसर्गाद्धत्ते मारकतीं द्युतिं H. Pr. 41, Mâl. 2. 10; R. 3. 64. 2 Light; a ray of light; Bh. 1. 61. 3 Majesty, dignity; Ms. 1 87.

द्युतित *a.* Illuminated, shining, bright.

द्युम्नं 1 Spendour, glory, lustre. 2 Energy, strength, power. 3 Wealth, property. 4. Inspiration.

द्युवन् *m.* The sun.

द्यूतः, –तं 1 Play, gambling, playing with dice; द्यूतं हि नाम पुरुषस्यासिंहासनं राज्यं Mk. 2; द्रव्यं लब्धं द्यूतेनैव दारामित्रं द्यूतेनैव । दत्तं भुक्तं द्यूतेनैव 2. 7.; अप्राणिभिर्यत्क्रियते तल्लोके द्यूतमुच्यते Ms. 9. 223. 2 The prize won. –COMP. –अधिकारिन् *m.* the keeper of a gambling house –करः,–कृत् *m.* a gamester, a gambler; अयं द्यूतिकरः सभिकेन खलीक्रियते Mk. 2. –कारः, –कारकः 1 the keeper of a gambling house. 2 a gambler. –क्रीडा playing at dice, gambling. –पूर्णिमा, –पौर्णिमा the day of full-moon in the month of Asvina (also called कोजागर) when people spend their time in games of chance in honour of Lakshmî, the goddess of wealth. -बीजं a *cowrie*, a shell used in playing. -वृत्तिः 1 a professional gambler. 2 the keeper of a gambling house. -सभा, -समाजः 1 a gambling house. 2 an assembly of gamblers.

द्यै 1. P. (द्यायति) 1 To despise, treat with contempt. 2 To disfigure.

द्यो *f.* (Nom. sing. द्यौः) Heaven, paradise, the sky; द्यौर्भूमिरापो हृदयं यमश्च Pt. 1 182; *S.* 2. 14. (In Dvandva compound द्यो is changed to द्यावा; *e. g.* द्यावापृथिव्यौ, द्यावाभूमी heaven and earth). -COMP. -भूमिः a bird. -सद् (द्योषद्) a god.

द्योतः 1 Light, lustre, brilliance; as in खद्योत. 2 Sunshine. 3 Heat.

द्योतक *a.* 1 Shining. 2 Illumination. 3 Explaining, making manifest, showing.

द्योतिस् *n.* 1 Light, brightness, lustre. 2 A star. -COMP. -इंगणः (द्योतिरिंगणः) a fire-fly.

द्रक्षणं A measure of weight, a *tola*.

द्रढयति Den. P. 1 To make firm, fasten, tighten (lit); as in जटाजूटग्रंथिं द्रढयति. 2 To strengthen, confirm, corroborate; निदेशः शैलानां तदिदमिति बुद्धिं द्रढयति U. 2. 27; विशुद्धेरुत्कर्षस्त्वयि तु मम भक्तिं द्रढयति 4. 11.

द्रढिमन् *m.* 1 Tightness, firmness; बधान द्रागेव द्रढिमरमणीयं परिकरं G. L. 47. 2 Confirmation, corroboration; उक्तस्यार्थस्य द्रढिम्ने *S*ankara. 3 Assertion, affirmation. 4 Heaviness

द्रप्सं Diluted sour milk, diluted curds (also द्रप्स्यं).

द्रम् 1. P. (द्रमति) To go about, run, run about; Bk. 14. 70.

द्रम्मं A drachma; (a word derived from the Greek drachma).

द्रव *a.* 1 Running (as a horse). 2 Dropping, oozing, wet, dripping, आक्षिप्य काचिद् द्रवरागमेव (पादं R. 7. 7. 3 Flowing, fluid. 4 Liquid (opp. कठिन); Ku. 2. 11. 5 Melted, liquefied. -वः 1 Going, walking about, motion. 2 Dropping, trickling, oozing, exudation. 3 Flight, retreat. 4 Play, amusement, sport. 5 Fluidity, liquefaction. 6 A liquid substance, fluid. 7 Juice, essence. 8 Decoction. 9 Speed, velocity. (द्रवीकृ means 'to melt, liquefy'; द्रवीभू to be melted, as with pity &c.; द्रवीभवति मे मनः Mv. 7. 34; द्रवीभूतं प्रेम्णा तव हृदयमस्मिन्क्षण इव U. 3. 13; द्रवीभूतं मन्ये पतति जलरूपेण गगनं Mk. 5. 25.) -COMP. -आधारः 1 a small vessel or receiver. 2 the hands joined together and hollowed (=चुलुक q. v.). -जः treacle. -द्रव्यं a fluid substance. -रसा 1 lac. 2 gum.

द्रवंती A river.

द्रविडः 1 N. of a country on the east coast of the Deccan; अस्ति द्रविडेषु कांची नाम नगरी Dk. 130. 2 An inhabitant or native of that country; जरद्द्रविडधार्मिकस्येच्छया निमुष्टिः K. 229. 3 N. of a degraded tribe; cf. Ms. 10. 22.

द्रविणं 1 Wealth, money, property, substance; Ve. 3. 20; Bv. 4. 29. 2 Gold; R 4. 70. 3 Strength, power. 4 Valour, prowess. 5 A thing, matter, material. -COMP. -अधिपतिः -ईश्वरः an epithet of Kubera.

द्रव्यं 1 A thing, substance, object, matter. 2 The ingredient or material of anything. 3 A material to work upon. 4 A fit or suitable object (to receive instruction &c.) Mu. 7. 14; see अद्रव्य also. 5 An elementary substance, the substratum of properties, one of the seven categories of the Vaiseshikas; (the *dravyas* are nine :-पृथिव्यप्तेजोवाय्वाकाशकालदिगात्ममनांसि). 6 Any possession, wealth, goods, property, money; तत्तस्य किमपि द्रव्यं यो हि यस्य प्रियो जनः U. 2. 19. 1 A medicinal substance or drug. 8 Modesty. 9 Bell-metal. 10 Spirituous liquor. 11 A wager, stake. -COMP. -अर्जनं, -वृद्धिः, -सिद्धिः *f.* acquisition of wealth. -ओघः affluence, abundance of wealth. -परिग्रहः the possession of property or wealth. -प्रकृतिः *f.* the nature of matter. -संस्कारः the consecration of articles for sacrifice &c -वाचकं a substantive.

द्रव्यवत् *a.* 1 Rich, wealthy. 2 Inherent in the substance.

द्रष्टव्य *a. pot. p.* 1 To be seen, visible. 2 Perceptible. 3 Fit to be seen, investigated or examined. 4 Lovely, pleasing to the sight, beautiful; त्वया द्रष्टव्यानां परं न दृष्टं *S.* 2; Bh. 1. 8.

द्रष्टृ *m.* 1 A seer, one who sees mentally; as in ऋषयो मंत्रद्रष्टारः 2 A Judge.

द्रहः A deep lake.

द्रा 2. 4. P. (द्राति, द्रायति) 1 To sleep. 2 To run, make haste. 3 To fly, run away. -WITH नि to sleep, go to sleep, be asleep; अथावलंब्य क्षणमेकपादिकां तदा निदद्राबुपपल्वलं खगः N. 1 21; नायं ते समयो रहस्यमधुना निद्राति नाथः Bh. 3. 97; Bv. 1. 41; Bk. 10. 74; *S*ânti. 4. 19. -वि to retreat, run away, fly.

द्राक् *ind.* Quickly, instantly, forth with, immediately. —COMP. -भृतकं water just drawn from a well.

द्राक्षा Vine, grape, (the creeper or the fruit); द्राक्षे द्रक्ष्यंति के त्वां Gît 12; R. 4. 65, Bv. 1. 14, 4. 39. -COMP. -रसः grape juice, wine.

द्राघयति Den. P. 1 To lengthen, stretch, extend. 2 To increase, intensify; द्राघयंति हि मे शोकं स्मर्यमाणा गुणास्तव Bk. 18. 33. 3 To tarry, delay.

द्राघिमन् *m.* 1 Length. 2 A degree of longitude.

द्राघिष्ठ 1. Longest, very long; (Superl. of दीर्घ).

द्राघियस् *a.* (सी *f.*) Longer, very long (compar. of दीर्घ q. v.); Bv. 1. 35.

द्राण *a.* 1 Flown, run away. 2 Sleeping, sleepy. -णं 1 Running away, flight, retreat. 2 Sleep.

द्रापः 1 Mud, mire. 2 Heaven, sky. 3 A fool, an idiot. 4 An epithet of *S*iva. 5 A small shell.

द्रामिलः N. of Châṇakya.

द्रावः 1 Flight, retreat. 2 Speed. 3 Running, flowing. 4 Heat. 5 Liquefaction, melting.

द्रावकः 1 A flux used to assist the fusion of metals. 2 The loadstone. 3 Moon-stone. 4 A thief. 5 A sharp or clever man, wit, wag. 6 A libertine, lecher. -कं Wax.

द्रावणं 1 Putting to flight. 2 Melting, fusing. 3 Distilling. 4 The clearing-nut.

द्राविडः 1 A Dravidian, Dravida. 2 A general name for a Brâhmaṇa of any of the five southern tribes (the पंचद्रविड), द्राविड, कर्णाट, गुर्जर, महाराष्ट्र and तैलंग. —डाः *pl.* The Dravida country and its people. —डी Cardamoms.

द्राविडकः Zedoary. -कं Black salt.

द्रु I. 1. P. (द्रवति, द्रुत; *desid.* दुद्रूषति) 1 To run; flow, run away, retreat, (often with acc.); यथा नदीनां बहवोंबुवेगाः समुद्रमेवाभिमुखं द्रवंति Bg. 11. 28; रक्षांसि भीतानि दिशो द्रवंति 36; द्रुतं द्रवत कौरवाः Mb. 2 To rush, attack, assault quickly Bk. 9. 59. 3 To become fluid, dissolve, melt, ooze (fig. also); द्रवति च हिमरश्मावुद्गते चंद्रकांतः Mâl. 1. 28; द्रवति हृदयमेतत् Ve. 5. 21; *S*i. 9. 9; Bk. 2. 12. 4 To go, move. —*Caus.* (द्रावयति-ते) 1 To cause to run away, put to flight. 2 To melt, fuse -WITH अनु 1 to run after, follow, accompany; R. 3. 38; 12. 67, 16. 25; *S*i. 1. 52. 2 to chase, pursue. -अभि 1 to attack, assail, march against; गजा इवाऽन्योन्यमभिद्रवंतः Mk. 5. 21. 2 to befall. 3 to pass or run over. -उप 1 to attack, assault; R. 15. 23. 2 to run towards. -प्र to run away, retreat or fly to (with acc. or abl.); रणात्प्रद्रवंति बलानि Ve. 4; Bk. 15. 79. -प्रति to run to, fly or go to; Bk. 6. 17. -वि to run, run away, retreat. (—*Caus.*) to put to flight, scare away, scatter; Bv. 1. 52; Mâl. 3. -II. 5 P. (द्रुणोति) 1 To hurt, injure; तं दुद्रावाद्रिणा कपिः Bk. 14. 81, 85. 2 To go. 3 To repent.

द्रु *m. n.* 1 Wood. 2 Any instrument made of wood. -*m.* 1 A tree; Ms. 7. 131. 2 A branch. -COMP.

-किलिमं the Devadâru tree. घण: 1 a mallet, wooden mace. 2 an iron weapon made like a carpenter's hammer. 3 an axe, hatchet. 4 an epithet of Brahmâ. -घ्नी a hatchet. -नख: a thorn. -नस a. (णस) large-nosed. -न (ण) हः a scabbard; see द्रण-ह also. -सल्लकः a kind of tree (पियाल).

द्रुणः 1 A scorpion. 2 A bee. 3 A rogue. -णं 1 A bow. 2 A sword. -COMP. -हः a sheath, scabbard.

द्रुणा A bow-string.

द्रुणिः -णी f. 1 A small or female tortoise. 2 A bucket. 3 A centipede.

द्रुत p. p. 1 Quick, swift, speedy. 2 Flown, run away, escaped. 3 Melted, liquid, dissolved; see द्रु. -तः 1 A scorpion. 2 A tree. 3 Acc तं ind. Quickly, swiftly, speedily, immediately. -COMP. -पद a. going quickly. -विलंबितं N. of a metre; See App.

द्रुतिः f. 1 Melting, dissolving. 2 Going, running away.

द्रुपदः N. of a king of the Pânchâlas. [He was a son of Prishata. He and Drona were school-fellows, as they learnt the science of archery from Drona's father Bharadvaja. After Drupada had succeeded to the throne, Drona, when in pecuniary difficulties, went to him on the strength of his former friendship, but the proud monarch disrespected and slighted him. For this Drona afterwards got him captured by his pupils the Pandavas, but was kind enough to spare his life, and allowed him to retain half his kingdom. But the defeat sustained by him at Drona's hands rankled in his soul, and with the desire of getting a son who would avenge the wrong done to him, he performed a sacrifice when a son named Dhrishtadyumna (and a daughter called Draupadi) sprang up from the fire. This son afterwards treacherously cut off the head of Drona; see Drona also].

द्रुमः 1 A tree; यत्र द्रुमा अपि मृगा अपि बंधवो मे U. 3. 8. 2 A tree of Paradise -COMP. -अरिः an elephant -आमयः lac, gum. --आश्रयः a lizard. -ईश्वरः 1 the palm tree. 2 the moon. 3 the पारिजात tree. -उत्पलः the Karnikâra tree. -नखः,-मरः a thorn. -व्याधिः lac, gum. -श्रेष्ठः the palm tree. -षंडं a grove of trees.

द्रुमिणी An assemblage of trees.

द्रुवयः A measure (मानं).

द्रुह् 4 P. (द्रुह्यति, द्रुग्ध) 1 To bear malice or hatred. 2 To seek to hurt or injure, plot maliciously or revengefully, meditate mischief; (generally with the dat. of the object of hatred); यान्वेति मां द्रुह्यति मह्यमेव सात्रेयुपालंभि तयालिवर्गः N. 3. 7; Bk. 4. 39. -WITH अभि to do injury, to seek to assail, plot against (with acc.); मच्छरीरमभिद्रोग्धुं यतते Mu. 1.

द्रुह् a. (At the end of comp). (Nom. Sing. ध्रुक्-ग्, ध्रुट्-ड्) Injuring, hurting, plotting or acting as an enemy against; Si. 2. 35; Ms. 5, 90. —f. Injury, damage.

द्रुहः 1 A son. 2 A lake.

द्रुहणः, द्रुहिणः N. of Brahmâ or Siva.

द्रूः Gold.

द्रूघणः A hammer, an iron club; see द्रुघण.

द्रूणः A scorpion.

द्रोणः 1 A lake 400 poles long. 2 A cloud (or a particular kind of cloud) abounding in water (from which rain streams forth as from a bucket); कोयमेवंविधे काले कालपाशस्थिते मयि । अनावृष्टिहते शस्ये द्रोणमेघ इवोदितः ॥ Mk. 10. 26. 3 A raven or a carrion crow. 4 A scorpion. 5 A tree (in general) 6 A tree bearing (white) flowers. 7 N. of the preceptor of the Kauravas and Pânadavas [Drona was the son of the sage Bharadvaja, and was so called because the seed, which fell at the sight of a nymph called Ghritachi, was preserved by the sage in a Drona. Though a Brahmana by birth, he was well versed in the science of arms which he learnt from Parasurama. He afterwards taught the Kauravas and Pandavas the science of arms and archery. When, however, the great war commenced, he attached himself to the side of the Kauravas, and after Bhishma had been mortally wounded–'lodged in the cage of darts'–he assumed the command of the Kaurava forces and maintained the struggle for four successive days, achieving wonderful exploits and killing thousands of warriors on the Pandava side. On the fifteenth day of the battle the fight continued even during the night, and it was on the morning of the 16th that Bhima at the suggestion of Krishna said within Drona's hearing that Asvatthaman was slain (the fact being that an elephant named Asvatthaman had fallen on the field). Being at a loss to understand how that could be, he appealed to Yudhishthira, 'the truthful', who also, at the advice of Krishna gave an evasive reply—uttered loudly the word Asvatthaman and added '*Gaja* or elephant' in a very low tone; see Ve. 3. 9. Sorely grieved at the death of his only son, the kind-hearted old father fell in a swoon, and Dhrishtadyumna, his avowed enemy, took advantage of this circumstance and cut off his head]. -णः,-णं A measure of capacity, either the same as an Adhaka or equal to 4 Adhakas or $\frac{1}{16}$ of a Khâri, or 64 or 32 *shers*. —णं 1 A wooden vessel or cup, bucket. 2 A tub. -COMP. -आचार्यः see द्रोण above. -काकः raven -क्षीरा, -घा, दुग्धा,-दुघा a cow yielding a drona of milk. -मुखं the capital of 400 villages.

द्रोणिः-णी f. 1 An oval vessel of wood used for holding or pouring out water, a bucket, basin, baling vessel. 2 A water reservoir (जलाधार). 3 A trough for feeding cattle. 4 A measure of capacity, equal to two Súrpas or 128 *shers*. 5 The valley or chasm between two mountains; बृहद्द्रोणीशैलकांतारप्रदेशमधितिष्ठनो माधवस्यांतिकं प्रयामि Mâl. 9; हिमवद्द्रोणी &c. -COMP. -दलः the Ketaka tree.

द्रोहः 1 Plotting against, seeking to hurt or assail, injury, mischief, malice; अद्रोहशपथं कृत्वा Pt. 2. 35; Bg. 1. 37; Ms. 2. 161. 7. 48. 9. 17. 2 Treachery, perfidy. 3 Wrong, offence 4 Rebellion. -COMP. -अटः 1 a religious impostor, hypocrite, impostor. 2 a hunter. 3 a false man. -चिंतनं a malicious thought, malice prepense, a thought or attempt to injure. -बुद्धि a. bent on mischief or evil design. (-द्धिः f.) a wicked or evil purpose.

द्रौणायनः, -निः, द्रौणिः An epithet of Asvatthâman; यद्रामेण कृतं तदेव कुरुते द्रौणायनिः क्रोधनः Ve. 3. 31.

द्रौपदी N. of the daughter of Drupada, king of the Pânchâlas. [She was won by Arjuna, at her Svayamvara ceremony, and when he and his brothers returned home they told their mother that they had that day made a great acquisition. Whereupon the mother said "Well, then my dear children, divide it amongst yourselves." As her words once uttered could not be changed, she became the common wife of the five brothers. When Yudhishthira lost his kingdom and even himself and Draupadi in gambling, she was grossly insulted by Duhsasana q. v. and by Duryodhana's wife. But these and the like insults she bore with uncommon patience and endurance; and on several occasions when she and her husbands were put to the test, she saved their credit (as on the occasion of Durvasas begging food at night for his 60,000 pupils). At last, however, her patience was exhausted and she taunted her husbands for the very tame way in which they put up with the insults and injuries inflicted upon them by their enemies (see Ki. 1. 29–46). It was then that the Pandavas resolved to enter upon the great Bharati war. She is one of the five very chaste women whose names one is recommended to repeat; see अहल्या].

द्रौपदेयः A son of Draupadí; Bg. 1. 6, 18.

द्वंद्वः A plate on which hours are struck. –द्वं A pair, couple of animals (including even men) of different sexes; *i. e.* male and female; द्वंद्वानि भावं क्रियया विवव्रुः Ku. 3. 35; Me. 46; न चेदिदं द्वंद्वमयोजयिष्यत् Ku. 7. 66; R. 1. 40; *S*. 2. 14, 7. 27. **3** A couple of any two things, a couple of opposite conditions or qualities (such as सुख and दुःख, शीत and उष्ण); द्वंद्वैरयोजयच्चेमाः सुखदुःखादिभिः प्रजाः Ms. 1. 26; 6. 81; सर्वर्त्तुनिर्वृतिकरे निवसन्नुपैति न द्वंद्वदुःखमिह किंचिदकिंचनोऽपि Si. 4. 64. **4** A strife, contention, quarrel, dispute, fight. **5** A duel. **6** Doubt, uncertainty. **7** A fortress, stronghold. **8** A secret. –द्वः (In gram.) One of the four principal kinds of compounds, in which two or more words are joined together which, if not compounded, would stand in the same case and be connected by the copulative conjunction 'and'; चार्थे द्वंद्वं P. II. 2. 29; द्वंद्वः सामासिकस्य च Bg. 10. 33. –Comp. –चर,–चारिन् *a.* living in couples. (–*m.*) the ruddy goose; दयिता द्वंद्वचरं पतत्रिणं R. 8. 56, 16. 63. –भावः antagonism, discord. –भिन्नं separation of the sexes. –भूत *a.* **1** forming a couple. **2** doubtful, uncertain. –युद्धं a duel, a single combat.

द्वंद्वशः *ind.* Two by two, in pairs or couples.

द्वय *a.* (यी *f.*) Two-fold, double, of two kinds or sorts; अनुपेक्षणे द्वयी गतिः Mu. 3; Bh. 2. 104 v. l.; sometimes used in pl. also; see *Si.* 3. 57. –यं **1** A pair, couple, brace; usually at the end of comp.; द्वितयेन द्वयमेव संगतं R. 8. 6; 1. 19, 3. 8, 4. 4. **2** Two-fold nature, duplicity. **3** Untruthfulness. –यी A pair, couple. –Comp. –अतिग *a.* one whose mind is freed from the influence of the two bad qualities रजस् and तमस्; a saint or a virtuous man. –आत्मक *a.* of a two-fold nature. –वादिन् *a.* double-tongued, insincere.

द्वयस *a.* (सी *f.*) A termination added to nouns in the sense of 'reaching to', 'as high or deep as', 'as far as'; गुल्फद्वयसमेदपयासि K. 114; नारीनितंबद्वयसं बभूव (अंभः) R. 16. 46; Si. 6. 55.

द्वापरः–रं **1** N. of the third Yuga of the world; Ms. 9. 301. **2** The side of a die marked with two points. **3** Doubt, suspense, uncertainty.

द्वामुष्यायण=द्व्यामुष्यायण q. v.

द्वार् *f.* **1** A door, gate; Y. 3. 12; Ms. 3. 38. **2** A means, an expedient; द्वारा 'by means of,' 'through'. –Comp. –स्थः, –स्थितः (द्वाःस्थः, द्वास्थः, द्वाःस्थितः, द्वास्थितः) a door-keeper, porter.

द्वारं **1** A door, gateway, gate. **2** A passage, entrance, ingress, opening; अथवा कृतवाग्द्वारे वंशेऽस्मिन् R. 1. 4; 11. 18. **3** An aperture of the human body; (they are nine; see खं) and Ku. 3. 50 and Bg. 8. 12 and Ms. 6. 48 also. **4** Way, medium, means; द्वारेण 'through' 'by means of'. –Comp. –अधिपः a porter, door-keeper. –कंटकः the bolt of a door. –कपाटः,–टं the leaf or pannel of a door. –गोपः, –नायकः, –पः, –पालः, –पालकः a door-keeper, porter, warder. –दारु: teak-wood. –पट्टः **1** the pannel of a door. **2** the curtain of a door. –पिंडी the threshold of a door –पिधानः the bolt of a door. –बलिभुज् *m.* **1** a crow. **2** a sparrow. –बाहुः a door-post, jamb. –यंत्रं a lock, bolt, –स्थः a door-keeper.

द्वार(रि)का N. of the capital of Krishṇa on the western point of Gujarâth (for a description of Dvârakâ, see *Si.* 3. 33-63.). –Comp. –ईशः an epithet of Krishṇa.

द्वारवती, द्वारावती=द्वारका q. v.

द्वारिकः, द्वारिन् *m.* A porter, door-keeper.

द्वि *num. a.* (Nom. du. द्वौ *m.*, द्वे *f.* द्वे *n.*) Two, both; सयः परस्परतुलामधिरोहतां द्वे R. 5. 68. (*N. B.* In comp. द्वा is substituted for द्वि necessarily before दशन्, विंशति and त्रिंशत्, and optionally before चत्वारिंशत्, पंचाशत्, षष्टि, सप्तति and नवति, द्वि remaining unchanged before अशीति). –Comp. –अक्ष *a.* two-eyed, binocular. –अक्षर *a.* dissyllabic. –अंगुल *a.* two fingers long. (–लं) two fingers length. –अणुकं an aggregate or molecule of two atoms. –अर्थ *a.* **1** having two senses. **2** ambiguous, equivocal. **3** having two objects in view. –अशीत *a.* eighty-second. –अशीतिः *f.* eighty-two. –अष्टं copper. –अहः a period of two days. –आत्मक *a.* **1** having a double nature. **2** being two. –आमुष्यायणः 'a son of two persons or fathers', an adopted son who remains heir to his natural father though adopted by another. –ऋचं (द्वृचं, or द्वयृचं) a collection of verses or *riks*. –कः–ककारः **1** a crow (there being two *Kas* in the word काक). **2** the ruddy goose (there being two *Kas* in the word कोक). –ककुद् *m.* a camel. –गु *a.* exchanged or bartered for two cows. (–गुः) a sub-division of the Tatpurusha compound in which the first member is a numeral; द्वंद्वो द्विगुरपि चाहं Udb. –गुण *a.* double, two-fold. (द्विगुणीकृ to plough twice; to double, increase) –गुणित *a.* **1** doubled, multiplied by two; Ki. 5. 46. **2** folded double. **3** enveloped. **4** doubly increased, doubled. –चरण *a.* having two legs, two legged; द्विचरणपशूनां क्षितिभुजां Sânti. 4. 15. –चत्वारिंश *a.* (द्वि-द्वा-चत्वारिंश) forty-second. –चत्वारिंशत् *f.* (द्वि-द्वा-चत्वारिंशत्) fortytwo. –जः twice-born' **1** a man of any of the first three castes of the Hindus (a Brâhmaṇa, Kshatriya or Vaisya); see Y. 1. 39. **2** a Brâhmaṇa (over whom the Samskâras or purificatory rites are performed जन्मना जायते शूद्रः संस्कारैर्द्विज उच्यते. **3** any oviparous animal, such as a bird, snake, fish &c.; स तमानंदमविंदत द्विजः N. 2. 1; *S*. 5. 21; R. 12. 22; Mu. 1. 11; Ms. 5. 17. **4** a tooth; कीर्णं द्विजानां गणैः Bh. 1. 13 where द्विज means 'a Brâhmaṇa also). °अग्र्यः a Brâhmana °अयनी the sacred thread worn by the first three castes of the Hindus. °आलय 1 the house of a *dvija*. °इंद्रः, °ईशः 1 the moon; *Si*. 12. 3. **2** an epithet of Garuḍa. **3** camphor. °दासः *S*ûdra. **3** पतिः,° राजः an epithet of **1** the moon; R. 5. 23. **2** Garuda. **3** camphor. °प्रपा **1** a trench or basin round the root of a tree for holding water. **2** a trough near a well for watering birds, cattle &c. °बंधुः, °ब्रुवः **1** a man who pretends to be a Brâhmaṇa. **2** one who is twice-born,' or a Brâhmaṇa by name and birth only and not by acts; cr. ब्रह्मबंधु. °लिंगिन् *m.* **1** Kshatriya. **2** a pseudo-Brâhmaṇa, one disguised as a Brâhmaṇa. °वाहनः an epithet of Vjshṇu, (having Grauda for his vehicle.).° सेवकः a Sûdra. –जन्मन्, -जातिः *m.* **1** a man of any of the first three castes of the Hindus; Ms. 2. 24. **2** a Brâhmaṇa; Ki. 1. 39; Ku. 5. 40. **3** a bird. **4** a tooth. –जातीय *a.* belonging to the first three castes of the Hindus. –जिह्वः **1** a snake; *Si*. 1. 63; R. 11. 64, 14. 41; Bv. 1. 20. **2** an informer, a slanderer, tale-bearer **3.** an insincere person. त्र *a.* pl. two or three; R. 5. 25; Bh. 2. 121. –त्रिंश (द्वात्रिंश) **1** thirty-second. **2** consisting of thirty-two. –त्रिंशत् (द्वात्रिंशत्) thirty-two. °लक्षण *a.* having thirty-two auspicious marks upon the body. —दंडि *ind.* stick against stick. –दत् *a.* having two teeth. –दश *a.* pl. twenty. –दश *a.* (द्वादश) **1** twelfth; Ms. 2. 36. **2** consisting of twelve. –दशन् (द्वादशन्) *a.* pl. twelve. अंशुः an epithet of **1** the planet Jupiter. **2** Brihaspati, the precepotr of the gods. अक्षः, °करः, °लोचनः epithets of Kârtikeya. °अंगुलः a measure of twelve fingers. °अहः **1** a period of twelve days; Ms. 5. 83, 11. 68. **2** a sacrifice lasting for or completed in twelve days; °आत्मन् *m.* the sun. °आदित्याः pl. the twelve suns; see आदित्य. आयुस् *m.* a dog. °सहस्र *a.* consisting of 12000. –दशी (द्वादशी) the twelfth day of a lunar fort-night. –देवतं the constellation विशाखा. –देहः an epithet of Ganesa. –धातुः an epithet of Ganesa. -नग्नकः a circumcised man. -नवत (द्वि-द्वा-नवत) *a*. ninety-second. -नवतिः *f*. (द्वि-द्वा-नवतिः) ninety-two. -पः an elephant. °आस्यः an epithet of Ganesa. -पक्षः 1 a bird. 2 a month. -पंचाश (द्वि-द्वा-पंचाश) *a*. fifty-second. -पंचाशत् (द्वि-द्वा-पंचाशत्) *f*. fifty-two. -पथं two ways. -पदः a biped man. -पदिका -पदी a kind of Prâkrita metre. -पाद्, -पादः 1 biped man. 2 a bird. 3 a god. -पाद्यः, -द्यं a double penalty. -पायिन् *m*. an elephant -बिंदुः a Visarga (:). -भुजः an angle. -भूम *a*. having two floors (as a palace). -मातृ,-मातृजः an epithet of 1 Ganesa. 2 king Jarâsandha. -मात्रः a long vowel (having two syllabic instants). -मार्गी a cross-way. -मुखा a leech. -रः 1 a bee; cf. द्विरेफ. 2=वर्बर q. v. -रदः an elephant; R. 4. 4; Me. 59. °अंतकः, °अरातिः, °अशनः a lion. -रसनः a snake. -रात्रं two nights. -रूप *a*. 1 biform. 2 bicolour, bipartite -रेतस् *m*. a mule. -रेफः a large black bee (there being two *ras* in the word भ्रमर); Ku. 1. 27, 3. 27, 36. -वचनं the dual number (in gram.). -वज्रकः a kind of house or structure with 16 angles (sides). -वाहिका a swing. -विंश (द्वाविंश) *a*. twenty-second. -विंशतिः (द्वाविंशतिः) *f*. twenty-two, -विध *a*. of two kinds or sorts; Ms. 7. 162. -वेशरा a kind of light carriage drawn by mules. -शतं 1 two hundred. 2 one hundred and two. -शत्य *a*. worth or bought for two hundred. -शफ *a*. cloven footed. (-फः) any cloven-footed animal. -शीर्षः an epithet of Agni. -षष् *a*. pl. twice six, twelve. -षष्ट (द्विषष्ट, द्वाषष्ट) sixty-second.-षष्टिः *f*. (द्विषष्टिः, द्वाषष्टिः) sixty-two. —सप्तत (द्वि-द्वा सप्तत *a*. seventy-second. -सप्ततिः *f*. (द्वि-द्वा-सप्ततिः) seventy-two. -सप्ताहः a fortnight. -सहस्र, -साहस्र *a*. consisting of 2000. (-स्रं) 2000. -सीत्य, -हल्य *a*. ploughed in two ways; *i. e.* first length-wise and then breadth-wise. -सुवर्ण *a*. worth or bought for two golden coins. -हन् *m*. an elephant. -हायन, -वर्ष *a*. two years old. -हीन *a*. of the neuter gender. -हृदया a pregnant woman. -होतृ *m*. an epithet of Agni.

द्विक *a*. 1 Two-fold, forming a pair, consisting of two. 2 Second. 3 Happening the second time. 4 Increased by two, two per cent; द्विकं शतं वृद्धिः Ms. 8. 141-2.

द्वितय *a*. (यी *f*.) Consisting of or divided into two, double, two-fold; sometimes used in pl.; द्रुमसानुमतां किमंतरं यदि वायौ द्वितयेऽपि ते चलाः R. 8. 90. -यं A pair, couple; R. 8. 6.

द्वितीय *a*. Second; त्वं जीवितं त्वमसि मे हृदयं द्वितीयं U. 3. 26; Me. 83; R. 3. 49. -यः 1 The second in a family, a son. 2 A companion, partner, friend; (usually at the end of comp.); प्रयतपरिग्रहद्वितीयः R. 1. 95; so छाया°, दुःख° &c. -या 1 The second day of a lunar fortnight. A wife, companion, partner. 3 (In gram.) The accusative case. -COMP. -आश्रमः the second stage or period of the religious life of a Brâhmaṇa; *i. e.* गार्हस्थ्य.

द्वितीयक *a*. Second.

द्वितीयाकृत *a*. Ploughed twice as a field).

द्वितीयिन् *a*. (नी *f*.) Occupying the second place.

द्विध *a*. Divided into two parts, split asunder.

द्विधा *ind*. 1 In two parts; द्विधा भिन्नाः शिखंडिभिः R. 1. 39; Ms. 1, 12, 32; द्विधेव हृदयं तस्य दुःखितस्याभवत्तदा Mb. 2 In two ways. -COMP. -करणं dividing into two parts, splitting. -गतिः 1 an amphibious animal. 2 a crab. 3 a crocodile.

द्विशस् *ind*. By twos, two by two, in couples.

द्विष् 2 U. (द्वेष्टि, द्विष्टे, द्विष्ट) To hate, dislike, be hostile towards. न द्वेक्षि यज्जनमतस्त्वमजातशत्रुः Ve. 3. 13; Bg. 2. 57, 18. 10; Bk. 17. 61; 18. 9; रम्यं द्वेष्टि *S*. 6. 4. (Prepositions like प्र, वि and सं are prefixed to this not without any change of meaning.

द्विष् *a*. Hostile, hating, inimical. —*m*. An enemy; रंध्रान्वेषणदक्षाणां द्विषामामिषतां ययौ R. 12. 11; 3. 45; Pt. 1. 70,

द्विषः An enemy. (द्विषंतप *a*. Harassing an enemy, retaliating).

द्विषत् *m*. An enemy (with acc. or gen.); ततः परं दुष्प्रसहं द्विषद्भिः R. 6. 31; *Si*. 2. 1; Bk 5. 97.

द्विष्ट *a*. 1 Hostile. 2 Hated, disliked. —ष्टं Copper.

द्विस् *ind*. Twice; द्विरिव प्रतिशब्देन व्याजहार हिमालयः Ku. 6. 64; Ms. 2. 60. -COMP. -आगमनं (द्विरागमनं) the ceremony of the second entrance of the bride to her husband's house. -आपः (द्विरापः) an elephant. -उक्त *a*. (द्विरुक्त) 1 spoken twice, repeated. 2 redundant, tautologous, superfluous -उक्तिः *f*. (द्विरुक्तिः). 1 repetition, tautology. 2 superfluity, uselessness. -ऊढा (द्विरूढा) a women married twice. -भावः; -वचनं reduplication.

द्वीपः, -पं 1 An island. 2 A place of refuge, shelter, production. 3 A division of the terrestrial world; (the number of these divisions varies according to different authorities, being four, seven, nine or thirteen, all situated round the mountain Meru like the petals of a lotus flower, and each being separated from the other by a distinct ocean. In N. 1. 5 the Dvîpas are said to be eighteen; but seven appears to be the usual number; cf. R. 1. 65 and *S*. 7. 33. The central one is जंबुद्वीप under which is included भरतखंड or India.) -COMP. -कर्पूरः camphor from China.

द्वीपवत् *a*. Full of islands. —*m*. The ocean. —ती The earth.

द्वीपिन् *m*. 1 A tiger in general! चर्षणि द्वीपिनं हंति Sk. 2 A leopard, panther. -COMP. -नखः, -खं 1 a tiger's nail. 2 a kind of perfume.

द्वेधा *ind*. In two parts, in two ways, twice.

द्वेषः 1 Hate, dislike, abhorrence, repugnance, distaste; *S*. 5. 18; Bg. 3. 34, 7, 27; so अन्नद्वेषः, भक्तद्वेषः &c. 2 Enmity, hostility, malignity; Ms. 8. 225.

द्वेषण *a*. Hating, disliking. -णः An enemy. -णं Hate, hatred, enmity, dislike.

द्वेषिन्, द्वेष्टृ *a*. Hating &c. —*m*. An enemy.

द्वेष्य *pot. p*. 1 To be hated. 2 Odious, hateful, disagreeable; R. 1. 28. -ष्यः An enemy; Bg. 6. 9; 9. 29; Ms. 9. 307.

द्वैगुणिकः A usurer who charges cent per cent interest.

द्वैगुण्यं 1 Double amount, value, or measure. 2 Duality. 3 The possession of two out of the three qualities (*i. e.* —सत्त्व, रजस् and तमस्).

द्वैतं 1 Duality. 2 Dualism in philosophy, the assertion of two distinct principles such as the maintenance of the doctrine that spirit and matter, Brahman and the universe, or the Individual and the Supreme Soul are different from each other; cf. अद्वैत; किं शास्त्रं श्रवणेन यस्य गलति द्वैतांधकारोत्करः Bv. 1. 86. 3 N. of a forest. -COMP.-वनं N. of a forest; Ki. 1. 1. -वादिन् *m*. a philosopher who maintains the *dvaita* doctrine.

द्वैतिन् *m*. A philosopher who maintains the *dvaita* doctrine.

द्वैतीयीक *a*. (की *f*.) Second; द्वैतीयीकतया मितोऽयमगमत्तस्य प्रबंधे महाकाव्ये चारुणि नैषधीयचरिते सर्गो निसर्गोज्ज्वलः N. 2. 110; cf. तार्तीयीक.

द्वैध *a*. (धी *f*.) Two-fold, double, (द्वैधीभू to become divided into two parts, be disunited, vacillate, be divided or uncertain, as mind).—धं 1 Duality, two-fold nature or state. 2 *S*eparation into two parts. 3 Double resource, seconddary reserve. 4 Diversity, difference, conflict, contest, variance; श्रुतिद्वैधं तु यत्र स्यात् तत्र धर्मावुभौ स्मृतौ Ms. 2. 14, 9 32; Y. 2. 78. 5 Doubt, uncertainty; Bg. 5. 25; Ve. 6. 44. 6 Double-dealing, duplicity; one of the six modes of foreign policy; see द्वैधीभाव below and गुण.

द्वैधीभावः 1 Duality, double state or nature. 2 Separation into two, difference, diversity. 3 Doubt, uncertainty, vacillation, suspense; धृतद्वैधीभावकातरं मे मनः S. 1. 4 A dilemma. 5 One of the six Guṇas or modes of foreign policy. (According to some authorities it means 'double-dealing, or 'duplicity,' keeping apparently friendly relations with the enemy; बलिनोर्द्विषतोर्मध्ये वाचात्मानं समर्पयन्। द्वैधीभावेन तिष्ठेत्तु काकाक्षिवदलक्षितः॥ According to others it means 'dividing one's army and encountering a superior enemy in detachments,' 'harassing the enemy by attacking them in small bands'; द्वैधीभावः स्वबलस्य द्विधाकरणं Mit. on Y. 1. 347; cf. also Ms. 7. 173 and 160.

द्वैध्यं 1 Duplicity. 2 Diversity, difference.

द्वैप *a.* (पी *f.*) 1 Relating to, living on, an island. 2 Belonging to a tiger, made of or covered with a tiger's skin. **-पः** A car covered with a tiger's skin.

द्वैपक्षं Two parties.

द्वैपायनः 'The island-born,' N. of Vyâsa.

द्वैप्य *a.* (प्या, प्यी *f.*) Living on or relating to an island; Si. 3. 76.

द्वैमातुर *a.* Having two mothers; *i. e.* a natural mother and a step-mother. **—रः** 1 N. of Gaṇesa. 2 N. of Jarâsandha; हते हिडिंबरिपुणा राज्ञि द्वैमातुरे युधि Si 2. 60.

द्वैमातृक *a.* (की *f.*) Nourished by rain and rivers (as a country); cf. देवमातृक.

द्वैरथं 1 A single combat in chariots. 2 A single combat in general. **—थः** An adversary.

द्वैराज्यं Dominion divided between two kings.

द्वैवर्षिक *a.* Biennial.

द्वैविध्यं 1 Duality, two-fold nature. 2 Variance, diversity, difference.

ध.

ध *a.* (At the end of comp.) Placing, holding &c. **-धः** 1 An epithet of Brahmâ. 2 N. of Kubera. 3 Virtue, moral, merit. **—धं** Wealth, property.

धक् An exclamation of anger; U. 4. 24.

धक्क 10 U. (धक्कयति-ते) To destroy or annihilate.

धटः 1 A balance, a pair of scales. 2 Ordeal by the balance. 3 The sign Libra of the zodiac.

धटकः A kind of weight equal to 42 Gunjas or Raktikas.

धटिका, धटी 1 Old cloth or raiment. 2 Strip of cloth fastened round the loins or over the privities.

धटिन् *m.* 1 An epithet of Siva. 2 The sign Libra of the zodiac. **—नी=**धटी.

धण् 1 P. (धणति) To sound.

धत्तूरः,-धत्तूरकाः-का The white thorn-apple; (Mar. धोतरा).

धन् 1 P. (धनति) To sound.

धन 1 Property, wealth, riches, treasure, money (gold, chattels &c.); धनं तावदसुलभं H. 1; (fig. also); as in तपोधन, विद्याधन &c. 2 (*a*) Any valued possession, an object of affection or endearment, dearest treasure; कष्टं जनः कुलधनैरनुरंजनीयः U. 1. 14; गुरोरपीदं धनमाहिताग्नेः R. 2. 44; मानधन; अभिमान° &c. (*b*) A valuable article; Ms. 8. 201, 202. 3 Capital (opp. वृद्धि or interest). 4 A booty, prey, spoil. 5 The reward given to a victor in a combat, the prize won in a game. 6 A contest for prizes, a match. 7 The lunar mansion called धनिष्ठा. 8 Surplus, residue. 9 (In math.) The affirmative quantity or plus (opp. ऋण). -COMP. **-अधिकारः** right to property, right of inheriting property. **-अधिकारिन्**, **-अधिकृतः** 1 a treasurer. 2 an heir. **-अधिगोप्तृ,-अधिपः, अधिपतिः -अध्यक्षः** 1 an epithet of Kubera; Ki. 5. 16. 2 a treasurer. **अपहारः** 1 fine. 2 plunder. **-आर्चित** *a.* 1 honoured with gifts of wealth, kept contented by valuable presents; मानधना धनार्चिताः Ki. 1. 19. 2 wealthy, opulent. **अर्थिन्** *a.* desiring or seeking for wealth, covetous, miserly. **-आढ्य** *a.* wealthy, rich, opulent. **-आधारः** a treasury. **-ईशः, ईश्वरः** 1 a treasurer. 1 an epithet of Kubera. **-उष्मन्** *m.* warmth of wealth; cf. अर्थोष्मन्. **-एषिन्** *m.* a creditor who claims his money. **-केलिः** an epithet of Kubera. **-क्षयः** loss of wealth; धनक्षये वर्धति जाठराग्निः Pt. 2. 178. **-गर्व, -गर्वित** *a* purse-proud. **-जातं** all kinds of valuable possessions, aggregate property. **-दः** 1 a liberal or munificent man. 2 an epithet of Kubera; R. 9. 25; 17. 80. 3 N. of fire. °**अनुजः** an epithet of Râvaṇa; R. 12. 52, 88. **-दंडः** punishment in the shape of a fine. **-दायिन्** *m.* fire. **-पतिः** an epithet of Kubera; तत्रागारं धनपतिगृहानुत्तरेणास्मदीयं Me. 75, 7. **-पालः** 1 a treasurer. 2 an epithet of Kubera. **-पिशाचिका, -पिशाची** 'the demon of wealth, an avaricious desire of wealth, greed, avarice. **-प्रयोगः** usury. **-मद** *a.* purse-proud. **-मूलं** principal, capital. **-लोभः** avarice, cupidity. **-व्ययः** 1 expenditure. 2 extravagance. **-स्थानं** a treasury. **-हरः** 1 an heir. 2 a thief. 3 a kind of perfume.

धनकः, धनाया Avarice, greed, covetuosness.

धनंजयः 1 N. of Arjuna; (the name is thus derived in Mb:—सर्वाञ्जनपदाञ्जित्वा वित्तमादाय केवलं। मध्ये धनस्य तिष्ठामि तेनाहुर्मां धनंजयं॥). 2 An epithet of fire.

धनवत् *a.* Rich, wealthy.

धनिकः 1 A rich or wealthy man. 2 A money-lender, creditor; दापयेद्धनिकस्यार्थं Ms. 8. 51; Y. 2. 55. 3 A husband. 4 An honest trader. 5 The प्रियंगु tree.

धनिन् *a.* (नी *f.*) Rich, opulent, wealthy. **-m** 1 A wealthy man. 2 A creditor; Y. 2. 18, 41; Ms. 8. 61.

धनिष्ठ *a.* Very rich; (superl. of धनिन् or धनवत्). **-ष्ठा** N. of the twenty-third lunar mansion (consisting of four stars).

धनी, धनीका A young girl or woman.

धनुः A bow (perhaps for धनुस् q. v.)

धनुस् *a* Armed with a bow. **-n.** 1 A bow; धनुष्यमोघं समधत्त बाणं Ku. 3. 66; so इंद्रधनुः &c. (At the end of Bah. comp. धनुस् is changed to धन्वन्; R. 2. 8.). 2 A measure of length equal to four *hastas*; Y. 2. 167; Ms. 8. 237. 3 An arc of a circle. 4 The sign Sagittarius of the zodiac. 5 A desert; cf. धन्वन्. -COMP. **-कर** (**धनुष्कर**) *a.* armed with a bow. (**-रः**) a bow-maker. **-कांड** (**धनुःकांड**) a bow and arrow. **-खंड** (**धनुः खंड**) part of a bow; Me. 15. **-गुणः** (**धनुर्गुणः**) a bow-string. **-ग्रहः** (**धनुर्ग्रहः**) an archer. **-ज्या** (**धनुर्ज्या**) a bow string; अनवरतधनुर्ज्यास्फालनक्रूरपूर्वं S. 2. 4 **-द्रुमः** (**धनुर्द्रुमः**) a bamboo **-धरः, -भृत्** *m.* (**धनुर्धर** &c). an archer; R. 2. 11, 29; 3. 31, 38, 39; 9. 11; 12. 97; 16. 77. **-पाणि** *a.* (**धनुष्पाणि**) armed with a bow, with a bow in hand. **-मार्गः** (**धनुर्मार्गः**) a line curved like a bow, a curve. **-विद्या** (**धनुर्विद्या**) the science of archery. **-वृक्षः** (**धनुर्वृक्षः**) 1 a bamboo. 2 the अश्वत्थ tree. **-वेदः** (**धनुर्वेदः**) the science of the four *upavedas* q. v.

धनू *f.* A bow.

धन्य *a.* **1** Bestowing or conferring wealth; Ms. 3. 106, 4. 19. **2** Wealthy, rich, opulent. **3** Blessed, fortunate, lucky, happy; धन्यं जीवनमस्य मार्गसरसः Bv. 1. 16, 4. 37; धन्या केयं स्थिता ते शिरसि Mu. 1. 1. **4** Excellent, good, virtuous. **–न्यः 1** A lucky or blessed man, a fortunate being; धन्यास्तदंगरजसा मलिनीभवंति *S.* 7. 17; Bh. 1. 41; धन्यः कोऽपि न विक्रियां कलयते प्राप्ते नवे यौवने 1. 72. **2** An infidel, an atheist. **3** N. of a spell. **–न्या 1** A murse. **2** Coriander. **–न्यं** Wealth, treasure. –COMP. **–वादः 1** expression of thanks, thanksgiving. **2** praise, applause.

धन्यंमन्य *a.* Considering onself to be blessed or fortunate.

धन्याकं 1 A plant bearing a small pungent seed used as a condiment. **2** The seed of this plant (coriander).

धन्वं A bow, (rarely used in classical literature). –COMP. **–धिः** a bow-case.

धन्वन् *m, n.* **1** A dry soil, desert, waste; एवं धन्वनि चंपकस्य सकले संहारहेतावपि Bv. 1. 31. Shore, firm land. –COMP. **–दुर्गं** a fort inaccessible on account of a surrounding desert; Ms. 7. 70.

धन्वंतरं A measure of distance or length equal to four *hastas*, cf. दंड.

धन्वंतरिः N. of the physician of the gods, said to have been produced at the churning of the ocean with a cup of nectar in his hand; cf. चतुर्दशरत्न.

धन्विन् *a.* (**नी** *f.*) Armed with a bow. **—***m.* **1** An archer; के मम धन्विनोऽन्ये Ku. 3. 10; उत्कर्षः स च धन्विनां यदिषवः सिध्यंति लक्ष्ये चले *S.* 2. 4. **2** An epithet of Arjuna. **3** Of *S*iva. **4** Of Vishṇu. **5** The sign Sagittarius of the zodiac.

धन्विनः A hog (शूकरः).

धम *a.* (**मा** or **मी** *f.*) (Usually at the end of a comp.) **1** Blowing; अग्निंधम, नाडिंधम. **2** Melting, fusing. **—मः 1** The moon. **2** An epithet of Krishna. **3** Of Yama, the god of death. **4** Of Brahmâ.

धमकः A blacksmith.

धमधमा An onomatopoetic word expressive of the sound made by blowing with a bellows or a trumpet.

धमन *a.* **1** Blowing. **2** Cruel. **—नः** A kind of reed.

धमनिः, –नी *f.* **1** A reed, pipe. **2** A tube or canal of the human body, any tubular vessel, as a vein, nerve &c. **3** Throat, neck.

धमिः *f.* The act of blowing.

धम्मलः, धम्मिलः, धम्मिल्लः The braided and ornamented hair of a woman tied over the head and intermixed with flowers, pearls &c.; आकुलाकुलगलद्धम्मिल्ल Gît. 2; उरसि निपतितानां स्रस्तधम्मिल्लकानां (वधूनां) Bh. 1. 49; *S.* Til. 1.

धय *a.* (Usually at the end of a comp.) Drinking, sucking; as in स्तनंधय.

धर *a.* (**रा** or **री** *f.*) (Usually at the end of a comp.) Holding, carrying, bearing, wearing, containing, possessing, endowed with, preserving, observing &c.; as in अक्षधर, अंशुधर, गदाधर, गंगाधर, महीधर, असृग्धर, विद्याधर &c. **—रः 1** A mountain; उत्कंधरं द्रष्टुमवेक्ष्य शौरिमुत्कंधरं दारुक इत्युवाच *Si.* 4. 18. **2** A flock of cotton. **3** A frivolous or dissolute man (विट). **4** The king of the tortoises; *i. e.* Vishnu in his Kurma incarnation. **5** N. of one of the Vasus.

धरण *a.* (**णी** *f.*) Bearing, preserving, holding &c. **—णः 1** A ridge of land serving the purpose of a brigde, the side of a mountain. **2** The world. **3** The sun. **4** The female breast. **5** Rice, corn. **6** The Himâlaya; (as king of mountains). **—णं 1** Supporting, sustaining, upholding; सारं धरित्रीधरणक्षमं च Ku. 1. 17; धरणिधरणकिणचक्रगरिष्ठे Gît. 1. **2** Possessing, bringing, procuring &c. **3** Prop, stay, support, **4** Security. **5** A measure of weight equal to ten Palas.

धरणिः, –णी *f.* The earth; लुठति धरणिशयने बहु विलपति तव नाम Gît. 5. **2** The ground, soil. **3** A beam for a roof. **4** A vein. –COMP. **–ईश्वरः 1** a king. **2** an epithet of Vishnu; **3** of *S*iva. **–कीलकः** a mountain. **–जः–पुत्रः, –सुतः 1** an epithet of Mars. **2** an epithet of the demon Naraka. **जा,–पुत्री. –सुता** an epithet of Sîtâ, daughter of Janaka (as born from the earth). **–धरः 1** an epithet of Sesha. **2** of Vishnu. **3** a mountain. **4** a tortoise. **5** a king. **6** an elephant fabled to support the earth. **–धृत्** *m.* **1** a mountain. **2** an epithet of Vishnu. **3** of *S*esha.

धरा 1 The earth; धरा धारापातैर्मणिमयशरैर्भिद्यत इव Mk. 5. 22. **2** A vein. **3** Marrow. **4** The womb or uterus. –COMP. **अधिपः** a king. **–अमरः, –देवः, –सुरः** a Brâhmana. **–आत्मजः, –पुत्रः, –सूनुः 1** epithets of the planet Mars. **2** epithets of the demon Naraka. **–आत्मजा** an epithet of Sîtâ. **–उद्धारः** deliverance of the earth. **–धरः 1** a mountain. **2** an epithet of Vishnu or Krishna. **3** of Sesha. **–पतिः 1** a king. **2** an epithet of Vishnu. **–भुज्** *m.* a king. **-भृत्** *m.* a mountain.

धरित्री 1 The earth; *S.* 2. 14; R. 14 54; Ku. 1. 2, 17. **2** Groud, soil.

धरिमन् *m.* A balance, pair of scales.

धर्त्तूरः The Dhattura plant.

धर्त्रं 1 A house. **2** A prop, stay. **3** A sacrifice. **4** Virtue, moral merit.

धर्मः 1 Religion, the customary observances of a caste, sect, &c. **2** Law, usage, practice, custom, ordinance, statute. **3** Religious or moral merit, virtue, righteousnass, good works (regarded as one of the four ends of human existence); Ku. 5. 38. and see त्रिवर्ग also; एक एव सुहृद्धर्मो निधनेऽप्यनुयाति यः H. 1. 65. **4** Duty, prescribed course of conduct; षष्ठांशवृत्तेरपि धर्म एषः *S.* 5. 4; Ms. 1. 114. **5** Right, justice, equity, impartiality. **6** Piety, propriety, decorum. **7** Morality, ethics. **8** Nature, disposition, character; Mâl. 1. 6; प्राणि°, जीव°. **9** An essential quality, peculiarity, characteristic property, (peculiar) attribute; वदंति वर्ण्यावर्ण्यानां धर्मैक्यं दीपकं बुधाः Chandr. 5. 45. **10** Manner, resemblance, likeness. **11** A sacrifice. **12** Good company, associating with the virtuous. **13** Devotion, religious abstraction. **14** Manner, mode, **15** An Upanishad q. v. **16** N. of Yudhishṭhira, the eldest Pândava. **17** N. of Yama, the god of death. —COMP. **अंगः, –गा** the Indian crane. **अधर्मौ** (*m.* du.) right and wrong, religion and irreligion. **°विद्** *m.* a Mîmâmsaka who knows the right and wrong course of action **-अधिकरणं 1** administration of the laws. **अधिकरणिन्** *m.* a judge, magistrate. **अधिकारः 1** superintendeuce of religious affairs; *S.* 1. **2** administration of justice. **3** the office of a judga. **–अधिष्ठानं** a court of justice. **–अध्यक्षः 1** a judge. **2** an epithet of Vishnu. **–अनुष्ठानं** acting according to religion, virtuous or moral conduct. **–अपेत** *a.* deviating from virtue, wicked, immoral, irreligious. (**–तं**) vice, immorality, injustice. **–अरण्यं** a sacred or penance grove, a wood inhabited by ascetics; धर्मारण्यं प्रविशति गजः *S.* 1. 33. **–अलीक** *a.* having a false character. **–आगमः** a religious statute, law-book. **–आचार्यः 1** a religious teacher. **2** a teacher of law or customs. **–आत्मजः** an epithet of Yudhishṭhira; q. v. **–आत्मन्** *a.* just, righteous, pious, virtuous. **–आसनं** the throne of justice, judgment-seat, tribunal; न संभावितमद्य धर्मासनमध्यासितुं *S.* 6; धर्मासनाद्विशति वासगृहं नरेंद्रः Ut. 1. 7. **–इंद्रः** an epithet of Yudhishṭhira. **–ईशः** an epithet of Yama **–उत्तर** *a.* 'rich in virtue', chiefly characterized by justice, eminently just and impartial; धर्मोत्तरं मध्यममाश्रयंते R. 13. 7. **–उपदेशः 1** instruction in law or duty religious or moral instruction. **2** the collective body of. laws. **–कर्मन्** *n,* **–कार्यं, –क्रिया 1** any act of duty or religion, any moral or religious observance, a religious act or rite. **2**

virtuous conduct. -कथादरिद्रः the *Kali* age. -कायः an epithet of Buddha. -कीलः a grant, royal edict or decree. -केतुः an epithet of Buddha. -कोशः, -षः the collective body of laws or duties; धर्मकोषस्य गुप्तये Ms. 1. 99. -क्षेत्रं 1 Bhâratavarsha (the land of religion). 2 N. of a plain near Delhi, the scene of the great battle between the Kauravas and Pândavas. धर्मक्षेत्रे कुरुक्षेत्रे समवेता युयुत्सवः Bg. 1. 1. -घटः a jar of fragrant water offered daily (to a Brâhmana) in the month of Vaisâkha. -चक्रभृत् *m.* a Buddha or Jaina. -चरणं, -चर्या observance of the law, performance of religious duties; Ku. 7. 83. -चारिन् *a.* practising virtue, observing the law, virtuons, righteous; R. 3. 45. (-*m.*) an ascetic. -चारिणी a wife. 2 a chaste or virtuous wife. -चिंतनं, -चिंता study of virtue, consideration of moral duties, moral reflection. -जः 1 'duly or lawfully born', a legitimate son: cf. Ms. 9. 107. 2 N. of युधिष्ठिर. -जन्मन् *m.* N. of युधिष्ठिर. -जिज्ञासा inquiry into religion or the proper course of conduct अथातो धर्मजिज्ञासा Jaimini Sutra. -जीवन *a.* one who acts according to the rules of his caste or fulfils prescribed duties. (-नः) a Brâhmana who maintains himself by assisting other men in the performance of their religious rites. -ज्ञ *a.* 1 knowing what is right, conversant with civil or religious law; Ms 7. 141, 8. 179, 10. 127. 2 just, righteous, pious. -त्यागः abandoning one's religion, apostacy. -दाराः (*m pl.*) a lawful wife; स्त्रीणां भर्ता धर्मदाराश्च पुंसां Mâl. 6. 18. -द्रोहिन् *m.* a demon. -धातुः an epithet ot Buddha. -ध्वजः, -ध्वजिन् *m.* a religious hypocrite, an impostor. -नंदनः an epithet of युधिष्ठिर. -नाथः a legal protector, rightful master. -नाभः an epithet of Vishnu. -निवेशः religious devotion. -निष्पत्तिः *f.* 1 discharge or fulfilment of duty. 2 moral or religious observance. -पत्नी a lawful wife; R. 2. 2. 20, 72; 8. 7; Y. 2. 128. -पथः the way of virtue, a virtuous course of conduct. -पर *a.* religiously-minded, pious, righteous. पाठकः a teacher of civil or religious law. -पालः 'protecter of the law', said metaphorically of दंड 'punishment or chastisement',' or 'sword'. -पीडा transgressing the law, an offence against law. -पुत्रः 1 lawful son, a son begotten from a sense of duty and not from mere lust or sensual pleasure. 2 an epithet of युधिष्ठिर. -प्रवक्तृ *m.* 1 an expounder of the law, a legal adviser. 2 a religious teacher, preacher. -प्रवचनं 1 the science of duty; U. 5. 23. 2 expounding the law. (-नः) an epithet of Buddha. वाणिजिकः, -वाणिजिकः 1 one who tries to make profit out of his virtue like a merchant. 2 one who performs religious rites with a view to reward, like a merchant dealing in transaction for profit. -भगिनी 1 a lawful sister. 2 a daughter of the spiritual preceptor. 3 a spiritual sister, any one regarded as a sister from discharging the same religious duties. -भागिनी a virtuous wife. -भाणकः a lecturer or public reader who reads and explains to audiences sacred books like the Bhârata, Bhâgavata &c. -भ्रातृ *m.* 1 a fellow-religious student, a spiritual brother. 2 any one regarded as a brother from discharging the same religious duties. -महामात्रः a minister of religion, a minister in charge of religious affairs. -मूलं the foundation of civil or religious law, Vedas. -युगं the Krita yuga. -यूपः an epithet of Vishṇu. -रति *a.* 'delighting in virtue or justice,' righteous, pious, just; R. 1 23. -राज् *m.* an epithet of Yama. -राजः an epithet of 1 Yama; 2 Jina; 3 युधिष्ठिर. 4 a king. -रोधिन् *a.* 1 apposed to law, illegal, unlawful. 2 immoral. -लक्षणं 1 the essential mark of law. 2 the Vedas. (-णा) the Mîmâmsâ philosophy. -लोपः 1 erreligion, immorality, violation of duty; R. 1. 76. -वत्सल *a.* loving piety or duty. -वर्तिन् *a.* just, virtuous. -वासरः the day of full moon. -वाहनः 1 an epithet of *S*iva. 2 a buffalo (being the vehicle of Yama.) -विद् *a.* familiar with the law (civil or religious). -विधिः a legal precept or injunction. -विप्लवः violetion of duty, immorality. -वीरः (in Rhet.) the sentiment of heroism arising out of virtue or piety, the sentiment of chivalrous piety; the following instance is given in R. G:.—सपदि विलयमेतु राज्यलक्ष्मीरुपरि पतंत्वथवा कृपाणधाराः । अपहरतुतरां शिरः कृतांतो मम तु मतिर्न मनागपैतु धर्मात् ॥ -वृद्ध *a.* advanced in virtue or piety; Ku. 5. 16. -वैतंसिकः one who gives away money unlawfully acquired in the hope of appearing generous. -शाला 1 a court of justice, tribunal. 2 any charitable institution. -शासनं, शास्त्रं a code of laws, jurisprudence; H. 1. 17; Y. 1. 5. -शील *a.* just, pious, virtuous. -संहिता a code of laws, (especially compiled by sages like Manu, Yâjnavalkya &c.) -संगः 1 attachmemnt to justice or virtue. 2 hypocrisy. -सभा a court of justice. -सहायः a partner or companion in the discharge of religious duties.

धर्मतः *ind.* 1 According to law or rule, rightly, religiously, justly. 2 Virtuously, righteously. 3 From a virtuous or religious motive.

धर्मयु *a.* Virtuous, just, pious, righteous.

धर्मिन् *a.* 1 Virtuous, just, pious. 2 Knowing one's duties. 3 Obeying the law. 4 Having the properties of having the nature, peculiar properties, or characteristics of anything (at the end of comp.); षट् सुता द्विजधर्मिणः Ms. 10. 14; कल्पवृक्षफलधर्मि कांक्षितं R. 11. 50. -*m.* An epithet of Vishṇu.

धर्मीपुत्रः An actor, player.

धर्म्य *a.* 1 Consistent with law, duty or religion, lawful, legal; Ms. 3. 22, 25-26. 2 Religious (as an act); Ku. 6. 13. 3 Just, righteous, fair, धर्म्याद्धि युद्धाच्छ्रेयोऽन्यत्क्षत्रियस्य न विद्यते Bg. 2. 31; 9. 2; Y. 3. 44. 4 Legitimate. Usual. 6 Endowed with particular qualities; as तद्धर्म्य.

धर्षः 1 Boldness, insolence, haughtiness, impudence. 2 Pride, arrogance. 3 Impatience. 4 Restraint. 5 Violation, seduction (of a woman). 6 Injury, wrong, insult. 7 A eunuch. Comp. -कारिणी a violated woman.

धर्षक *a.* 1 Assailing, attacking, assaulting. 2 Violating, seducing. 3 Impatient. -कः 1 A seducer, an adulterer, violater. 2 An actor, dancer.

धर्षणं, -णा 1 Boldness, insolence. 2 Insult, affront. 3 An assault, outrage, seduction, violation; नारी°. 4 Copulation. 5 Contempt, disrespect, 6 Abuse.

धर्षणिः -णी *f.* A disloyal or wanton woman, a harlot.

धर्षित *a.* 1 Seduced, outraged, violated. 2 Overpowered, overcome, defeated; N. 22. 155. 3 Ill-treated, abused, insulted. -तं 1 Contumely, pride. 2 Cohabitation, copulation. -ता A harlot, a disloyal or unchaste woman.

धर्षिन् *a.* 1 Proud, arrogant, overbearing. 2 Assaulting, seducing, outraging. 3 Insulting, ill-treating. 4 Audacious, impudent. 5 Cohabiting. -णी A harlot, an unchaste woman.

धवः 1 Shaking, trembling. 2 A man. 3 A husband, as in विधवा. 4 A master, lord. 5 A rogue, cheat. 6 A kind of tree.

धवल *a.* 1 White; धवलातपत्र, धवलगृहं &c. 2 Handsome. 3 Clear, pure. -लः 1 The white colour. 2 An excellent bull. 3 China camphor (चीनकर्पूर). 4 N. of a tree. (धव). -लं White-paper. -ला A woman with a white complexion. -ली A white cow (धवला also). Comp. -उत्पलं the white water-lily (said to open at moon-rise).

-गिरिः N. of the highest peak of the Himâlaya mountain. -गृहं a house whitened with chunam, a palace. -पक्षः 1 a goose. 2 the bright half of a lunar month: -मृत्तिका chalk.

धवलित *a.* Whitened, made white.

धवलिमन् *n.* 1 Whiteness, white colour. 2 Paleness; इयं भूतिर्नांगे प्रियविरहजन्मा धवलिमा Subhâsh.

धवित्रं A fan made of the deer's skin.

धा 3 U. (दधाति, धत्ते, हित; *Pass.* धीयते, *Caus.* धापयति-ते, *Desid.* धित्सति-ते) 1 To put, place, set, lay, put in, lay on or upon; विज्ञातदोषेषु दधाति दंडं Mb. निःशंकं धीयते (v. l. for दीयते) लोकैः पश्य भस्मचये पदं H. 2. 173. 2 To fix upon, direct (the mind or thoughts &c.) towards (with dat. or loc.); धत्ते चक्षुर्मुकुलिनि रणत्कोकिले बालचूते Mâl. 3. 12; दधुः कुमारानुगमे मनांसि Bk. 3. 11, 2. 7; Ms. 12. 23. 3 To bestow anything upon one, grant, give, confer, present (with dat., gen., or loc.); धुर्यां लक्ष्मीमथ मयि भृशं धेहि देव प्रसीद Mâl. 1. 3; यद्यस्य सोऽदधात्सर्गे तत्तस्य स्वयमाविशत् Ms. 1. 29. 4 To hold, contain; तानपि दधासि मातः Bv. 1. 68; *S*. 4. 1. 5 To seize, take hold of (as in the hand); Bk. 1. 26, 4. 26; Ki. 13. 54. 6 To wear, put on, bear; गुरूणि वासांसि विहाय तूर्णं तनूनि......धत्ते जनः काममदालसांगः Rs. 6. 13, 16; धत्ते भरं कुसुमपत्रफलावलीनां Bv. 1. 94; दधतो मंगलक्षौमे R. 12. 8, 9. 40; Bk. 18. 54. 7 To assume, take, have, show, exhibit, possess; (usually Atm.); काचः कांचनसंसर्गाद्धत्ते मारकतीं द्युतिं H. Pr. 41; शिरसि मसीपटलं दधाति दीपः Bv. 1. 74; R. 2. 7; Amaru. 23, 67; Me. 36; Bh. 3. 46; R. 3. 1; Bk. 2. 1, 4. 16-18; *Si*. 9. 3, 10, 86; Ki. 5. 5. 8 To hold up, sustain, bear up; गामधास्यत्कथं नागो मृणालमृदुभिः फणैः Ku. 6. 68. 9 To support, maintain; संपद्विनिमयेनोभौ दधतुर्भुवनद्वयं R. 1. 26. 10 To cause, create, produce, generate, make; मुग्धा कुड्मलिताननेन दधती वायुं स्थिता तस्य सा Amaru. 70. 11 To suffer, undergo, incur; *Si*. 9. 2, 32, 66. 12 To perform, do. [The meanings of this root, like those of दा, are variously modified according to the word with which it is connected; *e g*. मनः, मतिं, धियं &c. धा to fix the mind or thoughts upon, resolve upon; पदं धा to set foot on, to enter; कर्णे करं धा to place the hand on the ear &c.]. -WITH अतिसं to cheat, deceive; भगवन् कुसुमायुध त्वया चंद्रमसा च विश्वसनीयाभ्यामतिसंधीयते कामिजनसार्थः *S*. 3; V. 2. -अंतर् 1 to receive within oneself, admit, take in; तथा विश्वंभरे देवि मामंतर्धातुमर्हसि R. 15. 81. 2 to hide or conceal oneself from, avoid the sight of (with abl.); Bk. 5. 32, 8. 71. 3 to cover up, hide, obscure, wrap up, eclipse; (fig. also); पितुरंतर्दधे कीर्तिं शीलवृत्तसमाधिभिः Mb. -अनुसं 1 to search, inquire into, investigate, examine. 2 to collect or calm oneself. 3 to refer or allude to, aim at. 4 to plan, arrange, set in order. -अपि (the अ being sometimes dropped) 1 (*a*) close, shut; ध्वनति मधुपसमूहे श्रवणमपिदधाति Gît. 5; so कर्णौ नयने-पिदधाति (*b*) to cover, hide, conceal; प्रायो मूर्खः परिभवविधौ नाभिमानं पिधत्ते *S*. Til. 17; प्रभावपिहिता V. 4. 2; *Si*. 9. 76; Bk. 7. 69. 2 to hinder, obstruct, bar; भुजंगापिहितद्वारं पातालमधितिष्ठति R. 1. 80. -अभि 1 (*a*) to say, speak, tell; Ku. 3. 63; Ms. 1. 42; Bk. 7. 78; Bg; 18. 68. (*b*) to denote, express or convey directly or primarily, set forth; साक्षात्संकेतितं योऽर्थमभिधत्ते स वाचकः K. P. 2; तन्नाम येनाभिदधाति सत्त्वं. 2 to name, call. -अभ्या to put under, throw under. -अभिसं 1 to throw or shoot at, aim at (as an arrow.) 2 to have in view, aim at (in the mind), think of; ऋष्यमूकमभिसंधाय Mv. 5; अभिसंधाय तु फलं Bg. 17. 12, 25; V. 4. 28. 3 to deceive, cheat; जनं विद्वानिकः सकलमभिसंधाय Mâl. 1. 14. 4 to win over, make friendship, ally oneself with; तान् सर्वानभिसंदध्यात् सामादिभिरुपक्रमैः Ms. 7. 159 (वशीकुर्यात्). 5 to promise, declare solemnly. 6 to add. -अव to be attentive, attend to, give ear; इतोऽवधत्तां देवराजः Mv. 6. -आ (usually in the Atm.) 1 to place, put, lodge; जनपदे न गदः पदमादधौ R. 9. 4; Bg. 5. 40; *S*. 4. 3. 2 to apply, fix upon, direct towards; प्रतिपात्रमाधीयतां यत्नः *S*. 1; मय्येव मन आधत्स्व Bg. 12 8; आधीयतां धैर्ये धर्मे च धीः K. 63. 3 to take, possess, bear, have; गर्भमाधत्त राज्ञी R. 2. 75 bore conception; आधत्ते कनकमयातपत्रलक्ष्मीं Ki. 5. 39 takes or assumes; Ku. 7. 26. 4 to bear up, uphold, support; शेषः सदैवाहितभूमिभारः *S*. 5. 4. 5 to cause, produce, create, excite (fear, wonder &c.); छायाश्चरंति बहुधा भयमादधानाः *S*. 3. 27; Ki. 4. 12. 6 to give, impart; R. 1. 85. 7 to appoint, fix upon; तमेव चाधाय विवाहसाक्ष्ये R. 7. 20. 8 to consecrate; Ku. 1. 47. 9 to perform, practise (as a vow &c.). -आविस् to disclose, manifest (not usually used in classical literature). -उप 1 to place or lay upon, place under or in; अधिजानु बाहुमुपधाय *Si*. 9. 54; हृदि चैनामुपधातुमर्हसि R. 8. 77 lay to heart उपहितं शिशिरापगमश्रिया मुकुलजालमशोभत किंशुके R. 9. 31; Ku. 1. 44. 2 to place near, to put to or yoke (as a horse &c.); Mv. 4. 56. 3 to cause, bring on, produce; Mk. 1. 53. 4 to impose upon, entrust or charge with, commit to the care of; तदुपहितकुटुंबः R. 7. 71. to use as a pillow; वामभुजमुपधाय Dk. 111. 6 to employ, apply, bestow upon; क्रिया हि वस्तूपहिता प्रसीदति R. 3. 29. 7 to cover, conceal. 8 to give, impart, communicate. -उपा 1 to place near or upon. 2 to put on. 3 to cause, create, produce; Bh. 3. 85. -तिरस् 1 to hide, conceal. 2 (Atm.) to vanish, disappear; अभिवृष्यमरुत्सस्यं कृष्णमेघस्तिरोदधे R. 10. 48, 11. 91; see under तिरस् also. -नि 1 to place, put, put or set down; शिरसि निदधानोंजलिपुटं Bh. 3. 121; R. 3. 50, 62; 12. 52; *Si*. 1. 13. 2 to confide or entrust, commit to the care of; निदधे विजयाशंसां चापे सीतां च लक्ष्मणे R. 12. 44, 14. 36. 6 to give, impart to, deposit with; दिनांते निहितं तेजः सवित्रेव हुताशनः R. 4. 1. 4 to put down, allay, restrain; सलिलैर्निहितं रजः क्षितौ Ghat. 1. 5 to bury, conceal or hide (as under ground); Ms. 5. 68. -परि 1 to put or wear (as a garmant): त्वचं स मेध्यां परिधाय रौरवीं R. 3. 31. 2 to enclose, surround. 3 to direct towards. -पुरस् 1 to place or put at the head; तरासाह पुरोधाय धाम स्वायंभुवं ययुः Ku. 2. 1; R. 12. 43. 2 to make a family-priest of one. -प्रणि 1 to place, put or lay down, prostrate; प्रणिहितशिरसं वा कांतमार्द्रापराधं M. 3. 12; तस्मात्प्रणम्य प्रणिधाय कायं Bg. 11. 44. 2 to set, put in, inlay or incase; यदि मणिस्त्रपुणि प्रणिधीयते Pt. 1. 75. v. 1. 3 to apply, fix upon, direct towards; भर्तृप्रणिहितेक्षणा R. 15. 84; Bk. 6. 142. 4 to stretch out, extend; मामाकाशप्रणिहितभुजं निर्दयाश्लेषहेतोः Me 106; नीवीं प्रति प्रणिहिते तु करे प्रियेण सख्यः शपामि यदि किंचिदपि स्मरामि K. P. 4. 5 to send out (as spies). -प्रतिवि 1 to counteract, correct, repair, retaliate, remedy, take steps against; अर्थवाद एषः दोषं तु मे कंचित्कथय येन स प्रतिविधीयेत U. 1; क्षिप्रमेव कस्मान्न प्रतिविहितमार्येण Mu. 3. 2 to dispose, arrange, prepare. 3 to despatch, send. -प्रवि 1 to divide. 2 to do or make. -वि 1 to do, make, bring about, effect, accomplish, perform, cause, produce, occasion; यथाक्रमं पुंसवनादिकाः क्रिया धृतेश्च धीरः सदृशीर्व्यधत्त सः R. 3. 10; तन्नो दैवा विधेयासुः Bk. 19. 2; विधेयासुर्देवाः परमरमणीयां परिणतिं Mal. 6. 7. प्राग्; शुभं च विदधात्यशुभं च जंतोः सर्वंकषा भगवती भवितव्यतैव 1. 23; ये द्वे कालं विधत्तः *S*. 1. 1, cause, produce or regulate time; तस्य तस्याचलां श्रद्धां तामेव विदधाम्यहं Bg. 7. 21; R. 2. 38, 3. 66; (these senses may be further modified according to the noun with which विधा is used; cf. कृ). 2 to lay down, ordain, prescribe, fix, settle, command, enjoin; प्राङ्नाभिवर्धनात्पुंसो जातकर्म विधीयते Ms. 2. 29, 3. 19; Y. 1. 72; शूद्रस्य तु सवर्णैव नान्या भार्या विधीयते 9. 157; 3. 118. 3 to make form, shape, create, manufacture; तं वेधा विदधे नूनं महाभूतसमाधिना R. 1. 29; अंगानि चंपकदलैः स विधाय नूनं कांते कथं घटितवानुपलेन चेतः *S*. Til. 3. 4 to appoint, depute (as a minister). **5** to put on, wear; Pt. 1. 29. **6** to fix upon, direct towards (as mind &c.); Bg. 2. 44; Bh. 3. 54. **7** to arrange, put in order. **8** to make ready, prepare. **–व्यव** to place between, interpose, intervene; प्रेक्ष्य स्थितां सहचरीं व्यवधाय देहं R. 9. 57. **2** to hide, conceal, screen, शापव्यवहितस्मृतिः *S.* 5. **–श्रद्** to confide, believe, put faith in (with acc. of thing); कः श्रद्धास्यति भूतार्थं Mk. 3. 24; श्रद्दधे त्रिदशगोपमात्रके दाहशक्तिमिव कृष्णवर्त्मनि R. 11. 42. **–सं 1** to join, bring together, unite, combine; यानि उदकेन संधीयंते तानि भक्षणीयानि Kull. **2** to treat with, form friendship or alliance with, make peace with; शत्रुणा न हि संदध्यात्सुश्लिष्टेनापि संधिना H. 1. 88; Chân. 19; Kâm. 9. 41. **3** to fix upon, direct towards; संदधे दृशमुदग्रतारकां R. 11. 69. **4** to fit to or place upon the bow (as a missile, arrow &c.); धनुष्यमोघं समधत्त बाणं Ku. 3. 66; R. 3. 53, 12. 97. **5** to produce, cause; पर्याप्तं मयि रमणीयडामरत्वं संधत्ते गगनतलप्रयाणवेगः Mâl. 5. 3; संधत्ते भृशमरतिं हि सद्वियोगः Ki. 5. 51. **6** to hold out against, be a match for; शतमेकोऽपि संधत्ते प्राकारस्थो धनुर्धरः Pt. 1. 229. **7** to mend, repair, heal. **8** to inflict upon. **9** to grasp, support, take hold of. **10** to grant, yield.–**संनि 1** to place, put or keep together; Ms. 2. 186. **2** to place near; *S.* 3. 19. **3** to fix upon, direct towards; R. 13. 144. **4** to draw near, approach. (*–Caus.*) to bring near, collect together. **–समा 1** to place or put together, join, unite. **2** to place, put, put or place upon, apply to; पदं मूर्ध्नि समाधत्ते केसरी मत्तदंतिनः Pt. 1. 327. **3** to install, place on the throne; R. 17. 8. **4** to compose, collect (as the mind); मनः समाधाय निवृत्तशोकः Râm.; न शशाक समाधातुं मनो मदनवेपितं Bhâg. **5** to concentrate, fix or apply intently upon (as the eye, mind &c.); Bg. 12. 9; Bh. 3. 48. **6** to satisfy, clear or solve (a doubt), answer an objection; इति समाधत्ते (in commentaries). **7** to repair, redress, set right, remove; न ते शक्याः समाधातुं H. 3. 37; उत्पन्नामापदं यस्तु समाधत्ते स बुद्धिमान् 4. 7. **8** to think over; Bk. 12. 6. **9** to entrust, commit to, deliver over. **10** to produce, effect, accomplish. (The following verse illustrates the use of धा with some prepositions:—अपिहित कापि मुखं सलिलं सखी प्यधित कापि सरोजदलैः स्तनौ। व्यधित कापि हृदि व्यजनानिलं न्यधित कापि हिमं सुतनोस्तनौ N. 4. 111; or, better still, the following verse of Jagannâtha:– निधानं धर्माणां किमपि च विधानं नवमुदां प्रधानं तीर्थानाममलपरिधानं त्रिजगतः । समाधानं बुद्धेरथ खलु तिरोधानमधियां श्रियामाधानं नः परिहरतु तापं तव वपुः ॥ G. L. 18).

धाकः 1 An ox. **2** A receptacle, reservoir. **3** Food, boiled rice. **4** A post, pillar, column.

धाटी Assault, attacking.

धाणकः A gold coin (part of a Dînâra).

धातुः 1 Constituent or essential part, an ingredient. **2** An element, primary or elementary substance; *i. e.* पृथिवी, आप्, तेजस्, वायु and आकाश. **3** A secretion, primary fluid or juice, essential ingredient of the body (which are considered to be 7 :–रसासृङ्मांसमेदोऽस्थिमज्जाशुक्राणि धातवः or sometimes ten if केश, त्वच् and स्नायु be added). **4** A humour or affection of the body (*i. e.* वात, पित्त and कफ). **5** A mineral, metal, metallic ore; न्यस्ताक्षरा धातुरसेन यत्र Ku. 1. 7; त्वामालिख्य प्रणयकुपितां धातुरागैः शिलायां Me. 105; R. 4. 71; Ku. 6. 51. **6** A verbal root; भूवादयो धातवः P. I. 3. 1; पश्चादध्ययनार्थस्य धातोरधिरिवाभवत् R. 15. 9. **7** The soul. **8** The supreme spirit. **9** An organ of sense. **10** Any one of the properties of the five elements; *i. e.* रूप, रस, गंध, स्पर्श and शब्द. **11** A bone. –Comp. **–उपलः** chalk. **–काशीशं, –कासीसं** red sulphate of iron. **–कुशल** *a.* skilful in working in metals. **–क्रिया** metallurgy, mineralogy. **–क्षयः** waste of the bodily humours, a wasting disease, a kind of consumption. **–जं** bitumen. **–द्रावकः** borax. **–पः** the alimentary juice, the chief of the seven essential ingredients of the body. **–पाठः** a list of roots arranged according to Pâṇini's grammatical system; (the most important of these lists called धातुपाठ being supposed to be the work of Pâṇini himself, as supplementary to his Sútras). **–भृत्** *m.* a mountain. **–मलं 1** impure excretion of the essential fluids of the body. **2** lead. **–माक्षिकं 1** sulphuret of iron. **2** a mineral substance. **–मारिन्** *m.* sulphur. **–राजकः** semen. **–वल्लभं** borax. **–वादः** mineralogy, metallurgy. **–वादिन्** *m.* a mineralogist. **–वैरिन्** *m.* sulphur. **–शेखरं** green sulphate of iron, green vitriol. **–शोधनं, –संभवं** lead. **–साम्यं** good health; (equilibrium of the three humours).

धातुमत् *a.* Rich or abounding in metals. **°ता** richness in metals; Ku. 1. 4.

धातृ *m.* **1** A maker, creator, originator, author. **2** A bearer, preserver, supporter. **3** An epithet of Brâhma, the creator of the world; मन्ये दुर्जनचित्तवृत्तिहरणे धातापि भग्नोद्यमः H. 2. 165; R. 13. 6; Si. 1. 13; Ku. 7. 44; Ki. 12. 33. **4** An epithet of Vishṇu. **5** The soul. **6 N. for** the seven sages (सप्तर्षि), being **the first** creation of Brahmâ; cf. Ku. 6. 9. **7** A married woman's paramour, adulterer.

धात्रं A vessel for holding any thing, a receptacle.

धात्री 1 A nurse, wet-nurse, foster mother; उवाच धात्र्या प्रथमोदितं वचः R. 3. 25; Ku. 7. 25. **2** A mother; Y. 3. 82. **3** The earth. **4** The tree called आमलक. –Comp. **–पुत्रः 1** a foster-brother. **2** an actor. **–फलं** An âmalaka fruit.

धात्रेयिका, धात्रेयी 1 A fostersister; धात्रेयिकायाश्चतुरं वचश्च Mâl. 1. 33; कथितमेव नो मालतीधात्रेय्या लवंगिकया Mâl. 1. **2** A nurse, wet-nurse.

धानं, –नी A receptacle, seat; as in मसीधानी, राजधानी, यमधानी.

धानाः *f.* pl. **1** Fried-barley or rice. **2** Grain fried or powdered. **3** Corn, grain. **4** A bud, shoot.

धानुर्दंडिकः, धानुष्कः An archer (living by the bow), a bowman; निमित्तादपराद्धेषोर्धानुष्कस्येव वल्गितं Si. 2. 27.

धानुष्यः Bamboo.

धांधा Cardamoms.

धान्यं 1 Grain, corn, rice. **2** Coriander; (for the distinction between सस्य, धान्य, तंडुल and अन्न see under तंडुल). –Comp. **–अर्थः** wealth in rice or grain. **–अम्लं** sour gruel made of the fermentation of rice-water. **–अस्थि** *n.* husk, chaff. **–उत्तमः** the best of grain, *i. e.* rice. **–कल्कं 1** bran. **2** chaff, straw. **–कोशः, –कोष्ठकं** a granary. **–क्षेत्रं** a corn field. **–चमसः** rice flattened by threshing after it has been steeped and fried in the husk. **–त्वच्** *f.* the husk of corn. **–मायः** a corndealer. **–राजः** barley. **–वर्धनं** lending grain at interest, usury with grain. **–बीजं (बीजं)** coriander. **–वीरः** a sort of pulse (माष). **–शीर्षकं** the ear of corn. **–शूकं** the beard or awn of corn. **–सारः** threshed corn.

धान्या, धान्याकं Coriander.

धान्वन् *a.* (**नी** *f.*) Situated in a desert (धन्वन्).

धामकः A sort of weight; (माष q. v.)

धामन् *n.* **1** A dwelling-place, abode, residence, house; तुरासाहं पुरोधाय धाम स्वायंभुवं ययुः Ku. 2. 1; पुण्यं यायास्त्रिभुवनगुरोर्धाम चंडीश्वरस्य Me. 33; Bg. 8. 21; Bh. 1. 33. **2** A place, site, resort; श्रियो धाम. **3** The inmates of a house, members of a family. **4** A ray of light; सहस्रधामन् Mu. 3. 17; हिमधामन् Si. 9. 53. **5** Light, lustre, splendour; Mu. 3 17; Ki 2. 20 55, 59; 10. 6; Amaru. 86; R. 6. 6; 18. 22. **6** Majestic lustre, glory, dignity; R. 11 85. **7** Power, strength, energy (प्रताप); Ki. 2. 47. **8** Birth. **9** The body. **10** A troop, host. **11** State, condition. –Comp. **–केशिन्, –निधिः** the sun.

धामनिका, धामनी see धमनी.

धार *a.* 1 Holding, bearing, supporting. 2 Streaming, dripping, flowing. **रः** 1 An epithet of Vishnu. 2 A sudden and violent shower of rain, sharpdriving shower. 3 Snow, hail. 4 A deep place. 5 Debt. 6 A boundary, limit.

धारकः 1 A vessel of any kind (box, trunk &c.), a water-pot. 2 A debtor.

धारण *a.* (**णी** *f.*) Holding, bearing, carrying, preserving, sustaining, protecting, having, assuming &c. —**णं** 1 The act of holding, bearing, supporting, preserving or keeping back. 2 Possessing, possession. 3 Observing, holding fast. 4 Keeping in the memory; ग्रहणधारणपटुर्बालकः. 5 Being indebted (to any one). —**णी** 1 A row or line. 2 A vein or tubular vessel.

धारणकः A debtor.

धारणा 1 The act of holding, bearing, supporting, preserving &c. 2 The faculty of retaining in the mind, a good or retentive memory; धीर्धारणावती मेधा Ak. 3 Memory in general. 4 Keeping the mind collected, holding the breath suspended, steady abstraction of mind; परिचेतुमुपांशु धारणां R. 8. 18; Ms. 6. 72; Y. 3. 201; (धारणेत्युच्यते चेयं धार्यते यन्मनो तया). 5 Fortitude, firmness, steadiness. 6 A fixed precept or injunction, a settled rule, conclusion; इति धर्मस्य धारणा Ms. 8. 184, 4. 38, 9. 124. 7 Understanding, intellect. 8 Continuance in rectitude, propriety, decorum. 9 Conviction. –COMP. –**योगः** deep devotion or abstraction. **शक्तिः** *f.* a retentive memory.

धारयित्री The earth.

धारा 1 A stream or current of water, a line of descending fluid, stream, current; Bh. 2. 93; Me. 55; R. 16. 66; आबद्धधारमश्रु प्रावर्तत Dk. 74. 2 A shower, a hard or sharp-driving shower. 3 A continuous line or series; Bv. 2. 20. 4 A leak or hole in a pitcher. 5 The pace of a horse; धाराः प्रसाधयितुमव्यतिकीर्णरूपाः *Si.* 5. 60. 6 The margin, edge or border of anything; ध्रुवं स नीलोत्पलपत्रधारया शमीलतां छेत्तुमृषिर्व्यवस्यति *S.* 1. 18. 7 The sharp edge of a sword, axe, or of any cutting instrument; तर्जितः परशुधारया मम R. 11. 78; 6. 42; 10. 86, 41; Bh. 2. 28. 8 The edge of a mountain or precipice. 9 A wheel or the periphery of a wheel; R. 13. 15. 10 A garden-wall; fence, hedge. 11 The van or front line of an army. 12 The highest point, excellence. 13 A multitude. 14 Fame. 15 Night. 16 Turmeric. 17 Likeness. 18 The tip of the ear. –COMP. –**अग्रं** the broad-edged head of an arrow. –**अंकुरः** 1 a drop of rain. 2 hail. 3 advancing before the line of an army (to defy the enemy). –**अंगः** a sword. –**अटः** 1 the Châtaka bird. 2 a horse. 3 a cloud. 4 a furious elephant, one in rut. –**अधिरूढ** *a.* raised to the highest pitch. (–**अ**) **वनिः** *f.* wind. –**अश्रु** *n.* a flood of tears; Amaru. 10. –**आसारः** a heavy down-fall of rain, a hard or sharp-driving shower; धारासारैर्महती वृष्टिर्बभूव H. 3; V. 4. 1. –**उष्ण** *a.* warm from a cow (as milk). –**गृहं** a bath-room with water-jets, a shower-bath or a house furnished with artificial jets or fountains of water; R. 16. 49; Ratn. 1. 13. –**धरः** 1 a cloud. 2 a sword. –**निपातः** –**पातः** 1 a fall of rain, a hard or pelting shower; Me. 48. 2 a stream of water. –**यंत्रं** a fountain, jet (of water); Amaru. 59; Ratn. 1. 12. –**वर्षः**-**र्षं**, –**संपातः** a hard, sharp-driving or incessant shower; R. 4. 82. –**वाहिन्** *a.* incessant, continuous; U. 4. 3. –**विष** a crooked sword.

धारिणी The earth.

धारिन् *a.* (**णी** *f.*) 1 Carrying, bearing, sustaining, preserving, having, holding, supporting; पादांभोरुहधारि Gît. 12; कर° &c. 2 Keeping in one's memory, possessed of retentive memory; अज्ञेभ्यो ग्रंथिनः श्रेष्ठा ग्रंथिभ्यो धारिणो वराः Ms. 12. 103.

धार्तराष्ट्रः 1 A son of Dhritarâshtra. 2 A sort of goose with black legs and bill; निपतंति धार्तराष्ट्राः कालवशान्मेदिनीपृष्ठे Ve. 1. 6. (where the word is used in both the senses).

धार्मिक *a.* (**की** *f.*) 1 Righteous, pious, just, virtuous. 2 Resting on right, conformable to justice, equitable. 3 Religious.

धार्मिणं An assemblage of virtuous men.

धार्ष्ट्यं Arrogance, insolence, audacity, impudence, rudeness.

धाव् I. 1 P. (धावति, धावित) 1 To run, advance; अद्यापि धावति मनः Ch. P. 36; धावंत्यमी मृगजवाक्षमयेव रथ्याः *S.* 1. 8; गच्छति पुरः शरीरं धावति पश्चादसंस्तुतं चेतः 1. 34. 2 To run towards, advance against, assault, encounter; Bk. 16. 67. 3 To flow, stream or flow forth; धावत्यंभांसि तैलवत् Susr. 4 To run or flee away. –II 1 U. (धावति-ते, धौत or धावित) 1 To wash, clean, cleanse, purify, rub off; दधावाद्रिस्ततश्चक्षुः सुग्रीवस्य बिभीषणः। विदांचकार धौताक्षः स रिपुं खे ननर्द च ॥ Bk. 14. 50, *S.* 6. 25; *Si.* 17. 8. 2 To brighten, polish. 3 To rub into one's person (Atm.) –WITH **निस्** to wash off; निर्धौते सति हरिचंदने जलौघैः *Si.* 8. 51; निर्धौतदानामलगंडभित्तिः R. 5. 43, 70.

धावकः 1 A washerman. 2 N. of a poet; (said to have composed the Ratnâvalî for King Srîharsha); श्रीहर्षादेर्धावकादीनामिव यशः K. P. 1. v. 1.; प्रथितयशसां धावकसौमिल्लकविपुत्रादीनां प्रबंधानतिक्रम्य M. 1. v, 1.

धावनं 1 Running, galloping. 2 Flowing. 3 Attacking. 4 Cleansing, purifying, rubbing, washing off. 5 Rubbing with anything.

धावल्यं 1 Whiteness. 2 Paleness.

धि I. 6 P. (धियति) To hold, have, possess. –WITH **सं** to make peace with; of. संधा. –II. or धिन्व् 5 P. (धिनोति) To please, delight; satisfy; पश्यंती चात्मरूपं तदपि विलुलितस्रग्धरेयं धिनोति Gît. 12; धिनोति नास्माञ्जलजेन पूजा त्वयान्वहं तन्वि वितन्यमाना N. 8. 97; U. 5 27; Ki. 1. 22.

धिः (At the end of comp. only) A receptacle, store, reservoir &c.; उदधि, इषुधि, वारिधि, जलधि &c.

धिक् *ind.* An interjection of censure, menace or displeasure ('fie', 'shame', 'out upon', 'what a pity' &c. usually with acc.); धिक् तां च तं च मदनं च इमां च मां च Bh. 2. 2; धिगिमां देहभृतामसारतां R. 8. 50; धिक् तान् धिक् तान् धिगेतान् कथयति सततं कीर्तनस्थो मृदंगः; धिक् सानुजं कुरुपतिं धिगजातशत्रुं Ve. 3. 11, sometimes with nom., voc. and gen. also; धिङ् मूर्ख, धिगर्थाः कष्टसंश्रयाः Pt. 1; धिगस्तु हृदयस्यास्य &c. (**धिक्कृ** to despise, disregard, condemn, reproach). –COMP. –**कारः**, –**क्रिया** reproach, contempt, disregard. –**दंडः** reprimand, censure; Ms. 8. 129. –**पारुष्यं** abuse, reproach, reviling.

धिप्सु *a.* Wishing to deceive, deceptive; Bk. 9. 33.

धिन्व् See धि II.

धिषणः N. of Brihaspati, preceptor of the gods. —**णं** A dwelling place, an abode; residence. —**णा** 1 Speech 2 Praise, hymn. 3 Intellect, understanding; Mv. 6. 8. 4 Earth. 5 A cup, bowl.

धिष्ण्यः 1 A place for the sacrificial fire; अमी वेदिं परितः क्लृप्तधिष्ण्याः *S.* 4. 7. 2 N. of *S*ukra, preceptor of the demons, 3 The planet Venus. 4 Power, strength. —**ष्ण्यं** 1 A seat, an abode, site, place, house; न भौमान्येव धिष्ण्यानि हित्वा ज्योतिर्मयान्यपि R. 15. 59. 2 A meteor. 3 Fire. 4 A star, an asterism.

धीः *f.* 1 (*a*) Intellect, understanding; धियः समग्रैः स गुणैरुदारधीः R. 3. 30; cf. कुधी, सुधी &c. (*b*) Mind; दुष्टधी wicked-minded; Bg. 2. 54; R. 3. 30. 2 Idea, imagination, fancy, conception; न धियां पथि वर्तसे Ku. 6. 22. 3 A thought, intention, purpose, propensity Ki. 1. 37. 4 Devotion, prayer. 5 A sacrifice. –COMP. –**इंद्रियं** an organ of perception (ज्ञानेंद्रिय q. v.); मनः कर्णस्तथा नेत्रं रसना च त्वचा सह । नासिका चेति षट् तानि धींद्रियाणि प्रचक्षते ॥). –**गुणाः** (pl.) intellectual qualities: (they are :—

शुश्रूषा श्रवणं चैव ग्रहणं धारणं तथा । ऊहापोहार्थ-विज्ञानं तत्वज्ञानां च धीगुणाः ॥ Kâmandaka) –पतिः (धियांपतिः) Brihaspati, the preceptor of the gods. –मंत्रिन् *m.* –सचिवः 1 a minister for counsel (opp. कर्मसचिव a minister for action or execution). 2 a wise or prudent adviser. –शक्तिः *f.* intellectual quality or faculty.–सखः a counsellor, adviser, minister.

धीमत् *a.* Wise, intelligent, learned, —*m.* An epithet of Brihaspati.

धीत *a.* 1 Sucked, drunk; see धे.

धीतिः *f.* 1 Drinking, sucking. 2 Thirst.

धीर *a.* 1 Brave, bold, courageous; धीरोद्धता गतिः U. 6. 19. 2 Steady, steadfast, firm, durable, lasting, constant; R. 2. 6. 3 Strong-minded, persevering, self-possessed, resolute, of firm resolve or purpose; धीरा हि तरंत्यापदं K. 175; विकारहेतौ सति विक्रियंते येषां न चेतांसि त एव धीराः Ku. 1. 52 4 Composed, calm, collected. 5 Sedate, sober, grave, solemn; R. 18. 4. 6 Strong, energetic. 7 Wise, prudent, intelligent, sensible, learned, clever; धृतेश्च धीरः सदृशीर्व्यधत्त सः R. 3. 10; 5. 38; 16. 74; U. 5. 31. 8 Deep, grave, loud, hollow (as sound); स्वरेण धीरेण निवर्तयन्निव R. 3. 43, 52; U. 6. 17. 9 ed. 10 Gentle, soft, agreeable, pleasing (as a breeze); धीरसमीरे यमुनातीरे वसति वने वनमाली Gît. 5 11 Lazy, dull. 12 Daring. 13 Headstrong.—रः 1 The ocean. 2 An epithet of king Bali. —रं Saffron.—रं *ind.* Boldly, firmly, steadfastly, steadily, Bh. 2. 31; Amaru. 11. –COMP. –उदात्तः the hero of a poetic composition (*i.e.* a play or poem) who is brave and nobleminded; अविकत्थनः क्षमावानतिगंभीरो महासत्वः । स्थेयान्निगूढमानो धीरोदात्तो दृढव्रतः कथितः S. D. 66. —उद्धतः the hero of a poetic composition who is brave but haughty; मायापरः प्रचंडश्चपलोऽहंकारदर्पभूयिष्ठः । आत्मश्लाघानिरतो धीरैर्धीरोद्धतः कथितः S. D. 67. –चेतस् *a.* firm, resolute, strongminded, courageous. –प्रशांतः the hero of a poetic composition who is brave and calm: सामान्यगुणैर्भूयान् द्विजातिको धीरप्रशांतः स्यात् S. D. 69. –ललितः the hero of a poetic composition who is firm and brave, but sportive and reckless, निश्चिंतो मृदुरनिशं कलापरो धीरललितः स्यात् S. D. 68. –स्कंधः a buffalo.

धीरता 1 Fortitude, courage, strength of mind; विपत्तौ च महांल्लोके धीरतामनुगच्छति H. 3. 44. 2 Suppression of jealousy &c. 3 Gravity, solemnity (as shown by silence &c.); प्रत्यादेशान्न खलु भवती धीरतां कल्पयामि Me. 144. (For other meanings see धैर्य).

धीरा The heroine of a poetic composition who, though jealous of her husband or lover, suppresses all outward manifestation or expression of her resentment in his presence, or as the Rasamanjarî puts it व्यंग्यकोपप्रकाशिका धीरा; see S. D. 102-105 also. –COMP. –अधीरा the heroine of a poetic composition who, being jealous of her husband or lover, alternately expresses and conceals her jealousy (व्यंग्याव्यंग्यकोपप्रकाशिका-धीराधीरा Rasamanjarî).

धीलटिः–टी *f.* A daughter.

धीवरः A fisherman; मृगमीनसज्जनानां तृणजलसंतोषविहितवृत्तीनां । लुब्धकधीवरपिशुना निष्कारणवैरिणो जगति ॥ Bh. 2. 61, 1. 85. —रं Iron. –री 1 A fisherman's wife, 2 A fish-basket.

धु 5 U. (धुनोति, धुनुते, धुत) See धू.

धुक्ष् 1 A. (धुक्षते, धुक्षित) 1 To be kindled. 2 To live. 3 To be weary —*Caus* (धुक्षयति) To kindle, inflame. -WITH सं to be kindled or excited (fig. also); संदुधुक्षे तयोः कोपः Bk. 14. 109. (-*Caus.*) to kindle, inflame, excite; निर्वाणभूयिष्ठमथास्य वीर्यं संधुक्षयंतीव वपुर्गुणेन Ku. 3. 52.

धुत *a.* 1 Shaken; R 11. 16. 2 Left, abandoned.

धुनिः, –नी *f.* A river; पुराणां संहर्तुः सुरधुनि कपर्दोऽधिरुरुहे G. L. 22. –COMP. –नाथः the ocean.

धुर् (Nom. sing. धूः) 1 A yoke (lit.); न गर्दभा वाजिधुरं वहंति Mk. 4. 17; अत्रस्नुभिर्युक्तधुरं तुरंगैः R. 14. 47. 2 That part of a yoke which rests on the shoulder. 3 The pin at both ends of an exle for fastening the nave of the wheel. 4 The shaft or pole of a carriage. 5 A load, burden (fig. also); responsibility, duty, task, तेन धूर्जगतो गुर्वी सचिवेषु निचिक्षिपे R. 1. 34; 2. 74, 3. 35, 66; Ku. 6. 30; अतिरभ्यनवाप्तपौरुषफलैः कार्यस्य धूरुज्झिता Mu. 6. 5. 4. 6; Ki. 3. 50; 14. 6. 6 The foremost or highest place, van, front, top, head; अपांसुलानां धुरि कीर्तनीया R. 2. 2; धुरि स्थिता त्वं पतिदेवतानां 14. 74; अविघ्नमस्तु ते स्थेयाः पितेव धुरि पुत्रिणां 1. 91; धुरि प्रतिष्ठापयितव्य एव M. 1. 16, 5, 16. (धुरि कृ to place at the head or in front of; S. 7. 4). –COMP. –गत (धूर्गत) *a.* 1 standing on the pole of a chariot. 2 standing at the head, chief, head, foremost. –जटिः (धूर्जटिः) an epithet of Siva. –धर (धूर्धर, also धुरंधर) *a.* 1 bearing the yoke. 2 fit to be harnessed. 3 laden with good qualities or important duties 4 chief, head, foremost, prominent; कुलधुरंधरो भव V. 5. (-रः) 1 a beast of burden. 2 a man of business, 3 a chief, head, leader. –वह (धुर्वह) *a.* 1 carrying or bearing a burden. 2 managing affairs. (-हः) a beast of burden; so धूर्वोढृ.

धुरा A burden, lead; रणधुरा Ve. 3. 5.

धुरीण, धुरीय *a.* 1 Able to bear or carry a burden. 2 Fit to be harnessed. 3 Charged with important duties. (-णः, -यः) 1 A beast of burden. 2 A man of business, or one charged with important duties. 4 A chief, head, leader.

धुर्य *a.* 1 Fit for a burden, able to bear a burden &c. 2 Fit to be entrusted with important duties. 3 Standing at the head, chief, foremost; see below. –र्यः 1 A beast of burden. 2 A horse or bullock yoked to the pole or carriage; नाविनीतैर्व्रजेत् धुर्यैः Ms. 4. 67; येनेदं ध्रियते विश्वं धुर्यैर्यानमिवाध्वनि Ku. 6. 76; धुर्यान् विश्रामयेति R. 1. 54. 6. 78; 17. 12. 3 One who carries a burden (of responsibility); R. 5. 66. 4 A chief, leader, head; न हि सति कुलधुर्ये सूर्यवंश्या गृहाय R. 7. 71. 5 A minister, one charged with important duties.

धुस्तु (स्तू)रः N. of a plant (=धत्तुर q. v.)

धू 6. P., 1. 5. 9. 10. U. (धुवति, धवति-ते धूनोति, धुनुते, धुनोति, धुनीते, धूनयति-ते, धूत, धून) 1 To shake, agitate, cause to move or tremble; धुन्वंति पक्षपवनैर्न नभो बलाकाः Rs. 3. 12; धुन्वन् कल्पद्रुमकिसलयानि Me. 62; Ku. 7. 49; R. 4. 67; Bk. 5. 101, 9. 7; 10, 22. 2 To shake off, remove, throw off; स्रजमपि शिरस्यंधः क्षिप्तां धुनोत्यहिशंकया S. 7. 24. 3 To blow away, destroy. 4 To kindle, excite, fan (as fire); वायुना धूयमानो हि वनं दहति पावकः Mb.; पवनधुतः अग्निः Rs. 1. 26. 5 To treat roughly, hurt, injure; मा न धावीररिं रणे Bk. 9. 50; 15. 61. 6 To shake off from oneself, free oneself from; (सेवकाः) आरोहंति शनैः पश्चाद्धुन्वंतमपि पार्थिवं Pt. 1. 36. (The following stanza from Kavirahasya illustrates the root in its different conjugations :— धूनोति चंपकवनानि धुनोत्यशोकं चूतं धुनाति धुवति स्फुटितातिमुक्तं । वायुर्विधूनयति चंपकपुष्परेणून् यत्कानने धवति चंदनमंजरीश्च ॥). –WITH अव 1 to shake, move, cause to tremble, wave; रेणुः पवनावधूतः R. 7. 43; लीलावधूतैश्चामरैः Me. 35; Ki. 6. 3; Si. 13. 36. 2 to shake off, remove, overcome; राजसत्त्वमवधूय मातृकं R. 11. 90; सुरवधूरवधूतभयाः शरैः 9. 19; 3. 61; Ki. 1. 42. 3 to disregard, reject, spurn, treat with disrespect or contempt; चंडी मामवधूय पादपतितं V. 4. 38; पादानतः कोपनयाऽवधूतः Ku. 3. 8; V. 3. 5. –उद् 1 to shake up, raise, move or throw up, wave, कैर्नोद्धूतानि चामराणि K. 117; R. 1. 85, 9. 50; उद्धुनीयात सत्केतून् Bk. 19. 8; Ki. 5. 39; मारुतभरोद्धुतोपि धूलिव्रजः Dhan. V. 2 to shake or throw off, remove, dispel, destroy (fig. also); उद्धूतपापाः Me. 55; Si. 18. 8. 3 to disturb, excite, rouse up. –निस् 1 to shake or throw off, remove, dispel, expel, destroy; निर्धूतोऽधरशोणिमा Gît. 12; ज्ञाननिर्धूतकल्मषाः Bg. 5 16; R. 12. 57. **2** to spurn, treat with contempt, disregard. **3** to abandon, forsake, throw away. **-वि 1** to shake, move, cause to tremble; मृदुपवनविधूतान् Rs. 6. 29, 3. 10; दीर्घा वेणीं विधुन्वाना Mb. **2** to shake off, destroy, expel, drive away; कपेर्विधवितुं द्युतिं Bk. 9. 28; R. 9. 72. v. l. **3** to spurn, despise, treat with contempt; R. 11. 40. **4** to leave, give up, abandon; N. 1. 35.

धूः *f.* Shaking, trembling, agitating.

धूत *p p.* **1** Shaken. **2** Shaken off, removed. **3** Fanned. **4** Abandoned, deserted. **5** Reviled. **6** Judged. **7** Disregarded, treated with contempt. **8** Guessed. -COMP. **-कल्मष, -पाप** *a.* who has shaken off his sins, free from sin.

धूतिः *f.* **1** Shaking, moving. **2** Fanning.

धून *p. p.* Shaken, agitated &c.

धूनिः *f.* Shaking, agitating.

धूप् I. 1. P. (धूपायति, धूपायित) To heat or to be heated. II. 10. U. (धूपयति-ते) **1** To fumigate, perfume, incense, to make fragrant. **2** To shine **3** To speak.

धूपः **1** Incense, frankincense, perfume, any fragrant substance. **2** The vapour issuing from any fragrant substance (like gum, resin &c.) aromatic vapour or smoke; धूपोष्मणा त्याजितमार्द्रभावं Ku. 7. 14; Me. 33; V. 3. 2; R. 16. 50. **3** A fragrant powder. -COMP. **-अगुरु** *n.* a kind of agallochum used for incense. **-अंगः 1** turpentine. **2** the Sarala tree. **-अर्हं** a black kind of agallochum. **-पात्रं** a vessel for incense, censer. **-वासः** fumigating, perfuming. **-वृक्षः** a kind of pine, the Sarala tree.

धूपनं **1** Fumigating, perfuming. **2** Incense; Ms. 7. 219.

धूपित *a.* Fumigated, heated, perfumed, incensed.

धूमः **1** Smoke, vapour; धूमज्योतिःसलिलमरुतां सन्निपातः क्व मेघः Me. 5. **2** Mist, haze. **3** A meteor. **4** A cloud. **5** Smoke inhaled (as a sternutatory). **6** Belch, eructation. -COMP. **-आभ** *a.* of a smoky appearance, smoke-coloured. **-आवलिः** a wreath or cloud of smoke. **-उत्थं** ammoniac. **-उद्गारः 1** issuing of smoke or vapour; Me. 69. **2** eructation, belch. **-उर्णा** N. of the wife of Yama. **-°पतिः** an epithet of Yama. **-केतनः, -केतुः 1** fire; कोपस्य नंदकुलकाननधूमकेतोः Mu. 1. 10; R. 11. 81. **2** a meteor, comet, falling star; धूमकेतुमिव किमपि करालं Gît. 1; धूमकेतुरिवोत्थितः Ku. 2. 32. **3** Ketu. **-जः** a cloud. **-ध्वजः** fire. **-पानं** inhaling smoke or vapour. **-महिषी** fog, mist. **-योनिः** a cloud; cf. Me. 5.

धूमल *a.* Smoke-coloured, brownish-red, purple.

धूमायति-ते To cover or fill with smoke, vapour &c., darken; धूमायिताशदिशो दलितारविंदाः Bv. 1. 104; Mk. 5. 57.

धूमिका Vapour, fog, mist.

धूमित *a.* Obscured with smoke, darkened; Ku. 4. 30.

धूम्या A volume or cloud of smoke, thick smoke.

धूम्र *a.* **1** Smoke-coloured, smoky, grey; Bh. 3. 55; R. 15. 16. **2** Dark red. **3** Dark, obscured. **4** Purple. **—म्रः 1** A mixture of red and black. **2** Incense.**—म्रं** Sin, vice, wickedness. -COMP. **—अट** the fork-tailed shrike. **-रुच्** *a.* of a purple hue. **-लोचनः** a pigeon. **-लोहित** *a* dark-red, deep-purple. (**-तः**) an epithet of Siva. **-शूकः** a camel.

धूम्रकः A camel.

धूर्त *a.* **1** Cunning, knavish, rouguish, crafty, fraudulent. **2** Mischievous, injurious. **—र्तः 1** A cheat, rogue, swindler. **2** A gamester. **3** A lover, gallant, gay deceiver; तत्ते धूर्त हृदि स्थिता प्रियतमा काचिन्ममैवापरा Pt. 4. 6; धूर्तोऽपरां चुंबति Amaru. 16; so धूर्तानामभिसारसत्वरहृदां Gît. 11. **4** The thornapple (धत्तूर). -COMP. **-कृत** *a.* crafty, dishonest. (**-m.**) the Dhattûra plant. **-जंतुः** a man. **-रचना** a roguery.

धूर्तकः **1** A jackal. **2** A rogue.

धूर्वी The fore-part or pole of a carriage.

धूलकं Poison.

धूलिः-ली *m. f.* **1** Dust; अनीत्वापंकतां धूलिमुदकं नावतिष्ठते Si. 2. 34. **2** Powder. -COMP. **-कुट्टिमं, केदारः 1** a mound, rampart of earth. **2** a ploughed field. **-ध्वजः** wind. **-पटलः** a cloud of dust. **-पुष्पिका,-पुष्पी** the Ketaka plant.

धूलिका Fog, mist.

धूसर *a.* Of a dusty, greyish, or dusky-white colour, grey; शशी दिवसधूसर Bh. 2. 56; Ku. 4. 4, 46; R. 5. 42; 16. 17; Si. 17. 41.**—रः 1** The grey colour. **2** A donkey. **3** A camel. **4** A pigeon. **5** An oilman.

धृ I. 6 A (Supposed by some to be a passive form of धृ (ध्रियते, धृत) **1** To be or exist, live, continue to live, survive; आर्यपुत्र ध्रिये एषा ध्रिये U. 3; ध्रियते यावदेकोपि रिपुस्तावत्कुतः सुखं Si. 2. 35; 15. 89. **2** To be maintained or preserved, remain, continue; सुरतश्रमसंभृतो मुखे ध्रियते स्वेदलवोद्गमोऽपि ते R. 8. 51; Ku. 4. 18. **3** To resolve upon. -II 1. 10. U. (धरति, usually धारयति-ते, धृत, धारित) **1** To hold, bear, carry; भुजंगमपि कोपितं शिरसि पुष्पवद्धारयेत् Bh. 2. 4; बैणवीं धारयेद्यष्टिं सोदकं च कमंडलुं Ms. 4. 36; Bk. 17. 54; V. 4. 36. **2** To hold or bear up, maintain, support, sustain; धृतमंदर Gît. 1; यथा सर्वाणि भूतानि धरा धारयते समं Ms. 9. 311; Pt. 1. 126; प्रातः—कुंदप्रसवशिथिलं जीवितं धारयेथाः Me. 113; चिरमात्मना धृतां R. 3. 35. **3** To hold in one's possession, possess, have, keep; या संस्कृता धार्यते Bh. **2**. 19. **4** To assume, take (as a form, disguise &c.); केशव धृतशूकररूप Gît 1; धारयति कोकनदरूपं 10. **5** To wear, put on, use (clothes, ornaments &c.); श्रितकमलाकुचमंडल धृतकुंडल ए Gît. 1. **6** To hold in check, curb, restrain, stop, detain. **7** To fix upon, direct towards; (with dat. or loc.); ब्राम्हण्ये धृतमानसः, मनो दध्रे राजसूयाय &c. **8** To suffer, undergo. **9** To assign anything to any person, allot, assign. **10** To owe anything to a person (with dat.; rarely gen. of person, 10 only in this sense); वृक्षसेचने द्वे धारयसि मे *S.* 1; तस्मै-तस्य वा धनं धारयति &c. **11** To hold, contain. **12** To observe, practise. **13** To cite, quote. (The senses of this root may be variously modified according to the noun with which it is connected; *e. g.* मनसा धृ to bear in mind, remember; शिरसा,-मूर्ध्नि धृ to bear on the head, respect highly; अंतरे धृ to pledge, deposit anything as surety; समये धृ to bring to terms or agreement; दंडं धृ to punish, chastise, use force; जीवितं -प्राणान्, -शरीरं-गात्रं,-देहं &c. धृ to continue to live, maintain the soul &c.: preserve the vital spirits; व्रतं धृ to observe a vow; तुलया धृ to hold in a balance, weigh &c. मनः,-मतिं,-चित्तं, -बुद्धिं धृ to bend the mind to a thing, fix the mind upon, think of, resolve upon; गर्भं धृ to become pregnant, conceive; धारणां धृ to practise (concentration or self-control &c). -WITH **अव 1** to fix, determine, settle; *Si* 1. 3. **2** to know, ascertain, understand, know accurately; न विश्वमूर्तेरवधार्यते वपुः Ku. 5. 78; R. 13. 5. **-उद् 1** to lift up, raise. **2** to save, deliver **3** to draw out, extract. **4** to extirpate, root up; (the meaning, of धृ with उद् are the same as those of हृ with उद् q. v.). **-निस्** to determine accurately, settle, fix; निर्धारितेऽर्थे लेखेन खलूक्त्वा खलु वाचिकं Si. **2**. 70, 9. 20 **-वि 1** to seize, catch, catch or take hold of; अंशुकपल्लवेन विधृतः, Amaru 79, 85. **2** to put on, wear, use; R. **12**. 40. **3** to maintain, bear, support hold up; Pt. 1. 82; Bh. 3. 23. **4** to fix upon, direct towards. **-सं 1** to hold, bear, carry. **2** to hold up support, अरैः संधार्यते नाभि Pt. 1. 81. **3** to curb, restrain, check. **4** to keep in the mind, retain in memory **-समुद् 1** to pull up by the roots extirpate; see हृ with उद्. 2 to save, deliver. -सम् 1 to know, determine, ascertain; Si. 9. 60. 2 to reflect, think, consider, ponder over; Ms. 10. 73; एवं संप्रधार्य Pt. 1.

धृत *p. p.* 1 Held, carried, borne, supported. 2 Possessed. 3 Kept, preserved, retained. 4 Seized, grasped, laid hold of. 5 Worn, used. 6 Placed, deposited. 7 Practised, observed. 8 Weighed. 9 (Actively used) Holding, bearing. 10 Intent upon; see धृ above. -COMP. -आत्मन् *a.* firm-minded, steady, calm, collected. -दंड *a.* 1 inflicting punishment. 2 one on whom punishment is inflicted. -पट *a.* covered with a cloth. -राजन् *a.* ruled by a good king (as a country). -राष्ट्रः N. of the eldest son of Vyâsa by a widow of विचित्रवीर्य. [As the eldest son he was entitled to the throne, but being blind from birth, he renounced the sovereingty in favour of P*a*ndu, but on his retirement to the woods, he undertook it himself, making Duryodhana—his eldest son–the virtual ruler. When Duryodhana was killed by Bh*i*ma, the old king thirsted for revenge, and expressed his desire to embarce Yudhish*th*ira and Bh*i*ma. Krish*n*a readily discovered his object, and convinced that Bh*i*ma was marked out by the King as his prey, he caused an iron image of Bh*i*ma to be made. And when the blind king rushed forward to embrace Bh*i*ma, Krish*n*a substituted the iron image which the revengeful old man pressed with so much force that it was crushed to pieces and Bh*i*ma escaped. Thus discomfited, he, with his wife, repaired to the Himalaya and there died after some years]. -वर्मन् *a.* clad in armour, mailed. **धृतिः** *f.* Taking, holding, seizing. 2 Having, possessing, 3 Maintaining, supporting. 4 Firmness; steadiness, constancy. 5 Fortitude, energy, resolution, courage, self-command; भज धृतिं त्यज भीतिमहेतुकां N. 4. 105; Ki. 6. 11; R. 8. 66. 6 Satisfaction, contentment, pleasure, happiness, delight, joy; धृतेश्चधीरः सदृशीर्व्यधत्त सः R. 3. 10; 16. 82; चक्षुर्बध्नाति न धृतिं V. 2. 8; Si. 7. 10, 14. 7 Satisfaction considered as one of the 33 subordinate feelings in Rhetoric; ज्ञानाभीष्टागमाद्यैस्तु संपूर्णस्पृहता धृतिः। सौहित्यवचनोल्लाससहासप्रतिमादिकृत् S. D. 198, 168. 8 A sacrifice.

धृतिमत् *a.* Firm, steady, steadfast, resolute. 2 Satisfied, happy, glad, content; R. 13. 77.

धृत्वन् *m.* 1 An epithet of Vishnu. 2 Of Brahmâ. 3 Virtue, morality. 4 The sky. 5 The sea. 6 A clever man.

धृष् I. 1. P. (धर्षति, धर्षित) 1 To come together, be compact. 2 To hurt or injure. -II. 1 P., 10 U. (धर्षति, धर्षयति-ते) 1 To offend, hurt, injure. 2 To insult, treat with indignity. 3 To assail, overcome, overpower, conquer, destroy. 4 To dare to attack, challenge, defy. 5 To violate or outrage (as a woman). -III. 5. P. (धृष्णोति, धृष्ट) 1 To be bold or courageous. 2 To be confident 3 To be proud or overbearing. 4 To be impudent or impatient. 5 To dare, venture (with inf.) 6 To brave, challenge; Bk. 14. 102 -IV. 10. A. (धर्षयते) To assail, attack, outrage.

धृष्ट *a.* 1 Bold, courageous, confident. 2 Impudent, rude, shameless, saucy, insolent; धृष्टः पार्श्वे वसति H. 2. 26. 3 Forward, presumptuous. 4 Profligate, abandoned. -ष्टः A faithless husband or lover; कृतागा अपि निःशंकस्तर्जितोऽपि न लज्जितः। दृष्टदोषोऽपि मिथ्यावाक् कथितो धृष्टनायकः S. D. 72. -COMP. -द्युम्नः N. of a son of Drupada and brother of Draupadî. [He with his father fought on the side of the P*a*nd*a*vas, and for some days he acted as commander-in-chief of their forces. When Dro*n*a had killed Drupada after a hard struggle, Dh*r*ish*t*adyumna vowed that he would be revenged for the death of his father. And he was able to fulfilt his vow on the morning of the 16th day of the battle, when he unfairly cut off the head of Dro*n*a; (see Dro*n*a). He was afterwards surprised by Asvatthaman while lying asleep in the camp of the P*a*ndavas and was stamped to death.]. -धी *a.* presumptuous. -मानिन् *a.* having too high an opinion of himself, presumptuous.

धृष्णज् *a.* 1 Bold, confident. 2 Impudent, shameless.

धृष्णिः A ray of light.

धृष्णु *a.* Bold, confident, courageous, valiant, powerful (in a good sense). 2 Shameless, impudent.

धे 1 P. (धयति, धीत; *Caus.* धापयति; *desid.* धित्सति) 1 To suck, drink; drink in, absorb (fig. also); अधाद्रसामधासीच्च रुधिरं वनवासिनां Bk. 15. 29, 6. 18; Ms. 4. 59; Y. 1. 140. 2 To kiss; धन्यो धयत्याननं Gît. 12. 3 To suck out, draw or take away.

धेनः 1 The ocean. 2 A male river (नद).

धेनुः *f* 1 A cow, milch-cow; धेनुं धीराः सूनृतां वाचमाहुः U. 5. 31. 2 The female of a species (affixed to the names of other animals in this sense); as खड्गधेनुः, वडवधेनुः &c. 3 The earth. (Sometimes at the end of comp. धेनु forms a diminutive; as असिधेनुः, खड्धेनुः).

धेनुकः N. of a demon killed by Balarâma. -COMP. -सूदनः an epithet of Balarâm.

धेनुका 1 A female elephant. 2 A milch-cow.

धेनुष्या A cow who or whose milk has been pledged.

धैनुकं 1 A herd of cows. 2 particular mode of sexual enjoyment (रतिबंध).

धैर्यं 1 Firmness, durability, strength, constancy, steadiness, stability, fortitude, courage; धैर्यमवष्टभ्य Pt. 1; विपदि धैर्यं Bh. 2. 63; so धैर्यवृत्ति Si. 9. 59. 2 Calmness, composure. 3 Gravity, patience. 4 Inflexibility. 5 Boldness, forwardness; Me. 40 (धाष्ट्र्यं Malli.).

धैवतः The sixth of the seven primary notes of the Indian gamut.

धैवत्यं Cleverness.

धोडः = डुंडुभ q. v.

धोर् 1 P. (धोरति) To go quickly, have good paces, run, trot. 2 To be skilful (in general). **धोरणं** 1 A vehicle in general (as a horse, elephant &c.). 2 Going well or quickly. 3 A horse's trot.

धोरणिः. -णी *f.* 1 An uninterrupted series or continuity; यैर्माकंदवने मनोज्ञपवने सद्यः स्खलन्माधुरीधाराधोरणिधौतधामनि धराधीशत्वमालंब्यते। तेषां नित्यविनोदिनां सुकृतिनां माध्वीकपानां पुनः कालः किं न करोति केतकि यतस्त्वं चापि केलीस्थली॥ Udb. 2 Tradition.

धोरितं 1 Injuring, hurting, striking. 2 Going, motion. 3 A horse's trot.

धौत *p. p.* 1 Washed, washed off, cleaned, purified, laved; कुल्यांभोभिः पवनचपलैः शाखिनो धौतमूलाः *S*. 1. 15; *S*ik. 58. Ru. 1. 6, 6. 57; R. 16. 49; 19. 10. 2 Polished, brightened. 3 Bright, white, shining, brightened, glistening; हरशिरश्चंद्रिकाधौतहर्म्या Me. 7, 44; विकसद्दंतांशुधौताधरं Gît. 12. -तं Silver. -COMP. -कटः a bag of coarse cloth. -कोषजं, -कौषेयं bleached or purified silk. -शिलं rock-crystal.

धौम्रः 1 Greyness. 2 A place for building (prepared in a particular way).

धौरितकं A horse's trot; cf. धोरित.

धौरेय (यी *f.*) Fit for a burden. -यः 1 A beast of burden. 2 A horse.

धौर्तकं, धौर्तिकं, धौर्त्यं Fraud, dishonesty, roguery.

ध्मा 1. P. (धमति, ध्मात, *caus.* ध्मापयति) 1 To blow, breathe out, exhale. 2 To blow, (as a wind instrument), produce sound by blowing; शंखं दध्मौ प्रतापवान् Bg. 1. 12, 18; R. 7. 63; Bk. 3. 34; 17. 7. 3 To blow a fire, excite fire by blowing, excite sparks; को धमेच्छांतं च पावकं Mb. 4 To manufacture by blowing. 5 To cast, blow, or throw away. -WITH आ 1 to inflate, puff up. 2 to blow or fill with wind (as a conch &c.) -उप to excite by blowing, fan; नाग्निं मुखेनोपधमेत् Ms. 4. 53. -निस् to blow out of something. -प्र to blow (as a conch &c.); शंखौ प्रदध्मतुः Bg. 1. 14. -वि to scatter, disperse, destroy.

ध्माकारः A black-smith, smith.

ध्मांक्षः v. l. for ध्वांक्ष q. v.

ध्मात *p. p.* **1** Blown (as a wind instrument). **2** Blown up or into, inflamed, blown, fanned, excited. **3** Inflated, puffed, puffed up.

ध्मापित *a.* Reduced to ashes, burnt to cinder.

ध्यात *a.* Thought of, meditated upon; see ध्यै.

ध्यानं **1** Meditation, reflection, thought, contemplation; ज्ञानाद् ध्यानं विशिष्यते Bg. 12. 12; Ms. 1. 12, 6 72. **2** Especially abstract contemplation, religious meditation; तदैव ध्यानाद्रवगतोऽस्मि *S.* 7; R. 1. 73. **3** Divine intuition or discernment. **4** Mental representation of the personal attributes of a deity; इति ध्यानं. -Comp. -गम्य *a.* attainable by meditation only. -तत्पर, -निष्ठ,-पर *a.* lost in thought, absorbed in meditation, contemplative. -मात्रं mere thought or reflection. -योगः profound meditation. -स्थ *a.* absorbed in meditation, lost in thought.

ध्यानिक *a.* Sought or obtained by pious contemplation or abstract meditation.

ध्याम *a.* Unclean, dirty, black, soiled; Bk. 8. 71. —मं A kind of grass.

ध्यामन् *m.* **1** Measure. **2** Light —*n.* Meditation (less correctly ध्मामन्).

ध्यै 1 P. (ध्यायति, ध्यात; *desid* दिध्यासति; *pass.* ध्यायते) To think of, meditate upon, ponder over, contemplate, reflect upon, imagine, call to mind; ध्यायतो विषयान् पुंसः संगस्तेषूपजायते Bg. 2. 63; न ध्यातं पदमीश्वरस्य Bh. 3. 11; पितॄन् ध्यायन् Ms. 3. 224; ध्यायंति चान्यं धिया Pt. 1. 136; Mo. 3; Ms. 5. 47, 9. 21. -With अनु **1** to think of, muse. **2** to remember. **3** to wish well to, bless, favour; R. 14. 60; 17. 36. -अप to think ill of, curse mentally. -अभि **1** to wish, desire, covet; Y. 3. 134. **2** to think of. -अव to disregard. -वि **1** to think of, meditate upon, remember; Bk. 14. 65. **2** to meditate deeply upon, look steadfastly or intently at; अंगुलीयकं निध्यायंती **M. 1**; *Si.* 8. 69; 12 4; Ki. 10. 46. -निस् to think of, meditate upon.

ध्राडिः Gathering flowers.

ध्रुव *a.* **1** (*a.*) Fixed, firm, immoveable, stable, permanent, constant, unchangeable; इति ध्रुवेच्छामनुशासती सुतां Ku. 5. 5. (*b*) Perpetual, everlasting, eternal; ध्रुवेण भर्त्रा Ku. 7. 85; Ms. 7. 208. **2** Fixed (in astrology). **3** Certain, sure, inevitable; जातस्य हि ध्रुवो मृत्युर्ध्रुवं जन्म मृतस्य च Bg. 2. 27; यो ध्रुवाणि परित्यज्य अध्रुवाणि निषेवते Chân. 63. **4** Retentive, tenacious; as in ध्रुवा स्मृति **5** Strong, fixed, settled (as a day). -वः **1** The polar star; R. 17. 35; 18. 34; Ku. 7. 85. **2** The pole of any great circle. **3** The distance of a planet from the beginning of the sidereal zodiac, polar longitude. **4** The Indian fig tree. **5** A post, stake. **6** The stem or trunk (of a tree lopped off). **7** The introductory stanza of a song (repeated as a kind of chorus; see Gît.). **8** Time, epoch, era. **9** An epithet of Brahmâ. **10** Of Vishṇu. **11** Of *S*iva. **12** N. of the son of Uttânapâda and grandson of Manu. [Dhruva is the polar star, but personified in mythology as the son of Utt*a*n*a*p*a*da. The account of the elevation of an ordinary mortal to the position of the Polar star runs thus. Utt*a*nap*a*da had two wives, Suru*c*hi and Sun*i*ti, but the latter was disliked by him. Suruchi had a son named Uttama and Sun*i*ty gave birth to Dhruva. One day the boy tried, like his elder brother, to take a seat in his father's lap, but he was contemptuously treated both by the King and his favourite wife. The poor child went sobbing to its mother who told him in consolatory terms that fortune and favour were not attainable without hard exertions. At these words the youth left the paternal roof, retired to the woods, and, though quite a lad, performed such rigorous austerities that he was at last raised by Vish*n*u to the position of the Polar star]. —वं **1** The sky, atmosphere. **2** Heaven. -वा A sacrificial ladle (made of wood). **2** A virtuous woman. -वं *ind.* Certainly, surely, verily; R. 8. 49; S. 1. 18. -Comp -अक्षर: an epithet of Vishṇu. -आवर्तः the point on the crowd of the head from which the hair radiate. -तारा, -तारकं the Polar star.

-ध्रुवकः **1** The introductory stanza of a song (repeated as a sort of chorus); see ध्रुव. **2** A trunk, stem. **3** A post.

ध्रौव्यं **1** Fixedness, firmness, stability. **2** Duration. **3** Certainty.

ध्वंस् 1 A. (ध्वंसते, ध्वस्त) **1** To fall down, fall to pieces, be reduced to dust or powder; Bk. 15. 93; 14. 55. **2** To drop, sink, despond; Mâl. 9. 44. **3** To perish, be ruined or decayed. **4** To be eclipsed; Mu. 3. 8. -*Caus.* To destroy. -With प्र to perish, be destroyed. -वि **1** to fall to pieces **2** to be dispersed or scattered. **3** to perish, be destroyed, be ruined.

ध्वंसः, ध्वंसनं **1** Falling down, sinking, falling to pieces. **2** Loss, destruction, ruin. —सी A mote in the sun-beam.

ध्वंसिः The hundredth part of a Muhûrta.

ध्वजः **1** A flag, banner, standard, ensign; R. 7. 40; 17. 32; P. 1. 26. **2** A distinguished or eminent person, the flag or ornament (at the end of comp.); as in कुलध्वजः the head, ornament, or distinguished person of a family. **3** A flag-staff. **4** A mark, emblem, sign, a symbol; वृषभ°, मकर° &c. **5** The attribute of a deity. **6** The sign of a tavern. **7** The sign of a trade, any trademark. **8** The organ of generation, (of any animal, male or female). **9** One who prepares and sells liquors. **10** A house situated to the east of any object. **11** Pride. **12** Hypocrisy. (ध्वजीकृ to hoist a flag; fig. to use as a plea or pretext). -Comp. -अंशुकं, -पटः, -टं a flag; R. 12. 85. -आहृत *a.* seized on the battle-field. गृहं a room in which banners are kept. -द्रुमः the palm tree. -प्रहरणः air, wind. -यंत्रं any contrivance to which a flagstaff is fastened. -यष्टिः *f.* a flagstaff; Ms. 9. 285.

ध्वजवत् *a.* **1** Adorned with flags. **2** Having a mark. **3** Having the mark of a criminal, branded. —*m.* **1** A standard-bearer. **2** A vendor of spirituous liquors, distiller.

ध्वजिन् *a.* (नी *f.*) **1** Bearing or carrying a flag. **2** Having as a mark. **3** Having the mark of a liquor-vessel (सुराभाजनचिह्न); Ms. 11. 93. -*m.* **1** A standard bearer. **2** A distiller or vendor of spirituous liquors; Y. 1. 141. **3** A car, carriage, chariot. **4** A mountain. **5** A snake. **6** A peacock **7** A horse. **8** A Brâhmaṇa. -नी An army; R. 7. 40; *Si.* 12 66; Ki. 13. 9.

ध्वजीकरणं **1** Raising a standard, hoisting a flag. **2** Setting up as a pretext or claim, making anything a plea.

ध्वन् 1 P. (ध्वनति, ध्वनित) To sound, produce or utter sound, buzz, hum, echo, reverberate, thunder, roar; बिभियमाना इव दध्वनुर्दिशः Ki. 14. 46; अयं धीरं धीरं ध्वनति नवनीलो जलधरः Bv. 1. 60; कपिर्दध्वान मेघवत् Bk. 9. 5; 14. 3; ध्वनति मधुपसमूहे श्रवणमपिदधाति Gît. 5. -*Caus.* (ध्वनयति) To cause to sound, ring (as a bell); but ध्वानयति 'to cause to articulate indistinctly.'

ध्वनः **1** Sound, tune. **2** Hum, buzz.

ध्वननं **1** Sounding. **2** Hinting at, suggesting or implying (as a meaning). **3** (In Rhet.) The same as व्यंजना q. v., or that power of a word or sentence by virtue of which it conveys a sense different from its primary or secondary meaning, suggestive power; cf, अंजन also.

ध्वनिः 1 Sound, echo, noise in general; मृदंगधीरध्वानिमन्वगच्छत् R. 16. 13; 2. 72; U. 6. 17. 2 Tune, note, tone; Si. 6. 48. The sound of a musical instrument; R. 9. 71. 4 The roar or thunder of a cloud. 5 A mere empty sound. 6 A word. 7 (In Rhet.) The first and best of the three main divisions of काव्य or poetry, in which the implied or *suggested* sense of a passage is more striking than the *expressed* sense; or where the *expressed* sense is made subordinate to the *suggested* sense; इदमुत्तममतिशयिनि व्यंग्ये वाच्याद्ध्वनिर्बुधैः कथितः K. P. 1 (R. G. gives 5 kind of ध्वनि; see under ध्वनि) COMP.–ग्रहः 1 the ear. 2 hearign. 3 the sense of hearing. –नाला 1 a sort of trumpet. 2 a lute. 3 a fife, pipe. विकारः a change of voice caused by fear, grief &c.; see काकु.

ध्वनित *p. p.* 1 Sounded. 2 Implied, suggested, hinted at. —तं 1 A sound 2 The roar or thunder of a cloud; Ki. 5. 12.

ध्वस्तिः *f.* Destruction, ruin.

ध्वांक्षः 1 A crow. (Sometimes) used at the end of comp. to show contempt; *e. g.* तीर्थध्वांक्षः q. v.). 2 A beggar. 3 An impudent fellow. 4 A gull, crane. –COMP. –अरातिः an owl. –पुष्टः the (Indian) cuckoo.

ध्वानः 1 Sound (in general). 2 Buzzing, humming, murmuring.

ध्वांतं Darkness; ध्वांतं नीलनिचोलचारु सुदृशां प्रत्यंगमालिंगति Gît. 11; N. 19. 42; Si. 4. 62. –COMP. उन्मेषः,–वित्तः a fire-fly.–शात्रवः 1 the sun. 2 the moon. 3 fire. 4 the white colour.

ध्वृ 1 P. (ध्वरति) 1 To bend. 2 To kill.

न.

न *a.* 1 Thin, spare. 2 Vacant, empty. 3 Same, identical 4 Undivided.—नः 1 A pearl. 2 N. of Ganesa. 3 Wealth, prosperity. 4 A band. 5 War. —*ind.* (*a*) A particle of negation equivalent to 'not,' 'no,' 'nor,' 'neither' and used in wishing, requesting, or commanding, but not in prohibition before the imperative mood. (*b*) Used with the potential mood न may sometimes have the force of 'lest,' 'for fear lest,' 'that not;, क्षत्रियैर्धार्यते शस्त्रं नार्तशब्दो भवेदिति Ram. (*c*) In argumentative writings न often comes after इति चेत् and means 'not so'. (*d*) When a negative has to be repeated in successive clauses of the same sentence or in different sentences, न may be simply repeated or may be used with particles like उत, च, अपि, चापि, वा &c. नाधीयीताश्वमारूढो न वृक्षं न च हस्तिनं । न नावं न खरं नोष्ट्रं नेरिणस्थो न यानगः ॥ Ms. 4. 120; प्रविशंतं न मां कश्चिदपश्यन्नाप्यवारयत् Mb.; Ms. 2. 195; 3. 8, 9; 4. 15; S. 6. 17. Sometimes न may not be expressed in the second and other clauses, but represented only by च, वा, अपिवा; संपदि यस्य न हर्षो विपदि विषादो रणे च धीरत्वं H. 1. 33. (*e*) न is frequently joined with a second न or any other negative particle to intensify or emphasize an assertion; प्रत्युवाच तमृषिर्न तस्वतस्त्वां न वेद्मि पुरुषं पुरातनं R. 11. 85; न च न परिचितो न चाप्यगम्यः M. 1. 11; न पुनरलंकारश्रियं न पुष्यति S. 1; नादंडयो नाम राज्ञोऽस्ति Ms. 8. 335; Me. 63. 106; नासौ न काम्यो न च वेदसम्यग् द्रष्टुं न सा R. 6. 30. Si 1. 55; V. 2. 10. (*f.*) In a few cases न is retained at the beginning of a negative Tatpurusha compound; as नाक, नासत्य, नकुल; see P. VI. 3. 75. (*g*) न is often joined with other particles; नच, नवा, नैव, ननु, नचेद्, नखलु &c. &c.–COMP. असत्यौ (*m. du.*) Asvins, the twin physicians of the gods. –एक *a.* 'not one,' more than one, several, various. °आत्मन् *a.* of manifold or diverse nature. °चर *a.* 'not living,' gregarious, living in society, °भेद, °रूप *a.* various, multiform. °शस् *ind.* repeatedly, often. –किंचन *a.* very poor, beggarly.

नकुटं The nose.

नकुलः 1 The mungoose, an ichneumon; यद्वयं नकुलद्वेषी सकुलद्वेषी पुनः पिशुनः Vâs. 2 N. of the fourth Pândava prince; अहं तस्य अतिशयितदिव्यरूपिणो नकुलस्य दर्शनेनोत्सुका जाता Ve. 2 (where नकुल has really sense, 1 but is taken in sense 2 by Duryodhana).

नक्तं 1 Night. 2 Eating only at night, as a sort of religious vow or penance. –COMP. अंध *a.* blind at night. –चर्या wandering at night. –चारिन् *m.* 1 an owl. 2 a cat. 3 a thief. 4 a demon, goblin, evil spirit. –भोजनं supper. –मालः N. of a tree; R. 5. 42.–मुखा evening.–व्रतं 1 fasting by day and eating at night. 2 any penance or religious rite observed at night.

नक्तं *ind.* At night, by night; गच्छंतीनां रमणवसतिं योषितां तत्र नक्तं Me. 37; Ms. 6. 19. –COMP. –चरः 1 any animal that goes about at night. 2 a thief. –चारिन् *m.* =नक्तचारिन् q. v. –दिनं night and day.–दिनं-दिवं *ind.* at night and day.

नक्तकः Dirty or ragged cloth (कर्पट).

नक्रः A crocodile, an alligator; नक्रः स्वस्थानमासाद्य गजेंद्रमपि कर्षति Pt. 3. 46; R. 7. 30; 16. 55. —क्रं 1 The upper timber of a door. 2 The nose.—क्रा 1 The nose. 2 A swarm of bees or wasps.

नक्षत्रं 1 A star in general. 2 A constellation, an asterism in the moon's path, lunar mansion नक्षत्रताराग्रहसंकुलाऽपि R. 6. 22; (they are seventy -seven. 3 A pearl. –COMP. –ईशः,–ईश्वरः, –नाथः, –पः, –पतिः, –राजः the moon; R. 6. 66. –चक्रं 1 the sphere of the fixed stars. 2 the lunar asterisms taken collectively. —दर्शः an astronomer or astrologer.–नेमिः 1 the moon. 2 the pole-star. 3 an epithet of Vishnu. (–मिः *f.*) Revatî, the last asterism, –पथः the starry sky. –पाठकः an astrologer. –माला 1 a group of stars. 2 a necklace of twenty-seven pearls. 3 the table of the asterisms in the moon's path. 4 a kind of neck-ornament of elephants; अनंगवारणशिरोनक्षत्रमालायमानेन मेखलादाम्ना K. 11.–योगः the conjunction of the moon with the lunar mansion.–वर्त्मन् *m.* the sky.–विद्या astronomy or astrology. –वृष्टिः *f.* shooting or falling stars. –सूचकः a bad astrologer; तिथ्युत्पत्तिं न जानंति ग्रहाणां नव साधनं । परवाक्येन वर्तंते ते वै नक्षत्रसूचकाः ॥ or अविदित्वैव यः शास्त्रं दैवज्ञत्वं प्रपद्यते । स पंक्तिदूषकः पापो ज्ञेयो नक्षत्रसूचकः ॥ Bri. S. 2. 17. 18.

नक्षत्रिन् *m.* 1 The moon. 2 An pithet of Vishnu.

नखः–**खं** 1 A nail of a finger or of a toe, claw, talon; नखानां पांडित्यं प्रकटयतु करिमन्मृगपतिः Bv. 1. 2. 31; 12. 12. 2 The number 'twenty'. –खः A part, portion.–COMP.–अंकः a scratch, nail-mark; Bv. 2. 32. –आघातः a scratch, nail-wound; Mâl. 5. 23. –आयुधः 1 a tiger. 2 a lion. 3 a cock. –आशिन् *m.* an owl. –कुट्टः a barber.–जाहं the root of a nail.–दारणः a falcon, hawk. (–णं) a pair of a nail-scissors, –निकृंतनं, –रंजनी a pair of nail-scissors, nail-parer. –पदं, –व्रणः a nail-mark, or scratch; नखपदसुखान् प्राप्य वर्षाग्रबिंदून् Me. 35. –मुचः a bow. –लेखा 1 a nail-mark. 2 nail-painting. –विष्किरः a bird of prey (tearing with claws). –शंखः a small shell.

नखंपच *a.* Nail-scorching; *Si.* 9. 85.

नखरः **-रं** A finger-nail, claw, talon. Bv. 1. 52. -COMP. **-आयुधः** 1 a tiger. 2 a lion 3 a cock. **-आह्वः** fragrant oleander (करवीर).

नखानखि *ind*. Nail against nail.

नखिन् *a*. 1 Having or armed with nails, claws &c. 2 Thorny. *-m*. Any animal armed with claws, such as a tiger or lion.

नगः 1 A mountain; Ku. 1. 1 7. 72; *S*i. 6. 79. 2 A tree. 3 A plant in general. 4 The sun. 5 A serpent. 6 The number 'seven'. -COMP. **-अटनः** a monkey. **-अधिपः, -अधिराजः, -इंद्रः** 1 Himâlaya (the lord of mountains) 2 the Sumeru mountain **-अरि**: an epithet of Indra. **-उच्छ्रायः** the height of a mountain. **-ओकस्** *m*. 1 a bird (in general). 2 a crow. 3 a lion. 4 the fabulous animal called शरभ. **-ज** *a*. produced in a mountain, mountain-born; Bk. 19. (**-जः**) an elephant. **-जा, -नंदिनी** epithet of Pârvatî. **-पतिः** 1 the Himâlaya mountain. 2 the moon (as the lord of plants and herbs). **-भिद्** *m*. 1 an axe. 2 an epithet of Indra. **-मूर्धन्** *m*. the crest or brow of a mountain. **-रंध्रकरः** an epithet of Kârtikeya; R. 9. 2.

नगरं A town, city (opp. ग्राम); नगरगमनाय मतिं न करोति *S*. 2. COMP. **-अधिकृतः, -अधिपः, -अध्यक्षः** the chief magistrate of a town, head police-officer. 2 governor or superintendent of a town. **-उपांतः** a suburb, the skrit of a town. **-ओकस्** *m*. a townsman. **-काकः** ' a town-crow ', an expression of contempt. **-घातः** an elephant. **-जनः** 1 a townsfolk. 2 a citizen. **-प्रदक्षिणा** carrying an idol round a city in procession. **-प्रांतः** a suburb. **-मार्गः** a principal road, high-way. **-रक्षा** superitendence or government of a town. **-स्थः** a townsman, citizen.

नगरी=नगर. q. v. -COMP. **-काकः** the (India) crane. **-बकः** a crow.

नग्न *a*. 1 Naked, nude, bare; न नग्नः स्नानमाचरेत् Ms. 4. 45; नग्नक्षपणके देशे रजकः किं करिष्यति Châṇ. 110. 2 Uncultivated, uninhabited, desolate. **-ग्नः** A naked mendicant. 2 A Buddhist mendicant (क्षपणक). 3 A hypocrite. 4 A bard accompanying an army, or a wandering bard. **-ग्ना** 1 A naked, shameless (or wanton) woman. 2 A girl before menstruation, or less than 12 or 10 (and therefore may go about naked). -COMP. **-अटः** **-अटकः** 1 one who goes about naked. 2 epecially, a Jaina or Buddhist mendicant (of the दिगंबर class).

नग्नक *a*. (**ग्निका** *f*.) Naked, nude. **-कः** 1 A naked mendicant. 2 A Jaina or Buddhist mendicant (of the दिगंबर class). 3 A bard.

नग्नका,-नग्निका 1 A naked, shameless (or wanton) woman. 2 A girl before menstruation.

नग्नंकरणं Making naked.

नग्नंभविष्णु,-भावुक *a*. Becoming naked.

नंगः A lover, paramour.

नचिकेतस् *m*. An epithet of Agni.

नचिर *a*. see अचिर; Bg. 5. 6. 12. 7.

नञ् *ind*. The technical term for the negative particle न.

नट I. 1 P. (नटति, the न not changed to ण after प्र in the sense of ' hurting ') 1 To dance; यदि मनसा नटनीयं Gît. 4. 2 To act. 3 To injure (by a deceptive trick). —*Caus*. (नाटयति-ते) 1 To act, gesticulate, represent dramatically (in dramas); शरसंधानं नाटयति *S*. 1. &c. 2 To imitate, copy; स्फटिककटकभूमिर्नाटयत्येष शैलः ...अधिगतधवलिम्नः शूलपाणेरभिख्यां *S*. 4. 65. (Note. नट forms नटयति in the sense of ' causing to dance'; Bh. 3. 126). -II. 10 U. (नाटयति-ते) 1 To drop or fall. 2 To shine. 3 To injure.

नटः 1 A dancer ; न नटा न विटा न गायकाः Bh. 3. 27. 2 An actor; कुर्वन्नयं प्रहसनस्य नटः कृतोऽस्मि Bh. 3. 126, 112. 3 The son of a degraded Kshatriya. 4 The Asoka tree. 5 A kind of reed. -COMP. **-अंतिका** shame, modesty. **-ईश्वरः** an epithet of *S*iva. **-चर्या** the performance of an actor. **-भूषणः, मंडनः** (yellow) orpiment. **-रंगः** a theatrical stage. **-वरः** ' the chief actor ', the Sûtradhâra of a drama. **-संज्ञकं** yellow orpiment. (**-कः**) an actor, dancer.

नटनं 1 Dancing, dance. 2 Acting, gesticulation, dramatic representation.

नटी 1 An actress. 2 The chief actress (regarded as the wife of the Sûtradhâra). 3 A courtezan, harlot. -COMP. **-सुतः** the son of a dancing girl.

नट्या A company of actors.

नडः-डं A species of reed. -COMP. **-अगारं,-आगारं** a hut of reeds. **-प्राय** *a*. abounding in reeds. **-वनं** a thicket of reeds. **-संहतिः** *f*. a collection or quantity of reeds.

नडश *a*. (**शी** *f*.) Covered with reeds.

नडिनी 1 A quantity of reeds. 2 A reed-bed, a river abounding in reeds.

नडिल *a*. **नड्वत्** *a*. (**ती** *f*.) Abounding in or covered with reeds, reedy.

नड्या A quantity of reeds.

नड्वल *a*. Abounding in reeds. **-लं** A quantity or a bed of reeds; यो नड्वलानीव गजः परेषां बलान्यमृद्नान्नलिनाभवक्त्रः R. 18. 5.

नत *p. p*. 1 Bent, bowed, stooping, inclined. 2 Sunk, depressed. 3 Crooked, curved. **—तं** The distance of any planet from the meridian. -COMP. **-अंशः** zenith-distance. **-अंग** *a*. 1 bending the body. 2 stooping, bowed. (**-गी**) 1 a woman with stooping limbs. 2 a woman in general. **-नासिक** *a*. flat-nosed. **-भ्रूः** a woman with curved eye-brows.

नतिः *f*. 1. Bending, stooping, bowing. 2 Curvature, crookedness. 3 Bending the body in salutation, a bow, courtesy. 4 Parallax in latitude (in astronomy).

नद् 1 P. (नदति, नदित) 1 To sound, resound, thunder (as a cloud); वामश्चायं नदति मधुरं चातकस्ते सगंधः Me. 9; नदत्याकाशगंगायाः स्रोतस्युद्दामदिग्गजे R. 1. 78; *S*i. 5. 63; Bk. 2. 4. 2 To speak, shout, cry, roar, (often with words like शब्द, स्वन, नाद &c. as object); ननाद बलवन्नादं, शब्दं घोरतरं नदंति Mb. 3 To vibrate. —*Caus*. (नादयति-ते) 1 To fill with noise, make noisy or resonant. 2 To cause to make a sound. -WITH **उद्** to roar, cry (loudly), bellow (as a bull); Ku. 1. 56. **-नि** to sound, shout; R. 5. 75; M. 5. 10; Bk. 6. 117. **-प्र** (प्रणदति) to sound, resound, echo; क्रव्यादाः प्राणदन् घोराः Mb.; शिवाः प्रणदंति &c. **-प्रति** to resound, echo. (*-Caus*.) to fill with noise, make resonant; *S*ânti. 2. 16; Rs. 3. 14. **-वि** to sound, resound; Bg. 1. 12. (*-Caus*.) 1 to cause to cry or utter notes; अंबुदैः शिखिगणो विनाद्यते Ghaṭ. 10.

नदः 1 A river, great river (such as the Indus); *S*i. 66 (where Malli. remarks :—प्राक्स्रोतसो नद्यः प्रत्यक्स्रोतसो नदा नर्मदां विनेत्याहुः). 2 A stream, flowing stream, rivulet; Ki. 5. 27. 3 The ocean. -COMP. **-राजः** the ocean.

नदथुः 1 Noise, roaring. 2 The roaring of a bull.

नदी A river, any flowing stream; रविपीतजला तपात्यये पुनरोघेन हि युज्यते नदी Ku. 4. 44. -COMP. **-इनः,-ईशः,-कांतः** the ocean. **-कुलप्रियः** a kind of reed. **-ज** *a*. aquatic. (**-जः**) an epithet of Bhîshma (**-जं**) a lotus. **-तरस्थानं** a landing-place, ferry. **-दोहः** freight, river-toll, fare. **-धरः** an epithet of *S*iva. **-पतिः** 1 the ocean. 2 an epithet of Varuna. **-पूरः** a river which has overflown its banks. **-भवं** river-salt. **-मातृक** *a*. watered by rivers, irrigated, supplied with the water of rivers, canals &c. (as a country &c.); N. 3. 38; cf. देवमातृक. **-रयः** the current of a river. **-वंकः** the bend or arm of a river. **ष्णः** (**स्नः**) 1 bathing in rivers. 2 knowing the dangerous spots in rivers, their depth, course &c.; ततः समाज्ञापयदाशु सर्वानानायि-

नस्तद्विचये नदीष्णान् R. 16. 75; (hence) **3** experienced, clever. **-सर्जः** the Arjuna tree.

नद्ध *p. p.* **1** Tied, bound, fastened, bound round, put on. **2** Covered, inlaid, interwoven. **3** Joined, connected; see नह्. **-द्धं** A tie, band, bond, knot.

नद्ध्री A leather-strap.

ननंदृ, ननांदृ A husband's sister; ननांदुः पत्या च देव्याः संदिष्टमृष्यशृंगेण U. 1. Comp. **-ननांदृपतिः** (also **ननांदुःपतिः**) the husband of a husband's sister.

ननु *ind.* (Originally a combination of न and नु, now used as a separate word) A particle implying:—**1** Inquiry or interrogation; ननु समाप्तकृत्यो गौतमः M. 4. **2** Surely, certainly, indeed, is it not indeed (with an interrogative force); यदाऽमेधाविनी शिष्योपदेशं मलिनयति तदाचार्यस्य दोषो ननु M. 1. **3** Of course, indeed, certainly (अवधारण); उपपन्नं ननु शिवं सप्तस्वंगेषु R. 1. 60; त्रिलोकनाथेन सदा मखद्विषस्त्वया नियम्या ननु दिव्यचक्षुषा 3. 45. **4** It is used as a vocative particle meaning 'O', 'Oh'; ननु मानव Dk.; ननु मूर्खाः पठितमेव युष्माभिस्तत्कांडे U. 4. **5** It is used in propitiatory expressions in the sense of 'pray', 'be pleased'; ननु मां प्रापय प्रत्युरंतिकं Ku. 4. 32. **6** It is sometimes used as a corrective word like the English 'why' or 'I say'; ननु पदे परिवृत्य भण Mk. 5; ननु भवानग्रतो मे वर्तते *S.* 2; ननु विचिनोतु भवान् V. 2. **7** In argumentative discussions ननु is frequently used to head an objection or advance a contrary proposition (generally followed by उच्यते); नन्वचेतनान्येव वृश्चिकादिशरीराणि अचेतनानां च गोमयादीनां कार्याणीति उच्यते S. B.

नंद् 1 P. (नंदति, नंदित) To be glad, be pleased, delighted or satisfied, rejoice at (anything); ननंदतुस्तत्सदृशेन तत्समौ R. 3. 23, 11; 2. 22; 4. 3; Bk. 15. 28. *-Caus.* (नंदयति ते) To please, delight, gladden, make happy; अंतर्हिते शशिनि सैव कुमुद्वती मे दृष्टिं न नंदयति संस्मरणीयशोभा *S.* 4. 2; Bk. 2. 16; R. 9. 52. -With **अभि 1** to rejoice at, be glad or satisfied; आत्मविडंबनामभिनंदंति K. 108; नाभिनंदति न द्वेष्टि Bg. 2. 57. **2** to congratulate, hail with joy, welcome, greet; तापसीभिरभिनंद्यमाना तिष्ठति *S.* 4; तमभ्यनंदत्प्रथमं प्रबोधितः R. 3. 68; 2. 74; 7. 69; 11. 30; 16. 64. **3** To praise, applaud, commend, approve of; नाम यस्याभिनंदंति द्विषोपि स पुमान् पुमान् Ki. 11. 73; *S.* 3. 24; R. 12. 35; न ते वचोऽभिनंदामि *S.* 2. **4** to wish or desire for, like, care for (usually with न) नाभिनंदति केलिकलाः Mâl. 3; नाभिनंदेत मरणं नाभिनंदेत जीवितं Ms. 6. 45; H. 4. 4. **-आ** to be glad, be pleased or delighted; आनंदितारस्त्वां दृष्ट्वा Bk. 22. 14. (*-Caus.*) to gladden, delight, please; U. 3. 14; Y. 1. 356. **-प्रति 1** to bless; R. 1. 57, Ms. 7. 146; Ku. 7. 87. **2** to welcome, congratulate, hail with joy, receive gladly; प्रतिनंद्य स तां पूजां Mb. Ms. 2. 54.

नंदः 1 Happiness, pleasure, joy. **2** A kind of lute (11 inches long). **3** A frog. **4** N. of Vishṇu. **5** N. of a cowherd, husband of Yaśodâ and foster-father of Kṛishṇa (to whose care the child was committed when Kaṁsa wanted to destroy it). **6** N. of the founder of the Nanda dynasty; or of nine brother kings of Pâṭaliputra killed by the machinations of Châṇakya, the minister of Chandragupta; समुत्खाता नंदा नव हृदयरोगा इव भुवः Mu. 1. 13; अगृहीते राक्षसे किमुत्खातं नंदवंशस्य Mu. 1, 3. 27, 28. -Comp. **-आत्मजः, -नंदनः** an epithet of Krishṇa. **-पालः** an epithet of Varuṇa.

नंदक *a.* **1** Rejoicing, making happy, gladdening. **2** Delighting or rejoicing in. **3** Gladdening a family. **-कः 1** A frog. **2** N. of the sword of Krishṇa. **3** A sword in general. **4** Happiness.

नंदकिन् *m.* An epithet of Vishṇu.

नंदथुः Happiness, pleasure, delight.

नंदन *a.* Delighting, pleasing, gladdening. **-नः 1** A son; Y. 1. 274; R. 3. 41. **2** A frog. **3** An epithet of Vishṇu. **4** N. of *S*iva. **-नं** N. of the garden of Indra, the elysium; अभिज्ञाश्छेदपातानां क्रियंते नंदनद्रुमाः Ku. 2. 41; R. 8. 95. **2** Rejoicing, being glad. **3** Joy. -Comp. **-जं** yellow sandal-wood. (हरिचंदन).

नदंतः, नंदयंतः A son.

नंदा 1 Delight, joy, happiness. **2** Affluence, wealth, prosperity. A **3** A small earthen water-jar. **4** A husband's sister. **5** The first, sixth and eleventh days of a lunar fortnight (considered as auspicious *tithis.*)

नंदिः *m. f.* Joy, pleasure, delight; कौशल्यानंदिवर्धनः, **-दिः** *m.* **1** An epithet of Vishṇu. **2** of *S*iva. **3** N. of an attendant of *S*iva. **4** Gambling, gaming (*n* also in this sense).-Comp. **ईशः, ईश्वरः 1** an epithet of *S*iva. **2** N. of one of the chief attendants of *S*iva. **-ग्रामः** N. of a village where Bharata lived during Râma's banishment; R. 12. 18.**-घोषः** N. of the chariot of Arjuna. **-वर्धनः 1** an epithet of *S*iva. a friend. **2** the end of a lunar fortnight, *i. e.* the day of new or full moon.

नंदिकः 1 Joy, pleasure. **2** A small water-jar. **3** An attendant of *S*iva. -Comp. **-ईशः -ईश्वरः 1** N. of one of *S*iva's chief attendants. **2** N. of *S*iva.

नंदिन् *a.* **1** Happy, pleased, glad, delighted. **2** Making happy, gladdening. **—m. 1** A son. **2** The speaker of a prelude or benediction in a drama. **3** N. of the door-keeper of *S*iva, his chief attendant, or of the bull which he rides; लतागृहद्वारगतोऽथनंदी Ku. 3. 41; Mâl. 1. 1. **—नी 1** A daughter; U. 1. 9. **2** A husband's sister. **3** A fabulous cow, daughter of *Surabhi*, yielding all desires (कामधेनु) and in the possession of the sage Vasishtha; अनिंद्या नंदिनी नाम धेनुरावबृते वनात् R. 1. 82, 2 69. **4** An epithet of the Ganges. **5** The holy basil.

नपात् *m.* A grandson (usually restricted to the Vedas); as in तनूनपात्.

नपुंस् *m.* **नपुंसः** Not a man, a eunuch.

नपुंसकः,-कं 1 A hermaphrodite (neither man nor woman). **2** An impotent man, a eunuch. **3** A coward. **—कं 1** A word in the neuter gender. **2** The neuter gender.

नप्तृ *m.* A grandson (as son's or daughter's son).

नभः The month *S*râvaṇa. **—भं** The sky, atmosphere.

नभस् *n.* **1** The sky, atmosphere; R. 5. 29; Bg. 1. 19; Rs. 1. 11. **2** A cloud. **3** Fog, vapour. **4** Water. **5** Period of life, age.**—m. 1** The rains or rainy season. **2** The nose, smell. **3** N. of *S*râvaṇa (corresponding to July-August, said to be *n.* also in this sense); प्रत्यासन्ने नभसि दयिताजीविताळंबनार्थी Me. 4; R. 12, 29; 17. 41; 18. 5. **4** The fibres in the root of the lotus. 5 A spitting pot. -Comp. **-अंबुपः** the Châtaka bird. **-कांतिन्** *m.* a lion. **-गजः** a cloud. **-चक्षुस्** *m.* the sun. **-चमसः 1** the moon. **2** magic. **-चर** *a.* moving in the sky; Ku. 5. 23. **(-रः) 1** a god or demi god; R. 18. 6. **2** a bird. **-दुहः** a cloud. **-दृष्टि** *a.* **1** blind. **2** looking towards the sky. **-द्वीपः, -धूमः** a cloud. **-नदी** the celestial Ganges. **-प्राणः** wind. **-मणिः** the sun. **-मंडलं** the firmament, the atmosphere; नेदं नभोमंडलमंबुराशिः S. D. 10. °**दीपः** the moon. **-रजस्** *m.* darkness. **-रेणुः** *f.* fog, mist. **-लयः** smoke **-लिह्** *a.* licking the sky, lofty, very high; cf. अभ्रंलिह. **-सद्** *m.* a god; *S*i. 1. 11. **-सरित्** *f.* **1** the milky way. **2** the celestial Ganges. **-स्थली** the sky. **-स्पृश्** *a.* reaching the sky, lofty.

नभसः 1 The sky. **2** The rainy season. **3** The ocean.

नभसंगमः A bird.

नभस्यः N. of the month Bhâdrapada (corresponding to August-September); R. 9. 54, 12. 29, 17. 41.

नभस्वत् *a.* Vaporous, misty, cloudy. **—m.** The wind, air; N. 1. 97; R. 4. 8; 10. 73; *S*i. 1. 10.

नभाकः 1 Darkness. **2** An epithet of Râhu.

नभ्राज् *m.* A dark cloud.

नम् 1 P., sometimes A. (नमति-ते; नत; *Caus.* नमयति-ते or नामयति-ते, but with a preposition नमयति only; *desid* निनंसति) **1** To bow to, make obeisance to, sâlute (as a mark of respect) (with acc. or dat.); इयं नमति वः सर्वान् त्रिलोचनवधूरिति Ku. 6. 89; Bg. 11. 17; Bk. 9. 51, 10. 31; 12. 39; *S*i. 4. 57. To submit or subject oneself, bow down; अशक्तः संधिमान् नमेत् Kâm. 8. 55. **3** To bend, sink, go down; अनंसीद्भूर्भरेणास्य Bk. 15. 25; नेमुः सर्वदिशः K. 55. उन्नमति नमति वर्षति...मेघाः Mk. 5. 26. **4** To stop, be inclined. **5** To be bent or curved. **6** To Sound. –WITH **अभ्युद्** to rise, go up. **–अव 1** to bend or bow down, stoop; *S*i. 9. 74. **2** to bend oneself, hang down; त्वय्यादातुं जलमवनते Me. 46. **–उद् 1** (*a*) to rise, appear, spring up; उन्नम्योन्नम्य लीयंते दरिद्राणां मनोरथाः Pt. 2. 91. (*b*) to hang over, impend. उन्नमत्यकालदुर्दिनं Mk. 5. **2** to rise, ascend, go up (fig- also); उन्नमति नमति वर्षति गर्जति मेघः Mk. 5. 26; नम्रत्वेनोन्नमंतः Bh. 2. 69; 3. 24; *S*i. 9. 79. **3** to raise, elevate; Ki. 16. 35. (*-Cause.*) to raise, erect. **–उप 1** to come to, arrive, approach. **2** to befall, fall to the lot of, occur, happen, with gen. or by itself; कस्यात्यंतं सुखमुपनतं दुःखमेकांततो वा Me. 109; मत्संभोगः कथमुपनमेत् स्वप्नजोऽपि Me. 91; यदेवोपनतं दुःखात्सुखं तद्रसवत्तरं V. 3. 21; Bh. 2. 121; Me. 10; R. 10 39. **3** to present, give, offer; परलोकोपनतं जलांजलिं R. 8. 68. **–परि 1** to stoop, bend down (as an elephant to strike with his tusks); वप्रक्रीडापरिणतगजप्रेक्षणीयं ददर्श Me. 2; विष्के नागः पर्यणंसीत् स्व एव *S*i. 18. 27. **2** to bend or bow down, be inclined; लज्जापरिणतैः (वदनकमलैः) Bk. 1. 4. **3** to be changed or transformed into, assume the form of (with instr.) लताभावेन परिणतमस्या रूपं V. 4; 4. 28; क्षीरं जलं वा स्वयमेव दधिहिमभावेन परिणमते S. B.; Me. 45. **4** to be developed or matured, be ripe; परिणतप्रज्ञस्य वाणीं U. 7. 20; Me. 18; Ki. 5. 37; M. 3. 8; Rs. 1. 26. **5** to be advanced (in age), grow old, be aged, decay; परिणतशरच्चंद्रिकासु क्षपासु Me. 110; so जरापरिणत &c. **6** to set, decline in the west (as the sun); अनेन समयेन परिणतो दिवसः K. 47. **7** to be digested; ग्रस्तं परिणमेच्च यत् Mb. **–प्र** (प्रणमति) to bow down, salute, make a low obeisance to (with acc. or dat.); न प्रणमंति देवताभ्यः K. 108; तां प्रणनाम K. 219; Bg. 11. 44; R. 2. 21. (**साष्टांग प्रणम्** to fall down on the eight limbs; see साष्टांग; **दंडवत् प्रणम्** to bow by throwing oneself down on the ground quite prostrate and flat like a stick placed horizontally, touching the ground at all points; cf. दंडप्रणाम). **–वि 1** to bend oneself, stoop, be bent; विनमंति च स्य तरवः प्रचये Ki. 6. 34; Bh. 1. 67; Bk. 7 52; see विनत. **–विपरि 1** to be changed into. **2** to undergo a change for the worse. **–सं 1** to bend, stoop, incline; संनतांगी Ku. 1. 34; Bk. 2. 31; पर्वसु संनता V. 4. 26. **2** to submit or subject oneself to; संनमतामरीणां R. 18. 34.

नमत *a.* Bent, bowed, crooked, curved. **–तः 1** An actor. **2** Smoke. **3** Master, lord. **4** A cloud.

नमनं 1 Bowing down, bending, stooping. **2** Sinking. **3** A bow, salutation, obeisance.

नमस् *ind.* A bow, salutation, obeisance, adoration (this word is, by itself, invariably used with dat.; तस्मै वदान्यगुरवे तरवे नमोऽस्तु Bv. 1. 94; नमस्त्रिमूर्तये तुभ्यं Ku. 2. 4; but with कृ, generally with acc.; मुनित्रयं नमस्कृत्य Sk. but sometimes with dat. also; नमस्कुर्मो नृसिंहाय *ibid.* The word has the sense of a noun, but is treated as an indeclinable). –COMP. **-कारः**, **–कृतिः** *f.* **–करणं** bowing, respectful or reverential salutation, respectful obeisance (made by uttering the word नमस्). **–कृत** *a.* **1** bowed down to, saluted. **2** revered, adored, worshipped. **–गुरुः** a spiritual teacher. **–वाकं** *ind.* uttering the word नमस् *i. e.* making a low obeisance ; इदं कविभ्यः पूर्वेभ्यो नमोवाकं प्रशास्महे U. 1. 1.

नमस *a.* Favourable, kindly disposed.

नमसित, **नमस्यित** *a.* Revered, respected, saluted.

नमस्यति Den. P. To bow down to, pay homage to, worship; Bh. 2. 94.

नमस्य *a.* **1** Entitled to obeisance, revered, respectable, adorable. **2** Respectful, humble. **—स्या** Worship, adoration, reverence, obeisance.

नमुचिः 1 N. of a demon slain by Indra; वनमुचे नमुचेररये शिरः R. 9. 22. [When Indra conquered the Asuras, there was only one called Namuchi who strongly resisted and at last captured him. He offered to let Indra go provided he promised 'not to kill by day or by night, with wet or dry'. Indra promised to do so and was released, but he cut off Namuchi's head at twilight and with foam of water (which is neither wet nor dry). According to another version Namuchi was a friend of Indra, and once drank up his strength and made him quite imbecile. The Asvins (and Sarasvatî also, as the story goes) then supplied Indra with a *Vajra* with which he cut off the demon's head]. **2** N. of the god of love.

नमेरुः N. of a tree (रुद्राक्ष or सुरपुन्नाग); गणा नमेरुप्रसवावतंसाः Ku. 1. 55; 3. 43; R. 4. 74.

नम्र *a.* **1** Bowing, bowing down, bent, inclined, hanging down; भवंति नम्रास्तरवः फलागमैः *S*. 5. 12; स्तोकनम्रा स्तनाभ्यां Me. 82; Pt. 1. 106; Ratn. 1. 19. **2** Bowing down, making a low obeisance; अभूच्च नम्रः प्रणिपातशिक्षया R. 3. 25; इत्युच्यते ताभिरुमा स्म नम्रा Ku. 7. 28. **3** Lowly, submissive, humble, reverential as in भक्तिनम्रः Me. 55. **4** Crooked, curved. **5** Worshipping. **6** Devoted or attached to.

नय् 1 A. (नयते) **1** To go. **2** To protect.

नयः 1 Guiding, leading, managing. **2** Behaviour, course of conduct, conduct, way of life; as in दुर्नय. **3** Prudence, foresight. **4** Policy, political wisdom, statesmanship, civil administration, state policy ; नयप्रचारं व्यवहारदुष्टतां Mk. 1. 7; नयगुणोपचितामिव भूपतेः सदुपकारफलां श्रियमर्थिनः R. 9. **27**. **5** Morality, justice, rectitude, equity; चलति नयान्न जिगीषतां हि चेतः Ki. 10. 29. **2**.3; 6. 38, 16. 42. **6** A plan, design, scheme, Mu. 6. 11, 7. 9. **7** A maxim, principle. **8** Course, method, manner. **9** A system, doctrine, opinion. **10** A philosophical system; वैशेषिके नये Bhâshâ P. 105. –COMP. **–कोविद्**, **–ज्ञ** *a.* skilled in policy, prudent. **–चक्षुस्** *a.* having political foresight, wise, prudent; R. 1. 55. **–नेतृ** *m.* a master in politics. **–विद्** *m.*, **–विशारदः** a politician, statesman. **–शास्त्रं 1** the science of politics. **2** any work on politics or political economy. **3** a work on morality. **–शालिन्** *a.* just, righteous; Ki. 5. 24.

नयनं 1 Leading, guiding, conducting, managing. **2** Taking, bringing to or near, drawing. **3** Ruling, governing. **4** Obtaining. **5** The eye. –COMP. **–अभिराम** *a.* gladdening the sight, lovely to behold. (**–मः**) the moon. **–उत्सवः 1** a lamp. **2** delight of the eyes. **3** any lovely object. **–उपांतः** the corner of the eye; Ku. 4. 23. **–गोचर** *a.* visible, within the range of sight. **–छदः** an eyelid. **–पथः** the range of sight. **–पुटं** the cavity of the eye. **–विषयः 1** any visible object. **2** the horizon. **–सलिलं** tears; Me. 39.

नरः 1 A man, male, person ; संयोजयति विद्यैव नीचगापि नरं सरित् । समुद्रमिव दुर्धर्षं नृपं भाग्यमतः परं H. Pr. 5; Ms. 1. 96; **2**. **213**. **2** A man or piece at chess. **3** The pin of a sun-dial. **4** The Supreme spirit, the original or eternal man. **5** Man's length (=पुरुष q. v.). **6** N. of a primitive sage. **7** N. of Arjuna; see नरनारायण below. –COMP. **–अधिपः**, **–अधिपतिः**, **–ईशः**, **–ईश्वरः**, **–देवः**, **–पतिः**, **–पालः** a king; Bg. 10. 27; Ms. 7. 13; R. 2. 25, 3. 42; 7. 62; Me. 37; Y. **1**. 310. **–अंतकः** death. **–अयणः** an epithet of Vishṇu. **–अंशः** a demon, **goblin.**

-इंद्रः 1 a king; R. 2. 18, 3. 33, 6. 80; Ms. 9. 253. 2 a physician, dealer in antidotes, curer of poisons; तेषु कश्चिन्नरेंद्राभिमानी तां निर्वर्ण्य Dk. 51; सुनिग्रहा नरेंद्रेण फणींद्रा इव शत्रवः *Si.* 2. 88 (where the word is used in both senses). -उत्तमः an epithet of Vishnu. -ऋषभः 'the chief of men', a prince, king. -कपालः a man's skull. -कीलकः the murderer of a spiritual preceptor. -केशरिन् *m.* Vishnu in his fourth incarnation; cf. नृसिंह below. -द्विष् *m.* a demon, goblin; Bk. 15. 94. -नारायणः N. of Krishṇa (-णौ dual) originally regarded as identical, but in mythology and epic poetry, considered as distinct beings, Arjuna being identified with Nara and Krishna with Nârâyana. [In some places they are called देवौ, पूर्वदेवौ or ऋषी or ऋषिसत्तमौ. They are said to have been practising very austere penance on the Himalaya, which excited the fear of Indra, and he sent down several damsels to disturb their austerities. But *Narayana* put all of them to shame by creating a nymph called Urv*asi* from a flower placed on his thigh who excelled them in beauty; cf. स्थाने खलु नारायणमृषिं विलोभयंत्यस्तदूरुसंभवामिमां दृष्ट्वा व्रीडिताः सर्वा अप्सरस इति V. 1.]. -पशुः ' a beast-like man; a beast in human form. -पुंगवः 'best of men,' an excellent man-मानिका,-मानिनी, मालिनी 'man like woman with a beard', masculine woman or an amazon. -मेधः a human sacrifice. -यंत्रं sun-dial. -यानं, -रथः, -वाहनं a vehicle drawn by men. -लोकः 1 'the world of men', the earth, terrestrial world. 2 mankind. -वाहनः an epithet of Kubera; R. 9. 11. -वीरः a brave man, hero. -व्याघ्रः, -शार्दूलः an eminent man. -शृंगं 'man's horn', an impossibility, chimera, nonentity -संसर्गः human society. -सिंहः, -हरिः 'man-lion', Vishṇu in his fourth incarnation; cf. तव करकमलवरे नखमद्भुतशृंगं दलितहिरण्यकशिपुतनुभृंगं । केशव धृतनरहरिरूप जय जगदीश हरे ॥ Gît. 1. -स्कंधः a multitude or body of men.

नरकः, -कं Hell, infernal regions; (corresponding to the realm of Pluto; there are said to be 21 different parts of these regions where different kinds of tortures are inflicted upon sinners). -कः N. of a demon, king of Prâgjyotisha. [According to one account he carried off Aditi's ear-rings and Krish*na* at the request of the gods killed him in a single combat and recovered the jewels. According to another account, Naraka assumed the form of an elephant and carried off the daughter of Visvakarman and outraged her. He also seized the daughters of Gandharvas, gods, men and the nymphs themselves, and collected more than 16000 damsels in his harem. These it is related, were transfferred by Krish*na* to his own harem after he had slain Naraka. The demon was born of earth and hence called Bhauma.] -COMP. -अंतकः, -अरिः -जित् *m.* epithets of Krishṇa. -आमयः 1 the soul after death. 2 a ghost, spirit. -कुंडं a pit in hell where the wicked are tormented (86 such places are enumerated). -स्था the Vaitariṇî river.

नरंगं, नरांगः The penis.

नरंधिः Worldy life or existence.

नरी A woman; Bv. 3. 16.

नर्कुटकं Nose.

नर्तः Dancing, a dance.

नर्तकः 1 A dancer; sometimes a dancing preceptor. 2 An actor, mime, mummer. 3 A bard, herald. 4 An elephant. 5 A king. 6 A peacock. -की 1 A female dancer, a singing girl, an actress; रंगस्य दर्शयित्वा निवर्तते नर्तकी यथा नृत्यात् Sân. K. 59; Ki. 10. 41; R. 19. 14, 19. 2 A female elephant. 3 A pea-hen.

नर्तनः A dancer. -नं Gesticulation, dancing, dance. -COMP. -गृहं, -शाला a dancing hall. प्रियः an epithet of *Siva.*

नर्तित *a.* Danced, made to dance.

नर्द् 1 P. (नर्दति, नर्दित) 1 To bellow, roar, sound in general; अनर्दिषुः कपिव्याघ्राः Bk. 15. 35, 14. 40, 15. 28, 17. 40. 2 To go, move.

नर्द *a.* Bellowing, roawing.

नर्दनं 1 Bellowing, roaring. 2 Celebrating, praising aloud.

नर्दितः A kind of die or a throw at dice; नर्दितदर्शितमार्गः कटेन विनिपातितो यामि Mk. 2. 8. -तं Sound, roar, bellowing.

नर्मटः 1 A pot-sherd. 2 The sun.

नर्मठः 1 A jester. 2 A lecher, rake, libertine. 3 Sport, pastime, amusement. 4 Copulation, coition. 5 The chin. 6 The nipple.

नर्मन् *n.* 1 Sport, amusement, diversion, merriment, pleasure, amorous pastime or sport; जितकमले विमले परिकर्मय नर्मजनकमलकं मुखे Gît. 12 (कौतुकजनक); R. 19. 28. 2 Jest, joke, humour, wit; नर्मप्रायाभिः कथाभिः K. 70 jocular, humorous. -COMP. -कीलः a husband. -गर्भ *a.* humorous, full of humour, witty. (-र्भः) a secret lover. -द *a.* delighting, making happy. (-दः) a jester (=नर्मसचिव q. v.) -दा N. of a river which rises in the Vindhya mountain, and falls into the gulf of Cambay. -द्युति *a.* bright with joy, cheerful, merry. (-तिः *f.*) enjoyment of a joke. -सचिवः,-सुहृद् *m.* 'a pleasure-companion', an associate of the amusements of a prince or a man of rank; इदं त्वैदंपर्यं यदुत नृपतेर्नर्मसचिवः सुतादानान्मित्रं भवतु Mâl. 2. 7; तां याचते नरपतेर्नर्मसुहृन्नंदनो नृपमुखेन 1. 11; *Si.* 1. 59.

नर्मरा 1 A valley, cavity. 2 A bellows. 3 An old woman past menstruation. 4 The plant *Saralâ.*

नलः 1 A kind of reed. 2 N. of a celebrated king of the Nishadhas and hero of the poem called 'Naishadhacharita.' [Nala was a very noble-minded and virtuous King. He was chosen by Damayant*i* in spite of the opposition of gods, and they lived happily for some years. But Kali—who was disappointed in securing her hand—resolved to persecute Nala, and entered into his person. Thus affected he played at dice with his brother, and having lost every thing, he, with his wife, was banished from the kingdom. One day, while wandering through the wilderness, he abandoned his wife almost naked, and went away. Subsequently he was deformed by the serpent Karko*t*aka, and so deformed he entered the service of king Ri*t*upar*n*a of Ayodhy*a* as a horse-groom under the name of B*a*huka. Subsequently with the assistance of the king he regained his beloved, and they led happy life; see ऋतुपर्ण and दमयंती also]. 3 N. of a monkey-chief, son of Visvakarman, who, it is said, built the bridge of stones called Nalasetu or 'Adam's bridge' over which Râma passed to Lankâ with his army. —लं A lotus. -COMP. -कीलः the knee. -कूब (व:) रः N. of a son of Kubera. -दं a fragrant root (उशीर); Ki. 12. 50; N. 4. 116. -पट्टिका a sort of mat made of reeds. -मीनः, a shrimp or prawn.

नलकं 1 Any long bone of the body; Mv. 1. 35. 2 The radius of the arm.

नलकिनी 1 The knee-pan. 2 The leg.

नलिनः The (Indian) crane. —नं 1 A lotus flower, waterlily. 2 Water. 3 The indigo plant. (नलिनेशयः) an epithet of Vishnu.

नलिनी 1 A lotus-plant; न पर्वताग्रे नलिनी प्ररोहति Mk. 4. 17; नलिनीदलगतजलमतितरलं Moha M. 5; Ku. 4. 6. 2 An assemblage of lotuses. 3 A pond or place abounding in lotuses. -COMP. -खंड, -षंडं a group or assemblage of lotuses. -रुहः an epithet of Brahmâ. (-हं) a lotus-stalk, the fibres of a lotus.

नल्वः A measure of distance equal to 400 *hastas* or cubits.

नव *a.* 1 New, fresh, young, recent; चित्तयोनिरभवत्पुनर्नवः R. 19. 46; क्लेशः फलेन हि पुनर्नवतां विधत्ते Ku. 5. 86; U. 1. 19; R. 1. 83, 2. 47, 3. 53, 4. 3, 11; *Si.* 1. 4, 3. 31; Ki. 9. 43. 2 Modern. -वः A crow. -वं *ind.* Recently, newly, lately, not long ago. -COMP. -अन्नं new rice or grain. -अंबु *n.* fresh water. -अहः the first day of a fortnight. -इतर *a.* old; R. 8. 22. -उद्धृतं fresh butter. -ऊढा, -पाणिग्रहणा a newly married woman, a bride; H. 1. 212; Bh. 1. 4; R. 8. 7. -कारिका, -कालिका, -फलिका 1 a woman newly married. 2 a woman in whom menstruation has recently commenced. -छात्रः a fresh student, novice, tyro. -नी *f.*, -नीतं fresh butter; अहो नवनीतकल्पहृदय आर्यपुत्रः M. 3. -नीतकं 1 clarified butter. 2 fresh butter. -पाठकः new teacher. -मल्लिका, -मालिका a kind of jasmine. -यज्ञः an offering of the first fruits of the harvest. -यौवनं fresh youth, bloom or prime of youth. -रजस् *f.* a girl who has recently menstruated. -वधूः, -वरिका a newly married girl. -वल्लभं a kind of sandal. -वस्त्रं new cloth. -शशिभृत् *m.* an epithet of *S*iva; Me. 43. सूतिः *f.* -सूतिका 1 a milch-cow. 2 a woman recently delivered.

नवकं The aggregate of nine.

नवत *a.* (ती *f.*) Ninetieth. —तः 1 An elephant's painted housings. 2 A woollen cloth, blanket. 3 A cover, wrapper (in general).

नवतिः *f.* Ninety; नवनवतिशतद्रव्यकोटीश्वरास्ते Mu. 3. 27; R. 3. 69.

नवतिका 1 Ninety. 2 A paintbrush (said to contain 90 hairs).

नवन् *num a.* (always pl) Nine; नवतिं नवाधिकां R. 3. 69; see comp. below. (At the beginning of comp. नवन् drops its final न्). Comp. -अशीतिः *f.* eightynine. -अर्चिस् *m* , -दीधितिः the planet Mars. -कृत्वस् *ind.* nine times. -ग्रहाः (*m.* pl.) the nine planets; see under ग्रह. -चत्वारिंश *a.* forty-ninth. -चत्वारिंशत् *f.* forty-nine. -छिद्रं -द्वारं the body (having nine apertures; see ख) -त्रिंश *a.* thirty-ninth. -त्रिंशत् *f.* thirty-nine. -दश *a.* nineteenth. -दशन् pl. nineteen. -नवतिः *f.* ninety-nine. -निधिः *m.* pl. the nine treasures of Kubera; *i. e.* महापद्मश्च पद्मश्च शंखो मकरकच्छपौ । मुकुंदकुंदनीलाश्च खर्वश्च निधयो नव ॥. -पंचाश *a.* fifty-ninth. पंचाशत् *f.* fifty-nine. -रत्नं 1 the nine precious jewels; *i. e.* मुक्तामाणिक्यवैदूर्यगोमेदान् वज्रविद्रुमौ । पद्मरागं मरकतं नीलं चेति यथाक्रमं ॥. 2 'the nine gems' or poets at the court of king Vikramâditya : —धन्वंतरिक्षपणकामरसिंहशंकुवेतालभट्टघटकर्परकालिदासाः । ख्यातो वराहमिहिरो नृपतेः सभायां रत्नानि वै वररुचिर्नव विक्रमस्य ॥. -रसाः (*m. pl.*) the nine sentiments in poetry, see under अष्टरस and रस also. -रात्रं 1 a period of nine days. 2 the first nine days of the month of Asvina held sacred to Durgâ. -विंश *a.* twenty-ninth. -विंशतिः *f.* twenty-nine. -विध *a.* ninefold, of nine kinds or sorts. -शतं 1 one hundred and nine. 2 nine-hundred. -षष्टिः *f.* sixty-nine. -सप्ततिः seventy-nine.

नवधा *ind.* In nine ways, ninefold.

नवम *a.* (मी *f.*) Ninth.—मी The ninth day of a lunar fortnight.

नवशः *ind.* By nines.

नवीन, नव्य 1 New, fresh, recent 2 Modern.

नश् 4 P. (नश्यति, नष्ट; *Caus* नाशयति; *desid.* निनंक्षति, निनशिषति) 1 To be lost, disappear, vanish, become invisible; प्रवाणि तस्य नश्यंति H. 1; तथा सीमा न नश्यति Ms 8. 247; Y. 2. 58; क्षणनष्टदृष्टतिमिरं Mk. 5. 4. 2 To be destroyed, to perish, die, be ruined; जीवनाशं ननाश च Bk. 14. 31; Ms 8. 166, 7. 40; Mu. 6. 8. 3 To run away, fly away, escape; नश्यंति वृंदानि ददर्श कपींद्रः Bk. 10. 12; नंष्ट्राश्रित्रा निशाचराः 14. 112, Ratn. 2. 3. 4 To be frustrated, become unsuccessful. —*Caus.* 1 To cause to disappear. 2 To destroy, remove, efface, drive away, cause to fly away. -With प्र (प्रणश्यति) or वि to perish, die; Bk. 3 14; Bg. 8. 20.

नश् *f.*, नशः, नशनं Destruction, perishing, loss, disappearing.

नश्वर *a.* (री *f.*) 1 Perishable, transitory, evanescent, transient, frail; निखिलं जगदेव नश्वरं R. G. 2 Destructive, mischievous.

नष्ट *p. p.* 1 Lost, disappeared, vanished, invisible. 2 Dead, perished, destroyed. 3 Spoiled, wasted. 4 Fled or run away. 5 Deprived of, free from (in comp.). -Comp. -अर्थ *a.* reduced to poverty (having lost one's wealth). -आतंकं *ind.* without anxiety or fear; नष्टातंकं हरिणशिशवो मंदमंदं चरंति *S.* 1. 13 v. 1. -आत्मन् *a.* deprived of sense. -आसिसूत्रं booty, plunder. -आशंक *a.* fearless, secure, free from fear. -इंदुकला the day of full moon. -इंद्रिय *a.* deprived of senses. -चेतन, -चेष्ट, -संज्ञ *a.* one who has lost his senses, unconscious, insensible, fainted. -चेष्टता universal destruction.

नस् *f.* The nose (a word optionally substituted for नासिका after acc. dual). -Comp. -क्षुद्र *a.* small-nosed.

नस्तस् *ind.* From the nose; Y. 3. 127.

नसा The nose.

नस्तः The nose. -स्तं A sternutatory, snuff. —स्ता A hole bored in the septum of the nose. -Comp. -ऊतः an ox led by a string through the nose.

नस्तित *a.* Nozzled (with a string through the nose.

नस्य *a.* Nasal. —स्यं 1 The hairs in the nose. 2 A sternutatory. —स्या 1 The nose. 2 The string through the nose of an animal; *Si* 12. 10.

नह् 4 U. (नह्यति-ते, नद्ध; *desid.* निनत्सति-ते) 1 To tie, bind, bind on or round or together, gird round; शैलेयनद्धानि शिलातलानि Ku. 1. 56; R. 4. 57; 16. 41. 2 To put on (oneself), to dress, arm oneself (Atm.). -*Caus.* To cause to put on. -With अप to untie. -अपि (अपि being often changed to पि) 1 to fasten, gird round, bind; अतिपिनद्धेन वल्कलेन *S.* 1; मंदारमाला हरिणा पिनद्धा *S.* 7. 2. 2 to put on, wear; Bk. 3. 47. 3 to cover, envelop; कुसुममिव पिनद्धं पांडुपत्रोदरेण *S.* 1. 19. -उद् to tie or bind up, intertwine; R. 17. 23, 18. 50. -परि to surround, intertwine, encircle; स जगति परिणद्धः शक्तिभिः शक्तिनाथः Mâl. 5. 1; R. 6. 64; M. 5. 10; Rs. 6. 25. -सं 1 to tie, bind, fasten. 2 to wear, put on, dress. 3 to put on (as armour), arm oneself, be accoutred; समनात्सीत्ततो सैन्यं Bk. 15. 111, 112; 14. 7; 17. 4. 4 to make oneself (for any action) (Atm. in this sense); युद्धाय संनह्यते Mbh. छेत्तुं वज्रमणीञ् शिरिषकुसुमप्रांतेन संनह्यते Bh. 2. 6; see संनद्ध also.

नहि *ind.* Surely or certainly not, by no means, not at all; आशंसा नहि नः प्रेते जीवेम दशमूर्धनि Bk. 19. 5.

नहुषः N. of a king of the lunar race, son of Âyus and grandson of Purûravas and father of Yayâti. [He was a very wise and powerful king and when Indra lay concealed under waters to expiate the sin of having killed the demon Vritra, a Brahma*n*a, he was asked to occupy his seat. While there he thought of winning the love of Indra*n*i and caused the seven sages to convey him in a palanquin to her house. On his away he asked them to be quick using the words '*sarpa*', '*sarpa*' (move on, move on), when one of the sages (Agastya ?) cursed him to be a '*sarpa*' (serpent). He fell down from the sky and remained in that wretched state till he was relieved from it by Yudhish*th*ira].

ना No, not (न q. v.).

नाकः 1 Heaven; आनाकरथवर्त्मनां R. 1. 5; 15. 96. 2 Vault of heaven, upper sky, firmament. -Comp. -चरः 1 a god. 2 a demi-god. -नाथः, -नायकः an epithet of Indra. -वनिता an *Apsaras*. -सद् *m.* a god; Bk. 1. 4.

नाकिन् *m.* A god; *Si.* 1. 45.

नाकुः 1 An ant-hill. 2 A mountain.

नाक्षत्र *a.* (त्री *f.*) Starry, sidereal. -त्रं A month computed by the moon's passage through the 27 lunar mansions, a month of 30 days of sixty, Ghatîs each; नाडीषष्ट्या तु नाक्षत्रमहोरात्रं प्रकीर्तितं Sûrya. S.

नाक्षत्रिकः A month of 27 days (each day being the period of the moon's passage through a lunar asterism).

नागः 1 A snake in general; particularly, the cobra. 2 A fabuous serpent-demon or semidivine being, having the face of a man and the tail of a serpent and said to inhabit the Pâtâla; Bg 10. 29; R. 15. 83. 3 An elephant; Me. 14, 36; *Si.* 4. 63; V. 4. 63; V. 4. 25 4 A shark 5 A cruel or tyrannical person. 6 (At the end of comp.). Any pre-eminent or distinguished person; *i. g.* पुरुषनाग. 7 A cloud. 8 A peg projecting from a wall to hang anything upon. 9 Piper betel. 10 One of the five vital airs of the body, that which is expelled by eructation. 11 The number 'seven' **-गं** 1 Tin. 2. Lead. -COMP. **-अंगना** 1 a femal elephant. 2 the proboscis of an elephant. **-अंजना** a female elephant. **-अधिपः** an epithet of *Sesha*. **-अंतकः**, **-अरातिः**, **-अरिः** 1 an epithet of Garuda. 2 a peacock. 3 a lion. **-अशनः** 1 a peacock; Pt. 1. 159. 2 an epihet of Garuḍa. **-आननः** an epithet of Ganesa. **-आह्वः** Hastinâpura. **-इंद्रः** 1 a lordly or superior elephant; Ku. 1. 36. 2 Airâvata, Indra's elephant. 3 an epithet of Śesha. **-ईशः** 1 an epithet of *Sesha*. 2 N. of the author of Paribhâshendusekhara and several other works. 3 N. of Patanjali. **-उदरं** 1 a breast-plate. 2 a peculiar disease of pregnancy (गर्भोपद्रवभेद्). **-केसरः** N. of a tree with fragrant flowers. **-गर्भं** red lead. **-चूडः** an epithet of *Siva*. **-जं** 1 red lead. 2 tin. **-जिह्विका** red arsenic. **-जीवनं** tin. **-दंतः**, **-दंतकः** 1 ivory. 2 a peg or bracket projecting from a wall and used to hang things upon. **-तंती** 1 a kind of sun-flower. 2 a harlot. **-नक्षत्रं**, **-नायकं** the constellation called Âśleshâ. (**-कः**) the lord of serpents. **-नासा** the proboscis of an elephant. **-निर्यूहः** a large pin or bracket projecting from a wall. **-पंचमी** N. of a festival on the fifth day in the bright half of Srâvaṇa. **-पदः** a mode of sexul enjoyment (रतिबंध). **-पाशः** 1 a sort of magical noose used in battle to entangle an enemy. 2 N. of the noose or weapon of Varuṇa. **-पुष्पः** 1 the Champaka tree. 2 the Punnâga tree. **-बंधकः** an elephant-catcher. **-बंधुः** the holy fig-tree. **-बल** an epithet of Bhîma. **-भूषणः** an epithet or *Siva*. **-मंडलिकः** 1 a snake-keeper. 2 a snake-catcher. **-मल्लः** an epithet of Airâvata. **-यष्टिः** *f*., **-यष्टिका** 1 a graduated pole or pot for showing the depth of water in a newly dug pond. 2 a boring rod driven into the earth. **-रक्तं**, **-रेणुः** red lead. **-रंगः** the orange. **-राजः** an epithet of *Sesha*. **-लता**, **-वल्लरी**, **-वल्ली** piper betel. **-लोकः** the world of serpents, the race of serpents collectively, one of the regions below the earth called Pâtâla. **-वारिकः** 1 a a royal elephant. 2 an elephant-driver. 3 a peacock. 4 an epithet of Garuḍa. 5 the chief of a herd of elephants. 6 the chief person in an assembly. **-संभवं**, **-संभूतं** red lead. **-साह्वयं** Hastinâpura.

नागर *a.* (**री** *f.*) 1 Town-born, tonw-bred. 2 Relating to a town, civic. 3 Spoken in a town. 4 Polite, civil. 5 Clever, sharp. 6 Bad, vile, one who has contracted the vices of a town. **-रः** 1 A citizen (पौर); Me. 25, Sânti. 4. 19 2 A husband's brother. 3 A lecture. 4 An orange. 5 Fatigue. hardship, toil. 6 Denial of knowledge. **-री** 1 The character in which Sanskrit is generally written; cf. देवनागरी. 2 A clever, intriguing or shrewd woman; हंतार्मीरीः स्मरतु स कथं संवृत्तो नागरीभिः Ud. D. 16. 3 The plant स्नुही.

नागरक, **नागरिक** *a.* 1 Town-bred, town-born. 2 Polite, courteous, courtly; नागरिकवृत्त्या संज्ञापयैनां *S.* 5. 3 Clever, shrewd, cunning (विदग्ध). **-कः** 1 A citizen. 2 A polite or courteous man, a gallant; one who shows exaggerated attention to his first mistress while he is courting some one else. 3 One who has contracted the vices of a town. 4 A thief. 5 An artist. 6 The chief of the police; V. 5; *S.* 6.

नागरीटः, **नागवीटः** 1 A libertine, rake. 2 A paramour. 3 A match-maker.

नागरुकः Orange.

नागर्यं Shrewdness, cleverness.

नाचिकेतः Fire.

नाटः 1 Dancing, acting. 2 N. of the Karnâṭaka country.

नाटकं 1 A play, drama (in general). 2 The first of the 10 principal kinds of dramatic composition; for definition and other information see S. D. 277. **-कः** An actor, a dancer.

नाटकीय *a.* Pertaining to a drama. dramatic; पूर्वरंगः प्रसंगाय नाटकीयस्य वस्तुनः *Si.* 2. 8.

नाटारः The son of an actress.

नाटिका A short or light comedy, one of the Uparúpakas, q. v.; *e. g.* the Ratnâvalî, Priyadarsikâ or Viddhasâlabhanjikâ. The S. D. thus defines it:—नाटिका क्लृप्तवृत्ता स्यात्स्त्रीप्राया चतुरंकिका । प्रख्यातो धीरललितस्तत्र स्यान्नायको नृपः ।...स्यादंतःपुरसंबंधा संगीतव्यापृताऽथवा । नवानुरागा कन्याऽत्र नायिका नृपवंशजा । संप्रवर्तेत नेतास्यां देव्यास्त्रासेन शंकितः । देवी पुनर्भवेज्ज्येष्ठा प्रगल्भा नृपवंशजा । पदे पदे मानवती तद्वशः संगमो द्वयोः । वृत्तिः स्यात्कौशिकी स्वल्पविमर्षाः संधयः पुनः ॥ 539.

नाटितकं A mimic representation, a gesture, gesticulation; भीतिनाटितकेन *S.* 5.

नाटेयः, **-रः** The son of an actress or dancing girl.

नाट्यं 1 Dancing. 2 Dramatic representation, gesticulation, acting; नाट्ये च दक्षा वयं Ratn 1. 6; नूनं नाट्ये भवति च चिरं नोर्वशी गर्वशीला Vikr. 18. 29. 3 The science or art of dancing or acting, scenic art; नाट्यं भिन्नरुचेर्जनस्य बहुधाप्येकं समाराधनं M. 1. 4. **-ट्यः** An actor. -COMP. **-आचार्यः** a dancing preceptor. **-उक्तिः** *f.* dramatic phraseology. **-धर्मिका**, **-धर्मी** the rules of dramatic representatiou. **-प्रियः** an epithet of *Siva*. **-शाला** 1 a dancing-hall. 2 a theatre. **-शास्त्रं** 1 the dramatic science, dramaturgy. 2 a work on dramatic representation.

नाडिः, **-डी** *f.* 1 The tubular stalk of any plant. 2 The hollow stalk of a lotus &c. 3 Any tubular organ of the body (such as an artery, vein); षडधिकदशनाडीचक्रमध्यस्थितात्मा Mâl. 5. 1, 2. 4. A pipe, flute. 5 A fistulous sore, fistula, sinus. 6 The pulse at the hand or foot. 7 A measure of time equal to twenty-four minutes. 8 A period of time =½ Muhúrta. 9 A juggling trick. -COMP. **-चरणः** a bird. **-चीरं** a small reed. **-जंघः** a crow. **-परीक्षा** feeling the pulse. **-मंडलं** the celestial equator. **-यंत्रं** any tubular instrument. **-व्रणः** sinus, an ulcer, fistula.

नाडिका 1 Tubular organ &c.; see नाडि. 2 A Ghaṭikâ or 24 minutes; नाडिकाविच्छेदपटहः Mâl. 7; K. 13, 70.

नाडिं (डीं) धम *a.* Causing a movement of the tubular organs (as fright &c.); नाडिंधमेन श्वासेन K. 353. **-मः** A goldsmith.

नाणकं A coin, anything stamped with an impression; एषा नाणकमोषिका मकशिका Mk. 1. 23; Y. 2. 240.

नातिचर *a* Of no long duration, very long.

नातिदूर *a.* Not very far or distant.

नातिवादः Avoiding abusive language.

नाथ् 1 P. (नाथति, but sometimes A. also) 1 To ask, beg, solicit for anything (with dat. or two acc.); मोक्षाय नाथते मुनिः Vop.; नाथसे किमु पतिं न भूभृतः Ki. 13. 59; संतुष्टमिष्टानि तमिष्टदेवं नाथंति के नाम न लोकनाथं N. 3. 25. 2 To have power, be master, prevail. 3 To harass, trouble. 4 To bless, wish well to, give blessings to; (said to be Atm. only in this sense); नाथित-

शमे Mv. 1. 11; (Mammaṭa quotes the line दीनं त्वामनुनाथते कुचयुगं पत्रावृतं मा कृथाः to show that नाथ् here only means 'to ask or beg', and नाथते should therefore be नाथति); सर्पिषो नाथते Sk.

नाथः 1 A lord, master, protector, leader; नाथे कुतस्त्वय्यशुभं प्रजानां R. 5. 13, 2. 73, 3. 45; त्रिलोक°, कैलास° &c. 2 A husband. 3 A rope passed through the nose of a draft ox. –COMP. **-हरिः** a beast (पशु).

नाथवत् *a.* 1 Possessed of a lord or protector; नाथवंतस्त्वया लोकास्त्वमनाथा विपत्स्यसे U. 1. 43. 2 Dependent, subject.

नादः 1 A loud roar, cry, shout, sounding, roaring; सिंहनादः, घन° &c. 2 A sound in general; Mâl. 5. 20. 3 (In Yoga phil.) The nasal sound represented by a semi-circle (ँ)

नादिन् *a.* Sounding, resonant; अंबुदवृंदनादी रथः R. 3. 59; 19. 5. 2 Bellowing, roaring; खर°, सिंह° &c.

नादेय *a.* (**यी** *f.*) River-born, aquatic, marine. **-यं** Rocksalt.

नाना *ind.* 1 In different places, in different ways, manifoldly, variously. 2 Distinctly, separately. 3 Without (-विना); (with acc., instr. or abl); नाना नारीं निष्फला लोकयात्रा Vop.; (विश्वं) न नाना शंभुना रामात् वर्षेणाधोक्षजो वरः *ibid.* 4 (Used as an adjective at the beginning of comp.) Manifold, various, sundry, different, diverse; नानाफलैः फलति कल्पलतेव भूमिः Bh. 2. 46; Bg. 1. 9; Ms. 9. 148. –COMP. **-अत्यय** *a.* of different kinds, manifold. **-अर्थ** *a.* 1 having different aims or objects. 2 having different meanings, homonymous (as a word). **-कार** *ind.* having done variously. **-रस** *a.* of different or varying tastes; M. 1. 4, **-रूप** *a.* of different forms, diverse, multiform, various. **-वर्ण** *a.* of different colours. **-विध** *a.* of various sorts, diverse, manifold. **-विधं** *ind.* in various ways.

नानांद्रः A husband's sister's son.

नांत *a.* Endless, infinite.

नांतरीयक *a.* Inseparable, invariably connected.

नांत्रं Praise, eulogy.

नांदिकरः, नांदिन् *m.* The speaker of the नांदी or benediction.

नांदी 1 Joy, satisfaction, delight. 2 Prosperity. 3 Praise of a deity at the commencement of a religious rite or observance. 4 Particularly, the benedictory verse or verses recited as a sort of prologue at the beginning of a drama, benediction; आशीर्वचनसंयुक्ता नित्यं यस्मात्प्रयुज्यते । देवद्विजनृपादीनां तस्मान्नांदीति संज्ञिता ॥ or देवद्विजनृपादीनामाशीर्वचनपूर्विका । नदंति देवता यस्यां तस्मान्नांदीति कीर्तिता ॥. –COMP. **-करः** see नांदिन्. **-निनादः** a shout of joy or rejoicing; Mv. 2. 4. **-पटः** the lid or cover of a well. **-मुख** *a.* (the class of manes or deceased ancestors) to whom the नांदीमुखश्राद्ध is offered. (**-खं**). °**श्राद्धं** a Srâddha ceremony performed in memory of the manes, preliminary to any festive occasion such as marriage &c (**-खः**) the cover or lid of a well. **-वादिन्** *m.* 1 the speaker of a prologue to a drama. 2 a drummer. **-श्राद्धं** see नांदीमुखं above.

नापितः A barber, shaver; Pt 5. 1. –COMP. **-शाला** a barber's shop, a shaving house.

नापित्यं The trade of a barber.

नाभिः *m., f.* navel; गंगावर्तसनाभिर्नाभिः Dk. 2; &c.; निम्ननाभिः Me. 83; R. 6. 52; Me. 28. 2 Any navel like cavity. —*m.* 1 The nave of a wheel; Pt. 1. 81. 2 The centre, focus, chief point. 3 Chief, leader, head; कृत्स्नस्य नाभिर्नृपमंडलस्य R. 18. 20. 4 Near relationship, community (of race &c.); as in सनाभि q. v. 5 A paramount sovereign or lord; R. 9. 16. 6 A near relation. 7 A Kshatriya. 8 Home. **-भिः** *f.* Musk. (*i. e.* मृगनाभि). N. B. **नाभि** at the end of Bah. comp. becomes **नाभ** when the comp. is used as an epithet; as **पद्मनाभः**. –COMP. **-आवर्तः** the cavity of the navel. **-जः, -जन्मन्** *m.* **-भूः** epithets of Brahmâ. **-नाडी, -नालं** 1 the umbilical cord. 2 rupture of the navel.

नाभिल *a.* Relating to or coming from a navel.

नाभीलं 1 The cavity of the navel. 2 Pain. 3 A ruptured navel.

नाभ्य *a.* Relating to, proceeding from, being in, the navel, umbilical. **-भ्यः** An epithet of Siva.

नाम *ind.* A particle used in the following senses :—1 Named, called, by name; हिमालयो नाम नगाधिराजः Ku. 1. 1; तस्मिन्दिनें सुवृत्ता नाम Dk. 7. 2 Indeed, certainly, truly, forsooth, verily, to be sure; मया नाम जितं Ve. 2. 17; विनीतवेषेण प्रवेष्टव्यानि तपोवनानि नाम S. 1; आश्वासितस्य मम नाम V. 5. 16; when I was just consoled. 3 Probably, perhaps; oft. with मा; अये पदशब्दइव मा नाम रक्षिणः Mk. 3. perhaps (but I hope not) that of guards; मा नाम अकार्यं कुर्यात् Mk 4. 5 Possibility; तवैव नामास्त्रगतिः Ku. 3 19; त्वया नाम मुनिर्विमान्यः S. 5. 19 is it possible &c. (implying censure); frequantly used with अपि in the sense of 'I which,' 'would that,' 'is it likely that &c. '; see under अपि. 5 A feigned or pretended action, pretence (अलीक); कार्तांतिको नाम भूत्वा Dk. 130; so भीतो नामवप्लुत्य 104 as if afraid; परिश्रमं नाम विनीय च क्षणं Ku. 5. 32. 6 (With imperatives) Granted, though, it may be, well, it may be; तद्भवतु नाम शोकां···य K. 308; करोतु नाम नीतिशतो व्यवसायमिनस्ततः H. 2. 14 though he may exert himself; so Mâl. 10. 7; S. 5. 8. 7 Wonder; अंधो नाम पर्वतमारोहति G. M. 8 Anger or censure; ममापि नाम दशाननस्य परैः परिभवः G. M.; (the sentence may imply censure also); किं नाम विस्फुरं शस्त्राणि U. 4; ममापि नाम सत्त्वैरभिभूयंते गृहाः S. 6. **नाम** is often used with the interrogative pronoun and its derivatives कथं, कदा &c. in the sense of 'possibly,' 'indeed,' 'I should like to know,; अपि कथं नामैतत् U. 6; को नाम राज्ञां प्रियः Pt. 1. 146; को नाम पाकाभिमुखस्य जंतुर्द्वाराणि दैवस्य पिधातुमीष्टे U. 7. 4.

नामन् *n.* 1 A name, appellation, personal name (opp. गोत्र) किं नु नामैतदस्याः Mu. 1. 1; नाम ग्रह् to address or call upon by name; नामग्राहमरोदीत्सा Bk. 5 5; नाम कृ or दा, नाम्ना or नामतः कृ to give a name, call, name; चकार नाम्ना रघुमात्मसंभवं R. 3. 21, 5. 36; तौ कुशलवौ चकार किल नामतः 15. 32; चंद्रापीड इति नाम चक्रे K. 74; मातरं नामतः पृच्छेयं S. 7. 2 The mere name; संतप्तायसि संस्थितस्य पयसो नामापि न ज्ञायते Bh. 2. 67. 'not even the name, *i. e.* no trace or mark is seen' &c. 3 (In gram.) A noun, substantive (opp. आख्यात); तन्नाम येनाभिदधाति सत्त्वं or सत्त्वप्रधानानि नामानि Nir. 4 A word, name, synonymous word; इति वृक्षनामानि. 5 Substance (opp. गुण). –COMP. **-अंक** *a.* marked with a name; R. 12. 103. **-अनुशासनं, -अभिधानं** 1 declaring one's name. 2 a dictionary, lexicon. **—अपराधः** abusing (a respectable man) by name, calling names. **-आवली** a list of names (of a god). **-करणं, -कर्मन्** *n.* 1 giving a name, naming a child after birth. 2 a nominal affix. **-ग्रहः** addressing or mentioning by name, utterance of the name, calling to mind the name पुण्यानि नामग्रहणान्यपि महामुनीनां 43; Ms. 8. 271; R. 7. 41. **-त्यागः** abandonment of name स्वनामत्यागं करोमि Pt. 1. 'I shall forego my name.' **-धातुः** a nominal verb, denominative base (as पार्थायते, वृषस्यति &c.). **-धारक, -धारिन्** *a.* bearing only the name, in name only, nominal; Pt. 2. 84. **-धेयं** a name, appellation; वनज्योत्स्नेति कृतनामधेया S. 1; किं नामधेया सा M. 4; R. 1. 45, 10. 67, 11. 8; Ms. 2. 30. **-निर्देशः** indication by name **-मात्र** *a.* having only the name, nominal, in name; Pt. 1. 77; 2. 86. **-माला, -संग्रहः** a list of names, glossary (of nouns). **-मुद्रा** a seal-ring, signet-ring; उभे नाम मुद्राक्षराण्यनुवाच्य परस्परमवलोकयतः S. 1. **-लिंगं** gender of nouns. °**अनुशासनं** rules on the gender of nouns. **-वर्जित** *a.* 1 nameless. 2 stupid, foolish. **-वाचक** *a.* expressing a name. (**-कं**) a proper name. **-शेष** *a.* having only the name left, remaining in name only, dead, deceased; U. 2. 6.

नामिः An epithet of Vishṇu.

नामित *a.* Bent, bowed down &c.

नाम्य *a.* Pliable, flexible, pliant.

नायः 1 A leader, guide. 2 Guiding, directing. 3 Policy. 4 Means, expedient.

नायकः 1 A guide, leader, conductor. 2 A chief, master, head, lord. 3 A pre eminent or principal person, distinguished personage; सैन्यनायकः &c. 4 A general, commander. 5 (In Rhet). The hero of a poetic composition (a play or drama); (according to S. D. there are four main kinds of नायकः—धीरोदात्त, धीरोद्धत, धीरललित and धीरप्रशांत, and these are again subdivided, the total number of kinds being :40; *S.* D. 64-75. The Rasamanjarî mentions 3 classes पति, उपपति and वैशिकः 95-110). 6 The central gem of a necklace. 7 A paradigm or leading example; दृशैते स्त्रीषु नायकाः –COMP. **–अधिपः** a king, sovereign.

नायिका 1 A mistress. 2 A wife. 3 The heroine of a poetic composition. (According to S. D. a नायिका is of three kinds स्वा or स्वीया, अन्या or परकीया, and साधारणस्त्री. For further classification, see S. D. 97-112 and Rasamanjarî 3-94; cf. अन्यस्त्री. also.)

नारः Water (said to be *f.* also; cf. Ms. 1. 10.) **–रं** A multitude or assemblage of men. –COMP. **–जीवनं** gold.

नारक *a.* (**की** *f.*) Hellish, relating to hell, infernal. **–कः** 1 The infernal regions, hell. 2 An inhabitant of hell.

नारकिक, नारकिन्, नारकीय *a.* Hellish. *–m.* An inhabitant of hell.

नारंगः 1 The orange tree. 2 A lecher, libertine. 3 A living being. 4 A twin. **–गं, गकं** 1 The fruit of the orange trees; सद्योमुंडितमत्तहूणाचिबुकप्रस्पर्धि नारंगकं. 2 A carrot.

नारदः N. of a celebrated *Devarshi* (deified saint or divine sage). [He is one of the ten mind-born sons of Brahmà, being supposed to have sprung from his thigh. He is represented as a messenger from the gods to men and *vice versa*, and as being very fond of promoting discords among gods and men; hence his epithet of *Kalipriya.* He is said to have been the inventor of the lute or Vînà. He is also the author of a code of laws which goes by his name].

नारसिंह *a.* Pertaining to Narasimha. **–हः** An epithet of Vishṇu.

नाराचः 1 An iron arrow; तत्र नाराचदुर्दिने R. 4. 41. 2 An arrow in general; कनकनाराचपरंपराभिरिव K. 57. 3 Water-elephant.

नाराचिका, नाराची A goldsmith's scales (assay balance).

नारायणः 1 An epithet of Vishṇu; (the word is thus derived in Ms. 1. 10; आपो नारा इति प्रोक्ता आपो वै नरसूनवः। ता यदस्यायनं पूर्वं तेन नारायणः स्मृतः ॥) 2 N. of an ancient sage said to be a companion of *Nara* and to have produced Urvaśî from his thigh; cf. ऊरूद्भवा नरसखस्य मुनेः सुरस्त्री. V. 1. 2; see नरनारायण under नर also. **–णी** 1 An epithet of Lakshmî the goddess of wealth. 2 An epithet of Durgâ.

नारिकेरः, –लः The cocoa-nut; नारिकेलसमाकारा दृश्यंते हि सुहृज्जनाः H. 1. 94. (The word is also written नारिकेलि ली, नारिकेर-ल, नारिकेलि-ली, नाडि (डी) केर, नालिकेर, नालिकेलि-ली).

नारी 1 A woman; अर्थतः पुरुषो नारी या नारी सार्थतः पुमान् Mk. 3. 27. –COMP. **–तरंगकः** 1 a paramour. 2 a libertine **–दूषणं** a woman's vice; (they are:—पानं दुर्जनसंसर्गः पत्या च विरहोऽटनं। स्वप्नोऽन्यगृहवासश्च नारीणां दूषणानि षट् Ms. 9. 13. **–प्रसंगः** lechery, libertinism. **—रत्नं** a jewel of a woman, an excellent woman.

नार्यंगः The orange tree.

नाल *a.* Consisting or made of reeds. **–लं** 1 A hollow stalk, especially the stalk of the lotus; विकचकमलैः स्निग्धवैडूर्यनालैः Me. 76; R. 6. 13; Ku. 7. 89. (*-m.* also in this sense). 2 Any tubular vessel of the body. 3 Yellow orpiment. 4 A handle. **–लः** A canal, drain.

नालंबी The lute of Siva.

नाला A hollow stalk, especially that of the lotus.

नालिः, –ली *f.* 1 Any tubular vessel of the body. 2 A hollow stalk, especially that of the lotus. 3 A period of 24 minutes (घटिका). 4 An instrument for boring an elephant's ear. 5 A canal, drain. 6 A lotus flower.

नालिकः A buffalo. **–का** 1 The stalk of a lotus. 2 A tube. 3 An instrument for boring an elephant's ear. **–कं** 1 A lotus flower. 2 A kind of wind-instrument, a flute.

नालिकेर, नालिकेलि-ली See नारिकेर. &c.

नालीकः 1 An arrow. 2 A dart, javelin, 3 A lotus. 4 The fibrous stalk of a lotus. 4 The fibrous stalk of lotus flowers.

नालिकिनी 1 A multitude or assemblage of lotus flowers. 2 A lotus-pond.

नाविकः The helmsman of a vessel, a pilot; अख्यातिरिति ते कृष्ण मग्ना नौर्नाविके त्वयि; नाविकपुरुषे न विश्वासः Mb. 2 A navigator, sailor. 3 A passenger on board a ship.

नाविन् *m.* A boatman.

नाव्य *a.* 1 Accessible by a boat or ship, navigable (as a river &c.); नाव्याः सुप्रतरा नदीः R. 4. 31; नाव्यं पयः केचिदतारिषुर्भुजैः *Si.* 12. 76. 2 Praiseworthy. **–व्यं** Newness, novelty.

नाशः 1 Disappearance; गता नाशं तारा उपकृतमसाधाविव जने Mk. 5. 25. 2 Frustrations, destruction, ruin, loss; Bg. 2 40; R. 8. 88; 12. 67; so वित्त°, बुद्धि° &c. 3 Death. 4 Misfortune, calamity. 5 Abandonment, desertion. 6 Flight, retreat.

नाशक *a.* Destructive, destroying.

नाशन *a.* (**नी** *f.*) Destroying, causing to perish, removing (in comp). **–नं** 1 Destruction, ruin. 2 Removing, removal, expulsion. 4 Perishing, death.

नाशिन् *a.* (**नी** *f.*) 1 Destructive, destroying, removing. 2 Perishing, perishable; Bg. 2. 18; Ms. 8. 185.

नाष्टिकः The owner of anything lost.

नासा 1 the nose; स्फुरदधरनासापुटतया U. 1. 29; Bg. 5. 26. 2 The trunk of an elephant. 3 The upper timber of a door. –COMP. **–अग्रं** the tip of the nose; Mâl. 1. 1. **–छिद्रं, –रंध्रं, –विवरं** a nostril. **–दारु** *n.* the upper timber of a door frame. **–परिस्रावः** running at the nose, a running cold. **–पुटः, –पुटं** a nostrial. **–वंशः** the bridge of the nose. **–स्रावः** running cold.

नासिकंधय *a.* Drinking through the nose.

नासिका The nose; see नासा. –COMP. **–मलः** the mucus of the nose.

नासिक्य *a.* 1 Nasal. 2 Being in the nose. **–क्यः** A nasal sound. **–क्यं** The nose.

नासीरं Advancing or fighting in front of an army. **–रः** 1 The van or front (of an army &c.); नासीरचरयोर्भटयोः Mv. 6; N. 1. 68. 2 A champion who advances befor the line.

नास्ति *ind.* 'It is not', non-existence, as in नास्तिक्षीरा &c. –COMP. **–वादः** assertion of the non existence of God or a Supreme ruler, atheism, infidelity; बौद्धैनेव सर्वदा नास्तिवादादूरेण K. 49.

नास्तिक *a.* or **–कः** An atheist, unbeliever, one who denies the authority of the Vedas and a future life or the existence of a supreme ruler or creator of the universe; *Si.* 16. 7; Ms. 2. 11; 1. 22.

नास्तिक्यं Atheism, infidelity, heresy.

नास्तिदः The mango tree.

नास्यं A nose cord, the rein of a draught-ox.

नाहः 1 Binding, confinement. 2 A trap or snare. 3 Costiveness, constipation.

नाहुषः–षिः An epithet of Yayâti.

नि *ind.* (Mostly used as a prifix to verbs and nouns, rarely as an adverb or preposition. It is used in the following senses (according to G. M.) 1 Lowness, downward motion ('down', 'under', 'below'); निपत् निषद्. 2 A group or collection; निकर,

निकाय. 3 Intensity; निकाम, निगृहीत. 4 Command, order; निदेश. 5 Continuance, permanence; विविशित. 6 Skill; निपुण. 7 Restraint, confinement; निबंध. 8 Inclusion ('into', 'in'); निपीतमुदकं. 9 Proximity, nearness; निकट. 10 Insult, wrong, harm; निकृति; निकार. 11 Showing; निदर्शन. 12 Cessation; निवृत्. 13 Resort, refuge; निलय. 14 Doubt. 15 Certainty. 16 Affirmation. 17 Throwing, giving &c. (according to Durgâdâsa).

निःक्षेपः 1 Throwing, sending away. 2 Spending.

निःश्रयणी, निःश्रेणिः *f.* A ladder, a staircase; R. 15. 100.

निःश्वासः, निश्श्वासः 1 Breathing out, expiration. 2 Sighing, a sigh, breath.

निःसरणं 1 Going out, exit. 2 An egress or outlet from a house, a gate. 3 Final departure, death. 4 A means, expedient remedy. 5 Final beatitude.

निःसह *a.* 1 Unable to bear, resist or suffer, impatient. 2 Powerless, unnerved, spiritless, languid, fatigued; अयि विरम निःसहासि जाता Mâl. 2; so Mâl. 2, 7, U, 3. 3 Intolerable, unbearable, irresistible (in a passive sense).

निःसारणं 1 Expelling, driving or turning out. 2 The outlet from a house, ingress or egress.

निःस्रवः Remainder, surplus.

निःस्रावः 1 Expense, expending, expenditure. 2 The water of boiled rice.

निकट *a.* Near, close, hard by, proximate. —**टः,-टं** Proximity. (**निकटे** is used adverbially in the sense of 'near', 'at hand', 'hard or close by'; वहति निकटे कालस्रोतः समस्तभयावहं Sânti. 3. 2).

निकरः 1 A heap, pile. 2 A flock, multitude, collection; पपात स्वेदांबुप्रसर इव हर्षाश्रुनिकरः Gît. 11; *Si.* 4. 58; Rs. 6. 18. 3 A bundle. 4 Sap, pith, essence. 5 A suitable gift, honorarium. 6 A treasure.

निकर्तनं Cutting down or off.

निकर्षणं 1 An open space for recreation, or a play-ground in or near a town. 2 A court at the entrance of a house. 3 Neighbourhood. 4 An uncultivated or unploughed plot of ground.

निकषः 1 A touch-stone, whetstone; निकषे हेमरेखेव R. 17. 46; Mv. 1. 4. 2 (Fig.) Anything serving as a touch stone, a test; नन्वेव दर्पनिकषस्तव चंद्रकेतुः U. 5. 10; आदर्शः शिक्षितानां सुचरितनिकषः Mk. 1. 48; Dk. 1; K. 44. 3 A streak or line of gold made on a touchstone; कनकनिकषरुचिशुचिवसनेन श्वसिति न सा परिजनहसनेन Gît. 7; कनकनिकषस्निग्धा विद्युत्प्रिया न ममोर्वशी V. 4. 1; 5. 19. –Comp. –**उपलः, -ग्रावन्** *m.*, –**पाषाणः** a touchstone, whetstone; तदेमहेमनिकषोपलतां तनोति Gît. 11; तत्वनिकषग्रावा तु तेषां विपद् H. 1. 210; 2. 80.

निकषा N. of the mother of Râvaṇa or of imps in general.—*ind.* 1 Near, hard, close by, at hand (with occ.); निकषा सौधभित्तिं Dk.; विलंघ्य लंकां निकषा हनिष्यति *Si.* 1. 68. –Comp. –**आत्मजः** a demon.

निकाम *a.* 1 Plentiful, copious, abundant; निकामजला स्रोतोवहा *S.* 6. 16. 2 Desirous of. —**मः,-मं** Wish, desire. —**मं** *ind.* 1 According to one's wish or desire, agreeably to desire. 2 To one's satisfaction, to the heart's content; रात्रौ निकामं शयितव्यमपि नास्ति *S.* 2 'I cannot even sleep at ease or comfortably at night'. 3 Very much, exceedingly; निकामं क्षामांगी Mâl 2. 3; often used as the first member of comp. when it loses its final म्, निकामनिरंकुशः Gît. 7; Ku. 5. 23; *Si.* 4. 54.

निकायः 1 A heap, an assemblage, a class, multitude, flock, group in general; Mv. 1. 50. 2 A congregation, school, an association of persons who perform like duties 3 A house, habitation; dwelling-place; काशीनिकायः &c. 4 The body. 5 Aim, butt, mark. 6 The Supreme Being.

निकाय्यः A dwelling, habitation, house; न प्रणाय्यो जनः कच्चिन्निकाय्यं तेऽधितिष्ठति Bk. 6. 66.

निकारः 1 Winnowing corn. 2 Lifting up. 3 Killing, slaughter. 4 Humiliation, subjugation. 5 Insult, injury, wrong, offence; तीर्णो निकारार्णवः Ve. 6 43; Mv. 3. 41; 5. 14; 7. 8; Ki. 1. 43; 3. 44. 6 Abuse, reproach, disrespect. 7 Wickedness, malice. 8 Opposition, contradiction.

निकारणं Killing, slaughter.

निकाशः,-सः 1 Appearance, sight. 2 Horizon. 3 Proximity, vicinity. 4 Likeness, resemblance (at the end of comp.); Mâl. 5. 13.

निकाषः Scratching, rubbing; Ki. 7. 6.

निकुंचनः A measure of capacity equal to ¼ of a *Kudava* (also निकुंचक).

निकुंजः,-जं A bower, an arbour, a place over-grown with shrubs and creepers; यमुनातीरवानीरनिकुंजे मंदमास्थितं Gît. 4, 2, 11; Rs. 1. 23.

निकुंभः 1 N. of an attendant of *Siva*; R. 2. 35. 2 N. of the father of Sunda and Upasunda.

निकुरं (रुं) बं A flock, collection, mass, multitude; लतानिकुरुंबं Gît. 11; किरण° A. L. 20; चिकुर° 43.

निकुलीनिका A family art, one inherited by birth, any skill or art peculiar to a race.

निकृत *p. p.* 1 Humbled, cast down, humiliated. 2 Insulted, offended; U. 6. 14. 3 Deceived, cheated. 4 Removed. 5 Afflicted, injured. 6 Wicked, dishonest. 7 Base, low, vile.

निकृति *a.* Base, dishonest, wicked. (**-तिः** *f.* 1 Baseness, wickedness. 2 Dishonesty, fraud, deception; अनिकृतिनिपुणं ते चेष्टितं मानशौंड Ve. 5. 21; Ki. 1. 45. 3 Insult, offence, humiliation; Mu. 4. 11 4 Abuse, reproach. 5 Rejection, removal. 6 Poverty, indigence. –Comp. –**प्रज्ञ** *a.* wicked, evil-minded.

निकृंतन *a.* (**नी** *f.*) Cutting down, destroying; विरहिनिकृंतनकुंतमुखाकृतिकेतकिदंतुरिताशे (वसंते) Gît. 11. –**नं** Cutting, cutting off, destruction. 2 An instrument for cutting; एकेन नखनिकृंतनेन सर्वं कार्ष्णायसं विज्ञातं स्यात् S. B

निकृष्ट *a.* 1 Low, base, vile. 2 Outcast, despised. 3 Vulgar.

निकेतः A house, habitation, mansion, abode; श्रितगोकर्णनिकेतमीश्वरं R. 8 33; 14. 58; Bg. 12. 19; Ku. 5. 25; Ms. 6. 23; *Si.* 5 26.

निकेतनः Onion. –**नं** A mansion, house, abode; सिंजाना मंजुमंजीरं प्रविवेश निकेतनं Gît. 11; Ms. 6. 26, 11. 128. Ki. 1. 16.

निकोचनं Contraction, compression.

निक्कणः, निक्काणः 1 A musical tone or sound. 2 A sound in general.

निक्षा A nit (a wrong form for लिक्षा).

निक्षिप्त *p. p.* 1 Thrown or put down, thrown into. 2 Deposited, pledged, pawned. 3 Sent, sent off. 4 Rejected, abandoned.

निक्षेपः 1 Throwing or casting on (with acc.); अलं मान्यानां व्याख्यानेषु कटाक्षनिक्षेपेण S. D. 2. 2 A deposit, pledge, pawn in general; Pt. 1. 14; Ms. 8. 4. 3 Anything deposited without a seal in trust or as a compensation, an open deposit; समक्षं तु निक्षेपणं निक्षेपः Mit. on Y. 2. 67. 4 Sending away. 5 Throwing away, abandoning. 6 Wiping, drying.

निक्षेपणं 1 Putting down, placing down (the feet); Ku. 1. 33. 2 A means by which anything is kept.

निखननं Digging in, burying; as in स्थूणानिखनन्याय.

निखव *a.* Dwarfish. –**वं** A billion.

निखात *p. p.* 1 Dug up, excavated. 2 Fixed, planted (as a stake), infixed; शल्यं निखातमुदहारयतामुरस्तः R. 9. 78; अष्टादशद्वीपनिखातयूपः 6. 38; गाढं निखात इव मे हृदये कटाक्षः Mâl. 1. 29. 3 Dug in, buried.

निखिल *a.* Complete, whole, entire, all; प्रत्यक्षं ते निखिलमचिराद्भ्रातरुक्तं मया यत् Me. 94.

निगड *a.* Fettered, chained; वृद्धस्य निगडस्य च Ms. 4. 210. –**डः, –डं** 1 An iron chain for the feet of an elephant; बद्धापराणि परितो निगडान्यलावीत् *Si.* 5. 48; Bv. 4. 20. **2** A fetter, chain or shackle in general.

निगडित *a.* Fettered, put in irons, chained, bound.

निगण: The smoke of a sacrificial fire or burnt offering.

निगद:, निगाद: **1** Recitation, audible recitation of prayers. **2** A prayer repeated aloud. **3** Speech, discourse. **4** Learning the meaning; यदधीतमविज्ञातं निगदेनैव शब्द्यते Nir. **5** Mention, mentioning; इति निगदेनैव व्याख्यातं.

निगदितं A discourse, speech.

निगम: The Veda or Vedic text; साढ्यै साढ्वा साढेति निगमे P. VI. 3. 113, VII. 2. 64. **2** Any passage or word quoted from the Vedas, a Vedic sentence; तथापि च निगमो भवति (often found in Nirukta). **3** A work auxiliary to, and explanatory of, the Vedas; Ms. 4. 19 and Kull. thereon. **4** A sacred precept, the words of a god or holy man. **5** A root (as the source of a word). **6** Certainty, assurance. **7** Logic. **8** Trade, traffic. **9** A market, fair. **10** A caravan of wandering merchants. **11** A road, market-road. **12** A city.

निगमनं **1** Quotation of a word from the Veda or the word so quoted. **2** (In logic) The conclusion in a syllogism, a deduction (the fifth member of the five-membered Indian syllogism).

निगर:, निगार: Swallowing, devouring.

निगरणं **1** Swallowing, devouring. **2** (Fig.) Taking up, completely absorbing. **—ण:** **1** The throat. **2** The smoke of a sacrificial fire or burnt offering.

निग (गा) ल: **1** Swallowing, devouring. **2** The throat or neck of a horse; °वत् *m.* a horse.

निगीर्ण *p. p.* **1** Swallowed, devoured. **2** (Fig.) Completely swallowed or absorbed, hidden, concealed and hence to be supplied; उपमानेनान्तर्निगीर्णस्योपमेयस्य यदध्यवसानं सैका K. P. 10.

निगूढ *a.* **1** Hidden, concealed; Si. 13. 59. **2** Secret, private.—**ढं** *ind.* Secret, privately.

निगूहनं Concealing, hiding.

निग्रंथनं Killing, slaughter.

निग्रह: **1** Keeping in check, restraint, curbing, subjection; as in इंद्रियनिग्रह Ms. 6. 92; Y. 1, 222; Bh. 1. 66; Bg. 6. 34. **2** Suppression, obstruction, putting down; Ms. 6. 71. **3** Overtaking, capturing, arresting; त्वन्निग्रहे तु वरगात्रि न मे प्रयत्न: Mk. 1. 22; *Si.* 2. 88. **4** Confinement, imprisonment. **5** Defeat, overthrow, vanquishing. **6** Dispelling, destruction, removing; R. 9. 25, 15. 6; Ku. 5. 53. **7** Arresting of diseases, cure. **8** Punishment, chastisement (opp. अनुग्रह); निग्रहानुग्रहस्य कर्ता Pt. 1; निग्रहोऽप्ययमनुग्रहीकृत: R. 11. 90, 55; 12. 52, 63. **9** Rebuke, reprimand, blame. **10** Aversion, dislike, disgust. **11** (In Nyâya phil.) A flaw in an argument, a fault, a fault in a syllogism (by which a disputant is put down in argument); cf. Mu 5. 10. **12** A handle. **13** A limit, boundary.

निग्रहण *a.* Holding back or down, suppressing. **—णं** **1** Subduing, suppression. **2** Capture, confinement. **3** Chastisement, punishment in general. **4** Defeat.

निग्राह: **1** Punishment. **2** An imprecation; as in निग्राहस्ते भूयात् 'confusion seize thee!'; Bk. 7. 43.

निघ *a.* As high as broad. **—घ:** **1** A ball. **2** Sin.

निघंटु: **1** A vocabulary or glossary of words. **2** Particularly, the glossary of Vedic words explained by Yâska in his Nirukta.

निघर्ष:, निघर्षणं Rubbing, friction; Ki. 2. 51.

निघस: **1** Eating, dining. **2** Food.

निघात: **1** A blow, stroke; R. 11. 78. **2** Suppression or absence of accent.

निघाति: *f.* An iron club.

निघुष्टं Sound, noise.

निघ्न *a.* **1** Dependant, subservient, obedient (as a servant); तथापि निघ्नं नृप तावकीनै: प्रह्वीकृतं मे हृदयं गुणौघै: Ki. 3. 13. निघ्नस्य मे भर्तृनिदेशरौक्ष्यं देवि क्षमस्वेति बभूव नम्र: R. 14. 58. **2** Docile, tractable. **3** Dependent on (*i. e.* following the gender &c. of a substantive; इति विशेष्यनिघ्नवर्ग:. **4** (After a numeral) Multiplied with.

निचय: **1** A collection, heap, multitude; Ki. 4. 37. **2** An assemblage of parts constituting a whole; as in शरीरनिचय. **3** Certainty.

निचिकि: See नैचिकी.

निचाय: A heap.

निचित *p. p.* **1** Covered, overcast, over-spread; निचितं खमुपेत्य नीरदै: Ghat. 1; *Si.* 17 14. **2** Full of, filled. **3** Raised up.

निचुल: **1** A kind of reed. **2** N. of a poet and friend of Kâlidâsa; स्थानादस्मात् सरसनिचुलादुत्पतोदङ्मुख: खं Me. 14. (where Malli. observes:—निचुलो नाम महाकवि: कालिदासस्य सहाध्याय:; but this explanation is very doubtful). **3** An upper garment, cover; cf. निचोल.

निचुलकं A breast-plate, cuirass.

निचोल: **1** A cover, veil, wrapper; ध्वांतं नीलनिचोलचारु Git. 11; शीलय नीलनिचोलं 5. **2** A bedcover. **3** The cover of a litter (दोलिकावरणं).

निचोलक: **1** A jacket, bodice. **2** A soldier's jacket serving as a breast-plate.

निच्छवि: N. of a district, the modern Tirhut.

निच्छिवि: N. of one of the degraded castes (sprung from outcast Kshatriyas); see Ms. 10. 22.

निज् 3 U. (नेनेक्ति, नेनिक्ते, प्रणेनेक्ति, निक्त), To wash, cleanse, purify; सस्नु: पय: पपुरनेनिजुरंबराणि *Si.* 5. 28. **2** To wash or clean oneself, to be purified (A.) **3** To nourish.-WITH अव to wash, sprinkle water.-निस् to wash, clean, purify; R. 17. 22; Y. 1. 191; Ms. 5. 127.

निज *a.* **1** Innate, indigenous, native, inborn, congenial. **2** Own, one's own, relating to one-self, of one's own party or country; निजं वपु: पुनरनयन्निजां रुचिं *Si.* 17. 4; R. **3.** 15, **18**, Ms. 2. 50. **3** Peculiar. **4** Continual, perpetual.

निंज् **2** A. (निंक्ते) To wash.-WITH प्र to wash (प्रणिंक्ते).

निटलं (Sometimes written निटिल) The forehead; निटिलतटचुंबित Dk. 4, 15. -COMP.-अक्ष; N. of *S*iva.

निडीनं The downward flight or swoop of birds; see डीन.

नितंब: **1** The buttocks, posteriors (of a woman), (the circumference of the hip and loins); यातं यच्च नितंबयोर्गुरुतयामंदं विलासादिव *S.* 2. 1; R. 4. 52, 6. 17; Me. 41; Bh. 1. 5; M. **2**. **7**. **2** The slope, ridge, side, flank of a mountain; सनाकवनि तं नितंबरुचिरं (गिरं) Ki. 5. 27; सेव्या नितंबा: किमु भूधराणां किंवा स्मरस्मेरविलासिनीनां Bh. 1. 19; V. 4. 26; Bk. 2. 8; 7. 58. **3** A precipice. **4** The sloping bank of a river. **5** The shoulder. -COMP. -बिंब round or circular hips; Rs. 1. 4.

नितंबवत् *a.* Having beautiful hips. **-ती** A woman; चारु चुचुंब नितंबवती दयितं Gît. 1; V. 4. 26.

नितंबिन् *a.* **1** Having beautiful hips, having well-sloped buttocks (often applied to जघन); cf. M. **2**. 3; Ki. 8. 16; R. 19. 26. **6** Having beautiful sides (as a mountain). **-नी** **1** A woman with large and handsome hips; Ki. 8. 3; *Si.* 7. 68; Ku. 3. 7. **2** A woman in general.

नितरां *ind.* **1** Wholly, entirely, completely; प्राणांस्त्यजामि नितरां तदवाप्तिहेतो: Ch. P. 41; Bh. 1. 96. **2** Exceedingly, excessively, very much; तुदंति चेतो नितरां प्रवासिनां Rs. 2. 4; Amaru. 10; शोषितसरसि निदाघे नितरामेवोद्धत: सिंधु: Pt. 1. 104; नितरां नीचोऽस्मीति Bv. 1. 9. **3** Continually, always; eternally. **4** At all events. **5** Certainly.

नितलं One of the seven divisions of the lower regions; see पाताल.

नितांत *a*. Extraordinary, excessive, very much, intense; नितांतकठिनां रुजं मम न वेद सा मानसीं V. 2. 2. **-तं** *ind*. Excessively, very much, exceedingly, in a high degree.

नित्य *a*. 1 Continual, perpetual, constant, ever-lasting, eternal, uninterrupted; यदि नित्यमनित्येन लभ्येत H. 1. 48; नित्यज्योत्स्नाः प्रतिहततमोवृत्तिरम्याः प्रदोषाः Me. (regarded by Malli. as an interpolation); Ms. 2. 206. 2 Invariable, regular, fixed, not optional, regularly prescribed; (opp. काम्य) 3 Necessary, obligatory, essential. 4 Ordinary, usual (opp. नैमित्तिक). 5 (At the end of comp.) Constantly dwelling in, perpetually engaged in or busy with; जाह्नवीतीर°, अरण्य°, आदान°, ध्यान°, &c. **—त्यः** The ocean.—**त्यं** *ind*. Daily, constantly, always, ever, perpetually, eternally. –Comp. **-अनध्यायः** invariable suspens; Ms. 4. 107. **-अनित्य** *a*. eternal and perishable. **-ऋतु** *a*. regularly recurring at the seasons. **-कर्मन्** *n*., **-कृत्यं**. **-क्रिया** any daily and necessary rite, a constant act or duty, as the five daily Yaj*n*as. **-गतिः** air, wind **-दान** daily alms-giving. **-नियमः** an invariable rule. **-नैमित्तकं** an occasional act regularly recurring or any ceremony constantly performed to accomplish a particular object (*e. g.* a पर्वश्राद्ध). **-प्रलयः** sleep. **-मुक्तः** the Supreme spirit. **-यौवना** (ever youthful) an epithet of Draupadî. **-शंकित** *a*. perpetually alarmed, ever suspicious. **-समासः** 'a necessary compound', a compound the meaning of which cannot be expressed by its constituent members used separately (the separate ideas having merged in one); *e. g.* जमदग्नि, जयद्रथ &c; इवेन नित्यसमासः &c.

नित्यता,-त्वं 1 Invariableness, constancy, continuance, eternity, perpetuity. 2 Necessity.

नित्यदा *ind*. Perpetually, always, constantly, eternally.

नित्यशस् *ind*. Constantly, always, eternally; Bg. 8. 14; Ms. 2. 96; 4. 150.

निदद्रुः A man.

निदर्शक *a*. 1 Seeing. 2 Seeing into, perceiving. 3 Pointing out, proclaiming, indicating.

निदर्शनं 1 View, insight, looking into, sight, vision. 2 Pointing to, showing. 3 Proof, evidence; बलिना सह योद्धव्यमिति नास्ति निदर्शनं Pt. 3. 23. 4 An instance, example, illustration; ननु प्रभुरेव निदर्शनं S. 2; निदर्शनमसाराणां लघुर्बहुतृणं नरः Si. 2. 50; R. 8. 45. 5 A prognostic. 6 A sign, an omen. 7 A scheme, system. 8 A precept. scriptural authority, injunction. **-ना** A figure of speech in rhetoric; thus defined:—निदर्शना । अभवन्वस्तुसंबंध उपमापरिकल्पकः K. P. 10; *e. g.* R. 1. 2.

निदाघः 1 Heat, warmth. 2 The hot season, summer (the months of ज्येष्ठ and आषाढ); निदाघमिहिरज्वालाशतैः Bv. 1. 16; निदाघकालः समुपागतः प्रिये Rs. 1. 1; Pt. 1. 105; Ku. 7. 84. 3 Sweat, perspiration. –Comp. **-करः** the sun. **-कालः** summer.

निदानं 1 A band, rope, halter. 2 A rope for tying up a calf. 3 A primary cause, the first or essential cause; निदानमिक्ष्वाकुकुलस्य संततेः R. 3. 1; अथवा बलमारंभो निदानं क्षयसंपदः Si. 2. 94. 4 A cause in general; मुंच मयि मानमनिदानं Gît. 5. 5 (In medicine) Inquiry into the causes of a disease, pathology. 6 Diagnosis of a disease. 7 End, termination. 8 Purity, purification, correctness.

निदिग्ध *p. p.* 1 Smeared, anointed, 2 Increased, accumulated. **—ग्धा** Small cardamoms.

निदिध्यासः, निदिध्यासनं Profound and repeated meditation, constant musing.

निदेशः 1 Order, command, direction, instruction; वाक्येनेयं स्थापिता स्वे निदेशे M. 3. 14; स्थितं निदेशे पृथगादिदेश R. 14. 14. 2 Speech, narration, conversation. 3 Vicinity, neighbourhood. 4 A vessel, vase.

निदेशिन् *a*. Pointing &c. **-नी** 1 A quarter, point of the compass. 2 A region.

निद्रा 1 Sleep, sleepiness; प्रच्छायसुलभनिद्रा दिवसाः S. 1. 3. 2 Sloth. 3 Shutting, budding state. –Comp. **-भंगः** awaking. **-वृक्षः** darkness. **-संजननं** phlegm, phlegmatic humour.

निद्राणं *a*. Sleeping, sleepy.

निद्रालु *a*. Sleeping, sleepy. **-लुः** An epithet of Vishṇu.

निद्रित *a*. Asleep, slept.

निधन *a*. Poor, indigent; अहो निधनता सर्वापदामास्पदं Mk 1. 14. **-नः**: **-नं** 1 Destruction, annihilation, death, loss; स्वधर्मे निधनं श्रेयः Bg. 3. 35; म्लेच्छनिवहनिधने कलयसि करवालं Gît. 1; कल्पांतेष्वपि न प्रयाति निधनं विद्याख्यमंतर्धनं Bh. 2. 16. 2 Conclusion, end, termination. **-नं** Family, race.

निधानं 1 Putting down, laying down, depositing. 2 Keeping, preserving. 3 A place where anything is placed, a receptacle, reservoir; निधानं धर्माणां G. L. 18; 4 Treasure; निधानगर्भामिव सागरांबरां R. 3. 9; Bg. 9. 18; विद्यैव लोकस्य परं निधानं 5 Hoard, store, property, wealth.

निधिः 1 Abode, receptacle, reservoir; जल°, तोय°, तपोनिधिः &c. 2 A store-house, treasury. 3 A treasure, store, hoard; (for the nine treasures of Kubera, see नवनिधि). 4 The ocean. 5 An epithet of Vishṇu. 6 A man endowed with many good qualities. –Comp. **-ईशः**, **-नाथः** an epithet of Kubera.

निधुवनं 1 Agitation, trembling. 2 Sexual enjoyment, coition; अतिशयमधुरिपुनिधुवनशीलं Gît. 2; Si. 11. 18; Ch. P. 4, 9, 25. 3 Pleasure, enjoyment, sport.

निध्यानं Seeing, beholding, sight.

निध्वानः Sound.

निनंक्षु *a*. 1 Wishing to die. 2 Wishing to escape or fly away; Bk. 4. 33.

निन (ना) दः 1 Sound, noise; उच्चार निनदोऽम्भसि तस्याः R. 9. 73; 11. 15; Rs 1. 15. 2 Buzzing, humming (of bees &c.)

निनयनं 1 Performance. 2 Performing, accomplishing. 3 Pouring out.

निंद् 1. P. (निंदति, निंदित, प्रणिंदति) To blame, censure, find fault with, revile, reproach, condemn; निनिंद रूपं हृदयेन पार्वती Ku. 5. 1; सा निंदंती स्वानि भाग्यानि बाला S. 5. 30; Bg. 2. 36, Ms. 3. 42.

निंदक *a*. Blaming, censuring, abusing, defaming.

निंदनं, निंदा 1 Blame, censure, reproof, reproach, abuse, reviling, defamation; व्याजस्तुतिर्मुखे निंदा K. P. 10; पर°, वेद°. 2 Injury, wickedness. –Comp. **-स्तुतिः** *f*. 1 ironical praise, irony. 2 Covert praise.

निंदित *p. p.* Blamed, censured, abused, defamed &c.

निंदुः *f*. A woman bearing a dead child.

निंद्य *a*. 1 Blamable, censurable, reprehensible, bad, vile. 2 Forbidden, prohibited.

निपः -पं A water-jar. **-पः** The Kadamba tree.

निप (पा) ठः Reading, reciting, studying.

निपतनं 1 Falling down, descending, alighting. 2 Flying down.

निपत्या 1 Slippery ground. 2 A battle-field.

निपाकः Maturing, ripening.

निपातः 1 Falling or coming down; descending, alighting; पयोधरोत्सेधनिपातचूर्णिताः Ku. 5. 24; Rs. 5. 4. 2 Attacking, falling upon, spring, leap; R. 2. 60. 3 Casting, hurling, discharging; Ku. 3. 15. 4 Descent, fall; निशितनिपाताः शराः S. 1. 10. 5 Dying, death; Ms. 6. 31. 6 Accidental occurrence or mention. 7 An irregular form, irregularity, putting down as irregular or exceptional; एते निपाताः, निपातोयं &c. 8 A particle, an indeclinable; P. 1. 4. 56.

निपातनं 1 Throwing down, beating or knocking down; Ms. 11. 208. 2 Overthrowing, destroying, killing. 3 Touching with. 4 Putting down as irregular or exceptional. 5 An irregular form of a word, irregularity, exception.

निपानं 1 Drinking. 2 Any reservoir of water, pool, puddle; गाहंतां महिषा निपानसलिलं शृंगैर्मुहुस्ताडितं *S*. 2. 5; H. 1. 172; R. 9. 53. 3 A place or trough near a well for watering cattle. 4 A well. 5 A milk-pail.

निपीडनं 1 Squeezing, pressing;, *Si*. 1. 74, 13. 11. 2 Hurting, injuring. **—ना** Oppression, hurt, injury.

निपुण *a*. 1 Clever, sharp, shrewd, skilful; वयस्य निसर्गनिपुणाः स्त्रियः M. 3. 2 Proficient or skilled in, conversant or familiar with (with loc. or instr.); वाचि निपुणः, वाचा निपुणः. 3 Experienced. 4 Kindly or friendly towards. 5 Acute, fine, delicate. 6 Complete, perfect, accurate. **—णं** *ind*. or **निपुणेन** 1 Skilfully, cleverly. 2 Perfectly, completely, totally. 3 Exactly, carefully, accurately, minutely; निपुणमन्विष्यन्नुपलब्धवान् Dk. 59. 4 in a delicate manner.

निबद्ध *p. p*. 1 Bound, tied, fettered, stopped, closed &c. 2 Connected with, relating to. 3 Formed of. 4 Set or inlaid with. 5 Called as a witness.

निबंधः 1 Binding, tying, fastening. 2 Attachment, intentness; Bg. 16. 5. 3 Composing, writing down. 4 A literary composition or treatise, work; प्रत्यक्षरश्लेषमयप्रबंधविन्यासवैदग्ध्यनिधिर्निबंधं चक्रे Vâs. 5 A compendium. 6 Restraint, obstruction, confinement. 7 Suppression of urine. 8 A bond, fetter. 9 A grant of property, an assignment of cattle, money &c. for support; भूर्या पितामहोपात्त निबंधो द्रव्यमेव वा Y. 2. 121 fixed property. 10 Foundation, origin. 11 Cause, reason.

निबंधनं 1 The act of fastening, binding together. 2 Constructing, building. 3 Restraining, checking, confining. 4 A bond, fetter. 5 A tie, band, support, stay; आशानिबंधनं जाता जीवलोकस्य U. 3; यस्त्वामिव मामकीनस्य मनसो द्वितीयं निबंधनं Mâl. 3. 6 Dependence, connection; ते त्वदाशानिबंधनाः M. 4. 14; परस्परनिबंधनः Pt. 1. 79 inter-dependent. 7 Cause, origin, ground, motive, basis, foundation; वाक्प्रतिष्ठानिबंधनानि देहिनां व्यवहारतंत्राणि Mâl. 4 base on &c.-प्रत्याशा° 3; अनिबंधन causeless; accidental; U. 5, 7. 8 Abode, seat, receptacle; Mâl. 2. 6. 9 Composing, arrangement; Ku. 7. 90 (रचना). 10 A literary composition or work, a treatise. 11 A grant (of land), an assignment; सद्वृत्तिः, सन्निबंधना *Si*. 2. 112 (where निबंधन means 'a treatise' also). 12 The peg of a lute. 13 (In gram.) Syntax. 14 A commentary.

निबंधनी A bond, fetter, tie.

निब (व)र्हण *a*. Destroying, destoyer, enemy (in comp.); Ki. 2. 43; Mv. 3. 37. **—णं** Killing, destruction, annihilation, slaughter; N. 1. 131.

निबिड *a*. Dense, thick; see निविड.

निभ *a*. (At the end of comp. only) Like, similar, resembling; उद्बुद्धमुग्धकनकाब्जनिभं वहति Mâl. 1. 40; so चंद्रनिभानना &c. **-भः, भं** 1 Appearence, light, manifestation. 2 Pretence, disguise, pretext. 3 A trick, fraud.

निभालनं Seeing, sight, perception.

निभीत *a*. 1 Quite frightened (अत्यंतभीत). 2 Gone, past.

निभृत *a*. 1 Placed down, deposited, lowered. 2 Filled with, full of; चिंतया निभृतः Bhâg. 3 Concealed, hidden, out of sight, unperceived, unobserved; निभृतो भूत्वा Pt. 1; नभसा निभृतेंदुना R. 8. 15. with the moon become invisible, about to set or go down; *Si*. 6. 30. 4 Secret, covert; *Si*. 13. 42. 5 (*a*) Still, silent; निभृतद्विरेफं (काननं) Ku. 3. 42, 6. 2. (*b*) Steady, fixed, immoveable, motionless; *S*. 1. 8. 6 Mild. gentle; अनिभृता वायवः Ki. 13. 66. not gentle, violent or strong; Mâl. 2. 12. 7 Modest, humble; अनिभृतकरेषु प्रियेषु Me. 68; प्रणामनिभृता कुलवधूरिव Mu. Mu. 1 8 Firm, resolute. 9 Lonely, solitary; निभृतनिकुंजगृहं गतया Gît. 2. 10 Shut, closed (as a door). **—तं** *ind*. 1 Secretly, covertly, privately, unperceived; *S*. 3; *Si*. 3. 74; Ms. 9. 263. 2 Silently, quietly; K. 134.

निमग्न *p. p*. 1 Plunged, dipped into, immersed, submerged, sunk (fig. also); निमग्नस्य पयोराशौ, चिंतानिमग्न &c. 2 Gone down, set (as the sun). 3 Over-whelmed, covered. 4 Depressed, not prominent.

निमज्जथुः 1 The act of diving or entering into, plunging. 2 Plunging into the bed, sleeping, going to bed; तल्पे कांतांतरैः सार्धं मन्येऽहं विह्न् निमज्जथुं Bk. 5. 20.

निमज्जनं Bathing, diving, plunging, sinking (lit. and fig.); हृद्ग् निमज्जनमुपैति सुधायां N. 5. 94; एवं संसारगहने उन्मज्जननिमज्जने Mb.

निमंत्रणं 1 Invitation. 2 Summoning, calling. 3 A summons.

निमयः Barter, exchange.

निमानं 1 Measure. 2 Price (निमानं =मूल्यं Sk.).

निमिः 1 Winking, twinkling (of the eyes). 2 N. of one of the descendants of Ikshvâku, and ancestor of the line of kings who ruled in Mithilâ.

निमित्तं 1 A cause, motive, ground, reason; निमित्तनैमित्तकयोरयं क्रमः *S*. 7. 30. 2 The instrumental or efficient cause (opp. उपादान). 3 Any apparent cause, pretext; निमित्तमात्रं भव सव्यसाचिन् Bg. 11. 33; निमित्तमात्रेण पांडवक्रोधेन भवितव्यं Ve. 1. 4 A mark, sing, token. 5 A butt, mark, target: निमित्तादपराद्धेषोर्धानुष्कस्येव वल्गितं *Si*. 2. 27. 6 An omen, prognostic (good or bad); निमित्तं सूचयित्वा *S*. 1; निमित्तानि च पश्यामि विपरीतानि केशव Bg. 1. 30; R. 1. 86; Ms. 6. 50; Y. 1. 203, 3. 171. (**निमित्त** is used at the end of comp. in the sense of 'caused or occasioned by'; किन्निमित्तोयमातंकः *S*. 3. **निमित्तं, निमित्तेन, निमित्तात्** 'because of, 'on account of.).-Comp. **-अर्थः** the infinitive mood (in gram.). **-आवृत्तिः** *f*. dependence on a special cause. **-कारणं, -हेतुः** an instrumental or efficient cause. **-कृत्** *m*. a crow. **-धर्मः** 1 expiation. 2 an occasionl rite. **-विद्** *a*. knowing good or bad omens. (*-m*). an astrologer.

निमिषः 1 Winking, shutting the eye, twinkling. 2 Twinkling of the eyes as a measure of time, a moment. 3 The shutting of flowers. 4 Morbid twinkling of the eye. 5 N. of Vishṇu. -Comp. **-अंतरं** the interval of a moment.

निमिलनं 1 Shutting the eyelids, winking; नयननिमिलनखिन्नया यया ते Gît. 4; Amaru. 33. 2 Closing the eyes in death, death. 3 (In astr.) Total eclipse.

निमीला, निमीलिका 1 Shutting the eyes. 2 Winking, blinking, conniving at anything. 3 Fraud, pretence, trick.

निमूलं *ind*. Down to the root; मिमूलकाषं कषति.

निमेषः Twinkling of the eye, a moment &c.; see निमिष; हरति निमेषात् कालः सर्वं Moha M. 4; अनिमेषेण चक्षुषा with a steadfast or fixed look; R. 2. 19; 3 43, 61. -Comp. **-कृत्** *f*. lightning. **-रुच्** *m*. a fire-fly.

निम्न *a*. Deep (lit. and fig.); चकितहरिणीप्रेक्षणा निम्ननाभिः Me. 82; Rs. 5. 12; *Si*. 10. 58. 2 Low, depressed. **—म्नं** 1 Depth, low ground, low land; (कः) पयश्च निम्नाभिमुखं प्रतीपयेत् Ku. 5. 5; न च निम्नादिव सलिलं निवर्तते मे ततो हृदयं *S*. 3. 2; Y. 2. 151; Rs. 2. 13. 2 A slope, declivity. 3 A gap, chasm in the ground. 4 A depression, low part; जलनिबिडितवस्त्रव्यक्तनिम्नोन्नताभिः Mâl. 4. 10. -Comp. **-उन्नत** *a*. low and high, depressed and elevated, uneven. **-गतं** a low place. **-गा** a river, a mountain-stream: R. 8. 8.

निंबः A tree with bitter fruits; आम्रं छित्त्वा कुठारेण निंबं परिचरेत्तु यः। यश्चैनं पयसा सिंचेन्नैवास्य मधुरो भवेत् ॥ Râm.

निम्लोचः Sunset.

नियत *p. p*. 1 Curbed, restrained. 2 Subdued, controlled, self-possessed, self-governed. 3 Abstemious, temperate. 4 Attentive. 5 Fixed, permanent, constant, steady. 6 Certain, settled, sure. 7 Inevitable. 8 Positive, definite. 9 Forming the subject of consideration, relevant or irrelevant; see तुल्ययोगिता. -तं *ind.* 1 Always, constantly. 2 Positively, certainly, inevitably, surely.

नियतिः *f.* 1 Restraint, restriction. 2 Destiny, fate, luck, fortune (good or bad); नियतिबलान्नु Dk.; नियतेर्नियोगात् *Si.* 4. 34; Ki. 2. 12, 4. 21 3 A religious duty or obligation. 4 Self-command, self-restraint.

नियंतृ *m.* 1 A charioteer, driver; *Si.* 12. 24. 2 A gevernor, ruler, master, regulator; R. 1. 17, 15. 51. 3 A punisher, chastiser.

नियंत्रणं-णा 1 Checking, reserve, restraint; अनियंत्रणानुयोगो नाम तपस्विजनः *S.* 1. 2 Restricting, confining (to a particular sense) अनेकार्थस्य शब्दस्यैकार्थनियंत्रणं S. D 2. 3 Guiding, governing. 4 Defining.

नियंत्रित *p. p.* 1 Curbed, restrained. 3 Restricted, confined to (a particular sense, as a word.)

नियमः 1 Restraining, checking. 2 Taming, subduing. 3 Confining, preventing. 4 A restraint, check; Ms. 8. 122. 5 Restriction, limitation. 6 A rule or precept, law (in general), usage; नायमेकांततो नियमः S. B. 7 Regularity; Ratn. 1. 20. 8 Certainty, ascertainment. 9 An agreement, promise, vow, engagement. 10 Necessity, obligation. 11 Any voluntary or self-imposed religious observance (dependent on external conditions); R. 1. 94; (see Malli. on Si. 13. 33 and Ki. 5. 42) 12 Any minor observance or lesser vow, a duty prescribed to be done, but which is not so obligatory as a यम q. v.; शौचमिज्या तपो दानं स्वाध्यायोपस्थनिग्रहः। व्रतमौनोपवासं च स्नानं च नियमा दश ॥ Atri. 13 Penance, devotion, religious austerities; नियमविघ्नकारिणी *S.* 1; R. 15. 74. 14 (In Mim. phil.) A rule or precept which lays down or *specifies* something which, in the absence of that rule, would be *optional*; विधिरत्यंतमप्राप्तौ नियमः पाक्षिके सति. 15 (In Yoga phil.) Restraint of the mind, the second of the 8 principal steps of meditation in *yoga*. 16 (In Rhet.) A poetical commonplace or convention, as the description of the cuckoo in spring, peacocks in the rains &c. (नियमेन as a rule, invariably). -COMP. -निष्ठा rigid observance of prescribed rites. -पत्रं a written agreement. -स्थितिः *f.* steady observance of religious obligations, asceticism.

नियमनं 1 Checking, punishing, restraining, subduing; नियमनादसतां च नराधिपः R. 9. 6. 2 Restriction, limitation. 3 Humiliation. 4 A precept, fixed rule.

नियमवती A woman having the monthly courses.

नियमित *p. p.* 1 Checked, curbed, restrained. 2 Governed, guided. 3 Regulated, prescribed, laid down. 4 Fixed, agreed upon, stipulated.

नियामः 1 Restraint. 2 A religious vow.

नियातनं See निपातनं.

नियामक *a.* (मिका *f.*) 1 Restraining, checking. 2 Subduing, overpowering. 3 Limiting, restricting, defining more closely. 4 Guiding, governing. -कः 1 A master, ruler. 2 A charioteer. 3 A boatman, sailor. 4 A pilot.

नियुक्त *p. p.* 1 Directed, ordered, instructed, commanded. 2 Authorised, appointed. 3 Permitted to raise issue; see नियोग below. 4 Attached to. 5 Fastened to. 6 Ascertained.

नियुक्तिः *f.* 1 Injunction, order, command. 2 Appointment, commission, office, charge.

नियुतं 1 A million. 2 A hundred thousand. 3 Ten thousand crores or 100 Ayutas.

नियुद्धं Fighting on foot, close fight, personal struggle.

नियोगः 1 Employment, use, application. 2 An injunction, order, command, direction, commission, charge, appointed task or duty, any business committed to one's care; यः सावज्ञो माधवश्रीनियोगे M. 5. 8; मनो नियोगक्रिययोत्सुकं मे R. 5. 11; अथवा नियोगः खल्वीदृशो मंदभागस्य U. 1; आज्ञापयतु को नियोगोनुष्ठीयतामिति *S.* 1; त्वमपि स्वनियोगमशून्यं कुरु 'go about your own business', 'do your appointed duty', (frequently occurring in plays and used as a courteous way of asking servants to withdraw). 3 Fastening or attaching to. 4 Necessity, obligation; तत्सिषेवे नियोगेन स विकल्पपराङ्मुखः R. 19. 49. 5 Effort, exertion. 6 Certainty, ascertainment. 7 A practice prevalent in ancient times which permitted a childless widow to have intercourse with the brother or any near kinsman of her deceased husband to raise up issue to him, the son so born being called क्षेत्रज; cf. Ms. 9. 59:—देवराद्वा सपिंडाद्वा स्त्रिया सम्यङ्नियुक्तया। प्रजेप्सिताधिगंतव्या संतानस्य परिक्षये ॥; see 60, 65 also. (Vyâsa begot पांडु and धृतराष्ट्र on the widows of विचित्रवीर्य in this way).

नियोगिन् *m.* An officer, a dependent, minister, functionary.

नियोग्यः A lord, master.

नियोजनं 1 Fastening, attaching. 2 Ordering, prescribing. 3 Urging, impelling. 4 Appointing.

नियोज्यः One charged with any duty, a functionary, an officer, a servant, employe; सिध्यंति कर्मसु महत्स्वपि यन्नियोज्याः *S.* 7. 4.

नियोद्धृ *m.* 1 A combatant, wrestler. 2 A cock.

निर् *ind.* A substitute for निस् before vowels and soft consonants conveying the senses of 'out of', 'away from', 'without', 'free from', and may be frequently expressed by 'less', 'un', used with the noun; see the compounds given below; see निस् and cf. अ also. -COMP. -अंश *a.* 1 whole, entire. 2 not entitled to any share of the ancestral property. -अक्षः the place of no latitude (in astronomy). अग्नि *a.* having lost or neglected the consecrated fire. -अंकुश *a.* 'not curbed by a hook', unchecked, uncontrolled, unruly, independent, completely free, unfettered; निरंकुश इव द्विपः Bhâg.; कामो निकामनिरंकुशः Git. 7; निरंकुशाः कवयः Sk.; Bh. 3. 106; Mv. 3. 39. -अंग *a.* 1 having no parts. 2 deprived of expedients or resources. -अजिन *a.* skinless. -अंजन *a.* 1 without collyrium. 2 unstained, untinged. 3 free from falsehood. 4 simple, artless. (-नः) an epithet of *Siva*. (-ना) the day of full moon. -अतिशय *a.* unsurpassed. -अत्यय *a.* 1 free from danger, secure, safe; R. 17. 53. 2 free from fault, unblameable, faultless, disinterested; Ki. 1. 12, 13. 61. 3 completely successful. -अध्व *a.* one who has lost his way. -अनुक्रोश *a.* pitiless, merciless, hard-hearted. (-शः) mercilessness, hard-heartedness. -अनुग *a.* having no followers. -अनुनासिक *a.* not nasal. -अनुरोध *a.* 1 unfavourable, unfriendly. 2 unkind, unamiable; Mâl. 10. -अंतर *a.* 1 constant, perpetual, uninterrupted, incessant; निरंतराविपटलैः Bv. 1. 16; निरंतरास्वंतरवातवृष्टिषु Ku. 5. 25. 2 having no intervening or intermediate space, having no interval, close; मूढे निरंतरपयोधरया मयैव Mk. 5. 15. हृदयं निरंतरबृहत्कठिनस्तनमंडलावरणमप्यभिदन् *Si.* 9. 66. 3 compact, dense; *Si.* 16. 76. 4 coarse, gross. 5 faithful, true (as a friend). 6 not hidden from view. 7 not different, similar, identical. (-रं) *ind.* 1 without interruption, constantly, continually, incessantly. 2 without intervening space or interval. 3 closely, tightly, firmly; (परिष्वजस्व) कतिरिदं मम निरंतरमंगमंगैः Ve. 3. 27; परिष्वजेते शयने निरंतरं Rs. 2. 11. 4

immediately. °अभ्यासः constant study, diligent exercise or practice. -अंतराल a. 1 without an intervening space, close. 2 narrow. -अन्वय a. 1 having no progeny, childless. 2 unconnected, unrelated. 3 not agreeing with the context (as a word in a sentence). 4 without logical connection or regular sequence, unmethodical. 5 without being seen, out of sight; Ms. 8. 332. 6 without retinue, unaccompanied; see अन्वय. -अपत्रप a. 1 shameless, impudent. 2 bold. -अपराध a. guiltless, innocent, faultless, blameless. (-धः) innocence. -अपाय a. 1 free from harm or evil. 2 free from decay, imperishable. 3 infallible. -अपेक्ष a. 1 not depending on, irrespective or independent of, having no need of (with loc.); न्यायनिर्णीतसारत्वान्निरपेक्षमिवागमे Ki. 11. 39. 2 disregarding, taking no notice of. 3 free from desire, secure; H. 1. 83 4 careless, negligent, indifferent. 5 indifferent to worldly attachments or pursuits; Ms. 6. 41. 6 disinterested, not expecting any reward from another; Bv. 1. 5, 7 without purpose. (-क्षा) indifference, disregard. -अभिभव a. not subject to humiliation or disgrace. -अभिमान a. 1 free from self conceit, devoid of pride or egotism. 2 void of self-respect. -अभिलाष a. not intent upon, indifferent to; स्वसुखनिरभिलाषः खिद्यसे लोकहेतोः S. 5. 5. -अभ्र a. cloudless. -अमर्ष a. 1 void of anger, patient. 2 apathetic. -अंबु a. 1 abstaining from water. 2 waterless, destitute of water. -अर्गल a. without a bolt, unbarred, unobstructed; unrestrained, unimpeded, completely free; M. 5. (-लं) ind. freely. -अर्थ a. 1 void of wealth, poor, indigent. 2 meaningless, unmeaning (as a word or sentence). 3 nonsensical. 4 vain, useless, purposeless. -अर्थक a. 1 useless, vain, unprofitable. 2 unmeaning, nonsensical, conveying no reasonable meaning. (-कं) an expletive; निरर्थकं तु हीत्यादि पूरणैकप्रयोजनं Chandr. 2. 6. -अवकाश a. 1 without free space. 2 without leisure. -अवग्रह a. 'free from restraint,' unrestrained, unchecked, uncontrolled, irresistible. 2 free, independent. 3 self-willed, head-strong. -अवद्य a. blameless, faultless, unblameable, unobjectionable; हृद्यनिरवद्यरूपो भूपो बभूव Dk. 1. -अवधि a. having no end, unlimited; U. 3. 44. -अवयव a. 1 without parts. indivisible. 3 without limbs. -अवलंब a. 1 unsupported, without support; S. 6. 2 not affording support. -अवशेष a. whole, complete, entire. -अवशेषेण ind. completely, entirely, fully, totally. -अशन a. abstaining from food. (-नं) fasting. -अस्त्र a. weaponless, unarmed. -अस्थि a. boneless. -अहंकार, -अहंकृति a. free from egotism or pride, humble, lowly. -अहम् a. free from egotism or self-conceit. -आकांक्ष a. 1 wishing nothing, free from desire. 2 wanting nothing to fill up or complete (as the sense of a word or sentence). -आकार a. 1 devoid of form, formless, without from. 2 ugly, deformed. 3 disguised. 4 unassuming, modest. (-रः) 1 the uuiversal spirit, Almighty. 2 an epithet of Siva. 3 of Vishṇu. -आकृति a. 1 formless, shapeless. 2 deformed. (-तिः) 1 a religious student who has not duly gone through a course of study, or who has not properly read the Vedas. 2 especially, a Brâhmaṇa who has neglected the duties of his caste by not going through a regular course of study. -आकुल a. 1 unconfused, unperplexed, unbewildered. 2 steady, calm. 3 clear. -आक्रोश a. unaccused, unreviled. -आगस् a faultless, innocent, sinless; R. 8. 48. -आचार a. without approved customs or usages, lawless. -आडंबर a. without drums. -आतंक a. 1 free from fear; R. 1. 63. 2 without ailment, comfortable, healthy. -आतप a. sheltered from heat, shady, not penetrated by the sun's rays (-पा) the night. -आदर a. disrespectful. -आधार a. 1 without a receptacle. 2 without support, supportless (fig. also); निराधारो हा रोदिमि कथय केषामिह पुरः G L. 4, 39. -आधि a. secure, free from anxiety -आपद् a. free from misfortune or calamity. आबाध a. 1 unvexed, unmolested, undisturbed, free from disturbance. 2 unobstructed. 3 not molesting or disturbing. 4 (in law) frivolously vexatious (as s suit or cause of complaint); e. g. अस्मद्गृहप्रदीपप्रकाशेनायं स्वगृहे व्यवहरति Mit. -आमय a 1 free from disease or illness, sound, healthy, hale. 2 untainted, pure. 3 guileless. 4 free from defects or blemishes. 5 full, complete. 6 infallible. (-यः, यं) freedom from disease or illness, health, well-being, welfare, happiness. (यः) 1 a wild goat. 2 a hog or boar. -आमिष a. 1 fleshless. 2 having no sensual desires or covetousness. 3 receiving no wages or remuneration. -आय a. yielding no income or revenue, profitless. -आयास a. not fatiguing, easy. -आयुध a. unarmed, weaponless. -आलंब a 1 having no prop or support (fig. also); Mv. 4. 53. 2 not depending on another, independent. 3 self-supported, friendless, alone; निरालंबो लंबोदरजननि कं यामि शरणं Jag. -आलोक a. 1 not looking about or seeing. 2 deprived of sight. 3 deprived of light, dark; Mâl. 5. 30. -आश a. devoid of hope, despairing or despondent of; मनोबभूवेंदुमतीनिराशं R. 6. 2. -आशंक a. fearless. -आशिस् a. 1 without a boon or blessing. 2 without any desire, wish or hope, indifferent; जगच्छरण्यस्य निराशिषः सतः Ku. 5. 76. -आश्रय a. 1 without a prop or support, supportless, unsupported. 2 friendless, destitute, alone, without shelter or refuge; निराश्रयाधुना वत्सलता. -आस्वाद a. testless, insipid, unsavoury. -आहार a. 'foodless', fasting, abstaining from food. (-रः) fasting. -इच्छ a. without wish or desire, indifferent. -इंद्रिय a. 1 having lost a limb or the use of it. 2 mutilated, maimed, 3 weak, infirm, frail. 4 without प्रमाण or means of certain knowledge; Ms. 9. 18. -इंधन a. destitute of fuel. -इति a. free from the calamities of the season; R. 1. 63; see ईति -ईश्वर a. godless, atheistic. -ईष the body of a plough. -ईह a. 1 desireless, indifferent; 10 21. 2 inactive. -उच्छ्वास a. 1 breathless, without breathing. (-सः) absence of breath. -उत्तर a. 1 answerless, without a reply. 2 unable to answer, silenced. 3 having no superior. -उत्सव a. without festivities; विरतं गयमृतुर्निरुत्सवः R. 8. 66. -उत्साह a. inactive, indolent, devoid of energy. (-हः) absence of energy, indolence. -उत्सुक a. 1 indifferent. 2 calm, tranquil. -उदक a. waterless. -उद्यम, उद्योग a. effortless, inactive, lazy, idle. -उद्वेग a. free from excitement or perturbation, sedate, calm. -उपक्रम a. without a commencement. -उपद्रव a. 1 free from calamity or affliction, not visited by danger or adversity, lucky, happy, undisturbed, unmolested, free from hostile attacks. 2 free from national distress or tyranny. 3 causing no affliction. 4 secure, peaceful. -उपाधि a. guileless, honest. U. 2.: 2. -उपपत्ति a. unsuitable. -उपपद a. 1 without any title or designation; Mu. 3. 2 unconnected with a subordinate word. -उपप्लव a. free from disturbance, obstacle or calamity, unharmed; निरुपप्लवानि न कर्माणि संवृत्तानि S. 3. -उपम a. peerless, matchless, incomparable. -उपसर्ग a. free from portents. -उपाख्य a. 1 unreal, false, non-existent (as वंध्यापुत्र). 2 immaterial. 3 invisible. -उपाय a. without expedients, helpless. -उपेक्ष a. 1 free from trick or fraud. 2 not neglectful. -उष्मन् a. devoid of heat, cold. -गंध a. void of smell, scentless, unfragrant, inodorous; निर्गंधा इव किंशुकाः °पुष्पिः f. the Sâlmali tree. -गर्व a.

free from pride. -गवाक्ष *a.* windowless. -गुण *a.* 1 stringless (as a bow). 2 devoid of all properties. 3 devoid of good qualities, bad, worthless; निर्गुणः शोभते नैव विपुलाडंबरोऽपि ना Bv. 1. 115. 4 without attributes. 5 having no epithet. (णः) the Supreme spirit. गृह *a.* houseless, homeless; सुगृही निर्गृही कृता Pt. 1. 390. -गौरव *a.* 1 without dignity, undignified. -ग्रंथ *a.* 1 freed from all ties or hindrances. 2 poor, possessionless, beggar. 3 alone, unassisted. (-थः) 1 an idiot, a fool. 2 a gambler. 3 saint or devotee who has renounced all worldly attachments and wanders about naked and lives as a hermit. -ग्रंथिक *a.* 1 clever, expert. 2 unaccompanied, alone. 3 deserted, abandoned. 4 fruitless. (-कः) 1 a religious mendicant. 2 a naked devotee. 3 a gambler. -ग्रंथिक *a.* (कः) a naked mendicant, a Jaina mendicant of the Digambara class. -घटं 1 a free market. 2 a crowded market. -घृण *a.* 1 cruel, merciless, pitiless. 2 shameless, immodest. -जन *a.* tenantless, uninhabited, unfrequented, lonely, desolate. (-नं) a desert, solitude, lonely place. -जर *a.* 1 young, fresh. 2 imperishable. immortal. (-रः) a deity, god; (nom. pl. निर्जराः-निर्जरसः) (-रं) ambrosia, nectar. -जल *a.* 1 waterless, desert, destitute of water. 2 not mixed with water. (-लः) a waste, desert. -जिह्वः a frog.-जीव *a.* 1 lifeless. 2 dead. -ज्वर *a.* feverless, healthy. -दंडः a Sûdra. -दय *a.* 1 merciless, cruel, pitiless, unmerciful, unkind. 2 passionate. 3 very close, firm or fast, strong, excessive, violent; मुग्धे विदेहि मयि निर्दयदंतदंशं Gît. 10; निर्दयरतिश्रमालसाः R. 19. 32; निर्दयाश्लेषहेतोः Me. 106. -दयं *ind.* 1 unmercifully, cruelly. 2 violently, excessively; R. 11. 84. -दश *a.* more than ten days old. -दशन *a.* toothless. -दुःख *a.* 1 free from pain, painless. 2 not causing pain. -दोष *a.* 1 faultless, defectless; न निर्दोषं न निर्गुणं. 2 guiltless, innocent. -द्रव्य *a.* without property, poor. -द्रोह *a.* not hostile, friendly, well-disposed, not malicious. -द्वंद्व *a.* 1 indifferent in regard to opposite pairs of feelings (pleasure or pain); neither glad nor sorry; निर्द्वंद्वो नित्यसत्त्वस्थो निर्योगक्षेम आत्मवान् Bg. 2. 45. 2 not dependent upon another, independent. 3 free from jealousy or envy. 4 not double. 5 not contested, undisputed. 6 not acknowledging two principles. -धन *a.* without property, poor, indigent; शशिनस्तुल्यवंशोऽपि निर्धनः परिभूयते Chân. 82. (-नः) an old ox. -धर्म *a.* unrighteous, impious. -धूम *a.* smokeless. -नर *a.* abandoned by men, deserted. -नाथ *a.* without a guardian or master. -निद्र *a.* sleepless, wakeful. -निमित्त *a.* causeless. -निमेष *a.* not twinkling. -बंधु *a.* without kindred or relation, friendless. -बल *a.* powerless, weak, feeble. -बाध *a.* 1 unobstructed. 2 unfrequented, lonely, solitary. 3 unmolested. -बुद्धि *a.* stupid, ignorant, foolish. -बुष, -बुस *a.* unhusked, freed from chaff. -भय *a.* 1 fearless, undaunted. 2 free from danger, safe, secure; Ms. 9. 255. -भर *a.* 1 excessive, vehement, violent, much, strong; त्रपाभरनिर्भरस्मरशर &c. Gît. 12; Amaru. 42. 2 ardent. 3 fast, close (as embrace); कुचकुंभनिर्भरपरीरंभामृतं वांछति Gît. 5; परिरभ्य निर्भरं Gît. 1. 4 sound, deep (as sleep). 5 full of, filled with (at the end of comp.; आनंद°, गर्व° &c. (-रं) excess. (रं *ind.* 1 excessively, exceedingly, intensely,. 2 soundly. -भाग्य *a.* unfortunate, unlucky. -भृति *a.* without wages. -मक्षिक *a.* 'free from flies', undisturbed, private, lonely. (कं) *ind.* without flies; *i. e.* lonely, private; कृतं भवतेदानीं निर्मक्षिकं *S.* 2. 6; -मत्सर *a.* free from envy, unenvious. -मत्स्य *a.* fishless. -मद *a.* 1 not intoxicated, sober, quiet. 2 not proud, humble. 3 not in rut (as an elephant). -मनुज, -मनुष्य *a.* tenantless, nninhabited, deserted by men. -मन्यु *a.* free from all connection with the outer world, who has renounced all worldly ties; संसारमिव निर्ममः (ततार) R. 12. 60; Bg. 2. 71; 3. 30. 2 unselfish, disinterested. 3 indifferent to (with loc.); निर्ममे निर्ममोऽर्थेषु मधुरां मधुराकृतिः R. 15. 28; प्रांतेष्वर्थेषु निर्ममाः Mb. -मर्याद *a.* 1 boundless, immeasurable. 2 transgressing the limits of right or propriety, unrestrained, unruly, sinful, criminal; मनुजपशुभिर्निर्मर्यादैर्भवद्भिरुदायुधैः Ve. 3. 22. -मल *a.* 1 free from dirt or impurities, clear, pure, stainless, unsullied (fig. also); नीरान्निर्मलतो जनिः Bv. 1. 63. 2 resplendent, bright; Bh. 1. 56. 3 sinless, virtuous; Ms. 8. 318. (-लं) 1 tale. 2 the remaining of an offering made to a deity. °उपलः crystal. -मशक *a.* free from gnats. -मांस *a.* fleshless. -मानुष *a.* uninhabited, desolate. -मार्ग *a.* roadless, pathless. -मुटः 1 the sun. 2 a rogue. (-टं) a large free market or fair. -मूल *a.* 1 rootless (as a tree). 2 baseless, unfounded (as a statement, charge &c.) 3 eradicated. -मेघ *a.* cloudless. -मेध *a.* without understanding, stupid, foolish, dull. -मोह *a.* free from illusion. -यत्न *a.* inactive, lazy. -यंत्रण *a.* 1 unrestrained, unobsrructed, uncontrolled, unrestricted. 2 unruly, selfwilled, independent. (-णं) absense of restraint, independence. -यशस्क *a.* without fame, discreditable, inglorious. -यूथ *a.* separated from the herd, strayed from the flock (as an elephant). -रक्त, (नीरक्त) *a.* colourless, faded. -रज, -रजस्क *a.* (नीरज, नीरजस्क) 1 free from dust. 2 devoid of passion or darkness. -रजस् (नीरजस्) *a.* see नीरज (-*f.*) a woman not menstruating. °तमसा absence of passion or darkness. -रंध्र *a.* (नीरंध्र) 1 without holes or interstices, very close, or contiguous, thickly situated; U. 2. 3. 2 thick, dense. 3 coarse, gross -रव *a.* (नीरव) not making any nose, noiseless; R. 8. 58. -रस *a.* (नीरव) not making any noise, noiseless; R. 8. 58. -रस *a.* (नीरस) 1 tasteless, unsavoury, flavourless. 2 (fig.) insipid, without any poetic charm; नीरसानां पद्यानां S. D. 1. 3 sapless, without juice, withered or dried up; *S.* Til. 9. 4 vain, useless, fruitless; अलब्धफलनीरसान् मम विधाय तस्मिन् जने V. 2. 11. 5 disagreeable. 6 cruel, merciless. (-सः) the pomegranate. -रसन *a.* (नीरसन) having no girdle; (रसना) Ki. 5. 11. -रुच् *a.* (नीरुच्) without lustre, faded, dim. -रुज्, -रुज *a.* (नीरुज्, नीरुज) free from sickness, healthy, sound; नीरुजस्य किमौषधैः H. 1. -रूप *a.* (नीरूप) formless, shapeless. -रोग *a.* (नीरोग) free from sickness or disease, healthy, sound. -लक्षण *a.* 1 having no auspicious marks, ill-featured. 2 undistinguished. 3 unimportant, insignificant. 4 unspotted. -लज्ज *a.* shameless, impudent. -लिंग *a.* having no distinguishing or characteristic marks. -लेप *a.* 1 unsmeared, unanointed; Ms. 5. 112. 2 stainless, sinless. -लोभ *a.* free from desire or avarice, unavaricious. -लोमन् *a.* devoid of hair, hairless. -वंश *a.* without posterity, childless. -वण, -वन *a.* 1 being out of a wood. 2 free from woods, bare, open. -वसु *a.* destitute of wealth, poor. -वात *a.* free or sheltered from wind, calm, still; R. 15. 66. (-तः) a place sheltered from wind. -वानर *a.* free from monkeys. -वायस *a.* free from crows. -विकल्प, -विकल्पक 1 *a.* not admitting an alternative. 2 being without determination or resolution. 3 not capable of mutual relation. 4 conditioned. 5 recognizing no such distinction as that of subject and object, or of the knower and the known; as applied to समाधि or contemplation, it is 'an exclusive concentration upon the one entity without distinct and separate consciousness of the knower, the known, and the knowing, and without even self-consciousness'; निर्विकल्पकः ज्ञातृज्ञानादिविकल्पभेदलयापेक्षः; नोचेत्तेतः प्रविश सहसा निर्विकल्पे समाधौ Bh. 3. 61; Ve. 1. 23. (–ल्पं *ind.* without hesitation or wavering. –**विकार** *a.* **1** unchanged, unchangeable, immutable. **2** not disposed; M. 5. 14. **3** disinterested; Rs. 2. 28. –**विकास** *a.* unblown. –**विघ्न** *a.* uninterrupted, unobstructed, free from impediments. (–घ्नं) absence of impediments. –**विचार** *a.* not reflecting, thoughtless, inconsiderate; रे रे स्वैरिणि निर्विचारकविते मास्मत्प्रकाशीभव Chandr. 1. 2. (–रं) *ind.* thoughtlessly, unhesitatingly. –**विचिकित्स** *a.* free from doubt or reflection. –**विचेष्ट** *a.* motionless, insensible. –**वितर्क** *a.* unreflecting. –**विनोद** *a.* without amusement, void of pastime, diversion or solace; Me. 86. –**विंध्या** N. of a river in the Vindhya hills; Me. 28. –**विमर्श** *a.* void of reflection, thoughtless, unreflecting. –**विवर** *a.* **1** having no opening. **2** without interstices or interval, close; *Si.* 9. 45. –**विवाद** *a.* **1** not contending or disagreeing. **2** undisputed, not contradicted or disputed, universally acknowledged. –**विवेक** *a.* indiscreet, void of judgment, wanting discrimination, foolish. –**विशंक** *a.* fearless, undaunted, confident; Ms. 7. 176; Pt. 1. 85. –**विशेष** *a.* **1** showing or making no difference, undiscriminating, without distinction; निर्विशेषा वयं त्वयि Mb., निर्विशेषो विशेषः Bh. 3. 50, 'a difference without distinction'. **2** having no difference, same, like, not differing from (oft. in comp.) प्रवातनीलोत्पलनिर्विशेषं Ku. 1. 46; स निर्विशेषप्रतिपत्तिरासीत् R. 14. 22. **3** indiscriminate, promiscuous. (–षः) absence of difference. (**निर्विशेषं** and **निर्विशेषेण** are used adverbially in the sense of 'without difference', 'equally', 'indiscriminately'; स्वगृहनिर्विशेषमत्र स्थीयतां H. 1; R. 5. 6. –**विशेषण** *a.* without attributes. **विष** *a.* poisonless (as a snake); निर्विषा डुंडुभाः स्मृताः. –**विषय** *a.* **1** expelled or driven away from one's home, residence or proper place; मनोनिर्विषयार्थकामया Ku. 5. 38, R. 9. 28. **2** having no scope or sphere of action; किंच एवं काव्यं प्रविरलविषयं निर्विषयं वा स्यात् S. D. 1. **3** not attached to sensual objects, (as mind). –**विषाण** *a.* destitute of horns. –**विहार** *a.* having no pleasure. –**वीज**, –**बीज** *a.* **1** seedless. **2** impotent. **3** causeless. –**वीर** *a.* **1** deprived of heroes; निर्वीरमुर्वीतलं P. R. 1. 31. **2** cowardly. –**वीरा** a woman whose husband and children are dead. –**वीर्य** *a.* powerless, feeble, unmanly, impotent; निर्वीर्यं गुरुशापभाषितवशात् किं मे तवेवायुधं Ve. 3. 34. –**वृक्ष** *a.* treeless. –**वृष** *a.* deprived of bulls. –**वेग** *a.* not moving, quiet, calm. –**वेतन** *a.* honorary, unsalaried. –**वेष्टनं** a weaver's shuttle. –**वैर** *a.* free from enmity, amicable, peaceable. (–रं) absence of enmity. –**व्यंजन** *a.* **1** straight-forward. **2** without condiment. (–**नं** *ind.*) plainly, in a straight-forward or honest manner. –**व्यथ** *a.* **1** free from pain. **2** quiet, calm. –**व्यपेक्ष** *a.* indifferent to, regardless of; R. 13. 25; 14. 39. –**व्यलीक** *a.* **1** not hurting or offending. **2** without pain. **3** pleased, doing anything willingly. **4** sincere, genuine, undissembling. –**व्याघ्र** *a.* not haunted or infested by tigers. –**व्याज** *a* **1** candid, upright, honest, plain. **2** not hypocritical; Bh. 2. 82. (–जं *ind.*) plainly, honestly, candidly; Amaru. 79. **व्यापार** *a.* without employment or business, free from occupation; R. 15. 56. –**व्रण** *a.* **1** unhurt, without wounds. **2** without rents. –**व्रत** *a.* not observing vows. –**हिमं** cessation of winter. –**हेति** *a.* weaponless. –**हेतु** *a.* causeless, having no cause or reason. –**ह्रीक** *a.* **1** shameless, impudent, **2** bold, daring.

निरत *a.* **1** Engaged or interested in. **2** Devoted to, fond of, attached to; वनवासनिरतः K. 157; मृगया° &c. **3** Pleased, delighted. **4** Rested, ceased.

निरतिः *f.* Strong attachment, fondness, devotion.

निरयः *f.* Hell; निरयनगरद्वारमुद्घाटयंती Bh. 1. 63; Ms. 6. 61.

निरवहानि (लि) का A fence, an outer wall.

निरस *a.* Tasteless, insipid, dry. –**सः** **1** Want of flavour, insipidity, tastlessness. **2** Want of juice, dryness. **3** Want of passion or feeling.

निरसन *a.* (**नी** *f.*) Expelling, removing, driving away; *Si.* 6. 47. **2** Vomiting.—**नं** **1** Expelling, ejecting, expulsion, removal. **2** Denial, contradiction, rejection, refusal. **3** Vomiting forth, spitting out. **2** Checking, suppressing. **5** Destruction, killing, extirpation.

निरस्त *p. p.* **1** Cast off or away, thrown out or away, repudiated, driven, expelled, banished; कौलीनभीतेन गृहान्निरस्ता R. 14. 84. **2** Dispelled, destroyed; अह्नाय तावदरुणेन तमो निरस्तं R. 5. 71. **3** Abandoned, deserted. **4** Removed, deprived or void of; निरस्तपादपे देशे एरंडोऽपि द्रुमायते H. 1. 69. **5** Discharged (as an arrow). **6** Refuted. **7** Vomited, spit out. **8** Uttered rapidly. **9** Torn out or destroyed. **10** Suppressed, checked. **11** Broken (as an agreement &c.). —**स्तं** **1** Rejecting, refusal &c. **2** Dropping or leavieg out, rapid pronunciation. -COMP. –**भेद** *a.* having all differences removed, same, identical. –**राग** *a.* one who has renounced all worldly attachments.

निराकः **1** Cooking. **2** Sweat. **3** The recompense of a bad action (a v. l. for निपाक).

निराकरणं **1** Repudiating, expelling, turning away; निराकरणविक्लवा *S.* 6. **2** Banishing. **3** Obstruction, contradiction, opposition, rejection. **4** Refutation, reply. **5** Contempt. **6** Neglecting the chief sacrificial duties. **7** Forgetting.

निराकरिष्णु *a.* **1** Repudiating, turning out, expelling; R. 14. 57. **2** Hindering from, obstructive. **3** Spurning, disdaining. **4** Seeking to deprive one of a thing.

निराकुल *a.* **1** Full of, filled or covered with; अलिकुलसंकुलकुसुमसमूहनिराकुलबकुलकलापे Gît. 1. **2** Distressed; see under निर् also.

निराकृतिः *f.* **निराक्रिया** **1** Repudiation, expulsion, rejection. **2** Refusal. **3** Obstruction, obstacle, impediment, interruption. **4** Opposition.

निराग *a.* Passionless, dispassionate.

निरादिष्ट *a.* Paid off as a debt.

निरामालुः The wood-apple (कपित्थ).

निरासः **1** Ejection, expulsion, throwing out, removal. **2** Vomiting. **3** Refutation. **4** Opposition.

निरिंगिणी-नी A veil.

निरीक्षणं, निरीक्षा **1** A look. **2** Looking at, regarding, seeing, beholding. **3** Looking out for, searching. **4** Consideration, regard; निरीक्षया as to, in respect of. **5** Hope, expectation. **6** Aspect of planets.

निरीशं (षं) A plough-share.

निरुक्त *a.* **1** Expressed, pronounced, explained, defined. **2** Loud, distinct. —**क्तं** **1** Explanation, derivation, etymological interpretations **2** N. of one of the six Vedângas, that which contains glossarial explanation of obscure words, especially those occurring in the Vedas; नाम च धातुजमाह निरुक्ते Nir. **3** N. of a celebrated commentary on the Nighaṇṭus by Yâska.

निरुक्तिः *f.* **1** Derivation, etymological interpretation of words. **2** (In Rhet.) An artificial explanation of the derivation of a word, thus defined:—निरुक्तिर्योगतो नाम्नामन्यार्थत्वप्रकल्पनं। इदशैश्चरितैर्जाने सत्यं दोषाकरो भवान्॥ Chandr. 5. 168 (दोषाकरः is equal to दोषाणामाकरः).

निरुत्सुक *a.* 1 Exceedingly anxious. 2 Unconcerned, indifferent.

निरुद्ध *p.p.* 1 Obstructed, hindered, checked, restrained, curbed; U. 1. 27. 2 Confined, imprisoned. –COMP.. –**कंठ** *a*, having all the breath obstructed, suffocated. –**गुद:** obstruction of the rectum.

निरूढ *a.* 1 Conventional, become current in popular usage, accepted (as the meaning of a word, as opposed to its यौगिक or etymological sense); यौर्न काचिदर्थवास्ति निरूढा सैव सा चलति यत्र हि चित्तं N. 5. 57. 2 Unmarried. —**ढ:** Inherence (as of 'redness' in the word 'red') –COMP –**लक्षणा** a *lakshana* or secondary use of a word which is based not on the *vivaksha* or particular intention of the speaker, but on its accepted and popular usage.

निरूढि: *f.* 1 Fame. celebrity. 2 Familiarity, conversancy, proficiency; नृप विद्यासु निरूढिमागता K. i. 2. 6. 2 Confirmation.

निरूपणं,–णा 1 Form, shape. 2 Sight, seeing. 3 Looking for, searching. 4 Ascertaining, investigation, determination. 5 Definition.

निरूपित *p. p*. 1 Seen, discovered, marked, beheld. 2 Appointed, chosen, elected. 3 Weighed, considered. 4 Ascertained, determined.

निरूह: 1 An enema not of an oily kind. 2 Logic, disputation. 3 Certainty, ascertainment. 4 A sentence having no ellipsis, a complete sentence.

निर्ऋति: *f.* 1 Decay, destruction, dissolution. 2 A calamity, evil, bane, adversity; सा हि लोकस्य निर्ऋति: U. 5. 30. 3 An imprecation, curse. 4 Death or destruction personified, the goddess of death or destruction, the regent of the south-western quarter; Ms. 11. 119.

निरोध:, निरोधनं 1 Confinement, locking up, imprisonment; Ms. 8. 210, 375. 2 Enclosing, covering up; Amaru. 87. 3 Restraint, check, suppression, control; योगश्चित्तवृत्तिनिरोध: Yoga S.; Ku. 3. 48. 4 Hindrance, obstruction, opposition. 5 Hurting, punishing, injuring. 6 Annihilation, destruction. 7 Aversion; dislike. 8 Disappointment, frustration of hopes (in dramatic language).

निर्ग: Country, region, place.

निर्गंधनं Killing, slaughter.

निर्गम: 1 Going forth or out, going away; R. 11. 3. 2 Departure, vanishing away; R. 19. 46. 3 A door, an outlet, egress; कथमप्यवातनिर्गम: प्रययौ K. 159. 4 Exit, issue.

निर्गमनं Going out or forth.

निर्गूढ: The hollow of a tree.

निर्ग्रंथनं Killing, slaughter.

निर्घंट:–टं 1 A vocabulary, collection of words. 2 A table of contents (सूचीपत्र).

निर्घर्षणं Rubbing, friction.

निर्घात: 1 Destruction. 2 A whirlwind, a violent gust of wind, hurricane. 3 The noise of contending winds (vapours?) &c. in the sky; निर्घातोग्रै: कुंजलिनात्र् जिघांसुर्ज्यानिर्घोषै: क्षोभयामास सिंहान् R. 9. 64; Ms. 1. 38., 4. 105 7. Y. 1, 145 (वायुना निहतो वायुर्गगनाच्च पतत्यध: । प्रचंडघोरनिर्घोषो निर्घात इति कथ्यते ॥). 4 An earth-quake. 5 A thunder-stroke in general; अहह दारुणो दैवनिर्घात: U. 2.

निर्घातनं Forcing out, bringing out.

निर्घोष: 1 A sound in general; Ve. 4; R. 1. 36. 2 A loud noise, rattling, twanging; ज्यानिर्घोषै: क्षोभयामास सिंहान् R. 9. 64; भारतीनिर्घोष: U. 3.

निर्जय:, निर्जिति: *f.* Complete victory, subjugation, vanquishing.

निर्झर:,–रं A spring, waterfall, cataract, cascade, mountain torrent; शीतं निर्झरवारि पानं Nâg. 4; R. 2. 13; Sânti. 2. 17, 21; 4. 6. –**र:** 1 Burning chaff. 2 An elephant. 3 A horse of the sun.

निर्झरिन् *m.* A mountain.

निर्झरिणी, निर्झरी A river, mountain-torrent; स्खलनमुखरभूरिस्रोतसो निर्झरिण्य: U. 2. 20.

निर्णय: 1 Removing, removal. 2 Complete ascertainment, decision, affirmation, determination, settlement; संदेहनिर्णयो जात: S. 1. 27; Ms. 8. 301, 409; 9. 250; Y. 2. 10; हृदयं निर्णयमेव धावति Ki. 2. 29. 3 Deduction, inference, conclusion, demonstration (in logic). 4 Discussion, investigation, consideration. 5 Sentence, verdict, judgment; सर्वज्ञस्याप्येकाकिनो निर्णयाभ्युपगमो दोषाय M. 1. –COMP. –**पाप:** a sentence, decree, verdict (in law).

निर्णायक *a.* Settling, conclusive.

निर्णायनं 1 Making certain. 2 The outer angle of the elephant's ear.

निर्णिक्त *p. p.* Washed, purified, cleansed; R. 17. 22.

निर्णिक्ति: *f.* 1 Washing. 2 Expiation, atonement; Mv. 4. 25.

निर्णेक: 1 Washing, cleaning. 2 Ablution. 3 Atonement, expiation.

निर्णेजक: A washerman.

निर्णेजनं 1 Ablution. 2 Expiation, atonement (for an offence).

निर्णोद: Removal, banishment.

निर्दट,–ड *a.* 1 Unkind, unfeeling, unmerciful. 2 Rejoicing over the faults of others. 3 Envious. 4 Abusive, slanderous. 5 Useless, unnecessary. 6 Violent. 7 Mad, intoxicated.

निर्दर:,–रि: A cave, cavern.

निर्दलनं Splitting, breaking, destroying.

निर्दहनं Burning, consuming.

निर्दातृ *m.* 1 A digger up of weeds. 2 A donor. 3 A husbandman, reaper.

निर्दारित *a.* 1 Torn, rent. 2 Opened, split open; Si. 18.28.

निर्दिग्ध *p. p.* 1 Anointed, smeared. 2 Well-fed, corpulent, stout.

निर्दिष्ट *p. p.* 1 Pointed out, shown, indicated. 2 Specified, particularized. 3 Described. 4 Assigned, allotted. 5 Asserted, declared. 6 Ascertained, determined. 7 Ordered.

निर्देश: 1 Pointing out, showing, indicating. 2 Order, command, direction; R. 12. 17. 3 Advice, instruction. 4 Telling, saying, declaring. 5 Specifying, particularization, specification, specific mention; अयुक्तोयं निर्देश: Mbh ; Bg. 17. 33. 6 Ascertainment. 7 Vicinity, proximity.

निर्धार:,–निर्धारणं 1 Specifying or separating one out of many; यतश्च निर्धारणं P. II. 3. 41; V. 3. 92. 2 Determining, settling, deciding. 3 Certainty, ascertainment.

निर्धारित *p. p.* Determined, ascertained, fixed, settled; see धृ with निस्.

निर्धूत *p. p.* 1 Shaken off, removed; R. 12. 57. 2 Deserted, rejected. 3 Deprived of, bereft. 4 Avoided. 5 Refuted. 6 Destroyed; (see धू with निस्).

निर्धौत *p. p.* 1 Washed off; R. 5. 43. 2 Polished, bright.

निर्बंध: 1 Insisting upon, persistence, intentness, pertinacity; निर्बंधसंजातरुषा (गुरुणा) R. 5. 21; Ku. 5. 66. 2 Importunity, a pressing demand or request, urgency; निर्बंधपृष्ट: स जगाद सर्वं R. 14. 32; अत एव खलु निर्बंध: S. 3. 3 Obstinacy. 4 Accusation. 5 Contest, dispute.

निर्बर्हण See निबर्हण.

निर्भट *a.* Hard, firm (दृढ).

निर्भर्त्सनं, –ना 1 Threat, menace; Si. 6. 62. 2 Abuse, reproach, reviling, blame. 3 Malignity. 4 Red paint, lac.

निर्भेद: 1 Bursting, dividing, splitting asunder. 2 A split, rent. 3 Explicit mention or declaration; M. 4. 4 The bed of a river. 5 Determination of an affair, event.

निर्मथ:, निर्मथन, निर्मंथ:, निर्मंथनं 1 Rubbing, churning, stirring. 2 Rubbing two pieces of wood together to produce fire, or the wood so used.

निर्मंथ्य *a.* 1 To be stirred or churned. 2 To be produced by friction (as fire). –**थ्यं** The wood used for producing fire by friction.

निर्माणं 1 Measuring, meting out यतश्चाध्वकालनिर्माणं P. II. 3. 28. Vârt. 2 Measure, reach, extent; अयमप्राप्तनिर्माण: (बाल:) Râm. 'not having reached the full measure of growth.' 3 Producing, formation, manufacture; ईदृशो निर्माणभागः परिणतः U. 4. 4 A creation, created thing or object, form; निर्माणमेव हि तदादरलालनीयं Mâl. 9. 49. 5 A shape, make, figure; शरीरनिर्माणसदृशो नन्वस्यानुभावः Mv. 1. 6 Composition, work. 7 A building. -णा Fitness, propriety, decorum.

निर्माल्यं 1 Purity, clearness, stainlessness. 2 The remains of an offering to a deity, such as flowers, निर्माल्योज्झितपुष्पदामनिकरे का षट्पदानां रतिः S. Til. 10. 3 Flowers used and cast off, faded or withered flowers; निर्माल्यैरथ ननृतेऽवधीरितानां Si. 8. 60. 4 Remains in general.

निर्मितिः *f.* Production, creation, formation, any artistic production; नवरसरुचिरां निर्मितिमादधती भारती कवेर्जयति

निर्मुक्त *p. p.* 1 Set free, freed, liberated; R. 1. 46. 2 Freed from worldly attachments. 3 Separated, disjoined. -क्तः A snake which has lately cast off its skin.

निर्मूलनं Eradication, uprooting, extirpating (fig. also); कर्मनिर्मूलनक्षमः Bh. 3. 72.

निर्मृष्ट *p. p.* Wiped off, washed out, rubbed out; निर्मृष्टरागोऽधरः S. D. 1.

निर्मोकः 1 Setting free, liberating. 2 A hide, skin; especially the slough of a serpent; R. 16; 17; Si. 20. 47. 3 Armour, mail. 4 The sky, heaven. 5 Atmosphere.

निर्मोक्षः Liberation, deliverance; R. 10. 2.

निर्मोचनं Liberation, deliverance.

निर्याणं 1 Exit, issue, setting out, departure. 2 Vanishing, disappearing. 3 Dying, death. 4 Eternal emancipation, final beautitude. 5 The outer corner of the eye of an elephant; वारणं निर्याणभागेऽभिन्नन् Dk. 97; निर्याणनिर्यदसृजं चलितं निषादी Si. 5. 41. 6 A rope for tying cattle or the feet of a calf, a foot-rope in general; निर्याणहस्तस्य पुरो दुधुक्षतः Si. 12. 41.

निर्यातनं 1 Returning, restoring, delivering, restitution (as of a deposit). 2 Payment of a debt. 3 Gift, donation. 4 Retaliation, requital, revenge (as in वैरनिर्यातन). 5 Killing, slaughter.

निर्यातिः *f.* 1 Exit, departure. 2 Departure from life, dying, death.

निर्यामः A sailor, pilot, boatman.

निर्यासः, -सं 1 Exudation of trees or plants, gum, juice, resin; शालनिर्यासगंधिभिः R. 1. 38; Ms. 5. 6. 2 Extract, infusion, decoction. 3 Any thick fluid substance.

निर्यूहः 1 A pinnacle, turret, projection (on columns or gates); वितर्दिनिर्यूहविटंकनीडः Si. 3. 55. (where Malli. renders निर्यूह by मत्तवारणाख्यः उपाश्रयः and quotes Vaijayantî; perhaps it was so called from its resemblance to the shape of an elephant in rut); चारुतोरणनिर्यूहा Râm. 2 A chaplet, crest, head-ornament. 3 A peg projecting from a wall. 4 A door, gate. 5 Extract, decoction.

निर्लुंचनं Pulling out or off, tearing off, peeling.

निर्लुंठनं 1 Robbing, plundering. 2 Tearing off.

निर्लेखनं 1 Scraping, scratching. 2 An instrument for scraping, a scraper.

निर्ल्वयनी The slough of a snake.

निर्वचनं 1 Utterance, pronunciation. 2 A proverbial expression, proverb. 3 Etymological interpretation, etymology. 4 A vocabulary, an index.

निर्वपणं 1 Pouring out, offering. 2 2 Particularly, the presentation of funeral offerings to the Manes, a libation; Ms. 3. 248, 260. 3 Bestowing presents. 4 Gift, donation.

निर्वर्णनं 1 Looking at, seeing, sight. 2 Marking, observing carefully.

निर्वर्तक *a.* (र्तिका *f.*) Completing, accomplishment, finishing, executing, performing &c.

निर्वर्तनं Accomplishment, completion, execution.

निर्वहणं 1 End, completion; Si. 14. 63. 2 Maintaining, carrying to the end, sustaining; मानस्य निर्वहणं Amaru. 24. 3 Destruction, annihilation. 4 (In dramas) The catastrophe, the last stage in which the action of the play is brought to a head, the denouement; तत्किंनिमित्तं कुकविकृतनाटकस्येव अन्यन्मुखेऽन्यन्निर्वहणे Mu. 6.

निर्वाण *p. p.* 1 Blown or put out, extinguished (as a lamp or fire); निर्वाणवैरदहनाः प्रशमादरीणां Ve. 1. 7; Ku. 2. 23. 2 Lost, disappeared. 3 Dead, deceased. 4 Liberated from existence. 5 Set (as the sun). 6 Calmed, quieted. 7 Plunged. -णं 1 Extinction; H. 1. 131; शनैर्निर्वाणमाप्नोति निरिंधन इवानलः Mb. 2 Vanishing from sight, disappearance. 3 Dissolution, death. 4 Final liberation or emancipation from matter and reunion with the Supreme Spirit, eternal bliss; निर्वाणमपिमन्येऽहमंतरायं जयश्रियः Ki. 11. 69; R. 12. 1. 5 (With Buddhists) Absolute extinction or annihilation, complete extinction of individual or wordly existence. 6 Perfect and perpetual calm, repose; Ki. 18. 39. 7 Complete satisfaction or pleasure, supreme bliss, highest felicity; अये लब्धं नेत्रनिर्वाणं S. 3; M. 3 1; Si. 4. 23; V. 3. 21. 8 Cessation, desisting. 9 Vacuity. 10 Union, association, confluence. 11 The bathing of an elephant; see अनिर्वाण in R. 1. 71. 12 Instruction in sciences. -COMP. -भूयिष्ठ *a.* almost vanished or departed; निर्वाणभूयिष्ठमथास्य वीर्यं संधुक्षयंतीव वपुर्गुणेन Ku. 3. 52. -मस्तकः final emancipation or diliverance, final beatitude.

निर्वादः 1 Blame, reproch. 2 Scandal, bad rumour, obloquy; R. 14. 34. 3 Decision of a controversy. 4 Absence of dispute (वादाभाव).

निर्वापः See निर्वपण.

निर्वापणं 1 An offering, oblation; a funeral oblation. 2 A gift, donation. 3 Putting out, extinguishing. 4 Pouring out, scattering, sowing (as seed). 5 Offering, giving. 6 Allaying, alleviation, pacification; कर्तव्यानि दुःखितैर्दुःखिनिर्वापणानि U. 3. 7 Annihilation. 8 Killing, slaughter. 9 Cooling, refreshing; शरीरनिर्वापणाय S. 3. 10 A refrigerant or cooling application.

निर्वासः, निर्वासनं 1 Expulsion, banishment. 2 Killing, slaughter.

निर्वाहः 1 Carrying on, accomplishing, performing. 2 Completion, end. 3 Carrying to the end, supporting, steadfast adherence, perseverance; निर्वाहः प्रतिपन्नवस्तुषु सतामेतद्धि गोत्रव्रतं Mu. 2. 18. 4 Subsisting on, 5 Sufficiency, competent provision, competency. 6 Describing, narrating.

निर्वाहणं See निर्वहण.

निर्विण्ण *p. p.* 1 Despondent, depressed; Mk. 1. 14. 2 Overcome with fear or sorrow. 3 Emaciated with grief. 4 Abused, degraded. 5 Disgusted with anything; मत्स्याशनस्य निर्विण्णः Pt. 1. 6 Impaired, decayed. 7 Humble, modest.

निर्विष्ट *p. p.* 1 Enjoyed, attained, experienced. 2 Fully enjoyed or used; R. 12. 1. 3 Obtained as wages; निर्विष्टं वैश्यशूद्रयोः Gautama. 4 Married. 5 Engaged in.

निर्वृत *p. p.* 1 Satisfied, contented, happy; निर्वृतौ स्वः S. 2; S. 4. Free from care or anxiety, secure, at ease. 3 Ceased, ended.

निर्वृतिः *f.* 1 Satisfaction, happiness, pleasure, bliss; व्रजति निर्वृतिमेकपदे मनः V. 2. 9; R. 9. 38; 12. 65; S. 7. 19; Si. 4. 64, 10. 28; Ki. 3. 8. 2 Tranquility, rest, repose. 3 Final emancipation or liberation from worldly existence; द्वारं निर्वृतिसद्मनो विजयते कृष्णेति वर्णद्वयं Bv. 4. 14. 4 Completion, accomplishment. 5 Freedom. 6 Disappearance, death, destruction.

निर्वृत्त *p. p.* Accomplished, attained, performed &c.

निर्वृत्तिः *f.* Acccomplishment, fulfilment; Ms. 12. 1.

निर्वेदः 1 Disgust, loathing. 2 Satiety, cloy, 3 Depression of spirits, despair, despondency; परिभवान्निर्वेदमापद्यते Mk. 1. 14. Humiliation. 5 Grief. 6

Complete indifference to worldly objects; Bg. 2. 52 (regarded as the feeling which gives rise to the sentiment called शांत (quietude); निर्वेदस्थायिभावोस्ति शांतोऽपि नवमो रसः K. P. 4; see R. G. under निर्वेद. 7 Self-disparagement or humiliation, (regarded as one of the 33 subordinate feelings); cf. the definition in R. G. under; (the following is there given as an instance; यदि लक्ष्मण सा मृगेक्षणा न मदीक्षासरणिं समेष्यति। अमुना जडजीवितेन मे जगता वा विफलेन किं फलं ॥).

निर्वेशः 1 Gaining, obtaining. 2 Wages, hire, employment. 3 Eating, enjoyment, use. 4 Return of payment. 5 Expiation, atonement. 6 Marriage. 7 Fainting, swooning.

निर्व्यथनं 1 Extreme pain, paining, afflicting. 2 Freedom from pain. 3 A hole, chasm.

निर्व्यूढ *p. p.* 1 Completed, finished. 2 Grown, increased, developed; मुहूर्तनिर्व्यूढविस्मय Mâl. 7; निर्व्यूढसौहृदभरोति 6. 17 :(उपचित Jagaddhara). 3 Vindicated, fully shown, proved true, carried out faithfully or to the end; हा तात जटायो निर्व्यूढस्तेऽपत्यस्नेहः U. 3; निर्व्यूढः संभावनाभारो बुद्धरक्षितया Mâl. 8; निर्व्यूढं तातस्य कापालिकत्वं Mâl. 4, 9. 10; Mv. 7. 8. 4 Deserted, abandoned.

निर्व्यूढिः *f.* 1 End, completion. 2 The top, highest point.

निर्व्यूहः 1 A turret. 2 A helmet, crest. 3 A door, gate: 4 A peg or bracket projecting from a wall. 5 Decoction; cf. निर्यूह.

निर्हरणं 1 Carrying out dead bodies to be burnt, carrying corpses to the funeral pile. 2 Taking forth, carrying or drawing out, extracting, removal. 3 Rooting up, extirpation.

निर्हादः Evacuation, voiding excrement.

निर्हारः 1 Taking away, removing, removal. 2 Drawing out, extracting. 3 Rooting up, destruction. 4 Carrying out a dead body to be burnt. 5 Accumulation of a private store of wealth, private hoard; Ms. 9. 199. 6 Evacuation of the natural excrements of the body (opp. आहार).

निर्हारिन् *a.* Carrying out. 2 Diffuse, spreading wide (as fragrance). 3 Fragrant.

निर्हृतिः *f.* Taking out of one's way, removal.

निर्ह्रादः A sound in general; R. 1. 41.

निलयः 1 A hiding place, the lair or den of animals, a nest (of birds); Si. 9. 4. 4 An abode, residence, house, dwelling; oft. at the end of comp. in the sense of 'living or residing in.' 3 Setting, disappearance; दिनांतेनिलयाय गंतु R. 2. 15 (where the word is used in sense 1 also).

निलयनं 1 Settling in a place, alighting. 2 A place of refuge, house, dwelling, habitation.

निलिंपः 1 A god; निलिंपैर्निर्मुक्तानपि च निरयांतर्निपतितान् G. L. 15. 2 A troop of Maruts. –COMP. –**निर्झरी** the celestial Ganges-

निलिंपा, निलिंपिका A cow.

निलीन *p. p.* 1 Melted or fused into. 2 Shut or wrapt up, hidden into. 3 Involved, surrounded, encompassed. 4 Destroyed, perished. 5 Changed, transformed (see ली with नि).

निवचने *ind.* Not speaking, ceasing to speak, holding the tongue (regarded as a गति or preposition or a separate word when used with कृ; *e. g.* निवचने कृत्य, निवचने कृत्वा P. I. 4. 76).

निवपनं Scattering down, pouring out, throwing down. 2 Sowing. 3 An offering to the Manes, an oblation in honour of one's deceased ancestors; को नः कुले निवपनानि नियच्छतीति S. 6. 24.

निवरा A virgin, an unmarried girl.

निवर्तक *a.* 1 Returning, coming or turning back. 2 Stopping, seizing. 3 Abolishing, expelling, removing. 4 Bringing back.

निवर्तन *a.* 1 Causing to return. 2 Turning back, ceasing.—**नं** 1 Returning, turning or coming back, return; इह हि पततां नास्त्यालंबो न चापि निवर्तनं Sânti. 3. 2. 2 Not happening, ceasing. 3 Desisting or abstaining from (with abl.). 4 Desisting from work, inactivity (opp. प्रवर्तन); Kâm. 1. 28. 5 Bringing back; Amaru. 84. 6 Repenting, a desire to improve. 7 A measure of land (20 rods).

निवसतिः *f.* A house, habitation, abode, residence, dwelling.

निवसथः A village.

निवसनं 1 A house, habitation, dwelling 2 A garment, cloth, an undergarment; Si. 10. 60; R. 19. 41;

निवहः 1 A multitude, collection, quantity, heap; राजपुत्रनिवहः Bh. 3. 37. so घन°, दैत्य°, कपोत° &c. 2 N. of one of the seven winds.

निवात *a.* 1 Sheltered from the wind, not windy, calm; R. 19. 42. 2 Unhurt, uninjured, unobstructed. 3 Safe, secure. 4 Well-armed, accoutred in strong mail. —**तः** 1 A refuge, dwelling, an asylum. 2 An impenetrable coat of mail. –**तं** 1 A place sheltered from the wind; निवातनिष्कंपमिव प्रदीपं Ku. 3. 48; Ki. 14. 37; R. 13. 52, 3. 17; Bg. 6. 19. 2 Absence of wind, calm, stillness; R. 12. 36. 3 A secure spot. 4 A strong armour.

निवापः 1 Seed, grain, seed-corn. 2 An offering to the manes of deceased parents or other relatives, a libation of water &c. at the Srâddha ceremony; एको निवापसलिलं पिबसीत्ययुक्तं Mâl. 9. 40; निवापदत्तिभिः R. 8. 86; निवापांजलयः पितॄणां 5. 8, 15. 91. Mu. 4. 5. 3 A gift or offering; in general.

निवारः, निवारणं 1 Keeping off, preventing, warding off; दंशनिवारणैश्च R. 2. 5. 2 Prohibition, impediment.

निवासः 1 Living, dwelling, residing. 2 A house, abode, habitation, resting place; निवासश्रितायाः Mk. 1. 15; Si. 4. 63, 5. 21; Bg; 9. 18; Mk. 3. 23. 3 Passing the night. 4 A dress garment.

निवासिन् *a.* 1 Dwelling, residing. 2 Wearing, dressed or clothed in; Ku. 7. 26. –*m.* A resident, an inhabitant.

निवासनं 1 Residenee. 2 Sojourn. 3 Spending time.

निवि (बि) ड *a.* 1 Without space or interstices, close, compact. 2 Firm, tight, fast; निबिडो मुष्टिः R. 9. 58, 19. 44. 3 Thick, impervious, dense, impenetrable R. 11. 15. 4 Gross, coarse. 5 Bulky, large. 6 Crooked nosed.

निविरीस *a.* 1 Compact, close; उरुनिविरीसनितंबभारखेदि Si. 7. 20. 2 Coarse, gross. 3 Crooked-nosed.

निविशेष *a.* Not different, alike. –**षः** Want of difference.

निविष्ट *p. p.* 1 Seated, sitting upon. 2 Encamped; R. 12. 68. 3 Fixed or intent upon. 4 Concentrated, subdued, controlled; Ku. 5. 31. 5 Initiated. 6 Arranged.

निवीतं 1 Wearing the sacred thread round the neck (making it hang down like a garland); निवीतं मनुष्याणां प्राचीनावीतं पितृणामुपवीतं देवानां J. N. V. 2 The thread so worn. –**तः**, –**तं** A veil, mantle.

निवृत *p. p.* Surrounded, enclosed. —**तः**,–**तं** A veil, mantle, wrapper.

निवृतिः *f.* Covering, enclosing.

निवृत्त *p. p.* 1 Returned, turned back. 2 Gone, departed. 3 Ceased, refrained or abstained from, stopped, desisted. 4 Abstaining from worldly acts, abstracted from this world, quiet. 5 Repenting of improper conduct. 6 Finished, completed, whole; see वृत् with नि. –**त्तं** Return. –COMP. –**आत्मन्** *m.* 1 a sage. 2 an epithet of Vishnu. –**कारण** *a.* without further cause or motive. (–**णः**) a virtuous man, a man uninfluenced by worldly desires. –**मांस** *a.* one who abstains from eating meat; निवृत्तमांसस्तु जनकः U. 4. –**राग** *a.* of subdued passion. –**वृत्ति** *a.* quitting any practice or occupation. –**हृदय** *a.* with relenting heart.

निवृत्तिः *f.* 1 Returning or coming back, return; Si. 14. 64; R. 4. 87. 2 Disappearance, cessation, termination, suspension; शापनिवृत्तौ *S.* 7; R. 8. 82. **3** Abstaining from work, inactivity (opp. प्रवृत्ति). **4** Abstaining from, aversion; प्राणाघातान्निवृत्तिः Bh. 3. 63. **5** Leaving of, desisting from. **6** Resignation, discontinuance of worldly acts or emotions, quietism, separation from the world. **7** Repose, rest. **8** Felicity, beatitude. **9** Denial, refusal. **10** Abolition, prevention.

निवेदनं 1 Making known, relating, proclaiming; a communication, announcement. **2** Delivering, entrusting. **3** Dedication. **4** Representation. **5** An offering or oblation.

निवेद्यं Offering of food to an idol; cf. नैवेद्य.

निवेशः 1 Entering, entrance. **2** Encamping, halting. **3** A halting place, camp, encampment; सेनानिवेशं तुमुलं चकार R. 5. 49, 7. 2; *Si.* 17. 40; Ki. 7. 27. **4** A house, an abode, a dwelling; Ki. 4. 19. **5** Expanse, contour (of the breast); Ki. 4. 8. **6** Depositing, delivering. **7** Marrying, marriage, settling in life. **8** Impression, copy. **9** Military array. **10** Ornament, decoration.

निवेशनं 1 Entering, entrance. **2** Halting, encamping. **3** Marrying, marriage. **4** Entering in writing, inscribing. **5** An abode, dwelling, house, habitation. **6** A camp. **7** A town or city. **8** A nest.

निवेष्टः A cover, an envelope.

निवेष्टनं Covering, enveloping.

निश् *f.* (This word is optionally substituted for निशा in all cases after acc. dual; it has no forms for the first five inflections) 1 Night. **2** Turmeric.

निशमनं 1 Looking at, beholding. **2** Seeing, sight. **3** Hearing. **4** Becoming aware of.

निश (शा) रणं Killing, slaughter.

निशा 1 Night; या निशा सर्वभूतानां तस्यां जागर्ति संयमी Bg. 2. 69. **2** Turmeric. -COMP. **-अटः, -अटनः** 1 an owl. **2** a demon, ghost, goblin. **-अतिक्रमः, -अत्ययः, -अंतः, -अवसानं** 1 the passing away of night. **2** daybreak. **-अदः** = Nishâda q. v. **-अंध** *a.* blind at night. **-अधीशः, -ईशः, -नाथः, -पतिः, -मणिः, -रत्नं** the moon. **-अर्धकालः** the first part of the night. **-आख्या -आह्वा** turmeric. **-आदिः** the evening twilight. **-उत्सर्गः** end of night, daybreak. **-करः** 1 the moon; Ku. 4. 13. **2** a cock. **3** camphor. **-गृहं** a bed-chamber. **-चर** *a.* (**-रा-री** *f.*) moving about by night, night-stalker. (**-रः**) 1 a fiend, goblin, an evil spirit; R. 12. 69. **2** an epithet of *S*iva. **3** a jackal. **4** an owl. **5** a snake. **6** the ruddy goose. **7** a thief. °पतिः 1 an epithet of 1 *S*iva. **2** of Râvaṇa. (**-री**) 1 a female fiend. **2** a woman going to meet her lover at night by appointment; राममन्मथशरेण ताडिता दुःसहेन हृदये निशाचरी R. 11. 20. (where the word is used in sense 1 also). **3** a harlot. **-चर्मन्** *m.* darkness. **-जलं** dew, frost. **-दर्शिन्** *m.* an owl. **-निशं** *ind.* every night, always. **-पुष्पं** 1 the white water-lily (opening at night). **2** hoar-frost, dew. **-मुखं** the beginning of night. **-मृगः** a jackal. **-वनः** hemp (शण). **-विहारः** a demon, goblin, a demon, goblin, a Râkshasa; प्रचक्रतू रामनिशाविहारी Bk. 2. 36. **-वेदिन्** *m.* a cock. **-हसः** the white water-lily (opening at night).

निशात *p. p.* 1 Sharpened, whetted, sharp; Ki. 14. 30. **2** Polished, burinished, bright.

निशानं Sharpening, whetting.

निशांत *p. p.* Tranquil, calmed, quiet, patient. **—तं** A house, habitation, dwelling; R. 16. 40.

निशामः Observing, perceiving, seeing.

निशामनं 1 Seeing, beholding. **2** Sight. **3** Hearing. **4** Repeated observation. **5** A shadow, reflection.

निशित *a.* 1 Sharpened, whetted, sharp; निशितनिपाताः शराः *S.* 1. 10. **2** Stimulated. **—तं** Iron.

निशीथः 1 Midnight; निशीथदीपाः सहसा हतत्विषः R. 3. 15. Me. 88. **2** The time of sleep, night in general; शुचौ निशीथेऽनुभवंति कामिनः Rs. 1. 3; Amaru. 11.

निशीथिनि, निशीथ्या Night.

निशुंभः 1 Killing, slaughter; Mâl. 5. 22. **2** Breaking, bending (as of a bow); Mv. 2. 33. **3** N. of a demon killed by Durgâ. -COMP. **-मथनी, मर्दनी** an epithet of Durgâ.

निशुंभनं Killing, slaying.

निश्चयः 1 Ascertainment, investigation, inquiry. **2** A fixed opinion, settled or firm conviction, firm belief. **3** A determination, resolution, resolve; एष मे स्थिरो निश्चयः Mu. 1. **4** Certainty, positiveness, positive conclusion. **5** Fixed intention, design, purpose, aim; कैकेयी क्रूरनिश्चया R. 12. 4; Ku. 5. 5.

निश्चल *a.* 1 Immoveable, steady, fixed, still. **2** Invariable, unchangeable; Bg. 2. 53. **-ला** The earth. -COMP. **-अंग** *a.* firm-bodied, firm. (**-गः**) 1 a species of crane, **2** a rock or mountain.

निश्चायक *a.* Who or what ascertains or determines, decisive, conclusive.

निश्चारकं 1 Evacuation by stools. **2** Air, wind. **3** Obstinacy, wilful nature.

निश्चित *p. p* Ascertained, determined, decided, settled, concluded (used actively also); अरावणमरामं वा जगद्द्येति निश्चितः R. 12. 83. **-तं** Certainty, decision. **-तं** *ind.* Decidedly, positively, certainly.

निश्चितिः *f.* 1 Ascertainment, settling **2** A determination, resolution.

निश्रमः Labour bestowed upon anything, continued practice or labour.

निश्रयणी, निश्रेणि, निश्रेणी A ladder, a staircase; cf. निःश्रयणी &c.

निश्वासः Inspiration, inhealing, sighing; cf. निःश्वास.

निषंगः 1 Attachment, clinging to. **2** Union, association. **3** A quiver; *Si.* 10. 34; Ki. 17. 36; R. 2. 30, 3. 64.

निषंगथिः 1 An embrace. **2** A bowman. **3** A charioteer. **4** A car.

निषंगिन् *a.* 1 Attached or clinging to; *Si.* 12. 26. **2** Having a quiver. *—m.* 1 An archer, bowman. **2** A quiver. **3** A sword-bearer.

निषण्ण *p. p.* 1 Seated; sitting on or in, rested, reclined, resting or reclining on; R. 9. 76, 13. 75. **2** Supported. **3** Gone to. **4** Dejected, afflicted, down cast; cf. निषण्ण.

निषण्णकं A seat.

निषद्या 1 A small bed or couch. **2** The hall of a merchant, a trader's shop. **3** A market place, market; *Si.* 18. 15.

निषद्वरः Mud, mire. **2** The god of love. **—री** Night.

निषधः (pl.) N. of a people and their country governed by Nala. **-धः** 1 A ruler of the Nishadhas. **2** N. of a mountain.

निषादः 1 N. of one of the wild aboriginal tribes in India, such as hunters, fishermen &c.; a mountaineer मा निषाद प्रतिष्ठां त्वमगमः शाश्वतीः समाः Râm.; R. 14. 52, 70. **2** A man of a degraded tribe in general, an outcast, a *Chândâla*. **3** Especially, the son of a Brâhmana by a *S*ûdra woman; cf. Ms. 10. 8. **4** (In music) The first, (more properly the last or seventh) note of the Hindu gamut; गतिकलाविन्यासमिव निषादानुगतं K. 21 (where it has sense 1 also).

निषादित *a.* 1 Made to sit down. **2** Afflicted, distressed.

निषादिन् *p. p.* (**नी** *f.*) Sitting or lying down, resting, reclining; R. 1. 52, 4. 2. *—m.* An elephant-driver; *Si.* 5. 41.

निषिद्ध *a.* Forbidden, prohibited. warded off, prevented; see सिधु with नि.

निषिक्त *p. p.* 1 Sprinkled upon. **2** Infused, instilled, poured into; impregnated.

निषिद्धिः *f.* 1 Prohibition, warding or keeping off. **2** Defence.

निषूदनं Killing, slaughter. **—नः** A killer; as in बलवृत्रनिषूदन &c.

निषेकः 1 Sprinkling, infusion; सुखसलिलनिषेकः Rs. 1. 28. 2 Dripping, trickling, distilling; तैलनिषेकबिंदुना R. 8. 38 a drop of dripping oil. 3 Effusion, discharge. 4 Seminal effusion or discharge, infusion of semen, impregnation, seed; Ku. 2. 16; R. 14. 60. 5 Irrigation. 6 Water for washing. 7 Seminal impurity. 8 Dirty water.

निषेधः 1 Prohibition, warding or keeping off, stopping, prevention 2 Negation, denial. 3 The particle of negation; द्वौ निषेधौ प्रकृतार्थं गमयतः. 4 A prohibitive rule (opp. विधि). 5 Deviation from a rule, exception.

निषेवक *a.* 1 Practising, following, devoted to, fond of. 2 Frequenting, inhabiting, resorting to, 3 Enjoying.

निषेवणं, निषेवा 1 Serving, service, waiting upon. 2 Worship, adoration. 3 Practice, performance. 4 Attachment or adherence to. 5 Living in, inhabiting, enjoying, using. 6 Familiarity with, use.

निष्क् 10 A. (निष्कयते) To weigh, measure.

निष्कः -कं 1 A golden coin (of different values, but generally taken to be qual to one *Karsha* or Suvarna of 16 Mâshas). 2 A weight of gold equal to 108 or 150 or *S*uvarnas q. v. 3 A golden ornament for the neck or the breast. 4 Gold in general. **-ष्कः** A Chándâla.

निष्कर्षः 1 Drawing out, extraction. 2 The essence, the chief or main point, pith; इति निष्कर्षः (often used by commentators); Ms. 5. 125; Bhâshâ P. 138. 3 Measuring. 4 Certainty, ascertainment.

निष्कर्षणं 1 Drawing out, extracting, pulling off; R. 12. 97. 2 Deducting.

निष्कालनं Driving away (cattle &c.). 2 Killing, slaughter (मरण).

निष्कासः (शः) 1 Exit, egress, issue. 2 A portico. 3 Day-break. 4 Disappearance.

निष्कासित *p. p.* 1 Expelled, turned out, driven out 2 Gone forth or out, issued. 3 Placed, deposited. 4 Stationed, appointed. 5 Opened, blown, expanded. 6 Reviled, reproached.

निष्कासिनी A femal slave not restrained by her master.

निष्कुटः 1 A pleasure-grove near a house. 2 A field. 3 The female apartments, the harem of a king. 4 A door. 5 The hollow of a tree.

निष्कुटिः-टी *f.* Large cardamoms (एला).

निष्कुषित *p. p.* 1 Torn off, forced or drawn out, lacerated; R. 7. 50. 2 Expelled; see कुष् with निः.

निष्कुहः The hollow of a tree; cf. निष्कुट.

निष्कृत *p. p.* 1 Taken away, removed. 2 Expiated, absolved, pardoned. **-तं** Expiation, or atonement.

निष्कृतिः *f.* 1 Expiation, atonement; Pt. 3. 157. 2 Acquittance, requital, discharge of a debt or obligation; न तस्य निष्कृतिः शक्या कर्तुं वर्षशतैरपि Ms. 2. 227, 3. 19; 8. 105, 9. 19, 11. 27. 3 Removal. 4 Restoration, cure. 5 Avoiding, escaping from. 6 Neglecting. 7 Bad conduct, roguery.

निष्कृष्ट *p. p.* 1 Pulled or drawn out, extracted. 2 Summed up.

निष्कोषः, निष्कोषणं 1 Tearing, drawing off or out, extracting, extirpating. 2 Husking, shelling.

निष्कोषणकं A tooth-pick; Pt. 1. 71.

निष्क्रमः 1 Going out, coming forth. 2 Departure from, exit. 3 One of the Samskâras or religious rites; *i. e.* taking out a child for the first time into the open air (which is usually performed in the fourth month of its age); चतुर्थे मासि निष्क्रमः Y. 1. 12; cf. उपनिष्क्रमण also. 4 Degradation, loss of caste, inferiority of tribe. 5 Intellectual faculty.

निष्क्रमणं 1 Going forth or out. 2 =निष्क्रम (3) above; चतुर्थे मासि कर्तव्यं शिशोर्निष्क्रमणं गृहात् Ms. 2. 34.

निष्क्रमणिका See निष्क्रम (3).

निष्क्रयः 1 Redemption, ransom; ददौ दत्तं समुद्रेण पीतेनेवात्मनिष्क्रयं R. 15. 55; 2. 55, 5. 22; Mu. 6. 20. 2 Reward. 3 Hire, wages. 4 Return, aquittance; *S*i. 1. 50. 5 Exchange, barter.

निष्क्रयणं Redemption, ransom.

निष्क्राथः 1 Decoction. 2 Broth.

निष्टपनं Burning.

निष्टानकः Roar, murmur.

निष्ठः *a.* (Usually at the end of comp.) 1 Being in or on, situated on; तन्निष्ठे फेने. 2 Depending or resting on, referring or relating to; तमोनिष्ठाः Ms. 12. 95. 3 Devoted or attached to, practising, intention; सत्यनिष्ठ. 4 Skilled in. 5 Believing in; धर्मनिष्ठ. **-ष्ठा** 1 Position, condition. 3 Fixity, fixedness, steadiness; नमो निष्ठाशून्यं भ्रमति च किमप्यालिखति च Mâl. 1. 31. 4 Devotion or application, close attachment. 5 Belief, firm adherence, faith; शास्त्रेषु निष्ठा Mâl. 3. 11; Bg. 3. 3. 6 Excellence, skill, proficiency, perfection. 7 Conclusion, end, termination; अत्यारूढिर्भवति महतामप्यपभ्रंशनिष्ठा *S*. 4. v. l. 8 The catastrophe or end of a drama. 9 Accomplishment, completion (समाप्ति) Ms. 8. 227. 10 The culminating point. 11 Death, destruction, disappearance from the world at the fixed time. 12 Fixed or certain knowledge, certainty. 13 Begging. 14 Suffering, trouble, distress, anxiety. 15 (In gram.) A technical term for the past participial terminations क्त, क्तवतु (त and तवत्).

निष्ठानं Sauce, condiment.

निष्ठी (ष्ठे) वः -वं, निष्ठी (ष्ठे) वनं, निष्ठीवितं Spitting out, spitting; Bh. 1. 92.

निष्ठुर *a.* 1 Hard, rugged, coarse, rough. 2 Severe, sharp, smart (as a blow); *S*i. 5. 49. 3 Cruel, harsh, hard-hearted (said of persons or things); व्यवसायः प्रतिपत्तिनिष्ठुरः R. 8. 65, 3. 62. 4 Contumelious.

निष्ठ्यूत *p.p.* Spit out, exuded, cast or thrown out; निष्ठ्यूतश्चरणोपयोगसुलभो लाक्षारसः केनचित् *S*. 4. 5; R. 2. 75; *S*i. 3. 10.

निष्ठ्यूतिः *f.* Spitting, spitting out.

निष्ण, निष्णात *a.* Clever, skilful, versed, skilled, conversant, expert; निष्णातोपि च वेदांते साधुत्वं नैति दुर्जनः Bv. 1. 87; Bk. 2. 26; *S*i. 8. 63; Ms. 2 66, 6. 30. 2 Brought about, completed, fully accomplished; Mâl. 10. 24 (निःशंकं विहितः Jagaddhara). 3 Superior, perfect.

निष्पक्व *a.* 1 Decocted, infused. 2 Well-cooked.

निष्पतनं 1 Rushing out, issuing quickly.

निष्पत्तिः *f.* 1 Birth, production; शस्यनिष्पत्तिः. 2 Ripeness, maturity (परिपाक); Ku. 2. 37. 3 Perfection, consummation. 4 Completion, accomplishment, termination.

निष्पन्न *p.p.* 1 Born, arisen, sprung up, produced. 2 Effected, completed, accomplished. 3 Ready.

निष्पवनं Winnowing.

निष्पादनं 1 Effecting, accomplishing. 2 Concluding. 3 Producing, causing.

निष्पावः 1 Winnowing, cleaning corn &c. 2 The wind caused by the winnowing sieve or basket. 3 Wind.

निष्पीडितः *p. p.* Squeezed, pressed together or out, निष्पीडितेंदुकरकंदलजो नु सेकः U. 3. 11.

निष्पेषः, निष्पेषणं 1 Rubbing together, grinding, bruising, pulverizing; भुजांतरनिष्पेष Ve. 3. 2 Striking, clashing, hitting against, friction; R. 4. 77; Mv. 1. 34; K. 56.

निष्प्रवाणि,-णि *n.* New unbleached cloth; °युगलं Dk.

निस् *ind.* 1 As a prefix to verbs it implies separation (away from, outside of), certainty, completeness or fulness, enjoyment, crossing over, transgressing &c.; (for examples see under (निर्). 2 As a prefix to nouns, not directly derived from verbs, it forms nouns or adjectives, and has the sense of (*a*) 'out of,' 'away from'; as in निर्वन्, निष्कौशाम्बि; or (*b*) more usually, 'not', 'without', 'devoid of' (having a privative force); निःशेष without a remainder; निष्फल, निर्जल &c. *N. B* In compound the स् of निस् is changed to र् before vowels and soft consonants (see निर्), to a visarga before sibilants, to श् before च् and छ्, and to ष् before क् and प्; see दुस्. –COMP. –कंटक (निष्कंटक) *a.* 1 thornless. 2 free from thorns or enemies, free from danger or nuisance. –कंद (निष्कंद) *a.* without edible roots. –कपट (निष्कपट) *a.* guileless, sincere. –कंप (निष्कंप) *a.* motionless, steady, immoveable; निष्कंपचामरशिखाः *S.* 1. 8; Ku. 3. 48. –करुण (निष्करुण) *a.* merciless, pitiless, cruel. –कल (निष्कल) *a.* 1 without parts, undivided, whole 2 waned, decayed, diminished. 3 impotent, barren. 4 maimed. –(लः) 1 a receptacle. 2 the pudendum muliebre. 3 N. of Brahmâ. (–ला, –ली) an elderly woman, one who is past childbearing, or one in whom menstruation has ceased. –कलंक (निष्कलंक) *a.* stainless, spotless. –कषाय (निष्कषाय) *a.* free from dirt or impure passions. –काम (निष्काम) *a.* 1 free from wish or desire, desireless, disinterested, unselfish. 2 free from all worldly desires. (–मं *ind.*) 1 without wish or desire. 2 unwillingly. –कारण (निष्कारण) *a.* 1 causeless, unnecessary. 2 disinterested, free from any motive; निष्कारणो बंधुः 3 groundless, not proceeding from any cause. (–णं *ind.*) without any cause or reason, causelessly, needlessly. –कालकः (निष्कालकः) a. penitent shaven and smeared with clarified butter. –कालिक (निष्कालिक) *a.* 1 one whose term of life is over or elapsed, whose days are numbered. 2 one who has no conqueror, invincible. (अजय्य). –किंचन (निष्किंचन) *a.* penniless, poor, indigent. –कुल (निष्कुल) *a.* having no kindred, left alone in the world. (निष्कुलं कृ to cut off complelely, exterminate; निष्कुला कृ 1 to exterminate one's family. 2 to shell, strip off the husk; निष्कुलाकरोति दाडिमं Sk.) –कुलीन (निष्कुलीन). *a.* of low family. –कूट (निष्कूट a free from deceit, honest, guileless. –कृप (निष्कृप) pitiless, merciless, cruel. –कैवल्य (निष्कैवल्य) *a.* 1 mere, pure, absolute. 2 deprived of final beatitude (मोक्षहीन). –कौशांबि (निष्कौशांबि) *a.* who has gone out of Kausâmbi. –क्रिय (निष्क्रिय) *a.* 1 inactive. 2 not performing ceremonial rites. –क्षत्र (निःक्षत्र), –क्षत्रिय, (निःक्षत्रिय) *a.* destitute of the military tribe. –क्षेपः (निक्षेपः) =निक्षेप q. v. –चक्रं (निश्चक्रं) *ind.* completely. –चक्षुस् (निश्चक्षुस्) *a.* *a.* blind, eyeless. –चत्वारिंश (निश्चत्वारिंश *a.* past forty. –चिंत (निश्चिंत) *a.* 1 free from anxiety, unconcerned, secure, 2 thoughtless, unthinking. –चेतन (निश्चेतन) unconscious. चेतस् (निश्चेतस् *a.* not in one's right senses. –चेष्ट (निश्चेष्ट) *a.* motionless, powerless. –चेष्टाकरण (निश्चेष्टाकरण) *a.* depriving (one) of motion, causing motionlessness (said of one of the arrows of Cupid). –छंदस् (निश्छंदस्) *a.* not studying the Vedas (छंदस्). –छिद्र (निश्छिद्र) *a.* 1 without holes. 2 without defects or weak points. 3 uninterrupted, unhurt. –तंतु *a.* having no offspring, childless. –तंद्र *a.* not lazy, fresh, healthy. तमस्क, –तिमिर *a.* 1 free from darkness, light. 2 freed from sin or moral impurities. –तर्क्य *a.* unimaginable, inconceivable. –तल *a.* 1 round, globular; मुक्ताकलापस्य च निस्तलस्य Ku. 1. 42. 2 moving, trembling, shaking. 3 bottomless. –तुष *a.* 1 freed from chaff. 2 purified, cleansed, Simplified. °क्षीरः wheat. °रत्नं crystal –तेजस् *a.* destitute of fire, heat or energy, powerless, impotent. 2 spiritless, dull. 3 Obscure –त्रप *a.* impudent, shameless–त्रिंश *a.* 1 more than thirty; निस्त्रिंशानि वर्षाणि चैत्रस्य P. IV. 4. 73. Sk. 2 pitiless, merciless, cruel; Amaru. 5. (–शः) a sword. °भृत् *m.* a sword-bearer. –त्रैगुण्य *a.* destitute of the three qualities (सत्त्व, रजस्, and तमस्). –पंक (निष्पंक) *a.* free from mud, clear, pure. –पताक (निष्पताक) *a.* having no flag or banner. –पतिसुता (निष्पतिसुता) a woman having no husband and no sons. –पत्र (निष्पत्र) *a.* 1 leafless. 2 unfeathered, featherless. (निष्पत्रा कृ to pierce with an arrow so that the feathers come through on the other side, to cause excessive bodily pain (fig.); निष्पत्राकरोति (मृगं व्याधः) (सपुंखस्य शरस्य अपर पार्श्वे निर्गमनान्निष्पत्रं करोति Sk.); एकश्च मृगः सपत्राकृतोऽन्यश्च निष्पत्राकृतोऽपतत् Dk. 165; so याती गुरुजनैः साकं स्मयमानाननांबुजा तिर्यग्ग्रीवं यद्द्राक्षीत्तन्निष्पत्राकरोज्जगत् Bv. 2. 132. –पद (निष्पद) *a.* having no foot. (–दं) a vehicle moving without feet. –परिकर (निष्परिकर) *a.* without prepearations. –परिग्रह (निष्परिग्रह). *a.* having no property or possessions; Mu. 2. (–हः) an ascetic without family, dependents, or other belongings. –परिच्छद (निष्परिच्छद) *a.* having no retinue or train. –परीक्ष (निष्परीक्ष) *a.* not examining or testing accurately. –परीहार (निष्परीहार) *a.* not observing caution. –पर्यंत (निष्पर्यंत), –पार (निष्पार) *a.* boundless, unbounded. –पाप (निष्पाप) *a.* sinless, guiltless, pure. –पुत्र (निष्पुत्र) *a.* sonless, childless. –पुरुष (निष्पुरुष) *a.* 1 unpeopled, tenantless, desolate. 2 without male issue. 3 not male, feminine, neuter (–षः) 1 a eunuch. 2 a coward. –पुलाक (निष्पुलाक) *a.* freed from chaff. –पौरुष (निष्पौरुष) *a.* unmanly. –प्रकंप (निष्प्रकंप) *a.* steady, immoveable, motionless. –प्रकारक (निष्प्रकारक) *a.* without distinction of species, without specification, absolute; निष्प्रकारकं ज्ञानं निर्विकल्पकं T. S. –प्रकाश (निष्प्रकाश) *a.* not transparent, not clear, dark. –प्रचार (निष्प्रचार) *a.* 1 not moving away, remaining in one place. 2 concentrated, intently fixed. –प्रति (ती) कार (निष्प्रति (ती) कार), –प्रतिक्रिय (निष्प्रतिक्रिय) *a.* 1 incurable, irremediable; सर्वथा निष्प्रतीकारेयमापदुपस्थिता K. 151. 2 unobstructed, uninterrupted. (–रं) *ind.* uninterruptedly. –प्रतिघ (निष्प्रतिघ) *a.* unhindered, unobstructed, unimpeded; R 8. 71. –प्रतिद्वंद्व (निष्प्रतिद्वंद्व) *a.* 1 without enemies, unopposed. 2 matchless, unrivalled, unequalled. –प्रतिभ (निष्प्रतिभ) *a.* 1 devoid of splendour. 2 having no intelligence, not ready-witted, dull, stupid. 3 apathetic. –प्रतिभान (निष्प्रतिभान) *a.* cowardly, timid. –प्रतीप (निष्प्रतीप) *a.* 1 looking straight-forward, not turned backwards. 2 unconcerned (as a look). –प्रत्यूह (निष्प्रत्यूह) *a.* unobstructed, unimpeded. –प्रपंच (निष्प्रपंच) *a.* 1 without extension. 2 without deceit, honest. –प्रभ (निःप्रभ or निष्प्रभ) *a.* 1 lustreless, pale-looking; R. 11. 81. 2 powerless. 3 gloomy, obscure, dark. –प्रमाणक (निष्प्रमाणक) *a.* without authority. –प्रयोजन (निष्प्रयोजन) *a.* 1 without motive, not influenced by any motive. 2 causeless, groundless. 2 useless. 4 needless, unnecesary. (–नं) *ind.* causelessly, without reason, without any object; Mu. 3. –प्राण (निष्प्राण) *a.* lifeless, dead. –फल (निष्फल) *a.* 1 bearing no fruit, fruitless, (fig. also); unsuccessful; निष्फलारंभयत्नाः Me. 54. 2 useless, profitless, vain; Ku. 4. 13. 3 barren (as a tree). 4 meaningless (as a word). 5 seedless, impotent. (–ला, –ली) a woman past child-bearing.–फेन (निष्फेन) *a.* foamless. –शब्द (निःशब्द) *a.* not expressed in words, inaudible; निःशब्दं रोदितुमारेभे K. 143. –शलाक (निःशलाक) *a.* lonely, solitary, retired. (–कं) a retired place, solitude; अरण्ये निःशलाके वा मंत्रयेयुरविभाविताः Ms. 7. 147. –शेष (निःशेष) *a.* without any remainder, complete, whole, entire; निःशेषविश्राणितकोशजातं R. 5. 1 –शोध्य (निःशोध्य) *a.* washed; clean. –संशय (निःसंशय) *a.* 1 undoubted, certain 2 not doubtful, not suspeting or doubting; R. 15. 79. (-यं) *ind.* doubtlessly, undoubtedly, surely, certaintly. **-संग (निःसंग)** *a.* 1 not attached or devoted, regardless of, indifferent to; यन्निःसंगस्त्वं फलस्यानतेभ्यः Ki. 18. 24. 2 one who has renounced all worldy attachments. 3 unconnected, separated, detached. 4 unobstructed. (-गं) *ind.* unselfishly, **-संज्ञ (निःसंज्ञ)** *a.* unconscious. **-सत्त्व (निःसत्त्व)** *a.* 1 unenergetic, weak, impotent. 2 mean, insignificant, low. 3 non-existent, unsubstantial. 4 deprived of living beings. (-त्त्वं) 1 absence of power or energy. 2 non-existence. 3 insignificance. **-संतति (निःसंतति), -संतान (निःसंतान)** *a.* childless. **-संदिग्ध (निःसंदिग्ध), -संदेह (निःसंदेह)** *a.* see निःसंशय. **-संधि (निस्संधि, निःसंधि)** *a.* having no joints perceptible, compact, firm, close. **-सपत्न (निःसपत्न)** *a.* 1 having no rival or enemy; धनरुचिरकलापो निःसपत्नोद्य जातः V. 4. 10. 2 not claimed by another, belonging exclusively to one possessor. 3 having no foes. **-समं (निस्समं)** *ind.* 1 unseasonably, at a wrong time. 2 wickedly. **-संपात (निःसंपात)** *a.* affording no passage, blocked up. (-तः) the darkness of midnight, thick darkness. **-संबाध (निःसंबाध)** *a.* not contracted, spacious, large. **-संसार (निःसंसार)** *a.* 1 sapless, pithless. 2 worthless, unsubstantial. **-सीम (निःसीम), -सीमन् (निःसीमन्)** *a.* immeasurable, boundless; अहह महतां निःसीमानश्चरित्रविभूतयः Bh. 2. 35; निःसीमशर्मप्रदं 3. 97. **-स्नेह (निःस्नेह)** *a.* 1 not unctuous or greasy, without unction or oil, dry. 2 not showing affection, unfeeling, unkind, indifferent. 3 not loved, not cared for; Pt. 1. 82. **-स्पंद (निःस्पंद)** or **निस्स्पंद)** *a.* motionless, steady; R. 6. 40. **-स्पृह (निःस्पृहः)** *a.* 1 free from desire. 2 regardless of, indifferent to; ननु वक्तृविशेषनिःस्पृहाः Ki. 2 5; R. 8. 10. 3 content, unenvious. 4 free from any wordly ties **-स्व (निःस्व)** *a.* poor, indigent; निःस्वो वष्टि शतं *S*ânti. 2. 6. **-स्वादु (निःस्वादु)** *a.* tasteless, insipid.

निसंपात See निःसंपात.

निसर्गः 1 Bestowing, granting, presenting, giving away; Ms. 8. 143. 2 A grant. 3 Evacuation, voiding, excrement 4 Abandoning, relinquishing. 5 Creation; निसर्गदुर्बोधं Ki. 1. 6; 18. 31; R. 3. 35; Ku. 4. 16; **-निसर्गतः, निसर्गेण** 'by nature', or 'naturally'. 7 Exchange, barter. -Comp. **-ज, -सिद्ध** *a.* innate, inborn, natural. **-भिन्न** *a.* different by nature; निसर्गभिन्नास्पदमेकसंस्थं R. 6. 29. **-विनीत** *a.* 1 Naturally discreet. 2 well naturally-behaved.

निसारः A multitude (समूह).

निसूदन *p. p.* Killing, destroying. **—नं** Killing, slaughter.

निसृष्ट *p. p.* 1 Delivered, given, bestowed. 2 Abandoned, left. 3 Dismissed. 4 Permitted, allowed. 5 Central, middle.-Comp. **-अर्थ** *a* to whom the management of an affair is entrusted. (-र्थः) 1 an envoy, ambassador. 2 a messenger, an agent; see S. D. 86, 87. °**दूती** a female who having discovered the love of a youth and maiden for each other, brings about their union of her own accord; तन्निपुणं निसृष्टार्थदूतीकल्पः सूत्रयितव्यः Mâl. 1 (where Jagaddhara explains निसृष्टार्थदूती by नायिकाया नायकस्य वा मनोरथं ज्ञात्वा स्वमत्या कार्यं साधयति या)

निस्तरणं 1 Going out or forth, coming out of. 2 Crossing over. 3 Rescue, deliverance, getting rid of. 4 An expedient, a means, plan.

निस्तर्हणं Killing, slaughter.

निस्तारः 1 Crossing over; संसार तव निस्तारपदवी न दवीयसी Bk. 1. 69. 2 Getting rid of, release, escape, rescue. 3 Final emancipation. 4 Discharge or payment of a debt, acquittance, requital; वेतनस्य निस्तारः कृतः H. 3. 5 A means, expedient.

निस्तीर्ण *p. p.* 1 Rescued, delivered, saved. Crossed (fig.); Ve. 6. 36,

निस्तोदः Pricking, sting.

निस्पंदः Trembling, throbbing, motion.

निस्यं (ष्यं) दः 1 Flowing forth or down, trickling down, dropping, dripping, streaming, oozing; वल्कलशिखानिस्यंदरेखांकिताः *S*. 1. 14. 2 A discharge, flux, sop, juice; U. 2. 24; Mâl. 9. 6. 3 A flow, stream, fluid that trickles down; हिमाद्रिनिस्यंद इवावतीर्णः R. 14. 3. 41, 16. 70; मदनिस्यंदरेखयोः 10. 58; Me. 42.

निस्यंदिन् *a.* Trickling or flowing down, oozing.

निस्रवः, निस्रावः 1 A stream, torrent. 2 The scum of boiled rice.

निस्वनः, निस्वानः Noise, voice; R. 3. 19; Rs. 1. 8; Ki. 5 6.

निहत *p. p.* 1 Struck down, smitten, killed, slain. 2 Struck into, infixed. 3 Attached or devoted.

निहननं Killing, slaughter.

निहवः Invocation, summoning,

निहारः See नीहार.

निहिंसनं Killing, slaughter.

निहित *p. p.* 1 Placed, laid, lodged, situated, deposited. 2 Delivered, entrusted. 3 Bestowed upon; applied to. 4 Inserted, infixed. 5 Treasured up. 6 Held. 7 Laid (as dust). 8 Uttered in a deep tone.

निहीन *a.* Low, vile **—नः** A low man, one of vile origin.

निह्नवः 1 Denial, concealment of knowledge; कार्यः स्वमातिनिह्नवः Mâl. 1. 12; Chandr. 5. 27. 2 Secrecy, concealment in general; Y. 2. 11, 267. 3 A secret. 4 Mistrust, doubt, suspicion. 5 Wickedness. 6 Atonement, expiation. 7 Excuse, exculpation.

निह्नुतिः *f.* 1 Denial, concealment of knowledge; Amaru. 8. 2 Dissimulation, reserve. 3 Secrecy, concealment in general.

नी 1 U. (नयति-ते, नीत) (One of the roots that govern two accusatives, see examples below) 1 To carry, lead, bring, convey, take, conduct; अजां ग्रामं नयति Sk.; नय मां नवेन वसतिं पयोमुचा V 4. 43. 2 To guide, direct, govern; M. 1. 2. 3 To lead away to, carry or bring away; सीता लंकां नीता सुरारिणा Bk. 6. 49; R. 12. 103; Ms. 6. 88. 4 To carry off; *S*ânti. 3. 5. 5 To carry off for oneself (Atm.) 6 To spend, pass (as time); येनामंदमरंदे दलदरविंदे दिनान्यनायिषत Bv. 1. 10; नीत्वा मासान् कतिचित् Me. 2; संविष्टः कुशशयने निशां निनाय R. 1. 95. 7 To bring or reduce any person to any state or condition; तमपि तरलतामनयदनंगः K. 143; नीतस्त्वया पंचतां Ratn. 3. 3; R. 8. 19. (In this sense the root is used with substantives much in the same way as कृ q. v.; *e. g.* **दुःखं नी** to reduce to misery; **वशं नी** to reduce to subjection, win over; **अस्तं नी** to cause to set; **विनाशं नी** to destroy; **परितोषं नी** to gratify, please; **शूद्रतां-दासत्वं** &c. **नी** to reduce to the state of a *S*udra, slave &c.; **साक्ष्यं नी** to admit as a witness; **दंडं नी** to inflict punishment upon, to punish; **पुनरुक्ततां नी** to render superfluous; **विक्रयं नी** to sell; **भस्मतां-भस्मसात् नी** to reduce to ashes &c. &c). 8 To ascertain, investigate, inquire into, settle, decide; छलं निरस्य भूतेन व्यवहारान्नयेन्नृपः Y. 2. 19; एवं शास्त्रेषु भिन्नेषु बहुधा नीयते क्रिया Mb. 9 To trace, track, find out; प्रतीलिंगैर्नयेत् सीमां Ms. 8. 252, 256; यथा नयत्यसृक्पातैर्मृगस्य मृगयुः पदं 8. 44; Y. 2. 151. 10 To marry. 11 To exclude from. 12 (Atm.) To instruct, give instruction in; शास्त्रे नयते Sk. —*Caus.* (नाययति-ते) To cause to lead, carry &c. (with instr. of agent); तेन मां सरस्तीरमनाययत् K. 38. —*Desid.* (निनीषति-ते) To wish to carry &c. -With. **अनु** 1 to conciliate, win over, induce, persuade, entreat, propitiate, appease, pacify (anger &c.), please, wheedle, स चानुनीतः प्रणतेन पश्चात् R. 5. 54. विग्रहाच्च शयने पराङ्मुखीर्नानुनेतुमबलाः स तत्वरे 19. 38; Ki. 13. 67; Bk. 5. 46, 6. 137. 2 to cherish love; Bh. 2. 77. 3 to train, discipline. **-अप** 1 to lead or carry away, lead off, cause to retire; Ms. 3. 242. 2 (*a*) to remove, destroy, take away; *S*. 6. 26; शत्रूनपनेष्यामि Bk. 16. 30. (*b*) to rob, steal, plunder, seize or take away; R. 13. 24. 3 to extract, draw out; शल्यं हृदयादपनीतमिव V. 5. 4 to put away, take or pull off (as dress &c); चरणान्निगडमपनय Mk. 6; अपनयंतु भवत्यो मृगयावेषं *S*. 2; R. 4. 64. **-अभि** 1 to bring near, conduct or lead towards, carry to Ki. 8. 32; Mu. 1, 6. 15. 2 to act, represent or exhibit dramatically, gesticulate (mostly occurring in stage-directions); श्रुतिमाभिनीय *S*. 3; कुसुमावचनमभिनयंत्यौ सख्यौ *S*. 4; Mu. 1. 2; 3. 31. 3 to quote, adduce. **-अभिवि** to teach, instruct, train. **-आ** 1 to bring, fetch; भुवनं मत्पार्श्वमानीयते *S*. 7. 8; Ms. 8. 210. 2 to bring on, cause, produce; आनिनाय भुवः कंपं R. 15. 24. 3 to reduce or lead to any condition; आनीतया नम्रतां Ratn. 1. 1. 4 to lead near, convey. **-उद्** 1 to lead towards, bring up. 2 to raise, lift up, erect (Atm.); दंडमुन्नयते Sk. 3 to lead out or aside; एकांतमुन्नीय Mb. 4 to infer, ascertain, guess, conjecture; U. 1. 29; 3. 22. **-उप** 1 to bring near, fetch; विधिनैवोपनीतस्त्वं Mk. 7. 6; Ms. 3. 225; M. 2. 5; Ku 7. 72. 2 to lift up, raise, carry to; *S*i. 9. 72. 3 to offer, present; R. 2. 59; Ku. 3. 69. 4 to bring about, cause, produce ; उपनयन्नर्थान् Pt. 3. 180; उपनयन्नंगैरनंगोत्सवं Gît. 1. 5 to bring into any state, lead or reduce to; पुरोपनीतं नृप रामणीयकं Ki. 1. 39. 6 to invest with the sacred thread (Atm.); माणवकमुपनयते Sk.; Bk. 1. 15; R. 3. 29; Ms. 2. 49. 7 to hire, employ as hired servants: कर्मकरानुपनयते Sk. **-उपा** to lead to, reduce to. **-नि** 1 to take near or towards, carry near; Y. 3. 295. 2 to bend, incline; वक्त्रं निनीय. 3 to pour down. 3 to bring about, accomplish. **-निस्** 1 to carry away or off. 2 to ascertain, settle, decide, resolve upon, fix; कथमप्युपागमात्मनैव निर्णीय Dk.; Ki. 11. 39 **-परि** 1 to lead or carry round (the fire); तौ दंपती त्रिः परिणीय वह्निं (पुरोधाः) Ku. 7. 80; अग्निं पर्यणयं च यत् Râm. 2 to marry, espouse; परिणेष्यति पार्वतीं यदा तपसा तत्प्रवणीकृतो हरः Ku. 4. 42. 3 to ascertain, investigate; Ms. 7. 122. **-प्र** 1 to lead out or forth (as an army); वानरेंद्रेण प्रणीतेन (बलेन) Râm. 2 to offer, give, present: अर्घ्यं प्रणीय जनकात्मजा Bk. 5. 76. 3 to bring to, set (as fire); Pt. 3. 1. 4 to consecrate by reciting sacred Mantras, hallow, concecrate in general; त्रिधा प्रणीतो ज्वलनः Hariv. 5 to inflict (as punishment); Ms. 7. 20. 8. 238. 6 to lay down, teach, promulgate, institute, prescribe; स एव धर्मो मनुना प्रणीतः R. 14. 67; भवत्प्रणीतमाचारमामनंति हि साधवः Ku. 6. 31. 7 to write, compose; प्रणीतः न तु प्रकाशितः U. 4; उत्तरं रामचरितं तत्प्रणीतं प्रयुज्यते U. 1. 3. 8 to accomplish, effect, perform, bring about; N. 1. 15, 19; Bh. 3. 82. 9 to lead or reduce (to any condition) **-प्रति** to carry or take back. **-वि** 1 to remove, take away, destroy (said to be Atm. only except where it has 'a part of the body' for its object); पटुपटहध्वनिभिर्विनीतनिद्रः R. 9. 71; 5. 75, 13. 35, 46; 15. 48; Ku. 1. 9; विनयंते स्म तद्योधा मधुभिर्विजयश्रमं R. 4. 65, 67. 2 to teach, instruct, educate, train; विनिन्युरेनं गुरवो गुरुप्रियं R. 3. 29, 15. 69, 18. 51; Y. 1. 311. 3 to tame, subdue, govern, control; वन्यान् विनेष्यन्निव दुष्टसत्त्वान् R. 2. 8, 14. 75; Ki. 2. 41. 4 to appease, pacify (anger) (Atm.). 5 to pass away, spend (as time); कथमपि यामिनीं विनीय Gît. 8. 6 to carry through, perform, complete. 7 to spend, apply to, use (Atm.); शतं विनयते Sk. 8 to give, present, pay, pay off (as tribute) (Atm.); करं विनयते Sk. 9 to lead or conduct towards; Ku. 7. 9. **-सं** 1 to bring together. 2 to rule, govern, guide. 3 to restore, give back. 4 to bring near to. **-समा** 1 to join, unite, bring together; R. 2. 64, *S*. 5. 15. 2 to fetch, bring; R. 12. 78.

नी *m*. (Used at the end of comp.) A leader, guide; as in ग्रामणी, सेनानी, अग्रणी.

नीका A channel for irrigation.

नीकारः See निकार.

नीकाश *a*. See निकाश; *S*i. 5. 35.

नीच *a*. 1 Low, short, small, little, dwarfish. 2 Situated below, being in a low position; Bg. 6. 11; Ms. 2. 198; Y. 1. 131. 3 Lowered, deep (as a voice). 4 Low, mean, base, vile, worst; प्रारभ्यते न खलु विघ्नभयेन नीचैः Bh. 2. 27; नीचस्य गोचरगतैः सुखमास्यते कैः 59; Bv. 1. 48. 5 Worthless, insignificant. **-चा** An excellent cow. -Comp. **-गा** a river. **-भोज्यः** onion. **-योनिन्** *a*. of low origin, low-born; so नीचजाति. **-वज्रः, -ज्रं** a kind of gem (वैक्रांत).

नीच (चि) का An excellent cow (also नीचिकी).

नीचकिन् *m*. 1 The top of anything. 2 The head of an ox. 3 The owner of a good cow.

नीचकैस् *ind*. See नीचैस् below.

नीचैस् *ind*. (Often used with the force of an adjective) 1 Low, beneath, below, underneath, down, downwards; (opp. उपरि); नीचैर्गच्छत्युपरि च दशा चक्रनेमिक्रमेण Me. 109. 2 Bowing down, humbly, modestly; R. 5. 62. 3 Gently, softly; नीचैर्वास्यति Me. 42. 4 In a low tone, with a low or depressed tone; नीचैः शंस हृदि स्थितो ननु स मे प्राणेश्वरः श्रोष्यति Amaru. 67; नीचैरनुदात्तः P. I. 2. 30. 5 Short, small, dwarfish; तथापि नीचैर्विनयाददृश्यत R. 3. 24. *-m*. N. of a mountain; नीचैराख्यं गिरिमधिवसेस्तत्र विश्रामहेतोः Me. 26. -Comp. **-गतिः** *f*. slow pace. **-मुख** *a*. with downcast countenance.

नीडः, -डं 1 A bird's nest; *S*. 7. 11. 2 A bed, couch. 3 A lair, den. 4 The interior of a carriage. 5 A place in general, abode, resting-place. -Comp. **-उद्भवः, -जः** a bird.

नीडकः 1 A bird. 2 A nest.

नीत *p. p*. 1 Carried, conducted, led. 2 Gained, obtained. 3 Brought or reduced to. 4 Spent, passed away. 5 Well-behaved, correct; see नी. **-तं** 1 Wealth. 2 Corn, grain.

नीतिः *f*. 1 Guidance, direction, management. 2 Conduct, manner of conducting oneself, behaviour, course of action. 3 Propriety, decorum. 4 Policy, prudence, wisdom, right course; आर्जवं हि कुटिलेषु न नीतिः N. 5. 103; R. 12. 69; Ku. 1. 22. 5 A plan, contrivance, scheme; Mâl. 6. 3. 6 Politics, political science, statesmanship, political wisdom; आत्मोदयः परग्लानिर्द्वयं नीतिरितीयती *S*i. 2. 30; Bg. 10. 38. 7 The science of morality, morals, ethics, moral philosophy. 8 Acquirement, acquisition. 9 Giving, offering, presenting. 10 Relation, support. -Comp. **-कुशल, -ज्ञ, -निष्ण, -विद्** *a*. 1 one versed in politics, a statesman, politician. 2 prudent, wise. **-घोषः** N. of the car of Brihaspati. **-दोषः** error of conduct, mistake in policy. **-बीजं** a germ or source of intrigue; °निर्वापणं कृतं Pt. 1. **-विषयः** the sphere of morality or prudent conduct. **-व्यतिक्रमः** transgression of the rules of moral or political sience. 2 error of conduct, mistake in policy. **-शास्त्रं** the science of ethics or of politics, morality.

नीध्रं (**व्रं**) 1 The edge of the thatch or roof. 2 A wood. 3 The circumference of a wheel. 4 The moon. 5 The asterism रेवती.

नीपः 1 The foot of a mountain 2 The Kadamba tree (said to blossom in the rainy season); नीपः प्रदीपायते Mk. 5. 14; सीमंते च त्वदुपगमजं यत्र नीपं वधूनां Me. 6. 65. 3 A species of Asoka. 4 N. of a family of kings. R. 6. 46. **-पं** The flower of the Kadamba tree; Me. 21; R. 19, 37.

नीरं 1 Water; नीरान्निर्मलतो जनिः Bv. 1. 63 2 Juice, liquor. -Comp. **-ज** 1 a lotus. 2 a pearl. **-दः** a cloud. धीरध्वनिभिरलं ते नीरद मे मासिको गर्भः Bv. 1; 61; *S*i. 4. 52. **-धिः, -निधिः** the ocean. **-रुहं** a lotus.

नीराजना, -ना 1 Lustration of arms, a kind of military and religious ceremony performed by kings or generals of armies in the month of Asvina before they took the field; (it was, so to say, a general purification of the king's Purohita, the ministers, and all the various component parts of the army, together with the arms and implements of war, by means of sacred Mantras); R. 4. 25, 17. 12; N. 4. 144. 2 Waving lights before an idol as an act of adoration.

नील *a.* (**ला -ली** *f.* the former in relation to clothes &c., the latter in relation to animals, plants &c.) 1 Blue, darkblue; नीलस्निग्धः श्रयति शिखरं नूतनस्तोयवाहः U. 1. 33. 2 Dyed with indigo. **-लः** 1 The dark-blue or black colour. 2 Sapphire. 3 The Indian fig tree. 4 N. of a monkey-chief in the army of Râma 5 'The blue mountain', N. of one of the principal ranges or mountains **-लं** 1 Black-salt. 2 Blue vitriol. 3 Antimony. 4 Poison. -COMP. **-अंगः** the Sârasa bird. **-अंजनं** antimony. **-अंजना, -अंजसा** lightning. **-अब्जं -अंबुजं, -अंबुजन्मन्** *n.* **-उत्पलं** the blue lotus. **-अभ्रः** the dark-cloud. **-अंबर** *a.* dressed in dark-blue clothes (**-रः**) 1 a demon, goblin. 2 the planet Saturn. 3 an epithet of Balarâma. **-अरुणः** early dawn, the first dawn of day. **-अश्मन्** *m.* sapphire. **-कंठः** 1 a peacock; Mâl. 9. 30; Me. 79. 2 an epithet of Siva. 3 a kind of gallinule. 4 a blue necked jay. 5 a wagtail. 6 a sparrow. 7 a bee. **-केशी** the indigo plant. **-ग्रीवः** an epithet of Siva. **-छदः** 1 the date-tree 2 an epithet of Garuḍa. **-तरुः** the cocoanut tree. **-तालः** the Tamâl tree. **-पंकः, -कं** darkness. **-पटलं** 1 a dark mass, a black coating or covering. 2 a dark film over the eye of a blind man; Pt. 5. **पिच्छः** a falcon. **-पुष्पिका** 1 the indigo plant. 2 linseed. **-भः** 1 the moon. 2 a cloud. 3 a bee. **-मणिः, -रत्नं** the sapphire; नेपथ्योचितनीलरत्नं Gît. 5; Bv. 2. 42. **-मीलिकः** a fire fly. **-मृत्तिका** 1 iron pyrites. 2 black earth. **-राजिः** *f.* a line of darkness, dark mass, thick darkness; निशाशशांकक्षतनीलराजयः Rs. 1. 2. **-लोहितः** an epithet of Siva; S. 7. 37; Ku. 2. 57.

नीलकं 1 Black salt. 2 Blue steel. 3 Blue vitriol. **-कः** A dark-coloured horse.

नीलं (लां) गुः A kind of insect.

नीला See नीली.

नीलिका The indigo plant; (also नीलिनी).

नीलिमन् *m.* Blue colour, darkness, blueness.

नीली 1 The indigo plant; तत्र नीलीरसपरिपूर्णं महाभांडमासीत् Pt. 1; एको ग्रहस्तु मीनानां नीलीमद्यपयोर्यथा Pt. 1. 260. 2 A species of blue fly. 3 A kind of disease. -COMP. **-राग** *a.* firm in attachment. (**-गः**) 1 affection as unchangeable as the colour of indigo, unalterable or unswerving attachment. 2 a firm and constant friend. **-संधानं** fermentation of idigo. °**भांडं** an indigo vat.

नीवरः 1 Trade, traffic. 2 A trader. 3 A religious mendicant. 4 Mud. **-रं** Water.

नीवाकः 1 Increased demand for grain in times of dearth. 2 Famine, scarcity.

नीवारः Rice growing wild or without cultivation; नीवाराः शुकगर्भकोटरमुखभ्रष्टास्तरूणामधः S. 1. 14; R. 1. 50, 5. 9. 15.

नीविः, -वी *f.* 1 A cloth worn round a woman's waist, or more properly the ends of the cloth tied into a knot in front, the knot of the wearing garment, प्रस्थानभिन्नां न बबंध नीविं R. 7. 9; नीवीबंधोच्छ्वसनं Mâl. 2. 5; Ku. 1. 38; नीविं प्रति प्रणिहिते तु करे प्रियेण K. P. 4; Me. 68; Si. 10. 64. 2 Capital, principal stock. 3 A stake, wager.

नीवृत् *m.* Any inhabited country, realm, kingdom.

नीव्र See नीध्र.

नीशारः 1 A warm cloth, a blanket. 2 A mosquito-curtain. 3 An outer tent or screen.

नीहारः 1 Fog, mist; R. 7. 60; Y. 1. 150; Ms. 4. 113. 2 Hoar-frost, heavy-dew. 3 Evacuation.

नु *ind.* 1 A particle having an interrogative force and implying some 'doubt', 'uncertainty'; स्वप्नो नु माया नु मतिभ्रमो नु S. अस्तशैलगहनं नु विवस्वानाविवेश जलधिं नु महीं नु Ki. 9. 7; 5. 1; 8. 53, 9. 15, 54; 13. 4; Ku. 1. 47; Si. 10. 14; S. 2. 8. 2 It is very often compounded with the interrogative pronoun and its derivatives in the sense of 'posibly' 'indeed'; किं न्वेतत्स्यात्किमन्यदितोऽथवा Mâl. 1. 17; कथं नु गुणवद्विंदेयं कलत्रं Dk; see किंनु, also.

नु 2 P. (नौति, प्रणौति; नुत; *caus.* नावयति; *desid.* नुनूषति) 1 To praise, extol, commend; सरस्वती तन्मिथुनं नुनाव Ku. 7. 90; Bk. 14. 112; see नू.

नुतिः *f.* 1 Praise, eulogium, panegyric; परगुणनुतिभिः (v. l.) स्वान् गुणान् ख्यापयंतः Bh. 2. 69. 2 Worship, reverence.

नुद् 6 U. (नुदति-ते, नुत्त or नुन्न-प्रणुदति) 1 To push, push or drive on, impel, propel; मंदं मंदं नुदति पवनश्चानुकूलो यथा त्वां Me. 9. 2 To prompt, incite, urge on; Si. 11. 26. 3 To remove, drive away, cast away, dispel; अदृस्त्वया नुन्नमनुत्तमं तमः Si. 1. 27; केयूरबंधोच्छ्वसितैर्नुनोद R. 6. 68, 8. 40; 16. 85; Ki. 3. 33; 5. 28. 4 To throw, cast, send. —*Caus.* 1 To remove, drive away. 2 To prompt, incite, push on or urge forward. -WITH **अप** to drive away, remove; Bk. 10. 13. **-उप** to propel, drive onward; Si. 4. 61. **-निस्** 1 to throw back, reject; धाना मत्स्यान्पयो मांसं शाकं चैव न निर्णुदेत् Ms. 4. 250. 2 to remove, dispel. **-प्र** to dispel, drive off, remove; Si. 9. 71. **-वि** 1 to strike, pierce. 2 to play on a musical instrument, (वीणां, आतोद्यं &c.). (*-Caus.*) 1 to remove, drive away, dispel, cast off; तापं विनोदय दृष्टिभिः Gît. 10; Si. 4. 66. 2 to pass, spend (as time). 3 to divert, amuse, entertain; लतासु दृष्टिं विनोदयामि S. 6; R. 14. 77. 4 to amuse oneself with; R. 5. 67. **-सं** 1 to draw or bring together, collect. 2 to find, meet.

नूतन, नूत्न *a.* 1 New; नूतनो राजा समाज्ञापयति U. 1; R. 8. 15. 2 Fresh, young, 3 Present. 4 Instantaneous. 5 Recent, modern. 6 Curious, strange.

नूनं *ind.* Certainly, assuredly, surely, verily, indeed; अद्यापि नूनं हरकोपवह्निस्त्वयि ज्वलत्यौर्व इवांबुराशौ S. 3. 3; Me. 9, 18, 46; Bh. 1. 10; Ku. 1. 12, 5. 75; R. 1. 29. 2 Most probably, in all probability; U. 4. 23.

नूपुरः, -रं An anklet, an ornament for the feet; न हि चूडामणिः पादे नूपुरं मूर्ध्नि धार्यते H. 2. 71.

नृ *m.* (Nom. sing. ना, gen, pl. नृणां or नॄणां 1 A man, a person whether male or female; Ms. 3. 81; 4. 61, 7. 61; 10. 33. 2 Mankind. 3 A piece at chess. 4 The pin of a sundial. 5 A masculine word; संधिर्ना विग्रहो यानं Ak. -COMP. **-अस्थिमालिन्** *m.* an epithet of Siva. **-कपालं** man's skull. **-केसरिन्** *m.* 'man-lion', Vishṇu in his Narasimha incarnation; cf. नरसिंह. **-जलं** human urine. **-देवः** a king. **-धर्मन्** *m.* an epithet of Kubera. **-पः** a ruler of men, king, sovereign. °**अध्वरः** N. of a sacrifice (Râjasuya) performed by an emperor or lord paramount, in which all the offices are performed by tributary princes. °**आत्मजः** a prince, crown prince. °**आभीरं,** °**मानं** music played at the royal meals. °**आमयः** consumption. °**आसनं** 'royal-seat', a throne, the chair of state. °**गृहं** a royal palace. °**नीतिः** *f.* politics, royal policy, state-craft; वेश्यांगनेव नृपनीतिरनेकरूपा Bh. 2. 47. °**प्रियः** the mango tree. °**लक्ष्मन्** *n.* °**लिंगं** a royal symbol, an emblem of royalty, any one of the royal insignia; particularly, the white umbrella. °**शासनं** a royal edict. °**सभं,** °**सभा** an assembly of kings. **-पतिः, -पालः** a king. **-पशुः** a beast in the form of a man, a brute of a man. -मिथुनं the sign Gemini (twins) of the zodiac. -मेधः a human sacrifice. -यज्ञः 'the sacrifice to be offered to men', hospitality, reception of guests (one of the five daily Yajnas, see पंचयज्ञ). -लोकः the world of mortals, the earth. -वराहः Vishnu in the boar-incarnation. -वाहनः and epithet of Kubera. -वेष्टनः N. of Siva. -श्रृंगं 'man's horn'; *i. e.* an impossibility. -सिंहः 1 'a lion like man', a chief among men, an eminent or distiguished man. 2 Vishnu in his fourth incarnation; cf. नरसिंह. 3 a particular mode of sexual enjoyment. -सेनं,-सेना an army of men. -सोमः an illustrious man, great man; R. 5. 59.

नृगः A son of Manu Vaivasvata, who, it is said, was cursed by a Brâhmaṇa to be a lizard.

नृत् 4 P. (नृत्यति, प्रणृत्यति, नृत्त) To dance, move about; नृत्यति युवतिजनेन समं सखि Gît. 1; लोलोर्मौ पयसि महोत्पलं ननर्त *Si.* 8. 23; Bk. 3. 43. 2 To act on the stage. 3 To gesticulate, play. -*Caus.* (नर्तयति-ते) 1 To cause to dance; त्वमाशे मोघाशे किमपरमतो नर्तयसि मां Bh. 3. 6; तालैः शिंजावलयसुभगैर्नर्तितः कांतया मे Me. 79; U. 3. 19. 2 To cause to move. -WITH आ (*caus.*) 1 to cause to dance. 2 to cause to dance or move quickly, shake; मरुद्भिरानर्तितनक्तमाले R. 5. 42; Amaru. 32; Rs. 3. 10. -उप 1 to dance. 2 to dance before some body उपानृत्यंत देवेशं. -प्र to dance &c. -प्रति to ridicule by dancing in return.

नृतिः *f.* Dancing, dance.

नृत्तं, नृत्यं Dancing, acting, a dance, pantomime, gesticulation; नृत्तादस्याः स्थितमतितरां कांतं M. 2. 7; नृत्यं मयूरा विजहुः R. 14. 69; Me. 32, 36; R. 3. 19. -COMP. -प्रियः an epithet of Siva. -शाला a dancing hall. -स्थानं a stage, dancing room.

नृप, नृपति, नृपाल &c. See under नृ.

नृशंस *a.* Wicked, malicious, cruel, mischievous, base; Mk. 3. 25; Ms. 3. 41; Y. 1. 64.

नेजकः A washerman.

नेजनं Washing, cleansing.

नेतृ *m.* 1 One who leads or guides, a leader, conductor, manager, guide (of elephants, animals &c.); R. 4. 75, 14. 22, 16. 30; Me. 69; नेताश्वस्य स्रुघ्नं स्रुघ्नस्य वा Sk.; Mu. 7. 14. 2 A director, preceptor; Bh. 2. 88. 3 A chief, master, head. 4 An inflicter (as of punishment); Ms. 7. 25. 5 An owner. 6 The hero of a drama.

नेत्रं 1 Leading, conducting. 2 The eye; प्रायेण गृहिणीनेत्राः कन्यार्थेषु कुटुंबिनः Ku. 6. 85, 2. 29, 30; 7. 13. 3 The string of a churning stick. 4 Woven silk, a fine silken garment; नेत्रक्रमेणोपरुरोध सूर्यं R. 7. 39 (where some commentators take नेत्र in its ordinary sense of the 'eye'.) 5 The root of a tree. 6 An enema-pipe. 7 A carriage, conveyance in general. 8 The number 'two'. 9 A leader. 10 A constellation, star (said to be *m.* only in these two senses). -COMP. -अंजनं a collyrium for the eyes; *S.* Til. 7. -अंतः the outer corner of the eye. -अंबु,-अंभस् *n.* tears. -आमयः ophthalmia. -उत्सवः any pleasing or beautiful object. -उपमं the almond fruit. -कनीनिका the pupil of the eye. -कोषः 1 the eye-ball. 2 the bud of a flower. -गोचर *a.* within the range of sight. perceptible, visible. -छदः the eyelid. -जं, -जलं, -वारि *n.* tears. -पर्यंतः the outer corner of the eye. -पिंडः 1 the eye-ball. 2 a cat. -मलं the mucus of the eyes. -योनिः 1 an epithet of Indra (who had on his body a thousand marks resembling the female organ inflicted by the curse of Gautama). 2 the moon. -रंजनं a collyrium. -रोमन् *n.* the eye-lash. -वस्त्रं a veil over the eye. -स्तंभः rigidity of the eyes.

नेत्रिकं 1 A pipe. 2 A ladle.

नेत्री 1 A river. 2 A vein. 3 A female leader. 4 An epithet of Lakshmî.

नेदिष्ठ *a.* Nearest, next, very near (superl. of अंतिक q. v.).

नेदीयस् *a.* (सी *f.*) Nearer, very near (compar. of अंतिक q. v.). नेदीयसी भूत्वा Mâl. 1. drawing near, approaching.

नेपः A family-priest.

नेपथ्यं 1 Decoration, an ornament. 2 Dress, apparel, costume, attire; उदारनेपथ्यभृत् R. 6. 6; राजेंद्रनेपथ्यविधानशोभा 14. 9; उज्ज्वलनेपथ्यविरचना Mâl. 1; Ku. 7. 7; V. 5. 3 Particularly, the costume of an actor; विरलनेपथ्ययोः पात्रयोः प्रवेशोस्तु M. 1. 4 The tiring room, the space where the actors attire themselves (which is always behind the curtain), the post-scenium; नेपथ्ये behind the scenes. -COMP. -विधानं arrangements of the tiring room; *S.* 1.

नेपालः N. of a country in the north of India. -लाः pl. The people of this country. -लं Copper. -ली The wild date tree or its fruit. -COMP. -जा, -जाता red arsenic.

नेपालिका Red arsenic.

नेम *a.* (*Nom.* pl. नेमे-नेमाः) Half. -मः 1 A part. 2 A period, time, season. 3 A boundary, limit. 4 An enclosure, fence. 5 The foundation of a wall. 6 Fraud, deceit. 7 Evening. 8 A hole, ditch. 9 A root.

नेमिः -मी *f.* 1 The circumference, ring or felly of a wheel; उपोढशब्दा न रथांगनेमयः *S.* 7. 10; चक्रनेमिक्रमेण Me. 109; R. 1. 17, 39. 2 Edge, rim. 3 A windlass. 4 A circle or circumference (in general); उदधिनेमि R. 9. 10. 5 A thunderbolt. 6 The earth. -मिः The tree तिनिश.

नेष्टृ *m.* One of the chief officiating priests at a Soma sacrifice (whose number is 16).

नेष्टुः A clod of earth.

नैःश्रेयस *a.* (सी *f.*), नैःश्रेयसिक *a.* (की *f.*) Leading to happiness or final beatitude.

नैस्वं, नैःस्व्यं Destitution, poverty, indigence.

नैक *a.* (न+एक) Not one or alone; mostly in comp; °आत्मन् *m.*,: °रूपः, °श्रृंगः epithets of the Supreme Being.

नैकटिक *a.* (की *f.*) Adjacent, near, contiguous. -कः An ascetic or Bhikshu; Bk. 14. 12 (*vide* commentary).

नैकट्यं Proximity, neighbourhood.

नैकषेयः A demon, Râkshasa.

नैकृतिक *a.* (की *f.*) 1 Dishonest, false (or perhaps cruel); Ms. 4. 196. 2 Low, vile, wicked. 3 Morose.

नैगम *a.* (मी *f.*) Relating to or occurring in the Veda or holy writings; see °कांड. -मः 1 An interpreter of the Vedas or sacred writings; इति नैगमाः. 2 An Upanishad q. v. 3 A means, an expedient 4 Prudent conduct. 5 A citizen, towns-man. 6 A trader, merchant; धाराहारोपनयनपरा नैगमाः सानुमंतः V. 4. 4.

नैघंटुकं N. of the glossary of Vedic words (in five chapters) commented upon and explained by Yâska in his Nirukta.

नैचिकं The head of an ox.

नैचिकी An excellent cow.

नैतलं The lower or infernal regions -COMP. -सद्मन् *m.* Yama (Pluto); Mv. 5. 18.

नैत्यं Eternity, perpetuity.

नैत्यक *a.* (की *f.*) नैत्यिकं *a.* (की *f.*) 1 Regularly recurring, constantly repeated. 2 To be performed regularly (and not on particular occasions). 3 Indispensable, constant, obligatory.

नैदाघः Summer.

नैदानः An etymologist.

नैदानिकः A pathologist.

नैदेशिकः One who executes orders, a servant.

नैपातिक *a.* (की *f.*) Mention incidentally or by the way.

नैपुण्यं (ण्यं) 1 Dexterity, skill, cleverness, proficiency; नैपुणोन्नेयमस्ति U. 6. 26; Si. 16. 30. 3 Anything that requires skill, a delicate matter. 4 Totality, completeness; Ms. 10. 85.

नैभृत्यं 1 Modesty, humility. 2 Secrecy; नैभृत्यमवलंबितं M. 5.

नैमंत्रणकं A banquet, feast.

नैमयः A trader, merchant.

नैमित्तिक *a.* (की) 1 Produced by, connected with, or dependent on, any particular cause. 2 Unusual, occasional, accidental, produced by some cause (opp. नित्य). -कः An astrologer, prophet. -कं 1 An effect (opp. निमित्त 'cause'); निमित्तनैमित्तिकयोरयं क्रमः *S.* 7. 30. 2 An occasional rite, a periodical ceremony.

नैमिष *a.* (षी *f.*) Lasting for a Nimish or twinking, momentary, transient. -षं N. of a sacred forest celebrated as the residence of certain sages to whom Sauti related the Mahâbhârata; R. 19. 7; (the name is thus derived:—यतस्तु निमिषेणेदं निहतं दानवं बलं। अरण्येऽस्मिं ततस्तेन नैमिषारण्यसंज्ञितं ॥).

नैमेयः Barter, exchage.

नैयग्रोधं The fruit of न्यग्रोध, the Indian fig-tree.

नैयत्यं Restrain, self-command.

नैयमिक *a.* (की *f.*) Conformable to rule or precept, regular. -कं Regularity.

नैयायिकः A logician, a follower of the Nyâya system of philosophy.

नैरंतर्यं 1 Uninterruptedness, close succession, continuty. 2 Closeness, contiguity (in space).

नैरपेक्ष्यं Disregard, indifference.

नैरयिकः An inhabitant of hell.

नैरर्थ्यं Senselessness, nonsense.

नैराश्यं 1 Hopelessness, despair, despondency; तटस्थं नैराश्यात् U. 3. 13. 2 Absence of wish or expection; येनाशाः पृष्ठतः कृत्वा नैराश्यमवलंबितं H. 1. 144; Bv. 4.

नैरुक्तः One who knows the etymology of words, an etymologist.

नैरुज्यं Health.

नैर्ऋतः A demon; भयमप्रलयोद्वेगादाचख्युर्नैर्ऋतोदधेः K. 10. 34; 11. 21; 12. 43; 14, 4; 15. 20.

नैर्ऋती 1 An epithet of Durgâ. 2 The south-western direction.

नैर्गुण्यं 1 Absense of qualities or properties. 2 Want of excellence, absence of good qualities; नैर्गुण्यमेव साधीयो धिगस्तु गुणगौरवं Bv. 1. 88.

नैर्घृण्यं Pitilessness, cruelty; वैषम्यनैर्घृण्ये न सापेक्षत्वात् तथा हि दर्शयति Br. Sút. II. 1. 34.

नैर्मल्यं Cleanness, purity, spotlessness.

नैर्लज्ज्यं Shamelessness, impudence.

नैल्यं Blueness, dark-blue colour.

नैवि (बि) ड्यं Compactness, closeness, thickness, denseness.

नैवेद्यं An offering of eatables presented to a deity or idol.

नैश *a.* (शी *f.*), **नैशिक** *a.* (की *f.*) 1 Nocturnal, belonging to the night, nightly; तन्नैशं तिमिरमपाकरोति चंद्रः *S.* 6. 29; नैशस्यार्चिर्हुतभुज इव छिन्नभूयिष्ठधूमा V. 1. 8; Ki. 5. 2. 2 To be observed at night.

नैश्चल्यं Fixedness, immoveableness, fixity.

नैश्चित्यं 1 Determination, certainty. 2 A fixed ceremony.

नैषधः 1 A king of the Nishadhas. 2 Especially, an epithet of king Nala q. v. 3 A native or inhabitant of Nishadha.

नैष्कर्म्यं 1 Idleness, inactivity. 2 Exemption from acts or their consequences; Bg. 3. 4, 18. 49. 3 The salvation obtained by abstraction (as opposed to the salvation obtained by कर्ममार्ग q. v.).

नैष्किक *a.* (की *f.*) Bought with or made of a Nishka, q v. —कः A mint-master.

नैष्ठिक *a.* (की *f.*) 1 Final, last, concluding; विदधे विधिमस्य नैष्ठिकं R. 8. 25. 2 Decided, definitive, conclusive (as a reply.). 3 Fixed, firm, constant. 4 Highest, perfect. 5 Completely familiar with or versed in 6 Vowing perpetual abstinence and chastity. —कः A perpetual religious student who continues, with his spiritual preceptor even after the prescribed period, and vows life-long abstinence and chastity; Ku. 5. 62; cf. Y. 1. 49 and उपकुर्वाण also.

नैष्ठुर्यं Cruelty, harshness, severity.

नैष्ठ्यं Constancy, firmness.

नैसर्गिक *a.* (की *f.*) Natural, inborn, innate, inherent; नैसर्गिकी सुरभिणः कुसुमस्य सिद्धा मूर्ध्नि स्थितिर्न मुसलैरवताडनानि Mâl, 9. 49; R. 5. 37, 6. 46.

नैस्त्रिंशिकः A swordsman.

नो *ind.* (न-उ) No, not, often used like न q v.; Bg. 17. 28; Pt. 5. 24; Amaru. 5, 7, 10, 62.

नोचेत् If not, otherwise.

नोदनं 1 Impelling, driving, urging onward. 2 Removing, driving sway, dispelling.

नोधा *ind.* Ninefold, in nine parts.

नौः *f.* 1 A ship, boat, vessel; महता पुण्यपण्येन क्रीतेयं कायनौस्त्वया *S*ânti. 3. 1. 2 N. of a constellation. -Comp. -आरोहः (नावारोहः) 1 a passenger on board a ship. 2 a sailor. -कर्णधारः a helmsman, pilot. -कर्मन् *n.* the occupation of a sailor; Ms. 10. 34. -चरः,-जीविकः a sailor, boatman; R. 17. 81. -तार्य *a.* navigable, to be traversed in a ship. -दंडः an oar. -पानं navigable. -यायिन् *a.* going in a boat, a passenger; Ms. 8. 409. -वाहः a steersman, pilot, captain. -व्यसनं shipwreck, naufrage; नौव्यसने विपन्नः *S.* 6. -साधनं fleet, navy; वंगानुत्खाय तरसा नेता नौसाधनोद्यतान् R. 4. 36.

नौका A small boat, a boat in general; क्षणमिह सज्जनसंगतिरेका भवति भवार्णवतरणे नौका Moha M. 6. -Comp. -दंडः an oar.

न्यक् *ind.* An adverb, prefixed to कृ or भू, to imply 'contempt', 'degradation' or 'humiliation,. -Comp. -करणं, -कारः 1 humiliation, degradation, disrespect, contempt, insult; न्यक्कारो हृदि वज्रकील इव मे तीव्रं परिस्पंदते Mv. 5. 22, 3. 40; G. L. 32. -भावः 1 humiliation, degradation. 2 making inferior, subordination. -भावित *a.* 1 humiliated, degraded, slighted. 2 surpassed, excelled, made inferior or secondary (अप्रधानीकृत); न्यग्भावितवाच्यव्यंग्यव्यंजनक्षमस्य शब्दार्थयुगलस्य K. P. 1.

न्यक्ष *a.* Low, inferior, vile, mean. -क्षः 1 A buffalo. 2 An epithet of Paras'urâma. -क्षं The hole.

न्यग्रोधः 1 The (Indian) figtree. 2 A fathom (measured by the arms extended). -Comp. -परिमंडला an excellent woman; (she is thus described:—स्तनौ सुकठिनौ यस्या नितंबे च विशालता। मध्ये क्षीणा भवेद्या सा न्यग्रोधपरिमंडला Śabdak); दूर्वाकांडमिव श्यामा न्यग्रोधपरिमंडला Bk. 4. 18.

न्यंकुः A kind of antelope; R. 16. 15.

न्यंच् *a.* (नीची *f.*) 1 Going or turned downwards, turned or bent down. 2 Lying on the face. 3 Low, contemptible, base, mean, vile; Si. 15. 21. (where it also means निम्न or downward). 4 Slow, lazy. 5 Whole, entire.

न्यंचनं 1 A curve. 2 A hiding place. 3 A hollow.

न्ययः 1 Loss, destruction. 2 Waste, decay.

न्यसनं 1 Depositing, lying down. 2 Delivering, giving up.

न्यस्त *p. p.* 1 Cast down, thrown, or laid down, deposited. 2 Put in, inserted, applied; न्यस्ताक्षराः Ku. 1. 7. 3 Depicted, drawn; चित्रन्यस्त. 4 Consigned, delivered or transffered to; V. 5. 17; Ratn. 1. 10. 5 Living, resting on. 6 Given up, set aside, resigned. -Comp. -दंड *a.* giving up punishment. -देह *a.* one who lays down the body, dead. -शस्त्र *a.* 1 one who has resigned or laid down his arms; आचार्यस्य त्रिभुवनगुरोर्न्यस्तशस्त्रस्य शोकात् Ve. 3. 18. 2 unarmed, defenceless. 3 harmless.

न्याक्यं Fried, rice.

न्यादः Eating, feeding.

न्यायः 1 Method, manner, way, rule, system, plan; अधार्मिकं त्रिभिर्न्यायैर्निगृह्णीयात्प्रयत्नतः Ms. 8. 310. 2 Fitness, propriety, decorum; Ki. 11. 30. 3 Law, justice, virtue, equity, righteousness, honesty; याति न्यायप्रवृत्तस्य तिर्यंचोपि सहायतां A. R. 1. 4. 4 A law suit, legal proceeding. 5 Judicial sentence, judgment. 6 Policy, good government. 7 Likeness, analogy. 8 A popular maxim, an apposite illustration, illustration; as दंडापूपन्याय, काकतालीयन्याय, घुणाक्षरन्याय &c; see below. 9 A Vedic accent; न्यायैस्त्रिभिरुदीरणं Ku. 2. 12 (Malli. takes न्याय to mean स्वर; but it is quite open in our opinion to take न्याय in the sense of 'a system' or 'way' (which are manifested in three systems; *i. e.* ऋच्, युजस्, and सामन्); Bh. 3. 55. 10 (In gram.) A universal rule. 11 A system of Hindu philosophy founded by the sage Gautama. 12 The science of logic, logical philosophy. 13 A complete argument or syllogism (consisting of five members; *i. e.* प्रतिज्ञा, हेतु, उदाहरण, उपनय, and निगमन). –COMP. –पथः the Mîmamsâ philosophy. –वर्तिन् *a.* well-behaved, acting justly. –वादिन् *a.* one who speaks what is right or just. –शास्त्रं the science of logic. –सारिणी proper or suitable behaviour. –सूत्रं aphorisms of Nyâya philosophy by Gautama.

Note. A few of the common Nyâyas or popular maxims are here collected for ready reference and arranged in alphabetical order.

1. अंधचटकन्यायः The maxim of the blind man catching a sparrow, analogous in sense to घुणाक्षरन्यायः q. v.

2. अंधपरंपरान्यायः The maxim of the blind following the blind. It is used in those cases where people blindly or thoughtlessly follow others, not caring to see whether their doing so would not be a leap in the dark.

3. अरुंधतीदर्शनन्यायः The maxim of the view of the star Arundhatî. The following explanation of Sankarâchârya will make its use clear :—अरुंधतीं दिदर्शयिषुस्तत्समीपस्थां स्थूलां तारामनुख्यां प्रथममरुंधतीति ग्राहयित्वा तां प्रत्याख्याय पश्चादरुंधतीमेव ग्राहयति.

4. अशोकवनिकान्यायः The maxim of the grove of Asoka trees. Râvaṇa kept Sîta in the grove of Asoka trees, but it is not easy to account for his preference of that particular grove to any other one; so when a man finds several ways of doing a thing, any one of them is as good as another, and the preference of any particular one cannot be accounted for.

5. अश्मलोष्टन्यायः The maxim of the stone and clod of earth. A clod of earth may be considered to be hard as compared with cotton, but is soft as compared with a stone. So a person may be considered to be very important as compared with his inferiors, but sinks into insignificance when compared with his betters. The maxim पाषाणेष्टकन्याय is similarly used.

6. कदंबकोरक (गोलक) न्यायः The maxim of the Kadamba buds; used to denote simultaneous rise or action, like the bursting forth of the buds of the Kadamba tree at one and the same time.

7. काकतालीयन्यायः The maxim of the crow and the palm fruit. It takes its origin from the unexpected and sudden fall of a palm-fruit upon the head of a crow (so as to kill it) at the very moment of its sitting on a branch of that tree; and is used to denote a very unexpected and accidental occurrence, whether welcome or unwelcome; cf. Chandrâloka:—यत्तया मेलनं तत्र लाभो मे यश्च सुभ्रुवः । तदेतत्काकतालीयमवितर्कितसंभवं ॥ also Kuvalayânanda: पतत् तालफलं यथा काकेनोपभुक्तमेवं रहोदर्शनक्षुभितहृदया तन्वी मया भुक्ता । see काकतालीय also.

8. काकदंतगवेषणन्यायः The maxim of searching after a crow's teeth, used to denote any useless, unprofitable, or impossible task.

9. काकाक्षिगोलन्यायः The maxim of the crow's eyeball. It takes its origin from the supposition that the crow has but one eye (cf. words like एकदृष्टि, एकाक्ष &c.), and that it can move it, as occasion requires from the socket on one side into that of the other; and the maxim is applied to a word or phrase which, though used only once in a sentence may, if occasion requires, serve two purposes; *e. g.* द्वीपोऽस्त्रियामंतरीपः इत्यत्र अस्त्रियामित्यस्य काकाक्षिगोलकन्यायेन अंतरीपशब्देनाप्यन्वयः.

10. कूपयंत्रघटिकान्यायः The maxim of the buckets attached to the water-wheel. It takes its origin from the fact that while some of the buckets filled with water go up, some are emptied of their contents, while others go down quite empty; and is used to denote the various vicissitudes of worldly existence; cf , कांश्चित्तुच्छयति प्रपूरयति वा कांश्चिन्नयत्युन्नतिं कांश्चित्पातविधौ करोति च पुनः कांश्चिन्नयत्याकुलान् । अन्योन्यप्रतिपक्षसंहतिमिमां लोकस्थितिं बोधयन्नेष क्रीडति कूपयंत्रघटिकान्यायप्रसक्तो विधिः ॥ Mk. 10. 59.

11. घट्टकुटीप्रभातन्यायः The maxim of day-break near a toll-station. It takes its origin from the attempt of one (say, a cartman) who with the intention of avoiding a toll takes at night an unfrequented road, but unfortunately finds himself at day-break near that very toll-station and is obliged to pay the toll which he studiously tried to avoid. Thus the maxim is used to denote the occurrence of that which one studiously tries to avoid; cf. Srîharsha:—तदिदं घट्टकुटीप्रभातन्यायमनुवदति.

12. घुणाक्षरन्यायः The maxim of letters bored by an insect in wood. It takes its origin from the unexpected and chance resemblance of an incision in wood or in the leaf of a book made by an insect to the form of some letter, and is used to denote any fortuitous or chance occurrence.

13. दंडापूपन्यायः The maxim of the stick and cakes. When a stick and cakes are kept t gether and one says that 'the stick has been pulled down or eaten by a rat', we are naturally led to expect that the cakes also have been pulled down or eaten by the rat, as a matter of course, the two being so closely connected together ; so when one thing is closely connected with another in a particular way, and we say something of the one, it naturally follows that what we assert of the one can, as a matter of course, be asserted of the other; cf. मूषिकेण दंडो भक्षितः इत्यनेन तत्सहचरितमपूपभक्षणमर्थादायातं भवतीति नियतसमानन्यायादर्थांतरमापततीत्येष न्यायो दंडापूपिका ॥ S. D. 10.

14. देहलीदीपन्यायः The maxim of the lamp placed over the threshold. It takes its origin from a lamp hanging over the threshold of a house which, by its peculiar position, serves to light the rooms on both sides of the threshold; and is used to denote something which serves a two-fold purpose at the same time.

15. नृपनापितपुत्रन्यायः The maxim of the king and barber's son. It is used to donote a man's innate fondness for his own possession–howsoever ugly or despicable in the eyes of others. It takes its origin from a story which states that a king on one occasion asked his barber to bring to him the finest boy that he could see in his kingdom. The barber roamed for a long time over every part of the realm, but could discover no boy such as the king wanted. At last wearied and disappointed, he returned home; and being charmed with the beauty of his own boy, who, to do him justice, was a personification of ugliness and deformity–went to the king and presented the boy to him. The king was at first very angry with the barber for having trifled with him but on consideration excused him,

as he ascribed the barber's preference of his own ugly boy to the dominant desire of human beings to consider their own possessions as supremely good; cf. सर्वः कांतमात्मीयं पश्यति *S.* 2.

16. पंकप्रक्षालनन्यायः The maxim of washing off the mud. Just as it is more advisable for one to avoid getting into mud than to get into it and then wash it off, so it is more advisable for one to avoid getting into danger than to expose oneself to it and then try to get out of it somehow or other; cf. प्रक्षालनाद्धि पंकस्य दूरादस्पर्शनं वरं; and also "Prevention is better than cure".

17. पिष्टपेषणन्यायः The maxim of grinding flour or meal; used to denote a superfluous or unprofitable exertion like the attempt of a man to grind pounded flour; cf. कृतस्य करणं वृथा.

18. बीजांकुरन्यायः The maxim of seed and sprout. It takes its origin from the relation of mutual causation which subsists between seed and sprout, (*seed* being the cause of *sprout*, which in its turn is the cause of *seed*); and is used in those cases where two things stand to each other in the relation of both cause and effect.

19. लोहचुंबकन्यायः The maxim of iron and magnet; it is used to denote a very close affinity between two things, by virtue of which they are instinctively attracted towards each other.

20. वह्निधूमन्यायः The maxim of the invariable concomitance of fire and smoke; (wherever there is smoke there is fire.) It is used to denote such inveriable concomitance between two persons or things; (*e. g.* where there is A, there is B; where there is not B, there is not A.).

21. वृद्धकुमारीवाक्य (वर) न्यायः The maxim of the old virgin's boon; that is, asking such a boon as will cover all that one wishes to have. The Mahâbhâshya says that an old virgin, when asked by Indra to choose a boon, said:—पुत्रा मे बहुक्षीरघृतमोदनं कांचनपात्र्यां भुंजीरन्. This one boon, if granted, would give her a husband, progeny, abundance of corn, cattle &c. and gold.

22. शाखाचंद्रन्यायः The maxim of the bough and the moon. As the moon, though considerably distant from the bough of a tree, is spoken of as 'the moon on the bough' because she appears to be near it, so this maxim is used when the position of an object, though at a very great distance, is fixed by that of another object to which it appears to be contiguous.

23. सिंहावलोकनन्यायः The maxim of the lion's backward glance. It is used when one casts a retrospective glance at what he has left behind while at the same time he is proceeding, just as the lion, while going onward in search of prey, now and then bends his neck backwards to see if anything be within his reach.

24. सूचीकटाहन्यायः The maxim of the needle and the kettle. It is used to denote that when two things-the one easy and the other difficult-are required to be done, the easier should be first attended to, as when one has to prepare a needle and a kettle, he should first take in hand a needle as it is an easier work compared with the preparation of a kettle.

25. स्थूणानिखननन्यायः The maxim of digging or fixing in the post. As a stake or post to be firmly fixed in the ground is again and again moved and thrust inward, so this maxim is used when one (say, a disputant) adds several corroborative illustrations, arguments &c. to strengthen and confirm still more his strong position.

26. स्वामिभृत्यन्यायः The maxim of master and servant. It is used to mark the relation of the feeder and the fed, or the supporter and the supported, subsisting between any two objects.

न्याय्य *a.* 1 Just, proper, right, equitable, suitable, fit; न्याय्यात्पथः प्रविचलंति पदं न धीराः Bh. 2. 83; Bg. 18. 15; Ms. 2. 152, 9. 202; R. 2. 55; Ki. 14. 7; Ku. 6. 87. 2 Usual, customary.

न्यासः 1 Placing, putting down or upon, planting, तस्याः खुरन्यासपवित्रपांसुं R. 2. 2; Ku. 6. 50, चरणन्यास, अंगन्यास &c. 2 Hence, any impression, mark, stamp, print; अतिशस्त्रनखन्यासः R. 12. 73 'where the nailmarks surpassed those of weapons'; दंतन्यास. 3 Depositing. 4 A pledge, deposit; प्रत्यर्पितन्यास इवांतरात्मा *S.* 4. 21, R. 12. 8; Y. 2. 67. 5 Entrusting, committing, delivering, consigning. 6 Painting, writing down. 7 Giving up, resigning, abandoning, relinquishing; शस्त्र°, Bg. 18. 2. 8 Bringing forward, adducing. 9 Digging in, seizing (as with claws). 10 Assignment of the various parts of the body to different deities, which is usually accompanied with prayers and corresponding gesticulations. –Comp. –अपह्नवः repudiation of a deposit. –धारिन् *m.* the holder of a deposit, a mortgagee.

न्यासिन् *m.* One who has renounced all worldly ties, a Sannyâsin.

न्युं (न्यूं) ख *a.* 1 Charming, beautiful, lovely. 2 Proper, right.

न्युब्ज *a.* 1 Turned or bent downwards, lying on the face; ऊर्ध्वार्पितन्युब्जकटाहकल्पे (व्योम्नि) N. 22. 32. 2 Bent, crooked. 3 Convex. 4 Hump-backed. —ब्जः The Nyagrodha tree. –Comp. –खड्गः a crooked sword, sabre.

न्यून *a.* 1 Lessened, diminished, shortened. 2 Defective, inferior, deficient, wanting, destitute of; as in अर्थन्युन. 3 Less (opp. अधिक); Y. 2. 116. 4 Defective (in some organ); पाद°. 5 Low, wicked, vile, despicable. —नं *ind.* Less, in a less degree. –Comp. –अंग *a.* maimed, mutilated. –अधिक *a.* less or more, unequal. –धी *a.* deficient in intellect, ignorant, foolish.

न्यूनयति Den. P. To diminish, lessen.

प.

प *a.* (At the end of comp.) 1 Drinking; as in द्विप, अनेकप. 2 Guarding, protecting, ruling; as in गोप, नृप, क्षितिप. —पः 1 Air, wind. 2 A leaf. 3 An egg.

पक्कणः The hut of a चांडाल or barbarian.

पक्तिः *f.* 1 Cooking. 2 Digesting, digestion. 3 Ripening, becoming ripe, maturity, development. 4 Fame, dignity. –Comp. –शूलं violent pain of the bowels arising from indigestion, colic.

पक्तृ *a.* 1 Who or what cooks. 2 Cooking. 3 Stimulating, digesting. —*m.* Fire (especially in the stomach).

पक्त्रं 1 The state of a house-holder who maintains the sacred fire. 2 The sacred fire so maintained.

पक्वात्रिम *a.* 1 Ripe, ripened. 2 Matured. 3 Cooked.

पक्व *a.* 1 Cooked, roasted, boiled; as in पक्वान्न. 2 Digested. 3 Baked, burned, annealed (opp. आम); प्रकोष्ठकानामाकर्षणं Mk. 3. 4 Mature, ripe;

पक्वबिंबाधरोष्ठी Me. 82. 5 Fully developed, come to perfection, perfect, matured; as in पक्वधी. 6 Experienced, shrewd. 7 Ripe (as a boil), ready to suppurate. 8 Grey (as hair). 9 Perished, decaying, is the eve of destruction, ripe to meet one's doom. -COMP. -अतिसारः chronic dysentery. -अन्नं dressed or cooked food. -आधानं, -आशयः the stomach, abdomen. -इष्टका a baked brick. -इष्टकचितं a building constructed with baked bricks. -कृत् *a.* 1 cooking. 2 maturing. -रसः wine or any spirituous liquor. -वारि *n.* the water of boiled rice (कांजिक).

पक्वशः N. of a barbarous tribe, a Chândâla.

पक्ष् 1 P., 10 U. (पक्षति, पक्षयति-ते) 1 To take, seize. 2 To accept. 3 To take a side, side with.

पक्षः 1 A wing, pinion; अद्यापि पक्षावपि नोद्भिद्येते K. 347; so उद्भिन्नपक्षः pledged; पक्षच्छेदोद्यतं शक्रं R. 4. 40, 3. 42. 2 The feather or feathers on each side of an arrow. 3 The flank or side of a man or animal, the shoulder; स्तंबेरमा उभयपक्षविनीतनिद्राः R. 5. 72. 4 The side of anything, flank. 5 The wing or flank of an army. 6 The half of any thing. 7 The half of a lunar month, a fortnight (comprising 15 days); (there are two such *pakshas*, शुक्लपक्ष the bright or light half, and कृष्णत-मिस्र-पक्ष the dark half); तमिस्रपक्षेऽपि सहप्रियाभिर्ज्योत्स्नावतो निर्विशति प्रदोषात् R. 6. 34; Ms. 1. 66; Y. 3. 50; सीमा वृद्धिं समायाति शुक्लपक्ष इवोडुराट् Pt. 1. 92. 8 A party in general, faction, side; प्रमुदितवरपक्षं R. 6. 86; *Si.* 2. 117; Bg. 14. 25; R. 6. 53, 18. 9 One belonging to any party, a follower, partisan: शत्रुपक्षो भवान् H. 1. 10 A class, multitude, host, any number of adherents; as शत्रु° मित्र°. 11 One side of an argument, an alternative, one of two cases; पक्षे in the other case, on the other hand; पूर्वपक्षाभवत्पक्षस्तस्मिन्नाभवदुत्तरः R. 4. 10, 14. 34; cf. पूर्वपक्ष and उत्तरपक्ष. 12 A case or supposition in general; as in पक्षांतरे 13 A point under discussion, a thesis. 14 The subject of a syllogism or conclusion (the minor term); संदिग्धसाध्यवान् पक्षः T. S.; दधतः शुद्धिभृतो गृहीतपक्षाः *Si.* 20. 11 (where it means 'feathered' also). 15 A symbolical expression for the number 'two'. 16 A bird. 17 A state, condition. 18 The body. 19 A limb of the body. 20 A royal elephant. 21 An army. 22 A wall. 23 Opposition. 24 Rejoinder, reply. 25 A mass, quantity (when in composition with words meaning 'hair'); केशपक्षः; cf. हस्त. -COMP. -अंतः the 15th day of either half month, *i. e.* the day of new or full moon. -अंतरं 1 another side. 2 a different side or view of an argument. 3 another supposition. -आघातः 1 palsy or paralysis of one side, hemiplegia. 2 refutation of an argument. -आभासः a fallacious argument. 2 a false plaint. -आहारः eating food only once in a fortnight. -ग्रहणं choosing a party. -चरः 1 an elephant strayed from the herd. 2 the moon. -छिद् *m.* an epithet of Indra (clipper of the wings of mountains); Ku. 1. 20. -जः the moon. -द्वयं 1 both sides of an argument. 2 'a couple of fortnights', *i. e.* a month. -द्वारं a side-door, private entrance. -धर *a.* 1 winged. 2 adhering to the party of one, siding with any one. (-रः) 1 a bird. 2 the moon. 3 a partisan. 4 an elephant strayed from the herd -नाडी a quill. -पातः 1 siding with any one. 2 liking, desire, love, affection (for a thing); भवंति भव्येषु हि पक्षपाताः Ki. 3. 12, Ve. 3. 10; U 5. 17; रिपुपक्षे बद्धपक्षपातः Mu. 1. 3 attachment to a party, partisanship, partiality; पक्षपातमत्र देवी मन्यते M. 1; सत्त्वं जना बच्मि न पक्षपातात् Bh. 1. 47. 4 falling of wings, the moulting of birds. 5 a partisan. -पातिन् *a.* or *s.* 1 siding with, adhering to a party, attached or partial (to a particular cause); पक्षपातिनो देवा अपि पांडवानां Ve. 3. 2 sympathising; Ve. 3. 3 a follower, partisan, friend; यः सुरपक्षपाती V. 1; (पक्षपातिता in N. 2. 52 means 'movement of the wings' also). -पालिः a private door. -बिंदुः a heron. -भागः 1 the side or flank. 2 especially, the flank of an elephant. -भुक्तिः the course traversed by the sun in a fortnight. -मूलं the root of a wing. वादः 1 an exparte statement. 2 stating a case, expression of opinion. -वाहनः a bird. -हत *a.* paralysed on one side. -हरः a bird. -होमः 1 a sacrificial rite lasting for a fortnight. 2 a rite to be performed every fornight.

पक्षकः 1 A side-door. 2 A side. 3 An associate, partisan (at the end of comp.).

पक्षता 1 Alliance, partisanship. 2 Adherence to a party. 3 Taking up a side or argument.

पक्षतिः *f.* 1 The root of a wing; अलिखच्चंचुपुटेन पक्षती N. 2. 2; खड्गच्छिन्नजटायुपक्षतिः U. 3. 43; *Si.* 11. 26. 2 The first day of a lunar fortnight.

पक्षालुः A bird.

पक्षिणी 1 A female bird. 2 A night with the two days enclosing it; (द्वावह्नावेकरात्रिश्च पक्षिणीत्यभिधीयते). 3 The day of full moon.

पक्षिन् *a.* (णी *f.*) 1 Winged. 2 Furnished with wings. 3 Siding with, adhering to the party of.—*m.* 1 A bird. 2 An arrow. 3 An epithet of *Siva.* -COMP.-इंद्रः,-प्रवरः,-राज् *m.*, -राजः,-सिंहः,-स्वामिन् *m.* epithets of Garuḍa. -कीटः an insignificant bird. बालकः,-शावकः a young bird. -शाला 1 a nest. 2 an aviary.

पक्ष्मन् *n.* 1 An eyelash: सलिलगुरुभिः पक्ष्मभिः Me. 90, 47; R. 2. 19, 11. 36. 2 The filament of a flower. 3 The point of a thread, a thin thread. 4 A wing.

पक्ष्मल *a.* 1 Having strong, long or beautiful eyelashes; पक्ष्मलाक्ष्याः *S.* 3 25. 2 Hairy, shaggy; मृदितपक्ष्मलरल्लकांगः *Si.* 4. 61.

पक्ष्य *a.* 1 Produced or occurring in a fortnight. 2 Siding with. 3 Lateral. -क्ष्यः A partisan, follower, friend, ally; ननु वज्रिण एव वीर्यमेतद्विजयंते द्विषतो यदस्य पक्ष्याः V. 1. 16.

पंकः, कं 1 Mud, clay, mire; अनीत्वा पंकतां धूलिमुदकं नावतिष्ठते *Si.* 2. 34, Ki. 2. 6; R. 16. 30. 2 Hence, a thick mass, large quantity; कृष्णागुरुपंक K. 30. 3 A slough, quagmire. 4 Sin.-COMP. -कीरः a lapwing. -क्रीडः a hog. -ग्राहः a Makara or crocodile. -छिद् *m.* the clearing-nut tree, (कतक, the fruit of which is used in purifying muddy water); M. 2. 8. -जं a lotus. °जः, °जन्मन् *m.* an epithet of Brahmâ. °नाभः an epithet of Vishṇu; R. 18. 20. -जन्मन् *n.* a lotus. (-*m.*) the Sârasa bird. -मंडुकः a bivalve conch. -रुह् *n*, -रुहं a lotus. -वासः a crab.

पंकजिनी 1 A lotus-plant; Ki. 10. 33. 2 A group of lotus-plants or lotuses. 3 A place abounding with lotuses. 4 The flexible stalk of a water-lily.

पंकणः The hut of a चांडाल, see पक्कण.

पंकारः 1 Moss. 2 A dam, dike. 3 Stairs, a ladder, a flight of steps.

पंकिल *a.* Muddy, foul, turbid, dirty; *Si.* 17. 8.

पंकेज A lotus.

पंकेरुह् *n.* -हं A lotus. -हः The crane or Sârasa bird.

पंकेशय *a.* Dwelling in mud.

पंक्ति *f.* 1 A line, row, range, series; इश्येत चारुपदपंक्तिरलक्तकांका V. 4. 6; पक्ष्मपंक्ति R. 2. 19; अलिपंक्तिः Ku. 4. 15; R. 6. 5. 2 A group, collection, flock, troop. 3 A row of people (of the same caste) sitting down to a meal, a company or party at dinner of the same caste; cf. पंक्तिपावन below. 4 The living generation. 5 The earth. 6 Fame, celebrity. 7 A collection of five, or the number 'five'. 8 The number 'ten'; as in पंक्तिरथ, पंक्तिग्रीव. -COMP. -ग्रीवः an epithet of Râvaṇa. -चरः an osprey. -दूषः,-दूषकः a person defiling a society of persons, one with whom it is improper to associate at dinner-time. -पावनः a respectable or eminent person; especially, a respectable Brâhmaṇa who, being very learned, always gets the seat of honour at dinner parties, or who purifies by his presence the पंक्ति or persons who sit in the same row to dine with him; पंक्तिपावनाः पंचाग्नयः Mâl. 1, where Jagaddhara says:—पंक्तिपावनाः पंक्तौ भोजनादिगोष्ठ्यां पावनाः । अग्रभोजिनः पवित्रा वा । यद्वा । यजुषां पारगो यस्तु साम्नां यश्चापि पारगः । अथर्वशिरसोऽध्येता ब्राम्हणः पंक्तिपावनः ॥ or अग्र्याः सर्वेषु वेदेषु सर्वप्रवचनेषु च । यावदेते प्रपश्यंति पंक्त्यां तावत्पुनंति च ॥ ततो हि पावनात्पंक्त्या उच्यंते पंक्तिपावनाः. Manu explains the word thus:— अपांक्त्योपहता पंक्तिः पाव्यते यैर्द्विजोत्तमैः । तान्निबोधत कार्त्स्न्येन द्विजाग्र्यान् पंक्तिपावनान् Ms. 3. 184; see 3. 183, 186 also. -रथः N. of Dasaratha; R. 9. 74.

पंगु *a.* (गू or ग्वी *f.*) Lame, halt, crippled. -गुः 1 A lame man; मूकं करोति वाचालं पंगुं लंघयते गिरिं. 2 An epithet of Saturn. -Comp. -ग्राहः 1 a crocodile (मकर). 2 the tenth sign of the zodiac; Capricornus (मकर).

पंगुल *a.* Lame, crippled.

पच् I. 1 U. (पचति-ते, पक्व) 1 To cook, roast, dress (as food &c.) (said to govern two accusatives; as तंडुलानोदनं पचति, but this use is very rare in classical Sanskrit); यः पचत्यात्मकारणात् Ms. 3. 118; शूले मत्स्यानिवापक्ष्यन् दुर्बलान् बलवत्तराः 7. 20; Bh. 1. 85. 2 To bake, burn (as bricks); see पक्व. 3 To digest (as food); पचाम्यन्नं चतुर्विधं Bg. 15. 14. 4 To ripen, mature. 5 To bring to perfection, develop (as understanding). 6 To melt (as metals). 7 To cook (for oneself) (Atm.). *-Pass.* (पच्यते) 1 To be cooked. 2 To become ripe, matured or developed, ripen; (fig.) to bear fruit, attain perfection or fulfilment; R. 11. 50. *-Caus.* (पाचयति-ते) To cause to be cooked, cause to ripen or develop, bring to perfection. *-Desid.* (पिपक्षति) To wish to cook &c. -With परि to ripen, mature, develop. -वि 1 to mature, develop, ripen, bear fruit; R. 17. 53. 2 to digest. 3 to cook thoroughly. -II. 1. A. (पचते) To make clear or evident; see पंच् also.

पचतः 1 Fire 2 The sun. 3 N. of Indra.

पचन *a.* Cooking, dressing, maturing &c. —नः Fire. —नं 1 Cooking, dressing, maturing &c. 2 A means or instrument for cooking, a vessel, fuel &c.

पचपचः An epithet of Siva.

पचा The act of cooking.

पचिः Fire.

पचेलिम *a.* 1 Cooking or ripening quickly. 2 Fit to be matured. 3 Ripening spontaneously or naturally; ददर्श मालूरफलं पचेलिमं N. 1. 94. —मः 1 Fire. 2 The sun.

पचेलुकः A cook.

पज्झटिका A small bell.

पंचक *a.* Consisting of five. 2 Relating to five. 3 Made of five. 4 Bought with five. 5 Taking five per-cent. -कः, -कं A collection or aggregate of five; अम्लपंचक.

पंचत् *f.* A pentad, an aggregate of five.

पंचता,-त्वं 1 Five-fold state. 2 A collection of five. 3 The five elements taken collectively; hence पंचतां-त्वं गम्,-या &c. means 'to be resolved into the five elements of which the body consists', 'to die or perish'; पंचतां,-त्वं नी to kill or destroy; पंचभिर्निर्मिते देहे पंचत्वं च पुनर्गते । स्वां स्वां योनिमनुप्राप्ते तत्र का परिदेवना ॥; Ratn. 3. 3.

पंचथुः 1 Time. 2 The (Indian) cuckoo.

पंचधा *ind.* 1 In five parts. 2 In five ways.

पंचन् *num. a.* (Always pl.; nom. and acc. पंच) Five. (As the first member of comp. पंचन् drops its final न्). -Comp. -अंशः the fifth part, a fifth. -अग्निः 1 an aggregate of five sacred fires; *i. e.* अन्वाहार्यपचन or दक्षिण, गार्हपत्य, आहवनीय, सभ्य and आवसथ्य) 2 a householder who maintains the five sacred fires; पंचाग्नयो धृतव्रताः Mâl. 1; Ms. 3. 185. -अंग *a.* five-membered, having five parts or divisions as in पंचांगःप्रणामः (*i. e.* बाहुभ्यां चैव जानुभ्यां शिरसा वक्षसा दृशा); कृतपंचांगविनिर्णयो नयः Ki. 2. 12 (see Malli. and Kâmandaka quoted by him). (-गः) 1 a tortoise or turtle. 2 a kind of horse with five spots in different parts of his body. (-गी) a bit for horses (-गं) 1 a collection or aggregate of five parts. 2 five modes of devotion. 3 a calender or almanac, so called because it treats of five things:— तिथिर्वारश्च नक्षत्रं योगः करणमेव च; चतुरंगबलो राजा जगतीं वशमानयेत् । अहं पंचांगबलवानाकाशं वशमानये ॥ Subhâsh. °गुप्तः a turtle. °शुद्धिः *f.* the propitiousness or favourable state of five important points; *i. e.* तिथि, वार, नक्षत्र, योग, and करण (in astrology). -अंगुल *a.* (-ला or ली *f.*) measuring five fingers. -अ (आ) जं the five products of the goat. -अप्सरस् *n.* N. of a lake, said to have been created by the sage Maṇḍakarṇi; cf. R. 13. 38. -अमृतं the collection of five sweet things used in worshipping deities; (दुग्धं च शर्करा चैव घृतं दधि तथा मधु). -आर्चिस् *m.* the planet Mercury. -अवयव *a.* five-membered (as a syllogism, the five members being, प्रतिज्ञा, हेतु, उदाहरण, उपनय, and निगमन). -अवस्थः a corpse; (so called because it is resolved into the five elements); cf. पंचत्व above. -अविकं the five products of the sheep. -अशीतिः *f.* eighty-five. -अहः a period of five days. -आतपः *a.* doing penance with five fires (*i. e.* with four fires and the sun); cf. R. 13. 41. -आननः, -आस्यः, -मुखः, -वक्त्रः 1 an epithet of Siva. 2 a lion (so called because its mouth is generally wide open; पंचं आननं यस्य); (often used at the end of names of learned men to express great learning or respect; न्याय°, तर्क° &c., *e. g.* जगन्नाथतर्कपंचानन). -इंद्रिय an aggregate of the five organs (of sense or action; see इंद्रियं). -इषुः, -बाणः,-शरः epithets of the god of love; (so called because he has five arrows: their names are:—अरविंदमशोकं च चूतं च नवमल्लिका । नीलोत्पलं च पंचैते पंचबाणस्य सायकाः). -उष्मन् *m.* pl. the five digestive fires supposed to be in the body. -कर्मन् *n.* (in medicine) the five kinds of treatment; *i. e.* 1 वमन 'giving emetics'; 2 रेचन 'purging'; 3 नस्य 'giving sternutatories'; 4 अनुवासन 'administering an enema which is oily', and 5 निरूह 'administering an enema which is not oily'. -कृत्वस् *ind.* five times. -कोणः a pentagon. -कोलं the five spices taken collectively. -कोषाः (*m.* pl.) the five vestures or wrappers supposed to invest the soul; they are:— अन्नमयकोष or the earthly body (स्थूलशरीर); प्राणमयकोष the vesture of the vital airs; मनोमयकोष the sensorial vesture; विज्ञानमयकोष the cognitional vesture (these three form the लिंगशरीर;) and आनंदमयकोष the last vesture, that of beatitude. -क्रोशी a distance of five Krosas. -खट्वं, -खट्वी a colleciion of five beds. -गवं a collection of five cows. -गव्यं the five products of the cow taken collectively; *i. e.* milk, curds, clarified butter or ghee, urine, and cowdung (क्षीरं दधि तथा चाज्यं मूत्रं गोमयमेव च). -गु *a.* bought with five cows. -गुण *a.* fivefold. -गुप्तः 1 a tortoise. 2 the materialistic system of philosophy, the docrines of the Chârvâkas. -चत्वारिंश *a.* fortyfifth. -चत्वारिंशत् *f.* forty-five. -जनः 1 man, mankind. 2 N. of a demon who had assumed the form of a conch-shell and was slain by Krishṇa. 3 the soul. 4 the five classes of beings; *i. e.* gods, men, Gandharvas, serpents and pitṛis. 5 the four primary castes of the Hindus (ब्राम्हण, क्षत्रिय, वैश्य and शूद्र)

with the Nishâdas or barbarians as the fifth (pl. in these two senses); (for a full exposition see *S*ârîrabhâshya on Br. Sútras I. 4. 11-13) **-जनीन** *a.* devoted to the five races. (**-नः**) an actor, mimic, buffoon. **-ज्ञानः 1** an epithet of Buddha as possessing the five kinds of knowledge. **2** a man familiar with the doctrines of the Pâs'upatas. **-तक्षं, -क्षी** a collection of five carpenters. **-तत्त्वं 1** the five elements taken collectively; *i. e.* पृथ्वी, आप्, तेजस्, वायु and आकाश. **2** (in the Tantras) the five essentials of the Tântrikas, also called पंचमकार because they all begin with म; *i. e.* मद्य, मांस, मत्स्य, मुद्रा and मैथुन. **-तपस्** *m.* an ascetic who in summer practises penance sitting in the middle of four fires with the sun burning right over his head; cf. हविर्भुजामेधवतां चतुर्णां मध्ये ललाटंतपसप्तसप्तिः R. 13. 41 and Ku. 5. 23; and Ms 6. 23 and *Si.* 2. 51 also. **-तय** *a.* five-fold. (**-यः**) a pentad. **-त्रिंश** *a.* thirty fifth. **-त्रिंशत्, -त्रिंशतिः** *f.* thirty-five. **-दश** *a.* **1** fifteenth. **2** increased by fifteen; as in पंचदशं शतं 'one hundred and fifteen' **-दशन्** *a.* pl. fifteen. °अहः a period of fifteen days. **-दशिन्** *a.* made or consisting of fifteen. **-दशी** the fifteenth day of a lunar fortnight. **-दीर्घं** the five long parts of the body; बाहू नेत्रद्वयं कुक्षिर्द्वे तु नासे तथैव च । स्तनयोरंतरं चैव पंचदीर्घं प्रचक्षते ॥. **-नखः 1** any animal with five claws; पंच पंचनखा भक्ष्या ये प्रोक्ताः कृतजैर्द्विजैः Bk. 6. 131; Ms. 5. 17, 18. Y. 1. 177. **2** an elephant. **3** a turtle. **4** a lion or tiger. **-नदः**, 'the country of five rivers, the modern Panjab (the five river being शतद्रु, विपाशा, इरावती, चंद्रभागा and वितस्ता, or the modern names Sutlej, Beas, Ravee, Chenab and Jhelum). (**-दाः** pl) the people of this country. **-नवतिः** *f.* ninety-five. **-नीराजनं** waving five things before an idol and then falling prostrate before it; (the five things being:—a lamp, lotus, cloth, mango and betel-leaf). **-पंचाश** *a.* fifty-fifth. **-पंचाशत्** *f.* fifty-five. **-पदी** five steps; Pt. 2. 115. **-पात्रं 1** five vessels taken collectively. **2** a *S*râddha in which offerings are made in five vessels. **-प्राणाः** (*m.* pl.) the five life-winds or vital airs; प्राण, अपान, व्यान, उदान and समान. **-प्रासादः** a temple of a particular size) with four pinnacles and a steeple). **-बाणः, -वाणः, -शरः** epithets of the god of love; see पंचेषु. **-भुज** *a.* pentagonal. (**-जः**) a pentagon; cf. पंचकोण. **-भूतं** the five elements; पृथ्वी, अप्, तेजस्, वायु and आकाश. **-मकारं** the five essentials of the left-hand Tantra ritual of which the first letter is म; see पंचतत्त्व. (**2**). **-महापातकं** the five great sins; see महापातक. **-महायज्ञाः** (*m.* pl.) the five daily sacrifices enjoined to be performed by a Brâhmaṇa; see महायज्ञ. **-यामः** a day. **-रत्नं** a collection of five gems; (they are variously enumerated:—(1) नीलकं वज्रकं चेति पद्मरागश्च मौक्तिकं । प्रवालं चेति विज्ञेयं पंचरत्नं मनीषिभिः ॥ (2) सुवर्णं रजतं मुक्ता राजावर्तं प्रवालकं । रत्नपंचकमाख्यातम् ॥ (3) कनकं हीरकं नीलं पद्मरागश्च मौक्तिकं । पंचरत्नमिदं प्रोक्तमृषिभिः पूर्वदर्शिभिः ॥. **-रात्रं** a period of five nights. **-राशिकं** the rule of five (in math.) **-लक्षणं** a Purâṇa; so called because it deals with five important topics:—सर्गश्च प्रतिसर्गश्च वंशो मन्वंतराणिच । वंशानुचरितं चैव पुराणं पंचलक्षणं ॥ see पुराण also **-लवणं** five kinds of salts; *i. e.* काचक, सैंधव, सामुद्र, बिड and सौवर्चल. **-वटी 1** the five fig-tree; *i. e.* अश्वत्थ, बिल्व, वट, धात्री and अशोक. **2** N. of a part of the Daṇḍakâ forest where the Godâvarî rises and where Râma dwelt for a considerable time with his beloved; it is two miles from Nasik; U. 2. 28; R. 13. 31. **-वर्षदेशीय** *a.* about five years old. **-वर्षीय** *a.* five years old. **-वल्कलं** a collection of the barks of the five kinds of trees; (*i. e.* न्यग्रोध, उदुंबर, अश्वत्थ, प्लक्ष and वेतस). **-विंश** *a.* twenty-fifth. **-विंशतिः** *f.* twenty-five. **-विंशतिका** a collection of twenty-five; as in वेतालपंचविंशतिका. **-विध** *a.* five-fold, of five kinds **-शत** *a.* amounting to five hundred and five. **2** five hundred. (**-तं**) **1** one hundred and five. **2** five hundred **-शाखः 1** the hand. **2** an elephant. **-शिखः** a lion. **-ष** *a.* pl. five or six; संत्यन्येऽपि बृहस्पतिप्रभृतयः संभाविताः पंचषाः Bh. 2. 34. **-षष्ट** *a.* sixty-fifth. **-षष्टिः** *f.* sixty-five. **-सप्तत** *a.* seventy-fifth. **-सप्ततिः** *f.* seventy-five. **-सूनाः** *f.* the five things in a house by which animal life may be accidentally destroyed; they are:—पंचसूना गृहस्थस्य चुल्लीपेषण्युपस्करः कंडनी चोदकुंभश्च Ms. 3. 68. **-हायन** *a.* five years old.

पंचनी A chequered cloth for playing at draughts.

पंचम *a.* (**मी** *f.*) **1** The fifth. **2** Forming a fifth part. **3** Dexterous, clever. **4** Beautiful, brilliant. **-मः 1** The fifth (or in later times the seventh) note of the Indian gamut; it is said to be produced by the cuckoo (कोकिलो रौति पंचमं. Nârada), and is so called because it is produced from 5 parts of the body:—वायुः समुद्गतो नाभेरुरोहृत्कंठमूर्धसु । विचरन् पंचमस्थानप्राप्त्या पंचम उच्यते ॥. **2** N. of a Râga or musical mode (sung in the above note); व्यथयति वृथा मौनं तन्वि प्रपंचय पंचमं Gît. 10; so उदंचितपंचमरागं Gît. 1. **-मं** A fifth. **2** Sexual intercourse (मैथुन), the fifth मकार of the Tântrikas. **-मी 1** the fifth day of a lunar fortnight. **2** The ablative case (in gram). **3** An epithet of Draupadî. **4** A chequered board for playing at draughts. -Comp. **-आस्यः** the cuckoo.

पंचालाः (*m. pl.*) **1** N. of a country and its people. **-लः** A king of the Panchâlas.

पंचालिका A doll, puppet; cf. पांचालिका.

पंचाली 1 A doll, puppet. **2** A kind of song. **3** Chequered board for playing at draughts, chess-board &c.

पंचाश *a.* (**शी** *f.*) The fiftieth.

पंचाशत्, पंचाशतिः *f.* Fifty.

पंचाशिका 1 A collection of fifty verses; *i. e.* चौरपंचाशिका.

पंजरं A cage, an aviary; पंजरशुकः, भुजपंजरः &c. **—रः, -रं 1** Ribs. **2** A skeleton. **-रः 1** The body. **2** The Kaliyuga. -Comp **-आखेटः** a sort of basket or trap for catching fish. **-शुकः** a parrot in a cage, caged parrot; V. 2. 23.

पंजिः, -जी *f.* **1** The ball of cotton from which thread is spun. **2** A record, journal, register. **3** A calender, an almanac. -Comp. **-कारः -कारकः** a writer, scribe.

पट् 1 P. (पटति) To go or move. -*Caus.* or 10. U. (पाटयति-ते) **1** To split, cleave, tear up, tear asunder, tear open, divide; कंचिन्मध्यात्पाटयामास दंती *Si.* 18. 51; दुस्वर्णं पाटयेल्लेखं Y. 2. 94; Mk. 9. **2** To break, break open; अन्यासु भित्तिषु मया निशि पाटितासु Mk. 3. 14. **3** To pierce, prick, penetrate; दर्भपाटिततलेन पाणिना R. 11. 31. **4** To remove, eradicate. **5** To pluck out. -With **उद् 1** to tear up or out, draw out; दंतैर्नोत्पाटयेन्नखान् Ms. 4. 69; कीलमुत्पाटयितुमारभे Pt. 1. **2** to root up; eradicate; Ku. 2. 43; R. 15. 49. **3** to extract. **-वि 1** to tear up or out; (केतकबर्हं) विपाटयामासयुवा नखाग्रैः R. 6. 17. **2** to pull or draw out, extract. -II. 10. U. (पटयति-ते) **1** To string or weave; गुविंदस्त्वं तावत्पटयति गुणग्राममभितः K. P. 7. **2** To clothe, envelope. **3** To Surround, encircle.

पटः -टं 1 A garment, raiment, cloth, a piece of cloth; अयं पटः सूत्रदरिद्रतां गतो ह्ययं पटश्छिद्रशतैरलंकृतः &c. Mk. 2. 9; मेघाः स्रवंति बलदेवपटप्रकाशाः 5. 45. **2** Fine cloth. **3** A veil, screen. **4** A tablet, plate or piece of cloth for writing or painting upon. **-टं** A thatch, roof. -Comp. **-उटजं** a tent. **-कारः 1** a weaver. **2** a painter. **-कुटी** *f.* **-मंडपः, -वापः, -वेश्मन्** *n.* a tent; *Si.* 12 63. **-वासः 1** a tent. **2** a petticoat. **3** perfumed powder; Ratn. 1 **-वासकः** perfumed powder.

पटकः 1 A camp, an encampment. **2** Cotton-cloth.

पटच्चरः A thief; cf. पाटच्चर. **-रं** Old or ragged clothes.

पटत्कः A thief.

पटपटा *ind.* An imitative sound.

पटलं 1 A roof, thatch; विनमितपटलांतं दृश्यते जीर्णकुड्यं Mu. 3. 15. 2 A cover, covering, veil, coating (in general,) शिरसि मसीपटलं दधाति दीपः Bv. 1. 74. 3 A film or coating over the eyes. 4 A heap, multitude, mass, quantity; रथांगपाणेः पटलेन रोचिषां Si. 1. 21; जलदपटलानि Pt. 1. 361. क्षौद्रपटलैः R. 4. 63; मुक्तापटलं 13. 17; तारकपटलं Git. 7. 5 A basket. 6 Retinue, train. **-लः, -ली** 1 A tree. 2 A stalk. **-लः, -लं** A section or chapter of a book. -COMP. **-प्रांतः** the edge of a roof.

पटहः 1 A kettle-drum, a wardrum, drum, tabor; कुर्वन् संध्याबलिपटहतां शूलिनः श्लाघनीयां Me. 34; पटुपटहध्वनिभिर्विनीतनिद्रः R. 9. 71. 2 Begining, undertaking. 3 Injuring, killing. -COMP. **-घोषकः** a crier (who beats a drum and then makes the proclamation). **-भ्रमणं** going about with a drum to call people together.

पटालुका A leech.

पटिः -टी *f.* 1 The curtain of a stage. 2 A cloth. 3 Coarse cloth, canvas. 4 A screen of cloth surrounding a tent. -COMP. **-क्षेपः** tossing aside the curtain (of the stage); used as a stage-direction to denote the hurried entrance of a character on the stage; cf. अपटीक्षेप.

पटिमन् *m.* 1 Dexterity, cleverness. 2 Sharpness. 3 Acidity. 4 Sharpness. 5 Violence, intensity &c.

पटीरः 1 A ball for playing with. 2 Sandal-wood. 3 Cupid, the god of love. **-रं** 1 Catechu. 2 A sieve. 3 The belly. 4 A field. 5 A cloud. 6 Height. -COMP.**-जन्मन्** *m.* sandal-tree; वहति विषधरान् पटीरजन्मा Bv. 1. 74.

पटु *a.* (**टु** or **टी** *f.*; compar. पटीयस्, superl. पटिष्ठ) 1 Clever, skilful, dexterous, proficient (usually with a loc.); वाचि पटुः &c. 2 Sharp, acrid, pungent. 3 Sharp, smart (as intellect). 4 Violent, strong, sharp, intense; अयमपि पटुर्धारासारो न बाणपरंपरा V. 4. 1; U. 4. 3. 5 Shrill, clear, sharpsounding; किमिदं पटुपटहशंखमिश्रो नांदीनादः Mu. 6; पटुपटहध्वनिभिर्विनीतनिद्रः R. 9. 71, 73. 6 Apt, disposed; Si. 15. 43. 7 Harsh, cruel, hard-hearted. 8 Sly, cunning, crafty, roguish. 9 Healthy, sound. 10 Active, busy. 11 Eloquent, talkative. 12 Blown, expanded. **-टुः, -टु** *n.* A mushroom (छत्रा). **-टु** *n.* Salt. -COMP. **-कल्प, -देशीय** *a.* pretty clever, tolerably sharp.

पटोलः A species of cucumber (Mar. पडवळ). **-लं** A kind of cloth.

पटोलकः An oyster.

पट्टः, -ट्टं 1 A slab, tablet (for writing upon), plate in general; शिलापट्टमधिशयाना Si. 3; so भालपट्ट &c. 2 A royal grant or edict; Y. 1. 317. 3 A tiara, diadem; R. 18. 44. 4 A strip; निर्मोकपट्टाः फणिभिर्विमुक्ताः R. 16. 17. 5 silk; पट्टोपधानं K. 17; Bh. 3. 74; so पट्टांशुकं. 6 Fine or coloured cloth, cloth in general. 7 An upper garment; Bk. 10. 60. 8 A fillet or cloth worn round the head, a turban; especially, a coloured silk turban; Ratn. 1. 4. 9 A throne. 10 A chair or stool. 11 A shield. 12 A grinding stone. 13 A place where four roads meet. 14 A city, town. 15 A bandage, ligature. -COMP. **-अर्हा** the principal queen. **-उपाध्यायः** a writer of royal grants and other documents. **-जं** a sort of cloth. **-देवी, -महिषी, -राज्ञी** the principal queen. **-वस्त्र, -वासस्** *a.* attired in wove silk or coloured cloth.

पट्टनं -नी A city.

पट्टिका 1 A tablet, plate; as in हृत्पट्टिका. 2 A document. 3 A piece or fragment or cloth, वल्कलैकदेशाद्विपाटय पट्टिकां K. 149. 4 A piece of silken cloth. 5 A ligature, bandage. -COMP. **-वायकः** a silk-weave.

पट्टि (ट्टी) शः (सः) A kind of spear with a sharp edge (Mar. पट्टा), कणपप्रासपट्टिश &c. Dk; (पट्टिशो लौहदंडो यस्तीक्ष्णधारः क्षुरोपमः Vaijayanti).

पट्टोलिका A kind of bond or lease (भूमिकरग्रहणव्यवस्थापकः पत्रभेदः Tv.).

पठ् 1 P. (पठति, पठित) 1 To read or repeat aloud; recite, rehearse; यः पठेच्छृणुयादपि. 2 To read or recite to oneself, study, peruse; इत्येतन्मानवं शास्त्रं भृगुप्रोक्तं पठन् द्विजः Ms. 12. 126, 4. 98. 3 To invoke (as a deity). 4 To cite, quote, mention (as in a book); पतदिच्छाम्यहं श्रोतुं पुराणे यदि पठ्यते Mb. 5 To declare, describe, express; भार्या च परमो ह्यर्थः पुरुषस्येह पठ्यते; Mb. 6 To learn from (with abl.) *-Caus.* (पाठयति-ते) 1 To cause to read aloud. 2 To teach, instruct. *-Desid.* (पिपठिषति) To wish to recite &c. -WITH **परि** to mention, declare. (*-Caus*) to teach; तौ सर्वं विद्याः परिपाठितौ U. 2. **-सं** to read, learn; Ms. 4. 98.

पठकः A reader.

पठनं 1 Reading, reciting. 2 mentioning. 3 Studying, perusing.

पठिः *f.* Reading, studying, perusal.

पण् I. 1 A. (पणते, पणित) 1 To deal in, barter, purchase, buy; N. 2. 91. 2 To bargain, transact business. 3 To bet or stake at play (usually with gen. of the thing staked, but sometimes with acc.); प्राणानामपणिष्टासौ Bk. 8. 121; पणस्व कृष्णां पांचालीं Mb. 4 To risk or hazard (a battle). II. 1 A., 10. U. (पणते, पणायति-ते) 1 To praise. 2 To honour. -WITH **वि** to sell, barter; आभीरदेशे किल चंद्रकांतं त्रिभिर्वराटैर्विपणंति गोपाः Subhâsh.

पणः 1 Playing with dice or for a stake. 2 A game played for a stake, bet, wager; Y. 2. 18; दमयंत्याः पणः साधुर्वर्ततां Mb. 3 The thing staked. 4 A condition, compact, agreement; संधिं करोतु भवतां नृपतिः पणेन Ve. 1. 15; a stipulation, treaty; H. 4. 118, 112. 5 Wages, hire. 6 Reward. 7 A sum in coins or shells. 8 A particular coin equal in value to 80 *cowries*; अशीतिभिर्वराटकैः पण इत्यभिधीयते. 9 Price. 10 Wealth, property. 11 A commodity for sale. 12 Business, transaction. 13 A shop. 14 A seller, vendor. 15 A distiller. 16 A house. -COMP. **-अंगना, स्त्री** a prostitute, harlot. **-ग्रंथिः** a market, fair. **-बंधः** 1 making a treaty or peace (संधि); पणबंधमुखान् गुणानजः षड्डपायुंक्त समीक्ष्य तत्फलं R. 8. 21, 10. 86. 2 an agreement, stipulation; (यदि भवानिदं कुर्याचर्हीदमहं भवते दास्यामीति समयकरणं पणबंधः Manoramâ).

पणनं 1 Bartering, purchasing. 2 Betting. 3 Sale.

पणवः A sort of musical instrument; Bg. 1. 13; Si. 13. 5.

पणाया 1 Transaction, business, dealing. 2 A market-place. 3 Profits of a trade. 4 Gambling. 5 Praise.

पणिः *f.* A market. *-m.* 1 A miser, niggard. 2 An impious man.

पणित *p. p.* 1 Transacted (as business). 2 Betted; see पण्.

पंड् I. 1 A. (पंडते, पंडित) To go or move. -II. 10 U. (पंडयति-ते) To collect, pile up, heap together.

पंडः A eunuch.

पंडा 1 Wisdom, understanding. 2 Learning, science.

पंडावत् *m.* A learned man.

पंडित *a.* 1 Learned, wise; स्वस्थे को वा न पंडितः 2 Shrewd, clever. 3 Skilled in, proficient, skilful (generally with loc. or in comp.); मधुरालापनिसर्गपंडितां Ku. 4. 16; so रतिपंडित 4. 18; नयपंडित &c. **—तः** 1 A scholar, learned man, *Pandita*. 2 Incense. -COMP. **-जातीय** *a.* somewhat clever. **-मानिक, -मानिन्, पंडितंमन्य** *a.* fancying oneself to be learned, a conceited person, a pedant who fancies himself to be a *Pandita*.

पंडितिमन् *m.* Learning, scholarship, wisdom.

पण्य *a.* 1 Saleable, vendible. 2 To be transacted. **-ण्यः** 1 A ware, an article, a commodity; पुराबभासे विपणिस्थपण्या R. 16. 41; पण्यानां गांधिकं पण्यं Pt. 1. 13; Ms. 5. 129; Y, 2. 245; M. 1. 16.

2 Trade, business. **3** Price; महता पुण्यपण्येन क्रीतेयं कायनौस्त्वया *S*ânti. 3. 1. –Comp. **–अंगना, योषित्** *f*., **–विलासिनी, –स्त्री** *f*. a harlot, a courtezan; पण्यस्त्रीषु विवेककल्पलतिकाशस्त्रीषु रज्येत कः Bh. 1. 90; Me. 25. **–अजिरं** a market. **–आजीवः** a trader. **–आजीवकं** a market, fair. **–पतिः** a great merchant. **–भूमिः** *f*. a warehouse. **–वीथिका, –वीथी, –शाला** 1 a market. 2 a stall, shop.

पत् 1 P. (पतति, पतित) **1** To fall, fall down, come down, alight; अवाङ्मुखस्योपरि पुष्पवृष्टिः पपात विद्याधरहस्तमुक्ता R. 2. 60; वृष्टिर्भवने चास्यपेतुषी 10. 77; (रेणुः) पतति परिणतारुणप्रकाशः शलभसमूह इवाश्रमद्रुमेषु *S*. 1. 31; Me. 105; Bk. 7. 9, 21. 6. **2** To fly, move through the air, soar; हंतुं कलहकारोऽसौ शब्दकारः पपात खं Bk. 5. 100; see पतत् below. **3** To set, sink. (below the horizon); सोयं चंद्रः पतति गगनादल्पशेषैर्मयूखैः *S*. 4. v. l. पतत्पतंगप्रतिमस्तपोनिधिः *Si*. 1. 12. **4** To cast oneself at, throw oneself down; मयि ते पादपतिते किंकरत्वमुपागते Pt. 4. 7; so चरणपतितं Me, 105. **5** To fall (in a moral sense), lose one's caste, forfeit one's rank or position, fall off; परधर्मेण जीवन् हि सद्यः पतति जातितः Ms. 10. 97, 3. 16, 5. 19, 9. 200; Y. 1. 38. **6** To come down (as from heaven); पतंति पितरो ह्येषां लुप्तपिंडोदकक्रियाः Bg. 1. 41. **7** To fall, be reduced to wretchedness or misery; प्रायः कंदुकपातेनोत्पतत्यार्यः पतन्नपि Bh. 2. 123. **8** To go down into hell, go to perdition; Ms. 11. 37; Bg. 16. 16. **9** To fall, occur, come to pass, take place; लक्ष्मीर्यत्र पतंति तत्र विवृतद्वारा इव व्यापदः Subhâsh. **10** To be directed to, light or fall upon (with loc.); प्रसादसौम्यानि सतां सुहृज्जने पतंति चक्षूंषि न दारुणाः शराः *S*. 6. 28. **11** To fall to one's lot or share. **12** To be in, fall in or into. –*Caus*. (पातयति-ते, पतयति rarely) **1** To cause to fall down descend or sink &c; निपतंती पतिमप्यपातयत् R. 8. 38, 9. 61, 11. 76. **2** To let fall, throw or drop down, fell down, (as trees &c.). **3** To ruin, overthrow. **4** To shed (as tears). **5** To cast, direct (as the sight). –*Desid*. (पिपतिषति or पित्सति) To wish to fall &c. –With **अनु 1** to fly to or towards. **2** to fly or run after, follow, pursue, chase; मुहुरनुपतति स्यंदने दत्तदृष्टिः *S*. 1. 7, Mâl. 9. 8; *Si*. 11. 40. **–अभि 1** to fly near, go or hasten near, approach; अधिरोढुमस्तागिरिमभ्यपतत् *Si*. 9. 1; Ki. 12. 36. **2** to attack, assail, fall upon; R. 7. 37. **3** to overtake in flying. **4** to get back, retire, withdraw. **–अभ्युद्** to fall upon or attack. **–आ 1** to fall upon, attack, assail; R. 12. 44, 5. 50. **2** to fly towards, rush upon, come or drive in haste towards. **3** to approach. **4** to take place, occur, happen; कथमिदमापतितं U. 2; अहो न शोभनमापतितं Pt. 2. **5** to occur to, cross (the mind); इति हृदये नापतितं K. 288. **–उद् 1** to fly or jump up; मंक्षूदपाति परितः पटलैरलीनां *Si*. 5. 37; oft. with acc. or dat. of place; उत्पतोदङ्मुखः खं Me. 14; Bk. 5. 30; स्वर्गायोत्पतिता भवेत् V. 4. 2; Ku. 6. 36. **2** to start up, emerge into view; R. 13. 11. **3** to rebound (as a ball); Bh. 2. 85. **4** to rise, originate, spring or proceed from, be produced; निष्पेषोत्पतितानलं R. 4. 77; रसात्तस्माद्धरस्त्रिय उत्पेतुः Râm. **–नि 1** to fall or come down; descend, alight, sink down; निपतंती पतिमप्यपातयत् R. 8. 38; Bk. 15. 27. **2** to be cast at, be directed towards; R. 6. 11. **3** to throw oneself down (as at the feet), fall prostrate; देवास्तदंते हरमूढभार्यं किरीटबद्धांजलयो निपत्य Ku. 7. 92; Bh. 2. 31. **4** to fall or descend into, meet in; R. 10. 26. **5** to fall upon, attack, rush at or upon; सिंहो शिशुरपि निपतति मदमलिनकपोलभित्तिषु गजेषु Bh. 2. 38. **6** to happen, occur, take place, fall to one's lot; सकृदंशो निपतति Ms 9. 47. **7** to be placed, occupy a place; अभ्यर्हितं पूर्वं निपतति. (–*Caus*.) **1** to cause to fall down, throw or hurl down. **2** to kill, destroy, ruin. **–निस्** to issue or come out of, issue from, fly out of ; अरविंदरेण्यश्चातकैर्निष्पतद्भिः *S*. 7. 7; एषा विदूरीभवतः समुद्रात्सकानना निष्पततीव भूमिः R. 13. 18, Ms. 8. 55; Y. 2. 16; Ku. 3. 71; Me. 69. **–परा 1** to arrive, draw near, approach. **2** to return. **–परि 1** to fly round or about, wheel or whirl round, hover about; बिंदूत्क्षेपान् पिपासुः परिपतति शिखी भ्रांतिमद्वारियंत्रं M. 2. 13; Amaru. 48. **2** to spring down upon, attack, fall upon (as in battle). **3** to run in all directions; (हयाः) परिपेतुर्दिशो दश Mb. **4** to go to or fall into; *Si*. 11. 41. **–प्र 1** to come down, fall down, descend. **2** to fall off or away from. **3** to fly, fly or move about. **–प्रणि** to bow down to, salute (with acc. or dat.); प्रणिपत्य सुरास्तस्मै R. 10. 15; वागीशं वाग्भिरर्थ्याभिः प्रणिपत्योपतस्थिरे Ku. 2. 3. **–प्रोद्** to fly up, soar. **–विनि** to fly at, fall down, descend; Rs. 4. 18. (–*Caus*.) to cause to fall down, ruin, destroy; Mk. 2. 8. **–सं 1** to fly or meet together, assemble. **2** to go or roam about. **3** to attack, fall upon, assail. **4** to come to pass, happen. (–*Caus*.) **1** to bring near. **2** to collect or assemble together, bring or call together; R. 14. 36, 15. 75.

पतः 1 Flying, flight. **2** Going falling, alighting. –Comp. **–गः** a bird; Ms. 7. 23.

पतंगः 1 A bird; नृपः पतंगं समधत्त पाणिना N. 1. 124; Bv. 1. 17. **2** The sun ; विकसति हि पतंगस्योदये पुंडरीकं U. 6. 12; Mâl. 1. 12; *Si*. 1. 12; R. 2. 15. **3** A moth, locust, grass-hopper; पतंगवद्वह्निमुखं विविक्षुः Ku. 3. 64, 4. 20; Pt. 3. 126. **4** A bee. **–गं 1** Quicksilver. **2** A kind of sandal-wood.

पतंगमः 1 A bird. **2** A moth.

पतंगिका 1 A small bird. **2** A kind of small bee.

पतंगिन् *m*. A bird.

पतंचिका A bow-string.

पतंजलिः N. of the celebrated author of the Mahâbhashya, the great commentary on Pa*n*ini's Sûtras; also of a philosopher, the propounder of the Yoga philosophy.

पतत् *a*. (न्ती *f*.) Flying, descending, alighting, coming down &c. —*m*. A bird; परमः पुमानिव पतिं पततां Ki. 6. 1 ; क्वचित्पथा संचरते सुराणां क्वचिद्घनानां पततां क्वचिच्च R. 13. 19; *Si*. 9. 15. –Comp. **–ग्रहः 1** the reserve of an army. **2** a spitting pot, spittoon; तमेकमाणिक्यमयं महोन्नतं पतद्ग्रहं ग्राहितवान्नलेन सः N. 16. 27. **–भीरुः** a hawk, falcon.

पतत्रं 1 A wing, pinion. **2** A feather. **3** A vehicle.

पतत्रिः A bird.

पतत्रिन् *m*. **1** A bird; दयिता द्वंद्वचरं पतत्रिणं (पुनरेति) R. 8. 56, 9. 27, 11. 11, 12. 48; Ku. 5. 4. **2** An arrow. **3** A horse. –Comp. **–केतनः** an epithet of Vishnu.

पतनं 1 The act of flying or coming down, alighting, descending, throwing oneself down at. **2** Setting (as of the sun). **3** Going down to hell. **4** Apostacy. **5** Falling from dignity, virtue &c. **6** Fall, decline, ruin, adversity (opp. उदय or उच्छ्राय); ग्रहाधीना नरेंद्राणामुछ्रायाः पतनानि च Y. 1. 307. **7** Death. **8** Hanging down, becoming flaccid (as breasts). **9** Miscarriage.

पतनीय *a*. Causing a fall, causing the loss of caste. **–यं** A degrading crime or sin; Y. 3. 40, 298.

पतयः, पतसः 1 The moon. **2** A bird. **3** A grasshopper.

पतयालु *a*. Tending or prone to fall, liable to fall.

पताका 1 A flag, banner (fig. also); यं काममंजरी कामयते स हरतु सुभगपताकां Dk. 47 'let him carry the palm of beauty or good fortune'. **2** A flagstaff. **3** A sign, emblem, mark, symbol. **4** An episode or episodical incident in a drama, see पताकास्थानक below. **5** Auspiciousness, good fortune or luck. –Comp. **–अंशुकं** a flag. **–स्थानकं** (in dramaturgy) intimation of an episodical incident, when instead of the thing thought of or expected, another of the same character is brought in by some unexpected circumstance ; (यत्रार्थे चिंतितेऽन्यस्मिंस्तल्लिंगोऽन्यः प्रयुज्यते । आगंतुकेन भावेन पताकास्थानकं तु तत् ॥ S. D.

299); (for its different kinds, see 300-304).

पताकिक *a.* Having or carrying a banner.

पताकिन् *a.* Having or carrying a banner, adorned with flags. —*m.* 1 An ensign, standard-bearer. 2 A flag. —**नी** An army; (न प्रसेहे) रथवर्त्मरजोऽप्यस्य कुत एव पताकिनीं R. 4. 82; Ki. 14. 27.

पतिः 1 A master, lord; as in गृहपतिः. 2 An owner, possessor, proprietor; क्षेत्रपतिः. 3 Governor, ruler, one who presides over; ओषधीपतिः, वनस्पतिः, कुलपतिः &c. 4 A husband; प्रमदाः पतिवर्त्मगा इति प्रतिपन्नं हि विचेतनैरपि Ku. 4. 33. –COMP. **–घातिनी, -घ्नी** a woman who murders her husband. **–देवता –देवा** one who regards her husband as a divinity, a woman loyally devoted to her husband, chaste woman; कः पतिदेवतामन्यः परिमार्ष्टुमुत्सहेत *S.* 6; तमलभंत पतिं पतिदेवताः शिखरिणामिव सागरमापगाः R. 9. 17; धुरि स्थिता त्वं पतिदेवतानां 14. 74. **धर्मः** duty (of a wife) towards a husband. **–प्राणा** a chaste wife. **–लोकः** the world of husbands in a future life. **–व्रता** a devoted, faithful, and loyal wife, a chaste and virtuous wife; °त्वं fidelity to a husband. **–सेवा** devotion to a husband.

पतिंवरा A woman who is about to choose a husband; R. 6. 10. 67.

पतितः *p. p.* 1 Fallen, descended, alighted. 2 Dropped. 3 Fallen (in a moral sense), abandoned, wicked. 4 Apostate. 5 Degraded, outcast. 6 Fallen in battle, defeated or overthrown. 7 Being in, fallen into; as in अवंशपतित.

पतेरः 1 A bird. 2 A hole or pit.

पत्तनं A town, city (opp. ग्राम); पत्तने विद्यमानेऽपि ग्रामे रत्नपरीक्षा M. 1.

पत्तिः 1 A footman, a foot-solder; R. 7. 37. 2 A pedestrian. 3 A hero. —*f.* 1 The smallest division of an army, consisting of one chariot, one elephant, three horsemen and five foot-soldiers. 2 Going, walking. –COMP. **–कायः** infantry. **–गणकः** an officer whose business it is to muster the infantry. **–संहतिः** *f.* a body of infantry, infantry.

पत्तिन् *m.* A foot-soldier, footman.

पत्रं 1 A leaf (of a tree); धत्ते भरं कुसुमपत्रफलावलीनां Bv. 1. 94. 2 The leaf of a flower, lotus &c.; नीलोत्पलपत्रधारया *S.* 1. 17. 3 A leaf for writing upon, a paper, a leaf written upon; पत्रमारोप्य दीयता *S.* 6. 'commit to writing'; V. 2. 14. 4 A letter, document. 5 Any thin leaf or plate of metal, a gold-leaf. 6 The wing of a bird, a pinion, feather. 7 The feather of an arrow; R. 2. 31. 8 A vehicle in general (car, horse, camel &c.); दिशः पपात पत्रेण वेगनिष्कंपकेतुना R. 15. 48; N. 3. 16. 9 Painting the person (particularly the face) with musk, sandal-juice or other fragrant substances; रचय. कुचयोः पत्रं चित्रं कुरुष्व कपोलयोः Gît. 12; R. 13. 55. 10 The blade of a sword, knife &c. 11 A knife, dagger. –COMP. **–अंगं** 1 the Bhûrja tree. 2 red sanders. **–अंगुलिः** drawing lines of painting with the finger on the person (throat, forehead &c.) with coloured sandal, saffron, or any other fragrant substance. **–अंजनं** ink. **–आवलिः** *f.* 1 red chalk. 2 a row of leaves. 3 the lines of painting drawn on the body with cosmetics as a decoration. **–आवली** 1 a row of leaver. 2 =°आवली (3). **–आहारः** feeding on leaves. **–ऊर्णं** wovesilk, a silk-garment; स्नानीयवस्त्रक्रियया पत्रोर्णं वोपयुज्यते M. 5. 12. **–काहला** the noise or sound made by the flapping of wings or rustling of leaves. **–दारकः** a saw. **–नाडिका** the fibre of e leaf. **–परशुः** a file. **–पालः** a long dagger, large knife. (**-ली**) 1 the feathered part of an arrow. 2 a pair of scissors. **–पाइया** an ornament (a gold-leaf) on the forehead. **–पुटं** a vessel of leaves; R. 2. 65. **–बा (वा) लः** an oar. **–भंगः, –भंगिः –गी** *f.* drawing lines or figures of painting on the face and person with fragrant and coloured substances, such as musk, saffron, sandal-juice, yellow pigment &c., as a mark of decoration; कस्तूरीवरपत्रभंगनिकरो मृष्टो न गंडस्थले *S.* Til. 7 (used frequently in K.). **–यौवनं** a young leaf or sprout. **–रथः** a bird; व्यर्थीकृतं पत्ररथेन तेन N. 3. 6. °**इंद्रः** N. of Garuda. °**इंद्रकेतुः** N. of Vishnu; R. 18. 30 **–रे (ले) खा, –वल्लरी, –वल्लिः, वल्ली** *f.* see पत्रभंग above; R. 6. 72, 16. 67; Rs. 9. 7; *Si.* 8. 56, 59. **–वाज** *a.* furnished with feathers (as an arrow) **–वाहः** 1 a bird; *Si.* 18. 73. 2 an arrow. 3 a lettercarrier. **–विशेषकः** lines of painting &c.; see पत्रभंग; Ku. 3. 33; R. 3. 55, 9. 29. **–वेष्टः** a kind of ear-ring; R. 16. 67. **–शाकः** a vegetable consisting chiefly of leaves. **–श्रेष्ठः** the Bilva tree. **–सूचिः** *f.* a thorn. **–हिमं** wintry or snowy weather.

पत्रकं 1 A leaf. 2 Drawing lines or figures on the body as a decoration.

पत्रणा 1 A Drawing lines of figures of painting on the body as a decoration. 2 Feathering an arrow.

पत्रिका 1 A leaf for writing upon. 2 A letter, document.

पत्रिन् *a.* (**णी** *f.*) 1 Winged, feathered; मयूर° R. 3. 56. 6 Having leaves or pages. –*m.* 1 An arrow; तां विलोक्य वनितावधे घृणां पत्रिणा सह मुमोच राघवः R. 11. 17, 3. 53, 57; 9. 61. 2 A bird; R. 11. 29. 3 A falcon. 4 A mountain. 5 A chariot. 6 A tree. –Comp. **–वाहः** a bird.

पत्नी A wife. COMP. **–आटः** seraglio, women's apartments. **–सन्नहनं** the girdle of a wife.

पत्सलः A way, road.

पथः A way, road; reach, end (at the end of comp.). –COMP. **–कल्पना** juggling tricks. **–दर्शकः** a guide.

पथिकः 1 A traveller, way-farer; पथिकवनिताः Me. 8; Amaru. 93. 2 A guide. –COMP. **–संततिः, –संहतिः,** *f.* **–सार्थः** a company of travellers, a caravan.

पथिन् *m.* (Nom. पंथाः, पंथानौ, पंथानः; acc. pl. पथः, instr. pl. पथिभिः &c.; the word is changed to पथ at the end of comp.; तोयाधारपथाः, दृष्टिपथः, नष्टपथः, सत्पथः, प्रतिपथं &c.) 1 A road, way, path; श्रेयसामिष पंथाः Bh. 2. 26; वक्रः पंथाः Me. 27. 2 Journey, way-faring; as in शिवास्ते संतु पंथानः (I wish) a happy journey to you ! God speed you on your journey ! 3 Range, reach; as in कर्णपथ, श्रुति°, दर्शन°. 4 Manner of action, line of conduct, course of behaviour; पथः शुचेर्दर्शयितार ईश्वरा मलीमसामाददते न पद्धतिं R. 3. 46. 5 A sect, doctrine. 6 A division of hell. –COMP. **–देयं** a toll levied on public roads. **–द्रुमः** the Khadira tree. **–प्रज्ञ** *a.* acquainted with roads. **–वाहक** *a.* cruel. (**–कः**) 1 a hunter, fowler. 2 a burden-bearer, porter.

पथिलः A traveller, way-farer.

पथ्य *a.* 1 Salutary, wholesome, beneficial, agreeing with (said of a medicine, diet, advice &c.); अप्रियस्य तु पथ्यस्य वक्ता श्रोता च दुर्लभः Râm.; Y. 3 65; पथ्यमन्नं &c. 2 Fit, proper, suitable (in general). **–थ्यं** 1 wholesome diet; as in पथ्याशी स्वामी वर्तते. 2 Welfare, well-being; उत्तिष्ठमानस्तु परो नोपेक्ष्यः पथ्यमिच्छता *Si.* 2. 10. –COMP. **–अपथ्यं** the class of things that are considered wholesome or hurtful in disease.

पद् I. 10. A. (पदयते) To go or move –II. 4. A. (पद्यते, पन्न; *Caus.* पादयति-ते; *desid.* पित्सते) 1 To go, move. 2 To go to, approach (with acc.). 3 To attain, obtain, gain; ज्योतिषामाधिपत्यं च प्रभावं चाप्यपद्यत Mb. 4 To observe, practice; स्वधर्मं पद्यमानास्ते Mb. –WITH **अनु** 1 to go after, follow, attend. 2 to be fond of, be attached to. 3 to enter, go into. 4 to betake oneself to. 5 to find, notice, observe, understand. **–अभि** 1 to go to, draw near, approach; रावणावरजा तत्र राघवं मदनातुरा। अभिपेदे निदाघार्ता व्यालीव मलयद्रुमं R. 12. 32; 19. 11. 2 to enter into; *Si.* 3. 25. 3 to look upon, consider, regard, take or know to be; क्षणमभ्यपद्यत जनैर्न मृषा गगनं गणाधिपतिमूर्तिरिति *Si.* 9.

27. 4 to help, assist; मयाभिपन्नं तं Mb. 5 to seize, overpower, attack, catch hold of, take possession of, afflict; सर्वतश्चाभिपन्नैषा धार्तराष्ट्री महाचमूः; चंडवाताभिपन्नानामुदधीनामिव स्वनः Mb.; see अभिपन्न. 6 to take, assume; Ms. 1. 3. 7 to accept, receive. **-अभ्युप 1** to take pity on, console, comfort, pity, favour, deliver (from distress); Ku. 4. 25, 5. 61. 2 to ask for help, submit. 3 to agree or assent to. **-आ 1** to go near, walk towards, approach, Bk. 15. 89. 2 to enter into, go or attain to (a place, state &c.); निर्वेदमापद्यते Mk. 1. 14 becomes disgusted; आपेदिरेऽम्बरपथं परितः पतंगाः Bv. 1. 17; so क्षीरं दधिभावमापद्यते S. B. 3 to get into trouble, fall into misfortune; अर्थधर्मौ परित्यज्य यः काममनुवर्तते । एवमापद्यते क्षिप्रं राजा दशरथो यथा ॥ Râm. 4 to happen, occur; Bk. 6 31 (*-Caus*). 1 to bring about, bring to pass, effect, accomplish; K. 2 12. 2 to bring on, cause, produce; लघिमानमापादयति R. 105. 3 to reduce to, cause to suffer, lead or bring to; R. 55. 4 to change into. 5 to bring under control or subjection. **-उद् 1** to be born or produced, arise, originate, spring up; उत्पत्स्यतेऽस्ति मम कोऽपि समानधर्मा Mâl. 1. 6; Ms. 1. 77. 2 to occur, happen. (*-Caus.*) 1 to produce, create, beget, cause, effect, bring about; वस्त्राण्युत्पादयति Pt. 2. 2 to bring forward. **-उप 1** to reach, go near, approach, arrive at; यमुनातटमुपपेदे Pt. 1. 2 to be got or obtained, fall to one's share; Bg. 6. 39; 13. 18. 3 to take place, occur, happen, be produced; देवि एवमुपपद्यते M. 1; उपपन्ना हि दारेषु प्रभुता सर्वतोमुखी S. 5. 26; R. 1. 60. 4 to be possible or probable; नेश्वरो जगतः कारणमुपपद्यते S. B.; Ku. 6. 61, 3. 12. 5 to be suitable, be fit or adequate for, fit, suit (with loc.); मा क्लैब्यं गच्छ कौंतेय नैतत्त्वय्युपपद्यते Bg. 2. 3; 18. 7. 6 to attack. (*-Caus.*) 1 to bring into any state, cause to arrive or be obtained; विश्वासमुपपादयति. 2 to lead or take to. 3 to get ready; रथमुपपादय Ve. 2. 4 to give or offer, present any one with; R. 14. 8, 15. 13, 16. 32; Y. 1. 315. 5 to bring about, accomplish, achieve, effect, do, perform; यावत्तु मातुष्यके शक्यमुपपादयितुं K. 62; देवकार्यमुपपादयिष्यतः R. 11. 91; 17. 55. 6 to justify, give reasons for, demonstrate, prove. 7 to furnish or endow with. **-निस् 1** to issue out of, spring from. 2 to be produced, be brought about, arise, to be effected; निष्पद्यंते च सस्यानि Ms. 9. 247. (*-Caus.*) to produce, bring about, cause, effect, prepare; त्वं नित्यमेकमेव पटं निष्पादयसि Pt. 5. **-प्र 1** (*a*) to go to or towards, approach, resort or attain to, reach; तां जन्मने शैलवधूं प्रपेदे Ku. 1. 21; (क्षितीशं) कौत्सः प्रपेदे वरतंतुशिष्यः R. 5. 1; Bk. 4. 1; Ki. 1. 9; 11. 6, R. 8. 11. (*b*) to take shelter with; शरणार्थमन्यां कथं प्रपत्स्ये त्वयि दीप्यमाने R. 14. 64. 2 to go or come to a particular state, arrive at or be in a particular condition; रेणुः प्रपेदे पथि पंकभावं R. 16. 30; मुहूर्तकर्णोत्पलतां प्रपेदे Ku. 7. 81; इदृशीमवस्थां प्रपन्नोऽस्मि S. 5; ऋषिनिकरैरीति संशयः प्रपेदे Bv. 4. 33; Amaru. 27. 3 to get, find, secure, obtain, attain; सहकार न प्रपेदे मधुपेन भवत्समं जगति Bv. 1. 21; R. 5. 51. 4 to behave or act towards, deal with; किं प्रपद्यते वैदर्भः M. 1 'what does he propose to do;' पश्यामो नयि किं प्रपद्यते Amaru. 20. 5 to admit, allow, agree or consent to; Y. 2. 40. 6 to draw near, come on, approach (as time &c). 7 to be going on or proceed. 8 to perceive. **-प्रति 1** to step or go towards, approach, resort or betake oneself to; उमामुखं तु प्रतिपद्य लोला द्विसंश्रयां प्रीतिमवाप लक्ष्मीः Ku. 1. 43. 2 to enter upon, step upon, take, follow (as a way &c.); इतः पंथानं प्रतिपद्यस्व S. 4; प्रतिपत्स्ये पदवीमहं तव Ku. 4. 10. 3 to arrive at, reach, attain; Si. 6. 16. 4 to get, gain, obtain, share, partake; स हि तस्य न केवलां श्रियं प्रतिपेदे सकलान् गुणानपि R. 8. 5, 13; 4. 1, 44; 11. 34; 12. 7; 19. 55; Bg. 14. 14; Si. 10. 63. 5 to accept, take to; Si. 15. 22; 16. 24. 6 to recover, reobtain, regain; to receive; S. 6. 31; Ku. 4. 16; 7. 92. 7 to admit, acknowledge; न मासि प्रतिपद्यासे मां चेन्मर्तासि मैथिलि Bk. 8. 75; S. 5. 22; प्रमदाः पतिवर्त्मगा इति प्रतिपन्नं हि विचेतनैरपि Ku. 4. 33. 8 to hold, grasp, seize; सुमंत्रप्रतिपन्नरश्मिभिः R. 14. 47. 9 to consider, regard, deem, look upon; तद्धनुर्ग्रहणमेव राघवः प्रत्यपद्यत समर्थमुत्तरं R. 11. 79. 10 to undertake, promise to do, take in hand; निर्वाहः प्रतिपन्नवस्तुषु सतामेतद्धि गोत्रव्रतं Mu. 2. 18; कार्यं त्वया नः प्रतिपन्नकल्पं Ku. 3, 14; R. 10. 40. 11 to assent or agree to, consent; तथेति प्रतिपन्नाय R. 15. 93. 12 to do, perform, practise, observe; आचारं प्रतिपद्यस्व S. 4; V. 2 'do the formal obeisance'; शासनमर्हतां प्रतिपद्यध्वं Mu. 4. 18 act up to or obey. 13 to act or behave towards, deal, do anything to any one (with gen. or loc); स कालयवनश्चापि किं कृष्णे प्रत्यपद्यत Hariv.; स भवान् भातृपितृवदस्मासु प्रतिपद्यतां Mb.; कथमहं प्रतिपत्स्ये S. 5; न युक्तं भवतास्मासु प्रतिपत्तुमसांप्रतं Mb. 14 to give or return (as a reply); कथं प्रतिवचनमपि न प्रतिपद्यसे Mu. 6. 15 to perceive, become aware of. 16 to know, understand, become acquainted with, learn, discover. 17 to roam, wander. 18 to take place, occur. (*-Caus.*) 1 to give, present, bestow, confer upon, impart; आर्थिभ्यः प्रतिपाद्यमानमनिशं प्राप्नोति वृद्धिं परां Bh. 2. 18; Ms. 11. 4; गुणवते कन्या प्रतिपादनीया S. 4. 2 to substantiate, prove, establish by proof; उक्तमेवार्थमुदाहरणेन प्रतिपादयति. 3 to explain, expound. 4 to bring or lead back, convey or transport (to a place). 5 to regard, consider. 6 to declare to be, represent. 7 to procure. 8 to effect, accomplish. **-वि 1** to go badly, fail, miscarry (as a business &c.). 2 to fall into misfortune or bad state; स बंधुर्यो विपन्नानामापदुद्धरणक्षमः H. 1. 31. 3 to be disabled or incapacitated. 4 to die, perish; नाथवंतस्त्वया लोकास्त्वमनाथा विपत्स्यसे U. 1. 44; Mk 1. 38. **-व्या 1** to come down (to the earth), fall down. 2 to die, perish, see व्यापन्न. (*-Caus.*) to kill, slay. **-सं 1** to turn out well, succeed, prosper, be accomplished or fulfilled; संपत्स्यते वः कामोयं कालः कश्चित्प्रतीक्ष्यतां Ku. 2. 54; R. 14. 76; Ms. 3. 254; 6. 69. 2 to be completed, to amount to (as a number); त्र्याहताः पंच पंचदश संपद्यंते. 3 to turn out to be, become; संपत्स्यंते नभसि भवतो राजहंसाः सहायाः Me. 11, 23; संपेदे श्रमसलिलोद्गमो विभूषा Ki. 7. 5. 4 to arise, be born or produced. 5 to fall or come together, unite. 6 to be provided or furnished with, be possessed of; अशोक यदि सद्य एव कुसुमैर्न संपत्स्यसे M. 3. 16; see संपन्न. 7 to tend to, bring about, produce (with dat.); साधोः शिक्षा गुणाय संपद्यते नासाधोः Pt. 1; Mu. 3. 32. 8 to obtain, attain to, acquire, get. 9 to enter into, be absorbed in (with loc.). (*-Caus.*) 1 to cause to happen, bring about, produce, accomplish, fulfil, effect; इति स्वसुर्भोजकुलप्रदीपः संपाद्य पाणिग्रहणं स राजा R. 7. 29. 2 to procure, obtain, make ready, prepare. 3 to obtain, acquire, attain to. 4 to furnish, provide, endow with. 5 to change or transform into. 6 to make an agreement. **-संप्रति** 1 to go towards, approach. 2 to consider, regard; Ku. 5. 39. **-समा 1** to take place, happen, occur. 2 to get, obtain, attain to.

पद् *m.* (This word has no forms for the first five inflections; it is optionally substituted for पद् after acc. dual) 1 A foot. 2 A quarter., a fourth part (as of a stanza.) —Comp. **काशिन्** *m.* a footman. **-गः** footman **-जः, रथः**, (**पज्जः, पद्रथः**) a foot-soldier, footman. **-हतिः-ती** *f.* (**पद्धतिः-ती**) 1 a way, path, road, course (fig. also); इयं हि रघुसिंहानां वीरचारित्रपद्धतिः U. 5. 22; R. 4. 46; 6. 55; 11. 87; कविप्रथमपद्धतिं 15. 33; 'the first way shown to poets'. 2 a line, row, range. 3 a surname, title or epithet, a word denoting caste or profession in compounds which are used as proper names;

e. g. गुप्त, दास, दत्त &c. 4 N. of a class of writings. –हिमं (पद्धिमं) coldness of the feet.

पदं A foot (said to be *m.* also in this sense); पदेन on foot; शिखरिषु पदं न्यस्य Me. 13; अपथे पदमर्पयंति हि R. 9. 74 'set foot on (follow) a wrong road'; **3.** 50; 12. **52;** पदं हि सर्वत्र गुणै- र्निधीयते 3. 62 'good qualities set foot everywhere'; *i. e.* command notice or make themselves felt; जनपदे न गदः पदमादधौ 9. 4 'no disease stepped into the country'; यद्यवधि न पदं दधाति चित्ते Bv. 2. 14; **पदं कृ** (*a*) to set foot in, on or over (lit.); शांतिं करिष्यसि पदं पुनराश्रमेऽस्मिन् *S.* 4. 25; (*b*) to enter upon or into, take possession of, occupy (fig.); कृतं वपुषि नवयौवनेन पदं K. 137; कृतं हि मे कुतूहलेन प्रश्नावकाशया हृदि पदं 133; so Ku. 5. 21; Pt. 1. 240; कृत्वा पदं नो गले Mu. 3. 26 'in defiance of us'; (lit. planting his foot on our neck); **मूर्ध्नि पदं कृ** 'to mount on the head of', 'to humble'; Pt. **1.** 327; आकृतिविशेषेष्वादरः पदं करोति M. 1 'good forms attract attention (command respect);' जने सखी पदं कारिता *S.* 4 'made to have dealings with (to confide in);' धर्मेण शर्वे पार्वतीं प्रति पदं कारिते Ku. 6. 14. 2 A step, pace, stride; तन्वी स्थिता कतिचिदेव पदानि गत्वा *S.* **2.** 12; **पदे पदे** at every step; अक्षमा- लामदत्त्वा पदात्पदमपि न गंतव्यं or चालितव्यं, 'do not move even a step &c.; पितुः पदं मध्यममुत्पतंती V. 1. 19 'the middle pace or stride of Vishṇu'; *i. e.* the sky (for mythologically speaking the earth, sky and lower world are considered as the three paces of Vishṇu in his fifth or dwarf incarnation); so अथात्मनः शब्दगुणं गुणज्ञः पदं विमानेन विगाह- मानः R. 13. 1. **3** A foot-step, foot-print, foot-mark; पदपंक्तिः *S.* 3. 8; or पदावली foot-prints; पदमनुविधेयं च महतां Bh. 2. 28. 'the foot-steps of the great must be followed'. **4** A trace, mark, impression, vestige; रतिवलयप- दांके चापमासज्य कंठे Ku. 2. 64; Me. 35, **96;** M. **3. 5** A place, position, station; अधोधः पदं Bh. 2. 10; आत्मा परिश्रमस्य पदमुपनीतः *S.* 1. 'brought to the point of or exposed to trouble', तदलब्धपदं हृदि शोकघने R. 8. 91 'found no place in (left no impression on) the heart'; अपदे शंकितोस्मि M. 1 'My doubts were out of place'; *i. e.* groundless; कृशाकुटुंबेषु लोभः पदमधत्त Dk. **162;** Ku. 6. **72,** 3. 4; R. 2. 50; 9. 82; कृतपदं स्तनयुगलं U. 6. 35 'brought into relief or bursting forth'. **6** Dignity, rank, office, station or position; भगवत्या प्राश्निकपदमध्यासितव्यं M. 1; यांत्येवं गृहिणीपदं युवतयः *S.* 4. 18 'attain to the rank or position' &c; साचिव°, राज° &c. **7** Cause, subject, occasion, thing, matter; व्यवहारपदं हि तत् Y. 2. 5; occasion or matter of dispute, title of law, judicial proceeding सतां हि संदेहपदेषु वस्तुषु *S.* 1. **22;** वांछितफलप्राप्तेः पदं Ratn. 1. 6. **8** Abode, object, receptacle: पदं दृशः स्याः कथमीश मादृशां *Si.* 1. 37, 14. 22; अगरीयान्न पदं नृपश्रियः Ki. **2. 14;** अविवेकः परमापदां पदं **2.** 30; के वा न स्युः परिभवपदं निष्फलारंभयत्नाः Me. 54; H. 4. 69. **9** A quarter or line of a stanza, verse; विरचितपदं (गेयं) Me. 86; 133; M. 5. 2; S. 3. 16. **10** A complete or inflected word; सुप्तिङंतं पदं P. I. 4. 14; वर्णाः पदं प्रयोगार्हानन्वितैकार्थबोधकाः S. D. 9; R. 8. 77. **11** A name for the base of nouns before all consonantal case-terminations except nom. singular. **12** Detachment of the Vedic words from one another, separation of a Vedic text into its several constituent words. **13** A pretext; *Si.* 7. 14. **14** A square root. **15** A part, portion or division (as of a sentence). **16** A measure of length. **17** Protection, preservation. **18** A square or house on a chess-board. **—दः** A ray of light. –Comp. **–अंकः –चिह्नं** a foot-print. **–अंगुष्ठः** the great toe, thumb (of the foot). **–अनुगः** a follower, companion. **–अनुशासनं** the science of words, grammar. **–अंतः** the end of a word. **–अंतरं** another step, the interval of one step; **पदांतरे स्थित्वा** *S.* 1. **–अब्जं, –अंभोजं, –अरविंदं, –कमलं, –पंकजं, –पद्मं** a lotus-like foot. **–अर्थः 1** the meaning of a word. 2 a thing or object. **3** a head or topic (of which the Naiyâyikas enumerate 16 sub-heads). **4** anything which can be named (अभिधेय); a category or predicament; the number of such categories, according to the Vaiseshikas, is seven; according to the Sânkhyas, twenty-five (or twenty-seven according to the followers of Patanjali), and two according to the Vedântins. **–आघातः** 'a stroke with the foot,' a kick. **–आजिः** a foot soldier. **–आवली** a series of words, a continued arrangement of words or lines; (काव्यस्य शरीरं तावदिष्टार्थव्यवच्छिन्ना पदावली Kâv. 1. 10; मधुरकोमलकांतपदावलीं शृणु तदा जयदेवसर- स्वतीं Gît. 1. **–आसनं** a foot-stool **–क्रमः** walking, pace. **–गः** a foot-soldier. **–छेदः, –विच्छेदः, –विग्रहः** separation of words, resolution of a sentence into its constituent parts. **–च्युत** *a.* dismissed from office, deposed. **–न्यासः 1** stepping, tread, step. 2 a foot-mark. **3** position of the feet in a particular attitude. **4** the plant गोक्षुर. **–पंक्तिः** *f.* **1** a line of foot-steps; *S.* 3 9; V. 4. 6. 2 a line or arrangement of words; Ki. 10. 30. **3** an *ishṭakâ* or sacred brick. **–पाठः** an arrangement of the Vedic text in which each word is written and pronounced in its original form and indepedently of phonetic changes (opp. संहितापाठ). **–पातः, विक्षेपः** step, pace (of a horse also). **–भंजनं** analysis of words, etymology. **–भंजिका** a commentary which separates the words and analyses the compounds of a passage. **–माला** a magical formula. **–वृत्ति** *f.* the hiatus between two words.

पदकं A step, position, office; see पद. **–कः 1** An ornament of the neck. **2** One conversant with the पदपाठ. q. v.

पदविः –वी *f.* **1** A way, road, path, course (fig. also); पवनपदवीं Me. 8; अनुयाहि साधुपदवीं Bh. **2.** 77 'follow in the footsteps of the good'; *S.* 4. 13; R. 3. 50, 7. 7; 8. 11; 15. 99; Bh. 3. 46; Ve. 6. 27; so यौवनपदवीमारूढः Pt. **1** 'attained his majority' (grew up to man's estate) **2** Position, station, rank, dignity, office, post. **3** A place, site.

पदातः, पदातिः 1 A foot-soldier; R. 7. 37. **2** A pedestrian (walking on foot); U. 5. 12.

पदातिन् *a.* **1** Having foot soldiers (as an army). **2** Being or going on foot. *–m.* A foot-soldier.

पदिक *a.* Going on foot. **कः** A footman.

पद्मं 1 A lotus (*m* also in this sense); पद्मपत्रस्थितं तोयं धत्तेमुक्ताफलश्रियं. **2** A lotus-like ornament. **3** The form or figure of a lotus. **4** The root of a lotus. **5** The coloured marks on the trunk and face of an elephant. **6** An army arrayed in the form of a lotus. **7** A particular high number (one thousand billions). **8** Lead. **–द्मः 1** A kind of temple. **2** An elephant. **3** A species of serpent. **4** An epithet of Râma. **5** One of the nine treasures of Kubera, see नवनिधि. **6** A kind of coitus or mode of sexual enjoyment. **–द्मा** N. of Lakshmî, the goddess of fortune, and wife of Vishṇu; (तं) पद्मा पद्मातपत्रेण भेजे साम्राज्यदीक्षितं R. R. 5. –Comp. **–अक्ष** *a.* lotus-eyed. **(–क्षः)** an epithet of Vishṇu or the sun. **(–क्षं)** the seed of lotus. **–आकरः 1** a large tank or pond abounding in lotuses. **2** or pond or pool of water in general. **3** an assemblage of lotuses; Bh. **2.** 73. **–आलयः** an epithet of Brahman, the creator. **(–या)** an epithet of Lakshmî. **–आसनं 1** a lotus-seat; Ku. 7. 86. **2** a particular posture in religious meditation; ऊरूमूले वामपादं पुनस्तु दक्षिणं पदं। वामोरौ स्थापयित्वा तु पद्मासन- मिति स्मृतं ॥ **(–नः)** an epithet or Brahman, the creator. **–आह्वं** cloves. **–उद्भवः** an epithet of Brahmâ. **–करः, –हस्तः** an epithet of Vishṇu. **(–रा, –स्ता)** N. of Lakshmî. **–कर्णिका** the pericarp of a lotus. **–कीलका** an unblown lotus. -केशरः -कं the filament of a lotus. -कोशः, -कोषः 1 the calyx of a lotus. 2 a position of the fingers resembling the calyx of a lotus. -खंडं, -षंडं a multitude of lotuses. -गंध, -गंधि *a.* lotus-scented or as fragrant as or smelling like a lotus. -गर्भः 1 an epithet of Brahmâ. 2 of Vishṇu. 3 the sun. -गुणा, गृहा an epithet of Lakshmî, the goddess of wealth. -जः, -जातः, -भवः, -भूः- -योनिः, -संभवः epithets of Brahmâ, the lotus-born god. तंतुः the fibrous stalk of a lotus. -नाभः, -भिः an epithet of Vishṇu. -नालं a lotus stalk. पाणिः 1 an epithet of Brahmâ. 2 of Vishṇu. -पुष्पः the Karṇikâra plant. -बंधः a kind of artificial composition in which the words are arranged in the form of a lotus-flower; see K. P. 9 *ad. loc.* -बंधुः 1 the sun. 2 a bee. -रागः, गं a ruby; R. 13. 53; 17. 23; Ku. 3. 53. -रेखा a figure on the palm of the hand (of the form of a lotus-flower) which indicates the acquisition of great wealth. -लांछन 1 an epithet of Brahmâ. 2 of Kubera. 3 the sun. 4 a king. (ना) 1 an epithet of Lakshmî, the goddess of wealth. 2 or of Sarasvatî, the goddess of learning. -वासा an epithet of Lakshmî.

पद्मकं 1 An army arrayed in the form of a lotus-flower. 2 The coloured spots on the trunk and face of an elephant. 3 A particular posture in sitting.

पद्मकिन् *m.* 1 An elephnat 2 The *Bhûrja* or birch tree.

पद्मावती 1 An epithet of Lakshmî. 2 N. of a river; Mâl. 9. 1.

पद्मिन् *a.* 1 Possessing lotuses. 2 Spotted. -*m.* An elephant. -नी 1 The lotus plant; सुरगज इव बिभ्रत् पद्मिनीं दंतलग्नां Ku. 3. 76; R. 16. 88; Me. 33; M. 2. 13. 2 An assemblage of lotus-flowers. 3 A pond or lake abounding in lotuses. 4 The fibrous stalk of a lotus. 5 A female elephant. 6 A woman of the first of the four classes into which writers on erotical science divide women; the रतिमंजरी thus defines her:—भवति कमलनेत्रा नासिकाक्षुद्ररंध्रा अविरलकुचयुग्मा चारुकेशी कृशांगी। मृदुवचनसुशीला गीतवाद्यानुरक्ता सकलतनुसुवेशा पद्मिनी पद्मगंधा ॥

पद्मेशयः An epithet of Vishṇu.

पद्य *a.* 1 Consisting of Padas or lines. 2 Measuring a pada. -द्यः 1 A Sûdra. 2 A part of a word. -द्या A foot-path, path, way -द्यं 1 A stanza or verse (consisting of four lines); मदीयपद्यरत्नानां मंजूषैषा मया कृता Bv. 4. 45; पद्यं चतुष्पदी तच्च वृत्तं जातिरिति द्विधा Chand. M. 2. 2 Praise, panegyric (स्तुति).

पद्रः A village.

पद्वः 1 The world of human beings (भूलोक). 2 A car. 3 A road.

पन् 1 U. (पनायति-ते, पनायित or पनित) To praise, extol; cf. पण.

पनसः 1 The bread-fruit tree 2 A thorn. -सं The fruit of the bread-fruit-tree.

पंथक *a.* Produced in or on the way.

पन्न *p. p.* 1 Fallen, sunk, gone down, descended. 2 Gone; see पद्. -Comp. -गः a snake, serpent; विप्रकृतः पन्नगः फणां कुरुते *S* 6. 30. (-गं) lead. °अरिः, °अशनः, °नाशनः epithets of Garuḍa.

पपिः The moon.

पपीः 1 The sun. 2 The moon.

पपु *a.* Fostering, protecting. -पुः *f.* A foster-mother.

पंपा 1 N. of a lake in the Daṇḍakâ forest; इदं च पंपाभिधानं सरः U. 1; R. 13. 30; Bk. 6. 73. 2 N. of a river in the south of India.

पयस् *n.* 1 Water. 2 Milk; पयःपानं भुजंगानां केवलं विषवर्धनं H 3. 4; R. 2. 36. 63; 14. 78 (where both senses are intended) 3 Semen virile; (पयस् is changed to पयो before soft consonants). -Comp. -गलः, -ङः 1 hail. 2 an island. -घनं hail. -चयः a reservoir or lake. -जन्मन् *m.* a cloud. -दः a cloud; Me. 7; R. 14. 37. -सुहृद् *m.* a peacock, -धरः 1 a cloud. 2 a woman's breast; पद्मापयोधरतटी Gît. 1. विपांडुभिर्म्लानतया पयोधरैः Ki. 4. 24 (where the word means 'a cloud' also); R. 14. 22. 3 an udder; R. 2. 3. 4 the cocoanut tree. 5 the back bone or spine (कशेरुक). -धस् *m.* 1 the ocean. 2 a pond, lake, a piece of water. -धिः, -निधिः the ocean; Rs. 2. 7; N. 4. 50. -मुच् *m.* a cloud; R. 3. 3; 6. 5. -वाहः a cloud; R. 1. 36.

पयस्य *a.* 1 Milky, made of milk. 2 Watery. -स्यः A cat -स्या Curds.

पयस्वल *a.* Rich in milk, yielding copious milk. -लः A goat.

पयस्विन् *a.* Milky, juicy. -नी 1 A milch-cow; R. 2. 21, 54, 65. 2 A river. 3 A she-goat. 4 Night.

पयोधिकं The cuttle-fish bone.

पयोष्णी N. of a river rising in the Vindhya mountain (identified by some with the modern Taptî river, but more correctly with Purṇâ, a feeder of that river).

पर *a.* (Declined optionally like a pronoun in nom. and voc. pl., and abl. and loc. sing. when it denotes relative position) 1 Other, different, another; see पर *m.* also. 2 Distant, removed, remote. 3 Beyond, further, on the other side of; म्लेच्छदेशस्ततः परः Ms. 2. 23, 7. 158. 4 Subsequent, following, next to (usually with abl.); बाल्यात्परामिव दशां मदनोऽध्युवास R. 5. 63; Ku. 1. 31. 5 Higher, superior; सिकतात्वादपि परां प्रपेदे परमाणुतां R. 15. 22; इंद्रियाणि पराण्याहुरिंद्रियेभ्यः परं मनः। मनसस्तु परा बुद्धिर्यो बुद्धेः परतस्तु सः॥ Bg. 2. 43. 6 Highest, greatest, most distinguished, pre eminent, chief, best, principal; न त्वया द्रष्टव्यानां परं दृष्टं *S.* 2; Ki. 5. 28. 7 Having as a following letter or sound, followed by (in comp.). 8 Alien, estranged, stranger. 9 Hostile, inimical, adverse. 10 Exceeding, having a surplus or remainder, left over; as in परं शतं exceeding or more than a hundred. 11 Final, last. 12 (At the end of comp.) Having anything as the highest object, absorbed or engrossed in, intent on, solely devoted to, wholly engaged or occupied in; परिचर्यापरः R. 1. 91; so ध्यानपर, शोकपर, दैवपर, चिंतापर &c. -रः 1 Another person, a stranger, foreigner; oft. in pl. in this sense; यतः परेषां गुणग्रहीतासि Bv. 1. 9; *Si.* 20. 74; see एक, अन्य also. 2 A foe, an enemy, adversary; उत्तिष्ठमानस्तु परो नोपेक्ष्यः पथ्यमिच्छता *Si.* 2. 10; Pt. 2. 158; R. 3. 21. -रं 1 The highest point or pitch, culminating point. 2 The Supreme spirit. 3 Final beatitude.

Note—The acc., instr., and loc. singulars of पर are used adverbially; *e. g.* (*a*) परं 1 beyond, over, out of (with abl.); वर्त्मनः परं R. 1. 17. 2 after (with abl.); अस्मात्परं *S.* 4. 16; ततः परं &c. 3 thereupon, thereafter. 4 but, however. 5 otherwise. 6 in a high degree, excessively, very much, completely, quite; पर दुःखितोऽस्मि &c. 7 at the utmost. (*b*) परेण 1 farther, beyond, more than; किंवा मृत्योः परेण विधास्यति Mâl. 2. 2. 2 afterwards; मयि तु कृतनिधाने किं विदध्याः परेण Mv. 2. 49. 3 after (with abl.); स्तन्यत्यागात्परेण U. 2, 7. (*c*) परे 1 afterwards, thereupon; अथ तेन दशाहतः परे R. 8. 73. 2 in future. -Comp. -अंगं the hinder part of the body. -अंगदः an epithet of *S*iva. -अदनः a horse found in the country of Persia or Arabia. -अधीन *a.* dependent on another, subject, subservient; Ms. 10. 54, 83. -अंताः (*m.* pl.) N. of a people. -अंतकः an epithet of *S*iva. -अन्न *a.* living or subsisting on another's food. (-न्नं) the food of another. °परिपुष्टता being fed with the food of others; Y. 3. 241. °भोजिन् *a.* subsisting on the food of others; H. 1 139. -अपर *a.* 1 far and near, remote and proximate. 2 prior and posterior. 3 before and beyond, earlier and later. 4 higher and lower, best and worst. (-रं) (in logic) a property intermediate between the greatest and smallest numbers, a species (as existing between the genus and individual.) –अमृतं rain. –अयण (अयन) *a.* 1 attached or devoted to, adhering to. 2 depending on, subject to. 3 intent on, solely devoted to or absorbed in (at the end of comp.); प्रभुर्धनपरायणः Bh. 2. 56; so शोक° Ku. 4. 1; अग्निहोत्र° &c. (–णं) the principal or highest object, chief aim, best or last resort. –अर्थ *a.* 1 having another aim or meaning. 2 intended or designed for another, done for another. (–र्थः) 1 the highest interest or advantage. 2 the interest of another (opp. स्वार्थ); स्वार्थो यस्य परार्थ एव स पुमानेकः सतामग्रणीः Subhâsh.; R. 1. 29. 3 the chief or highest meaning. 4 the highest object (*i. e.* sexual intercourse). (–र्थं-र्थे) *ind.* for the sake of another. –अर्धं 1 the other part (opp. पूर्वार्ध); the latter half; दिनस्य पूर्वार्धपरार्धभिन्ना छायेव मैत्री खलसज्जनानां Bh. 2. 60. 2 a particular high number; *i. e* 100,000,000,000,000,000; एकत्वादिपरार्धपर्यंता संख्या T. S. –अर्ध्य *a.* 1 being on the farther side or half. 2 most distant in number; इमेतो वसंतात्परार्ध्यः Sat. Br. 3 most excellent, best, most exalted, highly esteemed, highest, supreme; R. 3. 27, 8. 27, 10. 64; 16. 39; *Si.* 8. 45. 4 most costly; *Si.* 4. 11. 5 most beautiful or lovely, finest; R. 6. 4; *Si.* 3. 58. (–र्ध्यं) 1 a maximum. 2 an infinite number. –अवर *a.* 1 far and near. 2 earlier and later. 3 prior and posterior or subsequent. 4 higher and lower. 5 traditional; Ms. 1. 105. 6 all-including. –अहः the next day. –अह्नः the afternoon, the latter part of the day. –आचित *a.* fostered or brought up by another. (–तः) a slave. –आत्मन् *m.* the Supreme spirit. –आयत्त *a.* dependent on another, subject, subservient; परायत्तः प्रीतिः कथमिव रसं वेत्तु पुरुषः Mu. 3. 4. –आयुस् *m.* an epithet of Brahmâ. –आविद्धः 1 an epithet of Kubera. 2 of Vishṇu. –आश्रयः, –आसंगः dependence upon another. –आस्कंदिन् *m.* a thief, robber. –इतर *a.* 1 other than inimical; *i. e.* friendly, kind. 2 one's own; Ki. 1. 14. –ईशः an epithet of Brahmâ –उत्कर्षः another's prosperity. –उपकारः doing good to others, benevolence, beneficence, charity; परोपकारः पुण्याय पापाय परपीडनं. –उपजापः causing dissension among enemies. –उपरुद्ध *a.* besieged by an enemy. –ऊढा another's wife. –एधित *a.* fostered or brought up by another. (–तः) 1 a servant. 2 the (Indian) cuckoo. –कलत्रं another's wife. °अभिगमनं adultery; H. 1. 135. –कार्यं another's business or work. –क्षेत्रं 1 another's body. 2 another's field; Ms. 9. 49. 3 anothers' wife; Ms. 3. 175. –गामिन् *a.* 1 being with another. 2 relating to another. 3 beneficial to another. –ग्रंथिः a joint (as of a finger.)–चक्रं 1 the army of an enemy. 2 invasion by an enemy, one of the six *itis*, q. v. –छंदः the will of another. °अनुवर्तनं following the will of another. –छिद्रं a weak or vulnerable point of another, a defect in another. –जात *a.* 1 born of another. 2 dependent on another for livelihood. (–तः) a servant. –जित *a.* conquered by another. (–तः) the (Indian) cuckoo. –तंत्र *a.* dependent on another, dependent, subservient. –दाराः (*m. pl*) another's wife. –दारिन् *m.* an adulterer. –दुःखं the sorrow or grief of another; विरलः परदुःखदुःखितो जनः; महदपि परदुःखं शीतलं सम्यगाहुः V. 4. 13. –देशः a foreign country. –देशिन् *m.* a foreigner- –द्रोहिन्-द्वेषिन् *a* hating others, hostile, inimical. –धनं another's property. –धर्मः 1 the religion of another; स्वधर्मे निधनं श्रेयः परधर्मो भयावहः Bg. 3. 35. 2 another's duty or business. 3 the duties of another caste; Ms. 10. 97. –निपातः the irregular posteriority of a word in a compound; *e. g.* भूतपूर्वः where the sense is पूर्वं भूतः; so राजदंतः, अग्न्याहितः &c. –पक्षः the side or party of an enemy. –पदं 1 the highest position, eminence. 2 final beatitude. –पिंडः another's food, food given by another. °अद् *a.* one who eats another's food or one who feeds at the cost of another (–*m.*) a servant. °रत *a.* feeding upon another's food. –पुरुषः 1 another man, a stranger. 2 the Supreme spirit, Vishṇu. 3 the husband of another woman. –पुष्ट *a.* fed or nourished by another. (–ष्टः) the (Indian) cuckoo. °महोत्सवः the mango tree. –पुष्टा 1 the (Indian) cuckoo. 2 a harlot, prostitute. –पूर्वा a woman who has had a former husband. –प्रेष्य a servant, menial slave. –ब्रह्मन् *n.* the Supreme spirit. –भागः 1 another's share. 2 superior merit. 3 good fortune, prosperity. 4 (*a*) excellence, superiority, supremacy; दुरधिगमः परभागो यावत्पुरुषेण पौरुषं न कृतं Pt. 1. 330; 5. 34. (*b*) excess, abundance, height; स्थलकमलगंजनं मम हृदयरंजनं जनितरतिरंगपरभागं Gît. 10; आभाति लब्धपरभागतयाधरोष्ठे R. 5. 79; Ku. 7. 17; Ki. 5. 30, 8. 42; *Si.* 7. 33, 8. 51; 10. 86. –भाषा a foreign tongue. –भुक्त *a.* enjoyed or used by another. –भृत् *m.* a crow (said to nourish the cuckoo) –भृतः ता the (Indian) cuckoo; (so called because she is nourished by another; *i. e.* by a crow); cf. *S.* 5. 22; Ku. 6. 2; R. 9. 43; *S.* 4. 9. –मृत्युः a crow. –रमणः a married woman's gallant or paramour; Pt. 1. 180. –लोकः the next (or future) world; Ku. 4. 10. °विधिः funeral rites; Ku. 4. 38. –वश, वश्य *a.* subject to another, dependent. –वाच्यं a fault or a defect. –वाणिः 1 a judge. 2 a year. 3 N. of the peacock of Kârtikeya. –वादः 1 rumour, report. 2 objection, controversy. –वादिन् *m.* a disputant, controversialist. –व्रतः an epithet of Dhritarâshtra. –श्वस् *ind.* the day after tomorrow. –संज्ञकः the soul. –सवर्ण *a.* homogeneous with a following letter (in gram.). –सेवा service of another. –स्त्री another's wife. –स्वं another's property; R. 1. 27; Ms. 7. 123. °हरणं seizing another's property. –हन् *a.* killing enemies. –हितं the welfare of another.

परकीय *a.* 1 Belonging to another; अर्थो हि कन्या परकीय एव *S.* 4. 21; Ms. 4. 201. –या Another's wife, a woman not one's own, one of the three main kinds of heroines; see अन्यस्त्री and S. D. 108 *et seq.*

परंजः 1 An oil-mill. 2 The blade of a sword.

परंजनः, परंजयः An epithet of Varuṇa.

परतस् *ind.* 1 From another; Bv. 1. 120. 2 From an enemy; R. 3. 48. 3 Further, more (than), beyond, after, over (often with able). बुद्धेः परतस्तु सः Bg. 3. 42. 4 Otherwise. 5 Differently.

परत्र *ind.* 1 In another world, in a future birth; परत्रेह च शर्मणे R. 1. 69; Ku. 4. 37; Ms. 3. 275, 5. 166; 8. 127. In the sequel, further or later on. 3 Hereafter, in future. –Comp. –भीरुः one who stands in awe of the future world, a pious or religious man.

परंतप *a.* Annoying or vexing others, subduing one's enemy; Bg. 4. 2; R. 15. 7. –पः A hero, conqueror.

परम *a.* 1 Most distant, last. 2 Highest, best, most excellent, greatest; प्राप्नोति परमां गतिं Ms. 4. 14; 7. 1, 2. 13. 3 Chief, principal, primary, supreme; Ms. 8. 302, 9. 319. 4 Exceeding, extreme. 5 Adequate, sufficient, –मं The utmost or highest, the chief or prominent part (at the end of comp.) consisting principally of, solely occupied with; कामोपभोगपरमा एतावदिति निश्चिताः Bg. 16. 11; Ms. 6. 96. –मं *ind.* 1 A particle of assent, acceptance or agreement (well, very well, yes, be it so); ततः परममित्युक्त्वा प्रतस्थे मुनिमंडलं Ku. 6. 35. 2 Exceedingly, very much; परमक्रुद्धः &c. –Comp. –अंगना an excellent woman.

-अणुः an infinitesimal particle, an atom; R. 15. 22; परमाणुपरमाणून् पर्वतीकृत्य नित्यं Bh. 2. 78; पृथ्वी नित्या परमाणुरूपा T. S; (a परमाणु is thus defined:—जालांतरगते रश्मौ यत्सूक्ष्मं दृश्यते रजः । तस्य त्रिंशत्तमो भागः परमाणुः स उच्यते ॥). -अद्वैतं 1 the Supreme spirit. 2 pure unitarianism. -अन्नं rice boiled in milk. -अर्थः 1 the highest or most sublime truth, true spiritual knowledge, knowledge about Brahman or the Supreme spirit; R. 8. 22; Mv. 7. 2. 2 truth, reality, earnestness; परिहासविजल्पितं सखे परमार्थेन न गृह्यतां वचः S. 2. 18; oft in comp. in the sense of 'true' or 'real'; °मत्स्याः R. 7. 40; Mv. 4. 30. 3 any excellent or important object. 4 the best sense. -अर्थतः *ind.* truly, really, exactly, accurately; विकारं खलु परमार्थतोऽज्ञात्वानारंभः प्रतीकारस्य S. 4; उवाच चैनं परमार्थतो हरं न वेत्सि नूनं यत एवमात्थ मां Ku. 5. 75; Pt. 1. 136. -अहः an excellent day. -आत्मन् *m.* the Supreme spirit or Brahman. -आपद् *f.* the greatest calamity or misfortune. -ईशः an epithet of Vishṇu. 2 of Indra. 3 of *S*iva. 4 the Almighty God, the Supreme Being. -ऋषिः a great sage. -ऐश्वर्यं supremacy. -गतिः *f.* final beatitude, emancipation. -गवः an excellent bull or cow. -पदं 1 the best position, highest rank. 2 final beatitude. -पुरुषः, -पूरुषः the Supreme spirit. -प्रख्य *a.* celebrated, renowned. -ब्रह्मन् *n.* the Supreme spirit हंसः an ascetic of the highest order, one who has controlled and subdued all his senses by abstract meditation; cf. कुटीचक.

परमेष्ठः An epithet of Brahmâ.

परमेष्ठिन् *m.* 1 An epithet of Brahmâ. 2 of *S*iva. 3 of Vishṇu. 4 of Garuḍa. 5 of Agni. 6 Any spiritual teacher.

परंपर *a.* 1 One following the other. 2 Successive, repeated. -रः A great-grandson. -रा 1 An uninterrupted series, regular series, succession; महतीयं खल्वनर्थपरंपरा K. 103; कर्णपरंपरया 'from ear to ear' by hearsay; परंपरया आगम् 'to be handed down in regular succession.' 2 A row, line, collection, assemblage (of regular things); तोयांतर्भास्करालीव रेजे मुनिपरंपरा Ku. 6. 49; R. 6. 5, 35, 40; 12. 50. 3 Method, order, due arragement. 4 Race, family, lineage. 5 Injury, hurting, killing.

परंपराक *a.* Immolating an animal at a sacrifice.

परंपरीण *a.* 1 Obtained by succession or descent, hereditary; लक्ष्मीं परंपरीणां त्वं पुत्रपौत्रीजितां नय Bk. 5. 15. 2 Traditional.

परवत् *a.* 1 Dependent upon or subject to another, ready to obey; सा बाला परवतीति मे विदितं S. 3. 2; भगवन्परवानयं जनः R. 8. 81; 2. 26; oft. with instr. or loc. of person; भ्रात्रा यदित्थं परवानसि त्वं R. 14. 59. 2 Deprived of strength, rendered powerless परवानिव शरीरोपतापेन Mâl. 3. 3 Completely under the influence of (another), not master of oneself, overpowered or overcome; विस्मयेन परवानस्मि U. 5; आनंदेन परवानस्मि U. 3; साध्वसेन Mâl. 6.

परवत्ता Subjection to another, dependence; V. 5. 17.

परशः A kind of stone or gem, the touch of which is said to turn other metals, such as iron, into gold; perhaps the philosopher's stone.

परशुः 1 An axe, a hatchet, a battle-axe; तर्जितः परशुधारया मम R. 11. 78. 2 A weapon in general. 3 A thunderbolt. -COMP. -धरः 1 an epithet of Parasurâma. 2 of Gaṇesa. 3 a soldier armed with an axe. -रामः 'Râma with axe', N. of a celebrated Brâhmaṇa warrior, son of Jamadagni and the sixth incarnation of Vishṇu. [While young he cut off with his axe, the head of his mother Re*n*uka at the command of his father when none of his other brothers was willing to do so: see Jamadagni. Some time after this, king K*a*rtav*i*rya went to the hermitage of his father, and carried off his cow. But Paras*u*r*a*ma, when he returned home, fought with the king and killed him. When his sons heard this, they became very angry and, repaired to the hermitage, and on finding Jamadagni alone, they shot him dead. When Paras*u*r*a*ma, who was not then also at home, returned, he became very much exasperated, and made the dreadful vow of exterminating the whole Kshatriya race. He succeeded in fulfilling this vow, and is said to have rid the earth thrice seven times of the royal race' He was afterwards, destroyer of the Kshatriyas as he was, defeated by R*a*ma, son of Das*a*ratha, though quite a boy of sixteen; (see R. 11. 68. 91). He is said to have at one time pierced through the Krauncha mountain, being jealous of the might of K*a*rtikeya; cf. Me. 57. He is one of the seven *chirajivins*, and is believed to be still practising penance on the Mehendra mountain cf. Gît. 1:—क्षत्रियरुधिरमये जगदपगतपापं स्नपयसि पयसि शमितभवतापम् । केशव धृतभृगुपतिरूप जय जगदीश हरे ।].

परश्व (स्व) धः A hatchet, a battle-axe; धारां शितां रामपरश्वधस्य संभावयत्युत्पलपत्रसारां R. 6. 42.

परस् *ind.* (Rarely used by itself in classical Sanskrit) 1 Beyond, further, more than. 2 On the other side of. 3 Far away, at a distance. 4 With the exception of. -COMP. -कृष्ण *a.* very black. -पुरुष *a.* higher than a man. -शत *a.* more than a hundred; Ki. 13. 26; Si. 12. 50. -श्वस् *ind.* the day after tomorrow. -सहस्र *a.* more than a thousand; परःसहस्राः शरदस्तपांसि तप्त्वा U. 1. 15; परःसहस्रैः पिशाचैः Mv. 5. 17.

परस्तात् *ind.* 1 Beyond, on the other side of, further than (with gen.); आदित्यवर्णं तमसः परस्तात् Bg. 8, 9. 2 Hereafter, afterwards. 3 Higher than.

परस्पर *a.* Mutual; परस्परां विस्मयवंति लक्ष्मीमालोकयांचक्रुरिवादरेण Bk. 2. 5. -*pron. a.* Each other, one another (used in the sign only; often in comp.) परस्परस्योपरि पर्यचीयत् R. 3. 24; 7. 35; अविज्ञातपरस्परैः अपसर्पैः 17. 51; परस्पराक्षिसादृश्यं 1. 40, 3. 24, *Note*. The acc., instr. and abl. singulars are often used adverbially in the sense of 'mutually', 'reciprocally', 'with one another,' 'by from, or to one another.' 'against one another' &c. ; see Bg. 3. 11, 10. 9; R. 4. 79; 6. 46; 7. 17, 53; 12. 94.

परस्मैपदं, परस्मैभाषा 'A voice for another', one of the two voices in which verbs in Sanskrit are conjugated.

परा *ind.* A prefix to verbs and nouns in the sense of away, back, in an inverted order, aside, towards. According to G. M. the senses of परा are– 1 Killing, injuring &c. (पराहतं) 2 going (परागत). 3 seeing, encountering (परावृष्ट). 4 prowess (पराक्रांत) 5 direction towards (परावृत्त) . 6 excess (पराजित) 7 dependence (पराधीन). 8 liberation (पराकृत). 9 inverted order, backwards (पराङ्मुख). 10 setting aside, disregarding.

पराकरणं The act of setting aside, rejecting, disregarding or disdaining.

पराक्रमः 1 Heroism, prowess, courage, valour; पराक्रमः परिभवे Si. 2. 44. 2 Marching against, attack. 3 Attempt, endeavour, enterprise. 4 N. of Vishṇu.

परागः 1 The pollen of a flower; स्फुटपरागपरागतपंकजं Si. 6. 2; Amaru. 54. 2 Dust in general; R. 4. 30. 3 Fragrant powder used after bathing. 4 Sandal. 5 An eclipse of the sun or moon. 6 Fame, celebrity. 7 Independence.

परांगवः The ocean.

परा (रां) च् *a.* (ची *f.*) 1 Situated beyond or on the other side; ये चामुष्मात्परांचो लोकाः Ch. Up. 2 Having the face turned away (पराङ्मुख); Si. 18. 18. 3 Unfavourable, adverse; दैवे परांचि Bv. 1. 105; or दैवे पराग्वदनशालिनि हंत जाते 3 1. 4 Distant. 5 Directed outwards. -COMP. -मुख *a* (पराङ्मुख)

1 having the face turned away or averted, turning the back upon; विग्रहाच्च शयने पराङ्मुखीर्नानुनेतुमबलाः स तत्वरे R. 19. 38; Amrau. 90; Ms. 2 195; 10. 119. 2 (*a*) averse from; मातुर्न केवलं स्वस्याः श्रियोऽप्यासीत् पराङ्मुखः R. 12. 13. (*b*) not disposed towards, shunning, avoiding; प्रवृत्तिपराङ्मुखो भावः V. 4. 20; *S*. 5. 28. 3 adverse, unfavourable; तनुरपि न ते दोषोऽस्माकं विधिस्तु पराङ्मुखः Amaru. 27. 4 not caring about, मर्त्येष्वास्थापराङ्मुखः R. 10. 43.

पराचीन *a*. 1 Turned in an opposite direction, averted. 2 Averse from, disinclined to. 3 Not minding, not caring about. 4 Happening subsequently or afterwards (उत्तरकालभव). 5 Situated on the other side, being beyond.

पराजयः 1 Overpowering, conquest, conquering, subjugating, defeat; R. 11. 19; Ms. 7. 199. 2 Being overcome by, not being able to suffer (with abl.); as in अध्ययनात्पराजयः' 3 Losing, loss, failure (as in a law-suit); अन्यथावादिनो (साक्षिणः) यस्य ध्रुवस्तस्यपराजयः Y. 2. 79. 4 Deprivation. 5 Desertion.

पराजित *p. p.* 1 Conquered, subjugated, defeated. 2 Condemned by law, cast or defeated (as in a lawsuit).

परान (ण) सा Medical treatment, practice of medicine.

पराभवः 1 (*a*) Defeat, discomfiture, overthrow; पराभवोऽप्युत्सव एव मानिनां Ki. 1. 41. (*b*) Mortification, humiliation; कुबेरस्य मनःशल्यं शंसतीव पराभवं Ku. 2. 22; तव पदपल्लववैरिपराभवमिदमनुभवतु सुवेशं Gît. 12. 3 Contempt, disregard, disrespect. 3 Destruction. 4 Disappearance, separation (sometimes written पराभव).

पराभूतिः *f*. See पराभव.

परामर्शः 1 Seizing, pulling; as in केशपरामर्शः 2 Bending or drawing (as a bow). 3 Violence, attack, assault, याज्ञसेन्याः परामर्शः Mb. 4 Disturbance, hindrance; तपः परामर्शविवृद्धमन्योः Ku. 3. 71. 5 Calling to mind, recollection. 6 Consideration, reflection, thought. 7 Judgment. 8 (In logic) Deduction, ascertaining that the पक्ष or subject possesses the हेतु; व्याप्तिविशिष्टपक्षधर्मताज्ञानं परामर्शः T. S.; or व्याप्तस्य पक्षधर्मत्वधीः परामर्श उच्यते Bhâshâ P. 66.

परामृष्ट *p. p.* Touched, handled, seized, grasped. 2 Roughly treated, violated. 3 Weighed, considered, judged. 4 Endured. 5 Connected with. 6 Afflicted by (as a disease); see मृश् with परा.

परारि *ind*. The year before last.

परायण See under पर (पर-अयन).

परावर्तः } **परावृत्तिः** } 1 Turning back, return, turn, retreat. 2 Exchange, barter. 3 Restoration. 4 Reversal of a sentence (in law).

पराशरः N. of a celebrated sage, father of Vyâsa and the author of a Smriti.

परासं Tin.

परासनं Killing, slaughter.

परासु *a*. Lifeless, dead; प्राङ् परासुर्द्विजात्मजः R. 15. 56; 9 78.

परास्त *p. p.* 1 Thrown or cast away. 2 Expelled, turned out. 3 Repudiated. 4 Refuted, rejected. 5 Defeated.

पराहत *p. p.* 1 Struck down or back. 2 Driven back, repelled.—**तं** A stroke.

परि *ind* (Sometimes changed to परि as परिवाह or परीवाह; परिहास or परीहास) 1 As a prefix to verbs and nouns derived from them, it means (*a*) round, round about, about. (*b*) in addition to, further. (*c*) opposite to, against. (*d*) much, excessively. 2 As a separable prepostion it means (*a*) towards, in the direction of, to, opposite to; (with an acc.);वृक्षं परि विद्योतते विद्युत्. (*b*) successively, severally (with an acc.); वृक्षं वृक्षं परि सिंचति 'he waters tree after tree.' (*c*) to the share or lot of (showing भाग or participation) (with acc यदत्र मां परि स्यात् 'what may fall to my lot'; or लक्ष्मीर्हरिं परि Sk. (*d*) from, out of, (*e*) exception of (with abl.); परि त्रिगर्तेभ्यो वृष्टो देवः, or पर्यनंतात्त्रयस्तापाः Vop. (*f*) after the lapse of. (*g*) in consequence of. 3 As an adverbial prefix to nouns not directly connected with verbs, it means 'very,''very much,' 'excessively'; as in पर्यश्रु 'bursting into tears'; परिचतुर्दशन्, परिदौर्बल्य. 4 At the beginning of adverbial compounds परि means (*a*) without, except, outside, with the exception of; as in परित्रिगर्तं वृष्टो देवः P. II. 1. 12; VI. 2. 33 According to P. II. 1. 10. परि may be used at the end of adverbial comp. after अक्ष, शलाका and a numeral to denote loss or defeat in a game by an unlucky or adverse cast of dice (द्यूतव्यवहारे पराजये एवायं समासः); *i g*. अक्षपरि, शलाकापरि, एकपरि; cf. अक्षपरि. (*b*) round about, all round, surrounded by; as in पर्यग्नि 'in the midst of flames' 5 At the end of an adjectival comp. परि has the sense of 'exhausted by,' or 'feeling repugnance for';as in पर्यध्ययनः=परिग्लानोऽध्ययनाय.

परिकथा A work giving the history and adventures of a fabulous person, a work of fiction.

परिकंपः 1 Great terror. 2 Violent tremour or trembling; Mv. 2. 27.

परिकरः 1 Retinue, train, attendants, followers, 2 A multitude, collection, crowd; Ratn. 3 5. 3 A beginning, commencement; Bh, 1. 6. 4 A girth, waist band, cloth worn round the loins; अहिपरिकरभाज *Si*. 4. 65; परिकरं बंधू or कृ to gird up one's loins, to make oneself ready, prepare oneself for any action; बध्नन्सधेगपरिकरं K. 170; कृतपरिकरस्य भवादृशस्य त्रैलोक्यमपि न क्षमं परिपंथीभवितुं Ve. 3; G. L. 47; Amaru. 92. 5 A sofa. 6 (In Rheti) N. of a figure of speech which consists in the use of significant epithets; विशेषणैर्यत्साकूतैरुक्तिः परिकरस्तु सः K. P. 10; *e. g*. सुधांशुकलितोत्तंसस्तापं हरतु वः शिवः Chandr. 5. 59. 7 (In dramaturgy) Covert or indirect intimation of coming events in the plot of a drama, the germ of the बीज q. v.; see S. D. 340. 8 Judgment.

परिकर्तृ *m*. A priest who performs the marriage ceremony of a younger brother whose elder brother is not yet mrrried; परिकर्ता याजकः Hârita; cf. परिवेत्तृ.

परिकर्मन् *m*. A servant.–*n*. 1 Painting or perfuming the body, personal decoration, dressing, toilet; कृताचारपरिकर्माणं *S*. 2. 2 Painting or dyeing the foot; Ku. 4. 19. 3 Preparation. 4 Worship, adoration. 5 (In Yoga phil.) Purifying, a means of purifying the mind; *Si*. 4. 55; (see Malli. thereon). 6 An arithmetical operation (of which there are 8 divisions.)

परिकर्षः,-कर्षणं Dragging out, extraction

परिकल्कन Deceit, cheating, roguery.

परिकल्पनं-ना 1 Settling, fixing, deciding, determining. 2 Contriving, inventing, forming, arranging; Mu. 7. 15. 3 Providing, furnishing, 4 Distributing.

परिकांक्षितः A religious mendicant or ascetic, a devotee.

परिकीर्ण *p. p* 1 Spread, diffused, scattered about. 2 Surrounded, crowded with, filled; *Si*. 16- 10; R. 8. 45.

परिकूटं A barrier, a trench before the gate of a town.

परिकोपः Great anger, fury.

परिक्रमः 1 Roaming about; moving about; Ki. 10. 2. -2 Roaming, walking or passing over. 3 Circumambulating. 4 Walking for pleasure. 5 Series, order. 6 Succession. 7 Penetrating. –Comp –**सहः** a goat.

परिक्रयः, –क्रियणं 1 Wages, hire. 2 Employing on wages. 3 Purchasing or buying off. 4 Barter, exchange. 5 A peace purchased with the payment of money; cf. H. 4. 122.

परिक्रिया 1 Enclosing with a fence or ditch, intrenching. 2 Encircling or surrounding in general. 3 (In dramaturgy) =परिकर (7) q. v.

परिक्लांत *p. p.* Exhausted, fatigued, tired out.

परिक्लेदः Wetness, dampness, moisture.

परिक्लेशः Hardship, fatigue, trouble.

परिक्षयः 1 Decay, waste, destruction; परिक्षयोऽपि आविकतरं रमणीयः Mk. 1; किरण° Ku. 4. 46. 2 Disappearing, ceasing. 3 Ruin, loss, failure; Ki. 16. 57, Ms. 9. 59.

परिक्षाम *a.* Ematiated, wasted away, lean.

परिक्षालनं 1 Washing, cleansing. 2 Water for washing.

परिक्षिप्त *p. p.* 1 Scattered, diffused. 2 Encircled, surrounded; वेतसपरिक्षिप्ते मंडपे *S.* 3; Ku. 6. 38. 3 Intrenched. 4 Overspread, overlaid. 5 Left, abandoned.

परिक्षीण *p. p.* 1 Vanished, disappeared. 2 Wasted, decayed. 3 Emaciated, worn away, exhausted. 4 Impoverished, entirely ruined: Bh. 2. 45. 5 Lost, destroyed. 6 Diminished, decreased. 7 (In law) Insolvent.

परिक्षीव *a.* Quite intoxicated.

परिक्षेपः 1 Moving about, walking to and fro. 2 Scattering, spreading. 3 Surrounding, encircling, circumfluence. 4 An enclosing belt or boundary, that by which anything is surrounded; R. 12. 66.

परिखा A moat, ditch, trench round a fort or town; R. 1. 30; 12. 66.

परिखातं 1 A moat, ditch. 2 A rut, furrow. 3 Digging round.

परिखेदः Fatigue, exhaustion, lassitude; Ku. 1. 60; Rs. 1. 27.

परिख्यातिः *f.* Fame, reputation.

परिगणनं-ना Complete enumeration, accurate statement or calculation; श्रेणीभूताः परिगणनया निर्दिशंतो बलाकाः Me. (considered as an interpolation or क्षेपक by Malli.).

परिगत *p. p.* 1 Surrounded, enclosed, encircled. 2 Diffused, spread around. 3 Known, understood; R. 7. 71; परिगतपरिगंतव्य एव भवान् Ve. 3; Mv. 3. 47. 4 Filled or covered with, possessed of (usually in comp.); *Si.* 9. 26. 5 Got, obtained; Bh. 3. 52. 6 Remembered.

परिगलित *p. p.* 1 Sunk. 2 Tumbled or dropped down. 3 Vanished 4 Melted. 5 Flowing.

परिगर्हणं Excessive blame.

परिगूढ *p. p.* 1 Quite secret. 2 Incomprehensible, very difficult to understand.

परिगृहीत *p. p.* 1 Grasped, seized, clutched. 2 Embraced, surrounded. 3 Accepted, taken, received. 4 Assented or consented to, admitted. 5 Patronized, favoured. 6 Followed, obeyed. 7 Opposed; see ग्रह् with परि.

परिगृह्या A married woman.

परिग्रहः 1 Seizing, holding, taking, grasping; आसनरज्जुपरिग्रहे R. 9. 46; शंकापरिग्रहः Mu. 1 'taking or entertaining a doubt'. 2 Surrounding, enclosing, encircling, fencing round. 3 Putting on, wrapping round (as a dress); मौलिपरिग्रहः R. 18. 38. 4 Assuming, taking; मानपरिग्रहः Amaru. 92; विवाहलक्ष्मी° U. 4. 5 Receiving, taking; accepting, acceptance; मौमो मुनेः स्थानपरिग्रहोऽयं R. 13. 36; अर्घ्यपरिग्रहांते 70; 12. 16; Ku. 6 53; विद्यापरिग्रहाय Mâl. 1; so आसनपरिग्रहं करोतु देवः U. 3 'your majesty will be pleased to take a seat or sit down'. 6 Possessions, property, belongings; त्यक्तसर्वपरिग्रहः Bg. 4. 21; R. 15. 55; V. 4. 26. 7 Taking in marriage, marriage; नवेदारपरिग्रहे U. 1. 19; Mâl. 5 27; *S.* 1. 22. 8 A wife, queen; प्रयतपरिग्रहद्वितीयः R. 1. 95. 92; 9. 14; 11. 33. 16. 8. *S.* 5. 27, 30; परिग्रहबहुत्वेऽपि *S.* 3. 21. 9 Taking under one's protection, favouring; U. 7. 11; M. 1. 13. 10 Attendants, followers, train, retinue, suite. 11 A household, family, members of a family. 12 The seraglio or a household of a king, harem. 13 Root, origin 14 The eclipse of the sun or moon. 15 An oath. 16 The rear of an army. 17 N. of Vishṇu. 18 Summing up, totality.

परिग्रहीतृ *m.* A husband, *S.* 4. 22.

परिग्लान *p. p.* 1 Languid, exhausted. 2 Averse from, disinclined to.

परिघः 1 An iron (or wooden) beam or bar used for locking or shutting a gate (अर्गल); एकः कृत्स्नां नगरपरिघप्रांशुबाहुर्भुनक्ति *S.* 2. 15; R. 16. 84; *Si.* 32; M. 5. 2. 2 (Hence) A bar, barrier, hindrance, obstacle; मार्गवस्य सुकृतोऽपि सोऽभवत्स्वर्गमार्गपरिघो दुरत्ययः R. 11. 88. 3 A stick or club studded or tipped with iron; R. 12. 73. 4 An iron club in general. 5 A water-jar, pitcher. 6 A glass pitcher. 7 A house. 8 Killing, destroying. 9 Striking, a stroke or blow.

परिघट्टनं Stirring up, stirring round.

परिघातः,-घातनं 1 Killing, striking, removing, getting rid of. 2 A club, an iron bludgeon.

परिघोषः 1 Noise. 2 Improper speech. 3 Thunder.

परिचतुर्दशन् *a.* Fully fourteen.

परिचयः 1 Heaping up, accumulation. 2 Acquaintance, familiarity, intimacy, conversancy; पुरुषपरिचयेन Mk. 1. 56; अतिपरिचयादवज्ञा 'familiarity breeds contempt'; परिचयं चललक्ष्यनिपातेन R. 9. 49; सकलकलापरिचयः K. 76. 3 Trial, study, practice, frequent repetition; हेतुः परिचयस्थैर्ये वक्तुर्गुणनिकैव सा *Si.* 2. 75; 11. 5; वर्णपरिचयं करोति *S.* 5. 4 Knowledge; Mv. 5. 10. 5 Recognition; Me. 9.

परिचरः 1 A servant, follower, an attendant. 2 A body-guard. 3 A guard or patrol in general. 4 Homage, service.

परिचरणः A servant, an attendant, assistant.—**णं** 1 Serving, attending or waiting upon. 2 Going about.

परिचर्या 1 Service, attendance; R. 1. 91; Bg. 18 44. 2 Adoration, worship; *Si.* 1. 17.

परिचाय्यः Sacrificial fire (arranged in a circle).

परिचारः 1 Service, attendance. 2 A servant. 3 A place for walking.

परिचारकः,परिचारिकः A servant, an attendant.

परिचित *p. p.* 1 Heaped up, accumulated. 2 Familiar, intimate or acquainted with. 3 Learnt, practised.

परिचितिः *f.* Acquaintance, familiarity, intimacy.

परिच्छद् *f.* 1 Retinue, train. 2 Paraphernalia.

परिच्छदः 1 A covering, cover. A garment, clothes, dress; शाखावसक्तकमनीयपरिच्छदानां Ki. 7. 40. 3 Train, retinue, attendents, circle of dependants; R. 9. 70. 4 Paraphernalia, external appendage; (as छत्र, चामर); सेना परिच्छदस्तस्य R. 1. 17. 5 Goods and chattels, personal property, all one's possessions or belongings (utensils, implements &c.); विवास्यो वा भवेद्राष्ट्रात्सद्रव्यः सपरिच्छदः Ms. 9. 241, 7. 40; 8. 405; 9. 78; 11. 76. 6 Necessaries for travelling.

परिच्छंदः Train, retinue.

परिच्छन्न *p. p.* 1 Enveloped, covered, clothed, clad. 2 Overspread or overlaid. 3 Surrounded with (a retinue). 4 Concealed.

परिच्छित्तिः *f.* 1 Accurate definition, limiting. 2 Partition, separation.

परिच्छिन्न *p. p.* 1 Cut off, divided. 2 Accurately defined, determined, ascertained; Ku. 2. 58. 3 Limited, circumscribed, confined; see छिद् with परि.

परिच्छितिः 1 Cutting, separating, dividing, discriminating (between right and wrong). 2 Accurate definition or distinction, decision, accurate determination, ascertainment; परिच्छेदव्यक्तिर्भवति न पुरस्थेऽपि विषये Mâl. 1. 31; परिच्छेदातीतः सकलवचनानामविषयः 1 30. 'transcending all definition or determination'; इत्यरूढबहुप्रतर्कमपरिच्छेदाकुलं मे मनः *S.* 5. 9. 3 Discrimination, judgment, discernment; परिच्छेदो हि पांडित्यं यदापन्ना विपत्तयः । अपरिच्छेदकर्तॄणां विपदः स्युः पदेपदे H. 1 148; किं पांडित्यं परिच्छेदः 1. 147. **4** A limit, boundary, setting limits to, circumscribing; अलमलं परिच्छेदेन M. 2. **5** A section, chapter or division of a work (for the other names for sections &c. see under अध्याय).

परिच्छेद्य *a.* **1** To be accurately defined, definable; Ms. 4. 9; R. 10. 28. **2** To be weighed or estimated.

परिजनः **1** Attendants, followers, servants taken collectively; परिजने राजानमभितः स्थितः M. 1. **2** Especially the retinue, suite, or train of females, the maids of a lady; R. 19. 23. **3** A single servant.

परिजल्पितं A covert indication (as by a servant) of one's own skill, superiority &c. by pointing out the cruelty, deceitfulness and such other faults of his master; Ujjvalamaṇi thus defines it:—प्रभोर्निर्दयताशाठ्यचापलाद्युपपादनात् । स्वविचक्षणताव्यक्तिर्भंग्या स्यात्परिजल्पितम् ॥ (Wilson renders the word by 'the covert reproaches of a mistress neglected or ill-used by her lover').

परिज्ञप्तिः **1** Conversation, discourse. **2** Recognition.

परिज्ञानं Thorough knowledge, complete acquaintance.

परिडीनं The flight of a bird in circles; see डीन.

परिणद्ध *p. p.* **1** Bound or wrapped round. **2** Broad, large; परिणद्धकंधरः R. 3. 34.

परिणत *p. p.* **1** Bent or bowed down, stooping; Me. 2. **2** Declining, old (as age); परिणते वयसि K. 35, 62, 63. **3** Ripe, matured, ripened, fully developed or formed शब्दब्रह्मविदः कवेः परिणतप्रज्ञस्य वाणीमिमां U. 7. 21; Me 23; परिणतमकरंदमार्मिकास्ते Bv. 1. 8; *Si.* 11. 49. **4** Full grown, advanced, perfected; परिणतशरच्चंद्रकिरणैः Bh. 3. 49; Me. 100. **5** Digested (as food). **6** Transformed or changed into (with instr.); V. 4. 28. **7** Ended, come to a close, terminated; अनेन समयेन परिणतो दिवसः K. 47. **8** Set (as the sun).—**तः** An elephant stooping to strike with his tusks, or giving a side blow with his tusks; (तिर्यग्दंतप्रहारश्च गजः परिणतो मतः Halây.); *Si* 2. 29; Ki. 6. 7.

परिणतिः *f.* **1** Bending or stooping down, bowing. **2** Ripeness, maturity, development; Mv. 2. 14. **3** Change, transformation, transmutation. **4** Fulfilment. **5** Result, consequence, issue; परिणतिरवधार्या यत्नतः पंडितेन Bh. 2. 94; 1. 20, 3. 17; Mv. 6. 28. **6** End, conclusion, close, termination; परिणतिरमणीयाः प्रीतयस्त्वद्विधानां Mâl. 6. 7, 16; *Si.* 11. 1. **7** Close of life, old age; सेवाकारा परिणतिरभूत् V. 3. 1; अभवद्गतः परिणतिं शिथिलः परिमंदसूर्यनयनो दिवसः *Si.* 9. 3 (where प° means 'end or conclusion' also). **8** Digestion (of food).

परिणयः,-णयनं Marriage; नवपरिणया वधूः शयने K. P. 10.

परिणहन Girding on, wrapping round.

परि(री)णामः **1** Alteration, change, transformation. **2** Digestion; अन्नं न सम्यक् परिणाममेति Susr.; भुक्तस्य परिणामहेतुरौदर्य T. S. **3** Result, consequence, issue, effect; अप्रियस्यापि पथ्यस्य परिणामः सुखावहः H. 2. 135. Mk. 3. 1; परिणामसुखे गरीयसि वचसि औषधे च Ki. 2. 4; Bg. 18. 37, 38. **4** Ripening, maturity, full development; उपैति शस्यं परिणामरम्यतां Ki. 4. 22. फलभरपरिणामश्यामजंबू &c. U. 2. 20; Mâl. 9. 24. **5** End, termination, conclusion, close, decline; दिवसाः परिणामरमणीयाः S. 1. 3, वयः परिणामपांडुरशिरसं K. 10; परिणाममुपैति दिवसः K 254 'the day is drawing to a close'. **6** Old age; परिणामे हि दिलीपवंशजाः R **8**. 11. **7** Lapse (of time.). **8** (In Rhet.) A figure of speech allied to रूपक, by which the properties of any object are transferred to that with which it is compared. (The Chandrâloka thus defines and illustrates it:—परिणामः क्रियार्थश्चेद्विषयी विषयात्मना । प्रसन्नेन दृगब्जेन वीक्षते मदिरेक्षणा 5. 18; see R. G. also under परिणाम). COMP. **-दर्शिन्** *a.* prudent, foresighted. **-दृष्टि** *a.* prudent. (**-ष्टिः** *f.*) prudence, providence. **-पथ्य** *a.* salutary in the end. **शूलं** violent or painful indigestion, colic, flatulence with pain.

परि(री)णायः **1** Moving a piece at chess, draughts &c **2** A move (at chess).

परिणायकः **1** A leader. **2** A husband; *Si.* 9. 73.

परी(री)णाहः **1** Circumference, compass, expanse, extent, breadth, width; स्तनयुगपरिणाहाच्छादिना वल्कलेन *S.* 1. 19; स्तनपरिणाहविलासवैजयंती Mâl. 3. 15. large or expansive breasts; ककुदे वृषस्य कृतबाहुमकृशपरिणामशालिनि Ki. 12. 20; Mk. 3. 9; Ratn. 2. 13; Mv. 7. 24. **2** Periphery or circumference of a circle.

परिणाहवत् *a.* Large, big, expansive.

परिणाहिन् *a.* Large, big; Ku. **1**. 26.

परिणिंसक *a.* Tasting, eating: पलानां परिणिंसकः Bk. 9. 106. **2** Kissing.

परिणिष्ठा Perfect skill.

परिणीत *p. p.* Married. **-ता** A married woman.

परिणेतृ *m.* A husband; *S.* 5. 17; R. 1. 25, 14. 26; Ku. 7. 31.

परितर्पणं Gratifying, satisfying.

परितस् *ind.* (Usually with a noun in the acc., sometimes by itself). **1** All around, on all sides, round about, in all directions, everywhere, on every side; रक्षांसि वेदिं परितो निरास्थत् Bk. 1. 12; *Si.* 5. 26, 9. 36; Ki **1** 14; गाहितमखिलं गहनं परितो दृष्टाश्च विटपिनः सर्वे Bv. 1. 21, 29. **2** Towards, in the direction of; आपिंदिंडिंबरपथं परितः पतंगाः Bv. 1. 17; R. 9. 66.

परितापः **1** Extreme or scorching heat; (पादपः) शमयति परितापं छायया संश्रितानां *S.* 5. 7; गुरुपरितापानि गात्राणि 3. 18; Rs. 1. 22. **2** Pain, agony, anguish, grief; प्रसक्ते निर्वाणे हृदय परितापं वहसि किं M. **3**. 1. **3** Lamentation, wailing; विरचितविविधविलापं सा परितापं चकारोच्चैः Gît. 7. **4** Trembling, fear.

परितुष्ट *p. p.* **1** Completely satisfied; वयमिह परितुष्टा वल्कलैस्त्वं च लक्ष्म्या Bh. 3. 50; स मनसि च परितुष्टे कोऽर्थवान् को दरिद्रः *ibid.* **2** Pleased, delighted.

परितुष्टिः *f.* **1** Contentment, complete satisfaction. **2** Delight, joy.

परितोषः **1** Contentment, absence of desire (opp. लोभ); सम इह परितोषो निर्विशेषो विशेषः Bh. 3. 50; **2** Complete satisfaction, gratification; आपरितोषाद्विदुषां न साधु मन्ये प्रयोगविज्ञानं *S.* **1. 2. 3.** Pleasure, delight, delight in, liking for (with loc.); Ku. 6. 59; R. 11. 92; गुणिनि परितोषः &c.

परितोषण *a.* Satisfying, gratifying. **—णं** Satisfaction.

परित्यक्त *p. p.* **1** Left, quitted, abandoned. **2** Deprived or bereft of (with instr.). **3** Let go, discharged (as an arrow). **4** Wanting.

परित्यागः **1** Leaving, quitting, abandonment, desertion, repudiation (as of a wife &c.); अपरित्यागमयाचदात्मनः R. 8. 12; कृतसीतापरित्यागः 15 1. **2** Giving up, renouncing, discarding, renunciation, abdication &c.; स्वनामपरित्यागं करोमि Pt. 1 'I shall forego my name'; Ms. 2. 25. **3** Neglect, omission; मोहात्तस्य (कर्मण) परित्यागस्तामसः परिकीर्तितः Bg. 18. 7. **4** Giving away, liberality. **5** Loss, privation.

परित्राणं Preservation, protection, rescue, defence, deliverance; परित्राणाय साधूनां विनाशाय च दुष्कृतां Bg. 4. 8; रामापरित्राणविहस्तयोधं सेनानिवेशं तुमुलं चकार R. 5. 49.

परित्रासः Terror, fright, fear.

परिदंशित *a.* Covered with mail, armed cap-a- pie (completely or from head to foot).

परिदानं **1** Barter, exchange. **2** Devotion. **3** Restitution or restoration of a deposit.

परिदायिन् *m.* A father who gives his daughter in marriage to a man whose elder brother is not yet married: cf. परिवेत्तृ.

परि (री) दाहः **1** Burning. **2** Anguish, pain, sorrow.

परिदेवः Wailing, lamentation.

परिदेवनं,-ना, परिदेवितं 1 Lamentation, complaint, bewailing; अथ तैः परिदेविताक्षरैः Ku. 4. 25. R. 14. 83; Bg. 2. 28; तत्र का परिदेवना Y. 3. 9; H. 4. 71. 2 Repentance, regret.

परिदेवन *a.* Sorrowful, sad, miserable.

परिद्रष्टृ *m.* A spectator, looker on.

परिधर्षणं 1 An assault, attack, outrage. 2 Insult, affront, abuse. 3 Ill-treatment, rough usage.

परि (री) धानं 1 Putting on a garment, dressing. 2 A garment, especially an under-garment, clothes in general; आत्तचित्रपरिधानविभूषाः Ki. 9. 1; *Si.* 1. 51, 61; 4. 61.

परिधानीयं An under-garment.

परिधायः 1 Train, retinue, attendants collectively. 2 A receptacle, a reservoir. 3 The posteriors.

परिधिः 1 A wall, fence, hedge, anything surrounding or enclosing another. 2 A misty halo round the sun or moon; परिधिर्मुक्त इवोष्णदीधितिः R. 8. 30; शशिपरिधिरिवोच्चैर्मंडलस्तेन तेने N. 2. 108. 3 A circle of light, 4 The horizon. 5 The circumference or compass in general. 6 The circumference of a circle. 7 The periphery of a wheel. 8 A stick (of a sacred tree like पलाश) laid round the sacrificial fire; सप्तास्यासन् परिधयः त्रिःसप्त समिधः कृताः Rv. 10. 90. 15.–COMP. –पतिखेचरः an epithet of *Siva*.-स्थः 1 a guard. 2 an officer attendant on a king or general (modern 'aide-de camp').

परिधूपित *a.* Richly perfumed or scented.

परिधूसर *a.* Quite grey; वसने परिधूसरे वसाना *S.* 7. 21; R. 11. 60.

परिधेयं An under-garment,

परिध्वंसः 1 Distress, disaster, ruin, trouble. 2 Failure. Destruction. 4 Loss of caste.

परिध्वंसिन् *a.* 1 Falling off. 2 Ruining, destroying; H. 2. 134,

परिनिर्वाण *a.* Completely extinguished.—**णं** Final extinction (of the individual).

परिनिर्वृत्तिः *f.* Final liberation or complete emancipation of the soul from the body and exemption from future transmigration.

परिनिष्ठा 1 Complete knowledge or acquaintance (of anything). 2 Complete accomplishment. 3 Extreme limit.

परिनिष्ठित *p. p.* 1 Completely skilled in. 2 Not well fixed; अपरिनिष्ठितस्योपदेशस्यान्याय्यं प्रकाशनं M. 1.

परिपक्व *p. p.* 1 Completely cooked. 2 Completely baked or burnt. 3 Quite ripe, mature, perfected (fig. also); प्रफुल्ललोध्रः परिपक्वशालिः Rs. 4. 1; so परिपक्वबुद्धिः 4 Highly cultivated, very sharp or shrewd. 5 Fully digested. 6 Decaying; on the point of decay or death.

परिपणं (नं) Capital, principal, stock.

परिपणनं Plighting, promising; Mu. 1.

परिपणित *p. p.* Plighted, pledged, promised; *Si.* 7. 9.

परिपंथकः An antagonist, adversary, foe.

परिपंथिन् *a.* Standing in the way, obstructing, opposing, hindering (said by Pâṇini to be admissible only in the Veda, but cf. the quotations given below) अर्थपरिपंथी महानरातिः Mu. 5; नाभविष्यमहं तत्र यदि तत्परिपंथिनी Mâl. 9 50; so Bv. 1. 62; Bg. 3. 34; Ms. 7. 108, 110.–*m.* An enemy; antagonist, opponent, a foe. 2 A robber, thief, highwayman.

परि (री) पाकः 1 Being completely cooked or dressed. 2 Digestion, as in अन्नपरिपाक. 3 Ripening, maturing, development, perfection; *Si.* 4. 48; Ku. 6 10. 4 Fruit, result, consequence; प्रपन्नानां मूर्तः सुकृतपरिपाको जनिमतां Mv. 7. 31; Bh. 2. Bh. 2. 132, 3. 135. 5 Cleverness, shrewdness, skilfulness.

परिपाटल *a.* Pale red; R. 19. 10; *Si.* 13. 42.

परिपाटिः-टी *f.* 1 Method, manner, course; पाटीर तव पटीयान्कः परिपाटीमिमामुरीकर्तुं Bv. 1. 12; कदंबानां वांटी रसिकपरिपाटीं स्फुटयति H. D. 24. 2 Arrangement, order, succession.

परिपाठः Complete enumeration, detail.

परिपार्श्व *a.* Near, at the side, close or hard by.

परिपालनं 1 Protecting, defending, maintaining, keeping, sustaining; क्लिश्नाति लब्धपरिपालनवृत्तिरेव *S.* 5. 6. 2 Nourishment, nurture; जातस्य परिपालनं Ms. 9. 27.

परिपिष्टकं Lead.

परिपीडनं 1 Squeezing, pressing out. 2 Injurying, hurting, doing harm.

परिपुटनं 1 Removing off. 2 Losing the bark or skin.

परिपूजनं, परिपूजा Honouring, worshipping, adoring.

परिपूत *p. p.* 1 Purified, quite pure; उत्पत्तिपरिपूतायाः किमस्याः पावनांतरैः U. 1. 13; *Si.* 2. 16. 2 Completely winnowed or threshed, freed from chaff.

परिपूरणं 1 Filling; *Si* 4. 61. 2 Perfecting, making complete.

परिपूर्ण *p. p.* 1 Quite full; ०इंदुः the full moon; entire, complete, completely filled. 2 Self satisfied, content.

परिपूर्तिः *f.* Completion, fulness.

परिपृच्छा Question.

परिपेलव *a.* Very delicate or fine, excessively tender.

परिपोटः,-पोटकः A particular disease of the ear (in medicine) (by which the ear loses its skin).

परिपोषणं 1 Feeding, nourishing. 2 Furthering, promoting.

परिप्रश्नः Inquiry, interrogation, question; कतरकतमौ जातिपरिप्रश्ने P. II. 1. 63; III. 3. 110, तद्विद्धि प्रणिपातेन परिप्रश्नेन सेवया Bg. 4. 34.

परिप्राप्तिः *f.* Acquisition, obtaining.

परिप्रेष्यः A servant.

परिप्लव *a.* 1 Floating. 2 Shaking, trembling, oscillating, undulating, tremulous. 3 Unsteady, restless; *Si.* 14. 68. –**वः** 1 Inundation. 2 Immersing, wetting. 3 A boat. 4 Oppression, tyranny.

परिप्लुत *p. p.* 1 Flooded, inundated. 2 Overwhelmed; as in शोक°. 3 Wetted, bathed. –**तं** A spring, jump. —**ता** Spirituous liquor.

परिप्लुष्ट *p. p.* Burnt, scorched, singed.

परिब (व) र्हः 1 Retinue, train, attendants; इयं प्रचुरपरिबर्हया भवत्या संवर्ध्यतां Dk. 108. 2 Furniture; परिबर्हवंति वेश्मानि R. 14. 15 'rooms properly furnished or provided with suitable furniture'. 3 Royal insignia. 4 Property, wealth.

परिब (व) र्हणं Retinue, train. 2 Attire, trim. 3 Growth. 4 Worship.

परिबाधा 1 Trouble, pain, annoyance. 2 Fatigue, hardship.

परिबृं (वृं) हणं 1 Prosperity, welfare. 2 Appendix, supplement.

परिबृं (वृं) हित *p. p.* 1 Increased, augmented. 2 Thriven, grown prosperous. 3 Accompanied by, furnished with. –**तं** The roar of an elephant.

परिभंगः Shattering, breaking to pieces.

परिभर्त्सनं Threatening, menacing.

परि (री) भवः 1 Insult, injury, humiliation, disrespect, degradation, disgrace; पराक्रमः परिभवे वैयात्यं सुरतेष्विव (भूषणं) *Si.* 2. 44; R. 12. 37; Ve. 1. 25; Mv. 1. 40, 3. 17. 2 Defeat, discomfiture. –COMP. –**आस्पदं, -पदं** 1 an object of contempt; H. 3. 51. 2 a disgrace or disgraceful situation. –**विधिः** humiliation; प्रायो मूर्खः परिभवविधौ नाभिमानं तनोति *S.* Til. 16.

परिभाविन *a.* (**नी** *f.*) 1 Humiliating, treating with disrespect or contempt. 2 Suffering disrespect.

परिभावः See परिभव.

परिभाविन् *a.* (**नी** *f.*) Humiliating, despising, treating with contempt; *S.* 4 2 Putting to shame, surpassing. excelling. 3 Setting at naught, defying; वैद्ययत्नपरिभाविनं गदं R. 19. 53 'defying medical remedies.'

परिभाषणं 1 Speaking, discourse, talking, chatting, gossiping. 2 Expression of censure, admonition, reproof, abuse. 3 Rule, precept.

परिभाषा: 1 Speech, discourse. 2 Censure, reproof, blame, abuse. 3 Terminology, technical phraseology, technical terms (used in a work); इति परिभाषाप्रकरणं Sk.; इको गुणवृद्धीत्यादिका परिभाषा Mbh. 4 (Hence) Any general rule, precept, or definition which is applicable throughout (अनियमनिवारको न्यायविशेषः); परितः प्रमिताक्षरापि सर्वं विषयं प्राप्तवती गता प्रतिष्ठां। न खलु प्रतिहन्यते कदाचित् परिभाषेव गरीयसी यदाज्ञा Si. 16. 80. 5 A list of abbreviations or signs used in any work. 6 (In gram.) An explanatory Sûtra mixed up with the other Sûtras of Pâṇini, which teaches the method of applying them.

परिभुक्त *p. p.* 1 Eaten, used. 2 Enjoyed. 3 Possessed.

परिभुग्न *a.* Bowed, curved, bent.

परिभूतिः *f.* Contempt, insult, disrespect, humiliation; Mu 4. 11.

परिभूषणः (*Scil* संधि) Peace obtained by cession of the whole revenue of a land.

परिभोगः 1 Enjoyment; R. 4. 45. 2 Especially sexual enjoyment; R. 11. 52, 19. 21, 28, 30. 3 Illegal use of another's goods.

परिभ्रंशः 1 Escape. 2 Falling from.

परिभ्रमः 1 Wandering, going about. 2 Rambling discourse, circumlocution, periphrasis. 3 Error, delusion.

परिभ्रमणं 1 Going about, roaming, wandering. 2 Revolving, turning round. 3 Circumference.

परिभ्रष्ट *p. p.* 1 Fallen or dropped off. 2 Escaped, 3 Cast down, degraded. 4 Deprived of, devoid of (with abl. or instr.). 5 Neglecting.

परिमंडल *a.* Globular, round, circular. –लं 1 A globe, sphere. 2 A ball. 3 A circle.

परिमंथर *a.* Extremely slow; Si. 9. 78.

परिमंद *a.* 1 Very dull or dim, quite faint; परिमंदसूर्यनयनो दिवसः Si. 9. 3. 2 Very slow. 3 Very tired or weak; Si. 9. 39. 4 Very little; Si. 9. 27.

परिमरः Destruction; चिरात्क्षत्रस्यास्तु प्रलयरव घोरः परिमरः Mv. 3. 41.

परिमर्दः, परिमर्दनं 1 Rubbing, grinding. 2 Crushing, trampling. 3 Destruction. 4 Hurting, injuring. 5 Embracing, pressing.

परिमर्षः 1 Envy, dislike. 2 Anger.

परिमलः 1 Fragrance, perfume, scent; परिमलो गीर्वाणचेतोहरः Bv 1. 63, 66, 70, 71; Me. 25. 2 Pounding or trituration of fragrant substances. 3 A fragrant substance. 4 Copulation; अथ परिमलजामवाप्य लक्ष्मीं Ki. 10. 1. 5 A meeting of learned men. 6 A stain, spot.

परिमलित *a.* Perfumed. 2 Soiled, despoiled of beauty.

परि (री) माणं 1 Measuring, measure (of strength, power &c.); सद्यः परात्मपरिमाणविवेकमूढः Mu. 1. 10; Ku. 2. 8; Ms. 8. 133. 2 Weight, number, value; Y. 2. 62; 1. 319.

परिमार्गः, परिमार्गणं 1 Searching or looking for, seeking out, tracing, tracking. 2 Touch, contact; Si. 7. 75. 3 Cleaning, wiping off.

परिमार्जनं 1 Cleaning, wiping off. 2 A dish of honey and oil.

परिमित *p. p.* 1 Moderate, sparing. 2 Limited. 3 Measured, meted out. 4 Regulated, adjusted. –COMP. –आभरण *a.* wearing a few ornaments, moderately adorned –आयुस् *a.* short-lived. –आहार, –भोजन *a.* abstemious, eating little food. –कथ *a.* saying or speaking little, using measured words; Me. 83.

परिमितिः *f.* 1 Measure, quantity. 2 Limitation.

परिमिलनं 1 Touch, contact; Ratn. 2. 12. 2 Combination, union.

परिमुखं *ind.* About the face, round or about (a person).

परिमुग्ध *a.* 1 Artlessly lovely, lovely yet simple. 2 Fascinating but foolish

परिमृदित *p. p.* 1 Trodden or trampled down, crushed, roughly handled; परिमृदितमृणालीम्लानमंगं Mâl. 1. 22; U. 1. 24. 2 Embraced, clasped. 3 Rubbed, ground.

परिमृष्ट *p. p.* 1 Washed, cleaned, purified. 2 Rubbed, touched, stroked. Ve. 3. 3 Embraced. 4 Spread, pervaded, filled with; Ki. 6. 23.

परिमेय *a.* 1 Few, limited; परिमेयपुरःसरौ R 1. 37. 2 Measureable, calculable. 3 Finite.

परिमोक्षः 1 Removing, relieving; प्रायो विषाणपरिमोक्षलघूतमांगान्खड्गांश्चकार नृपतिर्निशितैः क्षुरप्रैः R. 9. 62. removing the horns *i. e.* breaking them down. 2 Liberation, setting free, deliverance. 3 Emptying, evacuation. 4 Escape. 5 Final beatitude (निर्वाण).

परिमोक्षणं Liberation, deliverance. 2 Untying.

परिमोषः Stealing, robbing, theft.

परिमोषिन् *m.* A theif, robber.

परिमोहनं 1 Beguiling, alluring, enticing, facinating. 2 Bewildering, infatuating.

परिम्लान *p. p.* 1 Faded, fainted, withered; Ku. 2. 2. 2 Languid, faint. 3 Waned, impaired, diminished. 4 Soiled, stained.

परिरक्षकः A protector, guardian.

परिरक्षणं, परिरक्षा 1 Protection, preservation, guarding; Ms. 5. 94, 7. 2. 2 Keeping, maintaining, adhering to; न समयपरिरक्षणं क्षमं ते Ki. 1. 45. 3 Deliverance, rescuing.

परिरथ्या A street, road.

परि (री) रंभः, परिरंभणं Embracing, an embrace; द्रुतपरिरंभनिपीडनक्षमत्वं Si. 1. 74, 10. 52; U. 1. 24, 27; किं पुरेव ससंभ्रमं परिरंभणं न ददासि Gît. 3.

परिराटिन् *a.* Crying aloud, screaming.

परिलघु *a.* 1 Very light (lit.) (as clothes &c.). 2 Very light or easy to digest; क्षीणः क्षीणः परिलघु पयः स्रोतसां चोपभुज्य Me. 13. 3 Very small; U. 4. 21.

परिलुप्त *p. p.* 1 Interrupted, disturbed, diminished. 2 Lost, disappeared.

परिलेखः 1 An outline, a delineation, sketch. 2 A picture.

परिलोपः 1 Injury. 2 Neglect, omission.

परिवत्सरः A year, a full year, the revolution of one year; देव्या शून्यस्य जगतो द्वादशः परिवत्सरः U. 3. 33.

परिवर्जनं 1 Leaving, quitting, abandoning. 2 Giving up, resigning. 3 Killing, slaughter.

परि (री) वर्तः 1 Revolving, revolution (as of planet). 2 A period, lapse or expiration of time; युगशतपरिवर्तान् S. 7. 34. 3 The expiration of a Yuga; Si. 17. 12. 4 Repetition, recurrence. 5 Change, alteration; तदीदृशो जीवलोकस्य परिवर्तः U. 3. 'changed condition of life', 'change in circumstances'; so जीवलोकपरिवर्तमनुभवामि Mâl. 7; स्वरपरिवर्तः Mk. 1. 6 Retreat, flight, desertion. 7 A year 8 Repeated birth, transmigration. 9 Barter, exchange; Si. 5. 39. 10 Requital, return. 11 An abode. 12 A chapter or section of a work. 13 N. of the Kúrma or second incarnation of Vishṇu.

परिवर्तक *a.* 1 Causing to turn round or revolve. 2 Requiting, exchanging.

परिवर्तनं 1 Moving to and fro, turning about, relling about (as on the lap, bed &c.), Ku. 5. 12; R. 9. 13; Si. 4. 47. 2 Turning round, revolving, whirling round. 3 Revolution, end of a period of time. 4 Change; वेषपरिवर्तनं विधाय Pt. 3. 5 Exchange, barter. 6 Inverting.

परिवर्तिका Phimosis or contraction of the prepuce (in medicine).

परिवर्तिन् *a.* 1 Moving or turning round, revolving. 2 Ever-recurring, coming round again and again; परिवर्तिनि संसारे मृतः को वा न जायते Pt. 1. 27. 3 Changing. 4 Being or remaining near, moving round about. 5 Retreating, flying. 6 Exchanging. 7 Recompensing, requiting.

परिवर्धनं 1 Increasing, enlarging. 2 Rearing, breeding. 3 Growing, growth.

परिवसथः A village.

परिवहः N. of one of the seven courses of wind; it is the sixth course, and bears along the *Saptarshis* and the celestial Ganges; सप्तर्षिचक्रं स्वर्गंगां षष्ठः परिवहस्तथा; for the other courses of wind see under वायु; cf. the description of परिवह given by Kâlidâsa:—त्रिस्रोतसं वहति यो गगनप्रतिष्ठां ज्योतींषि वर्तयति च प्रविभक्तरश्मिः। तस्य द्वितीयहरिविक्रमनिस्तमस्कं वायोरिमं परिवहस्य वदंति मार्गं S. 7. 6.

परि (री) वादः 1 Blame, censure, detraction, abuse; अयमेव मयि प्रथमं परिवादरतः M. 1; Y. 1. 133. 2 Scandal, stain, stigma, illrepute; मा भूत्परीवादनवावतारः R. 5. 24; 14. 86; Mv. 5. 28. 3 Charge, accusation; Mk. 3. 30. 4 An instrument with which the lute is played.

परिवादकः 1 A plaintiff, complainant, accuser. 2 One who plays on the lute.

परिवादिन् *a.* 1 Reviling, censuring, abusing, slandering. 2 Accusing. 3 Screaming, crying aloud. 4 Censured, slandered. *–m.* An accuser, plaintiff, complainant. **–नी** A lute (वीणा) of seven strings; Si. 6. 9; R. 8. 35.

परि (रीं) वापः 1 Shaving, shearing. 2 Sowing. 3 A reservoir, pool, pond, a piece of water. 4 Furniture. 5 Train, retinue.

परिवापित *a.* Shaven, shorn.

परि (री) वारः 1 Train, retinue, attendants or followers collectively; (यानं) अध्यास्य कन्या परिवारशोभि R. 6. 10; 12. 16; ग्रहगणपरिवारो राजमार्गप्रदीपः Mk. 1. 57. 2 A cover, covering. 3 A sheath, scabbard.

परिवासः Residence, stay, sojourn.

परि (री) वाहः 1 Over-flowing, (of a tank &c.), inundation, overflow natural or artificial; प्रथमं (कौतूहलं) सपरिवाहमासीत् S. 2. 2 A water-course, drain or channel to carry off excess of water; पूरोत्पीडे तडागस्य परीवाहः प्रतिक्रिया U. 3. 29; Pt. 2. 105; Si. 16. 51; R. 8. 74.

परिवाहिन् *a.* Overflowing; as in आनंदपरिवाहिणा चक्षुषा S. 4.

परिविण्णः (न्नः), परिवित्तः, परिवित्तिः An unmarried elder brother whose younger brother is married; see Ms. 3. 171; and परिवेत्तृ also.

परिविद्धः An epithet of Kubera.

परिविंदकः, परिविंदत् *m.* A younger brother married before the elder.

परिविहारः Walking about, strolling, walking for pleasure.

परिविह्वल *a.* Extremely confused, agitated or bewildered.

परिवारणं 1 A cover, an envelope. 2 A train, retinue. 3 Keeping or warding off.

परिवारित् *p. p.* 1 Encircled, encompassed, surrounded, encompassed. 2 Pervaded, overspread; Si. 3. 34; Ki. 5. 42. **–तं** The bow of Brahmâ.

परिवृढः A master, lord, owner, head, chief (used adjectively also); किं भुवः परिवृढा न विवोढुं तत्र तामुपनता विवदंते N 5. 42; Ku. 12. 58; Mv. 6. 25, 31, 48.

परिवृत *p. p.* 1 Surrounded, encompassed, encircled, attended. 2 Hidden, concealed. 3 Pervaded, overspread. 4 Known.

परिवृत्त *p. p.* 1 Revolved, turned round; °अर्धमुखी V. 1. 17. 2 Retreated, turned back. 3 Exchanged, bartered. 4 Finished, ended. **–त्तं** An embrace.

परिवृत्तिः *f.* 1 Revolution; Si. 10. 91. 2 Return, turning back. 3 Barter, exchange. 4 End, termination. 5 Surrounding. 6 Staying or dwelling in a place. 7 (In Rhet) A figure of speech in which there is an exchange of a thing for what is equal, less or greater; परिवृत्तिर्विनिमयो योऽर्थानां स्यात्समासमैः K. P. 10; *e. g.* दत्वा कटाक्षमेणाक्षी जग्राह हृदयं मम। मया तु हृदयं दत्वा गृहीतो मदनज्वरः॥ S. D. 734. 8 Substitution of one word for another without affecting the sense; as in शब्दपरिवृत्तिसहत्वं K. P. 10; *e. g.* in वृषध्वज, ध्वज may be substituted by लाञ्छन or वाहन.

परिवृद्धिः *f.* Growth, increase.

परिवेत्तृ *m.*, **परिवेदकः** A younger brother married before the elder; R. 12. 16; ज्येष्ठे अनिर्विष्टे कनीयान् निर्विशन् परिवेत्ता भवति, परिविण्णो ज्येष्ठः, परिवेदनीया कन्या, परिदायी दाता, परिकर्ता याजकः, सर्वे ते पतिताः Hârîta.

परिवेदनं 1 The marriage of a younger brother before the elder 2 Marriage in general. 3 Complete or accurate knowledge. 4 Gain, acquisition 5 Maintaining the household fire; (अग्न्याधान); Ms. 11. 60. 6 Pervasion on all sides, universal pervasion or existence. **–ना** 1 Shrewdness, wit. 2 Prudence, foresight.

परिवेदनीया, परिवेदिनी The wife of a younger brother who is married before the elders.

परि (री) वेशः (षः) 1 Waiting at meals, distributing food, serving up meals. 2 A circle, circlet, halo (of lustre &c.); R. 5. 74, 6. 13; Si. 5. 52, 17. 9. 3 Especially, the halo round the sun or moon; लक्ष्यते स्म तदनंतरं रविर्बद्धभीमपरिवेषमंडलः R. 11. 59. 4 The circumference of a circle. 5 The disc of the sun or moon. 6 Any thing which surrounds or protects.

परिवेषकः A waiter at meals.

परिवेषणं 1 Serving up meals, waiting, distributing food. 2 Enclosing, surrounding. 3 A halo round the sun or moon. 4 Circumference.

परिवेष्टनं 1 Surrounding, enclosing. 2 Circumference. 3 A cover, covering.

परिवेष्टृ *m.* A waiter at meals, one who serves up meals; मरुतः परिवेष्टारो मरुत्तस्यावसन्गृहे Ait. Br.

परिव्ययः 1 Cost. 2 Condiment spices.

परिव्याधः A species of reed.

परिव्रज्या 1 Strolling, wandering from place to place. 2 Turning a recluse, leading the life of a religious mendicant or recluse. 3 Renunciation of the word, ascetic devotion, religious austerity.

परिव्राज् *m.*, **परिव्राजः–जकः** A wandering mendicant, vagrant, recluse, an ascetic (of the fourth religious order) who has renounced the word.

परिशाश्वत *a.* (**ती** *f.*) Perpetually the same.

परिशिष्ट *a.* Left, remaining.**—ष्टं** A supplement, an appendix; as in गृह्यपरिशिष्ट.

परिशीलनं 1 Touch, contact (lit.); ललितलवंगलतापरिशीलनकोमलमलयसमीरे Gît. 1; so वदनकमलपरिशीलनमिलित &c. 11. 2 Constant contact, intercourse or correspondence. 3 Study, application or attachment (to a thing), steady or fixed pursuit; काव्यार्थ° S. D.

परिशुद्धिः *f* 1 Complete purification, अग्नि° U. 4. 2 Justification, acquittal.

परिशुष्क *p. p.* 1 Thoroughly dried, completely dried or parched up; तृषा महत्या परिशुष्कतालवः Rs. 1. 11. 2 Withered, shriveled; hollow (as cheeks).**—ष्कं** A kind of fried meat.

परिशून्य 1 Quite empty; R. 8. 66. 2 Quite free from, completely devoid of; 19. 6.

परिशृतः Ardent spirits.

परि (री) शेषः 1 Remainder, remnant. 2 Supplement. 3 Termination, conclusion, completion.

परिशोधः, परिशोधनं 1 Purifying, cleansing. 3 Quittance, discharging or paying off (a debt or obligation).

परिशोषः Act of being completely dry or parched up.

परिश्रमः 1 Fatigue, exhaustion, trouble, pain; आत्मा परिश्रमस्य पदमुपनीतः

S. 1; R. 1. 58; 11. 12. 2 Exertion, labour. (Hence). 3 Close application to or study of, being constantly occupied with; आर्ये कृतपरिश्रमोस्मि चतुःषष्ट्यंगे ज्योतिःशास्त्रे Mu. 1.

परिश्रमः 1 A meeting, an assembly. 2 Refuge, asylum.

परिश्रयः 1 A meeting, an assembly. 2 Refuge, asylum.

परिश्रांतिः *f.* 1 Fatigue, weariness, trouble, exhaustion. 2 Labour, exertion.

परिश्लेषः An embrace.

परिषद् *f.* 1 An assembly, a meeting, council, audience; अभिरूपभूयिष्ठा परिषदियं *S.* 1. 2 A religious assembly or synod.

परिषदः, परिषद्यः A member of an assembly.

परिषेकः परिषेचनं Sprinkling or pouring over, moistening.

परिष्कण्ण (स्न) *a.* Fostered by another. **–ण्णः** A foster-child, one nourished by a stranger.

परिष्कं (स्कं) *a.* Fostered by another. **–दः** 1 A foster-child. 2 A servant.

परिष्करः Decoration, ornamentation.

परिष्कारः 1 Decoration, ornament, embellishment. 2 Dressing, cooking. 3 Initiation, purification by initiatory rites. 4 Furniture. (also **परिस्कार** in this sense).

परिष्कृत *p. p.* 1 Adorned, decorated; Ki. 7. 40. 2 Cooked, dressed. 3 Purified by initiatory ceremonies; (see कृ with परि). (Also परिस्कृत in this sense).

परिष्क्रिया Adorning, decorating, embelishment.

परिष्टो (स्तो) मः 1 The coloured housings of an elephant. 2 A coverlet in general.

परिष्पं (स्पं) दः 1 A train, retinue. 2 Decorating the hairs (with flowers &c.). 3 Ornament or decoration in general. 4 Throbbing, vibration, palpitation, movement. 5 Provision, maintenance. 6 Crushing.

परिष्वक्त *p. p.* Clasped, embraced.

परिष्वंगः 1 An embrace; Ki. 18. 19; H. 3. 67. 2 Touch, contact, union; Bh. 3. 17.

परिसंवत्सर *a.* A whole year old. **–रः** A whole year परिसंवत्सरात् after the expiration of one whole year; Ms. 3. 119.

परिसंख्या 1 Enumeration, computation. 2 Sum, total, number; वित्तस्य विद्यापरिसंख्यया मे R. 5. 21 3 (In Mîm. phil.) Exclusion, specification, limitation to that which is enumerated or expressly mentioned, so that everything else is excluded; (परिसंख्या is opposed to विधि which lays down a rule for the first time, and to नियम which restricts the choice to an alternative which is expressly stated when several such alternatives are possible; विधिरत्यंतमप्राप्तौ नियमः पाक्षिके सति। तत्र चान्यत्र च प्राप्तौ परिसंख्येति गीयते॥ *e. g.* पंच पंचनखा भक्ष्याः usually quoted by Mimâmsakas; अयं नियमविधिर्न तु परिसंख्या Kull. on Ms. 3. 45. 4 (In Rhet.) Special mention or exclusive specification; *i. e.* where with or without a query something is affirmed for the denial, expressed or understood, of something else similar to it; (this figure is particularly striking when it is based on a श्लेष or pun); यस्मिंश्च महीं शासति चित्रकर्मसु वर्णसंकराश्चापेषु गुणच्छेदाः &c. or यस्य नूपुरेषु मुखरता विवाहेषु करग्रहणं तुरंगेषु कशाभिघातः &c. K.; for other examples see S. D. 735.

परिसंख्यात *p. p.* 1 Enumerated, reckoned up. 2 Specified exclusively.

परिसंख्यानं 1 Enumeration, total, number. 3 Exclusive specification. 4 Correct judgment, proper estimate.

परिसंचरः Time of universal destruction.

परिसमापन, परिसमाप्तिः *f.* Finishing, completing.

परिसमूहनं 1 Heaping up. 2 Sprinkling water (in a particular way) round the sacrificial fire (अग्नेः समंतात् मार्जनं).

परिसरः 1 Verge, border, proximity, vicinity, neighbourhood, environs (of a river, mountain, town &c.); गोदावरीपारिसरस्य गिरेस्तटानि U. 3. 8; परिसरविषयेषु लीढमुक्ताः Ki 5. 38 2 Position, site. 3 Width, breadth. 4 Death. 5 A rule, precept.

परिसरणं Running about.

परिसर्पः 1 Going or moving about. 2 Going in search of, following, pursuing. 3 Surrounding, encirling.

परिसर्पणं 1 Walking or creeping about. 2 Running to and fro, flying about, constantly moving; पतगपतेः परिसर्पणे च तुल्यः Mk. 3. 21.

परि (री) सर्या, परि (री) सारः Wandering or moving about, perambulation.

परिस्तरणं 1 Strewing or spreading round, scattering about. 2 A covering, cover.

परिस्फुट *a.* 1 Quite plain, manifest, distinctly visible. 2 Fully developed, blown or grown.

परिस्फुरणं 1 Quivering, shooting. 2 Budding.

परिस्यंदः 1 Oozing, trickling, dropping. 2 A flow, stream. 3 A train &c.; see परिष्यंद.

परिस्रवः 1 Flowing, streaming. 2 Gliding down. 3 A river, torrent.

परिस्रावः Effluxion, efflux.

परिस्रुत् *f.* 1 kind of intoxicating liquor. 2 Trickling, dropping, flowing.

परिस्रुता A kind of intoxicating liquor. 2 Trickling, dropping, flowing.

परिहत *a.* Loosened.

परिहरणं 1 Leaving, quitting, abandoning. 2 Avoiding, shunning. 3 Refuting. 4 Seizing, taking away.

परि (री) हारः 1 Leaving, quitting, giving up, abandoning. 2 Removing, taking away; as in विरोधपरिहार. 4 Refuting, repelling. 5 Omitting to mention, omission, leaving out. 6 Reserve, concealment. 7 A tract of common land round a village or town; धनुःशतं परीहारो ग्रामस्य स्यात्समंततः Ms. 8. 237. 8 A special grant, immunity, privilege, exemption from taxes; Ms. 7. 201. 9 Contempt, disrespect. 10 An objection.

परिहाणिः (नि) *f.* 1 Decrease, deficincy, loss. 2 Decay, decline; R. 19. 50.

परिहार्य *a.* To be shunned or avoided, to be escaped from, to be taken off or away. **–र्यः** A bracelet.

परि (री) हासः 1 Joking, jesting, mirth; merriment; त्वराप्रस्तावोयं न खलु परिहासस्य विषयः Mâl. 6. 44. परिहासपूर्वं jokingly or in jest R. 6. 82; परिहासविजल्पितं *S.* 2. 18 uttered in jest; परीहासाश्चित्राः सततमभवन् येन भवतः Ve. 3. 14; Ku. 7. 19; R. 9. 8; *Si.* 10. 12- 2 Ridiculing, deriding. –Comp. **–वेदिन्** *m.* a buffoon, jester, a witty person.

परिहृत *p. p.* 1 Shunned, avoided. 2 Left, abandoned. 3 Refuted, repelled (as a charge, objection &c.). 4 Taken, seized; see हृ with परि.

परीक्षकः An examiner, investigator, a judge.

परीक्षणं Putting to test, testing, examining; Ms. 1. 117; Y. 2. 177.

परीक्षा 1 Examination, test, trial; पत्तने विद्यमानेपि ग्रामे रत्नपरीक्षा M. 1; Ms. 9. 19. 2 Trial by various kinds of ordeals (in law)

परीक्षित् *m.* N. of a king, son of Abhimanyu and grandson of Arjuna. He succeeded to the throne of Hastinâpura after Yudhishthira. He died of a snake-bite. The Kali age is said to have commenced with his reign.

परीक्षितं *p. p.* Examined, tried, परीक्षितं काव्यसुवर्णमेतत् Vikr. 1. 24.

परीत *p. p.* 1 Surrounded, encompassed. 2 Expired, elapsed. 3 Departed, gone forth. 4 Seized, taken possession of, filled with; कोपपरीतमानसं Ki. 2. 25; Mu. 3. 30.

परीताप, परीपाक, परीवार-ह, परीहास &c. see परिताप &c.

परीप्सा 1 Desire of obtaining. 2 Haste, hurry.

परीरं A fruit.

परीरणं 1 A tortoise. 2 A stick. 3 A garment (पट्टशाटक).

परीष्टिः *f.* 1 Research, inquiry, investigation. 2 Service, attendance. 3 Respect, worship, homage.

परुः 1 A joint, knot. 2 A limp, member. 3 The occasion. 4 Heaven, paradise. 5 A mountain.

परुत् *ind.* Last year.

परुद्वारः A horse.

परुष *a.* 1 Hard, rough, rugged, stiff (opp. मृदु or श्लक्ष्ण); परुषं चर्म, परुषा माला &c. 2 Harsh, abusive, severe, unkind, cruel, stern (as word); (वाक्) अपरुषा परुषाक्षरमीरिता R. 9. 8; Pt. 1. 50; said also of a person; Git. 9; Y. 1. 309. 3 Harsh or disagreeble to the ear (as a sound &c.); तेन वज्रपरुषस्वनं धनुः R. 11. 46; Me. 4 Rough, coarse, rough to the touch, shaggy (as hair); शुद्धस्नानात्परुषमलकं Me. 19. 5 Sharp, violent, strong, keen, piercing (wind &c.), परुषपवनवेगोत्क्षिप्तसंशुष्कपर्णः Rs. 1. 22; 2. 28. 6 Gross. 7 Dirty. **-षं** A harsh or abusive speech, abuse. -Comp. **-इतर** *a.* other than rough, soft, mild; R. 5. 68. **-उक्तिः, -वचनं** abusive or harsh language.

परुत् *n.* 1 A joint knot. 2 A limb or member of the body.

परेत *p. p.* Deceased, departed, dead. **-तः** A spirit, a ghost. -Comp. **-भर्तृ, -राज्** *m.* the god of death, Yama; Si. 1. 57. **-भूमिः** *f.*, **-वासः** a cemetery; Ku. 5. 68.

परेद्यवि, परेद्युस् *ind.* The other day.

परेष्टुः *f.*, **परेष्टुका** A cow that has often calved.

परोक्ष *a.* 1 Out of or beyond the range of sight, invisible, escaping observation, Absent; स्थाने वृता भूपतिभिः परोक्षैः R. 7. 13. 3 Secret, unknown, stronger; परोक्षमन्मथो जनः *S*. 2. 18 'a stranger to the influence of love'; H. Pr. 10. **-क्षः** An ascetic. **-क्षं** 1 Absence, invisibility. 2 (In gram.) Past time or tense (not witnessed by the speaker); परोक्षे लिट् P. III. 2. 115. *Note* The acc. and loc. singulars of **परोक्ष** (*i. e.* **परोक्षं, परोक्षे**) are used adverbially in the sense of 'in one's absence', 'out of sight', 'behind one's back,' with or witout a gen.; परोक्षे खलीकर्तुं शक्यते न ममाग्रतः M. 2; परोक्षे कार्यहंतारं प्रत्यक्षे प्रियवादिनं Chāṇ. 18; नोदाहरेदस्य नाम परोक्षमपि केवलं Ms. 2. 119. -Comp. **-भोगः** enjoyment of anything in the absence of the owner **-वृत्ति** *a.* living out of sight. (**-त्तिः** *f.*) an unseen or obscure life.

परोष्टिः, परोष्णी A cock-roach.

पर्जन्यः 1 A rain-cloud, thundering cloud, a cloud in general; प्रवृद्ध इव पर्जन्यः सारंगैरभिनंदितः R. 17. 15; यंतु नद्यो वर्षंतु पर्जन्याः Tait. *S*.; Mk. 10. 60. 2 Rain; अन्नाद्भवंति भूतानि पर्जन्यादन्नसंभवः Bg. 3. 14. 3 The god of rain, *i. e.* Indra.

पर्ण् 10. U. (पर्णयति-ते) To make green or verdant; वसंतः पर्णयति चंपकं.

पर्णं 1 A pinion, wing; as in सुपर्ण. 2 The feather of an arrow. 3 A leaf. 4 The betel-leaf. **-र्णः** The Palāsa tree. -Comp. **-अशनं** feeding on leaves. (**-नः**) a cloud. **-असिः** a kind of basil. **-आहार** *a.* feeding upon leaves. **-उटजं** a hut of leaves, a hermit's hut, a hermitage. **-कारः** a vendor of betel-leaves. **-टिका, -कुटी** a hut made of leaves. **-कृच्छ्रः** a kind of expiatory penance which consists in living upon an infusion of leaves and Kus'a grass only for five days; see. Y. 3. 317 and Mit. thereon. **-खंडः** a tree without apparent blosoms. (**-डं**) a collection of leaves. **-चीरपटः** an epithet of Siva. **-चोरकः** a kind of perfume. **-नरः** the figure of a man made of leaves and burnt in place of a lost corpse. **-मेदिनी** the Priyangu creeper. **-भोजनः** a goat. **-मुच्** *m.* the winter season (शिशिर). **-मृगः** any wild animal living in the boughs of trees. &c. **-रुह्** *m.* the spring season (वसंत) **-लता** the betel-plant. **-वीटिका** pieces of areca-nut mixed with other spices and rolled up in betelleaves. **-शय्या** a bed or couch of leaves. **-शाला** a hut made of leaves, a hermitage; निर्दिष्टां कुलपतिना स पर्णशालामध्यास्य R. 1. 95; 12. 40.

पर्णल *a.* Full of or abounding in leaves, leafy; Bk. 6. 143.

पर्णसिः 1 A house standing in the midst of water, a summerhouse. 2 A lotus. 3 A vegetable. 4 Decoration, toilet, adorning.

पर्णिन् *m.* A tree.

पर्णिल *a* See पर्णल.

पर्द् 1 A. (पर्दते) To break wind.

पर्दः 1 A quantity of hair, thick hair. 2 A fart, breaking wind.

पर्पः 1 Young grass. 2 A seat for criples (पंगुपीठं), a wheelcarriage in which cripples are moved about; येन पीठेन पंगवश्चरंति स पर्पः Sk. on P. IV. 4. 10. 3 A house.

पर्परीकः 1 The sun. 2 Fire. 3 A reservoir, tank.

पर्यक् *ind.* Round about, in every direction.

पर्यंकः 1 A bed, couch, sofa. 2 A cloth girt round the back, loins, and knees (by a person) when sitting on his hams; cf. अवसक्थिका. 3 A particular kind of posture practised by ascetics in meditation, sitting on the hams; it is the same as वीरासन which is thus defined by Vasistha:—एकं पादमथैकस्मिन् विन्यस्योरौ तु संस्थितं । इतरस्मिंस्तथैवोरुं वीरासनमुदाहृतं ॥ ; पर्यंकग्रंथिबंध &c. Mk. 1. 1.-Comp.**-बंधः** sitting on the hams, the posture called पर्यंक; पर्यंकबंधस्थिरपूर्वकायं Ku. 3. 45, 59.**-भोगिन्** *m.* a kind of serpent.

पर्यटनं, पर्यटितं Wandering or roaming about, travelling over.

पर्यनुयोगः An inquiry with the object of contradicting or refuting a statement (दूषणार्थं जिज्ञासा Halāy.); एतेनास्यपि पर्यनुयोगस्यानवकाशः Dāy. B.

पर्यंत *a.* Bounded by, extending as far as; समुद्रपर्यंता पृथ्वी the ocean-bounded earth. **—तः** 1 Circuit, circumference. 2 Skirt, edge, border, extremity, boundary; उटजपर्यंतचारिणी *S*. 4; पर्यंतवनं R. 13. 38; Rs. 3, 3. 3 Side, flank; Ratn 2. 3; R. 18. 43. 4 End, conclusion, termination; Pt. 1. 125.-Comp. **देशः, -भूः, -भूमिः** an adjoining district or region. **-पर्वतः** an adjoining hill.

पर्यंतिका Loss of good qualities, depravity, moral turpitude.

पर्ययः 1 Revolution, lapse, expiration; कालपर्ययात् Y. 3. 217; Ms. 1. 30; 11. 27. 2 Waste or loss (of time). 3 Change, alteration. 4 Inversion; confusion, irregularity. 5 Deviation from customary observances; neglect of duty. 6 Opposition.

पर्ययणं 1 Walking round, circumambulation. 2 A horse's saddle.

पर्यवदात *a.* Perfectly pure or clean.

पर्यवरोधः Obstruction, hinderance.

पर्यवसानं 1 End, termination, conclusion. 2 Determination, ascertainment.

पर्यवसित *p. p.* 1 Finished, ended, completed. 2 Perished, lost. 3 Determind.

पर्यवस्था, पर्यवस्थानं 1 Opposition, resistance, obstruction. 2 Contradiction.

पर्यश्रु *a.* Bathed in or suffused with tears, shedding tears, tearful; पर्यश्रुणी मंगलभंगभीरुर्न लोचने मीलयितुं विषेहे Ki. 3. 36; पयश्रुरस्वजत मूर्धनि चोपजघ्रौ R. 13. 70.

पर्यसनं 1 Casting, throwing about. 2 Sending forth, throwing. 3 Sending away. 4 Putting off or away.

पर्यस्त *p. p.* 1 Thrown round, scattered over or about; पर्यस्तो धनंजयस्योपरि शिलीमुखासारः Ve. 4; *Si*. 10. 91. 2 Surrounded, encompassed. 2 Upset, overturned. 4 Dismissed, laid aside. 5 Struck, hurt; killed.

पर्यस्तिः *f.*, **पर्यस्तिका** Sitting upon the hams; see पर्यंक 3.

पर्याकुल *a.* 1 Turbid, foul (as water). 2 Confused, confounded, frightened; *S.* 1. 3 Disordered, dishevelled; *S.* 1. 30. 4 Excited, agitated, bewildered; पर्याकुलोस्मि *S.* 6; Rs. 6. 22. 5 Full of, filled with; स्नेह°, क्रोध° &c.

पर्याणं A saddled; दत्तपर्याणं K. 126 saddled.

पर्याप्त *p. p.* 1 Obtained, got, gained. 2 Finshed, completed, 3 Full, whole, entire, complete, all; पर्याप्तचंद्रेव शरत्त्रियामा Ku. 7. 26; R. 6. 44. 4 Able, competent, adequate; R. 10. 55. 5 Enough, sufficient; R. 15. 18, 17. 17; Ms. 11. 7. –**तं** *ind.* 1 Willingly, readily. 2 To one's satisfaction, enough, sufficiently; पर्याप्तमाचामति U. 4. 1 drinks his fill. 3 Fully, adequately, ably, competently.

पर्याप्तिः *f.* 1 Obtaining, acquisition. 2 End, conclusion, close. 3 Enough, fulness, sufficiency. 4 Satiety. satisfaction. 5 Preserving, guarding, warding off a blow, 6 Fitness, competency.

पर्यायः 1 Going or winding round, revolution. 2 Lapse, course, expition (of time). 3 Regular recurrence or repetition. 4 Turn, succession, due or regular order; पर्यायसेवामुत्सृज्य Ku. 2. 36; Ms. 4. 87; Mu. 3. 27. 5 Method, arrangement. 6 Manner, way, method of proceeding. 7 A synonym, convertible term; पर्यायो निधनस्यायं निधनत्वं शरीरिणां Pt. 2. 99. पर्वतस्य पर्याया इमे &c. 8 An opportunity, occasion. 9 Creation, formation, preparation, manufacture. 10 Property, quality. 11 (In Rher.) A figure of speech; see K. P. 10; Chandr. 5. 108, 109; S. D. 733. (Note **पर्यायेण** is often used adverbially in the sense of 1 in turn or succession, by rotation, by regular gradation; 2 occasionally, now and then पर्यायेण हि दृश्यंते स्वप्नाः कामं शुभाशुभाः Ve. 2. 13. Comp.–**उक्तं** a figure of speech in Rhetoric; it is a circumlocutory or periphrastic way of speaking, when the fact to be intimated is expressed by a turn of speech or periphrasis *e. g* see Chandr. 5. 66 or S. D. 703. –**च्युत** *a.* supplanted, superseded. –**वचनं**, –**शब्दः** a synonym. –**शयनं** alternate sleeping and watching.

पर्याली *ind.* A particle expressing 'harm or injury' (हिंसन) used with कृ, भू or. अस्; पर्यालीकृत्य=हिंसित्वा.

पर्यालोचनं –**ना** 1 Circumspection, attentive observation, deliberation, mature reflection. 2 Knowing, recognition.

पर्यावर्तः, **पर्यावर्तनं** Coming back, return.

पर्याविल *a.* Very muddy or turbid, much soiled; R. 7. 40.

पर्यासः 1 End, conclusion, termination. 2 Rotation, revolution. 3 Inverted order or position.

पर्याहारः 1 A yoke worn across the shoulders in carrying a load. 2 Conveying. 3 A load or burden. 4 A pitcher. 5 Storing grain.

पर्युक्षणं Sprinkling round water silently and without uttering any ritual formulæ or Mantras.

पर्युत्थानं Standing up.

पर्युत्सुक *a.* Sorrowful, sorry, regretting, sad; °त्वं sorrow; R. 5. 67. 2 Eagerly desirous, anxious, anxiously longing for; स्मर पर्युत्सुक एष माधवः Ku. 4. 28; V. 2. 16.

पर्युदञ्चनं 1 Debt. 2 Raising up, drawing out (उद्धार).

पर्युदस्त *p. p.* 1 Excluded, excepted. 2 Prohibited, objected (as a ceremony).

पर्युदासः An exception, a prohibitive rule or precept.

पर्युपस्थानं Serving, waiting upon, attendance.

पर्युपासनं 1 Worship, honour, service. 2 Friendliness, courtesy. 3 Sitting round.

पर्युप्तिः *f.* Sowing.

पर्युषणं Worship, adoration, service.

पर्युषित *a.* Stale, not fresh; cf. अपर्युषित. 2 Insipid. 3 Stupid. 4 Vain.

पर्येषणं –**णा** 1 Investigation by reasoning. 2 Search, inquiry in general. 3 Homage, worship.

पर्येष्टिः *f.* Search, inquiry.

पर्वकं The knee-joint.

पर्वणी 1 The full-moon day or the day of new moon. 2 A festival 3 A particular disease of the juncture or संधि of the eye (in medicine).

पर्वतः 1 A mountain, hill; परगुणपरमाणून्पर्वतीकृत्य नित्यं Bh. 2. 78; न पर्वताग्रे नलिनी प्ररोहति. 2 A rock. 3 An artificial mountain or heap. 4 The number seven. 5 A tree.–Comp. –**अरिः** an epithet of Indra. –**आत्मजः** an epithet of the mountain Mainâka. –**आत्मजा** an epithet of Pârvatî. –**आधारा** the earth. –**आशयः** a cloud. –**आश्रयः** a fabulous animal called Sarabha q. v. –**काकः** a raven. –**जा** a river. –**पतिः** an epithet of the Himâlaya mountain. –**मोचा** a kind of plantain. –**राज्** *m.*, –**राजः** 1 a large mountain. 2 'the lord of mountains', the Himâlaya mountain. –**स्थ** *a.* situated on a hill or mountain.

पर्वन् *n.* 1 A knot, joint (sometimes changed to पर्व at the end of Bah. comp.; as in कर्कशाङ्गुलिपर्वया R. 12. 41). 2 A limb, member. 3 A portion, part, division. 4 A book, section (as of the Mahâbhârata). 5 The step of a staircase; R. 16. 46. 6 A period, fixed time. 7 Particularly, the days of the four changes of the moon; *i. e.* the eighth and fourteenth day of each half month, and the days of the full and new moon. 8 A sacrifice performed on the occasion of a change of the moon. 9 The day of new or full moon, the day of opposition or conjunction; अपर्वणि ग्रहकलुषेंदुमंडला विभावरी कथय कथं भविष्यति M. 4. 15; R. 7. 33; Ms. 4. 150; Bh. 2. 34. 10 An eclipse of the sun or moon. 11 A festival, holiday, an occasion of joy. 12 An opportunity or occasion in general. –Comp. –**कालः** 1 a periodic change of the moon. 2 the time at which the moon at its conjunction or opposition passes through the node. –**कारिन्** *m.* a Brâhmana who from motives of gain performs on common days ceremonies which ought to be performed on periodical occasions, such as अमावास्या. &c. –**गामिन्** *m.* one who has sexual intercourse with his wife on particular times or occasions when such intercourse is prohibited by the *S*âstras. –**धिः** the moon. –**योनिः** a cane or reed. –**रुहू** *m.* a pomegranate tree. –**संधिः** the junction of the fifteenth and first of a lunar fortnight, the full and change of the moon, or the exact moment of the full and change of the moon.

पर्शुः 1 An axe, a hatchet; cf. परशु. 2 A weapon in general. –Comp. –**पाणिः** 1 an epithet of Gaṇesa. 2 of Parasurâma.

पर्शुका A rib.

पर्श्वधः See परश्वध.

पर्षद् *f.* 1 An assembly, meeting, conclave. 2 Particularly, a religious synod or assembly; Y. 1. 9.

पलः Straw, husk. –**लं** 1 Flesh, meat. 2 A particular weight equal to four *karshas.* 3 A particular measure of fluids. 4 A particular measure of time. –Comp. –**अग्निः** bile. –**अंगः** a tortoise. –**अदः**, –**अशनः** a demon. Râkshasa. –**क्षारः** blood. –**गंडः** plasterer, mason. –**प्रियः** 1 a demon. 2 a raven. –**भा** the equinoctial shadow at mid-day.

पलंकट *a* Timid, bashful.

पलंकरः Bile.

पलंकषः 1 A demon, goblin, an evil spirit. –**लं** 1 Flesh. 2 Mire, mud. 3 A sweetmeat made of ground sesamum and sugar. –Comp. –**ज्वरः** gall, bile. –**प्रियः** 1 a ravan. 2 a demon.

पलवः A kind of net or basket for catching fish.

पलांडु *m. n.* An onion; Ms. 5. 5; Y. 1. 176.

पलापः 1 The temples of an elephant. 2 A halter, rope.

पलायनं Running away, retreat, flight, escape; Bg. 18, 43; R. 19. 31.

पलायित *p. p.* Fled, retreated, run away, escaped.

पलालः -लं Straw, husk; N. 8. 2. -COMP. **-दोहदः** the mango tree.

पलालिः A heap of flesh.

पलाशः N. of a tree, also called किंशुक; नवपलाशपलाशवनं पुरः Si. 6. 2. **-शं** 1 The flower or blossom of this tree; बालेंदुवक्राण्यविकाशभावाद्बभुः पलाशान्यतिलोहितानि Ku. 3. 29. 2 A leaf or petal in general; चलत्पलाशांतरगोचरास्तरोः Si. 1. 21, 6. 2. 3 The green colour.

पलाशिन् *m.* A tree.

पलिक्नि 1 An old, grey-haired woman. 2 A cow for the first time with calf (बालगर्भिणी).

पलिघः 1 A glass-vessel, pitcher. 2 A wall or rampart. 3 An iron club; cf. परिघ. 4 A cow-pen (गोगृह).

पलित *a.* Grey, hoary, grey-haired, old, aged; तातस्य मे पलितमौलिनिरस्तकाशे (शिरसि) Ve. 3. 19. **-तं** 1 Grey hair, hair, or the greyness of hair brought on by old age; कैकेयीशंकयेवाह पलितच्छद्मना जरा R. 12. 2; Ms. 6. 2. 2 Much or ornamented hair.

पलितंकरण *a.* Rendering grey.

पलितंभविष्णु *a.* Becoming grey.

पल्यंकः A bed; see पर्यंक.

पल्ययनं 1 A saddle. 2 A rein, bridle.

पल्लः A large granary.

पल्लवः -वं 1 A sprout, sprig, twig; करपल्लवः; लतेव संनद्धमनोज्ञपल्लवा R. 3. 7. 2 A bud, blossom. 3 Expansion, spreading, dilating. 4 The red dye called Alakta, q. v. 5 Strength, power. 6 The blade of grass. 7 A bracelet, an armlet. 8 Love, amorous sport. 9 Unsteadiness (चापलं). **-वः** A libertine. -COMP. **-अंकुरः, आधारः** a branch. **-अस्त्रः** an epithet of the god of love. **-द्रुः** the Asoka tree.

पल्लवकः 1 A libertine. 2 A catamite. 3 The paramour of a harlot. 4 The Asoka tree. 5 A kind of fish. 6 A sprout.

पल्लविकः 1 A libertine, a gallant. 2 A catamite.

पल्लवित *a.* 1 sprouting, having young shoots or sprouts. 2 Spread, extended; अलं पल्लवितेन 'enough of further amplification or expatiation.' 3 Dyed red with lac. **-तः** Lac-dye.

पल्लविन् *a.* (**-नी** *f.*) Having young shoots or leaves; Ku. 3. 54. *-m.* A tree.

पल्लिः -ल्ली *f.* 1 A small village, 2 A hut. 3 A house, station. 4 A city or town (at the end of names of towns; as त्रिशिरपल्लि). 5 A house-lizard.

पल्लिका 1 A small village, station. 2 A house-lizard.

पल्वलं A small pool or pond, a puddle, tank (अल्पं सरः); स पल्वलजलेऽधुना...कथं वर्ततां Bv. 1. 3; R. 2. 17; 3. 3. -COMP. **-आवासः** a tortoise. **-पंकः** the mud of a pool.

पवः 1 Wind. 2 Purification. 3 Winnowing corn. **-वं** Cow-dung.

पवनः Air, wind; सर्पाः पिबंति पवनं न च दुर्बलास्ते Subhâsh.; पवनपदवी, पवनसुतः &c. **-नं** 1 Purification. 2 Winowing. 3 A sieve, a strainer. 4 Water. 5 A potter's kiln (*m.* also). **-नी** A broom. COMP. **-अशनः, -भुज्** *m.* a serpent. **-आत्मजः** 1 an epithet of Hanumat. 2 of of Bhîma. 3 fire. **-आशः** a serpent, a snake. **नाशः** 1 an epithet of Garuḍa 2 a peacock. **तनयः -सुतः** 1 an epithet of Hanumat. 2 of Bhima. **-व्याधिः** 1 an epithet of Uddhava, a friend and counsellor of Krishṇa. 2 Rheumatism.

पवमानः 1 Air, wind; पवमानः पृथिवीरुहानिव R. 8. 9. 2 One of the sacred fires, considered to be the same as गार्हपत्य q. v.

पवाका A whirl-wind, a hurricane.

पविः The thunderbolt of Indra.

पवित *a.* Purified, cleansed. **-तं** Black pepper.

पवित्र *a.* 1 Sacred, holy, sinless, sanctified (persons or things); श्रीणि श्राद्धे पवित्राणि दौहित्रः कुतपस्तिलाः Ms. 3. 236; पवित्रो नरः, पवित्रं स्थानं &c. 2 Pure, cleansed. 3 Purified by the performance of ceremonial acts (such as sacrifices &c.). 4 Purifying, removing sin. **-त्रं** 1 An instrument for cleansing or purifying, such as a sieve or strainer &c. 2 Two blades of Kusa grass used at sacrifices in purifying and sprinkling ghee. 3 A ring of Kusa grass worn on the fourth finger on certain religious occasions. 4 The sacred thread worn by members of the first three castes of the Hindus. 5 Copper. 6 Rain. 7 Water. 8 Rubbing, cleansing 2 A vessel in which the *arghya* is presented. 10 Clarified butter. 11 Honey. -COMP. **-आरोपणं, आरोहणं** investiture with the sacred thread. **-पाणि** *a.* holding *darbha* grass in the hand. **-धान्यं** barley.

पवित्रकं A net or rope made of hemp or pack-thread.

पशव्य *a.* 1 Fit or suitable for cattle; Y. 1. 321. 2 Relating to cattle, or to a herd or drove. 3 Possessed of cattle. 4 Brutish.

पशुः 1 Cattle (both singly and collectively); Ms. 9. 327, 331. 2 An animal in general. 3 A sacrificial animal, such as a goat. 4 A brute, a beast; often added to words meaning 'man' to show contempt; पुरुषपशोश्च पशोश्च को विशेषः H. 1; cf. नृपशु, नरपशु. &c. 5 N. of a subordinate deity and one of Siva's followers. -COMP. **अवदानं** a sacrifice of animals. **-क्रिया** 1 the act of animal-sacrifice. 2 copulation. **-गायत्री** a Mantra whispered into the ear of an animal which is about to be sacrificed; it is a parody of the celebrated Gâyatrî q. v.; पशुपाशाय विद्महे शिरश्छेदाय (विश्वकर्मणे) धीमही। तन्नो जीवः प्रचोदयात्. **-घातः** slaughter of animals for sacrifice. **-चर्या** copulation. **-धर्मः** 1 the nature or characteristics of cattle. 2 treatment of cattle. 3 promiscuous cohabitation; Ms. 9. 66. 4 the marrying of widows. **-नाथः** an epithet of Siva. **-पः** a herdsman. **-पतिः** 1 an epithet of Siva; Me. 36, 56; Ku. 6. 95. 2 a herdsman, owner of cattle. 3 N. of a philosophy who taught the philosophical doctrines called पाशुपत; see Sarva. S. *ad. loc.* **-पालः, -पालकः** a herdsman. **-पालनं, -रक्षणं** the tending, or rearing of cattle. **-पाशकः** a kind of coitus or mode of sexual enjoyment. **-प्रेरणं** the driving of cattle. **-मारं** *ind.* according to the manner of slaughtering animals; इष्टिपशुमारं मारितः S. 6. **-यज्ञः, -यागः, -द्रव्यं** an animal sacrifice. **-रज्जुः** *f.* a cord for tethering cattle. **राजः** a lion.

पश्चात् *ind.* (Used by itself or with gen. or abl.) 1 From behind, from the back; पश्चाद्बद्धपुरुषमादाय S. 6; पश्चादुच्चैर्भवति हरिणः स्वांगमायच्छमानः S. 4. v. 1. 2 Behind, backwards, towards the back (opp. पुरः) गच्छति पुरः शरीरं धावति पश्चादसंस्तुतं चेतः S. 34; 3. 9. 3 After (in (time or space), then, afterwards, subsequently; लघ्वी पुरा वृद्धिमती च पश्चात् Bh. 2. 60; तस्य पश्चात् after him; R. 4. 30, 12. 7, 17, 39; 16. 29; Me. 36, 44. 4 At last, lastly, finally. 5 From the west. 6 Towards the west, westward. -COMP. **-कृत** *a.* left behind, surpassed, thrown into the background; पश्चात्कृताः स्निग्धजनाशिशोपि Ku. 7. 28; R. 17. 18. **-तापः** repentance, contrition; °पं कृ to repent.

पश्चार्धः 1 The hinder part or side (of the body); पश्चार्धेन प्रविष्टः शरपतनभयाद्भूयसा पूर्वकायं S. 1. 7. 2 Last (in time or space); पश्चिमे वयसि वर्तमानस्य K. 25; R. 19. 1. 56; पश्चिमायामिनीयामात्प्रसादमिव चेतना R. 17. 1; स्मरंतः पश्चिमामाज्ञा

17. 8 ; पत पश्चिमयोः पितुः पाद्योः Mu. 7. 3 Western, westerly; Ms. 2. 22; 5. 92. (पश्चिमेन is used adverbially in the sense of 'in the west;' or 'after, behind'; with acc. or gen.; so पश्चिमे in the west). –COMP. –अर्धः 1 the latter half. 2 the hinder part of the night ; उपारताः पश्चिमरात्रगोचरात् Ki. 4. 10 v. l.

पश्चिमा the west. –COMP. –उत्तरा the north-west.

पश्यत् *a*. (न्ती *f.*) Seeing, perceiving, beholding, looking at, observing &c.

पश्यतोहरः A thief, robber, highwayman (one who steals before a person's eyes, or in the very sight of the possessor ; as for instance a goldsmith.)

पश्यंती 1 A harlot, courtezan. 2 A particular sound.

पस्त्यं A house, habitation, abode ; पस्त्यं प्रयातुमथ तं प्रभुरापपृच्छे Kir. K. 9. 74.

पस्पशः 1 N. of the first *A*hnika of the first chapter of Patanjali's Mahabhashya ; शब्दविद्येव नो भाति राजनीतिरपस्पशा *Si*. 2. 112 (where अपस्पशा also means 'without 'spies'). 2 (fig.) An introductory chapter in general (उपोद्घात).

पह्ल (ह्न) वाः, पह्लिकाः (*m. pl.*) N. of a people ; (the Persians ?).

पा I. 1. P. (पिबति, पीत ; pass. पीयते) 1 To drink, quaff ; पिब स्तन्यं पोत Bv. 1. 60 ; दुःशासनस्य रुधिरं न पिबाम्युरस्तः Ve. 1. 15; R. 3. 54 ; Ku. 3. 36; Bk. 14. 92 ; 15. 6. 2 To kiss ; पिबत्यसौ पाययते च सिंधुः R. 13. 9 ; *S*. 1. 24, 3 To drink in, inhale ; R. 7. 63. 4 To drink in (with the eyes or ears), feast on, look at or listen to intently ; विवातपद्मस्तिमितेन चक्षुषा नृपस्य कांतं पिबतः सुताननं R 3. 17; 2. 19, 73; 11. 36; 13. 30; Me. 16; Ku. 7. 64. 5 To absorb, drink or swallow up; (बाणैः) आयुर्देहातिगैः पीतं रुधिरं तु पतत्रिभिः R. 12. 48. –*Caus*. (पाययति-ते) 1 To cause to drink, give to drink; R. 13. 9; Bk. 8. 41, 62. 2 To water. —*Desid*. (पिपासति) To wish to drink &c. हलाहलं खलु पिपासति कौतुकेन Bv. 1. 95. –WITH अनु to drink after, follow (one in drinking; अनुपास्यसि बाष्पदूषितं परलोकोपनतं जलांजलिं R. 8. 68. –आ 1 to drink; R. 14. 22. 2 to drink up, absorb, soak up: आपीतसूर्यं नभः Mk. 5. 20; उपैति सविता ह्यस्तं रसमापीय पार्थिवं Mb. 3 to feast on (with the eyes or ears); ता राघवं दृष्टिभिरापिबंत्यः R. 7. 12. –नि 1 to drink, kiss; अत एव निपीयतेऽधरः Pt. 1. 189; दंतच्छदं प्रियतमेन निपीतसारं Rs. 4. 13. 2 to feast on (with the eyes or ears). –परि to drink; उपनिषदः परिपीताः Bv. 2. 40. –II. 2 P. (पाति, पात) 1 To protect, guard, keep, defend, preserve; (oft. with abl.); पर्याप्तोसि प्रजाः पांतु R. 10. 25; पांतु R. 10. 25; पांतु त्वां......भूतेशस्य भुजंगवल्लिवलयस्रङ्नद्धजूटाजटाः Mâl. 1. 2; जीवन् पुरः शश्वदुपप्लवेभ्यः प्रजाः प्रजानाथ पितेव पासि R. 2. 48. 2 To rule, govern; पांतु पृथ्वीं......भूपाः Mk. 10. 60. –*Caus*. (पालयति-ते) 1 To protect, guard, keep, preserve; कथं सुहृः स्वयं धर्मे प्रजास्त्वं पालयिष्यसि Bk. 6. 132; Ms. 9. 108; R. 9. 2. 2 To rule, govern; तां पुरीं पालयामास Râm. 3 To observe, keep, adhere to, fulfil (as a vow or promise); पालितसंगराय R. 13. 65. 4 To bring up, nourish, maintain. 5 To wait for; अत्रोपविश्य मुहूर्तमार्यः पालयतु कृष्णागमनं Ve. 1. –WITH अनु to protect, guard &c.; Ms. 8. 27. –परि 1 to protect, preserve, guard, defend against; Y. 1. 334; Ms. 9 251. 2 to rule, govern; Mâl. 10. 25. 3 to bring up, nourish, support. 4 to keep to, observe, adhere to, persevere in; अंगीकृतं सुकृतिनः परिपालयंति Ch. P. 50. 5 to wait for, await; अथ मदनवधूरुपप्लवांतं व्यसनकृशा परिपालयांबभूव Ku. 4. 46. –प्रति 1 to protect, preserve. 2 to wait for, await. 3 to act up to, obey.

पा *a*. (At the end of comp.) 1 Drinking, quaffing; as in सोमपाः अग्रेपाः &c. 2 Protecting, guarding, keeping; गोपा.

पांस (श) न *a*. (ना or नी *f.*) (Usually at the end of comp.) 1 Disgracing, dishonouring, defiling; पौलस्त्यकुलपांसन Mv. 5. 2 Vitiating, spoiling. 3 Wicked, contemptible. 4 Infamous.

पांस (श) व *a*. Consisting of dust.

पांसुः (शुः) 1 Dust, dirt; crumbling soil; R. 2. 2; Rs. 1. 13; Y. 1. 150. 2 A particle of dust.. 3 Dung, manure. 4 A kind of camphor. –COMP. –कासीसं sulphate of iron. –कुली a highroad, highway. –कूलं 1 a dustheap. 2 a legal document not made out in any particular person's name (निरुपपदशासनं). –कृत *a*. covered with dust. –क्षारं-जं a kind of salt –चत्वरं hail. –चंदनः an epithet of *S*iva. –चामरः 1 a heap of dust. 2 a tent. 3 a bank covered with Dúrva grass. 4 praise. –जालिकः an epithet of Vishṇu. –पटलं a mass or coating of dust. –मर्दनः an excavation for water round the root of a tree, trench or basin.

पांसु (शु) रः 1 A gadfly. 2 A cripple moved about in a wheel-chair.

पांसु (शु) ल *a*. 1 Dusty, covered with dust; Mâl. 2. 4. 2 Polluted, defiled, sullied, stained; दारत्यागी भवाम्याहो परस्त्रीस्पर्शपांसुलः *S*. 5. 28. 3 Defiling, disgracing, dishonouring ; as in कुलपांसुल. –लः 1 A profligate or licentous person, libertine, gallant. 2 An epithet of *S*iva. –ला 1 A menstruous woman. 2 An unchaste or licentious woman ; अ° a chaste woman ; R. 2. 2. 3 The earth.

पाकः 1 Cooking, dressing; baking, boiling. 2 Burning (as bricks), baking ; Ms. 5. 122 Y. 1. 187. 3 Digestion (as of food). 4 Ripeness ; ओषध्यः फलपाकांताः Ms. 1. 46 ; फलमभिमुखपाकं राजजंबूद्रुमस्य V. 4. 13 ; Mâl. 9. 31. 5 Maturity, full or perfect development ; °धी मति°. 6 Completion, accomplishment, fulfilment: पुयोजपाकाभिमुखैर्भृत्यान् विज्ञापनाफलैः R. 17. 40. 7 Result, consequence, fruit, fruition (fig. also); आशीर्भिरेधयामासुः पुरःपाकाभिरंबिकां Ku. 6. 90 ; पाकाभिमुखस्य दैवस्य U. 7. 4 ; 14. 8 Development of the consequences of acts done. 9 Grain, corn ; नीवारपाकादि R. 5. 9 ; (पच्यते इति पाकः धान्यं). 10 Ripeness, suppuration (as of a boil). 11 Greyness of hair caused by old age. 12 A domestic fire. 13 An owl. 14 A child, young one. 15 N. of a demon killed by Indra. –COMP. –अगारः -रं, –आगारः -रं, –शाला, –स्थानं a kitchen. –अतीसारः chronic dysentery. –अभिमुख *a*. 1 ready for ripeness or development. 2 inclined to favour. –जं 1 black salt. 2 flatulence. –पात्रं a cooking utensil –पुटी a potters kiln. –यज्ञः a simple or domestic sacrifice ; (for some varities of it ; see Kull. on Ms. 2. 143). –शुक्ला chalk. –शासनः an epithet of Indra ; Ku. 2. 63. –शासनिः 1 an epithet of Jayanta, son of Indra. 2 of Vâli. 3 of Arjuna.

पाकलः 1 Fire. 2 Wind. 3 A fever to which elephants are subject ; cf. कूटपाकल.

पाकिम *a*. 1 Cooked, dressed. 2 Ripened (naturally or artificially). 3 Got by boiling (as salt).

पाकुः, पाकुकः A cook.

पाक्य *a*. To be cooked, dressed, matured &c. –क्यः Salt-petre.

पाक्ष *a*. (क्षी *f.*) 1 Belonging to a lunar fortnight, fortnightly. 2 Relating to a party.

पाक्षिक *a*. (की *f.*) 1 Belonging to a fortnight, fortnightly. 2 Belonging to a bird. 3 Favouring a party or faction. 4 Belonging to an argument. 5 Optional, subject to an alternative, allowed but not specifically laid down; नियमः पाक्षिके सति. –कः A fowler.

पाखंडः A heretic; पाखंडचंडालयोः पापारंभकयोर्मृगीव वृकयोर्भीर्गता गोचरं Mâl. 5. 24; दुरात्मन् पाखंडचंडाल Mâl. 5.

पागल *a*. Mad, deranged.

पांक्तेय, पांक्त्य *a.* 1 Fit to sit in the same row at a dinner-party. 2 Fit to be associated with.

पाचक *a.* 1 Cooking, baking. 2 Digestive, tonic. **-कः** 1 A cook. 2 Fire. **-कं** Gall, bile. -COMP. **-स्त्री** a female cook.

पाचन *a.* (**नी** *f.*) 1 Cooking. 2 Ripening. 3 Digestive. **-नः** 1 Fire. 2 Sourness, acidity. **-नं** 1 The act of cooking. 2 The act of ripening. 3 A dissolvent, digestive medicine. 4 Causing a wound to close. 5 Penance, expiation (प्रायश्चित्त).

पाचलः 1 A cook. 2 Fire. 3 Wind. **-लं** Cooking, maturing.

पाचा Cooking.

पांचकपाल *a.* (**ली** *f.*) Relating to an oblation offered in five cups (कपाल)

पांचजन्यः N. of the conch of Krishṇa; (दधानो) निध्वानमश्रूयत पांचजन्यः *Si.* 3. 21; Bg. 1. 15. -COMP. **-धरः** an epithet of Krishṇa.

पांचदश *a.* (**शी** *f*) Relating to the fifteenth day of a month.

पांचदश्यं A collection of fifteen.

पांचनद *a.* Prevalent in the पंचनद or Punjab.

पांचभौतिक *a.* (**की** *f.*) Composed of the five elements or containing them; पांचभौतिकी सृष्टिः Mv. 6; Y. 3. 175.

पांचवर्षिक *a.* (**की** *f.*) Five years old.

पांचशाब्दिकं 1 Music of five kinds. 2 Musical instruments in general.

पांचाल *a.* (**ली** *f.*) Belonging to or ruling over the Panchâlas. **-लः** 1 The country of the Panchâlas. 2 A prince of the Panchâlas. **-लाः** (*m. pl.*) The people of the Panchâlas.

पांचालिका A doll, puppet; स्तन्यत्यागात्प्रभृति सुमुखी दंतपांचालिकेव क्रीडायोगं तदनु विनयं प्रापिता वर्धिता च Mâl. 10. 5.

पांचाली 1 A woman or princess of the Panchâlas. 2 N. of Draupadî, the wife of the Pâṇḍavas. 3 A doll, puppet. 4 (In Rhet.) One of the four styles of composition. The S. D. thus defines it:—वर्णैः शेषैः (*i. e.* माधुर्यव्यंजकाजैः प्रकाशकाभ्यां भिन्नैः) पुनर्द्वयोः। समस्तपंचषपदो बंधः पांचालिको मतः॥ 628.

पाट् *ind.* An interjection used in calling.

पाटकः 1 A splitter, divider. 2 Part of a village. 3 The half of a village. 4 A kind of musical instrument. 5 A bank, shore. 6 A flight of steps leading to water. 7 Loss of capital or stock. 8 A long span. 9 Throwing dice.

पाटच्चरः A thief, robber, pilferer; कुसुमरसपाटच्चर S. 6; पद्मिनीपरिमलालिपाटच्चरैः Bv. 2. 75.

पाटनं Splitting, breaking, cleaving, destroying.

पाटल *a.* Pale-red, of a pink or pale-red colour; अग्रे स्त्रीनखपाटलं कुरबकं V. 2. 7; R. 1. 83; 2. 29; 7. 27; पाटलपाणिजांकितमुरः Gît. 12. **-लः** The pale-red or pink colour; कपोलपाटलादेशि बभूव रघुचेष्टितं R. 4. 68. 2 The trumpet flower; पाटलसंसर्गसुरभिवनवाताः *S.* 1. 3. **-लं** 1 The flower of this tree; R. 16. 59; 19. 46. 2 A kind of rice ripening in the rains. 3 Saffron. -COMP. **-उपलः** a ruby. **-द्रुमः** the trumpet flower.

पाटला 1 The red *lodhra.* 2 The trumpet flower (the tree or its blossom). 3 An epithet of Durgá.

पाटलिः *f.* The trumpet flower. -COMP. **-पुत्रं** N. of an ancient city, the capital of Magadha, situated near the confluence of the Soṇa and the Ganges, and identified by some with the modern Pâtnâ. It is also known by the names of पुष्पपुर, कुसुमपुर, see Mu. 2, 3, and 4. 16, and R. 6. 24 also.

पाटलिकः A pupil.

पाटलिमन् *m.* Pale-red colour.

पाटल्या A multitude of Pâṭala flowers.

पाटवं 1 Sharpness, acuteness. 2 Cleverness, skill, dexterity, proficiency; पाटवं संस्कृतोक्तिषु H. 1; Ki. 9. 54. 3 Energy. 4 Quickness, rashness.

पाटविक *a.* (**की** *f.*) 1 Clever, sharp, skilful. 2 Cunning, fraudulent, crafty.

पाटित *p. p.* 1 Torn, cleft, split, broken. 2 Pierced, pricked; R. 11. 31.

पाटी Arithmetic. -COMP. **-गणितं** arithmetic.

पाटीरः 1 Sandal; पाटीर तव पटीयान् कः परिपाटीमिमामुरीकर्तुं Bv. 1. 12. 2 A field. 3 Tin. 4 A cloud. 5 A sieve.

पाठः 1 Reciting, recitation, repeating. 2 Reading, perusal, study. 3 Studying or reciting the Vedas (ब्रम्हयज्ञ), one of the five daily Yajnas or sacrifices to be performed by Brâhmaṇas. 4 The text of a book, a reading, variant; अत्र गंधवद्गंधमादनः इति आगंतुकः पाठः। प्राचीन पाठस्तु सुगंधिर्गंधमादनः इति पुल्लिंगांतः Malli. on Ku. 6. 46. -COMP. **-अंतरं** another reading, a variant (v. l.). **-छेदः** a pause, cæsura. **-दोषः** a false reading. **-निश्चयः** determining the text of a passage. **-मंजरी, -शालिनी** the Sârikâ bird. **-शाला** a school, college, seminary.

पाठकः 1 A teacher, lecturer, preceptor. 2 A public reader of the Purâṇas or other sacred books. 3 A spiritual teacher. 4 A pupile, student, scholar.

पाठनं Teaching, lecturing.

पाठित *p. p.* Taught, instructed.

पाठिन् *a.* 1 One who has read or studied any subject. 2 Knowing or familiar with.

पाठीनः 1 A public reader of the Purâṇas or other mythological books. 2 A kind of fish; विवृत्तपाठीनपराहतं पयः Ki. 4. 5.

पाणः 1 Trade, traffic. 2 A trader. 3 A game. 4 A stake at play. 5 An agreement. 6 Praise. 7 The hand.

पाणिः The hand; दानेन पाणिर्न तु कंकणेन (विभाति) Bh. 2. 71. **-णिः** *f.* A market (**पाणौ कृ** to hold by the hand, marry; **पाणौकरणं** marriage); -COMP. **-गृहीती** 'espoused by the hand', a wife. **--ग्रहः, -ग्रहणं** marrying, marriage; R. 7. 29; 8. 7; Ku. 7. 4. **ग्रहीतृ** *m.*, **ग्राहः** a bridegroom, husband; ध्यायत्यनिष्टं यत्किंचित्पाणिग्राहस्य चेतस Ms. 9. 26; बाल्ये पितुर्वशे तिष्ठेत् पाणिग्राहस्य यौवने 5. 148. **घः** 1 a drummer. 2 a workman, handicraftsman. **-घातः** a blow with the hand. **-जः** a fingernail; तस्याः पाटलपाणिजांकितमुरः Gît. 12. **-तलं** the palm of the hand. **-धर्मः** due form of marriage. **-पीडनं** marriage; पाणिपीडनमहं दमयंत्याः कामयेमहि महीमहिकांशो N. 5. 99; पाणिपीडनविधेरनंतरं Ku. 8. 1. **-प्रणयिनी** a wife. **-बंधः** 'union of the hands', marriage. **-भुज्** *m.* the sacred fig-tree. **-मुक्तं** a missile thrown with the hand. **रुह्** *m.*, **-रुहः** a finger-nail. **-वादः** 1 clapping the hands together. 2 playing on a drum. **-सर्ग्या-या** a rope. **पाणिनिः** N. of a celebrated grammarian who is considered as an inspired *muni*, and is said to have derived the knowledge of this grammar from *Siva.*

पाणिनीय *a.* Relating to or composed by Pâṇini; *Si.* 19. 75. **-यः** A follower of Pâṇini; अकृतव्यूहाः पाणिनीयाः **-यं** The grammer of Pâṇini.

पाणिंधम-य *a.* Blowing through the hands.

पांडर *a.* Whitish, pale white. **-रं** 1 Red chalk. 2 The blossom of the jasmine.

पांडवः A son or descendant of Pandu. N. of any one of the five sons of Pâṇḍu; *i. e.* युधिष्ठिर, भीम, अर्जुन, नकुल, and सहदेव; हंसाः संप्रति पांडवा इव बनादज्ञातचर्यां गताः Mk. 5. 6. -COMP. **-आभीलः** N. of Krishṇa. **-श्रेष्ठः** N. of Yudhishṭhira.

पांडवीय *a.* Belonging to the Pâṇḍavas.

पांडवेय=पांडव q. v.

पांडित्यं 1 Scholarship, profound learning, erudition; तदेव गमकं पांडित्य-

वैदग्ध्ययोः Mâl. 1. 7. 2 Cleverness; skill, dexterity, sharpness; नखानां पांडित्यं प्रकटयतु कस्मिन् मृगपतिः Bv. 1. 2

पांडु *a.* Pale-white, whitish, pale, yellowish; विकलकरणः पांडुच्छायः शुचा परिदुर्बलः U. 3. 22. **-डुः** 1 The pale-white or yellowish-white colour. 2 Jaundice. 3 A white elephant. 4 N. of the father of the Pâṇḍavas. [He was begotten by Vyasa on Ambalikâ, one of the widows of Vichitravirya. He was called Pandu, because he was born pale (पांडु) by reason of his mother having become quite pale with fear when in private with the sage Vyasa; (यस्मात्पांडुत्वमापन्ना विरूपं प्रेक्ष्य मामिह । तस्मादेव सुतस्ते वै पांडुरेव भविष्यति Mb.). He was prevented by a curse from having progeny himself; so he allowed his first wife Kunti to make use of a charm she had acquired from Durvasas for the birth of sons. She gave birth to Yudhishṭhira, Bhima and Arjuna; and Madri, his other wife, by the use of the same charm, gave birth to Nakula and Sahadeva. One day Pandu forgot the curse under which he was labouring, and made bold to embrace Madri, but he fell immediately dead in her arms.]. -COMP. **-आमयः** jaundice. **-कंबलः** 1 a white blanket. 2 a warm upper garment. 3 the housings of a royal elephant. **-पुत्रः** a son of Pâṇḍu, any one of the five Pâṇḍavas. **-मृत्तिका** white or pale soil. **-रागः** whiteness, pallor. **-रोगः** jaundice. **-लेखः** a sketch made with chalk; a rough draft or sketch made on the ground, board &c. पांडुलेखेन फलके भूमौ वा प्रथमे लिखेत् । न्यूनाधिकं तु संशोध्य पश्चात्पत्रे निवेशयत् ॥ Vyâsa. **-शर्मिला** an epithet of Draupadî. **-सोपाकः** N. of a mixed tribe; चांडालात्पांडुसोपाकस्त्वक्सारव्यवहारवान् Ms. 10. 37.

पांडुर *a.* Whitish, pale-white, yellowish-white, pale; छविः पांडुरा S. 3. 10; R. 14. 26. Ku. 3. 33. **-रं** The white leprosy, -COMP. **-इक्षुः** a species of sugar-cane.

पांडुरिमन् *m.* Paleness, white or pale colour.

पांड्याः (*m. pl.*) N. of a country and its inhabitants; तस्यामेव रघोः पांड्याः प्रतापं न विषेहिरे R. 4. 49. **-ड्यः** A king of that country; R. 6. 60.

पात *a.* Protected, guarded, preserved. **-तः** 1 Flying, fight. 2 Alighting, descending, descent. 3 Falling down, fall, downfall (fig. also); द्रुम°, गृह°; चरणपातः falling down at the feet; R; 11. 92; पातोत्पातौ rise and fall. 4 Destruction, dissolution, ruin; Ku. 3. 44. 5 A blow, stroke; as in खड्गपातः 6 Shedding, discharging, emitting; असृक्पातः Ms. 8. 44. 7 A cast, throw, shot: दृष्टि° R. 13. 18. 8 An attack, inroad. 9 Happening, coming to pass; occurrence. 10 Failing, defect. 11 An epithet of Râhu.

पातकः -कं Sin, crime; (Hindu law-givers enumerate five geat sins: —ब्रह्महत्या सुरापानं स्तेयं गुर्वंगनागमः । महांति पातकान्याहुः संसर्गश्चापि तैस्सह ॥ Ms. 11. 54).

पातंगिः 1 An epithet of Saturn. 2 Of Yama. 3 Of Karṇa; 4 of Sugrîva.

पातंजल *a.* (**ली** *f.*) Composed by Patanjali; पातंजले महाभाष्ये कृतभूरिपरिश्रमः Paribhâshenduśekhara. **-लं** The Yoga system of philosophy taught by Patanjali. (It is generally believed that Patanjali, the author of the Mahâbhâshya, is the same as the auther of the Yoga system; but it is a dubious point).

पातनं 1 Causing to fall, felling, bringing or throwing down, knocking down. 2 Throwing, casting. 3 Humbling, lowering. 4 Romoving. *N. B.* पातनं may have different meanings according to the noun with which it is used; *e. g.* दंडस्य पातनं 'causing the rod to fall,' chastising; गर्भस्य पातनं 'causing the fœtus to fall', causing an abortion.

पातालं 1 The last of the seven regions or worlds under the earth, said to be peopled by Nâgas; the seven regions are:—अतल, वितल, सुतल, रसातल, तलातल, महातल and पाताल. 3 The lower regions or world in general; R. 15. 84; 1. 80. 3 An excavation, a hole. 4 Submarine-fire. -COMP. **-गंगा** the Ganges of the lower world. **-ओकस्** *m.* **-निलयः, -निरासः, -वासिन्** *m.* 1 a demon. 2 a Nâga or a serpent-demon.

पातिकः The Gangetic porpoise.

पातित *p. p.* 1 Cast down, thrown, of felled down, struck down. 2 Overthrown, humbled. 3 Lowered.

पातित्यं Loss of caste or position.

पातिन् *a.* (**नी** *f.*) 1 Going to, descending, alighting on. 2 Falling, sinking. 3 Being contained in. 4 Falling or throwing down. 5 Pouring forth, discharging, emitting.

पातिली 1 A snare, trap. 2 A small earthen vessel.

पातुक *a.* (**की** *f.*) 1 Falling habitually or frequently. 2 Apt or disposed to fall. **-कः** 1 The declivity of a mountain, precipice. 2 The water-elephat.

पात्रं 1 A drinking-vessel, cup, jar. 2 A vessel or pot in general; पात्रे निधायार्घ्यं R. 5. 2, 12. 3 A receptcle of any kind, recipient; Pt. 2. 97. 4 A reservoir. 5 A fit or worthy person, a person fit or worthy to receive gifts; वित्तस्य पात्रे व्ययः Bh. 2. 82 Bg. 17. 22; Y. 1. 201; R. 11. 86. 6 An actor, a *dramatis persona*; तत्प्रतिपात्रमाधीयतां यत्नः S. 1; उच्यतां पात्रवर्गः V. 1. *dramatis personae.* 7 A king's minister. 8 The channel or bed of a river. 9 Fitness, propriety. 10 An order, command. -COMP. **-उपकरणं** decoration of an inferior kind. **-पालः** 1 a large paddle used as a rudder. 2 the rod of a balance (तुलादंड). **-संस्कारः** 1 tho cleaning or purification of a vessel. 2 the current of a river.

पात्रिक *a.* (**की** *f.*) 1 Measured out with any vessel or a measure called आढक. 2 Fit, adequate, appropriate. **-कं** A vessel, cup, dish.

पात्रिय, पात्र्य *a.* Worthy to partake of a meal.

पात्रीयं A sacrificial vessel or utensil.

पात्रीरः -रं An oblation.

पात्रेबहुलः, पात्रेसमितः 1 'Constant at meals or dinner-time', a parasite. 2 A treacherous or hypocritical fellow.

पाथः 1 Fire. 2 The sun. **-थं** Water.

पाथस् *n.* 1 Water; G. L. 26. 2 Air, wind 3 Food. -COMP. **-जं** 1 a lotus. 2 a conch. **-दः, -धरः** a cloud. **-धिः, -निधिः, -पतिः** the ocean; N. 13 20.

पाथेयं 1 Provender or provisions for a journey, viaticum; जयाइ पाथेयमिवेंद्रसूनुः Ki. 3. 37; बिसकिसलयच्छेदपाथेयवंतः Me. 11; V. 4. 15. 2 The sign *virgo* of the zodiac.

पादः 1 The foot (whether of men or animals); तयोर्जगृहतुः पादान् R. 1. 57; पादयोर्निपत्य; पादपतित &c. (The word पाद at the end of comp. is changed to पाद् after सु and numerals; *e. g.* सुपाद्, द्विपाद्, त्रिपाद् &c.; and also when the first member is used as a standard of comparison, but is a word other than हस्तिन् &c.; see P. V. 4. 138-140; *e. g.* व्याघ्रपाद्. The nom. pl. of पाद is often added to names of persons or titles of address to show great respect or veneration; सृण्वंतु लवस्य बालिशतां तातपादाः U. 6; 1. 29; देवपादानां नास्माभिः प्रयोजनं Pt. 1; so एवमाराध्यपादा आज्ञापयंति Prab. 1; so कुमारिलपादाः &c.; 2 A ray of light; बालस्यापि रवेः पादाः पतंत्युपरि भूभृतां Pt. 1. 328; Si. 9. 34; R. 16. 53 (where the word has sense 1 also). 3 The foot or leg of an inanimate object, as of a bedstead. 4 The foot or root of a tree; as in पादप. 5 The foot of a mountain, a hill at the foot of a mountain (पादाः प्रत्यंतपर्वताः); Me. 19; S. 6. 16. 6 A quarter, fourth part; as in सपादो रूपकः one and one-fourth rupee; Ms. 8. 241; Y. 2. 174. 7 The fourth part of a stanza, a line. 8 The fourth part of a chapter or book, as of the Adhyâyas of Pâṇini, or of the Brahma Sûtras. 9 A part in general. 10 A column, pillar. –COMP. –अग्रं the point or extremity of the foot; Ratn. 1. 1. –अंकः a foot-mark. –अंगदं,-दी an ornament for the foot, an anklet. अंगुष्ठः the great toe. –अंतः the point or extremity of the feet. –अंतरं the interval of a step, the distance of a foot. (–रे) *ind.* 1 after the interval of a step. 2 close or near to. –अंबु *n.* butter-milk containing a fourth part of water. –अंभस् *n.* water in which the feet (of revered persons) have been washed. –अरविंदं, –कमलं, –पंकजं, –पद्मं a lotus-like foot. –अलिंदी a boat. –अवसेचनं 1 washing the feet. 2 the water used for washing the feet. –आघातः a kick. –आनत *a.* prostrate, fallen at the feet of; Ku. 3. 8. –आवर्तः a wheel worked by the feet for raising up water from a well. –आसनं a foot-stool. –आस्फालनं trampling or motion of the feet, floundering. –आहत *a.* kicked. –उदकं, –जलं 1 water for washing the feet. 2 water in which the feet of sacred and revered persons are washed and which is thus considered holy. –उदरः a serpent. –कटकः-कं, -कीलिका an anklet. –क्षेपः a foot-step. –ग्रंथिः the ankle. –ग्रहणं seizing or clasping the feet (as a mark of respectful salutation); Ku. 7. 27. –चतुरः,-चत्वरः 1 a slanderer. 2 a goat. 3 a sand-bank. 4 hail. –चारः going on foot, walking; यदि च विचरेत् पादचारेण गौरी Me. 60 'if Gaurî should walk on foot'; R. 11. 10. –चारिन् *a.* walking or fighting on foot. (–*m.*) 1 a pedestrian. 2 a foot-soldier. –जः a Sûdra. –जाहं the tarsus. –तलं the sole of the foot. –त्रः, -त्रा, -त्राणं a boot or shoe. –पः a tree; निरस्तपादपे देशे एरंडोऽपि द्रुमायते H. 1. 69; अनुभवति हि मूर्ध्ना पादपस्ती-व्रमुष्णं S. 5. 5. °खंडः,-डं a grove of trees. –पालिका an anklet. –पाशः a foot-rope for cattle. (–शी) 1 a fetter. 2 a mat. 3 creeper. –पीठः-ठं a foot-stool; R. 17. 28; Ku. 3. 11. –पूरणं 1 filling out a line. 2 an expletive; तु पादपूरणे भेदे समुच्चयेऽवधारणे Visva. –प्रक्षालनं washing the feet. –प्रतिष्ठानं a foot-stool. प्रहारः a kick. –बंधनं a fetter. –मुद्रा a foot-print. –मूलं 1 the tarsus. 2 the sole of the foot. 3 the heel. 4 the foot of a mountain. 5 a polite way of speaking of a person; देवपादमूलमागताहं K. 8. –रजस् *n.* the dust of the feet. –रज्जुः *f.* a leather for the foot of an elephant. –रथी a shoe, boot. –रोहः,-रोहणः the (Indian) fig-tree. –वंदनं saluting the feet. –विरजस् *n.* a shoe, boot. (–*m.*) a god. –शाखा a toe. –शैलः a hill at the foot of a mountain. –शोथः swelling of the foot. –शौचं cleaning the feet by washing, washing the feet. –सेवनं, –सेवा 1 showing respect by touching the feet. 2 service. –स्फोटः 'cracking of the feet', chilblain. –हत *a.* kicked.

पादविकः A traveller.

पादात् *m.* A foot-soldier, a footman.

पादातः A foot-soldier; Si. 18. 4. —तं Infantry.

पादातिः, पादाविकः A foot-soldier.

पादिक *a.* (की *f.*) Amounting to a quarter or fourth; पादिकं शतं 25 percent.

पादिन् *a.* 1 Footed, having feet. 2 Having four parts, as a stanza. 3 Receiving or entitled to a fourth part.

पादिनः A fourth part.

पादुकः *a.* (का-की *f.*) Going on foot. –का A wooden-shoe, sandal; व्रज भरत गृहीत्वा पादुके त्वं मदीये Bk. 3. 56; R. 12. 17. –COMP. –कारः a shoemaker.

पादू *f.* A shoe. –कृत् *m.* a shoemaker.

पाद्य *a.* Belonging to the foot. –द्यं Water for washing the feet; पादयोः पाद्यं समर्पयामि.

पानं 1 Drinking, quaffing, kissing (a lip); पयः पानं; देहि मुखकमलमधुपानं Gît. 10. 2 Drinking spirituous liquors; Ms. 7. 50, 9. 13, 12. 45. 3 A drink, beverage in general; Ms. 3. 227. 4 A drinking vessel. 5 Sharpening, whetting 6 Protection, defence. –नः A distiller.-COMP.-अगारः,-आगारः -रं. a tavern. –अत्ययः hard-drinking. –गोष्ठिका, –गोष्ठी 1 a drinking party. 2 a drum shop, tavern. –प *a.* drinking spirituous liquors. –पात्रं,-भाजनं, -भांडं a drinking vessel, a goblet. –भूः,-भूमिः. भूमी *f.* a drinking room; R. 7. 49; 19. 11. –मंगलं a drinking party. –रत *a.* addicted to drinking. –वणिज् *m.* vender of spirits. –विभ्रमः intoxication. –शौंडः a hard drinker.

पानकं A drink, beverage, potion.

पानिकः A vender of spiritual liquors, a distiller.

पानिलं A drinking vessel, goblet.

पानीयं 1 Water. 2 A drink, potion, beverage. –COMP. –नकुलः an otter. –वर्णिका sand. –क्षाला.-शालिका a place where water is distributed to travellers; cf. प्रपा.

पांथः A traveller, a way-farer; पांथ विह्वलमना नमनागपि स्याः Bv. 1. 37.

पाप *a.* 1 Evil, sinful, wicked, vicious; पापं कर्म च यत् परैरपि कृतं तत्तस्य संभाव्यते Mk. 1. 36; Bg. 6. 9. 2 Mischievous, destructive, accursed; पापेन मृत्युना गृहीतोऽस्मि M. 4 3 Low, vile, abandoned; Ms. 3. 52; 4. 171. 4 Inauspicious, malignant, foreboding evil; as in पापग्रह. –पं 1 Evil, bad fortune or state; पापं पापाः कथयथ कथं शौर्यराशेः पितुर्मे Ve. 3. 5; शांतं पापं 'may the evil be averted', 'god forbid' (often used in dramas). 2 Sin, crime, vice, guilt; अपापानां कुले जाते मयि पापं न विद्यते Mk. 9. 37; Ms. 11. 231; 4. 181; R. 12. 19. –पः A wretch, sinful person, wicked or profligate person. –COMP. –अधम *a.* exceedingly wicked, the vilest. –अपनुत्तिः *f.* expiation. –अहः an unlucky day. –आचार *a.* following evil or sinful courses, leading a sinful life, vicious, wicked. –आत्मन् *a.* evil-minded, sinful, wicked. (–*m.*) a sinner. –आशय, –चेतस् *a.* evil-intentioned, wicked-minded. –कर, –कारिन्, –कृत् &c. *a.* sinful, a sinner, villain. –क्षयः removal or destruction of sin. –ग्रहः a planet of evil or malignant aspect such as Mars, Saturn, Râhu or Ketu. –घ्न *a.* destroying sin, expiating. –चर्यः 1 a sinner. 2 a demon. –दृष्टि *a.* evil-eyed. –धी *a.* evilminded, wicked. –नापितः a cunning or vile barber. –नाशन *a.* destroying or expiating sin. –पतिः a paramour. –पुरुषः a villainous person. –फल *a.* evil, inauspicious. –बुद्धि, –भाव, –मति *a.* evil-minded, wicked, depraved. –भाज् *a.* sinful, a sinner; Ku. 5. 83. –मुक्त *a.* freed from sin, purified. –मोचनं, –विनाशनं destruction of sin. –योनि *a.* low-born. (निः *f.*) vile birth, birth in an inferior condition. –रोगः 1 any bad disease. 2 small-pox. –शील *a.* prone to evil, wicked by nature, evilminded. –संकल्प *a.* evil-minded, wicked. (–ल्पः) a wicked thought.

पापर्द्धिः Hunting, chase.

पापल *a.* Imparting or incurring sin.

पापिन् *a.* (नी *f.*) Sinful, wicked, bad. –*m.* A sinner.

पापिष्ठ *a.* Most sinful, worst, very wicked (superl. of पाप q. v.).

पापीयस् *a.* (सी *f.*) Worse, more vile or wicked (compar. of पाप q. v.)

पाप्मन् *m.* Sin, crime, wickedness, guilt; मया गृहीतनामानः स्पृश्यंत इव पाप्मना U. 1. 48; 7. 20; Mâl. 5. 26; Ms. 6. 85.

पामन् *m.* A kind of skin-disease, scab. –COMP. –घ्नः sulphur.

पामन *a.* Diseased with scab.

पामर *a.* (रा-री *f*) 1 Diseased with scab, scabby. 2 Vile, wicked. 3 Low, vulgar, base. 4 Foolish, stupid. 5 Poor, helpless; Ud. D. 5,

-र: 1 A fool, an idiot; बलंति चेत्पामराः Bv. 1. 72. 2 A wicked or low man. 3 One engaged in the most degrading occupation.

पामा See पामन् above. COMP. -अरिः sulphur.

पायना 1 Causing to drink. 2 Watering, moistening. 3 Sharpening, whetting.

पायस a. (सी f.) Made of water or milk -सः, -सं 1 Rice boiled in milk; Ms 3. 271. 5. 7; Y. 1. 173. 2 Turpentine. -सं Milk.

पायिकः A foot-soldier.

पायुः The anus; पायूपस्थं Ms. 2. 90, 91; Y. 3. 92.

पाय्यं 1 Water. 2 Drinking. 3 Protection. 4 A measure (परिमाण).

पारः, -रं 1 The further or opposite bank of a river or ocean; पारं दुःखोदधेर्गंतुं तर यावन्न भिद्यते Sânti. 3. 1; विरहजलधेः पारमासादयिष्ये Pad. D. 13; H. 1. 20½. 2 The further or opposite side of anything; Ku. 2 58. 3 The end or extremity of anything; furtherest or concluding limit; Ve. 3. 35. 4 The fullest extent, the totality of anything; स पूर्वजन्मांतरदृष्टपाराः स्मरन्निव R 18. 50; (पारं गम्, -इ, -या 1 to cross over, surmount. 2 to accomplish, fulfil; as in प्रतिज्ञायाः पारंगतः to master fully, become proficient in; सकलशास्त्रपारंगतः-रः Quick-silver. (पार meaning 'on the other side of' 'beyond' sometimes enters into comp; e. g. पारेगंगं, पारेसमुद्रं beyond the Ganges or the ocean). -COMP. -अपारं, अवारं both banks, the nearer and further bank. (-रः) the sea, ocean; शोकपारावारमुत्तर्तुमशक्नुवती Dk. 4; Bv. 4. 11. -अयणं 1 going across. 2 reading through, perusal, thorough study. 3 the whole, completeness, or totality of anything; as in ब्रम्हपारायण, मंत्रपारायण &c. -अयणी 1 N. of the goddess Sarasvati. 2 considering, meditation. 3 an act, action. 4 light. -काम a. desirous of going to the other end. -गः a. 1 crossing over, ferrying across. 2 one who has gone to the end of, one who has completely mastered anything, completely familiar or conversant with (with gen. or in comq.); Ms. 2. 148; Y. 1. 111 3 profoundly learned. -गत, -गामिन् a. one who has gone to the other side or shore. -दर्शक a. 1 showing the opposite bank. 2 transparent. -दृश्वन् a. 1 far-seeing, wise, prudent. 2 one who has seen the other side of anything, one who has completely mastered or has become familiar with anything; श्रुतिपारदृश्वा R. 5. 24.

पारक a. (की f.) 1 Enabling to cross. 2 Carrying over, saving, delivering. 3 Pleasing, satisfying.

पारक्य a. 1 Alien, belonging to another. 2 Intended for others. 3 Hostile, inimical. -क्यं Doing anything for future happiness (परलोकसाधन); pious conduct.

पारग्रामिक a. (की f.) Alien, hostile, inimical.

पारज़ m. Gold.

पारजायिकः An adulterer.

पारटीटः -नः A stone or rock.

पारण a 1 Carrying across, bringing over. 2 Saving, Delivering -णः 1 A cloud. 2 satisfaction. -णं 1 Accomplishing, fulfilling. 2 Reading through, perusal. 3 Eating after a fast, concluding a fast. -णा 1 Eating after a fast, concluding a fast; कारय चक्षुषी पारणां Vb. 1; 2. 39, 55, 70 2 Eating (in general) ; Ku. 5. 22; (अभ्यवहारकर्म Malli.).

पारतः Quick-silver.

पारतंत्र्यं Dependence, subjection, subservience.

पारत्रिक a. (की f.) 1 Belonging to the next world. 2 Useful in the future life.

पारतंड्यं Reward in a future life (परलोकफल) ; Ms. 2. 236.

पारदः Quick-silver; निदर्शनं पारदोऽत्र रसः Bv. 1. 82.

पारदारिकः An adulterer (intriguing with the wife of another); Y. 2. 295.

पारदार्यं Adultery, intriguing with another's wife; Ms. 11. 59; Y. 3. 235.

पारदेशिक a. (की f.) Foreign, out-landish. -कः 1 A foreigner, 2 A traveller.

पारदेश्य a. (श्यी f.) Belonging to a foreign country, foreign. -श्यः 1 A foreigner. 2 A traveller.

पारभृतं A present (prehaps a misreading for प्राभृत).

पारमहंस्यं Most sublime asceticism or meditation. -COMP. -परि and. relating to such asceticism.

पारमार्थिक a. (की f.) 1 Relating to परमार्थ or the highest truth or spiritual knowledge. 2 Real, essential, truly or really existent; सत्ता त्रिविधा पारमार्थिकी, व्यावहारिकी, प्रातीतिकी च Vedanta. 3 Caring for truth, loving truth or right; न लोकः पारमार्थिकः Pt. 1. 312. 3 Excellent, supremely good, best.

पारमिक a. (की f.) Supreme, best, chief, principal.

पारमित a, 1 Gone to the opposite bank or side. 2 Crossed, traversed. 3 Transcendent.

पारमेष्ठ्यं 1 Supremacy, highest position. 2 Royal insignia.

पारंपरीण a. (णी f.) Handed down from father to son, hereditary, ancestral.

पारंपरीय a. Handed down, traditionally, hereditary.

पारंपर्यं 1 Hereaditary succession, continuous order. 2 Traditional instruction, tradition. 3 Intermediation. -COMP. -उपदेशः traditional instruction, tradition, regarded by the Paurânikas as a प्रमाण or proof.

पारयिष्णु a. 1 Pleasing, gratifying 2 Able to go to the end of or accomplish anything.

पारलौकिक a. (की f.) Relating to or useful in the next world धर्म एको मनुष्याणां सहायः पारमार्थिकः Mb. ; N. 5. 92.

पारवतः A pigeon.

पारवश्यं Dependence, subjection, subservience.

पारशव a. (वी f.) 1 Made of iron. 2 Relating to or derived from an axe. -वः 1 Iron. 2 The son of a Brâhmana by a Sûdra women; यं ब्राम्हणस्तु शूद्रायां कामादुत्पादयेत्सुतं। स पारयन्नेव शवस्तस्मात्पारशवः स्मृतः Ms. 9. 178; or परं शवात् ब्राम्हणस्यैष पुत्रः शूद्रापुत्रं पारवशं तमाहुः Mb. 3 An adulterine, a bastard.

पारश्वधः, पारश्वधिकः A man armed with an axe, halberd-man.

पारस a. (सी f.) Persian.

पारासिकः 1 Persia. 2-पारसीक 2 p. v.

पारसी The Persian language.

पारसीकः 1 Persia. 2 A Persian horse. -काः (m. pl.) The Persians; पारसीकांस्ततो जेतुं प्रतस्थे स्थलवर्त्मना R. 4. 6.

पारस्त्रैणेयः An adulterine, a bastard (born from another's wife परस्त्री).

पारहंस्य a. Relating to an ascetic who has subdued all his senses.

पारा N. of a river; तदुचित्र पारासिंधुसंभेदमवगाह्य नगरीमेव प्रविशावः Mal. 4, 9. 1.

पारापतः 1 A pigeon.

पारायणिकः 1 A lecturer, reader of the Puranas or mythological works. 2 A pupil, scholar.

पारावतः 1 A pigeon, a turtledove, dove. पारावतः खरशिलाकणमात्रभोजी कामी भवत्यनुदिनं वद कोत्र हेतुः Bh. 3. 154; Me. 38. 2 A monkey. 3 A mountain. -COMP.-अंघ्रिः, -पिच्छः a kind of pigeon.

पारारुकः A stone, rock.

पारावारीण a. 1 One who goes to both sides. 2 Completely conversant with.

पाराशरः, पाराशर्यः An epithet of Vyâsa, son of Parâshara.

पाराशरिः 1 An epithet of Suka. 2 N. of Vyâsa.

पाराशरिन् m. 1 A religious mendicant. 2 Particularly, such religious mendicants or ascetics as study the Sârîra Sutras of Vyâsa (pl.).

पारिकांक्षिन् m. A contemplative

saint, an ascetic who devotes himself to abstract meditation.

पारिक्षतः A patronymic of Janamejaya, great-grandson of Arjuna, and son of परीक्षित्.

पारिखेय *a.* (यी *f.*) Surrounded by a ditch.

पारिजातः, पारिजातकः 1 N. of one of the five trees of Paradice (said to have been produced at the churning of the ocean and come into the possession of Indra, from whom it was wrested by Krishna and planted in the garden of his beloved Satyabhâmâ); कल्पद्रुमाणामिव पारिजातः R. 6. 6. 10. 11: 17. 7. 2 The coral tree. 3 Fragrance.

पारिणाय्य *a.* (य्यी *f.*) 1 Relating to marriage. 2 Obtained on the occasion of marriage. –य्यं 1 Property received by a woman at the time of marriage; मातुः पारिणाय्यं स्त्रियो विभजेरन् Vasistha. 2 Marriage-settlement.

पारिणाह्यं Household furniture and utensils; Ms 9. 11.

पारितथ्या A string of pearls for binding the hair.

पारितोषिक *a.* (की *f.*) Pleasing, gratifying, consolatory. –कं A present, reward; गृह्यतां पारितोषिकमिदमंगुलीयकं Mk. 5.

पारिध्वजिकः A standard-bearer.

पारिंद्रः A lion.

पारिपंथिकः A robber, highwayman.

पारिपाट्यं 1 Mode, method, manner (परिपाटी) 2 Regularity.

पारिपार्श्वं Retinue, attendants, followers.

पारिपार्श्वकः पारिपार्श्विकः 1 A servant or an attendant. 2 An assistant of the manager of a play, one of the interlocutors in the prologue; प्रविश्य पारिपार्श्वकः तत्किमिति पारिपार्श्विक नारंभयासि कुशीलवैः सह संगित Ve. 1.

पारिपार्श्विका A female-attendant, a chamber-maid.

पारिप्लव *a.* 1 Moving to and fro, rolling, shaking, unsteady, tremulous; ननंद पारिप्लवनेत्रया नृपः R. 3; 11. 2 Swimming, floating; R. 13. 30; 16. 61. 3 Agitated, bewildered, disturbed or perplexed; U. 4. 22. –वः A boat. –वं Restlessness, uneasiness; Mâl. 4. 3.

पारिप्लाव्यः A goose. –व्यं 1 Perplexity, uneasiness, agitation. 2 Tremour, tremulousness.

पारिबर्हः A wedding present.

पारिभद्रः 1 The coral tree. 2 The *Devadâru* tree. 3 The *Sarala* tree. 4 The *Nimba* tree.

पारिभाव्यं Bail, security, surety.

पारिभाषिक *a.* (की *f.*) 1 Current, common, universally received. 2 Technical (as a word &c.).

पारिमांडल्यं An atom, a mote in a sun-beam; Bhâshâ P. 15.

पारिमुखिक *a.* (की *f.*) Being before the face, being near or present.

पारिमुख्यं Presence.

पारिया (पा) त्रः N. of one of the seven principal mountain ranges; R. 18. 16; see कुलाचल.

पारिया (पा) त्रिकः 1 An inhabitant of the Pâriyâtra mountain. 2 The Pâriyâtra mountain itself.

पारियानिकः A travelling carriage.

पारिरक्षिकः A religious mendicant, an ascetic.

पारिवित्त्यं, पारिवेत्त्यं Being unmarried while a younger brother is married.

पारिव्राजकं, पारिव्राज्यं The wandering life of a religious mendicant, asceticism.

पारिशीलः A cake (अपूप q. v.).

पारिशेष्यं That which is left over, remainder.

पारिषद् *a.* (दी *f.*) Belonging to an assembly or council. –द्ः 1 A person present at an assembly, a member of an assembly such as an assessor. 2 A king's companion. –द्ाः (*m. pl.*) The retinue of a god.

पारिषद्यः One present at an assembly, a spectator.

पारिहारिकी A kind of riddle.

पारिहार्यः A bracelet. –र्यं Taking, seizing.

पारिहास्यं Jest, joke, fun.

पारी 1 A rope for tying an elephant's feet. 2 A quantity of water. 3 A drinking vessel, water-jar, cup. 4 A milk pail; *Si.* 12. 40.

पारीक्षितः=पारिक्षित q. v.

पारीण *a.* 1 Being on or going over to the other or opposite side. 2 (At the end of comp.) Thoroughly versed in, well-acquainted with; त्रिवर्गपारीणमसौ भवंतमध्यासयन्नासनमेकमिंद्रः Bk. 2. 46.

पारीणह्यं Household furniture or utensils.

पारींद्रः 1 A lion. 2 A large serpent, boa.

पारीरणः 1 A tortoise. 2 A strick, staff.

पारुः 1 The sun. 2 Fire.

पारुष्यं 1 Roughness, ruggedness, hardness. 2 Harshness, cruelty, unkindness (as of disposition). 3 Abusive language, abuse, reproach, scurrilous language, insult; Bg. 16. 4; Y. 2. 12, 72. 4 Violence (in word or deed); Ms. 8. 6, 72; 7. 48, 51. 5 The garden of Indra. 6 Aloewood. –ष्यः An epithet of Brihaspati.

पारोवर्यं Tradition.

पार्घटं Dust or ashes.

पार्जन्य *a.* Belonging to rain.

पार्ण *a.* (र्णी *f.*) 1 Relating to, or made of leaves, leafly. 2 Raised from leaves (as a tax).

पार्थः 1 A metronymic of Yudhishṭhira, Bhîma and Arjuna, but especially of Arjuna; Bg. 1. 25 and several other places. 2 A king. –COMP. –सारथिः an epithet of Krishṇa.

पार्थक्यं Severalty, separateness, separation, singleness, variety.

पार्थवं Greatness, immensity, width.

पार्थिव *a.* (वी *f.*) 1 Earthen, earthly, terrestrial relating to the earth; यतो रजः पार्थिवमुज्जिहीते R. 13. 64. 2 Ruling the earth. 3 Princely, royal. –वः 1 An inhabitant of the earth. 2 A king, sovereign; R. 8. 1. 3 An earthen vessel. –COMP. –नंदनः, –सुतः a prince, the son of a king. कन्या, –नंदिनी, –सुता the daughter of a king, princess.

पार्थिवी 1 An epithet of Sitâ, daughter of the earth; पार्थिवीमुद्वहद्रघूद्वहः R. 11. 54. 2 An epithet of Lakshmî.

पार्परः 1 A handful of rice. 2 Consumption (क्षयरोग)

पार्यंतिक *a.* (की *f.*) Final, last, conclusive.

पार्वण *a.* (णी *f.*) Belonging or relating to a *Parvan* q. v ; R. 11. 82. 2 Waxing, increasing (as the moon) –णं The general ceremony of offering oblations to all the Manes at a *Parvan*.

पार्वत *a.* (ती) 1 Being or living in a mountain. 2 Growing on or coming from a mountain. 3 Mountainous.

पार्वतिकं A multitude of mountains, a mountain-range.

पार्वती 1 N. of Durgâ, born as the daughter of the Himâlaya mountain (she was Satî in her former birth; cf. Ku. 1. 21); तां पार्वतीत्याभिजनेन नाम्ना बंधुप्रियां बंधुजनो जुहाव Ku. 1. 26. 2 A female cowherd. 3 An epithet of Draupadî. 4 A mountain stream. 5 A kind of fragrant earth. –COMP. –नंदनः 1 an epithet of Kârtikeya. 2 of Gaṇesa.

पार्वतीय *a.* (यी *f.*) Dwelling in a mountain. –यः A mountaineer. 2 N. of a particular mountain tribe (pl.); तत्र जन्यं रघोर्घोरं पार्वतीयैर्गणैरभूत् R. 4.

पार्वतेय *a.* (यी *f.*) Mountain-born. –यं Antimony.

पार्शवः A warrior armed with an axe.

पार्श्वः –र्श्वं 1 The part of the body below the arm-pit, the region of the ribs; शयने संनिषण्णैकपार्श्वां Me. 89. 2 The side, flank (in general) (of animate or inanimate objects); पिटरं क्रथदातिमात्रं निजपार्श्वानिव दहतितरां Pt. 1. 324.

3 Vicinity. -र्श्वः An epithet of Jina. -र्श्वं 1 A multitude of ribs. 2 A fraudulent expedient, a dishonourable means. (पार्श्वे is used adverbially in the sense of 'near to,' 'by the side of,' 'towards'; *S.* 7. 8; so पार्श्वात् 'from the side of', 'away from'; पार्श्वे 'near', 'at hand', 'at the side'; न मे दूरे किंचित्क्षणमपि न पार्श्वे रथजवात् *S.* 1. 9, Bh. 2. 37). -Comp. -अनुचरः an attendant, a servant; R. 2. 9. -अस्थि *n.* a rib. -आयात *a.* one who has come very near. -आसन्न *a.* standing by the side. -उदरप्रियः a crab. -गः an attendant, servant; R. 11. 43. -गत *a.* 1 being at the side, being near or close to, attending upon. 2 sheltered. -चरः a servant. an attendant; R. 9. 72; 14. 29. -द्रः an attendant, a servant. -देशः the side (of the human body). -परिवर्तनं 1 turning round from one side to the other in a bed. 2 N. of a festival on the eleventh day of the first half of Bhâdrapada (when Vishṇu is supposed to turn upon the other side in his sleep). -भागः the side or flank. -वर्तिन् *a.* 1 being by the side, attending, waiting upon. 2 adjacent. -शय *a.* sleeping on the side. 2 sleeping by the side. -शूलः-लं a shooting pain in the side. -सूत्रकः a kind of ornament. -स्थ *a.* being at the side, near, close, proximate. (-स्थः) 1 a companion. 2 an assistant of a stage-manager; cf. पारिपार्श्वक.

पार्श्वकः (की *f.*) A swindler, pilferer, thief.

पार्श्वतस् *ind.* Near, at hand, by the side, close to; R. 19. 31.

पार्श्विक *a.* (की *f.*) Belonging to the side.-कः 1 A sidesman, partisan. 2 A companion, an associate. 3 A juggler.

पार्षत *a.* (ती *f.*) Belonging to the spotted antelope; Ms. 3. 269; Y. 1. 257. -तः A patronymic of king Drupada, and of his son Dhṛishṭadyumna.

पार्षती 1 An epithet of Draupadî. 2 Of Durgâ.

पार्षद् *f.* An assembly.

पार्षदः 1 A companion, an associate, attendant. 2 A train, retinue (of a god). 3 One present at an assembly, a spectator, an assessor.

पार्षद्यः A member of an assembly, an assessor.

पार्ष्णिः *m. f.* 1 The heel; उद्वेजयत्यङ्गुलिपार्ष्णिभागान् Ku. 1. 11; पार्ष्णिप्रहार K. 119. 2 The rear of an army. 3 The back or rear in general; शुद्धपार्ष्णिरयान्वितः R. 4. 26 'with his rear cleared of foes'. 4 A kick.-*f.* 1 A licentious woman. 2 An epithet of Kuntî. -Comp. -ग्रहः a follower. -ग्रहणं attacking or threatening an enemy in the rear. -ग्राहः 1 an enemy in the rear. 2 a general commanding the rear of an army. 3 an ally who supports a prince; Ms. 7. 207. -घातः a kick; Ki. 17. 50. -त्रं a rear-guard, a body of forces in the rear, reserve. -वाहः an outside horse.

पालः 1 A protector, guardian, keeper; as in गोपालः, वृष्णिपालः &c. 2 A herdsman; विवादः स्वामिपालयोः Ms. 8. 5, 229, 240. 3 A king. 4 A spitting-pot. -Comp. -घ्नः a mushroom.

पालकः 1 A guardian, protector. 2 A prince, king, ruler, sovereign. 3 A groom, horsekeeper. 4 A horse. 5 The Chitraka tree. 6 A foster-father.

पालकाप्यः N. of a sage, son of Kareṇu (who first taught the science of elephants). -प्यं The science of elephants.

पालंकः 1 The olibanum tree. 2 A hawk. -की Incense.

पालंक्यः-क्या Incense.

पालन *a.* Protecting, guarding &c.; Ki. 1. 1. -नं 1 Protecting, guarding, nourishing, cherishing, fostering; लब्ध° R. 19. 3; so प्रजा°, क्षिति°, &c. 2 Maintaining, observing, keeping (as a promise, vow &c.). 3 The milk of a cow that has recently calved.

पालयितृ *m.* Protector, guardian; R. 2. 69; 8. 32.

पालाश *a.* (शी *f.*) 1 Belonging to or coming from the Palâsa tree. 2 Made of the wood of the Palâsa tree; Ms. 2. 45. 3 Green. -शः The green colour. -Comp. -खंडः, -षंडः an epithet of the Magadha country.

पालिः-ली *f.* 1 The tip of the ear; श्रवणपालिः Gît. 3. 2 The edge, skirt, margin; Bh. 3. 55. 3 The sharp side, edge or point of anything (अश्रि); Bv. 2. 3. 4 Boundary, limit. 5 A line, row; विपुलपुलकपाली Gît. 6; Si. 3. 51. 6 A spot, mark. 7 A causeway, bridge. 8 The lap, the bosom. 9 An oblong pond. 10 Maintenance of a pupil by his teacher during the period of his studies. 11 A louse. 12 Praise, eulogium. 13 A woman with a beard.

पालिका 1 The tip of the ear. 2 The sharp edge of a sword or of any cutting instrument. 3 A cheese or butter-knife.

पालित *p. p.* 1 Protected, guarded, preserved. 2 Observed, fulfilled.

पालित्यं Greyness of hair caused by old age, hoariness.

पाल्वल *a.* (ली *f.*) Coming from a pool.

पावकः 1 Fire; पावकस्य महिमा स गण्यते कक्षवज्ज्वलति सागरेऽपि यः R. 11. 75, 3. 9; 16. 87. 2 Agni or the god of fire. 3 The fire of lightning. 4 The Chitraka tree. 5 The number 'three'.-Comp. -आत्मजः 1 an epithet of Kârtikeya. 2 N. of a sage called सुदर्शन.

पावकिः An epithet of Kârtikeya.

पावन *a.* (नी *f.*) 1 Purifying, freeing from sin, purificatory, sanctifying; पादास्तामभितो निषण्णहरिणा गौरीगुरोः पावनाः *S.* 6. 17, R. 15. 101, 19. 53; Bg. 18. 5, Ms. 2. 26; Y. 3. 307. 2 Sacred, holy, pure, purified; Ku. 5. 17. -नः 1 Fire. 2 Incense. 3 A kind of demi-god or Siddha. 4 N. of the poet Vyâsa. -नं 1 Purifying, purification; पदनखनीरजनितजनपावन Gît. 1. 2 Penance. 3 Water. 4 Cow-dung. 5 A sectarial mark. -Comp. -ध्वनिः a conchshell.

पावनी 1 The holy basil. 2 A cow. 3 The river Ganges.

पावमानी An epithet of particular Vedic hymns.

पावरः The side of a die which is marked with two points; or a particular throw of this die; पावरपतनाच्च शोषितशरीरः Mk. 2. 8.

पाशः 1 A cord, chain, fetter, noose; पादाकृष्टव्रततिवलयासंगसंजातपाशः *S.* 1. 32; बाहुपाशेन व्यापादिता Mk. 9; R. 6. 84. 2 A snare, trap or net for catching birds and beasts. 3 A noose used as a weapon (as by Varuna); Ku. 2. 21. 4 A die, dice; Malli. on R. 6. 18. 5 The edge or border of anything woven. 6 (At the end of comp.) पाश expresses (*a*) contempt or depreciation; as in छत्रपाशः a bad pupil; वैयाकरण°, भिषक्° &c. (*b*) beauty or admiration; as in सैषोष्ठमुद्रा स च कर्णपाशः U. 6. 27. (*c*) abundance, mass, or quantity (aftar a word signifying 'hair'): केशपाश q. v.-Comp. -अंतः the back of a garment. -क्रीडा gambling, playing with dice. -धरः, -पाणिः an epithet of Varuṇa. -बद्ध *a.* entrapped, caught in a snare or net, noosed -बंधः a noose, snare, halter. -बंधकः a bird-catcher. -बंधनं a snare. -भृत् *m.* an epithet of Varuṇa; R. 2. 9. -रज्जुः *f.* a fetter, rope. -हस्तः 'holding a noose in hand', an epithet of Varuṇa.

पाशकः A die, dice. -Comp. -पीठं a gambling table.

पाशनं 1 A noose, share, net, sling. 2 A cord, lash. 3 Ensnaring, entrapping.

पाशव *a.* (वी *f.*) Relating to or derived from animals. -वं A flock, heard. -Comp. -पालनं pasturage or meadow grass.

पाशित *a.* Bound, ensnared, fettered.

पाशिन् *m.* 1 An epithet of Varuṇa. 2 Of Yama. 3 A deercatcher, fowler, trapper.

पाशुपत *a.* (ती *f.*) Coming from or relating or sacred to Paśupati. **-तः** 1 A follower and worshipper of Siva. 2 A follower of the doctrines of Pasupati. **-तं** The Pâsupata doctrines; (for the Pâsupata doctrines, see Sarva. S.).-Comp. **-अस्त्रं** N. of a missile presided over by **पशुपति** or Siva (which Arjuna acquired from Siva).

पाशुपाल्यं The breeding or rearing of cattle, a herdsman's occupation.

पाश्चात्य *a.* 1 hinder. 2 Western; R. 4. 62. 3 Posterior, later. 4 Subsequent. **-त्यं** The hinder part.

पाश्या 1 A net. 2 A collection of stairs or ropes.

पाषकः An ornament for the feet.

पाषंडः=पाखंड q. v.; Ms. 5. 90; 9. 225.

पाषंडकः, पाषंडिन् *m.* A heretic, a religious hypocrite; Y. 1. 130; 2. 70

पाषाणः A stone. **-णी** A small stone used as a weight. -Comp. **-दारकः, -दारणः** a stone-cutter's chisel. **-संधिः** a cave or chasm in a rock. **-हृदय** *a.* stonehearted, cruel, relentless.

पि 6 P. (पियति) To go, move.

पिकः The (Indian) cuckoo; कुसुमशरासनशासनवंदिनि पिकनिकरे भज भावं Git. 11; or उन्मीलंति कुहूः कुहूरिति कलोत्तालाः पिकानां गिरः Git. 1. -Comp. **-आनंदः, -बांधवः** the spring. **-बंधुः, -रागाः, -वल्लभः** the mango-tree.

पिकाः 1 An elephant twenty years old. 2 A young elephant in general.

पिंग *a.* Reddish-brown, tawny, yellow-red; अंतर्निविष्टामलपिंगतारं (विलोचनं) Ku 7. 33. **-गः** 1 The tawny colour. 2 A buffalo. 3 A rat. **-गा** 1 Turmeric. 2 Saffron. 3 A kind of yellow pigment. 4 An epithet of चंडिका. -Comp. **-अक्ष** *a.* having reddish-brown eyes, red-eyed. (**-क्षः**) 1 an ape. 2 an epithet of Siva. **-ईक्षणः** an epithet of Siva. **-ईशः** an epithet of fire. **-कापिशा** a species of cockroach. **-चक्षुस्** *m.* a crab **-जटः** an epithet of Siva. **-सारः** yellow orpiment. **-स्फटिकः** ' yellow crystal ', a kind of gem (**गोमेद**).

पिंगल *a.* Reddish-brown, yellowish, brown, tawny; R. 12. 71; Ms. 3. 8. **-लः** 1 The tawny colour. 2 Fire. 3 A monkey. 4 An ichneumon. 5 A small owl. 6 A kind of snake. 7 N. of an attendant on the sun. 8 N. of one of Kubera's treasures. 9 N. of a reputed sage, the father of Sanskrit prosody; his work being known as:—पिंगलच्छंदःशास्त्र; छंदोज्ञाननिधिं जघान मकरो वेलातटे पिंगलं Pt. 2. 33. **-लं** 1 brass. 2 Yellow orpiment. **-ला** 1 A kind of owl. 2 The Sisu tree (शिंशपा). 3 A kind of metal. 4 A particular vessel of the body. 4 The female elephant of the south. 5 N. of a courtezan who became remarkable for her piety and virtuous life; (the Bhâgavata mentions how she and Ajamîla were delivered from the trammels of the world). -Comp. **-अक्षः** an epithet of Siva.

पिंगलिका 1 A kind of crane. 2 A kind of owl.

पिंगाशः 1 The headman or proprietor of a village. 5 A kind of fish. **-शं** Virgin gold. **-शी** The Indigo plant.

पिचंडः-डं, पिचिंडः-डं The belly.

पिचंडकः A glutton (औदरिक).

पिचिंडिका The calf of the leg.

पिचिंडिल *a.* Big-bellied, corpulent.

पिचुः 1 Cotton. 2 A kind of weight, a Karsha (equal to two tolas). 3 A kind of leprosy. -Comp. **-तलं** cotton. **-मंदः,-मर्दः** the Nimba tree; Si. 5. 66.

पिचुलः 1 Cotton. 1 A kind of cormorant or sea-crow.

पिचट *a.* Pressed fist. **-टः** Inflammation of the eyes, ophthalmia. **-टं** 1 Tin. 2 Lead.

पिच्चा A string of 16 pearls weighing a *dharana* (a particular measure of pearls).

पिच्छं 1 A feather of a tail (as of a peacock). 2 The tail of a peacock Si. 4. 50. 3 The feathers of an arrow. 4 A wing. 5 A crest. **-च्छः** A tail in general. **-च्छाः** 1 A sheath, covering, coat. 2 The scum of boiled rice. 3 A row, line. 4 A heap, multitude. 5 The gum or exudation of the silk-cotton tree. 6 A plantain. 7 An armour. 8 The calf of the leg. 9 The venomous saliva of a snake. 10 A betelnut. -Comp. **-बाणः** a hawk.

पिच्छल *a.* Slimy, slippery.

पिच्छिका The feathers of a peacock's tail tied in a bunch, a feather-brush (used by conjurors &c.).

पिच्छिल *a.* 1 Slimy, lubricous, slippery, smeary; तरुणं सर्षपशाकं नवौदनं पिच्छिलानि च दधीनि Chand. M. 1. 2 Having a tail. **-लः -ला -लं** 1 The scum of boiled rice (भुक्तमंड). 2 sauce mixed with rice-gruel. 3 Curds with cream on the surface. -Comp. **-त्वच्** *m.* the orange tree or its peel.

पिंज् 1. 2 A. (पिंक्ते) 1 To tinge, dye. 2 To touch. 3 To adore. -11. 10 U. (पिंजयति-ते) 1 To give. 2 To take. 3 To shine. 4 To be strong or powerful. 5 To live, dwell. 6 To hurt, injure, kill.

पिंजः 1 The moon. 2 A species of camphor. 3 Killing, slaughter, 4 Heap. **-जं** Strength, power. **-जा** 1 Injury, hurting. 2 Turmeric. 3 Cotton.

पिंजटः The mucus or excretion of the eyes.

पिंजनं A bow-shaped instrument used for cleaning cotton.

पिंजर *a.* Reddish-yellow, tawny, gold-coloured; शिखा प्रदीपस्य सुवर्णपिंजरा Mk. 3. 17; R. 18. 40. **-रः** 1 The reddise-yellow or tawny-brown colour. 2 The yellow colour. **-रं** 1 Gold. 2 yellow orpiment. 3 A skeleton. 4 A cage (for पंजर).

पिंजरकं Orpiment.

पिंजरित *a.* Coloured yellow, tinged brown.

पिंजल *a.* 1 Overcome with grief or terror, extremely confounded or perplexed. 2 Panicstruck (as an army). **-लं** 1 Yellow orpiment. 2 The leaf of the Kusa grass.

पिंजालं Gold.

पिंजिका A roll of cotton from which threads are spun.

पिंजूषः The wax of the ear (कर्णमल).

पिंजेटः The excretion or mucus of the eyes.

पिंजोला The rusting of leaves, rustling noise of leaves.

पिटः A box, basket. **-टं** 1 A house, hovel. 2 A roof.

पिटकः-कं 1 A box, basket. 2 A granary. 3 A pimple, pustule, small boil or ulcer; (also पिटका or पिटिका in this sense); ततः गंडस्योपरि पिटका संवृत्ता S. 2. 4 kind of ornament on the banner of Indra.

पिटक्या A multitude of boxes.

पिटाकः A basket, box.

पिट्टकं The tartar of the teeth; (दंतकिट्ट).

पिठरः-रं A pot, pan, boiler (also पिठरी in this sense); पिठरं क्वथदतिमात्रं निजपार्श्वानेव दहतितरां Pt. 1. 324; जठरपिठरी दुष्पूरेयं करोति विडंबनां Bh. 3. 116 **-रं** A churning stick.

पिठरकः-कं A pot, pan. -Comp. **-कपालः-लं** a pot-sherd.

पिडकः-का A small boil, pimple, pustule.

पिंड् 1 A., 10. U. (पिंडते, पिंडयति-ते; पिंडित) 1 To roll into a lump or ball, put together. 2 To join, unite. 3 To heap or accumulate.

पिंड *a* (डी *f.*) 1 Solid (घन). 2 Compact, dense, close. **-डः-डं** 1 A round mass, ball, globe; (as अयःपिंडः, &c.). 2 A lump, clod (of earth &c.) 3 A round lump of food, morsel, mouthful; R. 2. 59. 4 A ball or lump of rice offered to the Manes at obsequial ceremonies or Srâddhas: R. 1. 66; 8. 26; Ms. 3. 216; 9. 132,

136, 140; Y. 1. 159. **5** Food in general; सफलीकृतभर्तृपिंडः M. 5 'who was true to his master's salt.' **6** Livelihood, sustenance, subsistence. **7** Alms; पिंडपातवेला Mâl. 2. **8** Flesh; meat. **9** The fætus or embryo in an early stage of gestation. **10** The body, corporeal frame; एकांतविध्वंसिषु मद्विधानां पिंडेष्वनास्था खलु भौतिकेषु R. 2. 57. **11** A heap, collection, multitude. **12** The calf of the leg; Mâl. 5. 16. **13** The frontal sinus of an elephant or its projection. **14** A portico or shed in front of the door. **15** Incense, frank-incense. **16** (In arith.) Sum, total amount. **17** (In geom.) Thickness. **-डं 1** Power, strength, might. **2** Iron. **3** Fresh butter. **4** An army. (**पिंडीकृ** to make into a lump or ball, press or heap together; **पिंडीभू** to be made into a ball or lump). -COMP. **-अन्वाहार्य** *a.* to be eaten after the funeral rice-ball has been offered to the Manes; Ms. 3. 123. **-अन्वाहार्यकं** a meal in honour of the Manes. **-अभ्रं** hail. **-अयसं** steel. **-अलक्तकः** a red dye. **-अशनः, आशः, -आशकः, -आशिन्** *m.* a beggar. **-उदकक्रिया** an oblation of obsequial rice-balls and water to the deceased. **-उद्धरणं** participating in funeral offerings. **-गोसः** gum myrrh. **-तैलं,-तैलकः** incense. **-द** *a.* **1** one who gives food, one who supplies with bread or with any other means of subsistence; श्वा पिंडदस्य कुरुते गजपुंगवस्तु धीरं विलोकयति चाटुशतैश्च भुंक्ते Bh. 2. 31. **2** one who is qualified to give the funeral rice-ball to deceâsed ancestors; Y. 2. 132 (**-दः**) **1** the nearest male relation who offers the funeral rice-ball. **2** a master, patron. **-दानं 1** presentation of the obsequial rice-ball. **2** the funeral oblattion made to deceased ancestors on the evening of new-moon. **-निर्वपणं** presenting obsequial rice-balls to the Manes. **-पातः** giving alms; Mal. 1. **-पातिकः** one who lives on alms. **-पादः, -पाद्यः** an elephant. **-पुष्पः 1** the Asoka tree. **2** the China rose. **3** the pomegranate. (**-ष्पं**) the blossom of the Asoka tree. **2** the flower of the China-rose. **3** a lotus. **-भाज्** *a.* receiving or entitled to a share in the funeral rice-ball. (*m. pl.*) the deceased ancestors or Manes; S. 6. 25. **-भृतिः** *f.* livelihood, means of subsistence. **-मूलं, -मूलकं** a carrot. **-यज्ञः** the presentetion of the obsequial rice-balls to the deceased ancestors; Y. 3. 16. **-लेपः** fragments of the obsequial rice-balls which cling to the hand; (these are presented to the three ancestors immediately preceding the great-grand-father.). **-लोपः** interruption in offering the funeral rice-balls (as the failure of issue). **-संबंधः** relationship between a living person and one deceased such as is sufficiently near to qualify the former to offer the obsequial rice-balls to the latter.

पिंडकः -कं 1 A lump, ball, globe. **2** A round swelling or protuberance. **3** A lump of food. **4** The calf of the leg. **5** Incense. **6** Carrot. **-कः** A goblin, demon (पिशाच).

पिंडनं Forming globes.

पिंडलः 1 A bridge, cause-way. **2** A mound, ridge.

पिंडसः A beggar, a mendicant living on alms.

पिंडातः Incense.

पिंडारः 1 A religious mendicant or beggar. **2** A cow-herd. **3** A buffalo-herdsman. **4** The *Vikankata* tree. **5** An expressien of censure.

पिंडिः-डी *f.* **1** A round mass, ball. **2** The nave of a wheel. **3** The calf of the leg. **4** The Asoka tree. **5** The long gourd (अलाबु). **6** A house. **7** A species of palm. -COMP. **-पुष्पः** the Asoka tree. **लेपः** a kind of unguent. **-शूरः** 'brave in the house', or 'a cake hero', a braggart, cowardly boaster, poltroon, cotquean; cf. गेहेनर्दिन्, गेहेशूर &c.

पिंडिका 1 A round or fleshy swelling. **2** The calf of the leg &c.; see पिंडि above.

पिंडित *a.* **1** Pressed or rolled into a ball or lump. **2** Thick, lumpish. **3** Heaped together, collected. **4** Mixed with. **5** Added, multiplied. **6** Counted, numbered.

पिंडिन् *a.* Receiving the funeral rice-balls (as ancestors). *-m.* **1** A beggar. **2** One who offers funeral rice-balls to the Manes.

पिंडिलः 1 A bridge, cause-way, mound. **2** An astronomer, a calculator of nativities.

पिंडीर *a.* Sapless, insipid, arid, dry. **-रः 1** The pomegranate tree. **2** Cuttle-fish-bone. **3** Foam of the sea; cf. डिंडीर.

पिंडोलिः *f.* Fragments dropped from the mouth, offal, leavings of a meal.

पिण्याकः -कं 1 Oil-cake. **2** Incense. **3** Saffron. **4** Asafœtida.

पितामहः (**हि** *f.*) **1** A paternal grandfather. **2** An epithet of Brahmâ.

पितृ *m.* A father; तेनास लोकः पितृमान् विनेत्रा R. 14. 23; 1. 24; 11. 67. **-रौ** (dual) Parents, father and mother; जगतः पितरौ वंदे पार्वतीपरमेश्वरौ R. 1. 1; Y. 2. 117. **-रः** (pl.) **1** Forefathers, ancestors, father; S. 6. 24. **2** Paternal ancestors taken collectively; Ms. 2. 151. **3** The Manes; R. 2. 16; 4. 20. Bg. 10. 29; Ms. 3. 81; 192. -COMP. **-अर्जित** *a.* acquired by a father, paternal (as property). **-कर्मन्** *n.*, **-कार्यं, -कृत्यं, क्रिया** oblation or sacrifice offered to deceased ancestors, obsequial rites. **-काननं** a cemetery; R. 11. 16. **-कुल्या** N. of a river rising in the Malaya mountain. **-गणः 1** the whole body of ancestors taken collectively. **2** a class of Manes or deceased progenitor who were sons of the Prajâpati; see Ms. 3. 194-195. **-गृहं 1** a paternal mansion. **2** cemetery, burial ground. **-घातकः, घातिन्** *m.* a parricide. **-तर्पणं 1** an oblation to the Manes. **2** the act of throwing water out of the right hand (as at the time of ablutions) as an offering to the Manes or deceased ancestors; Ms. 2. 176. **3** sesamum. **-तिथिः** *f.* the day of new-moon (अमावास्या). **-तीर्थं 1** N. of the place called Gayâ where the performance of funeral rites, such as Srâddhas in honour of the Manes, is held to be particularly meritorious. **2** the part of the hand between the fore-finger and the thumb (considered to be sacred to the Manes). **-दानं** an offering to the Manes. **-दायः** patrimony. **-दिनं** the day of new-moon (अमावास्या). **-देव** *a.* **1** worshipping a father. **2** relating to the worship of the Manes. (**-वाः**) the divine Manes. **-दैवत** *a.* presided over by the Manes. (**-तं**) N. of the tenth lunar mansion (मघा). **-द्रव्यं** patrimony; Y. 2. 118. **-पक्षः 1** the paternal side, paternal relationship **2** relatives by the father's side. **3** 'the fortnight of the manes', N. of the dark half of Bhâdrapada which is particularly appointed for the celebration of obsequial rites to the Manes. **-पतिः** an epithet of Yama. **-पदं** the world of the Manes. **-पितृ** *m.* paternal grandfather. **-पुत्रौ** (पितापुत्रौ dual) father and son. (पितुः पुत्रः means 'the son of a well-known and renowned father'). **-पूजनं** worship of the Manes. **-पैतामह** *a.* (**ही** *f.*) inherited from ancestors, ancestral, hereditary. (**-हाः** pl.) ancestors. **-प्रसूः** *f.* **1** paternal grandmother. **2** evening twilight. **-प्राप्त** *a.* **1** inherited from a father. **2** inherited patrimonially. **-बंधुः** a kinsman by the fathers side. (**-धु**) relationship by the father's side. **-भक्त** *a.* dutifully attached to a father. **-भक्तिः** *f.* filial duty. **-भोजनं** food offered to the Manes. **-भ्रातृ** *m.* a father's brother, paternal uncle. -मंदिरं 1 a paternal mansion 2 a cemetery -मेधः sacrifice offered to the Manes, obsequial offerings. -यज्ञः 1 obsequial offerings. 2 offering libations of water every day to the deceased ancestors; it is one of the five daily Yag*n*as enjoined to be performed by a Brâhma*n*a; पितृयज्ञस्तु तर्पणं Ms. 3. 70; also 122, 283. -राज् m. राजः, -राजन् m. an epithet of Yâma. -रूपः an epithet of *S*iva. -लोकः the world of the Manes. -वंशः the paternal family. -वनं a cemetery. (पितृवनेचरः 1 a demon, goblin. 2 an epithet of *S*iva). वसतिः *f.* -सद्मन् *n.* a cemetry; Ku. 5. 77. -व्रतं obsequial rites. -श्राद्धं obsequial rites in honour of a father or deceased ancestor. -स्वसृ *f.* (also पितृष्वसृ as well as पितुः स्वसृ or पितुः ष्वसृ) a father's sister. Ms. 2. 131. -ष्वस्रीयः a paternal aunt's son. संनिभ *a.* fatherly, paternal. -सूः 1 paternal grandmother. 2 evening twilight. -स्थानः -स्थानीयः a guardian (who is in the place of a father). -हत्या parricide. -हन् *m.* a parricide.

पितृक *a.* Paternal, ancestral, hereditary. 2 Obsequial.

पितृव्यः 1 A father's brother, paternal uncle. 2 Any elderly male relation; Ms. 2. 130.

पित्तं Bile, one of the three humours of the body (the other two being वात and कफ); पित्तं यदि शर्करया शाम्यति कोर्थः पटोलेन Pt. 1. 378. Comp. -अतीसारः a bilious form of diarrhœa. -उपहत *a.* affected by bile; पश्यति पित्तोपहतः शशिशुभ्रं शंखमपि पीतं K. P. 10. -कोषः the gall-bladder. -क्षोभः excess or derangement of the bilious humour. -ज्वरः a bilious fever. -प्रकृति *a.* of a bilious or choleric temperament -प्रकोपः excess and vitiation of the bilious humour. -रक्तं plethora. -वायुः flatulence caused by the excess and vitiation of the bilious humour. -विदग्ध *a.* impaired by bile. -शमन, -हर *a.* antibilious.

पित्तल *a.* Bilious. -लं 1 Brass. 2 A species of birch tree.

पित्र्य *a.* 1 Paternal, patrimonial, ancestral. 2 (*a*) Relating or sacred to the deceased ancestors; Ms. 2. 59. (*b*) Obsequial. -त्र्यः 1 The eldest brother. 2 The month of Mâgha. -त्र्या 1 The constellation called Maghâ. 2 The day of full as well as new moon. त्र्यं 1 The lunar mansion called Maghâ. 2 The part of the hand between the fore-finger and the thumb (sacred to the Mânes).

पित्सत् *m.* A bird.

पित्सलः A road, path.

पिधानं 1 Covering, concealing. 2 A sheath. 3 A wrapper, cloak. 4 A lid or top.

पिधानकं 1 A sheath, scabbard. 2 A lid.

पिधायक *a.* Covering, hiding, concealing.

पिनद्ध *p. p.* 1 Fastened, tied or put on. 2 Dressed. 3 Hid, concealed. 4 Pierced, penetrated. 5 Wrapped, covered, enveloped.

पिनाकः-कं 1 The bow of *S*iva. 2 A trident. 3 A bow in general. 4 A staff or stick. 5 A shower of dust. -Comp. -गोप्तृ, धृक्, धृत्, पाणिः *m.* epithets of *S*iva; Ku. 3. 10.

पिनाकिन् *m.* An epithet of *S*iva; Ku. 5. 77; *S*. 1. 6.

पिपतिषत् *m.* A bird.

पिपतिषु *a.* Being about to fall. -षुः A bird.

पिपासा Thirst.

पिपासित, पिपासिन्, पिपासु *a.* Thirsty.

पिपीलः, पिपीली An ant.

पिपीलकः A large black ant.

पिपीलिकः An ant. -कं A kind of gold (said to be collected by ants).

पिपीलिका A female ant. -Comp. -परिसर्पणं the running about of ants.

पिप्पलः 1 The holy fig-tree; Y. 1. 302. 2 A nipple. 3 The sleeve of a jacket or coat. -लं 1 A berry in general. 2 A berry of the holy fig-tree. 3 Sensual enjoyment. 4 Water.

पिप्पलिः -ली *f.* Long pepper.

पिप्पिका The tartar of the teeth.

पिप्लुः A mark, mole, freckle.

पियालः N. of a tree; Ku. 3. 31. -लं The fruit of this tree.

पिल् 10 P. (पेलयति-ते) 1 To throw, cast. 2 To send, direct. 3 To incite, prompt.

पिलुः See पीलु.

पिल्ल *a.* Blear-eyed. -ल्लं A bleared eye.

पिल्लका A female elephant.

पिश् 6 U. (पिंशति-ते) 1 To shape, fashion, form. 2 To be organised. 3 To light, irradiate.

पिशंग *a.* Reddish-brown, reddish, of a tawny colour; मध्येसमुद्रं ककुभः पिशंगीः *S*i. 3. 33; 1. 6; Ki. 4. 36. -गः The tawny colour.

पिशंगकः An epithet of Vish*n*u or his attendant.

पिशाचः A fiend, goblin, devil, spirit, malevolent being; नन्वाश्वासितः पिशाचोपि भोजनेन V. 2; Ms. I. 37; 12. 44. -Comp. -आलयः phosphorescence. -द्रुः a kind of tree. -बाधा -संचारः demoniacal possession. -भाषा 'the language of devils', a giberish or corruption of Sanskrit, one of the lowest Prâkrita dialects used in plays. -सभं 1 an assemblage of fiends. 2 pandemonium, the hall of their assembly.

पिशाचकिन् *m.* An epithet of Kubera, the god of wealth.

पिशाचिका 1 A she-demon, a female imp. 2 (At the end of comp.) Devilish or diabolical fondness for a thing; किमनया आयुधपिशाचिकया Mv. 3 devilish fondness for fighting; पिशाची is used in the same sense; तस्य खल्वियं यावज्जीवमायुधपिशाची न हृदयादपक्रामति B. R. 4, or कियच्चिरमियमतिनाटयिष्यति भवंतमायुधपिशाची A. R. 4.

पिशितं Flesh; कुत्रापि नापि खलु हा पिशितस्य लेशः Bv. 1. 105; R. 7. 50. Comp. -अशनः, -आशः, -आशिन्, -भुज् *m.* 1 flesh-eater, a demon, goblin; (छायाः) संध्यापयोदकपिशाः पिशिताशनानां चरंति *S*. 3. 27. 2 a man-eater, cannibal.

पिशुन *a.* 1 (*a*) Indicating, manifesting, evincing, displaying, indicative of; शत्रूणामनिशं विनाशपिशुनः *S*i. 1. 75; तुल्यानुरागपिशुनं V. 2. 14; R. 1. 53; Amaru. 97. (*b*) Memorable for, commemorating; क्षेत्रं क्षत्रप्रधनपिशुनं कौरवं तद्भजेथाः Me. 48. 2 Slanderous, back-biting, calumniating; पिशुनजनं खलु बिभ्रति क्षितींद्राः Bv. 1. 74. 3 Wicked, cruel, malignant. 4 Low, vile, contemptible. 5 Foolish, stupid. -नः 1 A slanderer, back-biter, tale-bearer, base informer, traitor, calumniator; H. 1. 135, Pt 1. 304; Ms. 3. 161. 2 Cotton. 3 An epithet of Nârada. 4 A crow. -Comp. -वचनं; -वाक्यं slander, detraction, calumny.

पिष् 7 P. (पिनष्टि, पिष्ट) 1 To pound, grind, pulverize, crush, अथवा भवतः प्रवर्तना न कथं पिष्टमियं पिनष्टि नः N. 2. 61; 13. 19; माषपेषं पिपेष Mv. 6. 45; Bk. 6. 37; 12. 18; Bv. 1. 12 2 To hurt, injure, destroy, kill (with gen.); क्रमेण पेष्टुं भुवनद्विषामसि *S*i. 1. 40. -With उद् to crush or grind down. -निस् 1 to pound, powder, pulverize, reduce to atoms; (तं) निष्पिपेष क्षितौ क्षिप्रं पूर्णं कुंभमिवांभसि Mb.; शिलानिष्पिष्टमुद्गरः R. 12. 73. 2 to hurt, injure, bruise; Bk. 6. 120.

पिष्ट *p. p.* 1 Ground, powdered, crushed; Bv. 1. 12. 73. 2 Rubbed together, squeezed or clasped (as the hands). -ष्टं 1 Anything ground, a ground substance. 2 Flour, meal; पिष्टं पिनष्टि 'he grinds flour'; *i. e.* does a useless work or a profitless repetition. 3 Lead. -Comp. -उदकं 'water mixed with flour' -पचनं a pan for parching flour, a boiler &c. -पशुः an effigy of a beast made with flour. -पिंड a cake or ball of flour. -पूरः see घृतपूर. -पेषः, -पेषणं 'grinding flour'; *i.e.* doing any useless work, a vain or profitless repetition. °न्यायः see under न्याय. -मेहः a variety of diabetes. -वर्तिः a kind of small ball made of the flour of barley, pulse or rice. –सौरभं (pounded) sandal-wood.

पिष्टकः –कं 1 A cake made of the flour of any grain. 2 A baked cake, bread. –कं Pounded sesamum seeds.

पिष्टपः –पं A division of the universe; cf. विष्टप.

पिष्टातः Scented or perfumed powder.

पिष्टिक A cake made of rice-flour.

पिस् I. 1 P. (पेसति) To go, move. –II. 10 U. (पेसयति ते) 1 To go. 2 To be strong. 3 To dwell. 4 To hurt, injure. 5 To give or take.

पिहित *p. p.* 1 Shut, closed, barred, fastened; see धा with अपि. 2 Covered, concealed, hidden; see अपिहित. 3 Filled or covered with.

पी 4 A. (पीयते) To drink तव वदनभवामृतं निपीय Mk. 10. 13; N. 1. 1.

पीचं The chin.

पीठं 1 A seat (a stool, chair, bench, sofa &c.); जवेन पीठादुदतिष्ठदच्युतः Si. 1. 12; R. 4 84; 6. 15. 2 The seat of a religious student made of Kusa grass. 3 The seat of a deity, an alter. 4 A pedestal in general, basis. 5 A particular posture in sitting. COMP. –केलिः a male confidant, a parasite. –गर्भः the cavity in the pedestal of an idol. –नायिका a girl of fourteen who represents Durgâ at the festival of that goddess. –भूः basis, basement. –मर्दः 1 a companion, parasite, one who assists the hero of a drama in great undertakings, *e. g.* in securing his mistress; so पीठमर्दिका 'a lady who assists the heroine in securing her lover'. 2 a dancing master who instructs courtezans in the art of dancing. –सर्प *a.* lame, crippled.

पीठिका 1 A seat (bench, stool). 2 A pedestal, base. 3 A section or division of a book, as the पूर्वपीठिका, and उत्तरपीठिका of दशकुमारचरित.

पीड् 10 U. (पीडयति-ते,पीडित) 1 To pain, torment, harm, hurt, injure, harass, annoy, molest; नलिं चापीपिडच्छरैः BK. 15. 82; Ms. 4. 67, 238; 7. 29. 2 To oppose, resist. 3 To besiege (as a city). 4 To press or squeeze together, compress, pinch; कंठे पीडयन् MK. 8; लभेत सिकतासु तैलमपि यत्नतः पीडयन् Bh. 2. 5; दशनपीडिताधरा R. 19. 35. 5 To suppress, destroy; Ms. 1. 51. 6 To neglect. 7 To cover with anything inauspicious. 8 To eclipse. –WITH अभि,-अव to press, squeeze, pain. –आ to press, weigh down; पयोधरभरेणापीडितः Git 12.–उद् 1 to press against, strike or rub against; अन्योन्यमुत्पीडयदुत्पलाक्ष्याः स्तनद्वयं पांडु तथा प्रवृद्धं Ku. 1. 40; Si. 3. 66 2 to press out, throw or strike upwards, propel, urge; R. 5. 46; 16 66. –उप 1 to hurt, injure, trouble, harass, molest; स्तनोपपीडं परिरब्धुकामा Ki. 3. 54; Si. 10. 47. 2 to oppress, lay waste; Ms. 8. 67; 7. 195. –नि 1 to harass, pain, molest, punish, trouble; Ms. 7. 23. 2 to squeeze, press together, hold fast, seize, grasp; गुरोः सदारस्य निपीड्य पादौ R. 2. 23; 5 65. –निस् to press or squeeze out; see निष्पीडित. –परि 1 to pain, trouble, molest. 2 to press, squeeze. –प्र 1 to pain excessively, torment, harass. 2 to press or squeeze. –सं to press together, pinch; कंठे जीर्णलताप्रतानवलयेनात्यर्थसंपीडितः S. 7. 11.; Ch. P. 3.

पीडकः An oppressor.

पीडनं 1 Paining, distressing, oppressing, inflicting pain; Ms. 9. 299. 2 Squeezing, pressing; दोर्वल्लिबंधनिबिडस्तनपीडनानि Git. 10; दंतौष्ठपीडननखक्षतरक्तसिक्ता Ch. P. 48. 3 An instrument for pressing. 4 Taking, holding, seizing; as in करपीडन or पाणिपीडन q v. 5 Laying waste, devastation. 6 Threshing corn. 7 An eclipse; as in ग्रहपीडन q. v. 8 Suppressing sounds, a fault in the pronunciation of vowels.

पीडा 1 Pain, trouble, suffering, annoyance, molestation, agony; आश्रमपीडा R. 1. 37 disturbance; 71; मदन°, दारिद्र्य° &c. 2 Injury, damage, harm; Bg. 17. 19; Ms. 7. 169. 3 Devastation, laying waste. 4 Violation, infringement. 5 Restriction. 6 Pity, compassion. 7 Eclipse. 8 A chaplet, garland for the head. 9 The *Sarala* tree. –COMP. –कर *a.* troublesome, painful.

पीडित *p. p.* 1 Pained, harassed, tormented, oppressed, pinched. 2 Squeezed, pressed. 3 Espoused, held. 4 Violated, broken. 5 Laid waste, devastated. 6 Eclipsed. 7 Bound, tied. –तं 1 Paining, injuring, harassing. 2 A particular mode of sexual enjoyment. –तं *ind.* Fast, closely, firmly.

पीत *a.* 1 Drunk, quaffed. 2 Steeped, soaked in, filled or saturated with. 3 Yellow; विद्युल्लेखारचितपीतपटोत्तरीयः MK. 5. 2. –तः 1 Yellow colour. 2 Topaz. 3 Safflower. –तं 1 Gold. 2 Yellow orpiment. –COMP. –अब्धिः an epithet of Agastya. –अंबरः 1 An epithet of Vishṇu; इति निगदितः प्रीतः पीतांबरोपि तथा करोत् Git 12. 2 an actor. 3 a religious mendicant wearing yellow garments. –अरुण *a.* yellowish-red. –अश्मन् *m.* topaz. –कदली a species of Banana (स्वर्णकदली). –कंदं the carrot. –कावेरं 1 saffron. 2 brass. –काष्ठं yellow sanders. –गंधं yellow sandal. –चंदनं 1 a species of sandal-wood. 2 saffron. 3 turmeric. –चंपकः a lamp. –तुंडः Kâraṇḍava bird. –दारु *n.* a kind of pine or *Sarala* tree. –दुग्धा a milch cow. –द्रुः the *Sarala* tree. –पादा a species of bird (Mar. मैना). –मणिः a topaz. –माक्षिकं a kind of mineral substance. –मूलकं the carrot. रक्त *a.* yellowish red, orange-coloured. (–क्तं) a kind of yellow gem, the topaz. –रागः 1 the yellow colour. 2 wax. 3 the fibres of a lotus. –वालुका turmeric. –वासस् *m.* an epithet of Krishṇa. –सारः 1 the topaz. 2 the sandal tree. (–रं) yellow sandal-wood. –सारि *n.* antimony. –स्कंधः a hog. –स्फटिकः the topaz. –हरित *a.* yellowish green.

पीतकं 1 Yellow orpiment. 2 Brass. 3 Saffron. 4 Honey. 5 Aloe-wood. 6 Sandal-wood.

पीतनः A species of fig tree (waved-leaf). —नं 1 Yellow orpiment. 2 Saffron.

पीतल *a.* Yellow. —लः The yellow colour. —लं Brass.

पीतिः A horse. —*f.* 1 Draught, drinking. 2 A tavern. 3 The proboscis of an elephant.

पीतिका 1 Saffron. 2 Turmeric. 3 Yellow jasmine.

पीतुः 1 The sun. 2 Fire. 3 The chief elephant of a herd.

पीथः 1 The sun. 2 Time. 3 Fire. 4 Drink. 5 Water.

पीथिः A horse.

पीन *a.* 1 Fat, fleshy, corpulent. 2 Plump, large, thick; as in पीनस्तनी. 3 Full, round. 4 Profuse, excessive. –COMP. –ऊधस् *f.* (पीनोघ्नी) a cow with full udders. –वक्षस् *a.* full-chested, having a full bosom.

पीनसः 1 Cold affecting the nose. 2 Cough, catarrh.

पीयुः 1 A crow. 2 The sun. 3 Fire. 4 An owl. 5 Time. 6 Gold.

पीयूषः-षं 1 Nectar, ambrosia; मनसि वचसि काये पुण्यपीयूषपूर्णाः Bh. 2. 78; इमां पीयूषलहरी G. L. 53. 2 Milk in general. 3 The Milk of a cow during the first seven days after calving.-COMP. -महस् *m.*, रुचिः 1 the moon. 2 camphor. -वर्षः 1 a shower of nectar, 2 the moon. 3 camphor.

पीलकः The large black ant.

पीलुः 1 An arrow. 2 An atom. 3 An insect. 4 An elephant. 5 The stem of the palm. 6 A flower. 7 A group of palm trees. 8 A kind of tree.

पीलुकः An ant.

पीव् 1 P. (पीवति) To be fat or corpulent.

पीवन् *a.* (पीवरी *f.*) 1 Full, fat, large. 2 Stout, strong.-*m.* Wind.

पीवर *a.* (रा or री *f.*) 1 Fat, large, stout, fleshy, corpulent; R. 3. 8. 5. 65; 19. 32. 2 Plump, thick. **-रः** 1 A tortoise. **-री** 1 A young woman. 2 A cow.

पीवा Water.

पुंस् 10 U. (पुंसयति-ते) 1 To crush, grind. 2 To pain, trouble, punish.

पुंस् *m.* (Nom. पुमान्, पुमांसौ, पुमांसः; Instr. Du; पुंभ्यां; Voc. sing. पुमन्.) 1 A male, male being; पुंसि विश्वसिति कुत्र कुमारी N. 5. 110. 2 A man, human being; यस्यार्थाः स पुमाँल्लोके H. 1. 3. man, mankind, people! वंद्यैः पुंसां रघुपतिपदैः Me. 12. 4 A servant, an attendant. 5 A word in the masculine gender. 6 The masculine gender; पुंसि वा हरिचंदनं Ak. 7 The soul. -COMP. **-अनुज** *a.* (पुंसानुज) having an elder brother. **-अनुजा** (पुमनुजा) a girl born after the male child; *i. e.* a girl having an elder brother. **-अपत्यं** (पुमपत्यं) a male child. **-अर्थः** (पुमर्थः) 1 the aim of man. 2 any one of the four ends of human existence; *i. e.* धर्म, अर्थ, काम and मोक्ष, see पुरुषार्थ. **-आख्या** (पुमाख्या) a designation of a male being. **-आचारः** (पुमाचारः) a usage of men. **-कटिः** *f.* a man's hip. **-कामा** a woman wishing for a husband. **-कोकिलः** a male cuckoo; Ku. 3. 32. **-खेटः** (पुंखेटः) a male planet. **-गवः** (पुंगवः) 1 a bull, an ox. 2 (at the end of comp.) chief, best, most excellent, distinguished or pre-eminent of any class; वाल्मीकिर्मुनिपुंगवः Râm; so गजपुंगवः Bh. 2. 31; नरपुंगवः &c. **-केतुः** an epithet of *S*iva; Ku. 7. 77. **-चली** (पुंश्चली) a harlot, an unchaste woman; Y. 1. 162. **-चलीयः** (पुंश्चलीयः) the son of a harlot. **-चिह्नं** (पुंश्चिह्नं) the characteristic of a male, the membrum virile. **-जन्मन्** (पुंजन्मन्) *n.* the brith of a male child. **योगः** a constellation under which male children are born. **-दासः** (पुंदासः) a male slave. **-ध्वजः** (पुंध्वजः) 1 the male of any species of animal. 2 a mouse. **-नक्षत्रं** (पुंनक्षत्रं) a male asterism. **-नागः** (पुंनागः) 1 'an elephant among men', a distinguished man. 2 a white elephant. 3 a white lotus. 4 nutmeg. 5 N. of a tree called नागकेशर; R. 6. 57. **-नाटः-ढः** (पुंनाटः-ढः) N. of a tree. **-नामधेयः** (पुंनामधेयः) a male. **-नामन्** (पुंनामन्) *a.* holding a masculine name. (*-m.*) the tree called पुंनाग. **-पुत्रः** a male child. **-प्रजननं** the male organ of generation. **-भूमन्** (पुंभूमन्) *m.* a word of the masculine gender used only in the plural number; दाराः पुंभूम्नि चाक्षताः Ak. **-योग** (पुंयोगः) 1 cohabitation with men. 2 reference to a male or husband; पुंयोगे क्षत्रियी. **-रत्नं** (पुंरत्नं) an excellent man. **-राशिः** (पुंराशिः) a male sign of the zodiac. **-रूपं** (पुंरूपं) the form of a man. **-लिंग** *a.* (पुल्लिंग) of the masculine gender, masculine. (**-गं**) 1 masculine gender. 2 virility, manhood. 3 the male organ **-वत्सः** (पुंवत्सः) a bull-calf. **-वृषः** (पुंवृषः) the musk-rat. **वेष** *a.* (पुंवेश) dressed like a male, clad in male attire. **-सवन** (पुंसवन) *a.* causing the birth of a male child. (**-नं**) the first of the purificatory Samskâras; it is a ceremony performed on a woman's perceiving the first signs of a living conception, with a view to the birth of a son; R. 3. 10. 2 foetus. 3 milk.

पुंस्त्वं 1 The characteristic of a male, virility, potency, masculinenss; यत्नात्पुंस्त्वे परीक्षितः Y. 1. 55. 2 Semen virile. 3 The masculine gender.

पुंवत् *ind.* 1 Like a man; R 6. 20. 2 In the masculine gender.

पुक्कश *a.* (शी *f.*), **पुक्कस** *a.* (सी *f.*) Low, vile. **-शः, -सः** N. of a degraded mixed caste, the offspring of a Nishâda by a *S*údra woman; जातो निषादाच्छूद्रायां जात्या भवति पुक्कसः Ms. 10. 18. **-शी-सी** 1 A bud. 2 The indigo plant. 3 A woman of the Pukkasa caste.

पुंखः खं 1 The feathered part of an arrow; R. 2. 31; 3. 64; 9. 61. 2 A falcon, heron.

पुंखित *a.* Furnished with feathers (as an arrow).

पुंगः, -गं A heap, collection, multitude.

पुंगलः The soul.

पुच्छः -च्छं 1 A tail in general; पश्चात्पुच्छे वहति विपुले U. 4. 27. 2 A hairy tail: 3 A peacock's tail. 4 The hinder part. 5 The end of anything. -COMP. **-अग्रं,-मूलं** the tip of the tail. **-कंटकः** a scorpion. **-जाहं** the root of the tail.

पुच्छटिः -टी *f.* Cracking the fingers (छोटिका).

पुच्छिन् *m.* A cock.

पुंजः A heap, multitude, quantity, mass, collection; क्षिरोदवेलेव सफेनपुंजा Ku. 7. 26; प्रत्युद्गच्छति मूर्छति स्थिरतमःपुंजे निकुंजे प्रियः Git. 11.

पुंजिः *f.* A heap, quantity, mass.

पुंजिकः Hail.

पुंजितः *a.* 1 Heaped, collected, heaped together. 2 Pressed together.

पुट् I. 6. P. (पुटति) 1 To embrace, clasp. 2 To intertwine.-11. 10 U. (पुटयति-ते) 1 To be in contact with. 2 To bind together, fasten. 3 (पोटयति-ते) (*a*) To grind, reduce to powder. (*b*) To speak. (*c*) To shine. -111. 1. P. (पोटति) 1 To grind. 2 To rub.

पुटः -टं 1 A fold. 2 A hollow space, cavity, concavity; भिन्नपल्लवपुटो वनानिलः R 9. 68, 11. 23; 17. 12; M. 3. 9; अंजलिपुट, नासापुट, कर्णपुट &c. 3 A cup made of a leaf folded or doubled; a vessel of leaves; दुग्ध्वा पयः पत्रपुटे मदीयं R. 2. 65; Ms. 6. 28; 4 Any shallow resceptacle 5 The pod or capsule which envelops young shoots. 6 A sheath, cover, covering. 7 An eyelid. (पुटी also in all these senses). 8 A horse's hoop. **-टः** A casket. **-टं** A nutmeg. -COMP. **-उटजं** a white umbrella. **-उदकः** a cocoa-nut. **-ग्रीवः** 1 a pot, jar, pitcher. 2 a copper-vessel. **-पाकः** a particular method of preparing drugs, in which the various ingredients are wrapped up in leaves, and being covered with clay are roasted in the fire; अनिर्भिन्नो गंभीरत्वादंतर्गूढघनव्यथः । पुटपाकप्रतीकाशो रामस्य करुणो रसः U. 3. 1. **-भेदः** 1 a town, city. 2 a kind of musical instrument (आतोद्य). 3 a whirl-pool or eddy. **-भेदनं** a town, city; *S*i. 13. 26.

पुटकं 1 A fold. 2 Any shllow cup or cavity. 3 A vessel made of a leaf. 4 A lotus. 5 Nutmeg.

पुटकिनी 1 A lotus 2 Group of lotuses.

पुटिका Cardamoms.

पुटित *a.* 1 Rubbed, ground. 2 Contracted. 3 Stitched, sewn. 4 Split.

पुटी See पुट.

पुड् 6 P. 1 To leave, quit, abandon. 2 To dismiss. 3 To emit, send forth. 4 To discover.

पुंड् 1 P. (पुंडति) To grind, reduce to powder, pound.

पुंड्रः A sign, mark.

पुंडरीकं 1 A lotus-flower, especially a white lotus; U. 6. 27; Mâl. 9. 14. 2 A white parasol. **-कः** 1 The white colour. 2 N. of the elephant presiding over the south-east direction; R. 18. 8. 3 A tiger. 4 A kind of serpent. 5 A species of rice. 6 A kind of leprosy. 7 A fever in an elephant. 8 A kind of mango-tree. 9 A pitcher, water-pot. 10 Fire. 11 A (sectarial) mark on the forehead. -COMP. **-अक्षः** an epithet of Vishnu; R. 18. 8. **-प्लवः** a kind of bird. **-मुखी** a kind of leech.

पुंड्रः 1 A kind of sugar-cane (red-variety). 2 A lotus in general. 3 A white lotus. 4 A mark or line (on the forehead) made with sandal &c. sectarial mark. 5 A worm. **-ड्राः** *pl.* N. of a country and its inhabitants. -COMP. **-केलिः** an elephant.

पुंड्रकः 1 A variety of sugar-cane (red-vâriety). 2 A sectatial mark.

पुण्य *a.* 1 Holy, sacred, pure; जनकतनयास्नानपुण्योदकेषु आश्रमेषु Me. 1; पुण्यं धाम चंडीश्वरस्य 33; R. 3. 41; *S*. 2. 14; Ms. 2. 68. 2 Good, meritorious virtuous, righteous, just. **3** Auspicious, propitious, lucky, favourable (as a day). Ms. 2. 30, 26. **5** Agreeable, pleasing, lovely, beautiful; प्रकृत्या पुण्यलक्ष्मीकौ Mv. 1. 16; **24**; U. 4. 19; so पुण्यदर्शनः &c. **5** sweet, fragrant (as odour). **6** solemn, festive. **-ण्यं 1** Virtue, religious or moral merit; अत्युत्कटैः पापपुण्यैरिहैव फलमश्नुते H. 1. 83; महता पुण्यपण्येन क्रीतेयं कायनौस्त्वया *S*ânti. 3. 1; R. 1. 69; N. **3.** 87. **2** A virtuous or meritorious act, good or virtuous works. **3** Purity, purification. **4** A trough for watering cattle. **-ण्या** The holy basil. -COMP. **-अहं** (for **अहन्**) a happy or auspicious day; पुण्याहं भवंतो ब्रुवंतु । अस्तु पुण्याहं; पुण्याहं व्रज मंगलं सुदिवसं प्रातः प्रयातस्य ते Amaru. 61. °**वाचनं** repeating 'this is an auspicious day' three times at the commencement of most religious ceremonies. **-उदयः** the dawn or resulting of good fortune. **-उद्यान** *a.* having lovely gardens. **-कर्तृ** *m.* a meritorious or virtuous man. **-कर्मन्** *a.* doing meritorious acts, upright, righteous. (*-n.*) a meritorious act. **-कालः** an auspicious time. **-कीर्ति** *a.* bearing a good or holy name, of auspicious fame, celebrated; Bk. 1. 5. **-कृत्** *a.* virtuous, meritorious. **-कृत्या** a meritorious work. **-क्षेत्रं 1** a holy place, place of pilgrimage. **2** 'the holy land', N. of *A*ryâvarta. **-गंध** *a.* sweetscented. **-गृहं 1** an alms-house. **2** a temple. **-जनः 1** a virtuous man. **2** a demon, goblin. **3** a Yaksha; R. 13. 60. **-ईश्वरः** an epithet of Kubera; अनुययौ यमपुण्यजनेश्वरौ R. 9. **6.** **-जित** *a.* won by merit or good works. **-तीर्थं** a holy place of pilgrimage. **-दर्शन** *a.* beautiful. (**-नः**) the blue jay. (**-नं**) visiting holy shrines. **-पुरुषः** a man rich in moral merit, a virtuous man. **-प्रतापः** the efficacy of virtue or moral merit. **-फलं** the reward of good works. (**-लः**) a grove. **-भाज्** *a.* blessed, virtuous, meritorious; पुण्यभाजः खल्वमी मुनयः K. 43. **-भूः**, **-भूमिः** *f.* 'the holy land'; *i. e. A*ryâvarta. **-रात्रः** an auspicious night. **-लोकः** heaven, paradise. **-शकुनं** an auspicious omen; (**-नः**) a bird of good omen. **-शील** *a.* of a virtuous disposition, inclined to pious acts, virtuous, pious, righteous. **-श्लोक** *a.* 'well-spoken of' or 'auspicious to repeat or utter the name of', of good fame. (**-कः**) an epithet of Nala, (of Nishadha), Yudhishthira and Janârdana; पुण्यश्लोको नलो राजा पुण्यश्लोको युधिष्ठिरः । पुण्यश्लोका च वैदेही पुण्यश्लोको जनार्दनः ॥ (**-का**) an epithet of Sîtâ and Draupadî. **-स्थानं** a sacred or holy place, a place of pilgrimage.

पुण्यवत् *a.* **1** Meritorious, virtuous. **2** Lucky, auspicious, fortunate. **3** Happy, blessed.

पुत् *n.* A particular division of Hell or the infernal regions to which childless persons are said to be condemned; see पुत्र below. -COMP. **-नामन्** *a.* called पुत्.

पुत्तलः—ली 1 An image, idol, a statue, effigy. **2** A doll, puppet. -COMP. **-दहनं**,**-विधिः** burning an effigy in place of the body of one who has died abroad or whose corpse is lost.

पुत्तलकः, **पुत्तलिका** A doll &c.

पुत्तिका 1 A small kind of bee. **2** The white ant.

पुत्रः 1 A son; (the word is thus derived:—पुन्नाम्नो नरकाद्यस्मात्त्रायते पितरं सुतः । तस्मात्पुत्र इति प्रोक्तः स्वयमेव स्वयंभुवा ॥ Ms. 9. 138; the word, therefore, should be strictly written पुत्त्रः). **2** A child, the young one of an animal. **3** A dear child (a term of endearment in addressing young persons). **4** (At the end of comp.) Anything little or small of its kind; as in असिपुत्रः, शिलापुत्रः &c. **-त्रौ** (bu.) A son and daughter. (**पुत्रीकृ** to adopt as a son; R. 2. 36.). -COMP. **-अन्नादः 1** one who lives at a son's expense, one who is maintained by his son. **2** a mendicant of a particular order; see कुटीचक. **-अर्थिन्** *a.* wishing for a son. **-इष्टिः**,**-इष्टिका** *f.* a sacrifice performed to obtain male issue. **-काम** *a.* desirous of sons. **-कार्यं** a ceremony relating to a son. **-कृतकः** one who is adopted as a son, an adopted son; श्यामाकमुष्टिपरिवर्धितको जहाति सोयं न पुत्रकृतकः पदवीं मृगस्ते *S*. 4. 13. **-जात** *a.* one to whom a son is born. **-दारं** son and wife. **-धर्मः** filial duty. **-पौत्रं** or **-त्राः** sons and grandsons. **-पौत्रिण** *a.* transmitted from son to son, hereditary; Bk. 5. 15. **-प्रतिनिधिः** a substitute for a son (*e. g.* an adopted son). **-लाभः** obtaining a son. **-वधूः** *f.* a daughter-in-law. **-सखः** 'a friend of children', one who is fond of childran. **-हीन** *a.* sonless, childless.

पुत्रकः 1 A little son or boy, boy, chap, lad (often used as a term of endearment). **2** A doll, puppet; Ku. 1. 29. **3** A rogue, cheat. **4** A locust, grasshopper. **5** A fabulous animal with eight feet (शरभ). **6** Hair.

पुत्रका, **पुत्रिका**, **पुत्री 1** A daughter. **2** A doll, puppet. **3** (At the end of comp.) Anything little or small of its kind; as in असिपुत्रिका, खड्गपुत्रिका &c. -COMP. **-पुत्रः**,**-सुतः 1** a daughter's son who by agreement becomes the son of her father; see Ms. 9. 127. **2** a daughter who, being regarded as a son, returns to her father's house; (पुत्रिकैव पुत्रः; अथवा पुत्रिकैव सुतः पुत्रिकासुतः सोऽप्यौरससम एव Mit. on Y. 2. 128). **3** a grandson. **-प्रसूः** a mother of daughters. **-भर्तृ** *m.* 'a daughter's husband,' a son-in-law.

पुत्रिन् *a.* (**णी** *f.*) Having a son or sons; R. 1. 91; V. 5. 14. *-m.* The father of a son.

पुत्रिय, **पुत्रीय**, **पुत्र्य** *a.* Relating to a son, filial.

पुत्रीया The desire of a son.

पुद्गल *a.* Beautiful, lovely, handsome, **-लः 1** An atom (परमाणुः); पुद्गलाः परमाणवः *S*ridhara. **2** The body, matter. **3** The soul. **4** An epithet of *S*iva.

पुनर् *ind.* **1** Again, once more, anew; न पुनरेवं प्रवर्तितव्यं *S*. 6; किमप्ययं बटुः पुनर्विवक्षुः स्फुरितोत्तराधरः Ku. 5. 82; so पुनर्भू to become a wife again. **2** Back, in an opposite direction (mostly with verbs); पुनर्दा to give back, restore; पुनर्या-इ गम् &c. to go back, return &c. **3** On the other hand, on the contrary, but, however, nevertheless, still (with an adversative force); प्रसाद इव मूर्तस्ते स्पर्शः स्नेहार्द्रशीतलः । अद्याप्यानंदयति मां त्वं पुनः क्वासि नंदिनि U. 3. 14; मम पुनः सर्वमेव तन्नास्ति U. 3. **पुनः पुनः** 'again and again,' 'repeatedly,' 'frequently'; पुनः पुनः सूतनिषिद्धचापलं R. 3. 42; **किंपुनः** 'how much more,' or 'how much less'; see under **किम्**; **पुनरपि** again, once more, and also; on the other hand. -COMP. **-अर्थिता** a repeated request. **-आगत** *a.* come back, return; भस्मीभूतस्य देहस्य पुनरागमनं कुतः *S*arva. S. **-आधानं**,**-आधेयं** renewing the consecrated fire. **-आवर्तः 1** return. **2** repeated birth. **-आवर्तिन्** *a.* returning to mundane existence. **-आवृत्** *f.* **आवृत्तिः** *f.* **1** repetition. **2** return to worldly existence, repetition of birth; Y. 3. 194. **3** revision, another edition (of a book &c.). **-उक्त** *a.* **1** said again, repeated, reiterated. **2** superfluous, unnecessary; शशंस वाचा पुनरुक्तयेव R. **2.** 68; *S*i. 9 64. (**-क्तं**), **पुनरुक्तता 1** repetition. **2** superfluity, redundancy, uselesseness, tautology; U. 5. 15; Bh. 3. 78. °**जन्मन्** *m.* a Brâhmana (द्विजन्मन्). **पुनरुक्तवदाभासः** seeming tautology, appearance of repetition, regarded as a figure of speech; *e. p.* भुजंगकुंडलीव्यक्तशशिशुभ्रांशुशीतगुः । जगंत्यपि सदा पायादव्याच्चेतोहरः शिवः S. D. 622; (here the first impression of the tautalogy is removed when the passage is rightly understood; cf. also K. P. 9 under पुनरुक्तवदाभास). **-उक्तिः** *f.* **1** repetition. **2** superfluity, uselessness, tautology. **-उत्थानं** rising again, resurrection. **-उत्पत्तिः** *f.* **1** reproduction. **2** return of birth, metempsychosis. **-उपगमः**

return; क्वायोध्यायाः पुनरुपगमो दंडकायां वने वः U. 2. 13. उपोढा,-ऊढा a woman married again. -गमनं return, going again. -जन्मन् *n.* repeated birth, metempsychosis. -जात *a.* born again. -णवः,-नवः ' growing again and again ', a fingernail. -दारक्रिया marrying again, taking a second wife. -प्रत्युपकारः returning one's obligations, repeated or recurring birth, metempsychosis; ममापि च क्षपयतु नीललोहितः पुनर्भवं परिगतशक्तिरात्मभूः *S.* 7. 35 Ku. 3. 5. 2 a finger-nail. -भावः new birth, repeated birth. -भूः 1 a widow remarried 2 re-existence. -यात्रा 1 going again. 2 repeated procession. -वचनं repetition. -वसुः (usually dual) 1 the seventh lunar mansion (consisting of two or four stars); गां गताविव दिवः पुनर्वसू R. 11. 36. 2 an epithet of Vishnu. 3 of *S*iva. -विवाहः remarriage. -संस्कारः (पुनः संस्कारः) repetition of any Samskâra or purificatory ceremony. -संगमः,-संधानं (पुनः संधानं &c.) reunion. -संभवः (पुनः संभव) being born again (into the world), metempsychosis.

पुष्फुलः Flatulency or wine (in the stomach).

पुप्फुसः 1 The lungs. 2 The pericarp of a lotus.

पुर् *f.* (Nom. sing. पूः instr. पूर्भ्यां) 1 A town, fortified town पूरभ्यामिव्यक्तमुखप्रसादा R. 16. 23. 2 A fortress, castle, stronghold. 3 A wall, rampart. 4 The body. 5 Intellect.--COMP. -द्वार *f.*, -द्वारं the gate of a city.

पुरं 1 A town, city (containing large buildings, surrounded by a ditch, and not less than one Krosa in extent); पुरे तावंतमेवास्य तनोति रविरातपं Ku. 2. 3. R. 1. 59. 2 A castle, fortress, stronghold. 3 A house, residence, abode. 4 The body. 5 The female apartments. 6 N. of the town पाटलिपुत्र. q. v. 7 The calyx of a flower or any cup formed of leaves. 8 A brothel. 9 The skin. 10 Bdellium, COMP. -अट्टः a turret on a city-wall. -अधिपः, -अध्यक्षः the governor of a town. -अरातिः, -अरिः, -असुहृद् *m.* -रिपुः epithets of *S*iva; पुरारातिभ्रांत्या कुसुमशर किं मा प्रहरसि Subhâsh; see त्रिपुर -उत्सवः a festival celebrated in a city. -उद्यानं a city-garden, park. -ओकस् *m.* an inhabitant of a town. -कोट्टं a citadel. -ग *a.* 1 going to a town, 2 favourably inclined. -जित्, -द्विष्, भिद् *m.* epithet of *S*iva. -ज्योतिस् *m.* 1 an epithet of fire 2 the world of Agni. -तटी a small market-town small village.-तोरणं the outer gate of a city. -द्वारं a city-gate. -निवेशः the founding of a city. -पालः 'city-governor', the commandant of a fortress. -मथनः an epithet of *S*iva. -मार्गः the street of a town; Ku. 4. 11; R. 11. 3. -रक्षः, -रक्षकः, रक्षिन् *m.* a constable, police-officer. -रोधः the siege of a fortress. -वासिन् *m.* a citizen, a townsman. -शासनः 1 an epithet of Vishṇu. 2 of *S*iva.

पुरटं Gold.

पुरणः The sea, ocean.

पुरतस् *ind.* Before, in front (opp. पश्चात्); पश्यामि तामित इतः पुरतश्च पश्चात् Mâl. 1. 40; in the presence of; यें यें पश्यति तस्य तस्य पुरतो मा ब्रूहि दीनं वचः Bh. 2. 51. 2 Afterwards; इयं च तेऽन्या पुरतो विडंबना Ku. 5. 70. (आद्यैव Malli.); Amaru.43.

पुरंदरः 1 N. of Indra; R. 2. 74. 2 An epithet of *S*iva. 3 Of Agni. 4 A thief, house-breaker. 2 -रा An epithet of the Ganges.

पुरंध्रिः, -ध्री *f.* 1 An elderly married woman, a respectable matron; पुरंध्रीणां चित्तं कुसुमसुकुमारं हि भवति U. 4. 12; Mu. 2. 7; Ku. 6. 32; 7. 2. 2 A woman whose husband and children are living.

पुरला An epithet of Durgâ.

पुरस् *ind.* 1 Before, in front, in the presence of, before the eyes of (by itself or with gen.); अमुं पुरः पश्यसि देवदारुं R. 2. 36; तस्य स्थित्वा कथमपि पुरः Me. 3; Ku 4. 3; Amaru. 43; often used with कृ, गम्, धा, भू (see the roots). 2 In the east, from the east. 3 Eastward. -COMP. -करणं, -कारः 1 placing before or in front. 2 preference. 3 treating with honour, showing respect, deference. 4 worshipping. 5 accompanying, attending. 6 preparing. 7 arranging. 8 making complete or perfect, 9 attacking. 10 accusation. -कृत *a.* placed in front; R. 2. 80. 2 honoured, treated with respect, distinguisded. 3 chosen, adopted, followed; पुरस्कृतमध्यमक्रमः R. 8. 9. 4 adored, worshipped. 5 attended or accompanied by, combined with. 6 prepared, got ready. 7 consecrated. 8 accused, calumniated. 9 made perfect. 10 anticipated. -क्रिया 1 showing respect, treating with honour. 2 a preparatory or initiatory rite. -ग, -गम (पुरोग-गम). *a.* 1 chief, leading, foremost, pre-eminent, oft. with the force of a noun; स किंवदंतीं वदतां पुरोगः R. 14. 31, 6. 55; Ku. 7. 40. 2 led or presided over by (at the end of comp.); इंद्रपुरोगमा देवाः 'the gods with Indra at the head'. -गति *f.* 1 precedence (-तिः) a dog. -गंतृ, -गामिन् *a.* 1 going before or in front. 2 chief, leading, a leader. (-*m.*) a dog. -चरणं 1 a preparatory or initiatory rite. 2 preparation, initiation. 3 repetition of the name of a deity accompanied with burnt offerings. -छदः a nipple. -जन्मन् (पुरोजन्मन्) *a.* born before. -डाश् *m.*, डाशः (पुरोडाश्-शः) a sacrificial oblation made of ground rice and offered in *Kapâlas* or vessel; Ms. 7. 21. -धस् (पुरोधस्) *m.* a family-priest (particularly) that of a king). -धानं (पुरोधानं) 1 placing in the front. 2 ministration by a priest. -धिका (पुरोधिका) a favourite wife (preferred to all others). -पाक *a.* near fulfilment, about to be fulfilled; Ku. 6. 90. -प्रहर्तृ *m.* one who fights in the van or front line; R. 13. 72. -फल *a.* having the fruit near or at hand, promising fruit (in the near future); R. 2. 22. -भाग (पुरोभाग) *a.* 1 obtrusive, officious. 2 fault-finding. 3 envious or jealous of; प्रायः समानविद्याः परस्परयशः पुरोभागाः M. 1. 20 (पुरोभाग may here mean 'envy' also). (-गः) 1 the front part, fore-part, van. 2 obtrusiveness, officiousness. 3 jealousy, envy. -भागिन् *a.* 1 forward, self-willed, naughty; *S.* 5. 2 obtrusive, officious; V. 3. 3 fault-finding. -मारुतः, -वातः (पुरोमारुतः -वातः) a forewind, wind blowing in front; M. 4. 3; R. 18. 38. -सर *a.* going or moving in front. (रः) 1 a fore-runner, harbinger; *S.* 4. 2. 2 a follower, attendant; servant; परिमेयपुरःसरौ R. 1. 37. 3 a leader, one who leads the way, foremost, pre-eminent; Ku. 6. 49. 4 (at the end of comp.) attended or preceded by, with; as मानपुरःसरं, प्रमाणपुरःसरं, वृकपुरःसराः &c. -स्थायिन् *a.* standing in front. -हित *a.* 1 placed in front. 2 appointed, charged, commissioned. (-तः) 1 one holding a charge, an agent. 2 a family-priest, one who conducts all the ceremonial rites of the family.

पुरस्तात् *ind.* 1 Before, in front (oft. with gen. or able.); R. 2. 44; Ku. 7. 30; Me. 15; or used by itself; अभ्युन्नता पुरस्तात् *S.* 3. 8. 2 At the head of, foremost; M. 1. 1. 3 In the first place, at the beginning. 4 Formerly, previously. 5 Eastward, in or towards the east. 6 Later or further on, in the sequel.

पुरा *ind.* 1 In former times, formerly, of yore, in the olden time; पुरा शक्रमुपस्थाय R. 1. 75; पुरा सरसि मानसे यस्य यातं वयः Bv. 1. 3; Ms. 1. 119; 5. 32. 2 Before, hitherto, up to the present time. 3 At first, in the first place. 4 In a short time, soon, ere-long, shortly, (in this sense usually with a present tense to which it gives a future sense); पुरा सप्तद्वीपां जयति वसुधामप्रतिरथः S. 7. 33; पुरा दूषयति

स्थली R. 12. 30; आलोके ते निपतति पुरा सा बलिव्याकुला वा Me. 85; N. 1. 18; Si. 15. 56; Ki. 10. 50; 11. 36. -COMP. -उपनीत *a.* formerly possessed. -कथा an old legend. -कल्पः 1 a former creation. 2 a story of the past. 3 a former age; द्यूतमेतत्पुराकल्पे दृष्टं वैरकरं महत् Ms. 9. 227. -कृत *a* done formerly. -योनि *a.* of ancient origin. -वसुः an epithet of Bhîshma. -विद् *a.* acquainted with the past, knowing the events of former times, conversant with former times or events; वदंत्यपर्णेति च तां पुराविदः Ku. 5. 28; 6. 9; R. 11. 10. -वृत्त *a.* occuring in, or relating to, ancient times. 2 old, ancient. °कथा an old legend. (-त्तं) 1 history. 2 an old or legendary event; पुरावृत्तोद्गारैरपि च कथिता कार्यपद्वी Mâl. 2. 13.

पुरा 1 An epithet of the Ganges 2 A kind of perfume. 3 The east. 4 A castle.

पुराण *a.* (णा or णी *f.*) 1 Old, ancient, belonging to olden times; पुराणमित्येव न साधु सर्वं न चापि काव्यं नवमित्यवद्यं M. 1. 2; पुराणपत्रापगमादनंतरं R. 3. 7. 2 Aged, primeval; अजो नित्यः शाश्वतोयं पुराणः Bg. 2. 20. 3 Decayed, worn out. -णं 1 A past event or occurrence. 2 A tale of the past, legend, ancient or legendary history. 3 N. of certain well-known sacred works; these are 18; they are supposed to have been composed by Vyâsa, and contain the whole body of Hindu mythology. A Purâṇa treats of five topics (or लक्षणानि), and is hence often called पंचलक्षणं; सर्गश्च प्रतिसर्गश्च वंशो मन्वंतराणिच । वंशानुचरितं चैव पुराणं पंचलक्षणं ॥ For the names of the 18 Purâṇas see under अष्टादशन्. -णः A coin equal to 80 cowries. -COMP. अंतः an epithet of Yama. -उक्त *a.* enjoined by or laid down in the Purâṇas. गः 1 an epithet of Brâhman. 2 a reciter or reader of the Purâṇas. -पुरुषः an epithet of Vishṇu.

पुरातन *a.* (नी *f.*) 1 Old, ancient; Si. 12. 60; Bg. 4. 3. 2 Aged, primeval; R. 11. 85; Ku. 6. 9. 3 Worn out, decayed. -नः An epithet of Vishṇu.

पुरिः *f.* 1 a town, city. 2 A river.

पुरिशय *a.* Reposing in the body.

पुरी 1 A city, town; शशासैकपुरीमिव R. 1. 30. 2 A stronghold. 3 The body. —COMP. मोहः the Dhattúra plant.

पुरीतत् *m.*, *n.* 1 A particular intestine near the heart. 2 The entrails in general; (also पुरीतत्, but it appears to be a wrong form).

पुरीषं 1 Feces, excrement, ordure; Ms. 3. 250, 5. 123, 6. 76; 4. 56. 2 Rubbish, dirt —COMP. -उत्सर्गः voiding excrement. -निग्रहणं obstruction of the bowels.

पुरीषणः Feces, ordure. -णं Evacuation by stool, voiding of excrement.

पुरीषमः The black kidney bean.

पुरू *a.* (रु-र्वी *f.*) Much, abundant, excessive, many; (in classical literature पुरु occurs usually at the beginning of proper names). -रुः 1 The pollen of flowers. 2 Heaven, the world of the immortals 3 N. of a prince, the sixth monarch of the lunar race. [He was the youngest son of Yayati and Sarmishtha. When his father asked his five sons if any one of them would exchange his youth and beauty, for his own decrepitude and infirmities, it was Puru alone who consented to make the exchange. After a thousand years Yayati restored to Puru his youth and beauty, and made him successor to the throne. Puru was the ancester of the Kauravas and Pandavas]. -COMP. -जित् *m.* 1 an epithet of Vishṇu. 2 N. of king Kuntibhoja or his brother. -दं gold. -दंशकः a goose. -लंपट *a.* very lustful or lascivious. -ह -हु much, many. -हूत *a.* invoked by many. (-तः) an epithet of Indra; R. 4. 3, 16 5; Ku. 7. 45; Ms. 11. 22. °द्विष् *m.* an epithet of Indrajit.

पुरुषः 1 A male, male being, man; अर्थतः पुरुषो नारी या नारी सार्थतः पुमान् Mk. 3. 27; Ms. 1. 32; 7. 17; 9. 2; R. 2. 41. 2 Men, mankind. 3 A member or representative of a generation. 4 An officer, functionary, agent, attendant, servant. 5 The height or measure of a man (considered as a measure of length); द्वौ पुरुषौ प्रमाणमस्याः सा द्विपुरुषा-षी परिखा Sk. 6 The soul; द्वाविमौ पुरुषौ लोके क्षरश्चाक्षर एव च Bg. 15. 16 &c. 7 The Supreme Being, God (soul of the universe) Si. 1. 33; R. 13. 6. 8 A person (in grammar); प्रथमपुरुषः the third person, मध्यमपुरुषः the second person, and उत्तमपुरुषः the first person, (this is the strict order in Sk.) 9 The pupil of the eye. 10 (In Sân. phil.) The soul (opp. प्रकृति); according to the Sânkhyas it is neither a production nor productive; it is passive and a looker-on of the Prakriti; cf. Ku. 2. 13 and the word सांख्य also. -षं An epithet of the mountain Meru. -COMP. -अंगं the male organ of generation. -अदः 'a man-eater', cannibal, goblin. -अधमः the vilest of men, a very low or despicable man. -अधिकारः 1 a manly office or duty. 2 calculation or estimation of men; Ki. 3. 51. -अंतरं another man; -अर्थः 1 any one of the four principal objects of human life; *i. e.* धर्म, अर्थ, काम and मोक्ष. 2 human effort or exertion (पुरुषकार); H. Pr. 35. -अस्थिमालिन् *m.* an epithet of Siva. -आद्यः an epithet of Vishṇu. -आयुषं, -आयुस् *n.* the duration of a man's life; अकृपणमतिः कामं जीव्याज्जनः पुरुषायुषं V. 6. 44; पुरुषायुषजीविन्यो निरातंका निरीतयः R. 1. 63. -आशिन् *m.* 'a man-eater', a demon, goblin. -इंद्रः a king. -उत्तमः 1 an excellent man. 2 the highest or Supreme Being, an epithet of Vishṇu or Krishṇa; यस्मात् क्षरमतीतोऽहमक्षरादपि चोत्तमः । अतोऽस्मि लोके वेदे च प्रथितः पुरुषोत्तमः ॥ Bg. 15. 18. -कारः 1 human effort or exertion, manly act, manliness, prowess (opp. दैव); एवं पुरुषकारेण विना दैवं न सिध्यति H. Pr. 32; दैवे पुरुषकारे च कर्मसिद्धिर्व्यवस्थिता Y. 349; cf. "god helps those who help themselves"; Pt. 5. 30; Ki. 5. 52. 2 manhood, virility. -कुणपः -पं a human corpse. -केसरिन् *m.* 'man-lion', an epithet of Vishṇu in his fourth incarnation; पुरुषकेसरिणश्च पुरा नखैः S. 7. 3. -ज्ञानं knowledge of mankind. -दघ्न, द्वयस *a.* of the height of a man. -द्विष् *m.* an enemy of Vishṇu. -नायः 1 a general, commander. 2 a king. -पशुः a beast of a man, brutish person; cf. नरपशुः -पुंगवः, -पुंडरिकः a superior or eminent man. -बहुमानः the esteem of mankind; Bh. 3. 9. -मेधः a human sacrifice. -वरः an epithet of Vishṇu. -वाहः 1 an epithet of Garuḍa. 2 an epithet of Kubera. -व्याघ्रः -शार्दूलः, -सिंहः 'a tiger or lion among men,' a distinguished or eminent man. 2 a hero, brave man. 2 -समवायः a number of men. -सूक्तं N. of the 90th hymn of the 10th Maṇḍala of the Rigveda (regarded as a very sacred hymn).

पुरुषकः -कं Standing on two feet like a man, the rearing of a horse; श्रीवृक्षकी पुरुषकोन्नमिताग्रकायः Si. 5. 56.

पुरुषता, त्वं 1 Manhood, manliness, prowess. 2 Virility.

पुरुषायित *a.* Acting like a man -तं 1 Playing the man, acting a manly part, conduct 2 A kind of coitus or mode of sexual enjoyment in which the woman plays the man; आकृतिमवलोक्य कयापि वितर्कितं पुरुषायित असिलतालिखनेन वैदग्ध्यादभिव्यक्तिमुपनीतम् K. P. 10.

पुरूरवस् *m.* The son of Budha and Ilâ and founder of the lunar race of kings. [He saw the nymph Urvasi, while descending upon earth owing to the curse of Mitra and Varuna and fell in love with her. Urvasi, too, was enmoured of the king who was as renowned for personal beauty as for truthfulness, devotion, and generosity, and became his wife. They lived happily together for many days, and after she had borne him a son, she returned to the heaven. The king heavily mourned her loss, and she was pleased to repeat her visits five successive times and bore him five sons. But the king, who wanted her life-long company, was not evidently satisfied with this; and he obtained his desired object after he had offered oblations as directed by the Gandharvas. The story told in Vikramorvasiya differs in many respects; so does the account given in the *S*atapatha Br*a*hma*n*a, based on a passage in the *R*igveda; where it is said that Urvas*i* agreed to live with Pur*u*ravas on two conditions:—namely that her two rams which she loved as children must be kept near her bed-side and never suffered to be carried away, and that he must take care never to be seen by her undressed. The Gandharvas, however, carried away the rams, and so Urvas*i* disappeared]-

पुरोटिः 1 The current of a river. 2 The rustling noise of leaves (पत्रशब्द).

पुरोडाश, पुरोधस् &c. See under पुरस्.

पुर्व् 1 P. (पुर्वति) 1 To fill. 2 To dwell, inhabit. 3 To invite (said to be 10 P. in the last two senses).

पुल *a*. Great, large, wide, extensive. –लः Horripilation.

पुलकः 1 Erection or bristling of the hairs of the body, a thrill (of joy or fear), horripilation; चारु चुचुंब नितंबवती दयितं पुलकैरनुकूले Gît. 1; मृगमदतिलकं लिखति सपुलकं मृगमिव रजनीकरे 7; Amaru. 57,77. 2 A kind of stone or gem. 3 A flaw or defect in a gem. A kind of mineral. 5 A ball of food with which elephants are fed (गजान्नपिंड). 6 Yellow orpiment. 7 A wine-glass. 8 A species of mustard. –Comp. –अंगः the noose of Varuṇa. –आलयः an epithet of Kubera. –उद्गमः erection of the hairs of the body, horripilation.

पुलकित *a*. Having the hairs of the body erect, thrilled with joy; hence rejoiced, enraptured.

पुलकिन् *a*. (नी *f*.) Having the hairs of the body erect &c. –*m*. A species of Kadamba tree.

पुलस्तिः –स्त्यः N. of a sage, one of the mind-born sons of Brahmâ; Ms. 1. 35.

पुला The soft palate, uvula.

पुलाकः –कं 1 Empty, bad or shrivelled grain. 2 A lump of boiled rice. 3 abridgment, compendium. 4 Brevity, conciseness. 5 Rice-water. 6 Despatch, celerity.

पुलाकिन् *m*. A tree.

पुलायितं A horse's gallop.

पुलिनः –नं 1 A sand-bank; a sandy beach; रमते यमुनापुलिनवने विजयी मुरारिरधुना Gît. 7; R. 14. 52; sometimes used in pl.; कालिंद्याः पुलिनेषु केलिकुपितामुत्सृज्य रासे रसं Ve. 1. 2. 2 A small island left in the bank of a river by the passing off of the water, an islet. 3 The bank of a river.

पुलिनवति A river.

पुलिंदकः 1 N. of a barbarous tribe (usually in pl.). 2 A man of this tribe, a savage, barbarian, mountaineer; R. 16. 19, 32.

पुलिरिकः A snake.

पुलोमन् *m*. N. of a demon, the father-in-law of Indra. –Comp. –अरिः, –जित्, –भिद्, –द्विष् *m* epithets of Indra. –जा –पुत्री Sachî, daughter of Puloman and wife of Indra.

पुष् 1. 4. 9. P. (पोषति, पुष्यति, पुष्णाति, पुष्ट or पुषित) 1 To nourish, foster, rear, bring up, nurture; तेनाद्य वत्समिव लोकममुं पुषाण Bh. 2. 46; Bg. 15. 13; Bk. 3. 13, 17. 32. 2 To support, maintain, bear. 3 To cause to thrive or grow, unfold, develop, bring into relief; पुपोष लावण्यमयान् विशेषान् Ku. 1. 25; R. 3. 32; न तिरोधीयते स्थायी तैरसौ पुष्यंते परं S. D. 3. 4 To increase, augment, further promote, enhance; पंचानामपि भूतानामुत्कर्षं पुपुषुर्गुणाः R. 4. 11; 9. 5. 5 To get, possess, have, enjoy; Bh. 3. 34. 6 To show, exihibit, bear, display; वपुरभिनवमस्याः पुष्यति स्वां न शोभां *S*. 1. 19; Ku. 7. 18, 78; R. 6. 58; R. 6. 58; 18. 32; न हीश्वरव्याहृतयः कदाचित्पुष्णंति लोके विपरीतमर्थं Ku. 3. 63; Me. 80. 7 To be increased or nourished, thrive, prosper. 8 To magnify, extol. –*Caus*. or 10 U. (पोषयति-ते) 1 To nourish, bring up, maintain &c. 2 To increase, promote.

पुष्करं 1 A blue lotus. 2 The tip of an elephant's tongue; *S*i. 5. 30. 3 The skin of a drum; *i. e*. the place where it is struck; पुष्करेष्वाहतेषु Me. 66; R. 17. 11. 4 The blade of a sword. 5 The sheath of a sword. 6 An arrow. 7 Air, sky, atmosphere. 8 A cage. 9 Water. 10 Intoxication. 11 The art of dancing. 12 War, battle. 13 Union. 14 N. of a celebrated place of pilgrimage in the district of Ajmere. –रः 1 A lake, pond. 2 A kind of serpent. 3 A kind of drum, kettle-drum. 4 The sun. 5 An epithet of a class of clouds said to cause dearth or famine; Me. 6; Ku. 2. 50. 6 An epithet of *S*iva. –रः रं N. of one of the seven great divisions of the universe. –Comp. –अक्षः an epithet of Vishṇu –आख्यः, –आह्वः the (Indian) crane. –तीर्थः N. of a sacred bathing-place; see पुष्कर above. –पत्रं a lotus-leaf. –प्रियः wax –बीजं lotus-seed. –व्याघ्रः an alligator. –शिखा the root of a lotus. –स्थपतिः an epithet of *S*iva. –स्रज् *f*. a garland of lotuses.

पुष्करिणी 1 A female elephant. 2 A lotus-pool. 3 A piece of water, a lake or pool in general. 4 The lotus-plant.

पुष्करिन् *a*. (णी *f*.) Abounding in lotuses. –*m*. An elephant.

पुष्कल *a*. 1 Much, copious, abundant; भक्षितेनापि भवता नाहारो मम पुष्कलः H. 1. 84; Ms. 3. 277. 2 Full, complete; Bg. 11. 21. 3 Rich, magnificent, splendid. 4 Excellent, best, eminent. 5 Near. 6 Loud, resonant, resounding. –लः 1 A kind of drum. 2 An epithet of mount Meru. –लं 1 A particular measure of capacity= 64 handfuls. 2 Alms to the extent of four morsels of food.

पुष्कलकः 1 The musk-deer; सीम्नि पुष्कलको हतः Sk. 2 A bolt, pin, wedge.

पुष्ट *p. p*. 1 Nourished, fed, reared, brought up. 2 Thriving, growing, strong, fat. 3 Tended, cared for. 4 Rich, magnificently provided. 5 Complete, perfect. 6 Full-sounding, loud. 7 Eminent.

पुष्टिः *f*. 1 Nourishing, breeding, or rearing. 2 Nourishment, growth, increase, advance; यद्विषितामपि नृणां पिष्टोपि तनोषि परिमलैः पुष्टिं Bv. 1. 12. 3 Strengthfulness, plumpness; अंधस्य दृष्टिरिव दृष्टिरिवातुरस्य Mk. 1. 49. 4 Wealth, property, means of comfort; R. 18. 32. 5 Richness, magnificence. 6 Development, perfection. –Comp. –कर *a*. nourishing, nutritive. –कर्मन् *n*. a religious ceremony performed for the attainment of worldly prosperity. –द *a*. causing growth or prosperity. –वर्धन *a*. promoting welfare, causing prosperity. (–नः) a cock.

पुष्प् 4 P. (पुष्प्यति) To open, blow, expand, bloom; पुष्प्यत्पुष्करवासितस्य पयसः U. 3. 16.

पुष्पं 1 A flower, blossom. 2 The menstrual discharge; as in पुष्पवती q. v. 3 A topaz. 5 A disease of the eyes (albugo). 5 The car or vehicle of Kubera, see पुष्पक. 6 Gallantry, politeness (in love language). 7 Expanding, blooming, blossoming (said to be *m*. in this sense).–Comp. –अंजनं calx of brass used as a collyrium. –अंजलिः a handful of flowers. –अभिषेकः = °स्नान q. v. –अंबुजं the sap of flowers. –अवचयः collecting or gathering flowers. –अस्त्रः an epithet of the god of love. –आकार *a*. rich or abounding in flowers; मासो नु पुष्पाकरः V. 1. 9. –आगमः the spring. –आजीवः a florist, garland-maker.

-आपीडः a chaplet of flowers. -आयुधः -इषुः the god of love. -आसवं honey. -आसारः a shower of flowers; Ms. 43. -उद्गमः appearance of flowers. -उद्यानं a flower-garden. -उपजीविन् *m.* a florist, gardener, garland-maker. -कालः 1 'flower-time, the spring. 2 the time of the menses. -कासीसं green (or black) sulphate of iron. -कीटः a large black bee. -केतनः the god of love. -केतुः the god of love. (-*n.*) 1 calx of flowers. 2 vitriol (used as a collyrium). -गृहं a flower-house, conservatory. -घातकः the bamboo. -चयः 1 gathering flowers. 2 a quantity of flowers. -चापः the god of love. -चामरः a kind of cone. -जं the juice of flowers. -द्रुः a tree. -दंतः 1 N. of an attendant of Siva. 2 N. of the author of the Mahimanstotra, 3 N. of the elephant presiding over the north-west. -दामन् *u.* a garland of flowers. -द्रवः 1 the sap or exudation of flowers. 2 an infusion of flowers. -द्रुमः a flowering tree. -धः the offspring of an outcast Brâhmaṇa; cf. Ms. 10. 21. -धनुस् -धन्वन् *m.* the god of love: Si. 9. 41; Ku. 2. 64. -धारणः an epithet of Vishṇu. -ध्वजः the god of love. -निक्षः a bee. -निर्यासः, -निर्यासकः the sap, nectar, or juice of flowers. -नेत्रं the tube of a flower. -पत्रिन् *m.* the god of love. -पथः the vulva. -पुरं N. of Pâtaliputra; R. 6. 24. -प्रचयः, प्रचायः the plucking or gathering of flowers. -प्रचायिका gathering of flowers. -प्रस्तारः a bed or couch of flowers. -बलिः an offering of flowers. -बाणः -वाणः an epithet of the god of love. -भवः the nectar or juice of flowers. -मंजरिका a blue lotus. -माला a garland of flowers. -मासः 1 the month of Chaitra. 2 the spring. -रजस् *n.* the pollen. -रथः a carriage for traveling or for pleasure (but not for war). -रसः the nectar or juice of flowers. °अह्वयं honey. -रागः,-राजः a topaz. -रेणुः pollen; वायुर्विधूनयति चंपकपुष्परेणून् Kavirahasya; R. 1. 38. -लोचन- the Nâgakesara tree, -लावः a flower-gatherer. (-वी) a female flower-gatherer; Me. 26. -लिक्षः -लिह् *m.* a bee. -वटुकः a gallent. -वर्षः, -वर्षणं a shower of flowers; R. 12. 102. -वाटिका, -वाटी *f.* a flower-garden. -वृक्षः a tree bearing flowers; R. 12. 94. -वेणि a garland of flowers. -शकटी a heavenly voice from heaven. -शय्या a flowery bed, a couch of flowers. -शरः -शरासनः, -सायकः the god of love. -समयः the spring. -सारः, स्वेदः the nectar or honey of flowers. -हासा a woman in her courses. -हीना a woman past child-bearing.

पुष्पकं 1 A flower. 2 Calx of brass. 3 A cup of iron. 4 The car of Kubera (snatched off from him by Râvana and from him by Râma); R. 13. 40; 16. 46. 5 A bracelet. 6 A kind of collyrium. 7 A particular disease of the eyes.

पुष्पंधयः A bee.

पुष्पवत् *a.* 1 Blooming, flowery. 2 Set off with flowers. -*m.* (dual) The snn and moon. -ती A woman in her courses; पुष्पवत्यपि पवित्रा K. 20.

पुष्पा N. of the town Champâ.

पुष्पिका 1 The tartar of the teeth. 2 The mucus of the penis. 3 The last words of a chapter, which state the subject treated therein; इति श्रीमहाभारते शतसाहस्त्र्यां संहितायां वनपर्वणि &c. ... अमुकोध्याय.

पुष्पिणी A woman in her courses.

पुष्पित *a.* 1 Flowered, full of flowers in bloom, blooming; चिरविरहेण विलोक्य पुष्पितायां Gît. 4 (where पुष्पिताग्रा is also the name of a metre). 2 Florid, flowery (as speech). 3 Abounding or rich in; as in सुवर्णपुष्पिता पृथ्वी Pt. 1. 45. 4 Full developed, completely manifested. -ता A woman in her courses.

पुष्पिन् *a.* 1 Bearing flowers, blooming. 2 Rich or abounding in flowers.

पुष्यः 1 The Kali age. 2 The month called पौष. 3 The eighth lunar mansion (consisting of three stars), written also तिष्य. Comp. -रथः =पुष्परथ q. v.

पुष्यलकः See पुष्पलक.

पुस्तं 1 Plastering, painting, anointing. 2 Working in clay, modelling. 3 Anything made of clay, wood or metal. 4 A book, manuscript. -Comp -कर्मन् *n.* plastering, painting.

पुस्तकः=कं, पुस्ती A book, manuscript.

पू 1. 4. A; 9 U. (पवते, पूयते, पुनाति, पुनीते; पूत; *caus.* पावयति; *desid*; पुपूषति, पिपविषते) 1 To make pure, cleanse, purify (lit. aud fig.); अवश्यपाव्यं पवसे Bk. 6. 64. 3. 18; पुण्याश्रमदर्शनेन तावदात्मानं पुनीमहे *S.* 1; Ms. 1. 105; 2. 62; Y. 1. 58. R. 1. 53; Bg. 10. 31. 2 To refine. 3 To clean from chaff, winnow. 4 To expiate, atone for. 5 To discern, discriminate. 6 To think out, devise, invent.

पूगः 1 A multitude, heap, collection, quantity; *Si.* 9. 64. 2 An association, corporation, union; Y. 2. 30; Ms. 3. 151. 3 The areca or betel-nut-tree (पूगी also); R. 4. 44; 6. 63; 13. 17. 4 Nature, property, disposition. -गं Areca-nut, betel-nut. -Comp. -पात्रं 1 a spitting-pot, spittoon. 2 a betel-box. -पीटः-ढं a spitting-pot. -फलं the areca-nut. -वैरं enmity against many men.

पूज् 10 U. (पूजयति-ते, पूजित) 1 To adore, worship, revere, honour, receive with respect; यदपूपुजस्त्वमिह पार्थ मुरजितमपूजितं सतां *Si.* 15. 14; Ms. 4. 31; Bk. 2. 26; Y. 2. 14. 2 To persent or honour with; Ms. 7. 203. -With सम् 1 to worship, revere, honour. 2 to present or honour with.

पूजक *v:* (जिका *f.*) Honouring, adoring, worshipping, respecting &c.

पूजनं Worshipping, honouring, adoring; Bg. 17. 14.

पूजा Worship, honour, adoration, respect, homage, R. 1. 79. -Comp. -अर्ह *a.* venerable, respectable, worshipful, worthy ef reverence.

पूजित *p. p.* 1 Honoured, respected. 2 Adored, revered. 3 Acknowledged. 4 Endowed. 5 Recommended.

पूजिल *a.* Venerable, respectable. -लः A god.

पूज्य *a.* Deserving respect, worthy of honour, respectable, venerable. -ज्यः 1 A father-in-law.

पूण् 10 U. (पूणयति-ते) To heap together, accumulate, amass.

पूत *ind.* An imitative word expressive of hard breathing or blowing.

पूत *p. p.* 1 Purified, cleansed, washed (fig. also); दृष्टीपूतं न्यसेत्पादं वस्त्रपूतं जलं पिबेत्। सत्यपूतां वदेद्वाचं मनःपूतं समाचरेत् Ms. 6. 46. 2 Threshed, winnowed. 3 Expiated. 4 Contrived, invented. 5 Stinking, putrid, fetid, foul-smelling. -तः 1 A conch-shell. 2 white Kusa grass. -तं Truth. -Comp. -आत्मन *a.* pure-minded. (-*m.*) an epithet of Vishṇu. -क्रतायी *Sachî*, the wife of Indra. -क्रतुः an epithet of Indra; Bk. 8. 29. तृणं white Kúsa grass. -द्रुः the tree called पलाश. --धान्यं sesamum. -पाप -पाप्मन् *a.* freed from sin. -फलः the bread-fruit-tree (पनस).

पूतना 1 N. of a female demon who, while attempting to kill Krishṇa when but an infant, was herself crushed by him. 2 A demoness or Râkshasî in general; मा पूतनात्वमुपगाः शिवतातिरेधि Mâl. 9. 49. --Comp -अरिः, -सूदनः -हन् *m.* epithets of Krishṇa.

पूति *a.* Putrid, stinking, fetid, foul smelling; Bg. 17. 10. -तिः *f.* 1 Purification. 2 Stink, stench. 3 Putrefaction. -*n.* 1 Filthy water. 2 Pus, matter. -Comp. -अंडः a musk-deer. -काष्ठं the Devadâru tree. -काष्ठकः the *Sarala* tree. -गंध *a.* putrid, fetid, foul-smelling, stinking. -धः 1 stench, fetid odour. 2 sulphur. (धं) 1 tin. 2 sulphur. -गंधि

a. strinking, foul-smelling. -नासिक *a.* having a fetid nose. -वक्त्र *a.* having offensive breath. -व्रणं a foul ulcer (discharging pus).

पूतिक *a.* Stinking, fetid, foul. -कं Ordure, excrement.

पूतिका A kind of herb. -Comp. -मुखः a bi-valve shell.

पून *a.* Destroyed (*p. p.* of ' पू to destroy ').

पूपः A sort of bread; see अपूप.

पूपला (ली), पूपालिका, पूपाली, पूपिका A sort of sweet cake.

पूयः -यं Pus, discharge from an ulcer or wound, suppuration, matter; Ms. 3. 180; 4. 220; 12 72. -Comp. -रक्तः a kind of disease of the nose (wherein purulent blood or sanies flows out). (क्तं) 1 ichor, sanies. 2 dicharge of sanies from the nostrils.

पूयनं =पूय q. v.

पूर् I. 4. A. (पूर्यते, पूर्ण) 1 To fill, fill out (allied in this sense with the pass. of पृ b. v.). 2 To please, satisfy. -II. 10 U. (पूरयति-ते, पूरित; strictly the caus. of पृ p. v.) 1 To fill को न याति वशं लोके मुखे पिंडेन पूरितः Bh. 2. 118; Si. 9. 64. 2 To blow into or fill with wind, blow (as a conch-shell). 3 To cover, surround; Bk. 7. 30. 4 To fulfil, satisfy; पूरयतु कुतूहलं वत्सः U. 4 ; आशां, मनोरथं &c. 5 To intensify, strengthen (as sound). 6 To make resonant. 6 To load or enrich with (gifts &c.). -With आ 1 to fill, make full or complete, fill up (fig. also); R. 16. 65 ; Bg. 11. 30; Bk. 6. 118. 2 to fill with wind, blow (as a conch) used in the *pass*. 3 to intertwine or cover with; Rs. 3. 18. -परि to fill, fill up or completely. -प्र 1 to fill. 2 to load with gifts, enrich; Mk. 9. 59 (where it has both senses). -सं to fill.

पूरः 1 Filling, making full. 2 Satisfying, pleasing, making content. 3 Pouring in, supplying ; अतैल-पूराः सुरतप्रदीपाः Ku. 1. 10. 4 The swelling or rising of a river or of the sea, flood; R. 3. 17. 5 A stream or flood in general ; °अंबु °बाष्प, शोणित° &c 6 A piece of water, lake, pond. 7 The healing or cleansing of wounds. 8 A kind of cake. -रं A kind of incense. -Comp. -उत्पीडः a flood or excess of water.

पूरक *a.* 1 Filling up, completing. 2 Satisfying, making content. -कः 1 The citron tree. 2 A ball of meal offered at the conclusion of the oblations to the Manes. 3 (In arith.) The multiplier.

पूरण *a.* (णी *f.*) 1 Filling up, completing. 2 Ordinal (as applied to numbers) (द्वितीय, तृतीय &c.); न पूरणी तं समुपैति संख्यां Ki. 3. 51. 3 Satisfying. -णः 1 A bridge, dam, causeway. 2 The ocean. -णं 1 Filling. 2 Filling up, completing ; R. 9. 73. 3 Puffing or swelling. 4 Fulfilling, accomplishing. 5 A sort of cake. 6 A funeral cake. 7 Rain, raining. 8 Warp. 9 Multiplication (in math.) -Comp. -प्रत्ययः an affix forming an ordinal number.

पूरिका A kind of cake.

पूरित *p. p.* 1 Filled, complete. 2 Overspread, covered over with. 3 Multiplied.

पूरुषः =पुरुष q. v.; Bv. 1. 75.

पूर्ण *p. p.* 1 Filled, filled with, full of; अश्रु,° शोक° &c. 2 Whole, full, entire, complete ; R 3. 38. 3 Fulfilled, accomplished. 4 Ended, completed. 5 Past, elapsed. 6 Satisfied, contented. 7 Full-sounding, sonorous. Strong, powerful. 9 Selfish, or self-indulgent. -Comp. -अंकः an integer. -अभिलाष *a.* satisfied, contented. -आनकं 1 a drum. 2 the sound of a drum. 3 a vessel. 4 a moon-beam. 5=पूर्णपात्र q. v.; (sometimes read पूर्णालक also). -इंदुः the full moon. -उपमा a full or complete simile, *i. e.* one in which the four requisites उपमान, उपमेय, साधारणधर्म and उपमाप्रतिपादक are all expressed ; (opp. लुप्तोपमा); *e. g.* अंभोरुहमिवाताम्रं मुग्धे करतलं तव ; see K. P. 10 under उपमा also. -ककुद् *a.* full-humped. -काम *a.* one whose desires are fulfilled, satisfied, contented. -कुंभः 1 a full jar. 2 a vessel full of water. 3 a particular mode of fighting. 4 a hole (in a wall) of the shape of a water-jar ; तदत्र पक्केष्टके पूर्णकुंभ एव शोभते Mk. 3. -पात्रं a full cup of jar. 2 a cup-ful. 3 a measure of capacity equal to 256 handfuls. 4 a vessel (or a box or basket) filled with valuable things (such as clothes, ornaments &c.) and scrambled for by servants or relatives on festive occasions or distributed as presents; hence the word is often used to denote 'a present made to one who brings a happy news'; कदा मे तनयजन्म-महोत्सवानंदनिर्भरो हरिष्यति पूर्णपात्रं परिजनः K. 62, 70, 73, 165 ; सखीजनेनापाह्रियमाणपूर्णपात्रां 299 ; तत्कामं प्रभवति पूर्णपात्रवृत्त्या स्वीकर्तुं मम हृदयं च जीवितं च Mâl. 4. 1. (पूर्णपात्र is defined :—हर्षादुत्सवकाले यदलंकारांशुकादिकं। आकृष्य गृह्यते पूर्णपात्रं स्यात्पूर्णकं च तत्। or वर्धापकं यदानंदादलंकारादिकं पुनः॥ आकृष्य गृह्यते पूर्णपात्रं पूर्णानकं च तत्॥ Hârâvalî). -बी (वी) जः a citron. -मासी the day of full moon.

पूर्णकः A kind of tree. 2 A cock. 3 The blue jay.

पूर्णिमा, पूर्णिमासी The day of full moon ; N. 2. 76.

पूर्त *a.* 1 Full, complete. 2 Concealed, covered. 3 Nourished, protected. -र्तं 1 Fulfilment. 2 Cherishing, nourishing. 3 A reward, merit. 4 An act of pious liberality; it is thus defined:—वापीकूपतटागादि देवतायतनानि च अन्नप्रदानमारामः पूर्तमित्यभिधीयते Ms. 4. 226 (opp. इष्ट which is thus defined by Atri:—अग्निहोत्रं तपः सत्यं वेदानां चैव पालनं। आतिथ्यं वैश्वदेवश्च इष्टमित्यभिधीयते) cf. इष्टपूर्त.

पूर्तिः *f.* 1 Filling. 2 Completion, fulfilment, accomplishment. 3 Satiety; satisfaction.

पूर्व *a.* (Declined like a pronoun when it implies relative position in time or space, but optionally so in nom. pl. ; and abl. and loc. sing.) 1 Being in front of, first, foremost. 2 Eastern, easterly, to the east of; ग्रामात्पर्वतः पूर्वः 3 Previous to, earlier than. 4 Old, ancient; पूर्वसूरिभिः R. 1. 4. 5 Former, previous, anterior, prior, antecedent (opp. उत्तर); in this sense often at the end of comp. and translated by 'formerly' or 'before,; श्रुतपूर्व &c. 6 Aforesaid, before-mentioned. 7 (At the end of comp.) Preceded by, accompanied by, attended with; संबंधमाभाषणपूर्वमाहुः R. 2. 58; पुण्यः शब्दो मुनिरिति मुहुः केवलं राजपूर्वः *S.* 2. 14. तान् स्मितपूर्वमाह Ku. 7. 47; 5. 31; दशपूर्वरथं यमाख्यया दश कंठारिगुरुं विदुर्बुधाः R. 8. 29; so मतिपूर्व Ms. 11. 147 'intentionally', 'knowingly', 12 89; अबोधपूर्वं 'unconsciously, *S*. 5. 3. &c. -र्वः An ancestor, forefather; पूर्वैः किलायं परिवर्धितो नः R. 13. 3; पयः पूर्वैः सनिश्वासैः कवोष्णमुपभुज्यते 1. 67; 5. 14 -र्वं The forepart. -र्वं *ind.* 1 Before (with abl.); मासात्पूर्वं. 2 Formerly, previously, at first, antecedently, beforehand; तं पूर्वमभिवादयेत् Ms. 2. 117; 3. 94; 8. 205; R. 12. 35. पूर्वेण 'to the east of'; with gen. or acc.; अद्य पूर्वं 'till-now'. hitherto'; पूर्वं -ततः-पश्चात्-उपरि 'first-then, first-afterwards', 'previously, subsequently', पूर्वं-अधुना or अद्य fromerly'-now.' -Comp. -अचलः, अद्रिः the eastern mountain behind which the sun and moon are supposed to rise. -अंतः the end of a preceding word. -अपर *a.* 1 eastern and western; पूर्वापरौ तोयनिधी वगाह्य Ku. 1. 1 2 first and last 3 prior and subsequent, preceding and following. 4 connected with another. (-रं) 1 what is before and behind. 2 connection. 3 the proof and the thing to be proved. °विरोधः inconsistency, incongruity. अभिमुख *a.* turned towards or facing the east. -अंबुधिः the eastern ocean. -अर्जित *a.* attained by former works. (तं) ancestral property. -अर्धः -र्धं 1 the first half; दिनस्य पूर्वार्धपरार्धभिन्ना छायेव मैत्री खलसज्जनानां Bh. 2. 60; समास पूर्वार्ध &c. 2 the upper part (of the body) R. R. 17. 6. **3** the first half of a hemistich. **अह्नः** the earlier part of the day, forenoon; Ms. 4. 96; 7. 87; (**पूर्वाह्णतन. पूर्वाह्णतेन** *a.* relating to the forenoon). **-आवेदकः** a plaintiff. **-आषाढा** N. of the 20th lunar mansion, consisting of two stars. **-इतर** *a.* before-mentioned, aforesaid. **-उत्तर** *a.* north-eastern. (-रे dual) the preceding and following, antecedent and subsequent. **-कर्मन्** *n.* **1** a former act or work. **2** the first thing to be done, a prior work. **3** actions done in a former life. **-कल्पः** former times. **-कायः** **1** the fore-part of the body of animals; पश्चार्धेन प्रविष्टः शरपतनभयाद् भूयसा पूर्वकायं *S.* 1. 7. **2** the upper part of the body of men; स्तुवन् करेणानतपूर्वकायं R. 5. 32; पर्यंकबंधस्थिरपूर्वकायं Ku. 3. 45. **-कालः** former or ancient times. **-कालिक, -कालीन** *a.* ancient. **-काष्ठा** the east, eastern quarter. **-कृतं** an act done in a former life. **-कोटिः** *f.* the starting point of a debate, the first statement or पूर्वपक्ष q. v. **-गंगा** N. of the river Narmadâ. **-चोदित** *a.* **1** afore-said, above-mentioned. **2** previously stated or advanced (as an objection). **-ज** *a.* **1** born or produced before or formerly, first-born. **2** ancient, old. **3** eastern. (-जः) **1** an elder brother; *Si.* 16. 44; R. 15. 36. **2** the son of the elder wife. **3** an ancestor, a forefather. **-जन्मन्** *n.* a former birth. (*-m.*) an elder brother; R. 14. 44. 15. 95. **-जा** an elder sister. **-जातिः** *f.* a former birth. **-ज्ञानं** knowledge of a former life. **-दक्षिण** *a.* south-eastern. (-णा) the south east. **-दिक्पतिः** Indra, the regent of the east. **-दिनं** the forenoon. **-दिश्** *f.* the east. **-दिष्टं** the award of destiny. **-देवः** **1** an ancient deity. **2** a demon or Asura. **3** a progenitor (पितृ). **-देशः** the eastern country or the eastern part of India. **-निपातः** the irregular priority of a word in a compound; cf. परनिपात. **-पक्षः** **1** the fore-part or side. **2** the first half of a lunar month. **3** the first part of an argument, the *prima facie* argument or view of a question. **3** the fist objection to an argument. **4** the statement of the plaintiff. **5** a suit at law. **-पदं** the first member of a compound or a sentence. **-पर्वतः** the eastern mountain behind which the sun is supposed to rise. **-पांचालक** *a.* belonging to the erstern Panchâlas. **-पाणिनीयाः** (*m. pl.*) the disciples of Pâṇini living in the east. **-पितामहः** a forefather, an ancestor. **-पुरुषः** **1** an epithet of Brahmâ. **2** any one of the first three ancestors beginning with the father; (पितृ, पितामह, and प्रपितामह). **3** an ancestor in general. **-पूर्व** *a.* each preceding one. **-फल्गुनी** the eleventh lunar mansion containing two stars. °**भवः** an epithet of the planet Jupiter. **-भागः** the fore-part. **-भाद्रपदा** the twenty-fifth lunar mansion containing two stars. **-भुक्तिः** *f.* prior occupation or possession. **-भूत** *a.* preceding, previous. **-मीमांसा** ' the first Mîmâmsâ ' ; an inquiry into the first or ritual portion of the Veda, as opposed to the उत्तरमीमांसा or वेदांत ; see मीमांसा. **-रंगः** the commencement or prelude of a drama, the prologue; पूर्वरंगं विधायैव सूत्रधारो निवर्तते S. D. 283; पूर्वरंगः प्रसंगाय नाटकीयस्य वस्तुनः *Si*, 2. 8 (see milli. thereon). **-रागः** the dawning or incipient love, love between two persons which springs (from some previous cause) before their meeting. **-रात्रः** the first part of the night. **-रूपं** **1** indication of approaching change. **2** a symptom of occurring disease. **3** the first of two concurrent vowels or consonants that is retained. **-वयस्** *a.* young. **-वर्तिन्** *a.* existing before, prior, previous. **-वादः** the first plea or commencement of an action at law. **-वादिन्** *m.* the complainant or Plaintiff. **-वृत्तं** **1** a former event; R. 11. 10. **2** previous conduct. **-शारद** *a.* relating to the first half of autumn. **-शैलः** see पूर्वपर्वत. **-सक्थं** the upper part of the thing. **-संध्या** day-break, dawn; *Si.* 11. 40. **-सर** *a.* going in front. **-सागरः** the eastern ocean; R. 4. 32. **-साहसः** the first or heaviest of the three fines. **-स्थितिः** *f.* former or first state.

पूर्वक *a.* (At the end of comp.) **1** Preceded by, attended with; आनामयप्रश्नपूर्वकमाह *S.* 5. **2** Preceding, antecedent. **-कः** An ancestor, a forefather.

पूर्वगम *a.* Going before, preceding.

पूर्वतस् *iud.* **1** In the east, to the east; R. 3. 42 **2** Before, in front of.

पूर्वत्र *and.* In the preceding part, previously.

पूर्ववत् *ind.* As before.

पूर्विन् *a.* (णी *f.*), **पूर्वीण** *a.* **1** Ancient. **2** Ancestral.

पूर्वेद्युस् *ind.* **1** On the former day. **2** On the day before, yesterday; Ms. 3. 187. **3** During the first part of the day, at dawn. **4** Early, betimes.

पूल् 1 P., 10 U. (पूलति, पूलयति-ते) To heap up, collect, gather.

पूलः, पूलकः A bundle, pack.

पूलाकः =पुलाक q v.

पूलिका A kind of cake.

पूषः, पूषकः The mulberry tree.

पूषन् *m.* (nom. पूषा,-षणौ,-षणः) The sun; सदापांथः पूषा गगनपरिमाणं कलयति Bh. 2. 114; इंधनौघधगप्यग्निस्त्विषा नात्येति पूषणं *Si.* 2. 23. -COMP. **-असुहृद्** *m.* an epithet of Siva. **-आत्मजः** **1** a cloud. **2** an epithet of Indra. **-भासा** the city of Indra.

पृ 6 A. (प्रियते, पृत) To be busy or active (mostly with व्या); कार्ये व्याप्रियते; see व्यापृत. —*Caus.* (पारयति-ते) **1** To cause to work, engage upon, entrust with, appoint to; (usually with loc.); व्यापारितः शूलभृता विधाय सिंहत्वमेकागतसत्त्ववृत्ति R. 2. 38. **2** To place, set, fix, direct, cast; व्यापारयामास करं किरीटे R. 6. 19; उमामुखे ...व्यापारयामास विलोचनानि Ku. 3. 67; व्यापारितं शिरसि शस्त्रमशस्त्रपाणेः Ve. 3. 19; R. 13. 25. -II 3 P. (पिपर्ति, पूर्ण) **1** To bring or carry over. **2** To deliver from, bring out of. **3** To fill. **4** To protect, maintain, sustain. **5** To promote, advance. -III. 9 P. (पृणाति). To protect. -IV. 10. U. (पारयति-ते; sometimes पार is regarded as a separate root) **1** To carry over or across, ferry over. **2** To reach the otherside of anything, acomplish, perform, achieve, bring to a conclusion (a vow &c.). **3** To be able or capable; अधिकं न हि पारयामि वक्तुं Bv. 2. 59; *S.* 4. **4** To deliver, save, extricate, rescue. -V. 5 P. (पृणोति) **1** To please or delight, gratify. **2** To be pleased or delighted.

पृक्त *p. p.* **1** Mixed, Mingled; R. 2. 12. **2** Touched, brought into contact, touching, united. **-क्तं** Property, wealth.

पृक्तिः *f.* Touch, contact, union.

पृक्थं Property, wealth, possessions.

पृच् 1. 2 A. (पृक्ते, पृक्य) To come in contact with. -II. 7 P. पृणक्ति, पृक्त) **1** To bring into contact with, join, unite; एवं वदन् दाशरथिरपृणग्धनुषा शरं Bk. 6. 39. **2** To mix, mingle. **3** To be in contact with, touch. **4** To satisfy, fill, satiate. **5** To augment, increase. -WITH **सं** to mix, bring in contact with, join, unite; वागर्थाविव संपृक्तौ R. 1. 1; Bk. 17. 106; see संपृक्त. -III. 1 P., 10 U. (पर्चति, पर्चयति-ते) **1** To touch, come in contact with. **2** To hinder, oppose.

पृच्छकः An inquirer, an investigator; पृच्छकेन सदा भाव्यं पुरुषेण विजानता Pt. 5. 93; Y. 2. 268.

पृच्छनं Asking, inquiring.

पृच्छा **1** Questioning, asking, inquiring. **2** An inquiry into the future.

पृज् 2 A. (पृंक्ते) To come in contact with, touch.

पृत् *f.* An army. (This word has no forms for the first five inflections, and is optionally substituted for पृतना after acc. dual).

पृतना **1** An army (in general). **2** A division of an army consisting of 243 elephants, as many chariots, 729 horse, and 1215 foot. 3 Battle, fight, encounter. –COMP. –साह: an epithet of Indra.

पृथ् 10 U. (पर्थयति-ते) 1 To extend. 2 To throw, cast. 3 To send, direct.

पृथक् *ind.* 1 Severally, separately, singly; शंखान् दध्मुः पृथक् पृथक् Bg. 1. 18; Ms. 3. 26; 7. 57. 2 Different, separate, differently; Bg. 5. 4; 13. 4; रचिता पृथगर्थता गिरां Ki. 2. 27. 3 Apart, aside, alone; V. 4. 20. 4 apart from, except, with the exception of, without; (with acc., instr., or abl.);पृथग्रामेण-रामात्-रामं वा Sk.; Bk. 8. 109. (पृथक् कृ to separate, divide, sever, analyse) –COMP. –आत्मता 1 severalty, separateness. 2 distinction, difference. 3 discrimination, judgment. आत्मन् *a.* distinct, separate. –आत्मिका individual existence, individuality.–करणं,-क्रिया 1 separating, distinguishing. 2 analysing. –कुल *a.* belonging to a different family. –क्षेत्राः (*m.* pl.). children of one father by different wives, or by wives of different classes. –चर *a.* going alone or separtely. –जनः 1 a low man, an unenlightened, vulgar man, the mob, low people; न पृथग्जनवच्छुचो वशं वशिनामुत्तम गंतुमर्हसि R. 8. 90; Ki. 14. 24. 2 a fool, a block-head. an ignorant man; Si. 16. 39. 3 a wicked man, sinner. –भावः separateness, individuality; (so पृथक्त्वं). –रूप *a.* of different shapes or kinds. –विध *a.* of different kinds, diverse, various. –शय्या sleeping apart. –स्थितिः *f.* separate existence.

पृथवीSee पृथिवी.

पृथा N. of Kuntî, one of the two wives cf Pâṇḍu. –COMP. –जः,-तनयः, सुतः,-सूनुः an epithet of the first three Pâṇḍava princes, but generally applied only to Arjuna; अश्वत्थामा हत, इति पृथासूनुना स्पष्टमुक्त्वा Ve. 3. 9; अभितस्तं पृथासूनुः स्नेहेन परितस्तरे Ki. 11. 8. –पतिः an epithet of Pâṇḍu.

पृथिका A centipede.

पृथिवी The earth; (sometimes written पृथिवी also.) –COMP. –इंद्रः, ईशः –क्षित् *m.*, –पालः, पालकः, –भुज् *m.*, –भुजः,–शक्रः a king. –तलं the surface of the earth. –पतिः 1 a king. 2 Yama, the god of death. –मंडलः-लं the circuit of the earth. –रुहः a tree; पथमानः पृथिवीरुहानिव R. 8. 9. –लोकः terrestrial world, the earth.

पृथु *a.* (थु or थ्वी *f.*; compar. प्रथीयस्; *superl.* प्रथिष्ठ) 1 Broad, wide, spacious, expansive; पृथुनितंब q. v. below; सिंधोः पृथुमपि तनुं Me. 46. 2 Copious, abundant, ample; V. 4. 25. 3 Large, great; दृशः पृथुतरीकृताः Ratn. 2. 15; Si. 12. 48; R. 11. 25. 4 Detailed, prolix. 5 Numerous. 6 Smart, sharp, clever. 7 Important. –थुः N. of Agni or fire. 2 N. of a king. [Prithu was the son of Vena, son of Anga. He was called the first king, from whom the earth received her name Prithvi. The Vishnu Purana relates that when Vena who was wicked by nature and prohibited worship and sacrifice, was beaten to death by the pious sages and when consequently robbery and anarchy prevailed in the absence of a King, the Munis rubbed the right arm of the dead king to produce a son, and from it sprang the majestic Prithu, glowing like Agni. He was immediately declared King, and his subjects who had suffered from famine, besought the monarch for the edible fruits and plants which the earth withheld from them. In anger Prithu took up his bow to compel her to yield the supply so much needed by his subjects. She assumed the form of a cow and began to flee chased by the King. But she at last yielded and requested him to spare her life, and at the same time promised to restore all the needed fruits, plants &c., 'if a calf were given to her through which she might be able to secrete milk'. Prithu thereupon made Svayambhuva Manu the calf, milked the earth and received the milk into his own hand, from which proceeded all kinds of corn, vegetables, fruits &c. for the maintenance of his subjects. The example of Prithu was afterwards followed by a variety of milkers gods, men, Rishis, mountains, Nagas, Asuras &c. who found out the proper milkman and calf from their own number, and milked the earth of whatever they wanted; cf. Ku. I. 2]. थुः *f.* Opium. –COMP. –उदर *a.* big-bellied, corpulent. (–रः) a ram. –जघन, –नितंब *a.* having large or broad hips or slopes; पृथुनितंब नितंबवती तव V. 4. 26. –पत्रः-त्रं red garlic. –प्रथ,–यशस् *a.* far-famed, widely renowned. –रोमन् *m.* a fish. °युग्मः the sign Pisces of the zodiac. –श्री *a.* highly prosperous. –श्रोणि *a.* having large hips. –संपद् *a.* rich, wealthy. –स्कंधः a hog.

पृथुकः-कं Rice parched and flattened (Mar. पोहे). —कः A child; निरयुर्जनन्यः पृथुकान् पथिभ्यः Si. 3. 30. –का A girl.

पृथुल *a.* Broad, large wide; श्रोणिषु प्रियकरः पृथुलासु स्पर्शमाप सकलेन तलेन Si. 10. 65.

पृथ्वी 1 The earth. 2 The earth as one of the five elements. 3 Large cardamoms. 4 N. of a metre; (see App. I.). –COMP. –ईशः, –पतिः, –पालः, –भुज् *m.* a king, sovereign. –खातं a cavern. –गर्भः an epithet of Ganesa. –गृहं a cave, grotto. –जः 1 a tree. 2 the planet Mars.

पृथ्वीका 1 Large cardamoms. 2 Small cardamoms.

पृदाकुः 1 A scorpion. 2 A tiger. 3 A serpent, adder. 4 A tree. 5 An elephant. 6 A panther (चित्रक).

पृश्नि (ष्णि) *a.* 1 short, small, dwarfish. 2 Delicate, feeble. 3 Diversified, spotted. –श्निः 1 A ray of light. 2 The earth. 3 The starry sky. 4 N. of Devakî, mother of Krishna. –COMP –गर्भः, -धरः, -भद्रः epithets of Krishna. –शृंगः 1 an epithet of Krishna. 2 of Ganesa.

पृश्नि (ष्णि) का, पृश्नी (ष्णी) N. of an aquatic plant.

पृषत् *n.* 1 A drop of water or of any other liquid; (said by some to be used only in pl.). –COMP. –अंशः, –अश्वः 1 wind, air. 2 an epithet of Siva. –आज्यं ghee mixed with coagulated milk. –पतिः (पृषतां पतिः) wind. –चलः N. of the horse of Wind.

पृषतः 1 The spotted antelope. 2 A drop of water; पृषतैरपां शमयता च रजः Ki. 6. 27; R. 3. 3; 4. 27; 6. 51. 3 A spot, mark. –COMP. –अश्वः air, wind.

पृषत्कः An arrow; तदुपोढैश्च नभश्चरैः पृषत्कैः Ki. 13. 23; Si 20. 18; Ub. 1. 1; धनुर्भृतां हस्तवतां पृषत्काः R. 7. 45.

पृषतिः A drop of water; पयःपृषतिभिः स्पृष्टा वांति वाताः शनैः शनैः Bharata on Ak.

पृषभाषा=पृषभासा. q. v.

पृषाकरा A small stone.

पृषातकं Mixture of ghee and coagulated milk.

पृषोदरः Wind, air. (The word is supposed to be compounded of पृषत् and उदर, the त् of पृषत् being dropped as an irregular case. The word is thus taken as the type of a whole class of such irregular compounds) ; पृषोदरादित्वात् साधुः; see Gana to P. IV. 3. 109.

पृष्ट *p. p.* 1 Asked, inquired, interrogated, questioned 2 Sprinkled.

पृष्टहायनः 1 A species of grain 2 An elephant.

पृष्टिः *f.* Inquiry, interrogation.

पृष्ठं 1 The back, hinder part, rear. 2 The back of an animal; अश्वपृष्ठमारूढः &c. 3 The surface or upper side; R. 4. 31, 12. 67; Ku. 7. 51; so अवनिपृष्ठचारिणीं U. 3. 4 The back or the other side (of a letter, document &c.); Y. 2. 93. 5 The flat roof of a house. 6 The page of a book. –COMP. –अस्थि *n.* the back-bone. –गोप; –रक्षः a soldier who protects the rear of a warrior while he is fighting –ग्रंथि *a.* hump-backed. –चक्षुस् *m.* a card. –तल्पनं the exterior muscles on the back of an elephant. –हृषिः 1 a crab. 2 a bear. –फलं the superficial contents of a figure. -भागः the back. –मांसं 1 fish on the back. 2 a fleshy protuberance on the back.

°अद, °अदन, *a.* back-biter, slanderer, calumniator. (-दं -दनं) back-biting; पृष्ठमांसादनं तद्यत् परोक्षे दोषकीर्तनं Hemachandra; cf. प्राङ् पादयोः पतति खादति पृष्ठमांसं H. 1. 81. -यानं riding. -वंश the backbone. -वास्तु *n.* the upper story of a house. -वाह् *m.*, वाह्यः a draught ox -शय *a.* sleeping on the back. -शृंगः a wild goat. -शृंगिन् *m.* 1 a ram. 2 a buffalo. 3 a eunuch. 4 an epithet of Bhîma.

पृष्ठकं The back.

पृष्ठतस् *ind* 1 Behind, behind the back, from behind; गच्छतः पृष्ठतोऽन्वियात् Ms. 4. 154; 8. 300; Bg. 11. 40. 2 Towards the back, backwards; गच्छ पृष्ठतः 3 On the back. 4 Behind the back, secretly, covertly. (**पृष्ठतः कृ** means 1 to place on the back, leave behind. 2 to neglect, forsake, abandon. 3 to renounce, desist from, leave off, resign; **पृष्ठतो गम्** to follow; **पृष्ठतो भू** 1 to stand at the back. 2 to be disregarded).

पृष्ठ्य *a.* Relating to the back -**ष्ठ्यः** A pack-horse.

पृष्णिः *f.* The heel.

पॄ 3. 9. P. (पिपर्ति, पृणाति, पूर्ण; *pass.* पूर्यते; *caus.* पूरयति-ते; *desid.* पिपरि-री-षति, पुपूर्षति) 1 To fill, fill up, complete. 2 To fulfil, gratify (as hopes &c.) 3 To fill with wind, blow (as a conch, flute &c.). 4 To satisfy, refresh, please; पितॄनपारीत् Bk. 1. 2. 5 To rear, bring up, nourish, nurture, cherish.

पेचकः 1 An owl. 2 The root of an elephant's tail. 3 A couch, bed. 4 A cloud. 5 A louse.

पेचकिन् *m.* **पेचिलः** An elephant.

पेंजूषः The wax of the ear; see पिंजूष

पेटः-टं 1 A bag, basket. 2 A chest. -**टः** The open hand with the fingers extended.

पेटकः-कं 1 A basket, box, bag. 2 A multitude, quantity.

पेटाकः A bag, basket, box.

पेटिका, पेटी A small bag, a basket.

पेडा A large bag.

पेय *a.* 1 Drinkable, fit to be quaffed or drunk. 2 Sapid. -**यं** A drink, beverage. -**या** Ricegruel.

पेयुः 1 The sea. 2 Fire. 3 sun.

पेयूषः-षं 1 Nectar. 2 The milk of a cow that has calved within seven days; सप्तरात्रप्रसूतायाः क्षीरं पेयूषमुच्यते Hârâvalî; Ms. 5. 6. 3 Fresh ghee.

पेरा A kind of musical instrument. Bk. 17. 7.

पेल् 1. P., 10 U. (पेलति, पेलयति-ते) 1 To go or move. 2 To shake or tremble.

पेलं, पेलकः A testicle.

पेलव *a.* 1 Delicate, fine, soft, tender; धनुष्यः पेलवपुष्पपत्रिणः Ku. 4. 29. 5. 4; 7. 65. 2 Lean, thin, slender; *S.* 3. 22.

पेलिः, पेलिन् *m.* A horse.

पेश (ष-स) ल *a.* 1 Soft, tender, delicate; R. 9. 40. 11. 45; Me. 93. 2 Thin, slender (as waist); R. 13. 34. 3 Lovely, beautiful, charming, good; Bv. 2. 2. 4 Expert, clever, skilful; Bh. 3. 56. 5 Crafty, fraudulent.

पेशिः -शी *f.* 1 A piece of flesh. 2 A ball or mass of flesh. 3 An egg. 4 A muscle; Y. 3. 100. 5 The foetus shortly after conception 6 A bud on the point of blowing. 7 The thunderbolt of Indra (said to be *m.* also). 8 A kind of musical instrument. -COMP. -**कोशः-षः** a bird's egg.

पेषः Grinding, pounding, crushing; *Si.* 11. 45.

पेषणं 1 Pounding, pulverizing. 2 A threshing-floor. 3 A stone and muller, any grinding or poundiag apparatus.

पेषणिः *f.* **पेषणी, पेषाकः** A millstone, a grind-stone, muller.

पेस्वर *a.* 1 Going, moving. 2 Destructive.

पै 1 P. (पायति) To dry, wither.

पैंगिः A patronymic of Yâska.

पैंजूषः The ear.

पैठर *a.* (**री** *f.*) Boiled in a पिठर q. v.

पैठीनसिः N. of an ancient sage, author of a system of laws.

पैंडिक्यं, पैंडिन्यं Living on alms, mendicity.

पैतामह (**ही** *f.*) 1 Relating to a paternal grand-father. 2 Inherited or derived from a paternal grandfather. 3 Derived from, presided over by, or relating, to Brahmâ; R. 15. 60. -**हाः** (pl.) Ancestors, forefathers.

पैतामहिक *a.* (**की** *f.*) Relating to a paternal grandfather.

पैतृक *a.* (**की** *f.*) 1 Relating to a father. 2 Coming or derived from a father, ancestral, paternal; R. 8. 6; 18. 40; Ms. 9. 104; Y. 2. 47. 3 Sacred to the Manes. -**कं** A Srâddha performed in honour of the Manes or deceassed ancestors.

पैतृमत्यः 1 The son of an unmarried woman (पितृमत्याः पुत्रः). 2 The son of an illustrious person (पितृमतः पुत्रः)

पैतृष्वसेयः, पैतृष्वस्रीयः The son of a paternal aunt.

पैत्त (**त्ती** *f.*); **पैत्तिक** *a.* (**की** *f.*) Bilious.

पैत्र *a.* (**त्री** *f.*) 1 Relating to a father or ancestors generally, paternal, ancestral. 2 Sacred to the Manes. -**त्रं** The part of the hand between the forefinger and the thumb. (Also पैत्र्य in this sense).

पैलव *a.* (**वी** *f.*) Made of the wood of the Pîlu tree; Ms. 2. 45.

पैशल्यं Mildness, affability, softness

पैशाच *a.* (**ची** *f.*) Demoniacal, infernal. -**चः** 1 The eighth or lowest of the eight forms of marriage in Hindu law, in which a lover ravishes a maiden without her consent when she is sleeping or intoxicated, or deranged in intellect; सुप्तां मत्तां प्रमत्तां वा रहो यत्रोपगच्छति । स पापिष्ठो विवाहानां पैशाचश्चाष्टमोऽधमः Ms. 3. 34; Y. 1. 61. 2 A kind of demon or पिशाच. -**ची** 1 A present made at a religious ceremony. 2 Night. 3 A sort of gibberish spoken on the stage by demons, one of the lowest forms of Prâkrita.

पैशाचिक *a.* (**की** *f.*) Infernal, demoniacal.

पैशुनं, -न्यं 1 Back-biting, slandering, tale-bearing, calumny; Ms. 7. 48; 11. 55; Bg. 16. 2. 2 Roguery, deprevity. 3 Wickedness, malignity.

पैष्ट *a.* (**ष्टी** *f.*) Made of flour or meal.

पैष्टिक *a.* (**की** *f.*) Made of flour or meal. -**कं** 1 A number of cakes. 2 A spirituous liquor distilled from meal.

पैष्टी A spirituous liquor distilled from meal; cf. **गौडी**.

पोगंड *a.* 1 Young, not adult or full-grown. 2 Having a deficient or redundant member. 3 Deformed. -**डः** A boy, one from his 5th to his 16th year; cf. अपागंड.

पोटः The foundation of a house. -COMP. -**गलः** 1 a kind of reed (नल). 2 kind of grass (काश). 3 a kind of fish.

पोटकः A servant.

पोटा 1 A masculine woman, a woman with a beard or such other maculine features. 2 A hermaphrodite. 3 A female servant.

पोटी A large alligator.

पोट्टलिका, पोट्टली A bundle, packet, parcel.

पोतः 1 The young of any animal, cub, colt, foal &c; पिब स्तन्यं पोत Bv. 1. 60; मृगपोतः, करिपोतः &c. वरिपोतः a young warrior; U. 5. 3. 2 An elephant ten years old. 3 A ship, raft, boat; पोतो दुस्तरवारिराशीतरणे H. 2. 164; Ms. 7. 32. 4 A garment, cloth. 5 The young shoot of a plant. 6 The site of house. -COMP. -**आच्छादनं** a tent. -**आधानं** a shoal of small fish. -**धारिन्** *m.* the master of a vessel. -**भंगः** a ship-wreck. -**रक्षः** the rudder of a boat or ship. -**वणिज्** *m.* a sea-faring merchant. -**वाहः** a rower, steersman,

पोतकः 1 The young of an animal. 2 A young plant. 3 The site of a house.

पोतासः A kind of camphor.

पोतृ *m.* One of the sixteen officiating priests at a sacrifice (assistant of the priest called ब्रह्मन्).

पोत्या A multitude of boats.

पोत्रं 1 The snout of a hog. 2 A boat, ship. 3 A ploughshare. 4 The thunderbolt. 5 A garment. 6 The office of the Potri. –COMP. –आयुधः a hog, boar.

पोत्रिन् *m.* A hog, boar.

पोलः 1 A A heap. 2 Bulk, magnitude.

पोलिका, पोली A kind of cake (of wheat).

पोलिंदः The mast of a ship.

पोषः 1 Nourishing, supporting, maintaining. 2 Nourishment, growth, increase, advance. 3 Prosperity, plenty, abundance.

पोषणं Nourishing, fostering, supporting, maintaining.

पोषयित्नुः The cuckoo.

पोशितृ *a.* One who feeds, nourishes &c. —*m.* A feeder.

पोषिन्, पोष्टृ *a.* One who feeds, nourishes &c. —*m.* A feeder, nourisher, protector.

पोष्य *a.* 1 To be fed, nourished or supported. 2 Well-fed, thriving. –COMP. –पुत्रः,-सुतः an adopted son. –वर्गः a class of relatives, who must be nourished and protected.

पौंश्चलीय *a.* (यी *f.*) Relating to harlots.

पौंश्चल्यं Harlotry, female incontinence; Ms. 9. 15.

पौंसवनं See पुंसवन.

पौंस्न *a* (स्त्री *f.*) 1 Fit for a man; Bk. 5. 91. 2 Manly, virile.—स्नं Manhood, virility.

पौगंड *a.* (डी) Boyish. —डं Boyhood (from the 5th to the 16th year).

पौंड्रः 1 N. of a country. 2 A king or inhabitant of that country. 3 kind of sugarcane. 4 A sectarial mark. 5 N. of the conch-shell of Bhîma; पौंड्रं दध्मौ महाशंखं भीमकर्मा वृकोदरः Bg. 1. 15.

पौंड्रकः 1 A kind of sugar-cane. 2 A mixed caste (of sugar-boilers); cf. Ms. 10. 44.

पौंड्किः A kind of sugar-cane

पौतवं A measure.

पौत्तिकं A kind of honey (pale-coloured).

पौत्र *a.* (त्री *f.*) Relating to or derived from a son.—त्रः A grandson, son's son. —त्री A granddaughter.

पौत्रिकेयः The son of a daughter appointed to raise issue for her father.

पौनःपुनिक *a* (की *f.*) Frequently repeated, recurring again and again.

पौनःपुन्यं Frequent or constant repetition.

पौनरुक्तं, पौनरुक्त्यं 1 Repetition; आतिप्रियोसीति पौनरुक्त्यं K. 237; R. 12. 40. 2 Superfluity, redundancy, uselessness; अभिव्यक्तायां चंद्रिकायां किं दीपिकापौनरुक्त्येन V. 3.

पौनर्भव *a.* 1 Relating to a widow who has married a second husband. 2 Repeated. —वः 1 The son of a widow remarried, one of the twelve sons recognised by the old Hindu law; Y. 2. 130; Ms. 3. 155. 2 The second husband of a woman; Ms. 9. 176.

पौर *a.*(री *f.*) Relating to a city or town. —रः A townsman, citizen; (opp. जानपद); Ku. 6. 41; Me 27; R. 2. 10, 74; 12. 3; 16. 9. –COMP. –अंगना, –योषित् *f.*,-स्त्री a woman living in a town. –जानपद *a.* belonging to town and country. (दाः pl.) citizens and rustics, townsmen and country people; कथं दुर्जनाः पौरजानपदाः U. 1. –वृद्धः an eminent citizen, an alderman.

पौरकं 1 A garden near a house. 2 A garden near a town.

पौरंदर *a.* (री *f.*) Derived from or sacred to, Indra. —रं The lunar mansion called ज्येष्ठा.

पौरव *a.* (वी *f.*) Descended from Puru. —वः 1 A descendant of Puru; S. 5. 2 N. of a country or people in the north of India. 2 An inhabitant or ruler of that country.

पौरवीय *a.* (यी *f.*) Devoted to Paurava.

पौरस्त्य *a* 1 Eastern; पौरस्त्यो वा सुखयति मरुत्साधुसंवाहनाभिः Mâl. 6. 25. पौरस्त्यझंझामरुत् 9. 17; R. 4. 34. 2 Foremost. 3 Prior, first, preceding.

पौराण *a.* (णी *f.*) 1 Belonging to the past, ancient, of the past. primeval. 2 Relating to the Purâṇas or derived from them.

पौराणिक *a* (की *f.*) 1 Belonging to the past, ancient. 2 Belonging to the Purâṇas or derived from them. 3 Versed in the legends of the past. —क Brâhmaṇa well-versed in the Purâṇas; a public reader of the Purâṇas. 2 A mythologist.

पौरुष *a* (षी *f.*) 1 Relating to a man or man in general, human. 2 Manly, virile. —षः A weight which can be carried by one man. —षी A woman. —षं 1 Human action, man's work, exertion, effort; धिग्धिग्वृथा पौरुषं Bh. 2. 88; दैवं निहत्य कुरु पौरुषमात्मशक्त्या Pt. 1. 2 Heroism, prowess, valour, manliness, courage; पौरुषभूषणः R. 15. 28; 8. 28. 3 Virility; Bg. 7. 8. 4 Semen virile. 5 Penis. 6 The full height of a man, the height to which he reaches with both arms elevated and the fingers extended. 7 Sun-dial.

पौरुषेय *a* (यी *f.*) 1 Derived from man; made, established or propounded by man; as in अपौरुषेया वै वेदाः. 2 Manly, virile. 3 Spiritual. –यः 1 Man-slaughter (पुरुषवध). 2 A crowd of men. 3 A day labourer, hireling. 4 Human action, man's work.

पौरुष्यं Manliness, courage, heroism.

पौड़गवः A superintendent of the royal household; especially, of the royal kitchen.

पौरोभाग्यं 1 Fault-finding, censoriousness; प्रियोपभोगचिह्नेषु पौरोभाग्यमिवाचरन् R. 12. 22. 2 Ill-will, envy, jealousy.

पौरोहित्यं The office of a family-priest.

पौर्णमास *a.* (सी *f.*) Relating to the full moon. —सः A ceremony performed on the fullmoon day by one who maintains the sacred fire (अग्निहोत्रिन्).

पौर्णमासी, पौर्णमी A day of full moon.

पौर्णमास्यं A sacrifice performed on the full-moon day.

पौर्णिमा A day of full moon.

पौर्तिक *a.* (की *f*) Relating to acts of pious charity; Ms. 3. 178; 4. 227.

पौर्व *a.* (र्वी *f.*) 1 Relating to the past. 2 Relating to the east, eastern.

पौर्वदे (दै) हिक *a.* (की *f.*) Relating to a former existence, done in a former existence, done in a former life; Bg. 6. 43; Y. 1. 348.

पौर्वपदिक *a.* (की *f.*) Relating to the first member of a compound.

पौर्वापर्यं 1 The relation of prior and posterior. 2 Due order, succession, continuity.

पौर्वाह्णिक *a.* (की *f.*) Relating to the forenoon.

पौर्विक *a.* (की *f.*) 1 Previous, former, prior. 2 Ancestral. 3 Old, ancient.

पौलस्त्यः 1 An epithet of Râvaṇ; पौलस्त्यः कथमन्यदारहरणे दोषं न विज्ञातवान् Pt. 2. 4; R. 4. 80; 10. 5; 12. 72. 2 Of Kubera. 3 Of Bibhishaṇa. 4 The moon.

पौलिः *m. f.* -पौली *f.* A kind of cake-

पौलोमी Sachî, daughter of Puloman and wife of Indra; आशीरन्या न ते युक्ता पौलोम्या सदृशी भव S. 7. 28. –COMP. संभवः an epithet of Jayanta.

पौष N. of a lunar month in which the moon is in the Pushya asterism (corresponing to December-January). —षी The day of full moon in the month of Pausha; R. 18. 32.

पौष्कर-रक (री-की *f.*), Relating to the blue lotus.

पौष्करिणी A lotus-pool or pond.

पौष्कलः A species of grain.

पौष्कल्यं 1 Maturity, complete development, full growth. 2 Abundance.

पौष्टिक *a.* (**की** *f.*) 1 Promoting growth or welfare. 2 Nourishing, nutritive. nutritious, invigorating.

पौष्णं The lunar mansion called Revatî.

पौष्प *a* (**ष्पी** *f.*) Relating to or coming from flowers, floral, flowery. **—ष्पी** 1 N. of the town पाटलिपुत्र q. v. 2 A kind of spirituous liquor (made from flowers).

प्याट् *ind.* A particle of calling (ho !, holla).

प्याय् 1 A. (प्यायते, प्यान or पीन) To swell, grow; see **प्यै** below.

प्यायनं Increase, growth.

प्यायित *a.* 1 Grown, increased. 2 Grown fat. 3 Refreshed, strengthened.

प्यै 1 A. (प्यायते पीन) 1 To grow, increase, swell; Bk. 6. 33. 2 To become full or exuberant. – *Caus.* (प्याययति-ते) 1 To increase, enlarge, make fat or comfortable; Ms, 9. 314. 2 To gratify, regale.

प्र *ind.* 1 As a prefix to verbs it means 'forward', 'forth', 'in front', 'onward', 'before', ' away', as in प्रगम्, प्रस्था, प्रचर, प्रया &c. 2 With adjectives it means 'very', 'excessively' 'very much' &c.; प्रकृष्ट, प्रमत्त &c., see further on. 3 With nouns whether derived from verbs or not, it is used in the following senses according to G. M.:—(*a*) beginning, commencement; (प्रयाणं प्रस्थानं, प्रह्न); (*b*) length; (प्रवालमूषिक); (*c*) power (प्रभु); (*d*) intensity, excess; (प्रवाद, प्रकर्ष, प्रच्छाय, प्रगुण); (*e*) source or origin; प्रभव, प्रपौत्र); (*f*) completion, perfectness, satisfaction (प्रभुक्तमन्नं); (*g*) destitution, separation, being without; (प्रोषिता, प्रपर्णवृक्षः); (*h*) apart; (प्रज्ञु); (*i*) excellence; (प्राचार्यः); (*j*) purity (प्रसन्नं जलं); (*k*) wish (प्रार्थना); (*l*) cessation (प्रशम); (*m.*) adoration, respect; (प्रांजलिः who respectfully folds his hands together); (*n*) prominence (प्रणस, प्रवाल).

प्रकट *a.* 1 Evident, plain, clear, apparent, manifest. 2 Undisguised, public. 3 Visible. **—टं** *ind.* Clearly, manifestly, publicly, visibly &c. (**प्रकटीकृ** to manifest, unfold, display; **प्रकटीभू** to become manifest, appear). Comp. **–प्रीतिवर्धनः** an epithet of *S*iva.

प्रकटनं The act of manifesting, disclosing, unfolding.

प्रकटित *p. p.* 1 Manifested, displayed, unfolded. 2 Publicly exhibited. 3 Apparent.

प्रकंपः Trembling, shaking, quivering, violent motion or tremour; बाला चाहं मनसिजवशात्प्रातगाढप्रकंपा Subhâsh; सशिरप्रकंपं *S*i. 13. 42.

प्रकंपन *a.* Causing to shake. **–नः** 1 Wind, violent wind or gust; प्रकंपनेनानुचकंपिरे सुराः *S*i 1. 61. 14. 43. 2 N. of a hell. **–नं** Excessive or violent trembling, violent motion.

प्रकरः 1 A heap, multitude, quantity, collection; मुक्ताफलप्रकरभांजि गुहागृहाणि *S*i. 5. 12; बाष्पप्रकरकलुषां दृष्टिं *S*. 6. 8; R. 9. 56; Ku. 5. 68. 2 A nosegay, bunch of flowers. 3 Aid, assistance, friendship. 4 Usage, practice. 5 Respect. 6 Seduction, abduction. **–रं** Aloewood.

प्रकरणं 1 Treating, explaining, discussing. 2 A subject, topic, department, a subject (of representation); कतमत्प्रकरणमाश्रित्य *S*. 1. 3 A section, chapter or any smaller division of a work. 4 An opportunity, occasion. 5 An affair, a matter. 6 An introduction, prologue. 7 A species of drama with invented or fictitious plot; as the मृच्छकटिक, मालतीमाधव, पुष्पभूषित &c. The S. D. thus defines it:— भवेत् प्रकरणे वृत्तं लौकिकं कविकल्पितं । शृंगारोऽगी नायकस्तु विप्रोऽमात्योऽथवा वणिक् । सापायधर्मकामार्थपरो धीरप्रशांतकः ॥ 511.

प्रकरणिका, प्रकरणी A drama of the same character as the प्रकरण. The *S*. D. thus defines it:—नाटिकैव प्रकरणिका सार्थवाहादिनायिका । सामानवंशजा नेतुर्भवेद्यत्र च नायिका ॥ 554.

प्रकरिका An interlude or episode inserted in a drama to explain what is to follow.

प्रकरी 1 An interlude or episode inserted in a drama to explain what is to follow. 2 Theatrical dress. 3 An open piece of ground. 4 A place where four roads meet. 5 A kind of song.

प्रकर्षः 1 Excellence, eminence, superiority; वपुःप्रकर्षादजयद्गुरुं रघुः R. 3. 34; वर्णप्रकर्षे सति Ku. 3. 28. 2 Intensity, high degree, excess; प्रकर्षगतेन शोकसंतानेन U. 3 3 Strength, power. 4 Absoluteness. 5 Length, protraction. (**प्रकर्षेण** and **प्रकर्षात्** are used adverbially in the sense of 'exceedingly', ' pre-eminently, ' ' in a high degree'.).

प्रकर्षणं 1 The act of drawing away; attracting. 2 Ploughing. 3 Duration, length, extension. 4 Excellence, superiority. 5 Distraction.

प्रकला A minute portion.

प्रकल्पना Settlement, fixing, allotment; Ms. 8. 211.

प्रकल्पित *p. p.* 1 Made, done, formed. 2 Settled, allotted. **–ता** A kind of riddle.

प्रकांडः-डं 1 The trunk of a tree from the root to the branches; *S*i. 9. 45. 2 A branch, shoot. 3 (At the end of comp.) Anything excellent or prominent of its kind; ऊरुप्रकांडद्वितयेन तस्याः N. 7. 93; क्षत्रप्रकांडः Mv. 4. 35; 5. 48. 3 The upper part of the arm.

प्रकांडकः See प्रकांड above; Bk. 5. 6.

प्रकांडरः A tree.

प्रकाम *a.* 1 Amorous. 2 Excessive, much, to the heart's content, at pleasure; प्रकामविस्तर R. 2. 11; प्रकामालोकनीयतां Ku. 2. 24. **–मः** Desire, pleasure, satisfaction. **–मं** *ind.* 1 Very much, exceedingly; जातो ममायं विशदः प्रकामं (अंतरात्मा) *S*. 4. 21; R. 6. 44; Mk. 5. 25. 2 Sufficiently, to the heart's content, according to the wish or desire. 3 Voluntarily, willingly. –Comp. **–भुज्** *a.* eating till satisfied or to the heart's content; R. 1. 66.

प्रकारः 1 Manner, mode, way, fashion; कः प्रकारः किमेतत् Mâl. 5. 20. 2 Sort, kind, variety, Species; oft. in comp.; बहुप्रकार manifold; त्रिप्रकार, नाना० &c. 3 Similitude. 4 Speciality, special property or quality.

प्रकाश *a.* 1 Bright, shining, brilliant; प्रकाशश्चाप्रकाशश्च लोकालोक इवाचलः R. 1. 68; 5. 2. 2 Clear, visible, manifest; *S*i. 12. 56; Bg. 7. 25. 3 Vivid, perspicuous; Ki. 14. 4. 4 Famous, renowned, celebrated, noted; R. 3. 48. 5 Open, public. 6 Cleared of trees, open; R. 4. 31. 7 Blown, expanded. 8 (At the end of comp.) Looking like, like, resembling. **–शः** 1 Light, lustre, splendour, brightness. 2 (Fig.) Light, elucidation, explanation (mostly at the end of titles of works); काव्यप्रकाश, भावप्रकाश, तर्कप्रकाश &c. 3 Sunshine. 4 Display, manifestation; *S*i. 9. 5. 5 Fame, renown, celebrity, glory. 6 Expansion, diffusion 7 Open spot or air; प्रकाशं निर्गतोऽवलोकयामि *S*. 4. 8 A golden mirror. 9 A chapter or section (of a book). **–शं** *ind.* 1 Openly, publicly; प्रतिभूर्दापितो यत्तु प्रकाशं धनिनो धनं Y. 2. 56; Ms. 8. 193; 9. 228. 2 Aloud, audibly (used as a stage-direction in dramas; opp. आत्मगतं). –Comp. **–आत्मक** *a.* shining, brilliant. **–आत्मन्** *a.* bright, shining. (**–m.**) an epithet of *S*iva. 2 the sun. **–इतर** *a.* invisible. **–क्रयः** an open purchase. **–नारी** a public woman, prostitute, harlot; अलं चतुःशालमिमं प्रवेश्य प्रकाशनारीधृत एष यस्मात् Mk. 3. 7.

प्रकाशक (**शिका** *f.*) 1 Making apparent, discovering, disclosing, evincing, betraying; displaying. 2 Expressing, indication. 3 Explaining. 4 Bright, shining, brilliant. 6 Noted, celebrated, renowned. -कः 1 The sun. 2 A discoverer. 3 A publisher. -COMP. -ज्ञातृ *m.* a cock.

प्रकाशन *a.* Illuminating, making known &c. -नं 1 Making known or manifest, bringing to light, disclosing. 2 Displaying, manifesting. 3 Illuminating, irradiating, making bright. -नः N. of Vishṇu.

प्रकाशित *p. p.* 1 Made clear or manifest, displayed, manifested. 2 Published; प्रणीतो न तु प्रकाशितः U. 4. 3 Illuminated, irradiated, enlightened. 4 Visible, evident, apparent.

प्रकाशिन् *a.* Clear, bright, shining &c.

प्रकिरणं Scattering about, strewing.

प्रकीर्ण *p. p.* 1 Scattered about, scattered forth, thrown about, dispersed; प्रकीर्णः पुष्पाणां हरिचरणयोरंजलिरयं Ve. 1. 1. 2 Spread, published, promulgated. 3 Waved, waving; *Si.* 12. 17. 4 Disordered, loose, dishevelled. 5 Confused, incoherent; बह्वपि स्वेच्छया कामं प्रकीर्णमभिधीयते *Si.* 2. 63. 6 Agitated, excited. 7 Miscellaneous, mixed; as the प्रकीर्णकांड of Bhattikâvya. -र्णं 1 A miscellany, any miscellaneous collection. 2 A chapter containing miscellaneous rules.

प्रकीर्णक *a.* Scattered or strewn about &c. -कः-कं A chowrie, fly-flap (चामर); *Si.* 12. 17. -कः A horse. -कं 1 A miscellany, any collection of miscellaneous things. 2 A miscellaneous chapter.

प्रकीर्तनं 1 Proclaiming, announcing. 2 Praising, extolling, lauding.

प्रकीर्तिः *f.* 1 Celebration, praise. 2 Fame, celebrity. 3 Declaration.

प्रकुंचः A particular measure of capacity.

प्रकुपित *p. p.* 1 Very angry, enraged, incensed. 2 Excited.

प्रकुलं A handsome body.

प्रकूष्मांडी An epithet of Durgâ.

प्रकृत *p p.* 1 Accomplished, completed. 2 Commenced, begun. 3 Appointed, charged. 4 Genuine, real. 5 Forming the subject of discussion, that which is under consideration, the subject in hand (often used in works on Alankâra for उपमेय); संभावनमथोत्प्रेक्षा प्रकृतस्य समेन यत् K. P. 10. 6 Important, interesting. -तं The original subject, the matter or subject in hand; यातु किमनेन प्रकृतमेव अनुसरामः. -COMP. -अर्थ *a.* having the original sense. (-र्थः) the original sense.

प्रकृतिः *f.* 1 The natural condition or state of anything, nature, natural form (opp. विकृति which is a change or effect); प्रकृत्या यद्वक्रं *S.* 1. 9; उष्णत्वमग्न्या तपसंप्रयोगात् शैत्यं हि यत्सा प्रकृतिर्जलस्य R. 5. 54; मरणं प्रकृतिः शरीरिणां विकृतिर्जीवितमुच्यते बुधैः R. 8. 87; अपेहि रे अत्रभवान् प्रकृतिमापन्नः *S.* 2 'has resumed his wonted nature'; प्रकृतिमापद् or प्रतिपद् or प्रकृतौस्था, 'to come to one's senses', 'regain one's consciousness'. 2 Natural disposition, temper, temperament, nature, constitution; प्रकृतिकृपण, प्रकृतिसिद्ध see below. 3 Make, form, figure; महानुभावप्रकृतिः Mâl. 1. 4 Extraction, descent; Mk 7. 5 Origin, source, original or material cause, the material of which anything is made; प्रकृतिश्चोपादानकारणं च ब्रह्माभ्युपगंतव्यं S. B. (see the full discussion on Br. Sût. I. 4. 23); यामाहुः सर्वभूतप्रकृतिरिति *S.* 1. 1. 6 (In Sân. phil.) Nature (as distinguished from पुरुष) the original source of the material world, consisting of the three essential qualities सत्व, रजस् and तमस् 7 (In gram.) The radical or crude form of a word to which case-terminations and other affixes are applied). 8 A model, pattern, standard, (especially in ritualistic works). 9 A woman. 10 The personified will of the Supreme Spirit in the creation (identified with माया or illusion); Bg. 9. 10. 11 The male or famale organ of generation. 12 A mother. *-pl.* 1 A king's ministers, the body of ministers or counsellors, ministry; R. 12. 12; Pt; 1. 48, 301. 2 The subjects (of a king); प्रवर्ततां प्रकृतिहिताय पार्थिवः *S* 7. 35. नृपतिः प्रकृतिरवेक्षितुं R. 8. 18, 10. 3 The constituent elements of the state (सप्तांगानि); *i e.* 1 the king; 2 the minister; 3 the allies; 4 treasure; 5 army; 6 territory; 7 fortresses; &c; 8 the corporations of citizens (which is sometimes added to the 7); स्वाम्यमात्यसुहृत्कोशराष्ट्रदुर्गबलानि च Ak. 4 The various sovereigns to be considered in case of war; (for full explanation see Kull, on Ms. 7. 155 and 157). 5 The eight primary elements out of which everything else is evolved according to the Sânkhyas; see Sân. K. 3. 6 The five primary elements of creation (पंचमहाभूतानि); *i. e.* पृथ्वी, अप्, तेजस्, वायु and आकाश. -COMP. -ईशः a king or magistarte. -कृपण a naturally slow or unable to discern; Me. 5. -तरल *a.* fickle by nature, naturally inconsistent; Amaru. 27. -पुरुषः a minister, a functionary (of the state); Me. 6. -मंडलं the whole territory or kingdom; R. 9. 2. -लयः absorption into the Prakriti, dissolution of the universe. -सिद्ध *a.* inborn, innate, natural; Bh. 2. 52. -सुभग *a.* naturally lovely or agreeable. -स्थ *a.* 1 being in the natural state or condition, natural, genuine. 2 inherent, innate, incidental to nature, R. 8. 21. 3 healthy, in good health. 4 recovered. 5 come to oneself. 6 stripped of everything, bare.

प्रकृष्ट *p. p.* 1 Drawn forth or out. 2 Protracted, long, lengthy. 3 Superior, distinguished, excellent, eminent, exalted. 4 Chief, principal. 5 Distracted, disquited.

प्रक्लृप्त *p. p.* Prepared, made ready, arranged.

प्रकोथः Putrefaction, putridity.

प्रकोष्ठः 1 The fore-arm, the part above the wrist; वामप्रकोष्ठार्पितहेमवेत्रः Ku. 3. 41. कनकवलयभ्रंशरिक्तप्रकोष्ठः Me. 2; R. 3. 59. *S.* 6. 6. 2 The room near the gate of a place. Mu. 1. 3 A court in a house, a quadrangle or square (surrounded by buildings); इमं प्रथमं प्रकोष्ठं प्रविशत्वार्यः &c. Mk. 4.

प्रकोष्ठकः A room near the gate of a place (=प्रकोष्ठक); तस्थुर्विनम्रक्षितिपालसंकुले तदंगनद्वारबहिःप्रकोष्ठके Ku. 15. 6.

प्रक्खरः 1 An armour for the defence of a horse or elephant. 2 A dog. 3 A mule.

प्रक्रमः 1 A step, stride. 2 A pace considered as a measure of distance. 3 Commencement, beginning. 4 Proceeding, course; Mâl. 5. 24. 5 The case in question. 6 Leisure, opportunity. 7 Regularity, order, method. 8 Degree, proportion, measure. -COMP. -भंगः want of symmetry or regularity, the breaking of arrangement, regarded as a fault of composition. (It is the same as भग्नप्रक्रमता mentioned in K. P, 7, the break of symmetry being either in expression or construction; नाथे निशाया नियतेर्नियोगादस्तं गते हंत निशापि याता is an instance of the former, where गता निशापि would relieve the irregularity of expression; and विश्रब्धं क्रियतां वराहततिभिर्मुस्ताक्षतिः पल्वले is an instance of the latter, where the symmetry of the verse requires the active instead of the passive construction, and the fault may be removed by reading the line as विश्रब्धा रचयंतु शूकरवरा मुस्ताक्षतिं पल्वले; see K. P. 7 under भग्नप्रक्रमता for further details.

प्रक्रांत *p. p.* 1 Commenced, begun. 2 Gone, proceeded. 3 In hand, under discussion. 4 Brave.

प्रक्रिया 1 Way, manner, conduct. 2 A rite, ceremony. 3 The bearing of royal insignia. 4 High position, precedance. 5 A chapter or section (of a book); as उणादिप्रक्रिया. 6 (In gram.) Etymological formation. 7 A privilege.

प्रक्रीड: Play, pastime, sport.

प्रक्लिन्न *p. p.* 1 Moist, humid, wet. 2 Satisfied (तृप्त). 3 Moved with pity.

प्रकणः, प्रकाणः The sound of a lute.

प्रक्षयः Ruin, destruction.

प्रक्षर See प्रक्खर.

प्रक्षरणं Trickling out, oozing, flowing.

प्रक्षालनं 1 Washing, washing off; R. 6. 48. 2 Cleansing, cleaning, purifying. 3 Bathing. 4 Anything used for purifying. 5 Water for washing.

प्रक्षालित *p. p.* 1 Washed, cleansed. 2 Purified. 3 Expiated.

प्रक्षिप्त *p. p.* 1 Thrown at, cast, hurled. 2 Thrown into; Mâl. 5. 22. 3 Projected. 4 Interpolated, spurious as in प्रक्षितोयं श्लोकः

प्रक्षीण *p. p.* 1 Decayed, wasting. 2 Destroyed. 3 Atoned. 4 Vanished, disappeared.

प्रक्षुण्ण *p. p.* 1 Crushed. 2 Pierced through. 3 Incited.

प्रक्षेपः 1 Throwing forward, projecting. 2 A throw, cast. 3 Scattering upon. 4 Spurious insertion, interpolation. 5 The box of a carriage. 6 The sum deposited by each member of a commercial company.

प्रक्षेपणं Throwing, casting, hurling.

प्रक्षोभणं Exciting, agitating.

प्रक्ष्वेडनः 1 An iron arrow. 2 Clamour, hubbub.

प्रक्ष्वेडित *a.* Clamorous, shouting, noisy.

प्रखर *a.* 1 Very hot; as in प्रखरकिरण. 2 Very acrid or pungent, sharp. 3 Very hard or rough. **-रः** See प्रक्खर.

प्रख्य *a.* 1 Clear, visible, distinct. 2 Looking like, resembling (at the end of comp.); अमृत°, शशांक° &c.

प्रख्या 1 Perceptibility, visibility. 2 Renown, fame, celebrity; न्यवसत्परमप्रख्यः संप्रत्येव पुरीमिमां Râm. 3 Disclosure. 4 Resemblance, similitude (in comp) Y. 3 10.

प्रख्यात *p. p.* 1 Famous, celebrated, renowned, noted. 2 Forestalled, claimed by right of pre-emption. 3 Happy, pleased. –COMP. **-वप्तृक** *a.* having a celebrated father.

प्रख्याति *f.* 1 Fame, renown, celebrity. 2 Praise, eulogium.

प्रगंडः The upper part of the arm from the elbow to the shoulder.

प्रगंडी The outer wall (of a city).

प्रगत *p. p.* 1 Gone forth or forward 2 Separate, apart. –COMP. **-जानु, -जानुक** *a.* bandy-legged, bow-legged.

प्रगमः The first advance in courtship, first manifestation of love.

प्रगमनं 1 Advance, progress. 2 The first advance in courtship; see प्रगम above.

प्रगर्जनं Roaring.

प्रगल्भ *a.* 1 Bold, confident. 2 Daring, brave, intrepid, spirited, courageous; R. 2. 41. 3 Bold in speech, eloquent; R. 6. 20. 4 Ready-witted, prompt. 5 Resolute, energetic. 6 Mature (as age); Ku. 1. 51. 7 Matured, developed, full-grown, strong; प्रगल्भवाक् Ku. 5. 30.(प्रौढवाक्) Mâl. 9. 29. U. 6. 35. 8 Skilful; K. 12. 9 Audacious, arrogant, officious, proud. 10 Shameless, impudent; R. 13. 9. 11 Illustrious, eminent. **-ल्भा** 1 A bold woman. 2 A shrew, scolding woman. 3 A bold or mature woman, one of the classes of heroines in poetic composition; she is versed in all kinds of caresses, lofty of demeanour, possessed of no great modesty; of mature age, and ruling her husband; see S. D. 101 and examples quoted *ad loc.*

प्रगाढ *p. p.* 1 Dipped into, soaked, steeped. 2 Much, excessive, intense. 3 Firm, strong. 4 Hard, difficult. **-ढं** 1 Privation. 2 Penance, bodily mortification. **-ढं** *ind.* 1 Very much, exceedingly. 2 Firmly.

प्रगातृ *m.* An excellent singer.

प्रगुण *a.* Straight, honest, upright (lit. and fig.); बहिः सर्वाकारप्रगुणरमणियं व्यवहरन् Mâl. 1. 14. 2 Being in the right state or condition, having excellent qualities; अमजयात्प्रगुणा च करोत्यसौ तनुमतोऽनुमतः सचिवैर्ययौ R. 9. 49. 3 (*a*) Worthy, suitable, meritorious; Mâl. 1. 16; (*b*) Efficient; 9. 45. 4 Skilful, clever. (प्रगुणीकृ means 1 to make straight, put in order, arrange. 2 to make smooth. 3 to nourish, bring up).

प्रगुणित *a.* 1 Made even or straight. 2 Made smooth.

प्रगृहीत *p. p.* 1 Held forth or out. 2 Received, accepted. 3 Not subject to the rules of euphony (संधि); see प्रगृह्य below.

प्रगृह्यं A vowel which is not liable to the rules of *Sandhi* or euphony and which is allowed to be written and pronounced separately; ईदूदेद्द्विवचनं प्रगृह्यं P. I. 1. 11.

प्रगे *ind.* Early in the morning, at day-break; इत्थं रथाश्वेभनिषादिनां प्रगे गणो नृपाणामथ तोरणाद्बहिः *Si.* 12. 1; सायं स्नायात्प्रगे तथा Ms. 6. 6; 4. 62. –COMP. **-तन** *a.* to be performed in the morning. **-निश-शय** *a.* who is asleep at day-break.

प्रगोपनं Protection, preservation.

प्रग्रथनं Stringing together, weaving.

प्रग्रहः 1 Holding or stretching forth, holding out. 2 Laying hold of, taking, grasping, seizing. 3 The commencement of an eclipse. 4 A rein, bridle; धृताः प्रग्रहाः अवतरत्वायुष्मान् *S.* 1; *Si.* 12. 31. 5 A check, rastraint. 6 Binding, confinement. 7 A prisoner, captive. 8 Taming, breaking (as an animal). 9 A ray of light. 10 The string of a balance. 11 A vowel not subject to the rules of *Sandhi* or euphony; see प्रगृह्य.

प्रग्रहणं 1 Taking, seizing, grasping. 2 The commencement of an eclipse. 3 A rein, bridle. 4 A check, restraint.

प्रग्राहः 1 Seizing, taking. 2 Bearing, carrying. 3 The string of a balance. 4 A rein, bridle.

प्रग्रीवः-वं 1 A painted turret. 2 A wooden fence round a building. 3 A stable. 5 The top of a tree.

प्रघटकः A rule, doctrine, precept.

प्रघटा The first elements or rudiments of a science. –COMP. **-विद्** *m.* a superficial reader, smatterer.

प्रघणः (नः), प्रघाणः (नः) 1 A porch before the door of a house; portico. 2 A copper-pot. 3 An iron mace, crow-bar

प्रघस *a.* Voracious, gluttonous. **-सः** 1 A demon. 2 Voracity, gluttony.

प्रघातः 1 Killing. 2 A combat, battle.

प्रघुणः A guest (v. l. for प्राघुण or प्राघूर्ण p. v.).

प्रघूर्णः A guest; see प्राघूर्ण.

प्रघोषः 1 Sound, noise. 2 Uproar.

प्रचक्रं An army in motion.

प्रचक्षस् *m.* 1 The planet Jupiter. 2 An epithet of Brihaspati.

प्रचंड *a.* 1 Vehement, excessively violent, impetuous. 2 Strong, powerful, fierce. 3 Very hot, stifling (as heat). 4 Furious, wrathful. 5 Bold, confident. 6 Terrible, terrific. 7 Intolerable, unbearable. –COMP. **-आतपः** fierce heat. **-घोण** *a.* large-nosed. **-सूर्य** *a.* having a hot or burning sun; Rs. 1. 1, 10.

प्रच (चा) यः 1 Collecting, gathering (as flowers). 2 A multitude, quantity, collection, number; Mv. 2. 15. 3 Growth, increase. 4 Slight union.

प्रचयनं Collecting, gathering.

प्रचरः 1 A road, path, way. 2 A custom, usage.

प्रचल *a.* 1 Trembling, shaking, tremulous; Ku. 5. 35. Mal. 1. 38. 2 Current, customary.

प्रचलाकः 1 Archery. 2 A peacock's tail. 3 A snake.

प्रचलाकिन् *m.* A peacock. U. 2. 29.

प्रचलायित *a.* Rolling about, tossing. **-तं** Nodding the head (while asleep in a sitting posture).

प्रचायिका 1 Gathering (flowers &c.) in turn. 2 A female who gathers.

प्रचारः 1 Going forth, ranging, walking about, wandering, Ku. 3. 42. 3 Appearance, coming in manifestation; U. 1; Mu. 1. 4 Currency, prevalence, use, being used or applied; विलोक्य तैरप्यधुना प्रचारं Trik. 5 Conduct, behaviour. 6 Custom, usage. 7 A play-ground, place of exercise. 8 A pasture-ground, pasturage, Y. 2. 166. 9 A passage, path; Ms. 9. 219.

प्रचालः The neck of the Indian lute.

प्रचालनं Stirring, shaking, a stir.

प्रचित *p. p.* 1 Gathered, collected, plucked. 2 Amassed, accumulated. 3 Covered, filled.

प्रचुर *a.* 1 Much, ample, abundant, plentiful; नित्यव्यया प्रचुरनित्यधनागमा च Bh. 2- 47. *Si.* 12. 72. 2 Great, large, extensive; प्रचुरपुरंदरधनुः Gît. 2. 3 (At the end of comp.) Abounding in, filled or replete with. **रः** A thief. -Comp. -**पुरुष** *a.*. populous. (-**षः**) a thief.

प्रचेतस् *m.* 1 An epithet of Varuṇa; Ku. 2. 21. 2 N. of an ancient sage and law-giver, Ms. 1. 35.

प्रचेतृ *m.* A charioteer, coachman.

प्रचेलं Yellow sandal-wood.

प्रचेलकः A horse.

प्रचोदः 1 Driving onward, urging, inciting. 2 Instigating.

प्रचोदनं 1 Driving onward, urging, inciting. 2 Instigating, setting on. 3 Ordering, enjoining. 4 A rule, precept, commandment.

प्रचोदित *p. p.* 1 Urged, incited. 2 Instigated. 3 Directed, ordered, prescribed; Ms. 2. 191. 4 Sent, despatched. 5 Decreed, determined.

प्रच्छ् 6. P. (पृच्छति, पृष्ट; *caus.* प्रच्छयति; *pass;* पृच्छयते; *desid.* पिपृच्छिषति) 1 To ask, question, interrogate, inquire of (with two acc.); पप्रच्छ रामां रमणोभिलाषं R. 14. 27; Bk. 6. 8; R. 3. 5. Bg. 2. 7; ब्राह्मणं कुशलं पृच्छेत् Ms. 2. 127. 2 To seek, seek for. -With **अनु** to inquire or question about. -**आ** 1 to ask or question. 2 to bid adieu to, take leave of (Atm.); आपृच्छस्व प्रियसखममुं तुंगमालिंग्य शैलं Me. 12. R. 8. 49; 12. 103. -**परि** to ask, question, inquire about.

प्रच्छदः A cover, wrapper, coverlet, bed-clothes, bed-cover; R. 19. 22. -Comp. -**पटः** bed-clothes, coverlet.

प्रच्छनं, प्रच्छना Inquiry, interrogation.

प्रच्छन्न *p. p.* 1 Covered, clothed, clad, wrapped, enveloped. 2 Private, secret; Bh. 2. 64. 3 Concealed, hidden. (see छद् with प्र). -**न्नं** 1 A private door. 2 A loop-hole, lattice, window. -**न्नं** *ind.* Secretly, covertly. -Comp. -**तस्करः** an unseen thief.

प्रच्छर्दनं 1 Vomiting. 2 Emiting, sending forth. 3 An emetic.

प्रच्छर्दिका Vomiting.

प्रच्छादनं 1 Covering, concealing. 2 An upper garment. -Comp. -**पटः** a wrapper, cover, coverlet.

प्रच्छादित *p. p.* 1 Covered, enveloped, clothed &c. 2 Hidden, concealed.

प्रच्छायं Thick or dense shade, a shadowy place; प्रच्छायसुलभनिद्रा दिवसाः परिणामरमणीयाः *S.* 1. 3; M. 3.

प्रच्छिल *a.* Dry, waterless (निर्जल).

प्रच्यवः 1 Fall, ruin. 2 Improvement, advancement, growth. 3 Withdrawal.

प्रच्यवनं 1 Departing, retreating, withdrawal. 2 Loss, deprivation. 3 Oozing, dropping (क्षरण).

प्रच्युत *p. p.* 1 Fallen off or from. 2 Strayed, deviated. 3 Dislodged, displaced, degraded. 4 Routed, put to flight.

प्रच्युतिः *f,* 1 Departing, withdrawal. 2 Loss, deprivation, falling down from; नित्यं प्रच्युतिशंकया क्षणमपि स्वर्गे न मोदामहे *S*ânti. 4. 20. 3 Fall, ruin.

प्रजः A husband.

प्रजनः 1 Impregnating, begetting, generating, production; Ms. 3. 61; 9. 61. 2 The impregnation of cattle. 3 Bringing forth, bearing; Ms. 9. 96.

प्रजननं 1 Procreation, generation, conception in the womb. 2 Production, birth, delivery. 3 Semen. 4 The male or female organ of generation (penis or vulva). 5 Offspring.

प्रजनिका A mother.

प्रजनुकः The body.

प्रजल्पः Prattle, gossip, heedless, or frivolous words (used in greeting a lover); असूयेर्षामदयुजा योवधीरणमुद्रया । प्रियस्य कौशलोद्गारः प्रजल्पः स तु कथ्यते ॥.

प्रजल्पनं 1 Talking, speaking. 2 Prattle, gossip.

प्रजविन् *a.* (**नी** *f.*) Rapid, swift, speedy. —*m.* An express, a courier.

प्रजा (Changed to प्रजस् at the end of a Bah. compound, when the first member is अ, सु or दुस्; see. R. 8. 32, 18. 29.) 1 Procreation, generation, propagation, birth, production. 2 Offspring, progeny, issue, children, brood (of animals); प्रजार्थव्रतकर्शितांगं R. 2, 73; प्रजायै गृहमेधिनां 1. 7; Ms. 3. 42; Y. 1. 269; so बकस्य प्रजा, सर्पप्रजा &c. 3 Subjects, people, mankind; ननंदुः सप्रजाः प्रजाः R. 4. 3; प्रजाः प्रजाः स्वा इव तंत्रयित्वा *S.* 5. 5; (where प्रजा has sense 2 also); R. 1. 7; 2. 73; Ms. 1. 8. 4 Semen. -Comp. -**अंतकः** Yama, the god of death; R. 8. 45. -**ईप्सु** *a.* desirous of progeny. -**ईशः**, -**ईश्वरः** the lord of men, a king, sovereign; R. 3. 68; 5. 32; 18. 29. -**उत्पत्तिः**, -**उत्पादनं** the raising up of progeny. -**काम** *a.* desirous of progeny. -**तंतुः** a line of descendants, race. -**दानं** silver. -**नाथः** 1 an epithet of Brahmâ. 2 a king, sovereign, prince; R. 2. 48; 10. 83. -**पः** a king. -**निषेकः** impregnation, seed (implanted in the womb); R. 14. 60. -**पतिः** 1 the god presiding over creation; Ms. 12. 121. 2 an epithet of Brahmâ; अस्याः सर्गविधौ प्रजापतिरभूच्चंद्रो नु कांतिप्रदः V. I. 9. 3 an epithet of the ten lords of created beings first created by Brahmâ; (see Ms. 1. 34). 4 an epithet of Visvakarman, the architect of gods. 5 the sun. 6 a king. 7 a son-in-law. 8 an epithet of Vishṇu. 9 a father, progenitor. 10 the penis. -**पालः**, -**पालकः** a king, sovereign. -**पालीः** an epithet of *S*iva. -**वृद्धिः** *f.* increase of progeny. -**सृज्** *m.* an epithet of Brahmâ; *S*i. 1. 28. -**हित** *a.* beneficial to children or people. (-**तं**) water.

प्रजागरः 1 Lying awake at night, sleeplessness; प्रजागरात्खिलीभूतस्तस्याः स्वप्ने समागमः *S.* 6. 21. 2 Vigilance, carefulness. 3 A guardian. 4 An epithet of Krishṇa.

प्रजात *p. p.* Born, produced &c. -**ता** A woman who has borne a child.

प्रजातिः *f.* 1 Procreation, production, propagation. 2 Delivery. 3 Procreative Power. 4 Travail, labour.

प्रजावत् *a.* 1 Having subjects or children. 2 Pregnant. -**ती** A brother's wife; (भ्रातृजाया); R. 14. 45; 15. 13. 2 A matron, mother.

प्रजिनः Wind, air.

प्रजीवनं Livelihood, subsistence.

प्रजुष्ट *a.* Attached or devoted to, intent on.

प्रज्ञ *a.* Wise, intelligent, learned.

प्रज्ञप्तिः *f.* 1 Agreement, engagement. 2 Teaching, informing, communicating. 3 A doctrine.

प्रज्ञा 1 Intelligence, understanding, intellect, wisdom; आकारसदृशप्रज्ञः प्रज्ञया सदृशागमः R. 1. 15; शस्त्रं निहंति पुरुषस्य शरीरमेकं प्रज्ञा कुलं च विभवं च यशश्च हंति ॥ Subhâsh. 2 Discernment, discrimination, judgment. 3 Device or design. 4 A wise or learned woman. -Comp. -**चक्षुस्** *a.* blind; (lit. having understanding as the only eyes). (-*m.*,) an epithet of Dhritarâshtra. (-*n*) the mind's eye, mental eye, the mind; M. 1. -**वृद्ध** *a.* old in wisdom. -**हीन** *a.* void of wisdom, silly, foolish.

प्रज्ञात *p. p.* 1 Known, understood. 2 Distinguished, discerned. 3 Distinct, clear. 4 Famous, well-known, renowned.

प्रज्ञानं 1 Intelligence, knowledge, wisdom. 2 A mark, token, sign.

प्रज्ञावत् *a.* Wise, intelligent.

प्रज्ञाल, प्रज्ञिन् (**नी** *f.*), **प्रज्ञिल** *a.* Wise, intelligent, prudent.

प्रज्ञु *a.* Bow-legged, bandy-legged; (also प्रज्ञ).

प्रज्वलनं Blazing up, flaming, burning.

प्रज्वलित *p. p.* 1 Being in flames, burning, flaming, blazing. 2 Bright, shining.

प्रडीनं 1 Flying in every direction. 2 Flying forward; see under डीन. 3 Taking flight.

प्रण *a.* Old, ancient.

प्रणखः The point of a nail.

प्रणत *p. p.* 1 Bending, inclined, stooping. 2 Bowing to, saluting. 3 Humble. 4 Skilful, clever; see नम् with प्र.

प्रणतिः *f.* 1 A bow, salutation, obeisance; तव सर्वविधेयवर्तिनः प्रणतिं बिभ्रति के न भूभृतः Si. 16. 5; R. 4. 88. 2 Submissiveness, humility, courtesy; स ददर्श वेतसवनाचरितां प्रणतिं बलीयसि समृद्धिकरीं Ki. 6. 5; निर्जितेषु तरसा तरस्विनां शत्रुषु प्रणतिरेव कीर्तये R. 11. 89.

प्रणदनं Sounding, a sound.

प्रणयः 1 Espousing, seizing (as in marriage); Mâl. 6. 14. 2 (*a*) Love, affection, fondness, attachment, liking, regard; साधारणोयमुभयोः प्रणयः स्मरस्य V. 2. 16; साधारणोयं प्रणयः *S.* 3; *S.* 6. 7; 5. 23; Me. 105; R. 6. 12; Bh. 2. 42. (*b*) A wish, desire, longing; Ku. 5. 85; Mâl. 8. 7; *S.* 7. 16. 3 Friendly acquaintance or regard, friendship, intimacy; Mâl. 1. 9. 4 Familiarity, confidence, trust; *S.* 6. 5 Favour, kindness, act of courtesy. अलंकृतोऽस्मि स्वयंग्राहप्रणयेन भवता Mk. 1; 1. 45. 6 An entreaty, request, solicitation; तद्भूतनाथानुग नार्हसि त्वं संबंधिनो मे प्रणयं विहंतुं R. 2. 28; V. 4. 13. 7 Reverence, obeisance. 8 Final beatitude. –COMP. **–अपराधः** an offence against friendship or love. **–उन्मुख** *a.* 1 disposed or about to declare one's love; M. 4. 13. 2 impatient through love. **–कलहः** a lover's quarrel, a mock or feigned quarrel; नाप्यन्यस्मात्प्रणयकलहाद्विप्रयोगोपपत्तिः Me. (considered spurious by Malli.). **–कुपित** *a.* angry througe love, feigning anger; Me. 105. **–कोपः** feigned anger of a mistress towards her lover, coquettish anger. **–प्रकर्षः** excessive love, intense attachment. **–भंगः** 1 breach of friendship. 2 faithlessness. **–वचनं** expression of love. **–विमुख** *a.* 1 averse from love. 2 disinclined to friendship; Me. 27. **–विहतिः, –विघातः** non-compliance, refusal (of a request &c.).

प्रणयनं 1 Bringing, fetching. 2 Conducting, conveying. 3 Carrying out, executing, performing; Ku. 6. 9. 4 Writing, composing. 5 Decreeing, sentencing; awarding; as दंडस्य प्रणयनं.

प्रणयवत् *a.* 1 Loving, fond, affectionate; R. 10. 57. 2 Candid, frank. 3 Earnestly desirous of, longing for.

प्रणयिन् *a.* 1 Loving, affectionate, kind, attached; Mâl. 3. 9. 2 Beloved, dearly loved. 3 Desirous of, longing for, fondly solicitous of; *S.* 7. 17; Me. 3; R. 9. 55, 11. 3. 4 Familiar, intimate. —*m.* 1 A friend, companion, favourite; Ku. 5. 11. 2 A husband, lover. 3 A supplicant, humble petitioner, suitor; स्वार्थात् सतां गुरुतरा प्रणयिक्रियैव V. 4. 15; 1. 2. 4 A worshipper; devotee; Ku. 3. 66. **–नी** 1 A mistress, beloved, wife. 2 A female friend.

प्रणवः 1 The sacred syllable *om*; आसीन्महीक्षितामाद्यः प्रणवश्छंदसामिव R. 1. 11; Ms. 2. 74; Ku. 2. 12; Bg. 7. 8. 2 A kind of musical instrument (drum or tabor). 3 An epithet of Vishnu or the Supreme Being.

प्रणस *v.* Having a prominent nose, large-nosed.

प्रणाडी Intervention, interposition, medium.

प्रणादः 1 A loud noise, shout, cry. 2 Roaring, a roar. 3 Neighing, braying. 4 A murmur or rapture; huzza. 5 A cry for help. 6 A particular disease of the ear (a buzzing sound in the ear).

प्रणामः 1 Bending, bowing, stooping. 2 A reverential salutation, obeisance, prostration, bow; as in साष्टांग प्रणाम; Ku. 6. 91.

प्रणायकः 1 A leader or commander (of an army). 2 A guide, head, chief.

प्रणाय्य *a.* 1 Dear, beloved. 2 Upright, honest, straightforward. 3 Disliked, disapproved; Bk. 6. 66. 4 Free from passion, indifferent to worldly attachments (विरक्त).

प्रणालः –ली, प्रणालिका 1 A channel, water-course, drain; कुर्वन् पूर्णां नयनपयसां चक्रवालैः प्रणालीः Ud. S. 2; Si. 3. 44. 2 Succession, uninterrupted series.

प्रणाशः 1 Cessation, loss, disappearance; Ki. 14. 9. 2 Death, destruction; R. 14. 1.

प्रणाशन *a.* Destroying, removing. **–नं** Destruction, annihilation; R. 3. 60.

प्रणिंसित *a.* Kissed.

प्रणिधानं 1 Applying, employing, application, use. 2 Great effort, energy. 3 Profound religious meditation, abstract contemplation; R. 1. 74; 8. 19; V. 2. 4 Respectful behaviour towards (with loc.). 5 Renunciation of the fruit of actions (कर्मफलत्याग).

प्रणिधिः 1 Observing, spying out. 2 Sending out spies. 3 A spy, an emissary; Ku. 3. 6; R. 17. 48; Ms. 7. 153; 8. 182. 4 An attendant, follower. 5 Care, attention. 6 Solicitation, entreaty, request.

प्रणिनादः A deep sound.

प्रणिपतनं, प्रणिपातः 1 Falling at one's feet, prostration, submission; R. 4. 64. 2 Obeisance, salutation, reverential bow; Ku. 3. 61, 4. 35; R. 3. 25. –COMP. **–रसः** a magical formula pronounced over weapons.

प्रणिहित *p. p.* 1 Laid on, applied. 2 Deposited. 3 Outstretched, stretched forth; Me. 105. 4 Consigned, delivered, entrusted. 5 Having the attention fixed upon one object, with the mind concentrated, intent. 6 Determined, decided. 7 Cautious, wary. 8 Obtained, attained. 9 Spied out; (see धा with प्रणि).

प्रणीत *p. p.* 1 Put forward, advanced, presented. 2 Delivered, given, offered, presented. 3 Brought into, reduced to. 4 Executed, effected, performed. 5 Taught, prescribed. 6 Cast, sent, discharged. (see नी with प्र). **–तः** Fire consecrated by prayers —**तं** Anything cooked or dressed, such as a condiment.

प्रणुत *p. p.* Praised, landed.

प्रणुत्त *p. p.* 1 Driven away, repelled. 2 Scared away.

प्रणुन्न *p. p.* 1 Driven or sent away. 2 Set in motion. 3 Scared away. 4 Shaking, trembling.

प्रणेतृ *m.* 1 A leader. 2 A maker, creator. 3 The promulgator of a doctrine, expounder, teacher. 4 An author.

प्रणेय *a.* 1 To be guided or led, tractable, yielding, submissive, obedient. 2 To be executed or accomplished. 3 To be settled or fixed.

प्रणोदः 1 Driving. 2 Directing.

प्रतत *p. p.* 1 Spread over, covered. 2 Stretched out, diffused.

प्रततिः *f.* 1 Extension, expansion, diffusion. 2 A creeper.

प्रतन *a.* (नी *f.*) Old, ancient.

प्रतनु *a.* (नु or न्वी *f.*) 1 Very thin or minute, delicate; Me. 29. 2 Very small, limited, narrow; प्रतनुतपसां K. 43; U. 1. 20; Me. 41. 3 Slender, emaciated. 4 Insignificant, trifling.

प्रतपनं Warming, making warm.

प्रतप्त *p. p.* 1 Heated. 2 Hot, ardent. 3 Tormented, tortured, pained.

प्रतरः Crossing, crossing or going over.

प्रतर्कः, प्रतर्कणं 1 Conjecture, supposition, guess. 2 Discussion.

प्रतलं One of the seven divisions of the lower world; see पाताल.—**लः** The open hand with the fingers extended.

प्रतानः 1 A shoot, tendril; लताप्रतानोद्ग्रथितैः स केशैः R. 2. 8; *S.* 7. 11. 2 A reeper, low spreading plant. 3 ranching out, ramification. 4 etanus or epilepsy.

प्रतानिन् *a.* 1 Spreading. 2 Having hoots or tendrils. —नी A spreading reeper.

प्रतापः 1 Heat, warmth; Pt. 1 107. Radiance, glowing heat; Ku. 2. 24. Splendour, brilliancy. 4 Dignity, ajesty, glory; Mv. 2. 4. 5 Courage, alour, heroism; प्रतापस्तस्य भानोश्च युगपद् ानशे दिशः R. 4. 15 (where प्रताप eans 'heat' also); 4. 30. 6 Spirit, igour, energy. 7 Ardour, zeal.

प्रतापन *a.* 1 Warming. 2 Distressing.—नं 1 Burning, heating, warming. 2 Paining, tormenting, inflicting punishment.—नः N. of a hell.

प्रतापवत् *a.* 1 Glorious, dignified. Valorous, powerful, mighty.—*m.* n epithet of Śiva.

प्रतारः 1 Carrying or bearing over, rossing. 2 Deceit, fraud.

प्रतारकः A cheat, an impostor.

प्रतारणं 1 Carrying over. 2 Deceiving, cheating, deception.—णा Fraud, eceit, knavery, trickery, roguery, eception, hypocrisy, यदीच्छसि वशीकर्तुं गदेकेन कर्मणा । उपास्यतां कलौ कल्पलतादेवी तारणा ॥; प्रतारणासमर्थस्य विद्यया किं प्रयोजनं Udb.

प्रतारित *a.* Deceived, defrauded.

प्रति *ind.* 1 As a prefix to verbs t means (*a*) towards, in the direcion of; (*b*) back, in return, again; c) in opposition to, against, counter; d) upon, down upon; (see the everal roots with this preposition). 2 As a prefix to nouns not directly derived from verbs it means (*a*) likeness, resemblance, equality; (*b*) rivalry; as in प्रतिचंद्रः a rival moon; तिपूरुषः &c. 3 As a separable preposition (with acc.) it means (*a*) towards, in the direction of, to; तौ दंपती वां प्रति राजधानीं प्रस्थापयामास वशी वसिष्ठः R. 2. 70, 1. 75; प्रत्यनिलं विचेरुः Ku. 3. 31; क्षं प्रति विद्योतते विद्युत् Sk.; (*b*) against, counter, in opposition to, opposite; दा यायाद्रिपुं प्रति Ms. 7. 171; प्रदुद्रुवुस्तं प्रति क्षसेंद्रं Râm.; ययावजः प्रत्यरिसैन्यमेव R. 7. 55; (*c*) in comparison with, on a par with, in proportion to, a match for; वं सहस्राणि प्रति Rv. 2. 1. 8; (*d*) near, in the vicinity of, by, at, in, on; समासेस्ततो गंगां शृंगवेरपुरं प्रति Râm.; गंगां प्रति; (*e*) at the time, about, during; आदित्यस्योये प्रति Mb.; फाल्गुनं वाथ चैत्रं वा मासौ प्रति Ms. 7. 182; (*f*) on the side of, in favour of, to the lot of; यदत्र मां प्रति यात् Sk.; हरं प्रति हलाहलं (अभवत्) Vop.; (*g*) in each, in or at every, severally used in a distributive sense); वर्षं ति, प्रतिवर्षं; यज्ञं प्रति Y. 1. 110; वृक्षं वृक्षं ति सिंचति Sk.; (*h*) with regard or reference to, in relation to, regarding, concerning, about, as to; न हि मे संशीतिरस्या दिव्यतां प्रति K. 132; चंद्रोपरागं प्रति तु केनापि विप्रलब्धासि Mu. 1; धर्मं प्रति *S.* 5; मंदौत्सुक्योऽस्मि नगरगमनं प्रति *S.* 1; Ku. 6. 27; 7. 83; Y. 1. 218; R. 6. 12; 10. 20; 12. 51; (*i*) according to, in conformity with; मां प्रति in my opinion; (*j*) before, in the presence of (*k*) for, on account of. 4 As a separable preposition (with abl.) it means either (*a*) a representative of, in place of, instead of; प्रद्युम्नः कृष्णात्प्रति Sk., संग्रामे यो नारायणतः प्रति Bk. 8. 89; or (*b*) in exchange or return for; तिलेभ्यः प्रति यच्छति माषान् Sk.; भक्तेः प्रत्यमृतं शंभोः Vop. 5 As the first member of Avyayîbhâva compounds it usually means (*a*) in or at every; as प्रतिसंवत्सरं every year; प्रतिक्षणं, प्रत्यहं &c.; (*b*) towards, in the direction of; प्रत्यग्नि शलभा डयंते. 6 प्रति is sometimes used as the last member of Avyayî. comp. in the sense of 'a little'; सूपप्रति, शाकप्रति. (*Note.* In the compounds given below all words the second members of which are words not immediately connected with verbs, are included; other words will be found in their proper places).–Comp. –अक्षरं *ind.* in every syllable or letter; प्रत्यक्षरश्लेषमयप्रबंध Vâs. –अग्नि *ind.* towards the fire. –अंगं 1 a secondary or minor limb (of the body), as the nose. 2 a division, chapter, section. 3 every limb. 4 a weapon. (–गं) *ind.* 1 on or at every limb of the body; as in प्रत्यंगमालिंगितः Gît. 1. 2 for every subdivision. –अनंतर *a.* 1 being in immediate neighbourhood. 2 standing nearest (as an heir). 3 immediately following, closely connected with; जीवेत् क्षत्रियधर्मेण स ह्यस्य (ब्राह्मणस्य) प्रत्यनंतरः Ms. 10. 82; 8. 185. –अनिलं *ind.* towards or against the wind. –अनीक *a.* 1 hostile, opposed, inimical. 2 resisting, opposing. (–कः) an enemy (–कं) 1 hostility, enmity; hostile attitude or position; न शक्ताः प्रत्यनीकेषु स्थातुं मम सुरासुराः Râm. 2 a hostile army; यस्य शूरा महेष्वासाः प्रत्यनीकगता रणे Mb.; येऽवस्थिताः प्रत्यनीकेषु योधाः Bg. 11. 32 (प्र० may have here sense 1 also). 3 (in Rhet.) a figure of speech in which one tries to injure a person or thing connected with an enemy, who himself cannot be injured; प्रतिपक्षमशक्तेन प्रतिकर्तुं तिरस्क्रिया । या तदीयस्य तत्स्तुत्यै प्रत्यनीकं तदुच्यते K. P. 10. –अनुमानं an opposite conclusion. –अंत *a.* contiguous, lying close to, adjacent, bordering (–तः) 1 a border, frontier; R. 4. 26. 2 a bordering country, especially, a country occupied by barbarians or Mlechchhas. °देशः a bordering country. °पर्वतः an adjacent hill; पादाः प्रत्यंतपर्वताः Ak. –अपकारः retaliation, injury in return; शाम्येत् प्रत्यपकारेण नोपकारेण दुर्जनः Ku. 2. 40. –अब्दं *ind.* every year. –अभियोगः a countercharge or accusation. –अमित्रं *ind.* towards an enemy. –अर्कः a mock sun. –अवयवं *ind.* 1 in every limb. 2 in every particular, in detail. –अवर *a.* 1 lower, less honoured. 2 very low or degrading, very insignificant. –अश्मन् *m.* red chalk. –अहं *ind.* every day, daily; day by day; गिरिशमुपचचार प्रत्यहं Ku. 1. 60. –आकारः a scabbard, sheath. –आघातः 1 a counterstroke. 2 reaction. –आचारः suitable conduct or behaviour. –आत्मं *ind.* singly, severally. –आदित्यः a mock sun. –आरंभः 1 recommencement, second beginning. 2 prohibition. –आशा 1 hope, expectation; Mâl. 9. 8. 2 trust, confidence. –उत्तरं a reply, rejoinder. –उलूकः 1 a crow. 2 a bird resembling an owl. –ऋचं *ind.* in each Rik. –एक *a.* each, each one, every single one. (–कं) *ind.* 1 one by by one, one at a time, severally; singly, in every one, to every one; oft. with the force of an adjective विवेश दंडकारण्यं प्रत्येकं च सतां मनः R. 12. 9 'entered the mind of every good man'; 12. 3; 7, 34; Ku. 2. 31. –कंचुकः an adversary. –कंठं *ind.* 1 severally, one by one. 2 near the throat. –कश *a.* not obeying the whip. –कायः 1 an effigy, image, picture, likeness. 2 an adversary; Ki. 13. 28. 3 a target, butt, mark. –कितवः an opponent in a game. –कुंजरः a hostile elephant. –कूपः a moat, ditch. –कूल *a.* unfavourable, adverse, contrary, hostile, opposite; प्रतिकूलतामुपगते हि विधौ विफलत्वमेति बहुसाधनता *Si.* 9. 6; Ku. 3. 24. 2 harsh, discordant, unpleasant, disagreeable; अप्यन्नपुष्टा प्रतिकूलशब्दा Ku. 1. 45. 3 inauspicious. 4 contradictory. 5 reverse, inverted. 6 perverse, cross, peevish, stubborn. °आचरितं any offensive or hostile action or conduct; R. 8. 81. °उक्त–क्तिः *f.* a contradiction. °कारिन् *a.* opposing. °दर्शन *a.* having an inauspicious or ungracious appearance. °प्रवर्तिन्–वर्तिन् *a.* acting adversely, taking an adverse course. °भाषिन् *a.* opposing, contradicting. °वचनं disagreeable or unpleasant speech. –कूलं *ind.* 1 adversely, contrarily. 2 inversely, in inverted order. –क्षणं *ind.* at every moment or instant; Ku. 3. 56. –गजः a hostile elephant. –गात्रं *ind.* in every limb. –गिरिः 1 an opposite mountain. 2 an inferior mountain. –गृहं, –गेहं *ind.* in every house. –ग्रामं *ind.* in every village. –चंद्रः a mock moon. –चरणं *ind.* 1 in every (Vedic) school or branch. 2 at every footstep. -छाया 1 a reflected image, reflection, shadow. 2 an image, picture. -जंघा the fore part of the leg. -जिह्वा, -जिह्विका the soft palate. -तंत्रं *ind.* according to each Tantra or opinion. -तंत्रसिद्धांतः a conclusion adopted by one of the disputants only; (वादिप्रतिवाद्येकतरमात्राभ्युपगतः) -त्र्यहं *ind.* for three days at a time. -दिनं *ind* in every direction, all round, everywhere; Me. 58. -देशं *ind* in every country. -देहं *ind.* in every body. दैवतं *ind.* for every deity. -द्वंद्वः 1 an antagonist, opponent, adversary, rival. 2 an enemy. (-द्वं) opposition, hostility. -द्वंद्विन् *a.* 1 hostile, inimical. 2 adverse (प्रतिकूल); Ki. 16. 29. 3 rivalling, vying with; *S.* 4. 4. (*-m.*) an opponent, adversary, rival; R. 7. 37; 15. 25. -द्वारं *ind.* at every gate. -धुरः a horse harnessed by the side of another.-नप्तृ *m.* a great-grand-son -नव *a.* 1 new, young, fresh. 2 newly blown or budded; Me. 36. -नाडी a branch-vein. -नायकः the adversary of the hero of any poetic composition; as रावण in the Râmâyaṇa,—शिशुपाल in Mâgha Kâvya &c. -पक्षः 1 the opposite side, party or faction, hostility. 2 an adversary, enemy, foe, rival; प्रतिपक्षकामिनी a rival wife; Bv. 2. 64, Vikr. 1. 70, 73; प्रतिपक्षमशक्तेन प्रतिकर्तुं K. P. 10; often used in comp. in the sense of 'equal' or 'similar'. 3 a defendant or respondent (in law). -पक्षित *a.* 1 containing a contradiction. 2 nullified by a contradictory premiss; (as a *hetu* in न्याय); cf. सत्प्रतिपक्ष. -पक्षिन् *m.* an opponent adversary. -पथं *ind.* along the road, towards the way; प्रतिपथगतिरासद्दिग्गदीर्घीकृतांगः Ku. 3. 76. -पदं *ind.* 1 at every step. 2 at every place, everywhere. 3 in every word.-पादं *ind.* in each quarter. -पात्रं *ind.* with regard to each part, of each character; प्रतिपात्रमाधीयतां यत्नः *S.* 1 'let care be taken of each character'. -पादपं *ind.* in every tree. -पाप *a.* returning sin for sin, requiting evil for evil. -पु (पू) रुषः 1 a like or similar man. 2 a substitute, deputy. 3 a companion. 4 the effigy of a man pushed by thieves into the interior of a house before entering it themselves (to ascertain if any body is awake.) 5 an effigy in general. -पूर्वाह्णं *ind.* every forenoon. -प्रभातं *ind.* every morning. -प्राकारः an outer wall or rampart. -प्रियं a kindness or service in return; R. 5. 56. -बंधुः an equal in rank or station -बल *a.* equal in strength, equally matched or powerful. (-लं) a hostile army; अस्त्रज्वालावलीढप्रतिबलजलधेरंतरौर्वायमाणे Ve. 3. 5. -बाहुः the forepart of the arm. -बिंं (विं) बः -बं 1 a reflection, reflected image; Ku. 6. 42; Si. 9. 18. 2 an image, a picture. -भट *a.* vying with, rivalling; घटप्रतिभटस्तनि N. 13. 5. (-टः) 1 a rival, an opponent. 2 a warrior on the opposite side; समालोक्याजौ त्वां विदधति विकल्पान् प्रतिभटाः K. P. 10. -भय *a.* 1 fearful, formidable, terrible, frightful. 2 dangerous; Pt. 2. 166. (-यं) a danger. -मंडलं an eccentric orbit. -मंदिरं *ind.* in every house. -मल्लः an antagonist, a rival; N. 1. 63; पातालप्रतिमल्लगल्ल &c. Mâl. 5. 22. -माया a counter spell or charm. -मासं *ind.* every month, monthly. —मित्रं an enemy, adversary. मुख *a.* 1 standing before the face, facing; प्रतिमुखागत Ms. 8. 291. 2 near, present. (-खं) a secondary plot or incident in a drama which tends either to hasten or retard the catastrophe; see S. D. 334 and 351-364. -मुद्रा a counter-seal. -मुहूर्तं *ind.* every moment. मूर्तिः *f.* an image, a likeness. -यूथपः the leader of a hostile herd of elephants -रथः an adversary in war (lit. in fighting in a war-chariot); दौष्यंतिमप्रतिरथं तनयं निवेश्य *S.* 4. 19. -राजः a hostile king. —रात्रं *ind.* every night. -रूप *a.* 1 corresponding, similar, having a counter-part in; चेष्टाप्रतिरूपिका मनोवृत्तिः *S.* 1. 2 suitable, proper. (-पं) a picture, an image, a likeness. -रूपकं a picture, an image. -लक्षणं a mark, sign, token. -लिपिः *f.* a transcript, a written copy. —लोम *a.* 1 'against the hair or grain', contrary to the natural order, inverted, reverse. 2 contrary to caste (said of the issue of a woman who is of a higher cast than her husband). 3 hostile. 4 low, vile, base 5 left (वाम). (-मं) *ind* 'against the hair or grain', inversely, invertedly. °ज *a.* born in the inverse order of the castes; *i. e.* born of a mother who is of a higher caste than the father. -लोमकं inverted order. -वत्सरं *ind.* every year. -वनं *ind.* in every forest. -वर्षं *ind.* every year. -वस्तु *n.* 1 an equivalent, a counter part. 2 anything given in return. 3 a parallel. °उपमा a figure of speech thus defined by Mâmmaṭa :—प्रतिवस्तूपमा तु सा । सामान्यस्य द्विरेकस्य यत्र वाक्यद्वये स्थितिः K. P. 10; *e. g.* तापेन भ्राजते सूर्यः शूरश्चापेन राजते Chandra. 5. 48. -वातः a contrary wind. (-तं) *ind.* against the wind; चीनांशुकमिव केतोः प्रतिवातं नीयमानस्य *S.* 1. 34. -वासरं *ind.* every day. -विटपं *ind.* 1 on every branch. 2 branch by branch. -वेदं *ind.* in or for every Veda. -विषं an antidote. -विष्णुकः a Muchakunda tree.-वीरः an opponent, antagonist. -वृषः a hostile bull.—वेलं *ind.* at each time, on every occasion. -वेशः 1 a neighbouring house, neighbourhood. 2 a neighbour -वेशिन् *a.* a neighbour. वेश्मन् *n.* a neighbour's house. —वेश्यः a neighbour. -वैरं requital of hostilities, revenge. -शब्दः 1 echo, reverberation; वसुधाधरकंदरराभिसर्पी प्रतिशब्दोऽपि हरेभिनत्ति नागान् V. 1. 16; Ku. 6. 64; R. 2 28. 2 a roar. -शशिन् *m.* a mock-moon. -संवत्सरं *ind* every year. -सम *a.* equal to, a match for. -सव्य *a* in an inverted order. -सायं *ind* every evening. -सूर्यः -सूर्यकः 1 a mock-sun. 2 a lizard, chameleon U. 2. 16. -सेना a hostile army -स्थानं *ind.* in every place, everywhere.-स्रोतस् *ind.* against the stream -हस्तः -हस्तकः a deputy, an agent substitute, proxy; आश्रितानां भृतौ स्वामिसेवायां धर्मसेवने । पुत्रस्योत्पादने चैव न संति प्रतिहस्तकाः ॥ H. 2. 33

प्रतिक *a.* Worth or brought for a Kârshâpaṇa, q. v.

प्रतिकरः Requital, compensation.

प्रतिकर्तृ *a.* (र्त्री *f.*) Requiting recompensing. —*m.* An opponent adversary.

प्रतिकर्मन् *n.* 1 Requital, retaliation 2 Redress, remedy, counteraction. Personal decoration, dress, toilet (अबलाः) प्रतिकर्म कर्तुमुपचक्रमिरे समये हि सर्वं मुपकारि कृतं Si. 9. 43; 5. 27; Ku. 7. 6 4 Opposition, hostility.

प्रतिकर्षः 1 Aggregation, drawing together. 2 Anticipation (of a word occurring later on.

प्रतिकषः 1 A leader. 2 An assistant. 3 A messenger (वार्ताहर).

प्रति (ती) कारः 1 Requital, reward return. 2 Revenge, retaliation, retribution. 3 Counter-action, obviating prevention, remedy, application of a remedy; विकारं खलु परमार्थतोऽज्ञात्वाऽनारंभः प्रतीकारस्य *S.* 3; प्रतीकारोव्याधेः सुखमिति विपर्यस्यति जनः Bh. 3. 92. 4 Opposition —Comp. -कर्मन् *n.* making reparation or amends. -विधानं application of remedy, medical treatment; प्रतिकारविधानमायुषः सति शेषे हि फलाय कल्पते R. 8. 40

प्रति (ती) काशः 1 A reflection. Look, appearance, resemblance; often at the end of comp. in this sense and translated by 'like,' 'resembling' पुटपाकप्रतीकाशः U. 3. 1.

प्रतिकुंचित *a.* Bent, curved.

प्रतिकृत *p. p.* 1 Returned, repaid requited, retaliated. 2 Counter-acted remedied.

प्रतिकृतिः *f.* 1 Revenge, retaliation 2 Return, requital. 3 A reflection reflected image. 4 A likeness picture, statue, an image; R. 8. 92 14. 87; 18 53. 5 A substitute.

प्रतिकृष्ट *p. p.* 1 Twice ploughed. 2 Repulsed, despised, rejected. 3 Hidden, concealed. 4 Low, vile, abject.

प्रतिकोपः, प्रतिक्रोधः Anger against any one.

प्रतिक्रमः Inverted order.

प्रतिक्रिया 1 Recompense, requital. 2 Retaliation, revenge, retribution. 3 Counteracting, remedying, removal; अहेतुः पक्षपातो यस्तस्य नास्ति प्रतिक्रिया U. 5. 17; R. 15. 4. 4 Opposition. 5 Personal decoration, embellishment, dress. 6 Protection. 7 Help, succour.

प्रतिकुष्ट *a.* Miserable, poor.

प्रतिक्षयः A guard, an attendant.

प्रतिक्षिप्त *p. p.* 1 Turned away, rejected, dismissed. 2 Repelled, resisted, repulsed, opposed. 3 Abused, reviled, traduced. 4 Sent, despatched.

प्रतिक्षुतं Sneezing.

प्रतिक्षेपः 1 Not acknowledging, rejection. 2 Opposing, controverting, contradiction. 3 Contest.

प्रतिख्यातिः *f.* Renown, fame.

प्रतिगत *p. p.* Flying backward and forward, wheeling about.

प्रतिगमनं Returning, going back, return.

प्रतिगर्हित *p. p.* Blamed, reviled.

प्रतिगर्जना Roaring against, answering roar.

प्रतिगृहीत *p. p.* 1 Taken, received, accepted. 2 Admitted, assented to. 3 Married.

प्रतिग्रहः 1 Receiving, accepting. 2 Receiving or accepting a donation. 3 The right of receiving or accepting a donation. 3 The right of receiving gifts (which is a peculiar prerogative of Brâhmaṇas); Ms. 1. 88; 4. 86; Y. 1. 118. 4 A gift, present, donation; राज्ञः प्रतिग्रहोऽयं *S.* 1; *Si.* 14. 35. 5 A receiver (of a gift). 6 Kind or friendly reception. 7 Favour, grace. 8 Marrying. 9 Listening to. 10 The rear of an army. 11 A spitting-pot.

प्रतिग्रहणं 1 Receiving presents. 2 Reception. 3 Marrying.

प्रतिगृहिन्, प्रतिग्रहीतृ *m.* A receiver.

प्रतिग्राहः 1 Accepting gifts. 2 A spitting-pot, spittoon.

प्रतिघः 1 Opposition, resistance. 2 Fighting, combat, mutual beating. 3 Anger, wrath. 4 Fainting. 5 An enemy.

प्रति (ती) घातः 1 Warding off, repulse. 7 Opposition, resistance. 3 A counterblow, blow in return. 4 Rebound, reaction. 5 Prohibiting.

प्रतिघातनं 1 Repulsing, warding off. 2 Killing, slaughter.

प्रतिघ्नं The body.

प्रतिचिकीर्षा Desire of retaliation or revenge, desire to be avenged.

प्रतिचिंतनं Meditating upon.

प्रतिच्छदनं A cover, a piece of cloth for a covering.

प्रतिच्छंदः, प्रतिच्छंदकः 1 A likeness, picture, statue, an image. 2 A substitute; *Si.* 12. 29.

प्रतिच्छन्न *p. p.* 1 Covered, covered over, enveloped. 2 Hidden, concealed. 3 Furnished or provided with. 4 Beset, hemmed in.

प्रतिच्छेदः Resistance, opposition.

प्रतिजल्पः An answer, reply.

प्रतिजल्पकः A respectful concurrence.

प्रतिजागरः Watchfulness, vigilance, attention.

प्रतिजीवनं Resuscitation.

प्रतिज्ञा 1 Admission, acknowledgment. 2 A vow, promise, engagement, solemn declaration; दैवात्तीर्णप्रतिज्ञः Mu. 4. 12; तीर्त्वा जवेनैव नितांतदुस्तरां नदीं प्रतिज्ञामिव तां गरीयसीं *Si.* 12. 74. 3 A statement, assertion, declaration, affirmation. 4 (In Nyâya phil.) A proposition, statement of the proposition to be proved, the first member of the five-membered Indian syllogism; see under न्याय; (पर्वतो वह्निमान् is the usual instance). 5 A plaint, an indictment. –COMP.–पत्रं a bond, written contract or document. –भंगः breach of promise. –विरोधः acting contrary to promise. –विवाहित *a* betrothed. संन्यासः 1 breaking a promise. 2 (in logic) abandonment of the original proposition; also प्रतिज्ञाहानि in this sense.

प्रतिज्ञात *p. p.* 1 Declared, stated, asserted. 2 Promised, agreed. 3 Admitted, acknowledged. –तं A promise.

प्रतिज्ञानं 1 Asserting, affirmation. 2 Agreement, promise. 3 Admission.

प्रतितरः An oarsman, a sailor.

प्रतिताली The key of a door.

प्रतिदर्शनं Seeing, perceiving.

प्रतिदानं 1 Restoration, giving back, restitution (as of a deposit). 2 Barter, exchange.

प्रतिदारणं 1 Fighting, battle. 2 Splitting.

प्रतिदिवन् *m.* 1 A day 2 The sun.

प्रतिदृष्ट *p. p.* 1 Beheld. 2 Come in sight, become visible.

प्रतिधावनं Assailing, attacking.

प्रतिध्वनिः, प्रतिध्वानः An echo, reverberation.

प्रतिध्वस्त *p. p.* Down-cast.

प्रतिनंदनं 1 Congratulating, welcoming. 2 Thanksgiving.

प्रतिनादः An echo, reverberation.

प्रति (ती) नाहः A flag, banner.

प्रतिनिधिः 1 A representative, substitute; सोऽभवत्प्रतिनिधिर्न कर्मणा R. 11. 13, 1. 81; 4. 54; 5 63; 9. 39. 2 A deputy, vicegerent. 3 Substitution. 4 A surety. 5 An image, likeness, picture.

प्रतिनियमः A general rule.

प्रतिनिर्जित *p. p.* 1 Vanquished, subdued. 2 Rescinded.

प्रतिनिर्देश्य *a.* That which, though before expressed, is repeated in order to state something more about it; cf. the instance give in K. P. 7; उदेति सविता ताम्रस्ताम्र एवास्तमेति च, where ताम्र is repeated to show that the sun that rises *red* sets also *red*.

प्रतिनिर्यातनं Retribution, retaliation.

प्रतिनिविष्ट *a.* Perverse, obstinate, hardened. –COMP. –मूर्खः a perverse fool, confirmed blockhead; न तु प्रतिनिविष्टमूर्खजनचित्तमाराधयेत् Bh. 2. 5.

प्रतिनिवर्तनं 1 Returning, return. 2 Turning away from.

प्रतिनोदः Repelling, repulse.

प्रतिपत्तिः *f.* 1 Getting, acquirement, gain; चंद्रलोकप्रतिपत्तिः; स्वर्ग° &c. 2 Perception, observation, consciousness, (right) knowledge; वागर्थप्रतिपत्तये R. 1. 1; तयोरभेदप्रतिपत्तिरास्ति मे Bh. 3. 99; गुणिनामपि निजरूपप्रतिपत्तिः परत एव संभवति Vâs. 3 Assent, compliance, acceptance; प्रतिपत्तिराङ्मुखी Bk. 8. 95 averse from compliance, unyielding. 4 Admission, acknowledgment. 5 Assertion, statement. 6 Undertaking, beginning, commencement. 7 Action, proceeding, course of action, procedure; वयस्य का प्रतिपत्तिरत्र M. 4; Ku. 5. 42; विषादलुप्तप्रतिपत्ति सैन्यं R. 3. 40 'which did not know what course of action to follow through dismay.' 8 Performance, doing, proceeding with; प्रस्तुतप्रतिपत्तये R. 15. 75. 9 Resolution, determination; व्यवसायः प्रतिपत्तिनिष्ठुरः R. 8. 65. 10 News, intelligence; कर्मसिद्धावाशु प्रतिपत्तिमानय Mu. 4; *S.* 6. 11 Honour, respect, mark of distinction, respectful behaviour; सामान्यप्रतिपत्तिपूर्वकमियं दारेषु दृश्या त्वया *S.* 4. 16; 7. 1; R. 14. 22; 15. 12. 12 A method, means. 13 Intellect, intelligence, 14 Use, application. 15 Promotion, preferment, exaltation. 16 Fame, renown, reputation. 17 Boldness, assurance, confidence. 18 Conviction, proof. –COMP. –दक्ष *a.* knowing how to act. –पटहः a kind of kettledrum. –भेदः difference of view.–विशारद *a.* knowing how to act, skilful, clever.

प्रतिपद् *f.* 1 Access, entrance, way. 2 Beginning, commencement. 3 Intelligence, intellect. 4 The first day of a lunar fortnight. 5 A kettledrum. –COMP. –चंद्रः the new moon (the moon on the first day) particulary revered and saluted by people; प्रतिपच्चंद्रनिभोयमात्मजः R. 8. 65. –तूर्यं a kind of kettle-drum.

प्रतिपदा-दी The first day of a lunar fortnight.

प्रतिपन्न *p. p.* 1 Gained, obtained. 2 Done, performed, effected, accomplished. 3 Undertaken, commenced. 4 Premised, engaged. 5 Agreed to, admitted, acknowledged. 6 Known, understood. 7 Answered, replied. 8 Proved, demonstrated (see पद् with प्रति).

प्रतिपादक *a.* (दिका *f.*) 1 Giving, granting, bestowing, imparting. 2 Demonstrating, supporting, proving, establishing. 3 Treating of, explaining, illustrating. 4 Promoting, furthering, advancing. 5 Effective, accomplishing.

प्रतिपादनं 1 Giving, granting, bestowing. 2 Demonstrating, proving, establishing. 3 Treating of, explaining, expounding, illustrating. 4 Effecting, accomplishing, fulfilment. 5 Causing, producing. 6 Repeated action, practice. 7 Commencement.

प्रतिपादित *p. p.* 1 Given, bestowed, granted, presented. 2 Established, proved, demonstrated. 3 Explained, expounded. 4 Declared, asserted. 5 Caused, produced.

प्रतिपालकः A protector, guardian.

प्रतिपालनं Guarding, protecting, defending, observing, practising.

प्रतिपीडनं Oppressing, molesting.

प्रतिपूजनं,-पूजा 1 Doing homage, showing respect. 2 Mutual salutation, exchange of courtesies.

प्रतिपूरणं 1 Filling, filling up. 2 Injecting (a fluid &c.).

प्रतिप्रणामः An obeisance in return.

प्रतिप्रदानं 1 Returning, restoring. 2 Giving in marriage.

प्रतिप्रयाणं Return, retreat.

प्रतिप्रश्नः 1 A question asked in return. 2 An answer.

प्रतिप्रसवः 1 A counter-exception, an exception to an exception (wherein the general rule is shown to be applicable to cases falling under the exception); तृजकाभ्यां कर्तरि इत्यस्य प्रतिप्रसवोऽयं (याजकादिभिश्च) Sk.

प्रतिप्रहारः A counter-blow, a blow in return.

प्रतिप्लवनं Leaping back.

प्रतिफलः, प्रतिफलनं 1 A reflection, reflected image, an image or shadow. 2 Remuneration, requital. 3 Retaliation, retribution.

प्रतिफुल्लक *a.* Blossoming, full-blown.

प्रतिबद्ध *p. p.* 1 Bound, tied, fastened to. 2 Connected with. 3 Hindered, obstructed, impeded. 4 Set, inlaid, *Si.* 9. 8. 5 Furnished with, possessing. 6 Entangled, involved. 7 Kept at a distance. 8 Disappointed. 9 (In phil.) Invariably and inseparably connected and implied (as fire in smoke).

प्रतिबंधः 1 Binding or tying to. 2 Obstruction, impediment, obstacle; स तपःप्रतिबंधमन्युना R. 8. 80. Mv. 5. 4. 3 Opposition, resistance. 4 Investment, blockade, siege. 5 Connection. 6 (In phil.) Invariable and inseparable connectien.

प्रतिबंधक *a.* (धिका *f.*) 1 Binding, fastening. 2 Impeding, obstructing, hindering. 3 Resisting, opposing. —**कः** A branch, shoot.

प्रतिबंधनं 1 Binding, tying. 2 Confinement, 3 Obstructing, impeding.

प्रतिबंधिः-धी 1 An objection. 2 An argument which equally affects the other side; (प्रतिबंदी also in this sense).

प्रतिबाधक *a.* 1 Repelling, keeping off. 2 Preventing, obstructing.

प्रतिबाधनं Repelling: keeping off, rejecting.

प्रतिबिंबनं 1 Reflection. 2 Comparison; दृष्टांतः पुनरेतेषा सर्वेषां प्रतिबिंबनं K. P. 10.

प्रतिबिंबित *a.* Reflected, mirrored.

प्रतिबुद्ध *p. p.* 1 Awakened, roused. 2 Recognized, observed. 3 Celebrated, known.

प्रतिबुद्धिः *f.* 1 Awakening. 2 Hostile purpose or intention.

प्रतिबोधः 1 Waking, awaking, being awakened; तदपोहितुमर्हसि प्रिये प्रतिबोधेन विषादमाशु मे R. 8. 54; अप्रतिबोधशायिनी 58 'sleeping not to wake again'; Ki. 6. 12; 12. 48. 2 Perception, knowledge. 3 Instruction. 4 Reason, reasoning, faculty; किमुत याः प्रतिबोधवत्यः *S.* 5. 22.

प्रतिबोधनं 1 Awakening. 2 Instructing, instruction.

प्रतिबोधित *p. p.* 1 Awakened. 2 Instructed, taught.

प्रतिभा 1 An appearance, look. 2 Light, splendour. 3 Intellect, understanding; Ki. 16. 2; Vikr. 1. 18, 23. 4 Genius, bright conception, vivid imagination; (प्रज्ञा नवनवोन्मेषशालिनी प्रतिभा मता). 5 An image, reflection. 6 Audacity, impudence. –Comp. –**अन्वित** *a.* 1 endowed with genius, intelligent. 2 audacious, bold. –**मुख** *a.* bold, confident. –**हानिः** *f.* 1 darkness. 2 absence of intellect or genius.

प्रतिभात *p. p.* 1 Bright, luminous. 2 Known, understood.

प्रतिभानं 1 Light, splendour. 2 Intellect, or understanding, brightness of conception; H. 3. 19. 3 Readiness of wit, presence of mind; कालावबोधाप्रतिभानवत्त्वं Mâl. 3. 11; दमघोषसुतेन कश्चन प्रतिशिष्टः प्रतिभानवानथ ॥ *Si.* 16. 1.

प्रतिभावः Corresponding disposition.

प्रतिभाषा An answer, a reply.

प्रतिभासः 1 Occurring to, flashing across, the mind at once, (sudden) perception; वाच्यवैचित्र्यप्रतिभासादेव K. P. 10. 2 A look, appearance. 3 Illusion.

प्रतिभासनं Look, appearance, semblance.

प्रतिभिन्न *p. p.* 1 Pierced through. 2 Closely connected with. 3 Divided.

प्रतिभूः A bail, surety, guarantee; सौभाग्यलाभप्रतिभूः पदानां Vikr. 1. 9; Y. 2. 10, 54; N. 14. 4.

प्रतिभेदनं 1 Piercing, penetrating. 2 Cutting, splitting, cleaving. 3 Putting out (as the eyes). 4 Dividing.

प्रतिभोगः Enjoyment.

प्रतिमा 1 An image, a likeness, statue, figure, an idol; R. 16. 39. 2 Resemblance, similitude; oft. in comp.; गुरोः कृशानुप्रतिमात् R. 2. 49. 3 A reflection, reflected image; सुखमिंदुरुज्ज्वलकपोलमतः प्रतिमाच्छलेन सुदृशामविशत् *Si.* 9. 48, 73; R. 7. 64; 12. 100. 4 A measure, extent. 5 The part of an elephant's head between the tusks. –Comp. –**गत** *a.* present in an idol. –**चंद्रः** the reflected moon, reflection of the moon; R. 10. 65; so **प्रतिमेंदुः, प्रतिमाशशांकः**. -**परिचारकः** an attendant upon an idol.

प्रतिमानं 1 A model, pattern. 2 An image, idol. 3 Likeness, similitude, similarity. 4 A weight. 5 The part of an elephant's head between the tusks; पृथुप्रतिमानभाग &c. *Si.* 5. 36. 6 A reflection.

प्रतिमुक्त *p. p.* 1 Put on, worn, applied. 2 Tied, bound, fastened. 3 Armed, accoutred. 4 Liberated, released. 5 Restored, returned. 6 Flung, hurled (see मुच् with प्रति).

प्रतिमोक्षः, प्रतिमोक्षणं Liberation, deliverance.

प्रतिमोचनं 1 Loosening. 2 Requital, retaliation, retribution; वैरप्रतिमोचनाय R. 14. 41. 3 Liberation, release.

प्रतियत्नः 1 An effort, endeavour, exertion. 2 Preparation, elaboration; *Si.* 3. 54. 3 Making complete or perfect. 4 Imparting a new quality or virtue; सतो गुणांतराधानं प्रतियत्नः Kâsi. on P. II. 3. 53. 5 Wish, desire. 6 Opposition, resistance. 7 Retaliation, retribution, revenge. 8 Making captive, taking prisoner. 9 Favour.

प्रतियातनं Requital, retaliation; as in वैरप्रतियातन.

प्रतियातना A picture, an image, statue; *Si.* 3. 34.

प्रतियानं Return, retreat.

प्रतियोगः 1 Being or forming a counter-part of anything. 2 Opposition, resistance. 3 Contradiction. 4 Co-operation. 5 An antidote, a remedy.

प्रतियोगिन् *a.* 1 Opposing, counteracting, impeding. 2 Related or corresponding to, being or forming a counter-part of (anything); often used in works on Nyâya. 3 Co-operating with. —*m*. 1 An adversary, opponent, enemy; दहत्यशेषं प्रतियोगिगर्वं Vikr. 1. 117. 2 A counter-part, match.

प्रतियोद्धृ *m*. **प्रतियोधः** An adversary, opponent.

प्रतिरक्षणं-रक्षा Safety, preservation, protection.

प्रतिरंभः Passion, rage.

प्रतिरवः 1 Quarrel, contest. 2 Echo.

प्रतिरुद्ध *p. p*. 1 Impeded, obstructed, hindered. 2 Interrupted. 3 Impaired. 4 Disabled. 5 Invested, blockaded.

प्रतिरोधः 1 Impediment, obstruction, hindrance. 2 Siege, blockade. 3 An opponent. 4 Concealing. 5 Theft, robbery. 6 Censure, despising.

प्रतिरोधकः, प्रतिरोधिन् *m*. 1 An opponent. 2 A robber, thief; M. 5. 10. 3 An obstacle.

प्रतिरोधनं Opposing, obstructing.

प्रतिलंभः 1 Getting, obtaining, receiving. 2 Censure, abuse, reviling.

प्रतिलाभः Taking or obtaining back, taking, getting.

प्रतिवचनं, प्रतिवचस् *n*. **प्रतिवाच्** *f*. **प्रतिवाक्यं** An answer, reply; प्रतिवाचमदत्त केशवः शपमानाय न चेदिभूभुजे Si. 16. 25; परभृतविरुतं कलं यथा प्रतिवचनीकृतमेभिरीदृशं S. 4. 9.

प्रतिवर्तनं Returning.

प्रतिवसथः A village.

प्रतिवहनं Leading back.

प्रतिवादः 1 An answer, a rejoinder, reply. 2 Refusal, rejection.

प्रतिवादिन् *m*. 1 An opponent. 2 A defendant, respondent (in law).

प्रतिवारः, प्रतिवारणं Warding or keeping off, keeping back.

प्रतिवार्ता Account, information, news, tidings.

प्रतिवासिन् *a*. (नी *f*.) Dwelling near, neighbouring. —*m*. A neighbour.

प्रतिविघातः Striking back, defending.

प्रतिविधानं 1 Counteracting, counter-working, taking measures against. 2 Arrangement, array. 3 Prevention. 4 Substituted ceremony, subsidiary rite.

प्रतिविधिः 1 Retaliation. 2 A remedy, means of counter-acting.

प्रतिविशिष्ट *a*. Most excellent.

प्रतिवेशः 1 A neighbour. 2 The residence of a neighbour, neighbourhood —COMP. —**वासिन्** *a*. living in the neighbourhood. (—*m*.) a neighbour.

प्रतिवेशिन् *a*. (नी *f*.) A neighbour; दृष्टिं हे प्रतिवेशिनि क्षणमिहाप्यस्मद्गृहे दास्यसि S. D.; Mk. 3. 14.

प्रतिवेश्यः A neighbour.

प्रतिवेष्टित *p. p*. Rolled back, reverted.

प्रतिव्यूढ *p. p*. Down out in battle-array.

प्रतिव्यूहः 1 Arraying an army against an enemy. 2 A multitude, collection.

प्रतिशमः Cessation.

प्रतिशयनं The act of lying down without food before a deity to secure some desired object.

प्रतिशयित *a*. One who lies down without food before a deity to secure his desired object; अनया च किलास्मै प्रतिशयिताय स्वप्ने समादिष्टं D. K. 121.

प्रतिशापः A curse for curse, a curse in return.

प्रतिशासनं 1 Giving orders, sending on an errand, ordering. 2 Ordering or despatching an inferior after calling him to attend. 3 Counter-manding. 4 A rival command or authority; अप्रतिशासनं जगत् R. 8. 27 'completely under the sway of one ruler'.

प्रतिशिष्ट *p. p*. 1 Ordered, sent; Si. 16. 1. 2 Dismissed, rejected. 3 Famous, celebrated.

प्रतिश्या, प्रतिश्यानं, प्रतिश्यायः A catarrh or cold.

प्रतिश्रयः 1 A shelter, asylum. 2 A house, dwelling, residence; Y. 1. 210; Ms. 10. 51. 3 An assembly. 4 A sacrificial hall. 5 Help, asssitance. 6 A promise.

प्रतिश्रवः 1 Assent, agreement, promise. 2 An echo.

प्रतिश्रवणं 1 Listening to; Ms. 2. 195. 2 Promising, assenting, agreeing. 3 A promise.

प्रतिश्रुत्, प्रतिश्रुतिः *f*. 1 A promise. 2 An echo, reverberation; R. 13. 40; 16. 31; Si. 17 42.

प्रतिश्रुत *p. p*. Promised, agreed, assented.

प्रतिषिद्ध *p. p*. 1 Forbidden, prohibited, disallowed, refused. 2 Contradicted.

प्रतिषेधः 1 Keeping or warding off, driving away, expulsion; Vikr. 1. 8. 2 Prohibition; as in शास्त्रप्रतिषेधः. 3 Denial, refusal. 4 Negation, contradiction. 5 A negative particle. —COMP. —**अक्षरं, —उक्तिः** *f*. words of denial, refusal; S. 3. 25. —**उपमा** one of the several kinds of Upamá mentioned by Daṇḍin. It is thus explained:—न जातु शक्तिरिंदोस्ते मुखेन प्रतिगर्जितुं । कलंकिनो जडस्येति प्रतिषेधोपमैव सा ॥ Kâv. 2. 34.

प्रतिषेधक, प्रतिषेद्धृ *a*. 1 Warding off, prohibiting, preventing. 2 Preventive. —*m*. A hinderer, prohibitor.

प्रतिषेधनं 1 Keeping or warding off, preventing. 2 Prohibition. 3 Denial, refusal.

प्रतिष्कः, प्रतिष्कसः A spy, messenger, an emissary.

प्रतिष्कशः 1 A spy, emissary. 2 A whip.

प्रतिष्कषः A whip, leather-thong.

प्रतिष्टंभः Obstruction, impediment, resistance, opposition, obstacle; बाहुप्रतिष्टंभविवृद्धमन्युः R. 2. 32, 59.

प्रतिष्ठा 1 Resting, remaining, situation, position; अपौरुषेयप्रतिष्ठं Mâl. 9; S. 7. 6. 2 A house, residence, home, habitation; R. 6. 2[illegible] 4. 5. 3 Fixity, stability, strength, permanence, firm basis; अप्रतिष्ठे रघुज्येष्ठे का प्रतिष्ठा कुलस्य नः U. 5. 25; अत्र खलु मे वंशप्रतिष्ठा S. 7; वंशः प्रतिष्ठां नीतः K. 280; Si. 2. 34. 4 Basis, foundation, site; as in गृहप्रतिष्ठा. 5 A prop, stay, support; (hence) an object of glory, a distinguished ornament; त्यक्ता मया नाम कुलप्रतिष्ठा S. 6. 24; द्वे प्रतिष्ठे कुलस्य नः 3. 21; Ku. 7. 27; Mv. 7. 21. 6 High position, pre-eminence, high authority; Mu. 2. 5. 7 Fame, glory, renown, celebrity; मा निषाद प्रतिष्ठां त्वमगमः शाश्वतीः समाः Râm (=U. 2. 5.). 8 Installation, inauguration; Mu. 1. 14. 9 Attainment of a desired object, accomplishment, fulfilment (of one's desire); औत्सुक्यमात्रमवसादयति प्रतिष्ठा S. 5 6. 10 Tranquillity, rest, repose. 11 A receptacle. 12 The earth. 13 The consecration of an idol or image. 14 A limit, boundary.

प्रतिष्ठानं 1 Basis, foundation. 2 Site, situation, position. 3 A leg, foot. 4 N. of a town at the confluence of the Ganges and Yamunâ and capital of the early kings of the lunar race; cf. V. 2. 5 N. of a town on the Godâvarî.

प्रतिष्ठित *p. p*. 1 Set up, erected. 2 Fixed, established. 3 Placed, situated. 4 Installed, inaugurated, consecrated. 5 Completed, effected. 6 Prized, valued. 7 Famous, celebrated; (see **स्था** with प्रति).

प्रतिसंविद् *f*. An accurate knowledge of the particulars of anything.

प्रतिसंहारः 1 Taking back, withdrawing. 2 Diminution, compression. 3 Comprehension, inclusion. 4 Yielding, giving up.

प्रतिसंहृत *p. p*. 1 Taken back, withdrawn; एष प्रतिसंहृतः S. 1. 2 Comprehended, included. 3 Compressed.

प्रतिसंक्रमः 1 Reabsorption. 2 Reflection (प्रतिच्छाया).

प्रतिसंख्या Consciousness.

प्रतिसंचरः 1 Moving backwards. 2 Reabsorption. 3 Especially, reabsorption (of the world) back into Prakṛiti.

प्रतिसंदेशः A message in return, an answer to a message.

प्रतिसंधानं 1 Joining together, uniting. 2 The period of transition between two ages. 3 A means, remedy. 4 Self-command, restraint of feelings or passions. 5 Praise.

प्रतिसंधिः 1 Reunion. 2 Entering into the womb. 3 The period of transition between two ages. 4 Stop, cessation (उपरम).

प्रतिसमाधानं Cure, remedy.

प्रतिसमासनं 1 Coping with, being a match for. 2 Resisting, opposing, withstanding.

प्रतिसरः-रं A cord or ribbon worn round the wrist or neck as an amulet. **-रः** 1 A servant, follower. 2 A bracelet, marriage-string; स्रस्तोरगप्रतिसरेण करेण पाणिः (अगृह्यत) Ki. 5. 33 (=कौतुकसूत्र Malli.). 3 A garland, wreath. 4 Day-break. 5 The rear of an army. 6 A form of incantation. 7 Healing or dressing a wound.

प्रतिसर्गः 1 Secondary creation (as by the agents of one Supreme Being). 2 Dissolution.

प्रतिसांधानिकः A bard, panegyrist.

प्रतिसारणं 1 Dressing the edges of a wound. 2 An instrument used for anointing a wound.

प्रतिसीरा A screen, a curtain, a wall of cloth.

प्रतिसृष्ट *p. p.* 1 Sent out, despatched. 2 Celebrated. 3 Repulsed, rejected. 4 Intoxicated (प्रमत्त according to धरणि).

प्रतिस्नात *p. p.* Bathed.

प्रतिस्नेहः Love in return, requital or reciprocation of love.

प्रतिस्पंदनं Throbbing.

प्रतिस्वनः,प्रतिस्वरः An echo, reverberation; *S*i. 13. 31.

प्रतिहत *p. p.* 1 Struck or beaten back; knocked back. 2 Driven away, repelled, repulsed. 3 Opposed, obstructed. 4 Sent, despatched. 5 Hated, disliked. 6 Disappointed, frustrated. -Comp. **-मति** *a.* hating, disliking.

प्रतिहतिः *f.* 1 Striking or knocking back, repelling. 2 Rebound, recoil. प्रतिहतिं ययुरर्जुनमुष्टयः Ki. 18. 5; *S*i. 9. 49. 3 Disappointment, frustration. 4 Anger.

प्रतिहननं Striking or knocking back, returning a blow.

प्रतिहर्तृ *m.* One who beats back or removes, repeller, remover.

प्रति (ती) हारः 1 *S*triking back. 2 A door, gate. 3 A porter, door-keeper. 4 A juggler. 5 Juggling, a juggling trick. -Comp. **-भूमिः** *f.* the threshold (of a house &c.); Ku. 3. 58. **-रक्षी** a female door-keeper; R. 6. 20.

प्रतिहारकः A juggler.

प्रतिहासः Returning a laugh.

प्रतिहिंसा Retaliation, revenge,

प्रतिहित *p. p.* 1 Fitted to, put close to.

प्रतीक *a.* 1 Directed or turned towards. 2 Inverted, reverse. 3 Contrary, unfavourable, adverse. **-कः** 1 A limb, member; *S*i. 18. 79. 2 A part, portion. **-कं** 1 An image. 2 Mouth, face. 3 The front (of anything). 4 The first word (of a verse, sentence &c.).

प्रतीक्षणं, प्रतीक्षा 1 Waiting for. 2 Expectation, hope. 3 Regard, consideration, attention.

प्रतीक्षित *p. p.* 1 Waited for, expected. 2 Considerd.

प्रतीक्ष्य *pot. p.* 1 To be waited for. 2 Worthy of consideration or regard. 3 Venerable, respectable; R. 5. 14; *S*i. 2 108. 4 To be adhered to or maintained, to be fulfilled; *S*i. 2. 180.

प्रतीची The west.

प्रतीचीन *a.* 1 Western, westerly. 2 Future, subsequent, following.

प्रतीच्छकः A receiver.

प्रतीच्य *a* Living in the west, western, westerly.

प्रतीत *p. p.* 1 Set forth, started. 2 Gone by, past, gone. 3 Believed, trusted. 4 Proved, established. 5 Acknowledged, recognised. 6 Called, known as, named; सोयं वटः श्याम इति प्रतीतः R. 13. 53. 7 Well-known, renowned, famous. 8 Firmly resolved. 9 Believing, trusting, confident. 10 Pleased, delighted; R. 3. 12; 5. 26; 14. 47; 16. 23. 11 Respectful. 12 Clever, learned, wise.

प्रतीतिः *f.* 1 Conviction, settled belief; *S*. 7. 31. 2 Belief. 3 Knowledge, ascertainment, clear or distinct perception or apprehension; अपि तु वाच्यवैचित्र्यप्रतिभासादेव चारुताप्रतीतिः K. P. 10. 4 Fame, renown. 5 Respect. 6 Delight.

प्रतीत्त *a.* Given back, restored.

प्रतीधकः N. of a country called विदेह q. v.

प्रतीप *a.* 1 Contrary, unfavourable, adverse, opposite. तत्प्रतीपपवनादि वैकृतं R. 11. 62. 2 Reverse, inverted, out of order. 3 Backward, retrograde. 4 Disagreeable, displeasing. 5 Refractory, disobedient, obstinate, perverse; Pt. 1. 424. 6 Hindering. **-पः** N. of a king, father of S'antanu and grandfather of Bhîshma. **-पं** N. of a figure of speech in which the usual form of comparison is inverted, the उपमान being compared with the उपमेय; प्रतीपमुपमानस्याप्युपमेयत्वकल्पनं । त्वल्लोचनसमं पद्मं त्वद्वक्त्रसदृशो विधुः ॥ Chandr. 5. 9. (for fuller definitions and explanation see K. P. 10 under प्रतीप). **-पं** *ind.* 1 On the contrary. 2 In an inverted order. 3 Against, in opposition to; भर्तुर्विप्रकृतापि रोषणतया मा स्म प्रतीपं गमः *S*. 4. 18. -Comp. **-ग** *a.* 1 going against. 2 adverse, unfavourable; R. 11. 58. **-गमनं, -गतीः** *f.* retrograde motion; Ku. 2. 25. **-तरणं** going or sailing against the stream; V. 2. 5. **-दर्शिनी** a woman. **-वचनं** 1 contradiction. 2 a perverse or evasive manner of speaking. **-विपाकिन्** *a.* producing the opposite result (recoiling on the doer); Mâl. 5. 26.

प्रतीरं A shore, bank.

प्रतीवापः 1 Adding to, inserting (as an ingredient). 2 calcining or fluxing metals. 3 An epidemic, disease, a plague.

प्रतीवेश, प्रतीहार, प्रतीहास &c. See प्रतिवेश &c.

प्रतीवेशिन् *a.* See प्रतिवेशिन्.

प्रतीहारी 1 A female door-keeper. 2 A door-keeper in general.

प्रतुदः 1 An epithet of a class of birds (such as hawks, parrots, crows &c.). 2 An instrument for pricking.

प्रतुष्टिः *f.* Gratification, satisfaction.

प्रतोदः 1 A goad. 2 A long whip. 3 A pricking instrument.

प्रतूर्ण *a.* Speedy, quick, fleet.

प्रतोली A street, main road, principal street through a town; प्राप्तप्रतोलीमतुलप्रतापः *S*i. 3. 64.

प्रत्त p. p. 1 Given, given away, presented, offered. 2 Given in marriage, married.

प्रत्न *a.* 1 Old, ancient. 2 Former. 3 Traditional, customary.

प्रत्यक् *ind.* 1 In an opposite direction, backwards. 2 Against. 3 Westward, to the west of (with abl) 4 In the interior, inwardly. 5 Formerly, in former times.

प्रत्यक्ष *a.* 1 Perceptible (to the eye), visible; प्रत्यक्षाभिः प्रपन्नस्तनुभिरवतु वस्ताभिरष्टाभिरीशः *S*. 1. 1. 2 Present, in sight, before the eye. 3 Cognizable by any organ of sense. 4 Distinct, evident, clear. 5 Direct, immediate. 6 Explicit, express. 7 Corporeal. **-क्षं** 1 Perception, ocular evidence, apprehension by the senses, considered as a प्रमाण or mode of proof; इंद्रियार्थसंनिकर्षजन्यं ज्ञानं प्रत्यक्षं T. S. 2 Explicitness, distinctness. (The forms प्रत्यक्ष, प्रत्यक्षेण, प्रत्यक्षतः, प्रत्यक्षात् are used adverbially in the sense of 1 Before, in the presence of, in the sight of. 2 Openly, publicly. 3 Directly, immediately. 4 Personally. 5 At sight. 6 Explicitly). -Comp. **-ज्ञानं** ocular evidence, knowledge obtained by direct perception. **-दर्शनः, -दर्शिन्** *m.* an eye-witness. **-दृष्ट** *a.* personally seen. **-प्रमा** correct or certain knowledge, such as is obtained by direct perception through the senses. -प्रमाणं ocular proof, evidence of the senses. -फल *a.* having evident or visible consequences. -वादिन् *m.* a Buddhist who admits no other evidence than ocular proof or perception. -विहित *a.* directly or explicitly enjoined.

प्रत्यक्षिन् *m.* An eye-witness.

प्रत्यग्र *a.* 1 Fresh, young, new, recent; प्रत्यग्रहतानां मांसं Ve. 3; कुसुमशयनं न प्रत्यग्रं V. 3. 10; Me. 4; R. 10. 54; Ratn. 1. 21. 2 Repeated. 3 Pure. -COMP. -वयस् *a.* young in age, in the prime of life, youthful.

प्रत्यंच् *a.* (प्रतीची *f.* or according to Vopadeva प्रत्यंची also) 1 Turned or directed towards. 2 Being behind. 3 Following, subsequent. 4 Averted, turned away. 5 Western, westerly. -COMP. -अक्षं (प्रत्यगक्षं) an inner organ. -आत्मन् *m.* (प्रत्यगात्मन्) the the individual soul. -आशापतिः (प्रत्यगाशापतिः) 'the lord of the western direction', an epithet of Varuṇa. -उदच् *f.* (प्रत्यगुदच्) the north-west. -दक्षिणतः (प्रत्यग्दक्षिणतः) *ind.* towards the south-west.-दृश् *f.* (प्रत्यग्दृश्) an inward glance, a glance directed inwards. -मुख *a.* (प्रत्यङ्मुख) 1 facing the west. 2 having the face averted. -स्रोतस् *a.* (प्रत्यक्स्रोतस्) flowing towards the west; Malli. on Si. 4. 66. (-*f.*) an epithet of the river Narmadâ.

प्रत्यंचित *a.* Honoured, worshipped.

प्रत्यदनं 1 Eating. 2 Food.

प्रत्यभिज्ञा Knowing, recognition; सप्रत्यभिज्ञमिव मामवलोक्य Mal. 1. 25.

प्रत्यभिज्ञानं 1 Recognition (in return); प्रत्यभिज्ञानरत्नं च रामायादर्शयत्कृती R. 12. 64.

प्रत्यभिज्ञात *p. p.* Recognised.

प्रत्यभिभूत *p. p.* Overcome, conquered.

प्रत्यभियुक्त *p. p.* Accused in return.

प्रत्यभियोगः A counter-charge, an accusation in return; Y. 2. 10.

प्रत्यभिवादः प्रत्यभिवादनं Returning a salutation; Ms. 2. 126.

प्रत्यभिस्कंदनं A counter-plaint or charge.

प्रत्ययः 1 Conviction, settled belief; मूढः परप्रत्ययनेयबुद्धिः M. 1. 2; संजातप्रत्ययः Pt. 4. 2 Trust, reliance, faith, confidence; Ku. 6. 20; Si. 18. 63; Bh. 3. 60. 3 Conception, idea, notion, opinion. 4 Surety, certainty. 5 Knowledge, experience, cognition; स्थानप्रत्ययात् S. 7 'judging by the place;' so आकृतिप्रत्ययात् M. 1. Me 8. 6 A cause, ground, means of action; Ku. 3. 18. 7 Celebrity, fame, renown. 8 A termination, an affix or suffix; Si. 14. 66. 9 An oath. 10 A dependant. 11 A usage, practice. 12 A hole. 13 Intellect, understanding (बुद्धि). -COMP. -कारक, -कारिन् *a.* producing assurance, convincing. (-णी) a seal, signet-ring.

प्रत्ययित *a.* 1 Relied upon, confided in. 2 Trusty, confidential.

प्रत्ययिन् *a.* 1 Relying upon, trusting, believing. 2 Trustworthy, confidential.

प्रत्यर्थ *a.* Useful, expedient. -र्थं 1 A reply, an answer. 2 Hostility, opposition.

प्रत्यर्थकः An opponent.

प्रत्यर्थिन् *a.* (नी *f.*) Hostile, opposing, inimical to; नास्मि भवत्योरीश्वरनियोगप्रत्यर्थी V. 2. -*m.* 1 An opponent, adversary, enemy. 2 A rival, equal, match; चंद्रो मुखस्य प्रत्यर्थी. 3 (In law) A defendant; स धर्मस्थसखः शश्वदर्थिप्रत्यर्थिनां स्वयं R. 17. 39; Ms. 8. 79; Y. 2. 6. -COMP. -भूत *a.* coming in the way, become an obstacle; Ku. 1. 59.

प्रत्यर्पणं Giving back, restoring; सीताप्रत्यर्पणैषिणः R. 15. 85.

प्रत्यर्पित *p. p.* Restored, given back.

प्रत्यवमर्शः-र्षः 1 Profound meditation or reflection. 2 Counsel, advice. 3 A counter-conclusion.

प्रत्यवरोधनं Obstruction, hindrance.

प्रत्यवसानं Eating, or drinking; P. I. 4. 52.

प्रत्यवसित *a.* Eaten, drunk.

प्रत्यवस्कंदः-दनं (In law) A special plea; admitting a fact, but qualifying it in such a manner that it may not appear as a count of accusation.

प्रत्यवस्थानं 1 Removal. 2 Hostility, opposition. 3 *Status quo.*

प्रत्यवहारः 1 Withdrawal. 2 Universal destruction, dissolution (of the world); सर्गस्थितिप्रत्यवहारहेतुः R. 2. 44.

प्रत्यवायः 1 Decrease, diminution. 2 An obstacle, impediment; U. 1. 9. 3 Contrary or opposite course, contrariety; Ms. 4. 245. 4 A sin, an offence, sinfulness, अनुत्पत्तिं तथा चान्ये प्रत्यवायस्य मन्वते Jâbali.

प्रत्यवेक्षणं, प्रत्यवेक्षा Taking care of, regard for, looking after R. 17. 53.

प्रत्यस्तमयः 1 Setting (of the sun). 2 End, cessation.

प्रत्याक्षेपक *a.* (पिका *f.*) Jeering, derisive, deriding, treating scornfully.

प्रत्याख्यात *p. p.* 1 Refused, denied. 2 Prohibited, forbidden. 4 Set aside, rejected. 4 Repulsed.

प्रत्याख्यानं 1 Repulse, rejection. 2 Denial, refusal, disavowal. 3 Disregard. 4 Reproach. 5 Refutation.

प्रत्यागतिः *f.* Coming back, return.

प्रत्यागमः, प्रत्यागमनं Return, coming back.

प्रत्यादानं Receiving back, resumption.

प्रत्यादिष्ट *p. p.* 1 Prescribed. 2 Informed. 3 Rejected, repulsed. 4 Removed, set aside. 5 Obscured, thrown into shade; R. 10 68. 6 Warned, cautioned.

प्रत्यादेशः 1 An order, command. 2 Information, declaration. 3 Refusal, denial, rejection, repulse, repudiation; प्रत्यादेशान्न खलु भवतो धीरतां कल्पयामि Me. 114. 95. S. 6. 9. 4 Obscuring, eclipsing, one that obscures, puts to shame or throws into shade; या प्रत्यादेशो रूपगर्वितायाः श्रियः V. 1; K. 5. 5 Caution, warning. 6 Particularly divine caution, supernatural warning.

प्रत्यानयनं Bringing back, recovery.

प्रत्यापत्तिः *f.* 1 Return. 2 Aversion from, or indifference to worldly objects (वैराग्य).

प्रत्याम्नायः The fifth member of a complete syllogism: *i. e.* निगमन (the repetition of the first proposition).

प्रत्यायः A toll, tax.

प्रत्यायक *a.* 1 Proving, explaining. 2 Convincing, producing assurance.

प्रत्यायनं 1 Leading home (a bride), marrying. 2 Setting (of the sun)

प्रत्यालीढं A particular attitude in shooting (opp. आलीढ q. v.).

प्रत्यावर्तनं Returning, coming back.

प्रत्याश्वस्त *p. p.* Consoled, revived, refreshed.

प्रत्याश्वासः Respiration, recovery (of breath).

प्रत्याश्वासनं Consolation.

प्रत्यासत्तिः *f.* 1 Close proximity or contiguity (in time or space). 2 Close contact. 3 An analogy.

प्रत्यासन्नः *p. p.* Proximate, near, contiguous.

प्रत्यास (सा) रः The rear of an army. 2 A form of array, one array behind another.

प्रत्याहरणं 1 Bringing or taking back, recovery. 2 Withholding. 3 Restraining the organs of sense.

प्रत्याहारः 1 Drawing back, marching back, retreat. 2 Keeping back, withholding. 3 Restraining the organs. 4 Dissolution of the world 5 (In gram) The comprehension of several letters or affixes into one syllable, effected by combining the first letter of a Sûtra with its final indicatory letter, or in the case of several Sûtras, with the final letter of the last member; thus अण् is the प्रत्याहार of the Sûtra अइउण्; अच् (vowels) of the four Sûtras अइउण, ऋलृक्, एओङ्, ऐऔच्; हल् of the consonants; अल् of all letters.

प्रत्युक्त *p. p.* Answered, said in return, replied.

प्रत्युक्तिः *f.* A reply, an answer.

प्रत्युच्चारः, -च्चारणं Repetition.

प्रत्युज्जीवनं Reviving, restoring to life, resuscitation (fig. also).

प्रत्युत *ind.* 1 On the contrary; कृतमपि महोपकारं पय इव पीत्वा निरातंकः। प्रत्युत हंतुं यतते काकोदरसोदरः खलो जगति Bv. 1. 76. 2 Rather, even. 3 On the other hand.

प्रत्युत्क्रमः, -क्रमणं, -क्रांतिः *f.* 1 An undertaking. 2 Preparations for war. 3 Marching out to attack an enemy. 4 A secondary act or effort tending to a main object. 5 The first step in any business.

प्रत्युत्थानं 1 Rising against. 2 Making preparations for war. 5 Rising from one's seat (as a mark of respect) to welcome a visitor; Ms. 2. 210.

प्रत्युत्थित *p. p.* Risen to meet or encounter (a friend, foe &c.)

प्रत्युत्पन्न *p. p.* 1 Reproduced, regenerated. 2 Prompt, ready, quick. 3 (In math.) Multiplied. **-न्नं** Multiplication. -Comp. **-मति** *a.* 1 possessed of presence of mind, ready-witted. 2 bold, confident. 3 Subtle, sharp.

प्रत्युदाहरणं A counter illustration, an example to the contrary.

प्रत्युद्गत *p. p.* 1 Risen from one's seat as a mark of respect to greet or welcome a guest; प्रत्युद्गतो मां भरतः ससैन्यः R. 13. 64; 12. 62. 2 Gone forth against.

प्रत्युद्गतिः *f.*, **प्रत्युद्गमः, प्रत्युद्गमनं** Going out or rising from one's seat to meet or greet a guest.

प्रत्युद्गमनीयं A clean pair of garments; गृहीतप्रत्युद्गमनीयवस्त्रा Ku. 7. 11. (v. l. for °प्रत्युद्गमनीय॰); see उद्गमनीय.

प्रत्युद्धरणं 1 Recovering, re-obtaining. 2 Raising up again.

प्रत्युद्यमः 1 Counterbalance, counterpoise. 2 An effort or measure against, counteraction; Bh 8. 88. v. l.

प्रत्युद्यात *a.* See प्रत्युद्गत.

प्रत्युन्नमनं Rising or springing up again, rebounding.

प्रत्युपकारः Returning a service or kindness, requital of an obligation, service in return.

प्रत्युपक्रिया Return of a service.

प्रत्युपदेशः Advice in return; Ku. 1. 34.

प्रत्युपपन्न *a.* See प्रत्युत्पन्न.

प्रत्युपमानं 1 A Counterpart of a resemblance. 2 A pattern, model. 3 A counter comparison; V. 2. 3.

प्रत्युपलब्ध *p. p.* Got back, recovered.

प्रत्युपवेशः -वेशनं Besetting any one in order to bring him to compliance.

प्रत्युपस्थान Vicinity, neighbourhood.

प्रत्युप्त *p. p.* 1 Inlaid, set with, studded. 2 Sown. 3 Fixed, implanted, firmly fixed or lodged; Mâl. 5. 10; U. 3. 35, 46.

प्रत्युषः, -प्रत्युषस् *n.* Morning, day-break, dawn.

प्रत्यूषः -षं Day-break, morning, dawn; प्रत्यूषेषु स्फुटितकमलामोदमैत्रीकषायः Me. 31. **-षः** 1 The sun. 2 N. of one of the eight Vasus.

प्रत्यूषस् *n.* Day-break, morning, dawn.

प्रत्यूहः Impediment, obstacle, hinderance; विस्मयः सर्वथा हेयः प्रत्यूहः सर्वकर्मणां H. 2. 15.

प्रथ् I 1 A. (प्रथते प्रथित) 1 To increase (wealth &c.). 2 To spread abroad (as fame, rumour &c.); तथा यशोऽस्य प्रथते Ms. 11. 15. 3 To become well-known, become famous or celebrated; अतस्तदाख्यया तीर्थं पावनं भुवि पप्रथे R. 15. 101; अतोऽस्मि लोके वेदे च प्रथितः पुरुषोत्तमः Bg. 15. 18; Si. 9, 16; 15. 23; Ku. 5. 7; Me. 24; R. 5. 65; 9. 76. 4 To appear, arise, come to light; श्रमो नु तासां मदनो नु पप्रथे Ki. 8. 53. -II. 10. U. (प्रथयति-ते, प्रथित) 1 To spread, proclaim; सज्जना एव साधूनां प्रथयंति गुणोत्करं Dri. S. 12; Bk. 17. 107. 2 To show, manifest, display, evince, indicate; परमं वपुः प्रथयतीव जयं Ki. 6. 35; 5. 3; Si. 10. 25; Ratn. 4. 13; S. 3. 16. 3 To increase, enlarge, enhance, augment, stretch; Bh. 2. 45. 4 To disclose.

प्रथनं 1 Spreading, extension. 2 Scattering. 3 Throwing, projecting 4 Showing, evincing, displaying. 5 A place where anything is spread.

प्रथम *a.* (Nom. pl. *-m.* प्रथमे or प्रथमाः) 1 First, foremost; R. 3. 44; H. 2. 36; Ki. 2. 44. 2 First, chief, principal, most excellent or eminent, matchless, incomparable; Si. 15. 42; Ms. 3. 147. 3 Earliest, most ancient, primeval, primary. 4 Prior, previous, former, earlier; प्रथमसुकृतापेक्षया Me. 17; R. 10. 67. 5 (In gram. The first person (=third person according to European phraseology). **-मः** 1 The first (=third) person. 2 The first consonant of a class. **-मा** The nominative case. **-मं** *ind.* 1 First, firstly, at first; Ku. 7. 24; R. 3. 4. 2 Already, previously, formerly; R. 3. 68. 3 At once, immediately. 4 Before; यात्रायै चोदयामास तं शक्तेः प्रथमं शरत् R. 4. 24; उत्तिष्ठेत्प्रथमं चास्य चरमं चैव संविशेत् Ms. 2. 194. 5 Newly, recently. **प्रथमं-अनंतरं** or **ततः** or **पश्चात्** first, afterwards. -Comp. **-अर्धः -र्धं** the first half. **-आश्रमः** the first of the four stages in the religious life of a Brâhmaṇa; *i. e.* Brahmacharya. **-इतर** *a.* 'other than first,' the second. **-उदित** *a.* first uttered; उवाच धात्र्या प्रथमोदितं वचः R. 3. 25. **-कल्पः** the best course to adopt, a primary rule. **-कल्पित** *a.* 1 first thought out. 2 first in rank or importance. **-ज** *a.* first-born. **-दर्शनं** first sight. **-दिवसः** the first day; Me. 2. **-पुरुषः** the first person (=the third person according to the English system of treating Sanskrit grammar). **-यौवनं** early youth or age. youthful state. **-वयस्** *n.* early age, -youth. **-विरहः** separation for the first time. **-वैयाकरणः** 1 the most distinguished grammarian. 2 a beginner in grammar. **-साहसः** the first or lowest of the three degrees of punishment or fine. **-सुकृतं** former kindness or service.

प्रथा Fame, celebrity; Si. 15. 27.

प्रथित *p. p.* 1 Increased, extended. 2 Published, proclaimed, spread, declared; प्रथितयशसां भासकविसौमिल्लकविमिश्रादीनां M. 1. 3 shown, displayed, manifested, evinced. 4 Famous, celebrated, renowned (see प्रथ् also).

प्रथिमन् *m.* Breadth, greatness, extension, magnitude; प्रथिमानं दधानेन जघनेन घनेन सा Bk. 4. 17; (गुणाः) प्रारंभसूक्ष्माः प्रथिमानमापुः R. 18. 48.

प्रथिविः *f.* The earth.

प्रथिष्ठ *a.* Largest, widest, broadest; (superl. of पृथु q. v.).

प्रथीयस् *a.* (**सी** *f.*) Larger, wider, broader; (compar. of पृथु q. v.).

प्रथु *a.* Wide, wide-spread.

प्रथुकः Rice parched and flattened (cf. पृथुक).

प्रदक्षिण *a.* Being placed or standing on the right, moving to the right. 2 Respectful, reverential. 3 Auspicious, of good omen. **-णः -णा, -णं** Circumambulation from left to right, so that the right side is always turned towards the person or object circumambulated, a reverential salutation made by walking in this manner; Ku. 7. 79; Y. 1. 232. **-णं** *ind.* 1 From left to right. 2 Towards the right side, so that the right side is always turned towards the person or object circumambulated. 3 In a southern direction, towards the south; Ms. 4. 87. (**प्रदक्षिणीकृ** means 'to go round from left to right' as a mark of respect; प्रदक्षिणीकुरुष्व सद्योहुताग्नीन् S. 4; प्रदक्षिणीकृत्य हुतं हुताशनं R. 2. 71). -Comp. **-अर्चिस्** *a.* flaming towards the right, having the flames turned towards the right; प्रदक्षिणार्चिर्हविरग्निराददे R. 3. 14. (*-f.*) flames turned towards the right; R. 4. 25. **-क्रिया** going round from left to right, keeping the right side towards one as a mark of respect; R. 1. 76. **-पट्टिका** a yard; court-yard.

प्रदग्ध *p. p.* Burnt up, consumed.

प्रदत्त *p. p.* See प्रत्त.

प्रदरः 1 Rending, tearing. 2 A fracture, crack, cleft, crevice, chasm. 3 The dispersion of an army. 4 An arrow. 5 A kind of disease of women.

प्रदर्पः Pride, arrogance.

प्रदर्शः 1 Look, appearance. 2 Direction, order.

प्रदर्शक *a.* Showing, manifesting &c.

प्रदर्शनं 1 Look, appearance; as in घोरप्रदर्शनः. 2 Manifesting, displaying, show, exhibition. 3 Teaching, explaining. 4 An example.

प्रदर्शित *p. p.* 1 Shown forth, exhibited, manifested, evinced, displayed. 2 Made known. 3 Taught. 4 Explained, declared.

प्रदलः An arrow.

प्रदवः Burning, inflaming.

प्रदातृ *m.* 1 A giver, donor. 2 A liberal man. 3 One who gives a daughter in marriage. 4 An epithet of Indra.

प्रदानं 1 Giving, granting, bestowing, offering; वर ०, अग्नि ०, काष्ठ ० &c. 2 Giving away in marriage; कन्या ०. 3 Imparting, teaching, instructing; विद्या ०. 4 A gift, donation, present. 5 A goad. –Comp. **–शूरः** a very munificent man, donor.

प्रदानकं An offering, a gift, donation, present.

प्रदायं A present, gift.

प्रदिः, प्रदेयः A present, gift.

प्रदिग्ध *p. p.* Besmeared, bedaubed, anointed. **–ग्धं** Meat fried in a particular way.

प्रदिश् *f.* 1 Pointing out. 2 An order, direction, command. 3 An intermediate point of the compass; such as नैर्ऋती, आग्नेयी, ऐशानी and वायवी.

प्रदिष्ट *p. p.* 1 Shown, pointed out. 2 Directed, ordered. 3 Fixed upon, ordained, appointed; R. 2. 39.

प्रदीपः 1 A lamp, light (fig. also); अतैलपूराः सुरतप्रदीपाः Ku 1. 10; R. 2. 24; 16. 4; कुलप्रदीपो नृपतिर्दिलीपः R. 6. 74 'light or ornament of the family'; 7. 29. 2 That which enlightens or elucidates, elucidation; especially at the end of titles of works; as in महाभाष्यप्रदीपः, काव्यप्रदीपः &c.

प्रदीपन *a.* (**नी** *f.*) 1 Kindling. 2 Stimulating, exciting. **–नं** The act of kindling, lighting, stimulating &c. **–नः** A kind of mineral poison.

प्रदीप्त *p. p.* 1 Kindled, lighted, inflamed, illuminated. 2 Blazing, burning, shining. 3 Raised, expanded; प्रदीप्तशिरसमाशीविषं Dk. 4 Stimulated, excited (hunger &c.)

प्रदुष्ट *p. p.* 1 Spoiled, corrupted. 2 Wicked, bad, sinful. 3 Licentious, wanton.

प्रदूषित *p. p* 1 Corrupted, vitiated, spoiled, depraved. 2 Polluted, defiled, contaminated.

प्रदेय *pot p.* To be given, imparted, communicated &c.; R. 5. 18, 31.

प्रदेशः 1 Pointing out, indicating. 2 A place, region, spot, country, territory, district; पितुः प्रदेशास्तव देवभूमयः Ku. 5. 45; R. 5. 60; so कंठ°, तालु°, हृदय° &c. 3 A span measured from the tip of the thumb to that of the fore-finger. 4 Decision, determination. 5 A wall. 6 An example (in grammar).

प्रदेशनं 1 Pointing out. 2 Advice, instruct. 3 A gift, present, an offering especially to gods, superiors &c.

प्रदेश (शि) नी The fore-finger, the index finger.

प्रदेहः 1 Applying a plaster, unction. 2 A plaster, thick ointment.

प्रदोष *a.* Bad, corrupt. **—षः** 1 A fault, defect, sin, offence. 2 Disordered condition, such as mutiny, rebellion. 3 Evening, nightfall, the first part of the night; तमःस्वभावास्तेऽप्यन्ये प्रदोषमनुयायिनः Si. 2. 78 (where प्रदोष primarily means 'corrupt' or 'bad'); व्रजसुंदरीजनमनस्तोषप्रदोषः Git. 5; Ku. 5. 44; R. 1. 93; Rs. 1. 12. —Comp. **-कालः** evening-time, night-fall. **-तिमिरं** evening darkness, the dusk of early night; कामं प्रदोषतिमिरेण न दृश्यसे त्वं Mk. 1. 35.

प्रदोहः Milking.

प्रद्युम्नः An epithet of Cupid, the god of love. [He was a son of Krish*n*a and Rukmi*n*i. When only six years old, he was stolen away by the demon *S*ambara, for he was foretold that Pradyumna would be his destroyer. *S*ambara cast the child into the roaring sea, and a large fish swallowed it. This fish was caught by a fisherman and taken to the demon; and when it was cut up, a beautiful child came out from the belly, and M*a*yavat*i*, the mistress of *S*amb*h*ar's household, at the desire of N*a*rada carefully reared him from childhood. As he grew up, she was fascinated by the beauty of his person, but Pradyumna reproved her for entertaining towards himself feelings so unbecoming a mother as he considered her. But when he was told that he was not her son, but of Vishnu and was cast into the sea by *S*ambara, he became enraged, and, challenging him to fight, succeeded in killing him by the force of illusions. He and M*a*yavat*i* afterwards repaired to the house of Krish*n*a, where N*a*rada told him and Rukmi*n*i that the boy was their own and that M*a*yavat*i* was his wife].

प्रद्योतः 1 Irradiating, lighting, illuminating. 2 Splendour, light, lustre. 3 A ray of light. 4 N. of a king of Ujjayini, whose daughter Vatsa married; प्रद्योतस्य प्रियदुहितरं वत्सराजोऽत्र जह्रे Me. (considered as an interpolation by Malli.); Ratn. 1. 10.

प्रद्योतनं 1 Blazing, shining. 2 Light. **—नः** The sun.

प्रद्रवः Running.

प्रद्रावः 1 Running away, flight, retreat, escape. 2 Going quickly or fast.

प्रद्वार, प्रद्वारं A place before a door or gate.

प्रद्वेषः, प्रद्वेषणं Dislike, hatred, aversion.

प्रधनं 1 A battle, fight, war, contest; प्रहितः प्रधनाय माधवानहमाकारयितुं महीभृता Si. 16. 52; क्षेत्रं क्षत्रप्रधनपिशुनं कौरवं तद्भजेथाः Me. 48; R. 11. 77; Mv. 6. 33. 2 Spoil taken in battle. 3 Destruction. 4 Tearing, rending.

प्रधमनं 1 Blowing in or into. 2 A sternutatory.

प्रधर्षः Assaulting, attacking, outrage.

प्रधर्षणं-णा 1 An assault, attack. 2 An outrage, ill-treatment, insult.

प्रधर्षित *p p.* 1 Assaulted, attacked. 2 Hurt, injured. 3 Haughty, arrogant.

प्रधान *a.* 1 Chief, principal, pre-eminent, main, best, most excellent; as in प्रधानामात्य, प्रधानपुरुष &c.; Ms. 7. 203. 2 Principally inherent, prevalent, predominant. **–नं** 1 The chief thing or object, most important thing; head, chief; न परिचया मलिनात्मनां प्रधानं Si. 7. 61; G. L. 18; प्रयोगप्रधानं हि नाट्यशास्त्रं M. 1; शमप्रधानेषु तपोधनेषु *S.* 2. 7; R. 6. 79. 2 The first evolver, originator, or source of the material world, the primary germ out of which all material appearances are evolved, according to the Sânkhya philosophy; न पुनरपि प्रधानवादी अशब्दत्वं प्रधानस्यासिद्धमित्याह *S.* B; see प्रकृति also. 3 The supreme Spirit. 4 Intellect. 5 The principal member of a compound. **–नः –नं** 1 The principal attendant or companion of a king (his minister or confidant). 2 A noble, courtier. 3 An elephant-driver. –Comp. **–अंगं** 1 the principal branch or part of anything. 2 the chief member of the body. 3 the principal or most eminent person in a state. **–अमात्यः** the prime minister, premier. **–आत्मन्** *m.* an epithet of Vishṇu. **–धातुः** the chief element of the body; *i. e.* semen virile. **–पुरुषः** 1 the principal or most eminent person (in a state &c.). 2 an epithet of *S*iva. **–मंत्रिन्** *m.* the prime-minister. **–वासस्** *n.* a principal garment **–वृष्टिः** *f.* a heavy shower of rain.

प्रधावनः Air, wind. **–नं** Rubbing; rubbing or washing off.

प्रधिः 1 The periphery of a wheel; Si. 15. 79; 17. 27. 2 A well.

प्रधी *a.* Pre-eminently intelligent. *–f.* Great intelligence.

प्रधूपित *p. p.* 1 Fumigated, perfumed. 2 Heated, burned, 3 Inflamed. 4 Afflicted. –ता 1 A woman in trouble. 2 The quarter to which the sun is proceeding.

प्रधृष्ट *p. p.* 1 Treated with contumely. 2 Proud, arrogant, haughty.

प्रध्यानं 1 Deep thought or reflection. 2 Reflection or thought in general.

प्रध्वंसः Utter destruction, annihilation. –COMP. अभावः 'non-existence caused by destruction,' one of the four kinds of अभाव or non-existence, in which the non-existence of a thing is caused by destruction, as of an effect subsequently to its production.

प्रध्वस्त *p. p.* Annihilated, completely destroyed.

प्रनप्तृ *m.* The son of a grand-son, a great-grandson.

प्रनष्ट *p. p.* 1 Disappeared, vanished, not to be seen. 2 Lost. 3 Perished, dead. 4 Ruined, destroyed, annihilated.

प्रनायक *a.* 1 One whose leader is away. 2 Destitute of a leader or guide.

प्रनालः-ली *f.* see प्रणाल and प्रणाली.

प्रनिपातनं Killing, slaughter.

प्रनृत्त *a.* Dancing. –त्तं A dance.

प्रपक्षः The extremity of a wing.

प्रपंचः 1 Display, manifestation; रागप्रायः प्रपंचः K. 141. 2 Development, expansion, extension; Si. 20. 44. 3 Amplification, expatiation, explanation, elucidation. 4 Prolixity, diffuseness, copiousness; अलं प्रपंचेन. 5 Manifoldness, diversity. 6 Heap, abundance, quantity. 7 An appearance, phenomenon. 8 Illusion, fraud. 9 The visible world or universe, which is illusory and the scene of manifold action. –COMP –बुद्धि *a.* cunning, deceitful. –वचनं a prolix discourse, diffuse talk.

प्रपंचयति Den. P. 1. To show forth, display; प्रपंचय पंचमं Gît. 10. 2 To expand, amplify.

प्रपंचित *p. p.* 1 Displayed. 2 Expanded, amplified, 3 Dilated upon, fully explained, expatiated upon. 4 Erring, mistaken. 5 Deceived, tricked.

प्रपतनं 1 Flying forth or away. 2 Throwing oneself into, falling down. 3 Alighting. 4 Death, destruction. 5 A precipice, a steep crag.

प्रपदं The fore-part of the foot.

प्रपदीन *a.* Relating or extending to the forepart of the foot.

प्रपन्न *p. p.* 1 Arriving at, reaching or going to. 2 Resorting to, betaking oneself to; Ku. 3. 5; 5. 59. 3 Taking refuge with, seeking protection with, suppliant or submissive to; शिष्यस्तेहं शाधि मां त्वां प्रपन्नं Bg. 2 7. 4 Adhering to. 5 Furnished or endowed with, possessed of; S. 1. 1. 6 Promised. 7 Got, obtained. 8 Poor, distressed.

प्रपन्नाडः See प्रपुनाट.

प्रपर्ण *a.* Devoid of leaves (as a tree; प्रपतितानि पर्णानि यस्य). –र्णं A fallen leaf.

प्रपलायनं Flight, retreat.

प्रपा 1 A place where water is distributed to travellers; व्याख्यास्थानान्यमलसलिला यस्य कूपाः प्रपाश्च Vikr. 18. 78. 2 A well, cistern; Ms. 8. 319. 3 A place for watering cattle. 4 A supply of water. –COMP. –पालिका a woman who distributes water to travellers; Vikr. 1. 89; 13. 10. –वनं a cool grove.

प्रपाठकः 1 A lesson, lecture. 2 A chapter or division of a work.

प्रपाणिः 1 The forepart of the hand. 2 The palm of the extended hand.

प्रपातः 1 Going forth or away, departure. 2 Falling down or into, a fall; मनोरथानाम तटप्रपातः S. 6. 9, Ku. 6. 57. 3 A sudden attack. 4 A cascade, waterfall, the place over which water falls down; R. 2. 26. 5 A bank, shore. 6 A precipice, steep rock. 7 Falling out or loss, as in केशप्रपात. 8 Emission, discharge, efflux, as in वीर्यप्रपात. 9 Throwing oneself down from a rock. 10 A particular mode of flight.

प्रपातनं Causing to fall, throwing down (on the ground).

प्रपादिकः A peacock.

प्रपानं Drinking.

प्रपानकं A kind of drink.

प्रपितामहः 1 A paternal great grandfather. 2 An epithet of Krishṇa; Bg. 11. 39. 3 Of Brahmâ. –ही A paternal great-grandmother.

प्रपितृव्य A paternal grand-uncle.

प्रपीडन 1 Pressing, squeezing. 2 An astringent.

प्रपीत (न) *a.* Swollen up, distended.

प्रपुना (न्ना) टः-डः N. of a tree (चक्रमर्द).

प्रपूरणं 1 Filling, filling up, completing. 2 Inserting, injecting. 3 Satisfying, satiating 4 Attaching to.

प्रपूरित *p. p.* Filled up.

प्रपृष्ठ *a.* Having a prominent back.

प्रपौत्रः A great-grandson; Y. 1. 78 –त्री A great-granddaughter.

प्रफुल्त *p. p.* Blooming, blossomed, full-blown; लोध्रद्रुमं सानुमतः प्रफुल्तं R. 2. 29 (v. l. for प्रफुल्ल.)

प्रफुल्तिः *f.* Blooming, expansion, blossoming,

प्रफुल्ल *p. p.* 1 Full-blown, blossoming; न हि प्रफुल्लं सहकारमेत्य वृक्षांतरं कांक्षति षट्पदाली R. 6. 69; 2. 29; Ku. 3. 45; 7. 11. 2 Expanded or dilated like a full-blown flower (as eyes). 3 Smiling. 4 Gay, cheerful, pleased. –COMP. –नयन,-नेत्र,-लोचन *a.* with eyes expanded with joy. –वदन *a.* having a beaming or cheerful countenance, looking cheerful.

प्रबद्ध *p. p.* 1 Bound, tied, fastened. 2 Stopped, obstructed, checked.

प्रबंद्धृ An author.

प्रबंधः 1 A bond, tie. 2 Uninterruptedness, continuance, continuity, uninterrupted series or succession; विच्छेदमाप भुवि यस्तु कथाप्रबंधः K. 239; क्रियाप्रबंधादयमध्वराणां R. 6. 23; 3. 58; Mál. 6. 3. 3 A continued or connected narrative or discourse; अनुज्झितार्थसंबंधः प्रबंधो दुरुदाहरः Si. 2. 73. 4 Any literary work or composition; especially, a poetical composition; प्रथितयशसां भासकविसौमिलकविमिश्रादीनां प्रबंधानतिक्रम्य M. 1; प्रत्यक्षरश्लेषमयप्रबंध &c. Vâs. 5 Arrangement, plan, scheme; as in कपटप्रबंध. –COMP. –कल्पना a feigned story, a work of imagination founded on a substratum of fact; प्रबंधकल्पनां स्तोकसत्यां प्राज्ञाः कथां विदुः.

प्रबंधनं Bond, tie.

प्रबभ्रः An epithet of Indra.

प्रब (व) र्ह *a.* Most excellent, best.

प्रबल *a.* 1 Very strong or powerful, mighty, valorous (as a man); R. 3. 60; Rs. 3. 23. 2 Violent, strong, intense, excessive, very great; प्रबलपुरोवातया वृष्ट्या M. 4. 2; प्रबला वेदना R. 8 50. 3 Important. 4 Abounding with. 5 Dangerous, destructive.

प्रब (व) ह्लिका See प्रहेलिका.

प्रबाधनं 1 Oppressing, tormenting. 2 Refusing, denying. 3 Keeping off.

प्रबा (वा) लः-लं 1 A sprout, shoot, new leaf; अपि...प्रवालमासामनुबंधि वीरुधां Ku. 5. 34; 1. 44; 3. 8; R. 6. 12; 13. 49. 2 Coral. 3 The neck of the Indian lute. –लः 1 A pupil. 2 An animal. –COMP. –अश्मंतकः 1 the red Asmantaka tree. 2 the coral tree. –पद्मं a red lotus. –फलं red sandalwood. –भस्मन् *n.* calx of coral.

प्रबाहुः The forearm.

प्रबाहुकं *ind.* 1 On high. 2 At the same time.

प्रबुद्ध *p. p.* 1 Awakened, roused. 2 Wise, learned, clever. 3 Knowing, conversant with. 4 Full-blown, expanded. 5 Beginning to work or take effect (as a charm).

प्रबोधः 1 Awaking (fig. also), awakening; regaining one's consciousness, consciousness; अप्रबोधाय सुष्वाप R. 12. 50; मोहादभूत्कष्टतरः प्रबोधः 14. 56. 2 Blowing; expanding (of flowers).

3 Wakefulness, sleeplessness; *S*. 6. 4 Vigilance, watchfulness. 5 Knowledge, understanding, wisdom, removal of delusion, real knowledge; as in प्रबोधचंद्रोदय. 6 Consolation. 7 Reviving the fragrance of a perfume.

प्रबोधन *a*. (नी *f*.) Awakening, rousing. **-नं** 1 Waking. 2 Awakening, rousing. 3 Regaining one's consciousness. 4 Knowledge, wisdom. 5 Instructing, advising. 6 Reviving the scent of a perfume.

प्रबोध (धि) नी The eleventh day of the bright half of Kârtika on which Vishṇu awakes from his four months' sleep.

प्रबोधित *p. p.* 1 Awakened, roused. 2 Instructed, informed.

प्रभंजनं Breaking to pieces. **-नः** Wind, especially, stormy wind, hurricane, N. 1. 61; Pt. 1. 122.

प्रभद्रः The Nimba tree.

प्रभवः 1 Source, origin; अनंतरत्नप्रभवस्य यस्य Ku. 1. 3; अकिंचनः सन् प्रभवः स संपदां 5. 77; R. 9. 75. 2 Birth, production. 3 The source of a river; तस्या एवं प्रभवमचलं प्राप्य गौरं तुषारैः Me. 52. 4 The operative cause, origin of being (as father, mother &c.); तमस्याः प्रभवमवगच्छ *S*. 1. 5 The author; creator; Ku. 2. 5. 6 Birth-place. 7 Power, strength, valour, majestic dignity (-प्रभाव q. v.) 8 An epithet of Vishṇu. 9 (At the end of comp.) Arising or originating from, derived from; सूर्यप्रभवो वंशः R. 1. 2, Ku. 3. 15.

प्रभवितृ *m*. A ruler, great lord.

प्रभविष्णु *a*. Strong, mighty, powerful. **-ष्णुः** 1 A lord, master; यत्प्रभविष्णवे रोचते *S*. 2. 2 An epithet of Vishṇu.

प्रभा 1 Light, splendour, lustre, effulgence, radiance; प्रभास्मि शशिसूर्ययोः Bg. 7. 8; प्रभा पतंगस्य R. 2. 15, 31; 6. 18; Rs. 1. 19; Me. 47. 2 A ray of light. 3 The shadow of the sun on a sundial. 4 An epithet of Durgâ. 5 N. of the city of Kubera. 6 N. of an Apsaras. -Comp. **-करः** 1 the sun; R. 10. 74. 2 the moon 3 fire. 4 the ocean. 5 an epithet of *S*iva. 6 N. of a learned writer, the founder of a school of Mîmâmsâ philosophy called after him. **-कीटः** a fire-fly. **-तरल** *a*. tremulously radiant; न प्रभातरलं ज्योतिरुदेति वसुधातलात् *S*. 1. 26. **-मंडलं** a circle or halo of light; Ku. 1. 24; 6. 4; R. 3. 60; 14. 14. **-लेपिन्** *a*. covered with lustre, emitting lustre; V. 4. 34.

प्रभागः 1 Division. 2 The fraction of a fraction (in math.).

प्रभात *p. p*. Begun to become clear or light; ननु प्रभाता रजनी *S*. 4. **-तं** Day-break, dawn.

प्रभानं Light, lustre, splendour, radiance.

प्रभावः 1 Lustre, splendour, brilliance. 2 Dignity, glory, majesty, grandeur, majestic lustre; प्रभाववानिव लक्ष्यते *S*. 1. 3 Strength, valour, power, efficacy; Pt. 1. 7. 4 Regal power (one of the three *S*aktis q. v.) 5 A superhuman power or faculty, miraculous power; R. 2. 41, 62; 3. 40; V. 1, 2, 5. 6 Magnanimity. -Comp. **-ज** *a*. proceeding from majesty or regal power.

प्रभाषणं Explanation, interpretation.

प्रभासः Splendour, beauty, lustre. **—सः-सं** N. of a well-known place of pilgrimage near Dvârkâ.

प्रभासनं Illumining, irradiating, brightening.

प्रभास्वर *a*. Brilliant, bright, shining.

प्रभिन्न *p. p*. 1 Severed, split, cleft, divided. 2 Broken to pieces. 3 Cut off, detached. 4 Budding, expanded, opened. 5 Changed, altered. 6 Deformed, disfigured. 7 Relaxed, loosened. 8 Intoxicated, in rut; Ku. 5. 80; (see भिद् with प्र). **-न्नः** An elephant in rut. -Comp. **-अंजनं** a kind of collyrium or eye-salve mixed with oil.

प्रभु *a*. (भु -भ्वी *f*.) 1 Mighty, strong, powerful 2 Able, competent, having power to (with inf. or in comp.); ऋषिप्रभावान्मयि नांतकोऽपि प्रभुः प्रहर्तुं किमुतान्यहिंस्राः R. 2. 62; समाधिभिद्प्रभवो भवंति Ku. 3. 40. 3 A match for; प्रभुर्मल्लो मल्लाय Mbh. **-भुः** 1 A lord, master; प्रभुर्बुभूषुर्भुवनत्रयस्य यः *S*i. 1. 49. 2 A governor, ruler, supreme authority. 3 An owner, proprietor. 4 Quick-silver. 5 N. of Vishṇu. 6 Of *S*iva. 7 Of Brahmâ. 8 Of Indra. -Comp. **-भक्त** *a*. attached or devoted to one's lord, loyal. (**-क्तः**) a good horse. **-भक्तिः** *f*. devotion to one's lord, loyalty, faithfulness.

प्रभुता-त्वं 1 Lordship, supremacy, mastery, ascendancy, authority; *S*. 5. 25; V. 4. 12. 2 Ownership.

प्रभूत *p. p.* 1 Sprung from, produced. 2 Much, abundant. 3 Numerous, many. 4 Mature, perfect. 5 High, lofty. 6 Long. 7 Presided over. -Comp. **-यवसेंधन** *a*. abounding in fresh grass and fuel. **-वयस्** *a*. advanced in age, old, aged.

प्रभूतिः *f*. 1 Source, origin. 2 Power, strength. 3 Sufficiency.

प्रभृतिः *f*. Beginning, commencement; generally used in this sense as the last member of Bah. compound; इंद्रप्रभृतयो देवाः &c, *-ind*. From, ever since, beginning with (with abl.); शैशवात्प्रभृति पोषितां प्रियां U. I. 45; R. 2. 28; अद्य प्रभृति henceforward; ततः प्रभृति, अतःप्रभृति &c.

प्रभेदः 1 Splitting, cleaving, opening. 2 Division, separation. 3 The flowing of rut or ichor from the temples of an elephant; R. 3. 37. 4 Difference, distinction. 5 A kind or sort.

प्रभ्रंशः Fall, falling off.

प्रभ्रंशथुः A disease of the nose.

प्रभ्रंशित *p. p.* 1 Thrown or cast down. 2 Deprived of.

प्रभ्रंशिन् *a*. Falling off or down.

प्रभ्रष्ट *p. p*. Fallen of, fallen or dropped down. **—ष्टं** A garland of flowers suspended from the lock on the crown of the head.

प्रभ्रष्टकं See प्रभ्रष्टं above.

प्रमग्न *p. p*. Drowned, immersed, dipped.

प्रमत *p. p*. Thought out.

प्रमत्त *p. p*. 1 Intoxicated, drunk; *S*. 4. 1. 2 Mad, insane. 3 Careless, negligent, inattentive, heedless, regardless (generally with loc.). 4 Swerving from, failing to do (with abl.); स्वाधिकारात् प्रमत्तः Me. 1. 5 Blundering. 6 Wanton, lascivious. -Comp. **-गीत** *a*. sung carelessly. **-चित्त** *a*. negligent, heedless, careless.

प्रमथः 1 A horse. 2 N. of a class of Beings (said to be goblins) attending on *S*iva; Ku. 7. 95.- Comp. **-अधिपः -नाथः, -पतिः** an epithet of *S*iva.

प्रमथनं 1 Hurting, injuring, tormenting. 2 Killing, slaughter. 3 Churning, stirring about.

प्रमथित *p. p*. 1 Tormented, distressed. 2 Trampled down. 3 Slain; killed; Mâl. 3. 18. 4 Properly churned. **-तं** Butter-milk without water.

प्रमद *a*. 1 Drunk, intoxicated (fig. also). 2 Impassioned. 3 Careless. 4 Wanton, dissolute. **—दः** 1 Joy, pleasure, delight; *S*i. 3. 54; 13 2. 5 The Dhattûra plant. -Comp. **-काननं, -वनं** a pleasure-garden attached to the royal harem.

प्रमदक *a*. Licentious, sensual.

प्रमदनं Amorous desire.

प्रमदा 1 A young handsome woman; R. 9. 31; *S*. 5. 17. 2 A wife or woman in general; Ku. 4. 12; R. 8. 72. 3 The sign *Virgo* of the zodiac. -Comp **-काननं-वनं** a pleasure garden attached to the royal harem (for the use of the wives of a king). **-जनः** a young woman. 2 womankind.

प्रमद्वर *a*. Careless, inattentive, heedless.

प्रमनस् *a.* Delighted, happy, cheerful, in good spirits.

प्रमन्यु *a.* 1 Enraged, irritated, incensed against (with loc.); R. 7. 34. 2 Distressed, sorrowful, sorely grieved.

प्रमयः 1 Death. 2 Ruin, downfall, fall. 3 Killing, slaughter.

प्रमर्दनं Crushing, destroying, trampling down.—**नः** An epithet of Vishṇu.

प्रमा 1 Consciousness, perception. 2 (In logic) Correct notion or apprehension, true and certain knowledge, accurate conception (यथा रंजते इदं रजतमिति ज्ञानं T. S.).

प्रमाणं 1 A measure in general (of length, breadth &c.); R. 18. 38. 2 Size, extent, magnitude. 3 Scale, standard; पृथिव्यां स्वामिभक्तानां प्रमाणे परमे स्थितः Mu. 2. 21. 4 Limit, quantity. 5 Testimony, evidence, proof. 6 Authority, warrant; one who judges or decides, one whose word is an authority; श्रुत्वा देवः प्रमाणं Pt. 1 'having heard this your Majesty will decide (what to do)'; आर्यमिश्राः प्रमाणं M. 1; Mu. 1. 1; *S.* 1. 22; व्याकरणे पाणिनिः प्रमाणं 7. A true or certain knowledge, accurate conception or notion. 8 A mode of proof, a means of getting correct knowledge (the Naiyâyikas recognize only four kinds; प्रत्यक्ष, अनुमान, उपमान and शब्द, the Vedântins and Mîmâmsakas add two more अनुपलब्धि and अर्थापत्ति; while the Sânkhyas admit प्रत्यक्ष, अनुमान and शब्द only; cf. अनुभव also. 9 Principal, capital. 10 Unity. 11. Scripture, sacred authority. 12 Cause, reason. (**प्रमाणीकृ** means 1 to hold or regard as an authority. 2 to obey, conform to. 3 to prove, establish. 4 to mete out or apportion). –COMP. **–अधिक** *a.* more than ordinary, inordinate, excessive; *S.* 1. 30. **–अंतरं** another mode of proof. **–अभावः** absence of authority. **–ज्ञ** *a.* knowing the modes of proof, (as a logician). (**–ज्ञः**) an epithet of *S*iva **–दृष्ट** *a.* sanctioned by authority. **–पत्रं** a written warrant. **–पुरुषः** an arbitrator, a judge, an umpire. **–वचनं, वाक्यं** an authoritative statement. **–शास्त्रं** 1 scripture. 2 the science of logic. **–सूत्रं** a measuring cord.

प्रमाणयति Den. P. To regard as an authority; H. 1. 10.

प्रमाणिक *a.* 1 Forming or being a measure. 2 Forming an authority.

प्रमातामहः A maternal greatgrandfather. **—ही** A maternal greatgrandmother.

प्रमाथः 1 Excessive paining, tormenting, torturing. 2 Agitating, churning. 3 Killing, slaughter, destruction; सैनिकानां प्रमाथेन सत्यमोजायितं त्वया U. 5. 31; 4. 4 Violence, outrage. 5 Rape, forcible abduction.

प्रमाथिन् *a.* 1 Tormenting, harassing, torturing, afflicting, harrowing; क्व रुजा हृदयप्रमाथिनी क्व च ते विश्वसनीयमायुधं M. 3. 2; Mâl. 2. 1; Ki. 3. 14. 2 Killing, destroying. 3 Agitating, setting in motion; Bg. 2. 60; 6 34. 4 Tearing or pulling down, striking down; R. 11. 58. 5 Cutting down; Ki. 17. 31.

प्रमादः 1 Carelessness, negligence, inattention, inadvertence, oversight; ज्ञातुं प्रमादस्खलितं न शक्यं *S.* 6. 26; Ch. P. 1. 2 Intoxication. 3 Insanity, madness. 4 A mistake, blunder, mistaken judgment. 5 An accident, mishap, calamity, danger. अहो प्रमादः Mâl. 3; U. 3.

प्रमापणं Killing, slaughter.

प्रमार्जनं Wiping off, rubbing or washing off.

प्रमित *p. p.* 1 Measured off, limited, few, little; प्रमितविषयां शक्तिं विंदन् Mv. 1. 51; *S*i. 16. 80. 3 Known, understood. 4 Proved, demonstrated.

प्रमितिः *f.* 1 Measurement, a measure. 2 True or certain knowledge, accurate notion or conception. 3 Knowledge obtained by any one of the Pramâṇas or sources of knowledge.

प्रमीढ *a.* 1 Thick, dense, compact. 2 Passed as urine.

प्रमीत *p. p*, Dead, deceased. **—तः** An animal immolated or killed at a sacrifice.

प्रमीतिः *f.* Death, destruction decease.

प्रमीला 1 Sleepiness, lassitude, enervation of spirits. 2 N. of a woman, sovereign of a kingdom of women. She fought with Arjuna when his horse entered her territory, but she was conquered and became his wife.

प्रमीलित *p. p.* With closed eyes.

प्रमुक्त *p. p.* 1 Loosened. 2 Liberated, set free. 3 Resigned, renounced. 4 Cast, hurled. –COMP. **–कंठं** *ind.* bitterly.

प्रमुख *a.* 1 Facing, turning the face towards. 2 Chief, principal, foremost, first. 3 (At the end of comp.) (*a*) Headed by, having as chief or at the head; वासुकिप्रमुखाः Ku. 2. 38. (*b*) Accompanied with; प्रीतिप्रमुखवचनं स्वागतं व्याजहार Me. 4. **–खः** 1 A respectable man. 2 A heap, multitude. **—खं** 1 The mouth 2 The beginning of a chapter or section. (प्रमुखतस् and प्रमुखे are used adverbially in the sense of 'in front of', 'before,' 'opposite to', Bg. 1. 25; *S.* 7. 22).

प्रमुग्ध *a.* 1 Fainting, unconscious. Very lovely.

प्रमुद् *f.* Extreme joy.

प्रमुदित *p. p.* Delighted, glad, pleased, happy. –COMP **–हृदय** *a.* delighted at heart.

प्रमुषित *p. p.* Stolen, taken away; *S*i. 17. 71. **—ता** A kind of riddle.

प्रमूढ *p. p.* 1 Perplexed, bewildered, infatuated. 2 Stupid, foolish.

प्रमृत *p. p.* Dead, deceased. **—तं** 1 Death Cultivation.

प्रमृष्ट *p. p.* 1 Rubbed off, washed or wiped off, cleared off; R. 6. 41, 44. 2 Polished, bright, clear.

प्रमेय *a.* 1 Measurable, finite. 2 To be proved, demonstrable. **—यं** 1 An object of certain knowledge, a demonstrated conclusion, theorem. 2 The thing to be proved, the topic to be proved or discussed.

प्रमेहः A general name for a urinary disease (such as gleet, diabetes &c).

प्रमोक्षः 1 Dropping, letting fall. 2 Discharging, liberating.

प्रमोचनं 1 Liberating, setting free. 2 Emitting, shedding.

प्रमोदः Joy, delight, rejoicing, pleasure; प्रमोदनृत्यैः सह वारयोषितां R. 3. 19; Ms. 3. 61.

प्रमोदनं 1 Gladdening, delighting, making glad. 2 Gladness. **—नः** An epithet of Vishṇu.

प्रमोदित *p. p.* Pleased, delighted, joyful, happy. **—तः** An epithet of Kubera.

प्रमोहः 1 Stupefaction, insensibility, stupor; तिरयति करणानां ग्राहकत्वं प्रमोहः Mâl 1. 41 2 Infatuation, bewilderment.

प्रमोहित *p. p.* Infatuated, bewildered.

प्रयत *p. p.* 1 Restrained, self-subdued, holy, pious, devout, purified by austerities or religious observances; keeping the organs of sense under restraint; R. 1. 95; 8. 11; 13. 70; Ku. 1. 58; 3. 16. 2 Zealous, intent. 3 Submissive.

प्रयत्नः 1 Effort, exertion, endeavour; R. 2. 56; Mu. 5. 20. 2 Persevering or continued effort; perseverance. 3 Labour, difficulty; प्रयत्नप्रेक्षणीयः संवृत्तः *S.* 1 'hardly visible', 'seen with difficulty'. 4 Great care, caution; कृतप्रयत्नोऽपि गृहे विनश्यति Pt. 1. 205. 5 (In gram.) Effort in uttering, effort of the mouth in the production of articulate sounds.

प्रयस्त *p. p.* Seasoned, dressed with condiments.

प्रयागः 1 A sacrifice. 2 N. of Indra. 3 A horse. 4 N. of a celebrated place of pilgrimage at the confluence of the Gangâ and Yamunâ near the modern Allahabad; Ms. 2. 21; (said to be *n.* also in this sense). -COMP. -भयः an epithet of Indra.

प्रयाचनं Begging, requesting, imploring.

प्रयाजः A principal sacrificial ceremony.

प्रयणं 1 Setting out, starting, departure. 2 A march, journey; मार्गं तावच्छृणु कथयतस्त्वत्प्रयाणानुरूपं Me. 13. 3 Progress, advance. 4 The march (of an enemy), an attack, invasion, expedition; कामं पुरः शुक्रमिव प्रयाणे Ku. 3. 43; R. 6. 33. 5 Beginning, commencement. 6 Death, departure (from the world); Bg. 7. 30. 7 The back of a horse. 8 The hinder part of any animal. -COMP. -भंगः a break in a journey, a halt; Pt. 1.

प्रयाणकं A journey, march; K. 118; 305.

प्रयात *p. p.* 1 Advanced, gone forth, departed. 2 Deceased, dead. —तः 1 An invasion. 2 A precipice, steep rock.

प्रयापित *p. p.* 1 Made to advance or go forward. 2 Made to go away.

प्रयामः 1 Dearth, scarcity, dearness of corn &c. 2 Checking, restraining. 3 Length.

प्रयासः 1 Effort, exertion, endeavour; R. 12. 53; 14. 51. 2 Labour, difficulty.

प्रयुक्त *p. p.* 1 Yoked, harnessed. 2 Used, employed (as a word). 3 Applied. 4 Appointed, nominated. 5 Acted, represented. 6 Arising or resulting from, produced by, consequent on. 7 Endowed with. 8 Lost in meditation, abstracted. 9 Lent or put to interest (as money) 10 Prompted, instigated; (see युज् with प्र).

प्रयुक्तिः *f.* 1 Use, employment, application. 2 Incitement, instigation. 3 Motive, main object or end, occasion. 4 Consequence, result.

प्रयुतं A million.

प्रयुत्सुः 1 A warrior. 2 A ram. 3 Wind, air. 4 An ascetic. 5 N. of Indra.

प्रयुद्धं War, battle.

प्रयोक्तृ *a.* 1 One who uses or employs (as a means, word &c.). 2 One who preforms or directs, an executor. 3 One who prompts or instigates, an instigator. 4 An author, an agent; U. 3. 48. 5 One who acts or represents (a drama). 6 One who lends money at interest, a money-lender. 7 One who shoots (an arrow).

प्रयोगः 1 Use, application, employment; as in शब्दप्रयोग; अयं शब्दो भूरिप्रयोगः -अल्पप्रयोगः 'this word is generally or rarely used'. 2 A usual form, general usage. 3 Hurling, throwing, discharging (opp. संहार); प्रयोगसंहारविभक्तमंत्रं R. 5. 57. 4 Exhibition, performance, representation (dramatic), acting; देव प्रयोगप्रधानं हि नाटयशास्त्रं M. 1; नाटिका न प्रयोगतो दृष्टा Ratn. 1 'not seen acted on the stage.' 5 Practice, experimental portion (of a subject); (opp. शास्त्र 'theory'); तदत्रभवानिमं मां च शास्त्रे प्रयोगे च विमृशतु M. 1. 6 Course of procedure, ceremonial form. 7 An act, action. 8 Recitation, dilivery. 9 Beginning, commencement. 10 A plan, contrivance, device, scheme. 11 A means, instrument. 12 Consequence, result. 13 Application of magic, magical rites. 14 Lending money on usury. 15 A horse. -COMP. -अतिशयः on of the five kinds of प्रस्तावना or prologue, in which a part or performance is superseded by another in such a manner that a character is suddenly brought on the stage; *i. e.* where the Sûtradhâra goes out hinting the entrance of a character and thus performs a part superseding that which he has apparently intended for his own, viz. dancing; the S. D. thus defines it:— यदि प्रयोग एकस्मिन् प्रयोगोऽन्यः प्रयुज्यते । तेन पात्रप्रवेशश्चेत् प्रयोगातिशयस्तदा ॥ 291. -निपुण *a.* skilled in practice; M. 3.

प्रयोजक *a.* Occasioning, causing, effecting, leading to, inciting, stimulating &c. -कः 1 An employer, one who uses or employs. 2 An author. 3 A founder, an institutor. 4 A money-lender. 5 A law-giver, legislator.

प्रयोजनं 1 Use, employment, application. 2 Use, need, necessity (with instr. of that which is needed and gen. of the user); सर्वैरपि राज्ञां प्रयोजनं Pt. 1; बाले किमनेन पृष्टेन प्रयोजनं K. 144; 3 End, aim, object, purpose; प्रयोजनमनुद्दिश्य न मंदोऽपि प्रवर्तते; पुत्रप्रयोजना दाराः पुत्रः पिंडप्रयोजनः । हितप्रयोजनं मित्रं धनं सर्वप्रयोजनं ॥ Subhâsh; गुणवत्तापि परप्रयोजना R. 8. 31. 4 A means of attaining; Ms. 7. 100. 5 A cause, motive, occasion. 6 Profit, interest.

प्रयोज्य *pot. p.* 1 To be used or employed. 2 To be practised. 3 To be produced or caused. 4 To be appointed. 5 To be thrown or discharged (as a missile). 6 To be set to work. -ज्यः A servant, an employé. -ज्यं Capital, principal.

प्ररुदित *p. p.* Crying bitterly, weeping.

प्ररूढ *p. p.* 1 Full-grown, developed. 2 Born, sprung, produced; यस्यायमंगात् कृतिनः प्ररूढः S. 7. 19. 3 Increased. 4 Gone deep, as in प्ररूढमूल. 5 Grown long; as in प्ररूढकेश, प्ररूढश्मश्रु.

प्ररूढिः *f.* Growth, increase.

प्ररोचनं 1 Exciting, stimulating. 2 Illustration, explanation. 3 Exhibition (of a person) for being seen and liked (by the people); अलोकसामान्यगुणस्तनूजः प्ररोचनार्थं प्रकटीकृतश्च Mâl. 1. 10 (where Jagaddhara interprets प्ररोचनार्थं by प्रवृत्तिपाटवार्थं 'in order to be thoroughly acquainted with the world'). 4 Favourable description of that which is to follow in a play. 5 Representation of the end as all but accomplished; see S. D. 383; (प्ररोचना also in the last two senses).

प्ररोहः 1 Sprouting, shooting or growing up, germination; as in यवांकुरप्ररोहः. 2 A sprout, shoot (fig. also); प्लक्षप्ररोह इव सौधतलं बिभेद R. 8. 93; प्लक्षान् प्ररोहजटिलानिव मंत्रिवृद्धान् 13. 71; Ku. 3. 60, 7. 17. 3 A scion, offspring; हा राधेयकुलप्ररोह Ve. 4; Mv. 6. 25. 4 A shoot of light; कुर्वंति सामंतशिखामणिनां प्रभाप्ररोहास्तमयं रजांसि R. 6. 33. 5 A new leaf or branch, twig, spray.

प्ररोहणं 1 Growing, shooting forth, germination. 2 Budding, sprouting. 3 A twig, sprout, shoot, spray.

प्रलपनं 1 Talking, speaking, talk, words, conversation. 2 Prating, Prattle, raving, incoherent or nonsensical talk; इदं कस्यापि प्रलपितं. 3 Lamentation, wailing; U. 3. 29.

प्रलपित *p. p.* Talked, prated, &c. -तं Talk; see प्रलपन above.

प्रलब्ध *p. p.* Deceived, cheated.

प्रलंब *a.* 1 Pendulous, hanging down; as in प्रलंबकेश. 2 Prominent; as in प्रलंबनासिकः. 3 Slow, dilatory. -बः 1 Hanging on or from, depending. 2 Any thing hanging down. 3 A branch. 4 A garland worn round the neck. 5 A kind of necklace. 6 The female breast. 7 Tin or lead. 8 N. of a demon killed by Balarâma. -COMP. -अंडः a man with hanging testicles. -घ्नः, -मथनः, -हन् *m.* an epithet of Balarâma.

प्रलंबनं Hanging down, depending.

प्रलंबित *a.* Pendulous, hanging down, suspended.

प्रलंभः 1 Obtaining, gaining, attaining. 2 Deceiving, imposing upon, cheating, overreaching.

प्रलयः 1 Destruction, annihilation, dissolution; स्थानानि किं हिमवतः प्रलयं गतानि Bh. 3. 70, 69; प्रलयं नीत्वा Si. 11. 66 'causing to disappear'. 2 The destruction of the whole universe (at the end of a *kalpa*), universal destruction; Ku. 2. 68; Bg. 7. 6. 3 Any extensive destruction or devastation. 4 Death, dying, destruction; प्रारब्धाः प्रलयाय मांसवदहो विक्रेतुमेते वयं Mu. 5. 21; 1. 14; Bg. 14. 14. 5 Swoon, fainting, loss of consciousness, syncope; Ku. 4. 2. 6 (In Rhet.)

Loss of consciousness, considered as one of the 33 subordinate feelings; प्रलयः सुखदुःखाद्यैर्गाढमिंद्रियमूर्छनं Pratâpa-rudra. 7 The mystic syllable *om*. –COMP. –कालः the time of universal destruction. –जलधरः a cloud at the dissolution of the world. –दहनः the fire at the dissolution of the world –पयोधिः the ocean at the dissolution of the world.

प्रललाट *a*. Having a prominent forehead.

प्रलवः A fragment, chip, bit.

प्रलवित्रं An instrument for cutting off.

प्रलापः 1 Talk, conversation, discourse. 2 Prating, prattling, an incoherent or nonsensical talk; Ms. 12. 6. 3 Lamentation, wailing; उत्तराप्रलापोपजनितकृपो भगवान् वासुदेवः K. 175; Ve. 5. 30. –COMP. –हन् *m*. a sort of collyrium.

प्रलापिन् *a*. 1 Talking, speaking; हा असंबद्धप्रलापिन् Ve. 3. 2 Prating, prattling.

प्रलीन *p. p*. 1 Melted, dissolved. 2 Annihilated, destroyed. 3 Insensible, unconscious.

प्रलून *p. p*. Cut off.

प्रलेपः An unguent, an ointment, a salve.

प्रलेपकः 1 An anointer, a plasterer. 2 A kind of slow fever.

प्रलेहः A kind of broth.

प्रलोठनं 1 Rolling (on the ground). 2 Heaving, tossing.

प्रलोभः 1 Cupidity, greediness, covetousness. 2 Allurement, seduction.

प्रलोभनं 1 Attracting. 2 An allurement, seduction, temptation. 3 A lure, bait.

प्रलोभनी Sand.

प्रलोल *a*. Greatly agitated or tremulous.

प्रवक्तृ *m*. 1 One who declares or relates, a speaker, declarer. 2 A teacher, expounder; Ms. 7. 20. 3 An orater, eloquent man.

प्रवगः, प्रवंगः, प्रवंगमः A monkey: see प्लवग, प्लवंग, प्लवंगम.

प्रवचनं 1 Speaking, declaration, announcement; Pt. 1- 190. 2 Teaching, expounding. 3 Exposition, explanation, interpretation; Mv. 4. 25. 4 Eloquence. 5 A sacred treatise or writing; Ms. 3. 184. –COMP. –पटु *a*. skilled in talking, eloquent.

प्रवटः Wheat.

प्रवण *a*. 1 Sloping down, inclined, shelving, flowing downwards. 2 Steep, abrupt, precipitous. 3 Crooked, bent. 4 Inclined, disposed to, tending to (oft. at the end of comp.); वंचनप्रवणः Ki. 3. 19. 5 Devoted or attached to, addicted to, intent on, prone to, full of; नृभिः प्राणत्राणप्रवणमतिभिः कैश्चिदधुना Bh. 3. 29; Si. 8. 35; Ms. 5. 21; Ki. 2. 44. 6 Favourably inclined or disposed towards; Ku. 4. 42. 7 Eager, ready; Ki. 2. 8. 8 Endowed with, possessed of. 9 Humbled, modestly humble, submissive. 10 Decayed, wasted, waning. –णः A place where four roads meet. –णं 1 A descent, a steep descent, precipice. 2 The side of a hill, slope, declivity.

प्रवत्स्यत् *a*. (ती or न्ती *f*.) About to go on a journey. –COMP. –पतिका the wife of one who intends to go on a journey (one of the 8 Nâyikâs in erotic poetry).

प्रवयणं 1 The upper part of a piece of woven cloth. 2 A goad; Si. 13. 19.

प्रवयस् *a*. Advanced in age, aged, old; केऽप्येते प्रवयसस्त्वां दिदृक्षवः U. 4; R. 8. 18.

प्रवर *a*. 1 Chief, principal, most excellent or distinguished, best, exalted; संकेतके चिरयति प्रवरो विनोदः Mk. 3. 3; Ms. 10. 27; Ghaṭ. 16. 2 Eldest. –रः 1 A call, summons. 2 A particular invocation addressed to Agni by a Brâhmaṇa at the consecration of his fire. 3 A line of ancestors. 4 A race, family, lineage. 5 An ancestor. 6 A Muni or noble ancestor who contributes to the credit of a particular *gotra* or family. 7 Offspring, descendants. 8 A cover, covering. –रं Aloe-wood. –COMP. –वाहनौ (du.) an epithet of the two Asvins.

प्रवर्गः 1 The sacrificial fire. 2 An epithet of Vishṇu.

प्रवर्ग्यः A ceremony preliminary to the *Soma* sacrifice.

प्रवर्तः Commencing, undertaking, engaging in

प्रवर्तक *a*. (र्तिका *f*.) 1 Setting on foot, founding. 2 Advancing, promoting, furthering. 3 Producing, causing. 4 Prompting, urging, inducing, instigating (in a bad sense). –कः 1 An originator, founder, author. 2 A prompter, instigator. 3 An arbiter, umpire.

प्रवर्तनं 1 Going on, moving forward. 2 Beginning, commencement. 3 Setting on foot, founding, establishing, instituting. 4 Prompting, urging, stimulating 5 Engaging in, applying oneself to. 6 Happening, coming to pass. 7 Activity, action. 8 Behaviour, conduct, procedure. –ना Inciting or prompting to action.

प्रवर्तयितृ *a*. One who sets in motion, urges, establishes, founds &c.

प्रवर्तित *p. p*. 1 Caused to turn, made to go or roll onwards, revolving; R. 9. 66. 2 Founded. 3 Prompted, incited, instigated. 4 Kindled. 5 Caused, made. 6 Purified, rendered pure; Ms. 11. 196.

प्रवर्तिन् *a*. 1 Proceeding, moving onward. 2 Being active. 3 Causing, effecting. 4 Using.

प्रवर्धनं Increasing, augmenting.

प्रवर्षः Heavy rain, heavy downpour.

प्रवर्षणं 1 Raining. 2 The first rain.

प्रवसनं Going or journeying abroad, going on a journey.

प्रवहः 1 Flowing or streaming forth. 2 Wind. 3 N. of on of the seven courses of wind (said to cause the motion of the planets).

प्रवहणं 1 A covered carriage or litter (for women). 2 A carriage, conveyance, vehicle in general. 3 A ship.

प्रवह्लि :-ह्ली See प्रहेलिका.

प्रवाच् *a*. Eloquent, oratorical;(कुर्वते) जडानप्यनुलोमार्थान् प्रवाचः कृतिनां गिरः Si. 2. 25. 2 Talkative, garrulous; Mu.3.16.

प्रवाचनं Proclamation, promulgation, declaration.

प्रवाणं The trimming or edging of a piece of woven cloth.

प्रवाणिः-णी *f*. A weaver's shuttle.

प्रवात *p. p*. Exposed to stormy wind. –तं 1 A current of air, fresh or free air; प्रवातशयनस्था देवी M. 4. 2 Strong or stormy wind; ननु प्रवातेऽपि निष्कंपा गिरयः S. 6. 3 An airy place; Ku. 1. 46.

प्रवादः 1 Uttering a word or sound. 2 Expressing, mentioning, declaring. 3 Discourse, conversation. 4 Talk, report, rumour, popular saying or belief; अनुरागप्रवादस्तु वत्सयोः सार्वलौकिकः Mâl. 1. 13; व्याघ्रो मानुषं खादतीति लोकप्रवादो दुर्निवारः H. 1. Ratn. 4. 15. 5 A fable, myth. 6 Litigious language. 7 Words of challenge, mutual defiance; इत्थं प्रवादं युधि संप्रहारं प्रचक्रतू रामनिशाविहारौ Bk. 2. 36.

प्रवारः, प्रवारकः A cover, covering.

प्रवारणं 1 Satisfying (a desire). 2 Priority of choice. 3 Prohibition, opposition. 4 A free-will offering (काम्यदानं).

प्रवाल See प्रबाल.

प्रवासः 1 Going or journeying abroad, being absent from one's home, foreign residence; R. 16. 4. –COMP.–गत,स्थ,–स्थित *a*. journeying abroad, being absent from home.

प्रवासनं 1 Living abroad, temporary sojourn. 2 Exile, banishment. 3 Killing, slaughter.

प्रवासिन् *m*. A traveller, wayfarer, sojourner.

प्रवाहः 1 Flowing or streaming forth. 2 A stream, course, current;

प्रवाहस्ते वारां श्रियमयमपारां दिशतु नः G. L. 2; R. 5. 46; 13. 10, 48; Ku. 1. 54; Me. 46. 3 Flow, running water. 4 Continuous flow, unbroken succession, continuity. 5 Course of events (rolling onward like a stream). 6 Activity, active occupation. 7 A pond, lake. 8 An excellent horse. (प्रवाहे मूत्रितं means (lit.) making water in a stream; (fig.) doing a useless action.)

प्रवाहकः A goblin, an imp.

प्रवाहनं 1 Driving forth. 2 Evacuation by stool.

प्रवाहिका Diarrhœa.

प्रवाही Sand.

प्रविकीर्ण p. p. 1 Scattered or strewed about. 2 Dispersed, diffused.

प्रविख्यात p. p. 1 Named, called. 2 Famous, renowned, celebrated.

प्रविख्यातिः f Fame, renown, celebrity.

प्रविचयः Examination, investigation.

प्रविचारः Discernment, discrimination.

प्रविचेतनं Understanding.

प्रवितत p. p. 1 spread out, expanded. 2 Dishevelled, disordered (hair).

प्रविदारः Bursting asunder, opening.

प्रविदारणं 1 Tearing, rending, breaking, bursting asunder. 2 Budding. 3 Conflict, war, battle. 4 Crowd, confusion, tumult.

प्रविद्ध p. p. Cast away, thrown off.

प्रविद्रुत p. p. Dispersed, put to flight, scattered.

प्रविभक्त p. p. 1 Severed, separated. 2 Apportioned, partitioned, divided, distributed; ज्योतींषि वर्तयति च प्रविभक्तरश्मिः S. 7. 6.

प्रविभागः 1 Division, distribution, classification; R. 16. 2. 2 A part, portion.

प्रविरल a. 1 Separated by a great interval, isolated, separate. 2 Very few or rare, very scanty; प्रविरला इव मुग्धवधूकथाः R. 9. 34.

प्रविलयः 1 Melting away. 2 Complete dissolution or absorption.

प्रविलुप्त p. p. Cut off, fallen or rubbed off, removed.

प्रविरः Yellow sandal.

प्रविवादः Dispute, quarrel, wrangling.

प्रविविक्त a. 1 Very solitary. 2 Separated, detached.

प्रविश्लेषः Separation.

प्रविषण्ण p. p. Dejected, spiritless.

प्रविष्ट p. p. 1 Gone or entered into; पश्चार्धेन प्रविष्टः शरपतनभयाद्भूयसा पूर्वकायं S. 1. 7. 2 Engaged in, occupied with. 3 Begun.

प्रविष्टकं Entrance on the stage.

प्रविस्त (स्ता) रः Extent, circumference, compass.

प्रवीण a. Clever, skilled or versed in, conversant with; आमोदानथ हरिदंतुराणि नेतुं नैवान्यो जगति समीरणात्प्रवीणः Bv. 1. 15; Ku. 7. 48.

प्रवीर a. 1 Foremost, best, most excellent or distinguished; R. 14. 29; 16. 1; Bg. 11. 48. 2 Strong, powerful, heroic. —रः 1 A brave person, hero, warrior. 2 A chief, distinguished personage.

प्रवृत p. p. Selected, picked, chosen.

प्रवृत्त p. p. 1 Begun, commenced, proceeded with. 2 Set in; अचिरप्रवृत्तं ग्रीष्मसमयमधिकृत्य S. 1. 3 Engaged in, occupied with. 4 Going to, bound for. 5 Fixed, settled, determined. 6 Unimpeded, undisputed. 7 Round. —त्तः A round ornament.

प्रवृत्तकं Entrance on the stage.

प्रवृत्तिः f. 1 Continued advance, progress, advance. 2 Rise, origin, source, flow (of words &c.); प्रवृत्तिरासीच्छब्दानां चरितार्था चतुष्टयी Ku. 2. 17. 3 Appearance, manifestation; कुसुमप्रवृत्तिसमये S. 4. 17; R. 11. 43; 14. 39; 15. 4. 4 Advent, setting in, commencement; आकालिकीं वीक्ष्य मधुप्रवृत्तिं Ku. 3. 34. 5 Application or addiction to, tendency, inclination, predilection, propensity; S. 1. 22. 6 Conduct; behaviour; R. 14. 73. 7 Employment, occupation, activity; Ku. 6. 26. 8 Use, employment, currency (as of a word). 9 Continued effort, perseverance. 10 Signification, sense, acceptation (of a word). 11 Continuance, permanence, prevalence. 12 Active worldly life, taking an active part in worldly affairs (opp. निवृत्ति). 13 News, tidings, intelligence; जीमूतेन स्वकुशलमयीं हारयिष्यन् प्रवृत्तिं Me. 4; V. 4. 20. 14 Applicability or validity of a rule. 15 Fate, destiny, luck. 16 Cognition, direct perception or apprehension. 17 Rutting juice, or ichor exuding from the temples of an elephant in rut. 18 N. of the city of उज्जयिनी q. v. –COMP. –ज्ञः a spy, secret emissary or agent. –निमित्तं a reason for the use of any term in a particular signification. –मार्गः active or worldly life, attachment to the business and pleasures of the world.

प्रवृद्ध p. p. 1 Full-grown. 2 Increased, augmented, expanded, enlarged 3 Full, deep. 4 Haughty, arrogant. 5 Violant. 6 Large.

प्रवृद्धिः f. 1 Increase, growth; R. 13. 71; 17. 71. 2 Rise, prosperity, preferment, promotion, elevation.

प्रवेक a. Best, chief, choicest, most excellent.

प्रवेगः Great speed, velocity.

प्रवेटः Barley.

प्रवेणिः-णी f. 1 A braid of hair (in general); R. 15. 30. 2 The hair twisted and unadorned (worn by wives in the absence of their husbands). 3 The housings of an elephant. 4 A piece of coloured woollen cloth. 5 The current or stream (of a river).

प्रवेतृ m. A charioteer.

प्रवेदनं Making known, announcing, proclaiming.

प्रवेपः, प्रवेपकः, प्रवेपथुः, प्रवेपनं Trembling, quivering, shaking, tremour.

प्रवेरित a. Cast hither and thither, thrown about.

प्रवेलः A kind of kidney-bean.

प्रवेशः 1 Entrance, penetration; पुरप्रवेशाभिमुखो बभूव R. 7. 1; Ku. 3. 40. 2 Ingress, access, approach. 3 Entrance on the stage; तेन पात्रप्रवेशश्चेत् S. D. 6. 4 The entrance or door (of a house &c.). 5 Income, revenue. 6 Close application (to a pursuit), intentness of purpose.

प्रवेशकः 'The introducer,' an interlude acted by inferior characters (such as servants, buffoon &c.) for the purpose of acquainting the audience with events not represented on the stage, but a knowledge of which is essential for the proper understanding of what follows; (like the Vishkambhaka it connects the story of the drama and the subdivisions of the plot, by briefly referring to what has occurred in the intervals of the acts, of what is likely to happen at the end; it never occurs at the beginning of the first act or at the end of the last). S. D. thus defines it :—प्रवेशकोनुदात्तोक्त्या नीचपात्रप्रयोजितः । अंकद्वयांतर्विज्ञेयः शेषं विष्कंभके यथा ॥ 308; see विष्कंभक.

प्रवेशनं 1 Entrance, penetration, going into. 2 Introducing, leading to, conducting. 3 An entrance or main door of a house, gate. 4 Sexual intercourse.

प्रवेशित p. p. Introduced, showed in, led or conducted to, brought in.

प्रवेष्टः 1 An arm. 2 The wrist or forearm.. 3 The fleshy part of an elephant's back (where the rider sits). 4 An elephant's gums. 5 An elephant's housings.

प्रव्यक्त p. p. Apparent, clear, manifest, evident.

प्रव्यक्तिः f. Manifestation, appearance.

प्रव्याहारः Prolongation of discourse.

प्रव्रजनं 1 Going abroad, sojourning. 2 Going into exile. 3 Turning a recluse.

प्रव्रजित *p. p.* 1 Gone abroad or into exile. 2 Turned a recluse.—**तः** 1 A religious mendicant or ascetic in general. 2 Especially, a Brâhmaṇa who has entered on the fourth (भिक्षु) order. 3 The pupil of a Jaina or Buddhist mendicant. —**तं** Turning a recluse, the life of a religious mendicant.

प्रव्रज्या 1 Going abroad, migration. 2 Roaming, wandering about as a religious mendicant. 3 The order of a religious mendicant, a mendicant's life, the fourth (or भिक्षु) order in the religious life of a Brâhmaṇa; प्रव्रज्यां कल्पवृक्षा इवाश्रिताः Ku. 6. 6 (where Malli. says प्रव्रज्या means the वानप्रस्थ or third order). -Comp. **-अवसितः** a religious mendicant who renounces his order.

प्रव्रश्चनः A knife for cutting wood.

प्रव्राज् *m.*, **प्रव्राजकः** A religious mendicant, recluse.

प्रव्राजनं Banishing, exile, sending into exile.

प्रशंसनं Praising, extolling.

प्रशंसा 1 Praise, eulogy, panegyric, applause; प्रशंसावचनं a complimentary or laudatory remark. 2 Description, reference to; as in अप्रस्तुतप्रशंसा q. v. 3 Glory, fame, reputation. -Comp. **-उपमा** one of the several kinds of उपमा mentioned by Daṇḍin; ब्रह्मणोऽप्युद्भवः पद्मश्चंद्रः शंभुशिरोधृतः । तौ तुल्यौ त्वन्मुखेनेति सा प्रशंसोपमोच्यते ॥ Kâv. 2. 31. **-मुखर** *a.* loudly praising.

प्रशंसित *p. p.* Praised, extolled, applauded.

प्रशाख्वन् *m.* The ocean.

प्रशाख्वरी A river.

प्रशमः 1 Calmness, tranquillity, composure; प्रशमस्थितपूर्वपार्थिवं R. 8. 15; Ki. 2. 32. 2 Peace, rest. 3 Extinction, abatement; Ku. 2. 20. 4 Cessation, end, destruction; Si. 20. 73. 5 Pacification, appeasement; Si. 16. 51.

प्रशमन *a.* (**नी** *f.*) Calming, tranquillizing, pacifying, removing &c. —**नं** 1 Calming, tranquillizing, pacifying. 2 Allaying, assuaging, soothing, mitigating आपन्नार्तिप्रशमनफलाः संपदो ह्युत्तमानां Me. 53. 3 Curing, healing; as in व्याधिप्रशमनं 4 Quenching, extinguishing, suppressing, quelling. 5 Cessation, abatement. 6 Bestowing fitly or on fit objects; Ms. 7. 56. (सत्पात्रे प्रतिपादनं Kull.; but others give it the next sense). 7 Securing, guarding, keeping safe; लब्धप्रशमनस्वस्थमथैनं समुपस्थिता R. 4. 14. 8 Killing, slaughter.

प्रशमित *p. p.* 1 Pacified, soothed, composed, appeased, allayed. 2 Extinguished, quenched. 3 Atoned for, expiated; U. 1. 40.

प्रशस्त *p. p.* 1 Praised, lauded, commended, eulogised. 2 Praiseworthy, commendable. 3 Best, excellent. 4 Blessed, happy, auspicious. -Comp. **-अद्रिः** N. of a mountain.

प्रशस्तिः *f.* 1 Praise, eulogy, laudation. 2 Description; U. 7. 3 A panegyric or small poem written in praise of any one (*e. g.* a patron.). 4 Excellence, eminence. 5 Benediction. 6 Guidance, instruction, rule for guidance; as in लेखप्रशस्तिः 'a form of writing'.

प्रशस्य *a.* (Compar. श्रेयस् or ज्यायस्, superl. श्रेष्ठ or ज्येष्ठ) Praiseworthy, commendable, excellent.

प्रशाख *a.* 1 Having many or spreading branches. 2 Being in the fifth stage of formation (said of the embryo when the hands and feet are formed).—**खा** A small branch or twig.

प्रशाखिका A small branch.

प्रशांत *p. p.* Calmed, tranquillized, composed. 2 Calm, serene, quiet, sedate, still; अहो प्रशांतरमणीयतोद्यानस्य. 3 Tamed, subdued, quelled. 4 Ended, ceased, over; तत्सर्वमेकपद एव मम प्रशांतं Mâl. 9. 36; प्रशांतमस्त्रं U. 6 'ceased to work or withdrawn.' 5 Dead, deceased (see शम् with प्र). -Comp. **-आत्मन्** *a.* composed in mind, peaceful, calm. **-ऊर्ज** *a.* weakened, enervated, prostrated, **-काम** *a.* content. **-चेष्ट** *a.* resting, ceased to work. **-बाध** *a.* having all obstacles or calamities removed; Ki. 1. 18.

प्रशांतिः *f.* 1 Calmness, tranquillity, composure, quiet, repose. 2 Rest, cessation, abatement. 3 Allaying, quenching, extinction.

प्रशामः 1 Tranquillity, calm, composure. 2 Quenching, extinction. allaying. 3 Cessation.

प्रशासनं 1 Governing, ruling. 2 Enjoining, exacting. 3 Government.

प्रशास्तृ *m.* A king, ruler, governor.

प्रशिथिल *a.* Very loose.

प्रशिष्यः The pupil of a pupil, the disciple of a disciple; शिष्यप्रशिष्यैरुपगीयमानमवेहि तन्मंडनमिश्रधाम *Sankaradigvijaya.*

प्रशुद्धिः *f.* Clearness, purity.

प्रशोषः Becoming dry, drying up, aridity.

प्रश्चोतनं Sprinkling, oozing; U. 3. 11.

प्रश्नः 1 A question, query, an inquiry, interrogation (अविज्ञातप्रवचनं प्रश्न इत्यभिधीयते); अनामयप्रश्नपूर्वकं *S.* 5. 'with an inquiry about (your) well-being or health.' 2 A judicial inquiry or investigation. 3 A point at issue, a subject of controversy, controverted or disputed point; इति प्रश्न उपस्थितः. 4 A problem for solution or calculation; अहं ते प्रश्नं दास्यामि Mk. 5. 5 Inquiry into the future. 6 A short section of a work. -Comp. **उपनिषद्** *n.* N. of an Upanishad consisting of six questions and six answers.-**दूतिः-ती** *f.* a riddle, an enigma.

प्रश्रथः Laxity, looseness, relaxation.

प्रश्रयः,प्रश्रयणं 1 Respect, courtesy, civility, politeness, respectful or courteous behaviour, humility; समागतैः प्रश्रयनम्रमूर्तिभिः Si. 12. 33; R. 10. 70, 83; U. 6. 23; सप्रश्रयं respectfully, modestly. 2 Love, affection, regard; Pt. 2. 2.

प्रश्रित *p. p.* Civil, polite, courteous, humble, well-behaved.

प्रश्लथ *a.* 1 Very loose or flaccid. 2 Spiritless, unnerved.

प्रश्लिष्ट *p p.* 1 Twisted, entwined. 2 Reasonable, well argued or reasoned (युक्तियुत).

प्रश्लेषः Close contact, pressing hard against.

प्रश्वास Breath, respiration.

प्रष्ठ *a.* 1 Standing or being in front; R. 15. 10. 2 Chief, principal, foremost, best; a leader; पुलस्त्यप्रष्ठः Mv. 1. 30; 6. 30; Si. 19. 30. -Comp. **वाह्** *m.* a young bull being trained for the plough.

प्रस् 1. 4. A. (प्रस-स्य-ते) 1 To bring forth young. 2 To spread, diffuse, expand, extend.

प्रसक्त *p. p.* 1 Attached to, connected with. 2 Excessively attached or fond; Pt. 1. 193. 3 Adhering or sticking to. 4 Fixed or intent upon, devoted or addicted to, engaged in, applied to; Si. 9. 63; so द्यूत°, निद्रा° &c. 5 Contiguous, near. 6 Constant, incessant, uninterrupted; Ki. 4. 18; R. 13. 40; Mâl. 4. 6; M. 3. 1. 7 Got, obtained, gained. —**क्तं** *ind.* Incessantly, continuously; Ki. 16. 55.

प्रसक्तिः *f.* 1 Attachment, devotion, addiction, devotedness; adherence. 2 Connection, union, association. 3 Applicability, bearing, application; as in अतिप्रसक्ति which is =अतिव्याप्ति q. v. 4 Energy, perseverance; संतापे दिशतु शिवः शिवां प्रसक्तिं Ki. 5. 50. 5 Conclusion, deduction. 6 A topic or subject of discourse. 7 Occurrence of a possibility.

प्रसंगः 1 Attachment, devotion, addiction, devotedness; स्वरूपयोग्ये सुरतप्रसंगे Ku. 1. 19, तस्यात्यायतकोमलस्य सततं द्यूतप्रसंगेन किं Mk. 2. 11; Si. 11. 22. 2 Union, intercourse, association, connection; निवर्ततामस्माद्गणिकाप्रसंगात् Mk. 4. 3 Illicit intercourse. 4 Occupation, intentness, being engaged or occupied with; भ्रविक्रियायां विरतप्रसंगैः Ku. 3. 47. 5 A subject or topic (of discourse or controversy). 6 An occasion, incident; दिग्विजयप्रसंगेन K. 191; यात्राप्रसंगेन

Mâl. 1. 7 Conjuncture, time, opportunity; Ms. 9. 5. 8 A contingency, event, case, occurrence of a possibility; नेश्वरो जगतः कारणमुपपद्यते कुतः वैषम्यनैर्घृण्यप्रसंगात् S. B.; एवं चानवस्थाप्रसंगः *ibid*; Ku. 7. 16. 8 Connected reasoning or argument. 9 A conclusion, inference. 10 Connected language. 11 Inseparable application or connection (=व्याप्ति q. v.). 12 Mention of parents. (**प्रसंगेन, प्रसंगतः, प्रसंगात्** are used adverbially in the sense of 1 in relation to. 2 in consequence of, on account of, because of, by way of. 3 occasionally. 4 in course of; (as in कथाप्रसंगेन in course of conversation). –COMP –**निवारणं** prevention or obviation of similar contingencies in future. –**वशात्** *ind.* according to the time, by the force of circumstances. –**विनिवृत्तिः** *f.* nonrecurrence of a contingency.

प्रसंख्या 1 Total number or sum. 2 Reflection.

प्रसंख्यानं 1 Enumeration. 2 Reflection, meditation; deep meditation; abstract contemplation; श्रुताप्सरोगीतिरपि क्षणेऽस्मिन् हरः प्रसंख्यानपरो बभूव Ku. 3. 40. 3 Fame, reputation, renown.—**नः** Payment, liquidation.

प्रसंजनं 1 Act of connecting, combining, uniting. 2 Applying, bringing to bear upon, bringing into use.

प्रसत्तिः *f.* 1 Favour, graciousness, complacency. 2 Clearness, purity, transparency.

प्रसंधानं Combination, union.

प्रसन्न *p. p.* 1 Pure, clear, bright, limpid, pellucid, transparent; Ku. 1. 23; 7. 74; *S.* 5. 20. 2 Pleased, delighted, propitiated, soothed; गंगां शरन्नयति सिंधुपतिं प्रसन्नां Mu. 3. 9; गंभीरायाः पयसि सरितश्चेतसीव प्रसन्ने Me. 40 (where the first sense is also intended); Ku. 5. 35; R. 2. 68. 3 Kind, kindly disposed, gracious, propitious; अवेहि मां कामदुघां R. 2. 63. 4 Plain, open, clear, easily intelligible (as meaning). 5 True, correct; प्रसन्ना प्रसन्नस्ते तर्कः V. 2; प्रसन्नप्रायस्ते तर्कः Mâl. I. —**न्ना** 1 Propitiation, pleasing. 2 Spirituous liquor. –COMP. –**आत्मन्** *a.* gracious-minded, propitious. –**ईरा** spirituous liquor. –**कल्प** *a.* 1 almost calm. 2 almost true. –**मुख, –वदन** *a.* gracious-looking, with a pleased countenance, smiling. –**सलिल** *a.* having clear water.

प्रसभः Force, violence, impetuosity; प्रसभोद्धृतारिः R. 2. 30. –**भं** *ind.* 1 Voilently, forcibly, perforce; इंद्रियाणि प्रमाथीनि हरंति प्रसभं मनः Bg. 2. 60; Ms. 8. 332. 2 Very much, exceedingly; तवास्मि गीतरागेण हारिणा प्रसभं हृतः *S.* 1. 5. Rs. 6. 25. 3 Importunately; Bg. 11. 41. –COMP. –**दमनं** subduing by force; *S.* 7. 33. –**हरणं** forcible abduction.

प्रसमीक्षणं, प्रसमीक्षा Consideration, deliberation, judgment.

प्रसयनं 1 Binding, fastening. 2 A net.

प्रसरः 1 Going forward, advancing *S.* 1. 29. 2 Free or unimpeded motion, free scope, access or course; R. 8. 23; 16. 20; Mu. 3. 5; H. 1. 186. 3 Spreading, diffusion, extension, expansion, dilation; *Si.* 9. 71. 4 Extent, dimention, great quantity; *Si.* 3. 35. 5 Prevalence, influence; *Si.* 3. 10. 6 A stream, flow, torrent, flood; पपात स्वेदांबुप्रसर इव हर्षाश्रुनिकरः Gît. 11. 7 A group, multitude. 8 War, battle. 9 An iron arrow. 10 Speed. 11 Affectionate solicitation.

प्रसरणं 1 Going forth, running or streaming forth. 2 Escaping, running away. 3 Spreading forth or abroad. 4 Surrounding an enemy. 5 Amiability.

प्रसरणिः-णी *f.* Surrounding an enemy.

प्रसर्पणं 1 Going or moving forward, advancing. 2 Pervading, spreading in all directions.

प्रस (श) लः The cold season (**हेमंत**).

प्रसवः 1 Begetting, generation, procreation, birth, production. 2 Child-birth, delivery, confinement; as in आसन्नप्रसवा. 3 Offspring, progeny, young ones, children; केवलं वीरप्रसवा भूयाः U. 1; Ku. 7. 87. 4 Source, origin, birth-place (fig. also); Ki. 2. 43. 5 Flower. blossom; प्रसवविभूतिषु भूरुहां विरक्तः *Si.* 7. 42; नीता लोध्रप्रसवरजसा पांडुतामानने श्रीः Me. 65; कुंदप्रसवशिथिलं जीवितं 113; R. 9. 28; Ku. 1. 55; 4. 4. 14; *S.* 5. 9; Mâl. 9. 27, 31; U. 2. 20. 6 A fruit, product. –COMP. –**उन्मुख** *a.* about to be delivered or confined; पतिः प्रतीतः प्रसवोन्मुखीं प्रियां ददर्श R. 3. 12. –**गृह** a lying-in-chamber. –**धर्मिन्** *a.* productive, prolific. –**बंधनं** the foot-stalk of a leaf or flower, peduncle. –**वेदना –व्यथा** pangs of child-birth, throes. –**स्थली** a mother. –**स्थानं** 1 a place for delivery. 2 a nest.

प्रसवकः The Piyâla tree.

प्रसवनं 1 Bringing forth. 2 Bearing children, **fecundity.**

प्रसवंतिः *f.* A **woman in** labour.

प्रसवितृ *m.* A father, procreator.

प्रसवित्री A mother.

प्रसव्य *a.* Contrary, inverted, reverse.

प्रसह *a.* Withstanding, enduring, bearing up. –**हः** 1 A beast or bird of prey. 2 Resistance, edurance, opposition.

प्रसहनः A beast or bird of prey. –**नं** 1 Withstanding, resisting. 2 Enduriug, bearing up. 3 Defeating, overcoming. 4 Embracing, an embrace

प्रसह्य *Ind.* 1 Forcibly, violently, by force; प्रसह्य मणिमुद्धरेन्मकरवक्त्रदंष्ट्रांकुरात् Bh. 2. 4; *Si.* 1 27. 2 Exceedingly, much.

प्रसातिका A kind of rice (with small grains)

प्रसादः 1 Favour, kindness, condescension, propitiousness; कुरु दृष्टिप्रसादं 'be pleased to show yourself'; इत्याप्रसादादस्यास्त्वं परिचर्यापरो भव R. 1. 91; 2. 22. 2 Good temper, graciousness of disposition. 3 Calmness, tranquillity, composure, serenity, sedateness, absence of excitement.; Bg. 2. 64. 4 Clearness, limpidness, bright ness, transparency, purity (as of water, mind &c.); गंगारोधपतनकलुषा गृह्णतीव प्रसादं V. 1. 8; *S.* 7. 32; प्रातबुद्धिप्रसादाः *Si.* 11. 6; R. 17. 1; Ki. 9. 25. 5 Perspicuity, clearness of style, one of the three Guṇas according to Mammaṭa, who thus defines it; शुष्केंधनाग्निवत् स्वच्छजलवत्सहसैव यः । व्याप्नोत्यन्यत्प्रसादोसौ सर्वत्र विहितास्थितिः K. P. 8; यावदर्थकपदत्वरूपमर्थवैमल्यं प्रसादः or श्रुतमात्रा वाक्यार्थं करतलबदरमिव निवेदयती घटना प्रसादस्य R. G.; see Kâv. 1. 45; S. D. 611 also 6 Food offered to idols &c., or the remnants of such food. 7 A free gift, gratuity. 8 Any propitiatory offering. 9 Well-being, welfare. –COMP. –**उन्मुख** *a.* disposed to favour. –**पराङ्मुख** *a.* 1 withdrawing favour from any one. 2 Not caring for anybody's favour. –**पात्रं** *a* an object of favour. –**स्थ** *a* 1 kind, propitious. 2 serene, pleased, happy.

प्रसादक *a.* (**दिका** *f.*) 1 Purifying, clearing, making pellucid. 2 Soothing, calming. 3 Gladdening, cheering. 4 Courting favour, propitiating.

प्रसादन *a.* (**नी** *f.*) 1 Purifying, clearing, rendering pure or clear; फलं कतकवृक्षस्य यद्यंबुप्रसादनं Ms. 6. 67. 2 Soothing, calming. 3 Cheering, gladdening. –**नः** A royal tent. –**नं** 1 Clearing from impurities, purifying. 2 Soothing, calming, tranquillizing, composing. 3 Pleasing, gratifying. 4 Propitiating, courting favour. –**ना** 1 Service, worship. 2 Purifying.

प्रसादित *p. p.* 1 Purified, cleared. 2 Appeased, propitiated. 3 Worshipped. 4 Calmed, soothed.

प्रसाधक *a.* (**धिका** *f.*) 1 Accomplishing, perfecting. 2 Purifying, cleansing. 3 Decorating, ornamenting.—**कः** A valet-de-chambre, an attendant who dresses his master. R. 17. 22.

प्रसाधनं 1 Accomplishing, effecting, bringing about. 2 Setting in order, arranging. 3 Decorating, ornamenting, embellishing; toilet, dress; Ku. 4. 18. 4 A decoration, ornament, means of decoration or ornament; Ku. 7. 13, 30.-**नः,-नं-नी** A comb. -COMP. **-विधिः** decoration, embellishment. **-विशेषः** the highest decoration; प्रसाधनविधेः प्रसाधनविशेषः V. 2. 3.

प्रसाधिका A lady's maid, a female attendant who looks to the toilet of her mistress; प्रसाधिकालंबितमग्रपादमाक्षिप्य R. 7. 7.

प्रसाधित *p. p.* 1 Accomplished, completed, perfected. 2 Ornamented, decorated.

प्रसारः 1 Spreading, extending. 2 Spread, diffusion, extension, expansion. 3 Stretching out. 4 Spreading over the country to forage.

प्रसारणं 1 Spreading abroad, extending, increase, diffusing, expanding. 2 Stretching out; as in बाहुप्रसारणं. 3 Surrounding an enemy. 4 Spreading over the country for fuel and grass. 5 The change of a semivowel (य्, र् and व्) into a vowel; see संप्रसारणं.

प्रसारिणी Surrounding an enemy.

प्रसारित *p. p.* 1 Expanded, spread, diffused, extended. 2 Stretched out (as hands.). 3 Exhibited, laid out, exposed (for sale).

प्रसाहः Overpowering, defeating.

प्रसित *p. p.* 1 Bound, fastened. 2 Devoted to, engaged in, occupied with. 3 Intent on, longing for, craving after (with instr. or loc); लक्ष्म्या लक्ष्म्यां वा प्रसितः Sk.; R. 8. 23. **-तं** Pus, matter.

प्रसितिः *f.* 1 A net. 2 A ligament. 3 A tie, fetter.

प्रसिद्धः *p. p.* 1 Renowned, famous, celebrated. 2 Decorated, ornamented, adorned, R. 18. 41; Ku. 5. 9; 7. 16.

प्रसिद्धिः *f.* 1 Fame, celebrity, publicity, renown. 2 Success, accomplishment, fulfilment; Ki. 3. 39; Ms. 4. 3. 3 Ornament, decoration.

प्रसीदिका A small garden.

प्रसुप्त *p. p.* 1 Asleep, sleepy. 2 Fast asleep.

प्रसुप्तिः *f.* 1 Sleepiness. 2 Paralysis.

प्रसू *a.* 1 Bringing forth, bearing, giving birth to; स्त्रीप्रसूश्चाधिवेत्तव्या Y 1. 73. -*f.* 1 A Mother; मातरपितरौ प्रसूजनयितारौ Ak. 'parents'. 2 A mare. 3 A spreading creeper. 4 The plantain.

प्रसूका A mare.

प्रसूत *p. p.* 1 Begotten, engendered. 2 Brought forth, born, produced. **-तं** 1 A flower. 2 Any productive source. **-ता** A woman recently delivered.

प्रसूतिः *f.* 1 Procreation, begetting, generation. 2 Bringing forth, bearing, delivering, giving birth to; R. 14. 66. 3 Calving. 4 Laying eggs; N. 1. 135. 5 Birth, production, generation; R. 10. 53. 6 Appearance, coming forth, growth (of flowers &c.); R 5. 15; Ku. 1. 42. 7 A product, production. 8 Offspring, progeny, issue; R. 1. 25, 77; 2. 4; 5. 7; Ku. 2. 7, *S.* 6. 24. 8 A producer, generator, procreator; R. 2. 63. 9. A mother.-COMP. **-जं** pain resulting as a necessary consequence of birth. **-वायुः** air produced in the womb during the pangs of travail.

प्रसूतिका A woman recently delivered.

प्रसून *p. p.* Produced, born. **—नं** 1 A flower; लतायां पूर्वलूनायां प्रसूनस्यागमः कुतः U. 5. 20; R. 2. 10. 2 A bud, blossom. 3 A fruit. -COMP. **-इषुः, -बाणः, -वाणः** an epithet of the god of love. **-वर्षः** a shower of flowers.

प्रसूनकं 1 A flower. 2 A bud, blossom.

प्रसृत *p. p.* 1 Gone forward. 2 Stretched out, extended. 3 Spread, diffused. 4 Long, lengthened. 5 Engaged in, attached to. 6 Swift, quick. 7 Modest, humble. **—तः** The palm of the hand stretched out and hollowed. **-तः, -तं** A measure equal to two *Palas*. **-ता** The leg. -COMP. **-जः** a particular class of sons, an adulterine (कुंडगोलकरूपः).

प्रसृतिः *f.* 1 Advance, progress. 2 Flowing. 3 The palm of the hand stretched out and hollowed. 4 A handful (considered as a measure equal to two *Palas*); परिक्षीणः कश्चित्स्पृहयति यवानां प्रसृतये Bh. 2. 45, Y. 2. 112.

प्रसृष्ट *p. p.* 1 Laid aside, dismissed. 2 Hurt, injured. **-ष्टा** A finger stretched forth or extended; (अंगुल्यः प्रसृता यास्तु ताः प्रसृष्टा उदीरिताः).

प्रसृत्वर *a.* Spreading about; Bv. 4. 1.

प्रसृमर *a.* Flowing forth, dropping, distilling.

प्रसेकः 1 Flowing forth, oozing, dropping. 2 Sprinkling, wetting. 3 Emission, discharge; Rs. 3. 6. 4 Vomiting.

प्रसेदिका A small garden.

प्रसेवः, प्रसेवकः 1 A sack, bag for grain. 2 A leathern bottle. 3 A small instrument of wood placed under the neck of the lute to make the sound deeper.

प्रस्कंदनं 1 Springing across or leaping over. 2 Evacuation by stool, diarrhœa. **-नः** An epithet of *Siva*.

प्रस्कन्न *p. p.* 1 Sprung forth, 2 Fallen, dropped. 3 Defeated. **-न्नः** 1 An outcast. 2 A sinner, transgressor.

प्रस्कुंदः An altar of a circular shape.

प्रस्खलनं 1 Staggering. 2 Stumbling, falling.

प्रस्तरः 1 A couch of leaves and flowers 2 A couch or bed in general. 3 A flat surface or top, level, plain. 4 A stone, rock. 5 A precious stone, gem.

प्रस्तरणं-णा 1 A bed, couch. 2 A seat.

प्रस्तारः 1 Strewing, spreading out, covering with. 2 A bed of leaves and flowers. 3 A bed or couch in general. 4 A flat surface, level, plain. 5 A thicket, wood. 6 (In prosody) A tabular representation of the long and short vowels of a metre with all possible varieties.

प्रस्तावः 1 Beginning, commencement. 2 An introduction. 3 Mention, allusion, reference; नाममात्रप्रस्तावः *S.* 7. 4 An occasion, opportunity, time, season; fit or proper time; त्वराप्रस्तावोयं न खलु परिहासस्य समयः Mâl. 9. 44; शिष्याय बृहतां पत्युः प्रस्तावमदिशद् दृशा *Si.* 2. 68. 5 The occasion of a discourse, subject, topic. 6 The prologue of a drama; see प्रस्तावना below. -COMP. **-यज्ञः** a conversation in which each interlocutor takes a part.

प्रस्तावना 1 Causing to be praised or mentioned, praising, praise 2 Beginning, commencement; आर्यबालचरितप्रस्तावनाडिंडिमः Mv: 1. 54. 3 An introduction, preface, exordium (in general): प्रस्तावना इयं कपटनाटकस्य Mal. 2 4 An introductory dialogue (the prologue) at the beginning of a drama between the manager and one of the actors, which, after giving an account of the author and his qualifications &c., introduces the audience to the incidents of the drama; for definition; see आमुख.

प्रस्तावित *a.* 1 Begun, commenced. 2 Mentioned, referred to; Mál. 3. 3.

प्रस्तिरः A bed of leaves and flowers.

प्रस्तीत-म *p. p.* 1 Making a noise, sounded. 2 Crowded together, swarming.

प्रस्तुत p. p. 1 Praised, eulogized. 2 Begun, commenced. 3 Accomplished, done, effected. 4 Happened. 5 Approached. 6 Proposed, declared, under discussion, taken in hand. (see स्तु with प्र). **-तं** 1 The matter in hand, the subject under discussion or consideration; अधुना प्रस्तुतमनुस्रियतां. 2 (In Rhet.) Forming the subject of discussion, the उपमेय; see प्रकृत; अप्रस्तुतप्रशंसा सा या सैव प्रस्तुताश्रया K.P.10. -COMP. **-अंकुरः** a figure of speech in which a reference is made to a passing circumstance to bring out something latent in the hearer's mind; see Chandr. 5. 64 and Kuval. under प्रस्तुतांकुरः

प्रस्थ *a.* 1 Going to, visiting, abiding in; as in वानप्रस्थ. 2 Going on a journey. 3 Spreading, expanding. 4 Firm, stable. **-स्थः,-स्थं** 1 A level expanse, level plain; as in औषधिप्रस्थ, इंद्रप्रस्थ &c. 2 Table land on the top of a mountain; प्रस्थं हिमाद्रेर्मृगनाभिगंधि किंचित् क्वणत्किंनरमध्युवास Ku. 1. 54; Me. 58. 3 The top or peak of a mountain; *Si.* 4. 11 (where it has sense 4 also). 4 A particular measure of capacity equal to thirty-two *palas.* 5 Anything measuring a *Prastha* -Comp. **-पुष्पः** a variety of holy basil.

प्रस्थंपच *a.* Cooking a *Prashtha.*

प्रस्थानं 1 Going or setting forth, departure, proceeding; प्रस्थानविक्लवगतेरवलंबनार्थं *S.* 5. 3; R. 4. 88; Me. 41; Amaru. 31. 2 Coming to; Ku. 6, 61. 3 A march, the march of an army or assailant. 4 A method, system. 5 Death, dying. 6 An inferior kind of drama; see S. D. 276, 544.

प्रस्थापनं 1 Sending away, dismissing, dispatching. 2 Appointment to an embassy. 3 Proving, demonstrating. 4 Using, employing. 5 Carrying off cattle.

प्रस्थापित *p. p.* 1 Sent away, dispatched. 2 Established, proved.

प्रस्थित *p. p.* Set out, gone forth, departed, gone on a journey; (see स्था with प्र).

प्रस्थितिः *f.* 1 Going forth, departure. 2 A march, journey.

प्रस्नः A vessel for bathing.

प्रस्नवः 1 Flowing, pouring forth, exudation; U. 6. 22. 2 A stream or flow (as of milk); R. 1. 84.

प्रस्नुत *p. p.* Dropping, oozing, pouring forth. -Comp. **-स्तनी** one whose breasts distil milk (through excess of maternal love); U. 3.

प्रस्नुषा The wife of a grandson.

प्रस्पंदनं Palpitating, vibrating, trembling.

प्रस्फुट *a.* 1 Blown, opened, expanded (as a flower). 2 Divulged, published, spread abroad (as a report). 3 Plain, clear, manifest, evident.

प्रस्फुरित *p. p.* Quivering, trembling, vibrating, tremulous.

प्रस्फोटनं 1 Expanding, blooming, opening. 2 Making clear or manifest, disclosing, revealing. 3 Splitting. 4 Causing to bloom or blow. 5 Threshing corn. 6 A winnowing basket. 7 Striking, beating.

प्रस्रंसिन् *a.* (**-नी** *f.*) Miscarrying.

प्रस्रवः 1 Trickling forth, pushing, flowing or oozing out. 2 A flow, stream. 3 Milk flowing from the breast or udder; प्रस्नवेन (v. 1. for प्रस्नवेन) अभिवर्षती वत्सालोकप्रवर्तिना R. 1. 84. 4 Urine. **-वाः** (pl.) Falling or gushing tears.

प्रस्रवणं 1 Flowing or gushing forth, trickling, oozing, dripping. 2 Flow or discharge of milk form the breast or udder; (वृक्षकान्) घटस्तनप्रस्रवणैर्व्यवर्धयत् Ku. 5. 14. 3 A fall of water, cascade, cataract. 4 A spring, fountain; समाचिता प्रस्रवणैः समंततः Rs. 2. 16; Ms. 8. 248; Y. 1. 159. 5 A spout. 6 A pool formed by the mountain streams. 7 Sweat, perspiration. 8 Voiding urine. **-णः** N. of a mountain; जनस्थानमध्यगो गिरिः प्रस्रवणो नाम U. 1.

प्रस्रावः 1 Flowing, oozing, 2 Urine.

प्रस्रुत *p. p.* Oozed, trickled, dropped, issued.

प्रस्व (स्वा) नः A loud noise.

प्रस्वापः 1 Sleep. 2 A dream. 3 A missile which induces sleep.

प्रस्वापनं 1 Causing or inducing sleep. 2 A missile which induces sleep in the person attacked; R.7.61.

प्रस्विन्न *p. p.* Sweated, perspired.

प्रस्वेदः Excessive perspiration.

प्रस्वेदित *p. p.* 1 Covered with sweat, perspired, sweating. 2 Causing perspiration, hot.

प्रहणनं Killing, slaughter.

प्रहत *p. p.* 1 Wounded, killed, slain. 2 Beaten, struck (as a drum); स स्वयं प्रहतपुष्करः कृती R. 19. 14; Me. 64. 3 Repulsed, overcome, defeated 4 Spread, expanded. 5 Contiguous. 6 Beaten, frequented (as a track). 7 Accomplished, learned.

प्रहरः The eighth part of a whole day, a watch (a period roughly reckoned at 3 hours); प्रहरे प्रहरेऽसहोच्चारितानि गामानयेत्यादिपदानि न प्रमाणं T. S.

प्रहरकः A watch.

प्रहरणं 1 Striking, beating. 2 Casting, throwing. 3 Assailing, attacking. 4 Hurting. 5 Removing, expelling. 6 A weapon, missile; या (उर्वशी) सुकुमारं प्रहरणं महेंद्रस्य V. 1; R. 13. 73; Bg. 1. 9; Mal. 8. 9. 7 War, battle, fight. 8 A covered litter or car.

प्रहरणीयं A missile, weapon.

प्रहरिन् *m.* 1 A watchman. 2 A bellman.

प्रहर्तृ *a.* or *s.* 1 One who strikes or beats, an assailant 2 Fighting, a combatant, fighter. 3 Shooting, a shooter, archer.

प्रहर्षः 1 Extreme joy, exultation, rapture; गुरुः प्रहर्षः प्रबभूव नात्मनि R. 3. 17. 2 Erection of the male organ.

प्रहर्षणं Enrapturing, making extremely glad. **-णः** The planet Mercury.

प्रहर्ष (र्षि) णी 1 Turmeric. 2 N. of a metre; see App. 1.

प्रहर्षुलः The planet Mercury.

प्रहसनं 1 Loud or violent laughter, laughing, mirth. 2 Ridicule, mockery. irony, joke; धिक् प्रहसनं U. 4. 3 Satire, satirical writing. 4 A farce, a kind of low comedy; S. D. thus defines it.—भाणवत्संधिसंध्यंगलास्यांगांकैर्विनिर्मितं । भवेत् प्रहसनं वृत्तं निंद्यानां कविकल्पितं ॥ 533 *et. seq. e. g.* कंदर्पकेलि.

प्रहसंती 1 A kind of Jasmine (यूथिका or वासंती q v.) 2 A large fire-pan.

प्रहसित *p. p.* 1 Laughing. **-तं** Laughter, mirth.

प्रहस्तः 1 The open hand with the fingers extended. 2 N. of a general of Râvaṇa.

प्रहाणं Abandoning, omitting, quitting; Ms. 5. 58.

प्रहाणिः *f.* 1 Abandoning. 2 Deficiency, want.

प्रहारः 1 Striking, beating, hitting; Y. 3. 248. 2 Wounding, killing. 3 A stroke, blow, hit, knock, thump; R. 7. 44; मुष्टिप्रहार, तलप्रहार &c. 4 A cut or thrust, as in खड्गप्रहार. 5 A kick; as in पादप्रहार; लत्ताप्रहार. 6 Shooting. -Comp. **-आर्त** *a.* wounded by a blow. (**-र्तं**) acute pain caused by a wound.

प्रहारणं A desirable gift.

प्रहासः 1 Violent or loud laughter. 2 Ridicule, derision. 3 Irony, satire. 4 A dancer, an actor. 5 N. of *Siva.* 6 Appearance, display; Ve. 2. 28. 7 N. of a place of pilgrimage; cf. प्रभास.

प्रहासिन् *m.* A jester, buffoon.

प्रहिः A well.

प्रहित *p. p.* 1 Placed, put forth. 2 Extended, stretched out. 3 Sent, despatched, directed; विचारमार्गप्रहितेन चेतसा Ku. 5. 42. 4 Discharged, shot (as an arrow). 5 Appointed. 6 Appropriate, suitable.—**तं** A sauce, condiment.

प्रहीण *p. p.* Left, quitted, abandoned. —**णं** Destruction, removal, loss.

प्रहुतः-तं An offering of food to all created beings (भूतयज्ञ), one of the five daily Yajnas to be performed by a householder; cf. Ms. 3. 74.

प्रहृत *p. p.* Beaten, struck, hit, wounded.—**तं** A blow, stroke, hit.

प्रहृष्ट *p. p.* 1 Delighted, pleased, glad, overjoyed, 2 Thrilling, bristling (as hair). -Comp.**-आत्मन्-चित्त, -मनस्** *a.* delighted in soul, rejoiced at heart.

प्रहृष्टकः A crow.

प्रहेलकः 1 A kind of cake or sweetmeat. 2 A riddle; see प्रहेलिका below.

प्रहेला Free or unrestrained behaviour, loose conduct, playful dalliance.

प्रहेलिः *f.*, **प्रहेलिका** A riddle, an enigma, a conundrum. It is thus defined in the विदग्धमुखमंडनः—व्यक्तीकृत्य कमप्यर्थं स्वरूपार्थस्य गोपनात् । यत्र बाह्यांतरावर्थौ कथ्येते सा प्रहेलिका. It is आर्थी or शाब्दी; तरुण्यालिंगितः कंठे नितंबस्थलमाश्रितः । गुरूणां सन्निधानेऽपि कः कूजति मुहुर्मुहुः (where the answer is ईषदूनजलपूर्णकुंभः) is an instance of the former kind; सदारिमध्यापि न वैरियुक्ता नितांतरक्ताप्यसितैव नित्यं । यथोक्तवादिन्यपि नैव दूती का नाम कांतेति निवेदयाशु ॥ (where the answer is सारिका), of the latter. Dandin, however, mentions 16 different kinds of प्रहेलिका; see Kâv. 3. 96-124.

प्रहृष्ट *p. p.* Delighted, joyful, pleased.

प्रह्ला (ह्ला) दः 1 Great joy, pleasure, delight, happiness. 2 Sound, noise 3 N. of a son of the Demon Hiranya-Kasipu [According to the Padma-Purana, he was a Brahmana in his previous existence, and when born as son of Hiranya-Kasipu, he still retained his ardent devotion to Vishnu. His father, of course, did not like that his own son should be such a devout worshipper of his mortal enemies, the gods, and with the object of getting rid of him, he subjected him to a variety of cruelties; but Prahlada, by the favour of Vishnu, was quite unscathed, and began to preach with even greater earnestness than before the doctrine that Vishnu filled all space and was omni-present, omniscient, omni-potent. Hiranya-Kasipu in a fit of exasperation asked him "If Vishnu is omni-present how do I not see him in the pillar of this hall". Whereupon Prahlada struck the pillar with his fist. (according to another account, Hiranya-Kasipu himself angrily kicked the pillar to convince his son of the absurdity of his faith), when Vishnu came out half-man and half-lion, and tore Hiranya-Kasipu to pieces. Prahlada succeeded his father, and reigned wisely and righteously.]

प्रह्ला (ह्ला) दन *a.* Gladdening, delighting; R. 13. 4. —**नं** Causing joy or delight, gladdening, delighting; यथा प्रह्लादनाच्चंद्रः R. 4. 12.

प्रह्व *a* 1 Sloping, slanting, inclined; Si. 12. 56. 2 Stooping, bent down; bowing humbly down; एष प्रह्वोऽस्मि भगवन् एषा विज्ञापना च न; Mv. 1. 47; 6. 37. 3 Submissive, humble, modestly submitting; प्रह्वेष्वनिर्बंधरुषो हि संतः R. 16. 80. 4 Devoted or attached to, engaged in, engrossed by.-COMP. -**अंजलि** *a.* bowing with the palms of the hand joined and put to the forehead as a mark of respect.

प्रह्वयति Den. P. To make humble, subdue; U. 6. 11.

प्रह्वलिका see प्रहेलिका.

प्रह्वायः A call, summons, invitation.

प्रांशु *a.* 1 High, tall, lofty, of lofty or great stature (as a man): शालप्रांशुर्महाभुजः R. 1. 13; 15. 19. 2 Long, extended; S. 2. 15.—**शुः** A tall man, a man of great stature; प्रांशुलभ्ये फले मोहादुद्बाहुरिव वामनः R. 1. 3.

प्राक् *ind.* 1 Before (usually with abl.), सफलानि निमित्तानि प्राक्प्रभातात्ततो मम Bk. 8. 10 6; प्राक् सृष्टेः केवलात्मने Ku. 2. 4; R. 14. 78; S. 5. 21. 2 At first, already; प्रमन्यवः प्रागपि कोशलेंद्रे R. 7. 34. 3 Before, previously, in a previous portion (as of a book): इति प्रागेव निर्दिष्टं; Ms. 1. 71. 4 In the east, to the east of; ग्रामात्प्राक् पर्वतः 5 In front. 6 As far as, up to; प्राक् कडारात्.

प्राकट्यं Manifestation, publicity, notoriety.

प्राकरणिक *a.* (**की** *f.*) Pertaining to the subject of discussion, relevant to the matter in hand (often used in the sense of उपमेय in works on Rhetoric); अप्राकरणिकस्याभिधानेन प्राकरणिकस्याक्षेपोऽप्रस्तुतप्रशंसा K. P. 10.

प्राकर्षिक *a.* (**की** *f.*) Entitled to preference or superiority.

प्राकषिकः 1 A catamite. 2 A man supported by another's wife.

प्राकाम्यं 1 Freedom of will; प्राकाम्यं ते विभूतिषु Ku. 2. 11. 2 Wilfulness. 3 Irresistible will, considered as one of the eight attributes or *Siddhis* of Siva or the Supreme Being; see सिद्धि.

प्राकृत *a.* (**ता-ती** *f.*) 1 Original, natural, unaltered, unmodified, स्यातामभित्रौ मित्रे च सहजप्राकृतावपि Si. 2. 36. (see Malli. thereon). 2 Usual, common, ordinary. 3 Uncultivated, vulgar, unrefined, illiterate; प्राकृत इव परिभूयमानमात्मानं न रुणत्सि K. 146; Bg. 18. 24 3 Insignificant, unimportant, trifling; Mu. 1. 4 Derived from Prakriti; q. v. प्राकृतो लयः reabsorption into Prakriti. 5 Provincial, vernacular (as a dialect); see below. —**तः** A low man, an ordinary or vulgar man.—**तं** A vernacular or provincial dialect derived from and akin to Sanskrit; प्रकृतिः संस्कृतं तत्र भवं तत आगतं च प्राकृतं Hemachandra. (Many of these dialects are spoken by the female characters and inferior personages of Sanskrit plays): तद्भवस्तत्समो देशीत्यनेकः प्राकृतक्रमः Kâv. 1. 33; also 34, 35; त्वमप्यस्मादृशजनयोग्ये प्राकृतमार्गे प्रवृत्तोऽसि Vb. 1. -COMP. -**अरिः** a natural enemy, *i. e.* the ruler of an adjacent country: see Malli. on Si. 2. 36. -**उदासीन**; a natural neutral; *i. e.* a ruler whose dominions lie beyond those of the natural ally. -**ज्वरः** a common or ordinary fever -**प्रलयः** complete dissolution of the universe.-**मित्रं** a natural ally; *i. e.* a ruler whose dominions lie immediately beyond those of the natural enemy (*i. e.* whose country is separated from the country with which he is allied by that of another).

प्राकृतिक *a.* (**की** *f.*) 1 Natural, derived from nature; Mv. 7. 39. 2 Illusory.

प्राक्तन *a.* (**नी** *f.*) 1 Former, previous, antecedent; प्रपेदिरे प्राक्तनजन्मविद्याः Ku. 1. 30. 2 Old, ancient, early. 3 Relating to a former life; or acts in a former life; संस्काराः प्राक्तना इव R. 1 20 Ku. 6. 10.

प्राखर्यं 1 Sharpness. 2 Pungency. 3 Wickedness.

प्रागल्भ्यं 1 Boldness, confidence; निःसाध्वसत्वं प्रागल्भ्यं S. D. 2 Pride, arrogance. 3 Proficiency, skill. 4 Development, greatners, maturity बुद्धिप्रागल्भ्य; तमः प्रागल्भ्य &c. 5 Manifestation, appearance; अवाप्तः प्रागल्भ्यं परिणतरुचः शैलतनये K. P. 10. 'which has appeared' 6 Eloquence; प्रागल्भ्यहीनस्य नरस्य विद्या शस्त्रं यथा कापुरुषस्य हस्ते (where प्र° may mean 'boldness' also); Mâl. 3. 11. 7 Pomp, rank. 8 Impudence.

प्रागारः A house, building.

प्राग्रं The highest point.-COMP. -**सर** *a.* first, foremost. -**हर** *a.* chief, principal; R. 16. 23.

प्राग्राटः Thin coagulated milk.

प्राग्र्य *a.* Chief, foremost, best, most excellent.

प्राघातः War, battle.

प्राघारः Trickling out, dropping, oozing.

प्राघुणः, **प्राघुणकः**, **प्राघुणिकः**, **प्राघूर्णकः**, **प्राघूर्णिकः** A guest, visitor; चिरापराधस्मृतिमांसलोऽपि रोषः क्षणप्राघुणिको बभूव Bv. 2. 66; श्रवणप्राघुणिकी कृता जनैः (कथा) N. 2. 56.

प्रांगं A small kind of drum (पणव)

प्रांगणं (नं) 1 A court, court-yard. 2 A floor (as of the house.). 3 A kind of drum.

प्राच्, **प्रांच्** *a.* (**ची** *f.*) 1 Turned towards the front, in front, foremost. 2 Eastern, easterly. 3 Prior, previous, former.—*m.* (pl.) 1 The people of the east. 2 Eastern grammarians. -COMP. *a.* -**अग्र** *a.* (**प्रागग्र**) having the point turned towards the east -**अभावः** (**प्रागभावः**) antecedent, non-existence, non-existence of a thing previous to its production, as of an effect previous to its production. -**अभिहित** (**प्रागभिहित**) *a.* mentioned before. -**अवस्था** (**प्रागवस्था**) the former state; न तर्हि प्रागवस्थायाः परिहीयसे Mâl. 4. 'you are none the worse for it'. -**आयत** (**प्रागायत**). *a.* extending towards the east. -**उक्ति**.

f. (प्राग्गुक्तिः) previous utterance. -उत्तर (प्रागुत्तर) *a*. north-eastern. -उदीची (प्रागुदीची) *f*. the north-east -कर्मन् (प्राक्कर्मन्) *n*. an action done in a former life. -कालः (प्राक्कालः) a former age. -कालीन (प्राक्कालीन) *a*. belonging to the former times, old, ancient. -कूल (प्राक्कूल) *a*. having the points turned towards the east (said of Kusa grass); Ms. 2. 75. -कृतं (प्राक्कृतं) an act done in a former life. -चरणा (प्राक्चरणा) the female organ of generation. -चिरं (प्राक्चिरं) *ind*. in due or good time, before too late -जन्मन् (प्राग्जन्मन्) *n*., -जातिः (प्राग्जातिः) *f*. a former birth. -ज्योतिषः (प्राग्ज्योतिषः) 1 N. of a country, also called Kâmarúpa. 2 the people of this country (pl.) (-षं) N. of a city.) °ज्येष्ठः an epithet of Vishṇu. -दक्षिण *a*. (प्राग्दक्षिण) south-eastern. -देशः (प्राग्देशः) the eastern country. -द्वार, -द्वारिक *a*. (प्राग्द्वार &c.) having doors facing the east. -न्यायः (प्राङ्न्यायः) the plea of a former trial, *resjudicata*; आचारेणावसन्नोपि पुनर्लेखयते यति। सोभिधेयो जितः पूर्वं प्राङ्न्यायस्तु स उच्यते ॥. -प्रहारः (प्राक्प्रहारः) the first blow. फलः (प्राक्फलः) the bread-fruit tree. -फ (फा) ल्गुनी (प्राक्फल्गुनी) the eleventh lunar mansion, (पूर्वा). °भवः 1 the planet Jupiter. 2 N. of Brihaspati. -फाल्गुनः, -फाल्गुनेयः (प्राक्फाल्गुनः &c.) the planet Jupiter. भक्तं (प्राग्भक्त) taking medicine before meals. -भागः (प्राग्भागः) 1 the front. 2 the fore-part. भारः (प्राग्भारः) 1 the top or summit of a mountain; Mal. 9. 15. 2 the front part, fore part or end (of any thing); क्रंदत्फेरवचंडडात्कृतिभृतप्राग्भारभीमैस्तटैः Mâl. 5. 19. 3 a large quantity, heap, multitude, flood; Bh. 3. 129, Mâl. 5. 29. —भावः (प्राग्भावः) 1 previous existence. 2 excellence, superiority. -मुख (प्राङ्मुख) *a*. turned towards or facing the east; Ku. 7. 13; Ms. 2. 51; 8. 87. 2 inclined towards, wishing, desirous of. -वंशः (प्राग्वंशः) 1 a kind of sacrificial room having its columns turned towards the east; R. 16. 61. (प्राचीनस्थूणो यज्ञशालाविशेषः Malli; but some interpret the word to mean 'a room in which the friends and family of the sacrificer assemble'). 2 a former dynasty or generation. वृत्तं =प्राङ्न्यायः q. v. -वृत्तांतः (प्राग्वृत्तांतः) a former event. शिरस्-स, -शिरस्क (प्राक्शिरस् &c.) *a*. having the head turned towards the east. -संध्या (प्राक्संध्या) the morning twilight. -सवनं (प्राक्सवनं) a morning libation or sacrifice. -स्रोतस् (प्राक्स्रोतस्) *a*. flowing eastward.

प्राचंड्यं 1 Vehemence, passion. 2 Fierceness, horrible look; Mâl. 3. 17.

प्राचिका 1 A mosquito. 2 A female falcon.

प्राची The east; तनयमचिरात् प्राचीवार्कं प्रसूय च पावनं *S*. 4. 18. -COMP. -पति an epithet of Indra. -मूलं the eastern horizon; प्राचीमूले तनुमिव कलामात्रशेषां हिमांशोः Me. 89.

प्राचीन *a*. 1 Turned towards the front or east, eastern, easterly. 2 Previous, former, previously mentioned. 3 Old, ancient. नः -नं A fence, wall. -COMP. -अग्र *a*. =प्रागग्र q. v. -आवीतं the sacred thread (यज्ञोपवीत) worn over the right shoulder and passed under the left arm, as at a *S*râddha). -आवीतिन्, उपवीत *a*. wearing the sacred thread over the right shoulder and under the left arm; Ms. 2. 63. कल्पः a former *Kalpa* q. v. गाथा an ancient story. -तिलकः the moon. -पनसः the Bilva tree. -बर्हिस् *m*. an epithet of Indra. —मतं an ancient opinion.

प्राचीरं An enclosure, fence, wall.

प्राचुर्यं 1 Abundance, copiousness, plenty. 2 Multitude.

प्राचेतसः A patronymic of Manu. 2 Of Daksha. 3 Of Vâlmîki.

प्राच्य *a*. 1 Being or situated in front. 2 Being or living in the east, eastern, easterly. 3 Prior, preceding, previous. 4 Ancient, old. -च्याः (pl.) 1 'The eastern country', the country south or east of the river Sarasvatî. 2 The people of this country. -COMP. भाषा the eastern dialect, language spoken in the east of India.

प्राच्यक *a*. Eastern, easterly.

प्राच्छ् *a*. (Nom. sing. प्राट्-ड्) Asking, inquiring, questioning; as in शब्दप्राट्. -COMP. -विवाकः (प्राड्विवाकः) a judge, the presiding officer in a court of law; Ms. 8. 79, 181; 9. 234.

प्राजकः A charioteer, driver, coachman; Ms. 8. 293.

प्राजनः -नं A whip, goad; त्यक्तप्राजनरश्मिरंकिततनुः पार्थांकितैर्मार्गणैः Ve. 5. 10.

प्राजापत्य *a*. Relating or sacred to Prajâpati.—त्यः 1 One of the eight forms of marriage in Hindu law, in which the father gives his daughter to the bridegroom without receiving any present from him in order that the two may live happily and faithfully together; सहोभौ चरतां धर्ममिति वाचानुभाष्य च। कन्याप्रदानमभ्यर्च्य प्राजापत्यो- विधिः स्मृतः ॥ Ms. 3. 30; or इत्युक्त्वाचरतां धर्मं सह या दीयतेऽर्थिने। स कायः (*i. e*. प्राजापत्यः) पावयेत्तज्जः षट् षड्वंश्यान्सहात्मना Y. 1. 60. 2 N. of the confluence of the Ganges and Yamunâ (प्रयाग). —त्यं 1 A kind of sacrifice performed before appointing a daughter to raise issue to her father failing male heirs. 2 Procreative energy or power. —त्या Giving away the whole of one's property before entering upon the life of an ascetic.

प्राजिकः A hawk.

प्राजितृ, प्राजिन् *m*. A charioteer, driver, coachman: *S*i. 18. 7.

प्राजेशं The constellation Rohiṇî.

प्राज्ञ *a*. (ज्ञा or ज्ञी *f*.). 1 Intellectual. 2 Wise, learned, clever; किमुच्यते प्राज्ञः खलु कुमारः U. 4. —ज्ञः 1 A wise or learned man; तेभ्यः प्राज्ञा न बिभ्यति Ve. 2. 14; Bg. 17. 14. 2 A kind of parrot.—ज्ञा 1 Intelligence, understanding. 2 A clever or intelligent woman.—ज्ञी 1 A clever or learned woman. 2 The wife of a learned man. 3 N. of a wife of the sun (सूर्यपत्नि).

प्राज्य *a*. 1 Abundant, copious, plentiful, much, many; तव भवतु बिडौजाः प्राज्यवृष्टिः प्रजासु *S*. 7. 34; R. 13. 62; *Si*. 14. 25. 2 Great, large, important; प्राज्यविक्रमाः Ku. 2. 18; अपि प्राज्यं राज्यं तृणमिव परित्यज्य सहसा G. L. 5.

प्रांजल *a*. Straightforward, candid, honest, sincere.

प्रांजलि *a*. Folding the hands in supplication, as a mark of respect or humility.

प्रांजलिक, प्रांजलिन् See प्रांजलि.

प्राणः 1 Breath, respiration. 2 The breath of life, vitality, life, vital air, principle of life (usually pl. in this sense, the Prânas being five; प्राण, अपान, समान, व्यान and उदान); प्राणैरुपक्रोशमलीमसैर्वा R. 2. 53; 12. 54. 3 The first of the five life-winds or vital airs (which has its seat in the lungs): Bg. 4. 20. 4 Wind, air inhaled. 5 Energy, vigour, strength, power; as in प्राणसार q. v. 6 The spirit or soul (opp. शरीर). 7 The Supreme Spirit. 8 An organ of sense; Ms. 4. 140. 9 Any person or thing as dear and necessary as life; a beloved person or object; कोशः कोशवतः प्राणाः प्राणाः प्राणा न भूपतेः H. 2. 92; अर्थप्रतेर्धिर्मद्को बहिश्चराः प्राणाः Dk. 10 The life or essence of poetry, poetical talent or genius, inspiration. 11 Aspiration; as in महाप्राण or अल्पप्राण q. v. 12 Digestion. 13 A breath as a measure of time. 14 Gum myrrh. -COMP. -अतिपातः killing a living being, taking away life. -अत्ययः loss of life. -अधिक *a*. 1 dearer than life. 2 superior in strength or vigour. -अधिनाथः a husband. -अधिपः the soul. -अंतः death. -अंतिकः *a*. 1 fatal, mortal. 2 lasting to the end of life, ending with life. 3 capital (as a sentence). (-कं) murder. -अपहारिन् *a*. fatal, destructive to life. -अयनं an organ of sense. -आघातः destruction of life, killing a living being; Bh. 3. 63. -आचार्यः a physician to a king. -आद् a. fatal, mortal, causing death. -आबाधः injury to life. -आयामः restraining or suspending the breath during the mental recitation of the names or attributes of a deity. -ईशः, ईश्वरः a lover, husband; Amaru. 67; Bv. 2. 57. -ईशा, -ईश्वरी a wife, beloved, mistress. -उत्क्रमणं, -उत्सर्गः departure of the soul, death. -उपहारः food. -कृच्छ्रं peril of life, a danger to life. -घातक a. destructive to life. -घ्न a. fatal, life-destroying. -छेदः murder. -त्यागः 1 suicide. 2 death. -दं 1 water. 2 blood. -दक्षिणा gift of life. -दंडः capital punishment. दयितः a husband. -दानं the gift of life, saving one's life. -द्रोहः an attempt upon any body's life. -धारः a living being. -धारणं 1 maintenance or support of life. 2 vitality. -नाथः 1 a lover, husband. 2 an epithet of Yama. -निग्रहः restraint of breath, checking the breath. -पतिः 1 a lover, husband. 2 the soul. -परिक्रयः staking one's life. -परिग्रहः possession of life, life, existence. -प्रद् a. restoring or saving life. -प्रयाणं departure of life, death. -प्रियः 'as dear as life', a a lover, husband. -भक्ष a. feeding on air only. -भास्वत् m. the ocean. -भृत् m. a living being; अंतर्गतं प्राणभृतां हि वेद R. 2. 43. -मोक्षणं 1 departure of life, death. 2 suicide. यात्रा support of life; maintenance, livelihood; पिंडपातमात्रप्राणयात्रां भगवतीं Mâl. 1. -योनिः f. the source of life. रंध्रं 1 the mouth. 2 a nostril. -रोधः 1 suppressing the breath. 2 danger to life, —विनाशः, -विप्लवः loss of life, death. -वियोगः separation of the soul from the body, death. -व्ययः cost or sacrifice of life. -संयमः suspension of breath. -संशयः,-संकटं, संदेहः risk or danger to life, peril of life, a very great peril. -सद्मन् n. the body. -सार a. 'having life as the essence', full of strength and vigour, muscular; गिरिचर इव नागः प्राणसारं (गात्रं) बिभर्ति S. 2. 4. —हर a. 1 causing death, taking away life, fatal; पुरो मम प्राणहरो भविष्यसि Gît. 7. 2 capital. -हारक a. fatal. (-कं) a kind of deadly poison.

प्राणकः 1 A living being, an animal or sentient being. 2 Myrrh.

प्राणथः 1 Air, wind. 2 A sacred bathing place. 3 The lord of created beings.

प्राणनः The throat. —नं 1 Respiration, breathing. 2 Life, living.

प्राणंतः Air, wind.

प्राणंती 1 Hunger. 2 Sobbing. 3 Hic-cough (हिक्का).

प्राणाय्य a. (य्यी f.) Proper, fit, suited.

प्राणित a. Kept alive; animated.

प्राणिन् a. Breathing, living, alive. —m. 1 A living or sentient being, a living creature; यया प्राणिनः प्राणवंत: S. 1. 1; Me. 5. 2 A man. -COMP. -अंगं a limb of an animal. -जातं a whole class of animals -द्यूतं gambling with fighting animals. (cock-fighting, ram-fighting &c). -पीडा cruelty to to animals -हिंसा injury to life, doing harm to living creatures.-हिता a shoe, boot.

प्राणीत्यं Debt.

प्रातर् ind. 1 At day-break, at dawn, early in the morning. 2 Early on the morrow, the next or to-morrow morning. -COMP. -अह्नः the early part of the day, forenoon -आशः morning meal, breakfast; अन्यथा प्रातराशाय कुर्याम त्वामलं वयं Bk. 8. 98. -आशिन् m. one who has breakfasted or taken his morning meal. -कर्मन् n. -कार्यं, -कृत्यं (प्रातःकर्म &c.) a morning ceremony. -कालः (प्रातःकालः) morning time. -गेयः a bard whose duty it is to wake the king or any great personage in the morning with appropriate songs. -त्रिवर्गा (प्रातस्त्रिवर्गा) the river Ganges. -दिनं forenoon. -प्रहरः the first watch of the day. -भोक्तृ m. a crow. -भोजनं morning meal, breakfast. -संध्या (प्रातःसंध्या) 1 the morning twilight. 2 the morning devotions or Sandhyâ adoration of a Brâhmaṇa. -समयः (प्रातःसमयः) morning-time, day-break. -सवः,-सवनं (प्रातःसवः &c.) the morning libation of *Soma*. -स्नानं (प्रातःस्नानं) morning ablution -होमः (प्रातर्होमः) morning sacrifice.

प्रातस्तन a. (नी f.) Relating to the morning, matutinal.

प्रातस्तरां ind. Very early in the morning; प्रातस्तरां पतत्रिभ्यः प्रबुद्धः प्रणमन् रविं Bk. 4. 14.

प्रातस्त्य a. Matutinal.

प्रातिः f. 1 The span of the thumb and the forefinger. 2 Filling.

प्रातिका The China rose (जवा).

प्रातिकूलिक a. (की f.) Opposed, opposing, contrary.

प्रातिकूल्यं Adverseness, opposition, hostility, unfavourableness, unfriendliness.

प्रातिजनीन (नी f.) Suitable against an adversary.

प्रातिज्ञं The subject under discussion.

प्रातिदैवसिक a. (की f.) Occurring daily.

प्रातिपक्ष a. (क्षी f.) 1 Contrary, adverse. 2 Hostile, inimical.

प्रातिपक्ष्यं Enmity, hostility.

प्रातिपद a. (दी f.) 1 Forming the commencement. 2 Produced in, or belonging to, the day called प्रतिपद् q.v.

प्रातिपदिकः Fire. -कं The crude form of a substantive, a noun in its uninflected state (before receiving the case-terminations); अर्थवदधातुरप्रत्ययः प्रातिपदिकं P. 1. 2. 45.

प्रातिपौरुषिक a. (की f.) Relating to manliness or valour.

प्रातिभ a. (भी f.) Relating to divination or genius. -भं Genius or vivid imagination.

प्रातिभाव्यं Becoming bail or security, suretiship, becoming answerable for the appearance of a debtor, for his being trustworthy, and for paying his debt.

प्रातिभासिक a. (की f.) 1 Existing only in appearance, not real. 2 Looking like.

प्रातिलोमिक a. (की f.) Against the gain, adverse, hostile, disagreeable.

प्रातिलोम्यं 1 Inversion, inverted or reverse order; Ms. 10. 13. 2 Hostility, opposition, hostile feeling.

प्रातिवेशिकः, प्रातिवेश्मकः, प्रातिवेश्यकः A neighbour.

प्रातिवेश्यः 1 A neighbour (in general). 2 A next-door neighbour; (निरंतरगृहवासी Kull.).

प्रातिशाख्यं A grammatical treatise laying down rules for the phonetic changes which words in any *Sâkhâ* of the Vedas undergo, and teaching the mode of pronouncing the accents &c. (There exist 4 Prâtisâkhyas, one for the *Sâkala* branch of *Rigveda*, one for each of the two branches of the Yajurveda, and one for the Atharvaveda).

प्रातिस्विक a. (की f.) Peculiar, not common to others, one's own.

प्रातिहंत्रं Vengeance, revenge.

प्रातिहारः, प्रातिहारकः, प्रातिहारिकः A juggler, conjurer.

प्रातीतिक a. (की f.) Mental, existing in the mind or imagination.

प्रातीपः A patronymic of Santanu.

प्रातीपिक a. (की f.) Reverse, contrary, retrograde.

प्रात्यंतिकः A prince of the Pratyantas; q. v.

प्रात्ययिक a. (की f.) 1 Confidential, trusty. 2 Standing bail for the trustworthiness of a debtor (as a प्रतिभू or surety).

प्रात्यहिक a. (की f.) Occurring every day, daily.

प्राथमिक a. (की f.) 1 Primary, first, initial. 2 Former, previous. 3 Happening for the first time.

प्राथम्यं Being first, precedence, priority.

प्रादक्षिण्यं Going round a person or object from left to right keeping the right-side towards the object circumambulated.

प्रादुस् *ind.* Visibly, evidently, manifestly, in sight (used chiefly with भू, कृ and अस्); प्रादुःष्यात्क इव जितः पुरः परेण *Si.* 8. 12; see under कृ; भू and अस् also). –COMP. **–करणं (प्रादुष्करणं)** manifestation, making visible. **–भावः (प्रादुर्भावः)** 1 coming into existence, arising; वपुःप्रादुर्भावात् K. P. 10. 2 becoming visible or manifest, manifestation, appearance. 3 Becoming audible. 4 the appearance of a deity on earth.

प्रादुष्यं Manifestation.

प्रादेशः 1 The span of the thumb and forefinger. 2 A spot, place, region.

प्रादेशनं A gift, donation.

प्रादेशिक *a.* (की *f.*) 1 Having precedents, precedented. 2 Limited, local. 3 Significant.– **कः** The owner of a district.

प्रादेशिनी The forefinger.

प्रादोष *a.* (षी *f.*), **प्रादोषिक** *a.* (की *f.*), Relating to the evening.

प्राधनिकं A destructive weapon, any war-implement.

प्राधानिक *a.* (की *f.*) 1 Most eminent or excellent, pre-eminent, supreme, most distinguished. 2 Relating to or derived from Pradhâna, q v.

प्राधान्यं 1 Pre-eminence, superiority, predominance, prominence. 2 Ascendancy, supremacy. 3 A chief or principal cause. (**प्राधान्येन, प्राधान्यात्, प्राधान्यतः** 'chiefly', 'especially', Principally'; Bg. 10. 19).

प्राधीत *a.* Well-read, highly educated (as a Brâhmaṇa).

प्राध्व *a.* Distant, remote, long. 2 Bent, inclined. 3 Fastened, bound (बद्ध). 4 Favourable. **–ध्वः** A carriage. **–ध्वं** *ind.* 1 Favourably, agreeably or conformably, suitably; सभाजने मे भुजमूर्ध्वबाहुः सव्येतरं प्राध्वमितः प्रयुंक्ते R. 13. 43. 2 Crookedly.

प्रांतः 1 Edge, margin, border, skirt, verge; प्रांतसंस्तीर्णदर्भाः S. 4. 7. 2 Corner (as of the lips, eyes &c.); Mâl. 4. 2; ओष्ठ°, नयन°. 3 Boundary, extremity. 4 Extreme verge, end; यौवनप्रांत Pt. 4. 5 A point, tip. –COMP. **–ग** *a.* living close by. **–दुर्गं** a suburb outside the walls of a town, a town near a fort. **–विरस** *a.* tasteless in the end. **–शून्य** *a.* see प्रांतरशून्य. **–स्थ** *a.* one who inhabits the borders.

प्रांतरं 1 A long, lonesome or solitary path, desolate road. 2 A road without shade, dreary tract of land. 3 A forest, wilderness. 4 The hollow of a tree. –COMP. **–शून्यः** a long dreary road (without trees, shade &c.).

प्रापक *a.* (पिका *f.*) 1 Leading to, Conveying. 2 Procuring, providing with. 3 Establishing, making valid.

प्रापणं 1 Reaching, extending to. 2 Obtaining, acquisition, attainment. 3 Bringing to, conveying, leading to. 4 Procuring.

प्रापणिकः A merchant, trader; आस्थादिव प्रापणिकादजस्रं *Si.* 4. 11.

प्राप्त *p. p.* 1 Got, obtained, won, acquired. 2 Reached, attained to. 3 Met with, found. 4 Incurred, suffered, endured. 5 Arrived, come, present. 6 Completed. 7 proper, right. 8 Following from a rule (see आप् with प्र). –COMP. **–अनुज्ञ** *a.* one who has got permission to go, allowed to depart. **–अर्थ** *a.* successful. (**–र्थः**) an object gained. **–अवसर** *a.* finding occasion or opportunity **–उदय** *a.* one who has attained rise or exaltation. **–कारिन्** *a.* doing what is right. **–काल** *a.* 1 opportune, seasonable, suitable; see अप्राप्तकाल. 2 marriageable. 3 fated, destined. (**–लः**) a fit time, suitable or favourable moment. **–पंचत्व** *a.* resolved into the five elements, *i. e.* dead; cf. पंचत्व. **–प्रसव** *a.* delivered of child. **–बुद्धि** *a.* instructed, enlightened. **–भारः** a beast of burden. **–मनोरथ** *a.* one who has obtained his desired object. **–यौवन** *a.* being in the bloom of youth, arrived at the age of puberty, youthful. **–रूप** *a.* 1 handsome, beautiful. 2 wise, learned. 3 fit, proper, worthy. **–व्यवहार** *a* come of age, being able and legally authorised to manage his own affairs (opp. 'minor'). **–श्री** *a.* one who owes his rise (to another); Ku. 2. 55.

प्राप्तिः *f.* 1 Obtaining, acquisition, gain, attainment, profit; °द्रव्य, यशः°, सुख° &c. 2 Reaching or attaining to. 3 Arrival, coming to. 4 Finding, meeting with 5 Range, reach. 6 A guess, conjecture. 7 Lot, share, portion. 8 Fortune, luck. 9 Rise, production. 10 The power of obtaining, anything (one of the eight Siddhis q. v.). 11 Union, collection (संहति). 12 The successful termination of a plot (सुखागम). –COMP. **आशा** the hope of obtaining anything (regarded as part of the development of the plot of a play); उपायापायशंकाभ्यां प्राप्त्याशा प्राप्तिसंभवा S. D. 6.

प्राबल्यं 1 Ascendancy, superiority, predominance. 2 Power, force, might.

प्राबा (वा) लिकः A dealer in coral.

प्राबोध (धि) कः 1 Dawn, daybreak. 2 A minstrel whose duty it is to wake the king in the morning by singing appropriate songs.

प्राभंजनं The lunar mansion Svâti.

प्राभंजनिः 1 An epithet of Hanumat. 2 Of Bhima.

प्राभवं Superiority, supremacy, predominance.

प्राभवत्यं Supremacy, authority, power; Ms. 8. 412.

प्राभाकरः 'A follower of Prabhâkar', a follower of that school of Mimâṃsâ philosophy which is known as प्राभाकर.

प्राभातिक (की *f.*) Relating to the morning, matutinal.

प्राभृतं, प्राभृतकं 1 A present, gift. 2 An offering to a deity or to a king (Nazerâ*n*â). 2 A bribe.

प्रामाणिक *a.* (की *f.*) 1 Established by proof, founded or resting on authority. 2 Founded on the authority of scriptures (शास्त्रसिद्ध). 3 Authentic, credible. 4 Relating to a प्रमाण q. v. **—कः** 1 One who accepts proof. 2 One who is conversant with the Pramâṇas of the Naiyâyikas, a logician. 3 The head of a trade.

प्रामाण्यं 1 Being a proof or resting on authority. 2 Credibility, authenticity. 3 Proof, evidence, authority.

प्रामादिक *a.* Due to carelessness or error, wrong, faulty, incorrect; इति प्रामादिकः प्रयोगः or पाठः &c.

प्रामाद्यं 1 Error, fault, blunder, mistake. 2 Madness, frenzy. 3 Intoxication.

प्रायः 1 Going away, departure, departure from life. 2 Seeking death by fasting, fasting, sitting down and abstaining from food with some object in view (generally with words like आस् उपविश् &c.); see प्रायोपवेशन below. 3 The largest portion, majority, plurality, majority of cases. 4 Excess, abundance, plenty. 5 A condition of life. *N. B.* At the end of comp. **प्राय** may be translated by (*a*) for the most part, generally, mostly, almost, nearly; पतनप्रायो about to fall; मृतप्रायः almost dead, a little less than dead, nearly dead; or (*b*) abounding or rich in, full of, excessive, abundant: कष्टप्रायं शरीरं U. 1; शालीप्रायो देशः Pt. 3: कमलमोदप्राया वनानिलाः U. 3. 24 'full of the fragrance' &c. or (*c*) like, resembling; वर्षशतप्रायं दिनं, अमृतप्रायं वचनं &c. –COMP. **–उपगमनं, –उपवेशः, –उपवेशनं, –उपवेशनिका** sitting down and abstaining from food and thus preparing oneself for death, fasting oneself to death; मया प्रायोपवेशनं कृतं विद्धि Pt. 4; प्रायोपवेशनमतिर्नृपतिर्बभूव R. 8. 94; प्रायोपवेशसदृशं व्रतमास्थितस्य Ve. 3. 19. **–उपेत** *a.* abstaining from food and thus awaiting the approach of death. **–उपविष्ट** *a.* fasting oneself to death. **–दर्शनं** an ordinary phenomenon.

प्रायणं 1 Entrance, beginning, commencement. 2 The path of life. 3 Voluntary death; Ms. 9. 323. 4 Taking refuge.

प्रायणीय *a.* Introductory, initial, initiatory. —यं The first day of a Soma sacrifice.

प्रायशस् *ind.* Generally, mostly, for the most part, in all probability; आशाबंधः कुसुमसदृशं प्रायशो ह्यंगनानां सद्यःपाति प्रणयि हृदयं विप्रयोगे रुणद्धि Me. 10.

प्रायश्चित्तं, प्रायश्चित्तिः *f.* 1 Atonement, expiation, indemnification, a religious act to atone for sin; मातुः पापस्य भरतः प्रायश्चित्तमिवाकरोत् R. 12. 19. (प्रायो नाम तपः प्रोक्तं चित्तं निश्चय उच्यते । तपोनिश्चयसंयोगात् प्रायश्चित्तमितीर्यते ॥ Hemâdri) 2 Satisfaction, amends (in general).

प्रायश्चित्तिन् *a.* One who makes an atonement.

प्रायस् *ind.* 1 Mostly, generally, as a general rule, for the most part; प्रायः प्रत्ययमाधत्ते स्वगुणेषूत्तमादरः Ku. 6. 20; प्रायो भृत्यास्त्यजंति प्रचलितविभवं स्वामिनं सेवमानाः Mu. 4. 21; or प्रायो गच्छति यत्र भार रहितस्तत्रैव यांत्यापदः Bh. 2. 93. 2. 2 In all probability, most likely, probably, perhaps: तव प्राज्ञ प्रसादाद्धि प्रायः प्राप्स्यामि जीवितं Mb.

प्रायाणिक, प्रायात्रिक *a.* (की *f.*) Necessary or suitable for a journey.

प्रायिक *a.* (की *f.*) Usual, common.

प्रायुद्धेषिन् *m.* A horse.

प्रायेण *ind.* 1 Mostly, as a general rule; प्रायेणैते रमणविरहेष्वंगनानां विनोदाः Me. 87; प्रायेण सत्यपि हितार्थकरे विधौ हि श्रेयांसि लब्धुमसुखानि विनांतरायैः Ki. 5. 49; Ku. 3. 28; Rs. 6. 23.

प्रायोगिक *a.* (की *f.*) 1 Applied. 2 Applicable.

प्रारब्ध *p. p.* Begun, commenced. –ब्धं 1 What is begun, an undertaking. 2 Fate, destiny.

प्रारब्धिः *f.* 1 Beginning, commencement. 2 A post to which an elephant is fastened; or a rope for fastening him.

प्रारंभः 1 Beginning, commencement; प्रारंभेपि त्रियामा तरुणयति निजं नीलिमानं वनेषु Mâl. 5. 6; R. 10. 9; 18. 49. 2 An undertaking, deed, enterprise; आगमैः सदृशारंभः प्रारंभसदृशोदयः R. 1. 15; फलानुमेयाः प्रारंभाः संस्काराः प्राक्तना इव 20.

प्रारंभणं Commencing, beginning.

प्रारोहः A shoot, sprout, new leaf; see प्ररोह.

प्रार्णं A chief debt.

प्रार्थक *a.* (र्थिका *f.*) Asking, begging, requesting, soliciting, entreating, desiring, wishing &c. —कः A suitor, petitioner.

प्रार्थनं-ना 1 A request, entreaty, prayer, solicitation; ये वर्धंते धनपतिपुरः प्रार्थनादुःखभाजः Bh. 3. 47. 2 A wish, desire; लब्धावकाशा मे प्रार्थना or न दुरवापेयं खलु प्रार्थना *S.* 1, उत्सर्पिणी खलु महतां प्रार्थना *S.* 7; 7. 2. 3 A suit, petition, supplication, a love-suit; कदाचिदस्मत्प्रार्थनामंतः पुरेभ्यः कथयेत् *S.* 2. –COMP. –भंगः refusal of a request. –सिद्धिः *f.* fulfilment of a desire; प्रार्थनासिद्धिशंसिनः R. 1. 42.

प्रार्थनीय *pot. p.* 1 To be prayed for or solicited. 2 To be wished or desired. —यं The third or Dvâpara age.

प्रार्थित *p. p.* 1 Begged, requested, asked for, solicited. 2 Wished, desired. 3 Attacked, opposed by an enemy; R. 9. 56. 4 Killed, hurt; (see अर्थ् with प्र.).

प्रार्थिन् *a.* 1 Begging, requesting. 2 Wishing, desiring: मंदः कवियशःप्रार्थी गमिष्याम्युपहास्यतां R. 1. 3.

प्रालंब *a.* 1 Pendent, hanging down प्रालंबद्विगुणितचामरप्रहासः Ve. 2. 20. —बः 1 A kind of pearl-ornament. 2 A female breast.—बं A garland worn round the neck and reaching to the breast; प्रालंबमुत्कृष्य यथावकाशं निनाय साचीकृतचारुवक्त्रः R. 6. 14; मुक्ताप्रालंबेषु K. 52.

प्रालंबकं See प्रालंब.

प्रालंबिका A king of golden necklace.

प्रालेयं Snow, frost, hoar frost, dew, ईशाचलप्रालेयप्लवनेच्छया Gît. 1; प्रालेयशीतमचलेश्वरमीश्वरोऽपि (अधिशेते) *Si.* 4. 64; Me 39. –COMP. –अद्रिः, –शैलः 'the snowy mountain', the Himâlaya; Me. 57. –अंशुः, करः, –रश्मिः 1 the moon. 2 comphor. –लेशः a hail-stone.

प्रावट: Barley.

प्रावणं A spade, hoe, shovel.

प्रावरः 1 A fence, an enclosure. 2 An upper garment (according to Hemachandra). 3 N. of a country.

प्रावरणं A garment, covering: especially, an upper garment, cloak, mantle.

प्रावरणीयं An upper garment.

प्रावारः 1 An upper garment, a cloak, mantle. 2 N. of a district. COMP. –कीटः a kind of white ant or moth.

प्रावारकः An upper garment, mantle; यदीच्छसि लंबदशाविशालं प्रावारकं सूत्रशतैर्हि Mk. 8. 22; जातीकुसुमवासितः प्रावारकोऽनुप्रेषितः Mk. 1.

प्रावारिकः A maker of upper garments.

प्रावास *a.* (सी *f.*) Relating to a journey, to be done or given in a journey.

प्रावासिक (की *f.*) Suitable or fit for a journey.

प्रावीण्यं Cleverness, skilfulness, proficiency, dexterity; आविष्कृतं कथाप्रावीण्यं वत्सेन U. 4; R. 15. 68.

प्रावृत *p. p.* Enclosed, surrounded, covered, screened. –तः, तं A veil, mantle, wrapper (*f.* also).

प्रावृतिः *f.* 1 An enclosure, a hedge, fence. 2 Spiritual darkness.

प्रावृत्तिक *a.* (की *f.*) Secondary –कः A messenger.

प्रावृष् *f.* The rainy season, monsoon, rains, (the months आषाढ and श्रावण); कलापिनां प्रावृषि पश्य नृत्यं R. 6. 51; 19. 37; प्रावृट् प्रावृडिति ब्रवीति शठधीः क्षारं क्षते प्रक्षिपन् Mk. 5. 18; Me. 115. –COMP. –अत्ययः (प्रावृडत्ययः) end of the rainy season. –कालः (प्रावृट्कालः) the rainy season.

प्रावृषः -षा The rainy season, monsoons.

प्रावृषिक *a.* (की *f.*) Produced in the rainy season. –कः A peacock.

प्रावृषिज *a.* Produced in the rainy season.

प्रावृषेण्य *a.* 1 Produced in, relating to the rainy season; सा किं शक्या जनयितुमिह प्रावृषेण्येन...वारिदेन Bv. 1. 30; 4. 6; R. 1. 36. 2 To be paid in the rainy season (as a debt &c.) –ण्यः 1 The Kadamba tree. 2 The Kutaja tree. –ण्यं Numerousness, abundance, plenty.

प्रावृष्यः 1 A kind of Kadamba tree. 2 The Kutaja tree. –ष्यं Lapis lazuli.

प्रावेण्यं A fine woollen covering.

प्रावेशन *a.* (ना *f.*) To be given or done on entering. –नं A worship.

प्रावेशिक *a.* (की *f.*) Relating to or connected with entrance (into a house or upon the stage).

प्राव्रज्यं, प्राव्राज्यं The life of a religious mendicant or recluse.

प्राशः 1 Eating, tasting, living or feeding on; Ms. 11. 143; धूम° &c. 2 Food.

प्राशनं 1 Eating, feeding upon, tasting. 2 Causing to eat, or taste; Ms. 2. 29. 3 Food.

प्राशनीयं Food.

प्राशस्त्यं Excellence, praiseworthiness, pre-eminence.

प्राशित *p. p.* Eaten, tasted, consumed. —तं An offering of rice and water to the Manes of deceased ancestors, daily obsequies to the Manes; प्राशितं पितृतर्पणं Ms. 3. 74.

प्राश्निकः 1 An examiner. 2 An umpire, an arbitrator, a judge; अहो प्रयोगाभ्यंतरः प्राश्निकः M. 2; तद्भगवत्या प्राश्निकपदमध्यासितव्यं M. 1.

प्रासः 1 Throwing, casting, discharging. 2 A dart, a barbed missile; Ms. 6. 32; Ki. 16. 4.

प्रासकः 1 A dart, barbed missile. 2 A die.

प्रासंगः A yoke for cattle.

प्रासंगिक *a.* (की *f*) 1 Derived from close connection. 2 Connected with, innate. 3 Incidental, casual, occasional; प्रासंगिकीनां विषयः कथानां U. 2. 6. 4 Relevant. 5 Seasonable, opportune. 6 Episodical.

प्रासंग्यः A draught-ox.

प्रासादः 1 A palace, mansion, any large palatial building; भिक्षुः कुटीयाति

प्रासादे Sk.; Me. 64. **2** A royal mansion. **3** A temple, shrine. -COMP. -अंगनं the court-yard of a palace or temple. -आरोहणं entering or going up into a palace. -कुक्कुटः a tame pigeon. तलं the surface or flat roof of a palace. -पृष्ठः a balcony on the top of a palace. -प्रतिष्ठा the consecration of a temple. -शायिन् *a.* sleeping in a palace. -शृंगं the spire or pinnacle of a palace or temple, a turret.

प्रासिकः A lancer, spearman.

प्रासूतिक *a* (की *f.*) Relating to delivery or child birth.

प्रास्त *p. p.* **1** Thrown, darted, hurled, cast, discharged. **2** Expelled, turned out.

प्रास्ताविक *a.* (की *f.*) **1** Serving as an introduction, introductory, prefactory; as in प्रास्ताविकविलास (the first or introductory part of Bhâminîvilâsa); प्रास्ताविकं वचनं prefatory remarks. **2** Seasonable, opportune, timely. **3** Pertinent, relevant (to the matter in hand); अप्रास्ताविकी महत्येषा कथा Mâl. 2.

प्रास्तुत्यं Being under discussion.

प्रास्थानिक *a.* (की *f.*) **1** Relating to or proper at the time of departure; R. 2. 70. **2** Favourable to a departure.

प्रास्थिक *a.* (की *f.*) **1** Weighing a *Prastha* q. v. **2** Bought for a *Prastha*. **3** Containing a *Prastha*. **4** Sown with a *Prastha*.

प्रास्रवण *a.* (णी *f.*) Derived from a spring.

प्राहः Instruction in the art of dancing.

प्राह्णः The forenoon.

प्राह्णेतन *a.* (नी *f.*) Relating to, or happening in, the forenoon.

प्राह्णेतरां -मां *ind.* Very early in the morning.

प्रिय *a.* (compar. प्रेयस्, superl. प्रेष्ठ) **1** Dear, beloved, liked, welcome, favourite; बंधुप्रियां Ku. 1. 26; R. 3. 29. **2** Pleasing, agreeable; तामूचतुस्ते प्रियमप्यमिथ्या R. 14. 6. **3** Fond of, devoted or attached to; प्रियमंडना *S.* 4. 9; प्रियारामा वैदेही U. 2. -यः **1** A lover, husband; स्त्रीणामाद्यं प्रणयवचनं विभ्रमो हि प्रियेषु Me. 28. **2** A kind of deer. -या **1** A beloved (wife), wife, mistress; प्रिये चारुशीले प्रिये रम्यशीले प्रिये Gît. 10. **2** A woman in general. **3** Small cardamoms. **4** News, information. **5** Spirituous liquor. **6** A kind of Jasmine. -यं **1** Love. **2** Kindness, service, favour; प्रियमाचरितं लते त्वया मे V. 1. 17; मत्प्रियार्थं यियासोः Me. 22; प्रियं मे प्रियं मे 'a good service done to me'; Bg. 1. 23; Pt. 1. 365, 193. **3** Pleasing or gladsome news; R. 12. 91; प्रियनिवेदयितारं *S.* 4. **4** Pleasure. -यं *ind.* In a pleasing or agreeable manner. -COMP. -अतिथि *a* hospitable. -अपायः absence or loss of a beloved object. -अप्रिय *a.* pleasant and unpleasant, agreeable and disagreeable (feelings &c.) (-यं) service and disservice, favour and injury. -अंबुः the mango tree. -अर्ह *a.* **1** deserving love or kindness; U. 3 **2** amiable. (-र्हः) N. of Vishṇu. -असु. *a.* fond of life. -आख्य *a.* announcing good news. -आख्यानं agreeable news. -आत्मन् *a.* amiable, pleasant, agreeable. -उक्तिः *f.*, -उदितं a kind or friendly speech, flattering remarks. -उपपत्तिः *f.* a happy or pleasant occurrence. -उपभोगः enjoyment of a lover or mistress; R. 12. 22. -एषिन् *a.* **1** desirous of pleasing or doing service. **2** friendly, affectionate. -कर *a.* giving or causing pleasure. -कर्मन् *a.* acting in a kind or friendly manner. -कलत्रः a husband who is fond of his wife, who loves her dearly. -काम *a.* friendly disposed, desirous of rendering service. -कार, -कारिन् *a.* acting kindly, doing good to. -कृत् *m.* one who does good, a friend, benefactor. -जनः a beloved or dear person. -जानिः a husband who dearly loves his wife. -तोषणः a kind of coitus or mode of sexual enjoyment. -दर्श *a.* pleasant to look at. -दर्शन *a.* pleasing to look at, of pleasing appearance, good-looking, lovely, handsome; अहो प्रियदर्शनः कुमारः U. 5; R. 1. 47; *S.* 3. 11. (-नः) **1** a parrot. **2** a kind of date tree. **3** N. of a prince of the Gandharvas; R. 5. 53 -दर्शिन् *a.* an epithet of king Asoka. -देवन *a.* fond of gambling. -धन्वः an epithet of *S*iva. -पुत्रः a kind of bird. -प्रसादनं propitiation of a husband -प्राय *a.* exceedingly kind or courteous; U. 2. 2. (-यं) eloquence in language. -प्रायस् *n.* a very agreeable speech, as of a lover to his mistress. -प्रेप्सु *a.* wishing to secure one's desired object. -भावः feeling of love; U. 6. 31. -भाषणं kind or agreeable words. -भाषिन् *a.* speaking sweet words. -मंडन *a.* fond of ornaments; *S.* 4. 9. -मधु *a.* fond of liquor. (-धुः) an epithet of Balarâma. -रण *a.* warlike, heroic. -वचन *a.* speaking kind or agreeable words. (-नं) kind, coaxing or endearing words; V. 2. 12. -वयस्यः a dear friend. -वर्णी the plant called प्रियंगु. -वस्तु *n.* a beloved object. -वाच् *a.* speaking kindly; affable in address. (-*f.*) kind or agreeable words. -वादिका a kind of musical instrument. -वादिन् *a.* speaking kind or pleasing words, a flatterer; सुलभाः पुरुषा राजन् सततं प्रियवादिनः Râm. -श्रवस् *m.* an epithet of Krishna. -संवासः the society of a beloved person. -सखः a dear friend. (-खी *f.*) a female friend, a lady's confidante. -सत्य *a.* **1** a lover of truth. **2** pleasant though true. संदेशः **1** a friendly message, the message of a lover. **2** the tree called चंपक. -समागमः union with a beloved object or person -सहचरी a beloved wife. -सुहृद् *m.* a dear or bosom friend. -स्वप्न *a.* fond of sleep; R. 12. 81.

प्रियंवद *a.* Sweet-speaking, speaking kindly, affable in address, agreeable; Ku. 5. 28; R. 3. 64. -दः A kind of bird **2** N. of a Gandharva.

प्रियकः **1** A kind of deer; *S*i. 4. 32. **2** The tree called नीप. **3** The creeper प्रियंगु. **4** A bee. **5** A kind of bird. **6** Saffron. -कं A flower of the *asana* tree; *S*i. 8. 28.

प्रियकर, प्रियंकरण, प्रियंकार *a.* **1** Showing kindness to, acting kindly or affectionately; प्रियंकरो मे प्रिय इत्यनंदत् R. 14. 48. **2** Agreeable. **3** Amiable.

प्रियंगुः **1** N. of a creeper (said to put forth blossoms at the touch of women); प्रियंगुश्यामांगप्रकृतिरपि Mâl. 3 9. (The following verse puts together all the conventions of poets about trees puting forth flowers under particular circumstances; पादाघातादशोकस्तिलककुरबकौ वीक्षणालिंगनाभ्यां स्त्रीणां स्पर्शात् प्रियंगुर्विकसति बकुलः सीधुगंडूषसेकात्। मंदारो नर्मवाक्यात् पटुमृदुहसनाच्चंपको वक्त्रवातात् चूतो गीतान्नमेरुर्विकसति च पुरो नर्तनात् कर्णिकारः ॥). **2** Long pepper. -गु *n* Saffron.

प्रियतम *a.* Most beloved, dearest. -मः A lover, husband; शिवाप्रातः प्रियतम इव प्रार्थनाचाटुकारः Me. 31, 70. -मा A wife, mistress, beloved.

प्रियतर *a.* Dearer, more beloved &c.

प्रियता, -त्वं **1** Being dear, dearness. **2** Love, affection.

प्रियंभविष्णु, प्रियंभावुक *a.* Become an object of affection, dearly loved.

प्रियालः The tree called Piyâl; see पियाल. -ला A vine.

प्री I 9 U. (प्रीणाति, प्रीणीते, प्रीत) **1** To please, delight, satisfy, gladden; प्रीणाति यः सुचरितैः पितरं स पुत्रः Bh. 2. 68; सस्नुः पितॄन् प्रियरापगासु Bk. 3. 38; 5. 104 7. 64. **2** To be pleased, take delight in कच्चित् मनस्ते प्रीणाति वनवासे Mb. **3** To act kindly towards, show kindness towards. **4** To be cheerful or gay. -*Caus.* (प्रीणयति-ते) To please, satisfy &c. -II. 4. A. (प्रीयते, strictly a passive voice of the root प्री). **1** To be satisfied or pleased, be gratified; प्रकाममप्रीयतयज्वनां प्रियः *S*i. 1. 17; R.15. 30; 19. 30; Y. 1. 245. **2** To feel affection for, love. **3** To assent, be satisfied.

प्रीण *a.* **1** Pleased, satisfied, gratified. **2** Old, ancient. **3** Previous.

प्रीणनं 1 Pleasing, satisfying. 2 That which pleases or satisfies.

प्रीत *p. p.* 1 Pleased, delighted, rejoiced, gladdened; प्रीतास्मि ते पुत्र वरं वृणीष्व R. 2. 63; 1. 81, 12. 94. 2 Glad, happy, joyful; Me. 4. 3 Content. 4 Dear, beloved. 5 Kind, affectionate –COMP. –आत्मन्, –चित्, –मनस् *a.* delighted at heart.

प्रीतिः *f.* 1 Pleasure, happiness, satisfaction, delight, gladness, joy, gratification; भुवनालोकनप्रीतिः Ku. 2. 45, 6. 21; R. 2. 21; Me 62. 2 Favour, kindness. 3 Love, affection, regard; Me. 4, 16; R. 1. 57; 12. 54. 4 Liking or fondness for, delight in, addiction to; द्यूत°, मृगया°. 5 Friendliness, amity. 6 N. of a wife of Cupid and rival of Ratî. (सपत्नी संजाता रत्याः प्रीतिरिति श्रुता). –COMP. –कर *a.* producing love, kind, agreeable.–कर्मन् *n.* an act of friendship or love, a kind action. –दः a jester or buffoon in a play. –दत्त *a.* given through affection. (–त्तं) property given to a female by her relatives, particularly by her father-in-law or mother-in-law at the time of marriage. –दानं, –दायः a gift of love, a friendly present; तदवसरोऽयं प्रीतिदायस्य Mâl. 4; R. 15. 68. –धनं money given through love or friendship. –पात्रं an object of love, any beloved person or object. –पूर्व, पूर्वकं *ind.* kindly, affectionately. –मनस् *a.* delighted in mind, pleased, happy. –युज् *a.* dear, affectionate, beloved; Ki. 1. 10. –वचस् *n.*, –वचनं a friendly or kind speech. –वर्धन *a.* increasing love or joy. (–नः) an epithet of Vishṇu. –वादः a friendly discussion. –विवाहः a love-marriage, love-match (based purely on love). –श्राद्धं a sort or *S*râddha or obsequial ceremony performed in honour of the Manes of both parents.

प्रु 1 A. (प्रवते) 1 To go, move. 2 To jump, spring.

प्रुष् I. 1 P. (प्रोषति, प्रुष्ट) 1 To burn, consume. 2 To reduce to ashes. –II. 9 P. (प्रुष्णाति) 1 To become wet or moist. 2 To pour out, sprinkle. 3 To fill.

प्रुष्ट *p. p.* Burnt, consumed, reduced to ashes.

प्रुष्वः 1 The rainy season. 2 The sun. 3 A drop of water (Sk.).

प्रेक्षकः A spectator, looker on, beholder, sight-seer.

प्रेक्षणं 1 Viewing, seeing. 2 A view, look, appearance. 3 The eye; चकितहरिणीप्रेक्षणा Me. 82. 4 Any public show or spectacle, sight, show. –COMP. –कूटं the eye-ball.

प्रेक्षणकं A show, spectacle.

प्रेक्षणिका A woman fond of seeing shows.

प्रेक्षणीय *pot. p.* 1 To be seen, viewed, or gazed at. 2 Fit to be seen, lovely to the sight, beautiful to look at; Me. 2; R. 14. 9. 3 To be considered or regarded.

प्रेक्षणीयकं A show, sight, spectacle; *S*i. 10. 83.

प्रेक्षा 1 Viewing, seeing, beholding. 2 A look, view, sight, appearance. 3 Being a looker-on. 4 Any public spectacle or show, sight. 5 Particularly a theatrical show, dramatic performance, play. 6 Intellect, understanding. 7 Reflection, consideration, deliberation. 8 The branch of a tree –COMP. –अ (आ) गारः-रं,-गृहं, -स्थानं 1 a theatre, a play-house. 2 a council-chamber. –समाजः an audience, crowd of spectators, assembly.

प्रेक्षावत् *a.* Considerate, wise, learned (as a man).

प्रेक्षित *p. p.* Seen, viewed, beheld, gazed or looked at.—तं A look, glance.

पेंखः,-खं A swing.

प्रेंखण *a.* Wandering, moving, going towards, entering; Bk. 9. 106. —णं 1 Swinging. 2 A swing. 3 A minor drama in one act, having no Sûtradhâra, hero &c;. S. D. thus defines it;: –गर्भविमर्षरहितं प्रेंखणं हीननायकं। असूत्रधारमेकांकमविष्कंभप्रवेशकम् । नियुद्धसंफोटयुतं सर्ववृत्तिसमाश्रितं ॥ 547. *e. g.* वालिवध.

प्रेंखा 1 A swing. 2 Dancing. 3 Roaming about, wandering, travelling. 4 A kind of building or house. 5 A particular pace of a horse.

प्रेंखित *p. p.* Swung, shaken, oscillated.

प्रेंखोल् 10 U. (प्रेंखोलयति-ते) To swing, shake, oscillate.

प्रेंखोलनं 1 Swinging, shaking, oscillating. 2 A swing.

प्रेत *p. p.* Departed from this world, dead, deceased; स्वजनाश्रु किलातिसंततं दहति प्रेतमिति प्रचक्षते R. 8. 86.—तः 1 The departed spirit, the spirit before obsequial rites are performed. 2 A ghost, evil-spirit; Bg. 17. 4; Ms. 12. 71. –COMP. –अधिपः an epithet of Yama. –अन्नं food offered to the Manes. –अस्थि *n.* the bone of a dead man, °धारिन् an epithet of *S*iva.–ईशः, –ईश्वरः an epithet of Yama. –उद्देशः an offering to the Manes. –कर्मन् *n.*, –कृत्यं, –कृत्या obsequial or funeral rites. गृहं a cemetery. –चारिन् *m.* an epithet of *S*iva. –दाहः the burning of the dead, cremation. –धूमः the smoke issusing from a funeral pile. –पक्षः 'the fortnight of the Manes', N. of the dark half of Bhâdrapada when offerings in honour of the Manes are usually performed; cf. पितृपक्ष –पटहः a drum beaten at a funeral- –पतिः an epithet of Yama. –पुरं the city of Yama. –भावः death –भूमिः *f.* a cemetery. –मेधः a funeral sacrifice. –राक्षसी the holy basil (तुलसी). -राजः an epithet of Yama. –लोकः the world of the dead. -वनं a cemetery. -शरीरं the body of the departed spirit. –शुद्धि *f.*, –शौचं purification after the death of a relative. –श्राद्धं an obsequial offering made to a departed relative during the year of his death. –हारः 1 one who carries out a dead body. 2 a near relative.

प्रेतिकः A ghost, spirit.

प्रेत्य *ind.* Having departed (from this world) after death in the next world; न च तत्प्रेत्य नो इह Bg. 17. 28; Ms. 2. 9. 26. COMP. –जातिः *f.* position in the world to come. –भावः the condition of soul after death.

प्रेत्वन् *m.* 1 Wind. 2 An epithet of Indra.

प्रेप्सा 1 Desire of obtaining. 2 Desire (in general).

प्रेप्सु *a.* 1 Desirous of obtaining, wishing, seeking, longing for. 2 Aiming at.

प्रेमन् *m., n.* 1 Love, affection; तत्प्रेमहेमनिकषोपलतां तनोति Gît. 11; Me. 44. 2 Favour, kindness, kind or tender regard. 3 Sport, pastime. 4 Joy, delight, gladness. –COMP. –अश्रु *n.* a tear of joy or affection. –ऋद्धिः *f.* increase of affection, ardent love. –पर *a.* affectionate, loving. –पातनं 1 tears (of joy). 2 the eye (that sheds them). –पात्रं 'an object of love,' any beloved person or thing. बंधः, –बंधनं a bond or tie of affection.

प्रेमिन् *a.* (णी *f.*) Loving, affectionate.

प्रेयस् *a.* (सी *f.*) Dearer, more beloved or agreeable &c. (compar. of प्रिय q. v.).—*m.* A lover, husband. —*m. -n.* Flattery. —सी A wife, mistress.

प्रेयोपत्यः A heron (fond of offspring).

प्रेरक *a.* (रिका *f.*) 1 Impelling, urging, stimulating. 2 Sending, directing.

प्रेरणं,-णा 1 Driving or urging on, impelling, inciting, instigation. 2 Impulse, passion. 3 Throwing, casting; भवति विफलप्रेरणा चूर्णमुष्टिः Me. 68 4 Sending, despatching. 5 Order, direction. 6 (In gram.) The sense of the causal form.

प्रेरित *p. p.* 1 Impelled, urged; instigated. 2 Excited, stimulated, prompted. 3 Sent, despatched. 4 Touched. —तः An envoy, a messenger.

प्रेष् 1 U. (प्रेषति-ते) To go, move.

प्रेषः 1 Urging on. 2 Affliction, pain, sorrow.

प्रेषणं,-णा 1 Sending, despatching. 2 Sending on a mission, directing, charging, commissioning.

प्रेषित *p. p.* Despatched (on an errand). 2 Ordered, directed. 3 Turned, fixed upon, directed towards, cast (as eyes). 4 Banished.

प्रेष्ठ *p. p.* Dearest, most beloved &c. (superl. of प्रिय q. v.). —ष्ठः A lover, husband. —ष्ठा A wife, mistress.

प्रेष्य *a.* To be ordered, sent, despatched &c. —ष्यः A servant, menial, slave. —ष्या A female servant, handmaid. —ष्यं 1 Sending on a mission. 2 Servitude. -COMP. -जनः servants taken collectively. -भावः capacity of a servant, servitude, bondage; M. 5. 12. -वधूः 1 the wife of a servant. 2 a female servant, hand-maid. -वर्गः body of servants, suite, train.

प्रेहि (Second person sing. of the imperative of इ with प्र q. v.).-COMP. -कटा a rite in which no mats are allowed. -कर्दमा a rite in which no impurity is allowed. -द्वितीया a rite at which no second person is allowed to be present. -वाणिजा a rite at which no merchants are allowed to be present. (See P. II. 1. 72).

प्रैयं Being kind, kindness, love.

प्रैषः 1 Sending, directing. 2 An order, command, invitation. 3 Affliction, distress. 4 Madness, frenzy. 5 Crushing, pressing, squeezing (मर्दन).

प्रैष्यः A servant, menial, slave.—ष्या A female servant. —ष्यं Servitude, slavery. -COMP. -भावः the capacity of a servant, being used as a servant, servitude; Ku. 6. 58.

प्रोक्त *p. p.* 1 Spoken, told, uttered. 2 Laid down, prescribed.

प्रोक्षणं 1 Sprinkling, sprinkling with water; Ms. 5. 118; Y. 1. 184. 2 Consecration by sprinkling. 3 Immolation (of animals) at a sacrifice. —णी Water used for sprinkling or consecrating, holy water (used in pl., and sometimes used to denote 'the vessel containing holy water,' in which sense the word generally used is प्रोक्षणीपात्र).

प्रोक्षणीयं Water for consecrating.

प्रोक्षित *p. p.* 1 Purified or consecrated by sprinkling. 2 Immolated at a sacrifice.

प्रोचंड *a.* Exceedingly frightful or terrible.

प्रोच्चैस् *ind.* 1 Very loudly, aloud. 2 In a very high degree.

प्रोच्छित *p. p.* High, lofty, elevated.

प्रोजासनं Killing, slaughter.

प्रोज्झनं Abandoning, quitting, leaving.

प्रोज्झित *p. p.* Abandoned, quitted, forsaken, avoided.

प्रोंछनं 1 Wiping away, wiping out, effacing; N. 5. 36. 2 Picking up the remnants.

प्रोड्डिन *a.* Flown up or away.

प्रोढ, प्रोढि See प्रौढ, प्रौढि.

प्रोत *p. p.* 1 Sewn, stitched; Ku. 7. 49. 2 Extended lengthwise or perpendicularly (opp. ओत). 3 Tied, bound, fastened; Mv. 6. 33. 4 Pierced, transfixed; R. 9 75. 5 Passed or come through; तरुच्छिद्रप्रोतान् *i. e.* (चंद्रकिरणान्) बिसमिति करी संकलयाति K. P. 10. 6 Set, inlaid; Mv. 1. 35. —तं A garment, woven cloth. -COMP. -उत्सादनं 1 an umbrella. 2 a cloth-house, tent.

प्रोत्कंठ *a.* Lifting up or stretching out the neck.

प्रोत्कुष्टं A loud noise or uproar.

प्रोत्खात *p. p.* Dug out.

प्रोत्तुंग *a.* Very high or lofty.

प्रोत्फुल्ल *a.* Full-blown, expanded.

प्रोत्सारणं Getting rid of, clearing away, removing, expelling.

प्रोत्सारित *p. p* 1 Removed, got rid of, expelled. 2 Urged forward, incited. 3 Relinquished.

प्रोत्साहः 1 Zeal, ardour. 2 An incentive, a stimulus.

प्रोत्साहकः An inciter, instigator.

प्रोत्साहनं Inciting, stimulating, instigating, prompting.

प्रोथ् 1 U. (प्रोथति ते) 1 To be equal to, be a match for, withstand (with dat.); पुम्प्रोथास्मै न कश्चन Bk. 14. 84; 15. 40. 2 To be able, adequate or competent. 3 To be full or complete.

प्रोथ *a.* 1 Famous, well-known. 2 Placed, fixed. 3 Travelling, going out on a journey, wayfaring; वृक्षांतमुदकांतं च प्रियं प्रोथमनुव्रजेत् Tv. —थः थं 1 The nose or notrils of a horse; N. 1. 60; *Si.* 11. 11. 12. 73. 2 The snout of a hog. —थः 1 The hip, buttock. 2 An excavation. 3 A garment, old clothes. 4 Embryo.

प्रोथिन् *m.* A horse.

प्रोद्घुष्ट *p. p.* 1 Resounding, resonant. 2 Making a loud noise.

प्रोद्घोषणं, -णा 1 Proclaiming, proclamation. 2 Sounding aloud.

प्रोद्दीप्त *p. p.* Set on fire, burning, blazing; Bh. 3. 88.

प्रोद्भिन्न *p. p.* 1 Germinated, shot up. 2 Burst forth.

प्रोद्भूत *p. p.* Sprung up, arisen.

प्रोद्यत *p. p.* 1 Lifted up. 2 Active, industrious.

प्रोद्वाहः Marriage.

प्रोन्नत *p. p.* 1 Very high or lofty. 2 Projecting.

प्रोल्लाघित *a.* 1 Recovered from sickness, convalescent. 2 Robust.

प्रोल्लेखनं Scratching; marking.

प्रोषित *p. p.* Gone abroad on a journey, living abroad, away from home, absent, living in a foreign country. -COMP. -भर्तृका a woman whose husband is gone abroad; one of the eight Nâyikâs in erotic poetry. She is thus defined in S. D.- नानाकार्यवशाद्यस्याः दूरदेशं गतः पतिः। सा मनोभवदुःखार्ता भवेत् प्रोषितभर्तृका ॥ 119.

प्रो (प्रौ) ष्ठः 1 A bull, an ox. 2 A bench, stool. 3 A kind of fish (ष्ठी also). -COMP. -पदः the month भाद्रपद. (-दा) the 25th and 26th lunar mansions; पूर्वाभाद्रपदा and उत्तराभाद्रपदा.

प्रो (प्रौ) ह *a.* A reasoner, disputant. -हः 1 Reasoning, logic. 2 An elephant's foot. 3 A knot, joint.

प्रौ (प्रो) ढ *a.* 1 Full-grown; fully developed, matured, ripened, perfected; full (as moon); प्रौढपुष्पैः कदंबैः Me. 25; प्रौढतालीविपांडु &c. Mâl. 8. 1; 9. 28. 2 Adult, old, grown up; वर्तते हि मन्मथप्रौढसुहृदो निशीथस्य यौवनश्रीः Mâl. 8; Si. 11. 39. 3 Thick, dense, pitchy; प्रौढं तमः कुरु कृतज्ञतयैव भद्रं Mâl. 7. 3; *Si.* 4. 62. 4 Grand, mighty, strong. 5 Violent, impetuous. 6 Confident, bold, audacious. 7 Proud. -ढा A bold and grown-up woman, no longer bashful or timid in the presence of her lord, one of the four principal female characters in poetic compositions; आषोडशाद्भवेद्बाला त्रिंशता तरुणी मता। पंचपंचाशता प्रौढा भवेद्वृद्धा ततः परम् ॥.-COMP. -अंगना a bold woman; see above. -उक्तिः *f.* a bold or pompous assertion. -प्रताप *a.* of great or mighty valour. -यौवन *a.* advanced in youth.

प्रौ (प्रो) ढिः *f.* 1 Full growth or development, maturity, perfection. 2 Growth, increase. 3 Greatness, grandeur, elevation, dignity; Vikr. 1. 15. 4 Boldness, audacity. 5 Pride, arrogance, self-confidence. 6 Zeal, exertion, enterprise. -COMP. -वादः 1 a grandiloquent or pompous speech. 2 a bold assertion.

प्रौण *a.* Clever, learned, skilful.

प्लक्षः 1 The Indian fig-tree; प्लक्षप्ररोह इव सौधतलं बिभेद R. 8. 93; 13. 71. 3 One of the seven Dvîpas or continents of the world 3 A side or back door, a private entrance. -COMP. -जाता, -समुद्रवाचका an epithet of the river Sarasvatî. -तीर्थं, -प्रस्रवणं,-राज् *m.* the place where the Sarasvatî rises.

प्लव *a.* 1 Swimming, floating. 2 Jumping, leaping. -वः 1 Swimming, floating. 2 Flood, swelling of a river. 3 A jump, leap. 4 A raft, float, canoe, small boat; नाशयेच्च शनैः पश्चात्प्लवं सलिलपूरवत् Pt. 2. 38; सर्वं ज्ञानप्लवेनैव वृजिनं संतरिष्यसि Bg. 4. 36; Ms. 4.

194; 11. 19; Ve. 3. 25. 5 A frog. 6 A monkey. 7 A declivity, slope. 8 An enemy. 9 A sheep. 10 A man of a low tribe; chândâla. 11 A net or snare for catching fish. 12 The fig tree. 13 The Kârandava bird, a kind of duck. 14 Five or more stanzas syntactically connected (=कुलक q. v.) 15 The prolated utterance of a vowel. –COMP. –गः 1 a monkey; R. 12. 78, 2 a frog. 3 an aquatic bird, the diver. 4 the tree शिरीष. 5. N. of the sun's charioteer. (–गा) the sign of the zodiac called *Virgo*. –गतिः a frog.

प्लवकः 1 A frog. 2 A jumper, tumbler, rope-dancer. 3 The holy fig-tree. 4 A Chândâla, outcast. 5 A monkey.

प्लवंगः 1 An ape, a monkey. 2 A deer. 3 The fig-tree.

प्लवंगमः 1 A monkey; Si. 12. 55. 2 A frog.

प्लवनं 1 Swimming. 2 Bathing, plunging into; Mâl. 1. 19. 3 Jumping, leaping. 5 A great flood, deluge, 5 A declivity.

प्लवाका A float, raft.

प्लाविक *a.* Taking over in a boat, a ferry-man.

प्लाक्षं The fruit of प्लक्ष.

प्लावः 1 Flowing over. 2 Jumping, leaping. 3 Filling to over-flowing. 4 Straining a liquid (to remove impurities &c.); Y. 1. 190; (see Mit. thereon).

प्लावनं 1 Bathing, ablution. 2 Overflowing, flooding, inundating. 3 A flood, deluge.

प्लावित *p. p.* 1 Made to smim, float, or over-flow. 2 Deluged, inundated, overflowed. 3 Moistened, wetted, sprinkled; Si. 12. 25; Ki. 11. 36. 4 Covered with.

प्लिह् 1 A. (प्लेहते). To go, move.

प्ली 9 P. (प्लीनाति) To go, move.

प्लीहन् *m.* The spleen, or its enlargement (प्लिहन् also). –COMP. –उदरं enlargement of the spleen. –उदरिन् *a.* suffering from enlargement of the spleen.

प्लीहा The spleen.

प्लु 1 A. (प्लवते, प्लुत) 1 To float, swim; किं नामैतत् मज्जंत्यलाबूनि ग्रावाणः प्लवंत इति Mv. 1; क्लेशोत्तरं रागवशात् प्लवंते R. 16. 60; प्लवंते धर्मलघवो लोकेऽम्भसि यथा प्लवाः Subhâsh. 2 To cross in a boat. 3 To swing to and fro, vibrate. 4 To leap, jump, spring; Bk. 5. 48; 14. 13, 15. 16. 5 To fly, soar, hover about. 6 To skip. 7 To be prolated or lengthened (as a vowel). –*Caus.* (प्लावयति-ते) 1 To cause to swim or float. 2 To remove, wash away. 3 To bathe. 4 To inundate, deluge, flood, submerge. 5 To cause to fluctuate. –WITH अभि 1 to over-flow. 2 to overwhelm, overcome (fig.). –अव to jump, jump or leap out. –उद् 1 to float, swim. 2 to spring, leap or jump upon; Ms. 8. 2363. to jump or bound away; Si. 12. 22. –उप 1 to float, swim. 2 to assault, assail, attack. 3 to oppress, trouble, harass, torment; निशाचरोपप्लुतभर्तृकाणां (तपस्विनीनां) R. 14. 64; 10. 5; Ms. 4. 188. –परि 1 to swim, float. 2 to bathe, plunge into. 3 to jump, spring. 4 to deluge, inundate, flood. 5 to cover with. 6 to overwhelm (fig.). –वि 1 to float about, swing to and fro, fluctuate. 2 to drift (in the sea), to be scattered; H. 3. 2. 3 to be confused (as mind). 4 to be ruined or destroyed. 5 to fail. (–*Caus.*) 1 to cause to float or swim. 2 to teach (to unworthy persons) Ms. 11. 199. 3 to confuse or confound, bewilder. –सं 1 to fluctuate, float about. 2 to flow together, meet (as waters); Bg. 2. 46.

प्लुत *p. p.* 1 Swimming, floating. 2 Inundated, submerged, overflowed. 3 Leaped, jumped. 4 Lengthened, protracted for prolated (as a vowel). 5 Covered with. (See प्लु). –तं 1 Jump, leap, spring. 2 Capering, one of the paces of a horse. –COMP. –गतिः a hare. (–*f.*) 1 going by leaps. 2 a gallop, bounding motion.

प्लुतिः *f.* 1 A flood, overflowing, inundation. 2 A leap, jump, spring; as in मंडूकप्लुति. 3 Capering, one of the paces of a horse. 4 Prolation or protraction of a vowel.

प्लुष् I. 1. 4. 9. P. प्लोषति, प्लुष्यति, प्लुष्णाति, प्लुष्ट) To burn, scorch, singe, sear Rs. 1. 22; Bk. 20. 34. –II. 9 P. (प्लुष्णाति) 1 To sprinkle, wet. 2 To anoint. 3 To fill.

प्लुष्ट *p. p.* Scorched, burnt, singed.

प्लेव् 1 A. (प्लेवते) To serve, attend or wait upon.

प्लोषः Burning, combustion (also प्रोष).

प्लोषण *a.* (णी *f.*) Burning, scorching, reducing to ashes; तार्तीयिकं पुरारेस्तद्वतु मदनप्लोषणं लोचनं वः Mâl. 1. v. 1. –णं Burning, scorching (प्रोषणं also).

प्सा 2 P. (प्साति, प्सात) To eat, devour.

प्सात *p. p.* 1 Eating. 2 Hungry.

प्सानं 1 Eaten. 2 Food.

फ.

फक्क् 1 P. (फक्कति, फक्कित) 1 To move slowly, go softly, glide, creep. 2 To act wrongly, behave ill. 3 To swell.

फक्किका 1 A position, an argument to be proved, a thesis or assertion to be maintained; फणिभाषितभाष्यफक्किका विषमा कुंडलनामवापिता N. 2. 95. 2 A prejudice, preconceived opinion.

फट् *ind.* An onomatopoetic word used mystically in uttering spells or incantations; अस्त्राय फट्.

फटः 1 The expanded hood of a snake (फटा also in this sense); निर्विषेणापि सर्पेण कर्तव्या महती फटा (फणा v. l.)। विषं भवतु मा भूद्वा फटाटोपो भयंकरः Pt. 1. 204. 2 A tooth. 3 A rogue, cheat (कितव).

फडिंगा A cricket, locust or grasshopper.

फण् I P. (फणति, फणित) 1 To move, move about; रुरुजुर्मेजिरे फेणुर्बहुधा हरिराक्षसाः Bk. 14. 78. 2 To produce easily or without exertion; (this sense according to some belongs to the *Caus.* of फण्).

फणः-णा The expanded hood of a cobra or any serpent; विप्रकृतः पन्नगः फणं (फणां) कुरुते S. 6. 30; मणिभिः फणस्थैः R. 13. 12; Ku. 6. 68; वहति भुवनश्रेणिं शेषः फणाफलकस्थितां Bh. 2. 35. –COMP. –करः a serpent. –धरः 1 a serpent. 2 N. of Siva. –भृत् *m.* a serpent. –मणिः a jewel said to be found in the hood of a serpent. –मंडलं the rounded body of a serpent; करालफणमंडलं R. 12. 98; तत्फणामंडलोदर्चिर्मणिद्योतितविग्रहं 10. 7.

फणिन् *m.* 1 A hooded serpent, serpent or snake in general; उद्गरितोद्गरलं फणिनः पुष्णासि परिमलोद्गारैः Bv. 1. 12, 58; फणी मयूरस्य तले निषीदति Rs. 1. 13; R. 16. 17; Ku. 3. 21. 2 An epithet of Râhu. 3 An epithet of Patanjali, the author of the Mahâbhâshya on Pâṇini's Sûtras; फणिभाषितभाष्यफक्किका N. 2. 95. –COMP. –इंद्रः, –ईश्वरः 1 an epithet of the serpent demon Sesha. 2 Of Ananta, the lord of serpents. 3 of Patanjali. –खेलः a quail. –तल्पगः an epithet of Vishṇu (who uses Sesha as his couch). –पतिः 1 an epithet of Sesha or of Vâsuki. 2 of Patanjali. –प्रियः wind. –फेनः opium. –भाष्यं Mahâbhâshya (the commentary of Patanjali on Pâṇini's Sûtras). –भुज् *m.* 1 a peacock. 2 an epithet of Garuḍa.

फत्कारिन् *m.* A bird.

फरं A shield; cf. फलक.

फरुवकं A betel-box.

फर्फरीकः The palm of the hand with the fingers extended. **–कं** 1 A young shoot or branch. 2 Softness. **–का** A shoe.

फल् I. 1 P. (फलति, फलित) 1 To bear fruit, yield or produce fruit; नानाफलैः फलति कल्पलतेव विद्या Bh. 2. 40; परोपकाराय द्रुमाः फलंति Subhâsh.; विधातुर्व्यापारः फलतु च मनोज्ञश्च भवतु Mâl. 1. 16; often used transitively in this sense; मौर्यस्यैव फलंति पश्य विविधश्रेयांसि मन्नीतयः Mu. 2. 16 'accomplish or bring about'; Si. 2. 89. 2 To be fruitful, to be successful, to be fulfilled or accomplished, to succeed; कैकेयि कामाः फलितास्तवेति R. 13. 59; 15. 78; यदा न फेलुः क्षणदाचराणां (मनोरथाः) Bk. 14. 113; 12. 66; नैवाकृतिः फलति नैव कुलं न शीलं Bh. 2. 96, 116. 3 To result, produce results or consequences; फलितमस्माकं कपटप्रबंधेन H. 1; फलितं नस्तर्हि भगवतीपादप्रसादेन Mâl. 6; Ki. 18. 25; खलः करोति दुर्वृत्तं नूनं फलति साधुषु H. 3. 21 'wicked men commit bad acts, and good men suffer their consequences'. 4 To become ripe, ripen. –II 1 P. (फलति, फुल्ल or फुल्त in the first sense, and फलित in other senses). 1 To burst open, split or cleave asunder, burst, cleave; तस्य मूर्धानमासाद्य पफालासिवरो हि सः Mb. 2 To shine back, be reflected; Ki 5. 38. 3 To go.

फलं 1 Fruit (fig. also); as of a tree; उदेति पूर्वं कुसुमं ततः फलं S. 7. 30, R. 4. 33; 1. 49. 2 Crop, produce; कृषिफलं Me. 16. 3 A result, fruit, consequence, effect; अत्युत्कटैः पापपुण्यैरिहैव फलमश्नुते H. 1. 83; फलेन ज्ञास्यसि Pt. 1; न नवः प्रभुराफलोदयात् स्थिरकर्मा विरराम कर्मणः R. 8. 22; 1. 33. 4 (Hence) Reward, recompense, meed, retribution (good or bad); फलमस्योपहासस्य सद्यः प्राप्स्यसि पश्य मां R. 12. 37. 5 A deed, an act (opp. words); ब्रुवते हि फलेन साधवो न तु कंठेन निजापयोगितां N. 2. 48 'good men prove their usefulness by deeds, not by words'. 6 Aim, object, purpose; परेंगितज्ञानफला हि बुद्धयः Pt. 1. 43; किमपेक्ष्य फलं Ki. 2. 21 'with what object in view'; Me. 54. 7 Use, good, profit, advantage; जगता वा विफलेन किं फलं Bv. 2. 61. 8 Profit or interest on capital. 9 Progeny, offspring; R. 14. 39. 10 A kernel (of a fruit). 11 A tablet or board (शारीफलं). 12 A blade (of a sword). 13 The point or head of an arrow, dart &c.; bard; Mu. 7. 10. 14 A shield. 15 A testicle. 16 A gift. 17 The result of a calculation (in Math.). 18 Product or quotient. 19 Menstrual discharge. 20 Nutmeg 21 A ploughshare. –COMP. **–अदनः** =फलाशन q. v. **–अनुबंधः** succession or sequence of fruits or results. **–अनुमेय** *a.* to be inferred from the results or consequences; फलानुमेयाः प्रारंभाः संस्काराः प्राक्तना इव R. 1. 20. **–अंतः** a bamboo. **–अन्वेषिन्** *a.* seeking for reward or recompense (of actions). **–अपेक्षा** expectation of the fruits or consequences (of acts), regard to results. **–अशनः** a parrot. **–अम्लं** tamarind. **–अस्थि** *n.* a cocoa-nut. **–आकांक्षा** expectation of (good) results; see फलापेक्षा. **–आगमः** 1 production of fruits, load of fruits; भवंति नम्रास्तरवः फलागमैः S. 5. 12. 2 the fruit season, autumn. **–आढ्या** a sort of grapes (having no stones). **–उत्पत्तिः** *f.* 1 production of fruit. 2 profit, gain. (**–त्तिः**) the mango tree (sometimes written फलोत्पति in this sense). **–उदयः** appearance of fruit, production of results or consequences, attainment of success or desired object; आफलोदयकर्मणां R. 1. 5. **–उद्देशः** regard to results; see फलापेक्षा. **–कामना** desire of fruits or consequences. **–कालः** fruit-season. **–केशरः** the cocoanut tree. **–ग्रहः** deriving benefit or advantage. **–ग्रहि, ग्राहिन्** *a.* (also **फलेग्रहि** and **फलेग्राहिन्**) fruitful, yielding or bearing fruit in season; श्लाघ्यतां कुलमुपैति पैतृकं स्यान्मनोरथतरुः फलेग्रहिः Kir. K. 3. 60; Mâl. 9. 39. **–द** *a.* 1 productive, fruitful, bearing fruit; Ms. 11. 142. 2 bringing in gain or profit. (**–दः**) a tree. **–निवृत्तिः** *f.* cessation of consequences. **निष्पत्तिः** *f.* production of fruit. **–पाकः** (फलेपाकः also) 1 the ripening of fruit. 2 the fulness of consequences. **–पादपः** a fruit-tree. **–पूरः, –पूरकः** the common citron tree. **–प्रदानं** 1 the giving of fruits. 2 a ceremony at weddings. **–बंधिन्** *a.* forming or developing fruit. **–भूमिः** *f.* a place where one receives the reward or recompense of his deeds (*i. e.* heaven or hell). **भृत्** *a.* bearing fruit, fruitful. **–भोगः** 1 enjoyment of consequences. 2 usufruct. **–योगः** 1 the attainment of fruit or the desired object, Mu. 7, 10. 2 wages, remuneration. **–राजन्** *m.* a water-melon. **–वर्तुलं** a water-melon. **–वृक्षः** a fruit-tree. **–वृक्षकः** the bread-fruit tree. **–शाडवः** the pomegranate tree. **–श्रेष्ठः** the mango tree. **संपद्** *f.* 1 abundance of fruit. 2 success. **–साधनं** a means of effecting any desired object, realization of an object. **–स्नेहः** a walnut tree. **–हारी** an epithet of Kâlî or Durgâ.

फलकं 1 A board, plank, slab, tablet; कालः काल्या भुवनफलके क्रीडति प्राणिशारैः Bh. 3. 39; द्यूत°, चित्र°, &c. 2 Any flat surface; चुंब्यमानकपोलफलकां K. 218; धुतमुग्धगंडफलकैर्विबभुः Si. 9. 47, 27; cf. तट. 3 A shield. 4 A leaf or page for writing upon. 5 The buttocks, hips. 6 The palm of the hand. –COMP. **–पाणि** *a.* armed with a shield (as a warrior). **–यंत्रं** an astronomical instrument invented by Bhâskarâchârya.

फलतस् *ind.* As a consequence, consequently, virtually.

फलनं 1 Bearing fruit, fructifying. 2 Producing results or consequences.

फलवत् *a.* 1 Fruitful, fruit-bearing. 2 Producing or yielding result, successful, profitable.—**ती** The plant called प्रियंगु.

फलिता A woman in her courses.

फलिन् *a.* Fruitful, bearing or yielding fruit (fig. also); पुष्पिणः फलिनश्चैव वृक्षास्तूभयतः स्मृताः Ms. 1. 47; Mk. 4. 10. —*m.* A tree.

फलिन *a.* Fruitful, bearing fruit. —**नः** The bread-fruit tree.

फलिनी, –फली The Priyangu creeper; (said by poets to be the 'wife' of the mango tree; cf. R. 8. 61).

फल्गु *a.* 1 Pithless, sapless, unessential; unsubstantial; सारं ततो ग्राह्यमपास्य फल्गु Pt. 1. 2 Worthless, useless, unimportant; Si. 3. 76. 3 Small, minute. 4 Vain, unmeaning. 5 Weak, feeble, flimsy. —**ल्गुः** *f.* 1 The spring season. 2 The opposite-leaved fig-tree. 3 N. of a river at Gayâ. –COMP. **–उत्सवः** the vernal festival, commonly called *holi*.

फल्गुनः 1 The month of फाल्गुन. 2 N. of Indra.—**नी** N. of a constellation; Ku. 7. 6.

फल्यं A flower.

फाणिः, फाणितं Molasses.

फांट *a.* Made by an easy process, readily or easily prepared (as a decoction)—**टः–टं** An infusion, decoction; फांटमनायाससाध्यः कषायविशेषः Sk.; फांट चित्राभ्रपाणयः Bk. 9. 17 (see the commentary.).

फालः–लं 1 A ploughshare; Ms. 6. 16. 2 Separation of the hair on each side of the head (सीमंतभाग); N. 1. 16. —**लः** 1 An epithet of Balarâma, 2 of Siva. 3 The citron tree.—**लं** 1 A garment of cotton. 2 A ploughed field.

फाल्गुनः 1 N. of a Hindu month (corresponding to February-March). 2 An epithet of Arjuna; Mb. thus explains the epithet:—उत्तराभ्यां फल्गुनीभ्यां नक्षत्राभ्यामहं दिवा । जातो हिमवतः पृष्ठे तेन मां फाल्गुनं विदुः ॥. 3 N. of a tree, also called अर्जुन. –COMP. **–अनुजः** 1 the month Chaitra. 2 the vernal season (वसंतकाल). 3 an epithet of नकुल and सहदेव.

फाल्गुनी The full-moon day of the month फाल्गुन. –COMP.**–भवः** an epithet of the planet Jupiter.

फिरंगः The country of the Franks (*i. e* of Europeans.)

फिरंगिन् *m.* A Frank, (*i. e.* a European).

फुकः A bird.

फु (फू) त् *ind.* An onomatopoetic word generally used in composition with कृ and imitative of the sound made by blowing into liquids &c.; sometimes it expresses disregard or contempt; फु (फू) त्कृ to blow into (a liquid); वालः पायसदग्धो दध्यपि फूत्कृत्य भक्षयति H. 4. 103. –COMP. **–कारः,–कृतं, –कृतिः** *f.* 1 blowing into. 2 hissing, whizzing. 3 the hiss of a serpent. 4 sobbing. 5 screaming, loud shriek, yell.

फुप्फुसः -सं The lungs.

फुल्ल् 1 P. (फुल्लति, फुल्लित) To bloom, expand, blow, open (as a flower)

फुल्ल *p. p.* (of फल्) 1 Expanded, opened, blown; पुष्पं च फुल्लं नवमल्लिकायाः प्रयाति कांतिं प्रमदाजनानां Rs. 6. 6. फुल्लारविंदवदनां Ch. P. 1. 2 Flowering, blossomed; R. 9. 63. 3 Expanded, dilated, wide opened (as eyes); Pt. 1. 136. –COMP. **–लोचन** *a.* having eyes dilated (with joy). (**–नः**) a kind of deer.

फेत्कारः A shriek, howl.

फेणः -नः 1 Foam, froth; गौरीवक्त्रभ्रुकुटिरचनां या विहस्येव फेनैः Me. 50; R. 13. 11; Ms. 2. 61. 2 Foam of the mouth. 3 Saliva. –COMP. **–पिंडः** 1 a mere bubble. 2 an empty idea, non-entity. **–वाहिन्** *m.* a filtering cloth.

फेण (न) क See फेन.

फेनिल *a.* Foamy, frothy; फेनिलमंबुराशि R. 13. 2.

फेरः, फेरंडः A jackal.

फेरवः 1 A jackal; क्रेदत्फेरवचंडडात्कृति &c. Mâl. 5. 19. 2 A rogue, rascal, cheat. 3 A demon, goblin.

फेरुः A jackal.

फेलं, फेला, फेलिका, फेली Remnants of food, leavings of a meal, orts.

ब.

बंह् 1 A. (बंहते, बंहित) To increase, grow.

बंहिमन् *m.* Abundance, multitude.

बंहिष्ठ *a.* Most abundant, very great, excessive; (superl. of बहुल q. v.).

बंहीयस् *a.* More numerous or abundant, much more, exceeding, (Compar. of बहुल q. v.).

बकः 1 The Indian crane. 2 A cheat, rogue, hypocrite (the crane being a very cunning bird that knows well how to draw others into its clutches). 3 N. of a demon killed by Bhîma. 4 N. of another demon killed by Krishṇa. 5 N. of Kubera –COMP. **–चरः, –वृत्तिः, –व्रतचरः, –व्रतिकः, –व्रतिन्** *m.* 'acting like a crane', a false devotee, religious hypocrite; अधोदृष्टिर्नैकृतिकः स्वार्थसाधनतत्परः । शठो मिथ्याविनीतश्च बकव्रतचरो द्विजः Ms. 4. 196. **–जित्** *m.* **–निषूदन**; epithet of 1 Bhîma. 2 of Krishṇa. **–व्रतं** 'crane-like conduct', hypocrisy.

बकुलः A kind of tree (said, according to the convention of poets, to put forth blossoms when sprinkled by young women with mouthfuls of wine); कांक्षत्यन्यो (*i. e.* केसरः or बकुलः) वदनमदिरां दोहदच्छद्मनाऽस्याः Me. 78; बकुलः सीधुगंडूषसेकात् (विकसति); (for similar conventions about other trees see the quotation under प्रियंगु). **–लं** The fragrant flower of this tree; Bv. 1. 54.

बकेरुका A small crane.

बकोटः A crane.

बटुः A boy, lad, chap, often used aa a depreciatory term or to show contempt; चाणक्यबटुः &c.; see वटु.

बडि (लि) शं A fish-hook; Bh. 3. 21.

बत *ind.* A particle expressing 1 sorrow, regret (alas!); वयं बत विदूरतः क्रमगता पशोः कन्यका Mâl. 3. 18; अहो बत महत्पापं कर्तुं व्यवसिता वयं Bg. 1. 45. 2 Pity or compassion; क्व बत हरिणकानां जीवितं चातिलोलं S. 1. 10. 3 Addressing, calling; बत वितरत तोयं तोयवाहा नितांतं G. M., R. 9. 47. 4 Joy or satisfaction; अहो बतासि स्पृहणीयवीर्यः Ku. 3. 20. 5 Wonder or surprise; अहो बत महच्चित्रं K. 154. 6 Censure. For the meanings of बत with अहो see under अहो.

बदरः The jujube tree. **–रं** The fruit of jujube; करबदरसदृशमखिलं भुवनतलं यत्प्रसादतः कवयः । पश्यंति सूक्ष्ममतयः सा जयति सरस्वती देवी Vâs. 1; Bv. 2. 8. –COMP. **–पाचनं** N. of a sacred bathing-place.

बदरिका 1 The jujube tree or its fruit; अन्ये बदरिकाकारा बहिरेव मनोहराः H. 1. 94. 2 N. of one of the many sources of the Ganges and of the neighbouring hermitage of the sages Nara and Narâyaṇa. –COMP. **–आश्रमः** the hermitage at Badarikâ.

बदरी 1 The jujube tree; see बादरायण. 2 =बादरिका (2) above. –COMP. **तपोवनं** the penance grove at Badarî; Ki. 12. 33. **–फलं** a fruit of the jujube tree. **–वनं (–णं)** a wood or thicket of jujube trees. **–शैलः** a rocky eminence at Badarî.

बद्ध *p. p.* 1 Bound, tied, fastened. 2 Chained, fettered. 3 Captured, caught. 4 Confined, imprisoned. 5 Put or girt on. 6 Restrained, suppressed, withheld. 7 Formed, built. 8 Cherished, entertained. 9 Combined, united. 10 Firmly rooted, firm. (see बंध्). –COMP. **–अंगुलित्र, अंगुलित्राण** *a.* having a finger-guard fastened. **–अंजलि** *a.* folding the hands together in supplication, with the hands joined in humble entreaty or raised to the forehead as a mark of respect. **–अनुराग** *a.* having the affection fixed upon, feeling or manifesting love for. **–अनुशय** *a.* feeling repentant. **–आशंक** *a.* one whose suspicions have been roused, grown suspicious. **–उत्सव** *a.* enjoying or observing a festival or holiday. **–उद्यम** *a.* making united efforts. **–कक्ष, –कक्ष्य** *a.* see बद्धपरिकर. **–कोप, –मन्यु, –रोष** *a.* 1 feeling anger, entertaining a feeling of anger. 2 suppressing or governing one's wrath. **–चित्त–मनस्** *a.* having the mind intently fixed on, rivetting the mind on. **–जिह्व** *a.* tongue-tied. **–दृष्टि, नेत्र-लोचन,** *a.* having the eyes intently fixed on, looking with a steadfast gaze at. **–धार** *a.* continuously or incessantly flowing. **–नेपथ्य** *a.* attired in a theatrical dress. **–परिकर** *a.* having the girdle girded on, one who has girded up his loins; *i. e.* ready, prepared. **–प्रतिज्ञ** *a.* 1 one who has made a vow or promise. 2 firmly resolved. **–भाव** *a.* having the affection or heart fixed upon, enamoured of (with loc.); दृढं त्वयि बद्धभावोर्वशी V. 2. **–मुष्टि** *a.* 1 having a closed fist. 2 closefisted, covetous. **–मूल** *a.* deep-rooted, striking root firmly; बद्धमूलस्य मूलं हि महद्वैरतरोः स्त्रियः Si. 2. 38. **–मौन** *a.* holding the tongue, keeping silence, silent; अदृश्यत त्वच्चरणारविंदविश्लेषदुःखादिव बद्धमौनं R. 13. 23. **–राग** *a.* having the desire fixed on, enamoured, impassioned; Pt. 1. 123. **–वसति** *a.* fixing an abode **–वाच्** *a.* tongue-tied, maintaining silence. **–वेपथु** *a.* seized with tremour. **–वैर** *a.* one who has conceived bitter hatred or contracted confirmed hostility. **–शिख** *a.* 1 one whose hair is tied up (into a knot on the crown of the head). 2 one who is still in childhood, young. **–स्नेह** *a.* forming an attachment, conceiving affection for.

बध् 1 A. (बीभत्सते; strictly desiderative base of बध् used in a primitive sense) To abhor, loathe, detest, shrink from, be disgusted with (with abl.); येभ्यो बीभत्समानाः U. 1.

बधिर *a*. Deaf; ध्वनिभिजनैस्य बधिरीकृतश्रुतेः *Si*. 13. 3; Ms. 7. 149.

बधिरयति Den. P. To deafen (fig. also); बधिरिताशेषदिगंतरालं K.; Mv. 6.80.

बधिरित *a*. Made deaf, deafened.

बधिरिमन् *m*. Deafness.

बंदिन् See वंदिन्.

बंदिः-दी *f*. **1** Bondage, confinement. **2** A prisoner, captive; Ku. 2. 91.

बंध् 9 P. (बध्नाति, बद्ध; *pass*. बध्यते) **1** To bind, tie, fasten; बद्धुं न संभावित एव तावत् करेण रुद्धोपि च केशपाशः Ku. 7. 57; R. 7. 9; Ku. 7. 25; Bk. 9. 75. **2** To catch, capture, imprison, ensnare, make captive; कर्मभिर्न स बद्ध्यते Bg. 4. 14; बलिर्बबंधे Bk. 2. 39; 14. 56. **3** To chain, fetter. **4** To check, stop, suppress; as in बद्धकोप, बद्धकोष्ठ &c. **5** To put on, wear; न हि चूडामणिः पादे प्रभवामीति बध्यते Pt. 1. 72; बबंधुरंगुलित्राणि Bk. 14. 7. **6** To attract, arrest (as eyes &c,); बबंध चक्षूंषि यवप्ररोहः Ku. 7. 17; or बध्नाति मे चक्षुः (चित्रकूटः) R. 13. 47. **7** To fix or set upon, direct towards (as the eyes or mind), cast upon (with loc.); दृष्टिं लक्ष्येषु बध्नन् Mu. 1. 2; R. 3. 4; 6. 36; Bk. 20. 22. **8** To bind or fasten together (as hair); Mu. 7. 17. **9** To build, construct, form, arrange; बद्धार्भिनाकवनितापरिभुक्तमुक्तं Ki. 8. 57; मृगकुलं रोमंथमभ्यस्यतु *S*. 2. 6; तस्यांजलिं बंधुमतो बबंध R. 16. 5; 4. 38; 11. 35, 78; Ku. 2. 47; 5. 30; Bk. 7. 77. **10** To put together, compose, construct (a poem, verse &c.); तुष्टैर्बद्धं तदलघु रघुस्वामिनः सच्चरित्रं Vikr. 18. 107; श्लोक एव त्वया बद्धः Râm. **11** To form, produce, bear (as fruit &c.); R. 12. 69; *S*. 6. 4. **12** To have, possess, entertain, cherish; U. 2, 8. (The senses of बंध् are variously modified according to the noun with which it is connected; *e. g*.; भ्रुकुटिं बंध् to knit or bend the eyebrows, to frown; मुष्टिं बंध् to clench the fist; अंजलिं बंध् to fold the hands together in supplication; चित्तं, -धियं,-मनः,-हृदयं बंध् to set the heart on; प्रीतिं,-भावं, -रागं बंध् to fall in love with, be enamoured of; सेतुं बंध् to construct or build a bridge; वैरं बंध् to conceive hatred, contract enmity; सख्यं, -सौहृदं बंध् to form friendship; गोलं बंध् to form a globe; मंडलं बंध् to form a circle, sit or stand in a circle; मौनं बंध् to maintain silence; परिकरं -कक्षां बंध् to gird up one's loins, prepare oneself for anything; see the compounds under बद्ध also). —*Caus*. To cause to bind, form, construct, build &c.; R. 12. 70. –WITH अनु **1** to bind or fasten to; *Si*. 8. 69. **2** to adhere or stick to, cling to; तान्येवाक्षराणि मामनुबध्नंति U. 3. **3** to attend or follow closely, follow at the heels of; मधुकरकुलैरनुबध्यमानं K. 139; को नु खल्वयमनुबध्यमानस्तपस्विनीभ्यामबालसत्त्वो बालः *S*. 7. **4** to press, urge, importune. –आ **1** to bind, fasten, tie; Ms. 11. 205. **2** to form, make, arrange; आबद्धमंडला ताप, सपरिषद् K. 49; आबद्धमालाः Me. 9; Bk. 3. 30; Ki. 5. 33; आबद्धरेखममितो नवमंजरीभिः Gît. 11. **3** **3** to fix on or upon, direct towards; R. 1. 40. –उद् to tie up, hang up, कंठमुद्बध्नाति Mu. 6; R. 16. 67, –नि **1** to bind, tie, fasten, chain, fetter; आत्मवंतं न कर्माणि निबध्नंति धनंजय Bg. 4. 41; 9. 9; 14. 7; 18. 17; Ms. 6. 74; Ku 5. 10. **2** to fix upon, rivet; त्वयि निबद्धरतेः V. 4. 29. **3** to form, build, construct, arrange; हेमनिबद्धं चक्रं, पाषाणचयबद्धः कूपः &c. **4** to write, compose; मया निबद्धेयमतिद्वयी कथा K. 5. निस् to press, urge, importune. –परि **1** to tie, bind. **2** to put on **3** to encircle, fasten round. **4** to arrest, stop. **5** to hinder, interrupt. –प्रति **1** to tie, fasten, bind (to); पीतप्रतिबद्धवत्सां (धेनुं) R. 2. 1. **2** to fix upon, direct towards; Ku. 7. 91. **3** to inlay, set, incase; यदि मणिस्त्रपुणि प्रतिबध्यते Pt. 1. 75; बहलानुरागकुरुविंददलप्रतिबद्धमध्यमिव दिग्वलयं *Si*. 9. 8. **4** to obstruct, hinder, keep off or back, exclude, shut out; प्रतिबध्नाति हि श्रेयः पूज्यपूजाव्यतिक्रमः R. 1. 79 **5** to stop, interrupt; मैनमंतरा प्रतिबध्नीत *S*. 6. सं **1** to bind or tie together, unite, connect, attach. **2** to construct, form; see संबद्ध.

बंधः **1** A tie, bond (in general) (आज्ञाबंध). **2** A hair-band, fillet; V. 4. 10; *S*. 1. 30. **3** A chain, fetter. **4** Fettering, confining, imprisoning; Ms. 8; 310. **5** Catching, capturing, catching hold of; गजबंध R. 16. 2. **6** Forming, constructing, arranging; सर्गबंधो महाकाव्यं S. D. 6. **7** Feeling, conceiving, cherishing; हे राजानस्त्यजत सुकविप्रेमबंधे विरोधं Vikr. 18. 107; R. 6. 81. **8** Connection, union, intercourse. **9** Joining or folding together, combining; R. 14. 13; अंजलिबंध &c. **10** A bandage, ligature. **11** Agreement, harmony. **12** Manifestation, display, exhibition; R. 18. 52. **13** Bondage, confinement to this world (opp. मुक्ति which is 'complete emancipation from the trammels of the word'); बंधं मोक्षं च या वेत्ति बुद्धिः सा पार्थ सात्त्विकी Bg. 18. 30; बंधोन्मुक्त्यै खलु मखमुखान्कुर्वते कर्मपाशान् Bv. 4. 21; R. 13. 58; 18. 7. **14** Result, consequence. **15** A position, posture in general; आसनबंध, धीरः R. 2. 6; Ku. 3. 45, 59. **16** A particular position in sexual intercourse, or a particular mode of sexual enjoyment (these are said in Ratimanjarî to be 16, but other writers increase the number to 84). **17** A border, frame-work. **18** Arrangement of a stanza in a particular shape; *e. g*. खड्गबंध, पद्मबंध, मुरजबंध (Vide K. P. 9. *ad loc*.). **19** A sinew, tendon **20** The body. **21** A deposit, pledge. –COMP. –करणं fettering, imprisoning. –तंत्रं a complete army containing the four necessary elements, *i. e*. elephants, horses, chariots and footmen. –पारुष्यं forced or unnatural construction of words. –स्तंभः a post to which an animal (*e. g*. an elephant) is tied.

बंधकः **1** One who binds or catches, a binder. **2** A catcher. **3** A band, tie, rope, leather. **4** A dike, bank, dam. **5** A pledge, deposit. **6** A posture of the body. **7** Barter, exchange. **8** A violator, ravisher. **9** A promise. **10** A city. **11** A part or portion (at the end of num. compounds) ऋणं सदशबंधकं Y. 2. 76. —कं Binding, confinement. —की **1** An unchaste woman; न मे त्वया कौमारबंधक्या प्रयोजनं Mâl. 7; Ve. 2. **2** A harlot, courtezan; बलात् धृतोसि मयेति बंधकीधाष्टर्यं K. 237. **3** A female elephant.

बंधनं **1** The act of binding, fastening, tying; Ku. 4. 8. **2** Binding on or round, throwing round, clasping; विनम्रशाखाभुजबंधनानि Ku. 3. 39; घटय भुजबंधनं Gît. 10; R. 19. 17. **3** A bond, tie (fig also); R. 12. 76; आशाबंधनं &c. **4** Fettering, chaining, confining. **5** A chain, fetter, tether, halter &c. **6** Capturing, catching. **7** Bondage, confinement, imprisonment, captivity; as in बंधनागार. **8** A place of confinement, prison, jail; त्वां कारयामि कमलोदरबंधनस्थं *S*. 6. 20; Ms. 9. 288. **9** Forming, building, construction; सेतुबंधनं Ku. 4. 6. **10** Connecting, uniting, joining. **11** Hurting, injuring. **12** A stalk, stem, peduncle (of a flower); *S*. 3. 7; 6. 18; Ku. 4. 14 **13** A sinew, muscle. **14** A bandage. –COMP. –अ (आ) गारः-रं,-आलयः a prison, jail. –ग्रंथिः **1** the knot of a bandage. **2** a noose. **3** a rope for tying cattle. –पालकः,-रक्षिन् *m*. a jailor. –वेश्मन् *n*. a prison. –स्थः a captive, prisoner. स्तंभः a tying post a post to which an animal (*e. g*. an elephant) is tied. –स्थानं a stable, stall (for horses &c.).

बंधित *a*. **1** Bound, fastened. **2** Confined, imprisoned.

बंधित्रः **1** The god of love. **2** A leathern fan (चर्मव्यजन). **3** A spot, mole.

बंधुः **1** A relation, kinsman, relative in general; यत्र द्रुमा अपि मृगा अपि बंधवो मे U. 3. 8; मातुर्बंधुमिवासन्नं R. 12. 12; *S*. 6. 22; Bg. 6. 9. **2** Any one connected or associated with another, a brother; प्रवासबंधुः a brother-traveller; धर्मबंधुः a spiritual brother; *S.* 4. 9.' **3** (In law) A cognate kinsman, one's own kindred or kinsmen generally; (three kinds are enumerated; आत्म° personal, पितृ° paternal, and मातृ° maternal; see these three words). **4** A friend (in general); as in बंधुकृत्य below; oft. at the end of comp; मकरंदगंधबंधो Mâl. 1. 36 'a friend of, (*i. e.*) charged with fragrance' &c; 9. 13. **5** A husband; वैदेहिबंधोर्हृदयं विदद्रे R. 14. 33. **6** A father. **7** A mother. **8** A brother. **9** The tree called बंधुजीव q. v. **10** One who belongs to or is connected with any tribe or profession only nominally; *i. e.* one who belongs to it, but does not do the duties pertaining thereto (often used by way of contempt); स्वयमेव ब्रह्मबंधुनोद्भिन्नो दुर्गप्रयोगः M. 4; cf. क्षत्रबंधु. -Comp. **-कृत्यं 1** The duty of a kinsman; त्वयि तु परिसमाप्तं बंधुकृत्यं प्रजानां S. 5. 8. **2** the business of a friendly act or service; कच्चित्सौम्य व्यवसितमिदं बंधुकृत्यं त्वया मे Me. 114. **-जनः 1** a relative, kinsman. **2** kindred, kinsmen taken collectively. **-जीवः,-जीवकः** N. of a tree; बंधुजीवमधुराधरपल्लवमुल्लसितस्मितशोभं Gît. 2; R. 11. 25. **-दत्तं** a kind of Strîdhana or woman's property, the property given to a girl by her relatives at the time of marriage; Y. 2. 144. **-प्रीतिः** *f.* 1 love of a relative; बंधुप्रीत्या Me. 49. 2 love for a friend. **-भावः 1** friendship. **2** relationship. **-वर्गः** kinsmen, kindred. **-हीन** *a.* destitute of relatives or friends.

बंधुकः 1 The tree called बंधुजीव. **2** A bastard. **-का-की** An unchaste woman (see बंधकी).

बंधुता 1 Relatives, kinsmen, kindred (taken collectively); Ki. 1 10. **2** Relationship, affinity.

बंधुदा An unchaste woman.

बंधुर *a.* **1** Undulating, wavy, uneven; *Si.* 7. 34; Ku. 1. 42. **2** Bent, inclined, bowed; बंधुरगात्रि R. 13. 47; (=संनतांगि). **3** Crooked, curved. **4** Pleasing, handsome, beautiful, lovely; *S.* 6. 13; (where it may mean 'undulating' also). **5** Deaf. **6** Injurious, mischievous. **—रः 1** A goose. **2** A crane. **3** A drug. **4** An oil-cake. **5** The vulva. **—राः** (*m. pl.*) Parched corn or meal thereof. **—रा** An unchaste woman. **—रं** A diadem.

बंधुल *a.* **1** Bent, curved, inclined. **2** Pleasing, delightful, attractive. beautiful**—लः 1** A bastard; परगृहललिताः परान्नपुष्टाः परपुरुषैर्जनिताः परांगनासु । परधननिरता गुणेष्ववाच्या गजकलभा इव बंधुला ललामः Mk. 4. 28 (which is an answer given by the *bandhulas* themselves to the Vidûshaka's question भोः के यूयं बंधुला नाम). **2** An attendant in a harlot's Chamber. **3** The tree called बंधूक q. v.

बंधूकः N. of a tree; तवकरनिकरेण स्पष्टबंधूकसूनस्तबकरचितमेते शेखरं बिभ्रतीव *Si.* 11. 46; Rs. 3. 5. **—कं** A flower of this tree; बंधूकद्युतिबांधवोऽयमधरः Gît. 10; Rs. 3. 25.

बंधूर *a.* **1** Undulating, uneven. **2** Bent, inclined, bowed. **3** Pleasing, delightful, lovely; cf. बंधुर **—रं** A hole.

बंधूलिः The बंधुजीव tree.

बंध्य *a.* **1** To be bound or fettered, to be confined or imprisoned; Y. 2. 243. **2** To be joined or bound together. **3** To be formed, built or constructed. **4** Detained, under arrest. **5** Barren, unproductive, fruitless, useless (said of persons or things); बंध्यश्रमास्ते R. 16. 75; अबंध्ययत्नाश्च बभूवुरत्र ते 3. 29; Ki. 1. 33. **6** Not having the menses or menstrual discharge. **7** (At the end of comp.) Deprived or destitute of. -Comp. **—फल** *a.* useless, vain, idle.

बंध्या 1 A barren woman; न हि बंध्या विजानाति गुर्वीं प्रसववेदनां Subâsh. **2** A barren cow. **3** A kind of perfume (बाल). -Comp. **-तनयः, पुत्रः, -सुतः,** or **-दुहितृ, -सुता** &c. the son or daughter of a barren woman; *i. e.* a wild impossibility, anything that does not and cannot exist; एषं वंध्यासुतो याति खपुष्पकृतशेखरः see खपुष्प.

बंभ्रं A bond, tie.

बभ्रवी *a.* An epithet of Durgâ.

बभ्रु *a.* **1** Deep-brown, tawny, reddish brown; ज्वालावभ्रुशिरोरुहः R. 15. 16; 19. 25; बबंध बालारुणबभ्रु वल्कलं Ku. 5. 8. **2** Baldheaded through disease. **—भ्रुः 1** Fire. **2** An ichneumon. **3** The tawny colour. **4** A man with tawny hair. **5** N. of a Yâdava; *Si.* 2. 40. **6** An epithet of *S*iva. **7** Of Vishṇu. -Comp. **-धातुः 1** gold. **2** red chalk (गैरिक), a kind of ochre.**-वाहनः** N. of a son of Arjuna by Chitrângada. [The sacrificial horse let loose by king Yudhish*th*ira and guarded by Arjuna entered, in the course of its wanderings, the country of Ma*n*ipura, which was then ruled by Babhruv*a*hana, unequalled in prowess. The horse was taken to the king; but when he read the writing on the plate on its head, he knew that it belonged to the P*a*ndavas, and that his father Arjuna had arrived in the kigndom; and, hastening to him, respectfully offered his kingdom and his treasures along with the horse. Arjuna, in an evil hour, struck the head of Babhruv*a*hana and upbraided him for his cowardice, saying that if he had possessed true valour and had been his true son, he should not have been afraid of his father and submitted to him so meekly. At these words the brave youth was exceedingly irritated and discharged a crescent-shaped arrow at Arjuna which severed his head from his body. He wa*s*, however, restored to life by Ul*u*pi who happened to be then with Chitr*a*ngad*a*; and having acknowledged Babhruv*a*hana as his true son, he resumed his journey.]

बंच् 1 P. (बंबति) To go, move.

बंभरः A bee.

बभराली A fly.

बरटः A kind of grain.

बर्ब् 1 P. (बर्बति) To go, move.

बर्बटः A kind of grain (राजमाष).

बर्बटी 1 A kind of grain (राजमाष). **2** A harlot, prostitute.

बर्बणा A blue fly.

बर्बरः 1 One not an Aryan, a barbarian, low fellow. **2** A fool, blockhead; शृणु रे बर्बर H. 2.

बर्बुरः N. of a tree (Mar. बाभळ); उपसर्पेम भवंतं बर्बुर वद कस्य लोभेन Bv. 1. 24.

बर्ह् 1 A. (बर्हते) **1** To speak. **2** To give. **3** To cover. **4** To hurt, kill, destroy. **5** To spread. -With नि to kill, destroy; *Si.* 1. 29.

बर्हः-र्हं 1 A peacock's tail; दवोल्काहतशेषबर्हाः R. 16. 14; (केशपाशे) सति कुसुमसनाथे कं हरेदेष बर्हः V. 4. 10 v. l. **2** The tail of a bird. **3** A tail-feather (especially of a peacock); Me. 44; Ku. 1. 15; *Si.* 8. 11. **4** A leaf; अपांडुरं केतकबर्हमन्यः R. 6. 17. **5** A train, retinue. Comp. **-भारः 1** a peacock's tail. **2** a tuft of peacock's feathers on the handle of a club &c.

बर्हणं A leaf.

बर्हिः Fire. **—*n.*** The Kusa grass.

बर्हिणः A peacock; आवासवृक्षोन्मुखबर्हिणानि (वनानि) R. 2. 17; 16. 14; 19. 37. -Comp. **-वाजः** an arrow feathered with a peacock's plumes. **-वाहनः** an epithet of Kâritikeya.

बर्हिन् *m.* A peacock; R. 16. 64; V. 3. 2. 4. 10. Rs. 2. 6. -Comp. **-कुसुमं, -पुष्पं** a kind of perfume. **-ध्वजा** an epithet of Durgâ. **-यानः, -वाहनः** an epithet of Kârtikeya.

बर्हिस् *m. n.* **1** Kusa grass; Ku. 1. 60. **2** A bed or layer of Kusa grass. **—*m.* 1** Fire. **2** Light, splendour. **—*n.* 1** Water. 2 Sacrifice. -Comp. **-केशः, -ज्योतिस्** *m.* an epithet of fire. **मुखः** (**बर्हिर्मुखः**) **1** an epithet of fire. **2** a god (whose mouth is fire). **-शुष्मन्** *m.* an epithet of fire. **-सद्** (**बर्हिषद्**) *a.* seated on a layer of Kusa grass. (*-m.*) the Manes (pl.).

बल् I. 1 P. (बलति) **1** To breathe or live. **2** To hoard grain. -II. 1. U. (बलति-ते) **1** To give- **2** To hurt, injure, kill. **3** To speak. **4** To see, mark. -*Caus.* (बालयति-ते) To nourish, support.

बलं 1 Strength, power, might, vigour. **2** Force, violence; as in बलात् q. v. **3** An army, host, forces, troops; भवेद्भीष्ममद्रोणं धृतराष्ट्रबलं कथं Ve. 3. 24, 43; Bg. 1. 10; R. 16. 37. 4 Bulkiness, stoutness (of the body), 5 Body, figure, shape. 6 Semen virile. 7 Blood. 8 Gum, myrrh. 9 A shoot, sprout. (बलेन means 'on the strength of', 'by means or virtue of'; बाहुबलेन जितः, वीर्यबलेन &c.; बलात् 'per-force', 'forcibly', 'violently,' 'against one's will'; बलान्निद्रा समायाता Pt. 1; हृदयमदये तस्मिन्नेवं पुनर्वलते बलात् Gît. 7).–लः crow. 2 N. of the elder brother of Krishṇa; see बलराम below. 3 N. of a demon killed by Indra. –COMP. –अग्रं excessive strength force or (–ग्रः) the head of an army.–अंगकः the spring (Hemachandra). अंचिता the lute of Balarâma. –अटः a kind of bean. –अधिक *a.* surpassing in strength, of superior strength or force. –अध्यक्षः 1 a general or commander of an army; Ms. 7. 182. 2 a war-minister. –अनुजः an epithet of Krishṇa. –अन्वित *a.* endowed with strength, mighty, powerful. –अबलं 1 comparative strength and want of strength, relative strength and weakness; R. 17. 59. 2 relative significance and insignificance, comparative importance and unimportance; समय एव करोति बलाबलं Si. 6. 44. –अभ्रः an army in the form of a cloud. –अरातिः an epithet of Indra. –अवलेपः pride of strength. –उशः –असः 1 consumption. 2 the phlegmatic humour (कफ). 3 a swelling in the throat (which stops the passage of food). –आत्मिका a kind of sunflower (हस्तिशुंडी). –आहः water. –उपपन्न, –उपेत *a.* endowed with strength, strong, powerful. –ओघः a multitude of troops, numerous army, Si. 5. 2. –क्षोभः disturbance in the army, mutiny, revolt. –चक्रं 1 dominion, sovereignty. 2 an army, host. –जं 1 city-gate, gate. 2 a field. 3 grain, a heap of grain; Si. 14. 7. 4 war, battle. 5 marrow, pith. (–जा) 1 the earth. 2 a handsome woman. 3 a kind of Jasmine (Arabian). –दः an ox, bullock. –दर्पः pride of strength. –देवः 1 air, wind. 2 N. of the elder brother of Krishṇa; see बलराम below. द्विष् *m.*, -निषूदनः epithets of Indra; बलनिषूदनमर्थपतिं च तं R. 9. 3. –पतिः 1 a general, commander. 2 an epithet of Indra. –प्रद *a.* giving strength, invigorating. –प्रसूः N. of Rohiṇî, mother of Balarâma. –भद्रः 1 a strong or powerful man. 2 a kind of ox. 3 N. of Balarâma; q. v. below. 4 the tree called लोध्र. –भिद् *m.* an epithet of Indra; S. 2. –भृत् *a.* strong, powerful. –रामः the strong Râma' N. of the elder brother of Krishṇa. [He was the seventh son of Vasudeva and Devakî; but transferred to the womb of Rohiṇî to save him from falling a prey to the cruelty of Kamsa. He and his brother Krishṇa were brought up by Nanda in Gokula. When quite young, he killed the powerful demons Dhenuka and Pralamba, and performed, like his brother, many feats of surprising strength. On one occasion Balarama under the influence of wine, of which he was very fond, called upon the Yamuna river to come to him that he might bathe; and on his command being unheeded, he plunged his ploughshare into the river and dragged the waters after him, until the river assumed a human form and asked his forgiveness. On another occasion he dragged towards himself the whole city of Hastinapura along with its walls. As Krishṇa was a friend and admirer of the Pandavas, so Balarama was of the Kauravas, as was seen in his desire of giving his sister Subhadra to Duryodhana rather than to Arjuna; yet he declined to take any part in the great Bharati war either with the Pandavas or the Kauravas. He is represented as dressed in blue clothes, and armed with a ploughshare which was his most effective weapon. His wife was Revati. He is sometimes regarded as an incarnation of the serpent Sesha and sometimes as the eighth incarnation of Vishṇu; cf. Gît. I.] –विन्यासः array or arrangement of troops. –व्यसनं the defeat of an army. –सूदनः an epithet of Indra. –स्थः a warrior, soldier. –स्थितिः *f.* 1 a camp, an encampment. 2 a royal camp. –हन् *m.* an epithet of Indra. –हीन *a.* destitute of strength, weak, feeble.

बलक्ष *a.* White; द्विरदृदंतबलक्षमलक्ष्यत स्फुरितभृंगमृगच्छवि केतकं Si. 6. 34. –COMP –गुः (for गो 'a ray') the moon; यथानत्यर्जुनाब्जन्मसदृक्षांको बलक्षगुः Kâv. 1. 46 (given as an instance of the प्रसाद quality of the Gauḍîyas).

बललः An epithet of Indra.

बलवत् *a.* 1 Strong, powerful, mighty; विविरहो बलवानिति मे मतिः Bh. 2 91. 2 Stout, robust. 3 Dense, thick (as darkness, &c.). 4 Getting the upper hand, predominant, prevailing; बलवानिंद्रियग्रामो विद्वांसमपि कर्षति Ms. 2. 215. 5 More important, of greater weight; R. 14 40. —*ind.* 1 Strongly, powerfully, पुनर्बशिखाद्बलवन्निगृह्य Ku. 3. 69. 2 Very much, excessively, in a high degree: बलवदपि शिक्षितानामात्मन्यप्रत्ययं चेतः S. 1. 2; शीतार्तिं बलवदुपेयुषेव नीरैः Si. 8. 62; S. 5. 31.

बला N. of a powerful lore or incantation (taught by Visvâmitra to Râma and Lakshmaṇa); तौ बलातिबलयोः प्रभावतः R. 11. 9.

बलाकः-का A crane; सेविष्यंते नयनसुभगं खे भवंतं बलाकाः Me 9; Mk. 5. 18 19. —का A mistress.

बलाकिका A small kind of crane.

बलाकिन् *a.* Abounding in cranes; कालिकेवनिबिडा बलाकिनी R. 11. 15; Ku. 7. 39.

बलात्कारः 1 Using violence, employing force. 2 Outrage, voilence, force, oppression, exaction; R. 10 47; बलात्कारेण निर्वर्त्य &c. 3 Injustice. 4 (In law) Detention of the person of a debtor by the creditor and the employment of forcible means to recover the debt.

बलात्कृत *a.* Forced, overcome.

बलाहकः 1 A cloud; बलाहकच्छेदविभक्तरागामकालसंध्यामिव धातुमत्तां Ku. 1. 4. 2 A kind of crane. 3 A mountain. 4 N. of one of the seven clouds appearing at the destruction of the world.

बलिः 1 An oblation, a gift or offering (usually religious); नीवारबलिं विलोकयतः S. 4. 20; U. 1. 49. 2 The offering of a portion of the daily meal (of rice, grain, ghee &c.) to all creatures, (also called भूतयज्ञ), one of the five daily Yajnas to be performed by a householder; (see Ms. 3. 67, 91); it is usually performed by throwing up into the air, near the house-door, portions of the daily meal before partaking of it; यासां बलिः सपदि मद्गृहदेहलीनां हंसैश्च सारसगणैश्च विलुप्तपूर्वः Mk. 1. 9. 3 Worship, adoration; Ku. 1. 60; Me. 55; S. 4. 4 Fragments of food left at a meal. 5 A victim offered a deity. 6 A tax, tribute, impost; प्रजानामेव भूत्यर्थं स ताभ्यो बलिमग्रहीत् R. 1. 18; Ms. 7. 80; 8. 307, 7 The handle of a *chowrie*. 8 N. of a celebrated demon. [He was a son of Virochana, the son of Prahlada. He was a very powerful demon and oppressed the gods very much. They, therefore, prayed to Vishṇu for succour, who descended on earth as a son of Kasyapa and Aditi in the form of a dwarf. He assumed the dress of a mendicant, and having gone to Bali prayed him to give him as much earth as he could cover in three steps. Bali, who was noted for his liberality, unhesitatingly acceded to this apparently simple request. But the dwarf soon assumed a mighty form, and began to measure the three steps. The first step covered the earth, the second the heavens; and not knowing where to place the third, he planted it on the head of Bali and sent him and all his legions to the Patala and allowed him to be its ruler. Thus the universe was once more restored to the rule of Indra]; छलयसि विक्रमेण बलिमद्भुतवामन

Gît. 1; R. 7. 35; Me. 57. –लिः *f.* A fold, wrinkle &c. (usually written वलि q. v.).–Comp. –कर्मन् *n.* 1 offering oblations to all creatures. 2 payment of tribute. –दानं 1 presentation of an offering to a deity. 2 offering oblations to all creatures. –ध्वंसिन् *m.* an epithet of Vishṇu. –नंदनः,पुत्रः,–सुतः epithets of Bâṇa, the son of Bali. –पुष्टः-भोजनः a crow, –प्रियः the *Lodhra* tree. –बंधनः an epithet of Vishṇu.–भुज् *m.* 1 a crow. 2 a sparrow. 3 a crane –मंदिरं –वेश्मन् –सद्मन् *n.* the lower regions, the abode of Bali. –व्याकुल *a.* engaged in worship or in offering oblations to all creatures; Me. 85. –हन् *m.* an epithet of Vishṇu. हरणं an offering of oblations to all creatures.

बलिन् *a.* Strong, powerful, mighty; R. 16. 37; Ms. 7. 1 4. –*m.* 1. A buffalo. 2 A hog. 3 A camel· 4 A bull. 5 A soldier. 6 A kind of Jasmine. 7 The phlegmatic humour. 8 An epithet of Balarâma.

बलिन, बलिभ See बलिन-भ.

बलिंदमः An epithet of Vishṇu.

बलिमत् *a.* 1 Having materials of worship or oblation ready; R. 14. 15. 2 Receiving taxes.

बलिमन् *m.* Strength, might, power.

बलिवर्द See बलीवर्द.

बलिष्ठ *a.* Most powerful, strongest, very powerful (superl. of बलवत् or बलिन् q. v.). –ष्ठः A camel.

बलिष्णु *a.* Dishonoured, degraded, despised (अपमानित).

बलीकः The edge of a thatched roof.

बलीयस् *a.* (सी *f.*) 1 Stronger, more powerful. 2 More effective 3 More important (compar. of बलवत् or बलिन् q. v.).

बली (री) वर्दः A bull, an ox; गारपत्य-पुमान् बलीवर्दः·

बल्य *a.* 1 Strong, powerful. 2 Giving strength. –ल्यः A Buddhist mendicant. –ल्यं Semen virile.

बल्लवः 1 A cowherd; कुंजेष्वाक्रांतवीरुन्निचयपरिचया बल्लवाः संचरंतु Ve. 6. 2; *Si.* 11. 8. 2 A cook. 3 The name assumed by Bhîma when serving as a cook at the court of Virâṭa. –वी A cowherdess; Ki. 4. 17. –Comp. युवतिः-ती *f.* a young cowherdess (गोपी); हरिविरहाकुलबल्लवयुवतिसखीवचनं पटनीयं Gît. 4.

बल्वजः-जा A kind of coarse grass Ms. 2. 43.

बल्हिकाः, बल्हीकाः (*pl.*) N. of a country and its inhabitants.

बष्कय *a.* Full-grown (as a calf,)

बष्कय (यि) णी (नी) *f.* 1 A cow whose calf is full-grown; N. 16. 92. 2 A prolific cow (one bearing many calves.).

बस्तः A goat.–Comp.–कर्णः the *Sâla* tree.

बहल *a.* 1 Very much, copious, abundant, plentiful, manifold, great, strong; U. 1. 38; 3 23; *Si.* 9. 8; Bv. 4. 27. 2 Thick, dense. 3 Shaggy (as a tail); Mâl 3. 4 Hard, firm, compact. –लः A kind of sugarcane. –ला Large cardamoms. –Comp. –गंधः a kind of sandal.

बहिस् *ind.* 1 Out of, outside, (with abl.); निवसन्नावसथे पुराद्बहिः R. 8. 15; 11. 29. 2 On the outside, out of doors; (opp. अंतः); बहिर्गच्छ. 3 Externally, outwardly; अंतर्बहिः पुरत एव विवर्तमानां Mâl. 1. 40, 14; H. 1. 94 (बहिष्कृ means 1 to place outside of, exclude from, drive out of; Ms. 8. 380; Y. 1. 93. 2 to excommunicate. बहिर्गम् or याइ &c. to go out of, leave). –Comp. –अंग *a.* outer, external. (–गं) 1 an external part. 2 outer limb. –उपाधिः (बहिरुपाधिः) an external condition or circumstance; Mâl. 1. 24. –चर *a.* outer, external, outward; बहिश्चराः प्राणाः Dk. –द्वारं an outer door, portal.

बहु (हु or ह्वी *f.*; compar. भूयस्; superl. भूयिष्ठ) 1 Much, plentiful, abundant, great; तस्मिन्बहु एतदपि *S.* 4; 'even this was much for him' (was too much to be expected of him); बहु प्रष्टव्यमत्र Mu. 3; अल्पस्य हेतोर्बहु हातुमिच्छन् R. 2. 47. 3 Many, numerous; as in बह्वक्षर, बहुप्रकार. 3 Frequented, repeated. 4 Large, great. 5 Abounding or rich in (as first member of comp.); बहुकंटको देशः &c. —*ind.* 1 Much, abundantly, very much, exceedingly greatly, in a high degree. 2 Somewhat, nearly, almost; as in बहुतृण. (किं बहुना 'why say much', 'in short'; बहु मन् to think or esteem highly, rate high, prize, value; त्वत्संभावितमात्मानं बहु मन्यामहे वयं Ku. 6. 20; ययातेरिव शर्मिष्ठा भर्तुर्बहुमता भव *S.* 4. 6.; 7. 1; R. 12. 89; Bg. 2. 35; Bk. 3. 53; 5. 84, 8. 12). —Comp —अक्षर *a.* having many syllables, pollysyllabic (as a word). –अच्,-अच्क *a.* having many vowels, pollysyllabic. –अप्,-अप *a.* watery. –अपत्य *a.* having a numerous progeny. (–त्यः) 1 a hog. 2 a mouse, rat. (–त्या) a cow that has often calved. –अर्थ *a.* 1 having many senses. 2 having many objects. 3 important. –आशिन् *a.* voracious, gluttonous. –उदकः a kind of mendicant who lives in a strange town and maintains himself with alms got by begging from door to door; cf. कुटीचक. –उपाय *a.* effective. –ऋच् *a.* having many verses. (*-f.*) a term applied to the *Rigveda*. –एनस् *a.* very sinful. –कर *a.* doing much, busy, industrious. (–रः) 1 a sweeper, cleaner. 2 a camel. (–री) a broom. –कालं *ind.* for a long time. –कालीन *a.* of a long standing, old, ancient. –कूर्चः a kind of cocoa-nut tree. –गंधदा musk. –गंधा 1 the Yûthikâ creeper. 2 a bud of the Champaka tree. –गुण *a.* 1 having many good qualities or virtues. 2 manifold, multifarious. 3 having many threads. –जल्प *a.* garrulous, talkative, loquacious. —ज्ञ *a.* knowing much, well-informed, possessed of great knowledge. –तृणं anything much like grass; (hence) what is unimportant or contemptible; निदर्शनमसाराणां लघुर्बहुतृणं नरः *Si.* 2. 50. –त्वक्कः,त्वच् *m.* a kind of birch tree. –दक्षिण *a.* 1 attended with many gifts or donations. 2 liberal, munificent.–दायिन् *a* liberal, munificent, liberal donor. –दुग्ध *a.* yielding much milk. (–ग्धः) wheat. (–ग्धा) a cow yielding much milk. –दृश्वन् *a.* greatly experienced, a great observer. –दोष *a.* 1 having many faults or defects, very wicked or sinful. 2 full of crimes or dangers; बहुदोषा हि शर्वरी Mk. 1. 58. –धन *a.* very rich, wealthy. –धारं the thunderbolt of Indra. –धेनुकं a great number of milch-cows.–नादः a conch-shell. –पत्रः an onion. (–त्रं) talc. (–त्री) the holy basil. –पद्, -पाद्, -पादः *m.* the fig-tree. –पुष्पः 1 the coral tree. 2 the Nimba tree. –प्रकार *a.* of many kinds, various, manifold. –प्रज *a.* having many children, prolific. (–जः) 1 a hog. 2 the *munja* grass. –प्रतिज्ञ *a.* 1 comprising many statements or assertions, complicated. 2 (in law) involving many counts, as a plaint. –प्रद *a.* exceedingly liberal, a munificent donor. –प्रसूः the mother of many children. –प्रेयसी *a.* having many loved ones. –फल *a.* rich in fruits. (–लः) the Kadamba tree. –बलः a lion. –भाग्य *a.* very lucky or fortunate. –भाषिन् *a.* garrulous, talkative. मंजरी the holy basil. –मत *a.* highly esteemed or prized, valued, respected. मतिः *f.* great value or estimation; Ki. 7. 15. –मलं lead. – मानः great respect or regard, high esteem; पुरुषबहुमानो विगलितः Bh. 3. 9; वर्तमानकवेः कालिदासस्य क्रियायां कथं परिषदो बहुमानः M. 1; V. 1. 1. 2; Ku. 5. 31. (–नं) a gift given by a superior to an inferior. –मान्य *a.* respectable, esteemable. माय *a.* artful, deceitful, treacherous; Pt. 1. 321. –मार्गगा N. of the river Ganges; Ratn. 1. 3. –मार्गी a place where several roads meet. –मूत्र *a.* suffering from diabetes. –मूर्धन् *m.* an epithet of Vishṇu. –मूल्य *a.* costly, high-priced. –मृग *a.* abounding in deer. –रत्न *a.* rich in jewels. –रूप *a.* 1 many-formed, multiform, manifold. 2 variegated, spotted, chequered. (–पः) 1 a lizard, chameleon. 2 hair. 3 the sun. 4 N. of Siva. 5 of Vishṇu. 6 of Brahmâ. 7 of the god of love. –रेतस् *m.* an epithet of Brahmâ. –रोमन् *a.* hairy, shaggy. (*–m.*) a sheep. –लवणं a soil impregnated with salt. –वचनं the plural number (in gram.) –वर्ण *a.* many-coloured. ०वार्षिक *a.* lasting for many years. –विघ्न *a.* presenting many difficulties, attended with many dangers. –विध *a.* of many kinds, manifold, diverse. –वी (बी) जं the custard apple. –व्रीहि *a.* possessing much rice; तत्पुरुष कर्मधारय येनाहं स्यां बहुव्रीहिः Udb. (where it is also the name of the compound). (–हिः–) one of the four principal kinds of compounds in Sanskrit. In it, two or more nouns in apposition to each other are compounded, the attributive member (whether a noun or an adjective) being placed first, and made to qualify another substantive, and neither of the two members separately, but the sense of the whole compound, qualifies that substantive. This compound is adjectival in character, but there are several instances of Bahuvrîhi compounds which have come to be regarded and used as nouns (their application being restricted by usage to particular individuals); *e. g.* चक्रपाणि, शशिशेखर, पीतांबर, चतुर्मुख, त्रिनेत्र, कुसुमशर &c. –शत्रुः a sparrow. –शल्यः a species of Khadira. –शृंगः an epithet of Vishṇu. –श्रुत *a.* 1 well-in-formed, very learned; H. 1. 1; Pt. 2. 1; Pt. 2. 1; R. 15. 36. 2 well-versed in the Vedas; Ms. 8. 350. –संतति *a.* having a numerous progeny. (–तिः) a kind of bamboo. –सार *a.* possessed of great pith or essence, substantial. (–रः) the Khadira tree. –सूः 1 a mother of many children. 2 a sow. –सूतिः *f.* 1 a mother of many children. 2 a cow that often calves. –स्वन *a.* vociferous. (–नः) an owl. –स्वामिक *a.* owned by many. बहुक *a.* Dear bought. –कः 1 The sun. 2 The sun-plant (अर्क). 3 A crab. 4 A kind of gallinule.

बहुतर *a.* More numerous, greater, larger.

बहुतम *a.* Most abundant, greatest.

बहुतः *ind.* From many sides.

बहुता,–त्वं Abundance, plenty, numerousness.

बहुतिथ *a.* Much, long, many; काले गते बहुतिथे *S.* 5. 3; तस्य भुवि बहुतिथास्तिथयः Ki. 12. 2.

बहुधा *ind.* 1 In many ways, variously, diversely, multifariously; बहुधाप्यागमैर्भिन्नाः R. 10. 26; Bg. 13. 4. 2 In different froms or ways, 3 Frequently, repeatedly. 4 In various places or directions.

बहुल *a.* (*compar* बंहीयस्; *superl.* बंहिष्ठ) 1 Thick, dense, compact. 2 Broad, wide, capacious, ample, large. 3 Abundant, copious, plentiful, much, numerous; अविनयबहुलतया K. 143. 4. Numerous, manifold, many; Mâl. 9. 18. 5. Full of, rich or abounding in; जन्मनि क्लेशबहुले किं नु दुःखमतःपरं H. 1. 184; Bg. 2. 43. 6 Accompanied or attended by. 7 Born under the Pleiades. 8 Black.—लः 1 The dark half of a month (कृष्णपक्ष); प्रादुरासबहुलक्षपाछविः R. 11. 15; करेण भानोर्बहुलावसाने संधुक्ष्यमाणेवशशांकरेखा Ku. 7. 8, 4. 13. 2 An epithet of fire.—ला 1 A cow. 2 Cardamoms. 3 The indigo plant. 4 The Pleiadas (pl.).—लं 1 The sky. 2 White-pepper. [बहुलीकृ means 1 to make public, disclose, divulge. 2 to make dense or compact; Si. 13. 44. 3 to increase, extend, aggrandize; भूतेषु किं च करुणां बहुली करोति Bv. 1. 122. 4 to thresh(?). बहुलीभू means 1 to spread, increase, multiply; छिद्रेष्वनर्था बहुलीभवंति Pt. 2. 175. 2 to get abroad, to become public or notorious, be generally known, become wild-spread; बहुलीभूतमेतत् किं न कथ्यते *S.* 6; पौरेषु सोऽहं बहुलीभवंतं...सोढुं न तत्पूर्वमवर्णमीशे R. 14. 38]. –COMP. –आलाप *a.* talkative, loquacious, garrulous. –गंधा cardamoms.

बहुलिका *f.* (pl.) The Pleiades.

बहुशस् *ind.* 1 Much, abundantly, plentifully; Me; 106. 2 Frequently, repeatedly, often times; चलापांगां दृष्टिं स्पृशसि बहुशो वेपथुमतीं *S.* 1. 23. Ku. 4. 35. 3 Generally, commonly.

बाकुलं The fruit of the Bakula tree.

बाड् 1 A. (बाडते) 1 To bathe. 2 To emerge.

बाडवः See वाडव.

बाडवेय See वाडवेय.

बाडव्यं See वाडव्य.

बाढ *a.* (*compar.* साधीयस्; *superal.* साधिष्ठ) 1 Firm, strong. 2 Loud. –ढं *ind.* 1 Assuredly, certainly, surely, really; oh yes (in answer to questions); चाणक्यः—चंदनदास एष न निश्चयः। चंदन० बाढं एष मे स्थिरो निश्चयः Mu. 1; बाढमेषु दिवसेषु पार्थिवः कर्म साधयति पुत्रजन्मने R. 19. 52. 2 Very well, be it so, good. 3 Exceedingly, very much; Si. 9. 77.

बाणः 1 An arrow, shaft, reed; धनुष्यमोघं समधत्त बाणं Ku. 3. 16. 2 An aim or mark for arrows. 3 The feathered end of an arrow. 4 The udder of a cow. 5 A kind of plant (निलाझिंटी; *f.* also); विकचबाणदलावलयोऽधिकं रुचिरे रुचिरेक्षणाविभ्रमाः Si. 6. 46. 6 N. of a demon, son of Bali; cf. उषा 7 N. of a celebrated poet who lived at the court of king Harshavardhana and flourished in the first half of the seventh century; (see App. II.) He is the author of कादम्बरी, हर्षचरित and of some other works (Govardhana in his *A*ryâsaptasati *v.* 37. speaks in these terms of Bâṇa:—जाता शिखंडिनी प्राग्यथा शिखंडी तथावगच्छामि। प्रागल्भ्यमधिकमाप्तुं वाणी बाणो बभूवेति ॥; So हृदयवसतिः पंचबाणस्तु बाणः P. R. 1. 22). 1 A symbolical expression for the number 'five'. –COMP. –असनं a bow. आवलिः–ली *f.* 1. a series of arrows. 2 a series of five verses forming one sentence. –आश्रयः a quiver. –गोचरः the range of an arrow. –जालं a number of arrows.–जित् *m.* an epithet of Vishṇu. –तूणः, धिः a quiver. –पंथः the range of an arrow. –पाणि *a* armed with arrows. –पातः 1 an arrow-shot (as a measure of distance). 2 the range of an arrow. –मुक्तिः, मोक्षणं discharging or shooting an arrow. –योजनं a quiver.–वृष्टिः *f.* a shower of arrows. –वारः a breast-plate, an armour, cuirass; cf. वारबाणः, –सुताः an epithet of Ushâ, daughter of Bâṇa; see उषा. हन् *m.* an epithet of Vishṇu.

बाणिनी See वाणिनी.

बादर *a.* (री *f.*) 1 Belonging to or coming from the jujube tree. 2 Made of cotton. –रः The cotton shrub –रं 1 The jujube. 2 Silk. 3 Water. 4 A garment of cotton. 5 A conch-shell winding from left to right.–रा The cotton shrub.

बादरायणः N. of a sage said to be the author of ths Sârîraka Sútras of the Vedânta philosophy (generally indentified with Vyâsa). –COMP. –सूत्रं the Vedanta aphorisms. –संबंधः (a modern formation) an imaginary or far-fetched relation.

बादरायणिः N. of Suka, son of Vyâsa.

बादरिक *a.* (की *f.*) One who gathers jujube fruits.

बाध् 1 A (बाधते, बाधित) 1 To harass, oppress, torment, press hard, annoy, trouble, disturb, vex, pain (persons or things); ऊनं न सत्त्वेष्वधिको बबाधे R. 2. 14 न तथा बाधते स्कंधो यथा बाधति बाधते Subhâsh; Me. 53 Ms. 9. 229; 10. 122, Bk. 14. 45. 2 To resist, oppose, thwart, check, obstruct, arrest, interfere with; Ki. 1. 11; U. 5. 12. 3 To attack, assault, assail. 4 To wrong, violate. 5 To hurt, injure. 6 To drive away, repel, remove. 7 To suspend, set aside, annul, annihilate, abolish (as a rules &c.), R. 17. 57. –With अभि 1 to hurt, injure. 2 to vex, harass, torment,. –आ to vex, torment, injure. -परि to trouble, afflict; *S*. 7. 25. -प्र 1 to trouble, torment, harass, tease, hurt समुच्छितानिव तरून् प्रबाधते (प्रभंजनः) H. 1; Bk. 12. 2. 2 to drive away, remove, get over, कथं नु दैवं शक्येत पौरुषेण प्रबाधितुं Mb. -सं to trouble, torment.

बाधः-धा 1 Pain, suffering, affliction, torment; रजन्या सह जृंभते मदनबाधा V. 3. 2 Disturbance, molestation, annoyance; इति भ्रमरबाधां निरूपयति *S*. 1. 3 Harm, injury, damage, hurt; चरणस्य बाधा M. 4, Y. 2. 156. 4 Danger, peril. 5 Resistance, opposition, 6 An objection. 7 Contradiction, refutation. 1 Suspension, annulment. 9 A flaw in a syllogism, one of tha five forms of हेत्वाभास or fallacious middle term; see बाधित below. -COMP. -अपवादः denial of an exception.

बाधक *a*. (धिका *f*.) 1 Troubling, tormenting, oppressing. 2 Vexing, annoying. 3 Annulling. 4 Hindering.

बाधनं 1 Harassing, oppression, annoyance, disturbance, pain; *S*. 1. 2 Annulment 3 Removal, suspension. 4 Refutation, contradiction.—ना Pain, trouble, anxiety, disturbance.

बाधित *p*. *p*. 1 Harassed, oppressed, annoyed. 2 Pained, troubled, afflicted. 3 Opposed, obstructed. 4 Checked, arrested. 5 Set aside, suspended. 6 Refuted. 7 (In logic) Contradicted, contradictory; inconsistent (and hence futile).

बाधिर्य Deafness.

बांधकिनेयः A bastard.

बांधवः 1 A relation, kinsman (in general); यस्यार्थास्तस्य बांधवाः H. 1; Ms. 5. 74, 101; 4. 179. 2 A maternal relation. 3 A friend ; धनेभ्यः परो बांधवो नास्ति लोके Subhâsh. 4 A brother.-COMP. -जनः relatives, kinsmen (taken collectively) ; दारिद्र्यात्पुरुषस्य बांधवजनो वाक्ये न संतिष्ठते Mk. 1. 36; Pt. 4. 78.

बाधव्यं Consanguinity, relationship.

बाभ्रवी An epithet of Durgâ.

बार्वटीरः 1 The kernel of the mango fruit. 2 Tin. 3 A young shoot. 4 The son of a harlot.

बार्ह *a*. (र्ही) Made of the feathers of a peacock's tail.

बार्हद्रथः, बार्हद्रथिः A patronymic of king Jarâsandha, q. v.

बार्हस्पत *a*. (ती *f*.) Related to, descended from or sacred to, Brihaspati.

बार्हस्पत्य *a*. Relating to Brihaspati -त्यः 1 A pupil of Brihaspati. 2 A follower of Brihrspati who taught the rankest form of materialism, a materialist. -त्यं The constellation Pushya.

बार्हिण *a*. (णी *f*.) Derived from or relating to a peacock.

बाल *a*. 1 Young , infantine, not full-grown or developed (of persons or things); बालेन स्थविरेण वा Ms. 8. 70. बालाशोकमुपोढरागसुभगं भेदोन्मुखं तिष्ठति V. 2. 7; so बालमंदारवृक्षः Me. 75; R. 2. 45; 13. 24. 2 Newly risen, young (as the sun or its rays); R. 12. 100. 3 New, waxing (as the moon) ; पुपोष वृद्धिं हरिदश्वदीधितेरनुप्रवेशादिव बालचंद्रमाः R. 3. 22, Ku, 3. 29 4 Puerile. 5 Ignorant, unwise. -लः 1 A child, an infant; बालादपि सुभाषितं ग्राह्यं Ms. 2. 239. 2 A boy, youth, young person. 3 A minor (under 16 years of age); बाल आषोडशाद्वर्षात् Nârada. 4 A colt, foal. 5 A fool, simpleton. 6 A tail. 7 Hair. 8 An elephant five years old. 9 A' kind of perfume. -COMP. -अग्रं the point of a hair. -अध्यापकः a tutor of youths or children -अभ्यासः study during childhood, early application (to study). -अरुण *a*. red like early dawn. (-णः) early dawn.—अर्कः the newly risen sun; R. 12. 100. -अवबोधः instruction of the young. -अवस्थ *a*. juvenile, young, V. 5. 18 -अवस्था childhood. -आतपः morning sunshine.-इंदुः the new or waxing moon; Ku. 3. 29. -इष्टः the jujube tree. -उपचारः (medical) treatment of children. -उपवीतं a piece of cloth used to cover the privities. -कदली a young plantain tree. -कुंदः-दं a kind of young Jasmine. (-दं) a young jasmine blossom; अलके बालकुंदानुविद्धं Me. 65. -कृमिः a louse. -कृष्णः Krishna as a boy. -क्रीडनं a child's play or toy. क्रीडनकं a child's toy. (-कः) 1 a ball. 2 an epithet of Siva. -क्रीडा a child's play, childish or juvenile sport. -खिल्यः a class of divine personrges of the size of a thumb and produced from the creator's body and said to precede the sun's chariot (their number is said to be sixty thousand); cf. R. 15. 10.-गर्भिणी a cow with calf for the first time. -गोपालः 'the youthful cowherd,' an epithet of Krishṇa, as the boy-cowherd. -ग्रहः any demon (or planetary influence) teasing or injuring children. -चंद्रः, चंद्रमस् *m*. the young or waxing moon; Mâl. 2. 10. -चरितं 1 juvenile sports. 2 early life or actions; U. 6. -चर्यः N. of Kârtikeya. (-र्या) the behaviour of a child. -ज *a*. produced from hair. -तनयः the Khadira tree. -तंत्रं midwifery -तृणं young grass. -दलकः the Khadira. -धिः a hairy tail; Si. 12. 73; Ki. 12. 47. -पाश्या 1 an ornament worn in the hair when parted. 2 a string of pearls binding or intertwining the braid of hair.-पुष्पिका -पुष्पी a kind of Jasmine. -बोधः 1 instructing the young. 2 any work adapted to the capacities of the young or inexperienced. -भद्रकः a kind of poison. -भारः a large bushy tail; बाधेतोल्काक्षपितचमरी बालभारो दवाग्निः Me. 53. -भावः childhood, infancy. -भैषज्यं a kind of collyrium. -भोज्यः pease. -मृगः a fawn. -यज्ञोपवीतकं the sacred thread worn across the breast. -राजं lapis lazuli. -रोगः a child's disease. -लता a young creeper; R. 2. 10. -लीला child's play, juvenile pastime. -वत्सः 1 a young calf. 2 a pigeon. -वायजं lapis lazuli. -वासस् *n*. a woollen garment. -वाह्यः a wild goat. -विधवा a child-widow. -वैधव्यं child-widowhood. -व्यजनं a *chowrie* or fly-flapper (usually made of the tail of the yâk or *Bos Grunniens* and used as one of the royal insignia); R. 9. 66; 14. 11; 16. 33. 57; Ku. 1. 13. -सखिः a friend from childhood. -संध्या early twilight. -सुहृद् *m*. a friend of one's youth. -सूर्यः, -सूर्यकः lapis lazuli. -हत्या infanticide. -हस्तः a hairy tail.

बालक *a*. (लिका *f*.) 1. Childlike, young, not yet fullgrown. 2 Ignorant. —कः 1 A child, boy. 2 A minor (in law). 3 A finger-ring. 4 A fool or blockhead. 5 A bracelet. 6 The tail of a horse or elephant. —कं A finger-ring. -COMP. -हत्या infanticide.

बाला 1 A girl, a female child. 2 A young woman under sixteen years of age. 3 A young woman (in general); जाने तपसो वीर्यं सा बाला परवतीति मे विदितं *S*. 3. 1: इयं बाला मां प्रत्यनवरतमिंदीवरदलप्रभाचोरं चक्षु क्षिपति Bh. 3. 67; Me. 83. 4 A varicty of Jasmine. 5 The cocoa-nut. 6 The plant घृतकुमारी. 7 Small cardamoms. 8 Turmeric. -COMP. -हत्या female infanticide.

बालिः N. of a celebrated monkey-king; see वालि. -COMP. -हन्, हंतृ *m*. an epithet of Râma.

बालिका 1 A girl. 2 The knot of an ear-ring. 3 Small cardamoms. 4 Sand. 5 The rustling of leaves.

बालिन् *m*. N. of a monkey; see वालि.

बालिनी The constellation Asvinî.

बालिमन् *m*. Childhood, boyhood, youth.

बालिश *a*. 1 Childish, puerile, silly. 2 Young. 3 Foolish, ignorant; Ms. 3. 176. 4 Careless.—शः 1 A fool, blockhead. 2 A child, boy. —शं A pillow.

बालीश्यं 1 Youth, boyhood. 2 Childishness, silliness, folly.

बाली A kind of ear-ring.

बालीशः Retention of urine.

बालुः,-बालुकं A kind of perfume.

बालुका see वालुका.

बालुकी-बालुंकी, बालुंगी A kind of cucumber.

बालूकः A kind of poison.

बालेय *a.* (यी *f.*) 1 Fit for an offering. 2 Tender, soft. 3 Descended from Bali. —**यः** An ass.

बाल्यं 1 Boyhood, childhood; बाल्यात्परामिव दशां मदनोध्युवास R 5. 63; Au. 1. 29. 2 The period or state of waxing (as of the moon); Ku. 7. 35. 3 Immaturity of understanding, folly, puerility.

बाल्हकाः, बाह्लिकाः, बाल्हीकाः (*m.* pl.) N. of a people. —**कः** 1 A king of the Bâlhikas. 2 A horse of the Balkh breed. —**कं** 1 Saffron. 2 Asa Fœtida.

बाल्हिः N. of a country (Balkh). -COMP. -**ज** *a.* bred in the Balkh country, of the Balkh breed.

बाष्पः-ष्पं 1 A tear, tears; कंठः स्तंभितबाष्पवृत्तिकलुषः S. 4. 5. 2 Vapour, steam, mist 3 Iron. -COMP. -**अंबु** *n.* tears. -**आकुल** *a.* dimmed or interrupted by tears. -**उद्भवः** the starting of tears. -**कंठ** *a.* having tears in the throat, choked with tears. -**दुर्दिनं** a flood of tears, -**पूरः** a gush or flood of tears; वारंवारं तिरयति दृशोरुद्गमं बाष्पपूरः Mâl. 1. 35. -**मोक्षः** -**मोचनं** shedding tears. -**बिंदुः** *m.* a tear-drop -**संदिग्ध** *a.* indistinct through suppressed tears.

बाष्पायते Den. A. To shed tears, weep; तत्किमिति बाष्पायितं भगवत्या Mâl. 6, V. 5. 9.

बास्त *a.* (स्ती *f.*) Coming or derived from a goat; Ms. 2. 41.

बाहः 1 The arm. 2 A horse.

बाहा The arm; मां प्रत्यालिंगितोगताभिः शाखाबाहाभिः S. 3. -COMP. -**बाहवि** *ind.* hand to hand, arm against arm; cf. बाहूबाहवि.

बाहीकाः (pl.) The people of the Punjab. —**कः** 1 An inhabitant of the Punjab. 2 An ox.

बाहुः 1 The arm; शांतमिदमाश्रमपदं स्फुरति च बाहुः कुतः फलमिहास्य S. 1. 16; so महाबाहुः &c. 2 The fore-arm. 3 The forefoot of an animal. 4 A door-post. 5 The base of a right-angled triangle (in geom.). —**हू** (du.) The lunar mansion Ardrâ. -COMP. -**उत्क्षेपं** *ind.* having raised or tossed up the arms; बाहूत्क्षेपं क्रंदितुं च प्रवृत्ता S. 5. 30. -**कुंठ**, -**कुब्ज** *a.* crippled in the arms. -**कुंथः** a wing (of a bird) -**चापः** the distance measured by the extended arms. -**जः** 1 a man of the Kshatriya caste; cf. बाहू राजन्यः कृतः Rv. 10. 90; 12; also Ms. 1. 31. 2 a parrot. -**ज्या** a sine (in math.). -**त्रः**, -**त्रं**, -**त्राणं** vantbrass (armour for the arms). -**दंडः** 1 a stafflike arm. 2 punishment with the arm or fist. -**पाशः** 1 a particular attitude in fighting. 2 the arm thrown round, as in the act of embracing. -**प्रहरणं** boxing, wrestling. -**बलं** strength of arm, muscular strength. -**भूषणं**, -**भूषा** an ornament worn on the arm, an armlet. -**भेदिन्** *m.* an epithet of Vishṇu. -**मूलं** 1 the armpit. 2 the shoulder-blade. -**युद्धं** a hand-to-hand or close fight, personal or pugilistic encounter, boxing. -**योधः**, -**योधिन्** *m.* a pugilist, boxer. -**लता** an armlike creeper. °**अंतरं** the breast, bosom. -**वीर्यं** strength of arm. -**व्यायाम** athletic exercise. -**शालिन्** *m.* 1 an epithet of Siva. 2 of Bhima. -**शिखरं** the upper part of the arm, the shoulder. -**संभवः** a man of the Kshatriya caste. -**सहस्रभृत्** *m.* an epithet of king Kârtavîrya (also called सहस्रार्जुन).

बाहुकः 1 A monkey. 2 A name assumed by Nala after his transformation into a dwarf by Karkoṭaka.

बाहुगुण्यं Possession of many virtues or excellences.

बाहुदंतकं A treatise on moral duties said to be composed or abridged by Indra.

बाहुदंतेयः An epithet of Indra.

बाहुदा N. of a river.

बाहुभाष्यं Garrulity, loquaciousness, talkativeness.

बाहुरूप्यं Manifoldness, variety.

बाहुलः 1 Fire. 2 The month Kârtika. —**लं** 1 Manifoldness. 2 An armour for the arms, vantbrass. COM. -**ग्रीवः** a peacock.

बाहुलकं Manifoldness. 2 The diverse or interminable applicability of a rule, of meanings or of forms; a term frequently used in grammar; बाहुलकाच्छंदसि.

बाहुलेयः An epithet of Kâtikeya.

बाहुल्यं 1 Abundance, plenty, copiousness. 2 Manifoldness, multiplicity, variety. 3 The usual course or common order of things.

बाहूबाहवि *ind.* Arm to arm, hand-to-hand, in close encounter.

बाह्य *a.* 1 Outer, outward, external, exterior, being or situated without; विरहः किमिवानुतापयेद्वद बाह्यैर्विषयैर्विपश्चितं R. 8. 89; बाह्योद्यान Me. 7; Ku. 6. 46; बाह्यनामन् 'the outer name' *i. e.* the address or superscription written on the back of a letter; Mu. 1. 2 Foreign, strange; Pt. 1. 3 Excluded from, out of the pale of; जातास्तद्वर्गोरुपमानबाह्याः Ku. 1. 36. 4 Expelled from society, outcast. -**ह्यः** 1 A stranger, foreigner. 2 One who is excommunicated, an outcast. —**ह्यं**,-**बाह्येन**, **बाह्ये** *ind.* Outside, on the outside, externally.

बाह्वृच्यं Traditional teaching of the Ṛigveda.

बिद् 1 P. (बेटति) 1 To swear. 2 curse. 3 To shout, exclaim.

बिटकः-कं, बिटका A boil.

बिडं A kind of salt.

बिडालः 1 A cat. 2 The eyeball. -COMP. -**पदः**,-**पदकं** a measure of weight equal to sixteen Mâshas.

बिडालकः 1 A cat. 2 Application of ointment to the exterior part of the eye. —**कं** Yellow ointment.

बिडौजस् *m.* An epithet of Indra; S. 7. 34.

बिद्, बिंद् I P. (बिंदति) 1 To split. 2 To divide.

बिदलं See विदल.

बिंदुः 1 A drop, small particle; जलबिंदुनिपातेन क्रमशः पूर्यते घटः 'small drops make a pool'; विस्तीर्यते यशो लोके तैलबिंदुरिवांभसि Ms. 7. 33; संक्षिप्यते यशो लोके घृतबिंदुरिवांभासि 7. 84; अधुना (कुतूहलस्य) बिंदुरपि नावशेषितः S. 2. 2. A dot, point. 3 A spot or mark of coloured paint on the body of an elephant; Ku. 1. 7. 4 A zero or cypher; न रोमकूपौघमिषाज्जगत्कृता कृताश्च किं दूषणशून्यबिंदवः N. 1. 21. -COMP. -**चित्रकः** the spotted antelope. **जालं**,-**जालकं** 1 a number of drops. 2 marks of coloured paint on the trunk and face of an elephant. -**तंत्रः** 1 a die. 2 a chess-board. -**देवः** an epithet of Siva. -**पत्रः** a kind of birch tree. -**फलं** a pearl. -**रेखकः** 1 an anusvâra. 2 a kind of bird. -**रेखा** a line of dots. -**वासरः** the day of conception.

बिब्बोकः 1 Affectation of indifference towards a beloved object through pride; मनाक्प्रियकथालापे बिब्बोकोऽनादरक्रिया Pratâparudra; or बिब्बोकस्त्वतिगर्वेण वस्तुनीष्टेऽप्यनादरः S. D. 139. 2 Haughty indifference in general. 3 Playful or amorous gestures; संशय्य क्षणमिति निश्चिकाय कश्चिद्बिब्बोकैर्बकसहवासिनां परोक्षैः Si. 8. 9. (विलासैः Mallî.). (Also written **विब्बोक** and **विब्वोक**).

बिभित्सा A wish to break through, a desire to pierce or penetrate.

बिभित्सु *a.* Desirous of piercing or penetrating.

बिभीषणः N. of a demon and brother of Râvaṇa. [Though a demon by birth, he was extremely sorry for the abduction of Sita by Ravana, and severely reprimanded him for his wicked act. He several times advised Ravana to restore Sita to Rama if he cared to live; but the proud demon turned a deaf ear to his warnings. At last seeing that the ruin of his brother was inevitable, he repaired to Rama and became his staunch friend. After the death of Ravana Rama installed him on the throne of Lanka. He is believed to be one of the seven Chirajivins; see चिरजीविन्].

बिभ्रक्षुः, बिभ्रजिषुः Fire.

बिंबः-बं 1 The disc of the sun or moon; वदनेन निर्जितं तव निलीयते चंद्रबिंबमंबुधरे Subhâsh.; so सूर्य°, रवि° &c. 2 Any round or disclike surface; disc or orb in general; as in नितंबबिंबं the round hip; श्रोणीबिंबः &c. 3 An image, shadow, reflection. 4 A mirror. 5 A jar. 6 An object compared (opp. प्रतिबिंब to which it is compared). -बं The fruit of a tree (which, when ripe, is ruddy and to which the lips of young women are often compared); रक्तशोकरुचा विशेषितगुणो बिंबाधरालक्तकः M. 3. 5; पक्वबिंबाधरोष्ठी Me. 82; cf. N. 2. 24. -COMP. -ओष्ठ *a.* (बिंबो-बौ-ष्ठ) having lips as ruddy or cherry as the Bimba fruit; M. 4. 14. (-ष्ठः) lip like, the Bimba fruit. -फलं the Bimba fruit; उमामुखे बिंबफलाधरोष्ठे Ku. 3. 67.

बिंबकं 1 The disc of the sun or moon. 2 The Bimba fruit.

बिंबिका 1 The disc of the sun or moon. 2 The Bimba plant.

बिंबित *a.* 1 Reflected, shadowed. 2 Pictured.

बिल् 6 P., 10 U. (बिलति, बेलयति-ते) To split, cleave, break, divide.

बिलं 1 A hole, cavity, burrow; खनन्नाखुबिलं सिंहः......प्राप्नोति नखभंगं हि Pt. 3. 17; R. 12. 5. 2 Agap, pit, chasm. 3 An aperture, opening, outlet. 4 A cave, hollow. -लः N. of उच्चैःश्रवस्, the horse of Indra. -COMP. -ओकस् *m.* any animal that lives in holes. -कारिन् *m.* a mouse. -योनि *a.* of the breed of Bila; सत्राश्वा बिलयोनयः Ku. 6. 39. -वासः a pole-cat. -वासिन् (also बिलेवासिन्) *m.* a snake.

बिलंगमः A serpent, snake.

बिलेशयः 1 A snake. 2 A mouse, rat. 3 Any animal living in burrows.

बिल्लः 1 A pit. 2 Particularly, a basin for water round the foot of a tree (आलवाल). -COMP. -सूः a mother of ten children.

बिल्वः A species of tree. -ल्वं 1 The fruit of this tree. 2 A particular weight (=one pala). -COMP. -दंडः an epithet of S'iva. -पेशिका -पेशी the shell of the Bilva fruit. -वनं a thicket or wood of Bilva trees.

बिल्वकीया A place planted with Bilva trees.

बिस् 4 P. (बिस्यति) 1 To go, move. 2 To incite, drive or urge on, instigate. 3 To throw, cast. 4 To split.

बिसं 1 The fibre of a lotus; 2 The fibrous stalk of a lotus; पाथेयमुत्सृज बिसं ग्रहणाय भूयः V. 4. 15; बिसमलमशनाय स्वादु पानाय तोयं Bh. 3. 22; Me. 11 Ku. 3. 17; 4. 29. -COMP. कंठिका, कंठिन् *m.* a small crane. -कुसुमं -पुष्पं -प्रसूनं a lotus; जक्षुर्बिसं धृतविकाशिबिसप्रसूनाः Si. 5. 58. -खादिका eating the fibres of a lotus. -ग्रंथिः a knot on the stalk of a lotus. -छेदः a bit of the fibrous stalk of a lotus. -जं a lotus flower, lotus. -तंतुः the lotus-fibre. -नाभिः *f.* the lotus-plant (पद्मिनी). -नासिका a sort of crane.

बिसलं A young shoot, sprout, bud.

बिसिनी 1 The lotus-plant; Bh. 3. 36. 2 Lotus-fibres. 3 An assemblage of lotuses.

बिसिल *a.* Coming from or relating to a Bisa.

बिस्तः A weight of gold (equal to 80 *Raktikas* or *gunjâs*).

बिह्लणः N. of a poet, the author of the Vikramânkadevacharita.

बीजं 1 Seed (fig. also), seed-corn, grain; अरण्यबीजांजलिदानलालिताः Ku. 5. 15; बीजांजलिः पतति कीटमुखावलीढः Mk. 1. 9; R. 19 57; Ms. 9. 33. 2 A germ, element. 3 Origin, source, cause; बीजप्रकृतिः S. 1. 1. v. l. 4 Semen virile; Ku. 2. 5, 60. 5 The seed or germ of the plot of a play; story &c.; see S. D. 318. 6 Marrow. 7 Algebra. 8 The mystical letter forming the essential part of the *Mantra* of a deity. -जः The citron tree. (बीजाकृ means 1 to sow with seed; व्योमनि बीजाकुरुते Bv. 1 98. 2 to plough over after sowing). -COMP. -अक्षरं the first syllable of a *Mantra*. -अंकुरः a seed-shoot; Au. 3. 18. °न्यायः the maxim of seed and sprout see under न्याय. -अध्यक्षः an epithet of Siva. -अश्वः a stallion. -आढ्यः -पूरः, -पूरकः common citron. (-रं-रकं) the fruit of. citron. -उत्कृष्टं good seed. -उदकं hail. -कर्तृ *m.* an epithet of Siva. -कोशः, -कोषः 1 the the seed-vessel 2 the seed-vessel of the lotus. -गणितं the science of Algebra. -गुप्तिः *f.* a pod, legume. -दर्शकः a stage-manager. -धान्यं coriander. -न्यासः making known the germ of the plot of a play. -पुरुषः the progenitor of a family. -फलकः the citron tree. -मंत्रः a mystical syllable with which a Mantra begins. -मातृका the pericarp of a lotus. -रुहः grain, corn. -वापः 1 a sower of seed. 2 sowing seed. -वाहनः an epithet of Siva. -सूः the earth. -सेक्तृ *m. a.* procreator, progenitor.

बीजकः 1 The common citron. 2 A lemon or citron. 3 The position of the arms of a child at birth. -कं Seed.

बीजल *a.* Furnished with seed, seedy.

बीजिक *a.* Abounding in seeds.

बीजिन् *a.* (नी *f.*) Possessed of seed, bearing seed. —*m.* 1 The real father or progenitor (sower of seed) (opp. क्षेत्रिन् the owner or husband of the क्षेत्र or woman); see Ms. 9. 51 *et seq.* 2 A father in general 3 The sun.

बीज्य *a.* 1 Born from seed. 2 Of a good or respectable family, nobly-born.

बीभत्स *a.* 1 Disgusting, loathsome, nauseous, hideous, revolting; हंत बीभत्समेवाग्रे वर्तते Mâl. 5 'Oh! it is indeed a loathsome sight.' 2 Envious, malignant, mischievous, 3 Savage, cruel, ferocious. 4 Estranged in mind. -त्सः 1 Disgust, abhorrence, detestation. 2 The disgusting sentiment, one of the 8 or 9 *rasas* in poetry; जुगुप्सास्थायिभावस्तु बीभत्सः कथ्यते रसः S. D. 236 (*e. g.* Mâl. 5. 16.). 3 N. of Arjuna.

बीभत्सुः An epithet of Arjuna; Mb. thus explains the word:—

न कुर्यां कर्म बीभत्सं युध्यमानः कथंचन। तेन देवमनुष्येषु बीभत्सुरिति विश्रुतः॥

बुक् *ind.* An imitative word. -COMP. -कारः the roaring of a lion.

बुक्क 1 P., 10 U. (बुक्कति, बुक्कयति-ते) 1 To bark; H. 3. 52. 2 To speak, talk.

बुक्कः-क्कं 1 The heart. 2 The bosom, chest; बुक्काघातैर्युवतिनिकटे प्रौढवाक्येन राधा Udb. 3 Blood. -क्कः 1 A goat. 2 Time (समय).

बुक्कन् *m.* The heart.

बुक्कनं Barking, yelping.

बुक्कसः A chând̤âla.

बुक्का -क्की The heart.

बुद् 1 U. (बोदति-ते) 1 To perceive, see, apprehend, discern. 2 To understand, know.

बुद्ध *p. p.* 1 Known, understood, perceived. 2 Awakened, awake. 3 Observed. 4 Enlightened, wise (see बुध्). -द्धः 1 A wise or learned man, a sage. 2 (With Buddhists) A wise or enlightened person who, by perfect knowledge of the truth, is absolved from all existence, and who reveals to the world the method of obtainning the Nirvâṇa or final emancipation before obtaining it himself. 3 'The enlightened', N. of Sâkyasimha, the celebrated founder of the Bauddha religion; (he is said to have been born at Kapilavastu and to have died in 543 B. C.; he is sometimes regarded as the ninth incarnation of Vishṇu; thus Jayadeva says:—निंदसि यज्ञविधेरहह श्रुतिजातं सदयहृदय दर्शितपशुघातं केशव धृतबुद्धशरीर जय जगदीश हरे Git. 1). -COMP. -आगमः the doctrines and tenets of the Baudha religion. -उपासकः a worshipper of Buddha. -गया N. of a sacred place of pilgrimage. -मार्गः the doctrines and tenets of Buddha, Buddhism.

बुद्धिः *f* 1 Perception, comprehension. 2 Intellect, understanding, intelligence, talent; तीक्ष्णा नारुंतुदा बुद्धिः *Si.* 2. 109; शास्त्रेष्वकुंठिता बुद्धिः R. 1 19. 3 Knowledge; बुद्धिर्यस्य बलं तस्य H. 2. 122. 'knowledge is power'. 4 Discrimination, judgment, discernment. 5 Mind; मूढः परप्रत्ययनेयबुद्धिः M. 1. 2; so कृपण°, पाप° &c. 6 Presence of mind, readiness of wit. 7 An impression, opinion, belief, idea, feeling, notion; दूरात्तमवलोक्य व्याघ्रबुद्ध्या पलायंते H. 3; अनया बुद्ध्या Mu. 1. in this belief; अनक्रोशबुद्ध्या Me 115. 8 Intention, purpose, design. (बुद्ध्या 'intentionally', 'purposely', 'deliberately'). 9 Returning to consciousness, recovery from a swoon; Mâl 4. 10 (In Sân. phil.) Intellect, the second of the 25 elements of the Sânkhyas. -COMP. -अतीत *a.* beyond the range or reach of the intellect. -अवज्ञानं contempt or low opinion for one's understanding; अप्राप्तकालं वचनं बृहस्पतिरपि ब्रुवन् । प्राप्नोति बुद्ध्यवज्ञानमपमानं च पुष्कलं ॥ Pt. 1. 63. -इंद्रियं an organ of perception (opp. कर्मेंद्रिय); (these are five—the ear, skin, eye, tongue, and nose; श्रोत्रं त्वक्चक्षुषी जिह्वा नासिका चैव पंचमी; to these sometimes मनस् is added). -गम्य, -ग्राह्य *a.* within the reach of, attainable to, intellect. -जीविन् *a.* employing the reason, rational. -पूर्वं, -पूर्वकं, पुरःसरं *ind.* intentionally, purposely, wilfully. -भ्रमः distraction or aberration of the mind. -योगः intellectual communion with the Supreme Spirit. -लक्षणं a sign of intellect or wisdom; प्रारब्धस्यांतगमनं द्वितीयं बुद्धिलक्षणम्. -वैभवं strength of intellect. -शस्त्र *a.* armed with understanding. -शालिन्, -संपन्न *a* intelligent, wise. -सखः, -सहायः a a counsellor. -हीन *a.* devoid of intellect, silly, foolish.

बुद्धिमत् *a.* 1 Endowed with understanding, intelligent, rational. 2 Wise, learned. 3 Sharp, clever, acute.

बुद्बुदः A bubble; सततं जातविनष्टाः पयसामिव बुद्बुदाः पयसि Pt. 5. 7.

बुध् 1 U., 4. A. (बोधति ते, बुध्यते, बुद्ध) 1 To know, understand, comprehend; क्रमादमुं नारद इत्यबोधि सः *Si.* 1. 3; 9. 24; नाबुद्ध कल्पद्रुमतां विहाय जातं तमात्मन्यसिपत्रवृक्षं R 14. 48; यदि बुध्यते हरिशिशुः स्तनंधयः Bv. 1. 53. 2 To perceive, notice, recognise, mark; हिरण्मयं हंसमबोधि नैषधः N. 1. 117; अपि लंघितमध्वानं बुबुधे न बुधोपमः R. 1. 47; 12. 39. 3 To deem, regard, consider, esteem &c. 4 To heed, attend to. 5 To think, reflect. 6 To wake up, awake, rise from sleep; ददृशुः गिरमंतर्बुध्यंते नो मनुष्यः *Si.* 11. 4; ते च प्रापुरुदन्वंतं बुबुधे चादिपुरुषः R. 10. 6. 7 To regain consciousness, to come to one's senses; शनैरबोधि सुग्रीवः सोऽलुंचीत्कर्णनासिकं Bk. 15. 57.—*Caus.* (बोधयति-ते) 1 To cause to know, make known, inform, acquaint with. 2 To teach, communicate, impart. 3 To advise, admonish; बोधयंतं हिताहितं Bk. 8. 82; Bg. 10 9. 4 To revive, restore to life, bring to senses or consciousness. 5 To remind, put in mind of: *S.* 4. 1. 6 To wake up, rouse, excite (fig.); अकाले बोधितो भ्रात्रा R. 12. 81, 5. 75 7 To revive the scent (of a perfume). 8 To cause to expand, open; मधुरया मधुबोधितमाधवी *Si.* 6. 20. 9 To signify, convey, indicate.—*Desid.* (बुबु -बो -धिषति-ते, बुभुत्सते) To wish to know &c.-WITH अनु 1 to know, understand. 2 to learn, be aware or conscious of. (*Caus.*) 1 to advise, admonish, R. 8. 75. 2 to remind, आर्ये सम्यगनुबोधितोस्मि *S.* 1. -अव to know, learn, understand; Ms. 8. 53; Bk. 15. 101. (*-Caus.*) 1 to make known, inform, acquaint with; ब्रह्मचोदनानुपुरुषमवबोधयत्येव केवलं S. B. 2 to rouse, awaken; R. 12. 23. -उद् 1 to awake, wake up. 2 to expand, bloom. (*-Caus.*) to awaken, excite, prompt, rouse.-नि 1 to know, understand, learn; निबोध साधो तव चेत्कुतूहलं Ku 5. 52; 3. 14; Ms. 1. 68; Y. 1 2. 2 to regard or consider as, deem. -प्र 1 to awake, wake up, rise from sleep; *S.* 5. 11; *Si.* 9 30 2 to blow, expand be blown; साभ्रे ह्नीव स्थलकमलिनीं न प्रबुद्धां न सुप्तां Me 90. (*-Caus*) 1 to inform, make known; R. 3. 68. 2 to awaken, rouse; R. 5. 65; 6. 56. 3 to cause to expand or open; Ku 1. 16. -प्रति to wake, wake up; Ms. 1 74; Y. 1 330. (*-Caus.*) 1 to inform, make known, acquaint with, communicate; R 1. 74; *Si.* 6. 8. 2 to awaken rouse; -वि to wake up, awake; Ku. 5. 57. (*-Caus.*) 1 to awaken, rouse 2 to restore to consciousness; अथ मोहपरायणा सती विवशा कामवधूर्विबोधिता Ku. 4. 1. -सं to know, understand, learn; become aware of; Bk. 19. 30 (*-Caus*) 1 to inform, acquaint with, give information about; तवागतिज्ञं समबोधयन्मां R. 13. 25 2 to address.

बुध *a.* Wise, clever, learned -धः 1 A wise or learned man; निपीय यस्य क्षितिरक्षिणः कथां तथाद्रियंते न बुधाः सुधामपि N. 1. 1. 2 A god; N. 1. 1. 3 The planet Mercury; रक्षत्येनं तु बुधयोगः Mu. 1. 6 (where बुध has sense 1 also); R. 1. 47; 13 76. -COMP. -जनः a wise or learned man. -तातः the moon. -दिनं, -वारः, -वासरः Wednesday. -रत्नं an emerald. -सुतः an epithet of Purûravas.

बुधानः 1 A wise man, sage. 2 A holy teacher, spiritual guide.

बुधित *a.* Known, understood.

बुधिल *a.* Learned, wise.

बुध्नः 1 The bottom of a vessel. 2 The foot of a tree. 3 The lowest part. 4 An epithet of *S*iva. (Also बुध्न्य in the last sense).

बुंद्, बुंध् 1 U. (बुंदति-ते, बुंधति-ते) 1 To perceive, see, descry. 2 To reflect, understand.

बुभुक्षा 1 Desire of eating, hunger. 2 The desire of enjoying anything.

बुभुक्षित *a* Hungry, starving, pinched with hunger; बुभुक्षितः किं न करोति पापं Pt. 4. 15, or बुभुक्षितः किं द्विकरेण भुंक्ते Udb.

बुभुक्षु *a.* 1 Hungry, desirous of worldly enjoyments (opp. मुमुक्षु)

बुभूषा Wish to be or become.

बुभूषु *a.* Wishing to be or become.

बुल् 10 U. (बोलयति-ते) 1 To sink, plunge; बोलयति प्लवः पयसि. 2 To cause to sink

बुलिः *f.* Fear (भय).

बुस् 4. P. (बुस्यति) To discharge, emit, pour forth.

बुसं (षं) 1 Chaff. 2 Rubbish, refuse. 3 Dry cowdung. 4 Wealth.

बुस्त् 10 U. (बुस्तयति-ते) 1 To honour, respect. 2 To disrespect, treat with disrespect or contempt.

बुस्तं The burnt crust of roast meat.

बूक्कं=बुक्क q. v.

बृशी, बृषी (सी) The seat of an ascetic or holy sage.

बृंह् 1. 6. P. (बृंहति, बृंहित) 1 To grow, increase; बृंहितमन्युवेग Bk. 3. 49. 2 To roar. -*Caus.* To cause to grow, nourish

बृंहणं The roaring noise (of an elephant); *Si.* 18. 3.

बृंहित *p. p.* 1 Grown, increased; Bv. 2. 109. 2 Roared &c.-तं The roaring of an elephant; *Si.* 12. 15; Ki. 7 39.

बृह् 1. 6. P. (बर्हति, बृहति) 1 To grow, increase, expand 2 To roar. WITH उद् 1 to lift, raise; Ms. 1 14; Bk. 14 9. -नि to destroy, remove; Si. 1. 29.

बृहत् *a.* (ती *f.*) 1 Large, great, big, bulky; Mâl. 9. 5. 2 Wide, broad, extensive, far-extended; दिलीपसूनोः स बृहद्भुजांतरं R. 3. 54. 3 Vast, ample, abundant. 4 Strong, powerful. 5 Long, tall ; देवदारुबृहद्भुजः Ku. 6. 51. 6 Full-grown. 7 Compact, dense. -*f*. Speech; *S*i. 2. 68. -*n*. 1 The Veda. 2 N. of a Sâman; Bg. 10. 35. 3 Brahma. -COMP.-अंग, काय *a*. large-bodied, gigantic. (-गः) a large elephant. -आरण्यं,-आरण्यकं N. of a celebrated Upanishad, forming the last six chapters of the *S*atapatha Brâhmaṇa. -एला large cardamoms -कुक्षि *a*. large-bellied. -केतुः an epithet of Agni. -गृहः N. of a country. -गोलं a water melon. -चित्तः the citron tree. -जघन *a*. broad-hipped. -जीवंतिका,-जीवंती a kind of plant. -ढक्का a large drum. -नटः,-नलः-ला the name assumed by Arjuna when residing as dancing and music master at the court of Virâṭa -नेत्र *a*. far-sighted, prudent. -पाटलिः the thorn-apple. -पालः the Indian fig-tree. -भट्टारिका an epithet of Durgâ. -भानुः fire. -रथः 1 an epithet of Indra. 2 N. of a king, father of Jarâsandha. -राविन् *m*. a kind of small owl. -स्फिच् *a*. broad-hipped, having large buttocks.

बृहतिका An upper garment, a mantle, wrapper.

बृहस्पतिः 1 N. of the preceptor of the gods; (for the abduction of his wife Târâ by the moon, see under तारा or सोम. 2 The planet Jupiter; बुधबृहस्पतियोगदृश्यः R. 13. 76. 3 N. of the author of a Smṛiti ; Y. 1. 4. -COMP. -पुरोहितः an epithet of Indra. -वारः वासरः Thursday.

बेडा A boat.

बेह् 1 A. (बेहते) To endeavour, strive, attempt.

बैजिक *a*. (की *f*.) 1 Seminal. 2 Original. 3 Relating to conception. 4 Relating to sexual union. -कः A sprout, young shoot. -कं Cause, source, origin.

बैडाल *a*. (ली *f*.) 1 Relating to a cat. 2 Peculiar to cats -COMP. -व्रतं 'a cat-like observance', concealing one's malice or evil designs under the garb of piety or virtue. -व्रतिः one who leads a chaste life simply from want of female company (and not because he has controlled his senses). -व्रतिकः,-व्रतिन् *m*. a religious hypocrite, impostor.

बैदल See बैदल.

बैंबिकः A man who is assiduous in his attentions to ladies, a gallant lover; दाक्षिण्यं नाम बिंबोष्ठि बैंबिकानां कुलव्रतं M. 4. 14.

बैल्व *a*. (ल्वी *f*.) 1 Relating to or made of the Bilva tree or its wood. 2 Covered with Bilva trees. -ल्वं The fruit of the Bilva trees.

बोधः 1 Perception, knowledge, apprehension, observation, conception; बालानां सुखबोधाय T. S. 2 Idea, thought. 3 Understanding, intellect, intelligence, wisdom 4 Waking up, becoming awake, waking state, consciousness. 5 Opening, blooming, expanding. 6 Instruction, advice, admonition. 7 Awakening, rousing. 8 An epithet, designation. -COMP. -अतीत *a*. unknowable, incomprehensible. -कर *a*. one who teaches or informs (-रः) 1 a bard or minstrel who wakes up his master by singing appropriate songs in the morning. 2 an instructor, a teacher. -गम्य *a*. intelligible. -पूर्व-*a*. intentional, conscious, cf. अबोधपूर्व. -वासरः the eleventh day in the bright half of Kârtika when Vishṇu is supposed to rise from his four month's sleep; see Me. 110, and प्रबोधिनी.

बोधक *a*. (धिका *f*.) 1 Informing, apprizing. 2 Instructing, teaching. 3 Indicative of. 4 Awakening, rousing. -कः A spy.

बोधनः The planet Mercury. -नं 1 Informing, teaching, instruction, giving a knowledge of; भयरूपोश्च तदिंगितबोधनं R 9. 49. 2 Denoting, signifying. 3 Arousing, awakening; समयेन तेन चिरसुप्तमनोभवबोधनं सममबोधिषत *S*i. 9. 24. 4 Burning incense. -नी 1 The eleventh day in the bright half of Kârtika when Vishṇu rises from his four months' sleep. 2 Long pepper.

बोधानः 1 A wise man. 2 An epithet of Bṛihaspati.

बोधिः 1 Perfect wisdom or enlightenment. 2 The enlightened intellect of a Buddha. 3 The sacred fig-tree. 4 A cock. 5 An epithet of Buddha. -COMP. -तरुः, -द्रुमः, -वृक्षः the sacred fig-tree. -दः an *arhat* (of the Jainas). -सत्त्वः a Buddhist saint, one who is on the way to the attainment of perfect knowledge and has only a certain number of births to undergo before attaining to the state of a Supreme Buddha and complete annihilation (this position could be attained by a long series of pious and virtuous deeds); एवंविधैर्बिलसितैरतिबोधिसत्त्वैः Mâl. 10. 21.

बोधित *p. p*. 1 Made known, informed, apprised. 2 Reminded. 3 Advised, instructed.

बौद्ध *a*. (द्धी *f*.) 1 Relating to the *Buddhi* or understanding. 2 Relating to *Buddha*. -द्धः A follower of the religion taught by Buddha.

बौधः 'Budha's son', an epithet of Purûravas.

बौधायनः N. of an ancient writer.

ब्रध्नः 1 The sun. 2 The root of a tree. 3 A day. 4 The *arka* plant. 5 Lead (*m*. ?). 6 A horse. 7 An epithet of *S*iva or Brahmâ.

ब्रह्मं The Supreme Spirit.

ब्रह्मण्य *a*. 1 Relating to Brahma. 2 Relating to Brahman or the creator. 3 Relating to the acquisition of sacred knowledge, holy, pious. 4 Fit for a Brâhmaṇa. 5 Friendly or hospitable to a Brâhmaṇa. -ण्यः 1 One well versed in the Veda ; Mv. 3 26. 2 The mulberry tree. 3 The palm tree. 4 Munja grass. 5 The planet Saturn. 6 An epithet of Vishṇu. 7 Of Kârtikeya. -ण्या An epithet of Durgâ. -COMP. -देवः an epithet of Vishṇu.

ब्रह्मण्वत् *n*. An epithet of Agni.

ब्रह्मता-त्वं 1 Absorption into the Supreme Spirit. 2 Divine nature.

ब्रह्मन् *n*. 1 The Supreme Being, regarded as impersonal and divested of all quality and action; (according the Vedântins, Brahman is both the efficient and the material cause of the visible universe, the all-pervading soul and spirit of the universe, the essence from which all created things are produced and into which they are absorbed; अस्ति तावन्नित्यशुद्धबुद्धमुक्तस्वभावं सर्वज्ञं सर्वशक्तिसमन्वितं ब्रह्म S. B.); समीभूता दृष्टिस्त्रिभुवनमपि ब्रह्म मनुते Bh. 3. 84; Ku. 3. 15. 2 A hymn of praise. 3 A sacred text. 4 The Vedas; Ku. 6. 16; U. 1. 15. 5 The sacred and mystic syllable *om*; एकाक्षरं परं ब्रह्म Ms 2. 83. 6 The priestly or Brâhmaṇical class (collectively); Ms. 9. 320. 7 The power or energy of a Brâhmaṇa; R. 8. 4. 8 Religious penance or austerities. 9 Celibacy, chastity; शाश्वते ब्रह्मणि वर्तते S. 1. 10 Final emancipation or beatitude. 11 Theology. 12 Brâhmaṇical portion of the Veda. 13 Wealth. -*m*. 1 The Supreme Being, the Creator, the first deity of the sacred Hindu Trinity, to whom is entrusted the work of creating the world. [The accounts of the creation of the world differ in many respects; but, according to Manu Smriti, the universe was enveloped in darkness, and the self-existent Lord manifested himself dispelling the gloom. He first created the waters and deposited in them a seed. This seed became a golden egg, in which he himself was born as Brahmâ—the progenitor of all the worlds. Then the Lord divided the egg into two parts, with which he constructed heaven and earth. He then created the ten Prajâpatis or mind-born sons who completed the work of creation. According to another account (*Ramayana*) Brahma sprang from ether; from him was descended Marichi, and his son was Kasyapa

From Kasyapa sprang Vivasvata, and Manu sprang from him Thus Manu was t e procreator of all human beings. According to a third acco nt. the Supreme deity, after dividing the golden egg, separated himself into two parts, male and female, from which sprang Viraj and from him Manu; cf. Ku 2. 7 and Ms. I 32 *et seq.*)- Mythologically Brahman is represented as being born in a lotus which sprang from the navel of Vishnu and as creating the world by an illicit connection with his own daughter Sarasvatî. Brahman had originally five heads, but one of them was cut down by *S*iva with the ring-finger or burnt down by the fire from his third eye. His vehicle is a swan. He has numerous epithets, most of which have reference to his birth in a lotus]. **2** A Brâh ana: *S*. 4. 4. **3** A devout man. **4** One of the four *Ritvijas* or priests employed at a Soma sacrifice. **5** One conversant with sacred knowledge. **6** The sun. **7** Intellect. **8** An epithet of the seven Prajâpatis:-मरीचि, अत्रि, अंगिरस्, पुलस्त्य, पुलह, क्रतु, and वसिष्ठ **9** An epithet of Brihaspati. **10** Of *S*iva. --Comp. **-अक्षरं** the sacred syllable *om*. **-अंगभूः** a horse. **-अंजलिः 1** respectful salutation with folded hands while repeating the Veda. **2** obeisance to a preceptor (at the beginning and conclusion of the repetition of Veda). **-अंडं** 'the egg of Brahman', the primordial egg from which the unvierse sprang, the world, universe; ब्रह्मांडच्छत्रदंडः Dk. 1. °**पुराणं** N. of one of the eighteen Purâṇas. **-अभिजाता** an epithet of the river Godâvarî. **-अधिगमः**, **-अधिगमनं** study of the Vedas. **-अभ्यासः** study of the Vedas. **-अंभस्** *n*. the urine of a cow. **-अयणः**, **-नः** an epithet of Nârâyaṇa. **-अर्पणं 1** the offering of sacred knowledge. **2** devoting oneself to the Supreme Spirit. **3** N. of a spell. **-अस्त्रं** a missile presided over by Brahman. **-आत्मभूः** a horse. **-आनंदः** bliss or rapture of absorption into Brahma; ब्रह्मानंदसाक्षात्क्रिया Mv. 7. 31 **-आरंभः** beginning to repeat the Vedas; Ms. 2. 71. **-आवर्तः** N. of the tract between the rivers Sarasvatî and Drishadvatî (north-west of Hastinâpura); सरस्वतीदृषद्वत्योर्देवनद्योर्यदंतरं। तं देवनिर्मितं देशं ब्रह्मावर्तं प्रचक्षते Ms. 2. 17, 19; Me. 48. **-आसनं** a particular position for profound meditation. **-आहुतिः** *f*. the offering of prayers; see ब्रह्मयज्ञ. **-उज्झता** forgetting or neglecting the Vedas; Ms 11 57 (अधितवेदस्यानभ्यासेन विस्मरणं Mull.) **-उद्य** explaining the Veda, treatment or discussion of theological problems. **उपदेशः** instruction in the Vedas or sacred knowledge. °**नेतृ** *m*. the Palâsa tree. **-ऋषिः** (**ब्रह्मर्षि** or **ब्रह्मऋषिः**) a Brahmanical sage. **-देशः** N. of a district; (कुरुक्षेत्रं च मत्स्याश्च पचालाः शूरसेनकाः। एष ब्रम्हर्षिदेशो वै ब्रम्हावर्तादनंतरः Ms. 2. 19) **-कन्यका** an epithet of Sarasvatî. **-करः** a tax paid to the priestly class. **-कर्मन्** *n*. **1** the religious duties of a Brâhmaṇa; **2** the office of Brahman, one of the four principal priests at a sacrifice. **-कल्पः** an age of Brahman. **-कांडं** the portion of the Veda relating to spiritual knowledge. **-काष्ठः** the mulberry tree. **-कूर्चं** a kind of penance; अहोरात्रोषितो भूत्वा पौर्णमास्यां विशेषतः। पंचगव्यं पिबेत् प्रातर्ब्रह्मकूर्चमिति स्मृतम्॥ **-कृत्** *a*. one who prays. (*-m*.) an epithet of Vishṇu. **-गुप्तः** N. of an astronomer born in 598 A. D. **-गोलः** the universe. **-गौरवं** respect for the missile presided over by Brahman; Bk. 9. 76 (मा भून्मोघो ब्राम्हःपाश इति). **-ग्रंथिः** N. of a particular joint of the body **-ग्रहः**, **-पिशाचः**, **-पुरुषः**, **-रक्षस्** *n* **-राक्षसः** a kind of ghost, the ghost of a Brâhmaṇa, who during his lifetime indulges in a disdainful spirit and carries away the wives of others and the property of Brâhmaṇas; (परस्य योषितं हृत्वा ब्रम्हस्वमपहृत्य च। अरण्ये निर्जले देशे भवति ब्रम्हराक्षसः॥ Y. 3. 212; cf. Ms. 12. 60 also) **-घातकः** the murderer of a Brâhmaṇa.. **-घातिनी** a woman on the second day of her courses. **-घोषः 1** recital of the Veda, **2** the sacred word, the Vedas collectively; U. 6. 9. v. 1. **-घ्नः** the murderer of a Brâhmaṇa. **-चर्यं 1** religious studentship, the life of celibacy passed by a Brâhmaṇa boy in studying the Vedas, the first stage or order of his life; अविप्लुतब्रह्मचर्यो गृहस्थाश्रममाचरेत् Ms. 3.2; 2. 249; Mv. 1. 24. **2** religious study, self-restraint. **3** celibacy, chastity, abstinence, continence. (**-र्यः**) a religious student; see ब्रम्हचारिन्. (**-र्या**) chastity, celibacy. °**व्रतं** a vow of chastity. °**स्खलनं** falling off from chastity, incontinence. **-चारिकं** the life of a religious student. **-चारिन्** *m*. **1** a religious student, a Brâhmaṇa in the first order of his life, who continues to live with his spiritual guide from the investiture with sacred thread and performs the duties pertaining to his order till he settles in life; Ms. 2. 41, 175; 6. 87. **2** one who vows to lead the life of a celibate. **-चारिणी 1** an epithet of Durgâ **2** a woman who observes the vow of chastity. **-जः** an epithet of Kârtikeya. **-जारः** the paramour of a Brâhmaṇa's wife. **-जीविन्** *m*. a Brâhmaṇa who lives by sacred knowledge. **-ज्ञ** *a*. one who knows Brahma. (**-ज्ञः**) **1** an epithet of Kartikeya. **2** of Vishṇu **-ज्ञानं** true or divine knowledge, knowledge of the identity of the universe with Brahma. **-ज्येष्ठः** the elder brother of Brâhmaṇa. **-ज्योतिस्** *n*. the light of Brahma or the Supreme Being. **-तत्त्वं** the true knowledge of the Supreme Spirit. **-तेजस्** *n*. **1** the glory of Brahman. **2** Brâhmanic lustre, the lustre or glory supposed to surround a Brâhmaṇa. **-दः** a spiritual preceptor. **-दंडः 1** the curse of a Brâhmaṇa. **2** a tribute paid to a Brâhmaṇa. **3** an epithet of *S*iva. **-दानं 1** the imparting of sacred knowledge. **2** sacred knowledge received as an inheritance or hereditary gift. **-दायादः 1** one who receives the Vedas as his hereditary gift, a Brâhmaṇa; **2** the son of a Brâhmaṇa. **-दारुः** the mulbery tree. **-दिनं** a day of Brahman. **-दैत्यः** a Brâhmaṇa changed into a demon; cf. **ब्रह्मग्रह**. **-द्विष्**, **द्वेषिन्** *a*. **1** hating Brahmaṇas. **2** hostile to religious acts or devotion, impious, godless. **-द्वेषः** hatred of Brâhmaṇas. **-नदी** an epithet of the river Sarasvatî. **-नाभः** an epithet of Vishṇu.**-निर्वाणं** absorption into the supreme spirit. **-निष्ठ** *a*. absorbed in or intent, on the contemplation of the Supreme Spirit. (**-ष्ठः**) the mulberry tree. **-पदं 1** the rank or position of a Brâhmaṇa. **2** the place of the Supreme Spirit. **-पवित्रः** the Kusa grass. **परिषद्** *f*. an assembly of Brâhmaṇas. **-पादपः** the Palâsa tree. **-पारायणं** complete study of the Vedas, the entire Vedas; U. 4. 9; Mv. 1. 14. **-पाशः** N of a missile presided over by Brahman; Bs. 9. 75 **-पितृ** *m*. an epithet of Vishṇu. **-पुत्रः 1** a son of Brahman. **2** N. of a (male) river which rises in the eastern extremity of the Himâlaya and falls with the Ganges into the Bay of Bengal. (**-त्री**) an epithet of the river Sarasvatî. **पुरं**,**-पुरी 1** the city of Brahman (in heaven). **2** N. of Benares. **-पुराणं** N. of one of the eighteen Purâṇas.**-प्रलयः** the universal destruction at the end of one hundred years of Brahman in which even the Supreme Being is supposed to be swallowed up. **-प्राप्तिः** *f*. absorption into the Supreme Spirit. **-बंधुः 1** a contemptuous term for a Brâhmaṇa, an unworthy Brâhmaṇa (cf. Mar. भट्टुर्गा); M. 4; V. 2. **2** One who is a Brâhmaṇa only by caste, a nominal Brâhmaṇa. **-बीजं** the mystic syllable *om*. **-ब्रुवाणः** one who pretends to be a Brâhmaṇa. **-भवनं** the abode of Brahman. -भागः the mulberry tree. -भावः absorption into the Supreme Spirit. -भुवनं the world of Brahman; Bg. 8. 16. -भूत *a.* become one with Brahma, absorbed into the Supreme Spirit. -भूतिः *f.* twilight. -भूयं 1 identity with Brahma, absorption or dissolution into Brahma, final emancipation; स ब्रह्मभूयं गतिमाजगाम R. 18. 28.; ब्रह्मभूयाय कल्पते Bg. 14. 26; Ms. 1. 98 2 Brâhmaṇhood; the state or rank of a Brâhmaṇa. -भूयस् *n.* absorption into Brahma. मंगलदेवता an epithet of Lakshmî. -मीमांसा the Vedânta philosophy which inquires into the nature of Brahma or Supreme Spirit. -मूर्ति *a.* having the form of Brahman. -मूर्धभृत् *m.* an epithet of *S*iva. -मेखलः the Muṇja plant. -यज्ञः one of the five daily Yaj*n*as or sacrifices (to be performed by a householder); teaching and reciting the Vedas; अध्यापनं ब्रह्मयज्ञः Ms. 3. 70 (अध्यापनशब्देन अध्ययनमपि गृह्यते Kull.) -योगः cultivation or acquisition of spiritual knowledge. -योनि *a.* sprung from Brahman. -रत्नं a valuable present made to a Brâhmaṇa. -रंध्रं an aperture in the crown of the head through which the soul is said to escape on its leaving the body. -राक्षसः see ब्रह्मग्रह. -रातः an epithet of *S*uka. -राशिः 1 the whole mass or circle of sacred knowledge. 2 an epithet of Parasurâma. -रीतिः *f.* a kind of brass. -रे (ले) खा-लिखितं, -लेखः lines written by the creator on the forehead of a man which indicate his destiny, the predestined lot of any man लोकः the world of Brahman. -वक्तृ *m.* an expounder of the Vedas. -वद्यं knowledge of Brahma. -वधः -वध्या,-हत्या the murder of a Brâhmanna. -वर्चस, *n.* —वर्चसं 1 divine glory or splendour, spiritual pre-eminence or holiness resulting from sacred knowledge; (तस्य हेतुस्त्वद्ब्रह्मवर्चसं R. 1. 63; Ms 2 37. 4. 94. 2 the inherent sanctity or power of a Brâhmaṇa; *S*. 6 -वर्चस्विन्, -वर्चसिन् *a* holy or sanctified by spiritual pre-eminence, holy. (*-m*) an eminent or holy Brâhmaṇa. -वर्तः see ब्रह्मावर्त, -वर्धनं copper. -वादिन् *m.* 1 one who teaches or expounds the Vedas: U. 1; Mâl. 1. 2 a follower of the Vedânta philospohy. -वासः the abode of Brahmaṇâ. -विद्, -विद *a.* knowing the Supreme *S*pirit (*-m.*) a sage, theologian, philosopher. -विद्या knowledge of the Supreme Spirit. -विं (बिं) दुः a drop of saliva sputtered while reciting the Vedas, -विवर्धनः an epithet of Indra. -वृक्षः 1 the Palâsa tree. 2 the Udumbara tree. -वृत्तिः *f* livelihood of Brâhmaṇa. -वृंद an assemblage of Brâhmaṇas. -वेदः 1 knowledge of the Vedas. 2 knowledge of Brahma. 3 N. of the Atharvaveda. -वेदिन् *a* knowing the Vedas; cf. ब्रह्मविद् -वैवर्त N of one of the eighteen Purâṇas. -व्रतं a vow of chastity. -शिरस्, -शीर्षन् *n.* N. of a particular missile. -संसद् *f.* an assembly of Brâhmaṇas. -सती an epithet of the river Sarasvatî. -सत्रं 1 repeating and teaching the Vedas (ब्रह्मयज्ञ q. v.). 2. absorption into the Supreme Spirit. -सदनस् *n.* the residence of Brahman. -सभा the hall or court of Brahman. -संभव *a.* sprung or coming from Brahman. (-वः) N. of Nârada.-सर्पः a kind of snake. -सायुज्यं complete identification with the Supreme Spirit; cf. ब्रह्मभूय. -सार्ष्टिता identification with Brahma; Ms. 4. 232. -सावर्णिः N. of the tenth Manu. -सुतः 1 N. of Nârada, Marîchi &c. 2 a kind of *Ketu*. -सूः 1 N. of Aniruddha. 2 N. of the god of love -सूत्रं 1 the sacred thread worn by the Brâhmaṇas or the twice-born over the shoulder. 2 the aphorisms of the Vedânta philosophy by Bâdarâyaṇa. -सूत्रिन् *a.* invested with the sacred thread. -सृज् *m.* an epithet of *S*iva. -स्तंबः the world, universe; Mv. 3. 48. -स्तेयं acquiring holy knowledge by unlawful means. -स्वं the property or possessions of a Brâhmaṇa; Y. 3. 212. °हारिन् *a.* stealing a Brâhmaṇa's property. -हन् *a.* murdering a Brâhmaṇa. -हुतं one of the five daily Yaj*n*as or sacrifices, which consists in offering the rites of hospitality to guests Ms 3. 74. -हृदयः-यं N. of a star (capella).

ब्रह्ममय *a.* Consisting of or derived from, the Veda, belonging to the Veda, or spiritual pre-eminence; ज्वलन्निव ब्रह्ममयेन तेजसा Ku 5. 30. 2 Fit for a Brâhmaṇa. —यं A missile presided over by Brahman.

ब्रह्मवत् *a.* Possessed of spiritual knowledge.

ब्रह्मसात् *ind.* 1 To the state of Brahma or the Supreme Spirit. 2 To the care of Brâhmaṇas.

ब्रह्माणी 1 The wife of Brahman 2 An epithet of Durgâ 3 A kind of perfume (रेणुका) 4 A kind of brass.

ब्राह्मन् *a.* Relating to Brahma.—*m.* An epithet of Vishṇu.

ब्रह्मिष्ठ *a* Thoroughly proficient in Vedas. very learned or pious; ब्रह्मिष्ठ माधाय निजेऽधिकारे ब्रह्मिष्ठमेव स्वतनुप्रसूतं R. 18. —ष्ठा An epithet of Durgâ.

ब्रह्मी N of a medicinal plant.

ब्रह्मण्यः 1 An epithet of Kârtikeya; 2 Of Vishṇu.

ब्राह्म *a* (ह्मी *f.*). 1 Relating to Brahman or the creator, or to the Supreme Spirit; R. 13 60; Ms. 2. 40, Bg. 2. 72. 2 Brâhmanical, belonging to Brâhmaṇas. 3 Relating to sacred knowledge or study. 4 Prescribed by the Vedas, Vedic. 5 Holy, sacred, divine 6 Presided over by Brahman as a मुहूर्त; (see ब्रह्ममुहूर्त), or a missile —ह्मः 1 One of the eight forms of marriage in Hindu law, in which the bride decorated with ornaments is given away to the bridegroom, without requiring any gift or present from him (this is the best of the 8 forms); ब्राह्मो विवाह आहूय दीयते शक्त्यलंकृता Y 1. 58; Ms. 3. 21, 27. 2 N of Nârada. —ह्मं 1 The part of the hand under the root of the thumb. 2 Holy or sacred study. —Comp. -अहोरात्रः a day and night of Brahman. -देयं a girl to be married according to the Brâhma form. -मुहूर्त a particular period of the day, the early part of the day (रात्रेश्च पश्चिमे यामे मुहूर्तो ब्राह्म उच्यते) ब्राह्मे मुहूर्ते किल तस्य देवी कुमारकल्पं सुषुवे कुमारं R. 5 36.

ब्राह्मण *a.* (णी *f.*) 1 Belonging to a Brâhmaṇa. 2 Befitting a Brâhmaṇa. 3 Given by a Brâhmaṇa. —णः 1 A man belonging to the first of the four original castes of the Hindus, a Brâhmaṇa (born form the mouth of the *Purusha*; ब्राह्मणोऽस्य मुखमासीत् Rv. 10 90. 12; Ms. 1. 31. 96.) जन्मना जायते शूद्रः संस्कारैर्द्विज उच्यते । विद्यया याति विप्रत्वं त्रिभिः श्रोत्रिय उच्यते ॥ or जात्या कुलेन वृत्तेन स्वाध्यायेन श्रुतेन च । एभिर्युक्तो हि यस्तिष्ठेन्नित्यं स द्विज उच्यते ॥). 2 A priest, theologian 3 An epithet of Agni. —णं 1 An assemblage or society of Brâhmaṇas. 2 That portion of the Veda which states rules for the employment of the hymns at the various sacrifices, their origin and detailed explanation with sometimes lengthy illustrations in the shape of legends or stories. It is distinct from the *Mantra* portion of the Veda. 3 N. of that class of Vedic works which contain the Brâhmaṇa portion (regarded as *S*ruti or part of the revelation like the hymns themselves). Each of the four Vedas has its own Brâhmaṇa or Brâhmaṇas —ऐतरेय or आश्वलायन and कौशीतकी or सांख्यायन belonging to the *R*igveda; शतपथ to the Yajurveda; पंचविंश and षड्विंश and six more, to the Sâmaveda and गोपथ to the Atharvaveda). —Comp.

-अतिक्रमः offensive or disrespectful conduct towards Brâhmaṇas, insult to Brâhmaṇas ब्राह्मणातिक्रमत्य गा भवतामेव भूतये Mv. 2. 80. -अपाश्रयः seeking shelter with Brahmaṇas, -अभ्युपपत्तिः *f.* protection or preservation of, or kindness shown to, a Brâhmaṇa; Ms. 9. 87. -घ्नः the slayer of a Brâhmaṇa. -जातं, जातिः *f.* the Brâhmaṇa caste. -जीविका the occupation or means of livelihood prescribed for a Brâhmaṇa. -द्रव्यं,-स्वं a Brâhmaṇa's property. -निंदकः a blasphemer or reviler of Brâhmaṇas. -ब्रुवः one who pretends to be a Brâhmaṇa, one who is a Brâhmaṇa only in name and neglects the duties of his caste; बहवो ब्राह्मणब्रुवा निवसंति Dk.; Ms. 7. 85; 8. 20. -भूयिष्ठ *a* consisting, for the most part, of Brâhmaṇas. -वधः the murder of a Brâhmaṇa, Brâhmanicide. -संतर्पणं feeding or satisfying Brâhmaṇas.

ब्राह्मणकः 1 A bad or unworthy Brâhmaṇa (only in name) 2 N. of a country inhabited by warlike Brâhmaṇas.

ब्राह्मणत्रा *ind.* 1 Among Brâhmaṇas. 2 To the state of a Brahmaṇa; as in ब्राह्मणसात् भवति धनं.

ब्राह्मणाच्छंसिन् *m.* N. of a priest, the assistant of the priest called *Barahmn* q. v.

ब्राह्मणी 1 A woman of the Brâhmaṇa caste. 2 The wife of a Brâhmaṇa. 3 Intellect; (बुद्धि according to नीलकंठ) 4 A kind of lizard. 5 A kind of wasp. 6 A kind of grass. Comp. -गामिन् *m.* the paramour of a Brâhmṇa woman.

ब्राह्मण्य *a.* Befitting a Brâhmaṇa. -ण्यः An epithet of the planet Saturn. -ण्यं 1 The station or rank of a Brâhmaṇa, priestly or sacerdotal character; सत्यं शपे ब्राह्मण्येन Mk. 5; Pt. 1. 66. Ms. 3, 17; 7. 42. 2 A collection of Brâhmaṇas.

ब्राह्मी 1 The personified female energy of Brahman. 2 Sarasvatî, the goddess of speech. 3 Speech. 4 A tale or narrative. 5 A pious usage or custom. 6 N. of the constellation Rohiṇî. 7 N. of Durgâ. 8 A woman married according to the *Brâhma* form of marriage. 9 The wife of a Brâhmaṇa. 10 A kind of medicinal plant. 11 A kind of brass. 12 N. of a river. -Comp. -कंदः a species of bulbous plant. -पुत्रः the son of a Brâhmî; see above; Ms. 3. 27, 37.

ब्राह्म्य *a.* (ह्मी *f.*) 1 Relating to Brahman, the creator. 2 Relating to the supreme Spirit. 3 Relating to the Brâhmaṇas. -ह्म्यं Wonder, astonishment (विस्मय). -Comp.— मुहूर्तः=ब्राह्ममुहूर्त q. v. -हुतं hospitality to guests; see ब्रह्मयज्ञ.

ब्रुव *a.* Professing or pretending to be, calling oneself by a name to which he has no real title; (at the end of comp.); as in ब्राह्मणब्रुव, क्षत्रियब्रुव.

ब्रू 2 U. (ब्रवीति, ब्रूते or आह; this root is defective in the non conjugational tenses, its forms being made up from वच्) 1 To say, tell, speak (with two acc.); तां......ब्रूया एवं Me. 104; रामं यथास्थितं सर्वं भ्राता ब्रूते स्म विह्वलः B. k. 6. 8. or माणवकं धर्मं ब्रूते Sk; किं त्वां प्रति ब्रूमहे Bv. 1. 46. 2 To say or speak about, refer to (a person or thing); अहं तु शकुंतलामधिकृत्य ब्रवीमि S. 2. 3 To declare, proclaim, publish, prove; ब्रवते हि फलेन साधवो न तु कंठेन निजोपयोगिता N. 2. 48; Ratn. 2. 13. 4 To name, call, designate; छंदांसि दक्षा ये कवयस्तन्मणिमध्यं ते ब्रुवते Srut. 15. 5 To answer; ब्रूहि मे प्रश्नान्. With अनु to say, speak, declare. -निस् to explain, derive. -प्र to say, speak, tell; Bk. 8. 85. -प्रति to speak in reply, answer or reply; प्रत्यब्रवीच्चैनं R. 2. 42. -वि 1 to say, speak. 2 to speak falsely or wrongly.

ब्लेष्कं A snare, net, noose.

भ.

भः 1 N. of the planet Venus. 2 Error, delusion, mere semblance. -भं 1 A star. 2 A lunar mansion or asterism. 3 A planet. 4 A sign of zodiac. 5 The number twenty seven. 6 A bee. Comp. -ईनः ईशः the sun. -गणः वर्गः 1 the group of star or asterisms. 2 the zodiac. 3 revolution of the planets in the zodiac. -गोलः the starry sphere.- चक्रं, मंडलं the zodiac. -पतिः the moon. -सूचकः an astrologer.

भक्किका A cricket.

भक्त *p. p.* 1 Distributed, alloted, assigned. 2 Divided. 3 Served, worshipped. 4 Engaged in, attentive to. 5 Attached or devoted to, loyal, faithful; Bg. 9. 34. 6 Dressed, cooked (as food); see (भज्). -क्तः A worshipper, adorer, devotee, votary, faithful attendant; भक्तोसि मे सखा चेति Bg. 4. 3; 9. 31; 7. 23. -क्तं 1 A share, portion. 2 Food; Bh. 3. 74. 3 Boiled rice; U. 4. 1. 4 Any eatable grain boiled with water. Comp. -अभिलाषः desire of food, appetite. उपसाधक-a cook. -कंसः a dish of food. -करः incense prepared from various fragrant resins and perfumes. -कारः a cook. -छंदः appetite. -दासः a slave who agrees to serve another for maintenance, or who receives his meals as a return for his services; Ms. 8. 415. -द्वेषः dislike of food, loss of appetite. -मंड the scum of boiled rice. -रोचन *a* stimulating appetite. -वत्सल *a.* kind to worshippers or devotees. -शाला 1 an audience chamber (to admit petitioners and hear them) 2 a dinning hall.

भक्तिः *f.* 1 Separation, partition, division. 2 A division, portion, share. 3 Devotion, attachment, loyalty, faithfulness; Ku. 7. 37; R. 2. 63; Mu. 1. 15. 4 Reverence, service, worship, homage. 5 Texture, arrangement; R. 5. 74. 6 Decoration, ornament, embellishment; आबद्धमुक्ताफलभक्तिचित्रे Ku. 7. 10, 91; भक्तिच्छेदैरिव विरचितां भूतिमंगे गजस्य Me. 19. R. 13. 59, 75. 15. 30. 7 An attribute. Comp.- नम्र *a* making a humble obliance.- पूर्वं,-पूर्वकं *ind.* devoutly, reverentially. -भाज् *a.* 1 devout, fervid. 2 firmly attached or devoted, faithful, loyal. -मार्गः the way of devotion; *i. e.* devotion to god, regarded as the way to the attaintment of final emancipation and eternal bliss. -योगः loving faith, loyal devotion. -वादः assurance of attachment.

भक्तिमत् *a.* 1 Devout, having pious faith. 2 Loyally devoted or attached, faithful, loyal.

भक्तिल *a.* Faithful, trusty (as a horse)

भक्ष 10 U. (भक्षयति-ते भक्षति) 1. To eat, devour यथामिषं जले मत्स्यैर्भक्ष्यते श्वापदैर्भुवि Pt. 1. 2 To use up, consume. 3 To waste, destroy. 4 To bite.

भक्षः 1 Eating. 2 Food.

भक्षक *a.* (क्षिका *f.*) 1 One who eats or lives upon. 2 Gluttonous, voracious.

भक्षण *a* (णी *f.*) Eating, one who eats, or devours. -णं Eating, feeding or living upon.

भक्ष्य *a* Eatable, fit for food. -क्ष्यं Anything eatable, an article of food, food (fig. also; भक्ष्यभक्षकयोः) प्रीतिर्विपत्तेरेव कारणं H. 1. 55; Ms. 1. 113. -Comp.

-कारः (also) भक्ष्यंकारः a baker, cook.

भगः One of the twelve forms of the sun; the sun. 2 The moon. 3 A form of Siva. 4 Good fortune, luck, happy lot, happiness; आस्ते भग आसीनस्य Ait. Br.; भगमिंद्रश्च वायुश्च भग सप्तर्षयो ददुः Y. 1. 282. 5 Affluence, prosperity. 6 Dignity, distinction. 7 Fame, glory. 8 Loveliness, beauty. 9 Excellence, distinction. 10 Love, affection. 11 Amorous dalliance or sport, pleasure. 12 The pudendum muliebre; Y. 3. 88; Ms. 9. 237. 13 Virtue, morality, religious merit (धर्म). 14 Effort, exertion. 15 Absence of desire indifference to worldly objects. 16 Final beatitude. 17 Strength. 18 Omnipotence; (said to be *n.* also in the last 15 senses). —**नं** The astersim called उत्तराफल्गुनी. COMP. -**अंकुरः** (in medicine) clitoris. -**आधानं** granting matrimonial happiness. -**घ्नः** an epithet of *S*iva. -**देवः** a thorough libertine, -**देवता** the deity presiding over marriage. -**दैवतं** the constellation उत्तराफल्गुनी. -**नंदनः** an epithet of Vishṇu -**भक्षकः** a pander procurer. -**वेदनं** proclaiming matrimonial felicity.

भगंदरः A fistula in the anus or pudendum.

भगवत् *a.* 1 Glorious, illustrious. 2 Revered, venerable, divine, holy, (an epithet applied to gods, demigods and other holy or respectable personages); अथ भगवान् कुशली काश्यपः *S*. 5. भगवत्परवानयं जनः R. 8. 81; so भगवान् वासुदेवः &c.—*m.* 1 A god, deity. 2 An epithet of Vishṇu. 3 Of Siva. 4 Of Jina. 5 Of a Buddha.

भगवद्दीयः A worshipper of Vishṇu.

भगालं A skull.

भगालिन् *m.* An epithet of *S*iva.

भगिन् *a.* (**नी** *f*) 1 Prosperous, happy, fortunate. 2 Grand, splendid.

भगिनिका A sister.

भगिनी 1 A sister. 2 A fortunate woman. 3 A woman in general. -COMP. -**पतिः**, **भर्तृ** *m.* a sister's husband.

भगिनीयः A sister's son.

भगीरथः N. of an ancient king of the solar dynasty, the greatgrandson of Sagara, who brought down, by practising the most austere penance, the celestial river Ganges from heaven to the earth and from earth to the lower regions to purify the ashes of his 60000 ancestors, the sons of Sagara. -COMP. -**पथः**, -**प्रयत्नः** the path or effort of Bhagîratha, used figuratively to denote any great or Herculean effort. -**सुता**, an epithet of the Ganges.

भग्न *p. p.* 1 Broken, fractured, shattered, torn. 2 Frustrated, foiled, disappointed. 3 Checked, arrested, suspended. 4 Marred, impaired. 5 Routed, completely defeated or vanquished; U. 5. 6 Demolished, destroyed. (see भंज्). —**ग्नं** Fracture of the leg. -COMP. -**आत्मन्** *m.* an epithet of the moon. -**आपद्** *a.* one who has surmounted difficulties or misfortunes. -**आश** *a.* disappointed; Bh. 2. 84; frustrated; Bh. 3. 52. -**उत्साह** *a.* broken in energy, depressed in spirits, discouraged, damped. -**उद्यम** *a.* foiled in one's endeavours, disappointed, baffled. -**क्रमः**, -**प्रक्रमः** violation of symmetry in construction or expression; see प्रक्रमभंग. -**चेष्ट** *a.* disappointed, frustrated. -**दर्प** *a.* humbled, crest-fallen -**निद्र** *a.* whose sleep is interrupted. -**पार्श्व** *a.* suffering from a pain in the sides. -**पृष्ठ** *a.* 1 having a broken back. 2 coming in front. -**प्रतिज्ञ** *a.* one who has broken his promises. -**मनस्** *a.* discouraged, disappointed. -**व्रत** *a.* faithless in one's vows. -**संकल्प** *a.* one whose designs are frustrated.

भग्नी A sister.

भंका (गा) री A gad-fly.

भंक्तिः *f.* Breaking, fracture.

भंगः 1 Breaking, breaking down, shattering, tearing down, splitting, dividing; वार्यर्गलाभंग इव प्रवृत्तः R. 5. 45 2 A break, fracture, breach. 3 Plucking off, lopping; आम्रकलिकाभंग *S*. 6. 4 Separation, analysis. 5 A portion, bit, fragment, detached portion: पुष्पोच्चय पल्लवभंगभिन्नः Ku. 3. 61. R 16. 16 6 Fall, downfall, decay, destruction, ruin; as in राज्य°, सत्त्व° &c. 7 Breaking up, dispersion; यात्राभंग Mâl. 1. 8 Defeat, overthrow, discomfiture, rout; Pt. 4. 41; *S*i. 16. 72. 9 Failure, disappointment, frustration; R. 2. 42 आशाभंग &c. 10 Rejection, refusal; Ku. 1. 42. 11 A chasm, fissure. 12 Interruption, obstacle, disturbance; निद्रा°, गति° &c. 13 Non-performance, suspension, stoppage. 14 Taking to flight, 15 A bend, fold, wave. 16 Contraction, bending, knitting; U. 5. 36. 17 Going, motion. 18 Paralysis. 19 Fraud, deceit. 20 A canal, water-course. 21 A circumlocutory or round-about way of speaking or acting; see; भंगि 22 Hemp. -COMP. -**नयः** removal of obstcles. **वासा** turmeric. -**सार्थ** *a.* dishonest, fraudulent.

भंगा 1 Hemp. 2 An intoxicating drink prepared from hemp. -COMP -**कटं** the pollen of hemp.

भंगिः -**गी** *f.* 1 Breaking, fracture, breach, division. 2 Undulation. 3 Bending, contracting; दृग्भंगीभिः प्रथममधुरासंगमे चुंबितोऽस्मि Ud. S. 13. 4 A wave. 5 A flood, current. 6 A crooked path, tortuous or winding course. 7 A circumlocutory or round-about way of speaking or acting, periphrasis; भंग्यंतरेण कथनात् K. P. 10; बहुभंगिविशारदः Dk. 8 A pretext, disguise, semblance; यः पांचजन्यप्रतिबिंबभंग्या धाराभसः फेनमिव व्यनक्ति Vikr. 1. 1. 9 Trick, fraud, deceit. 10 Irony. 11 Repartee, wit. 12 A step; R. 13; 69. 13 An interval. 14 Modesty. -COMP. -**भक्तिः** *f.* division into a series of waves or wave-like steps, a wavy staircase; Me 60.

भंगिन् *a.* 1 Frail, fragile, transient; तदपि तत्क्षणभंगि करोति चेत् Bh. 2. 92. 2 Cast in a suit.

भंगिमत् *a.* Wavy, crisped.

भंगिमन् *m.* 1 Fracture, breach. 2 Bending, undulation. 3 Curliness. 4 Disguise, deceit. 5 Wit, irony. 6 Perversity.

भंगिलं A defect in the organs of sense.

भंगुर *a.* 1 Apt to break, fragile, brittle. 2 Frail, transitory, transient, perishable: आमरणांताः प्रणयाः कोपास्तत्क्षणभंगुराः H. 1 188; *S*i. 16. 72. 3 Changeful, variable. 4 Crooked, bent. 5 Curved, curled; शशिमुखि तव भाति भंगुरभ्रूः Gît. 10. 6 Fraudulent, dishonest, crafty. -**रः** The bend of a river.

भज् I. 1. U. (भजति-ते, but usually Atm. only: भक्त) 1 (*a*) To share, distribute, divide; भजेरन् पैतृकं रिक्थं Ms. 9. 104; न तत्पुत्रैर्भजेत्सार्धं 209, 119. (*b*) To assign, allot, apportion; गायत्रीमग्नयेऽभजत् Ait. Br. 2 To obtain for oneself, share in, partake of; पित्र्यं वा भजते शीलं Ms. 10. 59. 3 To accept, receive; Mâl. 5. 25. 4 (*a*) To resort to, betake oneself to, have recourse to; शिलातलं भेजे K. 179; मातर्लक्ष्मि भजस्व कंचिदपरं Bh. 3. 64; न कश्चिद्वर्णानामपथमपकृष्टोपि भजते *S*. 5. 10; Bv. 1. 83; R. 17. 28. (*b*) To practise, follow, observe; भेजे धर्ममनातुरः R. 1. 21. 5 To enjoy, possess, have, suffer, experience, entertain; विधुरपि भजतेतरां कलंकं Bv 1. 74; न भेजिरे भीमविषेण भीतिं Bh. 2. 80; व्यक्तिं भजंत्यापगाः *S*. 7. 8.; अभितप्तमयोपि मार्दवं भजते कैव कथा शरीरिषु R. 8. 43; Mâl. 3 9; U. 1. 35. 6 To wait or attend upon, serve. R. 2. 23. Pt. 1 181; Mk 1. 32; 7 To adore, honour, worship. (as a god). 8 To choose, select, prefer, accept; संतःपरीक्ष्यान्यतरद्भजंते M. 1. 2. 9 To enjoy carnally; Pt. 4. 50. 10 To be attached or devoted to. 11 To take possession of. 12 To fall to the lot of any one. (The meanings of this root are variously modified according to the noun with which it is connected:—*e. g.* निद्रां भज् to go to sleep; मूर्च्छां भज् to swoon; भावं भज् to show love for &c. &c.). -WITH वि 1 to divide, distribute; विभज्य मेरुर्न यदर्थिसात्कृतः N. 1. 16; पत्रिणो व्यभजदा-श्रमाद्बहिः R. 11. 29; 10. 54; *Si*. 1. 3. 2 to separate. divide (as property, patrimony &c.); विभक्ता भ्रातरः divided brothers. 3 to distinguish. 4 to honour, worship. -संवि to share in common, admit (one) to a share; वित्तं यदा यस्य च संविभक्तम्. -II 10 U. (भाजयति-ते regarded by some as *caus.* of भज् I) 1 To cook. 2 To give.

भजकः A divider, distributer. 2 A worshipper, votary, devotee.

भजनं 1 Sharing, dividing. 2 Possession. 3 Service, adoration, worship.

भजमान *a.* 1 Dividing. 2 Enjoying. 3 Fit, right, proper.

भंज् I. 7. P. (भनक्ति, भग्न; *desid.* बिभंक्षति) 1 To break, tear down, shatter, shiver or break to pieces, split; भनज्मि सर्वमर्यादाः Bk. 6. 38; भंक्त्वा भुजौ 4 3: बभंजुर्वलयानि च 3. 22; धनुरभाजि यत्त्वया R. 11. 76. 2 To devastate, destroy by pulling down; भनक्त्युपवनं कपिः Bk. 9. 2. 3 To make a breach (in a fortress). 4 To frustrate, foil, disappoint, baffle; पिनाकिना भग्नमनोरथा सती Ku. 5. 1. 5 To arrest, check, interrupt, suspend; as in भग्ननिद्रः. 6 To defeat, vanquish; क्षत्राणि रामः परिभूय रामात्क्षत्रायथाऽभज्यत स द्विजेंद्रः N. 22. 133. -WITH अव to break down, shatter; Ku. 3. 74. -प्र 1 to break down, shatter, splinter. 2 to stop, arrest, suspend. 3 to frustrate, disappoint.-II. 10 U. (भंजयति-ते) To brighten, illuminate.

भंजक *a.* (जिका *f.*) Breaking, dividing.

भंजन *a.* (नी *f.*) 1 Breaking, splitting. 2 Arresting, checking. 3 Frustrating. 4 Causing violent pain. —नं 1 Breaking down, shattering, destroying. 2 Removing, dispelling, driving away; तदुदितभयभंजनाय यूनां Gît. 10. 3 Routing, vanquishing. 4 Frustrating. 5 Checking, interrupting, disturbing. 6 Afflicting, paining. —नः Decay of the teeth.

भंजनकः A particular disease of the mouth which consists in the decay of the teeth attended with contortion of the lips.

भंजरुः A tree growing near a temple.

भट् I. 1 P. (भटति, भटित) 1 To nourish, foster, maintain. 2 To hire. 3 To receive wages-II, 10 U. (भटयति-ते) To speak, converse.

भटः 1 A warrior, soldier, combatant; तद्भटचातुरीतुरी N. 1. 12; वादिव्रसद्विर्षेटते भटस्य 22. 22; Bk. 14. 101. 2 A mercenary, hired soldier, hireling. 3 An outcast, a barbarian. 4 A demon.

भटित्र *a.* Roasted on a spit.

भट्टः 1 A lord, master (used as a title of respect in addressing princes.). 2 A title used with the names of learned Brâhmaṇas; भट्टगोपालस्य पौत्रः Mâl. 1; so कुमारिलभट्टः &c. 3 Any learned man or philosopher. 4 A kind of mixed caste, whose occupation is that of bards or panegyrists; क्षत्रियाद्विप्रकन्यायां भट्टो जातोऽनुवाचकः, 5 A bard, panegyrist. -COMP. -आचार्यः 1 a title given to a learned man or any celebrated teacher. 2 a great doctor. प्रयागः= प्रयाग q. v.

भट्टार *a.* 1 Revered, worshipful. 2 A title of respect or distinction used with proper names; as in भट्टारहरिचंद्रस्य पद्यबंधो नृपायते Hch.

भट्टारक *a.* (रिका *f.*) Venerable, worshipful &c; see भट्टार above. -COMP. -वासरः Sunday.

भट्टिनी 1 A queen (not crowned), a princess; (often used in dramas by maid-servants in addressing a queen). 2 A lady of high rank. 3 The wife of a Brâhmaṇa.

भड्डः A particular mixed caste.

भडिलः 1 A hero, warrior. 2 An attendant, servant.

भण् 1 P. (भणति, भणित) 1 To say, speak; पुरुषोत्तम इति भणितव्ये V. 3; Bk. 14. 16 2 To describe; काव्यः स काव्येन सभामभाणीत् N. 10. 59. 3 To name, call.

भणनं, भणितं, भणितिः *f.* Speaking, speech, talk, words, discourse, conversation; न येषामानंदं जनयति जगन्नाथभणितिः Bv. 4. 39; 2. 77; श्रीजयदेवभणितं हरिरमितं Gît. 7; इह रसभणने *ibid*.

भंड् I. 1 A. (भंडते) 1 To chide, upbraid. 2 To mock, deride. 3 To speak. 4 To jest, joke. II. 10 U. (भंडयति-ते) 1 To make fortunate. 2 To cheat (properly भंद्).

भंडः A buffoon, jester, mime; त्रयो वेदस्य कर्तारो भंडधूर्तनिशाचकाः Sarv. S 2 N. of a mixed caste; cf. भड्ड. -COMP. -तपस्विन् *m.* a pseudo ascetic. -हासिनी a harlot, courtezan.

भंडकः A species of wag-tail.

भंडनं 1 Mail, armour, 2 War, battle. 3 Mischief, wickedness.

भंडिः -डी *f.* A wave.

भंडिल *a.* Happy, auspicious, prosperous, fortunate. —लः 1 Good fortune, happiness, welfare. 2 A messenger. 3 A workman, artisan.

भदंतः 1 A term of respect applied to a Buddhist; भदंत तिथिरेव न शुध्यति Mu. 4. 2 A Buddhist mendicant.

भदाकः Prosperity, good fortune.

भद्र *a* 1 Good, happy, prosperous. 2 Auspicious, blessed; as in भद्रमुख. 3 Foremost, best, chief, पप्रच्छ भद्रं विजितारिभद्रः R. 14. 31. 4 Favourable, propitious. 5 Kind, gracious, excellent, friendly, good; often used in voc. sing. in the sense of "my good sir' or 'my good friend', 'my good lady', 'my dear madam'. 6 Pleasant, enjoyable, lovely, beautiful; Pt. 1. 181. 7 Laudable, desirable, praiseworthy. 8 beloved, dear. 9 Specious, plausible, hypocritical. -द्रं 1 Happiness, Good fortune, welfare, blessing, prosperity; भद्रं भद्रं वितर भगवन् भूयसे मंगलाय Mâl. 1. 3; 6. 7; त्वयि वितरतु भद्रं भूयसे मंगलाय U. 3. 48; oft· used in pl. in this sense; सर्वो भद्राणि पश्यंतु; भद्रं ते 'god bless you', 'prosperity to you'. 2 Gold. 3 Iron, steel. 1 A bullock—द्रः. 2 A species of wagtail. 3 A term applied to a particular kind of elephants. 4 An impostor, hypocrite; Ms. 9. 258. 5 N. of *S*iva. 6 An epithet of mount Meru. 7 A kind of *Kadamba*. (भद्राकृ means 'to shave'; भद्राकरणं shaving).-COMP. -अंगः an epithet of Balarâma. -आकार,-आकृति *a.* of auspicious features.-आत्मजः a sword. -आसनं 1 a chair of state, splendid seat, a throne. 2 particular posture in meditation. -ईशः an epithet of *S*iva.-एला large cardamoms. -कपिलः an epithet of *S*iva. -कारक *a.* propitious. -काली N. of Durgâ. -कुंभः a golden jar filled with water from a holy place, particularly from the Ganges. -गणितं the construction of magical diagrams.-घटः घटकः a vessel from which a lottery is drawn. -दारु *m. n.* a sort of pine. नामन् *m.* a wagtail. -पीठं 1 a splendid seat, a chair of state, throne; R. 17. 10. 2 a kind of winged insect. -बलनः an epithet of Balarâma. -मुख *a.* 'of an auspicious face', used as a polite address, 'good sir,' 'gentle sir'; *S*. 7. -मृगः an epithet of a particular kind of elephant. -रेणुः N. of Indra's elephant. -वर्मन् *m.* a kind of jasmine. -शाखः an epithet of Kârtikeya.-श्रयं, -श्रियं sandal-wood.-श्रीः *f.* the sandal tree. -सोमा an epithet of the Ganges.

भद्रक *a.* (द्रिका *f*) 1 Good, auspicious. 2 Handsome, beautiful.—कः The *Devadâru* tree.

भद्रंकर *n.* One who confers prosperity.

भद्रवत् *a.* Auspicious. —*n.* The Devadâru tree.

भद्रा 1 A cow. 2 N. of the second, seventh, and twelfth days of a lunar fortnight. **3** The celestial Ganges **4** N. of various plants. –COMP. **श्रयं** sandal-wood.

भद्रिका 1 An amulet. **2** =भद्रा (2) above.

भद्रिलं 1 Prosperity, good fortune. **2** Tremulous motion.

भंभः 1 A fly. **2** Smoke.

भंभरालिका, भंभराली 1 A gad-fly. **2** A gnat.

भंभारवः The lowing of a cow.

भयं 1 Fear, alarm, dread, apprehension: (oft. with abl.); भोगे रोगभयं कुले च्युतिभयं वित्ते नृपालाद्भयं Bh. 3. 35; यदि समरमपास्य नास्ति मृत्योर्भयं Ve. 3 4. **2** Fright, terror; जगद्भयं &c. **3** A danger, risk, hazard; तावद्भयस्य भेतव्यं यावद्भयमनागतं । आगतं तु भयं वीक्ष्य नरः कुर्याद्यथोचितं H. 1. 57. **–यः** Sickness, disease.–COMP. **अन्वित, –आक्रांत** *a.* overcome with fear. **–आतुर, -आर्त** *a.* afraid, alarmed, frightened. **–आवह** *a.* **1** causing fear. **2** risky; स्वधर्मे निधनं श्रेयः परधर्मो भयावहः Bg. 3. 35. **–उत्तर** *a.* attended with or succeeded by fear. **–कर** (also **भयंकर**) *a.* **1** frightening, terrible, fearful. **2** dangerous, perilous; so **भयकारक, भयकृत् –डिंडिमः** a drum used in battle. **–द्रुत** *a.* fleeing from fear, routed, put to flight. **प्रतीकारः** warding off or removed of fears. **–प्रद** *a.* inspiring fear, fearful terrible. **प्रस्तावः** an occasion of fear. **–ब्राह्मणः** a timid Brâhmaṇa, a Brâhmaṇa who to save himself from danger declares his caste relying on the inviolability of a Brâhmaṇa. **–विप्लुत** *a.* panic-struck. **–व्यूहः** a particular array of troops when they are threatened with danger.

भयानक *a* Fearful, horrible, terrible, frightful; किमतः परं भयानकं स्यात् U. 2: Si. 17. 20; Bg. 11. 27. **–कः 1** A tiger. **2** N. of Râhu. **3** The sentiment of terror, one of the eight or nine sentiments in poetry see under रस.—**कं** Terror, fear.

भर *a.* Bearing, granting, supporting &c. **–रः 1** A burden, load, weight; खुरत्रये भरं कृत्वा Pt. 1 'supporting himself on his three hoofs'; फलभरपरिणामश्यामजम्बू &c. U. 2 20; भरव्यथा Mu 2. 18. **2** A great number, large quantity, collection, multitude; धत्ते भरं कुसुमपत्रफलावलीनां Bv. 1. 94, 54, Si. 9. 47 **3** Bulk, mass **4** Excess: निर्व्यूढसौहृदभरेति गुणोज्ज्वलेति Mal 6. 17; शोभाभरैः संभृताः Bv. 1. 103; कोपभरेण Git. 3. **6** A particular measure of weight.

भरटः 1 A potter. **2** A servant.

भरण *a.* (**णी** *f.*) Bearing, maintaining, supporting, nourishing. **–णं 1** The act of nourishing, maintaining or supporting; R. 1. 24; S. 7. 33. **2** The act of bearing or carrying. **3** Bringing or procuring. **4** Nutriment **5** Hire, wages **–णः** The constellation Bharaṇî.

भरणी N. of the second constellation containing three stars. COMP. **–भूः** an epithet of Râhu.

भरंडः 1 A master, lord. **2** A prince, king. **3** An ox, a bull. **4** A worm.

भरण्यं 1 Cherishing, supporting, maintaining. **2** Wages, hire. **3** The lunar mansion Bharaṇî. **–ण्या** Wages, hire. –COMP. **भुज्** *m.* a hired servant, hireling.

भरण्युः 1 A master. **2** A protector. **3** A friend. **4** Fire. **5** The moon. **6** The sun.

भरतः 1 N. of the son of Dushyanta and Sakuntalâ, who became a universal monarch (**चक्रवर्तिन्**), India being called *Bharatavarsha* after him. He was one of the remote ancestors of the Kauravas and Pâṇḍavas. **2** N. of a brother of Râma, son of Kaikeyî, the youngest wife of Das'aratha. He was very pious and righteous, and was so much devoted to Râma that when the latter prepared to go to the forest in accordance with the wicked demand of Kaikeyî, he was very much grieved to find that his own mother had sent his brother into exile, and refusing the sovereignty that was his own, ruled the kingdom in the name of Râma (by bringing from him his two sandals and making them the 'regents' of the realm) till he returned after his fourteen years' exile. **3** N. of an ancient sage who is supposed to have been the founder of the science of music and dramaturgy. **4** An actor, a stage player; तत्किमित्युदासते भरताः Mâl. 1. **5** A hired soldier, mercenary. **6** A barbarian, mountaineer. **7** An epithet of Agni. –COMP. **–अग्रजः** 'the elder brother of Bharata', an epithet of Râma; R. 14. 73. **–खंडं** N. of a part of India. **–ज्ञ** *a.* knowing the science of Bharata; or the dramatic science. **–पुत्रकः** an actor. **–वर्षः** 'the country of Bharata; *i. e.* India. **–वाक्यं** the last verse or verses in a drama, a sort of benediction (said to be in honour of Bharata, the founder of the dramatic science); तथापीदमस्तु भरतवाक्यं (occurring in every play).

भरथः 1 A sovereign king. **2** Fire. **3** A deity presiding over one of the regions of the world (लोकपाल).

भरद्वाजः 1 N. of one of the seven sages. **2** A sky-lark.

भरित *a.* **1** Nourished, maintained **2** Filled with, full of; जगज्जालं कर्तां कुसुमभरसौरभ्यभरितं Bv. 1. 54; 33.

भरुः 1 A husband. **2** A lord. **3** N. of Siva. **4** Of Vishṇu. **5** Gold. **6** The sea.

भरुजः (**जा** or **जी** *f.*) A jackal.

भरुटक Fried meat.

भर्गः 1 N. of Siva **2** Of Brahman.

भर्ग्यः An epithet of Siva.

भर्जन *a.* Roasting, frying, baking. **2** Annihilating **–नं 1** The act of roasting or frying. **2** A frying-pan.

भर्तृ *m.* **1** A husband; यद्भर्तुरेव हितमिच्छति तत्कलत्रं Bh. 2. 68; स्त्रीणां भर्ता धर्मदाराश्च पुंसां Mal. 6. 18. **2** A lord, master, superior; भर्तुः शापेन Me. 1; गण°, भूत° &c. **3** A leader, commander, chief; R 7, 41. **4** A supporter, bearer, protector –COMP. **–घ्नी** a woman who murders her husband. **–दारकः** a crown-prince, prince royal, young prince, an heir apparent (a term of address chiefly used in dramas). **–दारिका** a young princess (a term of address in dramas). **–व्रतं** fidelity or devotion to a husband. (**–ता**) a virtuous and devoted wife; cf. पतिव्रता **–शोकः** grief for the death of the husband **–हरिः** N. of a celebrated author to whom are ascribed the three Satakas (शृंगार, नीति, and वैराग्य) and also वाक्यप्रदीप and भट्टिकाव्य.

भर्तृमती A married woman whose husband is living.

भर्तृसात् *ind* In the possession of a husband; °**कृता** married.

भर्त्स् 10 A. (भर्त्सयते; P. also sometimes) **1** To menace, threaten. **2** To revile, reproach, abuse. **3** To deride. –WITH **निस् 1** to revile, censure, abuse. **2** to surpass, eclipse, put to shame; Ku. 3. 53.

भर्त्सकः A threatener, reviler.

भर्त्सनं, भर्त्सना, भर्त्सितं 1 Threatening, reviling. **2** A threat, menace. **3** Reproach, abuse. **4** A curse.

भर्मं 1 Wages, hire. **2** Gold. **3** The navel.

भर्मण्या Wages, hire.

भर्मन् *n.* **1** Support, maintenance, nourishment **2** Wages, hire. **3** Gold. **4** A gold coin. **5** The navel.

भल् I 10 A. (भालयते, भालित) To see, behold –With **नि** (also P.) **1** To see, behold, perceive, look at; निभाल्य भूयो निजगौरिमाणं मा नाम मानं सहसैव यासीः Bv 2 176; or यन्मां न भामिनि निभालयसि प्रभातनीलारविंदमदभंगिदृशा कटाक्षैः 3. 4. –II. 1 A. see भल्ल्.

भल्ल् 1 A. (भल्लते, भल्लित) **1** To describe, narrate, tell. **2** To wound, hurt, kill. **3** To give.

भल्लः-ल्ली-ल्लं A kind of missile or arrow; क्वचिदाकर्णविकृष्टभल्लवर्षी R. 9. 66; 4. 63; 7. 58. **—ल्लः** 1 A bear. 2 An epithet of *S*iva. 3 The marking-nut plant. (भल्ली also.)

भल्लकः A bear.

भल्लातः, -भल्लातकः The marking-nut plant.

भल्लुकः A bear.

भल्लूकः 1 A bear; दधति कुहरभाजामत्र भल्लूकयूनां U. 2. 21. 2 A dog.

भव *a.* (At the end of comp.) Arising or produced from, originating in. **-वः** 1 Being, state of being, existence, (सत्ता). 2 Birth, production; भवो हि लोकाभ्युदयाय तादृशां R. 3. 14; *S.* 7. 27. 3 Source, origin. 4 Worldly existence, worldly life, life; as in भवार्णव, भवसागर &c.; Ku. 2. 51. 5 The world. 6 Well-being, health, prosperity. 7 Excellence, superiority. 8 N. of *S*iva; दक्षस्य कन्या भवपूर्वपत्नी Ku. 1. 21; 3. 72. 9 A god, deity. 10 Acquisition (प्राप्ति). **-Comp. -अतिग** *a.* overcoming wordly existence. **-अंतकृत्** *m.* an epithet of Brahmâ. **-अंतरं** another existence (previous or future); Pt. 1. 121. **-अब्धिः, -अर्णवः, -समुद्रः, -सागरः, -सिंधुः** the ocean of worldly life. **-अयना -नी** the Ganges. **-अरण्यं** 'a forest of worldly life,' a dreary world. **-आत्मजः** an epithet of Gaṇesa or Kârtikeya. **-उच्छेदः** destruction of worldly existence, R. 14. 74. **-क्षितिः** *f.* the place of birth. **-घस्मरः** a forest-conflagration. **-छिद्** *a.* cutting the (bonds of) worldly life, preventing recurrence of birth; भवच्छिदस्त्र्यंबकपादपांशवः K. 1. **-छेदः** prevention of recurring birth: *S*i. 1. 35. **-दारु** *n.* the *devadâru* tree. **-भूतिः** N. of a celebrated poet (see App. II.); भवभूतेः संबंधाद्भूधरभूरेव भारती भाति। एतत्कृतकारुण्ये किमन्यथा रोदिति ग्रावा ॥ *Aryâ* S. 36. **-रुद्** *m.* a drum beaten at funeral ceremonies. **-वीतिः** *f.* liberation from worldly existence; Ki. 6. 41.

भवत् *a.* (**न्ती** *f.*) 1 Being, becoming, happening. 2 Present; समतीतं च भवच्च भावि च R. 8. 78. *-pron. a.* (**ती** *f.*) A respectful or honorific pronoun, translated by 'your honour,' 'your lordship, worship or highness'; (oft. used in the sense of the second personal pronoun, but with the third person of the verb); अथवा कथं भवान् मन्यते M. 1; भवंत एव जानंति रघूणां च कुलस्थितिं U. 5. 23; R. 2. 40, 3. 48; 5. 16. It is often joined to अत्र or तत्र (see the words), and sometimes to स also; यन्मां विधेयविषये सभवान्नियुंक्ते Mâl. 1. 9.

भवदीय *a.* Your honour's, your, thine.

भवनं 1 Being, existence. 2 Production, birth. 3 An abode, residence, dwelling, mansion; अथवा भवनं प्रत्ययात् प्रविष्टोस्मि Mk. 3; Me. 32. 4 A site, abode, receptacle; as in अविनयभवनं Pt. 1. 191. 5 A building. 6 Nature. **-Comp. -उदरं** the interior of a house. **-पतिः, स्वामिन्** *m.* the lord of the house, a *pater familias*.

भवंतः -तिः The time being, present time.

भवंती A virtuous wife.

भवानी N. of Pârvatî, wife of *S*iva आलंबताग्रकरमत्रभवो भवान्याः Ki. 5. 29; Ku. 7. 84; Me. 36, 44. **-Comp. -गुरुः** an epithet of the mountain Him'alaya. **-पतिः** an epithet of *S*iva; अधिवसति सदा यदेनं जनैरविदितविभवो भवानीपतिः Ki. 5. 21.

भवादृक्ष *a.* (**क्षी** *f.*), **भवादृश्** *a.* **भवादृश** *a.* (**शी**) Like your honour, like you.

भविक *a.* (**की** *f.*) 1 Beneficial, suitable, useful. 2 Happy, prosperous. **-कं** Prosperity, welfare.

भवितव्य *pot. p.* About to take place, about to happen, likely to be, often used like भाव्य impersonally, *i. e.* in the neuter gender and singular number, with instrumental of the subject and the predicative word, त्वया मम सहायेन भवितव्यं *S.* 2; गुरुणा कारणेन भवितव्यं *S.* 6. **-व्यं** What is destined to happen; भवितव्य भवत्येव यद्विधेर्मनसि स्थितं Subhâsh.

भवितव्यता Inevitable necessity, necessary consequence, fate, destiny; भवितव्यता बलवती *S.* 6; सर्वंकषा भगवती भवितव्यतैव Mâl. 1. 23.

भवितृ *a.* (**त्री** *f.*) About to become, future; R. 6. 52; Ku. 1. 50.

भविनः A poet; also **भविनिन्** *m.*

भविलः 1 A paramour. 2 A sensualist, voluptuary.

भविष्णु *a.* = भूष्णु q. v.

भविष्य *a.* 1 Future 2 Imminent, impending. **-ष्यं** The future, futurity. **-Comp. -कालः** the future tense. **-ज्ञानं** knowledge of futurity. **-पुराणं** N. of one of the 18 Purâṇas.

भविष्यत् *a.* (**ती** or **न्ती** *f.*) About to be. **-Comp. -कालः** futurity. **-वक्तृ, -वादिन्** *a.* predicting future events, prophesying.

भव्य *a.* 1 Existing, being, being present. 2 Future, about to be. 3 Likely to become. 4 Suitable, proper, fit, worthy; Ki. 11. 13. 5 Good, nice, excellent. 6 Auspicious, fortunate, happy; Ku I. 22; Ki. 3. 12; 10. 51. 7 Handsome, lovely, beautiful. 8 Calm, tranquil, palccid. 9 True. **-व्या** N. of Pârvatî. **-व्यं** 1 Existence. 2 Future time. 3 Result, fruit. 4 Good result, prosperity; R. 17. 53. 5 A bone.

भष् 1 P. (भषति) 1 To bark, growl, bark at. 2 To abuse, reproach, revile, rail at.

भषः, भषकः A dog.

भषणः A dog. **-णं** The barking of a dog, a growl.

भसद् *m.* 1 The sun. 2 Flesh. 3 A kind of duck. 4 Time. 5 A float (प्लव). 6 The hinder parts (said to be *f.* and *n.* also). 7 Pudendum Muliebre.

भसनः A bee.

भसंतः Time.

भसित *a.* Reduced to ashes. **—तं** Ashes; Bv. 1. 84.

भस्त्रका, भस्त्रा, भस्त्रि, *f.* 1 A bellows. 2 A leathern vessel for holding water. 3 A pouch, leathern bag.

भस्मकं 1 Gold or silver. 2 Morbid appetite from over-digestion of food. 3 A kind of disease of the eyes.

भस्मन् *n.* 1 Ashes; (**कल्पते**) ध्रुवं चिताभस्मरजो विशुद्धये Ku. 5. 79. 2 Sacred ashes (smeared on the body); (**भस्मनि हु** 'to sacrifice in ashes'; *i. e.* to do a useless work; **भस्मा** or **भस्मीकृ** to reduce to ashes; **भस्मीभू** to be reduced to ashes; भस्मीभूतस्य देहस्य पुनरागमनं कुतः Sarva. S.) **-Comp. -अग्निः** morbid appetite from rapid digestion of food. **-अवशेष** *a.* remaining in the form of ashes; Ku. 3. 72. **-आह्वयः** camphor. **-उद्धूलनं, -गुंठनं** smearing the body with ashes; भस्मोद्धूलन भद्रमस्तु भवते K. P. 10. **-कारः** a washerman. **-कूटः** a heap of ashes. **-गंधा, -गंधिका, गंधिनी** a kind of perfume. **-तूलं** 1 frost, snow. 2 a shower of dust. 3 a number of villages. **-प्रियः** an epithet of *S*iva. **-रोगः** a kind of disease; cf. भस्माग्नि. **-लेपनं** smearing the body with ashes. **-विधिः** any rite performed with ashes. **-वेधकः** camphor. **-स्नानं** purification by ashes.

भस्मता The state of ashes.

भस्मसात् *ind.* To the state of ashes; °कृ 'to reduce to ashes.'

भा 2 P. (भाति, भात; *caus.* भापयति-ते; *desid.* बिभासति) To shine, be bright or splendid, be luminous; पंकैर्विना सरो भाति सदः खलजनैर्विना। कटुवर्णैर्विना काव्यं मानसं विषयैर्विना Bv. 1. 116; समतीत्य भाति जगती जगती Ki. 5. 25; R. 3. 18. 2 To seem, appear; बुभुक्षितं न प्रति भाति किंचित् Mbh. 3 To be, exist. 4 To show oneself. -WITH **अभि** to shine forth; दिवि स्थितः सूर्य इवाभिभाति Mb. **-आ** 1 to shine, blaze, appear splendid; नरेंद्रकन्यास्तमवाप्य सत्पतिं तमोनुदं दक्षसुता इवाबभुः R. 3. 33. 2 to seem, appear; R. 5. 15, 70; 13. 14. **-निस्** 1 to shine forth, shine; अक्षबीजवलयेन निर्बभौ R. 11. 66. 2 to proceed, arise, start into view; वेदाद्धर्मो हि निर्बभौ Ms. 5. 44; 2. 10. **-प्र** 1 to appear. 2 to shine forth. 3 to begin to become light, begin to dawn (as night); ननु प्रभाता रजनी S. 4; प्रभातकल्पा शशिनेव शर्वरी R. 3. 2. -प्रति 1 to shine, appear bright or luminous; प्रतिभांत्यद्य वनानि केतकानां Ghat. 15. 2 to show oneself, become manifest. 3 to seem, appear; क्षीरत्नस्थिरपरा प्रतिभाति सा मे S. 2. 9; R. 2. 47; Ku. 5. 38, 6. 54. 4 to occur to, come into the mind of; as in नोत्तरं प्रतिभाति मे. -वि 1 to shine; Bh. 2.71. 2 to seem, appear. -व्यति (Atm.) to shine very much, shine forth (in prominent contrast); अपिलोकयुगं दृशावपि श्रुतदृष्टा रमणीगुणा अपि । श्रुतिगामितया दमस्वसुर्व्यतिभाते नितरां धरापते ॥ N. 2. 22 (where the verb can be construed equally with युगं, दृशौ and गुणाः; cf. P. I. 3. 14).

भा 1 Light, splendour, lustre, beauty; तावद्भा भारवेर्भाति यावन्माघस्य नोदयः Udb. 2 A shadow, reflection. -Comp. -कोशः-षः the sun. -गणः the whole group of constellations. -निकरः a mass of light, collection of rays. -नेमिः the sun. -मंडलं a halo of light.

भाःकर See भास्कर under भास्.

भाक्त a. 1 Regularly fed by another, a dependant, retainer. 2 Fit for food. 3 Inferior, secondary (opp. मुख्य). 4 Used in a secondary sense.

भाक्तिकः A retainer, dependant.

भाक्ष a. (क्षी f.) Voracious, gluttonous.

भागः 1 A part, portion, share, division; as in भागहर, भागशः &c. 2 Allotment, distribution, partition. 3 Lot, fate; निर्माणभागः परिणतः U. 4. 4 A part of any whole, a fraction. 5 The numerator of a fraction. 6 A quarter, one fourth part. 7 A degree or the 360th part of the circumference of a circle. 8 The 30th part of a zodiacal sign. 9 The quotient. 10 Room, space, spot, region, place; R. 18. 47. -Comp. -अर्ह a. entitled to a share or inheritance. -कल्पना allotment of shares. -जातिः f. reduction of fractions to a common denominator (in math.). -धेयं 1 a share, part, portion; नीवारभागधेयोचितमृगैः R. 1. 50. 2. fortune, destiny, luck. 3 good fortune or luck; तद्भागधेयं परमं पशूनां Bh. 2. 12. 4 property. 5 happiness. (-यः) 1 a tax; S. 2. 2 an heir. -भाज् a. interested, a sharer or partner. -भुज् m. a king, sovereign. -लक्षणा a kind of लक्षणा or secondary use of a word by which it partly loses and partly retains its primary meaning; also called जहदजहल्लक्षणा; e. g. सोयं देवदत्तः. -हरः 1 a co-heir. 2 division (in math.). -हारः division (in math.).

भागवत a. (ती f.) 1 Relating to or worshipping Vishṇu. 2 Pertaining to a god. 3 Holy, divine, sacred. -तः A follower or devotee of Vishṇu or Krishṇa. -तं N. of one of the 18 Purâṇas.

भागशस् ind. 1 In parts or portions, part by part. 2 According to the share.

भागिक a. 1 Relating to a part. 2 Forming a part. 3 Fractional. 4 Bearing interest. (भागिकं शतं 'one part in a hundred': i. e one per cent; so भागिक विंशतिः &c.)

भागिन् a. 1 Consisting of shares or parts. 2 Sharing, having a share. 3 Sharing or participating in, partaking of; as in दुःख°. 4 Concerned in, affected by. 5 A possessor, owner; Ms. 9. 53. 6 Entitled to a share; Ms. 9. 165; Y. 2. 125. 7 Lucky, fortunate. 8 Inferior, secondary.

भागिनेयः A sister's son. -यी A sister's daughter.

भागीरथी 1 N. of the river Ganges; भागीरथीनिर्झरशीकराणां Ku. 1. 15. 2 N. of one of the three main branches of the Ganges.

भाग्यं 1 Fate, destiny, luck, fortune; स्त्रियश्चरित्रं पुरुषस्य भाग्यं देवो न जानाति कुतो मनुष्यः Subhâsh. oft. in pl.; S. 5. 30. 2 Good fortune or luck; R. 3. 13. 3 Prosperity, affluence; भाग्येष्वनुत्सेकिनी S. 4. 17. 4 Happiness, welfare. -Comp. -आयत्त a. dependent on fate; भाग्यायत्तमतःपरं S. 4. 16. -उदयः dawn of good fortune, lucky occurrence. -क्रमः course or turn of fortune; भाग्यक्रमेण हि धनानि भवंति यांति Mk. 1. 13. -योगः a lucky or fortunate juncture. -विप्लवः ill luck, adverseness, of fate; R. 8. 47. -वशात् ind. through the will of fate, luckily, fortunately.

भाग्यवत् a. 1 Fortunate, blessed, happy. 2 Prosperous.

भांग a. (गी f.) Made of hemp, hempen.

भांगकः A tattered cloth, shred, rag.

भांगीनं A field of hemp.

भाज् 10 U. To divide, distribute; see भज् caus.

भाज a. (Usually at the end of Comp.) 1 Sharing or participating in, liable to. 2 Having, enjoying, possessing, obtaining; सुख°, रिक्थ°. 3 Entitled to. 4 Feeling, experiencing, being sensible of. 5 Devoting oneself to. 6 Living in, inhabiting, dwelling in; कुहरभाजां. 7 Going or resorting to, seeking. 8 Worshipping. 9 Falling to the lot of. 19 What must be done, a duty (कर्तव्य); Bk. 3. 21.

भाजकः 1 Dividing. 2 (In arith.) A divider.

भाजनं 1 Sharing, dividing. 2 Division (in arith.). 3 A vessel, pot, cup, plate; पुष्पभाजनं S. 4; R. 5. 22. 4 (Fig.) A receptacle, recipient, repository; स श्रियो भाजनं नरः Pt. 1. 143; कल्याणानां त्वमसि महसां भाजनं विश्वमूर्ते Mâl. 1. 3; U. 3. 15; M. 5. 8. 5 A fit or deserving person, a fit object or person; भवादृशा एव भवंति भाजनान्युपदेशानां K. 108. 6 Representation. 7 A measure equal to 64 *palas*.

भाजितं A share, portion.

भाजी Rice, gruel.

भाज्यं 1 A portion, share. 2 An inheritance. 3 (In arith.) The dividend.

भाटं, भाटकं Wages, hire, rent.

भाटिः f. 1 Wages, hire. 2 The earnings of harlots.

भाट्टः A follower of Bhaṭṭa, a follower of that school of the Mîmâmsâ philosophy which was founded by Kumârila Bhaṭṭa.

भाणः A species of dramatic composition; in it only one character is introduced on the stage which supplies the place of interlocutors by a copious use of आकाशभाषित q. v.; भाणः स्याद्धूर्तचरितो नानावस्थांतरात्मकः । एकांक एक एवात्र निपुणः पंडितो विटः ॥ S. D. 513; see the next stanzas also; e. g. वसंततिलक, मुकुंदानंद, लीलामधुकर &c.

भाणकः A declarer, proclaimer.

भांडं 1 A vessel, pot, utensil (plate, dish, can &c.); नीलीभांडं 'an indigo-vat'; so क्षीरभांडं 'a milk-pail'; सुरा°, मद्य° &c. 2 A box, trunk, chest, case; क्षुरभांड Pt. 1. 3 Any tool or instrument, an implement. 4 A musical instrument. 5 Goods, wares, merchandise, shopkeeper's stock; मथुरागामीनि भांडानि Pt. 1. 6 A bale of goods. 7 (Fig.) Any valued possession, treasure; शांतं वा रघुनंदने तदुभयं तत्पुत्रभांडं हि मे U. 4. 26. 8 The bed of a river. 9 Trappings or harness of a horse. 10 Buffoonery, mimicry (from भंड). -डाः (m. pl.) Wares, merchandise. -Comp. -अ(आ)गारः, -रं 1 a store-house, store-room (lit. where household goods and utensils &c. are kept); भांडागाराण्यकृत विदुषां सा स्वयं भोगभांजि Vikr. 18. 45. 2 treasury; ज्ञान°. 3 a collectoin, store, magazine. -पतिः a merchant. -पुटः a barber. -प्रतिभांडकं barter, computation of the exchange of goods. -भरकः the contents of a vessel. -मूल्यं capital in the form of wares. -शाला a storehouse, store.

भांडकः-कं A small vessel, cup. -कं Goods, merchandise. wares.

भांडारं A store-house, store.

भांडारिन् m. The keeper of a storehouse.

भांडिः f. A razor-case. -Comp. -वाहः a barber. -शाला a barber's shop.

भांडिकः-लः A barber.

भांडिका An implement, a tool, utensil.

भांडिनी A chest, basket.

भांडीरः The Indian fig-tree.

भात *p. p.* Shining, brilliant, bright. **-तः** Dawn, morning.

भातिः *f.* **1** Light, brightness, lustre, splendour. **2** Perception, knowledge (ज्ञान or प्रतीति).

भातुः The sun.

भाद्रः, भाद्रपदः N. of a lunar month (corresponding to August-September). **-दाः** (*f. pl.*) N. of the 25th and 26th lunar mansions (पूर्वाभाद्रपदा and उत्तराभाद्रपदा).

भाद्रपदी, भाद्री The day of full moon in the month of Bhâdrapada.

भाद्रमातुरः The son of a virtuous or good mother (भद्रमातृ).

भानं **1** Appearing, being visible. **2** Light, lustre. **3** Perception, knowledge.

भानुः **1** Light, lustre, brightness. **2** A ray of light; मंडिताखिलदिक्प्रांताश्चंडांशोः पांतु भानवः Bv. 1. 129; *Si.* 2. 53; Ms. 8. 132. **3** The sun; भानुः सकृद्युक्ततुरंग एव *S.* 5. 4; भीमभानौ निदाघे Bv. 1. 30. **4** Beauty. **5** A day. **6** A king, prince, sovereign. **7** An epithet of *Siva.* *-f.* A handsome woman. **-Comp. -केश(स)रः** the sun. **-जः** the planet Saturn. **-दिनं, -वारः** Sunday.

भानुमत् *a.* **1** Luminous, bright, splendid. **2** Beautiful, handsome. *-m.* The sun ; Ku. 3. 65; R. 6. 36. Rs. 5. 2. **-ती** N. of the wife of Duryodhana.

भामः **1** Brightness, lustre, splendour. **2** The sun. **3** Passion, wrath, anger. **4** A siser's husband. **-मा** **1** A passionate woman. **2** N. of one of the wives of Krishṇa, usually called सत्यभामा.

भामिनी **1** A beautiful young woman; (कामिनी); R. 8. 28. **2** A passionate woman (often used like चंडी as a term of endearment); उपचीयत एव कापि शोभा परितो भामिनि ते मुखस्य नित्यं Bv. 2. 1.

भारः **1** A load, burden, weight (fig. also); कुचभारानमिता न योषितः Bh. 3. 27; so श्रोणीभार Me. 82; भारः कायो जीवितं वज्रकीलं Mâl. 9. 37. **2** Brunt, thickest part (as of a battle); U. 5. 5. **3** Excess, pitch; R. 14. 68. **4** Labour, toil, trouble. **5** A mass, large quantity; कच°, जटा°. **6** A particular weight equal to 2000 *palas* of gold. **7** A yoke for carrying burdens. **-Comp. -आक्रांत** *a.* heavily laden, over-burdened. **-उद्वहः** a porter, burden-carrier. **-उपजीवनं** living by carrying burdens, a porter's life. **-यष्टिः** a pole for carrying burdens. **-वाह** *a.* (**भारौही** *f.*) bearer of burdens. **-वाहः** a burden-carrier, porter. **-वाहनः** a beast of burden. (**-नं**) a cart, waggon. **-वाहिकः** a porter. **-सह** *a.* 'able to carry a great load', very strong or powerful. **-हर, -हारः** a burden-bearer, porter. **-हारिन्** *m.* an epithet of Krishṇa.

भारंडः A kind of fabulous bird. (Also **भारुंड**); Pt. 5. 102.

भारत *a.* (**ती** *f.*) Belonging to or descended from Bharata. **-तः** **1** A descendant of Bharata. **2** An inhabitant of *Bharatavarsha* or India. **3** An actor. **-तं** **1** India, the country of Bharata; *Si.* 14. 5. **2** N. of the most celebrated epic poem in Sanskrit which gives the history of the descendants of Bharata with innumerable episodes. (It is attributed to Vyâsa or कृष्णद्वैपायन, but the work, as we have it at present, is evidently the production of many hands); श्रवणांजलिपुटपेयं विरचितवान् भारताख्यममृतं यः । तमहमरागमकृष्णं कृष्णद्वैपायनं वंदे Ve. 1. 4; व्यासगिरां निर्यासं सारं विश्वस्य भारतं वंदे । भूषणतयैव संज्ञां यदंकितां भारती वहति ॥ *Aryâ* S. 31. **-ती** **1** Speech, voice, words, eloquence; भारतीनिर्घोषः U. 3; तमर्थमिव भारत्या सुतया योक्तुमर्हसि Ku. 6. 79; नवरसरुचिरां निर्मितिमादधती भारती कवेर्जयति K. P. 1. **2** The goddess of speech, Sarasvatî. **3** N. of a particular kind of style; भारती संस्कृतप्रायो वाग्व्यापारो नटाश्रयः S. D. 285. **4** A quail.

भारद्वाजः **1** N. of Droṇa, the military preceptor of the Kauravas and Pâṇḍavas. **2** Of Agastya. **3** The planet Mars. **4** A sky-lark. **-जं** A bone.

भारवः A bow-string.

भारविः N. of the author of the Kirâtârjunîya; तावद्भा भारवेर्भाति यावन्माघस्य नोदयः । उदिते च पुनर्माघे भारवेर्भा रवेरिव ॥ भारवेरर्थगौरवं Udb.

भारिः A lion.

भारिक, भारिन् *a.* Heavy. *-m.* A burden-carrier, porter.

भार्गः A king of the Bhargas.

भार्गवः **1** N. of Sukra, regent of planet Venus and preceptor of the Asuras. **2** N. of Parasurâma; see परशुराम. **3** An epithet of *Siva.* **4** An archer. **5** An elephant. **-Comp. -प्रियः** a diamond.

भार्गवी **1** The Dûrvâ grass. **2** An epithet of Lakshmî.

भार्यः A servant, a dependant (to be supported).

भार्या **1** A lawful wife; सा भार्या या गृहे दक्षा सा भार्या या प्रजावती । सा भार्या या पतिप्राणा सा भार्या या पतिव्रता ॥ H. 1. 196. **2** The female of an animal. **-Comp. -आट** *a.* livig by the prostitution of his wife. **-ऊढ** *a.* married (as a man); भार्योढं तमवज्ञाय Bk. 4. 15. **-जितः** a hen-pecked husband.

भार्यारुः **1** A kind of deer. **2** The father of a child by another man's wife.

भालं **1** The forehead, brow ; यद्धात्रा निजभालपट्टलिखितं स्तोकं महद्वा धनं Bh. 2. 49 ; (स्मरस्य) वपुः सद्यो भालानलभसितजालास्पदमभूत् Bv. 1. 84. **2** Light. **3** Darkness. -Comp. **-अंकः** **1** a man born with lucky lines on his forehead. **2** an epithet of *Siva.* **3** a saw. **4** a tortoise. **-चंद्रः** **1** an epithet of *Siva.* **2** of Gaṇesa. **-दर्शनं** red lead. **-दर्शिन्** *a.* 'looking at or watching the brow', said of a servant who is attentive to his master's wishes. **-दृश्** *m.*, **-लोचनः** an epithet of *Siva.* **-पट्टः, -ट्टं** the forehead.

भालुः The sun.

भाल(.लू :)कः, भालु(लू)कः A bear.

भावः **1** Being, existing, existence ; नासतो विद्यते भावः Bg. 2. 16. **2** Becoming, occurring, taking place. **3** State, condition, state of being ; लताभावेन परिणतमस्या रूपं V. 4 ; कातरभावः, विवर्णभावः &c. **4** Manner, mode. **5** Rank, station, position, capacity ; देवभावं गमिता K. P. 10; so प्रेष्यभावं ; किंकरभावं &c. **6** (*a.*) True condition or state, truth, reality; Bg. 10. 8. (*b*) Sincerity, devotion ; त्वयि मे भावनिबंधना रतिः R. 8. 52 ; 2. 26. **7** Innate property, disposition; nature, temperament ; U. 6. 14. **8** Inclination or disposition of mind, idea, thought, opinion, supposition ; Pt. 3. 43 ; Ms. 8. 25 ; 4. 65. **9** Feeling, emotion, sentiment ; एको भावः Pt. 3. 66 ; Ku. 6. 95. (In the dramatic science or in poetic compositions generally, *Bhâvas* are either स्थायिन् primary, or व्यभिचारिन् subordinate. The former are eight or nine, according as the *Rasas* are taken to be 8 or 9 each *rasa* having its own स्थायिभाव. The latter are thirty-three or thirty-four in number and serve to develop and strengthen the prevailing sentiment ; for definition and enumeration of the several kinds, see R. G. first *ânana* or K. P. 4.). **10** Love, affection, attachment ; द्वंद्वानि भावं क्रियया विवव्रुः Ku. 3. 35; R. 6. 36. **11** Purport, drift, gist, substance ; इति भावः (often used by commentators). **12** Meaning, intention, sense, import ; Mâl. 1. 25. **13** Resolution, determination. **14** The heart, soul, mind ; तयोर्विवृतभावत्वात् Mâl. 1. 12 ; Bg. 18. 16. **15** Any existing thing, an object, a thing, substance ; जगति जयिनस्ते ते भावा नवेंदुकलादयः Mâl. 1. 17, 36 ; R. 3. 41 ; U. 3. 32. **16** A being, living creature. **17** Abstract meditation, contemplation (=भावना q. v.). **18** Conduct, movement, gesture. **19** Amorous gesture or expression of sentiment, gesture of love; *S*. 2. 1. **20** Birth. **21** The world, universe. **22** The womb., **23** Will. **24** Superhuman power. **25** Advice, instruction. **26** (In dramas) A learned or venerable man, worthy man, (A term of address): भाव अयमस्मि V. 1; तां खलु भविन तथैव सर्वे वर्गीः पाटिताः Mâl. 1. **27** (In gram.) The sense of an abstract noun, abstract idea conveyed by a word; भावे क्तः. **28** A term for an impersonal passive or neuter verb. **29** (In astr.) An astronomical house. **30** A lunar mansion. **–Comp. –अनुग** *a.* not forced, natural. (**–गा**) a shadow. **–अंतरं** a different state. **–अर्थः 1** the obvious meaning or import (of a word, phrase &c.) **2** The subject-matter. **–आकूतं** (secret) thoughts of the mind; Amaru. 4. **–आत्मक** *a.* real, actual. **–आभासः** simulation of a feeling, a feigned or false emotion. **–आलीना** a shadow. **–एकरस** *a.* influenced solely by the sentiment of (sincere) love; Ku. 5. 82. **–गंभीरं** *ind.* **1** heartily, from the bottom of the heart. **2** deeply, gravely. **–गम्य** *a.* conceived by the mind; Me. 85. **–ग्राहिन्** *a.* **1** understanding the sense. **2** appreciating the sentiment. **–जः** the god of love. **–ज्ञ, विद्** *a.* knowing the heart. **–दर्शिन्** *a.* see भालदर्शिन्. **–बंधन** *a.* enchanting or fettering the heart, linking together the hearts; R. 3. 24. **–बोधक** *a.* indicating or revealing any feeling. **–मिश्रः** a worthy person, a gentleman (used in dramas). **–रूप** *a.* real, actual. **–वचनं** denoting an abstract idea, conveying the abstract notion of a verb. **–वाचकं** an abstract noun. **–शबलत्वं** a mixture of various emotions; (भावानां बाध्यबाधकभावमापन्नानामुदासीनानां वा व्यामिश्रणं R. G., *vide* examples given *ad. loc.*). **–शून्य** *a.* devoid of real love. **–संधिः** the union or coexistence of two emotions, भावसंधिरन्योन्यानभिभूतयोरन्योन्याभिभावनयोग्ययोः सामानाधिकरण्यं R. G. see the examples there given). **–समाहित** *a.* abstracted in mind, devout. **–सर्गः** the mental or intellectual creation; *i. e.* the creation of the faculties of the human mind and their affections (opp. भौतिकसर्ग or material creation). **–स्थ** *a.* attached; devoted (to one); Ku. 5. 58. **–स्थिर** *a.* firmly rooted in the heart; *S*.5.2. **–स्निग्ध** *a.* affectionately disposed, sincerely attached; Pt. 1. 285.

भावक *a.* **1** Effecting, bringing about. **2** Promoting any one's welfare. **3** Fancying, imagining. **4** Having a taste for the sublime and beautiful, having a poetic taste. **–कः 1** A feeling, sentiment. **2** The external manifestation of one's sentiments (especially of love).

भावन *a.* (**नी** *f.*) Effecting &c.; see भावक above. **–नः 1** An efficient cause. **2** A creator; Mâl. 9. 4. **3** An epithet of *S*iva. **–नं,–ना 1** Creating, manifesting. **2** Promoting any one's interests. **3** Conception, imagination, fancy, thought, idea; मधुरिपुरहमिति भावनशीला Gît. 6; or भावनया त्वयि लीना 4; Pt. 3. 162. **4** Feeling of devotion, faith; Pt. 5. 105. **5** Meditation, contemplation, abstract meditation. **6** A supposition, hypothesis. **7** Observing, investigating. **8** Settling, determining. Y. 2. 149. **9** Remembering, recollection. **10** Direct knowledge, perception or cognition. **11** The cause of memory which arises from direct perception (in logic); see भावना and स्मृति in T. S. **12** Proof, demonstration, argument. **13** Steeping, infusion, saturating a dry powder with fluid. **14** Scenting, decorating with flowers and perfumes.

भावाटः 1 Emotion, passion, sentiment. **2** The external indication of the feeling of love. **3** A pious or holy man. **4** An amorous man. **5** An actor. **6** Decoration, dress.

भाविक *a.* (**की** *f.*) **1** Natural, real, inherent, innate. **2** Sentimental, pervaded by feeling or sentiment. **3** Future. **–कं 1** Language full of love or passion. **2** (In Rhet.) A figure of speech which consists in describing the past or future so vividly that it appears to be actually present. It is thus defined by **Mammaṭa**; प्रत्यक्षा इव यद्भावाः क्रियंते भूतभाविनः । तद्भाविकं K. P. 10.

भावित *p. p.* **1** Created, produced. **2** Manifested, displayed, exhibited; भावितविषवेगविक्रियः Dk. **3** Cherished, fostered. **4** Conceived, imagined, supposed, presented to the imagination. **5** Thought of, meditated upon. **6** Made to become, transformed into. **7** Sanctified by meditation, see भावितात्मन्. **8** Proved, established. **9** Pervaded by, filled or saturated with, inspired by. **10** Soaked, steeped, infused in. **11** Perfumed, scented. **12** Mixed with. **–तं** A product obtained by multiplication. **–Comp. –आत्मन्, –बुद्धि** *a.* **1** one whose soul is purified by meditating on the Supreme spirit, one who has perceived the Supreme soul. **2** pure, devout, holy; Pt. 3. 66. **3** thoughtful, meditative; R. 1. 74. **4** engaged in, occupied with; *S*i. 12. 38.

भावितकं The product of a multiplication, a factum.

भावित्रं The three worlds (heaven, earth, and lower regions).

भाविन् *a.* **1** Being, becoming; भूत्यभावि R. 11. 49. **2** To be or to come to pass in future, what will take place; लोकेन भावी पितुरेव तुल्यः R. 18. 38; Me. 41. **3** Future; समतीतं च भवच्च भावि च R. 8. 78; प्रत्यक्षा इव यद्भावाः क्रियंते भूतभाविनः K. P. 10; N. 3. 11. **4** Capable of taking place. **5** What must take place or is destined to happen, predestined: यदभावि न तद्भावि भावि चेन्न तदन्यथा H. 1. **6** Noble, beautiful, illustrious. **–नी 1** A handsome woman. **2** A noble or virtuous lady; Ku. 5. 38. **3** A wanton woman.

भावुक *a.* **1** About to be or happen. **2** Becoming. **3** Prosperous, happy. **4** Auspicious, blessed. **5** Having a poetic taste, appreciative. **–कः** A sister's husband (used chiefly in dramas). **–कं 1** Happiness, welfare prosperity; स रातु वो दुश्च्यवनो भावुकानां परंपरां K. P. 7 (given as an instance of the fault of composition called अप्रयुक्तत्व). **2** Language full of love and passion.

भाव्य *a.* **1** About to be or happen; oft. used impersonally like भवितव्यं q. v., किं तैर्भाव्यं मम सुदिवसैः Bh. 3. 41. **2** Future. **3** To be performed or accomplished. **4** To be conceived or imagined. **5** To be proved or demonstrated. **6** To be determined or investigated. **–व्यं 1** What is destined or sure to happen in the future. **2** Futurity.

भाष् 1 A (भाषते भाषित) **1** To say, speak, utter; त्वयेकमीशं प्रति साधु भाषितं Ku. 5. 81; oft. with two acc.; भीतां प्रियामेत्य वचो बभाषे R. 7. 66; आखंडलः; काममिदं बभाषे Ku. 3 11; Bk. 9. 122. **2** To speak to, address; किंचिद्विहस्यार्थपतिं बभाषे R. 2. 46; 3. 51. **3** To tell, announce, declare; क्षितिपालमुच्चैः प्रीत्या तमेवार्थमभाषतेव R. 2. 51. **4** To speak or talk about. **5** To name, call. **6** To describe. –WITH **अनु 1** To speak, say. **2** To communicate, announce; Ms. 11. 228. **–अप** to revile, abuse, defame, censure, speak ill of; अहमणुमात्रं न किंचिदपभाषे Bv. 4. 27; न केवलं यो महतोऽपभाषते शृणोति तस्मादपि यः स पापभाक् Ku. 5. 83. **–अभि 1** to speak to, address; Ms. 2 128. **2** to speak, say. **3** to proclaim, announce, tell, communicate. **4** to relate. **–आ 1** to speak to, address; वैशंपायनश्चंद्रापीडमाबभाषे K. 117. **2** to say or speak something. आभाषि रामेण वचः कनीयान् Bk. 3.51. **–परि** to lay down a convention, to speak conventionally. **–प्र** to say, speak to; स्थितधीः किं प्रभाषेत Bg. 2. 54. **–प्रति 1** to speak in return, reply or answer Bk. 5. 39. **2** to tell, relate. **3** to say after one, speak after hearing. **4** to name, call; कामिनि तामुपगीतिं प्रतिभाषंते महाकवयः Srut. 6. -वि to lay down as an optional rule. -सं to speak together, converse; Ms. 8. 55.

भाषणं 1 Speaking, talking, saying. **2** Speech, words, talk. **3** Kind words.

भाषा 1 Speech, talk; as in चारुभाषः. **2** Language, tongue; Ms. 8. 164. **3** A common or vernacular dialect; (*a.*) the *Spoken* Sanskrit language (opp. छंदस् or वेद); विभाषा भाषायां P. VI. 1. 181; (*b*) any Prâkrita dialect (opp. संस्कृत); Ms. 8. 332. **4** Definition, description; स्थितप्रज्ञस्य का भाषा Bg. 2. 54. **5** An epithet of Sarasvatî, the goddess of speech. **6** (In law) The first of the four stages of a law-suit; the plaint, charge or accusation. **-Comp. -अंतरं 1** another dialect or language. **2** translation. **-पादः** a charge, plaint; see भाषा (6) above. **-समः** a figure of speech, which consists in so arranging the words of a sentence that it may be considered and read either as Sanskrit or Prâkrita (one or more of its varieties); *e. g.* मंजुलमणिमंजीरे कलगंभीरे विहारसरसीतीरे। विरसासि केलिकीरे किमालि धीरे च गंधसारसमीरे॥ S. D. 642; (एष श्लोकः संस्कृतप्राकृतशौरसेनीप्राच्यावंतीनागरापभ्रंशेष्वेकविध एव); किं त्वां भणामि विच्छेददारुणायासकारिणि। कामं कुरु वरारोहे देहि मे परिरंभणं Mâl 6. 11 (which is in Sanskrit or *Saurasenî*); so 6. 10.

भाषिका Speech, language.

भाषित *p. p.* Spoken, said, uttered. **-तं** Speech, utterance, words, language; Ms 8. 26. **-Comp. -पुंस्कः =** उक्तपुंस्क q. v.

भाष्यं 1 Speaking, talking. **2** Any work in the common or vernacular language. **3** Exposition, gloss, commentary; as in वेदभाष्य. **4** Especially, a commentary which explains *Sûtras* or aphorisms word by word with comments of its own; (सूत्रार्थो वर्ण्यते यत्र पदैः सूत्रानुसारिभिः। स्वपदानि च वर्ण्यंते भाष्यं भाष्यविदो विदुः॥); संक्षिप्तस्याप्यतोऽस्यैव वाक्यस्यार्थगरीयसः। सुविस्तरतरा वाचो भाष्यभूता भवंतु मे *Si*. 2. 24. **5** N. of the great commentary of Patanjali on Pâṇini's Sûtras. **-Comp. -करः, -कारः, -कृत्** *m.* **1** a commentator, scholiast. **2** N. of Patanjali.

भास् 1 A. (भासते, भासित) **1** To shine, glitter, be bright; तावत्कामनृपातपत्रसुषमं बिंबं बभासे विधोः Bv. 2. 74; 4. 18; Ku. 6. 11; Bk. 10. 61. **2** To become clear or evident, come into the mind; त्वदंगमार्दवे दृष्टे कस्य चित्ते न भासते। मालतीशशभृल्लेखाकदलीनां कठोरता Chandr. 5. 42. **3** To appear. *-Caus.* (भासयति-ते) **1** To brighten, irradiate, illuminate: अधिवसंस्तनुमध्वरदीक्षितामसमभासमभासयदीश्वरः R. 9. 21; Bg. 15. 6. **2** To show, make clear or evident, manifest; Bk. 15. 42. -WITH **अव 1** to shine; Ki. 3. 46. **2** to appear, shine forth, become evident; आहोस्वित्प्रसवमवभासते युवत्याः Si. 8. 29. **-आ** to appear or shine like, seem like; स्थानांतरं स्वर्ग इवाबभासे Ku. 7. 3; R. 7. 43; 14. 12. **-उद् 1** to shine. **2** to seem like. **-निस्** to shine forth; Ki. 7. 36. **-प्रति** 1 to shine. **2** to appear or look like. **3** to become clear, manifest oneself. **-वि** to shine.

भास् *f.* **1** Light, lustre, brightness; दृशा निशेंदीवरचारुभासा N. 22. 43; R. 9. 21; Ku. 7. 3. **2** A ray of light; Ki. 5. 38, 46; 9. 6; Ratn. 1. 24; 4. 16. **3** A reflection, an image. **4** Majesty, glory, splendour. **5** Wish, desire. **-Comp. -करः** 1 the sun; *Si*. 11. 69; R. 11. 7; 12. 25; Ku. 6. 49. **2** a hero. **3** fire. **4** an epithet of *Siva*. **5** N. of a celebrated Hindu astronomer who is said to have flourished in the eleventh or twelfth century A. D. (**-रं**) gold. °**प्रियः** a ruby. °**सप्तमी** the seventh day in the bright half of Mâgha. **-करिः** the planet Saturn.

भासः 1 Brightness, light, lustre. **2** Fancy. **3** A cock. **4** A vulture. **5** A cow-shed (गोष्ठ). **6** N. of a poet. भासो हासः कविकुलगुरुः कालिदासो विलासः P. R. 1. 22; M. 1.

भासक *a.* (**सिका** *f.*) **1** Enlightening, brightening, illuminating. **2** Showing, making evident. **3** Making intelligible. **-कः** N. of a poet.

भासनं 1 Shining, glittering. **2** Illuminating.

भासंत *a.* (**ती** *f.*) 1 Shining. **2** Beautiful, handsome. **-तः 1** The sun. **2** The moon. **3** An asterism, a star. **-ती** An asterism (नक्षत्र).

भासुः The sun.

भासुर *a.* **1** Shining, bright, splendid; Ki. 5. 5; R. 5. 30. **2** Terrible. **-रः 1** A hero. **2** A crystal.

भास्मन a (**नी** *f.*) Consisting or made of ashes, ashy; *Si*. 4. 65.

भास्वत् *a.* Bright, shining, luminous, resplendent; Ku. 1. 2; 6. 60. *-m.* **1** The sun; भास्वानुदेष्यति हसिष्यति चक्रवालं Subhâsh.; R. 16. 44. **2** Light, lustre, splendour. **3** A hero. **-ती** The city of the sun.

भास्वर *a.* Shining, bright, radiant, brilliant. **-रः 1** The sun. **2** A day.

भिक्ष् 1 A. (भिक्षते, भिक्षित) **1** To ask, beg or ask for (with two acc.), भिक्षमाणो वनं प्रियां Bk. 6. 9. **2** To beg (as alms); न यज्ञार्थं धनं शूद्राद्विप्रो भिक्षेत कर्हिचित् Ms. 11. 24, 25. **3** To ask without obtaining. **4** To be weary or distressed.

भिक्षणं, भिक्षा Begging, begging alms, mendicancy.

भिक्षा 1 Asking, begging, soliciting; Ms. 6. 56. **2** Anything given as alms, alms; भवति भिक्षां देहि. **3** Wages, hire. **4** Service. **-Comp. -अटनं** wandering about begging for alms. (**-नः**) a beggar, mendicant. **-अन्नं** food obtained by begging, alms. **-अयनं** (**णं**) = भिक्षाटन q. v. **-अर्थिन्** *a.* begging for alms or charity (*-m.*) a beggar. **-अर्ह** *a.* worthy of alms, a fit object of charity. **-आशिन्** *a.* **1** living on alms. **2** dishonest. **-आहारः** begged food. -उपजीविन् *a.* living on alms, a beggar. **-करणं** asking alms, begging. **-चरणं, चर्यं,-र्या** wandering about begging for alms. **-पात्रं** a begging-bowl, an alms-dish; so भिक्षाभांडं, भिक्षाभाजनं. **-माणवः** a young beggar (used as a term of contempt). **-वृत्तिः** *f.* living by begging, a medicant's life.

भिक्षाकः (**की** *f.*) A beggar, mendicant.

भिक्षित *p. p.* Begged, asked &c.

भिक्षुः 1 A beggar, mendicant in general; भिक्षां च भिक्षवे दद्यात् Ms. 3. 94. **2** A religious mendicant, a Brâhmaṇa in the fourth order of his religious life (when he quits his house and family and lives only on alms), a *Sannyâsin*. **3** The fourth order or stage in the religious life of a Brâhmaṇa (संन्यास). **4** A Buddhist mendicant. **-Comp. -चर्या** begging, a mendicant's life. **-संघः** a society of Buddhist mendicants. **-संघाती** old or tattered clothes (चीवर).

भिक्षुकः A beggar, mendicant; Ms. 6. 51.

भित्तं 1 A part, portion. **2** A fragment, bit. **3** A wall, partition.

भित्तिः *f.* **1** Breaking, splitting, dividing. **2** A wall, partition; समया सौधभित्तिं Dk.; *Si*. 4. 67. **3** (Hence) Any place, spot or ground (आश्रय) to work anything upon; चित्रकर्मरचनाभित्तिं विना वर्तते Mu. 2. 4. **4** A fragment, bit, piece, portion. **5** Anything broken. **6** A rent, fissure. **7** A mat. **8** A flaw. **9** An opportunity. **-Comp. -खातनः** a rat. **-चौरः** a house-breaker. **-पातनः. 1** a kind of rat. **2** a rat.

भित्तिका 1 A wall, partition. **2** A small house-lizard.

भिद् I. 1 P. (भिंदति) To divide or cut into parts. -II. 7 U. (भिनत्ति, भिंत्ते, भिन्न) **1** To break, cleave, split, cut asunder, rend, pierce, break through or down; अतिशीतलमप्यंभः किं भिनत्ति न भूभृतः H. 3. 45; तेषां कथं नु हृदयं न भिनत्ति लज्जा Mu. 3. 34.; *Si* 8. 39. Ms. 3. 33; R. 8. 55; 12. 77. **2** To dig or tear up, excavate; U. 1. 23. **3** To pass through; Pt. 1. 211, 212. **4** To divide, separate; द्विधा भिन्ना शिखंडिभिः R. 1. 39; to displace; R. 14. 3. **5** To violate, transgress, break, infringe; समयं लक्ष्मणोऽभिनत् R. 15. 94; निदनश्च

स्थितिं भिंदन् दानवोऽसौ बलद्विषा Bk. 7. 68. 6 To remove, take away; *Si.* 15. 87. 7 To disturb, interrupt; as in समाधिभेदिन्. 8 To change, alter; (न) भिंदंति मंदां गतिमश्वमुख्यः Ku. 1. 11; or विश्वासोपगमादभिन्नगतयः शब्दं सहंते मृगाः *S.* 1. 14. 9 To expand, cause to open or blossom, open; सूर्यांशुभिर्भिन्नमिवारविंदं Ku. 1. 12; नवोषसा भिन्नमिवैकपंकजं *S.* 7. 16; Me. 107. 10 To disperse, scatter, scare away; भिन्नसारंगयूथः *S.* 1. 33; V. 1. 16. 11 To disjoin, disunite, set at variance; Mu. 3. 13. 12 To loosen, relax, dissolve; पर्यंकबंधं निबिडं बिभेद Ku. 3. 59. 13 To disclose, divulge. 14 To perplex, distract. 15 To distinguish, discriminate. –*Pass.* (भिद्यते) 1 To be split, rent or shivered; Mk. 5. 22. 2 To be divided or separated. 3 To expand, blossom, open. 4 To be loose or relaxed; प्रस्थानभिन्ना न बबंध नीविं R. 7. 9, 66. 5 To be different from (with abl.); R. 5. 37; U. 4. 6 To be destroyed. 7 To be divulged or betrayed, get abroad; षट्कर्णो भिद्यते मंत्रः &c. Pt. 1. 99. 8 To be harassed, pained or afflicted. –*Caus.* (भेदयति-ते) 1 To split, cleave, divide, tear &c. 2 To destroy, dissolve. 3 To disunite, set at variance. 4 To perplex. 5 To seduce. –*Desid.* (बिभित्सति-ते) To wish to break &c. –WITH अनु to divide, break down or through. –उद् to shoot up, germinate, grow (as a plant); Ku. 1. 24; R. 13. 21. –निस् 1 to tear up, burst or tear asunder, break through; Bk. 9. 67. 2 to disclose, betray; U. 3. 1. –प्र 1 to break, tear, break or tear asunder. 2 to exude (from the temples of an elephant); Ku. 5. 80. –प्रति 1 to break through, pierce, penetrate. 2 to disclose, betray. 3 to repoach, abuse, censure, प्रतिभिद्य कांतमपराधकृतं *Si.* 9. 58; R. 19. 22. 4 to reject, disown. 5 to touch, be in close contact with; Ku. 7. 35. –वि 1 to break, tear down. 2 to pierce, penetrate. 3 to divide; separate. 4 to interrupt. 5 to scatter, disperse. –सं 1 to break or tear asunder, break to pieces. 2 to mingle, meet, combine, mix, join, bring together; अन्योन्यसंभिन्नदृशां सखीनां Mâl. 1. 33; Bk. 7. 5.

भिदकः A sword. –कं 1 A diamond. 2 Indra's thunderbolt.

भिदा 1 Breaking, bursting, rending, tearing; *Si.* 6. 5. 2 Separation. 3 Difference. 4 Kind, species, sort.

भिदिः, भिदिरं, भिदुः Indra's thunderbolt.

भिदुर *a.* 1 Breaking, bursting, splitting. 2 Fragile, brittle. 3 Blended, variegated, mixed, mingled; नीलाश्मद्युतिभिदुराम्भसोऽपरत्र *Si.* 4. 26; 19. 58. –रः The *Plaksha* tree. –रं A thunderbolt.

भिद्यः 1 A rushing river. 2 N. of a particular river; तोयदागम इवोद्ध्यभिद्ययोर्नामधेयसदृशं विचेष्टितं R. 11. 8; (see Malli.)

भिद्रं A thunderbolt.

भिंद(न्दि)पालः 1 A small javelin thrown from the hand. 2 A sling, an instrument like a sling for throwing stones.

भिन्न *p. p.* 1 Broken, torn, split, rent. 2 Divided, separated. 3 Detached, disunited, disjoined. 4 Expanded, blown, opened. 5 Different from, other than (with abl.); तस्मादयं भिन्नः. 6 Different, varied. 7 Loosened. 8 Mingled, mixed, blended. 9 Deviating from. 10 Changed. 11 Furious, in rut. 12 Without, deprived of. (see भिद्). –न्नः A defect or flaw in a gem. –न्नं 1 A bit, fragment, part. 2 A blossom. 3 A wound, stab. 4 A fraction. –Comp. –अंजनं a kind of mixed collyrium, made of many pounded ingredients; प्रयाति...भिन्नांजनवर्णतां वनाः *Si.* 12. 68; Me. 59; Rs. 3. 5. –अर्थ *a.* clear, evident, intelligible. –उदरः 'born of a different womb or mother,' a half-brother. –करटः an elephant in rut (from whose temples ichor exudes). –कूट *a.* deprived of a leader (as an army). –क्रम *a.* out of order, disordered. –गति *a* 1 going with broken steps. 2 going quickly. –गर्भ *a.* broken up (in the centre), disorganized. –गुणनं multiplication of fracstions. –घनः the cube of a fraction. दार्शिन् *a.* –making or seeing a difference, partial. –प्रकार *a.* of a different kind or sort. –भाजनं a potsherd. –मर्मन् *a.* wounded in the vital parts, mortally wounded. –मर्याद *a.* 1 one who has transgressed the due limits, disrespectful; आस्ताताप्रवादभिन्नमर्याद U. 5. 2 unrestrained, uncontrolled. –रुचि *a.* having different tastes; भिन्नरुचिर्हि लोकः R. 6. 30. –लिंगं, –वचनं incongruity of gender or number in a composition; see K. P. 10. –वर्चस्, वर्चस्क *a.* voiding excrement. –वृत्त *a.* leading a bad life, abandoned. –वृत्ति *a.* 1 leading a bad life, followin evil courses. 2 having different feelings or tastes or emotions. 3 having different occupations. –संहति *a.* disunited, dissolved. –स्वर *a.* 1 having a changed voice, faltering. 2 discordant. –हृदय *a.* pierced through the heart; R. 11. 19.

भिरिंटिका N. of a plant (श्वेतगुंजा).

भिल्लः N. of a wild tribe. –Comp. –गवी the female of the *Bos gavæus.* –तरुः the *lodhra* tree. –भूषणं the *Gunja* plant.

भिल्लोटः –टकः The *lodhra* tree.

भिषज् *m.* 1 A physician, doctor; भिषजामसाध्यं R. 8. 93. 2 N. of Vishṇu. –Comp. –जितं a drug or medicine. –पाशः a quack doctor. –वरः an excellent physician.

भिस्मा, भिस्मिका–टा, भिस्सटा, भिस्सिटा, Parched or fried grain.

भिस्सा Boiled rice.

भी 3 P. (बिभेति, भीत) 1 To fear, dread, be afraid of; मृत्योर्बिभेषि किं बाल न स भीतं विमुंचति; रावणाद्बिभ्यती भृशं Bk. 8. 70; *Si.* 3. 45. 2 To be anxious or solicitous about (A.). –*Caus.* (भाययति) To frighten (any one) with anything; कुंचिकयैनं भाययति Sk.; (भापयते, भीषयते) to frighten, terrify, intimidate; मुंडो भापयते Sk.; स्तनितेन भीषयित्वा धाराहस्तैः परामृशसि Mk. 5. 28.

भी *f.* Fear, dread, alarm, fright, terror; अभीः 'fearless' R. 15. 8; वपुष्मान् वीतभीर्वाग्मी दूतो राज्ञः प्रशस्यते Ms. 7. 64.

भीत *p. p.* 1 Frightened, terrified, alarmed, afraid of (with abl.); न भीतो मरणादस्मि Mk. 10. 27. 2 Placed in danger, imperiled. –Comp. –भीत *a.* exceedingly afraid.

भीतंकार *a.* Making (one) afraid.

भीतंकारं *ind.* Calling (one) a coward.

भीतिः *f.* 1 Fear, apprehension, dread, terror. 2 Shaking, tremour. –Comp. –नाटितकं a gesticulation or representation of fear.

भीम *a.* Fearful, terrific, terrible, dreadful, formidable; न भेजिरे भीमविषेण भीतिं Bh. 2. 80; R. 1. 16; 3. 54. –मः 1 An epithet of Siva. 2 N. of the second Pâṇdava prince. [He was begotten on Kuntî by the god Wind. From a child he showed that he was possessed of extraordinary strength, and hence he was called Bhîma. He had also a most voracious appetite, and was called Vṛikodara, or 'wolf-bellied'. His most effective weapon was his mace. He played a very important part in the great war, and, on the last day of the battle, smashed the thigh of Duryodhana with his unfailing mace. Some of the principal events of his earlier life are his defeat of the demons Hidimba and Baka, the overthrow of Jarasandha, the fearful vow which he uttered against the Kauravas and particularly against Duhsasana for his insulting conduct towards Draupadî, the fulfilment of that vow by drinking Duhsasana's blood, the defeat of Jayadratha, his duel with Kîchaka while he was serving as head-cook to king Virata, and several other exploits in which he showed his usual extraordinary strength. His name has become proverbial for one who possesses immense strength and courage]. **–Comp.** –उदरी an epitht of Umā. –कर्मन् *a.* of terrific prowess ; Bg. 1. 15. –दर्शन *a.* frightful in appearance, hideous. –नाद *a.* Sounding dreadfully. (–दः) 1 a loud or dreadful sound ; *Si.* 15. 10. 2 a lion. 3 N. of one the seven clouds that will appear at the destruction of the world. –पराक्रम *a.* of terrific prowess. –रथी N. of the 7th night in the 7th month of the 77th year of a man's life (said to be a very dangerous period); (सप्तसप्ततिमे वर्षे सप्तमे मासि सप्तमी । रात्रिर्भीमरथी नाम नराणामतिदुस्तरा). –रूप *a.* of terrific form. –विक्रम *a.* of terrific prowess. –विक्रांतः a lion. –विग्रह *a.* gigantic, of terrific form. –शासनः an epithet of Yama. –सेनः 1 N. of the second Pandava prince. 2 a kind of camphor.

भीमरं War, battle.

भीमा 1 An epithet of Durgā. 2 A kind of perfume (रोचना). 3 A whip.

भीरु *a* (रु or रू *f.*) 1 Timid, cowardly, fearful ; क्षांत्या भीरुः H. 2. 26. 2 Afraid of ; (mostly in comp.); पाप,°अधर्म,°प्रतिज्ञाभंग° &c. –रुः 1 A jackal. 2 A tiger. –रु *n.* Silver. *–f.* 1 A timid woman. 2 A goat. 3 A shadow. 4 A centipede. **–Comp.** –चेतस् *m.* a deer. –रंध्रः an oven, a furnace. –सत्त्व *a.* timid, fearful. –हृदयः a deer.

भीरु(लु)क *a.* 1 Timid, cowardly, timorous. 2 Shy. –कः A bear. 2 An owl. 3 A kind of sugar-cane. –कं A forest, wood.

भीरू (लू) *f.* A timid woman; त्वं रक्षसा भीरु यतोऽपनीता R. 13. 24.

भीलु(लू)कः A bear.

भीषण *a.* Terrific, formidable, dreadful, horrible, frightening ; बिम्बुर्बिडालेक्षणभीषणाभ्यः *Si.* 3. 45. –णः 1 The sentiment of terror (in rhetoric); see भयानक. 2 N. of *Siva*. 3 A pigeon, dove. –णं Anything that excites terror.

भीषा 1 The act of terrifying or frightening, intimidating. 2 Fright, terror.

भीषित *a.* Frightened, terrified.

भीष्म *a.* Terrible, dreadful, frightful, fearful. –ष्मः 1 The sentiment of terror (in rhetoric), see भयानक. 2 A demon, an imp, a fiend, goblin. 3 An epithet of *Siva*. 4 N. of the son of *Santanu* by Gangâ. [He was the youngest of the eight sons of *Santanu* by Gang*a*; but all the others having died, he was the heir to the throne after his father. On one occasion while *Santanu* was walking by the side of a river, he beheld a charming young damsel named Satyavat*i*, the daughter of a fisherman, and, though bowed down with age, conceived a passion for her, and sent his son to negotiate the marriage. But the parents of the girl said that if their daughter bore sons to the king, they would not succeed to the throne, for after his death *Sa*ntanava, being the rightful heir, woutd be the king. But *Sa*ntanava, to please his father, made a vow to the parents that he would never accept the kingdom or marry a wife or become the father of children by any woman, so that if their daughter bore a son to Santanu, he would be the king. This ' dreadful ' vow soon became known abroad, and thenceforth he was called *Bhishma*. He remainad single, and, after the death of his father, he installed Vichitrav*i*rya, the son of Satyavat*i*, on the throne, got him married to the two daughters of king K*a*sir*a*ja (see Ambik*a*), and became the guardian of his sons and grandsons, the Kauravas and P*and*avas. In the great war he fought on the side of the Kauravas, but was wounded by Arjuna with the assistance of *Sikhandi*n and was lodged in a ' cage of darts ' But having got from his father the power of choosing his own time for death, he waited till the sun had crossed the vernal equinox, and then gave up his soul. He was remarkable for his continence, wisdom, firmness of resolve, and unflinching devotion to God]. **–Comp.** –जननी an epithet of the Ganges. –पंचकं N. of the five days from the eleventh to the fifteenth of the bright half of Kârtika (said to be sacred to Bhishma. –सूः *f.* an epithet of the river Ganges.

भीष्मकः 1 N. of a son of *S*antanu by Gangâ. 2 N. of a king of the Vidarbhas, whose daughter Rukmiṇī was carried off by Krishṇa.

भुक्त *p. p.* 1 Eaten. 2 Enjoyed, used. 3 Suffered, experienced. 4 Possessed, occupied (in law); (see भुज्). –क्तं 1 The act of eating or enjoying. 2 That which is eaten, food. 3 The place where any one has eaten. **–Comp.** –उच्छिष्टं, –शेषः, –समुज्झितं remnants of the food eaten, leavings of food, orts. –भोग *a.* 1 one who has enjoyed or suffered (anything). 2 that which has been used, enjoyed or employed. –सुप्त *a.* sleeping after a meal.

भुक्तिः *f.* 1 Eating, enjoyment. 2 (In law) Possession, fruition; Pt. 3. 94; Y. 2. 22. 3 Food. 4 The daily motion of a planet. **–Comp.** –प्रदः a kind of plant (मुद्ग). –वर्जित *a.* not allowed to be enjoyed.

भुग्न *p. p.* 1 Bent, bowed, stooping; वायुभुग्न, रुजाभुग्न &c. 2 Crooked, curved ; Bk. 11. 8 ; V. 4. 32. 3 Broken (for भग्न).

भुज् I. 6 P. (भुजति, भुग्न) 1 To bend. 2 To curve, make crooked. –II. 7 U. (भुनक्ति, भुंक्ते) 1 To eat, devour, consume (Atm.) ; शयनस्थो न भुंजीत Ms. 4. 74 ; 3. 146 ; Bk. 14. 92 ; Bg. 2. 5. 2 To enjoy, use, possess (property, land &c.) ; V. 3. 1 ; Ms. 8. 146 ; Y. 2. 24. 3 To enjoy carnally (Atm.) ; सदयं बुभुजे महाभुजः R. 8. 7, 4. 7, 15. 1, 18. 4; सुरूपं वा कुरूपं वा पुमानित्येव भुंजते Ms. 9. 14. 4 To rule, govern, protect, guard (Paras.); राज्यं न्यासमिवाभुनक् R. 12. 18 ; एकः कृत्स्नां (धरित्रीं) नगरपरिघप्रांशुबाहुर्भुनक्ति *S.* 2. 14. 5 To suffer, endure, experience ; वृद्धो नरो दुःखशतानि भुंक्ते Sk. 6 To pass, live through (as time). *–Caus.* (भोजयति–ते) To cause to eat, feed with. *–Desid.* (बुभुक्षति–ते) To wish to eat &c. –WITH अनु to enjoy, experience (good or bad things), suffer (bad consequences); मेघमुक्तविशदां स चंद्रिकां (अन्वभुंक्त) R. 19. 39 ; Ku. 7. 5. –उप 1 to enjoy, taste (in all senses) ; तपसामुपभुंजानाः फलानि Ku. 6. 10. 2 to enjoy (carnally), (as a woman). 3 to eat or drink ; अर्धोपभुक्तेन बिसेन Ku. 3. 37 ; पयः पुत्रोपभुंक्ष्व R. 2. 65, 1. 67 ; Bk. 8. 40. 4 to suffer, endure, bear ; Ms. 12. 8. 5 to possess, have. –परि 1 to eat. 2 to use, enjoy ; न खलु च परिभोक्तुं नैव शक्नोमि हातुं *S.* 5. 19 ; Ki. 5. 5, 8. 57. –सं 1 to eat. 2 to enjoy. 3 to enjoy carnally.

भुज् *a.* (At the end of comp.) Eating, enjoying, suffering, ruling, governing ; स्वधाभुज्, हुतभुज्, पाप°, क्षिति°, मही° &c. *–f.* 1 Enjoyment. 2 Profit, advantage.

भुजः 1 The arm ; ज्ञास्यसि कियद्भुजो मे रक्षति मौर्वीकिणांक इति *S.* 1. 13 ; R. 1. 34, 2. 74, 3. 5. 2 The hand. 3 The trunk of an elephant. 4 A bend, curve. 5 The side of a mathematical figure ; as in त्रिभुजः ' a triangle. ' 6 The base of a triangle. **–Comp.**–अंतरं–अंतरालं the bosom, breast, R. 3. 54, 19. 32 ; M. 5. 10. –आपीडः clasping or folding in the arms. –कोटरः the armpit. –ज्या the base-sine. –दंडः a stafflike arm. –दलः–लं the hand. –बंधनं clasping, an embrace (in the arms) घटय भुजबंधनं Gît. 10; Ku. 3. 39. –बलं;

-वीर्यं strength. of arm, muscular strength. -मध्यं the breast; R. 13. 73. -मूलं the shoulder. -शिखरं,-शिरस् *n.* the shoulder. -सूत्रं the base sine.

भुजगः A snake, serpent; भुजगाश्लेषसंवीतजानोः Mk. 1. 1; Me. 60. -Comp. -अंतकः,-अशनः, आभोजिन् *m.*, -दारणः, -भोजिन् *m.* epithets of 1 Garuda. 2 a peacock. 3 an ichneumon. -ईश्वरः, -राजः epithets of *S*esha.

भुजंगः 1 A serpent, snake, भुजंगमपि कोपितं शिरसि पुष्पवद्धारयेत् Bh. 2. 4. 2 A paramour, gallant; अधुनिरेषा भुजंगभंगिभाषितांना K. 196. 3 A husband or lord in general. 4 A catamite. 5 The dissolute friend of a king. 6 The constellation आश्लेषा. 7 The number 'eight'. -Comp. -इंद्रः an epithet of *S*esha, the lord of snakes. -ईशः an epithet of 1 Vâsuki. 2 of *S*esha. 3 of Patanjali. 4 of the sage Pingala. -कन्या a young female snake. -भं the asterism आश्लेषा. -भुज् *m.* 1 an epithet of Garuda. 2 a peacock. -लता betel-pepper (तांबूली). -हन् *m.* an epithet of Garuda; see भुजगांतक &c.

भुजंगमः 1 A snake. 2 An epithet of Râhu. 3 The number 'eight'.

भुजा 1 The arm; निहितभुजालतैकयोपकंठं *S*i. 7. 71. 2 The hand. 3 The coil of a snake (भोग). 4 Winding. -Comp. -कंटः a finger-nail. -दलः the hand. -मध्यः 1 the elbow. 2 the breast. -मूलं the shoulder.

भुजिष्यः 1 A slave, servant. 2 A companion. 3 The string worn round the wrist. 4 A disease (रोग). -ष्या 1 A hand-maid, maid-servant, female slave; अथांगदश्लिष्टभुजं भुजिष्या R. 6. 53; Mk. 4. 8; Y. 2. 90. 2 A harlot, prostitute.

भुंड् 1 A. (भुंडते) 1 To support, maintain. 2 To select.

भुर्भुरिका, भुर्भुरी A kind of sweatmeat.

भुवनं 1 A world (the number of worlds is either three; as in त्रिभुवन, or fourteen; इह हि भुवनान्यन्ये धीराश्चतुर्दश भुंजते Bh. 3. 23 (see लोक also); भुवनालोकनप्रीतिः Ku. 2. 45; भुवनविदितं Me. 6 2 The earth. 3 Heaven. 4 A being, living creature. 5 Man, mankind. 6 Water. 7 The number 'fourteen'. -Comp. -ईशः a lord of the earth, a king. -ईश्वरः 1 a king. 2 N. of *S*iva. -ओकस् *m.* a god. -त्रयं the three worlds (the earth, atmosphere and heaven; or heaven, earth and lower regions). -पावनी an epithet of the Ganges. -शासिन् *m.* a king, ruler.

भुवन्युः 1 A master, lord. 2 The sun. 3 Fire. 4 The moon.

भुवर्, भुवस् *ind.* 1 The atmosphere, ether (the second of the three orlds, the one immediately above the earth). 2 A mystic word, one of the three Vyâhritis, (भुर्भुवःस्व).

भुविस् *m.* The ocean.

भुशुंडिः -डी *f.* A sort of weapon or missile.

भू I. 1 P. (rarely A.) (भवति, भूत) 1 To be, become; कथमवं भवेन्नाम; अस्याः किमभवत् Mâl. 9. 29, 'what has become her fate,' 'what has become of her'; U. 3. 27; यद्भावि तद्भवतु U. 3 'come what may'; so दुःखितो भवति, हृष्टो भवति &c. 2 To be born or produced; यदपत्यं भवेदस्यां Ms. 9. 127; भाग्यक्रमेण हि धनानि भवंति यांति Mk. 1. 13. 3 To spring or proceed from, arise; क्रोधाद्भवति संमोहः Bg. 2. 63, 14. 17. 4 To happen; take place, occur; नाततायिवधे दोषो हंतुर्भवति कश्चन Ms. 8. 351; यदि संशयो भवेत् &c. 5 To live, exist; अभूद्भूतपूर्वः.... राजा चिंतामणिर्नाम Vâs.; अभून्नृपो विबुधसखः परंतपः Bk. 1. 1. 6 To be alive or living, breathe; त्वमिदानीं न भविष्यसि *S*. 6; आः चारुदत्तहतक अयं न भवसि Mk. 4; दुरात्मन् प्रहर नन्वयं न भवसि Mâl. 5; ('thou art a dead man'. 'thou shalt breathe no longer); Bg. 11. 32. 7 To remain or be in any state or condition, fare; भवान् स्थले कथं भविष्यति Pt. 2. 8 To stay, abide; remain, U. 3. 37. 9 To serve, do: इदं पादोदकं भविष्यति *S*. 1. 10 To be possible (usually with a future tense in this sense); भवति भवान् याजयिष्यति Sk. 11 To lead or tend to conduce to; bring about; (with dat.); वाताय कपिला विद्युत् ... पीता भवति सस्याय दुर्भिक्षाय सिता भवेत् Mbh.; सुखाय तज्जन्मदिनं बभूव Ku. 1. 23; संसृतिरिव भवत्यभवाय Ki. 18. 27; न तस्या रुचये बभूव R. 6. 44. 12 To be on the side of, assist; देवा अर्जुनतोऽभवत्. 13 To belong or pertain to (=often expressed by 'have'); तस्य ह शतं जाया बभूवुः Ait. Br.; Ms. 6. 39. 14 To be engaged in, be occupied (with loc.); चरणक्षालने कृष्णो ब्राह्मणानां स्वयं ह्यभूत् Mb. 15 Used with a preceding noun or adjective भू serves to form verbs in the sense of 'becoming what it previously is not' or 'becoming' in general; श्वेती भू to become white; कृष्णीभू to become black; पयोधरीभूत 'becoming or serving the purpose of teats'; so क्षपणीभू to be or become a mendicant; प्रणिधीभू to act the spy; आर्द्रीभू to melt; भस्मीभू to be reduced to ashes; विषयीभू to form the subject of; so एकमतीभू; तरुणीभू &c. &c. (*Note*—The senses of भू may be variously modified according to the adverbs with which it is connected; *e. g.* पुनर्भू to marry again; आविर्भू to appear, arise, to be evident or clear; see आविस्, तिरोभू to disappear. प्रादुर्भू to arise, be visible, appear; अग्रेभू to be in front, take the lead; अंतर्भू to be absorbed or included; ओजस्यंतर्भवंत्यन्ये K. P. 8; दोषाभू to grow evening or dusk-time; अन्यथा भू to be otherwise, be changed; न मे वचनमन्यथा भावितुमर्हति *S*. 4; पुरो भू to come forward, stand forth; मिथ्या भू to turn out false; वृथा भू to become useless &c. &c.). -*Caus.* (भावयति-ते) 1 To cause to be or become, call into existence, call into being. 2 To cause, produce, effect. 3 To manifest, display, exhibit. 4 To foster, cherish, support, preserve, enliven; पुनः सृजति वर्षाणि भगवान् भावयन्प्रजाः Mb.; देवान् भावयतानेन ते देवा भावयंतु वः। परस्परं भावयंतः श्रेयः परमवाप्स्यथ Bg. 3. 11; Bk. 16. 27. 5 To think or reflect, consider, fancy, imagine. 6 To look upon, consider or regard as; अर्थमनर्थं भावय नित्यं Moha. M. 2. 7 To prove, substantiate, establish; Y. 2. 11. 8 To purify. 9 To get, obtain. 10 To mingle or mix. 11 To change or transform into. 12 To soak, steep. -*Desid.* (बुभूषति) To wish to be or become &c. -WITH अति to be over and above, surpass, excel. -अनु 1 to enjoy, experience, feel, suffer (good or bad things); असक्तः सुखमन्वभूत् R. 1. 21; Ku. 2. 45; R. 7. 28; आत्मकृतानां हि दोषाणां फलमनुभवितव्यमात्मनैव K. 121; *S*. 5. 7. 2 to perceive, apprehend, understand. 3 to try, test. (-*Caus.*) to cause to enjoy, feel or experience; आमोदो न हि कस्तूर्याः शपथेनानुभाव्यते Bv. 1. 120. -अभि 1 to overcome, subdue, vanquish, surpass, excel; Bg 1. 39; Ki. 10. 23; R. 8. 36. 2 to attack assail, विपदोऽभिभवंत्यविक्रमं Ki. 2. 14; अभ्यभावि भरताग्रजस्तया R. 11. 16. 3 to humiliate, insult. 4 to predominate, prevail, spread. -उद् to arise, spring up; उद्भूत् ध्वनिः (-*Caus.*) to create, produce, generate; R. 2. 62. -परा 1 to defeat, vanquish, overcome. 2 to hurt, injure, tease. -परि 1 to defeat; subdue, conquer, overcome; (hence) to surpass, excel; लग्नद्विरेफं परिभूय पद्मं Mu. 7. 16; R. 10. 35. 2 to despise, slight, treat with contempt, disrespect, insult; मा मां महात्मन् परिभूः Bk. 1. 22; 4. 37. 3 to injure, destroy, ruin. 4 to afflict, grieve. 5 to humiliate, disgrace. -प्र 1 to arise, proceed, spring up, to be born or produced, originate (with abl.); लोभात्क्रोधः प्रभवति H. 1. 27; स्वायंभुवान्मरीचेर्यः प्रबभूव प्रजापतिः *S*. 7. 9; पुरुषः प्रबभूवाग्नेर्विस्मयेन सहर्त्विजा R. 10. 50; Bg. 8. 18. 2 to appear, become visible; H. 4. 84. 3 to multiply, increase; see प्रभूत. 4 to be strong or powerful, prevail, predominate, show one's power; प्रभवति हि महिम्ना स्वेन योगीश्वरीयं Mâl. 9. 52; प्रभवति भगवान् विधिः K. 5 to be able or equal, have power for (with inf.); कुसुमान्यपि गात्रसंगमात् प्रभवंत्यायुरपोहितुं यदि R. 8. 44; *S*. 6. 30; V. 1. 9; U. 2. 4. 6 to have control or power over, prevail over, be master of

(usually with gen.; sometimes with dat. or loc.) यदि प्रभविष्यास्यात्मनः S 1; U. 1 ; प्रभवति निजस्य कन्यकाजनस्य महाराजः Mâl. 4 : तत्प्रभवति अनुशासने देवी Ve. 2 **7** to be a match for ; प्रभवति मल्लो मल्लाय Mbh. **8** to be sufficient for, be able to contain ; Ku. 6. 59. **9** to be contained in (with loc.); गुरुः प्रहर्षः प्रबभूव नात्मनि R. 3. 17. **10** to be useful. **11** to implore, beseech. –वि (*caus.*) **1** to think of, reflect, contemplate. **2** to be aware of, know, perceive; see ; S. 4. **3** to decide, settle, make clear. –सं **1** to arise, to be born or produced, spring up ; कथमपि भुवनेऽस्मिंस्तादृशाः संभवंति Mâl. 2. 9 ; धर्मसंस्थापनार्थाय संभवामि युगे युगे Bg. 4. 8 ; Ki. 5. 22 ; Bk. **6.** 138 ; Ms. 8. 155. **2** to be, become, exist. **3** to occur, take place. **4** to be possible. **5** to be adequate for, be competent for (with inf.); न यन्नियंतुं समभावि भानुना Si. 1. 27. **6** to meet, be united or joined with ; संभूयांभोधिमभ्येति महानद्या नगापगा Si. 2. 100 ; संभूयैव सुखानि चेतसि Mâl. 5. 9. **7** to be consistent. **8** to be capable of holding. (–*Caus.*) **1** to produce, effect. **2** to imagine, conceive, fancy, think. **3** to guess or conjecture ; S. 2. **4** to consider, regard. **5** to honour, respect, show respect to ; प्राप्तोसि संभावयितुं वनान्मां R. 5. 11, 7. 8. **6** to honour or present with, treat with ; Ku. 3. 37. **7** to ascribe or impute to ; Mk. 1. 36. –II. I U. (भवति-ते) To get, obtain. –III. 10 A. (भावयते) To obtain, gain. –IV. 10 U. (भावयति-ते) **1** To think, reflect. **2** To mix, mingle. **3** To be purified (connected with caus. of भू q. v. above).

भू *a.* (At the end of Comp.) Being, existing, becoming, springing from, arising or produced from, &c.; चित्तभू, आत्मभू, कमलभू, वित्तभू &c. –*m.* An epithet of Vishṇu.

भूः *f.* **1** The earth (opp. अंतरीक्ष or स्वर्ग); दिवं मरुत्वानिव भोक्ष्यते भुवं R. 3. 4. 18. 4; Me. 18 ; मत्तेभकुंभदलने भुवि संति शूराः. **2** The universe, globe. **3** Ground, floor ; प्रासादोपरिभूमय; Mu. 3 ; मणिमयभुवः (प्रासादाः) Me 64. **4** Land, landed property. **5** A place, site, region, plot of ground ; काननभुवि, उपवनभुवि &c. **6** Matter, subject-matter. **7** A symbolical expression for the number 'one.' **8** The base of a geometrical figure. **9** The first of the three Vyâhritis or mystical syllables (representing the earth) repeated by every Brâhmana at the commencement of his daily Sandhyâ. –**Comp.** –उत्तमं gold. –कदंबः a kind of Kadamba tree. –कंपः an earthquake. –कर्णः the diameter of the earth. –कश्यपः an epithet of Vasudeva, Krishṇa's father. –काकः **1** a kind of heron. **2** the curlew. **3** a kind of pigeon. –केशः the fig-tree. –केशा a female demon, demoness. –क्षित् *m.* a hog. –गरं a particular poison. –गर्भः an epithet of Bhavabhûti. –गृहं, –गेहं a cellar, a room underground. –गोलः terrestrial globe; भूगोलमुद्विभ्रते Git. I. °विद्या geography. –घनः the body. –चक्रं the equator. चर *a.* moving or living on land. (–रः) an epithet of Siva. –छाया, छायं **1** earth's shadow (vulgarly called Râhu). **2** darkness. जंतुः **1** a kind of earth-worm. **2** an elephant. –जंबुः –जूः *f.* wheat. –तलं the surface of the earth. –तृणः, भूस्तृणः a kind of fragrant grass. –दारः a hog. –देवः –सुरः a Brâhmaṇa. –धनः a king. –धरः **1** a mountain. **2** an epithet of Siva. **3** of Krishṇa. **4** the number 'seven'. °ईश्वरः, °राजः an epithet of the mountain Himâlaya. °जः a tree. –नागः a kind of earth-worm. –नेतृ *m.* a sovereign, ruler, king. –पः a sovereign, ruler; king. –पतिः **1** a king. **2** an epithet of Siva. **3** of Indra. –पदः a tree. –पदी a particular kind of jasmine. –परिधिः the circumference of the earth. –पालः a king, sovereign. –पालनं sovereignty, dominion. –पुत्रः, –सुतः the planet Mars. –पुत्री, –सुता 'daughter of the earth,' an epithet of Sítâ. –प्रकंपः an earth-quake. –प्रदानं a gift of land. बिंबः –बं terrestrial globe. –भर्तृ *m.* a king, sovereign. –भागः a region, place, spot. –भुज् *m.* a kin . –भृत् *m.* a mountain ; दाता मे भूभृता नाथः प्रमाणीक्रियतामिति Ku. 6. 1; R. 17. 78. **2** a king, savereign ; निष्प्रभश्च रिपुरास भूभृतां R. 11. 81. **3** an epithet of Vishṇu. –मंडल 'the earth', terrestrial globe. –रुहम्. रुहः a tree. –लोकः(भूर्लोकः) the terrestrial globe. –वलयं the terrestrial globe. –वल्लभः a king, sovereign. –वृत्तं the equator. –शक्रः 'Indra on earth', a king, sovereign. –शयः an epithet of Vishṇu. –श्रवस् *m.* an ant-hill. –सुरः a Bra'hmaṇa. –स्पृश् *m.* 1 a man. **2** mankind. **3** a Vaisya. –स्वर्गः an epithet of the mountain Meru. –स्वामिन् *m.* a landlord.

भूकः-कं **1** A cavity, hole, chasm. **2** A spring. **3** Time.

भूकलः A restive horse.

भूत *p.p.* **1** Become, being, existing. **2** Produced, formed. **3** Actually being, really happened, true. **4** Right, proper, fit. **5** Past, gone. **6** Obtained. **7** Mixed or joined with. **8** Being like, similar. (see भू). –तः **1** A son, child. **2** An epithet of Siva. **3** The fourteenth day of the dark half of a lunar month. –तं **1** Any being (human, divine or even inanimate); Ku. 4. 45; Pt. 2. 87. **2** A living being, an animal, a creature भूतेषु किं च करुणां बहुलीकरोति Bv. 1. 122; U. 4 6 .**3** A spirit, ghost, an imp, a devil. **4** An element ; (they are five, *i.e.* पृथ्वी, अप्, तेजस् , वायु and आकाश); तं वेधाविदधे नूनं महाभूतसमाधिना R. 1. 29. **5** An actual occurrence, a fact, a matter of fact. **6** The past, past time. **7** The world. **8** Well-being, welfare. **9** A symbolical expression for the number 'five'. –**Comp.** –अनुकंपा compassion for all beings ; भूतानुकंपा तव चेत् R. 2. 48. –अंतकः the god of death, Yama. –अर्थः the fact, real fact, true state, truth, reality ; आर्ये कथयामि ते भूतार्थं S.1; भूतार्थशोभाह्रियमाणनेत्राः Ku. 7. 13; कः श्रद्धास्यति भूतार्थं सर्वो मां तुलयिष्यति Mk. 3. 24. °कथनं, °व्याहृतिः *f.* a statement of facts ; भूतार्थव्याहृतिः सा हि न स्तुतिः परमेष्ठिनः R.10. 33.–आत्मक *a.* consisting or composed of the elements. –आत्मन् *m.* **1** the individual, as opposed to the Supreme, soul. **2** an epithet of Brahmâ'. **3** of Siva. **4** an elementary substance. **5** the body. **6** war, conflict. –आदिः **1** the Supreme Spirit. **2** an epithet of *Ahanka'ra* (in Sa'nkhya phil.). –आर्त *a.* possessed by a devil. –आवासः **1** the body. **2** an epithet of Siva. **3** of Vishṇu. –आविष्ट *a.* possessed by a devil or evil spirit. –आवेशः demoniac possession. –इज्यं, –इज्या making oblations to the Bhûtas. –इष्टा the fourteenth day of a lunar fortnight. –ईशः **1** an epithet of Brahman. **2** of Vishṇu. **3** of Siva; भूतेशस्य भुजंगवल्लिवलयस्रङ्नद्धजूटा जटाः Mâl. 1. 2. –ईश्वरः an epithet of Siva; R. 2. 46. –उन्मादः demoniac possession. –उपसृष्ट, –उपहत *a.* possessed by a devil. –ओदनः a dish of rice. –कर्तृ, –कृत् *m.* an epithet of Brahman. –कालः **1** past time. **2** (in gram.) the past or preterite time. –केशी the holy basil. –क्रांतिः *f.* possession by a devil. –गणः **1** the collection of created beings. **2** the whole class of spirits or devils ; Bg. 18. 4. –ग्रस्त *a.* possessed by a devil. –ग्रामः **1** the whole multitude or aggregate of living beings ; U. 7, Bg. 8. 19. **2** a multitude of spirits. **3** the body. –घ्नः **1** a camel. **2** garlic. (–घ्नी) the holy basil. –चतुर्दशी the fourteenth day of the dark half. of Ka'rtika. –चारिन् *m.* an epithet of Siva. –जयः victory over the elements. –दया compassion towards all beings, universal benevolence. –धरा, –धात्री, –धारिणी the earth. –नाथः an epithet of Siva. –नायिका an epithet of Durgâ. –नाशनः **1** the marking-nut plant. **2** mustard. **3** pepper. –निचयः the body. –पतिः **1** an epithet of Siva. ; Ku. 3. 43, 74. **2** of Agni. **3** the sacred basil. –पत्री the holy basil. –पूर्णिमा the day of full-moon in the month of Asvina. –पूर्व *a.*

existed before, former; भूतपूर्वखरालयं U. 2. 17. -पूर्वं *ind.* formerly. -प्रकृतिः *f.* the origin of all beings. -बलिः =भूतयज्ञ q. v. -ब्रह्मन् *m.* a low Brâhmaṇa who maintains himself with the offerings made to an idol; see देवल. -भर्तृ *m.* an epithet of Siva. -भावनः 1 an epithet of Brahman. 2 of Vishṇu. -भाषा, -भाषित the language of devils. -महेश्वर, an epithet of Siva. -यज्ञः an oblation or offering to all created beings, one of the five daily Yajnas to be performed by a householder. -योनिः the origin of all created beings. -राजः an epithet of Siva. -वर्गः the whole class of spirits. -वासः the Bibhîtaka tree. -वाहनः an epithet of Siva. -विक्रिया 1 epilepsy. 2 possession by a devil. -विज्ञानं,-विद्या demonology. -वृक्षः the Bibhîtaka tree. -संसारः the world of mortals. -संचारः demoniac possession. -संप्लवः universal deluge or destruction. -सर्गः the creation of the world, the class or order of created beings. -सूक्ष्मं a subtle element. -स्थानं 1 the abode of living beings. 2 the abode of demons. -हत्या destruction of living beings.

भूतमय *a.* 1 Including all beings. 2 Formed out of the elements or created beings.

भूतिः *f.* 1 Being, existence. 2 Birth, production. 3 Well-being, welfare, happiness, prosperity; प्रजानामेव भूत्यर्थं स ताभ्यो बलिमग्रहीत् R. 1. 18; नरपतिकुलभूत्यै 2. 74; स वोऽस्तु भूत्यै भगवान् मुकुंदः Vikar. 1. 2. 4 Success, good fortune. 5 Wealth, riches, fortune, विपत्प्रतीकारपरेण मंगलं निषेव्यते भूतिसमुत्सुकेन वा Ku. 5. 76. 6 Grandeur, dignity, majesty. 7 Ashes; भूतभूतिरहीन भोगभाक् Si. 16. 71 (where भूति means 'riches' also); स्फुटोपमं भूतिसितेन शंभुना 1. 4. 8 Decoration of elephants with coloured stripes; भक्तिच्छेदैरिव विरचितां भूतिमंगे गजस्य Me. 19. 9 The superhuman power attainable by the practice of penance or magical rites. 10 Fried meat. 11 The rutting of elephants. -तिः 1 An epithet of Siva. 2 of Vishṇu. 3 of a class of Manes. -Comp. -कर्मन् *n.* any auspicious or festive rite. -काम *a.* desirous of prosperity. (-मः) 1 a minister of state. 2 an epithet of Bṛihaspti. -कालः a happy or auspicious hour. -कीलः 1 a hole, pit. 2 moat. 3 a cellar, underground room. -कृत् *m.* an epihet of Siva. -गर्भः an epithet of Bhavabhûti. -दः an epithet of Siva. निधानं the lunar mansion called धनिष्ठा. -भूषणः an epithet of Siva. -वाहनः an epithet of Siva.

भूतिकं 1 Camphor. 2 Sandal-wood. 3 N. of a medicinal plant (Mar. कायफळ).

भूमत् *a.* Possessed of land or earth. -*m.* A king, sovereign.

भूमन् *m.* 1 A great quantity, abundance, plenty, large number. भूम्ना रसानां गहनाः प्रयोगाः Mâl. 1. 4; संभूयेव सुखानि चेतसि परं भूमानमातन्वते 5. 9. 2 Wealth. -*n.* 1 The earth. 2 A territory, district, piece of ground. 3 A being, creature. 4 Plurality (of number); आपः स्त्रीभूम्नि Ak.; cf. पुंभूमन्,

भूमय *a.* (यी *f.*) Earthen, earthly. made of or produced from earth.

भूमिः *f.* 1 The earth (opp. स्वर्ग, गगन or पाताल); द्यौर्भूमिरापो हृदयं यमश्च Pt. 1. 182; R. 2. 74. 2 Soil, ground; उत्खातिनी भूमिः S. 1; Ku. 1. 24. 3 A territory, district, country, land; विदर्भभूमिः 4 A place, spot, ground, plot of ground; प्रमदवनभूमयः S. 6; अधित्यकाभूमिः. N. 22. 41; R. 1. 52, 3. 61; Ku. 3. 58. 5 A site, situation. 6 Land, landed property. 7 A story, the floor of a house; as in सप्तभूमिकः प्रासादः. 8 Attitude, pasture. 9 A character or part (in a play); cf. भूमिका. 10 Subject, object, receptacle; विश्वासभूमि, स्नेहभूमि &c. 11 Degree, extent, limit; Ki. 10. 58. 12 The tongue. -Comp. -अंतरः a king of an adjacent district. -इंद्रः, ईश्वरः a king, soverign. -कदंबः a kind of Kadamba. -कंपः an earth-quake. -गुहा a hole in the ground. -गृहं a cellar, an underground chamber. -चलः, चलनं an earth-quake. -जः 1 the planet Mars. 2 an epithet of the demon Naraka. 3 a man. 4 the plant भूनिंब. (-जा) an epithet of Sitâ. -जीविन् *m.* a Vaisya. -तलं the surface of the earth. -दानं a grant of land. -देवः a Brâhmaṇa. -धरः 1 a mountain. 2 a king. 3 the number 'seven'. -नाथः, -पः, -पतिः, -पालः, -भुज् *m.* a king, sovereign; R. 1. 47. -पक्षः a swift or fleet horse. -पिशाचं the wine palm. -पुत्रः the planet Mars. -पुरंदरः 1 a king. 2 N. of Dilîpa. -भृत् *m.* 1 a mountain. 2 a king. -मंडा a kind of jasmine. -रक्षकः a swift or fleet horse. -लाभः death (lit. returning to the dust of the earth). -लेपनं cow-dung. -वर्धनः -नं a dead body, corpse. -शय *a.* sleeping on the ground. (-यः) a wild pigeon. -शयनं, -शय्या sleeping on the ground. -संभवः, -सुतः 1 the planet Mars. 2 an epithet of the demon Naraka. (-वा, -ता) an epithet of Sitâ. -संनिवेशः the general appearance of a country. -स्पृश *m.* 1 a man. 2 mankind. 3 a Vaisya. 4 a thief.

भूमिका 1 Earth, ground, soil. 2 A place, region, spot (of ground). 3 A story, floor (of a house). 4 Step, degree, मधुमतीसंज्ञां भूमिकां साक्षात्कुर्वतः Yoga. S.; or नैयायिकादिभिरात्मा प्रथमभूमिकायामवतारितः Sânkhyapravachana-bhâshya. 5 A tablet or board as for writing; see अक्षरभूमिका. 6 A part or character in a play; या यस्य युज्यते भूमिका तां खलु तथैव भाविन सर्वे वर्ग्याः पाठिताः; कामंदक्याः प्रथमां भूमिकां भाव एवाधीते Mâl.; or लक्ष्मीभूमिकायां वर्तमानोर्वशी वारुणीभूमिकायां वर्तमानया मेनकया पृष्टा V. 3; Si. 1. 69. 7 Theatrical dress, an actor's costume. 8 Decoration (as of an image). 9 A preface or introduction to a book.

भूमी The earth; see भूमि. -Comp. -कदंबः=भूमिकदंबः. -पतिः, -भुज् *m.* a king, -रुह् *m.*, -रुहः a tree.

भूयं The state of being or becoming; as in ब्रह्मभूय; दाशरथिभूयं Si. 14. 81.

भूयशस् *ind.* 1 Mostly, generally, commonly, as a general rule. 2 Exceedingly, in a high degree. 3 Again, more further.

भूयस् *a.* (सी *f.*) 1 More, more numerous or abundant. 2 Greater, larger; Ku. 6. 13. 3 More important. 4 Very great or large, much, many, numerous; भवति च पुनर्भूयान्भेदः फलं प्रति तद्यथा U. 2. 4; भद्रं भद्रं वितर भगवन्भूयसे मंगलाय Mâl. 1. 3; U. 3. 48; R. 17. 41; U. 2. 3. 5 Rich or abounding in; एवंप्रायगुणभूयसीं स्वकृतिं Mâl. 1. -*ind.* 1 Much, very much, exceedingly, largely, greatly. 2 More, again, further, more, moreover; पाथेयमुत्सृज बिसं ग्रहणाय भूयः V. 4. 16; R. 2. 16; Me. 111. 3 Repeatedly, frequently. (The form भूयसा is often used adverbially in the sense of 1 very much, in a high degree, exceedingly, beyond measure, for greater part; न खरो न च भूयसा मृदुः R. 8. 8; पश्चार्धेन प्रविष्टः शरपतनभयात् भूयसा पूर्वकायं S. 1. 7; 2 generally, as a general rule; भूयसा जीविधर्म एषः U. 5). -Comp -दर्शनं 1 frequent observation. 2 an inference based on frequent and wide observation. -भूयस् *ind.* again and again, repeatedly; भूयोभूयः सविधनगरीरथ्यया पर्यटंतं Mâl. 1 15. -विद्य *a.* 1 more learned. 2 very learned.

भूयस्त्वं 1 Abundance, plentifulness. 2 Majority, preponderance.

भूयिष्ठ *a.* 1 Most, most numerous or abundant. 2 Most important, principal, chief. 3 Very great or large, very much, much, many, numerous. 4 Chiefly or for the most part composed of, mostly composed or consisting of, chiefly filled with or characterized by (at the end of Comp.) अभिरूपभूयिष्ठा परिषद् S. 1; शुल्वमांसभूयिष्ठ आहारोऽश्यते S. 2; R. 4. 70. 5 Almost, mostly, nearly all (usually after a past passive participle); अये उदितभूयिष्ठ एष तपनः Mâl. 1; निर्वाणभूयिष्ठमथास्य वीर्यं Ku. 3. 52; V. 1. 8. -ष्ठं *ind.* 1 For the most part, mostly; S. 1. 31. 2 Exceedingly, very much, in the highest degree; भू-

यिष्ठं भव दक्षिणा परिजने S. 4. 17; R. 6 4; 13. 14.

भूर् *ind.* One of the three Vyâhritis.

भूरि *a.* 1 Much, abundant, numerous, copious. 2 Great, large. *–m.* An epithet of 1 Vishnu, 2 of Brahmâ. 3 of *S*iva. 4 of Indra. *–n.* Gold. *–ind.* 1 Very much, exceedingly; नवांबुभिर्भूरि विलंबिनो घनाः S.5.12. 2 Frequently, often, repeatedly. **–Comp.** **–गमः** an ass. **–तेजस्** *a.* possessed of great lustre. (*–m.*) fire. **–दक्षिण** *a.* 1 attended with rich presents or rewards. 2 giving liberal rewards, munificent. **–दानं** liberality. **–धन** *a.* wealthy. **–धामन्** *a.* possessed of great lustre. **–प्रयोग** *a.* frequently used, in common use (as a word). **–प्रेमन्** *m.* the ruddy goose. **–भाग** *a.* wealthy, prosperous. **–मायः** a jackal or fox. **–रसः** the sugar-cane. **–लाभः** 1 a great gain. **–विक्रम** *a.* very brave, a great warrior. **–वृष्टिः** *f.* a heavy rain. **–श्रवस्** *m.* N. of a warrior on the Kaurava side slain by Satyaki.

भूरिज् *f.* The earth.

भूर्जः The birch-tree: भूर्जगतोऽक्षरविन्यासः V. 2; Ku. 1. 7. **–Comp.** **–कंटकः** a man of one of the mixed tribes, the offsrping of an outcast Brâhma*n*a by a woman of the same class; व्रात्यात्तु जायते विप्रात्पापात्मा भूर्जकंटकः Ms. 10. 21. **–पत्रः** the birch-tree.

भूर्णिः *f.* The earth.

भूष् 1 P., 10 U. (भूषति, भूषयति-ते, भूषित) 1 To adorn, deck, decorate; शुचि भूषयति श्रुतं वपुः Bk. 20. 15. 2 To decorate oneself (Atm.); भूषयते कन्या स्वयमेव. 3 To spread or strew with, overspread; R. 2. 31. –WITH **अभि** to adorn, grace, give beauty to; *S*i.7 38. **–वि** to adorn, decorate; केयूरा न विभूषयंति पुरुषं Bh. 2. 19; *S*i. 9. 33; Ku. 1. 28.

भूषणं 1 Ornamenting, decoration. 2 An ornament, decoration, an article of decoration; क्षीयंते खलु भूषणानि सततं वाग्भूषणं भूषणं Bh. 2. 19; R. 3. 2; 13. 57.

भूषा 1 Decorating, adorning. 2 An ornament, decoration; as in कर्णभूषा q. v. 3 A jewel.

भूषित *p. p.* Decorated, ornamented; मणिना भूषितः सर्पः किमसौ न भयंकरः.

भूष्णु *a.* 1 Being, becoming; as in अलंभूष्णु q. v. 2 Wishing for wealth or prosperity; Ms. 4. 135.

भृ 1. 3. U. (भरति-ते; बिभर्ति, बिभृते, भृत; *pass.* भ्रियते ; *desid.* बिभरिषति or बुभूर्षति) 1 To fill; जठरं को न बिभर्ति केवलं Pt. 1. 22. 2 To fill, pervade, fill with; अभार्षीद् ध्वनिना लोकान् Bk. 15. 24. 3 To bear, support, uphold, bear up; धुरं धरित्र्या बिभरांबभूव R. 18. 44; कूर्मो बिभर्ति धरणीं खलु पृष्ठकेन Ch. P. 50; Bk. 17. 16. 4 To maintain, foster, cherish, protect, take care of nourish; दरिद्रान् भर कौंतेय मा प्रयच्छेश्वरे धनं H. 1. 15. 5 To bear, have, possess; सिंधोर्बभार सलिलं शयनीयलक्ष्मीं Ki. 8. 57; पिशुनजनं खलु बिभ्रति क्षितींद्राः Bv. 1. 74; बलित्रयं चारु बभार बाला Ku. 1. 39; इंदोर्दैन्यं त्वदनुसरणक्लिष्टकांतेर्बिभर्ति Me. 84; *S*. 2. 4. 6 To wear; बिभ्रज्जटामंडलं *S*. 7. 11; 6. 5; विवाहकौतुकं ललितं बिभ्रत एव (तस्य) R. 8. 1, 10. 10; जटाश्च बिभृयान्नित्यं Ms. 6. 6. 7 To feel, experience, suffer, endure (joy, sorrow &c.); भावशुद्धिसहितैर्मुदं जनो नाटकैरिव बभार भोजनैः *S*i. 14. 50; संत्रासमबिभः शक्रः Bk. 17. 108; *S*. 7. 21. 8 To confer, bestow, give, produce; यौवने सदलंकाराः शोभां बिभ्रति सुभ्रुवः Subhâsh. 9 To keep, hold, retain (as in memory). 10 To hire; Ms. 11. 62; Y. 3. 235. 11 To bring or carry. –With **उद्** to bear, support, uphold; भूगोलमुद्बिभ्रते Gît. 1. **–सं** 1 to collect, hoard, place or bring together; त्यागाय संभृतार्थानां R. 1. 7; 5. 5, 8. 3; Bk. 6. 80. 2 to effect, produce bring on, accomplish; सुरतश्रमसंभृतो मुखे स्वेदलव; R. 8. 51; Ki. 9. 49; Me. 115. 3 to maintain, cherish, foster. 4 to make ready, prepare; V. 5; R. 19. 54. 5 to give, offer, present.

भृकुंशः (**सः**) A male actor in female attire.

भृकुटिः **–टी** See भ्रु(भ्रू)कुटि.

भृग् *ind.* An onomatopoetic word expressive of the crackling sound of fire.

भृगुः 1 N. of a sage, regarded as the ancestor of the family of the Bhrigus and described in Ms. 1. 35 as one of the ten patriarchs created by the first Manu. [On one occasion when the sages could not agree a as to which of three gods, Brahman, Vish*n*u and *S*iva, was best entitled to the worship of Brah*m*a as the sage Bhrigu was sent to test the character of the three gods. He first went to the abode of Brahman, and, on approaching him, purposely omitted an obeisance. Upon this the god reprehended him severely, but was pacified by apologies. Next he entered the abode of *S*iva in Kail*a*sa, and omitted, as before, all tokens of adoration. The vindictive deity was enraged and would have destroyed him, had he not conciliated him by mild words. (According to another account, Bhrigu was coldly received by Brahman, and he therefore cursed him that he would receive no worship or adoration; and condemned *S*iva to take the form of a *Linga*, as he got no access to the deity who was engaged in private with his wife). Lastly he went to Vish*n*u, and finding him asleep, he boldly gave the god a kick on his breast which at once awoke him. Instead of showing anger, however, the god arose and on seeing Bhrigu, inquired tenderly whether his foot was hurt, and then began to rub it gently. 'This' said Bhrigu, ' is the mightiest god. He overstops all by the most potent of all weapons–kindness end generosity', Vish*n*u was therefore, to be the god who was best entitled to the worship of all.] 2 N. of the sage Jamadagni. 3 An epithet of *S*ukra. 4 The planet Venus. 5 A cliff, precipice; भृगुपतनकारणमपृच्छं Dk. 6 Tableland, the level summit of a mountain. 7 N. of Krish*n*a. **–Comp.** **–उद्वहः** an epithet of Parasurâma. **–जः**, **–तनयः** an epithet of *S*ukra. **–नंदनः** 1 an epithet of Parasurâma; वीरो न यस्य भगवान् भृगुनंदनोपि U.5.34. 2 *S*ukra. **–पतिः** an epithet of Parasurama; भृगुपतियशोवर्त्मयत्क्रौंचरंध्रं Me. 57; so भृगूणां पतिः. **–वंशः** N. of a family descended from Parasurâma. **–वारः**, **–वासरः** Friday. **–शार्दूलः**, **–श्रेष्ठः**, **–सत्तमः** an epithet of Parasurama. **–सुतः**, **–सूनुः** 1 an epithet of Parasurâma. 2 of Venus.

भृंगः 1 A large black bee; Bv. 1. 5; R. 8. 53. 2 A kind of wasp. 3 A kind of bird. 4 A libertine, dissolute or lecherous man; cf. भ्रमर. 5 A Golden vase or jar. **–गं** Talc. **–गी** The female of the large black-bee; भृंगी पुष्पं पुरुषं स्त्री वांछति नवं नवम्. **–Comp.** **–अभीष्टः** the mango-tree. **–आनंदा** the Yûthikâ creeper. **–आवली** a flight of bees. **–जं** 1 aloe-wood. 2 talc. (**–जा**) the plant भार्गी. **–पर्णिका** small cardamoms. **–राज्** *m.* 1 a kind of large bee 2 N. of a shrub. **–रिटिः**, **–रीटिः** N. of one of the attendants of *S*iva (said to be very deformed). **–रोलः** a kind of wasp. **–वल्लभः** a species of Kadamba.

भृंगारः **–रं** 1 The A golden vase or pitcher. 2 A pitcher of a particular shape (Mar. झारी); शिशिरसुरभिसलिलपूर्णोयं भृंगारः Ve. 6. 3 A vase used at the coronation of a king. **–गं** 1 Gold 2 Cloves.

भृंगारिका, भृंगारी A cricket.

भृंगिन् *m* 1 The fig-tree. 2 N. of an attendant of *S*iva.

भृंगिरि(री)टिः See भृंगरिटि.

भृंगिरिटिः N. of an attendant of *S*iva.

भृज् 1 A. (भर्जते) To roast, fry.

भृंटिका A species of plant.

भृंडिः *f.* A wave.

भृत *p. p.* 1 Borne. 2 Supported, maintained, cherished, fostered. 3 Possessed, endowed or furnished with. 4 Full of, filled with. 5 Hired, paid. **–तः** A hired servant; hireling, mercenary; उत्तमस्त्वायुधीयो यो मध्यमस्तु कृषीवलः। अधमो भारवाही स्यादित्येवं त्रिविधो भृतः Mit.

भृतक *a.* Hired, paid. **–कः** A hired servant. **–Comp.** **–अध्यापकः** a hired teacher. **–अध्यापित** *a.* taught by a paid teacher. (-तः) a student who pays his teacher for his labour (='a paying student' of the modern days); Ms. 3. 156.

भृतिः *f.* 1 Bearing, upholding, supporting. 2 Supporting, maintaining. 3 Bringing, leading to. 4 Nourishment, support, maintenance. 5 Food. 6 Wages, hire. 7 Service for hire. 8 Capital, principal. -Comp. -अध्यापनं teaching (especially the Vedas) for hire. -भुज् *m.* a hired servant, a hireling. -रूपं a reward in place of the wages due, but not to be paid.

भृत्य *a.* To be nourished or maintained &c. -त्यः 1 Any one requiring to be supported. 2 A servant, dependant, slave. 3 A king's servant, minister of state. -त्या 1 Rearing, fostering, nourishing, taking care of ; as in कुमारभृत्या q. v. 2 Maintenance, support. 3 A means of sustenance, food. 4 Wages. 5 Service. -Comp. -जनः 1 a servant, dependant. 2 servant taken collectively. -भर्तृ *m.* the master of a family. -वर्गः the body of servants. -वात्सल्यं kindness to servants. -वृत्तिः *f.* maintenance of servants ; Ms. 11. 7.

भृत्रिम *a.* Supported, nourished.

भृमिः An eddy, a whirlpool.

भृश् 4 P. (भृश्यति To fall down ; see भ्रंश्.

भृश *a.* (compar. भ्रशीयस् superl. भ्रशिष्ठ) Strong, powerful, mighty, intense, excessive, very much. -शं *ind.* 1 Much, very much, exceedingly, intensely, violently, excessively, in a high degree, greatly ; त वेश्य रुरोद सा भृशं Ku. 4. 25 ; रघुर्भृशं वक्षसि तन ताडितः R. 3. 61 ; चुकोप तस्मै स भृशं 3. 56 ; Ms. 7. 170 ; Rs. 1. 11. 2 Often, repeatedly. 3 In a better or superior manner. -Comp. -कोपन *a.* highly choleric or irascible. -दुःखित, -पीडित *a.*exceedingly afflicted. -संहृष्ट *a.* very much delighted.

भृष्ट *p. p.* Fried, roasted, parched. -Comp. -अन्नं rice boiled and fried. -यवाः (pl.) parched rice.

भृष्टिः *f.* 1 Frying, parching, roasting. 2 A deserted garden or orchard.

भॄ 9 P. (भृणाति) 1 To bear; nourish, support, maintain. 2 To fry. 3 To blame, censure.

भेकः 1 A frog ; पंके निमग्ने कारिणि भेको भवति मूर्धगः 2 A timid man. 3 A cloud. -की 1 A small frog. 2 A female frog. -Comp. -भुज् *m.* a serpent. -रवः, -शब्दः the croaking of frogs.

भेडः 1 A ram, sheep. 2 A raft, flot.

भेड्रः A ram.

भेदः 1 Breaking splitting, cleaving; hitting (as a mark). 2 Rending, tearing. 3 Dividing, separating. 4 piecing through, perforation. 5 Breach, rupture. 6 Disturbance, interruption. 7 Division, separation. 8 A chasm, gap, fissure, cleft. 9 Hurt, injury, wound. 10 Difference, distinction ; तयोरभेदप्रतिपत्तिरस्ति मे Bh. 3. 99; अगोरवभेदेन Ku. 6 12; Bg. 18. 19, 29; रस°, काल° &c. 11 A change, modification ; बुद्धिभेद Bg. 3. 26. 12 Dissension, disuniod. 13 Disclosure, betrayal ; as in रहस्यभेदः. 14 Treachery, treason. 15 A kind, variety ; भेदाः पद्मशंखादयो निधेः Ak.; शिरिषं पुष्पभेदः &c. 16 Dualism. 17 (In politics) Sowing dissensions in an enemy's party and thus winning him over to one's side, one of the four Upâyas or means of success against an enemy; see उपाय and उपायचतुष्टय. 18 Defeat. 19 (In medicine) evacuation of the bowels. -Comp. -अभेदौ (dual) 1 disunion and union, dissagreement and agreement. 2 Difference and sameness ; भेदाभेदज्ञानं. -उन्मुख *a.* on the point of bursting forth or opening ; V. 2. 7. -कर, -कृत् *a.* sowing dissensions. -दर्शिन्, -दृष्टि, -बुद्धि *a.* considering the universe as distinct from the Supreme Spirit. -प्रत्ययः belief in dualism. -वादिन् *m.* one who maintains the doctrine of dualism. -सह *a.* 1 capable of being divided or separated. 2 corruptible, seducible.

भेदक *a.* (दिका *f.*) 1 Breaking, splitting, dividing, separating. 2 Breaking through, piercing. 3 Destroying, a destroyer. 4 Distinguishing, discriminating. 5 Defining. -कः An adjective or differentiating attribute.

भेदनं 1 Splitting, breaking, rending. 2 Dividing, separating. 3 Distinguishing. 4 Sowing dissensions, creating discord. 5 Dissolving, loosening. 6 Disclosing, betraying. -नः A hog.

भेदिन् *a.* reaking, dividing, distinguishing &c.

भेदिरं, भेदुर A thunderbolt.

भेद्यं A substantive. -Comp. -लिंग *a.* distinguished by the gender.

भेरः A kettle-drum.

भेरिः -री *f.* A kettle drum ; B . 1. 13.

भेरुंड *a.* Terrible, frightful, awful, fearful. -डः A species of bird. -डं Conception, pregnancy.

भेरुंडकः A jackal.

भेल *a.* 1 Timid, cowardly. 2 Foolish, ignorant. 3 Unsteady, inconstant. 4 Tall. 5 Agile, quick. -लः A boat, raft, float.

भेलकः -कं A boat, raft.

भेष् 1 U (भेषति-ते) To fear, dread be afraid.

भेषजं 1 A medicine, medicament, or drug ; नरानंब त्रातुं त्वमिह परमं भेषजमसि G. L. 15 ; अतिवीर्यवतीव भेषजे बहुरल्पीयसि दृश्यते गुणः Ki. 2. 4. 2 A remedy or cure in general. 3 A kind of fennel. -Comp. -अ(आ)गारः, -रं an apothecary's shop. -अंगं anything taken after medicine.

भैक्ष *a.* (क्षी *f*) Living on alms. -क्षं 1 Begging, mendicancy ; Ms. 6. 55; Y. 3. 42. 2 Anything got by begging, alms, charity ; भैक्षेण वर्तयन्नित्यं Ms. 2. 188; 4. 5. -Comp. -अन्नं alms, food obtained by begging. -आशिन् *a.* eating food obtained by begging. (-*m.*) a beggar, mendicant. -आहारः a beggar. -कालः the time for begging. -चरणं, -चर्यं, -चर्या going about begging, begging, collecting alms. -जीविका, -वृत्तिः *f.* mendicancy. -भुज् *m.* a beggar, mendicant.

भैक्षवं, भैक्षुक A number of beggars.

भैक्ष्यं Food got by begging, alms, charity ; see भैक्ष.

भैम *a.* (मी *f.*) Relating to Bhîma. -मी 1 'The daughter of Bhîma,' a patronymic of Damayantî, wife of Nala. 2 The eleventh day of the bright half of Mâgha or a festival performed on that day.

भैमसेनिः -न्यः A son of Bhîmasena.

भैरव *a.* (वी *f.*) 1 Terrible, frightful, horrible, formidable. 2 Relating to Bhairava. -वः A form of *S*iva (of which 8 kinds are enumerated). -वी 1 A form of the goddess Durgâ. 2 N. of a Rāgiṇi in the Hindu musical system. 3 A girl of 12 or a young girl representing the goddess Durgâ at the Durgâ festival. -वं Terror, horror. -Comp. -ईशः an epithet of Vishṇu (of *S*iva 2); so -तर्जकः -यातना a sort of purificatory torment inflicted by Bhairava of Benares on those who die there, to make their spirits fit for absorption into the Supreme Spirit.

भैषजं A medicine, drug. -जः The bird called लावक or quail.

भैषज्यं 1 Administering medicines medical treament. 2 A medicament, medicine, drug. 3 Healing power, curativeness.

भैष्मकी A patronymic of Rukminî, daughter of Bhîshmaka of Vidarbha.

भोक्तृ *a.* 1 One who enjoys or eats. 2 Possessing. 3 Employing or making use of. 4 Feeling, enduring, experiencing. -*m.* 1 A possessor, enjoyer, user. 2 A husband. 3 A king, ruler. 4 A lover,

भोगः **1** Eating, consuming. **2** Enjoyment, fruition. **3** Possession. **4** Utility, advantage. **5** Ruling, governing, govenment. **6** Use, application (as of a deposit). **7** Suffering, enduring, experiencing. **8** Feeling, perception. **9** Enjoyment of women, sexual enjoyment, carnal pleasures. **10** An enjoyment, an object of enjoyment or pleasure ! भोगे रोगभयं Bh. 3. 35; Bg. 1. 32. **11** A repast, feast, banquet. **12** Food. **13** Food offered to an idol. **14** Profit, gain. **15** Income, revenue. **16** Wealth. **17** The wages of prostitutes. **18** A curve, coil, winding. **19** The (expanded) hood of a snake; श्वसदसितभुजंगभोगांगदग्रंथि &c. Mâl. 5. 23; R. 10. 7. 11. 59. **21** A snake. **-Comp.** **-अर्ह** *a.* fit to be enjoyed. (-र्हं) property, wealth. **-अर्ह्यं** corn, grain. **-आधिः** a pledge which may be used until redeemed. **-आवली** the panegyric of a professional encomiast! नग्नः स्तुतिव्रतस्तस्य ग्रंथो भोगावली भवेत् Hemachandra. **-आवासः** the apartments of women, harem. **-कर** *a.* affording enjoyment or pleasure. **-गुच्छं** wages paid to prostitutes. **-गृहं** the women's apartments, harem, zenana. **-तृष्णा** **1** desire of worldly enjoyments; तदुपास्थितमग्रहीदजः पितुराज्ञेति न भोगतृष्णया R. 8. 2; selfish enjoyment; Mâl. 2. **-देहः** ' the body of suffering', the subtle body which a dead person is supposed to carry with him, and with which he experiences happiness or misery according to his good or bad works. **-धरः** a serpent. **-पतिः** the governor or ruler of a district or province. **-पाल** a groom. **-पिशाचिका** hunger. **-भृतकः** a servant who works only for livelihood. **-वस्तु** *n.* an object of enjoyment. **-सद्मन्** *n.* = भोगावास q. v. **-स्थानं** **1** the body, as the seat of enjoyment. **2** women's apartment.

भोगवत् *a.* **1** Giving pleasure or delight, delightful. **2** Happy, prosperous. **3** Having curves, ringed, coiled. *-m.* **1** A snake. **2** A mountain. **3** Dancing, acting, and singing together. *-f.* (ती) **1** An epithet of the Ganges of Pâtâla or the lower world (पातालगंगा). **2** A female snake-demon. **3** N. of the city of the snake-demons in the lower world. **4** The night of the second day of a lunar month.

भोगिकः A groom, horse-keeper.

भोगिन् *a.* **1** Eating. **2** Enjoying. **3** Suffering, experiencing, enduring. **4** Using, possessing; (at the end of Comp.) in these four senses). **5** Having curves. **6** Having hoods. **7** Devoted to enjoyment, indulging in sensual pleasures; Pt. 1. 65 (where it has sense 6 also). **8** Rich, opulent. *-m.* **1** A snake; गजाजिनालंबि पिनद्धभोगि वा Ku. 5. 78; R. 2. 32, 4. 48, 10. 7, 11. 59. **2** A king. **3** A voluptuary. **4** A barber. **5** The headman of a village. **6** The lunar mansion आश्लेषा. **-नी** A woman belonging to the king's harem, but not consecrated with him, the concubine of a king. **-Comp.** **-इंद्रः**, **ईशः** *Sesha* or *Vásuki*. **-कांतः** wind, air. -भुज् *m.* **1** an ichneumon. **2** a peocock. **-वल्लभं** sandal.

भोग्य *a.* **1** To be enjoyed, or turned to one's account; R. 8. 14. Pt. 1. 117. **2** To be suffered or endured; Me. 1. **3** Profitable. **-ग्यं** **1** Any object of enjoyment. **2** Wealth, property, possessions. **8** Corn, grain. **-ग्या** A harlot, courtezan.

भोजः N. of a celebrated king of Mâlvâ (or Dhârâ); (supposed to have flourished about the end of the tenth or the beginning of the eleventh century, and to have been a great patron of Sanskrit lerning; he is also supposed to have been the author of several learned works, such as सरस्वतीकंठाभरण &c.). **2** N. of a country. **3** N. of a King of the Vidarbhas; भोजेन दूतो रघवे विसृष्टः R. 5. 39; 7. 1-29, 35. **-जाः** (*m.* pl.) N. of a people. **-Comp.** **-अधिपः** an epithet of **1** Kamsa. **2** Karna. **-इंद्रः** King of the Bhojas. **-कटं** N. of a town founded by Rukmin. **-देवः**, **राजः** King Bhoja; see (1) above. **-पतिः** **1** king Bhoja. **2** an epithet of Kamsa.

भोजनं Eating, eating food; अजीर्णे भोजनं विषं. **2** Food. **3** Giving (food) to eat, feeding. **4** Using, enjoying. **5** Any object of enjoyment. **6** That which is enjoyed. **7** Property, wealth, possession. **-नः** An epithet of *Siva*. **-Comp.** **-अधिकारः** charge of provendor, superintendence over food or provisions, stewardship. **-आच्छादनं** food and raiment. **-कालः**, **-वेला**, **-समयः** meal-time, dinner or supper time. **-त्यागः** abstaining from food, fasting. **-भूमिः** *f.* a dining-hall **-विशेषः** a dainty, delicacy. **-वृत्तिः** *f.* a meal, food. **-व्यग्र** *a.* engaged in eating. **-व्ययः** expense for food.

भोजनीय *a* Eatable, edible. **-यं** Food.

भोजयितृ *a.* One who feeds, a feeder.

भोज्य *pot p.* **1** To be eaten. **2** To be enjoyed or possessed. **3** To be suffered or experienced. **4** To be enjoyed carnally. **-ज्यं** **1** Food, meal; त्वं भोक्ता अहं च भोज्यभूतः Pt. 2; Ku. 2. 15; Ms. 3. 240. **2** A store of provisions, eatables. **3** A dainty. **4** Enjoyment. **-Comp.** **-कालः** mealtime. **-संभवः** chyme, the primary juice of the body.

भोज्या A princess of the Bhojas; R. 6. 59; 7. 2, 13.

भोटः N. of a country (said to be the same as Tibet.) **-Comp.** **-अंगः** the country called Bhootâna.

भोटीय *a.* Tibetan.

भोमीरा Coral.

भोस् *ind.* A vocative particle used in addressing persons and translatable by 'oh,' 'sir,' 'ho,' 'halloo,' 'ah,' (it drops its final visarga before vowels and soft consonants); काः कोऽत्र भोः *S.* 2 अयि :भो महर्षिपुत्र *S.* **7**; it is sometimes repeated; भो भोः शंकरगृहाधिवासिनो जानपदाः Mâl. **3.** भोस् is said to have, in addition, the senses of 'sorrow' and 'interrogation.'

भौजंग *a.* (गी *f.*) Serpentine. **—गं** The lunar mansion called आश्लेषा.

भौट्टः A Tibetan.

भौत *a.* (ती *f.*) **1** Relating to living beings. **2** Elemental, material. **3** Demoniacal. **4** Mad, crazy. **-तः** **1** A worshipper of demons and spirits. **2** An attendant upon an idol (देवल). **-तं** A collection of evil spirits.

भौतिक *a.* (**की** *f.*) **1** Belonging to created or living beings; Ms. 3. 74. **2** Formed of coarse elements, elemental, material; पिंडेष्वनास्था खलु भौतिकेषु R. 2. 57. **3** Relating to evil spirits. **-कः** N. of *Siva*. **-कं** A pearl, **-Comp.** **-मठः** a monastery. **-विद्या** sorcery, witch-craft.

भौम *a.* (मी *f.*) **1** Belonging to the earth. **2** Being on the earth, earthly, terrestrial; भौमो मुनेः स्थानपरिग्रहोयं R. 13. 36; 15. 59. **3** Earthy, made of earth. **4** Relating to Mars. **-मः** **1** The planet Mars. **2** An epithet of the demon Naraka. **3** Water. **4** Light. **-Comp.** **-दिनं**, **वारः**, **-वासरः** Tuesday; Si. 15. 17. **-रत्नं** coral.

भौमनः N. of Visvakarman, architect of the gods.

भौमिक *a.* (**की** *f.*), **भौम्य** *a.* Earthly, terrestrial, living or existing on the earth.

भौरिकः The superintendent of gold in a royal treasury, a treasurer.

भौवनः See भौमन.

भौवादिक *a.* (**की** *f.*) Belonging to the class of roots which being with भू, *i. e.* to the first conjugation.

भ्रंश् 1 A., 4 P. (भ्रंशते, भ्रश्यति, भ्रष्ट; with abl. in most cases) **1** To fall or drop down, tumble; हस्ताद्भ्रष्टमिदं बिसाभरणं *S.* 3. 26. **2** To fall from, deviate or swerve from, stray from; यूथाद्भ्रष्टः H. 4; R. 14. 16. **3** To be deprived of, lose; बभ्रंशेऽसौ धृतेस्ततः Bk. 14. 71; Pt. 2. 108; 4. 37. **4** To escape, flee from; संग्रामात् बभ्रशुः केचित् Bk.

14. 105; 15. 59. **5** To decline, decay, decrease. **6** To disappear, vanish, depart; Mâl. 8. 12. –*Caus.* (भ्रंशयति-ते) **1** To cause to fall, to throw or cast down. **2** To deprive of. –WITH **परि 1** to fall or drop down, tumble, slip. **2** to stray from, go astray. **3** to fall away from, swerve, deviate. **4** to lose, be deprived of; Ms. 10. 20. **–प्र 1** to drop or fall down, slip; प्रभ्रश्यमानाभरणप्रसूना R. 14. 54. **2** to lose, be deprived of; प्रभ्रश्येते तेजसः Mk. 1. 14. (–*Caus.*) to throw or bring down from, cause to fall down from, R. 13. 36. **–वि 1** to drop or fall down. **2** to go to ruin, decay. **3** to fall off, stray from, go astray. **4** to lose.

भ्रंशः–सः 1 Falling off, dropping down, fall, slipping or falling down; सेहेऽस्य न भ्रंशमतो न लोभात् R. 16. 74; कनकवलयभ्रंशरिक्तप्रकोष्ठः Me. 2. **2** Decline, decrease, decay. **3** Fall, destruction, ruin, overthrow. **4** Running away. **5** Disappearance. **6** Losing, loss, deprivation; स्मृतिभ्रंशाद् बुद्धिनाशः Bg. 2. 63; so जातिभ्रंश, स्वार्थभ्रंश. **7** Straying, swerving or deviating from.

भ्रंशथुः see प्रभ्रंशथुः.

भ्रंश(स)न *a.* (नी *f.*) Throwing down.**–नं 1** The act of dropping down. **2** Falling from, being deprived of, losing.

भ्रंशिन् *a.* **1** Falling off or down, falling from. **2** Decaying. **3** Straying away from. **4** Ruining, destroying.

भ्रंस् = भ्रश् q. v.

भ्रंकुशः An actor in female dress.

भ्रक्ष् 1 U. (भ्रक्षति-ते) To eat, devour.

भ्रज्जनं The act of frying, roasting or parching.

भ्रण् 1 P. (भ्रणति) To sound.

भ्रभंगः = भ्रूभंग q. v.

भ्रम् 1. 4 P. (भ्रमति, भ्रम्यति, भ्राम्यति, भ्रांत) **1** To roam or wander about, move or go about, rove, ramble (fig. also); भ्रमति भुवने कंदर्पाज्ञा Mâl. 1. 17; मनो निद्राशून्यं भ्रमति च किमप्यालिखति च 31; oft. with acc. of place; भुवं बभ्राम Dk.; दिङ्मंडलं भ्रमसि मानस चापलेन Bh. 3. 77; so भिक्षां भ्रम् to go about begging. **2** To turn or whirl round, revolve, move round or in a circle; सूर्यो भ्राम्यति नित्यमेव गगने Bh. 2. 95; भ्रमता भ्रमेरण Gît. 3. **3** To go astray, stray, swerve, deviate. **4** To totter, reel, stagger, be in doubt or suspense, waver; Mâl. 5. 20. **5** To err, be in error or mistake, be mistaken; आभरणकारस्तु तालव्य इति बभ्राम. **6** To flicker, flutter, quiver, move unsteadily; चक्षुर्भ्रम्यति Pt. 4. 78. **7** To surround. –*Caus.* (भ्रमयति ते or भ्रामयति-ते) **1** To cause to rove or wander, cause to revolve or turn round, whirl round; भ्रमय जलदानंभोगर्भान् Mâl. 9. 41. **2** To cause to err, delude, mislead, perplex, confuse, embarrass, cause to reel or stagger; विकारश्चैतन्यं भ्रमयति च संमीलयति च U. 1. 35. **3** To wave, brandish, vibrate; लीलारविंदं भ्रमयांचकार R. 6. 13. –WITH **उद् 1** to wander, roam about, to be confused; धावत्युद्भ्रमति प्रमीलति पतत्युद्याति मूर्छत्यपि Gît. 4. **2** to err, be in error. **3** to be agitated or distracted; R. 12. 74. **–परि 1** to rove, wander about, ramble, move to and fro; परिभ्रमसि किं वृथा क्वचन चित्त विश्राम्यतां Bh. 3. 137. **2** to hover, whirl round; परिभ्रमन्मूर्धजषट्पदाकुलैः Ki. 5. 14. **3** to revolve, rotate, move or turn round. **4** to wander or roam over (with acc.). **5** to turn round (anything), circumambulate. **–वि 1** to roam, wander about. **2** to hover, whirl or wheel ronnd. **3** to scare away, disperse, scatter about. **4** to be confused or disordered, be bewildered or perplexed; Bg. 16. 16. (–*Caus.*) to confound, confuse; प्रभामत्तचंद्रां जगदिदमहो विभ्रमयति K. P. 10. **–सं 1** to roam, rove. **2** to be in error, be perplexed or confused, be bewildered.

भ्रमः 1 Moving or roaming about, roving. **2** Turning round, whirling, revolving. **3** Circular motion, rotation. **4** Straying, deviating. **5** An error, mistake, misapprehension, delusion; शुक्तौ रजतमिति ज्ञानं भ्रमः. **6** Confusion, perplexity, embarrassment. **7** An eddy, a whirlpool. **8** A potter's wheel. **9** A grind stone. **10** A lathe. **11** Giddiness. **12** A fountain, watercouse. **–Comp. –आकुल** *a.* confused. **–आसक्तः** a sword-cleaner, an armourer.

भ्रमणं 1 Moving or roving about, roaming about. **2** Turning round, revolution. 3 Deviation, swerving. **4** Shaking, tottering, unsteadiness, staggering. **5** Erring. **6** Giddiness, dizziness. **–णी 1** A kind of game. **2** A leech.

भ्रमत् *a.* Wandering, roving &c. **–Comp. –कुटी** a kind of umbrella.

भ्रमरः 1 A bee, large black bee; मलिनेऽपि रागपूर्णां विकसितवदनामनल्पजल्पेऽपि। त्वयि चपलेऽपि च सरसां भ्रमर कथं वा सरोजिनीं त्यजसि Bv. 1. 100 (where the next meaning is also suggested). **2** A lover, gallant, libertine. **3** A potter's wheel. **–रं** Giddiness, vertigo. **–Comp. –अतिथिः** the *Champaka* tree. **–अभिलीन** *a.* with bees clung or attached to; R. 3. 8. **–अलकः** a curl on the forehead. **–इष्टः** the tree called श्योनाक. **–उत्सवा** the Mâdhavî creeper. **–करंडकः** a small box containing bees (carried by thieves to extinguish light in a house by letting the bees escape). **–कीटः** a species of wasp. **–प्रियः** a kind of Kadamba tree. **–बाधा** molestation by a bee; *S.* 1. **–मंडलं** a swarm of bees.

भ्रमरकः 1 A bee. **2** A whirlpool, an eddy. **–कः-कं 1** A lock of hair or curl hanging down on the forehead. **2** A ball for playing with. **3** A humming-top.

भ्रमरिका Roving in all directions.

भ्रमिः *f.* **1** Whirling or turning round, circular movement, moving about or round, revolution; U. 3. 19; 6. 3; Mâl. 5. 23. **2** A potter's wheel. **3** A turner's lathe. **4** A whirlpool. **5** A whirlwind. **6** A circular arrangement of troops. **7** An error, a mistake.

भ्रश् See भ्रंश्.

भ्रशिमन् *m.* Violence, excessiveness, impetuosity, vehemence.

भ्रष्ट *p. p* **1** Fallen or dropped down. **2** Fallen from. **3** Strayed or deviated from. **4** Separated from, deprived of, expelled or turned out from; as in भ्रष्टाधिकार q.v. **5** Decayed, declined, ruined. **6** Disappeared, lost. **7** Vicious, depraved.**–Comp.–अधिकार** *a.* deprived of office or power, dismissed. **–क्रिय** *a.* one who has omitted prescribed rites. **–गुद** *a.* suffering from *prolapsus ani.* **योगः** a backslider.

भ्रस्ज् 6 U. (भृज्जति, भृष्ट; *caus.* भर्जयति ते, भ्रज्जयति ते; *desid.* बिभर्क्षति-बिभ्रक्षति, बिभर्जिषति बिभ्रज्जिषति) To fry, roast, parch, broil; (fig. also); बभ्रज्ज निहते तस्मिन् शोको रावणमाग्निवत् Bk. 14. 86.

भ्राज् 1 A. (भ्राजते) To shine, gleam, flash, glitter; रुरुजुर्बभ्रेजिरे फेणुर्बहुधा हरिराक्षसाः Bk. 14. 78; 15. 24. –WITH **वि** to shine brilliantly or intensely; विभ्राजसे मकरकेतनमर्चयंती Ratn. 1. 21.

भ्राजः N. of one of the seven suns. **–जं** N. of a Sa'man.

भ्राजक *a.* (जिका *f.*) Illuminating, irradiating. **–कं** Bile, gall.

भ्राजथुः Splendour, lustre, brilliance, beauty.

भ्राजिन् *a.* Shining, glittering.

भ्राजिष्णु *a.* Shining, resplendent, bright, radiant. **–ष्णुः 1** An epithet of *S*iva. **2** of Vishṇu.

भ्रातृ *m.* **1** A brother; uterine brother. **2** An intimate friend or relation. **3** A near relative in general. **4** A term of friendly address (my good friend); भ्रातः कष्टमहो Bh. 3. 37; 2. 34; तत्त्वं चिंतय तदिदं भ्रातः Moha M. 3. –*Dual.* A brother and sister. **–Comp. –गंधि, गंधिक** *a.* having only the name of a brother, a brother in mere name. **–जः** a brother's son. (–जा) a brother's daughter. **–जाया**

(also भ्रातृजाया) a brother's wife, a sister-in-law; Me. 10. -दत्तं property given by a brother to a sister at the time of her marriage. -द्वितीया the second day of the bright half of Kârtika (when sisters invite their brothers to their houses and entertain them, who in their turn give them presents; the day seems to have been so called on account of Yamunâ having entertained her brother Yama on that day; cf. यमद्वितीया). -पुत्रः (also भ्रातृष्पुत्रः) a brother's son. -वधूः a brother's wife. -श्वशुरः elder brother of the husband.-हत्या fratricide.

भ्रातृक *a.* Relating to a brother.

भ्रातृव्यः 1 A brother's son, nephew. 2 An enemy, adversary.

भ्रातृवल *a.* Having a brother or brothers.

भ्रात्रीयः, भ्रात्रेयः A brother's son, nephew.

भ्रात्र्यं Fraternity, brotherhood.

भ्रांत *p. p.* 1 Wandered or roamed about. 2 Turned round, whirled, revolved. 3 Erred, mistaken, gone astray. 4 Perplexed, confused. 5 Moving about, moving to and fro, wheeling. -तं 1 Roaming, moving about; वरं पर्वतदुर्गेषु भ्रांतं वनचरैः सह Bh. 2. 14. 2 A mistake, an error.

भ्रांतिः *f.* 1 Moving or wandering about. 2 Turning round, rolling. 3 A revolution, circular or rotatory movement; चक्रभ्रांतिररांतरेषु वितनोत्यन्यामिवारावलीं V. 1. 4. 4 An error, a mistake, delusion, wrong notion, false idea or impression; श्रितासि चंदनभ्रांत्या दुर्विपाकं विषद्रुमं U. 1. 46. 5 Confusion, perplexity. 6 Doubt, uncertainty, suspense. -Comp. -कर *a.* confounding, causing delusion. -नाशनः an eithet of *S*iva. -हर *a.* removing doubt or error.

भ्रांतिमत् *a.* 1 Revolving, turning round; भ्रांतिमद्वारियंत्रं M. 2. 13. 2 Erring, mistaking, being under a delusion. —*m.* A figure of speech in which one thing is represented as being mistaken for another on account of the close resemblance between the two; भ्रांतिमानन्यसंवित्तत्तुल्यदर्शने. K. P. 10 *e. g.* कपाले मार्जारः पय इति करालँढिशशिनः &c.; see V. 3. 2; Mâl. 1. 2 also.

भ्रामः 1 Roaming about. 2 Delusion, error, mistake.

भ्रामक *a.* (मिका *f.*) 1 Causing to move or whirl. 2 Perplexing, deceptive. -कः 1 A sunflower. 2 A kind of loadstone. 3 A deceiver, rogue, cheat. 4 A jackal.

भ्रामर *a.* (री *f.*) Relating to a bee. -रः-रं A kind of loadstone. -रं 1 Whirling round. 2 Giddiness. 3 Epilepsy. 4 Honey. 5 A kind of coitus or mode of sexual enjoyment. -री 1 An epithet of Durgâ. 2 Going round, walking round from left to right; (=प्रदक्षिणा q. v.); as in रांयंता भ्रामर्यः Karpûr. 4; Vb. 2.

भ्रा(भ्ला)श् 1. 4. A: (भ्राशते, भ्राश्यते, भ्लाशते भ्लाश्यते), To shine, glitter, blaze.

भ्राष्ट्रः-ष्ट्रं A frying-pan. -ष्ट्रः 1 Light. 2 Ether.

भ्राष्ट्रमिंध *a.* One who fries or roasts.

भ्रा(भ्ला)स् See भ्रा(भ्ला)श्.

भ्रु(भ्रू)कुंशः (सः) A male actor in female attire.

भ्रुकुटिः -टी See भृकुटि.

भ्रुड् 6 P. (भ्रुडति) 1 To collect, gather. 2 To cover.

भ्रू *f.* Brow, eyebrow; कांतिर्भुवोरायतलेखयोर्या Ku. 1. 47. -Comp. -कुटिः-टी *f.* contraction or knitting of the eyebrows, a frown. °बंधः, °रचना bending or knitting the eyebrows; भ्रुकुटिं बध्न् or रच् to knit the eyebrows, to frown. -क्षेपः contraction of the eyebrows; भ्रूक्षेपमात्रानुमतप्रवेशां Ku. 3. 60. -जाहं the root of the eyebrow. -भंगः, -भेदः, contraction or knitting of the eyebrows, a frown; तरंगभ्रूभंगा क्षुभितविहगश्रेणिरशना V. 4. 28; सभ्रूभंगं मुखमिव Me. 24; सभ्रूभंगं 'with a frown'. -भेदिन् *a.* frowning. -मध्यं the space between the eyebrows. -लता a creeper-like eyebrow, an arched or curving eyebrow. -विकारः, -विक्रिया, -विक्षेपः contraction of the eyebrows. -विचेष्टितं,-विभ्रमः,-विलासः graceful or playful movement of the eyebrows, amorous play of the brows; सभ्रूविलासमथ सोऽयमितीरयित्वा Mâl. 1. 24; Me. 16.

भ्रूणः 1 An embryo, fœtus. 2 A child, boy. -Comp. -घ्न,-हन् *a.* one who procures or causes abortion. -हातिः -हत्या killing an embryo, causing abortion; भ्रूणहत्यां वा एते घ्नंति; Y. 1. 64.

भ्रेज् 1 A. (भ्रेजते) To shine.

भ्रे(भ्ले)ष् 1 U. (भ्रेषति-ते, भ्लेषाते-ते) 1 To go, move. 2 To fall, totter, trip, slip. 3 To fear. 4 To be angry.

भ्रेषः 1 Moving, motion. 2 Tottering, wavering, slipping. 3 Deviation, swerving, aberration. 4 Deviation from rectitude, trespass, sin. 5 Loss, deprivation.

भ्रौणहत्यं The killing of an embryo.

भ्लक्ष् See भ्रक्ष्.

भ्लाश् See भ्राश्.

म.

मः 1 Time. 2 Poison. 3 A magical formula. 4 The moon. 5 N. of Brahman. 6 Of Vishṇu. 7 Of *S*iva. 8 Of Yama. -मं 1 Water. 2 Happiness, welfare.

मकरः 1 A kind of sea-animal, a crocodile, shark; झषाणां मकरश्चास्मि Bg. 10. 31; मकरवक्त्र Bh. 2. 4. (Makara is regarded as an emblem of Cupid; cf. comps. below). 2 The sign *Capricornus* of the zodiac. 3 An array of troops in the form of a Makara. 4 An ear-ring in the shape of a Makara. 5 The hands folded in the form of a Makara. 6 N. of one of the nine treasures of Kubera. -Comp -अंकः an epithet of 1 the god of love. 2 the ocean. -अश्वः an epithet of Varuṇa. -आकरः, -आलयः, -आवासः the ocean. -कुंडलं an ear-ring in the shape of a Makara. -केतनः, -केतुः, -केतुमत् *m.* an epithet of the god of love. -ध्वजः 1 an epithet of the god of love; ध्वजः 1 an epithet of the god of love, तल्पेमवारि मंकरध्वजतापहारि Ch. P. 41. 2 a particular array of troops. -राशिः *f.* the sign *Capricornus* of the zodiac. -संक्रमणं the passage of the sun into the sign *Capricornus*. -सप्तमी the seventh day in the bright half of Mâgha.

मकरंदः 1 The honey of flowers, flower-juice; मकरंदतुंदिलानामरविंदानामयं महामान्य Bv. 1. 6, 8. 2 A kind of jasmine. 3 The cuckoo. 4 A bee. 5 A kind of fragrant mango tree. -दं A filament.

मकरंदवत् *a.* Filled with honey. -ती The *Pâtala* creeper or its flower.

मकरिन् *m.* An epithet of the ocean.

मकरी The female of a crocodile -Comp. -पत्रं, लेखा the mark of a Market on the face of Lakshmî. -प्रस्थः N. of a town.

मकुटं A crown; cf. मुकुट.

मकुतिः 1 A government order addressed to the *S*ûdras (शूद्रशासनं).

मकुरः 1 A mirror. 2 The *Bakula* tree. 3 A bud. 4 The Arabian jasmine. 5 The rod or handle of a potter's wheel.

मकुलः 1 The *Bakula* tree. 2 A bud.

मकुष्टः, मकुष्टकः, मकुष्ठः A kind of kidney bean or rice.

मकूलकः 1 A bud. 2 The tree called दंती.

मक् 1 A. (मकते) To go, move.

मक्कुलः Benzoin, red chalk.

मक्कोलः Chalk

मक्ष् 1 P (मक्षति) 1 To accumulate, heap, collect. 2 To be angry.

मक्षः 1 Wrath. 2 ypocrisy. 3 A multitude, collection. -Comp. -वीर्यः the tree पियाल.

मक्षि(क्षी)का A fly, bee; भो उपस्थितं नयनमधु संनिहिता मक्षिका च M. 2.-Comp. -मलं wax.

मख् or मंख् 1 P. (मखति, मंखति) To go, move, creep.

मखः A sacrifice, a sacrificial rite; अकिंचनत्वं मखजं व्यनक्ति R. 5. 16; Ms. 4. 24; R. 3. 39.-Comp. -अग्निः,-अनलः sacrificial fire. -असुहृद् *m.* an epithet of *S*iva. -क्रिया a sacrificial rite. -त्रातृ *m.* an epithet of Râma. -द्विष् *m.* a demon, a Râkshasa; R. 11. 27. -द्वेषिन् *m.* an epithet of *S*iva. -हन् *n.* an epithet 1 of Indra. 2 of *S*iva.

मगधः 1 N. of a country, the southern part of Behar; अस्ति मगधेषु पुष्पपुरी नाम नगरी Dk. 1; अगाधसत्त्वो मगधप्रतिष्ठः R. 6. 21. 2 A bard, minstrel. -धाः (pl.) 1 The people of Magadha, the Magadhas. 2 Long pepper. -Comp. -उद्भवा long pepper. -पुरी the city of Magadha. -लिपिः *f.* writing or character of the Magadhas.

मग्न *p. p.* 1 Plunged, dived. 2 Immersed, sunk. 3 Absorbed (see मस्ज्).

मचः 1 N. of one of the Dvîpas or divisions of the universe. 2 N. of a country. 3 A kind of drug or medicine. ˆ Pleasure. 5 N. of the tenth lunar mansion; see मघा. -घं A kind of flower.

मघवः, मघवत् *m.* N. of Indra.

मघवन् *m.* (Nom. sing. मघवा; acc. pl. मघोनः) 1 N. of Indra; दुदोह गां स यज्ञाय सस्याय मघवा दिवं R. 1. 26, 3. 46; Ki. 3. 52; Ku. 3. 1. 2 An owl (पेचक) 3 N. of Vyâsa.

मघा N. of the tenth lunar mansion containing five stars. -Comp.-त्रयोदशी the thirteenth day of the dark half of Bhâdrapada. -भवः, -भूः the planet Venus.

मंक् 1 A. (मंकते) 1 To go, move. 2 To decorate, adorn.

मंकिलः A forest conflagration.

मंकुरः A mirror.

मंक्षणं An armour for the legs, greaves.

मंक्षु *ind.* 1 Immediately, quickly, soon; मंक्षूदपाति परितः पटलैरलीनां Si. 5. 37. 2 Exceedingly, very much.

मंखः 1 A royal bard. 2 A medicament of a particular class.

मंग् 1 U. (मंगति-ते) To go, move.

मंगः 1 The head of a boat. 2 A side of a ship.

मंगल *a.* 1 Auspicious, lucky, propitious, fortunate; as मंगलदिवसः, मंगलवृषभः &c. 2 Prosperous, doing or faring well. 3 Brave. -लं 1 (*a*) Auspiciousness, propitiousness; जनकानां रघूणां च यत्कृत्स्नं गोत्रमंगलं U. 6. 42; R. 6. 9. 10. 67. (*b*) Happiness, good luck or fortune. bliss, felicity; Mâl. 1. 3; U. 3. 48. (*c*) Well-being, welfare, good; संगः सतां किमु न मंगलमातनोति Bv. 1. 122. 2 A good omen, anything tending to an auspicious issue. 3 A blessing, benediction. 4 An auspicious or lucky object. 5 An auspicious occasion or event, festivity. 6 Any solemn or auspicious ceremony or rite (such as marriage). 7 Any ancient custom. 8 Turmeric. -लः The planet Mars. -ला A faithful wife. -Comp. -अक्षताः (*m. pl.*) rice thrown over persons by Brâhmṇas when pronouncing blessings. -अगुरु *n.* a variety of sandal. -अयनं the way to happiness or prosperity. -अलंकृत *a.* decorated with auspicious ornaments; Ku. 6. 87. -अष्टकं a benedictory verse or verses repeated by priests over a youth and maiden, when being married, to promote their good luck. -आह्निक any daily religious rite performed for good luck.-आचरणं an auspicious introduction in the form of a prayer (for the attainment of success) at the beginning of any undertaking or of any work of composition. -आचारः 1 an auspicious or pious ceremony or usage. 2 a benediction, pronouncing a blessing. -आतोद्यं a drum beaten on festive occasions. -आदेशवृत्तिः a fortune-teller. -आरंभः an epithet of Gaṇes'a. -आलंभनं touching anything auspicious. -आलयः, -आवासः a temple. -इच्छु *a.* desirous of happiness or prosperity. -करणं repeating a prayer for the success of any undertaking. -कारक, -कारिन् *a.* auspicious. -कार्यं any festive occasion, a religious or auspicious ceremony. -कालः an auspicious occasion; *S*. 4. -क्षौमं a silken cloth worn on occasions of festivity; R. 12. 8. -ग्रहः an auspicious planet. -घटः, -पात्रं a pot filled with water offered to the gods on festive occasions. -छायः the *plaksha* tree. -तूर्यं, -वाद्यं a musical instrument, such as a trumpet, drum &c., played on festive or auspicious occasions; R. 3. 20. -देवता an auspicious or tutelary deity. -पाठकः a bard, minstrel, professional panegyrist; आः दुरात्मन् वृथामंगलपाठक शैलूषापसद Ve. 1. -पुष्पं an auspicious flower. -प्रतिसरः, -सूत्रं 1 an auspicious cord or string, the auspicious thread worn by a married woman round her neck as long as her husband lives; अंत्रैः कल्पितमंगलप्रतिसराः (अंगनाः) Mâl. 5. 18. 2 the cord of an amulet. -प्रद *a.* auspicious. (-दा) turmeric. -प्रस्थः N. of a mountain.-मात्रभूषण *a.* decked in auspicious ornaments only, such as the auspicious thread, saffronmark &c. -वचस् *m.* -वादः a benedictory or congratulatory expression, benediction, blessing. -वाद्यं see मंगलतूर्य. -वारः-, -वासरः Tuesday. -विधिः a festive or auspicious rite. -शब्दः greeting, a benedictory expression. -सूत्र see मंगलप्रतिसर. -स्नानं solemn or auspicious ablution.

मंगलीय *a.* Auspicious, fortunate.

मंगल्य *a.* 1 Auspicious, fortunate, happy, lucky, prosperous; Ms. 2. 31. 2 Pleasing, agreeable, beautiful. 3 Holy, pure, pious; U. 4. 10. -ल्यः 1 The sacred fig-tree. 2 The cocoanut tree. 3 A sort of pulse. -ल्या 1 A species of fragrant sandal. 2 No. of Durgâ. 3 A kind of aloe-wood. 4 A particular perfume. 5 A particular yellow pigment. -ल्यं 1 Auspicious water for the coronation of a king (brought from various holy places). 2 Gold. 3 Sandal-wood. 4 Red lead. 5 Sour curds.

मंगल्यकः A kind of pulse (मसूर).

मंघ् I. 1 P. (मंघति) To adorn, decorate. -II. 1 A. (मंघते) 1 To cheat, deceive. 2 To begin. 3 To blame, censure. 4 To go, move quickly. 5 To start, set out.

मच् 1 A. (मचते) 1 To be wicked. 2 To cheat, deceive. 3 To boast. 4 To be vain or proud.

मचर्चिका A word used at the end of a noun to denote 'excellence' or 'the best of its kind'; as गोमचर्चिका an excellent cow or bull; cf. उद्ध.

मच्छः A fish (corrupted from मत्स्य).

मज्जन् *m.* 1 The marrow of the bones and flesh. The pith of plants. -Comp. -कृत् *n.* a bone. -समुद्भवः semen virile.

मज्जनं 1 Sinking, plunging, sinking under water, immersion. 2 Bathing, ablution; प्रत्ययमज्जनविशेषविविक्तकांतिः Ratn. 1. 21; R. 16. 57. 3 Drowning. 4 The marrow of the bones and flesh (=मज्जन.)

मज्जा 1 The marrow of the bones and flesh. 2 The pith of plants. -Comp. -जं semen virile. -रजस् *n.* 1 a particular hell. 2 bdellium. -रसः semen virile. -सारः a nutmeg.

मज्जूषा See मंजूषा.

मंच् 1 A. (मंचते) 1 To hold 2. To grow high or tall. 3 To go, move. 4 To shine. 5 To adore.

मंचः 1 A couch, bedstead, sofa, bed. 2 A raised seat, *dais*, a dlatfrom resting on columns, a seat of honour or state, throne तत्र मंचेषु मनोज्ञवेषान् R. 6. 1, 3 10. 3 An elevated shed in a field (for a watchman). 4 A pulpit.

मंचकं 1 A couch, bed, sofa. 2 A raised seat or platform. 3 A stan for holding fire. -**Comp.** -आश्रयः 'a bed-bug,' bug in general.

मंचिका 1 A chair. 2 A trough, tray.

मंजरं 1 A cluster of blossoms. 2 A pearl. 3 The plant *Tilaka*.

मंजरिः-री *f*. 1 A shoot, sprout, spring; निवपेः सहकारमंजरीः Ku. 4 38; सदृशकांतिरलक्ष्यत मंजरी R. 9. 44, 16. 51; so स्फुरतु कुचकुंभयोरुपरि मणिमंजरी Gît. 10; मुखं मुक्तारुचो धत्ते घर्माम्भःकणमंजरीः Kâv. 2. 71. 2 A cluster of blossoms. 3 A flower-bud. 4 A branching flower-stalk. 5 A (parallel) line or row. 6 A pearl. 7 A creeper. 8 The holy basil. 9 The plant *Tilaka*.-**Comp.**-चामरं a *Chowrie* in the form of a sprout, fan-like sprout; V. 4. 4. -नम्रः the plant called वेतस.

मंजरित *a*. 1 Furnished with or possessing clusters of blossoms. 2 Mounted on a stalk (as a bud).

मंजा 1 A she-goat. 2 A cluster of blossoms. 3 A creeper.

मंजिः-जी *f*. 1 A cluster of blossoms. 2 A creeper.-**Comp.**-फला the plantain tree

मंजिका A harlot, prostitute, courtezan.

मंजिमन् *m*. Beauty, loveliness.

मंजिष्ठा Bengal or Indian madder. -**Comp.** -मेहः a kind of urinary disease. -रागः 1 the colour of the Indian madder. 2 (fig.) attachment as charming and durable as the colour of the madder; *i. e.* durable or permanent attachment.

मंजीरः -रं An anklet or ornament for the foot (नूपुर); सिंजानमंजुमंजीरं प्रविवेश निकेतनं Gît. 11; or मुखरमधरिं त्यज मंजीरं रिपुमिवकेलिषु लोलं 5; Mâl. 1. -रं A post round which the string of the churning stick passes.

मंजीलः A village inhabited by washermen.

मंजु *a*. 1 Lovely, beautiful, charming, sweet, pleasing, agreeable, attracitve; स्खलदसमंजसमंजुजल्पितं ते (स्मरामि) U. 4. 4; अयि दलदरविंद स्यंदमानं मरंदं तव किमपि लिहंतो मंजु गुंजंतु भृंगाः Bv. 1. 5; तन्मंजु मंदहासितं श्वसितानि तानि 2. 5. -**Comp.** -केशिन् *m*. an epithet of Krishṇa. -गमन *a* having a lovely gait. (-ना) 1 a goose. 2 a flamingo. -गर्तः N. of the country called Nepâl. -गिर् *a*. sweet-voiced; पते मंजुगिरः शुकाः Kâv. 2. 9. -गुंजः a charming hum. -घोष *a*. uttering a sweet sound. -नाशी 1 a handsome woman. 2 an epithet of Durgâ. 3 of Sachî, wife of Indra. -पाठकः a parrot. -प्राणः an epithet of Brahmâ. -भाषिन्, -वाच् *a*. sweet-speaking; (गिरं अनुवदति शुकस्ते मंजुवाक् पंजरस्थः R. 5. 74, 12. 39. -वक्त्र *a*. having a beautiful face, handsome. -स्वन, -स्वर *a*. sweet-sounding.

मंजुल *a*. Lovely, beautiful, agreeable, charming, sweet, melodious (voice); संप्रति मंजुलवंजुलसीमनि केलिशयनमनुयातं Gît. 11; कूजितं राजहंसानां वर्धते. मदमंजुलं Kâv. 2. 334. -लः 1 A kind of gallinule. -लं 1 An arbour, bower. 2 A spring, well.

मंजूषा 1 A box, casket, chest, receptacle; मदीयपद्यरत्नानां मंजूषैषा मया कृता Bv. 4. 45. 2 A large basket, hamper. 3 Madder (= मंजिष्ठा) 4 A stone.

मटची, मटती Hail.

मटस्फटिः 'Beginning of pride', incipient pride.

मट्टकं The ridge of a roof.

मठ् 1 P. (मठति) 1 To dwell, inhabit. 2 To go. 3 To grind.

मठः -ठं 1 The hut of an ascetic, a small cell or room. 2 A monastery, convent. 3 A seminary, college, place of learning. 4 A temple. 5 A cart drawn by oxen. -ठी 1 A cell. 2 A cloister, convent. -**Comp.** -आयतनं a monastery, college.

मठर *a*. Intoxicated, drunk.

मठिका A small cell, a hut or cottage.

मड्डुः, मड्डुकः A kind of drum.

मण् 1 P. (मणति) To sound, murmur.

मणिः (said to be *f*. also, but rarely used) 1 A jewel, gem, precious stone; अलब्धशाणोत्कषणा नृपाणां न जातु मौलौ मणयो वसंति Bv. 1. 73; मणौ वज्रसमुत्कीर्णे सूत्रस्येवास्ति मे गतिः R. 1. 4, 3. 18. 2 An ornament in general. 3 Anything best of its kind; cf. रत्न. 4 A magnet, load-stone. 5 The wrist. 6 A water-pot. 7 Clitoris. 8 Glans-penis. (also written मणी in these senses). -**Comp.** -इंद्रः, -राजः a diamond. -कंठः the blue jay. -कंठकः a cock. -कर्णिका, -कर्णी N. of a sacred pool in Benares. -काचः the feathered part of an arrow. -काननं the neck. -कारः a lapidary, jeweller. -तारकः the crane or Sârasa bird. -दर्पणः a jewelled mirror. -द्वीपः 1 the hood of the serpent Ananta. 2 N. of a fabulous island in the ocean of nectar. -धनुः *m*., -धनुस् *n*. a rainbow. -पाली a female keeper of jewels. -पुष्पकः N. of the conch-shell of Sahadeva; Bg. 1. 16. -पूरः 1 the navel. 2 a kind of bodice richly adorned with jewels. (-रं) N. of a town in Kalinga. -बंधः 1 the wrist; S 7. 2 the fastening of jewels; R. 12.102. -बंधनं 1 fastening on of jewels, a string or ornament of pearls. 2 that part of a ring or bracelet where the jewels are set, collet; *S*. 6. 3 the wrist; *S*. 3. 13. -बीजः, -बीज: the pomegranate tree. -भित्तिः *f*. N. of the palace of *Sesha*. -भूः *f*. a floor set with jewels. -भूमिः *f*. 1 a mine of jewels. 2 a jewelled floor, floor inlaid with jewels. -मंथं rock-salt. -माला 1 a string or necklace of jewels. 2 lustre, splendour, beauty. 3 a circular impression left by a bite (in amorous sports). 4 N. of Lakshmî 5 N. of a metre. -यष्टिः *m*. *f*. a jewelled stick, a string of jewels. -रत्नं a jewel, gem. -रागः the colour of jewels. (-गं) vermilion. -शिला a jewelled slab. -सरः a necklace. -सूत्रं a string of pearls. -सोपानं a jewelled staircase. -स्तंभः a pillar inlaid with jewels. -हर्म्यं a jewelled or crystal palace.

मणिकः-कं A water-jar. -कः A jewel, gem.

मणितं An inarticulate murmuring sound uttered at cohabitation; *Si*. 10. 75.

मणिमत् *a*. Jewelled. -*m*. 1 The sun. 2 N of a mountain. 3 N. of a place of pilgrimage.

मणीचकः A king-fisher. -कं The moon-stone.

मणीवकं A flower.

मंठ् 1 A. (मंठते) 1 To long for. 2 To remember with regret, think of sorrowfully.

मंठः A kind of baked sweetmeat.

मंड् I. 1. P., 10 U. (मंडति, मंडयति-ते, मंडित) 1 To adorn, decorate; प्रभवति मंडयितुं वधूरनंगः Ki. 10. 59; Bk. 10. 23. 2 To rejoice. -II. 1 A. (मंडते) 1 To clothe, dress. 2 To surround, encompass. 3 To distribute, divide.

मंडः -डं 1 The thick oily matter or scum forming on the surface of any liquid. 2 The scum of boiled rice; नवीवारौदनमंडमुष्णमधुरं U. 4. 1. 3 Cream (of milk). 4 Foam, froth or scum in general. 5 Ferment. 6 Gruel. 7 Pith, essence. 8 The head. -डः 1 An ornament, decoration. 2 A frog. 3 The castor-oil tree. -डा 1 Spirituous liquor. 2 The emblic myrobalan tree.-**Comp**. -उदकं 1 barm. 2 decorating walls, floors &c. on festive occasions. 3 mental agitation or excitement. -प *a*. drinking scum or cream. -हारकः a distiller of spirits &c.

मंडकः 1 A kind of baked flour. 2 A very thin kind of cake (Mar. मांडे.)

मंडनं 1 The act of decorating or ornamenting, adorning; माम क्षमं मंडनकालहानेः R. 13. 16; मंडनविधिः *S*. 6. 5. 2 An ornament, decoration, embellishment; सा मंडनान्मडनमन्वभुंक्त Ku. 7. 5; Ki. 8. 40; R. 8. 71. -नः (or मंडनमिश्रः) N. of a philosopher who is said to have been defeated in controversy by Sankarâchârya.

मंडपः 1 A temporary hall erected on ceremonial occasions, an open hall; विवाहमंडप. 2 A tent, pavilion; R.

5. 73. 3 An arbour, bower; as in लतामंडप Me. 78. 4 A building consecrated to a deity. -Comp. -प्रतिष्ठा the consecration of a temple.

मंडयंतः 1 An ornament, decoration. 2 An actor. 3 Food. 4 An assembly of women. -ती A woman.

मंडरी A kind of cricket.

मंडल *a*. Round, circular. -लः 1 A circular array of troops. 2 A dog. 3 A kind of snake. -लं 1 A circular orb, globe, wheel, ring, circumference, any thing round or circular; करालफणमंडलं R. 12. 98; आदर्शमंडलनिभानि समुल्लसंति Ki. 5. 41; स्फुरत्प्रभामंडलया चकाशे Ku. 1. 24; so रेणुमंडल, छायामंडल, चापमंडल, मुखमंडल, स्तनमंडल &c. 2 The charmed circle (drawn by a conjurer); Mu. 2. 1. 3 A disc, especially of the sun or moon; अपर्वणि ग्रहकलुषेंदुमंडला (विभावरी) M. 4. 15; दिनमणिमंडलमंडन भयखंडन ए Gît. 1. 4 The halo round the sun or moon. 5 The path or orbit of a heavenly body. 6 A multitude, group, collection, assemblage, troop, company; एवं मिलितेन कुमारमंडलेन Dk.; अखिलं चारिमंडलं R. 4. 4. 7 Society, association. 8 A great circle. 9 The visible horizon. 10 A district or province. 11 A surrounding district or territory. 12 (In politics) The circle of a king's near and distant neighbours; उपगतोऽपि च मंडलनाभितां &c. R. 9. 15. (According to Kāmandaka quoted by Malli. the circle of a king's near and distant neighbours consists of twelve kings:-विजिगीषु or the central monarch, the five kings whose dominions are in the front, and the four kings whose dominions are in the rear of his kingdoms, the मध्यम or intermediate, and उदासीन or indifferent king. The kings in the front as well as in the rear are designated by particular names; see Malli. *ad loc*.; cf. also Śi. 2. 81 and Malli. thereon. According to some the number of such kings is four, six, eight, twelve or even more; see Mit. on Y. 1. 345. According to others, the circle consists of three kings only:—the प्राकृतारि or natural enemy, (the sovereign of an adjacent country), the प्राकृतमित्र natural ally, (the sovereign whose dominions are separated by those of another from the country of the central monarch with whom he is allied) and प्राकृतोदासीन or the nautral neutral the sovereign whose dominion lie beyond those of the natural ally). 13 A particular position of the feet in shooting. 14 A kind of mystical diagram used in invoking a divinity. 15 A division of the Ṛigveda (the whole collection being divided into 10 Mandalas or eight Ashṭakas). 16 A kind of leprosy with round spots. 17 A kind of perfume. -ली A circle, group, assemblage. (मंडलीकृ means 'to form into a ring or circle', 'to coil'; 'मंडलीभू' 'to form a circle'). -Comp. -अग्रः a bent or crooked sword, scimitar. -अधिपः, अधीशः -ईशः, -ईश्वरः 1 the ruler of governor of a district or province. 2 a king, sovereign. -आवृत्तिः *f*. circular movement; U. 3. 19. -कार्मुक *a*. having a circular bow. -नृत्यं a circular dance, dance in a ring. -न्यासः describing a circle. -पुच्छकः a kind of insect. -वटः the fig-tree forming a circle. -वर्तिन् *m*. a ruler of a small province. -वर्षः rain over the whole of a king's territory, general rainfall.

मंडलकं 1 A circle. 2 A disc. 3 A district, province. 4 A group, collection. 5 A circular array of troops. 6 A White leprosy with round spots. 7 A mirror.

मंडलयति Den. P. To make round or circular.

मंडलायित *a*. Round, circular. -तं A ball, globe.

मंडलित *a*. Rounded, made round or circular.

मंडलिन् *a*. 1 Forming a circle, made up into a coil. 2 Ruling a country. —*m*. 1 A particular kind of snake. 2 A snake in general. 3 A cat. 4 The pole-cat. 5 A dog. 6 The sun. 7 The fig-tree. 8 The ruler of a province.

मंडित *p. p*. Adorned, decorated.

मंडूकः A frog; निपानमिव मंडूकाः सरोवरं नरमायांति विवशाः सर्वसंपदः Subhash.—कं A kind of coitus or mode of sexual enjoyment. —की 1 A female frog 2 A wanton or unchaste woman. 3 N. of several plants. -Comp. -अनुवृत्तिः -प्लुतिः *f*. 'the leap of a frog', skipping over or omitting at intervals; (in grammar the word is used to denote the skipping of several Sûtras and supplying from a previous Sútra); क्रियाग्रहणं मंडूकप्लुत्यानुवर्तते Sk. -कुलं a collection of frogs. -योगः a kind of abstract meditation in which the person who meditates sits motionless like a frog. -सरस् *n*. a pond full of frogs.

मंडूरं Rust of iron, dross (used as a tonic).

मत *p. p*. 1 Thought, believed, supposed. 2 Considered, regarded, deemed, looked upon. 3 Esteemed, honoured, respected; R. 2. 16. 8. 8. 4 Commended, valued. 5 Conjectured, guessed. 6 Meditated upon, thought of, perceived, recognised. 7 Thought out. 8 Intended, aimed at. 9 Approved, sanctioned (see मन्). -तं A thought, idea, opinion, belief, view; निश्चितं मतमुत्तमं Bg. 18. 6; केषांचिन्मतेन &c. 2 Doctrine, tenet; creed, religious belief; ये मे मतमिदं नित्यमनुतिष्ठंति मानवाः Bg. 3. 31. 3 Advice, instruction, counsel. 4 Aim, design, intention, purpose. 5 Approbation, sanction, commendation. -Comp. -अक्ष *a*. well-versed in playing at dice. -अंतरं 1 a different view. 2 a different creed. -अवलंबनं adopting or holding a particular opinion.

मतंगः 1 An elephant. 2 A cloud. 3 N. of a sage; R. 5. 53.

मतंगजः An elephant; न हि कमलिनीं दृष्ट्वा ग्राहमवेक्षते मतंगजः M. 3; Ki. 5. 47; R. 12. 73.

मतल्लिका A word used at the end of nouns to denote 'excellence or anything best of its kind'; गोमतल्लिका 'an excellent cow'; cf. उद्ध.

मतल्ली See मतल्लिका.

मतिः *f*. 1 Intellect, understanding, sense, knowledge, judgment; मतिरेव बलाद्गरीयसी H. 2. 86; अल्पविषया मतिः R. 1. 2. 2 Mind, heart; मम तु मतिर्न मनागपैतु धर्मात् Bv. 4. 26; so दुर्मति, सुमति. 3 Thought, idea, belief, opinion, notion, supposition, impression, view; विधिरहो बलवानिति मे मतिः Bh. 2. 91; Bg. 18. 78. 4 Intention, design, purpose; see मत्या. 5 Resolution, determination. 6 Esteem, regard, respect; Ki. 10. 9. 7 Wish, desire, inclination; प्रायोपवेशनमतिर्नृपतिर्बभूव R. 8. 94. 8 Counsel, advice. 9 Remembrance, recollection; (मतिं कृ, -धा, -आधा 'to set the heart on', 'resolve upon', 'think of'. मत्या is used adverbially in the sense of 1 knowingly, intentionally, wilfully; मत्या भुक्त्वाचरेत् कृच्छ्रं Ms. 4. 223, 5. 19. 2 under the impression that; व्याघ्रमत्या पलायते). -Comp. -ईश्वरः an epithet of Visvakarman. -गर्भ *a*. full of intelligence, intelligent, clever. -द्वैधं difference of opinion. -निश्चयः a settled belief, firm conviction.-पूर्व *a*. intentional, wilful.-पूर्वं,-पूर्वकं *ind*. purposely, intentionally, wilfully, willingly. -प्रकर्षः superiority of intellect, cleverness. -भेदः change of views. -भ्रमः, -विपर्यासः 1 delusion, mental illusion, confusion of mind; Ś. 6. 9. 2 an error, a mistake, misapprehension. -विभ्रमः, विभ्रंशः confusion or infatuation of mind, madness, frenzy. -शालिन् *a*. intelligent, clever.-हीन *a*. stupid, senseless, foolish.

मत्क *a*. My, mine; संशृणुष्व कपे मत्कैः संगच्छस्व वनैः शुभैः Bk. 8. 16. -त्कः A bug.

मत्कुणः 1 A bug; मत्कुणाविव पुरापरिप्लवौ Śi. 14. 68. 2 An elephant without tusks. 3 A small elephant. 4 A beardless man. 5 A buffalo. 6 The cocoa-nut tree.-णं An armour for the legs or the thighs. –Comp. –अरिः hemp.

मत्त *p. p.* 1 Intoxicated, drunk, inebriated (fig. also); ज्योत्स्नापानमदालसेन वपुषा मत्ताश्चकोरांगनाः Vb. 1. 11; प्रभामत्तश्चंद्रो जगदिदमहो विभ्रमयति K. P. 10; so ऐश्वर्य°, धन° बल°, &c. 2 Mad, insane. 3 In rut, furious (as an elephant); R. 12. 93. 4 Proud, arrogant. 5 Delighted, overjoyed, excited with joy. 6 Amorous, sportive, wanton. –त्तः 1 A drunkard. 2 A mad man. 3 An elephant in rut. 4 A cuckoo. 5 A buffalo. 6 The thorn-apple or Dhattûra plant. –Comp. –आलंबः a fence round a large building (as of a rich man). –इभः an elephant in rut. °गमना a woman having the gait of an elephant in rut; *i. e.* with a lounging gait. –काशि(सि)नी a handsome and very fascinating woman. –दंतिन् *m.*, –नागः, –वारणः an elephant in rut. (–णः, –णं) 1 a fence round a large building or mansion. 2 a turret or small room on the top of a large building. 3 a veranda. 4 a pavilion. (–णं) pounded betel-nuts.

मत्यं 1 A harrow. 2 The means of acquiring knowledge. 3 The exercise of knowledge.

मत्सः 1 A fish. 2 A lord of the Matsyas.

मत्सर *a.* 1 Jealous, envious. 2 Insatiate, greedy, covetous. 3 Niggardly. 4 Wicked. –रः 1 Envy, jealousy; अदत्तावकाशो मत्सरस्य K. 45; परवृद्धिषु बद्धमत्सराणां Ki. 13. 7; Si. 9. 63; Ku. 5. 17. 2 Hostility, enmity; R. 3. 60. 3 Pride; Si. 8. 71. 4 Covetousness, greediness. 5 Anger, passion. 6 A gnat or mosquito.

मत्सरिन् *a.* 1 Envious, jealous; परवृद्धिमत्सरि मनो हि मानिनां Si. 15. 1; 2. 115; दुष्टात्मा परगुणमत्सरी मनुष्यः Mk. 9. 27; R. 18. 19. 2 Hostile, inimical. 3 Greedy after, selfishly addicted to (with loc.). 4 Wicked.

मत्स्यः 1 A fish; शूले मत्स्यानिवापक्ष्यन् दुर्बलान्बलवत्तराः Ms. 7. 20. 2 A particular variety of fish. 3 A king of the Matsyas. –त्स्यौ (dual) The sign *Pisces* of the zodiac. –त्स्याः (pl.) N. of a country and its inhabitants; Ms. 2. 19; Y. 1. 83. Comp. –अक्षका, अक्षी N. of a kind of Soma plant.–अद्, -अदन आद *a.* feeding on fish; fish-eater. –अवतारः the first of the ten incarnations of Vishṇu; (during the reign of the seventh Manu, the whole earth, which had become corrupt, was swept away by a flood, and all living beings perished except the pious Manu and the seven sages who were saved by Vishṇu in the form of a fish); cf. Jayadeva's description of this Avatâra; प्रलय पयोधिजले धृतवानासि वेदं विहितवहित्रचरित्रमखेदं केशव धृतमीनशरीर जय जगदीश हरे Gît. 1. –अशनः 1 a king- fisher. 2 one who eats fish. असुरः N. of a demon. –आधानी, –धानी a fishbasket (used by fishermen.) –उदारिन् *m.*an epithet of Virâta. –उदरी an epithet of Satyavatî. –उदरीयः an epithet of Vyâsa –उपजीविन् *m.* –आजीवः a fisherman. –करंडिका a fish-basket. –गंध *a.* having the smell of fish. (–धा) N. of Satyavatî. –घंटः a kind of fish-sauce. –घातिन्, जीवत्, जीविन् *m.* a fisherman. –जालं a fishing. net.–देशः the country of the Matsyas. –नारी an eptithet of Satyavatî. –नाशकः –नाशनः an ospray. पुराणं N. of one of the eighteen Purâṇas. –बंधः, –बंधिन् *m.* a fisherman. –बंधनं a fish-hook, an angle. –बंध(धि)नी a fish-basket. –रंकः, –रंगः, –रंगकः a halcyons, king-fisher. –वेधनं, –वेधनी an angle- –संघातः a shoal of fish. मत्स्यंडिका, मत्स्यंडी Coarse or unrefined sugar; ही ही इयं :सीधुपानोद्वेजितस्य मत्स्यंडिकोपनता M. 3.

मथ् See मंथ्.

मथ–माथ q. v.

मथन *a.* (नी *f.*) 1 Churning, stirring, up. 2 Hurting, injuring. 3 Killing, destroying a destroyer; मुग्धे मधुमथनमनुगतमनुसर राधिके Gît. 2 –नः N. of a tree. –नं 1 Churning, stirring round, agitating. 2 Rubbing, friction. 3 Injury, hurting, destruction –Comp. -अचलः,-पर्वतः –the,mountain Mandara used as churning-stick.

माथिः A churning-stick.

मथित *p. p.* 1 Churned, stirred round, agitated, shaken about. 2 Crushed, ground, pinched. 3 Afflicted, distressed, oppressed. 4 Killed, destroyed. 5 Dislocated; (see मंथ्.) –तं Pure butter-milk (without water.)

मथिन् *m.* (Nom. sing. मथाः, acc. pl. मथः) 1 A churning-stick; मुहुः प्रणुन्नेषु मथां विवर्तनैर्नदत्सु कुंभेषु मृदंगमंथरं Ki. 4. 16; N. 22. 44. 2 Wind. 3 A thunder bolt. 4 The penis.

मथु(थू)रा N. of an ancient town situated on the right bank of the Yamunâ, the birth-place of Krishṇa and the scene of his amours and exploits; it is one of the seven sacred cities in India (see अवंति), and is, to this day, the favourite resort of thousands of devotees. It is said to have been founded by Satrughna; निर्ममे निर्ममोऽर्थेषु मथुरां मथुराकृतिः R. 15. 28; कलिंदकन्या मथुरां गतापि गंगोर्मिसंसक्तजलेव भाति 6. 48. –Comp. –ईशः, -नाथः epithets of Krishṇa.

मद् A form of the first personal pronoun in the singular number used chiefly at the beginning of comps.; as मदर्थे 'for me', 'for my sake'; मच्चित thinking of me'; मद्वचनं, मत्संदेशः, मत्प्रियं &c. &c.

मद् I. 4 P. (माद्यति, मत्त) 1 To be drunk or intoxicated; वीक्ष्य मद्यमितरा तु ममाद Si. 10. 27. 2 To be mad. 3 To revel or delight in. 4 To be glad or rejoiced. –*Caus.* (मादयति) 1 To intoxicate; inebriate, madden. 2 ('मदयति) To exhilarate, gladden, delight; Mâl. 1. 36. 3 To inflame with passion; Mâl. 3. 6. –WITH उद् 1 to be drunk or intoxicated; (fig. also). 2 to be mad; Ms. 3. 161. (–*Caus.*) to intoxicate or inebriate; अद्यापि मे हृदयमुन्मदयंति हंत Bv. 2. 5. –प्र 1 to be intoxicated or drunk. 2 to be careless about, to be negligent or heedless (with loc.); अतोऽर्थान्न प्रमाद्यंति प्रमदासु विपश्चितः Ms. 2. 213. 3 to omit to do, swerve or deviate from; as in स्वाधिकारात्प्रमत्तः Me. 1. 4 to make a mistake, to err, go astray; Bk. 5. 8, 17. 39; 18. 8. –सं 1 to be intoxicated 2 to rejoice, be glad.–II. 10 A. (मादयते) To please, gratify.

मदः 1 Intoxication, drunkenness, inebriety; मदेनास्पृश्ये Dk.; मदविकाराणां दर्शकः K. 45, see comps. below. 2 Madness, insanity. 3 Ardent passion, wanton or lustful passion, lasciviousness, lust; इति मदमदनाभ्यां रागिणः स्पष्टरागान् Si. 10. 91. 4 Rut, ichor or the juice that exudes from the temples of an elephant in rut; मदेन भाति कलभः प्रतापेन महीपतिः Chandr. 5. 45; so see मदकल; मदोन्मत्त; Me. 20, R. 2. 7; 12. 102. 5 Love, desire, ardour. 6 Pride, arrogance, conceit; Pt. 1. 240. 7 Rapture, excessive delight. 8 Spirituous liquor. 9 Honey. 10 Musk. 11 Semen virile. –Comp. –अत्ययः, -आतंकः any distemper (such as head-ache) resulting from drunkenness. –अंधः *a.* 1 blinded by intoxication, dead drunk, drunk with passion; अधरमिव मदांधा पातुमेषा प्रवृत्ता V. 4. 13. 2 blinded by pride, arrogant. –अपनयनं removal of intoxication. –अंबरः 1 an elephant in rut. 2 N. of Airâvat, the elephant of Indra. –अलस *a.* languid with passion or intoxication. –अवस्था 1 a state of drunkenness. 2 wantonness, lustfulness. 3 rut, being in rut; R. 2. 7. –आकुल *a.* furious with rut. –आढ्य *a.* drunk, intoxicated. (–ढ्यः) the palm tree. –आम्नातः a kettle-drum carried on the back of an elephant. –आलापिन् *m.* a cuckoo. –आह्वः musk. –उत्कट *a.* 1 intoxicated, excited by drink. 2 furious with passion, lustful. 3 arrogant, proud, haughty. 4 ruttish, under the influence of rut; R. 6. 7. (–टः) 1 an elephant in rut. 2 a dove. (–टा) spirituous liquor. –उदग्र, उन्मत्त *a.* 1 drunk, intoxicated. 2 furious, drunk with passion; मदोदग्राः ककुद्मंतः सरितां कूलमुद्रुजाः R. 4. 22. 3 arrogant, proud, haughty. –उद्धत *a.* 1 drun

with passion; Ku. 3. 31. **2** inflated **with** pride. **–उल्लापिन्** *m.* the cuckoo. **–कर** *a.* intoxicating, causing intoxication. **–करिन्** *m.* an elephant in rut. **–कल** *a.* speaking softly or inarticulately, speaking indistinctly; R. 9. 37. **2** uttering low sounds of love. **3** drunk with passion: U. 1. 31; Mâl. 9. 14. **4** indistinct yet sweet; मदकलं कूजितं सारसानां Me. 31. **5** ruttish, furious, under the influence of rut, V. 4. 24. (**–लः**) an elephant in rut. **–कोहलः** a bull set at liberty (to roam at will). **–खेल** *a.* stately or sportive through passion, V. 4. 16. **–गंधा 1** an intoxicating drink. **2** hemp. **–गमनः** a buffalo. **–च्युत्** *a.* **1** distilling rut (as an elephant). **2** lustful, wanton, drunk. **3** gladdening, exhilarating. (*–m.*) an epithet of Indra. **–जलं,–वारि** *n.* rutting juice, ichor exuding from the temples of a ruttish elephant. **–ज्वरः** fever of pride or passion; Bh. 3. 23. **–द्विपः** a furious elephant, an elephant in rut. **–प्रयोगः, –प्रसेकः, –प्रस्रवणं, –स्रावः, –स्रुतिः** *f.* the exudation of ichor or rutting juice from the temples of an elephant. **–मुच्** *a.* 'dropping down ichor', furious, intoxicated; U. 3. 15. **–रक्त** *a.* affected with passion. **–रागः 1** Cupid. **2** a cock. **3** a drunkard. **–विक्षिप्त** *a.* **1** in rut, furious. **2** agitated by lust or passion. **–विह्वल** *a.* **1** maddened by lust or pride. **2** stupefied with intoxication. **–वृंदः** an elephant. **–शौंडकं** nutmeg. **–सारः** a cotton shrub. **–स्थलं, –स्थानं** an ale-house, a dram-shop, tavern.

मदन *a.* (**नी** *f.*) **1** Intoxicating, maddening. **2** Delighting, exhilarating. **–नः 1** The god of love, Cupid; व्यापाररोधि मदनस्य निषेवितव्यं *S.* 1. 27; हतमपि निहंत्येव मदनः Bh. 3. 18. **2** Love, passion, sexual love, lust; विनयवारितवृत्तिरतस्तया न विवृतो मदनो न च संवृतः *S.* 2. 11; सतंत्रिगीतं मदनस्य दीपकं Rs. 1. 3, R. 5. 63; so मदनातुर, मदनपीडित &c. **3** The spring season. **4** A bee. **5** Bees'-wax. **6** A kind of embrace. **7** The Dhattûra plant. **8** The Bakula tree. **–ना,–नी 1** Spirituous liquor. **2** Musk. **3** The *atimukta* creeper (**–नी** only in these two senses). **–नं 1** Intoxicating. **2** Gladdening, delighting. **–Comp. –अग्रकः** a species of grain (कोद्रव). **–अंकुशः 1** the penis. **2** a fingernail, or a wound inflicted by it in cohabitation. **–अंतकः, –अरिः, –दमनः, –दहनः, –नाशनः, –रिपुः** epithets of *S*iva. **–अवस्थ** *a.* in love, enamoured. **–आतुर, –आर्त, –क्लिष्ट, –पीडित** *a.* afflicted by love, smit with love, love-sick; R. 12. 32, *S.* 3 10. **–आयुधं 1** pudendum muliebre. **2** 'Cupid's missile', said of a very lovely woman. **–आलयः–यं 1** pudendum muliebre. **2** a lotus. **3** a king. **–इच्छाफलं** a kind of mango. **–उत्सवः** the vernal festival celebrated in honour of Cupid. (**–वा**) an *apsaras.* **–उत्सुक** *a.* pining or languid with love. **–उद्यानं** 'a pleasuregarden', N. of a garden. **–कंटकः 1** erection of hair caused by the feeling of love. **2** N. of a tree. **–कलहः** 'love's quarrel', sexual union, °छेदसुलभां Mâl. 2. 12. **–काकुरवः** a dove or pigeon. **–गोपालः** an epithet of Krishṇa. **–चतुर्दशी** the fourteenth day in the bright half of Chaitra, or the festival celebrated on that day in honour of Cupid. **–त्रयोदशी** the thirteenth day in the bright half of Chaitra, or the festival celebrated on that day in honour of Cupid. **–नालिका** a faithless wife. **–पक्षिन्** *m.* the Khanjana bird. **–पाठकः** the cuckoo. **–पीडा,–बाधा** pangs or torments of love. **–महोत्सवः** a festival celebrated in honour of Cupid. **मोहनः** an epithet of Krishṇa. **–ललितं** amorous sport or dalliance. **–लेखः** a love-letter. **–वश** *a.* influenced by love enamoured. **–शलाका 1** the female of the cuckoo. **2** an aphrodisiac.

मदनकः N. of a plant (दमनक).

मदयंतिका, मदयंती A kind of Jasmine (Arabian).

मदयित्नु *a.* 1 Intoxicating, maddening. 2 Gladdening. **–त्नुः 1** The god of love. **2** A cloud. **3** A distiller of spirituous liquors. **4** A drunken man. **5** Spirituous liquor (*n.* also in this sense).

मदारः 1 An elephant in rut. **2** A hog. **3** A thorn-apple or Dhattûra. **4** A lover, libertine. **5** A kind of perfume. **6** A cheat or rogue (?).

मदिः *f.* A kind of roller or harrow.

मदिर *a.* **1** Intoxicating, maddening. **2** Delighting, fascinating, gladdening (eyes &c.) **–रः** A kind of Khadira tree (red-flowered). –Comp. **–अक्षी, –ईक्षणा, –नयना, –लोचना** a woman with fascinating or bewitching eyes; मधुकर मदिराक्ष्याः शंस तस्याः प्रवृत्तिं V 4. 22; R. 8. 68. **–आयतनयन** *a.* having long and fascinating eyes; *S.* 3. 5. **–आसवः** an intoxicating drink.

मदिरा 1 Spirituous liquor; कांक्षत्यन्यो वदनमदिरां दोहदच्छद्मनास्याः Me. 78; *S*i. 11. 49. **2** A kind of wag-tail. **3** N. of Durgâ. –Comp. **–उत्कट, –उन्मत्त** *a.* intoxicated with spirituous liquor. **–गृहं, –शाला** an ale-house, dram-house, a tavern. **–सखः** the mango tree.

मदिष्ठा Spirituous liquor.

मदीय *a.* My, mine, belonging to me; R. 2. 45, 65, 5. 25.

मद्गुः A kind of aquatic bird, a cormorant or diver. **2** A kind of snake. **3** A kind of wild animal. **4** A kind of galley or vessel of war; कोपि मद्गुरस्यधावत् Dk. **5** N. of a degraded mixed tribe, the offspring of a Brâhmaṇa by a woman of the bard class; see Ms. 10. 48. **6** An outcast.

मद्गुरः 1 A diver, pearl-fisher. **2** A kind of sheat-fish. **3** N. of a degraded mixed tribe; see मद्गु (5).

मद्य *a.* 1 Intoxicating. **2** Gladdening, exhilarating. **–द्यं** Spirituous liquor, wine, any intoxicating drink; रणक्षितिः शोणितमद्यकुल्या R. 7. 49; Ms. 5. 56, 9. 84, 10. 89. **–Comp. –आमोदः** the *Bakula* tree. **–कीटः** a kind of insect. **–द्रुमः** a kind of tree (माडवृक्ष). **–पः** a drunkard, tippler, sot. **–पानं 1** drinking intoxicating liquor. **2** any intoxicating drink. **–पीत** *a.* intoxicated with drink. **–पुष्पा** the plant called Dhâtakî. **–बीज(वीज)जं** a drug used to cause fermentation, leaven. **–भाजनं** a wine-glass; so **मद्यभांडं**. **–मंडः** barm, yeast. **–वासिनी** the plant called धातकी. **–संधानं** distillation of spirit.

मद्रः 1 N. of a country. **2** A ruler of that country. **–द्राः** (pl.) The inhabitants of Madra. **–द्रं** Joy, happiness. (**मद्राकृ = भद्राकृ** 'to shave or shear'). **–Comp. –कार** *a.* (also **मद्रंकार**) producing delight.

मद्रकः A ruler or inhabitant of Madra. **–काः** (pl.) N. of a degraded tribe in the south.

मधव्यः The month called Vaisákha.

मधु *a.* (**धु** or **ध्वी** *f.*) Sweet, pleasant, agreeable, delightful. *–n.* (**धु**) **1** Honey; पतास्तामधुनो धाराश्चोतंति सविषास्त्वयि U. 3. 34; मधु तिष्ठति जिह्वाग्रे हृदये तु हलाहलम्. **2** The juice or nectar of flowers; Ku. 3. 36; देहि मुखकमलमधुपानं Gît. 10. **3** A sweet intoxicating drink, wine, spirituous liquor; विनयंते स्म तद्योधा मधुभिर्विजयश्रमं R. 4. 65; Rs. 1. 3. **4** Water. **5** Sugar. **6** Sweetness. *–m.* (**–धुः**) **1** The spring or vernal season; क्व नु हृदयंगमः सखा कुसुमायोजितकार्मुको मधुः Ku. 4. 24, 25; 3. 10, 30. **2** The month of Chaitra; भास्करस्य मधुमाधवाविव R. 11. 7; मासि मधौ मधुरकोकिलभृंगनादै रामा हरंति हृदयं प्रसभं नराणां Rs. 6. 24. **3** N. of a demon killed by Vishṇu. **4** N. of another demon, father of Lavaṇa and killed by *S*atrughna. **5** The Asoka tree. **6** N. of king Kártavîrya. **–Comp. –अष्ठीला** a lump of honey, clotted honey. **–आधारः** wax. **–आपात** *a.* having honey at the first taste; Ms. 11. 9. **–आम्रः** a kind of mango tree. **–आसवः** sweet spirituous liquor (made from honey). **–आस्वाद** *a.* having the taste of honey. **–आहुतिः** *f.* a sacrificial offering of sweet things. **–उच्छिष्टं, –उत्थं, –उत्थितं** bees' wax. **–उत्सवः** the spring or vernal festival. **–उदकं** 'honey-water', water mixed with honey, hydromel. **–उद्यानं** a spring-garden. **–उपघ्नं** 'the abode of Madhu,' an epithet of Mathurá; R. 15. 15. -कंठः the cuckoo. -करः 1 a large black bee; कुटजे खलु तेनेहा तेने हा मधुकरेण कथं Bv. 1. 10; R. 9. 30; Me. 35, 47. 2 a lover, libertine. °गणः, °श्रेणिः *f.* a swarm of bees. -कर्कटी 1 sweet lime, a kind of citron. 2 a kind of date. -काननं, वनं the forest of the demon Madhu. -कारः,-कारिन् *m.* a bee. -कुक्कुटिका, कुक्कुटी a sort of citron tree. -कुल्या a stream of honey. -कृत् *m.* a bee. -केशटः a bee. -कोशः, -षः a bee-hive. -क्रमः a bee-hive. (pl.). drinking-bout, carousals. -क्षीरः, क्षीरकः a Kharjûra tree. -गायनः the cuckoo. -ग्रहः a libation of honey. -घोषः the cuckoo. -जं bees'-wax. -जा 1 sugar-candy. 2 the earth. -जंबीरः a kind of citron. -जित्, -द्विष्, -निषूदनः, -निहतृ *m.*, -मथः, -मथनः, -रिपुः, -शत्रुः, -सूदनः epithets of Vishṇu; इति मधुरिपुणा सखी नियुक्ता Gît. 5; R. 9. 48; *Si.* 15. 1. -तृणः-णं sugar-cane. -त्रयं the three sweet things; *i. e.* sugar, honey, and clarrified butter. -दीपः the god of love. -दूतः the mango tree. -दोहः the extracting of sweetness or honey. -द्रुः 1 a bee. 2 a libertine. -द्रवः N. of a tree having red blossoms. -द्रुमः the mango tree. -धातुः a kind of yellow pyrites. -धारा a stream of honey. -धूलिः molasses. -नालिकेरकः a kind of cocoanut. -नेतृ *m.* a bee. -पः a bee or a drunkard; राजप्रियाः कैरविण्यौ रमंते मधुपैः सह Bv. 1. 126, 1. 63. (where both meanings are intended). -पटलं a beehive. -पतिः an epithet of Kṛishṇa. -पर्कः 'a mixture of honey', a respectful offering made to a guest or to the bridegroom on his arrival at the door of the father of the bride; its usual ingredients are five:—दधि सर्पिर्जलं क्षौद्रं सिता चैतैश्च पंचभिः | प्रोच्यते मधुपर्कः; समांसो मधुपर्कः U. 4; असिस्वदद्यन्मधुपर्कमर्पितं स तद् व्यधात्तर्कसुदर्कदर्शिनाम्। यदेष पास्यन्मधु भीमजाधरं मिषेण पुण्याहविधिं तदा कृतं N. 16. 13; Ms. 3. 119 *et seq.* -पर्क्य *a.* worthy of *madhuparka* q. v. -पर्णिका, -पर्णी the Indigo plant. -पायिन् *m.* a bee. -पुरं, -री an epithet of Mathurâ; संप्रत्युज्झितवासनं मधुपुरी मध्ये हरिः सेव्यते Bv. 4. 44. -पुष्पः 1 the Asoka tree. 2 the Bakula tree. 3 the Dantî tree. 4 the Sirîsha tree. -प्रणयः addiction to wine. -प्रमेहः diabetes, saccharine urine. -प्राशनं one of the sixteen purificatory Saṃskâras (which consists in putting a little honey into the mouth of a new-born male-child). -प्रियः an epithet of Balaráma. -फलः a kind of cocoa-nut. -फलिका a kind of date. -बहुला the Mádhavî creeper. -बी(वी)जः a pomegranate tree. -बी(वी)जपुरः a kind of citron. -मक्षः -क्षा, -माक्षिका a bee. -मज्जनः the reet called आखोट. -मदः the intoxication of liquor. -मल्लिः -ल्ली *f.* the Málatî creeper. -माधवी 1 a kind of intoxicating drink. 2 any springflower. -माध्वीकं a kind of intoxicating liquor. -मारकः a bee. -मेहः =मधुप्रमेह q. v. -यष्टिः *f.* sugar-cane. -रसः 1 the wine-palm. 2 sugar-cane. 3 sweetness. (-सा) 1 a bunch of grapes 2 vine. -लग्नः N. of a tree. -लिह्, -लेह् -लेहिन् *m.* -लोलुपः, a bee; so मधुनोलेहः -वनं N. of the forest inhabited by the demon Madhu where *S*atrughna founded Mathurá. (-नः) the cuckoo. -वाराः (*m.* pl.) drinking often and often, tippling, carousing जज्ञिरे बहुमताः प्रमदानामोष्ठयावकनुदो मधुवाराः Ki. 8. 59; क्षालितं नु शमितं नु वधूनां द्रावितं नु हृदयं मधुवारैः Si. 10. 14; sometimes in the sing. also; see Ki. 8. 57. -व्रतः a bee; मार्मिकः को मरंदानामंतरेण मधुव्रतं Bv. 1. 117; तस्मिन्नद्य मधुव्रते विधिवशान्माध्वीकमाकांक्षति 46. -शर्करा honey-sugar. -शाखः a kind of tree. -शिष्टं -शेषं wax. -सखः, -सहायः, -सारथिः, -सुहृद् *m.* the god of love. -सिक्थकः a kind of poison. -सूदनः a bee. -स्थानं a bee-hive. -स्वरः the cuckoo. -हन् *m.* 1 a destroyer or collector of honey. 2 a kind of bird of prey. 3 a sooth-sayer. 4 an epithet of Vishṇu.

मधुकः 1 N. of a tree (=मधूक q. v.) 2 The Asoka tree. 3 A kind of bird. —कं 1 Tin. 2 Liquorice.

मधुर *a.* 1 Sweet. 2 Honied, mellifluous. 3 Pleasant, charming, attractive, agreeable; अहो मधुरमासां दर्शनं *S.* 1; Ku. 5. 9; U. 1.20. 4 Melodious (as a sound). -रः 1 The red sugar-cane. 2 Rice. 3 A kind of sugar, molasses (गुड). 4 A kind of mango. -रं 1 Sweetness. 2 A sweet drink, syrup. 3 Poison. 4 Tin. -रं *ind.* Sweetly, pleasantly, agreeably. -Comp. -अक्षर *a.* sounding sweetly, uttering sweet sounds, melodious -आलाप *a.* uttering sweet sounds. (-पः) sweet or melodious notes; मधुरालापनिसर्गपंडितां. Ku. 4. 16. (-पा) a kind of thrush. -कंटकः a kind of fish. -जंबीरं a species of lime. -त्रयं = मधुत्रयं q. v. -फलः a sort of jujube tree (राजबदर). -भाषिन्, -वाच् *a.* sweet-speaking. -स्रवा a kind of date tree. -स्वर, स्वन *a.* warbling sweetly, sweet-voiced.

मधुरता-त्वं Sweetness, pleasantness, agreeableness.

मधुरिमन् *m.* Sweetness, agreeableness; मधुरिमातिशयेन वचोऽमृतं Bv. 1. 113.

मधुलिका Black mustard.

मधूकः 1 A bee. 2 N. of a tree. -कं A flower of the Madhûka tree; दूर्वावता पांडुमधूकदाम्ना Ku. 7. 14; स्निग्धो मधूकच्छाविगैडः Gît. 10. R. 6. 25.

मधूलः A kind of tree. -ली The mango tree.

मधूलिका A kind of tree.

मध्य *a.* 1 Middle, central, being in the middle or centre; Me. 46; Ms. 2. 21. 2 Intervening, intermediate. 3 Middling, moderate, of a middling size or quality, mediocre; प्रारभ्य विघ्नविहता विरमंति मध्याः Bh. 2. 27. 4 Neutral, impartial. 5 Just, right. 6 Mean (in astr.). -ध्यः, -ध्यं 1 The middle, centre, middle or central part; अह्नः मध्यं midday; सहस्रदीधितिरलंकरोति मध्यमह्नः Mâl. 1 'the sun is on the meridian' or 'right overhead,'; व्योममध्ये V. 2.1. 2 The middle of the body, the waist; मध्ये क्षामा Me. 82; वेदिविलग्नमध्या Ku. 1. 39. विशालववक्षास्तनुवृत्तमध्यः R. 6. 32. 3 The belly, abdomen; मध्येन... वलित्रयं चारु बभार बाला Ku. 1.39. 4 The inside or interior of anything. 5 A middle state or condition. 6 The flank of a horse. 7 Mean time in music. 8 The middle term of a progression. -ध्या The middle finger. -ध्यं Ten thousand billions [The acc., instr. abl. and loc. singulars of मध्य are used adverbially. (*a*) मध्य into the midst of, into; (*b*) मध्येन through or between. (*c*) मध्यात् out of, from among, from the midst (with gen.); तेषां मध्यात् काकः प्रोवाच Pt. 1. (*d*) मध्ये 1 in the middle, between, among, in the midst; R. 12. 29. 2. in, into, within, inside, oft. as the first member of adverbial compounds; *e. g.* मध्येगंगं into the Ganges; मध्येजठरं, in the belly; Bv. 1 61; मध्येनगरं inside the city; मध्येनादि in the middle of the river; मध्येपृष्ठं on the back; मध्येभक्तं a medicine taken in the middle of one's meals; मध्येरणं in the battle; Bv. 1. 128; मध्येसभं in or before an assembly; N. 6. 76; मध्येसमुद्रं in the midst of the sea; *Si.* 3. 33.] -Comp. -अंगुलिः, -ली *f.* the middle finger. -अह्नः (for अहन्). midday, noon. कृत्यं, °क्रिया a midday rite or observance. °कालः, °वेलाः, °समयः noon-time, midday. °स्नानं; midday ablution -कर्णः a radius. -ग *a.* being or going in the middle or among -गत *a.* central, middle, being in the middle. -गंधः the mango tree -ग्रहणं the middle of an eclipse. -दिनं (also मध्यंदिनं) 1 midday, noon. 2 a midday offering. -दीपकं a variety of the figure called Dîpaka, in which the common attribute that throws light on the whole description is placed in the middle; *e. g.* Bk. 10. 24. -देशः 1 the middle region or space, the middle part of anything. 2 the waist. 3 the belly. 4 the meridian. 5 the central region, the country lying between the Himâlaya and Vindhya mountains; हिमवद्विंध्ययोर्मध्यं यत्प्राग्विनशनादपि प्रत्यगेव प्रयागाच्च मध्यदेशः स कीर्तितः ॥ Ms. 2. 21.

-देहः the trunk of the body, the belly. -पदं the middle word. °लोपिन् see मध्यमपदलोपिन्. -पातः communion, intercourse. -भागः 1 the middle part. 2 the waist. -भावः middle state, mediocrity. -यवः a weight of six white mustard seeds.-रात्रः, -रात्रिः *f.* midnight. -रेखा the central or first meridian. -लोकः the middle of the three worlds; *i. e.* the earth or world of mortals. °ईशः, °ईश्वरः a king. -वयस् *a.* middle-aged. -वर्तिन् *a.* middle, central. (*-m.*) an arbitrator, a mediator. -वृत्तं the navel. -सूत्रं = मध्यरेखा q. v. -स्थ *a.* 1 being or standing in the middle, central. 2 intermediate, intervening. 3 middling. 4 mediating, acting as umpire between two parties. 5 impartial, neutral. 6 indifferent, unconcerned; *S.* 5. (-स्थः) 1 an umpire, arbitrator, a mediator. 2 an epithet of Śiva. -स्थलं 1 the middle or centre. 2 the middle space or region. 3 the waist. -स्थानं 1 the middle station 2 the middle space ; *i. e.* air. 3 a neutral region. -स्थित *a.* central, inter mediate.

मध्यतस् *ind.* 1 From the middle or midst, out of. 2 Among, between.

मध्यम *a.* 1 Being or standing in the middle, middle, central; पितुः पदं मध्यममुत्पतंती V. 1. 19; so मध्यमलोकपालः, मध्यमपदं, मध्यमरेखा q. q. v. v. 2 Intermediate, intervening. 3 Middling, of a middling condition or quality, mediocre ; as in उत्तमाधममध्यम. 4 Middling, moderate; तेन मध्यमशक्तीनि मित्राणि स्थापितान्यतः R. 17. 58. 5 Middle-sized. 6 Neither youngest nor oldest, the middle-born (as a brother); प्रणमति पितरौ वां मध्यमः पांडवोऽयं Ve. 5. 26. 7 Impartial, neutral. -मः 1 The fifth note in music. 2 A particular musical mode. 3 The midland country; see मध्यदेश. 4 The second person (in grammar). 5 A neutral sovereign; वर्मोत्तरं मध्यममाश्रयंते R. 13. 7. 6 The governor of a province. -मा 1 The middle finger. 2 A marriageable girl,one arrived at the age of puberty. 3 The pericarp of a lotus. 4 One of the classes of heroines (Nâyikás) in poetic compositions, a woman in the middle of her youth; cf. S. D. 100. -मं The waist. -Comp अंगुलिः the middle finger. -आहरणं (in alg.) elimination of the middle term in an equation. -कक्षा the middle courtyard. -जात *a.* middle-born. -पदं the middle member (of a compound). °लोपिन् *m.* a subdivision of the Tatpurusha compound in which the middle word is omitted in composition; the usual instance given is शाकपार्थिवः which is dissolved as शाकप्रियः पार्थिवः; here the middle word प्रिय is omitted ; so छायातरुः, गुडाधानाः &c., -पांडवः an epithet of Arjuna. -पुरुषः the second person (in grammar). -भृतकः a husbandman or cultivator (who works both for himself and his master or landord). -रात्रः midnight. -लोकः the middle world, the earth. °पालः a king ; R. 2. 16. -वयस् *n.* middle aged. -वयस्क middle-aged. -संग्रहः intrigue of a middling character, such as sending presents of flowers &c. to another's wife; it is thus defined by Vyása. -प्रेषणं गंधमाल्यानां धूपभूषणवाससां। प्रलोभनं चान्नपानैर्मध्यमः संग्रहः स्मृतः ॥. -साहसः the second of the three penalties or modes of punishment; see Ms. 8. 138. (-सः-सं) an outrage or offence to the middle class. -स्थ *a.* being in the middle.

मध्यमक *a.* (मिका *f.*) Middle, middlemost.

मध्यामिका A girl arrived at puberty.

मध्ये See under मध्य.

मध्वः N. of a celebrated preceptor and author, the founder of the sect of Vaishṇavas, and author of a Bhâshya on the Vedánta Sûtras.

मध्वकः A bee.

माध्विजा Any intoxicating drink, spirituous liquor.

मन् I. 1. P. (मनति) 1 To be proud. 2 To worship. -II. 10. A. (मानयते) To be proud -III. 4. 8. A. (मन्यते, मनुते, मत) 1 To think, believe, suppose, imagine, fancy, conceive; अंकं केऽपि शशंकिरे जलनिधेः पंकं परे मेनिरे Subhásh; वत्स मन्ये कुमारेणानेन जृंभकास्त्रमामंत्रितं U. 5; कथं भवान् मन्यते 'what is your opinion?' 2 To consider, regard, deem, look upon, take (one) for, take to be; समीभूता दृष्टिस्त्रिभुवनमपि ब्रह्म मनुते Bh. 3. 84; अमंस्त चानेन परार्ध्यजन्मना स्थितेरभेत्ता स्थितिमंतमन्वयं R. 3. 27; 1. 32. 6. 84. Bg. 2. 26. 35; Bk. 9. 117; स्तनविनिहितमपि हारमुदारं सा मनुते कृशतनुरिव भारं Git. 4. 3 To honour, respect, value, esteem, think highly of, prize यस्यानुषंगिण इमे भुवनाधिपत्यभोगादयः कृपणलोकमता भवंति Bh. 3. 76. 4 To know, understand, perceive, observe, have regard to; मत्वा देवं धनपतिसखं यत्र साक्षाद्वसंतं Me. 73. 5 To agree or consent to, act up to; तन्मन्यस्व मम वचनं Mk. 8. 6 To think or reflect upon. 7 To intend, wish or hope for. 8 To set the heart or mind on. The senses of मन् are variously modified according to the word with which it is used; *e. g.* बहु मन् to think highly or much of, value greatly, prize, esteem; बहु मनुते ननु ते तनुसंगतपवनचलितमपि रेणुं Git. 5; see under बहु also; लघु मन् to think lightly of; despise, slight; *S.* 7. 1; अन्यथा मन् to think otherwise, doubt; साधु मन् to think well of, approve, consider satisfactory; *S.* 1. 2; असाधु मन् to disapprove; तृणाय मन् or तृणवत् मन् to value at a straw, value lightly, make light of; हरिमप्यमंसत तृणाय Si. 15. 61; न मन् to disregard, not to mind. *-Caus.* (मानयति-ते) To honour, esteem, respect, pay respect, to value; मान्यान् मानय Bh. 2. 77. *-Desid.* (मीमांसते) 1 To reflect upon, examine, investigate, inquire into. 2 To doubt, call in question (with loc.). WITH अनु to agree or consent to, approve, grant, permit, allow, sanction; राजन्यान्स्वपुरनिवृत्तयेऽनुमेने R. 4. 87. 14. 20; तत्र नाहमनुमंतुमुत्सहे मोघवृत्ति कलभस्य चेष्टितं 11 39; Ku. 1. 59 ; 3. 60, 5. 68 ; Bh. 3 22; R. 16. 85. (*-Caus.*) to ask for leave or permission, ask the consent of ; अनुमान्यतां महाराज ; V. 2. -अभि 1 to wish or desire for, covet ; Ms. 10. 95. 2 to approve of, assent to. 3 to think, fancy, imagine, regard. -अव to despise, contemn, disregard, slight, think lightly of ; चतुर्दिगीशानवमत्य मानिनी Ku. 5. 53 ; Ms. 4. 135 ; V. 2. 11. -प्रति to think, reflect. (*-Caus.*) 1 to honour, hold in honour, respect. 2 to approve, applaud. 3 to allow, permit. -वि (*Caus.*) to disrespect, slight, disregard, contemn ; स्त्रीभिर्विमानितानां कापुरुषाणां विवर्धते मदनः Mk. 8. 9. -सं 1 to agree, concur, be of the same mind. 2 to assent or consent to, approve, like. 3 to think, suppose, regard. 4 to sanction, authorize. 5 to esteem, honour, value highly ; कच्चिदग्निमिवानाय्यं काले संमन्यसेऽतिथिं Bk. 6. 65 ; सममंस्त बंधून् 1. 2. 6 to allow, permit. (*Caus.*) to honour, respect, value highly.

मननं 1 Thinking, reflection, meditation, cogitation ; मननान्मुनिरेवासि Hariv. 2 Intelligence, understanding. 3 An inference arrived at by reasoning. 4 A guess, conjecture.

मनस् *n.* 1 The mind, heart, understanding, perception, intelligence ; as in सुमनस्, दुर्मनस् &c. 2 (In phil.) The mind or internal organ of perception and cognition, the instrument by which objects of sense affect the soul ; (in Nyáya phil. मनस् is regarded as a Dravya or substance and is distinct from आत्मन् or the soul); तदेव सुखदुःखाद्युपलब्धिसाधनमिंद्रियं प्रतिजीवं भिन्नमणु नित्यं च Tarka K. 3 Conscience, the faculty of discrimination or judgment. 4 Thought, idea, fancy, imagination, conception ; पश्यन्नदूरान्मनसाप्यधृष्यं Ku. 3. 51 ; R. 2. 27 ; कायेन वाचा मनसापि शश्वत् 5. 5. 5 Design, purpose, intention. 6 Will, wish, desire, inclination ; in this sense मनस् is fre quently used with the infinitive form with the final म् dropped and forms adjectives; अयं जनः प्रष्टुमनास्तपोधने Ku. 5. 40; cf. काम. 7 Reflection. 8 Disposition, temper, mood. 9 Spirit, energy, mettle. 10 N. of the lake called Mânasa. (मनसा गम् &c. to think of, contemplate, remember; Ku. 2. 63; मनः कृ to fix the mind upon, direct the thoughts towards; with dat. or loc.; मनो बंध् to fix the heart or affection upon; अभिलाषे मनो बबंधान्यरसान् विलंघ्य सा R. 3. 4; मनः समाधा to collect oneself; मनसि उद्भू to cross the mind; मनसिकृ to think, to bear in mind; to resolve, determine, think of). -Comp. -अधिनाथः a lover, husband. अनवस्थानं inattention. -अनुग a. suiting the mind, agreeable. -अपहारिन् a. captivating the heart. -अभिनिवेशः close application of mind, firmness of purpose. -अभिराम a. pleasing the mind, gratifying to the heart; R. 1. 39. -अभिलाषः the desire or longing of the heart. -आप a. gaining the heart, attractive, pleasing. -कांत a. (मनस्कांत or मनः कांत) dear to the mind, pleasant, agreeable. -कारः perfect perception, full consciousness (of pleasure or pain).-क्षेपः distraction of the mind, mental confusion. -गत a. 1 existing or passing in the mind, concealed in the breast, internal, inward, secret; नेयं न वक्ष्यति मनोगतमाधिहेतुं S. 3 12. 2 affecting the mind, desired. (-तं) 1 a wish, desire; मनोगतं सा न शशाक शंसितुं Ku. 5. 51. 2 an idea, thought, notion, opinion. -गतिः f. desire of the heart. -गवी wish, desire. -गुप्ता red arsenic. -ग्रहणं captivating the mind. -ग्राहिन् a. captivating or fascinating the mind. -ज, -जन्मन् a. mind-born. (-m.) the god of love. -जव a. 1 quick or swift as thought. 2 quick in thought or conception. 3 fatherly, paternal -जवस a. resembling a father, fatherly. -जात a. mind-born, arisen or produced in the mind. -जिघ्र a. scenting out, i. e. guessing the thoughts. -ज्ञ a. pleasing, lovely, agreeable, beautiful, charming; इयमधिकमनोज्ञा वल्कलेनापि तन्वी S. 1. 20; R. 3. 7; 6. 7. (-ज्ञः) N. of a Gandharva. (-ज्ञा) 1 red arsenic. 2 an intoxicating drink. 3 a princess. -तापः, -पीडा 1 mental pain or agony, anguish. 2 repentance, contrition. -तुष्टिः f. satisfaction of the mind. -तोका an epithet of Durgâ. -दंडः complete control over the mind or thoughts; Ms. 10. 10; cf. त्रिदंडिन्. -दत्त a. devoted in thought, mentally dedicated. -दाहः, -दुःखं mental distress or torment. -नाशः loss of the mind or understanding, dementedness. -नीत a. approved, chosen. -पतिः an epithet of Vishnu. -पूत a. 1 considered pure by the mind, approved by one's conscience; मनःपूतं समाचरेत् Ms. 6. 46. 2 of a pure mind, conscientious. -प्रणीत a. agreeable or pleasing to the mind. -प्रसादः composure of mind, mental calm. -प्रीतिः f. mental satisfaction, joy, delight. -भवः, -भूः 1 the god of love, cupid; रेरे मनो मम मनोभववशासनस्य पादांबुजद्वयमनारतमामनंत Bv. 4. 33; Ku. 3. 27; R. 7.22. 2 love, passion, lust; अत्यारूढो हि नारीणामकालज्ञो मनोभवः R. 12. 33. -मथनः the god of love. -मय see separately. -यायिन् a. 1 going at will or pleasure. 2 swift, quick as thought. -योगः close application of the mind, close attention. -योनिः the god of love. -रंजनं 1 pleasing the mind. 2 pleasantness. -रथः 1 'the car of the mind', a wish, desire; अवतरतः सिद्धिपथं शब्दः स्वमनोरथस्येव M. 1. 22; मनोरथानामगतिर्न विद्यते Ku. 5. 64; R. 3. 72, 12. 59. 2 a desired object; मनोरथाय नाशंसे S. 7. 13. 3 (in dramas) a hint, a wish expressed indirectly or covertly. °दायक a. fulfilling one's expectations.(-कः) N. of a Kalpataru. °सिद्धिः f. fulfilment of one's desires. °सृष्टिः f. a creation of the fancy, a castle in the air. -रम a. attractive, pleasing, agreeable, lovely, beautiful; अरुणनखमनोरमासु तस्याः (अंगुलीषु) S. 6. 10. (-मा) 1 a lovely woman. 2 a kind of pigment. -राज्यं 'kingdom of the fancy', a castle in the air; मनोराज्यविजृंभणमेतत् 'this is building castles in the air.' -लयः loss of consciousness. -लौल्यं freak, caprice. -वांछा, -वांछितं a wish of the heart, a desire. -विकारः,-विकृतिः f. emotion of the mind. -वृत्तिः f. 1 working of the mind, volition. 2 disposition, temper. -वेगः quickness of thought. -व्यथा mental pain or anguish. -शीलः, -ला red arsenic; मनःशिलाविच्छुरिता निषेदुः Ku. 1. 55; R. 12. 80. -शीघ्र a. quick as thought. -संगः attachment of the mind (to anything). -संतापः anguish of the mind. -स्थ a. being in the heart, mental. -स्थैर्यं firmness of mind. -हत a. disappointed. -हर a. pleasing, charming, attractive, fascinating, lovely; अव्याजमनोहरं वपुः S. 1. 17; Ku. 3. 39; R. 3. 32. (-रः) a kind of Jasmine. (-रं) gold. -हर्तृ,-हारिन् a. heart-stealing, captivating, agreeable, pleasing; हितं मनोहारिच दुर्लभं वचः Ki. 1. 4. -हारी an unchaste or unfaithful woman. -ह्लादः gladness of heart. -ह्वा red arsenic.

मनसा N. of a daughter of Kasyapa, sister of the serpent king Ananta and wife of the sage जरत्कारु; so मनसादेवी.

मनसिजः 1 The god of love; R. 18. 52. 2 Love, passion; मनसिजरुजं सा वा दिव्या ममालमपोहितुं V. 3. 10; S. 3. 9.

मनसिशयः The god of love; S. 7. 2.

मनस्तः ind. From the mind or heart; R. 14. 81.

मनस्विन् a. 1 Wise, intelligent, clever, high-souled, high-minded; R. 1. 32; Pt. 2. 120. 2 Steady-minded, resolute, determined; Ku. 5. 6. -नी 1 A high-minded or proud woman; मनस्विनीमानविघातदक्षं Ku. 3. 32; M. 1. 19. 2 A wise or virtuous woman. 3 N. of Durgâ.

मनाक् ind 1 A little, slightly, in a small degree; न मनाक् 'not at all'; रे पांथ विह्वलमना न मनागपि स्याः Bv. 1. 37, 111. 2 Slowly, tardily. -Comp. -कर a. doing little. (-रं) a kind of fragrant aloe-wood.

मनाका A female elephant.

मनित p. p. Known, perceived, understood.

मनीकं Collyrium, eye-salve.

मनीषा 1 Desire, wish; यो दुर्जनं वशयितुं तनुते मनीषां Bv. 1. 95. 2 Intelligence, understanding. 3 A thought, idea.

मनीषिका Understanding, intelligence.

मनीषित a. 1 Wished for, desired, liked, loved, dear; मनीषिताः संति गृहेषु देवताः Ku. 5. 4. 2 Agreeable. -तं A wish, desire, desired object; मनीषितं द्यौरपि येन दुग्धा R. 5. 33.

मनीषिन् a. Wise, learned, intelligent, clever, thoughtful, prudent; R. 1. 25. -m. A wise or learned person, a sage, a Pandit; माननीयो मनीषिणां R. 1. 11; संस्कारवत्येव गिरा मनीषी Ku. 1. 28, 5. 39; R. 3. 44.

मनुः 1 N. of a celebrated personage regarded as the representative man and father of the human race (sometimes regarded as one of the divine beings). 2 Particularly, the fourteen successive progenitors or sovereigns of the earth mentioned in Ms. 1. 63. (The first Manu called स्वायंभुवमनु is supposed to be a sort of secondary creator, who produced the ten *Prajâpatis* or *Maharshis* and to whom the code of laws known as *Manusmriti* is ascribed. The seventh Manu called वैवस्वतमनु, being supposed to be born from the sun, is regarded as the progenitor of the present race of living beings and was saved from a great flood by Vishnu in the form of a fish, cf. मत्स्यावतार ; he is also regarded as the founder of the solar race of kings who ruled at Ayodhyâ ; see U. 6. 18 ; R. 1. 11. The names of the fourteen Manus in order are :— 1 स्वायंभुव, 2 स्वारोचिष, 3 औत्तमि, 4 तामस, 5 रैवत, 6 चाक्षुष, 7 वैवस्वतः 8 सावर्णि, 9 दक्षसावर्णि, 10 ब्रह्मसावर्णि,

11 धर्मसावर्णि, 12 रुद्रसावर्णि, 13 रौच्य-देव-सावर्णि, and 14 इंद्रसावर्णि). **3** A symbolical expression for the number 'fourteen'. -**नुः** *f*. The wife of Manu. -**Comp.** -**अंतरं** the period or age of a Manu; (this period, according to Ms. 1. 79, comprises 4,320,000 human years or 1/14th day of Brahmā, the fourteen *Manvantaras* making up one whole day; each of these fourteen periods is supposed to be presided over by its own Manu; six such periods have already passed away; we are at present living in the seventh, and seven more are yet to come). -**जः** a man, mankind. °अधिपः, °अधिपतिः, °ईश्वरः, °पतिः, °राजः a king, sovereign. °लोकः the world of men, *i. e.* the earth. -**जातः** a man. -**ज्येष्ठः** a sword. -**प्रणीत** *a*. taught or expounded by Manu. -**भूः** a man, mankind. -**राज्** *m*. an epithet of Kubera. -**श्रेष्ठः** an epithet of Vishṇu. -**संहिता** the code of laws ascribed to the first Manu, the institutes of Manu.

मनुष्यः **1** A man, human being, mortal. **2** A male. -**Comp.** -**इंद्रः**, -**ईश्वरः** a king, sovereign; R. 2. 2. -**जातिः** mankind, human race. -**देवः** **1** a king; R. 2. 52. **2** a god among men, a Brāhmaṇa. -**धर्मः** **1** the duty of man. **2** the character of man, human character. -**धर्मन्** *m*. an epithet of Kubera. -**मारणं** homicide. -**यज्ञः** hospitality, hospitable reception of guests, one of the five daily acts of a house-holder; see नृयज्ञ. -**लोकः** the world of mortals, the earth. -**विश्**, -**विशा** *f*., -**विशं** human race, mankind. -**शोणितं** human blood; (पपौ) कुतूहलेनेव मनुष्यशोणितं R. 3. 54. -**सभा** 1 an assembly of men. **2** a crowd, multitude.

मनोमय *a*. Mental, spiritual. -**Comp.** -**कोशः** -**षः** the second of the five vestures or sheaths which are supposed to enshrine the soul.

मंतुः **1** A fault, an offence; मुधैव मंतुं परिकल्प्य Bv. 2. 13. **2** Man, mankind. -**तुः** *f*. Understanding.

मंतृ *m*. A sage, wise man, an adviser or counsellor.

मंत्र् 10 A. (मंत्रयते, but sometimes मंत्रयति also, मंत्रित) **1** To consult, deliberate, ponder over, hold consultation, take counsel; न हि स्त्रीभिः सह मंत्रयितुं युज्यते Pt. 5; Ms. 7. 146. **2** To advise; counsel, give advice; अतीतलाभस्य च रक्षणार्थं.. यन्मंत्र्यतेऽसौ परमो हि मंत्रः Pt. 2. 182. **3** To consecrate with sacred texts, enchant with spells or charms. **4** To say, speak, talk, mutter; किमपि हृदये कृत्वा मंत्रयेथे S 1; किमेकाकिनी मंत्रयसि S. 6; हला संगीतशालापरिसरेऽवलोकिताद्वितिया त्वं किं मंत्रयंत्यासीः Māl. 2. -WITH **अनु** **1** to consecrate or accompany with spells; विसृष्टश्च वामदेवानुमंत्रितोऽश्वः U. 2. **2** to dismiss with a blessing; रथमारोप्य कृष्णेन यत्र कर्णानुमंत्रितः Mb. -**अभि** **1** to consecrate or accompany with sacred hymns or spells; पशुरसौ योऽभिमंत्र्य क्रतौ हतः Ak.; Y. 2. 102, 3. 326. **2** to enchant, charm. -**आ** **1** to bid farewell, bid adieu; आमंत्रयस्व सहचरं S. 3; Ku. 6. 94. **2** to speak to, call out to, tell, address, converse; तमामंत्रयांबभूव K. 81, Ve. 1. **3** to say, speak; परिजनोप्येवमामंत्रयते K. 195; Bk. 9. 98. **4** to call, invite. -**उप** to advise, persuade, induce. -**नि** to invite, call; summon; द्विग्यो निमंत्रिताश्चैनमभिजग्मुर्महर्षयः R. 15-59; 11. 32; Y. 1. 225. -**परि** to consecrate by means of spell. -**सं** to consult or take counsel with; मम हृदयेन सह संमंत्र्योक्तवानासि Mu. 1.

मंत्रः **1** A Vedic hymn or sacred prayer (addressed to any deity), a sacred text; (it is of three kinds:—it is called ऋच् if metrical and intended to be loudly recited; यजुस् if in prose and muttered in a low tone; and सामन् if, being metrical, it is intended for chanting). **2** The portion of the Veda including the Samhitā and distinguished from the *Brāhmana* q. v. **3**. A charm, spell, an incantation; न हि जीवंति जना मनागमंत्राः Bv. 1. 111, अचिंत्यो हि मणिमंत्रौषधीनां प्रभावः Ratn. 2; R. 2. 32, 5. 57. **4** A formula (of prayer) sacred to any deity; ओं नमः शिवाय &c. **5** Consultation, deliberation, counsel, advice, resolution, plan; तस्य संवृतमंत्रस्य R. 1. 20; 17. 20; Pt. 2. 182; Ms. 7. 58. **6** Secret plan or consultation, a secret. -**Comp.** -**आराधनं** endeavouring to obtain by spells or incantations; मंत्राराधनतत्परेण मनसा नीताः श्मशाने निशाः Bh. 3. 4. -**उदकं**, -**जलं**, -**तोयं**, -**वारि** *n*. water consecrated by means of spells, charmed water. -**उपष्टंभः** backing up by advice. -**करणं** 1 Vedic texts. **2** composing or reciting sacred texts. -**कारः** the author of Vedic hymns. -**कालः** time of consultation or deliberation. **कुशल** *a*. skilled in giving advice. -**कृत्** *m*. **1** an author or composer of Vedic hymns; R. 5. 4, 1. 61, 15. 31. **2** one who recites a sacred text. **3** a counsellor, an adviser. **4** an ambassador. -**गंडकः** knowledge, science. -**गुप्तिः** *f*. secret counsel. -**गूढः** a spy, a secret emissary or agent. -**जिह्वः** fire; Si. 2. 107. -**ज्ञः** 1 a counsellor, adviser. **2** a learned Brāhmaṇa. **3** a spy. -**दः** -**दातृ** *m*. a spiritual preceptor or teacher. -**दर्शिन्** *m*. **1** a seer of Vedic hymns. **2**. a Brāhmaṇa versed in the Vedas. -**दीधितिः** fire. -**दृश्** *m*. **1** a seer of Vedic hymns **2** an adviser a counsellor. -**देवता** the deity invoked in a sacred text or *mantra*. —**धरः** a counsellor. -**निर्णयः** final decision after deliberation. -**पदं** the word of a sacred text. -**पूत** *a*. purified by *mantras*. -**प्रयोगः** application of spells. -**बीजं** (**वी**)**जं** the first syllable of a spell. -**भेदः** breach or betrayal of counsel. -**मूर्तिः** an epithet of Siva. -**मूलं** magic. -**यंत्रं** a mystical diagram with a magical formula. -**योगः** **1** employment or application of spells. **2** magic. -**वर्जं** *ind*. without the use of spells. -**विद्** see **मंत्रज्ञ** above. -**विद्या** the science of spells, magic. -**संस्कारः** any Samskāra or rite performed with sacred texts. -**संहिता** the whole body of Vedic hymns. -**साधकः** a magician, conjurer. -**साधनं** **1** effecting or subduing by magic. **2** a spell, an incantation. -**साध्य** *a*. **1** to be effected or subdued by magic spells. **2** attainable by consultation. -**सिद्धिः** *f*. **1** the working or accomplishment of a spell. **2** the power which the possession or knowledge of a spell gives to a person. -**स्पृश्** *a*. obtaining (anything) by means of spells. -**हीन** *a*. destitute of or contrary to sacred hymns.

मंत्रणं -**णा** Deliberation, consultation.

मंत्रवत् *a*. Attended with spells or incantations; R. 3. 31.

मांत्रिः = मंत्रिन् q. v.

मंत्रित *p. p.* **1** Consulted. **2** Counselled, advised. **3** Said, spoken. **4** Charmed, consecrated by *mantras*. **5** Settled, determined.

मंत्रिन् *m*. A minister, counsellor, a King's minister; R 8. 17; Ms. 8. 1. -**Comp.** -**धुर** *a*. able to bear the burden of a minister's office. -**पतिः** -**प्रधानः**, -**प्रमुखः**, -**मुख्यः**, -**वरः**, **श्रेष्ठः** the prime minister, premier. -**प्रकांडः** an excellent or eminent minister. -**श्रोत्रियः** a minister conversant with the Vedas.

मंथ्, मथ् **1**. 9. P. (मंथति, मथति, मथ्नाति, मथित; *pass*. मथ्यते) **1** To churn, produce by churning; (oft. with two acc.); सुधां सागरं ममंथुः, or देवासुरैरमृतमंबुनिधिर्ममंथे Ki. 5. 30. **2** To agitate, shake, stir round or up, turn up and down; तस्मात् समुद्रादिव मथ्यमानात् R. 16. 79. **3** To grind down, oppress, afflict, trouble, ditress sorely; मन्मथो मां मथ्नान्निजनाम सान्वयं करोति Dk.; जातां मन्ये शिशिरमथितां पद्मिनीं वान्यरूपां Me. 83. **4** To hurt, injure. **5** To destroy, kill, annihilate, crush down; मथ्नामि कौरवशतं समरे न कोपात् Ve. 1. 15; अमंथीच परानीकं Bk. 15. 46; 14. 36. **6** To tear off, dislocate. -WITH **उद्** **1** to strike, kill, destroy; मीमांसाकृतमुन्ममाथ सहसा हस्ती मुनिं जैमिनिं Pt. 2. 33; धैर्यमुन्मथ्य Māl. 1. 18 'destroying or uprooting.' **2** to shake, disturb. **3** to tear, cut or peel off; R. 2, 37. -**निस्** **1** to churn, shake, stir round; अमृतस्यार्थे निर्मथिष्यामहे

जलं Mb. 2 to produce or excite fire by rubbing. 3 to bruise, thresh. 4 to destroy completely, crush down. –प्र 1 to churn ; (समुद्रः) प्रमथ्यमानो गिरिणेव भूयः R. 13. 14. 2 to harass, trouble excessively, annoy, torment. 3 to strike down, bruise, hurt. 4 to tear off or cut. 5 to devastate. 6 to kill, destroy; Mál. 4. 9, 2. 9.

मंथः 1 Churning, shaking about, stirring, agitating; मैथादिव क्षुभ्यति गांगमंभः U. 7. 16; R. 10. 3. 2 Killing, destroying. 3 A mixed beverage. 4 A churning-stick (मंथा also). 5 The sun. 6 A ray of the sun. 7 Excretion of rheum from the eyes, mucus (from the eyes), cataract. 8 An instrument for kindling fire by attrition. –Comp. –अचलः, –अद्रिः, –गिरिः, –पर्वतः, –शैलः the Mandara mountain (used as a churning stick); Bv. 1. 55. –उदकः, –उदधिः the sea of milk. –गुणः a churning-cord. –जं butter. –दंडः, –दंडकः a churning-stick.

मंथनः A churning-stick. –नं 1 Churning, agitating, stirring or shaking about. 2 Kindling fire by attrition. –नी A churning-vessel. –Comp. –घटी a churning-vessel.

मंथर *a.* 1 Slow, dull, tardy, lazy, inactive; गर्भमंथरा *S.* 4; प्रत्यभिज्ञानमंथरो भवेत् *ibid*; दरमंथरचरणविहारं Gít. 11.; *Si.* 6. 40; 7. 18; 5. 62.; R. 19. 21. 2 Stupid, foolish, silly; मंथरकौलिकः. 3 Low, deep, hollow, having a low tone. 4 Large, broad, wide, big. 5 Bent, crooked, curved. –रः 1 A store, treasure. 2 The hair of the head. 3 Wrath, anger. 4 Fresh butter. 5 A churning-stick. 6 Hinderance, an obstacle. 7 A stronghold. 8 Fruit. 9 A spy, an informer. 10 The month Vaisákha. 11 The mountain Mandara. 12 an antelope. –रा N. of a hump-backed nurse or slave of Kaikeyî who instigated her mistress, on the eve of Ráma's coronation as heir-apparent, to beg of her husband by the two boons formerly promised to her by him, the banishment of Râma for fourteen years and the installation of Bharata on the throne. –रं Safflower. –Comp. –विवेक *a.* slow in judgment, void of discrimination; Mál. 1. 18.

मंथारुः The wind produced by the waving of a *chowrie*.

मंथानः 1 A churning stick. 2 An epithet of Siva.

मंथानकः A kind of grass.

मंथिन् *a.* 1 Churning, stirring. 2 Afflicting, annoying. –*m.* Semen virile. –नी A churning vessel.

मंद् 1 A. (मंदते) (mostly Vedic) 1 To be drunk. 2 To be glad, to rejoice. 3 To languish, be languid. 4 To shine. 5 To move slowly, loiter, tarry.

मंद *a.* 1 Slow, tardy, inactive, lazy, dull, loitering; (न) भिंदंति मंदां गतिमश्वमुख्यः Ku. 1. 11; तच्चरितं गोविंदे मनसिजमंदे सखी प्राह Gít. 6. 2 Cold, indifferent, apathetic. 3 Stupid, dull-witted, foolish, ignorant, weak-brained; मंदोप्यमंदतामेति संसर्गेण विपश्चितः M. 2. 8; मंद कवियशःप्रार्थी गमिष्याम्युपहास्यतां R. 1. 3; or द्विषंति मंदाश्चरितं महात्मनां Ku. 5. 75. 4 Low, deep, hollow (as sound). 5 Soft, faint; gentle; as in मंदस्मितं. 6 Small, little, slight; मंदोदरी; see अमंद also. 7 Weak, defective, feeble; as मंदाग्निः. 8 Unlucky, unhappy. 9 Faded. 10 Wicked, vile. 11 Addicted to drinking. –दः 1 The planet Saturn. 2 An epithet of Yama. 3 The dissolution of the world. 4 A kind of elephant; *Si.* 5 49. –दं *ind.* 1 Slowly, gradually, by degrees; यातं यच्च नितंबयोर्गुरुतया मंदं विलासादिव. *S.* 2. 1. 2 Gently, soft, not violently; मंदं मंदं नुदति पवनश्चानुकूलो यथा त्वां Me. 9. 3 Faintly, feebly, weakly, lightly. 4 In a low tone, deeply. (मंदीकृ to slacken; मंदीकृतो वेगः S. 1; मंदीभू to be slackened, grow less strong). –Comp. –अक्ष *a.* weak-eyed. (–क्षं) sense of shame, modesty, bashfulness. –अग्नि *a.* having a weak digestion. (–ग्निः) slowness of digestion. –अनिलः a gentle breeze. –असु *a.* having weak or faint breath. –आक्रांता N. of a meter; see App. I. –आत्मन् *a.* dull-witted, silly, ignorant; मंदात्मानुजिघृक्षया Malli. –आदर *a.* 1 having little respect for, disregarding, caring little for. 2 neglectful. –उत्साह *a.* discouraged, dispirited; मंदोत्साहः कृतोऽस्मि मृगयापवादिना माठव्येन *S.* 2. –उदरी N. of the wife of Râvaṇa, regarded as one of the five very chaste women cf. अहल्या. –उष्ण *a.* tepid, lukewarm. (–ष्णं) gentle heat. –औत्सुक्य *a.* slackened in eagerness, cast down, disinclined; मंदौत्सुक्योऽस्मि नगरगमनं प्रति *S.* 1. –कर्ण *a.* slightly deaf; Proverb; बधिरान्मंदकर्णः श्रेयान् 'something is better than nothing'. –कांतिः the moon. –कारिन् *a.* acting slowly or foolishly. –गः Saturn. –गति, –गामिन् *a.* walking slowly, slow of pace. –चेतस् *a.* 1 dull-witted, silly, foolish. 2 absent-minded. 3 fainting away, scarcely conscious. –छाय *a.* dim, faint, lustreless; Me. 80. –जननी the mother of Saturn. –धी, -प्रज्ञ, -बुद्धि, -मति, मेधस् *a.* dull-witted, silly, foolish. –भागिन्, -भाग्य *a.* unfortunate, ill-fated, wretched, miserable. –रश्मि *a.* dim. –वीर्य a weak. –वृष्टिः *f.* slight rain. –स्मितं, -हासः, -हास्यं a gentle laugh, a smile.

मंदटः The coral tree.

मंदनं Praise, eulogium.

मंदयंती An epithet of Durgâ.

मंदर *a.* 1 Slow, tardy, dull. 2 Thick, dense; firm. 3 Large, bulky. –रः 1 N. of a mountain (used by the gods and demons as a churning-stick when they churned the ocean for nectar); पृष्ठतैर्मंदरोद्धूतैः क्षीरोर्मय इवाच्युतं R. 4. 27; अभिनवजलधरसुंदर धृतमंदर ए Gít. 1. शोभैव मंदरक्षुब्धक्षुभितांभोधिवर्णना *Si.* 2. 107; Ki. 5. 80. 2 A necklace of pearls (of 8 or 16 strings). 3 Heaven. 4 A mirror. 5 One of the five trees in Indra's paradise; see मंदार. –Comp. –आवासा, –वासिनी an epithet of Durgâ.

मंदसानः 1 N. of fire. 2 Life. 3 Sleep. (also written मंदसानु).

मंदाकः A current, stream.

मंदाकिनी 1 The river Ganges; मंदाकिनी भाति नगोपकंठे मुक्तावली कंठगतेव भूमेः R. 13. 48; Ku. 1. 29. 2 The river of heaven, celestial Ganges (मंदाकिनी वियद्गंगा); मंदाकिन्याः सलिलशिशिरैः सेव्यमाना मरुद्भिः Me. 67.

मंदायते Den. A. 1 To go slowly, tarry, lag behind, loiter, delay; मंदायंते न खलु सुहृदामभ्युपेतार्थकृत्याः Me. 38; V. 3. 15. 2 To be weak or faint, grow dim; R. 4. 49.

मंदारः 1 The coral tree, one of the five trees in Indra's paradise हस्तप्राप्यस्तवकनमितो बालमंदारवृक्षः Me. 75, 67; V. 4. 35. 2 The plant called Arka. 3 The Dhattûra plant. 4 Heaven. 5 An elephant. –रं A flower of the coral tree; Ku. 5. 80; R. 6. 23. –Comp. –माला a garland of Mandâra flowers: मंदारमाला हरिणा पिनद्धा *S.* 7. 2. –षष्ठी the sixth day in the bright half of Mâgha.

मंदारकः, मंदारवः, मंदारुः The coral tree; see मंदार.

मंदिमन् *m.* 1 Slowness, tardiness. 2 Dulness, stupidity, folly.

मंदिरं A dwelling, house, habitation palace, mansion; Ku. 7. 55; Bk. 8. 96; R. 12. 83. 2 An abode, a dwelling in general; as in क्षीराब्धिमंदिरः. 3 A town. 4 A camp. 5 A temple. –Comp. –पशुः a cat. –मणिः an epithet of Siva.

मंदिरा A stable.

मंदुरा 1 A stable for horses, a stable in general; प्रभ्रष्टोयं प्लवंगः प्रविशति नृपतेर्मंदिरं मंदुरायाः Ratn. 2. 2; R. 16. 41. 2 A bed, mattress.

मंद्र *a.* Low, deep, grave, hollow, rumbling (as sound); पयोदमंद्रध्वनिना धरित्री Ki. 16. 3; 7. 22; Me. 99; R. 6. 56. –द्रः 1 A low tone. 2 A kind of drum. 3 A kind of elephant.

मन्मथः 1 Cupid, the god of love: मन्मथो मां मथ्नन्निजनाम सान्वयं करोति Dk. 21; Me. 73. 2 Love, passion; प्रबोध्यते सुप्त इवाद्य मन्मथः Rs. 1. 8; so परोक्षमन्मथः जनः *S.* 2. 18. 3 The wood-apple. –Comp.

-आनंदः a kind of mango tree. -आलयः 1 the mango tree. 2 pudendum muliebre. -कर a. exciting love. -युद्धं amorous strife, sexual union, compulation. -लेखः a love-letter; S. 3. 26.

मन्मनः 1 Confidential whispering (दंपत्योर्जल्पितं मंदं); करोति सहकारस्य कलिकोत्कलिकोत्तरं । मन्मनो मन्मनोऽप्येष मत्तकोकिलनिस्वनः Kâv. 3. 11. 2 The god of love.

मन्युः 1 Anger, wrath, resentment, indignation, rage; R. 2. 32, 49; 11. 46. 2 Grief, sorrow, affliction, distress; U.4. 3; Ki.1. 35; Bk. 3. 49. 3 Wretched or miserable state, meanness. 4 A sacrifice. 5 An epithet of Agni. 6 Of Siva.

मभ्र् 1 P. (मभ्राति) To go, move.

मम (gen. sing. of अस्मद् the first personal pronoun). -Comp. -कारः, -कृत्यं interesting oneself about anything, self-interest.

ममता 1 The feeling of '*meum*,' the sense of ownership, self-interest, selfishness. 2 Pride, arrogance, self-sufficiency. 3 Individuality.

ममत्वं 1 Regarding as 'mine' or one's own, sense of ownership. 2 Affectionate regard, attachment to, regard for; Ku. 1. 12. 3 Arrogance, pride.

ममापतालः An object of sense.

मंब् 1 P. To go, move.

मम्मटः N. of the author of the Kâvyaprakâsa.

मय् 1 A. (मयते) To go, move.

मय a. (यी f.) An affix used to indicate 'made of,' 'consisting or composed of,' 'full of', कनकमय, काष्ठमय, तेजोमय जलमय &c. -यः 1 N. of a demon, the architect of the demons.(He is said to have built a splendid hall for the Pâṇḍavas). 2 A horse. 3 A camel. 4 A mule.

मयटः A hut of grass or leaves.

मय(ु)ष्टकः A kind of bean.

मयुः 1 A *kinnara*, a celestial musician. 2 A deer, an antelope. -Comp. -राजः an epithet of Kubera.

मयूखः 1 A ray of light, beam, ray, lustre, brightness; विसृजति हिमगर्भैरग्निमिंदुर्मयूखैः S. 3. 2; R. 2. 46; Si. 4. 56; Ki. 5. 5, 8. 2 Beauty. 3 A flame. 4 The pin of a sun-dial.

मयूरः 1 A peacock; स्मरति गिरिमयूर एष दृव्याः U. 3. 20; फणी मयूरस्य तले निषीदति Rs. 1. 13. 2 A kind of flower. 3 N. of a poet (author of the सूर्यशतक); यस्याश्चोरश्चिकुरनिकरः कर्णपूरो मयूरः P. R. 1. 22. -री A pea-hen; Proverb -वरं तत्कालोपनता तित्तिरी न पुनर्दिवसांतरिता मयूरी Vb. 1. or वरमद्य कपोतो न श्वो मयूरः 'a bird in the eand is worth two in the bush.' -Comp. -अरिः a lizard. -केतुः an epithet of Kârtikeya. -ग्रीवकं blue vitriol. -चटकः the domestic cock. -चूडा a peacock's crest. -तुत्थं blue vitriol. -पत्रिन् a. feathered, with peacock's feathers (as an arrow); R. 3. 56. -रथः an epithet of Kârtikeya. -व्यंसकः a cunning peacock. -शिखा a peacock's crest.

मयूरकः A peacock. -कः -कं Blue vitriol.

मरकः A plague, murrain, pestilential disease, an epidemic.

मरकतं An emerald; वापी चास्मिन्मरकतशिलाबद्धसोपानमार्गा Me. 76; Si. 4. 56; Rs. 3. 21; (sometimes written मरकत). -Comp. -मणिः m., f. an emerald. -शिला an emerald slab.

मरणं 1 Dying, death; मरणं प्रकृतिः शरीरिणां R. 8. 87; or संभावितस्य चाकीर्तिर्मरणादतिरिच्यते Bg. 2. 34. 2 A kind of poison. -Comp. अंत,-अंतक a. ending in death. -अभिमुख,-उन्मुख a. on the point of death, near death, moribund. -धर्मन् a. mortal. -निश्चय a. determined to die; Pt. 1.

मरतः Death.

मरंदः-दकः The juice of flowers; Bv. 1. 5, 10, 15. -Comp. -ओकस् n. a flower.

मरारः A granary.

मराल a. 1 Soft, greasy, unctuous. 2 Bland, tender. -लः (ली f.) 1 A swan, flamingo, goose; मरालकुलनायकः कथय रे कथं वर्तताम् Bv. 1. 3; विधेहि मरालविकारं Git. 11; N. 6. 72. 2 A kind of duck (कारंडव). 3 A horse. 4 A cloud. 5 Collyrium. 6 A grove of pomegranate trees. 7 A rogue, cheat.

मरि(री)चः The pepper-shrub. -चं Black pepper.

मरीचिः m. f. 1 A ray of light; न चंद्रमरीचयः V. 3. 10; सवितुर्मरीचिभिः Rs. 1. 16; R. 9. 13, 13. 4. 2 A particle of light. 3 Mirage. -चिः 1 N. of a Prajâpati, one of the ten patriarchs created by the first Manu, or one of the ten mindborn sons of Brahman; he was father of Kasyapa. 2 N. of a law-giver. 3 N. of Krishṇa. 4 A miser. -Comp. -तोयं a mirage. -मालिन् a. encircled by rays, radiant, shining. (-m.) the sun.

मरीचिका Mirage.

मरीचिन् m. The sun.

मरीचिमत् m. The sun.

मरीमृज a. Repeatedly rubbing.

मरुः 1 A desert, sandy desert, a wilderness, any region destitute of water. 2 A mountain or rock. -m. pl. N. of a country or its inhabitants. -Comp. -उद्भवा 1 the cotton shrub. 2 a cucumber. -कच्छः N. of a district. -जः a kind of perfume. -देशः 1 N. of a district. 2 any region destitute of water. -द्विपः -प्रियः a camel. -धन्वः,धन्वन् m. a wilderness, desert. -पथः, -पृष्ठं a sandy desert, wilderness; R. 4. 31. -भूः (pl.) the country called Mârwâr. -भूमिः f. a desert, sandy desert. -संभवः a kind of horse-radish. -स्थलं, स्थली a wilderness, desert, waste; तत्प्राप्नोति मरुस्थलेऽपि नितरां मेरौ ततो नाधिकं Bh. 2. 49.

मरुकः A peacock.

मरुत् m. 1 Wind, air, breeze; दिशः प्रसेदुर्मरुतो ववुः सुखाः R. 3. 14. 2 The god of wind; Ki. 2. 25. 3 A god, deity; वैमानिकानां मरुतामपश्यदाकृष्टलीलान्नर लोकपालान् R. 6. 1; 12. 101. 4 A kind of plant (मरुवक). -n. A kind of plant (ग्रंथिपर्ण). -Comp. -आंदोलः a kind of fan (of a deer's or buffalo's skin). -करः a kind of bean. -कर्मन् m. -क्रिया flatulency. -कोणः the north-west quarter. -गणः the host of the gods. -तनयः, -पुत्रः, सुतः, -सूनुः 1 epithets of Hanumat. 2 of Bhîma. -ध्वजं the down of cotton floating in the air. -पटः a sail. -पतिः, -पालः an epithet of India. -पथः sky atmosphere. -प्लवः a lion. -फलं hail. -बद्धः 1 an epithet of Vishṇu. 2 a kind of sacrificial vessel. -रथः a car in which idols of gods are moved about. -लोकः the world of the Maruts. -वर्त्मन् n. sky, atmosphere. -वाहः 1 smoke. 2 fire. -सखः 1 an epithet of fire. 2 of India.

मरुतः 1 Wind. 2 A god.

मरुत्तः N. of a king of the solar race, who is said to have performed a sacrifice in which the Gods took the part of waiters &c.; cf. तदप्येष श्लोकोऽभि गीतो मरुतः परिवेष्टारो मरुत्तस्यावसन्गृहे । आविक्षितस्य कामप्रेर्विश्वेदेवाः सभासद इति.

मरुत्तकः Marubaka plant.

मरुत्वत् m. 1 A cloud. 2 N. of Indra. 3 N. of Hanumat.

मरुलः A kind of duck.

मरुवः 1 N. of a plant. 2 An epithet of Râhu.

मरुव(च)कः 1 A kind of plant (Marjoram). 2 a variety of lime. 3 A tiger. 4 Râhu. 5 A crane.

मरूकः 1 A peacock. 2 A kind of stag.

मर्कटः 1 An ape, a monkey; हारं वक्षसि केनापि दत्तमज्ञेन मर्कटः । लेढि जिघ्रति संक्षिप्य करोत्युन्नतमासनं Bv. 1. 99. 2 A spider. 3 A kind of crane. 4 A kind of coitus or mode of sexual enjoyment. 5 A kind of poison. -Comp. -आस्य a. monkey-faced. (-स्यं) copper. -इंदुः ebony. -तिंदुकः a kind of ebony. -पोतः a young monkey. -वासः a cobweb. -शीर्षं vermilion.

मर्कटकः 1 An ape. 2 A spider. 3 A kind of fish. 4 A kind of grain.

मर्करा 1 A pot, vessel. 2 A subterranean hole, cavity, cavern, hollow. 3 A barren woman.

मर्च् 10 U. (मर्चयति-ते) 1 To take. 2 To cleanse. 3 To sound.

मर्जूः 1 A washerman. 2 A catamite. f. Cleansing, washing, purification.

मर्तः 1 A man, human being, mortal. 2 The earth, the world of mortals.

मर्त्य *a*. Mortal. **-र्त्यः 1** A mortal, a human being, man; Ms. 5. 97. **2** The world of mortals, the earth. **-र्त्यं** The body. **-Comp. -धर्मः** mortality. **-धर्मन्** *a*. mortal. **-निवासिन्** *m*. a mortal, human being. **-भावः** human nature. **-भुवनं** the earth. **-महितः** a god. **-मुखः** a *kinnara*, a being having the face of a man and the figure of an animal, and regarded as an attendant of Kubera. **-लोकः** the world of mortals, the earth; क्षी पुण्ये मर्त्यलोकं विशंति Bg. 9 21.

मर्द *a*. Crushing, pounding, grinding, destroying &c. (at the end of comp.). **-र्दः 1** Grinding, pounding. **2** A violent stroke.

मर्दन *a* (**नी** *f*.) Crushing, grinding, destroying, tormenting &c. **-नं 1** Crushing, grinding **2** Rubbing, shampooing. **3** Anointing, (with unguents &c.). **4** Pressing, kneading. **5** Paining, tormenting, afflicting. **6** Destroying, devastating.

मर्दलः A kind of drum; *Si*. 6. 31; Rs. 2. 1.

मर्ब् 1. P. (मर्बति) To go, move.

मर्मन् *n*. **1** A vital part of the body, the vitals; तथैव तीव्रो हृदि शोकशंकुर्मर्माणि कृंतन्नपि किं न सोढः U 2. 35; Y. 1 153; Bk. 16. 15; स्वहृदयमर्मणि वर्म करोति Gît. 4. **2** Any weak or vulnerable point, a defect, failing. **3** The core, quick. **4** Any joint (of a limb). **5** The secret or hidden meaning, the pith or essence (of anything); काव्यमर्मप्रकाशिका टीका ; नत्वा गंगाधरं मर्मप्रकाशं तनुते गुरुं-नागेशभट्ट. **6** A secret, a mystery. **-Comp. -अतिग** *a*. piercing deeply into the vital parts; *Si*. 20. 77. **-अन्वेषणं 1** probing the vital Parts. **2** seeking weak or vulnerable points. **-आवरणं** an armour, a coat of mail. **-आविध्, उपघातिन्** *a*. piercing the vitals (of the heart); Mv. 3. 10. **-कीलः** a husband. **-ग** *a*. piercing to the quick, very acute, poignant. **-घ्न** *a*. Piercing the vitals, excessively painful. **-चरं** the heart. **-छिद्, -भिद्** (so **छेदिन्, भेदिन्**) *a*. **1** piercing the vitals, cutting to the quick, excessively painful; U. 3. 31. **2** wounding mortally, mortal. **-ज्ञ** *a*., **विद्** *a*. **1** knowing the weak or vlunerable points of another. **2** knowing the most secret portions of a subject. **3** having a deep insight into anything, exceedingly acute or clever. (**-ज्ञः**) any acute or learned man. **-त्रं** a coat of mail. **-पारग** *a*. having a deep insight into, thoroughly conversant with, one who has entered into the secret recesses of anything. **-भेदः 1** piercing the vitals. **2** disclosing the secrets or vulnerable points of another. **-भेदनः, भेदिन्** *m*. an arrow. **-विद्** see मर्मज्ञ. **-स्थलं, स्थानं 1** a sensitive or vital part. **2** a weak or vulnerable point. **-स्पृश् 1** piercing the vitals, stinging to the quick. **2** very cutting, poignant, sharp or stinging (words &c.).

मर्मर *a*. Rustling (leaves, garments &c.); तीरेषु तालीवनमर्मरेषु R. 6. 57, 4. 73; 19. 41; मदोद्धताः प्रत्यनिलं विचेरुर्वनस्थलीर्मर्मरपत्रमोक्षाः Ku. 3. 31. **-रः 1** A rustling sound. **2** A murmur.

मर्मरी 1 A species of pine tree **2** Turmeric.

मर्मरीकः 1 A poor man, pauper. **2** A wicked man.

मर्या 1 A limit, boundary.

मर्यादा 1 A limit, boundary (fig. also); bound, border, frontier, verge; मर्यादाव्यतिक्रमः Pt. 1. **2** End, termination, terminus. **3** A shore, bank. **4** A mark, land-mark. **5** The bounds of morality, any fixed usage or established rule, moral law. **6** A rule of propriety or decorum, bounds or limits of propriety, propriety of conduct; आस्तातापवादभिन्नमर्याद U. 5; Pt. 1. 142. **7** A contract, covenant, an agreement. **-Comp. -अचलः, गिरिः, पर्वतः** a frontier mountain. **-भेदकः** a destroyer of land-marks.

मर्यादिन् *m*. A neighbour, borderer.

मर्व् 1 P. (मर्वति) **1** To go, move. **2** To fill.

मर्शः 1 Deliberation. **2** Advice, counsel. **3** A sternutatory.

मर्शनं 1 Rubbing. **2** Examination, inquiry. **3** Consideration, deliberation. **4** Advising, counselling. **5** Removing, rubbing off.

मर्षः, मर्षणं Endurance, forbearance, patience.

मर्षित, *p. p*. **1** Endured, patiently borne or endured. **2** Excused, forgiven. **-तं** Endurance, patience.

मर्षिन् *a*. Enduring, forbearing.

मल् 1 A. 10 P. (मलते, मलयति) To hold, possess.

मलः -लं 1 Dirt, filth, impurity, dust, any impure matter; मलदायकाः खलाः K. 2; छाया न मूर्छति मलोपहतप्रसादे शुद्धे तु दर्पणतले सुलभावकाशा *S*. 7. 32. **2** Dress, refuse, sediment, feces, dunf. **3** Dross (of metals), rust, alloy. **4** Moral taint or impurity, sin. **5** Any impure secretion of the body; (according to Manu these excretions are twelve:- वसा शुक्रमसृङ् मज्जा मूत्रविड् घ्राणकर्णविट्। श्लेष्माश्रुदूषिका स्वेदो द्वादशैते नृणां मलाः Ms. 5. 135.) **6** Camphor. **7** Cuttle-fish bone. **8** Tanned leather; a leather-garment. **-लं** A kind of base metal. **Comp. -अपकर्षणं 1** removing the dirt, purification. **2** removal of sin. **-अरिः** a kind of natron. **-अवरोधः** constipation of the bowels. **-आकर्षिन्** *m*. a sweeper, scavenger. **-आवह** *a*. causing dirt, dirtying, soiling. **2** defiling, polluting. **-आशयः** the stomach. **-उत्सर्गः** evacuation of the feces, voiding the excrement. **-घ्न** *a*. cleaning, detergent. **-जं** pus, matter. **-दूषित** *a*. dirty, foul, soiled. **-द्रवः** purging, diarrhœa. **-धात्री** a nurse who attends to a child's necessities. **-पृष्ठं** the first (or outer) page of a book. **-भुज्** *m*. a crow. **-मल्लकः** a strip of cloth covering the privities (कौपीन). **-मासः** an intercalary month (so called because during that month religious ceremonies are not performed). **-वासस्** *f*. a woman in her courses. **-विसर्गः, -विसर्जनं, शुद्धिः** *f*. evacuation of the bowels. **-हारक** *a*. removing dirt or sin.

मलनं Crushing, grinding. **-नः** A tent.

मलयः 1 N. of a mountain range in the south of India, abounding in sandal trees; (Poets usually represent the breeze from the Malaya mountain as wafting the odour of sandal trees and other plants growing thereon, which peculiarly affects persons who are smit with love), स्तनाविवशिशस्तस्याः शैलौ मलयदर्दुरौ R. 4. 51; 9. 25; 13. 2; विना मलयमन्यत्र चंदनं न प्ररोहति Pt. 1. 41. **2** N. of the country lying to the east of the Malaya range, Malabar. **3** A garden. **4** The garden of Indra. **-Comp. -अचलः, -अद्रिः, -गिरिः, -पर्वतः** &c. the Malaya mountain. **-आनिलः, -वातः, समीरः** the wind blowing from the Malaya mountain, south-wind; ललितलवंगलतापरिशीलनकोमलमलयसमीरे Gît. 1; cf. अपगतदाक्षिण्य दक्षिणानिलहतक पूर्णास्ते मनोरथाः कृतं कर्तव्यं वहेदानीं यथेष्टं K. **-उद्भवं** sandalwood. **-जः** a sandal tree; अयि मलयज महिमायं कस्य गिरामस्तु विषयस्ते Bv. 1. 11. (**-जः -जं**) sandal-wood. (**-जं**) an epithet of Râhu. °**रजस्** *n*. the dust of sandal. **-द्रुमः** a sandal tree. **-वासिनी** an epithet of Durgâ.

मलाका 1 An amorous or lustful woman. **2** A female messenger, confidante. **3** A female elephant.

मलिन *a*. **1** Dirty, foul, filthy, impure, unclean, soiled, stained, sullied (fig. also); धन्यास्तदंगरजसा मलिनीभवंती *S*. 7. 17; किमिति सुधा मालिनं यशः कुरुध्वे Ve. 3. 4. **2** Black, dark (fig. also); मलिनमपि हिमांशोर्लक्ष्म लक्ष्मीं तनोति, *S*. 1. 20; अतिमालिने कर्तव्ये भवति, खलानामतीव निपुणा धीः Vâs.; *Si*. 9. 18. **3** Sinful, wicked, depraved; मलिनाचरितं कर्म सुरभेर्नन्वसांप्रतं Kâv. 2. 178. **4** Low, vile; base; लघवः प्रकटीभवंति मलिनाश्रयतः *Si*. 9. 23. **5** Clouded, obscured. **-नं 1** Sin, fault guilt. **2** Butter-milk. **3** Borax. **-ना, -नी** A woman during menstruation. **-Comp.**

-अंबु *n.* 'black water', ink. -आस्य *a.* 1 having a dirty or black face. 2 low, vulgar. 3 savage, cruel. -प्रभ *a.* obscured, soiled, clouded. -मुख *a.* =मलिनास्य q. v. (-खः) 1 fire. 2 a ghost, an evil spirit. 3 a kind of monkey (गोलांगूल).

मलिनयति Den. P. 1 To make dirty, soil, stain, defile, sully, spoil; यदा-मेधाविनी शिष्योपदेशं मलिनयति तदाचार्यस्य दोषो ननु M. 1. 'stains or brings discredit on' &c. 2 To corrupt, deprave.

मलिनिमन् *m.* 1 Dirtiness, foulness, impurity. 2 Blackness, darkness; मलिनिमालिनि माधवयोषितां Si. 6. 4. 3 Moral impurity, sin.

मलिम्लुचः 1 A robber, thief; Si 16. 52. 2 A demon. 3 A gnati, mosquito. 4 An intercalary month. 5 Air, wind. 6 Fire. 7 A Brâhmaṇa who neglects the five daily Yaj*n*as or sacrifices.

मलीमस *a.* 1 Dirty, foul, impure, unclean, stained, soiled; मा ते मलीमसविकारघना मतिर्भूत् Mâl. 1. 32; R 2. 53. 2 Dark, black, of a black colour; पणिता न जनारवैरवैदपि कूजंतमलिं मलीमसं N. 2. 92; विसारितामाजिहत कोकिलावलीमलीमसा जलदमदांबुराजयः Si. 17. 57, 1. 58. 3 Wicked, sinful, wrong; unrighteous; मलीमसामाददते न पद्धतिं R. 3. 46. -सः 1 Iron. 2 Green vitriol.

मल्ल् 1 A. (मल्लते) To hold, possess.

मल्ल *a.* 1 Strong, athletic, robust; Ki. 18. 8. 2 Good; excellent. -ल्लः 1 A strong man. 2 An athlete, a boxer, wrestler, प्रभुर्मल्लो मल्लाय Mbh. 3 A drinking-vessel, cup. 4 The remnants of an oblation. 5 The cheek of and temple. -Comp. -अरिः 1 an epithet of Krishṇa. 2 of Siva. -क्रीडा boxing or wrestling match. -जं blackpepper. -तूर्यं a kind of drum. -भूः, -भूमिः *f.* 1 an arena, a wrestling ground. 2 N. of a country. -युद्धं a wrestling or boxing match, pugilistic encounter. -विद्या the art of wrestling. -शाला a gymnasium.

मल्लकः 1 A lamp-stand. 2 An oil-vessel, a lamp-vessel. 3 A lamp. 4 A cup made out of a cocoa-nut shell. 5 A tooth. 6 A kind of jasmine.

मल्लिः -ल्ली *f.* A kind of Jasmine. -Comp. -गंधि *n.* a kind of agallochum. -नाथः N. of a celebrated commentator who probably lived in the fourteenth or fifteenth century; (he has written commentaries on रघुवंश, कुमारसंभव, मेघदूत, किरातार्जुनीय, नैषधचरित, and शिशुपालवध). -पत्रं a mushroom.

मल्लिकः 1 A kind of goose with brown legs and bill. 2 The month Mâgha. 3 A shuttle. -Comp. -अक्षः, -आख्यः a kind of goose with brown legs and bill; एतस्मिन्मदकलमल्लिकाक्षपक्षव्याधुतस्फुरदुरुदंडपुंडरीकाः (भुवो विभागाः) U. 1. 31; Mâl. 9. 14. -अर्जुनः N. of a Linga of Siva on the mountain Srîsaila. -आख्या a kind of jasmine.

मल्लिका 1 A kind of jasmine; वनेषु सायंतनमल्लिकानां विजृंभणोद्गंधिषु कड्मलेषु R. 16. 47. 2 A flower of this jasmine; विन्यस्तसायंतनमल्लिकेषु (केशेषु) R. 16. 50; Kâv. 2. 215. 3 A lamp-stand. 4 An earthen vessel of a particular form. -Comp. -गंधं a kind of agallochum.

मल्लीकरः A thief.

मल्लुः bear.

मव् 1 P. ((मवति) To fasten, bind.

मव्य् 1 P. (मव्यति) To bind.

मश् 1 P. (मशति) 1 To buzz, hum, make a sound. 2 To be angry.

मशः 1 A mosquito. 2 Hum, humming. 3 Anger. -Comp. -हरी a mosquito-curtain.

मशकः 1 A mosquito, gnat; सर्वं खलस्य चरितं मशकः करोति H. 81; Ms. 1. 85. 2 A particular disease of the skin. 3 A leather water-bag. -Comp. -कुटिः-टी *f.*, -वरणं a whisk for scaring away mosquitos. -हरी a mosquito-curtain.

मशकिन् *m.* The *udumbara* tree.

मशुनः A dog.

मष् 1 P. (मषति) To hurt, injure, kill, destroy.

मषिः-षी *f.* = मसी q. v.

मस् 4 P. (मस्यति) 1 To weigh, measure, mete. 2 To change form.

मसः A measure, weight.

मसनं 1 Measuring, weighing. 2 A species of medicinal plant.

मसरा A kind of pulse.

मसारः, मसारकः An emerald.

मसिः *m. f.* 1 Ink. 2 Lamp-black, soot. 3 A black powder used to paint the eyes. -Comp. -आधारः, -कूपी, -धानः, -धानी, -मणिः an ink-bottle, an ink-stand. -जलं ink. -पण्यः a writer, scribe. -पथः a pen. -प्रसूः *f.* 1 a pen. 2 an ink-bottle. -वर्धनं myrrh.

मसिकः A serpent's hole.

मसी *See* मसि above. -Comp. -जलं ink. -धानी an ink-stand. -पटलं a coating of soot; शिरसि मसीपटलं दधाति दीपः Bv. 1. 74.

मसु(-सू)रः 1 A kind of pulse. 2 A pillow. -रा 1 A lentil. 2 A harlot.

मसूरिका 1 A kind of small pox (erection of small pustules). 2 A mosquito-curtain. 3 A procuress bawd.

मसूरी A kind of small-pox.

मसृण *a.* 1 Unctuous, oily; मसृणचंदनचर्चितांगी Ch. P. 7; or सरसमसृणमपि मलयजपंकं Gît. 4. 2 Soft, tender, smooth; U. 1. 38. 3 Bland, mild, sweet, मसृणवाणि Gît. 10. 4 lovely, charming; विनयमसृणो वाचि नियमः U. 2. 2; 4. 21. 5 Beaming, glistening; Mâl. 1. 27; 4. 2. -णा Linseed.

मस्क् 1 P. (मस्कति) To go, move.

मस्करः 1 A bamboo. 2 A hollow bamboo. 3 Going, motion. 4 Knowledge (ज्ञान).

मस्करिन् *m.* 1 An ascetic or religious mendicant, a Brâhmaṇa in the fourth order; धारयन् मस्करिव्रतं Bk. 5. 63. 2 The moon.

मस्ज् 6 P. (मज्जति, मग्न; *caus.* मज्जयति; *desid.* मिमंक्षति) 1 To bathe, plunge, dip or throw oneself into water; R. 15. 101; Bv. 2. 95. 2 To sink, sink into or down, sink under, plunge (with loc. or acc.); सीदन्नंधे तमसि विधुरो मज्जतीवांतरात्मा U. 3. 38; Mâl. 9. 30; सोऽसंवृतं नाम तमः सह तेनैव मज्जति Ms. 4. 81; R. 16 52. 3 To be drowned, perish (in water). 4 To sink into misfortune. 5 To despond, be discouraged or disheartened. -WITH उद् to come out of water, emerge (into view), rise up; वन्यः सरितो गज उन्ममज्ज R. 5. 43. 16. 79; Ki. 9. 23; Si. 9. 30. -नि 1 to sink, sink down or under, sink. into (fig. also); यथा प्लवेनौपलेन निमज्जत्युदके तरन्। तथा निमज्जतोऽधस्तादज्ञौ दातृप्रतीच्छकौ Ms. 4. 194; 5. 73; शोके मुहुश्चाविरतं न्यमांक्षीत् Bk. 3. 30, 15. 31; Si. 9. 74; Gît. 1. 2 to be merged into, merge, disappear, escape observation; एको हि दोषो गुणसन्निपाते निमज्जतींदोः किरणेष्विवांकः Ku. 1. 3.

मस्तं The head. -Comp. -दारु *n.* the *devadâru* tree. -मूलकं the neck.

मस्तकः-कं 1 The head, skull; अतिलोभा(v. l. तृष्णा)भिभूतस्य चक्रं भ्रमति मस्तके Pt. 5. 22. 2 The head or top of anything; न च पर्वतमस्तके Ms. 4. 47; वृक्ष° चुली° &c. -Comp. -आख्यः the top of a tree. -ज्वरः, -शूलं an acute headache. -पिंडकः-कं a round protuberance on the temples of an elephant in rut. -मूलकं the neck. -स्नेहः the brain.

मस्तिकं The head.

मस्तिष्कं The brain. -Comp. -त्वच् *f.* the membrane which surrounds the brain.

मस्तु *n.* 1 Sour cream. 2 Whey. -Comp. -लुंगः,-गं, -लुंगकः-कं the brain.

मह् I. 1 P., 10 U. (महति, महयति-ते, महित) To honour; respect, hold in great esteem, worship, revere, value greatly; गोप्तारं न निधीनां महयंति महेश्वरं विबुधाः Subhâsh.; जयश्रीविन्यस्तैर्महित इव मंदारकुसुमैः Gît. 11; Ku. 5. 12; Ki. 5. 7, 24; Bk. 10. 2; R. 5. 25, 11. 49. -II. 1 A. (महते) To grow or increase.

महः 1 A festival, festive occasion; बंधुताहृदयकौमुदीमहः Mâl. 9. 21; स खलु दूरगतोऽप्यतिवर्तते महमसाविति बंधुतयोदितैः Si. 6. 19; मदनमहं Ratn. 1. 2 An offering, sacrifice. **3** A buffalo. **4** Light, lustre ; cf. महस् also.

महकः **1** An eminent man. **2** A tortoise. **3** N. of Vishṇu.

महत् *a.* (compar. महीयस् ; superl. महिष्ठ; Nom. महान्, महांतौ, महांतः ; acc. pl. महतः) **1** Great, big, large, huge, vast ; महान् सिंहः-व्याघ्रः &c. **2** Ample, copious, abundant, many, numerous; महाजनः, महान् द्रव्यराशिः. **3** Long, extended, extensive ; महांतौ बाहू यस्य स महाबाहुः; so महती कथा, महानध्वा. **4** Strong, powerful, mighty ; as महान् वीरः. **5** Violent, intense, excessive; महती शिरोवेदना, महती पिपासा. **6** Gross, thick, dense ; महानंधकारः. **7** Important, weighty, momentous ; महत्कार्यमुपस्थितं, महती वार्ता. **8** High, lofty, eminent, distinguished, noble ; महत्कुलं, महाञ्जनः. **9** Loud ; महान् घोषः -ध्वनिः. **10** Early or late; महति प्रत्यूषे 'early in the morning'; महत्यपराह्णे 'late in the afternoon.' **11** High; महार्घ. *-m.* **1** A camel. **2** An epithet of *S*iva. **3** (In Sân. phil.) The great principle, the intellect (distinguished from मनस्), the second of the twenty five elements or *tattvas* recognized by the Sânkhyas ; Ms. 12. 14 ; Sân. K. 3, 8, 22 &c. *-n.* **1** Greatness, infiniteness, numerousness. **2** Kingdom, dominion. **3** Sacred knowledge.*-ind.* Greatly, excessively, very much, exceedingly. (*Note.* **महत्** as the first member of a Tatpurusha compound and a few other cases, remains unchanged, while in Karmadhâraya and Bahuvrîhi compounds it is changed to महा q. v.) **-Comp.** **-आवासः** a spacious or large building. **-आशा** a high hope. **-आश्चर्य** *a.* very wonderful. **-आश्रयः** dependence on, or seeking protection with, the great. **-कथ** *a.* talked of or mentioned by the great, in great men's mouths. **-क्षेत्र** *a.* occupying a wide terrritory. **-तत्त्वं** the second of the 25 principles of the Sânkhyas. **-बिलं** the atmosphere. **-सेवा** service of the great. **-स्थानं** a high place, lofty station.

महती **1** A kind of lute. **2** N. of the lute of Nârada ; अवेक्षमाणं महतीं मुहुर्मुहुः *S*i. 1. 10. **3** The egg-plant. **4** Greatness, importance.

महत्तर *a.* Greater larger &c. **-रः** **1** The principal, chief, or oldest person, the most respectable person; U. 4. **2** A chamberlain. **3** A courtier. **4** The head or the oldest man of a village.

महत्तरकः A courtier, chamberlain.

महत्त्वं **1** Greatness, largeness, magnitude, great extent. **2** Mightiness, majesty. **3** Importance. **4** Exalted position, height, elevation. **5** Intensity, violence, high degree.

महनीय *a.* Worthy of honour, respectable, worthy, illustrious, glorious, noble, exalted ; महनीयशासनः R. 3. 69 ; महनीयकीर्तेः 2. 25.

महंतः The superior of a monastery.

महर् (**महस्**) *ind.* The fourth of the seven worlds which rise one above the other from the earth (being between *svar* and *janas*) ; (**महर्लोक** also in this sense).

महल्लः,-महल्लिकः A eunuch in a king's harem (a word derived from Arabic).

महल्लक *a.* Weak, feeble, old. **-कः** **1** A eunuch in a king's harem. **2** A large house, halatial building ; (cf. Mar. महाल.)

महस् *n.* **1** A festival, a festive occasion. **2** An offering, oblation, a sacrifice. **3** Light, lustre ; कल्याणानां त्वमसि महसां भाजनं विश्वमूर्ते Mâl. 1. 3 ; U. 4. 10. **4** The fourth of seven worlds; see महर्.

महस्वत्, महस्विन् *a.* Splendid, bright, brilliant, luminous, lustrous.

महा A cow.

महा The substitute of महत् at the beginning of Karmadhâraya and Bahuvrîhi compounds, and also at the beginning of some other irregular words. (*Note.* The number of compounds of which महा is the first member is very large and may be multiplied *ad infinitum* The more important of them, or such as have peculiar significations, are given below). **-Comp.** **-अक्षः** an epithet of *S*iva. **-अंग** *a.* huge, bulky. (**-गः**) **1** a camel. **2** a kind of rat. **3** N. of *S*iva. **-अंजनः** N. of a mountain. **-अत्ययः** a great danger of calamity. **-अध्वनिक** *a.* 'having gone a long way', dead. **-अध्वरः** a great sacrifice. **-अनसं** a heavy carriage. (**-सः-सं**) a kitchen. **-अनुभाव** *a.* **1** of great prowess, dignified, noble, glorious, magnanimous, exalted, illustrious; *S*i. 1. 17; *S*. 3. **2** virtuous, righteous, just. (**-वः**) a worthy or respectable person. **-अंतकः** **1** death. **2** an epithet of *S*iva. **-अंधकारः** **1** thick darkness. **2** gross (spiritual) ignorance. **-अंध्राः** (*pl.*) N. of a people and their country. **-अन्वय, -अभिजन** *a.* nobly born, of noble birth. (**-यः, -नः**) noble birth, high descent. **-अभिषवः** the great extraction of Soma. **-अमात्यः** the chief or prime minister (of a king). **-अंबुकः** an epithet of *S*iva. **-अंबुजं** a billion. **-अम्ल** *a.* very sour. (**-म्लं**) the fruit of the tamarind tree. **-अरण्यं** a great (dreary) forest, large forest. **-अर्घ** *a.* very costly, costing a high price. (**-र्घः**) a kind of quail. **-अर्घ्य** *a.* valuable, precious. **-अर्चिस्** *a.* flaming high. **अर्णवः** **1** the great ocean. **2** N. of *S*iva. **-अर्बुदं** one thousand millions. **-अर्ह** *a.* **1** very valuable, very costly; Ku. 5. 12. **2** invaluable, inestimable; U. 6. 11. (**-र्हं**) white sandal-wood. **अवरोहः** the fig-tree. **-अशनिध्वजः** a great banner in the form of the thunderbolt; R. 3. 56. **-अशन** *a.* voracious, gluttonous. **-अश्मन्** *m.* a precious stone, ruby. **-अष्टमी** the eighth day in the bright half of Asvina sacred to Durgâ. **-असिः** a large sword. **-असुरी** N. of Durgâ. **-अह्नः** the afternoon. **-आकार** *a.* extensive, large, great. **-आचार्यः** **1** a great teacher. **2** an epithet of *S*iva. **-आढ्य** *a.* wealthy, very rich. (**-ढ्यः**) the Kadamba tree. **-आत्मन्** *a.* **1** high-souled, high-minded, magnanimous, noble ; अयं दुरात्मा अथवा महात्मा कौटिल्यः Mu. 7; द्विषंति मंदाश्चरितं महात्मनां Ku. 5. 75; U. 1. 49. **2** illustrious, distinguished, exalted, eminent. (*-m.*) the Supreme Spirit; Ms. 1. 54 ; (**महात्मवत्** means the same as महात्मन्). **-आनकः** a kind of large drum. **-आनंदः, -नंदः** **1** a great joy or bliss. **2** especially, the great bliss of final beatitude. **-आपगा** a great river. **-आयुधः** an epithe of *S*iva. **-आरंभ** *a.* undertaking great works, enterprizing. (**-भः**) any great enterprize. **-आलयः** **1** a temple in general. **2** a sanctuary, an asylum. **3** a great dwelling. **4** a place of pilgrimage. **5** the world of Brahman. **6** the Supreme spirit. (**-या**) N. of a particular deity. **-आशय** *a.* high-souled, nobl-minded, magnanimous, noble; see महात्मन्. (**-यः**) **1** a noble-minded or magnanimous person; महाशयचक्रवर्ती Bv. 1. 70. **2** the ocean. **-आस्पद** *a.* **1** occupying a great position. **2** mighty, powerful. **-आहवः** a great or tumultuous fight. **-इच्छ** *a.* **1** magnanimous, noble-minded, high-souled, noble; R. 18. 33. **2** having lofty aims or aspirations, ambitious. **-इंद्रः** **1** 'the great Indra,' N. of Indra ; Ku. 5. 53; R. 13. 20; Ms. 7. 7. **2** a chief or leader in general. **3** N. of a mountain range; °**चापः** rain-bow. °**नगरी** N. of Amarâvatî, the capital of Indra. °**मंत्रिन्** *m.* an epithet of Brihaspati. **-इष्वासः** a great archer, a great warrior; Bg. 1. 4 **-ईशः, -ईशानः** N. of *S*iva. **-ईशानी** N. of Pârvatî. **-ईश्वरः** **1** a great lord, sovereign. **2** N. of *S*iva. **3** of Vishṇu. (**-री**) N. of Durgâ. **-उक्षः** (for उक्षन्) a large bull, a full grown or strong bull ; महोक्षतां वत्सतरः स्पृशन्निव R. 3. 32, 4. 22, 6. 72 ; *S*i. 5. 63. **-उत्पलं** a large blue lotus.

–उत्सवः 1 a great festival or occasion of joy. 2 the god of love. –उत्साह *a.* possessed of great energy, energetic persevering. (ः–हः) perseverance, –उदधिः 1 the great ocean ; R. 3. 17. 2 an epithet of Indra. °जः a conch-shell, shell. –उदय *a.* very prosperous or lucky, very glorious or splendid ; of great prosperity. (–यः) 1 great elevation or rise, greatness, prosperity ; R. 8. 16. 2 final beatitude. 3 a lord, master. 4 N. of the district called Kânyakubja or Kanouja. 5 N. of the capital of Kanouja. 6 sour milk mixed with honey. –उदर *a.* big-bellied, corpulent. (–रं) 1 a big belly. 2 dropsy. –उदार *a.* very generous or magnanimous. –उद्यम *a.* = महोत्साह q. v. –उद्योग *a.* very industrious or diligent, hard-working. –उन्नत *a.* exceedingly lofty. (–तः) the palmyra tree. –उन्नतिः *f.* great rise or elevation (fig. also), high rank. –उपकारः a great obligation. –उपाध्यायः a great preceptor, a learned teacher. –उरगः a great serpent ; R. 12. 98. –उरस्क *a.* broad-chested. (–स्कः) an epithet of *S*iva. –उल्का 1 a great meteor. 2 a great firebrand. –ऋद्धिः *f.* great prosperity or affluence. –ऋषभः a great bull. –ऋषिः 1 a great sage or saint; (the term is applied in Ms. 1. 34 to the ten *Prajâpatis* or patriarchs of mankind, but it is also used in the general sense of 'a great sage'). 2 N. of *S*iva. –ओष्ठ (महोष्ठ) *a.* having large lips. (–ष्ठः) an epithet of *S*iva. –ओजस *a.* very mighty or powerful possessed of great splendour or glory ; महौजसो मानधना धनार्चिताः Ki. 1. 19. (*–m.*) a great hero or warrior, a champion. –ओजसं the discus of Vishṇu. –ओषधिः *f.* 1 a very efficacious medicinal plant, a sovereign drug. 2 the Dûrvâ grass. –औषधं 1 a sovereign remedy, panacea. 2 ginger. 3 garlic. 4 a kind of poison (वत्सनाभ). –कच्छः 1 the sea. 2 N. of Varuṇa. 3 a mountain. –कंदः garlic. –कपर्दः a kiud of shell. –कपित्थः 1 the Bilva tree. 2 red garlic. –कंबु *a.* stark naked. (–बुः) an epithet of *S*iva. –कर *a.* 1 large-handed. 2 having a large revenue. –कर्णः an epithet of *S*iva. –कर्मन् *a.* doing great works. (*m.*) an epithet of *S*iva. –कला the night of the new moon. –कविः 1 a great poet, a classical poet such as कालिदास, भवभूति, बाण, भारवि &c. 2 an epithet of *S*ukra. –कांतः an epithet of *S*iva. (–ता) the earth. –काय *a.* big-bodied, big, gigantic, bulky. (–यः) 1 an elephant. 2 an epithet of *S*iva. 3 of Vishṇu. 4 of a being attending on *S*iva (= नंदि). –कार्तिकी the night of full-moon in the month of Kârtika. –कालः 1 a form of *S*iva in his character as the destroyer of the world. 2 N. of a celebrated shrine or temple of *S*iva (Mahâkâla), established at Ujjayinî (immortalized by Kâlidâsa in his Meghadûta, which gives a very beautiful description of the god, his temple, worship &c., together with a graphic picture of the city ; cf. Me. 30–38 ; also R. 6. 34). 3 an epithet of Vishṇu. 4 N. of a kind of gourd. °पुरं the city of Ujjayinî. –काली an epithet of Durgâ in her terrific form. –काव्यं a great or classical poem ; (for a full description of its nature, contents &c. according to Rhetoricians see S. D. 559). (The number of Mahâkâvyas is usually said to be five :—रघुवंश, कुमारसंभव, किरातार्जुनीय, शिशुपालवध and नैषधचरित, or six if मेघदूत—a very small poem or खंडकाव्य—be added to the list. But this enumeration is apparently only traditional, as there are several other poems, such as the भट्टिकाव्य, विक्रमांकदेवचरित, हरविजय &c. which have an equal claim to be considered as Mahâkâvyas :). –कुमारः the eldest son of a reigning prince, heir-apparent. –कुल *a.* of noble birth or descent, sprung from a noble family nobly-born. (–लं) a noble birth or family, high decent. –कृच्छ्रं a great penance. –कोशः an epithet of *S*iva. –क्रतुः a great sacrifice; *e. g.* a horse-sacrifice ; R. 3. 46. –क्रमः an epithet of Vishṇu. –क्रोधः an epithet of *S*iva. –क्षत्रपः a great satrap. –क्षीरः sugarcane. –खर्वः–र्वं a high number (ten billions ?). –गजः a great elephant ; see दिक्करिन्. –गणपतिः a form of the god Gaṇesa. –गंधः a kind of cane. (–धं) a kind of sandal-wood. –गवः *Bos gavæus.* –गुण *a.* very efficacious, sovereign (as a medicine). –गृष्टिः a cow with a large hump. –ग्रहः an epithet of Râhu. –ग्रीवः 1 a camel. 2 an epithet of *S*iva. –ग्रीविन् *m.* a camel. –घूर्णा spirituous liquor. –घोषं a market, fair. (–षः) a loud noise, clamour. –चक्रवर्तिन् *m.* a universal monarch. –चमूः *f.* a large army. –छायः the fig-tree. –जटः an epithet of *S*iva. –जत्रु *a.* having a great collar-bone. (–त्रुः) an epithet of *S*iva. –जनः 1 a multitude of men, a great many beings, the general populace or public ; महाजनो येन गतः स पंथाः Mb. 2 the populace, mob ; महाजनः स्मेरमुखो भविष्यति Ku. 5. 70. 3 a great man, a distinguished or eminent man ; महाजनस्य संसर्गः कस्य नो न्नतिकारकः । पद्मपत्रस्थितं तोयं धत्ते मुक्ताफलश्रियं Subhâsh. 4 the chief of a trade. 5 a merchant, tradesman. –जातीय *a.* 1 rather large. 2 of an excellent kind. –ज्योतिस् *m.* an epithet of *S*iva. –तपस् *m.* 1 a great ascetic. 2 an epithet of Vishṇu. –तलं N. of one of the seven lower regions ; see पाताल. –तिक्तः the *Nimba* tree. –तीक्ष्ण *a.* exceedingly sharp or pungent. (–क्ष्णा) the marking-nut plant. –तेजस् *a.* 1 possessed of great lustre or splendour. 2 very vigorous or powerful, heroic. (*–m.*) 1 a hero, warrior. 2 fire. 3 an epithet of Kârtikeya. (*–n.*) quick-silver. –दंतः 1 an elephant with large tusks. 2 an epithet of *S*iva. –दंडः 1 a long arm. 2 a severe punishment. –दशा the influence exercised (over a man's destiny) by a predominant planet. –दारू *n.* the *Devadaru* tree. –देवः N. of *S*iva. (–वी) N. of Pârvati. –द्रुमः the sacred fig tree. –धन *a.* 1 rich. 2 expensive, costly. (–नं) 1 gold. 2 incense. 3 a costly or rich dress. –धनुस् *m.* an epithet of *S*iva. –धातुः 1 gold. 2 an epithet of *S*iva. 3 of Meru. –नटः an epithet of *S*iva. –नदः a great river. –नदी 1 a great river ; such as Gangâ, Krishṇâ ; संभूयांभोधिमभ्येति महानद्या नगापगा Si. 2. 100. 2 N. of a river falling into the bay of Bengal. –नंदा 1 spirituous liquor. 2 N. of a river. –नरकः N. of one of the 21 hells. –नलः a kind of reed. –नवमी the ninth day in the bright half of Asvina, sacred to the worship of Durgâ. –नाटकं 'the great drama', N. of a drama, also called Hanumannâtaka, (being popularly ascribed to Hanumat.). –नादः a loud sound, uproar. 2 a great drum. 3 a thunder-cloud. 4 a shell. 5 an elephant. 6 a lion. 7 the ear. 8 a camel. 9 an epithet of *S*iva. (–दं) a musical instrument. –नासः an epithet of *S*iva. –निद्रा 'the great sleep', death. –नियमः an epithet of Vishṇu. –निर्वाणं total extinction of individuality (according to the Buddhists). –निशा 1 the dead of night, the second and third watches of the night; महानिशा तु विज्ञेया मध्यमं प्रहरद्वयम्. –नीचः a washerman. –नील *a.* dark-blue. (–लः) a kind of sapphire or emerald; Si. 1. 16, 4. 44; R. 18. 42. °उपलः a sapphire. –नृत्यः an epithet of *S*iva. –नेमिः a crow. –पक्षः 1 an epithet of Garuḍa. 2 a kind of duck. (–क्षी) an owl. –पंचमूल the five great roots:— बिल्वोग्निमंथः श्योनाकः काश्मरी पाटला तथा सर्वैस्तु मिलितैरेतैः स्यान्महापंचमूलकं ॥. –पंचविषं the five great or deadly poisons:--शृंगी च कालकूटश्च मुस्तको वत्सनाभकः । शंखकर्णीति योगीयं महापंचविषाभिधः ॥. --पथः 1 chief road, principal street, high or main road; Ku. 7. 3. 2 the passage into the next world, *i. e.* death. 3 N. of certain mountain-tops from which devout persons used to throw themselves down to secure entrance into heaven. 4 an epithet of *Siva*. --पद्मः 1 a particular high number. 2 N. of Nârada. 3 N. of one of the nine treasures of Kubera. (--द्मं) 1 a white lotus. 2 N. of a city. °पतिः N. of Nârada. --पराह्णः a late hour in the afternoon. --पातकं 1 a great sin, a heinous crime; ब्रह्महत्या सुरापानं स्तेयं गुर्वंगनागमः । महांति पातकान्याहुस्तत्संसर्गश्च पंचमम् ॥ Ms. 11. 54. 2 any great sin or transgression. --पात्रः a prime minister. --पादः an epithet of Siva. --पाप्मन् *a.* very sinful or wicked. --पुंसः a great man. --पुरुषः 1 a great man, an eminent or distinguished personage; शब्दं महापुरुषसंविहितं निशम्य U. 6. 7. 2 the Supreme Spirit. 3 an epithet of Vishṇu. --पुष्पः a kind of worm. --पूजा great worship; any solemn worship performed on extraordinary occasions. --पृष्ठः a camel. --प्रपंचः the great universe. --प्रभ *a.* of great lustre. (--भः) the light of a lamp. --प्रभुः 1 a great lord. 2 a king, sovereign. 3 a chief. 4 an epithet of Indra. 5 of *Siva*. 6 of Vishṇu. --प्रलयः 'the great dissolution,' the total annihilation of the universe at the end of the life of Brahman, when all the *lokas* with their inhabitants, the gods, saints &c. including Brahman himself, are annihilated. --प्रसादः 1 a great favour. 2 a great present (of food offered to an idol). --प्रस्थानं departing this life, death. --प्राणः 1 the hard breathing or aspirate sound made in the pronunciation of the aspirates. 2 the aspirated letters themselves (pl.); they are:--ख्, घ्, छ्, झ्, ठ्, ढ्, थ्, ध्, फ्, भ्, श्, ष्, स्, ह्. 3 a raven. --प्लवः a great flood, deluge. --फल *a.* bearing much fruit. (--ला) 1 a bitter gourd. 2 a kind of spear. (--लं) a great fruit or reward. --बल *a.* very strong. (--लः) wind. (--लं) lead. °ईश्वरः N. of a Linga of *Siva* near the modern Mahâblehwar. --बाहु *a.* long-armed, powerful. (--हुः) an epithet of Vishṇu. --बि-(वि)लं 1 the atmosphere. 2 the heart. 3 a water-jar, pitcher. 4 a hole, cave. --बी(वी)जः an epithet of *Siva*. --बी(वी)ज्यं the perinæum. --बोधिः a Buddha. --ब्रह्मं,--ब्रह्मन् *n.* the Supreme Spirit. --ब्राह्मणः 1 a great or learned Brâhmaṇa. 2 a low or contemptible Brâhmaṇa. --भागः *a.* 1 very fortunate or blessed, very lucky or prosperous. 2 illustrious, distinguished, glorious; महाभागः कामं नरपतिरभिन्नस्थितिरसौ *S.* 5. 10; Ms. 3. 192. 3 very pure or holy, highly virtuous. --भागिन् *a.* very fortunate or prosperous. --भारतं N. of the celebrated epic which describes the rivalries and contests of the sons of Dhritarâshṭra and Pâṇḍu. (It consists of 18 *parvans* or books, and is said to be the composition of Vyâsa; cf. the word भारत also). --भाष्यं 1 a great commentary. 2 particularly, the great commentary of Patanjali on the Sûtras of Paṇini. --भीमः an epithet of king *Santanu*. --भीरुः a sort of beetle or fly. --भुज *a.* long-armed, powerful. --भूतं a great or primary element; see भूत; तं वेधा विदधे नूनं महाभूतसमाधिना R. 1. 26; Ms. 1. 6. (--तः) a great creature. --भोगा an epithet of Durgâ. --मणिः a costly or precious jewel. --मति *a.* 1 high-minded. 2 clever. (--तिः) N. of Brihaspati or Jupiter. --मद *a.* greatly intoxicated. (--दः) an elephant in rut. --मनस्, मनस्क *a.* 1 high-minded, noble-minded, magnanimous. 2 liberal. 3 proud, haughty. (--*m.*) a fabulous animal called शरभ q. v. --मंत्रिन् *m.* the prime-minister, premier. --महोपाध्यायः 1 a very great preceptor. 2 a title given to learned men and reputed scholars; *e. g.* महामहोपाध्यायमल्लिनाथसूरि &c. --मांसं 'costly flesh', especially human flesh; Mâl. 5. 12. --मात्रः 1 a great officer of state, high state official, a chief minister; मंत्रे कर्मणि भूषायां वित्ते माने परिच्छदे । मात्रा च महती येषां महामात्रास्तु ते स्मृताः ॥; Ms. 9. 259. 2 an elephant-driver or keeper; Pt. 1. 161. 3 a superintendent of elephants. (--त्री) 1 the wife of a chief minister. 2 the wife of a spiritual teacher. --मायः an epithet of Vishṇu. --माया worldly illusion, which makes the material world appear really existent. --मारी cholera, an epidemic. --माहेश्वरः a great worshipper of Mahesvera or *Siva*. --मुखः a crocodile. --मुनिः 1 a great sage. 2 N. of Vyâsa. (--नि *n.*) any medicinal herb or drug. --मूर्धन् *m.* an epithet of *Siva*. --मूलं a large radish. (--लः) a kind of onion. --मूल्य *a.* very costly. (--ल्यः) a ruby. --मृगः 1 any large animal. 2 an elephant. --मेदः the coral tree. --मोहः great infatuation of mind. (--हा) an epithet of Durgâ. --यज्ञः 'a great sacrifice,' a term applied to the five daily sacrifices or acts of peity to be performed by a householder; अध्यापनं ब्रह्मयज्ञः पितृयज्ञस्तु तर्पणम् । होमो दैवो (or देवयज्ञः) बलिर्भौतो (or भूतयज्ञः) नृयज्ञोऽतिथिपूजनम् ॥ Ms. 3. 70, 71, 72. --यमकं 'a great *Yamaka*' *i. e.* a stanza all the four lines of which have exactly the same words, though different in sense; *e. g.* see Ki. 15. 52 where विकाशमीयुर्जगतीशमार्गणाः has four different senses; cf. also Bk. 10. 19. --यात्रा 'the great pilgrimage,' the pilgrimage to Benares. --याम्यः an epithet of Vishṇu. --युगं 'a great Yuga,' consisting of the four *Yugas* of mortals, or comprising 4,320,000 years of men. --योगिन् *m.* 1 an epithet of *Siva*. 2 of Vishṇu. 3 a cock. --रजतं 1 gold. 2 the thorn-apple. --रजनं 1 safflower. 2 gold. --रत्नं a precious jewel. --रथः 1 a great chariot. 2 a great warrior or hero; कुतः प्रभावो धनंजयस्य महारथजयद्रथस्य विपत्तिमुत्पादयितुं Ve. 2; R. 9. 1; *Si.* 3. 22; (a महारथ is thus defined: --एको दशसहस्राणि योधयेद्यस्तु धन्विनां । शस्त्रशास्त्रप्रवीणश्च विज्ञेयः स महारथः ॥). --रस *a.* very savoury. (--सः) 1 a sugar-cane. 2 quicksilver. 3 a precious mineral. (--सं) sour rice-water. --राजः 1 a great king, sovereign or supreme ruler. 2 a respectful mode of addressing kings or other great personages (my lord, your majesty, your highness). °चूतः a kind of mango tree. --राजिकाः (*m. pl.*) an epithet of a class of gods (said to be 220 or 236 in number). --राज्ञी the chief queen, principal wife of a king. --रात्रिः,--त्री *f.* see महाप्रलय. --राष्ट्रः 'the great kingdom', N. of a country in the west of India, the country of the Marâthâs. 2 the people of Mahârâshṭra; the Marâthâs (pl.). (--ष्ट्री) N. of the principal Prâkrita dialect, the language of the people of the Mahârâshṭra; cf. Daṇḍin:--महाराष्ट्राश्रयां भाषां प्रकृष्टं प्राकृतं विदुः Kâv. 1. 34. --रूप *a.* mighty in form. (--पः) 1 an epithet of *Siva*. 2 resin. --रेतस् *m.* an epithet of *Siva*. --रौद्र *a.* very dreadful. (--द्री) an epithet of Durga. --रौरवः N. of one of the 21 hells; Ms. 4. 88-90. --लक्ष्मी 1 the great Lakshmî, or *Sakti* of Nârâyaṇa. 2 a young girl who represents the goddess Durgâ at the Durgâ festival. --लिंगं the great *Linga* or Phalus. (--गः) an epithet of *Siva*. --लोलः a crow. --लोहं a magnet. --वनं 1 a large forest. 2 N. of a large forest in Vrindâvana. --वराहः 'the great boar', an epithet of Vishṇu in his third or boar incarnation. --वसः the porpoise. --वाक्यं 1 a long sentence. 2 any continuous composition or literary work. 3 a great proposition, principal sentence such as तत्वमसि, ब्रह्मैवेदं सर्वं &c. --वातः a stormy wind, violent wind. --वार्तिकं N. of the Vârtikas of Kâtyâyana on Pâṇini's Sûtras. --विदेहा N. of a certain वृत्ति or condition of the mind in the

Yoga system of philosophy. –विभाषा a rule giving a general option or alternative. –विषुवं the vernal equinox. °संक्रांतिः *f.* the vernal equinox (the sun's entering the sign Aries). –वीरः 1 a great hero or warrior. 2 a lion. 3 the thunderbolt of Indra. 4 an epithet of Vishṇu. 5 of Garuḍa. 6 of Hanumat. 7 a cuckoo. 8 a white horse. 9 a sacrificial fire. 10 a sacrificial vessel. 11 a kind of hawk. –वीर्या an epithet of संज्ञा, the wife of the sun. –वृषः a great bull. –वेग *a.* very swift or fleet. (–गः) 1 great speed, excessive velocity. 2 an ape. 3 the bird Garuḍa. –वेल *a.* billowy. –व्याधिः *f.* 1 a great disease. 2 a very bad kind of leprosy (black leprosy). –व्याहृतिः *f.* a great mystical word ; *i. e.* भूर्, भुवस् and स्वर्. –व्रत *a.* very devotional, rigidly observing vows. (–तं) 1 a great vow, a great religious observance. 2 any great or fundamental duty; प्राणैरपि हिता वृत्तिरद्रोहो व्याजवर्जनं । आत्मनीव प्रियाधानमेतन्मैत्रीमहाव्रतं Mv. 5. 59. –व्रतिन् *m.* 1 a devotee, an ascetic. 2 an epithet of *S*iva. –शक्तिः 1 an epithet of *S*iva. 2 of Kârtikeya. –शंखः 1 a great conch-shell; Bg. 1. 15. 2 the temporal bone, forehead. 3 a human bone. 4 a particular high number. –शठः a kind of thorn-apple. –शब्द *a.* making a loud sound, very noisy, boisterous. –शल्कः a kind of sea-crab or prawn ; Ms. 3. 272. –शालः a great householder. –शिरस् *m.* a kind of serpent. –शुक्तिः *f.* a pearl-shell. –शुक्ला an epithet of Sarasvatî. –शुभ्रं silver. –शूद्रः (द्री *f.*) 1 a *S*ûdra in a high position. 2 a cowherd. –श्मशानं an epithet of Benares. –श्रमणः an epithet of Buddha. –श्वासः a kind of asthma. –श्वेता 1 an epithet of Sarasvatî. 2 of Durgâ. 3 white sugar. –संक्रांतिः *f.* the winter solstice. –सती a very chaste woman. –सत्ता absolute existence. –सत्यः an epithet of Yama. –सत्त्वः an epithet of Kubera. –संधिविग्रहः the office of the minister of peace and war –सन्नः an epithet of Kubera. –सर्जः the bread-fruit of jacktree. –सांतपनः a kind of very rigid penance ; see Ms. 11. 212. –सांधिविग्रहिकः a minister of peace and war. –सारः a kind of Khadira tree. –सारथिः an epithet of Aruṇa. –साहसं great violence or outrage, great audacity. –साहसिकः a dacoit, highwayman, a daring robber. –सिंहः the fabulous animal called *S*arabha. –सिद्धिः *f.* a kind of magical power. –सुखं 1 great pleasure. 2 copulation. –सूक्ष्मा sand. –सूतः a military drum. –सेनः 1 an epithet of Kârtikeya. 2 the commander of a large army. (–ना) a great army. –स्कंधः a camel. –स्थली the earth. –स्थानं a great position. –स्वनः a kind of drum. –हंसः an epithet of Vishṇu. –हविस् *n.* clarified butter. –हिमवत् *m.* N. of a mountain.

महिका Frost, mist.

महित *p p.* Honoured, worshipped, esteemed, revered; see मह्. –तं The trident of *S*iva.

महिमन् *m.* 1 Greatness (fig. also), अयि मलयज महिमायं कस्य गिरामस्तु विषयस्ते Bv. 1. 11. 2 Glory, majesty, might, power ; Ku. 2. 6 ; U. 4. 21. 3 high rank, exalted rank, or position, dignity. 4 One of the *Siddhis*, the power of increasing size at will ; see सिद्धि.

महिरः The sun.

महिला 1 A woman. 2 An amorous or intoxicated woman ; विरहेण विकलहृदया निर्जलमीनायते महिला Bv. 2. 68. 3 The creeper called Priyangu. 4 A kind of perfume or fragrant plant (रेणुका). –Comp. –आह्वया the Priyangu creeper.

महिलारोप्यं N. of a city in the south.

महिषः 1 A buffalo ; (considered as the vehicle of Yama) ; गाहंतां महिषा निपानसलिलं शृंगैर्मुहुस्ताडितं *S*. 2. 6. 2 N. of a demon killed by Durgâ. –Comp. –अर्दनः an epithet of Kârtikeya. –असुरः the demon Mahisha. °घातिनी, °मथनी, °मर्दनी, °सूदनी epithets of Durgâ. –घ्नी an epithet of Durgâ. –ध्वजः an epithet of Yama. –पालः, –पालकः a buffalo-keeper. –वहनः, –वाहन epithets of Yama ; कृतांतः किं साक्षान्महिषवहनोऽसाविति पुनः K. P. 10.

महिषी 1 A she-buffalo, buffalo-cow ; Ms. 9. 55 ; Y. 2. 159. 2 The principal queen, queen-consort ; महिषिसखः R. 1. 48, 2. 25, 3. 9. 3 A queen in general. 4 The female of a bird. 5 A lady's maid, female servant (सैरंध्री). 6 An immoral woman. 7 Money acquired by the prostitution of one's wife ; cf. माहिषिक. –Comp. –पालः a keeper of she buffaloes. –स्तंभः a pillar adorned with a buffalo's head.

महिष्मत् *a.* Possessing, rich or abounding in buffaloes.

मही 1 Earth ; as in महीपाल, महीभृत् &c. ; मही रम्या शय्या Bh. 3. 79. 2 Ground, soil. 3 Landed property or estate, land. 4 A country, kingdom. 5 N. of a river, falling into the gulf of Cambay. 6 (In geom.) the base of any plane figure. –Comp. –इनः, ईश्वरः a king; न न मही नमहीनपराक्रमं R. 9. 5. –कंप an earthquake. –क्षित् *m.* a king, sovereign; R. 1. 11. 85; 19. 20. –जः 1 the planet Mars. 2 a tree. (–जं) wet ginger. –तलं surface of the earth. –दुर्गं an earth fort. –धरः 1 a mountain; R. 6. 52; Ku. 6. 89. 2 an epithet of Vishṇu. –ध्रः 1 a mountain ; Bh. 2. 10; *S*i. 15. 24, R. 3. 60, 13. 7. 2 an epithet of Vishṇu. –नाथः, –पः, –पतिः –भुज् *m.*, –मघवन् *m.*, –महेंद्रः a king; Bg. 1. 20; R. 2. 34, 6. 12. –पुत्रः, –सुतः, –सूनुः 1 the planet Mars. 2. epithets of the demon Naraka. –पुत्री, –सुता an epithet of Sitâ. –प्रकंपः an earthquake. –प्ररोहः –रुह् *m.*, –रुहः a tree, Ki. 5. 10; *S*i. 20. 49. –प्राचीरं, –प्रावरः the sea. –भर्तृ *m.* a king. –भृत् *m.* 1 a mountain; Ku. 1. 27, Ki. 5. 1. 2 a king, sovereign. –लता an earthworm. –सुरः a Brâhmaṇa

महीयस् *a.* Greater, larger, more powerful or weighty or important, mightier, stronger (compar. of महत् q. v.). –*m.* A great or noble-minded man ; प्रकृतिः खलु सा महीयसः सहते नान्यसमुन्नतिं यया Ki. 2. 21 ; *S*i. 2. 13.

महीला, महेला A woman, female.

मा *ind.* A particle of prohibition (rarely of negation) usually joined with the Imperative ; मद्वाणि मा कुरु विषादमनादरेण Bv. 4. 41 ; also (*a*) with the Aorist, when the augment अ is dropped ; पापे रतिं मा कृथाः Bh. 2. 77; मा मूमुहत् खलु भवंतमनन्यजन्मा मा ते मलीमसविकारघना मतिर्भूत् Mâl. 1. 32; (*b*) the Imperfect (the augment being dropped here also); मा चैनमभिभाषथाः Râm.; (*c*) the Future, or Potential mood; in the sense of 'lest', 'that not'; लघु एनां परित्रायस्व मा कस्यापि तपस्विनो हस्ते पतिष्यति *S*. 2; मा कश्चिन्ममाप्यनर्थो भवेत् Pt. 5; मा नाम देव्याः किमप्यनिष्टमुत्पन्नं भवेत् K. 307; (*d*) the present participle when a curse is implied; मा जीवन्यः परावज्ञादुःखदग्धोपि जीवति *S*i. 2. 45; or (*e*) with potential passive participles ; मैवं प्रार्थ्यम्. मा is sometimes used without any verb ; मा तावत् ' oh ! do not (say or do) so; मा मैवं ; मा नाम रक्षिणः Mk. 3 'may it not be the police'; see under नाम. Sometimes मा is followed by स्म and is used with the Aorist or Imperfect with the augment dropped and rarely with the potential mood ; क्लैब्यं मा स्म गमः पार्थ Bg. 2. 3; मा स्म प्रतीपं गमः *S*. 4. 17; मास्म सीमंतिनी काचिज्जनयेत्पुत्रमहिशम्.

मा 1 The goddess of wealth, Lakshmî ; तमाखुपत्रं राजेंद्र भज माज्ञानदायकं Subha'sh. 2 A mother. 3 A measure. –Comp. –पः, –पतिः epithets of Vishṇu.

मा 2 P., 3. 4. A (माति, मिमीते or मीयते, मित) 1 To measure ; न्यधित मिमान इवावनिं पदानि *S*i. 7. 13. 2 To measure or mark off, limit; see मित. 3 To compare with (in size), measure by any standard; Ku. 5. 15. 4 To be in, find room or space in, be contained or comprised in; तनौ ममुस्तत्र न कैटभद्विषस्तपोधनाभ्यागमसंभवा मुदः *S*i. 1. 23; वृद्धिं गतेप्यात्मनि नैव मांतीः 3. 73; 10. 50; माति मातुमशक्योऽपि यशोराशिर्यदत्र ते K. P. 10. –*Caus.*

(मापयति-ते) To cause to be measured, measure or mete out ; एतेन मापयाति भित्तिषु कर्ममार्ग Mk. 3. 16. *-Desid.* (मित्सति-ते) To wish to measure &c. -WITH अनु 1 to infer, deduce (from some premises &c.); धूमादग्निमनुमाय T. S.; Ku. 2. 25; to guess, conjecture ; अन्वमीयत शुद्धेति शांतेन वपुषैव सा R. 15. 77 ; 17. 11. 2 to reconcile. -उप to compare, liken ; तेनोपमीयेत तमालनीलं *Si.* 3. 8; स्तनौ मांसग्रंथी कनककलशावित्युपमितौ Bh. 3. 20. -निस् 1 to make, create, bring into existence ; निर्मातुं प्रभवेन्मनोहरमिदं रूपं पुराणो मुनिः V. 1. 4 ; यस्मादेष सुरेंद्राणां मात्राभ्यो निर्मितो नृपः Ms. 7. 5, 1. 13. 2 (*a*) to build, form, construct ; स्नायुनिर्मिता एते पाशाः H. 1. (*b*) to cause to be settled, colonize (as a town &c.); निर्ममे निर्ममोऽर्थेषु मथुरां मधुराकृतिः R. 15. 28. 3 to cause, produce ; शलाकांजननिर्मितेव Ku. 1. 48; निर्मातु मर्मव्यथां Gît. 3. 4 to compose, write ; स्वनिर्मितया टीकया समेतं काव्यं. 5 to prepare, manufacture (in general). -परि 1 to measure. 2 to measure off, limit. -प्र 1 to measure. 2 to prove, establish, demonstrate. -सं 1 to measure. 2 to make equal, equalize; कांतामंमिततयोपदेशयुजे K.P. 1; see संमित 3 to liken, compare. 4 to be comprised or contained in ; मृणालसूत्रमपि ते न संमाति स्तनांतरे Subhâsh.

मांस् *n.* 1 Flesh. (This word has no forms for the first five inflections, and is optionally substituted for मांस after acc. dual.).

मांसं Flesh, meat ; समांसो मधुपर्कः U. 4. (The word is thus fancifully derived in Ms. 5. 55.:—मां स भक्षयिताऽमुत्र यस्य मांसमिहाद्म्यहम् । एतन्मांसस्य मांसत्वं प्रवदंति मनीषिणः ॥). 2 The flesh of fish. 2 The fleshy part of a fruit. -सः 1 A worm. 2 N. of a mixed tribe, selling meat. -Comp. -अद्, -अद, -आदिन, -भक्षक *a.* flesh-eating, carnivorous (as an animal) ; Bk. 16. 28, Ms 5. 15. -अर्गलः-लं a piece of flesh hanging down from the mouth. -अशनं flesh-eating. आहारः animal food. -उपजीवित् *m.* a dealer in flesh. -ओदनः 1 meal of flesh. 2 rice boiled with flesh. -कारि *n.* blood. -ग्रंथिः a gland. -जं, तेजस् *n.* fat. -द्राविन् *m.* a kind of sorrel. -निर्यासः the hair of the body. -पिटकः-कं 1 a basket of flesh 2 a large quantity of flesh. -पित्तं a bone. -पेशी 1 a muscle. 2 a piece of flesh. 3 an epithet of the fœtus from the 8th to the 14th day. -भेत्तृ,-भेदिन् *a.* cutting the flesh. -योनिः a creature of flesh and blood. -विक्रयः sale of meat. -सारः, -स्नेहः fat. -हासा skin.

मांसल *a.* 1 Fleshy. 2 Muscular, lusty, brawny ; U. 1. 3 Fat, strong, powerful ; शाखाः शतं मांसलाः Bv. 1. 34 4 Deep (as sound) ; U. 6 25. 5 Increased in bulk or quantity ; Mâl. 9. 13.

मांसिकः A butcher.

माकंदः The mango tree ; Bv. 1. 29. -दी 1 The myrobalan tree. 2 Yellow sandal. 3 N. of a city on the Ganges.

माकर *a.* (री *f.*) Belonging to the sea-monster Makara q. v.

माकरंद *a.* (दी *f.*) Derived from, relating to, the juice of flowers; full of or mixed with honey, Mâl. 8. 1 ; 9. 12.

माकलिः 1 N. of Mâtali, the charioteer or Indra. 2 The moon.

माक्षि(क्षी)क *a.* (की *f.*) Coming or derived from a bee. -कं 1 Honey ; Bv. 4. 33. 2 A kind of honey-like mineral substance. -Comp. -आश्रयं, -जं bees'-wax. -फलः a kind of cocoa-nut. -शर्करा candied sugar.

मागध *a.* (धी *f.*) Relating to or living in the country of Magadha or the people of Magadha. -धः 1 A king of the Magadhas. 2 N. of a mixed tribe, said to have been the offspring of a Vaisya father and a Kshatriya Mother, (the duty of the members of this caste being that of professional bards); Ms. 10. 11, 17; Y. 1. 94. 3 A bard or panegyrist in general. -धाः (*pl.*) N. of a people, the Magadhas. -धी 1 A princess of the Magadhas ; R. 1. 57. 2 The language of the Magadhas, one of the four principal kinds of Prâkrita. 3 Long pepper. 4 White cumin. 5 Refined sugar. 6 A kind of jasmine. 7 A variety of cardamoms.

मागधा, मागधिका Long pepper.

मागधिकः A king of the Magadhas.

माघः 1 N. of a lunar month (corresponding to January-February). 2 N. of a poet, the author of the *Sisupâlavadha* or Mâgha-kâvya; (the poet describes his family in *Si.* 20. 80-84 and thus concludes:— श्रीशब्दरम्यकृतसर्गसमाप्तिलक्ष्म लक्ष्मीपतेश्चरितकीर्तनचारु माघः । तस्यात्मजः सुकविकीर्तिदुराशयादः काव्यं व्यधत्त शिशुपालवधाभिधानम् ॥); उपमा कालिदासस्य भारवेरर्थगौरवं। दंडिनः पदलालित्यं माघे संति त्रयो गुणाः ॥ Udb. -घी The day of full moon in the month of Ma'gha.

माघमा A female crab.

माघवत *a.* (ती *f.*) Belonging to Indra. -ती The east. -Comp. -चापं the rainbow ; U. 5. 11.

माघवन *a.* (नी *f.*) Belonging to or ruled by Indra; ककुभं समस्कुरुत माघवनीं *Si.* 9. 25; अवनीतलमेव साधु मन्ये न वनी माघवनी विलासहेतुः Jog.

माघ्यं The flower of the *kunda* creeper.

मांक्ष् 1. P. (मांक्षति) To wish or desire, long for.

मांगलिक *a.* (की *f.*) 1 Auspicious, tending to good fortune, indicative of auspiciousness; मुदमस्य मांगलिकतूर्यकृता ध्वनयः प्रतेनुरनुवप्रमपां Ki. 6. 4; Mv. 4. 35; Bv. 2. 57. 2 Fortunate.

मांगल्य *a.* Auspicious, indicative of good fortune ; *S.* 4. 5. -ल्यं 1 Auspiciousness, prosperity, welfare, good fortune. 2 A blessing or benediction. 3 A festivity, festival-any auspicious rite. -Comp. -मृदंगः a drum beaten on auspicious occasions; U. 6. 25.

माचः A way, road.

माचलः 1 A thief, robber. 2 A crocodile.

माचिका A fly.

मांजिष्ठ *a.* (ष्ठी *f.*) Red as madder. -ष्ठं Red colour.

मांजिष्ठिक (की *f.*) Dyed or tinged with madder ; U. 4 20; Mv. 1. 18.

माठरः 1 N. of Vyâsa. 2 A Brâhmaṇa. 3 A distiller (शौंडिक Sk.). 4 One of the attendants on the sun.

माठी An armour, mail.

माढः 1 A species of tree. 2 Weight, measure.

माढिः *f.* 1 The young leaf before it opens. 2 Honouring. 3 Sadness, dejection. 4 Poverty. 5 Anger, passion. 6 The border or hem of a garment. 7 A double tooth.

माणवः 1 A lad, boy, youth, youngster. 2 A little man, mannikin (used contemptuously). 3 A pearl-necklace of sixteen (of twenty) strings.

माणवकः 1 A youth, boy, lad, youngster. (oft. used contemptuously). 2 A little man, dwarf-mannikin ; मायामाणवकं हरिं Bhâg. 3 A, silly fellow. 4 A scholar, religious student. 5 A pearl-necklace of sixteen (or twenty) strings.

माणवीन *a.* Boyish, childish.

माणव्यं A company of lads or boys.

माणिका A particular weight (equal to eight *palas*).

माणिक्यं A ruby.

माणिक्या A small house-lizard.

माणिबंधं माणिमंथं, Rock-salt.

मांडलिक *a.* (की *f.*) Relating to, or ruling, a province. -कः The ruler of a province.

मातंगः 1 An elephant, *Si.* 1, 64. 2 A man of lowest caste, a Chânḍâla. 3 A Kirâta. a mountaineer or barbarian. 4 (At the end of comp.) Any thing the best of its kind ; *e. g.* बलाहकमातंगः. -Comp. -दिवाकरः N. of a poet. -नक्रः a crocodile as large as an elephant ; R. 13. 11.

मातरिपुरुषः 'One who can act like a man only against his mother', a poltroon, cowardly boaster.

मातरिश्वन् *m.* Wind ; पुनरुषसि विविक्तैर्मातरिश्वावचूर्ण्य ज्वलयति मदनाग्निं मालतीनां रजोभिः *Si*. 11. 17, Ki. 5. 36.

मातलिः N. of the charioteer of Indra **-Comp.** **-सारथिः** an epithet of Indra.

माता A mother.

मातामहः A maternal grand-father. **-हौ** (dual) The maternal grand-father and grandmother. **-ही** The maternal grand-mother.

मतिः *f.* **1** Measure. **2** A thought, idea, conception.

मातुलः **1** A maternal uncle; Bg. 1. 26; Ms. 2. 130, 5. 81. **2** The Dhattûra plant. **3** A kind of snake. **-Comp.** **-पुत्रकः** **1** the son of a maternal uncle. **2** the fruit of the Dhattûra plant.

मातुलंगः See मातुलिंग.

मातुला, मातुलानी, मातुली **1** The wife of a maternal uncle; Ms. 2. 131; Y. 3. 232. **2** Hemp.

मातुलिंगः, मातुलुंगः A kind of citron tree; (भुवो) भागाः प्रेंखितमातुलुंगवृतयः प्रेयो विधास्यंति वा Mâl. 6. 19. **-गं** The fruit of this tree, a citron.

मातुलेयः (**यी** *f.*) The son of a maternal uncle.

मातृ *f.* **1** A mother ; मातृवत्परदारेषु यः पश्यति स पश्यति; सहस्रं तु पितॄन् माता गौरवेणातिरिच्यते Subhâsh. **2** Mother, as a term of respect or endearment; मातर्लक्ष्मि भजस्व कंचिदपरं Bh. 3. 64, 87; अयि मातर्देवयजनसंभवे देवि सीते U. 4. **3** A cow. **4** An epithet of Lakshmî. **5** An epithet of Durgâ. **6** Ether, sky. **7** The earth. **8** A divine mother; मातृभ्यो बलिमुपहर Mk. 1. *-pl.* An epithet of the divine mothers, said to attend on Siva, but usually on Skanda. (They are usually said to be 8; ब्राह्मी माहेश्वरी चंडी वाराही वैष्णवी तथा । कौमारी चैव चामुंडा चर्चिकेत्यष्ट मातरः ॥ or, according to some, only seven; ब्राह्मी माहेश्वरी चैव कौमारी वैष्णवी तथा । माहेंद्री चैव वाराही चामुंडा सप्त मातरः ॥ Some increase the number to sixteen). **-Comp.** **-केशटः** a maternal uncle. **-गणः** the collection of the divine mothers. **-गंधिनी** an unnatural mother. **-गामिन्** *m.* one who has committed incest with his mother. **-गोत्रं** a mother's family. **-घातः,-घातकः,-घातिन्** *m.*, **-घ्नः** a matricide. **-घातुकः** **1** a matricide. **2** an epithet of Indra. **-चक्रं** the group of divine mothers. **-देव** *a.* having a mother for one's god, adoring mother like a god. **-नंदनः** an epithet of Kârtikeya. **-पक्ष** *a.* belonging to the mother's side or line. (**-क्षः**) maternal kinsmen. **-पितृ** (dual) (forming मातापितरौ or मातरपितरौ) parents. **-पुत्रौ** (मातापुत्रौ) a mother and sun. **-पूजनं** worship of the divine mothers. **-बंधुः,-बांधवः** a maternal kinsman; R. 12. 12. (*-pl.*) a class of relatives on the mother's side; they are thus specified:-मातुः पितुः स्वसुः पुत्रा मातुर्मातुः स्वसुः सुताः मातुर्मातुलपुत्राश्च विज्ञेया मातृबांधवाः ॥ **-मंडलं** the collection of the divine mothers. **-मातृ** *f.* an epithet of Pârvatî. **-मुखः** a foolish fellow, simpleton. **-यज्ञः** a sacrifice offered to the divine mothers. **-वत्सलः** an epithet of Kârtikeya. **स्वसृ** *f.* (मातृष्वसृ or मातुः स्वसृ) a mother's sister, a maternal aunt. **-स्वसेयः** (मातृष्वसेयः) a mother's sister's son. (**यी**) the daughter of a maternal aunt; so **मातृष्वस्रीयः -या.**

मातृकः *a.* **1** Coming or inherited from a mother; मातृकं च धनुरूर्जितं दधत् R. 11. 64, 90. **2** Maternal. **-कः** A maternal uncle. **-का** **1** A mother. **2** A grandmother. **3** A nurse. **4** A source, origin. **5** A divine mother. **6** N. of certain diagrams written in characters supposed to have a magical power. **7** The character or alphabet so used (pl.)

मात्र *a.* (**त्रा, -त्री** *f.*) An affix added to nouns in the sense of 'measuring as much as', 'as', high or long, or broad as, 'reaching as far as'; as in ऊरुमात्री भित्तिः (in this sense the word may as well be considered to be मात्रा at the end of comp. q. v. below). **-त्रं** **1** A measure, whether of length, breadth, height, size, space, distance or number; usually at the end of comp. ; *e. g.* अंगुलिमात्रं a finger's breadth ; किंचिन्मात्रं गत्वा to some distance ; क्रोशमात्रे at the distance of a Krosa; रेखामात्रमपि even the breadth of a line, as much as a line ; R. 1. 17; so क्षणमात्रं, निमिषमात्रं the space of an instant ; शतमात्रं a hundred in number; so गजमात्र as high or big as an elephant ; तालमात्र, यवमात्र &c. **2** The full measure of anything, the whole or entire class of things, totality ; जीवमात्रं or प्राणिमात्रं the entire class of living beings; मनुष्यमात्रो मर्त्यः every man is mortal. **3** The simple measure of anything, the one thing and no more, often translatable by 'mere,' 'only', 'even' ; जातिमात्रेण H. 1. 58 by mere caste ; टिट्टिभमात्रेण समुद्रो व्याकुलीकृतः 2. 149 by a mere wag-tail ; वाचामात्रेण जाप्यसे *S.* 2 'merely by words'; so अर्थमात्रं, संमानमात्रं Pt. 1. 83; used with past participles मात्र may be translated by 'as soon as', 'no sooner than', 'just' ; विद्धमात्रः R. 5. 51 'as soon as pierced', 'when just pierced' ; भुक्तमात्रे just after eating : प्रविष्टमात्र एव तत्रभवति *S.* 3. &c.

मात्रा **1** A measure; see मात्रं abovet **2** A standard of measure, standard, rule. **3** The correct measure. **4** A unit of measure, a foot. **5** A moment. **6** A particle, an atom. **7** A part, portion; नरेंद्रमात्राश्रितगौरवत्वात् R. 3. 11. **8** A small portion, a little quantity, a small measure only, see मात्र (**3**). **9** Account, consideration; राजेति कियती मात्रा Pt. 1. 40 'of what account or consideration is a king ', *i. e.* I hold him of no account ; कायस्थ इति लघ्वी मात्रा Mu. 1. **10** Money, wealth . **11** (In prosody) a prosodial or syllabic instant, the time required to pronounce a short vowel. **13** An element. **14** The material world, matter. **15** The upper part of the Nâgarî characters. **16** An ear-ring. **17** An ornament, jewel. **-Comp.** **-अर्धं** half of a prosodial instant. **-छंदस्, -वृत्तं** a metre regulated by the number of posodial instants it contains, *e. g.* the *Aryâ*. **-भस्त्रा** a money-bag. **-संगः** attachment to or regard for houcehold possessions or property; Ms. 6. 57. **-समकः** N. of a class of metres, see App. I. **-स्पर्शः** material contact, contact with material elements; Bg. 2. 14.

मात्रिका A syllable or prosodial instant (= मात्रा above.)

मात्सर *a.* (**री** *f.*); **मात्सरिक** *a.* (**की** *f.*) Jealous, envious, malicious, spiteful.

मात्सर्यं Envy, jealousy, spite, malice; अहो वस्तूनि मात्सर्यं Ks. 21. 49 ; Ki. 3. 53.

मात्स्यिकः A fisherman.

माथः **1** Stirring, churning, shaking about. **2** Killing, destruction. **3** A way, road.

माथुर *a.* (**री** *f.*) **1** Coming from Mathurâ. **2** Produced in Mathurâ. **3** Dwelling in Mathurâ.

मादः Intoxication, drunkenness. **2** Joy, delight. **3** Pride, arrogance.

मादक *a.* (**दिका** *f.*) **1** Intoxicating, maddening, stupefying. **2** Gladdening. **-नः** A gallinule.

मादन *a.* (**नी** *f.*) Intoxicating &c.; see मादक. **-नः** **1** The god of love. **2** The thorn-apple. **-नं** **1** Intoxication. **2** Delighting, exhilaration. **3** Cloves.

मादनीयं An intoxicating drink.

मादृक्ष *a.* (**क्षी** *f.*) , **मादृश्** *a.*, **मादृश** *a.* (**शी** *f.*) Like me, resembling me; प्रवृत्तिसाराः खलु मादृशां गिरः Ki. 1. 25 ; U. 2 ; उपचारो नैव कल्प्य हति तु मादृशाः R. G.

माद्रकः A Prince of the Madras.

माद्रवती N. of the second wife of Pâṇḍu.

माद्री N. of the second wife of Pâṇḍu.**-Comp.** **-नंदनः** an epithet of Nakula and Sahadeva. **-पतिः** an epithet of Pâṇḍu.

माद्रेयः An epithet of Nakula and Sahadeva.

माधव *a.* (**वी** *f.*) **1** Honey-like, sweet. **2** Made of honey. **3** Vernal. Relating to the descendants of Madhu.

-वः 1 N. of Krishṇa, राधामाधवयोर्जयंति यमुनाकूले रहःकेलयः Gît. 1; माधवे मा कुरु मानिनि मानमेय 9. 2 The spring season, a friend of Cupid; स्मर पर्युत्सुक एष माधवः Ku. 4. 28 ; स माधवेनाभिमेतेन सख्या (अनुप्रयातः) 3. 23. 3 The month called Vaisâkha ; भास्करस्य मधुमाधवाविव R.11 .7. 4 N. of Indra. 5 N. of Parasurâma. 6 N. of the Yâdavas (pl .) ; Si. 16. 52. 7 N. of a celebrated author, son of Mâyaṇa and brother of Sâyaṇa and Bhoganâth, and supposed to have lived in the fifteenth century. He was a very reputed scholar, numerous important works being ascribed to him ; he and Sâyaṇa are supposed to have jointly written the commentary on the Rigveda; श्रुतिस्मृतिसदाचारपालको माधवो बुधः । स्मार्तं व्याख्याय सर्वार्थं द्विजार्थं श्रौत उद्यतः । J. N. V -Comp. -वल्ली = माधवी q. v. -श्री vernal beauty.

माधवकः A kind of intoxicating liquor (produced from honey).

माधविका N. of a creeper ; माधविकापरिमलललिते Gît. 1.

माधवी 1 Candied sugar. 2 A kind of drink made from honey. 3 The spring-creeper (वासंती), with white fragrant flowers ; पत्राणामिव शोषणेन मरुता स्पृष्टा लता माधवी S. 3. 10; Me. 78. 4 The sacred basil. 5 A procuress, bawd. -Comp. -लता the spring creeper. -वनं a grove of Mâddhavî creepers.

माधवीय a. Relating to Mádhava.

माधुकर a. (री f.) Relating to or resembling a bee ; as in माधुकरी वृत्तिः. -री 1 Collecting alms by begging from door to door, as a bee collects honey by moving from flower to flower. 2 Alms obtained from five different places.

माधुरं The flower of the Mallikâ-creeper.

माधुरी 1 Sweetness, sweet or savoury taste ; वदने तव त्र माधुरी सा Bv. 2. 161; कामालसस्वर्वामाधरमाधुरीमधरयन् वाचा विपाकों मम 4. 42, 37, 43. 2 Spirituous liquor.

माधुर्यं 1 Sweetness, pleasantness ; माधुर्यमीष्टे हरिणान् ग्रहीतुं R.18. 13. 2 Attractive beauty, exquisite beauty : रूपं किमप्यनिर्वाच्यं तनोर्माधुर्यमुच्यते. 3 (In Rhet.) Sweetness, one of the three (according to Mammaṭa) chief Guṇas in poetic compositions: चित्तद्रवीभावमयो ह्लादो माधुर्यमुच्यते S. D. 606; see K. P. 8 also.

माध्य a. Central, middle.

माध्यंदिनः N. of a branch of Vâjasaneyins. -नं A branch of the शुक्ल or white Yajurveda (followed by the Mâdhyandinas).

माध्यम a. (मी f.) Belonging to the middle portion, central, middle, middle-most.

माध्यमक a. (मिका f.) **माध्यमिक** a, (की f.) Middle, central.

माध्यस्थं, माध्यस्थ्यं 1 Impartialit . 2 Indifference, unconcern; अभ्यर्थनाभंगभयेन साधुर्माध्यस्थ्यमिष्टेऽप्यवलंबतेर्थे Ku. 1. 52. 3 Intercession, mediation.

माध्याह्निक a. (की f.) Belonging to noon.

माध्व a. (ध्वी f.) Sweet. -ध्वः A follower of Madhva. -ध्वी A kind of liquor (made from honey).

माध्वीकं 1 A kind of spirituous liquor, distilled from the flowers of the tr e called Madhûka. चचाम मधु माध्वीकं Bk. 14. 94. 2 Wine distilled from grapes; साध्वी माध्वीक चिंता न भवति भवतः Gît. 12 (=मधो Com.) 3 A grape. -Comp. -फलं a kind of cocoa-nut.

मान् I. 1 A. (मीमांसते = desid. of मन् q. v.). -II. 1 P., 10 U. = *Caus.* of मन् q. v.

मानः 1 Respect, honour, regard, respectful consideration; मानद्रविणाल्पता Pt. 2. 159; Bg. 6. 7; so मानधन &c. 2 Pride (in a good sense), self-reliance, self-respect; जन्मिनो मानहीनस्य तृणस्य च समा गतिः Pt. 1. 106; R. 16. 81. 3 Haughtiness, pride, econceit, self-confidence. 4 A wounded sense of honour. 5 Jealous anger, anger excited by jealousy (especially in women); anger in general मुंच मयि मानमनिदानं Gît. 10; माधवे मा कुरु मानिनि मानमये 9 ; Si. 9. 84; Bv. 2. 56. -नं 1 Measuring. 2 A Measure, standard. 3 Dimension, computation. 4 A standard of measure, measuring rod, rule. 5 Proof, authority, means of proof or demonstration; येऽमी माधुर्योजः-प्रसादा रसमात्रधर्मतयोक्तास्तेषां रसधर्मत्वे किं मानं R. G.; मानाभावात् (frequently occurring in controversial language). 6 Likeness, resemblance. -Comp. आसक्त a. given to pride, haughty, proud. -उन्नतिः f. great respect or honour. -उन्मादः infatuation of pride. -कलहः, कलिः a quarrel caused by jealous anger. -क्षतिः f., भंगः,-हानिः f. injury to reputation or honour, humiliation, insult, indignity. -ग्रंथिः injury to honour or pride. -द a. 1 showing respect. 2 proud. -दंडः a measuring-rod; स्थितः पृथिव्या इव मानदंडः Ku. 1. 1. -धन a. rich in honour; महौजसो मानधना धनार्चिताः Ki. 1. 19. -धानिका a cucumber. -परिखंडनं mortification, humiliation. -भंग see मानक्षति. -महत् a. rich or great in pride, greatly proud; किं जीर्णं तृणमत्ति मानमहतामग्रेसरः केसरी Bh. 2. 29. -योगः the correct mode of measuring or weighing; Ms. 9. 330. -रंध्रा a sort of clepsydra, a perforated water-vessel, which, placed in water and gradually filling, serves to measure time. -सूत्रं 1 a measuring cord. 2 a chain (of gold &c) worn round the body.

मानःशिल a. Consisting of red arsenic (मनःशिला).

माननं-ना 1 Honouring, respecting. 2 Killing; Si. 16. 2.

माननीय a. Fit to be honoured, worthy of honour, deserving to be honoured (with gen.); मेनां मुनीनामपि माननीयां Ku. 1. 18; R. 1. 11.

मानव a. (वी f.) 1 Relating to or descended from Manui; मानवस्य राजर्षिवंशस्य प्रसवितारं सवितारं U. 3; Ms. 12. 107. 2 Human. -वः 1 A man, human being; मनोर्वंशो मानवानां ततोयं प्रथितोऽभवत् । ब्रह्मक्षत्रादयस्तस्मान्मनोर्जातास्तु मानवाः Mb.; Ms. 2. 9; 5. 35. 2 Mankind (pl.). -वं A particular fine. -Comp. -इंद्रः, -देवः -पतिः a lord of men, king, sovereign; R. 14. 32. -धर्मशास्त्रं the institutes of Manu. -राक्षसः a demon or fiend in the form of a man; तेऽमी मानवराक्षसाः परहितं स्वार्थाय निघ्नंति ये Bh. 2. 74.

मानवत् a. Proud, arrogant, haughty, high-spirited -ती A haughty or high-spirited woman (angry through jealous pride).

मानव्यं A number of boys or youths (माणव्यं).

मानस a. (सी f.) 1 Pertaining to the mind, mental, spiritual (opp. शारिर). 2 Produced from the mind, sprung at will; किं मानसी सृष्टिः S. 4; Ku. 1. 18; Bg. 10. 6. 3 Only to be conceived in the mind, conceivable. 4 Tacit, implied. 5 Dwelling on the lake Mânasa. -सः A form of Vishṇu. -सं 1 The mind, the heart; सपदि मदनानलो दहति मम मानसं Gît. 10; अपि च मानसमंबुनिधिः Bv. 1. 113; मानसं विषयैर्विना (भाति) 116. 2 N. of a sacred lake on the mountain Kailâsa; कैलासशिखरे राम मनसा निर्मितं सरः । ब्रह्मणा प्रागिदं यस्मात्तदभून्मानसं सरः॥ Râm.; (it is said to be the native place of swans, who are described as migrating to its shores every year at the commencement of the breeding season or the monsoons; मेघश्यामा दिशो दृष्ट्वा मानसोत्सुकचेतसां । कूजितं राजहंसानां नेदं नूपुरशिंजितं V. 4. 14. 15 ; यस्यास्तोये कृतवसतयो मानसं संनिकृष्टं नाध्यास्यंति व्यपगतशुचस्त्वामपि प्रेक्ष्य हंसाः Me. 76 ; see Me. 11; Ghaṭ. 9 also); R. 6. 26; Me. 62 ; Bv. 1. 3. 3 A kind of salt. -Comp. -आलयः a swan, goose. -उत्क a. eager to go to Mânasa; Me. 11. -ओकस्, -चारिन् m. a swan. -जन्मन् m. 1 the god of love. 2 a swan.

मानसिक a. (की f.) Mental, spiritual. -कः An epithet of Vishṇu.

मानिका 1 A kind of spirituous liquor. 2 A kind of weight.

मानित p. p. Honoured, respected, esteemed.

मानिन् a. 1 Fancying, considering, regarding, (at the end of comp.);

as in पंडितमानिन्. 2 Honouring, respecting; (at the end of comp.). 3 Haughty, proud, possessed of self-respect; पराभवोऽप्युत्सव एव मानिनां Ki. 1. 41 ; परवृद्धिमत्सरि मनो हि मानिनां Si. 15. 1. 4 Entitled to respect, highly honoured ; Bk. 19. 24. 5 Disdainful, angry, sulky. -*m*. A lion. -नी 1 A woman possessed of self-respect, strong-minded, resolute, proud (in a good sense); चतुर्दिगीशानवमत्यमानिनी Ku. 5. 53 ; R. 13. 38 2 An angry woman, or one offended with her husband (through jealous pride); माधवे मा कुरु मानिनि मानमये Gît. 9 ; Ki. 9. 36. 3 A kind of odoriferous plant.

मानुष *a*. (षी *f*.) 1 Human ; मानुषी तनुः, मानुषी वाक् &c. ; R. 1. 60, 16. 22 ; Bg. 4. 12 ; 9. 11 ; Ms. 4. 124. 2 Humane, kind. -षः 1 A man, human being. 2 An epithet of the three signs of the zodiac ; Gemini, Virgo and Libra. -षी A woman. -षं 1 Humanity. 2 Human effort or action.

मानुषक *a*. (की *f*.) Human, mortal.

मानुष्यं, मानुष्यकं 1 Human nature, humanity. 2 Mankind, the race of human beings. 3 A collection of men.

मानोज्ञकं Beauty, loveliness.

मांत्रिकः One who is conversant with charms or spells, a conjurer, sorcerer.

मांथर्यं 1 Slowness, dulness, tardiness. 2 Weakness.

मांदारः, मांदारवः A kind of tree.

मांद्यं 1 Dulness, laziness, slowness. 2 Stupidity. 3 Weakness, feeble state ; अग्निमांद्यं. 4 Apathy. 5 Sickness, illness, indisposition.

मांधातृ *m*. N. of a king of the solar race, son of Yuvanâsva (being born from his own belly). As soon as he came out of the belly, the sages said ' कं एष धास्यति '; whereupon Indra came down and said 'मां धास्यति'; the boy was, therefore, called Mândhâtṛi.

मान्मथ *a*. (थी *f*.) Relating to or caused by love ; आचार्यकं विजयि मान्मथमाविरासीत् Mâl. 1. 26 ; 2. 4.

मान्य *pot. p*. 1 To be revered or respected ; अहमपि तव मान्या हेतुभिस्तैश्च तैश्च Mâl. 6. 26. 2 Respectable, honourable, venerable ; R. 2. 45 ; Y. 1. 111.

मापनं 1 Measuring. 2 Forming, making. -नः A balance

मापत्यः The god of love.

माम *a*. (मी *f*.) 1 My, mine. 2 Uncle (used in voc.).

मामक *a*. (मिका *f*.) 1 My, mine, belonging to my side; मामकाः पांडवाश्चैव किमकुर्वत संजय Bg. 1. 1. 2 Selfish, covetous, greedy. -कः 1 A miser. 2 A maternal uncle.

मामकीन *a*. My, mine ; यो मामकीनस्य मनसो द्वितीयं निबंधनं Mâl. 2 ; Bv. 2. 32 ; 3. 6.

मायः 1 A conjurer, juggler. 2 A demon, an evil spirit.

माया 1 Deceit, fraud, trick, trickery ; a device, an artifice ; Pt. 1. 359. 2 Jugglery, witchcraft, enchantment, an illusion of magic ; स्वप्नो नु माया नु मतिभ्रमो नु *S*. 6. 7. 3 (Hence) A unreal or illusory image, a phantom, illusion, unreal apparition ; मायां मयोद्भाव्य परीक्षितोऽसि R. 2. 62 ; oft. as the first member of comp. in the sense of ' false ', ' phantom ', ' illusory '; *e. g*. मायावचनं false words; मायामृग &c. 4 A political trick or artifice, diplomatic feat. 5 (In Vedânta phil.) Unreality, the illusion by virtue of which one considers the unreal universe as really existent and as distinct from the Supreme Spirit. 6 (In Sân. phil.) The Pradhâna or Prakriti. 7 Wickedness. 8 Pity, compassion. 9 N. of the mother of Buddha. -Comp. आचार *a*. acting deceitfully. -आत्मक *a*. false, illusory. -उपजीविन् *a*. living by fraud ; Pt. 1. 288. -कारः, -कृत्, -जीविन् *m*. a conjurer, juggler. -दः a crocodile. -देवी N. of the mother of Buddha. °सुतः Buddha. -धर *a*. deceitful, illusive. -पटु *a*. skilled in deception, fraudulent, deceitful. -प्रयोगः 1 deceitfulness, employment of tricks or fraud. 2 employment of magic. -मृगः a phantom deer, an illusory or false deer. -यंत्रं an enchantment. -योगः employment of magic. -वचनं false or deceitful words. -वादः the doctrine of illusion, a term applied to Buddhism. -विद् *a*. skilled in deception or magical arts. -सुतः an epithet of Buddha.

मायावत् *a*. 1 Deceitful, fraudulent. 2 Illusory, unreal, deceptive. 3 Skilled in magical arts, employing magical powers. -*m*. An epithet of Kamsa. -ती N. of the wife of Pradyumna.

मायाविन् *a*. 1 Using deceits or tricks, employing stratagems, deceitful, fraudulent ; व्रजंति ते मूढधियः पराभवं भवंति मायाविषु ये न मायिनः Ki. 1. 30. 2 Skilled in magic. 3 Unreal, illusory. -*m*. A magician, conjurer. 2 A cat. -*n*. A gall-nut.

मायिक *a*. 1 Deceitful, fraudulent. 2 Illusory, unreal. -कः A juggler. -कं A gall-nut.

मायिन् See मायाविन्. -*m*. 1 A conjurer. 2 A rogue, cheat. 3 N. of Brahmâ or Kâma.

मायुः 1 The sun. 2 Bile, bilious humour; (*n*. also in this sense).

मायूर *a*. (री *f*.) 1 Belonging to or arising from a peacock. 2 Made of the feathers of a peacock. 3 Drawn by a peacock (as a car). 4 Dear to a peacock. -रं A flock of peacocks.

मायूरकः, मायूरिकः A peacock-catcher.

मारः 1 Killing, slaughter, slaying ; अशेषप्राणिनामासीदमारो दश वत्सरान् Râj. T. 5. 64. 2 An obstacle, hindrance, opposition. 3 The god of love; श्यामात्मा कुटिलः करोतु कबरीभारोऽपि मारोद्यमं Gît. 3; (where मार primarily means 'killing'); Nâg. 1. 1. 4 Love, passion. 5 The thorn-apple (धत्तूर). 6 An evil one, destroyer; (according to Buddhists). -Comp. -अंक *a*. 'marked by love', displaying signs of love; मारांके रतिकेलिसंकुलरणारंभे Gît. 12. -अभिभूः (भुः ?) an epithet of a Buddha. -अरिः, -रिपुः Siva. -आत्मक *a*. murderous ; कथं मारात्मके त्वयि विश्वासः कर्तव्यः H. 1. -जित् *m*. 1 an epithet of Siva. 2 of a Buddha.

मारकः 1 Any pestilential disease, plague epidemic. 2 The god of love. 3 A murderer, destroyer in general. 4 A hawk.

मारकत *a*. (ती *f*.) Belonging to an emerald; काचः कांचनसंसर्गाद्धत्ते मारकतीं द्युतिं H. Pr. 41.

मारणं 1 Killing, slaying, slaughter, destruction; पशुमारणकर्मदारुणः *S*. 6. 1. 2 A magical ceremony performed for the purpose of destroying an enemy. 3 Calcination. 4 A kind of poison.

मारिः *f*. 1 A pestilence, plague. 2 killing, ruin.

मारिच *a*. (ची *f*.) Made of pepper.

मारिषः A respectable, worthy or venerable man, used in dramas in the voc. as a respectful mode of address by the Sûtradhâra to one of the principal actors; see U. 1.; Mâl. 1.

मारी 1 Plague, pestilence, an epidemic. 2 Pestilence personified (the goddess presiding over plagues and identified with Durgâ).

मारीचः 1 N. of a demon, son of Sunda and Tâdakâ. He assumed the form of a golden deer, and thus enticed Râma to a considerable distance from Sîtâ; so that Râvaṇa found a good opportunity to carry her off. 2 A large or royal elephant. 3 A kind of plant. -चं A collection of pepper-shrubs.

मारुंडः 1 A serpent's egg.. 2 Cow-dung. 3 A way, road.

मारुत *a*. (ती *f*.) 1 Relating to or arising from the Maruts. 2 Relating to wind, aerial, windy. -तः 1 Wind; R. 2. 12, 34; 4. 54; Ms. 4. 122. 2 The god of wind, the deity presiding over wind. **3** Breathing. **4** Vital air, one of the three essential humours of the body. **5** The trunk of an elephant. **–तं** The lunar mansion called Svâti. **–Comp. –अशनः** a snake. **–आत्मजः, सुतः, सूनुः 1** epithets of Hanumat. **2** of Bhîma.

मारुतिः 1 An epithet of Hanumat; R. 12. 60. **2** Of Bhîma.

मार्कंडः, मार्कंडेयः N. of an ancient sage. **–Comp. –पुराणं** N. of one of the eighteen Purâṇas (composed) by this sage).

मार्ग् 1. 1 P., 10 U. (मार्गति, मार्गयति-ते) **1** To seek, seek for. **2** To hunt after, chase. **3** To strive to attain, strive after; आत्मोत्कर्षं न मार्गेत परेषां परिनिंदया। स्वगुणैरेव मार्गेत विप्रकर्षं पृथग्जनात् Subhâsh. **4** To solicit, beg, ask for; वरं वरेण्यो नृपते-रमार्गीत् Bk. 1. 12; Y. 2. 66. **5** To ask in marriage. –II. 10 U. (मार्गयति-ते) **1** To go, move. **2** To decorate, adorn. –WITH **परि** to seek, look out for.

मार्गः 1 A way, road, path (fig. also); अग्निशरणमार्गमादेशय *S*. 5; so विचारमार्गप्रहितेन चेतसा Ku. 5. 42; R. 2. 72. **2** A course, passage, the tract passed over; वायोरिमं परिवहस्य वदंति मार्गं *S*. 7. 7. **3** Reach, range; Ki. 18. 40. **4** A scar, mark (left by a wound &c.); R. 4. 48; 14. 4. **5** The path or course of a planet. **6** Search, inquiry, investigation. **7** A canal, channel, passage. **8** A means, way. **9** The right way or course, proper course; सुमार्ग, अमार्ग. **10** Mode, manner, method, course, usage, शांति° R. 7. 71.; so कुल°, शास्त्र°, धर्म° &c. **11** Style, diction; इति वैदर्भमार्गस्य प्राणा दश गुणाः स्मृताः Kâv. 1. 41; वाचां विचित्रमार्गाणां 1. 9. **12** The anus. **13** Musk. **14** The constellation called मृगशिरस्. **15** The month called मार्गशीर्ष. **–Comp. –तोरणं** a triumphal arch erected on a road; R. 11. 5. **–दर्शकः** a guide. **–धेनुः, -धेनुकं**, a measure of distance equal to 4 krosas. **–बंधनं** a barricade. **–रक्षकः** a road-keeper, guard. **–शोधकः** a pioneer. **–स्थ** *a*. travelling, wayfaring. **–हर्म्यं** a palace on a high road.

मार्गकः The month called मार्गशीर्ष.

मार्गणं-णा 1 Begging, requesting, soliciting. **2** Seeking, looking out for, searching. **3** Investigating, inquiry, examination. **–णः 1** A begger, supplicant, mendicant. **2** An arrow; दुर्वाराः स्मरमार्गणाः K. P. 10; अभेदि तचादृग-नंगमार्गणैर्यदस्य पौष्पैरपि धैर्यकंचुकं N. 1. 46; Vikr. 1. 77, R. 9. 17, 65. **3** The number 'five.'

मार्गशिरः, मार्गशिरस् *m*., **मार्गशीर्षः** N. of the ninth month of the Hindu year (corresponding to November-December) in which the full-moon is in the constellation मृगशिरस्.

मार्गशिरी, मार्गशीर्षी The full-moon day in the month of मार्गशीर्ष.

मार्गिकः 1 A traveller. **2** A hunter.

मार्गित *p. p.* **1** Sought, searched, inquired after. **2** Hunted after, desired, solicited.

मार्ज् 10 U. (मार्जयति-ते) **1** To purify, cleanse, wipe; cf. मृज्. **2** To sound.

मार्जः 1 Cleansing, purifying, scouring. **2** A washerman. **3** An epithet of Vishṇu.

मार्जक *a*. (**र्जिका** *f*.) Cleansing, purifying, scouring.

मार्जन *a*. (**नी** *f*.) Cleansing, purifying. **–नं 1** Cleansing, cleaning, purifying. **2** Wiping or rubbing off. **3** Effacing, wiping away. **4** Cleansing the person by rubbing it with unguents. **5** Sprinkling the person with water by means of the hand, a blade of Kusa grass &c. **–नः** The tree called *Lodhra*. **–ना 1** Cleansing, purifying, cleaning. **2** The sound of a drum; मायूरी मदयति मार्जना मनांसि M. 1. 18. **–नी** A broom, brush.

मार्जारः (**लः**) A cat; कपाले मार्जारः पय इति करॉल्लेढि शशिनः K. P. 10. **2** A pole-cat. **–Comp. –कंठः** a peacock. **–करणं** a kind of coitus or mode of sexual enjoyment.

मार्जारकः 1 A cat. **2** A peacock.

मार्जारी 1 A female cat. **2** A civet-cat. **3** Musk.

मार्जारीयः 1 A cat. **2** A *S*ûdra.

मार्जित *p. p.* **1** Cleansed, scoured, purified. **2** Swept, brushed. **3** Adorned.

मार्जिता Curds with sugar and spices.

मार्तंडः 1 The sun; अयं मार्तंडः किं स खलु तुरगैः सप्तभिरितः K. P. 10; U. 6. 3. **2** The Arka tree. **3** A hog. **4** The number twelve. (Also मार्तांड).

मार्तिक *a*. (**की** *f*.) Made of clay, earthen. **–कः 1** A kind of pitcher. **2** The lid of a pitcher. **–कं** A clod or lump of earth; गुरुमध्ये हरिणाक्षी मार्तिकशकलैर्निहंतुकामं मां Bv. 2. 49.

मार्त्यं Mortality.

मार्दंगः A drummer. **–गं** A city, town.

मार्दंगिकः A drummer.

मार्दवं Softness (lit. and fig.), pliancy, weakness; अभितप्तमयोऽपि मार्दवं भजते R. 8. 43 'becomes soft'; स्वशरीर-मार्दवं Ku. 5. 18. **2** Mildness, indulgence, gentleness, leniency; Bg. 16. 2.

मार्द्वीक *a*. (**की** *f*.) Made of grapes. **–कं** Wine; *S*i. 8. 30.

मार्मिक *a*. Having a deep insight into, fully conversant with the essence, beauty. &c.; (= मर्मज्ञ q. v.) मार्मिकः को मरंदानामंतरेण मधुव्रतं Bv. 1. 117. 1. 8, 4. 40.

मार्ष See मारिष.

मार्ष्टिः *f*. Cleansing, scouring, purifying.

मालः 1 N. of a district in the west or south-west of Bengal. **2** N. of a tribe of barbarians, a mountaineer. **3** N. of Vishṇu. **–लं 1** A field. **2** A high ground, rising or elevated ground; (मालमुन्नतभूतलं); क्षेत्रमारुह्य मालं Me. 16 (शैलप्रायमुन्नतस्थलं Malli.). **3** Deceit, fraud. **–Comp. –चक्रकं** the hip-joint.

मालकः 1 The *Nimba* tree. **2** A wood near a village. **3** A pot made of a cocoa-nut shell. **–कं** A garland.

मालतिः-ती *f*. **1** A kind of jasmine (with fragrant white flowers); तन्मन्ये क्वचिदंग भृंगतरुणेनास्वादिता मालती G. M.; जालकैर्मालतीनां Me. 98. **2** A flower of this jasmine; शिरसि बकुलमालां मालतीभिः समेतां Rs. 2. 24. **3** A bud, blossom (in general). **4** A virgin, young woman. **5** Night. **6** Moon-light. **–Comp. –क्षारकः** borax. **–पत्रिका** the shell of a nutmeg. **–फलं** a nutmeg. **–माला** a garland of jamine flowers.

मालय *a*. (**यी** *f*.) Coming from the Malaya mountain. **–यः** Sandal-wood.

मालवः 1 N. of a country, the modern Mâlva' in central India. **2** N. of a Râga or musical mode. **–वाः** (pl.) The people of Mâlvâ. **–Comp. –अधीशः, –इंद्रः, –नृपतिः** a king of Mâlvâ.

मालवकः 1 The country of the Mâlavas. **2** An inhabitant of Mâlvâ.

मालसी N. of a plant.

माला 1 A garland, wreath, chaplet; अनाघ्रितपरिमलापि हि हरति दृशं मालतीमाला Vâs. **2** A row, line, series, succession; गंडोड्डीनालिमाला Mâl. 1. 1; आबद्धमालाः Me. 9. **3** A group, cluster, collection. **4** A string, necklace; as in रत्नमाला. **5** A rosary, chain; as in अक्षमाला. **6** A streak; as in तडिन्माला, विद्युन्माला. **7** A series of epithets. **8** (In drama) The offering of several things to obtain a wish. **–Comp. –उपमा** a variety of Upamâ or simile, in which one *Upameya* is compared to several *Upamânas*; *e. g.* अनयेनेव. राज्यश्रीर्दैन्येनेव मनस्विता। मम्लौ साथ विषादेन पद्मिनीव हिमांभसा K. P. 10. **–करः; कारः 1** a garand-maker, florist, gardener; कुर्वी मालाकारो बकुलमपि कुत्रापि निदधे Bv. 1. 54; Pt. 1. 220. **2** the tribe of gardeners. **–तृणं** a kind of fragrant grass. **–दीपकं** a variety of दीपक; Mammaṭa thus defines it:—मालादीपकमाद्यं चेद्यथोत्तरगुणावहम् K. P. 10; see the example given *ad loc*.

मालिकः 1 A florist, gardener. **2** A dyer, painter.

मालिका 1 A garland. **2** A row, line, series. **3** A string, necklace. **4** A variety of jasmine. **5** Lin-seed. **6** A daughter. **7** A palace. **8** A kind of bird. **9** An intoxicating drink.

मालिन् *a.* **1** Wearing a garland. **2** (At the end of comp.) crowned or wreathed with, encircled by ; समुद्रमालिनी पृथ्वी ; अंशुमालिन्, मरीचिमालिन्, ऊर्मिमालिन् &c. –*m.* A florist, garland-maker. **–नी 1** A female florist, the wife of a garland-maker. **2** N. of the city of Champâ. **3** A girl seven years old representing Durgâ at the Durgâ festival. **4** N. of Durgâ. **5** The celestial Ganges. **6** N. of a metre ; see App I.

मालिन्यं 1 Dirtiness, foulness, impurity. **2** Pollution, defilement. **3** Sinfulness. **4** Blackness. **5** Trouble, affliction.

मालुः *f.* **1** A kind of creeper. **2** A woman. **–Comp. –धानः** a kind of snake.

मालूरः 1 The *Bilva* tree. **2** The *Kapittha* tree.

मालेया Large cardamoms.

माल्य *a.* Proper for or relating to a garland. **–ल्यं 1** A garland, wreath; माल्येन तां निर्वचनं जघान Ku. 7. 19 ; Ki. 1. 21. **2** A flower ; Bg. 11. 11 ; Ms. 4. 72. **3** A chaplet or garland worn on the head. **–Comp. –आपणः** a flower-market. **–जीवकः** a florist, garland-maker. **–पुष्पः** a king of hemp. **–वृत्तिः** a florist.

माल्यवत् *a.* Wreathed, crowned. –*m.* **1** N. of a mountain or mountain range ; U. 1. 33 ; R. 13. 26. **2** N. of a demon, son of Suketu. [He was the maternal uncle and minister of Ravan*a* and aided him in many of his schemes. In early times he propitiated the god Brahma by his austere penance, as a reward of which the splendid island of Lank*a* was caused to be built for him. He lived there with his brothers for some years, but afterwards left it, which was then occupied by Kubera. Afterwards when Ravan*a* ousted Kubera from the island, M*a*lyavat returned with his relatives and lived with him for a long time.]

माल्लः N. of a particular mixed tribe.

माल्लवी A wrestling or boxing match.

माषः 1 A bean ; (the sing. being used for the plant and the Pl. for the fruit or seed); तिलेभ्यः प्रति यच्छति माषान् Sk. **2** A particular weight of gold ; माषो विंशतिमो भागः पणस्य परिकीर्तितः or गुंजाभिर्दशभिर्माषः. **3** A fool, blockhead. **–Comp. –अदः, –आदः** a tortoise. **–आज्यं** a dish of beans cooked with ghee. **–आशः** a horse. **–ऊन** *a.* less by a Mâsha. **–वर्धकः** a goldsmith.

माषिक *a.* (**की** *f.*) Worth a Mâsha.

माषीणं, माष्यं A field of kidney-beans.

मास् *m.* = मास q. v (This word has no forms for the first five inflections, and is optionally substituted for मास after acc. dual).

मासः, सं 1 A month ; (it may be चांद्र, सौर, सावन, नाक्षत्र or बार्हस्पत्य); न मासे प्रतिपत्तासे मां चेन्मर्तासि मैथिलि Bk. 8. 95. **2** The number ' twelve '. **–Comp. –अनुमासिक** *a.* monthly. **–अंतः** the day of new moon. **–आहार** *a.* eating only once a month. **–उपवासिनी 1** a woman who fasts for a whole month. **2** a procuress, a lascivious or lewd woman (ironically). **–कालिक** *a.* monthly. **–जात** *a.* a month old, born a month ago. **–ज्ञः** a kind of gallinule. **–देय** *a.* to be paid in a month. **–प्रमितः** the new-moon. **प्रवेशः** the beginning of a month. **–मानः** a year.

मासकः A month.

मासरः The scum of boild rice, rice-gruel.

मासलः A year.

मासिक *a.* (**की** *f.*) **1** Relating to a month. **2** Happening every month, monthly. **3** Lasting for a month. **4** Payable in a month. **5** Engaged for a month. **–कं** A funeral rite or Srâddha performed every new-moon (during the first year of a man's death); पितॄणां मासिकं श्राद्धमन्वाहार्यं विदुर्बुधाः.

मासीन *a.* **1** One month old. **2** Monthly.

मासुरी A beard.

माह् 1. U. (माहति-ते) To measure.

माहाकुल *a.* (**ली** *f.*), **माहाकुलीन** *a.* (**नी** *f.*). **1** Nobly born, of noble family, of illustrious descent.

माहाजनिक *a.* (**की** *f.*) **माहाजनीन** *a.* (**नी** *f.*) **1** Fit for merchants. **2** Fit for great persons..

माहात्मिक *a.* (**की** *f.*) High-minded, magnanimous, noble, dignified, glorious.

माहात्म्यं 1 Magnanimity, noble-mindedness. **2** Majesty, dignity, exalted position. **3** The peculiar virtue of any divinity or sacred shrine ; or a work giving an account of the merits of such divinities or shrines; as देवीमाहात्म्य, शनिमाहात्म्य &c.

माहाराजिक *a.* (**की** *f.*) Fit for a great king, imperial, royal.

माहाराज्यं Sovereignty.

माहाराष्ट्री See महाराष्ट्री.

माहिरः An epithet of Indra.

माहिष *a.* (**षी** *f.*) Coming or derived from a buffalo or a buffalo cow ; ३s माहिषं दधि.

माहिषकः A buffalo-keeper.

माहिषिकः 1 A buffalo-keeper, a herdsman. **2** The paramour of an unchaste woman ; माहिषीत्युच्यते नारी या च स्याद् व्यभिचारिणी। तां दुष्टां कामयति यः स वै माहिषिकः स्मृतः ॥ Kâlikâ Purâṇa. **3** One who lives by the prostitution of his wife ; महिषीत्युच्यते नार्या भगेनोपार्जितं धनं। उपजीवति यस्तस्याः स वै माहिषिकः स्मृतः॥ Srîdhara on V. P.

माहिष्मती N. of a city, the hereditary capital of the Haihaya kings, R. 6. 43.

माहिष्यः A mixed caste sprung from a Kshatriya father and a Vaisya mother.

माहेंद्र *a.* (**द्री** *f.*) Relating to Indra ; Ku. 7. 84 ; R. 12. 86. **–द्री 1** The east. **2** A cow. **3** N. of Indrâṇî.

माहेय *a.* (**यी** *f.*) Terrestrial. **–यः 1** The planet Mars. **2** Coral.

माहेयी A cow.

माहेश्वरः A worshipper of Siva.

मि 5 U. (मिनोति, मिनुते; rarely used in classical literature). **1** To throw, cast, scatter. **2** To build, erect. **3** To measure. **4** To establish. **5**. To observe, perceive.

मिच्छ् 6 P. (मिच्छति) **1** To hinder, obstruct. **2** To annoy.

मित *p.p.* **1** Measured, meted or measured out. **2** Measured off, bounded, defined. **3** Limited, measured, moderate, little, scanty, sparing, brief (words &c.); पृष्टः सत्यं मितं ब्रूते स भृत्योर्हो महीभुजां Pt. 1. 87 ; R. 9. 34. **4** Measuring, of the measure of; (at the end of comp.) as in ग्रहवसुकरिचंद्रमिते वर्षे *i. e.* in 1889. **5** Investigated, examined ; (see मा). **–Comp. –अक्षर** *a.* **1** brief measured short, concise ; Ku. 5. 63. **2** composed in verse, metircal. **–अर्थ** *a.* of measured meaning. **–आहार** *a.* sparing in diet. **(–रः)** moderation in eating. **–भाषिन्, –वाच्** *a.* speaking little or measured words; महीयांसः प्रकृत्या मितभाषिणः Si. 2. 13.

मितंगम *a.* Going slowly. **–मः** An elephant.

मितंपच *a.* **1** Cooking a measured portion, cooking little. **2** Sparing, niggardly, stingy.

मितिः *f.* **1** Measuring, a measure, weight. **2** Accurate knowledge. **3** Proof, evidence.

मित्रः 1 The sun **2** N. of an *Aditya* and usually associated with Varuṇa. **–त्रं 1** A friend ; तन्मित्रमापदि सुखे च समक्रियं यत् Bh. 2. 68 ; Me. 17 **2** An ally, the next neighbour of a king ; cf. मंडल. **–Comp. –आचारः** conduct towards a friend. **–उदयः 1** sun-rise. **2** the welfare or prosperity of a friend. **–कर्मन्** *n.*, **–कार्यं, कृत्यं** the business of a friend, a friendly act or service; R. 19. 31. **–घ्न** *a.* treacherous. **–द्रुह्, –द्राहिन्** *a.* hating a friend, treacherous to a friend, a false or treacherous friend. **–भावः** friendship. **–भेदः**

breach of friendship. –वत्सल *a.* kind to friends, of winning manners. –हत्या the murder of a friend.

मित्रयु *a.* **1** Friendly-minded. **2** Winning friends.

मिथ् 1 U. (मेथति-ते) **1** To associate with. **2** To unite, pair, copulate. **3** To hurt, injure, strike, kill. **4** To understand, perceive, know. **5** To wrangle.

मिथस् *ind.* **1** Mutually, reciprocally, to each other ; Ms. 2.147 ; oft. in comp. ; मिथःप्रस्थाने *S.* 2; मिथःसमयात् *S.* 5. **2** In secret or private, secretly, privately ; भर्तुः प्रसादं प्रतिनंद्य मूर्ध्ना वक्तुं मिथः प्राक्रमतैवमेनं Ku. 3. 2; 6.1; R. 13.1.

मिथिलः N. of a king. –**लाः** (pl.) N. of a people. –**ला** N. of a city, capital of the country called Videha, q. v.

मिथुनं **1** A pair, couple ; मिथुनं परिकल्पितं त्वया सहकारः फलिनी च नन्विमौ R. 8. 61 ; Me. 18 ; U. 2. 6. **2** Twins. **3** Union, junction. **4** Sexual union. copulation, cohabitation. **5** The third sign of the zodiac. *Gemini*. **6** (In gram.) A root compounded with a preposition. –**Comp.** –**भावः** **1** forming a couple, state of being a pair. **2** copulation. –**व्रतिन्** *a.* practising cohabitation.

मिथुनेचरः The ruddy goose (चक्रवाक) cf. द्वंद्वचर.

मिथ्या *ind.* **1** Falsely, deceitfully, wrongly, incorrectly ; oft. with the force of an adjective ; मणौ महानील इति प्रभावादल्पप्रमाणेऽपि यथा न मिथ्या R. 18. 42 ; यदुवाच न तन्मिथ्या 17. 42 ; मिथ्यैव व्यसनं वदंति मृगयामीदृग्विनोदः कुतः *S.* 2. 5. **2** Invertedly, contrarily. **3** To no purpose, in vain, fruitlessly ; मिथ्या कारयते चारैर्घोषणां राक्षसाधिपः Bk. 8. 44 ; Bg. 18. 59. (मिथ्या वद्-वच् to tell a falsehood, lie ; मिथ्या कृ to falsify ; मिथ्या भू to turn out false, be false ; मिथ्या ग्रह् to misunderstand, mistake. At the beginning of comp. मिथ्या may be translated by 'false, untrue, unreal, sham, pretended, feigned' &c.) –**Comp.** –**अध्यवसितिः** *f.* a figure of speech, an expression of the impossibility of a thing by making it depend upon an impossible contingency ; किंचिन्मिथ्यात्वसिद्ध्यर्थं मिथ्यार्थांतरकल्पनम् । मिथ्याध्यवसितिर्वेश्यां वशयेत् खस्रजं वहन् ॥ Kuval. –**अपवादः** a false charge. –**आभधानं** a false assertion. –**अभियोगः** a falsse or groundless charge. –**अभिशंसनं** calumny, false accusation. –**अभिशापः** **1** a false prediction. **2** a false or unjust claim. –**आचारः** wrong or improper conduct. –**आहारः** wrong diet. –**उत्तरं** a false or prevaricating reply. –**उपचारः** pretended kindness or service. –**कर्मन्** *n.* a false act. –**कोपः**, –**क्रोधः** feigned anger. –**क्रयः** a false price. –**ग्रहः**, –**ग्रहणं** misconception, misunderstanding. –**चर्या** hypocrisy. –**ज्ञानं** a mistake, error, misapprehension. –**दर्शनं** heresy. –**दृष्टिः** *f.* heresy, holding heretic or atheistic doctrines. –**पुरुषः** a man only in appearance. –**प्रतिज्ञ** *a.* false to one's promise, perfidious. –**फलं** an imaginary advantage. –**मतिः** delusion, mistake, error. –**वचनं**, **वाक्यं** a falsehood, lie. –**वार्ता** a false report. –**साक्षिन्** *m.* a false witness.

मिद् I. 1 A., 4. 10. U. (मेदते, मेद्यति-ते, मेदयति ते) **1** To be unctuous or greasy. **2** To melt. **3** To be fat. **4** To love, feel affection. –II. 1 U. (मेदति-ते) see मिथ्.

मिद्धं **1** Sloth, indolence. **2** Torpor, sleepiness, dulness (of spirits also.).

मिंद् 1. 10. P. (मिंदति, मिंदयति) See मिद् II.

मिन्व् 1 P. (मिन्वति) **1** To sprinkle, moisten. **2** To honour, worship.

मिल् 6 U. (मिलति ते, generally मिलति; मिलित) **1** To join, be united with, accompany ; रुमण्वतो मिलितः Ratn. 4. **2** To come or meet together, meet, gather, assemble ; ये चान्ये सुहृदः समृद्धिसमये द्रव्याभिलाषाकुलास्ते सर्वत्र मिलंति H. 1. 210 ; यांतः किं न मिलंति Amaru. 10 ; मिलितशिलीमुख &c. Gīt. 1 ; स पात्रेसमितोऽन्यत्र भोजनान्मिलितो न यः Trik. **3** To be mixed or united with, come in contact with; मिलति तव तोयैर्मृगमदः G. L. 7. **4** To meet or encounter (as in fighting); close, close with. **5** To come to pass, happen. **6** To find, fall in with. –*Caus.* (मेलयति-ते) To bring together, assemble, convene.

मिलनं **1** Joining, meeting, assembling together. **2** Encountering. **3** Contact, being mixed with, coming in contact with ; व्यालनिलयमिलनेन गरलमिव कलयति मलयसमीरं Gīt. 4.

मिलित *p. p.* **1** Come together, assembled, encountered, combined. **2** Met, encountered. **3** Mixed. **4** Put together, taken in all.

मिलिंदः A bee ; परिणतमकरंदमार्मिकास्ते जगति भवंतु चिरायुषो मिलिंदाः Bv. 1. 8, 15.

मिलिंदकः A kind of snake.

मिश् 1 P. (मेशति) **1** To make a sound or noise. **2** To be angry.

मिश्र् 10 U. (मिश्रयति-ते ; strictly a denom. from मिश्र) To mix, mingle, unite, blend, combine, add ; वाचं न मिश्रयति यद्यपि मे वचोभिः *S.* 8. 31 ; न मिश्रयति लोचने Bv. 2. 140.

मिश्र *a.* **1** Mixed, blended, mingled, combined ; गद्यं पद्यं च मिश्रं च तत् त्रिधैव व्यवस्थितं Kâv. 1. 11, 31, 32 ; R. 16. 32. **2** Associated, connected. **3** Manifold, diverse. **4** Tangled, intertwined. **5** (At the end of comp.) Having a mixture of, consisting for the most part of. –**श्रः** **1** A respectable or worthy person ; usually affixed to the names of great men and scholars ; आर्यमिश्राः प्रमाणं M. 1; वसिष्ठमिश्रः, मंडनमिश्रः &c. **2** A kind of elephant. –**श्रं** **1** A mixture. **2** A kind of radish. –**Comp.** –**जः** a mule. –**वर्ण** *a.* of a mixed colour. (–**र्णं**) a kind of black aloewood. –**शब्दः** a mule.

मिश्रक *a.* **1** Mixed, mingled. **2** Miscellaneous. –**कः** **1** A compounder. **2** An adulterator of mercantile goods. –**कं** Salt produced from salt soil.

मिश्रणं Mixing, blending, combining.

मिश्रित *p. p.* **1** mixed, blended, combined. **2** Added. **3** Respectable.

मिष् I. 6 P. (मिषति) **1** To open the eyes, wink. **2** To look at, look helplessly ; जातवेदोमुखान्मायी मिषतामाच्छिनत्ति नः Ku. 2. 46. **3** To rival, contend, emulate. WITH **उद्** **1** to open the eyes ; उन्मिषन्निमिषन्नपि Bg. 5. 9. **2** to open (as the eyes); Ku. 4. 2. **3** to open, bloom, be expanded. **4** to rise. **5** to shine, glitter. –**नि** to shut the eyes ; Bg. 5. 9. –II. 1 P. (मेषति) To wet, moisten, sprinkle.

मिषः Emulation, rivalry. –**षं** Pretext, disguise, deceit, trick, fraud, false or outward appearance; बालमेनमेकेन मिषेणानीय Dk. (often used like छल q. v., to indicate an उत्प्रेक्षा); स रोमकूपौघमिषाज्जगत्कृता कृताश्च किं दूषणशून्यबिंदवः N. 1. 21. वदने विनिवेशिता भुजंगी पिशुनानां रसनामिषेण धात्रा Bv. 1. 111.

मिष्ट *a.* **1** Sweet. **2** Dainty, savoury; किं मिष्टमन्नं खरसूकराणां 'who cast pearls before swine.' **3** Moistened, wetted. –**ष्टं** A sweet-meat.

मिह् 1 P. (मेहति; मीढ) **1** To make water. **2** To wet, moisten, sprinkle. **3** To emit semen.

मिहिका Mist, snow.

मिहिरः **1** The sun ; मयि तावन्मिहिरोऽपि निर्दयोऽभूत् Bv. 2. 34 ; याते मय्यचिरान्निदाघमिहिरज्वालाशतैः शुष्कतां 1. 16; N. 2. 36 ; 13. 54. **2** A cloud. **3** The moon. **4** Wind, air. **5** An old man.

मिहिराणः An epithet of *S*iva.

मी I 9 U. (मीनाति, मीनीते ; seldom used in classical literature) **1** To kill, destroy, hurt, injure. **2** To lessen, diminish. **3** To change, alter. **4** To transgress, violate. –II. 1 P., 10 U. (मयति, माययति-ते) **1** To go, move. **2** To know, understand (गतिमत्ययोः). –III. 4 A. (मीयते) To die, perish.

मीढ *p. p.* **1** Urined, watered. **2** Passed (as urine).

मीढुष्टमः, **मीढुस्** *m.* An epithet of *S*iva.

मीनः **1** A fish; मुग्धमीन इव हृदः R. 1. 73; मीनो नु हंत कतमां गतिमभ्युपैतु Bv. 1.

17. **2** the twelfth sign of the zodiac (*Pisces*). **3** The first incarnation of Vishṇu; see मत्स्यावतार. **–Comp.–अंडं** roe, fish-sprawn. **–आघातिन्, घातिन्** *m.* **1** a fisherman; **2** a crane. **–आलयः** the sea. **–केतनः** the god of love. **–गधा** an epithet of Satyavatî. **–गंधिका** a pond, pool of water. **–रंकः, –रंगः** a king-fisher.

मीनरः The sea-monster called *Makara* q. v.

मीम् 1 P. (मीमति) **1** To go move. **2** To sound.

मीमांसकः **1** One who investigates or inquires into, an investigator, examiner. **2** A follower of the system of philosophy called मीमांसा q. v. below.

मीमांसनं Investigation, examination, inquiry.

मीमांसा **1** Deep reflection, inquiry, examination, investigation; रसगंगाधरनाम्नीं करोति कुतुकेन काव्यमीमांसां R. G.; so दत्तक°, अलंकार° &c. **2** N. of one of the six chief *Darsanas* or systems of Indian philosophy. It was originally divided into two systems:—the पूर्वमीमांसा or कर्ममीमांसा founded by Jaimini; and the उत्तरमीमांसा or ब्रह्ममीमांसा ascribed to Bâdarâyaṇa; but the two systems have very little in common between them, the first concerning itself chiefly with the correct interpretation of the ritual of the Veda and the settlement of dubious points in regard to Vedic texts; and the latter dealing chiefly with the nature of Brahman or the Supreme Spirit. The पूर्वमीमांसा is, therefore, usually styled only मीमांसा or *the* Mîmâmsâ, and the उत्तरमीमांसा, वेदांत which, being hardly a sequel of Jaimini's system, is now considered and ranked separately); मीमांसाकृतमुन्ममाथ सहसा हस्ती मुनिं जैमिनिं Pt. 2. 33.

मीरः **1** The ocean. **2** A limit, boundary.

मील् 1 P. (मीलति, मीलित) **1** To close (as the eyes), close or contract the eye-lids, wink, twinkle; पत्रे बिम्यति मीलति क्षणमपि क्षिप्रं तदालोकनात् Gît. 10. **2** To close, be closed or shut (as eyes or flowers); नयनयुगममीलत् *Si.* 11. 2; तस्यां मिमीलतुर्नेत्रे Bk. 14. 54. **3** To fade, disappear, vanish. **4** To meet or be collected (for मिल्). *–Caus.* (मीलयति-ते) To cause to shut, close, shut (eyes, flowers &c.); शेषान्मासान्गमय चतुरो लोचने मीलयित्वा Me. 110. –WITH. **–आ** *Caus.* to shut; नेत्रे चामीलयन् Kâv. 2. 11. **–उद्** **1** to open (as the eyes; उदमी लीच लोचने Bk. 15. 102, 16. 8. **2** To be awakened or roused, *Si.* 10.72. **3** to expand, blow; Ki. 4. 3; Mâl. 1. 38. **4** to be diffused or spread, cluster round; उन्मीलन्मधुगंध &c Gît. 1; U. 1. 20. **5** to appear, spring up, rise, become manifest; खं वायुर्ज्वलनो जलं क्षितिरिति त्रैलोक्यमुन्मीलति Prab. 1. 2; Bv. 2. 72 (*Caus.*) to open; तंदतदुन्मीलय चक्षुरायतं V. 1. 5; Mk. 1 33. **–नि** **1** to shut the eyes; R. 12. 65; Ms. 1. 52. **2** to close the eyes in death, die; निमिमील नरोत्तमप्रिया हतचंद्रा तमसेव कौमुदी R. 8. 38. **3** to obscure (fig.); प्रजालोपनिमीलितः R. 1. 68. **4** to be closed or shut (as eyes, flowers &c.); निमीलितानामिव पंकजानां R. 7. 64. **5** to disappear, vanish, set (fig. also); नरेशे जीवलोकोऽयं निमीलति निमीलति H. 3. 145; यैर्निमीलितनक्षत्रा Hariv. (*–Caus.*) to shut, close; उन्मीलितापि दृष्टिर्निमीलितेवांधकारेण Mk. 1. 33; न्यमिमीलदब्जनयनं नलिनी *Si.* 9. 11; ललिपद्मं न्यमीलयत् Kâv. 2. 261; Ku. 3. 36; 5. 57; R. 19. 28. **–सं** to be shut or closed. (*–Caus.*) **1** to shut or close; उपांतसंमीलितलोचनो नृपः R. 3. 26; 13. 10. **2** to obscure, darken, make dim; विकारश्चैतन्यं भ्रमयति च संमीलयति च U. 1. 36.

मीलनं **1** Closing of the eyes, winking, twinkling. **2** Closing the eyes. **3** The closing of a flower.

मीलित *p. p.* **1** Snut, closed. **2** Twinkled. **3** Half-opened, unblown. **4** Vanished, disappeared. **–तं** (In Rhet.) A figure of speech in which the difference or distinction between two objects is shown to be completely obscured on account of their similarity-whether natural or artificial-in some respects; it is thus defined by Mammaṭa:–समेन लक्ष्मणा वस्तु वस्तुना यन्निगूह्यते। निजेनागंतुना वापि तन्मीलितमिति स्मृतं ॥ K. P. 10.

मीव् 1 P. (मीवति) **1** To go, move. **2** To grow fat.

मीवरः The leader of an army, a general.

मीवा **1** The tapeworm. **2** Wind.

मुः **1** An epithet of *Siva.* **2** Bondage, confinement. **3** Final emancipation. **4** A funeral pile.

मुकुंदकः An onion.

मुकुः Liberation, deliverance; especially, final emancipation.

मुकुटं **1** A crown, tiara, diadem; मुकुटरत्नमरीचिभिरस्पृशत् R.9. 13. **2** A crest. **3** A peak, point.

मुकुटी Cracking or snaping the fingers.

मुकुंदः **1** N. of Vishṇu or Krisṇa. **2** Quicksilver. **3** A kind of precious stone. **4** N. of one of the nine treasures of Kubera. **5** A kind of drum.

मुकुरः **1** A mirror, looking-glass; गुणिनामपि निजरूपप्रतिपत्तिः परत एव संभवति। स्वमहिमदर्शनमक्ष्णोर्मुकुरतले जायते यस्मात् Vâs., *Si.* 9. 73; N. 22. 43. **2** A bud; see मुकुल. **3** The handle of a potter's wheel. **4** The Bakula tree.

मुकुलः-लं **1** A bud; आविर्भूतप्रथममुकुलाः कंदलीश्चानुकच्छं Me. 21; R. 9. 31; 15. 99. **2** Anything like a bud; आलक्ष्यदंतमुकुलान् (तनयान्) *S.* 7. 17. **3** The body. **4** The soul or spirit. (मुकुलीकृ means 'to close in the form of a bud,' Ku. 5. 63).

मुकुलित *a.* **1** Having buds, budded, blossoms. **2** Half-closed, half-shut; दरमुकुलितनयनसरोजं Gît. 2; Ku. 3. 76.

मुकुष्टः, मुकुष्ठकः A kind of bean.

मुक्त *p. p.* **1** Loosened, relaxed, slackened. **2** Set free, liberated, relaxed. **3** Abandoned, left, given up, set aside, taken off. **4** Thrown, cast, discharged, hurled. **5** Fallen down, dropped down from. **6** Drooping, unnerved; मुक्तैरवयवैरशायिषि Dk. **7** Given, bestowed. **8** Sent forth, emitted. **9** Finally saved or emancipated, (see मुच्). **–क्तः** One who is finally emancipated from the bonds of worldly existence, one who has renounced all worldly attachments and secured final beatitude, an absolved saint; सुभाषितेन गीतेन युवतीनां च लीलया मनो न भिद्यते यस्य स वै मुक्तोऽथवा पशुः ॥ Subha'sh. **–Comp. –अंबरः** a Jaina mendicant of the *digambara* class. **–आत्मन्** *a.* finally saved or emancipated. (*–m.*) **1** the soul absolved from sins or from worldly matter. **2** a person whose soul is absolved. **–आसन** *a.* rising from a seat. **–कच्छः** a Buddhist. **–कंचकः** a snake that has cast off its slough. **–कंठ** *a.* raising a cry. (**–ठं**) *ind.* bitterly, loudly, aloud; R. 14. 68. **–कर, –हस्त** *a.* open-handed, liberal, bountiful. **–चक्षुस्** *m.* a lion. **–वसन** see मुक्तांबर.

मुक्तकं **1** A missile, a missile weapon. **2** Simple prose. **3** A detached stanza, the meaning of which is complete in itself; see Kâv. 1. 13; मुक्तकं श्लोक एवैकश्चमत्कारक्षमः सताम्.

मुक्ता **1** A pearl; हारोयं हरिणाक्षीणां लुठति स्तनमंडले। मुक्तानामप्यवस्थेयं के वयं स्मरकिंकराः Amaru. 100 (where मुक्तानां means also 'of absolved saints'). Pearls are said to be produced from various sources, but particularly from oyster-shells:–करींद्रजीमूतवराहशंखमत्स्याहिशुक्त्युद्भववेणुजानि। मुक्ताफलानि प्रथितानि लोके तेषां तु शुक्त्युद्भवमेव भूरि ॥ Malli.). **2** A harlot, courtezan. **–Comp. –अगारः, आगारः** the pearl-oyster. **–आवलिः -ली** *f.* **–कलापः** a pearl-necklace. **–गुणः** a pearl-necklace, string of pearls; Me. 46; R. 16. 18. **–जालं** a string or zone of pearls. **–दामन्** *n.* a. string of pearls. **–पुष्पः** a kind of jasmine. **–प्रसूः** *f.* the pearl-oyter **–प्रालंबः** a string of pearls. **–फलं** **1** a pearl; Ku. 1. 6; R. 6. 28; 16. 62. **2** a kind of flower. **3** the custard-apple. **4** camphor. **–मणिः** a pearl. **–मातृ** *f.* the pearl-oyster. **–लता,**

-स्रज् *f.*, -हारः a pearl-necklace. -शुक्तिः, -स्फोटः the pearl-oyster.

मुक्तिः *f.* 1 Release, liberation, deliverance. 2 Freedom, emancipation. 3 Final beatitude or emancipation, absolution of the soul from metempsychosis. 4 Leaving, giving up, abandoning, avoiding; संसर्गमुक्तिः खलेषु Bh. 2. 62. 5 Throwing, hurling, letting off, discharging. 6 Unloosing-opening. 7 Discharge, paying off (as a debt). -Comp. -क्षेत्रं an epithet of Benares. -मार्गः the way to final beatitude. -मुक्तः frankincense.

मक्त्वा *ind.* 1 Having left, abandoned &c. 2 Excepting, except (with the force of a preposition.)

मुखं 1 The mouth (fig. also) ब्राह्मणोऽस्य मुखमासीत् Rv. 10. 90. 12; सुभ्रूभंगं मुखमिव Me. 24; त्वं मम मुखं भव V. 1 'be my mouth or spokesman'. 2 The face, countenance; परिवृत्तार्धमुखी मयाद्य दृष्टा V. 1. 17; नियमक्षाममुखी धृतैकवेणिः *S.* 7. 21; so चंद्रमुखी, मुखचंद्रः &c. 3 The snout or muzzle (of any animal). 4 The front, van, forepart. 5 The tip, point, barb (of an arrow), head; पुरारिमप्राप्तमुखः शिलीमुखः Ku. 5. 54; R. 3. 57. 59. 6 The edge or sharp point (of any instrument). 7 A teat, nipple; Ku. 1. 40; R. 3. 8. 8 The beak or bill of a bird. 9 A direction, quarter; as in दिङ्मुखं, अंतर्मुख. 10 Opening, entrance, mouth; नीवाराः शुकगर्भकोटरमुखभ्रष्टास्तरूणामधः *S.* 1. 14; नदीमुखेनेव समुद्रमाविशत् R. 3. 28; Ku. 1. 8. 11 An entrance to a house, a door, passage. 12 Beginning, commencement; सखीजनोद्वीक्षणकौमुदीमुखं R. 3. 1; दिनमुखानिरविर्हिमनिग्रहैर्विमलयन् मलयं नगमत्यजत् 9. 25; 5. 76; Ghaṭ 2. 13 Introduction. 14 The chief, the principal or prominent; (at the ond of comp. in this sense): बंधोन्मुक्त्यै खलु मखमुखान्कुर्वते कर्मपाशान् Bv. 4. 21; so इंद्रमुखा देवाः &c. 15 The surface or upper side. 16 A means. 17 A source, cause, occasion. 18 Utterance; as in मुखसुख. 19 The Vedas, scripture. 20 (In Rhet.) The original cause or source of the action in a drama. -Comp. -अग्निः 1 a forest-conflagration. 2 a sort of goblin with a face of fire. 3 the consecrated or sacrificial fire. 4 fire put into the mouth of a corpse at the time of lighting the funeral pile. -अनिलः, उच्छ्वासः breath. -अस्रः a crab. -आकारः look, mien, appearance. -आसवः nectar of the lips. -आस्रावः, -स्रावः spittle, saliva. -इंदुः a moon-like face, *i. e.* a round lovely face. -उल्का a forest-conflagration. -कमलं a lotus-like face. -खुरः a tooth. -गंधकः an onion. -चपल *a.* talkatise, garrulous. -चपेटिका a slap on the face. -चीरिः *f.* the tongue. -जः a Brâhmaṇa. -जाहं the root of the mouth. -दूषणः an onion. -दूषिका an eruption disfiguring the face. -निरीक्षकः a lazy fellow, an idler. -निवासिनी an epithet of Sarasvatî. -पटः a veil कुर्वन् कामं क्षणमुखपटप्रीतिमैरावतस्य Me. 62.-पिंडः a mouthful of food. -पूरणं 1 filling the mouth. 2 a mouthful of water, a mouthful in general. -प्रसादः a pleased countenance, graciousness of aspect. -प्रियः an orange. -बंधः a preface, an introduction. -बंधनं 1 a preface. 2 a lid, cover. -भूषणं a preparation of betel; see तांबूल. -भेदः distortion of the face. -मधु *a.* honey-mouthed, sweet-lipped. -मार्जनं washing the face. -यंत्रणं the bit of a bridle. -रागः the colour or complexion of the face; R. 12. 8; 17. 31. -लांगलः a hog. -लेपः 1 anointing the face or upper side (of a drum). 2 a disease of the phlegmatic humour. -वल्लभः the pomegranate tree. -वाद्यं 1 an instrument of music sounded with the mouth, any wind-instrument. 2 a sound made with the mouth. -वासः, -वासनः a perfume used to scent the breath. -विलुंठिका a she-goat. -व्यादानं gaping, yawning. -शफ *a.* abusive, foul-mouthed, scurrilous. -शुद्धिः *f.* washing or purifying the mouth. -शेषः an epithet of Râhu. -शोधन *a.* 1 cleansing the mouth. 2 pungent, sharp. (-नः) the sharp flavour, pungency. (-नं) cleansing the mouth. -श्रीः *f.* 'beauty of countenance', a lovely face. -सुखं facility of pronunciation, phonetic ease. -सुरं the moisture of the lips.

मुखंपच्चः A beggar, mendicant.

मुखर *a.* 1 Talkative, garrulous, loquacious; मुखरा खल्वेषा गर्भदासी Ratn. 2; मुखरतावत्सरे हि विराजते Ki. 5. 16. 2 Noisy, making a continuous sound, tinkling, jingling (as an anklet), स्तंबेरमा मुखरशृंखलकर्षिणस्ते R. 5. 72; अंतःकूजन्मुखरशकुनो यत्र रम्यो वनांतः U. 2. 25. 20; Mâl. 9. 5; मुखरमधीरं त्यज मंजीरं रिपुमिव केलिषु लोलं Gît. 5: Mk. 1 35. 3 Sounding, resonant or resounding with (usually at the end of comp.); स्थाने स्थाने मुखरककुभो झांकृतैर्निर्झराणां U. 2. 14; मंडलीमुखरशिखरे (लताकुंजे) Gît. 2; R. 13. 46. 4 Expressive or indicative of. 5 Foul-mouthed, abusive, scurrilous. 6 Mocking, ridiculing (मुखरीकृ 'to cause to sound or talk, make resonant with'). -रः 1 A crow. 2 A leader, the chief or principal person; यदि कार्यविपत्तिः स्यान्मुखरस्तत्र हन्यते H. 1. 29. 3 A conch-shell.

मुखरयति Den. P. 1 To make resonant or noisy, cause to sound or echo. 2 To make (one) talk or speak; अत एव शुश्रूषा मां मुखरयति Mu. 3. 3 To notify, declare, announce.

मुखरिका, मुखरी The bit of a bridle.

मुखरित *a.* Made noisy or resonant with, ringing or noisy with, गंडोड्डीनालिमाला मुखरितककुभस्तांडवे शूलपाणेः Mâl. 1. 1.

मुख्य *a.* 1 Relating to the mouth or the face. 2 Chief, principal, foremost, first, pre-eminent, prominent; द्विजातिमुख्यः, वारमुख्या, योधमुख्याः &c. -ख्यः A leader, guide. -ख्यं 1 A principal rite or ordinance. 2 Reading or teaching the Vedas. -Comp. -अर्थः the primary or original (as opp. गौण) meaning of a word. -चांद्रः the chief lunar month. -नृपः, -नृपतिः a sovereign monarch, paramount sovereign. -मंत्रिन् *m.* the prime minister.

मुगूहः A kind of gallinule.

मुग्ध *a.* 1 Stupefied, fainted. 2 Perplexed, infatuated. 3 Foolish, ignorant, silly, stupid; शशांक केन मुग्धेन सुधांशुरिति भाषितः Bv. 2. 29. 4 Simple, artless, innocent; U. 1. 46. 5 Erring, mistaken. 6 Attractive by youthful simplicity (not yet acquainted with love), childlike; (कः) अयमाचरत्यविनयं मुग्धासु तपस्विकन्यासु *S.* 1. 25; R. 9. 34. (Hence) Beautiful, lovely, charming, pretty; हरिरिह मुग्धवधूनिकरे विलासिनि विलसति केलिपरे Gît. 1; U. 3. 5. -ग्धा A young girl attractive by her youthful simplicity, a pretty young maiden; (regarded as a variety of Nâyikâ in poetic compositions). -Comp. अक्षी a lovely eyed woman; वियोगो मुग्धाक्ष्याः स खलु रिपुघातावधिरभूत् U. 3. 44. -आनना having a lovely face. -धी, -बुद्धि, -मति *a.* silly, foolish, stupid, simple. -भावः simplicity, silliness.

मुच् I. 1 A. (मोचते) To deceive, cheat; see मुंच्. -II. 6 U. -मुंचति-ते, मुक्त) 1 To loose, set free, release, let go, let loose, liberate, deliver (from captivity &c.); वनाय ... यशोधनो धेनुमृषेर्मुमोच R. 2. 1, 3. 20; Ms. 8.202; मोक्ष्यते सुरबंदीनां वेणीर्वीर्यविभूतिभिः Ku. 2. 61; R. 10 47; मा भवांगानि मुंचतु V. 2 'let not thy limbs droop', 'do not despond'. 2 To set free, loosen (as the voice); कंठं मुंचति बर्हिणः समदनः Mk. 5. 14, loosens his throat or voice, *i. e.* raises a cry. 3 To live, abandon, quit, give up, lay aside, relinquish; रात्रिर्गता मतिमतां वर मुंच शय्यां R. 5. 66; मुनिसुताप्रणयस्मृतिरोधिना मम च मुक्तमिदं तमसा मनः *S.* 6. 7; मौनं मुंचति किं च कैरवकुले Bv. 1. 4; आविर्भूते शशिनि तमसा मुच्यमानेव रात्रिः V. 1. 8; Me. 96, 41; R. 3. 11. 4 To set apart, take away, except, see मुक्त्वा. 5 To dismiss, send away. 6 To cast, throw, hurl, fling, discharge; मृगेषु शरान्मुमुक्षोः R. 9. 58; Bk. 15. 53. 7 To emit, drop, pour forth or down, shed, let fall (tears &c.); अपसृतपांडुपत्रा मुंचंत्यश्रूणीव लताः S. 4. 11 ; चिरविरहजं मुंचतो बाष्पमुष्णं Me. 12; Bk. 7. 2. 8 To utter, give forth; Mâl. 9. 5; Bk. 7. 57. 9 To give away, grant, bestow. 10 To put on (A). 11 To void (as excrement). *-Pass.* (मुच्यते) To be loosed or released, be freed or absolved from ; मुच्यते सर्वपापेभ्यः &c. *-Caus.* (मोचयति-ते) 1 To cause to be freed or liberated. 2 To cause to shed. 3 To loose, set at liberty, liberate. 4 To extricate, disentangle. 5 To unyoke, unharness. 6 To give away, bestow. 7 To gladden, delight. *-Desid.* 1 (मुमुक्षति) To wish to free or liberate. 2 (मुमुक्षते,-मोक्षते) To long for final emancipation. -WITH अव to take off or down, put away. -आ 1 to wear, put on, tie round or fasten ; आमुंचतीवाभरणं द्वितीयं R. 13. 21; 12. 86 ; 16. 74 ; Ki. 11. 15 ; आमुंचद्वर्म रत्नाढ्यं Bk. 17. 6. 2 to cast, throw, discharge ; आमोक्ष्यंते त्वयि कटाक्षान् Me. 35. -उद् 1 to unfasten ; R. 6. 28. 2 to loosen, liberate; free from. 3 to take or pull off, keep or put aside, give up, abandon Bk. 3. 22. निस् 1 to free, liberate; release ; हिमनिर्मुक्तयोर्योगे चित्राचंद्रमसोरिव R. 1. 46; Bg. 7. 28. 2 to leave, quit, abandon. -परि 1 to free, release, liberate ; मेघोपरोधपरिमुक्तशशांकवक्त्रा Rs. 3. 7; Ch. P. 9. 2 to leave, quit, abandon. -प्र 1 to free, liberate, release. 2 to throw, cast, hurl. 3 to shed, emit, seed forth. -प्रति 1 to free, liberate, release, set free, गृहीतप्रतिमुक्तस्य R. 4. 43; अमुं तुरंगं प्रतिमोक्तुमर्हसि 3. 46. 2 to put on, wear. 3 to quit, leave, abandon. 4 to throw, cast or discharge at. -वि 1 to free, liberate. 2 to give up, lay aside, abandon, quit; विमुच्य वासांसि गुरूणि सांप्रतं Rs. 1. 7. 3 to let go, let loose; Bk. 7. 50. 4 to except, leave apart ; Ku. 4. 31. 5 to shed, pour down (tears); चिरमश्रूणि विमुच्य राघवः R. 8. 25. 6 to throw, cast. -सं to shed, discharge.

मुचकः Lac.

मुच(चु)कुंदः 1 N. of a tree. 2 N. of an ancient king, son of Mândhâtri. [For having assisted the gods in their wars with the demons he got, as a reward, the boon of long and unbroken sleep. The gods also decreed that whosoever dared to interrupt his sleep should be burnt to ashes. When Krishna wanted to kill the mighty Kalayavana he cunningly decoyed him to the cave of Muchukunda and on his entering it he was burnt down by the fire which emanated from the king's eye]. -Comp. -प्रसादकः an epithet of Krishna.

मुचिरः 1 A deity. 2 Virtue. 3 Wind.

मुचिलिंदः A kind of flower.

मुचुटी 1 Snapping the fingers. 2 A fist.

मुज्, मुंज् 1 P. 10 U. (मोजति, मुंजति, मोजयति-ते, मुंजयति-ते) 1 To cleanse, purify. 2 To sound.

मुंजः 1 A sort of rush or grass (of which the girdle of a Brâhmaṇa should be made); Ms. 2. 43. 2 N. of a king of Dhârâ (said to be the uncle of the celebrated Bhoja). -Comp. -केशः 1 an epithet of Siva. 2 of Vishṇu. -केशिन् *m.* an epithet of Vishṇu. -बंधनं investiture with the sacred thread (or girdle). -वासस् *m.* an epithet of Siva.

मुंजरं The fibrous root of the lotus.

मुट् I. 1. P. 10 U. (मोटति, मोटयति-ते) 1 To crush, break, grind, powder. 2 To blame, rebuke (in this sense 6 P. also.)

मुण् 6 P. (मुणति) To promise.

मुंट् 1 P. (मुंटति) To crush, grind.

मुंड् I 1 P., (मुंडति) 1 To shave, shear. 2 To crush, grind. -II. 1 A. (मुंडते) To sink.

मुंड *a.* 1 Shaved. 2 Lopped. 3 Blunt. 4 Low, mean. -डः 1 A man with a shaved or bald head. 2 A bald or shaven head. 3 The forehead. 4 A barber. 5 The trunk of a tree stripped of its top branches. -डा A female mendicant of a particular order. -डं 1 The head. 2 Iron. -Comp. -अयसं iron. -फलः a cocoanut tree. -मंडली a number of shaven heads. -लोहं iron. -शालिः a kind of rice.

मुंडकः 1 A barber. 2 The trunk of a tree stripped of its top-branches, a pollard. -कं The head. -Comp. -उपनिषद् *f.* N. of an Upanishad of the Atharvaveda.

मुंडनं Shaving the head, tonsure.

मुंडित *p. p.* 1 Shaved. 2 Lopped. -तं Iron.

मुंडिन् *m.* 1 A barber. 2 An epithet of Siva.

मुत्यं A pearl.

मुद् I. 10 U. (मोदयति-ते) 1 To mix, blend. 2 To cleanse, purify. -II. 1 A. (मोदते, मुदित; *caus.* मोदयति-ते *desid.* मुमुदिषते or मुमोदिषते) To rejoice, be glad or happy, be joyful or delighted ; यक्ष्ये दास्यामि मोदिष्य इत्यज्ञानविमोहिताः Bg. 16. 15; Ms. 2. 232. 3. 191; Bk. 15. 97. -WITH अनु to approve of, allow, permit, sanction; R. 14. 43. -आ 1 to be glad or joyous, rejoice. 2 to be fragrant. (*-Caus.*) to scent, perfume; परिमलैरामोदयंती दिशः Bv. 1. 56. -प्र to be extremely glad, to be very much delighted; R. 6. 86, Mâl. 5. 23.

मुद्, मुदा *f.* Joy, delight, pleasure, gladness, satisfaction; पितुर्मुदं तेन ततान सोऽर्भकः R. 3. 25; अश्नन् पुरो हरितको मदमादधानः Si. 5. 58; 1. 23; विषादे कर्तव्ये विदधति जडाः प्रत्युत मुदं Bh. 3. 25; द्विपरणमुदा Gît. 11; Ki. 5. 25; R. 7. 30.

मुदित *p. p.* Pleased, rejoiced; delighted, glad, joyous. -तं 1 Pleasure, delighr, joy, happiness. 2 A kind of sexual embrace. -ता Joy, delight.

मुदिरः 1 A cloud; प्रचुरपुरंदरधनुरनुरंजितमेदुरमुदिरसुवेशं Gît. 2; or मुंचसि नाद्यापि रुषं भामिनि मुदिरालिरुदियाय Bv. 2. 88. 2 A lover, libertine. 3 A frog.

मुदी Moonlight.

मुद्गः 1 A kind of kidney-bean. 2 A lid, cover. 3 A kind of sea-bird. -Comp. -भुज्, -भोजिन् *m.* a horse.

मुद्गरः 1 A hammer, mallet ; as in मोहमुद्गरः (a small poem by Sankarâchârya) R. 12. 73. 2 A club, mace. 3 A staff for breaking clods of earth. 4 A kind of dumb-bell. 5 A bud. 6 A kind of jasmine (said to be *n.* also in this sense.)

मुद्गलः A kind of grass.

मुद्गष्टः A kind of bean.

मुद्रणं 1 Sealing, stamping, printing, marking. 2 Closing, shutting.

मुद्रयति Den. P. 1 To seal; अनया मुद्रया मुद्रयैनं Mu. 1. 2 To stamp, mark, impress. 3 To cover, close up (fig.); विवराणि मुद्रयन् द्रागूर्णायुरिव सज्जनो जयति Bv. 1. 90.

मुद्रा 1 A seal, an instrument for sealing or stamping; especially a seal-ring, signet ring; अनया मुद्रया मुद्रयैनं Mu. 1; नाममुद्राक्षराण्यनुवाच्य परस्परमवलोकयतः S. 1. 2 A stamp, print, mark, impression ; चतुःसमुद्रमुद्रः K. 191; सिंदूरमुद्रांकितः (बाहुः) Gît. 4. 3 A pass, pass-port (as given by a seal-ring); अगृहीतमुद्रः कटकान्निष्क्रामसि Mu. 5. 4 A stamped coin, piece of money. 5 A medal. 6 An image, sign, badge, token. 7 Shutting, closing, sealing ; सैवौष्ठमुद्रा स च कर्णपाशः U. 6. 27 ; क्षिपाक्षिद्रामुद्रां मदनकलहच्छेदसुलभां Mâl. 2. 12. 8 A mystery. 9 N. of certain positions of the fingers practised in devotion or religious worship. -Comp. -अक्षरं 1 a letter of the seal. 2 a type (modern use). -कारः a maker of seels. -मार्गः an opening believed to exist in the crown of the head through which the soul is said to escape at death ; cf. ब्रह्मरंध्र.

मुद्रिका A senl-ring; see मुद्रा.

मुद्रित *a.* 1 Sealed, marked, impressed, stamped; त्यागःसप्तसमुद्रमुद्रितमहीनिर्व्याजदानावधिः Mv. 2. 36; काश्मीरमुद्रितमुरो मधुसूदनस्य Gît. 1 ; स्वयं सिंदूरेण द्विपरणमुदा मुद्रित इव 11. 2 Closed, sealed up. 3 Unblown.

मुधा *ind.* 1 In vain, to no purpose, uselessly, unprofitably ; यत्किंचिदपि संवीक्ष्य कुरुते हसितं मुधा S. D. 2 wrongly, falsely, रात्रिः सैव पुनः स एव दिवसो मत्वा मुधा जंतवः Bh. 3. 78. v. l.

मुनिः 1 A sage, a holy man, saint, devote, an ascetic; मुनीनामप्यहं व्यासः Bg. 10. 37; पुण्यः शब्दो मुनिरिति मुहुः केवलं राजपूर्वः S. 2. 14; R. 1. 8, 3. 49; Bg. 2. 56. 2 N. of the sage Agastya. 3 Of Vyâsa. 4 Of Buddha. 5 The mango-tree. 6 The number 'seven'. -pl. The seven sages. **-Comp.** -अन्नं (pl.) the food of ascetics. -इंद्रः, ईशः, ईश्वरः a great sage. -त्रयं 'the triad of sages', *i. e.* Pâṇini, Kâtyâyana, and Patanjali (who are considered to be inspired saints); मुनित्रयं नमस्कृत्य, or त्रिमुनि व्याकरणं Sk. -पित्तलं copper. -पुंगवः a great or eminent sage. -पुत्रकः 1 a wagtail. 2 the *Damanaka* tree. -भेषजं 1 the fruit of the yellow myrobalan. 2 fasting. -व्रतं an ascetic vow; Ku. 5. 48.

मुंथ् 1 P. (मुंथति) To go, move.

मुमुक्षा Desire of liberation or of final emancipation.

मुमुक्षु *a.* 1 Desirous of releasing or liberating. 2 Wishing to discharge. 3 About to shoot (arrows &c.); R. 9. 58. 4 Wishing to be free from worldly existence, striving after final emancipation. -क्षुः A sage striving after final emancipation or beatitude; Ku. 2. 51; Bg. 4. 15; V. 1. 1.

मुमुचानः A cloud.

मुमूर्षा Desire of death; Bk. 5. 57.

मुमूर्षु *a.* Being on the point of death, about to die.

मुर् 6 P. (मुरति) To encircle, surround, encompass, entwine.

मुरः N. of a demon slain by Krishṇa. -रं Encompassing, surrounding. **-Comp.** -अरिः 1 an epithet of Krishṇa; मुरारिमारादुपदर्शयंत्यसौ Gît. 1. 2 N. of the author of Anargharâghava. -जित्, -द्विष्, -भिद्, -मर्दनः, -रिपुः, -वैरिन्, -हन् *m.* epithets of Krishṇa or Vishṇu; प्रकीर्णास्रग्बिंदुर्जयति भुजदंडो मुराजितः Gît. 1; मुरवैरिणो राधिकामाधि वचनजातं 10.

मुरजः 1 A kind of drum or tabour; सानंदं नंदिहस्ताहतमुरजरव &c. Mâl. 1. 1; संगीताय प्रहतमुरजाः Me. 64, 56; M. 1. 22; Ku. 6. 41. 2 A stanza artificially arranged in the form of a drum; also called मुरजबंध, see K. P. 9. *ad loc.* **-Comp.** -फलः the jack-fruit tree.

मुरजा 1 A large drum. 2 N. of Kubera's wife.

मुरंदला N. of a river (supposed to be the same as Narmadâ).

मुरला N. of a river rising in the country of the Keralas; (mentioned in U. 3 along with तमसा); मुरलामारुतोद्धूतमगमत्कैतकं रजः R. 4. 55.

मुरली A flute, pipe. **-Comp.** -धरः an epithet of Krishṇa.

मुर्छ् 1 P. (मूर्छति, मूर्छित or मूर्त; the word is written as मूर्छ् or मूर्च्छ्) 1 To settle into a solid form, coagulate, congeal. 2 To faint, swoon, faint away; loose consciousness, become senseless, पतत्युयाति मूर्च्छत्यपि Gît. 4; क्रीडानिर्जितविश्व मूर्च्छितजनाघातेन किं पौरुषं Gît. 3; Bk. 15. 55. 3 To grow, increase, become strong or powerful; मुमूर्च्छ सहजं तेजो हविषेव हविर्भुजः R. 10. 79; मुमूर्च्छ सख्यं रामस्य 12. 57; मूर्च्छंत्यमी विकाराः प्रायेणैश्वर्यमत्तेषु S. 5. 18; 4 To gather strength, thicken, become dense; तमसां निशि मूर्च्छतां V. 3. 7. 5 (*a*) To take effect on; छाया न मूर्छति मलोपहतप्रसादे शुद्धे तु दर्पणतले सुलभावकाशा S. 7. 32. (*b*) To prevail against, have power against; न पादपोन्मूलनशक्ति रंहः शिलोच्चये मूर्छति मारुतस्य R. 2. 34. 6 To fill, pervade, penetrate, spread over; Ku. 6. 59; R. 6. 9. 7 To be a match for. 8 To be frequent. 9 To cause to sound loudly. *-Caus.* (मूर्छयति-ते) To stupefy, cause to faint; म्लेच्छान्मूर्छयते Gît. 1. -WITH वि to faint, swoon. -सं 1 to faint, swoon. 2 to grow strong or powerful, gather strength, become intense; Ki. 5. 41.

मुर्मुरः 1 A fire made of chaff, chaff-fire; स्मरहुताशनमुर्मुरचूर्णतां दधुरिवाम्रवणस्य रजःकणाः Si. 6. 6. 2 The god of love. 3 N. of one of the horses of the sun.

मुर्व् 1 P. (मुर्वति) To bind, tie.

मुशटी A kind of grain.

मु (स) ली A small house-lizard.

मुष् I. 9 P. (मुष्णाति, मुषित; *desid.* मुमुषिषति) 1 To steal, filch, rob, plunder, carry off (said to govern two acc.; देवदत्तं शतं मुष्णाति, but very rarely used in classical literature); मुषाण रत्नानि Si. 1. 51; 3. 38; क्षत्रस्य मुष्णन् वसु जैत्रमोजः Ki. 3. 41. 2 To eclipse, cover, envelop, conceal; सैन्यरेणुमुषितार्कदीधितिः R. 11. 51. 3 To captivate, enrapture, ravish. 4 To surpass, excel; मुष्णन् श्रियमशोकानां रक्तैः परिजनांबरैः। गीतैर्वरांगनानां च कोकिलभ्रमरध्वनिं Ks. 55. 113; Ratn. 1. 24; Bk. 9. 32; Me. 47. -WITH परि to rob, deprive of; परिमुषितरत्नं त्रिभुवनं Mâl. 5. 30. -प्र to take away, obscure; Bk. 17. 60. -II. 1 P. (मोषति) To hurt, injure, kill. -III. 4 P. (मुष्यति) 1 To steal. 2 To break, destroy; Bk. 15. 16.

मुषकः A mouse.

मुषल See मुसल.

मुषा-षी A crucible.

मुषित *p. p.* 1 Robbed, stolen, plundered. 2 Taken away, carried off, ravished. 3 Deprived of, free from. 4 Cheated, deceived; दैवेन मुषितोऽस्मि K.

मुषितकं Stolen property.

मुष्कः 1 A testicle. 2 The scrotum. 3 A muscular or robust man. 4 A mass, heap, quantity, multitude. 5 A thief. **-Comp.** -देशः the region of the scrotum. -शून्यः a eunuch, a castrated person. -शोफः swelling of the testicles.

मुष्ट *p. p.* Stolen; S. 5. 20. -ष्टं Stolen property.

मुष्टिः *m. f.* 1 The clenched hand. first; कर्णांतमेत्य बिभिदे निबिडोऽपि मुष्टिः R. 9. 58; 15. 21; Si. 10. 59. 2 A handful; fistful श्यामाकमुष्टिपरिवर्धितकः S. 4 14; R. 19. 57; Ku. 7. 69; Me. 68. 3 A handle or hilt. 4 A particular measure (=a *pala*). 5 the penis. **-Comp.** -देशः the middle of a bow, that part of it which is grasped in the hand. -द्यूतं a kind of game. -पातः boxing. -बंधः 1 clenching the fist. 2 a handful. -युद्धं a pugilistic encounter, boxing.

मुष्टिकः 1 A goldsmith. 2 A particular position of the hands. 3 N. of a demon. -कं A pugilistic encounter, fisticuffs. **-Comp.** -अंतकः an epithet of Balarâma.

मुष्टिका The fist.

मुष्टिंधयः A child, baby, infant.

मुष्टीमुष्टि *ind.* Fist-to fist, hand-to-hand fighting.

मुष्ठकः Black mustard.

मुस् 4 P. (मुस्यति) To cleave, divide, break into pieces.

मुसलः-लं 1 A mace, club. 2 A pestle (used for cleaning rice); मुसलमिदमियं च पातकाले मुहुरनुयाति कलेन हुंकृतेन Mu. 1. 4; Ms. 6. 56. **-Comp.** -आयुधः an epithet of Balarâma. -उलूखलं a pestle and mortar.

मुसलामुसलि *ind.* Club against club.

मुसलिन् *m.* 1 An epithet of Balarâma. 2 Of Siva.

मुसल्य *a.* To be pounded or put to death with a club.

मुस्त् 10 U. (मुस्तयति-ते) To heap up, gather, collect, accumulate.

मुस्तः-स्ता-स्तं A kind of grass; विस्रब्धं क्रियतां वराहततिभिर्मुस्ताक्षतिः पल्वले S. 2. 6; R. 9. 59; 15. 19. **-Comp.** -अदः, -आदः hog.

मस्नं 1 A pestle. 2 A tear.

मुह् 4 P. (मुह्यति, मुग्ध or मूढ) 1 To faint, swoon, lose consciousness, become senseless; इहाहं द्रष्टुमाह्वं तां स्मरन्नेवं मुमोह सः Bk. 6. 21. 1. 20; 15. 15. 2 To be perplexed or bewildered, to be disturbed in mind. 3 To be foolish, stupid or infatuated. 4 To err, mistake. *-Caus.* (मोहयति-ते) 1 To stupefy, infatuate; मा मूमुहत्खलु भवंतमनन्यजन्मा Mâl. 1. 32. 2 To confound, bewilder, perplex; Bg. 3. 2, 4. 16. -WITH परि to be bewildered or perplexed. (*-Caus.* Atm.) to entice, beguile, allure; Bk. 8. 63. -प्र to be stupefied or infatuated. -वि 1 to be confused, bewildered, or perplexed, be embarrassed; Bg. 2. 72; 3. 6.

27. 2 to be foolish or infatuated. -सं 1 to be perplexed. 2 to be foolish or ignorant. (-*Caus.*) to infatuate, stupefy; अधरमधुस्यंदेन संमोहिता Gît. 12.

मुहिर *a.* Silly, foolish, stupid. -रः 1 The god of love. 2 A fool, blockhead.

मुहुस् *ind.* 1 Often, constantly, repeatedly, frequently ; ग्रीवाभंगाभिरामं मुहुरनुपतति स्यंदने दत्तदृष्टिः *S.* 1. 7, 2. 6; generally repeated in this sense; मुहुर्मुहुः over and over again, often and often ; गुरूणां सन्निधानेऽपि कः कूजति मुहुर्मुहुः. 2 For a time or moment, awhile ; Me. 115 ; generally used with successive clauses in the sense of 'now now', 'at one time-at another time'; मुहुरनुपतते बाला मुहुः पतति विह्वला । मुहुरालायते भीता मुहुः क्रोशति रोदिती॥ Subhâsh.; Mu. 5. 3. -Comp. -भाषा, -वचस् *n.* repetition, tautology. -भुज् *m.* a horse.

मुहूर्तः -र्तं 1 A moment, any short portion of time, an instant; नवांबुदानीकमुहूर्तलांछने R. 3. 53 ; संध्याभ्ररेखेव मुहूर्तरागाः Pt. 1. 194 ; Me. 19; Ku. 7. 50. 2 A period, time (auspicious or otherwise). 3 A period of 48 minutes. -र्तः An astrologer.

मुहूर्तकः 1 An instant, a moment. 2 A period of 48 minutes.

मू 1 P. (मवते) To bind, fasten, tie.

मूक *a.* 1 Dumb, silent, mute, speechless ; मूकं करोति वाचालं; मूकांडजं (काननं) Ku. 3. 42; सखीमियं वीक्ष्य विषादमूकां Gît. 7. 2 Poor, miserable, wretched. -कः 1 A mute; मौनान्मूकः H. 2. 26, v. l.; Ms. 7. 149. 2 A poor or miserable man. 3 A fish. -Comp. -अंबा a form of Durgâ. -भावः silence, muteness, dumbness.

मूकिमन् *m.* Muteness; dumbness, silence.

मूढ *p. p.* 1 Stupefied, infatuated. 2 Perplexed, bewildered; confounded, at a loss; किंकर्तव्यतामूढः 'being at a loss what to do'; so ह्रीमूढ Me. 68. 3 Foolish, silly, dull, stupid, ignorant; अल्पस्य हेतोर्बहु हातुमिच्छन्विचारमूढः प्रतिभासि मे त्वं R. 2. 47. 4 Mistaken, erring, deceived, gone astray. 5 Abortive. 6 Confounding. -ढः A fool, blockhead, dolt, an ignorant person; मूढः परप्रत्ययेनयबुद्धिः M. 1. 2. -Comp. -आत्मन् *a.* 1 stupefied in mind. 2 Foolish, stupid, silly -गर्भः a dead fœtus. -ग्राहः a wrong notion, misconception, misapprehension. -चेतन, चेतस् *a.* foolish, silly, ignorant; अवगच्छति मूढचेतनः प्रियनाशं हृदि शल्यमार्पितं R. 8. 88. -धी, -बुद्धि, -मति *a.* foolish, stupid, silly, simple; Ki. 1. 30. -सत्त्व *a.* infatuated, insane.

मूत *a.* 1 Bound, tied 2 Confined.

मूत्रं Urine; नाप्सु मूत्रं समुत्सृजेत् Ms. 4. 56; मूत्रं चकार made water. -Comp. -आघातः a urinary disease. -आशयः the lower belly. -उत्संग see मूत्रसंग. -कृच्छ्रं painful discharge of urine, strangury. -कोशः the scrotum. -क्षयः insufficient secretion of urine.-जठरः -रं the swelling of the belly caused by retention of urine.-दोषः a urinary disease. -निरोधः retention of urine. -पतनः a civet-cat. -पथः the urinary passage. -परीक्षा uroscopy or examination of urine. -पुटं the lower belly. -मार्गः the urethra. -वर्धक *a.* diuretic. -शूलः -लं urinary colic. -संगः urinary obstruction, a painful and bloody discharge of urine.

मूत्रयति Den. P. To make water; तिष्ठन्मूत्रयति Mbh.

मूत्रल *a.* Promoting the secretion of urine, diuretic.

मूत्रित *a.* Discharged or voided as urine.

मूर्ख *a.* Stupid, dull-headed, foolish, silly. -र्खः 1 A fool, blockhead; न तु प्रतिनिविष्टमूर्खजनचित्तमाराधयेत् Bh. 2. 6, 8; मूर्ख बलादपराधिनं मां प्रतिपादयिष्यासि V. 2. 2 A kind of bean. -Comp. -भूयं folly, stupidity, ignorance.

मूर्च्छन *a.* (नी *f.*) 1 Stupefying, producing insensibility or stupor (an epithet applied to one of the five arrows of Cupid). 2 Increasing, augmenting, strengthening. -नं 1 Fainting, swooning. 2 (In music) The rising of sounds, an intonation, a duly regulated rise and fall of sounds, conducting the air and the harmony through the keys in a pleasing manner, changing the key or passing from one key to another; modulation, melody; स्फुटीभवद्ग्रामविशेषमूर्च्छनां Si. 1. 10; भूयो भूयः स्वयमपि कृतां मूर्च्छनां विस्मरंती Me. 86; वर्णानामपि मूर्च्छनांतरगतं तारं विरामे मृदु Mk. 3. 5; सप्त स्वरास्त्रयो ग्रामा मूर्च्छनाश्चैकविंशतिः Pt. 5. 54; (a मूर्च्छा or मूर्च्छना is thus defined:— क्रमात्स्वराणां सप्तानामारोहश्चावरोहणम् । सा मूर्च्छेत्युच्यते ग्रामस्था एताः सप्त सप्त च ॥ see Malli. on *Si.* 1. 10 for further information).

मूर्च्छा 1 Fainting, swooning; R. 7. 44. 2 Spiritual ignorance or delusion. 3 A process in calcining metals ; मूर्च्छा गतो मृतो वा निदर्शनं पारदोऽत्र रसः Bv. 1. 82.

मूर्च्छाल *a.* Fainted, insensible, senseless.

मूर्छित *p. p.* 1 Fainted, swooning, insensible. 2 Foolish, stupid, silly. 3 Increased, augmented. 4 Made violent, intensified. 5 Perplexed, bewildered. 6 Filled. 7 Calcined.

मूर्त *a.* 1 Fainted, insensible. 2 Stupid, foolish. 3 Embodied, incarnate : मूर्तो विघ्नस्तपस इव नो भिन्नसारंगयूथः *S.* 1. 33 ; प्रसाद इव मूर्तस्ते स्पर्शः स्नेहार्द्रशीतलः U. 3. 14 ; R. 2. 69 ; 7. 70; Ku. 7. 42; Pt. 2. 99. 4 Material, corporeal. 5 Solid, hard.

मूर्तिः *f.* 1 Anything which has definite shape and limits, material element, matter, substance. 2 A form, visible shape, body, figure ; Mu. 2. 2 ; R. 3. 27; 14. 54. 3 An embodiment, incarnation, personification, manifestation; करुणस्य मूर्तिः V. 3. 4; Pt. 2. 159. 4 An image, idol, a statue. 5 Beauty. 6 Solidity, hardness. -Comp. -धर, -संचर *a.* embodied, incarnate ; U. 6. -पः a worshipper of an image, one who is in charge of an idol.

मूर्तिमत् *a.* 1 Material, corporeal. 2 Embodied, incarnate, personified ; शकुंतला मूर्तिमती च सत्क्रिया *S.* 5. 15 ; तव मूर्तिमानिव महोत्सवः करः U. 1. 18 ; R. 12. 64. 3 Hard, solid.

मूर्धन् *m.* 1 The forehead, brow. 2 The head in general ; नतेन मूर्ध्ना हरिरग्रहीद्पः Si. 1. 18; R. 16. 81; Ku. 3. 12. 3 The highest or most prominent part, top, summit, peak, head; अतिष्ठन्मनुजेंद्राणां मूर्ध्नि देवपतिर्यथा Mb. 'stood at the head of all kings' &c.; भूम्यां पर्वतमूर्धनि; *S.* 5. 7; Me. 17. 4 (Hence) A leader, head, chief, foremost, prominent. 5 Front, van, forepart; स किल संयुगमूर्ध्नि सहायतां मघवतः प्रतिपद्य महारथः R. 9. 19. -Comp. -अंतः the crown of the head. -अभिषिक्त *a* consecrated, crowned, inaugurated R. 16. 81. (-क्तः) 1 a consecrated king. 2 a man of the Kshatriya caste. 3 a minister. 4 =मूर्धावसिक्त (1) q. v. -अभिषेकः consecration, inauguration. -अवसिक्तः 1 N. of a particular mixed tribe sprung from a Brâhmaṇa father and a Kshatriya mother. 2 a consecrated king. -कर्णी, -कर्परी *f.* an umbrella. -जः 1 the hair (of the head); पर्याकुला मूर्धजाः *S.* 1. 30; विललाप विकीर्णमूर्धजा Ku. 4. 4 'she tore her hair for grief'. 2 The mane. -ज्योतिस् *n.* see ब्रह्मरंध्र or मुद्रामार्ग. -पुष्पः the Sirîsha tree. -रसः the scum of boiled rice. -वेष्टनं a turban, diadem.

मूर्धन्य *a.* 1 Being in or on the head. 2 Cerebral or lingual, a term applied to the letters ऋ, ॠ, ट्, ठ्, ड्, ढ्, ण्, र्, and ष्; ऋटुरषाणां मूर्धा. 3 Chief, pre-eminent, most excellent.

मूर्द्धन् See मूर्धन्.

मूर्वा -र्वी, **मूर्विका** A kind of creeper from the fibres of which bow-strings and the girdle of Kshatriyas are made.

मूल् I 1 U. (मूलति-ते) To take or strike root, be firm, stand fast. -II. 10 U. (मूलयति-ते,मूलित) To plant, cause to grow, rear. -WITH उद् to root out, extirpate, eradicate; Ki. 1. 41 ;

to destroy, annihilate. -निस् to root out, eradicate.

मूलं 1 A root (fig. also); तरुमूलानि गृहीभवंति तेषां S. 7. 20; or शाखिनो धौतमूलाः 1. 20; मूलं बंध् to take or strike root ; बद्धमूलस्य मूलं हि महद्वैरतरोः स्त्रियः Si. 2. 38. 2 The root, lowest edge or extremity of anything; कस्याश्चिदासीद्रशना तदानीमंगुष्ठमूलार्पितसूत्रशेषा R. 7. 10; so प्राचीमूले Me. 89. 3 The lower part or end, base, the end of anything by which it is joined to something else; बाहोर्मूलं Si. 7. 32; so पादमूलं, कर्णमूलं, ऊरूमूलं &c. 4 Beginning, commencement; आमूलाच्छ्रोतुमिच्छामि S. 1. 5 Basis, foundation, source, origin, cause ; सर्वं गार्हस्थ्यमूलकाः Mb. ; रक्षोगृहे स्थितिर्मूलं U. 1. 6 ; इति केनाप्युक्तं तत्र मूलं मृग्यं 'the source or authority should be found out.' 6 The foot or bottom of anything; पर्वतमूलं, गिरिमूलं &c. 7 The text, or original passage (as distinguished from the commentary or gloss). 8 Vicinity, neighbourhood. 9 Capital, principal stock. 10 A hereditary servant. 11 A square root. 12 A king's own territory; स गुप्तमूलप्रत्यंतः R. 4. 26; Ms. 7. 184. 13 A vendor who is not the true owner; Ms. 7. 202 (अस्वामिविक्रेता Kull.). 14 The nineteenth lunar mansion containing 11 Stars. 15 A thicket, copse. 16 The root of long pepper. 17 A particular position of the fingers. -Comp. आधारं 1 the navel. 2 a mystical circle above the organs of generation. -आभं a radish. -आयतनं original abode. -आशिन् a. living upon roots. -आह्वं a radish. -उच्छेदः utter destruction, total eradication. -कर्मन् n. magic. -कारणं the original or prime cause; Ku. 6. 13. -कारिका a furnace, an oven. -कच्छ्रः -कच्छ्रं a kind of penance, living only upon roots. -केशरः a citron. -गुणः the coefficient of a root. -जः a plant growing from a root. (-जं) green ginger. -देवः an epithet of Kamsa. -द्रव्यं, -धनं principal, stock, capital. -धातुः lymph. -निकृंतन a. destroying root and branch. -पुरुषः 'the stockman ', the male representative of a family. -प्रकृतिः f. the Prakrîti or Pradhâna of the Sânkhyas (q. v.). -फलदः the bread-fruit tree. -भद्रः an epithet of Kamsa. -भृत्यः an old or hereditary servant. -वचनं an original text. -वित्तं capital, stock. विभुजः a chariot. -शाकटः,-शाकिनं a field planted with edible roots. -स्थानं 1 base, foundation. 2 the Supreme Spirit. 3 wind, air. -स्रोतस् n. the principal current or fountain-head of a river.

मूलकः-कं 1 A radish. 2 An esculent root. -कः A kind of poison. -Comp. -पोतिका a radish.

मूला 1 N. of plant. 2 he asterism Mûla.

मूलिक a. Radical, original. -कः A devotee, an ascetic.

मूलिन् m. A tree.

मूलन a. Growing from a root.

मूली A small house-lizard.

मूलेरः 1 A king. 2 The Indian spikenard.

मूल्य a. 1 To be eradicated. 2 Purchasable. -ल्यं 1 Price, worth, cost; क्रीणंति स्म प्राणमूल्ययशांसि Si. 18. 15, Sânti. 1. 12. 2 Wages, hire, salary. 3 Gain. 4 Capital, principal.

मूष् 1 P. (मूषति, मूषित) To steal, rob, plunder.

मूषः 1 A rat, mouse. 2 A round window, an air-hole.

मूषकः 1 A rat, mouse. 2 A thief. -Comp. -अरातिः a cat. -वाहनः an epithet of Ganesa.

मूषणं Stealing, pilfering.

मूषा, मूषिका 1 A female rat. 2 A crucible.

मूषिकः 1 A rat. 2 A thief. 3 The Sirîsha tree. 4 N. of a country. -Comp. -अंकः, -अंचनः -रथः epithets of Ganesa. -अदः a cat. -अरातिः a cat. -उत्करः, -स्थलं a molehill.

मूषिकारः A male rat.

मूषी, मूषीकः मूषीका A rat, mouse.

मृ 6 A. (but P. in the Perfect, the two Futures and the Conditional) (म्रियते, मृत) To die, perish, decease, depart from life. -*Caus.* (मारयति-ते) To Kill, slay. -*Desid.* (मुमूर्षति) 1 To wish to die. 2 To be about to die, be on the point of death. -With अनु to die after, follow in death; R.8.85.

मृक्ष् See म्रक्ष्.

मृग् 4 P., 10 A. (मृग्यति, मृगयते, मृगित) 1 To seek, search for, seek after ; न रत्नमन्विष्यति मृग्यते हि तत् Ku. 5. 45; गता दुता दूर क्वचिदपि परेतान् मृगयितुं G. L. 25. 2 To hunt, chase, pursue. 3 To aim at, strive for. 4 To examine, investigate ; अविचलितमनोभिः साधकैर्मृग्यमाणः Mâl. 5. 1; अंतर्यश्च मुमुक्षुभिर्नियमितप्राणादिभिर्मृग्यते V. 1. 1 'inwardly sought or investigated'. 5 To ask for, beg of one; एतावदेव मृगये प्रतिपक्षहेतोः M. 5. 20.

मृगः 1 A quadruped, an animal in general; नाभिषेको न संस्कारो सिंहस्य क्रियते मृगैः। विक्रमार्जितराज्यस्य स्वयमेव मृगेंद्रता; see मृगाधिप below. 2 A deer, an antelope; विश्वासोपगमादभिन्नगतयः शब्दं सहंते मृगाः S. 1. 14; R. 1. 40, 50; आश्रममृगोयं न हंतव्यः S. 1. 3 Game in general. 4 The spots on the moon represented as an antelope. 5 Musk. 6 Seeking, search. 7 Pursuit, chase, hunting. 8 Inquiry, investigation. 9 Asking, soliciting. 10 A kind of elephant. 11 N. of a particular class of men; मृगे तुष्टा च चित्रिणी; वदति मधुरवाणीं दीर्घनेत्रोऽतिभीरुश्चपलमतिसुदेहः शीघ्रवेगो मृगोऽयम् Sabdak. 12 The lunar mansion called मृगशिरस्. 13 The lunar month called मार्गशीर्ष. 14 The sign *Capricornus* of the zodiac. -Comp. -अक्षी a fawn-eyed or deer-eyed woman. -अंकः 1 the moon. 2 camphor. 3 the wind. -अंगना a doe. -अजिनं a deer's skin. -अंडजा musk. -अद्,-अदनः,-अंतकः a small tiger or hunting leopard, hyena. -अधिपः,-अधिराजः a lion; केसरी निष्ठुरक्षितमृगयूथो मृगाधिपः Si.2.53; मृगाधिराजस्य वचो निशम्य R. 2. 41. -अरातिः 1 a lion. 2 a dog. -अरिः 1 a lion. 2 a dog. 3 a tiger. 4 N. of a tree. -अशनः a lion. -आविध् m. a hunter. -आस्यः the sign *Capricornus* of the zodiac. -इंद्रः 1 a lion; ततो मृगेंद्रस्य मृगेंद्रगामी R. 2. 30. 2 a tiger. 3 the sign *Leo* of the zodiac. °आसनं a throne. °आस्यः an epithet of Siva. °चटकः a hawk. -इष्टः a variety of jasmine. -ईक्षणा a fawn-eyed woman. -ईश्वरः 1 a lion. 2 the sign *Leo* of the zodiac. -उत्तमं -उत्तमांगं the constellation मृगशिरस्. -काननं a park. -गामिनी a kind of medicinal substance. -जलं mirage. °स्नानं bathing in the waters of the marage; *i.e.* an impossibility. -जीवनः a hunter, fowler. -तृष्,-तृषा,-तृष्णा,-तृष्णिका f. mirage ; मृगतृष्णांभसि स्नातः; see खपुष्प. -दंशः, दंशकः a dog -दृश् f. a fawn-eyed woman; तदीषद्विस्तारि स्तनयुगलमासीन्मृगदृशः U. 6. 35. -द्युः a hunter. -द्विष् m. a lion. -धरः the moon. -धूर्तः,-धूर्तकः a jackal. -नयना a fawn-eyed woman. -नाभिः 1 musk; Ku. 1. 54; Rs. 6. 12; Ch. P. 8; R. 17. 24. 2 the musk-deer; R. 4. 74. °जा musk. -पतिः 1 a lion. 2 a roe-buck. 3 a tiger. -पालिका the musk-deer. पिप्लुः the moon. -प्रभुः the lion. -ब(व)धाजीवः a hunter. -बंधिनी a net for catching deer. -मदः musk; कुचतटीगतो यावन्मातर्मिलति तव तोयैर्मृगमदः G. L. 7; मृगमदतिलकं लिखति सपुलकं मृगमिव रजनीकरे Gît. 7. °वासा a musk-bag. -मंद्रः N. of a class of elephants. -मातृका a doe. -मुखः the sign *Capricornus* of the zodiac. -यूथं a herd of deer. -राज् m. 1 a lion; Si. 9. 18. 2 a tiger. 3 the sign *Leo* of the zodiac. -राजः 1 as lion; R. 6. 3. 2 the sign *Leo* of the zodiac. 3 a tiger. 4 the moon. °धारिन्, °लक्ष्मन् m. the moon. -रिपुः a lion. -रोमं wool. °जं woollen cloth. -लांछनः the moon; अंकाधिरोपितमृगश्चंद्रमा मृगलांछनः Si. 2. 53. °जः the planet Mercury. -लेखा the deer like streak on the moon; मृगलेखामुषसीव चंद्रमाः R. 8. 42. -लोचनः the moon. (-ना,-नी) a fawn-eyed woman. -वाहनः Wind. -व्याधः 1 a hunter. 2 Sirius or the dog-star. 3 an epithet of Siva. -शावः a fawn; मृगशावैः सममेधितो जनः S. 2. 18. -शिरः, शिरस् n., -शिरा N. of the fifth lunar mansion consisting of three stars. -शीर्षं the constellation मृगशिरस् (-र्षः) the lunar month Mârgasîrsha.

-शीर्षन् *m.* the constellation मृगशिरस्. -श्रेष्ठः a tiger. -हन् *m.* a hunter.

मृगणा Searching, looking out for, inquiry, research.

मृगया Hunting, chase, मिथ्यैव व्यसनं वदंति मृगयामीदृग्विनोदः कुतः *S.* 2. 5 ; मृगवापधादिना माटव्येन *S.*2; मृगयावेष, मृगयाविहारिन् &c.

मृगयुः 1 A hunter, fowler ; हंति नोपशयस्थोऽपि शयालुर्मृगयुर्मृगान् *Si.* 2. 80. 2 A jackal. 3 An epithet of Brahman.

मृगव्यं 1 The chase, hunting ; Ki. 13. 9. 2 A target.

मृगी 1 A female deer, doe. 2 Epilepsy. 3 N. of a particular class of women. -**Comp.**-दृश् *f.* a woman with eyes like those of a doe or fawn. -पतिः an epithet of Krishṇa.

मृग्य *a.* To be sought or inquired. after to be hunted; तत्र मुलं तृग्यम्.

मृज् I. 1 P. (मार्जति) To sound. -II. 2 P. 10 U. (मार्ष्टि, (मार्जयति-ते; *desid.* मिमृक्षति or मिमार्जिषति) 1 To wipe, or wash off, cleanse, clean, sweep clean (fig. also); स्वेदलवान्ममार्ज *Si.* 3. 79; दोषप्रवादममृजन् 5. 28. 2 To rub, stroke. 3 To make smooth, curry (as a horse). 4 To deck, adorn. 5 To purify, wash with water, sharpen; लद्ः खड्गान् ममार्जुश्च ममृजुश्च परश्वधान् Bk. 14. 92 (शुद्धान् चक्रुः or शोधितवंतः)— WITH अव 1 to rub, stroke. 2 to wash off. -उद् to wipe off, remove ; R. 15. 32. -निस् to wipe off, wash out. -परि 1 to wipe off or away, wash out, remove ; (वाच्यं) त्यागेन पत्न्याः परिमार्ष्टुमैच्छत् R. 14. 35. 2 to rub, stroke. -प्र to wipe off or out, remove, atone for ; स्वभावलोलेत्ययशः प्रमृष्टं R. 6. 31 ; प्राणिपातलंघनं प्रमार्ष्टुकामा V. 3 ; M. 4.-वि 1 to wipe off or away, wipe out. 2 to purify, cleanse. -सं 1 to sweep clean, purify. 2 to wipe off or out, wipe away, remove. 3 to rub, stroke. 4 to strain, filter.

मृजः A kind of drum.

मृजा 1 Cleansing, purifying, washing, ablution. 2 Cleanliness, purity ; Bk. 2. 13 (शुद्धि). 3 Complexion, pure skin or clear complexion.

मृजित *a.* Wiped off or away, cleansed, removed.

मृडः An epithet of *Siva.*

मृडा, मृडानी, मृडी An epithet of Pârvatî; शंके सुं रेकालकूटमपिबन् मूढो मृडानापतिः Gît. 12.

मृण् 6 P. (मृणति) To kill, slay, destroy.

मृणालः-लं The fibrous root of a lotus, a lotus-fibre ; भंगेपि हि मृणालानामनुबध्नंति तंतवः H. 1. 95; सूत्रं मृणालादिव राजहंसी V. 1. 19; Rs. 1. 19; V. 3. 13. -लं The root of a fragrant grass (वरिणमूल). -**Comp.**-भंगः a bit of lotus-fibre. -सूत्रं the fibre of a lotus-stalk.

मृणालिका, मृणाली A lotus stalk or fibre ; परिम्रादितमृणालीम्लानमंगं Mâl. 1. 22; or परिमृदितमृणालीदुर्बलान्यंगकानि U. 1. 24.

मृणालिन् *m.* A lotus.

मृणालिनी 1 A lotus-plant. 2 An assemblage of lotuses. 3 A place abounding with lotuses.

मृत *p. p.* 1 ead, deceased. 2 As good as dead, useless, inefficacious ; मृतो दरिद्रः पुरुषो मृतं मैथुनमप्रजं । मृतमश्रोत्रियं श्राद्धं मृतो यज्ञस्त्वदक्षिणः ॥ Pt. 2. 94. 3 Calcined, reduced ; मूर्च्छा गतो मृतो वा निदर्शनं पारदोऽत्र रसः Bv. 1. 82. -तं 1 Death. 2 Food obtained by begging, alms; see अमृतं (8). -**Comp.** -अंगं a corpse. -अंडः the sun. -अशौचं impurity contracted through the death of a relation; see अशौच. -उद्भवः the sea, ocean. -कल्प *a.* almost dead, insensible. -गृहं a grave. -दारः a widower. -निर्यातकः one who carries out dead bodies to the cemetery. -मत्तः, -मत्तकः a jackal. -संस्कारः funeral or obsequial rites. -संजीवन *a.* reviving the dead. (-नं,-नी) the revival of a dead person. (-नी) a charm for reviving the dead. -सूतक bringing forth a stil-lborn child. -स्नानं ablution after a death. or funeral.

मृतकः-कं A dead person, a corpse; ध्रुवं ते जीवंतोप्यहह मृतका मंदमतयो न येषामानंदं जनयति जगन्नाथ मीणि'तः Bv. 4. 39. -कं Impurity contracted through the death of a relation. -**Comp.** -अंतकः a jackal.

मृतंडः The sun.

मृतालकं A kind of clay.

मृतिः *f.* Death, dying.

मृत्तिका 1 Clay, earth; Ms. 2. 182. 2 Fresh earth. 3 A kind of fragrant earth.

मृत्युः 1 Death, decease; जातस्य हि ध्रुवो मृत्युर्ध्रुवं जन्म मृतस्य च Bg. 2. 27. 2 Yama, the god of death. 3 An epithet of Brahmâ. 4 Of Vishṇu. 5 Of Mâyâ. 6 Of Kali. 7 The god of love. -**Comp.** -तूर्यं a kind of drum beaten at obsequial rites. -नाशकः quicksilver. -पः an epithet of *Siva.* -पाशः the noose of death or Yama. -पुष्पः the sugar-cane. -प्रतिबद्ध *a.* liable to death. -फला-ली the plantain. -बीजः, -वीजः a bamboo-cane. -राज् *m.* Yama, the god of death. -लोकः 1 the world of the dead, the world of Death or Yama. 2 earth, the world of mortals; cf. मर्त्यलोक. -वंचनः 1 an epithet of *Siva.* 2 a raven. -सूतिः *f.* a female crab.

मृत्युंजयः An epithet of *Siva.*

मृत्सा, मृत्स्ना 1 Earth, clay. 2 Good earth or clay. 3 A kind of fragrant earth.

मृद् 9 P. (मृद्नाति, मृदित) 1 To squeeze, press, rub; मम च : मृदितं क्षौमं बाल्ये त्वदंगविवर्तनैः Ve. 5. 40. 2 To trample or tread upon ; crush to pieces, kill, destroy, pound, bruise, ulverize, तावमर्दीदिखादीच्च Bk. 15 15 ; बलान्यमृद्नान्नलनाभवक्त्रः R. 18. 5. 3. To rub, stroke, rub against, touch; *Si.* 4. 61. 4 To overcome, surpass. 5 To wipe away, rub off, remove. -WITH अभि to squeeze, crush, trample upon. -अव to tread or trample upon. -उप 1 to squeeze, press. 2 to destroy, kill, crush; यामिकाननुपमृद्य N. 5. 110. -परि 1 to press, squeeze ; परिमृदितमृणालीदुर्बलान्यंगकानि U. 1. 24. 2 to kill, destroy. 3 to wipe away, rub off -प्र to crush, bruise, pound, kill. -वि 1 to press, squeeze. 2 to bruise, crush, pound; Ms. 4. 70. 3 to kill, destroy. -सं to squeeze together, bruise, pound, kill.

मृद् *f.* 1 Clay, earth, loam; आमोदं कुसुमभवं मदेव धत्ते मृद्गंधं न हि कुसुमानि धारयंति । Subhâsh.; प्रभवति शुचिर्बिंबोद्ग्राहे मणिर्न मृदां चयः U. 2. 4. 2 A piece of earth, lump of clay. 3 A mound of earth. 4 A kind of fragrant earth. -**Comp.** -कणः a small clod or lump of earth. -करः a potter. -कांस्यं an earthen vessel. -गः a kind of fish. -चयः (मृच्चयः) a heap of earth. -पचः a potter. -पात्रं,-भांडं earthenware, a vessel of clay. -पिंडः a clod of earth, a lump of clay. °बुद्धिः 'clod-poted', a blockhead; मया च मत्पिंडबुद्धिना तथैव गृहीतं *S.* 6. -लोष्टः a clod of earth. -शकटिका (मृच्छकटिका) a small car of earth, a toy-cart; (it is the name of a celebrated play by *Sûdraka*).

मृदंगः 1 A kind of drum or tabor. 2 A bamboo-cane. -**Comp.** -फलः the bread-fruit tree.

मृदर *a.* 1 Sporting, sportive. 2 Transient, evanescent.

मृदा See मृद् *f.*

मृदित *p. p.* 1 Pressed, squeezed; सुरतमृदिता बालवनिता Bh. 2. 44. 2 Crushed, pounded, ground down, trampled upon, killed. 3 Rubbed off, removed. (see मृद्.)

मृदिनी Good or soft earth.

मृदु *a.* (दु or द्वी *f.*; compar. म्रदीयस्; superl. म्रदिष्ठ) 1 Soft, tender, subtle, pliant, delicate: मृदु तीक्ष्णतरं यदुच्यते तदिदं मन्मथ दृश्यते त्वयि M. 3. 2; अथवा मृदु वस्तु हिंसितुं मृदुनैवारभते प्रजांतकः R. 8. 45, 57; *S.* 1. 10; 4. 10. 2 Soft, mild, gentle; न खरो न च भूयसा मृदुः R. 8. 9; बाणं कृपामृदुमानाः प्रतिसंजहार 9. 47 'with his mind softened with pity'; 11. 83; *S.* 6. 1; महर्षिर्मृदुतामगच्छत् R. 5. 54 'relented'; खातमूलमनिलो नदीरयैः पातयत्यपि मृदुस्तटद्रुमं 11. 76 'even a soft or gentle breeze' &c. 3 Weak, feeble; सर्वथा मृदुरसौ राजा H. 3; ततस्ते मृदवोऽभूवन गंधर्वाः शरपीडिताः Mb. 4 Moderate. -दुः The planet Saturn. -दु *ind.* Softly, gently, in a sweet manner ; स्वनसि मृदु कर्णांतिकचरः *S.* 1. 23; वादयते मृदु वेणुं Gît. 5. -**Comp.** -अंग *a.* of delicate limbs. (-गं) tin. (-गी) a delicate woman.

-उत्पलं the soft *i. e.* blue lotus. -कार्ष्णायसं lead. -कोष्ठ *a.* having bowels which are relaxed or easily affected by medicines. -गमन *a.* having a gentle or lounging gait. (-ना) a goose, female swan. -चर्मिन्, -छदः, -त्वच्, -त्वच *m.* a kind of birch tree. -पत्रः a rush or reed. -पर्वकः, -पर्वन् *n.* a reed, cane. -पुष्पः the *Siri 'sha* tree. -पूर्व *a.* gentle at first, bland, coaxing. -भाषिन् *a.* sweet speaking. -रोमन् *m.*, -रोमकः a hare. -स्पर्श *a.* soft to the touch.

मृदुत्वकं Gold.

मृदुल *a.* **1** Soft, tender, delicate. **2** Mild, gentle. -लं **1** Water. **2** A variety of aloewood.

मृद्वी, मृद्वीका A vine or bunch of grapes; वाचं तदीयां परिपीय मृद्वीं मृद्वीकया तुल्यरसां स हंसः N. 3. 60; Bv. 4. 13, 37.

मृध् 1 U. (मर्धति-ते) To be moist or to moisten.

मृधं War, battle, fight; सत्त्वविहितमतुलं भुजयोर्बलमस्य पश्यत मृधेऽधिकुप्यतः Ki. 12. 39; R. 13. 65; Mv. 5. 13.

मृन्मय *a.* Earthen; R. 5. 2.

मृश् 6 P. (मृशति, मृष्ट) **1** To touch, handle. **2** To rub, stroke. **3** To consider, reflect, deliberate. -WITH **अभि** to touch, handle. -**आ** **1** to touch, handle, lay hands on (fig. also); नवातपामृष्टसरोजचारुभिः Ki. 4. 14; शरासनज्यां मुहुराममर्श Ku. 3. 64; *Si.* 9. 34. **2** to seize upon, eat up; R. 5. 9. **3** to attack, assail; आमृष्टं नः पदं परैः Ku. 2. 31. -**परा** **1** to touch, rub or stroke gently; परामृशन् हर्षजडेन पाणिना तदीयमंगं कुलिशव्रणांकितं R. 3. 68; *Si.* 17. 11; Mk. 5. 28. **2** to lay hands on, attack, assail, seize.; Mk. 1. 39. **3** to defile, pollute. outrage. **4** to reflect-think, consider; किं भवितेति सशंकं पंकजनयना परामृशति Bv. 2. 53. **5** to think of mentally, praise (स्तु); ग्रंथारंभे विघ्नविघाताय समुचितेष्टदेवता ग्रंथकृत्परामृशति K. P. 1. -**परि** 1 to touch, graze; शिखरशतैः परिमृष्टदेवलोकं Bk. 10. 45. **2** to find. -**वि** **1** to touch. **2** to think, consider, reflect, ponder (over); वृणते हि विमृश्यकारिणं गुणलुब्धाः स्वयमेव संपदः Ki. 2. 30; रामप्रवासे व्यमृशन्न दोषं जनापवादं सनरेंद्रमृत्युं Bk. 3. 7, 12. 24; Ku. 6. 87; Bg. 18. 63. **3** to perceive, observe. **4** to examine, test; तदत्रभवानिमं मां च शास्त्रे प्रयोगे च विमृशतु M. 1.

मृष् I. 1 P. (मर्षति) To sprinkle. -II. 1 U. (मर्षति-ते) To bear, endure &c. (usually 4 U.) -III. 4. 10. U. (मृष्यति-ते, मर्षयति-ते, मर्षित) **1** To suffer, bear, endure, put up with; तत्किमिदमकार्यमनुष्ठितं देवेन-लोको न मृष्यतीति U. 3; *Si.* 9. 62. **2** To allow, permit. **3** To pardon, forgive, excuse; forbear; मृष्यंतु लवस्य बालिशतां तातपादाः U. 6; प्रथममिति प्रेक्ष्य दुहितृजनस्यैकोऽपराधो भगवता मर्षयितव्यः *S.* 4; आर्य मर्षय मर्षय Ve. 1; महाब्राह्मण मर्षय Mk. 1.

मृषा **1** Falsely, wrongly, untruly, lyingly; यद्वक्त्रं मुहुरीक्षसे न धनिनां ब्रूषे न चाटुं मृषा Bh. 3. 147; मृषाभाषासिंधो Bv. 2. 21. **2** In vain, to no purpose, uselessly. -Comp. -अध्यायिन् *m.* a kind of crane. -अर्थक *a.* **1** untrue. **2** absurd. (-कं) an absurdity, an impossibility. -उद्यं falsehood, lying, a false statement; तत्किं मन्यसे राजपुत्रि मृषोद्यं तदिति U. 4. -ज्ञानं ignorance, error. -भाषिन्, -वादिन् *m.* a liar. -वाच् *f.* an untrue or satirical speech, satire, irony. -वादः **1** an untrue speech; a lie, falsehood. **2** insincere speech, flattery. **3** irony, satire.

मृषालकः The mango tree.

मृष्ट *p. p.* **1** Cleansed, purified. **2** Besmeared. **3** Dressed, cooked. **4** Touched. **5** Considered, deliberated. **6** Savoury, agreeable. -Comp. -गंधः a savoury or agreeable smell.

मृष्टिः *f.* **1** Cleansing, cleaning, purifying. **2** Cooking, dressing, preparation. **3** Touch, contact.

मे 1 A. (मयते, मित; *desid.* मित्सते) To exchange or barter. -WITH **नि** or **विनि** to exchange or barter.

मेकः A goat.

मेकलः **1** N. of a mountain; (also मेखल). **2** A goat. -Comp. -अद्रिजा, -कन्यका, -कन्या epithets of the river Narmadâ.

मेखला **1** A belt, girdle, waistband, zone in general (fig. also); anything which girds or surrounds; महीसागरमेखला 'the sea-girt earth'; रत्नानुविद्धार्णवमेखलाया दिशः सपत्नी भव दक्षिणस्याः R. 6. 63; Rs. 6. 2. **2** Particularly, the girdle or zone of a woman; नितंबबिंबैः सदुकूलमेखलैः Rs. 1 4, 6; R. 8. 64; मेखलागुणैरुत गोत्रस्खलितेषु बंधनं Ku. 4. 8. **3** The triple girdle worn by the first three castes; cf. Ms. 2. 42. **4** The slope of a mountain (नितंब); आमेखलं संचरतां घनानां Ku. 1. 5; Me. 12. **5** The hips. **6** A sword-belt. **7** A sword-knot or string fastened to the hilt. **8** The girth of a horse. **9** N. of the river Narmadâ. -Comp. -पदं the hips. -बंधः investiture with the girdle.

मेखलालः An epithet of *Siva.*

मेखलिन् *m.* **1** An epithet of *Siva.* **2** A religious student, a Brahmachârin, q. v.

मेघः **1** A cloud; कुर्वन्नंजनमेचका इव दिशो मेघः समुत्तिष्ठते Mk. 5. 23, 2, 3 &c. **2** A mass, multitude. **3** A fragrant grass. -घं Talc. -Comp. -अध्वन् *m.*, -पथः, -मार्गः 'the path of clouds', atmosphere. -अंतः the autumn. -अरिः the wind. -अस्थि *n.* hail. -आख्यं talc. -आगमः the approach of rains, the rainy season. -आटोपः a dense or thick cloud. -आडंबरः thunder. -आनंदा a kind of crane. -आनंदिन् *m.* a peacock. -आलोकः the appearance or sight of clouds: मेघालोके भवति सुखिनोऽप्यन्यथावृत्ति चेतः Me. 3. -आस्पदं the sky, atmosphere. -उदकं rain. -उदयः the rising of clouds. -कफः hail. -कालः the rains, rainy season. -गर्जनं, गर्जना thunder. -चिंतकः the Châtaka bird. -जः a large pearl. -जालं **1** a dense mass of clouds. **2** talc. -जीवकः, -जीवनः the Châtaka bird. -ज्योतिस् *m. n.* lightning. -डंबरः thunder. -दीपः lightning. -द्वारं the sky, atmosphere. -नादः **1** the roar of clouds, thunder. **2** an epithet of Varuṇa. **3** of Indrajit, son of Râvaṇa. °अनुलासिन्, °अनुलासकः a peacock. °जित् *m.* an epithet of Lakshmaṇa. -निर्घोषः thunder. -पंक्तिः, -माला a line of clouds. -पुष्पं **1** water. **2** hail. **3** river-water. -प्रसवः water. -भूति a thunderbolt. -मंडलं the firmament, sky. -माल, -मालिन् *a.* cloud-capt. -योनिः fog, smoke. -रवः thunder. -वर्णा the Indigo plant. -वर्त्मन् *n.* the atmosphere. -वह्निः lightning. -वाहनः **1** an epithet of Indra; श्रयति स्म मेघमिव मेघवाहनः *Si.* 13. 18. **2** an epithet of *Siva.* -विस्फूर्जितं **1** thunder, rumbling of clouds. **2** N. of a metre; see App. I. -वेश्मन् *n.* the atmosphere. -सारः a kind of camphor. -सुहृद् *m.* a peacock. -स्तनितं thunder.

मेघंकर *a.* Producing clouds.

मेचक *a.* Black, dark-blue, dark-coloured; कुर्वन्नंजनमेचका इव दिशो मेघः समुत्तिष्ठते Mk. 5. 23; U. 6. 25; Me. 59. -कः **1** Blackness, the dark blue colour. **2** An eye of a peacock's tail. **3** A cloud. **4** Smoke. **5** A nipple. **6** A kind of gem. -कं Darkness. -Comp. -आपगा an epithet of the Yamunâ.

मेद्, मेड् 1 P. (मेटति, मेडति) To be mad.

मेडुला The myrobalan tree (आमलकी).

मेठः **1** A ram. **2** An elephant driver or keeper.

मेठिः, मेथिः **1** A pillar, post. **2** A pillar in the midst of a threshing-floor to which oxen are bound. **3** A prst to which cattle are bound. **4** A prop for supporting the shafts of a carriage.

मेढ्रः A ram. -ढ्रं The male organ of generation, penis; (यस्य) मेढ्रं चोन्मादशुक्राभ्यां हीनं क्लीबः स उच्यते. -Comp. -चर्मन् *n.* the prepuce. -जः an epithet of *Siva.* -रोगः a venereal disease.

मेढ्रकः **1** A arm. **2** The penis.

मेंठः, मेंडः An elehant-keeper.

मेंढः, मेंढकः A ram.

मेंढ्रः See मेढ्र.

मेथ् 1 U. (मेथति-ते) **1** To meet. **2** To meet one another (Atm.). **3** To revile. **4** To know, understand. **5** To hurt, injure, kill.

मेथिका, मेथिनी A kind of grass.

मेदः 1 Fat. 2 A particular mixed tribe. 3 N. of a serpent-demon. -Comp. -जं a species of bdellium. -भिल्लः N. of a degraded tribe.

मेदकः Liquor used for distillation.

मेदस् *n.* 1 Fat, marrow (one of the seven *dhâtus* of the body and supposed to lie in the abdomen); Ms. 3. 182; Y. 1. 44. 2 Corpulence, fat of the body; मेदश्छेदकृशोदरं लघु भवत्युत्थानयोग्यं वपुः *S*. 2. 5. -Comp. -अर्बुदं a fatty tumour. -कृत् *m. n.* flesh. -ग्रंथिः a fatty tumour -जं, -तेजस् *n.* a bone. -पिंडः a lump of fat. -वृद्धिः *f.* 1 increase of fat, corpulence. 2 enlargement of the scrotum.

मेदस्विन् *a.* 1 Fat, corpulent. 2 Strong, robust; *S*i. 5. 64.

मेदिनी 1 The earth; न मामवति सद्वीपा रत्नसूरपि मेदिनी R. 1. 65; चंचलं वसु नितांतमुन्नता मेदिनीमपि हरंत्यरातयः Ki. 13. 53. 2 Ground, land, soil. 3 Spot, place. 4 N. of a lexicon (मेदिनीकोश). -Comp. -ईशः, -पतिः a king. -द्रवः dust.

मेदुर *a.* 1 Fat. 2 Smooth, unctuous, soft. 3 Thick, dense; Mâl. 8. 11; thick with, full of, covered with, (usually with instr. or at the end of comp.); मेघैर्मेदुरमंबरं Gît. 1; मकरंदसुंदरगलन्मंदाकिनीमेदुरं (पदारविंदं) 7.

मेदुरित *a.* Thickened, made dense; U. 1.

मेद्य *a.* 1 Fat. 2 Dense, thick.

मेध् 1 U. *S*ee मेथ्.

मेधः 1 A sacrifice, as in नरमेध, अश्वमेध. 2 A sacrificial animal or victim. -Comp. -जः an epithet of Vishṇu.

मेधा (changed to मेधस् in Bah. comp. when preceded by सु, दुस् and the negative particle अ) 1 Retentive faculty, retentiveness (of memory); धीर्धारणावती मेधा Ak. 2 Intellect; intelligence in general; Bg 10. 34; Ms. 3. 263; Y. 3. 174. 3 A form of Sarasvatî. 4 A sacrifice. -Comp. -अतिथिः N. of a learned commentator on Manusmṛiti. -रुद्रः an epithet of Kâlidâsa.

मेधावत् *a.* Wise, intelligent.

मेधाविन् *a.* 1 Very intelligent, having a good memory. 2 Intelligent, wise, endowed with intellect. -*m*. 1 A learned man, sage, scholar. 2 A parrot. 3 An intoxicating drink.

मेधि See मेथि.

मेध्य *a.* 1 Fit for a sacrifice; Y. 1. 194; Ms. 5. 54. 2 Relating to a sacrifice, sacrificial; मेध्येनाश्वेनेजे; R. 13. 3. 3 Pure, sacred, holy; R. 1. 84, 3. 31, 14. 81. -ध्यः 1 A goat. 2 A Khadira tree. 3 Barley (according to Medinî). -ध्या N. of several plants.

मेनका 1 N. of an *Apsaras* (mother of *S*akuntalâ). 2 N. of the wife of Himâlaya. -Comp. -आत्मजा N. of Pârvatî.

मेना 1 N. of the wife of Himâlaya; मेनां मुनीनामपि माननीयां (उपयेमे) Ku. 1. 18, 5. 5. 2 N. of a river.

मेनादः 1 A peacock. 2 A cat. 3 A goat.

मेंधिका, मेंधी N. of a plant (Mar. मेंदी, from the leaves of which reddish dye is extracted, wherewith to colour the tips and nails of fingers, the soles of the feet and the palms of the hand).

मेप् 1 A. (मेपते) To go, move.

मेय *a.* 1 Measurable, to be measured. 2 Capable of being estimated. 3 Discernible, capable of being known (ज्ञेय).

मेरुः 1 N. of a fabulous mountain (round which all the planets are said to revolve; it is also said to consist of gold and gems); विभज्य मेरुर्न यदर्थिसात् कृतः N. 1. 16; स्वात्मन्येव समाप्तहेममहिमा मेरुर्न मे रोचते Bh. 3. 151. 2 The central bead in a rosary. 3 The central gem of a necklace. -Comp. -धामन् *m.* an epithet of *S*iva. -यंत्रं a figure shaped like a spindle.

मेरुकः Incense.

मेलः Meeting, union, intercourse, a company, an assembly. (Also मेलक.)

मेलनं 1 Union, junction, 2 Association. 3 Mixture.

मेला 1 Union, intercourse. 2 A company, an assembly, a society. 3 Antimony. 4 The indigo plant. 5 Ink. 6 A musical scale. -Comp. -अंधुकः, -अंबुः, -नंदः, -नंदा, -मंदा an inkstand, ink-bottle.

मेव् 1 A. (मेवते) To worship, serve, attend upon.

मेषः 1 A ram, sheep. 2 The sign *Aries* of the zodiac. -Comp. -अंडः an epithet of Indra. -कंबलः a woollen blanket or rug. -पालः, -पालकः a shepherd. -मांसं mutton. -यूथं a flock of sheep.

मेषा Small cardamoms.

मेषिका, मेषी A ewe.

मेहः 1 Making water, passing urine. 2 Urine. 3 A urinary disease. 4 A ram. 5 Goat. -Comp. -घ्नी turmeric.

मेहनं 1 Passing urine. 2 Urine. 3 The penis.

मैत्र *a.* (त्री *f.*) 1 Belonging to a friend. 2 Given by a friend. 3 Friendly, well-disposed, amicable, kind; Ms. 2. 87; Bg. 12. 13. 4 Relating to the god Mitra (as a Muhûrta); Ku. 7. 6. -त्रः 1 A high or perfect Brâhmaṇa. 2 N. of a particular mixed tribe; Ms. 10. 23. 3 The anus. -त्री 1 Friendship, good will. 2 Intimate connection or association, union, contact; प्रत्यूषेषु स्फुटितकमलामोदमैत्रीकषायः Me. 31. 3 The lunar mansion called अनुराधा. -त्रं 1 Friendship. 2 Voiding or evacuation of excrement; Ms. 4. 152. 3 The lunar mansion अनुराधा (मैत्रभं in the same sense.)

मैत्रकं Friendship.

मैत्रावरुणः 1 An epithet of Vâlmîki. 2 Of Agastya. 3 N. of one of the officiating priests at a sacrifice.

मैत्रावरुणिः 1 An epithet of Agastya. 2 Of Vasishṭha. 3 Of Vâlmîki.

मैत्रेय *a.* (यी *f.*) Relating to a friend, friendly. -यः N. of a mixed tribe.

मैत्रेयकः N. of a mixed tribe; Ms. 10. 33.

मैत्रेयिका A contest between friends or allies (मित्रयुद्धं).

मैत्र्यं Friendship, alliance.

मैथिलः A king of Mithilâ; R. 11. 32, 48. -ली N. of Sîtâ; R. 12. 29.

मैथुन *a.* (नी *f.*) 1 Paired, coupled. 2 United by marriage. 3 Relating to copulation. -नं 1 Copulation, sexual union; मृतं मैथुनमप्रजं Pt. 2. 94. 2 Marriage 3 Union, connection. -Comp. -ज्वरः the excitement of sexual passion. धर्मिन् *a.* copulating. -वैराग्यं abstinence from sexual intercourse.

मैथुनिका Union by marriage, matrimonial alliance.

मैधावकं Wisdom, intelligence.

मैनाकः N. of a mountain, son of Himâlaya and Menâ, who alone retained his wings (when Indra clipped those of other mountains) on account of his friendship with the ocean; cf. Ku. 1. 20. -Comp. -स्वसृ *f.* an epithet of Pârvatî.

मैनालः A fisherman.

मैंदः N. of a demon killed by Krishṇa. -Comp. -हन् *m.* an epithet of Krishṇa.

मैरेयः -य, मैरेयकः -कं A kind of intoxicating drink; अविरजनि वधूभिः पतिमैरेयरिक्तं *S*i. 11. 51; G. L. 34.

मैलिंदः A bee.

मोकं The cast-off skin of an animal.

मोक्ष् 1 P., 10 U. (मोक्षति, मोक्षयति-ते) 1 To release, set free, liberate, emancipate. 2 To loose, untie, undo. 3 To wrest away. 4 To cast, hurl, fling. 5 To shed.

मोक्षः 1 Liberation, release, escape freedom; साऽद्युना तव बंधे मोक्षे च प्रभवति K. Me. 61; लब्धमोक्षाः शुकादयः R. 17.20; धुर्याणां च धुरो मोक्षं 17. 19. 2 Rescue, deliverance, delivery. 3 Final emancipation, deliverance of the soul from recurring births or transmigration, the last of the four ends of human existence; see अर्थ; Bg. 5. 28, 18. 30; R. 10. 84; Ms. 6. 35. 4 Death. 5 Falling down, dropping down, falling off; वनस्थलीमर्मरपत्रमोक्षाः Ku. 3. 31. 6 Loosening, untying, unbinding; वेणिमोक्षोत्सुकानि Me. 99. 7 Shedding, causing to fall down or flow; बाष्पमोक्ष, अश्रुमोक्ष. 8 Shooting, casting, discharging, बाणमोक्षः S. 3. 5. 9 Scattering, strewing. 10 Acquittance or discharge of an obligation (debt &c.). 11 (In astr.) The liberation of an eclipsed planet, the end of an eclipse. -Comp.-उपायः a means of obtaining final emancipation. -देवः an epithet applied to Hiouen Thsang, the celebrated Chinese traveller. -द्वारं the sun. -पुरी an epithet of the town called कांची.

मोक्षणं 1 Releasing, liberating, emancipating, setting at liberty. 2 Rescuing, deliverance. 3 Loosening, untying. 4 Giving up, abandoning, resigning. 5 Shedding. 6 Squandering.

मोघ *a.* 1 Vain, useless, fruitless, unprofitable, unsuccessful; याञ्चा मोघा वरमधिगुणे नाधमे लब्धकामा Me. 6; मोघवृत्ति कलभस्य चेष्टितं R. 11. 39; 14. 65; Bg. 9. 12. 2 Aimless, purposeless, indefinite. 3 Left, abandoned. 4 Idle. -घः A fence, an enclosure, a hedge. -घं *ind.* In vain, to no purpose, uselessly. -Comp. -कर्मन् *a.* engaging in useless rites. -पुष्पा a barren woman.

मोघोलिः A hedge, fence.

मोचः 1 The plantain tree. 2 The tree called शोभांजन. -चा 1 The plantain tree. 2 The cotton shrub. 3 The indigo plant. -चं A plantain fruit.

मोचकः 1 A devotee, an ascetic. 2 Emancipation, deliverance. 3 A plantain tree.

मोचन *a.* (नी *f.*) Releasing, freeing from. -नं 1 Releasing, liberating, setting free, emancipating. 2 Unyoking. 3 Discharging, emitting. 4 Acquittance of a debt or obligation. -Comp. -पट्टकः a filter.

मोचयितृ *a.* Releasing, setting free.

मोचाटः 1 The pith or fruit of the banana. 2 Sandal wood.

मोटकः -कं A pill. -कं A couple of broken blades of Kusa grass given at a *S*râddha (भुग्नकुशपत्रद्वयं).

मोटनं, मोटनकं Crushing, pressing, grinding, breaking.

मोट्टायितं Silent involuntary expression of affection towards an absent lover, as when a woman, her mind being taken up by her lover, scratches the ear &c. when he is remembered or talked of; it is thus defined by उज्ज्वलमणिः—कांतस्मरणवार्तादौ हृदि तद्भावभावतः । प्राकट्यमभिलाषस्य मोट्टायितमुदीर्यते see S. D. 141 also.

मोदः 1 Delight, pleasure, joy, gladness; यत्रानंदाश्च मोदाश्च U. 2. 12; R. 5. 15. 2 Perfume, fragrance. -Comp. -आख्यः the mango tree.

मोदक *a.* (का,-की *f.*) Pleasing, delighting, gladdening. -कः, -कं A sweetmeat in general; Y. 1. 289. -कः N. of a mixed tribe (sprung from a Kshatriya father and a *S*ûdra mother).

मोदनं 1 Joy, pleasure. 2 The act of pleasing. 3 Wax.

मोदयंतिका, मोदयंती A kind of jasmine (Arabian).

मोदिन् *a.* 1 Glad, pleased, cheerful. 2 Gladdening, delighting. -नी 1 N. of various plants (अजमोदा, मल्लिका, यूथिका). 2 Musk. 3 An intoxicating or spirituous liquor.

मोरटः 1 A kind of plant with sweet juice. 2 The milk of a cow recently calved. -टं The root of the sugarcane.

मोषः 1 A thief, robber. 2 Theft, robbery. 3 Plundering, stealing, taking away, removing (fig. also); नं पुष्पमोषमर्हत्युद्यानलता Mk. 1, दृष्टिमोषे प्रदोषे Gît. 11. 4 Stolen property. -Comp. -कृत् *m.* a thief.

मोषकः A robber, thief.

मोषणं 1 Robbing, plundering, stealing, defrauding. 2 Cutting. 3 Destroying.

मोषा Theft, robbery.

मोहः 1 Loss of consciousness, fainting, a swoon, insensibility; मोहेनांतर्वरतनुरियं लक्ष्यते मुच्यमाना V. 1. 8; Ku. 3. 73. 2 Perplexity, delusion, embarrassment, confusion; यज्ज्ञात्वा न पुनर्मोहमेवं यास्यसि पांडव Bg. 4. 35. 3 Folly, ignorance, infatuation; तितीर्षुर्दुस्तरं मोहादुडुपेनास्मि सागरं R. 1. 2; *S*. 7. 25. 4 Error, mistake. 5 Wonder, astonishment. 6 Affliction, pain. 7 A magical art employed to confound an enemy 8 (In phil.) Delusion of mind which prevents one from discerning the truth (makes one believe in the reality of worldly objects and to be addicted to the gratification of sensual pleasures). -Comp. -कलिल the thick net or snare of delusion. -निद्रा overweening confidence. -मंत्रः a deluding spell. -रात्रिः *f.* the night when the whole universe will be destroyed. -शास्त्रं a false doctrine or precept.

मोहन *a.* (नी *f.*) 1 Stupefying. 2 Bewildering, perplexing, puzzling. 3 Deluding, infatuating. 4 Fascinating. -नः 1 An epithet of *S*iva. 2 N. of one of the five arrows of Cupid. 3 The thorn-apple (धत्तूर). -नं 1 Stupefying. 2 ilde. perplexing, puzzling. 3 Stupor; loss of sensation. 4 Infatuation, delusion, mistake. 5 A seduction, temptation. 6 Sexual intercourse; Mâl. 4. 7 A magical charm employed to bewilder an enemy. -Comp.-अस्त्रं a missile which fascinates or bewitches the person against whom it is used.

मोहनकः The month of Chaitra.

मोहित *p. p.* 1 Stupefied. 2 Perplexed, bewildered. 3 Deluded, fascinated, infatuated, beguiled.

मोहिनी 1 N. of an *Apsaras*. 2 A fascinating woman (the form assumed by Vishṇu at the time of cheating the demons of nectar.) 3 The flower of a kind of jasmine.

मौक(कु)लिः A crow; U. 2. 29.

मौक्तिकं A pearl; मौक्तिकं न गजे गजे Subhâsh. -Comp. -आवली a string of pearls. -गुंफिका a female who prepares pearl-necklaces. -दामन् *n.* a string of pearls. -प्रसवा a pearl-muscle. -शुक्तिः *f.* a pearl oyster -सरः a necklace or string of pearls.

मौक्यं Dumbness, muteness, speechlessness.

मौख्यं Precedence, superiority.

मौखरिः N. of a family; पदे पदे मौखरिभिः कृतार्चनं K.

मौखर्यं 1 Talkativeness, garrulity. 2 Abuse, defamation, calumny.

मौग्ध्यं 1 Silliness, foolishness. 2 Artlessness, simplicity, innocence. 3 Charm, beauty.

मौचं The fruit of the plantain tree.

मौंज *a.* (जी *f.*) Made of Munja grass. -जः A blade of Munja grass.

मौंजी The girdle of a Brâhmaṇa made of a triple string of Munja grass; Ku. 5. 10; Ms. 2. 42. -Comp. -निर्बंधनं, -बंधनं binding on the Munja grass girdle, investiture with the sacred thread; Ms. 2. 27, 169.

मौढ्यं 1 Ignorance, stupidity, folly. 2 Childishness.

मौत्रं A quantity of urine.

मौदकिकः A confectioner.

मौद्गलिः A crow.

मौद्गीन *a.* Fit for being sown with beans, or sown with beans (as a field).

मौनं Silence, taciturnity; मौनं सर्वार्थसाधनं; मौनं त्यज 'open your lips'; मौनं समाचर 'hold your tongue.' -Comp. -मुद्रा the attitude of silence. -व्रतं a vow of silence.

मौनिन् *a.* (नी *f.*) Observing a vow of silence, silent, taciturn; Bg. 12. 19. -*m.* A holy sage, an ascetic, a hermit.

मौरजिकः A drummer.

मौरूर्यं Folly, stupidity.

मौर्यः N. of a dynasty of kings beginning with Chandragupta; मौर्ये नवे राजनि Mu. 4. 15; मौर्यैर्हिरण्यार्थिभिरर्चाः

प्रकाल्पिता: Mbh.; (there is a difference of opinion among scholars as to the meaning of the word मौर्य in this passage).

मौर्वी 1 A bow-string; मौर्वीकिणांको भुजः S. 1. 13; मौर्वी धनुषि चातता R. 1. 19; 18. 48; Ku. 3. 55. 2 A girdle made of Mûrvâ grass (to be worn by a Kshatriya); Ms. 2. 42.

मौल *a*. (ला, -ली *f*.) 1 Radical, original. 2 Ancient, old, of long standing (as a custom). 3 Nobly born, of a good family. 4 Brought up in the service of a king for generations, holding office from ancient times, hereditary; Ms. 7. 54; R. 19. 57. -लः An old or hereditary minister; R. 12. 12, 14. 10; 18. 38.

मौलि *a*. Head, foremost, best; अखिलपार्मिलानां मौलिना सौरभेण Bv. 1. 121. -लिः 1 The head, the crown of the head; मौलौ वा रचयांजलिं Ve. 3. 40; R. 13. 59; Ku. 5. 79. 2 The head or top of anything, top-most point; U. 2. 30. 3 The Asoka tree. -लिः (*m*. or *f*.) 1 A crown, diadem, tiara; Bv. 1. 73. 2 Hair on the crown of the head, tuft or lock of hair; जटामौलि Ku. 2. 16 (जटाजूट Malli.). 3 Braided hair, hair-braided and ornamented; Ve. 6. 34. -लिः, -ली *f*. The earth. -Comp. -मणिः, -रत्नं a crest-jewel, a jewel worn in the crown. -मंडनं a head-ornament. -मुकुटं a crown, tiara.

मौलिक *a*. (की *f*.) 1 Radical. 2 Chief, principal. 3 Inferior.

मौल्यं Price.

मौष्टा Playing at fisticuffs, a boxing or pugilistic encounter.

मौष्टिकः A rogue, cheat, sharper.

मौसल *a*. (ली *f*.) 1 Formed like a club, club-shaped. 2 Fought with clubs (as a battle). 3 Relating to the battle with clubs (as a *parvan*).

मौहूर्तः, मौहूर्तिकः An astrologer.

म्ना 1 P. (मनति, म्नात) 1 To repeat (in the mind). 2 To learn diligently. 3 To remember. -With आ 1 to think of, meditate upon; पादांबुजद्वयमनारतमामनंतं Bv. 4. 32. 2 to hand down traditionally, lay down, mention, consider, speak of; त्वामामनंति प्रकृतिं पुरुषार्थप्रवर्तिनीं Ku. 2. 13, 5. 81, 6. 31. 3 To study, learn, commit to memory; यद् ब्रह्म सम्यगाम्नातं Ku. 6. 16; Bk. 17. 30. -समा 1 to repeat. 2 to lay down, prescribe; तं हि धर्मसूत्रकाराः समामनंति U. 4.

म्नात *p. p*. 1 Repeated. 2 Learnt, studied.

म्रक्ष् I. 1 P. (म्रक्षति) 1 To rub. 2 To heap, collect accumulate. II. 10 U. (म्रक्षयति-ते) 1 To heap, accumulate. 2 To smear, rub, anoint. 3 To mix, combine.

म्रक्षः Hypocrisy, dissimulation.

म्रक्षणं 1 Smearing the body with unguents. 2 Anointing, smearing in general. 3 Accumulating, heaping up. 4 Oil, ointment.

म्रद् 1 A. (म्रदते, *caus*. म्रदयति-ते) To pound, grind, crush, trample upon.

म्रदिमन् *m*. 1 Tenderness, softness. 2 Mildness, weakness; (स्वर्भानुः) हिमांशुमाशु ग्रसते तन्म्रादिम्नः स्फुटं फलं Si. 2. 49.

म्रुच् 1 P. (म्रोचती) To go, move.

म्रुंच 1 P. (म्रुंचति To go, move.

म्लक्ष् 10 U. (म्लक्षयति-ते) To cut or divide.

म्लात *p. p*. Faded, withered.

म्लान *p. p*. 1 Faded, withered. 2 Wearied, weary, languid. 3 Enfeebled, weak, feeble, faint. 4 Sad, dejected, melancholy. 5 Foul, dirty. -Comp. -अंग *a*. weak bodied. (-गी) a woman during her menses. -मनस् *a*. depressed in mind, dispirited, disheartened.

म्लानिः *f*. 1 Fading, withering, decay. 2 Languor, lassitude, weariness. 3 Sadness, dejection. 4 Foulness.

म्लायत्-म्लायिन् *a*. Withering, growing thin or emaciated.

म्लास्नु *a*. 1 Becoming faded or withered. 2 Growing thin or emaciated. 3 Growing languid or weary.

म्लिष्ट *a*. 1 Spoken indistinctly (as by barbarians), indistinct. 2 Barbarous. 3 Withered, faded. -ष्टं An indistinct or barbarous speech.

म्लुच, म्लुंच् See म्रुच्, म्रुंच्.

म्लेच्छ्, or **म्लेछ्** 1. P., 10 U. (म्लेच्छति म्लेच्छयति, म्लिष्ट, म्लेच्छित) To speak confusedly, indistincly, or barbarously.

म्लेच्छः 1 A barbarian, a nong Aryan (one not speaking the Sanskrit language or not conformin-to Hindu or Aryan institutions), a foreigner in general: ग्राह्या म्लेच्छप्रसिद्धिस्तु विरोधादर्शने. सति J. N. V.; म्लेच्छान् मूर्छयते, or म्लेच्छनिवहनिधने कलयसि करवालं Git. 1. 2 An outcast, a very low man, Baudhâyana thus defines the word:-गोमांसखादको यस्तु विरुद्धं बहु भाषते। सर्वाचारविहीनश्च म्लेच्छ इत्यभिधीयते। 3 A sinner, wicked person. -च्छं Copper. -Comp. -आस्यं copper. -आशः wheat. -आस्यं, -मुखं copper. -कंदः garlic. -जातिः *f*. a savage or barbarian race, a mountaineer, barbarian. -देशः, -मंडलं a country inhabited by Non-Aryans or barbarians, a foreign or barbarous country; Ms. 2. 23. -भाषा a foreign language. -भोजनः wheat. (-नं) barely. -वाच् *a*. speaking a barbarous or foreign language; Ms. 10. 45.

म्लेच्छित *p. p*. Spoken indistinctly or barbarously. -तं 1 A foreign tongue. 2 An ungrammatical word or speech.

म्लेट्, म्लेड् (म्लेट-ड-ति) To be mad.

म्लेव् 1 A (म्लेवते) To worship-serve.

म्लै 1 P. (म्लायति, म्लान) 1 To fade, wither; म्लायतां भूरुहाणां Bv. 1. 36; Si. 5. 43. 2 To grow weary or languid to be fatigued or exhausted; पथि... मम्लतुर्न मणिकुट्टिमोचितौ R. 11. 9; Bk. 14. 6. 3 To be sad or dejected; be downcast or dispirited; मम्लौ साथ विषादेन K. P. 10; म्लायते मे मनो हीदं Mb. 4 To become thin or emaciated. 5 To disappear, vanish. -With परि 1 to fade, wither; परिम्लानमुखश्रियां Ku. 2. 2; R. 14. 50. 2 to be dejected or dispirited. -प्र 1 to fade, wither. 2 to be sad or dejected. 3 to be languid. 4 to be dirty or foul, to be soiled.

य.

यः 1 One who goes or moves, a goer, mover. 2 A carriage. 3 Wind, air. 4 Union. 5 Fame. 6 Barley.

यकन् *n.* The liver. (This word has no forms for the first five inflections and is optionally substituted for यकृत् after acc. dual).

यकृत् *n.* The liver or any affection of it. **–Comp.** –आत्मिका a kind of cockroach. –उदरं enlargement of the liver. –कोषः the membrane enveloping the liver.

यक्षः 1 N. of a class of demi-gods who are described as attendants of Kubera, the god of riches and employed in guarding his gardens and treasures; यक्षोत्तमा यक्षपतिं धनेशं रक्षंति वै प्रासगदादिहस्ताः Hariv., Me. 1, 66; Bg. 10. 23, 11. 22. 2 A kind of ghost or spirit. 3 N. of the palace of Indra. 4 N. Of Kubera. –क्षी A female Yaksha. **–Comp.** –अधिपः, –अधिपतिः, –इंद्रः Kubera, the lord of Yakshas. –आवासः the fig-tree. –कर्दमः an ointment consisting of camphor, agallochum, musk and Kakkola (according to others, also sandal and saffron) mixed in equal proportions; (कर्पूरागुरुकस्तूरीकक्कोलैर्यक्षकर्दमः Ak.; कुंकुमागुरुकस्तूरी कर्पूरं चंदनं तथा। महासुगंधमित्युक्तं नामतो यक्षकर्दमः ॥). –ग्रहः the being possessed by Yakshas or evil spirits. –तरुः the fig-tree. –धूपः resin, incense. –रसः a kind of intoxicating drink. –राज *m.*, –राजः N. of Kubera. –रात्रिः *f.* the festival called Dîpâli, q. v. –वित्तः one who is like a Yaksha, *i. e.* the guardian of wealth, but who never uses it.

यक्षिणी 1 A female Yaksha. 2 N. of the wife of Kubera. 3 A certain female fiend in the service of Durgâ. 4 A sylph or fairy (holding intercourse with mortals).

यक्ष्मः, यक्ष्मन् *m.* 1 Pulmonary disease, consumption. 2 A disease in general. **–Comp.** –ग्रहः an attack of consumption. –ग्रस्त *a.* consumptive. –घ्नी grapes.

यक्ष्मिन् *a.* One who is affected by or suffers from consumption; Ms. 3. 154.

यज् 1 U. (यजति-ते, इष्ट; *pass.* इज्यते; *desid.* यियक्षति-ते) 1 To sacrifice, worship with sacrifices (often with instr. of words meaning 'a sacrifice'); यजेत राजा क्रतुभिः Ms. 7. 79; 5. 53, 6. 36, 11. 40; Bk. 14. 90; so अश्वमेधेनेजे, पाकयज्ञेनेजे &c. 2 To make an oblation to (with acc. of the deity and instr. of the means of sacrifice or oblation); पशुना रुद्रं यजते Sk.; यास्तिलैर्यजते पितॄन् Mb. Ms. 8. 105, 11. 118. 3 To worship, adore, honour, revere. –*Caus.* (याजयति-ते) 1 To cause to sacrifice. 2 To assist at a sacrifice. –WITH आ,-परि,-प्र to offer sacrifices, bring oblations to. –सं to adore, worship; समयष्टास्त्रमंडलं Bk. 15. 96.

यजतिः A technical name for those sacrificial ceremonies to which the verb यजति is applied; see जुहोति for further information.

यजत्रः A Brâhmaṇa who maintains consecrated fire (अग्निहोत्रिन्). –त्रं Maintenance of consecrated fire.

यजनं 1 The act of sacrificing. 2 A sacrifice; देवयजनसंभवे देवि सीते U. 4. 3 A place of sacrifice.

यजमानः 1 A person who perfoms a regular sacrifice and pays its expenses. 2 A person who employs a priest or priests to sacrifice for him. 3 (Hence) A host, patron, rich man. 4 The head of a family. **–Comp.** –शिष्यः the pupil of a sacrificing Brâhmaṇa (of one who himself performs a sacrifice); *S.* 4.

यजिः 1 A sacrificer. 2 The act of sacrificing. 3 A sacrifice; दानमध्ययनं याजिः Ms. 10. 79.

यजुस् *n.* 1 A sacrificial prayer or formula. 2 A text of the Yajurveda, or the body of sacred *Mantras* in prose muttered at sacrifices; cf. मंत्रं. 3 N. of the Yajurveda. **–Comp.** –विद् *a.* knowing the sacrificial formulæ. –वेदः the second of the three (or four, including the Atharvaveda) principal Vedas, which is a collection of sacred texts in prose relating to sacrifices; it has two chief branches or recensions:—the तैत्तिरीय or कृष्णयजुर्वेद and वाजसनेयि or शुक्लयजुर्वेद.

यज्ञः 1 A sacrifice, sacrificial rite; यज्ञेन यज्ञमयजंत देवाः; तस्माद्यज्ञात्सर्वहुतः &c. 2 An act of worship, any pious or devotional act. (Every householder, but particularly a Brâhmaṇa, has to perform five such devotional acts every day; their names are:—भूतयज्ञ, मनुष्ययज्ञ, पितृयज्ञ, देवयज्ञ, and ब्रह्मयज्ञ, which are collectively called the five 'great sacrifices', see महायज्ञ, and the five words separately). 3 N. of Agni. 4 of Vishṇu. **–Comp.** –अंशः a share of sacrifice. °भुज् *m.* a deity, god; Ku. 3. 14. –अ(आ)गारः-रं a sacrificial hall. –अंगं 1 a part of a sacrifice. 2 any sacrificial requisite, a means of a sacrifice; यज्ञांगयोनित्वमवेक्ष्य यस्य Ku. 1. 17. (–गः) 1 the glomerous fig-tree (उदुंबर). 2 N. of Vishṇu. –अरिः an epithet of Siva. –अशनः a god. –आत्मन् *m.*, –ईश्वरः N. of Vishṇu. –उपकरणं any utensil or implement necessary for a sacrifice. –उपवीतं the sacred thread worn by members of the first three classes (and now even of other lower castes) over the left shoulder and under the right arm; see Ms. 2. 63; (originally यज्ञोपवीत was the ceremony of investiture with the sacred thread). –कर्मन् *a.* engaged in a sacrifice. (–*n.*) a sacrificial rite. –कल्प *a.* of the nature of a sacrifice or sacrificial offering. –कीलकः the post to which the sacrificial victim is fastened. –कुंडं a hole in the ground made for receiving the sacrificial fire. –कृत् *a.* performing a sacrifice. (–*m.*) 1 N. of Vishṇu. 2 a priest conducting a sacrifice. –क्रतुः 1 a sacrificial rite. 2 a complete rite or chief ceremony. 3 an epithet of Vishṇu. –घ्नः a demon who interrupts sacrifices. –दक्षिणा a sacrificial gift, the fee given to the priests who perform a sacrifice. –दीक्षा 1 admission or initiation to a sacrificial rite. 2 performance of a sacrifice; Ms. 5. 169. –द्रव्यं anything (*e. g.* a vessel) used for a sacrifice. –पतिः 1 one who institutes a sacrifice, see यजमान. 2 N. of Vishṇu. –पशुः 1 an animal for sacrifice, a sacrificial victim. 2 a horse. –पुरुषः, –फलदः epithets of Vishṇu. –भागः 1 a portion of a sacrifice, a share in the sacrificial offerings. 2 a god, deity. –भुज् *m.* a god, deity. –भूमिः *f.* a place for sacrifice, a sacrificial ground. –भृत् *m.* an epithet of Vishṇu. –भोक्तृ *m.* an epithet of Vishṇu. or Kṛishṇa –रसः, रेतस् *n.* Soma. –वराहः Vishṇu in his boar-incarnation. –वल्लिः-ल्ली *f.* the Soma plant. –वाटः a place prepared and enclosed for a sacrifice. –वाहनः an epithet of Vishṇu. –वृक्षः the fig-tree. –वेदिः, दी *f.* a sacrificial altar. –शरणं a sacrificial shed or hall, a temporary structure under which a sacrifice is performed. –शाला a sacrificial hall. –शेषः-षं the remains of a sacrifice; यज्ञशेषं तथामृतं Ms. 3. 285. –श्रेष्ठा the Soma plant. –सदस् *n.* a number of people at a sacrifice. –संभारः materials necessary for a sacrifice. –सारः an epithet of Vishṇu. –सिद्धिः *f.* the completion of a sacrifice. –सूत्रं see यज्ञोपवीत. –सेनः an epithet of king Drupada. –स्थाणुः a sacrificial post. -हन् *m.*, -हनः an epithet of *S*iva.

यज्ञिकः The Palâsa tree.

यज्ञिय *a.* **1** Belonging to or fit for a sacrifice, sacrificial. **2** Sacred, holy, divine. **3** Adorable, worthy of worship. **4** Devout, pious. **-यः 1** A god, deity. **2** The third or Dvâpara age. **-Comp. -देशः** the land of sacrifices; कृष्णसारस्तु चरति मृगो यत्र स्वभावतः । स ज्ञेयो यज्ञियो देशो म्लेच्छदेशस्ततः परः ॥ Ms. 2. 23. **-शाला** a sacrificial hall.

यज्ञीय *a.* Sacrificial. **-यः** The *Udumbara* tree **-Comp. -ब्रह्मपादपः** the tree called विकंकत.

यज्वन् *a.* (**यज्वरी** *f.*) Sacrificing, worshipping, adoring &c. *-m.* **1** One who performs sacrifices in accordance with Vedic precepts, a performer of sacrifices; नृपान्वयः पार्थिव एष यज्वा R. 6. 46, 1. 44, 3. 39, 18. 11; Ku. 2. 46. **2** N. of Vishṇu.

यत् 1 A (यतते, यतित) **1** To attempt, endeavour, strive, try (usually with inf. or dat.); सर्वः कल्ये वयसि यतते लब्धुमर्थान् कुटुंबी V. 3. 1. **2** To strive after, be eager or anxious for, long for, या न ययौ प्रियमन्यवधूभ्यः सारतरागमना यतमानं Si. 4. 45; R. 9. 7. **3** To exert oneself, persevere, labour. **4** To observe caution, be watchful; Bg. 2. 60. *-Caus.* (यातयति-ते) **1** To return, repay, requite, recompense, restore. **2** To despise, censure. **3** To encourage, animate. **4** To torture, distress, annoy. **5** To prepare, elaborate. -WITH **आ 1** to strive, endeavour. **2** to rest or depend upon (with loc.); वयं त्वय्यायतामहे Mv. I. 49. **-निस्** *caus.* **1** to return, restore; निर्यातय हस्तन्यसं V. 5; Ms. 11. 164. **2** to requite, repay, retaliate; रामलक्ष्मणयोर्वरं स्वयं निर्यातयामि वै Râm. **-प्र** to try, attempt, strive. **-प्रति** to try, (*-Caus*). to restore, return; see यत् with निस्. **-सं** to struggle, contend; देवासुरा वा एषु लोकेषु संयेतिरे.

यत *p. p.* **1** Restrained, curbed, controlled, subdued. **2** Limited, moderate. **-तं** The spurring of an elephant by means of the rider's feet. **-Comp. -आत्मन्** *a.* governing oneself, self-restrained, curbing the senses; (तस्मै) यतात्मने रोचयितुं यतस्व Ku. 3. 16, 1. 55. **-आहार** *a.* moderate or temperate in eating, abstemious. **-इंद्रिय** *a.* one who has restrained his senses or subdued his passions, pure, chaste. **-चित्त, -मनस्, -मानस्** *a.* subdued in mind. **-वाच्** *a.* restraining one's speech, observing silence, reticent; see वाग्यत. **-व्रत** *a.* **1** observing vows. **2** keeping to one's engagements or promised observances.

यतनं Exertion, effort.

यतम *a.* (**-मत्** *n.*) Who or which of many.

यतर *a.* (**-रत्** *n.*) Which of two.

यतस् *ind.* (often used merely for the abl. of the relative pronoun यद्) **1** From whence (referring to persons or things), from what, from which place or quarter; यतस्त्वया ज्ञानमशेषमाप्तं R. 5. 4 (यतः = यस्मात् from whom); यतश्च भयमाशंकेत्प्राचीं तां कल्पयेद्दिशं Ms. 7. 189. **2** For which reason, wherefore. **3** As, since, for, because ; उवाच चैनं परमार्थतो हरं न वेत्सि नूनं यत एवमात्थ मां Ku. 5. 75; R. 8. 76; oft. with ततः as correlative; R. 16. 74. **4** From which time forward, ever since. **5** That, so that. (**यतस्ततः** means **1** from which place soever, from any quarter whatever. **2** from any person whatever. **3** anywhere soever, on all sides, in any direction; Ms. 4. 15. **यतो यतः 1** from whatever place. **2** from whomsoever, from any person whatever **3** wherever, in whatever direction ; यतो यतः षट्चरणोऽभिवर्तते S. 1. 24; Bg. 6. 26; **यतः प्रभृति** from which time forward). **-Comp. -भव** *a.* arising from which. **-मूल** *a.* originating in, or sprung from, which.

यति: *pron. a.* (declined only in pl.; nom. and acc. यति) As many, as often, how many.

यतिः *f.* **1** Restraint, check, control. **2** Stopping, ceasing, rest. **3** Guidance. **4** A pause in music. **5** (In prosody) A caesura; यतिर्जिह्वेष्टविश्रामस्थानं कविभिरुच्यते। सा विच्छेदविरामाद्यैः पदैर्वाच्या निजेच्छया ॥ Chand. M. 1; म्रभ्नैर्यानां त्रयेण त्रिमुनियतियुता स्रग्धरा कीर्तितेयम्. **6** A widow. **-तिः** An ascetic, one who has renounced the world and controlled his passions; यथा दानं विना हस्ती तथा ज्ञानं विना यतिः Bv. 1. 119.

यतित *a.* Tried, attempted, endeavoured, striven after.

यतिन् *m.* An ascetic.

यतिनी A widow.

यत्नः 1 An effort, exertion, attempt, endeavour, trial; यत्ने कृते यदि न सिध्यति कोऽत्र दोषः H. Pr. 31. **2** Diligence, assiduity, perseverance. **3** Care, zeal, watchfulness, vigilance; महान्हि यत्नस्तव देवदारौ R. 2. 56; प्रतिपात्रमाधीयतां यत्नः *S.* 1. **4** Pains, trouble, labour, difficulty ; शेषांगनिर्माणविधौ विधातुर्लावण्य उत्पाद्य इवास यत्नः Ku. 1. 35, 7. 66; R. 7. 14.

यत्र *ind.* **1** Where, in which place, whither; सैव सा (द्यौः) चलति यत्र हि चित्तं N. 5. 57; Ku. 1. 7, 10. **2** When; as in यत्र काल. **3** Whereas, because, since, as. (**यत्र यत्र** means wherever; यत्र यत्र धूमस्तत्र तत्र वह्निः T. S. **यत्रतत्र** in whatever place.; everywhere; **यत्रकुत्र यत्रक्वचन-क्वापि 1** wheresoever, in whatever place; **2** whensoever, at whatever time ; **3** whenever, as often as; **4** hither and thither.)

यत्रत्य *a.* Of which place, dwelling in which place.

यथा *ind.* **1** Used by itself यथा has the following senses:— (*a*) as, in the manner mentioned; यथाज्ञापयति महाराजः 'as your Majesty orders'; (*b*) namely, as follows; तद्यथानुश्रूयते; Pt. 1; U. 2. 4; (*c*) as, like (showing comparison and used to express the point of similarity); आसीदियं दशरथस्य गृहे यथा श्रीः U. 4. 8; Ku. 4. 34; प्रभावप्रभवं कांतं स्वाधीनपतिका यथा (न मुंचति) K. P. 10; (*d*) as, as for example, for instance; यत्र यत्र धूमस्तत्र तत्र वह्निर्यथा महानसे T. S.; Pt. 1. 288 ; 3. 68; (*e*) that (used to introduce direct assertions with or without इति at the end); अकथितोऽपि ज्ञायत एव यथायमाभोगस्तपोवनस्येति *S.* 1; विदितं खलु ते यथा स्मरः क्षणमप्युत्सहते न मां विना Ku. 4. 36; (*f*) so that, in order that; दर्शय तं चौरसिंहं यथा व्यापादयामि Pt. 1. **2** Used correlatively with **तथा, यथा** has the following senses:— (*a*) as, so (in which case एवं and तद्वत् often take the place of तथा); यथा वृक्षस्तथा फलं or यथा बीजं तथांकुरः; Bg. 11. 29; in this case एव is frequently added to either यथा or तथा or to both to make the equality of relation more marked or striking; वधूचतुष्केऽपि यथैव शांता प्रिया तनूजास्य तथैव सीता U. 4. 16; न तथा बाधते स्कंधो (or शीतं) यथा बाधति बाधते; (as much-as, as-as,); Ku. 6. 70; U. 2. 4, V. 4. 33. In this sense तथा is often omitted, in which case यथा has sense (*c*) in **1** above; (*b*) so-that (तथा standing for 'so' and यथा for 'that'; यथा बंधुजनशोच्या न भवति तथा निर्वाहय *S.* 3; तथा प्रयतेथा यथा नोपहस्यसे जनैः K. 109; तस्मान्मुच्ये यथा तात संविधातुं तथार्हसि R. 1. 72; 3. 66, 14. 66, 15. 68. (*c*) since-therefore, as (because); so; यथा इतो मुखागतैरपि कलकलः श्रुतस्तथा तर्कयामि &c. Mâl. 8; sometimes तथा is omitted; मंदं मंदं नुदति पवनश्चानुकूलो यथा त्वां...सेविष्यंते भवंतं बलाकाः Me. 9; (*d*) if-then, as surely as-so surely (a strong form of assertion or adjuration); वाङ्मनःकर्मभिः पत्यौ व्यभिचारो यथा न मे ।तथा विश्वंभरे देवि मामंतर्धातुमर्हसि R. 15. 81.; **यथायथा-तथातथा** the more-the more, the less-the less; यथायथा यौवनमतिचक्राम तथा तथावर्धतास्य संतापः K. 59; Ms. 8. 286; 12. 73; **यथा-तथा** in any manner, in whatever way; **यथा कथंचित्** any how, some how or other. *N. B.* As the first member of Avyayîbhâva comp. **यथा** is usually translated by 'according to, according as, in accordance with, in conformity to, in proportion to, not exceeding'; **see**

compounds below. -अंशं,-अंशतस् *ind.* in due proportions, proportionately. -अधिकारं *ind.* according to authority. -अधीत *a.* as read or studied, conformable to the text. -अनुपूर्वं, -अनुपूर्व्यं, -अनुपूर्व्या *ind.* in regular order or succession, successively. -अनुभूतं *ind.* 1 according to experience. 2 by previous experience. -अनुरूपं *ind.* in exact conformity, properly. -अभिप्रेत, -अभिमत,-अभिलषित,-अभीष्ट *a.* as wished, intended or desired, agreeably to desire. -अर्थ *a.* 1 conformable to truth, true, real, correct; सौम्येति च भाष्य यथार्थभाषी R. 14. 44; so यथार्थानुभवः correct or right perception; यथार्थवक्ता. 2 conformable to the true meaning, true to the sense, right, appropriate, significant; करिष्यान्निव नामास्य (*i. e.* शत्रुघ्न) यथार्थमरिनिग्रहात् R. 15. 6; युधि सद्यः शिशुपाल तां यथार्थां Si. 16. 85; Ki. 8. 49 Ku. 2. 16. 3 fit, suitable. (-र्थं, अथतः) truly, rightly, properly. °अक्षर *a.* significant or true to the syllable; V. 1. 1. °नामन् *a.* one whose name is true to its meaning, or fully significant. (Whose deeds are according to his name); ध्रुवासिद्धेरपि यथार्थनाम्नः सिद्धिं न मन्यते M. 4; परंतपो नामयथार्थनामा R. 6. 21. °वर्णः a spy (for यथार्हवर्ण). -अर्ह *a.* 1 according to merit, as deserving. 2 appropriate, suitable, just. °वर्णः a spy, an emissary. -अर्हं, -अर्हतः *ind.* according to merit or worth; R. 16. 40. -अर्हणं *ind.* 1 according to propriety. 2 according to worth or merit. -अवकाशं *ind.* 1 according to room or space. 2 as occasion may occur, according to occasion, leisure or propriety. 3 in the proper place; प्रालंबमुत्कृष्य यथावकाशं निनाय R. 6. 14. -अवस्थं *ind.* according to the condition or circumstances. -आख्यात *a.* as mentioned before, before-mentioned. -आख्यानं *ind.* as before stated -आगत *a.* foolish, stupid. (-तं) *ind.* as one came, by the same way as one came; यथागतं मातलिसारथिर्ययौ R. 3. 67. -आचारं *ind.* as customary or usual. -आम्नातं, आम्नायं *ind.* as laid down in the Vedas. -आरंभं *ind.* according to the beginning, in regular order or succession. -आवासं *ind.* according to one's dwelling, each to his own dwelling. -आशयं *ind.* 1 according to wish or intention. 2 according to the agreement. -आश्रमं *ind.* according to the Asrama or period in one's religious life. -इच्छा, -इष्ट, -ईप्सित *a.* according to wish or desire, agreeably to one's desire, as much as desired, as desired or wished for. (-च्छं, -ष्टं, -तं) *ind.* 1 according to wish or desire, at will or pleasure; R. 4. 51. 2 as much as may be wanted, to the heart's content; यथेष्टं बुभुजे मांसं; Ch. P. 3. -ईक्षितं *ind.* as personally seen, as actually perceived. -उक्त,-उदित *a.* as said or told above, aforesaid, above-mentioned; यथोक्ताः संवृत्ताः Pt. 1; यथोक्तव्यापारा S. 1; R. 2. 70. -उचित *a.* suitable, proper, due, fit. (-तं) *ind.* duly, suitably, properly. -उत्तरं *ind.* in regular order or succession, one after another; संबंधोत्र यथोत्तरं S. D. 729. -उत्साहं *ind.* 1 according to one's power or might. 2 with all one's might. -उद्दिष्ट *a.* as indicated or described. (-ष्टं) or उद्देशं *ind.* in the manner indicated. -उपजोषं *ind.* according to pleasure or desire. -उपदेशं *ind.* as advised or instructed. -उपयोगं *ind.* according to use or requirements, according to circumstances. -काम *a.* conformable to desire. (-मं) *ind.* agreeably to desire, at will or pleasure, to the heart's content; यथाकामार्चितार्थिनां R. 1. 6; 4. 51. -कामिन् *a.* free, unrestrained. -कालः the right or due time, proper time; R. 1. 6. (-लं) *ind.* at the right time, opportunely, seasonably; सोपसर्पैर्जजागार यथाकालं स्वपन्नपि R. 17. 51. -कृत *a.* as agreed upon, done according to rule or custom, customary; Ms. 8. 183. -क्रमं, -क्रमेण *ind.* in due order or succession, regularly, in due form, properly; R. 3. 10, 9. 26. -क्षमं *ind.* according to one's power, as much as possible. -जात *a.* foolish, senseless, stupid. -ज्ञानं *ind.* to the best of one's knowledge or judgment. -ज्येष्ठं *ind.* according to rank, by seniority. -तथ *a.* 1 true, right. 2 accurate, exact. (-थं) a narrative of the particulars or details of anything, a detailed or minute account. (-थं) *ind.* 1 exactly, precisely. 2 fitly, properly, as the case really may be. -दिक्, -दिशं *ind.* in all directions. -निर्दिष्ट *a.* as mentioned before, as specified above; यथानिर्दिष्टव्यापारा सखी&c. -न्यायं *ind.* justly, rightly, properly; Ms. 1. 1. -पुरं *ind.* as before, as on previous occasions. -पूर्व *a.* -पूर्वक *a.* being as before, former; R. 12. 48. (-र्वं), -पूर्वकं *ind.* 1 as before; Ms. 11. 187. 2 in due order or succession, one after another; एते मान्या यथापूर्व *Y.* 1. 35. -प्रदेशं *ind.* 1 in the proper or suitable place; यथाप्रदेशं विनिवेशितेन Ku. 1. 49. आसंजयामास यथाप्रदेशं कंठेगुणं R. 6. 83, 7. 34. 2 according to direction or precept. -प्रधानं,-प्रधानतः *ind.* according to rank or position, according to precedence; आलोकमात्रेण सुरानशेषान् संभावयामास यथाप्रधानं Ku. 7. 46. -प्राणं *ind.* according to strength, with all one's might. -प्राप्त *a.* suitable to circumstances. -प्रार्थितं *ind.* as requested. -बलं *ind.* to the best of one's power, with all one's might. -भागं, भागशः *ind.* 1 according to the share of each, proportionately. 2 each in his respective place; यथाभागमवस्थिताः Bg. 1. 11. 3 in the proper place; यथाभागमवास्थितापि R. 6. 19. -भूतं *ind.* according to what has taken place, according to truth, truly, exactly. -मुखीन *a.* looking straight at (with gen.); (मृगः) यथामुखीनः सीतायाः पुप्लुवे बहु लोभयन् Bk. 5. 48. -यथं *ind.* 1 as is fit, fitly, properly; Ki. 8 2. 2 in regular order, severally, by degrees. बीजवंतो मुखाद्यर्था विप्रकीर्णा यथायथं S. D. 337. -युक्तं, -योगं *ind.* according to circumstances, fitly, suitably. -योग्य *a.* suitable, fit, proper, right. -रुचं, -रुचि *ind.* according to one's liking or taste. -रूपं *ind.* 1 according to form or appearance. 2 duly, properly, fitly. -वस्तु *ind.* as the fact stands, exactly, accurately, truly. -विधि *ind.* according to rule or precept, duly, properly; यथाविधि हुताग्नीनां R. 1. 6; संचस्कारोभयप्रीत्या मैथिलेयौ यथाविधि 15. 31, 3. 70. -विभवं *ind.* in proportion to one's income, according to means. -वृत्त *a.* as happened, done or acted. (-त्तं) the actual facts, the circumstances or details of an event. -शक्ति, -शक्त्या *ind.* to the best of one's power, as far as possible. -शास्त्रं *ind.* according to the scriptures, as the law ordains; Ms. 6. 88. -श्रुतं *ind.* 1 as heard or reported. 2 (यथाश्रुति) according to Vedic precepts. -संख्यं a figure of speech in Rhetoric; यथासंख्यं क्रमेणैव क्रमिकाणां समन्वयः K. P. 10; *e. g.* शत्रुं मित्रं विपत्तिं च जय रंजय भंजय Chandr. 5. 107. (-ख्यं), -संख्येन *ind.* according to number, respectively, number for number; Y. 1. 21. -समयं *ind.* 1 at the proper time. 2 according to agreement or established usage. -संभव *a.* possible. -सुखं *ind.* 1 at will or pleasure. 2 at ease, comfortably, pleasantly, so as to give pleasure; अंके निधाय करभोरु यथासुखं ते संवाहयामि चरणावुत पद्मताम्रौ *S.* 3. 22; R. 8. 48, 4. 43. -स्थानं the right or proper place. (-नं) *ind.* in the proper place, duly -स्थित *a.* according to circumstances or actual facts, as it stands; Bk. 8. 8. 2 truly, properly. -स्वं *ind.* 1 each his own, respectively; अध्यासते चीरभृतो यथास्वं R. 13. 22; Ki. 14. 43. 2 Individually; R. 17. 65. 3 duly, properly, rightly.

यथावत् *ind.* 1 Duly, fitly, properly, rightly; oft. with the force of an adjective; अध्यापिपद्गाधिसुतो यथावत् Bk. 2. 21; लिपेर्यथावद्ग्रहणेन R. 3. 28. 2 According to rule or precept, as enjoined by rules; ततो यथावद्विहिताध्वराय R. 5. 19; Ms. 6. 1; 8. 214.

यद् *pron. a.* (Nom. sing. *m.* यः *f.* या, *n.* यत्-द्) The relative pronoun corresponding to 'who', 'which' or 'what' in English. (*a.*) Its proper correlative is तद्; यस्य बुद्धिर्बलं तस्य; but sometimes इदम्, अदस्, एतद्, take the place of तद्; sometimes the relative is used alone, its antecedent being supplied from the context. Not unfrequently two relatives are used in the same sentence; यद्वे रोचते यस्मै भवेत्तत्तस्य सुंदरं. (*b*) When repeated, the relative pronoun has the sense of 'totality', and may be translated by 'whoever', 'whatever', in which case the correlative pronoun is generally repeated; यो यः शस्त्रं बिभर्ति स्वभुजगुरुबलः पांडवानां चमूनां... क्रोधांधस्तस्य तस्य स्वयमिह जगतामंतकस्यांतकोहं Ve. 3. 30. (*c*) When joined with the interrogative pronoun or its derivatives with or without the particles चिद्, चन्, वा or अपि, it expresses the sense of 'whatever,' 'any whatsoever', 'any'; येन केन प्रकारेण anyhow, some how or other; यत्रकुत्रापि, यो वा कोवा, यः कश्चन &c.; यत्किंचिदेतद् 'this is a mere trifle'; यानि कानि च मित्राणि &c. *-ind.* As an indeclinable यद् is frequently used **1** to introduce a direct or subordinate assertion with or without इति at the end; सत्योयं जनप्रवादो यत्संपत्संपदमनुपबध्नातीति K. 73; तस्य कदाचिच्चिंता समुत्पन्ना यदर्थोत्पत्त्युपायाश्चिंतनीयाः कर्तव्याश्च Pt. 1. **2** or in the sense of 'because', 'since'; प्रियमाचरितं लते त्वया मे ... यदियं पुनरप्यपांगनेत्रा परिवृत्तार्धमुखी मयाद्य दृष्टा V. 1. 17; or किं शेषस्य भरव्यथा न वपुषि क्ष्मां न क्षिपत्येष यत् Mu. 2. 18; R. 1. 27, 87; in this sense यद् is often followed by तद् or ततः as its correlative; see N. 22. 46. **-Comp.** **-अपि** *ind.* although, though; वक्रः पंथा यदपि भवतः Me. 27. **-अर्थं -अर्थे** *ind.* **1** for which, wherefore, why, on which account; श्रूयतां यदर्थमस्मि हरिणा भवत्सकाशं प्रेषितः *S.* 6; Ku. 5. 52. **2** since, because; नूनं दैवं न शक्यं हि पुरुषेणातिवर्तितुम् यदर्थं यत्नवानेव न लभे विप्रतां विभो ॥ Mb. **-कारण, -कारणात्** *ind.* **1** wherefore, on which account. **2** since, because. **-कृते** *ind.* wherefore, why, for which person or thing. **-भविष्यः** a fatalist (one who says 'what will be will be', Pt. 1. 318. **-वा** *ind.* or else, whether; नैतद्विद्मः कतरन्नो गरीयो यद्वा जयेम यदि वा नो जयेयुः Bg. **2.** 6; (often used by commentators in suggesting an alternative meaning). **-वृत्तं** an adventure. **-सत्यं** *ind.* to be sure, to speak the truth, truly, forsooth; अमंगलाशंसया वो वचनस्य यत्सत्यं कंपितामिव मे हृदयं Ve. 1, Mu. 1; Mk. 4.

यदा *ind.* **1** When, at the time when; यदा यदा whenever; यदैवतदैव at the very time, as soon as; यदाप्रभृति -तदाप्रभृति from what time-from that time forward. **2** If (=यदि); पत्रं नैव यदा करीरविटपे दोषो वसंतस्य किं Bh. 2. 93. **3** Whereas, since, as.

यदि *ind.* **1** If, in case (showing condition and in this sense, generally used with the otential mood, but sometimes also with the future or present tense; it is usually followed by तर्हि and sometimes by ततः, तदा, तत् or अत्र); प्राणैस्तपोभिरथवाभिमतं मदीयैः कृत्यं घटेत सुहृदो यदि तत्कृतं स्यात् ॥ Mâl. 1. 9; वदसि यदि किंचिदपि दंतरुचिकौमुदी हरति दरतिमिरमतिघोरं Gît. 10; यत्ने कृते यदि न सिद्ध्यति कोत्र (= कस्तर्हि) दोषः H. Pr. 35. **2** Whether, if; वद प्रदोषे स्फुटचंद्रतारका विभावरी यद्यरुणाय कल्पते Ku. 5. 44. **3** Provided that, when. **4** If perchance, perhaps; यदि तावदेवं क्रियतां perhaps you might do so; पूर्वं स्पृष्टं यदि किल भवेदंगमेभिस्तवेति Me. 103; Y. 3. 104 (**यद्यपि**) means 'though' 'although;' *Si.* 16. 82; Bg. 1. 38; *S.* 1. 31; **यदिवा** or; यद्वा जयेम यदि वा नो जयेयुः Bg. 2. 6; Bh. 2. 83; or perhaps, or rather and if necessary; oft. expressed by the reflexive pronoun; U. 1. 12. 4. 5.

यदुः N. of an ancient king, the eldest son of Yayâti and Devayânî and ancestor of the Yâdavas. **-Comp.** **-कुलोद्वहः, -नंदनः, -श्रेष्ठः** epithets of Krishṇa.

यदृच्छा **1** Acting as one likes, self-will, independence (of action). **2** Chance, accident; usually used in the instrumental singular in this sense and translated by 'accidentally,' 'by chance; किंनरमिथुनं यदृच्छयाऽद्राक्षीत् K. 'chanced or happened to see' &c. वसिष्ठधेनुश्च यदृच्छयाऽऽगता श्रतप्रभावा ददृशेथ नंदिनी R. 3. 42; V. 1. 10; Ku. 1. 14. **-Comp.** **-अभिज्ञः** **1** voluntary or self-offered witness. **-संवादः** **1** accidental conversation. **2** spontaneous or incidental intercourse, accidental meeting.

यदृच्छातस् *ind.* Accidentally, by chance.

यतृ *m.* **1** A director, governor, ruler. **2** A driver (as of an elephant carriage); coachman, charioteer; यंतां गजस्याभ्यपतद्गजस्थं R. **7.** 37; अथ यंतारमादिश्य धुर्यान् विश्रामयेति सः 1. 54. **3** An elephant driver or rider.

यंत्र् 1. 10. U. (यंत्रति-ते, यंत्रयति-ते) To restrain, curb, check, bind, fasten, compel; शापयंत्रितपौलस्त्यबलात्कारकचग्रहैः R. 10. 47. -WITH **नि** **1** to curb, restrain, fetter. **2** to fasten, bind. **-सं** to check, restrain, stop; संयंत्रितो मया रथः *S.* 7.

यंत्रं **1** That which restrains or fastens, any prop or support, a stay; as in गृहयंत्र (see the quotation under this word). **2** A fetter, band, fastening, tie, thong. **3** A surgical instrument, especially a blunt instrument (opp. शस्त्र). **4** Any instrument or machine, an appliance, a contrivance, implement in general; कूपयंत्र Mk. 10. 59 'a machine for drawing up water from a well'; so तैल°, जल° &c. **5** A bolt, lock. **6** Restraint, force. **7** An amulet, a mystical or astronomical diagram used as an amulet. **-Comp.** **-उपलः** a mill, mill-stone. **-करंडिका** a kind of magical basket. **-कर्मकृत्** *m.* an artist, artisan. **-गृहं** **1** an oil-mill. **2** a manufactory. **-चेष्टितं** any magical work, an enchantment. **-दृढ** *a.* secured by a bolt (as a door). **-नालं** a mechanical pipe or tube. **-पुत्रकः**, **-पुत्रिका** a mechanical doll, a puppet furnished with contrivances, such as strings, for moving the limbs. **-प्रवाहः** an artificial stream of water; R. 16. 49. **-मार्गः** a canal or an aqueduct. **-शरः** an arrow or any missile shot off by means of machinery.

यंत्रकः **1** One well acquainted with machinery. **2** A mechanist. **-कं** **1** A bandage (in medic.) **2** A turner's wheel or lathe.

यंत्रणं-णा **1** Restraining, curbing, stopping; करयंत्रणदंतुरांतरे व्यलिखच्चंचुपुटेन पक्षती N. 2. 2. **2** A restraint, restriction; check; ह्रीयंत्रणां तत्क्षणमन्वभूवन्नन्योन्यलोलानि विलोचनानि Ku. 7. 75; R. 7. 23. **3** Fastening binding (बंध); निबिडपीनकुचद्वययंत्रणा तमपराधमधात् प्रतिबध्नती N. 4, 10. **4** Force, compulsion, constraint, trouble, pain or anguish (arising from compulsion). अलमलमुपचारयंत्रणया M. 4. **5** Guarding, protecting. **6** A bandage.

यंत्रणी, यंत्रिणी A wife's younger sister.

यंत्रिन् *a.* or *s.* **1** Furnished with harness or trappings (as a horse). **2** One who pains, a tormentor. **3** One who possesses an amulet.

यम् 1 P. (यच्छति, यत; *desid.* यियंसति), **1** To check, curb, restrain, control subdue, stop, suppress; यच्छेद्वाङ्मनसी प्रज्ञः Kaṭh.; यतचित्तात्मन् Bg. 4. 21; see यत. **2** To offer, give, bestow. *-Caus.* (यमयति-ते) To restrain, check &c. -WITH **आ** **1** to extend, lengthen, stretch out; वस्त्रं-पार्गि-आयच्छते Sk.; स्वागमायच्छमानः *S.* 4 v. l. **2** to draw up or back; आयच्छति कूपाद्रज्जुं Sk.; बाणमुद्यतमायंसीत् Bk. 6. 119. **3** to restrain, hold in, suppress, suspend (as breath). Ms. 3. 217, 11. 100, Y. 1. 24. **4** to stretch oneself, grow long (Atm.). **5** to grasp, possess, have; श्रियमायच्छमानाभिरुत्तमाभिरुत्तमां Bk. 8. 46. **6** to bring or lead towards. **-उद्** (usually Atm.) **1** to raise, list up, elevate; बाहू उद्यम्य *S.* 1; परस्य दंडं नोद्यच्छेत् Ms. 4. 104, R. 11. 17, 15. 23; Bk. 4. 31. **2**

to become ready, set about, begin (with dat. or inf.); उद्यच्छमाना गमनाय भूयः R. 16. 29; Bk. 8. 47. **3** to strive, strive hard for; उद्यच्छति वेदं Sk. **4** to reign, manage, govern. **–उप** (Atm.) **1** to marry; भवान्मिथःसमयादिमामुपायस्तं *S*. 5. (मेनां) आत्मानुरूपां विधिनोपयेमे Ku. 1. 18; R. 14. 87; *Si*. 15. 27. **2** to seize, hold, take, accept, possess; शस्त्राण्युपायंसत जित्वराणि Bk. 1. 16; 15. 21; 8. 33. **3** to show, indicate; Rk. 7. 101. **–नि** **1** to restrain, curb, check, control, govern; प्रकृत्या नियताः स्वया Bg. 7. 20; (सुतां) शशाक मेना न नियंतुमुद्यमात् Ku. 5. 5 'could not dissuade her' &c. **2** to suppress, suspend, hold in (as breath &c.); Ms. 2. 192; न कथंचन दुर्योनिः प्रकृतिं स्वां नियच्छति Ms. 10. 59. 'does not suprress or conceal' &c. **3** to offer, give; को नः कुले निवपनानि नियच्छतीति *S*. 6. 24. **4** to punish chastise; नियंतव्यश्च राजभिः Ms. 9. 213. **5** to regulate or direct in general. **6** to attain, obtain; तालज्ञश्चाप्रयासेन मोक्षमार्गं नियच्छति Y. 3. 115; Ms. 2. 93. **7** to assume. (*–Caus.*) **1** to restrain, control, regulate, check, punish; नियमयसि विमार्गप्रस्थितानात्तदंडः *S*. 5. 8. **2** to bind, fasten; *Si*. 7. 50; R. 5. 73. **3** to moderate, mitigate, relieve; Ku. 1. 61. **विनि** to curb, control; Bg. 6. 24. **–सं 1** to restrain, curb, check, control (Atm.); Bg. 6. 36; Ms. 2. 100. **2** to bind, imprison, fasten, confine, वानरं मा न संयसीः Bk. 9. 50; M. 1. 7; R. 3. 20; 42. **3** to gather (Atm.); व्रीहीन्संयच्छते Sk. **4** to shut, close; Bg. 8. 12.

यमः 1 Restraining, controlling, curbing. **2** Control, restraint. **3** Self-control. **4** Any great moral or religious duty or observance (opp. नियम); तवं यमेन नियमेन तपोऽस्मुनैव N. 13. 16. यम and नियम are thus distinguished:—शरीरसाधनापेक्षं नित्यं यत्कर्म तद्यमः । नियमस्तु स यत्कर्म नित्यमागंतुसाधनं ॥ Ak.; see Malli. on Ki. 10. 10 also. The *yamas* are usually said to be ten, but their names are given differently by different writers; *e. g.* ब्रह्मचर्यं दया क्षांतिर्दानं सत्यमकल्कता । अहिंसाऽस्तेयमाधुर्ये दमश्चेति यमाः स्मृताः ॥ Y. 3. 313 ; or आनृशंस्य दया सत्यमहिंसा क्षांतिरार्जवम् । प्रीतिः प्रसादो माधुर्यं मार्दवं च यमा दश॥; sometimes only five *yamas* are mentioned:—अहिंसा सत्यवचनं ब्रह्मचर्यमकल्कता । अस्तेयमिति पंचैते यमाख्यानि व्रतानि च ॥). **5** The first of the eight *angas* or means of attaining Yoga; the eight *angas* are:—यमनियमासनप्राणायामप्रत्याहारधारणाध्यानसमाधयोऽष्टावंगानि. **6** The god of death, death personified, regarded as a son of the sun; दत्ताभये त्वयि यमादपि दंडधारे U. 2. 11. **7** A twin; धर्मात्मजं प्रति यमौ च (*e. i.*) नकुलसहदेवौ कथैव नास्ति Ve. 2. 25; यमयोश्चैव गर्भेषु जन्मतो ज्येष्ठता मता Ms. 9. 126. **8** One of a pair or couple. **–मं** A pair or couple. **–Comp. –अनुगः, –अनुचरः** a servant or attendant of Yama. **–अंतकः** an epithet of **1** *Siva*. **2** of Yama. **–किंकरः** 'Yama's servant', a messenger of death. **–कीलः** N. of Vishṇu. **–ज** *a.* twin-born, twin; भ्रातरौ आवां यमजौ U. 6. **–दूतः 1** a messenger of death. **2** A crow. **–द्वितीया** the second day in the bright half of Kârtika when sisters entertain their brothers (Mar. भाऊबीज.); cf. भ्रातृद्वितीया. **–धानी** the abode of Yama; नरः संसारांते विशति यमधानीजवनिकां Bh. 3. 112. **–भगिनी** N. of the river Yamunâ. **–यातना** the tortures inflicted by Yama upon sinners after death; (the word is sometimes used to denote 'horrible tortures,' 'extreme pain'). **–राज्** *m.* Yama, the god of death. **–सभा** the tribunal of Yama. **–सूर्यं** a building with two halls, one facing the west and the other facing the north.

यमकः 1 Restraint, check. **2** A twin. **3** A great moral or religious duty see यम (4). **–कं 1** A double bandage. **2** (In Rhet.) Repetition in the same stanza (in any part of it) of words or syllables similar in sound, but different in meaning, a kind of rhyme; (of which various kinds are enumerated: see Kâv. 3. 2. 52); आवृत्तिं वर्णसंघातगोचरां यमकं विदुः Kâv. 1. 61, 3. 1; S. D. 640.

यमन *a.* (**नी** *f.*) Restraining, curbing, governing &c. **–नं 1** The act of restraining, curbing or binding. **2** Stopping, ceasing. **3** Cessation, rest. **–नः** The god of death, Yama.

यमनिका A curtain, screen; cf. जवनिका.

यमल *a.* Twin, one of a couple. **–लः** The number 'two'. **–लौ** (dual) A pair. **–लं, –ली** A pair, couple.

यमवत् *a.* One who has restrained his passions, self-controlled; यमवतामवतां च धुरि स्थितः R. 9. 1.

यमसात् *ind.* In the hands of Yama, to the power of Yama; यमसात् कृ 'to hand over to death.'

यमुना N. of a celebrated river (regarded as a sister of Yama). **–Comp. –भ्रातृ** *m.* Yama, the god of death.

ययातिः N. of a celebrated king of the lunar race, son of Nahusha.[He married Devay*a*ni, daughter of *S*ukra, and *S*armish*th*a, daughter of the king of Asuras, was told by her father to be her servant as a sort of recompense for her insulting conduct towards her on a previous occasion; (see Devay*a*ni). But Yay*a*ti fell in love with this servant and privately married her. Aggrieved at this Devay*a*ni went to her father and complained of the conduct of her husband, on whom, therefore, *S*ukra inflicted premature infirmity and old age. Yay*a*ti, however, propitiated him and obtained from him permission to transfer his decrepitude to any one who would consent to take it. He asked his five sons, but all refused except Puru, the youngest. Yay*a*ti accordingly transerred his infirmity to Puru, and being fonce more in the prime of youth, paseed his time in the enjoyment of sensual pleasures. This he did for 1000 years, and yet his desire was not satisfied. At last, however, with a vigorous effort he renounced his sensual life, restored his youth to Puru, and, having made him successor to the throne, repaired to the woods to lead a pious life and meditate upon the Supreme Spirit].

ययावरः =यायावर q. v.

ययिः–यी *m.* **1** A horse fit for the A*s*vamedha (or any) sacrifice; *Si*. 15. 69. **2** A horse in general.

यर्हि *ind.* **1** When, while, whenever. **2** Because, as, since; (its proper correlative is तर्हि or एतर्हि; but it is seldom used in classical literature).

यवः 1 Barley; यवाः प्रकीर्णा न भवंति शालयः Mk. 4. 17. **2** A barley-corn or the weight of a barley-corn. **3** A measure of length equal to $\frac{1}{6}$ or $\frac{1}{8}$ of an *angula*. **4** A mark on the fingers of the hand resembling a barley-corn and supposed according to its position to indicate **wealth,** progeny, good fortune &c. **–Comp. –अंकुरः, –प्ररोहः** a shoot or blade of barley. **–आग्रयणं** the first fruits of barley. **–क्षारः** saltpetre, nitre, nitrate of potash. **–क्षोदः, –चूर्णं, –पिष्टं** barley-meal. **–फलः** a bamboo. **–लासः** salt-petre, nitre. **–शूकः -शूकजः** an alkaline salt prepared from the ashes of burnt barley-straw, nitre. **–सुरं** malt-liquor, beer.

यवनः 1 A Greek, an Ionian. **2** Any foreigner, of barbarian; Ms. 10. 44; (the word is applied at present to a Mahomedan or a European also). **3** A carrot.

यवनानी The writing of the Yavanas.

यवनिका, यवनी 1 A Yavana female, a Greek or Mahomedan woman; यवनी नवनीतकोमलांगी Jag.; यवनीमुखपद्मानां सेहे मधुमदं न सः R. 4. 61; (from dramas it appears that Yavana girls were formery employed as attendants on kings, particularly to be in charge of their bows and quivers; cf. एष बाणासनहस्ताभिर्यवनीभिः परिवृत इत एवागच्छति प्रियवयस्यः *S*. 2; प्रविश्य शार्ङ्गहस्ता यवनी *S*.6; प्रविश्य चापहस्ता यवनी V. 5. &c.). **2** A curtain.

यवसं Grass, fodder, meadow grass; यवसेंधनं Pt. 1; Y. 3. 30; Ms. 7. 75.

यवागू *f.* Rice-gruel, sour-gruel made from rice or from any other kind of grain, such as barley; यवागूर्विरलद्रवा Susr.; मूत्राय कल्पते यवागूः Mbh.

यवानिका, यवानी A kind of bad barley; (दुष्टो यवो यवानी).

यविष्ठ *a.* Youngest, very young; (superl. of युवन् q. v.). -ष्ठः The youngest brother.

यवीयस् *a.* Younger, very young (compar. of युवन् q. v.) *-m.* 1 A younger brother. 2 A Sûdra.

यशस् *n* Fame, reputation, glory, renown; विस्तीर्यते यशो लोके तैलबिंदुरिवांभसि Ms. 7. 34; यशस्तु रक्ष्यं परतो यशोधनैः R. 3. 48, 2. 40. -Comp. -कर *a.* (यशस्कर) conferring glory, glorious; Ms. 8. 387. -काम *a.* (यशस्काम) 1 desirous of getting fame. 2 aspiring, ambitious. -कायं, -शरीरं body in the form of fame; यशःशरीरे भव मे दयालुः R. 2. 57; Bh. 2. 24. -द *a.* (यशोद) conferring fame. (-दः) quicksilver. (-दा) N. of the wife of Nanda and foster-mother of Krishṇa. -धन *a.* or *s.* one whose wealth or valued treasure is fame, rich in fame, very renowned; अपि स्वदेहात् किमुतेंद्रियार्थात् यशोधनानां हि यशो गरीयः R. 14. 35, 2. 1. -पटहः a double-drum. -शेष *a.* remaining only in fame, having nothing left behind except glory; *i. e.* dead; cf. कीर्तिशेष. (-षः) death.

यशस्य *a.* 1 Leading to glory or distinction; Ms. 2. 52. 2 Renowned, famous, glorious.

यशस्विन् *a.* Famous, glorious, renowned.

यष्टिः-ष्टी *f.* 1 A stick, staff. 2 A cudgel, mace, club. 3 A column, pillar, pole. 4 A perch, as in वासयष्टि. 5 A stem, support. 6 A flag-staff; as in ध्वजयष्टि. 7 A stalk, stem. 8 A branch, twig; कदंबयष्टिः स्फुटकोरकेव U. 3. 42; so चूतयष्टिः Ku 6. 2; सहकारयष्टिः &c. 9 A string, thread (as of pearls), a necklace; विमुच्य सा हारमहार्यनिश्चया विलोलयष्टिप्रविलुप्तचंदनं Ku. 5. 8; R. 13. 54. 10 Any creeping plant. 11 Anything thin, slim or slender (at the end of comp. ater words meaning 'the body'); तं वीक्ष्य वेपथुमती सरसांगयष्टिः Ku. 5. 85 'with her slender or delicate frame perspiring'. -Comp. -ग्रहः a club-bearer, staff-bearer. -निवासः 1 a stick or rod serving as a perch for peacocks &c.; वृक्षेशया यष्टिनिवासभंगात् R. 16. 14. 2 a pigeon-house resting on upright poles. -प्राण *a.* 1 feeble or powerless. 2 out of breath.

यष्टिकः A lapwing.

यष्टिका 1 A staff, stick, pole, club. 2 A pearl-necklace (of one string).

यष्टी see यष्टि.

यष्टृ *m.* A worshipper, sacrificer.

यस् 1. 4. P. (यसति, यस्यति, यस्त) To strive, endeavour, labour. *-Caus.* (यासयति-ते) To put to trouble. -With आ 1 to strive, endeavour, exert oneself, Mu. 3. 14. 2 to weary oneself, be fatigued or exhausted; नायस्यसि तपस्यंती Bk. 6. 69, 15. 54. (*-Caus.*) to trouble, torment, afflict. -प्र to strive, endeavour.

या 2 P. (याति, यात) 1 To go, move, walk, proceed; ययौ तदीयामवलंब्य चांगुलिं R. 3. 25; अन्वग्ययौ मध्यमलोकपालः 2. 16. 2 To march against, invade; Ms. 7. 183. 3 To go to, march towards, set out for (with acc., dat. or with प्रति). 4 To pass away, withdraw, depart. 5 To vanish, disappear; यातस्तवापि च विवेकः Bv. 1. 68; भाग्यक्रमेण हि धनानि भवंति यांति Mk. 1. 13. 6 To pass away or by, elapse (as time); योवनमनिवर्ति यातं तु K. P. 10. 7 To last. 8 To happen, come to pass. 9 To go or be reduced to any state, be or become (usually with the acc. of abstract noun). 10 To undertake; न त्वस्य सिद्धौ यास्यामि सर्गव्यापारमात्मना Ku. 2. 54. 11 To have carnal intercourse with. 12 To request, implore. 13 To find out, discover. (The meanings of या, like those of गम्, are variously modified according to the noun with which it is connected; *e. g.* नाशं या to be destroyed; वाच्यतां या to incur blame or censure; लघुतां या to be slighted; प्रकृतिं या to regain one's natural state; निद्रां या to fall asleep; वशं या to submit, go into one's possession; उदयं या to rise; अस्तं या to set, decline; पारं या to reach the other side of, to master, surmount, get over; पदं या to attain to the position of; अग्रे या to go before, take the lead, lead; अधो या to sink; विपर्यासं या to undergo a change, to be changed in appearance; शिरसा महीं या to bend the head down to the ground &c.). *-Caus.* (यापयति-ते) 1 To cause to go or proceed. 2 To remove, drive away; R. 9. 31. 3 To spend, pass (time); तावत्कोकिल विरसान् यापय दिवसान् Bv. 1. 7; Me. 89. 4 To support, nourish. *-Desid.* (यियासति) To wish to go, to be about to go &c. -With अति 1 to go beyond, transgress, violate. 2 to surpass. -अधि to go away or forth; escape; कुतोऽधियास्यसि क्रूर निहतंस्तेन पत्रिभिः Bk. 8. 90. -अनु 1 to follow, go after (fig. also); अनुयास्यन्मुनितनयां *S.* 1. 29; Ku. 4. 21; Bk. 2. 77. 2 to imitate, equal; न किलानुययुस्तस्य राजानो रक्षितुर्यशः R. 1. 27; 9. 6; Si. 12. 3. 3 to accompany. -अनुसं to go to in succession. -अप to go away, depart, retreat. -अभि 1 to approach, go or repair to; अभिययौ स हिमाचलमुच्छ्रितं Ki. 5. 1; R. 9. 27. 2 to march against, attack; R. 5. 30. 3 to devote oneself to. -आ 1 to come to, arrive, approach. 2 to reach or attain to, undergo, be in any particular state; क्षयं, तुलां, नाशं &c. -उप 1 to approach, go towards; Ki. 6. 16. 2 to attain (to a particular state); मृत्युं, तनुतां, रुजं &c. -निस् 1 to go out, go out of; R. 12. 83. 2 to pass, elapse (as time). -परि to walk round, go round, circumambulate. -प्र 1 to walk, go; त्रस्तास्त्रुतं नगरदैवतवत्प्रयासि Mk. 1. 27. 2 to walk on, set out. -प्रति to go back, return; R. 1. 75, 15. 18, 8. 90. -प्रत्युद् to go forth to meet (as a mark of respect), to greet, welcome; तानर्घ्यानर्घ्यमादाय दूरात्प्रत्युद्ययौ गिरिः Ku. 6. 50; Me. 22; R. 1. 49. -विनिस् to go out, go away, pass out of; प्राणास्तस्या विनिर्ययुः. -सं 1 to go away, depart, walk away; Bg. 15. 8. 2 to go to, go or enter into; तथा शरीराणि विहाय जीर्णान्यन्यानि संयाति नवानि देही Bg. 2. 22. 3 to reach to.

यागः 1 An offering, a sacrifice, an oblation. 2 Any ceremony in which oblations are presented; R. 8. 30.

याच् 1 A. (याचते; rarely याचति, याचित) To beg, ask, solicit, request, entreat; implore (with two acc.); बलिं याचते वसुधां Sk.; पितरं प्रणिपत्य पादयोरपरित्यागमयाचतात्मनः R. 8. 12; Bk. 14. 105. (With prepositions the meanings of this root are not materially changed.)

याचकः (की *f.*) A mendicant, beggar, petitioner; तृणादपि लघुस्तूलस्तूलादपि च याचकः Subhâsh.

याचनं-ना 1 Asking; begging, entreating, soliciting. 2 A request, an entreaty, a petition; याचना माननाशाय; बध्यतामभययाचनांजलिः R. 11. 78.

याचनकः A beggar, suitor, petitioner.

याचिष्णु *a.* Disposed to beg, habitually begging or soliciting.

याचित *p. p.* Asked, solicited, begged, entreated, requested.

याचितकं A thing got by begging, anything borrowed for use.

याच्ञा 1 Begging, asking. 2 Mendicancy. 3 Request, solicitation, entreaty; याच्ञा मोघा वरमधिगुणे नाधमे लब्धकामा Me. 6.

याजकः 1 A sacrificer, a sacrificing priest. 2 A royal elephant. 3 An elephant in rut.

याजनं The act of performing or conducting a sacrifice; Ms. 3. 65; 1. 88.

याज्ञसेनी A patronymic of Draupadî.

याज्ञिक *a.* (की *f.*) Belonging to a sacrifice. **–कः** A sacrificer or a sacrificing priest.

याज्य *a.* **1** To be sacrificed. **2** Sacrificial. **3** One for whom a sacrifice is performed. **4** One who is allowed by *S*âstras to sacrifice. **–ज्यः** A sacrificer, the institutor of a sacrifice. **–ज्यं** The presents or fee received for officiating at a sacrifice.

यात *p. p.* **1** Gone, marched, walked. **2** Passed, departed, gone away. (see या). **–तं 1** Going, motion. **2** A march. **3** The past time. **–Comp.** **–याम, –यामन्** *a.* **1** stale, used, spoiled, rejected, become useless; अयातयामं वयः Dk. **2** raw, halfcooked (as food); यातयामं गतरसं पूति पर्युषितं च यत् Bg. 17. 10. **3** aged, exhausted, worn out

यातनं 1 Return, requital, recompense, retaliation; as in वैरयातनं. **2** Vengeance, revenge. **–ना 1** Requital, recompense, return. **2** Torment, acute pain, anguish. **3** The torments inflicted by Yama upon sinners, the tortures of hell (pl.).

यातुः 1 A traveller, a way-farer. **2** Wind. **3** Time. *–m.*, *–n.* An evil spirit, a demon, Râkshasa. **–Comp.** **–धानः** an evil spirit, a demon; Bk. 2. 21; R. 12. 45.

यातृ *f.* A husband's brother's wife.

यात्रा 1 Going, motion, journey; Mv. 6. 1; R. 18. 16. **2** The march of an army, expedition, invasion; मार्गशीर्षे शुभे मासि यायाद्यात्रां महीपतिः Ms. 7. 182; Pt. 3. 37, R. 17. 56. **3** Going on a pilgrimage; as in तीर्थयात्रा. **4** A company of pilgrims. **5** A festival, fair, festive or solemn occasion; कालप्रियनाथस्य यात्राप्रसंगेन Mâl. 1; U. 1. **6** A procession, festive train; प्रवृत्ता खलु यात्राभिमुखं मालती Mâl. 6; 6. 2. **7** A road. **8** Support of life, livelihood, maintenance; यात्रामात्रप्रसिद्ध्यर्थं Ms. 4. 3; शरीरयात्रापि च ते न प्रसिध्येदकर्मणः Bg. 3. 8. **9** Passing away (time). **10** Intercourse;; यात्रा चैव हि लौकिकी Ms.11. 184;लोकयात्रा Ve.3; Ms.9. 27. **11** Way, means, expedient. **12** A custom, usage, practice, way; एषोदिता लोकयात्रा नित्यं स्त्रीपुंसयोः परा Ms. 9. 25. (लोकाचारः Kull.). **13** A vehicle in general.

यात्रिक *a.* (की *f.*) **1** Marching. **2** Relating to a journey or campaign. **3** Requisite for the support of life. **4** Usual, customary. **–कः** A traveller. **–कं 1** A march, an expedition or campaign. **2** Provisions, supplies (for a march).

याथातथ्यं 1 Reality, truth. **2** Rectitude, propriety.

याथार्थ्यं 1 Real or correct nature, truth, true character; न संति याथार्थ्यविदः पिनाकिनः Ku. 5. 77; R. 10. 24. **2** Justness, suitableness. **3** Accomplishment or attainment of an object.

यादवः A descendant of Yadu.

यादस् *n.* Any (large) aquatic animal, a sea-monster; यादांसि जलजंतवः Ak.; वरुणो यादसामहं Bg. 10. 29; Ki. 5 29; R. 1. 16. **–Comp.** **–पतिः, –नाथः** (also **यादसांपतिः** and **यादसांनाथः**) **1** the ocean. **2** N. of Varuṇa; R. 17. 81.

यादृक्ष *a.* (क्षी *f.*), **यादृश्, यादृश** *a.* (शी *f.*) What like, of which sort or nature; Ms. 1. 42; Bg. 13. 3.

यादृच्छिक *a.* (की *f.*) **1** Voluntary, spontaneous, independent. **2** Accidental, unexpected.

यानं 1 Going, moving, walking, riding; as गजयानं, उष्ट्र°, रथ° &c. **2** A voyage, journey; समुद्रयानकुशलाः Ms. 8. 157; Y. 1. 14. **3** Marching against, attacking (one of the six Guṇas or expedients in politics); अहितान्प्रत्यभीतस्य रणे यानं Ak.; Ms. 7. 160. **4** A procession, train. **5** A conveyance, vehicle, carriage, chariot; यानं सस्मार कौबेरं R. 15. 45, 13. 69; Ku. 6. 76; Ms. 4. 120. **–Comp.** **–पात्रं** a ship, boat. **–भंगः** shipwreck. **–मुखं** the forepart of a carriage, the part where the yoke is fixed.

यापनं-ना 1 Causing to go away, driving out, expulsion, removal. **2** Cure or alleviation (of a disease). **3** Spending or passing time, as in कालयापनं. **4** Delay, procrastination. **5** Support, maintenance. **6** Practice, exercise.

याप्य *a.* **1** To be removed, expelled or rejected. **2** Low, contemptible, trifling, unimportant. **–Comp.** **–यानं** a litter or palanquin.

यामः 1 Restraint, forbearance, control. **2** A watch, one-eighth part of a day, a period of three hours; पश्चिमाद्यामिनीयामात्प्रसादमिव चेतना R. 17. 1; so यामवती, त्रियामा &c. **–Comp.** **–घोषः 1** a cock. **2** a gong or metal-plate on which nightwatches are struck; मंद्रध्वनित्याजितयामतूर्यः R. 6. 56. **–यमः** a stated occupation for every hour. **–वृत्तिः** *f.* being on watch or guard.

यामलं A pair, couple.

यामवती Night; Ki. 8. 56.

यामिः-मी *f.* **1** A sister (see जामि); Si. 15. 53. **2** Night.

यामिकः A watchman, one on duty or guard at night; N. 5. 110.

यामिका, यामिनी Night; सविता विधवति विधुरपि सवितरति दिनंति यामिन्यः । यामिनयंति दिनानि च सुखदुःखवशीकृतं मनसि ॥ K. P. 10. **–Comp.** **–पतिः 1** the moon. **2** camphor.

यामुन *a.* (नी *f.*) Belonging to or coming from, or growing in, the Yamunâ. **–नं** A kind of collyrium.

यामुनेष्टकं Lead.

याम्य *a.* **1** Southern; द्वारं रंध्रतुर्याम्यं Bk. 14. 15. **2** Belonging to or resembling Yama. **–Comp.** **–अयनं** the winter solstice. **–उत्तर** *a.* going from south to north.

याम्या 1 The south. **2** Night.

यायजूकः A performer of frequent sacrifices, one who constantly performs sacrifices (इज्याशीलः); तं यायजूकः सह भिक्षुमुख्यैः Bk. 2. 20.

यायावरः A Vagrant mendicant, saint; यायावराः पुष्पफलेन चान्ये प्रानर्चुरर्च्या जगदर्चनियं Bk. 2. 20; महाभागस्तस्मिन्नयमजनि यायावरकुले B. R. 1. 13 (where यायावर is the name of a family).

यावः, यावकः-कं 1 Food prepared from barley. **2** Lac, red dye; लभ्यते स्म परिरब्धयात्मा यावकेन वियतापि युवत्याः Si. 10. 9, 15. 13; Ki. 5. 40.

यावत् *a.* (ती *f.*) (As a correlative of तावत्) **1** As much as, as many as, (यावत् standing for 'as' and तावत् for 'as much or as many'); पुरे तावंतमेवास्य तनोति रविरातपं । दीर्घिकाकमलोन्मेषो यावन्मात्रेण साध्यते Ku. 2. 33; ते तु यावंत एवाजौ तावांश्च ददृशे स तैः R. 12. 45, 17. 17. **2** As great, as large, how great or large; यावानार्थ उदपाने सर्वतः संप्लुतोदके । तावान्सर्वेषु वेदेषु ब्राह्मणस्य विजानतः Bg. 2. 46, 18. 55. **3** All, whole (where the two together have the sense of totality or साकल्य); यावद् दत्तं तावद्भुक्तं G. M. *–ind.* **1** Used by itself यावत् has the following senses; (*a*) as far as, for, upto, till; (with acc.); स्तन्यत्यागं यावत्पुत्रयोरवेक्षस्व U. 7; कियंतमवधिं यावदस्मच्चरितं चित्रकारेणालिखितं U. 1; सर्पकोटरं यावत् Pt. 1. (*b*) just, then, in the meantime (denoting an action intended to be done immediately); तद्यावत् गृहिणीमाहूय संगीतकमनुतिष्ठामि *S*. 1; यावदिमां छायामाश्रित्य प्रतिपालयामि *S*. 3. **2** Used correlatively यावत् and तावत् have these senses:– (*a*) as long as–long long as; यावद्वित्तोपार्जनशक्तस्तावन्निजपरिवारो रक्तः Moha M. 8. (*b*) as soon as, scarcely-when, no sooner-than; एकस्य दुःखस्य न यावदंतं गच्छामि ... तावद्द्वितीयं समुपस्थितं मे H. 1. 204; Me. 105; Ku. 3. 72. (*c*) while, by the time; आश्रमवासिनो यावदवेक्ष्याहमुपावर्ते तावदार्द्रपृष्ठाः क्रियंतां वाजिनः *S*. 1; often with न when यावन्न is translated by 'before'; यावदेते सरसो नोत्पतंति तावदेतेभ्यः प्रवृत्तिरवगमयितव्या V. 4. (*d*) when, as (=यदा); यावदुत्थाय निरीक्षते तावद्धंसोऽवलोकितः H. 3. **–Comp.** **–अंतं, –अंताय** *ind.* upto the end, to the last. **–अर्थ** *a.* corresponding to requirement, as many as may be required to convey the meaning (said of words); यावदर्थपदां वाचमेवमादाय माधवः विरराम Si. 2. 13. (**–र्थं**) *ind.* **1** as much as useful. **2** in all senses; वयमपि च गिरामीश्महे यावदर्थं Bh. 3. 30. v. l. **–इष्टं, –ईप्सितं** *ind.* as much as is desired. **–इत्थं** *ind.* as much as is necessary. **–जन्म, –जीवं, –जीवेन** *ind.* for life, throughout life, for the rest of one's life. **–बलं** *ind.* to the best of one's power. **–भाषित**

or उक्त *a.* as much as said. -मात्र *a.* **1** as large, extending as far, of which size or extent; Ku. 2. 33. **2** insignificant, trifling, little. -शक्यं, -शक्ति *ind.* as far as possible, to the best of one's power; so यावत्सत्त्वं.

यावन *a.* (नी *f.*) Belonging to the Yavanas; न वदेद्यावनीं भाषा प्राणैः कंठगतैरपि Subhâsh. -नः Incense.

यावसः **1** A heap of grass. **2** Fodder, provisions.

याष्टीक *a.* (की *f.*) Armed with a club. -कः A warrior armed with a club.

यास्कः N. of the author of the Nirukta.

यु I. 2 P. (यौति, युत; *caus.* यावयति; *desid* यियविषति or यूयूषति) **1** To join, unite. **2** To mix, combine. -II. 3 P. (युयोति) To separate. -III. 9 U. (युनाति, युनीते) To bind, fasten, join, unite. -With प्र to hold up, perform. -व्यति to mix; अन्योन्यं स्म व्यतियुतः शब्दाञ् शब्दैस्तु भीषणान् Bk. 8. 6.

युक्त *p. p.* **1** Joined, united. **2** Fastened, yoked, harnessed. **3** Fitted out, arranged. **4** Accompanied. **5** Furnished or endowed with, filled with, having, possessing (with instr. or in comp.). **6** Fixed or intent on, absorbed or engaged in (with loc.). **7** Active, diligent. **8** Skilful, experienced, clever. **9** Fit, proper, right, suitable (with gen. or loc.). **10** Primitive, not derived (from another word). -क्तः **1** A saint who has become one with the Supreme Spirit. -क्तं A team, yoke. -Comp. -अर्थ *a.* sensible, rational, significant. -कर्मन् *a.* entrusted with some duty. -दंड *a.* punishing justly; R. 4. 8. -मनस् *a.* attentive. -रूप *a.* fit, proper, worthy, suitable (with gen. or loc.); जन्म यस्य पुरोर्वंशे युक्तरूपमिदं तव *S.* 1. 7; अनुकारिणि पूर्वेषां युक्तरूपमिदं त्वयि 2. 16.

युक्तिः *f.* **1** Union, junction, combination. **2** Application, use, employment. **3** Yoking. **4** A practice, usage. **5** A means, an expedient, a plan, scheme. **6** A contrivance, device, trick. **7** Propriety, fitness, adjustment, aptness, suitableness. **8** Skill, art. **9** Reasoning, arguing, an argument. **10** Inference. deduction. **11** Reason, ground. **12** Arrangement (रचना) ; यत्र खल्वियं वाचोयुक्तिः Mâl. 1. **13** (In law) Probability, enumeration or specification of circumstances, such as time, place &c. युक्तिप्राप्तिक्रियाचिह्नसंबंधाभोगहेतुभिः Y. 2. 92. 212. **14** (In dramas). The regular chain or connection of events; cf. S. D. 343. **15** (In rhet.) Emblematical or covert expression of one's purpose or design. **16** Sum, total. **17** Alloying of metal. -Comp. -कथनं statement of reasons. -कर *a.* **1** suitable, fit. **2** proved. -ज्ञ *a.* skilled in expedients, invetive. -युक्त *a.* **1** suitable, fit. **2** expert, skilful. **3** eastablished, proved. **4** argumentative.

युगं **1** A yoke (*m.* also in this sense); युगव्यायतबाहुः R. 3. 34, 10. 57; *Si.* 3. 68. **2** A pair, couple, brace; कुचयोर्युगेन तरसा कलिता *Si.* 9. 72; स्तनयुग *S.* 1. 19. **3** A couple of stanzas forming one sentence; see युग्म. **4** An age of the world; (the Yugas are four:- कृत or सत्य, त्रेता, द्वापर and कलि; the duration of each is said to be respectively 1,728,000; 1,296,000; 864,000; and 432,000 years of men, the four together comprising 4,320,000 years of men which is equal to one Mahâyuga q. v.; it is also supposed that the regularly descending length of the Yugas represents a corresponding physical and moral deterioration in the people who live during each age, *Krita* being called the 'golden' and *Kali* or the present age the 'iron' age; धर्मसंस्थापनार्थाय संभवामि युगे युगे Bg. 4. 8; युगशतपरिवर्तान् *S.* 7. 34. **5** A generation, life; आसप्तमाद्युगात् Ms. 10. 64; जात्युत्कर्षो युगे ज्ञेयः पंचमे सप्तमेऽपि वा Y. 1. 96 (युगे = जन्मनि Mit.). **6** An expression for the number 'four', rarely for 'twelve'. -Comp. -अंतः **1** the end of the yoke. **2** the end of an age, end or destruction of the world; युगांतकालप्रतिसंहृतात्मनो जगंति यस्यां सविकाशमासत *Si.* 1. 23; R. 13. 6. **3** meridian, midday. -अवधिः end or destruction of the world; *Si.* 17. 40. -कीलकः the pin of a yoke. -पार्श्वग *a.* going to the side of the yoke, said of an ox while being broken in to the yoke. -बाहु *a.* long-armed; Ku. 2. 18.

युगंधरः -रं The pole of a carriage to which the yoke is fixed.

युगपद् *ind.* Simultaneously, all at once, all together, at the same time; Ku. 3. 1; oft. in comp.; *S.* 4. 2.

युगलं A pair, couple, बाहु°, हस्त°, चरण° &c.

युगलकं **1** A pair. **2** A couple of verses forming one sentence; see युग्म.

युग्म *a.* Even; युग्मासु पुत्रा जायंते स्त्रियोऽयुग्मासु रात्रिषु । तस्माद्युग्मासु पुत्रार्थी संविशेदार्तवे स्त्रियं Ms. 3. 48; Y. 1. 79. -ग्मं **1** A pair couple; see अयुग्म. **2** Junction, union. **3** Confluence (of rivers). **4** Twins. **5** A couple of stanzas forming one grammatical sentence; द्वाभ्यां युग्ममिति प्रोक्तं. **6** The sign *Gemini* of the zodiac.

युग्य *a.* **1** Fit to be yoked. **2** Yoked, harnessed. **3** Drawn by; as in अश्वयुग्यो रथः. -ग्यः Any yoked or draught animal, especially a chariot-horse; हरियुग्यं रथं तस्मै प्रजिघाय पुरंदरः R. 12. 84.

युज् I. 7 U. (युनक्ति, युंक्ते, युक्त) **1** To join, unite, attach, connect, add; तमर्थमिव भारत्या सुतया योक्तुमर्हसि Ku. 6. 79; see *pass.* below. **2** To yoke, harness, put to; भानुः सकृद्युक्ततुरंग एव *S.* 5. 4; Bg. 1. 14. **3** To furnish or endow with; as in गुणयुक्त. **4** To use, employ, apply; प्रशस्ते कर्मणि तथा सच्छब्दः पार्थ युज्यते Bg. 17. 26; Ms. 7. 204. **5** To appoint, set (with loc). **6** To direct, turn or fix upon (as the mind &c.). **7** To concentrate on'es attention upon; मनः संयम्य मच्चित्तो युक्त आसीत मत्परः Bg. 6. 14; युंजन्नेवं सदात्मानं 15. **8** To put, place or fix on (with loc.). **9** To prepare, arrange, make ready, fit. **10** To give, bestow, confer; आशिषं युयुजे. -*Pass.* (युज्यते) **1** To be joined or united with; रविपीतजला तपात्यये पुनरोघेन हि युज्यते नदी Ku. 4. 44; R. 8. 17. **2** To get, be possessed of; इष्टेन युज्यस्व *S.* 5; Mv. 7; R. 2. 65. **3** To be fit or right, be proper to, suit (with loc. or gen.); या यस्य युज्यते भूमिका तां खलु भावेन तथैव सर्वे वर्ग्याः पाठिताः Mâl. 1; त्रैलोक्यस्यापि प्रभुत्वं त्वयि युज्यते H. 1. **4** To be ready for; ततो युद्धाय युज्यस्व Bg. 2. 38, 50. **5** To be intent on, be absorbed in, be directed towards; Ms. 3. 75, 14. 35; Ki. 7. 13. -*Caus.* (योजयति-ते) **1** To join, unite, bring together; R. 7. 14. **2** To present, give, bestow; R. 10. 56. **3** To appoint, employ, use; शत्रुभिर्योजयेच्छत्रुं Pt. 4. 17. **4** To turn or direct towards; पापान्निवारयति योजयते हिताय Bh. 2. 72. **5** To excite, urge, instigate. **6** To perform, achieve. **7** To prepare, arrange, equip. -*Desid.* (युयुक्षति-ते) To wish to join, yoke, give &c. -With अनु (Atm.) **1** to ask, question; अन्वयुंक्त गुरुमीश्वरः क्षितेः R. 11. 62, 5. 18, *Si.* 13, 68. **2** to examine, put on trial; Ms. 8. 79. -अभि (Atm.) **1** to exert oneself, set about. **2** to attack, assail; भवंतमभियोक्तुमुद्युंक्ते Dk. **3** to accuse, charge; Ms. 8. 183. **4** to claim, demand (as in a law-suit); विभावितैकदेशेन देयं यदभियुज्यते V. 4. 17; Y. 2. 9. **5** say, speak. -उद् **1** to excite stimulate to exertion. **2** to endeavour, exert oneself, strive, भवंतमभियोक्तुमुद्युंक्ते Dk. **3** to prepare. -उप (Atm.). **1** to use, employ; षाड्गुण्यमुपयुंजीत *Si.* 2. 93; पणबंधमुखान्गुणानजः षडुपायुंक्त समीक्ष्य तत्फलं R. 8. 21; M. 5. 12. **2** to taste, enjoy, experience (fig. also); R. 18. 46, Bk. 8. 39. **4** to consume, eat; Ms. 8. 40. -नि (Atm.) **1** to appoint, depute, order (with loc.); यन्मां विधेयविषये सभवान्नियुंक्ते Mâl. 1. 9; असाधुदर्शी तत्रभवान् काश्यपः य इमामाश्रमधर्मे नियुंक्ते *S.* 1; Ku. 3. 13; R. 5. 29. **2** to join, unite. **3** to prescribe, ordain. (-*Caus.*) **1** to join, unite, provide or endow with give to; Ku. 4. 42. **2** to yoke, harness. **3** to incite, urge, Bg. 3. 1. -प्र (Atm.) 1 to use, employ; अयमपि

च गिरं नस्त्वत्प्रबोधयुक्तां R. 5. 75; सद्भावे साधुभाव च सदित्येतत्प्रयुज्यते Bg. 17. 26. **2** to appoint, employ, direct, order,; मा मां प्रयुंक्थाः कुलकीर्तिलोपे Bk. 3. 54; प्रायुक्त राज्ये बत दुष्करे त्वां 3. 51; Ku. 7. 85. **3** to give, bestow, confer; आशिषं प्रयुयुजे न वाहिनीं R. 11. 6, 2. 70, 5. 35; 15. 8. **4** to move, set in motion; गरुत्प्रयुक्ताः (बाललताः) R. 2. 10. **5** to excite, urge, prompt, drive on; Ku. 1. 21; Bg. 3. 36. **6** to perform, do; R. 7. 86, 17. 12. **7** to represent on the stage, act, perform; उत्तरं रामचरितं तत्प्रणीतंप्रयुज्यते U. 1. 2; परिषदि प्रयुंजानस्य मम Ku. 1. 8. to lend for use, put to interest (as money); Ms. 8. 146; **-वि** (Atm.) **1** to leave, abandon. Ki. 2. 49; R. R. 13. 63. **2** to separate; पुरो वियुक्ते मिथुने कृपावती Ku. 5. 26. **3** to relax, slacken. **-विनि 1** use, expend. **2** to appoint, employ. **3** to divide, apportion, distribute; प्रत्येकं विनियुक्तात्मा कथं न ज्ञास्यसि प्रभो Ku. 2. 31. **4** to disconnect, separate. **-सं** to be united with (in *pass.*); संयोक्ष्यसे स्वेन वपुर्महिम्ना. R. 5. 55. (*-Caus.*) to unite, join. -II. 1. 10 P. (योजति, योजयति) To unite, join, yoke &c.; see युज् above. -III. 4 A. (युज्यते) to concentrate the mind (identical with the *pass.* of युज् I)

युज् *a.* (At the end of comp.) **1** Joined or united with, yoked, drawn by &c. **2** Even, not odd. *-m.* **1** A joiner, one who unites or joins. **2** A sage, one who devotes himself to abstract meditation. **3** A pair, couple (*n.* also in this sense).

युंजानः 1 A driver, charioteer. **2** A Brâhmaṇa who is engaged in the practice of Yoga to obtain union with the Supreme Spirit.

युत *p. p.* **1** United, joined or united with. **2** Provided or endowed with; as in गुणगणयुतो नरः.

युतकं 1 A pair. **2** Union, friendship, alliance. **3** A nuptial gift. **4** A sort of dress worn by women. **5** The edge of a woman's garment.

युतिः *f.* **1** Union, junction. **2** Being endowed with. **3** Gaining possession of. **4** Sum, addition. **5** (In astr.) Conjunction.

युद्धं 1 War, battle, fight, engagement, contest, struggle, combat; वत्सं केयं वार्ता युद्धं युद्धमिति U.6. **2** (In astr.) The opposition or conflict of planets; **-Comp.** **-अवसानं** cessation of hostilities, a truce. **-आचार्यः** a military preceptor **-उन्मत** *a.* frantic in battle. **-कारिन्** *a.* fighting, contending. **-भूः -भूमिः** *f.* a battle-field. **-मार्गः** military stratagems or tactics, manœuvres. **-रंगः** battle-field, a battle-arena. **-वीरः 1** a warrior, hero, champion. **2** (in Rhet.) the sentiment of heroism arising out of military prowess, the sentiment of chivalrous heroism; see S. D. 234 and R G. under युद्धवीर. **-सारः** a horse.

युध् 4 A. (युध्यते, युद्ध) To fight, struggle, contend with, wage war; Bg. 1. 23; Bk. 5. 101. *-Caus.* (योधयति-ते) **1** To cause to fight. **2** To oppose or encounter in fight with; R. 12. 50. *-Desid.* (युयुत्सते) To wish to fight. -WITH **नि** to wrestle, box. **-प्रति** to encounter in fight, oppose.

युध् *f.* War, battle, fight, contest; निघातयिष्यन्युधि यातुधानान् Bk. 2. 21; सदसि वाक्पटुता युधि विक्रमः Bh. 2. 63.

युधानः A warrior, a man of the warrior caste.

युप् 4 P. (युप्यति) **1** To efface, blot out. **2** To trouble.

युयुः A horse.

युयुत्सा Desire of fighting, hostile intention.

युयुत्सु *a.* Wishing to fight, hostile, bellicose, धर्मक्षेत्रे कुरुक्षेत्रे समवेता युयुत्सवः Bg 1. 1.

युवतिः-ती *f.* **1** A young woman, any young female (whether of men or animals); सुरयुवतिसंभवं किल मुनेरपत्यं S. 2. 8; so इभयुवतिः.

युवन् *a.* (युवतिः-ती or यूनी *f.*; compar यवीयस् or कनीयस्; superl. यविष्ठ or कनिष्ठ) **1** Young, youthful, adult, arrived at puberty. **2** Strong, healthy. **3** Excellent, good. *-m.* (nom. युवा, युवानौ, युवानः acc. pl. यूनः, instr.pl. युवभिः &c.) **1** A young man, a youth; सा यूनि तस्मिन्नभिलाषबंधं शशाक शालीनतया न वक्तुं R. 6. 81. **2** A younger descendant (the elder being still alive); जीवति तु वंश्ये युवा P. IV. 1. 113. (see Sk. thereon). **-Comp.** **-खलति** *a.* (तिः -ती *f.*) bald in youth. **-जरत्** (-ती *f.*) appearing old in youth, prematurely old. **-राज्** *m.*, **-राजः** an heir-apparent, a prince-royal, crown-prince; (असौ) नृपेण चक्रे युवराजशब्दभाक् R. 3. 35.

युष्मद् The base of the second personal pronoun); (*Nom.* त्वं, युवां, यूयं) Thou, you; (at the beginning of several compounds).

युष्मादृश् -श *a.* Like you.

यूकः -का A louse; Ms. 1. 45.

यूतिः *f.* Mixing, union, junction, connection; करोमि यो वहिर्यूतीन पिधध्वं पाणि भिर्दशः Bk. 7. 69.

यूथं A herd, flock, multitude, a large number or troop (as of beasts); स्त्रीरत्नेषु ममोर्वशी प्रियतमा यूथे तवेयं वशा V. 4. 25; S. 5. 5. **-Comp.** **-नाथः, -पः, -पतिः** **1** the leader of a troop or band. **2** the head of a flock or herd (usually of elephants), a lordly elephant; गजयूथप यूथिकाशबलकेशी V. 4. 24.

यूथिका, -यूथी A kind of jasmine or its flower; यूथिकाशबलकेशी V. 4. 24; Me. 26.

यूपः 1 A sacrificial post (usually made of bamboo or Khadira wood) to which the victim is fastened at the time of immolation; अपेक्ष्यते साधुजनेन वैदिकी श्मशानशूलस्य न यूपसत्क्रिया Ku. 5. 73. **2** A trophy.

यूषः, -षं, यूषन् *m.*, *n.* Soup, broth, pease-soup. (यूषन् has no forms for the first five inflections and is optionally substituted for यूष after acc. dual).

येन *ind.* (Strictly instr. sing. of यद् used adverbially) **1** Whereby, by which, wherefore, on which account, by means of which; किं तद्येन मनो हर्तुमलं स्यातां न शृण्वतां R. 15. 64, 14. 74. **2** so that; दर्शय तं चौरसिंहं येन व्यापादयामि Pt. 4 **3** Since, because.

योक्त्रं 1 A cord, rope, thong, halter. **2** The tie of the yoke of a plough. **3** The rope by which an animal is tied to the pole of a carriage.

योगः 1 Joining, uniting. **2** Union, junction, combination; उपरागांते शशिनः समुपगता रोहिणी योगं S. 7. 22; गुणमहतां महते गुणाय योगः Ki. 10. 25; (वा) योगस्तडित्तोयदयोरिवास्तु R. 3. 25. **3** Contact, touch, connection; तमंकमारोप्य शरीरयोगजैः सुखैर्निषिंचंतमिवामृतं त्वचि R. 3. 26. **4** Employment, application, use; एतैरुपाययोगैस्तु शक्यास्ताः परिरक्षितुं Ms. 9. 10; R. 10. 86. **5** Mode, manner, course, means; कथायोगेन बुध्यते H. I 'in the course of conversation'. **6** Consequence, result; (mostly at the end of comp. or in abl.); रक्षायोगादयमपि तपः प्रत्यहं संचिनोति S. 2. 14; Ku. 7. 55. **7** A yoke. **8** A conveyance, vehicle, carriage. **9** An armour. **10** Fitness, propriety, suitableness. **11** An occupation, a work, business. **12** A trick, fraud, device. **13** An expedient, a plan, means in general. **14** Endeavour, zeal, diligence, assiduity; Ms. 7. 44. **15** Remedy, cure. **16** A charm, spell, incantation, magic, magical art. **17** Gaining, acquiring, acquisition. **18** Wealth, substance. **19** A rule, precept. **20** Dependence, relation, regular order or connection, dependence of one word upon another. **21** Etymology or derivation of the meaning of a word. **22** The etymological meaning of a word (opp. रूढि). **23** Deep and abstract meditation, concentration of the mind, contemplation of the Supreme Spirit, which in *Yoga* phil. is defined as चित्तवृत्तिनिरोध; सती सती योगविसृष्टदेहा Ku. 1. 21; योगेनांते तनुं त्यजां R. 1. 8. **24** The system of philosophy established by Patanjali, which is considered to be the second division of the Sânkhya philosophy, but is practically reckoned as a separate system. (The chief aim of the *Yoga* philosophy is to teach the means by which the human soul may be completely united with the Supreme Spirit and thus secure absolution; and deep abstract meditation is laid down as the chief means of securing this end, elaborate rules being given for the proper practice of such *Yoga* or concentration of mind). **25** (In arith.) Addition. **26** (In astr.) Conjunction, lucky conjunction. **27** A combination of stars. **28** N. of a particular astronomical division of time (27 such *Yogas* are usually enumerated). **29** The principal star in a lunar mansion. **30** Devotion, pious seeking after god. **31** A spy, secret agent. **32** A traitor, a violator of truth of confidence. **–Comp. –अंगं** a means or attaining *Yoga*; (these are eight; for their names see यम 5). **–आचारः 1** the practice or observance of *Yoga*. **2** a follower of that Buddhist school which maintains the eternel existence of intelligence or विज्ञान alone. **–आचार्यः 1** a teacher of magic. **2** a teacher of the *Yoga* philosophy. **–आधमनं** a fraudulent pledge; Ms. 8. 165. **–आरूढ** *a.* engaged in profound and abstract meditation. **–आसनं** a posture suited to profound and abstract meditation. **–इंद्रः, –ईशः, –ईश्वरः 1** an adept in or a master of *Yoga*. **2** One who has obtained superhuman faculties. **3** a magician. **4** a deity. **5** an epithet of *S*iva. **6** of Yâjnavalkya. **–क्षेमः 1** security of possession, keeping safe of property. **2** the charge for securing property from accidents, insurance. **3** welfare, well-being, security, prosperity; तेषां नित्याभियुक्तानां योगक्षेमं वहाम्यहं Bg. 9. 22; मुग्धाया मे जनन्या योगक्षेमं वहस्व M. 4. **4** property, profit, gain. (**–मौ, –मे** or **–मं** *i. e. m.* or *n.* dual or *n.* sing.) acquisition and preservation (of property), gain and security, preserving the old and acquiring the new (not previously obtained); अलब्धलाभो योगः स्यात् क्षेमो लब्धस्य पालनम्; see Y. 1. 100 and Mit. thereon. **–चूर्णं** a magical powder, a powder having magical virtues; कल्पितमनेन योगचूर्णमिश्रितमौषधं चंद्रगुप्ताय Mu. 2. **–तारका, –तारा** the chief star in a *Nakshatra* or constellation. **–दानं 1** communicating the *Yaga* doctrine. **2** a fraudulent gift. **–धारणा** perseverance or steady continuance in devotion. **–नाथः** an epithet of *S*iva. **–निद्रा 1** a state of half contemplation and half sleep, a state between sleep and wakefulness; *i. e.* light sleep; योगनिद्रां गतस्य मम Pt. 1; H. 3. 75; Bh. 3. 41. **2** particularly, the sleep of Vishṇu at the end of a Yuga; R. 10. 14, 13. 6. **–पट्टं** a cloth thrown over the back and knees of an ascetic during abstract meditation. **–पतिः** an epithet of Vishṇu. **–बलं 1** the power of devotion or abstract meditation, any supernatural power. **2** power of magic. **–माया 1** the magical power of the *Yoga*. **2** the power of God in the creation of the world personified as a deity; (भगवतः सर्जनार्था शक्तिः). **3** N. of Durgâ. **–रंगः** the orange. **–रूढ** *a.* having an etymological as well as a special or conventional meaning (said of a word); *e. g.* the word पंकज etymologically means 'anything produced in mud', but in usage or popular convention it is restricted to some things only produced in mud, such as the lotus; cf. the word आतपत्र or 'parasol'. **–रोचना** a kind of magical ointment said to have the power of making one invisible or invulnerable; तेन च अ परितुष्टेन योगरोचना मे दत्ता Mk. 3. **–वर्तिका** magical lamp or wick. **–वाहिन्** *m.*, *n.* a medium for mixing medicines; *e. g.* honey; नानाद्रव्यात्मकत्वाच्च योगवाहि परं मधु Susr. **–वाही 1** an alkali. **2** honey. **3** quicksilver. **–विक्रयः** a fraudulent sale. **–विद्** *a.* conversant with *Yoga*. (*–m.*) **1** an epithet of *S*iva. **2** a practiser of *Yoga*. **3** a follower of the *Yoga* doctrines. **4** a magician. **5** a compounder of medicines. **–विभागः** separation of that which is usually combined together into one; especially, the separation of the words of a Sûtra, the splitting of one rule into two or more (frequently used by Patanjali in his Mahâbhâshya; *e. g.* on अदसो मात् P. I. 1. 12). **–शास्त्रं** the *Yoga* philosophy. **–समाधिः** the absorption of the soul in profound and abstract contemplation; तमसः परमापदव्ययं पुरुषं योगसमाधिना रघुः R. 8. 24; योगविधि 8. 22. **–सारः** a universal remedy; a panacea. **–सेवा** the practice of abstract meditation.

योगिन् *a.* **1** Connected or endowed with. **2** Possessed of magical powers. *–m.* **1** A contemplative saint, a devotee, an ascetic; सेवाधर्मः परमगहनो योगिनामप्यगम्यः Pt. 1. 285; बभूव योगी किल कार्तवीर्यः R. 6. 38. **2** A magician, sorcerer. **3** A follower of the *Yoga* system of philosophy. **–नी 1** A female magician, witch, sorceress, fairy. **2** A female devotee. **3** N. of a class of female attendants on *S*iva, or Durgâ; (they are usually said to be eight).

योगेष्टं Lead.

योग्य *a.* **1** Fit, proper, suitatble, appropriate, qualified; योग्योयं दृश्यते नरः. **2** Fit or suitable for, qualified for capable of, able to (with loc, dat. or even gen. or in comp.). **3** Useful, serviceable. **4** Fit for *Yoga* or abstract meditation. **–ग्यः** A calculator of expedients. **–ग्या 1** Exercise or practice in general; अपरः प्रणिधानयोग्यया मरुतः पंचशरीरगोचरान् R. 8. 19; so मानयोग्या Kâv. 2. 243; धनुर्योग्या, अस्त्रयोग्या &c. **2** Martial exercise, drill. **–ग्यं 1** A conveyance, carriage, vehicle. **2** Sandal-wood. **3** A cake. **4** Milk.

योग्यता 1 Ability, capability; न युद्धयोग्यतामस्य पश्यामि सह राक्षसैः Râm. **2** Fitness, propriety. **3** Appropriateness. **4** (In Nyâya phil.) Fitness or compatibility of sense, the absence of absurdity in the mutual connection of the things signified by the words; *e. g.* in अग्निना सिंचति there is no योग्यता; it is thus defined: एकपदार्थेऽपरपदार्थसंसर्गो योग्यता Tarka. K.

योजनं 1 Joining, uniting, yoking. **2** Applying, fixing. **3** Preparation, arrangement. **4** Grammatical construction, construing the sense of a passage. **5** A measure of distance equal to four *Krosas* or eight or nine miles; न योजनशतं दूरं बाह्यमानस्य तृष्णया H. 1. 146. **6** Exciting, instigation. **7** Concentration of the mind, abstraction. (= योग q. v.). **–ना 1** Junction, union, connection. **2** Grammatical construction. **–Comp. –गंधा 1** musk. **2** N. of Satyavatî, mother of Vyâsa.

योत्रं See योक्त्र.

योधः 1 A warrior, soldier, combatant; सहास्मदीयैरपि योधमुख्यैः Mb. **2** War, battle. **–Comp. –अगारः –रं** a soldier's dwelling, a barrack. **–धर्मः** the law of soldiers, a military law. **–संरावः** mutual defiance of combatants, a challenge.

योधनं War, battle, contest.

योधिन् *m.* A warrior, soldier, combatant.

योनिः *m. f.* **1** Womb, uterus, vulva, the female organ of generation. **2** Any place of birth or origin, source, origin, generating cause, spring, fountain; सा योनिः सर्ववैराणां सा हि लोकस्य निर्ऋतिः U. 5. 30; Ku. 2. 9, 4. 43; oft. at the end of comp. in the sense of 'sprung or produced from'; Bg. 5. 22. **3** A mine. **4** An abode, a place, repository, seat, receptacle. **5** Home, lair. **6** A family, stock, race, birth, form of existence; as मनुष्ययोनि, पक्षि°, पशु°, &c. **7** Water. **–Comp. –गुणः** the quality of the womb or place of origin. **–ज** *a.* born of the womb, viviparous. **–देवता** the asterism पूर्वफल्गुनी. **–भ्रंशः** fall of the womb, *prolapsus uteri*. **–रंजनं** the menstrual discharge. **–लिंगं** the clitoris. **–संकरः**

mixture of caste by unlawful intermarriage; Ms. 10. 60.

यौनी See योनि.

योपनं 1 Effacing, blotting out. 2 Anything used for effacing. 3 Confusing, perplexing. 4 Molesting, oppressing, destroying.

योषा, योषित् *f.*, योषिता A woman, a girl, a young woman in general; गच्छंतीनां रमणवसतिं योषितां तत्र नक्तं Me. 37; Si. 4. 42, 8. 25.

यौक्तिक *a.* (की *f.*) 1 Suitable, fit, proper. 2 Logical, based on argument or reasoning. 3 Deducible. 4 Usual, customary. -कः A king's boon companion, cf. नर्मसचिव.

यौगः A follower of the *Yoga* system of philosophy.

यौगपद्यं Simultaneity.

यौगिक *a.* (की *f.*) 1 Useful, serviceable, proper. 2 Usual. 3 Derivative, etymological, agreeing with the derivation of the word (opp. रूढ or 'conventional'). 4 Remedial. 5 Relating to or derived from *Yoga*.

यौतक *a.* (की *f.*) Forming the rightful or exclusive property of any one, rightfully belonging to any one; विभागभावना ज्ञेया गृहक्षेत्रैश्च यौतकैः Y. 2. 149. -कं 1 Private property in general. 2 A woman's dowry, a woman's private property (given to her at marriage); मातुस्तु यौतकं यत्स्यात्कुमारीभाग एव सः Ms. 9. 131.

यौतवं A measure in general.

यौध *a.* (धी *f.*) Warlike.

यौन *a.* (नी *f.*) 1 Uterine. 2 Resulting from marriage, matrimonial; Ms. 2. 10. -नं Marriage, matrimonial alliance; Ms. 11. 180.

यौवतं 1 An assemblage of young women; अवधूत्य दिवोपि यौवतैर्न सहाधीतवतीमिमामहं N. 2. 41. 2 The quality of a young woman (beauty &c.), the state of being a young woman; अहो विबुधयौवतं वहसि तन्वि पृथ्वीगता Gît. 10 (सुरसुंदरीरूपं).

यौवनं 1 Youth (fig. also), youthfulness, prime or bloom of, youth, puberty; मुग्धत्वस्य च यौवनस्य च सखे मध्ये मधुश्रीः स्थिता V. 2. 7; यौवनेऽभ्यस्तविद्यानां R. 1. 8; 6. 50; दिनयौवनोत्थान् 13. 20. 2 A number of young persons, especially women. -Comp. -अंत *a.* ending in youth, being a prolonged youth; Ku. 6. 44. -आरंभः prime of youth, budding youth. -दर्पः 1 youthful pride. 2 indiscretion natural to youth. -लक्षणं 1 a sign of youth. 2 charm, loveliness. 3 the female breast..

यौवनकं Youth.

यौवनाश्वः N. of Mândhâtri, son of Yuvanâsva.

यौवराज्यं The rank or rights of an heir-apparent यौवराज्येऽभिषिक्तः crowned heir-apparent.

यौष्माक *a.* (की *f.*); यौष्माकीण *a.* Your, yours.

र.

रः 1 Fire. 2 Heat. 3 Love, desire. 4 Speed.

रंहु 1 P. (रंहति) To move or go with speed, hasten; न ररंहाश्वकुंजरं Bk. 14. 98. -*Caus.* (रंहयति-ते according to some 10 U.) 1 To cause to move rapidly, urge on. 2 To cause to flow. 3 To go. 4 To speak.

रंहतिः *f.* Speed, velocity.

रंहस् *m.* 1 Speed, velocity; R. 2. 34; Si. 12. 7. Ki. 2. 40. 2 Eagerness, violence, vehemence, impetuosity.

रक्त *p. p.* 1 Coloured, dyed, tinged, painted; आभाति बालातपरक्तसानुः R. 6. 60. 2 Red, crimson, blood-red; सांध्यं तेजः प्रतिनवजवापुष्परक्तं दधानः Me. 36; so रक्ताशोक, रक्तांशुक &c. 3 Enamoured, impassioned, attached, affected with love; अयमैंद्रीमुखं पश्य रक्तश्चुंबति चन्द्रमाः Chandr. 5. 58 (where it has sense 2 also). 4 Dear, beloved. 5 Lovely, charming, sweet, pleasant; श्रोत्रेषु संमूर्छति रक्तमासां गीतानुगं वारिमृदंगवाद्यं R. 16. 64. 6 Fond of play, sporting, playful. -क्तः 1 Red colour. 2 Safflower. -क्ता 1 Lac. 2 The plant गुंजा. -क्तं 1 Blood. 2 Copper. 3 Saffron. 4 Vermilion. -Comp. -अक्ष *a.* 1 red-eyed. 2 fearful. (-क्षः) 1 a buffalo. 2 a pigeon. -अंकः a coral. -अंगः 1 a bug. 2 the planet Mars. 3 the disc of the sun or moon. -अधिमंथः inflammation of the eyes. -अंबरं a red garment. (-रः) a vagrant devotee wearing red garments. -अर्बुदः a bloody tumour. -अशोकः the red-flowered Asoka; M. 3. 5. -आधारः the skin. -आभ *a.* red-looking. -आशयः any viscus containing or secreting blood (as the heart, spleen, or liver). -उत्पलं the red lotus. -उपलं red chalk, red earth. -कंठ, -कंठिन् *a.* sweet-voiced. (-*m.*) the cuckoo. -कंदः, -कंदलः coral. -कमलं the red lotus. -चंदनं 1 red-sandal. 2 saffron. -चूर्णं vermilion. -छर्दिः *f.* vomiting blood. -छर्दिः F. vomiting blood. -जिह्वः alion. -तुंडः a parrot. -दृश् *m.* a pigeon. -धातुः 1 red chalk or orpiment. 2 copper. -पः a demon, an evil sptirit. -पल्लवः the Asoka tree. -पा a leech. -पातः blood-shed. -पाद *a.* red-footed. (-दः) 1 a bird with red feet, a parrot. 2 a war-chariot. 3 an elephant. -पायिन् *m.* a bug. -पायिनी a leech. -पिंडं 1 a red pimple. 2 a spontaneous discharge of blood from the nose and mouth. -प्रमेहः the passing of blood in the urine. -भवं flesh. -मोक्षः, -मोक्षणं bleeding. -वटी, -वरटी small-pox. -वर्गः 1 lac. 2 the pomegranate tree. 3 safflower. -वर्ण *a.* red-coloured. (-र्णः) 1 red-colour. 2 cochineal insect. (-र्णं) gold -वसन, वासस् *a.* clothed in red. -शासनं vermilion. -शीर्षकः a species of heron. -संध्यकं the red lotus. -सारं red sandal.

रक्तक *a.* 1 Red. Impassioned, enamoured, fond of. 3 Pleasing, amusing. 4 Bloody. -कः 1 A red garment. 2 An impassioned man, amorous person. 3 A sporter.

रक्तिः *f.* 1 Pleasingness, loveliness, charmingness. 2 Attachment, affection, loyalty, devotion.

रक्तिका The *Gunjá* plant or its seed used as a weight.

रक्तिमन् *m.* Redness.

रक्ष् 1 P. (रक्षति, रक्षित) 1 To protect, guard, take care of, watch, tend (as cattle); rule, govern (as earth); भवानिमां प्रतिकृतिं रक्षतु *S.* 6; ज्ञास्यसि कियद्भुजो मे रक्षति मौर्वीकिणांक इति *S.* 1. 13. 2 To keep, not to divulge; रहस्यं रक्षति. 3 To preserve, save, spare (often with abl.); अलब्धं चैव लिप्सेत लब्धं रक्षेदवक्षयात् H. 2. 8; आपदर्थे धनं रक्षेत् H. 1. 42; R. 2. 50, 11. 87. 4 To avoid; Mu. 1. 2. (Prepositions like अभि, परि, सं are prefixed to this root without any material change in meaning).

रक्षक *a.* (क्षिका *f.*) Guarding, protecting. -कः A protector, guardian, guard, watchman.

रक्षणं Protecting, protection, preservation, watching, guarding &c. (Also रक्ष्णं). -णी A rein, bridle.

रक्षस *n.* An evil spirit, a demon, an imp, a goblin; चतुर्दशसहस्राणि रक्षसां भीमकर्मणाम् । त्रयश्च दूषणखरत्रिमूर्धानो रणे हताः ॥ U. 2. 15. -Comp. -ईशः, -नाथः an epithet of Râvaṇa. -जननी night. -सभं an assembly of demons.

रक्षा 1 Protection, preservation, guarding; मयि सृष्टिर्हि लोकानां रक्षा युष्मास्व-

वस्थिता Ku. 2. 28; Si. 18. 31; S. 1. 14; R. 2. 4, 8; Me. 43. **2** Care, security. **3** A guard, watch. **4** An amulet or mystical object used as a charm, any preservative; as in रक्षाकरंड q. v. below. **4** A tutelary deity. **5** Ashes. **6** A piece of silk or thread fastened round the wrist on particular occasions, especially on the full-moon day of Srâvaṇa, as an amulet or preservative; (रक्षी also in this sense). **–Comp.** **–अधिकृतः 1** one who is entrusted with protection or superintendence, a superintendent or governor. **2** a magistrate. **3** the chief police-officer. **–अपेक्षकः 1** a porter, door-keeper. **2** a guard of the women's apartments. **3** a catamite. **4** an actor. **–करंडः, -करंडकं** a preservative casket, an amulet, a magical or charmed casket; अहो रक्षाकरंडकमस्य मणिबंधे न दृश्यते S. 7. **–गृहं** a lying-in-chamber; रक्षागृहगता दीपाः प्रत्यादिष्टा इवाभवन् R. 10. 59. **–पत्रः** a species of birch tree. **–पालः,-पुरुषः** a watchman, guard, police. **–प्रदीपः** a lamp kept burning, as a sort of protection against evil-spirits. **–भूषणं, -मणिः, -रत्नं** an ornament or jewel worn as an amulet or preservative against evil spirits.

रक्षितृ, रक्षिन् *a.* Protecting, guarding, ruling &c.; N. 1. 1. *–m.* **1** A protector, guardian, saviour. **2** A guard, watchman, sentinel, policeman; अये पदशब्द इव मा नाम रक्षिणः Mk. 3.

रघुः N. of a celebrated king of the solar race, son of Dilîpa and father of Aja. [He appears to have been called *Raghu* from *ragh* or *rangh* 'to go', becaue his father foresaw that the boy would 'go' to the end of the holy learning as well as of his enemies in battle; cf. R. 3. 21. True to his name, he commenced the conquest of the directions, went over the whole of the then kuown world, overcame kings in battle, and returned, covered with glory and laden with spoils. He then performed the *Visvajit* sacrifice in which he gave away everything to Brahma*n*as and made his son Aja successor to the throne]. **–Comp.** **–नंदनः, –नाथः, –पतिः, -श्रेष्ठः, -सिंहः** &c. epithets of Râma.

रंक *a.* **1** Mean, poor, beggarly, wretched, miserable. **2** Slow. **–कः** A beggar, wetch, any hungry or half-starved being; प्रेतरंकः Mâl. 5. 16 'the famished or half-starved spirit'; Pt. 1. 254.

रंकुः A dear, an antelope; N. 2. 83.

रंगः 1 Colour, hue, dye, paint. **2** A stage, theatre, play-house, an arena, any place of public amusement, as in रंगविघ्नोपशांतये S. D. 281. **3** A place of assembly. **4** The members of an assembly, the audience; अहो रागबद्धचित्तवृत्तिरालिखित इव सर्वतो रंगः S. 1; रंगस्य दर्शयित्वा निवर्तते नर्तकी यथा नृत्यात् । पुरुषस्य तथात्मानं प्रकाश्य विनिवर्तते प्रकृतिः ॥ Sarva. S. **5** A field of battle. **6** Dancing, singing, acting. **7** Mirth, diversion. **8** Borax. **9** The nasal modification of a vowel; सरंगं कंपयेत्कंपं रथीवेति निदर्शनं Sik. 30; so, 26, 27, 28. **–गः,-गं** Tin. **–Comp.** **–अंगणं** an arena, an amphitheatre. **–अवतरणं 1** entrance on the stage. **2** an actor's profession. **–अवतारकः, -अवतारिन्** *m.* an actor. **–आजीवः 1** an actor. **2** a painter; so उपजीविन् *m.* **–कारः,-जीवकः** a painter. **–चरः 1** an actor, a player. **2** a gladiator. **–जं** red lead. **–देवता** the goddess supposed to preside over sports and public diversions generally. **–द्वारं 1** a stage-door. **2** the prologue of a play. **–भूतिः** *f.* the night of full moon in the month of Asvina. **–भूमिः** *f.* **1** a stage, theatre. **2** an arena, battle-field. **–मंडपः** a theatre. **–मातृ** *f.* **1** lac, red-dye; or the insect which produces it. **2** a bawd, procuress. **–वस्तु** *n.* a paint. **–वाटः** an arena, a place enclosed for plays, dancing &c. **–शाला** a dancing-hall, a theatre, play-house.

रंघ् 1. U. (रंघति-ते) **1** To go. **2** To go quickly, hasten; द्वारं ररंघतुर्यम्यं Bk. 14. 15.

रच् 10 U. (रचयति-ते, रचित) **1** To arrange prepare, make ready, contrive, plan; पुष्पाणां प्रकरः स्मितेन रचितो नो कुंदजात्यादिभिः Amaru. 40; रचयति शयनं सचकितनयनं Gît. 5. **2** To make, form, effect, create, produce; मायाविकल्परचितैः स्यंदनैः R. 13. 75; माधुर्यं मधुबिंदुना रचयितुं क्षारांबुधेरीहते Bh. 2. 6; मौलौ वा रचयांजलिं Ve. 3. 40. **3** To write, compose, put together (as a work); अश्वधाटीं जगन्नाथो विश्वहृद्यामरीरचत् Asvad. 26; S. 3. 15. **4** To place in or upon, fix on; रचयति चिकुरे कुरबककुसुमं Gît. 7; Ku. 4. 18, 34; S. 6. 17. **5** To adorn, decorate; Me. 66. **6** To direct (the mind &c.) towards. **–With आ** to arrange. **–वि 1** to arrange. **2** to compose. **3** to effect, produce, make; Me. 95.; Bv. 1. 30.

रचनं-ना 1 Arrangement, preparation, disposition; अभिषेक°, संगीत° &c. **2** Formation, creation, production; अन्यैव कापि रचना वचनावलीनां Bv. 1. 69; so भ्रुकुटिरचना Me. 50. **3** Performance, completion, accomplishment, effecting; कुरु मम वचनं सत्वररचनं Gît. 5; R. 10. 77. **4** A literary work or production, work, composition; संक्षिप्ता वस्तुरचना S. D. 422. **5** Dressing the hair. **6.** An array or arrangement of troops. **7** A creation of the mind, an artificial fancy.

रजः See रजस्.

रजकः A washerman.

रजका-की A washerwoman.

रजत *a.* **1** Silvery, made of silver. **2** Whitish. **–तं 1** Silver; शुक्तौ रजतमिदमिति ज्ञानं भ्रमः; Ki. 5. 41; N. 22. 52. **2** Gold. **3** A pearl-ornament or necklace. **4** Blood. **5** Ivory. **6** An asterism, a constellation.

रजनिः –नी *f.* Night; हरिरभिमानी रजनिरिदानीमियमपि याति विरामं Gît. 5. **–Comp.** **–करः** the moon. **–चरः** a night-stalker, demon, goblin. **–जलं** night-dew, hoar-frost. **–पतिः, –रमणः** the moon. **–मुखं** nightfall, evening.

रजनिंमन्य *a.* Passing for or looking like night (as a day); Bk. 7. 13.

रजस् *m.* **1** Dust, power, dirt; धन्यास्तदंगरजसा मलिनीभवंति S. 7. 17; आत्मोद्भवैरपि रजोभिरलंघनीयाः 1. 8; R. 1. 42; 6 32. **2** The dust or pollen of flowers; भूयात्कुशेशयरजोमृदुरेणुरस्याः (पंथाः) S. 4. 10; Me. 33, 65. **3** A mote in a sun-beam, any small particle (of matter); cf. Ms. 8. 132 and Y. 1. 362. **4** A ploughed or cultivated land, arabie field. **5** Gloom, darkness. **6** Foulness, passion, emotion, moral or mental darkness; अपथे पदमर्पयंति हि श्रुतवंतोऽपि रजोनिमीलिताः R. 9. 74. **7** The second of the three Guṇas or constituent qualities of all material substances (the other two being सत्व and तमस्, रजस् is supposed to be the cause of the great activity seen in creatures; it predominates in men, as *Sattva* and *Tamas* predominate in gods and demons); अंतर्गतमपास्तं मे रजसोऽपि परं तमः Ku. 6. 69; Bg. 6. 27; Mâl. 1. 20. **8** Menstrual discharge, menses; Ms. 4. 41, 5. 66. **–Comp.** **–गुणः** see (7) above. **–तमस्क** *a.* being under the influence of both *rajas* and *tamas*. **-तोकः –कं, -पुत्रः 1** greediness, avarice. **2** 'the child of passion', a term applied to a person to show that he is quite insignificant. **–दर्शनं** the first appearance of the menstrual excretion, first menstrual flow. **–बंधः** suppression of menstruation. **–रसः** darkness. **–शुद्धिः** pure condition of the menses. **–हरः** 'dirt-remover', a washerman.

रजसानुः 1 A could. **2** Soul, heart.

रजस्वल *a.* Dusty, covered with dust; R. 11. 60; Si. 17. 61; (where it also means 'being in menses.') **2** Full of passion (रजस्) or emotion; Ms. 6. 77. **–लः** A buffalo. **–ला 1** A woman during the menses; रजस्वलाः परिमालिनांबरश्रियः Si. 17. 61; Y. 3. 229; R. 11. 60. **2** A marriageable girl.

रज्जुः *f.* **1** A rope, cord, string. **2** N. of a sinew proceeding from the vertebral column. **3** A lock of braided hair. **–Comp.** **–दालकं** a kind of wild fowl; so रज्जुवालः. **–पेडा** a rope-basket.

रंज् 1. 4. U. (रजति-ते, रज्यति-ते, रक्त *pass.* रज्यते; *desid.* रिरंक्षति) **1** To be dyed or coloured, to redden, become red, glow; कोपरज्यन्मुखश्रीः U. 5. 2; नेत्रे स्वयं रज्यतः 5. 26; N. 3. 120; 7. 60, 22. 52. **2** To dye, tinge, colour, paint. **2** To be attached or devoted to (with loc.); देवानियं निषधराजरुचस्त्यजंती रूपादर-ज्यत नले न विदर्भसुभ्रूः N. 13. 38; S. D. 111. **4** To be enamoured of, fall in love with, feel passion or affection for. **5** To be pleased, satisfied or delighted. –*Caus.* (रंजयति-ते) **1** To dye, tinge, colour, redden, paint; सा रंजयित्वा चरणौ कृताशीः Ku. 7. 19, 6. 81; Ki. 1. 40, 4. 14. **2** To please, gratify, propitiate, satisfy; ज्ञानलवदुर्विदग्धं ब्रह्मापि नरं न रंजयति Bh. 2. 3. (रजयति also in this sense; see Ki. 6. 25); स्फुरतु कुचकुंभयोरुपरि मणिमंजरी रंजयतु तव हृदयेशं Git. 10. **3** To conciliate, win over, keep contented; Ms. 7. 19. **4** To hunt deer (रजयति only in this sense). –WITH अनु **1** to be red; Si. 9. 7. **2** to be fond of, be devoted or attached to, love, like (with loc., also acc.); Pt. 1. 301; Ms. 3. 173. **3** to be delighted; Bg. 11. 36. –अप **1** to be dissatisfied or discontented (with abl.); नयहीनादपरज्यते जनः Ki. 2. 49. **2** to become pale or colourless; श्वासापरक्ताधरः *S.* 6. 5. –उप **1** to be eclipsed; उपरज्यते भगवांश्चंद्रः Mu. 1. **2** to be tinged or coloured; *Si.* 2. 10. **3** to be afflicted or distressed. –वि **1** to grow discoloured or soiled, be coarse or rough; केशा अपि विरज्यंते निःस्नेहाः किं न सेवकाः Pt. 1. 82 (where it has sense 2 also). **2** to be discontented or disaffected, to dislike, hate; चिरानुरक्तोऽपि विरज्यते जनः Mk. 1. 53; यां चिंतयामि सततं मयि सा विरक्ता Bh. 2. 2; Bk. 18. 22. **3** to become disgusted with the world and hence to renounce all worldly attachments.

रंजकः **1** A painter, dyer. **2** An exciter, a stimulus. –**कं** **1** Red sandal. **2** Vermilion

रंजनं **1** Colouring, dyeing, painting. **2** Colour, dye. **3** Pleasing, delighting; keeping, contented, gratifying, giving pleasure; राजा प्रजारंजनलब्धवर्णः R. 6. 21; तथैव सोऽभूदन्वर्थो राजा प्रकृतिरंजनात् 4. 12. **4** Red sandal-wood.

रंजनी The Indigo plant.

रट् 1 P. (रटति, रटित) **1** To shout, scream, yell, cry, roar, howl; घोराश्चारेटिषुः शिवाः Bk. 15. 27; पपात राक्षसो भूमौ रराट च भयंकरं 14. 81. **2** To call out, proclaim loudly. **3** To shout with joy, applaud. –WITH आ to call to, shout at; प्रियसहचरमपश्यंत्यातुरा चक्रवाक्यारटति *S.* 4.

रटनं **1** The act of crying, screaming or shouting. **2** A shout of applause, approbation.

रण् 1 P. (रणति, रणित) To sound, ring, tinkle, jingle (as anklets &c.); रणद्भिराघट्टनया नमस्वतः पृथग्विभिन्नश्रुतिमंडलैः स्वरैः *Si.* 1. 10; चरणरणितमणिनूपुरया परिपूरितसुरतवितानं Git. 2.

रणः –**णं** **1** War, combat, battle, fight; रणः प्रववृते तत्र भीमः प्लवगरक्षसां R. 12. 72; वचोजीवितयोरासीद्बहिर्निःसरणे रणः Subhâsh. **2** A battle-field. –**णः** **1** Sound, noise. **2** The quill or bow of a lute. **3** Motion, going. –**Comp.** –**अग्रं** the front or van of a battle. –**अंगं** any weapon of war, a weapon, sword; सस्यंदे शोणितं व्योम रणांगानि प्रजज्वलुः Bk. 14, 98. –**अंगणं** –**नं** a battle-field. –**अपेत** *a.* flying away from battle, a fugitive; स बभार रणापेतां चमूं पश्चादवस्थितां Ki. 15. 33. –**आतोद्यं**, -**तूर्यं**, -**दुंदुभिः** a military drum. -**उत्साहः** prowess in battle. –**क्षितिः** *f.* क्षेत्रं, -**भूः** *f.* –**भूमिः** *f.*, –**स्थानं** a battle-field. -**धुरा** the front or van of battle, the brunt of battle; तातेचापद्वितीये वहति रणधुरां को भयस्यावकाशः Ve. 3. 5. –**प्रिय** *a.* fond of war, war-like. –**मत्तः** an elephant. -**मुखं**,-**मूर्धन्** *m.*, –**शिरस्** *n.* **1** the front of battle, the head or van of fight; *S.* 6. 30. 7. 26. **2** the van of an army. –**रंकः** the space between the tusks of an elephant. –**रंगः** a battle-field. –**रणः** a gnat, mosquito. (–**णं**) **1** longing, anxious desire **2** regret for a lost object. –**रणकः**. –**कं** **1** anxiety, uneasiness, regret (for a beloved object), affliction or torment (as caused by love); रणरणकविवृद्धिं बिभ्रदावर्तमानं Mâl. 1. 41; U. 1. **2** love, desire. (–**कः**) the god of love. –**वाद्यं** a military instrument of music. –**शिक्षा** military science, the art or science of war. –**संकुलं** the confusion of battle, a tumultuous fight, melée. –**सज्जा** military accoutrement. –**सहायः** an ally. -**स्तंभः** a monument of war, trophy.

रणत्कारः **1** A rattling, clanking, or jingling sound. **2** A sound in general. **3** Humming (as of bees).

रणितं Rattling, ringing, a rattling or jingling sound.

रंडः **1** A man who dies without male issue. **2** A barren tree. –**डा** **1** A slut, whore; a term of abuse used in addressing women; रंडे पंडितमानिनि Pt. 1. 392. v. l.; प्रतिकूलामकुलजां पापां पापानुवर्तिनीम्। केशेष्वाकृष्य तां रंडां पाखंडेषु नियोजय॥ Prab. 2. **2** A widow; रंडाः पीनपयोधराः कति मया नोद्गाढमालिंगिताः Prab. 3.

रत *p. p.* **1** Pleased, delighted, gratified. **2** Pleased or delighted with, fond of, enamoured of, fondly attached to. **3** Intent on, engaged in, devoted to; (see रम्). –**तं** **1** Pleasure. **2** Sexual union, coition; R. 19. 23, 25; Me. 89. **3** The private parts. –**Comp.** –**अयनी** a prostitute, harlot. –**अर्थिन्** *a.* lustful, lascivious. –**उद्वहः** the (Indian) cuckoo. –**ऋद्धिकं** **1** a day. **2** bathing for pleasure. –**कीलः** a dog. –**कूजितं** lustful or lascivious murmur. –**ज्वरः** a crow. –**तालिन्** *m.* a libertine, sensualist. –**ताली** a procuress, bawd. –**नारीचः** **1** a voluptuary. **2** the god of love, Cupid. **3** a dog. **4** lascivious murmur. –**बंधः** sexual union, coition. –**हिंडकः** **1** a ravisher or seducer of women. **2** a voluptuary.

रतिः *f.* **1** Pleasure, delight, satisfaction, joy; *S.* 2. 1. **2** Fondness for, devotion or attachment to, pleasure in (with loc..); पापे रतिं मा कृथाः Bh. 2. 77; स्वयोषिति रतिः 2. 62; R. 1. 23; Ku. 5. 65. **3** Love, affection; S. D. thus defines it:— रतिर्मनोनुकूलेऽर्थे मनसः प्रवणायितं 207; cf. 206 also. **4** Sexual pleasure; दाक्षिण्योदकवाहिनी विगलिता याता स्वदेशं रतिः Mk. 8. 38; so रतिसर्वस्वं q. v. below. **5** Sexual union, coition, copulation. **6** The goddess of love, the wife of Kâma or Cupid; साक्षात्कामं नवमिव रतिर्मालती माधवं यत् Mâl. 1. 16; Ku. 3. 23; 4. 45; R. 6. 2. **7** The pudenda. –**Comp.** –**अंगं**, –**कुहरं** pudendum muliebre. –**गृहं**, -**भवनं**, -**मंदिरं** **1** a pleasure-house. **2** a brothel. **3** pudendum muliebre. –**तस्करः** a seducer, ravisher. –**दूतिः**-**ती** *f.* a love-messenger; Ku. 4. 16. –**पतिः**, -**प्रियः**,-**रमणः** the god of love; अपि नाम मनागवतीर्णोऽसि रतिरमणबाणगोचरम् Mâl. 1; दधति स्फुटं रतिपतेरिषवः शिततां सदुत्पलपलाशदृशः Si. 9. 66. –**रसः** sexual pleasure. -**लंपट** *a.* lustful, libidinous, lascivious. –**सर्वस्वं** the all-in-all or highest essence of sexual pleasure; करं व्याधुन्वत्याः पिबसि रतिसर्वस्वमधुरं *S.* 1. 24.

रत्नं **1** A gem, jewel, a precious stone; किं रत्नमच्छा मतिः Bv. 1. 86; न रत्नमन्विष्यति मृग्यते हि तत् Ku. 5. 45. (The *ratnas* are said to be either five, nine, or fourteen, see the words पंचरत्न, नवरत्न and चतुर्दशरत्न respectively). **2** Anything valuabte or precious, any dear treasure. **3** Anything best or excellent of its kind; (mostly at the end of comp.); जातौ जातौ यदुत्कृष्टं तद्रत्नमभिधीयते Malli.; कन्यांरत्नमयोनिजन्म भवतामास्ते वयं चार्थिनः Mv. 1. 30; so पुत्र°, स्त्री°, अपत्य°, &c. **4** A magnet. –**Comp.** –**अनुविद्ध** *a.* set or studded with jewels. –**आकरः** **1** a mine of jewels. **2** the ocean; रत्नेषु लुप्तेषु बहुष्वमर्त्यैरद्यापि रत्नाकर एव सिंधुः Vikr. 1. 12; रत्नाकरं वीक्ष्य R. 13. 1. –**आलोकः** the lustre of a gem. –**आवली**, –**माला** a necklace of jewels. –**कंदलः** a coral. –**खचित** *a.* set or studded with gems. –**गर्भः** the sea. (–**र्भा**) the earth. –**दीपः**, -**प्रदीपः** **1** a jewel-lamp. **2** a gem serving as a lamp; अर्चिस्तुंगानभिमुखमपि प्राप्य रत्नप्रदीपान् Me. 68. –**मुख्यं** a diamond. –**राज्** *m.* a ruby. –**राशिः** **1** a heap of gems. **2** the ocean. –**सानुः** N. of the mountain Meru. –**सू** *a.* producing jewels; R. 1. 65. –**सू**, –**सूतिः** *f.* the earth.

रत्निः *m. f.* **1** The elbow. **2** The distance from the elbow to the end of the closed fist, a cubit. -*m*. The closed fist. (This word appears to be a corruption of अरत्नि q. v.).

रथः 1 A carriage, chariot, car, vehicle; especially, a war-chariot. 2 A hero (for रथिन्). 3 A foot. 4 A limb, part, member. 5 The body; cf. आत्मानं रथिनं विद्धि शरीरं रथमेव तु ॥ Kath. 6 A reed. -Comp. -अक्षः a carriage-axle. अंगं 1 any part of a carriage. 2 particularly, the wheels of a carriage; रथो रथांगध्वनिना विजज्ञे R. 7. 41; *S*. 7. 10. 3 A discus, especially of Vishṇu; चक्रधर रति रथांगमदः सततं बिभर्षि भुवनेषु रूढये *Si*. 15. 26. 4 a potter's wheel. °आह्वयः, °नामकः, °नामन् *m*. the ruddy goose (चक्रवाक); रथांगनामन् वियुतो रथांगश्रोणिबिंबया । अयं त्वां पृच्छति रथी मनोरथशतैर्वृतः ॥ V. 4. 18; Ku. 3. 37; R. 3. 24; (the male bird is said by poets to be separated from the female at night and to be united at sun-rise). °पाणिः N. of Vishṇu. -ईशः a warrior fighting from a chariot. -ईषा-षा the pole of a carriage. -उद्वहः, -उपस्थः the seat of a chariot, the driving-box. -कट्या, -कड्या an assemblage of chariots. -कल्पकः an officer who is in charge of a king's chariots. -कारः a coach-builder, carpenter, wheel-wright; रथकारः स्वकां भार्यां सजारां शिरसावहत् Pt. 4. 54. -कुटुंबिकः,-कुटुंबिन् *m*.a charioteer, coachman. -कूबरः-रं the pole or shaft of a carriage. -केतुः the flag of a chariot. -क्षोभः the jolting of a chariot; R. 1. 53. -गर्भकः a litter, palanquin. -गुप्तिः *f*. a fence of wood or iron with which a chariot is provided as a protection from collision. -चरणः,-पादः 1 a chariot-wheel. 2 the ruddy goose. -चर्या chariot-exercise, the use of chariot, travelling by carriage; अनभ्यस्तरथचर्याः U. 5. -धुर् *f*. the shaft or pole of a chariot. -नाभिः *f*. the nave of the wheel of chariot. -नीडः the inner part or seat of a chariot. -बंधः the fastenings or harness of a chariot. -महोत्सवः-यात्रा the solemn procession of an idol placed in a car (usually drawn by men). -मुखं the forepart of a carriage. -युद्धं 'a chariot-fight,' a fight between combatants mounted on chariots. -वर्त्मन् *n*., -वीथिः high way, main road. -वाहः 1 a carriage-horse. 2 a charioteer. -शक्तिः *f*. the staff which supports the banner of a war-chariot. -शाला a coach-house, carriage-shed. -सप्तमी the seventh day in the bright half of Mâgha.

रथिक *a*. (की *f*.) 1 Riding in a carriage. 2 The owner of a carriage.

रथिन् *a*. 1 Riding or driving in a carriage. 2 Possessing or owning a carriage. -*m*. 1 An owner of a carriage. 2 A warrior who fights from a chariot; R. 7. 37.

रथिन, रथिर *a*. See रथिन् above.

रथ्यः 1 A chariot-horse; धावंत्यमी मृगजवाक्षमयेव रथ्याः *S*. 1. 8. 2 A part of a chariot.

रथ्या 1 A road for carriages; (hence) a high way, main road; भूयो भूयः सविधनगरीरथ्यया पर्यटंतं Mâl. 1. 15. 2 A place where many roads meet. 3 A number of carriages or chariots; *Si*. 18. 3.

रद् 1. P. (रदति) 1 To split, rend. 2 To scratch.

रदः 1 Splitting, scratching. 2 A tooth; tusk (of an elephant); यातश्चेत्र परांचति द्विरदानां रदा इव Bv. 1. 65. -Comp. -खंडनं tooth-bite; जनय रदखंडनं Gît. 10. -छदः a lip.

रदनः A tooth. -Comp. -छदः A lip.

रध् 4 P. (रध्यति, रद्ध : *caus*. रंधयति ; *desid*. रिरधिषति or रिरत्सति) 1 To hurt, injure, torment, kill, destroy; अक्ष राधितुमारेभे Bk. 9. 29. 2 To dress, cook or prepare (as food).

रंतिदेवः N. of a king of the lunar race, sixth in descent from Bharata. [He was very pious and benevolent. He possessed enormous riches, but he spent them in performing grand sacrifices. So great was the number of animals slaughtered during his reign both in sacrifices as well as for use in his kitchen that a river of blood is supposed to have issued from their hides which was afterwards appropriately called चर्मण्वती ; cf. Me. 45. and Malli. thereon].

रंतुः 1 A way, road. 2 A river.

रंधनं, रंधिः *f*. 1 Injuring, tormenting, destroying. 2 Cooking.

रंध्रं 1 A hole, an aperture, a cavity, an opening, a chasm, fissure; रंध्रेष्विवालक्ष्यनभःप्रदेशा R. 13. 56, 15. 82.; नासाग्ररंध्रे Mâl. 1. 1; क्रौंचरंध्रं Me. 57. 2 (*a*) A weak or vulnerable point, assailable point; रंध्रोपनिपातिनोऽनर्थाः *S*. 6; रंध्रान्वेषणदक्षाणां द्विषामामिषतां ययौ R. 12. 11; R. 15. 17, 17. 61. (*b*) A defect, fault, an imperfection. -Comp. -अन्वेषिन्,-अनुसारिन् *a*. searching or watching for weak points; Mk. 8. 27. -बभ्रुः a rat. -वंशः a hollow bamboo.

रभ् 1. A. (रभते, रब्ध ; *caus*. रंभयति-ते ; *desid*. रिप्सते) To begin. -WITH आ or प्रा 1 to begin, commence, set about, undertake; प्रारभ्यते न खलु विघ्नभयेन नीचैः Bh. 2. 27; आरंभंतेऽल्पमेवाज्ञाः Subhâsh.; Bk. 5. 38; R. 8. 45. 2 to be busy or energetic; *Si*. 2. 91. -परि to clasp, embrace; इत्युक्तवंतं परिरभ्य दोर्भ्यां Ki. 11. 80; Bv. 1. 95; Ku. 5. 3; *Si*. 9. 72. -सं 1 to be agitated, be overwhelmed or affected. 2 to be exasperated or furious, be enraged or irritated (mostly in *p. p.*); R. 16. 16.

रभस् *n*. 1 Violence, zeal. 2 Force, strength.

रभस *a*. 1 Violent, impetuous, fierce, wild. 2 Strong, intense, vehement, powerful, ardent, eager (as desire &c.); रभसया नु दिगंतदिदृक्षया Ki. 5, 1; R. 9. 61, Mu. 5. 24. -सः 1 Violence, force, impetuosity, haste, speed, hurry, vehemence; आलीषु केलीरभसेन बाला मुहुर्ममालापमपालपंती Bv. 2. 12; त्वदभिसरणरभसेन वलंती Gît. 6; *Si*. 6. 13, 11. 23; Ki. 9. 47. 2 Rashness, precipitateness, headlong haste; अतिरभसकृतानां कर्मणामाविपत्तेर्भवति हृदयदाही शल्यतुल्यो विपाकः Bh. 2. 99. 3 Anger, passion, rage, fury. 4 Regret, sorrow. 5 Joy, pleasure, delight, मनसि रभसविभवे हरिरुदयतु सुकृतेन Gît. 5.

रम् 1 A. (रमते, but Paras. when preceded by वि, आ, परि and उप; रत) 1 To be pleased or delighted, rejoice, be gratified; रहसि रमते Mâl. 3. 2, Ms. 2. 223. 2 To rejoice at, be pleased with, take delight in, be fond of (with instr. or loc.); लोलापांगैर्यदि न रमसे लोचनैर्वंचितोऽसि Me. 27; व्यजेष्ट षड्वर्गमरंस्त नीतौ Bk. 1. 2. 3 To play, sport, dally, amuse oneself with; राजप्रियाः कैरविण्यो रमंते मधुपैः सह Bv. 1. 126 (where the next meaning is also hinted); Bk. 6. 15, 67. 4 To have sexual intercourse with; सा तत्पुत्रेण सह रमते H. 3. 5 To remain, stay, pause. -*Caus*. (रमयति-ते) To please, delight, satisfy. -*Desid*. (रिरंसते) To wish to sport &c.; *Si*. 15. 88. -WITH अभि to rejoice, be pleased or delighted, be fond of; Bk. 1. 7; Bg. 18. 45. -आ (Paras.) 1 to take pleasure in, delight in; Bk. 8. 52, 3. 38. 2 to cease, stop, leave off (speaking &c.), end; Ms. 2. 73. -उप (P. and A.) 1 to cease, end, terminate; संगतावुपरराम च लज्जा Ki. 9. 44, 13. 69. 2 to cease or desist from; भयाद्रणादुपरतं मंस्यंते त्वां महारथाः Bg. 2. 35; Bk. 8. 54, 55; Ki. 4. 17. 3 to be quiet or calm; Bg. 6. 20. 4 to die; see उपरत. -परि (Paras.) to be pleased or delighted; Bk. 8. 53. -वि (Paras.) 1 to end, terminate, come to an end; अविदितगतयामा रात्रिरेव व्यरंसीत् U. 1. 27. 2 to cease, desist, stop, leave off (speaking &c.); एतावदुक्त्वा विरते मृगेंद्रे R. 2. 51; *Si*. 2. 13; oft. with abl.; हा हंत किमिति चित्त विरमति नाद्यापि विषयेभ्यः Bv. 4. 25: U. 1. 33. -सं (Atm.) to be pleased, to rejoice; Bk. 19. 30.

रम *a*. Pleasing, delightful, gratifying &c. -मः 1 Joy, delight. 2 A lover, husband. 3 The god of love.

रमठं Asa Fœtida (हिंगु). -Comp. -ध्वनिः Asa Fœtida.

रमण *a.* (णी *f.*) Pleasing, gratifying, delightful, charming Bk. 6. 72. **-णः 1** A lover, husband ; पप्रच्छ रामां रमणोऽभिलाषं R. 14. 27; Me. 37, 87 ; Ku. 4. 21 ; *Si.* 9. 60. **2** The god of love. **3** An ass. **4** A testicle. **-णं 1** Sporting, **2** Dalliance, pastime, amorous sport. **3** Love, sexual union. **4** Joy or pleasure in general. **5** The hip and the loins.

रमणा, रमणी 1 A lovely young woman ; लता रम्या सेयं भ्रमरकुलरम्या न रमणी Bv. 2. 90. **2** A wife, mistress ; भोगः को रमणीं विना Subhâsh.

रमणीय *a.* Pleasant, delightful, lovely, charming, handsome ; स्मितं नैतत्किंतु प्रकृतिरमणीयं विकसितं Bv. 2. 90.

रमा 1 A wife, mistress. **2** N. of Lakshmî, the wife of Vishṇu and Goddess of wealth. **3** Riches. **-Comp. -कांतः, -नाथः, -पतिः** epithets of Vishṇu. **-वेष्टः** turpentine.

रंभा 1 A plantain tree ; विजितरंभमूरुद्वयं Gît. 10; पिबोरुंरंभातरुपीवरोरु N. 22. 43, 2 37. **2** N. of Gaurî. **3** N. of an *apsaras*, wife of Nalakûbara and considered as the most beautiful woman in the paradise of Indra ; तरुमूरुयुगेन सुंदरी किमु रंभां परिणाहिना परम् । तरुणीमपि जिष्णुरेव तां धनदापत्यतपःफलस्तनीं ॥ N. 2. 37. **-Comp. -ऊरु** *a.* (रु or रू *f.*) having thighs like the interior of a plantain, tree, *i. e.* full, round and hence lovely ; *Si.* 8. 19; R. 6. 35.

रम्य *a.* **1** Pleasing, pleasant, delightful, agreeable ; रम्यास्तपोधनानां क्रियाः समवलोक्य *S.* 1. 13 **2** Beautiful, lovely, handsome; सरसिजमनुविद्धं शैवलेनापि रम्यं *S.* 1. 20; 5. 2. **-म्यः** The tree called चंपक. **-म्यं** Semen virile.

रय् 1. A. (रयते, रयित) To go, move.

रयः 1 The stream of a river, current ; जंबूकुंजप्रतिहतरयं तोयमादाय गच्छेः Me. 20. **2** Force, speed, velocity; U. 3. 36. **3** Zeal; ardour, vehemence, impetuosity.

रल्लकः 1 A woollen cloth, blanket. **2** An eye-lash ; युवतिरल्लभल्लसमाहतो भवति को न युवा गतचेतनः. **3** A kind of deer.

रवः 1 A cry, shriek, scream, yell, roar (of animals &c.). **2** Singing; humming sound (of birds); R. 9. 29. **3** Clamour. **4** Noise or sound in general ; घंटा°, भूषण°, चाप° &c.

रवण *a.* **1** Crying, roaring, screaming. **2** Sonorous, sounding उत्कंठावर्धनैः शुभ्रं रवणैरंबरं ततं Bk. 7. 14. **3** Sharp, hot. **4** Fickle, unsteady. **-णः 1** A camel; *Si.* 12. 2. **2** The cuckoo. **-णं** Brass, bell-metal.

रविः The sun ; सहस्रगुणमुत्स्रष्टुमादत्ते हि रसं रविः R. 1. 18. **-Comp. -कांतः** the sun-stone (सूर्यकांत). **-जः,-तनयः,-पुत्रः, -सुतः 1** the planet Saturn. **2** epithets of Karṇa. **3** of Vâli. **4** of Manu Vaivasvata. **5** of Yama. **6**. of Sugrîva. **-दिनं, -वारः, -वासरः -रं** Sunday. **-संक्रांतिः** *f.* the sun's entrance into any zodiacal sign.

रशना, रसना 1 A rope, cord. **2** A rein, bridle. **3** A zone, girdle, woman's girdle; रसतु रसनापि तव घनजघनमंडले घोषयतु मन्मथनिदेशं Gît. 10 ; R. 7. 10, 8. 57; Me. 35. **4** The tongue ; Bv. 1. 111. **-Comp. -उपमा** a variety of the figure उपमा ; it is 'a string or series of comparisons, which consists in making the *Upameya* in the first comparison the *Upama'na* in the second and so forth; see S. D. 664.

रश्मिः 1 A string, cord, rope. **2** A bridle, rein ; मुक्तेषु रश्मिषु निरायतपूर्वकायाः *S.* 1. 8; रश्मिसंयमनात् *S.* 1. **3** A goad, whip. **4** A beam, ray of light ; *S.* 7. 6 ; N. 22. 56 ; so हिमरश्मि &c. **-Comp. -कलापः** a pearl-necklace of 54 threads.

रश्मिमत् *m.* The sun.

रस् I. 1 P. (रसति, रसित) **1** To roar, yell, cry out, scream ; करिव वन्यः परुषं ररास R. 16. 78 ; *Si.* 3. 48. **2** To sound, make a noise, tinkle, jingle &c. ; राजन्योपनिमंत्रणाय रसति स्फीतं यशोदुंदुभिः Ve. 1. 25 ; रसतु रसनापि तव घनजघनमंडले Gît. 10. **3** To resound, reverberate. -II. 10 U. (रसयति-ते, रसित) To taste, relish; मृद्वीका रसिता Bv. 4. 13 ; *Si.* 10. 27.

रसः 1 Sap, juice (of trees) ; इक्षुरसः, कुसुमरसः &c. **2** A liquid, fluid ; Ku. 1. 7. **3** Water ; सहस्रगुणमुत्स्रष्टुमादत्ते हि रसं रविः R. 1. 19 ; Bv. 2. 144. **4** Liquor, drink ; Ms. 2. 177. **5** A draught, potion. **6** Taste, flavour, relish (fig. also.) (considered in Vais. phil. as one of the 24 *gunas* ; the *rasas* are six; कटु, अम्ल, मधुर, लवण, तिक्त and कषाय; परायत्तः प्रीतेः कथमिव रसं वेत्तु पुरुषः Mu. 3. 4 ; U. 2. 2. **7** A sauce, condiment. **8** An object of taste ; R. 3. 4. **9** Taste or inclination for a thing, liking, desire ; इष्टे वस्तुन्युपचितरसाः प्रेमराशिभवंति Me 112. **10** Love, affection ; जरसा यस्मिन्नहार्यो रसः U. 1. 39; प्रसरति रसो निर्वृतिघनः 6. 11. 'a feeling, of love'; Ku. 3. 37. **11** Pleasure, delight, happiness ; R. 3. 26. **12** Charm, interest, elegance, beauty. **13** Pathos, emotion feeling. **14** (In poetic compositions) A sentiment ; नवरसरुचिरां निर्मितिमादधती भारती कवेर्जयति K. P. 1.(The *rasas* are usually eight:— शृंगारहास्यकरुणरौद्रवीरभयानकः । बीभत्साद्भुतसंज्ञौ चेत्यष्टौ नाट्ये रसाः स्मृताः; but sometimes शांतरस is added thus making the total number 9; निर्वेदस्थायिभावोस्ति शांतोपि नवमो रसः K. P. 4 ; sometimes a tenth, वात्सल्यरस, is also added. *Rasas* are more or less a necessary factor of every poetic composition, but, according to Visvanâtha, they constitute the very essence of poetry ; वाक्यं रसात्मकं काव्यं S D. 3.) **15** Essence, pith, best part. **16** A constituent fluid of the body. **17** Semen virile. **18** Mercury. **19** A poison, poisonous drink ; as in तीक्ष्णरसदायिनः. **20** Any mineral or metallic salt. **-Comp. -अंजनं** vitriol of copper, a sort of collyrium. **-अम्लः** sour sauce. **-अयनं 1** an elixir of life (elixir vitæ), any medicine supposed to prolong life and prevent old age ; निखिलरसायनमहितो गंधेनोग्रेण लशुन इव R. G. **2** (fig.) serving as an elixir vitæ ; *i. e.* that which gratifies or regales ; आनंदनानि हृदयैकरसायनानि Mâl. 6. 8. ; मनसश्च रसायनानि U. 1. 36 ; श्रोत्र°, कर्ण° &c. **3** alchemy or chemistry. °श्रेष्ठः mercury. **-आत्मक** *a.* **1** consisting of juice or sentiment. **2** fluid, liquid. **-आभासः 1** the semblance or mere appearance of a sentiment. **2** an improper manifestation of a sentiment. **-आस्वादः 1** tasting juices or flavours. **2** perception or appreciation of poetic sentiments, a perception of poetical charm ; as in काव्यामृतरसास्वादः. **-इंद्रः 1** mercury. **2** the philosopher's stone (the touch of which is said to turn iron into gold). **-उद्भवं, -उपलं** a pearl. **-कर्मन्** *n.* preparation of quicksilver. **-केसरं** camphor. **-गंधः-धं** gum-myrrh. **-ग्रह** *a.* **1** perceiving flavours. **2** appreciating or enjoying pleasures. **-जः** sugar molasses. **-जं** blood. **-ज्ञ** *a.* **1** one who appreciates the flavour or excellence of, one who knows the taste of ; सांसारिकेषु च सुखेषु वयं रसज्ञाः U. 2. 27. **2** capable of discerning the beauty of things. (**-ज्ञः**) **1** a man of taste or feeling, a critic, an appreciative person, a poet. **2** an alchemist. **3** a physician, or one who prepares mercurial or other chemical compounds. (**-ज्ञा**) the tongue ; Bv. 2. 59. **-तेजस्** *n.* blood. **-दः** a physician. **-धातु** *n.* quicksilver. **-प्रबंधः** any poetical composition, particularly a drama. **-फलः** the cocoa-nut tree. **-भंगः** the interruption or cessation of a sentiment. **-भवं** blood. **-राजः** quicksilver. **-विक्रयः** sale of liquors. **-शास्त्रं** the science of alchemy. **-सिद्ध** *a.* **1** accomplished in poetry, conversant with sentiments; जयंति ते सुकृतिनः रससिद्धाः कवीश्वराः Bh. 2. 24. **2** skilled in alchemy. **-सिद्धिः** *f.* skill in alchemy.

रसनं 1 Crying, screaming, roaring, sounding, tinkling, noise or sound in general. **2** Thunder, rumbling or muttering of clouds. **3** Taste, flavour. **4** The organ of taste, the tongue; इंद्रियं रसग्राहकं रसनं जिह्वाग्रवर्ति T. S.; Bg. 15. 9. **5** Perception, appreciation, sense; सर्वेऽपि रसनाद्रसाः S. D. 244.

रसना See रशना. **-Comp. -रदः** a bird. **-लिह्** *m.* a dog.

रसवत् *a.* **1** Juicy, succulent. **2** Tasteful, savoury, sapid, well-flavoured; संसारसुखवृक्षस्य द्वे एव रसवत्फले । काव्यामृतरसास्वादः संपर्कः सज्जनैः सह ॥. **3** Moist, well-watered. **4** Charming, graceful, elegant. **5** Full of feeling or sentiment, impassioned. **6** Full of affection, possessed of love. **7** Spirited, witty. -ती A kitchen.

रसा **1** The lower of infernal regions, hell. **2** The earth, ground, soil; Bv. 1. 59; स्मरस्य युद्धरंगतां रसारसारसारसा Nalod. 2. 10. **3** The tongue. **–Comp.** **-तलं 1** N. of one of the seven regions below the earth; see पाताल. **2** the lower world or hell in general; राज्यं यातु रसातलं पुनरिदं न प्राणितुं कामये Bv. 2. 63; or जातिर्यातु रसातलं Bh. 2. 39.

रसाल: **1** The mango tree; भृंगा रसालकुसुमानि समाश्रयंते Bv. 1. 17. **2** The sugar-cane. **-ला 1** The tongue. **2** Curds mixed with sugar and spices. **3** Dûrvâ grass. **4** A vine or grape. **-लं** Gum-myrrh, frankincense.

रसिक *a.* **1** Savoury, sapid, tasteful. **2** Graceful, elegant, beautiful. **3** Impassioned. **4** Apprehending flavour or excellence, possessed of taste, appreciative, discriminating; तद् वृत्तं प्रवदंति काव्यरसिकाः शार्दूलविक्रीडितं Śrut. 40. **5** Finding pleasure in, taking delight in, delighting in, devoted to (usually in comp.); यद् मालती भगवता सदृशसंयोगरसिकेन वेधसा मन्मथेन मया च तुभ्यं दीयते Mal. 6; so कामरसिकः Bh. 3. 112; परोपकाररसिकस्य Mk. 6. 19. **-कः 1** A man of taste or feeling, an appreciator of excellence or beauty; cf. अरसिक. **2** A libertine. **3** An elephant. **4** A horse. **-का 1** The juice of sugarcane, molasses. **2** The tongue. **3** A woman's girdle; see रसाला also.

रसित *p. p.* **1** Tasted. **2** Having flavour or sentiment. **3** Gilded. **-तं 1** Wine or liquor. **2** A cry, roar, thunder, roaring noise, sound or noise in general; दैरेककंठरसितप्रतिमानमेति Mâl. 9. 3.

रसोन: A kind of garlic; cf. लसुन.

रस्य *a.* Juicy, savoury, sapid, palatable; रस्याः स्निग्धाः स्थिरा हृद्या आहाराः सात्त्विकप्रियाः Bg. 17. 8.

रह् 1 P., 10 U.(रहति, रहयतिते, रहित) To quit, leave, abandon, forsake, desert; रहयत्यापदुपेतमायतिः Ki. 2. 14.

रहणं Desertion, quitting, separation; सहकारवृते समये सह कारहणस्य केन सस्मार पदं Nalod. 2. 14.

रहस् *n.* **1** Solitude, privacy, loneliness, retirement, secrecy; R. 3. 3, 15. 92; Pt. 1.138. **2** A deserted or lonely place, hiding-place. **3** A secret, mystery. **4** Copulation coition. **5** A privity. *-ind.* Secretly, clandestinely, privately, in private or secret; अतः परीक्ष्य कर्तव्यं विशेषात्संगतं रहः S. 5. 24; oft. in comp.; वृत्रे रहःप्रणयमप्रतिपद्यमाने 5. 22.

रहस्य *a.* **1** Secret, private, clandestine. **2** Mysterious. **-स्यं 1** A secret (fig. also); स्वय रहस्यभेदः कृतः V. 2. **2** A mystic spell or incantation, the mystery (of a missile); सरहस्यानि जृंभकास्त्राणि U. 1. **3** The mystery or secret of conduct, mystery; रहस्यं साधूनामनुपधि विशुद्धं विजयते U. 2. 2. **4** A secret or esotric teaching, a mystic doctrine; भक्तोसि मे सखा चेति रहस्यं ह्येतदुत्तमं Bg. 4. 3; Ms. 2. 150. **-स्यं** *ind.* Secretly, privately; Y. 3. 301; (where it may be taken as an adj. also). **–Comp.** **-आख्यायिन्** *a.* telling a secret; रहस्याख्यायीव स्वनसि मृदु कर्णांतिकचरः S. 1. 24. **-भेदः, -विभेदः** disclosure of a secret or mystery. **-व्रतं 1** a secret vow or penance. **2** the mystic science of obtaining command over magical weapons.

रहित *p. p.* **1** Quitted, left, abandoned, deserted. **2** Separated from, free from, deprived or destitute of, without (with instr. or at the end of comp.); रहिते भिक्षुभिर्ग्रामे Y. 3. 59; गुणरहितः, सत्त्वरहितः &c. **3** Lonely, solitary. **-तं** Secrecy, privacy.

रा 2 P. (राति, रात) To give, grant, bestow; स रातु वो दुश्च्यवनो भावुकानां परंपरां K. P. 7.

राका **1** The full-moon day, particularly the night; दारिद्र्यं भजते कलानिधिरयं राकाधुना म्लायति Bv. 2. 72, 54, 94, 150, 165, 175; 3. 11. **2** The goddess presiding over the full moon day. **3** A girl in whom menstruation has just commenced. **4** Itch, scab.

राक्षस *a.* (**सी** *f.*) Belonging to or like an evil spirit, demoniacal, partaking of a demon's nature; U. 5. 30; Bg. 9. 12. **-सः 1** A demon, an evil spirit, a goblin, fiend, imp. **2** One of the eight forms of marriage in Hindu Law, in which a girl is forcibly seized and carried away after the defeat or destruction of her relatives in battle; राक्षसो युद्धहरणात् Y. 1. 61; cf. Ms. 3. 33 also. (Krishṇa carried away Rukmiṇî in this manner). **3** One of the astronomical *Yogas.* **4** N. of a minister of Nanda, an important character in the Mudrârâkshasa. **-सी** A female demon.

राक्षा See लाक्षा; (perhaps an incorrect form).

राग: **1** Colour, hue, dye; Pt. 1. 33. **2** Red colour, redness; अधरः किसलयरागः S. 1. 21. **3** Red dye, red lac; रागेण बालारुणकोमलेन चूतप्रवालोष्ठमलंचकार Ku. 3. 30, 5 11. **4** Love, passion, affection, amorous or sexual feeling; मलिनेपि रागपूर्णां Bv. 1. 100 (where it means 'redness' also); अथ भवंतमंतरेण कीदृशोऽस्या दृष्टिरागः S. 2; see चक्षूराग also. **5** Feeling, emotion, sympathy, interest. **6** Joy, pleasure. **7** Anger, wrath. **8** Loveliness, beauty. **9** A musical mode or order of sound; (there are six primary *Ra'gas*; भरवः कौशिकश्चैव हिंदोलो दीपकस्तथा । श्रीरागो मेघरागश्च रागाः षडिति कीर्तिताः Bharata; other writers give different names. Each *ra'ga* has six *ra'giṇîs* regarded as its consorts, and their union gives rise to several musical modes). **10** Musical harmony, melody; तवास्मि गीतरागेण हारिणा प्रसभं हृतः S. 1. 5; अहो रागपरिवाहिणी गीतिः S. 5. **11** Regret, sorrow. **12** Greediness, envy. **–Comp.** **-आत्मक** *a.* impassioned. **-चूर्णः 1** Acacia Catechu or Khadira tree. **2** red lead. **3** lac. **4** red powder thrown by people over one another at the festival called *holi.* **5** the god of love. **-द्रव्यं** a colouring substance, a paint, dye. **-बंधः** manifestation of feeling, interest created by a proper representation (of various emotions); भावो भावं नुदति विषयाद्रागबंधः स एव M. 2. 9. **-युज्** *m.* a ruby. **-सूत्रं 1** any coloured thread. **2** a silk-thread. **3** the string of a balance.

रागिन् *a.* **1** Coloured, dyed. **2** Colouring, painting. **3** Red. **4** Full of passion or feeling, impassioned. **5** Full of love, subject to love. **6** Passionately fond of, devotedly attached to, desirous of, yearning after (at the end of comp.). *-m.* **1** A painter. **2** A lover. **3** A libertine, sensualist. **-णी 1** A modification of a musical mode (राग), of which 30 or 36 kinds are enumerated. **2** A wanton and intriguing woman, a lustful woman.

राघव: **1** A descendant of Raghu, especially Râma. **2** A kind of large fish; Bv. 1. 55.

रांकव *a.* (**वी** *f.*) Belonging to the species of deer called *ranku,* or made from its hair; woollen; Vikr. 18. 31. **-वं 1** A woollen cloth made of deer's hair, a woollen garment. **2** A blanket.

राज् 1 U. (राजतिते, राजित) **1** (*a*) To shine, glitter, appear splendid or beautiful, be eminent; रेजे ग्रहमयीव सा Bh. 1. 17; राजन् राजति वीरवैरिवनितावैधव्यदस्ते भुजः K. P. 10; R. 3. 7; Ki. 4. 24, 11. 6. (*b*) To appear or look (like), shine (like); तोयांतर्भास्करालीव रेजे मुनिपरंपरा Ku. 6. 49. **2** To rule, govern. *-Caus.* (राजयतिते) To cause to shine, illuminate, brighten. -WITH **निस्** (*Caus.*) **1** to cause to shine, illuminate, make brilliant, adorn, irradiate; विद्यासुस्फुरदुग्रदीधितिशिखानिराजितज्यं धनुः U. 6. 18; नीराजयंति भूपालाः पादपीठांतभूतलं Prab. 2. **2** to perform the ceremony called नीराजन (q. v.) over a person or thing (wave lights before one as a mark of respect or by way of worship); नानायोधसमाकीर्णे नीराजितहयद्विपः Kâm. 4. 66. **-वि 1** to shine; Bv. 1. 88. **2** to appear or look like; R. 2. 20.

राज् *m.* A king, chief, prince.

राजकः A little king, a petty prince. **-कं** A number of kings or princes, a collection of sovereigns; सहेते न जनोऽप्यधःक्रियां किमु लोकाधिकधाम राजकं Ki. 2. 47; Si. 14. 43.

राजत *a.* (**ती** *f.*) Silvery, made of silver; Si. 4. 13. **-तं** Silver.

राजन् *m.* **1** A king, ruler, prince, chief (changed to राजः at the end of Tat. comp.); वंगराजः, महाराजः &c.; तथैव सोऽभूदन्वर्थो राजा प्रकृतिरंजनात् R. 4. 12. **2** A man of the military caste, a Kshatriya; Si. 14. 14. **3** N. of Yudhishthira. **4** N. of Indra. **5** The moon; Bv. 1. 126. **6** A Yaksha.**-Comp. -अंगनं** a royal court, the court-yard of a palace. **-अधिकारिन्,-अधिकृतः 1** a government officer or official. **2** a judge. **-अधिराजः,-इंद्रः** a king of kings, a supreme king, paramount sovereign, an emperor. **-अनकः 1** an inferior king, a petty prince. **2** a title of respect formerly given to distinguished scholars and poets. **-अपसदः** an unworthy or degraded king. **-अभिषेकः** coronation of a king. **-अर्हं** aloe-wood, a species of sandal. **-अर्हणं** a royal gift of honour. **-आज्ञा** a king's edict, an ordinance, a royal decree. **-आभरणं** a king's ornament. **-आवलिः -ली** a royal dynasty or genealogy. **-उपकरणं** (pl.) the paraphernalia of a king, the insignia of royalty. **-ऋषिः (राजऋषिः** or **राजर्षिः)** a royal sage, a saint-like prince, a man of the Kshatriya caste who, by his pious life and austere devotion, comes to be regarded as a sage or *rishi*; *i. e.* पुरूरवस्, जनक, विश्वामित्र. **-करः** a tax or tribute paid to the king. **-कार्यं** state-affairs. **-कुमारः** a prince. **-कुलं 1** a royal family, a king's family. **2** the court of a king. **3** a court of justice; (राजकुले कथ् or निविद् *caus.* means 'to sue one in a court of law, lodge a complaint against'). **4** a royal palace. **5** a king, master (as a respectful mode of speaking). **-गामिन्** *a.* escheating to the sovereign (as the property of a person having no heir). **-गृहं 1** a royal dwelling, royal palace. **2** N. of a chief city in Magadha (about 75 or 80 miles from Pâtaliputra). **-चिह्नं** insignia of royalty, regalia **-तालः, -ताली** a belet-nut tree. **-दंडः 1** a king's sceptre. **2** royal authority. **3** punishment inflicted by a king. **-दंतः** (for दंतानां राजा) the front tooth; N. 7. 46. **-दूतः** a king's ambassador, an envoy. **द्रोहः** high treason, sedition, rebellion. **-द्वाः** *f.*, **-द्वारं** theg ate of a royal palace. **-द्वारिकः** a royal porter. **-धर्मः 1** a king's duty. **2** a law or rule relating to kings (oft. in pl.) **-धानं, -धानिका, -धानी** the king's residence, the capital, metropolis, the seat of government; R. 2. 10. **धुर्** *f.*, **-धुरा** the burden or responsibitity of government. **-नयः, नीतिः** *f.* administration of a state, administration of government, politics, statesmanship. **-नीलं** an emerald. **-पट्टः** a diamond of inferior quality. **-पथः, -पद्धतिः** *f.* = **राजमार्ग** q. v. **-पुत्रः 1** a prince. **2** a Kshatriya, a man of the military tribe. **3** the planet Mercury. **-पुत्री** a princess. **-पुरुषः 1** a king's servant. **2** a minister. **-प्रेष्यः** a king's servant. (**-ष्यं**) royal sevice (more correctly राजप्रैष्य). **-बीजिन्, -वंश्य** *a.* scion of royalty, of royal descent. **-भृतः** a king's soldier. **-भृत्यः 1** a royal servant or minister. **2** any public or government officer. **-भोगः** a king's meal, royal repast. **-भौतः** a king's fool or jester. **-मात्रधरः, -मंत्रिन्** *m.* a king's counsellor. **-मार्गः 1** a high way, high road, a royal or main road, principal street. **2** the way, method or procedure of kings. **-मुद्रा** the royal seal. **-यक्ष्मन्** *m.* ' consumption of the moon', pulmonary consumption, consumption in general; राजयक्ष्मपरिहानिराययौ कामयानसमवस्थ या तुला R. 19. 50; राजयक्ष्मेव रोगाणां समूहः स महीभृतां Si. 2. 96; (for explanation of the word see Malli. thereon, as well as on Si. 13. 29.) **-यानं** a royal vehicle, a palanquin. **-योगः 1** a configuration of planets, asterisms &c. at the brith of a man which indicates that he is destined to be a king. **2** an easy mode of religious meditation (fit for kings to practise) as distinguished from the more rigorous one called हठयोग. q. v. **-रंगं** silver. **-राजः 1** a supreme king, sovereign lord, an emperor. **2** N. of Kubera; अंतर्बाष्पश्चिरमनुचरो राजराजस्य दध्यौ Me. 3. **3** the moon. **-रीतिः** *f.* bell-metal. **-लक्षणं 1** any mark on a man's body indicating future royalty. **2** royal insignia, regalia. **-लक्ष्मीः, श्रीः** *f.* the fortune or prosperity of a king (personified as a goddess), the glory or majesty of a king R. 2. 7. **-वंशः** a dynasty of kings. **-वंशावली** genealogy of kings, royal pedigree. **-विद्या** ' royal policy', king-craft, state-policy, statesmanship; (cf. राजनय); so **राजशास्त्रं**. **-विहारः** a royal convnet. **-शासनं** a royal edict. **-शृंगं** a royal umbrella with a golden handle. **-ससद्** *f.* a court of justice. **-सदनं** a palace. **-सर्षपः** black mustard. **-सायुज्यं** sovereignty. **-सारसः** a peacock. **-सूयः -यं** a great sacrifice performed by a universal monarch (in which the tributary princes also took part) at the time of his coronation as a mark of his undisputed sovereinty; राजा वै राजसूयेनेष्ट्वा भवति Sat. Br.; cf. सम्राट् also. **-स्कंधः** a horse. **-स्वं 1** royal property. **2** tribute, revenue. **-हंसः** a flamingo (a sort of white goose with red legs and bill); संपत्स्यंते नभसि भवतो राजहंसाः सहायाः Me. 11. **-हस्तिन्** *m.* a royal elephant, *i. e.* a lordly and handsome elephant.

राजन्य *a.* Royal, kingly. **-न्यः 1** A man of the Kshatriya caste, royal personage; राजन्यान् स्वपुरनिवृत्तयेऽनुमेने R. 4. 87; 3. 48; Me. 48. **2** A noble or distinguished personage.

राजन्यकं A collection of warriors or Kshatriyas.

राजन्वत् *a.* Governed by a just or good king (as a country, as distinguished from राजवत् which simply means 'having a ruler'); सुराज्ञि देशे राजन्वान् स्यात्ततोऽन्यत्र राजवान् Ak.); राजन्वतीमाहुरनेन भूमिं R. 6. 22; Kâv. 3. 6.

राजस *a.* (**सी** *f.*) Relating to or influenced by the quality *rajas*, endowed with the quality *rajas* or passion; ऊर्ध्वं गच्छंति सत्त्वस्था मध्ये तिष्ठंति राजसाः Bg. 14. 18; 7. 12; 17. 2.

राजसात् *ind.* To the state or in the possession of a king.

राजिः -जी *f.* A streak, line, row, range; सर्वं पंडितराजराजितिलकेनाकारि लोकोत्तरं Bv. 4. 44; दानराजिः R. 2. 7; Ki. 5. 4.

राजिका 1 A line, row, range. **2** A field. **3** Black mustard. **4** Mustard (used as a weight).

राजिलः A species of innocent and poisonless snakes; किं महोरगविसर्पिविक्रमो राजिलेषु गरुडः प्रवर्तते R. 11. 27; cf. डुंडुभ.

राजीवः 1 A kind of deer. **2** A crane. **3** An elephant. **-वं** A blue lotus; Ku. 3. 46. **-Comp. -अक्ष** *a.* lotus-eyed.

राज्ञी A queen, the wife of a king.

राज्यं 1 Royalty, sovereignty, royal authority; राज्येन किं तद्विपरीतवृत्तेः R. 2. 53; 4. 1. **2** A kingdom, country, an empire; R. 1. 58. **3** Rule, reign, government, administration of a kingdom. **-Comp. -अंगं** a constituent member of the state, a requiste of regal administration; these are usually said to be seven :— स्वाम्यमात्यसुहृत्कोषराष्ट्रदुर्गबलानि च Ak. **-अधिकारः 1** authority over a kingdom. **2** a right to sovereignity. **-अपहरणं** usurpation. **-अभिषेकः** inauguration or coronation of a king. **-करः** the tribute paid by a tributary prince. **-च्युत** *a.* deposed, or dethroned. -तंत्रं the science of government, system of administration, the government or administration of a kingdom; Mu. 1. -धुरा, -भार: the yoke or burden of government, the responsibility or administration of government. -भंग: subversion of sovereignty. -लोभ: greed of dominion, desire of territorial aggrandisement. -व्यवहार: administration, government business. -सुखं the sweets of royalty.

राढा 1 Lustre. 2 N. of a district in Bengal, as also of its capital; गौडं राष्ट्रमनुत्तमं निरुपमा तत्रापि राढापुरी Prab. 2.

रात्रिः -त्री *f.* Night; रात्रिर्गता मतिमतां वर मुंच शय्यां R. 5. 63; दिवा काकरवाद्भीता रात्रौ तरति नर्मदाम्. -Comp. -अट: 1 a goblin, demon, ghost. 2 a thief. -अंध *a.* night-blind. -कर: the moon. -चर: (also -रात्रिंचर) (री *f.*) 1 'a night-rover', robber, thief. 2 a watchman, patrol, guard. 3 a demon, ghost, evil-spirit; (तं) यातं वने रात्रिचरी डुढौके Bk. 2. 23. -चर्या 1 night-roving. 2 a nightly act or ceremony. -जं a star, constellation. -जलं dew. -जागर: 1 night-watching, wakefulness or sitting up at night; R. 19. 34. 2 a dog. -तरा the dead of night. -पुष्पं a lotus-flower opening at night. -योग: night-fall.-रक्ष:,-रक्षक: a watchman, guard. -राग: darkness, obscurity. -वासस् *n.* 1 night-dress. 2 darkness. -विगम: 'end of night', break of day, dawn, day-light. -वेद:, -वेदिन् *m.* a cock.

रात्रिंदिवं, रात्रिंदिवा *ind.* By night and day, constantly, ceaselessly; रात्रिंदिवं गंधवहः प्रयाति S. 5. 4.

रात्रिंमन्य *a.* Looking like night (as a cloudy or dark-day); cf. रजनिंमन्य.

राद्ध *p. p.* 1 Propitiated, pleased, conciliated. 2 Effected, accomplished, achieved, performed. 3 Dressed, cooked (as food). 4 Prepared. 5 Obtained,got. 6 Successful, fortunate, happy. 7 Perfect in magical power; (see राध्). -Comp. -अंत: a proved or established fact, a demonstrated conclusion or truth, an ultimate conclusion, doctrine, dogma; सर्ववैनाशिकराद्धांतो नितरामनपेक्षितव्य इतीदानीमुपपादयामः S. B. -अंतित *a.* demonstrated, established by proof, logically proved.

राध् I. 5 P. (राध्नोति, राद्ध; *desid.* रिरात्सति, but रित्सति 'to wish to kill') 1 To propitiate, conciliate, please. 2 To accomplish, effect, complete, perform, achieve. 3 To prepare, make ready. 4 To injure, destroy, kill, exterminate; वानरा भूधरान् रेधुः Bk. 14. 19. -II. 4. P. (राध्यति, राद्ध) 1 To be favourable or mercifull. 2 To be accomplished or finished. 3 To be successful, to succeed, prosper. 4 To be ready. 5 To kill, destroy. -*Caus.* (राधयति-ते) 1 To propitiate. 2 accomplish, complete. -With अनु to propitiate, worship, conciliate. -अप 1 to offend, wrong, sin against (with gen. loc. or by itself); यास्मिन्कस्मिन्नपि पूजार्हेऽपराद्धा शकुंतला S. 4; अपराद्धोऽस्मि तत्रभवतः कण्वस्य S. 7. 2 to miss, not to hit the mark; Si. 2. 27. 3 to annoy, hurt, injure; न तु ग्रीष्मस्यैवं सुभगमपराद्धं युवतिषु S. 3. 9. -आ to propitiate. (-*Caus.*) 1 to propitiate, conciliate, please; परेषां चेतांसि प्रतिदिवसमाराध्य बहुधा Bh. 3. 34, 2. 4. 5. 2 to worship, serve ; Me. 45. -वि to hurt, injure, offend, worng; क्रियासमभिहारेण विराध्यंतं क्षमेत क: Si. 2. 43; विराद्ध एवं भवता विराद्धा बहुधा च नः 2. 41.

राध: The month called Vaisâkha.

राधा 1 Prosperity, success. 2 N. of a celebrated Gopî or cowherdess loved by Krishṇa (whose amours have been immortalized by Jayadeva in his Gîtagovind); तदिमं राधे गृहं प्रापय Gît. 1. 3 N. of the wife of Adhiratha and foster-mother cf Karṇa. 4 The lunar mansion called विशाखा. 5 Lightning.

राधिका See राधा.

राधेय: An epithet of Karṇa.

राम *a.* 1 Pleasing, delighting, rejoicing. 2 Beautiful, lovely, charming. 3 Obscure, dark-coloured, black. 4 White. -म: 1 N. of three celebrated personages; (*a*) Parasurâma, son of Jamadagni; (*b*) Balarâma, son of Vasudeva and brother of Krishṇa, q. q. v. v.; (*c*) Râmachandra or Sîtârâma, son of Dasaratha and Kausalyâ and the hero of the Râmâyaṇa. [When quite a boy, he with his brother was taken by Visvamitra, with the permission of Dasaratha, to his hermitage to protect his sacrifices from the demons that obstructed them. R*a*ma killed them all with perfect ease, and received from the sage several miraculous missiles as a reward. He then accompanied Visv*a*mitra to the capital of Janaka where he married S*i*ta by having performed the wonderful feat of bending *S*iva's bow, and then returned to Ayodhy*a*. Dasaratha, seeing that R*a*ma was growing fitter and fitter to rule the kingdom, resolved to install him as heir-apparent. But, on the eve of the day of coronation, his favourite wife Raikey*i*, at the instigation of her wicked nurse Manthar*a*, asked him to fulfil the two boons he had formerly promised to her, by one of which she demanded the exile of R*a*ma for fourteen years and by the other the installation of her own son Bharata as Yuvar*a*ja. The king was terribly shocked, and tried his best to dissuade her from her wicked demands, but was at last obliged to yield. The dutiful son immediately prepared to go into exile accompanied by his beautiful young wife S*i*ta and his devoted brother Lakshma*n*a. The period of his exile was very eventful, and the two brothers killed several powerful demons and at last roused the jealousy of R*a*va*n*a himseif. The wicked demon resolved to try R*a*ma by carrying off his beauteous wife for whom he had conceived an ardent passion, and accomplished his purpose being assisted by M*a*richa. After several fruitless inquiries as to her whereabouts, Hanumat ascertained that she was in Lank*a* and persuaded R*a*ma to invade the island and kill the ravisher. The monkeys built a bridge across the ocean over which R*a*ma with his numerous troops passed, conquered Lank*a* and killed R*a*vana along with his whole host of demons. R*a*ma, attended by his wife and friends in battle, triumphantly returned to Ayodhy*a* where he was crowned king by Vasish*t*ha. He reigned long and righteously and was succeeded by his son Kusa. R*a*ma is said to be the seventh incarnation of Vish*n*u; cf. Jayadeva:— वितरसि दिक्षु रणे दिक्पतिकमनीयं दशमुखमौलिबलिं रमणीयं । केशव धृतरघुपतिरूप जय जगदीश हरे Gît. 1.] 2 A kind of deer. -Comp. -अनुज: N. of a celebrated reformer, founder of a Vedântic sect and author of several works. He was a Vaish*n*ava. -अयनं (णं) 1 the adventures of Râma. 2 N. of a celebrated epic by Vâlmîki which contains about 24000 verses in seven Kâṇdas or books. -गिरि: N. of a mountain; (चक्रे) स्निग्धच्छायातरुषु वसतिं रामगिर्याश्रमेषु Me. 1. -चंद्र:, -भद्र: N. of Râma, son of Dasaratha. -दूत: N. of Hanumat. -नवमी the ninth day in the bright half of Chaitra, the anniversary of the birth of Râma. -सेतु: 'the bridge of Râma', a ridge of sand between the Indian peninsula and Ceylon now called Adam's bridge.

रामठ:-ठं Asa Foetida (हिंगु).

रामणीयक *a.* (की *f.*) Lovely, beautiful, pleassing. -कं Loveliness, beauty; सा रामणीयकनिधेरधिदेवता वा Mâl. 1. 21; 9. 47; तरुणस्तिन एव शोभते मणिहारावलिरामणीयकं N. 2. 44.; Ki. 1. 33; 4. 4.

रामा 1 A beautiful woman, a charming young woman; अथ रामा विकसन्मुखी बभूव Bv. 2. 16; 3. 6. 2 A beloved, wife, mistress; R. 12. 23, 14. 27. 3 A woman in general; रामा हरंति हृदयं प्रसभं नराणां Rs. 6. 25. 4 A woman of low origin. 5 Vermilion. 6 Asa Fœtida.

राभ: A bamboo-staff carried by a religious student or ascetic.

राव: 1 A cry, scream, shriek, roar, the cry of any animal. 2 sound in general.; मुरजवाद्यराव: M. 1. 21; मधुरिपुरावं Git. 11.

रावण *a.* Crying, screaming, roaring, bewailing. -ण: N. of a celebrated demon, king of Lankâ and the chief of the Râkshasas. [He was the son of Visravas by Kesini or Kaikasi and so halfbrother of Kubera. He is called *Paulastya* as being a grandson of the sage Pulastya. Lanka was originally occupied by Kubera, but Ravana ousted him from it and made it his own capital. He had ten heads (and hence his names Dasagriva, Dasavadana &c.) and twenty arms, and according to some, four legs (cf. R. 12. 88 and Malli). He is represented to have practised the most austere penance for ten thousand years in order to propitiate the god Brahman, and to have offered one head at the end of each one thousand years. Thus he offered nine of his heads and was going to offer the tenth when the God was pleased and granted him immunity from death by either god or man. On the strength of this boon he grew very tyrannical and oppressed all beings. His power became so great that even the gods are said to have acted as his domestic servants. He conquered almost all the kings of the day, but is said to have been imprisoned by Kartavirya for some time when he went to attack his territory. On one occasion he tried to uplift the Kailasa mountain, but Siva pressed it down so as to crush his fingers under it. He, therefore, hymned Siva for one thousand years so loudly that the God gave him the name Ravana, and freed him from his painful position. Bnt though he was so powerful and invincible, the day of retribution drew near. While Rama–who was Vishnu descended on earth for the destruction of this very demon–was passing his years of exile in the forest, Ravana carried off his wife Sita and urged her to become his wife; but she persistently refused and remained loyal to her husband. At last Rama assisted by his monkey-troops invaded Lanka, annihilated Ravana's troops and killed the demon himself. He was a worthy opponent of Rama, and hence the expression रामरावणयोर्युद्धं रामरावणयोरिव]

रावणिः 1 N. of Indrajit; रावणिश्चाप्यथो योद्धुमारब्ध च महीं गतः Bk. 15. 78, 89. 2 Any son of Râvaṇa; Bk. 15. 79, 80.

राशिः 1 A heap, mass, collection, quantity, multitude; धनराशिः, तोयराशिः, यशोराशिः &c. 2 The numbers or figures put down for any arithmetical operation (such as adding, multiplying &c.) 3 A sign of the zodiac. –Comp. –अधिपः the regent of an astrological house. –चक्रं the zodiac. –त्रयं the rule of three. –भागः a fraction. °अनुबंधः the addition of fractions. –भोगः the passage of the sun, moon or any planet through a sign of the zodiac.

राष्ट्रं 1 A kingdom, realm, empire; राष्ट्रदुर्गबलानि च Ak., Ms. 7. 109, 10. 61. 2 A district, territory, country, region; as in महाराष्ट्र; Ms. 7. 32. 3 The people, nation, subjects; Ms. 9. 254. –ष्ट्रः, –ष्ट्रं Any national or public calamity.

राष्ट्रिकः 1 A inhabitant of a kingdom or country, a subject ; Ms. 10. 61. 2 The ruler of a kingdom, governor.

राष्ट्रिय *a.* Belonging to a kingdom. –यः 1 The ruler of a kingdom, king; as in राष्ट्रियश्यालः Mk. 9. 2 The brother-in-law of a king (queen's brother); श्रुतं राष्ट्रियमुखाद्यावदंगुलीकदर्शनम् S. 6. (Also राष्ट्रीय.)

रास् 1 A. (रासते) To cry, scream, yell, sound, howl.

रासः 1 An uproar, a din, confused noise. 2 A sound in general. 3 A kind of dance practised by Krishṇa and the cowherds, but particularly the *gopi's* or cowherdesses of Vrindâvana, उत्सृज्य रासे रसं गच्छंती Ve. 1. 2; रासे हरिमिह विहितविलासं स्मरति मनो मम कृतपरिहासं Gît. 2; also Gît. 1. –Comp. –क्रीडा, –मंडलं a sportive dance, the circular dance of Krishṇa and the cowherdesses of Vrindâvana.

रासकं A kind of minor drama, See S. D. 548.

रासभः An ass, a donkey.

राहित्यं Being without anything, destitution; destituteness.

राहुः 1 N. of a demon, son of Viprachitti and Simhikâ and hence often called *Saimhikeya* [When the nectar, that was churned out of the ocean, was being served to the gods, Rahu disguised himself and attempted to drink it along with them. But he was detected by the sun and the moon who informed Vishnu of the fraud. Vishnu, thereupon, severed his head from the body, but as he had tasted a little quantity of nectar the head became immortal, and is supposed to wreak its vengeance on the sun and moon at the time of conjunction and opposition; cf. Bh. 2. 34. In astronomy Rahu is regarded, like Ketu, as one of the nine planets or only as the ascending node of the moon.] 2 An eclipse, or rather the moment of occultation. –Comp. –ग्रसनं, –ग्रासः –दर्शनं, –संस्पर्शः an eclipse (of the sun or moon). –सूतकं 'the birth of Râhu,' *i. e.* an eclipse (of the sun or moon); Y. 1. 146; cf. Ms. 4. 110.

रि I. 6. P. (रियति, रीण) To go move. –II. 9 U. see री.

रिक्त *p. p.* 1 Emptied, cleared, evacuated. 2 Empty, void. 3 Devoid or deprived of, without. 4 Hollowed (as hands). 5 Indigent. 6 Divided, separated; (see रिच्). –क्तं 1 An empty space, vacuum. 2 A forest, desert, wilderness. –Comp. –पाणि, –हस्त *a.* empty-handed, bringing no present (of flowers &c.), अहमपि देवीं प्रेक्षितुमरिक्तपाणिर्भवामि M. 4.

रिक्तक *a.* See रिक्त.

रिक्ता N. of the fourth, ninth, and fourteenth days of a lunar fortnight.

रिक्थं 1 Inheritance, bequest, property left at death; विभजेरन् सुताः पित्रोरूर्ध्वं रिक्थमृणं समं Y. 2. 117; Ms. 9. 104; ननु गर्भः पित्र्यं रिक्थमर्हति S. 6. 2 Property in general, wealth, possessions ; Ms. 8. 27. 3 Gold. –Comp. –आदः, –ग्राहः, –भागिन् *m.*, –हरः, –हारिन् *m.* an heir.

रिंख्, रिंग् (रिंखति, रिंगति) 1 To crawl, creep. 2 To go slowly.

रिंखणं, रिंगणं 1 Crawling, creeping (of children who creep on all fours). 2 Deviating (from rectitude) swerving.

रिच् I. 7. U. (रिणक्ति, रिंक्ते, रिक्त) 1 To empty, evacuate, clear, purge; रिणच्मि जलधेस्तोयं Bk. 6. 36 ; आविर्भूते शशिनि तमसा रिच्यमानेव रात्रिः V. 1. 8. 2 To deprive of, make destitute of ; usually in *p. p.*, see रिक्त. –With अति to excel, exceed, surpass (in *pass.* and with abl.) ; गृहं तु गृहिणीहीनं कांतारादतिरिच्यते Pt. 4. 81, H. 4. 131 ; Bg. 2. 36 ; वाचः कर्मातिरिच्यते 'example is better than precept.' –उद् 1 to excel, surpass, exceed. 2 to increase, expand. –व्यति to exceed, surpass ; स्तुतिभ्यो व्यतिरिच्यंते दूराणि चरितानि ते R. 10. 30. –II. 1. 10 P. (रेचति, रेचयति, रेचित). 1 To divide, separate, disjoin. 2 To abandon, leave. 3 To join, mix. –With आ to contract, move playfully or sportively ; आरेचितभ्रूचतुरैः कटाक्षैः Ku. 3. 5.

रिटिः 1 A musical instrument. 2 N. of an attendant of Siva; cf. भृंग- (गे)रिटि.

रिपुः An enemy, a foe, an opponent.

रिफ् 6 P. (रिफति, रिफित) 1 To utter a rough grating sound. 2 To revile, blame.

रिष् 1. P. (रेषति, रिष्ट) 1 To injure, hurt, harm ; तस्येहार्थो न रिष्यते Mb. ; तेन यायात्सतां मार्गं तेन गच्छन्न रिष्यते Ms. 4. 178. 2 To kill or destroy ; Bk. 9. 31.

रिष्ट *p. p.* 1 Injured, hurt. 2 Unlucky. –ष्टं 1 Mischief, injury, harm. 2 Misfortune, ill-luck. 3 Destruction, loss. 4 Sin. 5 Good luck, prosperity.

रिष्टिः *f* See रिष्टं above. –*m.* A sword.

री I. 4 A. (रीयते) To trickle, drip, distil, ooze, flow. –II. 9 U. (रिणाति, रिणीते, रीण ; *caus.* रेपयति-ते 1 To go, move. 2 To hurt, injure, kill. 3 To howl.

रीज्या 1 Censure, reproach, blame. 2 Shame, modesty.

रीढकः The back-bone.

रीढा Disrespect, contempt, irreverence.

रीण *p. p.* Oozed, flowed, dripped &c.

रीतिः *f.* 1 Moving, flowing. 2 Motion, course. 3 A stream, river. 4 A line, boundary. 5 A method, mode, manner, way, fashion, course, general way ; रीतिं गिराममृतवृष्टिकरीं तदीयां Bv. 3. 19 ; सर्वत्रैषा विहिता रीतिः Moha M. 2 ; उक्तरीत्या, अनयैव रीत्या &c. 6 Usage, custom, practice. 7 Style, diction ; पदसंघटना रीतिरंगसंस्थाविशेषवत् । उपकर्त्री रसादीनां सा पुनः स्याच्चतुर्विधा । वैदर्भी चाथ गाडी च पांचाली लाटिका तथा S. D. 624-5. 8 Brass, bell-metal; (रीती also in this sense). 9 Rust of iron. 10 The oxide formed on the surface of metals.

रु 2 P. (रौति, रवीति, रुत) To cry, howl, scream, yell, shout, roar, to hum (as bees); to sound in general; कर्णे कलं किमपि रौति शनैर्विचित्रं H. 1. 81; Bk. 3. 17, 12. 72, 14. 21. –WITH वि 1 to cry, bewail, lament ; ननु सहचरीं दूरे मत्वा विरौषि समुत्सुकः V. 4. 20 ; Bk. 5. 54 ; Rs. 6. 27. 2 to make a noise, sound in general ; न स विरौति न चापि स शोभते Pt. 1. 75. ; जीर्णत्वाद्गृहस्य विरौति कपाट Mk. 3 ; एते न एव गिरयो विरुवन्मयूराः U. 2. 23.

रुक्म *a.* Bright, radiant. **–क्मः** A golden ornament ; *Si.* 15. 78. **–क्मं** 1 Gold. 2 Iron. **–Comp. –कारकः** a goldsmith. **–पृष्ठक** *a.* gilded, coated with gold. **–वाहनः** N. of Droṇa.

रुक्मिन् *m.* N. of the eldest son of Bhîshmaka and brother of Rukmiṇî.

रुक्मिणी The daughter of Bhîshmaka of Vidarbha. [She was betrothed by her father to *S*isup*a*la, but she secretly loved Krish*n*a, and sent him a letter praying him to take her away. Krish*n*a with Balar*a*ma came and snatched her off after having defeated her brother in battle. She bore to Krish*n*a a son named Pradyumna.).

रुक्ष *a.* = रूक्ष q. v.

रुग्ण *p. p.* 1 Broken, shattered. 2 Thwarted. 3 Bent, curved. 4 Injured, hurt. 5 Diseased, sick (see रुज्). **–Comp. –रय** *a.* checked in an onset, foiled in an attack.

रुच् 1 A. (रोचते, रुचित) 1 To shine, look splendid or beautiful, be resplendent ; रुरुचिरे रुचिरेक्षणविभ्रमाः *Si.* 6. 46 ; Ms. 3. 62. 2 To like, be pleased with (said of persons), be agreeable to, please (of things) ; used with dat. of the person who is pleased and nom. of the thing; न स्रजो रुरुचिरे रमणीभ्यः Ki. 9. 35; यदेव रोचते यस्मै भवेत्तत्तस्य सुंदरं H. 2. 53 ; sometimes with gen. of person ; दारिद्र्यान्मरणाद्वा मरणं मम रोचते न दारिद्र्यं Mk. 1 11. *–Caus.* (रोचयति-ते) To cause to like, make pleasant or agreeable ; Ku. 3. 16. *–Desid.* (रुरु-रो चिषते) To wish to like &c. –WITH अभि to like, be agreeable ; यदभिरोचितं भवते V. 2. –प्र 1 to shine very much. 2 to be liked. –वि to shine, be resplendent ; R. 6. 5 ; 17. 14 ; Bk. 8. 66.

रुच्, रुचा *f.* 1 Light, lustre, brightness ; क्षणदासु यत्र च रुचैकतां गताः *Si.*13. 53, 9. 23, 25;शिखरमणिरुचः Ki. 5. 43 ; Me. 44. 2 Splendour, loveliness, beauty. 3 Colour, appearance (at the end of comp.) ; चलयन्भृंगरुचस्तवालकान् R. 8. 53 ; Ku. 3. 65 ; Ki. 5. 45. 4 Liking, desire.

रुचक *a.* 1 Agreeable, pleasing. 2 Stomachic. 3 Sharp, acrid. **–कः** 1 The citron. 2 A pigeon. **–कं** 1 A tooth. 2 A golden ornament especially for the neck. 3 A tonic, stomachic. 4 A wreath, garland. 5 Sochal salt.

रुचा See रुच्.

रुचिः *f.* 1 Light, lustre, splendour, brightness ; रुचिमिंदुदले करोत्यजः परिपूर्णेंदुरुचिर्महीपतिः *Si.* 16. 71 ; R. 5. 67 ; Me. 15. 2 A ray of light ; as in रुचिभर्तृ q. v. 3 Appearance, colour, beauty (usually at the end of comp.) ; पटलं बहिर्बहलपंकरुचि *Si.* 9. 19. 4 Taste, relish ; as in रुचिकर. 5 Zest, hunger, appetite. 6 Wish, desire, pleasure ; स्वरुच्या at will or pleasure. 7 Liking, taste ; विमार्गगायाश्च रुचिः स्वकांते Bv. 1. 125 'liking or love' ; न स क्षितीशो रुचये बभूव ; भिन्नरुचिर्हि लोकः R. 6. 30 ; नाट्यं भिन्नरुचेर्जनस्य बहुधाप्येकं समाराधनं M. 1. 4; oft. in comp. in the sense of 'indulging in', 'devoted or addicted to'; हिंसारुचेः Mâl. 5. 29. 8 Passion, close application to any object. **–Comp. –कर** *a.* 1 tasteful, savoury, palatable. 2 exciting desire. 3 stomachic, tonic. **–भर्तृ** *m.* 1 the sun ; *Si.* 9. 17. 2 a husband.

रुचिर *a.* 1 Bright, shining, brilliant, radiant ; हेमरुचिरांबर Ch. P. 14 ; कनकरुचिरं, रत्नरुचिरं &c. 2 Tasteful, palatable. 3 Sweet, dainty. 4 Stomachic, exciting appetite. 5 Cordial, restorative. **–रा** 1 A kind of yellow pigment. 2 N. of a metre ; see App. I. **–रं** 1 Saffron. 2 Cloves.

रुच्य *a.* Bright, lovely &c. ; see रुचिर.

रुज् 6 P. (रुजति, रुग्ण) 1 To break to pieces, destroy ; R. 9. 63, 12. 73, Bk. 4. 42. 2 To pain, injure, disorder, afflict with disease, sometimes with gen. ; रावणस्येह रोक्ष्यंति कपयो भीमविक्रमाः Bk. 8. 120. 3 To bend.

रुज्, रुजा *f.* 1 Breaking, fracture. 2 Pain, torment, pang, anguish ; अनिशमपि मकरकेतुर्मनसो रुजमावहन्नभिमतो मे *S.* 3. 4; क्व रुजा हृदयप्रमाथिनी M. 3. 2. ; चरणं रुजापरीतं 4. 3. 3 Sickness, malady, disease ; R. 49. 52. 4 Fatigue, toil, effort, trouble. **–Comp. –प्रतिक्रिया** counteraction or treatment of disease, curing, practice of medicine. **–भेषजं** a medicine. **–सद्मन्** *n.* feces, excrement.

रुंडः-डं A headless body, trunk; वेलद्वैरवरुंडमुंडनिकरैर्वीरो पिबत्ते भुवः U. 5. 6, Mâl. 3. 17.

रुतं A cry, yell, roar, sound or noise in general ; note (of birds), humming (of bees); पक्षि°, हंस°, कोकिल°, अलि°. **–Comp- –ज्ञः** an augur. **–व्याजः** 1 simulated cry. 2 mimicry.

रुद् 2 P. (रोदिति, रुदित ; *desid.* रुरुदिषति) 1 To cry, weep, lament, mourn, shed tears ; निराधारो हा रोदिमि कथय केषामिह पुरः G. L. 4 ; अपि ग्रावा रोदित्यपि दलति वज्रस्य हृदयं U. 1. 28. 2 To howl, roar, scream. –WITH प्र to weep bitterly.

रुदनं, रुदितं Weeping, crying, wailing, lamentation ; अत्यंतमासीद्रुदितं वनेऽपि R. 14. 69, 70, Me. 84.

रुद्ध *p. p.* 1 Obstructed, impeded, opposed. 2 Besieged, enclosed, hemmed.

रुद्र *a.* Dreadful, terrific, frightful, formidable. **–द्रः** 1 N. of a group of gods, eleven in number, supposed to be inferior manifestations of *S*iva or *S*ankara, who is said to be the head of the group ; रुद्राणां शंकरश्चास्मि Bg. 10. 23; रुद्राणामपि मूर्धानः क्षतहुंकारशंसिनः Ku. 2. 26. 2 N. of *S*iva. **–Comp. –अक्षः** a kind of tree. (**–क्षं**) the berry of this tree, used for rosaries; भस्मोद्धूलन भद्रमस्तु भवते रुद्राक्षमाले शुभं K. P. 10. **आवासः** 1 'the abode of Rudra' the mountain Kailâsa. 2 N. of Benares. 3 a cemetery ; cf. पितृसद्मगोचरः.

रुद्राणी The wife of Rudra, N. of Pârvatî.

रुध् 7 U. (रुणद्धि, रुंद्धे, रुद्ध; *desid.* रुरुत्सति-ते) 1 To obstruct, stop, arrest, check, oppose hinder ; impede, prevent, इदं रुणद्धि मां पद्ममंतःकूजितषट्पदं V. 4. 21 ; रुद्धालोके नरपतिपथे Me. 37, 91; प्राणापानगती रुद्ध्वा Bg. 4. 29. 2 To hold up, preserve, sustain (from falling); आशाबंधः कुसुमसदृशं प्रायशो ह्यंगनानां सद्यःपाति प्रणयि हृदयं विप्रयोगे रुणद्धि Me. 10. 3 To shut up, lock or block up, close up, shut or close ; with loc. ; but sometimes with two acc.; Bk. 6. 35; व्रजं रुणद्धि गां Sk. 4 To bind, confine ; व्यालं बालमृणालतंतुभिरसौ रोद्धुं समुज्जृंभते Bh. 2. 6. 5 To besiege, invest, blockade; रुंधंतु वारणघटा नगरं मदीयाः Mu. 4. 17 ; अरुणद्यवनः साकेतं or माध्यमिकान् Mbh.; Bk. 14. 29. 6 To hide, cover, obscure, conceal. 7 To oppress, torment, afflict excessively. –WITH अनु (often used as if the root belonged to the 4th class) **1** to observe, practise; Ms. 5. 63. **2** to love, be fond of attach oneself to; स्वधर्ममनुरुंधते Ki. 11. 78. नानुरोत्स्ये जगल्लक्ष्मी Bk. 16. 23. **3** to obey, follow, conform to; नियतिं लोक इवानुरुध्यते Ki. 2. 12 ; अनुरुध्यस्व चंद्रकेतोर्वचनं U. 5 ; मद्वचनमनुरुध्यते वा भवान् K. 181. **4** to assent or agree to, approve of. **5** to urge, press. -**अव 1** to obstruct, detain S. 2. 2. **2** to confine, lock up, shut up ; (sometimes with two acc.); शोकं चित्तमवारुधत् Bk. 6. 9. **3** to besiege. -**उप 1** to obstruct, interrupt, hinder; उपरुध्यते तपोनुष्ठानं S. **4. 2** to disturb, trouble, molest; पौरास्तपोवनमुपरुंधंति S. 1. **3** to overcome, subdue; R. 4. 83. **4** to lock up, confine, restrain. **5** To hide, conceal. -**नि 1** to obstruct, stop, oppose, block up; न्यरुंधंश्चास्य पंथानं Bk. 17. 49, 16. 20; Mk. 1. 22. **2** to confine, lock up; Ms. 11. 176; Bg. 8 12. **3** to cover, hide; Ms. 10. 16. -**प्रति** to obstruct &c. -**वि 1** to oppose, obstruct. **2** to contend or quarrel with. **3** to be at variance. -**सं 1** to obstruct, detain, stop; स चेत्तु पथि संरुद्धः पशुभिर्वा रथेन वा Ms. 8. 295. **2** to impede, obstruct, prevent; R. 2. 43. **3** to hold fast, enchain; तृणमिव लघु लक्ष्मीर्नैव तान्संरुणद्धि Bh. 2. 17. **4** to seize upon, grasp, catch hold of; Ms. 8. 235.

रुधिरं 1 Blood. **2** Saffron. -**रः** The planet Mars. -**Comp.** -**अशनः** 'a blood, eater', a demon, an evil spirit. -**आमयः** hemorrhage. -**पायिन्** *m.* a demon.

रुरुः A kind of deer; R. 9. 51, 72.

रुश् 6 P. (रुशति) To hurt, kill, destroy.

रुशत् *a.* Hurting, disagreeable, displeasing (as words).

रुष् 1. 4 P. (रुष्यति; rarely रुष्यते; रुषित, रुष्ट) To be angry, to be vexed or annoyed, be offended; ततोऽरुष्यदनर्दच्च Bk. 17. 40; मा त्रुहो मा रुषोऽधुना 15. 16, 9. 20. -II. 1 P. (रोषति) **1** To hurt, injure, kill. **2** To vex, annoy.

रुष्, रुषा *f.* Anger, wrath, rage; निर्बंधसंजातरुषा R. 5. 21; प्रहेष्वनिर्बंधरुषा हि सतः 16. 86. 19. 20.

रुह् 1 P. (रोहति, रूढ) **1** To grow, spring up, shoot forth, germinate; रूढरागप्रवालः M. 4. 1; केसरैरर्धरूढैः Me. 23; छिन्नोऽपि रोहति तरुः Bh. 2. 87. **2** To grow up, be developed, increase. **3** To rise, mount upwards, ascend. **4** To grow over, heal up (as a wound). -*Caus.* (रोपयति ते, रोहयति-ते) **1** To cause to grow, plant, put in the ground. **2** To raise up, elevate. **3** To entrust, devolve upon, commit to the care of; गुणवत्सुतरोपितश्रियः R. 8. 11. **4** To fix upon, direct towards, cast at; R. 9. 22. -*Desid.* (रुरुक्षति) To wish to grow &c. -WITH **अधि** to ascend, mount (in all senses), ride; R. 7. 37; Ku. 7. 52. (-*Caus.*) to elevate, raise, seat; R. 19. 44. -**अव** to go down, descend; S. 7. 8. -**आ** to ascend, mount, get upon, ride; (the senses of रुह् with आ are variously modified according to the noun with which it is used; *e. g.* प्रतिज्ञां आरुह् to enter upon or make a vow; तुलां आरुह् to rise to equality; संशयं आरुह् to run a risk or be in doubt &c.). (-*Caus.*) **1** to elevate, raise. **2** to place, fix, direct. **3** to ascribe, impute, attribute. **4** to string (as a bow). **5** to appoint to, charge or entrust with. -**प्र** to grow, rise ; न पर्वताग्रे नलिनी प्ररोहति Mk. 4. 17. -**वि** to grow, shoot up; R. 2. 26; Mk. 1. 9. (-*Caus.*) to heal (as a wound). -**सं** to grow; R. 6. 47.

रुह्, रुह *a.* (At the end of comp.) Growing or produced in; as in महीरुह्, पंकेरुह &c.

रुहा The Dūrvā grass,

रूक्ष *a.* **1** Rough, harsh, not smooth or soft (as touch, sound &c.); रूक्षस्वरं वाशति वायसोऽयं Mk. 9. 10; Ku. 7. 17. **2** Astringent (taste). **3** Rough, uneven, difficult, austere. **4** Sullied, soiled, dirtied; R. 7. 70; Mu. 4. 5. **5** Cruel, unkind, harsh; नितांतरूक्षाभिनिवेशमीशं R. 14. 43; S. 7. 32; Pt. 4. 91. **6** Arid, parched up, dry, dreary; स्निग्धश्यामाः क्वचिदपरतो भीषणाभोगरूक्षाः U. 2. 14. (रूक्षीकृ means 'to make rough', 'soil', ' besmear ').

रूक्षणं 1 Making dry or thin. **2** (In medic.) A treatment for reducing fat (of the body).

रूढ *p. p.* **1** Grown, sprung up, shot forth, germinated. **2** Born, produced. **3** Grown up, increased, developed. **4** Risen, ascended. **5** Large, great, grown strong. **6** Diffused, spread about. **7** Commonly known, become current or widely known; क्षतात्किल त्रायत इत्युदग्रः क्षत्रस्य शब्दो भुवनेषु रूढः R. 2. 53; (here क्षत्र has a sense which is योगरूढ q. v.). **8** Popularly accepted, traditional, conventional, popular (as the meaning of a word, or the word itself; as opposed to यौगिक or etymological sense); व्युत्पत्तिरहिताः शब्दा रूढा आखंडलादयः; नाम रूढमपि च व्युदपादि Si. 10. 23. **9** Certain, ascertained.

रूढिः *f.* **1** Growth; germination. **2** Birth, production. **3** Increase, development, growth, spread. **4** Rife, ascent. **5** Fame, celebrity, notoriety, Si. 15. 26. **6** A tradition, custom, customary or traditional usage; शास्त्राद् रूढिर्बलीयसी 'custom prevails over precept'. **7** General prevalence, common currency. **8** Popular meaning conventional acceptation of a word; मुख्यार्थबाधे तद्योगे रूढितोऽथ प्रयोजनात् K. P. 2.

रूप् 10 U. (रूपयति-ते, रूपित) **1** To form, fashion. **2** To represent on the stage, act, gesticulate; रथवेगं निरूप्य S. 1. **3** To mark, observe carefully, behold, look at. **4** To find out, seek. **5** To consider, ponder over. **6** To settle, fix upon. **7** To examine, investigate. **8** To appoint. -WITH **वि** to deform, disfigure.

रूपं 1 Form, figure, appearance; विरूपं रूपवंतं वा पुमानित्येव भुंजते Pt. 1. 143; so सुरूप, कुरूप. **2** Form or the quality of colour (one of the 24 guṇas of the Vaiseshikas); चक्षुर्मात्रग्राह्यजातिमान् गुणो रूपं Tarka. K.; (it is of six kinds:- शुक्ल, कृष्ण, पीत, रक्त, हरित, कपिल or of seven, if चित्र be added). **3** Any visible object or thing. **4** A handsome form or figure, beautiful form, beauty, elegance, grace; मानुषीषु कथं वा स्यादस्य रूपस्य संभवः S. 1. 26 ; विद्या नाम नरस्य रूपमधिकं Bh. 2. 20 ; रूपं जरा हंति &c. **5** Natural state or condition, nature, property, characteristic, essence. **6** Mode, manner. **7** A sign, feature. **8** Kind, sort, species. **9** An image, a reflected image. **10** Similitude, resemblance. **11** Specimen, type, pattern. **12** An inflected form, the form of a noun or a verb derived, from inflection (declension or conjugation). **13** The number one, an arithmetical unit. **14** An integer. **15** A drama, play, see रूपक. **16** Aquiring familiarity with any book by learning it by heart or by frequent recitation. **17** Cattle. **18** A sound, a word. (रूप is frequently used at the end of comp. in the sense of 'formed or composed of,' 'consisting of,' 'in the form of,' 'namely,' 'having the appearance or colour of', तपोरूपं धनं; धर्मरूपः सखा &c.) -**Comp.** -**अधिबोधः** the perception of form or colour of any object by the senses. -**अभिग्राहित** *a.* caught in the act, caught redhanded. -**आजीवा** a harlot, prostitute, courtezan. -**आश्रयः** an exceedingly beautiful person. -**इंद्रियं** the organ which perceives form and colour, the eye. -**उच्चयः** a collection of lovely forms; S. 2. 9. -**कारः**, -**कृत्** *m.* a sculptor. -**तत्त्वं** inherent property, essence. -**धर** *a.* of the form of, disguised as. -**नाशनः** an owl. -**लावण्यं** exquisiteness of form, elegance. -**विपर्ययः** disfigurement, morbid change of bodily form. -**शालिन्** *a.* beautiful. -**संपद्**, -**संपत्ति** *f.* perfection or excellence of form, richness of beauty, superb beauty.

रूपकः A particular coin, a *rupee.* -**कं 1** Form, figure, shape (at the end of comp.). **2** Any manifestation or representation. **3** A sign, feature. **4**

A kind, species. **5** A drama, play, a dramatic composition; (one of the two main subdivisions of dramatic compositions; it is divided into ten classes; there are eighteen minor divisions of it called उपरूपक); दृश्यं तत्राभिनेयं तद्रूपारोपात्तु रूपकं S. D. 272 3. **6** (In Rhet.) A figure of speech corresponding to the English *metaphor*, in which the *Upameya* is represented as being identical with the *Upamâna*; तद्रूपकमभेदो य उपमानोपमेययोः K. P. 10 (see *ad loc.* for details). **7** A kind of weight. **–Comp** –तालः a particular time in music. –शब्दः a figurative or metaphorical expression.

रूपणं **1** Metaphorical or figurative description. **2** Investigation, examination.

रूपवत् *a.* **1** Having form or colour. **2** Bodily, corporeal. **3** Embodied. **4** Handsome, beautiful. –ती A beautiful woman.

रूपिन् *a.* **1** Appearing like. **2** Embodied, incarnate. **3** Beautiful.

रूप्य *a.* Beautiful, lovely. –प्यं **1** Silver. **2** Silver (or gold) bearing a stamp, a stamped coin, a rupee. **3** Wrought gold.

रूष् I. 1 P. (रूषति, रूषित) **1** To adorn, decorate. **2** To smear, anoint, cover, overlay (as with dust). –II. 10 U. (रूषयति-ते) **1** To tremble. **2** To burst.

रूषित *p. p.* **1** Adorned. **2** Smeared, covered, overspread. **3** Soiled. **4** Made rough or rugged. **5** Pounded.

रे *ind.* A vocative particle; रेरेशंकरगृहाधिवासिनो जानपदाः Mâl. 3.

रेखा **1** A line, streak, मद्रेखा, दानरेखा, रागरेखा &c. **2** The mesasure of a line, a small portion, as much as a line; न रेखा मात्रमपि व्यतीयुः R. 1. 17. **3** A row, range, line, series. **4** Delineation, sketch, drawing; लावण्यं रेखया किंचिदन्वितं *S.* 6. 14. **5** The first or prime meridian of the Indian astronomers drawn from Lankâ to Meru and passing through Ujjayinî. **6** Fulness, satisfaction. **7** Deceit, fraud. **–Comp.** –अंशः a degree of longitude. –अंतरं distance east or west from the first meridian, longitude of a place. –आकार *a.* lineal, formed in lines, striped. –गणितं geometry.

रेच See रेचक.

रेचक *a.* (चिका *f.*) **1** Emptying, purging. **2** Purgative, aperient. **3** Emptying the lungs, emitting the breath. –कः **1** Emission of breath, breathing out, exhalation, especially through one of the nostrils (opp. पूरक which means 'inhaling breath,' and कुंभक 'suspending breath'). **2** A syringe. **3** Nitre, salt-petre. –कं A purgative, cathartic.

रेचनं, –ना **1** Emptying. **2** Lessening, diminishing. **3** Emitting the breath. **4** Purging. **5** Evacuation.

रेचित *a.* Emptied, cleared. –तं A horse's gallop.

रेणुः *m. f.* **1** Dust, an atom of dust, sand &c.; तुरगखुरहतस्तथा हि रेणुः *S.* 1. 31. **2** The pollen of flowers.

रेणुका The wife of Jamadagni and mother of Parasurâma; see जमदग्नि.

रेतस् *n.* Semen virile.

रेप *a* **1** Contemptible, low, vile. **2** Cruel.

रेफ *a.* Low, vile, contemptible. –फः **1** A burr, grating sound. **2** The letter र्. **3** Passion, affection.

रेवटः **1** A boar. **2** A bamboo cane. **3** A whirl-wind.

रेवतः The citron tree.

रेवती **1** N. of the 27th constellation which contains thirty-two stars. **2** N. of the wife of Balarâma; *Si.* 2. 16.

रेवा N. of the river Narmadâ; रेवारोधसि वेतसीतरुतले चेतः समुत्कंठते K. P. 1; R. 6. 43; Me. 19.

रेष् 1 A. (रेषते, रेषित) **1** To roar, howl, yell. **2** To neigh.

रेषणं, रेषा Roaring, neighing.

रै *m.* (Nom. राः, रायौ, रायः) Wealth, property, riches.

रैवतः, रैवतकः N. of a mountain near Dvârakâ; (for a description of this mountain, see *Si.* 4).

रोकं **1** A hole. **2** A boat, ship. **3** Moving, shaking.

रोगः A disease, sickness, malady, distemper, infirmity, संतापयंति कमपथ्यभुजं न रोगाः H. 3. 117; भोगे रोगभयं Bh. 3. 35. **–Comp.** –आयतनं the body. –आर्त *a.* afflicted with disease, sick. –शांतिः *f.* alleviation or cure of disease. –हर *a.* curative. (–रं) a medicine. –हारिन् *a.* curative. (*–m.*) a physician.

रोचक *a.* **1** Pleasant, agreeabl. **2** Exciting appetite. –कं **1** Hunger. **2** Any medicine serving as a tonic or restoring lost appetite, a stimulant, tonic. **3** A worker in glass or artificial ornaments.

रोचन *a.* (ना or नी *f.*) **1** Enlightening, illuminating, irradiating. **2** Bright splendid, beautiful, lovely, pleasing, agreeable; Bk. 6. 73. **3** Stomachic. –नः A stomachic. –नं The bright sky, firmament.

रोचना **1** The bright sky, firmament. **2** A handsome woman. **3** A kind of yellow pigment (= गोरोचना q. v.); R. 6. 65, 17. 24; *Si.* 11. 51.

रोचमान *a.* **1** Shining, bright. **2** Lovely, beautiful, charming. –नं A tuft of hair on a horse's neck.

रोचिष्णु *a.* **1** Bright, resplendent, shining, brilliant. **2** Gay, gaily or elegantly dressed, blooming. **3** Exciting appetite.

रोचिस् *n.* Light, splendour, brightness, flame; *Si.* 1. 5.

रोदनं **1** Weeping; see रुदन. **2** A tear or tears.

रोदस् *n.* (in dual), **रोदसी** *f.* Heaven and earth; रवः श्रवणभैरवः स्थगितरोदसीकंदरः Ve. 3. 2; वेदांतेषु यमाहुरेकपुरुषं व्याप्य स्थितं रोदसी V. 1. 1; *Si.* 8. 15.

रोधः **1** Stopping, arresting, hindering *Si.* 10. 89. **2** Obstruction, stoppage, hindrance, prevention, prohibition, suppression; शापादसि प्रतिहता स्मृतिरोधरूक्षे S. 7. 32; उपलरोध Ki. 5. 15; Y. 2. 220. **3** Closing, blocking up, blockade, siege; प्रीतिरोधमसहिष्ट सा पुरी R. 11. 52. **4** A dam.

रोधनः The planet Mercury. –नं Stopping, checking, confining, restraint, check &c.

रोधस् *n.* **1** A bank, an embankment, a dam; गंगा रोधः पतनकलुषा गृह्णतीव प्रसादं V. 1. 8; R. 5. 42; Me. 51. **2** A shore, high bank; R. 8. 33. **–Comp.** –वक्रा, –वती **1** a river. **2** A rapid river.

रोध्रः A kind of tree (=लोध्र q. v.). –ध्रः –ध्रं Sin. –ध्रं Offence, injury.

रोपः **1** The act of raising or setting up. **2** Planting. **3** An arrow; *Si.* 19. 120. **4** A hole, cavity.

रोपणं **1** The act of erecting, setting up or raising. **2** Planting. **3** Healing. **4** A healing application. (said of sores.)

रोमकः **1** The city of Rome. **2** A Roman, an inhabitant of Rome (usually in pl.). **–Comp.** –पत्तनं the city of Rome. –सिद्धांतः one of the five chief Siddhântas (so called because it was probably derived from the *Romans*).

रोमन् *n.* The hair on the body of men and animals; especially, short hair, bristles or down; Ms. 4. 144; 8. 116. **–Comp.** –अंकः a mark of hair; बिभ्रती श्वेतरोमांकं R. 1. 83. –अंचः a thrill (of repture, horror, surprise &c.), horripilation; हर्षाद्भुतभयादिभ्यो रोमांचो रोमविक्रिया S. D. 167. अंचित *a.* with the hair erect or thrilled with joy. –अंतः the hair on the back or upper side of the hand –आली, –आवलिः –ली *f.* a line of hair on the abdomen (above the navel); शिखा धूमस्येयं परिणमति रोमावलिवपुः U. P. 10; see रोमराजि also –उद्गमः –उद्भेदः erection of the hair (on the body), thrill, horripilation; Ku. 7. 77. –कूपः, –पं, –गर्तः a pore of the skin –केशरं, केसरं a whisk, *chowrie*, –पुलकः bristling of the hair, thrill Ch. P. 34. –भूमिः 'the place of the hair,' *i. e.* the skin. –रंध्रं a pore of the skin. –राजिः, –जीः, –लता *f.* a line of hair on the abdomen (above the navel); रराज तन्वी नवरो(लो)मराजिः Ku. 1. 38; *Si.* 9. 22. –विकारः, –विक्रिया –विभेदः thrill, horripilation; Ki. 9 46;

Ku. 5. 16. -हर्षः bristling of the hair, thrill; वेपथुश्च शरीरे मे रोमहर्षश्च जायते Bg. 1. 29. -हर्षण a. causing thrill or horripilation, thrilling, awe-inspiring; एतानि खलु सर्वभूतरो(लो)महर्षणानि दीर्घाण्यानि U. 2. संवादमिममश्रौषमद्भुतं रोमहर्षणं Bg. 18. 74. (-णः) N. of Sûta, a pupil of Vyâsa who narrated several Purâṇas to Saunaka. (-णं) erection of hair on, the body, thrill.

रोमंथ 1 Ruminating, chewing the cud; छायाबद्धकदंबकं मृगकुलं रोमंथमभ्यस्यतु S. 2. 8. **2** (Hence) Frequent repetition.

रोमश a. Hairy, shaggy, woolly. -**शः 1** A sheep, ram. **2** A hog, boar.

रोरुदा Violent weeping, excessive lamentation; लुठन् सशोको भुवि रोरुदावान् Bk. 3. 32.

रोलंबः A bee; तस्या रोलंबावली केशजालं Dk.; Bv. 1. 118.

रोषः Anger, wrath, rage; रोषोपि निर्मलधियं रमणीय एव Bv. 1. 71, 44.

रोषण a. (णी f.) Angry, irascible, wrathful, passionate. -**णः 1** A touchstone. **2** Quicksilver. **3** A desert soil containing salt.

रोहः 1 Rising, heeight, attitude. **2** The raising of anything (as of a number from a smaller to a higher denomination). **3** Growth, development (fig.). **4** Bud, blossom, shoot.

रोहणः N. of a mountain in Ceylon. -**णं** The act of mounting, riding, ascending, growing or healing. -**Comp.** -**द्रुमः** the sandal tree.

रोहंतः A tree in general. -**ती** A creeper.

रोहिः 1 A kind of deer. **2** A religious man. **3** A tree. **4** A seed.

रोहिणी 1 A red cow. **2** A cow in general; Si. 12. 40. **3** N. of the fourth lunar mansion (containing five stars) figured by a cart; she was one of the several daughters of Daksha and is regarded as the most favourite consort of the moon; उपरागांते शशिनः समुपगता रोहिणी योगं S. 7. 22. **4** N. of a wife of Vasudeva and mother of Balarâma. **5** A young girl in whom menstruation has just commenced; नववर्षा च रोहिणी. **6** Lightning. -**Comp.** -**पतिः**, -**प्रियः**, -**वल्लभः** the moon. -**रमणः 1** a bull. **2** the moon. -**शकटः** the constellation Rohiṇî figured by a cart; रोहिणीशकटमर्कनंदनश्चेद्भिनत्ति रुधिरोऽथवा शशी Pt. 1. 213 (=Bṛi. S. 47. 14.).

रोहित a. (**रोहिता** or **रोहिणी** f.) Red, red-coloured. -**तः 1** Red colour. **2** A fox. **3** A kind of deer. **4** A species of fish. -**तं 1** Blood. **2** Saffron. -**Comp.** -**अश्वः** fire.

रोहिषः 1 A kind of fish. **2** A kind of deer.

रौक्ष्यं 1 Hardness, dryness, aridity. **2** Roughness, harshness, cruelty; प्रतिषेधरौक्ष्यं R. 5. 58.; निदेश° 14. 58.

रौद्र a. (द्रा-द्री f.) **1** 'Rudra-like', violent, irascible, wrathful. **2** Fierce, savage, terrible, wild. -**द्रः 1** A worshipper of Rudra. **2** Heat, ardour, warmth, passion, warth. **3** The sentiment of wrath or furiousness; see S. D. 232 or K. P. 4. -**द्रं 1** Wrath, rage. **2** Formidableness, fierceness, savageness. **3** Heat, warmth, solar heat.

रौप्य a. Made of silver, silver, like silver. -**प्यं** Silver.

रौरव a. (वी f.) **1** Made of the hide of *Ruru*; R. 3. 31. **2** Dreadful, terrible. **3** Fraudulent, dishonest. -**वः 1** A sauage. **2** N. of one of the hells; Ms. 4. 88.

रौहिणः 1 The sandal tree. **2** The fig-tree.

रौहिणेयः 1 A calf. **2** N. of Balarâma. **3** The planet Mercury. -**यं** An emerald.

रौहिष् m. A kind of deer.

रौहिषः See रोहिष. -**षं** A kind of grass.

ल.

लः 1 An epithet of Indra. **2** A short syllable (in prosody). **3** A technical term used by Pâṇini for the ten tenses and moods (there being ten lakâras).

लक् 10 U. (लाकयति-ते) **1** To taste. **2** To obtain.

लकः 1 The forehead. **2** An ear of wild rice.

लकचः, लकुचः A kind of bread-fruit tree. -**चं** The fruit of this tree.

लकुटः A club, cudgel.

लक्तकः 1 Lac. **2** A tattered cloth, a rag.

लक्तिका A Lizard.

लक्ष् I. 1 A. (लक्षते, लक्षित) To perceive, apprehend, observe, see. -II. 10 U. (लक्षयति-ते, लक्षित) **1** To notice, observe, see, find, perceive; आर्यपुत्रः शून्यहृदय इव लक्ष्यते V. 2; R. 9. 72, 16. 7. **2** To mark, denote, characterize, indicate; सर्वभूतप्रसूतिर्हि बीजलक्षणलक्षिता Ms. 9. 35. **3** To define; इदानीं कारणं लक्षयति &c. **4** To indicate secondarily, mean or signify in a secondary sense; यथा गंगाशब्दः स्रोतसि सबाध इति तटं लक्षयति तद्वत् यदि तटेऽपि सबाधः स्याच्चत्प्रयोजनं लक्षयेत् K. P. 2.; अत्र गोशब्दो वाहीकार्यं लक्षयति S. D. 2. **5** To aim at. **6** To consider, regard, think. -WITH -**अभि** to mark, see. -**आ** to see, perceive, observe; आलक्ष्यदंतमुकुलान् S. 7. 17; नातिपर्याप्तमालक्ष्य मत्कुक्षेरद्य भोजनं R. 15. 18. -**उप 1** to look at, observe, behold, mark; सम्यगुपलक्षितं भवत्या S. 3. **2** to mark, put a sign upon; Y. 1. 30, 2. 151. **3** to denote, designate. **4** to imply in addition, include more than what is actually expressed; नक्षत्रशब्देन ज्योतिःशास्त्रमुपलक्ष्यते Kull. on Ms. 3 162. **5** to mind, have in view. **6** to consider, regard. -**वि 1** to observe, see, notice. **2** to characterize, distinguish. **3** to be confused or abashed, be bewildered; निर्व्यापारविलक्षितानि सांत्वय बलानि U. 6. -**सं 1** to observe, perceive, see, notice; आश्चर्यदर्शनः संलक्ष्यते मनुष्यलोकः S. 7; संलक्ष्यते न छिदुरोपि हारः R. 16. 62 'is not noticed or known'; 8. 42. **2** to test, prove, determine; हेम्नः संलक्ष्यते ह्यग्नौ विशुद्धिः श्यामिकापि वा R. 1. 10. **3** to hear, learn, understand. **4** to characterize, distinguish.

लक्षं 1 One hundred thousand (m. also in this sense); इच्छति शती सहस्रं सहस्री लक्षमीहते Subhâsh.; श्रयो लक्षास्तु विज्ञेयाः Y. 3. 102. **2** A mark, butt, aim, target; प्रत्यक्षवदाकाशे लक्षं बध्ध्वा Mu. 1. **3** A sign, token, mark. **4** Show, pretence, fraud, disguise; as in लक्षसुप्तः 'feigning sleep.' -**Comp.** -**अधीशः** a person possessing a *lac* or *lacs*.

लक्षक a. Indicating indirectly, expressing secondarily. -**कं** One hundred thousand.

लक्षणं 1 A mark, token, sign, indication, characteristic, distinctive mark; वधूदुकूलं कलहंसलक्षणं Ku. 5. 67; अनारंभो हि कार्याणां प्रथमं बुद्धिलक्षणं Subhâsh.; अव्याक्षेपो भविष्यंत्याः कार्यसिद्धेर्हि लक्षणं R. 10. 6, 19. 47; गर्भलक्षण S. 5; पुरुषलक्षणं 'the sign or organ of virility'. **2** A symptom (of a disease). **3** An attribute, a quality. **4** A definition, accurate description. **5** A lucky or auspicious mark on the body (these are considered to be 32); द्वात्रिंशल्लक्षणोपेतः. **6** Any mark or feature of the body (indicative of good or bad luck); क तद्विधस्त्वं क च पुण्यलक्षणा Ku. 5. 37; क्लेशावहा भर्तुरलक्षणाहं R. 14. 5. **7** A name, designation, appellation (oft. at the end of comp.); विदिशालक्षणां राजधानीं Me. 25, N. 22. 41. 8 Excellence, merit, good quality; as in अहितलक्षण R. 6. 71 (where Malli. renders it by प्रख्यातगुण and quotes Ak. गुणैः प्रतीते तु कृतलक्षणाहितलक्षणौ). 9 An aim, a scope, an object. 10 A fixed rate (as of duties); Ms. 8. 406. 11 Form, kind, nature. 12 Effect, operation. 13 Cause, occasion. 14 Head, topic, subject. 15 Pretence, disguise (=लक्ष); प्रसुप्तलक्षणः Mâl. 7. -णः The crane. -णा An aim, object. 2 (In Rhet.) 1 An indirect application or secondary signification of a word, one the of three powers of a word; it is thus defined:--मुख्यार्थबाधे तद्योगे रूढितोऽथ प्रयोजनात् । अन्योऽर्थो लक्ष्यते यत्सा लक्षणारोपितक्रिया K. P. 2; see S. D. 13 also. 3 A goose. -Comp. -अन्वित a. possessed of auspicious marks. -ज्ञ a. able to interpret or explain marks (as on the body). -भ्रष्ट a. ill-fated, unlucky. -लक्षणा = जहल्लक्षणा q. v. -संनिपातः branding, stigmatizing.

लक्षण्य a. 1 Serving as a mark. 2 Having good marks.

लक्षशस् ind. By hundreds of thousands; i. e. in large numbers.

लक्षित p. p. 1 Seen, observed, marked, beheld. 2 Denoted, indicated. 3 Characterized, marked, distinguished. 4 Defined. 5 Aimed at. 6 Indirectly expressed, indicated, hinted at. 7 Inquired into, examined.

लक्ष्मण a. 1 Having marks. 2 Possessed of good or auspicious marks, fortunate, lucky. 3 Prosperous, thriving. -णः 1 The crane. 2 N. of a son of Dasaratha by his wife Sumitrâ. [He was so much attached to Rama from his very childhood that he became ready to accompany him during his travels and took no small part in the several events that took place during the fourteen years of Rama's exile. In the war of Lanka he killed several powerful demons, but particularly Meghanada, the most heroic of the sons of Ravana. He was at first mortally wounded by Meghanada by means of a magical weapon, but was restored to life by Sushena by means of the medicinal drugs fetched by Maruti. One day Time in the disguise of a hermit came to Rama and said that he who should happen to see them converse in private should be immediately abandoned, which was agreed to Lakshmana on one occasion intruded on their privacy and made the word of his brother true by throwing himself into the Sarayu, (see R. 15. 92-95). He married Urmila by whom he had two sons Angada and Chandraketu]. -णा A goose. -णं 1 A name, an appellation. 2 A mark, sign, token. Comp. -प्रसूः N. of Sumitrâ, mother of Lakshmaṇa.

लक्ष्मन् m. 1 A mark, sign, token, characteristic; Si. 11. 30; Ki. 11. 28, 14. 64; R. 19. 30; Ku. 7. 43. 2 A speck, spot; मलिनमपि हिमांशोर्लक्ष्म लक्ष्मीं तनोति S. 1. 20; Mâl. 9. 25. 3 Definition -m. 1 The crane or Sârasa bird. 2 N. of Lakshmaṇa.

लक्ष्मीः f. 1 Fortune, prosperity, wealth; सा लक्ष्मीरुपकुरुते यया परेषां Ki. 8. 18; तृणमिव लघुलक्ष्मीर्नैव तान् संरुणद्धि Bh. 2. 17. 2 Good fortune, good luck. 3 Success, accomplishment; U. 4. 18. 4 Beauty, loveliness, grace, charm, splendour, lustre; मलिनमपि हिमांशोर्लक्ष्म लक्ष्मीं तनोति S. 1. 20; Mâl. 9. 25; लक्ष्मीमुवाह सकलस्य शशाङ्कमूर्तेः Ki. 2. 59, 5. 39, 52, 9. 2; Ku. 3. 49. 5 The goddess of fortune, prosperity and beauty, regarded as the wife of Vishṇu. (She is said to have sprung from the ocean along with the other precious things or 'jewels' when it was churned for nectar by the gods and demons); इयं गेहे लक्ष्मीः U. 1. 38. 6 Royal or sovereign power, dominion; (oft. personified as a wife of the king and regarded as a rival of the queen); तामेकभार्या परिवादभीरोः साध्वीमपि त्यक्तवतो नृपस्य । वक्षस्यसंघट्टसुखं वसंती रेजे सपत्नीरहितेव लक्ष्मीः ॥ R. 14. 86, 12. 26. 7 The wife of a hero. 8 A pearl. 9 N. of turmeric. -Comp. -ईशः 1 an epithet of Vishṇu. 2 the mango tree. 3 a prosperous or fortunate man. -कांतः 1 an epithet of Vishnu. 2 A king. -गृहं the red lotus flower. -तालः a kind of palm. -नाथः an epithet of Vishṇu. -पतिः 1 an epithet of Vishṇu. 2 a king; विहाय लक्ष्मीपतिलक्ष्म कार्मुकं Ki. 1. 44. 3 the betel-nut tree. 4 the clove tree. -पुत्रः 1 a horse. 2 N. of Cupid or Kâma. -पुष्पः a ruby. -पूजनं the ceremony of worshipping Lakshmî (performed by the bridegroom in company with his bride after she has been brought home). -पूजा the worship of Lakshmî performed on the day of new-moon in the month of Asvina (chiefly by bankers and traders whose commercial or official year closes on that day). -फलः the Bilva tree. -रमणः an epithet of Vishṇu. -वसति. f. 'Lakshmî's abode' the red lotus-flower. -वारः Thursday. वेष्टः turpentine. -सखः a favourite of Lakshmî. -सहजः, सहोदरः epithets of the moon.

लक्ष्मीवत् a. 1 Possessed of good fortune, fortunate, lucky. 2 Wealthy, rich, thriving. 3 Handsome, lovely, beautiful.

लक्ष्य pot. p. 1 To be looked at or observed, visible, observable, perceptible; दुर्लक्ष्यचिह्ना महतां हि वृत्तिः Ki. 17. 23. 2 Indicated or recognizable by (with instr. or in comp.) दूराल्लक्ष्यं सुरपतिधनुश्चारुणा तोरणेन Me. 75; प्रवेपमानाधरलक्ष्यकोपया Ku. 5. 74, R. 4. 5, 7. 60. 3 To be known or found out, traceable; Ku. 5. 72, 81. 4 To be marked or characterized. 5 To be defined. 6 To be aimed at. 7 To be expressed or denoted indirectly. 8 To be regarded or considered as. -क्ष्यं 1 An aim, a butt, mark, target, mark aimed at (fig. also); उत्कर्षः स च धन्विनां यदिषवः सिध्यंति लक्ष्ये चले S. 2. 5; दृष्टिं लक्ष्येषु बध्नन् Mu. 1. 2; R. 1. 61, 6. 11, 9. 67; Ku. 3. 47, 64; 5. 49. 2 A sign, token. 8 The thing defined (opp. लक्षण); लक्ष्यैकदेशे लक्षणस्यावर्तनमव्याप्तिः Taraka K. 4 An indirect or secondary meaning, that derived from लक्षणा q. v.; वाच्यलक्ष्यव्यंग्या अर्थाः K. P. 2. 5 A pretence, sham, disguise; इदानीं परीक्षे किं लक्ष्यसुप्तमुत परमार्थसुप्तमिदं द्वयं Mk. 3, 3. 18; कंदर्पप्रवणमनाः सखीसिसिक्षालक्ष्येण प्रतियुवमंजलिं चकार Si. 8. 35, R. 6. 58. 6 A lac, one hundred thousand. -Comp. -क्रम a. the method or order of which is (indirectly) preceptible, as a *dhvani*. -भेदः, -वेधः hitting the mrak ; Ki. 3. 27. -सुप्त a. feigning sleep. -हन् a. hitting the mark (-m.) an arrow.

लख्, लंख् 1 P. (लखति, लंखति) To go, move.

लग् I. 1 P. (लगति, लग्न) 1 To adhere or stick to, cling to, attach oneself to ; श्यामथ हंसस्य करानवाप्तैर्मंदाक्षलक्ष्या लगति स्म पश्चात् N. 3. 8 ; गमनसमये कंठे लग्ना निरुध्य निरुध्य मां Mâi 3. 2. 2 To touch, come in contact with ; कर्णे लगति चान्यस्य प्राणैरन्यो वियुज्यते Pt. 1. 305; यथा यथा लगति शीतवातः Mk. 5. 11. 3 To touch, affect, have an effect on, go home ; विदितेंगिते हि पुर एव जने सपदीरिताः खलु लगंति गिरः Si. 9. 69. 4 To become united, to meet, cut (as lines). 5 To follow closely, ensue or happen immediately; अनावृष्टिः संपद्यते लग्ना Pt. 1. 6 To engage, detain, occupy (one); तत्र दिनानि कतिचिल्लगिष्यंति Pt. 4 'I shall be detained there for some days'. -WITH अव to adhere or stick to ; R. 16. 68. -आ to stick to ; Kâv. 3. 50. -वि to stick or adhere to, cling to. -II. 10 U. (लागयति-ते) 1 To taste. 2 To obtain.

लगड a. Lovely, handsome, beautiful.

लगित a. 1 Adhered or clung to. 2 Connected with, attached to. 3 Got, obtained.

लगुडः, लगुरः, लगुलः A club, stick, staff, cudgel.

लग्न p. p. 1 Adhered or clung to, stuck, held fast ; लताविटपे एकावली लग्ना"

V. 1. 2 Touching, coming in contact with. 3 Attached to, connected with. 4 Clinging or sticking to, remaining on. 5 Cutting, meeting (as lines). 6 Following closely, impending. 7 Busy with, closely occupied about. 8 Auspicious. (See लग्). -ग्नः 1 A bard, minstrel. 2 An elephant in rut. -ग्नं 1 The point of contact or intersection, the point where the horizon and the ecliptic or the path of planets meet. 2 The point of the ecliptic whice at any given time is at the horizon or on the meridian. 3 The moment of the sun's entrance into a zodiacal sign. 4 A figure of the twelve zodiacal signs. 5 An auspicious or lucky moment. 6 (Hence) A decisive moment, time for action. -Comp. -अहः -दिनं, -दिवसः, -वासरः an auspicious day, a day chosen as lucky for the performance of any work.-कालः, -मुहूर्तः, -वेला, -समयः auspicious time, the time fixed upon (by astrologers &c.) as auspicious for the performance of any work (marriage &c.). -नक्षत्रं an auspicious asterism. -मंडलं the zodiac. -मासः an auspicious month. -शुद्धिः f. auspiciousness of the zodiacal signs etc. for the performance of any work.

लग्नकः A surety, bail, bondsman.

लग्निका Incorrect form of नग्निका q. v.

लघयति Den. P. 1 To make light, lighten (lit.); नितांतगुर्वी लघयिष्यता धुरं R. 13.35. 2 To alleviate, lighten, lessen, mitigate ; V. 3. 13 ; R. 11. 62. 3 To make light of, slight, despise ; Ki. 2. 18; make inferior or insignificant; Ki. 5. 4 ; 13. 38.

लघिमन् m. 1 Lightness, absence of weight. 2 Lightness, smallness, insignificance. 3 Litlleness, levity, lowness or meanness of spirit ; मानुषतासुलभो लघिमा प्रश्नकर्मणि मां नियोजयति K. 4 Thoughtlessness, frivolity. 5 The supernatural power of assuming excessive lightness at will, one of the eight *Siddhis* q. v.

लघिष्ठ a. Lightest, lowest, very light &c. (superl. of लघु q. v.).

लघीयस् a. Lighter, lower, very light &c.; (compar. of लघु q. v.).

लघु a. (घु or घ्वी f.) 1 Light, not heavy; तृणादपि लघुस्तूलस्तूलादपि च याचकः Subhâsh.; रिक्तः सर्वो भवति हि लघुः पूर्णता गौरवाय Me. 20 (where the word means 'contemptible' also); R. 9. 6. 2. 2 Little, small, diminutive; Pt. 1 253.; Si. 9. 38, 78. 3 Short, brief, concise; लघुसंदेशपदा सरस्वती R. 8. 77. 4 Trifling, trivial, insignificant, unimportant; कायस्थ इति लघ्वी मात्रा Mu. 1. 5 Low, mean, despicable, contemptible; Si. 9. 23; Pt. 1. 106. 6 Weak, feeble. 7 Wretched, frivolous. 8 Active, light, nimble, agile; S. 2. 5. 9 Swift, quick rapid; किंचित् पश्चाद् व्रज लघुगतिः Me. 16; R. 5. 45. 10 Easy, not difficult; R. 12. 66. 11 Easy. to be digested, light (as food). 12 Short (as a vowel in prosody). 13 Soft, low, gentle. 14 Pleasant, agreeable, desirable; R. 11. 12, 80. 15 Lovely, handsome, beautiful. 16 Pure, clean. -*ind.* 1 Lightly, meanly, contemptuously. 2 Quickly, swiftly ; लघु लघूत्थिता S. 4 'risen very early').-N. 1 Agallochum, a particular variety of it. 2 A partincular measure of time. -Comp. -आशिन्, -आहार a. eating little, moderate in diet, abstemious. -उक्तिः f. a brief mode of expression.-उत्थान, -समुत्थान a. working actively, doing work rapidly. -काय a. light bodied. (-यः) a goat. -क्रम a. having a quick step, going quickly. -खट्विका a small bed-stead. -गोधूमः a small kind of wheat. -चित्त,-चेतस्,-मनस्, -हृदय a. 1 light minded, low-hearted, little-minded, mean-hearted. 2 frivolous. 3 fickle, unsteady. -जंगलः a kind of quail (लावक). -द्राक्षा a small stoneless grape. -द्राविन् a. melting easily. -पाक a. easily digested. -पुष्पः a kind of Kadamba. -प्रयत्न a. 1 pronounced with slight articulation (as a letter). 2 indolent, lazy. -बदरः, -बदरी f. a kind of jujube. -भवः humble birth or origin. -भोजनं a light repast. -मांसः a kind of partridge. -मूलं the lesser root of an equation. -मूलकं a radish. -लयं a kind of fragrant root (वीरणमूल).-वासस् a. wearing light or pure clothes. -विक्रम a. having a quick step, quick-footed. -वृत्ति a. 1 ill-behaved, low, vile. 2 light, frivolous. 3 mismanaged, ill-done. -वेधिन् a. making a clever hit. -हस्त a. 1 light-handed, clever, dexterous, expert ; R. 9. 63. 2 active, agile. (-स्तः) an expert or skilful archer.

लघुता, -त्वं 1 Lightness, levity. 2 Smallness, littleness. 3 Insignificance, unimportance, contempt, absence of dignity; इंद्रोऽपि लघुतां याति स्वयं प्रख्यापितैर्गुणैः. 4 Dishonour, disrespect; Pt. 1. 140, 353. 5 Activity, quickness. 6 Shortness, brevity. 7 Ease, facility. 8 Thoughtlessness, frivolity. 9 Wantonness.

लघ्वी 1 A delicate woman. 2 A light carriage ; Si. 12. 24.

लंका 1 N. of the capital and residence of Râvaṇa and identified with the island of Ceylon or the chief town in it ; according to some Lankâ was much larger than the present island of Ceylon. It was originally built for Mâlyavat q. v. 2 An unchaste woman, a prostitute, harlot. 3 A branch. 4 A kind of grain. -Comp. -अधिपः,-अधिपतिः,-ईशः, ईश्वरः,-नाथः,-पतिः 'lord of Lankâ'; *i. e.* Râvaṇa or Bibhîshaṇa. -अरिः an epithet of Râma. -दाहिन् m. an epithet of Hanumat.

लंखनी The bit of a bridle.

लंगः 1 Lameness. 2 Union, association. 3 A lover, paramour.

लंगकः A lover, paramour.

लंगलं A plough.

लंगूलं The tail of an animal ; cf. लांगूल.

लंघ् 1 U. (लंघति-ते, लंघित ; *desid.* लिलंघिषति-ते) 1 To spring, leap, go by leaps. 2 To mount upon, ascend; अन्ये चाल्लंघिषुः शैलान् Bk. 15. 32. 3 To go beyond, transgress; लंघते स्म मुनिरेष विमानान् N. 5. 4. 4 To fast, abstain from food. 5 To dry, dry up (Paras.). 6 To seize upon, attack, eat up, injure; पल्लवान् हरिणो लंघितुमागच्छति M. 4. -*Caus.* or 10 U. (लंघयति-ते) 1 To leap or spring over, go beyond; सागरः पुत्रगेंद्रेण क्रमेणैकेन लंघितः Mb.; Ms. 4. 38. 2 To pass over, traverse (as distance); R. 1. 47. 3 To mount upon, ascend; R. 4. 52. 4 To violate, transgress, disobey; R. 9. 9; Y. 2. 187. 5 To offend, insult, disrespect, disregard; हस्त इव भूतिमलिनो यथा यथा लंघयति खलः सुजनं । दर्पणमिव तं कुरुते तथा तथा निर्मलच्छायं ॥ Vâs. 6 To prevent, oppose, stop, avoid, avert; भाग्यं न लंघयति कोपि विधिप्रणीतं Subhâsh.; Mk. 6. 2. 7 To attack, seize upon, injure, hurt; R. 11. 92. 8 To excel, surpass, outshine, eclipse; (यशः) जगत्प्रकाशं तदशेषमिज्यया भवद्गुरुर्लंघयितुं ममोद्यतः R. 3. 48. 9 To cause to fast. 10 To shine. 11 To speak. -WITH अभि 1 to go beyond, spring over. 2 to violate, transgress, disobey. -उद् 1 to go over, pass or cross over, go beyond; Si. 7. 74. 2 to mount upon, ascend. 3 to violate, transgress; Mu. 1. 10; Si. 12. 57. -वि 1 to pass or spring over, traverse; निवेशयामास विलंघिताध्वा R. 5. 42, 16. 32; Si. 12. 24. 2 to violate, transgress, overstep, disregard, neglect; गंतुं प्रवृत्ते समयं विलंघ्य Ku. 5. 25; R. 5.48. 3 to violate the limits of propriety; R. 9. 74. 4 to rise towards, ascend or go up to; Ki. 5. 1; N. 5. 2. 5 to give up, abandon, leave aside; मनो बबंधान्यरसान् विलंघ्य सा R. 3. 4. 6 to surpass, excel; इति कर्णोत्पलं प्रायस्तव दृष्ट्या विलंघ्यते Kâv. 2. 224. 7 to cause to fast.

लंघनं 1 Leaping, jumping. 2 Going by leaps, traversing, passing over, going, motion in general; यूयमेव पथि शीघ्रलंघनाः Ghat. 8. 3 Mounting, ascending, rising up to (fig. also) नभोलंघन R. 16. 33; जनेयमुच्चैः पदलंघनोत्सुकः Ku. 5. 64 ' wishing to attain or aspire to a high position'. 4 Assaulting, storming, capturing; as in दुर्गलंघनं. **5** Exceeding, going beyond, overstepping, violating, transgression; आज्ञालंघनं, नियमलंघनं &c. **6** Disregarding, despising, treating with contempt, slighting; प्रणिपातलंघनं प्रमार्ष्टुकामा V. 3; M. 3. 22. **7** An offence, affront, insult. **8** A harm, an injury; as in आतपलंघनं q. v. **9** Fasting, abstinence; Śi. 12. 25 (where it means 'leaping' also). **10** One of the paces of a horse.

लंघित *p. p.* **1** Lept over, passed over. **2** Traversed. **3** Transgressed, violated. **4** Disregarded, insulted, disrespected; (see लंघ्).

लछ् 1 P. (लच्छति) To mark, see; cf. लक्ष्.

लज् I. 6 A. (लजते) To be ashamed. –II. 1 P. (लजति) To blame &c.; see लंज् I. –III. 10 P. (लजयति) **1** To seem, appear, shine. **2** To cover, conceal; (according to some लाजयति also in this sense).

लज्ज् 6 A. (लज्जते, लज्जित) To be ashamed, to blush.

लज्जका The wild cotton tree.

लज्जा **1** Shame; कामातुराणां न भयं न लज्जा Subhâsh.; विहाय लज्जां R. 2. 40; Ku. 1. 48. **2** Bashfulness, modesty; शृंगारलज्जां निरूपयति Ś. 1; Ku. 3. 7; R. 7. 25. **3** N. of the sensitive plant. **–Comp.** –अन्वित *a.* modest, bashful. –आवह, –कर *a.* (रा or री *f.*) causing shame, shameful, disgraceful, ignominious. –शील *a.* bashful, modest –रहित, –शून्य, –हीन *a.* shameless, impudent, immodest.

लज्जालु *a.* Modest, bashful. –*m. f.* N. of the sensitive plant.

लज्जित *p. p.* **1** Modest, bashful. **2** Ashamed, abashed.

लंज् I. 1 P. (लंजति) **1** To blame, censure, traduce. **2** To roast, fry. –II. 10 U. (लंजयति-ते) **1** To injure, strike, kill. **2** To give. **3** To speak. **4** To be strong or powerful. **5** To dwell. **6** To shine.

लंजः **1** A foot. **2** The end of a lower garment tucked into the waistband; cf. कक्षा. **3** A tail.

लंजा **1** A current. **2** An adulteress. **3** N. of Lakshmî. **4** Sleep.

लंजिका A prostitute, harlot.

लट् 1 P. (लटति) **1** To be a child. **2** To act like a child. **3** to talk like a child, prattle. **4** To cry.

लटः **1** A fool, blockhead. **2** A fault, defect. **3** A robber.

लटकः A cheat, rogue, rascal, villain.

लटभ *a.* (Connected with the Prâkrita लडह which appears to be derived from it) Charming, handsome, beautiful, attractive, lovely; अतिक्रांतः कालो लटभललनाभोगसुलभः Bh. 3. 32 (where commentators render लटभ by सलावण्य) तस्याः पादनखश्रेणिः शोभते लटभभ्रुवः Vikr. 8. 6. Bilhaṇa has used this word in three more places of the same book, where it appears to mean 'a young pretty woman', 'a handsome woman'; *e. g.* किं वा वर्णनया समस्तलटभालंकारतामेष्यति 8. 86; अनर्घ्यलावण्यनिधानभूमिर्न कस्य लोभं लटभा तनोति 9. 68; केशबंधविभवैर्लटभानां पिंडितामिव जगाम तमिस्रं 11. 18.

लट्टः A rogue, rascal; see लटक.

लड्वः **1** A horse. **2** A dancing boy. **3** N. of a caste. –**द्वा** **1** A kind of bird. **2** A curl on the forehead. **3** A sparrow. **4** A kind of musical instrument. **5** A game. **6** Safflower. **7** An unchaste woman.

लड् I. 1 P. (लडति) To play, sport, dally. –II. 1 P., 10 P. (लडति, लडयति) **1** To throw, toss. **2** To blame. **3** To loll the tongue. **4** To harass, annoy. –III 10 U. (लाडयति-ते) **1** To fondle, caress. **2** To annoy.

लडह *a.* Beautiful, handsome (a Prâkrita word.

लड्डु = लटक q. v.

लड्डुः, लड्डुकः A kind of sweetmeat (a round ball of sugar, wheat or rice-flour, ghee and spices).

लंड् 1 P., 10 U. (लंडति, लंडयति-ते) **1** To toss upwards, throw up. **2** To speak.

लंडं Excrement, ordure.

लंडः London (a modern formation probably from the French *Londres*).

लता **1** A creeper, creeping plant; लताभावेन परिणतमस्या रूपं V. 4; लतेव संनद्धमनोज्ञपल्लवा R. 3. 7 (often used as the last member of compounds, especially with words meaning 'arm', 'eyebrow', 'lightning', to denote beauty, tenderness, thinness, &c.; भुजलता, बाहुलता, भ्रूलता, विद्युल्लता; so खड्ग°, अलक° &c.; cf. Ku. 2. 64; Me. 47; Ś. 3. 15; R. 9. 45. **2** A branch. **3** The creeper called *Priyangu*. **4** The Mâdhavî creeper. **5** Musk-creeper. **6** A whip or the lash of a whip. **7** A string of pearls. **8** A slender woman. **–Comp.** –अंतं a flower. –अंबुजं a kind of cucumber. –अर्कः a green onion. –अलकः an elephant. –आननः a particular position of the hands in dancing. –उद्गमः the upward winding or climbing of a creeper. –करः a particular position of the hands in dancing. –कस्तूरिका, कस्तूरि, musk-creeper. –गृहः, –हं a bower surrounded with creepers, an arbour; Ku. 4. 41. –जिह्वः, –रसनः a snake. –तरुः **1** the Sâla tree. **2** the ornage tree. –पनसः the water-melon. –प्रतानः the tendril of a creeper; R. 2. 8. –भवनं an arbour, a bower. –मणिः coral. –मंडपः a bower, an arbour. –मृगः a monkey. –यावकं a shoot, sprout. –वलयः, –यं an arbour. –वृक्षः the cocoanut tree. –वेष्टः a kind of coitus or mode of sexual enjoyment. –वेष्टनं, –वेष्टितकं a kind of embrace.

लतिका **1** A small creeper. **2** A string of pearls.

लत्तिका A kind of lizard.

लप् 1 P. (लपति) **1** To speak, talk in general. **2** To prate, chatter. **3** To whisper; कपोलतले मिलिता लपितुं किमपि श्रुतिमूले Gît. 1. –*Caus.* (लापयति-ते) To cause to talk &c.–With अनु to repeat, talk over and over again. –अप **1** to deny, disown, refuse; शतमपलपति Sk. **2** to conceal, hide. –आ **1** to talk to, converse with. **2** to talk, speak. **3** to prate, chatter. –उद् to call out loudly to. –प्र **1** to talk, speak; वचो वैदेहीति (वैदेहीति) प्रतिपदमुदश्रु प्रलपितं S. D. 6. **2** To talk at random or incoherently, prate, chatter, talk wildly or nonsensically. –वि **1** to say, speak. **2** to lament, bewail, cry, weep; विललाप विकीर्णमूर्धजा Ku. 4. 4; विललाप स बाष्पगद्गदं R. 8. 43, 70; Bk. 6. 11; तामिह वृथा किं विलपामि Gît. 3. –विप्र to dispute, contradict, wrangle, quarrel. –सं **1** to talk, converse; संलपतो जनसमाजात् Dk. **2** to name, call.

लपनं **1** Talking, speaking. **2** The mouth.

लपित *p. p.* Spoken, said, chattered &c. –तं Speech, voice.

लब्ध *p. p.* **1** Got, obtained, acquired. **2** Taken, received. **3** Perceived, apprehended. **4** Obtained (as by division &c.); see लभ्. –ब्धं That which is secured or got; लब्धं रक्षेद्वक्षयात् H. 2. 8; R. 19. 3. **–Comp.** –अंतर *a.* **1** one who has found an opportunity. **2** one who has got access or admission; R. 16. 7. –अवकाश, –अवसर *a.* **1** one who has found an opportunity. **2** (anything) that has gained a scope (for work); लब्धावकाशा मे प्रार्थना Ś. 1. **3** one who has obtained leisure, being at leisure; so लब्धक्षण. –आस्पद *a.* one who has gained a footing or secured a position; M. 1. 17. –उदय *a.* **1** born, produced, sprung; लब्धोदया चांद्रमसीव लेखा Ku. 1. 25. **2** one who has got prosperity or elevation; स त्वत्तो लब्धोदयः 'he owes his rise or elevation to you.' –काम *a.* one who has got desired object. –कीर्ति *a.* become widely known, famous, celebrated. –चेतस्, –संज्ञ *a.* one who has come to his senses, restored to consciousness. –जन्मन् *a.* born, produced. –नामन्, –शब्द *a.* renowned, celebrated. –नाशः the loss of what has been acquired; लब्धनाशो यथा मृत्युः. –प्रशमनं **1** securing or keeping safe what has been acquired. **2** bestowing on a worthly recipient; Kull. on Ms. 7. 56. –लक्ष, –क्ष्य *a.* **1** one who has hit the mark. **2** skilled in the use of missiles. –वर्ण *a.* **1** learned, wise; चित्र त्वदीये विषये समंतात् सर्वेऽपि लोकाः किल लब्धवर्णाः Râj. P. **2** famous, renowned, celebrated; Mk. 4. 26. °भाज् *a*. respecting the learned; कृच्छ्रलब्धमपि लब्धवर्णभाक् तं दिदेश मुनये सलक्ष्मणं R. 11. 2. **-विद्य** *a*. learned, educated, wise. **-सिद्धि** *a*. one who has attained perfection or his desired object.

लब्धिः *f*. **1** Acquisition, gaining, acquirement. **2** Profit, gain. **3** (In arith.) The quotient.

लब्धिम *a*. Obtained, acquired, received.

लभ् 1 A. (लभते, लब्ध) **1** To get, obtain, gain, acquire; लभेत सिकतासु तैलमपि यत्नतः पीडयन् Bh. 2. 5; चिराय याथार्थ्यमलंभि दिग्गजैः Si. 1. 64; R. 9. 29. **2** To have, possess, be in possession of. **3** To take, receive. **4** To catch, take or catch hold of; R. 1. 3. **5** To find, meet with; यत्किंचिल्लभते पथि. **6** To recover, regain. **7** To know, learn, perceive, understand; भ्रमणं...गमनादिव लभ्यते Bhâshâ. P. 6; सत्यमलभमानः Kull. on Ms. 8. 169. **8** To be able or be permitted (to do a thing) with (inf.); भर्तुमपि न लभ्यते; नाधर्मो लभ्यते कर्तुं लोके वैद्याधरे. (The senses of लभ् are modified according to the noun with which it is used; *i. e.* गर्भं लभ् to conceive, become pregnant; पदं or आस्पदं लभ् to gain a footing, take a hold on; see under पद; अंतरं लभ् to get a footing, enter into; लेभेऽतरं चेतसि नोपदेशः R. 6. 66. 'was not impressed on the mind;' चेतनां, -संज्ञां -लभ् to regain one's consciousness; जन्म लभ् to be born; Ki. 5. 43; स्वास्थ्यं लभ् to enjoy ease, be at ease; दर्शनं लभ् to get an audience of &c.). *-Caus.* (लंभयति-ते) **1** To cause to get or receive, cause to take; Ki. 2. 58. **2** To give, confer or bestow upon; मोदकशरावं माणवकं लंभय V. 3. **3** To cause to suffer. **4** To obtain, receive. **5** To find out, discover. *-Desid.* (लिप्सते) To wish to get, long for; अलब्धं चैव लिप्सेत H. 2. 8. -WITH **आ 1** to touch; गामालभ्यार्कमीक्ष्य वा Ms. 5. 87; Bk. 14. 91. **2** to get, obtain, attain to; येन श्यामं वपुरतितरां कांतिमालप्स्यते ते Me. 15. v. l. **3** to kill, immolate (as a victim in sacrifice); गर्दभं पशुमालभ्य Y. 3. 280. **-उप 1** to know, understand; see, perceive directly; Pt. 1. 76. **2** to ascertain, find out; ब्रूहि यदुपलब्धं U. 1; तत्त्वत एनामुपलप्स्ये S. 1. **3** to get, obtain, acquire, enjoy, experience; उपलब्धसुखस्तदा स्मरं वपुषा स्वेन नियोजयिष्यति Ku. 4. 42; V. 2. 10, R. 8. 82, 10. 2, 18. 21; Ms. 11. 17. **-उपा 1** to blame, chide, taunt, scold; पयोधरविस्तारयितृकमात्मनो यौवनमुपालभस्व मां किमुपालभसे S. 1; Ku. 5. 58, R. 7. 44; Si. 9. 60. **-प्रति 1** to recover, regain. **2** to get, obtain. **-विप्र 1** to cheat, deceive, impose upon. **2** to recover, regain. **3** to insult, disrespect. **-सं** to get, obtain.

लभनं 1 The act of getting, obtaining &c. **2** Act of conceiving.

लभसः 1 Wealth, riches. **2** One who solicits, a solicitor. **-सं** A rope for tying a horse (*-m.* also).

लभ्य *a*. **1** Capable of being acquired or obtained, attainable, obtainable, to be reached; प्रांशुलभ्ये फले मोहादुद्बाहुरिव वामनः R. 1. 3, 4. 88; Ku. 5. 18. **2** To be found; Ku. 1. 40. **3** Fit, suitable, proper. **4** Intelligible.

लमकः A lover, paramour.

लंपट *a*. **1** Greedy, covetous, hankering after. **2** Lustful, libidinous, dissolute, addicted to licentious pleasures. **-टः** A libertine, profligate, rake; (लंपाक in the same sense.)

लंफः A leap, jump, spring.

लंफनं Leaping, jumping.

लंब् 1 A (लंबते, लंबित) **1** To hang down, hang from, dangle; ऋषयो ह्यत्र लंबते Mb. **2** To be attached to, stick to, hold on to, rest on; ललंबिरे सदासिलताः प्रिया इव Si. 17. 25; प्रस्थानं ते कथमपि सखे लंबमानस्य भावि Me. 41 (where लं° means 'hanging down towards' or 'resting upon' the bank or hips). **3** To go down, sink, decline or hang down (as the sun), fall down; लंबमाने दिवाकरे; Si. 9. 30, Ki. 9. 1; त्वदधरचुंबनलंबितकज्जलमुज्ज्वलय प्रिय लोचने Gît. 12 (=गलित). **4** To fall or lag behind, stay behind. **5** To delay, tarry. **6** To sound. *-Caus.* (लंबयति-ते) **1** To let down, cause to hang down. **2** To hang up, suspend. **3** To stretch out, extend (as the hand); करेण वातायनलंबितेन R. 13. 21; कोलंबयेदाहरणाय हस्तं 6. 75. -WITH **अव 1** to hang, hang down, be suspended; कनकशृंखलावलंबिनी Mu. 2. **2** to sink down, descend. **3** to hold, cling to, lean or rest on, support oneself on; दंडकाष्ठमवलंब्य स्थितः S. 2; ययौ तदीयामवलंब्य चांगुलिं R. 3. 25. **4** to hold or bear up, support, sustain (fig. also), take up; हस्तेन तस्थाववलंब्य वासः R. 7. 9; Ku. 3. 55. 6. 68; हृदयं न त्ववलंबितुं क्षमाः R. 8. 60. **5** to depend upon, hinge on; व्यवहारोयं चारुदत्तमवलंबते Mk. 9; Bk. 18. 41. **6** to resort to, have recourse to, take to; धैर्यमवलंब्य to summon or pluck up courage; किं स्वातंत्र्यमवलंबसे S. 5; माध्यस्थ्यमिष्टेऽप्यवलंबतेऽर्थे Ku. 1. 52; Si. 2. 15. **-आ 1** to rest or lean upon. **2** to hang down from, be suspended; V. 5. 2. **3** to lay hold of, seize; अथालंब्य धनु रामः Bk. 6. 35, 14. 95. **4** to support, hold or take up; आवेरणालंबितं R. 18. 39. **5** to depend upon; तमालंब्य रसोद्गमान् S. D. 63. **6** to have recourse to, resort to, take, assume; अमुमेवार्थमालंब्य न जिजीविषा Mu. 2. 20; Ki. 17. 34. **-उद्** to stand up, stand erect; पादेनैकेन गगने द्वितीयेन च भूतले । तिष्ठाम्युल्लंबितस्तावद्यावत्तिष्ठति भास्करः Mk. 2. 10. **-वि 1** to hang down, hang from, be suspended from, R. 10. 62. **2** to set, decline (as the sun &c.) **3** to stay or lag behind stay or remain; Ku. 7. 13. **4** to delay, be retarded विलंबितफलैः कालं निनाय स मनोरथैः R. 1. 33; किं विलंब्यते त्वरितं तं प्रवेशय U. 1.

लंब *a*. **1** Hanging down, hanging from, pendent, dangling; पांडुचोयमंसार्पितलंबहारः R. 6. 60, 84 Me. 84. **2** Hanging upon, attached to. **3** Great, large. **4** Spacious. **5** Long, tall. **-बः 1** A perpendicular. **2** Co-latitude, the arc between the pole of any place and the zenith, complement of latitude. **-Comp. -उदर** *a*. big-bellied, pot-bellied, portly. (**-रः**) **1** N. of Ganesa. **2** a glutton. **-ओष्ठः** (लं-बो-बौ-ष्ठः) a camel. **-कर्णः 1** an ass. **2** a goat. **3** an elephant. **4** a falcon. **5** a demon or Râkshasa. **-जठर** *a*. pot-bellied, portly. **-पयोधरा** a woman with large pendent breasts. **-स्फिच्** *a*. having fat or protuberant buttocks.

लंबकः 1 A pernpendicular (in geom.). **2** The complement of latitude, coalatitude (in astr.).

लंबनः 1 an epithet of Siva. **2** The phlegmatic humour. **-नं 1** Hanging down, depending, descending &c. **2** Fringe. **3** The parallax in longitude (of the moon). **4** A sort of long necklace.

लंबा 1 An epithet of Durgâ. **2** of Lakshmî.

लंबिका The soft palate or uvula.

लंबित *p. p.* **1** Hanging down, pendent. **2** Suspended. **3** Sunk, gone down. **4** Resting on, attached to (see लंब्).

लंबुषा A nacklace of seven strings.

लंभः 1 Attainment, acquirement. **2** Meeting with. **3** Recovery. **4** Gain.

लंभनं 1 Attainment, acquirement. **2** Recovery.

लंभित *p. p.* **1** Procured, got, obtained. **2** Given. **3** Improved. **4** Employed, applied. **5** Cherished. **6** Spoken to, addressed.

लय् 1 A. (लयते) To go, move.

लयः 1 Sticking, union, adherence. **2** Lurking, hiding. **3** Fusion, melting, solution. **4** Disappearance, dissolution, extinction, destruction; लयं या 'to be dissolved or destroyed.' **5** Absorption of the mind, deep concentration, exclusive devotion (to any one object); पश्यंती शिवरूपिणं लयवशादात्मानमभ्यागता Mâl. 5. 2, 7; ध्यानलयेन Gît. 4. **6** Time in music (of three kinds द्रुत, मध्य and विलंबित); किसलयैः सलयैरिव पाणिभिः R. 9. 35; पादन्यासो लयमनुगतः M. 2. 9. **7** A pause in music. **8** Rest, repose **9** A place of rest, abode, habitation; अलया Si. 4. 57 'having no fixed abode, wandering'. **10** Slackness of mind, mental inactivity. **11** An embrace. **-Comp. -आरंभः, आलंभः** an actor, a danceer. **-कालः** the time of destruction (of the world). **-गत** *a.* dissolved, melted away. **-पुत्री** an actress, a female dancer.

लयनं 1 Adhering, clinging, sticking. **2** Rest, repose. **3** A place of rest, house.

लर्ब् 1 P. (लर्बति) To go, move.

लल् I. 1 U. (ललति-ते) To play, sport, dally, frolic; पनसफलानीव वानरा ललंति Mk. 8. 8; मजकलभा इव बंधुला ललामः 4. 28. -II 10. U. or *Caus.* (लालयति-ते, लालित) **1** To cause to sport or play, caress, fondle, coax, dangle ; लालने बहवो दोषास्ताडने बहवो गुणाः । तस्मात्पुत्रं च शिष्यं च ताडयेन्न तु लालयेत् ॥ Subhâsh.; Ku. 5. 15. **2** To desire. -III. 10 U. (ललयति-ते) **1** To fondle; Mk. 4. 28. **2** To loll the tongue. **3** To desire.

लल *a.* **1** Playful, sportive. **2** Lolling. **3** Wishing desirous. **-Comp. -जिह्व = ललज्जिह्व** q. v.

ललत् *a.* **1** Playing, sporting. **2** Lolling. **-Comp. -जिह्व** *a.* (ललजिह्व) **1** lolling the tongue. **2** savage, fierce. (**-ह्वः**) **1** a dog. **2** a camel.

ललनं 1 Sport, play, pleasure., dalliance. **2** Lolling the tongue.

ललना 1 A woman (in general); शठनाकलोकललनाभिरविरतरतं रिरंससे Si. 15. 88. **2** A wanton woman. **3** The tongue. **-Comp. -प्रियः** the *Kadamba* tree.

ललनिका A little or miserable woman; Kâv. 3. 50.

ललंतिका 1 A long necklace. **2** A lizard or chameleon.

ललाकः The penis.

ललाटं The forehead ; लिखितमपि ललाटे प्रोज्झितुं कः समर्थः H. 1. 21, N. 1. 15. **-Comp. -अक्षः** an epithet of Siva. **-तटं** the slope of the forehead, the forehead itself **-पट्टः, -पट्टिका 1** the flat surface of the forehead. **2** a tiara, fillet. **-लेखा** the line on the forehead.

ललाटकं 1 The forehead. **2** A beautiful forehead.

ललाटंतप *a.* **1** Burning or scorching the (fore) head; ललाटंतपस्तपति तपनः Mâl. 1; U. 6 'the sun is shining right overhead'; ललाटंतपसप्तसप्तिः R.13. 41. **2** (Hence) Very painful; लिपिर्ललाटंतपनिष्ठुराक्षरा N. 1. 138. **-पः** The sun.

ललाटिका 1 An ornament worn on the forehead. **2** A mark made with sandal or any other fragrant powder on the forehead ; Ku. 5. 55.

ललाटूल *a.* Having a high or handsome forehead.

ललाम *a.* (**मी** *f.*) Beautiful, lovely, charming. **-मं 1** An ornament for the forehead, an ornament or decoration in general; (*m.* also in this sense.); अहं तु तामाश्रमललामभूतां शकुंतलामधिकृत्य ब्रवीमि *S.* 2; *Si.* 4. 28. **2** Anything the best of its kind. **3** A mark on the forehead. **4** A sign, symbol, markin general. **5** A banner, flag. **6** A row, series, line. **7** A tail. **8** A mane. **9** Eminence, dignity, beauty. **10** A horn. **-मः** A horse.

ललामकं A chaplet of flowers worn on the forehead.

ललामन् *n.* **1** An ornament, a decoration. **2** (Hence) Anything the best of its kind; कन्याललाम कमनीयमजस्य लिप्सोः R. 5. 64 'the best or ornament of girls.' **3** A banner, flag. **4** a sectarial mark, token, sign, symbol. **6** A tail.

ललित *a.* **1** Playing, sporting, dallying. **2** Amorous, sportive, wanton, voluptuous. **3** Lovely, beautiful, handsome, elegant, graceful ; ललितललितैर्ज्योत्स्नाप्रायैरकृत्रिमविभ्रमैः (अंगकैः)U. 1. 20; बिधाय सृष्टिं ललितां विधातुः R. 6. 37, 19. 39; 8. 1; Mâl. 1. 15, Ku. 3. 75, 6. 45; Me. 32, 64. **4** Pleasing, charming, agreeable, fine; प्रियशिष्या ललिते कलाविधौ R. 8. 67; संदर्शितेव ललिताभिनयस्य शिक्षा M. 4. 9; V. 2. 18. **5** Desired. **6** Soft, gentle; *Si.* 7. 64. **7** Tremulous, trembling. **-तं 1** Sport, dalliance, play. **2** Amorous pastime, gracefulness of gait, any languid or amorous gesture in a woman; *Si.* 9. 79; Ki. 10. 52. **3** Beauty, grace, charm. **4** Any natural or artless act. **5** Simplicity, innocence. **-Comp. -अर्थ** *a.* having a pretty or amorous meaning; V. 2. 14. **-पद** *a.* elegantly composed; *S.* 3. **-प्रहारः** a soft or gentle blow.

ललिता 1 A woman (in general). **2** A wanton woman. **3** Musk. **4** A form of Durgâ. **5** N. of various metres. **-Comp. -पंचमी** the fifth day in the bright half of Asvina. **-सप्तमी** the seventh day in the bright half of Bhâdrapada.

लवः 1 Plucking, mowing. **2** Reaping, gathering (of corn). **3** A section, piece, fragment, bit. **4** A particle, drop, amall quantity, a little; oft. at the end of comp. in this sense ; जललवमुचः Me. 20, 70; आचामति स्वेदलवान् मुखे ते R. 13. 20, 6. 57, 16. 66; अश्रु° 15. 97; अमृत° Ki. 5. 44; भ्रूक्षेपलक्ष्मीलवक्रीते दास इव Gît. 11 ; so तृण°, अपराध°, ज्ञान°, सुख°, धन° &c. &c. **5** Wool, hair. **6** Sport. **7** A minute division of time (= the sixth part of a twinkling). **8** The numerator of a fraction. **9** A degree (in astr.). **10** Loss, destruction. **11** N. of a son of Râma, one of the twins, the other being Kusa q. v. He with his brother was brought up by the sage Vâlmiki, and they were taught by the poet to repeat his Râmâyaṇa at assemblies &c.; (for the derivation of his name, see R. 15. 32). **-वं 1** Cloves. **2** Nutmeg. **-वं** *ind.* A liltte; लवमपि लवंगे न रमते Sar. K. 1.

लवंगः The clove plant; द्वीपांतरानीतलवंगपुष्पैः R. 6. 57; ललितलवंगलतापरिशीलनकोमल मलयसमीरे Gît. 1. **-गं** Cloves. **-Comp. -कलिका** cloves.

लवंगकं Cloves.

लवण *a.* **1** Saline, saltish, briny **2** Lovely, handsome. **-णः 1** Saline taste. **2** The sea of salt water. **3** N. of a demon, son of Madhu, who was killed by Satrughna ; R. 15. 2, 5, 16, 26. **4** N. of a hell. **-णं 1** Salt sea-salt. **2** A factitious salt. **-Comp. -अंतकः** an epithet of Satrughna. **-अब्धिः** the salt ocean. **°जं** sea-salt. **-अंबुराशिः** the ocean; आभाति वेला लवणांबुराशेः R. 13. 15; V. 1. 15. **-अंभस्** *m.* the ocean ; R. 12. 70, 17. 54. (*-n.*) salt water. **-आकरः 1** a salt-mine. **2** a receptacle of salt water; *i. e.* the sea. **3** (fig.) a mine of beauty. **-आलयः** the ocean. **-उत्तमं 1** rock-salt. **2** nitre. **-उदः 1** the ocean. **2** the sea of salt water. **-उदकः, -उदधिः, -जलः** &c. the ocean. **-क्षारं** a kind of salt. **-मेहः** a kind of urinary disease. **-समुद्रः** the salt-sea, the ocean.

लवणा Lustre, beauty.

लवणिमन् *m.* **1** Saltness. **2** Beauty, loveliness, grace.

लवनं 1 Mowing, cutting, reaping (of corn &c.) **2** An instrument for mowing, a sickle, scythe.

लवली A kind of creeper; मया लब्धः पाणिर्ललितलवलीकंदलनिभः U. 3. 40.

लवित्रं An instrument for mowing, a sickle.

लश् 10 U. (लशयति-ते) To exercise or practise any art; cf. लस्.

लशु(शू)नः-नं Garlic ; निखिलरसायनमहितो गंधेनोग्रेण लशुन इव R. G. (= Bv. I. 81); यशः-सौरभ्यलशुनः Bv. 1. 93.

लष् 1. 4. P. (लषति-ते, लष्यति-ते, लषित) To wish, desire, long for, be eager for; (usually with the preposition अभि). -WITH **अभि** to wish, desire, long for &c.; मानुषानभिलषंति Bk. 4. 22; तेन दूतमभिलेषुरंगनाः R. 19. 12.

लषित *p. p.* Wished, desired.

लष्वः An actor, a dancer.

लस् I. 1 P. (लसति, लसित) **1** To shine, glitter, flash ; मुक्ताहारेण लसता हसतीव स्तनद्वयं K. P. 10; करवाणि चरणद्वयं सरसलसदलक्तकरागं Gît. 10; Amaru. 16; N. 22. 53. **2** To appear, arise, come to light. **3** To embrace. **4** To play, frolic about, skip about, dance. *-Caus.* (लासयति-ते) **1** To cause to shine, grace, adorn. **2** To cause to dance. **3** To exercise an art. -WITH **उद् 1** To sport, play, wave, flutter; Si. 5. 47.

2 to shine, flash, glitter; उलसत्काचनकुंडलाग्रं Si. 3. 5. 33; 5. 15 ; 20. 56. 3 to rise, appear forth; Si. 4. 58; 6. 11; Mâl. 9. 38. 4 to blow, open, be expanded. (-*Caus.*) to illuminate, brighten. **-परि** to shine forth, appear beautiful. **-वि 1** to shine, flash, glitter; वियति च विललास तद्वदिंदुर्विलसति चंद्रमसो न यद्वदन्यः Bk. 10. 68; Me. 47, R. 13. 76. 2 to appear, arise, become manifest; प्रेम विलसति महत्तद्हो Si. 15. 14; 9. 87. 3 to sport, amuse oneself, play, frolic about sportively; कापि चपला मधुरिपुणा विलसति युवतिरधिकगुणा Git. 7; or हरिरिह मुग्धवधूनिकरे विलासिनि विलसति केलिपरे Git. 1. 4 to sound, echo, reverberate.

लसा 1 Saffron. 2 Turmeric.

लसिका Spittle, saliva.

लसित *p. p.* Played, sported, appeared, manifested, skipping about &c.; See लस्.

लसीका 1 Saliva. 2 Pus, matter. 3 The juice of the sugarcane. 4 Lymph.

लस्ज् 1 A. (लज्जते, लज्जित) **1** To be ashamed, feel shame (oft. with instr. or inf.); स्त्रीजनं प्रहरस्कथं न लज्जसे Ratn. 2; Bk. 15. 33. **2** To blush. -*Caus.* (लज्जयति-ते) To put to shame; R. 19. 14. -WITH **-वि** to be bashful or modest, to blush; यात्रांशुकाक्षेपविलज्जितानां Ku. 1. 14; R. 14. 27.

लस्त *a.* **1** Embraced, clasped. **2** Skilful, skilled.

लस्तकः The middle of a bow, that part which is grasped.

लस्तकिन् *m.* A bow.

लहरिः-री *f.* A wave, a large wave or billow; करेणोक्षिप्तास्ते जननि विजयंतां लहरयः G. L. 40; इमां पीयूषलहरीं जगन्नाथेन निर्मितां 53; so आनंद°, करुणा°, सुधा°, &c.

ला 2 P. (लाति) To take, receive, obtain, take up; ललुः खड्गान् Bk. 14. 92, 15. 53.

लाकुटिक *a.* (**की** *f.*) Armed with a club or cudgel. **-कः** A sentinel, watchman; Pt. 4.

लाक्षकी N. of Sîtâ.

लाक्षणिक *a.* (**की** *f.*) **1** One who is acquainted with marks or signs. **2** Characteristic, indicatory. **3** Having a secondary sense, used in a secondary sense (as a word, as distinguished from वाच्य and व्यंजक q. v. v.); स्याद्वाचको लाक्षणिकः शब्दोऽत्र व्यंजकस्त्रिधा K. P. 2. 4 Secondary, inferior. **5** Technical. **-कः** A technical term.

लाक्षण्य *a.* **1** Relating to signs, indicative. **2** Conversant with, able to explain or interpret, signs.

लाक्षा 1 A kind of red dye, lac; (largely used by women in ancient times as an article of decoration, especially for the soles of the feet and lips; cf. अलक्त; it is said to be obtained from the cochineal insect and from the resin of a particular tree): निष्ठयूतश्चरणोपभोगसुलभो लाक्षारसः केनचित् (तरुणा) *S.* 4. 5; Rs. 6. 13, Ki. 5. 23. **2** The insect which produces the red dye. **-Comp. -तरुः, -वृक्षः** N. of a tree, *Butea Frondosa*. **-प्रसादः, -प्रसाधनः** the red *Lodhra* tree. **-रक्त** *a.* dyed with lac.

लाक्षिक *a.* (**की** *f.*) **1** Relating to, made of or dyed with, lac. **2** Relating to a *lac* (लक्ष).

लाख् 1 P. (लाखति) **1** To be dry or arid. **2** To adorn. **3** To suffice, be competent. **4** To give. **5** To prevent.

लागुडिक See लाकुटिक.

लाघ् 1 A. (लाघते) To be equal to, to suffice or be competent.

लाघवं 1 Smallness, littleness. **2** Levity, lightness. **3** Thoughtlessness, frivolity. **4** Insignificance. **5** Disrepect, contempt, dishonour, degradation; सेवां लाघवकारिणीं कृतधियः स्थाने श्ववृत्तिं विदुः Mu. 3. 14. Bg. 2. 35. **6** Quickness, speed, rapidity. **7** Activity, dexterity, readiness; हस्तलाघवं. **8** Versatility बुद्धिलाघवं **9** Brevity, conciseness (of expression). **10** Shortness of a syllable (in prosody).

लांगलं 1 A plough. **2** A plough-shaped beam or timber. **3** The palem tree. **4** Membrum virile. **5** A kind of flower. **-Comp. -ग्रहः** a ploughman, peasant. **-दंडः** the pole of a plough. **-ध्वजः** N. of Balarâma. **-पद्धतिः** *f.* a furrow. **-फालः** a ploughshare.

लांगलिन् *m.* **1** N. of Balarâma; बंधुप्रीत्या समरविमुखो लांगली याः सिषेवे Me. 49. **2** The cocoanut tree. **3** A snake.

लांगली The cocoanut tree.

लांगलीषा (for लांगल-ईषा) The pole of a plough.

लांगुलं 1 A tail. **2** Membrum virile.

लांगूलं 1 A tail; लांगूलचालनमधश्चरणावपातं... श्वा पिंडदस्य कुरुते Bh. 2. 31 'wags his tail.' **2** The membrum virile.

लांगूलिन् *m.* A monkey, an ape.

लाज्, लांज् 1 P. (लाजति, लांजति) **1** To blame, censure, **2** To roast, fry.

लाजः Wetted grain. **-जाः** (pl.) Parched or fried grain (*f.* also); (तं) अवाकिरन्बाललताः प्रसूनैराचारलाजैरिव पौरकन्याः R. 2. 10, 4. 27, 7. 25; Ku. 7. 69, 80.

लांछ् 1 P. (लांछति) 1 To distinguish, mark, characterize. **2** To deck, decorate.

लांछनं 1 A sign, mark, token, characteristic mark; नवांबुदानीकमुहूर्तलांछने (धनुषि) R. 3. 53; oft. at the end of comp. in the sense of 'marked with'; 'characterized by &c.'; जातिऽथ देवस्य तया विवाहमहोत्सवे साहसलांछनस्य Vikr. 10. 1; R. 6. 18, 16. 84; so श्रीकंटपद्लांछनः Mâl. 1 'bearing the characteristic epithet श्रीकंट' **2** A name, an appellation. **3** A stain, stigma, a mark of ignominy. **4** The spot on the moon; Ku. 7. 35. **5** A land mark.

लांछित *a.* **1** Marked, distinguished, characterised. **2** Named, called. **3** Decorated. **4** Furnished with.

लाट *m. pl.* N. of a country and its inhabitants एष च (लाटानुप्रासः) प्रायेण लाटजनप्रियत्वाल्लाटानुप्रासः S. D. 10. **-टः 1** A king of the Lâṭas. **2** Old, worn out or shabby clothes. **3** Clothes in general. **4** Childish language. **-Comp. -अनुप्रासः** one of the five kinds of अनुप्रास or alliteration, the repetition of a word or words in the same sense but in a different application; it is thus defined and illustrated by Mammaṭa:— शाब्दस्तु लाटानुप्रासो भेदे तात्पर्यमात्रतः, *e. g.* वदनं वरवर्णिन्यास्तस्याः सत्यं सुधाकरः । सुधाकरः क नु पुनः कलंकविकलो भवेत्; or यस्य न सविधे दयिता दवदहनस्तुहिनदीधितिस्तस्य । यस्य च सविधे दयिता दवदहनस्तुहिनदीधितिस्तस्य ॥ K. P. 9.

लाटक *a.* (**टिका** *f.*) Relating to the Lâṭas.

लाटिका, लाटी 1 A particular style of composition; see S. D. 629. **2** N. of a Prâkrita dialect; see Kâv. 1. 35.

लाड् 10 U. (लाडयति-ते) **1** To fondle, caress. **2** To blame, censure. **3** To throw, toss; cf. लड्.

लांठनी An unchaste woman (कुलटा).

लात *p. p.* Taken, received.

लापः 1 Speaking, talking. **2** Chattering, prating.

लाबः, लावकः A sort of quail.

लाबुः (**बूः**) A kind of gourd.

लाबुकी A kind of lute.

लाभः 1 Gaining, obtaining, acquirement, acquisition ; शरीरत्यागमात्रेण शुद्धिलाभममन्यत R. 12. 10; स्त्रीरत्नलाभं 7. 34, 11. 92 ; क्षणमप्यवतिष्ठते श्वसन्यादि जंतुर्ननु लाभवानसौ R. 8. 87. **2** Gain, profit, advantage ; सुखदुःखे समे कृत्वा लाभालाभौ जयाजयौ Bg. 2. 38 ; Y. 2. 259. **3** Enjoyment. **4** Capture, conquest. **5** Perception, knowledge, apprehension. **-Comp. -कर, -कृत्** *a.* profitable, advantageous. **-लिप्सा** desire of gain, avarice, covetousness.

लाभकः Gain, profit.

लांमज्जकं The root of a particular fragrant grass (वीरणमूल).

लांपट्यं Lasciviousness, lustfulness, lewdness.

लालनं 1 Caressing, fondling, coaxing; सुतलालनं &c. **2** Indulging, over-indulgence, fondling too much; लालने बहवो दोषास्ताडने बहवो गुणाः; see लल्.

लालस *a.* **1** Ardently longing for, eagerly desirous of, hankering after; प्रणामलालसाः K. 14; ईशानसंदर्शनलालसानां Ku. 7. 56, Si. 4. 6. **2** Taking

pleasure in, devoted to, fond of, absorbed in; विलासलालसं Gît. 1 ; शोक°, मृगया° &c.

लालसा 1 Longing or ardent desire, extreme desire, eagerness. **2** Asking, solicitation, entreaty. **3** Regret, sorrow. **4** The longing of a pregnant woman (दोहद).

लालसीकं Sauce.

लाला Saliva, spittle ; Bh. 2. 9. **–Comp.–स्रवः** a spider. **–स्रावः 1** a flow of saliva. **2** a spider.

लालाटिक *a.* (की *f.*) **1** Being on or relating to the forehead. **2** Arising from or dependent on fate ; प्रातिस्तु लालाटिकी Udb. **3** Useless, low, vile. **–कः 1** An attentive servant (lit. one who watches his master's countenance and learns by it what is necessary to be done). **2** An idler, a careless or useless person. **3** A kind of embrace.

लालाटी The forehead.

लालिकः A buffalo.

लालित *p. p.* **1** Caressed, fondled, coaxed, indulged. **2** Seduced. **3** Loved, desired. **–तं** Pleasure, love, joy.

लालितकः A fondling or darling, pet, little favourite.

लालित्यं 1 Loveliness, charm, beauty, grace, sweetness ; दंडिनः पद-लालित्यं Udb. **2** Amorous gestures.

लालिन् *m.* A seducer.

लालिनी A wanton woman.

लालुका A kind of necklace.

लाव *a.* (वी *f.*) **1** Cutting, lopping, cutting off ; कुशसूचिलावं R. 13. 43. **2** Plucking, gathering. **3** Cuttiing down, killing, destroying ; Bk. 6. 87. **–वः 1** Cutting. **2** A quail.

लावकः 1 A cutter, divider. **2** A reaper, gatherer. **3** A quail.

लावण *a.* (णी *f.*) **1** Salt. **2** Salted, dressed with salt.

लावणिक *a.* (की *f.*) **1** Salted, dressed with salt. **2** Dealing in salt. **3** Lovely, beautiful, charming ; *Si.* 10. 38 (where it means 'a salt-merchant' also). **–कः** A salt-merchant. **–कं** A salt-vessel, salt-cellar.

लावण्यं 1 Saltness. **2** Beauty, loveliness, charm, तथापि तस्या लावण्यं रेखया किंचिदन्वितं *S.* 6. 13; Ku. 7. 18; लावण्यं is thus defined in *S*abdak.:— मुक्ताफलेषु छायायास्तरलत्वमिवांतरा । प्रतिभाति यदंगेषु तल्लावण्यमिहोच्यते ॥. **–Comp. –आर्जितं** the private property of a married woman given to her at her marriage by her father or mother-in-law.

लावण्यमय, लावण्यवत् *a.* Lovely, handsome.

लावाणकः N. of a district near Magadha.

लाविकः A buffalo.

लाषुक *a.* (का or की *f.*) Covetous, greeedy, avaricious.

लासः 1 Jumping, sporting, skipping about, dancing. **2** Dalliance, wanton sport. **3** Dancing as practised by women. **4** Soup, broth.

लासक *a.* (सिका *f.*) **1** Playing, frolicking, sporting. **2** Moving hither and thither. **–कः 1** A dancer. **2** A peacock. **3** Embracing. **4** N. of *S*iva. **–कं** A room on the top of a building, turret.

लासकी A female dancer.

लासिका 1 A female dancer. **2** A harlot, wanton or unchaste woman.

लास्यं 1 Dancing, a dance ; आस्ये धास्यति कस्य लास्यमधुना...वाचां विपाको मम Bv. 4. 42; R. 16. 14. **2** A dance accompanied with singing and instrumental music. **3** A dance in which the emotions of love are represented by means of various gesticulations and attitudes. **–स्यः** A dancer, an actor. **–स्या** A dancing girl.

लिकुचः See लकुच.

लिक्षा 1 A nit, the egg of a louse. **2** A very minute measure of weight (said to be equal to 4 or 8 *trasa re-nus*); जालांतरगते भानौ यच्चाणु दृश्यते रजः तैश्चतुर्भिर्भवेल्लिक्षा; or त्रसरेणवोऽष्टौ विज्ञेया लिक्षैका परिमाणतः Ms. 8. 133 ; see Y. 1. 362 also.

लिक्षिका A nit.

लिख् 6 P. (लिखति, लिखित) **1** To write, write down, inscribe, draw a line, engrave ; अरसिकेषु कवित्वनिवेदनं शिरसि मा लिख मा लिख मा लिख Udb. ; ताराक्षैरर्यमसिते कठिन्या निशालिखद् व्योम्नि तमःप्रशस्तिं N. 22. 54; Y. 2. 87; *S*. 7. 5. **2** To sketch, draw, portray, delineate, paint ; मृगमदतिलकं लिखति सपुलकं मृगमिव रजनीकरे Gît. 7 ; मत्सादृश्यं विरहतनु वा भावगम्यं लिखंती Me. 85, 80 ; Ku. 6. 48 ; स्मितत्वा पाणौ खड्गलेखां लिलेख K. P. 10. **3** To scratch, rub, scrape, tear up ; न किंचिदूचे चरणेन केवलं लिलेख बाष्पाकुललोचना भुवं Ki. 8. 14. ; मूर्ध्नादिवामिवालिखन् Bk. 15. 22. **4** To lance, scarify. **5** To touch, graze. **6** To peck (as a bird). **7** To make smooth. **8** To unite sexually with a female. –WITH **आ 1** to write, delineate, draw lines ; Mâl. 1. 31. **2** to paint, draw in a picture; आलिखित इव सर्वतो रगः *Si.* 1; त्वामालिख्य प्रणयकुपितां Me. 105 ; R. 19. 19. **3** to scratch ; scrape. **–उद् 1** to scratch, scrape, tear or rip up ; *Si.* 5. 20 ; Ms. 1. 23. **2** to grind down, polish ; त्वष्टा विवस्वंतमिवोल्लिलेख Ki. 17. 48, R. 6. 32; *S.* 6. 5. **3** to paint, write, delineate ; Ku. 5. 58. **4** to carve. **–प्रति** to reply or write in return, write back. **–वि 1** to write, inscribe. **2** to draw, paint, delineate, portray; विलिखति रहसि कुरंगमदेन भवंतमसमशरभूतं Gît. 4. **3** to scratch, scrape, tear up ; मंदं शब्दायमानं विलिखति शयनादुत्थितः क्ष्मां खुरेण K. P. 10 ; व्यालिखच्चंचुपुटेन पक्षती N. 2. 2 ; पादेन हैमं विलिलेख पीठं R. 6. 15 ; Ku. 2. 23. **4** to implant, infix; H. 4. 72. v. l. **–सं** to scratch, scrape.

लिखनं 1 Writing, inscribing. **2** Drawing, painting. **3** Scratching. **4** A written document, a writing or manuscript.

लिखित *p. p.* Written, painted, scratched &c.; see लिख्. **–तः** N. of a writer on law (mentioned along with शंख). **–तं 1** A writing, document. **2** Any book or composition.

लिंख् 1. P. (लिंखति) To go, move.

लिगुः 1 A deer. **2** A fool, block-head. *–n.* The heart.

लिंग् I. 1 P. (लिंगति, लिंगित) To go, move. –WITH **आ** to embrace, clasp. –II. 10. U. (लिंगयति-ते) **1** To paint, variegate. **2** To inflect (a noun) according to its gender.

लिंगं 1 A mark, sign, token, an emblem, a badge, symbol, distinguishing mark, characteristic ; यतिपार्थिवलिंगधारिणौ R. 8. 16 ; मुनिर्दोहदलिंगदर्शी 14. 71. ; Ms. 1. 30 ; 8. 25, 252. **2** A false or unreal mark, a guise, disguise, a deceptive badge; लिंगैर्मुदः संवृतविक्रियास्ते R. 7. 30 ; क्षपणकलिंगधारी Mu. 1 ; न लिंगं धर्मकारणं H. 4. 85 ; see लिंगिन् below. **3** A symptom, mark of disease. **4** A means of proof, a proof, evidence. **5** (In logic) The predicate of a proposition. **6** The sign of gender or sex. **7** Sex ; गुणाः पूजास्थानं गुणिषु न च लिंगं न च वयः U. 4. 11. **8** The male organ of generation. **9** Gender (in gram.) **10** The genital organ of *S*iva worshipped in the form of a Phallus. **11** The image of a god, an idol. **12** One of the relations or indications (such as संयोग, वियोग, साहचर्य &c.) which serve to fix the meaning of a word in any particular passage; *e. g.* in कुपितो मकरध्वजः the word कुपित restricts the meaning of मकरध्वज to 'Kâma', see K. P. 2. and commentary *ad loc.* **13** (In Vedânta phil.) The subtle frame or body, the indestructible original of the original gross or visible body ; cf. पंचकोष. **–Comp. –अग्रं** the glans penis. **–अनुशासनं** the laws of grammatical gender. **–अर्चनं** the worship of *S*iva as a *linga*. **–देहः –शरीरं** the subtle frame or body; see लिंग (13) above. **–धारिन्** *a.* wearing a badge. **–नाशः 1** loss of the characteristic marks. **2** loss of penis. **3** loss of vision, a particular disease of the eye. **–परामर्शः** the finding out or consideration of a sign or characteristic (in logic); (*e. g.* that smoke is a sign of fire). **–पुराणं** N. of one of the 18 Purâṇas. **–प्रतिष्ठा** the establishment or consecration of a *linga.* -वर्धन *a.* causing erection of the male organ. -विपर्ययः change of gender. -वृत्ति *a.* hypocritical. (-वृत्तिः a religious hypocrite. -वेदी the base or pedestal of a *linga.*

लिंगकः The *Kapittha* tree.

लिंगनं Embracing.

लिंगिन् *a.* **1** Having a mark or sign. **2** Characterized by. **3** Wearing the marks or badges of, having the appearance of, disguised as, hypocritical, wearing false badges (at the end of comp.): स वर्णिलिंगी विदितः समाययौ युधिष्ठिरं द्वैतवने वनेचरः Ki. 1. 1; so आर्यलिंगिन्. **4** Furnished with a *linga.* **5** Having a subtle body. **-m.** **1** A religious student, Brâhmaṇa ascetic; Pt. 4. 39. **2** A worshipper of *Siva's linga.* **3** A hypocrite, pretending devotee, pseudo-ascetic. **4** An elephant. **5** (In logic) The subject of a preposition.

लिप् 6 U. (लिंपति-ते, लिप्त) **1** To anoint, smear, besmear; लिंपतीव तमोंगानि Mk. 1. 34. **2** To cover, overspread; *Si.* 3. 48. **3** To stain, pollute, defile, taint, contaminate; यः करोति स लिप्यते Pt. 4. 64.; न मां कर्माणि लिंपंति Bg. 4. 14, 18. 17; Ms. 10. 106. **4** To inflame, kindle; तस्यालिपत शोकाग्निः स्वांतं काष्ठमिव ज्वलन् Bk. 6. 22. -WITH **अनु 1** to anoint, besmear; वपुरन्वलिप्त न वधूः *Si.* 9. 51, 9. 15. **2** to cover, overspread, envelop; R. 10. 10; *S.* 7. 7. -अव to smear, anoint. (*-pass.*) to be puffed up or proud, be elated. -आ **1** to anoint, smear; U. 3. 39; Rs. 6. 12. **2** to defile, stain. -उप to stain, defile; Bg. 13. 32. -वि to anoint, smear, rub on; Ku. 5. 79; Bk. 3. 20, 15. 6; *Si.* 16. 62.

लिपिः-पी *f.* **1** Anointing, smearing. **2** Writing, hand-writing. **3** The written characters, letters, alphabet; यवनाल्लिप्यां Vârt.; लिपेर्यथावद्ग्रहणेन वाङ्मयं नदीमुखेनैव समुद्रमाविशत् R. 3. 28, 18. 46. **4** The art of writing. **5** A writing (as a letter, document, manuscript &c.); अयं दरिद्रो भवितेति वैधसीं लिपिं ललाटे-र्थिजनस्य जाग्रतीं N. 1. 15, 138. **6** Painting, drawing. **-Comp.** -करः **1** a plasterer, white-washer, mason. **2** a writer, scribe. **3** an engraver (also **लिंपिकर**). -कारः a writer, scribe. -ज्ञ *a.* one who can write. -न्यासः the art of writing or transcribling. -फलकं a writing-tablet or board. -शाला a writing school. -सज्जा writing materials or apparatus.

लिपिका See लिपी.

लिप्त *p. p.* **1** Anointed, smeared, besmeared, covered. **2** Stained, soiled, polluted, defiled. **3** Poisoned, envenomed (as an arrow). **4** Eaten. **5** United, joined.

लिप्तकः A poisoned arrow.

लिप्सा 1 Desire of getting or regaining; Bv. 1. 125. **2** Desire in general.

लिप्सु *a.* Desirous of getting &c.

लिविः-वी *f.* =लिपि q. v.

लिविंकरः A scribe, writer, copyist.

लिंपः Smearing, anointing, covering.

लिंपट *a.* Libidinous, lustful. -टः A libertine, lecher.

लिंपाकः 1 The citron or lime tree. **2** An ass. -कं A citron or lime.

लिश् I. 6 P. (लिशति) **1** To go, move. **2** To hurt; see रिश्. -II. 4 U. (लिश्यति-ते) To become small, be eased.

लिष्ट *p. p.* Become small, lessened, decreased.

लिष्वः An actor, a dancer.

लिह् 2 U. (लेढि, लीढे, लीढ; *desid.* लिलिक्षति-ते) **1** To lick; कपाले मार्जारः पय इति करॉल्लेढि शशिनः K. P. 19; Bv. 1. 99; Ki. 5. 38, *Si.* 12. 40. **2** to lick up, taste, sip, lap; N. 2. 99, 100. -WITH **अव 1** to lick, lap, bit; भवव्यालावलीढात्मनः G. L. 50; Ve. 3. 5; Bv. 1. 111. **2** To chew, eat; दर्भैरर्धावलीढैः *S.* 1. 7; Mk. 1. 9. -आ **1** to lick, lap. **2** to wound, hurt; सेनान्यमालीढमिवासुरास्त्रैः R. 2. 37. **3** to take in (with the eyes), see; न याम्यामालीढा परमरमणीया तव तनुः G. L. 32. -उद् to polish, grind, rub; मणिः शाणोल्लीढः Bh. 2. 44. -परि-सं to lick; Bk. 13. 42.

ली I. 1 P. (लयति) To melt, dissolve. -II. 9 P. (लिनाति) **1** To adhere. **2** To melt; usually with वि.- III. 4 A. (लीयते, लीन) **1** To stick or adhere firmly to, cling to; M. 3. 5. **2** To clasp, embrace. **3** To lie or rest on, recline, stay or dwell in, lurk, hide, cower; (भृंगांगनाः) लीयंते मुकुलांतरेषु शनकैः संजातलज्जा इव Ratn. 1. 26; R. 3. 9; *S.* 6. 16; Ku. 1. 12; 7. 21; Bk. 18. 13; Ki. 5. 26. **4** To be dissolved, melt away. **5** To be sticky or viscous. **6** To be absorbed in, be devoted or attached to; माधव मनसिजविशिखभयादिव भावनया त्वयि लीना Gît. 4. **7** To vanish, disappear. -*Caus.* (लापयति-ते, लाययति-ते, लीनयति-ते, लालयति-ते) To melt, dissolve, liquefy. (The form लापयते is used in the sense of 'to honour' 'cause to be honoured'; जटाभिर्लापयते = पूजामधिगच्छति; cf. P. I. 3. 70). -WITH **अभि 1** to cling or adhere to; R. 3. 8. **2** to shroud, spread over; पश्चादुच्चैर्भुजतरुवनं मंडलेनाभिलीनः Me. 56. -आ **1** to settle down upon, hide or lurk in; V. 2. 23. **2** to cling or stick to; R. 4. 51. -नि **1** to stick or adhere to, lie or rest upon, settle down or alight upon; निलिल्ये मूर्ध्नि गृध्रोऽस्य Bk. 14. 76; 2. 5. **2** to lurk or hide, hide oneself in; गुहास्वन्ये न्यलेषत Bk. 15. 22; निशि रहसि निलीय Gît. 2. **3** to hide or conceal oneself from (with abl.); मातुर्निलीयते कृष्णः Sk. **4** to die, perish. -प्र **1** to be absorbed or dissolved in, be resolved into; आत्मना कृतिना च त्वमात्मन्येव प्रलीयसे Ku. 2. 10; रात्र्यागमे प्रलीयंते तत्रैवाव्यक्तसंज्ञके Bg. 8. 18; Ms. 1. 54. **2** to vanish, disappear. **3** to be destroyed, to perish. -वि **1** to cling or stick to, adhere to. **2** to rest on, settle down or alight on; पुरोऽस्य यावन्न भुवि व्यलीयत *Si.* 1. 12. **3** to be dissolved, to melt away, be absorbed in; Mv. 6. 60, 7. 14. **4** to vanish, disappear. **5** to perish. -सं **1** to cling or stick to. **2** to lie down or settle upon, alight. **3** to lurk, hide in. 4 to melt away.

लीक्षा A nit; see लिक्षा.

लीढ *p. p.* Licked, sipped, tasted, eaten &c.; see लिह्.

लीन *p. p.* **1** Clung or adhered to, suck to. **2** Lurking, hid, concealed. **3** Resting or reclining on. **4** Melted, dissolved; Mâl. 5. 10. **5** Completely absorbed or swallowed up in, intimately united with; नद्यः सागरे लीना भवंति. **6** Devoted or given up to. **7** Disappeared, vanished; (see ली).

लीला 1 Play, sport, pastime, diversion, pleasure, amusement; क्रमं ययौ कंदुकलीलयापि या Ku. 5. 19; oft. used as the first member of comp.; लीलाकमलं, लीलाशुकः &c. **2** Amorous pastime, wanton, amorous or playful sport; उत्सृष्टलीलागतिः R. 7. 7; 4. 22; 5. 70; क्षुभ्यंति प्रसभमहो विनापि हेतोर्लीलाभिः किमु सति कारणे रमण्यः *Si.* 8. 24; Me. 35; (लीला in this sense is thus explained by उज्ज्वलमणिः-अप्राप्तवल्लभसमागमनायिकायाः सख्याः पुरोऽत्र निजचित्तविनोदबुद्ध्या। आलापवेशगतिहास्यविलोकनाद्यैः प्राणेश्वरानुकृतिमाकलयंति लीलाम्॥). **3** Ease, facility, mere sport, child's play; लीलया जघान killed with ease. **4** Appearance, semblance, air, mien; यः संयति प्राप्तपिनाकिलीलः R. 6. 72 'appearing like Pinâkin'. **5** Beauty charm, grace; मुहुरवलोकितमंडनलीला Gît. 6. R. 6. 1.; 16. 71. **6** Pretence, disguise, dissimulation, sham; as लीलामनुष्यः, लीलानटः &c. **-Comp.** -अ(आ)-गारः-रं, -गृहं, -गेहं, -वेश्मन् *n.* a pleasure-house; R. 8. 95. -अंग *a.* having graceful limbs. -अब्जं, -अंबुजं, -अरविंदं, -कमलं, -तामरसं, -पद्मं &c. 'a toy-lotus,' a lotus-flower held in the hand as a play-thing; R 6. 13; Me. 65, Ku. 6. 84. -अवतारः the descent (of Vishṇu) on the earth for amusement. -उद्यानं, **1** a pleasure-garden. **2** the garden of gods, Indra's paradise. -कलहः 'sportive quarrel; a sham or feignd quarrel; cf. प्रणयकलह. -चतुर *a.* sportively charming; Ku. 1. 47. -नटनं a sportive dance. -मनुष्यः a sham man, a man in disguise. -मात्रं mere sport or play, child's play, absence of the least effort. -रतिः *f.*

diversion, sport. -वापी a pleasure-tank.-शुकः a parrot kept for pleasure.

लीलायितं Play, sport, amusement, pleasure.

लीलावत् *a.* Sportive, playful.-ती **1** A charming or handsome woman. **2** An amorous or wanton woman. **3** N. of Durgâ.

लुक् *ind.* A technical term used by Pâ*n*ini to express the dropping or disappearance of affixes.

लुंच् 1 P. (लुंचति, लुंचित) **1** To pluck, pull, peel, pare. **2** To tear off, pluck or pull out.

लुंचः, -चनं Peeling, plucking out.

लुंचित *p. p.* **1** Peeled. **2** Plucked, plucked out, torn off.

लुट् I. 1 A. (लोटते) **1** To resist, repel, oppose. **2** To shine. **3** To suffer pain. -II. 10 U. (लोटयति-ते) **1** To speak. **2** To shine. -III 1. 4. P. (लोटति, लुटयति) **1** To roll, wallow on the ground; cf. लुट्. **2** To be connected with. **3** To take away, rob, plunder (perhaps for लुंट् or लुंड्.)

लुट् I. 1 P. (लोटति) To strike, knock-down. -II. 1 A. (लोटते) **1** To roll on the ground. **2** To suffer pain. **3** To go, move. **4** To resist, oppose. -III. 10 U. (लोटयति-ते) To rob, plunder. IV. 6 P. (लुटति) To roll about, roll on the ground, wallow, welter, move to and fro; मणिर्लुटति पादेषु काचः शिरसि धार्यते H. 2. 68; लुटति न सा हिमकराकिरणेन Gît. 7; हारोयं हरिणाक्षीणां लुठति स्तनमंडले Amaru. 100; Bk. 14. 54; Bv. 2. 176. -WITH प्र-वि to roll, wallow &c.; Bk. 5. 108.

लुठनं Rolling, wallowing, moving to and fro.

लुठित *p. p.* Rolled down, rolling or wallowing on the ground.

लुड् I. 1 P. (लोडति) To stir, agitate, churn, disturb.-*Caus.* (लोडयति-ते) To stir, churn, agitate (used with वि in the same sense); *Si.* 11. 8, 19. 69. -II. 6 P. (लुडति) **1** To adhere. **2** To cover.

लुंट् I 1 P. (लुंटति) **1** To go. **2** To steal, rob, plunder. **3** To be lame or crippled. **4** To be idle or lazy. -II- 1 P., 10 U. (लुंटयति-ते) **1** To rob, plunder, steal. **2** To disregard, despise.

लुंटाक *a.* (की *f.*) Stealing (fig. also), robbing, plundering; तरुणानां हृदयलुंटाकी परिष्वक्रमाणा निवारयति K. P. 10; आः सितशकुनयः केयं लुंटाकता B. R. 5.

लुंठ् 1 P. (लुंठति) **1** To go. **2** To stir up, agitate, set in motion. **3** To be idle. **4** To be lame. **5** To rob, plunder. **6** To resist.

लुंठकः A robber, plunderer, thief.

लुंठनं Plundering, robbing, stealing; यद्स्य दैत्या इव लुंठनाय काव्यार्थचौराः प्रगुणीभवंति Vikr. 1. 11.

लुंठा **1** Robbing, plundering. **2** Rolling.

लुंठाकः **1** A robber. **2** A crow.

लुंठिः-ठी *f.* Plundering, robbing, pillaging.

लुंड् 10 U. (लुंडयति-ते) To plunder, rob, pillage.

लुंडिका **1** A round mass or ball. **2** Proper conduct.

लुंडी Proper or becoming conduct.

लुंथ् 1 P. (लुंथति) **1** To strike, hurt, kill **2** To suffer, pain, be afflicted.

लुप् I. 4 P. (लुप्यति) **1** To confound, perplex. **2** To be perplexed or confounded. -II. 6. U. (लुंपति-ते, लुप्त) **1** To break, violate, cut off, destroy, injure; अनुभवं वचसा सखि लुंपसि N. 4. 105. **2** To take away, deprive of, rob, plunder. **3** To seize, pounce upon. **4** To elide, suppress, cause to disappear. -*Pass.* (लुप्यते) **1** To be broken or violated. **2** To be elided or lost, to disappear (in gram.). -*Caus.* (लोपयति-ते) **1** To break, violate, infringe, offend against. **2** To omit, neglect. **3** To cause to swerve from; R. 12. 9. -*Desid.* (लुलुप्सति, लुलोपिषति); *freq.* लोलुप्यते or लोलोप्ति. -WITH अव,-प्र to take away, destroy. -वि **1** to break off, pull out, cut off. **2** to seize, plunder, rob, carry off. **3** to impair. **4** to destroy, ruin, cause to disappear; प्रियमत्यंतविलुप्तदर्शनं Ku. 4. 2 'for ever lost to view'; U. 3. 28. **5** to wipe or rub off.

लुप्त *p. p.* **1** Broken, violated, injured, destroyed. **2** Lost, deprived of; R. 14. 56. **3** Robbed, plundered. **4** Dropped, elided, disappeared (in gram.). **5** Omitted, neglected. **6** Obsolete, disused, out of use; U. 3. 33; see लुप्. -प्तं Stolen property, booty. -**Comp.** -उपमा a mutilated or elliptical simile, *i. e.* an *upam'a* in which one, two or even three of the four requisites of a simile are omitted; see K. P. 10 under उपमा. -पद *a.* wanting in words. पिंडोदकक्रिय *a.* deprived of the funeral rites. -प्रतिज्ञ *a.* one who has broken his promise, faithless, perfidious. -प्रतिभ *a.* deprived of reason.

लुब्ध *p. p.* **1** Greedy, covetous, avaricious. **2** Desirous of, longing for, greedy of; as in धनलुब्ध, मांसलुब्ध, गुणलुब्ध &c. -ब्धः **1** A hunter. **2** A libertine, lecher.

लुब्धकः **1** A hunter, fowler; मृगमीनसज्जनानां तृणजलसंतोषविहितवृत्तीनाम् लुब्धकधीवरपिशुना निष्कारणवैरिणो जगति Bh. 2. 61. **2** A covetous or greedy man. **3** A libertine. **4** The star Sirius.

लुभ् 4 P. (लुभ्यति, लुब्ध) **1** To covet, long for, desire eagerly (with dat. or loc.); तथापि रामो लुलुभे मृगाय. **2** To allure, entice. **3** To be bewildered or perplexed, go astray. -*Caus.* (लोभयति-ते) **1** To make greedy, cause to long for, produce or excite desire for; पुपुवे बहु लोभयन् Bk. 5. 48. **2** To excite lust. **3** To entice, seduce, allure, attract; लोभ्यमाननयनः श्लथांशुकैर्मेखलागुणपदैर्नितंबिभिः R. 19. 26. **4** To derange, disorder, disturb. -WITH प्र to be greedy or desirous. (-*Caus.*) to allure, attract entice. -वि to be disturbed or deranged; Bk. 9. 40. (-*Caus.*) **1** to allure, enice, attract; स्मर यावन्न विलोभ्यसे दिवि Ku. 4. 20; अंगनास्तमधिकं व्यलोभयन् (मुखैः) R. 19. 10. **2** to divert, amuse, entertain; क्व दृष्टिं विलोभयामि *S.* 6.

लुंब् 1 P., 10 U. (लुंबति, लुंबयति-ते) To torment, harass.

लुंबिका A kind of musical instrument.

लुल् 1 P. (लोलति, लुलित) **1** To roll, roll about, move to and fro, toss about; लुलितदृष्टि मदादिव चस्खले Ki. 18. 6.; *Si.* 3. 72, 10. 36. **2** To shake, stir, agitate, make tremulous, disturb. **3** To press down, crush; see लुलित below. -*Caus.* (लोलयति-ते) To shake, stir up *Si.* 9. 4. -WITH आ to touch slightly; M. 2. 7. -वि **1** to move to and fro. **2** to shake, make tremulous. **3** to disorder, derange, dishevel (as hair).

लुलापः, लुलायः A buffalo; खुरविधुरधरित्रीचित्रकायो लुलायः.

लुलित *p. p.* **1** Shaken, tossed about, moved to and fro, tremulous, waving; सुरालयप्राप्तिनिमित्तमंभस्त्रैस्रोतसं नौलुलितं ववंदे R. 16. 34, 59. **2** Disturbed, touched; लुलितमकरंदो मधुकरैः Ve. 1. 1. **3** Disarranged, dishevelled (as hair); Rs. 4. 14. **4** Pressed down, crushed, injured; *S.* 3. 27. **5** Pressing on, touching; अनतिलुलितज्याघातांकं (कनकवलयं) *S.* 3. 14. **6** Fatigued, drooping; अलसलुलितमुग्धान्यध्वसंजातखेदात् (अंगकानि) U. 1. 24; Mâl. 1. 15, 3. 6. 4. 2. **7** Elegant, beautiful; वनं ललितपल्लवं Bk. 9. 56.

लुष् 1 P. (लोषति) See लूष्.

लुषभः An elephant in rut.

लुह् 1 P. (लोहति) To covet, desire or long for; cf. लुभ्.

लू 9 U. (लुनाति, लुनीते, लून, *caus.* लावयति-ते; *desid.* लुलूषति-ते) **1** To cut, lop, clip, sever, divide, pluck, reap, gather (flowers &c.) शरासनज्यामलुनाद्बिडोजसः R. 3. 59; 7. 45, 12. 43; पुरीमवस्कंद लुनीहि नंदनं Si. 1. 51; क्रीडति काकैरिव लूनपक्षैः Pt. 1. 187; Au. 3. 61; Bg. 9. 80. **2** To cut off, destroy completely, annihilate; लोकानलावीद्विजितांश्च तस्य Bk. 2. 53. -WITH आ to pluck (gently); Ku. 2. 41. -विप्र to cut, lop or pluck off; U. 3. 5.

लूता 1 A spider. 2 An ant. **-Comp.** **-तंतुः** a cobweb. **-मर्कटकः** 1 an ape. 2 a kind of jasmine.

लूतिका A spider.

लून *p. p.* 1 Cut, lopped, severed, cut off. 2 Plucked, gathered (flowers &c.). 3 Destroyed. 4 Bitten, nibbled at. 5 Wounded. **-नं** A tail.

लूमं A tail. **-Comp.** **-विषः** 'having poison in the tail', an animal that stings with its tail.

लूष् 1 P. (लूषति) 1 To hurt, injure. 2 To rob, plunder, steal.

लेखः 1 A writing, document, written document (of any kind), a letter; लेखोयं न ममेति नोत्तरमिदं मुद्रा मदीया यतः Mu. 5. 18; निर्धारितेऽर्थे लेखेन खल्वुक्त्वा खलु वाचिकं Si. 2. 70; अनंगलेख Ku. 1. 7; मन्मथलेख S. 3. 26. 2 A god, deity. **-Comp.** **-अधिकारिन्** *m.* one in charge of writing letters, the secretary (of a king &c.). **-अर्हः** a kind of palm tree. **-ऋषभः** N. of Indra. **-पत्रं, -पत्रिका** 1 an epistle, a letter, writing in general. 2 a deed, document (legal). **-संदेशः** a written message. **-हारः,-हारिन्** *m.* a letter-carrier.

लेखकः 1 A writer, scribe, copyist. 2 A painter. **-Comp.** **-दोषः -प्रमादः** a slip of the scribe, copyist's mistake.

लेखन *a.* (नी *f.*) Writing, painting, scratching &c. **-नः** A kind of reed of which pens are made. **-नं** 1 Writing, transcribing. 2 Scratching, scraping. 3 Grazing, touching. 4 Attenuating, making thin or emaciated. 5 A palm-leaf (for writing upon). **-नी** 1 A pen, writing reed, reed-pen. 2 A spoon. **-Comp.** **-साधनं** writing materials or apparatus.

लेखनिकः A letter-carrier.

लेखिनी 1 A pen. 2 A spoon.

लेखा 1 A line, streak; कांतिर्भ्रुवोरायतलेखयोर्या Ku. 1. 47; Ku. 7. 16, 87; Ki. 16. 2; Me. 44; विद्युल्लेखा, फेनलेखा, मदलेखा &c. 2 A stroke, furrow, row, stripe. 3 Writing, drawing lines, delineation, painting; पाणिर्लेखाविधिषु नितरां वर्तते किं करोमि Mâl. 4. 35. 4 The moon's crescent, a streak of the moon; लब्धोदया चांद्रमसीव लेखा Ku. 1. 25, 2. 34; Ki. 5. 44. 5 A figure, likeness, an impression, a mark; उषसि सयावकसव्यपादलेखा Ki. 5. 40. 6 Hem, border, edge, skirt. 7 The crest.

लेख्य *a.* To be drawn, written, painted, scratched &c. **-ख्यं** 1 The art of writing. 2 Writing, transcribing. 3 A writing, a letter, document, manuscript. 4 An inscription. 5 Painting, drawing. 6 A painted figure. **-Comp.** **-आरूढ,-कृत** *a.* committed to writing, done in writing. **-गत** *a.* painted, drawn in picture. **-चूर्णिका** a paint-brush, writing-pencil. **पत्रं पत्रकं** 1 a writing, letter, document. 2 a palm-leaf. **-प्रसंगः** a document. **-स्थानं** a writing-place.

लेंडं Excrement, feces.

लेतः -तं Tears.

लेप् 1 A. (लेपते) 1 To go, move. 2 To worship.

लेपः 1 Smearing, plastering, anointing; Y. 1. 188. 2 An unguent, ointment, salve. 3 A plaster in general (such as white-wash, mortar &c.). 4 The wipings of the hand (or the remnants of the food sticking to the hand), after offering funeral oblations to the first three ancestors पितृ, पितामह and प्रपितामह), (these wipings being offered to the three ancestors after the great-grand-father; *i. e.* to paternal ancestors in the 4th, 5th and 6th degrees); लेपभाजश्चतुर्थाद्याः पित्राद्याः पिंडभागिनः. 5 A spot, stain, defilement, pollution. 6 Moral impurity, sin. 7 Food. **-Comp.** **-करः** a plaster-maker, white-washer, bricklayer. **-भागिन्,-भुज्** *m.* a paternal ancestor in the 4th, 5th, and 6th degree; Ms. 3. 216.

लेपकः A plasterer, mason, white-washer.

लेपनः Incense. **-नं** 1 Anointing, smearing, plastering; Y. 1. 188. 2 A plaster, an ointment. 3 Mortar, white-wash. 4 Flesh.

लेप्य *a.* To be plastered, smeared &c. **-प्यं** 1 Plastering, smearing. 2 Moulding, modelling, making models. **-Comp.** **-कृत्** *m.* 1 a model-maker. 2 a bricklayer. **-स्त्री** a woman covered with unguents or perfumed ointments.

लेप्यमयी A doll, puppet.

लेलायमाना One of the seven tongues of fire.

लेलिहः A snake or serpent.

लेलिहानः 1 A snake or serpent. 2 An epithet of Siva.

लेशः 1 A small bit or portion, a particle, an atom, a very small quantity; क्लेश (v. l. स्वेद). लेशैरभिन्नं S. 2. 4; श्रमवारिलेशैः Ku. 3. 38; so भक्ति°, गुण° &c. 2 A measure of time (equal to two *kala's*). 3 (In Rhet.) A figure of speeh which consists in representing what is usually considered as an advantage to be a disadvantage and *vice versa*. It is thus defined in R. G.:—गुणस्यानिष्टसाधनतया दोषत्वेन दोषस्येष्टसाधनतया गुणत्वेन च वर्णनं लेशः; for examples see *ad loc.* (Mammaṭa appears to include this figure under विशेष, see K. P. 10 under विशेष and commentary). **-Comp.** **-उक्त** *a.* only suggested, or hinted at, insinuated.

लेश्या Light.

लेष्टुः A cold, lump of earth. **-Comp.** **-भेदनः** an instrument for breaking clods.

लेसिकः A rider of an elephant.

लेहः 1 Licking, sipper; as in मधुनो लेहः Bk. 6. 82. 2 Tasting. 3 A lambative, an electuary. 4 Food.

लेहनं Licking, sipping with the tongue.

लेहिनः Borax.

लेह्य *a.* To be licked, to be eaten by licking, to be lapped up. **-ह्यं** 1 Anything to be eaten by licking (as an article of food), a lambative. 2 Food in general.

लैंगं N. of one of the eighteen Purâṇas.

लैंगिक *a.* (की *f.*) 1 Depending on or relating to a sign or mark. 2 Inferred (अनुमित). **-कः** A maker of images, a statuary.

लोक् I. 1 A. (लोकते, लोकित) To see, view, perceive. —WITH **अव** to see, behold; नोलूकोप्यवलोकते यदि दिवा सूर्यस्य किं दूषणं Bh. 2. 93. **-आ** to see, look at, perceive; Bk. 2. 24. -II. 10 U. or *caus.* (लोकयति-ते, लोकित) 1 To look at, behold, view, perceive. 2 To know, be aware of. 3 To shine. 4 To speak. —WITH **अव** 1 to see, behold, look at; परिक्रम्यावलोक्य (in dramas). 2 to find; know, observe; अवलोकयामि कियदवशिष्टं रजन्याः S. 4. 3 to view, meditate or reflect upon; Ku. 8. 50; R. 8. 74. **-आ** 1 to see, perceive; behold, view. 2 to regard consider, look upon; तृणमिव जगज्जालमालोकयामः Bh. 3. 66. 3 to know, find out. 4 to greet, express congratulations. **-वि** 1 to see, behold, look at, perceive; विलोक्य वृद्धोक्षमधिष्ठितं त्वया महाजनः स्मेरमुखो भविष्यति Ku. 5. 70; R. 2. 11, 6. 59. 2 to search for, look out for.

लोकः 1 The world, a division of the universe; (roughly speaking there are three *lokas* स्वर्ग, पृथ्वी and पाताल, but according to fuller classification the *lokas* are fourteen, seven higher regions rising from the earth one above the other *i. e.* भूर्लोक, भुवर्लोक, स्वर्लोक, महर्लोक, जनर्लोक, तपर्लोक and सत्यलोक or ब्रह्मलोक; and seven lower regions, descending from the earth one below the other; *i. e.* अतल, वितल, सुतल, रसातल, तलातल, महातल and पाताल). 2 The earth, terrestrial world (भूलोक); इहलोके in this world (opp. परत्र). 3 The human race, mankind, men, as in लोकातिग, लोकोत्तर &c. q. v. 4 The people or subjects (opp. the king); स्वसुखनिरभिलाषः खिद्यसे लोकहेतोः S. 5. 7; R. 4. 8. 5 A collection, group, company; आकुंचलीलान्नरलोकपालान् R. 6. 1; or शशाम तेन क्षितिपाललोकः 7. 3. 6 A region, tract, district, province. 7 Common life, ordinary practice (of the world); लोकवत्तु लीलाकैवल्यं Br. Sût. II. 1. 33; यथा लोके कस्यचिदाप्तैषणस्य राज्ञः &c. S. B. (and diverse other places of the same work).' **8** Common or worldly usage (opp. Vedic usage or idiom ; वेदोक्ता वैदिका शब्दाः सिद्धा लोकाच्च लौकिकाः, प्रियतद्धिता दाक्षिणात्या यथा लोके वेदे चेति प्रयोक्तव्ये यथा लौकिकवैदिकेष्विति प्रयुंजते Mbh.; (and in diverse other places); अतोऽस्मि लोके वेदे च प्रथितः पुरुषोत्तमः Bg. 15. 18. **9** Sight, looking. **10** The number ' seven ', or ' fourteen '. **-Comp.** -अतिग *a.* extraordinary, supernatural. -अतिशय *a.* superior to the world, extraordinary. -अधिक *a.* extraordinary, uncommon; सर्वं पंडितराजराजितिलकेनाकारि लोकाधिकं Bv. 4. 44; Ki. 2. 47. -अधिपः **1** a king. **2** a god or deity. -अधिपतिः a lord of the world. -अनुरागः 'love of mankind', universal love, general benevolence, philanthropy. -अंतरं 'another world', the next world, future life; R. 1. 69; 6. 45; लोकांतरं गम्, प्राप् &c. to die. -अपवादः public scandal, popular censure; लोकापवादो बलवान्मतो मे R. 14. 40. -अभ्युदयः public weal or welfare. -अयनः N. of Nârâyaṇa. -अलोकः N. of a mythical mountain that encircles the earth and is situated beyond the sea of fresh water which surrounds the last of the seven continents; beyond लोकालोक there is complete darkness and to this side of it there is light; it thus divides the visible world from the regions of darkness; प्रकाशश्चाप्रकाशश्च लोकालोक इवाचलः R. 1. 68; (for further explanation see Dr. Bhândârkar's note on *l.* 79 of Mâl. 10th Act.). (-कौ) the visible and the invisible world. -आचारः common practice, popular or general custom, ways of the world. -आत्मन् *m.* the soul of the universe. -आदिः **1** the beginning of the world. **2** the creator of the world. -आयत *a.* atheistical, materialistic. (-तः) a materialist, an atheist, a follower of Chârvâka. (-तं) materialism, atheism; (for some account see the first chapter of the Sarvadarśanasangraha). -आयतिकः an atheist, a materialist. -ईशः **1** a king (lord of the world). **2** Brahman. **3** quick-silver. -उक्तिः *f.* **1** a proverb, popular saying. **2** common talk, public opinion. -उत्तर *a.* extraordinary, uncommon, unusual; लोकोत्तरा च कृतिः Bv. 1. 69, 70; U. 2. 7. (-रः) a king. -एषणा desire for heaven. -कंटकः a troublesome or wicked man, the curse of mankind, see कंटक. -कथा a popular legend. -कर्तृ, -कृत् *m.* the creator of the world. -गाथा a song handed down among people. -चक्षुस् *n.* the sun. -चारित्रं the ways of the world. -जननी an epithet of Lakshmî. -जित् *m.* **1** an epithet of Buddha. **2** any conqueror of the world. -ज्ञ *a.* knowing the world. -ज्येष्ठः an epithet of Buddha. -तत्त्वं knowledge of mankind. -तंत्रं course of the world. -तुषारः camphor. -त्रयं, -त्रयी the three worlds taken collectively; उत्खातलोकत्रयकंटकेऽपि R. 14. 73. -द्वारं the gate of heaven. -धातुः a particular division of the world. -धातृ *m.* an epithet of Śiva. -नाथः **1** Brahman. **2** Vishṇu. **3** Śiva. **4** a king, sovereign. **5** a Buddha. -नेतृ *m.* an epithet of Śiva. -पः, -पालः **1** a regent or guardian of a quarter of the world; ललिताभिनयं तमद्य भर्ता मरुतां द्रष्टुमनाः सलोकपालः V. 2. 18, R. 2. 75, 2. 89, 17. 78; (the *lokapâ'las* are eight; see अष्टदिक्पाल). **2** a king, sovereign. -पक्तिः *f.* esteem of mankind, general respectability. -पतिः **1** an epithet of Brahman. **2** of Vishṇu. **3** a king, sovereign. -पथः, -पद्धतिः *f.* the general or usual way, the universally accepted way. -पितामहः an epithet of Brahman. -प्रकाशनः the sun. -प्रवादः general rumour, current report, popular talk. -प्रसिद्ध *a.* well-known, universally known. -बंधुः बांधवः the sun. -बाह्य, -वाह्य *a.* **1** excluded from society, excommunicated. **2** differing from the world, eccentric, singular. (-ह्यः) an outcast. -मर्यादा an established or current custom. -मातृ *f.* an epithet of Lakshmî. -मार्गः an established custom. -यात्रा **1** worldly affairs, the course of worldly life, business of the world; एवं किलेयं लोकयात्रा Mv. 7; यावदयं संसारस्तावत्प्रसिद्धैवेयं लोकयात्रा Ve. 3. **2** worldly existence, career in life; Mâl. 4. **3** support of life, maintenance. -रक्षः a king, sovereign. -रंजनं pleasing the world, popularity. -रवः popular talk or report. -लोचनं the sun. -वचनं popular rumour or report. -वादः public rumour; common talk, popular report; मा लोकवादश्रवणादहासीः R. 14. 61. -वार्ता popular report, public rumour. -विद्विष्ट *a.* disliked by men, generally or universally disliked. -विधिः **1** a mode of proceeding prevalent in the world. **2** the creator of the world. -विश्रुत *a.* far-famed, universally known, famous, renowned. -वृत्तं **1** the way of the world, a custom prevalent in the world. **2** an idle talk, gossip. -वृत्तांतः, -व्यवहारः **1** the course or ways of the world, general custom; Ś. 5. **2** course of events. -श्रुतिः *f.* **1** a popular report. **2** world-wide fame. -संकरः general confusion in the world. -संग्रहः **1** the whole universe, the welfare of the world. **3** propitiation of mankind. -साक्षिन् *m.* **1** an epithet of Brahman. **2** fire. -सिद्ध *a.* **1** current among the people, usual, customary. **2** generally received or accepted. -स्थितिः *f.* **1** existence or conduct of the universe, worldly existence. **2** a universal law. -हास्य *a.* world-derided, the butt of general ridicule. -हित *a.* beneficial to mankind or to the world. (-तं) general welfare.

लोकनं Looking at, seeing, beholding &c.

लोकंपृण *a.* Filling or pervading the world: लोकंपृणैः परिमलैः परिपूरितस्य काश्मीरजस्य कटुतापि नितांतरम्या Bv. 1. 70.

लोच् I. 1 A. (लोचते) To see, view, perceive, observe. -II. 10 U. or *Caus.* (लोचयति-ते) To cause to see. -With आ **1** to see, perceive. **2** to consider, reflect, think, ponder; आलोचयंतो विस्तारमंभसां दक्षिणोदधेः Bk. 7. 40. -III. 10 U. (लोचयति-ते) **1** To speak. **2** To shine.

लोचं Tears.

लोचकः **1** A stupid person. **2** The pupil of the eye. **3** Lampblack, collyrium. **4** A kind of ear-ring. **5** A dark or blue garment. **6** A bowstring. **7** A particular ornament worn by women on the forehead. **8** A lump of flesh. **9** The slough of a snake. **10** A wrinkled skin. **11** The wrinkled brow. **12** A plantain tree.

लोचनं **1** Seeing, sight, viewing. **2** The eye; शेषान्मासान् गमय चतुरो लोचने मीलयित्वा Me. 110. **-Comp.** -गोचरः, -पथः, -मार्गः the range of sight, sphere of vision. -हिता blue vitriol.

लोट् 1 P. (लोटति) To be mad or foolish.

लोठः Rolling on the ground, wallowing.

लोड् 1 P. (लोडति) To be foolish or mad.

लोडनं Disturbing, agitating, shaking about.

लोणारः A kind of salt.

लोतः **1** Tears. **2** A mark, sign, token.

लोत्रं Stolen property, booty; लोत्रेण (or लोप्त्रेण) गृहीतस्य कुंभीलकस्यास्ति वा प्रतिवचनं V. 2.

लोधः, लोध्रः N. of a tree with red or white flowers; लोध्रद्रुमं सानुमतः प्रफुल्लं R. 2. 29; मुखेन सालक्ष्यत लोध्रपांडुना 3. 2; Ku. 7. 9.

लोपः **1** Taking away, deprivation. **2** Loss, destruction. **3** Abolition, cancellation, annulment (of customs), disappearance, disuse. 4 Violation, transgression; R. 1. 76. **5** want, failure, absence ; R. 1. 68. **6** Omission, dropping; तद्वद्धर्मस्य लोपे स्यात् K. P. 10. **7** Elision, dropping, (in (gram.); अदर्शनं लोपः P. I. 1. 60.

लोपनं 1 Violation, transgression. 2 Omission; dropping.

लोपा, लोपामुद्रा N. of a daughter of the king of Vidarbha and wife of the sage Agastya [She is said to have been formed by the sage himself from the most beautiful parts of different animals so as to have a wife after his own heart, and then secretly introduced into the palace of the king of Vidarbha where she grew up as his daughter. She was afterwards married by Agastya. He was asked by her to acquire immense riches before he thought of having any connection with her. The sage accordingly first went to king Srutarvan, and from him to several other persons till he went to the rich demon Ilvala and, having conquered him got immense wealth from him and satisfied his wife.]

लोपाकः, लोपापकः A kind of jackal.

लोपाशः, लोपाशकः A jackal, fox.

लोपिन् a. 1 Injuring, harming. 2 Subject to elision.

लोप्त्रं See लोत्रं.

लोभः 1 Covetousness, avarice, greed, cupidity; लोभश्चेद्गुणेन किं Bh. 2. 55. 2 Desire for, longing after (with gen. or in comp. कंकणस्य तु लोभेन H. 1. 5; आननस्पर्शलोभात् Me. 10. 3. –Comp. –आन्वित a. covetous, greedy, avaricious. –विरहः absence of avarice; H. 1.

लोभनं 1 Allurement, temptation, seduction, enticement. 2 Gold.

लोभनीय a. Enticing, alluring, attractive; so लोभ्य.

लोमः A tail.

लोमाकिन् m. A bird.

लोमन् n. The hair on the body of men or animals; see रोमन्. –Comp. –अचः =रोमाच q. v. –आलिः -ली, –आवलिः -ली, -राजिः f. a line of hair from the breast to the navel; see रोमावली &c. –कर्णः a hare. –कीटः a louse. –कूपः, -गर्तः, -रंध्रं, -विवरं a pore of the skin. –घ्नं morbid baldness. –मणिः an amulet made of hair. –वाहिन् a. feathered. –संहर्षण a. thrilling, causing horripilation. –सारः an emerald. –हर्ष, -हर्षण, -हर्षिन् see रोमहर्ष &c. –हृत् m. yellow orpiment.

लोम a. 1 Hairy, woolly, shaggy 2 Woollen. 3 Containing hair. –शः A sheep, ram. –शा 1 A fox. 2 A female jackal. 3 An ape. 4 Green vitriol. –Comp. –मार्जारः the civet-cat.

लोमाशः A jackal.

लोल a. 1 Shaking, rolling, tremulous, moving to and fro, quivering, dangling, trembling; flowing, waving, (as locks of hair); परिस्फुरल्लोलशिखाग्रजिह्वं जगज्जिघत्संतमिवांतवह्निं Ki. 3. 20; लोलांशुकस्य पवनाकुलितांशुकांतं Ve. 2. 22; लोलापांगैः लोचनैः Me. 27; R. 18. 43. 2 Agitated, disturbed, restless, uneasy. 3. Fickle, inconstant, changing, unsteady; येन श्रियः संश्रयदोषरूढं स्वभावलौलेत्ययशः प्रमृष्टं R. 6. 41; so Ku. 1. 43. 4 Frail, transient; S. 1. 10. 5 Longing or anxious for, eager for, eagerly desirous of (mostly in comp.); अये लोलः करिकलभको यः पुरा पोषितोऽभूत् U. 3. 6; कर्णे लोलः कथयितुमभूदाननस्पर्शलोभात् Me. 103; Si. 1. 61; 18. 46, 10. 66, Ki. 4. 20; Me. 61; R. 7. 23, 9. 37. 16. 54. 61. –ला 1 N. of Lakshmî. 2 Lightning. 3 The tongue. –Comp. –आक्षि n. a rolling eye. –आक्षिका a woman with rolling eyes. –जिह्व a. with a rolling or restless tongue, greedy. –लोल a. excessively tremulous, ever restless.

लोलुप a. Very eager or desirous, ardently longing for, greedy of; अभिनवमधुलोलुपस्त्वं तथा परिचुंब्य चूतमंजरीं कमलवसतिमात्रनिर्वृतो मधुकर विस्मृतोस्येनां कथं S. 5. 1; मिथस्त्वदाभाषणलोलुपं मनः Si. 1. 40; R. 19. 24. –पा Ardent longing, eager or earnest desire, eagerness.

लोलुभ a. Ardently desirous, covetous, see लोलुप.

लोष्ट् 1 A (लोष्टते) To heap up, accumulate.

लोष्टः, –ष्टं A clod, A lump of earth; परद्रव्येषु लोष्टवत् यः पश्यति स पश्यति; समलोष्टकांचनः R. 8. 21. –ष्टं Rust of iron. –Comp. –घ्नः, –भेदनः -नं an instrument for breaking clods, a harrow.

लोष्टुः A clod, lump of earth.

लोह a. 1 Red, reddish. 2 Made of copper, coppery. 3 Made of iron. –हः, –हं 1 Copper. 2 Iron. 3 Steel. 4 Any metal. 5 Gold. 6 Blood. 7 A weapon; Ms. 9. 321. 8 A fish-hook. –हः The red goat. –हं Aloewood. –Comp. –अजः the red goat. –अभिसारः, –अभिहारः N. of a military ceremony resembling नीराजन q. v. उत्तमं gold. –कांतः a loadstone, magnet. –कारः a blacksmith. –किट्टं rust of iron. –घातकः a blacksmith. –चूर्णं iron-filings, rust of iron. –जं 1 bell-metal. 2 iron-filings. –जालं a coat of mail. –जित् m. a diamond. –द्राविन् m. borax. –नालः an iron arrow. –पृष्ठः a heron. –प्रतिमा 1 an anvil. 2 an iron image. –बद्ध a. tipped or studded with iron. –मुक्तिका a red pearl. –रजस् n. rust of iron. –राजकं silver. –वरं gold. –शंकुः an iron spike. –श्लेषणः borax. –संकरं blue steel.

लोहल a. 1 Made of iron. 2 Speaking indistinctly, lisping.

लोहिका An iron vessel.

लोहित a. (लोहिता or लोहिनी f.) 1 Red, red-coloured; स्रस्तांसावतिमात्रलोहिततलौ बाहू घटोत्क्षेपणात् S. 1. 30; Ku. 3. 29; मुहुश्चलत्पल्लवलोहिनीभिरुच्चैः शिखाभिः शिखिनोवलीढाः Ki. 16. 53. 2 Copper, made of copper. –तः 1 The red colour. 2 The planet Mars. 3 A serpent. 4 A kind of deer. 5 A kind of rice. –ता N. of one of the seven tongues of fire. –तं 1 Copper. 2 Blood; Ms. 8. 284. 3 Saffron. 4 Battle. 5 Red sanders. 6 A kind of sandal. 7 An imperfect form of a rainbow. –Comp. –अक्षः 1 a red die. 2 a kind of snake. 3 the (Indian) cuckoo. 4 an epithet of Vishṇu. –अंगः the planet Mars. –अयस् n. copper. –अशोकः a variety of *Asoka* (having red flowers). –अश्वः fire. –आननः an ichneumon. –ईक्षण a. red-eyed. –उद a. having red or blood-red water. –कल्माष a red-spotted. –क्षयः loss of blood. –ग्रीवः an epithet of Agni. –चंदनं saffron. –पुष्पकः the granate tree. –मृत्तिका red chalk. –शतपत्रं a red lotus-flower.

लोहितक a. (तिका f.) Red. –कः 1 A ruby; Si. 13. 52. 2 The planet Mars. 3 A kind of rice. –कं Bell-metal.

लोहितिमन् m. Redness.

लोहिनी A woman with a red-coloured skin.

लौकायतिकः A follower of Chârvâka, an atheist, a materialist.

लौकिक a. (की f.) 1 Worldly, mundane, terrestrial, earthly. 2 General, common, usual, ordinary, vulgar; U. 1. 10. 3 Of every-day life, generally accepted, popular, customary; Ku. 7. 88. 4 Temporal, secular; (opp. आर्ष or शास्त्रीय); Ms. 3. 282. 5 Not sacred, profane (as a word or its sense); वाक्यं द्विविधं वैदिकं लौकिकं च T. S.; (see Mbh. quoted under लोक 8). 6 Belonging to the world of; as in ब्रह्मलौकिक. –काः (pl.) Ordinary men, men of the world. –कं Any general or worldly custom. –Comp. –ज्ञ a. knowing the ways of the world, acquainted with worldly customs; वनौकसोपि संतो लौकिकज्ञा वयं S. 4.

लौक्य a. 1 Worldly, terrestrial, mundane, human. 2 Common, ordinary, usual.

लौड् 1 P. (लौडति) To be foolish or mad.

लौल्यं 1 Fickleness, unsteadiness, inconstancy. 2 Eagerness, eager desire, greediness; lustfulness, excessive passion or desire; जिह्वालौल्यात् Pt. 1; R. 7. 61, 16. 76; 18. 30; Ku. 6. 30.

लौह a. (ही f.) 1 Made of iron, iron. 2 Coppery. 3 Metallic. 4 Copper-coloured, red. –हं Iron; Bk. 15. 54. –हा A kettle. –Comp. –आत्मन् m., –त्मा f. a boiler, kettle, caldron. –कारः, a blacksmith. –जं rust of iron. –बंधः, -धं an iron fetter, irons. –भांडं an iron vessel. –मलं rust of iron. –शंकुः an iron spike.

लौहितः The trident of Siva.

लौहित्यः N. of a river, the Brahmaputra; चकंपे तीर्णलौहित्ये तस्मिन् प्राग्ज्योतिषेश्वरः R. 4. 81; (where Malli. says तीर्णा लौहित्या नाम नदी येन, but quotes no authority). -त्यं Redness.

ल्पी, ल्यी 9 P. (ल्पिनाति, ल्यिनाति) To join, unite, be mixed with.

ल्वी 9 P. (ल्विनाति) To go, move, apporach.

व.

वः 1 Air, wind. 2 the arm. 3 N. of Varuṇa. 4 Conciliation. 5 Addressing. 6 Auspiciousness. 7 Residence, dwelling. 8 The ocean. 9 A tiger. 10 Cloth. 11 N. of Râhu. -वं N. of Varuṇa (Medinî). *-ind.* Like, as; as in मणी वोष्ट्रस्य लंबेते प्रियौ वत्सतरौ मम Sk.; where the word may be व or वा.

वंशः 1 A bamboo; धनुर्वंशविशुद्धोऽपि निर्गुणः किं करिष्यति H. Pr. 23; वंशभवो गुणवानपि संगविशेषेण पूज्यते पुरुषः Bv. 1. 80 (where वंश has sense 2 also); Me. 79. 2 A race, family, dynasty, lineage; स जातो येन जातेन याति वंशः समुन्नतिं H. 2; सूर्यप्रभवो वंशः R. 1. 2 &c.; see वंशकर, वंशस्थिति &c. 3 A shaft. 4 A flute, pipe, reed-pipe.; कूजद्भिरापादितवंशकृत्यं R. 2. 12. 5 A collection, assemblage, multitude (usually of similar things); सांद्रीकृतः स्यंदनवंशचक्रैः R. 7. 39. 6 A cross-beam. 7 A joint (in a bamboo). 8 A sort of sugar-cane. 9 The backbone. 10 The *S*âla tree. 11 A particular measure of length (equal to ten *hastas*). **-Comp.** -अंग, -अंकुरः 1 the tip or end of a bamboo-cane. 2 the shoot of a bamboo. -अनुकीर्तनं genealogy. -अनुक्रमः genealogy. -अनुचरितं the history of a dynasty or family. -आवली a pedigree, genealogy. -आह्वः bamboo-manna. -कठिनः a thicket of bamboos. -कर *a.* 1 founding a family. 2 perpetuating a race; R. 18. 31. (-रः) an ancestor. -कर्पूररोचना, -रोचना, -लोचना bamboo-manna. -कृत् *m.* the founder or perpetuator of a family. -क्रमः family succession. -क्षीरी bamboo-manna. -चरितं the history of a family. -चिंतकः a genealogist. -छेत्तृ *a.* the last of a family. -ज *a.* 1 born in the family of; R. 1. 31. 2 sprung from a good family. (-जः) 1 progeny, issue, lineal descendant. 2 the seed of the bamboo. (-जं) bamboo-manna. (-जा) bamboo-manna. -नर्तिन् *m.* a buffoon. -नाडि(ली)का a pipe made of bamboo. -नाथः the chief or head of a race. -नेत्रं the root of sugar-cane. -पत्रं a bamboo-leaf. (-त्रः) a reed. -पत्रकः 1 a reed. 2 a white kind of sugarcane. (-कं) yellow orpiment. -परंपरा lineal descent, family succession. -पूरकं the root of sugarcane. -भोज्य *a.* hereditary. (-ज्यं) a hereditary estate. -लक्ष्मीः *f.* the fortune of a family. -विततिः *f.* 1 a family, descent. 2 a thicket of bamboos. -शर्करा bamboo-manna. -शलाका a small bamboo peg at the lower end of a Vîṇâ. -स्थितिः *f.* the perpetuation of a family; R. 18. 31.

वंशकः 1 A kind of sugarcane. 2 The joint in a bamboo. 3 A kind of fish. -कं Aloewood.

वंशिका 1 A kind of flute. 2 Aloewood.

वंशी 1 A flute, pipe; न वंशी मज्ञासीत्त्रुवि करसरोजाद्विगलिता H. D. 108; कंसारिपोर्व्यपोहतु स वोऽश्रेयांसि वंशीरवः Gît. 9. 2 A vein or artery. 3 Bamboo-manna. 4 A particular weight. **-Comp.** -धरः, -धारिन् *m.* 1 an epithet of Krishṇa, 2 any flute-player or piper.

वंश्य *a.* 1 Relating to the main beam. 2 Connected with the spine. 3 Belonging to a family. 4 Of a good family, born in a good family. 5 Lineal, genealogical. -श्यः 1 A descendant, posterity (pl.); इतरेऽपि रघोर्वंश्याः R. 15. 35. 2 A forefather, an ancestor; नून मत्तः परं वंश्याः पिंडविच्छेददर्शिनः R. 1. 66. 3 Any member of a family. 4 A cross-beam. 5 A bone in the arm or leg. 6 A pupil.

वंह् See बंह्.

वक See बक.

वकुल See बकुल.

वक्क् 1 A. (वक्कते) To go, move.

वक्तव्य *pot. p.* 1 Fit to be said, told, spoken or declared; तत्तर्हि वक्तव्यं न वक्तव्यं (frequently occurring in Mbh.). 2 To be spoken about. 3 Reprehensible, blamable, censurable. 4 Low, vile, base. 5 Accountable, responsible. 6 Dependent. -व्यं 1 Speaking, speech. 2 A precept, rule, dictum. 3 Blame, censure, reproach.

वक्तृ *a.* or *m.* 1 Speaking, talking, a speaker. 2 Eloquent, an orator; किं करिष्यंति वक्तारः श्रोता यत्र न विद्यते; दर्दुरा यत्र वक्तारस्तत्र मौनं हि शोभनं Subhâsh. 3 A teacher, an expounder. 4 A learned or wise man in general.

वक्त्रं 1 The mouth. 2 The face; यद्वक्त्रं मुहुरीक्षसे न धनिनां ब्रूषे न चाटून्मृषा Bh. 3. 147. 3 Snout, muzzle, beak. 4 Beginning. 5 The point (of an arrow), the spout of a vessel. 6 A sort of garment. 7 N. of a metre similar to *anushtubh*; see S. D. 567; Kâv. 1. 26. **-Comp.** -आसवः saliva. -खुरः a tooth. -जः a Brâhmaṇa. -तालं a musical instrument played with the mouth. -दलं the palate. -पटः a veil. -रंध्रं the aperture of the mouth. -परिस्पंदः speech. -भेदिन् *a.* pungent, sharp. -वासः an orange. -शोधनं 1 cleansing the mouth. 2 a lime, citron. -शोधिन् *n.* a citron (*-m.*) a citron tree.

वक्र *a.* 1 Crooked (fig. also), bent, curved, winding, tortuous; वक्रः पंथा यदपि भवतः प्रस्थितस्योत्तराशां Me. 27; Ku. 3. 29. 2 Round about, indirect, evasive, circuitous, equivocating, ambiguous (as a speech); किमेतैर्वक्रभणितैः Ratn. 2; वक्रवाक्यरचनारमणीयः ...सुभ्रुवा प्रववृते परिहासः Si. 10. 12; see वक्रोक्ति also. 3 Curled, curling, crisped (as hair). 4 Retrograde (as motion). 5 Dishonest, fraudulent, crooked in disposition. 6 Cruel, malignant (as a planet). 7 Prosodially long. -क्रः 1 The planet Mars. 2 The planet Saturn. 3 N. of *S*iva. 4 N. of the demon Tripura. -क्रं 1 The bend or arm of a river. 2 Retrograde motion (of a planet). **-Comp.** -अंग a croocked limb. (-गः) 1 a goose. 2 the ruddy goose. 3 a snake. -उक्तिः *f.* 1 a figure of speech consisting in the use of evasive speech or reply, either by means of a pun, or by an affected change of tone; Mammaṭa thus defines it:—यदुक्तमन्यथा वाक्यमन्यथान्येन योज्यते श्लेषेण काक्वा वा ज्ञेया सा वक्रोक्तिस्तथा द्विधा K. P. 9; for example see the opening stanza in Mu. (धन्या केयं स्थिता ते &c.) 2 equivocation, insinuation, inuendo सुबंधुर्बाणभट्टश्च कविराज इति त्रयः । वक्रोक्तिमार्गनिपुणाश्चतुर्थो विद्यते न वा ॥ 3 sarcasm. -कंटः the jujube tree. -कंटकः the Khadira tree. -खड्गः, -खड्गकः a sabre, scimitar. -गति, -गामिन् *a.* 1 winding, meandering. 2 fraudulent, dishonest; -ग्रीवः a camel. -चंचुः a parrot. -तुंडः 1 an epithet of Gaṇesa. 2 a parrot. -दंष्ट्रः a boar. -दृष्टि *a.* 1 squint-eyed, squinting. 2 having a malignant or evil look. 3 envious. (*-f.*) squint, an oblique look. -नक्रः 1 a parrot. 2 a low man. -नासिकः an owl. -पुच्छः, -पुच्छिकः a dog. -पुष्पः the *pala'sa* tree.

-बालधिः, -लांगूलः a dog. -भावः 1 crookedness. 2 deceit. -वक्त्रः a hog.

वक्रयः Price (for अवक्रय q. v.).

वक्रिन् *a.* 1 Crooked. 2 Retrograde. -*m.* A Jaina or Buddha.

वक्रिमन् *m.* 1 Crookedness, curvature. 2 Equivocation, evasion, ambiguity, tortuous, round-about or indirect nature (as of a speech); तद्वक्त्रांबुजसौरभं स च सुधास्यंदी गिरा वक्रिमा Gît. 3. 3 Cunningness, duplicity, craftiness.

वक्रोष्टिः, -वक्रोष्टिका *f.* A gentle smile.

वक्ष् 1 P. (वक्षति) 1 To grow, increase. 2 To be powerful. 3 To be angry. 4 To accumulate.

वक्षस् *n.* The breast, bosom, chest; कपाटवक्षाः परिणद्धकंधरः R. 3. 34.-Comp. -जः, -रुह्, -रुहः, (वक्षोजः, वक्षोरुह्, वक्षोरुहः) the female breast; Bv. 2. 17. -स्थलं (वक्ष or वक्षःस्थलं) the breast or bosom.

वख्, वख् (वखति, वंखति) To go, move.

वगाहः See अवगाह.

वंकः The bend of a river.

वंका The pummel of a saddle.

वंकिलः A thorn.

वंक्रिः 1 A rib (of an animal or building (said to be *f.* only by some). 2 The timber of a roof. 3 A kind of musical instrument (said to be *n.* also in these two senses).

वंक्षुः A small arm or branch of the Ganges.

वंग् 1 P. (वंगति) 1 To go. 2 To limp, be lame.

वंगाः (pl.) N. of Bengal proper and its inhabitants; वंगानुत्खाय तरसा नेता नौसाधनोद्यतान् R. 4. 36; रत्नाकरं समारम्य ब्रह्मपुत्रांतगः प्रिये वंगदेश इति प्रोक्तः. -गः 1 Cotton. 2 The egg-plant. -गं 1 Lead. 2 Tin. -Comp. -अरिः yellow orpiment. -ज 1 brass. 2 red lead. -जीवनं silver. -शुल्यजं bell-metal (कांस्यं).

वंघ् 1 A. (वंघते) 1 To go. 2 To go swiftly. 3 to begin. 4 To censure, blame.

वच् 2 P. (A. also in non-conjugational tenses; in conjugational tenses it is said to be defective in the third person plural by some authorities, or in the whole plural by others; वक्ति, उक्त) 1 To say, speak; वैराग्यादिव वक्षि K. P. 10; (oft. with two. acc.); तामूचतुस्ते प्रियमप्यमिथ्या R. 14. 6; sometimes with accusative of words meaning 'speech'; उवाच धात्र्या प्रथमोदितं वचः R. 3. 25, 2. 59; क एवं वक्ष्यते वाक्यं Râm. 2 To relate, describe; रघूणामन्वयं वक्ष्ये R. 1. 9. 3 To tell, communicate, announce, declare; उच्यतां मद्वचनात्सारथिः *S.* 2, Me. 98. 4 To name, call; तदेकसप्ततिगुणं मन्वंतरमिहोच्यते Ms. 1. 79. -*Caus* (वाचयति-ते) 1 To cause to speak. 2 To go over, read, peruse. 3 To say, tell, declare. 4 To promise. -*Desid.* (विवक्षति) To wish to speak, intend to say (something). -With अनु to say after, repeat, recite. (-*Caus.*) to read to oneself; नाममुद्राक्षराण्यनुवाच्य *S.* 1. -निस् 1 to interpret, explain; वेदा निर्वक्तुमक्षमाः. 2 to relate, tell, declare, announce. 3 to name, call. -प्रति to speak in reply, answer, reply to; न चेद्रहस्यं प्रतिवक्तुमर्हसि Ku. 5. 42, R. 3. 47. -वि to explain. -सं to say, speak.

वंचः 1 A parrot. 2 The sun. -चा 1 A kind of talking bird. 2 A kind of aromatic root. -चं Speaking, talk.

वचनं 1 The act of speaking, uttering, saying. 2 Speech, an utterance, words (spoken), sentence, ननु वक्तृविशेषनिः स्पृहागुणगृह्या वचने विपश्चितः Ku. 2. 5; प्रीतः प्रीतिप्रमुखवचनं स्वागतं व्याजहार Me. 3. 3 Repeatting, recitation. 4 A text, diction, rule, precept, a passage of a sacred book; शास्त्रवचनं, श्रुतिवचनं, स्मृतिवचनं &c. 5 An order, a command, direction; मद्वचनात् 'in my name,' 'by my order. 6 Advice, counsel, instruction. 7 Declaration, affirmation. 8 Pronunciation (of a letter) (in gram.). 9 The signification or meaning of a word; अत्र पयोधरशब्द मेघवचनः 10 Number (in gram.): there are three numbers, singular, dual and plural. 11 Dry ginger. -Comp -उपक्रमः introduction, exordium. -कर *a.* obedient, doing what is ordered. -कारिन् *a.* obeying orders, obedient. -क्रमः discourse. -ग्राहिन् *a.* obedient, complaint, submissive. -पटु *a.* eloquent. -विरोधः inconsistency of precepts, contradiction or incongruity of texts. -शतं a hundred speeches, *i. e.* repeated declaration, reiterated assertion. -स्थित *a.* (वचनेस्थितः also) obedient, compliant.

वचनीय *a.* 1 To be said, spoken or related. 2 Censurable, blamable. -यं Blame, censure, reproach; न कामवृत्तिर्वचनीयमीक्षते Ku. 5. 82; वचनीयमिदं व्यवस्थितं रमण त्वामनुयामि यद्यपि 4. 21; भवंति योजयितुर्वचनीयता Pt. 1. 75, Ki. 9. 39, 65; Mk. 4. 1.

वचरः 1 A cock. 2 A rogue, low or wicked person (शठ).

वचस् *n.* 1 A speech, word, sentence; उवाच धात्र्या प्रथमोदितं वचः R. 3. 25, 47; इत्यव्यभिचारि तद्वचः Ku. 5. 36; वचस्तत्र प्रयोक्तव्यं यत्रोक्तं लभते फलं Subhâsh. 2 A command, order, precept, injunction. 3 Advice, counsel. 4 Number (in gram.). -Comp. -कर *a.* 1 obedient, complaint. 2 excuting the orders of another. -क्रमः discourse. -ग्रहः the car. -प्रवृत्तिः *f.* an attempt at speaking; *S.* 7. 17.

वचसांपतिः An epithet of Brihaspati, or the planet Jupiter.

वज् I. 1 P. (वजति) To go, move, roam about. -II. 10 U. (वाजयति-ते) 1 To trim, prepare. 2 To feather an arrow. 3 To go, move.

वज्रः-ज्रं 1 A thunderbolt, the weapon of Indra (said to have been formed out of the bones of the sage Dadhîchi. q. v.). आशंसंते समितिषु सुराः सक्तवैरा हि दैत्यैरस्याधिज्ये धनुषि विजयं पौरुहूते च वज्रे *S.* 2. 15. 2 Any destructive weapon like the thunderbolt. 3 A diamond-pin, an instrument for perforating jewels; मणौ वज्रसमुत्कीर्णे सूत्रस्येवास्ति मे गतिः R. 1. 4. 4 A diamond in general, an adamant; वज्रादपि कठोराणि मृदूनि कुसुमादपि U. 2. 7; R. 6. 19. 5 Sour-gruel. -ज्रः 1 A form of military array. 2 A kind of Kusa grass. 3 N. of various plants. -ज्रं 1 Steel. 2 A kind of talc. 3 Thunderlike or severe language. 4 A child. 5 Emblic myrobalan. -Comp. -अंगः a snake. -अभ्यासः cross multiplication. -अशनिः the thunderbolt of Indra. -आकरः a diamond mine; R. 18. 21. -आख्यः a kind of mineral spar. -आघातः 1 a stroke of thunder or lightning. 2 (hence fig.) any sudden shock or calamity. -आयुधः an epithet of Indra. -कंकटः an epithet of Hanumat. -कीलः a thunderbolt, an adamantine shaft; जीवितं वज्रकीलं Mâl. 9. 37; cf. U. 1. 47. -क्षारं an alkaline earth. -गोपः-इंद्रगोपः q. v. -चंचुः a vulture. -चर्मन् *m.* a rhinoceros. -जित् *m.* N. of Garuḍa. -ज्वलनं, -ज्वाला lightning. -तुंडः 1 a vulture. 2 mosquito, gnat. 3 N. of Garuḍa. 4 of Gaṇesa. -तुल्यः *lapis lazuli* or azure stone. -दंष्ट्रः a kind of insect. -दंतः 1 a hog. 2 a rat. -दशनः a rat. -देह, -देहिन् *a.* having an adamantine or hardy frame. -धरः an epithet of Indra; वज्रधरप्रभावः R. 18. 21. -नाभः the discus of Krishṇa. -निर्घोषः, -निष्पेषः a clap or peal of thunder. -पाणिः an epithet of Indra; वज्रं मुमुक्षन्निव वज्रपाणिः R. 2. 42. -पातः a stroke of lightning, fall of thunderbolt. -पुष्पं the blossom of sesamum. -भृत् *m.* an epithet of Indra. -मणिः a diamond, an adamant; Bh. 2. 6. -मुष्टिः an epithet of Indra. -रदः a hog. -लेपः a kind of very hard cement; वज्रलेपघटितेव Mâl. 5. 10, U. 4 (for its preparation see Bri. S. chapter 57). -लोहकः a magnet. -व्यूहः a kind of military array. -शल्यः a porcupine. -सार *a.* as hard as adamant, having the strength of the thunderbolt, adamantinet; क्व च निशितनिपाता वज्रसाराः शरास्ते *S.* 1. 10; त्वमपि कुसुमबाणान्वज्रसारीकरोषि 3. 3. -सूचिः, -ची *f.* a diamond-needle. -हृदयं an adamantine heart.

वज्रिन् *m.* 1 N. of Indra; तनु वज्रिण इव वीर्यमेतद्विजयंते द्विषतो यदस्य पक्ष्याः V. 1. 5: R. 9. 24. 2 An owl.

वंच् 1 P. (वंचति) 1 To go, to arrive at; ववंचुश्राहवक्षितिं Bk. 14. 74, 7. 106. 2 To wander over. 3 To go slyly or secretly, sneak. –*Caus.* (वंचयति-ते) 1 To avoid, escape from, evade; shun; अहिं वंचयति, अवंचयत मायाश्च स्वमायाभिर्नरद्विषा Bk. 8. 43. 2 To cheat, deceive, defraud (said to be A. only, but often P. also); मूर्खास्त्वामववंचत Bk. 15. 15; कथमथ वंचयसे जनमनुगतमसमशरज्वरदूनं Gît. 8; (वंचनं) वंचयन् प्रणयिनीरवाप सः R. 19. 17; Ku. 4. 10, 5. 49; R. 12. 53. 3 To deprive of, leave (one) destitute of; R. 7. 8.

वंचक *a.* 1 Fraudulent, deceitful, crafty. 2 Cheating, deceiving. –कः 1 A rogue, cheat, swindler. 2 A jackal. 3 Musk-rat. 4 A tame ichneumon.

वंचतिः Fire.

वंचथः 1 Cheating, roguery, deceit, trickery. 2 A cheat, rogue, swindler. 3 The cuckoo.

वंचनं-ना 1 Cheating. 2 A trick, deceit, fraud, deception, trickery; वंचना परिहर्तव्या बहुदोषा हि शर्वरी Mk. 1. 58; स्वर्गाभिसंधिसुकृतं वंचनामिव मेनिरे Ku. 5. 47. 3 An illusion, delusion. 4 Loss, deprivation, hinderance; दृष्टिपातवंचना Mâl. 3; R. 11. 36.

वंचित *p. p.* 1 Deceived, cheated. 2 Deprived of. –ता A sort of riddle or enigma.

वंचुक *a.* (की *f.*) Deceitful, fraudulent, crafty, dishonest. –कः A jackal.

वंजुलः 1 The common cane or reed; आमंजुवंजुललतानि च तान्यमूनि नीरन्ध्रनीलनिचुलानि सरित्तटानि U. 2. 23; or मंजुलवंजुलकुंजगतं विचकर्ष करेण दुकूले Gît. 1. 2 A kind of flower. 3 The Asoka tree. 4 A kind of bird. –Comp. –द्रुमः the Asoka tree. –प्रियः the ratan.

वट् I. 1 P. (वटति) To surround. –II. 10 U. (वाटयति-ते) 1 To tell. 2 To divide, partition. 3 To surround, encompass.

वटः 1 The fig-tree; अयं च चित्रकूटयायिनि वर्त्मनि वटः श्यामो नाम U. 1; R. 13. 53. 2 A small shell or *cowrie*. 3 A small ball, globule, pill. 4 A round figure, a cipher. 5 A kind of cake. 6 A string, rope (*n.* also in this sense). 7 Equality in shape. –Comp. –पत्रं a variety of the white basil. (–त्रा) a jasmine. –वासिन् *m.* a Yaksha.

वटकः 1 A kind of cake. 2 A small lump, ball, globule, pill.

वटरः 1 A cock. 2 A mat. 3 A turban. 4 A thief, robber. 5 A churning-stick. 6 Fragrant grass.

वटाकरः, वटारकः A cord, string.

वटिकः A pawn at chess.

वटिका 1 A pill. 2 A chessman.

वटिन् *a.* Stringed, circular. –*m.* = वटिक q. v.

वटी 1 A rope or string. 2 A pill, bolus.

वटुः 1 A boy, lad, youth, stripling; oft. used like the English word ' chap ' or ' fellow '; चपलोयं वटुः *S.* 2; निवार्यतामालि किमप्ययं वटुः पुनर्विवक्षुः स्फुरितोत्तराधरः Ku. 5. 83; cf. बटु also. 2 A religious student or Brahmachârin q. v.

वटुकः 1 A boy, lad. 2 A Brahmachârin. 3 A fool or blockhead.

वट्ट् 1 P. (वटति) 1 To be strong or powerful. 2 To be fat.

वठर *a.* 1 Dull, stupid. 2 Wicked. –रः 1 A fool or blockhead. 2 A rogue, wicked or vile fellow. 3 A physician. 4 A water-pot.

वडभिः-भी See वलभिः-भी.

वडवा 1 A mare. 2 The nymph Asvinî who in the form of a mare bore to the sun two sons, the Asvins; see संज्ञा. 3 A female slave. 4 A harlot, prostitute. 5 A woman of the Brâhmaṇa caste (द्विजयोषित्). –Comp. –अग्निः, –अनलः the submarine fire. –मुखः 1 the submarine fire. 2 N. of *Siva*.

वडा A kind of cake.

वडिशं See बडिश.

वड्ड *a.* Large, big, great.

वण् 1 P. (वणति) To sound.

वणिज् *m.* 1 A merchant, trader; यस्यागमः केवलजीविकायै तं ज्ञानपण्यं वणिजं वदंति M. 1. 17. 2 The sign *Libra* of the zodiac. –*f.* Merchandise, trade. –Comp. –कर्मन् *n.*, –क्रिया traffic, trade. –जनः 1 merchants (collectively). 2 a trader, merchant. –पथः 1 trade, traffic. 2 a merchant. 3 a merchant's shop, a stall. 4 the sign *Libra* of the zodiac. –वृत्तिः *f.* trade, traffic; Bh. 3. 81. –सार्थः a caravan.

वणिजः 1 A merchant, trader. 2 The sign *Libra* of the zodiac.

वणिजकः A merchant.

वणिज्यं, वणिज्या Trade, traffic.

वंट् 1 P., 10 (U. वंटति, वंटयति-ते) To divide, apportion, partition, share.

वंटः 1 A part, portion, share. 2 The handle of a sickle. 3 An unmarried man, a bachelor.

वंटकः 1 Dividing, distributing. 2 A distributer. 3 A part, portion, share.

वंटनं Partitioning, apportioning, dividing.

वंटालः, वंडालः 1 A contest of heroes. 2 A shovel, hoe. 3 A boat.

वंठ् 1 A. (वंठते) To go alone or unaccompanied.

वंठ *a.* 1 Unmarried. 2 Dwarfish. 3 Crippled. –ठः 1 An unmarried man, a bachelor. 2 A servant. 3 A dwarf. 4 A javelin, dart.

वंठरः 1 The sheath that envelops the young bamboo. 2 The new shoot of the palm tree. 3 A rope for tying (a goat &c.). 4 A dog. 5 The tail of a dog. 6 A cloud. 7 The female breast.

वंड् I. 1 A. (वंडते) 1 To divide, share, apportion. 2 To surround, encompass. –II. 10 U. (वंडयति-ते) To share, divide, apportion.

वंड *a.* 1 Maimed, crippled. 2 Unmarried. 3 Emasculated. –डः 1 A man who is circumcised or has no prepuce. 2 An ox without a tail. –डा An unchaste woman ; cf. रंडा.

वंडरः 1 A miser, stingy person. 2 A eunuch.

वत् *a.* 1 An affix added to nouns to show 'possession'; धनवत् possessed of wealth ; रूपवत् beautiful ; so भगवत्, भास्वत् &c. ; (the words so formed being adjectives). 2 Added to the base of the past passive participle वत् turns it into a past active participle ; इत्युक्तवंतं जनकात्मजायां R. 14. 43. –*ind.* An affix added to nouns or adjectives to denote ' likeness ' or ' resemblance ' and may be translated by ' like ', ' as '; आत्मवत्सर्वभूतानि यः पश्यति स पंडितः.

वत See बत.

वतंसः See अवतंस; कपोलविलोलवतंसं Gît. 2.

वतोका A barren or childless woman; a woman or cow miscarrying from accident.

वत्सः 1 A calf, the young of an animal ; तेनाद्य वत्समिव लोकममुं पुषाण Bh. 2. 56 ; यं सर्वशैलाः परिकल्प्य वत्सं Ku. 1. 2. 2 A boy, son; in this sense often used in the voc. as a term of endearment and translatable by ' my dear ', 'my darling', ' my dear child ' ; अयि वत्स कृतं कृतमातिविनयेन किमपराद्धं वत्सेन U. 6. 3 Offspring or children in general ; जीवद्वत्सा ' one whose children are living'. 4 A year. 5 N. of a country, (its chief town was कौशांबी and ruled over by Udayana) or the inhabitants of that country (pl.). –त्सा 1 A female calf. 2 A little girl; वत्से सीते 'dear Sîtâ' &c. –त्सं The breast. –Comp. –अक्षी a kind of cucumber. –अदनः a wolf. –ईशः, –राजः a king of the *Vatsas* ; लोके हारि च वत्सराजचरितं नाट्ये च दक्षा वयं Nâg. 1. –काम *a.* fond of children. (–मा) a cow longing for her calf. –नाभः 1 N. of a tree. 2 a kind of very strong poison. –पालः 'a keeper of calves', N. of Kṛishṇa or Balarâma. –शाला a cow-shed.

वत्सकः 1 A little calf, calf in general. 2 A child. 3 N. of a plant (कुटज). –कं Green or black sulphate of iron.

वत्सतरः A weaned calf, a steer, a young ox ; महोक्षतां वत्सतरः स्पृशन्निव R. 3.

32. -री A heifer ; श्रोत्रियायाभ्यागताय वत्सतरीं वा महोक्षं वा निर्वपति गृहमेधिनः U. 4.

वत्सरः 1 A year ; Y. 1. 205. 2 N. of Vishṇu. **-Comp.** **-अंतकः** the month *Phâlguna*. **-ऋणं** a debt to be paid by the end of a year.

वत्सल *a.* 1 Child-loving, affectionate towards children or offspring; as वत्सला धेनुः माता &c. 2 Affectionate towards, fondly loving, devoted to-fond of, kind or compassionate to, wards ; तद्वत्सलः क स तपस्विजनस्य हंता Mâl. 8. 8 ; 6. 14 ; R. 2. 69, 8. 41 ; so शरणागतवत्सल; दीनवत्सलः &c. **-लः** A fire fed with grass. **-ला** A cow fond of her calf. **-लं** Affection, fondness.

वत्सलयति Den. P. To cause to yearn, cause to feel yearning affection for; नूनमनपत्यता मां वत्सलयति *S.* 7.

वत्सा, वत्सिका A heifer.

वत्सिमन् *m.* Childhood, youth, early youth.

वत्सीयः A cowherd.

वद् 1 P (वदति) but Atm. in certain senses and with certain prepositions; see below ; उदित *pass.* उद्यते, *desid.* विवदिषति) 1 To say, speak, utter, address, speak to ; वद प्रदोषे स्फुटचंद्रतारका विभावरी यद्यरुणाय कल्पते Ku. 5. 44 ; वदतां वरः R. 1. 59 'the foremost of the eloquent'. 2 To announce, tell, communicate, inform; यो गात्रादि वदति स्वयं. 3 To speak of, describe ; Bg. 2. 29. 4 To lay down, prescribe, state ; Ms. 2. 9, 4. 14. 5 To name, call ; वदंति वर्ण्यावर्ण्यानां धर्मैक्यं दीपकं बुधाः Chandr. 5. 45. 6 To indicate, bespeak ; कृतज्ञतामस्य वदंति संपदः Ki. 1. 14. 7 To raise the voice, utter a cry, sing ; कोकिलः पंचमेन वदति ; वदति मधुरा वाचः &c. 8 To show brilliance or proficiency in, be an authority on (Atm.); शास्त्रे वदते Sk., पाणिनिर्वदते Vop. 9 To shine, look splendid or bright (Atm.); Bk. 8. 27. 10 To toil, exert, labour (Atm.); क्षेत्रे वदते Sk. *-Caus.* (वादयति-ते) 1 To cause to speak or say. 2 To cause to sound, play on a musical instrument ; वीणामिव वादयंती Vikr. 1. 10; वादयते मृदु वेणुं Gît. 5. -WITH **-अनु** 1 to imitate in speaking, repeat after (one) ; (गिरं नः) अनुवदती शुकस्ते मंजुवाक् पंजरस्थः R. 5. 74. 2 to echo, resound (P. and A.); अनुवदति वीणा. 3 to approve (by echoing back the same sentiment); *Si.* 2. 67. 4 to imitate (Atm.) ; Bk. 8. 29. 5 to repeat by way of corroboration. **-अप** (said to be Atm. only, but sometimes Paras. also) 1 to revile, abuse, censure ; *Si.* 17. 19 ; Ms. 4. 236 ; sometimes with dat.; Bk. 8. 45. 2 to disown. 3 to repute, contradict. **-अभि** 1 to express, utter, signify ; यद्वाचाऽनभ्युदितं येन वागभ्युद्यते तदेव ब्रह्म त्वं विद्धि नेदं यदिदमुपासते Ken. 2 to salute, greet respectfully. (*-Caus.*) to salute; भगवन्नभिवादये. **-उप** (Atm.) 1 to coax, flatter, cajole ; Bk. 8. 28. 2 to conciliate, talk (one) over. **-परि** to abuse, censure, revile. **-प्र** 1 to speak, utter. 2 to speak to, address; Bk. 7. 24. 3 to name, call. 4 to regard, consider. **-प्रति** 1 to speak, in reply, answer; R. 3. 64. 2 to speak, utter. 3 to repeat. **-वि** (Atm.) 1 to quarrel, dispute; परस्परं विवदमानौ भ्रातरौ. 2 to be at variance, to conflict, be in opposition; परस्परं विवदमानानां शास्त्राणां H. 1. 3 to contend (as in a court of law). **-विप्र** (P. and A). to dispute, quarrel, wrangle; Bk. 8. 42. **-विसं** 1 to be inconsistent, be at variance. 2 to fail. (*-Caus.*) to make inconsistent. **-सं** 1 to talk to, address. 2 to speak together, converse, discourse. 3 to resemble, correspond to, be like (with instr.); अस्य मुखं सीताया मुखचंद्रेण संवदत्येव U. 4. 4 to name, call. 5 to speak or utter in general. (*-Caus.*) 1 to consult, hold consultation (with instr.). 2 to cause to sound, play upon a musical instrument). **-संप्र** (Atm.) 1 to speak loudly or distinctly (as men); संप्रवदंते ब्राह्मणाः Sk. 2 to cry, utter a cry (Paras.); वरतनु संप्रवदंति कुक्कुटाः Mbh.

वद *a.* Speaking, talking, speaking well.

वदनं 1 The face; आसाद्रित्तवदना च विमोचयंती *S.* 2. 10; so सुवदना, कमलवदना &c. 2 The mouth; वदनं विनिवेशिता भुजंगी पिशुनानां रसनामिषेण धात्रा Bv. 1. 111. 3 Aspect, look, appearance. 4 The front point. 5 First term (in a series). **Comp.** **-आसवः** saliva.

वदंती Speech, discourse.

वदन्य *a.* See वदान्य.

वदरः See बदर.

वदालः 1 A whirlpool. 2 A kind of sheat-fish.

वदावद *a.* 1 A speaker, eloquent. 2 Talkative, garrulous.

वदान्य *a.* 1 Speaking fluently, eloquent. 2 Speaking kindly or affably. 3 Liberal, munificent, generous; Ms. 4. 224. **-न्यः** A liberal or generous person, munificent or bountiful man; शिरसा वदान्यगुरवः सादरमेनं वहंति सुरतरवः Bv. 1. 19; or तस्मै वदान्यगुरवे तरवे नमोऽस्तु 1. 94; N. 5. 11; R. 5. 24.

वदि *ind.* In the dark half (of a lunar-month); ज्येष्ठवदि (opp. सुदि).

वद्य 1 Fit to be spoken, not blamable ; cf. अवद्य. 2 Dark or second (said of the fortinght of a lunar month; वद्यपक्षः the dark fortnight). **-द्यं** Speech, speaking about.

वध् 1 P. (वधति) To slay, kill (not used in classical Sanskrit except as a substitute for हन् in the Aorist and Benedictive).

वधः 1 Killing, murder, slaughter, destruction; आत्मनो वधमाहर्ता क्वासौ विहगतस्करः V. 5. 1; मनुष्यवधः homicide; पशुवधः &c. 2 A blow, stroke. 3 Paralysis. 4 Disappearance. 5 Multiplication (in math.). **-Comp.** **-अंगकं** a poison. **-अर्ह** *a.* deserving capital punishment. **-उद्यत** *a.* 1 murderous. 2 an assassin. **-उपायः** a means of killing. **-कर्माधिकारिन्** *m.* a hangman, an executioner. **-जीविन्** *m.* 1 a hunter. 2 a butcher. **-दंडः** 1 corporeal punishment (as whipping &c.). 2 capital punishment. **-भूमिः** *f.*, **-स्थली** *f.*, **-स्थानं** 1 a place of execution. 2 a slaughter-house. **-स्तंभः** the gollows; Mk. 10.

वधकः 1 An executioner, a hangman. 2 A murderer, an assassin.

वधत्रं A deadly weapon.

वधित्रं 1 The god of love. 2 Sexual passion, lust.

वधुः, -वधुका 1 A daughter-in-law. 2 A young woman in general.

वधूः *f.* 1 A bride; वरः स वध्वा सह राजमार्गं प्राप ध्वजच्छायनिवारितोष्णं R. 7. 4, 19; समानयंस्तुल्यगुणं वधूवरं चिरस्य वाच्यं न गतः प्रजापतिः *S.* 5. 15; Ku. 6. 82. 2 A wife, spouse; इयं नमति वः सर्वास्त्रिलोचनवधूरिति Ku. 6. 89; R. 1. 90. 3 A daughter-in-law; इयाच रघुकुलमहत्तराणां वधूः U. 4; 4. 16; तेषां वधूस्त्वमसि नंदिनि पार्थिवानां 1. 9. 4 A female, maiden, woman in general; हरिरिह मुग्धवधूनिकरे विलासिनि विलसति केलिपरे Gît. 1; स्वयशांसि विक्रमवतामवतां नवधूष्वघानि विमृशंति धियः Ki. 6. 45; N. 22. 47; Me. 16, 47, 65. 5 The wife of a younger relation, a younger female relation. 6 The female of any animal; मृगवधूः a doe; व्याघ्रवधूः, गजवधूः &c. **-Comp.** **-गृहप्रवेशः**, **-प्रवेशः** the ceremony of a brides entrance into her husband's house. **-जनः** a wife; female-woman. **-पक्षः** the party of the bride (at a wedding). **-वस्त्रं** bridal apparel, nuptial attire.

वधूटी 1 A young woman or female; रथं वधूटीमारोप्य पापः क्वायं गच्छति Mv. 5. 17; गोपवधूटींदुकूलचौराय (कृष्णाय) Bhâshâ P. 1. 2 A daughter-in -law.

वध्य *a.* 1 To be killed or slain. 2 Sentenced to be killed. 3 To be subjected to corporeal punishment, to be corporeally punished. **-ध्यः** 1 A victim, one seeking his doom ; Mu. 1. 9. 2 An enemy. **-Comp.** **-पटहः** a drum beaten at the time of execution. **-भूः**, **-भूमिः** *f.*, **-स्थलं**, **-स्थानं** a place of execution. **-माला** a garland of flowers placed on a person who is about to be executed.

वध्या Killing, slaughter, murder.

वध्र 1 A leathern strap or thong; *Si.* 20. 50. 2 Lead. **-ध्री** A leathern thong.

वध्र्यः A shoe.

वन् I. 1 P. (वनति) 1 To honour, worship. 2 To aid. 3 To sound. 4 To be occupied or engaged. –II. 8 U. (वनोति, वनुति, usually वनुते only) 1 To beg, ask, request (said to govern two acc.); तोयदादितरं नैव चातको वनुते जलम्. 2 To seek for, seek to obtain. 3 To conquer, possess. –III. 1 P., 10 U. (वनति, वानयति-ते) 1 To favour, aid. 2 To hurt, injure. 3 To sound. 4 To confide in.

वनं 1 A forest, wood, thicket of trees ; एको वासः पत्तने वा वने वा Bh. 3. 120 ; वनेऽपि दोषाः प्रभवंति रागिणां. 2 A cluster, group, a quantity of lotuses or other plants growing in a thick bed; चित्रद्विपाः पद्मवनावतीर्णाः R. 16. 16, 6. 86. 3 A place of abode, residence, house. 4 A fountain, spring (of water). 5 Water in general; *Si.* 6. 73. 6 Wood, timber. (As the first member of comp. वन may be translated by 'wild', 'forest'; वनवराहः, वनकदली, वनपुष्पं &c. –**Comp.** –अग्निः a forest-conflagration. –अजः the wild goat. –अंतः 1 The skirts or borders of a forest; R. 2. 58. 2 The forest region itself, wood; U. 2. 25. –अंतरं 1 another wood. 2 the interior of a forest; V. 4. 26. –अरिष्टा wild turmeric. –अलक्तं red earth or ruddle. –अलिका a sun-flower. –आखुः a hare. –आखुकः a kind of bean. –आपगा 'wood-river,' a forest-stream. –आर्द्रका wild ginger. –आश्रमः abode in the woods, the third stage in the religious life of a Brâhmaṇa. –आश्रमिन् *m.* an anchorite, a hermit. –आश्रयः 1 an inhabitant of the wood. 2 a sort of crow or raven. –उत्साहः a rhinoceros. –उद्भवा the wild cotton plant. –उपप्लवः a forest-conflagration. –ओकस् *m.* 1 an inhabitant of a wood, a forester. 2 an anchorite, a hermit. 3 a wild animal such as a monkey, boar. –कणा wild pepper. –कदली wild plantain. –करिन् *m.*, –कुंजरः, –गजः a wild elephant. –कुक्कुटः a wild fowl. –खंडं a forest. –गवः the wild ox. –गहनं a thicket, the thick part of a forest. –गुप्तः a spy. –गुल्मः a wild or forest shrub. –गोचर *a.* frequenting woods. (–रः) 1 a hunter. 2 a forester. (–रं) a forest. –चंदनं 1 the Devadâru tree. 2 aloe-wood. –चंद्रिका, –ज्योत्स्ना a kind of jasmine. –चंपकः the wild Champaka tree. –चर *a.* living in a forest, haunting woods, sylvan. (–रः) 1 a forester, forest-dweller, woodman; उपतस्थुरास्थितविषादधियः शतयज्वनो वनचरा वसतिं Ki. 6. 29; Me. 12. 2 a wild animal. 3 the fabulous eight-legged animal called *Sarabha*. –चर्या roaming about or residence in a forest. –छागः 1 a wild goat. 2 a boar. –जः 1 an elephant. 2 a kind of fragrant grass. 3 the wild citron tree. (–जं) a blue lotus-flower. –जा 1 wild ginger. 2 the wild cotton tree. –जीविन् a forester, woodman. –दः a cloud. –दाहः a forest-conflagration. –देवता a sylvan deity, a dryad; R. 2. 12, 9. 52; *S.* 4. 4; Ku. 3. 52, 6. 39. –द्रुमः a tree growing wild in a forest. –धारा an avenue of trees. –धेनु *f.* the female of the wild ox or *Bos gavoeus*. –पांसुलः a hunter. –पार्श्वं the neighbourhood of a wood, the forest region itself. –पुष्पं a forest-flower. –पूरकः the wild citron tree. –प्रवेशः commencing a hermit's life. –प्रस्थः a wood situated on table-land. –प्रियः the cuckoo. (–यं) the cinnamon tree. –बर्हिणः, –बर्हिणः a wild peacock. –भूः forest-ground. –मक्षिका a gad-fly. –मल्ली wild-jasmine. –माला a garland of wood-flowers, such as was uaually worn by Krishṇa; R. 9. 51; it is thus described:—आजानुलंबिनी माला सर्वर्तुकुसुमोज्ज्वला मध्ये स्थूलकदंबाढ्या वनमालेति कीर्तिता. °धरः an epithet of Krishṇa. –मालिन् *m.* an epithet of Krishṇa; धीरसमीरे यमुनातीरे वसति वने वनमाली Git. 5; तव विरहे वनमाली सखि सीदति *ibid.* –मालिनी N. of the town of Dvârakâ. –मुच् *a.* pouring water; R. 9. 22. (–*m.*), –मूतः a cloud. –मुद्गः a kind of kidney-bean. –मोचा wild plantain. –रक्षकः a forest-keeper. –राजः the lion. –रुहं a lotus-flower. –लक्ष्मीः *f.* 1 an ornament or beauty of the wood. 2 the plantain. –लता a fores-creeper; दूरीकृताः खलु गुणैरुद्यानलता वनलताभिः *S.* 1. 17. –वह्निः –हुताशनः a forest-conflagration. –वासः 1 living in a wood, residence in a forest, *S.* 4; 10. 2 a wild or nomadic, life. 3 a forest-dweller, a forester –वासनः a civet-cat. –वासिन् *m.* 1 a forest-dweller, forester. 2 a hermit ; so. –वनस्थायिन्, –व्रीहिः wild rice. –शोभनं a lotus. –श्वन् *m.* 1 a jackal. 2 a tiger. 3 a civet-cat. –संकटः a kind of pulse. –सद्, –संवासिन् *m.* forester. –सरोजिनी *f.* the wild cotton plant. –स्थः 1 a deer. 2 a hermit. –स्था the holy fig-tree. –स्थली a wood, forest-ground. –स्रज् *f.* a garland of forest-flowers.

वनर See वानर.

वनस्पतिः 1 a large forest tree, especially one that bears fruit apparently without any blossoms. 2 A tree in general; तमाशु विघ्नं तपसस्तपस्वी वनस्पतिं वज्र इवावभज्य Ku. 3. 74.

वनायुः N. of a district; R. 5. 73. –**Comp.** –ज *n.* produced in Vanâyu, (as a horse).

वनिः *f.* Wish, desire.

वनिका A little wood, as in अशोकवनिका.

वनिता 1 A woman in general; वनितेति वदंत्येतां लोकाः सर्वे वदंतु ते । यूनां परिणता सेयं तपस्येति मतं मम Bv. 2. 117; पथिकवनिताः Me. 8. 2 A wife, mistress; वनेचराणां वनितासखानां Ku. 1. 10; R. 2. 19. 3 Any beloved woman. 4 The female of an animal. –**Comp.** –द्विष् *m.* a misogynist (woman-hater). –विलासः wanton pastime of women.

वनिन् *m.* 1 A tree. 2 The Soma plant. 3 A Brâhmaṇa in the third stage of his life, a Vânaprastha, q. v.

वनिष्णु *a.* Begging, requesting; (याचक).

वनी A forest, wood, grove or thicket (of trees); अवनीतलमेव साधु मन्ये न वनी माघवनी विलासहेतुः Jag.

वनीपकः, वनीयकः A beggar, mendicant; वनीयकानांस हि कल्पभूरुहः N. 15.60.

वनेकिंशुकाः (pl.) 'A Kimsuka in a wood.' anything found unexpectedly.

वनेचर *n.* Dwelling in a wood. –रः 1 A forester, woodman; वनेचराणां वनितासखानां Ku. 1. 10; Ki. 1. 1. 2 An ascetic, a hermit. 3 A wild beast. 4 A sylvan, satyr. 5 A demon.

वनेज्यः A kind of mango.

वंद् 1 A (वंदते, वंदित) 1 To salute, greet respectfully, pay homage to; जगतः पितरौ वंदे पार्वतीपरमेश्वरौ R. 1. 1, 13. 77, 14. 5. 2 To adore, worship. 3 To praise, extol. –WITH अभि to salute, greet respectfully; R. 16. 81.

वंदकः A praiser.

वंदथः A praiser, bard, panegyrist.

वंदनं 1 Salutation, obeisance. 2 Reverence, adoration. 3 Obeisance paid to a Brâhmaṇa &c. (by touching his feet.) 4 Praising, extolling. –ना 1 Worship, adoration. 2 Praise. –नी 1 A Worship, adoration. 2 Praise. 3 Solicitation. 4 A drug for reviving the dead. –**Comp.** –माला, –मालिका a garland suspended across gateways.

वंदनीय *a.* Fit to be saluted, adorable. –या Yellow pigment.

वंदा A female beggar.

वंदारु *a.* 1 Praising. 2 Reverential, respectful, polite, civil; परमनुगृहीतो महामुनिवंदारुः mu. 7. –*n.* Praise.

वंदिन् *m.* 1 A panegyrist, bard, an encomiast, a herald; (the bards form a distinct caste sprung from a Kshatriya father and a Sûdra mother). 2 A captive, prisoner.

वंदी *f.* See बंदी. –**Comp.** –पालः a keeper of prisoners, jailer.

वंद्य *a.* 1 Adorable, venerable. 2 To be respectfully saluted; R. 13. 78; Ku. 6. 83; Me. 12. 3 Laudable, commendable, praiseworthy.

वंद्रः A worshipper, votary. –द्रं Prosperity.

वंधुर *a.* See वंधुर.

वंध्य, वंध्या See वंध्य, वंध्या.

वन्य *a.* 1 Belonging to, growing or produced in, woods, wild; कल्पवित्कल्पयामास वन्यामेवास्य संविधां R. 1. 94; वन्यानां मार्गशाखिनां 45. 2 Savage, not tamed or domesticated; R. 2. 8, 37; 5. 43. **-न्यः** A wild animal. **-न्यं** Forest-produce (such as fruits, roots &c.); R. 12. 20. **-Comp. -इतर** *a.* tame, domesticated. **-गजः, -द्विपः** a wild elephant.

वन्या 1 A large forest, a number of thickets. 2 A mass of water, flood, deluge.

वप् 1 U (वपति, वपते, उप्तः; *pass.* उप्यते; *desid.* विवप्सति-ते) 1 To sow, scatter (as seed), plant; यथेरिणे बीजमुप्त्वा न वप्ता लभते फलं Ms. 3. 142; न विद्यामिरिणे वपेत् 2. 113; यादृशं वपते बीजं तादृशं लभते फलं Subhâsh.; Ku. 2. 5; *S.* 6. 23. 2 To throw, cast (as dice). 3 To beget, produce. 4 To weave. 5 To shear, shave (mostly Vedic). *-Caus.* (वापयति-ते) To sow, plant, put into the ground. -WITH **आ** 1 to scatter, throw about. 2 to sow. 3 to offer, as in a sacrifice. **-उद्.** to pour out. **-नि** 1 to scatter about (as seed). 2 to offer (as oblations), especially to the Manes; न्युप्य पिंडांस्ततः Ms. 3. 216; (स्मरमुद्दिश्य) निवपेः सहकारमंजरीः Ku. 4. 38. 3 to immolate, kill. **-निस्** 1 to scatter, strew (as seed). 2 to offer, present; श्रोत्रियायाभ्यागताय वत्सतरीं वा महोक्षं वा निर्वपंति गृहमेधिनः U. 4. 3 to offer libations, especially to the Manes. 4 to perform. **-प्रति** 1 to sow. 2 to plant or fix in implant; U. 3. 46; Mâl. 5. 10. 3 to set, stud (as with jewels). **-प्र** to throw, cast, offer; Bk. 9. 98.

वपः 1 Sowing seed. 2 One who sows, a sower. 3 Shaving. 4 Weaving.

वपनं 1 Sowing seed. 2 Shaving, shearing; Ms. 11. 151. 3 Semen virile, seed. **-नी** 1 A barber's shop. 2 A weaving instrument. 3 A weaver's shop (तंतुशाला).

वपा 1 Fat, marrow; Y. 3. 94. 2 A hole, cavity. 3 A mound of earth thrown up by ants. **-Comp. -कृत्** *m.* marrow.

वपिलः A procreator, father.

वपुषः A god, deity.

वपुष्मत् *a.* 1 Embodied, incarnate, corporeal; ददृशे जगतीभुजा मुनिः स वपुष्मानिव पुण्यसंचयः Ki. 2. 56. 2 Beautiful, handsome. *-m.* N. of one of the Visvedevas.

वपुस् *n.* 1 (*a*) Body, person; (स्मरं) वपुषा स्वेन नियोजयिष्यति Ku. 4. 42; नवं वयः कांतमिदं वपुश्च R. 2. 47; *Si.* 10. 50. (*b*) Form, figure, appearance; लिखितवपुषौ शंखपद्मौ च दृष्ट्वा Me. 80; परिवःक्षाजतुल्यवपुः Bri. S. 30. 25. 2 Essence, nature; Ms. 5. 96. 3 Beauty, a beautiful form or appearance. **-Comp. -गुणः, -प्रकर्षः** excellence of form, personal beauty; संधुक्षयंतीव वपुर्गुणेन Ku. 3. 52; वपुःप्रकर्षादजयद् गुरुं रघुः R. 3. 34; Ki. 3. 2. **-धर** *a.* 1 embodied. 2 beautiful. **-स्रवः** a humour of the body.

वप्तृ 1 A sower (of seed), planter, husbandman; न शालेः स्तंबकरिता वप्तुर्गुणमपेक्षते Mu. 1. 3; Ms. 3. 142. 2 A father, procreator. 3 A poet, an inspired sage.

वप्रः-प्रं 1 A rampart, earth-work, mud-wall; वेलावप्रवलयां (उर्वीं) R. 1. 30. 2 A bank or mound of any kind (against which bulls and elephants butt); R. 13. 47; see वप्रक्रीडा below. 3 The slope or declivity of a hill or rocky place; बृहच्छिलावप्रघनेन वक्षसा Ki. 14. 40. 4 A summit, peak, table-land on a mountain; तविं महाव्रतमिवात्र चरंति वप्राः *Si.* 4. 58, 3. 37; Ki. 5. 36, 6. 8. 5 The bank of a river, side, shore, bank in general; ध्वनयः प्रतेनुरनुवप्रमपां Ki. 6. 4, 7. 11, 17. 58. 6 The foundation of a building. 7 The gate of a fortified town. 8 A ditch. 9 The circumference of a sphere. 10 A field in general. 11 The butting of an elephant or bull. **-प्रः** A father. **-प्रं** Lead. **-Comp. -अभिघातः** butting against the bank or side (as of a hill, river &c.); Ki. 5. 42; cf. तटाघात. **-क्रिया, -क्रीडा** the playful butting of an elephant (or bull) against a bank or mound; वप्रक्रियामृक्षवतस्तटेषु R. 5. 44; वप्रक्रीडापरिणतगजप्रेक्षणीयं ददर्श Me. 2.

वप्रिः 1 A field. 2 The ocean.

वम्री A mound of earth, hillock.

वभ्र् 1 P. (वभ्रति) To go, move.

वम् 1 P. (वमति, वांत; *caus.* वामयति, वमयति; but wirh prepositions only वमयति) 1 To vomit, spit out, eject from the mouth; रक्तं चावमिषुर्मुखैः Bk. 15. 62, 9. 10, 14. 30. 2 To send forth or out, pour out, give out, give off, give forth, emit (fig. also); किमाग्नेयग्रावा निकृत इव तेजांसि वमति U. 6. 14; *S.* 2. 7; R. 16. 66; Me. 20; अविदितगुणापि सत्कविभणितिः कर्णेषु वमति मधुधारां Vâs. 3 To throw out or down; वांतमाल्यः R. 7. 6. 4 To reject. -WITH **उद्** 1 to spit out, vomit forth. 2 to emit, send forth, pour out; उद्वमेंद्रसिक्ता भूर्बिलमग्नाविवोरगौ R. 12. 5; Mu. 6. 13.

वमः Ejecting, vomiting, giving out.

वमथुः 1 Ejecting, vomiting, spitting out. 2 Water ejected by an elephant from his trunk.

वमनं 1 Ejecting, vomiting. 2 Drawing out, taking or getting out; as in स्वर्गाभिष्यंदवमनं R. 15. 29; Ku. 6. 37. 3 An emetic. 4 Offering oblations. **-नः** Hemp. **-नी** A leech.

वमनीया A fly.

वमिः 1 Fire. 2 A cheat, rogue. **-मिः** *f.* 1 Sickness, nausea. 2 An emetic.

वमी Vomiting.

वंभारवः The lowing of cattle

वम्रः-म्री An ant. **-Comp. -कूटं** an ant-hill.

वय् 1 A. (वयते) To go, move.

वयनं Weaving.

वयस् *n.* 1 Age, any time or period of life; गुणाः पूजास्थानं गुणिषु न च लिंगं न च वयः U. 4. 11; नवं वयः R. 2. 47; पश्चिमे वयसि 19. 1; न खलु वयस्तेजसो हेतुः Bh. 2. 38; तेजसां हि न वयः समीक्ष्यते R. 11. 1; Ku 5. 16. 2 Youth, the prime of life; वयो गते किं वनिताविलासः Subhâsh.; so अतिक्रांतवयाः. 3 A bird in general; स्मरणीयाः समये वयं वयः N. 2. 62; मृगवयोगवयोपचितं वनं R. 9. 53.; 2. 9; *Si.* 3. 55. 11. 47. 4 A crow; Pt. 1. 23 (here it may mean 'a bird' also. **-Comp. -अतिग, -अतीत** *a.* (**वयोतिग** &c.) advanced in age, aged, derepit. **-अधिक** *a.* (**वयोधिक**) older in age, senior. **-अवस्था** (**वयोवस्था**) stage or period of life, measure of age, Mâl. 9. 29. **-कर** *a.* causing health and vigour of life, prolonging life. **-गत** *a.* 1 come of age. 2 advanced in years. **-परिणतिः, -परिणामः** ripeness of age, advanced or old age. **-प्रमाणं** 1 measure or length of life. 2 duration of life. **-वृद्ध** *a.* (**वयोवृद्ध**) old, advanced in years. **-संधिः** 1 transition from one period of life to another; त्रयो वयःसंधयः. 2 puberty, maturity (period of coming of age). **-स्थ** *a.* (**वयःस्थ** or **वयस्थ**) 1 youthful. 2 grown up, mature. 3 strong, powerful. (**-स्था**) a female companion. **-हानिः** (**वयोहानिः**) 1 loss or decline of youth. 2 loss of youthful vigour.

वयस्य *a.* 1 Being of the same age. 2 Contemporary. **-स्यः** A friend, companion, an associate (usually of the same age). **-स्या** A female companion or friend, a woman's confidante.

वयुनं 1 Knowledge, wisdom, faculty of perception. 2 A temple (said to be *m.* also in this sense in Uṇadisûtras).

वयोधस् *m.* A young or middle-aged man.

वयोरंगं Lead.

वर् 10 U. (वरयति-ते, strictly *caus.* of वृ, or वृ of class 10) To ask for, choose, seek to get; see वृ.

वर *a.* 1 Best, excellent, most beautiful or precious, choicest, finest; with gen. or loc. or usually at the end of comp.; वदतां वरः R. 1. 59; वदीवदां वरेण 5. 23, 11. 54; Ku. 6. 18; नृवरः; तरुवराः, सरिद्वरा &c. 2 Better than preferable to ; ग्रंथिभ्यो धारिणो वराः Ms. 12. 103 ; Y. 1. 351. -रः 1 The act of choosing, selecting. 2 Choice, selection. 3 A boon, blessing, favour ; वरं वृ or याच् 'to ask a boon'; प्रीतास्मि ते पुत्र वरं वृणीष्व R. 2. 63; भवलब्धवरोदीर्णः Ku. 2. 32 ; (for the distinction between वर and आशिस् see आशिस्). 4 A gift, present, reward, recompense. 5 A wish, desire in general. 6 Solicitation, entreaty. 7 A bridegroom, husband; वरं वरयते कन्या ; see under वधू (2) also· 8 A suitor, wooer. 9 A dowry. 10 A son-in-law. 11 A dissolute man, libertine. 12 A sparrow. -रं Saffron; (for वरम् see separately). -Comp. -अंग a. having an excellent form. (-गः) an elephant. (-गी) turmeric. (-गं) 1 the head. 2 the best part. 3 an elegant form. 4 pudendum muliebre. 5 green cinnamon. -अंगना a lovely woman. -अर्ह a. worthy of a boon. -आजीविन् m. an astrologer. -आरोह a. having fine hips. (-हः) an excellent rider. (-हा) a beautiful woman. -आलिः the moon. -आसनं 1 an excellent seat. 2 the chief seat, a seat of honour. 3 the China rose. -उरुः-रूः f. a beautiful woman (lit. having beautiful thighs.) -क्रतुः an epithet of Indra. -चंदनं 1 a kind of sandal wood. 2 the pine tree. -तनु a. fair-limbed. (-नुः f.) a beautiful woman ; वरतनुरथवासौ नैव दृष्टा त्वया मे V. 4. 22. -तंतुः N. of an ancient sage ; R. 5. 1. -त्वचः the *Nimba* tree. -द a. 1 conferring a boon, granting or fulfilling a boon. 2 propitious. (-दः) 1 a benefactor. 2. N. of a class of Manes. (-दा) 1 N. of a river ; M. 5. 1. 2 a Maiden, girl. -दक्षिणा a present made to the bridegroom by the father of the bride. -दानं the granting of a boon. -द्रुमः agallochum. -निश्चयः the choice of a bridegroom. -पक्षः the party of the bridegroom (at a wedding) ; R. 6. 86. -प्रस्थानं, -यात्रा the setting out of the bridegroom in procession towards the house of the bride for the celebration of marriage. -फलः the cocoanut tree. -बाह्लिकं saffron. -युवतिः, -ती f. a beautiful young woman. -रुचि N. of a poet and grammarian (one of the 'nine gems' at the court of king Vikrama ; see नवरत्न ; he is identified by some with Kâtyâyana, the celebrated author of the Vârtikas on Pâṇini's Sûtras). -लब्ध a. received as a boon. (-ब्धः) the *Champaka* tree. -वत्सला a mother-in-law. -वर्ण gold. -वर्णिनी 1 an excellent or fair-complexioned woman. 2 a woman in general. 3 turmeric. 4 lac. 5 N. of Lakshmî. 6 of Durgâ. 7 of Sarasvatî. 8 the creeper called *Priyangu*. -स्रज् f. 'the bridegroom's garland', the garland put by the bride round the neck of the bridegroom.

वरकः 1 A wish, request, boon. 2 A cloak. 3 A kind of wild bean. -कं 1 The cover of a boast. 2 A towel, wiper.

वरटः 1 Gander. 2 A kind of grain. 3 A kind of wasp. -टा,-टी 1 A goose; नवप्रसूतिर्वरटा तपस्विनी N. 1. 135. 2 A wasp or a variety of it ; भो वयस्य एते खलु दास्याःपुत्रा अर्थकल्यवर्ता वरटाभीता इव गोपालदारका अरण्ये यत्र यत्र न खाद्यंते तत्र तत्र गच्छंति Mk. 1. -टं A jasmine flower (कुंदपुष्प.).

वरणं 1 Choosing, selecting. 2 Begging, soliciting, requesting. 3 Surrounding, encircling. 4 Covering, screening, protecting. 5 The choice of a bride. -णः 1 A rampart, surrounding wall. 2 A bridge. 3 The tree called Varuṇa. 4 A tree in general ; इह सिंधवश्च वरणावरणाः करिणां मुदे सनलदानलदाः Ki. 5. 25. 5 A camel. -Comp. -माला, -स्रज् see वरस्रज्.

वरणसी More usually written वाराणसी q. v.

वरंडः 1 A multitude, group. 2 A pimple or eruption on the face. 3 A veranda. 4 A heap of grass. 5 A pocket. (The word वरंडलंबुक in यदिदानीमहं वरंडलंबुक इव दूरमुत्क्षिप्य पातितः Mk. 1 is of doubtful meaning ; it seems to mean 'an over-hanging or projecting wall', which if raised high is sure to topple down ; so in the case of the Sûtradhâra whose expectations were raised very high only to be cruelly disappointed).

वरंडकः 1 A mound of earth. 2 The seat on an elephant, a *howdah*. 3 A wall. 4 An eruption on the face

वरंडा 1 A dagger, knife. 2 A kind of bird (सारिका). 3 the wick of a lamp.

वरत्रा 1 A strap, thong or girth (of leather ; Si. 11. 44. 2 the girth of an elephant or horse.

वरम् *ind.* Rather or better than, preferably to, it is better that &c. It is sometimes used with the ablative; समुन्नयन् भूतिमनार्यसंगमाद्वरं विरोधोपि समं महात्मभिः Ki. 1. 8. But it is generally used absolutely, वरं being used with the clause containing the thing preferred, and न च, न तु or न पुनः with the clause containing the thing to which the firt the is preferred, (both being put in the nominative case); वरं मौनं कार्यं न च वचनमुक्तं यदनृतं... वरं भिक्षाशित्वं न च परधनास्वादनसुखं H. 1; वरं प्राणत्यागो न पुनरधमानामुपगमः *ibid.*; sometimes न is used without च, तु or पुनः; याच्ञा मोघा वरमधिगुणे नाधमे लब्धकामा Me. 6.

वरलः A kind of wasp. -ला 1 A goose. 2 A kind of wasp.

वरा 1 The three kinds of myrobalan. 2 A kind of perfume. 3 Turmeric. 4 N. of Pârvatî.

वराक a. (-की f.) Poor, pitiable, miserable, wretched, unhappy, unfortunate (often used to show pity); तन्मया न युक्तं कृतं यत्स वराकोऽपमानितः Pt. 1; तत्किमुज्झिहानजीवितां वराकीं नानुकंपसे Mâl. 10. -कः 1 N. of Siva. 2 War, battle.

वराटः 1 A *cowrie*. 2 A rope, cord.

वराटकः 1 A *cowrie*, प्रातः काणवराटकोपि न मया तृष्णेऽधुना मुंच मां Bh. 3. 4. 2 The seed-vessel of the lotus-flower. 3 A string, rope (*n.* also in this sense). -Comp. -रजस् *m.* the tree called नागकेशर.

वराटिका A *cowrie* ; Bv. 2. 42.

वराणः An epithet of Indra.

वराणसी See वाराणसी.

वरारकं A diamond.

वरांलः,-वरालकः Cloves.

वराशिः-सिः A coarse cloth.

वराहः 1 A boar, hog: विस्रब्धं क्रियतां वराहततिभिर्मुस्ताक्षतिः पल्वले *S*. 2. 6. 2 A ram. 3 A bull. 4 A cloud. 5 A crocodile. 6 An array of troops in the form of a boar. 7 N. of Vishṇu in the third or boar incarnation; cf. वसति दशनशिखरे धरणी तव लग्ना शशिनि कलंककलेव निमग्ना। केशव धृतशूकररूप जय जगदीश हरे Gît. 1. 8 A particular measure. 9 N. of Varâhamihira. 10 N. of one of the 18 Purâṇas. -Comp. -अवतारः the boar or third incarnation of Vishṇu. -कंदः a kind of esculent root. -कर्णः a kind of arrow. -कर्णिका a kind of missile. -कल्पः the period of the boar-incarnation, the period during which Vishṇu assumed the form of a boar. -मिहिरः N. of a celebrated astronomer, author of बृहत्संहिता (supposed to be one of the 'nine gems' at the court of king Vikrama). -शृंगः N. of Siva.

वरिमन् *m.* Excellence, superiority, pre-eminence.

वरिवसि(स्वि)त a. Worshipped, honoured, adored, revered.

वरिवस्या Worship, honour, adoraion, devotion.

वरिष्ठ a. 1 Best, most excellent, most distinguished or pre-eminent. 2 Largest, greatest. 3 Widest. 4 Heaviest; superl. of उरु q. v.). -ष्ठः 1 The francoline partridge. 2 The orrange tree. -ष्ठं 1 Copper. 2 Pepper.

वरी 1 N. of Chhâyâ, wife of the sun. 2 The plant called (शतावरी).

वरीयस् a. 1 Better, more excellent, preferable. 2 Most excellent, very good; Mâl. 1. 16. 3 Larger, wider, more extentsive (compar. of उरु q. v.).

वरी(ली)वर्दः An ox, a bull.

वरीषुः N. of Cupid, tne god of love.

वरुटः N. of a class of Mlechchhas.

वरुडः N. of a low caste.

वरुणः 1 N. of an *Aditya* (usually associated with Mitra). 2 (In later mythology) The regent of the ocean and of the western quarter (represented with a noose in hand); यासां राजा वरुणो याति मध्ये सत्यानृते अवपश्यञ्जनानाम्; वरुणो यादसामहं Bg. 10. 29; प्रतीचीं वरुणः पाति Mb.; अतिसक्तिमेत्य वरुणस्य दिशा भृशमन्वरज्यदतुषारकरः Si. 9. 7. 3 The ocean. 4 Firmament. -Comp. -अंगरुहः an epithet of Agastya. -आत्मजा spirituous liquor (so called being produced from the sea). -आलयः,-आवासः the ocean. -पाशः a shark. -लोकः 1 the worln of Varuṇa. 2 water.

वरुणानी Varuṇa's wife.

वरुत्रं A cloak, mantle.

वरूथं 1 A sort of a wooden fence or fender with which a chariot is provided as a defence against collision (*m.* also in this sense); वरूथो रथगुप्तिर्या तिरोधत्ते रथास्थितिम्. 2 An armour, a coat of mail. 3 A shield. 4 A group, multitude, an assemblage. -थः 1 The cuckoo. 2 Time.

वरूथिन् *a.* 1 Wearing an armour, mailed 2 Furnished with a fender or protecting plank; अवनिमेकरथेन वरूथिना जितवतः किल तस्य धनुर्भृतः R. 9. 11. 3 Protecting, sheltering. 4 Being or seated in a carriage. *-m.* 1 A chariot. 2 A guard, defender. -थी An army; स्खलितसालिलामुल्लंघ्यैनां जगाम वरूथिनी Si. 12. 77; R. 12. 50.

वरेण्य *a.* 1 To be wished for, desirable, eligible ; अनेन चेदिच्छसि गृह्यमाणं पाणिं वरेण्येन R. 6. 24. 2 (Hence) Best, most excellent, pre-eminent, most worthy or distinguished, chief ; वेधा विधाय पुनरुक्तमिवेंदुबिंबं दूरीकरोति न कथं विदुषां वरेण्यः Bv. 2. 158; तत्सवितुर्वरेण्यं भर्गो देवस्य धीमहि Rv. 3. 62. 10; R. 6. 84; Bk. 1. 4; Ku. 7. 90. -ण्यं Saffron.

वरोटः The Marubaka plant. -टं Its flower.

वरोलः A kind of wasp.

वर्करः 1 A lamb, kid. 2 A goat. 3 Any young domestic animal. 4 Mirth, sport, pastime. -Comp. -कर्करः a strap tor rope of leather (कर्कर) to bind a lamb or goal with.

वर्कराटः 1 A side-glance, leer. 2 The marks of a lover's finger-nails on the bosom of a woman.

वर्कुटः A pin, bolt.

वर्गः 1 A class, division, group, company, society, tribe, collection (of similar things); न्यषेधि शेषोऽप्यनुयायिवर्गः R. 2. 4, 11. 7; so पौरवर्गः, नक्षत्रवर्गः &c. 2 A party, side; Ku. 7. 73. 3 A category. 4 A class of words grouped to gether; as मनुष्यवर्गः, वनस्पतिवर्गः &c. 5 A class of consonants in the alphabet. 6 A section, chapter, division of a book. 7 Particularly, a subdivision of an Adhyâya in *Rigveda.* 8 The square power. 9 Strength. -Comp. -अन्त्यं, -उत्तमं the last letter of each of the first five classes of consonants; *i. e.* a nasal. -घनः the cube of a square. -पदं, -मूलं the square root. -वर्गः the square of a square.

वर्गणा Multiplication.

वर्गशस् *ind.* In groups, according to class.

वर्गीय *a.* Belonging to a class or category. -यः A class-fellow.

वर्ग्य *a.* Belonging to the same class. -र्ग्यः One belonging to the same class or company, a colleague, class-fellow, fellow-student (in learing); या गस्य युज्यते भूमिका तां खलु भावन तथैव सर्वे वर्ग्याः पाठिताः Mâl. 1; Si. 5. 15.

वर्च् 1 A. (वर्चते) To shine, be bright or splendid.

वर्चस् *n.* 1 Vigour, energy, power. 2 Light, lustre, brilliance, splendour. 3 Form, figure, shape. 4 Ordure, feces. -Comp. -ग्रहः constipation.

वर्चस्कः 1 Brightness, lusture. 2 Vigour. 3 Feces.

वर्चस्विन् *a.* 1 Vigorous, energetic, active. 2 Bright, brilliant, radiant.

वर्जः Leaving, abandoning.

वर्जनं 1 Leaving, giving up, abandoning. 2 Renouncing. 3 Exception, exclusion. 4 Hurt, injury, killing.

वर्जं *ind.* To the exclusion of, excluding, except (at the end of comp.); गौतमीवर्जमितरा निष्क्रांताः S. 4; Ku. 7. 72.

वर्जित *p. p.* 1 Left out, excepted. 2 Abandoned, relinquished. 3 Excluded. 4 Deprived of, destitute of, without; as in गुणवर्जित.

वर्ज्य *a.* 1 To be avoided or shunned. 2 To be excuded or left out. 3 With the exception of.

वर्ण् 10 U. (वर्णयति-ते, वर्णित) 1 To colour, paint, dye; यथा हि भरता वर्णैर्वर्णयंत्यात्मनस्तनुं Subhâsh. 2 To describe, relate, explain, write, depict, delineate, illustrate; वर्णितं जयदेवेन हरेरिदं प्रणतेन Gît. 3; Ki. 5. 10. 3 To praise; extol. 4 To spread, extend. 5 To illuminate. -WITH उप to describe, narrate. -निस् 1 to look at carefully, mark attentively. 2 to see, behold.

वर्णः 1 A colour, hue ; अंतःशुद्धस्त्वमपि भविता वर्णमात्रेण कृष्णः Me. 49. 2 A paint, dye, paint-colour; see वर्ण् (1). 3 Colour, complexion, beauty; त्वय्यादातुं जलमवनते शार्ङ्गिणो वर्णचौरे Me. 46; R. 8. 42. 4 A class of men, tribe, caste (especially applied to the four principal castes, ब्राह्मण, क्षत्रिय, वैश्य, and शूद्र): वर्णानामानुपूर्व्येण Vârt.; न कश्चिद्वर्णानामपथमपकृष्टोऽपि भजते S. 5. 10; R. 5. 19. 5 A class, race, tribe; kind, species; as in सवर्णं अक्षरं. 6 (*a*) A letter, character, sound; न मे वर्णविचारक्षमा दृष्टिः V. 5. (*b*) A word, syllable; S. D. 9. 7 Fame, glory, celebrity, renown; राजा प्रजारंजनलब्धवर्णः R. 6. 21. 8 Praise. 9 Dress, decoration. 10 Outward appearance, form, figure. 11 A cloak, mantle. 12 covering, lid. 13 The order or arrangement of a subject in a song (गीतक्रम); उपात्तवर्णे चरिते पिनाकिनः Ku. 5. 56, 'celebrated in song,' made the subject of a song. 14 The housings of an elephant. 15 A quality, property. 16 A religious observance. 17 An unknown quantity. -र्णं 1 Saffron. 2 A coloured unguent or perfume. -Comp. -अंका a pen. -अपसदः an outcast. -अपेत *a.* devoid of any caste, outcast, degraded. -अर्हः a kind of bean. -आगमः the addition of a letter; भवेद्वर्णागमाद्धंसः Sk. -आत्मन् *m.* word. -उदकं coloured water ; R. 16. 70. -कूपिका an ink-stand. -क्रमः 1 the order of castes or colours. 2 alphabetical order or arrangement. -चारकः a painter. -ज्येष्ठः a Brâhmaṇa. -तुलिः तूलिका,-तूली *f.* a pencil, paint-brush. -द *a.* colouring. (-दं) kind of fragrant yellow wood. -दात्री turmeric. -दूतः a letter. -धर्मः the peculiar duties of a caste. -पातः the omission of a letter. -पुष्पं the flower of the globe-amaranth. -पुष्पकः the globe-amaranth. -प्रकर्षः excellence of colour. -प्रसादनं aloe-wood. -मातृ *f.* a pen, pencil. -मातृका N. of Sarasvatî. -माला,-राशिः *f.* the alphabet. -वर्तिः,-वर्तिका *f.* a paint-brush. -विपर्ययः the substitution or change of letters; (भवेत्) सिंहो वर्णविपर्ययात् Sk. -विलासिनी turmeric. -विलोडकः 1 a house-breaker. 2 a plagiarist (lit. word-stealer). -वृत्तं a metre regulated by the number of syllables it contains (opp. मात्रावृत्त). -व्यवस्थितिः *f.* the institution of caste. -शिक्षा instruction in letters. -श्रेष्ठः a Brâhmaṇa. -संयोगः marriage between persons of the same caste. -संकरः 1 confusion of castes through intermarriage. 2 mixture or blending of colours; चित्रेषु वर्णसंकरः K. (where both senses are intended); Si. 14. 37. -संघातः, -समाम्नायः the alphabet.

वर्णकः 1 A mask, the dress of an actor. 2 A paint, colour for painting; Si. 16. 62. 3 A paint, or anything used as an unguent or pigment; एतैः पिष्टतमालवर्णकनिभैरालिप्तमंभोधरैः Mk. 5. 46; Bk. 19. 11. 4 A bard, panegyrist. 5 Sandal (the tree). -का 1 A musk. 2 A paint, colour for painting. 3 A cloak, mantle. -कं 1 A paint, colour, pigment; S. 6. 15. 2 Sandal. 3 A chapter, division.

वर्णनं-ना 1 Painting. 2 Description, delineation, representation; स्वभावोक्तिस्तु डिंभादेः स्वक्रियारूपवर्णनं K. P.

10. **3** Writing. **4** A statement, an assertion. **5** Praise, commendation. (**-ना** only in this sense.)

वर्णसिः Water.

वर्णाटः **1** A painter. **2** A singer. **3** One who maintains himself by his wife (स्त्रीकृताजीव).

वर्णिका **1** The mask or dress of an actor. **2** A colour, paint. **3** Ink. **4** A pen, pencil. **-Comp. -परिग्रहः** the assumption of a character or mask; ततः प्रकरणनायकस्य मालतीवल्लभस्य माधवस्य वर्णिकापरिग्रहः कथं Mâl. 1.

वर्णित *p.p.* **1** Painted. **2** Described, represented. **3** Extolled, praised.

वर्णिन् *a.* (At the end of comp.) **1** Having the colour or appearance of. **2** Belonging to the caste of. *-m.* **1** A painter. **2** A scribe, writer. **3** A religious student, a Brahmachârin q. v.; अथाह वर्णी Ku. 5. 65, 52; वर्णाश्रमाणां गुरवे स वर्णी विचक्षणः प्रस्तुतमाचचक्षे R. 5. 19. **4** A person of any one of the four principal castes. **-Comp. -लिंगिन्** *a.* disguised as, or wearing the marks of, a religious student; स वर्णिलिंगी विदितः समाययौ युधिष्ठिरं द्वैतवने वनेचरः Ki. 1. 1.

वर्णिनी **1** A woman (in general). **2** A woman belonging to any one of the four principal castes. **3** Turmeric.

वर्णुः The sun.

वर्ण्य *a.* To be described; (often used in rhetorical works like प्रकृत or प्रस्तुत q. v.). **-र्ण्यं** Saffron.

वर्तः (Usually at the end of comp.) Living, livelihood; as in कल्यवर्त **-Comp. -जन्मन्** *m.* a cloud. **-लोहं** bell-metal, a kind of brass.

वर्तक *a.* Living, being, existing. **-कः** **1** A quail. **2** A horse's hoof. **-कं** A sort of brass or bell-metal.

वर्तका A kind of quail.

वर्तकी A kind of quail.

वर्तन *a.* **1** Abiding, living, staying, being, &c. **2** Stationary. **-नः** A dwarf. **-नी** 1 A road, way. **2** Living, life. **3** Pounding, grinding. **4** A spindle. **-नं** **1** Living, being. **2** Staying, abiding, residing. **3** Action, movement, mode or manner of living; स्मरसि च तदुपांतेष्वावयोर्वर्तनानि U. 1. 26; (the word may here mean 'abode or residence', also). **4** Living on, subsisting (at the end of comp.) **5** Livelihood, maintenance, subsistence. **6** A means of subsistence, profession, occupation. **7** Conduct, behaviour, proceeding. **8** Wages, salary, hire. **9** Commerce, traffic. **10** A spindle. **11** A globe, ball.

वर्तनिः **1** The eastern part of India, the eastern country. **2** A hymn, praise, eulogium (स्तोत्र). **-निः** *f.* A way, road.

वर्तमान *a.* **1** Being, existing. **2** Living, being alive, contemporary; प्रथितयशसां भासकविसौमिल्लकविमिश्रादीनां प्रबंधानतिक्रम्य वर्तमानकवेः कालिदासस्य क्रियायां कथं परिषदो बहुमानः M. 1. **3** Turning or moving round, revolving. **-नः** The present tense (in gram.) वर्तमानसामीप्ये वर्तमानवद्वा P. III. 3. 131.

वर्तरूकः **1** A pool, puddle. **2** An eddy, a whirlpool. **3** A crow's nest. **4** A door-keeper. **5** N. of a river.

वर्तिः **-र्ती** *f.* **1** Anything wrapped round, a pad, roll. **2** An unguent, ointment, eye-salve, collyrium or any cosmetic (in the form of a ball or pill); सा पुनर्मम प्रथमदर्शनात्प्रभृत्यमृतवर्तिरिव चक्षुषोरानंदमुत्पादयंती Mâl. 1; इयममृतवर्तिर्नयनयोः U. 1. 38; कर्पूरवर्तिरिव लोचनतापहंत्री Bv. 3. 16; Vb. 1. **3** The wick of a lamp; Mâl. 10. 4. **4** The projecting threads or unwoven ends (of a cloth), the fringe. **5** A magical lamp. **6** The protuberance round a vessel. **7** A surgical instrument (such as a bougie). **8** A streak, line.

वर्तिकः A kind of quail.

वर्तिका **1** A paint-brush तदुपनय चित्रफलकं चित्रवर्तिकाश्च Mâl. 1; अंगुलिक्षरणसन्नवर्तिकः R. 19. 19. **2** The wick of a lamp. **3** Colour, paint. **4** A quail.

वर्तिन् *a.* (**-नी** *f.*) (Usually at the end of comp.) **1** A Abiding, being, resting, staying, situated. **2** Going, moving, turning. **3** Acting, behaving. **4** Performing, practising.

वर्ति(र्ती)रः A kind of quail.

वर्तिष्णु *a.* **1** Revolving. **2** Being, abiding. **3** Circular.

वर्तुल *a.* Round, circular, globular. **-लः** **1** A kind of pulse, a pea. **2** A ball. **-लं** A circle.

वर्त्मन् *n.* **1** A way, road, path, passage, track; वर्त्म भानोस्त्यजाशु Me. 39; पारसीकांस्ततो जेतुं प्रतस्थे स्थलवर्त्मना 'by land'; आकाशवर्त्मना 'through the air'. **2** (Fig.) A way, course, an established or prescribed usage, the usual manner or course of conduct; मम वर्त्मानुवर्तंते मनुष्याः पार्थ सर्वशः Bg. 3. 23; रेखामात्रमपि क्षुण्णादामनोर्वर्त्मनः परम् । न व्यतीयुः प्रजास्तस्य नियंतुर्नेमिवृत्तयः R. 1. 17 (where the literal sense is also intended); अहमेत्य पतंगवर्त्मना पुनरंकाश्रयिणी भवामि ते Ku. 4. 20 'after the manner of a moth.' **3** Room, scope for action; न वर्त्म कस्मैचिदपि प्रदीयतां Ki. 14. 14. **4** An eye-lid. **5** An edge, a border. **-Comp. -पातः** deviation from the road. **-बंधः**, **बंधकः** an affection of the eye-lids.

वर्त्मनिः -नी *f* A road, way.

वर्ध् 10 U. (वर्धयति ते, also वर्धापयति) **1** To cut, divide, shear. **2** To fill

वर्धः **1** Cutting, dividing. **2** Increasing, causing increase or prosperity. **3** Increase, augmentation. **-र्धं** **1** Lead. **2** Red-lead.

वर्धकः, **वर्धकिः**, **वर्धकिन्** *m.* A carpenter.

वर्धन *a.* **1** Increasing, growing. **2** Causing to increase, enlarging, magnifying. **-नः** **1** A bestower of prosperity. **2** A tooth growing over another tooth. **3** N. of *Siva*. **-नी** 1 A broom. **2** A water-jar of a particular shape. **-नं** **1** Growing, thriving. **2** Growth, increase, prosperity, magnifying, enlargement. **3** Elevation. **4** Exhilaration (of spirits), animation. **5** Educating, rearing. **6** Cutting, dividing; as in नाभिवर्धनं.

वर्धमान *a.* Growing, increasing. **-नः** **1** The castor-oil plant. **2** A kind of riddle. **3** N. of Vishṇu. **4** N. of a district (said to be the same as the modern Bardvâna). **-नः**, **-नं** 1 A pot or dish of a particular shape, lid. **2** A kind of mystical diagram. **3** A house having no door on the south side. **-ना** N. of a district (the modern Bardvâna). **-Comp. -पुरं** the city of Bardvâna.

वर्धमानकः A kind of dish or pot, lid or cover.

वर्धापनं **1** Cutting, dividing. **2** Cutting the umbilical cord, or the ceremony connected with this act. **3** A festival on a birth-day. **4** Any festival in general when wishes for prosperity and other congratulatory expressions are offered.

वर्धित *p.p.* **1** Grown, increased. **2** Enlarged, magnified.

वर्धिष्णु *a.* Growing, increasing, thriving.

वर्ध्री **1** A leather strap or thong. **2** Leather. **3** Lead.

वर्ध्रिका, **वर्ध्री** A leather strap or thong.

वर्मन् *n.* **1** An armour, a coat of mail; स्वहृदयमर्मणि वर्म करोति सजलनलिनीदलजालं Git. 4; R. 4. 56; Mu. 2. 8. **2** Bark, rind. *-m.* An affix added to the names of Kshatriyas; as चंडवर्मन्, प्रहारवर्मन्; cf. दास. **-Comp. -हर** *a.* **1** wearing armour. **2** old enough to wear armour (*i. e.* to take part in battle); सम्यग्विनीतमथ वर्महरं कुमारं R. 8. 94.

वर्मणः The orange tree.

वर्मिः A kind of fish.

वर्मित *a.* Mailed, furnished with armour.

वर्य *a.* **1** To be chosen or selected, eligible. **2** Best, most excellent, chief, principal (mostly at the end of comp.); अन्वीतः स कतिपयैः किरातवर्यैः Ki. 12. 54. **-र्यः** The god of love. **-र्या** **1** A girl choosing her own husband. **2** A girl in general.

वर्वट See बर्बट.

वर्वणा See बर्वणा.

वर्वर *a.* **1** Stammering. **2** Curled. **-रः 1** A barbarian. **2** A blockhead, babbling fool. **3** An outcast. **4** Curly hair. **5** The clash of weapons. **6** A mode of dancing. **-रा, -री 1** A kind of fly. **2** A kind of basil. **-रं 1** Yellow sandal-wood. **2** Vermilion. **3** Gum-myrrh.

वर्वरकं A variety of sandal-wood.

वर्वरीकः 1 Curly hair. **2** A kind of basil. **3** A kind of shrub.

वर्वु(र्वु)रः A kind of tree.

वर्षः, -र्षं 1 Raining, rain, a shower of rain; विद्युत्स्तनितवर्षेषु Ms. 4. 103; Me. 35. **2** Sprinkling, effusion, throwing down, a shower of anything; सुरभि सुरविमुक्तं पुष्पवर्षं पपात R. 12. 102; so शरवर्षः, शिलावर्षः &c.; लाजवर्षः &c. **3** Seminal effusion. **4** A year (usually only *n.*); इयंति वर्षाणि तया सहोग्रमभ्यस्यतीव व्रतमासिधारं R. 13. 67; न ववर्ष वर्षाणि द्वादश दक्षशताक्षः Dk.; वर्षभोग्येण शापेन Me. 1. **5** A division of the world, a continent; (nine such divisions are usually enumerated--1 कुरु; 2 हिरण्मय; 3 रम्यक; 4 इलावृत; 5 हरि; 6 केतुमाला; 7 भद्राश्व; 8 किंनर; and 9 भारत); एतदूढगुरुभार भारतं वर्षमद्य मम वर्तते वशे *Si.* 14. 5. **6** India (= भारतवर्ष). **7** A cloud (only *m.* according to Hemachandra).**-Comp.** **-अंशः, -अंशकः, -अंगः** a month. **-अंबु** *n.* rain-water. **-अयुतं** ten thousand years. **-आर्चिस्** *m.* the planet Mars. **-अवसानं** the autumn or *S*arat season. **-आघोषः** a frog. **-आमदः** a peacock. **-उपलः** hail. **-करः** a cloud. (**-री**) a cricket. **-कोशः -षः 1** a month. **2** an astrologer. **-गिरिः, -पर्वतः** 'a Varsha mountain', *i. e.* one of the mountain ranges supposed to separate the different divisions of the world from one another. **-ज** *a.* (**वर्षेज** also) produced in the rainy season. **-धरः 1** a cloud. **2** a eunuch, an attendant on the women's apartments; M. 4; (**वर्षधर्ष** in the same sense). **-पूगः** a series or collection of years. **-प्रतिबंधः** a drought. **-प्रियः** the Châtaka bird. **-वरः** a eunuch, an attendant on the women's apartments. **-वृद्धिः** *f.* birthday. **-शतं** a century, one hundred years. **-सहस्रं** a thousand years.

वर्षक *a.* Raining.

वर्षणं 1 Raining, rain. **2** Sprinkling, showering down (fig. also): द्रव्यवर्षणं showering or bestowing wealth.

वर्षणिः 1 *f.* Raining. **2** A sacrifice, a sacrificial rite. **3** An act, action. **4** Staying, living, abiding (वर्तनं).

वर्षा (Usually *f. pl.*) **1** The rainy season, the rains, the monsoon; ग्रीष्मे पञ्चाग्निमध्यस्थो वर्षासु स्थण्डिलेशयः Y. 3. 52; Bk. 7. 1. **2** Rain (sing. in this sense). **-Comp.** **-कालः** the rains, the rainy season; so **-वर्षासमयः -कालीन** *a.* belonging to or produced in the rainy season. **-भू** *m.* **1** a frog. **2** a kind of insect (इंद्रगोप). **-भूः, -भ्वी** *f.* a female frog or a little frog. **-रात्रः 1** a night in the rainy season. **2** the rainy season.

वार्षिक *a.* Raining, showering. **-कं** Aloe-wood.

वर्षितं Rain.

वर्षिष्ठ *a.* **1** Oldest, very old. **2** Strongest. **3** Largest (superl. of वृद्ध q. v.)

वर्षीयस् *a.* (**सी** *f.*) **1** Older; very old. **2** Stronger (compar. of वृद्ध q. v.)

वर्षुक *a.* (**की** *f.*) Raining, watery, pouring down water; वर्षुकस्य किमपः कृतोन्नतेरंबुदस्य परिहार्यमूषरं *Si.* 14. 46; Bk. 2. 37. **-Comp.** **-अब्दः, -अंबुदः** a rain-cloud.

वर्ष्मं The body; see below.

वर्ष्मन् *n.* **1** Body, form. **2** A measure, height; वर्ष्म द्विपानां विरुवंत उच्चकैर्वने-चरेभ्यश्चिरमाचचक्षिरे *Si.* 12. 64; R. 4. 76. **3** A handsome or lovely form.

वर्ह्, **वर्ह**, **वर्हण**, **वर्हिण**, **वर्हिन्**, **वर्हिस्** } See बर्ह्, बर्ह, बर्हण, बर्हिण, बर्हिन्, बर्हिस्.

वल् 1 A. (वलते); but sometimes वलति also; वलित) **1** To go, approach, hasten; अन्योन्यं शरवृष्टिरेव वलते Mv. 6. 41; प्रणयिनं परिरब्धुमथांगना ववलिरे वलिरेचितमध्यमाः *Si.* 6. 31, 6. 11, 19. 42; त्वदभिसरणरभसेन वलंती पतति पदानि कियंति चलंती Gît. 6. **2** To move, turn, move or turn round; वलितकंधर Mâl. 1. **3** To turn to, be drawn or attracted towards, be attached to; हृदयमदये तस्मिन्नेवं पुनर्वलते बलात् Gît. 7; Nalod. 3. 5. **4** To increase; वलत्पुरनिस्वना S. D. 116; अमंदं कंदर्पज्वरजनितचिंताकुलतया वलद्बाधां राधां सरसमिदमूचे सहचरी Gît. 1. **5** To cover, enclose. **6** To be covered, enclosed or surrounded. -With **वि** to move to and fro, roll about; स्विद्यति कूणति वेल्लति विवलति निमिषति विलोकयति तिर्यक् K. P. 10. **-सं 1** to mix, blend. **2** to connect, unite with (mostly in *p. p.* see संवलित).

वल See बल.

वलक्ष See बलक्ष.

वलग्नः, -ग्नं The waist.

वलनं 1 Moving, turning towards. **2** Moving round in a circle. **3** (In astr.) Deflection.

वलभिः-भी *f.* (Also frequently written वलभिः **-भी**) **1** The sloping roof, the wooden frame of a thatch; धूपैर्जालविनिःसृतैर्वलभयः संदिग्धपारावताः V. 3. 2; M. 2. 13. **2** The topmost part (of a house), दृष्टा दृष्टा भव ।वलभीतुंगवातायनस्था Mâl. 1. 15; Me. 38; *Si.* 3, 53. **3** N. of a town in Saurâshtra; अस्ति सौराष्ट्रेषु वलभी नाम नगरी Dk., Bk. 22. 35.

वलंब See अवलंब.

वलयः -यं 1 A bracelet, armlet; विहितविशदबिसकिसलयवलयाजीवति परमिह तव रतिकलया Gît. 6; Bk. 3. 22; Me. 2, 60. R. 13. 21, 43. **2** A ring, coil; *S.* 1. 33, 7. 11. **3** The zone or girdle of a married woman. **4** A circle, circumference (oft. at the end of comp.); भ्रांतभ्रूवलयः Dk.; वेलावप्रवलयां (उर्वी) R. 1. 30; दिग्वलय *Si.* 9. 8. **4** An enclosure, bower; as in लतावलयमंडप **-यः 1** A fence, hedge. **2** A sore throat. (**वलयीकृ** 'to form into a bracelet;' **वलयीभू** 'to serve as a bracelet or girdle').

वलयित *a.* Surrounded, encircled, enclosed; Bh. 3. 26.

वलाक *S*ee बलाक.

वलाकिन् See बलाकिन्.

वलासकः 1 The cuckoo. **2** A frog.

वलाहक See बलाहक.

वलिः-ली *f.* (Also written बलिः **-ली**) **1** A fold or wrinkle (on the skin); वलिभिर्मुखमाक्रांतम्. **2** A fold of skin on the upper part of the belly (especially of females, regarded as a mark of beauty); मध्येन सा वेदिविलग्नमध्या वलित्रयं चारु बभार बाला Ku. 1. 39. **3** The ridge of a thatched roof. **-Comp.** **-भृत्** *a.* curled, having curls (as hair); कुसुमोत्खचितान् वलीभृतश्चलयन् भृंगरुचस्तवालकान् R. 8. 53. **-मुखः, -वदनः** a monkey; Mâl. 9. 31.

वलिकः-कं The edge of a thatched roof.

वलित *p. p.* **1** Moving. **2** Moved, turned round, bent round. **3** Surrounded, enclosed. **4** Wrinkled; Ki. 11. 4.

वलिन, वलिभ *a.* Wrinkled, shrivelled, contracted into wrinkles, flaccid; *Si.* 6. 13.

वलिमत् *a.* Wrinkled.

वलिर *a.* Squint-eyed, squinting, ogling.

वलिशं-शी A fish-hook.

वलीकं The edge of a thatched roof; *Si.* 3. 53.

वलूकः A kind of bird. **-कं** The root of a lotus.

वलूल *a.* Strong, robust, powerful.

वल्क् 10 U. (वल्कयति-ते) To speak.

वल्कः-ल्कं 1 The bark of a tree; स वल्कवासांसि तवाधुना हरन् करोति मन्युं न कथं धनंजयः Ki. 1. 35; R. 8. 11; Bk. 10. 1. **2** The scales of a fish. **3** A part, fragment (खंड). **-Comp.** **-तरुः** a kind of tree. **-लोध्रः** a variety of the Lodhra.

वल्कलः -लं 1 The bark of a tree. **2** A garment made of bark, bark-garment, इयमधिकमनोज्ञा वल्कलेनापि तन्वी

S. 1. 20, 19. R. 12. 8; Ku. 5 8; हेमवल्कला: 6. 6 'wearing golden bark-dresses'; (cf. चीरपरिग्रहाः in Ku. 6. 92). –Comp. –संवीत *a.* clad in bark.

वल्कवत् *a.* A fish (having scales).

वल्किल: A thorn.

वल्कुटं Bark, rind.

वल्ग् 1 U. (वल्गति-ते, वल्गित) **1** To go, move, shake; *Si.* 12. 20. **2** To leap, bounce, bound, go by leaps, gallop (fig. also); Pt. 1. 62. **3** To dance; Bh. 3. 125. *Si.* 18. 53. **4** To be pleased; Bk. 13. 28. **5** To eat; *Si.* 14. 29. **6** To swagger, vaunt; Bv. 1. 72.

वल्गनं Leaping, jumping, galloping; R. 9. 51.

वल्गा A bridle, rein; आलाने गृह्यते हस्ती वाजी वल्गासु गृह्यते Mk. 1. 50.

वल्गित *p.p.* **1** Jumped, bounded, leaped &c. **2** Moved, made to dance; Kâv. 2. 73. –तं **1** A gallop, one of the paces of a horse. **2** Swaggering, boasting, vaunt; निमित्तादपराद्धेषोर्धानुष्कस्येव वल्गितं *Si.* 2. 27.

वल्गु *a.* **1** Lovely, beautiful, handsome, attractive; R. 5. 68, *Si.* 5. 29; Ki. 18. 11. **2** Sweet; Bv. 2. 136. **3** Precious. –ल्गुः A goat. –Comp. –पत्रः a kind of wild pulse.

वल्गुक *a.* Handsome, lovely, beautiful. –कं **1** Sandal. **2** Price. **3** A wood.

वल्गुल: The flying fox.

वल्गुलिका 1 A cockroach. **2** A chest.

वल्भ् 1 A. (वल्भते) To eat, devour.

वल्मिक, –वल्मिकि *m. n.* See वल्मीक.

वल्मी An ant. –Comp. –कूटं an ant-hill.

वल्मीकः-कं An ant.hill, a hillock thrown up by white ants, moles &c.; धर्मं शनैः संचिनुयाद्वल्मीकमिव पुत्तिकाः Subhâsh.; Me. 15; *S.* 7. 11. –कः **1** Swelling of certain parts of the body, elephantiasis. **2** The poet Vâlmîki. –Comp. –शीर्षं a kind of antimony (used as collyrium).

वल्यु(ल्यू)ल् 10 P. (वल्युलयति) **1** To cut oft. **2** To purify.

वल्ल् 1 A. (वल्लते) **1** To cover. **2** To be covered. **3** To go, move.

वल्लः **1** Covering. **2** A weight of three *Gunja's*. **3** Another weight of one *Gunja'* and a half; or of two *Gunja's* (in medicine). **4** Prohibiting.

वल्लकी The (Indian) lute; अजस्रमास्फालितवल्लकीगुणक्षतोज्ज्वलांगुष्ठनखांशुभिन्नया *Si.* 1. 9. 4. 57, Rs. 1. 8; R. 8. 41, 19. 13.

वल्लभ *a.* **1** Beloved, desired, dear. **2** Supreme. –भः **1** A lover, husband; Mâl. 3. 8, *Si.* 11. 33. **2** A favourite; Pt. 1. 53. **3** A superintendent, an overseer. **4** A chief herdsman. **5** A good horse (one with auspicious marks). –Comp. –आचार्यः N. of the celebrated founder of a Vaishnava sect. –पालः a groom.

वल्लभायितं A mode of sexual enjoyment; cf. पुरुषायित.

वल्लरं **1** A loe-wood. **2** A bower. **3** A thicket (गहन).

वल्लरिः-री *f.* **1** A creeping plant; अनपायिनि संश्रयद्रुमे गजभग्ने पतनाय वल्लरी Ku. 4. 31; तमोवल्लरी Mâl. 5. 6. **2** A branching foot-stalk.

वल्लवः (वी *f.*) See बल्लवः, *Si.* 12. 39.

वल्लिः *f.* **1** A creeper, creeping or winding plant; भूतेशस्य भुजंगवल्लिवलयस्रङ्नद्धजूटा जटाः Mâl. 1. 2. **2** The earth. –Comp. –दूर्वा a kind of grass.

वल्ली *f.* A creeping plant, winding plant, creeper. –Comp. –जं pepper. –वृक्षः the *Sâla* tree.

वल्लूरं **1** A bower, an arbour. **2** A wood, thicket. **3** A branching foot-stalk. **4** An uncultivated field. **5** A desert, wild, wilderness. **6** Dried flesh.

वल्लूरः **1** Dried flesh. **2** The flesh of the (wild) hog. –रं **1** A thicket. **2** A desert, wilderness. **3** An uncultivated field.

वल्ह् I. 1 A (वल्हते) **1** To be pre-eminent or excellent. **2** To cover. **3** To kill, hurt. **4** To speak. **5** To give. –II. 10 U. (वल्हयति-ते) **1** To speak. **2** To shine.

वल्हिक, वल्हीक See बल्हिक, बल्हीक.

वश् 2 P. (वष्टि, उशीत) **1** To wish, desire, long for; निःस्वो वष्टि शतं शती दशशतं Sânti. 2. 6; अमी हि वीर्यप्रभवं भवस्य जयाय सेनान्यमुशंति देवाः Ku. 3. 15; *S.* 7. 20. **2** To favour. **3** To shine (कांतौ).

वश *a.* **1** Subject to, influenced by, under the influence or control of, usually in comp.; शोकवशः, मृत्युवशः &c. **2** Obedient, submissive, compliant. **3** Humbled, tamed. **4** Charmed, fascinated. **5** Subdued by charms. –शः, –शं **1** Wish, desire, will. **2** Power, influence, control, mastership, authority, subjection, submission; स्ववशः 'subject to oneself'; independent; परवशः 'under the influence of others;' अनयत् प्रभुशक्तिसंपदा वशमेको नृपतीननंतरान् R. 8. 19; वशं नी, आनी to reduce to subjection, subdue, win over; वशं गम्-ई-या &c. to become subject to, give way, yield, submit; न शुचो वशं वशिनामुत्तम गंतुमर्हसि R. 8. 90; वशे कृ or वशी कृ to subdue, overcome, win over; to fascinate, bewitch. वशात् (abl.) is frequently used adverbially in the sense of through the force, power or influence of', 'on account of', 'for the purpose of'; दैववशात्, वायुवशात् कार्यवशात् &c. **3** Being tamed. **4** Birth. –शः The residence of harlots. –Comp. –अनुग, –वर्तिन् (so वशंगत) *a.* obedient to the will of another, submissive, subject. (–*m.*) a servant. –आढ्यकः a porpoise. –क्रिया winning over, subjection. –ग *a.* subject, obedient; Bh. 2. 94. (–गा) an obedient wife.

वशंवद *a.* Obedient to the will of, compliant, submissive, subject, under the influence of (lit. and fig.); कोपस्य किं नु करभोरु वशंवदाऽभूः Bv. 3. 9, 2. 136, 157; N. 1. 33; सा ददर्श गुरुहर्षवशंवदवदनमनंगनिवासं Git. 11.

वशका An obedient wife.

वशा **1** A woman. **2** A wife. **3** A daughter. **4** A husband's sister. **5** A cow. **6** A barren woman. **7** A barren cow. **8** A female elephant; स्त्रीरत्नेषु ममोर्वशी प्रियतमा यूथे तवेयं वशा V. 4. 25.

वशिः **1** Subjugation. **2** Fascinating; bewitching. –*n.* Subjection.

वशिक *a.* Void, empty. –का Aloe-wood.

वशिन् *a.* (नी *f.*) **1** Powerful. **2** Being under control, subdued, subject, submissive. **3** One who has subdued his passions (used like a noun also); R. 2. 70, 8. 90, 19. 1; *S* 5. 28.

वशिनी The *Sami* tree.

वशिरः A sort of pepper. –रं Seasalt.

वशिष्ठ See वसिष्ठ.

वश्य *a.* **1** Capable of being subdued, controllable, governable; आत्मवश्यैर्विधेयात्मा प्रसादमधिगच्छति Bg. 2. 64. **2** Subdued, conquered, tamed, humbled; Bg. 6. 36. **3** Under influence or control, subject, dependent, obedient; तस्य पुत्रो भवेद्वश्यः समृद्धो धार्मिकः सुधीः H. Pr. 18; oft. in comp.; (मनः) हृदि व्यवस्थाप्य समाधिवश्यं Ku. 3. 50. –श्यः A servant, dependant. –श्या An humble or obedient wife; यं ब्राह्मणमियं देवी वाग्वश्येवानुवर्तते U. 1. 2 (who has full command of language). –श्यं Cloves.

वश्यका See वश्या.

वष् 1 P. (वषति) To injure, hurt, kill.

वषट् *ind.* An exclamation used on making an oblation to a deity, (with dat. of the deity); इंद्राय वषट्; पूष्णे वषट् &c. –Comp. –कर्तृ *m.* the priest, who makes the oblation with the exclamation वषट्. –कारः the formula or exclamation वषट्.

वष्क 1 A (वष्कते) To go, move.

वष्कयः A calf one year old.

वष्कयणी, वष्कयिणी *f.* A cow that has full-grown calves; (चिरप्रसूता गौः).

वस् I. 1 P. (वसति, some times वसते; उषित) **1** To dwell, inhabit, live, stay, abide, reside (usually with loc.; but sometimes acc.); धीरसमीरे यमुनातीरे वसति वने वनमाली Git. 5. **2** To be, exist, be; found in; वसंति हि प्रेम्णि गुणा न वस्तुनि Ki. 8. 37; यत्राकृतिस्तत्र गुणा वसंति; भूतिः श्रीर्ह्रीर्धृतिः कीर्तिर्दक्षे वसति नालसे Subhâsh. **3** To speed, pass. (as time) (with acc.). –*Caus.* To cause to dwell, lodge, people. –*Desid.* (विवत्सति) To wish to dwell. –With अधि (with acc.) **1** to dwell or reside in, inhabit, settle ; यानि प्रियासहचरश्चिरमध्यवात्सं U. 3. 8 ; बाल्यात्परामिव दशां मदनोऽध्युवास R. 5. 63, 11. 61 ; *Si.* 3. 59 ; Me. 25 ; Bk. 1. 3. **2** to alight or perch on.-अनु (with acc.) to dwell. -आ (with acc.) **1** to dwell, inhabit ; रविमावसते सतां क्रियायै V. 3. 7 ; Ms. 7. 69. **2** to enter upon ; Ms. 3. 2. **3** to spend, pass (as time). -उप **1** to dwell in, stay (with acc. in this sense). **2** to fast, abstain from food ; Ms. 2. 220, 5. 20 ; (fig. also);उपोषिताभ्यामिव नेत्राभ्यां पिबंती Dk. -नि **1** to live, dwell, stay ; आहो निवत्स्यति समं हरिणांगनाभिः *S.* 1. 27 ; निवसिष्यसि मय्येव Bg. 12. 8. **2** to be, exist ; Pt. 1. 31. **3** to occupy, settle in, take possession of. -निस् to live out, *i. e.* go to the end of (as a period). (*-Caus.*) to banish, drive away, expel ; R. 14. 67. -परि **1** to dwell, stay. **2** to stay over night, see पर्युषित. -प्र **1** to live, dwell. **2** to go abroad, sojourn, be absent from home, travel ; विधाय वृत्तिं भार्यायाः प्रवसेत्कार्यवान्नरः Ms. 9. 74 ; R. 11. 4 (*-Caus.*) to banish, send into exile. -प्रति to dwell near, be near. -वि to dwell abroad. (*-Caus.*) to banish, send into exile ; Bk. 4. 35. -विप्र to sojourn, be absent from home, R. 12. 11. -सं **1** to live, dwell. **2** to live with, associate ; Ms. 4. 79 ; Y. 3. 15. -II. 2. A (वस्ते) To wear, put on ; वसने परिधूसरे वसाना *S.* 7. 21, *Si.* 9. 75 ; R. 12. 8 ; Ku. 3. 54, 7. 9 ; Bk. 4. 10. *-Caus.* (वासयति-ते) To cause to put on.-WITH नि to dress oneself; Bk. 15. 7. -वि to put on, wear ; Bk. 3. 20. -III. 4 P. (वस्यति) **1** To be straight. **2** To be firm. **3** To fix. -IV. 10 U. (वासयति-ते) **1** To cut, divide; cut off. **2** To live. **3** To take, accept. **4** To hurt, kill. -V. 10 U. (वसयति-ते) To scent, perfume.

वसतिः-ती *f.* **1** Dwelling, residing, abiding ; आश्रमेषु वसतिं चक्रे Me. 1 'fixed his residence in' ; *S.* 5. 1. **2** A house, dwelling, residence, habitation; हर्षो हर्षो हृदयवसतिः पंचबाणस्तु बाणः P. R. 1. 22 ; *S.* 2. 14. **3** A receptacle, reservoir, an abode (fig.); Ku. 6. 37 ; so विनयवसतिः, धर्मैकवसतिः. **4** A camp, halting place (शिबिर). **5** The time when one halts or stays to rest, *i. e.* night ; तस्य मार्गवशादेका बभूव वसतिर्यतः R. 15. 11. (वसतिः =रात्रिः Malli.) 'he halted at night' &c. ; तिस्रो वसतीरुषित्वा 7. 33 ; 11. 33.

वसनं **1** Dwelling, residing, staying. **2** A house, residence. **3** Dressing, clothing, covering. **4** A garment, cloth, dress, clothes; वसने परिधूसरे वसाना *S.* 7. 21 ; उत्संगे वा मलिनवसने सौम्य निक्षिप्य वीणां Me. 86, 41. **5** An ornament worn (by women) round the loins (probably for रसना).

वसंतः **1** The spring, vernal season (comprising the two months चैत्र and वैशाख); मधुमाधवौ वसंतः Susr. ; सर्वं प्रिये चारुतरं वसंते Rs. 6. 2 ; विहरति हरिरिह सरसवसंते Gît. 1. **2** Spring personified as a deity and regarded as a companion of Kâmadeva; सुहृदः पश्य वसंत किं स्थितं Ku. 4. 27. **3** Dysentery. **4** Small-pox. -Comp. -उत्सवः the vernal festival, spring-festivities, formerly held on the full-moon day of Chaitra, but now on the full-moon day of Phalguna and identified with the *Holi* festival. -कालः the spring-tide vernal season. -घोषिन् *m.* a cuckoo. -जा **1** the Vâsantî or Mâdhavî creeper. **2** the spring festival ; see वसंतोत्सव. -तिलकः-कं the ornament of the spring ; फुल्लं वसंततिलकं तिलकं वनाल्याः Chand. M. 5. (-कः, -का, -कं) N. of a metre; see App. I.-दूतः **1** the cuckoo. **2** the month called Chaitra. **3** the musical mode हिंदोल. **4** the mango tree. -दूती the trumpet flower. -द्रुः, -द्रुमः the mango tree. -पंचमी the fifth day in the bright half of Mâgha. -बंधुः, -सखः epithets of the god of love.

वसा **1** The marrow of the flesh, fat, marrow; adeps, suet ; Mu. 3. 28 ; R. 15. 15. **2** Any oily or fatty exudation. **3** Brain. -Comp. -आढ्यः, -आढ्यकः the Gangetic porpoise. -छटा the mass of the brain. -पायिन् *m.* a dog.

वासिः **1** Clothes. **2** A dwelling, an abode.

वासित *p. p.* **1** Worn, put on. **2** Dwelling. **3** Stored (as grain).

वसिरं Sea-salt.

वसिष्ठः (also written वशिष्ठ) **1** N. of a celebrated sage, the family priest of the solar race of kings and author of several Vedic hymns, particularly of the seventh Mandala of the *Rigveda*. He was the typical representative of true Brâhmanic dignity and power, and the efforts of Visvâmitra to rise to his level form the subject of many legends; cf. विश्वामित्र. **2** N. of the author of a Smriti (sometimes ascribed to the sage himself).

वसु *n.* **1** Wealth, riches ; स्वयं प्रदुग्धेऽस्य गुणैरुपस्नुता वसूपमानस्य वसूनि मेदिनी Ki. 1. 18; R. 8. 31, 9. 6. **2** A jewel, gem. **3** Gold. **4** Water. **5** A thing, substance. **6** A kind of salt. **7** A medicinal root (वृद्धि). *-m.* **1** N. of a class of deities (*pl.* in this sense); the *Vasus* are eight in number :— 1 आप, 2 ध्रुव, 3 सोम, 4 धर or धव, 5 अनिल, 6 अनल, 7 प्रत्यूष, and 8 प्रभास; sometimes अह is substituted for आप; धरो ध्रुवश्च सोमश्च अहश्चैवानिलोऽनलः । प्रत्यूषश्च प्रभासश्च वसवोऽष्टाविति स्मृताः. **2** The number 'eight'. **3** N. of Kubera. **4** of Siva. **5** of Agni. **6** A tree. **7** A lake, pond. **8** A rein. **9** The tie of a yoke. **10** A halter. **11** A ray of light; निरकाशयद्रविमपेतवसुं वियदालयादपरदिग्गणिका *Si.* 9. 10; शिथिलवसुमगाधे मग्नमापत्पयोधौ Ki. 1. 46 (in both cases वसु means 'wealth' also). **12** The sun. *-f.* A ray of light. -Comp. -ओकसारा **1** N. of Amarâvatî, the city of Indra. **2** of Alakâ, the city of Kubera. **3** of a river attached to Amarâvatî and Alakâ. -कीटः, -कृमिः a beggar. -दा the earth. -देवः N. of the father of Krishna and son of Sûra, a descendant of Yadu. °भूः, -सुतः &c. epithets of Krishna. -देवता, -देव्या the asterism called Dhanishthâ. -धर्मिका crystal. -धा **1** the earth; वसुधेयमवेक्ष्यतां त्वया R. 8. 83. **2** the ground, Ku. 4. 4. °अधिपः a king. °धरः a mountain; V. 1. 7. °नगरं the capital of Varuna. -धारा, भारा the capital of Kubera. -प्रभा one of the seven tongues of fire. -प्राणः an epithet of Agni. -रेतस् *m.* fire. -श्रेष्ठं **1** wrought gold. **2** silver. -षेणः N. of Karna. -स्थली an epithet of the city of Kubera.

वसु(सू)कः The plant called Arka. -कं **1** Sea-salt. **2** Fossil-salt.

वसुंधरा The earth; नानारत्ना वसुंधरा; R. 4. 7.

वसुमत् *a.* Wealthy, rich. -ती The earth; वसुमत्या हि नृपाः कलत्रिणः R. 8. 82; *S.* 1. 25.

वसुलः A god, deity.

वसूरा A harlot, prostitute, courtezan.

वस्क् 1 A. (वस्कते) To go, move.

वस्कय See वष्कय.

वस्कयणी See वष्कयणी.

वस्करादिका A scorpion.

वस्त् 10 U. (वस्तयति ते) **1** To hurt, kill. **2** To ask, beg, solicit. **3** To go, move.

वस्तं An abode. -स्तः A goat; see बस्त.

वस्तकं An artificial salt (कृत्रिमलवण)

वस्तिः *m. f.* **1** Residing, dwelling, staying. **2** The abdomen, the lower belly. **3** The pelvis. **4** The bladder. **5** A syringe, clyster. -Comp. -मलं urine. -शिरस् *n.* **1** the pipe of a clyster. -शोधनं a diuretic (which clears the bladder.)

वस्तु *n.* **1** A really existing thing, the real, a reality; वस्तुन्यवस्त्वारोपोऽज्ञानम्. **2** A thing in general, an object, article, substance, matter; अथवा मृदु वस्तु हिंसितुं मृदुनैवारभते कृतांतकः R 8. 45; किं वस्तु विद्वन् गुरवे प्रदेयं 5. 18, 3. 5; वस्तुनीष्टेप्यनादरः S. D. **3** Wealth, property, possessions. **4** Essence, nature, natural or essential property. **5** Stuff (of which a thing is made), materials, ingredients (fig. also); आकृतिप्रत्ययादेवैनामनूनवस्तुकां संभावयामि M. 1. **6** The plot (of a drama), the subject-matter of any poetic composition; कालिदासग्रथितवस्तुना नवेनाभिज्ञानशकुंतलाख्येन नाटकेनोपस्थातव्यमस्माभिः S. 1. अथवा सद्वस्तुपुरुषबहुमानात् V. 1. 2; आशीर्नमस्क्रिया वस्तुनिर्देशो वापि तन्मुखं S. D. 6; Ve. 1. **7** The pith of a thing. **8** A plan, design. **–Comp. –अभावः 1** absence of reality. **2** loss of property or possessions. **–उत्थापनं** the production of any incident in a drama by means of magic, conjuration; see S. D. 420. **–उपमा** a variety of Upamâ according to Daṇḍin who thus illustrates it; राजीवमिव ते वक्त्रं नेत्रे नीलोत्पले इव । इयं प्रतीयमानैकधर्मा वस्तूपमैव सा ॥ Kâv. 2. 16; (it is a case of Upamâ where the साधारणधर्म or common quality is omitted). **–उपहित** *a.* applied to a proper object, bestowed on proper material; क्रिया हि वस्तूपहिता प्रसीदति R. 3. 29. **–मात्रं** the mere outline or skeleton of any subject (to be afterwards developed). **–रचना** style, arrangement of matter.

वस्तुतस् *ind.* **1** In fact, in reality, really, actually. **2** Essentially, virtually, substantially. **3** As a natural consequence, as a matter of course, indeed.

वस्त्यं A house, an abode, a residence; Śi. 13. 63.

वस्त्रं 1 A garment, cloth, clothes, raiment. **2** Dress, apparel. **–Comp –अगारः-रं, -गृहं** a tent **–अंचलः,-अंतः** the hem of a garment. **–कुट्टिमं 1** a tent. **2** an umbrella. **–ग्रंथिः** the knot of the lower garment (which fastens it neat the navel); cf. नीवि. **–निर्णेजकः** a washerman. **–परिधानं** putting on garments, dressing. **–पुत्रिका** a doll, puppet. **–पूत** *a.* filtered through a cloth; वस्त्रपूतं पिबेज्जलं Ms. 6. 46. **–भेदकः -भेदिन्** *m.* a tailor. **–योनिः** the material of cloth (as cotton). **–रंजनं** safflower.

वस्नं 1 Hire, wages in this sense *m.* also). **2** Dwelling, abiding. **3** Wealth, substance. **4** A cloth, clothes. **5** A skin. **6** Price. **7** Death.

वस्ननं A girdle, zone.

वस्नसा A tendon, nerve.

वह् 10 U. (वंहयति-ते) To make bright, illuminate, cause to shine.

वह् 1 U. (वहति-ते, ऊढ ; *pass.* उह्यते) **1** To carry, lead, bear, convey, transport (oft. with two acc.); अजां ग्रामं वहति; वहति विधिहुतं या हविः S 1. 1 ; न च हव्यं वहत्यग्निः Ms. 4. 249. **2** To bear along, cause to move onward, waft, propel ; जलानि या तीरनिखातयूपा वहत्ययोध्यामनु राजधानीं R. 13. 61 ; त्रिस्रोतसं वहति यो गगनप्रतिष्ठां S. 7. 7; R. 11. 10. **3** To fetch, bring ; वहति जलमियं Mu. 1. 4. **4** To bear, support, hold up, sustain ; न गर्दभा वाजिधुरं वहंति Mk. 4. 17. ; ताते चापद्वितीये वहति रणधुरां को भयस्यावकाशः Ve. 3. 5 ' when my father is leading the van &c. '; वहति भुवनश्रेणीं शेषः फणाफलकस्थितां Bh. 2. 35, *S.* 7. 17 ; Me. 17. **5** To carry off; take away ; अद्रेः शृंगं वहति (v. l. for हरति) पवनः किं स्विद् Me. 14. **6** To marry ; यदूढया वारणराजहार्यया Ku. 5. 70 ; Ms. 3. 38. **7** To have, possess, bear ; वहासि हि धनहार्यं पण्यभूतं शरीरं Mk 1. 31 ; वहति विषधरान् पटीरजन्मा Bv. 1. 74. **8** To assume, exhibit, show ; लक्ष्मीमुवाह सकलस्य शशांकमूर्तेः Ki. 5. 92, 9. 2. **9** To look to, attend to, take care of; मुग्धाया मे जनन्या योगक्षेमं वहस्व M. 4; तेषां नित्याभियुक्तानां योगक्षेमं वहाम्यहं Bg. 9 22. **10** To suffer; feel, experience ; Bv. 1. 94; so दुःखं, हर्षं, शोकं, तोषं &c. **11** (Intransitive in this and the following senses) To be borne or carried on, move or walk on ; वहतं बलीवर्दौ वहतं Mk. 6 ; उत्थाय पुनरवहत् K. ; Pt. 1. 43, 291. **12** To flow (as rivers) ; प्रत्यगूहुर्महानद्यः Mb.; परोपकाराय वहंति नद्यः Subhâsh. **13** To blow (as wind); मंदं वहति मारुतः Râm. ; वहति मलयसमीरे मदनमुपनिधाय Gît. 5. *–Caus.* (वाहयति-ते) **1** To cause to bear or carry, cause to be brought or led. **2** To drive, impel, direct. **3** To traverse, pass or go over ; स वाह्यते राजपथः शिवाभिः R. 16. 12 ; भवान्वाहयदध्वशेषं Me. 38. **4** To use, carry ; Bk. 14. 23. *–Desid* (विवक्षति-ते) To wish to carry &c. –WITH **अति** to pass, spend (as time); chiefly in *caus.* ; Mâl. 6. 13 ; R. 9. 70. **–अप 1** to drive away, remove, take away ; R. 13. 22, 16. 6. **2** to leave, give up, abandon ; R. 11. 25. **3** to subtract, deduct. **–आ 1** to bring home. **2** to cause, produce, lead or tend to ; व्रीडमावहति मे स संप्रति R. 11. 73 ; *S.* 3. 4. **3** to bear, possess, have ; Ch. P. 18. **4** to flow. **5** to apply, use. (*–Caus.*) to invoke (as a deity). **–उद् 1** to marry ; पार्थिवीमुदवहद्रघूद्वहः R. 11. 54 ; Ms. 3. 8 ; Bk. 2. 48. **2** to bear up, elevate. **3** to hold up, sustain, raise, support ; R. 16. 60. **4** to suffer, experience. **5** to possess, have, wear, put on ; Ku. 1. 19, V. 4. 42. **6** to finish, complete. **–उप 1** to bring near. **2** to bring about, commence. **–नि** to bear up, sustain, support ; वेदानुद्धरते जगन्निवहते Gît. 1. **–निस् 1** to be finished. **2** to live upon, live by the aid of. (*–Caus.*) to take to the end, complete, finish, manage, *S.* 3. **–परि** to overflow. **–प्र 1** to bear, carry, draw along. **2** to waft, carry or bear along ; Bk. 8. 52. **3** to support, bear up (as a burden). **4** to flow. **5** to blow. **6** to have, possess, feel. **–वि** to marry. **–सं 1** to carry or bear along. **2** to rub, press, see *Caus.* **3** to marry. **4** to show, display, exhibit. (*–Caus.*) to rub or press together shampoo ; *S.* 3. 21.

वहः 1 Bearing, carrying, supporting &c. **2** The shoulder of an ox. **3** A vehicle or conveyance in general. **4** Particularly, a horse. **5** Air, wind. **6** A way, road. **7** A male river(नद) **8** A measure of four *Droṇas.*

वहतः 1 A traveller. **2** An ox.

वहतिः 1 An ox. **2** Air, wind. **3** A friend, counsellor, adviser.

वहती, वहा A river, stream in general.

वहतुः An ox.

वहनं 1 Carrying, bearing, conveying. **2** Supporting. **3** Flowing. **4** A vehicle, conveyance **5** A boat, raft.

वहंतः 1 Wind. **2** An infant.

वहल *a.* See बहल.

वहित्रं, वहित्रकं, वहिनी A raft, float, boat, vessel; प्रत्यूषस्यदृश्यत किमपि वहित्रं Dk.; प्रलयपयोधिजले धृतवानसि वेदं विहितवहित्रचरित्रमखेदम् Gît. 1.

वहिस् See बहिस्.

वहिष्क *a* Outer, external.

वहेडुकः The Bibhitaka tree.

वह्निः 1 Fire ; अतृणे पतितो वह्निः स्वयमेवोपशाम्यति Subhâsh. **2** The digestive faculty, gastric fluid. **3** Digestion, appetite. **4** A vehicle. **–Comp. –कर** *a.* **1** igniting. **2** stimulating digestion, stomachic. **–काष्ठं** a kind of agallochum. **–गंधः** incense. **–गर्भः 1** a bamboo. **2** the Śamî tree ; cf. अग्निगर्भ. **–दीपकः** safflower. **–भोग्यं** clarified butter. **–मित्रः** air, wind. **–रेतस्** *m.* an epithet of Śiva. **–लोहं, लोहकं** copper. **–वर्णं** the red water-lily. **–वल्लभः** resin. **–बीजं 1** gold. **2** the common lime. **–शिखं 1** saffron. **2** safflower. **–सखः** the wind. **–संज्ञकः** the *Chitraka* tre.

वह्यं 1 A carriage. **2** A vehicle or conveyance in general. **–ह्या** The wife of a sage.

वह्लिक, -वह्लीक see बाह्लिक, बह्लीक.

वा *ind.* **1** As an alternative conjunction it means ' or '; but its position is different in Sanskrit, being used either with each word or assertion or only with the last, but it is never used at the beginning of a clause; cf. च. **2** It has also the following senses:— (*a*) and, as well as, also; वायुर्वा दहनो वा G. M.; अस्ति ते माता स्मरसि वा तातं U. 4. (*b*) like, as; जातां मन्ये तुहिनमथितां पद्मिनीं वान्यरूपां Me. 83; मणी वोष्ट्रस्य लंबेते Sk.; दृष्टो गर्जति चातिदर्पितबलो दुर्योधनो वा शिखी Mk. 5. 6, M. 5. 12; Śi. 3. 63, 4. 35, 7. 64; Ki. 3. 13. (*c.*) optionally; (in this sense mostly in grammatical rules, as of Pâṇini); दोषो णौ वा चित्तविरागे P. VI. 4. 90. 91. (*d*) Possibility; (in this sense वा is usually added to the interrogative pronoun and its derivatives like इव or नाम) and may be translated by ' possibly, ' ' I should liked to know ' ; कस्य वान्यस्य वचसि मया स्थातव्यं K.; परिवर्तिनि संसारे मृतः को वा न जायते Pt. 1. 27. (*e*) Sometimes used merely as an expletive. 3 When repeated वा has the sense of either-or, ' ' whether-or '; सा वा शंभोस्तदीया वा मूर्तिर्जलमयी मम Ku. 2. 60; तत्र परिश्रमानुरोधाद्वा उचा नकथावस्तुगौरवाद्वा नवनाटकदर्शनकुतूहलाद्वा भवद्भिरवधानं दयिमानं प्रार्थये V. 1. (अथवा or, or rather, or else, see under अथ; न वा not, neither, nor; यदि वा or if; यद्वा or, or else; किं वा whether &c.)

वा I. 2 P. (वाति, वात or वान) 1 To blow; वाता वाता दिशि दिशि न वा सप्तधा सप्तभिन्नाः Ve. 3. 6; दिशः प्रसेदुर्मरुतो ववुः सुखा, R. 3. 14; Me. 42; Bk. 7. 1, 8. 61. 2 To go, move. 3 To strike, hurt, injure. –*Caus.* (वापयति-ते) 1 To cause to blow. 2 (वाजयति-ते) To shake. –WITH आ to blow; बद्धां बद्धां भित्तिशंकामुष्मिन्नावानावान्मातरिश्वा निहंति Ki. 5. 36; Bk. 14. 97. –निस् 1 to blow. 2 to be cooled, be cool or assuaged (fig. also); वपुर्जलार्द्रापवनैर्न निर्ववौ Si. 1. 65; त्वयि दृष्ट एव तस्या निर्वाति मनो मनोभवज्वलितं Subhâsh. 3 to blow out, be extinguished, be extinct; निर्वाणदीपे किमु तैलदानम्; निर्वाणभूयिष्ठमथास्य वीर्यं संधुक्षयंतीव वपुर्गुणेन Ku. 3. 52, Si. 14. 85. –*Caus.*) 1 to blow or put out, extinguish. 2 to cool, alleviate the heat of, act as a refrigerant; Ratn; 3. 11; R. 19. 56. 3 to gratify, soothe, comfort; R. 12. 63. –प्र,–वि to blow. वायुर्विवाति हृदयानि हरन्नराणां Rs. 6. 23.

वांश *a.* (शी *f.*) Made of bamboo. -शी Bamboo manna.

वांशिकः 1 A bamboo-cutter. 2 A flute-player, a piper.

वाकं A flight of cranes.

वाकुल See बाकुल.

वाक्यं 1 Speech, words, a sentence, saying, what is spoken; शृणु मे वाक्यं 'hear my words', 'hear me'; वाक्ये न तिष्ठते 'does not obey'; Si. 2. 24. 2 A sentence, period (complete utterance of a thought); वाक्यं स्याद्योग्यताकांक्षासत्तियुक्तो पदोच्चयः S. D. 6; श्रौत्यार्थी च भवेद्वाक्ये समासे तद्धिते तथा K. P. 10. 3 An argument or syllogism (in logic). 4 A precept, rule, an aphorism. –Comp. –अर्थः the meaning of a sentence. –उपमा a variety of Upamâ according to Dandin; see Kâv. 2. 43. –आलापः conversation, discourse. –खंडनं refutation of an assertion or argument. –पदीयं N. of a work attributed to Bhartrihari. –पद्धतिः *f.* the manner of composing sentences, diction, style. –प्रबंधः 1 a treatise, connected composition. 2 the flow of sentences. –प्रयोगः employment of speech, use of language. –भेदः a different assertion, a divergent statement; Mu. 2. –रचना, –विन्यासः arrangement of words in a sentence, syntax. –शेषः 1 the remainder of a speech, an unfinished or incomplete sentence; सदोषावकाश इव ते वाक्यशेषः V. 3. 2 an eliptical sentence.

वागरः 1 A sage, holy man. 2 A learned Brâhmaṇa, scholar. 3 A brave man, hero. 4 A whet-stone. 5 An impediment, obstacle. 6 Certainty. 7 Sub-marine fire. 8 A wolf.

वागा A bridle.

वागुरा A trap, net, snare, toils, meshet; को वा दुर्जनवागुरासु पतितः क्षेमेण यातः पुमान् Pt. 1. 146. –Comp. –वृत्तिः *f.* livelihood obtained by catching wild animals. (–त्तिः) a fowler, huntsman.

वागुरिकः A fowler, hunter, deer-catcher; R. 9. 53.

वाग्मिन् *a.* 1 Eloquent, oratorical. 2 Talkative. 3 Verbose wordy. –*m.* 1 An orator, an eloquent man; अनिर्लोडितकार्यस्य वाग्जालं वाग्मिनो वृथा Si. 2. 27, 109; Ki. 14. 6; Pt. 4. 86. 2 N. of Brihaspati.

वाग्य *a.* 1 Speaking little, speaking cautiously. 2 Speaking truly. –य्यः Modesty, humility.

वांकः The ocean.

वांक्ष् 1 P. (वांक्षति) To wish, desire.

वाङ्मय *a.* (यी *f.*) 1 Consisting of words; R. 3. 28. 2 Relating to speech or words. Ms. 12. 6; Bg. 17. 15. 3 Endowed with speech. 4 Eloquent, rhetorical, oratorical. –यं 1 Speech, language; म्यरस्तजम्नैर्लोतिरोभिर्दशाभिरक्षरैः समस्तं वाङ्मयं व्याप्तं त्रैलोक्यमिव विष्णुना Chand. M. 1; Ku. 7. 90; Si. 2. 72. 2 Eloquence. 3 Rhetoric. –यी The goddess Sarasvatî.

वाच् *f.* 1 A word, sound, an expression (opp. अर्थ); वागर्थाविव संपृक्तौ वागर्थप्रतिपत्तये R. 1. 1. 2 Words, talk, language, speech; वाचि पुण्यापुण्यहेतवः Mâl. 4; लौकिकानां हि साधूनमर्थं वागनुवर्तते 1 ऋषीणां पुनराद्यानां वाचमर्थोनुधावति U. 1. 10; विनिश्चितार्थामिति वाचमाददे Ki. 1. 10 'spoke these words', 'spoke as follows'; 14. 2; R. 1. 59; Si. 2. 13, 23; Ku. 2. 3. 3 A voice, sound; अशरीरिणी वागुदचरत् U. 2; मनुष्यवाचा R. 3. 53. 4 An assertion, a statement. 5 An assurance, a promise. 6 A phrase, proverb, saying. 7 N. of Sarasvatî, the goddess of speech. –Comp. –अर्थः (वागर्थः) a word and its meaning; R. 1. 1; see above. –आडंबरः (वागाडंबरः) verbosity, bombast. –आत्मन्(वागात्मन्) *a.* consisting of words; U. 2. –ईशः (वागीशः) 1 an orator, an eloquent man. 2 an epithet of Brihaspati, the preceptor of the gods. 3 an epithet of Brahman; Ku. 2. 3. (–शा) N. of Sarasvatî. –ईश्वरः (वागीश्वरः) 1 an orator, eloquent man. 2 an epithet of Brahman. (–री) Sarasvatî, the goddess of speech. –ऋषभः (वागृषभः) 'eminent in speech', an eloquent or learned man. –कलहः (वाक्कलहः) a quarrel, strife, –कीरः (वाक्कीरः) a wife's brother. –गुदः (वाग्गुदः) a kind of bird. –गुलिः, –गुलिकः (वाग्गुलिः &c.) the betel-bearer of a king &c.; cf. तांबूलकरंकवाहिन्. –चपल *a.* (वाक्चपल) chattering, frivolous or inconsiderate in talk. –चापल्यं (वाक्चापल्यं) idle or frivolous talk, chattering, gossiping. –छलं (वाक्छलं) 'dishonesty in words', an evasive reply, a prevarication; Mu. 1. –जालं (वाग्जालं) bombast, empty talk; Si. 2. 27. –डंबरः (वाग्डंबरः) 1 bombast. 2 eloquent language. –दंडः (वाग्दंडः) 1 reproachful words, reprimand, reproof. 2 restraint of speech, control over words; cf. त्रिदंड. –दत्त (वाग्दत्त) *a.* promised, affianced, betrothed. (–त्ता) an affianced or betrothed virgin. –दरिद्र (वाग्दरिद्र) *a.* 'poor in words', *i. e.* speaking little. –दलं (वाग्दलं) a lip. –दानं (वाग्दानं) betrothal. –दुष्ट (वाग्दुष्ट) *a.* 1 abusive, scurrilous, using abusive words. 2 using ungrammatical language. (–ष्टः) 1 a defamer. 2 a Brâhmaṇa not invested with the sacred thread at the proper time of his life. –देवता, -देवी (वाग्देवता, वाग्देवी) Sarasvatî, the goddess of speech; वाग्देवतायाः सांमुख्यमाधत्ते S. D. 1. –दोषः (वाग्दोषः) 1 the utterance of a (disagreeable) sound; वागदोषाद् गर्दभो हतः H. 3. 2 abuse, defamation. 3 an ungrammatical speech. –निबंधन (वाग्निबंधन) *a.* depending on words. –निश्चयः (वाङ्निश्चयः) affiance by word of mouth, marriage contract. –निष्ठा (वाङ्निष्ठा) faithfulness (to one's word or promise). –पटु *a.* (वाक्पटु) skilful in speech, eloquent. –पति *a.* (वाक्पति) eloquent, oratorical. (–तिः) N. of Brihaspati (in this sense वाचसांपतिः is also used). –पारुष्यं (वाक्पारुष्यं) 1 severity of language. 2 violence in words, abusive or scurrilous language, defamation. –प्रचोदनं (वाक्प्रचोदनं) an order expressed in words. –प्रतोदः (वाक्प्रतोदः) 'the goad of words', goading or taunting language. –प्रलापः (वाक्प्रलापः) eloquence. –बंधनं (वाग्बंधनं) stopping the speech, silencing; Amaru. 13. –मनसे dual (वाङ्मनसी in Vedic language) speech and mind. –मात्रं (वाङ्मात्रं) mere words. –मुखं (वाङ्मुखं) the beginning or introduction of a speech, an exordium, a preface. –यत *a.* (वाग्यत) one who has controlled or curbed his speech silent. –यमः (वाग्यमः) one who has controlled his speech, a sage. –यामः (वाग्यामः) a dumb man. –युद्धं (वाग्युद्धं) a war of words, (hot) debate or discussion, controversy. –वज्रः (वाग्वज्रः) 1 adamantine words; अहह दारुणो वाग्वज्रः U. 1. 2 harsh or severe language. –विदग्ध (वाग्विदग्ध) *a.* skilled in speech. (–ग्धा) a sweet-speaking or fascinating woman. –विभवः

(वाग्विभवः) stock or provision of words, power of description, command of language; Mâl. 1. 26; R. 1. 9. -विलासः (वाग्विलासः) graceful or elegant speech. -व्यवहारः (वाग्व्यवहारः) verbal or oral discussion; प्रयोगप्रधानं हि नाटयशास्त्रं किमत्र वाग्व्यवहारेण M. 1. -व्ययः (वाग्व्ययः) waste of words or breath. -व्यापारः (वाग्व्यापारः) 1 the manner of speaking. 2 the style or habit of speaking. -संयमः (वाक्संयमः) restraint or control of speech.

वाचः 1 A kind of fish. 2 The plant मदन.

वाचंयम *a*. Holding the tongue, maintaining perfect silence, silent, taciturn; उपस्थिता देवी तद्वाचंयमो भव V. 3; विद्वांसो वसुधातले परवचःश्लाघासु वाचंयमाः Bv. 4. 42; R. 13. 44. -मः A sage who maintains rigid silence.

वाचक *a*. 1 Speaking, declaring, explanatory. 2 Expressing, signifying, denoting directly (as a word, distinguished from लाक्षणिक and व्यंजक); see K. P. 2. 3 Verbal. -कः 1 A speaker. 2 A reader. 3 A significant word. 4 A messenger.

वाचनं 1 Reading, reciting. 2 Declaration, proclamation, utterance; as in वस्तिवाचनं, पुण्याहवाचनं.

वाचनकं A riddle.

वाचनिक *a*. (की *f*.) Verbal, expressed by words.

वाचस्पतिः 'The lord of speech', an epithet of Brihaspati, preceptor of the gods.

वाचस्पत्यं An eloquent speech, oration, a harangue; तदूरीकृत्य कृतिभिर्वाचस्पत्यं प्रतायते H. 3. 96 (=Si. 2. 30).

वाचा 1 Speech. 2 A sacred text, a text or aphorism. 3 An oath.

वाचाट *a*. Talkative, garrulous; talking much or idly; अरेरे वाचाट Ve. 3; Mv. 6; Bk. 5. 23.

वाचाल *a*. 1 Noisy, making a sound, crying. 2 Talkative, garrulous; see वाचाट; Si. 1. 40.

वाचिक *a*. (का-की) 1 Consisting of or expressed by words ; वाचिकं पारुष्यम्. 2 Oral, verbal, expressed by word of mouth. -कं 1 A message, an oral or verbal communication; वाचिकमप्यार्येण सिद्धार्थकाच्छ्रोतव्यमिति लिखितं Mu. 5; निर्धारितेऽर्थे लेखेन खलूक्त्वा खलु वाचिकं Si. 2. 70. 2 News, tidings, intelligence in general.

वाचोयुक्ति *a*. Skilled in speech, eloquent. -क्तिः *f*. 'Arrangement of words', a declaration, announcement, speech; यत्र खल्वियं वाचोयुक्तिः Mâl. 1.

वाच्य *a*. 1 To be spoken, told or said, to be spoken to or addressed; वाच्यस्त्वया मद्वचनात्स राजा R. 14. 61 'say to the king in my name'. 2 to be predicated, attributive. 3 Expressed (as the meaning of a word); cf. लक्ष्य and व्यंग्य. 4 Blamable, censurable, reprehensible; Si. 20. 34; H. 3. 129. -च्यं 1 Blame, censure, reproach; प्रमदामनु संस्थितः शुचा नृपतिः सन्निति वाच्यदर्शनात् R. 8. 72, 84; चिरस्य वाच्यं न गतः प्रजापतिः S. 5. 15, Si. 3. 58. 2 The expressed meaning; that derived by means of अभिधा q. v. cf. लक्ष्य and व्यंग्य; अपि तु वाच्यवैचित्र्यप्रतिभासादेव चारुताप्रतीतिः K. P. 10. 3 A predicate. 4 The voice of a verb. K. -Comp. -अर्थः expressed meaning. -चित्रं one of the two kinds of the third or lowest (अधम) division of *Ka'vya* or poetry, in which the charm lies in the expression of a striking or fanciful idea (opp. शब्दचित्र); see चित्र also. -वज्रं severe or harsh language.

वाजः 1 A wing. 2 A feather. 3 The feather of an arrow. 4 Battle, conflict. 5 Sound. -जं 1 Clarified butter. 2 An oblation of rice offered at a Srâddha or obsequial ceremony. 3 Food in general. 4 Water. 5 A prayer or *mantra* with which a sacrifice is concluded. -Comp. -पेयः -यं N. of a particular sacrifice. -सनः 1 N. of Vishṇu. 2 of Siva. -सनिः the sun.

वाजसनेयः N. of Yâj*n*avalkya, the author of the Vâjasaneyi Samhitâ or the Sukla Yajurveda.

वाजसनेयिन् *m*. 1 N. of the sage Yâj*n*avalkya, the author and founder of the white or Sukla Yajurveda. 2 A follower of the white Yajurveda, one belonging to the sect of the Vâjasaneyins.

वाजिन् *m*. 1 A horse; न गर्दभा वाजिधुरं वहंति Mk. 4. 17 ; R. 3. 43 ; 4. 25, 67; Si. 18. 31. 2 An arrow. 3 A bird. 4 A follower of the Vâjasaneyin branch of the Yajurveda. -Comp. -पृष्ठः the globe amaranth. -भक्षः a chick-pea. -भोजनः a kind of kidney-bean. -मेधः a horse-sacrifice. -शाला a stable.

वाजिकर *a*. Stimulating amorous desires.

वाजीकरण Stimulating or exciting desire by aphrodisiacs.

वांछ् 1 P. (वांछति, वांछित) To wish, desire; न संहतास्तस्य न भिन्नवृत्तयः प्रियाणि वांछत्यसुभिः समीहितुं Ki. 1. 19. -WITH -अभि,-सं to wish, desire or long for; Bk. 17. 53.

वांछनं Wishing, desiring.

वांछा A wish, desire, longing; वांछा सज्जनसंगमे Bh. 2. 62.

वांछित *p. p*. Wished, desired. -तं A wish, desire.

वांछिन् *a*. 1 Wishing. 2 Lustful.

वाटः -टं 1 An enclosure, a piece of enclosed ground, court; स्ववाटकुक्कटविजयहृष्टः Dk.; so वेश°, श्मशान° &c. 2 A garden, park, an orchard. 3 A road. 4 The groin. 5 A sort of grain. -Comp. -धानः the descendant of an outcast Brâhmaṇa by a Brâhmaṇa female; see Ms. 10. 21.

वाटिका 1 The site of a house. 2 An orchard, a garden; अथे दक्षिणेन वृक्षवाटिकामालाप इव श्रूयते Si. 1; so पुष्प°, अशोक° &c.

वाटी 1 The site of a house. 2 A house, dwelling. 3 A court, an enclosure. 4 A garden, park, orchard; वाटीभुवि क्षितिभुजां Asvad 5. 5 A road. 6 The groin. 7 A kind of grain.

वाट्या, वाट्यालः, वाट्यालो N. of a plant (अतिबला).

वाड् 1 A. (वाडते) To bathe, dive.

वाडवः 1 Submarine fire. 2 A Brâhmaṇa. -वं A stud or collection of mares. -Comp. -अग्निः, -अनलः the submarine fire.

वाडवेयः A bull. -यौ (*m*. dual) the two Asvins.

वाडव्यं A collection of Brâhmaṇas.

वाढ See बाढ.

वाण See बाण.

वाणिः *f*. 1 Weaving. 2 A weaver's loom.

वाणिजः A merchant.

वाणिज्यं Trade, traffic.

वाणिनी 1 A clever or intriguing woman. 2 A dancing girl, an actress. 3 A drunken woman (literally or figuratively), an amorous and wanton woman ; R. 6. 75.

वाणी 1 Speech, words, language, वाण्येका समलंकरोति पुरुषं या संस्कृता धार्यते Bh. 2. 19. 2 Power of speech. 3 Sound, voice; केका वाणी मयूरस्य Ak.; so आकाशवाणी. 4 A literary production, a work or composition ; मद्वाणि मा कुरु विषादमनादरेण मात्सर्यमग्नमनसां सहसा खलानां Bv. 4. 41; U. 7. 21. 5 Praise. 6 Sarasvatî, the goddess of learning.

वात् 10 U. (वातयति-ते) 1 To blow. 2 To fan, ventilate. 3 To serve. 4 To make happy. 5 To go.

वात *p. p*. 1 Blown. 2 Desired or wished for, solicited. -तः 1 Air, wind. 2 The god of wind, the deity presiding over wind. 3 Wind, as one of the three humours of the body. 4 Gout, rheumatism. -Comp. -अटः 1 an antelope (वातमृग). 2 a horse of the sun. -अंडः a disease of the testicles. -अतिसारः dysentery caused by some derangement or vitiation of the bodily wind. -अयं a leaf. -अयनः a horse. (-नं) 1 a window, an air-hole; Mâl. 2. 11; Ku. 7. 59; R. 6. 24, 13. 21. 2 a porch, portico. 3 a pavilion. -अयुः an antelope. -अरिः the castor-oil tree. -अश्वः a very fleet or swift horse. -आमोदा musk. -आलिः *f*. a whirlwind. -आहत *a.* 1 shaken by the wind. 2 affected by gout. -आहतिः *f.* a violent gust of wind. -ऋद्धिः *f.* 1 excess of wind. 2 a mace, a club, stick tipped with iron. -कर्मन् *n.* breaking wind. -कुंडलिका scanty and painful flow of urine. -कुंभः the part of an elephant's forehead below the frontal sinuses. -केतुः dust. -केलिः 1 amorous discourse, the low whispering of lovers. 2 the marks of finger-nails on the person of a lover. -गुल्मः 1 a high wind, strong gale. 2 rheumatism. -ज्वरः fever arising from vitiated wind. -ध्वजः a cloud. -पुत्रः N. of Bhîma or Hanumat. -पोथः, -पोथकः the tree called पलाश. -प्रकोपः excess of wind. -प्रमी *m. f.* a swift antelope. -मंडली whirl-wind. -मृगः a swift antelope. -रक्तं, -शोणितं acute gout. -रंगः the fig-tree. -रूषः 1 a storm, violent wind, tempest. 2 the rain-bow. 3 a bribe. -रोगः, -व्याधिः gout or rheumatism. -वस्तिः *f.* suppression of urine. -वृद्धिः *f.* swelled testicle. -शीर्षं the lower belly. -शूलं colic with flatulence. -सारथिः fire.

वातकः 1 A paramour (जार). 2 N. of a plant.

वाताकिन् *a.* (नी *f.*) Gouty.

वातमजः A swift antelope.

वातर *a.* 1 Stormy, windy. 2 Swift. -Comp. -अयणः 1 an arrow. 2 an arrow's flight, bow-shot. 3 a peak, summit. 4 a saw. 5 a mad or intoxicated man. 6 an idler. 7 the Sarala or pine tree.

वातलः *a.* (ली *f.*) 1 Stormy, windy. 2 Flatulent. -लः 1 Wind. 2 The chick-pea (चणक).

वातापिः N. of a demon said to have been eaten up and digested by Agastya. -Comp. -द्विष् *m.*, -सूदनः, -हन् *m.* epithets of Agastya..

वातिः 1 The sun. 2 Wind, air. 3 The moon. -Comp. -गः, -गमः the egg-plant; (वातिंगणः in the same sense).

वातिक *a.* (की *f.*) 1 Stormy, windy. 2 Gouty, rheumatic. 3 Mad. -कः Fever caused by a vitiated state of the wind.

वातीय *a.* Windy. -यं Rice-gruel.

वातुल *a.* 1 Affected by wind disease, gouty. 2 Mad, crazy-headed; H. 2. 26. -लः A whirl wind.

वातुलिः A large bat.

वातूल *a.* See वातुल.

वातृ *m.* Air, wind.

वात्या A storm, hurricane, whirlwind, stormy or tempestuous wind; वात्याभिः परुषीकृता दश दिशश्चंडातपो दुःसह Bv. 1. 13; R. 11. 16; Ki. 5. 39; Ve. 2. 21.

वात्सकं A herd of calves.

वात्सल्यं 1 Affection (towards one's offspring,) affection or tenderness in general; न पुत्रवात्सल्यमपाकरिष्यति Ku. 5. 14; पतिवात्सल्यात् R. 15. 98; so भार्या°) प्रजा°, शरणागत°, &c. 2 Fond affection or partiality.

वात्सिः-सी *f.* The daughter of a Sûdra woman by a Brâhmaṇa.

वात्स्यायनः 1 N. of the author of the Kâmasûtras (a work on erotic subjects). 2 N. of the author of a commentary on the Nyâya Sûtras.

वादः 1 Talking, speaking. 2 Speech, words, talk; सामवादाः सकोपस्य तस्य प्रत्युत दीपिकाः Si. 2. 55; so कैतववाद Gît. 8; सांत्ववादः &c. 3 A statement, an assertion, allegation; अवाच्यवादांश्च बहून् वदिष्यंति तवाहिताः Bg. 2. 36. 4 Narration, account; शाकुंतलादीनितिहासवादान् Mâl. 3. 3. 5 Discussion, dispute, controversy; वादे वादे जायते तत्त्वबोधः Subhâsh.; सीमा° Ms. 8. 265. 6 A reply. 7 An exposition, explanation. 8 A demonstrated conclusion, theory, doctrine; इदानीं परमाणुकारणवादं निराकरोति S. B. (and in diverse other places of the work). 9 Sounding, sound. 10 Report, rumour. 11 A plaint (in law). -Comp. -अनुवादौ (*m.* du.) 1 assertion and reply, plaint and reply, accusation and defence. 2 dispute, controversy. -कर, -कृत् *a.* causing a dispute. -ग्रस्त *a.* disputed, in dispute; वादग्रस्तोऽयं विषयः. -चंचु *a.* clever in repartees or witty replies. -प्रतिवादः controversy. -युद्धं a dispute, controversy. -विवादः disputation, discussion, debate.

वादकः A musician.

वादनं 1 Sounding. 2 Instrumental music.

वादर *a.* (री *f.*) Made or consisting of cotton. -रा The cotton shrub. -रं Cotton cloth.

वादरंगः The sacred fig-tree.

वादरायण See बादरायण.

वादालः The sheat-fish.

वादि *a.* Wise, learned, skilful.

वादित *p. p.* 1 Caused to be uttered, made to speak. 2 Played, sounded.

वादित्रं 1 A musical instrument; N. 22. 22. 2 Instrumental music.

वादिन् *a.* 1 Speaking, talking, discoursing. 2 Asserting. 3 Disputing. -*m.* 1 A speaker. 2 A disputant, an antagonist; Mu. 5. 10; R. 12. 92. 3 An accuser, a plaintiff. 4 An expounder, a teacher.

वादिशः A learned man, sage, scholar.

वाद्यं 1 A musical instrument. 2 The sound of a musical instrument; R. 16. 64 (वाद्यध्वनिः Malli.). -Comp. -करः a musician. -भांडं 1 a band of music, a number of musical instruments. 2 a musical instrument.

वाध्, वाध, वाधक, वाधन-ना, वाधा See बाध्, बाध, बाधक, बाधन-ना, बाधा.

वाधु(धू)क्यं Marriage.

वाध्रीणसः A rhinoceros.

वान *a.* 1 Blown. 2 Dried (by wind), dried up. 3 Belonging to a forest. -नं 1 Dry or dried fruit (-*m.* also). 2 Blowing. 3 Living. 4 Rolling, moving. 5 A perfume, fragrance. 6 A number of groves or thickets. 7 Weaving. 8 A mat of straw. 9 A hole in the wall of a house.

वानप्रस्थः 1 A Brâhmaṇa in the third stage of his religious life. 2 An anchorite, a hermit. 3 The Madhûka tree. 4 The Palâsa tree.

वानरः A monkey, an ape. -Comp. -अक्षः a wild goat. -आघातः the tree called Lodhra. -इंद्रः N. of Sugrîva or of Hanumat. -प्रियः the tree called क्षीरिन्.

वानलः A kind of holy basil (the black variety).

वानस्पत्यः A tree the fruit of which is produced from blossom; *e. g.* the mango.

वाना A quail.

वानायुः N. of a country to the north-west of India. -Comp. -जः a Vanâyu horse, *i. e.* a horse produced in the Vanâyu country.

वानीरः A sort of cane or ratan; स्मरामि वानीरगृहेषु सुप्तः R. 13. 35; Me. 41; Mâl. 9. 15; R. 13. 30, 16. 21.

वानीरकः The *Munja* grass, a kind of rush.

वानेयं N. of a fragrant grass (मुस्ता).

वांत *p. p.* 1 Vomited, spitted out. 2 Emitted, ejected, effused. -Comp. -अदः a dog.

वांतिः *f.* 1 Vomiting. 2 Ejecting, emitting. -Comp. -कृत, -द *a.* emetic.

वान्या A multitude of groves or woods.

वापः 1 Sowing seed. 2 Weaving. 3 Shaving, shearing; Ms. 11. 108. -Comp. -दंडः a weaver's loom.

वापनं 1 Causing to sow. 2 Shaving.

वापित *p. p.* 1 Sown. 2 Shaven.

वापिः-पी *f.* A well, any large oblong or circular reservoir of water; वापी चास्मिन्मरकतशिलाबद्धसोपानमार्गा Me. 76. -Comp. -हः the *Cha'taka* bird.

वाम *a.* 1 Left (opp. दक्षिण); विलोचनं दक्षिणमंजनेन संभाव्य तद्वंचितवामनेत्रा R. 7. 8; Me. 78, 96. 2 Being or situated on the left side; वामश्चायं नदति मधुरं चातकस्ते सगंधः Me. 9; (वामेन is used adverbially in the same sense; *e. g.* वामेनात्र वटस्तमध्वगजनः सर्वात्मना सेवते K. P. 10). 3 (*a*) Reverse, contrary, opposite, adverse, unfavourable; तदहो कामस्य वामा गतिः Gît. 12; Mâl. 9. 8, Bk. 6. 17. (*b*) Acting contrary, of an opposite nature; S. 4. 18. (*c*) Perverse, crooked-natured, refractory; *S*. 6. **4** Vile, wicked, base, low, bad; Ki. 11. 24. **5** Lovely, beautiful, charming; as in वामलोचना q. v. **-मः** **1** A sentient being, an animal. **2** N. of *Siva*. **3** Of Cupid, the god of love. **4** A snake. **5** An udder, a breast. **-मं** Wealth, possessions. **-Comp.** **-आचारः** **-मार्गः** the left hand ritual of the *Tantras*. **-आवर्तः** a conch-shell, the spiral of which runs from right to left. **-उरु, ऊरू** *f*. a woman with handsome thighs. **-दृश्** *f*. a woman (with lovely eyes). **-देवः** **1** N. of a sage. **2** N. of *Siva*. **-लोचना** a woman with lovely eyes; विरूपाक्षस्य जयिनीस्ताः स्तुवे वामलोचनाः K. P. 10; R. 19 13. **-शील** *a*. of a perverse or crooked nature. (**-लः**) an epithet of the god of love.

वामक *a*. **1** Left. **2** Adverse, contrary; Mâl. 1. 8. (where both senses are intended).

वामन *a*. **1** (*a*) Short in stature, dwarfish, pigmy; छलवामनं *Si*. 13. 12. (*b*) (Hence) Small, short, little, reduced in length; वामनार्चिरिव दीपभाजनं R. 19. 51; कथं कथं तानि (दिनानि) च वामनानि N. 22. 57. **2** Bent down, bent low (नम्र); *Si*. 13. 12. **3** Vile, low, base. **-नः** **1** A dwarf, pigmy; प्रांशुलभ्ये फले मोहादुद्बाहुरिव वामनः R. 1. 3, 10. 60. **2** N. of Vishṇu in his fifth incarnation, when he was born as a dwarf to humble the demon Bali,, (see बलि); छलयसि विक्रमणे बलिमद्भुतवामन पदनखनीरजनितजनपावन । केशव धृतवामनरूप जय जगदीश हरे Gît. 1. 3 N. of the elephant that presides over the south. **4** N. of the author of the Kâsikâvritti, a commentary on Pâṇini's *Sûtras*. **5** The tree called अंकोट. **-Comp.** **-आकृति** *a*. dwarfish. **-पुराणं** N. of one of the 18 Purâṇas.

वामनिका A female dwarf.

वामनी **1** A female dwarf. **2** A mare. **3** A kind of woman.

वामलूरः An ant-hill, a mole-hill.

वामा **1** A woman. **2** A lovely woman; Bv. 4. 39, 42. **3** N. of Gaurî **4** Of Lakshmî. **5** Of Sarasvatî.

वामिल *a*. **1** Beautiful, handsome. **2** Proud, haughty. **3** Cunning, deceitful.

वामी **1** A mare; अथोष्ट्रवामीशतवाहितार्थं R. 5. 32. **2** A she-ass. **3** A female elephant. **4** The female of the jackal.

वायः Weaving, sewing. **-Comp.** **-दंडः** a weaver's loom.

वायकः **1** A weaver. **2** A heap, multitude, collection.

वायनं, -वायनकं A present of sweetmeats made to a deity, particularly to a Brâhmaṇa, on festive occasions, observance of fasts &c.

वायव *a*. (**वी** *f*.) **1** Relating to or given by the wind or Vâyu. **2** Aerial.

वायवीय, वायव्य *a* Relating to the wind, aerial **Comp.** **-पुराणं** N. of a Purâṇa.

वायसः **1** A crow; बलिमिव परिभोक्तुं वायसास्तर्कयंति Mk. 10. 3. **2** Fragrant aloe-wood, agallochum. **3** Turpentine. **-Comp.** **-अरातिः, अरिः** an owl. **-आह्वा** a kind of esculent vegetable. **-इक्षुः** a kind of long grass.

वायुः **1** Air, wind; वायुर्विधूनयति चंपकपुष्परेणून् K. R. (for its production, see Ms. 1. 76. (There are seven courses of wind:--आवहः प्रवहश्चैव संवहश्चोद्वहस्तथा । विवहाख्यः परिवहः परावह इति क्रमात्). **2** The god of wind, the deity supposed to preside over wind. **3** A life-wind or vital air, of which five kinds are enumerated:-- प्राण, अपान, समान, व्यान, and उदान. **4** Morbid affection or vitiation of the windy humour. **-Comp.** **-आस्पदं** the sky, atmosphere. **-केतुः** dust. **-कोणः** the north-west. **-गंडः** flatulence (caused by indigestion). **-गुल्मः** **1** a hurricane, storm. **2** a whirlpool. **-गोचरः** the range of the wind. **-ग्रस्त** *a*. **1** affected by wind, flatulent. **2** gouty. **-जातः, -तनयः, -नंदनः, -पुत्रः, -सुतः, -सूनुः** epithets of Hanumat or Bhîma. **-दारुः** a cloud. **-निघ्न** *a*. affected by wind, crazy, mad, frantic. **-पुराणं** N. of one of the 18 Purâṇas. **-फलं** **1** hail. **2** the rainbow. **-भक्षः; -भक्षणः, भुज्** *m*. **1** one who feeds only on air, as an ascetic. **2** a snake; cf. पवनाशन. **-रोषा** night. **-रुग्ण** *a*. broken down by wind; R. 9. 63. **-वर्त्मन्** *m*., *n*. the sky, atmosphere. **-वाहः** smoke. **-वाहिनी** a vein, an artery, a vessel of the body. **-वेग, -सम** *a*. swift as wind. **-सखः, -सखिः** *m*. fire.

वार् *n*. Water; Bv. 1. 30. **-Comp.** **-आसनं** a reservoir of water. **-किटिः** (**वाःकिटिः**) a porpoise. **-चः** a oose, gander. **-दः** a cloud. **-दरं** **1** water. **2** silk. **3** speech. **4** the seed of the mango **5** a curl on a horse's neck. **6** a conch-shell. **-धिः** the ocean. °**भवं** a kind of salt. **-पुष्पं** (**वाःपुष्पं**) cloves. **-भटः** an alligator. **-मुच्** *m*. a cloud. **-राशिः** the ocean. **-वटः** a ship, boat. **-सदनं** (**वाःसदनं**) a reservoir of water, a cistern. **-स्थ** *a*. (**वाःस्थ**) being in water.

वारः **1** That which covers, a cover. **2** A multitude, large number; as in वारयुवति. **3** A heap, quantity. **4** A herd, flock; Si. 18. 56. **5** A day of the week ; as in बुधवार, शनिवार. **6** Time, turn ; शशकस्य वारः समायातः Pt. 1; R. 19. 18 ; often used in pl. like the English 'times'; बहुवारान् 'many times,' कतिवारान् 'how many times'. **7** An occasion, opportunity. **8** A door, gate. **9** The opposite bank of a river. **10** N. of *Siva*. **-रं** **1** A vessel for holding spirituous liquor. **2** A mass of water (जलसंघ). **-Comp** **-अंगना, -नारी, -युवति** *f*. **-योषित्** *f*. **-वनिता, -विलासिनी -सुंदरी, -स्त्री** ' a woman of the multitude ', a common woman, harlot, courtezan, prostitute ; Ratn. 1. 26 ; *S*. Til. 16. **-कीरः** **1** a wife's brother (according to Trik.) **2** the submarine fire. **3** a hair-dresser or comb **4** a louse. **5** a courser, (these meanings are given in Medinî). **-बु(बू)षा** the plantain tree. **-मुख्या** the chief of a number of harlots. **-वा(वा)णः-णं** an armour, a coat of mail; R. 4. 85. **-वाणिः** **1** a piper, player on a flute. **2** a musician. **3** a year. **4** a judge. (**-णिः** *f*.) a harlot. **-वाणी** a harlot. **-सेवा** **1** harlotry, prostitution. **2** a number of harlots.

वारक *a*. Obstructing, opposing. **-कः** **1** A kind of horse. **2** A horse in general. **3** One of the paces of a horse. **-कं** **1** The seat of pain. **2** A kind of perfume (वाल or ह्रीवेर).

वारकिन् *m*. **1** An opposer, enemy. **2** The ocean. **3** A kind of horse, one with good marks. **4** An ascetic living on leaves.

वारंकः A bird.

वारंगः The handle of a sword, knife &c.

वारटं **1** A field. **2** A number of fields. **-टा** A goose.

वारण *a*. (**णी** *f*.) Warding off, resisting, opposing. **-णं** **1** Warding off, restraining, obstructing ; न भवति बिसतंतुर्वारणं वारणानां Bh. 2. 17. **2** An obstacle, impediment. **3** Resistance, opposition. **4** Defending, guarding, protecting. **-णः** **1** An elephant ; न भवति बिसतंतुर्वारणं वारणानां Bh. **2**. 17 ; Ku. 5. 70 ; R. 12. 93 ; Si. 18. 56. **2** An armour, mail-coat. **-Comp.** **-बुषा-सा, -वल्लभा** the plantain tree. **-साह्वयं** N. of Hastinâpura.

वारणसी See वाराणसी.

वारणावत *m*. *n*. N. of a town.

वारत्रं A leather thong.

वारंवारं *ind*. Often times, repeatedly, again and again ; वारंवारं तिरयति दृशोरुद्गमं बाष्पपूरः Mâl. 1. 35.

वारला **1** A wasp. **2** A goose ; cf. वरटा.

वाराणसी The holy city of Benares.

वाराणिधिः The ocean.

वाराह *a*. (**ही** *f*.) Relating to a boar; Mu. 7. 19 ; Y. 1. 259. **-हः** **1** A boar. **2** A kind of tree. **-Comp.** **-कल्पः** N. of the present *Kalpa* (that in which we are at present living). **-पुराणं** N. of one of the eighteen Purâṇas.

वाराही 1 A sow. 2 The earth. 3 The Sakti of Vishṇu in the form of a boar. 4 A measure. **–Comp.** –कंदः N. of a bulbous plant.

वारि *n.* 1 Water ; यथा खनन् खनित्रेण नरो वार्यधिगच्छति Subhâsh. 2 A fluid. 3 A kind of perfume (बाल or ह्रीवेर). –रिः, –री *f.* 1 A lace for fastening an elephant ; वारी वारिः सस्मेर वारणानां *Si.* 18. 56; R. 5. 45. 2 A rope for fastening an elephant. 3 A hole or trap for catching elephants. 4 A captive, prisoner. 5 A water-pot. 6 N. of Sarasvatî. **–Comp.** –ईशः the ocean –उद्भवं a lotus. –ओकः a leech. –कर्पूरः a kind of fish (इलीश) –कुब्जकः the plant शृंगाटक. –क्रिमिः a leech. –चत्वरः a piece of water. –चर *a.* aquatic. (–रः) 1 a fish. 2 any aquatic animal. –ज *a.* produced in water. (–जः) 1 a conch-shell ; *Si.* 15. 72. 2 any bivalve or shell. (–जं) 1 a lotus ; *Si.* 4. 66. 2 a kind of salt. 3 a kind of plant (गौरसुवर्ण). 4 cloves. –तस्करः a cloud. –त्रा an umbrella. –दः a cloud; वितर वारिद वारि दवातुरे Subhâsh.; Bv. 1. 30. (–दं) a kind of perfume. –द्रः the *Chat'aka* bird. –धरः a cloud; नववारिधरोदयादहोभिर्भवितव्यं च निरातपत्वरम्यैः V. 4. 3. –धारा a shower of rain. –धिः the ocean ; वारिधिसुतामक्ष्णां दिदृक्षुः शतैः Gît. 12. –नाथः 1 the ocean. 2 an epithet of Varuṇa. 3 a cloud. –निधिः the ocean. –पथः,-थं 'journey by sea', a voyage. –प्रवाहः a cascade, waterfall. –मसिः, –मुच् *m.*, –रः a cloud. –यंत्रं a water-wheel, a machine for drawing up water ; M. 2. 13. –रथः a raft, boat, float. –राशिः 1 the ocean. 2 a lake. –रुहं a lotus. –वासः a dealer in spirituous liquors. –वाहः, -वाहनः a cloud. –शः N. of Vishṇu. –संभवः 1 cloves. 2 a kind of antimony. 3 the fragrant root उशीर q. v.

वारित *p. p.* 1 Warded off, prevented, obstructed. 2 Defended, protected.

वारी See वारि (*f.*).

वारीटः An elephant.

वारुः A war-elephant (विजयकुंजर).

वारुठः A bier.

वारुण *a.* (णी *f.*) 1 Belonging to Varuṇa. 2 Dedicated or sacred to Varuṇa. 3 Given to Varuṇa. –णः N. of one of the nine divisions of Bharatavarsha. –णं Water.

वारुणिः 1 N. of Agastya. 2 Of Bhrigu.

वारुणी 1 The west (the quarter presided over by Varṇa). 2 Any spirituous liquor ; पयोपि शौंडिकीहस्ते वारुणीत्यभिधीयते H. 3. 11. ; Pt. 1. 178. (where both senses are intended); Ku. 4. 12. 3 The asterism शतभिषज्. 4 A kind of Dûrvâ. **–Comp.** –वल्लभः an epithet of Varuṇa.

वारुंडः The chief of the serpent-race. –डः,-डं 1 The rheum or excretion of the eyes. 2 The ear-wax. 3 A vessel for bailing water out of a boat.

वारेंद्री N. of a part of Bengal (and Behar) now called राजशाही.

वार्क्ष *a.* (क्षी *f.*) Consisting of trees. –क्षं A forest.

वार्णिकः A scribe, writer.

वार्ताकः, **वार्ताकिः** *f.*, **वार्ताकिन्** *m.*, **वार्ताकी** *f.*, **वार्ताकुः** *m. f.* The egg-plant.

वार्तिका A kind of quail.

वार्त्त *a.* 1 Healthy, hale, doing well, 2 Light, weak, unsubstantial (असार). 3 Following a profession. –र्त्तं 1 Welfare, good health ; सर्वत्र नो वार्त्तमवेहि राजन् R. 5. 1, 3, 13, 71 ; स पृष्टः सर्वतो वार्त्तमाख्यद्राज्ञे न संततिं 15, 41 ; *Si.* 3. 68. 2 Skill, dexterity ; अनुयुक्त इव स्ववार्त्तमुच्चैः Ki. 13. 34. 3 Chaff.

वार्त्ता 1 Staying, abiding. 2 Tidings, news, intelligence ; सागरिकायाः का वार्ता Ratn. 4. 3 Livelihood, profession. 4 Agriculture, the occupation of a Vaisya ; R. 16. 2 ; Ms. 10. 80 ; Y. 1. 310. 5 The egg-plant. **–Comp.** –आरंभः a commercial undertaking or business. –वहः,-हरः 1 a messenger. 2 a chandler. –वृत्तिः one who lives on agriculture. –व्यतिकरः general or common report.

वार्त्तायनः A news-bearer, spy, an emissary.

वार्त्तिक *a.* (की *f.*) 1 Relating to news. 2 Bringing news. 3 Explanatory, glossarial. –कः 1 As emissary, a spy. 2 A husbandman (a man of the third tribe). –कं An explanatory or supplementary rule which explains the meaning of that which is said, of that which is left unsaid, and of that which is imperfectly said ; or a rule which explains what is said or but imperfectly said and supplies omissions ; उक्तानुक्तदुरुक्तार्थव्यक्ति (चिंता)कारि तु वार्त्तिकम् (the term is particularly applied to the explanatory rules of Kâtyâyana on Pâṇini's Sûtras).

वार्त्रघ्नः N. of Arjuna ; Ku. 15. 1.

वार्द्धकं 1 Old age ; किमित्यपास्याभरणानि यौवने धृतं त्वया वार्द्धकशोभि वल्कलं Ku. 5. 44; R. 1. 8 ; N. 1. 77. 2 The infirmity of old age. 3 A collection of old men.

वार्द्धक्यं 1 Old age. 2 The infirmity of old age.

वार्द्धुषिः, **वार्द्धुषिकः**, **वार्द्धुषिन्** *m.* A usurer.

वार्द्धुष्यं Usury, high or exorbitant interest.

वार्ध्रं, **वार्ध्री** *f* A leather thong.

वार्ध्रीणसः A rhinoceros ; see वाध्रीणस also.

वार्मणं A collection of men in armour.

वार्यं A blessing, boon. –(pl.) Posessions.

वार्वणा A kind of blue fly.

वार्ष *a.* (र्षी *f.*) 1 Belonging to the rains. 2 Annual.

वार्षिक *a.* (की *f.*) 1 Belonging to the rains or rainy season ; वार्षिकं संजहारेंद्रो धनुर्जैत्रं रघुर्दधौ R. 4. 16. 2 Annual, yearly. 3 Lasting for one year ; मातुषाणां प्रमाणं स्याद्भुक्तिर्वै दशवार्षिकी ; so वार्षिकमन्नं Y. 1. 124. –कं N. of a medicinal plant.

वार्षिला Hail.

वार्ष्णेयः 1 A descendant of Vrishṇi. 2 Particularly Krishṇa. 3 N. of the charioteer of Nala.

वार्ह, **वार्हद्रथ**, **वार्हद्रथि**, **वार्हस्पत**, **वार्हस्पत्य**, **वार्हिण**, **वाल**, **वालक** } See बार्ह, बार्हद्रथ, बार्हद्रथि, बार्हस्पत, बार्हस्पत्य, बार्हिण, बाल, बालक.

वालखिल्य See बालखिल्य.

वालिः N. of a celebrated monkey-chief, who was slain by Râma at the desire of Sugrîva, his younger brother.

[He is represented as a very powerful monkey and is said to have placed under his armpit even *Ravana* when he went to fight with him. During his absence from Kishkindh*a* to slay the brother of Dundubhi, Sugr*i*va usurped the throne considering him to be dead, but when V*a*li returned, he had to run away to *R*ishyam*u*ka. T*a*r*a*, wife of Sugr*i*va, was seized by V*a*li, but she was restored to her husband when R*a*ma slew him.]

वालुका 1 Sand, gravel ; अकृतज्ञस्योपकृतं वालुकास्विव मूत्रितम्. 2 Powder. 3 Camphor in general. –का-की A kind of cucumber. **–Comp.** –आत्मिका sugar.

वालेय See बालेय.

वाल्क *a.* (ल्की *f.*) Made of the bark of trees.

वाल्कल *a.* (ली *f.*) Made of the bark of trees. –लं A bark-garment. –ली Spirituous liquor.

वाल्मीकः, **वाल्मीकिः** N. of a celebrated sage, and author of the Râmâyaṇa. [He was a Brahma*n*a by birth, but being abandoned by his parents in his child-hood, he was found by some wild mountaineers who taught him the art of thieving. He soon became an adept in the art, and pursued his business of plundering and killing (where necessary) travellers for several years. One day he saw a great sage whom he asked on pain of death to deliver up his possessions. But the sage told him to go home and asked his wife and children if they were ready to become his partners in the innumerable iniquities that he had committed. He accordingly went home, but returned dismayed at their unwillingness. The sage then told him to repeat the word *mara* (which is *Rama* inverted) and disappeared. The robber continued to repeat it for years together without moving from the place, so that his body was covered up with ant-hills. But the same sage reappeared and got him out, and as he issued from the *valmika* he was called *Valmiki*, and became afterwards an eminent sage. One day while he was performing his ablutions, he saw one of a pair of *Krauncha* birds being killed by a fowler, at which he cursed the wretch in words which unconsciously took the form of a verse in the Anush*t*ubh metre. This was a new mode of composition, and at the command of the god Brahman he composed the first poem the R*a*may*a*na. When S*i*ta was abandoned by R*a*ma, he gave her shelter under his roof, and brought up her two sons. He afterwards restored them all to R*a*ma.]

वाल्लभ्यं Being beloved or favourite.

वावदूक *a.* **1** Talkative, garrulous. **2** Eloquent.

वाक्य: A kind of basil.

वावुट: A boat, raft.

वावृत् 4 A. (वावृत्यते) **1** To choose, prefer, select, love; ततो वावृत्यमानासौ रामशालां न्यविक्षत Bk. 4. 28. **2** To serve.

वावृत्त *a.* Chosen, selected, preferred.

वाश् I. 4 A. (वाश्यते, वाशित) **1** To roar, cry, scream, shriek, howl; hum (as birds), sound in general; (शिवाः) तां श्रिताः प्रतिभयं ववाशिरे R. 11. 61, *S*i. 18. 75, 76; Bk. 14. 14, 76. **2** To call.

वाशक *a.* Roaring, sounding.

वाशनं **1** Roaring, howling, growling, yelling &c. **2** The warbling or cry of birds, humming (of bees &c.).

वाशि: Fire, the god of fire.

वाशितं The cry of birds.

वाशिता **1** A female elephant; अभ्यपद्यत स वाशितासखः पुष्पिताः कमलिनीरिव द्विपः R. 19. 11; (also written वासिता in this sense). **2** A woman.

वाश्र: A day. **-श्रं** **1** A dwelling, house. **2** A place where four roads meet. **3** Dung.

वाष्प:, -ष्पं See बाष्प.

वास् I. 10 U. (वासयति-ते) **1** To scent, perfume, incense, fumigate, make fragrant; वासिताननविशेषितगंधा Ki. 9 80; प्रकटितपटवासैर्वासयन् काननानि Git. 1; U. 3. 16; R. 4. 74; Me. 20; Rs. 5. 5. **2** To steep, infuse. **3** To spice, season. -II. 4 A. See वाश्.

वास: **1** Perfume. **2** Living, dwelling; वासो यस्य हरेः करे Bv. 1. 63; R. 19. 2 Bg. 1. 44. **3** An abode, a habitation, house. **4** Site, situation. **5** Clothes, dress. **-Comp.** -अ(आ)-गार: -रं, -गृहं, -वेश्मन् *n.* the inner apartments of a house; particularly bed chamber; धर्मासनाद्विशति वासगृहं नरेंद्रः U. 1. 7; V. 3. -कर्णी a hall where public exhibitions (such as dancing, wrestling matches &c.) are held. -तांबूलं betel mixed with other fragrant spices. -भवनं, -मंदिरं, -सदन a dwelling-place, house. -यष्टि: *f.* a roosting perch, a rod for a bird to perch on; Ve. 2. 3; Me. 79. -योग: a kind of fragrant powder. -सज्जा = वासकसज्जा q. v.

वासक *a.* (का or सिका *f.*) **1** Scenting, perfuming, infusing, fumigating &c. **2** Causing to dwell, populating. -कं Clothes. **-Comp.** -सज्जा, -सज्जिका a woman who dresses herself in all her ornaments and keeps herself (and her house) ready to receive her lover, especially when he has made an appointment with her; an expectant heroine, one of the several classes of a Nâyikâ; S. D. thus defines her;— कुरुते मंडनं यास्याः (या तु) सज्जिते वासवेश्मनि । सा तु वासकसज्जा स्यादि्वदितप्रियसंगमा 120; भवति विलंबिनि विगलितलज्जा विलपति रोदिति वासकसज्जा Git. 6.

वासत: An ass.

वासतेय *a.* (यी *f.*) Habitable. -यी Night.

वासनं **1** Perfuming, fumigating. **2** Infusing. **3** Dwelling, abiding. **4** An abode, a dwelling. **5** Any receptacle, a basket, box, vessel &c.; Y. 2. 65 (वासनं निक्षेपाधारभूतं संपुटादिकं समुद्रं ग्रंथ्यादियुतम्). **6** Knowledge. **7** Clothes, dress. **8** A cover, an envelope.

वासना **1** Knowledge derived from memory; cf. भावना. **2** Particularly, the impression unconsciously left on the mind by past good or bad actions, which therefore produces pleasure or pain. **3** Fancy, imagination, idea. **4** False idea, ignorance. **5** A wish; desire, inclination; संसारवासनाबद्धशृंखला Git. 3. **6** Regard, liking, respectful regard; तेषां (पाक्षिणां) मध्येन मम तु महती वासना चातकेषु Bv. 4. 17.

वासंत *a.* (ती *f.*) **1** Vernal, suitable to or produced in spring. **2** In the spring or prime of life, youthful. **3** Diligent, attentive (in the performance of duties) -त: **1** A camel. **2** A young elephant. **3** Any young animal. **4** A cuckoo. **5** The south wind, the breeze blowing from the Malaya mountain; cf. मलयसमीर. **6** A kind of bean. **7** A dissolute man. -ती **1** A kind of jasmine (with fragrant flowers); वसंते वासंतीकुसुमसुकुमारैरवयवैः Git. 1. **2** Long pepper. **3** The trumpet flower **4** N. of a festival held in honour of Cupid; cf. वसंतोत्सव.

वासंतिक *a.* (की *f.*) Vernal. **-क:** **1** The Vidûshaka or buffoon in a drama. **2** An actor.

वासर:, -रं A day (of the week). **-Comp.** -संग: morning.

वासव *a.* (वी *f.*) Belonging to Indra; पांडुतां वासवी दिग्यासीत् K.; वासवीनां चमूनां Me. 43. -व: N. of Indra; Ku. 3. 2, R. 5. 5. **-Comp.** -दत्ता **1** N. of a work by Subandhu. **2** N. of a heroine of several stories. [Different writers give different accounts of this lady. According to Kathasaritsagara she was the daughter of king Cha*nd*amahasena of Ujjayin*i* and was carried off by Udayana king of Vatsa. *S*r*i*harsha represents her to be the daughter of king Pradyota (see Ratn. I. 10), and according to Mallinatha's comment on the line प्रद्योतस्य प्रियदुहितरं वत्सराजोऽत्र जह्रे she was the daughter of Pradyota king of Ujjayin*i*. Bhavabh*u*ti says that she was betrothed by her father to king Sanjaya, but that she offered herself to Udayana; (see Mâl. 2) But the V*a*savadatt*a* of Subandhu has nothing in common with the story of Vatsa, except the name of the heroine, as she is represented to have been betrothed by her father to Pushpaketu but carried off by Kandarpaketu. It is probable that there were several heroines bearing the name V*a*savadatt*a*]

वासवी N. of the mother of Vyâsa.

वासस् *n.* A cloth, garment, clothes; वासांसि जीर्णानि यथा विहाय नवानि गृह्णाति नरोऽपराणि Bg. 2. 22, Ku. 7. 9; Me. 59

वासि: *m. f.* An adze, a small hatchet, chisel. -सि: Dwelling, abiding.

वासित *p. p.* **1** Perfumed, scented. **2** Steeped, infused. **3** Seasoned, spiced. **4** Dressed, clothed. **5** Peopled, populous. **6** Famous, celebrated. -तं **1** The cry or hum of birds. **2** Knowledge; cf. वासना (2).

वासिता See वाशिता.

वासि(शि)ष्ठ (ष्ठी *f.*) *a.* Belonging to or composed by (rather revealed to) Vasishṭha, as a Maṇdala of the *R*igveda -ष्ठ: A descendant of Vasishṭha.

वासु: 1 The soul. **2** The soul of the universe, supreme being. **3** N. of Vishṇu.

वासुकि:, वासुकेय: N. of a celebrated serpent, king of snakes (said to be a son of Kasyapa); Ku. 2. 38, Bg. 10. 28.

वासुदेव: 1 Any descendant of Vasudeva. **2** Particularly, Krishṇa.

वासुरा **1** The earth. **2** Night. **3** A woman. **4** A female elephant.

वासू: *f.* A young girl, maiden (used chiefly in dramas): एषासि वासु शिरासि गृहीता Mk. 1. 41; वासु प्रसीद Mk.

वास्त See बास्त.

वास्तव *a.* (वी *f.*) 1 Real, true, substantial. 2 Determined, fixed. -वं Anything fixed or determined.

वास्तवा Dawn.

वास्तविक *a.* (की *f.*) True, real, substantial, genuine.

वास्तिकं A collection of goats.

वास्तव्य *a.* 1 Dwelling, inhabiting, resident; पुरेऽस्य वास्तव्यकुटुंबितां ययुः Si. 1. 66. 2 Fit to be inhabited, habitable. -व्यः 1 A dweller, resident, an inhabitant; नानादिगंतवास्तव्यो महाजनसमाजः Mâl. 1. -व्यं 1 A habitable place, house. 2 Habitation, residence (वसति).

वास्तु *m. n.* 1 The site of a house, building ground, site. 2 A house, an abode, a dwelliug place; रवेरविषये वास्तु किं न दीपः प्रकाशयेत् Subhâsh., Ms. 3. 89. -Comp. -यागः a sacrifice performed on the occasion of laying the foundation of a house.

वास्तेय *a.* (यी *f.*) 1 Habitable, fit to be inhabited. 2 Abdominal.

वास्तोष्पतिः 1 N. of a Vedic deity (supposed to preside over the foundation of a house.) 2 N. of Indra.

वास्त्र *a.* Made of cloth. -स्त्रः A carriage covered with cloth.

वास्प See बाष्प.

वास्पेयः The tree called नागकेशर.

वाहृ 1 A (वाहते) To try, exert oneself, endeavour.

वाह *a.* Bearing, carrying &c. (at the end of comp.); as in अंबुवाह, तायवाह &c. -हः 1 Carrying, bearing. 2 A porter. 3 A draught animal, a beast of burden. 4 A horse; R. 4. 56, 5. 73, 14. 52. 5 A bull; Ku. 7. 49. 6 A buffalo. 7 A carriage, conveyance in general. 8 The arm. 9 Air, wind. 10 A measure equal to ten Kumbhas or four Bhâras; वाहो भारचतुष्टयं. -Comp. -द्विषत् *m.* a buffalo. -श्रेष्ठः a horse.

वाहकः 1 A porter. 2 A coach-driver. 3 A horseman.

वाहनं 1 Bearing, carrying, conveying. 2 Driving (as a horse). 3 A vehicle, conveyance of any kind ; Ms. 7. 75; N. 22. 45. 4 An animal used in riding or draught, as a horse; स दुष्प्रापयशाः प्रापदाश्रमं श्रांतवाहनः R. 1. 48, 9. 25. 60. 5 An elephant.

वाहसः 1 A water-course. 2 A large serpent, the boa.

वाहिकः 1 A large drum. 2 A car drawn by oxen. 3 A carrier of loads.

वाहितं A heavy burden.

वाहित्थं The part of an elephant's forehead below the frontal globes.

वाहिनी 1 An army; आशिषं प्रयुयुजे न वाहिनीं R. 11. 6, 13. 66. 2 A division of an army consisting of 81 elephants, as many chariots, 243 horse, and 405 foot. 3 A river. -Comp. -निवेशः the camp of an army. -पतिः 1 a general, a commanding officer. 2 the ocean (lord of rivers.)

वाहीक See बाहीक.

वाहुक See बाहुक.

वाह्य See बाह्य.

वाह्लिः N. of a country (the modern Balkh). -Comp. -जः a Balkh-bred horse.

वाह्लि(ह्ली)कः 1 N. of a country (the modern Balkh). 2 A horse from this country, a Balkh-bred horse. -कं 1 Saffron. 2 Asa Fœtida.

वि *ind.* 1 As a prefix to verbs and nouns it expresses:—(*a*) separaion, disjunction (apart, asunder, away, off &c.). as वियुज्, विहृ, विचल &c.; (*b*) the reverse of an action; as क्री 'to buy', विक्री 'to sell'; स्मृ 'to remember; विस्मृ 'to forget'; (*c*) division; as विभज् विभाग; (*d*) distinction; as विशिष्, विशेष, विविच्, विवेक; (*e*) discrimination व्यवच्छेद; (*f*) order, arrangement, as विधा, विरच्; (*g*) opposition; as विरुध्, विरोध; privation; as विनी, विनयन; (*i*) deliberation, as विचर्, विचार; (*j*) intensity; विध्वंस. 2 As a prefix to nouns or adjectives not immediately connected with roots वि expresses (*a*) negation or privation, in which case it is used much in the same way as अ or निर्, *i. e.* it forms Bah. comp., विधवा व्यसुः &c.; (*b*) intensity, greatness; as विकराल; (*c*) variety, as विचित्र; (*d*) difference; as विलक्षण; (*e*) manifoldness, as विविध; (*f*) contrariety, opposition, as विलोम; (*g*) change, as विकार; (*h*) impropriety, as विजन्मन्.

विः *m. f.* 1 A bird. 2 A horse.

विंश *a.* (शी *f.*) Twentieth. -शः A twentieth part.

विंशक *a.* (की *f.*) Twenty.

विंशतिः *f.* Twenty, a score.- Comp. -ईशः, -ईशिन् *m.* a ruler of twenty villages.

विंशतितम *a.* (मी *f.*) Twentieth.

विंशिन् *m.* 1 Twenty, a score. 2 A lord or ruler of twenty villages.

विकं The milk of a cow that has recently calved.

विकंकटः -तः A kind of tree (of the wood of which ladles were made) ; R. 11. 25.

विकच *a.* 1 Blown, expanded, opened (as a lotus flower &c.); विकचकिंशुकसंहतिरुच्चकैः Si 6. 21; R. 9. 37. 2 Spread about, scattered over; Bv. 1. 3. 3 Destitute of hair. -चः 1 A Buddhist mendicant. 2 N. of Ketu.

विकट *a.* 1 Hideous, ugly. 2 (*a*) Formidable, frightful, horrible, dreadful; पृथुललाटतटघटितविकटभ्रूकुटिना Ve. 1. विधुमिव विकटविधुंतुददंतदलनगलितामृतधारे Git. 4. (*b*) Fierce, savage. 3 Great, large, broad, spacious, wide; जृंभाविडंबि विकटोदरमस्तु चापं U. 4. 29; आवरिष्ट विकटेन विवोढुर्वक्षसैव कुचमंडलमान्या Si. 10. 42, 13. 10; Mâl. 7. 4 Proud, haughty; विकटं परिक्रामति U. 6. Mv. 6. 32. 5 Beautiful ; Mk. 2. 6 Frowning. 7 Obscure. 8 Changed in appearance. -टं A boil, tumour.

विकत्थन *a.* 1 Boasting, swaggering, vaunting, bragging; विद्वांसोऽप्यविकत्थना भवंति Mu. 3.; R. 14. 73. 2 Praising ironically. - नं 1 Vaunting, boasting. 2 Irony, false praise.

विकत्था 1 Boasting, vaunt, brag, boast. 2 Praise. 3 False praise, irony.

विकंप *a.* 1 Heaving. 2 Unsteady inconstant.

विकरः Sickness, disease.

विकरणः The inserted conjugational affix, the conjugational sign placed between the root and the terminations.

विकराल *a.* Very dreadful or formidable, frightful.

विकर्णः N. of a Kuru prince ; Bg. 1. 8.

विकर्तनः 1 The sun ; U. 5. 2 The *Arka* plant. 3 A son who has usurped his father's kingdom.

विकर्मन् *a.* Acting wrongly. -*n.* An unlawful or prohibited act, an impious act ; Bg. 4. 17; Ms. 9. 226. -Comp. -क्रिया an illegal act, irreligious conduct. -स्थ *a.* doing prohibited acts, addicted to vice.

विकर्षः 1 Drawing asunder, pulling apart. 2 An arrow.

विकर्षणः N. of one of the five arrows of Cupid. -णं 1 Drawing, dragging, pulling asunder. 2 A cross throw.

विकल *a.* 1 Deprived of a part or member, defective, imperfect, maimed, mutilated; कूटकृद्वि कलेंद्रियाः Y. 2. 70; Ms. 8. 66; U. 4. 24. 2 Frightened, alarmed; Mâl. 5. 20. 3 Devoid or destitute of (in comp.); आरामाधिपतिर्विवेकविकलः Bv. 1. 31; Mk. 5. 41. 4 Agitated, weakened, dispirited, unnerved drooping, sinking, languid; किमिति विषीदसि रोदिषि विकला विहसीत युवतिसभा तव सकला Git. 9; विरहेण विकलहृदया Bv. 2. 71, 164. श्रुतियुगले पिकरुतविकले Git. 12; U. 3. 31; Mâl. 7. 1, 9. 12. 5 Withered, decayed. -Comp.- अंग *a.* having a redundant or deficient limb. -इंद्रिय *a.* having impaired or defective organs of sense. -पाणिकः a cripple.

विकला The sixtieth par of a *Kalâ* q. v.

विकल्पः 1 Doubt, uncertainty, indecision, hesitation ; तत्तिरेषेवे नियोगेन स विकल्पपराङ्मुखः R. 17. 49. 2 Suspicion; Mu. 1. 3 Contrivance, art; मायविकल्परचितैः R. 13. 75. 4 Option, alternative (in gram.). **5** Sort, variety. **6** An error, a mistake, ignorance. **–Comp.** –उपहारः an optional offering. –जालं a netlike indecision, a dilemma.

विकल्पनं **1** Admitting of doubt. **2** Allowing an option. **3** Indecision.

विकल्मष *a.* Sinless, stainless, guiltless.

विकषा (सा) Bengal madder.

विकसः The moon.

विकसित *p. p.* Blown, fully opened or expanded; Bv. 1. 100.

विकस्व(इव)र *a.* **1** Opening, expanding; कुशेशयैरत्र जलाशयोषिता मुदा रमंते कलभा विकस्वरैः *Si*. 4. 33. **2** Loud, distinctly audible (as a sound); उदडीयत वैकृतात्करग्रहजादस्य विकस्वरस्वरैः N. 2. 5.

विकारः **1** Change of form or nature, transformation, deviation from the naturalt sate; cf. विकृति. **2** A change, an alteration, a modification; Pt. 1. 44. **3** Sickness, disease malady; विकरं खलु परमार्थतोऽज्ञात्वाऽनारंभः प्रतीकारस्य *S*. 4; Ku. 2. 38. **4** Change of mind or purpose; मूर्छंत्यमी विकाराः प्रायेणैश्वर्यमत्तेषु *S*. 5. 19. **5** A feeling, an emotion; U. 1. 35, 3. 25, 36. **6** Agitation, excitement perturbation; Ki. 17. 23. **7** Contortion, contraction, (as of the features of the face); प्रमथमुखविकारैर्हासयामास गूढं Ku. 7. 95. **8** (In Sân. phil.) That which is evolved from a previous source or Prakṛiti. **–Comp.** –हेतुः a temptation, seduction, cause of perturbation; विकारहेतौ सति विक्रियंते येषा न चेतांसि त एव धीराः Ku. 1. 59.

विकारित *a.* Changed, perverted, corrupted.

विकारिन् *a.* Liable to change, susceptible of emotions or impressions; भ्रमति भुवने कंदर्पाज्ञा विकारि च यौवनं Mâl. 1. 17.

विकालः, **विकालकः** Evening, evening twilight, the close of day.

विकालिका A perforated copper vessel which, placed in water, marks the time by gradually filling; cf. मानरंध्रा.

विकाशः **1** Manifestation, display, exhibition. **2** Blowing, expanding (usually written विकास in this sense); Ku. 3. 29. **3** An open or direct course; Ki. 15. 52. **4** An oblique course; Ki. 15. 52. **5** Joy, pleasure; Ki. 15. 52. **6** Sky, heaven (आकाश); Ki. 15. 52. **7** Eagerness, ardent desire; *Si*. 9. 41 (where it means 'blowing' also). **8** Retreat, solitude, privacy.

विकाशक *a.* (शिका *f.*) **1** Displaying. **2** Opening.

विकाशनं **1** Manifestation, display, exhibition. **2** Blowing, expanding (of flowers &c.)

विकाशि(सि)न् *a.* (नी *f.*) **1** Becoming visible, shining forth. **2** Expanding, opening, blowing.

विकासः Blowing, expanding; see विकाश above.

विकासनं Expansion, opening, blowing.

विकिरः **1** A scattered portion or fallen bit. **2** One who tears or scatters, a bird; कंकोलीफलजग्धिमुग्धविकिरव्याहारिणस्तद्भुवो भागाः Mâl. 6. 19. **3** A well. **4** A tree.

विकिरण **1** Scattering, throwing, about, dispersing. **2** Spreading abroad. **3** Tearing up. **4** Killing (हिंसन). **5** Knowledge.

विकीर्ण *p. p.* **1** Scattered, dispersed. **2** Diffused. **3** Celebrated. **–Comp.** –केश, –मूर्धज *a.* tearing the hair, having dishevelled hair. –र्णं a kind of perfume.

विकुंठः N. of Vishṇu's heaven.

विकुर्वाण *a.* **1** Undergoing or causing a change. **2** Feeling glad, delighted, rejoiced.

विकुस्रः The moon.

विकूजनं **1** Cooing, humming. **2** Rumbling (as of the bowels).

विकूणनं A side-glance, leer.

विकूणिका The nose.

विकृत *p. p.* **1** Changed; altered, modified. **2** Sick, diseased. **3** Mutilated, deformed, disfigured. **4** Incomplete, imperfect. **5** Affected by passion or emotion. **6** Averse from, disgusted with. **7** Loathsome. **8** Strange, extraordinary; (see कृ with वि). –तं **1** Change, modification. **2** Change for the worse, sickness. **3** Aversion, disgust.

विकृतिः *f.* **1** Change (as of purpose, mind, form &c.); चित्तविकृतिः, अंगुलीयकं सुवर्णस्य विकृतिः &c. **2** An unnatural or accidental circumstance, an accident; मरणं प्रकृतिः शरीरिणां विकृतिर्जीवितमुच्यते बुधैः R. 8. 87. **3** Sickness. **4** Excitement, perturbation, anger, rage; Ki. 13. 56; *Si*. 15. 11, 40; see विकार and विक्रिया also.

विकृष्ट *p. p.* **1** Dragged asunder, pulled hither and thither. **2** Drawn, pulled, drawn towards or attracted. **3** Extended protracted. **4** Making a noise; (see कृष् with वि).

विकेश *a.* (शी *f.*) **1** Having loose hair. **2** Having no hair, bald (as head). –शी **1** A woman with loose hair. **2** A woman without hair. **3** A small tress of hair tied up separately and then collected into the larger braid or *Veni'*.

विकोश –ष *a.* **1** Without a husk. **2** Unsheathed, uncovered; Ki. 17. 45; R. 7. .

विक्कः A young elephant.

विक्रमः **1** A step, stride, pace; *S*. 7. 6; cf. त्रिविक्रम. **2** Stepping over, walking. **3** Overcoming, overpowering. **4** Heroism, prowess, heroic valour; अनुत्सेकः खलु विक्रमालंकारः V. 1; R. 12. 87, 93. **5** N. of a celebrated king of Ujjayinî; See App. II. **6** N. of Vishṇu. **–Comp.** –अर्कः, –आदित्यः see विक्रम. –कर्मन् *n.* a heroic deed, feat of valour.

विक्रमणं A stride (of Vishṇu); छलयसि विक्रमणे बलिमद्भुतवामन Gît. 1.

विक्रमिन् *a* Chivalrous, heroic. –*m.* **1** A lion. **2** A hero. **3** An epithet of Vishṇu.

विक्रयः Sale, selling; Ms. 3. 54. **–Comp.** –अनुशयः rescission of a sale. –पत्रं a bill of sale, sale-deed.

विक्रयिकः, **विक्रयिन्** *m.* A dealer, seller, vendor.

विक्रस्रः The moon.

विक्रांत *p. p.* **1** Stepped or passed beyond. **2** Powerful, heroic, valiant, chivalrous. **3** Victorious, overpowering (one's enemies). –तः **1** A hero, warrior. **2** A lion. –तं **1** Space, stride. **2** Heroism, valour, prowess.

विक्रांतिः *f.* **1** Stepping, striding. **2** A horse's gallop or canter. **3** Heroism, valour, prowess.

विक्रांतृ *a.* Valiant, victorious. –*m.* A lion.

विक्रिया **1** Change, modification, alteration; श्रुप्रवृद्धिजनितानन विक्रियान् R. 13. 71, 10. 17. **2** Agitation, excitement, perturbation, excitement of passion; अथ तेन निगृह्य विक्रियामभिशप्तः फलमेतदन्वभूत् Ku. 4. 41, 3. 34. **3** Anger, wrath, displeasure; स धोः प्रकोपितस्यापि मनो नायाति विक्रियां Subhâsh.; लिंगैर्मुदः संवृतविक्रियास्ते R. 7. 30. **4** Reverse, evil; Ku. 6. 29 (वैकल्यं Malli. ' defect '.) **5** Knitting, contraction (of the eyebrows); भ्रूविक्रियायां विरतप्रसंगैः Ku. 3. 47. **6** Any sudden movement, as in रोमविक्रिया V. 1. 12. ' thrill '. **7** A sudden affection or seizure, disease. **8** Violation, vitiation (of the proper duties); R. 15. 48. **–Comp.** –उपमा a kind of Upamâ mentioned by Daṇḍin; See Kâv. 2. 41.

विक्रुष्ट *p. p.* **1** Exclaimed, cried out. **2** Harsh, cruel, unkind. –ष्टं **1** A cry for help. **2** Abuse.

विक्रेय *a.* Saleable, vendible (as an article).

विक्रोशनं **1** Calling out, exclaiming. **2** Abusing.

विक्लव *a.* **1** Overcome with fear, startled, alarmed, frightened; आचकांक्ष घनशब्दविक्लवा R. 19. 38; Ku. 4. 11. **2** Timid; *Si*. 7. 43; Me. 37. **3** Affected by, overcome with; Ki. 1. 6. **4** Agitated, excited, confused, bewildered; *S*. 3. 26. **5** Distressed afflicted; grieved; *Si*. 12. 63; Ku. 4.

39. 6 Disgusted with, averse from; मृगयाविक्लवं चेतः S. 2. 7 Faltering; प्रस्थानविक्लवगतेरवलंबनार्थं S. 5. 3.

विक्लिन्न *p. p.* 1 Very moist, thoroughly wetted. 2 Decayed, withered up. 3 Old.

विक्लिष्ट *p. p.* 1 Excessively afflicted, distressed. 2 Injured, destroyed. **-ष्टं** A fault in pronunciation.

विक्षत *p. p.* Torn asunder, wounded, hurt, struck.

विक्षावः 1 Cough, sneezing. 2 A sound.

विक्षिप्त *p. p.* 1 Scattered, thrown about, dispersed, cast about. 2 Discarded, dismissed. 3 Sent, despatched. 4 Distracted, bewildered, agitated. 5 Refuted (see क्षिप् with वि).

विक्षीणकः 1 N. of the chief of a class of beings attending on *S*iva. 2 An assembly of the gods.

विक्षीरः The *Arka* tree.

विक्षेपः 1 Throwing away or asunder, scattering about. 2 Casting, throwing, discharging (opp. संहार); R. 5. 45. 3 Waving, moving about, shaking, moving to and fro; लांगूल° Ku. 1. 13. 4 Sending, despatching. 5 Distraction, confusion, perplexity; Mâl. 1. 6 Alarm, fear. 7 Refutation of an argument. 8 Polar latitude.

विक्षेपणं 1 Throwing, casting, discharging. 2 Despatching, sending. 3 Scattering, dispersing. 4 Confusion, perplexity.

विक्षोभः 1 Shaking, agitation, movement ; वीचि° R. 1. 43. 2 Agitation of mind, distraction, alarm. 3 Conflict, struggle.

विख, **विखु**, **विख्य**, **विख्र**, **विख्र**, **विग्र** } *a.* Noseless.

विखंडित *p. p.* 1 Broken up, divided. 2 Cleft in two.

विखानसः A kind of hermit.

विखुरः 1 A demon, goblin. 2 A thief.

विख्यात *p. p.* 1 Renowned, well-known, celebrated, famous. 2 Called, named. 3 Avowed, confessed.

विख्यातिः *f.* Celebrity, fame, reputation.

विगणनं 1 Reckoning, computing, calculation. 2 Considering, deliberating. 3 Paying off a debt.

विगत *p. p.* 1 Departed, gone away, disappeared. 2 Parted, separated. 3 Dead. 4 Destitute or devoid of, free from (in comp.) ; विगतमदः. 5 Lost. 6 Dark, obscured. **-Comp. -आर्तवा** a woman past child-bearing (in whom the menstrual discharge has ceased). **-कल्मष** *a.* sinless, pure. **-भी** *a.* fearless, intrepid. **-लक्षणं** *a.* unlucky, inauspicious.

विगंधकः The tree called इंगुदी.

विगमः 1 Departure, disappearance, cessation, end; चारुनृत्यविगमे च तन्मुखं R. 19. 15; ईतिविगम M. 5. 20; Rs. 6. 22. 2 Abandoning; करणविगमात् Me. 55 (देहत्यागात्). 3 Loss, destruction. 4 Death.

विगरः 1 A naked ascetic. 2 A mountain. 3 An abstemious man (abstaining from eating).

विगर्हणं-णा Censure, blame, reproach, abuse; Ve. 1. 12.

विगर्हित *p. p.* 1 Censured, reviled, abused. 2 Disdained. 3 Condemned, reprobated, prohibited. 4 Low, vile. 5 Bad, wicked.

विगलित *p. p.* 1 Trickled, oozed. 2 Disappeared, gone away. 3 Fallen of dropped down. 4 Melted away, dissolved. 5 Dispersed. 6 Slackened, untied; V. 4. 10. 7 Loose, dishevelled, disordered (as hair) ; (see गल् with वि).

विगानं 1 Censure, reproach, defamation, scandal. 2 A contradictory statement, contradiction, inconsistency (frequently occurring in *S*ânkarabhâshya).

विगाहः Plunging into, bathing, diving.

विगीत *p. p.* 1 Censured, abused, reviled. 2 Contradictory, inconsistent.

विगीतिः *f.* 1 Censure, abuse, reproach. 2 Contradictory statement, contradiction.

विगुण *a.* 1 Destitute of merits, worthless, bad; Bg. 3. 35, *S*i. 9. 12, Mu. 6. 11. 2 Destitute of qualities. 3 Having no string; Mu. 7. 11.

विगूढ *p. p.* 1 Secret, concealed, hidden. 2 Reproached, censured.

विगृहीत *p. p.* 1 Divided, dissolved, analysed, resolved (as a compound). 2 Seized. 3 Encountered, opposed; (see ग्रह् with वि).

विग्रहः 1 Stretching out, extension, expansion. 2 Form, figure, shape. 3 The body; त्रयी विग्रहवत्येव सममध्यात्मविद्यया M. 1. 14; गूढविग्रहः R. 3. 39, 9. 52. Ki. 4. 11, 12. 43. 4 Resolution, dissolution, analysis, separation (as of a compound word into its component parts) ; वृत्त्यर्थ (समासार्थ) बोधकं वाक्यं विग्रहः. 5 Quarrel, strife (often, love-quarrel or प्रणयकलह) ; विग्रहाच्च शयने पराङ्मुखीर्नानुनेतुमबलाः स त्वरे R. 19. 38, 9. 47; *S*i. 11. 35. 6 War, hostilities, fighting, battle (opp. संधि), one of the six Guṇas or modes of policy; see गुण. 7 Disfavour. 8 A part, portion, division.

विघटनं Breaking up, ruin, destruction.

विघटिका A measure of time equal to one-sixtieth part of a Ghaṭikâ (or nearly equal to 24 seconds).

विघटित *p. p.* 1 Separated, severed. 2 Divided.

विघट्टनं-ना 1 Striking asunder. 2 Striking against, friction. 3 Separating, undoing, untying. 5 Offending, hurting.

विघट्टित *p. p.* 1 Struck apart, severed, separated, dispersed; Bh. 3. 54. 2 Untied, loosened, opened. 3 Rubbed; touched. 4 Shaken about, churned. 5 Hurt, offended.

विघनः A mallet, hammer.

विघसः 1 Half-chewed morsel, the residue or leavings of food eaten, विघसो भुक्तशेषं तु Ms. 3. 285; U. 5. 6; Mâl. 5. 14. 2 Food in general. **-सं** Bees'-wax.**-Comp. -आशः** - **आशिन्** *m.* one who eats the remains of an offering or of food eaten.

विघातः 1 Destruction, removing, warding off; क्रियाद्धानां मघवा विघातं Ki. 3. 52. 2 Killing, slaying. 3 An obstacle, impediment, interruption; क्रियाविघाताय कथं प्रवर्तसे R. 3. 44; अध्वरविघातशांतये 11. 1. 4 A blow, stroke. 5 Abandoning, leaving. **-Comp. -सिद्धिः** *f.* the removal of obstacles.

विघूर्णित *p. p.* Rolled, shaken about, rolling (as eyes).

विघृष्ट *p. p.* 1 Rubbed excessively. 2 Sore.

विघ्नः (rarely *n.*) 1 An obstacle, interruption, impediment, a hindrance; कुतो धर्मक्रियाविघ्नः सतां रक्षितरि त्वयि *S.* 5. 14, 1. 33; Ku. 3. 40. 2 Difficulty, trouble. **-Comp. -ईशः, -ईशानः, -ईश्वरः** epithets of Gaṇesa. **°वाहनं** a rat. **-कर, -कर्तृ, -कारिन्** *a.* opposing, obstructing. **-ध्वंसः, -विघातः** removal of obstacles. **-नायकः, -नाशकः, -नाशनः** epithets of Gaṇesa. **-प्रतिक्रिया** removal of impediments ; R. 15. 4. **-राजः -विनायकः, -हारिन्** *m.* epithets of Gaṇesa. **-सिद्धिः** *f.* removal of obstacles.

विघ्नित *a.* Impeded, hindered, obstructed, impeded.

विंखः A horse's hoof.

विच् 3. 7. U. (वेवेक्ति, वेविक्ते, विनक्ति, विंक्ते, विक्त) 1 To separate, divide, sever. 2 To discriminate, distinguish, discern. 3 To deprive of, remove from (with instr.); Bk. 14. 103. -WITH **वि** 1 to separate, divide, remove from; विविनच्मि दिवः सुरान् Bk. 6. 36. 2 to discern, discriminate. 3 to judge, ascertain, determine ; रे खल तव खलु चरितं विदुषामग्रे विविच्य वक्ष्यामि Bv. 1. 108. 4 to describe, treat of. 5 to tear up.

विचकिलः 1 A kind of jasmine. 2 N. of the tree called *Madana*.

विचक्षण *a.* 1 Clear-sighted, far-seeing, circumspect. 2 Wise, clever, learned ; R 5. 19. 3 Expert, skilful, able ; R. 13. 69. **–णः** A learned man, wise man ; न दत्वा कस्यचित्कन्यां पुनर्दद्याद्विचक्षणः Ms. 9. 71.

विचक्षुस् *a.* 1 Blind, sightless. 2 Perplexed, sad.

विचयः 1 Search, seeking, looking out ; U. 1. 23. 2 Investigation.

विचयनं Searching, seeking &c.

विचर्चिका Itch, herpes, scab.

विचर्चित *a.* Anointed, rubbed, smeared.

विचल *a.* 1 Moving about, shaking, wavering, tottering, unsteady. 2 Conceited, proud.

विचलनं 1 Moving. 2 Deviation. 3 Unsteadiness, fickleness. 4 Conceit.

विचारः 1 Reflection, deliberation, thought, consideration ; विचारमार्गप्रहितेन चक्षुषा Ku. 5. 42. 2 Examination, discussion, investigation ; तत्त्वार्थविचार. 3 Trial (of a case) ; Mk. 9. 43. 4 Judgment, discrimination, discernment, exercise of reason ; विचारमूढः प्रतिभासि मे त्वं R. 2. 47. 5 Decision, determination. 6 Selection. 7 Doubt, hesitation. 8 Prudence, circumspection. **–Comp.** **–ज्ञ** *a.* able to decide, a judge. **–भूः** *f.* 1 a tribunal, seat of justice. 2 particularly, the judgment seat of Yama. **–शील** *a.* thoughtful, considerate, prudent. **–स्थलं** 1 a tribunal. 2 a logical discussion.

विचारकः An investigator, a judge.

विचारणं 1 Discussion, consideration, examination, deliberation, investigation. 2 Doubt, hesitation.

विचारणा 1 Examination, discussion, invsetigation. 2 Reflection, consideration, thought. 3 Doubt. 4 The Mîmâmsâ system of philosophy.

विचारित *p. p.* 1 Considered, inquired into, examined, discussed. 2 Decided, determined.

विचिः *m f.*, **विचीः** *f.* A wave.

विचिकित्सा 1 Doubt, uncertainty. 2 Mistake, error.

विचित *p. p.* 1 Searched, searched through.

विचितिः *f.* Searching, search, seeking for.

विचित्र *a.* 1 Diversified, variegated, spotted, speckled. 2 Various, varied. 3 Painted. 4 Beautiful, lovely ; क्वचिद्विचित्रं जलयंत्रमंदिरं Rs. 1. 2. 5 Wonderful, surprising, strange ; हतविधिलसितानां ही विचित्रो विपाकः Si. 11. 64. **–त्रं** 1 Variegated colour. 2 Surprise. **–Comp.** **–अंग** *a.* having a spotted body. (**–गः**) 1 a peacock. 2 a tiger. **–देह** *a.* having a lovely body. (**–हः**) a cloud. **–रूप** *a.* diverse. **–वीर्यः** N. of a king of the lunar race. [He was a son of *S*antanu by his wife Satyavat*i* and so half-brother of Bh*i*shma. When he died childless, his mother called Vy*a*sa (her own son before her marriage), and requested him to raise up issue to Vichitrav*i*rya in accordance with the practice of *Niyoga.* He complied with the request, and begot on Ambik*a* and Amb*a*lik*a*, the two widows of his brother, two sons Dh*r*itar*a*sh*t*ra and Pa*n*du respectively].

विचित्रकः The birch tree. **–कं** Wonder, astonishment, surprise.

विचिन्वत्कः 1 Search. 2 Investigation. 3 A hero.

विचिर्ण *a.* 1 Occupied by, wandered through. 2 Entered.

विचेतन *a.* 1 Senseless, lifeless, unconscious, dead. 2 Inanimate.

विचेतस् *a.* 1 Senseless, stupid, ignorant. 2 Perplexed, confounded, sad.

विचेष्टा Effort, exertion.

विचेष्टित *p. p.* 1 Striven, tried, struggled. 2 Examined, investigated. 3 Misdone, done foolishly. **–तं** 1 An act, a deed. 2 Effort, movement, undertaking, enterprise. 3 Gesture. 4 Working, sensation, play ; V. 2. 9. 5 Machination.

विच्छ् I. 6 P. (विच्छति, also विच्छयति-ते) To go, move. –II. 10 U. (विच्छयति-ते) 1 To shine. 2 To speak.

विच्छंदः, विच्छंदकः A palace, a large building having several stories.

विच्छर्दकः A palace ; see विच्छंद above.

विच्छर्दनं Vomiting, ejecting.

विच्छर्दित *p. p.* 1 Vomited, ejected. 2 Disregarded, neglected. 3 Impaired, lessened.

विच्छाय *a.* Pale, dim ; Ratn. 1. 26. **–यः** A gem, jewel.

विच्छित्तिः *f.* 1 Cutting off or asunder, tearing off; Bh. 3. 11. 2 Dividing, separating. 3 Disappearance, absence, loss. 4 Cessation. 5 Colouring the body with paints and unguents, painting colours, rouge ; S. 7.5; Si. 16. 84. 6 Limit, boundary (of a house &c.). 7 A pause in a verse, cæsura. 8 A particular kind of amorous gesture, consisting in carelessness in dress and decoration (through pride of personal beauty); स्तोका प्याकल्परचना विच्छित्तिः कांतिपोषकृत् S. D. 138.

विच्छिन्न *p. p.* 1 Torn asunder, cut off. 2 Broken, severed, divided, separated ; अर्धेविच्छिन्नं S. 1. 9. 3 Interrupted, prevented. 4 Ended, ceased, terminated. 5 Variegated. 6 Hidden. 7 Smeared or painted with unguents ; (see छिद् with वि).

विच्छुरित *p.p.* 1 Covered, overspread, coated. 2 Inlaid. 3 Besmeared, anointed.

विच्छेदः 1 Cutting asunder, cutting, dividing, separation ; Mâl. 6. 11. 2 Breaking ; Si. 6. 51. 3 Break, interruption, cessation, discontinuance विच्छेदमाप भुवि यस्तु कथाप्रबंधः K.; पिंडविच्छेददर्शिनः R. 1. 66. 4 Removal, prohibition. 5 Dissension. 6 A section, or division of a book. 7 Interval, space.

विच्छेदनं Cutting off, breaking &c. see विच्छेद.

विच्युत *p. p.* 1 Fallen down, slipped off. 2 Displaced, thrown down from, 3 Deviated or swerving from.

विच्युतिः *f.* 1 Falling down from, severance, separation. 2 Decline, decay, downfall. 3 Deviation. 4 Miscarriage, failure; as in गर्भविच्युतिः.

विज् I. 3 U. (वेवेक्ति, वेविक्ते, विक्त) 1 To separate, divide. 2 To distinguish, discern, discriminate (usually with वि and allied to विच् with वि q. v.). –II. 6 A., 7 P. (विजते, विनक्ति, विग्न) 1 To shake, tremble. 2 To be agitated, tremble with fear. 3 To fear, be afraid ; चक्रंद विग्ना कुररीव भूयः R. 14. 68. 4 To be distressed or afflicted. *–Caus.* (वेजयति-ते) To terrify, frighten. –WITH आ to be afraid. **–उद्** 1 to be afraid of, to fear (usually with abl. sometimes also gen.); तीक्ष्णादुद्विजते Mu. 3. 5 ; यस्मान्नोद्विजते लोको लोकान्नोद्विजते च यः Bg. 12. 5 ; Bk. 7. 92. 2 to be grieved or afflicted, be sorry ; न प्रहृष्येत्प्रियं प्राप्य नोद्विजेत्प्राप्य चाप्रियं Bg. 5. 20; 3 to be disgusted with (with abl.). जीवितादुद्विजमानेन Mâl. 3 ; मनो नोद्विजते तस्य ददतोऽर्थमहर्निशम् । उद्विजनंति तु संसारादसारात्तत्त्ववेदिनः ॥ K. R. 4 to frighten, afflict. (*–Caus.*). 1 to trouble, afflict ; Ku. 1. 5, 11. 2 to frighten.

विजन *a.* Lonely, retired, solitary. **–नं** A solitary place, retreat (**विजने** means 'privately').

विजनन Birth, procreation, delivery.

विजन्मन् *a.* or *m.* A bastard, one born illegitimately.

विजपिलं Mud.

विजयः 1 Overcoming, vanquishing, defeating. 2 Conqest, victory, triumph ; Ki. 10. 35 ; R. 12. 44 ; Ku. 3. 19 ; S. 2. 14. 3 A chariot of the gods, celestial chariot. 4 N. of Arjuna ; the Mb thus explains the name:—अभिप्रयामि संग्रामे यदहं युद्धदुर्मदान् नाजित्वा विनिवर्तामि तेन मां विजयं विदुः ॥. 5 An epithet of Yama. 6 N. of the first year of Jupiter's cycle. 7 N. of an attendant of Vishṇu. **–Comp.** **–अभ्युपायः** a means of victory. **–कुंजरः** a war-elephant **–छंदः** a necklace of 500 strings. **–डिंडिमः** a large military drum. **–नगरं** N. of a town. **–मर्दलः** a large military drum. **–सिद्धिः** *f.* success, victory, triumph.

विजयंतः N. of Indra.

विजया 1 N. of Durgâ. **2** N. of one of her female attendants ; Mu- 1. 1. **3** N. of a lore taught by Visvâ. mitra to Râma Bk. 2. 21. **4** Hemp **5** N. of a festival =विजयोत्सव,see below. **6** Yellow myrobalan. **–Comp. –उत्सवः** a festival in honour of Durgâ held on the 10th day of the bright half of Asvina. **–दशमी**:the tenth day of the bright half of Asvina.

विजयिन् *m.* A conqueror, victor.

विजरं A stalk.

विजल्पः 1 Prattle, idle or foolish talk. **2** Talk or speech in general. **3** A malignant or spiteful speech.

विजल्पित *p. p.* **1** Spoken, talked. **2** Prated, babbled.

विजात *p. p.* **1** Base-born, of mixed origin. **2** Born, produced. **3** Transformed. **–ता** A mother, matron, a woman who has given birth to children.

विजातिः *f.* **1** Different origin. **2** Different kind, species or tribe.

विजातीय *a.* **1** Of a different kind or species, dissimilar, unlike. **2** Of different caste or tribe. **3**:Of mixed origin.

विजिगीषा 1 Desire to conquer or overcome. **2** Desire to surpass, emulation, competition, ambition.

विजिगीषु *a.* **1** Desirous of victory, wishing to conquer ; यशसे विजिगीषूणां R. 1. 7. **2** Emulous, ambitious. **–षुः 1** A warrior, a hero. **2** An antagonist, a disputant, an opponent.

विजिज्ञासा Desire to know clearly.

विजित *p. p.* Subdued, conquered, overcome, defeated. **–Comp. –आत्मन्** *a.* self-subdued, self-controlled. **–इंद्रिय** *a.* having the organs of sense subdued or controlled.

विजितिः *f.* Conquest, victory, triumph ; Kâv. 3. 85.

विजिनः –नं (लः –लं) A sauce (mixed with gruel).

विजिह्म *a.* **1** Crooked, bent, turned away; Ki. 1. 21; R. 19. 35. **2** Dishonest.

विजुलः The silk-cotton tree.

विजृंभणं 1 Gaping, yawning. **2** Blossoming, budding, blowing, opening; वनेषु सायंतनमल्लिकानां विजृंभणोद्गंधिषु कुड्मलेषु R. 16. 47. **3** Exhibiting, displaying, unfolding. **4** Expanding. **5** Pastime, amorous sport.

विजृंभित *p. p.* **1** Gaped, yawned; Mk. 5. 51. **2** Opened, blown, expanded. **3** Displayed, exhibited, manifested; R. 7. 42. **4** Appeared. **5** Sported. **–तं 1** Sport, pastime. **2** Wish, desire. **3** Display, exhibition; अज्ञानविजृंभितमेतत्. **4** An act, action, conduct; Mâl. 10. 21.

विज्जनं-लं 1 A kind of sauce; see बिजुल. **2** An arrow.

विज्जुलं Cinnamon.

विज्ञ *a.* **1** Knowing, intelligent, wise, learned. **2** Clever, skilful, proficient. **–ज्ञः** A wise or learned man.

विज्ञप्त *p. p.* Respectfully told, requested.

विज्ञप्तिः *f.* **1** A respectful statement or communication, a request, an entreaty. **2** An announcement.

विज्ञात *p. p.* **1** Known, understood, perceived. **2** Well-known, celebrated, famous.

विज्ञानं 1 Knowledge, wisdom, intelligence, understanding; विज्ञानमयः कोशः 'the sheath of intelligence' (the first of the five sheaths of the soul). **2** Discrimination, discernment. **3** Skill, proficiency; प्रयोगविज्ञान S. 1. 2. **4** Worldly or profane knowledge, knowledge derived from worldly experience (opp. ज्ञान which is 'knowledge of Brahma or Supreme Spirit'); Bg. 3. 41, 7. 2; (the whole of the 7th Adhyâya of Bg. explains ज्ञान and विज्ञान). **5** Business, employment. **6** Music. **–Comp. –ईश्वरः** N. of the author of the Mitâkshara, a commentary on Yâj*n*avalkya's Smriti. **–पादः** N. of Vpâsa. **–मातृकः** an epithet of Buddha. **–वादः** the theory of knowledge, the doctrine taught by Buddha.

विज्ञानिक *a.* Wise, learned; see विज्ञ.

विज्ञापकः 1 An informant. **2** A teacher, an instructor.

विज्ञापनं –ना 1 Respectful statement or communication, a request, an entreaty; कालप्रयुक्ता खलु कार्यविद्भिर्विज्ञापना भर्तृषु सिद्धिमेति Ku. 7. 93; R. 17. 40. **2** Information, representation. **3** Instruction.

विज्ञापित *p. p.* **1** Respectfully told or communicated. **2** Requested. **3** Informed. **4** Instructed.

विज्ञाप्ति See विज्ञप्ति.

विज्ञाप्यं A request; U. 1.

विज्वर *a.* Free from fever, anxiety or distress.

विंजामरं The white of the eye.

विंजोलि-ली *f.* A line, row.

विंट् 1 P. (वेटति) **1** To sound. **2** To curse, rail.

विटः 1 A paramour; Mâl. 8. 8; *Si.* 4. 48. **2** A voluptuary, sensualist. **3** (In dramas) The companion of a prince or dissolute young man, or of a courtezan (who is described as being skilled in the arts of singing, music, and poetry and as a parasite on familiar terms with his associate to whom he nearly serves the purpose of the Vidûshaka; see *inter alia* Mk. acts 1. 5,and 8); for definition see S. D. 78. **4** A rogue, cheat. **5** A catamite. **6** A rat. **7** The Khadira tree. **8** The orange tree. **9** A branch together with its shoot. **–Comp. –माक्षिकं** a kind of mineral. **–लवणं** a medicinal salt.

विटंकः 1 An aviary, dove-cot. **2** The loftiest point, pinnacle, alevation, अयमेव महीधरविटंकः Mâl. 10; Vikr. 5. 77.

विटंकक See विटंक.

विटंकित *a.* Marked, stamped.

विटपः 1 A branch, bough (of a creeper or tree); कोमलविटपानुकारिणौ बाहू *S.* 1. 21, 31; यदनेन तरुर्न पातितः क्षपिता तद्विटपाश्रिता लता R. **8.** 47; *Si.* 4. 48; Ku. 6. 41. **2** A bush. **3** A new shoot or sprout; *Si.* 7. 53. **4** A cluster, clump, thicket. **5** Extension. **6** The septum of the scrotum.

विटपिन् *m.* **1** A tree; परितो दृष्टाश्च विटपिनः सर्वे Bv. 1. 21, 29. **2** The fig-tree. **–Comp. –मृगः** a monkey, an ape.

विठ(ठ)लः N. of a form of Vishṇu or Krishṇa (worshipped at Pandharpur in the Bombay presidency).

विठंक *a.* Bad, vile, base, low.

विठरः N. of Brihaspati.

विड् 1 P. (वेडति) **1** To curse, rail at, revile. **2** To cry out loudly.

विडं A kind of artificial salt.

विडंगः -गं N. of a vegetable and medicinal substance (largely used as a vermifuge).

विडंबः 1 Imitation. **2** Distressing, afflicting, molesting.

विडंबनं-ना 1 Imitation. **2** Disguise, imposture. **3** Deception, fraud. **4** Vexation, mortification. **5** Paining, distressing. **6** Disappointing. **7** Ridiculousness, mockery, a matter for laughter; इयं च तेऽन्यापुरतो विडंबना Ku. 5. 70; असति त्वयि वारुणीमदः प्रमदानामधुना विडंबना 4. 12.

विडंबित *p. p.* **1** Imitated, copied. **2** Mocked, ridiculed. **3** Deceived. **4** Vexed, mortified. **5** Frustrated. **6** Low, abject, poor.

विडारकः A cat.

विडाल, विडालक See बिडाल, बिडालक.

विडीनं One of the several modes of flight of birds; see डीन.

विडुलः A sort of cane.

विडूरजं *Lapis lazuli.*

विडो(डौ)जस् *m.* N. of Indra; see बिडौजस्.

वितसः 1 A bird-cage. **2** A rope, chain, fetter &c. to confine beasts or birds.

वितंडः 1 An elephant. **2** A sort of lock or bolt.

वितंडा 1 A captious objection, idle carping, a frivolous or fallacious argument or controversy; स (जल्पः) प्रतिपक्षस्थापनाहीनो वितंडा Gaut. S. **2** Wrangling, captious criticism in general. **3** A spoon, ladle. **4** Benzoin.

वितत *p. p.* **1** Spread out, extended, stretched. **2** Elongated, large, broad. 3 Performed, accomplishsd, effected; विततयज्ञः S. 7. 34. 4 Covered. 5 Diffused (see तन् with वि). -तं Any stringed instrument, such as a lute &c. -Comp. -धन्वन् a. one who has fully drawn or stretched his bow.

विततिः *f.* 1 Extension, expansion. 2 Quantity, collection, cluster, clump. 3 A line, row; Mâl. 9. 47.

वितथ *a.* 1 Untrue, false; आजन्मनो न भवता वितथं किलोक्तं Ve. 3. 13, 5. 41; R. 9. 8. 2 Vain, futile; as in वितथप्रयत्न.

वितथ्य *a.* False; see above.

वितद्रुः *f.* N. of a river in the Panjab.

वितंतुः A good horse. -*f.* A widow.

वितरणं 1 Crossing over. 2 Gift, donation. 3 Leaving, giving up, abandoning.

वितर्कः 1 Argument, reasoning, inference. 2 Guess, conjecture, supposition, belief; शिरीषपुष्पाधिकसौकुमार्यौ बाहू तदीयाविति मे वितर्कः Ku. 1. 41. 3 Fancy, thought; Bh. 3. 45. 4 Doubt; Ki. 4. 5, 13. 2. 5 Deliberation, discussion.

वितर्कणं 1 Reasoning. 2 Conjecturing, guessing. 3 Doubt. 4 Discussion.

वितर्दिः, -र्दी, वितर्दिका *f.* 1 A raised seat of a quadrangular shape in a courtyard. 2 A balcony, verandah.

वितर्द्धिः -र्द्धी, वितर्द्धिका *f.* See वितर्दि &c.

वितलं The second of the seven lower regions under the earth, see पाताल or लोक.

वितस्ता N. of a river in the Punjab called Hydaspes by the Greeks and now called Jhelum or Betustâ.

वितस्तिः A measure of length equal to 12 *angulas* (being the distance between the extended thumb and the little finger).

वितान *a.* 1 Vacant, empty. 2 Pithless. 3 Dismayed, sad; R. 6. 86. 4 Dull, stupid. 5 Wicked, abandoned. -नः, -नं 1 Spreading out, expansion, extension; Si. 11. 28. 2 An awning, a canopy; विद्युल्लेखाकनकरुचिरश्रीवितानं ममाद्रः V. 4. 4; R. 19. 39; Ki. 3. 42; Si. 3. 50. 3 A cushion. 4 A collection, quantity, an assemblage; Ki. 17. 61; Mâl. 6. 5. 5 A sacrifice, an oblation; वितानिष्वप्येवं तव मम च सोमे विधिरभूत् Ve. 6. 30, 3. 16, Si. 14. 10. 6 The sacrificial hearth or altar. 7 Season, opportunity. -नं Leisure, rest.

वितानकः-कं 1 An expanse. 2 A heap, quantity, collection, mass; Si. 3. 6. 3 An awning, a canopy. 4 The tree called Mâda.

वितीर्ण *p. p.* 1 Crossed or passed over. 2 Given, bestowed, imparted; Si. 7. 67, 17. 65. 3 Gone down, descended; R. 6. 77. 4 Conveyed. 5 Subdued, overcome (see तृ with वि).

वितुन्नं 1 The pot-herb called सुनिषण्णक. 2 The plant called शैवाल.

वितुन्नकं 1 Coriander seed. 2 Blue vitriol. -कः The plant called तामलकी.

वितुष्ट *p. p.* Dissatisfied, displeased, discontented.

वितृष्ण *a.* Free from desire, content.

वित्त् 10 U. (वित्तयति-ते; वित्तापयति-ते also according to some) To give away, give as alms.

वित्त *p. p.* 1 Found, discovered. 2 Gained, acquired. 3 Examined, investigated. 4 Known, famous. -त्तं 1 Wealth, possessions, property, substance. 2 Power. -Comp. -आगमः, -उपार्जनं acquisition of wealth. -ईशः an epithet of Kubera; Bg. 10. 23; Ms. 7. 4. -दः a donor, benefactor. -मात्रा property.

वित्तवत् *a.* Rich, wealthy.

वित्तिः *f.* 1 Knowledge. 2 Judgment, discrimination, thought. 3 Gain, acquisition. 4 Likelihood.

वित्रासः Fear, alarm, terror.

वित्सनः An ox, a bull.

विथ् 1 A. (वेथते) To beg, ask.

विथुरः 1 A demon. 2 A thief.

विद् I. 2 P. (वेत्ति or वेद, विदित; *desid.* विविदिषति) 1 To know, understand, learn, find out, ascertain, discover; अवैलवणतोयस्य स्थिता दाक्षिणतः कथं Bk. 8. 107; तं मोहांधः कथमयममुं वेत्तु देवं पुराणं Ve. 1. 23, 3. 39; S. 5. 27; Bg. 4. 35, 18. 1. 2 To feel, experience; Mu. 3. 4. 3 To look upon, regard, consider, know or take to be; विद्धि व्याधिव्यालग्रस्तं लोकं शोकहतं च समस्तं Moha M. 5; Bg. 2. 17; R. 3. 39; Ms. 1. 33; Ku. 6. 30. -*Caus.* (वेदयति-ते) 1 To make known, communicate, inform, apprise, tell. 2 To teach, expound; वेदार्थं स्वानवेदयत् Sk. 3 To feel, experience; Ms. 12. 13. -WITH आ (*Caus.*) 1 to announce, tell, declare, किमिति नावेदयसि अथवा किमावेदितेन Ve. 1; R. 12. 55; Ku. 6. 21; Bk. 3. 49. 2 to display, show, indicate; आवेदयंति प्रत्यासन्नमानंदमग्रजातानि शुभानि निमित्तानि K. 3 to offer, give. -नि (*Caus.*) 1 to tell, communicate, inform (with dat.); R. 2. 68. 2 to declare or announce oneself; कथमात्मानं निवेदयामि S. 1. 3 to indicate or show; दिगंबरत्वेन निवेदितं वसु Ku. 5. 72. 4 to offer, present, make an offering of; Ms. 2. 51, Y. 1. 27. 5 to entrust to. the care of, make or deliver over to -प्रति (*Caus.*) to communicate, inform. -सं (Atm.) 1 to know, be aware of; Bk. 5. 37, 8. 17. 2 to recognise. (-*Caus.*) to cause to know or perceive; Bk. 17. 63. -II. 4 A. (विद्यते, वित्त) To be, to exist; अपापानां कुले जाते मयि पापं न विद्यते Mk. 9. 37; नासतो विद्यते भावो नाभावो विद्यते सतः Bg. 2. 16; (cf. the root अस्). -III. 6 U. (विंदति-ते, वित्त) 1 To get, obtain, acquire, gain; एकमप्यास्थितः सम्यगुभयोर्विंदते फलं Bg. 5. 4; Y. 3. 192. 2 to find, discover, recognise; यथा धेनुसहस्रेषु वत्सो विंदति मातरं Subhâsh.; Ku. 1. 6, Ms. 8. 109. 3 To feel, experience; R. 14. 56; Bg. 5. 21, 11. 24, 18. 45. 4 To marry; Ms. 9. 69. -WITH अनु 1 to get, obtain. 2 to suffer, experience, feel; पांथ मंदमते किं वा संतापमनुविंदसि Bv. 2. 112; Gît. 4. -IV. 7 A. (विंत्ते, वित्त or विन्न). 1 To know, understand. 2 To consider, regard, take for; न तृणेह्मीति लोकोयं विंत्ते मां निष्पराक्रमं Bk. 6. 39. 3 To find, meet with. 4 To reason, reflect. 5 To examine, inquire into. -V. 10 A. (वेदयते) 1 To tell, declare, announce, communicate. 2 To feel, experience. 3 To dwell. (The following verse illustrates the root in some of its conjugations:—वेत्ति सर्वाणि शास्त्राणि गर्वस्तस्य न विद्यते। विंत्ते धर्मं सदा सद्भिस्तेषु पूजां च विंदति ॥).

विद् *a.* (At the end of comp.) Knowing, conversant with; वेदविद् &c. -*m.* 1 The planet Mercury. 2 A learned man, wise man. -*f.* 1 Knowledge. 2 Understanding, intellect.

विदः 1 A learned man, wise man or Pandita. 2 The planet Mercury. -दा 1 Knowledge, learning. 2 Understanding.

विदंशः Pungent food such as excites thirst.

विदग्ध *p. p.* 1 Burnt up, consumed by fire. 2 Cooked. 3 Digested. 4 Destroyed, decomposed. 5 Clever, shrewd, sharp, subtle. 6 Crafty, artful, intriguing. 7 Unburnt or ill-digested. -ग्धः 1 A wise or learned man, scholar. 2 A libertine. -ग्धा A shrewd and clever woman, an artful woman.

विदथः 1 A learned man, scholar. 2 An ascetic, a sage.

विदरः Breaking, bursting, rending. -रं The prickly pear.

विदर्भाः (*m. pl.*) 1 N. of a district, the modern Berar; अस्ति विदर्भेषु नाम जनपदः Dk.; अस्ति विदर्भो पद्मपुरं नाम नगरं Mâl. 1; R. 5. 40, 60; N. 1. 50. 2 The natives of Vidarbha. -र्भः 1 A king of the Vidarbhas. 2 Any dry or desert soil. -Comp. -जा-तनया, -राजतनया, -सुभ्रूः epithets of Damayanti, daughter of the king of the Vidarbhas.

विदल *a.* 1 Split, rent asunder. 2 Opened, blown (as a flower &c.). -लः 1 Dividing, separating. 2 Rending, splitting. 3 A cake. 4 Mountain ebony. -लं 1 A basket of split bomboos or any vessel of wicker-work. **2** The bark of pomegranate. **3** A twig. **4** The chips of a substance.

विदलनं Splitting, rending asunder, cutting, dividing.

विदारः **1** Rending or cutting asunder, splitting. **2** War, battle. **3** An inundation, overflowing (of a tank, river &c.).

विदारकः **1** A tearer, divider. **2** A tree or rock in the middle of a stream (which divides its course). **3** A hole sunk for water in the bed of a dry river.

विदारणः **1** A tree or rock in the middle of a stream (to which a boat is fastened). **2** War, battle. **3** The Karṇikâra tree. **–णा** War, battle. **–णं** **1** Rending, splitting, tearing, ripping up, breaking; श्रुतं सखे श्रवणविदारणं वचः Mu. 5. 6; युवजनहृदयविदारणमनसिजनखरुचिकिंशुकजाले Gît. 1., Ki. 14. 54; (where विदारण has the force of an adjective). **2** Afflicting, tormenting. **3** Killing, slaughter.

विदारुः a lizard.

विदित *p. p.* **1** Known, understood, learnt. **2** Informed. **3** Renowned, celebrated, well-known; भुवनविदिते वंशे Me. 6. **4** Promised, agreed to. **–तः** A learned man, scholar. **–तं** Knowledge, information.

विदिश् *f.* An intermediate point of the compass.

विदिशा **1** N. of the capital of the district called दशार्ण; तेषां (दशार्णानां) दिक्षु प्रथितविदिशालक्षणां राजधानीं Me. 24. **2** N. of a river in Mâlvâ. **3**=विदिश् q. v.

विदीर्ण *p. p.* **1** Torn, split, rent asunder, split open. **2** Opened expanded (see दृ with वि).

विदुः The middle of the frontal globes on an elephant's forehead (हस्तिकुंभमध्यभागः).

विदुर *a.* Wise, intelligent. **–रः** **1** A wise or learned man. **2** A crafty man, an intriguer. **3** N. of the younger brother of Pâṇḍu. [When Satyavatî found that both the sons begotten by Vyâsa upon her two daughters-in-law were physically incapacitated for the throne--Dhṛitarâshṭra being blind and Pâṇḍu pale and sickly--she asked them to seek the assistance of Vyâsa once more. But being frightened by the austere look of the sage, the elder widow sent one of her slave-girls dressed in her own clothes, and this girl became the mother of Vidura. He is remarkable for his great wisdom, righteousness, and strict impartiality. He particularly loved the Pâṇḍavas, and saved them from several critical dangers].

विदुलः **1** A kind of reed or ratan. **2** Gum-myrrh.

विदून *p. p.* Afflicted, tormented, distressed (see दु with वि).

विदूर *a.* Remote, distant; सरिद्विदूरांतरभावतन्वी R. 13. 48. **–रः** N. of a mountain or city from which the Vaidûrya jewel or *lapis lazuli* is brought; विदूरभूमिर्नवमेघशब्दादुद्भिन्नया रत्नशलाकयेव Ku. 1. 24; see Malli. thereon, as well as on Si. 3. 45. (The forms **विदूरं, विदूरेण, विदूरतस्** or **विदूरात्** are often used adverbially in the sense of 'from a distance', 'from afar', 'at a distance,' 'far off'). **–Comp.** **–ग** *a.* spreading far and wide. **–जं** the *lapis lazuli.*

विदूषक *a.* (**की** *f.*) **1** Defiling, polluting, contaminating, corrupting. **2** Detracting, abusing. **3** Witty, humorous, jocular. **–कः** **1** A jester, buffoon. **2** Particularly, the humorous companion and confidential friend of the hero in a play, who excites mirth by his quaint dress, speeches, gestures, appearances &c., and by allowing himself to be made the butt of ridicule by almost every body); the S. D. thus defines him :— कुसुमवसंताद्यभिधः कर्मवपुर्वेशभाषाद्यैः । हास्यकरः कलहरतिर्विदूषकः स्यात्स्वकर्मज्ञः ॥ 79. **3** A libertine, lecher.

विदूषणं **1** Pollution, corruption. **2** Abuse, reproach, detraction.

विदृतिः A seam.

विदेशः Another country, foreign land or country; भजते विदेशमधिकेन जितस्तदनुप्रवेशमथवा कुशलः Si. 9. 48. **–Comp.** **–ज** *a.* exotic, foreign.

विदेशीय Foreign, exotic.

विदेहाः (*m. pl.*) **1** N. of a country, the ancient Mithilâ (see App. III); R. 11. 36, 12. 26. **2** The natives of this country. **–हः** The disrtict Videha. **–हा** The same as विदेह.

विद्धं *p. p.* **1** Pierced, penetrated; wounded, stabbed. **2** Beaten, whipped, lashed. **3** Thrown, Directed, sent. **4** Opposed. **5** Resembling. **–द्धं** A wound. **–Comp.** **–कर्ण** *a.* having bored ears.

विद्या **1** Knowledge, learning, lore; science; (तां) विद्यामभ्यसनेनेव प्रसादयितुमर्हसि R. 1. 88; विद्या नाम नरस्य रूपमधिकं प्रच्छन्नगुप्तं धनं &c. Bh. 2. 20. (According to some *Vidyâs* are four:— आन्वीक्षिकी त्रयी वार्ता दंडनीतिश्च शाश्वती Kâmandaka; Ki. 2. 6; to these four Manu adds a fifth आत्मविद्या; see Ms. **7.** 43. But the usual number of *Vidyâs* is stated to be fourteen, *i. e.* the four *Vedas*, the six *Angas*, *Dharma*, *Mîmâmsâ*, *Tarka* or *Nyâya* and the *Purânas*; see चतुर्दशविद्या under चतुर्; and N. 1. 4). **2** Right knowledge; spiritual knowledge; U. 6. 6; cf. अविद्या. **3** A spell, an incantation. **4** The goddess Durgâ. **5** Magical skill. **–Comp.** **–अनुपालिन्, अनुसेविन्** *a.* acquiring knowledge. **–अभ्यासः, -अर्जनं,-आगमः** acquisition of knowledge, pursuit of learning, study. **–अर्थः** seeking for knowledge. **–अर्थिन्** *m* a student, scholar, pupil. **–आलयः** a school, college, any place of learning. **–उपार्जनं** = विद्यार्जनं q. v. **–करः** a learned man. **–चण, -चंचु** *a.* famous for one's learning. **–देवी** the goddess of learning. **–धनं** wealth in the form of learning. **–धरः** (**री** *f.*) a class of demigods or semi-divine beings. **–प्राप्तिः** =विद्यार्जन q. v. **–लाभः** **1** acquisition of learning. **2** wealth or any other acquisition made by learning. **–विहीन** *a.* illiterate, ignorant. **–वृद्ध** *a.* old in knowledge, advanced in learning. **–व्यसनं,-व्यवसायः** pursuit of knowledge.

विद्युत् *f.* **1** Lightning; वाताय कपिला विद्युत् Mbh.; Me. 38, 115. **2** A thunderbolt. **–Comp.** **–उन्मेषः** a flash of lightning. **–जिह्वः** a kind of demon or Râkshasa. **–ज्वाला, -द्योतः** a flash or lustre of lightning. **–दामन्** *n.* a flash of zigzag or forked lightning. **–पातः** falling or stroke of lightning. **–प्रियं** bell-metal. **–लता, –लेखा** (**विद्युल्लता, विद्युल्लेखा**) **1** a streak of lightning. **2** forked or zigzag lightning.

विद्युत्वत् *a.* Having lightning; Me. 64. *–m.* A cloud; Ku. 6. 27.

विद्योतन *a.* (**नी** *f.*) **1** Illuminating, irradiating. **2** Illustrating, elucidating.

विद्रः **1** Tearing, splitting, piercing. **2** A fissure, hole, cavity.

विद्रधिः An abscess.

विद्रवः **1** Running away, flight, retreat. **2** Panic. **3** Flowing out. **4** Melting, liquefaction.

विद्राण *a.* Roused from sleep, awakened.

विद्रावणं **1** Driving or scaring away, putting to flight, defeating. **2** Liquefying.

विद्रुमः **1** The coral tree (bearing reddish precious gems called corals). **2** A coral; तवाधरस्पर्धिषु विद्रुमेषु R. 13. 13; Ku. 1. 44. **3** A young shoot or sprout. **–Comp.** **–लता** **1** a branch of coral. **2** a kind of perfume. **–लतिका** a kind of perfume (नलिका).

विद्वस् *a.* (Nom. sing. *m.* विद्वान्; *f.* विदुषी; *n.* विद्वत्) **1** Knowing (with acc.) ; आनंदं ब्रह्मणो विद्वान् न बिभेति कदाचन; तव विद्वानपि तापकारणं R. 8. 76; Ki. 11. 30. **2** Wise, learned. *–m.* A learned or wise man, scholar; किं वस्तु विद्वन् गुरवे प्रदेयं R. 5. 18. **–Comp.** **–कल्प, –देशीय, –देश्य** *a* (**विद्वत्कल्प, विद्वद्देशीय, विद्वद्देश्य**) slightly learned, a little learned. **–जनः** (**विद्वज्जनः**) a learned or wise man, sage.

विद्विष् *m.*, **विद्विषः** An enemy, a foe; विद्विषोऽप्यनुनय Bh. 2. 77; R. 3. 60; Y. 1. 162.

विद्विष्ट *p. p.* Hated, disliked, odious.

विद्वेषः 1 Enmity, hatred, odium; Ms. 8. 346. 2 Disdainful pride, contempt; विद्वेषोऽभिमतप्रातावपि गर्वादनादरः Bharata.

विद्वेषणः A hater, an enemy. -**णी** A woman of a resentful temper. -**णं** 1 Causing hatred or enmity. 2 Enmity, hatred.

विद्वेषिन्, विद्वेष्टृ *a.* Hating, inimical. -*m.* A hater, an enemy.

विध् 6 P. (विधति) 1 To pierce, cut. 2 To honour, worship. 3 To rule, govern, administer.

विधः 1 Kind, sort ; as in बहुविध, नानाविध. 2 Mode, manner, form. 3 Fold (at the end of comp. especially after numerals) ; त्रिविध, अष्टविध &c. 4 The food of elephants. 5 Prosperity. 6 Penetration.

विधवनं 1 Shaking, agitating. 2 Tremor, trembling.

विधव्यं Tremor, agitation.

विधवा A widow; सा नारी विधवा जाता गृहे रोदिति तत्पतिः Subhâsh. -**Comp.** -**आवेदनं** marrying a widow. -**गामिन्** *m.* one who has sexual intercourse with a widow.

विधस् *m.* N. of Brahman, the creator.

विधा 1 Mode, manner, form. 2 Kind, sort. 3 Prosperity, affluence. 4 The food of elephants, horses &c. 5 Penetration. 6 Hire, wages.

विधातृ *m.* 1 A maker, creator; Ku. 7. 36. 2 The creator, N. of Brahman; विधाता भद्रं नो वितरतु मनोज्ञाय विधये Mâl. 6. 7, R. 1. 35, 6. 11; 7. 25. 3 Granter, giver, bestower; Ku. 1. 57. 4 Fate, destiny; H. 1. 40. 5 N. of Visvakarman. 6 N. of Kâma, the god of love. 7 Spirituous liquor. -**Comp.** -**आयुस्** *m.* 1 sunshine. 2 the sunflower. -**भूः** an epithet of Nârada.

विधानं 1 Arranging, disposing. 2 Performing, making, doing, executing; नेपथ्यविधानं *S.* 1; आज्ञा°, यज्ञ° &c. 3 Creation, creating; R. 6. 11, 7. 14; Ku. 7. 66. 4 Employment, use, application; प्रतिकारविधानं R. 8. 40. 5 Prescribing, enjoining, ordering. 6 A rule, precept, ordinance, sacred rule or precept, sacred injunction ; Ms. 9. 148 ; Bg, 16. 24, 17. 24. 7 Mode, manner. 8 A means or expedient. 9 The food given to elephants (to make them intoxicated); विधानसंपादितदानशोभितैः K. (where विधान means 'rule' also) ; *Si.* 5. 51. 10 Wealth. 11 Pain, agony, torment, distress. 12 An act of hostility. -**Comp.** -**गः, ज्ञः** a wise or learned man. -**युक्त** *a.* in accordance with or conformable to sacred precept.

विधानकं Distress, affliction, pain.

विधायक *a.* (**यिका** *f.*) 1 Arranging, disposing. 2 Doing, making, performing, executing. 3 Creating. 4 Enjoying, prescribing, laying down. 5 Consigning, committing, delivering (to the care of).

विधिः 1 Doing, performance, practice, an act or action ; ब्रह्माभ्यासनविधिना योगनिद्रां गतस्य Bh. 3. 41; योगविधि R. 8. 22; लेखाविधि Mâl. 1. 35. 2 Method, manner, way, means, mode ; Pt. 1. 376. 3 A rule, commandment, any precept which enjoins something for the first time (as distinguished from नियम and परिसंख्या q. q. v. v.) ; विधिरत्यंतमप्राप्तौ. 4 A sacred precept or rule, ordinance, injunction, law, a sacred command, religious commandment (opp. अर्थवाद which means an explanatory statement coupled with legends and illustrations ; See अर्थवाद) ; श्रद्धा वित्तं विधिश्चेति त्रितयं तत्समागतं *S.* 7. 29; R. 2. 16. 5 Any religious act or ceremony, a rite, ceremony; स चेत् स्वयं कर्मसु धर्मचारिणां त्वमंतरायो भवसि च्युतो विधिः R. 3. 45, 1. 34. 6 Behaviour, conduct. 7 Condition; V. 4. 8 Creation, formation; सामग्र्यविधौ Ku. 3. 28; कल्याणी विधिषु विचित्रता विधातुः Ki. 7. 7. 9 The creator. 10 Fate, destiny, luck; विधौ वामारंभे मम समुचितैषा परिणतिः Mâl. 4. 4. 11 The food of elephants. 12 Time. 13 A physician. 14 N. of Vishṇu. -**Comp.** -**ज्ञ** *a.* knowing the ritual. (-**ज्ञः**) a Brâhmaṇa versed in the ritual, a ritualist. -**दृष्ट, -विहित** *a.* prescribed by rule, enjoined by law. -**द्वैधं** diversity of rules, variance of precept or commandment. -**पूर्वकं** *ind.* according to rule -**प्रयोगः** application of a rule. -**योगः** the force or influence of fate, -**वधूः** *f.* an epithet of Sarasvatî. -**हीन** *a.* devoid of rule, unauthorised, irregular.

विधित्सा 1 Desire to do or perform. 2 Design, purpose, desire in general.

विधित्सित *a.* Intended to be done. **तं**- Intention, design.

विधुः 1 The moon ; सविता विधवति विधुरपि सवितरति दिनंति यामिन्यः K. P. 10. 2 Camphor. 3 A demon, fiend. 4 An expiatory oblation. 5 N. of Vishṇu. 6 N. of Brahman. -**Comp.** -**क्षयः** waning of the moon, the period of the dark fortnight of a month. -**पंजरः** (also **पिंजरः**) a scimitar, sabre. -**प्रिया** a *Nakshatra* or lunar mansion.

विधुत See विधूत.

विधुतिः *f.* Shaking, trepidation, tremor; वैनायक्यश्चिरं वो वदनविधुतयः पांतु चीत्कारवत्यः Mâl. 1. 1.

विधुननं 1 Shaking or tossing about, agitating. 2 Trembling, tremor.

विधुंतुदः N. of Râhu; विधुमिव विकटविधुंतुददंतदलनगलितामृतधारं Gît. 4; N. 4. 71; *Si.* 2. 61.

विधुर *a.* 1 Distressed, troubled, afflicted, overwhelmed with grief, miserable; Mâl. 2 3, 9. 11, U. 3. 38, 6. 41, Ki. 11. 26. 2 Love-lorn, bereaved, suffering separation from a wife or husband ; मयि च विधुरे भावः कांताप्रवृत्तिपराङ्मुखः V. 4. 20; विधुरा ज्वलनातिसर्जनान्ननु मां प्रापय पत्युरंतिकं Ku. 4. 32; *Si.* 6. 29. 12. 8. 3 Devoid, deprived, or destitute of, free from; सावि कलंकविधुरा मधुराननश्रीः Bv. 2. 5. 4 Adverse, hostile, unfriendly; Pt. 2. 81. -**रः** A widower. -**रं** 1 Alarm, fear, anxiety. 2 Separation from a wife or husband, bereavement suffered by a lover or mistress.

विधुरा Curds mixed with sugar and spices.

विधुवनं Shaking, tremor, trembling.

विधुत *p. p.* 1 Shaken or tossed about, waved. 2 Tremulous. 3 Shaken off, dispelled, removed. 4 Unsteady. 5 Abandoned. -**तं** Repugnance.

विधूतिः *f.*, **विधूननं** Shaking, tremor, agitation.

विधृत *p. p.* 1 Seized, held, grasped. 2 Separated, kept asunder or separate. 3 Assumed, possessed. 4 Checked, restrained. 5 Supported, protected, borne up. (See धृ with वि). -**तं** 1 Disregard of a command. 2 Dissatisfaction.

विधेय *pot. p.* 1 To be done or performed. 2 To be enjoined or prescribed. 3 (*a*) Dependent on, at the disposal of; अथ विधिविधेयः परिचयः Mâl. 2. 13. (*b*) Subject to, influenced or controlled by, subdued or overpowered by (usually in comp.); निद्राविधेयं नरदेवसैन्यं R. 7. 62; संभाव्यमानस्नेहरसेनाभिसंधिना विधेयीकृतोऽपि Mâl. 1; Bg. 2. 64; Mu. 3. 1; *Si.* 3. 20; R. 19. 4. 4 Obedient, tractable, compliant, submissive; अविधेयेंद्रियः पुंसां गौरिवैति विधेयतां Ki. 11. 33. 5 To be predicated (in gram, &c.) ; अत्र मिथ्यामहिमत्वं नानुवाद्यं अपि तु विधेयं K. P. 7. -**यं** 1 What ought to be done, a duty; Ki. 16. 62. 2 The predicate of a proposition. -**यः** A servant, dependant. -**Comp.** -**अविमर्शः** a fault of composition which consists in assigning to the predicate a subordinate position or in expressing it imperfectly अविमृष्टः प्राधान्येनानिर्दिष्टो विधेयांशो यत्र K. P. 7; see examples *ad loc.*). -**आत्मन्** *m.* N. of Vishṇu. -**ज्ञ** *a.* one who knows one's duty; Pt. 1. 337. -**पदं** 1 the object to be accomplished. 2 the predicate.

विध्वंसः 1 Ruin, destruction. 2 Enmity, aversion; dislike. 3 An insult, offence.

विध्वंसिन् *a.* Being ruined, falling to pieces.

विध्वस्त *p. p.* **1** Ruined, destroyed. **2** Scattered about, tossed up. **3** Obscured, darkened. **4** Eclipsed.

विनत *p. p.* **1** Bent down, bowed. **2** Stooping, drooping, inclined; *S.* 3. 11. **3** Sunk down, depressed. **4** Bent, crooked, curved. **5** Humble, modest; (see नम् with वि).

विनता **1** N. of the mother of Aruṇa and Garuḍa, said to be one of the wives of Kasyapa; see गरुड. **2** A kind of basket. **–Comp. –नंदनः, –सुतः, –सूनुः** epithets of Garuḍa or Aruṇa.

विनतिः *f.* **1** Bowing down, bending, stooping. **2** Modesty, humility. **3** A request.

विनदः **1** Sound, noise. **2** N. of a tree.

विनमनं Bending, bowing, stooping.

विनम्र *a.* **1** Bent down, stooping; Ki. 4. 2. **2** Depressed, sunk down. **3** Modest, humble.

विनम्रकं The flower of the *Tagara* tree.

विनय *a.* **1** Cast, thrown. **2** Secret. **3** Ill-behaved. **–यः 1** Guidance, discipline, instruction (in one's duties), moral training; R. 1. 24; Mâl. 10. 5. **2** Sense of propriety, decorum, decency; *S.* 1. 29. **3** Polite conduct, gentlemanlike bearing, good breeding or manners; R. 6. 79; Mâl. 1. 18. **4** Modesty, humility; सुष्ठु शोभसे आर्यपुत्र एतेन विनयमाहात्म्येन U. 1; विद्या ददाति विनयम्; तथापि नीचैर्विनयाददृश्यत R. 3. 34; 10. 71 (where Malli. renders विनय by इंद्रियजय or restraint of passions, unnecessarily in our opinion). **5** Reverence, courtesy, obeisance. **6** Conduct in general. **7** Drawing off, taking away, removing; *Si.* 10. 42. **8** A man who has subdued his senses. **9** A trader, merchant. **–Comp. –अवनत** *a.* stooping humbly. **–ग्राहिन्** *a.* tractable, obedient, submissive. **–वाच्** *a.* speaking mildly or affably. **–स्थ** *a.* modest.

विनयनं **1** Removing, taking away; Me. 52. **2** Education, instruction, training, discipline.

विनशनं Perishing, loss, destruction, disappearance. **–नः** N. of the place where the river Sarasvatî is lost in the sand; cf. Ms. 2. 21.

विनष्ट *p. p.* **1** Perished, destroyed, ruined. **2** Disappeared, lost. **3** Spoiled, corrupted.

विनस *a.* (**सा –सी** *f.*) Noseless; Bk. 5. 8.

विना *ind.* Without, except (with acc.; instr. or abl.); यथा तानं विना रागो यथा मानं विना नृपः। यथा दानं विना हस्ती तथा ज्ञानं विना यतिः Bv. 1. 119; पंकैर्विना सरो भाति सदः खलजनैर्विना। कटुवर्णैर्विना काव्यं मानसं विषयैर्विना 1. 116; विना वातैर्हस्तिभ्यः क्रियतां सर्वमेक्षः Mu. 7; *Si.* 2. 9 (**विनाकृ** means 'to leave, abandon, bereave, deprive of'; मदनेन विनाकृता रतिः Ku. 4. 21 'bereft of Cupid'). **–Comp. –उक्तिः** *f.* a figure of speech in which विना is used in a poetically charming way; विनार्थसंबंध एव विनोक्तिः R. G.; see K. P. 10 also.

विनाडिः, विनाडिका A measure of time equal to one-sixtieth part of a Ghaṭikâ or equal to 24 seconds.

विनायकः **1** A remover (of obstacles). **2** N. of Gaṇesa. **3** A Buddhist deified teacher. **4** N. of Garuḍa. **5** Obstacle, impediment.

विनाशः **1** Destruction ruin, utter loss, decay. **2** Removal. **–Comp. –उन्मुख** *a.* about to perish, ripe to meet one's doom. **–धर्मन्, –धर्मिन्** *a.* subject to decay, perishable, transient, विषयेषु विनाशधर्मसु त्रिदिवस्थेष्वपि निःस्पृहोऽभवत R. 8. 10.

विनाशनं Destruction, ruin, annihilation. **–नः** A destroyer.

विनाहः A cover for the mouth of a well; cf वीनाह.

विनिक्षेपः Throwing down, sending forth.

विनिग्रहः **1** Restraining, curbing, subduing; Bg. 13. 7, 17. 16; Ms. 9. 263. **2** Mutual opposition or antithesis.

विनिद्र *a.* **1** Sleepless, awake (fig. also); R. 5. 65. **2** Budded, opened, full-blown, expanded; विनिद्रमंदाररजोरुणांगुली Ku. 5. 80.

विनिपातः **1** Falling down, a fall. **2** A great fall, calamity, an evil, loss, ruin, destruction; विवेकभ्रष्टानां भवति विनिपातः शतमुखः Bh. 2. 10 (where it has sense 1 also); Ki. 2. 34. **3** Decay, death. **4** Hell, perdition; *S.* 5. **5** Occurrence, happening. **6** Pain, distress. **7** Disrespect.

विनिमयः **1** Exchange, barter; कार्यविनिमयेन M. 1; संपद्विनिमयेनोभौ दधतुर्भुवनद्वयं R. 1. 26. **2** A pledge, deposit, security.

विनिमेषः Twinkling (of the eyes).

विनियत *p. p.* Controlled, checked, restrained, regulated; as in विनियताहार, विनियतवाच् &c.

विनियमः Control, restraint, check.

विनियुक्त *p. p.* **1** Separated, loosed, detached. **2** Attached to, appointed. **3** Applied to. **4** Commanded, enjoined.

विनियोगः **1** Separation parting, detachment. **2** Leaving, giving up, abandoning. **3** Employment, use, application, disposal; बभूव विनियोगज्ञः साधनीयेषु तस्तुषु R. 17. 67; प्राणायामे विनियोगः. **4** Appointment to a duty, commission, charge; विनियोगप्रसादा हि किंकराः प्रभविष्णुषु Ku. 6. 62. **5** An obstacle, impediment.

विनिर्जयः Complete victory.

विनिर्णयः **1** Complete settlement or ascertainment, full decision. **2** Certainty. **3** A settled rule.

विनिर्बंधः Persistence, pertinacity.

विनिर्मित *p. p.* **1** Formed or made of. **2** Made, created.

विनिवृत्त *p. p.* **1** Returned, turned away. **2** Stopped, ceased, desisted from. **3** Retired.

विनिवृत्तिः *f.* **1** Cessation, stopping, removing; शक्राभ्यसूयाविनिवृत्तये R. 6. 74. **2** End, stop, termination.

विनिश्चयः **1** Fixing, settling, ascertainment. **2** A decision, resolution.

विनिश्वासः Hard breathing or respiration, sighing, a sigh.

विनिष्पेषः Bruising, crushing, grinding.

विनिहत *p. p.* **1** Struck down, wounded. **2** Killed. **3** Completely overcome. **–तः 1** Any great or unavoidable calamity, such as that inflicted by fate or heaven. **2** A portent, comet.

विनीत *p. p.* **1** Taken away, removed. **2** Well trained, educated, disciplined. **3** Refined, well-behaved. **4** Modest, humble, meek, gentle. **5** Decent, decorous, gentlemanly. **6** Sent away, dismissed. **7** Tamed, broken in. **8** Plain, simple, (as a dress). **9** Having the passions under control, self-subdued. **10** Chastised, punished. **11** Tractable, governable. **12** Lovely, handsome. (See नी with वि). **–तः 1** A trained horse. **2** A trader.

विनीतकं **1** A vehicle or conveyance (a litter &c.) **2** A carrier, bearer.

विनेतृ *m.* **1** A leder, guide. **2** A teacher, an instructor; R. 8. 91. **3** A king, ruler. **4** A chastiser, punisher; अयं विनेता दृप्तानां Mv. 3. 46. 4. 1, R. 6. 39, 14. 23.

विनोदः **1** Removing, driving away; श्रमविनोदः. **2** A diversion, an amusement, any interesting or amusing pursuit or occupation; प्रायेणैते रमणविरहेष्वंगनानां विनोदाः Me. 87; *S.* 2. 5. **3** Play, sport, pastime. **4** Eagerness, vehement desire. **5** Pleasure, happiness, gratification; विलपनविनोदोऽप्यसुलभः U. 3. 30; जनयतु रसिकजनेषु मनोरमरतिरसभावविनोदं Gît. 12. **6** A particular mode of sexual enjoyment.

विनोदनं **1** Removing. **2** A diversion &c.; see विनोद.

विंदु *a.* **1** Intelligent, wise. **2** Liberal. **–दुः** A drop; see बिंदु.

विंध्यः **1** N. of a range of mountains which separates Hindustân proper from the Deccan or south; it is one of the seven *Kulaparvatas* q. v., and forms the southern limit of Madhyadesa; see Ms. 2. 21.

[According to a legend, the Vindhya mountain, being jealous of the mount Meru (or Himalaya) demanded that the sun should revolve round himself as about Meru, which the sun declined to do ; whereupon the Vindhya began to ise higher and higher so as to obstruct the path of the sun and moon The gods being alarmed sought the aid of the sage Agastya, who approached the mountain and requested that by bending down he would give him an easy passage to the south, and that he would retain the same position till his return. This Vindhya consented to do (because according to one account, he regarded Agastya as his teacher); but Agastya never returned from the south, and Vindhya never attained the height of Meru]. **2** A hunter. **-Comp.** **-अटवी** the great Vindhya forest. **-कूटः,-कूटनं** epithets of the sage Agastya. **-वासिन्** *m.* an epithet of the grammarian व्याडि.(**-नी**) an epithet of Durgâ.

विन्न *p. p.* **1** Known. **2** Got, obtained. **3** Discussed, investigated. **4** Placed, fixed. **5** Married. (See विद्).

विन्नकः N. of Agastya.

विन्यस्त *p. p.* **1** Placed or put down. **2** Inlaid, paved. **3** Fixed. **4** Arranged. **5** Delivered. **6** Presented, offered. **7** Deposited.

विन्यासः **1** Entrusting, depositing, **2** A deposit. **3** Arrangement, adjustment, disposition; अक्षरविन्यासः inscribing letters ; प्रत्यक्षरश्लेषमयप्रबंधविन्यासवैदग्ध्यनिधिः Vâs. 'composition of a work &c.' **4** A collection, an assemblage. **5** A site or receptacle.

विपक्त्रिम *a.* **1** Fully ripened or matured. **2** Developed, fulfilled (as the consequences of former acts).

विपक्व *a.* **1** Fully ripened or matured. **2** Developed, fulfilled ; Ki. 6. 16. **3** Cooked.

विपक्ष *a.* Hostile, inimical, adverse, contrary. **-क्षः** **1** An enemy, adversary, opponent ; R. 17. 75, *Si.* 11. 59. **2** A rival or fellow wife ; R. 19. 20. **3** A disputant ; Ki. 17. 43. **4** (In logic) A negative instance, an instance on the opposite side (*i. e.* that in which the *hetu* or major term is not found) ; निश्चितसाध्याभाववान् विपक्षः T. S. ; Mu. 5. 10.

विपंच्विका, विपंची **1** A lute. **2** Play, sport, pastime.

विपणः, विपणनं **1** Sale ; Ma. 3. 152. **2** Petty trade.

विपणिः, -णी *f.* **1** A market, market-place, stall ; हा हा नश्यति मन्मथस्य विपणिः सौभाग्यपण्याकरः Mk. 8. 38; *Si.* 5. 24 ; R. 16. 41. **2** An article or commodity for sale. **3** Trade, traffic; Ms. 10. 116.

विपणिन् *m.* A trader, merchant, shop-keeper ; *Si.* 5. 24.

विपत्तिः *f.* **1** A calamity, misfortune, disaster, mishap, adversity ; संपत्तौ च विपत्तौ च महतामेकरूपता Subhâsh. **2** Death, destruction; अतिरभसकृतानां कर्मणामाविपत्तेर्भवति हृदयदाही शल्यतुल्यो विपाकः Bh. 2. 99 ; R. 19. 56; Ve. 4. 6; हिमसेकविपत्तिः नलिनी R. 8. 45. **3** Agony, torment (यातना). **-त्तिः** (*m.*) An excellent or distinguished foot-soldier; Ki. 15. 16.

विपथः A wrong road, bad way (lit. and fig.).

विपद् *f.* **1** A calamity, misfortune, adversity, distress; तत्स्वनिकषग्रावा तु तेषां (मित्राणां) विपद् H. 1. 210. **2** Death; सिंहादवापद्विपदं नृसिंहः R. 18. 35. **-Comp.** **-उद्धरणं, उद्धारः** relieving or extricating (one) from misfortune. **-कालः** times of need, season of calamity, adversity. **-युक्त** *a.* unfortunate, unhappy.

विपदा See विपद्.

विपन्न *p. p.* **1** Dead. **2** Lost, destroyed. **3** Unfortunate, afflicted, distressed, fallen into adversity. **4** Declined. **5** Disabled, incapacitated. (see पद् with वि). **-न्नः** A snake.

विपरिणमनं, विपरिणामः **1** A change, an alteration. **2** Change of form, transformation.

विपरिवर्तनं Turning about, rolling.

विपरीत *a.* **1** Reversed, inverted. **2** Contrary, opposite, reverse, inverse; R. 2. 53. **3** Wrong, contrary to rule. **4** False, untrue; Bv. 2. 177. **5** Unfavourable, adverse. **6** Cross, acting in an opposite manner. **7** Disagreeable, inauspicious. **-तः** A particular mode of sexual enjoyment. **-ता** **1** An unchaste or faithless wife. **2** A perverse woman. **-Comp.** **-कर, -कारक, -कारिन्, -कृत्** *a.* perverse, acting in a contrary manner; *Si.* 14. 66. **-चेतस्, -मति** *a.* having a perverted mind. **-रतं** inverted sexual intercourse; cf. पुरुषायित.

विपर्णकः The Palâsa tree.

विपर्ययः **1** Contrariety, reverse, inversion; आहितो जयविपर्ययोपि मे श्लाघ्य एव परमेष्ठिना त्वया R. 11. 86, 8. 89; नभसः स्फुटतारस्य रात्रेरिव विपर्ययः (न भाजनं); Ki. 11. 44; विपर्यये तु *S.* 5. 'if it be otherwise', 'if contrary be the case.' **2** Change (of purpose, dress &c.); कथमेत्य मतिर्विपर्ययं करिणी पंकमिवावसीदति Ki. 2. 6; so वेषविपर्ययः Pt. 1. **3** Absence or non-existence; समुद्रगारूपविपर्ययेऽदि Ku. 7. 42; त्यागे श्लाघाविपर्ययः R. 1. 22. **4** Loss; निद्रा संज्ञाविपर्ययः Ku. 6. 44 'loss of consciousness'. **5** Complete destruction, annihilation. **6** Exchange, barter. **7** Error, trespass, mistake, misapprehension. **8** A calamity, misfortune, adverse fate. **9** Hostility, enmity.

विपर्यस्त *p. p.* **1** Changed, inverted, reversed; हंत विपर्यस्तः संप्रति जीवलोकः U. 1. **2** Opposite, contrary. **3** Wrongly considered to be real.

विपर्यायः Reverse, contrariety; see विपर्यय.

विपर्यासः **1** Change, contrariety, reverse; विपर्यासं यातो घनविरलभावः क्षितिरुहां U. 2. 27. **2** Adverseness, unfavourableness; as in दैवविपर्यासात्. **3** Interchange, exchange ; प्रवहणविपर्यासेनागता Mk. 8. **4** An error, a mistake.

विपलं A moment, an extremely small division of time (said to be equal to one-sixth or one-sixtieth part of a *pala*).

विपलायनं Running away, fleeing in different directions.

विपश्चित् *a.* Learned, wise; विपश्चितो विनिन्युरेनं गुरवो गुरुप्रियं R 3. 29. **-m.** A learned or wise man, sage; भवति ते सभ्यतमा विपश्चितां मनोगतं वाचि निवेशयंति ये Ki. 14. 4.

विपाकः **1** Cooking, dressing. **2** Digestion. **3** Ripening, ripeness, maturity, development (fig. also); अमी पृथुस्तंबभृतः पिशंगतां गता विपाकेन फलस्य शालयः Ki. 4. 26; वाचो विपाको मम Bv. 4. 42 'my mature, full-developed or dignified words'. **4** Consequence, fruit, result, the result of actions either in this or in a former birth, अहो मे दारुणतरः कर्मणां विपाकः K. 354; ममैव जन्मांतरपातकानां विपाकविस्फूर्जथुरप्रसह्यः R. 14. 62; Bh. 2. 99 ; Mv. 5. 56. **5** (*a*) Change of state; U. 4. 6. (*b*) An unexpected event or occurrence, a reverse, adverse turn of fate, distress, alcamity ; U. 3. 3, 4. 12. **6** Difficulty, embarrassment. **7** Flavour, taste.

विपाटनं **1** Splitting, tearing open. **2** Eradication. **3** Spoliation.

विपाठः A kind of large arrow.

विपांडु *a.* Pale, pallid; Ki. 5. 6; *Si.* 9. 3; so **विपांडुर** *Si.* 4. 5; Ratn. 2. 4.

विपादिका **1** A sore or tumour on the foot. **2** An enigma, a riddle.

विपाश्, विपाशा *f.* N. of one of the five rivers in the Panjab (now called Beas).

विपिनं A wood, forest, grove, thicket; वृंदावनविपिने ललितं वितनोतु शुभानि यशस्यं Gît. 1.; विपिनानि प्रकाशानि शक्तिमत्वाच्चकार सः R. 4. 31.

विपुल *a.* **1** Large, extensive, capacious, broad, wide, spacious ; विपुलं नितंबदेशे M. 3. 7; शिरसि तनुर्विपुलश्च मध्यदेशे Mk. 3. 22; so विपुलं, पृष्ठं विपुलः कुक्षिः &c. **2** Much, ample, copious, abundant ; Ki. 18. 14. **3** Deep, profound; Mv. 1. 2. **4** With the hair standing on end, thrilling ; *Si.* 16. 3 (where it has sense **1** also). **-लः** **1** N. of the mountain Meru. **2** Of Himâlaya. **3** A respectable man. **-Comp.** **-छाय** *a.*

shady, umbrageous. -जघना a woman with large hips. -मति a. endowed with great talent or understanding. -रसः the sugar-cane.

विपुला The earth.

विपूयः The *Munja* grass.

विप्रः 1 A Brâhmaṇa; see the quotations under ब्राह्मण. 2 A sage, wise man. 3 The Asvattha tree. -Comp. -ऋषिः = ब्रह्मर्षि q. v. -काष्ठं the cotton plant. -प्रियः the Palâsa tree. -समागमः a concourse or synod of Brâhmaṇas. -स्वं the property of a Brâhmaṇa.

विप्रकर्षः Distance, remoteness.

विप्रकारः 1 Insult, contumely, abuse, treating with disrespect ; Ki. 3. 55. 2 Injury, offence. 3 Wickedness. 4 Opposition, counteraction. 5 Retaliation.

विप्रकीर्ण p. p. 1 Spread about, dispersed, scattered. 2 Loose, dishevelled (as hair). 3 Expanded, outstretched. 4 Wide, broad.

विप्रकृत p. p. 1 Hurt, offended, injured. 2 Insulted, abused, treated with contumely. 3 Opposed. 4 Rataliated, requitted; (see कृ with विप्र).

विप्रकृतिः f. 1 Injury, offence. 2 An insult, abuse, contumely. 3 Retaliation, retort.

विप्रकृष्ट p. p. 1 Drawn away, removed. 2 Distant, remote. 3 Protracted, lengthened, extended.

विप्रकृष्टक a. Remote, distant.

विप्रतिकारः 1 Counteraction, opposition, contradiction. 2 Retaliation.

विप्रतिपत्तिः f. 1 Mutual discrepancy, contest, conflict, dispute, opposition (as of opinions or interests). 2 Dissent, objection. 3 Perplexity, confusion. 4 Mutual relation. 5 Conversancy.

विप्रतिपन्न p. p. 1 Mutually opposed, opposite, dissentient. 2 Confused, bewildered, perplexed. 3 Contested, disputed. 4 Mutually connected or related.

विप्रतिषेधः 1 Keeping under control, controlling. 2 The opposition of two courses of action which are equally important, the conflict of two even-matched interests; हरिर्विप्रतिषेधं तमाचचक्षे विचक्षणः Si. 2. 6; (तुल्यबलविरोधो विप्रतिषेधः Malli.). 3 (In gram.) The conflict of two rules by which two different grammatical operations become possible according to two different rules, conflict of two equally important rules; विप्रतिषेधे परं कार्यं P. I. 4. 2; see Kâsikâ or Mbh. thereon). 4 Prohibition.

विप्रति(ती)सारः 1 Repentance; Si. 10. 20. 2 Anger, rage, wrath. 3 Wickedness, evil.

विप्रदुष्ट p. p. 1 Vitiated, spoiled, dissolute. 2 Corrupt.

विप्रनष्ट p. p. 1 Lost. 2 Vain, useless.

विप्रमुक्त p. p. 1 Set free, liberated, loosened. 2 Shot, discharged. 3 Free from (in comp.)

विप्रयुक्त p. p. 1 Separated, severed, detached. 2 Separated from, being absent or away from; Me. 2. 3 Freed or released from. 4 Deprived or destitute of, without (in comp.).

विप्रयोगः 1 Disunion, severance, separation, dissociation; as प्रिय°. 2 Especially, separation of lovers, मा भूदेवं क्षणमपि च ते विद्युता विप्रयोगः Me. 115, 10; R. 13. 26, 14. 66. 3 Quarrel, disagreement.

विप्रलब्ध p. p. 1 Deceived; cheated. 2 Disappointed. 3 Hurt, injured. -ब्धा A woman disappointed by her lover's breaking his appointment; (one of the several classes of a Nâyikâ in poetic composition); she is thus defined in S. D. :—प्रियः कृत्वापि संकेतं यस्या नायाति संनिधिम्। विप्रलब्धेति सा ज्ञेया नितांतमवमानिता ॥ 118.

विप्रलंभः 1 Deceiving, deceit, tricking; Ki. 11. 27. 2 Especially, deceiving by false statements or by not keeping promises. 3 Quarrel, Disagreement. 4 Disunion, separation, disjunction. 5 The separation of lovers; शुश्रुवे प्रियजनस्य कातरं विप्रलंभपरिशंकिनो वचः R. 19. 18; Ve. 2. 12. 6 (In Rhet.) The feeling or sentiment of love in separation, one of the two main kinds of शृंगार (opp. संभोग); अपरः (विप्रलंभः) अभिलाषविरहेर्ष्याप्रवासशापहेतुक इति पंचविधः K. P. 4; यूनोरयुक्तयोर्भावो युक्तयोर्वाथवा मिथः। अभीष्टालिंगनादीनामनवाप्तौ प्रहृष्यते। विप्रलंभः स विज्ञेयः— उज्ज्वलमणिः—; cf. S. D. 212 *et seq.*

विप्रलापः 1 Idle or unmeaning talk, prattle, gibberish, nonsense. 2 Mutual contradiction, contradictory statement. 3 A dispute, wrangling. 4 Violation of one's promise, breaking one's word.

विप्रलयः Complete destruction or dissolution, annihilation; वियाकल्पेन मरुता मेघानां भूयसामपि। ब्रह्मणीव विवर्तानां क्वापि विप्रलयः कृतः U. 6. 6.

विप्रलुप्त p. p. 1 Carried away, snatched away. 2 Disturbed, interrupted.

विप्रलोभिन् m. N. of two trees ; किंकिरात and अशोक.

विप्रवासः Staying abroad, dwelling in a foreign country (away from one's home.)

विप्रश्निका A female fortune-teller.

विप्रहीण a. Deprived or destitute of.

विप्रिय a. Disagreeable, disliked, unpleasant, distasteful. -यं Offence, wrong, a disgreeable act; मनसापि न विप्रियं मया कृतपूर्वं तव किं जहासि मां R. 8. 52, Ku. 4. 7; Ki. 9. 39; Si. 15. 11.

विप्रुष् f. 1 A drop (of water or any other liquid); संतापं नवजलविप्रुषो गृहीत्वा Si. 8. 40; स्वेदविप्रुषः 2. 18. 2 A mark, dot, spot.

विप्रोषित p. p. 1 Staying abroad, away from, absent. 2 Banished, being in exile; R. 12. 11. -Comp. -भर्तृका a woman whose husband is absent from home.

विप्लवः 1 Floating or drifting about, floatinag in different directions. 2 Opposition, contrariety. 3 Confusion, perplexity. 4 Tumult, scuffle, affray; M. 1. 5 Devastation, predatory warfare; danger from an enemy. 6 Extortion. 7 Loss, destruction; सत्त्वविप्लवात् R. 8. 41. 8 Adverseness, evil turn; अथवा मम भाग्यविप्लवात् R. 8. 47. 9 The rust on a mirror (dust accumulating on its surface); अपवर्जितविप्लवे शुचौ... मतिरादर्श इवाभिदृश्यते Ki. 2. 26 (where विप्लव also means प्रमाणबाधः absence of reasoning). 10 Transgression, violation ; Ki. 1. 13. 11 An evil, a calamity. 12 Sin, wickedness, sinfulness.

विप्लावः 1 Deluging, inundating. 2 Causing tumult. 3 A horse's canter or gallop.

विप्लुत p. p. 1 Drifted about. 2 Drowned, submerged, deluged, overflowed. 3 Confounded, distrubed. 4 Ravaged, devastated. 5 Lost, disappeared. 6 Disgraced, dishonoured. 7 Ruined. 8 Obscured, disfigured. 9 Depraved, dissolute, profligate, guilty of lewdness. 10 Contrary, reverse. 11 Turning out false, untrue, U. 4. 18.

विप्लुष् See विप्रुष्.

विफल a. 1 Fruitless, useless, vain, ineffectual, unprofitable; मम विफलमेतदनुरूपमपि यौवनं Gît. 7; जगता वा विफलेन किं फलं R. G.; Si. 9. 6; Ku. 7. 66; Me. 68. 2 Idle, unmeaning.

विबंधः 1 Constipation. 2 Obstruction.

विबाधा Pain, anguish, tornment, agony.

विबुद्ध p. p. 1 Aroused, awakened, wide awake, S. 2. 2 Expanded, blossomed, full-blown. 3 Clever, skilful.

विबुधः 1 A wise or learned man, sage; सख्यं साप्तपदीनं भो इत्याहुर्विबुधा जनाः Pt. 2. 43. 2 A god, deity; अभूनृपो विबुधसखः परंतपः Bk. 1. 1; गोप्तारं न निधीनां महयंति महेश्वरं विबुधाः Subhâsh. 3 The moon. -Comp. -अधिपतिः, -इंद्रः, -ईश्वरः epithets of Indra. -द्विष्, -शत्रुः a demon; V. 1. 3.

विबुधानः 1 A learned man. 2 A teacher.

विबोधः 1 A wakening, being awake. **2** Perceiving, discovering. **3** Intelligence. **4** Awaking, becoming conscious, one of the 33 or 34 subordinate feelings (or व्यभिचारिभाव) in Rhetoric; निद्रानाशोत्तरं जायमानो बोधो विबोधः R G.

विब्बोक See बिब्बोक.

विभक्त *p. p.* **1** Divided, partitioned (as property &c.). **2** Divided, separated in interest, as in विभक्ता भ्रातरः. **3** Parted, separated, made distinct; *Si.* 1. 3. **4** Different, multifarious. **5** Retired, secluded. **6** Regular, symmetrical. **7** Ornamented. (See भज् with वि). **-क्तः** N. of Kârtikeya.

विभक्तिः *f.* **1** Separation, division, partition, apportionment. **2** Division, separation in interest. **3** A portion or share of inheritance. **4** (In gram.) Inflection of nouns, a case or case-termination.

विभंगः 1 Breaking, fracture. **2** Stopping, obstruction, stoppage; Bg. 2. 26. **3** Bending, contraction (as of the eye-brows); भ्रूविभंगकुटिलं च वीक्षितं R. 19. 17. **4** A fold, wrinkle. **5** A step, stair; R. 6. 3. **6** Breaking out; manifestation; विविधविकारविभंगं Gît. 11.

विभवः 1 Wealth, riches, property; अतनुषु विभवेषु ज्ञातयः संतु नाम *S.* 5. 8; R. 8. 69. **2** Might, power, prowess, greatness; एतावान्मम मतिविभवः V. 2; वाग्विभवः Mâl. 1. 20, R. 1. 9; Ki. 5. 21. **3** Exalted position, rank, dignity. **4** Magnanimity. **5** Final beatitude, absolution.

विभा 1 Light, lustre. **2** A ray of light. **3** Beauty. **-Comp. -करः 1** the sun; बत बत लसत्तेजःपुंजो विभाति विभाकरः K. P. 10. **2** the *arka* plant. **3** the moon. **-वसुः 1** the sun. **2** fire ; रचयिष्यामि तनुं विभावसौ Ku. 4. 34; R. 3. 37, 10. 83; Bg. 7. 9. **3** the moon. **4** a kind of necklace.

विभागः 1 Division, partition, apportionment (as of inheritance); समस्तत्र विभागः स्यात् Ms. 9. 120, 210; Y. 2. 114. **2** The share of an inheritance. **3** A part or share in general. **4** Division, separation, disjunction (regarded in Nyâya phil. as a Guṇa); Ku. 24; Bg. 3. 29. **5** The numerator of a fraction. **6** A section. **-Comp. -कल्पना** allotment of shares; Y. 2. 149. **-धर्मः** the law of inheritance. **-पत्रिका** a deed of partition. **-भाज्** *m.* one who shares in a portion of property already distributed ; Y. 1. 122.

विभाजनं Dividing, distributing.

विभाज्य *a.* **1** Portionable, to be divided. **2** Divisible.

विभातं Day-break, dawn.

विभावः 1 (In Rhet.) Any condition which produces or develops a particular state of body or mind (one of the three main divisions of *Bha'vas* the other two being अनुभाव and व्यभिचारिभाव q. q. v. v.); रत्याद्युद्बोधका लोके विभावाः काव्यनाट्ययोः S. D. 61; its chief subdivisions are आलंबन and उद्दीपक; see आलंबन. **2** A friend, an acquaintance.

विभावनं-ना 1 Clear perception or ascertainment, discrimination, judgment. **2** Discussion, investigation, examination. **3** Conception, imagination. **-ना** (In Rhet.) A figure of speech in which effects are represented as taking place though their usual causes are absent; क्रियायाः प्रतिषेधेपि फलव्यक्तिर्विभावना K. P. 10.

विभावरी 1 Night; अपर्वणि ग्रहकलुषेंदुमंडला विभावरी कथय कथं भविष्यति M. 4. 15, 5. 7; Ku. 5. 44. **2** Turmeric. **3** A bawd. **4** A harlot. **5** A perverse woman. **6** A talkative woman (मुखरस्त्री).

विभावित *p. p.* **1** Manifested, made clearly visible. **2** Known, understood, ascertained. **3** Seen, conceived. **4** Judged, discriminated. **5** Inferred, indicated. **6** Proved, established. **-Comp. -एकदेश** *a.* 'with whom a part has been discoverd', who has been found guilty with regard to a part (of what is in dispute); विभावितैकदेशेन देयं यदभियुज्यते V. 4.17.

विभाषा 1 An option, alternative. **2** Optionality of a rule.

विभासा Light, lustre.

विभिन्न *p. p.* **1** Broken asunder, divided, split. **2** Pierced, wounded. **3** Dispelled, driven away, dispersed. **4** Perplexed, bewildered. **5** Moved to and fro. **6** Disappointed. **7** Different, various. **8** Mixed, blended, variegated; विभिन्नवर्णा गरुडाग्रजेन सूर्यस्य रथ्याः परितः स्फुरंत्या *Si.* 4. 14; (see भिद् with वि). **-जः** N. of *Siva.*

विभीतः, -तं, विभीतकः -कं, विभीतकी, विभीता N. of tree, Terminalia Belerica, one of the three myrobalans.

विभीषक *a.* Frightening, terrifying.

विभीषिका 1 Terror. **2** A means of terrifying, a scare (a scare-crow); यदि ते संति संत्येव केयमन्या विभीषिका U. 4. 29.

विभु *a.* (भु -भ्वी *f.*) **1** Mighty, powerful. **2** Eminent, supreme. **3** Able to, capable of (with inf.), (धनुः) पूरयितुं भवंति विभवः शिखरमणिरुचः Ki. 5. 43. **4** Self-subduded, firm; self-controlled; कमपरमवशं न विप्रकुर्युर्विभुमपि तं यदमी स्पृशंति भावाः Ku. 6. 95. **5** (In Nyâya phil.) Eternal, existing everywhere, pervading all material things. **-भुः 1** Ether. **2** Space. **3** Time. **4** The soul. **5** A lord, ruler, master, sovereign, king. **6** The supreme ruler; Bg. 5. 14; 10. 12. **7** A servant. **8** N. of Brahman. **9** Of *Siva*; Ku. **7**. 31. **10** Of Vishṇu.

विभुग्न *a.* Curved, bent, crooked.

विभूतिः *f.* **1** Might, power, greatness; *Si.* 14. 5, Ku. 2. 61. **2** Prosperity, welfare. **3** Dignity, exalted rank. **4** Riches, plenty, magnificence, splendour; अहो राजाधिराजमंत्रिणो विभूतिः Mu. 3- R. 8. 36. **5** Wealth, riches ; R. 4. 19, 6. 76; 17. 43. **6** Superhuman power (which consists of eight faculties; अणिमन्, लघिमन्, प्राप्ति, प्राकाम्य, महिमन्, ईशिता, वशिता and कामावसायिता); Ku. 2. 11. **7** Ashes of cow-dung.

विभूषणं Ornament, decoration; विशेषतः सर्वविदां समाजे विभूषणं मौनमपंडितानां Bh. 2. 7; R. 16. 80.

विभूषा 1 Ornament, decoration; संपेदे श्रमसलिलोद्गमो विभूषा Ki. 7. 5, R. 4. 54. **2** Light, lustre. **3** Beauty, splendour.

विभूषित *p. p.* Adorned, decorated, ornamented.

विभृत *p. p.* Upheld, supported, maintained.

विभ्रंशः 1 Falling away or off. **2** Decay, decline, ruin. **3** A precipice.

विभ्रंशित *p. p.* **1** Led astray, seduced. **2** Deprived of.

विभ्रमः 1 Roaming or wandering about. **2** Whirling or going round, rolling about. **3** Error, mistake, blunder. **4** Hurry, confusion, flurry, perturbation.; especially, the flurry of mind caused by love; चित्तवृत्त्यनवस्थानं शृंगाराद्विभ्रमो भवेत्. **5** (Hence) Putting on of ornaments &c. in the wrong places through flurry; विभ्रमस्त्वरयाऽकाले भूषास्थानविपर्ययः; see Ku. 1. 4 and Malli. thereon. **6** Any amorous or sportive action, amorous play or movement; Mâl. 1. 26, 9. 38. **7** Beauty, grace, charm; N. 15. 25, U. 1. 20, 34, 6. 4; *Si.* 6. 46, 7. 15, 16. 64. **8** Doubt apprehension. **9** Caprice, whim.

विभ्रमा Old age.

विभ्रष्ट *p. p.* **1** Fallen off or away, separated. **2** Decayed, lost, fallen, ruined. **3** Dissappeared, vanished.

विभ्राज् *a.* Shining, splendid, luminous.

विभ्रांत *p. p.* **1** Whirled about. **2** Agitated, bewildered, confused, flurried. **3** Mistaken, erring. **-Comp. -नयन** *a.* with rolling eyes. **-शील** *a.* **1** confused in mind. **2** intoxicated, drunk. (**-लः**) **1** a monkey. **2** the disc of the sun or moon.

विभ्रांतिः *f.* **1** Whirling, going round. **2** Flurry, error, confusion. **3** Hurry, precipation.

विमत *p. p.* **1** Disagreeing, dissenting, differing in opinion. **2** At variance, in consistent. **3** Slighted. despised, neglected. **-तः** An enemy.

विमति *a.* Stupid, devoid of intelligence, foolish. **-तिः** *f.* **1** Dissent, desagreement, difference of opinion. **2** Dislike. **3** Stupidity.

विमत्सर *a.* Free from jealousy, unenvious; Bg. 4. 22.

विमद *a.* **1** Free from intoxication. **2** Devoid of joy, jealous.

विमनस्, विमनस्क *a.* **1** Sad, disconsolate, depressed in mind or spirits, sorry, discomposed; U. 1. 7. **2** Absent-minded. **3** Perplexed, bewildered. **4** Displeased. **5** Changed in mind or feeling.

विमन्यु *a.* **1** Free from anger. **2** Free from grief.

विमयः Exchange, barter.

विमर्दः **1** Pounding, crushing, bruising. **2** Rubbing together, friction; विमर्दसुरभिर्बकुलावलिका खल्वहं M. 3; R. 5. 65. **3** Touch. **4** Rubbing the person with saffron or other unguents. **5** War, battle, fight, encounter; विमर्दक्षमां भूमिमवतराव: U. 5. **6** Destruction, devastation; R. 6. 62. **7** Conjunction of the sun and moon. **8** An eclipse.

विमर्दकः **1** Grinding, pounding, bruising. **2** The trituration of perfumes. **3** An eclipse. **4** The conjunction of the sun and moon.

विमर्दनं,-ना **1** Pounding, crushing, trampling. **2** Rubbing together, friction. **3** Destruction, killing. **4** Trituration of perfumes. **5** An eclipse.

विमर्शः **1** Deliberation, consideration, examination, discussion. **2**. Reasoning. **3** A conflicting judgment. **4** Hesitation, doubt. **5** The impression left on the mind by past good or bad actions ; see वासना.

विमर्षः **1** Thought, deliberation. **2** Impatience, non-forbearance. **3** Dissatisfaction, displeasure. **4** (In dramas) A change in the successful progress of a dramatic plot, a change in the prosperous course of a love-story caused by some unforeseen reverse or accident, one of the five *Sandhis* in a drama; it is thus defined in S.D.; यत्र मुख्यफलोपाय उद्भिन्नो गर्भतोऽधिकः । शापाद्यैः सांतरायश्च स विमर्ष इति स्मृतः 336; see Mu. 4. 3; (often written विमर्श in all these senses.)

विमल *a.* **1** Pure, stainless, spotless, clean (fig. also). **2** Clear, limpid, pellucid, transparent (as water); विमलं जलं. **3** White, bright. **–लं** **1** Silver-gilt. **2** Talc. **–Comp. –दानं** an offering to a deity. **–मणिः** a crystal.

विमांसः -सं Unclean meat (as of dogs.).

विमातृ *f.* A step-mother. **–Comp. –जः** a step-mother's son.

विमानः -नं **1** Disrespect, dishonour. **2** A measure. **3** A balloon, a heavenly car (moving through the skies); पदं विमानेन विगाहमानः R. 13. 1, 7. 51; 12. 104; Ku. 2. 45, 7. 40, V. 4. 43; Ki. 7. 11. **4** A vehicle or conveyance in general; R. 16. 68. **5** A hall, splendid room or assembly-hall; R. 17. 9. **6** A palace (with seven stories); नेत्रा नीताः सततगतिना यद्विमानाग्रभूमीः Me. 69. **7** A horse. **–Comp. –चारिन्, –यान** *a.* moving in a balloon. **–राजः** **1** an excellent heavenly car; U. 3. **2** the driver of a heavenly car.

विमानना Disrespect, dishonour, contempt, humiliation; विमाननना सुभ्रु कुतः पितुर्गृहे Ku. 5. 43; अभवन्नास्य विमानना क्वचित् R. 8. 8.

विमानित *p. p.* Disrespected, dishonoured.

विमार्गः **1** A bad road. **2** A wrong road, evil conduct or course, immorality. **3** A broom. **–Comp. –गा** an unchaste woman ; विमार्गगायाश्च रुचिः स्वकांते Bv. 1. 125. **–गामिन्, –प्रस्थित** *a.* following evil courses; S. 5. 8.

विमार्गणं Searching, looking out for, seeking for.

विमिश्र, विमिश्रित *a.* Mixed, blended, mingled (with instr. or in comp.); पुंभिर्विमिश्रा नार्यश्च Mb.; दंपत्योरिह को न को न तमसि व्रीडाविमिश्रो रसः Gīt. 5.

विमुक्त *p. p.* **1** Set free, released, liberated. **2** Abandoned, given up, quitted, left. **3** Freed from. **4** Hurled, discharged. **5** Given vent to. **–Comp. –कंठ** *a.* raising a loud cry, weeping bitterly.

विमुक्तिः *f.* **1** Released, liberation. **2** Separation. **3** Absolution, final liberation.

विमुख *a.* (**खी** *f.*) **1** With the face averted or turned away from. **2** Averse, disinclined, opposed; न क्षुद्रोऽपि प्रथमसुकृतापेक्षया संश्रयाय प्राप्ते मित्रे भवति विमुखः किं पुनर्यस्तथोच्चैः Me. 17, 27; (रघूणां) मनः परस्त्रीविमुखप्रवृत्ति R. 16. 8, 19. 47. **3** Adverse; H. 1. 130. **4** Without, devoid of (in comp.); करुणाविमुखेन मृत्युना हरता त्वां वद किं न मे हृतं R. 8. 67.

विमुग्ध *a.* Confused, confounded, bewildered.

विमुद्र *a.* **1** Unsealed. **2** Opened, budded, blown.

विमूढ *p. p.* **1** Confounded, bewildered. **2** Seduced, tempted, beguiled. **3** Stupid.

विमृष्ट *p. p.* **1** Rubbed off, wiped, cleansed. **2** Considered, reflected upon, pondered over.

विमोक्षः **1** Release, liberation, freeing. **2** Discharging, shooting. **3** Final emancipation or beatitude.

विमोक्षणं-णा **1** Liberating, releasing, setting free. **2** Discharging. **3** Quitting, leaving, abandoning. **4** Laying (as eggs).

विमोचनं **1** Unloosing, unyoking. **2** Release, freedom. **3** Liberation, emancipation.

विमोहन *a.* (**ना** or **नी** *f.*) Alluring, tempting, fascinating. **–नः-नं** N. of a division of Hell. **–नं** Seducing, tempting, fascinating.

विंबः-बं See बिंब.

विंबकः See बिंबक.

विंबटः The mustard plant.

विंबिका: See बिंबिका.

विंबा-बी *f.* N. of a creeper.

विंबित See बिंबित.

विंबुः The betel-nut tree.

वियत् *n.* The sky, atmosphere, ether; पश्योदग्रप्लुतत्वाद्वियति बहुतरं स्तोकमुर्व्यां प्रयाति S. 1. 7; R. 13. 40. **–Comp. –गंगा** **1** the heavenly Ganges. **2** the galaxy. **–चारिन्** (**वियच्चारिन्**) *m.* a kite. **–भूतिः** *f.* darkness. **–मणिः** (**वियन्मणिः**) the sun.

वियतिः A bird.

वियमः **1** Restraint, check, control. **2** Distress, pain, affliction. **3** Cessation, stop.

वियात *a.* **1** Bold (**धृष्ट**). **2** Audacious, shameless, impudent.

वियाम See वियम.

वियुक्त *p. p.* **1** Detached, severed, separated. **2** Separated from, deserted by. **3** Free from, deprived of (with instr. or in comp.).

वियुत *p. p.* Separated from, being deprived of; V. 4. 18.

वियोगः **1** Separation, disunion; अयमेकपदे तया वियोगः सहसा चोपनतः सुदुःसहो मे V. 4. 3; त्वयोपस्थितवियोगस्य तपोवनस्यापि समवस्था दृश्यते S. 4; संधत्ते भृशमरतिं हि सद्वियोगः Ki. 5. 41; R. 12. 10; Me. 83, 88; Si. 12. 63. **2** Absence, loss. **3** Subtraction.

वियोगिन् *a.* Separated. **–m.** The ruddy goose.

वियोगिनी **1** A woman separated from her lover or husband; **गुरुनिः-** श्वसितैः कपिर्मनीषी निरणैषीदथनां वियोगिनीति Bv. 4. 35. **2** N. of a metre; (see App. I.)

वियोजित *p. p.* **1** Separated. **2** Separated from, deprived of.

वियोनिः-नी **1** Manifold birth. **2** The womb of animals (Kull. on Ms. 12. 77). **3** A debased or ignominious birth.

विरक्त *p. p.* **1** Very red, ruddy; R. 13. 64. **2** Discoloured. **3** Changed in mind, disaffected, displeased; Bh. 2. 2. **4** Free from passion or worldly attachment, indifferent. **5** Impassioned.

विरक्तिः *f.* **1** Change of disposition, dissatisfaction, discontent, disaffection. **2** Estrangement. **3** Indifference, absence of desire, freedom from passion or worldly attachment.

विरचनं-ना **1** Arrangement, disposition; Si. 5. 21. **2** Contriving, constructing. **3** Formation, creation. **4** Composition, compilation.

विरचित *p. p.* 1 Arranged, made, formed, prepared. 2 Contrived; constructed. 3 Written, composed. 4 Trimmed, dressed, embellished, ornamented. 5 Put on, worn. 6 Set, inlaid.

विरज *a.* Free from dust or passion. –**जः** An epithet of Vishṇu.

विरजस्, विरजस्क *a.* 1 Free from dust. 2 Free from passion; *Si.* 20. 80. 3 From menstrual excretion.

विरजस्का A woman in whom the menstrual secretion has ceased.

विरंचः,-चिः N. of Brahman.

विरटः A kind of black agallochum.

विरणं A kind of fragrant grass; cf. वीरण.

विरत *p. p.* 1 Ceased or desisting from (with abl.). 2 Rested, stopped, ceased. 3 Ended, concluded, at an end; विरतं गेयमृतुर्निरुत्सवः R. 8. 66.

विरतिः *f.* 1 Cessation, stop, discontinuance. 2 Rest, end, pause. 3 Indifference to worldly attachments; Bh. 3. 79.

विरमः 1 Cessation, stop. 2 Sunset.

विरल *a.* 1 Having interstices, separated by intervals, thin, not thick or compact; विपर्यासं यातो घनविरलभावः क्षितिरुहां U. 2. 27; भवति विरलभक्तिर्म्लानपुष्पोपहारः R. 5. 74. 2 Fine delicate. 3 Loose, wide apart. 4 Rare, scarcely found, unfrequent; Pt. 1. 29. 5 Few, little (referring to number or quantity); तत्त्वं किमपि काव्यानां जानाति विरलो भुवि B. v. 1. 117; विरलातपच्छविः *Si.* 9. 3. 6 Remote, distant, long (as time, distance &c.). –लं Curds, coagulated milk. –लं *ind.* Scarcely, rarely, not frequently. –**Comp.** –जानुक *a.* bandy-legged, bow-kneed. –द्रवा a kind of gruel.

विरस *a.* 1 Tasteless, insipid, flavourless. 2 Unpleasant; disagreeable, painful; तावत्कोकिल विरसान् यापय दिवसान् वनांतरे निवसन् Bv. 1. 7. 3 Cruel, unfeeling. –सः Pain.

विरहः 1 Parting with, separation. 2 Especially the separation of lovers; सा विरहे तव दीना Gît. 4; क्षणमपि विरहः पुरा न सेहे *ibid.*; Me. 8, 12, 29, 85, 87. 3 Absence. 4 Want. 5 Desertion, abandonment, relinquishment. –**Comp.** –अनलः the fire of separation. –अवस्था the state of separation. –आर्त, –उत्कंठ, –उत्सुक *a.* suffering from separation, pining away in separation. –उत्कंठिता a woman distrssed by the absence of her lover or husband, one of the several classes of a Nâyikâ in poetic compositions; see S. D. 121. –ज्वरः the fever or anguish of separation.

विरहिणी 1 A woman separated from her lover or husband. 2 Wages, hire.

विरहित *p. p.* 1 Deserted, abandoned, forsaken. 2 Separated from. 3 Lonely, solitary. 4 Bereft of, devoid or destitute of, free from (mostly in comp.).

विरहिन् *a.* (णी *f.*) Absent from, being separated from a mistress or lover; नृत्यति युवतिजनेन समं सखि विरहिजनस्य दुरंते Gît. 1.

विरागः 1 Change of colour. 2 Change of disposition, disaffection, discontent, dissatisfaction; विरागकारणेषु परिहृतेषु Mu. 1. 3 Aversion, disinclination. 4 Indifference to worldly attachments, freedom from passion.

विराज् *m.* 1 Beauty, splendour. 2 A man of the Kshatriya or warrior tribe. 3 The first progeny of Brahman; cf. Ms. 1. 32; तस्मात् विराजायत Rv. 10. 90. 5. (where विराज् is represented as born from *Purusha*). 4 The body. –*f.* N. of a Vedic metre.

विराज See विराज्.

विराजित *p. p.* 1 Irradiated, illuminated. 2 Displayed, manifested.

विराटः 1 N. of a district in India. 2 N. of a king of the Matsyas. The Pâṇḍavas lived *incognito* in the service of this king for one year, (the thirteenth of their exile) having assumed different disguises. His daughter Uttarâ was married to Abhimanyu and was mother of Parîkshit who succeeded Yudhishthira to the throne of Hastinâpura. –**Comp.** –जः a sort of inferior diamond. –पर्वन् *n.* the fourth book of the Mahâbhârata.

विराटकः A sort of inferior diamond, a diamond of inferior quality.

विराणिन् *m.* An elephant.

विराद्ध *p. p.* 1 Opposed, counteracted. 2 Offended, injured, treated with contempt; see the quotations under राध् with वि.

विराधः 1 Opposition. 2 Annoyance, vexation, molestation. 3 N. of a powerful Râkshasa slain by Râma.

विराधनं 1 Opposing. 2 Hurting, injuring, offending. 3 Pain, anguish.

विरामः 1 Cessation, discontinuance. 2 End, termination, conclusion; रजनिरिदानीमियमपि याति विरामं Gît. 5; U. 3. 16, Mâl. 9. 34. 3 Pause, stop. 4 The stop or pause of the voice; Mk. 3. 5. 5 A small oblique stroke placed under a consonant, usually at the end of a sentence. 6 N. of Vishṇu.

विराल See बिडाल.

विराव Clamour, noise, sound; आलोकशब्दं वयसां विरावैः R. 2. 9, 16. 31.

विराविन् *a.* 1 Weeping, crying, shouting. 2 Lamenting. –णी 1 Weeping, crying. 2 A broom.

विरिंचः, विरिंचनः N. of Brahman.

विरिंचिः 1 N. of Brahman; Vikr. 1. 46.; N. 3. 44; *Si.* 9. 9. 2 Of Vishṇu. 3 Of *Siva*.

विरुग्ण *p. p.* 1 Broken to pieces. 2 Destroyed. 3 Bent. 4 Blunted.

विरुत *p. p.* 1 Screamed, shouted. 2 Resounding, filled with cries –तं 1 Crying, shrieking, roaring &c. 2 Cry, sound, noise, clamour, din. 3 Singing, humming, chirping, buzzing; परभृतविरुतं कलं यथा प्रतिवचनीकृतमेभिरीदृशं S. 4. 9.

विरुदः-दं 1 Proclaiming. 2 Crying aloud. 3 A panegyric laudatory poem; गद्यपद्यमयी राजस्तुतिर्विरुदमुच्यते S. D. 570; नदंति मददंतिनः परिलसंति वाजिव्रजाः पठंति विरुदावलीमहितमंदिरे वंदिनः ॥ R. G.

विरुदितं Loud cry or lamentation; U. 3. 30. v. l.

विरुद्ध *p. p.* 1 Hindered, checked, opposed, obstructed. 2 Blocked up, confined or shut up. 3 Besieged, blockaded. 4 Opposed to, inconsistent with, incongruous, incompatible. 5 Contrary, opposite, opposed in quality. 6 Contradictory, proving the reverse, (as a *hetu* in Logic); *e. g.* शब्दो नित्यः कृतकत्वात् T. S. 7 Hostile, adverse, inimical. 8 Unfavourable, unpropitious. 9 Prohibited, forbidden (as food.) 10 Wrong, improper –द्धं 1 Opposition, contraraiety, hostility. 2 Discord, disagreement.

विरूक्षणं 1 Roughening. 2 Acting as an astringent. 3 Blame, censure. 4 A curse, an imprecation.

विरूढ *p. p.* 1 Grown, germinated, shot up; Mk. 1. 9. 2 Produced, born, arisen. 3 Grown, increased. 4 Budded, blossomed. 5 Ascended, mounted.

विरूप *a.* (पा or पी *f.*) 1 Deformed, ugly, misshapen, disfigured; Pt. 1. 143. 2 Unnatural, monstrous. 3 Multiform, diverse –पं 1 Deformity, ugliness. 2 Variety of form, nature or character. –**Comp.** –अक्ष *a.* having deformed eyes, वपुर्विरूपाक्षं Ku. 5. 72. (-क्षः) N. of *Siva* (having an unusual number of eyes); दृशा दग्धं मनसिजं जीवयंति दृशैव याः विरूपाक्षस्य जयिनीस्ताः स्तुवे वामलोचनाः Vb. 1. 2; Ku. 6. 21. –करणं 1 disfiguring. 2 injuring. –चक्षुस् *m.* an epithet of *Siva*. –रूप *a.* deformed.

विरूपिन् *a.* (णी *f.*) Deformed, ugly, disfigured.

विरेकः 1 Evacuation of the bowels, purging. 2 A purgative.

विरेचनं See विरेक.

विरेचित *a.* Purged, evacuated.

विरेफः 1 A river, stream. 2 Absence of the letter र.

विरोकः-कं A hole, pit, chasm. –कः A ray of light.

विरोचनः 1 The sun. 2 The moon 3 Fire 4 N. of the son of Prarhâda and father of Bali. -Comp. -सुतः an epithet of Bali.

विरोधः 1 Opposition, obstruction, impediment. 2 Blockade, siege, investment. 3 Restraint, check. 4 Inconsistency, incongruity, contradiction. 5 Antithesis, contrast. 6 Enmity, hostility ; विरोधो विश्रांतः U. 6. 11 ; Pt. 1. 332 ; R. 10. 13. 7 A quarrel, disagreement. 8 A calamity, misfortune. 9 (In Rhet.) An apparent incongruity which is merely verbal and is explained away by properly construing the passage ; it consists in representing objects as antithetical to one another though in the nature of things they are not so:—representing things as being together though really they cannot be together ; (this figure is largely used by Bâṇa and Subandhu; पुष्पवत्यपि पवित्रा, कृष्णोप्यसुदर्शनः, भरतोपि शत्रुघ्नः being familiar instances); it is thus defined by Mammata :—विरोधः सोऽविरोधेऽपि विरुद्धत्वेन यद्वचः K. P. 10; this figure is also called विरोधाभास. -Comp.-उक्तिः *f.*,-वचनं contradiction, opposition. -कारिन् *a.* fomenting quarrels. -कृत् *a.* opposing. (-*m.*) an enemy.

विरोधनं 1 Hindering, opposing, obstructing. 2 Besieging, blockading. 3 Opposition, resistance. 4 Contradiction, inconsistency.

विरोधिन् *a.* (नी *f.*) 1 Resisting, opposing, obstructing. 2 Besieging. 3 Contradictory, opposed to, inconsistent with ; तपोवन° *S.* 1. 4 Hostile, inimical, adverse ; विरोधिसत्त्वोज्झितपूर्वमत्सरं Ku. 5. 17. 5 Quarrelsome. -*m.* An enemy ; *Si.* 16. 64.

विरोप(ह)णं Healing (as a sore); व्रणविरोपणं तैलं *S.* 4. 14.

विल् I. 6 P. (विलति) 1 To cover, conceal. 2 To break, divide. -II. 10. U. (वेलयति-ते) To throw, send forth.

विलं See बिल.

विलक्ष *a.* 1 Having no characteristic or distinguishing marks. 2 Bewildered, embarrassed. 3 Surprised, astonished. 4 Ashamed, abashed, disconcerted ; गोत्रेषु स्खलितस्तदा भवति च व्रीडाविलक्षश्चिरं *S.* 6. 5. 5 Strange, unusual.

विलक्षण *a.* 1 Having no characteristic or distinguishing marks. 2 Different, other. 3 Strange, extraordinary, unusual. 4 Possessed of inauspicious marks. -णं A vain or useless state.

विलक्षित *p. p.* 1 Distinguished, perceived, seen, discovered. 2 Discernible by. 3 Dismayed, perplexed, embarrassed, puzzled. 4 Vexed, annoyed.

विलग्न *a.* 1 Clinging or sticking to, resting on, fastened on ; *S.* 7. 25 ; *Si.* 9. 20. 2 Cast, fixed, directed ; Ku. 7. 50. 3 Gone by, elapsed (as time). 4 Thin, slender, delicate ; मध्येन सा वेदिविलग्नमध्या Ku. 1. 39 ; V. 4. 37. -ग्नं 1 The waist. 2 The hips. 3 The rising of constellations.

विलंघनं 1 Transgressing, overstepping. 2 Offence, transgression, injury.

विलंघित *p. p.* 1 Passed over or beyond, gone over. 2 Transgressed. 3 Surpassed, excelled. 4 Overcome, defeated.

विलज्ज *a.* Shameless, unabashed.

विलपनं 1 Talking. 2 Talking idly, chattering, prattle. 3 Lamenting, wailing ; विलपनविनोदोऽप्यसुलभः U. 3. 30. 4 The sediment of any oily substance.

विलपितं 1 Lamentation, wailing. 2 A wail.

विलंबः 1 Hanging over, pendulousness. 2 Tardiness, delay, procrastination.

विलंबनं 1 Hanging down, depending. 2 Delay, procrastination ; न कुरु नितंबिनि गमनविलंबनं Gît. 5 ; or तन्मुग्धे विफलं विलंबनमसौ रम्योऽभिसारक्षणः *ibid.*

विलंबिका Constipation.

विलंबित *p. p.* 1 Hanging, depending. 2 Pendent, pendulous. 3 Depending on. closely connected with. 4 Tardy, delayed, retarded. 5 Slow (as time in music). See लंब् with वि). -तं Delay.

विलंबिन् *a.* (नी *f.*) 1 Hanging down, depending, pendent ; नवांबुभिर्भूरिविलंबिनो घनाः *S.* 5. 12:; अलघुविलंबिपयोधरोपरुद्धाः *Si.* 4. 29,. 59 ; Ku. 1. 14 ; Ki. 5. 6 ; R. 16. 84, 18. 25 ; Mk. 5. 13. 2 Delaying, dilatory, being slow; भवति विलंबिनि विगलितलज्जा विलपति रोदिति वासकसज्जा Gît. 6.

विलंभः 1 Liberality. 2 A gift, donation.

विलयः 1 Dissolution, liquefaction. 2 Destruction, death, end, U.7. 3 Destruction or dissolution of the world; (विलयं गम् to be dissolved, to end, to be terminated ; दिवसोऽनुमित्रमगमद्विलयं *Si* 9. 17).

विलयनं 1 Dissolving liquefying, dissolution. 2 Corroding. 3 Removing, taking away. 4 Attenuating. 5 An attenuant.

विलसत् *pres. a.* (न्ती *f.*) 1 Glittering, shining, bright. 2 Flashing, darting. 3 Waving. 4 Sportive; playful.

विलसनं 1 Glittering, flashing, gleaming. 2 Sporting, dallying.

विलसित *p. p.* 1 Glittering, shining, gleaming. 2 Appeared, manifested. 3 Sportive, wanton. -तं 1 Glittering, gleaming. 2 A gleam, flash; रोषोभुवां मुहुरमुत्र हिरण्मयीनां भासस्तडिद्विलसितानि विडंबयंति Ki. 5. 46, Me. 81, V. 4. 3 Appearance, manifestation; as in अज्ञानविलसितं &c. 4 Sport, play, dalliance, amorous or wanton gesture.

विलापः Wailing, lamentation, a wail, moan; लंकास्त्रीणां पुनश्चक्रे विलापाचार्यकं शरैः R. 12. 78.

विलालः 1 A cat (for बिडाल). 2 An instrument, a machine.

विलासः 1 Sport, play, pastime. 2 Amorous pastime, diversion, pleasure, as in विलासमेखला R. 8. 64; so विलासकाननं, विलासमंदिरं &c. 3 Coquetry, dalliance, affectation, wantonness, graceful movement or play, any feminine gesture indicative of amorous sentiment; *S.* 2. 2; Ku. 5. 13; *Si.* 9. 26. 4 Grace, beauty, elegance, charm; Mâl. 2. 6. 5 Flash, gleam.

विलासनं 1 Sport, play, pastime. 2 Wantonness, dalliance.

विलासवती A wanton or amorous woman; R. 9. 48; Rs. 1. 12.

विलासिका A drama in one act full of love-incidents; it is thus defined in S. D. :—शृंगारबहुलैकांका दशलास्यांगसंयुता। विदूषकविटाभ्यां च पीटमर्देन भूषिता। हीना गर्भविमर्षाभ्यां संधिभ्यां हीननायका। स्वल्पवृत्ता सुनेपथ्या विख्याता सा विलासिका 552.

विलासिन् *a.* (नी *f.*) Sportive, playful, dallying, wanton, coquettish, R. 6. 14. -*m.* 1 A sensualist, voluptuary, an amorous person; उपमानमभूद्विलासिनां करणं यत्तव कांतिमत्तया Ku. 4. 5. 2 Fire. 3 The moon. 4 A snake. 5 An epithet of Krishṇa or Vishṇu. 6 Of *S*iva. 7 Of the god of love.

विलासिनी 1 A woman (in general). 2 A coquettish or wanton woman; हरिरिह मुग्धवधूनिकरे विलासिनी विलसति केलिपरे Gît. 1; Ku. 7. 59; *Si.* 8. 70; R. 6. 17. 3 A wanton, harlot.

विलिखनं Scratching, scraping, writing.

विलिप्त *p. p.* Anointed, besmeared, smeared over.

विलीन *p. p.* 1 Sticking to, clung or attached to. 2 Perched or settled on, alighting on. 3 Contiguous to, in contact with. 4 Melted, dissolved, liquefied. 5 Disappeared, vanished. 6 Dead, perished.

विलुंचनं Tearing off, peeling.

विलुंठनं Robbing, plundering.

विलुप्त *p. p.* 1 Broken or torn off; Pt. 2. 2. 2 Seized, snatched away, carried off. 3 Robbed, plundered. 4 Destroyed, ruined. 5 Impaired, mutilated.

विलुंपकः A thief, robber, ravisher.

विलुलित *p. p.* 1 Moving to and fro, unsteady, shaken, tossed about, tremulous. 2 Disordered, disarranged; गलितकुसुमदलविलुलितकेशा Gît. 7.

विलून *p. p.* Cut off, lopped off, clipt, cut asunder.

विलेखनं 1 Scratching, scraping, making a mark or furrow. 2 Digging. 3 Uprooting.

विलेपः 1 Unguent, an ointment. 2 Mortar. 3 Plaster (in general).

विलेपनं 1 Smearing, anointing. 2 An ointment, unguent, any cosmetic or perfume for the body (such as saffron, sandal &c.), यान्येव सुरभिकुसुमधूपविलेपनादीनि K.

विलेपनी 1 A woman scented with perfumes. 2 A woman beautifully dressed or attired. (सुवेशा). 3 Rice-gruel.

विलेपिका, विलेपी, विलेप्यः Rice-gruel.

विलोकनं 1 Seeing, looking at, observing; Ki. 5. 16. 2 Sight, observation; Si. 1. 29.

विलोकित *p. p.* 1 Seen, observed, viewed, beheld. 2 Examined, thought about. -तं A look, glance; *S.* 2. 3.

विलोचनं The eye; R. 7. 8; Ku. 4. 2. 3. 67. -Comp. -अंबु *n.* tears.

विलोडनं Agitating, shaking about, stirring up, churning; Si. 14. 83.

विलोडित *p. p.* Shaken, churned, stirred, agitated. -तं Buttermilk.

विलोपः 1 Taking away, carrying off, seizure, plunder. 2 Loss, destruction, disappearance.

विलोपनं 1 Cutting off. 2 Carrying away. 3 Destroying, desrtuction.

विलोभः Attraction, seduction, allurement.

विलोभनं 1 Enticing, alluring. 2 An allurement, temptation, seduction. 3 Praise, flattering.

विलोम *a.* (मी *f.*) 1 Inverted, reverse, inverse, contrary, opposite. 2 Produced in the reverse order. 3 Backward. -मः 1 Reverse order, inversion. 2 A dog. 3 A snake. 4 N. of Varuṇa. -मं A waterwheel, a machine for raising water from a well. -Comp. -उत्पन्न, -ज, -जात, -वर्ण *a.* 'born in the reverse order'; *i. e.* 'born of a mother whose caste is superior to the father's; cf. प्रतिलोमक also. -क्रिया, -विधिः 1 a reverse action. 2 A rule of inversion (in math.). -जिह्वः an elephant.

विलोमी The emblic myrobalan.

विलोल *a.* 1 Shaking about, trembling, tremulous, unsteady, rolling, waving, tossing about; पृषतीषु विलोलमीक्षितं R. 8. 59; Si. 9. 8, 15. 62, 20. 42; Ve. 2. 28; R. 7. 41, 16. 68. 2 Loose, disordered, dishevelled (as hair); U 3. 4.

विलोहितः N. of Rudra.

विल्ल See बिल्ल.

विल्व See बिल्व.

विवक्षा 1 A desire to speak. 2 Wish, desire. 3 Meaning, sense. 4 Intention, purpose.

विवक्षित *a.* 1 Intended to be said or spoken; विवक्षितं ह्यनुक्तमनुतापं जनयति *S.* 3. 2 Meant, intended, purposed. 3 Wished, desired. 4 Favourite. -तं 1 Purpose, intention. 2 Sense, meaning.

विवक्षु *a.* Wishing or about to speak; Ku. 5. 83.

विवत्सा A calfless cow.

विवधः 1 A yoke for carrying burdens. 2 A road, highway. 3 A load, burden. 4 Storing grain. 5 A pitcher.

विवधिकः 1 A carrier of loads, porter. 2 A pedlar, hawker.

विवरं 1 A fissure, hole, cavity, hollow, vacuity: यश्चकार विवरं शिलाघने ताडकोरसि स रामसायकः R. 11. 18, 9. 61, 19. 7. 2 An interstice, interval, intervening space; *S.* 7. 7. 3 A solitary place; Ki. 12. 37. 4 A fault, flaw, defect, weak point. 5 A breach, wound. 6 The number 'nine'. -Comp. -नालिका a flute, fife, pipe.

विवरणं 1 Displaying, expressing, unfolding, opening. 2 Exposing, laying bare or open. 3 Exposition, explanation, gloss, comment, interpretation.

विवर्जनं Leaving, excluding, abandoning; Y. 1. 181.

विवर्जित *p. p.* 1 Left, abandoned. 2 Shunned. 3 Deprived of, destitute of, without (usually in comp.). 4 Given, distributed.

विवर्ण *a.* 1 Colourless, pale, wan, pallid; नरेंद्रमार्गाट्ट इव प्रपेदे विवर्णभावं स स भूमिपालः R. 6. 67. 2 Discoloured, deprived of water; *S.* 3. 14. 3 Low, vile. 4 Ignorant, stupid, unlettered. -र्णः An outcast, a man belonging to low caste.

विवर्तः 1 Turning round, revolving, whirling. 2 Rolling onward. 3 Rolling back, returning. 4 Dancing. 5 Alteration, modification, change of form, altered condition or state; शब्दब्रह्मणस्तादृशं विवर्तमितिहासं रामायणं प्रणिनाय U. 2; एको रसः करुण एव निमित्तभेदाद्भिन्नः पृथक् पृथगिवाश्रयते विवर्तान् U. 3. 47; Mv. 5. 57. 6 (In Vedānta phil.) An apparent or illusory form, an unreal appearance caused by अविद्या or human error; (this is a favourite doctrine of the Vedāntins according to whom the whole visible world is a mere illusion—an unreal and illusory appearance—while Brahman or Supreme spirit is the only real entity; as a serpent (सर्प) is a *vivarta* of a rope (रज्जु), so is the world a *vivarta* of the real entity Brahman, and the illusion is removed by *Vidyā* or true knowledge; cf. Bhavabhûti; विद्याकल्पेन मरुता मेघानां भूयसामपि । ब्रह्मणीव विवर्तानां क्वापि विप्रलयः कृतः ॥ U. 6. 6. 7 A heap, multitude, collection, an assemblage. -Comp. -वादः the doctrine of the Vedāntins that the visible world is illusory and Brahman alone is the real entity.

विवर्तनं 1 Revolving, revolution, whirling round. 2 Rolling about, turning round; *S.* 5. 6. 3 Rolling back, returning. 4 Rolling down, descending. 5 Existing, abiding. 6 Reverential salutation. 7 Passing through various states or existences. 8 An altered condition; U. 4. 15; Mâl. 4. 7.

विवर्धनं 1 Increasing. 2 Increase, augmentation, growth. 3 Enlargement, aggrandisement.

विवर्धित *p. p.* 1 Increased, augmented. 2 Advanced, promoted, furthered. 3 Gratified, satisfied.

विवश *a.* 1 Uncontrolled, unsubdued. 2 Having lost control over oneself, dependent, subject, under control (of another), helpless; परीता रक्षोभिः श्रयति विवशा कामपि दशां Bv. 1. 83, Mu. 6. 18; Si. 20. 58, H. 1. 172; Mv. 6. 32, 63. 3 Insensible, not master of oneself; विवशा कामवधूर्विबोधिता Ku. 4. 1. 4 Dead, perished; उपलब्धवती दिवश्च्युतं विवशा शापनिवृत्तिकारणं R. 8. 82. 5 Desirous or apprehensive of death.

विवसन *a.* Naked, unclothed. -नः A Jaina mendicant.

विवस्वत् *m.* 1 The sun; त्वष्टा विवस्वंतमिवोल्लिलेख Ki. 17. 48, 5. 48, R. 10. 30, 17. 48. 2 N. of Aruṇa. 3 N. of the present Manu. 4 A god. 5 The *Arka* plant.

विवहः N. of one of the seven tongues of fire.

विवाकः A judge; cf. प्राड्विवाक.

विवादः 1 (*a*) A dispute, contest, contention, controversy, discussion, debate, quarrel, strife; अलं विवादेन Ku. 5. 83; एतयोर्विवाद एव मे न रोचते M. 1; एकाप्सरः- प्रार्थितयोर्विवादः R. 7. 53. (*b*) Argument, argumentation, discussion. 2 Contradiction; एष विवाद एव प्रत्याययति *S.* 7. 3 A litigation, lawsuit, contest at law; सीमाविवादः, विवादपदं &c.; it is thus defined :—ऋणादिदायकलहे द्वयोर्बहुतरस्य वा विवादो व्यवहारश्च; see व्यवहार also. 4 Crying aloud, sounding. 5 An order, command; R. 18. 43. -Comp. -अर्थिन् *m.* 1 a litigant. 2 a plaintiff, complainant, prosecutor. -पदं a title of dispute. -वस्तु *n.* the subject of dispute, the matter at issue.

विवादिन् *a.* 1 Disputing, contending, disputations, quarrelling. 2

Litigating. *-m.* A litigant, party in a law-suit.

विवारः 1 Opening, expansion. 2 Expansion of the throat in the articulation of letters, (one of the Abhyantara Prayatnas, opp. संवार, see Sk. on P. I. 1. 9).

विवासः, विवासनं Banishment, sending into exile, expulsion ; रामस्य गात्रमसि दुर्वहगर्भखिन्नसीताविवासनपटोः करुणा कुतस्ते U. 2. 10.

विवासित *p. p.* Banished, exiled, expelled.

विवाहः Marriage ; (Hindu lawgivers enumerate eight forms of marriage; ब्राह्मो दैवस्तथैवार्षः प्राजापत्यस्तथासुरः। गांधर्वो राक्षसश्चैव पैशाचश्चाष्टमोऽधमः Ms. 3. 21 ; see Y. 1. 58-61 also ; for explanation of these forms see s. v.) **-Comp.** **-चतुष्टयं** marrying four wives. **-दीक्षा** the marriage ceremony or rite.

विवाहित *p. p.* Married.

विवाह्यः 1 A son-in-law. 2 A bridegroom.

विविक्त *p. p.* 1 Separated, detached, disjoined, abstracted. 2 Lonely, solitary, retired, sequestered. 3 Single, alone. 4 Distinguished, discriminated. 5 Judicious. 6 Pure, faultless ; Ratn. 1. 21. **-क्तं** 1 A lonely or solitary place ; *Si.* 8. 70. 2 Loneliness, privacy, seclusion. **-क्ता** An unlucky or ill-fated woman, one disliked by her husband (दुर्भगा).

विविग्न *a.* Very much agitated or terrified ; R. 18. 13.

विविध *a.* Various, diverse, manifold, multiform, sundry ; Ms. 1. 8, 39.

विवीतः An enclosed or preserved spot of ground, such as pasture-land.

विवृक्त *p. p.* Left, abandoned, deserted.

विवृक्ता A woman disliked by her husband ; cf. विविक्ता.

विवृत *p. p.* 1 Displayed, manifested, expressed. 2 Evident, open. 3 Uncovered, exposed, laid bare. 4 Opened, unclosed, bare, open. 5 Proclaimed. 6 Expounded, explained, commented upon. 7 Expanded, spread out. 8 Extensive, large, spacious. **तं** Open articulation. **-Comp.** **-अक्ष** *a.* large-eyed. (**-क्षः**) a cock. **-द्वार** *a.* with the gates thrown open Ku. 4. 26.

विवृतिः *f.* 1 Display, manifestation. 2 Expansion. 3 Exposure, discovery. 4 Exposition, comment, interpretation, gloss.

विवृत्त *p. p.* 1 Turned round. 2 Turning round, revolving, rolling whirling.

विवृत्तिः *f.* 1 Turning round, whirling, revolution. 2 (In gram.) A hiatus.

विवृद्ध *p. p.* 1 Grown up. 2 Increased, augmented, heightened, enhanced, intensified (as grief, joy &c.). 3 Copious, large, plentiful.

विवृद्धिः *f.* 1 Growth, increase, augmentation, development ; ययुः शरीरावयवा विवृद्धिं R. 18. 49 ; विवृद्धिमत्राश्नुवते वचांसि 13. 4 ; so शोक,° हर्ष° &c. 2 Prosperity.

विवेकः 1 Discrimination, judgment, discernment, discretion ; काश्यपि यातस्तथापि च विवेकः Bv. 1. 68, 66 ; ज्ञातोयं जलधर तावको विवेकः 96. 2 Consideration, discussion, investigation; यच्छृंगारविवेकतत्त्वमपि यत्काव्येषु लीलायितं Gît. 12, so द्वैत°, धर्म.° 3 Distinction, difference, discriminating, (between two things) ; नीरक्षीरविवेके हंसालस्यं त्वमेव तनुषे चेत् Bv. 1. 53 ; Bk. 17. 60. 4 (In Vedânta phil.) The power of distinguishing between the visible world and the invisible spirit, or of separating reality from mere semblance or illusion. 5 True knowledge. 6 A receptacle for water, basin, reservoir. **-Comp.** **-ज्ञ** *a* judicious, discriminative. **-ज्ञानं** the faculty of discrimination. **-दृश्वन्** *m.* a discerning man. **-पदवी** reflection, consideration.

विवेकिन् *a.* Discriminating, discreet, judicious. *-m.* 1 A judge, discriminator. 2 A philosopher

विवेक्तृ *m.* 1 A judge. 2 A sage, philosopher.

विवेचनं-ना 1 Discrimination. 2 Discussion, consideration. 3 Settlement, decision.

विवोढ़ *m.* A bridegroom, husband.

विव्वोक See बिब्बोक ; विब्बोकस्ते सुरविजयिनो वर्त्मपाती बभूव Ud. S. 43.

विश् 6 P. (विशति, विष्ट) 1 To enter, go or enter into ; विवेश कश्चिज्जटिलस्तपोवनं Ku. 5. 30 ; R. 6. 10, 12 ; Me. 102 ; Bg. 11. 29. 2 To go or come to, come into the possession of, fall to the share of ; उपदा विविशुः शश्वन्नोत्सेकाः कोशलेश्वरं R. 4. 70. 3 To sit or settle down upon. 4 To penetrate, pervade. 5 To enter upon, undertake. *-Caus.* (वेशयति-ते) To cause to enter. *-Desid.* (विविक्षति) To wish to enter -WITH **अनु** 1 to enter into. 2 to enter after some one else, follow in entering. **-अनुप्र** to enter into; (fig.) to adapt or accommodate oneself to the will of; यस्य यस्य हि यो भावतस्य तस्य हि तं नरः। अनुप्रविश्य मेधावी क्षिप्रमात्मवशं नयेत् Pt. 1. 68. **-अभिनि** (Atm.) 1 to enter into, occupy. 2 to resort to, take possession of ; अभिनिविशते सन्मार्गे Sk. ; भयं तावत्सेव्याद्भिनिविशते सेवकजनं Mu. 5. 12 ; Bk. 8. 80. **-आ** 1 to enter ; R. 2. 26. 2 to possess, occupy, take possession of. 3 to approach. 4 to go or attain to a particular state. **-उप** 1 to sit down, take a seat ; Bg. 1. 46. 2 to encamp. 3 to enter upon, practise ; प्रायमुपविशति. 4 to abstain from food ; Bk. 7. 7. 5. **-नि** (Atm.) 1 to sit down, take a seat ; नवांबुदश्याममवुर्न्यविक्षत (आसने) *Si.* 1. 19. 2 to halt, encamp ; R. 12. 68. 3 to enter ; रामशालां न्यविक्षत Bk. 4. 28, 6. 143, 8. 7, R. 9. 82. 4 to be fixed on, be directed towards ; सूर्यानिविष्टदृष्टिः R. 14. 66. 5 to be devoted or attached to, be intent on, practise ; श्रुतिप्रामाण्यतो विद्वान्स्वधर्मे निविशेत वै Ms. 2. 8. 6 to marry (for निर्विश्). (*-Caus.*) 1 to fix or direct upon, apply to (as thoughts, mind &c.) ; Bg. 12. 8. 2 to put, place, keep ; R. 6. 16, 4. 39, 7. 63. 3 to seat, install ; R. 15. 97. 4 to cause to settle in life, get married; *S.* 4. 19. 5 to encamp (as an army); R. 5. 42, 16. 37. 6 to draw, paint, portray ; चित्रे निवेश्य परिकल्पितसत्त्वयोगा *S.* 2. 9 ; M. 3. 11. 7 to commit to (writing), inscribe on ; V. 2. 14. 8 to entrust or commit to ; R. 19. 4. **-निस्** 1 to enjoy ; ज्योत्स्नावतो निर्विशति प्रदोषान् R. 6. 34 ; निर्विष्टविषयस्नेहः स दशान्तमुपेयिवान् R. 12. 1, 4. 51, 6, 50, 9. 35, 13 60, 14. 80, 18. 3, 19. 47 ; Me. 110. 2 to adorn, embellish. 3 to marry. **-प्र** 1 to enter. 2 to enter upon, begin. (*-Caus.*) to introduce, usher. **-विनि** to be placed in, be seated in. (*-Caus.*) 1 to fix, place ; Ku. 1. 49, R. 6. 63 ; मदुरसि कुचकलशं विनिवेशय Gît. 12. 2 to populate; colonize; Ku. 6. 37. **-सं** 1 to enter. 2 to sleep, lie down to rest ; संविष्टः कुशशयने निशां निनाय R. 1. 95 ; Ms. 4. 55, 7. 225. 3 to cohabit, have sexual intercourse with ; षोडशर्तुनिशाः स्त्रीणां तस्मिन् युग्मासु संविशेत् Y. 1. 79 ; Ms. 3. 48. 4 to enjoy. **-समा** 1 to enter ; Bk. 8. 27. 2 to approach. 3 to be devoted to, be intent on. **-संनि** (*Caus.*) 1 to place, put. 2 to install or place on ; R. 12. 58.

विश् *m.* 1 A man of the third caste, a Vaisya. 2 A man in general. 3 People. *-f* 1 People, subjects. 2 A daughter. **-Comp.** **-पण्यं** goods, merchandise. **-पतिः** (also **विशांपतिः**) a king, lord of subjects.

विशं The fibres of the stalk of a lotus ; cf. बिस **-Comp.** **-आकरः** a kind of plant (भद्रचूड). **-कंठा** a crane.

विशंकट *a.* (**टा-टी** *f.*) 1 Great, large, big ; विशंकटो वक्षसि बाणपाणिः Bk. 2. 50, *Si.* 13. 34. 2 Strong, vehement, powerful.

विशंका Fear, suspicion.

विशद *a.* 1 Clear, pure, pellucid, clean, spotless ; योगनिद्रांतविशदैः पावनैरवलोकनैः R. 10. 14, 19. 39 ; Ratn. 3. 9, Ki. 5. 12. 2 White, of a pure, white colour ; निर्धौतहारगुलिकाविशदं हिमांभः R. 5. 70 ; Ku. 1. 44, 6. 25, *Si.* 9. 26, Ki. 4. 23. 3 Bright, shining, beautiful ; Ku. 3. 33 ; *Si.* 8. 70. 4 Clear, evident, manifest. **5** Calm, free from anxiety, at ease; जातो ममायं विशदः प्रकामं (अंतरात्मा) *S*. 4. 22.

विशयः 1 Doubt, uncertainty, the second of the five members of an Adhikaraṇa, q. v. **2** Refuse, asylum.

विशरः 1 Splitting, bursting. **2** Slaughter, killing, destruction.

विशल्य *a*. Free from trouble or anxiety, secure.

विशसनं 1 Killing, slaughter, immolation; U. 4. 5. **2** Ruin. **-नः 1** A sabre, crooked sword. **2** A sword in general.

विशस्त *p. p*. **1** Cut up, hacked. **2** Rude, ill-mannered. **3** Praised, celebrated.

विशस्तृ *m*. **1** An immolator. **2** A Châṇḍâla.

विशस्त्र *a*. Weaponless, unarmed, defenceless.

विशाखः 1 N. of Kârtikeya; Mv. 2. 38. **2** An attitude in shooting (in which the archer stands with the feet a span apart). **3** A beggar petitioner. **4** A spindle. **5** N. of Siva. **-Comp. -जः** the orange tree.

विशाखल See विशाख (2).

विशाखा (Usually in the dual) N. of the 16th lunar mansion consisting of two stars; किमत्र चित्रं यदि विशाखे शशांकलेखामनुवर्तेते *S*. 3.

विशायः Sleeping in rotation, the rest enjoyed in rotation by the sentinels on watch.

विशारणं 1 Splitting, rending. **2** Killing, slaughter.

विशारद *a*. **1** Clever, skilful or proficient in, versed in, conversant with (usually in comp.); मधुरालापविशारदाः R. 9. 29, 8. 17. **2** Learned, wise. **3** Famous, celebrated. **4** Bold, confident. **-दः** The Bakula tree.

विशाल *a*. **1** Large, great, extensive, spacious, broad, wide; गृहैर्विशालैरपि भूरिशालैः Si. 3. 50, 11. 23; R. 2. 21, 6. 32. Bg. 9. 21. **2** Rich or abounding in; श्रीविशालां विशालां Me. 30. **3** Eminent, illustrious, great, noble, celebrated. **-लः 1** A kind of deer. **2** A kind of bird. **-ला 1** N. of the town Ujjayinî; पूर्वोद्दिष्टामनुसर पुरीं श्रीविशालां विशालां Me. 30. **2** N. of a river. **-Comp. -अक्ष** *a*. large-eyed. (**-क्षः**) an epithet of Siva. (**-क्षी**) an epithet of Pârvatî.

विशिख *a*. Crownless, crestless, pointless. **-खः 1** An arrow; माधव मनसिजविशिखभयादिव भावनया त्वयि लीना Gît. 4; R. 5. 50; Mv. 2. 38. **2** A kind of reed. **3** An iron crow.

विशिखा 1 A spade. **2** A spindle. **3** A needle or pin. **4** A minute arrow. **5** A highway. **6** A barber's wife.

विशित *a*. Sharp, acute.

विशिनं 1 A temple. **2** An abode, a house.

विशिष्ट *p. p*. **1** Distinguished, distinct. **2** Particular, special, peculiar, distinctive. **3** Characterized by, endowed with, possessed of, having. **4** Superior, best (of all), eminent, excellent, choice. **-Comp. अद्वैतवादः** a doctrine of Râmânuja which regards Brahman and Prakṛiti as identical and real entities. **-बुद्धिः** *f*. a distinguishing knowledge, differentiation. **-वर्ण** *a*. of an eminent or excellent colour.

विशीर्ण *p. p*. **1** Shattered, broken to pieces. **2** Decayed, withered. **3** Dropped or fallen down; Ku. 5. 28. **4** Shrunk, shrivelled. **-Comp. -पर्णः** the Nimba tree. **-मूर्ति** *a*. having the body destroyed; Ku. 5. 54. (**-र्तिः**) an epithet of the god of love.

विशुद्ध *a*. **1** Purified, cleansed. **2** Pure, free from vice, sin or imperfection. **3** Spotless, stainless. **4** Correct, accurate. **5** Virtuous, pious, straightforward; Mâl. 7. 1. **6** Humble.

विशुद्धिः *f*. **1** Purification, sanctification; तदंगसंसर्गमवाप्य कल्पते ध्रुवं चिताभस्मरजो विशुद्धये Ku. 5. 79, Bg. 6. 12; Ms. 6. 69, 11. 53. **2** Purity, complete purity; R. 1. 10, 12. 48. **3** Correctness, accuracy. **4** Rectification, removal of error. **5** Similarity, equality.

विशूल *a*. Without (*i. e*. not possessing) a spear; R. 15. 5.

विशृंखल *a*. **1** Without fetters (lit.). **2** Unfettered, unchecked, unrestrained, uncurbed (fig.); Si. 12. 7; Bv. 2. 177. **3** Free from all moral bonds, dissolute; Bh. 2. 59.

विशेष *a*. **1** Peculiar. **2** Copious, abundant; R. 2. 14. **-षः 1** Discrimination, distinguishing between. **2** Distinction, difference; निर्विशेषो विशेषः Bh. 3. 50. **3** Characteristic difference, peculiar mark, special property, speciality, differentia; oft. in comp. and translated by 'special', 'peculiar' &c.; *S*. 6. 6. **4** A favourable turn or crisis in sickness, a change for the better; अस्ति मे विशेषः *S*. 3; 'I feel better'. **5** A limb, member; पुपोष लावण्यमयान् विशेषान् Ku. 1. 25. **6** A species, sort, variety, kind, mode (usually at the end of comp.); भूतविशेषः U. 4; परिमलविशेषान् Pt. 1; कदलीविशेषाः Ku. 1. 36. **7** A different or various object, various particulars, (pl.); Me. 58, 64. **8** Excellence, superiority, distinction; usually at the end of comp. and translated by 'excellent', 'distinguished', 'pre-eminent', 'choice' &c. अनुभावविशेषात्तु R. 1. 37; वपुर्विशेषेण Ku. 5. 31, R. 2. 7, 6. 5; Ki. 9. 58; so आकृतिविशेषाः 'excellent forms'; अतिथिविशेषः 'a distinguished guest' &c. **9** A peculiar attribute, the eternal distinguishing nature of each of the nine *dravyas*. **10** (In logic) Individuality (opp. सामान्य), particularity. **11** A category, predicament. **12** A mark on the forehead with sandal, saffron &c. **13** A word which limits or qualifies the sense of another; see विशेषण. **14** N. of the mundane egg. **15** (In Rhet.) A figure of speech, said to be of three kinds; it is thus defined by Mammaṭa:-- विना प्रसिद्धमाधारमाधेयस्य व्यवस्थितिः। एकात्मा युगपद्वृत्तिरेकस्यानेकगोचरा। अन्यत्प्रकुर्वतः कार्यमशक्यान्यस्य वस्तुनः। तथैव करणं चेति विशेषस्त्रिविधः स्मृतः॥ K. P. 10. **-Comp. -अतिदेशः** a special supplementary rule, special extended application. **-उक्तिः** *f*. a figure of speech in which an effect is represented as not taking place though the usual necessary causes exist; विशेषोक्तिरखंडेषु कारणेषु फलावचः K. P. 10; *e. g*. हृदि स्नेहक्षयो नाभूत्स्मरदीपे ज्वलत्यपि. **-ज्ञ, -विद्** *a*. **1** knowing distinctions, critical, connoisseur. **2** learned, wise; Bh. 2. 3. **-लक्षणं, -लिंगं** a special or characteristic mark. **-वचनं** a special text or precept. **-विधिः, -शास्त्रं** a special rule.

विशेषक *a*. Distinguishing, distinctive. **-कः, -कं 1** A distinguishing feature or characteristic, an attribute. **2** A mark on the forehead with sandal, saffron &c.; M. 3. 5. **3** Drawing lines of painting on the face and person with coloured unguents and cosmetics; स्वेदोद्गमः किंपुरुषांगनानां चक्रे पदं पत्रविशेषकेषु Ku. 3. 33, R. 9. 29, Si. 3. 63, 10. 14. **-कं** A group of three stanzas forming one grammatical sentence; द्वाभ्यां युग्ममिति प्रोक्तं त्रिभिः श्लोकैर्विशेषकम्। कलापकं चतुर्भिः स्यात्तदूर्ध्वं कुलकं स्मृतम्॥.

विशेषण *a*. Attributive. **-णं 1** Distinguishing, discrimination. **2** Distinction, difference. **3** A word which particularizes or defines another, an adjective, attribute, epithet (opp. विशेष्य). (विशेषण is said to be of three kinds व्यावर्तक, विधेय and हेतुगर्भ) **4** A distinguishing feature or mark. **5** Species, kind.

विशेषतस् *ind*. Especially, particularly.

विशेषित *p. p*. **1** Distinguished. **2** Defined, particularized. **3** Distinguished by an attribute. **4** Superior, excellent.

विशेष्य *a*. **1** To be distinguished. **2** Chief, superior. **-ष्यं** The word qualified or limited by an adjective, the object to be defined or particularized by another word; a noun; विशेष्यं नाभिधा गच्छेत्क्षीणशक्तिर्विशेषणे K. P. 2.

विशोक *a*. Free from grief, happy. -कः The Asoka tree. -का Exemption from grief.

विशोधनं 1 Cleaning, clearing (fig. also); राज्यकंटकविशोधनोद्यतः Vikr. 5. 1. 2 Purifying, freeing from sin, defect &c. 3 Expiation, atonement.

विशोध्य *a*. To be purified, cleansed or corrected. -ध्यं A debt.

विशोषणं Drying up, desiccation.

विश्रणनं, विश्राणनं Giving away, bestowing, grant, gift, donation; विश्राणनाच्चान्यपयस्विनीनां R. 2. 54.

विश्रब्ध *p. p*. (Also written विस्रब्ध) 1 Confined in, confided to, entrusted. 2 Confident, fearless, confiding; Mu. 3. 3. 3 Trusty, confidential. 4 Quiet, calm, tranquil, free from anxiety. 5 Firm, steady. 6 Meek, lowly. 7 Excessive, exceeding. -ब्धं *ind*. Confidently, fearlessly, without fear or hesitation; विश्रब्धं क्रियतां वराहततिभिर्मुस्ताक्षतिः पल्वले S. 2. 6.

विश्रमः 1 Rest, repose. 2 Relaxation, cessation.

विश्रंभः 1 Trust, confidence, familiar confidence, perfect intimacy or familiarity; विश्रंभादुरसि निपत्य लब्धनिद्रां U. 1. 49, Mâl. 3. 1. 2 A confidential matter, secret; विश्रंभेष्वभ्यंतरीकरणीया K. 3 Rest, relaxation. 4 An affectionate inquiry. 5 A love-quarrel, an amorous dispute. 6 Killing. -Comp. -आलापः, -भाषणं confidential or familiar conversation. -पात्रं, -भूमिः, -स्थानं an object of confidence, a confidant, trusty person.

विश्रवः A shelter, an asylum.

विश्रवस् *m*. N. of a son of Pulastya, and father of Râvaṇa, Kumbhakarṇa, Bibhîshaṇa and Sûrpaṇakhâ by his wife Keikasî, and of Kubera by his wife Iḍâvidâ.

विश्राणित *p*. p. Given away, bestowed; निःशेषविश्राणितकोशजातं R. 5. 1.

विश्रांत *p. p*. 1 Ceased, stopped. 2 Rested, reposed. 3 Calm, tranquil composed.

विश्रांतिः *f*. 1 Rest, repose. 2 Cessation.

विश्रामः 1 Cessation, stop. 2 Rest, repose; विश्रामो हृदयस्य यत्र U. 1. 39. 3 Tranquillity, calm, composure.

विश्रावः 1 Dropping, flowing forth (for विस्राव q. v.). 2 Celebrity, renown.

विश्रुत *p. p*. 1 Well-known, renowned, celebrated. 2 Pleased, delighted, happy. 3 Flowing forth.

विश्रुतिः *f*. Fame, celebrity.

विश्लथ *a*. 1 Loose, relaxed, untied; R. 6. 73. 2 Languid.

विश्लिष्ट *p. p*. Disjoined, separated, disunited; R. 12. 76.

विश्लेषः 1 Disunion, disjunction. 2 Especially separation of lovers, or of husband and wife. 3 Separation (in general); तनयाविश्लेषदुःखैः *S*. 4. 5; चरणारविंदविश्लेष R. 13. 23. 4 Absence, loss, bereavement. 5 A chasm.

विश्लेषित *p. p*. Severed, separated, disunited.

विश्व *pron. a*. 1 All, whole, entire, universal. 2 Every, every one. -*m. pl*. N. of a particular group of deities ten in number and supposed to be sons of विश्वा; their names are:—वसुः सत्यः क्रतुर्दक्षः कालः कामो धृतिः कुरुः। पुरूरवा माद्रवाश्च विश्वेदेवाः प्रकीर्तिताः ॥ -श्वं 1 The universe, the (whole) world; इदं विश्वं पाल्यं U. 3. 30; विश्वस्मिन्नधुनान्यः कुलव्रतं पालयिष्यति कः Bv. 1. 13. 2 Dry ginger. -Comp. -आत्मन् *m*. 1 the Supreme Being (soul of the universe). 2 an epithet of Brahman. 3 of *S*iva; अथ विश्वात्मने गौरी संदिदेश मिथः सखीं Ku. 6. 1. 4 of Vishṇu. -ईशः, -ईश्वरः 1 the Supreme Being, lord of the universe. 2 an epithet of *S*iva. -कद्रु *a*. wicked low, vile. (-द्रुः) 1 a hound, dog trained for the chase. 2 sound. -कर्मन् *m*. 1 N. of the architect of gods; cf. त्वष्टृ. 2 an epithet of the sun. °जा, °सुता an epithet of संज्ञा, one of the wives of the sun. -कृत् *m*. 1 the creator of all beings. 2 an epithet of Visvakarman. -केतुः an epithet of Aniruddha. -गंधः an onion. (-धं) myrrh.-गंधा the earth. -जनं mankind. जनीन, -जन्य *a*. good for all men, suitable to all mankind, beneficial to all men; Bk. 2. 48, 21. 17. -जित् *m*. 1 N. of a particular sacrifice; R. 5. 1. 2 the noose of Varuṇa. -देव See under विश्व *m*. -धारिणी the earth. -धारिन् *m*. a deity. -नाथः lord of the universe, an epithet of *S*iva. -प *m*. 1 the protector of all. 2 the sun. 3 the moon. 4 fire. -पावनी, -पूजिता holy basil. -प्सन् *m*. 1 a god. 2 the sun. 3 the moon. 4 an epithet of Agni. -भुज् *a*. all-enjoying, all-eating. (-*m*.) an epithet of Indra. -भेषजं dry ginger. -मूर्ति *a*. existing in all forms, all-pervading, omnipresent; Mâl. 1. 3. -योनिः 1 an epithet of Brahman. 2 of Vishṇu. -राज्, -राजः a universal sovereign. -रूप *a*. omnipresent, existing everywhere. (-पः) an epithet of Vishṇu. (-पं) agallochum.-रेतस् *m*. an epithet of Brahman. -वाह *a*. (विश्वौही *f*.) all-sustaining. -सहा the earth. -सृज् *m*. an epithet of Brahman, the creator; प्रायेण सामग्र्यविधौ गुणानां पराङ्मुखी विश्वसृजः प्रवृत्तिः Ku. 3. 28, 1. 49.

विश्वंकरः The eye (*n*. according to some).

विश्वतस् *ind*. On all sides, all round, everywhere; Bv. 1. 30. -Comp. -मुख *a*. having a face on every side; Bg. 9. 15.

विश्वथा *ind*. Everywhere.

विश्वंभर *a*. All-sustaining. -रः 1 The all-pervading being, the Supreme Spirit. 2 An epithet of Vishṇu. 3 of Indra. -रा The earth; विश्वंभरा भगवती भवतीमसूत U. 1. 9; विश्वंभराप्यतिलघुर्नरनाथ तवांतिके नियतं K. P. 10.

विश्वसनीय *pot. p*. 1 To be relied upon, trustworthy, reliable. 2 Capable of inspiring confidence; *S*. 2, M. 3. 2.

विश्वस्त *p. p*. 1 Believed in, trusted, relied on. 2 Confiding, relying on. 3 Fearless, confident. 4 Trustworthy, reliable. -स्ता A widow.

विश्वाधायस् *m*. A god, deity.

विश्वानरः An epithet of Savitṛi.

विश्वामित्रः N. of a celebrated sage. [He was originally a Kshatriya, being the king of Kanyakubja and son of Gadhi. One day while out hunting, he went to the hermitage of the great sage Vasish*t*ha, and seeing there the cow of plenty, offered the sage untold treasure in exchange for it, but being refused he tried to take it by force. A long context thereupon ensued in which king Visvamitra was signally defeated; and so great was his vexation, and withal so greatly was he impressed with the power inherent in Brahmanism that he devoted himself to the most rigorous austerities till he successively got the titles *Rajarshi*, *Rishi*, *Maharshi*, and *Brahmarshi*, but he was not contented till Vasish*t*ha himself called him by the name *Brahmarshi*-which, however, took place after several thousands of years. Visvamitra several times tried to excite Vasish*t*ha—for example by killing his one hundred sons—but the great sage was not in the least perturbed. His power, even before he finally became a Brahmarshi was very great, as was seen in his transporting Trishanku to the skies, in saving *S*unah*s*epha from the hands of Indra, in creating things after the style of Brahman &c. &c. He was the companion and counsellor of young Rama to whom he gave several miraculous missiles.]

विश्वावसुः N. of a Gandharva.

विश्वासः 1 Trust, confidence, faith, reliance; दुर्जनः प्रियवादीति नैतद्विश्वासकारणं; *S*. 1. 14; R. 1. 51, H. 4. 103. 2 A secret, confidential communication. -Comp. -घातः, -भंगः breach of faith, treachery, perfidy. -घातिन् *m*. a treacherous fellow, traitor. -पात्रं, -भूमिः, -स्थानं an object of confidence, a reliable or trusty person, a confidant.

विष् I. 3 U. (वेवेष्टि, वेविष्टे, विष्ट) 1 To surround. 2 To spread through, extend, pervade. **3** To go to, go against, encounter ; (not gen rally used in classical literature). –II. 9 P. (विष्णाति) To separate, disjoin. –III. 1 P. (वेषति) To sprinkle, pour out.

विष् *f*. **1** Feces, excrement, ordure. **2** Spreading, diffusion. **3** A girl, as in विट्पति. –**Comp.**–कारिका (विड्कारिका) a kind of bird. –ग्रहः (विड्ग्रहः constipation.–चरः,-वराहः(विड्चरः,विड्वराहः) a tame or village hog (eating ordure). –लवणं (विड्लवणं) a kind of medicinal salt. –गंगः (विड्संगः) constipation. –सारिका, (विड्सारिका) a kind of bird.

विषं **1** Poison, venom (said to be *m*. also in this sense ; विषं भवतु मा भूद्वा फटाटोपो भयंकरः Pt. 1. 204. **2** Water ; विषं जलधरैः पीतं मूर्छिताः पथिकांगनाः Chandr. 5. 82. (where both senses are intended). **3** The fibres of a lotus-stalk. **4** Gum-myrrh. –**Comp**. –अक्त, –दिग्ध *a*. poisoned, envenomed. –अंकुरः **1** a spear. **2** a poisoned arrow. –अंतकः an epithet of *S*iva. –अपह, -घ्न *a*. repelling poison, antidotic. –आननः, –आयुधः, -आस्यः a snake. –आस्वाद *a*. tasting poison. –कुंभः a jar filled with poison. –कृमिः a worm bred in poison. °न्याय see under न्याय. –ज्वरः a buffalo. –दः a cloud. (–दं) green vitriol. –दंतकः a snake. –दर्शनमृत्युकः –मृत्युः a kind of bird (said to be Chakora). -धरः a snake ; Bv. 1. 74. °निलयः the lower regions, the abode of snakes. –पुष्पं the blue lotus. –प्रयोगः use of poison; administering poison. –भिषज् *m*.– वैद्यः a dealer in antidotes, curer of snake-bites; संप्रति विषवैद्यानां कर्म M. 4.–मंत्रः **1** a spell for curing snake-bites. **2** a snake-charmer, conjurer. –वृक्षः a poisonous tree ; विषवृक्षोपि संवर्ध्य स्वयं छेत्तुमसांप्रतं Ku. 2. 55. °न्याय see under न्याय. –वेगः the circulation or effect of poison.–शालूकः the root of the lotus. –शूकः, –शृंगिन्, –सृक्कन् *m*. a wasp. –हृदय *a*. ' poison-hearted ', malicious.

विषक्त *p. p*. **1** Fixed firmly or closely. **2** Adhering or clinging closely to.

विषंड The fibres of the lotus-stalk.

विषण्ण *p. p*. Dejected, cast down, sad, sorrowful, spiritless, despondent. –**Comp.** –मुख, –वदन *a*. looking sad. –रूप *a*. in a sad mood.

विषम *a*. **1** Uneven, rough, rugged; पथिषु विषमेष्वप्यचलता Mu. 3. 3 ; Pt. 1. 64, Me. 19. **2** Irregular, unequal ; Mâl. 9. 43. **3** Odd, not even. **4** Difficult, hard to understand, mysterious ; Ki. 2. 3. **5** Impassable, inaccessible ; Ki. 2. 3. **6** Coarse, rough. **7** Oblique ; Mâl. 4. 2. **8** Painful, troublesome ; Bh. 3. 105. **9** Very strong, vehement ; Mâl. 3. 9. **10** Dangerous, fearful ; Mk. 8. 127. Mu. 1. 18, 2. 20. **11** Bad, adverse, unfavourable ; Pt. 4. 16. **12** Odd, unusual, unparalleled. **13** Dishonest, artful. –मं **1** Unevenness. **2** Oddness. **3** An inaccessible place, precipice, pit &c. **4** A difficult or dangerous position, difficulty; misfortune; सुप्तं प्रमत्तं विषमस्थितं वा रक्षंति पुण्यानि पुरा कृतानि Bh. 2. 97; Bg. 2. 2. **5** N. of a figure of speech in which some unusual or incompatible relation between cause and effect is described ; said to be of four kinds ; see K. P. Kârikâs 126 and 127. –मः N. of Vishṇu. –**Comp.** –अक्षः, –ईक्षणः, –नयनः, –नेत्रः, –लोचनः epithets of *S*iva. –अन्नं unusual or irregular food. –आयुधः, -इषुः, -शरः epithets of the god of love. –कालः an unfavourable season. –चतुरस्रः, –चतुर्भुजः an unequal quadrilateral figure. –छदः the tree सप्तपर्ण q. v –ज्वरः remittent fever. –लक्ष्मीः ill-luck. –विभागः unequal distribution of property. –स्थ *a*. **1** being in an inaccessible position. **2** being in difficulty or misfortune.

विषमित *a*. **1** Made rough, uneven or crooked. **2** Contracted, frowning. **3** Made difficult or inaccessible.

विषयः **1** An object of sense; (these are five, corresponding to the five organs of sense ; रूप, रस, गंध, स्पर्श and शब्द corresponding to the eye, tongue, nose, skin and ear); श्रुतिविषयगुणा या स्थिता व्याप्य विश्वं *S*. 1. 1. **2** A worldly object or concern, an affair, a transaction. **3** The pleasures of sense, worldly or sensual enjoyments, sensual objects (usually in pl.) ; यौवने विषयैषिणां R. 1. 8 ; निर्विष्टविषयस्नेहः 12. 1, 3. 70, 8. 10, 19. 49 ; V. 1. 9 ; Bg. 2. 59. **4** An object, a thing, matter ; नार्यो न जग्मुर्विषयांतराणि R. 7. 12, 8. 89. **5** An object or thing aimed at, mark, object; भूयिष्ठमन्यविषया न तु दृष्टिरस्याः *S*. 1. 31 ; *S*i. 9. 40. **6** Scope, range, reach, compass; सौमित्रेरपि पत्रिणामविषये तत्र प्रिये क्वासि भोः U. 3. 45; सकलवचनानामविषयः Mâl. 1. 30, 36 ; U. 5. 19 ; Ku. 6. 17. **7** Department, sphere, province, field, element ; सर्वत्रौदरिकस्याभ्यवहार्यमेव विषयः V 3. **8** A subject, subject-matter, topic ; Bv. 1. 10 ; so शृंगारविषयको ग्रंथः ' treating of love '. **9** The topic or subject to be explained, general head ; the first of the five members of an Adhikaraṇa. q. v. **10** A place, spot ; परिसरविषयेषु लीढमुक्ताः Ki. 5. 35. **11** A country, realm, domain, territory, district, kingdom. **12** A refuge, an asylum. **13** A collection of villages. **14** A lover, husband. **15** Semen virile. **16** A religous observance. (विषये means ' with regard or reference to, ' ' in respect of, ' ' in the case of ', 'reagarding, ' concerning ' ; या तत्रास्ते युवतिविषये सृष्टिराद्येव धातुः Me. 82 ; स्त्रीणां विषये ; धनविषये &c.). –**Comp.**–अभिरतिः **1** attachment to objects of sense or worldly pleasures ; Ki. 6. 44 ; so –अभिलाषः Ki. 3. 13. –आत्मक *a*. consisting of worldly objects. –आसक्त, -निरत *a*. addicted to sensual objects, sensualist, worldly-minded. –आसक्तिः –उपसेवा, –निरतिः *f*., –प्रसंगः addiction to pleasures of sense, sensuality. –ग्रामः the collection of the objects of sense. –सुखं the pleasures of sense.

विषयायिन् *m*. **1** One addicted to pleasures of sense, a sensualist. **2** A man of the world. **3** The god of love. **4** A king. **5** An organ of sense. **6** A materialist.

विषयिन् *a*. Sensual, carnal. –*m*. **1** A man of the world, worldling. **2** A king. **3** The god of love. **4** A sensualist, voluptuary ; Pt. 1. 146 ; *S*. 5. –*n*. **1** An organ of sense. **2** Knowledge (ज्ञान).

विषलः Poison, venom.

विषह्य *a*. **1** Endurable, bearable ; अविषह्यव्यसनेन धूमितां Ku. 4. 30, R. 6. 47. **2** Possible to be settled or determined ; Ms. 8. 265. **3** Possible.

विषा **1** Ordure, feces. **2** Intellect, understanding.

विषाणः-णं,-णी **1** A horn ; साहित्यसंगीतकलाविहीनः साक्षात्पशुः पुच्छविषाणहीनः Bh. 2. 12 ; कदाचिदपि पर्यटञ्छशविषाणमासादयेत् 2. 5. **2** The tusk of an elephant or boar ; ततानामुपदधिरे विषाणभिन्नाः प्रह्लादं सुरकरिणां घनाः क्षरंतः Ki. 7. 13 ; *S*i. 1. 60.

विषाणिन् *a*. Having horns or tusks. –*m*. **1** Any animal having horns or tusks. **2** An elephant; *S*i. 4. 63, 12. 77. **3** A bull.

विषादः **1** Dejection, sadness, depression of spirits, grief, sorrow ; मद्वाणि मा कुरु विषादं Bv. 4. 41 ; विषादे कर्तव्ये विदधाति जडाः प्रत्युत मुदं Bh. 3. 25, R. 8. 54. **2** Disappointment, despondency, despair, विषादलुप्तप्रतिपत्तिसैन्यं R. 3. 40 ; (विषादश्चेतसो भंग उपायाभावनाशयोः). **3** Languor, drooping state ; Mâl. 2. 5. **4** Dulness, stupidity, insensibility.

विषादिन् *a*. Dejected, dismayed, sad, disconsolate.

विषारः A snake.

विषालु *a*. Poisonous, venomous.

विषु *ind*. **1** In two equal parts ; equally. **2** Differently, variously. **3** Same, like.

विषुपं The equinox.

विषुवं The first point of *Aries* or *Libra* into which the sun enters at the vernal or autumnal equinox, the equinoctial point. –**Comp.** –छाया the shadow of the gnomon at noon. –दिनं the day of the equinox. –रेखा

the equinoctial line. -संक्रांतिः f. the sun's equinoctial passage.

विषूचिका Cholera.

विष्क् 10 U. (विष्कयति-ते) 1 To kill, hurt, injure (Atm. only in this sense). 2 To see, perceive.

विष्कंदः 1 Dispersing. 2 Going away.

विष्कंभः 1 Obstacle, hindrance, impediment. 2 The bolt or bar of a door. 3 The supporting beam of a house. 4 A post, pillar. 5 A tree. 6 (In dramas). An interlude between the acts of a drama and performed by one or more characters-middling or inferior-who connect the story of the drama and the subdivisions of the plot by briefly explaining to the audience what has occurred in the intervals of the acts or what is likely to happen later on :- S. D. thus defines it :—वृत्तवर्तिष्यमाणानां कथांशानां निदर्शकः । संक्षिप्तार्थस्तु विष्कंभः आदावंकस्य दर्शितः । मध्येन मध्यमाभ्यां वा पात्राभ्यां संप्रयोजितः । शुद्धः स्यात् स तु संकीर्णो नीचमध्यमकल्पितः 3. 8. 7 The diameter of a circle. 8 A particular posture practised by Yogins. 9 Extension, length.

विष्कंभक See विष्कंभ.

विष्कंभित a. Hindered, obstructed.

विष्कंभिन् m. The bolt of a door.

विष्किरः 1 Scattering about, tearing up. 2 A cock. 3 A bird, gallinaceous-bird; छायापस्किरमाणविष्किरमुखव्याकृष्टकीटत्वचः U. 2. 9.

विष्टपः -पं A world; Ku. 3. 20; cf. त्रिविष्टप. -Comp. -हारिन् a. one who pleases the world; Bh. 2. 25.

विष्टब्ध p. p. 1 Fixed firmly; well supported. 2 Propped up, supported. 3 Obstructed; hindered. 4 Paralysed, made motionless.

विष्टंभः 1 Fixing firmly. 2 Obstruction, hindrance, an impediment. 3 Obstruction of the urine or ordure, constipation. 4 Paralysis. 5 Stopping, staying.

विष्टरः 1 A seat (a stool, chair &c.); R. 8. 18. 2 A layer, bed (as of Kusa grass.). 3 A handful of Kusa grass. 4 The seat of the presiding priest (or Brahman) at a sacrifice. 5 A tree. -Comp. -भाज् a. seated on or occupying a seat; Ku. 7. 72. -श्रवस् m. an epithet of Vishṇu or Krishṇa; Si. 14. 12.

विष्टिः f. 1 Pervading. 2 An act, occupation. 3 Hire, wages. 4 Unpaid labour. 5 Sending. 6 Residence in hell to which one is condemned.

विष्ठलं A remote place, one situated at a distance.

विष्ठा 1 Feces, ordure, excrement; Ms. 3. 180, 10. 91. 2 The belly.

विष्णुः 1 The second deity of the sacred Triad, entrusted with the preservation of the world, which duty he is represented to have duly discharged by his various incarnations; (for, their descriptions see the several avatâras s. v. and also under अवतार); the word is thus popularly derived :—यस्माद्विश्वमिदं सर्वं तस्य शक्त्या महात्मनः । तस्माद्वेवोच्यते विष्णुर्विशधातोः प्रवेशनात् ॥. 2 N. of Agni. 3 A pious man. 4 N. of a law-giver, author of a Smriti called विष्णुस्मृति. -Comp. -कांची N. of a town. -क्रमः the step or stride of Vishṇu. -गुप्तः N. of Chāṇakya. -तैलं a kind of medicinal oil. -दैवत्या N. of the eleventh and twelfth day of each fortnight (of a lunar month). -पदं 1 the sky, atmosphere. 2 the sea of milk. 3 a lotus. -पदी an epithet of the Ganges. -पुराणं N. of one of the most celebrated of the eighteen Purāṇas. -प्रीतिः f. land granted rent-free to Brâhmaṇas to maintain Vishṇu's worship. -रथः an epithet of Garuḍa. -रिंगी a quail. -लोकः Vishṇu's world. -वल्लभा 1 an epithet of Lakshmî. 2 the holy basil. -वाहनः, -वाह्यः epithets of Garuḍa.

विष्पंदः Throbbing, palpitation.

विष्फारः 1 The twang of a bow. 2 Vibration.

विष्य a. Deserving death by poison.

विष्यंदः Flowing, trickling.

विष्व a. Hurtful, injurious, mischievous.

विष्वच्, विष्वंच् a. (Nom. sing. m. विष्वङ्, f. विषूची, n. विष्वक्) 1 Going or being every where, all-pervading; विष्वङ्मोहः स्थगयति कथं मंदभाग्यः करोमि U. 3. 38, Mâl. 9. 20. 2 Separating into parts. 3 Different. (विष्वक् is used adverbially in the sense of ' everywhere, on all sides, all around '; Ki. 15. 59; Pt. 2. 2; Mâl. 5. 4, 9. 25) -Comp. -सेनः (विश्वक्सेनः or विष्वक्सेनः) an epithet of Vishṇu; साम्यमाप कमलासखविष्वक्सेनसेवितयुगांतपयोधेः Si. 10. 55; विष्वक्सेनः स्तवनुमविशत्सर्वलोकप्रतिष्ठा R. 15. 103. -प्रिया N. of Lakshmî.

विष्वणनं, विष्वाणः Eating.

विष्वद्र्य(ग्रं)च् a. (विष्वद्रीची f.) Going everywhere, all pervading; विष्वद्रीचीर्विक्षिपन् सैन्यवीचीः Si. 18. 25; विष्वद्रीच्या भुवनमभितो भासते यस्य भासा Bv. 4. 18.

विस् I. 4 P. (विस्यति) To cast, throw, send. -II. 1 P. (वेसति) To go, move.

विस See बिस.

विसंयुक्त p. p. Disjoined, separated.

विसंयोगः Disjunction, separation.

विसंवादः 1 Deception, breaking one's promise, disappointment. 2 Inconsistency, incongruity, disagreement. 3 Contradiction.

विसंवादिन् a. 1 Disappointing, deceiving. 2 Inconsistent, contradictory. 3 Differing, disagreeing; R. 15. 67. 4 Fraudulent, crafty.

विसंष्ठुल a. 1 Unsteady, agitated. 2 Uneven.

विसंकट a. Frightful; dreadful, Mâl. 5. 13; cf. विशंकट. -टः 1 A lion. 2 The Ingudi tree.

विसंगत a. Ill-fitted, incongruous, unharmonious.

विसंधिः Bad or disagreeable *Sandhi* (euphony) or absence of Sandhi, regarded as a fault in composition; see K. P. 7.

विसरः 1 Going forth. 2 Spreading, extending. 3 Crowd, multitude, herd, flock. 4 A large quantity, heap; Mâl. 1. 37.

विसर्गः 1 Sending forth, emission. 2 Shedding, pouring down, dropping; R. 16. 38. 3 Casting, discharge. 4 Giving away, a gift, donation; आदानं हि विसर्गाय सतां वारिमुचामिव R. 4. 86 (where the word means ' pouring down ' also). 5 Sending away, dismissal. 6 Abandonment, relinquishment. 7 Voiding, evacuation; as in पुरीषविसर्ग. 8 Departure, separation. 9 Final beatitude. 10 Light, splendour. 11 A symbol in writing, representing a distinct hard aspiration and marked by two perpendicular dots (:). 12 The southern course of the sun. 13 The penis.

विसर्जनं 1 Emitting, sending forth, pouring down; समतया वसुवृष्टिविसर्जनैः R. 9. 6. 2 Giving away, a gift, donation; R. 9. 6. 3 Voiding; Ms. 4. 48. 4 Casting off, quitting, abandoning; R. 8. 25. 5 Sending away, dismissal. 6 Allowing (the deity invoked) to go (opp. आवाहन). 7 Setting a bull at liberty on certain occasions.

विसर्जनीय a. To be abandoned &c. -यः = विसर्ग. (11) q. v.

विसर्जित p. p. 1 Emitted, sent forth. 2 Given away. 3 Left, quitted, abandoned. 4 Sent, dispatched. 5 Dismissed.

विसर्पः 1 Creeping about, gliding. 2 Moving to and fro. 3 Spread, circulation; U. 1. 35. 4 An unexpected or unwished for consequence of an act. 5 A sort of disease, dry spreading itch. -Comp. -घ्नं wax.

विसर्पणं 1 Creeping along, gliding, going gently. 2 Diffusion, spreading, extending.

विसर्पिः, विसर्पिका See विसर्प (5) above.

विसल See बिसल.

विसारः 1 Spreading out, expansion, diffusion. 2 Creeping, gliding. 3 A fish. -रं 1 A wood. 2 Timber.

विसारिन् *a.* (णी *f.*) 1 Spreading, diffusing. 2 Creeping, gliding. *-m.* A fish.

विसिनी See बिसिनी.

विसेल See बिसिल.

विसूचिका Cholera.

विसूरणं-णा Distress, sorrow.

विसूरितं Repentance, distress. -ता Fever.

विसृत *p. p.* 1 Spread out, extended, diffused. 2 Extended, stretched. 3 Uttered.

विसृत्वर *a.* (री *f.*) 1 Spreading about, being diffused ; विसृत्वरैरंबुरुहां रजोभिः *Si.* 3. 11. 2 Creeping, gliding.

विसृमर *a.* Creeping along, gliding, moving gently ; विसृमरस्त्रेषितहयः Ve. 4.

विसृष्ट *p. p* 1 Emitted, sent forth. 2 Created, emanated. 3 Shed, cast. 4 Sent, dispatched ; R. 5. 39. 5 Dismissed, let go, discharged ; R. 2. 9. 6 Discharged, hurled. 7 Given, bestowed, granted ; ग्रामेष्वात्मविसृष्टेषु R. 1. 44. 8 A. bandoned, quitted, removed. (See सृज् with वि.)

विस्त See बिस्त.

विस्तरः 1 Extension, expansion. 2 Minute details, detailed description, minute particulars ; संक्षिप्तस्याप्यतोऽस्यैव वाक्यस्यार्थगरीयसः । सुविस्तरतरा वाचो भाष्यभूता भवंतु मे *Si.* 2. 24 ; (**विस्तरेण, विस्तरतः, विस्तरशः** 'in detail, at length, fully, with minute details, with full particulars' ; अंगुलिसुद्राधिगमं विस्तरेण श्रोतुमिच्छामि Mu. 1, Bg. 10. 18.) 3 Prolixity, diffuseness ; अलं विस्तरेण. 4 Abundance, quantity, multitude, number 5 A bed, layer. 6 A seat, stool.

विस्तारः 1 Spreading, extension, expansion ; प्रांतविस्तारमाजा Mâl. 1. 27. 2 Amplitude, bredth ; विलोकयंत्यो वपुरापुरक्ष्णां प्रकामविस्तारफलं हरिण्यः R. 2. 11 ; Bg. 13. 30. 3 Expanse, vastness, magnitude; मध्यः श्यामः स्तन इव भुवः शेषविस्तारपांडुः Me. 18. 4 Details, full particulars ; कण्वोऽपि तावच्छ्रुतविस्तारः क्रियतां *S.* 7. 5 The diameter of a circle. 6 A shrub. 7 The branch of a tree with new shoots.

विस्तीर्ण *p. p.* 1 Spread out, expanded, extended. 2 Wide, broad. 3 Large, great, extensive. -Comp. -पर्णं a kind of root (मानक).

विस्तृत *p. p.* 1 Diffused, spread, extended. 2 Broad, expanded. 3 Ample. 4 Diffuse, prolix.

विस्तृतिः *f.* 1 Extension, expansion. 2 Breadth, width, magnitude. 3 The daimeter of a circle.

विस्पष्ट *a.* 1 Plain, clear, intelligible. 2 Manifest, evident, obvious, open, apparent.

विस्फारः 1 Vibration, trembling, throbbing. 2 The twang of a bow.

विस्फारित *p. p.* 1 Made to vibrate 2 Trembling, tremulous. 3 Twanged 4 Dilated, expanded. 5 Manifested, displayed.

विस्फुरित *p. p.* 1 Tremulous, quivering. 2 Swollen, enlarged.

विस्फुलिंगः 1 A spark of fire ; अग्रेर्ज्वलतो विस्फुलिंगा विप्रतिष्ठेरन् S. B. 2 A kind of poison.

विस्फूर्जथुः 1 Roaring, thundering, rumbling. 2 A clap or peal of thunder. 3 (Hence) A thunder-like manifestation or rise, any sudden appearance or stroke ; ममैव जन्मांतरपातकानां विपाकविस्फूर्जथुरप्रसह्यः R. 14. 62. 4 Rolling (as of waves) ; swell surging appearance ; महोर्मिविस्फूर्जथुनिर्विशेषाः R. 13. 12.

विस्फूर्जितं 1 Roar, shout. 2 Rolling. 3 Fruit, result ; Bh. 2 125, 3. 148

विस्फोटः-टा 1 A boil, tumour. 2 Small-pox.

विस्मयः 1 Wonder, surprise, astonishment, amazement ; पुरुषः प्रबभूवाग्नेर्विस्मयेन सहर्त्विजां R. 10. 51. 2 Astonishment or wonder, being the feeling which produces the *adbhuta* sentiment ; S. D. thus defines it:—विविधेषु पदार्थेषु लोकसीमातिवर्तिषु । विस्फारश्चेतसो यस्तु स विस्मय उदाहृतः ॥ 207. 3 Pride ; arrongance ; तपः क्षरति विस्मयात् Ms. 4. 237. 4 Uncertainty, doubt. -Comp. -आकुल, -आविष्ट *a.* astonished, struck with wonder.

विस्मयंगम *a.* Astonishing, producing wonder.

विस्मरणं Forgetting, forgetfulness, oblivion ; *S* 5. 23.

विस्मापन *a.* (नी *f.*) Astonishing. -नः 1 The god of love. 2 Trick, deceit, illusion. -नं 1 Causing wonder. 2 Anything causing wonder. 3 A city of the Gandharvas (said to be *m.* also).

विस्मित *p. p.* 1 Astonished, surprised, amazed, wonder-struck. 2 Disconcerted. 3 Proud.

विस्मृत *p. p.* Forgotten.

विस्मृतिः *f.* Forgetfulness, oblivion, loss of memory.

विस्मेर *a.* Surprised, struck with wonder, astoniseed.

विस्रं A smell like that of raw meat. -Comp. -गंधिः yellow orpiment.

विस्रंसः सा 1 Falling down. 2 Decay, laxness, weakness, debility.

विस्रंसन *a.* 1 Causing to fall or drop down ; अंतर्मोहनमौलिघूर्णनचलन्मंदारविस्रंसनः Gît. 3. 2 Untying, loosening ; नीविविस्रंसनः करः K. P. 7. -नं 1 Falling down. 2 Flowing, dropping. 3 Untying, loosening. 4 A laxative, purgative.

विस्रब्ध, विस्रंभ Se विश्रब्ध, विश्रंभ.

विस्रसा Decay, debility, decrepitude.

विस्रस्त *p. p.* 1 Loosened. 2 Weak, infirm.

विस्रवः, विस्रावः, Flowing, dropping, trickling.

विस्रावणं Bleeding.

विस्रुतिः *f.* Flowing forth, trickling, oozing.

विस्वर *a.* Discordant.

विहगः 1 bird ; Me. 28 ; Rs. 1. 23. 2 A cloud. 3 An arrow. 4 The sun. 5 The moon. 6 A planet in general.

विहंगः 1 A bird ; R. 1. 51, Ms. 9. 55. 2 A cloud. 3 An arrow. 4 The sun. 5 The moon. -Comp. इंद्रः, -ईश्वरः, -राजः epithets of Garuḍa.

विहंगमः A bird ; (गृहदीर्घिकाः) मदकलोदकलोलविहंगमाः R. 9. 37 ; Ms. 1. 39, H. 1. 37.

विहंगमा, विहंगिका A pole for carrying burdens.

विहत *p. p.* 1 Struck completely, killed. 2 Hurt. 3 Opposed, impeded, resisted.

विहतिः A friend, companion. -*f.* 1 killing, striking. 2 Failure. 3 Defeat, rout.

विहननं 1 Killing, striking. 2 Hurt, injury. 3 Obstruction, obstacle, impediment. 4 A bow for cleaning cotton.

विहरः 1 Taking away, removing. 2 Separation, disunion.

विहरणं 1 Removing, taking away. 2 Taking a walk, airing, going about or rambling for pleasure. 3 Pleasure, pastime.

विहर्तृ *m.* 1 A roamer. 2 A robber.

विहर्षः Great joy, rapture.

विहसनं, विहसितं, विहासः A gentle laugh, smile.

विहस्त *a.* 1 Handless. 2 Confounded, bewildered, overpowered, made powerless ; Mâl. 1, R. 5. 49. 3 Disabled, incapacitated (for doing the proper work) ; रुजा विहस्तचरणं M. 4. 4 Learned, wise.

विहा *ind.* Heaven, paradise.

विहापित *p. p.* 1 Caused to abandon. 2 Extorted, caused to be given up. -तं A gift, donation.

विहायस् *m. n.* Sky, atmosphere ; Ki. 16. 43. -*m.* A bird ; N. 3. 99.

विहायस See विहा स्.

विहारः 1 Removing, taking away. 2 Roaming or walking for pleasure, airing, a stroll, taking a walk. 3 Sport, play, pastime, recreation, diversion, pleasure ; विहारशैलानुगतेव नागैः R. 16. 26, 67 ; 5. 41 ; 9. 68, 13. 38, 19. 37. 4 Tread, stepping; दरमंथरचरणविहारं Gît. 11 ; Ki. 4. 15. 5 A park, garden ; especially a pleasure-garden. 6 The shoulder. 7 A Jaina or Buddhist temple, convent, monastery. 8 A temple in general. 9 Great expansion of the organs of speach. -Comp. -गृहं a pleasure-house. -दासी a nun.

विहारिका A convent.

विहारिन् *a.* Diverting or amusing oneself by ; मृगयाविहारिणः *S.* 1.

विहित *p. p.* 1 Done, performed, made, acted. 2 Arranged, fixed, settled, appointed, determined. 3 Orderd, prescribed, decreed. 4 Framed, constructed 5 Placed, deposited. 6 Furnished with, possessed of. 7 Fit to be done. 8 Distributed, apportioned. (See धा with वि.) –तं An order, a command.

विहितिः *f.* 1 Performance, doing, action. 2 Arrangement.

विहीन *p. p.* 1 Left, abandoned, forsaken. 2 Devoid of, destitute or deprived of, without (usually in comp.) ; विद्याविहीनः पशुः Bh. 2. 20. 3 Base, low, inferior. **–Comp.** –जाति, –योनि *a.* base-born, low-born.

विहृत *p. p.* 1 Sported, played. 2 Expanded. –तं One of the ten modes of indicating love used by women ; see S. D. 125, 146 ; (written विकृत also in this sense).

विहृतिः *f.* 1 Removal, taking away. 2 Sport, pastime, pleasure. 3 Expansion.

विहेठकः An injurer.

विहेठनं 1 Injuring, hurting. 2 Rubbing, grinding. 3 Afflicting. 4 Pain, sorrow, torment.

विह्वल *a.* 1 Agitated, disquieted, perturbed, confused ; R. 8. 37. 2 Overcome with fear, alarmed. 3 Delirious, beside oneself. 4 Afflicted, distressed ; Ku. 4. 4. 5 Desponding. 6 Fused, liquid.

वी 2 P. (वेति, rarely used in classical literature) 1 To go, move. 2 To approach. 3 To prevade. 4 To bring, convey. 5 To throw, cast. 6 To eat, consume. 7 To obtain. 8 To conceive, bring forth. 9 To be born or produced. 10 To shine, be beautiful.

वीकः 1 Wind. 2 A bird. 3 The mind.

वीकाश See विकाश.

वीक्षं 1 A visible object. 2 Surprise, astonishment. –क्षः–क्षा Seeing, gazing at.

वीक्षणं-णा Seeing, looking at, sight.

वीक्षितं A look, glance.

वीक्ष्य *a.* 1 To be looked at. 2 Visible, perceptible. –क्ष्यः 1 A dancer, an actor. 2 A horse. –क्ष्यं 1 Anything to be looked at, a visible object. 2 Wonder, surprise.

वींखा 1 Going, moving, progress. 2 One of the paces of a horse. 3 Dancing. 4 Junction, union.

वीचिः *m. f.*, वीची 1 A wave ; समुद्रवीचीव चलस्वभावाः Pt. 1. 194, R. 6 56, 12. 100. Me. 28. 2 Inconstancy, thoughtlessness. 3 Pleasure, delight. 4 Rest, leisure. 5 A ray of light. 6 Little. **–Comp.** –मालिन् *m.* the ocean.

वीची = वीचि q. v.

वीज् I. 1 A (वीजते) To go. –II. 10 U. (वीजयति-ते) To fan, cool by fanning; स्वं वीज्यते मणिमयैरिव तालवृंतैः Mk. 5. 13 ; Ku. 2. 42. –With अभि, उप, परि to fan ; Rs. 3. 4 ; *S.* 3.

वीज, वीजक, वीजल, वीजिक, वीजिन्, वीज्य — See बीज, बीजक, बीजल, बीजिक, बीजिन् and बीज्य.

वीजनः 1 The ruddy goose. 2 A sort of pheasant. –नं 1 Fanning; Ku. 4. 36. 2 A fan.

वीटा A small piece of wood (about a span long) struck with a stick or bat in a game played by boys (called in Marâthî विटीदांडूचा खेळ).

वीटिः, -वीटिका, वीटी *f.* 1 The betel-plant. 2 A preparation of betel (Mar. विडा = तांबूल q. v.). 3 A tie, fastening, knot (of a wearing garment). 4 The knot of a bodice ; Amaru. 23.

वीणा 1 The (Indian) lute ; मूकीभूतायां वीणायां K.; Me. 86. 2 Lightning. **–Comp.** –आस्यः an epithet of Nârada. –दंडः the neck of a lute ; Bv. 1. 80. –वादः, –वादकः a lutanist.

वीत *p. p.* 1 Gone, disappeared. 2 Gone away, departed. 3 Let go, loosed, set free. 4 Excepted, exempt. 5 Approved, liked. 6 Unfit for war. 7 Tame, quiet. 8 Freed from, devoid of (mostly in comp.); वीतचिंत, वीतस्पृह, वीतभी, वीतशंक &c. –तः An elephant or horse unfit or untrained for war. –तं Pricking (an elephant) with the goad and striking with the legs ; वीतवीतभया नागाः Ku. 6. 39 v. l. (see Malli. thereon) ; Si. 5. 47. **–Comp.** –दंभ *a.* humble, lowly. –भय *a.* fearless, intrepid. (–यः) an epithet of Vishṇu. –मल *a.* pure. –राग *a.* 1 free from desire ; Ku. 6. 43. 2 free from passion, calm, tranquil. 3 colourless. (–गः) a sage who has subdued his passions. –शोकः (= अशोकः) the Asoka tree.

वीतंसः 1 A cage, a cage or net for confining beasts or birds. 2 An aviary. 3 A place for preserving game.

वीतनौ (*m.* dual) The sides of the larynx or throat.

वीतिः A horse. –तिः *f.* 1 Going, motion. 2 Producing, production. 3 Enjoyment. 4 Eating. 5 Light, lustre. **–Comp.** –होत्रः 1 fire. 2 the sun.

वीथिः-थी *f.* 1 A road, way ; Ki. 7. 17. 2 A row, line. 3 A market, stall, shop in a market ; Si. 9. 32. 4 A variety of drama ; it is thus defined in S. D.:—वीथ्यामेको भवेदंकः कश्चिदेकोऽत्र कल्प्यते । आकाशभाषितैरुक्तैश्चित्रां प्रत्युक्तिमाश्रितः । सूचयेद्भूरि शृंगारं किंचिदन्यान् रसानपि । मुखनिर्वहणे संधी अर्थप्रकृतयोऽखिलाः ॥ 520.

वीथिका 1 A road &c. 2 A picture-gallery ; or a large scroll of paper (on which pictures are drawn) (according to some); a wall (according to others); आर्यस्य चरित्रमस्यां वीथिकायामालिखितं U. 1.

वीध्र *a.* Pure, clean. –ध्रं 1 The sky. 2 Wind, air. 3 Fire.

वीनाहः The top or cover of a well.

वीपा Lightning.

वीप्सा 1 Pervasion. 2 Repetition of words to imply continuous o successive action ; as in the example वृक्षं वृक्षं सिंचति ; वीप्सायां द्विरुक्तिः. 3 Repetition in general.

वीभ् 1 A (वीभते) To boast, brag.

वीर *a.* 1 Heroic, brave. 2 Mighty, powerful. –रः 1 A hero, warrior, champion ; कोप्येष संप्रति नवः पुरुषावतारो वीरो न यस्य भगवान् भृगुनंदनोऽपि U. 5. 34. 2 The sentiment of heroism (in rhetoric); it is distinguished under four heads; दानवीर, धर्मवीर, दयावीर and युद्धवीर, for explanations see these words s. v.). 3 An actor. 4 Fire. 5 The sacrificial fire. 6 A son. 7 A husband. 8 The tree Arjuna. 9 N. of Vishṇu. –रं 1 A reed. 2 Pepper. 3 Rice-gruel. 4 The root of Usîra q. v. **–Comp.** –आशंसनं 1 keeping watch. 2 the post of danger in battle. 3 a forlorn hope. –आसनं 1 a kind of posture practised in meditation ; for definition see पर्यंक (3). 2 kneeling on one knee. 3 a field of battle. 4 the station of a sentinel. ईशः, –ईश्वरः 1 epithets of *S*iva. 2 a great hero. –उज्झः a Brâhmaṇa who omits to offer oblations to the sacrificial fire. –कीटः an insignificant of contemptible warrior. –जयंतिका 1 a war-dance. 2 war, battle. –तरुः the Arjuna tree. –धन्वन् *m.* an epithet or the god of love. –पानं (णं) an exciting or refreshing drink taken by soldiers either before or after a battle. –भद्रः 1 N. of a powerful hero created by *S*iva from his matted hair , see दक्ष. 2 a distinguished hero. 3 a horse fit for the Asvamedha sacrifice. 4 a kind of fragrant grass. –मुद्रिका a ring worn on the middle toe. –रजस् *n.* red lead. –रस 1 the senti ment of heroism. 2 a warlike feeling. –रेणुः N. of Bhîmasena. –विप्लावकः = विरोज्झः q. v. –वृक्षः 1 the Arjuna tree. 2 the marking-nut plant. –सूः *f.* the mother of a hero ; (so वीरप्रसवा, –प्रसूः, –प्रसविनी). –सैन्यं garlic. –स्कंधः a buffalo. –हन् *m.* 1 a Brâhmaṇa who has neglected his domestic fire. 2 N. of Vishṇu.

वीरणं N. of a fragrant grass (the root of which is used as a refrigerant.)

वीरणी 1 A side-look. 2 A deep place.

वीरतरः 1 A great hero 2 An arrow· -रं A kind of fragrant grass.

वीरंधरः 1 A peacock. 2 Fighting with beasts. 3 A leather-jacket.

वीरवत् *a.* Full of heroes. -ती A woman whose husband and sons are living.

वीरा 1 The wife of a hero. 2 A wife. 3 A mother, matron. 4 A kind of perfume (called Murâ). 5 Spirituous liquor. 6 An aloe. 7 The plantain tree.

वीरिणं See ईरिण.

वीरुध्-धा *f.* 1 A spreading creeper; लता प्रतानिनी वीरुत् Bk; आहेास्वित्प्रसवेा ममापचरितैर्विष्टंभितेा वीरुधां *S.* 5. 9, Ku. 4. 34, R. 8. 36. 2 A branch, shoot. 3 A plant which grows after being cut. 4 A creeper, a shrub in general ; Ki 4. 19.

वीर्यं 1 Heroism, prowess, valour ; वीर्यावदानेषु कृतावमर्षः Ki. 3. 43, R. 2. 4, 3. 62, 11. 78, Ve. 3. 3. 2 Vigour, strength. 3 Virility. 4 Energy, firmness, courage. 5 Power, potency; *S.* 3. 2. 6 Efficacy (of medicines) ; अतिवीर्यवतीव भेषजे बहुरल्पयीसि दृश्यते गुणः Ki. 2. 24; Ku. 2. 48. 7 Semen virile; Ku. 3. 15, Pt. 4. 50. 8 Splendour, lustre. 9 Dignity, consequence. -**Comp**. -जः a son. -प्रपातः seminal effusion, discharge of semen.

वीर्यवत् *a.* 1 Strong, stout, vigorous. 2 Efficacious.

वीवधः 1 A yoke for carrying burdens. 2 A burden. 3 Storing corn. 4 A way, road.

ववीधिकः A man who carries loads by means of a yoke.

वीहारः 1 A Buddhist or Jaina convent. 2 A sanctuary.

वुंग् 1 P (वुंगति) To leave, abandon.

वुंद् 10 U. (वुंटयति-ते) 1 To hurt, kill. 2 To perish.

वुवूर्षु *a.* Desirous of choosing.

वुस् See बुस्.

वूर्ण *a.* Chosen, selected.

वृ I. 1. 5. 9 U. (वरति-ते, वृणेाति-वृणुते, वृणाति -वृणीते, वृत ; *pass.* व्रियते) 1 To choose, select, select as a boon ; वृतं तेनेदमेव प्राक् Ku. 2. 56 ; ववार रामस्य वनप्रयाणं Bk. 3. 6. 2 To choose for oneself (Atm.) ; वृणते हि विमृश्यकारिणं गुणलुब्धाः स्वयमेव संपदः Ki. 2. 30, R. 3. 6. 3 To choose in marriage, woo, court ; Mv. 1. 28, A. R. 3. 42 4 To beg, solicit, ask for. 5 To cover, conceal, hide, screen, envelop ; मेघैर्वृतश्चंद्रमाः Mk. 5 14 6 To surround, encompass; Bk. 5. 10, R. 12. 61. 7 To ward off, keep away, restrain, check. 8 To hinder, oppose, obstruct. -*Caus.* (वारयति-ते) 1 To cover, conceal. 2 To avert from (with abl.). 3 To prevent, ward off, restrain, suppress, check, hinder ; शक्यो वारयितुं जलेन हुतभुक् Bh. 2. 11. -*Desid.* वुवूर्षति-ते, विवरिषति-ते, विवरीषति-ते) To wish to choose. -WITH अप to open. (-*Caus.*) to cover, conceal. -अपा to open. -आ 1 to cover, conceal, hide ; आवृणेाद्‌ात्मनो रंध्रं रंध्रेषु प्रहरन् रिपून् R. 17. 61 ; Bk. 9. 24. 2 to fill, pervade ; Bg. 13. 13, Ms. 2. 144. 3 to choose, desire. 4 to solicit, beg. 5 to enclose, block up, obstruct ; R. 7. 31. 6 to keep off ; Bk. 14. 109. -नि to surround, enclose; Bk. 14. 29. (-*Caus.*) to ward off, keep away from, avert from (with abl.); पापान्निवारयति येाजयते हिताय Bh. 2. 72. -निस् (usually in *p. p.* only) to feel happy, be pleased or satisfied ; निर्ववार मधुनींद्रियवर्गः *Si.* 10. 3, see निर्वृत. -परि to surround. -प्र 1 to cover, envelop ; प्रावारिषुरिव क्षेाणीं क्षिता वृक्षाः समंततः Bk. 9. 25. 2 to wear, put on. 3 to select, choose. -प्रा to wear, put on. -वि 1 to cover up, stop. 2 to open ; Ku. 4. 26. 3 to unfold, disclose, reveal, show, display; N. 9. 1; Ku. 3. 15, R. 6. 85 ; Bk. 7. 73. 4 to teach, explain, expound ; Mv. 2. 43. 5 to spread ; Bv. 1. 5. 6 to choose. -विनि (*Caus.*) to prevent, ward off, suppress ; विनयं विनिवार्य Mâl. 1. 18. -सं 1 to hide, cover, conceal ; मुहुरंगुलिसंवृताधरोष्ठं *S.* 3. 25, 2. 10 ; R. 1. 20, 7. 30. 2 to suppress, restrain, oppose; Bk. 9. 27. 3 to shut. -II. 10 U. (वरयति-ते) 1 To choose, select ; वरं वरयते कन्या माता वित्तं पिता श्रुतं Pt. 4. 67. 2 To choose in marriage. 3 To ask for, beg, solicit.

वृंह, वृंहित See बृंह, बृंहित.

वृक् 1 A. (वर्कते) To seize, take, grasp.

वृकः 1 A wolf. 2 A hyena. 3 A jackal. 4 A crow. 5 An owl. 6 A robber. 7 A Kshatriya. 8 Turpentine. 9 A compound perfume, a mixture of various fragrant articles. 10 N. of a demon. 11 N. of a tree (बकवृक्ष). 12 N. of a fire in the stomach. -**Comp.** -अरातिः, -अरिः a dog. -उदरः 1 an epithet of Brahman. 2 of Bhîma, the second Pândava prince; Bg. 1. 15, Ki. 2. 1. -दंशः a dog. -धूपः 1 turpentine. 2 a compound perfume. -धूर्तः a jackal.

वृक्कः-क्का 1 The heart. 2 A kidney (in dual in this sense).

वृक्ण *p. p.* 1 Cut, divided. 2 Torn. 3 Broken.

वृक्त *p. p.* Cleaned, cleared, purified.

वृक्ष् 1 A. (वृक्षते) 1 To accept, select. 2 To cover.

वृक्षः A tree; आत्मापराधवृक्षाणां फलान्येतानि देहिनाम्. -**Comp.** -अदनः 1 a carpenter's chisel. 2 a hatchet. 3 the fig-tree. 4 the *Piyâla* tree. -अम्लः the hog-plum. -आलयः a bird. -आवासः 1 a bird. 2 an ascetic. -आश्रयिन् *m.* a kind of small owl. -कुक्कुटः a wild cock. -खंडं a grove or clump of trees. -चरः a monkey. -छाया the shade of a tree. (-यं) thick shade; the shade of many trees. -धूपः turpentine. -नाथः the fig-tree. -निर्यासः gum, resin. -पाकः the fig-tree. -भिद् *f.* an axe. -मर्कटिका a squirrel. -वाटिका, -वाटी a garden, grove of trees. -शः a lizard. -शायिका a squirrel.

वृक्षकः 1 A small tree ; Ku. 5. 14. 2 A tree (in general).

वृच् 7 P. (वृणक्ति) To choose.

वृज् 1. 2. A. (वृक्ते) To avoid, shun, abandon. -II. 7 P. (वृणक्ति) 1 To avoid, shun, give up, abandon 2 To choose; आसमिकतमां वृंग्धि सवर्णां स्वर्गभूषणां Bhâg. 3 To atone for, efface, purify; तन्मे रेतः पिता वृंक्तामित्यस्यैतन्निदर्शनं Ms. 9. 20. 4 To turn away, avert. -III. 1 P., 10 U. (वर्जति, वर्जयति-ते, वर्जित) 1 To shun, avoid. 2 To give up; abandon. 3 To exclude, set aside. 4 To abstain from. 5 To cut to pieces. (The following verse from K. R. illustrates the root in its different conjugations:— वृणक्ति वृजिनैः संगं वृंक्ते च वृषैलः सह। वर्जत्यनार्जवोपेतैः स वर्जयति दुर्जनैः ॥. -With अप to destroy. 2 to finish. 3 to leave, quit; R. 17. 79, Ki. 1. 29. 4 to pour, throw; *Si.* 13. 37. -आ 1 to bend, incline; आवर्ज्य शाखाः सदयं च यासां R. 16. 19, 13. 17; आवर्ज्य दृष्टीः Me. 46. 2 to offer, give; R. 1. 62, 67; 8. 26; Ku. 5. 34. 3 to subdue, win over. -परि to avoid, shun. -वि 1 to shun, avoid. 2 to make destitute of, deprive of.

वृजनः 1 Hair. 2 Curled hair. -नं 1 Sin. 2 A calamity. 3 Sky. 4 An enclosed piece of ground, an enclosure ; especially a field cleared for pasture or agriculture.

वृजिन *a.* 1 Crooked, bent, curved. 2 Wicked, sinful. -नः 1 Hair, curled hair. 2 A wicked man ; वृणक्ति वृजिनैः संगं K. R. -नं 1 Sin ; सर्वं ज्ञानप्लवेनैव वृजिनं संतरिष्यसि Bg. 4. 36, R. 14. 57. 2 Pain, distress (said be *m.* also in this sense).

वृण् 8 U. (वृणेाति, वृणुते) To eat, consume.

वृत् I. 4 A (वृत्यते) To choose, like; cf. व्यावृत्. 2 To distribute, divide. -II. 10 U. (वर्तयति-ते) To shine. -III. 1 A. (वर्तते, but Paras. also in the Aorist, the two Futures and the Conditional; also in the Desiderative; वृत्त) 1 To be, exist, abide, remain, subsist, stay ; इदं मे मनसि वर्तते *S.* 1; अत्र विषयेऽस्माकं महत्कुतूहलं वर्तते Pt. 1; मरालकुलनायकः कथय रे कथं वर्तता Bv. 1. 3; often used merely as a copula ; अतीत्य हरितो हरींश्च वर्तंते वाजिनः *S.* 1. 2 To be in any particular condition or circumstances; पश्चिमे वयसि वर्तमानस्य K.; so दुःखे, हर्षे, विषादे &c. वर्तते. **3** To happen, take place, occur, come to pass; सीतादेव्याः किं वृत्तमित्यस्ति काचित्प्रवृत्तिः U. 2; सायं संप्रति वर्तते पथिक रे स्थानांतरं गम्यतां Subhâsh. 'now it is evening' &c.; *S*. Til. 6; Bg. 5. 26 **4** To move on, proceed in regular course; सर्वथा वर्तते यज्ञः Ms. 2. 15; निर्व्याजमिज्या ववृते Bk. 2. 37; R. 12. 56. **5** To be maintained or supported by, live on, subsist by (fig. also); फलमूलवारिभिर्वर्तमाना K. 172; Ms. 3. 77. **6** To turn, roll on, revolve; यावदियं लोकयात्रा वर्तते Ve. 3. **7** To occupy or engage oneself, be occupied or engaged in, set about (with loc.); भगवान् काश्यपः शाश्वते ब्रह्मणि वर्तते *S*. 1; इतरो दहने स्वकर्मणां ववृते ज्ञानमयेन वह्निना R. 8. 20; Ms. 8. 346; Bg. 3. 22. **8** To act, behave, conduct or demean oneself towards, do, perform, practise (usually with loc. or by itself); आर्योऽस्मिन् विनयेन वर्ततां U. 6; कविर्निसर्गसौहृदेन भरतेषु वर्तमानः Mâl. 1; औदासीन्येन वर्तितुं R. 10. 25; Ms. 7. 104, 8. 173, 11. 30. **9** To act a part, enter upon a course of conduct; साध्वीं वृत्तिं वर्तते 'he acts an honest part'. **10** To have the sense of, signify, be used in the sense of; पुष्यसमीपस्थे चंद्रमसि पुष्यशब्दो वर्तते Mbh. on P. IV. 2. 3. (often used in lexicons in this sense). **11** To tend or conduce to (with dat.); पुत्रेण किं फलं यो वै पितृदुःखाय वर्तते. **12** To rest or depend upon. *-Caus.* (वर्तयति-ते) **1** To cause to be or exist. **2** To cause to move or turn round cause to revolve, *S*. 7. 6. **3** To brandish, flourish, whirl round; Bk. 15. 37. **4** To do, practise exhibit; Mâl. 9. 33. **5** To perform, discharge, attend or look to; सोधिकारमभिकः कुलोचितं काश्चन स्वयमवर्तयत्समाः R. 19. 4; Mv. 3. 23. **6** To spend, pass (as time). **7** To live on, subsist; Ki. 2. 18; R. 12. 20. **8** To relate, describe. *-Desid.* (विवृत्सति, विवर्तिषते).-WITH अति **1** to go beyond, exceed; Mâl. 1. 26. **2** to surpass, excel; Ki. 3. 40; *Si*. 14. 59. **3** to violate, overstep, transgress; *Si*. 6. 19. **4** to neglect, disregard; Ms. 5. 16 **5** to hurt, injure, offend. **6** to overcome, subdue. **7** to pass away (as time). **8** to be late or delay; Ms. 2. 38. **-अनु 1** to follow, conform to, act according to; प्रभुचित्तमेव हि जनोऽनुवर्तते *Si*. 15. 41, Mâl. 3. 2. **2** to humour, adapt oneself to the will of, be guided by. **3** to obey. **4** to resemble, imitate. **5** to please, gratify. **6** to be repeated or supplied from a preceding rule or Sûtra (intransitive). (*-Caus.*) **1** to turn round. **2** to follow, obey. **-अप 1** to turn away from, turn back; तस्मादपावर्तत दूरकृष्टा नीत्येव लक्ष्मीः प्रतिकूलदैवात् R. 6. 58, 7. 33. **2** to be reversed or inverted, to be overturned; Ki. 12. 49. **3** to have the face downward; Mâl. 3. 17. (*-Caus.*) to turn away or aside, bend; Mâl. 1. 40, Ki. 4. 15. **-अभि 1** to go up to, go towards, go near, approach, turn to; इत एवाभिवर्तते *S*. 1; R. 2. 10. **2** to attack, assail, rush at or upon; Ki. 13. 3. **3** to commence, break (as day). **4** to stand supreme, be over all. **5** to be, exist, chance to be. **-आ 1** to revolve. **2** to return; R. 1. 89, 2. 19. **3** to go to or towards. **4** to be restless or uneasy, whirl round; Mâl. 1. 41. **-उद् 1** to ascend. **2** to rise, increase **3** to be haughty or proud. **4** to overflow, be swollen; उद्वृत्तः क इव सुखावहः परेषां *Si*. 8. 18; Mu. 3. 8, R. 7. 56. **-उप 1** to approach. **2** to return. **-नि 1** to come back, return; न च निम्नादिव सलिलं निवर्तते मे ततो हृदयं *S*. 3. 1; Ku. 4. 30, R. 2. 43; Bg. 8, 21, 15. 4. **2** to flee from, retreat; Bk. 5. 102. **3** to turn away from, be averse to; R. 5. 23, 7. 61. **4** to abstain from; प्रसमीक्ष्य निवर्तेत सर्वमांसस्य भक्षणात् Ms. 5. 49, 1. 53; Bk. 1. 18; निवृत्तमांसस्तु जनकः U. 4. **5** to be freed or absolved from, to escape; Bg. 1. 39 **6** to leave off speaking, cease, stop. **7** to be removed, come to an end, cease, disappear; Bg. 2. 59, 14. 22; Ms. 11. 185, 186. **8** to be withheld or withdrawn from. (*-Caus.*) **1** to cause to return, send back; R. 2. 3, 3. 47, 7. 44. **2** to withdraw, keep away from; turn away, divert, R. 2. 28; Ku. 5. 11. **-निस् 1** to cease, come to an end; Bk. 8. 69. **2** to be got or accomplished; R. 17. 68; Ms. 7. 161. **3** to be withheld, not to happen; Bk. 16. 6. (*-Caus.*) **1** to perform; accomplish, finish, complete; R. 2. 45, 3. 33, 11. 30. **-परा** to return, turn back. **-परि 1** to turn round, revolve; Ku. 1. 16. **2** to roam about, move hither and thither. **3** to change, barter, exchange. **4** to turn back; R. 4. 72, V. 1. 17. **5** to be, fall into; Mâl. 9. 8. **6** to decay, perish, disappear; Mâl. 10. 6. **-प्र 1** to go forward, move on, proceed; Pt. 1. 81. **2** to arise, be produced, spring. **3** to happen; come to pass, take place. **4** to begin, commence (usually with inf.); हंत प्रवृत्तं संगीतकं M. 1; Ku. 3. 25. **5** to strive, exert oneself; प्रवर्ततां प्रकृतिहिताय पार्थिवः *S*. 7. 35. **6** to act up to, follow; Pt. 1. 116. **7** to engage in, be occupied with; *S*. 1; Ku. 5. 23. **8** to act, do; *S*. 6. **9** to act or behave towards. **10** to prevail, exist; राजन् प्रजासु ते कश्चिदपचारः प्रवर्तते R. 15. 47. **11** to hold good. **12** to proceed uninterruptedly, thrive; Bg. 17. 24, Ms. 3. 61. (*-Caus.*) **1** to proceed with, continue; Mu. 1. **2** to introduce. **3** to set on foot, establish, found. **4** to drive, propel, urge, stimulate. **5** to promote, advance. **-प्रतिनि 1** to turn back, return; गत्वेव पुनः प्रतिनिवृत्तः *S*. 1. 29, V. 1. **2** to turn round. **-वि 1** to turn round, roll, revolve, move round; Mâl. 1. 40. **2** to turn aside, bend; R. 6. 16; *S*. 2. 11. **3** to be, become. **-विनि 1** to return. **2** to cease, come to an end; Bg. 2. 59; Ms. 5. 7. **3** to desist, turn away, abstain (from); देवनात्, युद्धात्, &c. **-विपरि** to revolve (fig. also); Bg. 9. 10. **-व्यप 1** to return, turn back; चेतः कथं कथमपि व्यपवर्तते मे Mâl. 1. 18. **2** to desist from, leave; U. 5. 8. **-व्या 1** to turn back, turn away from; सहभुवा व्यावर्तमाना ह्रिया Ratn. 1. 2. **2** to be turned or withdrawn from, to be averse to; विषयव्यावृत्तकौतूहलः V. 1. 9. (*-Caus.*) to restrict, limit, exclude, arrest; तुशब्दः पूर्वपक्षं व्यावर्तयति S. B.; अपवाद इवोत्सर्गं व्यावर्तयितुमीश्वरः R. 15. 7. **-सं 1** to be or become; ते यथोक्ताः संवृत्ताः Pt. 1. **2** to be produced, arise, spring. **3** to happen, take place. **4** to be accomplished.

वृत *p. p.* **1** Chosen, selected. **2** Covered, screened. **3** Hidden. **4** Surrounded, encompassed. **5** Agreed or assented to. **6** Hired. **7** Spoiled, vitiated. **8** Served.

वृतिः *f.* **1** Choosing, selecting. **2** Hiding, covering, concealing. **3** Asking, soliciting. **4** An entreaty, a request. **5** Surrounding, encompassing. **6** A hedge, fence, an enclosure, Me. 78.

वृतिंकर *a.* Surrounding, encompassing. **-रः** The tree called विकंकत.

वृत्त *p. p.* **1** Lived, existed. **2** Occurred, happened. **3** Completed, finished. **4** Performed, done, acted. **5** Past, gone. **6** Round, circular, R. 6. 32. **7** Dead, deceased. **8** Firm, fixed. **9** Read through, studied. **10** Derived from. **11** Famous :— (See वृत्). **-त्तः** A tortoise. **-त्तं 1** An event, occurrence. **2** History, account; R. 15. 64. **3** News, tidings. **4** Practice, profession, mode of life, occupation; सतां वृत्तमनुष्ठिताः Ms. 10, 127, v. 1., 7. 122; Y. 3. 44. **5** Conduct, behaviour, manner, act, action; as in सद्वृत्त, दुर्वृत्त. **6** Good or virtuous conduct; Pt. 4. 28. **7** An established rule or usage, law, custom; observance of such rule or usage, duty; R. 5. 33. **8** A circle;

circumference of a circle. **9** A metre in general, especially a metre regulated by the number of syllables it contains (opp. जाति), see App. I. **–Comp.** **–अनुपूर्व** *a.* taperingly round; Ku. 1. 35. **–अनुसारः** **1** conformity to prescribed rules. **2** conformity to metre. **–अंतः** **1** an occasion, incident, event; अनेनारण्यकवृत्तांतेन पर्याकुलाः स्मः *S.* 1; R. 3. 66, U. 2. 17. **2** news, tidings, intelligence; को नु खलु वृत्तांतः V. 4; R. 14. 87. **3** account, history, tale, narrative, story. **4** a subject, topic. **5** kind, sort. **6** mode, manner. **7** state, condition. **8** the whole, totality. **9** rest, leisure. **10** property, nature. **–इर्वारुः**, **–कर्कटी** the water-melon. **–गंधि** *n.* N. of a kind of prose (having only the name of metre). **–चूड**, **–चौल** *a.* tonsured, whose tonsure ceremony has been performed; U. 2. **–पुष्पः** **1** a cane (वानीर). **2** the *Siri'sha* tree. **3** the *kadamba* tree. **–फलः** **1** the jujube tree. **2** the pomegranate tree. **–शस्त्र** *a.* one who has mastered the science of arms; Bk. 9. 19.

वृत्तिः *f.* **1** Being, existence. **2** Abiding, remaining, attitude, being in a particular state; as in विरुद्धवृत्ति, विपक्षवृत्ति &c. **3** State, condition. **4** Action, movement, function, operation; शतैस्तमक्ष्णामनिमेषवृत्तिभिः R. 3. 43, Ku. 3. 73, *S.* 4. 15. **5** Course, method; *S.* 2. 11. **6** Conduct, behaviour, course of conduct, mode of action; कुरु प्रियसखीवृत्तिं सपत्नीजने *S.* 4. 18, Me. 8; वैतसीवृत्तिः, बकवृत्तिः &c. **7** Profession, occupation, business, employment, mode of leading life (often at the end of comp.); वार्धके मुनिवृत्तीनां R. 1. 8; *S.* 5. 6; Pt. 3. 125. **8** Livelihood, maintenance, means of subsistence or livelihood; oft. in comp.; R. 2. 38, *S.* 7. 12, Ku. 5. 28; (for the several means of subsistence, see Ms. 4. 4-6). **9** Wages, hire. **10** Cause of activity. **11** Respectful treatment. **12** Gloss, commentary, exposition; सद्वृत्तिः सन्निबंधना *Si.* 2. 112, काशिकावृत्तिः &c. **13** Revolving, turning round. **14** The circumference of a wheel or circle. **15** (In gram.) A complex formation requiring resolution or explanation. **16** The power or force of a word by which it expresses, indicates or suggests a meaning; (these are three अभिधा, लक्षणा and व्यंजना q. q. v. v.) **17** A style in composition (these are four; कैशिकी, भारती, सात्वती and आरभटी q. q. v. v.) **–Comp.** **–अनुप्रासः** a kind of alliteration; see K. P. 9. **–उपायः** a means of subsistence. **–कर्षित** *a.* badly off or distressed for want of livelihood; Ms. 8. 411. **–चक्रं** the wheel of state; Pt. 1. 81. **–छेदः** deprivation of the means of subsistence. **–भंगः**, **–वैकल्यं** want of a livelihood; Pt. 1. 153. **–स्थ** *a.* **1** being in any state or employment. **2** well-conducted, of good behaviour. (**–स्थः**) a lizard, chameleon.

वृत्रः **1** N. of a demon killed by Indra; (he is supposed to be a personification of darkness); see इंद्र. **2** A cloud. **3** Darkness. **4** An enemy. **5** Sound. **6** A mountain. **–Comp.** **–अरिः**, **–द्विष्** *m.*, **–शत्रुः**, **–हन्** *m.* epithets of Indra; क्रुद्धेऽपि पक्षाच्छिदि वृत्रशत्रौ Ku. 1. 20; वाचा हरिं वृत्रहणं स्मितेन 7. 46.

वृथा *ind.* **1** To no purpose, in vain, uselessly, unprofitably; often with the force an adjective; व्यर्थं यत्र कपींद्रसख्यमपि मे वीर्यं हरीणां वृथा U. 3. 45; दिवं यदि प्रार्थयसे वृथा श्रमः Ku. 5. 45. **2** Unnecessarily. **3** Foolishly, idly, wantonly. **4** Wrongly, improperly. (At the beginning of comp. वृथा may be translated by 'vain, useless, improper, false, idle' &c.). **–Comp.** **–अट्या** strolling about idly, walking for pleasure. **–आकारः** a false form, an empty show. **–कथा** idle talk. **–जन्मन्** *n.* unprofitable or vain birth. **–दानं** a gift that may be revoked or not made good if promised. **–मति** *a.* foolish-minded. **–मांसं** flesh not intended for the Gods or Manes. **–वादिन्** *a.* speakin falsely. **–श्रमः** useless exertion or trouble.

वृद्ध *a.* (compar. ज्यायस् or वर्षीयस् superl. ज्येष्ठः or वर्षिष्ठ) **1** Increased, augmented. **2** Full-grow ,grown up. **3** Old, aged, advanced in years; वृद्धास्ते न विचारणीयचरिताः U. 5. 35. **4** Advanced or grown up (at the end of comp.), cf. वयोवृद्ध, धर्मवृद्ध, ज्ञानवृद्ध, आगमवृद्ध &c. **5** Great, large. **6** Accumulated, heaped. **7** Wise, learned. **–द्धः** **1** An old man; हैयंगवीनमादाय घोषवृद्धानुपस्थितान् R. 1. 45, 9. 78; Me. 30. **2** A worthy or venerable man. **3** A sage, saint. **4** A male descendant. **–द्धं** Benzoin. **–Comp.** **–अंगुलिः**, *f.* great toe. **–अवस्था** old age. **–आचारः** an ancient or long-standing custom. **–उक्षः** an old bull. **–काकः** a raven. **–नाभि** *a.* corpulent, pot-bellied. **–भावः** old age. **–मतं** the precept of ancient sages. **–वाहनः** the mango tree. **–श्रवस्** *m.* an epithet of Indra. **–संघः** a council of elders. **–सूत्रकं** a flock of cotton.

वृद्धा **1** An old woman. **2** A female descendant.

वृद्धिः **1** Growth, increase, augmentation, development; पुपोष वृद्धिं हरिदश्वदीधितेरनुप्रवेशादिव बालचंद्रमाः R. 3. 22; तपोवृद्धिः; ज्ञानवृद्धिः &c. **2** Waxing, increase of the digits of the moon; पर्यायपतितस्य सुरैर्हिमांशोः कलाक्षयः श्लाघ्यतरो हि वृद्धेः R. 5. 16, Ku. 7. 1. **3** Increase in wealth, prosperity, affluence; Pt. 2. 112. **4** Success, advancement, rise, progress; परवृद्धिमत्सरि मनो हि मानिनां *Si.* 15. 1. **5** Wealth, property. **6** A heap, quantity, multitude. **7** Interest; सरला वृद्धिः and चक्रवृद्धिः **8** Usury. **9** Profit, gain. **10** Enlargement of the scrotum. **11** Extension of power or revenue. **12** (In gram.) The increase or lengthening of vowels, the change of अ, इ, उ, ऋ, short or long and ऌ to आ, ऐ, औ, आर् and आल् respectively. **13** The impurity caused by child-birth in a family (called जननाशौच q. v.). **–Comp.** **–आजीवः**, **–आजीविन्** *m.* a usurer, money-lender. **–जीवनं**, **–जीविका** the profession of usury. **–द** *a.* promoting prosperity. **–पत्रं** a kind of razor. **–श्राद्धं** an offering made to the Manes on prosperous occasions such as the birth of a son.

वृध् I. 1 A. (but Paras. also in the two Futures, the Aorist and the Conditional, also in the Desiderative (वर्धते, वृद्ध; *desid.* विवृत्सति or विवर्धिषते) **1** To grow, increase, become larger, stronger or greater, thrive, prosper; अन्योन्यजयसंरंभो ववृधे वादिनोरिव R. 12. 92, 10. 78; धनक्षये वर्धति जाठराग्निः Subhâsh.; Bk. 14 13, 19. 26. **2** To continue, last. **3** To rise, ascend. **4** To have cause for congratulation, usually with दिष्ट्या; दिष्ट्या धर्मपत्नीसमागमेन पुत्रमुखदर्शनेन चायुष्मान् वर्धते *S.* 7. 'your honour is to be congratulated upon your union' &c. *–Caus.* (वर्धयति-ते, also वर्धापयति-ते) **1** To cause to grow, increase, augment, heighten, amplify, enhance; वर्धयन्निव तत्कूटानुद्धतैर्धातुरेणुभिः R. 4. 71. **2** To cause to prosper, glorify, magnify, exalt; H. 3. 3. **3** To congratulate, felicitate (वर्धापयति in this sense). –WITH अभि to grow, increase; क्षीणः क्षीणोऽपि शशी भूयो भूयोभिवर्धते नित्यं K. P. 10. **–परि,–प्र,–वि** to grow, increase, prosper &c. **–सं** to increase. (*–Caus.*) to rear, bring up; R. 5. 6. –II. 10 U. (वर्धयति-ते) **1** To speak. **2** To shine.

वृधसानः A man.

वृधासानुः **1** A man. **2** A leaf. **3** An act or action.

वृंतं **1** The foot-stalk of a leaf or fruit, a stalk; वृंताच्छ्लथं हरति पुष्पमनोकहानां R. 5. 69. **2** The stand of a water-jar. **3** A teat, nipple.

वृंताकः-की The egg-plant.

वृंतिका A small stalk.

वृंदं **1** A multitude, host, large number, group; अनुगतमलिवृंदैर्गंडभित्तीर्विहाय R. 12. 102; Me. 99; so अभ्र°. **2** A heap, quantity.

वृंदा **1** The holy basil. **2** N. of a forest near *Gokula*. **–Comp.** **–अरण्यं,**

-वनं N. of a forest near Gokula; वृंदारऽण्ये वसतिरधुना केवलं दुःखहेतुः Pad. D. 38, 41, R. 6. 50. -वनी the holy basil.

वृंदार *a.* 1 Much, great, large. 2 Eminent, best, excellent. 3 Pleasing, attractive, beautiful.

वृंदारक *a.* (का or रिका *f.*) 1 Much, great, many. 2 Eminent, best, excellent. 3 Pleasing, attractive, handsome, lovely. 4 Respectable, venerable. -कः 1 A god, deity; श्रितो वृंदारण्यं नतनिखिलवृंदारकवृतः Bv. 4. 5. 2 The chief of anything (at the end of comp.) see (2) above.

वृंदिष्ठ *a.* 1 Very great or large. 2 Very handsome (superl. of वृंदारक, q. v.).

वृंदीयस् *a.* 1 Greater, larger. 2 More handsome or beautiful (compar. of वृंदारक q. v.).

वृश् 4 P. (वृश्यति) To choose, select.

वृशः A rat. -शा A drug. -शं Ginger.

वृश्चिकः 1 A scorpion. 2 The sign *scorpio* of the zodiac. 3 A crab. 4 A centipede. 5 A kind of beetle. 6 A hairy caterpillar.

वृष् I. 1 P. (वर्षति, वृष्ट) 1 To rain (usually with words signifying 'Indra', 'Parjanya', 'cloud', &c. as the subject of the verb, or sometimes used impersonally); द्वादश वर्षाणि नववर्ष दशशताक्षः Dk.; कालि वर्षतु मेघाः; गर्ज वा वर्ष वा शक्र Mk. 5. 31; मेघा वर्षतु गर्जंतु मुंचंत्वशनिमेव वा 5. 16. 2 To rain or pour down, shower down; वर्षतीवांजनं नभः Mk. 1. 34; so शरवृष्टिं, -कुसुमवृष्टिं-वर्षति &c., 3 To pour forth, shed. 4 To grant, bestow. 5 To moisten. 6 To produce, engender. 7 To have supreme power. 8 To strike, hurt. -WITH अभि 1 to shower, rain or pour down, sprinkle; R. 1. 84, 10. 48. 2 to give, bestow. -प्र to rain, shower; यस्यायमभितः पुष्पैः प्रवृष्ट इव केसरः Râm. (=U. 6. 36). -II. 10 A. (वर्षयते) 1 To be powerful or eminent. 2 To have the power of production.

वृषः 1 A bull; असपदस्तस्य वृषेण गच्छतः Ku. 5. 80, Me. 52, R. 2. 35, Ms. 9. 123. 2 The sign *Taurus* of the zodiac. 3 The chief or best of a class, the best of its kind; (at the end of comp.); मुनिवृषः, कपिवृषः &c. 4 The god of love. 5 A strong or athletic man. 6 A lustful man, a man of one of the four classes into which men are divided in erotic works; see Ratimanjarî 37. 7 An enemy, adversary. 8 A rat. 9 The bull of *Siva*. 10 Morality, justice. 11 Virtue, a pious or meritorious act; न सद्वृत्तिः स्याद् वृषवर्जितानां Kir. K. 9. 62 (where वृष means a 'bull' also). 12 N. of Kaṇa. 13 N. of Vishṇu. 14 N. of a particular drug. -र्षं A peacock's plumage. -Comp. -अंकः 1 an epithet of *Siva*; R. 3. 23. 2 a pious or virtuous man. 3 the markintg-nut plant. 4 a eunuch. °जः a small drum. -अंचनः an epithet of *Siva*. -अंतकः an epithet of Vishṇu. -आहारः a cat. -उत्सर्गः setting free a bull on the occasion of a funeral rite, or as a religious act generally. -दंशः,-दंशकः a cat. -ध्वजः 1 an epithet of *Siva*; R. 11. 44. 2 an epithet of Gaṇesa. 3 a pious or virtuous man. -पतिः an epithet of *Siva*. -पर्वन् *m.* 1 an epithet of *Siva*. 2 N. of a demon who with the aid of *Sukra*, preceptor of the Asuras, maintained struggle with the gods for a long time. His daughter *Sarmi shthâ* was married by Yayâti; see Yayâti and Devayânî. 3 a wasp. -भासा the residence of Indra and the gods; *i. e.* Amarâvatî. -लोचनः a cat. -वाहनः an epithet of *Siva*.

वृषणः The scrotum, the bag containing the testicles.

वृषणश्वः A horse of Indra.

वृषन् *m.* 1 A bull. 2 The sign *Taurus* of the zodiac. 3 The chief of a class; Mv. 1. 7. 4 A stallion, horse. 5 Pain, sorrow. 6 Insensibility to pain. 7 N. of Indra; वृषेव सीतां तदवग्रहक्षतां Ku. 5. 61, 80; R. 10. 52, 17. 77. 8 N. of Karṇa. 9 of Agni.

वृषभः 1 A bull. 2 Any male animal. 3 Anything best or eminent of its class (at the end of comp.); द्विजवृषभः Ratn. 1. 5, 4. 21. 4 The sign *Taurus* of the zodiac. 5 A kind of drug; cf. ऋषभ. 6 An elephant's ear. 7 The orifice or hollow of the ear. -Comp. -गतिः,-ध्वजः epithets of *Siva*; R. 2. 36; Ku. 3. 62.

वृषभी *f.* 1 A widow. 2 Cowach.

वृषलः 1 A *Sûdra*. 2 A horse. 3 Garlic. 4 A sinner, wicked or irreligious man. 5 An outcast. 6 N. of Chandragupta (particularly used by Châṇakya, see *inter alia* Mu. acts 1 and 3).

वृषलकः A contemptible *Sûdra*.

वृषली 1 An unmarried girl twelve years old; particularly, a girl remaining unmarried at her father's house in whom menstruation has commenced; पितर्गेहे च या नारी रजः पश्यत्यसंस्कृता। भ्रूणहत्या पितुस्तस्याः सा कन्या वृषली स्मृता॥ 2 A woman during menstruation. 3 A barren woman. 4 The mother of a still-born child. 5 A Sûdra female or the wife of a *Sûdra*. -Comp. -पतिः the husband of a Sûdra woman. -सेवनं intercourse with a *Sûdra* female.

वृषस्त्री A wasp.

वृषस्यंती 1 A woman longing for sexual intercourse (with acc. of male; रघुनंदनं वृषस्यंती शूर्पणखा प्राप्ता Mv. 5; Bk. 4. 30, R. 12. 34. 2 A libidinous or lascivious woman. 3 A cow in heat.

वृषाकपायी 1 An epithet of Lakshmî. 2 Of Gaurî. 3 Of *Sachî*. 4 Of Svâhâ; wife of Agni. 5 Of the dawn, wife of the sun.

वृषाकपिः 1 An epithet of the sun. 2 Of Vishṇu. 3 Of *Siva*. 4 Of Indra. 5 Of Agni.

वृषायणः 1 An epithet of *Siva*. 2 A sparrow.

वृषिन् *m.* A peacock.

वृषी The seat of an ascetic or religious student (made of Kusa grass).

वृष्ट *p. p.* 1 Rained, 2 Raining. 3 Showering, pouring down.

वृष्टिः *f.* 1 Rain, a shower of rain; आदित्याज्जायते वृष्टिर्वृष्टेर ततः प्रजाः Ms. 3. 76. 2 A shower (of anything); अस्त्रवृष्टि R. 3. 58; पुष्पवृष्टि 2. 60; so शर,° धन°, उपल° &c. -Comp. -कालः the rainy season. -जीवन *a.* nourished or watered by rain (as a country); cf. देवमातृक. -भूः a frog.

वृष्टिमत् *a.* Raining, rainy. -*m.* A cloud.

वृष्णि *a.* 1 Heretical, heterodox. 2 Angry, passionate. -*m.* 1 A cloud. 2 A ram. 3 A ray of light. 4 N. of an ancestor of Krishṇa. 5 N. of Krishṇa. 6 Of Indra. 7 Of Agni. -Comp. -गर्भः an epithet of Krishṇa.

वृष्य *a.* 1 To be rained or showered down. 2 Stimulating amorous desire, provocative of sexual vigour, aphrodisiac. -ष्यः A kind of kidney-bean.

वृह, वृहत्, वृहतिका } See बृह्, बृहत्, and बृहतिका.

वृहती 1 The lute of Nârada. 2 The number 'thirty-six'. 3 A mantle, cloak, wrapper. 4 Speech. 5 A reservoir (as of water); see बृहती also -Comp. -पतिः an epithet of Brihaspati.

वृहस्पति See बृहस्पति.

वॄ 9 U. (वृणाति, वृणीते, वूर्ण; *pass.* वूर्य; *desid.* वुवूर्षति-ते or विवरिषति-ते or विवरीषति-ते) To choose, select; (see वृ I.).

वे 1 U. (वयति-ते, उत; *caus.* वाययति-ते) 1 To weave; सितांशुवर्णैर्वयति स्म तद्गुणैः N. 1. 12. 2 To braid, plant. 3 To sew. 4 To make, compose, string together. -WITH प्र 1 to weave. 2 to tie, fasten. 3 to set, fix. 4 to interweave; interlace; see प्रोत.

वेकटः 1 A buffoon. 2 A jeweller. 3 A youth.

वेगः 1 Impulse, impetus. 2 Speed, velocity, rapidity. 3 Agitation. 4 Impetuosity, violence, force. 5 A stream, current; as in अंबुवेगः. 6 Energy, activity, determination. 7 Power, strength; मदनज्वरस्य वेगात् K. 8 Circulation, orking, effect (as of poison);

U. 2. 26, V. 5. 18. **9** Haste, rashness, sudden impulse ; Pt. 1. 109. **10** The flight of an arrow ; Ki. 13. 24. **11** Love, passion. **12** The external manifestation of an internal emotion. **13** Delight, pleasure. **14** Evacuation of the feces. **15** Semen virile.–**Comp.** **–अनिलः** **1** blast caused by speed ; V. 1. 4. **2** strong or violent wind.–**आघातः** **1** sudden arresting of velocity, check of speed. **2** obstruction of excretion, constipation. **–नाशनः** the phlegmatic humour. **–वाहिन्** *a* swift. **–विधारणं** checking of speed. **–सरः** a mule.

वेगिन् *a.* (**नी** *f.*) Swift, fleet, impetuous, violent, rapid. *–m.* **1** A courier. **2** A hawk. **–नी** A river.

वेंकटः N. of a mountain.

वेच्चा Hire, wages.

वेडं A kind of sandal.

वेडा A boat.

वण्, वेन् 1 U. (वेणति-ते, वेनति ते) **1** To go, move. **2** To know, recognize, perceive. **3** To reflect, consider. **4** To take. **5** To play on an instrument.

वेणः **1** A musician by caste ; cf. Ms. 10. 19 ; वेणानां भांडवादनं 10. 49. **2** N. of a king, son of Anga and said to be a descendant of Manu Svâyambhuva. [When he became king he issued a proclamation prohibiting all worship and sacrifices. The sages strongly remonstrated with him, but when he turned a deaf ear to their words, they killed him with 'blades of consecrated Kus*a* grass.' The kingdom was now without a ruler. So they rubbed the thigh of the dead body, until a Nish*a*da came forth, short in stature and with a flat face. They then rubbed the right arm, and from it sprang the majestic Prithu (see Prithu). According to the Padma Puran*a*, Ven*a* began his reign well, but subsequently fell into Jaina heresy. He is also said to have caused confusion of castes ; cf. Ms, 7. 41, 9. 66-67.].

वेणा N. of a river (joining the Krishnâ).

वेणिः -णी *f.* **1** Braided hair, a braid of hair ; तरंगिणी वेणिरिवायता भुवः *S*i. 12. 75 ; Me. 18. **2** Hair twisted into a single unornamented braid and allowed to fall on the back (said to be worn by women whose husbands are absent from them); बनान्निवृत्तेन रघूत्तमेन मुक्ता स्वयं वेणिरिवाबभासे R. 14. 12 ; अबलावेणिमोक्षोत्सुकानि Me. 99, Ku. 2. 61. **3** Continuous flow, current, stream ; जलवेणिरम्यां रेवां यदि प्रेक्षितुमास्ति कामः R. 6. 43 ; Me. 29 ; cf. the word त्रिवेणी also. **4** The confluence of two or more rivers. **5** The confluence of the Ganges, Yamunâ and Sarasvatî. **6** N. of a river. **–Comp.** **–बंधः** hair twisted into a braid ; R. 10. 47. **–वेधनी** a leech. **–वेधिनी** a comb. **–संहारः** **1** tying the hair into a braid ; Ve. 6. **2** N. of a drama by Bhatta Nârâyana.

वेणुः **1** A bamboo ; मलयेऽपि स्थितो वेणुर्वेणुरेव न चंदनं Subhâsh., R. 12. 41. **2** A reed. **3** A flute pipe ; नामसमेतं कृतसंकेतं वादयते मृदु वेणुं Gît. 5. **–Comp.** **–जः** bamboo seed. **–ध्मः** a flute-player, piper. **–निस्रुतिः** the sugar-cane. **–यवः** bamboo-seed. **–यष्टिः** *f.* a bamboo stick. **–वादः**, **–वादकः** a piper, flute-player. **–बीजं** bamboo-seed.

वेणुकं A goad with a bamboo handle.

वेणुनं Black pepper.

वेतं(दं)डः An elephant ; Bv. 1. 62.

वेतनं **1** Hire, wages, salary, pay, stipend ; R. 17. 66. **2** Livelihood, subsistence. **–Comp** **–अदानं, -अनपाकर्मन्** *n.*, **–अनपक्रिया** **1** non-payment of wages **2** an action for non-payment of wages. **–जीविन्** *m.* a stipendiary.

वेतसः **1** The ratan, reed, cane ; अविलंबितमेधि वेतसस्तरुवन्माधव मा स्म भज्यथाः *S*i. 16. 53; R. 9. 75. **2** The citron.

वेतसी The ratan; वेतसीतरुतले K. P. 1.

वेतस्वत् *a.* (**ती** *f.*) Abounding in reeds.

वेतालः **1** A kind of ghost, a goblin, vampire ; particularly a ghost occupying a dead body ; Mâl. 5. 23, *S*i. 20. 60. **2** A door-keeper.

वेत्तृ *m.* **1** A knower. **2** A sage. **3** A husband, an espouser.

वेत्रः **1** The cane, ratan. **2** A stick, staff, particularly the staff of a door-keeper ; वामप्रकोष्ठार्पितहेमवेत्रः Ku. 3. 41. **Comp.** **–आसनं** a cane-seat. **–धरः**, **–धारकः** **1** a door-keeper. **2** a mace-bearer, staff-bearer.

वेत्रकीय *a.* Reedy, abounding in reeds.

वेत्रवती **1** A female door-keeper. **2** N. of a river ; Me. 24.

वेत्रिन् *m.* **1** A door-keeper, warder. **2** staff-bearer.

वेथ् 1 A (वेथते) To beg, solicit, ask.

वेदः **1** Knowledge. **2** Sacred knowledge, holy learning, the scriptures of the Hindus. (Originally there were only three *Vedas*: ऋग्वेद, यजुर्वेद and सामवेद, which are collectively called त्रयी 'the sacred triad'; but a fourth, the अथर्ववेद, was subsequently added to them. Each of the *Vedas* has two distinct parts, the *Mantra* or *Samhita'* and the *Bra'hmana*. According to the strict orthodox faith of the Hindus the Vedas are *a-paurusheya*, 'not human compositions', being supposed to have been directly revealed by the Supreme Being Brahman, and are called Sruti *i. e.* 'what is heard or revealed', as distinguished from Smriti, *i. e.* what is remembered or is the work of human origin ; see श्रुति, स्मृति also ; and the several sages to whom the hymns of the Vedas are ascribed are, therefore, called द्रष्टारः 'seers,' and not कर्तारः or स्रष्टारः 'composers'). **3** A bundle of Kusa grass ; Ms. 4. 36. **4** N. of Vishnu. **–Comp.** **–अंगं** 'a member of the Veda,' N. of certain classes of works regarded as auxiliary to the Vedas and designed to aid in the correct pronunciation and interpretation of the text and the right employment of the *Mantras* in ceremonials ; (the *Vedângas* are six in number:— 1 शिक्षा 'the science of proper articulation and pronunciation;' 2 छंदस् 'the science of prosody'; 3 व्याकरण 'grammar'; 4 निरुक्त 'etymological explanation of difficult Vedic words'; 5 ज्योतिष 'astronomy', and 6 कल्प 'ritual or ceremonial). **–अधिगमः**, **–अध्ययनं** holy study, study of the Vedas. **–अध्यापकः** a teacher of the Vedas, a holy preceptor. **–अंतः** **1** 'the end of the Veda', an *Upanishad* (which comes at the end of the Veda.) **2** the last of the six principal *Darsanas* or systems of Hindu philosophy ; (so called because it teaches the ultimate aim and scope of the Veda, or because it is based on the *Upanishads* which come at the end of the Veda) ; (this system of philosophy is sometimes called उत्तरमीमांसा being regarded as a sequel to Jaimini's पूर्वमीमांसा, but it is practically quite a distinct system ; see मीमांसा. It represents the popular pantheistic creed of the Hindus, regarding, as it does, the whole world as synthetically derived from one eternal principle, the Brahman or Supreme Spirit ; see ब्रह्मन् also). °गः, °ज्ञः a follower of the Vedânta philosophy. **–अंतिन्** *m.* a follower of the Vedânta philosophy. **–अर्थः** the meaning of the Vedas. **–अवतारः** revelation of the Vedas. **–आदि** *n.*, **–आदिवर्णः**, **–आदिबीजं** the sacred syllable *om.* **–उक्त** *a.* scriptural, taught in the Vedas. **–कौलेयकः** an epithet of *S*iva. **–गर्भः** **1** an epithet of Brahman. **2** a Brâhmana versed in the Vedas. **–ज्ञः** a Brâhmana versed in the Vedas. **–त्रयं**, **-त्रयी** the three Vedas collectively. **–निंदकः** an atheist, a heretic, an unbeliever (one who rejects the divine origin and character of the Vedas). **–निंदा** unbelief, heresy. **–पारगः** a Brâhmana skilled in the Vedas. **–मातृ** *f.* N. of a very sacred Vedic verse called

Gâyatri' q. v. –वचनं, –वाक्यं a Vedic text. –वदनं grammar. –वासः a Brâhmaṇa. –वाह्य *a.* contrary to, or not founded on, the Veda. –विद् *m.* a Brâhmaṇa versed in the Vedas. –विहित *a.* enjoined by the Vedas. –व्यासः an epithet of Vyâsa who is regarded as the 'arranger' of the Vedas in their present form; see व्यास. –संन्यासः giving up the ritual of the Vedas.

वेदनं, वेदना 1 Knowledge, perception. 2 Feeling, sensation. 3 Pain, torment, agony, anguish; अवेदनाज्ञं कुलिशक्षतानां Ku. 1. 20, R. 8. 50. 4 Acquisition, wealth, property. 5 Marriage; Ms. 3. 44, 9. 65; Y. 1. 62.

वेदारः A chameleon.

वेदिः A learned man, sage, Paṇḍit. –दिः–दी *f.* 1 An altar, especially one prepared for a sacrifice. 2 An altar of a particular shape, the middle points of which come very close to each other; मध्येन सा वेदिविलग्नमध्या Ku. 1. 37; (some propose to take वेदि in this passage as meaning 'a seal-ring'). 3 A quadrangular spot in the court-yard of a temple or palace. 4 A seal-ring. 5 N. of Sarasvatî. 6 A tract or region. –**Comp.** –जा an epithet of Draupadî who was born from the midst of the sacrificial altar of king Drupada.

वेदिका 1 A sacrificial altar or ground. 2 A raised seat; an elevated spot of ground (usually for sacred purposes); सप्तपर्णवेदिका *S.* 1; Ku. 3. 44. 3 A seat in general. 4 An altar, heap, mound; मंदाकिनीसैकतवेदिकाभिः Ku. 1. 29 'by making altars or heaps of sand &c'. 5 A quadrangular open shed in the middle of a courtyard. 6 An arbour, a bower.

वेदिन् *a.* 1 Knowing; as in कृतवेदिन्. 2 Marrying. –*m.* 1 A knower. 2 A teacher. 3 A learned Brâhmaṇa. 4 An epithet of Brâhman.

वेदी see वेदि *f.*

वेद्य *a.* 1 To be known. 2 To be taught or explained. 3 To be married.

वेधः 1 Penetrating, piercing, perforation. 2 Wounding, a wound. 3 A hole, an excavation. 4 The depth (of an excavation). 5 A particular measure of time.

वेधकः 1 N. of one of the divisions of hell. 2 Camphor. –कं Rice in the ear.

वेधनं 1 The act of piercing, perforating. 2 Penetration. 3 Evacuation. 4 Pricking, wounding 5 Depth (of an evacuation).

वेधनिका A sharp-pointed instrument for perforating shells and jewels, a gimblet.

वेधनी 1 An instrument for piercing an elephant's ear. 2 A sharp-pointed instrument for perforating shells and jewels, a gimblet.

वेधस् *m.* 1 A creator; Mâl. 1. 21. 2 N. of Brahman, the creator; तं वेधा विदधे नूनं महाभूतसमाधिना R. 1. 29; Ku. 2. 16, 5. 41. 3 A secondary creator (such as Daksha, sprung from Brahman); Ku. 2. 14. 4 N. of Siva. 5 Of Vishṇu. 6 The sun. 7 The *Arka* plant. 8 A learned man.

वेधसं The part of the hand under the root of the thumb.

वेधित *p. p.* Pierced, perforated.

वेन् 1 U. (वेनति-ते) see वेणृ.

वेन See वेण (2).

वेन्ना See वेणा.

वेप् 1 A (वेपते, वेपित) To tremble, shake, quiver, quake; कृतांजलिर्वेपमानः किरीटी Bg. 11. 35; R. 11. 65. –WITH –प्र to quiver, throb, tremble; Ku. 5. 27, 74.

वेपथुः Tremor, trembling, heaving (of breasts); अद्यापि स्तनवेपथुं जनयति श्वासः प्रमाणाधिकः *S.* 1. 30, *Si.* 9. 22, 73; R. 19. 23; Ku. 4. 17, 5. 85.

वेपनं Tremor, trembling.

वेमः, वेमन् *m. n.* A loom; महासिवेम्नः सहकृत्वरी बहुं N. 1. 12; तुरीवेमादिकं T. S.

वेरः–रं 1 The body. 2 Saffron. 3 The egg-plant.

वेरटः A low man, one belonging to an inferior caste. –टं The fruit of the jujube.

वेल् I. 1 P. (वेलति) 1 To go, move. 2 To shake, move about, tremble. –II. 10 U. (वेलयति ते) To count the time.

वेलं A garden, grove.

वेला 1 Time; वेलोपलक्षणार्थमादिष्टोस्मि *S.* 4. 2 Season, opportunity. 3 Interval of repose, leisure. 4 Tide, flow, current. 5 The sea-coast, seashore; वेलानिलाय प्रसृता भुजंगाः R. 13. 12, 15; 1. 30, 8. 80, 17. 37; *Si.* 3. 79; 9. 38. 6 Limit, boundary. 7 Speech. 8 Sickness. 9 Easy death. 10 The gums. –**Comp.** –कुलं N. of a district called Tâmralipta. –मूलं the seashore. –वनं a wood on the sea-coast.

वेल्ल् 1 P. (वेलति) 1 To go, move. 2 To shake, tremble, move about; Bv. 1. 55; *Si.* 7. 72.

वेल्लः, वेल्लनं 1 Shaking, moving, 2 Rolling (on the ground).

वेल्लहलः *f.* A libertine.

वेल्लिः *f* A creeper; cf. वल्लि.

वेल्लित *p. p.* 1 Trembling, tremulous, shaken. 2 Crooked. –तं 1 Going, moving. 2 Shaking.

वेवी 2 A. (वेवीते) 1 To go. 2 To obtain. 3 To conceive, be pregnant. 4 To pervade. 5 To cast, throw. 6 To eat. 7 To wish, desire; (seldom used in classical literature).

वेशः 1 Entrance. 2 Ingress, access. 3 A house, dwelling. 4 A house or residence of prostitutes; तरुणजनसहायश्चिंत्यतां वेशवासः Mk. 1. 31. 5 Dress, apparel (also written वेष in this sense); मृगयावेषधारी; विनीतवेषेण *S.* 1; कृतवेशे केशवे Gît. 11. –**Comp.** –दानं the sun-flower. –धारिन् *a.* disguised. –नारी,–वनिता a harlot; Mu. 3. 10. –वासः the residence of harlots.

वेशकः A house.

वेशनं 1 Entering, entrance. 2 A house.

वेशंतः 1 A small pond, pool. 2 Fire.

वेशरः A mule.

वेश्मन् *n.* A house, dwelling, an abode, a mansion, palace; R. 14. 15; Me. 25, Ms. 4. 73, 9. 85. –**Comp.** –कर्मन् *n.* house-building. –कलिंगः a kind of sparrow. –नकुलः the musk-rat. –भूः *f.* the site of a habitation, building-ground.

वेश्यं The habitation of harlots.

वेश्या A harlot, prostitute, courtezan, concubine; Mk. 1. 32; Me. 35, Y. 1. 141. –**Comp.** –आचार्यः 1 the master or keeper of prostitutes. 2 a pimp. 3 a catamite. –आश्रयः habitation of harlots. –गमनं debauchery, whoring. –गृहं a brothel. –जनः a harlot. –पणः the wages given to a prostitute.

वेश्वरः A mule.

वेष See वेश.

वेषणं Occupation, possession.

वेष्ट् 1 A. (वेष्टते) 1 To surround, enclose, encompass, envelop. 2 To wind or twist round. 3 To dress. –*Caus.* (वेष्टयति-ते) 1 To surround. &c. 2 To blockade. –With –आ to fold. –परि, –सं to fold together, clasp or wind round.

वेष्टः 1 Surrounding, enclosing. 2 An enclosure, a fence. 3 A turban. 4 Gum, resin, exudation. 5 Turpentine. –**Comp.** –वंशः a kind of bamboo. –सारः turpentine.

वेष्टकः 1 An enclosure, a fence. 2 A pumpkin-gourd. –कं 1 A turban. 2 A wrapper, mantle. 3 Gum, exudation. 4 Turpentine.

वेष्टनं 1 Encompassing, encircling surrounding; अंगुलिवेष्टनं a finger-ring. 2 Coiling round, twisting round; R. 4. 48. 3 An envelope, a wrapper, cover, covering, case. 4 A turban, tiara; अस्पृष्टालकवेष्टनौ R. 1. 42; शिरसा वेष्टनशोभिना 8. 12. 5 An enclosure, a fence; क्रीडाशैलः कनककदलीवेष्टनप्रेक्षणीयः Me. 77. 6 A girdle, zone. 7 A bandage. 8 The outer ear. 9 Bdellium. 10 A particular attitude in dancing.

वेष्टनकः A particular position in copulation.

वेष्टित *p. p.* **1** Surrounded, enclosed, encircled, enveloped. **2** Wrapped up, dressed. **3** Stopped, blocked, impeded. **4** Blockaded.

वेष्प:, वेष्य: Water.

वेष्या See वेश्या.

वेसर: A mule ; *S*i. 12. 19.

वेस(श)वार: A particular condiment (consisting of ground coriander, mustard, pepper, ginger &c).

वेह् 1 A. (वेहते) See बेह्.

वेहत् *f.* A barren cow.

वेहार: N. of a country (Behâr).

वेल्ल् 1 P. (वेल्लते) To go, move.

वै 1 P. (वायति) **1** To dry, be dried. **2** To be languid or weary, be exhausted.

वै *ind.* A particle of affirmation or certainty (indeed, truly, forsooth), but it is generally used as an expletive ; आपो वै नरसूनवः Ms. 1. 10 ; 2. 231, 9. 49, 11. 77. &c. It is also said to be a vocative particle and sometimes shows entreaty or persuasion (अनुनय).

वैंशतिक *a.* (की *f.*) Bought for twenty.

वैकक्षं **1** A garland worn over one shoulder and under the other, like the यज्ञोपवीत. **2** An upper garment, a mantle.

वैकक्षकं, वैकक्षिकं A garland worn over the left shoulder and under the right arm (like the यज्ञोपवीत q. v.).

वैकटिक: A jeweller.

वैकर्तन: N. of Karṇa.

वैकल्पं **1** Optionality. **2** Dubiousness, ambiguity. **3** Uncertainty, indecision.

वैकल्पिक *a.* (की *f.*) **1** Optional. **2** Dubious, doubtful, uncertain, undecided.

वैकल्यं **1** Defect, deficiency, imperfection. **2** Mutilation, being crippled or lame. **3** Incompetency. **4** Agitation, flurry, excitement. **5** Non-existence.

वैकारिक *a.* (की *f.*) **1** Relating to modification. **2** Modifying. **3** Modified.

वैकाल: Afternoon, evening.

वैकालिक *a.* (की *f.*), **वैकालीन** *a.* (नी *f.*) Relating to or occurring in the evening.

वैकुंठ: **1** An epithet of Vishṇu. **2** of Indra. **3** Holy basil. **–ठं** **1** The heaven of Vishṇu. **2** Talc. **–Comp.** **–चतुर्दशी** the fourteenth day of the bright half of Kârtika. **–लोक:** the world of Vishṇu.

वैकृत *a.* (ती *f.*) **1** Changed. **2** Modified. **–तं** **1** Change, alteration, modification. **2** Aversion, disgust, loathing. **3** Change in state, appearance &c., disfigurement ; N. 4. 5. **4** A portent, any event foreboding evil ; तत्प्रतीपपवनादि वैकृतं प्रेक्ष्य R. 11. 62. **–Comp.** **–विवर्त:** a woful plight, miserable condition, suffering ; वैकृतविवर्तदारुणः Mâl. 1. 39.

वैकृतिक *a.* (की *f.*) **1** Changed modified. **2** Belonging to a Vikṛiti q. v. (in Sânkhya phil.).

वैकृत्यं **1** Change, alteration. **2** Woful state, miserable plight. **3** Disgust.

वैक्रांतं A kind of gem.

वैक्लवं, वैक्लव्यं **1** Confusion, agitation, bewilderment. **2** Commotion, tumult. **3** Affliction, distress, grief ; *S*. 4. 6, Ve. 5 : Mk. 3.

वैखरी **1** Articulate utterance, production of sound ; see Malli. on Ku. 2. 17. **2** The faculty of speech. **3** Speech in general.

वैखानस *a.* (सी *f.*) Relating to a hermit, ascetic, monastic ; वैखानसं किमनया व्रतमा प्रदानाद् व्यापाररोधि मदनस्य निषेवितव्यं *S*. 1. 27. **–स:** An anchorite, a hermit (वानप्रस्थ) ; a Brâhmaṇa in the third order of his religious life ; R. 14. 28 ; Bk. 3. 46.

वैगुण्यं **1** Absence of qualities or attributes. **2** Absence of good qualities, a defect, fault, an imperfection. **3** Difference of properties, diversity, contrariety. **4** Inferiority, lowness. **5** Unskilfulness.

वैचक्षण्यं Skill, cleverness, proficiency.

वैचित्त्यं Grief, mental distraction, sorrow ; Mâl. 3. 1.

वैचित्र्यं **1** Variety, diversity. **2** Manifoldness. **3** Strangeness. **4** Strikingness ; as in वाच्यवैचित्र्य K. P. 10. **5** Surprise.

वैजननं The last month of pregnancy.

वैजयंत: **1** The palace of Indra. **2** The banner of Indra. **3** A banner or flag in general. **4** A house.

वैजयंतिक: A standard-bearer.

वैजयंतिका **1** A banner, flag (fig. also) ; संचारिणीव देवस्य मकरकेतोर्जगद्विजयवैजयंतिका काप्यागतवती Mâl. 1. **2** A kind of necklace of pearls.

वैजयंती **1** A banner, flag ; स्तनपरिणाहविलासवैजयंती Mâl. 3. 15. **2** An ensign. **3** A garland, necklace. **4** The necklace of Vishṇu. **5** N. of a lexicon.

वैजात्यं **1** Difference of kind or species. **2** Difference of, caste. **3** Strangeness. **4** Exclusion from caste. **5** Looseness, wantonness.

वैजिक *a.* See बैजिक.

वैज्ञानिक *a.* (की *f.*) Clever, skilful, proficient.

वैडाल See बैडाल.

वैण: A maker of bamboo-work.

वैणव *a.* (वी) **1** Made of or produced from, a bamboo. **–व:** **1** A bamboo-staff. **2** A worker in bamboo or wicker-work. **–वी** Bamboo-manna. **–वं** The seed or fruit of the bamboo.

वैणविक: A piper, flute player.

वैणविन् *m.* An epithet of *S*iva.

वैणिक: A lutanist.

वैणुक: A piper, flute-player. **–कं** A goad ; See वेणुक.

वैतंसिक: A vendor of flesh.

वैतंडिक: A disputatious man, captious person.

वैतनिक *a.* (की *f.*) Living on wages. **–क:** **1** A hired labourer, labourer. **2** A stipendiary.

वैतरणि:-णी *f.* **1** N. of the river of hell. **2** N. of a river in the country of the Kalingas.

वैतस *a.* (सी *f.*) **1** Pertaining to a cane. **2** Reed-like, *i. e.* yielding to a superior foe, bowing down to a stronger enemy; as in वैतसी वृत्तिः R. 4. 35, Pt. 3. 19.

वैतान *a.* (नी *f.*) Sacrificial, sacred; वैतानास्त्वां वह्नयः पावयंतु *S*. 4. 7. **–नं** **1** A sacrificial rite. **2** A sacrificial oblation.

वैतानिक *a.* (की *f.*) See वैतान.

वैतालिक: **1** A bard, minstrel. **2** A magician, conjurer ; especially one who is a votary of Vetâla q. v.

वैत्रक *a.* (की *f.*) Cany, reedy.

वैद: A wise man, learned man.

वैदग्धं, वैदग्धी, वैदग्ध्यं **1** Skill, dexterity, proficiency, cleverness ; अहो वैदग्ध्यं Mâl. 1; प्रबंधविन्यासवैदग्ध्यनिधिः Vâs.; *S*i. 4. 26. **2** Skill in arrangement, beauty ; Mâl. 1. 37. **3** Shrewdness, smartness, cunningness ; Ratn. 2. **4** Wit.

वैदर्भ: A king of Vidarbha. **–र्भी** **1** N. of Damayantî. **2** of Rukmiṇî. **3** A particular style of composition ; thus defined in S. D.:—माधुर्यव्यंजकैर्वर्णै रचना ललितात्मिका । अवृत्तिरल्पवृत्तिर्वा वैदर्भी रीतिरिष्यते ॥ 626. Daṇḍin very minutely distinguishes this style from the *Gauḍí'ya* ; see Kâv. 1. 41–53.

वैदल *a.* (ली *f.*) **1** Made of wicker or cane. **–ल:** A kind of cake. **2** Any leguminous vegetable or grain. **–लं** **1** A shallow cup of a religious mendicant. **2** Any seat or vessel of wicker-work.

वैदिक *a.* (की *f.*) **1** Derived from or conformable to the Vedas, Vedic. **2** Sacred, scriptural, holy ; Ku. 5. 73. **–क:** A Brâhmaṇa well-versed in the Vedas. **–Comp.** **–पाश:** a smatterer in Veda, one possessing an imperfect knowledge of the Vedas.

वैदुषी *f.*, **वैदुष्यं** Learning, wisdom.

वैदूर्य *a.* (री or र्यी *f.*) Brought, from or produced in Vidûra. **–र्यं** *Lapis lazuli* ; Ku. 7. 10, *S*i. 3. 45.

वैदेशिक *a.* (की *f.*) Belonging to another country, foreign, exotic. **–क:** A stranger, foreigner ; U. 1.

वैदेश्यं Foreignness.

वैदेहः 1 A king of Videha. **2** An inhabitant of Videha. **3** A trader by caste. **4** The son of a Vaisya by a Brâhmaṇa woman; Ms. 10. 11. **-हाः** (*m. pl.*) The people of Videha. **-ही** N. of Sîtâ; वैदेहिबंधोर्हृदयं विदद्रे R. 14. 33 (The final vowel in वैदेही being shortened.)

वैदेहकः 1 A trader. **2 = वैदेह** (4) q. v.

वैदेहिकः A merchant.

वैद्य *a.* (**द्यी** *f.*) **1** Reltaing to the Vedas, spiritual. **2** Relating to medicine, medical. **-द्यः 1** A learned man, scholar, doctor. **2** A medical man, physician; वैद्ययत्नपरिभाविनं गदं न प्रदीप इव वायुमत्यगात् R. 19. 53; वैद्यानामातुरः श्रेयान् Subhâsh. **2** A man of the medical caste, supposed to be one of the mixed classes; (the offspring of a Brâhmaṇa by a Vaisya woman). **-Comp. -क्रिया** a doctor's profession, practice of medicine. **-नाथः 1** N. of Dhanvantari. **2** of Siva.

वैद्यकः A doctor, physician. **-कं** The science of medicine.

वैद्युत *a.* (**ती** *f.*) Belonging to or proceeding from lightning, electric; वृक्षस्य वैद्युत इवाग्निरुपस्थितोऽयं V. 5. 16, U. 5. 13. **-Comp. -अग्निः, -अनलः, -वह्निः** the fire of lightning.

वैध *a.* (**धी** *f.*), **वैधिक** *a.* (**की** *f.*) **1** Conformable to rule, settled, fixed, ritual. **2** Legal, lawful.

वैधर्म्यं 1 Dissimilarity, difference. **2** Difference of characteristic qualities. **3** Difference of duty or obligation. **4** Contrariety. **5** Unlawfulness, impropriety, injustice. **6** Heterodoxy.

वैधवेयः The son of a widow.

वैधव्यं Widowhood; Ku. 4. 1, M. 5.

वैधुर्यं 1 Bereavement. **2** Agitation, tremor.

वैधेय *a.* (**यी** *f.*) **1** According to rule, prescribed. **2** Foolish, silly, stupid. **-यः** A fool, an idiot; प्रलपत्येष वैधेयः S. 2, V. 2.

वैनतेयः 1 N. of Garuḍa; वैनतेय इव विनतानंदनः K.; R. 11. 59, 16. 88; Bg. 10. 30. **2** N. of Aruṇa.

वैनयिक *a.* (**की** *f.*) **1** Pertaining to modesty, decorum, moral conduct or discipline. **2** Enforcing proper conduct. **-कः** A war-carriage.

वैनायक *a.* (**की** *f.*) Belonging to Gaṇesa; Mâl. 1. 1.

वैनायिकः 1 The doctrines of a Buddhist school of philosophy. **2** A follower of that school.

वैनाशिकः 1 A slave. **2** A spider. **3** An astrologer. **4** The doctrines of the Buddhists. **5** A follower of those doctrines.

वैनीतक See विनीतक.

वैपरीत्यं 1 Contrariety, opposition. **2** Inconsistency.

वैपुल्यं 1 Spaciousness, largeness. **2** Plenty, abundance.

वैफल्यं Uselessness, fruitlessness.

वैबोधिकः 1 A watchman. **2** Especially, one who awakens sleepers by announcing the time; Ki 9. 74.

वैभवं 1 Greatness, glory, grandeur, magnificence, splendour, wealth. **2** Power, might; Ki. 12. 3.

वैभाषिक *a.* (**की** *f.*) Optional.

वैभ्रं The heaven of Vishṇu.

वैभ्राजं N. of a celestial grove or garden.

वैमत्यं 1 Dissension, dissent. **2** Dislike, aversion.

वैमनस्यं 1 Distraction of mind, mental depression, sorrow, sadness; *S.* 6. **2** Sickness.

वैमात्रः, वैमात्रेयः A step-mother's son.

वैमात्रा, वैमात्री, वैमात्रेयी A step-mother's daughter.

वैमानिक *a.* (**की** *f.*) Borne in divine cars. **-कः** An aeronaut.

वैमुख्यं 1 Turning away the face, flight, retreat. **2** Aversion, disgust.

वैमेयः Exchange, barter.

वैयग्र्यं, वैयग्रयं 1 Distraction, perplexity, bewilderment. **2** Exclusive devotion, complete absorption in any object; Mv. 7. 38.

वैयर्थ्यं Uselessness, unproductiveness.

वैयधिकरण्यं The state of being in different case-relations or positions; see व्यधिकरण.

वैयाकरण *a.* (**णी** *f.*) Grammatical. **-णः** A grammarian; वैयाकरणकिरातादपशब्दमृगाः क्व यांतु संत्रस्ताः Subhâsh. **-Comp. -पाशः** a bad grammarian. **-भार्यः** one whose wife is a grammarian.

वैयाघ्र *a.* (**घ्री** *f.*) **1** Tiger like. **2** Covered with a tiger's skin. **-घ्रः** A cart covered with a tiger's skin.

वैयात्यं 1 Boldness, immodesty, absence of shame; अन्यदा भूषणं पुंसां क्षमा लज्जेव योषितां। पराक्रमः परिभवे वैयात्यं सुरतेष्विव Si. 2. 44. **2** Rudeness in general.

वैयासिकः A son of Vyâsa.

वैरं 1 Hostility, enmity, animosity, spite, grudge, opposition, quarrel; दानेन वैराण्यपि यांति नाशं Subhâsh.; अज्ञातहृदयेष्वेवं वैरीभवति सौहृदं *S.* 5. 23 'turns into enmity'; विधाय वैरं सामर्षे नरोऽरौ य उदासते। प्रक्षिप्योदर्चिषं कक्षे शेरते तेऽभिमारुतं *Si.* 2. 42. **2** Hatred, revenge. **3** Heroism, prowess. **-Comp. -अनुबंधः** commencement of hostilities. **-अनुबंधिन्** *a.* leading to enmity. **-आतंकः** the Arjuna tree. **-आनृण्यं, -उद्धारः, -निर्यातनं, -प्रतिक्रिया, -प्रतिकारः. -यातना, -शुद्धिः** *f.*, **साधनं** requital of enmity, taking revenge, retaliation. **-करः, -कारः, -कृत्** *m.* an enemy. **-भावः** hostile attitude. **-रक्षिन्** *a.* guarding against hostilities.

वैरक्तं-क्त्यं 1 Indifference to worldly attachments, absence of desire. **2** Displeasure, dislike, aversion.

वैरंगिकः One who has subdued all his passions and desires, an ascetic.

वैरल्यं 1 Scarceness, rareness. **2** Looseness. **3** Fineness.

वैराग See वैराग्य.

वैरागिकः, वैरागिन् *m.* An ascetic who has subdued all his passions and desires.

वैराग्यं 1 Absence of worldly desires or passions, indifference to the world, asceticism; Bg. 6. 35, 13. 8. **2** Dissatisfaction, displeasure, discontent; कामं प्रकृतिवैराग्यं सद्यः शमयितुं क्षमः R. 17. 55. **3** Aversion, dislike. **4** Grief, sorrow.

वैराज *a.* (**जी** *f.*) Belonging to Brahman; U. 2.

वैराट *a.* (**टी** *f.*) Belonging to Virâṭa. **-टः** A kind of earthworm (इंद्रगोप).

वैरिन् *a.* Hostile, inimical. **-m.** An enemy, शौर्ये वैरिणि वज्रमाशु निपतत्वर्थोऽस्तु नः केवलं Bh. 2. 39; Bg. 3. 27; R. 12. 104.

वैरूप्यं 1 Deformity, ugliness; R. 12. 40. **2** Difference or diversity of form.

वैरोचनः, वैरोचनिः. वैरोचिः Epithets of the demon Bali, son of Virochana.

वैलक्षण्यं 1 Strangeness. **2** Contrariety, opposition. **3** Difference, disparity.

वैलक्ष्यं 1 Embarrassment, confusion. **2** Unnaturalness, affectation; वैलक्ष्यस्मितं 'a forced or affected smile'. **3** Shame. **4** Contrariety, inversion.

वैलोम्यं Opposition, inversion, contrariety.

वैल्व *a.* See बैल्व.

वैवधिकः 1 A pedlar, hawker. **2** A carrier of loads on a pole.

वैवर्ण्यं 1 Change of colour or a complexion, paleness. **2** Difference, diversity. **3** Deviation from caste.

वैवस्वतः 1 N. of the seventh Manu who is supposed to preside over the present age, see under Manu; वैवस्वतो मनुर्नाम माननीयो मनीषिणां R. 1. 11; U. 6. 18. **2** N. of Yama; R. 15. 45. **3** The planet Saturn. **-तं** The present age or Manvantara, as presided over by Manu Vaivasvata or the seventh manu.

वैवस्वती 1 The southern quarter. **2** N. of Yamunâ.

वैवाहिक *a.* (**की** *f.*) Relating to marriage, matrimonial, nuptial; Ku. 7. 2. **-कः -कं** A marriage, wedding. –कः The father of a son's wife or daughter's husband.

वैशद्यं 1 Clearness, purity (fig. also). 2 Perspicuity. 3 Whiteness. 4 Calmness, composure (of mind).

वैशसं 1 Destruction, slaughter, butchery, Ku. 4. 31; U. 4. 24, 6. 40. 2 Distress, torment, pain, suffering, hardship; उपरोधवैशसं Mu. 2; Mâl. 9. 35.

वैशस्त्रं 1 Defencelessness. 2 Government rule.

वैशाखः 1 N. of the second lunar month (corresponding to April–May). 2 A churning stick; द्रुततरकरदक्षाः क्षिप्तवैशाखशैले...कलशिमुदधिगुर्वीं वल्लवा लोडयंति Si. 11. 8. –खं A kind of attitude in shooting; see विशाख. –खी The full-moon day in the month of Vaisâkha.

वैशिक *a.* Practised by harlots; वैशिकीं कला Mk. 1. 3 'arts practised by harlots'. –कः A person who associates with harlots; a kind of hero in erotic works. –कं Harlotry, arts of harlots.

वैशिष्ट्यं 1 Distinction, difference. 2 Peculiarity, speciality, particularity; वैशिष्ट्यादन्यमर्थं या बोधयेत्सार्थसंभवा S. D. 27. 3 Excellence; S. D. 78. 4 Possession or endowment with some characteristic attribute.

वैशेषिक *a.* (की *f.*) 1 Characteristic. 2 Belonging to the Vaiseshika doctrine. –कं One of the six principal Darsanas or systems of Hindu philosophy founded by Kanâda; it differs from the Nyâya philosophy of Gautama in that it recognizes only seven instead of sixteen categories or heads of predicables and lays particular stress upon Visesha.

वैशेष्यं Excellence, pre-eminence, superiority.

वैश्यः A man of the third tribe, his business being trade and agriculture; विशत्याशु पिशुभ्यश्च कृष्यादावरुचिः शुचिः। वेदाध्ययनसंपन्नः स वैश्य इति संज्ञितः Padma Purâṇa. –Comp. –कर्मन् *n.*, –वृत्तिः *f.* the business or occupation of a Vaisya; trade, agriculture &c.

वैश्रवणः 1 N. of Kubera, the god of wealth; विभाति यस्यां ललितालकायां मनोहरा वैश्रवणस्य लक्ष्मीः Bv. 2. 10. 2 N. of Râvaṇa. –Comp. –आलयः, -आवासः 1 the abode of Kubera. 2 the fig-tree. –उदयः the fig-tree.

वैश्वदेव *a.* (वी *f.*) Belonging to the Visvedevas, q. v. –वं 1 An offering made to the Visvedevas. 2 An offering to all deities (made by presenting oblations to fire before meals).

वैश्वानरः 1 An epithet of fire; स्वस्तः खांडवरंगतांडवनटो दूरेऽस्तु वैश्वानरः Bv. 1. 57. 2 The fire of digestion (in the stomach); अहं वैश्वानरो भूत्वा प्राणिनां देहमाश्रितः। प्राणापानसमायुक्तः पचाम्यन्नं चतुर्विधं Bg. 15. 14. 3 General consciousness (in Vedânta phil.). 4 The Supreme Being.

वैश्वासिक *a.* (की *f.*) Trusty, confidential.

वैषम्यं 1 Unevenness. 2 Roughness, harshness. 3 Inequality. 4 Injustice. 5 Difficulty, misery, calamity. 6 Solitariness.

वैषयिक *a.* (की *f.*) 1 Relating to an object. 2 Pertaining to objects of sense, sensual, carnal. –कः A sensualist, voluptuary.

वैष्टुतं The ashes of a burnt offering.

वैष्टः 1 Heaven, sky. 2 Air, wind. 3 A world, a division of the universe.

वैष्णव *a.* (वी *f.*) 1 Relating to Vishṇu; R. 11. 85. 2 Worshipping Vishṇu. –वः One of the three important modern Hindu sects, the other two being Saiva and Sâkta sects. –वं The ashes of a burnt offering. –Comp. –पुराणं N. of one of the 18 Purâṇas.

वैसारिणः A fish.

वैहायस *a.* (सी *f.*) Being in the air, aerial.

वैहार्य *a.* To be sported with, to be made the subject of jokes or pleasantry (said of the brother of one's wife or of the wife's relatives in general).

वैहासिकः A jester, buffoon.

वोड्रः 1 A kind of snake. 2 A kind of fish.

वोड्री The fourth part of a Paṇa, q. v.

वोढ्ढ *m.* 1 A bearer, porter. 2 A leader. 3 A husband. 4 A bull. 5 A charioteer. 6 A draugh-thorse.

वोंटः A stalk, stem.

वोद *a.* Moist, wet, damp.

वोदालः The sheat-fish.

वोर(ल)कः A scribe, writer.

वोरटः A kind of jasmine (कुंद).

वोलः Gum-myrrh.

वोल्लाहः A kind of horse.

वौद्ध *a* See बौद्ध.

वौषट् *ind.* An exclamation or formula used in offering an oblation to the gods or Manes.

व्यंशकः A mountain.

व्यंशुक *a.* Undressed, naked; Ki. 9. 24.

व्यंसकः A rogue, cheat; as in मयूरव्यंसकः 'a roguish peacock', 'a rogue of a peacock'.

व्यंसनं Cheating, deceiving.

व्यक्त *p. p.* 1 Manifested, displayed. 2 Developed, created; Ku. 2. 11. 3 Evident, manifest, clear, plain, distinct, clearly visible. 4 Specified, known, distinguished. 5 Individual. 6 Wise, learned. –क्तं *ind.* Clearly, evidently, certainly. –Comp. –गणितं arithmetic. –दृष्टार्थः an eye-witness, a witness in general. –राशिः a known quantity. –रूपः an epithet of Vishṇu. –विक्रम *a.* displaying valour.

व्यक्तिः *f.* 1 Manifestation, visibility, clear perception; राज्ञः समक्षमेवाधरोत्तरव्यक्तिर्भविष्यति M. 1, स्नेहव्यक्तिः Me. 12. 2 Visible appearance, clearness, distinctness; S. 7. 8. 3 Distinction, discrimination; तं संतः श्रोतुमर्हंति सदसद्व्यक्तिहेतवः R. 1. 10. 4 Real form or nature, true character; न हि ते भगवन् व्यक्तिं विदुर्देवा न दानवाः Bg. 10. 14. 5 Individuality (opp. जाति); Bg. 8. 18. 6 An individual, a person. 7 Gender (in gram.) 8 Inflection.

व्यग्र *a.* 1 Bewildered, perplexed, distracted. 2 Alarmed, frightened. 3 Eagerly or intently occupied (with loc., instr. or in comp.); R. 17. 27, Mv. 1. 13, 4. 28, Ku. 7. 2, U. 1. 23; Bv. 1. 123, Si. 2. 79.

व्यंग *a.* 1 Bodiless. 2 Wanting a limb, deformed, mutilated, maimed, crippled. –गः 1 A cripple. 2 A frog. 3 Dark spots on the cheek.

व्यंगुलं An extremely small measure of length equal to one-sixtieth part of an *angula*.

व्यंग्य *a.* 1 Indicated by implication, indicated by covert or indirect allusion. 2 Suggested (as sense). –ग्यं Suggested sense, insinuation, the meaning hinted at (opp. वाच्य 'the primary or expressed meaning', and लक्ष्य 'the secondary or indicated meaning'); इदमुत्तममतिशयिनि व्यंग्ये वाच्याद्ध्वनिर्बुधैः कथितः K. P. 1.

व्यच् 6 P. (विचति, *pass.* विच्यते) To cheat, deceive, trick.

व्यजः A fan.

व्यजनं A fan; निर्वाति व्यजनं H. 2. 165; R. 8. 40, 10. 52; cf. बालव्यजन.

व्यंजक *a.* (जिका *f.*) 1 Making clear, indicating, showing, manifesting. 2 Suggesting or insinuating a meaning (as a word, opp. वाचक and लाक्षणिक q. q. v. v.) –कः 1 Dramatic action or gesture, external indication of an internal feeling by suitable gesticulation. 2 A sign, symbol.

व्यंजनं 1 Making clear, indicating, manifesting. 2 A mark, token, sign. 3 A reminder; Mâl. 9. 4 Disguise, garb; Si. 2. 56; तपस्विव्यंजनोपेताः &c. 5 A consonant. 6 A mark of the sex, *i. e.* the male or female organ. 7 Insignia. 8 A mark or sign of puberty. 9 The beard. 10 A limb, member. 11 A condiment, sauce, a seasoned article; N. 16. 104. 12 The last of the three powers of a word by virtue of which it suggests or insinuates a sense; see अंजनना (8) (written

व्यंजना also in this sense). -**Comp.** -**उदय** *a.* followed by a consonant. -**संधिः** the junction or coalition of consonants.

व्यंजना See व्यंजन (12) above.

व्यंजित *p. p.* **1** Made clear, manifested, indicated. **2** Marked, distinguished, characterized. **3** Suggested, insinuated.

व्यडंवकः, व्यडंबनः The castor-oil plant.

व्यतिकरः 1 Mixture, inter mixture, mixing or blending together; तीर्थे तोयव्यतिकरभवे जह्नुकन्यासरय्वोः R. 8. 95; व्यतिकर इव भीमस्तामसो वैद्युतश्च U. 5. 12, Mâl. 9. 52. **2** Contact, union, combination; M. 1. 4, Si. 4. 53. 7. 28. **3** Striking against; Mâl. 5. 34. **4** Obstruction; Ku. 5. 85. **5** An incident, occurrence, affair, a thing, matter; एवंविधे व्यतिकरे 'such being the case.' **6** An opportunity. **7** Misfortune, calamity. **8** Mutual relation, reciprocity. **9** Exchange, interchange.

व्यतिकीर्ण *p.p.* **1** Mixed or blended together. **2** United.

व्यतिक्रमः 1 Transgressing, deviating, swerving. **2** Violation, breach, non-performance; as in संविद्व्यतिक्रमः; R. 1. 79. **3** Disregard, neglect, omission. **4** Contrariety, inversion, reverse. **5** Sin, vice, crime. **6** Adversity, misfortune.

व्यतिक्रांत *p. p.* **1** Passed over transgressed, violated, neglected. **2** Inverted, reversed. **3** Elapsed, passed away (as time).

व्यतिरिक्त *p. p.* **1** Separated or distinct from; अव्यतिरिक्तेयमस्मच्छरीरात् K., Ku. 1. 31, 5. 22. **2** Surpassing, excelling, going beyond. **3** Withdrawn, withheld. **4** Excepted.

व्यतिरेकः 1 Distinction, difference. **2** Separation from. **3** Exclusion, exception. **4** Excellence, surpassing, excelling. **5** Contrast, dissimilarity. **6** (In logic) Logical discontinuance (opp. अन्वय q. v.); *e. g.* यत्र वह्निर्नास्ति तत्र धूमो नास्ति is an instance of व्यतिरेकव्याप्ति. **7** (In Rhet.) A figure of speech which consists in representing the *Upameya* as superior to the *Upamâna* in some particular respects; उपमानाद्यदन्यस्य व्यतिरेकः स एव सः K. P. 10.

व्यतिरेकिन् *a.* **1** Different. **2** Surpassing, excelling. **3** Excluding, excepting. **4** Showing negation or non-existence; as in व्यतिरेकि लिंगं.

व्यतिषक्त *p. p.* **1** Mutually connected or related, linked or joined together. **2** Intermixed. **3** Inter-marrying.

व्यतिषंगः 1 Mutual relation, reciprocal connection. **2** Intermixure. **3** Union, junction in general.

व्यति(ती)हारः 1 Exchange, barter. **2** Reciprocity, interchange; R. 12. 93.

व्यतीत *p. p.* **1** Passed, gone, elapsed, passed over; R. 5. 14. **2** Dead. **3** Left, abandoned, departed from. **4** Disregarded.

व्यतीपातः 1 Total departure, complete deviation. **2** Any great portentous calamity, or a portent foreboding a great calamity. **3** Disrespect, contempt.

व्यत्ययः 1 Passing over. **2** Opposition, contrariety. **3** Inverted order, inversion. **4** Interchange, transmutation. **5** Obstruction, hindrance.

व्यत्यस्त *p. p.* **1** Reversed, inverted. **2** Contrary, opposite. **3** Incoherent; व्यत्यस्तं लपति Bv. 2. 84. **4** Crossed, placed crosswise; व्यत्यस्तपादः, व्यत्यस्तभुजः &c.

व्यत्यासः 1 Inverted position or order. **2** Opposition, contrariety.

व्यथ् 1 A. (व्यथते, व्यथित) **1** To be sorry, to be pained, vexed or afflicted, be agitated or disquieted; विश्वंभरापि नाम व्यथते इति जितमपत्यस्नेहेन U. 7, न विव्यथे तस्य मनः Ki. 1. 2, 24. **2** To be ruffled or agitated; Ki. 5. 11. **3** To tremble. **4** To be afraid. **5** To dry, become dry. -*Caus.* (व्यथयति-ते) To pain, distress, vex, annoy; U. 1. 28. -WITH **प्र** to be excessively vexed; Bg. 11. 20.

व्यथक *a.* (**थिका** *f.*) Painful, distressing; Ki. 2. 4.

व्यथनं Giving pain, tormenting.

व्यथा 1 Pain, agony, anguish; तां च व्यथां प्रसवकालकृतामवाप्य U. 4. 23, 1. 12. **2** Fear, alarm, anxiety; स्वंतामित्यलघयत्स तदुव्यथ R. 11. 62. **3** Agitation, disquietude. **4** Disease.

व्यथित *p. p.* **1** Afflicted, distressed, pained. **2** Alarmed. **3** Agitated, disquieted, troubled.

व्यध् 4 P. (विध्यति, विद्ध) **1** To pierce, hurt, strike, stab, kill; आक्षितारासु विव्याध द्विषतः स तनुत्रिणः Si. 19. 99; विद्धमात्रः R. 5.51, 9. 60, 14.70; Bk. 5. 52, 9. 66, 15. 69. **2** To bore, perforate, pierce through. **3** To pick. -WITH **अनु 1** to pierce, hurt, wound. **2** to intertwine, surround. **3** to set, inlay; see **अनुविद्ध**. -**अप 1** to throw, cast, toss or throw away; Mv. 2. 23; R. 19. 44. **2** to pierce through; हृदयमशरणं मे पक्ष्मलाक्ष्याः कटाक्षैरपहृतमपविद्धं पीतमुन्मूलितं च Mâl. 1. 28. **3** to desert, abandon. -**आ 1** to pierce. **2** to throw, cast; see आविद्ध. -**परि, -सं** to pierce through, wound.

व्यधः 1 Piercing, splitting, hitting; Si. 7. 24. **2** Smiting, wounding, striking. **3** Perforating.

व्यधिकरणं Subsisting in different receptacles or substrata; (as in व्यधिकरणबहुव्रीहि which means 'a Bahuvrîhi' compound, the first member of which is not in apposition or stands in a different case-relation to the second, in the dissolution of the compound; *e. g.* चक्रपाणिः, चंद्रमौलिः &c.).

व्यध्यः A butt, target, a mark to aim at.

व्यध्वः A bad or wrong road.

व्यनुनादः Reverberation, loud echo.

व्यंतरः A spirit, a kind of supernatural being.

व्यप् 10 U. (व्यपयति-ते) **1** To throw. **2** To diminish, waste, decrease.

व्यपकृष्ट *p. p.* Drawn aside, taken away, removed.

व्यपगत *p. p.* **1** Gone away, departed, disappeared; मदो मे व्यपगतः Bh. 2. 8; Me. 76. **2** Removed. **3** Fallen away from.

व्यपगमः Departure, disappearance.

व्यपत्रप *a.* Shameless, impudent.

व्यपदिष्ट *p. p.* **1** Named. **2** Shown, represented, signified. **3** Pleaded as a pretext or excuse.

व्यपदेशः 1 Representation, information, notice. **2** Designation by name, naming. **3** A name, an appellation, a title; एवंव्यपदेशभाजः U. 6. **4** A family, race; अथ कोस्य व्यपदेशः *S.* 7; व्यपदेशमाविलयितुं किमीहसे जनमिमं च पातयितुं *S.* 5. 20. **5** Fame, reputation, renown. **6** A trick, pretext, excuse, device. **7** Fraud, craft.

व्यपदेष्टृ *m.* A cheat.

व्यपरोपणं 1 Extirpating, uprooting. **2** Expelling, removing, driving away. **3** Cutting off, tearing out, plucking; चुकोप तस्मै स भृशं सुरश्रियः प्रसह्यकेशव्यपरोपणादिव R. 3. 56.

व्यपाकृतिः *f.* **1** Expelling, driving away. **2** Denial.

व्यपायः End, disappearance, close; Ku. 3. 33, R. 3. 37.

व्यपाश्रयः 1 Succession. **2** Taking refuge with, having recourse to, trusting to; Bg. 3. 18. **3** Depending on; धर्मो रामव्यपाश्रयः Râm.

व्यपेक्षा 1 Expectation, hope. **2** Regard, consideration; R. 8. 24. **3** Mutual relation, interdependence. **4** Mutual regard. **5** Application. **6** (In gram.) The Mutual application of two rules.

व्यपेत *p. p.* **1** Separated, severed. **2** Gone away, departed, oft. in comp.; व्यपेतकल्मषः, व्यपेतभी, व्यपेतहर्ष &c.

व्यपोढ *p. p.* **1** Expelled, removed. **2** Contrary, opposite; Ki. 4. 15. **3** Manifested, displayed, shown.

व्यपोहः Expelling, driving away, keeping off.

व्यभि(भी)चारः 1 Going away from, deviation, leaving the right course, following improper courses,

मंत्रज्ञमव्यसनिनं व्यभिचारविवर्जितं H. 3. 16, Bg. 14. 26. **2** Transgression, violation, Ms. 10. 24. **3** Error, crime, sin. **4** Separableness. **5** Infidelity, faithlessness (of a wife or husband), unchastity ; व्यभिचारात्तु भर्तुः स्त्री लोके प्राप्नोति गर्ह्यतां Ms. 5. 164 ; वाङ्मनःकर्मभिः पत्यौ व्यभिचारो यथा न मे R. 15. 81 ; Y. 1. 71. **6** An anomaly, irregularity, exception (to a rule.) **7** (In logic) A fallacious *hetu*, the presence of the *hetu* without the *sa'dhya*.

व्यभिचारिणी An unchaste wife, adulteress.

व्यभिचारिन् *a.* **1** Straying or deviating from, going astray, erring, tresspassing. **2** Irregular, anomalous. **3** Untrue, false; अव्यभिचारिन्. **4** Faithless, unchaste, adulterous. *-m.* -**व्यभिचारिभावः** A transitory feeling, an accessory (opp. स्थायिन् or स्थायिभाव). (Though like the Sthâyibhâvas these accessories do not form a necessary substratum of any *Rasa*, still they act as *feeders* to the prevailing sentiment, and strengthen it in various ways, whether openly or covertly. They are said to be 33 or 34 in number; for an enumeration of these, see K. P. 4 Kârikâs 31-34, S. D. 169; or R. G. first *Anana* ; cf. विभाव and स्थायिभाव also).

व्यय् I. 10 U. (व्ययति-ते) 1 To go, move. **2** To expend, give away, bestow. -II. 1 U. (व्ययति-ते) To go, move. -III. 10 U. (व्याययति-ते, also व्यापयति-ते) **1** To throw, cast. **2** To drive.

व्यय *a.* Liable to change, mutable, perishable ; cf. अव्यय. -**यः** **1** (*a*) Loss, disappearance, destruction ; आपाद्यते न व्ययमंतरायैः कच्चिन्महर्षेस्त्रिविधं तपस्तत् R. 5. 5, 12. 33. (*b*) Cost, sacrifice ; प्राणव्ययेनापि मया विधेयः Mâl. 4. 4 ; Ku. 3. 23. **2** Hindrance, obstacle, R. 15. 37. **3** Decay, decline, overthrow, downfall. **4** Expenditure, expense, outlay, spending, applying to use (opp. आय); अये दुःखं व्यये दुःखं धिगर्थाः कष्टसंश्रयाः Pt. 1. 163; आयाधिकं व्ययं करोति 'he lives beyond his means'; R. 5. 12, 15. 3; Ms. 9. 11. **5**. Extravagance, prodigality. -**Comp.** -**पर** *a.* lavish in expenditure. -**पराङ्मुख** *a.* stingy, niggardly. -**शील** *a.* spendthrift, prodigal. -**शुद्धिः** *f.* defraying of expenses.

व्ययनं **1** Spending. **2** Wasting, destroying.

व्ययित *p. p.* **1** Expended, spent. **2** Wasted, fallen into decay.

व्यर्थ *a.* 1 Useless, vain, fruitless, unprofitable ; व्यर्थं यत्र कपींद्रसख्यमपि मे U. 3. 45. **2** Meaningless, unmeaning, idle.

व्यलीक *a.* **1** False, untrue. **2** Offensive, disagreeable, displeasing. **3** Not false ; *Si.* 5. 1. -**कः** **1** A libertine. **2** A catamite. -**कं** **1** Anything disagreeable or displeasing, disagreeableness ; इत्थं गिरः प्रियतमा इव सोऽव्यलीकाः शुश्राव सूततनयस्य तदा व्यलीकाः *Si.* 5. 1. **2** Any cause of grief or uneasiness, pain, sorrow, grief ; सुतनु हृदयात्प्रत्यादेशव्यलीकमपैतु ते *S.* 7. 24; Ki. 3. 19 ; Ku. 3. 25 ; R. 4. 87. **3** A fault, an offence, a transgression, any improper act ; सव्यलीकमवधीरितखिन्नं प्रस्थितं सपदि कोपपदेन Ki. 9. 45 ; *Si.* 9. 85 ; Ratn. 3. 5. **4** Fraud, trick, deception ; Pt. 1. 120, 242. **5** Falsehood. **6** Inversion, contrariety.

व्यवकलनं **1** Separation. **2** (In math.) Subtraction, deduction.

व्यवक्रोशनं Wrangling, Mutual abuse.

व्यवच्छिन्न *p. p.* **1** Cut, off, rent, asunder, torn off. **2** Separated, divided. **3** Particularized, specified. **4** Marked, distinguished ; शरीरं तावदिष्टार्थव्यवच्छिन्ना पदावली Kâv. 1. 10. **5** Interrupted.

व्यवच्छेदः **1** Cutting off, rending asunder. **2** Dividing, separating. **3** Dissection. **4** Particularizing. **5** Distinguishing. **6** Contrast, distinction. **7** Determination. **8** Shooting, letting fly (as an arrow). **9** A chapter or section of a work.

व्यवधा **1** That which intervenes. **2** A cover, screen, partition. **3** Concealment.

व्यवधानं **1** Intervention, interposition, separation. **2** Obstruction, hiding from view ; दृष्टिं विमानव्यवधानमुक्तां पुनः सहस्रार्चिषि संनिधत्ते R. 13. 44. **3** Concealment, disappearance. **4** A screen, partition. **5** A cover, covering ; Ku. 3. 44. **6** Interval, space. **7** (In gram.) The intervention of a syllable or letter.

व्यवधायक *a.* (यिका *f.*) **1** Intervening, screening, covering. **2** Obstructing, hiding **3** Intermediate.

व्यवधिः Covering, intervention &c.; see व्यवधान.

व्यवसायः **1** Effort, exertion, energy, industry, perseverance ; करोतु नाम नीतिज्ञो व्यवसायमितस्ततः H. 2. 14. **2** Resolve, resolution, determination; मंदीचकार मरणव्यवसायबुद्धिं Ku. 4. 45 'the thought of resolving to die'; Bg. 2. 41, 10. 36. **3** An act, action, performance ; व्यवसायः प्रतिपत्तिनिष्ठुरः R. 8. 65. **4** Business, employment, trade. **5** Conduct, behaviour **6** Device, stratagem, artifice. **7** Boasting. **8** N. of Vishṇu.

व्यवसायिन् *a.* **1** Energetic, industrious, diligent. **2** Resolute, persevering.

व्यवसित *p. p.* **1** Endeavoured, attempted ; *S.* 6. 9. **2** Undertaken. **3** Resolved, determined, settled. **4** Devised, planned. **5** Endeavouring, resolving. **6** Persevering, energetic. **7** Cheated, deceived. -**तं** Ascertainment, determination.

व्यवस्था **1** Adjustment, arrangement, settlement ; as in वर्णाश्रमव्यवस्था. **2** Fixity, definiteness ; R. 7. 54. **3** Fixity, firm basis ; आजह्रतुस्तच्चरणौ पृथिव्यां स्थलारविंदश्रियमव्यवस्थां Ku. 1. 33. **4** Relative position. **5** A settled rule, law, statute, decree, decision, legal opinion, written declaration of the law (especially on doubtful points or where contradictory texts have to be properly adjusted). **6** An agreement, a contract. **7** State, condition.

व्यवस्थानं, व्यवस्थितिः *f.* **1** Arrangement, settlement, determination, decision. **2** A rule, statute, decision. **3** Steadiness, constancy. **4** Firmness, perseverance. **5** Separation.

व्यवस्थापक *a.* (पिका *f.*) **1** Arranging, putting in proper order, adjusting ; settling, establishing, deciding. **2** One who gives a legal opinion. **3** A manager (modern use).

व्यवस्थापनं **1** Arranging, proper adjustment. **2** Fixing, determining, settling, deciding.

व्यवस्थापित *p. p.* Arranged, settled &c. ; °वाच् Ku. 5. 68.

व्यवस्थित *p. p.* **1** Placed in order, adjusted, arranged. **2** Settled, fixed; किं व्यवस्थितविषयाः क्षात्रधर्माः U. 5. **3** Decided, determined, declared by law. **4** Stood aside, separated. **5** Extracted. **6** Based on, resting on. -**Comp.** -**विभाषा** a fixed option.

व्यवस्थिति See व्यवस्थान.

व्यवहर्तृ *m.* 1 The manager of a business. **2** A suer, litigant, plaintiff. **3** A judge. **4** An associate.

व्यवहारः **1** Conduct, behaviour, action. **2** Affair, business, work. **3** Profession, occupation. **4** Dealing, transaction. **5** Commerce, trade, traffic. **6** Dealing in money, usury. **7** Usage, custom, an established rule or practice. **8** Relation, connection; Pt. 1. 79. **9** Judicial procedure, trial or investigation of a case, administration of justice ; व्यवहारस्तमाह्वयतिः ; अलं लज्जया व्यवहारस्त्वां पृच्छति Mk. 9. **10** A legal dispute, complaint, suit, law suit, litigation ; व्यवहारोऽयं चारुदत्तमवलंबते, इति लिख्यतां व्यवहारस्य प्रथमः पादः, केन सह मम व्यवहारः Mk. 9 ; R. 17. 39. **11** A title of legal procedure, any occasion of litigation. -**Comp.** -**अंगं** the body of civil and criminal law. -**अभिशस्त** *a.* prosecuted, charged. -**आसनं** tribunal of justice, judgment-seat ; R. 8. 18. -**ज्ञः** **1** one who understands business. **2** a youth come of age, one who is no longer a minor. **3** one who is acquainted with judicial procedure. **-तंत्रं** course of conduct; Mâl. 4. **-दर्शनं** trial, judicial investigation. **-पदं** = व्यवहारविषय q. v. **-पादः 1** any one of the four stages of a legal proceeding. **2** the fourth stage; *i. e.* निर्णयपाद that part which concerns the verdict or decision. **-मातृका 1** a legal process in general. **2** any act or subject relating to the administration of justice or formation of courts (of which hirty heads are enumerated). **-विधिः** a rule of law, any code of law. **-विषयः** (so **-पदं**, **-मार्गः**, **-स्थानं**) a subject or head of legal procedure. an actionable business, a matter which may be made the subject of litigation (these are eighteen; for enumeration of names, see Ms. 8. 4-7).

व्यवहारकः A dealer, trader, merchant.

व्यवहारिक *a.* (**का** or **की** *f.*) **1** Relating to business. **2** Engaged in business, practical. **3** Judicial, legal. **4** Litigant. **5** Usual, customary.

व्यवहारिका 1 Usage, custom. **2** A broom. **3** The *Ingudi* plant.

व्यवहारिन् *a.* **1** Transacting business, acting, practising. **2** Engaged in a law-suit, litigant. **3** Usual, customary.

व्यवहित *p. p.* **1** Placed apart. **2** Separated by anything intervening; Si. 2 85. **3** Interrupted, stopped, obstructed, impeded. **4** Screened from view, hidden, concealed **5** Not immediately connected. **6** Done, performed. **7** Passed over, omitted. **8** Surpassed, excelled. **9** Hostile, opposed.

व्यवहृतिः *f.* **1** Practice, process. **2** Action, performance.

व्यवायः 1 Separation, decomposition, resolution (into components). **2** Dissolution. **3** Covering, concealment. **4** Intervention, interval; अट्कुप्वाङ्नुम्व्यवायेऽपि. **5** An impediment, obstacle. **6** Copulation, sexual intercourse. **7** Purity. **-यं** Light, lustre.

व्यवायिन् *m.* **1** A sensualist, libertine. **2** An aphrodisiac.

व्यवेत *p. p.* **1** Separated, decomposed. **2** Different.

व्यष्टि *f.* **1** Individuality, singleness. **2** Distributive pervasion. **3** (In Vedânta phil.) An aggregate or whole viewed as made up of many separate bodies (opp. समष्टि q. v.).

व्यसनं 1 Casting away, dispelling. **2** Separating, dividing. **3** Violation, infraction, **4** Loss, destruction, defeat, fall; defection, weak point; अमात्यव्यसनं Pt. 3; स्वबलव्यसने Ki. 13. 15. **5** (*a*) A calamity, misfortune, distress, evil, disaster, ill-luck; अज्ञातभर्तृव्यसना मुहूर्तं कृतोपकारेव रतिर्बभूव Ku. 3. 73, 4. 30, R. 12. 57. (*b*) Adversity, need; स सुहृद्व्यसने यः स्यात् Pt. 1. 337 'a friend in need is a friend indeed'. **6** Setting (as of the sun &c.): तेजोद्वयस्य युगपद् व्यसनोदयाभ्यां S. 4. 1 (where व्यसन means 'a fall' also). **7** Vice, bad practice, evil habit; मिथ्यैव व्यसनं वदन्ति मृगयामीदृग् विनोदः कुतः S. 4. 5, R. 18. 14; Y. 1. 309; (these vices are usually said to be ten; see Ms. 7. 47—48); समानशीलव्यसनेषु सख्यं Subhâsh. **8** Close or intent application, assiduous devotion; विद्यायां व्यसनं Bh. 2. 62, 63. **9** Inordinate addiction. **10** Crime, sin. **11** Punishment. **12** Inability, incompetency. **13** Fruitless effort. **14** Air, wind. **-Comp. -अतिभारः** heavy calamity or distress; R. 14. 68. **अन्वित, -आर्त, -पीडित** *a.* overtaken by calamity, involved in distress.

व्यसनिन् *a.* **1** Addicted to any vice, vicious. **2** Unlucky, unfortunate. **3** Intently attached or excessively devoted to anything (usually in comp.).

व्यसु *a.* Lifeless, dead; Si. 20. 3.

व्यस्त *p. p.* **1** Cast or thrown asunder, tossed about: Mâl. 5. 23. **2** Dispersed, scattered; U. 5. 14. **3** Dispelled, cast away. **4** Separated, divided, severed: V. 5 23. **5** Taken or considered separately, taken singly (opp. समस्त); एभिः समस्तैरपि किमस्य किं पुनर्व्यस्तैः U. 5; तदस्ति किं व्यस्तमपि त्रिलोचने Ku. 5. 72. **6** Simple, uncompounded (as words). **7** Manifold, different. **8** Removed, expelled. **9** Agitated, troubled, confused. **10** Disordered, out of order, disarranged. **11** Reversed upset. **12** Inverse (as ratio).

व्यस्तारः The issue of rut or ichor from the temples of an elephant.

व्याकरणं 1 Analysis, decomposition. **2** Grammatical analysis, grammar, one of the six *Vedângas* q. v.; सिंहो व्याकरणस्य कर्तुरहरत् प्राणान् प्रियान् पाणिनेः Pt. 2. 33.

व्याकारः 1 Transformation, change of form. **2** Deformity.

व्याकीर्ण *p. p.* **1** Scattered or thrown about. **2** Disordered.

व्याकुल *a.* **1** Agitated, perplexed, bewildered, distracted; शोकव्याकुल, बाष्प°. **2** Alarmed, troubled, frightened; वृष्टिव्याकुलगोकुल Git. 4 **3** Full of, overtaken by. **4** Intently engaged in, busy with; आलोके ते निपतति पुरा सा बलिव्याकुला वा Me. 85. **5** Flashing, moving about; U. 3. 43.

व्याकुलित *a.* Agitated, distracted, confounded, perplexed &c.

व्याकूतिः *f.* Fraud, disguise, deception.

व्याकृत *p. p.* **1** Analyzed, separated. **2** Explained, expounded. **3** Disfigured, distorted, deformed.

व्याकृतिः *f.* **1** Analysis. **2** Exposition, explanation. **3** Change of form, development. **4** Grammar.

व्याकोश (ष) *a* **1** Expanded, blown, blossomed; व्याकोशकोकनदतां दधते नलिन्यः Si. 4. 46. **2** Developed; Bh. 3. 17.

व्याक्षेपः 1 Tossing about. **2** Obstruction, hindrance. **3** Delay; अव्याक्षेपो भविष्यन्त्याः कार्यसिद्धेर्हि लक्षणं R. 10. 6. **4** Distraction.

व्याख्या 1 Relation, narration. **2** Explanation, exposition, comment, gloss.

व्याख्यात *p. p.* **1** Related, narrated. **2** Explained, expounded, commented upon.

व्याख्यातृ *m.* An expounder, a commentator.

व्याख्यानं 1 Communication, narration. **2** Speech, lecture. **3** Explanation, exposition, interpretation, comment.

व्याघट्टनं 1 Churning. **2** Rubbing together, friction.

व्याघातः 1 Striking against. **2** A blow, stroke. **3** An impediment, obstacle. **4** Contradiction. **5** A figure of speech in which opposite effects are shown to be produced from the same cause or by the same agency; it is thus defined by Mammaṭa:—तद्यथा साधितं केनाप्यपरेण तदन्यथा । तथैव यद्विधीयेत स व्याघात इति स्मृतः ॥ K. P. 10; *e. g.* see Vb. 1. 2. or the quotation under विरूपाक्ष.

व्याघ्रः 1 A tiger. **2** (At the end of comp.) Best, pre-eminent, chief; as in नरव्याघ्र, पुरुषव्याघ्र. **3** The red variety of the castor-oil plant. **-घ्री** A tigress; व्याघ्रीव तिष्ठति जरा परितर्जयंती Bh. 3. 109. **-Comp. -अटः** a sky-lark. **-आस्यः** a cat. **-नखः-खं 1** a tiger's claw. **2** a kind of perfume. **3** a scratch, the impression of a finger-nail. **-नायकः** a jackal.

व्याजः 1 Deceit, trick, deception, fraud. **2** Art, cunning; अव्याजमनोहरं वपुः S. 1. 18 'artlessly lovely'. **3** A pretext, pretence, semblance; ध्यानव्याजमुपेत्य Nâg. 1. 1; R. 4. 25, 58; 10. 66; 11. 66. **4** An artifice, a device, contrivance; व्याजार्धसंदर्शितमेखलानि R. 13. 42. **-Comp. -उक्तिः** *f.* **1** a figure of speech in which what is apparenty the effect of one cause is intentionally ascribed to another; in other words, where a feeling is dissembled by being attributed to a different cause; see K. P. 10 under व्याजोक्ति. **2** covert allusion, insinuation. **-निंदा** artful censure. **-सुप्त** *a* feigning to be asleep. -स्तुति: *f.* a figure of speech resembling the English 'irony', wherein censure is implied by apparent praise, or praise by apparent censure ; व्याजस्तुतिर्मुखे भिंदान्तुतिर्वा रूढिरन्यथा K. P. 10.

व्याडः 1 A carnivorous animal, such as a tiger. 2 A villain, rogue. 3 A snake. 4 N. of Indra ; cf. व्याल.

व्याडिः N. of a celebrated grammarian.

व्यात्युक्षी Mutual splashing and sporting in water.

व्यात्त *p. p.* Opened, spread, expanded.

व्यादानं Opening.

व्यादिशः An epithet of Vishṇu.

व्याधः 1 A hunter, fowler (by caste or profession). 2 A wicked or low man. -Comp. -भीतः a deer.

व्याधामः, व्याधावः Indra's thunderbolt.

व्याधिः 1 Sickness, ailment, disease, illness (usually physical, and opp. आधि which means 'mental distress or anxiety'); रिपुरुन्नतधीरचेतसः सततव्याधिरनीतिरस्तु ते Si. 16. 11 (where व्याधि means free from आधि' also) ; cf. आधि. 2 Leprosy. -Comp. -कर *a.* unwholesome. -ग्रस्त *a.* seized with disease, or diseased.

व्याधित *a.* Diseased, sick.

व्याधूत *p. p.* Shaken about, trembling, tremulous.

व्यानः One of the five life-winds or vital airs in the body, that which is diffused through the whole body.

व्यानतं A particular kind of coitus or mode of sexual enjoyment.

व्यापक *a.* (पिका *f.*) 1 Pervading, comprehensive, diffusive, widely extending over the whole of anything; तिर्यगूर्ध्वमधस्ताच्च व्यापको महिमा हरेः Ku. 6. 71. 2 Invariably concomitant. -कः An attribute which is invariably concomitant or inherent. -कं An invariably concomitant or inherent property.

व्यापत्तिः *f.* 1 Ruin, calamity, misfortune ; Ms. 6. 20. 2 Substitution of one thing for another. 3 Death ; R. 12. 56.

व्यापद् *f.* 1 Calamity, misfortune ; Bh. 3. 105. 2 Disease. 3 Derangement. 4 Death, decease.

व्यापनं Pervading, penetrating, spreading throughout.

व्यापन्न *p. p.* 1 Fallen into misfortune, ruined. 2 Failed, miscarried. 3 Hurt, injured. 4 Dead, expired, deceased ; as in अव्यापन्न q. v. 5 Deranged, disordered. 6 Substituted, changed.

व्यापादः, व्यापादनं 1 Killing, slaying. 2 Ruin, destruction. 3 Evil design, malice.

व्यापादित *p. p.* 1 Killed, slain, destroyed. 2 Ruined, injured, hurt.

व्यापारः 1 Employment, engagement, business, occupation ; ततः प्रविशति यथोक्तव्यापारा शकुंतला *S.* 1; Ku. 2. 54. 2 Application, employment ; Mu. 2. 4. 3 Profession, trade, practice, exercise; as in शस्त्रव्यापार. 4 An act, doing, performance. 5 Working, operation, action, influence ; (व्रतं) व्यापाररोधि मदनस्य निषेवितव्यं *S.* 1. 27 ; तस्यानुमेने भगवान् विमन्युर्व्यापारमात्मन्यपि सायकानां Ku. 7. 93 ; V. 3. 17. 6 Being placed on ; M. 4. 14. 7 Exertion, effort ; आर्याप्यरुंधती तत्र व्यापारं कर्तुमर्हति Ku. 6 32. 'will be pleased to exert herself in that behalf.' (व्यापारं कृ 1 to take part in. 2 to have effect on 3 to meddle ; as in अव्यापारेषु व्यापारं यो नरः कर्तुमिच्छति Pt. 1. 21.)

व्यापारित *p. p.* 1 Engaged, occupied, employed, appointed ; R. 2. 38. 2 Placed, fixed, set ; Ve. 3. 19

व्यापारिन् *m.* 1 A dealer, trader. 2 One who exercises or practises anything.

व्यापिन् *a.* 1 Pervading, filling, occupying (at the end of comp.). 2 All-pervading, coextensive, invariably concomitant. 3 Covering. *-m.* An epithet of Vishṇu.

व्यापृत *p. p.* 1 Engaged in, occupied or busy with, employed in (with loc.). 2 Placed, fixed. *-m.* An employé, a minister.

व्यापृतिः *f.* 1 Employment, engagement, business ; स्वस्वव्यापृतिमग्नमानसतया Bv. 1. 57. 2 Operation, action. 3 Exertion. 4 Profession, practice ; see व्यापार.

व्याप्त *p. p.* 1 Spread through, penetrated, pervaded, extended over, permeated, covered. 2 Pervading, extending over all. 3 Filled with, full of. 4 Encompassed, surrounded. 5 Placed, fixed. 6 Obtained, possessed. 7 Comprehended, included. 8 Invariably accompanied (in logic). 9 Famous, celebrated. 10 Expanded, stretched out.

व्याप्तिः *f.* 1 Pervasion, permeation. 2 (In logic) Universal pervasion, invariable concomitance, universal accompaniment of the middle term by the major ; यत्र यत्र धूमस्तत्र तत्राग्निरिति साहचर्यनियमो व्याप्तिः T. S. 3 A universal rule, universality. 4 Fulness. 5 Obtaining. -Comp. -ग्रहः apprehension of universal concomitance. -ज्ञानं knowledge of invariable or universal concomitance.

व्याप्य *a.* To be pervaded, filled &c. -प्यं The sign or middle term of a syllogism (= हेतु, साधन q. v.), (in logic.).

व्याप्यत्वं Invariableness. -Comp -असिद्धिः *f.* imperfect inference.

व्याम्युक्षी = व्यात्युक्षी q. v.

व्यामः, व्यामनं A measure of length equal to the space between the tips of the fingers of either hand when the arms are extended.

व्यामिश्र *a.* Mingled, intermixed.

व्यामोहः 1 Infatuation. 2 Bewilderment, embarrassment, perplexity ; कंसस्यालमभूज्जितं जितमिति व्यामोहकोलाहलः Gīt. 10 ; Kâv. 3. 101.

व्यायत *p. p.* 1 Long, extended ; युवा युगव्यायतबाहुरंसलः R. 3. 34. 2 Expanded, wide open. 3 Exercised, disciplined. 4 Busy, engaged, occupied. 5 Hard, firm. 6 Strong, intense, excessive. 7 Mighty, powerful. 8 Deep ; Ku. 5. 54.

व्यायतत्वं Muscular development ; *S.* 2. 4.

व्यायामः 1 Extending, stretching out. 2 Exercise, gymnastic or athletic exercise ; *Si.* 2. 94. 3 Fatigue, labour. 4 Effort, exertion. 5 Contention, struggle. 6 A measure of distance (= व्याम q. v.).

व्यायामिक *a.* (की *f.*) Athletic, gymnastic.

व्यायोगः A kind of dramatic composition in one act; it is thus described by S. D. :—ख्यातेतिवृत्तो व्यायोगः स्वल्पस्त्रीजनसंयुतः। हीनो गर्भविमर्शाभ्यां नरैर्बहुभिराश्रितः। एकांकश्च भवेदस्त्रीनिमित्तसमरोदयः। कौशिकीवृत्तिरहितः प्रख्यातस्तत्र नायकः। राजर्षिरथ दिव्यो वा भवेद्धीरोद्धतश्च सः। हास्यशृंगारशांतेभ्य इतरेऽत्रांगिनो रसाः॥ 514.

व्याल *a.* 1 Wicked, vicious ; व्यालद्विपा यंतृभिरुन्मदिष्णवः *Si.* 12. 28 ; यंता गजं व्यालमिवापराद्धः Ki. 17. 25. 2 Bad, villainous. 3 Cruel, fierce, savage ; Ki 13. 4. -लः 1 A vicious elephant ; व्यालं बालमृणालतंतुभिरसौ रोद्धुं समुज्जृंभते Bh. 2. 6. 2 A beast of prey. 3 A snake ; H. 3. 29. 4 A tiger ; Mâl. 3. 5 A leopard. 6 A king. 7 A cheat, rogue. 8 N. of Vishṇu. -Comp. -खड्गः, -नखः a kind of herb. -ग्राहः, -ग्राहिन् *m.* a snake-catcher. -मृगः 1 a wild animal. 2 a hunting leopard. -रूपः an epithet of Siva.

व्यालकः A vicious or wicked elephant.

व्यालंबः A kind of caster-oil plant.

व्यालोल *a.* 1 Shaking about, tremulous. 2 Disordered, dishevelled ; व्यालोलः केशपाशः Gīt. 11.

व्यावकलनं Subtraction.

व्यावक्रोशी, व्यावभाषी Mutual abuse, reciprocal imprecation.

व्यावर्तः 1 Surrounding, encompassing. 2 Revolution, going round. 3 Ruptured navel.

व्यावर्तक *a.* (र्तिका *f.*) 1 Encompassing, surrounding. 2 Excluding, excepting, separating. 3 Turning away from. 4 Turning round.

व्यावर्तनं 1 Surrounding, encompassing. 2 Revolving, turning round; Ki. 5. 30. 3 A fold, band.

व्यावल्गित *p. p.* Moved, agitated.

व्यावहारिक *a.* (**की** *f.*) 1 Relating to business, practical. 2 Legal, judicial. 3 Customary, usual. 4 Relating to the world of illusion; cf. प्रातिभासिक. **-कः** A counsellor, minister.

व्यावहारी Mutual seizing.

व्यावहासी Mutual derision or laughter.

व्यावृत्तिः *f.* 1 Covering, screening. 2 Exclusion.

व्यावृत्त *p. p.* 1 Turned away from, withdrawn from; व्यावृत्ता यत्परस्वेभ्यः श्रुतौ तस्करता स्थिता R. 1. 21; V. 1. 9. 2 Separated from, singled out. 3 Excluded, set aside. 4 Revolved, turned round. 5 Encompassed, surrounded. 6 Desisting, ceased from; Ku. 2, 35. 7 Split asunder.

व्यासः 1 Distribution, separation into parts. 2 Dissolution or analysis of a compound. 3 Severalty, distinction. 4 Diffusion, extension. 5 Width, breadth. 6 The diameter of a circle. 7 A fault in pronunciation. 8 Arrangement, compilation. 9 An arranger, a compiler. 10 N. of a celebrated sage. [He was the son of the sage Parasara by Satyavati (born before her marriage with Santanu q. v.); but he retired to the wilderness as soon as he was born, and there led the life a hermit, practising the most rigid austerities until he was called by his mother Satyavati to beget sons on the widows of her son Vichitravirya. He was thus the father of Pandu and Dhritarashtra and also of Vidura; q. q. v. v. He was at first called 'Krishnadvaipayana from his dark complexion and from his having been brought forth by Satyavati on a Dvipa or island; but he afterwards came to be called Vyasa or 'the *arranger*', as he was supposed to have arranged the Vedas in ther present form; विव्यास वेदान् यस्मात्स तस्माद्व्यास इति स्मृतः. He isbelieved to be the author of the great epic the Mahabharata which he is said to have composed with Ganapati for his scribe. The eighteen Pnranas, as also the Brahma-sutras and several other works are also ascribed to him. He is one of the seven *chirajivins* or deathless persons; cf. चिरजीविन्.]. 11 A Brâhmaṇa who recites or expounds the Purâṇas in public.

व्यासक्त *p. p.* 1 Closely adhering to. 2 Attached or devoted to, intent on, occupied or busy with (with loc.). 3 Separated, detached, disjoined. 4 Confused, bewildered.

व्यासंगः 1 Close adherence, intent attachment or application. 2 Intentness, devotion; Bv. 1. 79. 3 Diligent study. 4 Attention. 5 Detachment, separation.

व्यासिद्ध *p. p.* 1 Prohibited, forbidden. 2 Contraband (said of goods &c.).

व्याहत *p. p.* 1 Obstructed, impeded. 2 Repelled, repulsed, 3 Foiled, disappointed; Si. 3; 40. 4 Confused, bewildered, alarmed. **-Comp.** **-अर्थता** one of the faults of composition; see K. P. 7.

व्याहरणं 1 Utterance, pronunciation. 2 Speech, narration.

व्याहारः 1 Speech, utterance, words U. 4. 18, 5. 29. 2 Voice, note, sound; M. 5. 1.

व्याहृत *p. p.* Said, spoken, uttered.

व्याहृतिः *f.* 1 Utterance, speech, words; न हीश्वरव्याहृतयः कदाचित्पुष्णंति लोके विपरीतमर्थं Ku. 3. 63. 2 Statement, expression; भूतार्थव्याहृतिः सा हि न स्तुतिः परमेष्ठिनः R. 10. 33. 3 A mystic word uttered by every Brâhmaṇa in performing his daily sandhyâ-adoration; (these Vyâhritis are three भूर्, भुवम् and स्वम् or स्वर् usually repeated after *om*; cf. Ms. 2. 76; according to some they are seven in number).

व्युच्छित्ति *f.* **व्युच्छेदः**, Cutting off; extermination, complete destruction.

व्युत्क्रमः 1 Transgression, going astray. 2 Inverted order, contrariety. 3 Confusion, disorder.

व्युत्क्रांत *p. p.* 1 Transgressed, overstepped. 2 Departed, left, gone forth.

व्युत्थानं, **व्युत्थितिः** *f.* 1 Great activity. 2 Rising up against, opposition, obstruction. 3 Independent action, following one's own bent of mind. 4 The completion of religious abstraction or abstract meditation (in Yoga phil.). 5 A kind of dance. 6 Causing (an elephhant) to rise; Si. 18. 26.

व्युत्पत्तिः *f.* 1 Origin, production 2 Derivation, etymology. 3 Perfect proficiency, conversancy. 4 Scholarship, learning; व्युत्पत्तिरावर्जितकोविदापि न रंजनाय क्रमते जडानां Vikr. 1. 15, 18. 103.

व्युत्पन्न *p. p.* 1 Produced, begotten. 2 Formed by derivation. 3 Derived, traced to its etymology, as a word (opp. अव्युत्पन्न or 'primitive'). 4 Completed, perfected; Mv. 4. 57. 5 Thoroughly proficient in, learned, erudite.

व्युत्त *p. p.* Wetted, drenched.

व्युदस्त *p. p.* Thrown aside, rejected, cast off.

व्युदासः 1 Throwing aside, rejection. 2 Exclusion (in gram.) 3 Prohibition. 4 Disregard, indifference. 5 Killing, destruction; Si. 15. 37.

व्युपदेशः Pretext, pretence.

व्युपरमः Cessation, stop, close.

व्युपशमः 1 Non-cessation. 2 Inquietude. 3 Complete cessation (where वि shows intensity .)

व्युष्ट *p. p.* 1 Burnt. 2 Dawned, become day-light. 3 Become bright or clear. 4 Dwelt. **-ष्टं** 1 Day-break, dawn; Si. 12. 4. 2 Day. 3 Fruit.

व्युष्टिः *f.* 1 Dawn. 2 Prosperity. 3 Praise. 4 Fruit, consequence.

व्यूढ *p. p.* 1 Expanded, developed, broad, wide; व्यूढोरस्को वृषस्कंधः R. 1. 13. 2 Firm, compact. 3 Placed in order, arranged, marshalled (as an army); Bg. 1. 3. 4 Disarranged, placed out of order. 5 Married. **-Comp.** **-कंकट** *a.* mailed, clad in armour.

व्यूत *a.* Interwoven, sewn, interlaced.

व्यूतिः *f.* 1 Weaving, sewing. 2 The wages of weaving.

व्यूहः 1 A military array; Ms. 7. 187. 2 An army, host, squadron; व्यूहावुभौ तावितरेतरस्मात् भंगं जयं चापतुरव्यवस्थं R. 7. 54. 3 A large quantity, an assemblage, a multitude, collection. 4 A part, portion, sub-head. 5 The body. 6 Structure, formation. 7 Reasoning, logic. **-Comp.** **-पार्ष्णिः** *f.* the rear of an army. **-भंगः**, **भेदः** breaking an array.

व्यूहनं 1 Arraying of troops, marshalling. 2 Structure of the members of the body.

व्यृद्धिः *f.* Non-prosperity, ill-luck, misfortune (विगता ऋद्धिर्व्यृद्धिः); as in यवनानां व्यृद्धिर्दुर्यवनं Sk.

व्ये 1 U. (व्ययति-ते, ऊत; *caus.* व्याययति-ते *desid.* विव्यासति) 1 To cover. 2 To sew.

व्योकारः A blacksmith.

व्योमन् *n.* 1 The sky, atmosphere; अस्त्येवं जडधामता तु भवतो यद् व्योम्नि विस्फूर्जसे K. P. 10, Me. 51; R. 12. 67; N. 22. 54. 2 Water. 3 A temple sacred to the sun. 4 Talc. **-Comp.** **-उदकं** rain-water, dew. **-केशः**, **-केशिन्** *m.* an epithet of Siva. **-गंगा** the heavenly Ganges. **-चारिन्** *m.* 1 a god. 2 a bird. 3 a saint. 4 a Brâhmaṇa. 5 a heavenly body. **-धूमः** a cloud. **-नाशिका** a kind of quail. **मंजरं**, **-मंडलं** a flag, banner. **-मुद्गरः** a gust of wind. **-यानं** a celestial car. **-सद्** *m.* 1 a deity, god 2 a *Gandharva*. 3 a spirit. **-स्थली** the earth. **-स्पृश्** *a.* 'sky-touching', very lofty.

व्रज् 1 P. (व्रजति) 1 To go, walk, proceed; नाविनीतैर्व्रजेद् धुर्यैः Ms. 4. 67. 2 To go to, approach, visit; मामेकं शरणं व्रज Bg. 18. 66. 3 To depart, retire, withdraw. 4 To pass away (as time); इयं व्रजति यामिनी त्यज नरेंद्र निद्रारसं Vikr. 11. 74. (This root is used much in the same way as गम् or या q.v.). -WITH अनु 1 to go after, follow Ms. 11. 111, Ku. 7. 38. 2 to practise, perform. 3 to resort to. -आ to come, appoach. -परि to wander about as a religious mendicant, turn out a recluse. -प्र 1 to go into exile. 2 to renounce all worldly attachments enter on the fourth stage of life; *i. e.* to become a *Sannyâsin* ; Ms. 6. 38, 8. 363. –प्रति to go to or towards, approach ; Bk. 8. 98. –प्रत्युद् to go forth to meet or receive ; R. 1. 90 ; 13. 33.

व्रजः 1 A multitude, collection, flock, group ; नेत्रव्रजाः पौरजनस्य तस्मिन् विहाय सर्वान्नपतीन्निपेतुः R. 6. 7 ; 7. 60, *Si.* 6. 6, 14. 33. 2 A station of cowherds. 3 A cowpen, cowshed ; *Si.* 2. 64. 4 An abode, a resting-place 5 A road. 6 A cloud. 7 N. of a district near Mathurâ. –Comp. –अंगना, युवतिः *f.* a woman of Vraja, a cowherdess ; Bv. 2. 165. –अजिरं a cowpen. –किशोरः, -नाथः, -मोहनः, वरः, -वल्लभः epithets of Krishṇa.

व्रजनं 1 Roaming, wandering, travelling. 2 Exile.

व्रज्या 1 Wandering about as a religious mendicant. 2 An attack, invasion, a march. 3 A flock, multitude tribe, class. 4 A theatre.

व्रण् I. 1 P. (व्रणति) To sound.–II. 10 U. (व्रणयति-ते) To hurt ; wound.

व्रणः-णं 1 A wound, sore, bruise, hurt ; R. 12. 55. 2 A boil, an ulcer –Comp. –अरिः gum-myrrh. –कृत् *a.* wounding. (*–m.*) the marking-nut tree. –विरोपण *a.* sore-healing ; *S.* 4. 13. –शोधनं the cleansing or dressing of a wound. –हः the castor-oil plant.

व्रणित *a.* Wounded, bruised ; U. 4. 3.

व्रतः-तं 1 A religious act of devotion or austerity, vowed observance, a vow in general ; अभ्यस्यतीव व्रतमासिधारं R. 13. 67, 2 4, 25 ; (there are several *vratas* enjoined in the different Purâṇas ; but their number cannot be said to be fixed, as new ones *e. g.* सत्यनारायणव्रत, are being added every day.). 2 A vow, promise, resolve ; सोऽर्हं मधुव्रतः शत्रूनुद्धृत्य प्रतिरोपयन् R. 17. 42 ; so सत्यव्रत, दृढव्रत &c. 3 Object of devotion or faith, devotion ; as in पतिव्रता (पातिर्व्रतं यस्याः सा); यांति देवव्रता देवान् पितॄन् यांति पितृव्रताः Bg. 9. 25. 4 A rite, an observance, practice, as in अर्कव्रत q. v. 5 Mode of life, course of conduct ; *S.* 5. 26. 6 An ordinance, a law, rule. 7 Sacrifice. 8 An act, a deed, work. –Comp. –आचरणं the observance of a vow. –आदेशः investiture of a youth (of ony one of the three classes) with the sacred thread. –उपवासः a fast for a vow. –ग्रहणं initiation into a vow for a religious performance. –चर्यः a religious student ; see ब्रह्मचारिन्. –चर्या observance or practice of a religious vow. –पारणं, -णा conclusion of a vow or fast, eating after a fast. –भंगः 1 breach of a vow. 2 breach of a promise. –भिक्षा begging alms as a part of a ceremony of investiture with the sacred thread. –लोपनं breaking a vow. –वैकल्यं the incompletion of a religious vow. –संग्रहः initiation into a vow. –स्नातकः a Brâhmaṇa who has completed the first stage of his religious life, *i. e.* that of a Brahmachârin or religious student ; see स्नातक.

व्रततिः, -ती *f.* 1 A creeper ; पादाकृष्टव्रततिवलयासंगसंजातपाशः *S.*1. 33, R. 14. 1. 2 Expansion, extension.

व्रतिन् *a.* Observing a vow, practising penance, devout, pious. *–m.* 1 A religious student. 2 An ascetic, a devotee ; *S.* 5. 9. 3 One who institutes a sacrifice ; cf. यजमान.

व्रध्न See ब्रध्न.

व्रह्मन् See ब्रह्मन्.

व्रश्च् 6 P. (वृश्चति, वृक्ण ; *caus.* व्रश्चयति -ते ; *desid.* विव्रश्चिषति or विवक्षति) 1 To cut, cut up of asunder, tear, lacerate. 2 To wound.

व्रश्चनः 1 A small saw. 2 A fine file used by goldsmiths. –नं Cutting, tearing, wounding.

व्राजिः *f.* A gust or gale of wind, stormy wind.

व्रातः A multitude, flock, an assemblage ; श्वपाकानां व्रातैः G. L. 29 ; R. 12. 94 ; *Si.* 4. 35. –तं 1 Bodily or manual labour. 2 Day-labour. 3 Casual employment.

व्रातीन *a.* Living by day-labour, a hired labourer, coolie.

व्रात्यः 1 A man of the first three classes who has lost caste owing to the non-performance of the principal Samskâras or purificatory rites (especially investiture with the sacred thread) over him, an outcast ; भवत्या हि व्रात्याधमपतितपाखंडपरिषत्परित्राणस्नेहः G. L. 37. 2 A low or vile person in general. 3 A man of a particular inferior tribe (the descendant of a Sûdra father and Kshatriya mother). –Comp. –ब्रुवः one who calls himself a Vrâtya. –स्तोमः N. of a sacrifice performed to recover the rights forfeited by the non-performance of the due Samaskâras.

व्री I. 9 P. (व्रिणाति- व्रीणाति) To choose, select ; cf. वृ.–II. 4 A. (व्रीयते, व्रीण) 1 To go, move. 2 To be chosen.

व्रीड् 4 P. (व्रीड्यति) 1 To be ashamed, feel shame. 2 To throw, cast, send forth.

व्रीडः-डा 1 Shame, व्रीडादिवाभ्यासगतैर्विलिल्ये *Si.* 3. 40 ; व्रीडमावहति मे स (शब्दः) संप्रति R. 11. 73. 2 Modesty, bashfulness ; *Si.* 10. 18.

व्रीडित *p. p.* Put to shame, ashamed, abashed.

व्रीस् 1 P., 10 U. (व्रीसति, व्रीसयति-ते) To injure, kill.

व्रीहिः 1 Rice ; as in बहुव्रीहि q. v. 2 A grain of rice. –Comp. –अगारं a granary. –कांचनं a kind of pulse. –राजिकं panic seed (कंगू q. v.).

व्रुड् 6 P. (व्रुडति) 1 To cover. 2 To be heaped or gathered. 3 To heap, accumulate. 4 To sink, go down.

व्रूस् 1 P., 10 U. See व्रीस्.

व्रैहेय *a.* (यी *f.*) 1 Fit for rice. 2 Sown with rice. –यं A field of rice, one fit for growing rice.

व्ली 9P. (व्लिनाति, rarely व्लीनाति, *caus.* व्लेपयति). 1 To go, move. 2 To support, hold, maintain. 3 To choose, select.

व्लेक्ष् 10 U. (व्लेक्षयति-ते) To see.

श

शः 1 A cutter, destroyer ; Ki. 15. 45. **2** A weapon. **3** N. of *S*iva. **-शं** Happiness ; Bh. 2. 16.

शंयु *a.* Happy, prosperous ; Bk. 4. 18.

शंवः 1 Ploughing in the regular direction. **2** The thunderbolt of Indra. **3** The iron head of a pestle.

शंस् 1 P. (शंसति, शस्त ; *pass.* शस्यते) **1** To praise, extol, approve of ; साधु साध्विति भूतानि शशंसुर्मारुतात्मजं Râm.; Bg. 5. 1. **2** To tell, relate, express, declare, communicate, announce, report (with dat. or sometimes gen. of person or by itself) ; शशंस सीतापरिदेवनांतमनुष्ठितं शासनमग्रजाय R. 14. 83 ; न मे ह्रिया शंसति किंचिदीप्सितं 3. 5, 2. 68, 4. 72, 9 77, 11. 84 ; Ku. 3. 60, 5. 51. **3** To indicate, bespeak, show ; गः (अशोकः) सावज्ञो माधवश्रीनियोगे पुष्पैः शंसत्यादरं त्वत्प्रयत्ने M. 5. 8 ; Ki. 5. 23, Ku. 2. 22. **4** To repeat, recite. **5** To hurt, injure. **6** To revile, traduce. -WITH **अभि 1** to curse. **2** to charge, defame, traduce ; Y. 3. 286. **3** to praise. **-आ** (usually Atm.) **1** to hope for, expect, desire, wish or long for ; स्वकार्यसिद्धिं पुनराशशंसे Ku. 3. 57 ; संग्रामं चाशशंसिरे Bk. 14. 70, 90 ; मनोरथाय नाशंसे किं बाहो स्पंदसे वृथा *S*. 7. 13, 2. 15. **2** to bless, express a pious wish, wish well ; एवं ते देवा आशंसतुं Mk. 1 ; राज्ञः शिवं सावरजस्य भूयादित्याशशंसे करणैरबाह्यैः R. 14. 50. **3** to tell, relate (Paras.); आशंसता बाणगतिं वृषांके कार्यं त्वया नः प्रतिपन्नकल्पं Ku. 3. 14. **4** to praise. **5** to repeat. **-प्र** to praise, extol, approve, speak approvingly of, command ; हरिणा युवतिः प्रशशंसे Gît. 1 ; यच्च वाचा प्रशस्यते Ms. 5. 127 ; प्राशंसीत्तं निशाचरः Bk. 12. 65 ; R. 5. 25, 17. 36.

शंसनं 1 Praising. **2** Telling, relating. **3** Reciting.

शंसा 1 Praise. **2** Wish, desire, hope. **3** Repeating, narrating.

शंसित *p. p.* **1** Praised, extolled. **2** Told, said, spoken, declared. **3** Wished, desired. **4** Ascertained, established, determined. **5** Falsely accused, calumniated.

शंसिन् *a.* (Usually at the end of comp.). **1** Praising. **2** Telling, announcing, communicating ; प्रजावती दोहदशंसिनी ते R. 14. 45. **3** Indicating, bespeaking ; मूर्वानः क्षतहुंकारशंसिनः Ku. 2. 26 ; प्रार्थनासिद्धिशंसिनः R 1. 42, *S*i. 9. 77. **4** Presaging, foretelling ; R. 3. 14, 12. 90.

शक् 1. 5 P. (शक्नोति, शक्त) **1** To be able, be competent for, have power to, effect (usually with an inf. and translateable by 'can') ; अदर्शयन् वक्तुमशक्नुवत्यः शाखाभिरावर्जितपल्लवाभिः R. 13. 24, Bk. 3. 6 ; Me. 20 ; sometimes with acc. or dat.; Ms. 11. 194. **2** To bear, endure. **3** To be powerful. —*Pass.* To be able, be possible or practicable (giving a passive sense to a following infinitive) ; तत्कर्तुं शक्यते 'it can be done'. *-Desid.* (शिक्षति) **1** To wish to be able. **2** To learn. -II. 4 U. (शक्यति ते, शक्त) **1** To be able, have power to effect. **2** To bear, endure.

शकः 1 N. of a king (especially applied to *S*âlivâhana ; but scholars do not seem to have yet agreed as to the precise meaning and scope of the word.) **2** An epoch, era (the term is especially applied to the era of Sâlivâhana which commences 78 years after the Christian era). **-काः** (*m. pl.*) **1** N. of a country. **2** N. of a particular tribe or race of people (mentioned in Ms. 10. 44 along with the Paundrakas, &c.). **-Comp. -अंतकः, -अरिः** epithets of king Vikramâditya who is said to have exterminated the *S*akas. **-अब्दः** a year of the *S*aka era. **-कर्तृ,-कृत्** *m.* the founder of an era.

शकटः-टं A cart, carriage, waggon; रोहिणिशकटं Pt. 1. 213, 211, 212 ; Y. 3. 42. **-टः 1** A form of military array resembling a wedge ; Ms. 7. 187. **2** A measure of capacity, cart-load equal to 2000 *palas.* **3** N. of a demon slain by Krishna when quite a boy. **4** N. of a tree (तिनिश). **-Comp. -अरिः,-हन्** *m.* epithets of Krishna. **-आह्वा** the lunar asterism Rohinî (so called because it is figured by a cart). **-बिलः** a gallinule.

शकटिका A small cart, a toy-cart ; as in मृच्छकटिका.

शकन् *n.* Ordure, fæces, especially of animals ; (this word has no forms for the first five inflections, and is optionally substituted for शकृत् after acc. dual).

शकलः 1 A part, portion, piece, fragment, bit (*n.* also in this sense) ; उपलशकलमेतद्भेदकं गोमयानां Mu. 3. 15 ; R. 2. 46, 5. 73. **2** Bark. **3** The scales (of a fish.)

शकलित *a.* Reduced to fragments, shattered to pieces.

शकलिन् *m.* A fish.

शकारः The brother of a king's concubine, the brother-in-law of a king by a wife not regularly married (अनूढाभ्रातृ) ; (he is usually represented as a strange mixture of pride, folly and vanity, of low family and raised to power by reason of his relation to the king. In the Mrichchhakatika of *S*ûdraka where he plays a prominent part, his character is well exhibited in his lightness and frivolity of spirit, vain-glory, constant references to his high connection, his blundering and ludicrous folly, but withal cruelty enough to throttle the heroine when she refused to yield to his desire ; S. D. thus defines him:— मदमूर्खताभिमानी दुष्कुलतैश्वर्यसंयुक्तः । सोयमनूढाभ्राता राज्ञः श्यालः शकार इत्युक्तः ॥ 81).

शकुनः 1 A bird (in general) ; शकुनोच्छिष्टं Y. 1. 168. **2** A kind of bird, a vulture or kite. **-नं 1** An omen, a prognostic, any omen presaging good or evil; *S*i. 9. 83. **2** An auspicious omen. **-Comp. -ज्ञ** *a.* knowing omens. **-ज्ञानं** knowledge of omens, augury. **-शास्त्रं** 'the science of omens', N. of a work.

शकुनिः 1 A bird; U. 2. 25; Ms. 12. 63. **2** A vulture, kite or eagle. **3** A cock. **4** N. of a son of Subala, king of Gândhâra and brother of Gândhâri, wife of Dhritarâshtra ; he was thus the maternal uncle of Duryodhan whom he assisted in many of his wicked schemes to exterminate the Pândavas The name is now usually applied to an old wicked-minded relative whose counsels tend to ruin. **-Comp. -ईश्वरः** N. of Garuda. **-प्रपा** a trough for watering birds. **-वादः 1** the cry or sound of a bird. **2** the crowing of a cock.

शकुनी 1 A hen-sparrow. **2** A kind of bird.

शकुंतः 1 A bird in general ; अंसव्यापिशकुंतनीडनिचितं बिभ्रज्जटामंडलं *S*. 7. 11. **2** The blue jay. **3** A kind of bird.

शकुंतकः A bird.

शकुंतला N. of the daughter of Visvâmitra by the nymph Menakâ who was sent down by Indra to disturb the sage's austerities. [When Menak*a* went up to the heaven she left the child in a solitary forest where she was taken care of by '*S*akuntas' or birds, whence she was called *S*akuntal*a*. " She was afterwards found by the sage Ka*n*va and brought up as his own daughter. When Dushyanta in the course of his hunting came to the sage's hermitage, he was fascinated by her charms and prevailed on her to become his wife by the Gandharva form of marriage ; (see Dushyanta). She bore to him a son named Bharata, who became a universal monarch, and gave his name to India which came to be called Bharatavarsha].

शकुंतिः A bird ; कलमविरलं रत्सुत्कंठाः क्वणंतु शकुंतयः U. 3. 24.

शकुंतिका 1 A bird ; U. 1. 45. **2** A kind of bird. **3** A locust, cricket.

शकुलः-ली A kind of fish. **–Comp.** **–अदनी** a kind of medicinal plant (called Katki). **–अर्भकः** a kind of fish.

शकृत् *n.* Ordure, excrement, especially of animals. **-Comp.** **–करिः** *m. f.*, **–करी** a calf ; शकृत्करिर्वत्सः Sk. **–द्वारं** the anus. **–पिंडः, –पिंडकः** a ball or lump of dung ; शष्पाण्यत्ति प्रकिरति शकृत्पिंडकानाम्रमात्रान् U. 4. 27.

शक्करः, शक्करिः A bull.

शक्करी 1 A river. **2** A girdle, zone. **3** A woman of impure caste.

शक्त *p. p.* **1** Able, capable, competent (with gen. or loc. or inf.) ; बहवोऽस्य कर्मणः शक्ताः Ve. 3 ; तस्योपकारे शक्तस्त्वं किं जीवन् किमुतान्यथा *ibid.* **2** Strong, mighty, powerful. **3** Rich, opulent, Ms. 11. 9. **4** Significant, expressive (as a word). **5** Clever, intelligent. **6** Speaking kindly or agreeably.

शक्तिः *f.* **1** Power, ability, capacity, strength, energy, prowess ; दैवं निहत्य कुरु पौरुषमात्मशक्त्या Pt. 1. 361 ; ज्ञाने मौनं क्षमा शक्तौ R. 1. 22 ; so यथाशक्ति, स्वशक्ति &c. Regal power ; (it has three parts or elements; 1 प्रभुशक्ति or प्रभावशक्ति 'the majesty or pre-eminent position of the king himself' ; 2 मंत्रशक्ति 'the power of good-counsel', and 3 उत्साहशक्ति 'the power of energy') ; राज्यं नाम शक्तित्रयायत्तं Dk. ; त्रिसाधना शक्तिरिवार्थसंचयं R. 3. 13, 6. 33, 17-63 ; *Si.* **2.** 26. **2** The power of composition, poetic power or genius ; शक्तिर्निपुणता लोकशास्त्रकाव्याद्यवेक्षणात् K. P. 1 ; see explanation *ad. loc.* **3** The active power of a deity, regarded as his wife, female divinity ; (these are variously enumerated, 8, 9 or even 50 being mentioned) ; स जयति परिणद्धः शक्तिभिः शक्तिनाथः Mâl. 5. 1; *S.* 7. 35. **4** A kind of missile ; शक्तिखंडामर्षितेन गांडीविनोक्तं Ve. 3 ; ततो बिभेद पौलस्त्यः शक्त्या वक्षसि लक्ष्मणं R. 12. 77. **5** A spear, dart, pike, lance. **6** (In Nyâya phil.) The relation of a term to the thing designated. **7** The power inherent in cause to produce its necessary effect. **8** (In Rhet.) The power or signification of a word ; (these are three अभिधा, लक्षणा and व्यंजना) ; S. D. 11. **9** The expressive power or denotation of a word (opp. लक्षणा and व्यंजना). **10** The female organ, the counterpart of the Phallus of Siva worshipped by a sect of people called Sâktas. **–Comp.** **–अर्धः** perspiring and panting through fatigue or exertion. **–अपेक्ष, –अपेक्षिन्** *a.* having regard to strength. **–कुंठनं** the deadening of a power. **–ग्रह** *a.* **1** apprehending the force or meaning. **2** armed with a spear. (**–हः**) **1** apprehension of the force, meaning, or acceptation of a word. **2** a spearman, lancer. **3** an epithet of Siva. 4 of Kârtikeya. **–ग्राहक** *a.* determining or establishing the meaning of a word. (**–कः**) an epithet of Kârtikeya. **–त्रयं** the three constituent elements of regal power; see शक्ति (2) above. **–धर** *a* strong, powerful. (**–रः**) **1** a spearman. **2** an epithet of Kârtikeya. **–पाणिः, –भृत्** *m.* **1** a spearman. **2** an epithet of Kârtikeya. **–पातः** prostration of strength. **–पूजकः** a Sâkta q. v. **–पूजा** the worship of Sakti. **–वैकल्यं** loss of strength, debility, incapacity. **–हीन** *a.* powerless, weak, impotent. **–हेतिकः** a lancer, spearman.

शक्तितस् *ind.* According to power, to the best of one's power or ability.

शक्न, शक्र, शक्व *a.* Speaking kindly or agreeably.

शक्य *pot. p.* **1** Possible, practicable, capable of being done or effected (usually with an inf.) ; शक्यो वारयितुं जलेन हुतभुक् Bh. 2. 11, R. 2. 49, 54. **2** Fit to be effected **3** Easy to be effected. **4** Directly conveyed or expressed (as the meaning of a word) ; शक्योऽर्थोऽभिधया ज्ञेयः S. D. 11. **5** Potential. (The form शक्यं is sometimes used as a predicative word with an inf. in a passive sense, the real object of the infinitive being in the nom. case ; एवं हि प्रणयवती सा शक्यमुपेक्षितुं कुपित M. 3. 22 ; शक्यं...अविरलमालिंगितुं पवनः *S.* 3. 8 ; विभूतयः शक्यमवाप्तुमूर्जिताः Subhâsh. ; Bg. 18. 11. **–Comp.** **–अर्थः** the meaning directly expressed.

शक्रः 1 N. of Indra ; पकः कृती शकुंतेषु योऽन्यं शक्रान्न याचते Kuval. **2** The Arjuna tree. **3** The Kutaja tree. **4** An owl. **5** The asterism ज्येष्ठा. **6** The number 'fourteen'. **–Comp.** **–अशनः** the Kutaja tree. **–आख्यः** an owl. **–आत्मजः** **1** Jayanta, son of Indra. **2** Arjuna. **–उत्थानं, –उत्सवः** a festival in honour of Indra on the 12th day of the bright half of Bhâdrapada. **–गोपः** a kind of red insect; cf. इंद्रगोप. **–जः, –जातः** a crow. **–जित्, –भिद्** *m.* epithets of Meghanâda, son of Râvana. **–द्रुमः** the Devadâru tree. **–धनुस्** *n.*, **–शरासनं** the rain-bow. **–ध्वजः** a flag set up in honour of Indra. **–पर्यायः** the Kutaja tree. **–पादपः 1** the Kutaja tree. **2** the Devadâru tree. **–प्रस्थ=इंद्रप्रस्थ** q. v. **–भवनं, –भुवनं, वासः** heaven, paradise. **–मूर्धन्**, *n.*, **–शिरस्** *m.* an ant-hill, a hillock. **–लोकः** the world of Indra. **–वाहनं** a cloud. **–शाखिन्** *m.* the Kutaja tree. **–सारथिः** 'the charioteer of Indra', an epithet of Mâtali. **–सुतः 1** an epithet of Jayanta. **2** of Arjuna. **3** of Vâli.

शक्राणी N. of Sachî, wife of Indra.

शक्रिः 1 A cloud. **2** The thunderbolt of Indra. **3** A mountain. **4** An elephant.

शक्वरः A bull, an ox ; cf. शक्कर.

शंक् 1 A. (शंकते, शंकित) **1** To doubt, be uncertain, hesitate, be doubtful ; शंके जीवति वा न वा Râm. **2** To dread, fear, be afraid (with abl.) ; नाशंकिष्ट विवस्वतः Bk. 15. 39 ; अशंकितेभ्यः शंकेत शंकितेभ्यश्च सर्वतः Subhâsh. **3** To suspect, mistrust, distrust ; स्वैर्दोषैर्भवति हि शंकितो मनुष्यः Mk. ; 4. 2. **4** To think, believe, fancy, imagine, think probable, suspect, fear ; त्वय्यासन्ने नयनमुपरि स्पंदि शंके मृगाक्ष्याः Me. 95 ; नाहं पुनस्तथा त्वयि यथा हि मां शंकसे भीरु V. 3. 14, Bk. 3. 26, N. 22. 42. **5** To start an objection, raise a doubt or objection (about) ; अत्रेदं शंक्यते (often used in controversial language) ; न च ब्रह्मणः प्रमाणांतरगम्यत्वं शंकितं शक्यं Sarva. S. –WITH **अभि 1** to suspect. **2** to be doubtful, or uncertain ; Ms. 8. 66. **–आ 1** to suspect, distrust, have doubts about ; Bk. 21. 1. **2** to suspect, believe to be, think ; आशंकसे यदग्निं तदिदं स्पर्शक्षमं रत्नं *S.* 1. 28 ; *Si.* 3. 72 ; Rk. 6. 6 ; Ms. 7. 185. **3** to fear, apprehend ; भरतागमनं पुनः आशंक्य R. 12. 24 ; Pt. 1. 392. **4** to raise an objection, start a doubt ; अत एव न ब्रह्मशब्दस्य जात्याद्यर्थांतरमाशंकितव्यं S. B. (and in several other places). **–परि 1** to suspect, believe, fancy (to be); पत्रेऽपि संचारिणि प्राप्तं त्वां परिशंकते Gît. 6. **2** to doubt, have doubts about. **3** to fear, be afraid of ; R. 8. 78. **–वि 1** to suspect, fear, have doubts or suspicious about ; विशंकसे भीरु यतोऽवधीरणां *S.* 3. 14 ; सतीमपि ज्ञातिकुलैकसंश्रयां जनोऽन्यथा भर्तृमती विशंकते 5.17. **2** to think to be, fancy, imagine ; विशंकमाना रमितं कयापि जनार्दनं दृष्टवदेतदाह Gît. 7.

शंकः A draught-ox.

शंकर *a.* (**रा-री** *f.*) Conferring happiness or prosperity, auspicious, propitious. **–रः 1** N. of Siva. **2** N. of a celebrated teacher and author ; see App. II. **–री 1** N. of Pârvatî, wife of Siva. **2** Bengal madder. **3** The Samî tree.

शंका 1 Doubt, uncertainty. **2** Hesitation, scruple. **3** Suspicion, distrust, misgiving ; अपायशंका ; अरिष्टशंका &c. **4** Fear, apprehension, dread, alarm ; जातशंकैर्देवैर्मेनका नामाप्सराः प्रेषिता *S.* 1 ; कैकेयीशंकयेवाह R. 12. 2, 13. 42 ; Me. 69. **5** Hope, expectation. **6** (Mistaken) belief, suspicion, (wrong) impression ; स्रजमपि शिरस्यंधः क्षिप्तां धुनोत्यहिशंकया *S.* 7. 24 ; कुर्वन् वधूजनमनःसु शशांकशंका Ki. 5. 42 ; हरितृणोद्गमशंकया 5. 38.

शंकित *p. p.* 1 Doubted, suspected, feared. 2 Suspicious, suspecting, distrustful. 3 Uncertain, doubtful. 4 Fearful, apprehensive, alarmed. (See शंक्). **-Comp.-चित्त, -मनस्** *a.* 1 timid, faint-hearted. 2 suspicious, distrustful. 3 doubtful.

शंकिन् *a.* Doubting, suspecting, fearing, believing (at the end of comp.); त्वदुपावर्तनशंकि मे मनः R. 8. 53; अतिस्नेहः पापशंकी *S.* 4.

शंकुः 1 A dart, spear, spike, javelin, dagger ; oft. at the end of comp. ; शोकशंकुः 'the dart of grief ; *i. e.* sharp, poignant, grief ; U. 3. 35 ; R. 8. 93. 2 A stake, pillar, post, pale. 3 A nail, pin, peg ; R. 12. 95. 4 The sharp head or point of an arrow, barb. 5 The trunk (of a lopped tree), stump, pollard. 6 The pin of a dial. 7 A measure of twelve fingers. 8 A measuring-rod. 9 The sine or altitude (in astr.). 10 Ten billions. 11 The fibres of a leaf. 12 An ant-hill. 13 The penis. 14 The skate-fish. 15 A demon. 16 Poison. 17 Sin. 18 An aquatic animal, particularly, a goose. 19 N. of *S*iva. 20 The *S*âla tree. **-Comp.** **-कर्ण** *a.* spike-eared. (**-र्णः**) an ass. **-तरुः, -वृक्षः** The *S*âla tree.

शंकुला 1 A kind of knife or lancet. 2 A pair of scissors. **-Comp.** **-खंडः** a piece cut off with a pair of scissors.

शंखः -खं 1 The conch-shell, a shell; न श्वेतभावमुज्झाति शंखः शिखिभुक्तमुक्तोपि Pt. 4. 110. ; शंखान् दध्मुः पृथक् पृथक् Bg. 1. 18. 2 The bone on the forehead : Ku. 7. 33. 3 The temporal bone. 4 The part between the tusks of an elephant. 5 A hundred billions. 6 A military drum or other martial instrument. 7 A kind of perfume (नखी). 8 One of the nine treasures of Kubera. 9 N. of a demon slain by Vishṇu. 10 N. of the author of a Smriti (mentioned in conjunction with लिखित q. v.). **-Comp.** **-उदकं** the water poured into a conch-shell. **-कारः, -कारकः** a shell-cutter, described as a kind of mixed caste. **-चरी, चर्ची** a mark made with sandal (on the forehead.) **-चूर्णं** powder produced from shells. **-द्रावः, -द्रावकः** a solvent for dissolving shells. **-ध्मः, -ध्मा** *m.* a shell-blower, conch-blower. **-ध्वनिः** the sound of a conch (sometimes, but erroneously, used to denote a cry of alarm or despair). **-प्रस्थः** a spot on the moon. **-भृत्** *m.* an epithet of Vishṇu. **-मुखः** an alligator. **-स्वनः** the sound of a conch.

शंखकः -कं 1 A conch-shell. 2 The temporal bone. **-कः** A bracelet (made of conch-shell) ; Si. 13. 41.

शंखनकः (**खः**) A small conch or shell.

शंखिन् *m.* 1 The ocean. 2 An epithet of Vishṇu. 3 A conch-blower.

शंखिनी 1 A woman of one of the four classes into which writers on erotical science divide women ; the Ratimanjarî thus describes her:— दीर्घातिदीर्घनयना वरसुंदरीया कामोपभोगरसिका गुणशीलयुक्ता । रेखात्रयेण च विभूषितकंठदेशा संभोगकेलिरसिका किल शंखिनी सा ॥ 6 ; cf. चित्रिणी, हस्तिणी and पद्मिनी also. 2 A female spirit, or a kind of fairy.

शच् 1 A. (शचते) To speak, say, tell.

शचिः-ची *f.* N. of the wife of Indra ; R. 3. 13, 23. **-Comp.** **-पतिः, -भर्तृ** *m.* epithets of Indra.

शंच् 1 A. (शंचते) To go, move.

शट 1 P. (शटति) 1 To be sick. 2 To divide, separate.

शट *a.* Sour, acid, astringent.

शटा The matted hair of an ascetic; cf. जटा.

शटिः *f.* The plant called zedoary.

शठ् I. 1 P. (शठति) 1 To deceive, cheat, defraud. 2 To hurt, kill. 3 To suffer pain. -II. 10. P. (शाठयति) 1 To finish. 2 To leave unfinished. 3 To go, move. 4 To be idle or lazy. 5 To deceive, cheat (शठयति in this sense).

शठ *a.* 1 Crafty, deceitful, fraudulent, dishonest, perfidious. 2 Wicked, depraved. **-ठः** 1 A rogue, cheat, knave, swindler ; Ms. 4. 30, Bg. 18. 28. 2 A false or deceitful lover (who pretends to love one woman while his heart is fixed on another); ध्रुवमस्मि शठः शुचिस्मिते विदितः कैतववत्सलस्तव R. 8. 49, 19. 31 ; M. 3. 19 ; S. D. thus defines a शठः—शठोयमेकत्र बद्धभावो यः दर्शितबहिरनुरागो विप्रियमन्यत्र गूढमाचरति ॥ 74. 3 A fool, blockhead. 4 A mediator, arbitrator. 5 The Dhattûra plant. 6 An idler, a lazy fellow. **-ठं** 1 Iron. 2 Saffron.

शणं Hemp. **-Comp.** **-सूत्रं** 1 a hempen cord or string. 2 a net made of hemp. 3 cordage.

शंडः 1 An impotent man, a eunuch. 2 A bull. 3 A bull at liberty to move. **-डं** A collection, multitude ; cf. षंड or खंड.

शंढः 1 A eunuch, an impotent man. 2 A male attendant in the women's apartments (chosen from the class of eunuchs or emasculated persons). 3 A bull. 4 A bull at liberty to move. 5 A madman.

शतं 1 A hundred; निःस्वो वष्टि शतं Sânti. 2. 6; शतमेकोपि संधत्ते प्राकारस्थो धनुर्धरः Pt. 1. 229 ; (शत is used in the singular with a plural noun of any gender ; शतं नराः, शतं गावः; or शतं गृहाणि, in which case it is treated as a numeral adjective ; but sometimes in dual and plural also ; द्वे शते; दश शतानि &c. It is also used with a noun in the genitive ; गवां शतं, वर्षाणां शतं 'a century of cows, years ' &c. At the end of comp., it may remain unchanged ; भव भर्ता शरच्छतं, or may be changed into शती ; as in आर्यासप्तशती a work of Govardhanâchârya.). 2 Any large number. **-Comp.** **-अक्षी** 1 night. 2 the goddess Durgâ. **-अंगः** a car, carriage; especially, a war-chariot. **-अनीकः** an old man. **-अरं, -आरं** the thunderbolt of Indra. **-आननं** a cemetery. **-आनंदः** 1 N. of Brahman. 2 of Vishṇu or Krishṇa. 3 of the car of Vishṇu. 4 of a son of Gotama and Ahalyâ, the family-priest of Janaka; U. 1. 16. **-आयुस्** *a.* lasting or living for a hundred years. **-आवर्तः-आवर्तिम्** *n.* N. of Vishṇu. **-ईशः** 1 the ruler of a hundred. 2 the ruler of a hundred villages ; Ms. 7. 115. **-कुंभः** N. of a mountain (where gold is said to be found). (**-भं**) gold. **-कृत्वस्** *ind.* a hundred times. **-कोटि** *a.* hundred-edged. (**-टिः**) Indra's thunderbolt. (*-f.*) a hundred crores. **-क्रतुः** an epithet of Indra ; R. 3. 38. **-खंडं** gold. **-गु** *a.* possessed of a hundred cows. **-गुण, -गुणित** *a.* hundred-fold, increased a hundred times ; V. 3. 22. **-ग्रंथिः** *f.* the Dûrvâ grass. **-घ्नी** 1 A kind of weapon used as a missile (supposed by some to be a sort of rocket, but described by others as a huge stone studded with iron spikes and four *ta'las* in length ; शतघ्नी च चतुस्ताला लोहकंटकसंचिता; or अयःकंटकसंच्छन्ना शतघ्नी महती शिला); R. 12. 95. 2 a female scorpion. 3 a disease of the throat. **-जिह्वः** an epithet of *S*iva. **-तारका, -भिषज्, -भिषा** *f.* N. of the 24th lunar mansion containing one hundred stars. **-दला** the white rose. **-द्रुः** *f.* N. of a river in the Panjab now called Sutlej. **-धामन्** *m.* an epithet of Vishṇu. **-धार** *a.* having a hundred edges. (**-रं**) the thunderbolt of Indra. **-धृतिः** 1 an epithet of Indra. 2 of Brahman. 3 heaven or *Svarga*. **-पत्रः** 1 a peacock. 2 the (Indian) crane. 3 A wood-pecker. 4 a parrot or a species of it. (**-त्रा**) a woman. (**-त्रं**) a lotus ; आवृत्तवृंतशतपत्रनिभं (आननं) वहंत्या Mâl. 1. 29. °**योनिः** an epithet of Brahman ; कंपेन मूर्ध्नः शतपत्रयोनिं (संभावयामास); Ku. 7. 46. **-पत्रकः** the wood-pecker. **-पद्, -पाद्** *a.* having a hundred feet. **-पदी** a centipede. **-पत्रं** 1 a lotus with a hundred petals. 2 the white lotus. **-पर्वन्** *m.* a bamboo. (*-f.*) 1 the full-moon day in the month of Asvina. 2 Dûrvâ-grass. 3 the plant Katukâ. °**ईशः** the planet Venus. **-भीरुः** *f.* the Arabian jasmine. **-मखः, -मन्युः** 1 epithets of Indra ; Ki. 2. 23 ; Bk. 1. 5 ; Ku. 2. 64 ; R. 9.

13. 2 an owl. **–मुख** *a.* 1 having a hundred ways. 2 having a hundred outlets, mouths or openings; विवेकभ्रष्टानां भवति विनिपातः शतमुखः Bh. 2. 10. (where the word has sense 1 also). (**–खं**) a hundred ways or openings. (**–खी**) a brush, broom. **–मूला** the Dûrvâ grass. **–यज्वन्** *m.* an epithet of Indra. **–यष्टिकः** a necklace of one hundred strings. **–रूपा** N. of a daughter of Brahman (who is supposed to be also his wife, from whose incestuous connection with her father is said to have sprung Manu *S*vâyambhuva). **–वर्षं** one hundred years, a century. **–वेधिन्** *m.* a kind of sorrel. **–सहस्रं** 1 a hundred thousand. 2 several hundreds, *i. e.* a large number. **–साहस्र** *a.* 1 consisting of or containing a hundred thousand. 2 bought with a hundred thousand. **–ह्रदा** 1 lightning; Ku. 7. 39; Mk. 5. 48. 2 the thunderbolt of Indra.

शतक *a.* 1 A hundred. 2 Containing a hundred. **–कं** 1 A century. 2 A collection of one hundred stanzas; as in नीति°, वैराग्य°, शृंगार° a collection of one hundred stanzas on Nîti &c.

शततम *a.* (**मी** *f.*) One-hundredth.

शतधा *ind.* 1 In a hundred ways. 2 Into a hundred parts or pieces. 3 A hundred-fold.

शतशस् *ind.* 1 By hundreds. 2 A hundred times; शतशः शपे Prab. 3.; Ms. 12. 58. 3 A hundred-fold, variously, multifariously; Bg. 11. 5.

शतिक *a.* (**की** *f.*) **शत्य** *a.* 1 Containing or consisting of a hundred; Y. 2. 208. 2 Relating to a hundred. 3 Effected with a hundred. 4 Bought with a hundred. 5 Changed with or for a hundred. 6 Bearing tax or interest per hundred. 7 Indicative of (the acquisition of) a hundred.

शतिन् *a.* 1 A hundred-fold. 2 Numerous. *–m.* The owner of a hundred; निःस्वो वष्टि शतं शती दशशतं Sânti. 2. 6, Pt. 5. 82.

शात्रिः An elephant.

शत्रुः 1 An overthrower, a destroyer, conqueror. 2 An enemy, a foe, an adversary; क्षमा शत्रौ च मित्रे च यतीनामेव भूषणं Subbâsh. 3 A political rival, a rival neighbouring king. **–Comp.** **–उपजापः** the secret whisperings of a foe, treacherous overture of an enemy. **–कर्षण, –दमन, –निबर्हण** *a.* subduing, overpowering or destroying enemies. **–घ्नः** 'destroyer of enemies', an epithet of a brother of Râma and twin brother of Lakshmaṇa being a son of Sumitrâ. He killed the demon Lavaṇa and colonized Mathurâ. He had two sons named Subâhu and Bahusruta; see R. 15. **–पक्षः** 1 the party or side of an enemy. 2 an opponent, antagonist. **–विनाशनः** an epithet of *S*iva. **–हत्या** foe-slaughter. **–हन्** *a.* foe-slayer.

शत्रुंजयः 1 An elephant. 2 N. of a mountain.

शत्रुंतप *a.* Overcoming or destroying one's foes.

शत्वरी Night.

शद् I. 1 P. (but A. in conjugational tenses) (शीयते, शन्न) 1 To fall, perish, decay, wither. 2 To go. *–Caus.* (शादयति-ते) 1 To cause to go, impel. 2 (शातयति-ते) (*a*) To fell, throw down, cut down; *S*i. 14. 80, 15. 24. (*b*) To kill, destroy.–II. 1 P. (शदति) To go (usually with आ).

शदः An eatable vegetable product (fruit, root &c.).

शद्रिः 1 An elephant. 2 A cloud. 3 N. of Arjuna. **–द्रिः** *f.* Lightning.

शद्रु *a.* 1 Going, moving. 2 Falling, perishing, decaying.

शनकैस् *ind.* Slowly; see शनैस्.

शनिः 1 The planet Saturn (the son of the sun and represented as of a black colour or dressed in dark-coloured clothes. 2 Saturday. 3 N. of *S*iva. **–Comp.** **–जं** black pepper. **–प्रदोषः** a term for the (evening) worship of *S*iva performed on the thirteenth day of a lunar fortnight when it falls on a Saturday. **–प्रियं** a sapphire. **–वारः, –वासरः** Saturday.

शनैस् *ind.* 1 Slowly, gently, quietly. 2 Gradually, by degrees, little by little; धर्मं संचिनुयाच्छनैः; Ku. 3. 59; Ms. 3. 217. 3 Successively, in due order; Ms. 1. 15. 4 Mildly, softly. 5 Tardily, sluggishly. (शनैः शनैः slowly, by slow degrees). **–Comp.** **–चर** *a.* going or moving slowly; शनैश्चराभ्यां पादाभ्यां रेजे ग्रहमयीव सा Bh. 1. 17. (where it means 'Saturn' also). (**–रः**) the planet Saturn.

शंतनुः N. of a king of the lunar race. He married Gangâ and Satyavatî; by the former wife he had a son named Bhîshma and by the latter Chitrângada and Vichitravîrya. Bhîshma remained a celibate all his life, and his younger brothers died childless; cf. भीष्म.

शप् I. 4 U. (शपति-ते, शप्यति-ते, शप्त) 1 To curse, execrate; अशपद्भव मानुषीति तां R. 8. 80; सोऽभूत्पराह्मुरथ भूमिपतिं शशाप (वृद्धः) 9. 78, 1; 77. 2 To swear, take an oath, promise by oath, say on oath (usually with dat. of the person to whom a promise &c. is made and instr. of the object by which it is made); भरतेनात्मना चाहं शपे ते मनुजाधिप । यथा नान्येन तुष्येयमृते रामविवासनात् Râm; when used without an object it generally governs the instr. of the thing and dat. of the person by whcih or whom the oath is taken; सत्यं शपामि ते पादपंकजस्पर्शेन K.; Ghaṭ. 22; अशप्त सिद्धं शनोऽसौ सीतायै स्मरमोहितः K. 8. 74, 33; sometimes शप governs a cognate accusative; सहस्रशोऽसौ शपथानशप्यत् Bk. 3. 32. 3 To blame, scold, revile, abuse (with dat. or by itself); द्विषद्भ्यश्चाशपंस्तथा Bk. 17. 4; प्रतिवाचमदत्त केशवः शपमानाय न चेदिभूभुजे *S*i. 4. 25. *–Caus.* (शापयति-ते) To bind by an oath, conjure; शापितोऽसि गोब्राह्मणकाम्यया Mk. 3; Mâl. 8.

शपः 1 A curse, imprecation. 2 An oath.

शपथः 1 Cursing. 2 A curse, an imprecation, anathema. 3 An oath, swearing, taking or administering on oath, asseveration by oath or ordeal; आमोदो न हि कस्तूर्याः शपथेनानुभाव्यते Rv. 1. 120; Ms. 8. 109. 4 Conjuration, binding by oaths; Mâl. 3. 2.

शपन See शपथ.

शप्त *p. p.* 1 Cursed. 2 Sworn. 3 Revil d, abused (see शप्).

शफः-फं 1 A hoof. 2 The root of a tree.

शफरः (**री** *f.*) A kind of small glittering fish; मोघीकर्तुं चटुलशफरोद्वर्तनप्रेक्षितानि Me. 40; *S*i. 8. 24; Ku. 4. 39. **–Comp.** **–अधिपः** the fish called Ilisha.

शब(व)रः 1 A mountaineer, barbarian, savage; राजन् गुंजाफलानां स्रज इति शबरा नैव हारं हरंति K. P. 10. 2 N. of *S*iva. 3 The hand. 4 Water. 5 A particular *S*âstra or sacred treatise. 6 N. of a celebrated commentator and writer on Mîmâmsâ. **–री** 1 A *S*abara female. 2 A female *Kira ta* who was an ardent devotee of Râma. **–Comp.** **–आलयः** the abode of wild mountaineers or barbarians. **–लोध्रः** the wild *Lodhra* tree.

शब(व)ल *a.* 1 Spotted, brindled, variegated; R. 5. 44, 13. 56; Mv. 7. 26. 2 Varied, divided into various parts. **–लः** A variegated colour. **–ला, –ली** 1 A spotted or brindled cow. 2 The cow of plenty or Kâmadhenu q. v. **–लं** Water.

शब्द् 10 U. (शब्दयति-ते, शब्दित) 1 To sound, make a noise. 2 To speak, call out, call out to; विततमृदुकराग्रः शब्दयंत्या वयोभिः परिपतति दिवोऽङ्के हेलया बालसूर्यः *S*i. 11. 47. 3 To name, call; अत एव सागारिकेति शब्द्यते Ratn. 4. **–With** अभि to name. **–प्र** to explain. **–सं** to call out to.

शब्दः 1 Sound (the object of the sense of hearing and property of आकाश); R. 13. 1. 2 Sound, note (of birds; men &c.), noise in general, विश्वासोपगमादभिन्नगतयः शब्दं सहंते मृगाः *S*. 1. 14; Bg. 1. 13; *S*. 3. 1; Ms. 4. 113; Ku. 1. 45. 3 The sound of a musical instrument; वाद्यशब्दः Pt. 2. 24,

Ku. 1. 45. **4** A word, sound, significant word (for def. &c. see Mbh. introduction); एकः शब्दः सम्यग्धीतः सम्यक् प्रयुक्तः स्वर्गे लोके कामधुग्भवति; so शब्दार्थौ. **5** A declinable word, a noun, substantive. **6** A title, an epithet; यस्यार्थयुक्तं गिरिराजशब्दं कुर्वंति बालव्यजनैश्चमर्यः Ku. 1. 13; *S*. 2. 14; नृपेण चक्रे युवराजशब्दभाक् R. 3. 35, 2. 53, 64, 3. 49, 5. 22; 18. 41; V. 1. 1. **7** The name, mere name; as in शब्दपति q. v. **8** Verbal authority (regarded by the Naiyâyikas as a Pramâṇa). **–Comp.** **–अतीत** *a.* beyond the power or reach of words, indescribable. **–अधिष्ठानं** the ear. **–अध्याहारः** supplying a word (to complete an ellipsis). **–अनुशासनं** the science of words; *i. e.* grammar. **–अर्थः** the meaning of a word. (**र्थौ** dual) a word and its meaning; अदोषौ शब्दार्थौ K. P. 1. **–अलंकारः** a figure of speech depending for its charmingness on sound or words and disappearing (as soon as the words which constitute the figure are replaced by others of the same meaning (opp. अर्थालंकार); *e. g.* see K. P. 9. **–आख्येय** *a.* to be communicated in words; Me. 103. (**–यं**) an oral or verbal communication. **–आडंबरः** bombast, verbosity, high-sounding or grandiloquent words. **–आदि** *a.* beginning with शब्द (as the objects of sense); R. 10. 25. **–कोशः** a lexicon, dictionary. **–गत** *a.* inherent or residing in a word. **–ग्रहः** **1** catching the sound. **2** the ear. **–चातुर्यं** cleverness of style, eloquence. **–चित्रं** one of the two subdivisions of the last (अवर or अधम) class of poetry (wherein the charm lies in the use of words which please the ear simply by their sound; see the example given under the word चित्र). **–चोरः** 'a word-thief,' a plagiarist. **–तन्मात्रं** the subtle element of sound. **–पतिः** a lord in name only, nominal lord; ननु शब्दपतिः क्षितेरहं त्वयि मे भावनिबंधना रतिः R. 8. 52. **–पातिन्** *a.* hitting an invisible mark, the sound of which is only heard, tracing a sound; R. 9. 73. **–प्रमाणं** verbal or oral evidence. **–बोधः** knowledge derived from verbal testimony. **–ब्रह्मन्** *n.* **1** the Vedas. **2** spiritual knowledge consisting in words, knowledge of the Supreme Spirit or the Spirit itself; U. 2. 7. 20. **3** a property of words called स्फोट q. v. **–भेदिन्** *a.* hitting a mark merely by its sound. (**–m.**) **1** an epithet of Arjuna. **2** the anus. **3** a kind of arrow. **–योनिः** *f.* a root, radical word. **–विद्या, –शासन, –शास्त्रं** the science of words; *i. e.* grammar.; अनंतपारं किल शब्दशास्त्रं Pt. 1; *Si.* **2.** 112, 14. 24. **–विरोध** opposition of words (in a sentence). **–विशेषः** a variety of sound. **–वृत्तिः** *f.* the function of a word (in Rhet.). **–वेधिन्** *a.* hitting an invisible mark the sound of which is only heard; see शब्दपातिन्. (**–m.**) **1** an epithet of Arjuna. **2** a kind of arrow. **–शक्तिः** *f.* the force or expressive power of a word; signification of a word; see शक्ति. **–शुद्धिः** *f.* **1** purity of words. **2** correct use of words. **–श्लेषः** a play or pun upon words, a verbal equivoque; (it differs from अर्थश्लेष in-as-much as the pun disappears as soon as the words which constitute it are replaced by others of the same signification, whereas in अर्थश्लेष the pun remains unchanged; शब्दपरिवृत्तिसहत्वमर्थश्लेषः). **–संग्रहः** a vocabulary, lexicon **–सौष्ठवं** elegance of words, a graceful or elegant style. **–सौकर्यं** ease of expression.

शब्दन *a.* Sounding, making a sound. **–नं** **1** Sounding, making a noise, uttering a sound. **2** A sound, noise. **3** Calling out, calling. **4** Naming.

शब्दायते Den. A. **1** To make a noise, sound; शब्दायंते मधुरमनिलैः कीचकाः पूर्यमाणाः Me. 56. **2** To cry, roar, scream, yell; Bk. 5. 52; 17. 91. **3** To call, call out to; एते हास्तिनापुरगामिन ऋषयेः शब्दायंते *S*. 4, Mu. 1; Mk. 1; Ve. 3.

शब्दित *p. p.* **1** Sounded, made to give out a sound, played upon (as a musical instrument). **2** Uttered, articulated. **3** Called, called out to. **4** Named; designated.

शम् *ind.* A particle meaning welfare, happiness, prosperity, health, and generally used to express a blessing or pious wish; (with dat. or gen.); शं देवदत्ताय or देवदत्तस्य (often used in modern letters as an auspicious conclusion; इति शम्). **–Comp.** **–कर** see s. v. **–ताति** *n.* conferring happiness, propitious, auspicious. **–पाकः** **1** lac, red dye. **2** cooking, maturing. **–भु** see s. v.

शम् I. 4 P. (शाम्यति, शांत) **1** To be calm, quiet or tranquil, be appeased or pacified; (as a person); शाम्येत्प्रत्यपकारेण नोपकारेण दुर्जनः Ku. 2. 40; R. 7. 3; शांतो लवः U. 6. 7. **2** To cease, stop, come to an end; चिंता शशाम सकलाऽपि सरोरुहाणां Bv. 3. 7; न जातु कामः कामानामुपभोगेन शाम्यति Ms. 2. 94 'is not satisfied'. **3** To be quelled, be extinguished or quenched; शशाम वृष्ट्यापि विना दवाग्निः R. 2. 14. U. 5. 7. **4** To put an end to, destroy, kill (also 9 P. in this sense). *–Caus.* (शमयति-ते, but शामयति-ते in the sense of 'seeing' see शम् II). **1** To appease, allay, calm, tranquillizie, pacify, soothe; कः शीतलैः शमयिता वचनैस्तवाधिं Bv. 3. 1; *S*. 5. 7. **2** To put an end, to stop; Ku. **2.** 56. **3** To remove, avert; प्रतिकूलं दैवं शमयितुं *S*. 1. **4** To subdue, tame, defeat, conquer, vanquish; शमयति गजानन्यान् गंधद्विपः कलभोऽपि सन् V. 5. 18; R. 9. 12, 11. 59. **5** To kill, destroy, slay; Ve. 5. 5. **6** To quench, extinguish; Me. 53; H. 1. 88. **7** To leave off, desist, cease. –With उप **1** to be clam or tranquil; Bk. 20. 5. **2** to cease, stop, be extinguished. **3** to cease, leave off speaking. **–नि** to hear, listen to, come to know; निशम्य चैनां तपसे कृतोद्यमां Ku. 5. 3; R. 2. 41, 52, 61; 3. 47; 4. 2; 5. 12; Bk. 2. 9. **–प्र** **1** to become calm or tranquil. **2** to be soothed or appeased. **3** to stop, cease. **4** to be allayed, be quenched or extinguished; प्रशांतपावकास्त्रं U. 6. **5** to decay, wither away. (*–Caus.*) **1** to soothe, appease, pacify; Ms. 8. 391. **2** to allay, extinguish, quench, put down; त्वामासारप्रशमितवनोपप्लवं Me. 17. **3** to remove, put an end to: तं (अपचारं) आन्विष्य प्रशमयेः R. 15. 47. **4** to conquer, vanquish, subdue; Mk. 10. 60. **5** to settle, adjust, compose; प्रशमयसि विवादं कल्पसे रक्षणाय *S*. 5. 8. **–सं** **1** to clam. **2** to be allayed or extinguished, disappear; सत्त्वं संशाम्यतीव मे Bk. 18. 28. **3** to be removed. –II. 10 U. (शामयति-ते) **1** To see, look at, inspect. **2** To show, display. –With नि **1** to see, observe. **2** to hear, listen; निशामय प्रियसखि Mâl. 7.

शमः **1** Quiet, tranquillity, calmness. **2** Rest, calm, repose, cessation. **3** Absence or restraint of passions, mental quietness, quietism; शमरतेऽमरतेजसि पार्थिवे R. 9. 4; Ki. 10. 10; 16. 48, *Si*. 2. 94; *S*. 2. 7; Bg. 10. 4. **4** Allayment, mitigalion, alleviation, satisfaction, pacification (of grief, thirst, hunger &c.); शमुपयातु ममापि चित्तदाहः U. 6. 8; शममेष्यति मम शोकः कथं नु वत्से *S*. 4. 20. **5** Peace; as in शमोपन्यास Ve. 5. **6** Final emancipation (from all worldly illusions and attachments). **7** The hand. **–Comp.** **–अंतकः** the god of love (a destroyer of mental tranquillity). **–पर** *a.* tranquil, quiet, stoical.

शमथः **1** Tranquillity, calmness; especially mental calmness, absence of passion. **2** A counsellor, minister.

शमन *a.* (**नी** *f.*) Quelling, allaying, subduing &c. **–नं** **1** Appeasing, allaying, soothing, conquering, alleviating, &c. **2** Calmness, tranquillity. **3** End, stop, cessation, destruction. **4** Hurting, injuring. **5** Killing animals for sacrifice, immolation. **6** Swallowing, chewing. **–नः** **1** A kind of deer, an antelope. **2** N of Yama, the god of death. **–Comp.** **–स्वसृ** *f.* 'Yama's sister,' epithet of the river Yamunâ.

शमनी Night. **–Comp.** **–सदः** (**–षदः**) a demon, goblin.

शमलं 1 Feces, ordure, excrement. 2 Impurity, sediment. 3 Sin, moral impurity.

शमित *p. p.* 1 Appeased, allayed, soothed, calmed. 2 Alleviated, cured, relieved. 3 Relaxed. 4 Calm, sedate. 5 Moderated, tempered.

शमिन् *a.* 1 Calm, tranquil, pacific. 2 One who has subdued his passions, self-controlled; Rk. 7. 5.

शमी (शमि sometimes) 1 N. of a tree (said to contain fire); अग्निगर्भां शमीमिव *S.* 4. 2; Ms. 8. 247; Y. 1. 302. 2 A pod, legume. –Comp. –गर्भः 1 an epithet of fire. 2 a Brâhmaṇa, one belonging to the sacerdotal or priestly class. –धान्यं any pulse or grain growing in pods, leguminous grain.

शंपा Lightning.

शंब् I. 1 P. (शंबति) To go, move. –II. 10 P. (शंबयति) To collect, heap together.

शंब (व) *a.* 1 Happy, fortunate. 2 Poor, unfortunate. –बः 1 The thunderbolt of Indra. 2 The iron head of a pestle. 3 An iron chain worn round the loins. 4 Ploughing 'with the grain' or in the regular direction. 5 The second ploughing of a field. (शंबाकृ means 'to plough twice').

शंबरः 1 N. of a demon slain by Pradyumna, q. v. 2 A mountain. 3 A kind of deer. 4 A kind of fish. 5 War. –रं 1 Water. 2 A cloud. 3 Wealth. 4 A rite or religious observance. –Comp. –अरिः, –सूदनः epithets of Pradyumna or the god of love. –असुरः the demon *S*ambara.

शंबरी 1 Illusion, jugglery. 2 A female juggler.

शंबलः-लं 1 A bank, shore. 2 Provisions for a journey, viaticum. 3 Envy, jealousy.

शंबली A procuress.

शंबुः, शंबुकः, शंबूकः A bivalve shell.

शंबूकः 1 A bivalve shell. 2 A small conch-shell. 3 A snail. 4 The edge of the frontal protuberance of an elephant. 5 N. of a *S*ûdra (who practised penance though forbidden to his caste and was in consequence slain by Râma; see *inter alia* U. 2 and R. 15.)

शंभः 1 A happy man. 2 The thunderbolt of Indra.

शंभली A bawd, procuress.

शंभु *a.* Causing happiness, granting prosperity. –भुः 1 N. of *S*iva. 2 Of Brahman. 3 A sage, venerable man. 4 A kind of Siddha. –Comp. –तनयः, –नंदनः, –सुतः epithets of Kârtikeya or Gaṇesa. –प्रिया 1 N. of Durgâ. 2 emblic myrobalan (आमलकी). –वल्लभं the white lotus.

शम्या 1 A wooden stick or post. 2 A staff. 3 The pin of a yoke. 4 A Kind of cymbal. 5 A sacrificial vessel.

शय *a.* (या-यी *f.*) Lying down, sleeping (usually at the end of comp.); रात्रिजागरपरो दिवाशयः R. 19. 34; so उत्तानशय, पार्श्वशय, वृक्षेशय, बिलेशय &c. –यः 1 Sleep. 2 A bed, couch. 3 A hand. 4 A snake, especially the boa. 5 A buse, imprecation, curse.

शयंड *a.* Sleepy, sleeping.

शयथ *a.* Sleepy, asleep. –थः 1 Death. 2 A kind of snake, the boa-constrictor. 3 A boar. 4 A fish.

शयनं 1 Sleeping, sleep, lying down. 2 A bed, couch; शयनस्थो न भुंजीत Ms. 4. 74, R. 1. 95; V. 3. 10. 3 Copulation, sexual union. –Comp. अ(आ)गारः-रं, –गृहं a bed-chamber, sleeping apartments. –एकादशी the eleventh day of the bright half of Ashâḍha when Vishṇu lies down to enjoy his four months' repose. –सखी a bed-fellow. –स्थानं a sleeping apartment, bed-chamber.

शयनीयं A bed, couch; परिशून्यं शयनीयमद्य मे R. 8. 66; कांतासखस्य शयनीयशिलातलं ते U. 3. 21; (शयनीयकं in the same sense).

शयानकः 1 A chameleon. 2 A kind of snake, the boa.

शयालु *a.* Sleepy, slothful; *Si.* 2. 80. –लुः 1 A kind of snake, the boa-constrictor. 2 A dog. 3 A jackal.

शयित *p. p.* 1 Sleeping, reposed, asleep. 2 Lying down.

शयुः A large snake, the boa.

शय्या 1 A bed, couch; शय्या भूमितलं *S*ânti. 4. 9; मही रम्या शय्या Bh. 3. 79; R. 5. 66. 2 Tying, stringing together. –Comp. –अध्यक्षः, –पालः the superintendent or guardian of a king's bed-chamber. –उत्संगः the side of a bed. –गत *a.* 1 lying in a bed. 2 confined to a bed. –गृहं a bed-chamber; R. 16. 4.

शरः 1 An arrow, a shaft; क्व च निशितनिपाता वज्रसाराः शरास्ते *S.* 1. 10. 2 A kind of white reed or grass; शरकांडपांडुगंडस्थला M. 3. 8; मुखेन सीता शरपांडुरेण R. 14. 26; *Si.* 11. 30. 3 The cream of slightly curdled milk, cream. 4 Hurt, injury, wound. 5 The number 'five.' –रं Water. –Comp. –अग्र्यः an excellent arrow. –अभ्यासः archery. –असनं, आस्यं an arrow-shooter, a bow; R. 3. 52; Ku. 3. 64. –आक्षेपः flight of arrows. –आरोपः, –आवापः a bow. –आश्रयः a quiver. –आहत *a.* struck by an arrow. –ईषिका an arrow. –इष्टः the mango tree. –ओघः a shower or multitude of arrows. –कांडः 1 a reed stalk. 2 a shaft of an arrow. –घातः shooting with arrows, archery. –जं fresh butter. –जन्मन् *m.* an epithet of Kârtikeya; R. 3. 28. –जालं a multitude or dense or dense mass of arrows. –धिः a quiver. –पातः an arrow's flight. °स्थानं a bow-shot. –पुंखः, पुंखा the feathered end of an arrow. –फलं the blade or barb of an arrow. –भंगः N. of a sage whom Râma visited in the Daṇḍaka forest; R. 13. 45. –भूः N. of Kârtikeya. –मल्लः a bow-man, an archer. –वनं (–वणं) a thicket of reeds; Me. 45. °उद्भवः, °भवः epithets of Kârtikeya. –वर्षः a shower or volley of arrows. –वाणिः 1 the head of an arrow. 2 an archer. 3 a maker of arrows. 4 a foot-soldier. –वृष्टिः *f.* a shower of arrows. –व्रातः a mass or multitude of arrows. –संधानं taking aim with an arrow; शरसंधानं नाटयति *S.* 1. –संबाध *a.* covered with arrows. –स्तंबः a clump of reeds.

शरटः 1 A chameleon. 2 A safflower.

शरणं 1 Protection, help, succour, defence; R. 14. 64, V. 1. 3; U. 4. 23. 2 Refuge, shelter; Ku. 3. 8; Pt. 2. 23. 3 A place of refuge, resort, asylum (applied to persons also); सं मुरासुरस्य जगतः शरणं Ki. 18. 22; संतप्तानां त्वमसि शरणं Me. 7; शरणं गम्–इ–या &c. to go to for protection, take shelter with, to submit to; यामि हे कमिह शरणं Gît. 7. 4 A sanctuary, closet, an apartment; अग्निशरणमार्गमादेशय *S.* 5. 5 An abode, a house, habitation; Mu. 3. 15; Bk. 6. 9. 6 Lair, resting-place. 7 Injuring, killing. –Comp. –आर्थिन् *a.*, –एषिन् *a.* seeking refuge or protection; Bh. 2. 76. –आगत, –आपन्न *a.* gone to for refuge or protection, taking shelter with, fugitive. –उन्मुख *a.* looking up to for protection; R. 6. 21.

शरंडः 1 A bird. 2 A chameleon. 3 A cheat, rogue. 4 A lecher, libertine. 5 A kind of ornament.

शरण्य *a.* 1 Fit to protect, yielding protection, a protector, refuge; असौ शरण्यः शरणोन्मुखानां R. 6. 21; शरण्यो लोकानां Mv. 4. 1; R. 2. 30; 14. 64, 15. 2; Ku. 5. 76. 2 Needing protection, poor, miserable. –ण्यः An epithet of *S*iva. –ण्यं 1 A place of refuge, shelter. 2 A protector, who or what affords protection. 3 protection, defence. 4 Injury, hurt.

शरण्युः 1 A protector. 2 A cloud. 3 Wind.

शरद् *f.* 1 The autumn, autumnal season (comprising the two months आश्विन and कार्तिक); यात्रायै चोदयामास तं शक्तेः प्रथमं शरद् R. 4. 24. 2 A year; त्वं जीव शरदः शतं; R. 10. 1; U. 1. 15; M. 1. 15. –Comp. –अंतः the end of autumn, winter. –अंबुधरः an autumnal cloud. –उदाशयः an autumnal lake. –कामिन् *m.* a dog. –कालः the autumnal season. -घनः, मेघः an autumnal cloud. -चंद्रः (शरच्चंद्रः) the autumnal moon. -त्रियामा an autumnal night. -पद्मः -द्मं the white lotus. -पर्वन् *n.* the festival called *Kojâgara* ; q. v. -मुखं the commencement of autumn.

शरदा 1 Autumn. 2 A year.

शरदिज *a.* Autumnal.

शरभः 1 A yong elephant. 2 A fabulous animal said to have 8 legs and to be stronger than a lion ; शरभकुलमजिह्मं प्रोद्धरत्यंबु कूपात् Rs. 1. 23 ; अष्टपादः शरभः सिंहघाती Mb. 3 A camel. 4 A grass-hopper. 5 A locust.

शरयु (यूः) *f.* N. of a river ; see सरयु (यू).

शरल *a.* See सरल.

शरलकं Water.

शरव्यं A butt or mark (for arrows), target ; (fig. also) ; तौ शरव्यमकरोत्स नेतरान् R. 11. 27 ; कृताः शरव्यं हरिणा तवासुराः *S.* 6. 29 ; R. 7. 45 ; *Si.* 7. 24 ; व्यसनशतशरव्यतां गताः K.

शराटि-तिः A kind of bird.

शरारु *a.* Noxious, hurtful, injurious.

शरावः-वं 1 A shallow dish, platter, an eathenware vessel, tray ; मोदकशरावं गृहीत्वा V. 3; Ms. 6. 56. 2 A cover, lid. 3 A measure equal to 2 *Kudavas.*

शरावती N. of a town of which Lava was made ruler by Râma ; R. 15. 97.

शरिमन् *m.* Bearing, bringing forth.

शरीरं 1 The body (of animate or inanimate objects) ; शरीरमाद्यं खलु धर्मसाधनं Ku. 5. 33. 2 The constituent element ; Kâv. 1. 10. 3 Bodily strength. 4 Dead body. **-Comp.** -अंतरं 1 the interior of the body. 2 another body. -आवरणं the skin. -कर्तृ *m.* a father. -कर्षणं emaciation of the body. -जः 1 sickness. 2 lust, passion. 3 the god of love. 4 a son, offspring ; Ki. 4. 31. -तुल्य *a.* equal to ; *i. e.* as dear as one's own person. -दंडः 1 corporal punishment. 2 mortification of the body (as in penance). -धृक् *a.* having a body. -पतनं, -पातः shuffling off the mortal coil, death. -पाकः emaciation (of the body). -बद्ध *a* endowed with a body, embodied, incarnate ; Ku. 5. 30. -बंधः 1 the bodily frame ; R. 16. 23. 2 being endowed with a body ; *i. e.* birth as an embodied being ; R. 13. 58. -बंधकः a hostage. -भाज् *a.* embodied, incarnate. (*-m.*) a creature, an embodied being. -भेदः separation of the body (from the soul), death. -यष्टिः *f.* a slender body, slim or delicate figure. -यात्रा means of bodily sustenance. -विमोक्षणं the emancipation of the soul from the body. -वृत्तिः *f.* maintenance or support of the body ; R. 2. 45. -वैकल्यं bodily ailment, sickness, disease. -शुश्रूषा personal attendance. -संस्कारः 1 decoration of the person. 2 purification of the body by the performance of the several purificatory *Samska'ras* -संपत्तिः *f* the prosperity of body, (good) health. -सादः leanness of body, emaciation ; R. 3. 2. -स्थितिः *f.* 1 the maintenance or support of the body ; R. 5. 9. 2 taking one's meals, eating (frequently used in Kâdambarî).

शरीरकं 1 The body. 2 A small body. -कः The soul.

शरीरिन् *a.* 1 (णी *f.*) Embodied, corporeal, incarnate ; करुणस्य मूर्तिरथवा शरीरिणी विरहव्यथैव वनमेति जानकी U. 3. 4, M. 1. 10. 2 Living. *-m.* 1 Anything endowed with a body (whether animate or inanimate) ; शरीरिणां स्थावरजंगमानां सुखाय तज्जन्मदिनं बभूव Ku. 1. 23 ; R. 8. 43. 2 A sentient being. 3 A mad. 4 The soul (clad with the body) ; R. 8. 89 ; Bg. 2. 18.

शर्करजा Candied sugar.

शर्करा 1 Candied sugar. 2 A pebble, gravel, small stone; Mk. 5. 3 Gravelly mould. 4 Soil abounding in stony fragments, sand. 5 A piece, fragment. 6 A potsherd. 7 Any hard particle, as in जलशर्करा a nodule of water, *i. e.* hail. 8 The disease called gravel. **-Comp.** -उदकं sugar water, water sweetened with sugar. -सप्तमी N. of an observance on the 7th day in the bright half of Vaisâkha.

शर्करिक *a.* (की *f.*), **शर्करिल** *a.* Stony, gravelly, gritty.

शर्करी 1 A river. 2 A girdle.

शर्धः 1 Breaking wind, flatulence (said to be *n.* also in this sense). 2 A troop, multitude. 3 Strength, power.

शर्धजह *a.* Causing flatulence -हः A kind of pulse or bean.

शर्धनं The act of breaking wind.

शर्ब् 1 P. (शर्बति) 1 To go. 2 To injure, kill.

शर्मन् *m.* An affix added to the name of a Brâhmaṇa ; as विष्णुशर्मन् ; cf. बर्मन्, दास, गुप्त. *-n.* 1 Pleasure, happiness, delight ; त्यजंत्यसून् शर्म च मानिनो वरं त्यजंति न त्वेकमयाचितं व्रतं N. 1. 50 ; R. 1. 69 ; Bh. 3. 97. 2 A blessing. 3 A house, receptacle (mostly Vedic in this sense). **-Comp.** -द *a.* conferring happiness. (-दः) an epithet of Vishṇu.

शर्मरः A sort of garment.

शर्या 1 Night. 2 A finger.

शर्व 1 P. (शर्वति) 1 To go. 2 To hurt, injure, kill.

शर्वः 1 N. of Siva ; R. 11. 93 ; Ku. 6 14. 2 N. of Vishṇu.

शर्वरः N. of the god of love. -रं Darkness.

शर्वरी 1 A night ; शशिनं पुनरेति शर्वरी R. 8. 56, 3. 2 ; 11. 93 ; *Si.* 11. 5. 2 Turmeric. 3 A woman. **-Comp.** -ईशः the moon.

शर्वाणी N. of Pârvatî or Durgâ, wife of Siva.

शर्शरीक *a.* Mischievous, cruel. -कः A rogue, wretch, mischievous man.

शल् I. 1 A (शलते) 1 To shake, stir, agitate. 2 To tremble. -II. 1 P. (शलति) 1 To go. 2 To run fast. -III. 10 A. (शालयते) To praise.

शलः 1 A dart, spear. 2 A stake. 3 N. of भृंगि an attendant of Siva. 4 N. of Brahman. -लं The quill of a porcupine (*m.* also according to some).

शलकः A spider.

शलंगः A king, sovereign.

शलभः 1 A grass-hopper, locust ; *S.* 1. 32. 2 A moth ; कौरव्यवंशदावेऽस्मिन्क एष शलभायते Ve. 1. 19 ; *Si.* 2. 117 ; Ku. 4. 40.

शललं The quill of a porcupine. -ली 1 The quill of a porcupine. 2 A small porcupine.

शलाका 1 A small stick, peg, rod, pin, piece, thin bar (of anything) ; अयस्कांतमणिशलाका Mâl. 1. 2 A pencil, small stick (used in painting the eyes with collyrium) ; अज्ञानांधस्य लोकस्य ज्ञानांजनशलाकया । चक्षुरुन्मीलितं येन तस्मै पाणिनये नमः ॥ Sik. 58 ; Ku. 1. 47 ; R. 7. 8. 3 An arrow. 4 A dart, javelin. 5 A probe or a kind of pointed surgical instrument. 6 A rib (as of an umbrella). 7 A bone (forming the root of the fingers and toes); Y. 3. 85. 8 A sprout, sprig, shoot ; Ku. 1. 24. 9 A paint-brush. 10 A tooth- brush, tooth-pick. 11 A porcupine. 12 An oblong piece of ivory or bone used in gambling. **-Comp.** -धूर्तः (forming शलाकधूर्तः) a swindler, sharper. -परि *ind.* an unlucky throw or movement of one of the pieces at a game played with Salâkâs ; cf. परि or अक्षपरि.

शलाटु *a.* Unripe. -टुः A kind of root.

शलाभोलिः A camel.

शल्कं, शल्कलं 1 The scale of a fish ; Ms. 5. 16 ; Y. 1. 178. 2 Bark, rind (of trees). 3 A part, portion, fragment.

शल्कलिन्, शल्किन् *m.* A fish.

शल्भ् 1 A. (शल्भते) To praise.

शल्मलिः -ली *f.* The silk-cotton tree.

शल्यं 1 A spear, javelin, dart. 2 An arrow, a shaft ; शल्यं निखातमुदहारयतामुरस्तः R. 9. 78 ; शल्यप्रोतं 9. 75 ; *S.* 6. 9. 3 A thorn, splinter. 4 A pin, peg, stake (said to be *m.* also in these four senses). 5 Any extraneous substance lodged in the body and giving it very great pain ; अलातशल्यं U. 3. 35. 6 (Fig.) Any cause of poignant or heart-rending grief ; उद्धृतविषादशल्यः कथयिष्यामि S. 7. 7 A bone. 8 Difficulty, distress. 9 Sin, crime. 10 Poison. -ल्यः 1 A porcupine, hedge-hog. 2 The thorny shrub. 3 (In medicine) Extraction of splinters in surgery. 4 A fence, boundary. 5 A kind of fish. 6 N. of a king of Madra and brother of Mâdrî, the second wife of Pându, and thus maternal uncle of Nakula and Sahadeva. [In the great war he at first intended to fight on the side of the Pandavas, but he was artfully won over by Duryodhana and subsequently fought in his behalf. He acted as charioteer to Karna when he, was generalissimo of the Kaurava forces, and after his death was appointed commander. He maintained the field for one day, but was at last slain by Yudhishthira]. -Comp. -अरिः an epithet of Yudhishthira. -आहरणं, -उद्धरणं, -उद्धारः, -क्रिया, -शास्त्रं extraction of thorns or splinters, or that part of surgery which relates to the extraction of extraneous matter from the body. -कंठः a porcupine. -लोमन् n. the quill of a porcupine. -हर्तृ m. a weeder.

शल्यकः 1 A dart, javelin, spike. 2 A splinter, thorn. 3 A porcupine.

शल्लः A frog. -ल्लं Bark, rind.

शल्लकः N. of a tree. -कं Bark, rind.

शल्लकी 1 A porcupine. 2 A kind of tree of which elephants are very fond ; cf. U. 2. 21 ; 3. 6 ; Mâl. 9. 6; V. 4. 23. -Comp. -द्रवः incense.

शल्वः N. of a country ; see शाल्व.

शव् 1 P. (शवति) 1 To go, approach. 2 To alter, change, transform.

शवः-वं A corpse, dead body ; Ms. 10. 55. -वं Water. -Comp. -आच्छादनं covering of a corpse, shroud. -आश a. feeding on corpses ; Bk. 12. 75. -काम्यः a dog. -यानं, -रथः a hearse, bier, a sort of litter for carrying a corpse.

शवर, **शवल** } See शबर, शबल.

शवसानः 1 A traveller. 2 A way, road. -नं A cemetery.

शशः 1 A hare, rabbit ; Ms. 3. 270, 5. 18. 2 The spots on the moon (which are popularly considered to resemble the form of a hare). 3 One of the four classes into which men are divided by erotic writers ; thus defined :—मृदुवचनसुशीलः कोमलांगः सुकेशः सकलगुणनिधानं सत्यवादी शशोऽयं Sabdak ; see Ratimanjarî 35 also. 4 The Lodhra tree. 5 Gum-myrrh. -Comp. -अंकः 1 the moon. 2 camphor. °अर्धमुख a. crescent-headed (as an arrow). °मूर्तिः an epithet of the moon. °लेखा the digit of the moon, lunar crescent. -अदः 1 a hawk. falcon. 2 N. of a son o[f Ikshv]âku father of पुरंजय. -अदनः a hawk, falcon, -ऊर्णं.-लोमं the hair of a rabbit, hair-skin. -धरः 1 the moon ; प्रसरति शशधरबिंबे Git. 7. 2 camphor. °मौलिः an epithet of Siva. -प्लुतकं a scratch with a finger-nail. -भृत् m. the moon. °भृत् m. an epithet of Siva. -लक्ष्मण an epithet of the moon. -लांछनः 1 the moon ; Ku. 7. 6. 2 camphor. -विं-(विं)दुः 1 the moon. 2 an epithet of Vishnu. -विषाणं, -शृंगं a hair's horn ; used to denote anything impossible, an utter impossibility ; कदाचिदपि पर्यटञ्शशविषाणमासादयेत् Bh. 2. 5 ; शशशृंगधनुर्धरः ; see खपुष्प. -स्थली the country between the Ganges and the Yamunâ, Doab.

शशकः 1 A hare, rabbit. 2 =शश (3) q. v.

शशिन् m. 1 The moon ; शशिनं पुनरेति शर्वरी R. 8. 56, 6. 85 ; Me. 41. 2 Camphor. -Comp. -ईशः an epithet of Siva. -कला a digit of the moon , Mu. 1. 1. -कांतः the moon-gem. (-तं) a lotus. -कोटिः a horn of the moon. -ग्रहः an eclipse of the moon. -जः an epithet of Budha or Mercury (son of the moon). -प्रभ a. having the lustre of the moon, as bright and white as the moon ; R. 3. 16. (-भं) a water lily. -प्रभा moon-light. -भूषणः, -भृत् m., -मौलिः, -शेखरः epithets of Siva. -लेखा a digit of the moon.

शश्वत् ind. 1 Perpetually, eternally. for ever. 2 Constantly, repeatedly, always, frequently, again and again; R. 2. 48, 4. 70 ; Me. 55. 3 In comp. शश्वत् may be translated by 'lasting, eternal'; as शश्वच्छांति eternal tranquillity.

शष्कु(स्कु)ली 1 The orifice of the ear, auditory passage ; अवलंबितकर्णशष्कुलीकलसीकं रचयन्नवोचत N. 2. 8 ; Y. 3. 96. 2 A kind of baked cake ; Y. 1. 173. 3 Rice gruel. 4 A disease of the ear.

शष्पः (स्पः) Loss of intellect or presence of mind (प्रतिभाक्षय). -ष्पं Young grass ; U. 4. 27 ; R. 2. 26.

शस् 1 P. (शसति) To cut up, kill, destroy. -WITH वि to cut up, kill; U. 4. -II. 1 P. (शास्ति) To sleep, cf; शंस् also.

शसनं 1 Wounding, killing. 2 Immolation (of an animal at sacrifice).

शस्त p. p. 1 Praised, extolled. 2 Auspicious, happy. 3 Right, best. 4 Injured, wounded. 5 Killed. -स्तं 1 Happiness, welfare. 2 Excellence, auspiciousness. 3 The body. 4 A finger-guard (अंगुलित्राण q. v.; also शस्तकं in the sense).

शस्तिः f. Praise, eulogy.

शस्त्रं 1 A weapon, arms ; क्षमाशस्त्रं करे यस्य दुर्जनः किं करिष्यति Subhâsh. ; R. 2. 40, 3. 51, 62 ; 5. 28. 2 An instr[u]ment, a tool in general. 3 Iron. 4 steel. 5 A hymn of praise (स्तोत्र). -Comp. -अभ्यासः the practice of arms, military exercise. -अयसं 1 steel. 2 iron. -अस्त्रं 1 weapons for striking and throwing, arms and missiles. 2 arms or weapons generally. -आजीवः, -उपजीविन् m. a professional soldier. -उद्यमः lifting up a weapon (to strike). -उपकरणं arms or instruments of war, military apparatus. -कारः an armourer. -कोषः the sheath or scabbard of any weapon. -ग्राहिन् a. taking up or wearing arms (for battle); U. 5. 33. -जीविन्, -व्राति m. one living by the use of arms, a professional soldier. -देवता 1 a deity presiding over weapons. 2 A deified weapon. -धरः = शस्त्रभृत् q. v. -न्यासः laying down arms : so शस्त्र-(परि)त्यागः. -पाणि a. bearing arms, armed. (-m.) an armed warrior. -पूत a. 'purified by arms ', rendered pure or absolved from guilt by being killed with a weapon on the battlefield ; अशस्त्रपूतं निर्व्याजं (महामांसं) Mâl. 5. 13 ; (see Jagaddhara's explanation of the word); अहमपि तस्य मिथ्याप्रतिज्ञविलक्ष्यसंपादितमशस्त्रपूतं मरणमुपादिशामि Ve. 2. -प्रहारः a wound inflicted with a weapon. -भृत् m. a soldier, warrior; R. 2. 40. -मार्जः a weapon-cleaner, an armourer, a furbisher. -विद्या, -शास्त्रं the science of arms. -संहतिः f 1 a collection of arms. 2 an arsenal. -संपातः a sudden fall of a number of weapons. -हत a. killed by a weapon. -हस्त a. armed. (-स्तः) an armed man.

शस्त्रकं 1 Steel. 2 Iron

शस्त्रिका A knife.

शस्त्रिन् a. Bearing arms or weapons, armed, accoutred.

शस्त्री A knife ; पण्यस्त्रीषु विवेककल्पलतिकाशस्त्रीषु रज्यते कः Subhâsh. ; Si. 4. 44.

शस्यं 1 Corn or grain in general ; दुदोह गां स यज्ञाय शस्याय मघवा दिवं R. 1. 26. 2 The produce or fruit of a plant or tree ; शस्यं क्षेत्रगतं प्राहुः सतुषं धान्यमुच्यते ; see तंडुल also. 3 A merit. -Comp. -क्षेत्रं a corn field. -भक्षक a. granivorous. -मंजरी an ear of corn. -मालिन् a. crowned with harvests. -शालिन्, संपन्न a. abounding in corn. -शूकं a beard of corn. -संपद् f. abundance of corn. -संव(व)रः the Sâla tree.

शाकः-कं A vegetable, pot-herb, herb, any edible leaf, fruit or root used as a vegetable ; दिल्लीश्वरो वा जगदीश्वरो वा मनोरथान् पूरयितुं समर्थः । अन्यैर्नृपालैः परिदीयमानं शाकाय वा स्याल्लवणाय वा स्यात् Jag. -कः 1 Power, strength, energy. 2 The teak tree. 3 The Sirîsha tree. 4 N. of a people ; see शक 5 An era ; especially the era of Sâlivâhana. -Comp. -अंगं pepper. -अम्लं ho plum. –आख्यः the teak tree. (–ख्यं) a vegetable. –आहारः a vegetarian (living only on herbs &c.). –चुक्रिका the tamarind. –तरुः the teak tree. –पणः 1 a measure equal to a handful. 2 a handful of vegetables. –पार्थिवः a king fond of an era; see मध्यमपदलोपिन् –प्रति ind. a little of herbs. –योग्यः coriander. –वृक्षः the teak tree. –शाकटं, –शाकिनं a field of vegetables, a kitchen-garden.

शाकट a. (टी f.) 1 Relating to a cart. 2 Going in a cart. –टः 1 A draught-ox. 2 The tree called श्लेष्मातक. –टं A field; cf. शाकशाकटं.

शाकटायनः N. of a philologist and grammarian often referred to by Pâṇini and Yâska; cf. व्याकरणे शकटस्य च तोकं Nir.

शाकटिक a. (की f.) 1 Belonging to a car. 2 Going in a car.

शाकटीनः A cart-load, a measure of load equal to 20 *tula's*.

शाकल a. (ली f.) Relating to a piece (शकल). –लः A school of the *R*igved or the followers of this school (pl.) –Comp. –प्रातिशाख्यं N. of the *R*igveda Prâtisâkhya. –शाखा the recension or traditional text of the *R*igveda as represented by the Sâkalas

शाकल्यः N. of an ancient grammarian mentioned by Pâṇini; (he is supposed to have arranged the *Pada* text of the *R*igveda.)

शाकारी One of the lowest forms of Prâkrita, the dialect spoken by the Sakâra; as in the Mrichchhakaṭika.

शाकिनं A field; as in शाकशाकिनं.

शाकिनी 1 A field of vegetables. 2 A kind of female being attendant on Durgâ (supposed to be a demon or fairy.)

शाकुन a. (नी f.) 1 Relating to birds; Ms. 3. 268. 2 Relating to omens. 3 Ominous.

शाकुनिकः A fowler, bird-catcher; Mk. 6; Ms. 8. 260. –कं The interpretation of omens.

शाकुनेयः A small owl.

शाकुंतलः A metronymic of Bharata (son of Sakuntalâ). –लं The drama called अभिज्ञानशकुंतला of Kâlidâsa.

शाकुलिकः A fisherman.

शाक्करः An ox.

शाक्त a. (क्ती f.) 1 Relating to power. 2 Relating to Sakti or the female personification of divine energy. –क्तः A worshipper of Sakti; (the Sâktas are generally worshippers of Durgâ representing the female personification of divine energy, and the ritual enjoined to them is of two kinds, the pure or right-hand ritual दक्षिणाचार, and impure or left-hand ritual वामाचार q. q. v. v.).

शाक्तिकः 1 A worshipper of S*a*kti. 2 A spearman, lancer.

शाक्तीकः A spearman, lancer.

शाक्तेयः A worshipper of Sakti.

शाक्यः 1 N. of the family of Buddha. 2 N. of Buddha. –Comp. –भिक्षुकः a Buddhist religious mendicant. –मुनिः, –सिंहः epithets of Buddha.

शाक्री 1 N. of Sachî, wife of Indra. 2 Of Durgâ.

शाक्करः An ox; cf. शाक्कर.

शाखा 1 A branch (as of a tree); आवर्ज्य शाखाः R. 16. 19. 2 An arm. 3 A party, section, faction. 4 A part or subdivision of a work. 5 A school, branch, sect. 6 A school or traditional recension of the Veda, the traditional text followed by a school; as in शाकलशाखा, आश्वलायन शाखा, बाष्कल-शाखा &c. –Comp. –चंद्रन्यायः see under न्याय. –नगरं, –पुरं a suburb. –पित्तः inflammation of the extremities of the body *e. g.* hands, shoulders &c. –भृत् *m.* a tree. –भेदः difference of (Vedic) school. –मृगः 1 a monkey; an ape. 2 a squirrel. –रंडः 'a traitor to his Sâkhâ', a Brâhmana who has changed his own school of the Vedas. –रथ्या a branch-road.

शाखालः A sort of cane (वानीर).

शाखिन् a. 1 Having branches (fig. also). 2 Branching, ramifying. 3 Belonging to any branch or school (as of the Veda). –*m*. 1 A tree; S. 1. 15. 2 A Veda. 3 A follower of any Vedic school or recension.

शाखोटः, शाखोटकः N. of a tree; कस्त्वं भोः कथयामि दैवहतकं मां विद्धि शाखोटकं K. P. 10.

शांकरः A bull.

शांकरिः 1 N. of Kârtikeya. 2 Of Gaṇesa. 3 Fire.

शांखिकः 1 A shell-cutter, worker in shells. 2 N. of a mixed tribe. 3 A shell-blower; Si. 15. 72.

शाटः, शाटी 1 A garment, cloth. 2 A petticoat.

शाटकः –कं Cloth, garment, petticoat; Pt. 1. 144.

शाठ्यं Dishonesty, perfidy, guile, trickery, fraud, villainy; आजन्मनः शाठ्यमशिक्षितो यः S. 5. 25, Mu. 1. 1.

शाण a. (णी f.) Hempen, flaxen. –णः 1 A touchstone; Bv. 1. 73; Bh. 2. 44. 2 A whetstone. 3 A saw. 4 A weight of four Mâshas. –णं 1 Sackcloth, coarse cloth. 2 A hempen garment; Ms. 2. 41, 10. 87. –Comp. –आजीवः an armourer.

शाणिः A plant from the fibres of which a coarse cloth is prepared.

शाणित p. p. Whetted, ground, sharpened (on a whetstone).

शाणी 1 A touchstone. 2 A whetstone. 3 A saw. 4 A hempen garment. 5 A ragged garment. 6 A small screen or tent. 7 Gesticulation, a sign made with the hands or eyes.

शाणीरं A bank or spot or ground in the Soṇa river.

शांडिल्यः 1 N. of a sage, the author of a law-book. 2 The *Bilva* tree. 3 A form of Agni. –Comp. –गोत्रं the family of Sâṇḍilya.

शात p. p. 1 Sharpened, whetted. 2 Thin, slender. 3 Weak, feeble. 4 Beautiful, handsome. 5 Happy, thriving. –तः The Dhattûra plant. –तं Happiness, pleasure, delight; मानिनीजनजनितशातं Gît. 10. –Comp. –उदरी a woman with a slender waist; Si. 5. 23; R. 10. 69. –शिख a. sharp-pointed.

शातकुंभं 1 Gold; Si. 9. 9; N. 16. 34. 2 The thorn-apple (धत्तूर).

शातकौंभं Gold.

शातनं 1 Whetting, sharpening. 2 Cutting down, destroyer; R. 3. 42. 3 Causing to fall or perish. 4 Causing to decay or wither. 5 Becoming thin or small, thinness. 6 Withering, decaying.

शातपत्रकः –की Moonlight.

शातभीरुः A kind of Mallikâ.

शातमान a. (नी f.) Bought, for one hundred.

शात्रव a. (वी f.) 1 Relating to an enemy; R. 4. 42. 2 Hostile, inimical. –वः An enemy; Si. 14. 44, 18. 20; Ve. 5. 1; Bk. 5. 81; Ki. 14. 2; Mu. 2. 5. –वं 1 A collection of enemies. 2 Enmity, hostility; त्रयीशात्रवशात्रवे R.G.

शात्रवीय a. 1 Relating to an enemy. 2 Hostile, inimical.

शादः 1 Young grass. 2 Mud. –Comp. –हरितः –तं a place green with young grass, a place clad in verdure.

शाद्वल a. 1 Grassy. 2 Abounding in young, green grass. 3 Green, verdant. –लः–लं A grass-plot, green, meadow; शय्या शाद्वलं Sânti. 2 21; R. 2. 17, Ki. 5. 37; Y. 3. 7.

शान् 1 U. (शीशांसति-ते, strictly a desiderative of शान् used in a primitive sense) To sharpen, whet.

शानः 1 A touch-stone. 2 A whetstone. –Comp. –पादः 1 a stone for grinding sandal. 2 the Pâriyâtra mountain.

शांत p. p. 1 Appeased, allayed, calmed, satisfied, pacified; R. 12. 20. 2 Cured, alleviated; शांतरोगः. 3 Abated, subsided, put an end to, removed, extinguished; शांतरथक्षोभपरिश्रमं R. 1. 58; 5. 47; शांतार्चिषं दपिमिव प्रकाशः Ki. 17. 16. 4 Ceased, stopped; Ku. 3. 42. 5 Dead, deceased. 6 Stilled, hushed. 7 Calm, quiet, undisturbed, tranquil, still; शांतमिदमाश्रमपदं S. 1. 16; 4. 19. 8 Tamed; R. 14. 79. 9 Free from passions, at ease, contented. 10 Shaded. 11 Purified. 12 Auspicious (in augury); (the phrase शांतं पापं, which is sometimes repeated, means 'oh, no!' 'how can it be', 'God forbid such an untoward or unlucky event' *S.* 5; Mu. 1). –तः 1 A man who has subdued his passions, an ascetic. 2 Tranquillity, quietism, the sentiment of quietism, the predominant feeling of which is indifference to worldly objects and pleasures; see निर्वेद and रस.–तं *ind.* Enough, not more, not so, for shame, hush!, god(heaven) forbid;; शांतं कथं दुर्जनाः पौरजानपदाः U. 1; तामेव शांतमथवा किमिहोत्तरेण 3. 26. –**Comp.** –आत्मन्, –चेतस् *a.* calm, tranquil-minded, sedate or composed in mind. –तोय *a.* having still waters. –रसः the sentiment of quietism; see शांतं above.

शांतनवः 'The son of *S*antanu', No. of Bhîshma.

शांता N. of the daughter of Da*s*aratha, adopted by the sage Lomapâda and subsequently married by *R*ishya*s*ringa; see U. 1. 4 and ऋष्यशृंग also.

शांतिः *f.* 1 Pacification, allayment, alleviation, removal; अध्वरविघातशांतये R. 11. 1, 62. 2 Calmness, tranquillity, quiet, ease, rest, repose; Ku. 4. 17; Mâl. 6. 1. 3 Cessation of hostility; Bv. 1. 125. 4 Cessation, stop. 5 Absence of passion, quietism, complete indifference to all worldly enjoyments; R. 7. 71. 6 Consolation, solace. 7 Settlement of differences, reconciliation. 8 Satisfaction of hunger. 9 An expiatory rite, a propitiatory rite for averting evil. 10 Good fortune, felicity, auspiciousness. 11 Exculpation or absolution from blame. 12 preservation.–**Comp.** –उदं, उदकं, –जलं soothing or propitiatory water; *S.* 3. –कर, –कारिन् *a.* soothing, pacifying. –गृहं a room for rest or retirement. –होमः a sacrifice or burnt offering to avert or remove an evil; Ms. 4. 150.

शांतिक *a.* (की *f.*) Expiatory, propitiatory. –कं Observances or ceremonies calculated to remove calamities.

शांत्व् &c. See सांत्व् &c.

शापः 1 A curse, an imprecation, anathoma; शापेनास्तं गमितमहिमा वर्षभोग्येण भर्तुः Me. 1, 92; R. 1. 78, 5, 56, 59; 11. 14. 2 An oath, asseveration. 3 Abuse, calumny. –**Comp.** –अंतः, –अवसानं, –निवृत्तिः *f.* the end of a curse; Me. 110; R. 8. 82. –अस्त्रः 'having a curse for a weapon', sage, saint; R. 15. 3. –उत्सर्गः the utterance of a curse. –उद्धारः, –मुक्तिः *f.*, –मोक्षः releas eor deliverance from a curse. –ग्रस्त *a.* labouring under a curse. –मुक्त *a.* released from a curse. –यंत्रित *a.* restrained by a curse.

शापित *p. p.* 1 Bound by an oath, conjured. 2 Sworn, adjured.

शाफरिकः A fisherman.

शाब(व)र *a.* (री *f.*) 1 Savage, barbarous. 2 Low, vile, base. –रः 1 An offence, a fault. 2 Sin, wickedness. 3 The tree called *Lodhra*. –री A low form of the Prâkrita dialect (spoken by mountaineers &c.). –**Comp.** –भेदाख्यं (also भेदाक्षं) copper.

शाब्द *a.* (ब्दी *f.*) 1 Relating to or derived from a word. 2 Relating to or depending on sound (opp. आर्थ). 3 Verbal, oral. 4 Sounding, sonorous. –ब्दः A grammarian. –**Comp.** –बोधः perception or apprehension of the sense of words. –व्यंजना insinuation founded on words.

शाब्दिक *a.* (की *f.*) 1 Verbal, oral. 2 Sounding. –कः A grammarian.

शामनः N. of Yama. –नं 1 Killing, slaughter. 2 Tranquillity, peace. 3 End. –नी The southern direction.

शामित्रं 1 Sacrificing. 2 Immolating, killing animals at a sacrifice. 3 Tying up cattle for sacrifice. 4 A sacrificial vessel.

शामिलं Ashes.

शामिली A sacrificial ladle; (स्रुच्).

शांबरी 1 Jugglery, sorcery. 2 A sorceress.

शांबविकः A dealer in shells.

शांबु(बू)कः A bivalve-shell.

शांभव *a.* (वी *f.*) Belonging to *S*iva; अत्तुं वांछति शांभवो गणपतेराखुं क्षुधार्तः फणी Pt. 1. 159. –वः A worshipper of *S*iva. 2 A son of *S*iva. 3 Camphor. 4 A kind of poison. –वं The *Devada'ru* tree.

शांभवी 1 N. of Pârvatî. 2 N. of a plant (नलिदूर्वा).

शायकः 1 An arrow. 2 A sword; cf. सायक.

शार् 10 U. (शारयति-ते) 1 To weaken. 2 To be weak.

शार *a.* Variegated, speckled, mottled, spotted. –रः 1 A variegated colour. 2 Green colour. 3 Air, wind. 4 A piece used at chess, a chessman; Bh. 3. 39. 5 Injuring, hurting.

शारंगः 1 The *Châtaka* bird. 2 A peacock. 3 A bee. 4 A deer. 5 An elephant; cf. सारंग.

शारंगी A particular musical instrument (played with a bow); cf. सारंगी.

शारद *a.* 1 Belonging to autumn, autumnal; (the *f.* is शारदी in this sense); विमलशारदचंद्रिरचंद्रिका Bv. 1. 113; R. 10. 9. 2 Annual. 3 New, recent. 4 Young, fresh. 5 Modest, shy, bashful. 6 diffident, not bold. –दः 1 A year. 2 An autumnal sickness. 3 Autumnal sunshine. 4 A kind of kidney-bean. 5 The Bakula tree. –दी The full-moon day in the month of Kârtika. –दं 1 Corn, grain. 2 The white lotus. –दा 1 A kind of Vînâ or lute. 2 N. of Durgâ. 3 of Sarasvatî.

शारदिकः 1 Autumnal sickness. 2 Autumnal sunshine or heat. –कं An autumnal or annual *S*râddha.

शारदीय *a.* Autumnal.

शारिः 1 A chessman, a piece at chess &c. 2 A small round ball. 3 A kind of die. –रिः *f.* 1 The bird called Sârikâ. 2 Fraud, trick. 3 An elephant's housings. –**Comp.** –पट्टः, –फलं, –फलकः-कं a chequered cloth for playing at chess, draughts &c.

शारिका 1 A kind of bird. 2 A bow or stick for playing any stringed instrument. 3 Playing at chess &c. 4 A chessman, a piece at chess.

शारी A kind of bird.

शारीर *a.* (री *f.*) 1 Relating to the body, bodily, corporeal. 2 Incorporate, embodied. –रः 1 The incorporate or embodied spirit (जीवात्मन्); human or individual soul. 2 A bull. 3 A kind of drug.

शारीरक *a.* (की *f.*) Relating to the body &c. –कं 1 the embodied spirit. 2 The inquiry into the nature of that spirit (a term applied to the Bhâshya of *S*ankarâchârya on the Brahma-sûtras). –**Comp.** –सूत्रं the aphorisms of the Vedânta philosophy.

शारीरिक *a.* (की *f.*) Bodily, corporeal, material.

शारुक *a.* (की *f.*) Noxious, hurtful, mischievous.

शार्कक: Candied sugar.

शार्कर *a.* (री *f.*) 1 Made of sugar, sugary. 2 Stony, gravelly. –रः 1 A gravelly place. 2 The froth or skum of Milk. 3 Cream.

शार्ग *a.* (शार्ङ्ग strictly) 1 Made of horn, horny. 2 Having a bow, armed with a bow; Bk. 8. 123. –र्गः –र्गं 1 A bow (in general. 2 The bow of Vishṇu. –**Comp.** –धन्वन् *m.*, –धरः, पाणिः, –भृत् *m.* epithets of Vishṇu.

शार्गिन् *m.* 1 An archer, a bowman. 2 An epithet of Vishṇu; धर्मसंरक्षणार्थैव प्रवृत्तिर्भुवि शार्गिणः R. 15. 4, 12. 70; Me. 46.

शार्दूलः 1 A tiger. 2 A leopard or panther. 3 A demon, *Ra'kshasa*. 4 A kind of bird. 5 (At the end of comp) An eminent or distinguished person, foremost; as in –नरशार्दूल; cf. कुंजर. –**Comp.** –चर्मन् *n.* a tiger's skin. –विक्रीडितं 1 a tiger's play; कंदर्पोऽपि यमायते विरचयन् शार्दूलविक्रीडितं Git. 4. 2 N. of a metre; see App. 1.

शार्वर *a.* (री *f.*) 1 Nocturnal ; Ku. 8. 58. 2 Mischievous, pernicious. –रं Darkness, thick gloom. –री Night.

शाल् 1 A. (शालते) 1 To praise, flatter. 2 To shine. 3 To be endowed with ; Malli. on Ki. 5. 44. 4 To tell.

शालः 1 N. of a tree (very tall and stately); R. 1. 38 ; Si. 3. 40. 2 A tree in general ; R. 1. 13 ; Ve. 4. 3. 3 An enclosure, a fence. 4 A kind of fish. 5 N. of king Sâlivâhana. **–Comp.** –ग्रामः a kind of sacred stone said to be typical of Vishṇu, as the Phallus is of Siva, °गिरि N. of a mountain. °शिला the *Salagra'ma* stone. –जः, –निर्यासः exudation of the Sâla tree, resin ; R. 1. 31. –भंजिका 1 a doll, puppet, statue ; Vb. 1 ; N. 2. 83. 2 a courtezan, harlot. –भंजी a doll, puppet. –वेष्टः the resin of the Sâla tree. ; cf. साल. –सारः 1 a superior tree. 2 Asa fœtida.

शालवः The *Lodhra* tree.

शाला 1 An apartment, a room, saloon, hall ; गृहैर्विशालैरपि भूरिशालैः Si. 3. 50 ; so संगीतशाला, रंगशाला &c. 2 A house, an abode ; R. 16. 41. 3 The upper or main branch of a tree. 4 The trunk of a tree. **–Comp.** –अजिरः, –रं a hollow earthen cup. –मृगः a jackal. –वृकः 1 a dog ; Bv. 1. 72. 2 a wolf. 3 a deer. 4 a cat. 5 a jackal. 6 a monkey.

शालाकः N. of Pâṇini.

शालाकिन् *m.* 1 A lancer spearman. 2 A surgeon. 3 A barber.

शालातुरीयः An epithet of Pâṇini (written also शालोत्तरीय ; so called from शलातुर the place of his birth).

शालारं 1 A flight of steps, ladder. 2 A bird-cage.

शालिः 1 Rice ; न शालेः स्तंबकरिता वप्तुर्गुणमपेक्षते Mu. 1. 13 ; यवाः प्रकीर्णा न भवंति शालयः Mk. 4. 16. 2 The civet-cat. **–Comp.** –ओदनः –नं boiled rice (of a superior kind). –गोपी a female appointed to watch a rice field ; R. 4. 20. –चूर्णः –र्णं rice-flour. –पिष्टं crystal. –भवनं a rice-field. –वाहनः N. of a celebrated sovereign of India whose era commences with 78 A. D. –होत्रः 1 N. of a writer on veterinary subjects. 2 a horse. होत्रिन् *m.* a horse.

शालिकः 1 A weaver. 2 A toll, tax.

शालिन् *a.* (नी *f.*) (Usually at the end of comp.) 1 Endowed with, possessed of, possessing, shining or resplendent with ; Ki. 8. 17, 55 ; Bk. 4. 2. 2 Domestic.

शालिनी 1 A mistress of the house, housewife. 2 N. of a metre ; see App. I.

शालीन *a.* 1 Modest, bashful, shy, retiring ; निसर्गशालीनः स्त्रीजनः M. 4 ; R. 6. 81, 18. 17 ; Si 16. 83. 2 Like, resembling. –नः A householder. (शालीनीकृ 'to make humble, humiliate').

शालुः 1 A frog. 2 A kind of perfume. –लु *n.* The root of the water-lily.

शालु(लू)कं 1 The root of the water-lily. 2 Nutmeg. –कः A frog.

शालु(लू)रः A frog.

शालेयं A field of rice.

शालोत्तरीयः An epithet of Pâṇini ; see शालातुरीय.

शाल्मलः 1 The silk-cotton tree. 2 One of the seven great divisions of the earth.

शाल्मलिः 1 The silk-cotton tree ; Bv. 1. 115 ; Ms. 8. 246. 2 One of the seven great divisions of the earth. 3 N. of a kind of hell. **–Comp.** –स्थः an epithet of Garuḍa.

शाल्मली 1 The silk-cotton tree. 2 N. of a river in Pâtâla. 3 A kind of hell. **–Comp.** –वेष्टः, –वेष्टकः the gum of the silk-cotton tree.

शाल्वः 1 N. of a country. 2 A king of Sâlva.

शाव *a.* (वी *f.*) 1 Relating to a dead body ; caused by the death (of a relative); दशाहं शावमाशौचं सपिंडेषु विधीयते Ms. 5. 59, 61. 2 Tawny, dark-yellowish. –वः The young of any animal, a fawn, cub ; क वयं क परोक्षमन्मथो मृगशावैः सममेधितो जनः S. 2. 18; मृगराजशावः R. 6. 3, 18. 37.

शावकः The young of any animal.

शावर See शाबर.

शाश्वत *a.* (ती *f.*) Eternal, perpetual, ever-lasting ; शाश्वतीः समाः Râm. (=U. 2. 5) 'for eternal years', 'ever more', 'for all time to come'; U. 5. 27; R. 14. 14. –तः 1 N. of Siva. 2 Of Vyâsa. 3 The sun. –तं *ind.* Eternally, perpetually, for ever.

शाश्वतिक *a.* (की *f.*) Eternal, permanent, perpetual, constant ; शाश्वतिको विरोधः 'natural antipathy'.

शाश्वती The earth.

शाष्कुल *a.* (ली *f.*) Eating flesh (or fish).

शाष्कुलिकं A quantity of baked cakes (शष्कुली).

शास् 2 P. (शास्ति, शिष्ट) 1 To teach, instruct, train (governing two accusatives in this sense); माणवकं धर्मं शास्ति Sk. ; Bk. 6. 10 ; शिष्यस्तेऽहं शाधि मां त्वां प्रपन्नं Bg. 2. 7. 2 To rule, govern ; अनन्यशासनामुर्वीं शशासैकपुरीमिव R. 1. 30 ; 10. 1 ; 14. 85, 19. 57 ; S. 1. 14 ; Bk. 3. 53. 3 To order, command, direct, enjoin ; R. 12. 34 ; Ku. 6. 24 ; Bk. 9. 68. 4 To tell, communicate, inform (with dat.); तस्मिन्नायोधनं वृत्तं लक्ष्मणायाशिषन्महत् Bk. 6. 27 ; Ms. 11. 82. 5 To advise ; स किंसखा साधु न शास्ति योऽधिपं Ki. 1. 5. 6 To decree, enact. 7 To punish, chastise, correct ; Ms. 4. 175 ; 8. 29. 8 To tame, subdue ; Mv. 6. 20. –WITH अनु 1 (*a*) to advise, persuade ; Ku. 5. 5. (*b*) to teach, instruct (how to act), order, command ; R. 6. 59, 13. 75 ; Bk. 20. 17. 2 to rule, govern. 3 to chastise, punish ; Ve. 2. 4 to praise, extol. –आ (usually Atm.) 1 to bless, pronounce a blessing; ऋक्छंदसा आशास्ते S. 4 ; U. 1. 2 to order, command, direct (P. in this sense) ; Bk. 6. 4. 3 to desire, seek for, hope, expect ; सर्वमस्मिन्वयमाशास्महे S. 7; आशासतं ततः शांतिमस्तुरग्नीनहावयत् Bk. 17. 1, 5. 16 ; Ms. 3. 80. 4 to praise. –प्र 1 to teach, instruct, advise ; Bk. 19. 19. 2 to order, command ; प्रशाधि यन्मया कार्यं Mârk. P. 3 to rule, govern, be lord of ; यां प्रशाधि गलितावधिकालं N. 5. 24 ; R. 6. 76 ; 9. 1. 4 to punish, chastise. 5 to pray or ask for, seek for (Atm.) ; इदं कविभ्यः पूर्वेभ्यो नमोवाकं प्रशास्महे U. 1. 1, (used in the sense of शास् with आ).

शासनं 1 Instruction, teaching, discipline. 2 Rule, sway, government ; अनन्यशासनामुर्वीं R. 1. 30 ;. so अप्रतिशासन. 3 An order, command, direction ; तरुभिरपि देवस्य शासनं प्रमाणीकृतं S. 6 ; R. 3. 69, 14. 83, 18. 18. 4 An edict, enactment, a decree. 5 A precept, rule. 6 A royal grant (of land &c.); charter ; अहं त्वां शासनशतेन योजयिष्यामि Pt. 1 ; Y. 2. 240, 295. 7 A deed, writing, written agreement. 8 Control of passions. (At the end of comp. शासन often means 'punisher, destroyer, killer', as in स्मरशासनः, पाकशासनः). **–Comp.** –पत्रं 1 a plate (usually of copper), on which a grant of land &c. is inscribed. 2 a sheet of paper on which an order is written. –हरः a royal messenger. –हारिन् *m.* an envoy, a messenger ; R. 3. 68.

शासित *p. p.* 1 Ruled, governed. 2 Punished.

शासितृ *m.* 1 A ruler, governor. 2 A chastiser ; S. 1. 25.

शास्तृ *m.* 1 A teacher, an instructor. 2 A ruler, king, sovereign. 3 A father. 4 A Buddha or Jaina ; or a deified teacher of the Bauddhas or Jainas.

शास्त्रं 1 An order, a command, rule, precept. 2 A sacred precept or rule, scriptural injunction. 3 A religious or sacred treatise, sacred book, scripture ; see comps. below. 4 Any department of knowledge, science ; इति गुह्यतमं शास्त्रं Bg. 15. 20 ; शास्त्रेष्वकुंठिता बुद्धिः ; R. 1. 19 ; often at the end of comp. after the word denoting the subject, or applied collectively to the whole body of teaching on that subject ; वेदांतशास्त्र, न्यायशास्त्र, तर्कशास्त्र, अलंकारशास्त्र &c. 5 A work, treatise; तंत्रैः पंचभिरेतच्चकार सुमनोहरं शास्त्रं Pt. 1. 6 Theory (opp. प्रयोग or practice); M 1.

-Comp. -अतिक्रमः, -अननुष्ठानं violation of sacred precepts, disregard of religious authority. -अनुष्ठानं conformity to or observance of sacred precepts. -अभिज्ञ *a*. versed in the *S*âstras. -अर्थः 1 the meaning of a sacred precept. 2 a scriptural precept or statement. -आचरणं observance of sacred precepts. -उक्त *a*. prescribed by sacred laws, enjoined by the *S*âstras, lawful, legal. -कारः, -कृत् *m*. 1 the author of a *S*âstra or sacred book. 2 an author in general. -कोविद *a*. versed in the *S*âstras. -गंडः a superficial reader of books, a superficial scholar. -चक्षुस् *n*. grammar (as being the 'eye', as it were, with which to understand any *S*âstra). -ज्ञ, -विद् *a*. conversant with the *S*âstras. -ज्ञानं knowledge of sacred books, conversancy with scriptures. -तत्त्वं truth as taught in the *S*âstras, scriptural truth. -दर्शिन् *a*. stated or enjoined in sacred books. -दृष्टिः *f*. scriptural point of view. -योनिः the source of the *S*âstras. -विधानं, -विधिः a sacred precept, scriptural injunction. -विप्रतिषेधः, -विरोधः 1 mutual contradiction of sacred precepts, inconsistency or precepts. 2 any act contrary to sacred precepts. -विमुख *a*. averse from study ; Pt. 1. -विरुद्ध *a*. contrary to the *S*âstras, illegal, unlawful. -व्युत्पत्तिः *f*. intimate knowledge of the sacred writings, proficiency in the *S*âstras. -शिल्पिन् *m*. the country of Kâshmira. -सिद्ध *a*. established by sacred authority.

शास्त्रिन् *a*. (णी *f*.) Versed or skilled in the *S*âstras. -*m*. One who has mastered the *S*âstras, a learned man, a great Paṇdit.

शास्त्रीय *a*. 1 Scriptural. 2 Scientific.

शास्य *a*. 1 To be taught or advised. 2 To be regulated or governed. 3 Deserving punishment, punishable.

शि 5 U. (शिनोति, शिनुते) 1 To whet, sharpen. 2 To attenuate, make thin. 3 To axcite. 4 To be attentive. 5 To be sharp.

शिः 1 Auspiciousness, good for tune. 2 Composure, calm, tranquillity, peace. 3 An epithet of *S*iva.

शिंशपा 1 N. of a tree (शिंशु). 2 The Asoka tree.

शिक्क *a*. Idle, lazy, indolent.

शिक्थ Bees'-wax ; cf. सिक्थ.

शिक्यं,-क्या 1 A loop or swing (made of rope). 2 A burden or load carried in a sling.

शिक्यित *a*. Suspended or carried in a loop.

शिक्ष् 1 A. (शिक्षते, शिक्षित) To learn, study, acquire knowledge of ; अशिक्षतास्त्रं पितुरेव मंत्रवत् R. 3. 31.

शिक्षकः (शिक्षका or शिक्षिका *f*.) 1 A learner. 2 A teacher, instructor ; यस्योभयं (*i. e*. क्रिया and संक्रांति) साधु स शिक्षकाणां धुरि प्रतिष्ठापयितव्य एव M. 1. 16.

शिक्षणं 1 Learning, acquiring knowledge. 2 Teaching, instruction.

शिक्षा 1 Learning, study, acquisition of knowledge ; R. 9. 63. 2 Desire of being able to do anything, wish to prevail ; Ki. 15. 37, 3 Teaching, instruction, training ; काव्यज्ञशिक्षयाऽभ्यासः K. P. 1 ; अभूच्च नम्रः प्रणिपातशिक्षया R. 3. 25 ; M. 4. 9 ; रणशिक्षा 'the science of war'. 4 One of the six Vedângas, the science which teaches the proper pronunciation of words and laws of euphony. 5 Modesty, humility. -Comp. -करः 1 a teacher, an instructor. 2 N. of Vyâsa. -नरः an epithet of Indra. -शक्तिः *f*. skill.

शिक्षित *p*. *p*. 1 Learnt studied. 2 Taught, instructed; अशिक्षितपटुत्वं *S*. 5. 21. 3 Trained, disciplined. 4 Tame, docile. 5 Skilful, clever. 6 Modest, diffident. -Comp. -अक्षरः a pupil. -आयुध *a*. versed in the use of weapons.

शिक्ष्मागः A pupil, scholar.

शिखंडः 1 A lock of hair left on the crown or sides of the head at tonsure. 2 A peacock's tail.

शिखंडकः 1 A lock of hair left on the crown of the head at tonsure. 2 Locks or tufts of hair left on the sides of the head ; (these are three or five in the case of the Kshatriyas) ; U. 4. 19. 3 A crest, tuft, plume. 4 A peacock's tail.

शिखंडिकः A cock.

शिखंडिका See शिखंड (1).

शिखंडिन् *a*. Crested, tufted. -*m*. 1 A peacock ; नदति स एष वधूसखः शिखंडी U. 3. 18 ; R. 1. 39; Ku. 1. 15. 2 A cock. 3 An arrow. 4 A peacock's tail. 5 A kind of jasmine. 6 N. of Vishṇu. 7 N. of a son of Drupada. [*S*ikhandin was originally a female, being Amb*a* born in the family of Drupada for wreaking her revenge upon Bhîshma ; (see Amb*a*). But from her very birth the girl was given out as a male-child and brought up as such. In due course she was married to the daughter of Hira*u*yavarman, who was extremely sorry to find that she had got a veritable woman for her husband. Her father, therefore, resolved to attack the kingdom of Drupada for his having deceived him ; but *S*ikhandin contrived, by practising austere penance in a forest, to exchange her sex with a Yaksha, and thus averted the calamity which threatened Drupada. Afterwards in the great Bharat*i* war he proved a means of killing Bhîshma, who declined to fight with a woman, when Arjuna put him forward as his hero. He was afterwards killed by Asvatth*a*man].

शिखंडिनी 1 A pea-hen. 2 A kind of jasmine 3 N. of the daughter of Drupada ; see शिखंडिन् above.

शिखरः-रं 1 The top, summit or peak of a mountain ; जगाम गौरी शिखरं शिखंडिमत् Ku. 5. 7, 1. 4 ; Me. 18. 2 The top of a tree. 3 Crest, tuf . 4 The point or edge of a sword. 5 Top, peak, point in general. 6 The arm-pit. 7 Bristling of the hair. 8 The bud of the Arabian jasmine. 9 A kind of ruby-like gem. -Comp. -वासिनी an epithet of Durgâ.

शिखरिणी 1 An excellent woman. 2 A dish of curds and sugar with spices. 3 A line of hair extending across the navel. 4 N. of a metre ; see App. I.

शिखरिन् *a*. (णी *f*.) 1 Crested, tufted. 2 Pointed, peaked ; शिखरिदशना Me. 82. -*m*. 1 A mountain ; इतश्च शरणार्थिनां शिखरिणां गणाः शेरते Bh. 2. 76 ; Me. 13 ; R. 9. 12, 22. 2 A hill-fort. 3 A tree. 4 The lapwing. 5 The plant अपामार्ग.

शिखा 1 A lock of hair on the crown of the head ; Mu. 3. 30 ; *S*i. 4. 50; Mâl. 10. 6. 2 A crest, topknot. 3 Tuft, plume. 4 Top, summit, peak; Ki. 6. 17. 5 Sharp end, edge, point or end in general ; *S*. 1. 4 ; Bv. 1. 2. 6 The end of a garment ; *S*. 1. 14. 7 A flame ; प्रभामहत्या शिखयेव दीपः Ku. 1. 28, R. 17. 34. 8 A ray of light ; Ku. 2. 38. 9 A peacock's crest or comb. 10 A fibrous root. 11 A branch in general ; especially one taking root. 12 The head or chief of anything. 13 The fever of love. -Comp. -तरुः a lamp-stand. -धरः a peacock. -°जं a peacock's feather. -धारः a peacock. -मणिः a crest-jewel. -मूलं 1 a carrot. 2 a turnip. -वरः the jack-fruit tree. -वल *a*. pointed, crested. (-लः) a peacock. -वृक्षः a lamp-stand. -वृद्धिः *f*. a kind of usurious interest, daily increasing.

शिखालुः The crest of a peacock.

शिखावत् *a*. 1 Crested. 2 Flaming. -*m*. 1 A lamp 2 Fire.

शिखिन् *a*. 1 Pointed. 2 Crested, tufted. 3 Proud. -*m*. 1 A peacock ; Pt. 1. 159 ; V. 2. 23 ; *S*i. 4. 50. 2 Fire ; रिपुरिव सखी संवासोयं शिखीव हिमानिलः Git. 7 ; Pt. 4. 110 ; R. 19. 54 ; *S*i. 15. 7. 3 A cock. 4 An arrow. 5 A tree. 6 A lamp. 7 A bull. 8 A horse. 9 A mountain. 10 A Brâhmaṇa. 11 A religious mendicant. 12 N. of Ketu. 13 The number 'three.' 14 The *Chitraka* tree. -Comp. -कंठ, ग्रीव blue vitriol. -ध्वजः 1 an epithet of धे Kârtikeya. 2 smoke. -पिच्छं, -पुच्छं a peacock's tail. -यूपः an antelope. -वर्धकः a gourd. -वाहनः an epithet of Kârtikeya. -शिखा 1 a flame. 2 a peacock's crest.

शिग्रुः 1 A pot-herb. 2 A kind of tree.

शिंख् 1 P. (शिंखति) To go, move.

शिंघ् 1 P. (शिंघति) To smell.

शिंघाणः 1 Froth, foam. 2 Phlegm. -णं 1 The mucus of the nose. 2 Rust of iron. 3 A glass-vessel.

शिंघाणकः-कं The mucus of the nose. -कः Phlegm.

शिंज् 1. 2. A., 10. U. (शिंजते, शिंक्ते, शिंजयति-ते, शिंजित) To tinkle, jingle, rattle ; *Si*. 10. 62.

शिंजः Tinkle, jingle, tinkling or jingling sound ; especially of ornaments such as anklets.

शिंजंजिका A chain worn round the loins.

शिंजा 1 Tinkle, jingle &c. 2 A bow-string.

शिंजित *p. p.* Tinkling, jingling. -तं Tinkling, jingling (cf anklets &c.) ; कूजितं राजहंसानां नेदं नूपुरशिंजितं V. 4. 14.

शिंजिनी 1 A bow-string. 2 An anklet (worn-ound the feet).

शिट् 1 P. (शेटति) To slight, despise, disregard.

शित *p. p.* 1 Sharpened, whetted. 2 Thin, emaciated. 3 Wasted, declined. 4 Weak, feeble. -Comp. -अग्रः a thorn. -धार *a.* sharp-edged. -शूकः 1 barley. 2 wheat.

शितद्रुः *f.* The river Sutlej ; see शतद्रु.

शिति *a.* 1 White. 2 Black ; *Si*. 15. 48. -तिः The birch tree. -Comp. -कंठः 1 an epithet of *Siva* ; तस्यात्मा शितिकंठस्य सैनापत्यमुपेत्य वः Ku. 2. 61, 6. 81. 2 a peacock ; अवनतशितिकंठकंठलक्ष्मीमिह दधति स्फुरिताणुरेणजालाः Si. 4. 56. 3 a gallinule. -छदः, -पक्षः a goose. -रत्नं a sapphire. -वाससू *m.* an epithet of Râma ; विडंबयंतं शितिवाससस्तनुं *Si*. 1. 6.

शिथिल *a.* 1 Loose, loosened, slackened, relaxed. 2 Untied, unfastened ; *S*. 2. 6. 3 Severed, fallen from the stalk ; *S*. 2. 8. 4 Languid, enfeebled, unnerved. 5 Weak, feeble ; अशिथिलपरिरंभ U. 1. 24, 27 ' fast or close embrace '. 6 Flaccid, flabby. 7 Dissolved. 8 Decayed. 9 Ineffective, futile, vain. 10 Careless. 11 Loosely done, not strictly or rigidly performed. 12 Cast off, abandoned. -लं 1 Laxity, looseness. 2 Slowness. (शिथिलीकृ means 1 to loosen, unfasten, untie. 2 to relax, slacken. 3 to weaken, impair, enfeeble. 4 to give up, abandon ; R. 2. 41 ; शिथिलीभू 1 to be slackened or relaxed. 2 to fall off from ; Mk. 1. 13).

शिथिलयति Den P. 1 To relax, slacken, loosen. 2 To give up, abandon ; Ve. 5. 6. 3 To lessen, allow to cool down ; V. 2.

शिथिलित *a.* 1 Loosed. 2 Relaxed, loosened. 3 Dissolvedt-

शिनिः N. of a warrior belonging to the side of the Yâdavas. (शिनेर्नप्तृ *m.* N. of Sâtyaki).

शिपिः A ray of light. -*f*. Skin, leather. -*n*. Water ; शैत्याच्छयनयोगाच्च शिपि वारि प्रचक्षते Vyâsa. -Comp. -विष्ट *a.* (written शिपिविष्ट or शिविपिष्ट also) 1 pervaded by rays. 2 bald, bald-headed. 3 leprous. (-ष्टः) 1 an epithet of Vishṇu. 2 of *Siva*. 3 a bold man. 4 a man without prepuce. 5 a leper.

शिप्रः N. of a lake on the Himâlaya.

शिप्रा N. of a river which issues from the *Sipra* lake and on the bank of which stands Ujjayinî ; शिप्रावातः प्रियतम इव प्रार्थनाचाटुकारः Me. 31.

शिफः See शिफा.

शिफा 1 A fibrous root. 2 The root of a water-lily. 3 A root in general. 4 A stroke with a whip. 5 A mother. 6 A river. -Comp. -धरः a branch. -रुहः the (Indian) fig-tree.

शिफाकः The root of a water-lily.

शिबिः (विः) 1 A beast of prey. 2 The birch tree. 3 N. of a country (pl.). 4 N. of a king (who is said to have saved *Agni* in the form of a dove from Indra in the form of a hawk by offering an equal quantity of his own flesh weighed in a balance) ; cf. Mu. 6. 17.

शिबि(वि)का 1 A palanquin, litter. 2 A bier.

शिबि(वि)रं 1 A camp ; धृष्टद्युम्नः स्वशिबिरमयं याति सर्वे सहध्वं Ve. 3. 18 ; *Si*. 5. 68. 2 A royal camp or residence. 3 An intrenchment for the protection of an army. 4 A kind of grain.

शिबि(वि)रथः A palanquin, litter.

शिंबा A pod, legume.

शिंबिका 1 A pod, legume. 2 A kind of kidney-bean. (*m.* also according to some.).

शिंबी 1 A pod, legume. 2 A kind of plant.

शिरं 1 The head. 2 The root of the pepper plant (*m.* also, according to some, in these senses) -रः 1 A bed. 2 A large serpent. -Comp. -ज hair.

शिरस् *n.* 1 The head ; शिरसा श्लाघते पूर्व (गुणं) परं (दोषं) कंठे नियच्छति Subhash. 2 Skull. 3 A peak, summit, top (as of a mountain) ; हिमगौरैरशलाधिपः शिरोभिः Ki. 5. 17 ; *Si*. 4. 54. 4 The top of a tree. 5 The head or top of anything; शिरसि मसीपटलं दधाति दीपः Bv. 1. 74. 6 Pinnacle, acme, highest point. 7 Front, forepart, van (as of an army); *S*. 7. 26 ; U. 5. 3. 8 Chief, principal, head (usually at the end of comp.). (Before soft consonants शिरस् is changed to शिरो in comp.). -Comp. -अस्थि *n.* (शिरोऽस्थि) the skull. -कपालिन् *m.* an ascetic who carries about a human skull. -गृहं a room on the top of a house, turret, garret. -ग्रहः affection of the head, head-ache. -छेदः, -छेदनं (शिरश्छेदः &c.) beheading, decapitation. -तापिन् *m.* an elephant. -त्रं, -त्राणं 1 A helmet ; च्युतैः शिरस्त्रैश्चषकोत्तरेव R. 7. 49, 66; अपनीतशिरस्त्राणाः 4. 64. 2 head-dress. -धरा, -धिः the neck ; *Si*. 4. 52, 5. 65. -पीडा headache. -फलः the cocoanut tree. -भूषणं an ornament for the head. -मणिः 1 a jewel worn on the head. 2 a crest-jewel. 3 a title of respect conferred on learned men. -मर्मन् *m.* a hog. -मालिन् *m.* an epithet of *Siva*. -रत्नं a jewel worn on the head. -रुजा head-ache. -रुह् *m.* -रुहः (also शिरसिरुह्-हः) the hair of the head, Rs. 1. 4, Ku. 5. 9 ; R. 15. 16. -वर्तिन् *a.* being at the head. (-*m.*) a chief, any one at the head of affairs. -वृत्तं pepper. -वेष्टः, -वेष्टनं a head-dress, turban. -शूलं headache. -हारिन् *m.* an epithet of *Siva*.

शिरसिजः The hair of the head ; *Si*. 7. 62.

शिरस्कं 1 A helmet. 2 A turban, head-dress.

शिरस्का A palanquin.

शिरस्तस् *ind.* From the head ; Ku. 3. 49 ; Bh. 2. 10.

शिरस्य *a.* Belonging to or being on the head. -स्यः Clean hair.

शिरा Any tubular vessel of the body, a nerve, vein, artery, blood-vessel. -Comp. -पत्रः the wood-apple वृत्तं lead.

शिराल *a.* Sinewy, tendinous, veiny.

शिरिः 1 A sword. 2 A killer, murderer. 3 An arrow. 4 A locust.

शिरीषः N. of a tree. -षं A flower of this tree (regarded as the type of delicacy) ; शिरीषपुष्पाधिकसौकुमार्यौ बाहू तदीयाविति मे वितर्कः Ku. 1. 41, 5. 4, R. 16. 48 ; Me. 65.

शिल् 6 P. (शिलति) To glean.

शिलः-लं Gleaning ears of corn (more than one at a time) ; see Kull. on Ms. 10. 112. -Comp. -उंछः 1 gleaning ears of corn. 2 irregular occupation.

शिला 1 A stone, rock. 2 A grind-stone. 3 The lower timber of a door. 4 The top of a column. 5 A tendon, vein (for शिरा). 6 Red arsenic. 7 Camphor. -Comp. -अष्टकः 1 a hole. 2 a fence, an enclosure. 3 a room on the top of a house. -आत्मजं iron. -आत्मिका a crucible. -आरंभा the wild plantain. -आसनं 1 a slab of stone used as a seat. 2 benzoin. -आह्वं bitumen. -उच्चयः a mountain, huge rock ; R. 2. 34. -उत्थं benzoin. -उद्भवं 1 benzoin. 2 a superior kind of sandal-wood. -ओकस् *m.*

an epithet of Garuḍa. –कुट्टकः a stone-cutter's chisel. –कुसुमं, –पुष्पं benzoin. –ज a. fossil, mineral. (–जं) 1 bitumen. 2 benzoin. 3 petroleum. 4 iron. 5 any fossil production. –जतु n. 1 bitumen. 2 red chalk. –जित् f. –दद्रुः bitumen. –धातुः 1 chalk. 2 red chalk. 3 a white fossil substance. –पट्टः a slab (of stone) used as a seat, stone-seat. –पुत्रः,-पुत्रकः a small flat stone for grinding condiments upon. –प्रतिकृतिः f. an image of stone. –फलकं a stone-slab. –भवं benzoin. –भेदः a stone-cutter's chisel. –रसः 1 benzoin. 2 incense. –वल्कलं a kind of moss. –वृष्टिः f. 1 a shower of stones. 2 hail. –वेश्मन् n. a grotto, rocky recess. –व्याधिः bitumen.

शिलिः The birch tree. –f. The lower timber of a door.

शिलिंद: A kind of fish.

शिलीः 1 The lower timber of a door. 2 A kind of earthworm. 3 The top of a pillar. 4 A dart. 5 An arrow. 6 A kind of earthworm. 7 A female frog. –Comp. –मुखः a bee; मिलिताशिलीमुखपाटलिपटलकृतस्मरतूणविलासे Gît. 1. ; R. 4. 57. 2 an arrow; सा कुसुमघटितशिलीमुखमनोहरान्मदनचापादिव प्रमदवनात्त्रस्यति K. 225 ; or युगपद्रिका शमुदयाद्गमिते शशिनः शिलीमुखगणोऽलभत Si. 9. 41 (in both passages the word is used in senses 1 and 2). 3 a fool.

शिलींध्रः 1 A kind of fish. 2 A kind of tree. –ध्रं A mushroom, fungus ; as in उच्छिलींध्र q. v. 2 The flower of the plantain tree ; अधिपुरंध्रि शिलींध्रसुगंधिभिः Si. 6. 32, or अलिनारमतालिनी शिलींध्रे 72. 3 Hail.

शिलींध्रकं A mushroom, fungus.

शिलींध्री 1 Earth, clay. 2 A small earthworm.

शिल्पं 1 An art, a fine or mechanical art ; (64 such arts are enumerated). 2 Skill (in any art) ; craft; M. 1. 6 ; Mk. 3. 15. 3 Ingenuity, cleverness. 4 Work, manual work or labour. 5 A rite, ceremony. 6 A kind of ladle or spoon used at sacrifices. –Comp. –कर्मन् n., –क्रिया any manual labour, handicraft. –कारः, –कारकः, –कारिन् m. an artisan, a mechanic. –शालं,-ला a workshop, manufactory (a technical school). –शास्त्रं 1 a book on any art, fine or mechanical. 2 mechanics.

शिल्पिन् a. 1 Relating to a fine or mechanical art. 2 Mechanical. –m. 1 An artisan, artist, a mechanic. 2 One who is skilled in any art.

शिव a. 1 Auspicious, propitious, lucky ; इयं शिवाया नियतेरिवायतिः Ki. 4. 21 ; 1. 38 ; R. 11. 33. 2 In good health or condition, happy, prosperous, fortunate ; शिवानि वस्तर्थिजलानि कच्चित् R. 5. 8 ; (अनुपप्लवानि ' undisturbed ') ; शिवास्ते पंथानः संतु ' a happy journey to you ', ' God bless (or speed) you on your journey ' –वः 1 N. of the third god of the sacred Hindu Trinity, who is entrusted with the work of destruction, as Brahman and Vishṇu are with the creation and preservation, of the world ; एको देवः केशवो वा शिवो वा Bh. 2. 115. 2 The male organ of generation, penis. 3 An auspicious planetary conjunction. 4 The Veda. 5 Final beatitude. 6 A post to which cattle are tied. 7 A god, deity. 8 Quicksilver. 9 Bdellium. 10 The black variety of thorn-apple. –वौ (m. dual) Siva and Pârvatî ; Ki. 5. 40. –वं 1 Prosperity, welfare, well-being, happiness ; तव वर्त्मनि वर्ततां शिवं N. 2. 62 ; Ratn. 1. 2 ; R. 1. 60. 2 Bliss, auspiciousness. 3 Final beatitude. 4 Water. 5 Sea salt. 6 Rock-salt. 7 Refined borax. –Comp. –अक्षं =रुद्राक्ष q. v. –आत्मकं rock-salt. –आदेशकः 1 the bearer of auspicious news. 2 a fortune-teller. –आलयः 1 Siva's abode. 2 the red basil. (–यं) 1 a temple of Siva. 2 a cemetery. –इतर a. inauspicious, unlucky ; शिवेतरक्षतये K. P. 1. –कर (शिवंकर also) a. conferring happiness, auspicious. –कीर्तनः N. of Bhringi. –गति a. prosperous, happy. –घर्मजः the planet Mars. –ताति a. 1 having an auspicious end, conferring or conducive to happiness, propitious ; प्रयत्नः कृत्स्नोयं फलतु शिवतातिश्च भवतु Mâl. 6. 7. 2 tender, not demoniacal ; मा :पूतनात्वमुपगाः शिवतातिरेधि 9. 49. (–तिः) auspiciousness, happiness. –दत्तं the discus of Vishṇu. –दारु n. the Devadâru tree. –द्रुमः the Bilva tree. –द्विष्टा the Ketaka tree. –धातुः quick-silver. –पुरं, –पुरी N. of Benares. –पुराणं N. of one of the eighteen Purâṇas. –प्रियः 1 a crystal. 2 the Baka tree. 3 the thorn-apple. –वल्लकः the Arjuna tree. –राजधानी N. of Benares. –रात्रिः f. the fourteenth day of the dark half of Mâgha on which a rigorous fast is observed in honour of Siva. -लिंगं Siva, worshipped in the form of a Phallus. –लोकः the world of Siva. –वल्लभः the mango tree. (–भा) Pârvatî. –वाहनः a bull. –वीजं quick-silver. -शेखरः 1 the moon. 2 the thorn-apple. –सुंदरी an epithet of Durgâ.

शिवकः 1 A post to which cows or cattle in general are tied. 2 A post for cattle to rub against, scratching-post.

शिवा 1 N. of Pârvatî. 2 A jackal (in general); जहासि निद्रामशिवैः शिवारुतैः Ki. 1. 38 ; हरेरद्य द्वारे शिव शिव शिवानां कलकलः Bv. 1. 32 ; R. 7. 50, 11. 61, 12. 39. 3 Final beatitude. 4 The Samî tree. 5 The yellow myrobalan. 6 Dûrvâ grass. 7 A kind of yellow pigment. 8 Turmeric. –Comp.–अरातिः a dog. –प्रियः a goat. –फला the Samî tree. –रुतं the howling of a jackal ; Ki. 1. 38.

शिवानी Pârvatî, wife of Siva.

शिवालुः A jackal.

शिशिर a. Cool, cold, chill, frigid ; कुरु यदुनंदनचंदनाशिशिरतरेण करेण पयोधरे Gît. 12 ; R. 9. 59 ; 14. 3, 16. 49. –रः –रं 1 Dew. hoarfrost ; पद्मानां शिशिराद्ध्रयं; जातां मन्ये शिशिरमथितां पद्मिनीं वान्यरूपां Me. 83. 2 The cold season (comprising the two months Mâgha and Phâlguna) ; कंठेषु स्खलितं गतेऽपि शिशिरे पुंस्कोकिलानां रुतं S. 6. 3. 3 Coldness, frigidity. –Comp. –अंशुः, –करः, –किरणः, –दीधितिः, –रश्मिः the moon ; बुध इव शिशिरांशोः V. 5. 21 ; शिशिराकिरणकांतं वासरांतेऽभिसार्य Si. 11. 21 ; शिशिरदीधितिना रजन्यः Rs. 3. 2. –अत्ययः, –अपगमः 'the close of the cold season,' spring season ; स्वहस्तलूनः शिशिरात्ययस्य (पुष्पोच्चयः) Ku. 3. 61 ; उपहितं शिशिरापगमश्रिया R. 9. 31 . –कालः, –समयः the cold season. –घ्नः an epithet of Agni.

शिशुः 1 A child, an infant ; शिशुर्वा शिष्या वा U. 4. 11. 2 The young of any animal (as a calf, puppy, fawn &c.) ; S. 1. 14 ; 7. 14, 18. 3 A boy under eight or sixteen years of age. –Comp. –क्रंदः, –क्रंदनं the cry or weeping of a child. –गंधा a kind of jasmine double jasmine). –पालः N. of a king of the Chedis and son of Damaghosha. [According to the Vishṇu Puraṇa this monarch was, in a previous existence, the unrighteous Hiraṇyakasipu, king of the Asuras who was killed by Vishṇu in the form of Narasimha. He was next born as the ten-headed Ravaṇa who was killed by Rama Then he was born as the son of Damaghosha, and continued his enmity to Krishṇa, the eighth incarnation of Vishṇu, with even greater implacability ; (see Si. 1). He denounced Krishṇa when they met at the Rajasuya sacrifice of Yudhishṭhira, but his head was cut off by Krishṇa with his discus. His death forms the subject of a celebrated poem by Magha]. °हन् m. an epithet of Krishṇa. –मारः the Gangetic porpoise. –वाहकः, –वाह्यकः a wild goat.

शिशुकः 1 A child, an infant. 2 The young of any animal. 3 A tree. 4 A porpoise.

शिश्नं, शिस्नं The penis or male organ of generation ; Y. 1. 17 ; Ms. 11. 104.

शिश्विदान a. 1 Pious in conduct, virtuous, holy. 2 Wicked, sinful.

शिष् I. 1 P. (शेषति) To hurt, kill. –II. 1 P., 10 U., (शेषति, शेषयति-ते) To leave as a remainder, spare. –III. 7 P. (शिनष्टि, शिष्ट) 1 To leave as a remainder, leave, leave remaining. 2 To distinguish or discriminate from others. -*Caus.* (शेषयति-ते) To leave &c. अव to leave as a remainder ; leave behind (mostly in *pass.*), स्तंबेन नीवार इवावाशिष्टः R. 5. 15 ; कियद्वशिष्टं रजन्याः *S.* 4 ; निद्रागमसीम्नः कियद्वाशिष्ट Mv. 6; Bg. 7. 2. -उद् to leave as a remainder ; see उच्छिष्ट. -परि to leave remaining (*caus.* also); भविता करेणुपरिशेषिता मही Bv. 1, 53. -वि 1 to particularize, individualize, specify, define. 2 to distinguish, discriminate. 3 to aggravate, heighten, enhance, intensify; पुनरकांडविवर्तनदारुणो विधिरहो विशिनष्टि मनोरुजं Mâl. 4. 7 ; U. 4. 15. (-*pass.*) 1 to be different from; R. 17. 62. 2 to be better or higher than, surpass, excel, be preferable or superior to (with abl.) ; Ms. 2. 83, 3. 203. (-*Caus.*) to surpass, excel ; Mk. 4. 4 ; M. 3. 5.

शिष्ट *p. p.* 1 Left, remaining, residual, rest 2 Ordered, commanded. 3 Trained, educated, disciplined. 4 Tamed, docile, tractable. 5 Wise, learned ; *S*i. 2. 10. 6 Virtuous, respectable. 7 Civil, polite. 8 Chief, principal, superior, excellent, distinguished, eminent. -ष्टः 1 An eminent or distinguished person. 2 A wise man. 3 A counsellor. -**Comp.** -आचारः 1 the practice of wise men. 2 Good manners, good breeding. -सभा an assembly of chief or learned men, a council of state.

शिष्टिः *f.* 1 Rule, government. 2 Order, command. 3 Chastisement, punishment.

शिष्यः 1 A pupil, disciple, scholar ; शिष्यस्तेऽहं शाधि मां त्वां प्रपन्नं Bg. 2. 7. 2 Anger, passion. -**Comp.** -परंपरा a succession of pupils. -शिष्टिः *f.* the correction of a pupil.

शिह्लः, शिह्लकः Benzoin.

शी 2 A. (शेते, शयित; *pass.* शय्यते ; *desid.* शिशयिषते) 1 To lie, lie down, recline, rest ; इतश्च शरणार्थिनः शिखरिणां गणाः शेरते Bh. 2. 76. 2 To sleep (fig. also); किं निःशंके शेषे शेषे वयसः समागतो मृत्युः । अथवा सुखं शयीथा निकटे जागर्ति जाह्नवी जननी Bv. 4. 30; Bh. 3. 79, Ku. 5. 12. -*Caus.* (शाययति-ते) To cause to sleep or lie down. -With अति 1 to precede in sleeping. 2 to sleep after or longer than one ; अहं पतीन्नातिशये Mb. 3 to excel, surpass ; पूर्वान्महाभागतयातिशेषे R. 5. 14 ; चरितेन चातिशायिता मुनयः Ki. 6. 32; Bk. 7. 46. (-*Caus.*) to cause to excel ; धाम्यातिशाययति धाम सहस्रधाम्नः Mu. 3. 17. -अधि (with acc. of place) 1 to lie or sleep on or in, rest upon ; अध्यशयिष्ट गां Bk. 15. 14 ; अमुं युगांतोचितयोगनिद्रः संहृत्य लोकान् पुरुषोऽधिशेते R. 13. 6, 16. 49, 19. 32 ; Ki. 1. 38. 2 to inhabit, dwell in ; Bk. 10. 35. -उप to sleep or lie near. -सं to doubt, be in doubt ; संशय्य कर्णादिषु तिष्ठते यः Ki. 3. 14, 42 ; Bv. 2. 115.

शी 1 Sleep, repose. 2 Tranquillity.

शीक् I. 1 A. (शीकते) 1 To wet, sprinkle. 2 To go or move gently. II. 1 P., 10 U. (शीकति, शीकयति-ते) 1 To be angry. 2 To moisten, wet.

शीकरः 1 Spray, thin rain, drizzle, mist ; Ku. 1. 15, 2. 52 ; R. 5. 42, 9. 68; Ki. 5. 15. 2 A drop of water or rain; गतमुपरि घनानां वारिगर्भोदराणां पिशुनयति रथस्ते शीकरक्लिन्ननेमिः *S.* 7. 7; R. 17. 62. -रं 1 The *Sarala* tree. 2 The resin of this tree.

शीघ्र *a.* Quick, rapid, speedy ; विभ्रमणि मंडलचारशीघ्रः V. 5. 2. -घ्रः Conjunction (iu astr.) -घ्रं *ind.* Quickly, swiftly, rapidly. -**Comp.** -उच्चः conjunction (in astr.). -कारिन् *a.* expeditious, quick. -कोपिन् *a.* choleric, irascible. -चेतनः a dog. -बुद्धिः *a.* acute, sharp-witted. -लंघन *a.* going rapidly, swift of foot, Ghaṭ. 8. -वेधिन् *m.* a good archer.

शीघ्रिन् *a.* Sppeedy, expeditious.

शीघ्रिय *a.* Quick. -यः 1 N. of Vishṇu. 2 Of *S*iva. 3 The fighting of cats.

शीघ्र्यं Quickness, rapidity.

शीत् *ind.* A sound made to express a sudden thrill of pleasure or pain, (particularly applied to the sound of pleasure during sexual enjoyment). -**Comp.** -कारः, कृत् *m.* the above sound.

शीत *a.* 1 Cool, cold, frigid ; तव कुसुमशरत्वं शीतरश्मित्वमिंदोः *S.* 3. 2. 2 Dull, sluggish, apathetic, sleepy. 3 Dull, lazy, stupid. -तः 1 A kind of reed. 2 The Nimba tree. 3 The cold season (*n.* also). 4 Camphor. -तं 1 Cold, coldness, chillness ; आः शीतं तुहिनाचलस्य करयोः K. P. 10. 2 Water. 3 Cinnamon. -**Comp**.-अंशुः 1 the moon; वक्त्रदौ तव सत्ययं यदपरः शीतांशुरुज्जृंभते K. P. 10. 2 camphor. -अदः a kind of affection or diseased state of the gums.-अद्रिः the Himâlaya mountain. -अश्मन् *m.* the moon-stone. -आर्त *a.* pinched or benumbed with cold, shivering. -उत्तमं water. -कालः the cold season, winter. -कालीन *a.* wintry. -कृच्छ्रः -च्छ्रं a kind of religious penance. -गंधं white sandal. -गुः 1 the moon. 2 camphor. -चंपकः 1 a lamp. 2 a mirror. -दीधितिः the moon. -पुष्पः the *Siri'sha* tree.-पुष्पकं benzoin. -प्रभः camphor. -भानुः the moon. -भीरुः a kind of jasmine (Arabian). -मयूखः, -मरीचिः, -रश्मिः 1 the moon. 2 camphor. -रम्यः a lamp. -रुच् *m.* the moon. -वल्कः the *udumbara* tree. -वीर्यकः the fig-tree. -शिवः the *Sami'* tree. (-वं) 1 rock-salt. 2 borax. -शूकः berley. -स्पर्श *a.* cooling.

शीतक *a.* Cold ; see शीतः -कः 1 Any cold thing. 2 Winter, the cold season. 3 A dull or dilatory person. 4 A happy man, one free from cares or anxieties. 5 A scorpion.

शीतल *a.* Cool, cold, chill, frigid (fig also); अतिशीतलमप्यंभः किं भिनत्ति न भूभृतः Subhâsh. ; महदपि परदुःखं शीतलं सम्यगाहुः V. 4. 13. -लः 1 The moon. 2 A kind of camphor. 3 Turpentine. 4 The Champaka tree. 5 A kind of religious observance. -लं 1 Cold, coolness. 2 The cold season. 3 Benzoin. 4 White sandal, or sandal in general. 5 A pearl. 6 Green sulphate of iron. 7 A lotus. 8 The root called वीरण q. v. -**Comp.** -छद् the Champaka tree. -जलं a lotus. -प्रदः -दं sandal. -षष्ठी the sixth day of the bright half of Mâgha.

शीतलकं A white lotus.

शीतला 1 Small-pox. 2 The goddess presiding over small-pox. -**Comp.** -पूजा worship of the goddess *S*italâ.

शीतली Small-pox.

शीता See सीता.

शीतालु *a.* Suffering from or shivering with cold, chilled, pinched ; *S*i. 8. 19.

शीत्य See सीत्य.

शीधु *m. n.* 1 Any spirituous liquor, rum. 2 Wine. -**Comp.** -गंधः the *Bakula* tree. -पः a drinker of spirits.

शीन *a.* Thick, congealed. -नः 1 A dolt, blockhead. 2 A large snake (अजगर).

शीभ् 1 A. (शीभते) 1 To boast. 2 To tell, say, speak (कथने ?).

शीभ्यः 1 A bull. 2 N. of *S*iva.

शीरः A large snake ; see सीर also.

शीर्ण *p.p.* 1 Withered ; decayed, rotten. 2 Dry, sere. 3 Shattered ; shivered. 4 Thin, emaciated, (see शॄ). -र्णं A kind of perfume. -**Comp.** -अंघ्रिः, -पादः 1 epithets of Yama. 2 of the planet Saturn. -पर्णं withered leaf ; (so शीर्णपत्रं). (-र्णः) the *Nimba* tree. -वृंतं a water melon.

शीर्वि *a.* Destructive, hurtful, noxious, injurious.

शीर्षं 1 The head ; शीर्षे सर्पो देशांतरे वैद्यः Karpûr., Mu. 1. 21. 2 The black variety of aloe-wood. -**Comp.** अवशेषः the head only as the remainder. -आमयः any affection or disease of the head. -छेदः decapitation. -छेद्य *a.* fit to be beheaded, deserving death by decapitation ; U. 2. 8; R. 15. 51. -रक्षकं a helmet.

शीर्षकः An epithet of Râhu. -कं 1 The head. 2 Skull. 3 A helmet. 4 A head-dress, (cap, hat &c). 5 Verdict, judgment, judicial sentence.

शीर्षण्यः Clean or unentangled hair· **-ण्यं 1** A helmet. **2** A hat, cap.

शीर्षन् *n.* The head. (This word has no forms for the first five inflections, and is opitionally substituted for शिरस् or शीर्ष after acc. dual.)

शील् I. 1 P. (शीलति)**1** To meditate, contemplate. **2** To serve, honour, worship. **3** To do, practise. -II. 10. U. (शीलयति-ते) **1** To honour, woship. **2** To practise repeatedly, exercise, study, think of, ponder over ; श्रुतिशतमपि भूयः शीलितं भारतं वा Bv. 2. 35 ; शीलयंति मुनयः सुशीलतां Ki. 13. 43. **3** To put on, wear; चल सखि कुंजं सतिमिरपुंजं शीलय नीलनिचोलं Gît. 5. **4** To go to, visit, frequent ; यदनुगमनाय निशि गहनमपि शीलितं Gît. 7 ; स्मेरानना सपदि शीलय सौध मौलिं Bv. 2. 4. -WITH **अनु**, **-परि** to practis reepeatedly, cultivate, think of: शश्वच्छतोसि मनसा परिशीलितोऽसि Râj. P.

शीलः A large serpent (the boa). **-लं 1** Disposition, nature, character, tendency, inclination, habit, custom ; समानशीलव्यसनेषु सख्यं Subhâsh. ; frequently at the end of comp. in the sense of 'disposed or habituated to,' 'indulging in', 'prone to,' 'addicted to,' 'attached' &c.; as कलहशील 'disposed to quarrel,' 'quarrelsome' ; भावनशील 'disposed or apt to think'; so दान°, मृगया°, दया°, पुण्य°, आश्वासन° &c. **2** Conduct, behaviour in general. **3** Good disposition or character ; good nature ; शीलं परं भूषणं Bh. 2. 82 ; Pt. 5. 2. **4** Virtue ; morality, good conduct, virtucus life, chastity, uprightness ; दौर्मंत्र्यान्नृपतिर्विनश्यति...शीलं खलोपासनात् Bh. 2. 42, 39 ; तथा हि ते शीलमुदारदर्शने तपस्विनामप्युपदेशतां गतं Ku. 5. 36, Ki. 11. 25; R. 10. 70. **5** Beauty, good form. **-Comp. -खंडनं** violation of morality or chastity ; Pt. 1. **-धारिन्** *m.* an epithet of *S*iva. **-वंचना** violation of chastity ; प्रातेयं शीलवंचना Mk. 1. 44.

शीलनं 1 Repeated practice, exercise, study, cultivation. **2** Constant application. **3** Honouring, serving. **4** Wearing.

शीलित *p. p.* **1** Practised, exercised. **2** Put on. **3** Frequented, visited. **4** Skilled in. **5** Endowed with, possessed of.

शीवन् *m.* A large snake (boa.)

शुंशुमारः A porpoise, (a corruption of शिशुमार q. v.).

शुक् 1 P. (शोकति) To go, move.

शुकः 1 A parrot ; आत्मनो मुखदोषेण बध्यंते शुकसारिकाः Subhâsh. ; तुंडैराताम्रकुटिलैः पक्षैर्हरितकोमलैः । त्रिवर्णराजिभिः कंठैरेते मंजुगिरः शुकाः ॥ Kâv. 2. 9. **2** the *S*irîsha tree. **3** N. of a son of Vyâsa. [He is said to have been born from the seed of Vy*a*sa which fell at the sight of the heavenly nymph Ghrit*a*ch*i* while roaming over the earth in the form of a female parrot. *S*uka was a born philosopher, and by his moral eloquence successfully resisted all the attempts of the nymph Rambh*a* to win him over to the path of love. He is said to have narrated the Bh*a*gavata Pur*a*n*a* to king Par*i*kshit. His name has become proverbial for the most rigid observer of continence]. **-कं 1** Cloth, clothes. **2** A helmet. **3** A turban. **4** End or hem of a garment. **-Comp. -अदनः** the pomegranate tree. **-तरुः,-द्रुमः** the *S*irîsha tree. **-नास** *a.* having an aquiline, nose. **-नासिका** an aquiline nose. **-पुच्छः** sulphur. **-पुष्पः,-प्रियः** the *S*irîsha tree. **-पुष्पा** the rose-apple. **-वल्लभः** the pomegranate. **-वाहः** an epithet of Cupid.

शुक्त *p. p.* **1** Bright, pure, clean. **2** Acid, sour. **3** Harsh, rough, hard, severe. **4** United, joined. **5** Deserted, lonely. **-क्तं 1** Flesh. **2** Sour gruel. **3** A kind of acid liquid.

शुक्तिः *f.* **1** An oyster-shell, pearl-oyster ; पात्रविशेषन्यस्तं गुणांतरं व्रजति शिल्पमाधातुः । जलमिव समुद्रशुक्तौ मुक्ताफलतां पयोदस्य M. 1. 6 ; Bh. 2. 67 ; R. 13. 17. **2** A conch-shell. **3** A small shell, muscle. **4** A portion of the skull. **5** A curl of hair on a horse's breast (or neck); *S*i. 5. 4, see Malli. thereon. **6** A kind of perfume. **7** A particular weight equal to two *Karshas*. **-Comp. -उद्भवं, -जं** a pearl. **-पुटं,-पेशी** a pearl-oyster shell. **-वधूः** the pearl-oyster. **-वीजं** a pearl.

शुक्तिका A pearl-oyster.

शुक्रः 1 The planet Venus. **2** N. of the preceptor of the Asuras, who, by means of his magical charm, restored to life the demons killed in battle ; see कच, देवयानी and ययाति. **3** The month of Jyesh*t*ha. **4** N. of Agni or fire. **-क्रं 1** Seman virile ; पुमान् पुंसोऽधिके शुक्रे स्त्री भवत्यधिके स्त्रियाः Ms. 3. 69 ; 5. 63. **2** The essence of anything. **-Comp. -अंगः** a peacock. **-कर** *a.* spermatic. (**-रः**) the marrow of the bones. **-वारः -वासरः** Friday. **-शिष्यः** a demon.

शुक्रल, -शुक्रिय *a.* **1** Seminal. **2** Increasing the seminal flow.

शुक्ल *a.* White, pure, bright ; as in शुक्लापांग q. v. **-क्लः 1** A white colour. **2** The bright or light half of a lunar month. **3** N. of *S*iva. **-क्लं 1** Silver. **2** A disease of the white part of the eye. **3** Fresh butter. **4** Sour gruel. **-Comp. -अंगः, -अपांगः** a peacock (having white corners of the eye); शुक्लापांगैः सजलनयनैः स्वागतकृत्य केकाः Me. 22. **-अम्लं** a kind of sorrel. **-उपला** candied sugar. **-कंठकः** a kind of gallinule. **-कर्मन्** *a.* pure in conduct, virtuous. **-कुष्ठं** white leprosy. **-धातुः** chalk. **-पक्षः** the light half of a month. **-वस्त्र** *a.* dressed in white. **-वायसः** a crane.

शुक्लक *a.* White. **-कः 1** White colour. **2** The bright half of a lunar month.

शुक्लल *a.* White.

शुक्ला 1 N. of Sarasvatî, **2** Candied sugar. **3** A woman having a white complexion. **4** The plant Kâkolî.

शुक्लिमन् *m.* Whiteness.

शुक्षिः 1 Air, wind. **2** Li-ght, lustre. **3** Fire.

शुंगः 1 The (Indian) fig-tree. **2** The hog-plum. **3** The awn of corn.

शुंगा 1 The sheath of a young bud. **2** The awn of barley or corn.

शुंगिन् *m.* The (Indian) fig tree.

शुच् I. 1 P. (शोचति) **1** To be sorry, grieve for, bewail, mourn ; अरोदीद्रावणोऽशोचीन्मोहं चाशिश्रियत्परं Bk. 15. 71 ; 21. 6 ; Bg. 16. 5. **2** To regret, repent. -WITH **-अनु** to bewail, mourn over, regret ; नष्टं मृतमतिक्रांतं नानुशोचंति पंडिताः Pt. 1. 333 ; Bg. 2. 11, Ve. 5. 4 ; U. 3. 32. **-परि** to lament, mourn. -II. 4 U. (शुच्यति-ते) **1** To be sorry or afflicted. **2** To be wet. **3** To shine. **4** To be pure or clean. **5** To decay, become fetid.

शुच्, शुचा *f.* Grief, sorrow, affliction, distress ; विकलकरणः पांडुच्छायः शुचा परिदुर्बलः U. 3. 22 ; कामं जीवति मे नाथ इति सा विजही शुचं R. 12. 75, 8. 72, Me. 88, *S*. 4. 18.

शुचि *a.* **1** Clear, pure, clear ; सकलहंसगणं शुचि मानसं Ki. 5. 13. **2** White; Ki. 18. 14. **3** Bright, resplendent ; प्रभवति शुचिर्बिंबोद्ग्राहे मणिर्न मृदां चयः U. 2. 4. **4** Virtuous, pious, holy, undefiled, unsullied ; अथ तु वेत्सि शुचि व्रतमात्मनः *S*. 5. 27 ; पथः शुचेर्दर्शयितार ईश्वराः R. 3. 46, Ki. 5. 13. **5** Purified, cleansed, hallowed ; R. 1. 81 ; Ms. 4. 71. **6** Honest, upright, faithful, true, guileless ; Pt. 1. 200. **7** Correct, accurate. **-चिः 1** The white colour. **2** Purity, purification. **3** Innocence, virtue, goodness, uprightness. **4** Correctness, accuracy. **5** The condition of a religious student. **6** A pure man. **7** A Brâhma*n*a. **8** The hot season ; उपययौ विदधन्नवमल्लिकाः शुचिरसौ चिरसौरभसंपदः *S*i. 6. 22, 1. 58, R. 3. 3 ; Ku. 5. 20. **9** The months of Jyesh*t*ha and Ash*a*dha. **10** A faithful or true friend. **11** The sun. **12** The moon. **13** Fire. **14** The sentiment of love (शृंगार). **15** The planet Venus **16** The Chitraka tree. **-Comp. -द्रुमः** the sacred fig-tree. **-मणिः** a crystal. **-मल्लिका** a kind of jasmine (Arabian) **-रोचिस्** *m.* the moon. **-व्रत** *a.* holy, virtuous. **-स्मित** *a.* having a sweet or pleasant smile ; Ku. 5. 20, R. 8. 48.

शुचिस् *n.* Light, lustre.

शुच्य् 1 P. (शुच्यति) **1** To bathe, perform ablutions. **2** To squeeze, express (as juice). **3** To distil. **4** To churn.

शुटीरः A hero.

शुठ् I. 1 P. (शोठति) **1** To be impeded or hindered. **2** To limp, be lame. **3** To resist. –II. 10 U. (शोठयति-ते) To be idle, lazy or dull.

शुंठ् 1 P., 10 U. (शुंठति शुंठयति-ते) **1** To purify. **2** To become dry ; see शुठ् I. also.

शुंठिः -ठी *f.*, **शुंठ्यं** Dry, ginger.

शुंडः **1** The juice issuing from the temples of an elephant in rut. **2** An elephant's trunk.

शुंडकः **1** Distiller. **2** A kind of military music or musical instrument.

शुंडा **1** An elephant's trunk. **2** Spirituous liquor. **3** A tavern, dram-shop. **4** The stalk of the lotus. **5** A courtezan, harlot. **6** A bawd, procuress. **–Comp.** **–पानं** a tavern, dram-shop.

शुंडारः **1** A distiller. **2** An elephant's trunk or proboscis ; Mv. 1. 53.

शुंडालः An elephant.

शुंडिका See शुंडा.

शुंडिन् *m.* **1** A distiller. **2** An elephant. **–Comp.** **–मूषिका** the musk-rat.

शुतद्रिः-द्रुः *f.* The river Sutlej ; cf. शतद्रु.

शुद्ध *p. p.* **1** Pure, clean, purified ; अंतःशुद्धस्त्वमपि भविता वर्णमात्रेण कृष्णः Me. 49. **2** Holy, undefiled, chaste, innocent ; अन्वमीयत शुद्धेति शांतेन वपुषैव सा R. 15. 77, 14. 14. **3** White, bright. **4** Stainless, spotless. **5** Innocent, simple, guileless. **6** Honest, upright. **7** Correct, faultless, right. **8** Cleared, acquitted. **9** Mere, only. **10** Simple, pure, unmixed ; (opp. मिश्र). **11** Unequalled. **12** Authorized. **13** Whetted, sharpened. **14** Not, nasal. **–द्धः** An epithet of *S*iva. **–द्धं** **1** Anything pure. **2** The pure spirit. **3** Rock-salt. **4** Black pepper. **–Comp.** **–अंतः** a king's female apartments, harem, seraglio ; शुद्धांतदुर्लभमिदं वपुराश्रमवासिनो यदि जनस्य *S*. 1. 17 ; Ku. 6. 52. °**चारिन्** *m.* an attendant in the harem, a chamberlain ; U. 1. °**पालकः,-रक्षकः** a guard of the harem. **–आत्मन्** *a.* pure-minded, honest. **–ओदनः** (**शुद्धोदनः**) N. of the father of the celebrated Buddha. °**सुतः** N. of Buddha. **–चैतन्यं** pure intelligence **–जंघः** an ass. **–धी,–भाव,–मति** *a.* pure-minded, guileless, honest.

शुद्धिः *f.* **1** Purity, cleanness. **2** Brightness, lustre ; मुक्तागुणशुद्धयोपि (चंद्रपादाः) R. 16. 18. **3** Sanctity, holiness ; तीर्थाभिषेकजां शुद्धिमादधाना महीक्षितः R. 1. 85. **4** Purification, expiation, atonement, expiatory act ; शरीरत्यागमात्रेण शुद्धिलाभममन्यत R. 12. 10. **5** A purificatory or expiatory rite. **6** Paying off or clearing (of expenses). **7** Retaliation, requital. **8** Acquittal, innocence (established by trial). **9** Truth, accuracy, correctness. **10** Rectification, correction. **11** Subtraction. **12** N. of Durgâ **–Comp.** **–पत्रं** **1** a list of errata or corrigenda. **2** a certificate of purification by penance or atonement.

शुध् 4 P. (शुध्यति, शुद्ध) **1** To become pure or purified ; (fig. also) ; मृत्तोयैः शुध्यते शोध्यं नदी वेगेन शुध्यति । अद्भिर्गात्राणि शुध्यंति मनः सत्येन शुध्यति Ms. 5.108-9 **2** To be auspicious, favourable or eligible ; तिथिरिव तावन्न शुध्यति Mu. 5. **3** To be made clear, have the doubts removed ; न शुध्यति मेऽतरात्मा Mk. 8. **4** To be defrayed or cleared; व्ययः शुध्यति Pt. 5. *–Caus.* (शोधयति-ते) **1** To purify, cleanse, wash off. **2** To clear, pay off (as a debt). –WITH –परि,-वि,-सं to be purified ; R. 12. 104; Ms. 5. 64.

शुन् 6 P. (शुनति) To go, move.

शुनःशेपः (**फः**) N. of a Vedic sage, son of Ajîgarta. [In the Aitareya Brahma*n*a it is related that king Harischandra, being childless, made a vow that on obtaining a son he would sacrifice him to the god Varu*n*a. A son was born who has named Rohita, but the king put off the fulfilment of the vow under various pretexts. At last Rohita purchased for one hundred cows *S*unahsepha, the middle son of Ajîgarta, as a substitute for himself to be offered to Varu*n*a. But the boy praised Vish*n*u. Indra and other deities and escaped death. He was then adopted by Visvamitra in his own family and called by the name Devarata].

शुनकः **1** N. of a sage, descendant of Bhrigu. **2** A dog.

शुनाशी(सी)रः **1** An epithet of Indra. **2** An owl.

शुनिः A dog.

शुनी *f.* A female dog, a bitch.

शुनीरः A number of female dogs.

शुंध् 1. 10 U. (शुंधति-ते, शुंधयति-ते) **1** To be purified or cleansed. **2** To cleanse, purify.

शुंध्युः Air, wind.

शुभ् 1 A. (शोभते) **1** To shine, be splendid, look beautiful or handsome ; सुष्टु शोभसे एतेन विनयमाहात्म्येन U. 1; R. 8. 6. **2** To appear to advantage ; सुखं हि दुःखान्यनुभूय शोभते Mk. 1. 10. **3** To suit, become, befit (with gen.); रामभद्र इत्येवोपचारः शोभते तातपारिजनस्य U. 1. *-Caus.* (शोभयति-ते). To decorate, adorn, grace. –WITH परि, -वि to shine, look splendid.

शुभ *a.* **1** Shining, bright. **2** Beautiful, handsome ; जंघे शुभे सृष्टवतस्तदीये Ku. 1. 35. **3** Auspicious, lucky, happy, fortunate. **4** Eminent, good, virtuous ; Pt. 1. 358. **–भं** **1** Auspiciousness, welfare, good fortune, happiness, good, prosperity ; Mâl. 1. 23. **2** An ornament. **3** Water. **4** A kind of fragrant wood. **–Comp.** **–अक्षः** an epithet of *S*iva. **–अंग** *a.* handsome. (**–गी**) **1** a handsome woman. **2** N. of Rati, wife of Cupid. **–अपांगा** a beautiful woman. **–अशुभं** weal and woe, good and evil. **–आचार** *a.* virtuous. **–आनना** a handsome woman. **–इतर** *a.* **1** evil, bad. **2** inauspicious. **–उदर्क** *a.* having a happy end. **–कर** *a.* auspicious, propitious. **–कर्मन्** *n.* a virtuous act. **–गंधकं** gum-myrrh. **–ग्रहः** an auspicious planet. **–द्रुः** the sacred fig-tree. **–दंती** a woman with good teeth. **–लग्नः –ग्नं** a lucky or auspicious moment. **–वार्ता** good news. **–वासनः** perfume for the mouth. **–शंसिन्** *a.* presaging good, indicative of auspiciousness ; R. 3. 14. **–स्थली** **1** a hall in which sacrifices are performed. **2** an auspicious place.

शुभंयु *a.* Auspicious, lucky, fortunate, blessed ; अधिकं शुशुभे शुभंयुना द्वितयेन द्वयमेव संगतं R. 8. 6.

शुभंकर *a.* **1** Auspicious. **2** Promoting happiness.

शुभंभावुक *a.* Decorated, ornamented, bright.

शुभा **1** Lustre, light. **2** Beauty. **3** Desire. **4** Yellow pigment. **5** The *S*âmi tree. **6** An assembly of gods. **7** Dûrvâ grass. **8** The Priyangu creeper.

शुभ्र *a.* **1** Shining, bright, radiant. **2** White ; पश्यति पित्तोपहतः शशिशुभ्रं शंखमपि पीतं K. P. 10 ; R. 2. 69. **–भ्रः** **1** The white colour. **2** Sandal (said to be *n.*). **–भ्रं** **1** Silver. **2** Talc. **3** Rock-salt. **4** Green vitriol. **–Comp.** **–अंशुः, -करः** **1** the moon. **2** camphor. **–रश्मिः** the moon.

शुभ्रा **1** The Ganges. **2** A crystal. **3** Bamboo-manna.

शुभ्रिः An epithet of Brahman.

शुंभ् 1 P. (शुंभति) **1** To shine. **2** To speak. **3** To hurt, injure.

शुंभः N. of a demon killed by Durgâ. **–Comp.** **–घातिनी, -मर्दिनी** an epithet of Durgâ.

शु(शू)र् 4 A. (शूर्यते) **1** To hurt, kill. **2** To make firm or steady, stop.

शुल्क् 10 U. (शुल्कयति ते) **1** To gain. **2** To pay, give. **3** To create. **4** To tell, narrate. **5** To leave, forsake, abandon.

शुल्कः, –ल्कं **1** A toll, tax, customs, duty ; particularly levied at ferries, passes, roads &c. ; कः सुधीः संत्यजेद्भांडं शुल्कस्यैवातिसाध्वसात् H. 3.125; Ms. 8. 159;

Y. 2. 47. **2** Gain, profit. **3** Money advanced to ratify a bargain. **4** Purchase-price (of a girl); money given to the parents of a bride; पीडितो दुहितृशुल्कसंस्थया R. 11. 47 ; न कन्यायाः पिता विद्वान् गृह्णीयाच्छुल्कमण्वपि Ms. 3. 51, 8. 204, 9. 93, 98. **5** A nuptial present. **6** Marriage settlement or dowry. **7** Present given by the bridegroom to his bride. **-Comp.** -ग्राहक, -ग्राहिन् *a.* toll-collector. -दः **1** the giver of a nuptial present. **2** an affianced suitor. -शाला, -स्थानं a toll-station, custom-house.

शुल्लं **1** A cord, rope, spring. **2** Copper.

शुल्व् (ल्व्): 10 U. (शुल्व-ल्ब-यति-ते) **1** To give, bestow. **2** To send away, dismiss. **3** To measure.

शुल्वं (ल्बं) **1** A rope, string. **2** Copper. **3** A sacrificial rite or act. **4** The proximity of water, a place near it. **5** A rule, law, an institute. -ल्बा, -ल्बी See above.

शुश्रू *f.* A mother.

शुश्रूषक *a.* Attentive, obedient. -कः A servant, an attendant.

शुश्रूषणं-णा **1** Desire to hear. **2** Service, attendance. **3** Obedience, dutifulness.

शुश्रूषा **1** Desire to hear; अत एव शुश्रूषा मां मुखरयति Mu. 3. **2** Service, attendance. **3** Dutifulness, obedience. **4** Reverence. **5** Telling, saying.

शुश्रूषु *a.* **1** Desirous to hear. **2** Desirous of serving or attending. **3** Obedient, attentive.

शुष् 4 P. (शुष्यति, शुष्क) **1** To be dried, become dry or parched up; तृषा शुष्यत्यास्ये पिबति सलिलं स्वादु सुरभि Bh. 3. 92. **2** To be withered. -*Caus.* (शोषयति-ते) **1** To dry up, wither, parch. **2** To emaciate. -WITH उद्, -परि **1** to be dried up, dry up; Bk. 10. 41; Bg. 1. 29. **2** to pine, decay, wither. -वि, -सं to be dried up.

शुषः, शुषी **1** Drying, drying up. **2** A hole in the ground.

शुषिः *f.* **1** Drying up. **2** A hole. **3** The hollow in the fang of a snake.

शुषिर *a.* Full of holes, perforated. -रः **1** Fire. **2** A rat or mouse. -रं **1** A hole. **2** The atmosphere. **3** A wind-instrument.

शुषिरा **1** A river. **2** A sort of perfume.

शुषिलः Air, wind.

शुष्क *p. p.* **1** Dry, dried up; शाखायां शुष्कं करिष्यामि Mk. 8. **2** Parched up, sear. **3** Shrivelled, shrunk up, emaciated. **4** Feigned, pretended, mock; कामिनः स्म कुरुते करभोरूर्हारि शुष्करुदितं च सुखेऽपि Si. 10. 69. **5** Empty, vain, useless, unproductive; M. 2. **6** Groundless. causeless. **7** Offensive, harsh; तस्मै नाकुशलं ब्रूयान्न शुष्कां गिरमीरयेत् Ms. 11. 35. **-Comp.** -अंग *a.* emaciated. (-गी) a lizard. -अन्नं rice in the husk. -कलहः **1** a vain or groundless quarrel. **2** a mock quarrel; Mu. 3. -वैरं groundless enmity. -व्रण a healed wound, scar.

शुष्कलः, -लं **1** Dried flesh. **2** Flesh in general.

शुष्मः **1** The sun. **2** Fire. **3** Air, wind. **4** A bird. -ष्मं **1** Prowess, strength. **2** Light, lustre.

शुष्मन् *m.* Fire; Si. 14. 22. -*n.* **1** Strength, prowess. **2** Light, lustre.

शूकः -कं **1** The awn of barley &c., beard. **2** A bristle; वृंतं च खलु शूकैः Bv. 1. 24. **3** Point, tip, sharp end. **4** Tenderness, compassion. **5** A kind of poisonous insect. **-Comp.** -कीटः, -कीटकः a kind of insect or worm covered with bristles. -धान्यं any awned grain, (as barley). -पिंडिः-डी, -शिंबा, -शिंबिका, -शिंबी cowach (कपिकच्छु).

शूककः **1** A kind of grain. **2** Tenderness, compassion.

शूकरः A hog; गच्छ शूकर भद्रं ते वद सिंहो मया हतः। पंडिता एव जानंति सिंहशूकरयोर्बलम् Subhâsh. **-Comp.** -इष्टः a kind of grass (मुस्ता).

शूकलः A restive horse.

शूद्रः A man of the fourth or the last of the four principal tribes of the Hindus; (he is said to have been born from the feet of *Purusha*; पद्भ्यां शूद्रो अजायत Rv. 10. 90. 12, or of Brahman; Ms. 1. 87, and his principal business was to serve the three higher castes; cf. Ms. 1. 91). -Comp. -आह्निकं the daily ceremonies of observances of a Sûdra. -उदकं water polluted by the touch of a Sûdra. -कृत्यं, -धर्मः the duties of a Sûdra. -प्रियः an onion. -प्रेष्यः a man of any of the three higher castes who has become a servant to a Sûdra. -भूयिष्ठ *a.* consisting mostly of Sûdras. -याजकः one who conducts a sacrifice for a Sûdra. -वर्गः the Sûdra or servile class. -सेवनं serving a Sûdra, being the servant of a Sûdra.

शूद्रकः N. of a king, the reputed author of the Mrichchhakaṭika.

शूद्रा A woman of the Sûdra tribe. -Comp. -भार्यः one who has Sûdra woman for his wife. -वेदनं marrying a Sûdra woman. -सुतः the son of a Sûdra woman (the father being of any caste).

शूद्राणी, शूद्री The wife of a Sûdra.

शून *p. p.* **1** Swollen. **2** Increased, grown, prospered.

शूना **1** The soft palate, uvula. **2** A slaughter-house in general. **3** Anything (such as a piece of household furniture), whereby life is likely to be destroyed; (these are five; a fire-place, a grindstone, a broom, a mortar, and a waterpot; पंच शूना गृहस्थस्य चुल्ली पेषण्युपस्करः। कंडनी चोदकुंभश्च बध्यते यास्तु वाहयन् Ms. 3. 68.

शून्य *a.* **1** Empty, void. **2** Vacant (applied also to the heart, glances &c.), absent, listless; गमनम स शून्य दृष्टिः Mâl. 1. 17; see शून्यहृदय below. **3** Non existent. **4** Lonely, desolate, secluded, deserted; शून्येषु शूरा न के K. P. 7; Bk. 6. 9; U. 3. 38; Mâl. 9. 20. **5** Dejected, downcast, dispirited; शून्या जगाम भवनाभिमुखी कथंचित् Ku. 3. 75; Ki. 17. 39. **6** Utterly devoid or deprived of, without, wanting in (with instr. or in comp.); अंगुलीयकशून्या मे अंगुलिः S. 5; दया°, ज्ञान° &c. **7** Indifferent. **8** Guileless. **9** Non-sensical, unmeaning; Si. 11. 4. **10** Bare, naked. -न्यं **1** A vacuum, void, blank. **2** The sky, space atmosphere. **3** A cipher, dot. **4** Non-entity, (absolute) non-existence; दूषणशून्यबिंदवः N. 1. 21. **-Comp.** -मध्यः a hollow reed. -मनस्, -मनस्क *a.* absent-minded, listless. -मुख, -वदन *a.* with a blank face, with a downcast countenance. -वादः the doctrine of the non-existence of anything, the doctrine of a Buddhist sect. -वादिन् *m.* **1** an atheist. **2** a Budhist. -हृदय *a.* **1** absent-minded; V. 2; S. 4. **2** open-hearted, unsuspecting.

शून्या **1** A hollow reed. **2** A barren woman.

शूर् 10 U. (शूरयति-ते) **1** To act the hero, be powerful. **2** To make vigorous exertions.

शूर *a.* Brave, heroic, valiant, mighty; शून्येषु शूरा न के K. P. 7. -रः **1** A hero, warrior, valiant man. **2** A lion. **3** A boar. **4** The sun. **5** The Sâla tree. **6** N. of a Yâdava, the grandfather of Krishṇa. **-Comp.** -कीटः a contemptible warrior; Mv. 6. 32. -मानं arrogance, vaunting. -सेन *m.* pl. N. of the country about Mathurâ or the inhabitants of that country; R. 6. 45.

शूरणः A kind of esculent root.

शूरंमन्य *a.* One who fancies himself to be a hero.

शूर्पः-र्पं A winnowing-basket. -र्पः A measure of two Droṇas. **-Comp.** -कर्णः an elephant. -णखा-खी (for नखा) 'having finger-nails like winnowingbaskets.', N. of a sister of Râvaṇa. [She was attracted by the beauty of *Rama*, and solicited him to marry her. But he said that as he had already got a wife she had better go to Lakshmana and try him. But he too rejected her and back, she came to Rama. This circumstance excited Sita's laughter, and the revengeful demoness, feeling herself grossly insulted, assumed a hideous form and threatened to eat her up. But Lakshmana cut off her ears and nose, and thus doubly deformed her; see R. 12. 32-40]. –वातः wind produced by shaking a winnowing basket. –श्रुतिः an elephant.

शूर्पी 1 A small winnowing-basket or fan. 2 N. of Sûrpaṇakhâ.

शूर्मः –शूर्मिः *m.f.*, शूर्मिका, शूर्मी 1 An iron-image. 2 An anvil.

शूल् 1 P. (शूलति) 1 To be ill. 2 To make a loud noise. 3 To make ill, disorder.

शूलः –लं 1 A sharp or pointed weapon, pike, dart, spear, lance. 2 The trident of Siva. 3 An iron-spit (for roasting meat upon); शूले संस्कृतं शूल्यम् cf. अयः शूल. 4 A stake for im paling criminals; (बिभ्रत्) स्कंधेन शूलं हृदयेन शोकं Mk. 10. 21, Ku. 5. 73. 5 Any acute or sharp pain. 6 Colic. 7 Gout, rheumatism. 8 Death. 9 A banner, an ensign. (शूलाकृ ' to roast on an iron-spit '). –Comp. –अग्रं the point of a pike. –ग्रंथिः *f.* a kind of Dûrvâ grass. –घातनं iron-filings. –घ्न *a.* sedative, anodyne. –धन्वन्, –धर, –धारिन्, –धृक्, –पाणि, –भृत् *m.* epithets of Siva; अधिगतधवलिम्नः शूलपाणेरभिख्यां Si. 4. 65; R. 2. 38. –शत्रुः the castor-oil plant. –स्थ *a.* impaled. –हंत्री a kind of barley. –हस्तः a lancer.

शूलकः A restive horse.

शूला 1 A stake for impaling criminals. 2 A harlot.

शूलाकृतं Roasted meat.

शूलिक *a.* 1 Having a spike. 2 Roasted on a spit. –कः A hare. –कं Roasted meat.

शूलिन् *a.* 1 Armed with a spear; धुर्जयो लवणः शूली R. 15. 5. 2 Suffering from colic. –*m.* 1 A spearman. 2 A hare. 3 N. of Siva; कुर्वन्संध्याबलिपटहतां शूलिनः श्लाघनीयां Me. 34; Ku. 3. 57.

शूलिनः The (Indian) fig-tree.

शूल्य *a.* 1 Roasted on a spit; S. 2. 2 Deserving impalement. –ल्यं Roasted meat.

शूष् 1 P. (शूषति) 1 To produce, beget. 2 To bring forth.

शृकालः A jackal; see शृगाल below.

शृगालः 1 A jackal. 2 A cheat, rogue, swindler. 3 A coward. 4 An ill-natured man, one using harsh words. 5 N. of Krishṇa. –Comp. –केलिः a kind of jujube. –जंबुः –बूः *f* a kind of cucumber. –योनिः birth in a future life as a jackal. –रूपः an epithet of Siva.

शृगालिका, शृगाली 1 A female jackal. 2 A fox. 3 Flight, retreat.

शृंखलः-ला-लं 1 An iron-chain, fetter. 2 A chain, fetter in general (fig. also); Bk. 9. 90; लीलाकटाक्षमालाशृंखलाभिः Dk.; संसारवासनाबद्धशृंखला Git. 3. 3 A chain for tying the feet of an elephant; स्तंबेरमा हस्तशृंखलकर्षिणस्ते R. 5. 72; Ki. 7. 31. 4 A chain or belt worn round the waist. 5 A measuring chain. 6 A chain, series, succession. –Comp. –यमकं a variety of *Yamaka*; see Ki. 15. 42.

शृंखलकः 1 A chain. 2 A camel in general.

शृंखलित *a.* Chained, fettered, bound.

शृंगं 1 A horn; वन्यैरिदानीं महिषैस्तदंभः शृंगाहतं क्रोशति दीर्घिकाणां R. 16. 13; गाहंतां महिषा निपानसलिलं शृंगैर्मुहुस्ताडितं *S.* 2. 6. 2 The top or summit of a mountain; अद्रेः शृंगं हरति पवनः किं स्विदित्युन्मुखीभिः Me. 14, 52; Ki. 15. 42; R. 13. 26. 3 The top of a building, turret. 4 Elevation, height. 5 Lordship, sovereignty, supremacy; eminence; शृंगं स दृप्तविनयाधिकृतः परेषामत्युच्छ्रितं न ममृषे न तु दीर्घमायुः R. 9. 62 (where the word means a ' horn ' also). 6 A cusp or horn of the moon. 7 Any peak, point or projection in general. 8 A horn (of a buffalo &c.) used for blowing. 9 A syringe; वर्णोदकैः काचनशृंगमुक्तैः R. 16. 70. 10 Excess of love, rising of desire. 11 A mark, sign. 12 A lotus. –Comp. –अंतरं the space or interval between the horns (of a cow &c.). –उच्चयः a lofty summit. –जः an arrow. (–जं) aloe-wood. –प्रहारिन् *a.* butting. –प्रियः an epithet of Siva. –मोहिन् *m.* the Champaka tree. –वेरं 1 N. of a town on the Ganges near the modern Mirzâpura; U. 1. 21. 2 ginger.

शृंगकः-कं 1 A horn. 2 A horn of the moon. 3 Any pointed thing. 4 A syringe; Ratn. 1.

शृंगवत् *a.* Peaked. –*m.* A mountain.

शृंगाटः, शृंगाटकः 1 N. of a mountain. 2 N. of a plant. –टं, –कं A place where four roads meet.

शृंगारः 1 The sentiment of love or sexual passion, the erotic sentiment (the first of the eight or nine sentiments in poetical compositions; it is of two kinds :—संभोगशृंगार and विप्रलंभशृंगार q. q. v. v.); शृंगारः सखि मूर्तिमानिव मधौ मुग्धो हरिः क्रीडति Git. 1; (it is thus defined:—पुंसः स्त्रियां स्त्रियाः पुंसि संभोगं प्रति या स्पृहा । स शृंगार इति ख्यातः क्रीडारत्यादिकारकः ॥ see S. D. 210 also). 2 Love, passion, sexual love; V. 1. 9. 3 A dress suited to amorous interviews, an elegant dress. 4 Coition, sexual union. 5 Marks made with red-lead on the body of an elephant. 6 A mark in general. –रं 1 Cloves. 2 Red lead. 3 Undried ginger. 4 A fragrant powder for the dress or body. 5 Agallochum. –Comp. –चेष्टा an amorous or love gesture; R. 6. 12. –भाषितं amorous talk. –भूषणं red lead. –योनिः an epithet of the god of love. –रसः the sentiment of love. –विधिः –वेशः a dress suited to amorous interviews and other purposes. –सहायः an assistant in love-affairs, a confident of the hero of a play; cf. नर्मसचिव.

शृंगारकः Love. –कं Red-lead.

शृंगारित *a.* 1 Impassioned, affected by love. 2 Reddened. 3 Adorned.

शृंगारिन् *a.* Amorous, impassioned, enamoured. –*m.* 1 An impassioned lover. 2 A ruby. 3 An elephant. 4 Dress, decoration. 5 The betal-nut tree. 6 A preparation of betel-leaves and pieces of areca-nut, see तांबूल.

शृंगिः Gold for ornaments. –*f.* The sheat-fish.

शृंगिकं A kind of poison. –का A kind of birch tree.

शृंगिणः A ram.

शृंगिणी 1 A cow. 2 The Arabian jasmine.

शृंगिन् *a.* (णी *f.*) 1 Horned. 2 Crested, peaked. –*m.* 1 A mountain. 2 An elephant. 3 A tree. 4 N. of Siva. 5 N. of one of Siva's attendants; शृंगी भृंगी रिटिस्तुंडी Ak.

शृंगी 1 Gold used for ornaments. 2 A kind of medicinal root. 3 A kind of poison. 4 The sheat-fish. –Comp. –कनकं gold used for ornaments.

शृणिः *f.* A hook for pricking an elephant, a goad.

शृत *p. p.* 1 Cooked. 2 Boiled (water, milk &c.).

शृध् I. 1 A. (but Paras. also in the Second Future, Aorist and Conditional), (शर्धते) To break wind downwards. –II. 1 U. (शर्धति-ते) 1 To moisten, wet. 2 To cut off. –III. 10 U. (शर्धयति-ते) 1 To strive. 2 To take, grasp. 3 To insult (as by breaking wind), mock, ridicule.

शृधुः 1 Intellect (बुद्धि). 2 The anus.

शॄ 9 P. (शृणाति, शीर्ण) 1 To tear asunder, tear to pieces. 2 To hurt, injure. 3 To kill, destroy; Ki. 14. 13. –*pass.* (शीर्यते) 1 To be shattered. 2 To wither, decay, waste away. –With अव to seize away. (–*pass.*) to fade or wither; मूर्ध्नि वा सर्वलोकस्य विशीर्येत वनेऽथवा Bh. 2. 104.

शेखरः 1 A crest, chaplet, tuft, a garland of flowers worn on the head; कपाले वा स्यादथवेंदुशेखरं Ku. 5. 98, 7. 32; नवकरनिकरेण स्पष्टबंधूकसूनस्तबकरचितमेते. शेखरं बिभ्रतीव Si. 11. 46, 4. 50; मगधदेशशेखरीभूता पुष्पपुरी नाम नगरी Dk. 2 A diadem; crown. 3 A peak, summit. 4 The best or most distinguished of a class (at the end of comp.). 5 A kind of *Dhruva* or burden of a song. –रं Cloves.

शेपः, शेपस् *n.*, शेफः-फं, शेफस् *n.* 1 The penis. 2 A testicle. 3 A tail.

शेफालिः-ली, शेफालिका *f.* A kind of plant; शेफालिकाकुसुमगंधमनोहराणि Rs. 3. 14.

शेमुषी Intellect, understanding.

शेल् 1 P. (शेलति) 1 To go, move. 2 To tremble.

शेवः 1 A snake. 2 The penis. 3 Height, elevation. 4 Happiness. 5 Wealth, treasure. -वं 1 The penis. 2 Happiness. -Comp. -धिः 1 a valuable treasure ; विद्या ब्राह्मणमेत्याह शेवधिस्तेऽस्मि रक्ष मां Ms. 2. 114 ; सर्वे कामाः शेवधिर्जीवितं वा स्त्रीणां भर्ता धर्मदाराश्च पुंसां Mâl. 6. 18. 2 one of the 9 treasures of Kubera.

शेवलं 1 The green moss-like substance growing on the surface of water. 2 A kind of plant.

शेवलिनी A river.

शेवालः See शेवल.

शेष *a.* Remaining, rest, all the other ; न्यषेधि शेषोऽप्यनुयायिवर्गः R. 2. 4, 4. 64, 10. 30 ; Me. 30. 87 ; Ms. 3. 47 ; Ku. 2. 44 ; oft. at the end of comp. in this sense ; भक्षितशेष, आलेख्यशेष &c. -षः-षं 1 Remainder, rest, residue ; ऋणशेषोऽग्निशेषश्च व्याधिशेषस्तथैव च । पुनश्च वर्धते यस्मात्तस्माच्छेषं न कारयेत् Chân. 40 ; अध्वशेष Me. 38 ; विभागशेष Ku. 5. 57 ; वाक्यशेषः V. 3 &c. 2 Anything left out or omitted to be said, (इति शेषः is often used by commentators in supplying an ellipsis or words necessary to complete the construction). 3 Escape, salvation, respite. -षः 1 Result, effect. 2 End, termination, conclusion. 3 Death, destruction. 4 N. of a celebrated serpent, said to have one thousand heads, and represented as forming the couch of Vishṇu or as supporting the entire world on his head ; किं शेषस्य भरव्यथा न वपुषि क्ष्मां न क्षिपत्येष यत् Mu. 2. 18, Ku. 3. 13, 6. 68 ; Me. 110, R. 10. 13. 5 N. of Balarâma (supposed to be an incarnation of Sesha). -षा The remains of flowers or other offerings made to an idol and distributed among the worshippers as a holy relique ; *S*. 3, Ku. 3. 22. -षं The remnants of food, remains of an offering. (शेषे is used adverbially in the sense of 1 at last, finally. 2 in other cases). -Comp. -अन्नं leavings of food. -अवस्था old age. -भागः the remainder. -भोजनं the eating of leavings. -रात्रिः the last watch of the night. -शयनः, -शायिन् *m.* epithets of Vishṇu.

शैक्षः 1 A student who studies *S*ikshâ or the science of pronunciation, one who has just entered upon the study of the Vedas. 2 (Hence) A novice, tyro.

शैक्षिकः One skilled in *S*ikshâ.

शैक्ष्यं Learning, proficiency.

शैघ्र्यं Quickness, rapidity.

शैत्यं Cold, coldness, frigidity ; शैत्यं हि यत्सा प्रकृतिर्जलस्य R. 5. 64, Ku. 1. 36.

शैथिल्यं 1 Looseness, laxity. 2 Slackness. 3 Dilatoriness, inattention. 4 Weakness ; cowardice.

शैनेयः N. of Sâtyaki.

शैन्याः (*m.* pl.) The descendants of *S*ini.

शैब्य See शैब्य.

शैलः 1 A mountain, hill ; शैले शैले न माणिक्यं मौक्तिकं न गजे गजे Chân. 55 ; शैलो मलयदर्दुरौ R. 4. 51. 2 A rock, big stone. -लं 1 Borax, benzoin. 2 Bitumen. 3 A kind of collyrium. -Comp. -अंशः N. of a country. -अग्रं the peak of a mountain. -अटः 1 a mountaineer, a barbarian. 2 an attendant on an idol. 3 a lion. 4 a crystal. -अधिपः, -अधिराजः, -इंद्रः -पतिः, -राजः epithets of the Himâlaya. -आढ्यं benzoin. -कटकः the side or slope of a mountain. -गंधं a kind of sandal. -जं 1 benzoin. 2 bitumen. -जा,-तनया,-पुत्री,-सुता epithets of Pârvatî; अवाप्तः प्रागल्भ्यं परिणतरुचः शैलतनये K. P. 10 ; Ku. 3. 68. -धन्वन् *m.* an epithet of *S*iva. -धरः an epithet of Krishṇa. -निर्यासः benzoin. -पत्रः the Bilva tree. -भित्ति *f.* an instrument for cutting stones, a stone-cutter's chisel. -रंध्रं a cave, cavern. -शिबिरं the ocean. -सार *a.* as strong as a mountain, firm as a rock; Ki. 10. 14.

शैलकं 1 Benzoin. 2 Bitumen.

शैलादिः N. of Nandin, *S*iva's attendant.

शैलालिन् *m.* An actor, a dancer.

शैलिक्यः A hypocrite, an impostor, cheat.

शैली 1 A short explanation of a grammatical aphorism. 2 A mode of expression or interpretation ; प्रायेणाचार्याणामियं शैली यत्स्वाभिप्रायमपि परोपदेशमिव वर्णयंति Kull. on Ms. 1. 4. 3 Behaviour, manner of acting, conduct, course.

शैलूषः 1 An actor, a dancer ; आः शैलूषापसद Ve. 1 ; एते पुरुषाः सर्वमेव शैलूषजनं व्याहरंति *ibid.* ; अवाप्य शैलूष इवैष भूमिकां *Si.* 1. 69. 2 A musician, leader of a band. 3 One who beats time at a concert. 4 A rogue. 5 The *Bilva* tree.

शैलूषिकः One who follows the profession of an actor.

शैलेय *a.* (यी *f.*) 1 Mountainous. 2 Produced from rocks. 3 Mountain-like, hard, stony. -यः 1 A lion. 2 A bee -यं 1 Benzoin ; शैलेयगंधीनि शिलातलानि R. 6. 51 ; Ku. 1. 55. 2 Fragrant resin. 3 Rock salt.

शैल्य *a.* (ली *f.*) Stony. -ल्यं Rockiness, hardness.

शैव *a.* (वी *f.*) Relating to the god *Siva*. -वः 1 N. of one of the three principal Hindu sects. 2 A member of the *S*aiva sect. -वं N. of one of the eighteen Purâṇas.

शैवलः A kind of aquatic plant, moss; सरसिजमनुविद्धं शैवलेनापि रम्यं *S*. 1. 20. -लं A kind of fragrant wood.

शैवलिनी A river.

शैवाल See शैवल.

शैब्यः 1 N. of one of the four horses of Krishṇa. 2 N. of a king and warrior in the Pâṇḍava army. 3 A horse (in general).

शैशवं Childhood, infancy (period under sixteen.); शैशवात्प्रभृति पोषितां प्रियां U. 1. 45 ; शैशवेऽभ्यस्तविद्यानां R. 1. 8.

शैशिर *a.* (री *f.*) Belonging to the cold or dewy season. -रः A black kind of the Châtaka bird.

शैयोपाध्यायिका Instruction or tuition of youth.

शो 4 P. (श्यति, शात or शित, *pass.* शायते; *caus.* शाययति ; *desid.* शिशासति) 1 To sharpen, whet. 2 To make thin, attenuate. -WITH नि to sharpen.

शोकः Sorrow, grief, distress, affliction, lamentation, wailing, deep anguish ; श्लोकत्वमापद्यत यस्य शोकः R. 14. 70 ; Bg. 1. 6. -Comp. -अग्निः, -अनलः the fire of grief. -अपनोदः removal of grief. -अभिभूत, -आकुल, -आविष्ट, -उपहत, -विह्वल *a.* afflicted or agonized by grief. -चर्चा indulgence in grief. -नाशः the Asoka tree. -परायण, -लालस *a.* engrossed in grief, wholly given up to grief. -विकल *a.* overwhelmed with grief. -स्थानं any cause of sorrow.

शोचनं Grief, sorrow, lamentation.

शोचनीय *a.* Lamentable; deplorable, mournful.

शोच्य *a.* 1 To be lamented or mourned, deplorable; pitiable. *S*. 3. 10. 2 Vile, wicked.

शोचिस् *n.* 1 Light, lustre, radiance. 2 A flame. -Comp. -केशः (शोचिष्केशः) an epithet of fire.

शोटीर्यं Valour, heroism.

शोठ *a.* 1 Foolish. 2 Low, wicked. 3 Idle, lazy. -ठः 1 A fool. 2 An idler, a sluggard. 3 A low or wicked man. 4 A rogue, cheat.

शोण् 1 P. (शोणति) 1 To go, move. 2 To become red.

शोण *a.* (णा or णी *f.*) 1 Red, crimson, tinged red ; स्त्यानावनद्धघनशोणितशोणपाणिरुत्तंसयिष्यति कचांस्तव देवि भीमः Ve. 1. 21 ; Mu. 1. 8 ; Ku. 1. 7. 2 Bay, reddish-brown. -णः 1 Crimson, the red colour. 2 Fire. 3 A kind of red sugarcane. 4 A bay horse. 5 N. of a male river, rising in Gondavana and falling into the Ganges near Pâtaliputra q. v. ; प्रत्यग्रहीत्पार्थिववाहिनीं तां भागीरथीं शोण इवोत्तरंगः R. 7. 36. 6 The planet Mars ; cf. लोहित. -णं 1 Blood. 2 Red lead. -Comp -अंबुः N. of a cloud which is said to rise at the destruction of the world. -अश्मन् *m.*, -उपलः 1 a red stone. 2 a ruby. -पद्मं a red lotus. -रत्नं a ruby.

शोणित *a.* **1** Red, purple,, crimson. **-तं 1** Blood ; उपस्थिता शोणितपारणा मे R. 2. 39 ; Ve. 1. 21; Mu. 1. 8. **2** Saffron. **-Comp.** -आह्वयं saffron. -उक्षित *a.* blood stained. -उपलः a ruby. **-चंदनं** red sandal. -प *a.* blood-sucking. **-पुरं** N. of the city of the demon Bâṇa.

शोणिमन् *m.* Redness.

शोथः Swelling, intumescence. **-Comp.** -घ्न, -जित् *a.* removing swellings, discutient. -जिह्वः hog-weed. -रोगः dropsy. -हृत् *a.* discutient. (*-m.*) the marking-nut plant.

शोधः 1 Purification. **2** Correction, rectification. **3** Acquittance, paying off (as of debts). **4** Retaliation, requital.

शोधक *a.* (का or धिका *f.*) **1** Purificatory. **2** Purgative. **3** Corrective. **-कः** A Purifier. **-कं** A kind of earth.

शोधन *a.* (नी *f.*) Purifying, cleansing &c. **-नं 1** Purifying, cleansing. **2** Correction, clearing away errors. **3** Exact determination. **4** Payment, discharge, acquittance. **5** Expiation, atonement. **6** Refining of metals. **7** Retaliation, requital, punishment. **8** Subtraction (in math). **9** Green vitriol. **10** Feces, ordure.

शोधनी A broom.

शोधनकः An officer in a criminal court ; Mk. 9.

शोधित *p. p.* **1** Purified, cleansed. **2** Refined. **3** Filtered. **4** Corrected, rectified. **5** Paid off, discharged. **6** Requited, retaliated.

शोध्य *a.* To be purified, refined, paid off &c. **-ध्यः** An accused person, one who has to clear himself of the charge brought against him.

शोफः Swelling, tumour, intumescence. **-Comp.** -जित्, -हृत् *m.* the marking-nut plant.

शोभन *a.* (नी *f.*) **1** Shining, splendid. **2** Handsome, beautiful, lovely. **3** Good, auspicious, fortunate. **4** Richly decorated. **5** Moral, virtuous. **-नः 1** N. of *S*iva. **2** A planet. **3** A burnt offering for the production of happy results. **-ना 1** Turmeric. **2** A beautiful or virtuous woman ; Ku. 4. 44. **3** A sort of yellow pigment (=गोरोचना q. v.). **-नं 1** Beauty, lustre, brilliance. **2** A lotus.

शोभा 1 Light, lustre, brilliance, radiance. **2** (*a*) Splendour, beauty, elegance, grace, loveliness ; वपुरभिनवमस्याः पुष्यति स्वान शोभां *S.* 1 19 ; Me. 52, 59. (*b*) Natural beauty, grandeur (as of a mountain) ; अद्रिशोभा R. 2. 27. **3** An ornament graceful expression ; शोभैव मदरशुब्धक्षुभिताम्भोधिवर्णना *Si.* 2. 107. **4** Turmeric. **5** A kind of pigment (=गोरोचना q. v.). **-Comp.** -अंजनः N. of a very useful tree.

शोभित *p. p.* **1** Adorned, graced, decorated. **2** Beautiful, lovely.

शोषः 1 Drying up, dryness ; हृदशोषविक्लवा Ku. 4. 39 ; so आस्यशोषः, कंठशोषः &c. **2** Emaciation, withering up ; शरीरशोषः, कुसुमशोषः &c. **3** Pulmonary consumption or consumption in general ; संशोषणाद्रसादीनां शोष इत्याभिधीयते Susr. **-Comp.** -संभवं the root of long pepper.

शोषण *a.* (णी *f.*) **1** Drying up, desiccating. **2** Causing to wither up, emaciating. **-णः** N. of one of the arrows of Cupid. **-णं 1** Drying up, desiccation. **2** Suction, sucking up, absorption. **3** Exhaustion. **4** Emaciation, withering up. **5** Dry ginger.

शोषित *p. p.* **1** Dried up. **2** Emaciated, withered up. **3** Exhausted.

शोषिन् *a.* (णी *f.*) Drying up, withering, emaciating.

शौकं A flock of parrots.

शौक्त *a.* (क्ती *f.*) Acid, acetic.

शौक्तिक *a.* (की *f.*) **1** Relating to a pearl. **2** Acid, acetic.

शौक्तिकेयं, शौक्तेयं A pearl.

शौक्लिकेयः A sort of poison.

शौक्ल्यं Whiteness, clearness.

शौचं 1 Purity, clearness; Pt. 1. 147. **2** Purification from personal defilement caused by voiding excrement, but particularly by the death of a relative. **3** Cleansing, purifying. **4** Voiding of excrement. **5** Uprightness, honesty. **-Comp.**-आचारः,-कर्मन् *n.*, -कल्पः a purificatory rite. **-कूपः** a privy.

शौचेयः A washerman.

शौट् 1 P. (शौटति) To be proud or haughty.

शौटीर *a.* Proud, haughty. **-रः 1** A hero, champion. **2** A proud man. **3** An ascetic.

शौटीर्यं, शौंडर्यं Pride, arrogance, haughtiness.

शौड् 1 P. (शौडति) See शौट्.

शौंड *a.* (डी *f.*) **1** Addicted to drinking, fond of liquor. **2** Excited, intoxicated, drunk &c. (fig.); अनिकृतिनिपुणं ते चेष्टितं मानशौंड Ve. 5. 21 'drunk with pride or very proud'. **3** Skilled in with loc. or in comp.); अक्षशौंड, दानशौंड &c.

शौंडिकः, शौंडिन् *m.* A distiller and seller of spirituous liquors, a vintner. **-की,-नी** A female vintner ; पयोपि शौंडिकीहस्ते वारुणीत्यभिधीयते H. 3. 11.

शौंडिकेयः A demon.

शौंडी Long pepper.

शौंडीर *a.* **1** proud, haughty. **2** Elevated, raised up.

शौद्धोदनिः An epithet of Buddha, son of शुद्धोदन.

शौद्र *a.* (द्री *f.*) Relating to a Sûdra or his tribe. **-द्रः** The son of a man of any of the first three castes by a Sûdra woman ; see Ms. 9. 160.

शौनं Meat kept at a slaughte house.

शौनक N. of a great sage, the reputed author of the *R*igveda Prâtisâkhya and various other Vedic compositions.

शौनिकः 1 A butcher ; छद्मना परिददामि मृत्यवे शौनिको गृहशकुंतिकामिव U. 1. 45 **2** A bird-catcher, hunter. **3** Hunting, chase.

शौभः 1 God, divinity. **2** The betel-nut tree.

शौभांजनः N. of a tree ; see शोभांजन.

शौभिकः 1 A juggler, conjurer. **2** A hunter, fowler; इति चिंतयतो हृदये पिकस्य समधायि शौभिकेन शरः Bv. 1. 114.

शौरसेनी N. of a Prâkrit dialect.

शौरिः 1 N of Vishṇu or Kṛishṇa. **2** Of Balarâma. **3** The planet Saturn.

शौर्यं 1 Prowess, heroism, valour ; शौर्ये वैरिणि वज्रमाशु निपतत्वर्थोऽस्तु नः केवलं Bh. 2. 39; नये च शौर्ये च वसति संपदः Subhâsh. **2** Strength, power, might **3** Representation of war and supernatural events on the stage ; cf. आरभटी.

शौल्कः, शौल्किकः A superintendent of tolls, customs -officer.

शौल्वि(ल्वि)कः A coppersmith.

शौव *a.* (वी *f.*) Relating to dogs, canine. **-वं 1** A pack of dogs. **2** The state or nature of a dog.

शौवन *a.* (नी *f.*) **1** Canine. **2** Having the qualities of a dog. **-नं 1** The nature of a dog. **2** The progeny of a dog.

शौवस्तिक *a.* (की *f.*) Belonging to or lasting till tomorrow, ephemeral.

शौष्कलः 1 A vendor of flesh. **2** A habitual eater of flesh. **-लं** The price of dried meat.

श्चुत् see श्च्युत् below.

श्च्युत् 1 P. (श्च्योतति) **1** To trickle, ooze, flow, exude ; *Si.* 8. 63 ; Ki. 5. 29. **2** To shed, pour out, diffuse, scatter. -With नि to flow, ooze, trickle ; निश्च्योतंते सुतनु कबरीबिंदवो यावदेते Mâl. 8. 2.

श्च्यो(श्चो)तः, श्चो(श्च्यो)तनं Oozing, flowing, exuding.

श्मशानं A cemetery, a burial or burning ground ; राजद्वारे श्मशाने च यस्तिष्ठति स बांधवः Subhâsh. **-Comp.** -अग्निः the fire of a burning ground -आलयः a cemetery. -गोचर *a.* frequenting burning grounds ; Ms. 11. 39. -निवासिन्, -वर्तिन् *m.* a ghost. -भाज्, -वासिन् *m.* epithets of *S*iva. -वेश्मन् *m.* **1** an epithet of *S*iva. **2** a spirit, ghost.-वैराग्यं temporary despondency, momentary renouncement of the world as at the sight of a cemetery. -शूलः-लं an impaling stake in a cemetery ; Ku. 5. 73. -साधनं performance of magical rites in cemetery to acquire control over ghosts.

श्मश्रु *n.* The beard ; ज्योतिष्कणाहतश्मश्रु कंठनालादपातयत् R. 15. 52. **-Comp.** -प्रवृद्धिः the growth of a beard ; R.

13. 71. –मुखी a woman with a beard –वर्धकः a barber.

श्मश्रुल *a.* Having a beard, bearded ; मल्लापवर्जितैस्तेषां शिरोभिः श्मश्रुलैर्महीं (तस्तार) R. 4. 63.

श्मील् 1 P. (श्मीलति) To wink, contract the eyelids, twinkle.

श्मीलनं Winking, twinkling.

श्यान *p. p.* **1** Gone. **2** Coagulated, congealed. **3** Thick, sticky, viscous. **4** Shrunk, dry ; Bh. 2. 44. –नं Smoke.

श्याम *a.* **1** Black, dark-blue, dark-coloured ; प्रत्याख्यातविशेषकं कुरबकं श्यामावदातारुणं M. 3. 5 ; V. 2. 7 ; कुवलयदलश्यामस्निग्धः U. 4. 19; Me. 15, 23. **2** Brown. **3** Dark-green. –मः **1** The black colour. **2** A cloud. **3** The cuckoo. **4** N. of a sacred fig-tree at Allahabad on the bank of the Yamunâ ; अयं च कालिंदीतटे वटः श्यामो नाम U. 1; सोऽयमटः श्याम इति प्रतीतः R. 13. 53. –मं **1** Sea-salt. **2** Black pepper. **–Comp.** –अंग *a.* dark. (–गः) the planet Mercury. –कंठः **1** an epithet of *S*iva (नीलकंठ); a peacock. –कर्णः a horse suitable for a horse-sacrifice. –पत्रः the *tama'la* tree –भास्. –रुचि a glossy black. –सुंदरः an epithet of Krishṇa.

श्यामल *a.* Black, dark-blue, blackish ; निशितश्यामलस्निग्धमुखी शक्तिः Ve. 4; *S*i. 18. 36 ; U. 2. 25. –लः **1** Black colour. **2** Black pepper. **3** A large bee. **4** The sacred fig-tree.

श्यामलिका The indigo plant.

श्यामलिमन् *m.* Blackness, darkness ; श्यामां श्यामलिमानमानयत भोः सांद्रैर्मषीकूर्चकैः Vb. 3. 1.

श्यामा **1** Night, particularly a dark night ; श्यामां श्यामलिमानमानयत भोः सांद्रैर्मषीकूर्चकैः Vb. 3. 1. **2** Shade, shadow. **3** A dark woman. **4** A kind of woman (यौवनमध्यस्था according to Malli. on N. 3. 8, *S*i. 8. 36, Me. 82 ; or शीते सुखोष्णसर्वांगी ग्रीष्मे या सुखशीतला । तप्तकांचनवर्णाभा सा स्त्री श्यामेति कथ्यते according to one commentator on Bk. 5. 18 and 8. 100). **5** A woman who has borne no children. **6** A cow. **7** Turmeric. **8** The female cuckoo. **9** The Priyangu creeper ; M. 2. 7 ; Me. 104. **10** The indigo plant. **11** The holy basil. **12** The seed of the lotus. **13** N. of the Yamunâ. **14** N. of several plants.

श्यामाकः A kind of grain or corn ; (न) श्यामाकमुष्टिपरिवर्धितको जहाति *S*. 4. 13 (Also श्यामक).

श्यामिका **1** Blackness, darkness ; Ku. 5. 21. **2** Impurity, alloy, (of metals &c.) ; हेम्नः संलक्ष्यते ह्यग्नौ विशुद्धिः श्यामिकापि वा R. 1. 10.

श्यामित *a.* Blackened, darkened.

श्यालः A wife's brother, brother-in-law.

श्यालकः **1** A wife's brother. **2** A wretched brother-in-law.

श्यालकी, श्यालिका, श्याली A wife's sister.

श्याव *a.* (वा or वी *f.*) **1** Darkbrown, dark, dusty. **2** Bay, brown. –वः The brown colour. **–Comp.** –तैलः the mango tree.

श्येत *a.* (ता or नी *f.*) White. –तः The white colour.

श्येनः **1** The white colour. **2** Whiteness. **3** A hawk, falcon. **4** Violence. **–Comp.** –करणं, –करणिका **1** burning on a separate funeral pile. **2** a hawk-like, *i. e.* rash and desperate act. –चित्, जीविन् *m.* a falconer.

श्यै 1 A. (श्यायते, श्यान, शीत or शीन) **1** To go, move. **2** To be congealed or coagulated. **3** To dry up, wither. –With आ to become dry ; R. 17. 37; see आश्यान also.

श्यैनंपाता Hawking, hunting, chase.

श्योणाकः, श्योनाकः N. of a tree.

श्रंक् 1 A (श्रंकते) To go, creep.

श्रंग् 1 P. (श्रंगति) To go, move, creep.

श्रण् 1 P., 10 U. (श्रणति, श्राणयति,-ते) To give, give away, bestow (usually with वि) ; R. 5. 1.

श्रत् *ind.* A prefix used with the root धा ; see under धा.

श्रथ् (श्रथति, श्रथ्नाति) To hurt, injure, kill. –II. 1 P., 10 U. (श्रथति, श्राथयति-ते) **1** To hurt, kill. **2** To untie, loosen, liberate, release. –III. 10 U. (श्रथयति-ते) **1** To make efforts, be occupied or busy. **2** To be weak or infirm. **3** To be glad.

श्रथनं **1** Killing, destruction. **2** Untying, loosening, release. **3** Effort, exertion. **4** Tying, binding.

श्रद्धा **1** Trust, faith, belief, confidence. **2** Belief in divine revelation, religious faith ; श्रद्धा वित्तं विधिश्चेति त्रितयं तत्समागतं *S*. 7. 29, R. 2. 16 ; Bg. 6. 37 ; 17. 3. **3** Sedateness, composure of mind. **4** Intimacy, familiarity. **5** Respect, reverence. **6** Strong or vehement desire ; तथापि वैचित्र्यरहस्यलुब्धाः श्रद्धां विधास्यंति सचेतसोऽत्र Vikr. 1. 13, M. 6. 18. **7** The longing of a pregnant woman.

श्रद्धालु *a.* **1** Believing, full of faith. **2** Desirous, longing or wishing for (anything). –लुः *f.* A pregnant woman longing for anything.

श्रंथ् I. 1 A. (श्रंथते) **1** To be weak. **2** To be loose or relaxed. **3** To loosen, relax. –II. 9 P. (श्रथ्नाति) **1** To loosen, liberate, release. **2** To delight repeatedly.

श्रंथः **1** Loosening, liberating. **2** Looseness. **3** N. of Vishṇu.

श्रंथनं **1** Loosening, untying. **2** Hurting, killing, destroying. **3** Tying, binding.

श्रपण –णा Causing to boil, boiling.

श्रपित *p. p.* Boiled or caused to be boiled. –ता Rice-gruel.

श्रम् 4 P. (श्राम्यति, श्रांत) **1** To exert oneself, take pains, toil, labour. **2** To perform austerities, mortify the body (by acts of penance) ; कियच्चिरं श्राम्यसि गौरि Ku. 5. 50. **3** To be wearied or fatigued, be exhausted ; रतिश्रांता शेते रजनिरमणी गाढमुरसि K. P. 10 ; *S*i. 14. 38 ; Bk. 14. 110. **4** To be afflicted or distressed ; यो वृंदानि त्वरयति पथि श्राम्यतां प्रोषितानां Me. 99. –*Caus.* (श्र-श्रा-मयति-ते) To cause to be fatigued &c. –With परि to be fatigued very much ; *S*. 1. –वि **1** to take rest, repose, stop ; Ku. 3. 9. **2** to cease, come to an end ; see विश्रांत also. (–*Caus.*) **1** to give rest to, rest ; R. 1. 54. **2** to cause to alight or settle on ; R. 4. 85.

श्रमः **1** Toil, labour, exertion, effort ; अलं महीपाल तव श्रमेण R. 2. 34 ; जानाति हि पुनः सम्यक् कविरेव कवेः श्रमं Subhâsh, R. 16. 75 ; Ms. 9. 208. **2** Weariness, fatigue, exhaustion ; विनयंते स्म तद्योधा मधुभिर्विजयश्रमं R. 4. 65, 67, Me. 17, 52; Ki. 5. 28. **3** Affliction, distress. **4** Penance, austerity, mortification of the body ; दिवं यदि प्रार्थयसे वृथा श्रमः Ku. 5. 45. **5** Exercise ; especially military exercise, drill. **6** Hard study. **–Comp.** –अंबु *n.* –जलं perspiration, sweat. –कर्षित *a.* worn out by fatigue. –साध्य *a.* to be accomplished by dint of labour.

श्रमण *a.* (णा–णी *f.*) **1** Labouring, toiling. **2** Low, base, vile. –णः **1** An ascetic, a devotee, religious mendicant in general. **2** A Buddhist ascetic. –णा–णी **1** A female devotee or mendicant. **2** A lovely woman. **3** A woman of low caste. **4** Bengal madder. **5** The spikenard.

श्रंभ् 1 A. (श्रंभते, श्रब्ध) **1** To be careless or inattentive, be negligent. **2** To err. –With वि to confide, place confidence in ; see विश्रब्ध.

श्रयः, श्रयणं Refuge, shelter, protection, asylum.

श्रवः **1** Hearing ; as in सुखश्रव. **2** The ear. **3** The hypotenuse of a triangle.

श्रवणः -णं **1** The ear ; ध्वनति मधुपसमूहे श्रवणमपिदधाति Gît. 5. **2** The hypotenuse of a triangle. –णः–णा N. of a lunar mansion containing three stars. –णं **1** The act of hearing ; श्रवणसुभगं Me. 11. **2** Study. **3** Fame, glory. **4** That which is heard or revealed, the Veda ; इति श्रवणात् 'because of such a Vedic text'. **5** Wealth. **–Comp.** –इन्द्रियं the sense of hearing, the ear. –उदरं the hollow of the outer ear. –गोचर *a.* within the range of hearing. (–रः) ear-shot ; as in श्रवणगोचरे तिष्ठ 'be within ear-shot'. –पथः, –विषयः the reach or range of the ear ; वृत्तांतेन श्रवणविषयप्रापिणा

R. 14. 87. -पालिः -ली *f.* the tip of the ear. -सुभग *a.* pleasing to the ear.

श्रवस् *n.* **1** The ear. **2** Fame, glory. **3** Wealth. **4** Hymn.

श्रवस्यं Fame, glory, renown.

श्रवाय्यः-य्यः An animal fit for sacrifice.

श्रविष्ठा 1 N. of a lunar asterism, also called *Dhanishtha'*. **2** The asterism called श्रवणा. **-Comp.** -जः the planet Mercury.

श्रा 2 P. (श्राति, श्राण or शृत, *caus.* श्रपयाति-ते) To cook, boil, dress, mature, ripen.

श्राण *a.* **1** Cooked, dressed, boiled. **2** Wet, moist.

श्राणा Rice-gruel.

श्राद्ध *a.* Faithful, believing. **-द्धं 1** A funeral rite or ceremony performed in honour of the departed spirits of dead relatives; श्रद्धया दीयते यस्माचस्माच्छ्राद्धं निगद्यते; it is of three kinds:—नित्य, नैमित्तिक and काम्य. **2** An obsequial oblation, a gift or offering at a *S*râddha. **-Comp.** **-कर्मन्** *n.*, -क्रिया a funeral ceremony. **-कृत्** *m.* the performer of a funeral rite. **-दः** the offerer of a *S*râddha or funeral oblation. **-दिनः -नं** the anniversary of the death of a relative in whose honoura *S*râddha is performed. **-देवः**, -देवता **1** a deity presiding over funeral rites. **2** an epithet of Yama. **3** a Visvadeva q. v. **4** a pitṛi or progenitor. **-भुज्**, **-भोक्तृ** *m.* a deceased ancestor.

श्राद्धिक *a.* (की *f.*) Relating to a *S*râddha. **-कः** The recipient of an obsequial offering. **-कं** A present given at a *S*râddha.

श्राद्धीय *a.* Relating to a *S*râddha.

श्रांत *p. p.* **1** Wearied, tired, fatigued, exhausted. **2** Calmed, tranquil. **-तः** An ascetic.

श्रांतिः *f.* Fatigue, exhaustion, weariness.

श्रामः 1 A month. **2** Time. **3** A temporary shed.

श्रायः Shelter, protection, refuge, asylum.

श्रावः Hearing, listening.

श्रावकः 1 A hearer. **2** A pupil disciple; श्रावकावस्थायां Mâl. 10. ' in their pupilage, *in statu pupilari* '. **3** A class of Buddhist saints or votaries. **4** A Buddhist votary in general. **5** A heretic. **6** A crow.

श्रावण *a.* (णी *f.*) **1** Relating to the ear. **2** Born under the asterism *S*ravaṇa. **-णः 1** N. of a lunar month; (corresponding to July-August). **2** A heretic. **3** An impostor. **4** N. of a Vaisya ascetic unwittingly shot dead by king Dasaratha who was in consequence cursed by his old parents that he would die of broken heart separated from his sons.

श्रावणिक *a.* Relating to the month *S*râvaṇa. **-कः** the month called *S*râvaṇa.

श्रावणी 1 The day of full moon in *S*râvaṇa. **2** N. of an annual ceremony performed on this day when the sacred thread is put on anew.

श्रावस्तिः -स्ती *f.* N. of a city north of the Ganges said to have been founded by king *S*râvasta.

श्रावित *a.* Told, narrated, related.

श्राव्य *a.* **1** To be heard (opp. दृश्य). **2** Audible, distinct.

श्रि 1 U. (श्रयति-ते, श्रित; *caus.* श्रिपयति-ते; *desid.* शिश्रयिषति ते, शिश्रइशति-ते) **1** To go to, approach, resort to, have recourse to, approach for protection; यं देशं श्रयते तमेव कुरुते बाहुप्रतापार्जितं H. 1. 171; R. 3. 70; 19. 1. **2** To go or attain to, reach, undergo, assume (as a state); परीता रक्षोभिः श्रयति विवशा कामपि दशां Bv. 1. 83; द्विपेंद्रभावं कलभः श्रयेन्निव R. 3. 32. **3** To cling to, lean or rest on, depend on; U. 1. 33. **4** To dwell in, inhabit. **5** To honour, serve, worship. **6** To use, employ. **7** To devote oneself to, be attached to. -WITH अधि **1** to dwell in. **2** to mount, ascend. -आ **1** to resort or betake oneself to, have recourse to; V. 5. 17; Bk. 14. 111. **2** to follow; R. 4. 35. **3** to seek refuge with, dwell in, inhabit; R. 13. 7; Pt. 1. 51. **4** to depend on; Ms. 3 77. **5** to go through, experience, undergo, assume; एको रसः करुण एव निमित्तभेदाद्भिन्नः पृथक् पृथगिवाश्रयते विवर्तान् U. 3. 47. **6** to stick or adhere to **7** to choose, prefer. **8** to help, assist. -उद् to lift up, raise, elevate. -उपा to have recourse to; Bg. 14. 2; U. 1. 37. -सं **1** to have recourse to, resort to, fly to for refuge or succour. **2** to rest on, dependent on; U. 6. 12; Mâl. 1. 24. **3** to attain, obtain. **4** to approach for sexual union. **5** to serve.

श्रित *p. p.* **1** Gone to, approached, approached for refuge or protection. **2** Clung to, resting or sitting on. **3** United or joined with, connected with. **4** Protected. **5** Honoured, served. **6** Subservient, auxiliary. **7** Covered with, overspread. **8** Contained. **9** Assembled, collected. **10** Having, possessing.

श्रितिः *f.* Resort, recourse, approach.

श्रियंमन्य *a.* **1** Thinking oneself worthy. **2** Proud.

श्रियापतिः an epithet of *S*iva.

श्रिष् 1 P. (श्रेषति) To burn.

श्री 9 U. (श्रीणाति, श्रीणीते) To cook, dress, boil, prepare.

श्री *f.* **1** Wealth, riches, affluence, prosperity, plenty; अनिर्वेदः श्रियो मूलं Râm; साहसे श्रीः प्रतिवसति Mk. 4; 'fortune favours the brave'; Ms. 9. 300. **2** Royalty, majesty, royal wealth; Ki. 1. 1. **3** Dignity, high position, state; श्रीलक्षण Ku. 7. 46 ' the marks or insignia of greatness or dignity'. **4** Beauty, grace, splendour, lustre; (मुखं) कमलश्रियं दधौ Ku. 5. 21, 7. 32; R. 3. 8; Ki. 1. 75. **5** Colour, aspect; Ku. 2. 2. **6** The goddess of wealth, Lakshmî, the wife of Vishṇu; आसीदियं दशरथस्य गृहे यथा श्रीः U. 4. 6; *S*. 3. 14; *S*i. 1. 1. **7** Any virtue or excellence. **8** Decoration. **9** Intellect, understanding. **10** Superhuman power. **11** The three objects of human existence taken collectively (धर्म, अर्थ and काम). **12** The Sarala tree. **13** The Bilva tree. **14** Cloves. **15** A lotus. (The word श्री is often used as an honorific prefix to the names of deities and eminent persons; श्रीकृष्णः, श्रीरामः, श्रीवाल्मीकिः, श्रीजयदेवः; also celebrated works, generally of a sacred character; श्रीभागवत, श्रीरामायण &c.; it is also used as an auspicious sign at the commencement of letters, manuscripts &c.; Mâgha has used this word in the last stanza of each canto of his *S*isupâlavadha, as Bhâravi has used लक्ष्मी). **-Comp.** **-आह्वं** a lotus. **-ईशः** an epithet of Vishṇu. **-कंठः 1** an epithet of *S*iva. **2** of the poet Bhavabhûti; श्रीकंठपदलांछनः U. 1. °सखः an epithet of Kubera. **-करः** an epithet of Vishṇu. (-रं) the red lotus. **-करणं** a pen. **-कांतः** an epithet of Vishṇu. **-कारिन्** *m.* a kind of antelope. **-खंडः-डं** sandal-wood; श्रीखंडविलेपनं सुखयति H. 1. 97. **-गदितं** a kind of minor drama. **-गर्भः 1** an epithet of Vishṇu. **2** a sword. **-ग्रहः** a trough or place for watering birds. **-घनं** sour curds. (**-नः**) Budhhist saint. **-चक्रं 1** the circle of the earth, the globe. **2** a wheel of Indra's car. **-जः** an epithet of Kâma. **-दः** an epithet of Kubera. **-दयितः- धरः** epithets of Vishṇu. **-नगरं** N. of a city. **-नंदनः** an epithet of Râma. **-निकेतनः**, **-निवासः** epithets of Vishṇu. **-पतिः 1** an epithet of Vishṇu; *S*i. 13. 69. **2** a king, sovereign. **-पथः** a main road, high-way. **-पर्णं** a lotus. **-पर्वतः** N. of a mountain; Mâl. 1. **-पिष्टः** turpentine. **-पुष्पं** cloves. **-फलः** the *Bilva* tree. (**-लं**) the *Bilva* fruit. **-फला**, **-फली 1** the indigo plant. **2** emblic myrobalan. **-भ्रातृ** *m.* **1** the moon. **2** a horse. **-मस्तकः** garlic. **-मुद्रा** a particular mark on the forehead by the Vaishṇavas. **-मूर्तिः** *f.* **1** an idol of Vishṇu or Lakshmî. **2** any idol. **-युक्त**, -युत *a.* **1** fortunate, happy. **2** wealthy, prosperous (often used as an honorific prefix to the names of men). **-रंगः** an epithet of Vishṇu

–रसः 1 turpentine. 2 resin. –वत्सः 1 an epithet of Vishṇu. 2 a mark or curl of hair on the breast of Vishṇu प्रभानुलिप्तश्रीवत्सं लक्ष्मीविभ्रमदर्पणं R. 10. 10. °अंकः °धा-,रिन्, °भृत्, °लक्ष्मन्, °लांछन *m.* epithets of Vishṇu; Ku. 7. 43. –वत्सकिन् *m.* a horse having a curl of hair on his breast. –वरः, –वल्लभः epithets of Vishṇu. –वल्लभः a favourite of fortune, a happy or fortunate person. –वासः 1 an epithet of Vishṇu. 2 of *S*iva. 3 a lotus. 4 turpentine. –वासस् *m.* turpentine. –वृक्षः 1 the *Bilva* tree. 2 the Asvattha or sacred fig-tree. 3 a curl of hair on the breast and forehead of a horse. –वेष्टः 1 turpentine. 2 resin. –संज्ञं cloves –सहोदरः the moon. –सूक्तं N. of a Vedic hymn. –हरिः an epithet of Vishṇu. –हस्तिनी the sun-flower.

श्रीमत् *a.* 1 Wealthy, rich. 2 Happy, fortunate, prosperous, thriving. 3 Beautiful, pleasing ; Ki. 1. 1. 4 Famous, celebrated, glorious, dig nified ; (the word is often used as a respectful affix to celebrated or revered names of persons and things). –*m.* 1 An epithet of Vishṇu. 2 Of Kubera. 3 Of *S*iva. 4 The *Tilaka* tree. 5 The Asvattha tree.

श्रील *a.* 1 Rich, wealthy. 2 Fortunate, prosperous. 3 Beautiful. 4 Famous, celebrated.

श्रु I. 1 P. (श्रवति) To go, move; cf. स्रु. –II. 5. P (शृणोति, श्रुत) 1 To hear, listen to, give ear to ; शृणु मे सावशेषं वचः V. 2 ; रुतानि चाश्रोषत षट्पदानां Bk. 2. 10 ; संदेशं मे तदनु जलद श्रोष्यसि श्रोत्रपेयं Me. 13. 2 To learn, study ; द्वादशवर्षैर्व्याकरणं श्रूयते Pt. 1. 3 To be attentive, to obey ; (इतिश्रूयते ' it is so heard ', *i. e.* is enjoined in the scriptures, such is the sacred precept).–*Caus.* (श्रावयति-ते) To cause to hear, communicate, tell, relate. –*Desid* (शुश्रूषते) 1 To wish to hear. 2 To be attentive, or obedient, obey ; Pt. 4. 78. 3 To serve, wait or attend upon ; शुश्रूषस्व गुरून् *S.* 4. 17 ; Ku. 1. 59 ; Ms. 2. 44. –WITH अनु 1 to hear ; Ms. 9. 100 ; तयथानुश्रूयंत Pt. 1. 2 to hand down as by sacred tradition. –अभि to hear, listen to. –आ 1 to hear. 2 to promise (with dat. of person) ; Y. 2. 196 ; cf. P. I. 4. 40. –उप 1 to hear. 2 to learn, ascertain ; केशिना हृतामुर्वशीं नारदादुपश्रुत्य गंधर्वसेना समादिष्टा V. 1. –परि to hear. –प्रति to promise (with dat. of person to whom the promise is made) ; तस्मै प्रतिश्रुत्य रघुप्रवीरस्तदीप्सितं R. 14. 29, 2. 56; 3. 67 ; 15. 4. –वि to hear (usually in p. p. q. v.). –सं to hear, listen to संशृणोति न चोक्तानि Bk. 5. 19 ; 6. 5 ; (but Atm. when used intransitively; हिताम्न यः संशृणुते स किं प्रभुः Ki. 1. 5.

श्रुघ्निका Natron.

श्रुत *p. p.* 1 Heard, listened to. 2 Reported, heard of. 3 Learnt, ascertained, understood. 4 Well-known, famous, celebrated, renowned ; R. 3. 40; 14. 61. 5 Named, called. –तं 1 The object of hearing. 2 That which was heard by revelation ; *i. e.* the Veda, holy learning, sacred knowledge ; श्रुतप्रकाशं R. 5. 2. 3 Learning in general (विद्या); श्रोत्रं श्रुतेनैव न कुंडलेन (विभाति). Bh. 2. 71, R. 3. 21, 5. 22 ; Pt. 2. 147 ; 4. 61. –Comp. –अध्ययनं study of the Vedas. –अन्वित *a.* conversant with the Vedas. –अर्थः a fact verbally or orally communicated. –कीर्ति *a.* famous, renowned. (–*m.*) 1 a generous man. 2 a divine sage. (–*f.*) N. of the wife of *S*atrughna. –देवी N. of Sarasvatî. –धर *a.* remembering what is heard, retentive.

श्रुतवत् *a.* Knowing the Veda, proficient in sacred knowledge or learning in general ; R. 9. 74.

श्रुतिः *f.* 1 Hearing ; चंद्रस्य ग्रहणमिति श्रुतेः Mu. 1. 7 ; R. 1. 27. 2 The ear ; श्रुतिसुखभ्रमरस्वनगीतयः R. 9. 35 ; *S.* 1. 1 ; Ve. 3. 23. 3 Report, rumour, news, oral intelligence. 4 A sound in general. 5 The Veda (known by revelation, opp. स्मृति ; see under वेद). 6 A Vedic or sacred text ; इति श्रुतेः or इति श्रुतिः ' so says a sacred text '. 7 Vedic or sacred knowledge, holy learning. 8 (In music) A division of the octavo, a quarter tone or interval ; *S*i. 1. 10, 11. 1 ; (see Malli. *ad loc.*). 9. The constellation *S*ravaṇa. –Comp. –अनुप्रासः a kind of alliteration ; see K. P. 9. –उक्त, –उदित *a.* enjoined by the Vedas. –कटः 1 a snake. 2 penance, expiation. –कटु *a.* harsh to hear. (–टुः) a harsh or unmelodious sound, regarded as a fault of composition. –चोदनं –ना a scriptural injunction, Vedic precept. –जीविका a law-book or code of laws. –द्वैधं disagreement or contradiction of Vedas or Vedic precepts. –धर *a.* hearing. –निदर्शनं evidence of the Vedas. –पथः the range of the ear ; M. 4. 1. –प्रसादन *a.* grateful to the ear. –प्रामाण्यं authority or sanction of the Vedas. –मंडलं the outer ear. –मूलं 1 the root of the ear ; लापितुं किमपि श्रुतिमूले Gît. 1. 2 Vedic text. –मूलक *a.* founded on the Veda.–विषयः 1 the object of the sense of hearing, *i. e.* sound ; *S.* 1. 1. 2 the reach or range of the ear ; पतत्रयेण श्रुतिविषयमापतितमेव K. 3 the subject-matter of the Veda. 4 any sacred ordinance. –वेधः boring the ear. –स्मृति *f.* (dual) revelation and legal institutes, Veda and law.

श्रुवः 1 A sacrifice. 2 A sacrificial ladle.

श्रुवा A sacrificial ladle ; cf. स्रुवा. –Comp. –वृक्षः the *Vikankata* tree.

श्रेढी A progression (in math). –Comp. –फल the sum of a progression.

श्रेणिः *m. f.*, श्रेणी *f.* 1 A line, series, row ; तरंगभ्रूभंगा क्षुभितविहगश्रेणिरसना Ve. 4. 28 ; न षट्पदश्रेणिभिरेव पंकजं सशैवलासंगमपि प्रकाशते Ku. 5. 9 ; Me. 28, 35. 2 A flock, multitude, group ; U. 4. 3 A guild or company of traders, artisans &c., corporate body. 4 A bucket. –Comp. –धर्माः (*m. pl.*) the customs or trades or guilds.

श्रेणिका A tent.

श्रेयस् *a.* 1 Better, preferable, superior ; वर्धनाद्रक्षणं श्रेयः H. 3. 3, 33. Bg. 3. 35, 2. 5. 2 Best, most excellent. 3 More happy or fortunate. 4 More blessed, dearer (compar. of प्रशस्य q. v.). –*m.* 1 Virtue, righteous deeds, moral or religious merit. 2 Bliss, good fortune, blessing, good, welfare; felicity, a good or auspicious result, पूर्वावधीरितं श्रेयो दुःखं हि परिवर्तते *S.* 7. 13 ; प्रतिबध्नाति हि श्रेयः पूज्यपूजाव्यतिक्रमः R. 1. 79 ; U. 5. 27, 7. 20 ; R. 5. 34. 3 Any good or auspicious occasion ; *S.* 7. 4 Final beatitude, absolution. –Comp.–अर्थिन् *a.*1 seeking happiness, desirous of felicity. 2 wishing well. –कर 1 promoting happiness, favourble. 2 propitious, auspicious. –परिश्रमः striving after absolution.

श्रेष्ठ *a.* 1 Best, most excellent, pre-eminent (with gen. or loc.). 2 Most happy or prosperous. 3 Most beloved, dearest. 4 Oldest, senior. –ष्ठः 1 A Brâhmaṇa. 2 A king. 3 N. of Kubera. 4 N. of Vishṇu. –ष्ठं Cow's milk. –Comp. –आश्रमः 1 the best order of one's religous life, *i. e.* that of a householder. 2 A householder. –वाच् *a.* eloquent.

श्रेष्ठिन् *m.* The head or president of a mercantile or other guild ; निक्षेपे पतिते हर्म्ये श्रेष्ठी स्तौति स्वदेवता Pt. 1. 14.

श्रै 1 P. (श्रायति) 1 To sweat, perspire. 2 To cook, boil.

श्रोण् 1 P. (श्रोणति) 1 To collect, heap. 2 To be collected or accumulated.

श्रोण *a.* Crippled, lame. –णः A kind of disease.

श्रोणा 1 Rice-gruel. 2 The constellation *S*ravaṇa.

श्रोणिः -णी *f.* 1 The hip or loins, the buttocks ; श्रोणीभारादलसगमना Me. 82 ; श्रोणीभारस्त्यजति तनुतां K. P. 10. 2 A road, way. –Comp. –तटः the slope of the hips. –फलकं 1 the broad hips. 2 the buttocks. –बिंबं 1 the round hips; V. 4. 18. 2 a waist-band. –सूत्रं 1 a string worn round the loins. **2** a word-belt.

श्रोतस् *n.* **1** The ear. **2** The trunk of an elephant. **3** An organ of sense. **4** The stream or current (for स्रोतस् q. v.). **-Comp.** -रंध्रं an aperture of the trunk, a nostril ; Me. 42. (also written स्रोतोरंध्र).

श्रोतृ *m.* **1** A hearer. **2** A pupil.

श्रोत्रं **1** The ear ; Bh. 2. 71. **2** Proficiency in the Vedas. **3** The Veda. **-Comp.** -पेय *a.* to be imbibed by the ear, to be attentively heard ; संदेशं मे तदनु जलद श्रोष्यसि श्रोत्रपेयं Me. 13. -मूलं the root of the ear.

श्रोत्रिय *a.* **1** Proficient or versed in the Veda. **2** Teachable, tractable. -यः A learned Brâhmaṇa, one well-versed in sacred learning : जन्मना ब्राह्मणो ज्ञेयः संस्कारैर्द्विज उच्यते । विद्यया याति विप्रत्वं त्रिभिः श्रोत्रिय उच्यते ॥ ; Mâl. 1. 5 ; R. 16. 25. **-Comp.** -स्वं the property of a learned Brâhmaṇa.

श्रौत *a.* (ती *f.*) **1** Relating to the ear. **2** Relating to, founded on, or prescribed by the Veda. -तं **1** Any observance prescribed by the Vedas. **2** Ritual enjoined by the Veda. **3** Preservation or maintenance of the sacred fire. **4** The three sacred fires collectively ; (*i. e.* गार्हपत्य, आहवनीय and दक्षिण). **-Comp.** -कर्मन् *n.* a Vedic rite. -सूत्रं N. of a class of Sûtra works based on the Veda (ascribed to आश्वलायन, सांख्यायन, कात्यायन &c.).

श्रौत्रं **1** The ear. **2** Proficiency in the Vedas.

श्रौषट् *ind.* An exclamation or formula used in making an offering with fire to the gods or departed spirits ; cf. वषट् or वौषट्.

श्लक्ष्ण *a.* **1** Soft, gentle, mild, bland (as words &c.). **2** Smooth, polished ; Si. 3. 46. **3** Small, fine, thin, delicate. **4** Beautiful, charming. **5** Candid, honest, frank.

श्लक्ष्णकं The Areca nut.

श्लंक् 1. A. (श्लंकते) To go, move.

श्लंग् 1 A. (श्लंगते) To go, move.

श्लथ् 10 U. (श्लथयति-ते) **1** To be loose or slackened. **2** To be weak or infirm. **3** To slacken, loosen, relax (fig. also) ; श्लथयितुं क्षणमक्षमतांगना न सहसा सहसा कृतवेपथुः Si. 6. 57 ; परित्राणस्नेहः श्लथयितुमशक्यः खलु यथा G. L. 37. **4** To hurt, kill.

श्लथ *a.* **1** Untied, unfastened. **2** Loose, relaxed, loosened, slipped off; वृंताच्छ्लथं हरति पुष्पमनोकहानां R. 5. 37, 19. 26. **3** Dishevelled (as hair). **-Comp.** -उद्यम *a.* relaxing one's efforts. -लंबिन् *a.* hanging loosely down ; Ku. 5. 47.

श्लाख् 1 P. (श्लाखति) To pervade, penetrate.

श्लाघ् 1 A. (श्लाघते) **1** To praise, extol, commend, applaud ; शिरसा श्लाघते पूर्वं (गुणं) परं (दोषं) कंठे नियाच्छति Suphâsh. यथैव श्लाघ्य ते गंगा पादेन परमेष्ठिनः Ku. 6. 70 (some read श्लाघते for श्लाघ्यते and give it the next sense). **2** To boast of, be proud of ; श्लाघिष्ये केन को बंधूश्चेत्युन्नतिमुन्नतः Bk. 16. 4. **3** To flatter, coax (with dat.) ; गोपी कृष्णाय श्लाघते Sk. ; Bk. 8. 73.

श्लाघनं **1** Praising, eulogizing. **2** Flattering.

श्लाघा **1** Praise, eulogy, commendation ; कर्णजयद्रथयोर्वा कात्र श्लाघा Ve. 2. **2** Self-praise, boast ; हते जरति गांगेये पुरस्कृत्य शिखंडिनं । या श्लाघा पांडुपुत्राणां सैवास्माकं भविष्यति Ve. 2. 4. **3** Flattery. **4** Service. **5** Wish, desire. **-Comp.** -विपर्ययः absence of boasting ; त्यागे श्लाघाविपर्ययः R. 1. 22.

श्लाघित *p. p.* Praised, eulogized, commended.

श्लाघ्य *a.* **1** Praiseworthy, worthy ; U. 4. 9, 13. **2** Respectable, venerable.

श्लिकुः **1** A debauchee, libertine. **2** A slave, dependant. -*n.* The science of astronomy, astrology.

श्लिक्युः **1** A libertine. **2** A servant.

श्लिष् I. 1 P. (श्लेषति) To burn. -II. 4 P. (श्लिष्यति, श्लिष्ट) **1** To embrace ; श्लिष्यति चुंबति जलधरकल्पं हरिरुपगत इति तिमिरमनल्पं Gît. 6. **2** To stick, cling or adhere to. **3** To unite, join. **4** To grasp, take, understand ; N. 3. 69. -With आ, -उप to embrace, clasp. -वि **1** to be separated, to be away from. **2** to burst, fly asunder ; Bk, 14. 67. (-*Caus.*) to separate ; Me. 7. -सं **1** To adhere or cling to. **2** to join, unite. -III. 10 U. (श्लेषयति-ते) To unite, join, connect.

श्लिषा **1** An embrace. **2** Clinging, adherence.

श्लिष्ट *p. p.* **1** Embraced. **2** Clung, adhered to. **3** Resting or leaning on. **4** Involving a pun, susceptible of a double interpretation ; अत्र विषमादयः शब्दाः श्लिष्टाः K. P. 10.

श्लिष्टिः *f.* **1** Embrace. **2** Adherence.

श्लीपदं Swelled leg, elephantiasis. -**Comp.** -प्रभवः the mango tree.

श्लील *a.* **1** Lucky, prosperous, see श्रील. **2** Decent ; cf. अश्लील.

श्लेषः **1** An embrace. **2** Clinging or adhering to. **3** Union. junction, contact; निरंतरश्लेषघनाः K. (where it has the next sense also). **4** Pun, paronomasia, *double entendre*, susceptibility of a word or sentence to yield two or more interpretations (regarded as a figure of speech and very commonly used by poets ; for def. see K. P. Kârikâs 84 and 96) ; अश्लेषि न श्लेषकवेर्भवत्याः श्लोकद्वयार्थः सुधिया मया किं N. 3. 69 ; see शब्दश्लेष also. **-Comp.** -अर्थः a pun, *double entendre*. -भिन्नक *a.*

resting on (lit. having for its basis) a Slesha.

श्लेष्मकः Phlegm.

श्लेष्मण *a.* Phlegmatic.

श्लेष्मन् *m.* Phlegm, the phlegmatic humour. **-Comp.** -अतिसारः dysentery produced by vitiated phlegm. -ओजस् *n.* the phlegmatic humour. -घ्ना, -घ्नी **1** the Arabian jasmine. **2** the hog-weed.

श्लेष्मल *a.* Phlegmatic.

श्लेष्मातः, श्लेष्मातकः A kind of tree.

श्लोक् 1 A. (श्लोकते) **1** To praise or compose in verse, versify. **2** To acquire. **3** To abandon, give up.

श्लोकः **1** Praising in verse, extolling. **2** A hymn or verse of praise ; Ms. 7. 26. **3** Celebrity, fame, renown, name ; as in पुण्यश्लोक q. v. **4** An object of praise. **5** A proverb or saying. **6** A stanza or verse in general ; R. 14 70. **7** A stanza or verse in the Anushṭubh metre.

श्लोण् 1 P. (श्लोणति) To heap together, collect, gather ; cf. श्रोण्.

श्लोणः A lame man, cripple.

श्वंक् 1 A. (श्वंकते) To go, move.

श्वच्, श्वंच् 1 A. (श्वचते, श्वंचते) **1** To go, move. **2** To be opened, gape, be split or cleft.

श्वज् 1 A. (श्वजते) To go, move.

श्वट् 10 U. (श्वटयति-ते) **1** To speak ill; (श्वाटयति only according to some.). **2** (श्वाटयति-ते) (*a*) To go, move. (*b*) To adorn. (*c*) To finish, accomplish ; (only श्वटयति in these senses according to some).

श्वंठ् 10 U. (श्वंठयति) To speak ill.

श्वन् *m.* (Nom. श्वा, श्वानौ, श्वानः ; acc. pl. शुनः, शुनी *f.*) A dog ; श्वा यदि क्रियते राजा स किं नाश्नात्युपानहं Subhâsh. ; Bh. 2. 31 ; Ms. 2. 201. **-Comp.** -क्रीडिन् *m.* a keeper or breeder of sporting dogs. -गणः a pack of hounds. -गणिकः **1** a hunter. **2** a dog-feeder. -धूर्तः a jackal. -नरः a snappish or currish fellow. -निशं-निशा a night on which dogs bark. -पच् *m.*, -पचः **1** a man of a very low and degraded caste, an outcast, a Chânḍâla ; Bv. 4. 23. **2** a dog-feeder. -पदं a dog's foot. -पाकः an outcast, a Chânḍâla ; G. L. 29. -फलं lime or citron. -फल्कः N. of the father of Akrûra. -भीरुः a jackal. -यूथ्यं a pack of dogs -वृत्तिः *f.* **1** the life of a dog (to which survitude is often likened) ; सेवां लाघवकारिणीं कृतधियः स्थाने श्ववृत्तिं विदुः Mu. 3. 14 ; Ms. 4. 6. **2** Servitude, service ; Ms. 4. 4. -व्याघ्रः **1** a beast of prey. **2** a tiger. **3** a leopard. -हन् *m.* a hunter.

श्वभ्र् 10 U. (श्वभ्रयति-ते) **1** To go, move. **2** To pierce, make a hole, bore. **3** To live in misery.

श्वभ्रं A hole, chasm ; V. 1. 18 ; Ki. 14. 33.

श्वयः Swelling, increase.

श्वयथुः Swelling, intumescence.

श्वयीची Sickness, disease.

श्वल् 1 P. (श्वलति) To run, go quickly.

श्वल्क् 10 U. (श्वल्कयति-ते) To tell, narrate.

श्वल्ल् 1 P. (श्वल्लति) To run ; see श्वल्.

श्वशुरः A father-in-law, wife's or husband's father ; Ms. 3. 119.

श्वशुरकः A father-in-law.

श्वशुर्यः 1 A brother-in-law, a wife's or husband's brother. 2 The younger brother of a husband.

श्वश्रूः f. A mother-in-law, a wife's or husband's mother ; R. 14. 13. –Comp. –श्वशुर m. du. the mother and father-in-law.

श्वस् 2 P. (श्वसिति, स्वस्त or श्वसित) 1 To breathe, respire, draw breath ; स कर्मकारभस्त्रेव श्वसन्नपि न जीवति H. 2. 11 ; R. 8. 87. 2 To sign, pant, heave ; श्वसिति विहगवर्गः Rs. 1. 13. 3 To hiss, snort. –*Caus.* (श्वासयति-ते) To cause to breathe or live. –WITH आ 1 to breathe ; Mv. 5. 51. 2 to recover breath, take courage, take heart ; Me. 8. 3 to revive ; Bk. 9. 56. (–*Caus.*) to console, comfort, cheer up. –उद् 1 to breathe, live ; Ve. 5. 15, Ms. 3. 72. 2 to cheer up, revive, take heart ; Ki. 3. 8 ; *S*i. 18. 58. 3 to open, bloom (as a lotus) ; *S*i. 10. 58, 11. 15. 4 to pant, sigh deeply ; Bk. 6. 120; 14. 55. 5 to heave, throb. 6 to be loosened or relaxed. –नि,-निस् to sigh, heave. –वि 1 to confide in, trust, rely on, place confidence in (usually with loc.) ; पुंसि विश्वसिति कुत्र कुमारी N. 5. 110 ; Ku. 5. 15; sometimes with gen. 2 to rest secure, be fearless or confident ; विशश्वसे पक्षिगणैः समंतात् Bk. 2. 25. (–*Caus.*) to cause to believe, to inspire confidence ; Bk. 8. 105. –समा to take courage, take heart, calm or compose oneself. (–*Caus.*) to console, encourage, cheer up.

श्वस् *ind.* 1 Tomorrow ; वरमद्य कपोतो न श्वो मयूरः Subhâsh. 2 Future (at the beginning of comp.). –Comp. –भूत *a.* (श्वोभूत) being tomorrow. –वसीय, -वसीयस् (श्वोवसीय, श्वोवसीयस्) *a.* happy, auspicious, fortunate (–*n.*) happiness, good fortune. –श्रेयस (श्वःश्रेयस) *a.* happy, prosperous. (–सं) 1 happiness, prosperity. 2 an epithet of Brahman or the Supreme Spirit.

श्वसनः 1 Air, wind ; स्वसनसुरभिगंधिः *S*i. 11. 21. 2 N. of a demon killed by Indra. –नं 1 Breath, breathing, respiration ; श्वसनचलितपल्लवाधरोष्ठे Ki. 10. 34 ; Ratn. 2. 4 (where it has sense 1 also) ; *S*i. 9. 52. 2 Sighing ; Ki. 2. 45. –Comp. –अशनः a serpent. –ईश्वरः the Arjuna tree. –उत्सुकः a serpent. –ऊर्मिः *f.* gust of wind.

श्वसित *p. p.* 1 Breathed, sighed. 2 Breathing. –तं 1 Breathing, respiration. 2 Sighing.

श्वस्तन *a.* (नी *f.*), श्वस्त्य *a.* Relating to the morrow, future.

श्वाकर्णः The ear of a dog.

श्वागणिकः A dog-keeper, one living by keeping dogs.

श्वादंतः A dog's tooth.

श्वानः A dog. –Comp. –निद्रा ' a dog's sleep ', a very light sleep. –वैखरी angry or currish snarling.

श्वापद *a.* (दी *f.*) Savage, ferocious. –दः 1 A beast of prey, wild beast. 2 A tiger.

श्वापुच्छः-च्छं A dog's tail.

श्वाविध् *m.* A porcupine.

श्वासः 1 Breathing, breath, respiration, heaving ; अद्यापि स्तनवेपथुं जनयति श्वासः प्रमाणाधिकः *S*. 1. 29 ; Ku. 2. 42. 2 A sigh, panting. 3 Air, wind. 3 Air, wind. 4 Asthma. –Comp. –कासः asthma. –रोधः suspension or obstruction of breath. –हिक्का a kind of hiccough. –हेतिः *f.* sleep.

श्वासिन् *a.* Breathing. –*m.* 1 Air, wind. 2 A breathing animal, living being. 3 One who pronounces (letters) with a hissing sound.

श्वि 1 P. (श्वयति, शून) 1 To grow, increase (fig. also), to swell (as the eye); रुदतोऽशिश्वियच्चक्षुरास्यं हेतोस्तवाश्वयीत् Bk. 6. 19, 31 ; 14. 79, 15. 30. 2 To thrive, prosper. 3 To go, approach, move towards. –WITH उद् 1 to swell, increase, grow ; प्रबलरुदितोच्छूननेत्रं (मुखं) Me. 84. 2 to be proud, be puffed up with pride.

श्वित् 1 A. (श्वेतते) To become white, be white ; व्यतिकरितदिगंताः श्वेतमानैर्यशोभिः Mâl. 2. 9.

श्वित *a.* White.

श्वितिः *f.* Whiteness.

श्वित्य *a.* White.

श्वित्रं 1 White leprosy. 2 A leprous spot (on the skin) ; तदल्पमपि नोपेक्ष्यं काव्ये दुष्टं कथंचन । स्याद्वपुः सुंदरमपि श्वित्रेणैकेन दुर्भगं Kâv. 1. 7.

श्वित्रिन् *a.* (णी *f.*) Leprous. –*m.* A leper.

श्विंद् 1 A. (श्विंदते) To become white.

श्वेत *a.* (श्वेता or श्वेती *f.*) White ; ततः श्वेतैर्हयैर्युक्ते महति स्यंदने स्थितौ Bg. 1. 14. –तः 1 The white colour. 2 A conch-shell. 3 A cowrie. 4 The planet Venus. 5 *S*ukra, the regent of the planet. 6 A white cloud. 7 Cumin seed. 8 N. of a range of mountains ; see कुलाचल or कुलपर्वत. 9 N. of a division of the world. –तं Silver. –Comp. –अंबरः,-वासस् *m.* a class of Jaina ascetics. –इक्षुः a kind of sugarcane. –उदरः an epithet of Kubera. –कमलं, -पद्मं a white lotus. –कुंजरः an epithet of Airâvata, the elephant of Indra. –कुष्ठं white leprosy. –केतुः a Bauddha or Jaina saint. –कोलः a kind of fish (शफर). –गजः,-द्विपः 1 a white elephant. 2 the elephant of Indra. –गरुत् *m.*, –गरुतः a goose. –छदः 1 a goose. 2 a kind of basil. –द्विपः N. of one of the eighteen minor divisions of the known continent. –धातुः 1 a white mineral. 2 chalk. 3 the milk-stone. –धामन् *m.* 1 the moon. 2 camphor. 3 cuttle-fish bone. –नीलः a cloud. –पत्रः a goose. °रथः an epithet of Brahman. –पाटला the white trumpet flower. –पिंगः a lion. –पिंगलः 1 a lion. 2 an epithet of *S*iva. –मरिचं white pepper. –मालः 1 a cloud. 2 smoke. –रक्तः the pink or rosy colour. –रंजनं lead. –रथः the planet Venus. –रोचिस् *m.* the moon. –रोहितः an epithet of Garuḍa. –वल्कलः the glomerous fig-tree. –वाजिन् *m.* 1 the moon. 2 an epithet of Arjuna. –बाहु *m.* an epithet of Indra. –वाहः 1 an epithet Arjuna. 2 of Indra. –वाहनः 1 an epithet of Arjuna. 2 the moon. 3 a marine monster (मकर). –वाहिन् *m.* an epithet of Arjuna. –शुंगः, –शृंगः barley. –हयः 1 a horse of Indra. 2 an epithet of Arjuna. –हस्तिन् *m.* Airâvata, Indra's elephant.

श्वेतकः A cowrie. –कं Silver.

श्वेता 1 A cowrie. 2 Hog weed. 3 White Dûrvâ grass. 4 A crystal. 5 Candied sugar. 6 Bamboo-manna. 7 N. of various plants.

श्वेतौही N. of *S*achi, wife of Indra.

श्वेत्रं White leprosy.

श्वैत्यं 1 Whiteness. 2 White leprosy.

श्वैत्रं, -श्वैत्र्यं White leprosy.

ष.

Many roots which begin with स् are written in the Dhâtupâtha with ष् to show that the स् is changed to ष् after certain prepositions. Such roots will be found under स in their proper places.

ष *a.* Best, excellent. **-षः** 1 Loss, destruction. 2 End. 3 Rest, remainder. 4 Final emancipation.

षट्क *a.* Sixfold. **-कं** An aggregate of six ; मासषट्क, पूर्वषट्क, उत्तरषट्क &c.

षड्धा See षोढा.

षंडः 1 A bull. 2 A eunuch ; (14 or 20 classes of eunuchs are mentioned by different writers). 3 A group, multitude ; collection, heap, quantity (*n.* also in this sense); कलरवमुपगीते षट्पदौघेन धत्तः कुमुदकमलषंडे तुल्यरूपामवस्थां Si. 11. 15 ; cf. खंड also.

षंडकः A eununch.

षंडाली 1 A pond, pool. 2 A wanton or unchaste woman.

षंढः 1 A eunuch ; Y. 1. 215. 2 The neuter gender ; निवेशः शिबिरं षंढे Ak. **-Comp. -तिलः** barren sesamum.

षष् *num. a.* (used in pl.; Nom. षट् gen. षण्णां); Ms. 1. 16, 8. 403.-**Comp. -अक्षीणः** (**षडक्षीणः**) a fish. **-अंगं** (**षडंगं**) 1 six parts of the body taken collectively :—जंघे बाहू शिरो मध्यं षडंगानीदमुच्यते. 2 the six works auxiliary to the Veda ; शिक्षा कल्पो व्याकरणं निरुक्तं छंदसां चितिः । ज्योतिषामयनं चैव षडंगो वेद उच्यते; see वेदांग also. 3 six suspicious things, *i. e.* the six things obtained from a cow :—गोमूत्रं गोमयं क्षीरं सर्पिर्दधि च रोचना । षडंगमेतन् मांगल्यं पठितं सर्वदा गवाम्. **-अंघ्रिः** (**षडंघ्रिः**) a bee. **-अधिक** *a.* (**षडधिक**) exceeded by six ; Mal. 5. 1. **-अभिज्ञः** (**षडभिज्ञः**) a Buddhist deified saint. **-अशीत** *a.* (**षडशीत**) eighty-sixth. **-अशीतिः** *f.* (**षडशीतिः**) eighty-six. **-अहः** (**षडहः**) a period of six days. **-आननः, -वक्त्रः, -वदनः** (**षडाननः, षड्वक्त्रः, षड्वदनः**) epithets of Kârtikeya; षडाननापीतपयोधरासु नेता चमूनामिव कृत्तिकासु R. 14. 22. **-आम्नायः** (**षडाम्नायः**) the six-fold Tantra. **-ऊषणं** (**षडूषणं**) six spices taken collectively ; पंचकोलं स मरिचं षडूषणमुदाहृतम्. **-कर्ण** *a.* (**षट्कर्ण**) heard by six ears ; *i. e.* by a third person other than the speaker and the person spoken to, told to more than one listener (as a counsel, secret &c.) षट्कर्णो भिद्यते मंत्रः Pt. 1. 99. (**-र्णः**) a kind of lute. **-कर्मन्** *n.* (**षट्कर्मन्**) 1 the six acts or duties enjoined on a Brâhmaṇa ; they are:—अध्यापनमध्ययनं यजनं याजनं तथा । दानं प्रतिग्रहश्चैव षट्कर्माण्यग्रजन्मनः Ms. 10. 75. 2 the six acts allowable to a Brâhmaṇa for his subsistence ; उंछं प्रतिग्रहो भिक्षा वाणिज्यं पशुपालनं । कृषिकर्म तथा चेति षट्कर्माण्यग्रजन्मनः ॥. 3 the six acts that may be performed by means of magic ; शांति, वशीकरण, स्तंभन, विद्वेष, उच्चाटन and मारण. 4 the six acts belonging to the practice of Yoga ; धौतिर्वस्ती तथा नेती (नौलिकी) त्राटकस्तथा । कपालभातीः चैतानि षट्कर्माणि समाचरेत्. (**-m.**) a Brâhmaṇa. **-कोण** *a.* (**षट्कोण**) hexangular. (**-णं**) 1 a hexagon. 2 the thunderbolt of Indra. **-गवं** (**षड्गवं**) 1 a team or yoke of six oxen. 2 a yoke of six (sometimes after the names ' of other animals); *e. g.* °हस्ति, °अश्व° six elephants, horses &c.' **-गुण** *a.* (**षड्गुण**) 1 sixfold. 2 having six attributes. (**-णं**) 1 an assemblage of six qualities. 2 the six expendients to be used by a king in foreign politics; see under गुण (21); cf. षाड्गुण्य also. **-ग्रंथि** *a.* (**षड्ग्रंथि**) the root of long pepper. **-ग्रंथिका** (**षड्ग्रंथिका**) zedoary (शटी). **-चक्रं** (**षट्चक्रं**) the six mystical circles of the body. **-चत्वारिंशत्** (**षट्चत्वारिंशत्**) forty-six. **-चरणः** (**षट्चरणः**) 1 a bee. 2 a locust. 3 a louse. **-जः** (**षड्जः**) the fourth (or first according to some) of the seven primary notes of the Indian gamut ; so called because it is derived from the six organs :—नासां कंठमुरस्तालु जिह्वां दंतांश्च संस्पृशन् । षड्जः संजायते (षड्भ्यः संजायते) यस्मात्तस्मात् षड्ज इति स्मृतः ; it is said to resemble the note of peacocks ; षड्जं रौति मयूरस्तु Nârada ; षड्जसंवादिनीः केकाः द्विधा भिन्नाः शिखंडिभिः R. 1. 39. **-त्रिंशत्** *f.* (**षट्त्रिंशत्**) thirty-six ; (**षट्त्रिंश** *a.* thirty-sixth). **-दर्शनं** (**षड्दर्शनं**) the six principal systems of Hindu philosophy; they are:—सांख्य, योग, न्याय, वैशेषिक, मीमांसा and वेदांत. **-दुर्गं** (**षड्दुर्गं**) the six kinds of forts taken collectively; धन्वदुर्गं महीदुर्गं गिरिदुर्गं तथैव च । मनुष्यदुर्गं मृद्दुर्गं वनदुर्गमिति क्रमात्. **-नवतिः** (**षण्णवतिः**) ninety-six. **-पंचाशत्** *f.* (**षट्पंचाशत्**) fifty-six. **-पदः** (**षट्पदः**) 1 a bee ; न पंकजं तद्यदलीनषट्पदं न षट्पदोऽसौ न जुगुंज यः कलं Bk. 2. 19 ; Ku. 5. 9 ; R. 6. 69. 2 a louse. °अतिथिः the mango tree. °आनंदवर्धनः the Asoka or Kinkirâta tree. °ज्य *a.* heving bees for the bow-string (as the bow of Cupid); प्रायश्चापं न वहति भयान्मन्मथः षट्पदज्यं Me. 73. °प्रियः the tree called नागकेशर. **-पदी** (**षट्पदी**) 1 a stanza consisting of six lines 2 a female bee. 3 a louse. **-प्रज्ञः** (**षट्प्रज्ञः**) 1 one who is well acquainted with six subjects; *i. e.* the four *Purushârthas* or objects of human existence, the nature of the world, and the nature of the Supreme Spirit ; धर्मार्थकाममोक्षेषु लोकतत्त्वार्थयोरपि । षट्सु प्रज्ञा तु यस्यासौ षट्प्रज्ञः परिकीर्तितः ॥. 2 a lustful or licentious man. **-बिंदुः** (**षड्बिंदुः**) an epithet of Vishṇu. **-भागः** (**षड्भागः**) a sixth part, one-sixth ; *S.* 2. 13 ; Ms. 7. 131. 8. 33. **-भुज** *a.* (**षड्भुज**) 1 six-armed. 2 six-sided, hexagonal. (**-जः**) a hexagon. (**-जा**) 1 an epithet of Durgâ. 2 the water-melon. **-मासः** (**षण्मासः** &c.) a period of six months. **-मासिक** *a.* (**षण्मासिक**) half-yearly, occurring every six months. **-मुखः** (**षण्मुखः**) an epithet of Kârtikeya ; R. 17. 67. (**-खा**) a water-melon. **-रसं, -रसाः** (*m. pl.*) (**षड्रसं** &c.) the six flavours taken collectively ; see under रस. **-रात्रं** (**षड्रात्रं**) a period of six nights. **-वर्गः** (**षड्वर्गः**) 1 an aggregate of six things. 2 especially, the six enemies of mankind ; (also called षड्रिपु) ; कामः क्रोधस्तथा लोभो मदमोहौ च मत्सरः कृतारिषड्वर्गजयेन Ki. 1. 9 ; व्यजेष्ट षड्वर्गं Bk. 1. 2. **-विंशतिः** *f.* (**षड्विंशतिः**) twenty-six ; **षड्विंश** twenty-sixth. **-विध** (**षड्विध**) *a.* of six kinds, six fold ; R. 4. 26. **-षष्टिः** *f.* (**षट्षष्टिः**) sixty-six. **-सप्ततिः** (**षट्सप्ततिः**) seventy-six.

षष्टिः *f.* Sixty ; Ms. 3. 177 ; Y. 3. 84. °तम sixtieth. **-Comp. -भागः** an epithet of *Siva*. **-मत्तः** an elephant who has reached the age of sixty and is in rut at that time. **-योजनी** *f.* a journey or extent of sixty *Yojanas*. **-संवत्सरः** a period of sixty years. **-हायनः** 1 an elephant (sixty years old). 2 a kind of rice.

षष्ठ *a.* (**-ष्ठी** *f.*) Sixth, the sixth ; षष्ठं तु क्षेत्रजस्यांशं प्रदद्यात्पैतृकाद्धनात् Ms. 9. 164, 7 130 ; षष्ठे भागे V. 2. 1 ; R. 17, 78. **-Comp. -अंशः** 1 sixth part in general ; Y. 3 35. 2 particularly, the sixth part of the produce of fields &c. which the king takes from his subjects as land tax; ऊधस्यमिच्छामि तवोपभोक्तुं षष्ठांशमुर्व्या इव रक्षितायाः R. 2. 66 ; (the different kinds of produce to the sixth part of which a king is entitled are specified in Ms. 7. 131 132). °वृत्तिः a king entitled to the sixth part of the produce) ; षष्ठांशवृत्तेरपि धर्म एषः S. 5. 4. **-अन्नं** the sixth meal. °कालः taking food once in three days, as an expiatory act.

षष्ठी 1 The sixth day of a lunar fortnight. 2 The sixth or genitive case (in gram.). 3 An epithet of Durgâ in the form of Kâtyâyanî, one of the 16 divine mothers. **-Comp. -तत्पुरुषः** the genitive Tatpurusha compound, one in which, when dissolved, the first member usually stands in the genitive case. -पूजनं, -पूजा worship of the goddes षष्ठी performed on the sixth day after a woman's delivery.

षहसाद्धः 1 A peacock. 2 A sacrifice.

षाड् *ind.* A vocative particle.

षाड्कौशिक *a.* (की *f.*) Incased or enveloped in six sheaths.

षाडवः 1 Passion, sentiment. 2 Singing, music. 3 (In music) A *Ra'ga* in which six of the seven primary notes are used ; औडवः पंचभिः प्रोक्तः स्वरैः षड्भिस्तु षाडवः.

षाड्गुण्यं 1 The collection of six qualities. 2 Six expedients to be used by a king, six measures of royal policy ; *Si.* 2. 93, see under गुण also. 3 Multiplication of anythig by six. -Comp. -प्रयोगः employment of the six expedients or meansures of royal policy.

षाण्मातुरः 'Having six mothers,' an epithet of Kârtikeya.

षाण्मासिक *a.* (की *f.*) 1 Six-monthly, half-yearly. 2 Six months ' old ; मौक्तिकानां षाण्मासिकानां Vb. 1. 17.

षाष्ठ (ष्ठी *f.*) Sixth.

षिड्गः 1 A lustful or libidinous man, libertine, lecher. 2 A gallant, an inconsistent lover (विट); षिड्गैरगयत ससंभ्रममिव काचित् *Si.* 5. 34.

षुः Delivery, child-bearing.

षोडश *a.* (शी *f.* Sixteenth ; Ms. 2. 65, 86.

षोडशन् *num. a.* (pl.) Sixteen. -Comp. -अंशु the planet Venus. -अंग *a.* having 16 parts or ingredients. (-गः) a kind of perfume. -अंगुलक *a.* having the breadth of 16 fingers. -अंघ्रिः a crab. -अर्चिस् *m.* the planet Venus. -आवर्तः a conch-shell. -उपचार *m.* pl. the sixteen ways of doing homage to a deity &c. ; they are thus enumerated:—आसनं स्वागतं पाद्यमर्घ्यमाचमनीयकम् । मधुपर्काचमस्नानं वसनाभरणानि च । गंधपुष्पे धूपदीपौ नैवेद्यं वंदनं तथा. -कलाः the sixteen digits of the moon, thus named :—अमृता मानदा पूषा तुष्टिः पुष्टी रतिर्धृतिः । शशिनी चन्द्रिका कांतिर्ज्योत्स्ना श्रीः प्रीतिरेव च । अंगदा च तथा पूर्णामृता षोडश वै कलाः॥. -भुजा a form of Durgâ. -मातृका *f.* pl. the sixteen divine mothers ; they are:—गौरी पद्मा शची मेधा सावित्री विजया जया। देवसेना स्वधा स्वाहा मातरो लोकमातरः । शांतिः पुष्टिर्धृतिस्तुष्टिः कुलदेवात्मदेवताः.

षोडशधा *ind.* In sixteen ways.

षोडशिक *a.* (की *f.* Consisting of sixteen parats, sixteenfold; षोडशिको देवतोपचारः.

षोडशिन् *m.* A modification of the Agnishṭoma sacrifice.

षोढा *ind.* In six ways. -Comp. -न्यासः the six ways of touching the body with mystical texts. -मुखः 'six-faced', N. of Kârtikeya ; द्रोढा जनोर्जनितषोढामुखः समिति षोढा स हाटकगिरेः Asvad. 7.

ष्ठिव् 1.4. P. (ष्ठीवति, ष्ठीव्यति, ष्ठ्यत) 1 To spit, eject saliva from the month. 2 To sputter ; Bk. 12. 18. -WITH नि 1 to eject, emit, send forth ; *S.* 4. 4 ; R, 2. 75 ; Bk. 14. 100, 17. 10. 18. 14 ; Kâv. 1. 95. 2 to eject saliva from the mouth ; Ms. 4. 132; Y. 2. 213.

ष्ठीवनं, ष्ठेवनं 1 Spitting out. 2 Saliva, spittle.

ष्ठ्यत *p. p.* Spit, ejected.

ष्वक्क्, ष्वस्क् 1 A. (ष्वक्कते, ष्वस्कते). To go, move.

स.

स *ind.* A prefix substituted for सह or सम्, सम, तुल्य or सदृश and एक or समान, and compounded with nouns to form adjectives and adverbs in the sense of(*a*)with, together with, along with, accompanied by, having, possessed of ; सपुत्र, सभार्य, सतृष्ण, सधन, सरोष, सकोप, सहरि &c. ; (*b*) similar, like ; सधर्मन् 'of a similar nature' ; so सजाति, सवर्ण ; (*c*) same ; सोदर, सपक्ष, सपिंड, सनाभि &c. -*m.* 1 A snake. 2 Air, wind. 3 A bird. 4 A short name for the musical note षड्ज q. v. 5 N. of *Siva.* 6 Of Vishnu.

संयः A skeleton.

संयत् *f.* A battle, war, fight; यः संयति प्राप्तपिनाकिलीलः R. 6. 72, 7. 39, 18. 20 ; Ki. 1. 19 ; *Si.* 16. 15. -Comp. -वरः a king, prince.

संयत *p. p.* 1 Restrained, curbed, subdued. 2 Tied up, bound together. 3 Fettered. 4 Captive, imprisoned, a prisoner ; R. 3. 20. 5 Ready. 6 Arranged ; see यम् with सं. -Comp. -अंजलि *a.* one who has folded his hands in supplication. -आत्मन् *a.* self-subdued, self-controlled. -आहार *a.* temperate in eating. -उपस्कर *a.* one who has a well-regulated house, whose house-furniture is kpet in good order. -चेतस्, -मनस् *a.* controlled in mind. -प्राण *a.* one whose breath is suppressed. -वाच् *a.* silent, taciturn, one who has held his tongue.

संयत्त 1 *a.* Ready, prepared; Mv. 5. 51. 2 Being on guard.

संयमः 1 Restraint, check, control ; श्रोत्रादीनींद्रियाण्यन्ये संयमाग्निषु जुह्वति Bg. 4. 26, 27. 2 Concentration of mind, a term applied to the last three stages of *Yoga* ; धारणाध्यानसमाधित्रयमेतरंगं संयमपद्वाच्यं Sarva. S., Ku. 2. 59. 3 A religious vow. 4 Religious devotion, practice of penance ; *S.* 4. 19. 5 Humanity, feeling of compassion.

संयमनं 1 Restraining, checking. 2 Drawing in ; *S.* 1. 3 Binding up ; U. 1 ; V. 3. 6. 4 Confinement. 5 A Self-denial, control. 6 A religious vow or obligation. 7 A square of four houses. -नः One who restrains or regulates, a ruler. -नी N. of the city of Yama.

संयमित *p.p.* 1 Restrained. 2 Bound, fettered. 3 Detained.

संयमिन् *a.* One who curbs or restrains, controlling. -*m.* One who controls or subdues his passions, a sage, an ascetic, R. 8. 11 ; Bg, 2. 69.

संयानः A mould. -नं 1 Going along with, accompanying. 2 Travelling, proceeding. 3 Carrying out a dead body.

संयाम See संयम.

संयावः A kind of cake of wheaten flour ; Ms. 5. 7.

संयुक्त *p. p.* 1 Joined, connected, united. 2 Blended, mixed, mingled. 3 Accompanied by. 4 Possessed of, endowed with. 5 Consisting of.

संयुगः 1 Conjunction, union, mixture. 2 Fight, war, battle, contest ; संयुगे सांयुगीनं तमुद्यतं प्रसहेत कः Ku. 2. 57 ; R. 9. 19. -Comp. -गोष्पदं ' a contest in a cow's footstep' ; *i. e.* an insignificant or trifling quarrel ; cf. the English ' a storm in a teapot.

संयुज् *a.* Connected, relating to; *Si.* 14. 55.

संयुत *p. p.* 1 Joined, united together, connected. 2 Endowed or furnished with ; see यु with सं.

संयोगः 1 Conjunction, union, combination, junction, association, intimate union ; संयोगो हि वियोगस्य संसूचयति संभवं Subhâsh. 2 Conjunction (as one of the 24 guṇas of the Vaiseshikas). 3 Addition, annexation. 4 A set; आभरणसंयोगाः Mâl. 6. 5 Alliance between two kings for a common object. 6 (In gram.) A conjunct consonant. 7 (In astr.) The conjunction of two heavenly bodies. 8 An epithet of Siva. -Comp. -पृथक्त्वं severalty of conjunction. -विरुद्धं any eatables causing disease by being mixed.

संयोगिन् a. 1 United, conjoined. 2 Joining.

संयोजनं 1 Union, conjunction. 2 Copulation, sexual union.

संरक्षः Protection, care, preservation.

संरक्षणं 1 Protection, preservation. 2 Charge, custody.

संरक्त p. p. 1 Coloured, red. 2 Impassioned, fired with passion. 3 Angry, irritated, inflamed with anger. 4 Enamoured, charmed. 5 Charming, beautiful.

संरब्ध p. p. 1 Excited, agitated. 2 Inflamed, exasperated, enraged, furious. 3 Augmented. 4 Swelled. 5 Overwhelmed.

संरंभः 1 Beginning. 2 Turbulence, impetuosity, violence ; S. 7. 3 Agitation, excitement, flurry ; Ku. 3. 48. 4 Energy, zeal, ardent desire ; R. 12. 96. 5 Anger, rage, wrath ; प्राणिपातप्रतीकारः संरंभो हि महात्मनां R. 4. 64 ; 12. 36 ; V. 2. 21 ; 4. 28. 6 Pride, arrogance. 7 Swelling with heat and inflammation. -Comp. -परुष a. harsh through rage. -रस a. excessively enraged. -वेगः the impetuosity of anger.

संरंभिन् a. (णी f.) 1 Excited, agitated, flurried ; Si. 2. 67. 2 Angry, furious, enraged. 3 Proud, arrogant.

संरागः 1 Colouring. 2 Passion, affection. 3 Rage, anger.

संराधनं 1 Propitiation, conciliation, pleasing by worship. 2 Accomplishing. 3 Profound or deep meditation.

संरावः 1 Clamour, tumult, uproar. 2 Sound or noise in general.

संरुग्ण p. p. Shattered, broken to pieces.

संरुद्ध p. p. 1 Checked, impeded, opposed. 2 Blocked up, filled up. 3 Blockaded, invested, besieged. 4 Covered over, concealed. 5 Refused, withheld ; see रुध् with सं.

संरूढ p. p. 1 Grown together. 2 Cicatrized, healed ; as in संरूढव्रण. 3 Shot forth, sprouted, budded, germinated ; R. 6. 47. 4 Firmly grown, striking firm root. 5 Bold, confident.

संरोधः 1 Complete obstruction or impediment, hindrance, prevention, check. 2 Blockade, siege. 3 Bond, fetter. 4 Throwing, sending forth.

संरोधनं Obstructing, stopping.

संलक्षणं Marking, distinguishing or characterizing.

संलग्न p. p. 1 Closely attached, stuck together, united with, adhering to. 2 Come to blows or close contest.

संलयः 1 Lying down, sleep. 2 Dissolution. 3 Universal destruction (प्रलय).

संलयनं 1 Adhering or clinging to. 2 Dissolution.

संललित p. p. Fondled, caressed.

संलापः 1 Conversation, chat, discourse. 2 Especially familiar or confidential talk, secret conversation. 3 (In dramas) A kind of dialogue.

संलापकः A kind of minor drama, said to be of a controversial kind ; see S. D. 549.

संलीढ p. p. Licked up, enjoyed,

संलीन p. p. 1 Clung, adhered to. 2 Joined together. 3 Hidden, concealed. 4 Cowering down. 5 Contracted, shrunk. -Comp. -कर्ण a. with the ears hanging down. -मानस a. depressed in mind, in drooping spirits.

संलोडनं Disturbing, confusing.

संवत् ind. 1 A year. 2 Especially a year of the Vikramâditya's era (commencing 56 years before the Christian era).

संवत्सरः 1 A year. 2 A year of Vikramâditya's era. 3 N. of Siva. -Comp. -करः an epithet of Siva. -भ्रमि a. revolving in a year, completing one revolution in a year (said of the sun). -रथः a year's course.

संवदनं 1 Conversing, talking together. 2 Communication of tidings. 3 Examination, consideration. 4 Subduing or overpowering by magic or charms. 5 A charm, an amulet.

संवरः 1 Covering. 2 Comprehension. 3 Compression, contraction. 4 A dam, bridge, causeway. 5 A kind of deer. 6 N. of a demon ; see शंबर. -रं 1 Concealment. 2 Forbearance, self-control. 3 Water. 4 A particular religious observance (practised by Buddhists).

संवरणं 1 Covering, screening. 2 Hiding, concealment ; Mâl. 1. 3 A pretext, disguise ; see संवर also.

संवर्जनं 1 Appropriating to oneself. 2 Consuming, devouring.

संवर्तः 1 Turning towards. 2 Dissolution, destruction. 3 The periodical destruction of the world ; Mv. 6. 26. 4 A cloud. 5 A cloud of a particular class (abounding in water). 6 N. of one of the seven clouds that rise at the dissolution of the world. 7 A year. 8 A collection, multitude.

संवर्तकः 1 A kind of cloud. 2 The fire of destruction, the fire that is to destroy the world at the period of universal destruction ; इतोऽपि वडवानलः सह समस्तसंवर्तकैः Bh. 2. 76. 3 Sub-marine fire. 4 N. of Balarâma.

संवर्तकिन् m. N. of Balarâma.

संवर्तिका 1 The new leaf of a water-lily. 2 The petal near the filament. 3 The flame of a lamp &c. ; (दीपादेः शिखा Tv.).

संवर्धक a. (र्धिका f.) 1 Causing complete growth or prosperity, augmenting. 2 Greeting, welcoming (guests &c.), hospitable.

संवर्धित p. p. 1 Brought up, reared. 2 Increased.

संवलित p. p. 1 Met together, mingled, mixed ; Mâl. 6. 5. 2 Sprinkled with ; Mâl. 4. 9. 3 Connected, associated. 4 Broken ; उदितोपलस्खलनसंवलिताः (ध्वनयः) Ki. 6. 4.

संवल्गित a. Overrun. -तं Sound ; Mâl. 5. 19.

संवसथः A place where people live together, a village, an inhabited place.

संवहः N. of the third of the seven courses or Mârgas of the wind ; see वायु.

संवादः 1 Speaking together, conversation, dialogue, colloquy ; Mv. 1. 12. 2 Discussion, debate. 3 Communication of tidings. 4 Information, news 5 Assent, concurrence. 6 Speaking likeness, agreement, similarity, correspondence ; रूपसंवादाच्च संशयादनया पृष्टः Dk. ; (नादः) चित्ताकर्षी परिचित इव श्रोत्रसंवादमेति Mâl. 5. 20.

संवादिन् a. 1 Speaking, conversing. 2 Like, similar, resembling, corresponding to ; षड्जसंवादिनीः ककाः R. 1. 39 ; अस्मदंगसंवादिन्याकृतिः U. 6.

संवारः 1 Covering, closing up. 2 Contraction of the throat &c. in the pronunciation of letters, obtuse articulation (opp. विवार q. v.). 3 Diminution 4 Protecting, securing. 5 Arranging.

संवासः 1 Dwelling together. 2 Association, company ; Pt. 1. 250. 3 Domestic intercourse. 4 A house, dwelling. 5 An open space for meeting or recreation.

संवाहः 1 Bearing or carrying along. 2 Pressing together. 3 Shampooing, stroking gently. 4 A servant employed to rub and shampoo the body.

संवाहकः A shampooer ; see संवाह (4) above.

संवाहनं, -ना 1 Carrying or bearing a burden. 2 Shampooing, gentle rubbing ; U. 1. 24 ; Mâl. 9. 25.

संविक्तं What is separated or individualized.

संविग्न p. p. 1 Agitated, excited, disturbed, distracted, flurried ; as in संविग्नमानस. 2 Terrified, frightened.

संविज्ञात p. p. Universally known, generally recognised or allowed.

संवित्ति *f.* **1** Knowledge, perception, consciousness, feeling; श्वस्त्वया सुखसंवित्तिः स्मरणीयाऽधुनातनी Ki. 11. 34, 16. 32. **2** Understanding, intellect. **3** Recognition, recollection. **4** Harmony (of feeling), mental reconciliation.

संविद् *f.* **1** Knowledge, understanding, intellect; Ki. 18. 42. **2** Consciousness, perception; Mâl. 6. 13. **3** An agreement, engagement, contract, covenant, promise; R. 7. 31. **4** Assent, consent. **5** An established usage, a prescribed custom. **6** War, battle, fight. **7** A warcry, watch-word. **8** A name, an appellation. **9** A sign, signal. **10** Pleasing, delighting, gratification; *Si*. 16. 47. **11** Sympathy, participation. **12** Meditation. **13** Conversation. **14** Hemp. **–Comp.** **–व्यतिक्रमः** breach of promise, violation of a contract.

संविदा An agreement or promise, covenant.

संविदात *a.* **1** Knowing, intelligent. **2** Harmonious.

संविदित *p. p.* **1** Known, understood. **2** Recognised. **3** Well-known, renowned. **4** Explored. **5** Agreed upon. **6** Advised, admonished; see विद् with सं. **–तं** An agreement.

संविधा **1** Arrangement, preparation, plan; R. 7. 16, 14. 17. **2** Mode of life, means of leading life; R. 1. 94.

संविधानं **1** Arrangement, disposition; Mâl. 6. **2** Performance. **3** Plan, mode. **4** A rite. **5** Arrangement of incidents (in a plot); Mâl. 6.

संविधानकं **1** Arrangement of incidents (in a plot), the plot of a drama &c.; अहो संविधानकं U. 3. **2** A strange act, an unusual occurrence.

संविभागः **1** Partition, dividing. **2** A part, portion, share.

संविभागिन् *m.* A partner, sharer, participator.

संविष्ट *p. p.* **1** Sleeping, lying down; R. 1. 95. **2** Entered together. **3** Seated together. **4** Dressed, clothed.

संवीक्षणं Looking about in all directions, search, looking for anything lost.

संवीत *p. p.* **1** Clothed, dressed. **2** Covered over, coated, overlaid. **3** Adorned. **4** Invested, surrounded, shut in, hemmed. **5** Overwhelmed.

संवृक्त *p. p.* **1** Devoured, consumed. **2** Destroyed.

संवृत *p. p.* **1** Covered, covered up; मुहुरंगुलिसंवृताधरोष्ठं (मुखं) *S*. 3. 26. **2** Hidden, concealed; *S*. 2. 11. **3** Secret. **4** Closed, shut up, secured. **5** Retired, secluded. **6** Contracted, compressed. **7** Confiscated, sequestered. **8** Filled with, full of. **9** Accompanied by; see वृ with सं. **–तं** **1** A secret or retired place, secrecy. **2** A mode of pronunciation. **–Comp.** **–आकार** *a.* one who conceals all outward manifestation of internal feeling, one who gives no clue to his internal thoughts. **–मंत्र** *a.* one who keeps his plans secret; R. 1. 20.

संवृतिः *f.* **1** Covering, covering up. **2** Concealment, suppression, hiding; Ki. 10. 44. **3** Secret purpose, covert design.

संवृत्त *p. p.* **1** Become, happened, occurred. **2** Fulfilled, accomplished. **3** Collected; heaped together. **4** Past, gone. **5** Covered. **6** Furnished with. **–त्तः** N. of Varuṇa.

संवृत्तिः *f.* **1** Becoming, happening, occurrence. **2** Accomplishment. **3** Covering.

संवृद्ध *p. p.* **1** Full-grown, increased, augmented. **2** Grown tall or high, big, large. **3** Prospering, blooming, flourishing.

संवेगः **1** Agitation, flurry, excitement; Mv. 1. 39. **2** Violent speed, impetuosity, vehemence; U. 2. 24; Mâl. 5. 6. **3** Haste, speed. **4** Agonising pain, poignancy.

संवेद्यः Perception, knowledge, consciousness, feeling.

संवेदनं-ना **1** Perception, knowledge. **2** Sensation, feeling, experiencing, suffering; दुःखसंवेदनायैव रामे चैतन्यमर्पितं U. 1. 47. **3** Giving, surrendering; Mu. 1. 23.

संवेशः **1** Sleep, retiring to rest; R. 1. 93. **2** A dream. **3** A seat (chair, stool &c.). **4** Cohabitation, copulation or a particular mode thereof.

संवेशनं Coition, sexual union.

संव्यानं Covering, wrapping. **2** Cloth, vesture, garment. **3** An upper garment; *Si*. 18. 69.

संशप्तकः **1** A warrior sworn never to recede from a contest and kept to prevent the flight of others. **2** A picked warrior. **3** A brother in arms. **4** A conspirator who has taken an oath to kill another.

संशयः **1** Doubt, uncertainty, irresolution, hesitation; मनस्तु मे संशयमेव गाहते Ku. 5. 46; त्वदन्यः संशयस्यास्य छेत्ता न ह्युपपद्यते Bg. 6. 39. **2** Misgiving, suspicion. **3** Doubt or indecision (in Nyâya), one of the 16 categories mentioned in the Nyâya philosophy; एकधार्मिकविरुद्धभावाभावप्रकारकं ज्ञानं संशयः. **4** Danger, peril, risk; न संशयमनारुह्य नरो भद्राणि पश्यति H. 1. 7; याता पुनः संशयमन्यथैव Mâl. 10. 13; Ki. 13. 16, Ve. 6. 1. **5** Possibility. **–Comp.** **–आत्मन्** *a.* doubting, sceptical. **–आपन्न, -उपेत, -स्थ** *a.* doubtful, uncertain, irresolute. **–गत** *a.* fallen into danger; *S*. 6. **–छेदः** solution of a doubt, decision. **–छेदिन्** *a.* clearing all doubt, decisive; *S*. 3.

संशयान, संशयालु *a.* Doubtful, irresolute, uncertain, wavering.

संशरणं Commencement of a combat, attack, charge.

संशित *p. p.* **1** Sharpened, aroused. **2** Sharp, acute. **3** Thoroughly completed, effected, accomplished. **4** Decided, well-ascertained, determined, certain. **–Comp.** **–आत्मन्** *a.* one whose mind is thoroughly matured or disciplined. **–व्रत** *a.* one who has fulfilled his vow.

संशुद्ध *p. p.* **1** Completely purified, pure. **2** Polished, refined. **3** Expiated.

संशुद्धिः *f.* **1** Complete purification; Bg. 15. 1. **2** Cleansing or purifying in general. **3** Correction, rectification. **4** Clearance. **5** Acquittance (of debt).

संशोधनं Purification, clearness &c.

संश्चत् *n.* Trick, jugglery, illusion. *–m.* A juggler.

संश्यान *p. p.* **1** Contracted, shrunk up. **2** Frozen, congealed. **3** Rolled up. **4** Collapsed.

संश्रयः **1** A resting or dwelling place, residence, habitation; परस्परविरोधिन्योरेकसंश्रयदुर्लभं V. 5. 24; R. 6. 41; oft. at the end of comp. in this sense and translated by 'residing with', 'relating or pertaining to', 'with reference to'; ज्ञातिकुलैकसंश्रया *S*. 5. 17; नौसंश्रयः R. 16. 57; मनोरथोऽस्या शशिमौलिसंश्रयः Ku. 5. 60; द्विसंश्रयां प्रीतिमवाप लक्ष्मीः 1. 43; एकार्थसंश्रयमुभयोः प्रयोगं M. 1. **2** Seeking protection or shelter with, fleeing for refuge, forming or seeking alliance, leaguing together for mutual protection; one of the 6 guṇas or expedients in politics; see under गुण also; Ms. 7. 160. **3** Resort, refuge, asylum, protection, shelter; अनपायिनि संश्रयद्रुमे गजभग्ने पतनाय वल्लरी Ku. 4. 31.; Me. 17; Pt. 1. 22.

संश्रवः **1** Hearing attentively. **2** A promise, an agreement, engagement.

संश्रवणं **1** Hearing. **2** The ear.

संश्रित *p. p.* **1** Gone to for refuge. **2** Supported, sheltered.

संश्रुत *p. p.* **1** Promised, agreed to. **2** Well-heard.

संश्लिष्ट *p. p.* **1** Clasped or pressed together, joined, united. **2** Embraced. **3** Related, connected together. **4** Adjoining, lying close or contiguous to. **5** Furnished or endowed with, having.

संश्लेषः **1** Embracing, an embrace. **2** Union, connection, contact.

संश्लेषण-णा **1** Pressing together. **2** Means of binding together.

संसक्त *p. p.* **1** Adhered or stuck together. **2** Adhering or clinging to attached to, sticking close to. 3 Joined or linked together, closely connected ; R. 7. 24. 4 Near, contiguous, adjoining. 5 Confused, mixed, mingled, blended ; मदमुखरमयूरीमुक्तसंसक्तकेकः Mâl 9. 5 ; कलिंदकन्या मथुरां गताऽपि गंगोर्मिसंसक्तजलेव भाति R. 6. 48. ; Mâl. 5. 11. 6 Intent on. 7 Endowed with, possessed of. 8 Fastened, restrained. –Comp. –मनस् *a.* having the mind fixed or attached. –युग *a.* yoked, harnessed ; *Si.* 3. 68.

संसक्तिः *f.* 1 Close adherence, intimate union or junction ; Ki. 7. 27. 2 Close contact, proximity. 3 Intercourse, intimacy, intimate acquaintance ; *Si.* 8. 67. 4 Tying, fastening together. 5 Devotion, addiction (to anything).

संसद् *f.* 1 An assembly, meeting, circle, संसत्सुजाते पुरुषाधिकारे Ki. 3. 51; छत्रसंसदि लब्धकीर्तिः Pt. 1 ; R. 16. 24. 2 A court of justice ; Ms. 8. 52.

संसरणं 1 Going, proceeding, revolution. 2 The world, worldly life, mundane existence ; ग्रीष्मचंडकरमंडलभीष्मज्वालसंसरणतापितमूर्तेः Bv. 4. 6. 3 Birth and rebirth. 4 The unresisted march of troops. 5 The commencement of battle. 6 A highway. 7 A resting place for passengers near the gates of a city.

संसर्गः 1 Commixture, junction, union. 2 Contact, company, asscoiation, society ; संसर्गमुक्तिः खलेषु Bh. 2. 62 ; *S.* 2. 3. 3 Proximity, touch. 4 Intercourse, familiarity. 5 Copulation, sexual union ; Ms. 6. 72. 6 Co-existence, intimate relation. –Comp. –अभावः one of the two main kinds of non-existence, relative non-existence, which is of three kinds :—प्रागभाव antecedent, प्रध्वंसाभाव emergent, and अत्यंताभाव absolute, non-existence. –दोषः the fault or evil consequences resulting from association, especially with bad people.

संसर्गिन् *a.* United, associated with. –*m.* An associate, a companion.

संसर्जनं 1 Commingling. 2 Leaving, abandoning. 3 Discharging, voiding.

संसर्पः 1 Creeping along, gliding or gentle motion. 2 The intercalary month occurring in a year in which there occurs a *Kshaya-ma'sa* (क्षयमास).

संसर्पणं 1 Creeping along. 2 Surprise, unexpected attack, sally.

संसर्पिन् *a.* Creeping along, moving or winding near ; Ku. 7. 81.

संसावः An assembly.

संसारः 1 Course, passage. 2 The course or circuit of worldly life, secular life, mundane existence, the world ; असारः संसारः U. 1 ; Mâl. 5. 30; संसारधन्वभुवि किं सारमासृशासि शंसाधुना शुभमते Asvad. 22 ; or परिवर्तिनि संसारे मृतः को वा न जायते Pt. 1. 27. 3 Transmigration. metempsychosis, succession or births, 4 Worldly illusion. –Comp. –गमनं transmigration. –गुरुः an epithet of the god of love. –मार्गः 1 the course of worldly affairs, worldly life. 2 the vulva. मोक्षः, –मोक्षणं final liberation or emancipation from worldly life.

संसारिन् *a.* (णी *f.*): Mundane, worldly, transmigratory. –*m.* 1 A sentient being, creature. 2 The embodied spirit, individual soul (जीवात्मन्).

संसिद्ध *p. p.* 1 Fully accomplished, perfected. 2 One who has secured final emancipation.

संसिद्धिः *f.* 1 Completion, complete accomplishment or attainment ; स्वनुष्ठितस्य धर्मस्य संसिद्धिर्हरितोषणं Bhâg. ; Ku. 2. 63. 2 Absolution, final beatitude ; संसिद्धिं परमां गताः Bg. 8. 15 ; 3. 20. 3 Nature, natural disposition, state or quality. 4 A passionate or intoxicated woman.

संसूचनं 1 Showing plainly, proving. 2 Informing, telling. 3 Hinting, intimating ; अर्थस्य संसूचनं. 4 Reproaching, acusing.

संसृतिः *f.* 1 Course, current, flow. 2 The worldly life, course of the world. 3 Metempsychosis, transmigration ; किं मां निपातयसि संसृतिगर्तमध्ये Bv. 4. 32 ; *Si.* 14. 63 ; cf. संसार.

संसृष्ट *p. p.* 1 Commingled, mixed or united together, conjoined. 2 Associated or connected together as partners. 3 Composed. 4 Reunited. 5 Involved in. 6 Created. 7 Cleanly dressed.

संसृष्टता, –त्वं 1 Association, union. 2 (In law) Voluntary reunion in pecuniary interest of kinsmen (as of father and son or of brothers after the partition of property).

संसृष्टिः *f.* 1 Combination, union. 2 Association, intercourse, co partnership. 3 Living in one family, see संसृष्टता (2) above. 4 A collection. 5 Collecting, assembling. 6 (In Rhet.) The combination or co-existence of two or more independent figures of speech in one passage ; मिथोऽन पेक्षयैतेषां (शब्दार्थालंकाराणां) स्थितिः संसृष्टिरुच्यते S. D. 756.

संसेकः Sprinkling, watering.

संस्कर्तृ *m.* 1 One who dresses, cooks, prepares &c. ; Ms. 5. 51. 2 One who consecrates, initiates &c. ; U. 7. 13.

संस्कारः 1 Making perfect, refining, polishing ; (मणिः) प्रयुक्तसंस्कार इवाधिकं बभौ R. 3. 18. 2 Refinement, perfection, grammatical purity (as of words) ; Ku. 1. 28 ; (where Malli. renders the word by व्याकरणजन्या शुद्धिः) R. 15. 76. 3 Education, cultivation, training (as of the mind) ; निसर्गसंस्कारविनीत इत्यसौ नृपेण चक्रे युवराजशब्दभाक् R. 3. 35 ; Ku. 7. 20. 4 Making ready, preparation. 5 Cooking, dressing (as of food &c.) 6 Embellishment, decoration, ornament स्वभावसुंदरं वस्तु न संस्कारमपेक्षते Dri. *S.* 49 ; *S.* 7. 23 ; Mu. 2. 10. 7 Consecration, sanctification, hallowing. 8 Impression, form, mould, operation, influence ; यन्नवे भाजने लग्नः संस्कारो नान्यथा भवेत् H. Pr. 8 ; Bh. 3. 84. 9 Idea, notion, conception. 10 Any faculty or capacity. 11 Effect of work, merit of action ; R. 1. 20. 12 The self-reproductive quality, faculty of impression ; one of the 24 qualities or guṇas recognised by the Vaiseshikas ; it is of three kinds:— भावना, वेग and स्थितिस्थापकता q. q. v. v. 13 The faculty of recollection, impression on the memory ; संस्कारमात्रजन्यं ज्ञानं स्मृतिः T. S. 14 A purificatory rite, a sacred rite or ceremony ; संस्कारार्थं शरीरस्य Ms. 2. 66. ; R. 10. 79 ; (Manu mentions 12 such Samskâras ; see Ms. 2.27; some writers increase the number to sixteen). 15 A rite or ceremony in general. 16 Investiture with the sacred thread. 17 Obsequial ceremonies. 18 A polishing stone ; *S.* 6. 6. (where संस्कार may mean 'polishing' also). –Comp. –पूत *a.* 1 purified by sacred rites. 2 purified by refinement or education. –रहित, –वर्जित, –हीन *a.* (a person of one of the three higher castes) over whom the purificatory ceremonies, particularly the thread-ceremony, have not been performed, and who therefore becomes a Vrâtya or outcast ; cf. व्रात्य.

संस्कृत *p. p.* 1 Made perfect, refined, polished, cultivated ; वाण्येका समलंकरोति पुरुषं या संस्कृता धार्यते Bh. 2. 19. 2. Artificially made, highly wrought, carefully or accurately formed, elaborated. 3 Made ready, dressed, prepared, cooked. 4 Consecrated, hallowed. 5 Initiated into worldly life, married. 6 Cleansed, purified. 7 Adorned, decorated. 8 Excellent, best. –तः 1 A word formed regularly according to the rules of grammar, a regular derivative. 2 A man of any one of the first three castes over whom all the purificatory rites have been performed. 3 A learned man. –तं 1 Refined or highly polished speech, the Sanskrit language. 2 A sacred usage. 3 An offering, oblation (mostly Vedic).

संस्क्रिया 1 A purificatory rite. 2 Consecration. 3 Obsequies, a funeral ceremony.

संस्तंभः 1 Support, prop. 2 Confirming, strengthening, fixing. 3 Stop, stay. 4 Stupefaction, paralysis.

संस्तरः 1 A bed, couch, layer ; नवपल्लवसंस्तरेपि ते R. 8. 57 ; नवपल्लवसंस्तरे यथा रचयिष्यामि तनुं विभावसौ Ku. 4. 34. 2 A sacrifice.

संस्तवः 1 Praise, eulogium. 2 Acquaintance, intimacy, familiarity; गुणाः प्रियत्वेऽधिकृता न संस्तवः Ki. 4. 25 ; नवैर्गुणैः संप्रति संस्तवस्थिरं तिरोहितं प्रेम घनागमश्रियः 4. 22 ; Si. 7. 31.

संस्तावः 1 Praise, celebration. 2 Hymning in chorus. 3 The place which Brâhmaṇas repeating hymns and prayers occupy at a sacrifice.

संस्तुत *p. p.* 1 Praised, eulogized. 2 Praised together. 3 Agreeing, together, harmonious. 4 Intimate, familiar.

संस्तुतिः *f.* Praise, eulogy.

संस्त्यायः 1 A collection, heap, an assemblage. 2 Vicinity. 3 Spreading, diffusion, expansion. 4 A house, residence, habitation ; संस्त्यायमेव गच्छावः Mâl 1. 9. 5 Familiarity, fomiliar talk.

संस्थ *a.* 1 Staying, abiding, lasting. 2 Dwelling, being, existing, situated (at the end of comp.) शिष्टा क्रिया कस्यचिदात्मसंस्था M. 1. 16 ; Ku. 6. 60 ; Mâl. 5. 16. 3 Tame, domesticated. 4 Fixed, stationary. 5 Endedi perished, dead. -स्थः 1 A dweller, an inhabitant. 2 A neighbour, countryman. 3 A spy.

संस्था 1 An assemblage, assembly. 2 Situation, state or condition of being. 3 Form, nature ; R. 11. 38. 4 Occupation, business, settled mode of life ; पृथक्संस्थाश्च निर्ममे Ms. 1. 21. 5 Correct or proper conduct. 6 End, completion. 7 Stop, stay. 8 Loss, destruction. 9 Destruction of the world. 10 Resemblance. 11 A royal decree or ordinance. 12 A form of Soma sacrifice.

संस्थानं 1 A collection, heap, quantity. 2 The aggregation of primary atoms. 3 Configuration, position ; आकृतिरवयवसंस्थानविशेषः. 4 Form, figure, appearance, shape ; स्त्रीसंस्थानं चाप्सरस्तीर्थमारादुत्क्षिप्यैनां ज्योतिरेकं जगाम S. 5. 29; Ms. 9. 261. 5 Construction, formation. 6 Vicinity. 7 Common place of abode. 8 Situation, position. 9 Any place or station. 10 A place where four roads meet. 11 A mark, sign, characteristic sign. 12 Death.

संस्थापनं 1 Placing or keeping together, collecting. 2 Fixing, determining, regulating ; कुर्वीत चैषां प्रत्यक्षमर्घसंस्थापनं नृपः Ms. 8. 422. 3 Establishment, confirmation. 4 Restraining, curbing. -ना 1 Restraining, curbing. 2 A means of calming or composing ; संस्थापना प्रियतरा विरहातुराणां Mk. 3. 3.

संस्थित *p. p.* 1 Being or standing together. 2 Being, staying ; नियोगसंस्थित Pt. 1. 92. 3 Adjacent, contiguous. 4 Resembling, like. 5 Collected, heaped. 6 Settled, fixed, established. 7 Placed in or on, being in. 8 Stationary. 9 Stopped, completed, ended, finished ; *S*. 3. 10 Dead, deceased ; see स्था with सं.

संस्थितिः *f.* 1 Being together, staying with. 2 Contiguity, nearness, vicinity. 3 Residence, abode, resting-place ; यथा नदीनदाः सर्वे सागरे यांति संस्थितिम्। तथैवाश्रमिणः सर्वे गृहस्थे यांति संस्थितिं Ms. 6. 90. 4 Accumulation, heap. 5 Duration, continuance ; H. 1. 43. 6 Station, state, condition of life. 7 Restraint. 8 Death.

संस्पर्शः 1 Contact, touch, conjunction, mixture. 2 Being touched or affected. 3 Perception, sense.

संस्पर्शा A kind of fragrant plant.

संस्फालः 1 A ram. 2 A cloud.

संस्फेटः, संस्फोटः War, battle.

संस्मरणं Remembering, calling to mind.

संस्मृतिः *f.* Remembrance, recollection ; संस्मृतिमेव भवत्यभवाय Ki. 18. 27.

संस्रवः, संस्रावः 1 Flowing, trickling, oozing. 2 A stream. 3 The remains of a libation. 4 A kind of offering or libation.

संहत *p. p.* 1 Struck together, wounded. 2 Closed, shut. 3 Well-knit, firmly united. 4 Closely joined, or allied ; Ki. 1. 19. 5 Compact, firm, solid. 6 Combined, joined, keeping together, being in a body, being very close ; जालमादाय गच्छंति संहताः पक्षिणोऽप्यमी Pt. 2. 9 ; 5. 101 ; H. 1. 37. 7 Of one accord. 8 Assembled, collected. -Comp. -जानु *a.* knock-kneed. -भ्रू *a.* knitting the eyebrows. -स्तनी a woman whose breasts are very close to each other.

संहतता-त्वं 1 Close contact, conjunction. 2 Compactness. 3 Agreement, union. 4 Harmony, concord.

संहतिः *f.* 1 Firm or close contact, close union ; Ku. 5. 8. 2 Union, combination ; संहतिः कार्यसाधिका, संहतिः श्रेयसी पुंसां H. 1 ; cf. "Union is strength". 3 Compactness, firmness, solidity. 4 Bulk, mass ; गुरुतां नयंति हि गुणा न संहतिः Ki. 12. 10. 5 Agreement, harmony. 6 A collection, heap, assemblage, multitude ; वनान्यवांचीव चकार संहतिः Ki. 14. 34, 27 ; 3. 20 ; 5. 4, Mu. 3. 2. 7 Strength. 8 The body.

संहननं 1 Compactness, firmness. 2 The body, person ; अमृताध्मातजीमूतस्निग्धसंहननस्य ते U. 6. 21 ; Mv. 2. 46. 3 Strength ; see संहति also.

संहरणं 1 Gathering, bringing together, collecting. 2 Taking, seizing. 3 Contracting. 4 Restraining. 5 Destroying, ruining.

संहर्तृ *m.* A destroyer.

संहर्षः 1 Horripilation, a thrill of joy or fear. 2 Pleasure, joy, delight. 3 Emulation, rivalry. 4 Wind. 5 Rubbing together.

संहातः One of the 21 hells ; Ms. 4. 89.

संहारः 1 Drawing or bringing together, collecting ; अनुभवतु वेणीसंहारमहोत्सवं Ve. 6. 2 Contraction, compression, abridgment. 3 Withholding, drawing back, withdrawal (opp. प्रयोग or विक्षेप) ; प्रयोगसंहारविभक्तमंत्रं R. 5. 57, 45. 4 Restraining, holding back. 5 Destruction, especially of the universe, universal destruction. 6 Close, end, conclusion. 7 An assemblage, a group. 8 A fault in pronunciation. 9 A charm or spell for withdrawing magical weapons. 10 Practice, skill. 11 A division of hell. -Comp. -भैरवः one of the forms of Bhairava. -मुद्रा N. of a particular posture in the *Tantra* worship ; it is thus defined :—अधोमुखे वामहस्ते ऊर्ध्वास्यं दक्षहस्तकं । क्षिप्त्वांगुलीरंगुलीभिः संगृह्य परिवर्तयेत्.

संहित *p. p.* 1 Placed together, joined, united. 2 Agreeing with, conformable to, in accordance with. 3 Relating to. 4 Collected. 5 Provided, furnished, endowed, accompanied. 6 Caused by ; see धा with सं.

संहिता 1 Combination, union, conjunction. 2 A collection, compilation, compendium. 3 Any systematically arranged collection of texts or verses. 4 A compendium or compilation of laws, code, digest ; मनुसंहिता. 5 The continuous hymnical text of the Veda as formed out of the Padas or individual words by proper phonetic changes according to different *S*âkhas or schools ; पदप्रकृतिः संहिता Nir. 6 (In gram.) Combination or junction of letters according to rules of Sandhi or euphony ; परः संनिकर्षः संहिता P. I. 4. 109 ; वर्णानामतिशयितः संनिधिः संहितासंज्ञः स्यात् Sk ; or वर्णानामेकप्राणयोगः संहिता 7. The Supreme Being who holds and supports the universe.

संहूतिः *f.* General shout, loud uproar, tumultuous exultation.

संहृत *p. p.* 1 Drawn together. 2 Contracted, abriged. 3 Withdrawn, drawn back. 4 Collected, assembled. 5 Seized, laid hold of. 6 Curbed, restrained. 7 Destroyed.

संहृतिः *f.* 1 Contraction, compression. 2 Destruction, loss. 3 Taking, seizure. 4 Restraint. 5 Collection.

संहृष्ट *p. p.* **1** Thrilled or horripilated with joy, delighted. **2** Bristling, shuddering. **3** Fired with emulation.

संह्रादः **1** A loud noise, an uproar. **2** Noise in general.

संह्रीण *a.* **1** Modest, bashful. **2** Completely abashed.

सकट *a.* Bad, vile.

सकंटक *a.* **1** Thorny, prickly. **2** Troublesome, dangerous. **–कः** The aquatic plant शैवल q. v.

सकप, सकंपन *a.* Trembling, tremulous.

सकरुण *a.* Tender, compassionate.

सकर्ण *a.* (र्णा or र्णी) Having ears. **2** Hearing, listening.

सकर्मक *a.* **1** Having or performing any act. **2** (In gram.) Having an object, transitive (as a verb).

सकल *a.* **1** Together with the parts. **2** All, whole, entire, complete. **3** Having all the digits, full (as the moon); as in सकलेंदुमुखी. **4** Having a soft or low sound. **–Comp. –वर्ण** *a.* (*i. e.* पद or वाक्य) having the letters क & ल, *i. e.* quarrelling ; Nalod. 2. 14.

सकल्प *a.* Attended with the ritual or ceremonial part of the Veda ; Ms. 2. 140. **–ल्पः** N. of *S*iva.

सकाकोलः N. of one of the 21 hells ; see **Ms.** 4. 89.

सकाम *a.* **1** Full of love, impassioned, loving. **2** Lustful, amorous. **3** One who has got his desired object, satisfied, contented ; काम इदानीं सकामो भवतु *S*. 4. **–मं** *ind.* **1** With pleasure. **2** Contentedly. **3** Assuredly, indeed.

सकाल *a.* Seasonable, opportune. **–ले** *ind.* Seasonably, betimes, early in the morning.

सकाश *a.* Having appearance, visible, present, near. **–शः** Presence, vicinity, nearness. (**सकाशम्** and **सकाशात्** are used adverbially in the sense of **1** near. **2** from near, from, from the presence of).

सकुक्षि *a.* Having the same womb, born of the same mother, unterine (as a brother &c.)

सकुल *a.* **1** Belonging to a noble family. **2** Belonging to the same family. **3** Having a family. **4** Along with the family. **–लः** **1** A kinsman. **2** A kind of fish (सकुली also.)

सकुल्यः **1** One of the same family. **2** A distant relation ; such as a descendant in the 4th, 5th, or 6th, or even in the 7th, 8th, or 9th degree. **3** A distant relation in general.

सकृत् *ind.* **1** Once; सकृदंशो निपतति सकृत्कन्या प्रदीयते । सकृदाह ददानीति त्रीण्येतानि सतां सकृत् Ms. 9. 47. **2** At one time, on one occasion, formerly, once ; सकृत्कृतप्रणयोऽयं जनः *S*. 5. **3** At once. **4** Together with. *–m. –f.* Feces, excrement (usually written शकृत् q. v.). **–Comp. –गर्भा** **1** a mule. **2** a woman who is pregnant only once. **–प्रजः** a crow. **–प्रसूता, –प्रसूतिका** **1** a woman who has borne only one child. **2** a cow that has calved once. **–फला** the plantain tree.

सकैतव *a.* Deceitful, fraudulent. **–वः** A cheat, rogue.

सकोप *a.* Angry, enraged. **–पं** *ind.* Angrily.

सक्त *p. p.* **1** Stuck or attached to, in contact with. **2** Addicted, devoted or attached to, fond of ; सक्तासि किं कथय वैरिणि मौर्यपुत्रे Mu. 2. 6. **3** Fixed or rivetted on ; R. 2. 28. **4** Relating to. **–Comp. –वैर** *a.* engaged in hostilities, constant in enmity ; *S*. 2. 14.

सक्तिः *f.* **1** Contact, touch. **2** Union, junction ; सक्तिं जवादपनयत्यनिलो लतानां Ki. 5. 46. **3** Attachment, addiction, devotion (to anything.)

सक्तु *m. pl.* The flour of barley first fried and then ground, barley-meal ; भिक्षासक्तुभिरेव संप्रति वयं वृत्तिं समीहामहे Bh. 3. 64.

सक्थि *n.* **1** The thigh ; (changed in comp. to सक्थ after उत्तर, पूर्व and मृग or when the compound implies comparison ; see P. V. 4. 98.). **2** A bone. **3** The pole or shafts of a carriage.

सक्रिय *a.* Active, moveable.

सक्षण *a.* Being at leisure.

सखि *m.* (nom. सखा, सखायौ, सखायः ; acc. सखायं,सखायौ ; सख्युः gen. sing ; सख्यौ loc. sing.) A friend, companion, an associate ; तस्मात्सखा त्वमसि यन्मम तत्तवैव U. 5. 10 ; सखीनिव प्रीतियुजोऽनुजीविनः Ki. 1. 10. (At the end of comp. सखि is changed to सख ; वनितासखानां Ku. 1. 10; सचिवसखः R. 4. 87 ; 1. 48, 12. 9 ; Bk. 1. 1.)

सखी A female friend or companion, a lay's maid ; नृत्यति युवतिजनेन समं सखि विरहिजनस्य दुरंते Gît. 1.

सख्यं **1** Friendship, intimacy, alliance ; मुमूर्च्छ सख्यं रामस्य समानव्यसने हरौ R. 12. 57 ; समानशीलव्यसनेषु सख्यम् Subhâsh. **2** Equality. **–ख्यः** A friend.

सगण *a.* Attended by troops or flocks. **–णः** An epithet of *S*iva.

सगर *a.* Poisonous, having poison. **–रः** N. of a king of the Solar race. [He was a son of Bahu and was called *Sagara*: because he was born together with *gara* or poison given to his mother by the other wife of his father. By his wife Sumati he had 60000 sons. He successfully performed 99 sacrifices, but when he commenced the hundredth, his sacrificial horse was stolen by Indra and carried down to the Patala. Sagara thereupon commanded his 60000 sons to search it out. Finding no trace of the animal on earth they began to dig down towards the Patala, and in doing this they naturally increased the boundaries of the ocean which was therefore called *Sagara*; cf. R. 13. 3. Meeting with the sage Kapila they rashly accused him of having stolen their horse, as a punishment for which they were instantly reduced to ashes by that sage. It was after several thousand of years that Bhag*i*ratha (q. v.) succeeded in bringing down to the P*a*tala the celestial river Ganges to water and purify their ashes and thus to covey their souls to heaven].

सगर्भः,–र्भ्यः A brother of whole blood ; Mv. 6. 27.

सगुण *a.* **1** Possessed of qualities or attributes. **2** Possessed of good qualities, virtuous. **3** Worldly. **4** Furnished with a string (as a bow). **5** Possessed of the qualities in rhetoric.

सगोत्र *a.* Being of the same family or kin, related. **–त्रः** **1** A kinsman sprung from a common ancestor ; *S*. 7. **2** A kinsman of the same family, one connected by funeral oblations of food and water. **3** A distant kinsman. **4** Family, race, lineage.

सग्धिः *f.* Eating together.

संकट *a.* **1** Contracted, narrow, strait. **2** Impervious, impassable. **3** Full of, crowded with, beset with, hemmedin; संकटा ह्याहिताग्नीनां प्रत्यवायैर्गृहस्थता **Mv. 4.** 33 ; U. 1. 8. **–टं** **1** A narrow passage, defile, pass. **2** A difficulty, strait, risk, peril, danger; संकटेष्वविषण्णधीः K.; संकटे हि परीक्ष्यते प्राज्ञाः शूराश्च संगरे Ks. 31. 93.

संकथा Conversation, talk.

संकरः **1** Commingling, mixture, intermixture ; *S*. 2. **2** Blending together, union. **3** Confusion or mixture (of castes), unlawful intermarriage resulting in mixed castes ; चित्रेषु वर्णसंकरः K., Bg. 1. 42 ; Ms. 10. 40. **4** (In Rhet.) The combination of two or more *dependent* figures of speech in one and the same passage (opp. संसृष्टि where the figures are *independent*) ; अविश्रांतिजुषामात्मन्यंगांगित्वं तु संकरः K. P. 10 ; or अंगागित्वेऽलंकृतीनां तद्वदेकाश्रयस्थितौ । संदिग्धत्वे च भवति संकरास्त्रिविधः पुनः *S*. D. 757. **5** Dust, sweepings. **–री** See संकारी below.

संकर्षणं **1** The act of drawing together, contracting. **2** Attracting. **3** Ploughing, furrowing. **–णः** N. of Balarâma ; संकर्षणात्तु गर्भस्य स हि संकर्षणो युवा Hariv.

संकलः **1** Accumulation, collection. **2** Addition.

संकलनं –ना **1** The act of heaping together. **2** Contact, junction. **3** Collision. **4** Bending, twining. **5** Addition (in math.).

संकलित *p. p.* **1** Heaped up, piled up, collected. **2** Blended together, intermixed. **3** Seized, laid hold of. **4** Added.

संकल्पः 1 Will, volition, mental resolve : कः कामः संकल्पः Dk. 2 Purpose, aim, intention, determination. 3 Wish, desire ; संकल्पमात्रोदितसिद्धयस्ते R. 14. 17. 4 Thought, idea, reflection, fancy, imagination ; तत्संकल्पोपहितजडिम स्तंभमभ्येति गात्रं Mâl. 1. 35 ; वृथैव संकल्पशतैरजस्रमनंग नतोसि मया विवृद्धिं S. 3. 4. 5 The mind, heart ; Mâl. 7. 2. 6 A solemn vow to perform an observance. 7 Expectation of advantage from a holy voluntary act. -Comp. -जः, -जन्मन् *m.*, -योनिः epithets of the god of love; भगवन्संकल्पयोने M. 4 ; Ku. 3. 24. -रूप *a.* 1 volitional. 2 conformable to will.

संकसुक *a.* 1 Unsteady, fickle, changeable, inconstant. 2 Uncertain, doubtful. 3 Bad, wicked. 4 Weak, feeble.

संकारः 1 Dust, sweepings. 2 The crackling of flames.

संकारी A girl recently deflowered.

संकाश *a.* 1 Like, similar, resembling (at the end of comp.), अग्नि°, हिरण्य°. 2 Near, close, at hand. -शः 1 Appearance, presence. 2 Vicinity.

संकिलः A fire-brand, burning torch.

संकीर्ण *p. p.* 1 Mixed together, intermingled. 2 Confused, miscellaneous. 3 Shattered, spread, crowded. 4 Indistinct. 5 In rut, intoxicated ; H. 4. 17. 6 Of mixed caste, of impure origin. 7 Impure, adulterated. 8 Narrow, contracted. -र्णः 1 A man of a mixed caste. 2 A mixed note or mode. 3 An elephant in rut, an intoxicated elephant. -र्णं A difficulty. -Comp. -जाति, -योनि *a.* of mixed birth, of a mongrel breed (as a mule). -युद्ध a confused fight, melee.

संकीर्तनं -ना 1 Praising, applauding, extolling. 2 Glorification (of a deity). 3 Repeating the name of a deity as a pious or devotional act.

संकुचित *p. p.* 1 Contracted, abridged ; लंकापतेः संकुचितं यशो यत् Vikr. 1. 27. 2 Shrunk, wrinkled. 3 Closed, shut. 4 Covering.

संकुल *a.* 1 Confused. 2 Thronged with, crowded or filled with, full of; नक्षत्रताराग्रहसंकुलापि ज्योतिष्मती चंद्रमसैव रात्रिः R. 6. 22; Mal. 1. 2. 3 Disordered. 4 Inconsistent. -लं 1 A crowd, mob, throng, collection, swarm, flock ; महतः पौरजनस्य संकुलेन विघटितायां तस्यामागतेऽस्मि Mâl. 1. 2 A confused fight, melee. 3 An inconsistent or contradictory speech ; *e. g.* यावज्जीवमहं मौनी ब्रह्मचारी च मे पिता । माता तु मम वंध्यैव पुत्रहीनः पितामहः.

संकेतः 1 An instimation, allusion. 2 A sign, gesture, hint ; Mu. 1. 3 An indicatory sign, mark, token. 4 Agreement, convention; संकेतो गृह्यते जातौ गुणद्रव्यक्रियासु च S. D. 12. 5 Engagement, appointment, assignation (made by a mistress or lover) ; नामसमेतं कृतसंकेतं वादयते मृदु वेणुं Git. 5. 6 A place of meeting (for lovers), rendezvous ; कांतार्थिनी तु या याति संकेतं साभिसारिका Ak. 7 Condition, provision. 8 A short explanatory rule (in gram.). -Comp. -गृहं, -निकेतनं, -स्थानं a place of appointment or assignation, rendezvous.

संकेतकः 1 Agreement, convention. 2 Appointment, assignation. 3 Rendezvous. 4 A lover or mistress who makes an appointment ; संकेतके चिरयति प्रवरो विनोदः Mk. 3. 3.

संकेतित *a.* 1 Agreed upon, fixed by convention ; साक्षात्संकेतितं योऽर्थमभिधत्ते स वाचकः K. P. 2. 2 Invited, called.

संकोचः 1 Contraction, shrinking up. 2 Abridgment, diminution, compression. 3 Terror, fear. 4 Shutting up, closing. 5 Binding. 6 A kind of skatefish. -चं Saffron.

संक्रंदनः N. of Krishṇa.

संक्रमः 1 Concurrence, going together. 2 Transition, traversing, transfer, progress. 3 The passage of a planetary body through the zodiacal signs. 4 Moving, travelling. -मः -मं 1 A difficult or narrow passage. 2 A causeway, bridge ; नदीमार्गेषु च तथा संक्रमानवसादयेत् Mb. 3 A Medium or means of attaining any object ; तामिव संक्रमीकृत्य Dk.; सोऽतिथिः स्वर्गसंक्रमः Pt. 4. 2.

संक्रमणं 1 Concurrence. 2 Transition, progress, passing from one point to another. 3 The sun's passage from one zodiacal sign to another. 4 The day on which the summer solstice begins. 5 Concurrence, a certain class of problems.

संक्रांत *p. p.* 1 Passed through or into, entered into. 2 Transferred, devolved, entrusted ; U. 1. 22. 3 Seized, affected. 4 Reflected, imaged. 5 Depicted.

संक्रांतिः *f.* 1 Going together, union. 2 Passage from one point to another, transition. 3 The passage of the sun or any planetary body from one zodiacal sign into another. 4 Transference, giving over (to another) ; संपातिताः...पयसो गंडूषसंक्रांतयः U. 3. 16. 5 Transferring or communicating (one's knowledge to another), power of imparting (instruction to others) ; विवादे दर्शयिष्यंतं क्रियासंक्रांतिमात्मनः M. 1. 18 ; शिष्टा क्रिया कस्यचिदात्मसंस्था संक्रांतिरन्यस्य विशेषयुक्ता 1. 16. 6 Image, reflection. 7 Depicting.

संक्राम See संक्रम.

संक्रीडनं Sporting together.

संक्लेदः 1 Dampness, moisture. 2 The fluid secretion supposed to form in the first month after conception and which constitutes the rudiment of the foetus.

संक्षयः 1 Destruction. 2 Complete destruction or consumption. 3 Loss, ruin. 4 End. 5 Destruction of the world.

संक्षिप्तिः *f.* 1 Throwing together. 2 Compressing, abridging. 3 Throwing, sending. 4 Ambuscade.

संक्षेपः 1 Throwing together. 2 Compression, abridgment. 3 Brevity, conciseness. 4 An epitome, a brief exposition. 5 Throwing, sending. 6 Taking away. 7 Assisting (in another's duty. (संक्षेपेण, संक्षेपतस् are used adverbially in the sense of ' briefly , concisely, shortly '.).

संक्षेपणं 1 Heaping together. 2 Abridgment, abbreviation. 3 Sending.

संक्षोभः 1 Agitation, trembling 2 Disturbance, commotion ; Mk. 2. 3 Upsetting, overturning 4 Pride, haughtiness.

संख्यं War, battle, fight ; संख्ये द्विषां वीररसं चकार Vikr. 1. 68, 70 ; Ve. 3. 25 ; Si. 18. 70.

संख्या 1 Enumeration, reckoning, calculation ; संख्यामिवैषां भ्रमरश्चकार R. 16. 47. 2 A number. 3 A numeral. 4 Sum. 5 Reason, understanding, intellect. 6 Deliberation, reflection. 7 Manner. -Comp. अतिग,-अतीत *a.* beyond number, innumerable, countless. -वाचक *a.* expressive of number. (-कः) a numeral.

संख्यात *p. p.* 1 Enumerated. 2 Calculated, reckoned up. -तं A number. -ता A kind of riddle.

संख्यावत् *a.* 1 Numbered. 2 Possessed of reason. -*m.* A learned man.

संगः 1 Coming together, joining. 2 Meeting, union, confluence (as of rivers.) 3 Touch, contact. 4 Company, association, friendship, friendly intercourse ; सतां सद्भिः संगः कथमपि हि पुण्येन भवति U. 2. 1 ; संगमनुव्रज् ' to keep company with, herd with ' मृगाः मृगैः संगमनुव्रजंति Subhâsh. 5 Attachment, fondness, desire ; ध्यायतो विषयान्पुंसः संगस्तेषूपजायते Bg. 2. 62. 6 Attachment to worldly ties, association with men ; दौर्मंत्र्यान्नृपतिर्विनश्यति यतिः संगात् Bh. 2. 42. 7 Encounter, fight.

संगणिका An excellent or incomparable discourse.

संगत *p. p.* 1 Joined or united with, come together, associated with. 2 Assembled, collected, convened, met together. 3 Joined in wedlock, married. 4 Sexually united. 5 Filled together, appropriate, proper, harmonious ; S. 3. 6 In conjunction with (as planets). 7 Shrunk up, contracted ; see गम् with सं. -तं 1 Union, meeting, alliance ; V. 5. 24, S. 5. 23. 2 Association, company. 3 Acquaintance, friendship, intimacy ; Ku. 5. 39. 4 A harmonious or consistent speech, well-reasoned remarks.

संगतिः *f.* 1 Union, meeting, conjunction. 2 Company, society, association, intercourse ; मनो हि जन्मांतरसंगतिज्ञं R. 7. 15. 3 Sexual union. 4 Visiting, frequenting. 5 Fitness, appropriateness, applicability, consistent relation. 6 Accident, chance, accidental occurrence. 7 Knowledge. 8 Questioning for further knowledge.

संगमः 1 Meeting, union ; V. 4. 37 ; R. 12. 66, 90. 2 Association, companny, society, intercourse ; as in सद्भिः संगमः. 3 Contact, touch ; R. 8. 44. 4 Sexual union or intercourse, अयं स ते तिष्ठति संगमोत्सुकः S. 3. 14 ; R. 19. 33. 5 Confluence (of rivers) ; गंगायमुनयोः संगमः. 6 Fitness, adaptation. 7 Encounter, fight. 8 Conjunction (of planets).

संगमनं Meeting, union ; see संगम.

संगरः 1 A promise, an agreement ; तथेति तस्यावितथं प्रतीतः प्रत्यग्रहीत्संगरमग्रजन्मा R. 5. 26, 11. 48, 13. 65. 2 Accepting, undertaking. 3 A bargain. 4 War, battle, fight ; अतरत्स्वभुजौजसा मुहुर्महतः संगरसागरानसौ Si. 16. 67. 5 Knowledge. 6 Devouring. 7 Misfortune, calamity. 8 Poison.

संगवः N. of a particular part of the day, said to be three Muhûrtas after Prâtastana or early dawn and to form the second of the five divisions of the day.

संगादः Discourse, conversation.

संगिन् *a.* 1 United with, meeting. 2 Attached or devoted to, fond of ; S. 5. 11 ; R. 19. 16 ; M. 4. 2 ; Bg. 3. 26 ; 14. 15.

संगीत *p. p.* Sung together, sung in chorus. -तं 1 Chorus, a song sung by many voices ; जगुः सुकंठ्यो गंधर्व्यः संगीतं सहभर्तृकाः Bhâg. 2 Music, harmonious singing, especially singing accompanied by instrumental music and dancing, triple symphony ; गीतं वाद्यं नर्तनं च त्रयं संगीतमुच्यते ; किमन्यदस्याः परिषदः श्रुतिप्रसादनतः संगीतात् S. 1 ; Mk. 1. 3 A concert. 4 The art of singing with music and dancing ; Bh. 2. 12. -Comp. -अर्थः 1 The subject of a musical performance. 2 the materials or necessary apparatus for a musical concert ; Me. 56. -शाला a concert-hall ; Mâl. 2. -शास्त्रं the science of music.

संगीतकं 1 Concert, symphony. 2 A public entertainment consisting of songs attended with music and dancing.

संगीर्ण *p p.* 1 Agreed or assented. 2 Promised.

संग्रहः 1 Seizing, grasping. 2 Clenching the fist, grasp, grip. 3 Reception, admission. 4 Guarding, protection ; तथा ग्रामशतानां च कुर्याद्राष्ट्रस्य संग्रहं Ms. 7. 114. 5 Favouring, propitiating, entertaining, supporting ; Ms. 3. 138 ; 8. 311. 6 Storing, accumulation, gathering, collecting ; तैः कृतप्रकृतिसंग्रहैः R. 19. 55 ; 17. 60. 7 Governing, restraining, controlling. 8 Conglomeration. 9 Conjunction. 10 Agglomeration (a kind of संयोग). 11 Inclusion, comprehension. 12 Compilation. 13 Epitome, summary, abridgment, compendium ; संग्रहेण प्रवक्ष्ये Bg. 8. 11 ; so तर्कसंग्रहः, 14 Sum, amount, totality ; करणं कर्म कर्तेति त्रिविधः कर्मसंग्रहः Bg. 18. 18. 15 A catalogue, list. 16 A store-room. 17 An effort, exertion. 18 Mention, reference. 19 Greatness, elevation. 20 Velocity. 21 N. of Siva.

संग्रहणं 1 Seizing, grasping. 2 Supporting, encouraging. 3 Compiling, collecting. 4 Blending. 5 Incasing, setting ; कनकभूषणसंग्रहणोचितः (मणिः) Pt. 1. 75. 6 Sexual union, intercourse with a female. 7 Adultery ; Ms. 8. 6, 72 ; Y. 2. 72. 8 Hoping. 9 Accepting, receiving. -णी Dysentery.

संग्रहीतृ *m.* A charioteer.

संग्रामः War, battle, fight ; संग्रामांगणमागतेन भवता चापे समारोपिते K. P. 10. -Comp. -जित् *a.* conquering in battle. -पटहः a large military drum.

संग्राहः 1 Laying hold of, grasping. 2 Forcible seizure. 3 Clenching the fist. 4 The handle of a shield.

संघः 1 A group, collection, multitude, flock ; as महर्षिसंघ, मनुष्यसंघ &c. 2 A number of people living together. -Comp -चारिन् *m.* a fish. -जीविन् *m.* a hired labourer, *coolie*. -वृत्तिः *f.* close combination.

संघटना Joining together, union, combination ; Ratn. 4. 20.

संघट्टः 1 Friction, rubbing together, सरलस्कंधसंघट्टजन्मा (दवाग्निः) Me. 53 ; Mâl. 5. 3. 2 Collision, clashing together, encounter ; Si. 20. 26. 3 Encounter, conflict. 4 Meeting, joining, collision or rivalry (as of wives) ; R. 14. 86. 5 Embracing. -ट्टा A large creeper.

संघट्टनं -ना 1 Rubbing together, friction. 2 Collision, clash. 3 Close contact, adherence to. 4 Contact, union, cohesion. 5 The intertwining of wrestlers. 6 Meeting, encounter in general.

संघशस् *ind.* In flocks or troops.

संघर्षः 1 Rubbing together, friction. 2 Grinding, trituration. 3 Collision, clash 4 Emulation, rivalry, contest for superiority ; तस्याश्च मम च कस्मिंश्चित्संघर्षे Dk. ; नाट्याचार्ययोर्महान् ज्ञानसंघर्षो जातः M. 1. 5 Envy, jealousy. 6 Gliding, gently flowing.

संघाटिका 1 A pair, couple. 2 A bawd, procuress. 3 Smell.

संघाणकः -कं The mucus of the nose

संघातः 1 Union, combination, an association. 2 A multitude, an assemblage, a collection ; उपायसंघात इव प्रवृद्धः R. 14. 11 ; Ku. 4. 6. 3 Killing, slaughter. 4 Phlegm. 5 Formation of compounds. 6 N. of a division of hell.

सचकित *a.* Startlled, timid. -तं *ind.* Tremblingly, in an alarmed or startled manner.

सचिः 1 A friend. 2 Friendship, intimacy. -*f.* The wife of Indra ; see शची.

सचिल्लक *a.* Blear-eyed.

सचिवः 1 A friend, companion. 2 A minister, counsellor ; सचिवान्सप्त चाष्टौ वा प्रकुर्वीत परीक्षितान् Ms. 7. 54 ; R. 1. 34, 4. 87; कार्यांतरसचिवः M. 1.

सची See शची.

सचेतन *a.* Sentient, animate, rational.

सचेतस् *a.* 1 Intelligent. 2 Possessed of feeling. 3 Unanimous.

सचेल *a.* Dressed.

सचेष्टः The mango tree.

सजन *a.* Having men or living beings. -नः A man of the same family, a kinsman.

सजल *a.* Watery, wet, humid.

सजाति, सजातीय *a.* 1 Of the same kind, tribe, class or species. 2 Like, similar. -*m.* A son of a man and woman of the same caste.

सजुष् (स्) *a.* 1 Loving, attached to. 2 Associated together. -*m.* (Nom. सजूः, सजुषौ, सजुषः instr. dual सजूर्भ्याम्) A friend, companion. -*ind.* With, together with.

सज्ज *a.* 1 Ready, made or got ready, prepared ; सज्जो रथः U. 1. 2 Dressed, clothed. 3 Accoutred, trimmed. 4 Fully equipped, armed. 5 Fortified.

सज्जनं 1 Fastening, tying on. 2 Dressing. 3 Preparing, arming, equipping. 4 A guard, sentry. 5 A ferry, *ghât*. -नः A good man ; see under सत्. -ना 1 Decoration, accoutrement, equipment. 2 Dressing, ornamenting.

सज्जा 1 Dress, decoration. 2 Equipment, apparatus. 3 Military accoutrement, armour,

सज्जित *a.* 1 Dressed. 2 Decorated. 3 Made ready, equipped. 4 Accoutred, armed.

सज्य *a.* **1** Furnished with a bow-string. **2** Strung (as a bow).

सज्योत्स्ना A moonlight night.

संचः A collection of leaves for writing upon.

संचत् *m.* A cheat, rogue, juggler.

संचयः **1** Heaping up, gathering. **2** Hoard, heap, accumulation, stock, store ; कर्तव्यः संचयो नित्यं कर्तव्यो नातिसंचयः Subhâsh. **3** A large quantity, collection.

संचयनं **1** Gathering, collecting. **2** Collecting the ashes and bones of a body after it has been burnt.

संचरः **1** Passage, transit from one zodiacal sign to another. **2** A way, path ; यत्रौषधिप्रकाशेन नक्तं दर्शितसंचराः Ku. 6. 43 ; R. 16. 12. **3** A narrow road, defile, difficult passage. **4** Entrance, gate. **5** The body. **6** Killing. **7** Development.

संचरणं Going, motion, travelling.

संचल *a.* Trembling, quivering.

संचलनं Agitation, trembling, shaking ; अचलसंचलनाहरणो रणः Ki. 18. 8.

संचाय्यः N. of a particular sacrifice.

संचारः **1** Going, movement, travelling or roaming through ; स पुनः पार्थिसंचारं संचरत्यवनीपतिः K. P. 10; R. 2. 15. **2** Passing through, passage, transit. **3** A course, way, road, pass. **4** Difficult progress or journey. **5** Difficulty, distress. **6** Setting in motion. **7** Inciting. **8** Leading, guiding. **9** Transmission, contagion. **10** A gem said to be found in the hood of serpents.

संचारक *a.* Conveying, transmitting. **-कः** **1** A leader, guide. **2** An instigator.

संचारिका **1** A female messenger, go-between. **2** A bawd, procuress. **3** A pair, couple. **4** Smell, odour.

संचारणं Moving, impelling, conveying, leading &c.

संचारिन् *a.* (णी *f.*) **1** Moving, moveable; संचारिणी नगरदेवतेव Mâl. 1; Ku. 3. 54 ; 6. 67. **2** Roaming, wandering. **3** Changing, unsteady, fickle. **4** Difficult to be passed, inaccessible. **5** Evanescent, as a Bhâva ; see below. **6** Influencing. **7** Hereditary, successively communicated (as a disease). **8** Contagious. **9** Impelling. **-*m.*** **1** Wind, air. **2** Incense. **3** A transient or evanescent feeling which serves to strengthen the prevailing sentiment, see व्यभिचारिन्.

संचाली The Gunjâ shrub.

संचित *p. p.* **1** Heaped up, accumulated, hoarded, collected. **2** Laid by, stored. **3** Enumerated, reckoned. **4** Full of, furnished or provided with. **5** Impeded, obstructed. **6** Dense, thick (as a wood).

संचितिः *f.* A collection.

संचिंतनं Consideration, reflection.

संचूर्णनं Crushing to pieces.

संछन्न *p. p.* **1** Enveloped, concealed, hidden. **2** Clothed.

संछादनं Obscuring, hiding.

संज् 1 P. (सजति, सक्त; the स् of the root being changed to ष्, after a preposition ending in इ or उ) **1** To stick or adhere to, cling to ; तुल्यगंधिषु मत्तेभकटेषु फलरेणवः (ससंजुः) ; R. 4. 47. **2** To fasten. *-Pass.* (सज्यते) To be attached to, cling or adhere to. *-Caus.* (संजयति-ते). *-Desid.* (सिसंक्षति). -WITH **अनु** **1** to stick or adhere to. **2** to be united with, to accompany ; मृत्युर्जरा च व्याधिश्च दुःखं चानेककारणम् । अनुषक्तं सदा देहे Mb. ; U. 4. 2. (*-Pass.*) to stick or adhere to (fig. also) ; धर्मपूते च मनसि नभसीव न जातु रजोऽनुषज्यते Dk. ; Bg. 6. 4 ; 18. 10. **-अव** **1** to suspend, attach, cling to, throw, place ; *Si.* 5. 16, 7. 16, 9. 7 ; Ku. 7. 23. **2** to entrust to, throw on, assign to. (*-Pass.*) **1** to be in contact with, touch ; Mk. 1. 54. **2** to be engaged in or intent on, be eager. **-आ** **1** to fasten, fix on, join or add to, place or put on ; चापमासज्य कंठे Ku. 2. 64 ; *S.* 3. 26 ; (भुजे) भूयः स भूमेर्धुरमाससंज R. 2. 74. **2** to confer upon, conduce to ; Ki. 13. 44. **3** to throw upon, assign to. **4** to stick or adhere to. **-नि** **1** to adhere or stick to, be thrown round or placed on ; कंठे स्वयंग्राहनिषक्तबाहुं Ku. 3. 7 ; R. 9. 50, 11. 70, 19. 45. **2** to be reflected ; Ku. 1. 10, 7. 36. **3** to be attached to. **-प्र** **1** to cling or adhere to. **2** to apply, follow, be applicable, hold good in the case of (pass. also in the same sense) ; इतरेतराश्रयः प्रसज्येत, वैषम्यनैर्घृण्ये नेश्वरस्य प्रसज्येते S. B. **3** to be attached to ; तस्यामसौ प्रासजत् Dk. **-व्यति** to join or link together ; व्यतिषजति पदार्थानांतरः कोऽपि हेतुः U. 6. 12.

संजः **1** N. of Brahman. **2** Of *S*iva.

संजयः N. of the charioteer of king Dhritarâshtra. He tried to bring about a peaceful settlement of the dispute between the Kauravas and Pândavas, but failed. It was he who narrated the events of the great Bhâratî war to the blind king Dhritarâshtra ; cf. Bg. 1. 1.

संजल्पः **1** Conversation. **2** Confused talk, chattering, confusion. **3** An uproar.

संजवनं A quadrangle, a group of four houses forming a court.

संजा A she-goat.

संजीवनं **1** Living together. **2** Bringing to life, life-restoring, reanimation, resuscitation. **3** N. of one of the 21 hells ; see Ms. 4. 89. **4** A group of four houses, quadrangle **-नी** A kind of elixir (said to restore the dead to life).

संज्ञ *a.* **1** Knock-kneed. **2** Being conscious. **3** Named, called ; see संज्ञा below. **-ज्ञं** A yellow fragrant wood.

संज्ञपनं Killing.

संज्ञा **1** Consciousness ; संज्ञां लभ्, आपद् or प्रतिपद् to regain or recover one's consciousness, come to one's senses. **2** Knowledge, understanding. **3** Intellect, mind. **4** A hint, sign, token, gesture ; मुखार्पितैकांगुलिसंज्ञयैव मा चापलायेति गणान् व्यनैषीत् Ku. 3. 41. **5** A name, designation, an appellation ; oft. at the end of comp. in this sense ; द्वंद्वैर्विमुक्ताः सुखदुःखसंज्ञैः Bg. 15. 5. **6** (In gram.) Any name or noun having a special meaning, a proper name. **7** The technical name for an affix. **8** The Gâyatrî Mantra, see गायत्री. **9** N. of the daughter of Visvakarman and wife of the sun, and mother of Yama, Yamî and the two Asvins. [A legend relates that संज्ञा on one occasion wished to go to her father's house and asked her father's permission, which was not granted. Resolved to carry out her purpose, she created, by means of her superhuman power, a woman exactly like herself—who was, as it were, her own shadow (and was therefore called Chhaya),—and putting her in her own place, went away without the knowledge of the sun. Chhaya bore to the sun three children (see छाया), and lived quite happily with him, so that when Sanjna re urned, he would not admit her. Thus repudiated and disappointed, she assumed the form of a mare and roamed over the earth. The sun, however, in course of time, came to know the real state of things, and discovered that his wife had assumed the form of a mare. He accordingly assumed the form of a horse and was united with his wife, who bore to him two sons—the Asvinikumaras or Asvins q. v.]. **-Comp.** **-अधिकारः** a leading rule which gives a particular name to the rules falling under it, and which exercises influence over them. **-विषयः** an epithet, an attribute. **-सुतः** an epithet of Saturn.

संज्ञानं Knowledge, understanding.

संज्ञापनं **1** Informing. **2** Teaching. **3** Killing, slaughter.

संज्ञावत् *a.* **1** Having consciousness, become sensible, revived. **2** Having a name.

संज्ञित *a.* Named, called, denominated.

संज्ञिन् *a.* **1** Named. **2** That which receives a name.

संज्ञु *a.* Knock-kneed.

संज्वरः 1 Great heat, fever. 2 Heat. 3 Indignation.

सट् I. 1 P. (सटति) To form a part. –II. 10 U. (साटयति-ते) To show, display, manifest.

सटं, सटा 1 An ascetic's matted hair. 2 A mane (of a lion); Mu. 7. 6; Si. 1. 47. 3 Bristles of a boar; विध्यंतमुद्धूतसटाः प्रतिहंतुमीषुः R. 9. 60. 4 A crest. –Comp. –अंकः a lion.

सट्ट् 10 U. (सट्टयति-ते) 1 To injure, kill. 2 To be strong. 3 To give. 4 To take. 5 To dwell.

सट्टकं A kind of minor drama in Prâkrita; e. g. कर्पूरमंजरी; see S. D. 542.

सट्वा f. 1 A kind of bird. 2 A musical instrument.

सठ् 10 U. (साठयति-ते) 1 To finish, complete. 2 To leave unfinished. 3 To go, move. 4 To adorn, decorate.

सणसूत्रं A hempen cord or thread.

संड See षंढ.

संडिशः A pair of tongs or nippers.

संडीनं One of the several modes of flight of birds; see डीन.

सत् a. (ती f.) 1 Being, existing, existent; संतः स्वनः प्रकाशंते गुणा न परतो नृणां BV. 1. 120; S. 7. 12. 2 Real, essential, true. 3 Good, virtuous, chaste; सती सती योगविसृष्टदेहा Ku. 1. 21; S. 5. 17. 4 Noble, worthy, high; as in सत्कुलम्. 5 Right, proper. 6 Best, excellent. 7 Venerable, respectable. 8 Wise, learned. 9 Handsome, beautiful. 10 Firm, steady. –m. A Good or virtuous man, a sage; आदानं हि विसर्गाय सतां वारिमुचामिव R. 4. 86; अविरतं परकार्यकृतां सतां मधुरिमातिशयेन वचोऽमृतं Bv. 1. 113; Bh. 2. 18; R. 1. 10. –n. 1 That which really exists, entity, existence, essence. 2 The really existent truth, reality. 3 Good; as in सदसत् q. v. 4 Brahman or the Supreme Spirit. (सत्कृ means 'to respect', 'treat with respect', 'receive hospitably'). –Comp. –असत् (सदसत्) a. 1 existent and non-existent, being and not being. 2 real and unreal. 3 true and false. 4 good and bad, right and wrong. 5 virtuous and, wicked. (-n. du). 1 entity and non-entity. 2 good and evil, right and wrong. °विवेकः discrimination between good and evil or truth and false hood. °व्यक्तिहेतुः the cause of discrimination between the good and bad; तं संतः श्रोतुमर्हंति सदसद्व्यक्तिहेतवः R. 1. 10. –आचारः (सदाचारः) 1 good manners, virtuous or moral conduct. 2 approved usage, traditionary observances, immemorial custom; Ms. 2. 18. –आत्मन् a. virtuous, good. –उत्तरं a proper or good reply. –कर्मन् n. 1 a virtuous or pious act. 2 virtue, piety. 3 hospitality. –कांडः a hawk, kite. –कारः 1 a kind or hospitable treatment, hospitable reception. 2 reverence, respect. 3 care, attention. 4 a meal. 5 a festival, religious observance. –कुलं a good or noble family. –कुलीन a. nobly born, of noble descent. –कृत a. 1 done well or properly. 2 hospitably received or treated. 3 revered, respectad, honoured. 4 worshipped, adored. 5 welcomed. (–तः) an epithet of Siva. (–तं) 1 hospitality. 2 A virtue, piety. –कृतिः f. 1 treating with respect, hospitality, hospitable reception. 2 virtue, morality. –क्रिया 1 virtue, goodness; शकुंतला मूर्तिमती च सत्क्रिया S. 5. 15. 2 charity, good or virtuous action. 3 hospitality, hospitable reception. 4 courtesy, salutation. 5 any purificatory ceremony. 6 funeral ceremonies, obsequies. -गति f. (सद्गतिः) a good or happy state, felicity, beatitude. –गुण a. possessed of good qualities, virtuous. (–णः) virtue, excellence, goodness, good quality. –चरित, चरित्र a. (सच्चरित-त्र) well-conducted, honest, virtuous, righteous; सूनुः सच्चरितः Bh. 2. 25. (-n.) 1 good or virtuous conduct. 2 history or account of the good; S. 1. –चारा (सच्चारा) turmeric. –चिद् n. (सच्चिद्) the Supreme Spirit. °अंशः portion of existence and thought. °आत्मन् m. the soul consisting of entity and thought. °आनंदः 'existence or entity, knowledge and joy'; an epithet of the Supreme Spirit. –जनः (सज्जनः) a good or virtuous man. -पत्रं the new leaf of a water-lily. –पथः 1 a good road. 2 right path of duty, correct or virtuous conduct. 3 an orthodox doctrine. –परिग्रहः acceptance (of gifts) from a proper person. -पशुः a victim fit for a sacrifice, a good sacrificial victim. -पात्रं a worthy or virtuous person. °वर्षः bestowing favours on worthy recipients, judicious liberality. °वर्षिन् a. having judicious liberality. –पुत्रः 1 a good or virtuous son. 2 a son who performs all the prescribed rites in honour of his ancestors. –प्रतिपक्षः (in logic) one of the five kinds of *hetva'bha'sas* or fallacious *hetus*, a counterbalanced *hetu*, one along which there exists another equal *hetu* on the opposite side, *e. g.* 'sound is eternal because it is audible'; and also 'sound is non-eternal, because it is a product.' –फलः the pomegranate tree. –भावः (सद्भावः) 1 existence, being, entity. 2 actual existence, reality. 3 good disposition or nature, amiability. 4 quality of goodness. -मातुरः (सन्मातुरः) the son of a virtuous mother. –मात्रः (सन्मात्रः) 'consisting of mere entity', the soul. –मानः (सन्मानः) esteem of the good. –मित्रं (सन्मित्रं) a good or faithful friend. –युवतिः f. a virtuous maiden. -वंश a. of high birth. –वचस् n. an agreeable or pleasing speech. –वस्तु n. 1 a good thing. 2 a good plot or story; V. 1. 2. –विद्य a. well-educated, having good learning. –वृत्त a. 1 well-behaved, well-conducted, virtuous, upright. 2 perfectly circular, well-rounded; सद्वृत्तः स्तनमंडलस्तव कथं प्राणैर्मम क्रीडति Git. 3 (where both senses are intended). (–त्तं) 1 good or virtuous conduct. 2 an agreeable or amiable disposition. –संसर्गः, –संनिधानं, –संगः, –संगतिः, –समागमः company or society of the good, association with the good; तथा सत्संनिधानेन मूर्खो याति प्रवीणतां H. 1. –संप्रयोगः right application. –सहाय a. having vitruous friends. (–यः) a good companion. –सार a. having good sap or essence. (–रः) 1 a kind of tree. 2 a poet. 3 a painter. –हेतुः (सद्धेतुः) a faultless or valid *hetu* or middle term.

सतत a. Constant, eternal, everlasting, perpetual. –तं ind. Constantly, contiually, eternally, always; सुलभाः पुरुषा राजन् सततं प्रियवादिनः Râm. –Comp. –गः, –गतिः wind; सलिलतले सततगतीनंतः संचारिणः संनिगृह्य शय्या कार्या Dk.; सततगास्ततगानगिरोऽलिभिः Si. 6. 5; नेत्रा नीताः सततगतिना यद्विमानाग्रभूमीः Me. 69. –यायिन् a. 1 always moving. 2 constantly tending to decay.

सतर्क a. 1 Versed in reasoning. 2 Considerate.

सातिः f. 1 A gift, donation. 2 End, destruction.

सती f. 1 A virtuous or good woman (or wife); Ku. 1. 21. 2 A female ascetic. 3 N. of the goddess Durgâ; Ku. 1. 21.

सतीत्वं Chastity.

सतीनः 1 A kind of pulse or pease. 2 A bamboo.

सतीर्थः, –सतीर्थ्यः A fellow religious student.

सतीलः 1 A bamboo. 2 Air, wind. 3 Pease, pulse (f. also).

सतेरः Husk, chaff.

सत्ता 1 Existence, entity, being. 2 Actual existence, reality. 3 The highest Jâti or generality. 4 Goodness, excellence.

सत्त्र (usually written सत्रं) 1 A sacrificial session, especially one lasting from 13 to 100 days. 2 A sacrifice in general. 3 An oblation, offering, gift. 4 Liberality, munif cence. 5 Virtue. 6 A house, residence. 7 Covering. 8 Wealth. 9 A wood, forest ; Ki. 13. 9. 10 A tank, pond. 11 Fraud, cheating. 12 A place of refuge, asylum, covert. –Comp. –अयनं (णं) a long sacrificial session.

सत्त्रा *ind.* With, together with. –Comp. –हन् *m.* an epithet of Indra.

सत्त्रिः 1 A cloud. 2 An elephant.

सत्त्रिन् *m.* One who constantly performs sacrifices, a liberal householder ; *S*i. 14. 32.

सत्त्वं (Said to be *m.* also in the first ten senses) 1 Being, existence, entity. 2 Nature, essence. 3 Natural character, inborn disposition. 4 Life, spirit, breath, vitality, principle of vitality ; *S.* 2. 9. 5 Consciousness, mind, sense. 6 An embryo. 7 Substance, thing, wealth. 8 An elementary substance, such as earth, air, fire &c. 9 A living or sentient being, animal, beast ; वन्यान् विनेष्यन्निव दुष्टसत्त्वान् R. 2. 8, 15. 15 ; *S.* 2. 7. 10 An evil spirit, a demon, ghost. 11 Goodness, virtue, excellence. 12 Truth, reality, certainty. 13 Strength, energy, courage, vigour, power, inherent power, the stuff of which a person is made ; क्रियासिद्धिः सत्त्वे भवति महतां नोपकरणे Subhâsh. ; R. 5. 31 ; Mu. 3. 22. 14 Wisdom, good sense. 15 The quality of goodness or purity regarded as the highest of the three Guṇas q. v.; (it is said to perdominate most in gods and heavenly beings). 16 A natural property or quality, characteristic. 17 A noun, substantive. –Comp. –अनुरूप *a.* 1 according to one's inborn disposition or inherent character ; Bh. 2. 30. 2 according to one's means or wealth ; R. 7. 32 (Malli.'s interpretation does not appear to suit the context). –उद्रेकः 1 excess of the quality of goodness. 2 pre-eminence in strength or courage. –लक्षणं signs of pregnancy ; *S.* 5. –विप्लवः loss of consciousness. –विहित *a.* 1 caused by nature. 2 caused by goodness, virtuous, upright. –संशुद्धिः *f.* purity or uprightness of nature. –संपन्न *a.* endowed with goodness, virtuous. –संप्लवः 1 loss of strength or vigour. 2 universal destruction. –सारः 1 essence of strength. 2 a very powerful person. –स्थ *a.* 1 being in the nature of things. 2 inherent in animals. 3 animate. 4 characterized by goodness, good, excellent.

सत्त्वमेजय *a.* Terrifying animals or living beings.

सत्य *a.* 1 True, real, genuine ; as in सत्यव्रत, सत्यसंध. 2 Honest, sincere, truthful, faithful. 3 Virtuous, upright. –त्यः 1 The abode of Brahman and of truth, the uppermost of the seven worlds or *lokas* above the earth ; see लोक. 2 The Asvattha tree. 3 N. of Râma. 4 Of Vishṇu. 5 The deity presiding over नांदीमुखश्राद्ध q. v. –त्यं 1 Truth ; मौनात्सत्यं विशिष्यते Ms. 2. 83; सत्यं ब्रू 'to speak the truth.' 2 Sincerity. 3 Goodness, virtue, purity. 4 An oath, a promise, solemn asseveration ; सत्यादुरुगलोयन् R. 12. 9 ; Ms. 8. 113. 5 A truism, demonstrated truth or dogma. 6 The first of the four Yugas or ages of the world, the golden age, the age of truth and purity. 7 Water. –त्यं *ind.* Truly, really, indeed, verily, forsooth ; सत्यं शपामि ते पादपंकजस्पर्शेन K. ; Ku. 6. 19. –Comp. –अनृत *a.* 1 true and false ; सत्यानृता च परुषा H. 2. 183. 2 apparently true, but really false. (–तं–ते) 1 truth and falsehood. 2 practice of truth and falsehood ; *i. e.* trade, commerce ; Ms. 4. 4. and 6. –अभिसंध *a.* true to one's promise, sincere. –उत्कर्षः 1 pre-eminence in truth. 2 true excellence. –उद्य *a.* speaking the truth. –उपयाचन *a.* fulfilling a request. –कामः a lover of truth. –तपस् *m.* N. of a sage. –दर्शिन् *a.* truth-seeing, foreseeing truth. –धन *a.* rich in truth, exceedingly truthful. –धृति *a.* strictly truthful. –पुरं the world of Vishṇu. –पूत *a.* purified by truth (as words) ; सत्यपूतां वदेद्वाणीं Ms. 6. 46. –प्रतिज्ञ *a.* true to one's promise. –भामा N. of the daughter of Satrâjit and the favourite wife of Krishṇa ; (it was for her that Krishṇa fought with Indra and brought the Pârijâta tree from the Nandana garden and planted it in her garden). –युगं the golden age ; see सत्य (6) above. –वचस् *a.* truthful, veracious. (–*m.*) 1 a saint, *R*ishi. 2 a seer. (–*n.*) truth, veracity. –वद्य *a.* veracious. (–द्यं) truth, veracity. –वाच् *a.* truthful, veracious, candid. (–*m.*) 1 a saint, seer. 2 a crow. (–*f.*), –वाक्यं truth speaking, veracity. –वादिन् *a.* 1 truth-speaking. 2 sincere, outspoken, candid. –व्रत, –संगर, –संध *a.* 1 true or faithful to an agreement, promise or word, adhering to truth, veracious. 2 honest, sincere. –श्रावणं taking a solemn oath. –संकाश *a* specious, plausible.

सत्यंकारः 1 Making true or good, ratification of a contract or bargain. 2 Earnest money, advance payment, something given in advance as an earnest for the performance of a contract ; Ki. 11. 50.

सत्यवत् *a.* Truthful, veracious. –*m.* N. of a king, husband of Sâvitrî, q. v. –ती N. of the daughter of a fisherman, who became mother of Vyâsa by the sage Parâsara. °सुत Vyâsa.

सत्या 1 Truthfulness, veracity. 2 N. of Sîtâ. 3 Of Draupadî ; Ki. 11. 50. 4 Of Satyavatî, mother of Vyâsa. 5 Of Durgâ. 6 Of Satyabhâmâ, wife of Krishṇa.

सत्यापनं 1 Speaking or observing the truth. 2 Ratification (of a contract, bargain &c.).

सत्र See सत्त्र.

सत्रप *a.* Ashamed, modest.

सत्राजित् *m.* Son of Nighna and father of Satyabhâmâ. [He got the *Syamantaka* jewel from the sun and always wore it round his neck. He afterwards gave it to his brother Prasena, from whom it passed into the hands of the monkey-chief Jambavat, who got possession of it after having killed Prasena. Krish*n*a, however, overtook Jambavat and vanquished him in fight after a long struggle. The monkey-chief thereupon presented it along with his daughter to Krish*n*a ; see जांबवत्. Krish*n*a then gave the jewel back to its proper owner Satrajit, who out of gratitude presented it along with his daughter Satyabh*a*m*a* to him. Afterwards when Satyabh*a*m*a* was at her father's house with the jewel, *S*atadhanvan, at the instigation of a Y*a*dava named Akr*u*ra who desired the jewel for himself, killed Satr*a*jit and gave it to Akr*u*ra. *S*atadhanvan was afterwards killed by Krish*n*a, but when he found that the jewel was with Akr*u*ra he allowed him to retain it with himself after having once shown it to the people.]

सत्वर *a.* Quick, speedy, expeditious. –रं *ind.* Quickly, speedily.

सथूत्कार *a.* Sputtered. –रः Speech accompanied with sputtering.

सद् 1 P. (6. P. also according to some) (सीदति, सन्न; the स् of सद् is changed to ष् after any preposition ending in इ or उ except प्रति) 1 To sit, sit down, recline, lie, lie down, rest, settle; अमदाः सेदुरेकस्मिन् नितंबे निखिला गिरेः Bk. 9. 58. 2 To sink down, plunge into ; तेन त्वं विदुषां मध्ये पंके गौरिव सीदसि H. Pr. 24 ; (where the word has sense 4 also). 3 To live, remain, reside, dwell. 4 To be dejected or low-spirited, despond, despair, sink into despondency ; नाथ हरे जय नाथ हरे सीदति राधा वासगृहे Gît. 6. 5 To decay, perish, go to ruin, waste away, be destroyed ; विपन्नायां नीतौ सकलमवशं सीदति जगत् H. 2. 77 ; R. 7. 64, H. 2. 130. 6 To be in distress, be pained or afflicted, be helpless ; Ki.

13. 60, Ms. 8. 21. 7 To be impeded or hindered ; Ms. 9. 94. 8 To be languid, be wearied or fatigued, droop, sink ; सीदति मे हृदयं K. ; सीदंति मम गात्राणि Bg. 1. 28. 9 To go. -*Caus.* (सादयति ते) 1 To cause to sit down, rest &c.-*Desid.* (सिषत्सति) To wish to sit &c.-WITH अव 1 To sink down, faint, fail, give way ; करिणी पंकमिवावसीदति Ki. 2. 6, 4. 20 ; Bk. 6. 24. 2 to suffer, be neglected. 3 to become disheartened or exhausted. 4 to perish, decay, come to an end ; नास्त्युद्यमसमो बंधुः कृत्वायं नावसीदति. (-*Caus.*) 1 to cause to sink, dispirit, ruin ; Bg. 6. 5. 2 to remove, allay ; औत्सुक्यमात्रमवसादयति प्रतिष्ठा *S*. 5. 6. 3 to destroy, kill. -आ 1 to sit down or near. 2 to lie in wait for. 3 to approach, reach, go to ; हिमालयस्यालयमाससाद Ku. 7. 69, *Si*. 2. 2, R. 6. 4. 4 to meet with, find, form ; R. 5. 60, 14. 25. 5 to suffer ; Bk. 3. 26. 6 to encounter, attack. 7 to place. (-*Caus.*) 1 to meet with, find, get, obtain ; अमरगणनालेख्यमासाद्य R. 8. 95. 2 to approach, go to, reach, be in possession of ; नक्रः स्वस्थानमासाद्य गजेंद्रमपि कर्षति Pt. 3. 46; Me. 34; Bk. 8. 37. 3 to overtake; अनेन रथवेगेन पूर्वप्रस्थितं वैनतेयमप्यासादयेयं V. 1. 4 to encounter, attack ; Bk. 6. 95. -उद् 1 to sink (fig. also), fall into ruin or decay ; उत्सीदेयुरिमे लोकाः Bg. 3. 24. 2 to leave off, quit. 3 to rise up. (-*Caus*). 1 to destroy, annihilate ; उत्साद्यंते जातिधर्माः Bg. 1. 42, Ms. 9. 267. 2 to overturn. 3 to rub, anoint. -उप 1 to sit near to, go to, approach ; उपसेदुर्दशग्रीवं Bk. 9. 92, 6. 135. 2 to wait upon, serve ; आकल्पसाधनैस्तैस्तैरुपसेदुः प्रसाधकाः R. 17. 22 ; *Si*. 13. 24. 3 to march against. -नि 1 to sit down, lie, recline ; उष्णालुः शिशिरे निषीदति तरोर्मूलालवाले शिखी V. 2. 23. 2 to sink down, fail, be disappointed. -प्र 1 to be pleased, be gracious or propitious, oft. with inf.; तमालपत्रास्तरणासु रंतुं प्रसीद शश्वन्मलयस्थलीषु R. 6. 64. 2 to be appeased or soothed, be satisfied ; निमित्तमुद्दिश्य हि यः प्रकुप्यति ध्रुवं स तस्यापगमे प्रसीदति Pt. 1. 283. 3 to be pure or clear, clear up, brighten up (lit. and fig.) ; दिशः प्रसेदुर्मरुतो ववुः सुखाः R. 3. 14; प्रससादोदयादंभः कुंभयोनेर्महौजसः 4. 21. 4 to bear fruit, succeed, be successful ; क्रिया हि वस्तूपहिता प्रसीदति R. 3. 29 ; see प्रसन्न. (-*Caus.*) 1 to propitiate, to secure the favour of, pray, beseech; तस्मात्प्रणम्य प्रणिधाय कायं प्रसादये त्वामहमीशमीड्यं Bg. 11. 44, R. 1. 88, Y. 3. 283. 2 to make clear ; चेतः प्रसादयति Bh. 2. 23. -वि 1 to sink down, be exhausted. 2 to be dispirited or cast down, be afflicted or sorrowful, despond, despair ; विलपति हसति विषीदति रोदिति चंचति मुंचति तापं Gît. 4, Bg. 2. 1 ; Bk. 7. 89 ; R. 9. 75. (-*Caus.*) 1 to cause to despond or despair. 2 to make afflicted, pain.

सदः The fruit of trees.

सदंशकः A crab.

सदंशवदनः A heron.

सदनं 1 A house, palace, mansion. 2 Sinking down, decaying, perishing. 3 Languor, exhaustion, fatigue. 4 Water.' 5 A sacrificial hall. 6 The abode of Yama.

सदय *a.* Kind, tender, merciful.-यं *ind.* Kindly, mercifully.

सदस् *n.* 1 Seat, abode, residence, dwelling. 2 An assembly ; पंक्तैर्विना सरो भाति सदः खलजनैर्विना Bv. 1. 116 ; Bh. 2. 63. -Comp. -गत *a.* seated in an assembly ; R. 3. 66. -गृहं an assembly-hall, council-room ; R. 3. 67.

सदस्यः 1 Any person present at or belonging to an assembly, a member of an assembly (an assessor, juror &c.) 2 An assistant at a sacrifice, superintending or assisting priest ; *S*. 3.

सदा *ind.* Always, ever, perpetually, at all times. -Comp. -आनंद *a.* ever happy. (-दः) an epithet of *Siva*. -गतिः 1 wind. 2 the sun 3 everlasting happiness, final beatitude -तोया, -नीरा 1 N. of the *Karatoyá* river. 2 a river always bearing water, a running stream. -दान *a.* always making gifts or exuding rut; Pt. 2. 79. (-नः) 1 a ruttish elephant. 2 a scentelephant (गंधद्विप q. v.). 3 N. of the elephant of Indra. 4 N. of Gaṇesa. -नर्तः a kind of bird, the wagtail. -फल *a.* always bearing fruit. (-लः) 1 the Bilva tree. 2 the jack tree. 3 the glomerous fig-tree. 4 the cocoanut tree -योगिन् *m.* an epithet of Krishṇa. -शिवः N. of *Siva*.

सदृक्ष (क्षी *f.*), **सदृश्**, **सदृश**, (शी *f.*) *a.* 1 Like, resembling, similar, of the same rank, (with gen. or loc., but usually in comp.) ; वज्रपातसदृश, कुसुमसदृश &c. 2 Fit, right, suitable, conformable, as in प्रस्तावसदृशं वाक्यं H. 2. 51. 3 Worthy, befitting, becoming श्रुतस्य किं तत्सदृशं कुलस्य R. 14. 61, 1. 15.

सदेश *a.* 1 Possessing a country. 2 Belonging to the same place or country. 3 Proximate, neighbouring.

सद्मन् *n.* 1 A house, dwelling, abode ; चकितनतनतांगी सद्म सद्यो विवेश Bv. 2. 32. 2 A place, station. 3 A temple. 4 An altar. 5 Water.

सद्यस् *ind.* 1 To-day, the same day; गवादीनां पयोऽन्येद्युः सद्यो वा जायते दधि, पापस्य हि फलं सद्यः Subhâsh. 2 Instantly, forthwith, immediately, on a sudden: चकितनतनतांगी सद्म सद्यो विवेश Bv. 2. 32 ; Ku. 3. 29 ; Me. 16. 3 Recently, a short time back ; as in सद्यो हुताग्नीन् *S*. 4.-Comp. -कालः the present time. -कालीन *a.* recent. -जात *a.* (सद्योजात) newly born. (-तः) 1 a calf. 2 an epithet of *Siva*. -पातिन् *a.* quickly perishing, frail ; Me 10. -शुद्धिः, -शौचं immediate purification.

सद्यस्क *a.* 1 New, recent. 2 Instantaneous.

सद्रु *a.* 1 Resting, staying. 2 Going.

सद्वंद्व *a.* Quarrelsome, fond of strife, contentious.

सद्वसथः A village.

सधर्मन् *a.* 1 Having similar properties. 2 Having similar duties. 3 Of the same sect or caste. 4 Like, resembling. -Comp. -चारिणी a legal wife, a legally married wife.

सधर्मिणी See सधर्मचारिणी above.

सधर्मिन् *a.* (णी *f.*) See सधर्मन्.

सधिस् *m.* An ox, a bull.

सध्रीची A female companion, confidante ; Bk. 6. 7.

सध्रीचीन *a.* Accompanying, associated with.

सध्र्यंच् *a.* (सध्रीची *f.*) Going along with, associated with, accompanying.-*m.* A companion (husband); *Si*. 8. 44.

सन् 1 P., 8 U. (सनति, सनोति, सनुते, सात ; *pass.* सन्यते, सायते, ; *desid.* सिसनिषति, सिषासति) 1 To love, like. 2 To worship, honour. 3 To acquire, obtain. 4 To receive graciously. 5 To honour with gifts, give, bestow, distribute.

सनः The flapping of an elephant's ears.

सनत् *m.* An epithet of Brahman. -*ind.* Always, perpetually. -Comp. -कुमारः N. of one of the four sons of Brahman.

सनसूत्र See सणसूत्र.

सना *ind.* Always, perpetually.

सनात् *ind.* Always.

सनातन *a.* (नी *f.*) 1 Perpetual, constant, eternal, permanent ; एष धर्मः सनातनः. 2 Firm, fixed, settled ; U. 5. 22. 3 Primeval, ancient. -तः 1 The primeval being, Vishṇu ; सनातनः पितरमुपागमत् स्वयं Bk. 1. 1. 2 N. of *Siva*, 3 Of Brahman. -नी 1 N. of Lakshmî. 2 Of Durgâ or Pârvatî. 3 Of Sarasvatî.

सनाथ *a.* 1 Having a master, lord or husband ; त्वया नाथेन वैदेही सनाथा ह्यद्य वर्तते Râm. 2 Possessed of a guardian or protector ; सनाथा इदानीं धर्मचारिणः *S*. 1. 3 Occupied by, possessed by. 4 Provided or furnished with, having, possessing, endowed with, full of, usually in comp. ; लतासनाथ इव प्रतिभाति *S*. 1 ; शिलातलसनाथो लतामंडपः V. 2 ; Me. 98; Ku. 7. 94 ; R. 9. 42, V. 4. 10.

सनाभि *a.* 1 Connected by the ame navel or womb, uterine. 2 Kindred, related. 3 Like resembling ; गंगावर्तसनाभिर्नाभिः Dk. **4** Affectionate. **-भिः 1** A uterine brother ; a near kinsman. **2** A relation, kinsman ; Ki. 13. 11. **3** A relation as far as the seventh degree.

सनाभ्यः A relation as far as the 7th degree.

सनिः 1 Worship, service. **2** A gift, donation. **3** An entreaty, a respectful solicitation (*f.* also in this sense).

सनिष्ठीवं, सनिष्ठेवं Speech accompanied with emission of saliva, sputtered speech.

सनी 1 A respectful entreaty. **2** A quarter or point of the compass. **3** Flapping of the elephant's ears.

सनीड (ल) *a.* **1** Living in the same nest, dwelling together. **2** Near, proximate.

संतः The two hands opened and the palms joined together.

संतक्षणं Sarcastic or cutting language, scoff, sarcasm.

संतत *p. p.* **1** Stretched, extended. **2** Uninterrupted, continual, constant, regular. **3** Lasting, eternal. **4** Much, many. **-तं** *ind.* Always, constantly, eternally, continually, perpetually.

संततिः *f.* **1** Stretching across, spreading along. **2** Extent, expanse, extension ; *S.* 7. 8. **3** Continuous line or flow, series, row, range, succession, continuity ; चिंतासंततितंतुजालनिबिडस्यूतेव लग्ना प्रिया Mâl. 5. 10 ; कुसुमसंततिसंततसंगिभिः *Si.* 6. 36. **5** Perpetuation, uninterrupted continuance ; R. 3. 1. **6** A race, lineage, family. **7** Offspring, progeny ; संततिः शुद्धवंश्या हि परत्रेह च शर्मणे R. 1. 69. **8** A heap, mass ; (अलं) सहसा संततिमंहसां विहंतुं Ki. 5. 17.

संतपनं 1 Heating, inflaming. **2** Torturing.

संतप्त *p. p.* **1** Heated, inflamed, red-hot, glowing. **2** Distressed, afflicted, tormented ; Me. 7. **-Comp. -अयस्** *n.* red-hot iron. **-वक्षस्** *n.* short-breathed.

संतमस् *n.* **संतमसं** All-pervading or universal darkness, great darkness ; निमज्जयन्संतमसे पराशयं N. 9. 98 ; *Si.* 9. 22 ; Bk. 5. 2.

संतर्जनं Threatening, reviling.

संतर्पणं 1 Satisfying, satiating. **2** Gratifying delighting. **3** That which gives delight. **4** A kind of sweet dish.

संतानः-नं 1 Stretching, extending, extension, expanse, spread. **2** Continuity, continuous flow or line, succession, continuance; अच्छिन्नामलसंतानाः Ku. 6. 69 ; संतानवाहीनि दुःखानि U. 4. 8. **3** Family, race. **4** Progeny, offspring, issue ; संतानार्थाय विधये R. 1. 34 ; संतानकामाय राज्ञे 2. 65, 18. 52. **5** One of the five trees of Indra's paradise.

संतानकः One of the five trees of Indra's paradise or its flower ; Ku. 6. 46, 7. 3 ; *Si.* 6. 67.

संतानिका 1 Froth, foam. **2** Cream. **3** A cob-web. **4** the blade of a knife or sword.

संतापः 1 Heat, great heat, inflammation ; Mâl. 3. 4. **2** Distress, torment, suffering, torture, agony, anguish ; संतापसंततिमहाव्यसनाय तस्यामासक्तमेतदनपेक्षितहेतु चेतः Mâl. 1. 23, *S.* 3. **3** Passion, rage. **4** Remorse, repentance ; Pt. 1. 109. **5** Penance, fatigues of penance, mortification of the body ; संतापे दिशतु शिवः शिवां प्रसक्तिं Ki. 5. 50.

संतापन *a.* (**-नी** *f.*) Burning, inflaming. **-नः** N. of one of the 5 arrows of Cupid. **-नं 1** Burning, scorching. **2** Paining, afflicting. **3** Exciting passion.

संतापित *p. p.* Heated, afflicted, tormented &c.

संतिः 1 End, destruction. **2** A gift; cf. सनि.

संतुष्टिः *f.* Complete satisfaction.

संतोषः 1 Satisfaction, contentment; संतोष एव पुरुषस्य परं निधानं Subhâsh. **2** Pleasure, delight, joy. **3** The thumb or fore-finger.

संतोषणं Pleasing, gratifying, comforting.

संत्यजनं Leaving, renouncing.

संत्रासः Fear, terror, alarm.

संदंशः 1 A pair of tongs. **2** Too great compression of the teeth in the pronunciation of vowels (or letters). **3** N. of a bell.

संदंशकः A pair of tongs.

संदर्भः 1 Stringing together, weaving, arranging. **2** Collection, uniting, mixture. **3** Consistency, continuity, regular connection, coherence ; संदर्भशुद्धिं गिरां Gît. 1. **4** Construction. **5** A composition, literary work ; रसगंगाधरनामा संदर्भोऽयं चिरं जयतु R. G. ; U. 4.

संदर्शनं A Seeing, beholding, viewing. **2** Gazing, looking steadfastly. **3** Meeting, seeing one another. **4** Sight, appearance, vision. **5** Regard, consideration.

संदानं 1 A rope, cord. **2** A chain, fetter. **-नः** That part of an elephant's temples whence ichor exudes.

संदानित *a.* **1** Bound, tied. **2** Fettered, chained.

संदानिनी A cow-pen (गोष्ठ).

संदावः Flight, retreat.

संदाहः Burning up, consuming.

संदिग्ध *p. p.* **1** Besmeared, covered. **2** Dubious, doubtful, uncertain ; as in संदिग्धमति-बुद्धि &c. **3** Mistaken for, confounded with ; Mâl. 1. 2. **4** Doubted, questioned. **5** Confused, obscure, unintelligible (as a sentence) **6** Dangerous, risky, unsafe. **7** Envenomed.

संदिष्ट *p. p.* **1** Pointed out, indicated. **2** Assigned. **3** Told, narrated, communicated. **4** Agreed to, promised. **-ष्टः** One entrusted with a message, a messenger, herald, courier (संदिष्टार्थ also). **-ष्टं** Information, news, tidings.

संदित *a.* Bound, chained, fettered.

संदी A small bed-stead, cot, couch.

संदीपन *a.* (**-नी** *f.*) **1** Kindling, inflaming, exciting ; U. 3. **2** Provoking ; U. 4. **-नः 1** One of the five arrows of Cupid. **-नं 1** Kindling, inflaming. **2** Exciting, stimulating ; अनंगसंदीपनमाशु कुर्वते Rs. 1. 12.

संदीप्त *p. p.* **1** Kindled or inflamed. **2** Excited, stimulated. **3** Instigated, stirred up, prompted.

संदुष्ट *p. p.* **1** Polluted, defiled. **2** Wicked, depraved.

संदूषणं Defiling, corrupting, vitiating.

संदेशः 1 Information, news, tidings. **2** Message, errand ; संदेशं मे हर धनपतिक्रोधविश्लेषितस्य Me. 7, 13 ; R. 12. 63 ; Ku. 6. 2. **3** Commission, command ; अनुष्ठितो गुरोः संदेशः *S.* 5. **-Comp. -अर्थः** the subject of a message. **-वाच्** a message. **-हरः 1** a news-bearer, messenger. **2** an envoy, ambassador.

संदेहः 1 Doubt, uncertainty, suspense ; अत्र कः संदेहः. **2** Risk; danger, peril ; जीवितसंदेहदोलामारोपितः K. ; अर्थार्जने प्रवृत्तिः ससंदेहः H. 1. **3** (In Rhet.) Doubt, regarded as a figure of speech, in which the close resemblance between two objects leads to one of them being mistaken for the other (this figure is also called ससंदेह by Mammaṭa and others); ससंदेहस्तु भेदोक्तौ तदनुक्तौ च संशयः K. P. 10 ; *e. g.* see Mâl. 1. 2 (*l.* 3.); V. 3. 2. **-Comp. -दोला** the swing of uncertainty, a state of suspense, dilemma, fix.

संदोहः 1 Milking. **2** The whole quantity of anything, a multitude, heap, mass, assemblage; कुंदमाकंदमधुबिंदुसंदोहवाहिना मारुतेनोत्ताम्यति Mâl. 3 ; Bv. 4. 9.

संद्रावः Flight, retreat.

संधा 1 Union, association. **2** Intimate union, close connection. **3** State, condition. **4** An agreement, a promise, stipulation, compact ; ततार संधामिव सत्यसंधः R. 14. 52 ; Mv. 7. 8. **5** Limit, boundary. **6** Fixity, steadiness. **7** Twilight. **8** Distillation (for संधान q. v.).

संधानं 1 Joining, uniting. **2** Union, junction, combination; यदर्धे विच्छिन्नं भवति कृतसंधानमिव तत् *S.* 1. 9 ; Ku. 5. 27 ; R. 12. 101. **3** Mixing, compounding (of medicines &c.). 4 Restoration, repairing. 5 Fitting, fixing (as an arrow to the bow-string); तत्साधुकृतसंधानं प्रतिसंहर सायकं S. 1. 11 ; Si. 20. 8. 6 Alliance, league, friendship, peace ; सुदृढघटबत्सुखभेद्यो दुःसंधानश्च दुर्जनो भवति H. 1. 92 (where it has sense 1 also). 7 A joint ; पादजंघयोः संधाने गुल्फः Susr. 8 Attention. 9 Direction. 10 Supporting. 11 Distillation (of liquors). 12 Spirituous liquor or a kind of it. 13 A kind of relish eaten to excite thirst. 14 Preparation of pickles. 15 Contraction of the skin by means of astringents. 16 Sour rice-gruel.

संधानित *a.* 1 United, strung together. 2 Bound, tied.

संधानी 1 Distillation. 2 Braziery, foundery.

संधिः 1 Union, junction, combination, connection ; संधये सरला सूची वक्रा छेदाय कर्तरी Subhâsh. ; Me. 58. 2 A compact, agreement. 3 Alliance, league, friendship, peace, treaty of peace (one of the six expedients to be used in foreign politics) ; कति प्रकाराः संधीनां भवंति H 4 ; (the several kinds are described in H. 4. 106-125); शत्रूणां न हि संदध्यात्सुश्लिष्टेनापि संधिना H. 1. 88. 4 A joint, articulation (of the body); तुरगानुधावनकंडित संधेः S. 2. 5 A fold (of a garment). 6 A breach, hole, chasm 7 Especially a mine, chasm or opening made by thieves in a wall or underneath a building ; वृक्षवाटिकापरिसरे संधिं कृत्वा प्रविष्टोऽस्मि मध्यमकं Mk. 3 ; Ms. 9. 276. 8 Separation, division. 9 Euphony, euphonic junction or coalition (in gram). 10 An interval, a pause. 11 A critical juncture. 12 An opportune moment. 13 A period at the expiration of each *Yuga* or age. 14 A division or joint (in a drama); they are five, see S. D. 330-332); Ku. 7. 91. 15 The vulva. **-Comp.** **-अक्षरं** a diphthong. **-चोरः** a house-breaker, a thief who breaks into a house **-छेदः** making holes or breaches. (in a wall &c.). **-जं** spirituous liquor. **-जीवकः** one who lives by dishonest means (particularly as a go-between). **-दूषणं** violation of a treaty ; अरिषु हि विजयार्थिनः क्षितीशा विदधति सोपधि संधिदूषणानि Ki. 1. 45. **-बंधः** the tissues of joints ; *S.* 2. **-बंधनं** a ligament, tendon, nerve. **-भंगः,-मुक्तिः** *f.* dislocation of a joint. **-विग्रह** *m.* du. peace and war. °**अधिकारः** the office of the minister for foreign affairs. **-विचक्षणः** one skilled in negotiating peaces. **-विद्** *m.* a negotiator of treaties. **-वेला** 1 the time of twilight. 2 Any connecting period. **-हारकः** a house-breaker.

संधिकः A kind of fever.

संधिका Distillation (of liquors).

संधित *a.* 1 United, joined. 2 Bound, tied. 3 Reconciled, allied. 4 Fixed, fitted. 5 Mixed together. 6 Pickled, preserved. **-तं** 1 Pickles. 2 Spirituous liquor.

संधिनी 1 A cow in heat (united with the bull or impregnated by him). 2 A cow milked unseasonably.

संधिला 1 A hole or breach made in a wall, pit, chasm. 2 A river. 3 Spirituous liquor.

संधुक्षणं 1 Kindling, inflaming. 2 Exciting, stimulating.

संधुक्षित *p. p.* Kindled, inflamed, excited.

संधेय *a.* 1 To be united or joined. 2 Capable of being reconciled ; सुजनस्तु कनकघटवद् दुर्भेद्यश्चाशुसंधेयः H. 1. 92. 3 To be made peace with. 4 To be aimed at.

संध्या 1 Union. 2 Joint, division. 3 Morning or evening twilight ; अनुरागवती संध्या दिवसस्तत्पुरस्सरः । अहो दैवगतिश्चित्रा तथापि न समागमः K. P. 7. 4 Early morning. 5 Evening, dusk. 6 The period which precedes a *Yuga*, the time intervening between the expiration of one *Yuga* and the commencement of another ; Ms. 1. 69. 7 The morning, noon and evening prayers of a Brâhmaṇa ; Ms. 2. 69, 4. 93. 8 A promise, an agreement. 9 A boundary, limit. 10 Thinking, meditation. 11 A kind of flower. 12 N. of a river. 13 N. of the wife of Brahman. **-Comp.** **-अभ्रं** 1 an evening cloud (tinged with the sun's rays); संध्याभ्ररेखेव मुहूर्तरागाः Pt. 1. 194. 2 a kind of red-chalk. **-कालः** 1 the period of twilight. 2 evening. **-नाटिन्** *m.* an epithet of *Siva.* **-पुष्पी** 1 a kind of jasmine. 2 a nutmeg. **-बलः** a demon (राक्षस). **-रागः** red lead. **रामः** (some take आराम as the word here) an epithet of Brahman. **-वंदनं** the morning and evening prayers.

सन्न *p. p.* 1 Sitting down, settling down, lying. 2 Dejected, sunk down, downcast. 3 Drooping, relaxed. 4 Weak, low, feeble. 5 Wasted away, decayed. 6 Perished, destroyed. 7 Still, motionless. 8 Shrunk. 9 Adjacent, near. **-न्नः** The tree called पियाल. **-न्नं** A little, a small quantity.

सन्नक *a.* Low, dwarfish. **-Comp.** **-द्रुः** the Piyâla tree.

सन्नतर *a.* Lower, more depressed (as a tone).

संनत *p. p.* 1 Bent down, stooping. 2 Downcast. 3 Contracted.

संनतिः *f.* 1 Obeisance, respectful salutation, reverence. 2 Humility. 3 A kind of sacrifice. 4 A sound, noise.

संनद्ध *p. p.* 1 Tied or bound together, girded or put on. 2 Clad or dressed in armour, accoutred, mailed. 3 Arranged, ready, or prepared for battle, armed, fully equipped ; नवजलधरः संनद्धोऽयं न दृप्तनिशाचरः V. 4. 1 ; Me. 8. 4 Ready, prepared, formed, arranged in general ; R. 3. 7. 5 Pervading ; कुसुममिव लोभनीयं यौवनमंगेषु संनद्धं S. 1. 21. 6 Well-provided with anything. 7 Murderous. 8 Closely attached, bordering, near.

संनयः 1 A collection, multitude, quantity, number. 2 Rear, rear-guard (of an army).

संनहनं 1 Preparing, equipping, arming oneself. 2 Preparation. 3 Fastening tightly. 4 Industry, effort.

संनाहः 1 Arming (oneself) or preparation for battle, putting on armour. 2 Warlike preparation, equipment. 3 Armour, mail ; आस्मिन्कलौ खलोत्सृष्टदुष्टवाग्बाणदारुणे । कथं जीवेज्जगन्न स्युः संनाहाः सज्जना यदि Kîr. K. 1. 36, Ki. 16. 12.

संनाह्यः A war-elephant.

संनिकर्षः 1 Drawing near. bringing near. 2 Vicinity, proximity ; presence ; उत्कंठते च युष्मत्संनिकर्षस्य U. 6 ; 3. 74 ; R. 7. 8, 6. 20. 3 Connection, relation. 4 (In Nyâya phil.) Connection of an organ of sense (इंद्रिय) with its object (विषय) ; this is of six kinds.

संनिकर्षणं 1 Bringing near. 2 Approaching, approximating. 3 Proximity, vicinity.

संनिकृष्ट *p. p.* 1 Approximate. 2 Proximate, adjacent, near. **-ष्टं** Proximity, vicinity.

संनिचयः A collection.

संनिधातृ *m.* 1 One who brings near. 2 One who deposits. 3 A receiver of stolen goods ; Ms. 9. 278. 4 An officer who introduces people at court.

संनिधानं, संनिधिः 1 Putting down together, juxta-position. 2 Proximity, vicinity, presence ; N. 2. 53. 3 Perceptibility, appearance. 4 A receptacle. 5 Receiving, taking charge of. 6 Combination, aggregate.

संनिपातः 1 Falling down, alighting, descent. 2 Falling together, meeting ; Ki. 13. 58. 3 Collision, contact. 4 Union, conjunction, combination, mixture, miscellaneous collection ; धूमज्योतिःसलिलमरुतां संनिपातः क्व मेघः Me. 5. 5 An assemblage, a collection, multitude, number ; नानारत्नज्योतिषां संनिपातैः Ki. 5. 36 ; एको हि दोषो गुणसंनिपाते निमज्जति Ku. 1. 3. 6 Arrival. 7 A combined derangement of the three humours of the body causing fever which is of a dangerous kind. 8 A kind of musical time or measure.

–Comp. –ज्वर: fever arising from a vitiated state of the three humours of the body.

संनिबंधः 1 Binding firmly. 2 Connection, attachment. 3 Effectiveness.

संनिभ *a*. Like, similar (at the end of comp.) ; Rs. 1. 11.

संनियोगः 1 Union, attachment. 2 Appointment.

संनिरोधः Obstruction, hindrance.

संनिवृत्तिः *f*. 1 Return ; *S*. 6. 10 ; R. 8. 49, 10. 27. 2 Desisting from. 3 Restraint, forbearance.

संनिवेशः 1 Deep entrance into, ardent devotion or attachment, close application. 2 A collection, multitude, assemblage. 3 Union, combination, arrangement ; रमणीय एष वः सुमनसां संनिवेशः Mâl. 1, 9. 4 Site, place, situation, position ; Ku. 7. 25; R 6. 19. 5 Vicinity, proximity. 6 Form, figure ; उद्दामशरीरसंनिवेशः Mâl. 3. निर्माणसंनिवेशः K. 7 A hut, dwelling-place ; R. 14. 76. 8 Seating in the proper places, giving seats to ; क्रियतां समाजसंनिवेशः U. 7. 9 Insertion. 10 An open space near a town where people assemble for amusement, exercise &c.

संनिहित *p. p*. 1 Placed near, lying close, near, contiguous, neighbouring ; *S*. 4. 2 Close, Proximate, at hand. 3 Present ; अपि संनिहितोऽत्र कुलपतिः *S*. 1 ; हृदयसंनिहिते *S*. 3. 20. 4 Fixed, placed, deposited. 5 Prepared, ready; Mu. 1. 6 Staying or being in –Comp. –अपाय *a*. having destruction close at hand, frail, perishable, transitory ; कायः संनिहितापायः Pt. 2. 177.

संन्यसनं 1 Resignation, laying down. 2 Complete renunciation of the world and its attachments ; न च संन्यासनादेव सिद्धिं समधिगच्छति Bg. 3. 4. 3 Consigning, entrusting to the care of.

संन्यस्त *p. p*. 1 Laid or placed down. 2 Deposited. 3 Entrusted, consigned. 4 Laid aside, relinquished, renounced.

संन्यासः 1 Leaving, abandonment. 2 Complete renunciation of the world and its possessions and attachments, abandonment of temporal ; concerns ; Bg. 6. 2, 18. 2 ; Ms. 1. 114 ; 5. 108. 3 A deposit, trust. 4 A stake or wager in a game. 5 Giving up the body, death. 6 Indian spikenard.

संन्यासिन् *m*. 1 One who lays down and deposits. 2 One who completely renounces the world and its attachments, an ascetic, a Brâhmana in the fourth order of his religious life ; ज्ञेयः स नित्यसंन्यासी यो न द्वेष्टि न कांक्षति Bg. 5. 3. 3 One who abstains from food (त्यक्ताहार) ; Bk. 7. 76.

सप् 1 P. (सपति) 1 To honour, worship. 2 To connect.

सपक्ष *a*. 1 Winged, having wings. 2 Having a side or party. 3 Belonging to the same side or party. 4 (Hence) Kindred, like, similar (fig.); दलद्द्राक्षानिर्यद्रसमरसपक्षा भणितयः Bv. 2. 77. 5 Containing the पक्ष or subject of an inference. –क्षः 1 An adherent, a follower, partisan. 2 A kindred, a kinsman ; M. 4. 3 (In logic). An instance on the same side, a similar instance ; निश्चितसाध्यवान् सपक्षः T. S.

सपत्नः An enemy, adversary, a rival ; R. 9. 8.

सपत्नी A rival or fellow wife, rival mistress, co-wife (having the same husband with another) ; दिशः सपत्नी भव दक्षिणस्याः R. 6. 63, 14. 86.

सपत्नीक *a*. Attended by a wife.

सपत्राकरणं 1 Wounding in such a manner that the feathered part of the arrow enters the body. 2 Causing excessive pain ; cf. निष्पत्राकरण.

सपत्राकृतिः *f*. Great agony or pain, excessive affliction or torment.

सपदि *ind*. Instantly, in a moment, immediately ; सपदि मदनानलो दहति मम मानसं Gît. 10 ; Ku. 3. 76 ; 6. 4.

सपर्या 1 Worship, honouring; सोऽहं सपर्याविधिभाजनेन R. 5. 22, 2. 22, 11. 35, 13. 46 ; Si. 1. 14. 2 Service, attendance.

सपाद *a*. 1 Having feet. 2 Increased by a fourth part.

सपिंडः 'Having the same पिंड or funeral rice-ball offering', a kinsman connected by the offering of the funeral rice-ball to the Manes of certain relations ; Y. 1. 52 ; Ms. 2. 247, 5. 59.

सापिंडीकरणं The performance of a particular Srâddha in honour of deceased relatives called सपिंड q. v., to be performed at the end of one full year after the death of a relative, but now usually performed on the 12th day after death as part of the funeral obsequies.

सपीतिः *f*. Drinking together or in company., compotation.

सप्तक *a*. (का or की *f*.) 1 Containing seven. 2 Seven. 3 Seventh. –कं A collection of seven things, (verses &c.)

सप्तकी A woman's girdle or zone.

सप्ततिः *f*. Seventy. °तम *a*. 70th.

सप्तधा *ind*. Seven-fold.

सप्तन् *num. a*. (always pl. सप्त nom. and acc.) Seven. –Comp. –अंग *a*. see सप्तप्रकृति below.–आर्चिस् *a*. 1 having seven tongues or flames. 2 evil-eyed, of inauspicious look. (–*m*.) 1 N. of fire. 2 of Saturn. –अशीतिः *f*. eighty-seven.–अश्रं a heptagon.–अश्वः the sun. °वाहनः the sun. –अहः seven days, *i. e*. a week. –आत्मन् *m*. an epithet of Brahman. –ऋषि (सप्तर्षि) *m*. pl. 1 the seven sages ; *i. e*. मरीचि, अत्रि, अंगिरस्, पुलस्त्य, पुलह, क्रतु and वसिष्ठ. 2 the constellation called Ursa Major (the seven stars of which are said to be the seven sages mentioned above). –चत्वारिंशत् *f*. forty-seven. –जिह्वः –ज्वालः fire. –तंतुः a sacrifice ; Si. 14. 6. –त्रिंशत् *f*. thirty-seven. –दशन् *a*. seventeen. –दीधितिः N. of fire. –द्वीप an epithet of the earth. –धातु *m*. pl. the seven constituent elements of the body ; *i. e*. chyle, blood, flesh, fat, bone, marrow, and semen. –नवतिः *f*. ninety-seven. –नाडीचक्रं a kind of astrological diagram used as a means of foretelling rain. –पर्णः (so सप्तच्छदः सप्तपत्रः) N. of a tree. –पदी the seven steps at a marriage (the bride and bridegroom walk together seven steps, after which the marriage becomes irrevocable). –प्रकृतिः *f*. pl. the seven constituent parts of a kingdom ; स्वाम्यमात्यसुहृत्कोशराष्ट्रदुर्गबलानि च Ak.; see प्रकृति also. –भद्रः the Sirîsha tree –भूमिक, -भौम *a*. seven stories high (as a palace). –रात्रं a period of seven nights. –विंशतिः *f*. twenty-seven. –विध *a*. seven-fold, of seven sorts. –शतं 1 700. 2 107. (–ती) an aggregate or collection of 700 verses or stanzas. –सप्तिः an epithet of the sun ; सर्वैरुस्रैः समग्रैस्त्वमिव नृपगुणैर्दीप्यते सप्तसप्तिः M. 2. 13.

सप्तम *a*. (मी *f*.) 1 The seventh. –मी *f*. The seventh or locative case (in gram.). 2 The seventh day of a lunar fort-night.

सप्तला A kind of jasmine (double jasmine).

सप्तिः 1 A yoke. 2 A horse ; जवो हि सप्तेः परमं विभूषणं Subhâsh. ; see सप्तसप्ति also.

सप्रणय *a*. Affectionate, friendly.

सप्रत्यय *a*. 1 Placing confidence in. 2 Certain, sure.

सफरः –री A small glittering fish ; cf. शफर.

सफल *a*. 1 Fruitful, bearing or yielding fruit, productive (fig. also). 2 Accomplished, fulfilled, succesful.

सबंधु *a*. 1 Closely connected. 2 Having a friend, befreinded. –धुः A relation, kinsman.

सबालिः Evening twilight.

सबाध *a*. 1 Hurtful. 2 Oppressive.

सब्रह्मचर्यं Fellow-studentship (being disciples of the same teacher).

सब्रह्मचारिन् *m*. 1 A fellow-student, one going through the same studies and observing the same austerities. 2 A fellow-sufferer, sympathiser ; दुःखसब्रह्मचारिणी तरलिका क गता K.; हे व्यसनसब्रह्मचारिन् गद्दि न गुह्यं तत श्रोतुमिच्छामि Mu. 6.

सभा 1 An assembly, a council, conclave; पंडितसभां कारितवान् Pt. 1 ; न सा सभा यत्र न संति वृद्धाः H. 1. 2 Company, society, meeting, large number. 3 Council-chamber or hall. 4 A court of justice. 5 A public audience (modern *levee*). 6 A gambling house. 7 Any room or place much frequented. –Comp. –आस्तारः 1 an assistant at an assembly. 2 a member of a society. –पतिः 1 the president of of a society, chairman. 2 the keeper of a gaming-house. –पूजा worship or reverence paid to the audience. –सद् *m.* 1 an assistant at an assembly or meeting. 2 a member of an assembly or meeting. 3 an assessor, a juror.

सभाज् 10 U. (सभाजयति-ते) 1 To salute, pay respects, greet, render homage to, congatulate ; स्नेहात्सभाजयितुमेत्य U. 1. 7 ; *Si*. 13. 14 ; *S*. 5. 2 To honour, worship, respect. 3 To please, gratify. 4 To beautify, adorn, grace ; U. 4. 19. 5 To show.

सभाजनं 1 (*a*) Paying respects to, salutation, honouring, worshipping ; *Si*. 13. 14. (*b*) Welcoming, congratulation ; R. 13. 43, 14. 18. 2 Civility, courtesy, politeness. 3 Service.

सभावनः N. of *Siva*.

सभि(भी)कः The keeper of a gaming house ; अयमस्माकं पूर्वसभिको माथुर इत एवागच्छति Mk. 3 ; Y. 2. 139.

सभ्य *a*. 1 Belonging to an assembly. 2 Fit for society. 3 Refined, polished, civilized. 4 Well-bred, polite, courteous ; R. 1. 55, Ku. 7. 29. 5 Confidential, trusty, faithful. –भ्यः 1 An assessor. 2 An assistant at an assembly. 3 A person of honourable parentage. 4 The keeper of a gaming-house. 5 The servant of the keeper of a gaming-house.

सभ्यता, -त्वं Politeness, good manners or breeding.

सम् I. 1 P. (समति) 1 To be confused or agitated. 2 Not to be confused or agitated. –II. 10 U. (समयति-ते) To be agitated.

सम् *ind*. 1 As a prefix to verbs and verbal derivatives it means (*a*) with, together with, together ; as in संगम्, संभाषण, संधा, संयुज् &c. (*b*) Sometimes it intensifies the meaning of the simple root, and may be translated by 'very, quite, greatly, thoroughly, very much' ; संतुष्, संतोष, संन्यस्, संन्यास, संताप &c. 2 As prefixed to nouns to form comp it means, 'like, same, similar,' as in समर्थ. 3 Sometimes it means 'near', 'before' ; as in समक्ष.

सम *a*. 1 Same, identical. 2 Equal, as in समलोष्टकांचनः R. 8. 21 ; Bg. 2. 38. 3 Like, similar, resembling with instr. or gen. or in comp. ; गुणयुक्तो दरिद्रोपि नेश्वरैरगुणैः समः Subhâsh. ; Ku. 3. 13, 23. 4 Even, level, plain ; समदेशवर्तिनस्ते न दुरासदो भविष्यति *S*. 1. 5 Even (as number). 6 Impartial, fair. 7 Just, honest, upright. 8 Good, virtuous. 9 Ordinary, common. 10 Mean, middling. 11 Straight. 12 Suitable, convenient. 13 Indifferent, unmoved, unaffected by passion. 14 All, every one. 15 All, whole, entire, complete. –मं A level plain, flat country ; Ki. 9. 11. –मं *ind*. 1 With, together with, in company with, accompanied by ; (with instr.) आहो निवत्स्यति समं हरिणांगनाभिः *S*. 1. 27 ; R. 2. 25, 8. 63, 16. 72. 2 Equally ; यथा सर्वाणि भूतानि धरा धारयते समं Ms. 9. 311. 3 Like, similarly, in the same manner ; Pt. 1. 78. 4 Entirely. 5 Simultaneously, all at once, at the same time, together ; नवं पयो यत्र घनैर्मया च त्वद्विप्रयोगाश्रु समं विसृष्टं R. 13. 26, 4. 4 ; 10. 60 ; 14. 1. –Comp. –अंशः an equal share. °हारिन् *m*. a co-heir. –अंतर *a*. parallel. –आचारः 1 equal or similar conduct. 2 proper practice. –उदकं a mixture of half buttermilk and half water. –उपमा a kind of Upamâ or simile. –कन्या a fit or suitable girl (fit to be married). –कर्णः an equi-diagonal tetragon. –कालः the sam time or moment. (–लं) *ind*. at the same time, simultaneously. –कालीन *a*. contemporary, coeval. –कोलः a serpent, snake. –क्षेत्रं (in astr.) an epithet of a particular arrangement of the Nakshatras. –खातः an equal excavation, a parallelopipedon. –गंधकः incense. –चतुरस्र *a*. square. (स्रं) an equilateral tetragon. –चतुर्भुजः -जं a rhombus. –चित्त *a*. 1 even-minded, equable, equanimous. 2 indifferent. –छेद्, –छेदनं *a*. having the same denominator. –जाति *a*. homogeneous. –ज्ञा fame. –त्रिभुजः -जं an equilateral triangle. –दर्शन,-दर्शिन् *a*. viewing equally, impartial ; विद्याविनयसंपन्ने ब्राह्मणे गवि हस्तिनि । शुनि चैव श्वपाके च पंडिताः समदर्शिनः Bg. 5. 17. –दुःख *a*. feeling for another's woe, sympathising (with another) ; a fellow-sufferer ; Ku. 4. 4. °सुख *a*. a companion or partner in joy and sorrow; *S*. 3. 12. –दृश्, –दृष्टि *a*. impartial. –बुद्धि *a*. 1 impartial. 2 indifferent, stoical. –भाव *a*. having the same nature or property. (–वः) sameness, equability. –मंडलं (in astr.) the prime vertical line. –मय *a*. of like origin. –रंजित *a*. tinged. –रभः a particular mode of sexual enjoyment –रेख *a*. straight ; प्रकृत्या यद्वक्रं तदपि समरेखं नयनयोः *S*. 1. 9. –लंबः -बं a trapezoid. –वर्णः community of caste. –वर्तिन् *a*. equal-minded, impartial. (–*m*.) Yama, the god of death. –वृत्तं 1 an even metre, *i. e*. a stanza the lines of which have all the same number of feet. 2 see सममंडल. –वृत्ति *a*. equable, fair. –वेधः mean depth. -शोधनं equal subtraction, *i. e*. subtraction of the same quantity on both sides of an equation. –संधिः peace on equal terms. –सुप्तिः *f*. universal sleep (as at the end of a Kalpa). –स्थ *a*. 1 equal, uniform. 2 level. 3 like. –स्थलं an even ground.

समक्ष *a*. Being before the eyes, visible, present. –क्षं *ind*. In the presence of, visibly, before the very eyes ; Ku. 5. 1.

समग्र *a*. All, whole, entire, complete ; M. 2. 13.

समंगा Bengal madder (मंजिष्ठा).

समजः 1 A multitude of beasts, animals or birds, a herd, flock. 2 A number of fools. –जं A wood, forest.

समज्या 1 A meeting, an assembly. 2 Fame, renown, celebrity.

समंजस *a*. 1 Proper, reasonable, right, fit. 2 Correct, true, accurate. 3 Clear, intelligible ; as in असमंजस q. v. 4 Virtuous, good, just ; भूज्ञाधिरूढस्य समंजसं जनं Ki. 10. 12. 5 Practised, experienced. 6 Healthy. –सं 1 Propriety, fitness. 2 Accuracy. 3 Correct evidence.

समता-त्वं 1 Sameness, identity. 2 Likeness, similarity. 3 Equality. 4 Impartiality, fairness ; समतां नी 'to treat as equal' Ms. 9. 218. 5 Equanimity. 6 Perfectness. 7 Commonness. 8 Evenness.

समतिक्रमः Transgression, omission.

समतीत *a*. Past, gone by ; R. 8 78.

समद *a*. 1 Intoxicated, furious. 2 Mad with rut. 3 Drunk with passion; U. 2. 20.

समधिक *a*. 1 Exceeding. 2 Excessive, abundant, plentiful ; U. 4. –कं *ind*. Very much, exceedingly.

समधिगमनं Surpassing, overcoming.

समध्व *a*. Travelling in company.

समनुज्ञानं 1 Assent, consent. 2 Entire approval, full concurrence.

समंत *a*. 1 Being on every side, universal 2 Complete, entire. –तः Limit, boundary, term. (समंतं, समंततः समंतात् are used adverbially in the sense of 'from every side', 'all around', 'on all sides', 'wholly', (completely'). –Comp. –दुग्धा the plant called स्नुही q. v. –पंचकं N. of the district called Kurukshetra or of a place near it ; Ve. 6. –भद्रः a Budd a or the Buddha. –भुज् *m*. fire.

समन्यु *a*. 1 Sorrowful. 2 Enraged.

समन्वयः 1 Regular succession or order. 2 Connected sequence, mutual connection, applicability (तात्पर्य) ; तत्तु समन्वयात् Br. Sût. I. 1.

4 ; न च तद्गताना पदानां ब्रह्मस्वरूपविषये निश्चिते समन्वयेऽर्थांतरकल्पना युक्ता S. B. 3 Conjunction.

समन्वित p. p. 1 Connected with, connected in natural order. 2 Followed. 3 Endowed with, possessing, full of. 4 Affected by.

समभिप्लुत p. p. 1 Inundated. 2 Eclipsed.

समभिव्याहारः 1 Mentioning together. 2 Association, company. 3 Proximity to or association with a word, the meaning of which is clearly ascertained or understood.

समभिसरणं 1 Approaching. 2 Seeking, wishing for.

समभिहारः 1 Taking together. 2 Repetition. 3 Surplus, excess.

समभ्यर्चनं Worshipping, reverencing.

समभ्याहारः Accomponiment, association.

समयः 1 Time in general. 2 Occasion, opportunity. 3 Fit time, proper time or season, right moment , Ku. 3. 25. 4 An agreement, a compact, contract, engagement ; मिथःसमयात् S. 5. 5 Convention, conventional usage. 6 An established rule of conduct, a ceremonial custom, usual practice ; Ki. 1. 28 ; U. 1. 7 The convention of poets ; (e. g. that persons separated from their beloveds are affected at the sight of clouds). 8 An appointment, assignation. 9 A condition, stipulation ; V. 5. 10 A law, rule, regulation ; Y. 3. 19. 11 Direction, order, instruction, precept. 12 Emergency, exigency. 13 An oath. 14 A sign, hint, indication. 15 Limit, boundary. 16 A demonstrated conclusion, doctrine, tenet ; बौद्ध°, वैशेषिक° &c. 17 End, conclusion, termination 18 Success, prosperity. 19 End of trouble. -Comp. -अध्युषितं a time at which neither the stars nor the sun is visible. -अनुवर्तिन् a. following established customs. -अनुसारेण, -उचितं ind. suitably to the occasion, as the occasion demands. -आचारः conventional practice, established usage. -क्रिया making an agreement. -परिरक्षणं observance of a compact, treaty or agreement; समयपरिरक्षणं क्षमं ते Ki. 1. 45. -व्यभिचारः breaking an agreement, violation or breach of contract. -व्यभिचारिन् a. breaking an agreement.

समया ind. 1 Duly, seasonably, in due time. 2 At a fixed or appointed time. 3 In the midst, within, between. 4 Near (with acc.) ; समया सौधभित्तिं Dk. ; Si. 6. 73, 15. 9, Nolad. 4. 8.

समरः-रं War, battle, fight ; कर्णादयोऽपि समरात्परा इमुखीभवंति Ve. 3. -Comp. -उद्देशः, -भूमिः battle-field. -मूर्धन् m., -शिरस् n. the front or van of battle.

समर्चनं Worshipping, honouring, adoration.

समर्ण a. 1 Afflicted, pained, wounded. 2 Asked, solicited.

समर्थ a. 1 Strong, powerful. 2 Competent, allowed, qualified ; प्रतिग्रहसमर्थोऽपि Ms. 4. 186, Y. 1. 213. 3 Fit, suitable, proper ; तद्धनुर्ग्रहणमेव राघवः प्रत्यपद्यत समर्थमुत्तरं R. 11. 79. 4 Made fit or proper, prepared. 5 Having the same meaning. 6 Significant. 7 Having proper aim or force, very forcible. 8 Being in apposition. 9 Connected in sense. -र्थः 1 A significant word (in gram.). 2 The coherence of words together in a significant sentence.

समर्थकं Aloe-wood.

समर्थनं 1 Establishing, supporting, corroborating 2 Defending, vindicating, justifying ; स्थिनेष्वेतत्समर्थनं K. P. 7. 3 Pleading, advocating. 4 Judging, considering, imagining. 5 Deliberation, determination, deciding on the propriety or otherwise of anything. 6 Adequacy, efficacy, force, capability. 7 Energy, perseverance. 8 Reconciling differences, allaying disputes. 9 Objection.

समर्धक a. 1 Granting a boon. 2 Causing to prosper.

समर्पणं Giving or handing over to, delivering, consigning.

समर्याद a. 1 Limited, bounded. 2 Near, proximite. 3 Correct in conduct, keeping within bounds of propriety. 4 Respectful, courteous.

समल a. 1 Dirty, foul, filthy, impure. 2 Sinful. -लं Excrement, ordure, feces.

समवकारः A kind of drama ; (thus described in S. D. :—वृत्तं समवकारे तु ख्यातं देवासुराश्रय। सेधय। निर्विमर्शास्तु त्रयोंकाः &c. 515).

समवतारः 1 A descent. 2 A descent into a river or sacred bathing place ; समवतारसमैरसमैस्तटैः Ki. 5. 7.

समवस्था 1 Fixed condition. 2 Similar condition or state ; S. 4. 3 State or condition in general ; R. 19. 50 ; M. 4. 7.

समवस्थित p. p. 1 Remaining fixed. 2 Steady.

समवाप्तिः f. Obtaining, acquisition.

समवायः 1 Combination, union, conjunction, aggregate, collection ; सर्वाविनयानामेकैकमप्येषामायतनं किमुत समवायः K. ; बहूनामप्यसाराणां समवायो हि दुर्जयः Subbâsh. 2 A number, multitude, heap. 3 Close connection, cohesion. 4 (In Vais. phil.) Intimate union, constant and inseparable connection, inseparable inherence or existence of one thing in another, one of the seven categories of the Vaiseshikas.

समवायिन् a. 1 Closely or intimately connected. 2 Multitudinous. -Comp. -कारणं inseparable cause, the material cause (one of the three kinds of कारण mentioned in Vaiseshikha phil.).

समवेत p. p. 1 Come together, met, united, joined. 2 Intimately united or inherent, inseparably connected. 3 Comprised or contained in a larger number.

समष्टिः f. Collective pervasion or aggregate, an aggregate which is considered as made up of parts each of which is consubstantially the same with the whole (opp. व्यष्टि q. v.). समष्टिरीशः सर्वेषां स्वात्मतादात्म्यवेदनात्। तदभावात्ततोऽन्ये तु ज्ञायंते व्यष्टिसंज्ञया ॥ Panchdasi.

समसनं 1 Joining together, combination. 2 Compounding, formation of compound words. 3 Contraction.

समस्त p. p. 1 Thrown together, combined. 2 Compounded. 3 Pervading the whole of anything. 4 Abridged, contracted, condensed. 5 All, whole, entire.

समस्या 1 Proposing part of a stanza to another to be completed, the part of a stanza so given to be completed ; कः श्रीपतिः का विषमा समस्या Subhâsh. ; thus the lines वागर्थाविव संपृक्तौ, शतकोटिप्रविस्तरं, तुरासाहं पुरोधाय are completed by नेमुः सर्वे सुराः शिवौ. 2 (Hence) Completing or filling up what is incomplete ; गौरीव पत्या सुभगा कदाचित्कर्त्रीयमप्यर्धतनुसमस्यां N. 7. 83. (समस्या = संघटनं).

समा (Generally in pl. but used by Pâṇini in sing. also, e. g. समां समां P. V. 2. 12.) A year ; तेनाष्टौ परिगमिताः समाः कथंचित् R. 8. 92 ; तयोश्चतुर्दशैकेन रामं प्राव्राजयत्समाः 12. 6 ; 19. 4 ; Mv. 4. 41. -ind. With, together with.

समांसमीना A cow bearing a calf every year.

समाकर्षिन् a (णी f.) 1 Attracting. 2 Spreading far, diffusing fragrance. -m. Diffused odour, a scent spreading afar.

समाकुल a. 1 Full of, thronged, crowded. 2 Greatly agitated, bewildered, confused, flurried.

समाख्या 1 Fame, reputation, celebrity. 2 A name, appellation.

समाख्यात p. p. 1 Reckoned up, counted, summed up. 2 Fully related, declared, proclaimed. 3 Celebrated, famous.

समागत p. p. 1 Come together, met, joined, united. 2 Arrived. 3 Being in conjunction.

समागतिः *f.* 1 Coming together, union, meeting. 2 Arrival, approach. 3 Similar condition or progress.

समागमः 1 Union, meeting, encountering, combination ; अहो दैवगतिश्चित्रा तथापि न समागमः K. P. 7 ; R. 8. 4, 92, 19. 16. 2 Intercourse, association, society ; as in सत्समागमः. 3 Approach, arrival. 4 Conjunction (in astr.).

समाघातः 1 Killing, slaughter. 2 War, battle.

समाचयनं Accumulation.

समाचरणं Practising, observing, behaving.

समाचारः 1 Proceeding, going. 2 Practice, conduct, behaviour. 3 Proper conduct or behaviour. 4 News, information, report, tidings.

समाजः 1 An assembly, a meeting; विशेषतः सर्वविदां समाजे विभूषणं मौनमपंडितानां Bh. 2. 7. 2 A society, club, an association. 3 A number, multitude, collection. 4 A party, convivial meeting. 5 An elephant.

समाजिकः A member of an assembly ; see सामाजिक.

समाज्ञा Fame, reputation.

समादानं 1 Receiving fully. 2 Receiving suitable gifts. 3 The daily observances of the Jaina sect.

समादेशः Command, order, direction, instruction.

समाधा See समाधान below.

समाधानं 1 Putting together, uniting. 2 Fixing the mind in abstract contemplation on the true nature of spirit. 3 Profound or abstract meditation, deep contemplation. 4 Intentness. 5 Steadiness, composure, peace (as of mind), satisfaction ; चित्तस्य समाधानं ; बुद्धेः समाधानं G. L. 18. 6 Clearing up a doubt, replying to the Pûrvapaksha ; answering an objection. 7 Agreeing, promising. 8 (In dramas) A leading incident which unexpectedly gives rise to the whole plot.

समाधिः 1 Collecting, composing, concentrating (as mind). 2 Profound or abstract meditation, concentration of mind on one object, perfect absorption of thought into the one object of meditation, *i. e.* the Supreme Spirit, (the 8th and last stage of Yoga); आत्मेश्वराणां न हि जातु विघ्नाः समाधिभेदप्रभवो भवंति Ku. 3. 40, 50 ; Mk. 1. 1 ; Bh. 3. 54 ; R. 8. 78 ; Si. 4. 55. 3 Intentness, concentration (in general), fixing of thoughts ; तस्यां लग्नसमाधि (मानसं) Gît. 3. 4 Penance, religious obligation, devotion (to penance) ; अस्त्येतत्समाधिभीरुत्वं देवानां *S.* 1 ; तपःसमाधि Ku. 3. 24, 5. 6 ; 1. 59, 5. 45. 5 Bringing together, concentration, combination, collection ; तं वेधा विदधे नूनं महाभूतसमाधिना R. 1. 29. 6 Reconciliation, settling or composing differences. 7 Silence. 8 Agreement, assent, promise. 9 Requital. 10 Completion ; accomplishment. 11 Perseverance in extreme difficulties. 12 Attempting impossibilities. 13 Laying up corn (in times of famine), storing grain. 14 A tomb. 15 The joint of the neck, a particular position of the neck ; Ki. 16. 21. 16 (In Rhet.) A figure of speech thus defined by Mammaṭa ; समाधिः सुकरं कार्यं कारणांतरयोगतः K. P. 10 ; see S. D. 614. 17 One of the ten Guṇas or merits of style; see Kâv. 1. 93.

समाध्मात *p. p.* 1 Blown into. 2 Elated, puffed up, inflated.

समान *a.* 1 Same, equal, like similar ; समानशीलव्यसनेषु सख्यं Subhâsh. 2 One, uniform. 3 Good, virtuous, just. 4 Common, general. 5 Honoured. **–नः** 1 A friend, an equal. 2 One of the five life-winds or vital airs, which has its seat in the cavity of the navel and is essential to digestion. **–नं** *ind.* Equally with, like (with instr.); जलधरेण समानमुमापतिः Ki. 18. 4. **–Comp.** **–अधिकरण** *a.* 1 having a common substratum. 2 being in the same category or predicament. 3 being in the same case-relation or government (in gram.); (**–णं**) 1 same location or predicament. 2 agreement in case, apposition. 3 a predicament including several things, a generic property. **–अर्थः** *a.* having the same meaning, synonymous. **–उदकः** a relative connected by the libations of water to the Manes of common ancestors ; this relationship extends from the seventh (or eleventh) to the thirteenth (or fourteenth according to some) degree ; समानोदकभावस्तु निवर्तेताचतुर्दशात् ; see Ms. 5. 60. also. **–उदर्यः** a brother of whole blood, uterine brother. **–उपमा** a kind of Upamâ ; see Kâv. 2. 29. **–काल, –कालीन** *a.* synchronous. **–गोत्र** = सगोत्र q. v. **–दुःख** *a.* sympathising. **–धर्मन्** *a.* possessed of the same qualities, sympathiser, appreciator of merits ; Mâl. 1. 6. **–यमः** the same pitch of voice. **–रुचि** *a.* agreeing in tastes.

समानयनं Bringing, together, collecting, conducting.

समाप Offering sacrifices or oblations to the gods.

समापत्तिः *f.* 1 Meeting, encountering. 2 Accident, chance, accidental encounter ; समापत्तिदृष्टेन केशिना दानवेन V. 1. ; क्रियासमापत्तिनिवर्तितानि R. 7. 23 ; Ku. 7. 75.

समापक *a.* (**पिका** *f.*) Finishing, accomplishing, fulfilling.

समापनं 1 Completion, conclusion, bringing to an end ; Ms. 5. 88. 2 Acquisition. 3 Killing, destroying. 4 A section, chapter. 5 Profound meditation.

समापन्न *p. p.* 1 Attained, obtained. 2 Occurred, happened. 3 Come, arrived. 4 Finished, completed, accomplished. 5 Proficient. 6 Endowed with. 7 Distressed, afflicted. 8 Killed.

समापादनं Accomplishing, restoring.

समाप्त *p. p.* 1 Finished, concluded, completed. 2 Clever.

समाप्तालः A lord, husband.

समाप्तिः *f.* 1 End, conclusion, completion, termination. 2 Accomplishment, fulfilment, Perfection. 3 Reconciling or settling differences, making up quarrels.

समाप्तिक *a.* 1 Final, concluding. 2 Finite. 3 One who has finished the whole of anything. **–कः** 1 A finisher. 2 One who has completed the whole course of holy studies.

समाप्लुत *p. p.* 1 Flooded, inundated 2 Filled with.

समाभाषणं Conversation, talking with ; R. 6. 16.

समाम्नानं 1 Repetition, mention. 2 Enumeration. 3 Traditional repetition or mention.

समाम्नायः 1 Traditional repetition or mention, handing down traditionally. 2 A traditional collection (of words &c.); अथ इति पशुसमाम्नाये पठ्यते U. 4. 3 Tradition, repetition (in general). 4 Reading, recitation, enumeration. 5 Totality, an aggregate, a collection ; अक्षरसमाम्नायं Sik. 57 ; (*i. e.* the letters from अ to ह which are said to have been revealed by Siva to Pâṇini).

समायः 1 Arrival, coming. 2 A visit.

समायत *p. p.* Drawn out, extended, lengthened.

समायुक्त *p. p.* 1 Joined, connected, united. 2 Intent on, devoted to. 3 Made ready, prepared. 4 Endowed or furnished with, filled with, provided, supplied. 5 Charged, appointed.

समायुत *p. p.* 1 Connected or united together, joined. 2 Collected. brought together. 3 Endowed or furnished with, having, possessed of.

समायोगः 1 Union, connection, conjunction. 2 Preparation. 3 Fitting (an arrow). 4 A collection, heap, multitude. 5 A cause, motive, object.

समारंभः 1 Beginning, commencement. 2 An enterprise, undertaking, a work, an action: भव्यमुख्याः समारंभाः ...तस्य गूढं विपेचिरे R. 17. 53; Bg. 4. 19. 3 An unguent; see समालंभ.

समाराधनं 1 A means of satisfying, gratification, delight; नाट्यं भिन्नरुचेर्जनस्य बहुधाप्येकं समाराधनं M. 1. 4. 2 Attendance, service; R. 2. 5, 18. 10.

समारोपणं 1 Depositing, placing in or upon. 2 Delivering over, consigning.

समारोपित p. p. 1 Caused to mount or ascend. 2 Strung (as a bow), भवता चापि समारोपिते K. P. 10. 3 Deposited, planted, lodged. 4 Consigned, delivered over.

समारोहः 1 Ascending, mounting. 2 Riding upon. 3 Agreeing.

समालंबनं Resting on, clinging to.

समालंबिन् a. Clinging to. -नी A kind of grass.

समालंभः, समालंभनं 1 Taking hold of, seizing. 2 Seizing a victim for sacrifice. 3 Smearing the body with unguents or coloured cosmetics; मंगलसमालंभनं विरचयावः S. 4.

समावर्तनं 1 Return. 2 Especially, a pupil's return home after finishing his course of holy study.

समावायः 1 Association, connection. 2 Inseparable connection; see समवाय. 3 Aggregation. 4 A multitude, number, heap.

समावासः A residence, habitation, dwelling-place.

समाविष्ट p. p. 1 Entered thoroughly, completely occupied, pervaded. 2 Seized, overcome, engrossed. 3 Possessed by an evil spirit. 4 Endowed with. 5 Settled, fixed, seated. 6 Well instructed.

समावृत p. p. 1 Encompassed, surrounded, enclosed, beset. 2 Screened, veiled. 3 Hidden, concealed. 4 Protected. 5 Shut out, excluded. 6 Stopped.

समावृत्तः, समावृत्तकः A pupil who has returned home after finishing his course of holy study.

समावेशः 1 Entering or abiding together. 2 Meeting, association. 3 Inclusion, comprehension. 4 Penetration. 5 Possession by an evil-spirit. 6 Passion, emotion.

समाश्रयः 1 Seeking protection or shelter. 2 Refuge, shelter, protection. 3 A place of refuge, asylum, resting or dwelling place. 4 Dwelling, residence.

समाश्लेषः A close embrace.

समाश्वासः 1 Recovering breath, breathing a sigh of relief. 2 Relief, encouragement, consolation. 3 Trust, confidence, belief.

समाश्वासनं 1 Reviving, encouraging, comforting. 2 Consolation; V. 2.

समासः 1 Aggregation, union, composition. 2 Composition of words, a compound; (the principal kinds of compounds are four:- द्वंद्व, तत्पुरुष, बहुव्रीहि and अव्ययीभाव q. q. v. v.). 3 Reconciliation, composition of differences. 4 A collection, an assemblage. 5 Whole, totality. 6 Contraction, conciseness, brevity. (समासेन, समासतः means 'in short', 'briefly', 'succinctly', एषा धर्मस्य वो योनिः समासेन प्रकीर्तिता Ms. 2. 25, 3. 20; Bg. 13. 18; समासतः श्रूयतां V. 2). -Comp. -उक्तिः f. a figure of speech thus defined by Mammaṭa:--परोक्तिर्भेदकैः श्लिष्टैः समासोक्तिः K. P. 10.

समासक्तिः f., समासंगः Union, adhering together, attachment.

समासंजनं 1 Joining, uniting. 2 Fixing or placing on. 3 Contact, combination, connection.

समासर्जनं 1 Abandoning completely. 2 Consigning.

समासादनं 1 Approaching. 2 Finding, meeting with, obtaining. 3 Accomplishing, effecting.

समाहरणं Uniting, collecting, combining, accumulating.

समाहर्तृ m. 1 One who is accustomed to collect or get together. 2 A collector (as of taxes).

समाहारः 1 A collection, an aggregate, assemblage; Mâl. 9. 2 Composition of words. 3 Conjunction of words or sentences. 4 A subdivision of *Dvandva* and *Dvigu* compounds, expressing an aggregate. 5 Abridgment, contraction, conciseness.

समाहित p. p. 1 Brought together, assembled. 2 Adjusted, settled. 3 Composed, collected, calm (as mind). 4 Intent on, absorbed in, concentrated. 5 Finished. 6 Agreed upon.

समाहृत p. p. 1 Brought together, collected, accumulated. 2 Abundant, excessive, much. 3 Received, accepted, taken. 4 Abridged, curtailed.

समाहृति f. Compilation, abridgment.

समाह्वः Challenge, defiance.

समाह्वयः 1 Calling out, challenging. 2 War, battle. 3 A single combat. 4 Setting animals to fight for sport, betting with living creatures; Y. 2. 203; Ms. 9. 221. 5 A name, an appellation.

समाह्वा A name, an appellation; Si. 11. 26.

समाह्वानं 1 Calling together, convocation. 2 Challenge.

समिकं A javelin, dart.

समित् f. War, battle; समिति पतिनिपाताकर्णन &c. N. 12. 75.

समिता Wheat-flour.

समितिः 1 Meeting, union, association. 2 An assembly. 3 Flock, herd; Ki. 4. 32. 4 War, battle; *S*. 2. 14; Ki. 3. 15; Si. 16. 13. 5 Likeness, equality. 6 Moderation.

समितिंजय a. Victorious in battle.

समिथः 1 War, battle. 2 Fire.

समिद्ध p. p. 1 Lighted up, kindled. 2 Set on fire. 3 Inflamed, excited.

समिध् f. Wood, fuel; especially fuel or sacrificial sticks for the sacred fire; समिदाहरणाय *S*. 1; Ku. 1. 57; 5. 33.

समिधः Fire.

समिंधनं 1 Kindling. 2 Fuel.

समिरः Wind.

समीकं War, battle; Si. 15. 83.

समीकरणं 1 Complete investigation. 2 The Sânkhya system of philosophy; Si. 2. 59.

समीक्षा 1 Investigation, search. 2 Consideration. 3 Close or thorough inspection. 4 Understanding, intellect. 5 Essential nature or truth. 6 An essential principle. 7 The Mîmâmsâ system of philosophy.

समीचः The ocean.

समीचकः Copulation, sexual union.

समीची 1 A doe. 2 Praise.

समीचीन 1 Good, right. 2 True, correct. 3 Fit, proper. 4 Consistent. -नं 1 Truth 2 Propriety.

समीदः Fine wheat-flour.

समीन a. 1 Yearly, annual. 2 Hired for a year. 3 A year hence.

समीनिका A cow calving every year.

समीप a. Near, close by, adjacent, at hand. -पं Proximity, vicinity. (समीपं, समीपतस् and समीपे are used adverbially in the sense of 'near, before, in the presence of'; अतः समीपे परिणेतु रिष्यते *S*. 5. 17.

समीरः 1 Air, wind; धीरसमीरे यमुनातीरे Gît. 5. 2 The *Samî* tree.

समीरणः 1 Air, wind; समीरणो नोदयिताभवेति व्यादिश्यते केन हुताशनस्य Ku. 3. 21; 1. 8. 2 The breath. 3 A traveller. 4 N. of plant (मरुबक). -णं Throwing, sending forth.

समीहा Longing, desire, striving after.

समीहित p. p. 1 Longed for, desired, wished. 2 Undertaken. -तं Wish, longing, desire.

समुक्षणं Shedding, effusion.

समुच्चयः 1 Collection, assemblage, aggregation, mass, multitude. 2 Conjunction of words or sentences; see च. 3 A figure of speech; K. P. 10. (Kârikâs 115 and 116).

समुच्चरः 1 Ascending. 2 Traversing.

समुच्छेदः Complete destruction, extermination, eradication.

समुच्छ्रयः 1 Elevation, height. 2 Opposition, enmity.

समुच्छ्रायः Elevation, height.

समुच्छ्वसितं, समुच्छ्वासः Sighing deeply, a heavy or deep sigh.

समुज्झित *a*. 1 Abandoned, left. 2 Let go. 3 Free from.

समुत्कर्षः 1 Exaltation. 2 Setting oneself up, belonging to a tribe higher than his own ; Ms. 11. 56.

समुत्क्रमः 1 Rising upwards, ascent. 2 Transgression of proper bounds.

समुत्क्रोशः 1 Crying aloud. 2 A loud uproar. 3 An osprey.

समुत्थ *a*. 1 Rising, getting up. 2 Sprung or produced from, born from (at the end of comp.) ; अथ नयनसमुत्थं ज्योतिरत्रेरिव द्योः R. 2. 75 ; Bg. 7. 27. 3 Occurring, occasioned.

समुत्थानं 1 Rising, getting up. 2 Resurrection. 3 Perfect cure, complete recovery. 4 Healing (as of a wound) ; Ms. 8. 287 ; Y. 2. 222. 5 A symptom of disease. 6 Engaging in industry, active occupation ; as in संभूयसमुत्थानं Ms. 8. 4.

समुत्पतनं 1 Flying up, ascending. 2 Effort, exertion.

समुत्पत्तिः *f*. 1 Production, birth, origin 2 Occurrence.

समुत्पिंज, समुत्पिंजल *a*. Excessively confused or bewildered, disorganised. -जः -लः 1 An army in great disorder. 2 Great confusion.

समुत्सवः A great festival.

समुत्सर्गः 1 Abandoning, leaving. 2 Shedding or casting forth, giving away. 3 Discharge of feces, voiding of excrement ; Ms. 4. 50.

समुत्सारणं 1 Driving away. 2 Pursuing, hunting.

समुत्सुक *a*. 1 Very uneasy or anxious, impatient ; विरोषि समुत्सुकः V. 4. 20, R. 1. 33 ; Ku. 5. 76. 2 Longing or eager for, fond of. 3 Sorrowful, regretting.

समुत्सेधः 1 Height, elevation. 2 Fatness, thickness.

समुदक्त *p. p.* Raised or drawn up (as water from a well).

समुदयः 1 Ascent, rising up (of the sun). 2 Rise (in general). 3 A collection, multitude, number, heap; सामर्थ्यानामिव समुदयः संचयो वा गुणानां U. 6. 9. 4 Combination. 5 The whole. 6 Revenue. 7 Effort, exertion. 8 War, battle. 9 Day. 10 The rear of an army.

समुदागमः Full knowledge.

समुदाचारः 1 Proper practise or usage. 2 Proper mode of address. 3 Purpose, intention, design.

समुदायः A collection, multitude &c. ; see समुदय.

समुदाहरणं 1 Declaring, pronouncing. 2 Illustration.

समुदित *p. p.* 1 Gone up, risen, ascended. 2 Lofty, elevated 3 Produced, arisen, occasioned. 4 Assembled, collected, united ; मद्भाग्योपचयादयं समुदितः सर्वो गुणानां गणः Ratn. 1. 6. 5 Possessed of, furnished with.

समुदीरणं 1 Uttering, speaking, pronouncing. 2 Repeating.

समुद्ग *a*. 1 Rising, ascending. 2 Completely pervading. 3 Having a covering or lid. 4 Having beans. -द्गः 1 A covered box or casket. 2 A kind of artificial stanza ; see समुद्गक below.

समुद्गकः 1 A covered box or casket; *S*. 4. 2 A kind of artificial stanza, the two halves of which exactly correspond in sound, though they differ in meaning ; *e. g.* Ki. 15. 16.

समुद्गमः 1 Rising, ascent. 2 Arising, issuing. 3 Birth, Production.

समुद्गिरणं 1 Vomiting, ejecting. 2 That which is vomited. 3 Raising, lifting up.

समुद्गीतं A loud song.

समुद्देशः 1 Fully pointing out. 2 Full description. Particularising, enumeration.

समुद्धत *p. p* 1 Upraised, uplifted, elevated. 2 Excited, drawn up. 3 Puffed up with pride, proud, arrogant. 4 Ill-mannered, ill-behaved. 5 Impudent, rude.

समुद्धरणं 1 Upraising, lifting up. 2 Picking up. 3 Drawing or lifting out. 4 Extrication, deliverance. 5 Eradication, extirpation. 6 Taking out from (a shore). 7 Food thrown up or vomited.

समुद्धर्तृ *m*. A deliverer, redeemer.

समुद्भवः Origin, production.

समुद्यमः 1 Lifting up. 2 Great effort or exertion ; कैर्मया सह योद्धव्यमस्मिन्रणसमुद्यमे Bg. 1. 22 ; समुद्यमः कार्यः &c. 3 An undertaking, commencement. 4 An onset.

समुद्योगः Active exertion, energy.

समुद्र *a* Sealed, bearing a seal, stamped ; समुद्रो लेखः. -द्रः 1 The sea, ocean. 2 An epithet of Siva. 3 The number ' four. ' -Comp. -अंतं 1 the sea-shore. 2 nutmeg. -अंता 1 the cotton-plant. 2 the earth. -अंबरा the earth. -अरुः, आरुः 1 a crocodile. 2 a large fabulous fish. 3 Râmâ's bridge; cf. रामसेतु. -कफः, -फेनः the cuttle-fish-bone. -ग *a*. sea-faring. (-गः) 1 a sea-trader. 2 a seaman, a sea-farer ; so समुद्रगामिन्, -यायिन् &c. (-गा) a river. -गृहं a summer-house built in the midst of water. -चुलुकः an epithet of Agastya. -नवनीतं 1 the moon. 2 ambrosia, nectar. -नेखला, -रसना, -वसना the earth. -यानं 1 a sea-voyage. 2 a vessel, ship, boat. -यात्रा a sea-voyage. -यायिन् *a*. see समुद्रग. -योषित् *f*. a river. -वह्नि submarine fire. -सुभगा the Ganges.

समुद्वहः 1 Bearing up. 2 One who lifts up.

समुद्वाहः 1 Bearing up. 2 Marriage.

समुद्वेगः Great fear, alarm, terror.

समुंदनं 1 Moistening. 2 Wetness, moisture.

समुन्न *a*. Wet, moist.

समुन्नत *p. p.* 1 Upraised, lifted up. 2 Elevated, high, lofty. 3 Exalted, sublime. 4 Proud. 5 Projecting. 6 Upright, just.

समुन्नतिः *f*. 1 Lifting up, raising. 2 Height, loftiness, elevation (mental also) ; मनसः शिखराणां च सदृशी ते समुन्नतिः Ku 6. 66 ; R. 3. 10. 3 Eminence, high position or dignity, exaltation ; उच्चैः सह संगेन को न याति समुन्नतिं; स जातो येन जातेन याति वंशः समुन्नतिं Subhâsh. 4 Rise, prosperity, increase, success ; विनिपातोपि समः समुन्नतेः Ki. 2. 34, or प्रकृतिः खलु सा महीयसः सहते नान्यसमुन्नतिं यया 2. 21. 5 Pride, arrogance.

समुन्नद्ध *p. p.* 1 Elevated, exalted. 2 Swollen. 3 Full. 4 Proud, arrogant, overbearing. 5 Conceited, thinking oneself to be learned. 6 Unfettered.

समुन्नयः 1 Getting, obtaining. 2 Occurrence, event.

समुन्मूलनं Uprooting, eradication, complete destruction.

समुपगमः Approach, contact.

समुपजोषम् *ind*. 1 Entirely according to wish. 2 Happily.

समुपभोगः Sexual union, coition.

समुपवेशनं 1 A building, habitation, residence. 2 Seating down.

समुपस्था, समुपस्थानं 1 Approach, approximation. 2 Proximity, nearness. 3 Happening, befalling, occurrence.

समुपस्थितिः = समुपस्थान q. v.

समुपार्जनं Acquiring together, simultaneous acquisition.

समुपेत *p. p.* 1 Come together, assembled, collected. 2 Arrived at. 3 Furnished or endowed with, possessed of.

समुपोढ *p. p.* 1 Gone upwards, risen. 2 Increased. 3 Brought near. 4 Restrained.

समुल्लासः 1 Excessive brilliance. 2 Great joy, exhilaration.

समूढ *p. p.* 1 Brought together, assembled. 2 Accumulated, collected. 3 Enveloped. 4 Associated with. 5 Produced quickly. 6 Calmed, tamed down, tranquillized. 7 Crooked, bent. 8 Purified, cleansed. 9 Borne along. 10 Led, conducted. 11 Married.

समूरः, समूरुः, समूरकः A kind of deer.

समूल *a*. Along with the roots ; as in समूलघातं 'having completely exterminated, tearing up root and branch'.

समूहः 1 A multitude, collection, assemblage, aggregate, number ; जन-

समूहः, विघ्नसमूहः, पदसमूहः &c. **2** A flock, troop.

समूहनं **1** Bringing together. **2** A collection, plenty.

समूहनी A broom.

समूह्यः A kind of sacrificial fire.

समृद्ध *p. p.* **1** Prosperous, flourishing, thriving. **2** Happy, fortunate **3** Rich, wealthy. **4** Rich in, richly endowedwith, abounding in. **5** Fruitful.

समृद्धिः *f.* **1** Great growth, increase, thriving. **2** Prosperity, opulence, affluence. **3** Wealth, riches. **4** Exuberance, profusion, abundance; as in धनधान्यसमृद्धिरस्तु. **5** Power, supremacy.

समेत *p. p.* **1** Come or met together, assembled. **2** United, combined. **3** Come near, approached. **4** Accompanied by. **5** Endowed or furnished with, having, possessed. of. **6** Come into collision, encountered. **7** Agreed upon.

संपत्तिः *f.* **1** Prosperity, increase of wealth; संपत्तौ च विपत्तौ च महतामेकरूपता Subhâsh. **2** Success, fulfilment, accomplishment. **3** Perfection, excellence; as in रूपसंपत्ति. **4** Exuberance, plenty, abundance.

संपद् *f.* **1** Wealth, riches; नीताविवोत्साहगुणेन संपद् Ku.1.32; आपन्नार्तिप्रशमनफलाः संपदो ह्युत्तमानां Me. 53. **2** Prosperity, affluence, advencement; (opp. विपद् or आपद्); ते भृत्या नृपतेः कलत्रमितरे संपत्सु चापत्सु च Mu.1.15. **3** Good fortune, happiness, luck. **4** Success, fulfilment, accomplishment of desired object; *S*.7. 30. **5** Perfection, excellence; as in रूपसंपद्; *Si*. 3. 35. **6** Richness, plenty, exuberance, abundance, excess; तुषारवृष्टिक्षतपद्मसंपदां Ku. 5. 27; R. 10. 59 **7** Treasure. **8** An advantage, benefit, blessing. **9** Advancement in good qualities. **10** Decoration. **11** Right method. **12** A necklace of pearls. **–Comp. –वरः** a king. **–विनिमयः** an interchange or reciprocity of benefits or services; R. 1. 26.

संपन्न *p. p.* **1** Prosperous, thriving, rich. **2** Fortunate, successful, happy. **3** Effected, brought about, accomplished. **4** Finished, completed. **5** Perfect. **6** Full-grown, mature. **7** Procured, obtained. **8** Right, correct. **9** Endowed with, possessed of. **10** Turned out, become. **–न्नः** An epithet of *S*iva. **–न्नं** **1** Riches, wealth. **2** A dainty, delicacy.

संपरायः **1** Conflict, encounter, war, battle. **2** A calamity, misfortune. **3** Future state, futurity. **4** A son.

संपराय(यि)कं Encounter, war, battle.

संपर्कः **1** Mixture. **2** Union, contact, touch; पादेन नापेक्षत सुंदरीणां संपर्कमाशिंजितनूपुरेण Ku. 3. 26; Me. 25, V. 1. 13. **3** Society, association, company; न मूर्खजनसंपर्कः सुरेंद्रभवनेष्वपि Bh. 2. 14. **4** Sexual union, copulation.

संपा Lightning.

संपाक *a.* **1** Reasoning well, a reasoner. **2** Cunning, subtle. **3** Lustful, lewd. **4** Small, little. **–कः** **1** Maturing. **2** N. of a tree (आरग्वध).

संपाटः **1** Intersection. **2** A spindle.

संपातः **1** Falling together, concurrence. **2** Meeting together, encountering. **3** Collision, butting against. **4** Falling down, descending; Bg. 1. 20. **5** Alighting (as of a bird). **6** Flight (of an arrow). **7** Going, moving. **8** Being removed, removal; Ms. 6. 56. **9** A particular mode of the flight of birds; cf. डीन. **10** The residue (of an offering).

संपातिः N. of a fabulous bird, son of Garuda and elder brother of Jatâyu.

संपादः **1** Completion, acccomplishment. **2** Acquisition.

संपादनं **1** Accomplishing, effecting, fulfilment. **2** Gaining, obtaining, acquiring. **3** Cleaning, clearing, preparing (as ground); Ms. 3. 225.

संपिंडित *p. p.* **1** Formed into a mass. **2** Contracted.

संपीडः **1** Squeezing together, compression. **2** Pain, torture. **3** Agitating, disturbing. **4** Sending, directing, driving onward, propelling; संपीडक्षुभितजलेषु तोयदेषु Ki. 7. 12.

संपीडनं **1** Squeezing, pressing together. **2** Sending. **3** Punishment, castigation. **4** Stirring up, agitating.

संपीतिः *f.* Drinking together, compotation.

संपुटः **1** A cavity; स्वात्यां सागरशुक्तिसंपुटगतं (पयः) सन्मौक्तिकं जायते Bh. 2. 67 v. l.; Kâv. 2. 288; Rs. 1. 21. **2** A casket, covered box. **3** The Kuravaka flower.

संपुटकः; **संपुटिका** A box, casket.

संपूर्ण *a.* **1** Filled &c. **2** All, whole; see पूर्ण. **–र्णं** Ether.

संपृक्त *p. p.* **1** Blended, mixed. **2** Connected together, related, in close relation; वागर्थाविव संपृक्तौ R. 1. 1. **3** Touching.

संप्रक्षालनं **1** Complete ablution. **2** Bathing. **3** Inundation.

संप्रणेतृ *m.* A ruler, judge.

संप्रति *ind.* Now, at present, at this time; अयि संप्रति देहि दर्शनं Ku. 4. 28.

संप्रतिपत्तिः *f.* **1** Approach, arrival. **2** Presence. **3** Gain, obtaining, acquiring. **4** An agreement. **5** Admission, confession; Mu. 5. 18. **6** Admission of a fact, a particular kind of reply in law. **7** Assault, attack. **8** Occurrence. **9** Co-operation. **10** Doing, performing.

संप्रतिरोधकः–कं **1** Complete obstruction. **2** Confinement, imprisonment.

संप्रतीत *p. p.* **1** Returned. **2** Fully convinced. **3** Proved, admitted. **4** Renowned. **5** Respectful.

संप्रतीतिः *f.* **1** Full ascertainment. **2** Compliance, fame, celebrity, notoriety; Ki. 3. 43.

संप्रत्ययः **1** Firm conviction. **2** Agreement.

संप्रतीक्षा Expectation.

संप्रदानं **1** Giving or handing over completely. **2** Bestowal, gift, donation. **3** Giving in marriage. **4** The sense expressed by the dative case.

संप्रदानीयं A gift, donation.

संप्रदायः **1** Tradition, traditional doctrine or knowledge, traditional handing down of instruction; U. 5. 15. **2** A peculiar system of religious teaching, a religious doctrine inculcating the worship of one peculiar deity. **3** An established custom, usage.

संप्रधानं Ascertainment.

संप्रधारणं–णा **1** Deliberation. **2** Determining the propriety or otherwise of anything.

संप्रपदः Roaming about.

संप्रभिन्न *p. p.* **1** Split open, cleft. **2** In rut.

संप्रमोदः Great joy, jubilee.

संप्रमोषः Loss, destruction, abstraction.

संप्रयाणं Departure.

संप्रयोगः **1** Union, connection, meeting, conjuction, contact; (जलस्य) उष्णत्वमग्न्यातपसंप्रयोगात् R. 5. 54; M. 5. 3. **2** A connecting link, fastening; पतेन मोचयति भूषणसंप्रयोगान् Mk. 3. 16. **3** Relation, dependence. **4** Mutual relation or proportion. **5** Connected series or order. **6** Sexual union, coition. **7** Application. **8** Magic.

संप्रयोगिन् *a.* Joining together. **–m.** **1** A joiner, uniter. **2** A conjuror. **3** A libertine. **4** A catamite.

संप्रवृष्टं Complete rain-fall.

संप्रश्नः Full or courteous inquiry. **2** An inquiry.

संप्रसादः **1** Propitiation. **2** Favour, grace. **3** Serenity, sedateness. **4** Trust, confidence. **5** The soul.

संप्रसारणं The change of य्, व्, र्, and ल्, to इ, उ, ऋ and ऌ respectively. इग्यणः संप्रसारणं P. I. 1. 45.

संप्रहारः **1** Mutual striking. **2** Encounter, war, battle, conflict; U. 6. 7.

संप्राप्तिः *f.* Attainment, acquisition.

संप्रीतिः *f.* **1** Attachment, affection. **2** Friendly assent. **3** Delight, joy.

संप्रेक्षणं **1** Observing, beholding. **2** Considering, investigating.

संप्रेषः 1 Sending away, dismissing. 2 Direction, command, order.

संप्रोक्षणं Sprinkling over, consecration.

संप्लवः 1 Submersion, tnundation. 2 Surge. 3 Flood. 4 Falling into ruin. 5 Subversion.

संफालः A ram, sheep.

संफेटः An angry or unultuous conflict, an incident describing the mutual encounter of angry persons ; see S. D. 379, 420 ; *e. g.* the encounter between माधव and अघोरघंट in Mâl. act 5.

संब् I. 1 P. (संबति) To go, move. -II. 10 U. (संबयति-ते) To collect, accumulate.

संबं The second ploughing of a field ; (संबाकृ to plough twice) see शंब also.

संबद्ध *p. p.* 1 Bound or fastened together. 2 Attached to. 3 Connected with, related to, belonging to. 4 Endowed with.

संबंधः 1 Connection, union, association. 2 Relation, relationship. 3 Relation, as the meaning of the genitive case. 4 Matrimonial alliance; Ku. 6. 29, 30. 5 Friendly connection, friendship ; संबंधमाभाषणपूर्वमाहुः R. 2. 58. 6 Fitness, propriety. 7 Prosperity, success.

संबंधक *a.* 1 Relating, concerning. 2 Fit, suitable. -कः 1 A friend. 2 A relation by birth or marriage. 3 A kind of peace.

संबंधिन् *a.* 1 Relating or belonging to. 2 Connected with, serving as an adjunct, inherent. 3 Possessing good qualities. *-m.* 1 A relation by marriage ; U. 4. 9. 2 A relation, kinsman (in general).

संबरः 1 A dam, bridge. 2 A kind of deer. 3 N. of a demon slain by Pradyumna ; see शंबर and प्रद्युम्न. 4 N. of a mountain. -रं 1 Restraint. 2 Water. -Comp. -अरिः, -रिपुः Cupid.

संबलः-लं Provisions for a journey, viaticum. -लं Water.

संबाध *a.* Thronged or crowned with, blocked up, narrow ; संबाधं बृहदपि तद्बभूव वर्त्म Si. 8. 2; व्योम्नि संबाधवर्त्मभिः R. 12. 67. -धः 1 Being thronged with. 2 Pressing on, striking, hurting ; स्तनसंबाधमुरो जघान च Ku. 4. 26. 3 Obstruction, difficulty, danger, impediment ; Ki. 3. 53. 4 The road to hell. 5 Fear, dread. 6 The vulva.

संबाधनं 1 Blocking up, obstructing. 2 Compressing. 3 A barrier, gate. 4 The vulva. 5 The point of a stake. 6 A door-keeper.

संबुद्धिः *f.* 1 Perfect knowledge or perception. 2 Full consciousness. 3 Calling to, addressing. 4 (In gram.) The vocativcase ; एङ्ह्रस्वात्संबुद्धेः P. VI. 1. 69.

संबोधः 1 Explaining, instructing, informing. 2 Full or correct perception. 3 Sending, throwing. 4 Loss, destruction.

संबोधनं 1 Explaining. 2 Addressing. 3 The vocative case. 4 An epithet (used in calling a person) ; Bv. 3. 13.

संभक्तिः *f.* 1 Sharing in, possessing. 2 Distributing.

संभग्न *p. p.* Shattered, dispersed. -ग्नः An epithet of *S*iva.

संभली A procuress ; see शंभली.

संभवः 1 Birth, production, springing up, arising, existence ; प्रियस्य सुहृदो यत्र मम तत्रैव संभवो भूयात् Mal. 9; मानुषीषु कथं वास्यादस्य रूपस्य संभवः *S.* 1. 26; Bg. 3. 14 ; oft. at the end of comp. in this sense ; अप्सरःसंभवैषा *S.* 1. 2 Production and bringing up ; Ms. 2. 227, (see Kull. thereon). 3 Cause, origin, motive. 4 Mixing, union, combination. 5 Possibility ; संयोगोहि वियोगस्य संसूचयति संभवं Subhâsh. 6 Compatibility, consistency. 7 Adaptation, appropriateness. 8 Agreement, conformity. 9 Capacity. 10 Equivalence (one of the Pramâṇas). 11 Acquaintance. 12 Loss, destruction.

संभारः 1 Bringing together, collecing. 2 Preparation, provisions, necessaries, requisites, apparatus, things requisite for any act ; सविशेषमद्य पूजासंभारो मया संनिध पनीयः Mâl. 5 ; R. 12. 4 ; V. 2. 3 An ingredient, a constituent part. 4 Multitude, heap, quantity, assemblage ; as in शस्त्रास्त्रसंभार. 5 Fulness. 6 Wealth, affluence. 7 Maintenance, support.

संभावनं-ना 1 Considering, reflecting ; R. 5. 28. 2 Fancying, suppostion ; संभावनमथोत्प्रेक्षा प्रकृतस्य समेन यत् K. P. 10. 3 An idea, fancy, thought. 4 Respect, honour, esteem, regard ; संभावनागुणमवेहि तमीश्वराणां *S.* 7. 3. 5 Possibility. 6 Fitness, adequacy; Ki. 3. 39. 7 Competency, ability. 8 Doubt. 9 Affection; love. 10 Celebrity.

संभावित *p. p.* 1 Considered, supposed, imagined ; पित्राहं दोषेषु संभावितः K. 2 Esteemed, honoured, respected ; Bh. 2. 34. 3 Suited, fitted, adequate, fit. 4 Possible.

संभाषः Conversation; Ms. 2. 195 ; 8. 354.

संभाषा 1 Discourse, conversation. 2 Greeting. 3 Criminal connection. 4 An agreement, a contract. 5 A watch-word, war-cry.

संभूतिः *f.* 1 Birth, origin, production ; Ms. 2. 147. 2 Combination, union. 3 Fitness, suitability. 4 Power.

संभृत *p. p.* 1 Brought together, collected, concentrated. 2 Got ready, prepared, provided, equipped. 3 Furnished or endowed with, possessed of. 4 Placed, deposited. 5 Full, complete, entire. 6 Gained, obtained. 7 Carried, borne. 8 Nourished. 9 Produced, caused.

संभृतिः *f.* 1 Collection. 2 Preparation, equipment, provision. 3 Fulness. 4 Support, maintenance, nourishment.

संभेदः 1 Breaking, splitting. 2 Union, mixture, combination; आलोकतिमिरसंभेदं Mâl. 10. 11 ; हर्षोद्वेगसंभेद् उपनतः Mâl. 8. 3 Meeting (as of glances). 4 Confluence, junction (of two rivers) ; तद्ववतिष्ठ पारासिंधुसंभेदमवगाह्य नगरीमेव प्रविशावः ; अयमसौ महानद्योः संभेदः Mâl. 4 ; मधुमतीसिंधुसंभेदपावनः 9.

संभोगः 1 Enjoyment (in general) ; संसंभोगफलाः श्रियः Subhâsh. 2 Possession, use, occupation ; Ms. 8. 200. 3 Carnal enjoyment, sexual union, copulation ; संभोगाते मम समुचितो हस्तसंवाहनानां Me. 95. 4 A lecher, catamite. 5 A subdivision of the sentiment of love ; see under शृंगार.

संभ्रमः 1 Turning round, whirling, revolving. 2 Haste, hurry. 3 Confusion, agitation, flurry; Ku. 3. 48. 4 Fear, alarm, fright ; *S.* 1; Ki. 15. 2. 5 Error, mistake, ignorance, 6 Zeal, activity. 7 Respect, reverence ; गृहमुपगते संभ्रमविधिः Bh. 2. 63 ; तव वर्यिवतः काश्चिद्यास्ति मयि संभ्रमः Râm. -Comp. -ज्वलित *a.* excited by agitation. -भृत् *a.* embarrassed, flurried.

संभ्रांत *p. p.* 1 Whirled about. 2 Flurried, agitated, perplexed, bewildered.

संमत *p. p.* 1 Agreed or consented to, approved of. 2 Liked, dear, beloved. 3 Like, resembling. 4 Regarded, considered, thought. 5 Highly respected, honoured, esteemed. -तं Agreement ; see संमति.

संमतिः *f.* 1 Agreement. 2 Concurrence, assent, approbation, approval, 3 Wish, desire. 4 Knowledge of self, or knowledge of the soul, true knowledge. 5 Regard, respect-esteem ; कथमिव तव संमतिर्भवित्रा सममृतुभिर्मुनिनावधीरितस्य Ki. 10. 36. 6 Love, affection.

संमदः Great joy, delight, happiness ; *S*i. 15. 77.

संमर्दः 1 Rubbing together, friction. 2 Throng, crowd, concourse ; यद्रोधप्रतरकल्लोऽभूत्संमर्दस्तत्र मज्जता R. 15. 101; Mâl. 10. 3 Treading or trampling on. 4 War, battle.

संमातुर=सन्मातुर q. v. under सत्.

संमादः Intoxication, frenzy.

संमानः Respect, honour. -नं 1 Measure. 2 Comparing.

संमार्जकः A sweeper.

संमार्जनं 1 Sweeping, cleansing. 2 Purifying, cleaning, brushing.

संमार्जनी A broom.

संमित *p. p.* 1 Meted, measured out. 2 Of equal measure, extent or value, equal, similar, like, resembling; कांतासंमिततयोपदेशयुजे K. P. 1; R. 3. 16. 3 As large as, reaching to. 4 Conformable, corresponding, commensurate. 5 Provided or furnished with.

संमिश्र, संमिश्रित *a.* Mixed together, intermixed.

संमिश्लः An epithet of Indra.

संमीलनं Closing up (of a flower &c.), covering, enveloping.

संमुख *a.* (खा or खी *f.*), संमुखीन *a.* 1 Facing, fronting, face to face, opposite, confronting; कामं न तिष्ठति मदाननसंमुखी सा S. 1. 31; R. 15. 17; Si. 10. 86. 2 Encountering, meeting. 3 Disposed to.

संमुखिन् *m.* A mirror, looking-glass.

संमूर्छनं 1 Fainting, insensibility, 2 Congealing, becoming dense. 3 Thickening, increasing. 4 Height. 5 Universal pervasion, co-extension, complete permeation.

संमृष्ट *p. p.* 1 Well swept, cleansed. 2 Strained, filtered.

संमेलनं 1 Meeting together, union. 2 Mixture. 3 Assembling, collecting.

संमोहः 1 Bewilderment, confusion. infatuation. 2 Insensibility, swoon. 3 Ignorance, folly. 4 Fascination.

संमोहनं Fascinating, fascination. -नः N. of one of the five arrows of Cupid; Ku. 3. 66.

सम्यच्, सम्यंच् *a.* (समीची *f.*) 1 Going with, accompanying. 2 Right, fit, proper, due. 3 Correct, true, accurate. 4 Pleasant, agreeable; किं च कुलानि कवीनां निसर्गसम्यंचि रंजयतु R. G. 5 Same, uniform. 6 All, whole, entire. -*ind.* (सम्यक्) 1 With, together with. 2 Well, properly, rightly, correctly, truly; सम्यगियमाह S. 1; Ms. 2. 5, 14. 3 Duly, suitably, correctly, truly. 4 Honourably. 5 Completely, thoroughly. 6 Distinctly.

सम्राज् *m.* A paramount sovereign, universal lord; especially one who rules over other princes and has performed the Râjasûya sacrifice; येनेष्टं राजसूयेन मंडलस्येश्वरश्च यः। शास्ति यश्चाज्ञया राज्ञः स सम्राट् Ak.; R. 2. 5.

सय् 1 A. (सयते) To go, move.

सयूथ्यः One of the same flock or tribe.

सयोनि *a.* Having the same womb, uterine. -निः 1 A whole or uterine brother. 2 A pair of nippers for cutting betel-nut. 3 N. of Indra.

सर *a.* 1 Going or moving. 2 Cathartic, purgative. -रः 1 Going, motion. 2 An arrow. 3 The coagulum of curds or milk, cream. 4 Salt. 5 A string, necklace; अयं कंठे बाहुः शिशिरमसृणो मौक्तिकसरः U. 1. 39, 29. 6 A water-fall. -रं 1 Water. 2 A lake, pool. -Comp. -उत्सवः a crane. -जं fresh butter; cf. शरज.

सरकः-कं 1 A continuous line of road. 2 Spirituous liquor, spirits. 3 Drinking spirits; चक्रुरथ सह पुरंध्रिजनैरयथार्थसिद्धि सरकं महीभृतः Si 15. 80, 10. 12. 4 A drinking vessel, wine-glass, goblet; Si. 10. 20. 5 Distribution of spirituous liquor. -कं 1 Going. 2 A pond, lake. 3 Heaven.

सरघा 1 A bee; तस्तार सरघाव्याप्तैः स क्षौद्रपटलैरिव R. 4. 63; Si. 15. 23.

सरंगः 1 A quadruped. 2 A bird.

सरजस् -सा *f.*, सरजस्का A woman during menstruation.

सरट् *m.* 1 Air, wind. 2 A cloud. 3 A lizard. 4 A bee.

सरटिः 1 Wind. 2 A lizard; लूताहिसरटानां च तिरश्चां चांबुचारिणां Ms. 12. 57.

सरडिः 1 Wind. 2 A cloud.

सरडुः A lizard, chameleon.

सरण *a.* Going, moving, flowing. -णं 1 Proceeding, going or flowing. 2 Iron rust.

सरणिः, -णी *f.* 1 A Path, way, road, course; A. L. 18. 2 Arrangement, mode. 3 A straight or continuous line. 4 A disease of the throat.

सरंडः 1 A bird. 2 A libertine, dissolute man. 3 A lizard. 4 A rogue. 5 A kind of ornament.

सरण्युः 1 Air, wind. 2 A cloud. 3 Water. 4 The spring. 5 Fire. 6 N. of Yama.

सरत्निः *m. f.* A kind of cubit-measure; cf. रत्नि or अरत्नि.

सरथ *a.* Riding in the same car -थः A warrior riding in a chariot.

सरभस *a.* 1 Speedy, quick. 2 Violent, impetuous. 3 Passionate. 4 Delighted. -सं *ind.* Impetuously hurriedly &c.

सरमा 1 The bitch of the gods. 2 N. of a daughter of Daksha. 3 N. of the wife of Bibhîshaṇa, brother of Râvaṇa.

सरयुः Air, wind. -युः -यूः *f.* N. of a river on which stands Ayodhyâ, or Oude; R. 8. 95, 13. 61, 63, 14. 30.

सरल *a.* 1 Straight, not crooked. 2 Honest, upright, sincere, candid. 3 Simple, artless, simple minded; सरले साहसरागं परिहर Mâl. 6. 10; अयि सरले किमत्र भया भगवत्या शक्यं 2. -लः 1 A kind of pine tree; विघट्टितानां सरलद्रुमाणां Ku. 1. 9; Me. 53; R. 4. 75. 2 Fire. -Comp. -अंगः 'the exudation of Sarala', resin, turpentine. -द्रवः fragrant resin.

सरव्य See शरव्य.

सरस् *n.* 1 A lake, pond, pool, a large sheet of water; सरसामस्मि सागरः Bg. 10. 21. 2 Water. -Comp. -जं, -जन्मन् *n.*, -रुहं, (सरोजं, सरोजन्मन्, सरोरुहं) also सरसिजं, सरसिरुहं a lotus; सरसिजमनुविद्धं शैवलेनापि रम्यं S. 1. 20; सरोरुहद्युतिमुषः पादांस्तवासेविनुं Ratn. 1. 24. -जिनी, -रुहिणी 1 a lotus-plant; भ्रमर कथं वा सरोजिनीं त्यजसि Bv. 1. 100. 2 a pond abounding in lotuses. -रक्षः (सरोरक्षः) the guardian of a pool. -रुह (सरोरुह) *n.* a lotus. -वरः (सरोवरः) a lake.

सरस *a.* 1 Juicy, succulent. 2 Tasty, sapid. 3 Wet; Si. 11. 54. 4 Wet with perspiration; Ku. 5. 85. 5 Full of love, impassioned; Bv. 1. 100 (where it means 'full of honey' also). 6 Charming, lovely, agreeable, beautiful; सरसवसंत Git. 1. 7 Fresh, new. -सं 1 A lake, pond. 2 Alchemy.

सरसी A lake, pool; Bv. 2. 144. -Comp. -रुहं a lotus.

सरस्वत् *a.* 1 Having water, watery. 2 Juicy, succulent. 3 Elegant. 4 Sentimental. -*m.* 1 The ocean. 2 A lake. 3 A male river (नद). 4 A buffalo. 5 N. of Vâyu.

सरस्वती 1 N. of the goddess of speech and learning, and represented as the wife of Brahman. 2 Speech, voice, words; Ku. 4. 39, 43; R. 15. 46. 3 N. of a river (which is lost in the sands of the great desert). 4 A river in general. 5 A cow. 6 An excellent woman. 7 N. of Durgâ. 8 N. of a female divinity peculiar to the Buddhists. 9 The Soma plant. 10 The plant called ज्योतिष्मति.

सराग *a.* 1 Coloured, tinged, tinted. (अकारि) सरागमस्या रसनागुणास्पदं Ku. 5, 10. 2 Dyed with red lac; R. 16 10. 3 Impassioned, full of love, enamoured; मुनेरपि मनोऽवश्यं सरागं कुरुतेऽङ्गना Subbâsh.

सराव *a.* Sounding, making a noise. -वः 1 A lid, cover. 2 A shallow dish, saucer; cf. शराव.

सरिः *f.* A spring, fountain.

सरित् *f.* 1 A river; अभ्यासरितो शतानि हि समुद्रगाः प्राप्यर्यत्याब्धिं M. 5. 19. 2 A thread, string. -Comp. -नाथः, -पतिः (also सरितांपतिः), -भर्तृ *m.* the ocean. -वरा (also सरितांवरा) N. of the Ganges. -सुतः an epithet of Bhîshma.

सरि(री)मन् *m.* 1 Motion, creeping. 2 Wind.

सरिलं Water; cf. सलिल.

सरीसृपः A serpent.

सरुः The handle of a sword.

सरूप *a.* 1 Having the same form. 2 Like, resembling, similar; R. 6. 59.

सरूपता, -त्वं 1 Likeness. 2 Assimilation to the deity, one of the four states of *Mukti*.

सरोष *a.* Angry, wrathful. 2 Enraged.

सर्कः 1 Wind, air. 2 The mind.

सर्गः 1 Relinquishment, abandonment. 2 Creation ; अस्याः सर्गविधौ प्रजापतिरभूच्चंद्रो नु कांतप्रभः V. 1. 9. 3 The creation of the world ; Ku. 2. 6 ; R. 3. 27. 4 Nature, the universe. 5 Natural property, nature. 6 Determination, resolve; गृहाण शस्त्रं यदि सर्ग एष ते R. 3. 51 ; 14. 42 ; *Si.* 19. 38. 7 Assent, agreement. 8 A section, chapter, canto (as of a poem) 9 Rush, onset, advance (of troops). 10 Voiding of excrement. 11 N. of *Siva*. **-Comp.** -क्रमः the order of creation. -बंधः a great poem having several cantos, a Mahâkâvya ; सर्गबंधो महाकाव्यं S. D.

सर्ज् 1 P. (सर्जति) 1 To acquire, gain. 2 To earn by labour.

सर्जः 1 N. of a tree (साल). 2 The resinous exudation of the Sâla tree. **-Comp.** -निर्यासकः, -मणिः -रसः, resin.

सर्जकः The Sâla tree.

सर्जनं 1 Abandoning, quitting. 2 Letting loose. 3 Creating. 4 Voiding. 5 The rear of an army.

सर्जिः, सर्जिका, सर्जी *f.* Natron.

सर्जूः A trader. *-f.* 1 Lightning. 2 Necklace. 3 Going, following.

सर्पः 1 Serpentine or winding motion, sliding. 2 Flowing, going. 3 A snake, serpent. **-Comp.** -अरातिः -अरिः 1 an ichneumon. 2 a peacock. 3 an epithet of Garuda. -अशनः a peacock. -आवासं, -इष्टं the sandal tree. -छत्रं a mushroom. -तृणः an ichneumon. -दंष्ट्रः a snake's fang. -धारकः a snake-charmer. -भुज् *m.* 1 a peacock. 2 a crane. 3 a large snake. -मणिः a snake-gem. -राजः N. of Vâsuki.

सर्पणं 1 Creeping, gliding. 2 Tortuous motion. 3 The flight of an arrow nearly parallel to the ground.

सर्पिणी 1 A female serpent. 2 N. of a small medicinal herb.

सर्पिन् *a.* 1 Creeping, gliding, winding, going tortuously. 2 Moving, going (in general); यूका मंदविसर्पिणी Pt. 1. 252.

सर्पिस् *n.* Clarified butter (for the difference between घृत and सर्पिस्, see आज्य). **-Comp.** -समुद्रः the sea of clarified butter, one of the seven seas.

सर्पिष्मत् *a.* Dressed with clarified butter.

सर्ब् 1 P. (सर्बति) To go, move.

सर्मः 1 Going, motion. 2 The sky.

सर्व् 1 P. (सर्वति) To hurt, injure, kill.

सर्व *pron. a.* (nom. pl. सर्वे *m.*) 1 All, every ; उपर्युपरि पश्यंतः सर्व एव दरिद्रति R. 2. 2 ; रिक्तः सर्वो भवति हि लघुः पूर्णता गौरवाय Me. 20, 93. 2 Whole, entire, complete. -र्वः 1 N. of Vishṇu. 2 Of *Siva*. **-Comp.** -अंगं the whole body. -अंगीण *a.* pervading or thrilling through the whole body ; सर्वांगीणःस्पर्शः सुतस्य किल V. 5. 11. -अधिकारिन् *m.*, -अध्यक्षः a general superintendent. -अन्नीन *a.* eating every kind of food; सर्वान्नभोजिन् &c. -आकारं (in comp.) entirely, thoroughly, completely. -आत्मन् *m.* the whole soul ; सर्वात्मना entirely, completely, thoroughly. -ईश्वरः a paramount lord. -ग, -गामिन् *a.* all-pervading, omnipresent. -जित् *a* all-conquering, invincible. -ज्ञ, -विद् *a.* all-knowing, omniscient. (*-m.*) 1 an epithet of *Siva*. 2 of Buddha. -दमन *a.* all-subduing, irresistible. -नामन् *n.* a class of pronominal words. -मंगला an epithet of Parvatî. -रसः resin. -लिंगिन् *m.* a heretic, an impostor. -व्यापिन् *a.* all-pervading. -वेदस् *m.* one who performs a sacrifice by giving away all his wealth. -सहा (also सर्वंसहा) the earth. -स्वं 1 every thing, the whole of one's possessions ; as in सर्वस्वदंडः; °हरणं 'confiscation of the whole property'. 2 the very essence, the all-in-all of anything ; see *S.* 1. 24, 6. 2 ; Mâl. 8. 6 ; Bv. 1. 63.

सर्वंकष *a.* 'All-destroying', all-powerful ; सर्वंकषा भगवती भवितव्यतैव Mâl. 1. 23 ; Bv. 4. 2. -षः A villain, rogue.

सर्वतस् *ind.* 1 From every side or quarter. 2 On all sides, everywhere, all round. 3 Completely, entirely. **-Comp.** -गामिन् *a.* 1 having access everywhere ; Ku. 3 12. -भद्रः 1 the car of Vishṇu. 2 a bamboo. 3 a kind of verse artificially arranged ; *e. g.* Ki. 15. 25. 4 a temple or palace having openings on four sides ; (*n.* also in this sense). (-द्रा) a dancing girl, an actress. -मुख *a.* of every kind, complete, unlimited ; *S.* 5. 25. (-खः) 1 an epithet of *Siva*. 2 of Brahman ; Ku. 2. 3. (having faces on all sides). 3 the Supreme Being. 4 the soul. 5 a Brâhmaṇa. 6 fire. 7 heaven or Svarga (of Indra).

सर्वत्र *ind.* 1 Everywhere, in all places. 2 At all times.

सर्वथा *ind.* 1 In every way, by all means ; U. 1. 5. 2 At all, altogether (usually with negation). 3 Completely, entirely, utterly. 4 At all times.

सर्वदा *ind.* At all times, always for ever.

सर्वरी See शर्वरी.

सर्वशस् *ind.* 1 Wholly, entirely, completely. 2 Everywhere. 3 On all sides.

सर्वाणी See शर्वाणी.

सर्षपः 1 Mustard; खलः सर्षपमात्राणि परच्छिद्राणि पश्यति Subhâsh. ; Mâl. 10. 6. 2 A small measure of weight. 3 A sort of poison.

सल् 1 P. (सलति) To go, move.

सलं Water.

सलिलं Water ; सुभगसलिलावगाहाः *S.* 1. 3. **-Comp.** -अर्थिन् *a.* thirsty. -आशयः a tank, reservoir of water. -इंधनः the submarine fire. -उपप्लवः inundation, deluge, flood of water. -क्रिया the funeral rite of washing a corpse. 2 = उदकक्रिया q. v. -जं a lotus. -निधिः the ocean.

सलज्ज *a.* Modest, bashful.

सलील *a.* Sportive, wanton, amorous.

सलोकता Being in the same world, residence in the same heaven with a particular deity, (one of the four states of *Mukti*).

सल्लकी A kind of tree ; cf. शल्लकी.

सवः 1 Extraction of Soma juice. 2 An offering, a libation. 3 A sacrifice. 4 The sun. 5 The moon. 6 Progeny. -वं 1 Water. 2 The honey of flowers.

सवनं 1 Extracting the Soma juice or drinking it. 2 A sacrifice ; अथ तं सवनाय दीक्षितः R. 8. 75 ; *S.* 3. 28. 3 Bathing, purificatory ablution. 4 Generation, bearing or bringing forth children.

सवयस् *a.* Of the same age. *-m.* 1 A contemporary, coeval. 2 A companion of the same age. *-f.* A woman's female companion or confidante.

सवरः 1 N. of *Siva* 2 Water.

सवर्ण *a.* 1 Of the same colour. 2 Of like appearance, like, resembling; दुर्वर्णभित्तिरिह सांद्रसुधासवर्णा *Si.* 4. 28 ; Me. 18 ; R. 9. 51. 3 Of the same caste or tribe. 4 Of the same kind, similar. 5 Belonging to the same class of letters, requiring the same effort (of the organs of speech) in pronunciation ; तुल्यास्यप्रयत्नं सवर्णं P. I. 1. 9

सविकल्प, -सविकल्पक *a.* 1 Optional. 2 Doubtful. 3 Recognizing a distinction as that of subject and object, or of the knower and the known (opp. निर्विकल्पक q. v.).

सविग्रह *a.* 1 Possessing a body, embodied. 2 Having meaning or import. 3 Engaged in strife, quarrelling.

सवितर्क, सविमर्श *a.* Thoughtful. -र्कं, -र्शं *ind.* Thoughtfully.

सवितृ *a.* (त्री *f.*) Generating, producing, yielding ; सवित्री कामानां यदि जगति जागर्ति भवती G. L. 23. *-m.* 1 The sun ; उदेति सविता ताम्रस्ताम्र एवास्तमेति च K. P. 7. 2 N. of *Siva*. 3 Of Indra. 4 The *Arka* tree.

सवित्री 1 A mother ; Ku. 1. 24. **2** a cow.

सविध *a.* **1** Of the same kind or sort. **2** Near, adjacent, proximate ; भूयो भूयः सविधनगरीरथ्यया पर्यटंतं Mâl. 1. 15. **-धं** Proximity, vicinity ; यस्य न सविधे दयिता दवदहनस्तुहिनदीधितिस्तस्य K. P. 9 ; किमासेव्यं पुंसा सविधमनवद्यं द्युसरितः 10 ; N. 2. 47, *Si.* 14. 69 ; Bv. 2. 182.

सविनय *a.* Modest, humble. **-यं** *ind.* Modestly.

सविभ्रम *a.* Sportive, coquettish.

सविशेष *a.* **1** Possessing characteristic qualities. **2** Peculiar, extraordinary. **3** Special, particular ; U. 4. **4** Pre-eminent, superior, excellent. **5** Discriminative. (**सविशेषं** and **सविशेषतस्** are used adverbially in the sense of 'especially', 'particularly', 'exceedingly'; अनेन धर्मः सविशेषमद्य मे त्रिवर्गसारः प्रतिभाति भामिनि Ku. 5. 38 ; oft. in comp.; Ku. 1. 27, R. 16. 53).

सविस्तर *a.* Detailed, minute, complete. **-रं** *ind.* In detail, *in extenso*.

सविस्मय *a.* Surprised, astonished.

सवृद्धिक *a.* Bearing interest.

सवेश *a.* **1** Decorated, ornamented, dressed. **2** Near, proximete.

सव्य *a.* **1** Left, left-hand. **2** Southern. **3** Contrary, backward, reverse. **4** Right. **-व्यं** *ind.* The usual position of the sacred thread when it hangs down over the left shoulder; cf. अपसव्य. **-Comp. -इतर** *a.* right. **-साचिन्** *m.* an epithet of Arjuna ; निमित्तमात्रं भव सव्यसाचिन् Bg. 11. 33 ; (the name is thus derived in Mb.:-- उभौ मे दाक्षिणौ पाणी गांडीवस्य विकर्षणे । तेन देवमनुष्येषु सव्यसाचीति मां विदुः ॥).

सव्यपेक्ष *a.* Connected with, dependent on; स्नेहश्च निमित्तसव्यपेक्षश्चेति विप्रतिषिद्धमेतत् Mâl. 1 ; U. 6.

सव्यभिचारः One of the five main divisions of *Hetva'bha'sa* (in logic), a too general middle term ; for explanation, see अनैकांतिक.

सव्याज *a.* **1** Artful. **2** Plausible; cunning.

सव्यापार *a.* Engaged, employed.

सव्रीड *a.* **1** Bashful. **2** Ashamed.

सव्येष्ठृ *m.*, **सव्येष्ठः** A charioteer.

सशल्य *a.* **1** Thorny. **2** Pierced by darts or thorns.

सशस्य *a.* Having or yielding corn. **-स्या** A variety of sun-flower.

सश्मश्रु *a.* Bearded. *-f.* A woman with a beard.

सश्रीक *a.* **1** Prosperous, fortunate. **2** Lovely, beautiful.

सस् 2 P. (सस्ति) To sleep.

ससत्त्व *a.* **1** Possessed of vitality, energy, vigour, courage &c. **2** Pregnant. **-त्त्वा** A pregnant woman.

ससंदेह *a.* Doubtful. **-हः** N. of a figure of speech ; see संदेह.

ससनं Immolation.

ससंध्य *a.* Evening, vespertine.

ससाध्वस *a.* Alarmed, frightened, timid.

सस्ज् See सज्ज्.

सस्यं 1 Corn, grain ; (पतानि) सस्यैः पूर्णे जठरपिठरे प्राणिनां संभवंति Pt. 5. 27 ; see शस्य also. **2** Fruit or produce of any plant. **3** A weapon. **4** A good quality, merit. **-Comp. -इष्टिः** *f.* a sacrifice made on the ripening of new grain. **-प्रद** *a.* fertile. **-मारिन्** *a.* destructive of grain. (*-m.*) a kind of rat or mouse. **-संवरः** the Sâla tree.

सस्यक *a.* Possessed of good qualities, meritorious. **-कः 1** A sword. **2** A weapon. **3** A kind of precious stone.

सस्वेद *a.* Covered over or moist with sweat, perspired. **-दा** A girl recently, deflowered.

सह् I. 4. P. (सह्यति) **1** To satisfy. **2** To be pleased. **3** To endure, bear. -II. 1 A. (सहते, epic Paras. also ; सोढ the स् of सह् is changed to ष् after prepositions ending in इ, as नि, परि, वि, except when ह् is changed to ढ) **1** (*a*) To bear, endure, suffer, put up with ; खलोल्लापाः सोढाः Bh. 3. 6 ; पदं सहेत भ्रमरस्य पेलवं शिरीषपुष्पं न पुनः पतत्रिणः Ku. 5. 4 ; so दुःखं, संतापं,-क्लेशं &c. ; R. 12. 63 ; 11. 52 ; Bk. 17. 59. (*b*) To tolerate, allow ; प्रकृतिः खलु सा महीयसः सहते नान्यसमुन्नतिं यया Ki. 2. 21 ; Me. 105; R. 14. 63. **2** To forgive, forbear ; वारंवारं मयैतस्यापराधः सोढः H. 3 ; Bg. 11. 44. **3** To wait, be patient ; द्वित्राण्यहान्यर्हसि सोढुमर्हन् R. 5. 25, 15. 45. **4** To bear, support, bear up ; *S.* 3. **5** To conquer, defeat, oppose, be able to resist. **6** To suppress, stop. **7** To be able (with inf.). -*Caus.* (साहयति-ते) **1** To cause to bear or suffer. **2** To make bearable or supportable; गुर्वपि विरहदुःखमाशाबंधः साहयति *S.* 4. 16. -*Desid.* (सिसहिषते) To wish to bear &c. -WITH **उद्** 1 to be able, have power or energy for, dare, venture ; तवानुवृत्तिं न च कर्तुमुत्सहे Ku. 5. 65 'I cannot approve &c'.; Bk. 3. 54, 5. 54, 14. 89 ; *Si.* 14. 83. **2** (*a*) to attempt, be prompted to ; Ki. 1. 36. (*b*) to cheer up, not to sink or give way ; Bk. 19. 16. **3** To be at ease ; Ku. 4. 36. **4** to go forward, march on. (*-Caus.*) to stir up, rouse, Bk. 9 69. **-परि** to bear ; Bk. 9. 73. **-प्र 1** to bear, endure ; न तेजस्तेजस्वी प्रसृतमपरेषां प्रसहते U. 6. 14. **2** to withstand, resist, overpower ; संयुगे सांयुगीन तमद्यतं प्रसहेत कः Ku. 2. 57 **3** to exert oneself, attempt. **4** to be able. **5** to have power or energy ; see प्रसह्य also. **-वि 1** to bear, endure ; R. 3. 63, 8. 56. **2** to resist, withstand, be able to resist ; R. 4. 49. **3** to be able. **4** to allow. **5** to wish, like.

सह *a.* **1** Bearing, enduring, suffering. **2** Patient. **3** Able ; see असह. **-हः** The month मार्गशीर्ष. **-हः, हं** Power, strength.

सह *ind.* **1** With, together with, along with, accompanied by (with instr.) शशिना सह याति कौमुदी सह मेघेन तडित्प्रलीयते Ku. 4. 33. **2** Together, simultaneously, at the same time ; अस्तौदयौ सहैवासौ कुरुते नृपतिर्द्विषां Subhâsh. **-Comp. -अध्यायिन्** *m.* a fellow-student. **-अर्थ** *a.* synonymous. (**-र्थः**) the same or common object. **-उक्तिः** *f.* a figure of speech in rhetoric ; सा सहोक्तिः सहार्थस्य बलादेकं द्विवाचकं K. P. 10 ; *e. g.* पपात भूमौ सह सैनिकाश्रुभिः R. 3. 61. **-उटजः** a hut made of leaves. **-उदरः** a uterine brother, brother of whole blood ; Vikr. 1. 21. -उपमा a kind of Upamâ. **-ऊढः**, **-ऊढजः** the son of a woman pregnant at marriage ; (one of the 12 kinds of sons recognised in old Hindu law). **-कार** *a.* having the sound ह ; Nalod. 2. 14. (**-रः**) **1** co-operation. **2** a mango tree ; क इदानीं सहकारमंतरेण पल्लवितामतिमुक्तलतां सहते *S.* 3. **-भंजिका** a kind of game. **-कारिन्**, **-कृत्** *a.* co-operating. (*-m.*) a co-adjutor, associate, colleague. **-कृत** *a.* co-operated with, assisted or aided by. **-गमनं 1** accompanying. **2** a woman's burning herself with her deceased husband's body, self immolation of a widow. **-चर** *a.* accompanying, going or living with ; U. 3. 8. (**रः**) **1** a companion, friend, associate. **2** a husband. **3** a surety. (**री** *f.*) **1** a female companion. **2** a wife, mate. **-चरित** *a.* accompanying, attending, associating with. **-चारः 1** accompaniment. **2** agreement, harmony. **3** (in logic) the invariable accompaniment of the *hetu* (middle term) by the *Sa'dhya* (major term). **-चारिन्** see सहचर. **-ज** *a.* **1** inborn, natural, innate. **2** hereditary. (**-जः**) **1** a brother of whole blood. **2** the natural state or disposition. °**अरिः** a natural enemy. °**मित्रं** a natural friend. **-जात** *a.* natural ; see सहज. **-दार** *a.* **1** with a wife. **2** married. **-देवः** N. of the youngest of the five Pândavas ; the twin brother of Nakula, born of Mâdrî by the gods Asvins. He is regarded as the type of manly beauty. **-धर्मः** same duties. °**चारिन्** *m.* a husband. °**चारिणी 1** a lawful wife, one legally married. **2** a fellow-worker. **-पांशुक्रीडिन्**, **-पांशुकिल** *m.* a friend from the earliest childhood. **-भाविन्** *m.* a friend, partisan, follower. **-भू** *a.* natural, innate ; Ratn. 1. 2. **-भोजनं** eating in company with friends. **मरणं** see सहगमन. **-युध्वन्** *m.* a brother in arms. **-वसतिः**, **-वासः** dwelling together ; सहवसतिमुपेत्य यैः प्रियायाः कृत इव मुग्धविलोकितोपदेशः *S.* 2. 3.

सहता, -त्वं Union, association.

सहन *a.* Bearing, enduring. **-नं 1** Bearing, enduring. **2** Patience, forbearance.

सहस् *m.* **1** The month called Mârgaśîrsha; *Si.* 6. 57; 16. 47. **2** The winter season. *-n.* **1** Power, might, strength. **2** Force, violence. **3** Victory, conquering. **4** Lustre, brightness.

सहसा *ind.* **1** With force, forcibly. **2** Rashly, precipitately, inconsiderately; सहसा विदधीत न क्रियामविवेकः परमापदां पदं Ki. 2. 30. **3** Suddenly, all at once; मातंगनक्रैः सहसोत्पतद्भिः R. 13. 11.

सहसानः 1 A peacock. **2** A sacrifice, an oblation.

सहस्यः The month called Pausha; सहस्यरात्रीरुदवासतत्परा Kn. 5. 26.

सहस्रं A thousand. **-Comp. -अंशु, -अर्चिस्, -कर, -किरण, -दीधिति, -धामन्, -पाद्, -मरीचि, -रश्मि** *m.* the sun; *S.* 7. 4; R. 13. 44; Mu. 3. 17. **-अक्ष** *a.* **1** thousand-eyed. **2** vigilant. (**-क्षः**) **1** an epithet of Indra. **2** of Pûrusha; Rv. 10. 90. **3** of Vishṇu. **-कांडा** white Dûrvâ grass. **-कृत्वस्** *ind.* a thousand times. **-द** *a.* liberal. (**-दः**) an epithet of *S*iva. **-दंष्ट्रः** a kind of fish. **-दृश्, -नयन, -नेत्र, -लोचन** *m.* **1** epithet of Indra. **2** of Vishṇu. **-धारः** the discus of Vishṇu. **-पत्रं** a lotus; R. 7. 11. **-बाहुः 1** an epithet of king Kârtavîrya q. v. **2** of the demon Bâṇa. **3** of *S*iva (or of Vishṇu according to some). **-भुजः, -मूर्धन्, -मौलि** *m.* epithets of Vishṇu. **-रोमन्** *n.* a blanket. **-वीर्या** asa fœtida. **-शिखरः** an epithet of the Vindhya mountain.

सहस्रधा *ind.* In a thousand parts, a thousand-fold; दीर्यें किं न सहस्रधाहमथवा रामेण किं दुष्करं U. 6. 40.

सहस्रशस् *ind.* By thousands.

सहस्रिन् *a.* **1** Possessed of a thousand; सहस्री लक्ष्मीहिते Pt 5. 82. **2** Consisting of thousands. **3** Amounting to a thousand (as a fine); Ms. 8. 376. *-m.* **1** A body of a thousand men &c. **2** The commander of a thousand.

सहस्वत् *a.* Strong, powerful.

सहा 1 The earth. **2** The aloeplant or flower.

सहायः 1 A friend, companion; सहायसाध्याः प्रदिशंति सिद्धयः Ki. 14. 44; Ku. 3. 21. **2** A follower, an adherent. **3** An ally. **4** A helper, patron. **5** The ruddy goose. **6** A kind of perfume. **7** N. of *S*iva.

सहायता -त्वं 1 A number of companions. **2** Companionship, union, friendship. **3** Help, assistance; कुसुमास्तरणे सहायतां बहुशः सौम्य गतस्त्वभावयोः Ku. 4. 25; R. 9. 19.

सहायवत् *a.* **1** Having a friend. **2** Befriended, assisted.

सहारः 1 The mango tree. **2** Universal destruction.

सहित *a.* Accompanied or attended by, together with, united or associated with; पवनाग्निसमागमो ह्ययं सहितं ब्रह्म यदस्त्रतेजसा R. 8. 4. **-तं** *ind.* Together with, with.

सहितृ *a.* Enduring, patient.

सहिष्णु *a.* **1** Able to bear or endure, capable of enduring; रविकिरणसहिष्णु क्लेशलेशैरभिन्नं *S.* 2. 4. **2** Patient, resigned, forbearing; सुकरस्तरुवत्सहिष्णुना रिपुरुन्मूलयितुं महानपि Ki. 2. 50.

सहिष्णुता -त्वं 1 Power to bear or support. **2** Patience, resignation.

सहुरिः The sun. *-f.* The earth.

सहृदय *a.* **1** Good-hearted, kind, compassionate. **2** Sincere. **-यः 1** A learned man. **2** An appreciator (of merits &c.), a man of taste, a man of critical faculty; इत्युपदेशं कवेः सहृदयस्य च करोति K. P. 1; परिष्कुर्वंत्यन्ये सहृदयधुरीणाः कतिपये R. G.

सहृल्लेख *a.* Questionable, doubtful. **-खं** Questionable food.

सहेल *a.* Sportive, playful.

सहोढः A thief caught with the stolen property in his possession.

सहोर *a.* Good, excellent. **-रः** A saint, sage.

सह्य *a.* **1** Bearable, supportable, endurable; अपि सह्या ते शिरोवेदना Mu. 5; M. 3. 4. **2** To be borne or endured; कथं तूष्णीं सह्यो निरवधिरिदानीं तु विरहः U. 3. 44. **3** Able to bear. **4** Adequate or equal to, able to bear. **5** Strong, powerful. **-ह्यः** N. of one of the seven principal mountain ranges in India, a part of the western Ghats at some distance from the sea; रामास्त्रोत्सारितोप्यासीत्सह्यलग्न इवार्णवः R. 4. 53, 52; Ki. 18. 5. **-ह्यं 1** Health, convalescence. **2** Assistance. **3** Fitness, adequacy.

सा 1 N. of Lakshmî. **2** Of Pârvatî.

सांयात्रिकः A sea-trader, a merchant trading by sea; (पोतवणिक्); Pt. 1. 316.

सांयुगीन *a.* Warlike, skilled in war; R. 11. 30; V. 5. **-नः** A great warrior, a soldier skilled in war; Ku. 2. 57.

सांराविणं A general or loud shout, tumultuous uproar; उत्तालाः कटपूतनाप्रभृतयः सांराविणं कुर्वते Mâl. 5. 11; Bk. 7. 43.

सांवत्सर (**री** *f.*), **सांवत्सरिक** (**की** *f.*) *a.* Annual, yearly. **-कः** An astrologer.

सांवादिक *a.* (**की** *f.*) **1** Colloquial. **2** Controversial. **-कः** A disputant.

सांवृत्तिक A. (**की** *f.*) Illusory, phenomenal.

सांशयिक *a.* (**की** *f.*) **1** Doubtful. **2** Uncertain, irresolute.

सांसारिक *a.* (**की** *f.*) Worldly, mundane; संसारिकेषु च सुखेषु वयं रसज्ञाः U. 2. 22.

सांसिद्धिक *a.* **1** Natural, existing naturally, innate, inherent. **2** Effected naturally, spontaneous. **3** Absolute. **4** Effected by supernatural means **-Comp. -द्रवः** natural fluidity (opp. नैमित्तिक 'generated'); belonging to water only).

सांस्थानिकः A fellow-countryman.

सांस्राविणं A general flow or stream.

सांहननिक *a.* (**की** *f.*) Bodily, corporeal.

साकम् *ind.* **1** With, together with (with instr.); यांती गुरुजनैः साकं स्मयमाना नतांबुजा Bv. 2. 132, 1. 41. **2** At the same time, simultaneously.

साकल्यं Entirety, totality, the whole or entire part of a thing; यावत्साकल्यं; Nalod. 3. 19. (**साकल्येन** 'entirely, completely, thoroughly'; Ms. 12. 25).

साकूत *a.* **1** Having meaning, significant, meaning; साकूतस्मितं Gît. 2; साकूतं वचनं &c. **2** Intentional. **3** Amorous, wanton. **-तं** *ind.* **1** Meaningly, significantly; as in साकूतं मां निर्वर्ण्य. **2** Amorously. **3** Feelingly, pathetically.

साकेतं N. of the city of Ayodhyâ; साकेत नार्योऽञ्जलिभिः प्रणेमुः R. 14. 13. 13. 79, 18. 35; अरुणद्यवनः साकेतं Mbh. **-ताः** (*m. pl.*) The inhabitants of Ayodhyâ.

साकेतकः An inhabitant of Ayodhyâ.

साक्तकं A quantity of fried grain (सक्तु). **-कः** Barley.

साक्षात् *ind.* **1** In the presence of before the very eyes, visibly, openly, evidently. **2** In person, actually, in bodily form; साक्षात् प्रियामुपगतामपहाय पूर्वं *S.* 6. 16, 1. 6. **3** Directly. In comp. often translated by 'incarnate'; साक्षाद्यमः; or by 'open, direct'; तत्साक्षात्प्रतिषेधः कोपाय Mâl. 1. 11. (**साक्षात्कृ** 'to see with one's own eyes, realise personally'). **-Comp. -करणं 1** causing to be visibly present. **2** making evident to the senses. **3** intuitive perception. **-कारः** perception, apprehension, knowledge.

साक्षिन् *a.* (**णी** *f.*) **1** Seeing, observing, witnessing. **2** Attesting, testifying. *-m.* A witness, an observer, an eye-witness; फलं तपः साक्षिषु दृष्टमेष्वपि Ku. 5. 60.

साक्ष्यं 1 Evidence, testimony; तमेव चाधाय विवाहसाक्ष्ये R. 7. 20. **2** Attestation.

साक्षेप *a.* Taunting, abusive.

साखेय *a.* (**यी** *f.*) **1** Relating to a friend. **2** Friendly, amicable.

साख्यं Friendship.

सागरः 1 The ocean, sea; सागरः सागरोपमः; (fig also;) दयासागर, विद्यासागर &c.; cf. सगर. **2** The number 'four' or 'seven'. **3** A kind of deer. **–Comp.** –अनुकूल *a.* situated along the sea-coast. –अंत *a.* bounded by the sea, sea-girt. –अंबरा, –नेमिः, –मेखला the earth. –आलयः N. of Varuṇa. –उत्थं sea-salt. –गा the Ganges. –गामिनी a river.

साग्नि *a.* **1** Having fire. **2** Taking the sacred fire.

साग्निक *a.* **1** Maintaining or possessing fire. **2** Attended by fire. **–कः** A house-holder who maintains a sacred fire.

साग्र *a.* **1** Entire. **2** With a surplus, more than.

सांकर्य Mixture, confusion, promiscuous or confused mixture.

सांकल *a.* (ली *f.*) Produced or effected by addition.

सांकाश्यं-श्या N. of the capital of Kusadhvaja, brother of Janaka.

सांकेतिक *a.* (की *f.*) **1** Symbolical, indicatory. **2** Conventional.

सांक्षेपिक *a.* (की *f.*) Abridged, short, concise.

सांख्य *a.* **1** Relating to number. **2** Calculating, enumerating. **3** Discriminative. **4** Deliberating, reasoning, a reasoner ; त्वं गतिः सर्वसांख्यानां योगिनां त्वं परायणं Mb. **–ख्यः, –ख्यं** N. of one of the six systems of Hindu philosophy, attributed to the sage Kapila ; (this philosophy is so called because it 'enumerates' twenty-five *Tattvas* or true principles ; and its chief object is to effect the final emancipation of the twenty-fifth *Tattva*, *i. e.* the *Purusha* or soul from the bonds of this worldly existence—the fetters of phenomenal creation—by conveying a correct knowledge of the twenty-four other *Tattvas* and by properly discriminating the Soul from them. It regards the whole universe to be a development of an inanimate principle called Prakṛiti q. v., while the *Purusha* is altogether passive and simply a looker-on. It agrees with the Vedânta in being synthetical and so differs from the analytical Nyâya or Vaiseshika ; but its great point of divergence from the Vedânta is that it maintains two principles which the Vedânta denies, and that it does not admit God as the creator and controller of the universe, which the Vedânta affirms). **–ख्यः** A follower of the Sânkya philosophy ; Bg. 3. 5, 5. 11. **–Comp.** –प्रसादः, –मुख्यः epithets of *S*iva.

सांग *a.* **1** Having members. **2** Complete in every part. **3** Together with the *angas* or auxiliary members.

सांगतिक *a.* (की *f.*) Relating to union or society, associating. **–कः** A visitor, guest, new-comer.

सांगमः Union, meeting ; cf. संगम.

सांग्रामिक *a.* (की *f.*) Relating to war, warlike, martial ; U. 5. 22. **–कः** A general, commander.

साचि *ind.* Obliquely, crookedly, awry, in a sidelong manner ; साचि लोचनयुगं नमयंती Ki. 9. 44, 10. 57. (**साचीकृ** means 'to turn or bend aside, make crooked' ; निनाय साचीकृतचारुवक्त्रः R. 6. 14 ; Ku. 3. 68 ; साचीकरोत्याननं M. 4. 14.

साचिव्यं 1 The office of a minister, ministership. **2** Ministry, administration. Friendship.

साजात्यं 1 Sameness of caste, class, or kind. **2** Community of genus, homogeneousness.

सांजनः A lizard.

साट् 10 U. (साटयति-ते) To show, manifest.

साटोप *a.* **1** Elated or puffed up with pride, haughty. **2** Majestic, stately. **3** Swollen (as with water); Pt. 1. **–पं** *ind.* Proudly, arrogantly, in a stately manner, struttingly.

सात् *ind.* A Taddhita affix added to a word to show that something is completely changed into the thing expressed by that word, or that it is left at the complete disposal or control of that thing ; **भस्मसात् भू** 'to be completely reduced to ashes'; अग्निसात्कृत्वा M. 5 ; भस्मसात्कृतवतः पितृद्विषः पात्रसाच्च वसुधां ससागरां R. 11. 86 ; विभज्य मेरुर्न यदर्थिसात्कृतः N. 1. 16 ; so ब्राह्मणसात्, राजसात् &c. ; *S*i. 14. 36.

सातत्यं Continuity, permanence.

सातिः *f.* **1** Giving, a gift, donation. **2** Gaining, obtaining. **3** Help. **4** Destruction. **5** End, conclusion. **6** Sharp or acute pain.

सातीनः, सातीनकः Pease.

सात्त्विक *a.* (की *f.*) **1** Real, essential. **2** True, genuine, natural. **3** Honest, sincere, good. **4** Virtuous, amiable. **5** Vigorous. **6** Endowed with the quality *Sattva* (goodness). **7** Belonging to or derived from the *Sattva* quality ; ये चैव सात्त्विका भावाः Bg. 7. 12, 14. 16. **8** Caused by internal feeling or sentiment (as of love), internal ; तद्भूरिसात्त्विकविकारमपास्तधैर्यमाचार्यकं विजयि मान्मथमाविरासीत् Mâl. 1. 26. **–कः 1** An external indication of (internal) feeling or emotion, one of the kinds of *Bhâvas* in poetry ; (these are eight:— स्तंभः स्वेदोऽथ रोमांचः स्वरभंगोऽथ वेपथुः । वैवर्ण्यमश्रु प्रलय इत्यष्टौ सात्त्विकाः स्मृताः ॥ S. D. 116. **2** A Brâhmaṇa. **3** N. of Brahman.

सात्यकिः N. of a Yâdava warrior, who acted as charioteer to Kṛishṇa, and took part with the Pāṇḍavas in the great war.

सात्यवतः, सात्यवतेयः A metronymic of the sage Vyâsa.

सात्वत् *m.* A follower, worshipper (of Kṛishṇa &c.)

सात्वतः 1 N. of Vishṇu. **2** Of Balarâma. **3** The son of an outcast Vaisya. **–ताः** (*m. pl.*) N. of a people; *S*i. 16. 14.

सात्वती 1 N. of one of the four dramatic styles ; see S. D. 416. **2** N. of the mother of *S*isupâla ; *S*i. 2. 11.

सादः 1 Sinking, settling down. **2** Exhaustion, weariness ; उदितोरुसादमतिवेपथुमत् *S*i. 9. 77. **3** Leanness, thinness emaciation; शरीरसादादसमग्रभूषणा R. 3. 2. **4** Perishing, decay, loss, destruction, cessation; गतिविभ्रमसादनीरवा R 8. 56; Nalod. 3. 24. **5** Pain, torment. Clearness, purity.

सादनं 1 Wearying, exhausting. **2** Destroying. **3** Exhaustion. **4** A house, dwelling.

सादिः 1 A charioteer. **2** A warrior.

सादिन् *a.* **1** Sitting down. **2** Exhausting, destroying &c. **–m. 1** A horseman. **2** One riding on an elephant or seated in a car.

सादृश्यं 1 Likeness, resemblance, similarity ; संतिपुनर्नामधेयसादृश्यानि *S.* 7 ; तवाक्षिसादृश्यमिव प्रयुंजते Ku. 5. 35, 7. 16 ; R. 1. 40 ; 15. 67. **2** A likeness, a portrait, an image ; मत्सादृश्यं विरहतनु वा भावगम्यं लिखंती Me. 85.

साद्यंत *a.* Entire, complete.

साद्यस्क *a.* (स्की *f.*) Quick, instantaneous.

साध् I. 5 P. (साध्नोति) **1** To complete, finish, accomplish. **2** To conquer. –II. 4 P. (साध्यति) To be completed or accomplished. –*Caus.* **1** To accomplish, effect, bring about, perform ; अपि साधय साधयेप्सितं N. 2. 62 ; Ku. 2. 33 ; R. 5. 25. **2** To complete, finish, conclude. **3** To gain, secure, obtain ; R. 17. 38, Ms. 6. 75. **4** To prove, substantiate. **5** To subdue, overpower, conquer (as a foe &c.), win over ; न हि साम्ना न दानेन न भेदेन च पांडवाः । शक्याः साधयितुं Mb. **6** To kill, destroy ; सुग्रीवांतक मासेदुः साधयिष्याम इत्या Bk. 7. 31. **7** To learn, understand. **8** To cure, heal. **9** To go, depart, go one's way ; साधयाम्यहमविघ्नमस्तु ते R. 11. 91 ; *S.* 1, 7 ; प्रायेणाण्यंतकः साधिर्गमेरर्थे प्रयुज्यते S. D. 340. **10** To recover (as a debt). **11** To make perfect. –With प्र (*caus.*) **1** to advance, promote. **2** to accomplish, effect. **3** to gain, obtain, **4** to overcome, subdue. **5** to dress, decorate. –सं **1** to be successful (Atm.). **2** to accomplish, complete; Ms. 2, 100. **3** to secure, obtain. **4** to settle. **5** to regain ; Ms. 8. 50. **6** to cause to be settled or paid ; Ms. 8. 213. **7** to destroy, kill. **8** to extinguish.

साधक *a.* (धका or धिका *f.*) **1** Accomplishing, fulfilling, effecting, completing. **2** Efficient, effective ; Ku. 3. 12. **3** Skilful, adapt. **4** Effecting by magic, magical. **5** Assisting, helping.

साधन *a.* (नी *f.*) Accomplishing, effecting &c. **–नं 1** Accomplishing, effecting, performing ; as in स्वार्थसाधनं. **2** Fulfilment, accomplishment, complete attainment of an object ; प्रसार्थसाधने तौ हि पर्यायोद्यतकार्मुक R. 4. 16. **3** A means, an expedient, a means of accomplishing anything ; शरीरमाद्यं खलु धर्मसाधनं Ku. 5. 33, 52 ; R. 1. 9, 3. 12, 4. 36, 62. **4** An instrument, agent ; कुठारः छिदिक्रियासाधनम्. **5** The efficient cause, source, cause in general. **6** The instrumental case. **7** Implement, apparatus. **8** Appliance, materials. **9** Matter, ingredients, substance. **10** An army or a part thereof ; Mu. 5. 10. **11** Aid, help, assistance (in general). **12** Proof, substantiation, demonstration. **13** The *hetu* or middle term in a syllogism, reason, that which leads to a conclusion ; साध्ये निश्चितमन्वयेन घटितं बिभ्रत्सपक्षे स्थितिं व्यावृत्तं च विपक्षतो भवति यत्तत्साधनं सिद्धये Mu. 5. 10. **14** Subduing, overcoming. **15** Subduing by charms. **16** Accomplishing anything by charms or magic. **17** Healing, curing. **18** Killing, destroying; फलं च तस्य प्रतिसाधनं Ki. 14. 17. **19** Conciliating, propitiating, winning over. **20** Going out, setting forward, departure. **21** Going after, following. **22** Penance, self mortification. **23** Attainment of final beatitude. **24** Medicinal preparation, drug, medicine. **25** (In law) Enforcement of the delivery of anything, or of the payment of debt, infliction of fine. **26** A bodily organ. **27** The penis. **28** An udder. **29** Wealth. **30** Friendship. **31** Profit, advantage. **32** Burning a dead body. **33** Obsequies. **34** Killing or oxydation of metals. **–Comp. –क्रिया** a finite verb. **–पत्रं** a document used as evidence.

साधनता–त्वं The state of having means, possession of means to accomplish a desired object ; प्रतिकूलतामुपगते हि विधौ विफलत्वमेति बहुसाधनता Si. 9. 6.

साधना 1 Accomplishment, fulfilment, completion. **2** Worship, adoration. **3** Conciliation, propitiat ion.

साधंतः A mendicantr, beggar.

साधर्म्यं 1 Sameness or community of duty, office &c. ; पंचमं लोकपालानामूचुः साधर्म्ययोगतः R. 17. 78. **2** Sameness of nature, common character, likeness, community of properties ; साधर्म्यमुपमा भेदे K. P. 10 ; Bg. 14, 2 ; Bhâsha P. 12.

साधारण *a.* (णा or णी *f.*) **1** Common (to two or more) joint ; साधारणोऽयं प्रणयः S. 3 ; साधारणं भूषणभूष्यभावः Ku. 1. 43 ; R. 16. 5, V. 2. 16. **2** Ordinary, common ; साधारणी न खलु बाधा भवस्य Asvad. 10. **3** General, universal. **4** Mingled, mixed with, in common with ; उत्कंठासाधारणं परितोषमनुभवामि S. 4 ; वीज्यते स हि संसुप्तः श्वाससाधारणानिलैः Ku. 2. 42. **5** Equal, similar, like. **6** (In logic) Belonging to more than one instance alleged, one of the three divisions of the fallacy called अनैकांतिक q. v. **–णं 1** A common or general rule, a rule or precept generally applicable. **2** A generic property **–Comp. –धनं** joint property. **–स्त्री** a common woman, harlot, prostitute.

साधारणता–त्वं 1 Community, universality. **2** Joint interest.

साधारण्यं Commonness; see साधारणता.

साधिका 1 A skilful or accomplished woman. **2** Deep sleep.

साधित *p. p.* **1** Accomplished, effected, achieved. **2** Completed, finished. **3** Proved, demonstrated. **4** Obtained, secured. **5** Discharged. **6** Overcome, subdued. **7** Made good, recovered. **8** Fined. **9** Made to pay. **10** Awarded (as fine or punishment).

साधिमन् *m.* Goodness, excellence, perfection.

साधिष्ठ *a.* **1** Best, most excellent, most proper. **2** Very strong, hard or firm (superl. of साधु or बाढ q. v.).

साधीयस् *a.* **1** Better, more excellent ; Bv. 1. 88. **2** Harder, stronger; (compar. of साधु or बाढ q. v.).

साधु *a.* (धु or ध्वी *f.* ; compar. साधीयस् ; superl. साधिष्ठ) **1** Good, excellent, perfect ; यद्यत्साधु न चित्रे स्यात्क्रियते तत्तदन्यथा S. 6. 13 ; आपरितोषाद्विदुषां न साधु मन्ये प्रयोगविज्ञानं 1. 2. **2** Fit, proper, right ; as in साधुवृत्त, साधुसमाचार. **3** Virtuous, righteous, honourable, pious. **4** (*a*) Kind, well disposed ; R. 2. 28 ; Pt. 1. 247. (*b*) Well-behaved (with loc.); मातरि साधुः Sk. **5** Correct, pure, classical (as language). **6** Pleasing, agreeable, pleasant ; अतोऽर्हसि क्षंतुमसाधु साधु वा Ki. 1. 4. **7** Noble, well-born, of noble descent. **–धुः 1** A good or virtuous man ; R. 13. 65, 2. 62 ; Me. 80. **2** A sage, saint ; साधोः प्रकोपितस्यापि मनो नायाति विक्रियां Subhâsh. **3** A merchant ; H. 2. 73. **4** A Jaina saint. **5** A usurer, money-lender. **–*ind.* 1** Well, well done, very nice, bravo ; साधु गीतं S. 1; साधु रे पिंगलवानर साधु M. 4. **2** Enough, away with. **–Comp. –धी** *a.* well-disposed. **–वादः** a cry of 'well done', a cry of approbation ; Si. 18. 55. **–वृत्त** *a.* **1** well-conducted, upright, virtuous ; प्रायेण साधुवृत्तानामस्थायिन्यो विपत्तयः Bh. 2. 85 ; (where the next sense is also intended). **2** well rounded. (**–त्तः**) a virtuous man. (**–त्तं**) good conduct, virtue, piety ; righteousness ; so साधुवृत्ति.

साधृतं 1 A stall, shop. **2** An umbrella. **3** A flock of peacocks.

साध्य *a.* **1** To be effected or accomplished, to be brought about ; साध्ये सिद्धिर्विधेयिता H. 2. 15. **2** Feasible, practicable, attainable. **3** To be proved or demonstrated ; आप्तवागनुमानाभ्यां साध्यं त्वां प्रति का कथा R. 10. 28. **4** To be established or made good. **5** To be inferred or concluded ; अनुमानं तदुक्तं यत्साध्यसाधनयोर्वचः K. P. 10. **6** To be conquered or subdued, conquerable ; Ku. 3. 15. **7** Curable. **8** To be killed or destroyed. **–ध्यः 1** A particular class of celestial beings; cf. Ms. 1. 22, 3. 195. **2** A deity in general. **3** N. of a Mantra. **–ध्यं 1** Accomplishment, perfection. **2** The thing to be proved or established, the matter at issue. **3** (In logic) The predicate of a proposition, the major term in a syllogism ; साध्ये निश्चितमन्वयेन घटितं...&c.; यत्साध्यं स्वयमेव तुल्यमुभयोः पक्षे विरुद्धं च यत् Mu. 5. 10. **–Comp. –अभावः** the absence of the major term. **–सिद्धिः** *f.* **1** accomplishment. **2** conclusion.

साध्यता 1 Feasibility, practicableness. **2** Curableness. **–Comp. –अवच्छेदकं** that which marks out or measures the साध्य or major term, its characteristic property.

साध्वसं 1 Fear, alarm, fright, terror ; कुसुमस्तेयसाध्वसात् Ku. 2. 35, 3. 51. **2** Torpor. **3** Agitation, perturbation.

साध्वी 1 A virtuous or chaste woman. **2** A faithful wife. **3** N. of a kind of root.

सानंद *a.* Happy, delighted.

सानसिः Gold.

सानिका, सानेयिका, सानेयी A pipe, flute.

सानु *m. n.* **1** A peak, summit, ridge ; सानूनि गंधः सुरभीकरोति Ku. 1. 9; Me. 2 ; Ku. 1. 6 ; Ki. 5. 36. **2** A level ground on the top of a mountain, table-land. **3** A shoot, sprout. **4** A forest, wood. **5** A road. **6** Any surface, point, end. **7** A precipice. **8** A gale of wind. **9** A learned man. **10** The sun.

सानुमत् *m.* A mountain. **–ती** N. of an Apsaras ; S. 6.

सानुक्रोश *a.* Tender, compassionate.

सानुनय *a.* Courteous, civil.

सानुबंध *a.* Uninterrupted, continuous.

सानुराग *a.* Attached, enamoured, in love.

सांतपनं A kind of rigid penance; cf. Ms. 11. 212.

सांतर *a.* **1** Having interstices or intervals. **2** Open in texture.

सांतानिक *a.* (**की** *f.*) **1** Stretching, spreading, extending (as a tree). **2** Relating to offspring or descendants. **3** Relating to the tree Santâna, q. v. **–कः** A Brâhmaṇa who wishes to marry for the sake of issue.

सांत्व् 10 U. (सांत्वयति-ते) To pacify, appease, conciliate, soothe, comfort; Bk. 3. 23.

सांत्वः, सांत्वनं -ना **1** Appeasing, pacification, consolation. **2** Conciliation, mild or gentle means. **3** Kind or conciliatory words. **4** Mildness. **5** Friendly salutation and inquiry.

सांदीपनिः N. of a sage. [According to Vish*n*u Pur*a*na, he was the tutor of Krish*n*a and Balar*a*ma, and asked as his preceptor's fee that his son, who was kept by a demon named Panchajana underneath the waters, should be restored to him. Krish*n*a, having undertaken to get him up, plunged into the sea, killed the demon, and brought back the boy to his father].

सांदृष्टिक *a.* (**की** *f.*) Relating to present perception, visible at the same time. **–कं** Immediate consequence.

सांद्र *a.* **1** Close, compact, having no interstices. **2** Coarse, gross, thick, dense; दुर्वर्णभित्तिरिह सांद्रसुधासवर्णा *Si.* 4. 28, 64; 9. 15; R. 7. 41; Rs. 1. 20. **3** Clustered together, collected. **4** Stout, strong, robust. **5** Excessive, abundant, much; सांद्रा नंदक्षुभितहृदयप्रस्रवेणेव सिक्तः U. 6. 22. **6** Intense, strong, vehement; व्यापांतराः सांद्रकुतूहलानां R. 7. 11; *Si.* 9. 37. **7** Unctuous, oily, viscid. **8** Bland, soft, smooth. **9** Pleasing, agreeable. **–द्रः** A heap, cluster.

सांधिकः A distiller.

सांधिविग्रहिकः A minister (or Secretary of State) for foreign affairs (deciding upon peace and war).

सांध्य *a.* (**ध्यी** *f.*) Relating to the twilight or evening; सांध्यं तेजः प्रतिनवजवापुष्परक्तं दधानः Me. 36; Ki. 5. 8; R. 11. 60; *Si.* 9. 15.

सांनहनिक *a.* (**की** *f.*) **1** Bearing or putting on an armour. **2** Calling to arms, encouraging to prepare for battle; *Si.* 15. 72. **–कः** An armour-bearer.

सांनाय्य Any substance mixed with clarified butter and offered as an oblation to fire; *Si.* 11. 41.

सांनिध्यं **1** Vicinity, proximity; वदनामलेंदुसांनिध्यतः Mâl. 3. 5. **2** Presence, attendance; R. 4. 6, 7. 3; Ku. 7. 33.

सांनिपातिक *a.* (**की** *f.*) **1** Miscellaneous. **2** Complicated. **3** Having a complicated derangement of the three bodily humours; Ku. 2. 48; Pt. 1. 127.

सांन्यासिकः **1** A Brâhmaṇa in the fourth order of his religious life; see संन्यासिन्. **2** A mendicant in general.

सान्वय *a.* Hereditary.

सापत्न *a.* (**त्नी** *f.*) Born from or belonging to a rival wife. **–त्नाः** (*m. pl.*) The children of different wives of the same husband.

सापत्न्यं **1** The state or condition of a rival wife. **2** Rivalry, ambition, enmity. **–त्न्यः** **1** The son of a rival wife. **2** An enemy.

सापराध *a.* Guilty, criminal.

सापिंड्यं Connection by the offering of rice-balls to the same Manes, kindred, consanguinity.

सापेक्ष *a.* Having regard to, dependent on.

साप्तपद *a.* (**दी** *f.*) **साप्तपदीन** *a.* Formed by walking together seven steps, or by talking together seven words: यतः सतां संनतगात्रि संगतं मनीषिभिः साप्तपदीनमुच्यते Ku. 5. 39 (where the latter sense appears better); Pt. 2. 43, 4. 103. **–दं, –नं** **1** Circumambulation of the nuptial fire by the bride and bridegroom in seven steps (which makes the marriage tie irrevocable). **2** Friendship, intimacy.

साप्तपौरुष *a.* (**षी** *f.*) Extending to or including seven generations; Ms. 3. 146.

साफल्यं **1** Fruitfulness, usefulness, productiveness. **2** Profit, advantage. **3** Success.

साब्दी A kind of grape.

साभ्यसूय *a.* Envious, jealous.

साम् 10 U. (सामयति-ते) To appease, conciliate, soothe.

सामकं The principal of a debt. **–कः** A whet-stone.

सामग्री **1** Collection or assemblage of materials, apparatus, furniture; Bh. 3. 155. **2** Stock, provision.

सामग्र्यं **1** Entireness, perfection, completeness, totality; प्रायेण सामग्र्यविधौ गुणानां पराङ्मुखी विश्वसृजः प्रवृत्तिः Ku. 3. 28. **2** Train, retinue. **3** A collection of implements, apparatus. **4** Stock, effects.

सामंजस्यं **1** Fitness, consistency, propriety; cf. असमंजस. **2** Accuracy, xorrectness.

सामन् *n.* **1** Appeasing, calming, comforting, soothing. **2** Conciliation, pacific measures, negotiation, (the first of the four *upa'yas* or expendients to be used by a king against an enemy); सामदंडौ प्रशंसंति नित्यं राष्ट्राभिवृद्धये Ms. 7. 109. **3** Conciliatory or mild means, pacific or conciliatory conduct, gentle words; Pt. 4. 26, 48. **4** Mildness, gentleness. **5** A metrical hymn or song of praise; सततसामोपगीतं त्वां R. 10. 21, Bg. 10. 35. **6** A verse or text of the Sâmaveda. **7** The Sâmaveda itself (said to have been produced from the sun; cf. Ms. 1. 23). **–Comp.** **–उद्भवः** an elephant. **–उपचारः, –उपायः** mild or conciliatory means, gentle or pacific measures. **–गः** a Brâhmaṇa who chants the Sâmaveda. **–ज, –जात** *a.* **1** produced by the Sâmaveda. **2** produced by conciliatory means. (**–जः, –तः**) an elephant; *Si.* 12. 11, 18. 33. **–योनिः** **1** Brahman. **2** an elephant. **–वादः** kind words, conciliatory words; *Si.* 2. 55. **–वेदः** the third of the four Vedas.

सामंत *a.* **1** Bordering, bounding, neighbouring. **2** Universal. **–तः** **1** A neighbour. **2** A neighbouring king. **3** A feudatory or tributary prince; सामंतमौलिमणिरंजितपादपीठं V. 3. 19, R. 5. 28, 6. 32. **4** A leader, general. **–तं** Neigh-bourhood.

सामयिक *a.* (**की** *f.*) **1** Customary, conventional. **2** Agreed upon, stipulated. **3** Conforming to agreement, keeping an appointment or engagement; देवि सामयिका भवामः M. 1. **4** Punctual, exact. **5** Seasonable, timely; Ki. 2. 10. **6** Periodical. **7** Temporary. **–Comp.** **–अभावः** temporary non-existence.

सामर्थ्यं **1** Power, force, capacity, ability, strength. **2** Sameness of aim or object. **3** Oneness of meaning or signification. **4** Adequacy, fitness. **5** The force or sense of words, the signifying power of a word. **6** Interest, advantage. **7** Wealth.

सामवायिक *a.* (**की** *f.*) **1** Belonging to an assembly or collection. **2** Belonging to inseparable connection. **–कः** A minister, counsellor.

सामाजिक *a.* (**की** *f.*) Belonging to an assembly. **–कः** A member of an audience or assembly, a spectator at an assembly or meeting; तेन हि तत्प्रयोगादेवात्रभवतः सामाजिकानुपास्महे Mâl. 1.

सामानाधिकरण्यं **1** Being in the same predicament or situation. **2** Common office, function or government, common relationship (as of case).

3 The state of relating to the same object.

सामान्य *a.* **1** Common, general ; सामान्यमेषां प्रथमावरत्वं Ku. 7. 44 ; आहारनिद्राभयमैथुनं च सामान्यमेतत्पशुभिर्नराणां Subhâsh. ; R. 14. 67 ; Ku. 2. 36. **2** Alike, equal, same. **3** Ordinary, of an average or middle degree ; Bh. 2. 74. **4** Vulgar, commonplace, insignificant. **5** Entire, whole. **-न्यं 1** Community, generality, universality. **2** Common or generic property, general characteristic. **3** Totality, entireness. **4** Kind, sort. **5** Identity. **6** Equanimity, equability. **7** Public affairs. **8** A general proposition ; उक्तिरर्थान्तरन्यासः स्यात्सामान्यविशेषयोः Chandr. 5. 120. **9** (In Rhet.) A figure of speech thus defined by Mammaṭa :— प्रस्तुतस्य यदन्येन गुणसाम्यविवक्षया । एकात्म्यं बध्यते योगात्तत्सामान्यमिति स्मृतम् ॥ K. P. 10. **-Comp. -ज्ञानं** knowledge or perception of generic properties. **-पक्षः** the mean. **-लक्षणं** a generic definition ; इति द्रव्यसामान्यलक्षणानि Tarka. K. **-वनिता** a common woman, prostitute. **-शास्त्रं** a general rule.

सामासिक *a.* (की *f.*) 1 Comprehensive, comprehending the whole, collective. **2** Condensed, concise, brief. **3** Relating to a compound word. **-कं** The whole class of compounds ; द्वंद्वः सामासिकस्य च Bg. 10. 33.

सामि *ind.* **1** Half ; *i. e.* unfinished; अभिवीक्ष्य सामिकृतमंडनं यतीः कररुद्धनीविगलदंशुकाः स्त्रियः Si. 13. 31, R. 19. 16. **2** Blamable, vile, contemptible.

सामिधेनी 1 A kind of prayer recited while the sacrificial fire is being kindled or fed with fuel. **2** Fuel.

सामीची Praise, eulogium.

सामीप्यं Vicinity, nearness, proximity. **-प्यः** A neighbour.

सामुद्र *a.* (द्री *f.*) Sea-born, marine, as in सामुद्रं लवणं. **-द्रः** A mariner, voyager. **-द्रं 1** Sea-salt. **2** The cuttle-fishbone. **3** A mark or spot on the body.

सामुद्रकं Sea-salt.

सामुद्रिक *a.* (की *f.*) **1** Sea-born ; oceanic. **2** Relating to marks on the body (which are supposed to indicate good or bad fortune). **-कः** One who is acquainted with palmistry, who knows how to interpret the various marks on the body. **-कं** The science of palmistry.

सांपराय *a.* (यी *f.*) **1** Relating to war, warlike. **2** Relating to the other world, future. **-यः, -यं 1** Conflict, contention. **2** Future life, the future. **3** The means of attaining the future world. **4** Inquiry into the future. **5** Inquiry, investigation. **6** Uncertainty.

सांपरायिक *a.* (की *f.*) **1** Warlike. **2** Military, strategic. **3** Calamitous. **4** Relating to the other world. **-कं** War, battle, conflict ; Si. 18. 1. **-कः** A war-chariot. **-Comp. -कल्पः** a strategic array (of troops).

सांप्रत *a.* **1** Fit, proper, suitable ; Ve. 3. 3. **2** Relevant. **-तं** *ind.* **1** Now, at this time ; हंत स्थानं क्रोधस्य सांप्रतं देव्याः Ve. 1. **2** Immediately. **3** Fitly, properly, seasonably.

सांप्रतिक *a.* (की *f.*) **1** Belonging to the present time. **2** Fit, proper, right ; U. 3.

सांप्रदायिक *a.* (की *f.*) Relating to the traditional doctrine, handed down by successive tradition, traditional.

सांबः N. of Siva.

सांबंधिक *a.* (की *f.*) Arising from relationship. **-कं** Relationship, alliance.

सांबरी A sorceress.

सांभवी 1 The red Lodhra tree. **2** Possibility.

साम्यं 1 Equality, sameness, evenness ; Ku. 5. 31. **2** Likeness, resemblance, similarity ; स्पष्टं प्राप्तसाम्यमुर्वीधरस्य Si. 18. 38 ; H. 1. 45 ; Ki. 17. 51. **3** Equability. **4** Concord, harmony. **5** Indifference, impartiality, sameness of view ; येषां साम्ये मनः स्थितं Bg. 5. 19.

साम्राज्यं 1 Universal or complete sovereignty, imperial sway ; साम्राज्यशंसिनो भावाः कुशस्य च लवस्य च U. 6. 23 ; R. 4. 5. **2** Empire, dominion.

सायः 1 End, close, termination. **2** Close of day, evening. **3** An arrow. **-Comp. -अहन्** *m.* (forming सायाह्नः) evening, evening time ; Bv. 2. 157.

सायकः An arrow ; तत्साधुकृतसंधानं प्रतिसंहार सायकं S. 1.11. **2** A sword. **-Comp. -पुंखः** the feathered part of an arrow; सक्त ग्रालिः सायकपुंख एव R. 2. 31.

सायनं The longitude of a planet reckoned from the vernal equinoctial point.

सायंतन *a.* (नी *f.*) Belonging to the evening, evening; सायंतने सवनकर्मणि संप्रवृत्ते S. 3. 27.

सायम् *ind.* In the evening ; प्रयता प्रातरन्वेतु सायं प्रत्युद्व्रजेदपि R. 1. 90. **-Comp. -कालः** evening. **-मंडनं 1** sunset. **2** the sun. **-संध्या** the evening twilight, **3** the evening prayer.

सायिन् *m.* A horseman.

सायुज्यं 1 Intimate union, identification, absorption, especially into a deity (one of the four states of *Mukti*). **2** Similarity, likeness.

सार *a.* **1** Essential. **2** Best, highest, most excellent ; Mu. 1. 13. **3** Real, true, genuine. **4** Strong, vigorous. **5** Sound, thoroughly proved. **-रः, -रं** (but usually *m.* only except in the first 4 senses). **1** Essence, essential part, quintessence ; स्नेहस्य तत्फलमसौ प्रणयस्य सारः Mâl. 1. 9; असारे खलु संसारे सारमेतच्चतुष्टयम् । काश्यां वासः सतां संगो गंगांभः शंभुसेवनं॥ Dharm. 14. **2** Substance, pith. **3** Marrow. **4** Real truth, main point. **5** The sap or essence of trees ; as in खदिरसार, सर्जसार. **6** Summary, epitome, compendium. **7** Strength, vigour, power, energy ; सारं धरित्रीधरणक्षमं च Ku. 1. 17; R. 2. 74. **8** Prowess, heroism, courage ; R. 4. 79. **9** Firmness, hardness. **10** Wealth, riches ; R. 5. 26. **11** Nectar. **12** Fresh butter. **13** Air, wind. **14** Cream, coagulum of curds. **15** Disease. **16** Matter, pus. **17** Worth, excellence, highest perception. **18** A man at chess. **19** Impure carbonate of soda. **20** A figure of speech corresponding to English ' climax ' ; उत्तरोत्तरमुत्कर्षो भवेत्सारः परावधिः K. P. 10. **-रं 1** Water. **2** Fitness, propriety. **3** Wood, thicket. **4** Steel. **-Comp. -असार** *a.* valuable and worthless, strong and weak. (**-रं**) **1** worth and worthlessness. **2** substance and emptiness. **3** strength and weakness. **-गंधः** sandal wood. **-ग्रीवः** N. of Siva. **-जं** fresh butter. **-तरुः** the plantain tree **-दा 1** N. of Sarasvatî. **2** of Durgâ. **द्रुमः** the Khadira tree. **-भंगः** loss of vigour. **-भांडं 1** a natural vessel. **2** a bale of goods, merchandise. **3** implements. **-लोहं** steel.

सारघं Honey.

सारंग *a.* (गी *f.*) spotted, variegated. **-गः 1** The variegated colour. **2** The spotted deer, an antelope ; एष राजेव दुष्यंतः सारंगेणातिरंहसा S. 1. 5. **3** A deer in general ; सारंगास्ते जललवमुचः सूचयिष्यंति मार्गं Me. 20 (where it is preferable to take this sense rather than that of ' elephant ' or ' bee '). **4** A lion. **5** An elephant. **6** A large black bee. **7** The cuckoo. **8** A large crane. **9** The flamingo. **10** A peacock. **11** An umbrella. **12** A cloud. **13** A garment. **14** Hair. **15** A conch-shell. **16** N. of Siva. **17** The god of love **18** A lotus. **19** Camphor. **20** A bow **21** Sandal. **22** A kind of musical instrument. **23** An ornament. **24** Gold. **25** The earth. **26** Night. **27** Light.

सारंगिकः A fowler, bird-catcher.

सारंगी 1 A kind of stringed instrument, violin. **2** A kind of spotted deer.

सारण *a.* (णी) Causing to go or flow. **-णः** 1 Dysentery. **2** The hogplum. **-णं** A kind of perfume.

सारणा A kind of process to which metals—particularly mercury—are subjected.

सारणिः -णी *f.* 1 A canal, drain ;

water-course, channel 2 A small river.

सारंड: The egg of a serpent.

सारतस् *ind*. 1 According to wealth. 2 Vigorously.

सारथिः 1 A charioteer ; स शापो न त्वया राजन् न च सारथिना श्रुतः R. 1. 78 ; मातलिसारथिर्ययौ 3. 67. 2 A companion, helper ; R. 3. 37. 3 The ocean.

सारथ्यं The office of a charioteership, coachmanship.

सारमेयः A dog. -यी A bitch.

सारल्यं Straightness (fig. also), artlessness, honesty, uprightness.

सारवत् *a*. 1 Substantial. 2 Fertile. 3 Having sap.

सारस *a*. (सी *f*.) Belonging to a lake ; Kâv. 3. 14 ; Nalod. 2. 40. -सः 1 The (Indian) crane ; or swan (according to some ; विभिद्यमाना विससार सारसानुदस्य तीरेषु तीरंगसंहतिः Ki. 8. 31, *Si*. 6. 75, 12. 44, Me. 31 ; R. 1. 41. 2 A bird in general. 3 The moon. -सं 1 A lotus. 2 The zone or girdle of a woman.

सारस(श)नं 1 A girdle or zone ; सारशनं महानहिः Ki. 18. 32. 2 A military girdle.

सारस्वत *a*. (ती *f*.) 1 Relating to the godddess Sarasvatî. 2 Belonging to the river Sarasvatî ; कृत्वा तासामभिगममपां सौम्य सारस्वतीनां Me. 49. 3 Eloquent. -तः 1 N. of a country about the river Sarasvatî. 2 N. of a particular class of Brâhmaṇas. 3 A particular ceremonial used in the worship of Sarasvatî. 4 A staff of the Bilva tree. -ताः (*m*. *pl*.) The people of the Sârasvata country. -तं Speech, eloquence ; शृंगारसारस्वतं Git. 12.

सारालः Sesamum.

सारिः-री *f*. 1 A man at chess, chessman. 2 A kind of bird. -Comp. -फलकः a chess-board.

सारिका A kind of bird ; आत्मनो मुखदोषेण बध्यंते शुकसारिकाः Subhâsh. ; सारिकां पंजरस्थां Me. 85.

सारिन् *a*. (णी *f*.) 1 Going, resorting to. 2 Having the essence or substance of.

सारूप्यं 1 Sameness of form, similarity, likeness, conformity, resemblance ; Mâl. 5. 2 Assimilation to the deity (one of the four states of *Mukti*). 3 (In dramas) An angry treatment of one mistaken for another through resemblance ; see S. D. 464. 4 Surprise at seeing an object or its likeness seen elsewhere.

सारेष्टिकः Kind of poison.

सार्गल *a*. Barred, obstructed, impeded ; R. 1. 79.

सार्थ *a*. 1 Having meaning, significant. 2 Having an aim or object. 3 Of like meaning or import. 4 Useful, serviceable. 5 Wealthy, rich, opulent. -र्थः 1 A rich man. 2 A company of merchants, caravan (of traders) ; सार्थाः स्वैरं स्वकीयेषु चेरुर्वेश्मस्विवाद्रिषु R. 17. 64 ; see सार्थवाह. 3 A troop. 4 A herd, flock (of animals of the same species) ; अथ कदाचित्तैरितस्ततो भ्रमद्भिः सार्थाद् भ्रष्टः कथनको नामोष्ट्रो दृष्टः Pt. 1. 5 A collection or multitude in general ; अर्थिसार्थः Pt. 1 ; त्वया चंद्रमसा चातिसंधीयते कामिजनसार्थः *S*. 3. 6 One of a company of pilgrims. -Comp. -ज *a*. bred in a caravan. -वाहः the leader of a caravan, a merchant, trader ; *S*. 6.

सार्थक *a*. 1 Having sense, significant. 2 Useful, serviceable advantageous.

सार्थवत् *a*. 1 Having meaning, significant. 2 Having a large company.

सार्थिकः A merchant, trader.

सार्द्र *a*. Wet, moist, humid, damp.

सार्ध *a*. Increased by half, plus one-half, having a half over ; सार्धशतं &c.

सार्धम् *ind*. Together with, with, in company with (with instr.) ; वनं मया सार्धमसि प्रपन्नः R. 14. 63, Ms. 4. 43 ; Bk. 6. 26 ; Me. 89.

सार्पः (र्प्यः) N. of the constellation Asleshâ.

सार्पिष *a*. (षी *f*.), सार्पिष्क *a*. (ष्की *f*.) Dressed or cooked with clarified butter.

सार्वकामिक *a*. (की *f*.) Satisfying every desire, granting all wishes ; Ki. 18. 25.

सार्वकालिक *a*. (की *f*.) Eternal, everlasting.

सार्वजनिक *a*. (की *f*.) सार्वजनीन *a*. (नी *f*.) Public, universal, general.

सार्वज्ञं Omniscience.

सार्वत्रिक *a*. (की *f*.) Belonging to every place, general, applicable to all places or circumstances ; as in सार्वत्रिको नियमः.

सार्वधातुक *a*. (की *f*.) Applicable to the whole of a radical term, or to the complete form of the verbal base after the conjugational characteristics have been affixed, *i. e*. to the four conjugational or special tenses. -कं N. of the verbal terminations of the four conjugational tenses (strictly, the personal terminations of all tenses and moods except the Perfect and Benedictive and the affixes distinguished by a mute श्).

सार्वभौतिक *a*. (की *f*.) 1 Belonging or relating to all elements or beings. 2 Comprising all animate beings.

सार्वभौम *a*. (मी *f*.) Relating to consisting of, the whole earth universal. -मः 1 An emperor, a universal monarch ; नाज्ञाभंगं सहंते नृवर नृपतयस्त्वादृशाः सार्वभौमाः Mu. 3. 22. 2 N. of the elephant presiding over the north, the quarter of Kubera.

सार्वलौकिक *a*. (की *f*.) Known to all people, prevailling throughout the whole world, public, universal ; अनुरागप्रवादस्तु वत्सयोः सार्वलौकिकः Mâl. 1. 13.

सार्ववर्णिक *a*. (की *f*.) 1 Of every kind or sort. 2 Belonging to every tribe or class.

सार्वविभक्तिक *a*. (की *f*.) Applicable or belonging to all the cases of a noun.

सार्ववेदसः One who gives away all his wealth at a sacrifice or sacred rite.

सार्ववैद्यः A Brâhmaṇa conversant with all the Vedas.

सार्षप *a*. (पी *f*.) Made of mustard -पं Mustard-oil.

सार्ष्टि *a*. Possessing the same station, condition or rank, having the same power.

सार्ष्टिता 1 Equality in rank, condition or power. 2 Equality with the Supreme Being in power and all the divine attributes, the last of the four states or grades of *Mukti* ; ब्रह्मदे ब्रह्मसार्ष्टितां (प्राप्नोति) ; Ms. 4. 232.

सार्ष्ट्यं The fourth grade of *Mukti*, see above.

सालः 1 N. of a tree or its resin. 2 A tree in general, as in कल्पसाल, रसालसाल. 3 A rampart, a fence or wall round a building. 4 A wall in general. 5 A kind of fish. (For compounds see under शाल).

सालनः The resin of the Sâla tree.

साला 1 A wall, rampart. 2 A house, an apartment ; see शाला. -Comp. -करी 1 a house-worker. 2 a male captive (particularly one taken in battle). -वृकः see शालावृक.

सालारं A peg projecting from a wall, bracket.

सालूरः A frog ; see शालूर.

सालेयं A kind of fennel ; see शालेय.

सालोक्यं 1 Being in the same world or sphere with another. 2 Residence in the same heaven with any deity.

साल्वः 1 N. of a country, or its inhabitants (pl. in this sense). 2 N. of a demon slain by Vishṇu. -Comp. -हन् *m*. an epithet of Vishṇu.

साल्विकः The bird called सारिका q. v.

सावः A libation.

सावक *a*. (विका *f*.) Productive, generative, causing birth, obstetric. -कः The young of an animal; (for शावक q. v.).

सावकाश *a.* Having leisure, at leisure, unengaged. -शं *ind.* Leisurely, at one's convenience.

सावग्रह *a.* Having the mark called *avagraha* q. v.

सावज्ञ *a.* Despising, disdainful, feeling contempt.

सावद्यं (*i. e.* ऐश्वर्यं) One of the three kinds of power attainable by an ascetic, (the other two being निरवद्य and सूक्ष्म).

सावधान *a.* 1 Attentive, bestowing attention, careful, heedful. 2 Cautious. 3 Diligent. -नं *ind.* Carefully, attentively, cautiously.

सावधि *a.* Having a bound or limit, limited, finite, defined, circumscribed ; सावधिस्तोयराशिस्ते यशोराशेस्तु नावधिः Subhâsh.

सावन *a.* (नी *f.*) Relating to, or comprising, the three *savanas*. -नः 1 An institutor of a sacrifice, or one who employs priests at a sacrifice. 2 The conclusion of a sacrifice, or the ceremony by which it is concluded. 3 N. of Varuṇa. 4 A month of thirty solar days. 5 A natural day from sunrise to sunset. 6 A particular kind of year.

सावयव *a.* Composed of parts ; सावयवत्वे चानित्यप्रसंगः, न ह्यविद्याकल्पितेन रूपभेदेन सावयवं वस्तु संपद्यते S. B.

सावरः 1 Fault, offence. 2 Sin, wickedness, crime. 3 The Lodhra tree.

सावरण *a.* 1 Clandestine, concealed, secret. 2 Covered, closed.

सावर्ण *a.* (र्णी *f.*) Relating or belonging to one of the same colour, tribe or caste. -र्णः A metronymic of the eighth Manu ; see सावर्णि. -Comp. -लक्ष्यं 1 the mark of the sameness of colour or caste. 2 the skin.

सावर्णिः A metronymic of the eighth Manu (son of the sun by Savarṇâ).

सावर्ण्यं 1 Sameness of colour. 2 Identity of class or caste. 3 The age or *Manvantara* presided over by the eighth Manu.

सावलेप *a.* Full of pride, proud, haughty. -पं *ind.* Proudly, haughtily, arrogantly.

सावशेष *a.* 1 Having a remainder, leaving a remainder or residue. 2 Imperfect, incomplete, unfinished.

सावष्टंभ *a.* 1 Proud, dignified, noble, majestic. 2 Courageous, resolute. 3 Full of firmness. -भं *ind* Resolutely, firmly, courageously.

सावहेल *a.* Disdainful, disdaining, despising. -लं *ind.* Disdainfully, scornfully.

साविका A midwife.

सावित्र *a.* (त्री *f.*) 1 Belonging to the sun. 2 Descended from the sun, belonging to the solar dynasty (of kings) ; यत्सावित्रैर्दीपितं भूमिपालैः U. 1. 42. 3 Accompained by the *Gâyatrî*. -त्रः 1 The sun. 2 An embryo or foetus. 3 A Brâhmaṇa. 4 An epithet of *S*iva. 5 Of Karṇa. -त्रं The sacrificial thread (so called because the repetition of the *Gâyatri* forms a principal part of the ceremony of putting on the sacred thread)

सावित्री 1 A ray of light. 2 N. of a celebrated verse of the *Rigveda*, so called because it is addressed to the sun ; it is also called गायत्री q. v. for further information. 3 The ceremony of investiture with the sacred thread. 4 N. of a wife of Brâhman. 5 N. of Pârvatî. 6 N. of a wife of Kasyapa. 7 N. of the wife of Satyavat, king of *S*âlva. [She was the only daughter of king Asvapati. She was so lovely that all the suitors that came to woo her were repulsed by her superior lustre, and thus though she reached a marriageable age, she found no one ready to espouse her. At last her father asked her to go and find out a husband of her own choice. She did so, and having made her selection returned to her father, and told him that she had chosen Satyavat, son of Dyumatsena, King of *S*alva, who being driven out from his kingdom was then leading a hermit's life along with his wife. When Narada, who happened to be present there, heard this, he told her as well as Asvapati that he was very sorry to hear of the choice she had made for though Satyavat was in every way, worthy of her, yet he was fated to die in a year from that date, and in choosing him, therefore, Savitri would be only choosing life-long widow-hood and misery. Her parents, therefore, naturally tried te dissuade her mind, but the high-souled maiden told them that her choice was unalterably fixed. Accordingly the marriage took place in due time, and Savitri laid aside her jewels and rich apparel, and putting on the coarse garments of hermits, spent her time in serving her old father and mother-in-law. Still, though outwardly happy, she could not forget the words of Narada, and as she counted, the days seemed to fly swiftly like moments, and the fated time, when her husband was to die, drew near. ' I have yet three days ', thought she, ' and for these three days I shall observe a rigid fast '. She maintained her vow, and on the fourth day, when Satyavat was about to go to the woods to bring sacrificial fuel, she accompanied him. After having collected some fuel, Satyavat being fatigued, sat down, and reposing his head on the bosom of Savitri fell asleep. Just then Yama came down, snatched off his soul, and proceeded towards the south. Savitri saw this and followed the god who told her to return as her husband's term of life was over. But the faithful wife besought Yama in so pathetic a strain that he granted her boon after boon, except the life of her husband, until, being quite subdued by her devotion to her husband and the force of her eloquent appeal, the god relented and restored even the spirit of Satyavat to her. Delighted she returned, and found her husband as if roused from deep sleep, and informing him of all that had occurred, went to the hermitage of her father-in-law who soon reaped the fruits of the boons of Yama. Savitri is regarded as the *beau ideal* or highest pattern of conjugal fidelity, and a young married woman is usually blessed by elderly females with the words जन्मसावित्री भव thus placing before her the example of Savitri for lifelong imitation]. -Comp. -पतित, -परिभ्रष्टः, a man of any one of the first three castes not invested with the sacred thread at the proper time ; cf. व्रात्य. -व्रतं N. of a particular fast kept by Hindu women on the last three days of the bright half of Jyeshtha to preserve them from widowhood.

साविष्कार *a.* 1 Proud, haughty. 2 Manifest.

साशंस *a.* Full of desire or passion, desirous, hopeful, expectant. -सं *ind.* Wishfully, hopefully.

साशंक *a.* Feeling fear, apprehensive, afraid, dismayed.

साशयंदकः A small house-lizard.

साशूकः A blanket.

साश्चर्य *a.* 1 Wonderful, marvellous. 2 Struck with wonder. -र्यं *ind.* With wonder or astonishment.

साश्र (स्र) *a.* 1 Having angles or corners, angular. 2 Tearful, weeping.

साश्रुधी A wife's or husband's mother, a mother-in-law.

साष्टांगम् *ind.* With humble pronstration of the body (by touching the earth with the eight members ; see अष्टांगप्रणाम under अष्टन्).

सास *a.* Having a bow ; Ki. 15. 5

सासुस् *a.* Having arrows ; Ki. 15. 5

सासूय *a.* Envious, jealous, disdainful. -यं *ind.* Jealously, angrily, disdainfully ; *S.* 2. 2.

सास्ना The dew-lap of an ox ; गोः सास्नादिमत्त्वं लक्षणं T. S.; रोमंथमंथरचलद्गुरुसास्नमासांचके निमीलदलसेक्षणमौक्षकेण *S*i. 5. 62.

साहचर्यं Companionship, (constant) fellowship or association, living together, concomitance ; किं न स्मरसि यदेकत्र नो विद्यापरिग्रहाय नानादिगंतवासिनां साहचर्यमासीत् Mal. 1 ; Ku. 3. 21, R. 16. 87, Ve. 1. 20, *S*i. 15. 24.

साहनं Endurance, suffering,

साहसं 1 Violence, force, rapine ; Ms. 7. 48, 8. 6. 2 Any crimiaal act (such as robbery, rape, felony &c.), a heinous crime, an aggressive act. 3 Cruelty, oppression ; Si. 9. 59. 4 Boldness, daring, daring courage ; साहसे श्रीः प्रतिवसति Mk. 4. 5 Precipitation, rashness, temerity, an inconsiderate or reckless act, rash or daring act ; तदपि साहसाभासं Mâl. 2 ; किमपरमतो निर्व्यूढं यत्करार्पणसाहसं 9. 10 ; Ki. 17. 42. 6 Punishment, chastisement, fine (*m.* also in this sense), see Ms. 8. 138 ; Y. 1. 66, 365. **-Comp.** -अंकः 1 an epithet of king Vikramâditya. 2 of a poet. 3 of a lexicographer. -अध्यवसायिन् *a.* acting rashly or with inconside ate haste. -ऐकरसिक *a.* wholly intent on violence, ferocious, brutal. -कारिन् *a.* 1 bold, audacious. 2 rash, inconsiderate -लांछन *a.* characterized by boldness.

साहसिक *a.* (की *f.*) 1 Using great force or violence, brutal, violent, rapacious, cruel, felonious. 2 Bold, daring, rash, inconsidarate, reckless; न सह्यास्मि साहसमसाहसिकी *Si.* 9. 59 ; केचित्तु साहासिकास्त्रिलोचनमिति पेठुः Malli. on Ku. 3. 44. 3 Castigatory, punitive. -कः 1 A bold or adventurous person, an enterpriising man ; Pt. 5 31. 2 A desperado, desperate or dangerous person ; या किल विविधजीवोपहारप्रियेति साहासि, कानां प्रवादः Mâl. 1. ; साहसिकः खल्वेषः 6. 3 A felon, freebooter, robber.

साहसिन् *a.* 1 Violent, ferocious, cruel. 2 Bold, daring, rash, impetuous.

साहस्र *a.* (स्री *f.*) 1 Relating to a thousand. 2 Consisting of a thousand. 3 Bought with a thousand. 4 Paid per thousand (as interest &c.). 5 A thousand-fold. -स्रः An army or detachment consisting of a thousand men. -स्रं An aggregate of a thousand.

साहायकं 1 Assistance, help, aid ; सकुलोचितमिंद्रस्य साहायकमुपेयिवान् R. 17. 5. 2 Fellowship, alliance, friendship. 3 A number of companions or associates. 4 Auxiliary troops.

साहाय्यं 1 Assistance, help, succour. 2 Friendship, alliance.

साहित्यं 1 Association, fellowship, combination, society. 2 Literary or rhetorical composition ; साहित्यसंगीतकलाविहीनः साक्षात्पशुः पुच्छविषाणहीनः Bh. 3. 12. 3 The science of rhetoric, art of poetry ; Vikr. 1. 11 ; साहित्यदर्पण &c. 4 A collection of materials for the production or perfomance of anything (a doubtful sense.)

साह्यं 1 Conjunction, union, fellowship, society. 2 Assistance, help. **-Comp.** -कृत् *m.* a companion.

साह्वयः Gambling with fighting animals.

सि 5. 9. U. (सिनोति, सिनुते, सिनाति, सिनीते) 1 To bind, tie, fasten. 2 To ensnare.

सिंहः 1 A lion ; (it is said to be derived from हिंस् ; cf. भवेद्वर्णागमाद्धंसः सिंहो वर्णविपर्ययात् Sk.) ; न हि सुप्तस्य सिंहस्य प्रविशंति मुखे मृगाः Subhâsh. 2 The sign *Leo* of the zodiac. 3 (At the end of comp.) Best, pre-eminent of a class; *e. g.* रघुसिंह, पुरुषसिंह. **-Comp.** -अवलोकनं the (backward) glance of a lion. °न्यायः the maxim of the lion's (backward) glance, generally used to mark the connection of a thing with what precedes and follows ; for explanation see under न्याय. -आसनं a throne, a seat of honour. (नः) a particular mode of sexual enjoyment. -आस्यः a particular position of the hands. -गः an epithet of *Siva.* -तलं the palms of the hand, opened and joined together. -तुंडः a kind of fish. -दंष्ट्रः an epithet of *Siva.* -दर्प *a.* as proud as a lion. -ध्वानिः, -नादः 1 the roar of a lion ; Ku. 1. 56 ; Mk. 5. 29. 2 a war-cry. -द्वारं the main or principal gate. -यानाा, -रथा N. of the goddess Pârvatî. -लीलः a kind of coitus. -वाहनः an epithet of *Siva.* -संहनन *a.* 1 as strong as a lion. 2 handsome. (-नं) the killing of a lion.

सिंहलं 1 Tin. 2 Brass. 3 Bark, rind. 4 The island or country of Ceylon (oft. in pl.); सिंहलेभ्यः प्रत्यागच्छता, सिंहलेश्वरदुहितुः फलकासादनं Ratn 1. -लाः (*m. pl.*) The people of Ceylon.

सिंहलकं The island of Ceylon.

सिंहाणं (नं) 1 Rust of iron. 2 The mucus of the nose.

सिंहिका The mother of Râhu. **-Comp.** -तनयः, -पुत्रः, -सुतः, -सूनुः epithets of Râhu.

सिंही 1 A lioness. 2 N. of the mother of Râhu.

सिकता 1 Sandy soil. 2 Sand (generally in pl.). लभेत सिकतासु तैलमपि यत्नतः पडियन् Bh. 2. 5. 3 Gravel or stone (the disease).

सिकतिल *a.* Sandy; Bh. 3. 38.

सिक्त *p. p.* 1 Sprinkled, watered. 2 Wetted, moistened, soaked. 3 Impregnated : see सिच्.

सिक्थः 1 Boiled rice. 2 A ball or lump of boiled rice ; ग्रासोद्गलितसिक्थेन का हानिः करिणो भवेत् Subhâsh. -क्थं 1 Bees'-wax. 2 Indigo.

सिक्यं See शिक्य.

सिक्ष्यः Crystal, glass.

सिंघ(घा)णं 1 The mucus of the nose. 2 Rust of iron.

सिंघिणी The nose.

सिच् 6 U. (सिंचति-ते, सिक्त ; स् of सिच् is generally changed to ष् after a preposition ending in इ or उ) 1 To sprinkle, scatter in small drops ; Bk. 19. 23. 2 To water, moisten, soak, wet ; Me. 26; Ms. 9. 255. 3 To pour out, emit, discharge, shed ; R. 16. 66. 4 To infuse, instil, pour in ; जाड्यं धियो हरति सिंचति वाचि सत्यं Bh. 2. 23. 5 To pour out for, offer to ; अन्यथा तिलोदकं मे सिंचतं *S.* 3. *-Caus.* (सेचयति-ते) To cause to sprinkle. *-Desid.* (सिसिक्षति-ते) To wish to sprinkle. -WITH अभि 1 to sprinkle, pour down, water, wet, shower upon (fig. also) ; अथ वपुरभिषेक्तुं तास्तदांभोभिरीशुः *Si.* 7. 75 ; Bk. 6. 21. 15. 3. 2 to anoint, consecrate, appoint (by sprinkling water over the head), to crown, inaugurate, install ; अग्निवर्णमभिषिच्य राघवः स्वे पदे R. 19. 1; 17. 13, V. 5. 23. (*-Caus.*) to cause to be crowned or inaugurated. -आ to sprinkle. (*-Caus.*) to cause to be poured or sprinkled ; तप्तमासेचयेत्तैलं वक्त्रे श्रोत्रे च पार्थिवः Ms. 8. 272. -उद् to sprinkle, pour upon, spread. *(-Pass.)* 1 to spout or foam up, be thrown upwards. 2 to be puffed up or elated be proud ; न तस्योत्सिषिचे मनः R. 17. 43. 3 to be disturbed ; Ms. 8. 71. (*-Caus.*) to fill with pride. -नि 1 to sprinkle, pour down or upon, pour in ; R. 3. 26 ; *S.* 4. 13 ; Ku. 2. 57. 2 to impregnate ; निषिंचन्माधवीमेतां लतां कौंदीं च नर्तयन् V. 2. 4. (where the first sense is also intended). -परि to sprinkle or pour.

सिंचयः Cloth, garment.

सिंचिता Long pepper.

सिंजा The jingling sound of metallic ornaments.

सिंजितं Tinkling, jingling ; आदित्सुभिर्नूपुरसिंजितानि Ku. 1. 34, V. 4. 14.

सिट् 1 P. (सेटति) To disregard, despise.

सित *a.* 1 White. 2 Bound, tied, fastened, fettered. 3 Surrounded. 4 Finished, ended. -तः 1 White colour. 2 The bright half of a lunar month. 3 The planet Venus. 4 An arrow. -तं 1 Silver. 2 Sandal. 3 Radish. **-Comp.** -अग्रः a thorn. -अपांगः a peacock. -अभ्रः, -भ्रं camphor. -अंबरः an ascetic dressed in white garments. -अर्जकः white basil. अश्वः an epithet of Arjuna. -असितः an epithet of Balarâma. -आदिः molasses. -आलिका a cockle. -इतर *a.* other than white ; *i. e.* black. -उद्भवं white sandal. -उपलः a crystal. -उपला candied sugar. -करः 1 the moon. 2 camphor. -धातुः a white mineral, chalk. -रश्मिः the moon. -वाजिन् *m.* N. of Arjuna. -शर्करा candied sugar. -शिंबिकः wheat. -शिवं rock-salt. -शूकः barley.

सिता 1 Candied suar, sugar ; चित्तेन दूने रसने सितापि तिक्तायते हंसकुलावतंस N. 3. 94 ; Bv. 4. 13. **2** Moonlight. **3** A lovely woman. **4** Spirituous liquor. **5** White Dûrvâ grass. **6** Arabian Jasmine.

सिति *a.* **1** White. **2** Black. **-तिः** White or black colour. **-Comp. -कंठ, -वासस्** see शितिकंठ ; शितिवासस्.

सिद्ध *p. p.* **1** Accomplished, effected, performed, achieved, completed. **2** Gained, obtained, acquired. **3** Succeeded, successful. **4** Settled, established ; नैसर्गिकी सुरभिणः कुसुमस्य सिद्धा मूर्ध्नि स्थितिर्न चरणैरवताडनानि U. 1. 14. **5** Proved, demonstrated, substantiated ; तस्मादिंद्रियं प्रत्यक्षप्रमाणामिति सिद्धं T. S., Ms. 8. 178. **6** Valid, sound (as a rule). **7** Admitted to be true. **8** Decided, adjudicated (as a lawsuit). **9** Paid, discharged, liquidated (as debt). **10** Cooked, dressed (as food). **11** Matured, ripened. **12** Thoroughly prepared, compounded, cooked together (as drugs). **13** Ready (as money). **14** Subdued, won over, subjugated (as by magic) **15** Brought under subjection, become propitious. **16** Thoroughly conversant with or skilled in, proient in ; as in रससिद्ध q. v. **17** Perfected, sanctified (as by penance). **18** Emancipated. **19** Endowed with supernatural powers or faculties. **20** Pious, sacred, holy. **21** Divine, immortal, eternal. **22** Celebrated, well-known, illustrious. **23** Shining, splendid. **-द्धः 1** A semi divine being supposed to be of great purity and holiness, and said to be particularly characterized by eight supernatural faculties called *Siddhis* q. v. ; उद्वेजिता वृष्टिभिराश्रयंते शृंगाणि यस्यातपवंति सिद्धाः Ku. 1. 5. **2** An inspired sage or seer (like Vyâsa). **3** Any sage or seer, a prophet ; सिद्धादेश Ratn. 1. **4** One skilled in magical arts, a magician. **5** A law-suit, judicial trial. **6** A kind of hard sugar. **-द्धं** Sea-salt. **-Comp. -अंतः 1** the established end. **2** the demonstrated conclusion of an argument, established view of any question, the true logical conclusion (following on the refutaion of the Pûrvapaksha). **3** a proved fact, established truth, dogma, settled doctrine. **4** any established text-book resting on conclusive evidence. °**कोटिः** *f.* the point in an argument which is regarded as a logical conclusion. °**पक्षः** the logically correct side of an argument. **-अन्नं** cooked food. **-अर्थ** *a.* one who has accomplished his desired object, successful. (**-र्थः**) **1** white mustard. **2** N. of Siva. **3** of the great Buddha. **-आसनं** a particular posture in religious meditation. **-गंगा, -नदी, -सिंधुः** the celestial Ganges. **-ग्रहः** N. of a particular kind of madness or dementia. **-जलं** sour-rice gruel. **-धातुः** quick silver. **-पक्षः** the established or logical side of an argument. **-प्रयोजनः** white mustard. **-योगिन्** *m.* an epithet of Siva. **-रस** *a.* mineral, metallic. (**-सः**) **1** quick-silver. **2** an alchemist. **-संकल्प** *a.* one who has accomplished his desired objects. **-सेनः** N. of Kârtikeya. **-स्थाली** the boiler or pot of a seer (it is supposed to be a vessel which is gifted with the property of overflowing with any kind of food at the desire of the possessor).

सिद्धता-त्वं Accomplishment, fulfilment, perfection.

सिद्धिः *f.* **1** Accomplishment, fulfilment, completion, perfection, complete attainment (of an object) क्रियासिद्धिः सत्त्वे भवति महतां नोपकरणे Subhâsh. **2** Success, prosperity, welfare, well-being. **3** Establishment, settlement. **4** Substantiation, demonstration, proof, indisputable conclusion. **5** Validity (of a rule, law &c.). **6** Decision, adjudication, settlement (of a lawsuit). **7** Certainty, truth, accuracy, correctness. **8** Payment, liquidation (of a debt). **9** Preparing, cooking (as of drugs &c.). **10** The solution of a problem. **11** Readiness. **12** Complete purity or sanctification. **13** A superhuman power or faculty); these faculties are eight :—अणिमा लघिमा प्राप्तिः प्राकाम्यं महिमा तथा । ईशित्वं च वशित्वं च तथा कामावसायिता ॥ **14** The acquisition of supernatural powers by magical means. **15** Marvellous skill or capability. **16** Good effect or result. **17** Final beatitude, final emancipation. **18** Understanding, intellect. **19** Concealment, vanishing, making oneself invisible. **20** A magical shoe. **21** A kind of Yoga. **22** N. of Durgâ. **-Comp. -द** *a.* granting success or supreme felicity. (**-दः**) an epithet of Siva. **-दात्री** an epithet of Durgâ. **-योगः** a particular auspicious conjunction of planets.

सिध् I. 4 P. (सिध्यति, सिद्ध; *caus.* साधयति or सेधयति ; *desid.* सिषित्सति) **1** To be accomplished or fulfilled ; यत्ने कृते यदि न सिध्यति कोऽत्र दोषः H. Pr. 31 ; उद्यमेन हि सिध्यंति कार्याणि न मनोरथैः 36. **2** To be successful, succeed ; सिध्यंति कर्मसु महत्स्वपि यन्नियोज्याः *S.* 7. 4. **3** To reach, hit, fall true on ; *S.* 2. 5. **4** To attain one's object. **5** To be proved or established, to become valid ; यदि वचनमात्रेणैवाधिपत्यं सिध्यति H. 3. **6** To be settled or adjudicated. **7** To be thoroughly prepared or cooked. **8** To be won or conquered ; Pt. 2. 36. -With प्र **1** to be accomplished or effected, to succeed ; शरीरयात्रापि च ते न प्रसिध्येदकर्मणः Bg. 3. 8 ; तपसैव प्रसिध्यंति Ms. 11. 231. **2** to be gained or acquired. **3** to be known ; see प्रसिद्ध. **-सं 1** to be made perfect. **2** to be fully accomplished or effected, to be performed thoroughly. **3** to attain supreme felicity, to become happy ; जप्येनैव तु संसिध्येद् ब्राह्मणो नात्र संशयः Ms. 2. 87. -II. 1 P. (सेधति, सिद्ध ; the स् of सिध् is generally changed to ष् after a preposition ending in इ or उ) **1** To go. **2** To ward or drive off. **3** To restrain, hinder, prevent. **4** To interdict, prohibit. **5** To ordain, command, instruct. **6** To turn out well or auspiciously. -With अप to drive off, remove ; संवत्सरं यवाहारस्तत्पापमपसेधति Ms. 11. 199. **-नि 1** to ward off, prevent, restrain, keep back ; न्यषेधि शेषोऽप्यनुयायिवर्गः R. 2. 4, 3. 42, 5. 18. **2** to oppose, contradict, object to ; R. 14. 43. **3** to prohibit, forbid ; निषिद्धो भाषमाणस्तु सुवर्णं दंडमर्हति Ms. 8. 361. **4** to defeat, conquer ; R. 18. 1. **5** to remove, drive off, counteract ; न्यषेधत्पावकास्त्रेण राभस्तद्राक्षसस्ततः Bk. 17. 87, 1. 15. **-प्रति 1** to prevent, ward off, restrain ; Ms. 2. 206, R. 8. 23. **2** to forbid, prohibit ; नृपतेः प्रतिषिद्धमेव तत्कृतवान् पंक्तिरथो विलंघ्य यत् R. 9. 74. -विप्रति to contradict, oppose ; स्नेहश्च निमित्तसव्यपेक्षश्चेति विप्रतिषिद्धमेतत् Mâl. 1.

सिध्मं, सिध्मन् *n.* **1** Blotch, scab. **2** Leprosy. **3** A leprous spot.

सिध्मल *a.* Scabby, tinted with leprosy, leprous.

सिध्मा 1 A blotch, scab, leprous spot. **2** Leprosy.

सिध्यः The asterism Pashya.

सिध्रः 1 A pious or virtuous man. **2** A tree.

सिध्रकावणं N. of one of the celestial gardens.

सिनः A morsel, mouthful.

सिनी A woman having a white complexion.

सिनीवाली The day preceding that of new moon, or that day on which the moon rises with a scarcely visible crescent; या पूर्वामावास्या सा सिनीवालायोत्तरा सा कुहूः Ait. Br. ; or सा दृष्टेंदुः सिनीवाली सा नष्टेंदुकला कुहूः Ak.

सिंदुकः सिंदुवारः N. of a tree.

सिंदूरः A kind of tree. **-रं** Red lead ; स्वयं सिंदूरेण द्विपरणमुद्रा मुद्रित इव Git. 11 ; N. 22. 45.

सिंधुः 1 The sea, ocean. **2** The Indus. **3** The country around the Indus. **4** N. of a river in Mâlvâ ; Me. 29 (where Malli.'s remark सिंधुनाम नदी तु कुत्रापि नास्ति is gratuitous);

Mâl. 4. 9 (see Dr. Bhândârkar's note *ad loc.*). **5** The water ejected from an elephant's trunk. **6** The juice exuding from the temples of an elephant. **7** An elephant. –*m. pl.* The inhabitants of the *Sindhu* country. –*f.* A great river or river in general ; पिबत्यसौ पाययते च सिंधूः R. 13. 9 ; Me. 46. –**Comp.** –ज *a.* **1** river-born. **2** sea-born. **3** born in the *Sindh* country. (–जः) the moon. (–जं) rock-salt. -नाथः the ocean.

सिंधुकः, सिंधुवारः N. of a tree.

सिंधुरः An elephant.

सिन्व् 1 P. (सिन्वति) To wet, moisten.

सिप्रः 1 Perspiration, sweat. **2** The moon.

सिप्रा 1 A woman's zone or girdle. **2** A female buffalo. **3** A river near Ujjayinî ; see शिप्रा.

सिम *a.* Every, all, whole, entire.

सिंबा-बी See शिंबा-बी.

सिरः The root of long pepper.

सिरा 1 Any tubular vessel of the body (as a vein, artery, nerve &c.). **2** A bucket, bailing vessel.

सिव् 4 P. (सीव्यति, स्यूत) **1** To sew, darn, stitch together ; मनोभवः सीव्यति दुर्यशः पटौ N. 1. 80 ; Mâl. 5. 10. **2** To unite, bring or join together ; स हि स्नेहात्मकस्तुंतुरंतर्मर्माणि सीव्यति U. 5. 17. –WITH –अनु to string together, connect very closely or uninterruptedly.

सिवरः An elephant.

सिषाधयिषा **1** Wish to effect or accomplish. **2** Desire to establish, prove or demonstrate.

सिसृक्षा Desire to create.

सिहुंडः The milk-hedge plant.

सिह्लः, सिह्लकः Benzoin, incense.

सिह्लकी, सिह्ली The olibanum tree.

सीक् I. 1 A. (सीकते) **1** To sprinkle, scatter in small drops. **2** To go, move. –II. 1 P, 10 U. (सीकति, सीकयति-ते) **1** To be impatient. **2** To be patient. **3** To touch.

सीकरः **1** Drizzling rain, drizzle, mist. **2** Spray, thin drops of water. See शीकर.

सीता **1** A furrow, track or line of a ploughshare. **2** (Hence) A tilled or furrowed ground, ploughed land; वृषेव सीतां तदवग्रहक्षतां Ku. 5. 61. **3** Husbandry, agriculture ; as in सीताद्रव्य q. v. **4** N. of the daughter of Janaka, king of Mithilâ, and wife of Râma. [She was so called because she was supposed to have sprung from a furrow made by king Janaka while ploughing the ground to prepare it for a sacrifice which he had instituted to obtain progeny, and hence also her epithets, 'Ayonij*a*', 'Dharaputr*i* &c. She was married to Rama and accompanied him to the forest. While there she was once carried off by Rav*a*n*a* who tried to violate her chastity, but she scornfully rejected his suit. When Rama came to know that she was in Lank*a*, he attacked the place, killed Rav*a*n*a* and his host of demons, and recovered S*i*ta. She had, however, to pass through the terrible ordeal of fire before she could be received by her husband as his wife. Though thus convinced of her chastity, he had afterwards to abandon her, when far advanced in pregnancy, because the people continued to suspect her fidelity. She, however, found a protector in the sage Valm*i*ki, at whose hermitage she was delivered of Kusa and Lava, and who brought them up. She was ultimately restored to Rama by the sage.] **5** N. of a goddess, wife of Indra. **6** N. of Umâ. **7** N. of Lakshmî. **8** N. of one of the fabulous branches of the Ganges. **9** Spirituous liquor. –**Comp.** –द्रव्यं implements of agriculture, tools of husbandry ; Ms. 9. 293. –पतिः N. of Râmachandra. –फलः the custard-apple tree. (–लं) its fruit.

सीतानकः Pease.

सीत्कारः, सीत्कृतिः *f.* A sound made by drawing in the breath, (expressive of sighing, shivering with cold, murmuring &c.); मया दृष्टाधरं तस्याः ससीत्कारमिवाननं V. 4. 21.

सीत्य *a.* Measured out by furrows, tilled, ploughed. –त्यं Rice, corn, grain.

सीद्यं Indolence, slothfulness, idleness.

सीधु *m.* Spirit distilled from molasses, rum ; स्फुरदधरसीधवे तव वदनचंद्रमा रोचयति लोचनचकोरं Gît. 10 ; Si. 9. 87 ; R. 16. 52. –**Comp.** –गंधः the Bakula tree. –पुष्पः **1** the Kadamba tree. **2** the Bakula tree. –रसः the mango tree. –संज्ञः the Bakula tree.

सीध्रं The anus.

सीपः A sacrificial vessel in the shape of a boat.

सीमन् *f.* **1** A boundary &c. ; see सीमा ; सीमानमत्यायतयोऽस्यजंतः *Si.* 3. 57 ; see निःसीमन् also. **2** The scrotum ; सीम्नि पुष्कलको हतः Sk.

सीमंतः **1** A boundary-line, landmark. **2** The parting line of the hair, the hair parted on each side of the head so as to leave a line ; सीमंते च त्वदुपगमजं यत्र नीपं वधूनां Me. 65 ; Si. 8. 69 ; Mv. 5. 44. –**Comp.** –उन्नयनं 'parting of the hair', one of the twelve Samskâras or purificatory rites observed by woman in the fourth, sixth, or eighth month of their pregnancy.

सीमंतकः N. of a particular kind of inhabitant of hell. –कं Red lead.

सीमंतयति Den. P. **1** To part as hair. **2** To part or mark by a line (in general); सेना सीमंतयन्निरे Kir. K. 5. 44.

सीमंतित *a.* **1** Parted (as hair). **2** Parted or marked by a line ; समीरसीमंतितकेतकीकाः (प्रदेशाः) *S*i. 3. 80 ; रथांगसीमंतितसांद्रकर्दमान् (पथः) Ki. 4. 18.

सीमंतिनी A woman ; मा स्म सीमंतिनी काचिज्जनयेत्पुत्रमीदृशं H. 2. 7 ; Me. 110 ; Bk. 5. 22.

सीमा **1** Boundary, limit, border, margin, frontier. **2** A mound or ridge serving to mark the boundary of a field, village &c. ; सीमां प्रतिसमुत्पन्ने विवादे Ms. 8. 245 ; Y. 2. 152. **3** A mark, land-mark. **4** A bank, shore, coast. **5** The horizon. **6** A suture (as of a skull). **7** The bounds of morality or decorum, limits of propriety. **8** The highest or utmost limit, highest point, climax; सीमेव पद्मासनकौशलस्य Bk 1. 6. **9** A field. **10** The nape of the neck. **11** The scrotum. –**Comp.** –अधिपः a neighbouring prince. –अंतः **1** a boundary-line, border, frontier-line. **2** the utmost limit. °पूजनं **1** the ceremony of worshipping or honouring a village-boundary. **2** worshipping the bridegroom when he arrives at the village-boundary. –उल्लंघनं transgressing or leaping over a boundary, crossing a frontier (now performed on the *Dasarâ* day). –निश्चयः a legal decision with respect to landmarks or boundaries. –लिंगं a boundary-mark, a land-mark. –वादः a dispute about boundaries.–विनिर्णयः settlement of disputed boundary questions. –विवादः litigation about boundaries. °धर्मः the law regarding disputes about boundaries. –वृक्षः a tree serving as a boundary-mark. –संधिः the meeting of two boundaries.

सीमिकः **1** A kind of tree. **2** An ant-hill. **3** An ant or a similar small insect.

सीरः **1** A plough; सद्यः सीरोत्कषणसुरभि क्षेत्रमारुह्य मालं Me 16. **2** The sun. **3** The *Arka* plant. –**Comp.** –ध्वजः an epithet of Janaka. –पाणिः, –भृत् *m.* epithets of Balarâma. –योगः the yoking of cattle to a plough, or a team so yoked.

सीरकः See सीर.

सीरिन् *m.* An epithet of Balarâma : *Si.* 2. 2.

सीलंदः (धः) A kind of fish.

सीव् See सिव्.

सीवनं **1** Sewing, stitching. **2** A seam, suture.

सीवनी **1** A needle. **2** The frenum of the prepuce.

सीसं, सीसकं, सीसपत्रकं Lead ; M. 5. 144 ; Y. 1. 190.

सीहुंडः The milk-hedge plant,

सु I. 1 U. (सुवति-ते) To go, move. -II. 1. 2 P (सवति, सौति) To possess power or supremacy. -III. 5 U. (सुनोति, सुनुते, सुत ; the स् of सु is changed to ष् after any preposition ending in इ or उ) 1 To press out or extract juice. 2 To distil. 3 To pour out, sprinkle, make a libation. 4 To perform a sacrifice, especially the Soma sacrifice. 5 To bathe. -*Desid.* (सुषूसति-ते). -With अभि to extract (Soma) juice. 2 to mix, mingle, compound ; यानि चैवाभिषूयंते पुष्पमूलफलैः शुभैः Ms. 5. 10. 3 to sprinkle ; Bk. 9. 90. -उद् to excite, agitate. -प्र to produce, beget.

सु *ind.* A particle often used with nouns to form Karmadhâraya and Bahuvrîhi compounds, and with adjectives and adverbs. It has the following senses :—1 Well, good, excellent ; as in सुगंधिः. 2 beautiful, handsome ; as in सुमध्यमा, सुकेशी &c. 3 well, perfectly, thoroughly, properly ; सुजीर्णमन्नं सुविचक्षणः सुतः सुशासिता स्त्री नृपतिः सुसेवितः &c.... सुदीर्घकालेऽपि न याति विक्रियां H. 1. 22. 4 easily, readily, as in सुकर or सुलभ q. v. 5 much, very much, exceedingly ; सुदारुण, सुदीर्घ &c. -Comp. -अक्ष *a.* 1 having good eyes. 2 having keen organs, acute. -अंग *a.* well-shaped, handsome, lovely. -अच्छ *a.* see s. v. -अंत *a.* having a happy end, ending well. -अल्प, -अल्पक *a.* see s. v. -अस्ति, -आस्तिक see s. v. -आकार, -आकृति *a.* well-formed, handsome, beautiful. -आगत see s. v. -आभास *a.* very splendid or illustrious ; Ki. 15. 22. -इष्ट *a.* properly sacrificed. °कृत् *m.* a form of fire. -उक्त *a.* well-spoken, well-said ; अथवा सूक्तं खलु केनापि Ve. 3. (-क्तं) 1 a good or wise saying; नेतुं वांछति यः खलान् पथि सतां सूक्तैः सुधास्यंदिभिः Bh. 2. 6, R. 15. 95. 2 a Vedic hymn, as पुरुषसूक्त &c. °दर्शिन् *m.* a hymn seer, Vedic sage. °वाच् *f.* 1 a hymn. 2 praise, a word of praise. -उक्तिः *f.* 1 a good or friendly speech. 2 a good or clever saying. 3 a correct sentence. -उत्तर *a.* 1 very superior. 2 well towards the north. -उत्थान *a.* making good efforts, vigorous, active. (-नं) vigorous effort or exertion. -उन्मद, -उन्माद *a.* quite mad or frantic. -उपसदन *a.* easy to be approached. -उपस्कर *a.* furnished with good instruments. -कंडुः itch. -कंदः 1 an onion. 2 a yam. 3 a sort of grass. -कंदकः onion. -कर *a.* (रा or री *f.*) 1 easy to be done, practicabl, feasible ; वक्तुं सुकरं कर्तुं (अध्यवसितुं) दुष्करं Ve. 3 'sooner said than done'. 2 easy to be managed. (-रा) a tractable cow. (-रं) charity, benevolence. -कर्मन् *a.* 1 one whose deeds are righteous, virtuous, good. 2 active, diligent. (*-m.*) N. of Visvakarman. -कल *a.* one who has acquired a great reputation for liberality in giving and using (money &c.). -कांडिन् *a.* 1 having beautiful stems. 2 beautifully joined. (*-m.*) a bee. -कालुका the plant called डोडी. -काष्ठं fire wood. -कुंदकः an onion. -कुमार *a.* 1 very delicate or soft, smooth. 2 beautifully young or youthful. (-रः) 1 a beautiful youth. 2 a kind of sugar-cane -कुमारकः 1 a beautiful youth. 2 rice (शालि). (-कं) the Tamâlapatra. -कृत् *a.* 1 doing good, benevolent. 2 pious virtuous, righteous. 3 wise, learned. 4 fortunate, lucky. 5 making good sacrifices or offerings. (*-m.*) 1 a skilful worker. 2 N. of Tvashṭri. -कृत *a.* 1 done well or properly. 2 thoroughly done 3 well made or constructed. 4 treated with kindness, assisted, befriended. 5 virtuous, righteous, pious. 6 lucky, fortunate. (-तं) 1 any good or virtuous act, kindness, favour, service ; नादत्ते कस्यचित्पापं कस्यापि सुकृतं विभुः Bg. 5. 15, Me. 17. 2 virtue, moral or religious merit ; स्वर्गाभिसंधिसुकृतं वंचनामिव मेनिरे Ku. 6. 47 ; तच्चिंत्यमानं सुकृतं तवेति R. 14. 16. 3 fortune, auspiciousness. 4 recompense, reward. -कृतिः *f.* 1 kindness, virtue. 2 practice of penance. -कृतिन् *a.* 1 acting well or kindly. 2 virtuous, pious, good, righteous ; संतः संतु निरापदः सुकृतिनां कीर्तिश्चिरं वर्धतां H. 4. 132 ; Bg. 7. 16. 3 wise, learned. 4 benevolent. 5 fortunate, lucky. -केश(स)रः the citron tree. -क्रतुः 1 N. of Agni. 2 of *S*iva. 3 of Indra. 4 of Mitra and Varuṇa. 5 of the sun. -ग *a.* 1 going gracefully or well. 2 graceful, elegant. 3 easy of access ; Pt. 2. 141. 4 intelligible, easy to be understood (opp. दुर्ग). (-गं) 1 ordure, feces. 2 happiness. -गत *a.* 1 well-gone or passed. 2 well-bestowed. (-तः) an epithet of Buddha. -गंधः 1 fragrance, odour, perfume. 2 sulphur. 3 a trader. (-धं) 1 sandal. 2 small cumin seed. 3 blue lotus. 4 a kind of fragrant grass. (-धा) sacred basil. -गंधकः 1 sulphur. 2 the red *Tulasî*. 3 the orange. 4 a kind of gourd. -गंधि *a.* 1 sweet-smelling, fragrant, redolent with perfumes. 2 virtuous, pious. (-धिः) 1 perfume, fragrance. 2 the Supreme Being. 3 a kind of sweet-smelling mango. (-धि *n.*) 1 The root of long pepper. 2 A kind of fragrant grass. 3 Coriander seed. °त्रिफला 1 nutmeg. 2 cloves. -गंधिकः 1 incense. 2 sulphur. 3 a kind of rice. (-कं) the white lotus. -गम *a.* 1 easy of access, accessible. 2 easy. 3 plain, intelligible. -गहना an enclosure round a place of sacrifice to exclude profane access. °वृत्तिः *f.* the same as above. -गृह *a.* (ही *f.*) having a beautiful house or abode, well-lodged ; सुगृही निर्गृहीकृता Pt. 1. 390. -गृहीत *a.* 1 held well or firmly, grasped. 2 used or applied properly or auspiciously. °नामन् *a.* 1 one whose name is auspiciously invoked, one whose name it is auspicious to utter (as Bali, Yudhishṭhira), a term used as a respectful mode of speaking ; सुगृहीतनाम्नः भट्टगोपालस्य पौत्रः Mâl. 1. -ग्रासः a dainty morsel. -ग्रीव *a.* having a beautiful neck. (-वः) 1 a hero. 2 a swan. 3 a kind of weapon. 4 N. of a monkey-chief and brother of Vâli. [By the advice of Kabandha R*a*ma went to Sugr*i*va who told him how his brother had treated him and besought his assistance in recovering his wife, promising at the same time that he would assist R*a*ma in recovering his wife S*i*t*a*. R*a*ma, therefore, killed V*a*li, and installed Sugr*i*va on the throne. He then assisted R*a*ma with his hosts of monkeys in conquering R*a*va*n*a and recovering S*i*ta.] °ईशः N. of Râma. -ग्ल *a.* very weary or fatigued. -चक्षुस् *a.* having good eyes, seeing well. (*-m.*) 1 a discerning or wise man, learned man. 2 the glomerous fig-tree. -चरित -चरित्र *a.* well-conducted, well-behaved. (-तं, -त्रं) 1 good conduct, virtuous deeds. 2 merit ; तव सुचरितमंगुलीय नूनं प्रतनु *S*. 6. 11. (-ता, -त्रा) a well-conducted, devoted, and virtuous wife. -चित्रकः 1 a king-fisher. 2 a kind of speckled snake. -चित्रा a kind of gourd. -चिंता deep thought, deep reflection or consideration. -चिरम् *ind.* for a very long time, very long. -चिरायुस् *m.* a god, deity. -जनः 1 a good or virtuous man, benevolent man. 2 a gentleman. -जनता 1 goodness, kindness, benevolence, virtue; ऐश्वर्यस्य विभूषणं सुजनता Bh. 2. 82. 2 a number of good men. -जन्मन् *a.* of noble or respectable birth ; या कौमुदी नयनयोर्भवतः सुजन्मा Mâl. 1. 34. -जल्पः a good speech. -जात *a.* 1 of high birth 2 beautiful, lovely ; Mâl. 1. 16 R. 3. 8. -तनु *a.* 1 having a beautiful body 2 extremely delicate or slender, very thin. 3 emaciated. (-नुः, -नूः *f.*) a lovely body ; एताः सुतनु मुखं ते सख्यः पश्यंति हेमकूटगताः V. 1. 11. -तपस् *a.* 1 one who practises austere penance. 2 having great heat. (*-m.*) 1 an ascetic, a devotee, hermit, an anchorite. 2 the sun (*-n.*) austere penance. -तराम् *ind.* 1 better, more excellently. 2 exceedingly, very, very much, excessively; तया दुहित्रा सुतरां सवित्री स्फुरत्प्रभामंडलया चकाशे Ku. 1. 24 ; सुतरां दयालुः R 2. 53, 4. 9, 18. 24. 3 more so, much more so ; मय्यप्यास्था न ते चेत्त्वयि मम सुतरामेष राजन् गतोस्मि Bh. 3. 30. -तर्दनः the (Indian) cuckoo. -तलं 1 'immense depth', N. of one of the seven regions below the earth; see पाताल. 2 the foundation of a large building. -तिक्तकः the coral tree. -तीक्ष्ण *a.* 1 very sharp. 2 very pungent. 3 acutely painful. (-क्ष्णः) 1 the Sigru tree. 2 N. of a sage ; नाम्ना सुतीक्ष्णश्चरितेन दांतः R. 13. 41. °दशनः an epithet of *S*iva. -तीर्थः 1 a good preceptor. 2 N. of *S*iva. -तुंग *a.* very lofty or tall. (-गः) the cocoa-nut tree. -दक्षिण *a.* 1 very sincere or upright. 2 liberal or rich in sacrificial gifts ; Pt. 1. 30. (-णा) N. of the wife of Dilîpa ; तस्य दाक्षिण्यरूढेन नाम्ना मगधवंशजा । पत्नी सुदक्षिणेत्यासीत् R. 1. 31, 3. 1. -दंडः a cane, ratan. -दत् *a.* (ती *f.*) having handsome teeth. -दंतः 1 a good tooth. 2 an actor, a dancer. (-ती) the female elephant of the north-west quarter. -दर्शन *a.* (ना or नी *f.*) 1 good looking, beautiful, handsome. 2 easily seen. (-नः) the discus of Vishṇu ; as in कृष्णोप्यसुदर्शनः K. 2 N. of *S*iva. 3 a vulture. (-नं) N. of Jambudvîpa. -दर्शना 1 a handsome woman. 2 a woman. 3 an order, a command. 4 a kind of drug. -दा *a.* very bountiful. -दामन् *a.* one who gives liberally. (*-m.*) 1 a cloud. 2 a mountain. 3 the sea. 4 N. of Indra's elephant. 5 N. of a very poor Brâhmaṇa who came to Dvârakâ with only a small quantity of parched rice as a present to his friend Kṛishṇa, and was raised by him to wealth and glory. -दायः 1 a good or auspicious gift. 2 a special gift given on particular solemn occasions. -दिनं 1 a happy or auspicious day. 2 a fine day or weather (opp. दुर्दिन); so सुदिनाहं in the same sense. -दीर्घ *a.* very long or extended. (-र्घा) a kind of cucumber. -दुर्लभ *a.* very scarce or rare. -दूर *a.* very distant or remote. (सुदूरं means 1 to a great distance 2 to a very high degree, very much सुदूरात् 'from afar, from a distance'). -दृश् *a* having beautiful eyes. *(-f.)* a pretty woman. -धन्वन् *a.* having an excellent bow. (*-m.*) 1 a good archer or bowman. 2 N. of Visvakarman. -धर्मन् *a.* attentive to duties. (*-f.*) the council or assembly of gods. -धर्मा-र्मी the council or assembly of gods (देवसभा); ययावुदीरितालोकः सुधर्मानवमां सभां R. 17. 28. -धी *a.* having a good understanding, wise, clever, intelligent. (-धीः) a wise or intelligent man, learned man or *pandit*. (*-f.*) a good understanding, good sense, intelligence. -उपास्यः 1 a particular kind of royal palace. 2 N. of an attendant on Kṛishṇa. (-स्यं) the club of Balarâma. -उपास्या 1 a woman. 2 N. of Umâ, or of one of her female companions. 3 a sort of pigment. -नंदा a woman. -नयः 1 good conduct. 2 good policy. -नयन *a* having beautiful eyes. (-नः) a deer. (-ना) 1 a woman having beautiful eyes. 2 a woman in general. -नाभ *a.* 1 having a beautiful navel. 2 having a good nave or centre. (-भः) 1 a mountain. 2 the Mainâka mountain q. v. -निभृत *a.* very lonely or private. (-तं) *ind.* very secretly or closely, very narrowly, privately. -निश्चलः an epithet of *S*iva. -नीत 1 well-conducted, well-behaved. 2 Polite, civil. (-तं) 1 good conduct or behaviour. 2 good policy or prudence. -नीतिः *f.* 1 good conduct, good manners, propriety. 2 good policy. 3 N. of the mother of Dhruva ; q. v. -नीथ *a.* well-disposed, well-conducted, righteous, virtuous, good. (-थः) 1 a Brâhmaṇa. 2 N. of *S*isupâla q. v. -नील *a.* very black or blue. (-लः) the pomegranate tree. (-ला) common flax. -नेत्र *a.* having beautiful eyes. -पक्व *a.* 1 well-cooked. 2 thoroughly matured or ripe. (-क्वः) a sort of fragrant mango. -पत्नी a woman having a good husband. -पथः 1 a good road. 2 a good course. 3 good conduct. -पथिन् *m.* (nom. sing. -सुपंथाः) a good road. -पर्ण *a.* (र्णा or र्णी *f.*) 1 well-winged. 2 having good or beautiful leaves. (-र्णः) 1 a ray of the sun. 2 a class of bird-like beings of a semi-divine character. 3 any supernatural bird. 4 an epithet of Garuḍa. 5 a cock. -पर्णा, -पर्णी *f.* 1 a number of lotuses. 2 a pool abounding with lotuses. 3 N. of the mother of Garuḍa. -पर्यास *a.* 1 very spacious. 2 well-fitted. -पर्वन् *a.* well-jointed, having many joints or knots. (*-m.*) 1 a bamboo. 2 an arrow. 3 a god, deity. 4 a special lunar day (as the day of full or new moon, and the 8th and 14th day of each fortnight). 5 smoke. -पात्रं 1 a good or suitable vessel, a worthy receptacle. 2 a fit or competent person, any one well-fitted for an office, an able person. -पाद् (पाद् or पदी *f.*) having good or handsome feet. -पार्श्वः the waved leaf fig-tree. (प्लक्ष.) -पीतं a carrot. (-तः) the fifth Muhûrta. (-पुंसी) a woman having a good husband. -पुष्प *a.* (ष्पा or ष्पी *f.*) having beautiful flowers. (-ष्पः) the coral tree. (-ष्पं) 1 cloves. 2 the menstrual excretion. -प्रतर्कः a sound judgment. -प्रतिभा spirituous liquor. -प्रतिष्ठ *a.* 1 standing well. 2 very celebrated, renowned, glorious, famous. (-ष्ठा) 1 good position. 2 good reputation, fame, celebrity. 3 establishment, erection. 4 installation, consecration. -प्रतिष्ठित *a.* 1 well-established. 2 consecrated. 3 celebrated. (-तः) the Udumbara tree. -प्रतिष्णात *a.* 1 thoroughly purified. 2 well-versed in. -प्रतीक *a.* 1 having a beautiful shape, lovely, handsome. 2 having a beautiful trunk. (-कः) 1 an epithet of Kâmadeva. 2 of *S*iva. 3 of the elephant of the north-east quarter. -प्रपाणं a good tank. -प्रभ *a.* very brilliant, glorious. (-भा) one of the seven tongues of fire. -प्रभातं 1 an auspicious dawn or daybreak ; दिष्ट्या सुप्रभातमद्य यदयं देवो दृष्टः U. 6. 2 the earliest dawn. -प्रयोगः 1 good management or application. 2 dexterity. -प्रसाद *a.* very gracious or propitious. (-दः) N. of *S*iva. -प्रिय *a.* very much liked, agreeable. (-या) 1 a charming woman. 2 a beloved mistress. -फल *a.* 1 very fruitful, very productive. 2 very fertile. (-लः) 1 the pomegranate tree. 2 the jujube. 3 a kind of bean. (-ला) 1 a pumpkin, gourd. 2 the plantain tree. 3 a variety of brown grape. -बंधः sesamum. -बल *a.* very powerful. (-लः) N. of *S*iva. -बोध *a.* easily apprehended or understood. (-धः) good information or advice. -ब्रह्मण्यः 1 an epithet of Kârtikeya. 2 N. of one of the sixteen priests employed at a sacrifice. -भग *a.* 1 very fortunate or prosperous, happy, blessed, highly favoured. 2 lovely, charming, beautiful, pretty; न तु ग्रीष्मस्यैवं सुभगमपराद्धं युवतिषु *S*. 3. 9 ; Ku. 4. 34, R. 11. 80 ; Mâl. 9. 3 pleasant, grateful, agreeable, sweet; श्रवणसुभग M. 3. 4, *S*. 1. 3. 4 beloved, liked, amiable, dear ; सुभ्रासि सुभगः पश्यन् स त्वामुपैतु कृतार्थतां Gît. 5. 5 illustrious. (-गः) 1 borax. 2 the Asoka tree. 3 the Champaka tree. 4 red amaranth. (-गं) good fortune. °मानिन्, सुभगंमन्य *a.* considering oneself fortunate, amiable, pleasing ; वाचालं मां न खलु सुभगंमन्यभावः करोति Me. 94. -भगा 1 a woman beloved by her husband, a favourite wife. 2 an honoured mother. 3 a kind of wild jasmine. 4 turmeric. 5 the holy basil. °सुतः the son of a favourite wife. -भंगः the cocoa-nut tree. -भद्र *a.* very happy or fortunate. (-द्रः) N. of Vishṇu. (-द्रा) N. of the sister of Balarâma and Kṛishṇa, married to Arjuna q. v. She bore to him a son named Abhimanyu. -भाषित *a.* 1 spoken well or eloquently. 2 speaking well, eloquent. (-तं) 1 fine speech, eloquence, learning ; जीर्णमंगे सुभाषितं Bh. 3. 2. 2 a witty saying, an apophthegm, an apposite saying ; सुभाषितेन गतिन युवतीनां च लीलया । मनो न भिद्यते यस्य स वै मुक्तोऽथवा पशुः Subhâsh. 3 a good remark ; बालादपि सुभाषितं (ग्राह्यं). -भिक्षं 1 good alms, successful begging. 2 abundance of food, an abundant supply of provisions, plenty of corn &c. -भ्रू *a.* having beautiful eyebrows. (-भ्रूः *f.*) a lovely woman. (*N. B.* The vocative singular of this word is strictly सुभ्रूः; but सुभ्रू is used by writers like Bhaṭṭi, Kâlidâsa, and Bhavabhûti ; cf. Bk. 6. 11 ; Ku. 5. 43 ; Mâl. 3. 8. -मति *a.* very wise. (-तिः *f.*) 1 a good mind or disposition, kindness, benevolence, friendship. 2 a favour of the gods. 3 a gift, blessing. 4 a prayer, hymn. 5 a wish or desire. 6 N. of the wife of Sagara and mother of 60,000 sons. -मदनः the mango tree. -मध्य,-मध्यम *a.* slender-waisted. -मध्या, -मध्यमा a graceful woman. -मन *a* very charming, lovely, beautiful. (-नः) 1 wheat. 2 the thorn-apple. (-ना) the great-flowered jasmine. -मनस् *a.* 1 good-minded, of a good disposition, benevolent. 2 well-pleased, satisfied. (*-m.*) 1 a god, divinity. 2 a learned man. 3 a student of the Vedas. 4 wheat. 6 Nimba tree. (*-f.*, *n.*; said to be pl. only by some) a flower ; रमणीय एष वः सुमनसां संनिवेशः Mâl. 1. (where the adjectival sense in 1 is also intended); किं सेव्यते सुमनसां मनसापि गंधः कस्तूरिकाजननशक्तिभृता मृगेण R. G. ; Si. 6. 66. °फलः the wood-apple. °फलं nutmeg. -मित्रा N. of one of the wives of Dasaratha and mother of Laksmaṇa and Satrughna. -मुख *a.* (खा or खी *f.*) 1 having a beautiful face, lovely. 2 pleasing. 3 disposed to, eager for ; Ki. 6. 42. (-खः) 1 a learned man. 2 an epithet of Garuḍa. 3 of Gaṇesa. 4 of Siva. (-खं) the scratch of a finger-nail. (-खा, खी) 1 a handsome woman. 2 a mirror. -मूलकं a carrot. -मेधस् *a.* having a good understanding, wise, intelligent. (*-m.*) a wise man. -मेरुः 1 the sacred mountain Meru, q. v. 2 N. of Siva. -यवसं beautiful grass, good pasturage -याधनः an epithet of Duryodhana q. v. -रक्तकः 1 a kind of red chalk. 2 a kind of mango tree. -रंगः 1 good colour. 2 the orange. °धातुः red chalk. -रंजनः the betel-nut-tree. -रत *a.* 1 much sported. 2 playful. 3 much enjoyed. 4 compassionate, tender (-तं) 1 great delight or enjoyment. 2 copulation, sexual union or intercourse, coition; सुरतमृदिता बालवनिता Bh. 2. 44. °ताली 1 a female-messenger, a go between. 2 a chaplet, garland for the head. °प्रसंगः addiction to amorous pleasures; Ku 1. 19. -रतिः *f.* great enjoyment or satisfaction. -रस *a.* 1 well-flavoured, juicy, savoury. 2 sweet. 3 elegant (as a composition). (-सः, -सा) the plant सिंधुवार. (-सा) N. of Durgâ. -रूप *a.* 1 well-formed, handsome, lovely ; सुरूपा कन्या. 2 wise, learned. (-पः) an epithet of Siva. -रेभ *a.* fine-voiced ; Ki. 15. 16. (-भं) tin. -लक्षण *a.* 1 having auspicious or beautiful marks ; 2 fortunate. (-णं) 1 observing, examining carefully, determining, ascertaining. 2 a good or auspicious mark. -लभ *a.* 1 easy to be obtained, easy of attainment, attainable, feasible ; न सुलभा सकलेंदुमुखी च सा V. 2. 9 ; इदमसुलभवस्तुप्रार्थनादुर्निवारं 2. 6. 2 ready for, adapted to, fit, suitable ; निष्ठ्यतश्चरणोपभोगसुलभो लाक्षारसः केनचित् *S.* 4. 5. 3 natural to, proper for; मानुषतासुलभो लघिमा K. °कोप *a.* easily provoked, irascible. -लोचन *a.* fine-eyed. (-नः) a deer. (-ना) a beautiful woman. -लोहकं brass. -लोहित *a.* very red. (-ता) one of the seven tongues of fire. -वक्त्रं 1 a good face or mouth. 2 correct utterance. -वचनं, वचस् *n.* eloquence. -वार्चिकः -का natron, alkali. -वर्ण see s. v. -वह *a.* 1 bearing well, patient. 2 patient, enduring. 3 easy to be borne. -वासिनी 1 a woman married or single who resides in her father's house. 2 a married woman whose husband is alive -विक्रांत *a.* very valiant or bold, chivalrous. (-तं) heroism. -विद् *m.* a learned man, shrewd person. (*-f.*) a shrewd or clever woman. -विदः an attendant on the women's apartments. -विदत् *m.* a king. -विदल्लः an attendant on the women's apartments (wrongly for सौविदल्ल q. v.). (-ल्लं) the women's apartments, harem. -विदल्ला a married woman. -विध *a.* of a good kind. -विधम् *ind.* easily. -विनीत *a.* well-trained, modest. (-ता) a tractable cow. -विहित *a.* 1 well-placed, well-deposited. 2 well-furnished, well-supplied, well-provided, well-arranged ; सुविहितप्रयोगतयाऽर्यस्य न किमपि परिहास्यते *S.* 1 ; कलहंसमकरंदप्रवेशावसरे तत्सुविहितं Mâl. 1. -वी(बी)ज *a.* having good seed. (-जः) 1 N. of Siva. 2 the poppy. (-जं) good seed. -वीराम्लं sour-rice gruel. -वीर्य *a.* 1 having great vigour. 2 of heroic strength, heroic, chivalrous. (-र्यं) 1 great heroism. 2 abundance of heroes. 3 the fruit of the jujube. (र्या) wild cotton. -वृत्त *a.* 1 well-behaved, virtuous, good ; मयि तस्य सुवृत्त वर्तते लघुसंदेशपदा सरस्वती R. 8. 77. 2 well-rounded, beautifully globular or round ; मृदुनातिसुवृत्तेन सुमृष्टेनातिहारिणा । मोदकेनापि किं तेन निष्पात्तिर्यस्य सेवया ; or सुमुखोऽपि सुवृत्तोपि सन्मार्गपातितोऽपि च । महतां पादलग्नोऽपि व्यथयत्येव कंटकः (where all the adjectives are used in a double sense). -वेल *a.* 1 tranquil, still. 2 humble, quiet. (-लः) N. of the Trikûṭa mountain. -व्रत *a.* strict in the observance of religious vows, stricty religious or virtuous. (-तः) a religious student. (-ता) 1 a virtuous wife. 2 a tractable cow, one easily milked. -शंस *a.* well-spoken of, famous, glorious, commendable. -शक *a.* capable of being easily done. -शल्यः the Khadira tree. -शाकं undried ginger. -शासित *a.* kept under control, well-controlled. -शिक्षित *a.* well-taught or trained, well-disciplined. -शिखः fire (-खा) 1 a peacock's crest. 2 a cock's comb. -शील *a.* good-tempered, amiable. (-ला) 1 N. of the wife of Yama. 2 N. of one of the eight favourite wives of Krishṇa. -श्रुत *a.* 1 well-heard. 2 versed in the Vedas. (-तः) N. of the author of a system of medicine, whose work, together with that of Charaka, is regarded as the oldest medical authority, and held in great esteem in India even to this day. -श्लिष्ट 1 well-arranged or united. 2 well-fitted; Mâl. 1. -श्लेषः close union or embrace. -संदृश् *a.* agreeable to look at. -सन्नत *a.* well-directed (as an arrow). -सह *a.* 1 easy to be borne. 2 bearing or enduring well. (-हः) an epithet of Siva. -सार *a.* having good sap or essence. (-रः) 1 good sap, essence or substance. 2 competence. 3 the red-flowering Khadira tree. -स्थ *a.* 1 well-suited, being in a good sense. 2 in health, healthy, faring well. 3 in good or prosperous circumstances, prosperous. 4 happy, fortunate. (-स्थं) a happy state, well-being ; सुस्थे को वा न पंडितः H. 3. 21. (सुस्थित in the same sense). -स्थता, -स्थितिः *f.* 1 good condition, well-being, welfare, happiness. 2 health, convalescence. -स्मित *a.* pleasantly smiling. (-ता) a woman with a pleased or smiling countenance. -स्वर *a.* 1 melodious, harmonious. 2 loud. -हित *a.* 1 very fit or suitable, appropriate. 2 beneficial, salutary. 3 friendly, affectionate. 4 satisfied. (-ता) one of the seven tongues of fire. -हृद् *a.* having a kind heart, cordial, friendly, loving, affectionate. (*-m.*) 1 a friend ; सुहृदः पश्य वसंत किं

स्थितं Ku. 4. 27 ; मंदायंते न खलु सुहृदामभ्युपेतार्थकृत्याः Me. 38. 2 an ally. °भेदः the separation of friends. °वाक्यं the counsel of a friend. -हृदः a friend. -हृदय *a.* 1 good-hearted. 2 dear, affectionate, loving.

सुख *a.* 1 Happy, delighted, joyful, pleased. 2 Agreeable, sweet, charming, pleasant ; दिशः प्रसेदुर्मरुतो ववुः सुखाः R 3. 14 ; so सुखश्रवा निस्वनाः 3. 19. 3 Virtuous, pious. 4 Taking delight in, favourable to ; *S.* 7. 18. 5 Easy, practicable ; Ku. 5. 49. 6 Fit, suitable. -खं 1 Happiness, joy, delight, pleasure, comfort ; यदेवोपनतं दुःखात्सुखं तद्रसवत्तरं V. 3. 21. 2 Prosperity ; अद्वैतं सुखदुःखयोरनुगुणं सर्वास्ववस्थासु यत् U. 1. 39. 3 Well-being, welfare, health ; देवीं सुखं प्रष्टुं गता M. 4. 4 Ease, comfort, alleviation (of sorrow &c.) ; oft. in comp. ; as in सुखशयित, सुखोपविष्ट, सुखाश्रय &c. 5 Facility, easiness, ease. 6 Heaven, paradise. 7 Water. -खं *ind.* 1 Happily, joyfully. 2 Well ; सुखमास्तां भवान् 'may you fare well'. 3 At ease, comfortably ; असंजातकिणस्कंधः सुखं स्वपिति गौगेडिः K. P. 10. 4 Easily, with ease, अज्ञः सुखमाराध्यः सुखतरमाराध्यते विशेषज्ञः Bh 2. 3. 5 Rather, willingly. 6 Quietly, placidly. -Comp. -आधारः paradise. -आप्लव *a.* suitable for bathing. -आयतः, -आयनः a good or well-trained horse. -आरोह *a.* of easy ascent. -आलोक *a* good-looking, lovely, charming. -आवह *a.* conducing to happiness, pleasant, comfortable. -आशः N. of Varuṇa. -आशकः a cucumber. -आस्वाद *a.* 1 having a sweet taste, sweet-flavoured. 2 agreeable, delightful. (-दः) 1 a pleasant flavour. 2 enjoyment (of pleasure). -उत्सवः 1 merry-making, pleasure, festival, jubilee. 2 a husband. -उदकं warm water. -उदयः dawn or realization of happiness. -उदर्क *a.* resulting in happiness. -उद्य *a.* to be spoken easily or agreeably. -उपविष्ट *a.* comfortably seated, sitting at ease. -एषिन् *a.* desiring happiness, wishing well to. -कर, -कार, -दायक *a.* giving pleasure, pleasant. -द *a.* giving pleasure. (-दा) a courtezan of Indras's heaven. (दं) the seat of Vishṇu. -बोधः 1 sensation of pleasure. 2 easy knowledge. -भागिन्, -भाज् *a.* happy. -श्रव, -श्रुति *a.* sweet to the ear, melodious ; Ki. 14. 3. -संगिन् *a.* attached to pleasure -स्पर्श *a.* agreeable to the touch.

सुत *p. p.* 1 Poured out. 2 Extracted or expressed (as Soma juice). 3 Begotten, produced, brought forth. -तः 1 A son. 2 A king. -Comp. आत्मजः a grandson. (-जा) a granddaughter. -उत्पत्तिः *f.* birth of a son. -निर्विशेषम् *ind.* 'not differently from a son', 'just like a son'; R. 5. 6. -वस्करा the mother of seven children. -स्नेहः paternal affection.

सुतवत् *a.* Having sons. -*m.* The father of a son.

सुता A daughter ; तमर्थमिव भारत्या सुतया योक्तुमर्हसि Ku. 6. 79.

सुतिः *f.* Extraction of Soma juice.

सुतिन् *a.* (नी *f.*) Having a child or children. -*m.* A father.

सुतिनी A mother ; तेनांबा यदि सुतिनी वद वंध्या कीदृशी भवति Subhâsh.

सुतुस् *a.* Well-sounding.

सुत्या 1 Extraction or preparation of Soma juice. 2 A sacrificial oblation. 3 Parturition.

सुत्रामन् *m.* N. of Indra.

सुत्वन् *m.* 1 An offerer or drinker of Soma juice. 2 A student who has performed his ablutions (subsequent or preparatory to a sacrifice).

सुदि *ind.* In the bright fortnight of a lunar month ; cf. वदि.

सुधन्वाचार्यः The son of an outcast Vaisya by a woman of the same class ; cf. Ms. 10. 23.

सुधा 1 The beverage of the gods, nectar, ambrosia ; निपीय यस्य क्षितिरक्षिणः कथां तथाद्रियंते न बुधाः सुधामपि N. 1. 1. 2 The nectar or honey of flowers. 3 Juice. 4 Water. 5 N. of the Ganges. 6 White-wash, plaster, mortar ; कैलासगिरिणेव सुधासितेन प्राकारेण परिगता K., R. 16. 18. 7 A brick. 8 Lightning. 9 The milk-hedge plant. -Comp. -अंशुः 1 the moon. 2 camphor. °रत्नं a pearl. -अंगः, -आकारः, -आधारः the moon. -जीविन् *m.* a plasterer, bricklayer. -द्रवः a nectar-like fluid. -धवलित *a.* plastered, white-washed. -निधिः 1 the moon. 2 camphor. -भवनं a stuccoed house. -भित्तिः *f.* 1 a plastered wall. 2 a brickwall. 3 the fifth Muhûrta or hour after noon. -भुज् *m.* a god, deity. -भूतिः 1 the moon. 2 a sacrifice, an oblation. -मयं 1 a brick or stone building. 2 a royal palace. -वर्षः a shower of nectar. -वर्षिन् *m.* an epithet of Brahman. -वासः 1 the moon. 2 camphor. -वासा a kind of cucumber. -सित *a.* 1 white as mortar. 2 bright as nectar. 3 bound by nectar ; जगतीशरणे युक्तो हरिकांतः सुधासितः Ki. 15. 45. (where it has senses 1 and 2 also). -सूतिः 1 the moon. 2 a sacrifice. 3 a lotus. -स्यंदिन् *a.* ambrosial, flowing with nectar ; Bh. 2. 6. -स्रवा uvula or soft palate. -हरः an epithet of Garuḍa ; see गरुड.

सुधितिः *m. f.* An axe.

सुनारः 1 The udder of a bitch. 2 The egg of a snake 3 A sparrow.

सुनासी(शी)रः An epithet of Indra.

सुंदः N. of a demon and brother of Upasunda, who were sons of Nikumbha. [They got a boon from the Creator that they would not die until they should kill themselves. On the strength of this boon they grew very oppressive, and Indra had at last to send down a lovely nymph named Tilottama, and while quarrelling for her, they killed each other].

सुंदर *a.* (री *f.*) 1 Lovely, beautiful, handsome, charming. 2 Right. -र N. of Cupid. -री A beautiful woman ; एका भार्या सुंदरी वा दरी वा Bh. 2. 115 ; विद्याधरसुंदरीणां Ku. 1. 7.

सुप्त *p. p.* 1 Slept, sleeping, asleep; न हि सुप्तस्य सिंहस्य प्रविशंति मुखे मृगाः H. Pr. 36. 2 Paralyzed, benumbed, insensible ; see स्वप्. -प्तं Sleep, sound sleep. -Comp. -जनः midnight. -ज्ञानं a dream. -त्वच् *a.* paralytic.

सुप्तिः *f.* 1 Sleep, sleepiness drowsiness. 2 Insensibility, paralysis, numbness. 3 Trust, confidence.

सुमः 1 The moon. 2 Camphor. 3 Sky. -मं A flower ; Bv. 1. 84.

सुरः 1 A god, deity ; सुराप्रतिग्रहाद् देवाः सुरा इत्यभिविश्रुताः Râm. ; सुधया तर्पयते सुरान् पितॄंश्च V. 3. 7 ; R. 5. 16. 2 The number ' thirty-three '. 3 The sun. 4 A sage, learned man. -Comp. -अंगना a celestial woman or damsel, an *apsaras* ; R. 8. 79. -अधिपः an epithet of Indra. -अरिः 1 an enemy of gods, a demon. 2 the chirp of a cricket. -अर्हं 1 gold. 2 saffron. -आचार्यः an epithet of Bṛihaspati. -आपगा ' the heavenly river ', an epithet of the Ganges. -आलयः 1 the mountain Meru. 2 heaven, paradise. -इज्यः N. of Bṛihaspati. -इज्या the sacred basil. -इंद्रः, -ईशः, -ईश्वरः N. of Indra. -उत्तमः 1 the sun. 2 Indra. -उत्तरः sandal-wood. -ऋषिः (सुरर्षिः) a divine sage. -कारुः an epithet of Visvakarman. -कार्मुकं rainbow. -गुरुः an epithet of Bṛihaspati. -ग्रामणी *m.* N. of Indra. -ज्येष्ठः an epithet of Brahman. -तरुः a tree of paradise. -तोषकः the jewel called Kaustubha ; q. v. -दारु *n.* the Devadâru tree. -दीर्घिका an epithet of the Ganges. दुंदुभी the sacred basil. -द्विपः 1 an elephant of the gods. 2 N. of Airâvata. -द्विष् *m.* a demon ; R. 10. 15. -धनुस् *n.* rainbow ; सुरधनुरिदं दूराकृष्टं न नाम शरासनं V. 4. 1. -धूपः turpentine, resin. -निम्नगा an epithet of the Ganges. -पतिः an epithet of Indra. -पथं the sky, heaven. -पर्वतः the mountain Meru ; q. v. -पादपः a tree of paradise, such as the कल्पतरु. -प्रियः 1 N. of Indra. 2 of Bṛihaspati. -भूयं identification with a deity, deification, apotheosis. -भूरुहः the Devadâru tree. -युवतिः *f.* a celestial damsel. -लासिका a flute, pipe -लोकः heaven. -वर्त्मन् *n.* the sky. -वल्ली the sacred basil. -विद्विष्, -वैरिन्, शत्रु *m.* an evil spirit, a demon. -सद्मन् *n.* heaven, paradise. सरित्, -सिंधु *f.* the Ganges ; सुरसरिदिव तेजो वह्निनिष्ठ्यूतमैशम् R 2. 75. -सुंदरी, -स्त्री a celestial woman ; V. 1. 3.

सुरंगः-गा 1 A hole cut in a wall for the purpose of breaking into a house. 2 A subterranean passage, a mine dug underneath a building ; ऐकागारिकेण तावतीं सुरंगां कारयित्वा Dk , सुरंगया बहिरपगतेषु युष्मासु Mu. 2 ; (written also सरुंगा).

सुरभि *a.* 1 Sweet-smelling, fragrant, odorous ; पाटलसंसर्गसुरभिवनवाताः S. 1. 3, Me. 16, 20, 22. 2 Pleasing, agreeable. 3 Shining, handsome ; तां सौरभेयीं सुरभिर्यशोभिः 4 Beloved, friendly. 5 Celebrated, famous. 6 Wise, learned. 7 Good, virtuous. -भिः 1 Fragrance, odour, perfume. 2 Nutmeg. 3 Resin of Sâla, or resin in general. 4 The Champaka tree. 5 The *Samî* tree. 6 The Kadamba tree. 7 A kind of fragrant grass. 8 The season of spring ; V. 2. 20. -*f.* 1 The gum olibanum tree. 2 The sacred basil. 3 Jasmine. 4 A sort of perfume or fragrant plint. 5 Spirituous liquor. 6 The earth. 7 A cow. 8 N. of the famous cow of plenty ; सुतां तदीयां सुरभेः कृत्वा प्रतिनिधिं R. 1. 81, 75. 9 N. of one of the Mâtris. -*n.* 1 A fragrant smell, perfume, fragrance. 2 Sulphur. 3 Gold. -Comp. -घृतं fragrant butter, well-seasoned ghee. -त्रिफला 1 nutmeg. 2 cloves. 3 areca nut. -बाणः an epithet of Cupid. -मासः the spring. -मुखं the commencement of spring.

सुरभिका A kind of plantain.

सुरभिमत् *m.* N. of fire.

सुरा 1 A spirituous liquor, wine ; सुरा वै मलमन्नानां Ms. 11. 93 ; गौडी पैष्टी च माध्वी च विज्ञेया त्रिविधा सुरा 94. 2 Water. 3 A drinking vessel. 4 A snake. -Comp. -आकारः a distillery. -आजीवः, -आजीविन् *m.* a distiller. -आलयः a tavern, dram-shop. -उदः the sea of spirituous liquor. -ग्रहः a vessel for holding liquor. -ध्वजः a flag or sign hung outside a tavern. -प *a.* 1 a drinker of spirituous liquor. 2 pleasant, agreeable. 3 wise, sage. -पाणं, -पानं the drinking of wine or liquor. -पात्रं, -भांडं a wine-glass or cup. -भागः yeast. -मंडः the froth or scum of spirituous liquor, during fermentation. -संधानं distillation of spirituous liquor.

सुवर्ण *a.* 1 Of good or beautiful colour, brilliant in hue, bright, yellow, golden. 2 Of a good tribe or caste. 3 Of good fame, glorious, celebrated. -र्णः 1 A good colour. 2 A good tribe or caste. 3 A sort of sacrifice. 4 An epithet of *Siva.* 5 The thorn-apple. -र्णं 1 Gold. 2 A golden coin (-*m.* also) ; नन्वहं दशसुवर्णान् प्रयच्छामि Mk. 2. 3 A weight of gold equal to 16 Mâshas or about 175 grains Troy (-*m.* also). 4 Money, wealth, riches. 5 A sort of yellow sandal wood. 6 A kind of red chalk. -Comp. -अभिषेकः sprinkling the bride and bridegroom with water into which a piece of gold has been dropped. -कदली a variety of plantain. -कर्तृ, -कार, -कृत *m.* a goldsmith. -गणितं a particular method of calculation in arithmetic. -पुष्पित *a.* abounding in gold ; *e. g.* सुवर्णपुष्पितां पृथ्वीं विचिन्वंति त्रयो जनाः । शूरश्च कृतविद्यश्च यश्च जानाति सेवितुं Pt. 1. 45. -पृष्ठ *a.* coated with gold, gilded. -माक्षिकं a kind of mineral substance. -यूथी yellow jasmine. -रूप्यक *a.* abounding in gold and silver. -रेतस् *m.* an epithet of *Siva.* -वर्णा turmeric. -सिद्धः an adept who has acquired gold by magical means. -स्तेयं stealing of gold (one of the five Mahâpâtakas q. v.).

सुवर्णकं 1 Brass, bell-metal. 2 Lead.

सुवर्णवत् *a.* 1 Golden. 2 Having a golden colour, beautiful, handsome.

सुषम *a.* Very lovely or beautiful, very pleasing. -मा Exquisite beauty, great lustre or splendour ; कुरबककुसुमं चपलासुषमं Gît. 7 ; सुषमाविषये परीक्षणे निखिलं पद्ममभाजि त खात् N. 2. 37 ; Bv. 1. 26, 2. 12.

सुषवी 1 A sort of gourd. 2 Black cumin. 3 Cumin-seed.

सुषाढः An epithet of *Siva.*

सुषिः *f.* A hole ; cf. शुषि.

सुषि(षी)म् *a.* 1 Cold, frigid. 2 Pleasant, agreeable. -मः 1 Cold. 2 A kind of snake. 3 The moon-stone.

सुषिर *a.* 1 Full of holes, hollow, perforated. 2 Slow in articulation. -रं 1 A hole, an aperture, a cavity. 2 Any wind-instrument.

सुषुप्तिः *f.* 1 Deep or profound sleep, profound repose. 2 Great insensibility, spirtual ignorance ; अविद्यात्मिका हि बीजशक्तिरव्यक्तशब्दनिर्देश्या परमेश्वराश्रया मायामयी महासुषुप्तिर्यस्यां स्वरूपप्रतिबोधरहिताः शेरते संसारिणो जीवाः S. B. on Br. Sût. 1. 4. 3.

सुषुम्णः N. of one of the principal rays of the sun -म्णा A particular artery of the human body, said to lie between इडा and पिंगला, two of the vessels of the body.

सुष्ठु *ind.* 1 Well, excellently, beautifully. 2 Very much, exceedingly ; सुष्ठु शोभसे आर्यपुत्र एतेन विनयमाहात्म्येन U. 1. 3 Truly, rightly ; शब्दे सुष्ठु प्रयुक्तः Sarv. S; अथवा सुष्ठु खल्विदमुच्यते.

सुप्मं A rope, cord, string.

सुह्माः (*m.* pl.) N. of a people ; आत्मा संरक्षितः सुह्मैर्वृत्तिमाश्रित्य वैतसीम् R. 4. 35.

सू I. 2. 4. A. (सूते, सूयते, सूत) To bring forth, produce, beget, yield (fig. also) ; असूत सा नागवधूपभोग्यं Ku. 1. 20 ; कीर्तिं सूते दुष्कृते या हिनस्ति U. 5. 31. -With प्र to bring forth, beget, produce. -II. 6 P. (सुवति) 1 To excite, incite, impel. 2 To remit (as debt).

सू *a.* (At the end of comp.) Bringing forth, producing, yielding &c. -*f.* 1 Birth. 2 A mother.

सूकः 1 An arrow. 2 Air, wind. 3 A lotus.

सूकरः 1 A hog, pig ; see शूकर. 2 A sort of deer. 3 A potter -री 1 A sow. 2 A sort of moss.

सूक्ष्म *a.* 1 Subtle, minute, atomic ; जालांतरस्थसूर्यांशौ यत्सूक्ष्मं दृश्यते रजः. 2 Little, small ; इदमुपहितसूक्ष्मग्रंथिना स्कंधदेशे S. 1. 18 ; R. 18. 49. 3 Fine, thin, delicate, exquisite. 4 Nice. 5 Sharp, acute, penetrating. 6 Crafty, artful, subtle, ingenious. 7 Exact, precise, accurate, correct. -क्ष्मः 1 An atom. 2 The Ketaka plant. 3 An epithet of *Siva.* -क्ष्मं 1 The subtle all-pervading spirit, the Supreme Soul. 2 Minuteness. 3 One of the three kinds of power attainable by an ascetic ; cf. सावद्य. 4 Craft, ingenuity. 5 Fraud, cheating. 6 Fine thread &c. 7 N. of a figure of speech, thus defined by Mammaṭa:—कुतोऽपि लक्षितः सूक्ष्मोऽप्यर्थोऽन्यस्मै प्रकाश्यते । धर्मेण केनचिद्यत्र तत्सूक्ष्मं परिचक्षते K. P. 10. -Comp. -एला small cardamoms. -तंडुलः the poppy. -तंडुला 1 long pepper. 2 a kind of grass. -दर्शिता quick-sightedness, acuteness, foresight, wisdom. -दर्शिन्, -दृष्टि *a.* 1 sharp-sighted, eagle-eyed. 2 of acute discernment. 3 acute, sharp-minded. -दारु *n.* a thin plank of wood, a board. -देहः, -शरीरं the subtle body which is invested by the grosser material frame(=लिंगशरीर q. v.). -पत्रः 1 coriander seed. 2 a kind of wild cumin. 3 a sort of red sugarcane. 4 the gum arabic tree. 5 a sort of mustard. -पर्णी a kind of basil. -पिप्पली wild pepper. -बुद्धि *a.* sharp-witted, acute, shrewd, intelligent. (-द्धिः *f.*) sharp wit, acute intellect, mental acumen. -मक्षिकं,-का a mosquito, gnat. -मानं a nice or exact measurement, precise computation (opp. स्थूलमान which means ' broad measurement, ' ' rough calculation '). -शर्करा small gravel, sand. -शालिः a kind of fine rice. -षट्चरणः a sort of louse.

सच् 10 U. (सूचयति-ते, सूचित) **1** To pierce. **2** To point out, indicate, show, manifest, prove ; त्वां सूचयिष्यति तु माल्य, समुद्भवोयं (गंधः) Mk. 1. 35 ; Me. 21 ; *S*. 1. 14. **3** To betray, reveal, divulge ; स जातु सेव्यमानोऽपि गुप्तद्वारो न सूच्यते R. 17. 50. **4** To gesticulate, act, indicate by gestures or signs ; वामाक्षिस्पंदनं सूचयति, रथवेगं सूचयति &c. **5** To trace out, spy, ascertain. –WITH **अभि** to show, indicate ; अमन्यत नलं प्राप्तं कर्मचेष्टाभिसूचितं Mb. –**प्र**, -**सं** to indicate, forebode ; संयोगो हि वियोगस्य संसूचयति संभवं Subhâsh.

सूचः A pointed shoot or blade of Kusa grass.

सूचक *a*. (**चिका** *f*.) **1** Indicative, indicating, proving, showing. **2** Betraying, informing. –**कः 1** A piercer. **2** A needle, any instrument for perforating or sewing. **3** An informer, a tale-bearer, traducer, spy. **4** A narrator, teacher, an instructor. **5** The manager or chief actor of a company. **6** A Buddha. **7** A *Siddha*. **8** A villain, scoundrel. **9** A demon, goblin. **10** A dog. **11** A crow. **12** A cat. **13** A kind of fine rice. –**Comp.** –**वाक्यं** the information given by an informer.

सूचनं –**ना 1** The act of piercing or perforating, boring, perforation. **2** Pointing out, indication, intimation. **3** Informing against, betraying, calumniating, traducing. **4** Gesticulation, indicating by proper signs or gesture. **5** Hinting, hint. **6** Information. **7** Teaching, showing, describing. **8** Spying out, spying, seeing, ascertaining. **9** Villainy, wickedness.

सूचा 1 Piercing. **2** Gesticulation. **3** Spying out, seeing, sight.

सूचिः –**ची** *f*. **1** Piercing, perforating. **2** A needle. **3** Sharp point or pointed blade (as of Kusa grass) ; अभिनवकुशसूच्या परिक्षतं मे चरणं *S*. 1 ; so मुखे कुशसूचिविद्धे *S*. 4. 14. **4** The sharp point or tip of anything ; कः करं प्रसारयेत् पन्नगरत्नसूचये Ku. 5. 43. **5** The point of a bud. **6** A kind of military array, a sharp column or file ; दंडव्यूहेन तन्मार्गं यायात्तु शकटेन वा वराहमकराभ्यां वा सूच्या वा गरुडेन वा Ms. 7. 187. **7** A triangle formed by the sides of a trapezium produced till they meet. **8** A cone, pyramid. **9** Indication by gesture, communicating by signs, gesticulation. **10** A particular mode of dancing. **11** Dramatic action. **12** An index, a table of contents. **13** A list, catalogue. **14** The earth's disc in computing eclipses (in astr.). –**Comp.** –**अग्र** *a*. needle-pointed, having a sharp needlelike point, acuminated. (–**ग्रं**) the point of a needle. –**आस्यः** a rat. –**कटाहन्याय** see under न्याय. –**खातः** a sharp pyramid or pyramidal excavation, a cone. –**पत्रकं** an index, a table of contents. (–**कः**) a kind of pot-herb. –**पुष्पः** the Ketaka tree. –**भिन्न** *a*. bursting open at the points of the buds ; पांडुच्छायोपवनवृतयः केतकैः सूचिभिन्नैः Me. 28.–**भेद्य** *a*. **1** to be pierced or penetrated by a needle. **2** thick, dense, pitchy, gross, utter ; रुद्धालोके नरपति पथे सूचिभेद्यैस्तमोभिः Me. 37. **3** palpable, tangible. –**मुख** *a*. **1** needle-mouthed, having a pointed beak. **2** pointed. (–**खः**) **1** a bird. **2** white Kusa grass. **3** a particular position of the hands. (–**खं**) a diamond. –**रोमन्** *m*. a hog. –**वदन** *a*. needle-faced, having a pointed beak. (–**नः**) **1** a gnat, mosquito. **2** a mungoose. –**शालिः** a kind of fine rice.

सूचिकः A tailor.

सूचिका 1 A needle. **2** An elephant's trunk. –**Comp.** –**धरः** an elephant. –**मुख** *a*. having a pointed mouth or head. (–**खं**) a shell, the conch-shell.

सूचित *p. p.* **1** Pierced, bored, perforated. **2** Pointed out, shown, intimated, indicated, hinted. **3** Made known or indicated by signs or gestures. **4** Communicated, told, revealed. **5** Ascertained, known.

सूचिन् *a*. (**नी** *f*.) **1** Piercing, perforating. **2** Pointing out, intimating, indicating. **3** Informing against. **4** Spying out. –*m*. A spy, an informer.

सूचिनी 1 A needle. **2** A night.

सूची See सूचि.

सूच्य *a*. Communicable, fit to be made known.

सूत् *ind*. An imitative sound (snorting, snoring &c.).

सूत *p. p.* **1** Born, begotten, engendered, produced. **2** Impelled, emitted. –**तः 1** A charioteer ; सूत चोदयाश्वान् पुण्याश्रमदर्शनेन तावदात्मानं पुनीमहे *S*. 1. **2** The son of a Kshatriya by a woman of the Brâhmaṇa caste (his business being that of a charioteer) ; क्षत्रियाद्विप्रकन्यायां सूतो भवति जातितः Ms. 10. 11 ; सूतो वा सूतपुत्रो वा यो वा को वा भवाम्यहं Ve. 3. 33. **3** A bard. **4** A carpenter. **5** The sun. **6** N. of a pupil of Vyâsa. –**तः**-**तं** Quicksilver. –**Comp.** –**तनयः** an epithet of Karṇa.–**राज्** *m*. quicksilver.

सूतकं 1 Birth, production ; Ms. 4. 112. **2** Impurity caused by child-birth (or miscarriage) in a family ; (also called जननाशौचं q. v.). –**कः**-**कं** Quicksilver.

सूतका A woman recently delivered, a lying-in woman ; Ms. 5. 85.

सूता A woman recently delivered.

सूतिः *f*. **1** Birth, production, parturition, delivery, child-bearing. **2** Offspring, progeny. **3** Source, fountain-head ; तपसा सूतिरसूतिरापदां Ki. 2. 56. **4** A place where Soma juice is extracted. –**Comp.** –**अशौचं** impurity caused by childbirth in a family (which lasts for 10 days) –**गृहं** the lying-in chamber. –**मासः** (also –**सूतीमासः**) the month of delivery, the last month of pregnancy.

सूतिका A woman recently delivered. –**Comp.** –**अगारं**, –**गृहं**, –**गेहं**, –**भवनं** the lying-in chamber. –**रोगः** sickness subsequent to child-birth, puerperal sickness. –**षष्ठी** N. of a particular goddess worshipped on the sixth day after child-birth.

सूत्वरं The distillation of spirituous liquor.

सूत्या See सुत्या.

सूत्र् 10 U. (सूत्रयति-ते, सूत्रित) **1** To tie, bind, thread, string together. **2** To write or compose in the form of a Sûtra or short rule ; तथा च सूत्र्यते हि भगवता पिंगलेन; जैमिनिरपि इदमपि धर्मलक्षणमसूत्रयत् &c. **3** To plan, arrange, systematize ; तन्निपुणं मया निसृष्टार्थदूतीकल्पः सूत्रयितव्यः Mâl. 1. **4** To relax, unbind.

सूत्रं 1 A thread, string, line, cord ; पुष्पमालानुषंगेण सूत्रं शिरसि धार्यते Subhâsh. ; मणौ वज्रसमुत्कीर्णे सूत्रस्येवास्ति मे गतिः R. 1. 4. **2** A fibre ; सुरांगनां कर्षति खंडिताग्रात्सूत्रं मृणालादिव राजहंसी V. 1. 19, Ku. 1. 40, 49. **3** A wire. **4** A collection of threads. **5** The sacred thread or sacrificial cord worn by members of the first three classes ; शिखासूत्रवान् ब्राह्मणः Tarka. K. **6** The string or wire of a puppet. **7** A short rule or precept, an aphorism. **8** A short or concise technical sentence used as a memorial rule ; it is thus defined:— स्वल्पाक्षरमसंदिग्धं सारवद्विश्वतोमुखम् । अस्तोभमनवद्यं च सूत्रं सूत्रविदो विदुः. **9** Any work or manual containing such aphoristic rules ; *e. g.* मानवकल्पसूत्र, आपस्तंबसूत्र, गृह्यसूत्र &c. **10** A rule, canon, decree (in law). –**Comp.** –**आत्मन्** *a*. having the nature of a string or thread. (–*m*.) the soul. –**आली** a string of beads &c. worn round the neck, a necklace. –**कंठः 1** a Brâhmaṇa. **2** a pigeon, dove. **3** a wag-tail. –**कर्मन्** *n*. carpentry. –**कारः**, –**कृत्** *m*. an author or composer of Sûtras. –**कोणः**, –**कोणकः** a small drum shaped like an hour-glass (डमरु). –**गंडिका** a kind of stick used by weavers in spinning threads. –**चरणं** N. of a class of *charaṇas* or Vedic schools which introduced various Sûtra works. –**दरिद्र** *a*. 'poor in threads', having a small number of threads, thread-bare ; अयं पटः सूत्रदरिद्रतां गतः Mk. 2. 9. –**धरः**, –**धारः 1** 'the thread-holder', a stage-manager, a principal actor who arranges the cast of characters and instructs them, and takes a prominent part in the Prastâvanâ or prelude ; he is thus defined :— नाट्यस्य यदनुष्ठानं तत्सूत्रं स्यात्सबीजकम् । रंगदैवतपूजाकृत् सूत्रधार इति स्मृतः ॥ **2** a carpenter, an artisan. **3** the author of a set of aphorisms **4** an epithet of Indra. **-पिटकः** N. of one of the three collections of Buddhistic writings. **-पुष्पः** the cotton plant. **-भिद्** *m.* a tailor. **-भृत्** *m.* = सूत्रधार q. v. **-यंत्रं 1** 'a thread-machine', shuttle. **2** a weaver's loom. **-वीणा** a kind of lute. **-वेष्टनं** a weaver's shuttle.

सूत्रणं 1 The act of stringing together, putting in order, arranging. **2** Arranging in aphorisms.

सूत्रला A spindle or distaff.

सूत्रामन् = सुत्रमन् q. v.

सूत्रिका A kind of dish (Mar. शेवया).

सूत्रित *p. p.* **1** Strung, arranged, methodised, systematized. **2** Prescribed in Sûtras, delivered in aphorisms.

सूत्रिन् *a.* (**णी** *f.*) **1** Having threads. **2** Having rules. *-m.* A crow.

सूद् I. 1 A. (सूदते) **1** To strike, hurt, wound, kill, destroy. **2** To effuse, pour out. **3** To deposit **4** To eject, throw away. –II. 10 U. (सूदयति-ते) **1** To incite, prompt, excite, urge on, animate. **2** To strike, hurt, kill. **3** To cook, dress, season, prepare. **4** To pour out, effuse. **5** To assent, agree, promise. **6** To eject, throw away. –WITH नि (निषूदयति-ते) to kill.

सूदः 1 Destroying, destruction, massacre. **2** Pouring out, distilling. **3** A well, spring. **4** A cook. **5** Sauce, soup. **6** Anything seasoned, a prepared dish. **7** Split pease. **8** Mud, mire. **9** Sin, fault. **10** The Lodhra tree. **-Comp. -कर्मन्** *n.* cookery. **-शाला** a kitchen.

सूदन *a.* (**नी** *f.*) **1** Destroying, killing, destructive ; दानवसूदन; अरिगणसूदन &c. **2** Dear, beloved. **-नं 1** Destroying, destruction, massacre. **2** Assenting to, promising. **3** Ejecting, throwing away.

सून *p. p.* **1** Born, produced. **2** Blown, blossomed, opened, budded. **3** Empty, vacant ; (perhaps for शून or शून्य in this sense). **-नं 1** Bringing forth, parturition. **2** A bud, blossom. **3** A flower.

सूनरी A happy woman.

सूना 1 A slaughter-house, butcher's house ; भवानपि सूनापरिचर इव गृध्र आमिषलोलुपो भीरुकश्च M. 2. **2** The sale of meat. **3** Hurting, killing, destroying. **4** The soft palate, uvula. **5** A girdle, zone. **6** Inflammation of the glands of the neck called mumps. **7** A ray of light. **8** A river. **9** A daughter. **-नाः** (*f. pl.*) The five things in a house by which animal life is likely to be destroyed ; see under शूना or पंचशूना.

सूनिन् *m.* **1** A butcher, flesh-seller. **2** A hunter.

सूनुः 1 A son ; पितुरद्धमेवैको सूनुरमर्व K. **2** A child, an offspring. **3** A grandson (daughter's son). **4** A younger brother. **5** The sun. **6** The Arka plant.

सूनू *f.* A daughter.

सूनृत *a.* **1** True and pleasant, kind and sincere ; तत्र सूनृतगिरश्च सूरयः पुण्यमृग्यजुषमध्यगीषत Si. 14. 21, R. 1. 93. **2** Kind, affable, gentle, courteous ; तां चाप्येतां मातरं मंगलानां धेनुं धीराः सूनृतां वाचमाहुः U. 5. 31 ; तृणानि भूमिरुदकं वाक् चतुर्थी च सूनृता । एतान्यपि सतं गेहे नोच्छिद्यंते कदाचन Ms. 3. 101 ; R. 6. 29. **3** Auspicious, fortunate. **4** Beloved, dear. **-तं 1** True and agreeable speech. **2** Kind and pleasant discourse, courteous language ; R. 8. 92. **3** Auspiciousness.

सूपः 1 Broth, soup ; न स जानाति शास्त्रार्थं दर्वी सूपरसानिव Subhâsh. ; Ms. 3. 226 **2** A sauce, condiment. **3** A cook. **4** A pan, vessel. **5** An arrow. **-Comp. -कारः** a cook. **-धूपनं, -धूपकं** asa fœtida.

सूमः 1 Water. **2** Milk. **3** Sky or heaven.

सूर् 4 A. (सूर्यते) **1** To hurt, kill. **2** To make firm or be firm.

सूर्ण *a.* Hurt, injured.

सूरः 1 The sun. **2** The Arka plant. **3** The Soma. **4** A wise or learned man. **5** A hero, king. **-Comp. -चक्षुस्** *a.* radiant as the sun. **-सुतः** an epithet of Saturn. **-सूतः** the charioteer of the sun ; *i. e.* Aruṇa.

सूरणः N. of an esculent root.

सूरत *a.* **1** Kindly-disposed, compassionate, tender. **2** Calm, tranquil.

सूरिः 1 The sun. **2** A learned or wise man, a sage ; अथवा कृतवाग्द्वारे वंशेऽस्मिन्पूर्वसूरिभिः R. 1. 4 ; Si. 14. 21. **3** A priest. **4** A worshipper. **5** A title of respect given to Jaina teachers ; *e. g.* मल्लिनाथसूरि. **6** N. of Krishṇa.

सूरिन् *a.* (**णी** *f.*) Wise, learned. *-m.* A wise or learned man, scholar, *pandit.*

सूरी 1 N. of the wife of the sun. **2** N. of Kuntî, q. v.

सूर्क्ष् I. 4 P. (सूर्क्षति, सूर्क्ष्यति) **1** To respect, honour. **2** To disrespect, disregard, slight.

सूर्क्ष (**क्ष्य**)**णं** Disrespect.

सूर्क्ष्यः A kind of bean.

सूर्प See शूर्प.

सूर्मिः, -र्मी *f.* **1** An iron or metallic image ; Ms. 11. 3. **2** The pillar of a house. **3** Radiance, lustre. **4** A flame.

सूर्यः 1 The sun ; सूर्ये तपत्यावरणाय दृष्टेः कल्पेत लोकस्य कथं तमिस्रा R. 5. 13. [In mythology, the sun is regarded as a son of Kasyapa and Aditi ; cf. *S.* 7. 20. He is represented as moving in a chariot drawn by seven horses, with Aruṇa for his charioteer. He is represented as all-seeing, the constant beholder of the good and bad deeds of mortals. Sanjṇa (or Chhaya or Asvini) was his principal wife, by whom he had Yama and Yamuna, the two Asvins and Saturn. He is also represented as having been the father of Manu Vaivasvata, the founder of the solar race of kings.]. **2** The tree called *Arka.* **3** The number 'twelve' (derived from the twelve forms of the sun). **-Comp. -अपायः** sunset ; Me. 80. **-अर्घ्यं** the presentation of an offering to the sun. **-अश्मन्** *m.* the sun-stone. **-अश्वः** a horse of the sun. **-अस्तं** sunset. **-आतपः** heat or glare of the sun, sunshine. **-आलोकः** sunshine. **-आवर्तः** a kind of sun-flower. **-आह्व** *a.* named after the sun. (**-ह्वः**) the gigantic swallow-wort. (**-ह्वं**) copper. **-इंदुसंगमः;** the day of the new moon (the conjunction of the sun and moon); दर्शः सूर्येंदुसंगमः Ak. **-उत्थानं, -उदयः** sun-rise. **-ऊढः 1** 'brought by the sun', an evening guest ; Pt. 1. **2** the time of sunset. **-कांतः** the sun-stone, sun crystal ; *S.* 2. 7. **-कांतिः** *f.* **1** sunlight. **2** a particular flower. **3** the flower of sesamum. **-कालः** day-time, day. **°अनलचक्रं** a particular astrological diagram for indicating good and bad fortune. **-ग्रहः 1** the sun. **2** an eclipse of the sun. **3** an epithet of Râhu and Ketu. **4** the bottom of a water-jar. **-ग्रहणं** a solar eclipse. **-चंद्रौ** (so **सूर्याचंद्रमसौ**) *m. du.* the sun and moon. **-जः, -तनयः, -पुत्रः 1** epithets of Sugrîva. **2** of Karṇa. **3** of the planet Saturn. **4** of Yama. **-जा, -तनया** the river Yamunâ. **-तेजस्** *n.* the radiance or heat of the sun. **-नक्षत्रं** that constellation (out of the 27) in which the sun happens to be. **-पर्वन्** *n.* a solar festival, (on the days of the solstices, equinoxes, eclipses &c.). **-प्रभव** *a.* sprung or descended from the sun ; R. 1. 2. **-फणिचक्रं** = सूर्यकालानलचक्रं q. v. above. **-भक्त** *a.* one who worships the sun. (**-क्तः**) the tree Bandhûka or its flower. **-मणिः** the sun-stone. **-मंडलं** the orb of the sun. **-यंत्रं 1** a representation of the sun (used in worshipping him). **2** an instrument used in taking solar observations. **-रश्मिः** a ray of the sun, sun-beam. **-लोकः** the heaven of the sun. **-वंशः** the Solar race of kings (who ruled at Ayodhyâ). **-वर्चस्** *a.* resplendent as the sun. -विलोकनं the ceremony of taking a child out to see the sun when four months old ; cf. उपनिष्क्रमणं. -संक्रमः, -संक्रांतिः *f.* the sun's passage from one zodiacal sign to another. -संज्ञं saffron. -सारथिः an epithet of Aruṇa. -स्तुतिः *f.*, -स्तोत्रं a hymn addressed to the sun. -हृदयं N. of a hymn to the sun.

सूर्या The wife of the sun.

सूष् 1 P. (सूषति) To bring forth, bear, produce, beget.

सूषणा A mother.

सूष्यंती A woman about to be confined, one who is parturient.

सृ 1. 3 P. (सरति, सिसर्ति, also धावति, सृत) 1 To go, move, proceed; मृगाः प्रदक्षिणं सस्रुः Bk. 14. 14. 2 To go towards, approach ; निष्पाद्य हरयः सेतुं प्रतीताः सस्रुरर्णवं Râm. 3 To rush upon, assail ; (तं) ससाराभिमुखः शूरः शार्दूल इव कुंजरं Mb. 4 To run, go fast, slip away from ; सरति सहसा बाह्वोर्मध्यं गताप्यबला सती M. 4 11. 5 To blow (as wind) : तं चेद्वायौ सरति सरलस्कंधसंघट्टजन्मा Me. 53. 6 To flow. *-Caus.* (सारयति-ते) 1 To cause to go or move. 2 To extend. 3 To rub, touch gently (with the fingers); तंत्रीमार्द्रां नयनसलिलैः सारयित्वा कथंचित् Me. 86. 4 To push back or away, remove ; सारयंतीं गंडाभोगात्कठिनविषमामेकवेणीं करेण Me. 92. *-Desid.* (सिसीर्षति) To wish to go &c. -WITH अनु 1 to follow (in all senses), go after, attend, pursue. 2 to go to, betake oneself to; पूर्वोद्दिष्टामनुसर पुरीं Me. 30 ; तेनोदीचीं दिशमनुसरेः 57. 3 to go over or through. (*-Caus.*) 1 to lead forward ; वायुरनुसारयतीव मां Râm. 2 to follow. -अप 1 to go away, retire, withdraw ; यदपसरति मेषः कारणं तत्प्रहर्तुं Pt. 3. 43. 2 to vanish, disappear. (*-Caus.*) to cause to go away, take or put away , remove, withdraw, drive off ; अपसारय घनसारं K. P. 9 ; Ms. 7. 149. -अभि 1 to go to, approach ; Ki. 8. 4. 2 to go or advance to meet (as at an appointed place); meet by appointment; सुंदरीरभिससार K.; Si. 6. 26. 3 to assail, attack. (*-Caus.*) to meet by appointment, go to meet ; बल्लभानभिसिसारयिषूणां Si. 10. 20 ; Ki. 9. 38 ; S. D. 115. -उद् (*-Caus.*) to drive away, expel. -उप 1 to go to, approach ; R. 19. 16. 2 to wait upon, visit ; कैलासनाथमुपसृत्य निवर्तमाना V. 1. 3. 3 to go against, attack. 4 to have intercourse with. -निस् 1 to go away from, go forth or out, slip away from ; issue from; बाणैः खरकार्मुकनिःसृतैः Râm. ; so वसुधांतनिःसृतमिवाहिपतेः Si. 9. 25. 2 to depart, set-out for ; Ms. 6. 4. 3 to flow forth, ooze out, exude ; यो हेमकुंभस्तननिःसृतानां स्कंदस्य मातुः पयसां रसज्ञः R. 2. 36. (*-Caus.*) to drive away, expel, turn out. -परि 1 to flow round ; एनं सरस्वती परिससार Ait. Br. ; परिसस्रुरापः Mb. 2 to move round; whirl round ; प्रदक्षिणं तं परिसृत्य Bhâg. ; परिसरति v. l. for परिपतति) शिखी भ्रांतिमद्वारियंत्र M. 2. 13. -प्र 1 to flow forth, spring, arise, proceed; लोहिताद्या महानद्यः प्रसस्रुस्तत्र चासकृत् Mb. 2 to go forth, advance ; वेलानिलाय प्रसृता भुजंगाः R. 13. 12 ; अन्वेषणप्रसृते च मित्रगणे Dk. 3 to spread, spread round ; कृशानुः किं साक्षात्प्रसरति दिशो नैष नियतं K. P. 10 ; प्रसरति तृणमध्ये लब्धवृद्धिः क्षणेन (दवाग्निः) Rs. 1. 25. 4 to spread, prevail, pervade ; प्रसरति परिमाथी कोप्ययं देहदाहः Mâl. 1. 41 ; भित्त्वा भित्त्वा प्रसरति बलात्कोपि चेतोविकारः U. 3. 36. 5 to be stretched, to extend ; न मे हस्तौ प्रसरतः S. 2. 6 to be disposed or inclined to (do a thing), move ; न मे उचितेषु करणीयेषु हस्तपादं प्रसरति S. 4 ; प्रसरति मनः कार्यारंभे. 7 to prevail, begin, commence ; प्रससार चोत्सवः Ks. 16. 85. 8 to be long, be lengthened ; V. 3. 22. 9 to grow strong or intense ; प्रसृततरं सख्यं Dk. 10 to pass away (as time). (*-Caus.*) 1 to spread, stretch ; Bk. 10. 44. 2 to stretch forward, extend, hold out (as the hand) : कालः सर्वजनान् प्रसारितकरो गृह्णाति दूरादपि Pt. 2. 20. 3 to spread out or expose for sale ; क्रेतारः क्रीणीयुरिति बुद्ध्यापणे प्रसारितं क्रय्यं Sk. ; Ms. 5. 129. 4 to open wide, expand (as eyes). 5 to publish, promulgate, circulate. -प्रति 1 to go back, return. 2 to go towards, rush upon, attack, assail ; दैत्यः प्रत्यसरद्देवं मत्तो मत्तमिव द्विपम् Hariv. (*-Caus.*) to push backwards, replace ; कनकवलयं स्रस्तं स्रस्तं मया प्रतिसार्यते S. 3. 13. -वि to spread, be extended, be diffused ; चक्रीवदंगरुहधूम्ररुचो विसस्रुः Si. 5 8, 9. 19, 37 ; Ki. 10. 53. (*-Caus.*) 1 to spread, stretch. 2 to cause to prevail. -सं 1 to spread. 2 to move. 3 to go or flow together. 4 to go to, obtain ; पापान् संसृत्य संसारान् प्रेष्यतां यांति शत्रुषु Ms. 12. 70. (*-Caus.*) 1 to spread over, 2 to cause to revolve or turn round ; जन्मवृद्धिक्षयैर्नित्यं संसारयति चक्रवत् Ms. 12. 124.

सृकः 1 Air, wind. 2 An arrow. 3 A thunderbolt. 4 A lotus (कैरव).

सृकंडुः *f.* Itch.

सृकालः A jackal ; see शृगाल.

सृक्कं, **सृक्कणी**, **सृक्कन्** *n.*, **सृक्किणी**, **सृक्किन्** *n.*, **सृकं**, **सृकणी**, **सृकन्** *n.*, **सृकिणी**, **सृकिन्** *n.* — The corner of the mouth ; सृक्कणी परिलोलिहन् Pt. 1.

सृगः A sort of arrow or javelin, a sling (भिंदिपाल).

सृगालः A jackal ; see शृगाल.

सृका A kind of garland made of jewels.

सृज् I. 6 P. (सृजति, सृष्ट) 1 To create, produce, make (in general) ; to procreate, beget (progeny &c.) ; अर्धेन नारी तस्यां स विराजमसृजत् प्रभुः Ms. 1. 32, 33, 34, 36 ; तंतुनाभः स्वत एव तंतून् सृजति S. B. 2 To put on, place on, apply. 3 To let go, let loose, release. 4 To emit, shed, effuse, pour forth or out ; अस्राक्षुरस्रं करुणं रुवंतः Bk. 3. 17 ; आनंदशीतामिव बाष्पवृष्टिं हिमस्रुतिं हैमवतीं ससर्ज R. 16. 44, 8. 35. 5 To send forth, utter (as words) ; Ku. 2. 53, 7. 47. 6 To throw, cast. 7 To leave, quit, abandon, send away. -II. 4 A. (सृज्यते) To be let loose or sent forth. *-Desid.* (सिसृक्षति) To wish to create &c. -WITH अति 1 to give, bestow ; V. 1. 15 ; R. 11. 48. 2 to abandon, dismiss. 3 to emit. 4 to permit, allow. -अभि to give, grant. -अव 1 to cast, throw, sow, plant (as seed) ; अप एव ससर्जादौ तासु बीजमवासृजत् Ms. 1. 8. 2 to shed, drop down ; U. 3. 23. 3 to let loose. -उद् 1 to pour out, emit, send forth or down ; व्यलीकनिःश्वासमिवोत्ससर्ज Ku. 3. 25 ; सहस्रगुणमुत्स्रष्टुमादत्ते हि रसं रविः R. 1. 18 ' to pour down, give back or return '. 2 (*a*) to quit, leave, abandon ; R. 5. 51, 6. 46 ; Ku. 2. 36. (*b*) to lay aside, put off ; स च चापमुत्सृज्य विवृद्धमन्युः R. 3. 60, 4. 54. 3 to let loose, allow to roam at liberty; तुरंगमुत्सृष्टमनर्गलं पुनः R. 3. 39. 4 to discharge, throw, shoot ; Bk. 14. 45. 5 to sow, scatter (as seed). 6 to present, give. 7 to stretch out, extend. 8 to dismiss. 9 to send away. 10 to abolish, restrict. -उप 1 to pour out or on, offer (water &c). 2 to add to, annex, join, attach, connect ; सुखं दुःखोपसृष्टम्. 3 to beset with, oppress, infest ; रोगोपसृष्टतनुदुर्वसतिं मुमुक्षुः R. 8. 94. 4 to eclipse ; Ms. 4. 37 ; Y. 1. 272. 5 to produce, effect. 6 to destroy. -नि 1 to set free, release ; न स्वामिना निसृष्टोपि शूद्रो दास्याद्विमुच्यते Ms. 8. 414. 2 to deliver over, consign, entrust ; cf. निसृष्ट. -प्र 1 to leave, abandon. 2 to let loose. 3 to sow, scatter. 4 to injure, hurt. -वि 1 to abandon, leave, give up ; विसृज सुंदरि संगमसाध्वसं M. 4. 13; पूर्वार्धविसृष्टतल्पः R.16.6; Bv.1. 78. 2 to let go, to let loose. 3 to shed, pour down ; R. 13. 26. 4 to send, despatch ; भोजेन दूतो रघवे विसृष्टः R. 5. 39. 5 to dismiss, allow to go, send away ; R. 8. 91, 14. 19. 6 to give ; R. 13. 67, 18. 7. 7 to send or cast forth, omit, dart;

विसृजति हिमगर्भैरग्निमिन्दुर्मयूखैः S. 3. 2. 8 to drop, let fall, strike ; विसृज शुभ्रमुनौ कृपाणं U. 2. 10. 9 to utter ; Si. 15. 62. 10 to cast off, repudiate. –सं 1 to mix, mingle, unite with, bring in contact with ; संसृज्यते सरसिजैररुणांशुभिन्नैः R. 5. 69 ; अस्ना रक्षः संसृजतात् Ait. Br. 2 to join, meet ; सौमित्रिणा तदनु संससृजे R. 13. 73 ; Ku. 7. 74. 3 to create.

सृजिकाक्षारः Natron, alkali.

सृंजयाः *m. pl.* N. of a people.

सृणिः *f.* A goad, a hook to drive an elephant ; मदांधकरिणां दर्पोपशान्त्यै सृणिः H. 2. 165 ; Si. 5. 5. –**णिः** 1 An enemy. 2 The moon.

सृणि(णी)का Saliva, spittle.

सृतिः *f.* 1 Going, gliding ; Ms. 6. 63. 2 A way, road, path (fig. also); (नैते सृती पार्थ जानन् योगी मुह्यति कश्चन Bg. 8. 27. 3 Hurting, injuring.

सृत्वर *a.* (**री** *f.*) Going, moving. –**री** 1 A stream, river. 2 A mother.

सृदरः A snake.

सृदाकुः 1 Air, wind. 2 Fire. 3 A deer. 4 The thunderbolt of Indra. 5 The sun's disc or orb. –*f.* A river, stream.

सृप् 1 P. (सर्पति, सृप्त ; *desid.* सिसृप्सति) 1 To creep, crawl, glide gently. 2 To go, move. –With **अनु** 1 to go towards, approach ; गिरिमन्वसृपद्रामः Bk. 6. 27. 2 to follow ; Bk. 15. 59. –**अप** 1 to go away, withdraw, retire ; तत्त्वारितमनेन तरुगहनेनापसर्पत U. 4. 2 to glide away, move gently along. 3 to observe closely (as a spy) ; U. 1. 4 to swerve from, leave. –**उद्** 1 to glide or soar upwards. 2 to go up to, approach ; सरित्प्रवाहस्तटमुत्ससर्प R. 5. 46. –**उप** 1 to approach, go near ; M. 1. 12. 2 to move, go ; Pt. 3. 23. 3 to go to, attain to, undergo ; दुःखं, सुखं &c. 4 to begin ; Ms. 10. 105. 5 to attack. –**परि** 1 to move round about, hover. 2 to move to and fro. –**प्र** 1 to go forth, come out or forth, proceed ; Bk. 14. 20. 2 to spread, circulate (fig. also) ; रुधिरेण प्रसर्पता Mb. ; आलर्कं विषमिव सर्वतः प्रसृप्तं U. 1. 40. –**वि** 1 to move, march, proceed ; यः सुबाहुरिति राक्षसोऽपरस्तत्र तत्र विससर्प मायया R. 11. 29, 4. 53. 2 to fly or roam about. 3 to spread ; मनोरागस्तीव्रं विषमिव विसर्पत्यविरतं Mâl 2. 1. 4 to flow along, fall down ; (बाष्पौघः) विसर्पन् धाराभिर्लुठति धरणीं जर्जरकणः U. 1. 26. 5 to sneak off, escape. 6 to hover about. 7 to wind, meander. 8 to go about in different directions. –**सं** 1 to move ; संसर्पत्या सपदि भवतः स्रोतसि च्छाययासौ Me. 51. 2 to move along, flow ; Me. 29.

सृपाटः A kind of measure.

सृपाटिका The beak of a bird.

सृपाटी A kind of measure.

सृमः The moon.

सृभ्, सृंभ् 1 P. (सर्भति, सृंभति) To hurt, injure, kill.

सृमर *a.* (**री** *f.*) Going, moving. –**रः** A kind of deer.

सृष्ट *p. p.* 1 Created, produced. 2 Poured out, emitted. 3 Let loose. 4 Left, abandoned. 5 Dismissed, sent away. 6 Ascertained, determined. 7 Connected, joined. 8 Much, abundant, numerous. 9 Ornamented; see सृज्.

सृष्टिः *f.* 1 Creation, anything created, किं मानसी सृष्टिः S. 4 ; या सृष्टिः स्रष्टुराद्या S. 1. 1 ; स्त्रीरत्नसृष्टिरपरा प्रतिभाति सा मे S. 2. 9 ; सृष्टिराद्येव धातुः Me. 82. 2 The creation of the world. 3 Nature, natural property. 4 Letting loose, emission. 5 Giving away, a gift. 6 The existence of properties or qualities. 7 The absence of properties. –**Comp.** –**कर्तृ** *m.* the creator.

सॄ 9 P. (सृणाति) To hurt, injure, kill.

सेक् 1 A. (सेकते) To go, move.

सेकः 1 Sprinkling, watering (trees) सेकः सीकरिणा करेण विहितः कामं U. 3. 16, R. 1. 51, 8. 45, 16. 30, 17. 16. 2 Emission, effusion. 3 Seminal effusion. 4 A libation, an offering. –**Comp.** –**पात्रं** 1 a pot for sprinkling water, a watering-pot. 2 a bucket.

सेकिमं A radish.

सेक्तृ *a.* (**क्त्री** *f.*) One who sprinkles &c. –*m.* 1 A sprinkler. 2 A husband.

सेक्त्रं A bucket, watering-pot.

सेचक *a.* (**चिका** *f.*) Sprinkling. –**कः** A cloud.

सेचनं 1 Sprinkling, watering ; वृक्षसेचने द्वे धारयसि मे S. 1. 2 Effusion, aspersion. 3 Oozing, dripping. 4 A bucket. –**Comp.** –**घटः** a watering pot.

सेचनी A bucket.

सेडुः 1 Water melon. 2 A kind of cucumber.

सेतिका N. of Ayodhyâ.

सेतुः 1 A ridge of earth, mound, bank, causeway, dam ; नलिनीं क्षतसेतुबंधनो जलसंघात इवासि विद्रुतः Ku. 4. 6, R. 16. 2. 2 A bridge in general ; वैदेहि पश्यामलयाद्विभक्तं मत्सेतुना फेनिलमंबराशिं R. 13. 2 ; सैन्यैर्बद्धद्विरदसेतुभिः 4. 38, 12. 70 ; Ku. 7. 53. 3 A land-mark ; Ms. 8. 245. 4 A defile, pass, a narrow mountain-road. 5 A boundary, limit. 6 A barrier, limitation, obstruction of any kind ; दूष्येयुः सर्ववर्णाश्च भिद्येरन् सर्वसेतवः Subhâsh. 7 A fixed rule or law, an established institution. 8 The sacred syllable *om.* मंत्राणां प्रणवः सेतुस्तत्सेतुः प्रणवः स्मृतः । स्रवत्यनोंकृतं पूर्वं परस्ताच्च विदीर्यते Kâlikâ. P. –**Comp.** –**बंधः** 1 the forming or construction of a bridge, causeway &c. ; वयोगते किं वनिताविलासो जले गते किं खलु सेतुबंधः Subhâsh. ; Ku. 4. 6. 2 the ridge of rocks extending from the southern extremity of the Coromandel coast towards Ceylon (said to have been built for Râma's passage to Lankâ by Nala and the other monkeys). 3 any bridge or causeway. –**भेदिन्** *a.* 1 breaking down barriers. 2 removing obstructions. (–*m.*) N. of a tree (दंती).

सेतुकः 1 A bank, cause-way, bridge. 2 A pass.

सेत्रं A bond, fetter.

सेदिवस् *a.* (**सेदुषी** *f.*) Sitting.

सेन *a.* Having a lord, possessing a master or leader.

सेना 1 Army ; सेना परिच्छदस्तस्य द्वयमेवार्थसाधनं R. 1. 19. 2 Army personified as the wife of Kârtikeya, the god of war ; cf. देवसेना. –**Comp.** –**अग्रं** the van or front of an army. °**गः** the leader or general of an army. –**अंगं** a component part of an army ; (these are four:—हस्त्यश्वरथपादातं सेनांगं स्याच्चतुष्टयं). –**चरः** 1 a soldier. 2 a camp-follower. –**निवेशः** the camp of an army ; R. 5. 49.–**नी** *m.* 1 a leader of an army, commander, general ; सेनानीनामहं स्कंदः Bg. 10. 24 ; Ku. 2. 51. 2 N. of Kârtikeya; अथैनमद्रेस्तनया शुशोच सेनान्यमालीढमिवासुरास्त्रैः R. 2. 37. –**पतिः** 1 a general. 2 N. of Kârtikeya. –**परिच्छद्** *a.* surrounded by an army ; (in R. 1. 19 सेनापरिच्छदः is sometimes taken as one word and is interpreted in this way, but it is much better to take them as separate words). –**पृष्ठं** the rear of an army. –**भंगः** the breaking of an army, complete rout, disorderly flight. –**मुखं** 1 a division of an army. 2 particularly, a division of an army consisting of three elephants, as many chariots, nine horse and fifteen foot. 3 a mound in front of a city-gate. –**योगः** the equipment of an army. –**रक्षः** a guard, sentinel.

सेफः The penis ; cf. शेफ.

सेमंती The Indian white rose.

सेरः A kind of measure (Mar. शेर); it is thus defined in Lîlâvatî :—पादोनगद्याणकतुल्यटंकैर्द्विसप्ततुल्यैः कथितोऽत्र सेरः ॥.

सेराहः A horse of a milk-white colour.

सेरु *a.* Binding, fastening.

सेल् 1 P. (सेलति) To go, move.

सेव् 1 A. (सेवते, सेवित ; *caus.* सेवयति-ते, *desid.* सिसेविषते; the स् of सेव् is generally changed to ष् after prepositions ending in इ such as नि, परि, वि) 1 To serve, wait or attend upon, honour, worship, obey ; प्रायो भृत्यास्त्यजंति प्रचलितविभवं स्वामिनं सेवमानाः Mu. 4. 21 ; or ऐश्वर्यादनपेतमीश्वरमयं लोकोऽर्थतः सेवते 1. 14. 2 To go after, pursue, follow. 3 To use, enjoy ; किं सेव्यते सुमनसां मनसापि गंधः कस्तूरिकाजननशक्तिभृता मृगेण R. G. 4 To enjoy carnally ; Bv. 1. 118. 5 To attach or devote oneself to, attend to, cultivate, practise, perform; Ms. 2. 1; Ku. 5. 38, R. 17. 49. 6 To resort to, betake oneself to, dwell in, frequent, inhabit; तत्तं वारि विहाय तीरनलिनीं कारंडवः सेवते V. 2. 23, Pt. 1. 9. 7 To watch over, guard, protect. –WITH आ 1 to enjoy; यद्वायुरेन्विष्टमृगैः किरातैरासेव्यते भिन्नशिखंडिबर्हः Ku. 1. 15; प्रवातमासेवमानां तिष्ठति M.1. 2 to practise, perform. 3 to resort to. –उप 1 to serve, worship, honour; Ms. 4. 133. 2 o practise, follow, cultivate, pursue. 3 to be addicted to, enjoy; Bg. 15. 9. 4 to frequent, inhabit. 5 to rub or anoint with. –नि 1 to pursue, follow, attach oneself to, practise; S. 1. 27. 2 to enjoy; निषेवते श्रांतमना विविक्तं S. 5. 5; Ku. 1. 6. 3 to enjoy carnally; यथा यथा तामरसेक्षणा मया पुनः सरागं नितरां निषेविता Bv. 2. 155. 4 to resort to, inhabit, frequent; Ku. 5. 76. 5 to use, employ; विषतां निषेवितमपाक्रियया समुपैति सर्वमिति सत्यमदः Si. 9. 68. 6 to wait upon, attend. 7 to draw near, approach. 8 to suffer, experience. –परि 1 to resort to. 2 to enjoy, take.

सेव See सेवन.

सेवक *a.* 1 Serving, worshipping, honouring. 2 Practising, following. 3 Dependent, servile. –**कः** 1 A servant, dependant; सेवया धनमिच्छद्भिः सेवकैः पश्य किं कृतम्। स्वातंत्र्यं यच्छरीरस्य मूढैस्तदपि हारितं H. 2. 20. 2 A votary, worshipper. 3 A sewer. 4 A sack.

सेवधि *ind.* See शेवधि under शेव.

सेवनं 1 The act of serving, service, attendance upon, worship; पात्रीकृतात्मा गुरुसेवनेन R. 18. 30. 2 Following, practising, employing; Ms. 12. 52. 3 Using, enjoying. 4 Enjoying carnally; यत्करोत्येकरात्रेण वृषलीसेवनाद्द्विजः Ms. 11. 179. 5 Sewing, stitching. 6 A sack.

सेवनी 1 A needle. 2 A seam. 3 A suture or seam-like union of parts of the body.

सेवा 1 Service, servitude, dependence; attendance; सेवां लाघवकारिणीं कृतधियः स्थाने श्ववृत्तिं विदुः Mu. 3. 14; हीनसेवा न कर्तव्या H. 3. 11. 2 Worship, homage, honouring. 3 Addiction or devotion to, fondness for. 4 Use, practice, employment, exercise. 5 Frequenting, resorting to. 6 Flattery, coaxing or flattering words; अलं सेवया मध्यस्थतां गृहीत्वा भण M. 3. –**Comp.** –**आकार** *a.* in the form of servitude; V. 3. 1. –**काकुः** change of voice in service; (this is a variant in V. 3. 1 for सेवाकारा). –**धर्मः** 1 the duty of service; सेवाधर्मः परमगहनो योगिनामप्यगम्यः Pt. 1. 285. 2 the obligations of service. –**व्यवहारः** the practice or law of service.

सेवि *n.* 1 The jujube. 2 An apple.

सेवित *p. p.* 1 Served, attended upon, worshipped. 2 Followed, practised, pursued. 3 Frequented by, resorted to, inhabited by, haunted by. 4 Enjoyed, used. –**तं** 1 An apple. 2 The jujube.

सेवितृ *m.* An attendant, a dependant.

सेविन् *a.* 1 Serving, worshipping. 2 Following, practising, using. 3 Inhabiting, dwelling. –*m.* A servant.

सेव्य *a.* 1 To be served or waited upon. 2 To be used or employed. 3 To be enjoyed. 4 To be taken care of or guarded. –**व्यः** 1 A master (opp. सेवक); भयं तावत् सेव्यादभिनिविशते सेवकजनं Mu. 5. 12, Pt. 1. 48. 2 The Asvattha tree. –**व्यं** A kind of root. –**Comp.** –**सेवकौ** *m. dual* master and servant.

सै 1 P. (सायति) To waste away, decline, perish.

सैंह *a.* (**ही** *f.*) Belonging to a lion, leonine; द्युतिं सैंहीं किं श्वा धृतकनकमालोऽपि लभते H. 1. 175.

सैंहल *a.* Belonging to, growing or produced in, Ceylon.

सैंहिकः, –**सैंहिकेयः** A metronymic of Râhu, q. v.

सैकत *a.* (**ती** *f.*) 1 Consisting or made of sand, sandy, gravelly; तोयस्येवाप्रतिहतरयः सैकतं सेतुमोघः U. 3. 36. 2 Having sandy soil –**तं** 1 A sand-bank; सुरगज इव गांगं सैकतं सुप्रतीकः R. 5. 75, 5. 8; 10. 69, 13. 17, 62; 14. 76; 16. 21; Ku. 1. 29; S. 6 17. 2 An island with sandy shores. 3 A bank or shore (in general). –**Comp.** –**इष्टं** ginger.

सैकतिक *a.* (**की** *f.*) 1 Belonging or relating to a sand-bank. 2 Fluctuating, wavering, living in doubt and error (संदेहजीविन्). –**कः** 1 A religious mendicant. 2 An ascetic. –**कं** A thread worn round the wrist or neck to secure good fortune.

सैद्धांतिकः *a.* (**की** *f.*) 1 Relating to a dogma or demonstrated trutn. 2 One who knows the real truth.

सैनापत्यं The command of an army, generalship; Ku. 2. 61.

सैनिक *a.* (**की** *f.*) 1 Relating to army. 2 Martial, military. –**कः** 1 A soldier; पपात भूमौ सह सैनिकाश्रुभिः R. 3. 61. 2 A guard, sentinel. 3 The body of troops drawn up in battle-array; R. 3. 57.

सैंधव *a.* (**वी** *f.*) 1 Produced or born in the Sindhu-territory. 2 Belonging to the Indus. 3 River-born. 4 Belonging to the sea, oceanic, marine. –**वः** 1 A horse, especially, one bred in *Sindhu*; N. 1. 71. 2 N. of a sage. 3 N. of a country. –**वः**, –**वं** A kind of rock-salt. –**वाः** *m.* pl. The people inhabiting the *Sindhu*-territory. –**Comp.** –**घनः** a lump of salt. –**शिला** a kind of rock or fossil salt.

सैंधवक *a.* (**की** *f.*) Relating to the Saindhavas. –**कः** A miserable inhabitant of *Sindhu*.

सैंधी A sort of spirituous liquor (perhaps from palm-juice.)

सैन्यः 1 A soldier; Si. 5. 28. 2 A guard, sentinel. –**न्यं** An army, a troop; स प्रतस्थेऽरिनाशाय हरिसैन्यैरनुद्रुतः R. 12. 67.

सैमंतिकं Red lead.

सैरंध्री, **सैरिंध्रः** 1 A menial servant or attendant. 2 A mixed tribe, the offspring of a *Dasgu* and an *Ayogava* female; सैरिंध्रं वागुरावृत्तिं सूते दस्युरयोगवे Ms. 10. 32.

सैरंध्री, **सैरिंध्री** 1 A maid-servant or female attendant in the women's apartments (a woman of the mixed tribe describeb in सैरंध्र (2). 2 An independent female artizan working in another person's house. 3 An epithet of Draupadî (assumed by her when she acted as servant to Sudheshṇâ, queen of Virâṭa.).

सैरिक *a.* (**की** *f.*) 1 Relating to a plough. 2 Having furrows. –**कः** 1 A plough-ox. 2 A ploughman.

सैरिभः 1 A buffalo; अवमानित इव कुलीनो दीर्घं निःश्वसिति सैरिभः Mk. 4. 2 Indra's heaven or Svarga.

सैवाल See शैवाल.

सैसक *a.* (**की** *f.*) Leaden, of lead.

सो 4 P. (स्यति, सित; *caus.* साययति-ते, *desid.* सिषासति; *pass.* सीयते; the स् of सो is changed to ष् after prepositions ending in इ or उ) 1 To kill, destroy. 2 To finish, complete, bring to an end. –WITH अव 1 to finish, complete; यूपवत्यवसिते क्रियाविधौ R. 11. 37; अवसितमंडनासि S. 4. 2 to destroy. 3 to know; Bk. 19. 29. 4 to fail, be at an end (intrans.); शक्तिर्ममावस्यति हीनयुद्धे Ki. 16. 17. –**अध्यव** 1 to resolve, determine, make up one's mind; कथमिदानीं दुर्जनवचनादध्यवसितं देवेन U. 1; अभिघातुमध्यवससौ न गिरा Si. 9. 76. 2 to attempt, undertake, perform; मा साहसमध्यवस्यः Dk.; वक्तुं सुकरमध्यवसातुं दुष्करं Ve. 3 'sooner said than done.' 3 to grapple with. 4 to think, reflect. –**पर्यव** 1 to complete; finish. 2 to determine, resolve. 3 to result in, be reduced to, to end in; एष एव समुच्चयः सद्योगेऽसद्योगे सदसद्योगे च पर्यवस्यतीति न पृथक् लक्ष्यते K. P. 10. 4 to perish, be lost, decline. 5 to attempt. –**व्यव** 1 to strive, endeavour, try, seek, attempt, set about; ध्रुवं स नीलोत्पलपत्रधारया शमीलतां छेत्तुमृषिर्व्यवस्यति S. 1. 18. 2 to think of, wish, desire; पातुं न प्रथमं व्यवस्यति जलं युष्मास्वपीतेषु या S. 4. 9. 3 to exert strenuously, be industrious or diligent. 4 to resolve, determine, settle, decide; S. 5. 18. 5 to accept, undertake; कच्चित्सौम्य व्यवसितमिदं बंधुकृत्यं त्वया मे Me. 114. 6 to do, perform. 7 to believe, be convinced or persuaded. 8 to reflect. -समव to decide, decree ; Ms. 7. 13.

सोढ *p. p.* Borne, suffered, endured, put up with &c. ; see सह्.

सोढृ *a.* (ढ्री *f.*) **1** Enduring, bearing, patient. **2** Powerful, able.

सोत्क, सोत्कंठ *a.* **1** Ardently longing, impatiently eager, anxious ; as in सोत्कंठमालिंगनम्. **2** Regretful. **3** Bewailing, sorrowing. -ठं *ind.* **1** With ardent or eager longing, anxiously ; प्रोड्डीयेव बलाकया सरभसं सोत्कंठमालिंगितः Mk. 5. 23. **2** Regretfully, sorrowfully.

सोत्प्रास *a.* **1** Excessive. **2** Exaggerated. **3** Ironical, sarcastic. -सः Violent laughter. -सः -सं Ironical exaggeration, sarcasm, irony ; cf. व्याजस्तुति.

सोत्सव *a.* Festive, making merry, joyous.

सोत्साह *a* Vigorous, active, energetic, persevering. -हं *ind.* Actively, energetically, carefully.

सोत्सुक *a.* Regretful, repining, anxious, sorrowful.

सोत्सेध *a.* Raised, elevated, high, lofty ; सोत्सेधैः स्कंधदेशैः Mu. 4. 7.

सोदर *a.* Born from the same womb, uterine -रः A uterine brother. -रा A uterine sister.

सोदर्यः A co-uterine brother, brother of whole blood ; (fig. also) ; भ्रातुः सोदर्यमात्मानमिंद्रजिद्वधशोभिनः R. 15. 26 ; अवज्ञासोदर्यं दारिद्र्यं Dk.

सोद्योग *a.* Making vigorous exertions diligent, active, persevering industrious.

सोद्वेग *a.* **1** Anxious, anprehensive. **2** Sorrowful. -गं *ind.* Anxiously, eagerly.

सोनहः Garlic.

सोन्माद *a.* Mad, insane, frantic.

सोपकरण *a.* Provided with all requisite materials or implements, properly equipped ; so **सोपकार.**

सोपद्रव *a.* Visited with calamities or afflictions.

सोपध *a.* Full of fraud or deceit, deceitful.

सोपाधि *a.* Fraudulent. -*ind.* Deceitfully, fraudulently ; अरिषु हि विजयार्थिनः क्षितीशा विदधति सोपधि संधिदूषणानि Ki. 1. 45.

सोपप्लव *a.* **1** Afflicted with any great calamity. **2** Invaded or overrun by enemies. **3** Eclipsed (as the sun or moon).

सोपरोध *a.* **1** Obstructed, impeded. **2** Favoured. -धं *ind.* Obligingly, respectfully.

सोपसर्ग *a.* **1** Afflicted or visited by any great calamity or misfortune. **2** Portentous. **3** Possessed by an evil spirit. **4** Preceded by a prepositional prefix (in gram.).

सोपहास *a.* Accompanied with derisive laughter, sneering, sarcastic. -सं *ind.* Sneeringly, with a sneer.

सोपाकः A man of a degraded caste ; see Ms. 10. 38.

सोपाधि *a.*, **सोपाधिक** *a.* (की *f.*) **1** Restricted by some conditions or limitations, qualified by particular characteristics, limited, qualified (in phil.). **2** Having some peculiar attribute.

सोपानं Steps, stairs, a staircase, ladder ; आरोहणार्थं नवयौवनेन कामस्य सोपानमिव प्रयुक्तं Ku. 1. 39. **-Comp.** पंक्तिः *f.*, -पथः, -पद्धतिः *f.*, -परंपरा, -मार्गः a flight of steps, a staircase; वापी चास्मिन् मरकतशिलाबद्धसोपानमार्गा Me. 76 ; समारुरुक्षुर्दिवमायुषः क्षये ततान सोपानपरंपरामिव R. 3. 69, 6. 3, 16. 56.

सोमः **1** N. of a plant, the most important ingredient in ancient sacrificial offerings. **2** The juice of the plant ; as in सोमपा, सोमपीथिन्. **3** Nectar, beverage of the gods. **4** The moon. [In mythology, the moon is represented as having sprung from the eye of the sage Atri ; (cf, R. 2. 75). or as produced from the sea at the time of churning. The twenty-seven asterisms-mythologically represented as so many daughters of Daksha q. v.—are said to be his wives. The phenomenon of the periodical waning of the moon is explained by a myth which states that his nectareous digits are drunk up by different gods in regular rotation, or by the invention of another legend which says that the moon, on account of his particular fondness and partiality for Rohini, one of the 27 daughters of Daksha, was cursed by his father-in-law to be consumptive, but that at the intercession of his wives the sentence of eternal consumption was commuted to one of periodical consumption. Soma is also represented as having carried off *Tara*, the wife of Brihaspati, by whom he had a son named Budha, who afterwards became the founder of the lunar race of kings; see *Tara* (*b*) also]. **5** A ray of light. **6** Camphor. **7** Water. **8** Air, wind. **9** N. of Kubera. **10** Of *Siva*. **11** Of Yama. **12** (As the last member of comp.) Chief, principal, best ; as in नृसोम q. v. -मं **1** Rice-gruel. **2** Sky, heaven. **-Comp.** -अभिषवः the extraction of Soma juice. -अहः Monday. -आख्यं the red lotus. -ईश्वरः a celebrated representation of *Siva*. -उद्भवा N. of the river Narmadâ ; R. 5. 59 ; (where Malli. quotes Ak. रेवा तु नर्मदा सोमोद्भवा मेकलकन्यका). -कांतः the moon-stone. -क्षयः disappearance or waning of the moon. -ग्रहः a vessel for holding Soma. -ज *a.* moon-born. (-जः) an epithet of the planet Mercury. (-जं) milk. -धारा the sky, heaven. -नाथः N. of a celebrated *Linga*, or the place where it was set up ; (which by its splendour and enormous wealth attracted the attention of Mahomad of Ghazani who in 1024 A. D. destroyed the image and carried off the treasures) ; तेषां मार्गे परिचयवशादर्जितं गुर्जराणां यः संतापं शिथिलमकरोत् सोमनाथं विलोक्य ॥ Vikr. 18. 87. -प, -पा, *m.* one who drinks the Soma. **2** a Soma-sacrificer. **3** a particular class of Pitris. -पतिः N. of Indra. -पानं drinking Soma juice. -पायिन्, -पीथिन् *m.* a drinker of Soma juice ; तत्र केचित् ...सोमपीथिन उदुंबरनामानो ब्रह्मवादिनः प्रतिवसति स्म Mâl. 1. -पुत्रः, -भूः, -सुतः epithets of Budha or Mercury. -प्रवाकः a person commissioned to engage sacrificial priests (श्रोत्रिय) for a Soma sacrifice. -बंधुः the white water-lily. -यज्ञः, -यागः the Soma sacrifice. -योनिः a sort of yellow and fragrant sandal. -रोगः a particular disease of women. -लता, -वल्लरी **1** the Soma plant. **2** N. of the river Godâvarî. -वंशः the lunar race of kings founded by Budha. -वारः, -वासरः Monday. -विक्रयिन् *m.* a vendor of Soma juice. -वृक्षः, -सारः the white Khadira. -शकला a kind of cucumber. -संज्ञं camphor. -सद् *m.* a particular class of Manes or Pitris ; Ms. 3. 195. -सिंधुः an epithet of Vishnu. -सुत् *m.* a Soma distiller. -सुता the river Narmadâ ; cf. सोमोद्भवा above. -सूत्रं a channel for conveying water from a *Siva-linga*. °प्रदक्षिणा circumambulation around a *Siva-linga* so as not to cross the *Soma-su'tra*.

सोमन् *m.* The moon.

सोमिन् *a.* (नी *f.*) Performing the Soma sacrifice. -*m.* A performer of Soma sacrifice.

सोम्य *a.* **1** Worthy of Soma. **2** Offering Soma. **3** Resembling or shaped like Soma. **4** Soft, good, amiable.

सोल्लुंठः, सोल्लुंठनं Irony, ridicule, sarcasm. -ठं, -नं *ind.* Ironically ; U. 5.

सोष्मन् *a.* **1** Warm, hot. **2** (In gram.) Aspirated. -*m.* An aspirate.

सौकर *a.* (री *f.*) Hoggish, of a hog ; Ki. 12. 53.

सौकर्यं **1** Hoggishness. **2** Ease, facility ; सौकर्यं च कार्यस्यानागासेन सिद्ध्या सांगासिद्ध्या च बोधम्. **3** Practicability, feasibility. **4** Adroitness, skill. **5** An easy or *extempore* preparation of food or medicine.

सौकुमार्यं **1** Softness, delicacy, tenderness ; शिरीषपुष्पाधिकसौकुमार्यौ बाहू तदीयाविति मे वितर्कः Ku. 1. 14. **2** Youthfulness.

सौक्ष्म्यं Minuteness, fineness, subtility.

सौखशायनिकः, सौखशायिकः One who asks another person whether he has slept well or has had comfortable sleep ; भ्रुवादीनतुगृह्णंतं सौखशायनिकान्नृपीन् R. 10. 14.

सौखसुप्तिकः 1 One who asks another person whether he has slept well. 2 A bard whose duty it is to waken a king or any other great personage with song and music.

सौखिक *a* (की *f.*), **सौखीय** *a.* (यी *f.*) Relating to pleasure, pleasurable, delightful.

सौख्यं Pleasure, happiness, satisfaction, felicity, enjoyment.

सौगतः A Buddhist ; (a follower of Sugata or Buddha) ; (the Buddhists are divided into four great schools ; माध्यमिक, सौत्रांतिक, योगाचार and वैभाषिक) ; सौगतजरत्परिव्राजिकयास्तु कामंद्क्याः प्रथमा भूमिकां भाव एवाधीते Mâl. 1.

सौगतिकः 1 A Buddhist. 2 A Buddhist mendicant. 3 An atheist, a heretic, an unbeliever. -कं Unbelief, heresy, atheism, scepticism.

सौगंध *a.* (धी *f.*) Sweet-scented, fragrant. -धं 1 Sweet-scentedness, fragrance. 2 A kind of fragrant grass (कत्तृण).

सौगंधिक *a.* (का or की *f.*) Sweet-scented, fragrant. -कः 1 A dealer in perfumes, perfumer. 2 Sulphur. -कं 1 The white water-lily. 2 The blue lotus 3 A kind of fragrant grass (कत्तृण). 4 A ruby.

सौगंध्यं Sweetness of odour, fragrance, perfume.

सौचिः, सौचिकः A tailor ; Kull. on Ms. 4. 214.

सौजन्यं 1 Goodness, kindness of spirit, gentility ; U. 3. 13 ; Mk. 8. 38. 2 Magnanimousness, generosity. 3 Kindness, compassion, clemency. 4 Friendship, love.

सौडी Long pepper.

सौतिः An epithet of Karṇa.

सौत्यं The office of a charioteer ; Nalod. 4. 9.

सौत्र *a.* (त्री *f.*) 1 Belonging to or having a thread or string. 2 Belonging to, mentioned, occurring or declared in, a Sûtra q. v. -त्रः 1 A Brâhmaṇa. 2 An artificial root occurring in grammatical Sûtras which cannot be conjugated like a regular verb, but is used only to form derivative words.

सौत्रांतिकाः *m. pl.* N. of one of the four great schools of Buddhism ; cf. सौगत.

सौत्रामणी The east ; चकोरनयनारुणा भवति दिक् च सौत्रामणी Vb. 4. 1.

सौदर्यं Brotherhood.

सौदामनी, सौदामिनी, सौदाम्नी Lightning ; सौदामन्या कनकनिकषस्निग्धया दर्शयोर्वीं Me. 37 ; सौदामिनीव जलदोदरसंधिलीना Mk. 1. 35.

सौदायिक *a.* (की *f.*) Whatever is given to woman at her marriage by her parents, or a relative in general, which becomes her own property -कं A nuptial present so made.

सौध *a.* (धी *f.*) 1 Relating to, or having, nectar. 2 Having plaster, or plastered. -धं 1 A white-washed mansion, any stuccoed house. 2 Any great mansion or palace, large house; सौधवासमुटजेन विस्मृतः संचिकाय फलनिःस्पृहस्तपः R. 19. 2, 7. 5, 13. 40. 3 Silver. 4 Opal. **Comp.** कारः 1 a plasterer. 2 a builder of a house. वासः a palatial building.

सौन *a.* (नी *f.*) Relating to butchery or a slaughter-house. -नं Bucher's meat. -**Comp.** -धर्म्य a state of deadly hostility.

सौनिकः A buacher ; cf. शौनिक.

सौनंदं The club of Balarâma.

सौनंदिन् *m.* An epithet of Balarâma.

सौंदर्यं Beauty, loveliness, gracefulness, elegance ; सौंदर्यसारसमुदायनिकेतनं वा Mâl. 1. 21 ; Ku. 1. 42, 5. 41.

सौपर्णं 1 Dry ginger. 2 Emerald.

सौपर्णेयः An epithet of Garuḍa.

सौप्तिक *a.* (की *f.*) 1 Connected with or relating to sleep. 2 Somniferous. -कं A night-attack, an attack on sleeping men. -**Comp.** -पर्वन् *n.* N. of the tenth *parvan* or book of the Mahâbhârata which relates how Asvatthâman, Kṛitavarman and Kṛipa—the only surviving Kuru warriers-attacked by night the Pâṇḍava camp and slaughtered thousands of warriors while asleep. -वधः the great nocturnal slaughter of the Pâṇḍava camp (above referred to) ; मार्गो ह्येष नरेंद्रसौप्तिकवधे पूर्वं कृतो द्राणिना Mk. 3. 11.

सौबलः N. of Sakuni, q. v.

सौबली, सौबलेयी N. of Gândhârî, wife of Dhṛitarâshṭra.

सौभं N. of Harischandra's city (said to be suspended in air).

सौभगं 1 Good luck, happiness. 2 Prosperity, riches, wealth.

सौभद्रः, सौभद्रेयः Epithets of Abhimanyu, son of Subhadrâ.

सौभागिनेयः The sun of a favourite wife.

सौभाग्यं 1 Good fortune or luck, fortunateness (chiefly consisting in a man's and woman's securing the favour and firm devotion of each other); प्रियेषु सौभाग्यफला हि चारुता Ku. 5. 1 ; सौभाग्यं ते सुभग विरहावस्थया व्यंजयंती Me. 29 ; (see Malli's remarks on सौभाग्य in both places). 2 Blessedness, auspiciousness. 3 Beauty, charm, grace ; (यस्य) हिमं न सौभाग्यविलोपि जातं Ku. 1. 3 ; 2. 53, 5. 49; R. 18. 19, U. 6. 27. 4 Grandeur, sublimity. 5 The auspicious state of wifehood (opp. widowhood), 6 Congratulation ; good wishes. 7 Red lead. 8 Borax. -**Comp.** -चिह्नं 1 any mark of good fortune or happiness. 2 any sign of the blessed state of wifehood (such as the saffron-mark on the forehead.) -तंतुः the marriage-string (put round the neck of the bride by the bridegroom at the time of marriage and worn by her till widowhood ; also called मंगलसूत्र q. v.). -तृतीया the third day of the bright half of Bhâdrapada. -देवता an auspicious or tutelary deity. -वायनं an auspicious offering of sweet-meats &c.

सौभाग्यवत् *a.* Fortunate, auspicious. -ती A married woman whose husband is alive, a married unwidowed woman.

सौभिकः A juggler.

सौभ्रात्रं Good brotherhood, fraternity ; सौभ्रात्रमेषां हि कुलानुसारि R. 16. 1 ; 10. 81.

सौमनस *a.* (सा or सी *f.*) 1 Agreeable to the feelings, pleasing. 2 Relating to flowers, floral -सं 1 Kindliness of spirit, benevolence, kindness. 2 Pleasure, satisfaction.

सौमनसा The outer skin of the nutmeg.

सौमनस्यं 1 Satisfaction of mind pleasure, delight ; R. 15. 14, 17. 40. 2 A particular offering of flowers made to a Brâhmaṇa at a Srâddha.

सौमनस्यायनी The blossom of the Mâlatî creeper.

सौमायनः A patronymic of Budha.

सौमिक *a.* (की *f.*) 1 Performed with or relating to the Soma juice. 2 Relating to the moon lunar.

सौमित्रः -सौमित्रिः 1 An epithet of Lakshmaṇa ; सौमित्रेरपि पत्रिणामविषये तत्र प्रिये क्वासि भोः U. 3. 45.

सौमिल्लः N. of a dramatist who preceded Kâlidâsa ; भासकविसौमिल्लकविमिश्रादीनां M. 1.

सौमेचकं Gold.

सौमेधिकः A sage, seer, one possessed of supernatural wisdom.

सौमेरुक *a.* (की *f.*) Relating to or coming from Sumeru. -कं Gold.

सौम्य *a.* (म्या or म्यी *f.*) 1 Relating or sacred to the moon. 2 Having the properties of Soma. 3 Handsome, pleasing, agreeable. 4 Gentle, soft, mild, placid ; सरभं मैथिलीहासः क्षणसौम्यां निनाय तां R. 12. 36 ; (the voc. सौम्य is often used in the sense of ' good sir, ' ' gentle sir, ' ' good man' ; प्रीतास्मि ते सौम्य चिराय जीव R. 14. 59 ; सौम्येति

चाभाष्य यथार्थवादी 14. 44, Me. 49, Ku. 4. 35, Mâl. 9. 25.) **5** Auspicious. **-म्यः** **1** N. of Budha or the planet by mercury. **2** A proper epithet which a Brâhmaṇa should be addressed; आयुष्मान्भव सौम्येति वाच्यो विप्रोऽभिवादने Ms. 2. 125. **3** A Brâhmaṇa. **4** The Udumbara tree. **5** Blood before it becomes red, rerum. **6** The gastric juice. **7** N. of one of the nine divisions of the earth. *-m. pl.* **1** N. of the five stars in Orion's head. **2** A particular class of Pitṛis or Manes; Ms. 3. 199. **-Comp. -उपचारः** a gentle measure, mild remedy. **-कृच्छ्रः -च्छ्रं** a kind of religious penance; cf. Y. 3. 322. **-गंधी** the Indian white rose. **-ग्रहः** a benign or auspicious planet. **-धातुः** the phlegmatic humour, phlegm. **-नामन्** *a.* having a pleasing or agreeable name; Ms. 3. 10 **-वारः, -वासरः** Wednesday.

सौर *a.* (**री** *f.*) **1** Relating to the sun, solar. **2** Sacred or dedicated to the sun. **3** Celestial, divine. **4** Relating to spirituous liquor. **-रः** **1** A worshipper of the sun. **2** The planet Saturn. **3** A solar month. **4** A solar day. **5** The plant called Tumburu. **-रं** N. of a collection of hymns (extracted from the *Rigveda*) addressed to *Su'rya*. **-Comp. -नक्तं** a particular religious observance. **-मासः** a solar month (comprising thirty risings and settings of the sun). **-लोकः** the sun's sphere.

सौरथः A hero, warrior.

सौरभ *a.* (**भी** *f.*) Fragrant. **-भं** **1** Fragrance; Bv. 1. 18, 121. **2** Saffron.

सौरभेय *a.* (**यी** *f.*) Relating to *Surabhi*. **-यः** An ox.

सौरभी, सौरभेयी **1** A cow. **2** N. of the daughter of the cow called *Surabhi*; तां सौरभेयीं सुरभिर्यशोभिः R. 2. 3.

सौरभ्यं **1** Fragrance, odour, sweet scent; सौरभ्यं भुवनत्रयेऽपि विदितं Bv. 1. 38; पुनाना सौरभ्यैः G. L. 43, R. 5. 69. **2** Agreeableness, beauty. **3** Good character, reputation, glory, fame.

सौरसेनाः *m. pl.* N. of a district and its people. **-नी** See शौरसेनी.

सौरसैयः An epithet of Skanda.

सौरसैंधव *a.* (**वी** *f.*) Belonging to the celestial river or Ganges angetic; Si. 13. 27. **-वः** A horse of the sun.

सौराज्यं Good government or rule; एको ययौ चैत्ररथप्रदेशान् सौराज्यरम्यानपरो विदर्भान् R. 5. 60.

सौराष्ट्र *a.* (**ष्ट्री** or **ष्ट्री** *f.*) Coming from or relating to the district called Surâshṭra (or Surat). **-ष्ट्रः** The district or Surâshtra. *-m. pl.* The people of Surâshtra. **-ष्ट्रं** Brass, bell-metal.

सौराष्ट्रकः A kind of bell-metal.

सौराष्ट्रिकं A kind of poison.

सौरिः **1** N. of the planet Saturn. **2** The Asana tree. **-Comp. -रत्नं** a kind of gem (sapphire).

सौरिक *a.* (**की** *f.*) **1** Celestial. **2** Spirituous, vinous. **3** Due for spirits (such as duty or money.) **-कः** **1** Saturn. **2** Heaven, paradise. **3** A vendor of spirituous liquor.

सौरी The wife of the sun.

सौरीय *a.* (**यी** *f.*) **1** Solar. **2** Fit for, or suitable to, the sun.

सौर्य *a.* (**र्यी** *f.*) Belonging to the sun, or solar.

सौलभ्यं **1** Easiness of acquisition. **2** Feasibility, facility, ease.

सौल्विकः A coppersmith.

सौव *a.* (**वी** *f.*) **1** Relating to one's own property. **2** Being in or belonging to heaven. **-वं** An order, edict.

सौवग्रामिक *a.* (**की** *f.*) Belonging to one's own village.

सौवर *a.* (**री** *f.*) **1** Relating to sound or a musical note. **2** Treating of accents.

सौवर्चल *a.* (**ली** *f.*) Coming from the country called सुवर्चल q. v. **-लं** **1** Sochal salt. **2** Natron.

सौवर्ण *a.* (**र्णी** *f.*) **1** Golden. **2** Weighing one *Suvarna* q. v.

सौवस्तिक *a.* (**की** *f.*) Benedictive. **-कः** A family-priest, or Brâhmaṇa.

सौवाध्यायिक *a.* (**की** *f.*) Belonging to sacred study (स्वाध्याय q. v.).

सौवास्तव *a.* (**वी** *f.*) Having a good site, pleasantly situated or placed.

सौविदः, सौविदल्लः An attendant on the women's apartments; Si. 5. 17.

सौवीरं **1** The fruit of the jujube. **2** Antimony. **3** Sour gruel. **-रः** N. of a district or its people (pl. in the latter sense). **-Comp. -अंजनं** a kind of antimony or collyrium.

सौवीरकः **1** The jujube tree. **2** An inhabitant of Suvira. **3** N. of Jayadratha. **-कं** Sour barley-gruel.

सौवीर्यं Great heroism or prowess.

सौशील्यं Excellence of disposition, good morals or character.

सौश्रवसं Celebrity, renown.

सौष्ठवं **1** Excellence, goodness, beauty, elegance, superior beauty; सर्वांगसौष्ठवाभिव्यक्तये विरलनेपथ्ययोः पात्रयोः प्रवेशोऽस्तु M. 1; शरीरसौष्ठवं Mâl. 1. 17 'not in good trim'. **2** Extreme skilfulness, cleverness. **3** Excess. **4** Suppleness, lightness.

सौस्नातिकः One who asks another or whether an ablution has been auspicious or successfully performed सौस्नातिको यस्य भवत्यगस्त्यः R. 6. 61.

सौहार्दः The son of a friend. **-र्दं** Good-heartedness, affection, friendliness, friendship; (वेश्मानि) विश्राण्य सौहार्दनिधिः सुहृद्भ्यः R. 14. 15; सौहार्दहृद्यानि विचेष्टितानि Mâl. 1. 4; Me. 115

सौहार्द्यं, सौहृदं-द्यं Friendship, affection; यत्सौहृदादपि जनाः शिथिलीभवंति Mk. 1. 13; सखीजनस्ते किमु रूढसौहृदः V. 1. 10; Mâl. 1.

सौहित्यं **1** Satiety, satisfaction; *Si.* 5. 62. **2** Fulness, completion. **3** Kindness, friendliness.

स्कंद् 1 A. (स्कंदते) **1** To jump. **2** To raise. **3** To pour out, emit.

स्कंद् I. 1 P. (स्कंदति, स्कन्न) **1** To leap, jump. **2** To raise, scend, jump upwards. **3** To fall, drop; Bk. 22. 11. **4** To burst or leap out. **5** To perish, come to an end; चस्कंदे तप ऐश्वरम्. **6** To be spilled, ooze. **7** To emit, shed. *-Caus.* (स्कंदयति-ते) **1** To pour out, effuse, shed, emit (as the seminal fluid); एकः शयीत सर्वत्र न रेतः स्कंदयेत् क्वचित् Ms. 2. 180; 9. 50. **2** To omit, neglect, pass by. -WITH **अव** to attack, assail, storm; पुरीमवस्कंद लुनीहि नंदनं *Si.* 1. 51. **-आ** to attack, assail; आस्कंदलक्ष्मणं बाणैरत्यक्रामच्च तं द्रुतं Bk. 17. 82. **-परि** to leap about; मेघनादः परिस्कंदम् परिस्कंदंतमाश्वरिम्। अबध्नादपरिस्कंदं ब्रह्मपाशेन विस्फुरन् Bk. 9. 75. **-प्र** **1** to leap forward. **2** to fall upon, attack. -II. 10 U. (स्कंदयति-ते) To collect.

स्कंदः **1** Leaping. **2** Quicksilver. **3** N. of Kârtikeya; सेनानीनामहं स्कंदः Bg. 10. 24, R. 2. 36, 7. 1; Me. 43. **4** N. of *Siva*. **5** The body. **6** A king. **7** The bank of a river. **8** A clever man. **-Comp. -पुराणं** one of the 18 Purâṇas **-षष्ठी** *f.* a festival in honour of Kârtikeya on the sixth day of Chaitra.

स्कंदकः **1** One who leaps. **2** A soldier.

स्कंदनं **1** Emission, effusion. **2** Purging, looseness, relaxation (of the bowels). **3** Going, moving. **4** Drying up. **5** The suppression of bleeding by cold applications.

स्कंध् 10 U. (स्कंधयति-ते) To collect.

स्कंधः **1** The shoulder. **2** The body. **3** The trunk or stem of a tree; तीव्राघातप्रतिहततरुस्कंधलग्नैकदंतः *S.* 1. 34, R. 4. 57, Me. 53. **4** A branch or large bough. **5** A department or branch of human knowledge. **6** A chapter, section, divison (of a book). **7** A division or detachment of an army. **8** A troop, multitude, group. **9** The five objects of sense. **10** The five forms of mundane consciousness (in Buddhistic phil.); सर्वकार्यशरीरेषु मुक्त्वांगस्कंधपंचकं *Si.* 2. 28. **11** War, battle. **12** A king. **13** An agreement. **14** A road, way. **15** A wise or learned man. **16** A heron. **-Comp. -आवारः** **1** an army or a division of it. **2** a royal capital or residence. **3** a camp. **-उपानेय** *a.* to be carried on the shoulders. (**-यः**) a form of peace-offering in which fruit or grain is presented, as a mark of submission. -चापः a sort of pole or yoke for carrying burdens; cf. शिक्य. -तरुः the cocoa-nut tree. -देशः the shoulder; इदमुपहितसूक्ष्मग्रंथिना स्कंधदेशे S. 1. 18. -परिनिर्वाणं the annihilation of the elements of being (with Buddhists). -फलः 1 the cocoa-nut tree. 2 the Bilva tree. 3 the glomerous fig-tree. -बंधना a sort of fennel. -मल्लकः a heron. -रुहः the (Indian) fig-tree. -वाहः, -वाहकः an ox trained to carry burdens, pack-bullock. -शाखा a principal branch, the forked branch issuing from the upper stem of a tree. -शृंगः a buffalo. -स्कंधः every shoulder.

स्कंधस् *n.* 1 The shoulder. 2 The trunk of a tree.

स्कंधिकः An ox trained to carry burdens; cf. स्कंधवाह.

स्कंधिन् *a.* (नी *f.*) 1 Having shoulders. 2 Having branches or stem. *-m.* A tree.

स्कन्न *p. p.* 1 Fallen, fallen down, descended. 2 Oozed out, or trickled down. 3 Emitted, effused, sprinkled. 4 Gone. 5 Dried up.

स्कंभ् 1 A., 5. 9. P. (स्कंभते, स्कम्नाति, स्कम्नाति) 1 To create. 2 To stop, hinder, impede, obstruct, curb, restrain. *-Caus.* (स्कभयति-ते or स्कंभयति-ते).-WITH वि to impede, obstruct.

स्कंभः 1 Support, prop, stay. 2 Fulcrum. 3 The Supreme Being.

स्कंभनं The act of supporting, support, prop.

स्कांद *a.* (न्दी *f.*) 1 Relating to Skanda. 2 Relating to Śiva. -न्दं The Skanda Purâṇa.

स्कु 5. 9. U. (स्कुनोति, स्कुनुते, स्कुनाति, स्कुनीते) 1 To go by leaps, jump, bound. 2 To raise, lift. 3 To cover, overspread; Bk. 17. 32. 4 To approach. -WITH प्रति to cover; Bk. 18. 73.

स्कुंद् 1 A. (स्कुंदते) 1 To jump. 2 To raise, lift.

स्कोटिका A kind of bird.

स्खद् 1 A. (स्खदते) 1 To cut, cut or tear to pieces. 2 To destroy. 3 To hurt, injure, kill. 4 To rout, defeat completely. 5 To fatigue, exhaust, trouble. 6 To make firm.

स्खदनं 1 Cutting, tearing to pieces. 2 Hurting, injuring, killing. 3 Troubling, harassing.

स्खल् 1 P. (स्खलति, स्खलित) 1 To stumble, tumble, fall down, slip, trip; स्खलति चरणं भूमौ न्यस्तं न चार्द्रतमा मही Mk. 9. 13; Ku. 5. 24. 2 To totter, waver, shake, fluctuate. 3 To be disobeyed or violated (as an order); Mu. 3. 25; R. 18. 43. 4 To fall or deviate from the right course; Ki. 9. 37. 5 To be affected or excited; Ki. 3. 53, 13. 5. 6 To err, blunder, commit mistakes; स्खलतो हि करालंबः सुहृत्साचिवचेष्टितं H. 3. 134. (where it has sense 1 also). 7 To stammer, lisp, falter; वदनकमलकं शिशोः स्मरामि स्खलदसमंजसमंजुजल्पितं ते U. 4. 4; R. 9. 76, Ku. 5. 56. 8 To fail, have no effect, R. 11. 83. 9 To drop, drip, trickle. 10 To go, move. 11 To disappear. 12 To collect, gather. *-Caus.* (स्खलयति-ते) 1 To cause to stumble or trip. 2 To cause to err or blunder, cause to falter or stammer; वचनानि स्खलयन् पदे पदे Ku. 4. 12; स्खलयति वचनं ते संश्रयत्यंगमंगं Mâl. 3. 8. -WITH प्र to jostle; रथाः प्रचस्खलुश्वाश्वाः Bk. 14. 98. -वि to err, blunder; R. 19. 24.

स्खलनं 1 Stumbling, slipping, tripping, falling down. 2 Tottering. 3 Deviating from the right course. Blundering, error, mistake. 5 Failure, disappointment, unsuccessfulness. 6 Stammering, blundering in speech or pronunciation, faltering. 7 Trickling, dripping. 8 Dashing against, clashing; U. 2. 20, Mv. 5. 40. 9 Mutual striking or rubbing together.

स्खलित *p. p.* 1 Stumbled, slipped, tripped. 2 Fallen, dropped down. 3 Shaking, wavering, fluctuating, unsteady. 4 Intoxicated, drunk. 5 Stam-mering; faltering. 6 Agitated, disturbed. 7 Erring, blundering. 8 Dropped, emitted. 9 Dripping, trickling down. 10 Interrupted, stopped. 11 Confounded. 12 Gone. -तं 1 Stumbling, tripping, a fall. 2 Deviation from the right course. 3 Error, blunder, mistake; गोत्रस्खलित Ku. 4. 8. 4 Fault, sin, transgression. 5 Deceit, treachery. 6 Circumvention, stratagem. -Comp. सुभगं *ind.* dashing or flowing along in a charming manner; Me. 28.

स्खुड् 6 P. (स्खुडति) To cover.

स्तक् 1 P. (स्तकति) 1 To resist. 2 To strike against, repel, push back.

स्तन् 1 P., 10 U. (स्तनति, स्तनयति-ते, स्तनित) 1 To sound, make a sound, resound, reverberate. 2 To groan, breathe hard, sigh. 3 To thunder, roar loudly; तस्तनुर्जेज्वलुर्मम्लुर्जग्लुर्लुलुठिरे क्षताः Bk. 14. 30. -WITH नि 1 to sound. 2 sigh. 3 to mourn. -वि to roar.

स्तनः 1 The female breast; स्तनौ मांसग्रंथी कनककलशावित्युपमितौ Bh. 3. 20; (दारिद्र्याणां मनोरथाः) हृदयष्वेव लीयंते विधवास्त्रीस्तनाविव Pt. 2. 91. 2 The breast, udder or dug of any female animal; अर्धपीतस्तनं मातुरामर्दक्लिष्टकेशरं S. 7 14. -Comp. -अंशुकं a cloth covering the breasts or bosom. -अग्रः a nipple. -अंगरागः a paint or pigment smeared on the breasts of women. -अंतरं 1 the heart. 2 the space between the breasts; (न) मृणालसूत्रं रचितं स्तनांतरे S. 6. 17, R. 10. 62. 3 a mark on the breast (said to indicate future widowhood). -आभोग 1 fulness or expanding of the breasts. 2 the circumference or orb of the breast. 3 a man with large breasts like those of a woman. -तटः, -टं the slope of the breast; cf. तट. -प, -पा, -पायक, -पायिन् *a.* sucking the breast, a suckling.-पानं sucking of the breast. -भरः 1 the weight or heaviness of breasts; पादाग्रास्थितया मुहुः स्तनभरेणानीतया नम्रतां Ratn. 1. 1. 2 a man having breasts like those of a woman. -भवः a particular position in sexual union. -मुखं, -वृंतं, -शिखा a nipple.

स्तननं 1 Sounding, sound, noise. 2 Roaring, thundering, rumbling (of clouds). 3 Groaning. 4 Breathing hard.

स्तनंधय *a.* Sucking the breast; यदि बुध्येत हारीशिशुः स्तनंधयो भविता करेणुपरिशेषिता मही Bv. 1. 53; तवांकशायी परिवृत्तभाग्यया मया न दृष्टस्तनयः स्तनंधयः Mâl. 10. 6. -यः An infant, suckling; R. 14. 78, Śi. 12. 40.

स्तनयित्नुः 1 Thundering, thunder, the muttering of clouds. 2 A cloud; U. 3. 7, 5. 8. 3 Lightning. 4 Sickness. 5 Death. 6 A kind of grass.

स्तनित *p. p.* 1 Sounded, sounding, noisy; Me. 28. 2 Thundering, roaring. -तं 1 The rattling of thunder, rumbling of thunder-clouds; तोयोत्सर्गस्तनितमुखरो मास्म भूर्विक्लवास्ताः Me. 37. 2 Thunder, noise. 3 The noise of clapping the hands.

स्तन्यं Mother's milk, milk; पिब स्तन्यं पोत Bv. 1. 60. -Comp. -त्यागः leaving off the mother's milk, weaning; स्तन्यत्यागात्प्रभृति सुमुखी दंतपांचालिकेव Mâl. 10. 5.; स्तन्यत्यागं यावत् पुत्रयोरवेक्षस्व U. 7.

स्तबकः Bunch, cluster; कुसुमस्तबकस्येव द्वे गती स्तो मनस्विनां Bh. 2. 104, R. 13. 32; Me. 75, Ku. 3. 39.

स्तब्ध *p. p.* 1 Stopped, blocked up, obstructed. 2 Paralysed, senseless, stupefied, benumbed. 3 Motionless, immoveable. 4 Fixed, firm, hard, rigid, stiff. 5 Obstinate, stubborn, hard-hearted, stern. 6 Coarse. -Comp. -कर्ण *a.* pricking up the ears. -रोमन् *m.* a hog, boar. -लोचन *a.* having motionless or unwinking eyes (said of gods).

स्तब्धता-त्वं 1 Rigidity, firmness, hardness. 2 Stupor, insensibility.

स्तब्धिः *f.* 1 Fixedness, hardness, stiffness, rigidity. 2 Firmness, immoveableness. 3 Stupor, insensibility, numbness. 4 Obstinacy.

स्तभ् See स्तंभ्.

स्तभः A goat, ram.

स्तभु *n.* = **स्तंभन** q. v.

स्तम् 1 P. (स्तमति) To be confused or agitated.

स्तंबः 1 A clump of grass &c. ; R. 5. 15. 2 A sheaf of corn, as in स्तंबकरिता q. v. 3 A cluster, clump or bunch (in general); U. 2. 29, R. 15. 19. 4 A bush, thicket. 5 A shrub or plant having no decided stem. 6 The post to which an elephant is tied. 7 A post. 8 Stupefaction, insensibility ; (probably for स्तंभ in these two senses). 9 A mountain. **-Comp. -करि** *a.* forming sheaves or clusters. (**-रिः**) corn, rice. **-करिता** forming sheaves or clusters, abundant or luxuriant growth ; न शालेः स्तंबकरिता वप्तर्गुणमपेक्षते Mu. 1. 3. **-घनः** 1 a small hoe for weeding clumps of grass. 2 a sickle for cutting corn. 3 a basket for holding the heads of wild rice. **-घ्नः** a sickle for cutting corn, a hoe.

स्तंबेरमः An elephant ; स्तंबेरमा मुखरशृंखलकर्षिणस्ते R. 5. 82 ; Si. 5. 34.

स्तंभ् 1 A., 5. 9 P. (स्तंभते, स्तभ्नोति, स्तभ्नाति, स्तंभित or स्तब्ध ; the स् of the root being changed to ष् after prepositions ending in इ or उ and also after अव) 1 To stop, hinder, arrest, suppress ; कंठः स्तंभितबाष्पवृत्तिकलुषः S. 4. 5. 2 To make firm or stiff, to make immoveable. 3 To stupefy, paralyze, benumb ; प्राणा दध्वंसिरे गात्रं तस्तंभे च हते प्रिये Bk. 14. 55. 4 To prop, support, uphold, sustain. 5 To become stiff, rigid or immoveable. 6 To be proud or elated, be stiff-necked. (The following verse illustrates the root in its different conjugations :—स्तंभते पुरुषः प्रायो यौवनेन धनेन च । न स्तभ्नाति क्षितीशोऽपि न स्तभ्नोति युवाप्यसौ ॥). *-Caus.* (स्तंभयति-ते) 1 To stop, arrest. 2 To make firm or rigid. 3 To paralyze. 4 To prop, support. -WITH **-अव** 1 to lean or rest upon ; प्रकृतिं स्वामवष्टभ्य Bg. 9. 8. 2 to block up. 3 to support, prop up. 4 to hold, clasp, embrace. 5 to warp, envelop. 6 to hinder, stop, arrest, restrain. **-उद्** 1 to stop, hinder, arrest. 2 to support, prop up, uphold. **-उप,-नि** to stop, arrest. **-पर्यव** to surround ; पर्यवष्टभ्यतामेतत्करालायतनं Mâl. 5. **-वि** 1 to stop. 2 to fix, plant, rest on ; अत्युच्छ्रिते मंत्रिणि पार्थिवे च विष्टभ्य पादावुपतिष्ठते श्रीः Mu. 4. 13. **-सं** (*-caus.* also) 1 to stop, restrain, control ; प्रयत्नसंस्तंभितविक्रियाणां कथंचिदीशा मनसा बभूवुः Ku. 3. 34. 2 to paralyze, benumb ; Ku. 3. 73. 3 to take heart or courage, cheer up, compose, collect (oneself); देवि संस्तंभयात्मानं U. 4. 4 to make firm or immoveable ; Bg. 3. 43. **-समव** 1 to support, prop. 2 to comfort, encourage.

स्तंभः 1 Fixedness, stiffness, rigidity, motionlessness ; रंभा स्तंभं भजति Vikr. 18. 29 ; गात्रस्तंभः स्तनमुकुलयोरुत्प्रबंधः प्रकंपः Mâl. 2. 5 ; तत्संकल्पोपहितजडिम स्तंभमभ्येति गात्रं 1. 35, 4. 2. 2 Insensibility, stupefaction, stupor, numbness, paralysis. 3 Stoppage, obstruction, hindrance ; सोऽपश्यत्प्रणिधानेन संततेः स्तंभकारणं R. 1. 79 ; वाक्स्तंभं नाटयति Mâl. 8. 4 Restraint, curbing, suppressing ; कृतश्चित्तस्तंभः प्रतिहतधियामंजलिरपि Bh. 3. 6. 5 Prop, support, fulcrum. 6 A pillar, column, post. 7 A stem, trunk (of a tree). 8 Stupidity. 9 Absence of feeling or excitability. 10 The suppression of any force or feeling by supernatural or magical means. **-Comp. -उत्कीर्ण** *a.* carved out of a post of wood (as a statue). **-कर** *a.* 1 paralysing, benumbing. 2 obstructing. (**-रः**) a fence. **-कारणं** cause of obstruction or impediment. **-पूजा** worship of the posts of temporary pavilions erected for marriages or other occasions of solemnity.

स्तंभकिन् *m.* A kind of musical instrument covered with leather.

स्तंभनं 1 Stopping, obstructing, hindering, arresting, suppressing, restraining ; लोलोल्लोलक्षुभितकरणोज्जृंभणस्तंभनार्थं U. 3. 36. 2 Paralysing, benumbing, stupefying. 3 Quieting, composure ; Pt. 1. 360. 4 Making firm or stiff, fixing firmly. 5 Propping, supporting. 6 Stopping the flow of blood. 7 Anything employed as an astringent. 8 A particular magical art or faculty ; see स्तंभ (10). **-नः** N. of one of the five arrows of Cupid.

स्तर *a.* Spreading, extending, covering. **-रः** 1 Anything spread, a layer, stratum. 2 A bed, couch.

स्तरणं The act of spreading, strewing, scattering &c.

स्तरि(री)मन् *m.* A bed, couch.

स्तरी 1 Smoke, vapour. 2 A heifer. 3 A barren cow.

स्तवः 1 Praising, celebrating, eulogizing. 2 Praise, eulogium, panegyric.

स्तवक *a.* (**विका** *f.*) Praising, eulogizing. **-कः** 1 A panegyrist, praiser. 2 Praise, eulogium. 3 A cluster of blossoms. 4 Bunch of flowers, nosegay, tuft, boquet. 5 A chapter or section of a book. 6 A multitude ; cf. स्तबक also.

स्तवनं 1 Praising, praise. 2 A hymn.

स्तावः Praise, eulogy.

स्तावकः A praiser, panegyrist, flatterer.

स्तिघ् 5 A. (स्तिघ्नुते) 1 To ascend. 2 To assail. 3 To ooze.

स्तिप् 1 A. (स्तेपते) To ooze, drop, drip.

स्तिभिः 1 An obstacle, obstruction. 2 The ocean. 3 A cluster, bunch, clump.

स्तिम्, स्तीम् 4 P. (स्तिम्यति, स्तीम्यति) 1 To become wet or moist. 2 To become fixed or immoveable, be rigid.

स्तिमित *a.* 1 Wet, moist. 2 (*a*) Still, unruffled, calm ; क्षुभितमुत्कलिकातरलं मनः पय इव स्तिमितस्य महोदधेः Mâl. 3. 10. (*b*) Fixed, rigid, unmoved, motionless, steady ; वाचस्पतिः सन्नपि सोऽष्टमूर्तौ त्वाशास्यचिंतास्तिमितो बभूव Ku. 7. 87 ; 2. 59 ; Mâl. 1. 27 ; R. 2. 22, 3. 17, 13. 48, 79 ; U. 6. 25. 3 Closed, shut ; R. 1. 73. 4 Benumbed, paralysed. 5 Soft, tender. 6 Gratified, satisfied. **-Comp. -वायुः** still air. **-समाधिः** steady contemplation.

स्तिमितत्वं Steadiness, stillness.

स्तीर्विः 1 An officiating priest at a sacrifice. 2 Grass. 3 Sky, atmosphere. 4 Water. 5 Blood. 6 An epithet of Indra.

स्तु 2 U. (स्तौति-स्तवीति, स्तुते-स्तुवीते, स्तुत; *Desid.* तुष्टूषति-ते ; the स् of स्तु is changed to ष् after a preposition ending in इ or उ) 1 To praise, laud, eulogize, extol, glorify, celebrate ; Bv. 1. 41 ; Mu. 3. 16 ; Bk. 8. 92,15. 70, 21. 3. 2 To celebrate or praise in song, to hymn, worship by hymns. -WITH **अभि** to praise, extol. **-प्र** 1 to praise. 2 to begin, commence ; प्रस्तुयतां विवादवस्तु M. 1. 3 to cause, produce ; Mâl. 5. 9. **-सं** 1 to praise ; R. 13. 6. 2 to be acquainted with, be familiar or intimate with (chiefly in p. p. in this sense); अनेकशः संस्तुतमप्यनल्पा नवं नवं प्रीतिरहो करोति Si. 3. 31, Ki. 3. 2 ; see संस्तुत also.

स्तुकः A collection of hair, a knot or braid of hair.

स्तुका 1 A knot or braid of hair. 2 A bunch of curly hair between the horns of a bull. 3 Hip, thigh.

स्तुच् 1 A. (स्तोचते) 1 To be bright, to shine, be pellucid. 2 To be propicious or pleased.

स्तुत *p. p.* 1 Praised, lauded, eulogized. 2 Flattered.

स्तुतिः *f.* 1 Praise, eulogy, commendation, laudation ; स्तुतिभ्यो व्यतिरिच्यंते दूराणि चरितानि ते R. 10. 30. 2 A hymn of praise, panegyric ; R. 4. 6. 3 Adulation ; flattery, empty or false praise ; भूतार्थव्याहृतिः सा हि न स्तुतिः परमेष्ठिनः R. 10. 33. 4 N. of Durgâ. **-Comp. -गीतं** a panegyric, hymn. **-पदं** an object of praise. **-पाठकः** a panegyrist, an encomiast, a minstrel, bard, herald. -वादः a laudatory speech, panegyric. -व्रतः a bard.

स्तुत्य *a.* Laudable, commendable, praiseworthy ; R. 4. 6.

स्तुनकः A goat.

स्तुभ् I. 1 P. (स्तोभति) **1** To praise. **2** To celebrate, extol, worship. -II. 1 A. (स्तोभते) **1** To stop, suppress. **2** To paralyse, benumb, stupefy.

स्तुभः A goat.

स्तुंभ् 5. 9 P. (स्तुम्नोति; स्तुम्नाति) **1** To stop. **2** To benumb, stupefy. **3** To expel.

स्तुप् 4 P., 10 U. (स्तुप्यति; स्तुपयति-ते) **1** To heap up, accumulate, pile, collect. **2** To erect, raise.

स्तूपः **1** A heap, pile, mound (of earth &c.). **2** A Buddhistic monument, or a kind of Tope erected for keeping sacred relics, as those of Buddha. **3** A funeral pile.

स्तृ I. 5 U. (स्तृणोति, स्तृणुते, स्तृत ;*pass.* स्तर्यते) **1** To spread, strew, cover, spread on or over ; (महीं) तस्तार सरघाव्यातैः स क्षौद्रपटलैरिव R. 4. 63, 7. 58. **2** To spread, expand, diffuse. **3** To scatter, spread about. **4** To clothe, cover, overspread, envelop. **5** To (स्तारयति ते) To overspread, cover, strew ; रक्तेनाचिक्रिदन्भूमिं सैन्यैश्चातस्तरद्धतैः Bk. 15. 48. -*Desid.* (तुस्तूर्षति-ते) (For prepositions see under स्तॄ below). -II. 5. P. (स्तृणोति To please, gratify

स्तृ *m.* A star.

स्तृक्ष् 1 P. (स्तृक्षति) To go.

स्तृतिः *f.* **1** Spreading, stretching, expansion. **2** Covering, clothing.

स्तृह्, स्तृंह् 6 P. (स्तृहति, स्तृंहति) To strike, hurt, kill.

स्तॄ 9 P. (स्तृणाति, स्तृणीते, स्तीर्ण ; *desid.* तिस्तरि-री-षति-ते, तिस्तीर्षति-ते) To cover, strew &c. ; see स्तृ. -WITH **अव** to cover, fill, overspread ; प्रकंपयन् गामवतस्तरे दिशः Ki. 16. 29. -**आ** to cover, spread over ; R. 4. 65. -**उप** **1** to strew. **2** to arrange, place in order. -**परि** **1** to spread, diffuse, extend ; Bk. 14. 11. **2** to cover (fig. also) ; अथ नागयूथमलिनानि जगत्परितस्तमांसि परितस्तरिरे Si. 9. 18 ; अभितस्तं पृथासूनुः स्नेहेन परितस्तरे Ki. 11. 8. **3** to place in order. -**वि** **1** to spread, diffuse. **2** to cover. (-*Caus.*) **1** to cause to spread or expand ; as in पयोधरविस्तारयितृकं यौवनं *S.* 1. **2** to increase ; R. 7. 39. **3** to stretch, extend. -**सं** **1** to spread, strew : प्रातसंस्तीर्णदर्भाः *S.* 4. 7. **2** to overspread.

स्तेन् 10 U. (Strictly a denom. from स्तेन ; स्तेनयति-ते) To steal, rob ; Ms. 8. 333.

स्तेनः A thief, robber ; न तं स्तेना न चामित्रा हरंति न च नश्यति Ms. 7. 83. -**नं** Thieving, stealing. -Comp. -**निग्रहः** **1** the punishment of thieves. **2** suppression of theft.

स्तेप् I. 1 A (स्तेपते) To ooze. -II. 10 U. (स्तेपयति-ते) To send, throw.

स्तेमः Moisture, wetness.

स्तेयं **1** Theft, robbery ; Ku. 2. 35. **2** Anything stolen or liable to be stolen. **3** Any thing private or secret.

स्तेयिन् *m.* **1** A thief, robber. **2** A goldsmith.

स्तै 1 P. (स्तायति) To put on, adorn.

स्तैनं Theft, robbery.

स्तैन्यं Theft, robbery. -**न्यः** A thief.

स्तैमित्यं **1** Fixedness, rigidity, immobility. **2** Numbness.

स्तोक *a.* **1** Little, small ; स्तोकेनोन्नतिमायाति स्तोकेनायात्यधोगतिं Pt. 1. 150 ; स्तोकं महद्वा धनं Bh. 2. 49. **2** Short. **3** Few. **4** Low, abject. -**कः** **1** A small quantity, drop. **2** The Châtaka bird. -**कं** *ind.* A little, less ; पश्योदग्रप्लुतत्वाद्वियति बहुतरं स्तोकमुर्व्यां प्रयाति *S.* 1. 7. -Comp. -**काय** *a.* little-bodied, small, dwarfish, diminutive. -**नम्र** *a.* a little bent down,slightly stooping or depressed; श्रोणीभारादलसगमना स्तोकनम्रा स्तनाभ्यां Me. 82.

स्तोककः The Châtaka bird ; Ms. 12. 67.

स्तोकशस् *ind.* By little, sparingly.

स्तोतव्य *a.* Fit to be praised, laudable, praiseworthy ; स्तोतव्यगुणसंपन्नः केषां न स्यात्प्रियो जनः.

स्तोतृ *m.* A praiser, panegyrist.

स्तोत्रं **1** Praise, eulogium. **2** A hymn of praise, panegyric.

स्तोत्रियः -या A particular kind of verse.

स्तोभः **1** Stopping, obstructing. **2** A stop pause. **3** Disrespect, contumely. **4** Hymn, praise. **5** A division of the Sâmaveda. **6** Anything inserted.

स्तोमः **1** Praise, eulogium, hymn. **2** Sacrifice, oblation ; *as* in ज्योतिष्टोम, अग्निष्टोम. **3** A *Soma* libation. 4 A collection, multitude, number, group, assemblage ; U. 1. 50. **5** A large quantity, mass ; भस्मस्तोमपवित्रलांछनमुरो धत्ते त्वचं रौरवीं U. 4. 20. Mv. 1. 18. -**मं** **1** The head. **2** Riches, wealth. **3** Grain, corn. **4** An iron pointed stick or shaft.

स्तोम्य *a.* Laudable, praiseworthy.

स्त्यान *a.* **1** Collected into a mass ; Mâl. 5. 11, Ve. 1. 21. **2** Thick, bulky, gross. **3** Soft, bland, smooth, unctuous. **4** Sounding. -**नं** **1** Thickness, grossness, increase in magnitude or bulk ; दधति कुहरभाजामत्र भल्लूकयूनामनुरसितगुरूणि स्त्यानमंबूकृतानि Mâl **9. 6** ; U. 2. 21, Mv. 5. 41. **2** Unctuousness. **3** Nectar. **4** Sloth, idleness. **4** Echo, sound.

स्त्यायनं Collecting into a mass, crowding together, aggregation.

स्त्यैनः **1** Nectar. **2** A thief.

स्त्यै 1 U. (स्त्यायति-ते) **1** To be collected into a heap or mass. **2** To spread about, be diffused ; शिशिरकटुकषायः स्त्यायते सल्लकीनां Mâl. 9. 6, 2. 21 ; Mv. 5. 41. **3** Sound, echo.

स्त्री **1** A woman. **2** A female of any animal ; गजस्त्री, हरिणस्त्री &c.; *S.* **5.** 22. **3** A wife ; स्त्रीणां भर्ता धर्मदाराश्च पुंसां Mâl. 6. 18 ; Me. 28. **4** The feminine gender, or a word taking that gender ; आपः स्त्रीभूम्नि Ak. -Comp.-**अगारः**, -**रं** a harem, the women's apartments. -**अध्यक्षः** a chamberlain. -**अभिगमः** sexual intercourse. -**आजीवः** **1** one who lives by his wife. **2** one who lives by keeping women for prostitution. -**कामः** **1** desire of intercourse with women, fondness for women. **2** desire of a wife. -**कार्यं** **1** the business of women. **2** attendance on women or women's apartments. -**कुमारं** a woman and child. -**कुसुमं** menses, the menstrual excretion in women. -**क्षीरं** mother's milk ; Ms. 5. 9. -**ग** *a.* co-habiting with women. -**गवी** a milch cow. -**गुरुः** a female *Guru* or priestess. -**गृहं** =स्त्र्यगार q. v. -**घोषः** dawn, daybreak. -**घ्नः** the murderer of a woman -**चरितं-त्रं** the doings of women. -**चिह्नं** **1** any mark or characteristic of the female sex. **2** the female organ, vulva. -**चौरः** a seducer of women, a libertine, -**जननी** a woman who brings forth only daughters. -**जातिः** *f.* womankind, female sex. -**जितः** a hen-pecked husband ; स्त्रीजितस्पर्शमात्रेण सर्वं पुण्यं विनश्यति Sabdak. ; Ms. 4. 217. -**धनं** a woman's private property over which she exercises independent control. -**धर्मः** **1** the duty of a woman or wife. **2** the laws concerning women. **3** menstruation. -**धर्मिणी** a woman in her courses. -**ध्वजः** the female of any animal. -**नाथ** *a.* one protected by a woman. -**निबंधनं** a woman's peculiar sphere of action or province ; domestic duty, housewifery. -**पण्योपजीविन्** *m.* see स्त्र्याजीव above. -**परः** a woman-lover, lecher, libertine. -**पिशाची** a fiend-like wife. -**पुंसौ** *m. du.* **1** wife and husband. **2** male and female ; Ku. 2. 7. -**पुंसलक्षणा** a hermaphrodite. -**प्रत्ययः** a feminine affix (in gram.). -**प्रसंगः** (excessive) intercourse with women. -**प्रसूः** *f.* a woman who brings forth only daughters ; Y. 1. 73. -**प्रिय** *a.* loved by women. (-**यः**) the mango tree. -**बाध्यः** one who suffers himself to be troubled by a woman. -**बुद्धिः** *f.* **1** the female understanding. **2** the counsel of a woman, female advice. -**भोगः** sexual intercourse. -**मंत्रः** a female stratagem, woman's counsel. -**मुखपः** the Asoka tree. -**यंत्रं**

a machine like woman, a machine in the form of a woman ; स्त्रीयंत्रं केन लोके विषममृतमयं धर्मनाशाय सृष्टं Pt. 1. 191. -रंजनं betel. -रत्नं an excellent woman ; स्त्रीरत्नेषु ममोर्वशी प्रियतमा यूथे तवेयं वशा V. 4. 25. -राज्यं the kingdom of women. -लिंगं 1 the feminine gender (in gram.). 2 the female organ. -वश: submissiveness to a wife, subjection to women. -विधेय *a.* governed by a wife, uxorious ; R. 19. 4. -विवाह: contracting marriage with a woman. -संसर्ग: female company. -संस्थान *a.* having a female shape ; *S.* 5. 39. -संग्रहणं 1 the act of embracing a woman (improperly). 2 adultery, seduction. -सभं an assembly of women. -संबंध: 1 matrimonial alliance with a woman ; 2 connection by marriage. 3 relation to women. -स्वभाव: 1 the nature of women. 2 a eunuch. -हत्या the murder of a woman. -हरणं 1 the forcible abduction of women. 2 rape.

स्त्रीतमा, स्त्रीतरा A thorough woman, more thoroughly a woman.

स्त्रीता, -त्वं 1 Womanhood. 2 Wifehood. 3 Effeminacy, feminineness.

स्त्रैण *a.* (णी *f.*) 1 Female, feminine. 2 Suited or belonging to women. 3 Being among women. -णं 1 Womanhood, nature of women, feminineness ; U. 4. 11. 2 The female sex, womanhood ; तृणे वा स्त्रैणे वा मम समदृशो यांति दिवसाः Bh. 3. 113 ; इदं तत्प्रत्युत्पन्नमति स्त्रैणमिति यदुच्यते *S.* 5 ; तस्य तृणमिव लघुवृत्ति स्त्रैणमाकलयतः K. 3 A collection of women.

स्त्रैणता, -त्वं 1 Feminineness, effeminacy. 2 Excessive fondness for women.

स्थ *a.* (At the end of comp.) Standing, staying, abiding, being, existing &c.; तत्रस्थ, अंकस्थ, प्रकृतिस्थ, तटस्थ, q q. v. v.

स्थकरं A betel-nut.

स्थग् 1 P. or *Caus.* (स्थगति, स्थगयति) 1 To cover, conceal, hide, veil ; पराम्रष्टुस्थानान्यापि तनुतराणि स्थगयति Mâl. 1. 14. 2 To cover, pervade, fill ; स्वः श्रवणभैरवः स्थगितरोदसीकंदरः K. P. 7.

स्थग *a.* 1 Fraudulent, dishonest. 2 Abandoned, impudent, reckless. -ग: A rogue, cheat.

स्थगनं Concealment, hiding.

स्थगरं A betel-nut.

स्थगिका 1 A courtezan. 2 The office of betel-bearer. 3 A kind of bandage.

स्थगित *a.* Covered, hidden, concealed.

स्थगी A betel-box.

स्थगु: A hump.

स्थंडिलं 1 A piece of ground (levelled, squared and prepared for a sacrifice), an altar ; निषेदुषी स्थंडिल एव केवले Ku. 5. 12. 2 A barren field. 3 A heap of clods. 4 A limit, boundary. 5 A land-mark. -Comp. -शायिन् *m.*, also स्थंडिलेशय: an ascetic who sleeps on the bare *Sthandila* or sacrificial ground. -सितकं an altar.

स्थपति: 1 A king, sovereign. 2 An architect. 3 A wheel-wright, master-carpenter. 4 A charioteer. 5 One who offers a sacrifice to Brihaspati. 6 An attendant on the women's apartments. 7 N. of Kubera.

स्थपुट *a.* 1 Being in contracted or difficult circumstances. 2 Unevenly raised, elevated and depressed. -Comp. -गत *a.* being in contracted or uneven parts, being in difficult places ; अंकस्थादस्थिसंस्थं स्थपुटगतमपि क्रव्यमव्यग्रमत्ति Mâl. 5. 16.

स्थल् 1 P. (स्थलति) To stand firm, be firm.

स्थलं 1 Firm or dry ground, dry land, *terra firma* (opp. जल) ; भो दुरात्मन् (समुद्र) दीयतां टिट्टिभांडानि नो चेत्स्थलतां त्वां नयामि Pt. 1 ; so स्थलकमलिनी or स्थलवर्त्मन् q. v. 2 Shore, strand, beach. 3 Ground, land, soil (in general). 4 Place, spot. 5 Field, tract, district. 6 Station. 7 A piece of raised ground, mound. 8 A topic, case, subject, the point under discussion ; विवाद°, विचार° &c. 9 A part (as of a book). 10 A tent. -Comp. -अंतरं another place. -आरूढ *a.* alighted on the ground. -अरविंद, -कमलं, -कमलिनी a land growing lotus ; Me. 90 ; Ku. 1. 33. -चर *a.* land-going, not aquatic. -च्युत *a.* fallen or removed from a place or position. -देवता a local or rural deity. -पद्मिनी the shrub *Hibiscus Mutabilis*. -मार्ग:, -वर्त्मन् *n.* a road by land ; स्थलवर्त्मना ' by land '; R. 4. 60. -विग्रह: a battle on level ground. -शुद्धि *f.* purification or clearance of a place from impurity.

स्थला A spot of dry ground artificially raised and drained (opp. स्थली q. v. below).

स्थली 1 Dry ground, firm land. 2 A natural spot of ground, ground or land (as of a forest) ; विललाप विकीर्णमूर्धजा समदुःखामिव कुर्वती स्थलीं Ku. 4. 4, -Comp. -देवता a deity of the soil, a tutelary deity ; Me. 106.

स्थलेशय *a.* Sleeping on dry ground. -य: Any amphibious animal.

स्थवि: 1 A weaver. 2 Heaven.

स्थविर *a.* 1 Fixed, firm, steady. 2 Old, aged, ancient. -र: 1 An old man. 2 A begger. 3 N. of Brahman. -रा An old woman ; स्थविरे का त्वं अयमर्भकः कस्य नयनानंदकरः Dk.

स्थविष्ठ *a.* Greatest, very strong, largest (superl. of स्थूल q. v.).

स्थवीयस् Greatest, larger (compar. of स्थूल q. v.).

स्था 1 P. (Atm. also in certain senses ; तिष्ठति-ते, स्थित ; *pass.* स्थीयते ; the स् of this root is changed to ष् after a preposition ending in इ or उ). 1 To stand ; चलत्येकेन पादेन तिष्ठत्येकेन बुद्धिमान् Subhâsh. 2 To stay, abide, dwell, live ; ग्रामे गृहे or तिष्ठति. 3 To remain, be left ; एको गंगदत्तस्तिष्ठति Pt. 4. 4 To delay, wait ; किमिति स्थीयते *S.* 2. 5 To stop, cease, desist, stand still ; तिष्ठत्येष क्षणमधिपतिर्ज्योतिषां व्योममध्ये V. 2 1. 6 To be kept aside; तिष्ठतु तावत् पत्रलेखागमनवृत्तांतः K. 'never mind the account of.' &c. 7 To be, exist, be in any state or position ; often with participles ; मेरौ स्थिते दोग्धरि दोहदक्षे Ku. 1. 2 ; *S.* 1. 1 ; V. 1. 1 ; कालं नयमाना तिष्ठति Pt. 1 ; Ms. 7. 8. 8 To abide by, conform to, obey (with loc.) ; शासने तिष्ठ भर्तुः V. 5. 17, R. 11. 65. 9 To be restrained; यदि ते तु न तिष्ठेयुरुपायैः प्रथमैस्त्रिभिः Ms. 7. 108. 10 To be at hand, be obtainable ; न विप्रं स्वेषु तिष्ठत्सु मृतं शूद्रेण नाययेत् Ms. 5. 104. 11 To live, breathe ; आः क एष मयि स्थिते चंद्रगुप्तमभिभवितुमिच्छति Mu. 1. 12 To stand by or near, stand at one's side, help ; उत्सवे व्यसने चैव दुर्भिक्षे शत्रुसंकटे। राजद्वारे श्मशाने च यस्तिष्ठति स बांधवः ॥ H. 1. 73. 13 To rest or depend on. 14 To do, perform, occupy oneself with. 15 (Atm.) To resort or go to (as an umpire), be guided by the advice of ; संशय्य कर्णादिषु तिष्ठते यः Ki. 3. 13. 16 (Atm.) To offer oneself to (for sexual embrace), stand as a prostitute (with dat.); गोपी स्मरात् कृष्णाय तिष्ठते Sk. on P. I. 4. 34. -*Caus.* (स्थापयति-ते). 1 To cause to stand. 2 To lay, set, place, put. 3 To found, establish. 4 To stop. 5 To arrest, check. -*desid.* (तिष्ठासति) To wish to stand &c. -WITH अति to remain over and above, exceed by ; अत्यतिष्ठद् दशांगुलं. -अधि 1 to stand on or upon, occupy (with acc.) अर्धासनं गोत्रभिदोऽधितष्ठौ R. 6. 73 ; Bk. 15. 31. 2 to practise (as penance) ; Ki. 10. 16. 3 to be in, dwell in, inhabit, reside ; पातालमधितिष्ठति R. 1. 80 ; श्रीजयदेवभणितमधितिष्ठतु कंठतटीमविरतं Git. 11. 4 to take possession, conquer, overcome, overpower; संग्रामे तानधिष्ठास्यन् Bk. 9. 72, 16. 40. 5 to obtain ; Ki. 2. 31. 6 to lead, conduct, beat the head of, govern, direct, preside over; दशरथदारानधिष्ठाय U. 4. 7 to rule, govern, control ; Bg. 4. 6. 8 to use, employ. 9 to ascend, be established or installed on ; अचिराधिष्ठितराज्यः शत्रुः M. 1. 8. -अनु 1 to do, perform, excute, attend to; अनुतिष्ठस्वात्मनो नियोगं M. 1. 2 to follow, practise, observe ; Bg. 3. 31. 3 to give, grant to, do something for; (यस्य) शैलाधिपत्यं स्वयमन्वतिष्ठत् Ku. 1. 17. 4 to stand by or near ; Ms. 11. 112. 5 to rule, govern. 6 to imitate. 7 to present oneself. -अव (usually Atm.) 1 to remain, stay, abide ; जोषं जोषं जोषमेवा-

वतस्थे Bv. 2. 17 ; अनीत्वा पंकतां धूलिमुदकं नावतिष्ठते Si. 2. 34 ; R. 2. 31. **2** to stay, wait ; Bk. 8. 11. **3** to abide by, conform to ; Bk. 3. 14. **4** to live ; R. 8. 87. **5** to stand still, make a halt, stop ; Bg. 1. 30. **6** to fall to, devolve on, rest with ; मयि सृष्टिर्हि लोकानां रक्षा युष्मास्ववस्थिता Ku. 2. 28. **7** to stand apart, withdraw. **8** to be settled or decided. (*-Caus.*) **1** to cause to stand or stop, station. **2** to establish or found. **3** to compose, collect. **-आ** **1** to occupy. **2** to ascend, mount ; as in एकस्यंदनमास्थितौ R. 1. 36. **3** to use, have recourse to, resort to, follow, practise, take, assume ; यथा हि सद्वृत्तमास्थितुद्गत्यनसूयकः Ms. 10. 128, 2. 133. 10. 101 ; (these senses are variously modified according to the noun with which the word is used ; see Ku. 5. 2, 84 ; Mu. 7. 19 ; R. 6. 72, 15. 79 ; Ku. 6. 72, 7. 29 ; Pt. 3. 21 &c.). **4** to do, perform, carry out. **5** to own. **6** to aim at. **7** to undertake. **8** to deport, behave. **9** to stand near. **-उद्** **1** to stand up, rise, get up ; उत्तिष्ठेत् प्रथमं चास्य Ms. 2. 194 ; वचो निशम्योत्थितमुत्थितः सन् R. 2. 61. **2** to leave, give up. **3** to rebound ; R. 16. 83. **4** to come forth, arise, proceed, spring or accrue from ; यदुत्तिष्ठति वर्णेभ्यो नृपाणां क्षयि तत्फलं S. 2. 13. **5** to rise, grow, increase in strength ; Si. 2. 10. **6** to be active or brave, rise up, stir oneself ; क्षुद्रं हृदयदौर्बल्यं त्यक्त्वोत्तिष्ठ परंतप Bg. 2. 3, 37. **7** to strive, try (Atm.); Ki. 11. 13, Si. 14. 17. (*-Caus.*) **1** to raise, lift up. **2** to rouse to action, excite. **-उप** **1** to stand near, to fall to one's share ; नादत्तमुपतिष्ठति Pt. 2. 123. **2** to come near, approach ; Ku. 2. 64, R. 15. 76. **3** to wait or attend upon, serve ; Ms. 2. 48. **4** to worship, attend upon with prayers, serve, or pay respects to (Atm.) ; न त्र्यंबकादन्यमुपास्थितासौ Bk. 1. 3 ; उदितभूयिष्ठ एष भगवांस्तपनस्तमुपतिष्ठे Mâl. 1 ; R. 4. 6.10. 63, 17.10, 18. 22. **5** to stand near. **6** to approach for intercourse. **7** to meet, join (Atm.); गंगा यमुनामुपतिष्ठते Sk. **8** to lead to (Atm.) **9** to make a friend of (Atm.) **10** to approach, draw near, be imminent. **11** to approach with hostile intentions. **12** to be present (Atm.). **13** to occur, arise. **-परि** to surround, stand round about. **-पर्यव** (*caus.*) to compose or collect oneself ; पर्यवस्थापयात्मानं V. 1. **-प्र** (Atm.) **1** to set out, depart ; पारसीकांस्ततो जेतुं प्रतस्थे स्थलवर्त्मना R. 4. 60. **2** to stand firmly. **3** to be established. **4** to approach, come near. (*-Caus.*) **1** to cause to retire. **2** to send away, dismiss ; तौ दंपती स्वां प्रति राजधानीं प्रस्थापयामास वशी वशिष्ठः R. 2. 70. **-प्रति** **1** to stand firm, be established. **2** to be supported. **3** to rest or depend upon. **4** to stay, abide, be situated. **-प्रत्यव** (Atm.) to oppose, act hotilely, object (in argument) ; अत्र केचित्प्रत्यवतिष्ठंते S. B. Bv. 1. 77. (*-Caus.*) to collect or compose oneself. **-वि** (Atm.) **1** to stand apart. **2** to remain, abide, dwell, remain fixed or stationary. **3** to spread, be diffused. **-विप्र** (Atm.) **1** to start. **2** to spread. **-व्यव** (Atm.) **1** to be placed asunder. **2** to be arranged in due order. **3** to be settled or fixed, become permanent ; वचनीयमिदं व्यवस्थितं Ku. 4. 21. **4** to rest or depend upon. (*-Caus.*) **1** to arrange, manage, adjust. **2** to settle, establish. **3** to separate, place apart. **-सं** (Atm.) **1** to dwell or live in, stand close together ; तीक्ष्णादुद्विजते मृदौ परिभवत्रासान्न संतिष्ठते Mu. 3. 5. **2** to stand on. **3** to be, exist, live. **4** to abide by, obey, act up to ; दारिद्र्यात्पुरुषस्य बांधवजनो वाक्ये न संतिष्ठते Mk. 1. 36. **5** to be completed ; सद्यः संतिष्ठते यज्ञस्तथाशौचमिति स्थितिः Ms. 5. 98. (यज्ञपुण्येन युज्यते Kull.). **6** to come to an end, be interrupted ; Bk. 8. 11. **7** to stand still, come to a stand (Paras.); क्षणं न संतिष्ठति जीवलोकः क्षयोदयाभ्यां परिवर्तमानः Hariv. **8** to die, perish. (*-Caus.*) **1** to establish, settle. **2** to place. **3** to compose, collect (oneself) ; देवि संस्थापयात्मानं U. 4. **4** to subject, keep under control ; Ms. 9. 2. **5** to stop, restrain. **6** to kill. **-समधि** to preside over, govern, administer, superintend. **-समव** (Atm.) **1** to remain fixed, stand immoveable. **2** to stand still. **3** to stand ready. (*-Caus.*) **1** to found. **2** to stop. **-समा** **1** to undergo, practise ; तपो महत्समास्थाय. **2** to engage in, perform. **3** to apply, employ. **4** to follow, observe ; Ms. 4. 2, 7. 44. **-समुद्** **1** to stand up, rise. **2** to rise together with. **3** to rise from death or sensibility, return to life or consciousness. **4** to arise or spring from. **-समुप** **1** to come near, go to, approach. **2** to attack. **3** to befall, occur. **4** to stand in close contact. **-संप्र** (Atm.) to set out, depart. **-संप्रति** **1** to hang or rest on, depend on. **2** to stand firm or fixed.

स्थाणु *a.* Firm, fixed, steady, table, immoveable, motionless.**-णुः** **1** An epithet of Siva ; स स्थाणुः स्थिरभक्तियोगसुलभो निःश्रेयसायास्तु वः V. 1. 1. **2** A stake, post, pillar; किं स्थाणुरयमुत पुरुषः **3** A peg, pin. **4** The gnomon of a dial. **5** A spear, dart. **6** A nest of white ants. **7** The drug or perfume called *Ji'vaka*. *-m. n.* A branchless trunk or stem, any bare stalk or stem, pollard. **-Comp. -छेदः** one who cuts down the trunks of trees, one who clears away timber ; स्थाणुच्छेदस्य केदारमाहुः शल्यवतो मृगं Ms. 9. 44. **-भ्रमः** mistaking anything for a post.

स्थांडिलः **1** An ascetic who sleeps on the bare ground or on a place prepared for sacrifice. **2** A religious mendicant or beggar.

स्थानं **1** The act of standing or remaining, stay, continuance, residence ; U. 3. 32. **2** Being fixed or stationary. **3** A state, condition. **4** A place, spot, site, locality ; अक्षमालामदत्वास्मात्स्थानात्पदात्पदमपि न गंतव्यं K. **5** Station, situation, position. **6** Relation, capacity ; पितृस्थाने ' in the place or capacity of a father '. **7** An abode, a house, dwelling-house ; स एव (नक्र.) प्रच्युतः स्थानाच्छुनापि परिभूयते Pt. 3. 46. **8** A country, region, district, town. **9** Office, rank, dignity ; अमात्यस्थाने नियोजितः. **10** Object ; गुणाः पूजास्थानं गुणिषु न च लिंगं न च वयः U. 4. 11. **11** An occasion, a matter, subject, cause ; पराम्यूहस्थानान्यपि तनुतराणि स्थगयति Mâl. 1. 14 ; स्थानं जरापरिभवस्य तदेव पुंसां Subhâsh. ; so कलह°, कोप°, विवाद° &c. **12** A fit or proper place ; स्थानेष्वेव नियोज्यंते भृत्याश्चाभरणानि च Pt. 1. 72. **13** A fit or worthy object ; स्थाने खलु सज्जति दृष्टिः M. 1 ; see स्थाने also. **14** The place or organ of utterance of any letter, (these are eight :— अष्टौ स्थानानि वर्णानामुरः कंठः शिरस्तथा जिह्वामूलं च दंताश्च नासिकोष्ठौ च तालु च Sik. 13. **15** A holy place. **16** An altar. **17** A place in a town. **18** The place or sphere assigned after death to persons according as they perform or neglect their prescribed duties. **19** (In politics, war &c.) The firm attitude or bearing of troops, standing firm so as to repel a charge ; Ms. 7. 190. **20** A halt. **21** A stationary condition, a neutral or middle state. **22** That which constitutes the chief strength or the very existence of a kingdom ; a stamina of a kingdom ; *i. e.* army, treasure, town and territory ; Ms. 7. 56 (where Kull. renders स्थानं by दंडकोषपुरराष्ट्रात्मकं चतुर्विधं). **23** Likeness, resemblance. **24** Part or division of a work, section, chapter &c. **25** The character or part of an actor. **26** Interval, opportunity, leisure. **27** (In music) A note, tone, modulation of the voice. **-Comp. -अध्यक्षः** a local governor, the superintendent of a place. **-आसन** *n. du.* standing and sitting down. **-आसेधः** confinement to a place, imprisonment, arrest ; cf. आसेध. **-चिंतकः** a kind of quarter-master. **-च्युत** see स्थानभ्रष्ट. **-पालः** a watchman, sentinel, policeman. **-भ्रष्ट** *a.* ejected from an office, displaced, dismissed, out of employ.

–माहात्म्यं 1 the greatness or glory of any place. 2 a kind of divine virtue or uncommon sanctity supposed to be inherent in a sacred spot. –योगः assignment of proper places ; द्रव्याणां स्थानयोगांश्च क्रयविक्रयमेव च Ms. 9. 332. –स्थ *a.* being in one's abode at home.

स्थानकं 1 A position, situation. 2 A particular point or situation in dramatic action ; *e. g.* पताकास्थानक q. v. 3 A city, town. 4 A basin. 5 Froth, a kind of scum on spirits or wine. 6 A mode of recitation. 7 A division or section of the Taittirîya, a branch of the *Yajurveda*.

स्थानतस् *ind.* 1 According to one's place or position. 2 From one's proper place. 3 With reference to the organ of utterance.

स्थानिक *a.* (की *f.*) 1 Belonging to a place, local. 2 (In gram.) That which takes the place of a thing, or is substituted for it. –कः 1 Any one holding an office, placeman. 2 The governor of a place.

स्थानिन् 1 Having place. 2 Having fixedness, permanent. 3 Having a substitute. –*m.* 1 The original form or primitive element, that for which anything else is substituted ; स्थानिवदादेशोऽनल्विधौ P. I. 1. 56. 2 That which has a place, or is actually expressed.

स्थानीय *a.* 1 Belonging to a place, local. 2 Suitable to a place. –यं A town, city.

स्थाने *ind.* (loc. of स्थान) 1 In the right or proper place, rightly, properly, justly, truly, appropriately ; स्थाने वृता भूपतिभिः परोक्षैः R. 7. 13 ; स्थाने प्राणाः कामिनां दूत्यधीनाः M. 3. 14 ; Ku. 6 67, 7. 65. 2 In place of, instead of, in lieu of ; as a substitute for ; धातोः स्थाने इवादेशं सुग्रीवं संन्यवेशयत् R. 12. 58. 3 On account of, because of. 4 Similarly, like as.

स्थापक *a.* Causing to stand, fixing, founding, establishing, regulating. –कः 1 Tha director of the stage-business, a stage-manager. 2 The founder of a temple, or erector of an image.

स्थापत्यः A guard of the women's apartments. –त्यं Architecture, building.

स्थापनं 1 The act of causing to stand, fixing, founding, directing, establishing, instituting. 2 Fixing the thoughts, concentration of the mind, steady application, abstraction. 3 A dwelling, habitation. 4 A ceremony performed on a woman's perceiving the first signs of living conception ; cf. पुंसवन.

स्थापना 1 Placing, fixing, founding, establishing. 2 Arranging, regulating (as a drama), stage-management.

स्थापित *p. p.* 1 Placed, fixed, located, deposited. 2 Founded, instituted. 3 Set up, raised, erected. 4 Directed, regulated, ordered, enacted. 5 Determined, settled, ascertained. 6 Appointed to, entrusted with any duty, post &c. 7 Wedded, married ; Mâl. 10. 5. 8 Firm, steady.

स्थाप्य *a.* 1 To be placed or deposited. 2 To be founded, fixed or established. –प्यं A pledge, deposit. –Comp. –अपहरणं the embezzlement of a deposit.

स्थामन् *n.* 1 Strength, power. stamina, as in the word अश्वत्थामन्, see the quotation from Mb. under अश्वत्थामन्. 2 Fixity, stability.

स्थायिन् *a.* 1 Standing, staying, being situated (at the end of comp.) 2 Enduring, continuing, lasting, abiding ; शरीरं क्षणविध्वंसि कल्पान्तस्थायिनो गुणाः Subhâsh. ; कतिपयदिवसस्थायिनी यौवनश्रीः Bh. 2. 82 ; Mv. 7. 15. 3 Living, dwelling, remaining ; Me. 23. 4 Permanent, firm, steady, invariable, unchangeable ; स्थायीभवति 'becomes permanent'. –*m.* 1 A lasting or permanent feeling ; (see स्थायिभाव below); *Si.* 2. 87. –*n.* Anything lasting, a permanent state or condition. –Comp. –भावः a fixed or permanent condition of mind, a lasting or permanent feeling ; (these feelings being said to give rise to the different *rasas* or sentiments in poetry, each *rasa* having its own Sthâyibhâva); they are eight or nine ; रतिर्हासश्च शोकश्च क्रोधोत्साहौ भयं तथा । जुगुप्सा विस्मयश्चेत्थमष्टौ प्रोक्तः शमोऽपि च S. D. 206 ; cf. व्यभिचारभाव, भाव, विभाव also.

स्थायुक *a.* (का or की *f.*) 1 Likely to last, enduring. 2 Firm, steady, stationary. –कः The superintendent or head of a village.

स्थालं 1 A plate or dish. 2 A cooking-pot, any culinary vessel. –Comp. –रूपं the form or representation of a pot.

स्थाली 1 An earthen pot or pan, a cooking-pot, caldron, kettle ; न हि भिक्षुकाः संतीति स्थाल्यो नाधिश्रीयते Sarva. S.; स्थाल्यां वैडूर्यमय्यां पचति तिलखलीमिंधनैश्चंदनाद्यैः Bh. 2. 100. 2 A particular vessel used in the preparation of Soma. 3 The trumpet-flower. –Comp. –पाकः a particular religious act performed by a householder. –पुरीषं the sediment or dirt sticking to a cooking-pot. –पुलाकः boiled rice in a cooking-pot. °न्यायः see under न्याय. –विलं the interior or hollow of a caldron.

स्थावर *a.* 1 Fixed to one spot, stable, stationary, immoveable, inanimate (opp. जंगम); शरीराणां स्थावरजंगमानां सुखाय तज्जन्मदिनं बभूव Ku. 1. 23, 6. 67, 73. 2 Inert, inactive, slow. 3 Regular, established. –रः A mountain ; स्थावराणां हिमालयः Bg. 10. 25 –रं 1 Any stationary or inanimate object (such as clay, stones, trees &c. which formed the seventh creation of Brahman ; cf. Ms. 1. 41); मान्यः स मे स्थावरजंगमानां सर्गस्थितिप्रत्यवहारहेतुः R. 2. 44; Ku, 6. 58. 2 A bow-string. 3 Immoveable property, real estate. 4 A heir-loom. –Comp. –अस्थावरं, –जंगमं 1 moveable and immoveable property. 2 animate and inanimate things.

स्थाविर *a.* (रा or री *f.*) Thick, firm. –रं Old age.

स्थासकः 1 Perfuming or smearing the body with fragrant unguents. 2 A bubble of water or any fluid ; *Si.* 18. 5.

स्थासु *n.* Bodily strength.

स्थास्नु *a.* 1 Disposed to stand, firm, immoveable. 2 Permanent, eternal, lasting, durable ; *Si.* 2. 93, Ki. 2. 19.

स्थित *p. p.* 1 Stood, remained, stayed. 2 Standing. 3 Standing up, risen ; स्थितः स्थितामुच्चलितः प्रयातां ...छायेव तां भूपतिरन्वगच्छत् R. 2. 6. 4 Staying, resting, living, being, existing, situated ; धन्या केयं स्थिता ते शिरसि Mu. 1. 1. Me. 7 ; oft. with gerunds merely as a copula ; V. 1. 1 ; *S.* 1. 1, Ku. 1. 1. 5 Happened, occurred ; Ku. 4. 27. 6 Stationed in, occupying, appointed to ; *S.* 4. 18. 7 Acting upto, abiding by, conforming to ; R. 5. 33. 8 Stood still, stopped, desisted. 9 Fixed on, firmly attached to ; Ku. 5. 82. 10 Steady, firm ; as in स्थितधी or स्थितप्रज्ञ q. v. 11 Determined, resolved ; Ku. 4. 39. 12 Established, decreed. 13 Steadfast in conduct, steady-minded. 14 Upright, virtuous. 15 Faithful to a promise or agreement. 16 Agreed, engaged, contracted. 17 Ready, being close or at hand. –तं A word standing by itself. –Comp. –उपस्थित *a.* with and without the particle '*iti*' (as a word). –धी *a.* firm-minded, steady-minded, cool. –पाठ्यं recitation in Prâkṛita by a woman while standing. –प्रज्ञ *a.* firm in judgment or wisdom, free from any hallucination, contented ; प्रजहाति यदा कामान् सर्वान् पार्थ मनोगतान् । आत्मन्येवात्मना तुष्टः स्थितप्रज्ञस्तदोच्यते Bg. 2. 55. –प्रेमन् *m.* a staunch or faithful friend.

स्थितिः *f.* 1 Standing, remaining, staying, abiding, living, stay residence ; स्थितिं नो रे दध्याः क्षणमपि मदांधेक्षण सखे Bv. 1. 52 ; रक्षो गृहे स्थितिर्मूलमग्निशुद्धौ त्वनिश्चयः U. 1. 6. **2** Stopping, standing still, continuance in one state ; प्रस्थितायां प्रतिष्ठेथाः स्थितायां स्थितिमाचरेः R. 1. 89. **3** Remaining stationary, fixity, steadiness, firmness, steady application or devotion ; मम भूयात् परमात्मनि स्थितिः Bv. 4. 23. **4** A state, position, situation, condition. **5** Natural state, nature, habit ; अथ वा स्थितिरियं मंदमतीनां H. 4. **6** Stability, permanence, perpetuation, continuance ; वंशस्थितेरधिगमान्महति प्रमोदे V. 5. 15 ; कन्यां कुलस्य स्थितये स्थितिज्ञः Ku. 1. 18 ; R. 3. 27. **7** Correctness of conduct, steadfastness in the path of duty, decorum, duty, moral rectitude, propriety ; R. 3. 27, 11. 65, 12. 31 ; Ku. 1. 18. **8** Maintenance of discipline, establishment of good order (in a state) ; R. 1. 25. **9** Rank, dignity, high station or rank. **10** Maintenance, sustenance ; Mâl. 9. 32, R. 5. 9. **11** Continuance in life, preservation (one of the three states of human beings); सर्गस्थितिप्रत्यवहारहेतुः R. 2. 44 ; Ku. 2. 6. **12** Cessation, pause, stop. **13** Well-being, welfare. **14** Consistency. **15** A settled rule; ordinance, decree, an axiom or maxim. **16** Settled determination. **17** Term, limit, boundary. **18** Inertia, resistance to motion. **19** Duration of an eclipse. -**Comp.** -**स्थापक** *a.* fixing in the original position, having the power of restoring to a previous state, having elastic properties. (-**कः**) elasticity, capability of recovering the former position.

स्थिर *a.* (compar. स्थेयस् ; superl. स्थेष्ठ) **1** Firm, steady, fixed ; भावस्थिराणि जननांतरसौहृदानि *S.* 5. 2 ; स स्थाणुः स्थिरभक्तियोगसुलभो निःश्रेयसायास्तु वः V. 1. 1 ; Ku. 1. 30 ; R. 11. 19. **2** Immoveable, still, motionless ; Ku. 2. 38. **3** Immoveably fixed ; U. 1. 40. **4** Parmanent, eternal, everlasting ; Me. 55 ; Mâl. 1. 25. **5** Cool, collected, composed, placid, calm. **6** Quiescent, free from passion. **7** Steady in conduct, stead-fast. **8** Constant, faithful, determined. **9** Certain, sure. **10** Hard, solid. **11** Strong, intense. **12** Stern, relentless, hard-hearted ; Ku. 5. 47. -**रः** **1** A god, deity. **2** A tree. **3** A mountain. **4** A bull. **5** N. of *S*iva. **6** N. of Kârtikeya. **7** Final beatitude or absolution. **8** The planet Saturn. (-**स्थिरीकृ** means **1** to confirm, strengthen, corroborate. **2** to stop, make fast. **3** to cheer up, console, comfort ; *S*. 4. -**स्थिरीभू** means **1** to become firm or steady. **2** to become calm or tranquil). -**Comp.** -**अनुराग** *a.* firm in attachment, constant in affection. -**आत्मन्**, -**चित्त**, -**चेतस्**, -**धी**, -**बुद्धि**, -**मति** *a.* **1** firm-minded, steady in thought or resolve, resolute ; R. 8. 22. **2** cool, calm, dispassionate. -**आयुस्**, -**जीविन्** *a.* long-lived, lasting. -**आरंभ** *a.* firm in undertakings, persevering. -**कुट्टकः** **1** a steady pulverizer. **2** a kind of common divisor(in algebra). -**गंधः** the *champaka* flower. -**छदः** the birch tree. -**छायः** **1** a tree which gives shelter to travellers. **2** a tree. (in general). -**जिह्वः** a fish. -**जीविता** the silk-cotton tree. -**दंष्ट्रः** a snake. -**पुष्पः** **1** the *champaka* tree. **2** the *Bakula* tree. -**प्रतिज्ञ** *a.* **1** persisting in an assertion, obstinate, pertinacious. **2** faithful to a promise. -**प्रतिबंध** *a.* firm in opposition, obstinate ; *S*. 2. -**फला** a kind of gourd. -**योनिः** a large tree which gives shade and shelter. -**यौवन** *a.* ever youthful. (-**नः**) a kind of good or evil genius, a fairy. -**श्री** *a.* having everlasting prosperity. -**संगर** *a.* faithful to a promise, true, veracious. -**सौहृद** *a.* firm in friendship. -**स्थायिन्** *a.* remaining firm or steady, keeping perfectly still (as in meditation).

स्थिरता-त्वं **1** Firmness, steadiness, stability. **2** Firm or vigorous effort, fortitude ; *S.* 4. 14. **3** Constancy, firmness of mind. **4** Fixity.

स्थिरा The earth.

स्थुड् 6 P. (स्थुडति) To cover.

स्थुलं A sort of long tent.

स्थूणा **1** The post or pillar of a house. **2** A post or pillar in general ; स्थूणानिखननन्यायेन S. B. **3** An iron image or statue. **4** An anvil. -**Comp.** -**निखननन्याय** see under न्याय.

स्थूमः **1** Light. **2** The moon.

स्थूरः **1** A bull. **2** A man.

स्थूल *a.* (compar. स्थवीयस्, superl. स्थविष्ठ) **1** Large, great, big, bulky, huge ; बहुसपृशापि स्थूलेन स्थीयते बहिरश्मवत् *S*i. 2. 78. (where it has sense 6 also); स्थूलहस्तावलेपान् Me. 14, 106 ; R. 6. 28. **2** Fat, corpulent, stout. **3** Strong, powerful ; स्थूलं स्थूलं श्वसिति K. ' breathes hard '. **4** Thick, clumsy. **5** Gross, coarse, rough (fig. also); as in स्थूलमानं q. v. **6** Foolish, doltish, silly, ignorant. **7** Stolid, dull, thick-headed. **8** Not exact. -**लः** The jack tree. -**लं** **1** A heap, quantity. **2** A tent. **3** The summit of a mountain (कूट). -**Comp.** -**अंत्रं** the larger intestine near the anus. -**आस्यः** a snake. -**उच्चयः** **1** a large fragment of a crag or rock fallen from mountain and forming an irregular mound. **2** incompleteness, deficiency, defect. **3** the middle pace of elephants. **4** an eruption of pimples on the face. **5** a hollow at the root of an elephant's tusks. -**काय** *a.* fat, corpulent. -**क्षेडः**, -**क्ष्वेडः** an arrow. -**चापः** a large bow-like instrument used in cleaning cotton. -**तालः** the marshy date-tree. -**धी**, -**मति** *a.* foolish, doltish. -**नालः** a kind of large reed. -**नास**, -**नासिक** *a.* thick-nosed. (-**सः**, -**कः**) a hog, boar. -**पटः**-**टं** coarse cloth. -**पट्टः** cotton. -**पाद** *a.* club-footed, having swelled legs. (-**दः**) **1** an elephant. **2** a man with elephantiasis. -**फलः** the silk cotton tree. -**मानं** rough or inexact calculation, gross or rough computation. -**मूलं** a kind of radish. -**लक्ष-क्ष्य** *a.* **1** munificent, liberal, generous. **2** wise, learned. **3** inclined to recollect both benefits and injuries. -**शंखा** a woman having a large vulva. -**शरीरं** the grosser or material and perishable body. (opp. सूक्ष्म or लिंग-शरीर q. v. (-**शाटकः**, -**शाटिः** thick or coarse cloth. -**शीर्षिका** a small ant having a large head in proportion to its size. -**षट्-पदः** **1** a large bee. **2** a wasp. -**स्कंधः** the *lakucha* tree. -**हस्तं** an elephant's trunk.

स्थूलक *a.* Large, big, huge, bulky. -**कः** A sort of grass or reed.

स्थूलता-त्वं **1** Largeness, bulkiness, bigness. **2** Dullness, stupidity.

स्थूलयति Den. P. To become big or stout, grow bulky or fat.

स्थूलिन् *m.* A camel.

स्थेमन् *m.* Firmness, stability, fixity, fixedness ; द्राघीयसः संहताः स्थेमभाजः *S*i. 18. 33 ; न यत्र स्थेमानं दधुरतिभयभ्रांतनयनाः Bv. 1. 32.

स्थेय *a.* To be fixed or placed, to be settled or determined. -**यः** **1** A person chosen to settle a dispute (between two parties), an arbitrator, umpire, a judge. **2** A domestic priest.

स्थेयस् *a.* (**सी** *f.*) More firm, stronger ; (compar. of स्थिर q. v.).

स्थेष्ठ *a.* Very firm, strongest ; (superl. of स्थिर q. v.).

स्थैर्यं **1** Firmness, stability, fixity, steadiness. **2** Continuance. **3** Firmness of mind, resolution, constancy; Bg. 13. 7. **4** Patience. **5** Hardness, solidity.

स्थौणेयः, **स्थौणेयकः** A kind of perfume.

स्थौरं **1** Firmness, strength, power. **2** A load sufficient for a horse or ass.

स्थौरिन् *n.* **1** A horse carrying burdens on his back, pack-horse. **2** A strong horse.

स्थौल्यं Bigness, bulkiness, stoutness.

स्नपनं 1 Sprinkling, washing. 2 Bathing, ablution ; रेजे जनैः स्नपनसांद्रतरार्द्रमूर्तिः Si. 5. 57.

स्नवः Trickling, oozing, dripping.

स्नस् 1. 4 P. (स्नसति, स्नस्यति) 1 To inhabit. 2 To eject (as from the mouth), reject.

स्ना 2 P. (स्नाति, स्नात) 1 To bathe, perform ablution मृगतृष्णाम्भसि स्नातः. 2 To perform the ceremony of bathing at the time of leaving the house of one's spiritual preceptor. -*Caus.* (स्नापयति-ते, स्नपयति-ते) To cause to bathe, wet, moisten, sprinkle ; (तोयैः) सतूर्यमेनां स्नपयांबभूवुः Ku. 7. 10 ; स्मितस्नापिताधरा Git. 12. U. 3. 23, Ki. 5. 44. 47 ; Si. 2. 7, 8. 3, Me. 43. -*Desid* (सिस्नासति) To wish to bathe. -WITH अप to bathe after mourning. -नि to plunge deep into ; *i. e.* to be perfect or thoroughly versed in ; see निष्णात.

स्नातकः 1 A Brâhmaṇa who has performed the ceremony of ablution which has to be performed on his finishing his first Asrama (that of a Brahmachârin). 2 A Brâhmaṇa just returned from the house of his preceptor and become an initiated householder (गृहस्थ). 3 A Brâhmaṇa who is a *Bhikshu* (beggar of alms) for any religious object ; Ms. 11. 1. 4 Any man of the first three classes who is an initiated householder.

स्नानं 1 Bathing, washing, ablution, immersion in water ; ततः प्रविशति स्नानोत्तीर्णः काश्यपः S. 4. 2 Purification by bathing, any religious or ceremonial ablution. 3 The ceremony of bathing or anointing an idol. 4 Anything used in ablution. -Comp. -अगारं a bath-room -द्रोणी a bathing tub. -यात्रा the festival held on the full-moon day in the month of Jyeshṭha -वस्त्रं a bathing-garment ; सकृत् किं पीडितं स्नानवस्त्रं मुंचेत् द्रुतं पयः H. 2. 106 -विधिः 1 the act of ablution. 2 the proper manner or rules of ablution.

स्नानीय *a*. Fit or suitable for bathing or ablution, worn during bathing, स्नानीयवस्त्रक्रियया पत्रोर्णं वोपयुज्यते M. 5. 12. -यं Water or any other article (such as unguents, perfumed powders &c.) proper for bathing ; R. 16. 21.

स्नापकः A servant who bathes his master, or brings bathing water for him.

स्नापनं The act of causing to bathe or attending a person while bathing. Ms. 2. 209.

स्नायुः 1 A tendon, muscle, sinew, स्वल्पं स्नायुवसावशेषमलिनं निर्मांसमप्यस्थि गोः Bh. 2. 30. 2 The string of a bow. -Comp. -अर्मन् *n*. a kind of disease of the eyes.

स्नायुकः See स्नायु.

स्नावः स्नावन् *m*. A tendon, muscle.

स्निग्ध *a*. 1 Loving, affectionate, friendly, attached, tender ; Mâl. 5. 20. 2 Oily, unctuous, greasy, wetted with oil ; उत्पश्यामि त्वयि तटगते स्निग्धभिन्नांजनाभे Me. 59 स्निग्धवेणीसवर्णे 18 ; Si. 12. 63 ; Mâl. 10. 4. 3 Sticky, viscid, adhesive, cohesive. 4 Glistening, shining, glossy, resplendent ; कनकनिकषस्निग्धा विद्युत् प्रिया न ममोर्वशी V. 4. 1 ; Me. 37 ; U. 1. 33, 6. 21. 5 Smooth, emollient. 6 Moist, wet. 7 Cooling. 8 Kind, soft, bland, amiable ; प्रीतिस्निग्धैर्जनपदवधूलोचनैः पयिमानः Me. 16. 9 Lovely, agreeable, charming ; R. 1. 36 ; U. 2. 14, 3. 22. 10 Thick, dense, compact ; स्निग्धच्छायातरुषु वसतिं रामगिर्याश्रमेषु (चक्रे) Me. 1. 11 Intent, fixed, steadfast (as a gaze or look). -ग्धः 1 A friend, an affectionate or friendly, person ; विज्ञैः स्निग्धैरुपकृतमपि द्वेष्यतां याति किंचित् H. 2. 160; or स स्निग्धोऽकुशलान्निवारयति यः Subhâsh. ; Pt. 2. 166. 2 The red castor-oil plant. 3 A kind of pine. -ग्धं 1 Oil. 2 Bee's-wax. 3 Light, lustre. 4 Thickness, coarseness. -Comp. -जनः an affectionate or friendly person, a friend ; स्निग्धजनसंविभक्तं हि दुःखं सह्यवेदनं भवति S. 3. -तंडुलः a kind of rice of quick growth -दृष्टि *a*. looking intently or with a fixed gaze.

स्निग्धता-त्वं 1 Oiliness. 2 Blandness. 3 Tenderness, affection, love.

स्निग्धा Marrow.

स्निह् 4 P. (स्निह्यति स्निग्ध) 1 To feel or have affection for, love, be fond of (with loc. of the person or thing that is loved or liked) ; किं नु खलु बालेऽस्मिन्नौरस इव पुत्रे स्निह्यति मे मनः S. 7 ; स च स्निह्यत्यावयो U. 6. (where आवयोः may be genitive also). 2 To be easily attached 3 To be pleased with, be kind to. 4 To be sticky, viscid or adhesive. 5 To be smooth or bland. -*Caus* (स्नेहयति-ते) 1 To make unctuous, anoint, besmear, lubricate. 2 To cause to love. 3 To dissolve, destroy, kill.

स्नु 2 P. (स्नौति, स्नुत) 1 To drip, trickle, fall in drops, distil, drop, ooze or run out, leak out. 2 To flow, stream. -WITH प्र to flow out, pour forth ; प्रस्नुतस्तनी U. 3.

स्नु *m. n.* 1 Table-land. 2 Top, surface (in general). (This word has no forms for the first five inflections and is optionally substituted for सानु after acc. dual.)

स्नुः *f*. A sinew, tendon, muscle.

स्नुत *a*. Oozed, dropped, flowed &c.

स्नुषा A daughter-in-law ; स्नुषयत पुत्रभोग्यया स्नुषयेवाविकृतेंद्रियः श्रिया R. 8. 14, 15. 72.

स्नुह् 4 P. (स्नुह्यति, स्नुग्ध or स्नूढ) To vomit.

स्नेहः 1 Affection, love, kindness, tenderness ; स्नेहदाक्षिण्ययोर्योगात् कामीव प्रतिभाति मे V. 2. 4 (where it has sense 6 also) ; अस्ति मे सोदरस्नेहोप्येतेषु S. 1. 2 Oiliness, viscidity, unctuousness, lubricity (one of the 24 Guṇas according to the Vaiseshikas). 3 Moisture. 4 Grease, fat, any unctuous substance. 5 Oil ; निर्विष्टविषयस्नेहः स दशांतमुपेयिवान् R. 12. 1, Pt. 1. 87. (where the word has sense 1 also); R. 4. 75. 6 any fluid of the body, such as semen. -Comp. -अक्त *a*. oiled, lubricated, greased. -अनुवृत्तिः *f*. affectionate or friendly intercourse. -आशः a lamp. -छेदः, -भंगः breach or loss of friendship -पूर्वं *ind*. affectionately -प्रवृत्तिः *f* flow or course of love ; S. 4. 16. -प्रिय *a*. fond of oil, (-यः) a lamp. -भूः phlegm. -रंगः sesamum. -बस्तिः *f*. injection of oil, an oily enema. -विमर्दित *a*. anointed with oil. -व्यक्तिः *f* manifestation of love, display of friendship : (भवति) स्नेहव्यक्तिश्चिरविरहजं मुंचतो बाष्पमुष्णं Me. 12.

स्नेहन् *m*. 1 A friend. 2 The moon. 3 A kind of disease.

स्नेहन *a*. 1 Anointing, lubricating. 2 Destroying. -नं 1 Anointing, unction, rubbing or smearing with oil or unguents. 2 Unctuousness. 3 An unguent, emollient.

स्नेहित *p. p.* 1 Loved. 2 Kind, affectionate. 3 Anointed, lubricated; -तः A friend, a beloved person.

स्नेहिन् *a*. (-नी *f*) 1 Attached, affectionate, friendly. 2 Oily, unctuous, fat. -*m*. 1 A friend. 2 An anointer, a smearer. 3 A painter.

स्नेहुः 1 The moon. 2 A kind of disease.

स्नै 1 P. (स्नायति) To dress, wrap round, envelop.

स्नैग्ध्यं 1 Unctuousness, oiliness, lubricity. 2 Tenderness, fondness. 3 Smoothness, blandness.

स्पंद् 1 A. (स्पंदते स्पंदित) 1 To throb, palpitate ; अस्पंदिष्टाक्षि वामं च Bk. 15. 27, 14. 83. 2 To shake, tremble, quiver 3 To go, move. -WITH परि to throb, tremble. -वि to move about, struggle.

स्पंदः 1 Throbbing, palpitation. 2 Vibration, tremor, motion, मनो मंदस्पंदं बहिरपि चिरस्यापि विमृशन् Bh. 3. 51.

स्पंदनं 1 Throbbing, pulsation, palpitation, quivering ; वामाक्षिस्पंदनं सूचयित्वा Mâl. 1 ; so अधर,° बाहु°, शरीर° &c. 2 Tremor, vibration. 3 The quickening of a child in the womb.

स्पंदित *p. p.* 1 Throbbed, quivered. 2 Gone. -तं A pulsation, throb, palpitation.

स्पर्ध् 1 A. (स्पर्धते) 1 To contend or vie with, emulate, rival, compete, be equal with ; अस्पर्धिष्ट च रामेण Bk. 15. 65 ; कस्तैस्सह स्पर्धते Bh. 2. 16. 2 To challenge, defy, bid defiance to. –WITH प्रति, –वि to bid defiance, challenge.

स्पर्धा 1 Emulation, rivalry, competition ; आत्मनस्तु बुधैः स्पर्धा शुद्धयोर्बह्मन्यत. 2 Jealousy, envy. 3 Defiance. 4 Equality with.

स्पर्धिन् *a.* (नी *f.*) 1 Rivalling, emulating, competing, vying with ; तवाधरस्पर्धिषु विद्रुमेषु R. 13. 13, 16. 62. 2 Emulous, envious. 3 Proud. –*m.* A competitor, an equal.

स्पर्श् 10 A. (स्पर्शयते) 1 To take, take hold of, touch. 2 To unite, join. 3 To embrace, clasp.

स्पर्शः 1 Touch, contact (in all senses) ; तदिदं स्पर्शक्षमं रत्नं *S.* 1. 28, 2. 7. 2 Contact (in astr.). 3 Conflict, encounter. 4 Feeling, sensation, the sense of touch. 5 The quality of touch or tangibility, touch, the object or विषय of skin (त्वच्) ; स्पर्शगुणो वायुः T. S. 6 That which affects or influences, affection, seizure 7 Disease, illness, disorder, distemper. 8 A consonant of any of the five classes of letters (from क् to म्) ; कादयो मांताः स्पर्शाः. 9 A gift, donation, presentation. 10 Air, wind. 11 The sky. 12 Sexual union. –र्शा An unchaste woman. –Comp. –अज्ञ *a.* senseless, insensible. –इंद्रियं the organ or sense of touch. –उदय *a.* followed by a consonant. –उपलः, –मणिः a kind of jewel considerd to be the same as 'philosopher's stone'. –तन्मात्रं the subtile element of tangibility. –लज्जा the sensitive plant. –वेद्य *a.* to be apprehended by the sense of touch. –संचारिन् *a.* contagious, infectious. –स्नानं ablution at the entrance of the sun or moon into an eclipse. –स्पंदः, –स्यंदः a frog.

स्पर्शन *a.* (नी *f.*) 1 Touching, handling. 2 Affecting, influencing. –नः Air, wind. –नं 1 Touching, touch, contact. 2 Sensation, feeling. 3 Sense or oragan of touch. 4 Gift, donation.

स्पर्शनकं A term used in Sânkhya philosophy for the ' skin '.

स्पर्शवत् *a.* 1 Tangible. 2 Soft, soft or agreeable to the touch ; Ku. 1. 55.

स्पर्ध् 1 A (स्पर्धते) To become wet or moist.

स्पर्ष्ट् *m.* A distemper, disorder of the body, disease.

स्पश् 1 U. (स्पशति-ते) 1 To obstruct. 2 To undertake, perform. 3 To string together. 4 To touch. 5 To see, behold, perceive clearly, spy out, espy.

स्पशः 1 A spy, a secret emissary or agent ; स्पशे शनैर्गतवति तत्र विद्विषां *Si.* 17. 20 ; see अपस्पश also. 2 Fight, war, battle. 3 One who fights with savage animals (for reward), or the fight itself.

स्पष्ट *a.* 1 Distinctly visible, evident, clearly perceived, clear, plain, manifest ; स्पष्टे जाति प्रत्यूषे K. ' when it was broad day-break ' ; स्पष्टाकृतिः R. 18. 30 ; स्पष्टार्थः &c. 2 Real, true. 3 Full-blown, expanded. 4 One who sees clearly. –ष्टं *ind.* 1 Clearly, distinetly, plainly. 2 Openly, boldly. (स्पष्टीकृ means 'to make clear or distinct, explain, elucidate'). –Comp. –गर्भा a woman who shows evident signs of pregnancy. –प्रतिपत्तिः *f.* distinct notion, clear perception. –भाषिन्,–वक्तृ *a.* plain-spoken, outspoken, candid.

स्पृ 5 P. (स्पृणोति) 1 To deliver or extricate from. 2 To gratify, grant, bestow. 3 To protect. 4 To live.

स्पृक्का N. of a wild plant.

स्पृश् 6 P. (स्पृशति, स्पृष्ट) 1 To touch; स्पृशन्नपि गजो हंति H. 3. 14 ; कर्णे परं स्पृशति हंति परं समूलं Pt. 1. 304. 2 To lay the hand on, stroke gently with, touch ; Ku. 3. 22. 3 To adhere or cling to, come in contact with. 4 To wash or sprinkle with water ; Ms. 2. 60. 5 To go to, reach ; *S.* 2. 14 ; R. 3. 43. 6 To attain to, obtain, reach a particular state ; महोक्षतां वत्सतरः स्पृशन्निव R. 3. 32. 7 To act upon, influence, affect, move, touch ; Mu. 7. 16 ; Ku. 6. 95. 8 To refer or allude to. –*Caus.* (स्पर्शयति ते) 1 To cause to touch. 2 To give, present ; गाः कोटिशः स्पर्शः यता घटोध्नीः R. 2. 49. WITH अप= उपस्पृश्. –अभि to touch. –उप 1 to touch. 2 to wash or sprinkle with water ; Ms. 4. 143. 3 to sip, water, rinse the mouth ; स नव्यवस्कंदमुपास्पृशच्च Bk. 2. 11 ; Ms. 2. 53, 5. 63 ; अप उपस्पृश्य. 4 to bathe; R. 5. 59, 18. 31. –परि to touch. –सं 1 to touch. 2 to sprinkle with water ; Ms. 2. 53. 3 to bring in contact with.

स्पृश् *a.* (At the end of comp.) Who or what touches, touching, affecting, piercing ; मर्मस्पृश् ˜ पृ श् &c.

स्पृष्ट *p. p.* 1 Touched, felt with the hand. 2 Come in contact with, touching. 3 Not reaching, applying or extending to; अस्पृष्टपुरुषांतरं Ku. 6. 75. 4 Affected, seized ; Me. 69 ; अनघस्पृष्ट R. 10. 19. 5 Tainted, defiled ; Ms. 8. 205. 6 Formed by the complete contact of the organs of speech (the letters of the five classes); अचोऽस्पृष्टा यणस्त्वीषन्नेमस्पृष्टाः शलः स्मृताः शेषाः स्पृष्टा हलः प्रोक्ता निबोधानुप्रदानतः *Sik.* 38.

स्पृष्टिः, -स्पृष्टिका *f.* Touch, contact ; तद्रूपस्य अस्मच्छारीरस्पृष्टिकया शापितोसि Mk. 3.

स्पृह् 10 U. (स्पृहयति-ते) To wish, long for, desire for, yearn, envy (with dat.); स्पृहयामि खलु दुर्ललितायास्मै S. 7 ; तपःक्लेशायापि स्पृहयंती K ; न मैथिलेयः स्पृहयांबभूव भर्त्रे दिवो नाप्यलकेश्वराय R. 16. 42, Bh. 2. 45.

स्पृहणं The act of desiring or wishing, longing for.

स्पृहणीय *a.* To be desired or longed for, enviable, desirable ; अहो बतासि स्पृहणीयवीर्यः Ku. 3. 20 ; वंद्या त्वमेव जगतः स्पृहणीयसिद्धिः Mâl. 10. 21; परस्परेण स्पृहणीयशोभं न चेदिदं द्वंद्वमयोजयिष्यत् R. 7. 14, Ku. 7. 60 ; U. 6. 40.

स्पृहयालु *a.* Disposed to be desirous or envious of, longing or eager for, covetous (with dat. or loc. ; भोगेभ्यः स्पृहयालवो न हि वयं Bh. 3. 64 ; तपोवनेषु स्पृहयालुरेव R. 14. 45.

स्पृहा Desire, eager desire, ardent wish, longing, envy, covetousness ; कथमन्ये करिष्यंति पुत्रेभ्यः पुत्रिणः स्पृहां Ve. 3. 29, R. 8. 34.

स्पृह्य *a.* Desirable, enviable. –ह्यः The wild citron tree.

स्पॄ 9 P. (स्पृणाति) To hurt, kill.

स्पष्ट् *m.* See स्पर्ष्ट्.

स्फट् 1 P. (स्फटति) To burst, expand.

स्फटः A snake's expanded hood ; cf. फट-टा.

स्फटा 1 A snake's expanded hood. 2 Alum.

स्फटिकः A crystal, quartz ; अपगतमले हि मनसि स्फटिकमणाविव रजनिकरगभस्तयः सुखं प्राविशंत्युपदेशगुणाः K. –Comp. –अचलः the mount Meru. –अद्रिः the mount Kailâsa. °भिद् *m.* camphor. –अश्मन्, -आत्मन्, -मणि *m.*, -शिला a crystal stone.

स्फटिकारिः, स्फटिकारिका *f.* Sulphate of alumina.

स्फटिकी Alum.

स्फंद् I. 1 P. (स्फंटति) To burst, open, expand. –II. 10 U. (स्फंटयति-ते) To jest or joke with, laugh at.

स्फर् See स्फुर्.

स्फरणं Trembling, quivering, throbbing.

स्फल् 1 P. (स्फलति) To tremble, quiver, throb, palpitate. –10. U. or *caus.* (स्फालयति-ते) To cause to tremble or shake. WITH आ 1 to cause to tremble, cause to flap, shake, rock. 2 to strike or press against, splash आस्फालितं यत्प्रमदाकराग्रैः R. 16. 13, U. 5. 9. 3 to strike, play upon ; *Si.* 1. 9. 4 to twang (as a bow.)

स्फाटिक *a.* (की *f.*) Crystalline. –कं A crystal.

स्फाटित *p. p.* Split open, burst, expanded, made to gape.

स्फातिः *f.* 1 Swelling, intumescence. 2 Increase, growth.

स्फाय् 1 A. (स्फायते, स्फीत) 1 To grow large or fat, to become big or bulky. 2 To swell, increase, expand; संदुधुक्षे तयोः कोपः पस्फाये शस्त्रलाघवं Bk. 14. 109. *-Caus.* (स्फावयति-ते) To cause to grow large, augment, increase; तावस्फावयता शक्तीर्बाणांश्चाकिरतां मुहुः Bk. 17. 43, 4. 33, 12. 76, 15. 99.

स्फार *a.* 1 Large, great, increased, expanded; स्फारफुल्लफणापीठनिर्यत् &c.; Mâl. 5 23, Mv. 6. 32. 2 Much, abundant; Mv. 5. 2; Bh. 3. 42. 3 Loud. **-रः** 1 Swelling, increase, enlargement, growth. 2 A bubble (in gold). 3 A protuberance. 4 Throbbing, quivering palpitation, vibration. 5 Twanging. **-रं** Abundance, much, plenty. (**स्फारीभू** means 'to swell out, expand, spread out, increase, multiply'; सुस्निग्धा विमुखीभवंति सुहृदः स्फारीभवंत्यापदः Mk. 1. 36.

स्फारण Throbbing, shaking, trembling.

स्फालः Throbbing, palpitation, beat, trembling.

स्फालनं 1 Quivering, palpitating. 2 Causing to shake about or move. 3 Rubbing, friction. 4 Patting or stroking (as a horse), gentle rubbing.

स्फिच् *f.* Buttocks, hips; अंसास्फिक्पृष्ठपिंडाद्यवयवसुलभान्युग्रपूतानि जग्ध्वा Mâl. 5.16.

स्फिट् 10 U. (स्फेटयति-ते) 1 To hurt, injure, kill. 2 To despise. 3 To love. 4 To cover.

स्फिट्ट 10 U. (स्फिट्टयति-ते) To hurt &c.; see स्फिट् above.

स्फिर *a.* (compar. स्फेयस्, superl. स्फेष्ठ) 1 Abundant, much, large. 2 Many, numerous. 3 Vast, capacious.

स्फीत *p. p.* 1 Swollen, increased; Ve. 5. 40. 2 Fat, thick, big, large, bulky. 3 Many, numerous, much, copious, plentiful, abundant. 4 Pure, Bv. 4. 13. 5 Successaful, prosperous, thriving. 6 Affected by hereditary disease. (**स्फीतीकृत** means 'to augment or enlarge').

स्फीतिः *f.* 1 Growth, increase, enlargement. 2 Abundance, copiousness, plenty; धनधान्यस्य च स्फीतिः सदा मे वर्ततां गृहे. 3 Prosperity.

स्फुट् I. 6 P., 1 U. (स्फुटति, स्फोटति-ते, स्फुटित) 1 To burst or split open, break forth, be suddenly rent asunder, cleave split, break; हाहा देवि स्फुटति हृदयं ध्वंसते देहबंधः U. 3. 38; स्फुटति न सा मनसिजविशिखेन Gît. 7; Bk. 14. 56, 15. 77. 2 To expand, open, blow, blossom; स्फुटति कुसुमनिकरे विरहिहृदयदलनाय Gît. 5; Pt. 1. 136, Kâv. 3. 167. 3 To run or bound away, disperse; तुरंगाः पुस्फुटुर्भीताः Bk. 14. 6, 10. 8. 4 To become visible, burst into view, become evident or manifest. -II. 10 U. (स्फुटयति-ते) 1 To burst, crack, break open. 2 To burst into view. *-Caus.* (स्फोटयति-ते) 1 To burst or rend asunder, split, tear open, cleave, divide. 2 To manifest, show, make clear. 3 To disclose, divulge, make public 4 To hurt, destroy, kill. 5 To winnow.

स्फुट *a.* 1 Burst, rent asunder, broken, split. 2 Opened, expanded, full-blown; स्फुटपरागपरागतपंकजं Si. 6. 2, 5. 3 Manifested, displayed, made clear, 4 Clear, plain, distinctly visible or manifest; अत्र स्फुटो न कश्चिदलंकारः K. P. 1; Ku. 5. 44; Me. 70; Ki. 11. 44. 5 Bursting into view; U. 3. 42. 6 White, bright, pure; मुक्ताफलं वा स्फुटविद्रुमस्थं Ku. 1.44. 7 Well-known, famous; स्फुटंनृत्यलीलमभवत्सुतनोः Si. 9. 79 (प्रथित). 8 Spread, diffused. 9 Loud. 10 Apparent, true. **-टं** *ind.* Clearly, evidently, distinctly, certainly, manifestly. **-Comp.** **-अर्थ** *a.* 1 intelligible, obvious. 2 significant. **-तार** *a.* bright or gemmed with stars. **-फलं** (in geom.). 1 distinct or precise area of a triangle. 2 the clear or net result of any calculation. **-सारः** the true latitude of a star or planet (?). **-सूर्यगतिः** *f.* the apparent or true motion of the sun.

स्फुटनं 1 Breaking open, rending, bursting forth, tearing open. 2 Expanding, opening, blossoming.

स्फुटिः **-टी** *f.* Cracking of the skin of the feet, sores or swelling of the feet.

स्फुटिका A small bit broken off, a slice.

स्फुटित *p. p.* 1 Burst, broken open, split, cracked. 2 Budded, blown, expanded (as a flower). 3 Made clear, manifested, shown. 4 Torn, destroyed. 5 Laughed at. **-Comp.** **-चरण** *a.* having wide feet, splay-footed.

स्फुट्ट 10 U. (स्फुट्टयति-ते) To despise, slight, disrespect.

स्फुड् 6 P. (स्फुडति) To cover.

स्फुंड् I. 1. P. (स्फुंटति) To open, expand. -II. 10 U. (स्फुंटयति-ते) To jest, joke, laugh at.

स्फुंड् 1 A., 10 U. (स्फुंडते, स्फुंडयति-ते) See स्फुंट्.

स्फुत् *ind.* An imitative sound. **-Comp.** **-करः** fire. **-कारः** the sound स्फुत्, a crackling noise.

स्फुर् 6. P. (स्फुरति, स्फुरित) 1 (*a*) To throb, palpitate (as eyes); शांतमिदमाश्रमपदं स्फुरति च बाहुः कुतः फलमिहास्य S. 1. 15; स्फुरता वामकेनापि दाक्षिण्यमवलंब्यते Mâl. 1. 8. (*b*) To shake, tremble, quiver, vibrate in general; स्फुरदधरनासापुटतया U. 1. 29, 6. 33. 2 To twitch, struggle, become agitated; हतं पृथिव्यां करुणं स्फुरंतं Râm. 3 To start, dart, spring forward; पुस्फुरुर्वृषभाः परं Bk. 14. 6. 4 To spring back, rebound (as a bow) 5 To spring or break forth, shoot out, spring up, rise forth; धर्मतः स्फुराति निर्मलं यशः. 6 To start into view, become visible or manifest, appear clearly, become displayed; मुखात्स्फुरंतीं को हर्तुमिच्छति हरेः परिभूय दंष्ट्रा Mu. 1. 8; रचितरुचिरभूषां दृष्टिमोषे प्रदोषे स्फुरति निरवसादां कापि राधां जगाद Gît. 11. 7 To flash, scintillate, sparkle, glitter, gleam, shine; स्फुरतु कुचकुंभयोरुपरि मणिमंजरी रंजयतु तव हृदयेशं Gît. 10; (तया) स्फुरत्प्रभामंडलया चकाशे Ku. 1. 24, R. 3. 60, 5. 51; Me. 15, 27. 8 To shine, distinguish oneself, become eminent; Pt. 1. 27. 9 To flash on the mind, rush suddenly into memory. 10 To go tremulously. 11 To bruise, destroy. *-Caus.* (स्फारयति ते, स्फोरय ति-ते) 1 To cause to throb or vibrate. 2 To cause to shine, irradiate. 3 To throw, cast. -WITH अप to shine forth or out. **-अभि** 1 to spread or be diffused, expand. 2 to become known. **-परि** to throb, quiver, palpitate; तस्याः परिस्फुरितगर्भभरालसायाः U. 3. 28. **-प्र** 1 to quiver, tremble. 2 to expand, be dilated; प्रास्फुरन्नयनं Mb. 2 to spread far and wide, become known; संस्थितस्य गुणोत्कर्षः प्रायः प्रस्फुरति स्फुटं Subhâsh. **-वि** 1 to quiver, tremble. 2 to struggle. 3 to shine, gleam; U. 4. 4 to draw or twang (as a bow, used in *caus.* in the same sense); एकोपि विस्फुरितमंडलचापचक्रः सिंधुराजमभिषेणयितुं समर्थः Ve. 2. 25; Ki. 14. 31.

स्फुरः 1 Throbbing, trembling, quivering. 2 Swelling. 3 A shield.

स्फुरणं 1 Throbbing, quivering, trembling (in general). 2 Throbbing or quivering or certain parts of the body (indicating good or bad luck). 3 Breaking forth, arising, starting into view. 4 Gleaming, flashing, glittering, shining, twinkling. 5 Flashing on the mind, crossing the memory.

स्फुरत् *a.* Throbbing, shining &c. **-Comp.** **-उल्का** a shooting meteor, aerolite.

स्फुरित *p. p.* 1 Trembling, throbbing. 2 Shaken. 3 Glittering, shining. 4 Unsteady. 5 Swollen. **-तं** 1 A throb, palpitation, tremor. 2 Agitation or emotion of the mind.

स्फुर्च्छ् 1 P. (स्फूर्च्छति) 1 To spread, extend. 2 To forget.

स्फुर्ज् 1 P. (स्फूर्जति) 1 To thunder, make a sound like thunder-clap, crash, explode; Ms. 1. 53. 2 To glitter, shine. 3 To burst or break forth; स्फूर्जत्येष स एष संप्रति मम न्यक्कारमिच्छस्थितेः Mv. 3. 40. -WITH वि 1 to roar, thunder. 2 to resound. 3 to increase. 4 to shine, appear; अस्त्येवं जडधामता तु भवतो यद् व्योम्नि विस्फूर्जसे K. P. 10.

स्फुल् 6. P. (स्फुलति) 1 To tremble, throb, vibrate. **2** To dart forth, appear. **3** To collect. **4** To kill, destroy.

स्फुलं A tent.

स्फुलनं Trembling, Throbbing, palpitation.

स्फुलिंगः, -गं, स्फुलिंगा A spark of fire ; स्फुलिंगावस्थया वह्निरेधापेक्ष इव स्थितः S. 7. 15, Ve. 6. 8.

स्फूर्जः 1 The crashing sound of a thunder-clap. **2** Indra's thunderbolt. **3** Sudden burst or rise, as in नर्मस्फूर्ज. **4** First union of lovers characterized by joy in the beginning and some expectation of a fear in the end.

स्फूर्जथुः A clap or peal of thunder.

स्फूर्तिः *f.* **1** Throbbing, shaking, vibration. **2** Spring, bound. **3** Blooming, opening. **4** Manifestation, display. **5** Flashing on the mind. **6** Poetical inspiration.

स्फूर्तिमत् *a.* 1 Throbbing, tremulous, agitated. **2** Tenderhearted.

स्फेयस् *a.* More abundant, larger (compar. of स्फिर q. v.)

स्फेष्ठ *a.* Most abundant, largest (superl. of स्फिर q. v.)

स्फोटः 1 Breaking forth, splitting open, bursting. **2** Disclosure ; as in नर्मस्फोट. **3** A swelling, boil, tumor. **4** The idea which bursts out or flashes on the mind when a sound is uttered, the impression produced on the mind at hearings a sound; बुधैर्वैयाकरणैः प्रधानभूतस्फोटरूपव्यंग्यव्यंजकस्य शब्दस्य ध्वनिरिति व्यवहारः कृतः K. P. 1, also see Sarva. S. (पाणिनीयदर्शन). **5** The eternal sound recongnised by the Mîmâmsakas. **-Comp.** -बीजकः the marking-nut plant.

स्फोटन *a.* (नी *f.*) Breaking asunder, manifesting, disclosing, making clear. -नः Separated utterance of a close combination of consonants. -नं **1** Rending, suddenly bursting, splitting, cracking. **2** Winnowing grain. **3** Cracking the fingerjoints, snapping the fingers. **4** The separation of a double consonant.

स्फोटनी The boring tool, an auger, gimlet.

स्फोटा The expanded hood of a serpent.

स्फोटिका A kind of bird.

स्फोरणं See स्फुरणं.

स्फ्यं A sword-shaped implement used in sacrifices ; Ms. 5. 117 ; Y. 1. 184. **-Comp.** -वर्तनिः the furrow made by this implement.

स्म् See स्मृ.

स्म *ind.* 1 A particle added to the present tense of verbs (or to present participles) and giving them the sense of the past tense ; भासुरको नाम सिंहः प्रतिवसति स्म Pt. 1; क्रीणंति स्म प्राणमूल्यैर्यशांसि Si. 17. 15. **2** A pleonastic particle (generally added to the prohibitive particle मा q. v.); भर्तुर्विप्रकृतापि रोषणतया मास्म प्रतीपं गमः S. 4. 17 ; मास्म सीमंतिनी काचिज्जनयेत्पुत्रमीदृशं H. 2. 7.

स्मयः 1 Astonishment, wonder, surprise. **2** Arrogance, pride, haughtiness, conceit ; तस्मै स्मयावेशविवर्जिताय R. 5. 19, Bh. 3. 2, 69.

स्मरः 1 Recollection, remembrance. **2** Love. **3** Cupid, the god of love ; स्मर पर्युत्सुक एष माधवः Ku. 4. 28, 42, 43. **-Comp.** -अंकुशः **1** a finger-nail. **2** a lover, lascivious person. -अगारं, -कूपकः,-गृहं,-मंदिरं female organ. -अंध *a.* blinded by love, infatuated with passion. -आतुर, -आर्त, -उत्सुक *a.* pining with love, love-sick, smit with love. -आसवः saliva. -कर्मन् *n.* any amorous action, a wanton act. -गुरुः an epithet of Vishṇu. -छत्रं the clitoris. -दशा state of love, state of the body produced by being in love (these are ten). -ध्वजः **1** the male organ. **2** a fabulous fish. **3** N. of a musical instrument. (-जं) the female organ. (-जा) a bright moon-light night. -प्रिया an epithet of Rati. -भासित *a.* inflamed by love. -मोहः infatuation of love, passion. -लेखनी the Sârikâ bird. -वल्लभः **1** an epithet of Spring. **2** of Aniruddha. -वीथिका a prostitute, harlot. -शासनः an epithet of Siva. -सखः the moon. -स्तंभः the male organ. -स्मर्यः a donkey, an ass. -हरः an epithet of Siva.

स्मरणं 1 Remembering, remembrance, recollection; केवलं स्मरणेनैव पुनासि पुरुषं यतः R. 10. 30. **2** Thinking of or about ; यदि हरिस्मरणे सरसं मनः Git. 1 **3** Memory. **4** Tradition, traditional precept ; इति भृगुस्मरणात् (opp. श्रुति). **5** Mental recitation of the name of a deity **6** Remembering with regret: regretting: **7** Rhetorical recollection, regarded as a figure of speech ; thus defined :—यथानुभवमर्थस्य दृष्टे तत्सदृशे स्मृतिः स्मरणं K. P. 10. **-Comp.** -अनुग्रहः **1** a kind remembrance. **2** the favour of remembrance ; Ku. 6. 19. -अपत्यतर्पकः a turtle, tortoise. -अयौगपद्यं the non-simultaneousness of recollections. -पदवी death.

स्मार *a.* Relating to Smara or the god of love ; स्मारं पुष्पमयं चापं बाणाः पुष्पमया अपि । तथाप्यनंगस्त्रैलोक्यं करोति वशमात्मनः ॥ -रं Recollection, memory.

स्मारक *a.* (रिका *f.*) Reminding. -कं A memorial (a modern use).

स्मारणं Calling to mind, raminding, causing to remember.

स्मार्त *a.* **1** Relating to memory, remembered, memorial. **2** Being within memory. **3** Based on or recorded in a Smriti, prescribed in a code of laws ; कर्मस्मार्तं विवाहाग्नौ कुर्वीत प्रत्यहं गृही Y. 1. 97 ; Ms. 1. 108. **4** Legal. **5** Following or professing the law-books. **6** Domestic (as fire). -र्तः **1** A Brâhmaṇa well-versed in traditional law. **2** One who follows the traditional law. **3** N. of a sect.

स्मि 1 A. (स्मयते, स्मित) **1** To smile, laugh (gently); काकुत्स्थ ईषत्स्मयमान आस्त Bk. 2. 11, 15. 8 स्मयमानं वदनांबुजं स्मरामि Bv. 2. 27. **2** To bloom, expand ; Pt. 1. 136 *-Caus.* (स्मापयति ते) **1** To cause a smile by, cause to smile. **2** To laugh at, deride. **3** To astonish (स्मापयते in this sense). *-Desid* (सिस्मयिषते) To wish to smile. -WITH उद् to smile, laugh.-वि **1** to wonder or be surprised at ; उभयोर्न तथा लोकः प्रावीण्येन विसिस्मिये R. 15. 65 ; Bk. 5. 51. **2** to admire. **3** to be proud or conceited ; न विस्मयेत तपसा Ms. 4. 236. (*-Caus.*) to cause to smile, cause to be surprised, fill with wonder or astonishment ; विस्माययन् विस्मितमात्मवृत्तौ R. 2. 33, Bk. 5. 58, 8. 42.

स्मिट् 10 U. (स्मेटयति-ते) **1** To slight, scorn, despise. **2** To love. **3** To go.

स्मित *p. p.* **1** Smiled, smiling. **2** Expanded, blown, blossomed. -तं A smile, gentle laugh ; सस्मितं ' with a smile ' ; सविलक्षस्मितं &c -**Comp.** -दृश् *a.* having a smiling look. (-*f.*) a handsome woman. -पूर्वम् *ind.* smilingly, with a smile ; सप्तर्षिभिस्तान् स्मितपूर्वमाह Ku. 7. 47.

स्मील् 1 P. (स्मीलति) To wink, blink.

स्मृ I. 5 P. (स्मृणोति) **1** To please, gratify. **2** To protect, defend. **3** To live. -II. 1 P. (Atm. also in epic poetry) (स्मरति, स्मृत; *pass.* स्मर्यते) **1** *(a)* To remember, bear or keep in mind, recollect, call to mind, be aware of ; स्मरसि सुतनु तस्मिन् पर्वते लक्ष्मणेन ... स्मरसि गोदावरीं वा स्मरसि च तदुपांतेष्वावयोर्वर्तनानि U. 1 26. *(b)* To call to mind, call upon mentally, think of ; स्मरात्मनोऽभीष्टदेवता Pt. 1 ; R. 15. 45. **2** To recite mentally or call upon the name of a deity &c. ; यः स्मरेत्पुंडरीकाक्षं सबाह्याभ्यंतरः शुचिः **3** To lay down or record in a Smriti ; तथा च स्मरंति. **4** To declare, regard, consider ; Pt. 1. 30. **5** To remember with regret, yearn after, long or desire for (oft. with gen.); स्मर्तुं दिशंति न दिवः सुरसुंदरीभ्यः Ki. 5. 28 ; कच्चिद्भर्तुः स्मरसि रसिके त्वं हि तस्य प्रियेति Me 85 ; Mu. 5. 14. *-Caus.* (स्मारयति-ते, but स्मरयति-ते in the last sense) **1** To cause to remember, remind, put in mind of, call to mind ; अनेन मल्लियामियोगेन स्मारयसि मे पूर्वशिष्यां सौदामिनीं Mâl. 1: sometimes with two acc. ; अपि चंद्रगुप्तदोषा अतिक्रांतपार्थिवगुणान् स्मारयंति प्रकृतीः Mu. 1; य एव दुःस्मरः कालस्त-

मेव स्मारिता वयं U. 6. 34. **2** To give information **3** To cause to remember with regret, cause to long or desire for; Si 6. 56, 8. 64. *-Desid* (सुस्मूर्षते) To wish to recollect. -WITH **अनु** to remember, recollect, call to mind. **-अप** to forget. **-प्र** to forget. **-वि** to forget; मधुकर विस्मृतोस्येनां कथं *S* 5. 1 (*-Caus.*) to cause to forget; U. 1. **-सं** to remember, think of; Bg. 18. 76, Ms. 4. 149. (*-Caus.*) to remind, put in mind of; (पाताल) मामद्य संस्मरयतीव भुजंगलोकः Ratn. 1. 13.

स्मृतिः *f.* **1** Remembrance, recollection, memory; अश्वत्थामा करधृतधनुः किं न यातः स्मृतिं ते Ve 3. 21; संस्कारमात्रजन्यं ज्ञानं स्मृतिः T. S; स्मृत्युपस्थितौ इमौ द्वौ श्लोकौ U. 6. **2** Thinking of, calling to mind. **3** What was delivered by human authors, law, traditional law, the body of traditional or memorial law (civil or religious) (opp. श्रुति). **4** A code of laws, law-book. **5** A text of Smriti, canon, rule, of law; इति स्मृतेः. **6** Desire, wish. **7** Understanding. **-Comp. -अंतरं** another law-book. **-अपेत** *a.* **1** forgotten **2** inconsistent with Smriti. **3** (hence) illegal, unjust. **-उक्त** *a.* prescribed or enjoined in the codes of law, canonical. **-पथः, -विषयः** the object of memory; स्मृतिपथं, विषयंगम to be dead; Bh. 3. 37, 38. **-प्रत्यवमर्षः** retentiveness of memory, accuracy of recollection. **-प्रबंधः** a legal work. **-भ्रंशः** loss or failure of memory. **-रोधः** temporary interruption of memory; loss or failure of memory; *S.* 7. 32. **-विभ्रमः** confusion of memory. **-विरुद्ध** *a.* illegal. **-विरोधः** **1** opposition to law, illegality. **2** Deisagreement between two or more Smṛities or legal texts : स्मृतिविरोधं परिहरति S. B. **-शास्त्रं** **1** a law book, code, digest. **2** legal science. **-शेष** *a.* deceased, dead (as person). **-शैथिल्यं** temporary loss of memory. **-साध्य** *a.* capable of being proved by law **-हेतुः** a cause of recollection, impression on the mind, association of ideas.

स्मेर *a.* **1** Smiling; विलोक्य वृद्धोक्षमधिष्ठितं त्वया महाजनः स्मेरमुखो भविष्यति Ku. 5. 70; Bv. 2. 4; 3. 2; Mâl. 10. 6. **2** Blown, expanded, dilated, blooming; अधिकविकसदंतर्विस्मयस्मेरतारैः Mâl. 1. 28. **3** Proud. **4** Evident. **-Comp. -विष्किरः** a peacock.

स्यदः Speed, rapid motion, rush, velocity.

स्यंद् 1 A. (स्यंदते, स्यन्न; *desid.* सिस्यंदिषते, सिस्यंत्सति-ते; the स् of स्यंद् is changed to ष् after a preposition ending in इ or उ) **1** To ooze, trickle, drop, drip, distil, flow; अपि दलदरविंदस्यंदमानं मरंदं तव किमपि लिहंतो मंजु गुंजंतु भृंगाः Bv. 1. 5 **2** To shed, pour forth. **3** To run, flee. -WITH **अनु** to flow. **-अभि** **1** to ooze, flow. **2** to rain, pour down water; अभिष्यंदमानमिवमंदुरितनीलिमा गिरः U. 2. 3 to be melted; U. 6. **-नि,-परि** to flow out or forth. **-प्र** to flow forth. **-वि** to flow; Bk. 9. 74.

स्यंदः **1** Flowing, trickling. **2** Going rapidly, moving. **3** A car, chariot.

स्यंदन *a.* (ना or नी *f.*) **1** Going quickly, fleet; flowing. **2** Quick, swift of foot, fleet; स्यंदना नो चतुरगाः Ki. 15. 16. **-नः** **1** A war-chariot, a car or chariot in general; धर्मारण्यं प्रविशति गजः स्यंदनालोकभीतः *S.* 1. 33. **2** Air, wind. **3** A kind of tree. (तिनिश). **-नं** **1** Flowing, trickling, oozing. **2** Rushing, going or flowing quickly. **3** Water. **-Comp. -आरोहः** a warrior who fights while seated in a chariot.

स्यंदनिका A drop, of saliva.

स्यंदिन् *a.* (नी *f.*) **1** Oozing, flowing, trickling. **2** Rushing. **3** Going.

स्यंदिनी **1** Saliva. **2** A cow bearing two calves at the same time.

स्यन्न *p. p.* Oozed, trickled, dropped.

स्यम् 1 P., 10 U. (स्यमति, स्यमयति-ते) **1** To sound, to cry aloud, shout. **2** To go. **3** To consider, reflect (Atm. only in this sense).

स्यमंतक A kind of valuable jem (said to yield daily eight loads of gold and to preserve from all kinds of dangers and portents). For some account, see the word सत्राजित्.

स्यमि(मी)कः **1** A cloud. **2** An ant-hill. **3** A kind of tree. **4** Time.

स्यानिका Indigo.

स्यात् *ind.* (Strictly 3rd. pers. sing. of the Potential of अस् ' to be '). It may be, perhaps, perchance. **-Comp. -वादः** an assertion of probability (in phil.) a form of scepticism. **-वादिन्** *m.* a sceptic.

स्यालः See श्याल.

स्यूत *p. p.* **1** Sewn with a needle, stitched, woven (fig. also); चिंतासंततितंतुजालनिबिडस्यूतेव लग्ना प्रिया Mâl. 5. 10. **2** Pierced. **-तः** A sack.

स्यूतिः **1** Sewing, stitching. **2** Needle-word. **3** A sack. **4** Lineage, family. **5** Offspring.

स्यूतः **1** A ray of light. **2** The sun. **3** A bag, sack.

स्यूमः A ray of light.

स्योतः A sack, bag.

स्योन *a.* **1** Beautiful, pleasing. **2** Auspicious, propitious. **-नः** **1** A ray of light **2** The sun. **3** A sack. **-नं** Happiness, pleasure.

स्रंस् 1 A. (स्रंसते, स्रस्त) **1** To fall, fall or drop down, slip off or down; नाल्पसत्कारिणी ग्रैवं त्रिपदीच्छेदिनामपि R. 4. 48; गांडीवं स्रंसते हस्तात् Bg. 1. 29; Bk. 14. 72. 15. 61. **2** To sink, drop, fall asunder; हाहा देवि स्फुटति हृदयं स्रंसते देहबंधः U. 3. 38; Mâl. 9. 20. **3** To hang down. **4** To go. *-Caus.* (स्रंसयति ते) **1** To cause to fall or slip down, move, ditsurb; वातोपि नास्रंसयदंशुकानि R. 6. 75 **2** To relax, loosen -WITH **वि** to slip down, become loosened, (*-Caus.*) **1** to cause to fall down, let fall; विस्रंसयंती नवकर्णिकारं Ku. 3. 62. **2** to loosen, relax.

स्रंसः Falling, slipping.

स्रंसनं **1** Falling. **2** Causing to fall, or bringing down.

स्रंसिन् *a.* (नी *f.*) **1** Falling or slipping down, hanging down, being loosened, giving way; बंधे स्रंसिनि चैकहस्तयमिताः पर्याकुला मूर्धजाः *S.* 1. 30. **2** Depending, pendulous, hanging loosely.

स्रंह् 1 A. (स्रंहते) To confide or trust.

स्रग्विन् *a.* (णी *f.*) (compar. स्रजीयस् superl. स्रजिष्ठ) Wearing a garland or chaplet; आमुक्ताभरणः स्रग्वी हंसचिह्नदुकूलवान् R. 17. 25.

स्रज् *f.* **1** A chaplet, wreath or garland of flowers (especially one worn on the head); स्रजमपि शिरस्यंधः क्षिप्तां धुनोत्यहिशंकया *S.* 7. 24. **2** A garland (in general). **-Comp. -दामन्,** (स्रग्दामन्) *n.* the tie or fillet of a garland. **-धर** *a.* wearing a garland; Gît. 12. (**-रा**) N. of a metre.

स्रज्वा A rope, string, cord.

स्रद्धू *f.* Breaking wind downwards (अपानवायु).

स्रंभ् 1 A. (स्रंभते, स्रब्ध) To confide; see श्रंभ्. -WITH **वि** **1** to be confident. **2** to rest secure.

स्रवः **1** Trickling, oozing, flowing. **2** A drop, flow, stream; विपुलौ स्नपयंती सा स्तनौ नेत्रजलस्रवैः Râm. **3** A fountain, spring.

स्रवणं **1** Flowing, trickling, oozing. **2** Sweat. **3** Urine.

स्रवत् *a.* (स्रवंती *f.*) Flowing, oozing, trickling &c. **-Comp. -गर्भा** **1** a woman that miscarries. **2** a cow miscarrying by accident.

स्रवंती A stream, river; वापीष्विव स्रवंतीषु R. 17. 63.

स्रष्टृ *m.* **1** A maker. **2** A creator. **3** The creator, an epithet of Brahman; या सृष्टिः स्रष्टुराद्या *S.* 1. 1; तत्स्रष्टुरेकांतरं 7. 27. **4** N. of Siva.

स्रस्त *p. p.* **1** Fallen or dropped down; slipped off, fallen off; स्रस्तं शारं चापमपि स्वहस्तात् Ku. 3 51; कनकवलयं स्रस्त स्रस्तं मया प्रतिसार्यते *S.* 3. 13; Ki. 5. 33, Me. 63. **2** Drooping, hanging loosely down; विषादस्रस्तसर्वांगी Mk. 4. 8; स्रस्तांसावतिमात्रलोहिततलौ बाहू घटोत्क्षेपणात् *S.* 1. 30. **3** Loosed. **4** Let go, relaxed. **5** Pendulous, hanging down. **6** Separated. **-Comp. -अंग** *a*

1 having the limbs relaxed. 2 swooning, fainting.

स्रस्तरः A couch or sofa (for reclining), bed; शिलातले स्रस्तरमास्तीर्य निषसाद K., Ms. 2. 204.

स्राक् *ind.* Quickly, speedily.

स्रावः Flow, flowing, oozing, dropping.

स्रावक *a.* (विका *f.*) Causing to flow, pouring out, exuding. **–कं** Black pepper.

स्रिभ् 1 P. (स्रेभति) To hurt, kill.

स्रिंभ् 1 P. (स्रिंभति) To hurt, kill.

स्रिव् 4 P. (स्रीव्यति, स्रुत) 1 To go. 2 To become dry.

स्रु 1 P. (स्रवति, स्रुत) 1 To flow, stream, trickle, ooze, drop, exude; न हि निंबात्स्रवेत्क्षौद्रं Râm. 2 To pour out, shed, let flow; अलोदिष्ट च भूपृष्ठे शोणितं चाप्यसुस्रुवत् Bk. 15. 76, 17. 18. 3 To go, move. 4 To trickle or slip away, wastle away, perish, come to nothing; स्रवते ब्रह्म तस्यापि भिन्नभांडात्पयो यथा Bhâg.; Bk. 6. 18; Ms. 2. 74. 5 To spread about, get abroad, transpire (as a secret). *–Caus.* (स्रावयति-ते) To cause to flow, pour out, shed, spill (blood &c.); न गात्रात्स्रावयेदसृक् Ms. 4. 169. (With prepositions the root retains nearly the same meanings).

स्रुघ्नः N. of a district; पंथाः स्रुघ्नमुपतिष्ठते Sk.; (it was situated at some distance-at least one day's journey–from Pâtaliputra q. v.; cf. न हि देवदत्तः स्रुघ्ने संनिधीयमानस्तदहरेव पाटलिपुत्रे संनिधीयते युगपदनेकत्र वृत्तावनेकत्वप्रसंगात् S. B.

स्रुघ्नी Natron.

स्रुच् *f.* A sort of wooden ladle, used for pouring clarified butter on sacrificial fire; (usually made of trees like Palâsa or Khadira); R. 11. 25; Ms. 5. 117; Y. 1. 183. **–Comp. –प्रणालिका** the spout of a ladle.

स्रुत् *a.* (Usually at the end of comp.) Flowing, dropping, pouring forth; स्वरेण तस्याममृतस्रुतेव Ku. 1. 4, 5; Si. 9. 68.

स्रुतिः *f.* 1 Flowing, oozing, distilling, trickling out; कीटक्षतिस्रुतिभिरस्रमिवोद्वमंतः Mu. 6. 13; पदं तुषारस्रुतिधौतरक्तं Ku. 1. 5; R. 16. 44; Ki. 5. 44, 16. 2; क्षीरस्रुतिसुरभयः (वाताः) Me. 107. 'exudation or flow of the sap.' 2 Exudation, resin. 3 A stream.

स्रुवः-वा 1 A sacrifical ladle. 2 A spring, cascade.

स्रेक् 1 A. (स्रेकते) To go, move.

स्रै 1 P. (स्रायति) 1 To boil. 2 To sweat; see श्रै.

स्रोतं A stream; see स्रोतस्.

स्रोतस् *n.* 1 (*a*) A stream, current flow or course of water; यत्र स्रोतः पुरा पुलिनमधुना तत्र सरितां U. 2. 27, Ms. 3 163. (*b*) A torrent, rapid stream; नद्याकाशगंगायाः स्रोतस्युद्दामदिग्गजे R. 1. 78; स्रोतसेवोह्यमानस्य प्रतीपतरणं हि तत् V. 2. 5. 2 A stream, river (in general); स्रोतसामस्मि जाह्नवी Bg. 10. 31. 3 A wave. 4 Water. 5 The canal of nutriment in the body. 6 An organ of sense; निगृह्य सर्वस्रोतांसि Râm. 7 The trunk of an elephant. **–Comp. –अंजनं (स्रोतोंजनं)** antimony. **–ईशः** the ocean. **–रंध्र** an aperture of the proboscis or trunk of an elephant, a nostril; स्रोतोरंध्रध्वनितसुभगं दंतिभिः पीयमानः Me. 42 (see Malli. thereon); (written श्रोतोरंध्र also q. v.). **–वहा** a river; स्रोतोवहां पथि निकामजलामतीत्य जातः सखे प्रणयवान् मृगतृष्णिकायां S. 6. 15; कार्या सैकतलीनहंसमिथुना स्रोतोवहा मालिनी 6. 16, R. 6. 52.

स्रोतस्यः 1 N. of Siva. 2 A thief.

स्रोतस्वती, स्रोतास्विनी A river.

स्व *pron. a.* 1 One's own, belonging to oneself, often serving as a reflexive pronoun; स्वनियोगमशून्यं कुरु S. 2; प्रजाः प्रजाः स्वा इव तंत्रयित्वा 5. 5; oft. in comp. in this sense; स्वपुत्र, स्वकलत्र, स्वद्रव्य. 2 Innate, natural, inherent, peculiar, inborn; सूर्यापाये न खलु कमलं पुष्यति स्वामभिख्यां Me. 80; S. 1. 18; स तस्य स्वो भावः प्रकृतिनियतत्वादकृतकः U. 6. 14. 3 Belonging to one's own caste or tribe; शूद्रैव भार्या शूद्रस्य सा च स्वा च विशः स्मृते: Ms. 3. 13, 5. 104. **–स्वः** 1 A relative, kinsman; Pt. 2. 96; Ms. 2. 109. 2 The soul. **–स्वः,-स्वं** Wealth, property, as in निःस्व q. v. **–Comp. –अक्षपादः** a follower of the Nyâya system of philosophy. **–अक्षरं** one's own hand-writing. **–अधिकारः** one's own duty or sway; स्वाधिकारात्प्रमत्तः Me. 1., स्वाधिकारभूमौ S. 7. **–अधिष्ठानं** one of the six Chakras or mystical circles of the body. **–अधीन** *a.* 1 dependent on oneself, self-dependent. 2 independent. 3 one's own subject. 4 in one's own power; स्वाधीना वचनीयतापि हि वरं बद्धो न सेवांजलिः Mk. 3. 11. **°कुशल** *a.* having prosperity in one's own power; स्वाधीनकुशलाः सिद्धिमंतः S. 4. **°पतिका, °भर्तृका** a woman who has full control over her husband, one whose husband is subject to her; अथ सा निर्गताबाधा राधा स्वाधीनभर्तृका निजगाद। रतिक्लांतं कांतं मंडनवांछया. Gît. 12; see S. D. 112 *et seq.* **–अध्यायः** 1 self-recitation, muttering to one-self. 2 study of the Vedas, sacred study. **–अनुभूतिः** *f.* 1 self-experience. 2 self-knowledge; स्वानुभूत्येकसाराय नमः शांताय तेजसे Bh. 2. 1. **–अंतं** 1 the mind; Bv. 4. 5: Mv. 7. 17. 2 a cavern. **–अर्थः** 1 one's own interest, self-interest; सर्वः स्वार्थं समीहते Si. 2. 65. 2 own meaning; Bv. 1. 79 (where both senses are intended). **°अनुमानं** inference for oneself, a kind of inductive reasoning, one of the two main kinds of अनुमान; the other being परार्थानुमान. **°पंडित** *a.* 1 clever in one's own affairs. 2 expert in attending to own interests. **°पर, °परायण** *a.* intent on securing one's own interests, selfish. **°विघातः** frustration of one's object. **°सिद्धिः** *f.* fulfilment of one's own object. **–आयत्त** *a.* subject to, or dependent upon, oneself; Bh. 2 7. **–इच्छा** self-will, own inclination. **°मृत्युः** an epithet of Bhishma. **–उदयः** the rising of a sign or heavenly body at any particular place. **–उपधिः** a fixed star. **–कंपनः** air, wind. **–कर्मिन्** *a.* selfish. **–कार्यं** one's own business or interest **गतम्** *ind.* to oneself, aside (in theatrical language). **–छंद** *a.* 1 self-willed, uncontrolled, wanton. 2 wild. (**–दः**) one's own will or choice, own fancy or pleasure, independence. (**–दं**) *ind.* at one's own will or pleasure, wantonly, voluntarily; स्वच्छंदं दलदरविंद ते मरंदं विंदंतो विदधतु गुंजितं मिलिंदाः Bv. 1. 5. **–ज** *a.* self-born. (**–जः**) 1 a son or child. 2 sweat, perspiration. (**–जं**) blood. **–जनः** 1 a kinsman, srelative; इतः प्रत्यादेशात् स्वजनमनुगंतुं व्यवसिता S. 6. 8, Pt. 1. 5. 2 one's own people or kindred, one's household. **तंत्र** *a.* self-dependent, uncontrolled, independent, self-willed. (**–त्रः**) a blind man. **-देशः** one's own country, native country. **°जः, °बंधुः** a fellow-countryman. **–धर्मः** 1 one's own religion. 2 one's own duty, the duties of one's own class; Ms. 1. 88-91. 3 peculiarity, one's own property. **–पक्षः** one's own side or party. **–परमंडलं** one's own and an enemy's country. **–प्रकाश** *a* 1 self-evident. 2 self-luminous. **–प्रयोगात्** *ind.* by means of one's own efforts. **–भटः** 1 one's own warrior. 2 body-guard. **–भावः** 1 own state. 2 an essential or inherent property, natural constitution, innate or peculiar disposition, nature; as in स्वभावो दुरतिक्रमः Subhâsh.; so कुटिल°, शुद्ध°, °मृदु, °चपल, °कठिन &c. **°उक्तिः** *f.* 1 spontaneous declaration. 2 (in Rhet.) a figure of speech which consists in describing a thing to the life, or with exact resemblance; स्वभावोक्तिस्तु डिंभादेः स्वक्रियारूपवर्णनं K. P. 10, or नानावस्थं पदार्थानां रूपं साक्षाद्विवृण्वती Kâv. 2. 8. **°वादः** the doctrine that the universe was produced and is sustained by the natural and necessary action of substances according to their inherent properties, (and not by the agency of a Supreme Being). **°सिद्ध** *a.* natural, spontaneous, inborn. **–भूः** 1 an epithet of Brahman. 2 of Siva. 3 of Vishnu. **–योनि** *a.* related on the mother's side. (**–m. f.**) own womb, one's own place of birth. (**–f.**) a sister or near female relative. -रसः 1 natural taste. 2 proper taste or sentiment in composition. -राज् *m.* the Supreme Being. -रूप *a.* 1 similar, like. 2 handsome, pleasing, lovely. 3 learned, wise (-पं) 1 one's own form or shape, natural state or condition. 2 natural character or form, true constitution. 3 nature. 4 peculiar aim. 5 kind, sort, species. °असिद्धि *f.* one of the three forms of fallacy called असिद्ध q. v. -वश *a.* 1 self-controlled. 2 independent. -वासिनी a woman whether married or unmarried who continues to live after maturity in her father's house. -वृत्ति *a.* living by one's own exertions. -संवृत्त *a.* self-protected, self-guarded. -संस्था 1 self-abiding. 2 self-possession. 3 absorption in one's own self. -स्थ *a.* 1 self-abiding. 2 self-dependent, relying on one's own exertions, confident, firm, resolute. 3 independent. 4 doing well, well, in health, at ease, comfortable; स्वस्थ एवास्मि Mâl. 4; स्वस्थे को वा न पंडितः Pt. 1. 127; see अस्वस्थ also. 5 contented, happy. (-स्थं) *ind.* at ease, comfortably, composedly. -स्थानं one's own place or home; one's own abode; नक्रः स्वस्थानमासाद्य गजेंद्रमपि कर्षति Pt. 3. 46. -हस्त one's own hand or handwriting, an autograph; see under हस्त. -हस्तिका an axe. -हित *a.* beneficial to oneself. (-तं) one's own good or advantage, one's own welfare.

स्वक *a.* One's own, own.

स्वकीय *a.* 1 One's own, own. 2 Of one's own family.

स्वंग् 1 P. (स्वंगति) To go, move.

स्वंगः An embrace.

स्वच्छ *a.* 1 Very clear or transparent, pure, bright, pellucid; स्वच्छस्फटिक, स्वच्छमुक्ताफलं &c. 2 White. 3 Beautiful. 4 Healthy. -च्छः A crystal. -च्छं A pearl. -Comp.-पत्रं talc. -वालुकं pure chalk. -मणिः a crystal.

स्वंज् 1 A (स्वंजते; the स् being changed to ष् after prepositions ending in इ or उ) 1 To embrace, clasp; कयाचिदाचुंब्य चिराय सस्वजे Bv. 2. 178; पर्यश्रुरस्वजत मूर्धनि चोपजघ्रौ R. 13. 70. 2 To encircle, twist round. -WITH परि to embrace; वत्से परिष्वजस्व मा सखीजनं च *S.* 4; Bv. 2. 178.

स्वट्ट् 10 U. (स्व-स्वा-ट्टयति-ते) 1 To go. 2 To finish.

स्वतस् *ind.* Of oneself, by oneself (used reflexively).

स्वत्वं 1 Self-existence. 2 Ownership, proprietory right.

स्वद् I. 1 A (स्वदते, स्वदित) 1 To be liked, be sweet, be pleasant to the taste (with dat. of person); यज्ञदत्ताय स्वदतेऽपूपः Kâsikâ; अपांहि तृप्ताय न वारिधारा स्वादुः सुगंधिः स्वदते तुषारा N. 3. 93; सस्वदे मुखसुरं प्रमदाभ्यः Si. 10. 23. 2 To taste, relish, eat. 3 To please. 4 To sweeten. -II. 10 U. or *Caus.* (स्वादयति-ते) 1 To cause to taste or eat. 2 To taste. 3 To sweeten. -WITH आ 1 to taste, eat (fig. also); पपावनास्वादितपूर्वमाशुगः R. 3. 54. 2 to enjoy; Me. 87.

स्वदनं Tasting, eating.

स्वदित *p. p.* Tasted, eaten. -तं An exclamation meaning 'may it be well tasted or relished', uttered at a *S*râddha ceremony after the presentation of rice-balls or oblations of food to the Manes; Ms. 3. 251, 254.

स्वधा 1 One's own nature or determination, spontaneity. 2 One's own will or pleasure. 3 The oblation of food offered to the Pitris or Manes of deceased ancestors; स्वधासंग्रहतत्पराः R. 1. 66, Ms. 9. 142, Y. 1. 102. 4 The food offered to the Manes personified. 5 Food or oblation in general. 6 N. of Mâyâ or worldly illusion. -*ind.* An exclamation uttered on offering an oblation to the Manes (with dat.); पितृभ्यः स्वधा Sk. -Comp. -कर *a.* offering oblations to the Pitris. -कारः 1 the exclamation Svadhâ; पूतं हि तद् गृहं यत्र स्वधाकारः प्रवर्तते. -प्रियः Agni or fire. -भुज् *m.* 1 a deceased or deified ancestor. 2 a god, deity.

स्वधितिः *m. f.* स्वधिती An axe.

स्वन् 1 P. (स्वनति) 1 To sound, make a noise; पूर्णाः पेराश्च सस्वनुः Bk. 14. 3; वेणव कीचकास्ते स्युर्ये स्वनंत्यनिलोद्धताः Ak. 2 To sing. -*Caus.* (स्वनयति-ते) 1 To cause to resound. 2 To sound. 3 To adorn (स्वानयति in this sense).

स्वनः Sound, noise, शिवाघोरस्वनां पश्चाद् बुबुधे विकृतेति तां R. 12. 39; शंखस्वनः &c. -Comp. -उत्साहः a rhinoceros.

स्वनिः Sound, noise.

स्वनिक *a.* Sounding; as in पाणिस्वनिकः 'one who claps his hands'.

स्वनित *a.* Sounded, sounding, making a noise. -तं The noise of thunder, thunder-clap; cf. स्तनित.

स्वप् 2 P. (स्वपिति, सुप्त; *pass.* सुप्यते; *desid.* सुषुप्सति) (rarely 1 U स्वपति-ते) 1 To sleep, fall asleep, go to sleep; असंजातकिणस्कंधः सुखं स्वपिति गौर्गडिः K. P. 10; इतः स्वपिति केशवः Bh. 2. 76. 2 To recline, repose, lie down, rest. 3 To be absorbed in; Bv. 4. 19. -*Caus.* (स्वापयति-ते) To cause to sleep, rock to sleep. -WITH अव, -नि, -प्र or सं to sleep, lie down; प्रसुप्तलक्षणः Mâl. 7; Ku. 2. 42; R. 11. 44.

स्वप्नः 1 Sleeping, sleep; अकाले बोधितो भ्रात्रा प्रियस्वप्नो वृथा भवान् R 12. 81, 7. 61, 12. 70. 2 A dream, dreaming; स्वप्नेंद्रजालसदृशः खलु जीवलोकः Sânti 2. 3; स्वप्नो नु माया नु मतिभ्रमो नु *S.* 6. 9, R. 10. 60. 3 Sloth, indolence, sleepiness. -Comp. -अवस्था a state of dreaming. -उपम *a.* 1 resembling a dream. 2 unreal or illusory (like a dream). -कर, -कृत् *a.* inducing sleep, soporific, narcotic -गृहं, -निकेतनं a sleeping-room, bedchamber. -दोषः involuntary seminal discharge, *pollutio nocturna.* -धीगम्य *a.* perceptible by the intellect only when it is in a state of sleep-like abstraction; Ms. 12. 122. -प्रपंचः the illusion of sleep, the world as appearing in a dream. -विचारः interpretation of dreams. -शील *a.* disposed to sleep, sleepy, drowsy. -सृष्टिः *f.* the creation of dreams or illusions in sleep.

स्वप्नज् *a.* Sleepy, sleeping, drowsy.

स्वयम् *ind.* 1 Oneself, in one's own person (used reflexively and applicable to all persons, such as myself, ourselves, thyself, himself &c. &c., and sometimes used with other pronouns for the sake of emphasis); विषवृक्षोपि संवर्ध्य स्वयं छेत्तुमसांप्रतं Ku. 2. 55; यस्य नास्ति स्वयं प्रज्ञा शास्त्रं तस्य करोति किं Subhâsh.; R. 1. 17, 2. 56; Ms. 5. 39. 2 Spontaneously, of one's own accord, without trouble or exertion; स्वयमेवोत्पद्यंत एवंविधाः कुलपांशवो निःस्नेहाः पशवः K. -Comp. -अर्जित *a.* self-acquired. -उक्तिः *f.* 1 voluntary declaration. 2 information, deposition (in law). -ग्रहः taking for oneself (without leave). -ग्राह *a.* voluntary, self-choosing. (-हः) self-choice, self-election; Ku. 2. 7, Mâl. 6, 7. -जात *a.* self-born. -दत्त *a.* self-given. (-त्तः) a boy who has given himself to be adopted (by his adoptive parents); one of the twelve kinds of sons recognised in Hindu law). -भुः N. of Brahman; शंभुस्वयंभुहरयो हरिणेक्षणानां येनाक्रियंत सततं गृहकर्मदासाः Bh. 1. 1. -भुवः the first Manu. 2 N. of Brahman. 3 of Siva. -भू *a.* self-existent. (-भूः) 1 N. of Brahman. 2 of Vishnu. 3 of Siva. 4 of *Kâla* or time personified. 5 of Kâmadeva. -वरः self-choice, self-election (of a husband by the bride herself), choice-marriage. -वरा a maiden who chooses her own husband.

स्वर् 10 U. (स्वरयति-ते) To find fault, blame, reprove, censure.

स्वर् *ind.* 1 Heaven, paradise; as in स्वर्लोक, स्वर्वेश्या &c. 2 The heaven of Indra and the temporary abode of the virtuous after death. 3 The sky, ether. 4 The space above the sun or between the sun and the polar star. 5 The third of the three Vyâhritis, pronounced by every Brâhmana in his daily prayers, see व्याहृति. -Comp. -आपगा, -गंगा. 1 the celestial Gange.

2 the galaxy or milky way. -गतिः *f.*, -गमनं 1 going to heaven, future felicity. 2 death. -तरुः (स्वस्तरुः) a tree of paradise. -द्रुह् *m.* 1 an epithet of Indra. 2 of *Agni*. 3 of *Soma*. -नदी (forming -स्वर्णदी) the celestial Ganges. -मानवः a kind of precious stone. -भानुः N. of Râhu ; तुलेऽपराधे स्वर्भानुभानुमंतं चिरेण यत् । हिमांशुमाशु ग्रसते तन्म्रदिम्नः स्फुटं फलं Si. 2. 49 °सूदनः the sun. -मध्यं the central point of the sky, the zenith. -लोकः the celestial world, heaven. -वधूः *f* a celestial damsel, an *apsaras*. -वापी the Ganges. -वेश्या 'a courtezan of heaven', a celestial nymph, an *apsaras*. -वैद्य *m. du.* an epithet of the two Asvins. -षा 1 an epithet of *Soma*. 2 of the thunderbolt of Indra. -सिंधु=स्वर्गंगा q. v.

स्वरः 1 Sound, noise. 2 Voice ; स्वरेण तस्यामभृतस्रुतेव प्रजल्पितायामभिजातवाचि Ku. 1. 45. 3 A note of the musical scale or gamut, a tone, tune ; (these are seven :— निषादर्षभगांधारषड्जमध्यमधैवताः । पंचमश्चेत्यमी सप्त तंत्रीकंठोत्थिताः स्वराः Ak.). 4 The number 'seven', 5 A vowel. 6 An accent ; (these are three ; उदात्त अनुदात्त and स्वरित q. q. v. v.). 7 Air breathed through the nostrils. 8 Snoring. -Comp -अंशः a half or quarter tone (in music). -अंतरं the interval between two vowels, hiatus. -उदय *a.* followed by a vowel. -उपध *a.* preceded by a vowel. -ग्रामः the musical scale, gamut. -बद्ध *a.* composed in musical measure. -भक्तिः *f.* a vowel sound phonetically inserted in the pronunciation of ऋ or ऌ when these letters are followed by a sibilant or any single consonant ; (*e. g.* वर्ष pronounced as वरिष). -भंगः 1 indistinctness of utterance, broken articulation. 2 hoarseness or cracking of voice -मंडलिका a kind of lute (वीणा). -लासिका a flute, pipe -शून्य *a.* without musical notes, unmelodious, unmusical. -संयोगः 1 the junction of vowels. 2 the union of notes or sounds, *i. e.* voice ; अन्य एवैष स्वरसंयोगः Mk. 1, 3 ; U. 3 ; पंडितकौशिक्या इव स्वरसंयोगः श्रूयते M. 5. -संक्रमः 1 a transition or succession of notes ; तं तस्य स्वरसंक्रमं मृदुगिरः श्लिष्टं च तंत्रीस्वनम् Mk 3. 5. 2 the gamut. -संधिः the coalition of vowels. -सामन् *m. pl.* epithets of particular day in a sacrificial session.

स्वरवत् *a.* 1 Having sound, sonorous. 2 Having a voice. 3 Vocal. 4 Having an accent, accented.

स्वरित *a.* 1 Sounded. 2 Sounded as a note, pitched. 3 Articulated. 4 Circumflexed. -तः The third or mixed tone lying between high and low ; समाहारः स्वरितः P. I. 2. 31 ; see Sk. thereon.

स्वरुः 1 Sunshine. 2 A part of a sacrificial post. 3 A sacrifice. 4 A thunderbolt. 5 An arrow.

स्वरुस् *m.* A thunderbolt.

स्वर्गः Heaven, Indra's paradise ; अहो स्वर्गादधिकतरं निर्वृतिस्थानं *S.* 7. -Comp. -आपगा the celestial Ganges. -ओकस् *m.* a god, deity. -गिरिः the heavenly mountain *Sumeru* -द, -प्रद *a.* procuring (entrance into) paradise. -द्वारं heaven's gate, the door of paradise, entrance into heaven ; स्वर्गद्वारकपाटपाटनपटुर्धर्मोऽपि नोपार्जितः Bh 3. 10. -पतिः, भर्तृ *m.* Indra. -लोकः 1 the celestial region. 2 paradise -वधूः, स्त्री *f.* a celestial damsel, heavenly nymph, or *apsaras* ; स्वर्गस्त्रीणां परिष्वंगः कथं मर्त्येन लभ्यते. -साधनं the means of attaining heaven.

स्वर्गिन् *m* 1 A god, deity, an immortal ; त्वमपि विततयज्ञः स्वर्गिणः प्रीणयालं *S.* 7. 34 ; Me. 30. 2 A dead or deceased man.

स्वर्गीय, स्वर्ग्य *a.* 1 Heavenly, celestial, divine. 2 Leading to heaven, procuring entrance into heaven; Ms. 4. 13, 5. 48.

स्वर्णं 1 Gold. 2 A golden coin. -Comp. -अरिः sulphur. -कणः, -कणिका a grain of gold. -काय *a* golden-bodied. (-यः) N. of Garuda -कारः a goldsmith. -गैरिकं a kind of red chalk. -चूडः 1 the blue jay 2 a cock. -जं tin -दीधितिः fire. -पक्षः N. of Garuḍa. -पाठकः borax -पुष्पः the *Champaka* tree. -बंधः a deposit of gold. -भृंगारः a golden vase. -माक्षिकं a kind of mineral substance. -रेखा, -लेखा a streak of gold -वणिज् *m.* 1 a gold-merchant. 2 a money-changer. -वर्णा turmeric.

स्वर्द् 1 A. (स्वर्दते) To taste, relish.

स्वल् 1 P. (स्वलति) To go, move.

स्वल्प *a.* (compar. स्वल्पीयस् superl. स्वल्पिष्ठ) 1 Very small or little, minute, insignificant. 2 Very few. -Comp. -आहार *a.* eating very little, most abstemious. -कंकः a species of heron. -चल *a.* very feeble or weak. -विषयः 1 an insignificant matter. 2 a small part. -व्ययः very little expenditure, stinginess. -व्रीड *a.* having little shame, shameless, impudent. -शरीर *a.* diminutive, dwarfish.

स्वल्पक *a.* Very little, very small or few.

स्वल्पीयस् *a.* Much less, smaller, more minute (compar. of स्वल्प q. v.).

स्वल्पिष्ठ *a.* Smallest, least, most minute (superl. of स्वल्प q. v.).

स्वशुरः A father-in-law ; cf. श्वशुर.

स्वसृ *f.* a sister ; स्वसारमादाय विदर्भनाथः पुरप्रवेशाभिमुखो बभूव R. 7. 1, 20.

स्वस्त *a.* Going or moving at will or pleasure.

स्वस्क् 1 A. (स्वस्कते) See ष्वक्.

स्वस्ति *ind.* A particle meaning 'may it be well with (one)', 'farewell,' 'hail', 'adieu' (with dat.); स्वास्ति भवते *S.* 2 ; स्वस्त्यस्तु ते R. 5. 17 ; (often used at the beginning of letters). -Comp. -अयनं 1 a means of securing prosperity. 2 the averting of evil by the recitation of *mantras* or performance of expiatory rites. 3 the benediction of a Brâhmaṇa after presentation of offerings ; प्रास्थाः निकं स्वस्त्ययनं प्रयुज्य R 2. 70. -दः, -भाव an epithet of Siva. -मुखः 1 a letter. 2 a Brâhmaṇa. 3 a bard, panegyrist. -वाचनं, -वाचनकं, -वाचानिकं 1 a religious rite preparatory to a sacrifice or any religious or solemn observance. 2 a complimentary or congratulatory present of flowers &c. to any one attended with good wishes and blessings -वाच्यं congratulation, invoking blessings.

स्वस्तिकः 1 A kind of mystical mark on persons or things denoting good luck. 2 A lucky object. 3 The meeting of four roads. 4 The crossing of the arms, making a sign like the cross ; स्तनविनिहितहस्तस्वस्तिकाभिर्वधूभिः Mâl. 4. 10 ; Si. 10. 43. 5 A palace of a particular form. 6 A particular symbol made with ground rice and shaped like a triangle. 7 A kind of cake. 8 A voluptuary, libertine. 9 Garlic. कः, -कं 1 A mansion or temple of a particular form with a terrace in front. 2 A particular mode of sitting practised by *Yogins*.

स्वस्रीयः, स्वस्रेयः A sister's son.

स्वस्रीया, स्वस्रेयी A sister's daughter.

स्वागतं Welcome, happy arrival (used chiefly in greeting a person who is put in the dative case) ; स्वागतं देव्यै M. 1 ; (तस्मै) प्रीतः प्रीतिप्रमुखवचनं स्वागतं व्याजहार Me. 4 ; स्वागतं स्वानधीकारान् प्रभावैरवलंब्य वः । युगपद्युगबाहुभ्यः प्राप्तेभ्यः प्राज्यविक्रमाः Ku. 2. 18.

स्वांकिकः A drummer.

स्वाच्छंद्यं The power of following one's own will or fancy, wilfulness, independence ; कन्याप्रदानं स्वाच्छंद्यादासुरो धर्म उच्यते Ms. 3. 31. (स्वाच्छंद्येन, स्वाच्छंद्यतस् mean 'wilfully,' 'voluntarily').

स्वातंत्र्यं Freedom of will, independence ; न स्त्री स्वातंत्र्यमर्हति Ms. 9. 3 ; न स्वातंत्र्यं क्वचित् स्त्रियाः Y. 1. 85.

स्वातिः-ती *f.* 1 One of the wives of the sun. 2 A sword. 3 An auspicious constellation. 4 The star *Arcturus*, considered as forming the fifteenth lunar asterism ; स्वात्यां सागरशुक्तिसंपुटगतं सन्मौक्तिकं जायते Bh. 2. 67 -Comp. -योगः conjunction with Svâti.

स्वाद् See स्वद्.

स्वादः, स्वादनं 1 Taste, flavour. 2 Tasting, eating, drinking. 3 Liking, relishing, enjoyment. 4 Sweetening

स्वादिमन् *m.* Savouriness, sweetness.

स्वादिष्ठ *a.* Very sweet, sweetest (superl. of स्वादु q. v.) ; किं स्वादिष्ठं जगत्यस्मिन् सदा सद्भिः समागमः.

स्वादीयस् *a.* Sweeter, very sweet ; (compar. of स्वादु q. v.) ; काव्यामृतरसास्वादः स्वादीयानमृतादपि.

स्वादु *a.* (दु or द्वी *f.*; compar. स्वादीयस्, superl. स्वादिष्ठ) **1** Sweet, pleasant to the taste, sapid, savoury, dainty, tasteful ; तृषा शुष्यत्यास्ये पिबति सलिलं स्वादु सुरभि Bh. 3. 92, Me. 24. **2** Pleasing, agreeable, attractive, lovely, charming. –*m.* **1** Sweet flavour, sweetness of taste, relish. **2** Treacle, molasses. –*n.* Sweetness, relish, taste ; कविः करोति काव्यानि स्वादु जानाति पंडितः Subhâsh. –दु *f.* A grape. –Comp. –अन्नं sweet or choice food, dainties, delicacies. –अम्लः the pomegranate tree. –खंडः **1** a piece of any sweet substance. **2** molasses. –फलं the jujube. –मूलं a carrot. –रसा **1** the fruit of the hog-plum. **2** the Satâvarî plant. **3** the root काकोली. **4** spirituous liquor. **5** a grape. –शुद्धं **1** rock-salt. **2** marine-salt.

स्वाद्वी Vine, grape.

स्वानः Sound, noise.

स्वापः **1** Sleep, sleeping ; U. 1. 37. **2** Dreaming, dream. **3** Sleepiness, sloth. **4** Paralysis, palsy, insensibility. **5** Temporary or partial loss of sensation from pressure on a nerve, numbness.

स्वापतेयं Wealth, property स्वापतेयकृते मर्त्याः किं किं नाम न कुर्वते Pt. 2. 156 ; Si. 14. 9.

स्वापदः See श्वापद.

स्वाभाविक *a.* (की *f.*) Belonging to one's own nature, innate, inherent, peculiar, natural ; स्वाभाविकं विनीतत्वं तेषां विनयकर्मणा । मुमूर्च्छ सहजं तेजो हविषेव हविर्भुजा R. 10. 79, 5. 69, Ku. 6. 71. –काः *m. pl.* A sect of Buddhists who accounted for all things by the laws of nature.

स्वामिता–त्वं **1** Ownership, mastership, proprietory right. **2** Lordship, sovereignty.

स्वामिन् *a.* (नी *f.*) Possessing proprietory rights. –*m.* **1** A proprietor, an owner. **2** A lord, master ; रघुस्वामिनः सच्चरित्रं Vikr. 18. 107. **3** A sovereign, king, monarch. **4** A husband. **5** A spiritual preceptor. **6** A learned Brâhmaṇa, an ascetic or religious man of the highest order ; (in this sense usually added to proper names). **7** An epithet of Kârtikeya. **8** Of Vishnu. **9** Of Siva. **10** of the sage Vâtsyâyana. **11** Of Garuda. –Comp. –उपकारकः a horse. –कार्यं the business of a king or master. –पाल *m. du.* the owner and the keeper (of cattle) ; Ms. 8. 5. –भावः the state of a lord or owner, ownership. –वात्सल्यं affection for the husband or lord. –सद्भावः **1** existence of a master or owner. **2** goodness of a master or lord. सेवा **1** the service of a master. **2** respect for a husband.

स्वाम्यं **1** Mastership, lordship, ownership. **2** Right or title to property. **3** Rule, supremacy, dominion.

स्वायंभुव *a.* (वी *f.*) **1** Relating to Brahman ; Ku. 2. 1. **2** Descended from Brahman. –वः An epithet of the first Manu (as he was a son of Brahman).

स्वारसिक *a.* (की *f.*) Possessing inherent flavour or sweetness (said of a poetical composition).

स्वारस्यं **1** Possessing natural flavour or excellence. **2** Elegance, fitness.

स्वाराज् *m.* An epithet of Indra.

स्वाराज्यं **1** The dominion of heaven, Indra's heaven. **2** Indentification with the self-refulgent (Brahman).

स्वारोचिषः, स्वारोचिस् *m.* N. of the second Manu ; see under मनु.

स्वालक्षण्यं Peculiar characteristics, natural disposition ; Ms. 9. 19.

स्वाल्प *a.* (ल्पी *f.*) **1** Little, small. **2** Few. –ल्पं **1** Littleness, smallness. **3** Smallness of number.

स्वास्थ्यं **1** Self-reliance, self-dependence. **2** Fortitude, resoluteness, firmness. **3** Sound state, health. **4** Prosperity, well-being, comfortableness **5** Ease, satisfaction, spirits ; लब्धं मया स्वास्थ्यं *S.* 4.

स्वाहा **1** An oblation or offering made to all gods indiscriminately. **2** N. of the wife of *Agni*. –*ind.* An exclamation used in offering oblations to the gods (with dat.) ; इंद्राय स्वाहा, अग्नये स्वाहा &c. –Comp. –कारः utterance of the exclamation Svâhâ; स्वाहास्वधाकारविवर्जितानि श्मशानतुल्यानि गृहाणि तानि. –पतिः, –प्रियः *Agni* or fire. –भुज् *m.* a god, deity.

स्विद् *ind.* A particle of interrogation or inquiry, often implying 'doubt', or 'surprise', and translateable by 'what', 'hey', 'hallo', 'can it be that' &c. It is added to interrogative pronouns in this sense or to give an indefinite sense ; कास्विदवगुंठनवती नातिपरिस्फुटशरीरलावण्या *S.* 5. 13; Me. 14. It is sometimes used disjunctively in the sense of 'either', 'or', with नु, उत, वा &c. ; see Ki. 8. 35, 12. 15, 13. 8, 14. 60 ; आहो also.

स्विद् I. 4 P. (स्विद्यति, स्विदित or स्विन्न) To sweat, perspire ; स्विद्यति कूणति वेल्लति K. P. 10 ; U. 3. 41, Ku. 7. 77 ; Mâl. 1. 35 ; स त्वां पश्यति कंपते पुलकयत्यानंदति स्विद्यति Gît. 11. –II. 1 A (स्वेदते, स्विन्न or स्वेदित) **1** To be anointed. **2** To be greasy or unctuous. **3** To be disturbed. –*Caus.* (स्वेदयति-ते) **1** To cause to perspire. **2** To heat.

स्वीकरणं, **स्वीकारः**, **स्वीकृतिः** *f.* **1** Taking, accepting **2** Assenting, agreeing, promising, an assent, a promise. **3** Espousal, wedding, marriage.

स्वीय *a.* Own, one's own ; लोकालोकविसारि तेन विहितं स्वीयं विशुद्धं यशः S. D. 97.

स्वृ 1 P. (स्वरति; *desid.* सिस्वरिषति, सुस्वूर्षति) **1** To sound, recite. **2** To praise. **3** To pain or be pained. **4** To go. –WITH अभि, –प्र to sound. –सं to pain (Atm.) ; Bk. 9. 28.

स्वॄ 9 P. (स्वृणाति) To hurt, kill.

स्वेक् 1 A. (स्वेकते) To go.

स्वेदः Sweat, perspiration ; अंगुलिस्वेदेन दूष्येरन्नक्षराणि V. 2. –Comp. –उदं, –उदकं, जलं perspiration. –चषकः a cooling breeze (sucking up sweat). –ज *a.* generated by warm vapour or sweat (said of insects.)

स्वैर *a.* **1** Following one's own will or fancy, self-willed, wanton, uncontrolled, unrestrained ; बद्धमिव स्वैरगतिर्जनमिह सुखसंगिनमवैमि *S.* 5. 11, अभ्याहतैः स्वैरगतैः स तस्याः R.2. 5. **2** Free; unreserved, confidential ; as in स्वैरालाप Mu. 4. 8. **3** Slow, mild, gentle ; Mu. 1. 2. **4** Dull, lazy. **5** Dependent on one's will, voluntary, optional. –रं Wilfulness, wantonness. –रं *ind.* **1** At will or pleasure, as one likes, at perfect ease ; सार्थाः स्वैरं स्वकीयेषु चेरुर्वेश्मस्विवाद्रिषु R. 17. 64. **2** Of one's own accord, spontaneously. **3** Slowly, gently, mildly ; U. 3. 2. **4** Lowly, in an under-tone, inaudibly, (opp. स्पष्ट); पश्चात्स्वैरं गज इति किल व्याहृतं सत्यवाचा Ve. 3. 9.

स्वैरता –त्वं Wantonness, freedom of will and action, independence.

स्वैरिणी A loose or unchaste woman, a wanton woman, an adulteress ; Y. 1. 67.

स्वैरिन् *a.* Self-willed, wanton, unrestrained, uncontrolled.

स्वैरिंध्री See. सैरंध्री.

स्वोरसः The residue or sediment of oily substances ground with a stone.

स्वोवशीयं Happiness, prosperity (especially as regards future life).

ह

ह *ind.* An emphatic particle used to lay stress on the preceding word and translateable by 'verily', 'indeed', 'certainly', &c.; but it is often used expletively without any particular signification, especially in a Vedic literature ; तस्य ह शतं जाया बभूवुः; तस्य ह पर्वतनारदौ गृह ऊषतुः &c. Ait. Br. It is sometimes used as a vocative particle and rarely of disdain or laughter. *-m.* 1 A form of Śiva. 2 Water. 3 Sky. 4 Blood.

हंसः (Said to be derived from हस्; cf. भवेद्वर्णागमाद् हंसः Sk.) 1 A swan, goose, duck, flamingo ; हंसाः संप्रति पांडवा इव वनादज्ञातचर्यां गताः Mk. 5. 6; न शोभते सभामध्ये हंसमध्ये बको यथा Subhâsh., R. 3. 10, 5. 12, 17. 25 ; (the description of this bird, as given by Sanskrit writers, is more poetical than real ; he is described as forming the vehicle of the god Brahman, and as ready to fly towards the Mânasa lake at the approach of rains ; cf. मानस. According to a very general poetical convention he is represented as being gifted with the peculiar power of separating milk from water ; *e. g.* सारं ततो ग्राह्यमपास्य फल्गु हंसो यथा क्षीरमिवांबुमध्यात् Pt. 1 ; हंसो हि क्षीरमादत्ते तन्मिश्रा वर्जयत्यपः *S.* 6. 27 ; नीरक्षीरविवेके हंसालस्यं त्वमेव तनुषे चेत् । विश्वस्मिन्नधुनान्यः कुलव्रतं पालयिष्यति कः Bv. 1. 13 ; see Bh. 2. 18 also). 2 The Supreme Soul, Brahman. 3 The individual soul, (जीवात्मन). 4 One of the vital airs. 5 The sun. 6 Śiva. 7 Vishṇu. 8 Kâmadeva. 9 An unambitious monarch. 10 An ascetic of a particular order. 11 A spiritual preceptor. 12 One free from malice, a pure person. 13 A mountain. **-Comp.** **-अंघ्रिः** vermilion. **-अधिरूढा** an epithet of Sarasvatî. **-अभिख्यं** silver. **-कांता** a female goose. **-कीलकः** a particular mode of sexual enjoyment. **-गति** *a.* having a swan's gait, stalking in a stately manner. **-गद्गदा** a sweetly speaking woman. **-गामिनी** 1 a woman having graceful gait like that of a swan ; Ms. 3. 10. 2 N. of Brahmâṇî. **-तूलः-लं** the soft feathers or down of a goose. **-दाहनं** aloe-wood. **-नादः** the cackling of a goose. **-नादिनी** a woman of a particular class (described as having a slender waist, large hips, the gait of an elephant and the voice of a cuckoo ; गजेंद्रगमना तन्वी कोकिलालापसंयुता नितंबे गुर्विणी या स्यात् सा स्मृता हंसनादिनी). **-माला** a flight of swans ; Ku. 1. 30. **-युवन्** *m.* a young goose or swan. **-रथः**, **-वाहनः** epithets of Brahman. **-राजः** a king of geese. **-लोमशं** green sulphate of iron. **-लोहकं** brass. **-श्रेणी** a line of geese.

हंसकः 1 A goose, flamingo. 2 An ornament for the ankles (नूपुर or पादकटक); सरित इव सविभ्रमप्रपातप्रणादितहंसकभूषणा विरेजुः *Si.* 7. 23. (where the word is used in the first sense also ; see हंस above for other senses).

हंसिका, हंसी A female goose.

हंहो *ind.* 1 A vocative purticles corresponding to, 'ho,' 'hallo'; हंहो चिन्मयचित्तचंद्रमणयः संवर्धयध्वं रसान् Chandr. 1. 2. 2 A particle expressing haughtiness or contempt. 3 A particle of interrogation. (In dramas it is mostly used as a form of address by characters of the middling class ; हंहो ब्रह्मण मा कुप्य Mu. 1.

हक्कः The calling of elephants.

हंजा, हंजे *ind.* A vocative particle used in addressing a female attendant or maid-servant ; हंजे कंचणमलि अहं ईदिसी कडुभासिणी Ratn. 3.

हट् 1 P. (हटति, हाटित) To shine, be bright.

हट्टः A market, a fair. **-Comp.** **-चौरकः** a thief who steals from fair; and markets. **-विलासिनी** 1 a wanton woman, prostitute, common woman. 2 a sort of perfume.

हठः 1 Violence, force. 2 Oppression, rapine. (**हठेन** and **हठात्** are used adverbially in the sense of 'forcibly', 'violently', 'suddenly', 'against one's will' ; अंबालिका च चंडवर्मणा हठात् परिणेतुमात्मभवनमनीयत Dk. ; वानरान् वारयामास हठेन मधुरेण च Râm. **-Comp.** **-योगः** a particular mode of Yoga or practising abstract meditation, (so called, distinguished from राजयोग q. v., because it is very difficult to practise ; it may be performed in various ways, such as by standing on one leg, holding up the arms, inhaling smoke with the head inverted &c.). **-विद्या** the science of forced meditation.

हडिः Wooden fetters or stocks.

हडि(ड्डि)कः, हड्डिः A man of the lowest caste.

हड्डं A bone. **-Comp.** **-जं** marrow.

हंडा *ind.* A vocative particle used in addressing a female of inferior rank, or by equals of the lowest caste in addressing each other ; हंडे हंजे हलाह्वाने नीचां चेटीं सखीं प्रति Ak. *-f.* A large earthen vessel (?).

हंडिका, हंडी An earthen pot.

हंडे *ind.* See हंडा *ind.*

हत *p. p.* 1 Killed, slain. 2 Hurt, struck, injured. 3 Lost, perished. 4 Deprived or bereft of. 5 Disappointed, frustrated. 6 Multiplied ; see हन्. It is often used as the first member of comp. in the sense of 'wretched', 'miserable' 'accursed', 'worthless'; अनुशयदुःखायेदं हतहृदयं संप्रति विबुद्धं *S.* 6. 6 ; कुर्यामुपेक्षां हतजीवितेऽस्मिन् R. 14. 65 ; हतविधिलसितानां ही विचित्रो विपाकः *Si.* 11. 64. **-Comp.** **-आश** *a.* 1 bereft of hope, hopeless, desponding. 2 weak, powerless. 3 cruel, merciless. 4 barren. 5 law, vile, wretched, accursed, villainous. **-कंटक** *a.* freed from thorns or foes. **-चित्त** *a.* bewildered, confounded. **-त्विष्** *a.* dimmed in lustre ; R. 3. 15. **-दैव** *a.* ill-fated, luckless, ill-starred. **-प्रभाव** *a.*, **-वीर्य** *a.* bereft of power or vigour. **-बुद्धि** *a.* deprived of sense, senseless. **-भाग**, **-भाग्य** *a.* ill-fated, unfortunate. **-मूर्खः** a dolt, blockhead. **-लक्षण** *a.* devoid of auspicious marks, unlucky. **-शेष** *a.* surviving. **-श्री**, **-संपद्** *a.* reduced to indigence, improverished. **-साध्वस** *a.* freed from fear.

हतक *a.* Miserable, ill-bred, wretched, low, vile ; (mostly at the end of comp.); न खलु विदितास्ते तत्र निवसंतश्चाणक्यहतकेन Mu. 2 ; दूषिताः स्थ परिभूताः स्थ रामहतकेन U. 1. **-कः** a low person, coward.

हतिः *f.* 1 Killing, destruction. 2 Striking, wounding. 3 A blow, stroke. 4 Loss, failure. 5 A defect. 6 Multiplication.

हत्नुः 1 A weapon. 2 A disease or sickness.

हत्या Killing, slaying, slaughter, murder, particularly criminal killing ; as in भ्रूणहत्या, गोहत्या &c.

हद् 1 A. (हदते, हन्न) To void excrement, evacuate or discharge feces. *-Desid.* (जिहत्सते).

हदनं Voiding excrement, evacuation of ordure.

हन् 2 P. (हंति, हत; *pass.* हन्यते; *caus.* घातयति-ते ; *desid.* जिघांसति) 1 To kill, slay, destroy, strike down; त्रयश्च दूषणखरत्रिमूर्धानो रणे हताः U. 2. 15 ; हतमपि च हंत्येव मदनः Bh. 3. 18. 2 To strike, beat ; चंडी चंड हंतुमभ्युद्यता मां विद्युद्दाम्ना मेघराजीवविंध्यं M. 3. 20, *Si.* 7. 56. 3 To hurt, injure, afflict, torment ; as in कामहत. 4 To put down, abandon ; Bh. 2. 77. 5 To remove, take away, destroy ; अंभोजिनीवननिवासविलासमेव हंसस्य हंति नितरां कुपितो विधाता Bh. 2. 18. 6 To conquer, overthrow, defeat, overcome ; विघ्नैः सहस्रगुणितैरपि हन्यमानाः प्रारब्धमुत्तमजना न परित्यजंति Subhâsh. **7** To hinder, obstruct. **8** To mar, spoil ; Ki. 2. 37. **9** To raise ; तुरगखुरहतस्तथा हि रेणुः S. 1. 32. **10** To multiply (in math.). **11** To go (rarely used in classical literature in this sense ; and when used it is regarded as a fault of composition); *e. g.* कुंजं हंति कृशोदरी S. D. 7 ; or तीर्थांतरेषु स्नानेन समुपार्जितसत्कृतिः । सुरस्रोतस्विनीमेष हंति संप्रति सादरं K. P. 7 (given as an instance of the दोष called असमर्थत्व). –WITH **अति** to injure excessively. **–अंतर** to strike in the middle. **–अप 1** to ward off, repel, destroy, kill. **2** to take away, remove ; न तु खलु तयोर्ज्ञाने शक्तिं करोत्यपहंति वा U. 2. 4, *S.* 4. 7. **3** to attack, seize, **–अभि 1** to strike, smite (fig. also); beat ; Mâl. 1. 39, M. 5. 3. **2** to hurt, injure, kill, destroy. **3** to strike or beat (as a drum &c.) ; Bg. 1. 13. **4** to attack, affect, overpower. **–अव 1** to strike, hit, kill. **2** to destroy, remove. **3** to thresh (as corn). **–आ 1** to hit, strike, beat ; कुट्टिममाजघान K.; *Si.* 7. 17 ; (said to be Atm. when the object is some limb of one's own body ; as आहते शिरः Sk. ; but Bhâravi says आजघ्ने विषमविलोचनस्य वक्षः Ki. 17. 63, Bk. 8. 15, 5. 102) ; R. 4. 23, 12. 77, Ku. 4. 25, 30. **2** to strike, ring, beat (as a bell, drum &c.); Bk. 1. 27, 17. 7, Me. 66, R. 17. 11. **–उद् 1** to raise up, elevate, uplift. **2** to be puffed up, become proud ; see उद्धत. **–उप 1** to strike, smite. **2** to waste, injure, destroy, kill ; लंका चोपहनिष्यते Bk. 16. 12, 5. 12, Bg. 3. 24. **3** to pain, affect, overpower, strike with ; दारिद्र्योपहत, भक्तोपहत, कामोपहत &c. Ku. 5. 76 ; Bh. 2. 26. **–नि 1** to kill, destroy; Bk. 2. 34, 6. 10, R. 11. 71 ; Y. 3. 262. **2** to strike, hit ; तानेव सामर्षतया निजघ्नुः R. 7. 44 ; Ms. 7. 27. **3** to conquer, overcome ; दैवं निहत्य कुरु पौरुषमात्मशक्त्या Pt. 1. 361. **4** to beat, strike (as a drum) ; Bk. 14. 2. **5** to counteract, render void, frustrate ; R. 12. 92. **6** to cure (as a disease). **7** to disregard. **8** to remove, dispel ; Ki. 5. 36. **–परा 1** to strike or beat back, strike down, repulse, repel, overthrow, drive back ; दैवं मत्पौरुषपराहतं Râm. **2** to attack, as sail ; कटाक्षपराहतं वदनपंकजं Mâl. 7. **3** To dash against, strike. **–प्र 1** to kill, slay ; प्राघानिषत रक्षांसि येनातानि बने मम । न प्रहण्मः कथं पापं वद पूर्वापकारिणं Bk. 9. 102. **2** to strike, beat, hit ; गदाप्रहततनुः. **3** to strike, beat (a drum &c.); R. 19. 15, Me. 64. **–प्राणि** to kill ; Bk. 2. 35. **–प्रति 1** to strike back or in return ; (तं) विध्यंतमुद्धतसटाः प्रतिहंतुमीषुः R. 9. 60. **2** to ward off, keep off, prevent, oppose, resist; तोयस्येवाप्रतिहतरयः सैकतं सेतुमोघः U. 3. 36 ; प्रतिहतविघ्नाः क्रियाः समवलोक्य S. 1. 13, Me. 20 ; Ku. 2. 48, V. 2. 1. **3** to repel, drive back, repulse. **4** to remove, destroy ; यदूत्पातं प्रतिजहि जगन्नाथ नम्रस्य तन्मे Mâl. 1. 3. **5** to counteract, remedy. **–वि 1** to kill, slay, destroy, destroy completely, annihilate ; (अलं) सहसा संहतिमंहसां विहंतुं Ki. 5. 17. **2** to strike, beat violently. **3** to obstruct, impede, oppose, resist ; विघ्नंति रक्षांसि वने क्रतुंश्च Bk. 1. 19 ; R. 5. 27. **4** to reject, refuse, decline ; R. 2. 58, 11. 2. **5** to dis ppoint, frustrate. **–सं 1** to unite closely together, join together ; हस्तौ संहत्य Ms. 2. 71 ; दूत एव हि संधत्ते भिनत्त्येव च संहतान् 7. 66 ; see संहत. **2** to heap, collect, accumulate. **3** to contract, diminish. **4** to clash. **5** to strike, kill, destroy. **–समा** to strike, hurt, injure.

हन् *a.* Killing, slaying, destroying (at the end of comp.); as in वृत्रहन्, पितृहन्, मातृहन्, ब्रह्महन् &c.

हनः Killing, slaying.

हननं 1 Killing, slaying, striking. **2** Hurting, injuring. **3** Multiplication.

हनु-नू *m. f.* The chin. **–नु** *f.* **1** That which injures life. **2** A weapon. **3** A disease, sickness. **4** Death. **5** A kind of drug. **6** A wanton woman, prostitute. **–Comp. –ग्रहः** locked jaw. **–मूलं** the root of the jaw.

हनु(नू)मत् *m.* N. of a powerful monkey-chief. [He was the son of Anjan*a* by the god Wind or Marut and hence called M*a*ruti. He is represented as a monkey of extraordinary strength and prowess which he manifested on several critical occasions on behalf of R*a*ma whom he regarded as the idol of his heart. When S*i*ta was carried off by R*a*vana, he crossed the sea and brought news about her to his lord. He played a very important part in the great war at Lank*a*.].

हंत *ind.* **1** A particle implying **1** Joy, surprise, flurry (oh !); हंत भो लब्धं मया स्वास्थ्यं S. 4. हंत प्रवृत्तं संगीतकं M. 1. **2** Compassion, pity ; पुत्रक हंत ते धानाकाः G. M. **3** Grief (oh !, alas); हंत धिङ् मामधन्यं U. 1. 43 ; स्मरामि हंत स्मरामि U. 1 ; काचमूल्येन विक्रीतो हंत चिंतामणिर्मया Sânti. 1. 12, Me. 104. **4** Good luck or benediction. **5** It is often used as an inceptive particle ; हंत ते कथयिष्यामि Râm. **–Comp. –उक्तिः** *f.* uttering the word 'alas !', tenderness, compassion. **–कारः 1** the exclamation 'hanta'. **2** an offering to be presented to a guest ; निवीती हंतकारेण मनुष्यांस्तर्पयेदथ.

हंतृ *a.* (**त्री** *f.*) **1** One who strikes or kills, striking, killer ; Ms. 5. 34 ; Ku. 2. 20. **2** One who removes, destroys, counteracts &c. **–m. 1** A slayer, killer. **2** A thief, robber.

हम् *ind.* An exclamation expressive of **1** anger; **2** courtesy or respect.

हंबा (भा) The lowing of cattle. **–Comp. –रवः** lowing of cattle.

हय् 1 P. (हयति, हयित) **1** To go. **2** To worship. **3** To sound. **4** To be weary.

हयः 1 A horse ; Bg. 1. 14, Ms. 8. 226, R. 9. 10. **2** A man of a particular class ; see under अश्व. **3** The number 'seven'. **4** N. of Indra. **–Comp. –अध्यक्षः** a superintendent of horses. **–आयुर्वेदः** veterinary science. **–आरूढः** a horseman, rider. **–आरोहः 1** a rider. **2** riding. **–इष्टः** barley. **–उत्तमः** an excellent horse. **–कोविद** *a.* versed in the science of horses-their management, training &c. **–ज्ञः** a horse-dealer, groom, jockey. **–द्विषत्** *m.* the buffalo. **–प्रियः** barley. **–प्रिया** *Kharju'ri'* tree. **–मारः, -मारकः** the fragrant oleander. **–मारणः** the sacred fig-tree. **–मेधः** a horse-sacrifice ; Y. 1. 181. **–वाहनः** an epithet of Kubera. **–शाला** a stable for horses. **–शास्त्रं** the art or science of training and managing horses. **–संग्रहणं** the restraining or curbing of horses.

हयंकषः A driver, charioteer.

हयी A female horse, mare.

हर *a.* (**रा-री** *f.*) **1** Taking away, removing, depriving one of ; खेदहर, शोकहर. **2** Bringing, conveying, carrying, taking ; अपथहराः Ki. 5. 50. R. 12. 51. **3** Seizing, grasping. **4** Attracting, captivating. **5** Claiming, entitled to; Mu. 2. 19. **6** Occupying; Ku. 1. 50. **7** Dividing. **–रः 1** Siva ; Ku. 1. 50, 3. 40, 67, Me. 7. **2** N. of Agni or fire. **3** An ass. **4** A divisor. **5** The denominator of a fraction. **–Comp. –गौरी** one of the forms of Siva and Pârvati conjoined (अर्धनारीनटेश्वर). **–चूडामणिः** 'Siva's crest-gem', the moon. **–तेजस्** *n.* quicksilver. **–नेत्रं 1** Siva's eye. **2** the number 'three'. **–बीजं** 'Siva's seed'. quicksilver. **–शेखरा** 'Siva's crest', the Ganges. **–सूनुः** Skanda ; R. 11. 83.

हरकः 1 A stealer, thief. **2** A rogue. **3** A divisor.

हरणं 1 Seizing, taking. **2** Carrying away, carrying off, removing, stealing ; कन्याहरणं Ms. 3. 33, R. 11. 74. **3** Depriving of, destroying ; as in प्राणहरणं. **4** Dividing. **5** A gift to a student. **6** The arm. **7** Semen virile. **8** Gold.

हरि *a.* **1** Green, greenish-yellow. **2** Tawny, bay, reddish-brown (कपिल); हरियुग्यं हरिस्तस्मै प्रजिघाय पुरंदरः R. 12. 14, 3. 43. **3** Yellow. **–रिः 1** N. of Vishṇu ; हरिर्यथैकः पुरुषोत्तमः स्मृतः R.

3. 49. **2** N. of Indra ; R. 3. 55, 68, 8. 79. **3** N. of *S*iva. **4** N. of Brahman. **5** N. of Yama. **6** The sun. **7** The moon. **8** A man. **9** A ray of light. **10** Fire. **11** Wind. **12** A lion ; Bv. 1. 50, 51. **13** A horse. **14** A horse of Indra ; सत्यमतीत्य हरितो हरींश्च वर्तते वाजिनः S.1, 7. 7. **15** An ape, a monkey ; U. 3. 48, R. 12. 57. **16** The cuckoo. **17** A frog. **18** A parrot. **19** A snake. **20** The tawny or yellow colour. **21** A peacock. **22** N. of the poet Bhartrihari. **–Comp.** –अक्षः **1** a lion. **2** N. of Kubera. **3** of *S*iva. –अश्वः **1** Indra. **2** *S*iva. –कांत *a.* **1** dear to Indra. **2** beautiful as a lion. –केलीयः the country called वंग q. v. –गंधः a kind of sandal. –चंदनः, –नं **1** a kind of yellow sandal (the wood or tree); R. 3. 59, 6. 60 ; *S.* 7. 2 ; Ku. 5. 69. **2** one of the five trees of paradise ; पंचैते देवतरवो मंदारः पारिजातकः । संतानः कल्पवृक्षश्च पुंसि वा हरिचंदनं Ak. (–नं) **1** moonlight. **2** saffron. **3** the filament of a lotus. –तालः (by some regarded as derived from हरित) a kind of yellow-coloured pigeon. (–लं) yellow orpiment ; H. D. 1 ; *S*i. 4. 21 ; Ku. 7. 23, 33. (–ली) the Dûrvâ grass. –तालिका **1** the fourth day of the bright half of Bhâdrapada. **2** the Dûrvâ plant. –तुरंगमः N. of Indra. –दासः a worshipper or votary of Vishṇu. –दिनं a particular day sacred to Vishṇu. –देवः the asterism *S*ravaṇa. –द्रवः a green fluid. –द्वारं N. of a celebrated Tîrtha or sacred bathing-place. –नेत्रं **1** the eye of Vishṇu. **2** the white lotus. (–त्रः) an owl. –पदं the vernal equinox. –प्रियः **1** the *Kadamba* tree. **2** a conchshell. **3** a fool. **4** a madman. **5** *S*iva. (–यं) a sort of sandal. –प्रिया **1** Lakshmî. **2** the sacred basil. **3** the earth. **4** the twelfth day of a lunar fortnight. –भुज् *m.* a snake. –मंथः, –मंथकः a chick-pea. –लोचनः **1** a crab. **2** an owl. –वल्लभा **1** Lakshmî. **2** the sacred basil. –वासरः 'Vishṇu's day', the eleventh day of a lunar fortnight. (एकादशी). –वाहनः **1** Garuḍa. **2** Indra. °दिश् *f.* the east. –शरः an epithet of *S*iva (Vishṇu having served *S*iva as the shaft which burnt down 'the three cities' or cities of the demon Tripura°. –सखः a *Gandharva*. –संकीर्तनं repeating the name of Vishṇu. –सुतः, –सूनुः N. of Arjuna. –हयः **1** Indra ; R. 9. 18. **2** the sun. –हरः a particular form of deity consisting of Vishṇu and *S*iva conjoined. –हेतिः *f.* **1** the rainbow ; कथमवलोकयेयमधुना हरिहेतिमतीः (ककुभः) Mâl. 9. 18. **2** the discus of Vishṇu. °हूतिः the ruddy goose ; *S*i. 9. 15.

हरिकः **1** A horse of a yellowish or tawny colour. **2** A thief. **3** A gambler (with dice).

हरिण *a.* (णी *f.*) **1** Pale, whitish. **2** Reddish or yellowish, white. –णः **1** A deer, an antelope ; (said to be of five kinds :—हरिणश्चापि विज्ञेयः पंचभेदोऽत्र भैरव । ऋष्यः खड्गो रुरुश्चव पृषतश्च मृगस्तथा (Kâlikâ P.); अपि प्रसन्नं हरिणेषु ते मनः Ku. 5. 35. **2** The white colour. **3** A goose. **4** The sun. **5** Vishṇu. **6** *S*iva. **–Comp.** –अक्ष *a.* deer-eyed, fawn-eyed. (–क्षी) 'deer-eyed', a woman with beautiful eyes. –अंकः **1** the moon. **2** camphor. –कलंकः, –धामन् *m.* the moon. –नयन, –नेत्र, –लोचन *a.* deer-eyed, fawn-eyed. –हृदय *a.* deer-hearted, timid.

हरिणकः A deer ; ॡ बत हरिणकानां जीवितं चातिलोलं *S.* 1. 10.

हरिणी **1** A female deer, doe ; चकितहरिणीप्रेक्षणा Me. 82, R. 9. 55, 14. 69. **2** One of the four classes of women (also called चित्रिणी q. v.). **3** Yellow jasmine. **4** A good golden image. **5** N. of a metre. **–Comp.** –दृश् *a.* deer-eyed. (*–f.*) a deer-eyed woman ; किमभवद्विपिने हरिणीदृशः U. 3. 27.

हरित् *a.* **1** Green, greenish. **2** Yellow, yellowish. **3** Greenish-yellow. *–m.* **1** The green or yellow colour. **2** A horse of the sun, a bay horse ; सत्यमतीत्य हरितो हरींश्च वर्तते वाजिनः *S.* 1.; दिशो हरिद्भिर्हरितामिवेश्वरः R. 3. 30, Ku. 2. 43. **3** A swift horse. **4** A lion. **5** The sun. **6** Vishṇu. *–m., n.* **1** Grass. **2** A quarter or point of the compass ; R. 3. 30. **–Comp.** –अंतः the end of the quarters (दिगंत); Bv. 1. 60. –अंतरं different regions, various quarters ; Bv. 1. 15. –अश्वः **1** the sun ; Ki. 2. 46, R. 3. 22, 18. 23, *S*i. 11. 56. **2** the *arka* plant. –गर्भः green or yellowish Kusa grass with broad leaves. –मणिः (हरिन्मणिः) an emerald ; *S*i. 3. 49. –वर्ण *a.* greenish, green-coloured.

हरित *a.* (ता or हरिणी *f.*) **1** Green, of a green colour, verdant ; रम्यांतरः कमलिनीहरितैः सरोभिः *S.* 4. 10 ; Ku. 4. 14; Me. 21 ; Ki. 5. 38. **2** Tawny. –तः **1** The green colour. **2** A lion. **3** A kind of grass. **–Comp.** –अश्मन् *m.* **1** an emerald. **2** blue vitriol. –छद *a.* green leaved.

हरितकं **1** A pot-herb, green grass; *S*i. 5. 58.

हरिता **1** The Dûrvâ grass. **2** Turmeric. **3** A brown-coloured grape.

हरिताल &c. See under हरि.

हरिद्रा **1** Turmeric. **2** The root of turmeric powdered ; see Malli. on N. 22. 49. **–Comp.** –आभ *a.* of a yellow colour. –गणपतिः, –गणेशः a particular form of the god Gaṇesa. –राग, रागक *a.* **1** turmeric-coloured. **2** unsteady in attachment or affection, fickle-minded (as a love) ; (thus defined by Halâyudha :—क्षणमात्रानुरागश्च हरिद्राराग (उच्यते).

हरियः A yellow-coloured horse.

हरिश्चंद्रः N. of a king of the solar dynasty. [He was the son of Trisanku and was famous for his liberality, probity, and unflinching adherence to truth. On one occasion his family-priest Vasis*t*ha commended his qualities in the presence of Vis*v*amitra, who refused to believe them. A quarrel thereupon ensued and it was at last dacided that Vis*v*amitra should himself test the king. The sage accordingly subjected him to the most crucial test with a view to see if he could be but once made to swerve from his plighted word. The king, however, stood the test with exemplary courage—adhering to his word though he had to forego the kingdom, to sell off his wife and son, and at last even his own self to a low caste man, and—as the last test, as it were, of his truthfulness and courage—to be even ready to put his own wife to death as a witch, Vis*v*amitra thereupon acknowledged himself vanquished and the worthy king was elevated along with his subjects to heaven.]

हरीतकी The yellow myrobalan tree.

हर्तृ *a.* (र्त्री *f.*) One who takes away, seizes, robs, accepts &c. *–m.* A thief, robber; Bh. 2 16. **2** The sun.

हर्मन् *n.* Gaping, yawning.

हर्मित *p. p.* **1** A Gaped, yawned. **2** Cast, thrown. **3** Burnt.

हर्म्यं **1** A palace, mansion, any large or palatial building ; हर्म्यपृष्ठं समारूढः काकोऽपि गरुडायते Subhâsh. ; बाह्योद्यानस्थितहरशिरश्चंद्रिकाधौतहर्म्या Me. 7 ; Rs. 1. 28 ; Bk. 8. 36, R. 6. 47 ; Ku. 6. 42. **2** An oven, a fire-place, hearth. **3** A fiery pit, abode of evil spirits, the infernal regions. –Comp. –अंगनं –णं the court-yard of a palace. –स्थलं the room of a palace.

हर्षः **1** Joy, delight, pleasure, satisfaction, gladness, rapture, glee, exultation ; हर्षो हर्षो हृदयवसतिः पंचबाणस्तु बाणः P. R. 1. 22 ; सहोत्थितः सैनिकहर्षनिःस्वनैः R. 3. 61. **2** Thrilling, bristling, erection (of the hair of the body) ; as in रोमहर्ष q. v. **3** Joy, considered as one of the 33 or 34 subordinate feelings; हर्षस्त्विष्टावाप्तेर्मनः प्रसादोऽश्रुगद्गदादिकरः S. D. 195 ; or इष्टप्राप्त्यादिजन्मा सुखविशेषो हर्षः R. G. –Comp. –आन्वित *a.* full of joy, happy ; so हर्षाविष्ट. –उत्कर्षः excess of happiness; or joy, ecstacy. –उदयः rise of joy. –कर *a.* gratifying, delighting. –जड *a.* dull or paralyzed with joy ; R. 3. 68. –विवर्धन *a.* increasing joy. –स्वनः a cry or shout of joy.

हर्षक *a.* (र्षका or र्षिका *f.*) Delighting, gladdening, delightful, pleasing.

हर्षण *a.* (णा or णी *f.*) Causing delight, gladdening, delightful, pleasant. –णः 1 N. of one of the five arrows of Kâmadeva. 2 A morbid affection of the eyes. 3 A deity presiding over rhe funeral ceremonies. –णं Joy, delight, happiness, gladdening, delighting ; दुर्हृदामप्रहर्षाय सुहृदां हर्षणाय च Mb.

हर्षयित्नु *a.* Gladdening, pleasing, delighting. –*n.* Gold. –*m.* A son.

हर्षुलः 1 A deer. 2 A lover.

हल् 1 P. (हलति, हलित) To plough.

हलं A plough ; वहसि वपुषि विशदे वसनं जलदाभम् । हलहतिभीतिमिलितयमुनाभम् or हलं कलयते Gît. 1. –Comp. –आयुधः an epithet of Balarâma. –धर, –भृत् *m.* 1 a ploughman. 2 N. of Balarâma ; केशव धृतहलधररूप जय जगदीश हरे Gît. ; अंसन्यस्ते सति हलभृतो मेचके वाससीव Me. 59. –भूतिः –भृतिः *f.* ploughing, agriculture, husbandry. –हतिः *f.* 1 striking or drawing along with a plough. 2 ploughing.

हलहला Halloo, hallooing.

हला 1 A female friend. 2 The earth. 3 Water. 4 Spirituous liquor. –*ind.* A vocative particle used in addressing a female friend ; (only in theatrical language) ; हला शकुंतले अत्रैव तावन्मुहूर्तं तिष्ठ *S.* 1 ; cf. हंडा also.

हलाहल See हाल(ला)हल.

हलिः 1 A large plough. 2 A furrow. 3 Agriculture.

हलिन् *m.* 1 A ploughman, an agriculturist. 2 N. of Balarâma. –Comp. –प्रियः the *Kadamba* tree. (–या) spirituous liquor.

हलिनी A number of ploughs.

हलीनः The teak tree.

हलीषा The handle of a plough.

हल्य *a.* 1 Arable, to be ploughed. 2 Ugly, deformed.

हल्या A multitude of ploughs.

हल्लकं The red lotus.

हल्लनं Rolling or tossing about (as in sleep).

हल्लीशं (षं) 1 One of the 18 Uparûpakas or minor dramatic compositions; (described as a piece in one act and consistsing mainly of singing and dancing by one male and seven, eight, or ten female performers see S. D. 555. 2 A kind of circular dance.

हल्लीशकः Dancing in a ring.

हवः 1 An oblation, a sacrifice. 2 Invocation, prayer. 3 Calling, call. 4 Order, command. 5 Challenge.

हवनं 1 Offering an oblation with fire. 2 A sacrifice, an oblation. 3 Invocation. 4 Calliug, summoning. 5 Challenging to fight. –Comp. –आयुस् *m.* fire.

हवनीयं 1 Anything fit for an oblation. 2 Clarified butter or ghee.

हविर्त्री A hole made in the ground for holding the sacred fire (to which oblations are offered).

हविष्मत् *a.* Possessed of oblation.

हविष्यं 1 Anything fit for an oblation ; Ms. 3. 256, 11. 77. 106 ; Y. 2. 239. 2 Clarified butter. –Comp. –अन्नं food fit to be eaten during certain holidays or days of fast. –आशिन्, –भुज् *m.* fire.

हविस् *n.* 1 An oblation or burnt offering in general ; वहति विधिहुतं या हविः *S.* 1. 1 ; Ms. 3. 87, 132 ; 5. 7, 6. 12 2 Clarified butter. 3 Water. –Comp. –अशनं (हविरशनं) devouring clarified butter or oblations. (–नः) fire. –गंधा (हविर्गंधा) the *Samî* tree. –गेहं (हविर्गेहं) a house in which sacrificial oblations are offered. –भुज् *m.* (हविर्भुज्) fire ; अन्वासितमरुंधत्या स्वाहयेव हविर्भुजा R. 1. 56, 10. 80, 13. 41; Ku. 5. 20, *Si.* 1. 2 ; Kâv. 2. 168. –यज्ञः (हविर्यज्ञः) a kind of sacrifice. –याजिन् (हविर्याजिन्) *m.* a priest.

हव्य *a.* To be offered in oblations. –व्यं 1 Clarified butter. 2 An oblation or offering to the gods (opp. कव्य q. v.). 3 An oblation in general. –Comp. –आशः fire. –कव्यं oblations to the gods and to the Manes, or spirits of deceased ancestors ; Ms. 1. 94, 3. 97, 128 ; *et seq.* –वाह्, –वाह, –वाहन *m.* 'the bearer oblations', fire.

हस् 1 P. (हसति, हसित) 1 To smile, laugh (gently) ; हसासि यदि किंचिदपि दंतरुचिकौमुदी हरति दरतिमिरमतिघोरं Gît. 10, Bk. 7. 63, 14. 93. 2 To laugh at; mock, ridicule (with acc.) ; गमवाप्य विद्रुमभुः प्रभुं हसति यामपि शक्रभर्तृकां N. 2. 16 3 (Hence) To surpass, excel, throw into the back-ground ; यो जहासेव वासुदेवं K. ; *Si.* 1. 71. 4 To resemble ; श्रिया हसद्भिः कमलानि सस्मितैः Ki. 8. 44. 5 To jest, joke. 6 To open, bloom, blow ; हसद्बंधुजीवप्रसूनैः. 7 To brighten up, or to clear up ; भास्वानुदेष्यति हसिष्यति चक्रवालं Subhâsh. –*Caus.* (हासयति–ते) To cause to smile ; Ku. 7. 95. –With अप to laugh at, deride, scoff at. –अव 1 to deride, ridicule. 2 to surpass, excel ; स्थितावहस्येव पुरं मघोनः Bk. 1. 6. –उप to laugh at, deride, ridicule ; तथा प्रयतेथा यथा नोपहस्यसे जनैः K. ; Ghaṭ. 17. –परि 1 to jest, joke. 2 to laugh at, ridicule ; (hence) to surpass, excel ; जनानामानंदः परिहसति निर्वाणपदवीं G. L. 5. –प्र 1 to laugh, smile ; ततः प्रहस्यापभयः पुरंदरं R. 3. 51. 3 to deride, ridicule, mock ; हसंतं प्रहसंत्येता रुदंतं प्ररुदंति च Subhâsh. 4 to brighten up, look splendid. –वि. 1 to smile, laugh gently ; किंचिद्विहस्यार्थपतिं बभाषे R. 2. 46. 2 to laugh at, deride, ridicule; किमिति विषीदसि रोदिषि विकला विहसति युवतिसभा तव विकला Gît. 9 ; गौरीवक्त्रभ्रुकुटिरचना या विहस्येव फेनैः Me. 50.

हसः 1 Laugh, laughter. 2 Derision. 3 Merriment, mirth.

हसनं Laughing, laughter.

हसती A portable fire-place.

हसंती 1 A portable fire-place. 2 A kind of Mallikâ.

हासिका Laughter, derision.

हसित *p. p.* 1 Laughed, laughing. 2 Blown, expanded. –तं 1 Laughter. 2 Joke, jesting 3 The bow of the god of love.

हस्तः 1 The hand ; हस्तं गत 'fallen in the hand or possession of.'; गौतमीहस्ते विसर्जयिष्यामि *S.* 3. 'I shall send it by Gautamî'; so हस्ते पतिता; हस्तेसनिहिता कुरु &c. ; शंभुना दत्तहस्ता Me. 60 'leaning on Sambha's hand'; हस्ते-कृ (हस्तेकृत्य/कृत्वा) 'to take or seize by the hand, take hold of the hand, take in hand, take possession of'; Prov. :—हस्तकंकणं किं दर्पणे प्रक्ष्यते Karpûr. 'sight requires no mirror'. 2 The trunk of an elephant, Ku. 1. 36. 3 N. of the 13th lunar mansioa consisting of five stars. 4 The fore-arm, cubit, a measure of length (equal to 24 *angulas* or about 18 inches, being the distance be tween the elbow and the tip of the middle finger). 5 Hand writing, signature ; धनी बोपगतं दद्यात् स्वहस्तपरिचिह्नितं Y. 3. 93 ; स्वहस्तकालसंपन्नं शासनं 1-320 'bearing date and signature'; धार्यतामयं प्रियायाः स्वहस्तः V. 2. 'the autograph of my beloved' ; 2. 20. 6 (Hence fig.) Proof, indication ; Mu. 3. 7 Help, assistance, support ; वाप्या खेदं कृशांग्याः सुचिरमवयवैर्दत्तहस्ता करोति Ve. 2. 21. 8 A mass, quantity, abundance (of hair), in comp. with केश, कच &c.; पाशः पक्षश्च हस्तश्च कलापार्थाः कचात्परे Ak. ; सनिविगलितबंधे केशहस्ते सुकेश्याः सति कुसुमसनाथे कं हरेदेष बर्हः V. 4. 10. –स्तं A pair of leather-bellows. –Comp.–अक्षरं one's own hand or signature, one's own sign-manual. –अग्रं the finger (being the extremity of the hand). –अंगुलि *f.* any finger of the hand. –अभ्यासः contact with the hand. –अवलंबः, –आलंबनं support of the hand ; दत्तहस्तावलंबे प्रारंभे Ratn.1. 8. 'being aided or helped on '. –आमलकं 'the fruit of the myrobalan held in the hand,' a phrase used to denote that which can be clearly and easily seen or understood. –आवापः a finger-guard (ज्याघातवारणं); V. 5, *S.* 6. –कमलं 1 a lotus carried in the hand. 2 a lotus-like hand. –कौशलं manual dexterity. –क्रिया manual work or performance, handicraft. –गत, –गामिन् *a.* come to hand, fallen into one's possession, obtained, secured ; त्वं प्रार्थ्यसे हस्तगता ममैभिः R. 7. 67, 8. 1. –ग्राहः taking by the hand. –चापल्यं

= हस्तकौशल q. v. -तलं 1 the palm of the hand. 2 the tip of an elephant's trunk. -तालः striking the palms together, clapping the hands. -दोषः a slip of the hand. -धारणं-वारणं warding off a blow (with the hand). -पादं the hands and feet ; न मे हस्तपादं प्रसरति S. 4. -पुच्छं the hand below the wrist. -पृष्ठं the back of the hand. -प्राप्त a. 1 held in the hand. 2 gained, secured. -प्राप्य a. easily accessible to the hand, that can be reached with the hand ; हस्तप्राप्यस्तबकनमितो बालमंदारवृक्षः Me. 75. -बिंबं perfuming the body with unguents. -मणिः a jewel worn on the wrist. -लाघवं 1 manual readiness or skill. 2 a sleight of the hand, legerdemain. -संवाहनं rubbing or shampooing with the hands ; Me. 96. -सिद्धिः f. 1 manual labour, doing with the hands 2 hire, wages. -सूत्रं a bracelet or thread-string worn on the wrist ; Ku. 7. 25.

हस्तकः 1 A hand. 2 The position of the hand.

हस्तिंवत् a. Dexterous, skilful, clever.

हस्ताहस्ति ind. Hand to hand ; हस्ताहस्ति जन्यमजनि Dk.

हस्तिकं A multitude of elephants.

हस्तिन् a. (नी f.) 1 Having hands. 2 Having a trunk. -m. An elephant; Ms. 7. 96, 12. 43; (elephants are said to be of foua kinds ; भद्र, मंद्र, मृग, and मिश्र). -Comp. -अध्यक्षः a superintendent of elephants. -आयुर्वेदः a work dealing with the treatment of elephants' diseases. -आरोहः an elephant-driver or rider. -कक्ष्यः 1 a lion. 2 a tiger. -कर्णः the castor-oil plant. -घ्नः 1 an elephant-killer. 2 a man. -चारिन् m. an elephant-driver. -दंतः 1 the tusk of an elephant. 2 a peg projecting from a wall. (-तं) 1 ivory. 2 a radish. -दंतकं a radish. -नखं a sort of turret projecting the approach to the gate of a city or fort. -पः, -पकः an elephant-driver or rider ; इति घोषयतीव डिंडिमः करिणो हस्तिपकाहतः क्वणन् H. 2. 86. -मदः the ichor issuing from the temples of an elephant in rut. -मल्लः 1 N. of *Airâvata*. 2 of Gaṇesa. 3 a heap of ashes. 4 a shower of dust. 5 frost. -यूथः, -थं a herd of elephants. -वर्चसं the splendour or magnificence of an elephant. -वाहः 1 an elephant-driver. 2 a hook for driving elephants. -षड्गवं a collection of six elephants. -स्नानं = गजस्नानं q. v. ; अवशेंद्रियचित्तानां हस्तिस्नानमिव क्रिया H. 1. 18. -हस्तः an elephant's trunk.

हस्तिन(ना)पुरं N. of a city founded by king Hastin, said to be situa.ed some fifty miles north-east of the modern Delhi ; it forms a central scene of action in the Mahâbhârata ; its other names are :— गजाह्वय, नागसाह्वय, नागाह्व, हास्तिन.

हस्तिनी 1 A female elephant. 2 A kind of drug and perfume. 3 A woman of a particular class, one of the four classes into which writers on erotical science divide women (described as having thick lips, thick hips, thick fingers, large breasts, dark complextion, and libidinous appetite); the Ratimanjarî thus describes her :—स्थूलाधरा स्थूलनितंबबिंबा स्थूलांगुलिः स्थूलकुचा सुशीला। कामोत्सुका गाढरतिप्रिया च नितांतभोक्त्री (नितंबखर्वा) खलु हस्तिनी स्यात् (करिणी मता सा) 1.

हस्त्य a. 1 Belonging to the hand. 2 Done with the hand, manual. 3 Given with the hand.

हहलं A kind of deadly poison.

हहा m. A kind of Gandarva ; cf. हाहा.

हा ind. A particle expressing. 1 Grief, dejection, pain, as expressed by 'ah,' 'alas !,' 'woe me', in English ; हा प्रिये जानाकि U. 3 ; हा हा देवि स्फुटति हृदयं U. 3. 38 ; हा पित क्वासि हे सुभ्रु Bk. 6. 11 ; हा वत्से मालति क्वासि Mâl. 10. &c.; (in this sense हा is often used with the acc. of person ; हा कृष्णाभक्तं Sk.) 2 Surprise ; हा कथं महाराजदशरथस्य धर्मदाराः प्रियसखी मे कौसल्या U. 4. 3 Anger or reproach.

हा I. 3 A. (जिहीते, हान ; *pass*. हायते ; *desid*. जिहासते) 1 To go, move ; जिहीर्षां विख्याता स्फुटमिह भवद्ध्वांधवरथं H. D. 28 ; Ki. 13. 23 ; Nalod. 1. 38. 2 To get, attain. -WITH उद् 1 to go or move upwards, rise (in all senses); यतो रजः पार्थिवमुज्जिहीते R. 13. 64 ; आविर्भूतानुरागाः क्षणमुदयगिरे रुज्जिहानस्य भानोः Mu. 4. 21, N. 22. 45, 55 ; उज्जिहीषे महाराज त्वं प्रशांतो न किं पुनः Bk. 18. 27 'why do you not rise ; *i. e.* come to life'; कोलाहलो लोकस्यादोजिहीत Dk. 'a noise rose from the people'. 2 to depart, go away ; उज्जिहानजीविता वराकी नानुकंपसे Mâl. 10. 3 to raise ; शिरसा यूपमुज्जिहीते Katy. 4 to throw up, contract (as eyebrows); Bk. 3. 47. -उप to come down to, descend ; निजौजसोज्जासयितुं जगद्द्रुहामुपाजिहीथा न महीतलं यदि Si. 1. 31. -सं to go to, attain to, enjoy ; जनता ...समहास्त मुदं Nalod. 1. 54. -II. 2 P. (जहाति, हीन) 1 To leave, abandon, quit, give up, forsake, relinquish, dismiss ; मूढ जहीहि धनागमतृष्णां कुरु तनुबुद्धे मनसि वितृष्णां Moha. M. 1 ; सा स्त्रीस्वभावादसहा भरस्य तयोर्द्वयोरेकतरं जहाति Mu. 4. 13, R. 5. 72, 8. 52, 12. 24, 14. 61, 87, 15. 59 ; S. 4. 13, Bg. 2. 50 ; Bk 3. 53, 5. 91, 10. 71, 20. 10. Me. 49, 60 ; Bv. 2. 129 ; Rs. 1. 38. 2 To resign, forego. 3 To let fall. 4 To omit, disregard, neglect. 5 To avoid, shun. -*pass*. (हीयते) 1 To be left or forsaken ; Ki. 12. 12. 2 To be excluded from, be deprived of, lose (with instr. or abl.); विरूपाक्षो जहे प्राणैः Bk. 14. 35 ; जनयित्वा सुतं तस्यां ब्राह्मण्यादेव हीयते Ms. 3. 17. 5. 161, 9. 211. 3 To be deficient or wanting in ; usually with परि q.v. 4 To diminish, decrease, decay, decline, wane (fig. also); प्रवृद्धो हीयते चंद्रः समुद्रोऽपि तथाविधः R. 17. 71 ; H. Pr. 42. 5 To fail (as in a law-suit); भूपमप्यनुपन्यस्तं हीयते व्यवहारतः Y. 2. 19. 6 To be left out or omitted. 7 To be weakened. -*Caus*. (हापयति-ते) 1 To cause to leave, abandon &c. 2 To neglect, omit. delay the performance of ; Si. 16. 33, Ms. 3. 71 ; 4. 21 ; Y. 1. 121. -*desid*. (जिहासति) To wish to leave &c. -WITH अप to leave, abandon, give up; विललाप स बाष्पगद्गदं सहजामप्यसहाय धीरता R. 8. 43. -अपा to leave, abandon. -अव to leave, be deprived of, (pass.).-परि 1 to leave, abandon, quit. 2 to omit, neglect ; यथोक्तान्यपि कर्माणि परिहाय Ms. 12. 92. (-*pass*.) 1 to be wanting or deficient in ; आर्यस्य सुविहितप्रयोगतया न किमपि परिहास्यते S. 1. 2 to be inferior to ; ओजस्वितया न परिहीयते शच्याः V. 3 ; M. 2. -प्र 1 to give up, forsake, abandon, relinquish. प्रजहाति यदा कामान् Bg. 2. 55, 39, मोहमेतौ प्रहास्येते Râm. 2 to let go, cast, discharge ; प्रजहुः शूलपट्टिशान् Bk. 14. 23. -वि to leave, abandon, forsake, give up ; विहाय लक्ष्मीपतिलक्ष्म कार्मुकं जटाधरः सन् जुहुधीह पावकं Ki. 1. 44 ; Me. 41, R. 2. 40 ; 5. 67, 73 ; 6. 7 ; 12. 102, 14. 48, 69 ; Ku. 3. 1. (-*Caus*.) to give away.

हांगर A large fish.

हाटक a. (की f.) Golden. -कं Gold. -Comp. -गिरिः the mountain Meru.

हात्रं Wages, hire.

हानं 1 Leaving, abandoning, loss, failure. 2 Escaping. 3 Prowess, power.

हानिः f. 1 Abandonment, relinquishment. 2 Loss, failure, absence, non-existence ; क्वचित्तु स्फुटालंकारविरहेऽपि न काव्यत्वहानिः K. P. 1 'it does not cease to be a Kâvya' &c. 3 Loss, damage, detriment ; ग्रासोद्गलितसिक्थेन का हानिः करिणो भवेत् Subhâsh. ; का नो हानिः Sarva.S. 4 Decrease, deficiency; यथा हानिः क्रमप्राप्ता तथा वृद्धिः क्रमागता Hariv. Y. 2. 207, 244. 5 Neglect, omission, breach ; प्रतिज्ञा°, कार्य°. 6 Passing away, waste, loss ; कालहानि R. 13. 16.

हाफिका Yawning, gaping.

हायनः, -नं A year. -नः 1 A kind of rice. 2 A flame.

हारः 1 Taking away, removal, seizing. 2 Conveying. 3 Abstraction, deprivation. 4 A carrier, porter. 5 A garland or necklace of pearls &c. ; a necklace in general ; हारोयं हरिणाक्षीणां लुठति स्तनमंडले Amaru. 100 ; पाण्ड्योयमंसार्पितलंबहारः R. 6. 60, 5. 52, 6. 16; Me. 67 ; Rs. 1. 4 ; 2. 18. 6 War, battle. 7 (In math.) The denominator of a fraction. 8 A divisor. –Comp. –आवलिः-ली *f.* a string of pearls ; तरुणीस्तन एव शोभते मणिहारावलिरामणीयकं N. 2. 44; हारावलीतरलकांचितकांचिदाम Gît. 11. –गुटि(लि)-का the bead or pearl of a necklace ; R. 5. 70. –यष्टिः *f.* a necklace, string of pearls ; दधति पृथुकुचाग्रैरुन्नतैर्हारयष्टिं Rs. 2. 25, 1. 8. –हारा a kind of reddish-brown grape.

हारकः 1 A thief, plunderer ; Y. 3. 215. 2 A cheat, rogue. 3 A string of pearls. 4 A divisor (in math.). 5 A kind of prose composition.

हारि *a.* Attracting, captivating, pleasing, charming. –रिः *f.* 1 Defeat. 2 Losing a game. 3 A body of travellers, caravan. –Comp. –कंठः a cuckoo.

हारिणिकः A deer-catcher, hunter.

हारित *p. p.* 1 Caused to be taken or seized. 2 Presented, offered. 3 Attracted. –तः 1 The green colour. 2 A kind of pigeon.

हारिन् *a.* (णी *f.*) 1 Taking, conveying, carrying. 2 Robbing, taking away; वाजिकुंजराणां च हारिणः Y. 2. 273, 3. 208. 3 Seizing, disturbing, Ms. 12. 28. 4 Obtaining, securing. 5 Attracting, captivating, pleasing, delighting, ravishing ; तवास्मि गीतरागेण हारिणा प्रसभं हृतः S. 1. 5 ; Si. 10. 13, 69 ; विश्वपहारिणि हरौ Bh. 2. 25. 6 Surpassing, excelling. 7 Having a necklace.

हारिद्रः 1 A yellow colour. 2 The Kadamba tree.

हारीतः 1 A kind of pigeon ; R. 4. 46. 2 A rogue, cheat. 3 N. of a writer of a Smriti or code of laws ; Y. 1. 4.

हार्द 1 Affection, love ; अमर्षशून्येन जनस्य जंतुना न जातहार्देन न विद्विषादरः Ki. 33 ; Si. 9. 69 ; V. 5. 10. 2 Kindness, tenderness. 3 Will. 4 Intention, meaning.

हार्य *a.* 1 To be taken or conveyed. 2 To be borne or carried on ; यदृच्छया वारणराजहार्यया Ku. 5. 70. 3 To be taken away or snatched off ; R. 7. 67. 4 To be displaced or borne away (as by wind); R. 16. 43. 5 To be shaken (as one's resolution); Ku. 5. 8. 6 To be secured or won over, to be attracted, conquered or influenced ; वहसि हि धनहार्यं पुण्यभूतं शरीरं Mk. 1. 31 ; Ku. 5. 53; Ms. 7. 217. 7 To be seized or robbed ; Ms. 8. 417. –र्यः 1 A snake. 2 The tree called Bibhîtaka. 3 The dividend (in math.).

हालः 1 A plough. 2 N. of Balarâma. 3 N. of Salivâhana. –Comp. –भृत् *m.* an epithet of Balarâma.

हालकः A horse of a yellowish-brown colour.

हाल(ला)हलं 1 A sort of deadly poison produced at the churning of the ocean ; (being of a very virulent character it began to burn up everything when it was swallowed by the god Siva); अहमेव गुरुः सुदारुणानामिति हालाहल मास्म तात दृप्यः । ननु संति भवादृशानि भूयो भुवनेऽस्मिन् वचनानि दुर्जनानां Subhâsh. 2 (Hence) A deadly poison or poison in general ; see Bv. 1. 95, 2. 73, Pt. 1. 183. (Also written हलाहल or हालहाल).

हालहली, हाला Wine, sipirituous liquor ; हित्वा हालामभिमतरसां रेवतीलोचनांकां Me. 49 ; Pt. 1. 58 ; Si. 10. 21.

हालिकः 1 A ploughman, an agriculturist. 2 One that draws a plough (as a plough-ox). 3 One who fights with a plough.

हालिनी A kind of large house-lizard.

हाली A wife's younger sister.

हालुः A tooth.

हावः 1 A call, calling. 2 Any feminine coquettish gesture calculated to excite amorous sensations, dalliance (of love), blandishments ; हावहारि हसितं वचनानां कौशलं दृशि विकारविशेषाः Si. 10. 13; जगुः सरागं ननृतुः सहावं Bk. 3. 43 ; (हाव is thus defined by उज्ज्वलमणिः—ग्रीवारेचकसंयुक्तो भ्रूनेत्रादिविकासकृत् । भावादीषत्प्रकाशो यः स हाव इति कथ्यते ॥ see S. D. 127 also.

हासः 1 Laughter, laughing, smile; मासो हासः P. R. 1. 22. 2 Joy, mirth, merriment. 3 Laughter, as the prevailing feeling of the *rasa* called हास्य; see S. D. 207. 4 Derisive laughter, R. 12. 36. 5 Opening, blowing, expanding (as of lotuses &c.); कूलानि सामर्षतयेव तेनुः सरोजलक्ष्मीं स्थलपद्महासैः Bk. 2. 3.

हासिका 1 Laughter. 2 Mirth, merriment.

हास्य *a.* Laughable, ridiculous ; R. 2. 43. –स्यं 1 Laughter ; Y. 1. 84. 2 Mirth, amusement, sport ; Ms. 9. 227. 3 Jest, joke. 4 Derision, ridicule. –स्यः The sentiment of mirth or humour, one of the eight or nine sentiments in poetry ; it is thus defined :—विकृताकारवाग्वेषचेष्टादेः कुहकाद्भवेत । हास्यो हासस्थायिभावः (so must the line be read instead of हासो हास्यस्थायिभावः); श्वेतः प्रथमदैवतः S. D. 228. –Comp. –आस्पदं a butt (of ridicule), laughing-stock. –पदवी, –मार्गः ridicule, derision ; कुड्रैर्नीतस्त्रिभुवनजयी हास्यमार्गं दशास्यः Vikar. 18. 107. –रसः the sentiment of mirth or humour ; see हास्य above.

हास्तिकः An elephant-driver or rider. –कं A herd of elephants ; Si. 5. 30.

हास्तिनं N. of Hastinâpura, q. v.

हाहा *m.* N. of a Gandharva. –*ind.* An exclamation denoting pain, grief or surprise, (it is simply हा repeated for the sake of emphasis ; see हा). –Comp. –कारः 1 a grief, lamentation, loud wailing. 2 the din or up-roar of battle. –रवः the cry हाहा.

हि *ind.* (Never used at the beginning of a sentence) It has the following senses :—1 For, because (expressing a strict or logical reason) ; अग्निरिहास्ति धूमो हि दृश्यते G. M.; R. 5. 10. 2 Indeed, surely ; देव प्रयोगप्रधानं हि नाट्यशास्त्रं M. 1 ; न हि कमलिनीं दृष्ट्वा ग्राहमवेक्षते मतंगजः M. 3. 3 For instance, as is well known ; प्रजानामेव भूत्यर्थं स ताभ्यो बलिमग्रहीत् । सहस्रगुणमुत्स्रष्टुमादत्ते हि रसं रविः R. 1. 18. 4 Only, alone (to emphasize an idea); मूढो हि मदनेनायास्यते K. 155. 5 Sometimes it is used merely as an expletive.

हि 5 P. (हिनोति, हित ; –*caus.* हाययति ; *desid.* जिघीषति) 1 To send forth impel. 2 To cast, throw, discharge, shoot ; गदां शक्रजिता जिघ्ये Bk. 14. 36. 3 To excite, incite, urge. 4 To promote, further. 5 To gratify, please, exhilarate. 6 To go or proceed. –WITH प्र 1 to send forth, propel. 2 to throw, discharge, shoot; विनाशात्तस्य वृक्षस्य रक्षस्तस्मै महोपलं प्रजिघाय R. 15. 21 ; Bk. 15. 121. 3 To send, despatch ; Mâl. 1 ; R. 8. 79 ; 11. 49, 12. 84 ; Bk. 15. 104.

हिंस् 1. 7. P., 10 U. (हिंसति, हिनस्ति, हिंसयति-ते, हिंसित) 1 To strike, hit. 2 To hurt, injure, harm. 3 To afflict, torment ; Mâl. 2. 1. 4 To kill, slay, destroy completely; कीर्तिं सूते दुष्कृतं या हिनस्ति U. 5. 31 ; R. 8. 45 ; Bg. 13, 28 ; Bk. 6. 38, 14. 57, 15. 78.

हिंसक *a.* Injurious, noxious, hurtful. –कः 1 A savage animal, a beast of prey. 2 An enemy. 3 A Brâhmaṇa skilled in the Atharvaveda.

हिंसनं-ना Striking, hurting, killing; Ms. 2. 177, 10. 48 ; Y. 1. 33.

हिंसा 1 Injury, mischief, wrong, harm, hurt (said to be of three kinds:- कायिक 'personal', वाचिक 'verbal', and मानसिक 'mental'); अहिंसा परमो धर्मः. 2 Killing, slaying, destruction ; R. 5. 57 ; Y. 3. 313 ; Ms. 10. 63. 3 Robbery, plunder. –Comp. –आत्मक *a.* injurious, destructive. –कर्मन् *n.* 1 any hurtful or injurious act. 2 magic used to effect the ruin or injury of an enemy (=अभिचार q. v.). –प्राणिन् *m.* a noxious animal. –रत *a.* delighting in mischief. –रुचि *a.*

intent on or delighting in mischief. -समुद्भव *a.* arising from injury.

हिंसारुः **1** A tiger. **2** Any noxious animal.

हिंसालु *a.* **1** Injurious,mischievous, hurtful. **2** Murderous. *-m.* A mischievous or savage dog (हिंसालुक also).

हिंसारः **1** A tiger. **2** A bird (खग). **3** A mischievous fellow.

हिंस्य *a.* Liable to be injured or killed ; R. 2. 57 ; Ms. 5. 41.

हिंस्र *a.* **1** Injurious, noxious, mischievous, hurtful, murderous) ; Ms. 9. 80, 12. 56. **2** Terrible. **3** Cruel, fierce, savage. -स्रः **1** A fierce animal, beast of prey ; R. 2. 27. **2** A destroyer. **3** N. of *Siva.* **4** N. of Bhîma. -**Comp.** -पशुः a beast of prey. -यंत्रं **1** a trap. **2** a mystical text used for malevolent purposes.

हिक् I. 1 U. (हिकति-ते, हिकित) **1** To make an indistinct or inarticulate sound. **2** To hiccough. -II. 10 A. (हिकयते) To hurt, injure, kill.

हिक्का **1** An indistinct sound. **2** Hiccough.

हिंकारः **1** A kind of low roar or sound like *'him'*. **2** A tiger.

हिंगु *m., n.* **1** The plant called Asa fœtida. **2** The substance prepared from this plant (asa fœtida) for household use, especially in seasoning articles of food. -**Comp.** -निर्यासः **1** the gummy exudation of the *hingu* tree. **2** The *nimba* tree. -पत्रः the *ingudi'* tree.

हिंगुलः-लं
हिंगुलिः } Vermilion.
हिंगुलु *m. n.*

हिंजीरः A rope or fetter for fastening an elephant's foot.

हिडिंबः N. of a demon slain by Bhîma. -बा The sister of Hidimba who married Bhîma. -**Comp.** -जित्, निषूदन, -भिद्,-रिपु *m.* epithets of Bhîma.

हिड् 1 A. (हिंडते, हिंडित) To go, wander, roam over. -With आ to wander or roam about ; *S.* 2.

हिंडनं **1** Wandering, roaming about. **2** Sexul intercourse, **3** Writing.

हिंडिकः An astrologer.

हिंडि(डी)रः **1** Cuttle-fish bone. **2** A man, a male. **3** The egg-plant.

हिंडी N. of Durgâ.

हित *a.* **1** Put, laid, placed. **2** Held, taken. **3** Suitable, fit, proper, good (with dat.); गोभ्यो हितं गोहितम्. **4** Useful, advantageous. **5** Beneficial, advantageous, wholesome, salutary (said of words, diet &c.); हितं मनोहारि च दुर्लभं वचः Ki. 1. 4; 14. 63. **6** Friendly, kind, affectionate, well-disposed (generally with loc.). -तः A friend, benefactor, friendly adviser ; हितान्नयः संशृणुते स किं प्रभुः Ki. 1. 5 ; H. 1. 30. -तं **1** Benefit, profit, advantage. **2** Anything proper or suitable. **3** Well-being, walfare, good. -**Comp.** -अनुबंधिन् *a.* involving or causing welfare. -अन्वेषिन्, -अर्थिन् *a.* seeking welfare -इच्छा good will, good wishes. -उक्तिः *f.* salutary instruction, friendly or kind advice. -उपदेशः friendly advice, salutary instruction. -एषिन् *a.* desiring another's welfare, well-wisher, benevolent. -कर *a.* doing a kind act or service, friendly, favourable. -काम *a.* desirous of befriending or benefiting. -काम्या desire for another's welfare, good will. -कारिन्, कृत् *m.* a benefactor. -प्रणी *m.* a spy. -बुद्धि *a.* friendly-minded, a well-wisher. -वाक्यं friendly advice. -वादिन् *m.* a friendly counsellor.

हितकः **1** A child. **2** The young of an animal.

हितालः A kind of palm.

हिंदोलः **1** A swing. **2** The swing on which the figures of Krishṇa are carried about during the swing-festival in the bright half of *S*râvana, or the festival itself.

हिंदोलकः, हिंदोला A swing.

हिम *a.* Cold, frigid, frosty, dewy. -मः **1** The cold season, winter. **2** The moon. **3** The Himâlaya mountain. **4** The sandal tree. **5** Camphor. -मं **1** Frost, hoar-frost; R. 1. 46, 9. 25; Ku. 2. 19. **2** Ice, snow ; Ku. 1. 3, 11 ; R. 9. 28, 15. 66, 16. 44, Ki. 5. 12. **3** Cold, coldness. **4** A lotus. **5** Fresh butter. **6** A pearl. **7** Night. **8** Sandal wood, -**Comp.** -अंशुः **1** the moon : Me. 89, R. 5. 16, 6. 47, 14. 80; *Si.* 2. 49. **2** camphor. °अभिख्य silver. -अचलः, -अद्रिः the Himâlaya mountain ; Ku. 1. 54; R. 4. 79, 14. 3. °जा, °तनया **1** Pârvatî. **2** the Ganges. -अंबु, -अंभस् *n.* **1** cold water. **2** dew; R. 5. 70. -अनिलः a cold wind. -अब्जं a lotus. -अरातिः **1** fire. **2** the sun. -आगमः the cold or winter-season. -आर्त *a.* pinched or shivering with call, chilled. -आलयः the Himâlaya mountain ; Ku. 1. 1. °सुता an epithet of Pârvatî. -आह्वः, -आह्वयः camphor. -उस्रः the moon. -करः **1** the moon ; लुठति न सा हिमकरकिरणेन Gît.7.**2** camphor. -कूटः **1** the winter season. **2** the Himâlaya mountain. -गिरिः the Himâlaya. -गुः the moon. -जः the Mainâka mountain. -जा **1** the plant zedoary. **2** Pârvatî. -तैलं a kind of camphor ointment. -दीधितिः the moon ; *Si.* 9. 29. -दुर्दिनं wintry weather, cold and bad weather. -द्युतिः the moon. -द्रुह् *m.* the sun. -ध्वस्त *a.* bitten, nipped, or blighted by frost. -प्रस्थः the Himâlaya mountain. -भास्, -रश्मि *m.* the moon. -वालुका camphor. -शीतल *a.* ice-cold. -शैलः the Himâlaya mountain. -संहतिः *f.* a mass of ice or snow. -सरस् *n.* ' a lake of snow ', cold water; Mâl. 1. 31. -हासकः the marshy date tree.

हिमवत् *a.* Snowy, icy, frosty. *-m.* The Himâlaya mountain; R. 4. 79, V. 5. 22. -**Comp.** -कुक्षिः a valley of the Himâlaya. -पुरं N. of Oshadhiprastha, the capital of Himâlaya; Ku. 6. 33. -सुतः the Mainâka mountain. -सुता **1** Pârvatî. **2** the Ganges.

हिमानी A mass or collection of snow, snow-drift ; नगमुपरि हिमानीगौरमासाद्य जिष्णुः Ki. 4. 38 ; Bv. I. 25.

हिरणं 1 Gold. **2** Semen. **3** A cowrie.

हिरण्मय *a* (यी *f.*) Made of gold. golden, हिरण्मयी सीतायाः प्रतिकृतिः U. **2**, R. 15. 61. -यः The god Brahman.

हिरण्यं **1** Gold ; Ms. 2. 246, 8. 182. **2** Any vessel of gold; Ms. 2. 29. **3** Silver. **4** Any precious metal. **5** Wealth, property. **6** Semen virile. **7** A *cowrie.* **8** A particular measure. **9** A substance. **10** The thorn-apple (धत्तूर). -**Comp.** -कक्ष *a.* wearing a golden girdle. -कशिपुः N. of a celebrated king of demons. [He was a son of Kasyapa and Diti, and by virtue of a boon from Brahman, he became so powerful that he usurped the sovereignty of Indra and oppressed the three worlds. He freely blasphemed the great god and subjected his son Prahrada to untold cruelties for acknowledging Vishnu as the Supreme deity. But he was eventually torn to pieces by Vishnu in the form of Narasimha ; see प्रह्लाद.] -कोशः gold and siver (whether wrought or unwrought). -गर्भः **1** N. of Brahman (as born from a golden-egg) **2** N. of Vishṇu. **3** the soul invested by the subtile body or सूक्ष्मशरीर q. v. -द *a* giving or granting gold, Ms. 4. 230. (-दः) the ocean. (-दा) the earth. -नाभः the mountain Mainâka. -बाहुः **1** an epithet of *Siva.* **2** the river *Soṇa.* -रेतस् *m.* **1** fire, R. 18. 25. **2** the sun. **3** N. of *Siva.* **4** the *Chitraka* or *Arka* plant. -वर्णा a river. -वाहः the river *So*ṇa.

हिरण्यय *a.* (यी *f.*) Golden.

हिरुक् *ind.* **1** Without, except. **2** Amongst, in the midst of. **3** Near. **4** Below.

हिल् 6 P. (हिलति) To sport amorously, wanton, dally, express amorous desire.

हिल्लः A kind of bird.

हिलोलः **1** A wave, billow. **2** The musical mode called Hindola. **3** A caprice, whim. **4** A kind of coitus.

हिल्वलाः *f. pl.* N. of five small stars in the head of the lunar mansion called मृगशिरस्.

ही *ind.* An interjection of **1** Surprise (ah !) ; हतविधिलसितानां ही विचित्रो विपाकः *Si.* 11. 64 ; or ही चित्रं लक्ष्मणेनोचे Bk. 14. 39 ; (often repeated in theatrical language in this sense). **2** Fatigue, despondency or sorrow. **3** Reason ; (cf. हि.)

हीन *p. p.* **1** Left, abandoned, forsaken &c. **2** Destitute or deprived of, bereft of, without ; (with instr. or in comp.) ; गुणैर्हीना न शोभंते निर्गंधा इव किंशुकाः Subhâsh. ; so द्रव्य°, मति°, उत्साह° &c. **3** Decayed, wasted. **4** Deficient, defective ; हीनातिरिक्तगात्रो वा तमप्यपनयेत्ततः Ms. 3. 242. **5** Subtracted. **6** Less, lower ; Ms. 2. 194. **7** Low, base, mean, vile. **–नः** **1** A defective witness. **2** A faulty respondent ; (Nârada enumerates five kinds :— अन्यवादी क्रियाद्वेषी नोपस्थायी निरुत्तरः । आहूतप्रपलायी च हीनः पंचविधः स्मृतः). **–Comp. –अंग** *a.* deficient in a limb, crippled, maimed, defective ; Ms. 4. 141 ; Y. 1. 222. **–कुल, –ज** *a.* base-born, of low family. **–क्रतु** *a.* one who neglects his sacrifice. **–जाति** *a.* **1** of a low caste. **2** excommunicated, outcaste, degraded. **–योनिः** *f.* low birth or origin. **–वर्ण** *a.* **1** of low caste. **2** of inferior rank. **–वादिन्** *a.* **1** making a defective statement. **2** prevaricating. **3** dumb, speechless. **–सख्यं** associating with low persons. **–सेवा** attendance on base persons.

हिंतालः The marshy date tree.

हीरः **1** A snake. **2** A necklace. **3** A lion. **4** N. of the father of Srîharsha, the author of the Naishadha-charita. **–रः, –रं** **1** The thunderbolt of Indra. **2** A diamond ; (occurring in the concluding stanza of each canto of नैषधचरित.). **–Comp. –अंगः** the thunder-bolt of Indra.

हीरकः A diamond.

हीरा **1** An epithet of Lakshmî. **2** An ant.

हीलं Semen virile.

हीही *ind.* A particle expressive of surprise or merriment ; see ही.

हु 3 P. (जुहोति, हुत ; *pass.* हूयते ; *caus.* हावयति-ते, *desid.* जुहूषति) **1** To offer or present (as an oblation to fire), make an offering to or in honor of a deity (with acc.), sacrifice ; यो मंत्रपूतां तनुमप्यहौषीत् R. 13. 45 ; जटाधरः सन् जुहुधीह पावकं Ki. 1. 44 ; हविर्जुहधि पावके Bk. 20. 11 ; Ms. 3. 87 ; Y. 1. 99. **2** To perform a sacrifice. **3** To eat.

हुड् I. 1 P. (होडति) To go. –II. 6 P. (हुडति) To collect.

हुडः **1** A ram. **2** An iron stake for keeping out thieves. **3** A kind of fence. **4** An iron club.

हुडुः A ram ; जंबुको हुडुयुद्धेन Pt. 1. 162.

हुडुक्कः **1** A small hour-glass shaped drum ; N. 15. 17. **2** A kind of bird (दात्यूह). **3** The bolt of a door. **4** A drunken man.

हुडुत् *n.* **1** Noise of a bull. **2** A sound of threat.

हुडः **1** A tiger. **2** A ram. **3** A blockhead. **4** A village-hog. **5** A demon.

हुत *p. p.* **1** Offered as an oblation to fire, burnt as a sacrificial offering. **2** One to whom an oblation is offered ; *S.* 4 ; R. 2. 71, 9. 33. **–तः** N. of *S*iva. **–तं** An oblation, offering. **–Comp. –अग्नि** *a.* who has made an oblation to fire ; R. 1. 6. **–अशनः** **1** fire ; समीरणो नोदयिता भवेति व्यादिश्यते केन हुताशनस्य Ku. 3. 21, R. 4. 1. **2** N. of *S*iva. **°सहायः** an epithet of *S*iva. **–अशनी** the full-moon day in the month of Phâlguna (होलाका). **–आशः** fire ; प्रदक्षिणीकृत्य हुतं हुताशं R. 2. 71. **–जातवेदस्** *a.* one who has made an oblation to fire. **–भुज्** *m.* fire ; नैशस्यार्चिर्हुतभुज इव च्छिन्नभूयिष्ठधूमा V. 1. 9 ; U. 5. 9. **°प्रिया** *S*vâhâ, the wife of Agni. **–वहः** fire ; जनाकीर्णं मन्ये हुतवहपरीतं गृहमिव *S.* 5. 10 ; शीतांशुस्तपनो हिमं हुतवहः Gît. 9 ; Me. 43 ; Rs. 1. 27. **–होमः** a Brâhmaṇa who has offered oblations to fire. (**–मं**) a burnt offering.

हुम् *ind.* A particle (originally an imitative sound) expressing. **1** Remembrance or recollection ; हुं ज्ञातं, or रामो नाम बभूव हुं तदबला सीतेति हुम्. **2** doubt ; चैत्रो हुं मैत्रो हुं. **3** Assent ; U. 5. 35. **4** Anger. **5** Aversion. **6** Reproach. **7** Interrogation. (In spells and incantations हुं is often found used with dat. ; *e. g.* ओं कवचाय हुम्). (**हुंकृ** means 'to utter the sound *hum*', to roar, grunt, bellow, as in **अनुहुंकृ** 'to roar in return;' अनुहुंकुरुते घनध्वनिं न हि गोमायुरुतानि केसरी *Si.* 16. 25.). **–Comp. –कारः –कृतिः** *f.* **1** uttering the sound 'hum' ; पृष्टा पुनः पुनः कांता हुंकारैरेव भाषते. **2** a menacing sound, sound of defiance ; क्षतहुंकारशंसिनः Ku. 2. 26 ; हुंकारेणेव धनुषः स हि विघ्नानपोहति *S.* 3. 1, R. 7. 58 ; Ku. 5. 54. **3** roaring, bellowing in general. **4** the grunting of a boar. **5** the twang of a bow.

हुर्छ् 1 P. (हुर्छति) To be crooked.

हुल् 1 P. (होलति) **1** To go. **2** To cover or conceal.

हुलहुली A kind of inarticulate sound, uttered by women on joyful occasions.

हुहु (**हू**) *m.* A kind of Gandharva.

हूड् 1 A. (हूडते) To go.

हूणः (**नः**) **1** A barbarian, foreigner ; सद्यो मुंडितमत्तहूणचिबुकप्रस्पर्धि नारंगकम्. **2** A kind of golden coin, (probably current in the country of the Hûṇas). **–णाः** *m. pl.* N. of a country or its people ; हूणावरोधानां R. 4. 68.

हूत *p. p.* Called, summoned, invited &c. ; see ह्वे.

हूतिः *f.* **1** Calling, inviting. **2** Challenging. **3** A name ; as in हरिहेतुहूति q. v.

हूम् &c. See हुम्.

हूरवः A jackal.

हूहू *m.* A kind of Gandharva.

हृ 1 U. (हरति-ते, हृत ; *pass.* ह्रियते) **1** To take, carry, convey, lead, (often used with two accusatives in this sense) ; अजां ग्रामं हरति Sk. ; संदेशं मे हर धनपतिक्रोधविश्लेषितस्य Me. 7 ; Ms. 4. 74. **2** To carry off or away, take or draw to a distance ; Bk. 5. 47. **3** To take away, rob, plunder, steal ; दुर्वृत्ता जारजन्मानो हरिष्यंतीति शंकया Bv. 4. 45 ; R. 3. 39, Ku. 2. 47, Bk. 2. 39 ; Ms. 7. 43. **4** To strip off, deprive of, despoil, take away ; वृंताच्छ्लथं हरति पुष्पमनोकहानां R. 5. 69, 3. 54, Bk. 15. 116 ; Ms. 8. 334. **5** To take away, cure, destroy ; तथापि हरते तापं लोकानामुन्नतो घनः Bv. 1. 49 ; R. 15. 24 ; Me. 31. **6** To attract, captivate, win over, influence, subdue ; enchant ; चेतो न कस्य हरते गतिरंगनायाः Bv. 2. 157. ये भावा हृदयं हरंति 1. 103 ; तवास्मि गीतरागेण हारिणा प्रसभं हृतः S. 1. 5 ; मृगया जहार चतुरेव कामिनी R. 9. 69, 10. 83, V. 4. 10 ; Rs. 6. 20, Bg. 6. 44, 2. 60 ; Ms. 6. 59. **7** To gain, acquire, take, obtain ; ततो विंशं नृपो हरेत् Ms. 8. 391, 153 ; स हरतु सुभगपताकां Dk. **8** To have, possess ; Bv. 2. 163. **9** To surpass, eclipse ; Bk. 5. 71 ; *Si.* 9. 63. **10** To marry ; Ms. 9. 93. **11** To divide. –*Caus.* (हारयति-ते) **1** To cause to take, carry or convey, send (something) by one ; (with acc. of instr) ; भृत्यं भृत्येन वा भारं हारयति Sk. ; जीमूतेन स्वकुशलमयीं हारयिष्यन् प्रवृत्तिं Me. 4 ; Ms. 8. 114 ; Ku. 2. 39. **2** To cause to be taken away, to lose, be deprived of. **3** To give away. –*Desid.* (जिहीर्षति-ते) To wish to take &c. –WITH **अध्या** to supply an ellipsis. **–अनु** **1** to imitate, resemble ; देहबंधेन स्वरेण च रामभद्रमनुहरति U. 4 ; so Ki. 9. 67. **2** to take after (one's parents), (Atm. in this sense) ; see P. 1 3. 21. Vârt. **–अप** **1** to bear or snatch off, take away ; पश्चात्पुत्रैरपहृतभरः कल्पते विश्रमाय V. 3. 1. **2** to avert, turn away ; वदनमपहरंतीं (गौरीं) Ku. 7. 95. **3** to rob, plunder, steal. **4** to deprive (one) of, take away, destroy ; त्वं च कीर्तिमपहर्तुमुद्यतः R. 11. 74. **5** to attract. affect, influence, overpower, subdue ; (न) प्रियतमा यतमानमपाहरत् R. 9. 7 ; so अपह्रियै निद्रया U. 1. (–*Caus.*) to cause (others) to take away ; Ki. 1. 31. **–अभि** to carry off, remove. **–अभ्यव** to eat. (–*Caus.*) to cause to eat, feed. **–आ** **1** (*a*) to bring, fetch ; यदेव वव्रे तदपश्यदाहृतं R. 3. 9, 14. 77. (*b*) to carry, convey ; Ms. 9. 54. **2** to bring near, give ; अयाचिताहृतं Y. 1. 215. **3** to obtain, get, receive ; Ms. 2. 183, 7. 80, 8. 151. **4** to have, assume ; आजह्रतुस्तच्चरणौ पृथिव्यां स्थलारविंदश्रियमव्यवस्थां Ku. 1. 33. **6** to perform (a sacrifice); स विश्वजितमाजह्रे यज्ञं सर्वस्वदक्षिणं R. 4. 86, 14. 37. **7** to recover, bring back. **8** to cause, produce, beget. **9** to wear, put on. **10** to attract. **11** to remove, draw off from. (*–Caus.*) **1** to cause to bring or fetch. **2** to cause to give or pay. **3** to collect, bring together. **–उद्** **1** to save, deliver, extricate, rescue ; मां तावदुद्धर शुचो दयितात्रवृत्त्या V. 4. 15. **2** to draw or take out ; (शरं) उद्धर्तुमैच्छत्प्रसभोद्धृतारिः R. 2. 30, 3. 64. **3** to uproot, eradicate, extricate ; नमयामास नृपानुद्धरन् R. 8. 9, 4. 66, त्रिदिवमुद्धृतदानवकंटकं *S.* 7. 3. **4** to raise, lift up, elevate, extend (as hands); Ms. 4. 62 ; Pt. 1. 363. **5** to pluck (as flowers). **6** to absorb ; *Si.* 3. 75. **7** to deduct, subtract. **8** to select, pick out, extract, as इदं पद्यं रामायणादुद्धृतम्. (*–Caus.*) to cause to take out ; R. 9. 74. **–उदा** **1** to relate, narrate, declare, say, speak, utter ; उदाजहार द्रुपदात्मजा गिरः Ki. 1. 27 ; Mk. 9. 4 ; चिकित्सका दोषमुदाहरंति M. 2 ; Mâl. 1. **2** to call, name; त्वां कामिनो मदनदूतिमुदाहरंति V. 4, 11 ; श्रुतान्वितो दशरथ इत्युदाहृतः Bk. 1. 1. **3** to illustrate, exemplify, cite as an instance or illustration ; त्वमुदाह्रियस्व कथमन्यथा जनैः *Si.* 15. 29. **–उप** **1** to fetch, bring near ; *S.* 1. **2** to offer, give, present ; नीवारभागधेयमस्माकमुपहरंतु *S.* 2 ; मातृभ्यो बलिमुपहर Mk. 1 ; Mv. 6. 22 ; R. 14. 19, 16. 80, 19. 12 ; *S.* 3. **3** to offer (as a victim). **–उपा** to bring, fetch. **–निस्** **1** to take or draw out from, extract ; R. 14. 42. **2** to carry out the dead body ; Ms. 5. 91; Y. 3. 15. **3** to remove (as a fault &c.). **–परि** **1** to avoid, shun ; स्त्रीसंनिकर्षं परिहर्तुमिच्छन्नंतर्दधे भूतपतिः सभूतः Ku. 3. 74 ; Ms. 8. 400 ; Ku. 3. 43. **2** to forsake, abandon, leave, desert ; कति न कथितमिदमनुपदमचिरं मा परिहर हरिमतिशयरुचिरं Gît. 9. **3** to remove, destroy ; answer, refute (as objections, charges &c.); ब्रह्मास्य जगतो निमित्तं कारणं प्रकृतिश्चेत्यस्य पक्षस्याक्षेपः स्मृतिनिमित्तः परिहृतः । तर्कनिमित्त इदानीमाक्षेपः परिह्रियते S. B. ; Me. 14. **–प्र** **1** to strike at, strike, beat लत्तया प्रहरति ' kicks'; R. 5. 68 ; Ku. 3. 70 ; Bk. 9. 7. **2** to hurt, injure, wound (with loc.); आर्तत्राणाय वः शस्त्रं न प्रहर्तुमनागसि *S.* 1. 11 ; R. 2. 62, 7. 59, 11. 84, 15. 3. **3** to attack, assault. **4** to throw, cast, hurl ; (with loc. or dat.). **5** to seize upon. **–वि** **1** to take away, seize away. **2** to remove, destroy. **3** to let fall, shed (as tears). **4** to pass (as time). **5** to amuse or divert oneself, sport, play ; विहरति हरिरिह सरसवसंते Gît. 1. **व्यव** **1** to deal in any transaction or business. **2** to act, behave, deal with. **3** to go to law, sue (one) in a court of law ; अर्थपतिर्व्यवहर्तुमर्थगौरवादाभियोक्ष्यते Dk. **–व्या** to speak, say, tell, narrate, declare ; Ku. 2. 62, 6. 2 ; R. 11. 83. **–सं** **1** to bring or draw together. **2** (*a*) to contract, abridge, compress ; R. 10. 32. (*b*) to drop ; संह्रियतामियं K. **3** to bring together, collect, accumulate. **4** to destroy, annihilate (opp. सृज्); अमुं युगांतोचितकालनिद्रः संहृत्य लोकान् पुरुषोऽधिशेते R. 13. 6. **5** to withdraw, withhold, draw or take back ; अभिमुखे मयि संहृतमीक्षितं *S.* 2. 11, 6. 4 ; न हि संहरते ज्योत्स्नां चंद्रश्चांडालवेश्मनि H. 1. 61 ; R. 4. 16, 12. 103 ; Bg. 2. 28. **6** to curb, restrain, suppress ; क्रोधं प्रभो संहर संहरेति यावद्गिरः खे मरुतां चरंति Ku. 3. 72. **7** to wind up, close. **–समा** **1** to bring, convey, carry ; सर्वे एव समाहारि तदा शैलः सहौषधिः Bk. 15. 107. **2** to collect, bring together, convene ; तत्र स्वयंवरसमाहृतराजलोकं R. 5. 62 ; Bk. 8. 63. **3** to draw, attract. **4** to destroy, annihilate ; Bg. 11. 32. **5** to complete (as a sacrifice). **6** to return, restore to one's proper place; Ms. 8. 319. **7** to curb, restrain.

हृ (ह्रि) णीयते Den. A. **1** To be angry. **2** to feel ashamed (with instr. or gen.); त्वयाद्य तस्मिन्नपि दंडधारिणा कथं न पत्या धरणी हृणीयते N. 1. 133 ; दिवोपि वज्रायुधभूषणाया हृणीयते वीरवती न भूमिः Bk. 2. 38.

हृणी (णि) या **1** Censure, reproach. **2** Shame. **3** Compassion.

हृत् *a.* (At the end of comp. only) Taking away, seizing, removing, carrying off, attracting &c.

हृत *p. p.* **1** Taken or carried away. **2** Seized. **3** Captivated. **4** Accepted. **5** Divided, see हृ. **–Comp.** **–अधिकार** *a.* **1** dismissed from authority, turned out. **2** deprived of one's due rights. **–उत्तरीय** *a.* having the upper garments stripped off. **–द्रव्य, -धन** *a.* spoiled of wealth. **–सर्वस्व** *a.* stripped of all one's property, utterly ruined.

हृतिः *f.* **1** Seizure. **2** Robbing, spoilation. **3** Destruction.

हृद् *n.* (This word has no forms for the first five inflections and is optionally substituted for हृदय after acc. dual) **1** The mind, heart. **2** The chest, bosom, breast ; इमां हृदि व्यायतपातमक्षिणोत् Ku. 3. 54. **–Comp.** **–आवर्तः** a lock or curl of hair on a horse's chest. **–कंपः** tremor of the heart, palpitation. **–गत** *a.* **1** seated in the mind, conceived, designed. **2** cherished. (**–तं**) design, meaning, intent. **–देशः** the region of the heart. **–पिंडः-डं** the heart. **–रोगः** **1** heart-disease, heart-burn. **2** sorrow, grief, anguish. **3** love. **4** the sign Aquarius of the zodiac. **–लासः** (**–हृल्लासः**) **1** hiccough. **2** disquietude, grief. **–लेखः** (**–हृल्लेखः**) **1** knowledge, reasoning. **2** heart-ache. **–लेखा** (**–हृल्लेखा**) grief, anxiety. **–वंटकः** the stomach. **–शोकः** heart-burn or anguish.

हृदयं **1** The heart, soul, mind ; हृदये दिग्धशरैरिवाहतः Ku. 4. 25 ; so अयोहृदयः R. 9. 9 ; पाषाणहृदय &c. **2** The bosom, chest, breast ; बाणभिन्नहृदया निपेतुषी R. 11. 19. **3** Love, affection. **4** The interior or essence of anything. **5** The secret science; अश्व°, अक्ष° &c. **–Comp.** **–आत्मन्** *m.* a heron. **–आविध्** *a.* heart-rending, heart-piercing ; Bk. 6. 73. **–ईशः, –ईश्वरः** a husband. (**–शा, –री** *f.*) **1** a wife. **2** a mistress. **–कंपः** tremor of the heart, palpitation. **–ग्राहिन्** *a.* heart-captivating. **–चौरः** one who steals the heart or affections. **–छिद्** *a.* heart-rending, heart piercing **–विध्**; **–वेधिन्** *a.* heart-piercing. **–वृत्ति** *f.* disposition of the heart. **–स्थ** *a.* being or cherished in the heart. **–स्थानं** the breast, bosom.

हृदयंगम *a.* **1** Heart-stirring, touching, thrilling. **2** Lovely, handsome ; Mâl. 1. **3** Sweet, attractive, pleasant agreeable ; अहो हृदयंगमः परिहासः Mâl. 3. वल्गुकी च हृदयंगमस्वना R. 19. 13, Ku. 2. 16. **4** Fit, appropriate. **5** Dear, beloved, cherished ; क्व नु ते हृदयंगमः सखा Ku. 4. 24.

हृदयालु, हृदयिक, हृदयिन् *a.* Tender-hearted, good-hearted, affectionate.

हृदि (दी) कः N. of a Yâdava prince.

हृदिस्पृश् *a.* **1** Touching the heart. **2** Dear, beloved. **3** Agreeable, charming, beautiful.

हृद्य *a.* **1** Hearty, cordial, sincere. **2** Dear to the heart, cherished, dear, desired, beloved ; Bv. 1. 69. **3** Agreeable, pleasant ; charming ; Mâl. 4, R. 11. 68. **–Comp.** **–गंधः** the Bilva tree. **–गंधा** the great-flowered jasmine.

हृष् 1, 4. P. (हर्षति, हृष्यति, हृष्ट or हृषित) **1** To be delighted or rejoiced, be pleased or glad, to exult, rejoice ; अद्वितीयं रुचात्मानं मत्वा किं चंद्र हृष्यसि Bv. 2. 105 ; Bk. 15. 104, Ms. 2. 54. **2** To bristle or stand erect, stand on end (as the hair of the body); हृषितास्तनूरुहाः Dk.; हृष्यंति रोमकूपानि Mb. **3** To become erect (said of other things, *e. g.* the penis). *–Caus.* (हर्षयति-ते) To please, delight, fill with pleasure. **–WITH प्र** **1** to be glad, to rejoice ; न प्रहृष्येत् प्रियं प्राप्य Bg. 5. 20, 11. 36. 2 to stand on end, bristle (as hair of the body). -वि to rejoice, be glad or delighted.

हृषित *p. p.* 1 Pleased, delighted, glad, happy, rejoiced, enraptured. 2 Thrilled ; having the hair bristling. 3 Astonished. 4 Bent, bowed. 5 Disappointed. 6 Fresh.

हृषीकं An organ of sense. -Comp. -ईशः an epithet of Vishṇu or Krishṇa ; Bg. 1. 15 ; *et seg.* ; (हृषीकाणींद्रियाण्याहुस्तेषामीशो यतो भवान् । हृषीकेशस्ततो विष्णो ख्यातो देवेषु केशव ॥ Mb.).

हृष्ट *p.p.* Pleased, rejoiced,(=हृषित). -Comp. -चित्त, -मानस *a.* rejoiced in mind, glad at heart, happy. -रोमन् *a.* having the hair on the body bristling or thrilling (with joy). -वदन *a.* having a cheerful countenance. -संकल्प *a.* contented, pleased. -हृदय *a.* joyous-hearted, cheerful, merry.

हृष्टिः *f.* 1 Delight, happiness, joy, pleasure. 2 Pride.

हे *ind.* 1 A vocative particle (oh !, ho !); हे कृष्ण हे यादव हे सखेति Bg. 11. 41 ; हे राजानस्त्यजत सुकविप्रेमबंधे विरोधं Vikr. 18. 107. 2 An interjection expressing defiance, envy, ill-will or disapprobation.

हेक्का Hiccough.

हेठः 1 Vexation. 2 Hindrance, obstruction, opposition. 3 Injury, hurt.

हेड् 1 A. (हेडते) To disregard, slight, neglect.– II. 1 P. (हेडति) 1 To surround. 2 To attire.

हेडः Disregard, slight. -Comp. -जः anger, displeasure.

हेडावुक्कः A horse-dealer.

हेतिः *m. f.* 1 A weapon, missile ; समरविजयी हेतिदलितः Bh. 2. 44 ; R. 10. 12 ; Ki. 3. 56, 14. 30. 2 A stroke, injury. 3 A ray of the sun. 4 Light, splendour. 5 Flame.

हेतुः 1 Cause, reason, object, motive; इति हेतुस्तदुद्भवे K. P. 1 ; Mâl. 1. 23, R. 1. 10 ; Me. 25 ; *S.* 3. 11. 2 Source, origin ; स पिता पितरस्तासां केवलं जन्महेतवः R. 1. 24 ' authors of their being '. 3 A means or instrument. 4 The logical reason, the reason for an inference, middle term (forming the second member of the five-membered syllogism). 5 Logic, science of reasoning. 6 Any logical proof or argument. 7 A rhetorical reason (regarded by some writers as a figure of speech); it is thus defined :-हेतोर्हेतुमता सार्धमभेदो हेतुरुच्यते. (N. B. The forms हेतुना, हेतोः rarely हेतौ are used adverbially in the sense of ' by reason of ', ' on account of ', ' because of ', with gen. or in comp. शास्त्रविज्ञानहेतुना, अल्पस्य हेतोर्बहु हातुमिच्छन् R. 2. 47 ; विस्मृतं कस्य हेतोः Mu. 1. 1. &c.). -Comp. -अपदेशः adducing the *hetu* (in the form of the five-membered syllogism). -आभासः 'the semblance of a reason,' a fallacious middle term, fallacy ; (it is of five kinds :- सव्यभिचार or अनैकांतिक, विरुद्ध, असिद्ध, सत्प्रतिपक्ष and बाधित). -उपक्षेपः, उपन्यासः adducing a reason, statment of an argument. -वादः disputation, controversy. -शास्त्रं a logically-treated work, any heretical work questioning the authority of Smritis or revelation ; Ms. 2. 11. -हेतुमत् *m. du.* cause and effect.°भावः the relation existing between cause and effect.

हेतुक *a.* Causing, producing (at the end of comp.). -कः 1 A cause, reason. 2 An intrument. 3 A logician.

हेतुता-त्वं Causation, the existence of cause.

हेतुमत् *a.* 1 Having a reason or cause. 2 Having the *hetu*. -*m.* An effect.

हेमं Gold. -मः 1 A dark or brown coloured horse. 2 A particular weight of gold. 3 The planet Mercury.

हेमन् *n.* 1 Gold. 2 Water. 3 Snow. 4 The thorn-apple. 5 The Kesara flower. -Comp. -अंग *a.* golden. (-गः) 1 Garuḍu. 2 a lion. 3 the mountain *Sumeru*. 4 N. of Brahman. 5 of Vishṇu. 6 *Champaka* tree. -अंगदं a gold-bracelet. -अद्रिः the mountain *Sumerun*. -अंभोजं a golden lotus ; हेमांभोजप्रसवि सलिलं मानसस्याददानः Me. 62. -अंभोरुहं a golden lotus ; Ku. 2. 44. -आह्वः 1 the wild *Champaka* tree. 2 the *Dhattu'ra* plant. -कंदलः coral. -करः, -कर्तृ, -कारः, -कारकः a goldsmith ; Ms. 12. 61, Y. 3. 147. -किंजल्कं the Nâgakesara flower. -कुंभः a golden jar. -कूटः N. of a mountain ; *S.* 7. -केतकी the *Keteka* plant, bearing yellow flowers (स्वर्णकेतकी). -गंधिनी the perfume named Reṇukâ. -गिरिः the mountain *Sumeru*. -गौरः The Asoka tree. -छन्न *a.* covered with gold. (-न्नं) gold covering. -ज्वालः fire. -तारं blue vitriol. -दुग्धः,-दुग्धकः the glomerous fig-tree -पर्वतः the mountain Meru. -पुष्प, -पुष्पकः 1 the Asoka tree. 2 the Lodhra tree. 3 the Champaka tree. (-*n.*) the Asoka flower. 2 the flower of China rose. -च(व)लं a pearl. -मालिन् *m.* the sun. -यूथिका the golden or yellow jasmine. -रागिणी *f.* turmeric. -शंखः N. of Vishṇu. -शृंगं 1 a golden horn. 2 a golden summit. -सारं blue vitriol. -सूत्रं, -सूत्रकं a kind of necklace ; (Mar. गोफ).

हेमंतः-तं One of the six seasons, cold or winter season (comprising the months मार्गशीर्ष and पौष); नवप्रवालो द्गमसस्यरम्यः प्रफुल्ललोध्रः परिपक्वशालिः । विलीनपद्मः प्रपतत्तुषारो हेमंतकालः समुपागतः प्रिये Rs. 4. 1.

हेमलः 1 A goldsmith. 2 A touchstone. 3 A chameleon.

हेय *a.* Fit to be left or abandoned.

हेरं 1 A kind of crown or diadem. 2 Turmeric

हेरंबः 1 N. of Gaṇesa. 2 A buffalo. 3 A boastful hero. -Comp. -जननी N. of Pârvatî (mother of Gaṇesa).

हेरिकः A spy, secret emissary.

हेलनं-ना Disregarding, slighting, contempt, insulting.

हेला 1 Contempt, disrespect ; insult ; *Si.* 12. 72. 2 Amorous sport or dalliance, wanton sport ; see S. D. 128 ; D. R. 2. 32. 3 Strong sexual desire ; प्रौढेच्छयाऽतिरूढानां नारीणां सुरतोत्सवे । शृंगारशास्त्रतत्त्वज्ञैर्हेला सा परिकीर्तिता ॥ 4 Ease, facility ; *Si.* 1. 34 ; हेलया ' easily ', without any difficulty or trouble. 5 Moonlight.

हेलावुक्कः A horse-dealer.

हेलिः The sun. -*f.* Wanton or amorous sport, dalliance.

हेवाकः Ardent or intense desire, eagerness ; (this word, like the word लटभ q. v., is used only by later writers like Kalhaṇa, Bilhaṇa, and is probably derived from Persian or Arabic); अस्मिन्नासीचदनु निबिडाश्लेषहेवाकलीलावेलद्बाहुक्वणितवलया संततं राजलक्ष्मीः Vikr. 18. 101 ; cf. हेवाकिन् below.

हेवाकस *a.* High, intense, ardent ; हेवाकसस्तु शृंगारो हावोक्षिप्तभ्रूविकारकृत् D. R. 2. 31 (might the word here not be derived from हेवाक ?)

हेवाकिन् *a.* Ardently desirous of, eager for, (in comp.); जायंते महतामहो निरुपमप्रस्थानहेवाकिनां निःसामान्यमहत्त्वयोगपिशुना वार्ता विपत्तावपि Kalhaṇa.

हेष् 1 A. (हेषते, हेषित) To neight (as a horse); to bray, roar (in general).

हेषः, हेषा, हेषितं Neighing, braying ; रथांगसंक्रीडितनप्रवहेषः Ki. 16. 8.

हेषिन् *m.* A horse.

हेहे *ind* A vocative particle used in addressing or calling out loudly.

है *ind.* A vocative particle.

हैतुक *a.* (की *f.*) 1 Causal, causative. 2 Argumentative, rationalistic. -कः 1 A logical reasoner, an arguer. 2 A follower of the Mîmâmsâ doctrines. 3 A rationalist, sceptic. 4 A heretic.

हैम *a.* (मी *f.*) 1 Cold, wintry, frigid. 2 Caused by frost ; मृणालिनी हैममिवोपरागं R. 16. 7. 2 Golden, made of gold ; पादेन हैमं विलिलेख पीठं R. 6. 15 ; Bk. 5. 89 ; Ku. 6. 6. -मं Hoarfrost, dew. -मः An epithet of Siva. -Comp. -मुद्रा,-मुद्रिका a golden coin.

हैमन a. (नी f.) 1 Wintry, cold ; Si. 6. 55, Ki. 17. 12. 2 Pertaining to winter, i. e. long (as nights); Si. 6. 77. 3 Growing in or suitable for winter ; हैमनैर्निवसनैः सुमध्यमाः R. 19. 41. 4 Golden, made of gold. -नः 1 The month Mârgasîrsha. 2 The winter season (= हेमंत q. v.).

हैमंतिक a. 1 Wintry, cold. 2 Growing in winter. -कं A kind of rice.

हैमल See हेमंत.

हैमवत a. (ती f.) 1 Snowy. 2 Flowing from the snowy, i. e. Himâlaya mountain ; R. 16. 44. 3 Bred in, belonging to, or situated on, the Himâlaya mountain ; Ku. 3. 23, 2. 67. -तं Bhâratavarsha or India.

हैमवती 1 N. of Pârvatî. 2 Of the river Ganges. 3 A kind of myrobalan. 4 A kind of drug. 5 Common flax. 6 A tawny grape.

हैयंगवीनं 1 Clarified butter prepared from the preceding day's milk, fresh ghee ; हैयंगवीनमादाय घोषवृद्धानुपस्थितान् R. 1. 45 ; Bk. 5. 12. 2 Butter prepared a day before it is used, fresh butter.

हैरिकः A thief.

हैहय m. pl. N. of a people and their country. -यः 1 N. of the great-grandson of Yadu. 2 N. of Arjuna Kârtavîrya (who had a thousand arms and was slain by Parasurâma q. v.); धेनुवत्सहरणाच्च हैहयस्त्वं च कीर्तिमपहर्तुमुद्यतः R. 11. 74.

हो ind. A vocative particle used in calling to a person (ho ! hallo !)

होड् I. 1 A. (होडते) To disregard, disrespect. -II. 1 P. (होडति) To go.

होडः A raft, float.

होतृ a. (त्री f.) Sacrificing, offering oblations with fire; वहति विधिहुतं या हविर्या च होत्री S. 1. 1. -m. 1 A sacrificial priest, especially one who recites the prayers of the Rigveda at a sacrifice. 2 A sacrificer ; R. 1. 62, 82 ; Ms. 11. 36.

होत्रं 1 Anything fit to be offered as an oblation (as ghee). 2 A burnt offering. 3 A sacrifice.

होत्रा 1 A sacrifice. 2 Praise.

होत्रीयः The priest who offers oblations to gods. -यं The sacrificial hall.

होमः 1 Offering oblations to gods by throwing ghee into the consecrated fire, (one of the five daily Yajnas, to be performed by a Brâhmaṇa, called देवयज्ञ q. v.). 2 A burnt offering. 3 A sacrifice. -Comp. -अग्निः sacrificial fire. -कुंडं a hole in the ground for receiving the consecrated fire. -तुरंगः a sacrificial horse ; R. 3. 38. धान्यं sesasum. -धूमः the smoke of a burnt offering or sacrificial fire. -भस्मन् n. the ashes of a burnt offering. -वेला the time for offering oblations ; S. 4. -शाला a sacrificial hall or chamber.

होमक See होतृ.

होमिः 1 Clarified butter. 2 Water. 3 Fire.

होमिन् m. The offerer of an oblation, a sacrificer in general.

होमीय, होम्य a. Belonging to or fit for an oblation. -म्यं Ghee.

होरा 1 The rising of a zodiacal sign. 2 Part of the duration of a sign. 3 An hour. 4 A mark, line.

होलाका 1 The spring-festival celebrated at the approach of the spring season, during the ten-but particularly three or four-days preceding the full-moon day in the month of Phâlguna (commonly called *Holi*). 2 The full-moon day in the month of Phâlguna.

होलिका, होली The festival called होलाका q. v. above.

हो, होहो ind. A vocative particle (ho !, hallo !).

हौत्र The office of the priest called होतृ q. v.

हौम्यं Clarified butter.

ह्नु 2 A. (ह्नुते, ह्नुत) 1 To take away, rob, abstract, deprive (one) of ; अध्यगीष्टार्थशास्त्राणि यमस्याह्नोष्ट विक्रमं Bk. 15. 88. 2 To conceal, hide, withhold ; Mâl. 1. 3 To hide from any one (with dat.) ; गोपी कृष्णाय ह्नुते Sk. -WITH अप 1 to conceal, hide; Ms. 8. 53; Ratn. 2. 2 to deny, disown, conceal before one ; गुणांश्चापह्नुषेऽस्माकं Bk. 5. 44; अपह्नुवानस्य जनाय यन्निजां (अधीरतां) N. 1. 49. -नि 1 to hide, conceal ; Bk, 10. 36. 2 to conceal or hide from, dissimulate or deny before any one (with dat.) ; Bk. 8. 74.

ह्यस् ind. Yesterday. -Comp. -भव a. what occurred yester-day.

ह्यस्तन a. (नी f.) Belonging to yesterday ; as in ह्यस्तनी वृत्तिः. -Comp. -दिनं yesterday, the previous day.

ह्यस्त्य a. Belonging to yesterday, hesternal.

ह्रदः 1 A deep lake, a large and deep pool of water; N. 3. 53. 2 A deep hole or cavity ; Si. 5. 29. 3 A ray of light. -Comp. -ग्रहः a crocodile.

ह्रदिनी 1 A river. 2 Lightning.

ह्रद्रोगः The sign *Aguarius* of the zodiac (derived from Greek.)

ह्रस् 1. P. (ह्रसति, ह्रसित) 1 To sound. 2 To become small.

ह्रसिमन् m. Smallness, shortness.

ह्रस्व a. (compar. ह्रसीयस्, superl. ह्रसिष्ठ) 1 Short, small, little. 2 Dwarfish, low or short in stature. 3 Short (opp. दीर्घ in prosody). -स्वः A dwarf. -Comp. -अंग a. dwarfish, short-bodied. (-गः) a dwarf. -गर्भः the Kusa grass. -दर्भः the short or white Kusa grass. -बाहुक a.) short armed. -मूर्ति a. short in stature, dwarfish, pigmy.

ह्राद् 1 A. (ह्रादते) 1 To sound. 2 To roar.

ह्रादः Noise, sound ; दुंदुभीनां ह्रादः Ki. 16. 8 ; so धनुर्ह्रादः &c.

ह्रादिन् a. Sounding, roaring.

ह्रादिनी 1 The thunderbolt of Indra. 2 Lightning. 3 A river. 4 The tree called शल्लकी.

ह्रासः 1 Sound, noise. 2 Decrease, diminution, decline, deterioration, decay ; Ms. 1. 85 ; Y. 2. 249. 3 Small number.

ह्रिणीयते See हृणीयते ; Mv. 1. 51.

ह्रिणीया 1 Reproach, censure. 2 Shame, bashfulness. 3 Pity ; cf. हृणीया.

ह्री 3 P. जिह्रेति, ह्रीण, ह्रीत) 1 To blush, be modest. 2 To be ashamed (used by itself or with abl. or gen.) जिह्रेम्यार्यपुत्रेण सह गुरुसमीपं गंतु S. 7 ; अन्योन्यस्यापि जिह्रीमः किं पुनः सहवासिना Ki. 11. 58 ; R. 15. 44, 17. 73; Bk. 3. 53, 5. 102, 6. 132. -*Caus.* (ह्रेपयति-ते) To put to shame (fig. also); cause to blush, make ashamed ; सकौस्तुभं ह्रेपयतीव कृष्णं R. 6. 49 ; ह्रेपिता हि बहवो नरेश्वराः 11. 40 ; किं वा जात्या स्वामिनो ह्रेपयंति Si. 18. 23 ; Ki. 11. 64, 13. 41 ; Ve. 1. 17.

ह्री f. 1 Shame; रतेरपि ह्रीपदमादधाना Ku. 3. 57 ; दारिद्र्याद् ह्रियमेति ह्रीपरिगतः प्रभ्रश्यते तेजसः Mk. 1. 14, R. 4. 80. 2 Bashfulness, modesty ; ह्रीसन्नकंठी कथमप्युवाच Ku. 7. 85. -Comp. -जित, -मूढ a. overcome or confounded by shame ; ह्रीमूढानां भवति विफलप्रेरणा चूर्णमुष्टिः Me. 68. -यंत्रणा the constraint of bashfulness ; R. 7. 63.

ह्रीका 1 Bashfulness, coyness, shyness. 2 Timidity, fear.

ह्रीकु a. 1 Bashful, modest, shy. 2 Timd. -कुः 1 Tin. 2 Lac.

ह्रीण, ह्रीत p. p. 1 Ashamed; Ve. 2. 11. 2 Bashful, modest; N. 3. 53.

ह्रीबेरं-लं A kind of perfume.

ह्रेष् 1 A. (ह्रेषते) 1 To neigh (as a horse), whinny. 2 To go, creep.

ह्रेषा Neighing.

ह्लग् 1 P. (ह्लगति) To cover.

ह्लत्तिः f. Joy, gladness.

ह्लस् 1 P. (ह्लसति) To sound.

ह्लाद् 1 A. (ह्लादते, ह्लन्न ह्लादित) 1 To be glad or delighted, rejoice. 2 To sound. -WITH आ, -प्र to rejoice, be delighted.

ह्लादः, ह्लादकः Pleasure, joy, delight.

ह्लादनं The act of rejoicing, joy delight.

ह्लादिन् *a.* Delighting, pleasing &c.

ह्लादिनी See ह्रादिनी.

ह्वल् 1 P. (ह्वलति) **1** To go, move. **2** To shake, tremble. –*Caus.* (ह्वलयति-ते, ह्वालयति-ते, but the former only with prepositons) To shake, move cause, to tremble (especially with वि).

ह्वानं **1** Calling. **2** A cry, sound.

ह्वृ 1 P. (ह्वरति) **1** To be crooked. **2** To be crooked in conduct, cheat, deceive. **3** To be afflicted or injured.

ह्वे I. U. (ह्वयति-ते हूतः *pass.* हूयते ; *caus.* ह्वाययति-ते; *desid.* जुहूषति -ते) **1** To call; तां पार्वतीत्याभिजनेन नाम्ना बंधुप्रिया बंधुजनो जुहाव Ku. 1. 26. **2** To call out to invoke, call upon. **3** To name, call. **4** To challenge. **5** To vie with, emulate. **6** To ask, beg. –WITH आ **1** to call, invite; वत्स-इत एवाह्वयैनं U. 6. **2** to challenge (Atm.) गतभीराह्वत चेदिराण्मुरारिं *S.* 20. 1 ; कृष्णश्चाणूरमाह्वयते Sk. ; Bk. 8. 18. 15. 89. –उप, -उपा to call ; Bk. 8. 17. –सं, -समा to call together.

FINIS.

SUPPLEMENT.

अक्रूरः N. of a Yâdava, a friend and uncle of Krishṇa. It was he who indueed Râma and Krishṇa to go to Mathurâ and kill Kamsa. He told the two brothers how their father *A*nakadundubhi, the princess Devakî and even his own father Ugrasena had been insulted by the iniquitous demon Kamsa, and told them why he had been despatched to them. Krishṇa consented to go and promised to slay the demon within 3 nights, which he succeeded in doing. See सत्राजित् also.

अगस्तिः, अगस्त्यः N. of a celebrated *R*ishi or sage. In the *R*igveda he and Vashisṭha are said to be the offspring of Mitra and Varuṇa, whose seed fell from them at the sight of the lovely nymph Urvasî. Part of the seed fell into a jar and part into water ; from the former arose Agastya who is, therefore, called Kumbhyoni, Kumbhajanman, Ghaṭodbhava, Kalasayoni &c. He is represented to have humbled the Vindhya mountain by making them prostrate themselves before him when they tried to rise higher and higher till they well-nigh occupied the sun's disc and obstructed his path ; See Vindhya. (This fable is supposed by some to typify the progress of the Aryas towards the south in their conquest and civilization of India). He is also known by the names of Pîtâbdhi, Samudra-chuluka &c., from another fable according to which he drank up the ocean because he wished to help Indra and the gods in their wars with a class of demons called Kâleyas who had hid themselves in the waters and oppressed the three worlds in various ways. His wife was Lopâmudrâ. He dwelt in a hermitage on mount Kunjara to the south of the Vindhya, and kept under control the evil spirits who infested the south ; and a legend relates how he once ate up a Râkshasa named Vâtâpi, who had assumed the form of a ram, and destroyed by a flash of his eye the Rakshasa's brother who attempted to avenge him. In the course of his wanderings Râma with his wife and brother came to the hermitage of Agastya who received him with the greatest kindness and became his friend, adviser and protector. He gave Râma the bow of Vishṇu and some other things ; (see R. 15. 55). In astronomy he is the Star Canopus ; cf. R. 4. 21 also.)

अग्निः The god of fire, and represented as the eldest son of Brahman. His wife was Svâhâ ; by her he had 3 sons—Pâvaka, Pavamâna and *S*uchi. The Harivamsa describes him as clothed in black, having smoke for his standard and head-piece, and carrying a flaming javelin. He is borne in a chariot drawn by red horses. He is accompanied by a ram and sometimes he is represented as riding on that animal. The Mahâbbârata represents Agni as having exhausted his vigour and become dull by devouring many oblations at the several sacrifices made by king *S*vetaki, but he recruited his strength by devouring the whole Khâṇḍava forest with the assistance of Arjuna, for which service he gave him the Gâṇḍîva bow.

अघः N. of a demon, brother of Baka and Pûtanâ ; and commander-in-chief of Kamsa. Being sent by Kamsa to Gokula to kill Krishṇa and Balarâma, he assumed the form of a huge serpent 4 yojanas long, and spread himself on the way of the cowherds, keeping his horrid mouth open. The cowherds mistook it for a mountain-cavern and entered it, cows and all. But Krishṇa saw it, and having entered the mouth so stretched himself that he tore it to pieces and rescued his companions.

अंगदः N. of a son of Vâli by his wife Târâ. When the whole host of Râma went to Lankâ Angada was despatched to Râvaṇa as a messenger of peace to give him a chance of saving himself in time. But Râvaṇa scornfully rejected his advice and met his doom. After Sugrîva, Angada became king of Kishkindhâ. In common parlance a man is said to act the part of Angada when he endeavours to mediate between two contending parties, but without any success.

अंजना N. of the mother of Mâruti or Hanûmat. She was the daughter of a monkey named Kunjara, and wife of Kesarin, another monkey. One day while she was seated on the summit of a mountain, her garment was slightly displaced, and the God of Wind being enamoured of her beauty assumed a visible form, and asked her to yield to his desires. She requested him not to violate her chastity, to which he consented ; but he told her that she would conceive a son equal to himself in strength and lustre by virtue of his amorous desire fixed on her, and then disappeared. This son was Mâruti.

अत्रि N. of a great sage. He is one of the ten Prajâpatis or mind-born sons of Brahman, being born from his eye. Anasûya was his wife and bore him three sons, Datta, Durvâsa, and Soma. In the Râmâyaṇa an account is given of the visit paid by Râma and Sîtâ to Atri and Anasûya in their hermitage, when they both received them most kindly (See अनसूया). As a *R*ishi or sage he is one of the seven sages, and represents in Astronomy one of the stars of the Great Bear. The moon is said to have been produced from his eye ; cf. R. 2. 75.

अदिति N. of one of the daughters of Daksha and wife of Kasyapa by whom she was mother of Vishṇu in his dwarf incarnation, of Indra, and of the other gods who are called *aditi-nandanas*.

अनिरुद्धः N. of a son of Pradyumna. Aniruddha was the son of Kâma and grandson of Krishṇa. Ushâ, the daughter of a demon named Bâṇa, fell in love with him, and had him brought by magic influence to her apartments in her father's city of *S*oṇitapura ; see उषा or चित्रलेखा. Bâṇa sent some guards to seize him, but the brave youth slew his assailants with only an iron club. At last, however, he was secured by means of magic powers. On discovering where Aniruddha had been carried, Krishṇa, Balarâma and Kâma went to rescue him and a great battle was fought. Bâṇa, though aided by *S*iva and Skanda, was vanquished, but his life was spared at the intercession of *S*iva, and Aniruddha was carried home to Dvârakâ with Ushâ as his wife.

अंधकः N. of an Asura, son of Kasyapa and Diti and killed by *S*iva. He is represented as a demon with 1,000 arms and heads, 2,000 eyes and feet, and called *Andhaka* because he walked like a blind man, though he could see very well. He was slain by *S*iva when he attempted to carry off the Pârijâta tree from heaven.

अभिमन्युः N. of a son of Arjuna by his wife Subhadrâ, sister of Krishṇa and Balarâma. When the Kauravas, at the advice of Droṇa, formed the peculiar battle array called 'Chakravyûha,' hoping that as Arjuna was away, none of the Paṇḍavas would be able to break through it, Abhimanyu assured his uncles that he was ready to try, if they only assisted him. He accordingly entered the Vyûha, killed many warriors on the Kaurava side, and was for a time more than a match even for such veteran and elderly heroes as Droṇa, Karṇa, Duryodhana &c. He could not, however, hold out long against fearful odds, and was at last overpowered and slain. He was very handsome. He had two wives, Vatsalâ daughter of Balarâma, and Uttarâ daughter of the king Viraṭa. Uttarā was pregnant when he was slain, and gave birth to a son named Parîkshita who succeeded to the throne of Hastinâpura.

अरुणः Aruṇa is represented as the elder brother of Garuḍa being, the son of Vinatâ by Kasyapa. Vinatâ prematurely hatched the egg and the child was born without thighs, and hence he is called *Anûru* 'thighless', or *Vipa'da* 'footless'. Aruṇa now holds the office of the charioteer of the sun. His wife was *S*yenî, who bore him two sons Sampâti and Jaṭâyu.

अश्वत्थामन् See द्रोण also.

अश्विनीकुमार See संज्ञा.

अष्टावक्रः N. of the son of Kahoḍa. This sage was so much devoted to study that he generally neglected his wife, and the unborn son, while yet in the womb, being provoked at this, rebuked his father, who being enraged, cursed him that he would be born crooked in eight limbs. When Kahoḍa was drowned into a river as the result of a wager in a dispute with a Buddhist, the young Ashtâvakra defeated the Buddhist, and delivered his father, by whose favour he became straight.

न्याय

1 विषकृमिन्यायः The maxim of the worms bred in poison It is used to denote a state of things which, though fatal to others, is not so to those who being bred in it, are inured or naturalized to it, like poison which, though fatal to others, is not so to the worms bred in it.

2 विषवृक्षन्यायः The maxim of the poison-tree ; used to denote that a thing, though hurtful and mischievous, does not deserve to be destroyed by the very person who has reared it, just as even a poison-tree ought not to be cut down by the planter himself.

3 स्थालीपुलाकन्यायः The maxim of the cooking-pot and boiled rice. In a cooking-pot all the grains being equally moistened by the heated water, when one grain is found to be well cooked, the same may be inferred with regard to the other grains. So the maxim is used when the condition of the hole class is inferred from that of a part. Cf. Mar. 'शितावरून भाताची परिक्षा'.

पंडावत् *a.* Wise ; पंडावदग्निम Asvad. 6.

प्रकोपः Anger, excitement, provocation.

प्राकारः 1 An encircling wall, exclosure, a fence. **2** A surrounding wall, rampart ; शतमेकोपि संधत्ते प्राकारस्थो धनुर्धरः Pt. 1. 229.

बाली A kind of ear-ornament ; Asvad. 24.

युधिष्ठिरः 'Firm in battle', N. of the eldest Pâṇḍava prince, also called 'Dharma', 'Dharmarâja', 'Ajâtasatru' &c. He was begotten on Kuntî by the god Yama. He is known more for his truthfulness and righteousness than for any military achievements or feats of arms. He was formally crowned emperor of Hastinâpura at the conclusion of the great Bhâratî war after eighteen days' severe fighting, and reigned righteously for many years. (For further particulars of his life see दुर्योधन.)

वैशंपायनः N. of a celebrated pupil of Vyâsa. It was he who made Yâj*n*avalkya disgorge the whole of the Yajurveda he had learnt from him which was picked up by his other pupils in the form of *Tittiris* or partridges, and hence the Veda was called 'Taittirîya'. Vaisampâyana was celebrated for his great skill in narrating Purâṇas, and is said to have recounted the whole of the Mahâbhârata to king Janmejaya.

हिरण्याक्षः N. of a celebrated demon, twin brother of Hiraṇyakasipu. On the strength of a boon from Brahman he became insolent and oppressive, seized upon the earth, and carried it with him into the depths of the ocean. Vishṇu, therefore, became incarnate as a boar, killed the demon, and lifted up the earth.

APPENDIX I.

SANSKRIT PROSODY.

Introduction.

The earliest and most important work in Sanskrit prosody is the Pingala-chhandas-sâstra, attributed to the sage Pingala, which consists of Sûtras distributed over eight books. The Agni Purâṇa also gives complete system of prosody founded apparently on Pingala's. Several other original treatises have likewise been composed by various authors, such as the *S*rutabodha, Vâṇîbhûshaṇa, Vṛitta-darpaṇa, Vṛitta-ratnâkara, Vṛitta-Kaumudî, Chhandomanjarî &c. In the following pages the Chhandomanjarî and Vṛitta-ratnâkara have been chiefly drawn upon. Vedic as well as Prâkṛita metres have been ignored in this Appendix.

Sanskrit composition may be in the form of गद्य 'prose' or पद्य 'verse' or poetry expressed in the form of stanzas.

A stanza or *padya* is a combination of four *pa'das* or quarters, which are regulated either by the number of syllables (अक्षर), or by the number of syllabic instants मात्रा).

A पद्य is a वृत्त or जाति.

A वृत्त is a stanza the metre of which is regulated by the number and position of syllables in each Pâda or quarter. A जाति is a stanza the metre of which is regulated by the number of syllabic instants in each quarter.

Vṛittas are divided into three classes :—समवृत्त in which the Pâdas or quarters composing the stanza are all similar ; अर्धसमवृत्त in which the alternate quarters are similar ; and विषमवृत्त in which the quarters are all dissimilar.

A syllable is as much of a word as can be pronounced at once, that is, a vowel with or without one or more consonants.

A syllable is लघु 'short' or गुरु 'long' according as its vowel is 'short' or 'long'. The vowels अ, इ, उ, ऋ, & ऌ are short ; and आ, ई, ऊ, ॠ, ए ऐ, ओ & औ are long. But a short vowel becomes long in prosody when it is followed by an *Anusva'ra* or *Visarga*, or by a conjunct consonant; as the vowel अ in गंध or गः. (The consonants प्र & ह्र as also ब्र & क्र, are said to be exceptions, before which the vowel may be short by a sort of poetical license; e. g. in Ku. 7. 11, or *Si*. 10.60, where, however, emendations have been proposed by critics to render the metre comformable to the general laws of prosody). So also the last syllable of a *pa'da* is either long or short, according to the exigence of the metre, whatever be its natural length.

सानुस्वारश्च दीर्घश्च विसर्गी च गुरुर्भवेत् ।
वर्णः संयोगपूर्वश्च तथा पादान्तगोऽपि वा ॥

In metres regulated by the number of syllabic instants one instant or Mâtrâ is allotted to a short vowel, and two to a long one.

For the purpose of scanning metres regulated by the number of syllables, writers on prosody have devised eight 'Gaṇas' or syllabic feet, each consisting of three syllables, and distinguished from one another by particular syllables being short or long. They are given in the following verse :—

मस्त्रिगुरुस्त्रिलघुश्च नकारो
भादिगुरुः पुनरादिलघुर्यः ।
जो गुरुमध्यगतो रलमध्यः
सोऽन्तगुरुः कथितोऽन्तलघुस्तः ॥
आदिमध्यावसानेषु यरता यांति लाघवम् ।
भजसा गौरवं यांति मनौ तु गुरुलाघवम् ॥

Expressed in symbols (the symbol ⌣ denoting a short syllable, and — a long one) the different Gaṇas may be represented as follows :—

य	⌣ — —	(Bacchius)
र	— ⌣ —	(Amphimacer)
त	— — ⌣	(Anti-bacchius)
भ	— ⌣ ⌣	(Dactylus)
ज	⌣ — ⌣	(Amphibrachys)
स	⌣ ⌣ —	(Anapæstus)
म	— — —	(Mollosus)
न	⌣ ⌣ ⌣	(Tribrachys)

Similarly ल (⌣) is used to denote a short syllable, and ग (—) a long one.

N. B.—Sanskrit prosodists classify Vṛittas according to the number of syllables contained in each quarter. Thus they enumerate twenty-six classes of 'Samavṛittas', as the number of syllables in each quarter of a regular metre may vary from one to twenty-six. Each of these classes comprehends a great number of possible metres according to the different modes in which long and short syllables may be distributed. For example, in the class where each quarter contains six syllables, each of the six syllables may be either short or long, and thus the number of *possible* combinations is $2 \times 2 \times 2 \times 2 \times 2 \times 2$ or $2^6 = 64$, though not even half a dozen are in general use ; so in the case of the twenty-six syllabled class, the possible varieties are 2^{26} or 87, 108, 864 ! But if we consider the cases where the alternate quarters are similar or all dissimilar, the variety of possible metres is almost infinite. Pingala, as also Lîlâvatî and the last chapter of Vṛitta-ratnâkara, give directions for computing the number of possible varieties and for finding their places, or that of any single one, in a regular enumeration of them. The different varieties, however, which have been used by poets are few when compared with the vast multitude of possible metres. But even these are too many to be dealt with in an Appendix like this, and we shall, therefore, only give such kinds as are most frequently employed or require particular notice, in the following order :—

Section A	समवृत्त
Section B	अर्धवृत्त
Section C	विषमवृत्त
Section D	जाति &c.

Note.—In the following definitions the letters representing the Gaṇas such as भ, म, स, &c. as also ल, ग will often be found to have dropped their vowels for the exigence of metre ; *e. g.* म्र, भ्र stands for म, र, म, न ; so स्तौ, for म, त &c. The first line gives the *Definition* of a metre; the second, the *Scheme in Gaṇas* with the *Yati* or Cæsura–the pause that may be made in reciting a quarter or verse, and which is usually indicated by the words in the Definition standing in the Instrumental case–denoted in brackets by Arabic figures, and then comes the example (many of these examples are drawn from the works of Mâgha, Bhâravi, Kâlidâsa, Daṇḍin &c.).

SECTION A.

Metres with 4 Syllables in a quarter.

(प्रतिष्ठा.)

कन्या.

Def. ग्मौ चेत् कन्या ।
Sch. G. ग, म.
Ex. भास्वत्कन्यों सैका धन्या यस्याः कूले कृष्णोऽखेलत् ॥

Metres with 5 Syllables in a quarter.

(सुप्रतिष्ठा.)

पंक्ति.

Def. भ्गौ गिति पंक्तिः ।
Sch. G. भ, ग, ग.
Ex. कृष्णसनाथा तर्णकपंक्तिः ।
यामुनकच्छे चारु चचार ॥

Metres with 6 Syllables in a quarter.

(गायत्री.)

(1) तनुमध्यमा.

Def. त्यौ चेत्तनुमध्यमा ।
Sch. G. त, य.
Ex. मूर्तिर्मुरशत्रोरत्यद्भुतरूपा ।
आस्तां मम चित्ते नित्यं तनुमध्या ॥

(2) विद्युल्लेखा.

(Also called वाणी.)

Def. विद्युल्लेखा मो मः ।
Sch. G. म, म. (3. 3)
Ex. श्रीद्वीती ह्रीकीर्ती धीनीती गीःप्रीती ।
एधेते द्वे द्वे ते ये नेमे देवेशे ॥ Kâv. 3. 36.

(3) शशिवदना.

Def. शशिवदना न्यौ ।
Sch. G. न, य.
Ex. **शशिवदनानां** व्रजतरुणीनाम् ।
अधरसुधोर्मि मधुरिपुरैच्छत् ॥

(4) सोमराजी.

Def. द्विया सोमराजी.
Sch. G. य, य. (2. 4)
Ex. हरे **सोमराजी**-समा ते यशःश्रीः ।
जगन्मंडलस्य छिनत्त्यंधकारम् ॥

Metres with 7 Syllables in a quarter.

(उष्णिक्.)

(1) कुमारललिता.

Def. कुमारललिता ज्सू गाः ।
Sch. G. ज, स, ग. (3. 4.)
Ex. मुरारितनुवल्ली **कुमारललिता** सा ।
व्रजैणनयनानां ततान मुदमुच्चैः ॥

(2) मदलेखा.

Def. मस्गौ स्यान्मदलेखा ।
Sch. G. म, स, ग. (3. 4.)
Ex. रेंगे बाहुविरुग्णाद् दंतींद्रान्**मदलेखा** ।
लग्नाभून्पुरशत्रौ कस्तूरीरसचर्चा ॥

(3) मधुमती.

Def. ननगि मधुमती ।
Sch. G. न, न, ग (5. 2)
Ex. रविदुहितृतटे वनकुसुमततिः ।
व्यधित मधुमती मधुमथनमुदम् ॥

Metres with 8 Syllables in a quarter.

(अनुष्टुभ्)

(1) अनुष्टुभ् (also called श्लोक .)

There are several varieties of this metre, but that which is most in use has eight syllables in each quarter, but of variable quantity. Thus the fifth syllable of each quarter should be short, the sixth long, and the seventh alternately long and short.

श्लोके षष्ठं गुरु ज्ञेयं सर्वत्र लघुपंचमम् ।
द्विचतुःपादयोर्ह्रस्वं सप्तमं दीर्घमन्ययोः ॥

Ex. वागर्थाविव संपृक्तौ वागर्थप्रतिपत्तये ।
जगतः पितरौ वंदे पार्वतीपरमेश्वरौ ॥ R. 1. 1.

य ⏑ — —; र — ⏑ —; त — — ⏑; भ — ⏑ ⏑; ज ⏑ — ⏑; स ⏑ ⏑ —; म — — —; न ⏑ ⏑ ⏑; ल ⏑; ग —

(2) गजगति.

Def. नभलगा। गजगतिः।
Sch. G. न, भ, ल, ग (4. 4.)
Ex. रविसुतापरिसरे विहरतो दृशि हरेः।
व्रजवधूगजगतिर्मुदमलं व्यतनुत ॥

(3) प्रमाणिका.

Def. प्रमाणिका जरौ लगौ।
Sch. G. ज, र, ल, ग (4. 4.)
Ex. पुनातु भक्तिरच्युता सदाच्युतांघ्रिपद्मयोः।
श्रुतिस्मृतिप्रमाणिका भवांबुराशितारिका ॥

(4) माणवक.

Def. भात्तलगा माणवकम्।
Sch. G. भ, त, ल, ग (4. 4.)
Ex. चंचलचूडं चपलैर्वत्सकुलैः केलिपरम्।
ध्याय सखे स्मेरमुखं नंदसुतं माणवकम्।

(5) विद्युन्माला.

Def. मो मो गो गो विद्युन्माला।
Sch. G. म, म, ग, ग, (4. 4.)
Ex. वासोवल्ली विद्युन्माला बर्हश्रेणी शाक्रश्चापः।
यस्मिन्नास्तां तापोच्छित्त्यैगामध्यस्थःकृष्णांभोदः ।।

(6) समानिका.

Def. ग्लौ रजौ समानिका तु।
Sch. G. र, ज, ग, ल (4. 4.)
Ex. यस्य कृष्णपादपद्ममस्ति हृत्तडागसद्म।
धीः समानिका परेण नोचितात्र मत्सरेण ॥

Metres with 9 Syllables in a quarter.

(बृहती)

(1) भुजगशिशुभृता.

Def. भुजगशिशुभृता नौ मः।
Sch. G. न, न, म (7. 2.)
Ex. ह्रदतटनिकटक्षौणी भुजगशिशुभृता याऽसीत्।
मररिपुदलिते नागे व्रजजनसुखदा साऽभूत्।

(2) भुजंगसंगता.

Def. सजरैर्भुजंगसंगता।
Sch. G. स, ज, र (3. 6.)
Ex. तरला तरंगिरिंगितैर्यमुना भुजंगसंगता।
कथमेति वत्सचारकश्चपलः सदैव तां हरिः ।।

(3) मणिमध्य.

Def. स्यान्मणिमध्यं चेद्भमसाः।
Sch. G. भ, म, स (5. 4.)
Ex. कालियभोगाभोगगतस्तन्मणिमध्यस्फीतरुचा।
चित्रपदाभो नंदसुतश्चारु ननर्त स्मेरमुखः ॥

Metres with 10 Syllables in a quarter.

(पंक्ति.)

(1) त्वरितगति.

Def. त्वरितगतिश्च नजनगैः।
Sch. G. न, ज, न, ग (5. 5.)
Ex. त्वरितगतिर्व्रजयुवतिस्तरणिसुता विपिनगता।
मुररिपुणा रतिगुरुणा परिरमिता प्रमदमिता ॥

(2) मत्ता.

Def. ज्ञेया मत्ता मभसगसृष्टा।
Sch. G. म, भ, स, ग (4. 6.)
Ex. पीत्वा मत्ता मधु मधुपाली
कालिंदीये तटवनकुंजे।
उद्दीव्यंतीर्व्रजजनरामाः
कामासक्ता मधुजिति चक्रे ॥

(3) रुक्मवती.

(Also called चंपकमाला.)

Def. रुक्मवती सा यत्र भमस्गाः।
Sch. G. भ, म, स, ग (5. 5.)
Ex. कायमनोवाक्यैः परिशुद्धै-
र्यस्य सदा कंसद्विषि भक्तिः।
राज्यपदे हर्म्यालिरुदारा
रुक्मवती विघ्नः खलु तस्य ॥

Metres with 11 Syllables in a quarter.

(त्रिष्टुभ्).

(1) इंद्रवज्रा.

Def. स्यादिंद्रवज्रा यदि तौ जगौ गः।
Sch. G. त, त, ज, ग, ग (5. 6.)
Ex. गोष्ठे गिरिं सव्यकरेण धृत्वा
रुष्टेंद्रवज्राहतिमुक्तवृष्टौ।
यो गोकुलं गोपकुलं च सुस्थं
चक्रे स नो रक्षतु चक्रपाणिः ॥

(2) उपेंद्रवज्रा.

Def. उपेंद्रवज्रा प्रथमे लघौ सा।
Sch. G. ज, त, ज, ग, ग (5, 6.)
Ex. उपेंद्रवज्रादिमणिच्छटाभि-
र्विभूषणानां छुरितं वपुस्ते।
स्मरामि गोपीभिरुपास्यमानं
सुरद्रुमूले मणिमंडपस्थम् ॥

(3) उपजाति.

Def. अनंतरोदीरितलक्ष्मभाजौ
पादौ यदीयावुपजातयस्ताः।
इत्थं किलान्यास्वपि मिश्रितासु
वदंति जातिष्विदमेव नाम ॥

Sch. G. When इंद्रवज्रा and उपेंद्रवज्रा are mixed in one stanza, the metre is called उपजाति. It is said to have 14 varieties.

Ex. अस्त्युत्तरस्यां दिशि देवतात्मा
हिमालयो नाम नगाधिराजः।
पूर्वापरौ तोयनिधी वगाह्य
स्थितः पृथिव्या इव मानदंडः ॥ Ku. 1. 1.

See R. 2, 5, 6, 7, 13, 14, 16, 18, Ku. 3; Ki. 17. &c.

When other metres also are mixed in one stanza, the metre is still called उपजाति; *e. g.* in the following verse from Magha there is a combination of वंशस्थ and इंद्रवंशा.

इत्थं रथाश्वेभनिषादिनां प्रगे
गजो नृपाणामथ तोरणाद्बहिः।

प्रस्थानकालक्षमवेशकल्पना-
कृतक्षणक्षेपमुदैक्षताच्युतम् ॥

(4) दोधक.

Def. दोधकमिच्छति भत्रितयाद्गौ ।
Sch. G. भ, भ, भ, ग, ग (6. 5.)
Ex. या न ययौ प्रियमन्यवधूभ्यः
सारतरागमना यतमानम् ।
तेन सहेह बिभर्ति रहः स्त्री
सा रतरागमनायतमानम् ॥ *S*i. 4. 45.

(5) भ्रमरविलसितं.

(भ्रमरविलसिता)

Def. म्भौ न्लौ गः स्याद् भ्रमरविलसितम् ।
Sch. G. म, भ, न, ल, ग (4. 7.)
Ex. प्रीत्यै यूनां व्यवहिततपनाः
प्रौढध्वांतं दिनमिह जलदाः ।
दोषामन्यं विदधति सुरत-
क्रीडायासश्रमशमपटवः ॥ *S*i. 4. 62.

(6) रथोद्धता.

Def. रात्परैर्नरलगै रथोद्धता ।
Sch. G. र, न, र, ल, ग (3. 8, or 4. 8.)
Ex. कौशिकेन स किल क्षितीश्वरो
राममध्वरविघातशांतये ।
काकपक्षधरमेत्य याचित-
स्तेजसां हि न वयः समीक्ष्यते ॥ R. 11. 1.
See Ku. 8 also.

(7) वातोर्मी.

Def. वातोर्मीयं गदिता म्भौ तगौ गः ।
Sch. G. म, भ, त, ग, ग (4. 7.)
Ex. ध्याता मूर्तिः क्षणमप्यच्युतस्य
श्रेणी नाम्नां गदिता हेलयापि ।
संसारेऽस्मिन् दुरितं हंति पुंसां
वातोर्मी पोतमिवांभोधिमध्ये ॥

(8) शालिनी.

Def. मात्तौ गौ चेच्छालिनी वेदलोकैः ।
Sch. G. म, त, त, ग, ग (4. 7.)
Ex. अंघो हंति ज्ञानवृद्धिं विधत्ते
धर्मं दत्ते काममर्थं च सूते ।
मुक्तिं दत्ते सर्वदोपास्यमाना
पुंसां श्रद्धाशालिनी विष्णुभक्तिः ॥

(9) स्वागता.

Def. स्वागता रनभगैर्गुरुणा च
Sch. G. र, न, भ, ग, ग (3. 8.)
Ex. यावदागमयतेऽथ नरेंद्रान्
स स्वयंवरमहाय महींद्रः ।
तावदेव ऋषिरिंद्रदिदृक्षु-
र्नारदस्त्रिदशधाम जगाम ॥ N. 5. 1.
See Ki. 9, *S*i. 10.

Metres with 12 Syllables in a quarter.

(जगती)

(1) इंद्रवंशा.

Def. तच्चेंद्रवंशा प्रथमाक्षरे गुरौ ।
Sch. G. इंद्रवंशा is the same as वंशस्थविल or वंशस्थ (See 13 Below) except that its first syllable is long:-Gaṇas are, त, ज, ज, र.
Ex. दैत्येंद्रवंशाग्निरुदीर्णदीधितिः
पीतांबरोऽसौ जगतां तमोपहः ।
यस्मिन्ममज्जुः शलभा इव स्वयं
ते कंसचाणूरमुखा मखद्विषः ॥

(2) चंद्रवर्त्म.

Def. चंद्रवर्त्म निगदंति रनभसैः ।
Sch. G. र, न. भ, स (4. 8)
Ex. चंद्रवर्त्म विहितं घनतिमिरै
राजवर्त्म रहितं जनगमनैः ।
इष्टवर्त्म तदलंकुरु सरसे
कुंजवर्त्मनि हरिस्तव कुतुकी ॥

(3) जलधरमाला.

Def. अब्ध्यंगैः स्याज्जलधरमालाम्भौ स्मौ ।
Sch. G. म, भ, स, म (4. 8.)
Ex. या भक्तानां कलिदुरितोत्तप्तानां
तापच्छेदे जलधरमाला नव्या ।
भव्याकारा दिनकरपुत्रीकूले
केलीलोला हरितनुरव्यात्सा वः ॥
See Ki. 5. 23.

(4) जलोद्धतगति.

Def. रसैर्जसजसा जलोद्धतगतिः ।
Sch. G. ज, स, ज, स (6. 6.)
Ex. समीरशिशिरः शिरस्सु वसतां
सतां जवनिका निकामसुखिनाम् ।
बिभर्ति जनयन्नयं मुदमपा-
मपायधवला बलाहकततीः ॥ *S*i. 4. 54

(5) तामरस.

Def. इह वद तामरसं नजजा यः ।
Sch. G. न, ज, ज, य (5. 7.)
Ex. स्फुटसुषमामकरंदमनोज्ञं
व्रजललनानयनालि निपीतम् ।
तव मुखतामरसं मुरशत्रो
हृदयतडागविकाशि ममास्तु ॥

(6) तोटक.

Def. वद तोटकमब्धिसकारयुतम् ।
Sch. G. स, स, स, स (4. 4. 3)
Ex. स तथेति विनेतुरुदारमतेः
प्रतिगृह्य वचो विससर्ज मुनिम् ।
तदलब्धपदं हृदि शोकघने
प्रतियातमिवांतिकमस्य गुरोः ॥ R. 8. 91.
See *S*i. 6. 71.

(7) द्रुतविलंबित.

Def. द्रुतविलंबितमाह नभौ जरौ ।

Sch. G. न, भ, ज, र (4. 8. or 4. 4. 4)
Ex.
मुनिसुताप्रणयस्मृतिरोधिना
मम च मुक्तमिदं तमसा मनः ।
मनसिजेन सखे प्रहरिष्यता
धनुषि चूतशरश्च निवेशितः ॥ S. 6 ;
See R. 9, Si. 6 also.

(8) प्रभा.
(Also called मंदाकिनी).

Def. स्वरशरविरतिर्ननौ रौ प्रभा ।
Sch. G. न, न, र, र (7. 5.)
Ex.
अतिसुरभिरभाजि पुष्पश्रिया-
मतनुत रतयेव संतानकः ।
तरुणपरभृतः स्वनं रागिणा-
मतनुत रतये वसंतानकः ॥ *S*i. 6. 67 ;
also Ki. 5. 21.

(9) प्रमिताक्षरा.

Def. प्रमिताक्षरा सजससैः कथिता ।
Sch. G. स, ज, स, स (5. 7.)
Ex.
विहगाः कदंबसुरभाविह गाः
कलयंत्यनुक्षणमनेकलयम् ।
भ्रमयन्नुपैति मुहुरभ्रमयं
पवनश्च धूतनवनीपवनः ॥ *S*i. 4. 36.
Ki. 6, *S*i. 9 also.

(10) भुजंगप्रयात.

Def. भुजंगप्रयातं चतुर्भिर्यकारैः ।
Sch. G. य, य, य, य (6. 6.)
Ex.
धनैर्निष्कुलीनाः कुलीना भवंति
धनैरापदं मानवा निस्तरंति ।
धनेभ्यः परो बांधवो नास्ति लोके
धनान्यर्जयध्वं धनान्यर्जयध्वम् ॥

(11) मणिमाला.

Def. त्यौ त्यौ मणिमाला छिन्ना गुहवक्त्रैः ।
Sch. G. त, य, त, य (6. 6.)
Ex.
प्रह्वामरमौलौ रत्नोपलक्लृप्ते
जातप्रतिबिंबा शोणा मणिमाला ।
गोविंदपदाब्जे राजी नखराणां-
मास्तां मम चित्ते ध्वांतं शमयंती ॥

(12) मालती.
(Also called यमुना.)

Def. भवति न जावथ मालती जरौ ।
Sch. G. न, ज, ज, र (5. 7.)
Ex.
इह कलयाच्युतकेलिकानने
मधुरससौरभसारलोलुपः ।
कुसुमकृतस्मितचारुविभ्रमा-
मलिरपि चुंबति मालतीं मुहुः ॥

(13) वंशस्थविल.
(Also called वंशस्थ and वंशस्तनित)

Def. वदंति वंशस्थविलं जतौ जरौ ।
Sch. G. ज, त, ज, र (5. 7.)
Ex.
तथा समक्षं दहता मनोभवं
पिनाकिना भग्नमनोरथा सती ।
निनिंद रूपं हृदयेन पार्वती
प्रियेषु सौभाग्यफला हि चारुता ॥ Ku. 5. 1 ;
See R. 3 also.

(14) वैश्वदेवी.

Def. बाणाश्वैश्छिन्ना वैश्वदेवी ममौ यौ ।
Sch. G. म, म, य, य (5. 7.)
Ex.
अर्चामन्येषां त्वं विहायामराणा-
मद्वैतेनैकं जिष्णुमभ्यर्च्य भक्त्या ।
तत्राशेषात्मन्यर्चिते भाविनी ते
भ्रातः संपन्नाराधना वैश्वदेवी ॥

(15) स्रग्विणी.

Def. कीर्तितैषा चतूरेफिका स्रग्विणी ।
Sch. G. र, र, र, र (6. 6.)
Ex.
इंद्रनीलोपलीनेव या निर्मिता
शातकुंभद्रवालंकृता शोभते ।
नव्यमेघच्छविः पीतवासा हरे-
मूर्तिरास्तां जयायोरसि स्रग्विणी ॥
See *S*i. 4. 42.

Metres with 13 Syllables in a quarter.

(अतिजगती.)

(1) कलहंस.
(Also called सिंहनाद and कुटजा.)

Def. सजसाः सगौ च कथितः कलहंसः ।
Sch. G. स, ज, स, स, ग (6. 7.)
Ex.
यमुनाविहारकुतुके कलहंसो
व्रजकामिनीकमलिनीकृतकेलिः ।
जनचित्तहारिकलकंठनिनादः
प्रमदं तनोतु तव नंदतनूजः ॥
See *S*i. 6. 73.

(2) क्षमा.
(Also called चंद्रिका and उत्पलिनी.)

Def. तुरगरसयतिर्नौ ततौ गः क्षमा ।
Sch. G. न, न, त, त, ग (7. 6.)
Ex.
इह दुरधिगमैः किंचिदेवागमैः
सततमसुतरं वर्णयंत्यंतरम् ।
अमुमतिविपिनं वेददिग्व्यापिनं
पुरुषमिव परं पद्मयोनिः परम् ॥ Ki. 5. 18.

(3) प्रहर्षिणी.

Def. म्नौ ज्रौ गस्त्रिदशयतिः प्रहर्षिणीयम् ।
Sch. G. म, न, ज, र, ग (3. 10.)
Ex.
ते रेखाध्वजकुलिशातपत्रचिह्नं
सम्राजश्चरणयुगं प्रसादलभ्यम् ।
प्रस्थानप्रणतिभिरंगुलीषु चक्रु-
र्मौलिस्रक्च्युतमकरंदरेणुगौरम् ॥ R. 4. 88.
See Ki. 7, *S*i. 8.

(4) मंजुभाषिणी.
(Also called सुनंदिनी and प्रबोधिता.)

Def. सजसा जगौ च यदि मंजुभाषिणी ।

Sch. G. स, ज, स, ज, ग (6. 7.)

Ex. यमुनामतीतमथ शुश्रुवानमुं
तपसस्तनूज इति नाधुनोच्यते ।
स यदाऽचलन्निजपुरादहर्निशं
नृपतेस्तदादि समचारि वार्तया ॥ Si. 13. 1.

(5) मत्तमयूरी.

Def. वेदैरंध्रैर्म्तौ यसगा मत्तमयूरः ।

Sch. G. म, त, य, स, ग (4. 9.)

Ex. दृष्ट्वा दृश्यान्याचरणीयानि विधाय
प्रेक्षाकारी याति पदं मुक्तमपायैः ।
सम्यग्दृष्टिस्तस्य परं पश्यति यस्त्वां
यश्चोपास्ते साधु विधेयं स विधत्ते ॥ Ki. 18. 28 ;
Si. 4. 44, 9. 76, also R. 9. 75.

(6) रुचिरा.

(Also called प्रभावती.)

Def. जभौ सजौ गिति रुचिरा चतुर्ग्रहैः ।

Sch. G. ज, भ, स, ज, ग (4. 9.)

Ex. कदा मुखं वरतनु कारणादृते
तवागतं क्षणमपि कोपपात्रताम् ।
अपर्वणि ग्रहकलुषेंदुमंडला
विभावरी कथय कथं भविष्यति ॥ M. 4. 13.
See Bk. 1. 1. Si. 17.

Metres with 14 Syllables in a quarter.

(शक्करी.)

(1) अपराजिता.

Def. ननरसलघुगैः स्वरैरपराजिता ।

Sch. G. न, न, र, स, ल, ग (7. 7.)

Ex. यदनवधि भुजप्रतापकृतास्पदा
यदुनिचयचमूः परैरपराजिता ।
व्यजयत समरे समस्तरिपुव्रजं
स जयति जगतां गतिर्गरुडध्वजः ।

(2) असंबाधा.

Def. म्तौ न्सौ गावक्षग्रहविरतिरसंबाधा ।

Sch. G. म, त, न, स, ग, ग (5. 9.)

Ex. वीर्याग्नौ येन ज्वलति रणवशात्क्षिप्ते
दैत्येंद्रे जाता धरणिरियमसंबाधा ।
धर्मस्थित्यर्थं प्रकटिततनुसंबंधः
साधूनां बाधां प्रशमयतु स कंसारिः ॥

(3) पथ्या.

(Also called मंजरी.)

Def. सजसा यलौ च सह गेन पथ्या मता ।

Sch. G. स, ज, स, य, ल, ग (5. 9.)

Ex. स्थगयंत्यमूः शमितचातकार्तस्वराः
जलदास्तडित्तुलितकांतकार्तस्वराः ।
जगतीरिह स्फुरितचारुचामीकराः
सवितुः क्वचित्कपिशयंति चामी कराः ॥
Si. 4. 24.

(4) प्रमदा.

(Also called कुररीरुता.)

Def. नजमजला गुरुश्च भवति प्रमदा ।

Sch. G. न, ज, म, ज, ल, ग (6. 8.)

Ex. अनतिचिरोज्झितस्य जलदेवचिर-
स्थितबहुबुद्बुदस्य पयसोऽनुकृतिम् ।
विरलविकीर्णवज्रशकला सकला-
मिह विदधाति धौतकलधौतमही ॥ Si. 4. 4

(5) प्रहरणकलिका.

Def. ननभनलगिति प्रहरणकलिका ।

Sch. G. न, न, भ, न, ल, ग (7. 7.)

Ex. व्यथयति कुसुमप्रहरणकलिका
प्रमदवनभवा तव धनुषि तता ।
विरहविपदि मे शरणमिह ततो
मधुमथनगुणस्मरणमविरतम् ॥

(6) मध्यक्षामा.

(Also called हंसश्येनी or कुटिल.)

Def. मध्यक्षामा युगदशविरमा म्भौ न्यौ गौ ।

Sch. G. म, भ, न, य, ग, ग (4. 10.)

Ex. नीतोच्छ्रायं मुहुरशिशिररश्मेरुस्रै-
रानीलाभैर्विरचितपरभागा रत्नैः ।
ज्योत्स्नाशंकामिह वितरति हंसश्येनी
मध्येप्यह्नः स्फटिकरजतभित्तिच्छाया ॥ Ki. 5. 31.

(7) वसंततिलका.

(Also called वसंततिलक,
उद्धर्षिणी, सिंहोन्नता.)

Def. उक्ता वसंततिलका तभजाः जगौ गः ।

Sch. G. त, भ, ज, ज, ग, ग (8. 6.)

Ex. यात्येकतोऽस्तशिखरं पतिरोषधीना-
माविष्कृतारुणपुरःसर एकतोऽर्कः ।
तेजोद्वयस्य युगपद्व्यसनोदयाभ्यां
लोको नियम्यत इवात्मदशांतरेषु ॥ S. 4. 1.

(8) वासंती.

Def. मात्तो नौ मो गौ यदि गदिता वासंतीयम् ।

Sch. G. म, त, न, म, ग, ग (4. 6. 4.)

Ex. भ्राम्यद्भृंगीनिर्भरमधुरालापोद्गीतैः
श्रीखंडाद्रेरद्भुतपवनैर्मंदांदोला ।
लीलालोला पल्लवविलसद्धस्तोल्लासैः
कंसारातौ नृत्यति सदृशी वासंतीयम् ।

Metres with 15 Syllables in a quarter.

(अतिशक्करी.)

(1) तूणक.

Def. तूणकं समानिका पदद्वयं विनांतिमम् ।

Sch. G. र, ज, र, ज, र (4. 4. 4. 3, or 7. 8.)

Ex. सा सुवर्णकेतकं विकाशि भृंगपूरितं
पंचबाणबाणजालपूर्णहेततुणकम् ।
राधिका वितर्क्य माधवाद्य मासि माधवे
मोहमेति निर्भरं त्वया विना कलानिधे ॥

(2) मालिनी.

Def. ननमयययुतेयं मालिनी भोगिलोकैः ।

Sch. G. न, न, म, य, य (8. 7.)

य ⏑ — —; र — ⏑ —; त — — ⏑; भ — ⏑ ⏑; ज ⏑ — ⏑; स ⏑ ⏑ —; म — — —; न ⏑ ⏑ ⏑; ल ⏑; ग —

Ex. शशिनमुपगतेयं कौमुदी मेघमुक्तं
जलनिधिमनुरूपं जह्नुकन्यावतीर्णा ।
इति समगुणयोगप्रीतयस्तत्र पौराः
श्रवणकटु नृपाणामेकवाक्यं विवव्रुः ॥ R. 6. 85.

(3) लीलाखेल.

Def. एकन्यूनौ विद्युन्मालापादौ चेल्लीलाखेलः ।
Sch. G. म, म, म, म, म.
Ex. मा कांते पक्षस्यांते पर्याकाशे देशे स्वाप्सीः
कांतं वक्त्रं वृत्तं पूर्णं चंद्रं मत्वा रात्रौ चेत् ।
क्षुत्क्षामः प्राटंश्चेतश्चेतो राहुः क्रूरः प्राद्यात्
तस्माद् ध्वांते हर्म्यस्यांते शय्यैकांते कर्तव्या ॥
Sar. K.

(4) शशिकला.

Def. गुरुनिधनमनुलघुरिह शशिकला
Sch. G. न, न, न, न, स (all short syllables except the last.)
Ex. मलयजतिलकसमुदितशशिकला
व्रजयुवतिलसदलिकगमनगता ।
सरसिजनयनहृदयसलिलनिधिं
व्यतनुत विततरभसपारितरलम् ॥

Metres with 16 Syllables in a quarter.

(अष्टि.)

(1) चित्र.

Def. चित्रसंज्ञमीरितं रजौ रजौ रगौ च वृत्तम् ।
Sch. G. र, ज, र, ज, र, ग (8. 8, or 4. 4. 4. 4.)
Ex. विद्रुमारुणाधरौष्ठशोभिवेणुवाद्यहृष्ट-
वल्लवीजनांगसंगजातमुग्धकंठकांग ।
त्वां सदैव वासुदेव पुण्यलभ्यपाद देव
वन्यपुष्पचित्रकेश संस्मरामि गोपवेश ॥

(2) पंचचामर.

Def. प्रमाणिकापदद्वयं वदंति पंचचामरम् ।
or जरौ जरौ ततो जगौ च पंचचामरं वदेत्
Sch. G. ज, र, ज, र, ज, ग (8. 8, or 4. 4. 4. 4.)
Ex. सुरद्रुमूलमंडपे विचित्ररत्ननिर्मिते
लसद्वितानभूषिते सलीलविभ्रमालसम् ।
सुरांगनाभवल्लवीकरप्रपंचचामर-
स्फुरत्समीरवीजितं सदाच्युतं भजामि तम् ।

(3) वाणिनी.

Def. नजरभजरैर्यदा भवति वाणिनी गयुक्तैः ।
Sch. G. न, ज, भ, ज, र, ग.
Ex. स्फुरतु ममाननेऽद्य ननु वाणि नीतिरम्यं
तवचरणप्रसादपरिपाकतः कवित्वम् ।
भवजलराशिपारकरणक्षमं मुकुंदं
सततमहं स्तवैः स्वचरितैः स्तवामि नित्यम् ॥

Metres with 17 Syllables in a quarter

(अत्यष्टि.)

(1) चित्रलेखा.

(Also called अतिशायिनी.)

Def. ससजा भजगा गु दिक्स्वरैर्भवति चित्रलेखा ।
Sch. G. स, स, ज, भ, ज, ग, ग (10. 7.)
Ex. इति धौतपुरंध्रिमत्सरान् सरासि मज्जनेन
श्रियमाप्तवतोऽतिशायिनीमपमलांगभासः ।
अवलोक्य तदैव यादवानपरवारिराशेः
शिशिरेतररोचिषाप्यपां ततिषु मङ्क्तुं मीषे ॥ Si. 8.

(2) नर्दटक.

(Also called कोकिकल.)

Def. यदि भवतो नजौ भजजला गुरु नर्दटकम् ।
Sch. G. न, ज, भ, ज, ज, ल, ग (8. 9.)
Ex. तरुणतमालनीलबहुलोन्नमंदम्बुधराः
शिशिरसमीरणाबधूतनूतनवारिकणाः ।
कथमवलोकयेयमधुना हरिहेतिमती-
मंदकलनीलकंठकलहैर्मुखराः कुकुभः ॥
Mâl. 9. 18, See 5. 31.

(3) पृथ्वी.

Def. जसौ जसयला वसुग्रहयतिश्च पृथ्वी गुरुः ।
Sch. G. ज, स, ज, स, य, ल, ग (8. 9.),
Ex. इतः स्वपिति केशवः कुलमितस्तदीयद्विषा-
मितश्च शरणार्थिनः शिखरिणां गणाः शेरते ।
इतोपि बडवानलः सह समस्तसंवर्तकै-
रहो विततमूर्जितं भरसहं च सिन्धोर्वपुः ॥
Bh. 2. 76.

(4) मंदाक्रांता.

Def. मंदाक्रांतांबुधिरसनगैर्मो भनौ तौ गयुग्मम् ।
Sch. G. म, भ, न, त, त, ग, ग (4. 6. 7.)
Ex. गोपी भर्तुर्विरहविधुरा काचिदिंदीवराक्षी
उन्मत्तेव स्खलितकवरी निःश्वसंती विशालम् ।
अत्रैवास्ते मुररिपुरिति भ्रांतिदूतीसहाया
त्यक्त्वा गेहं झटिति यमुनामंजुकुंजं जगाम ।
Pad. D. 1.

(The whole of the "Meghadûta" is written in this metre.)

(5) वंशपत्रपतित.

Def. दिङ्मुनिवंशपत्रपतितं भरनभनलगैः ।
Sch. G. भ, र, न, भ, न, ल, ग (10. 7.)
Ex. दर्पणनिर्मलासु पतिते धनतिमिरमुषि
ज्योतिषि रौप्यभित्तिषु पुरः प्रतिफलति मुहुः ।
व्रीडमसंमुखोपि रमणैरपहृतवसनाः
कांचनकंदरासु तरुणीरिह नयति रविः ॥ Si. 4. 67.

(6) शिखरिणी.

Def. रसै रुद्रैश्छिन्ना यमनसभलागः शिखरिणी
Sch. G. य, म, न, स, भ, ल, ग (6. 11.)
Ex. दिगंते श्रूयंते मदमलितगंडाः करटिनः
करिण्यः कारुण्यास्पदमसमशीलाः खलु मृगाः ।

इदानीं लोकेऽस्मिन्ननुपमशिखानां पुनरयं
नखानां पांडित्यं प्रकटयतु कस्मिन् मृगपतिः ॥
Bv. 1. 2.

(7) हरिणी.

Def. नसमरसलागः षड्वेदैर्हयैर्हरिणी मता ।
Sch. G. न, स, म, र, स, ल, ग (6. 4. 7.)
Ex. सुतनु हृदयात्प्रत्यादेशव्यलीकमपैतु ते
किमपि मनसः संमोहो मे तदा बलवानभूत् ।
प्रबलतमसामेवंप्रायाः शुभेषु हि वृत्तयः
स्रजमपि शिरस्यंधः क्षिप्तां धुनोत्यहिशंकया ॥
S. 7. 24.

Metres with 18 Syllables in a quarter.

(धृति)

(1) कुसुमलतावेल्लिता.

Def. स्याद्भूतर्त्वश्वैः कुसुमितलतावेल्लिता म्तौ न यौ यौ ।
Sch. G. म, त, न, य, य, य (5. 6. 7.)
Ex. क्रीडत्कालिंदीललितलहरीवारिभिर्दाक्षिणात्यै-
र्वातैः खेलद्भिः कुसुमितलतावेल्लिता मंदमंदम् ।
भृंगालीगीतैः किसलयकरोल्लासितैर्लास्यलक्ष्मीं
तन्वाना चेतो रभसतरलं चक्रपाणेश्चकार ॥

(2) चित्रलेखा.

Def. मंदाक्रांता नपरलघुयुता कीर्तिता चित्रलेखा ।
Sch. G. त, भ, न, य, य, य (4. 7. 7.)
Ex. शंकेऽमुष्मिन् जगति मृगदृशां साररूपं यदासी-
दाकृष्येदं व्रजयुवतिसभा वेधसा सा व्यधायि ।
नैतादृक् चेत् कथमुदधिसुतामंतरेणाच्युतस्य
प्रीतं तस्या नयनयुगमभूच्चित्रलेखाद्भुतायाम् ॥

(3) नंदन.

Def. नजभजरैस्तु रेफसहितैः शिवैर्हयैर्नंदनम् ।
Sch. G. न, ज, भ, ज, र, र (11. 7.)
Ex. तरणिसुतातरंगपवनैः सलीलमांदोलितं
मधुरिपुपादपंकजरजः सुपूतपृथ्वीतलम् ।
मुरहरचित्रचेष्टितकलाकलापसंस्मारकं
क्षितितलनंदनं व्रज सखे सुखाय वृंदावनम् ॥

(4) नाराच.

(Also called महामालिका or महामालिनी.)

Def. इह ननरचतुष्कसृष्टं तु नाराचमाचक्षते ।
Sch. G. न, न, र, र, र, र (8. 5, 5.)
Ex. रघुपतिरपि जातवेदोविशुद्धां प्रगृह्य प्रियां
प्रियसुहृदि बिभीषणे संक्रमय्य श्रियं वैरिणः ।
रविसुतसहितेन तेनानुयातः ससौमित्रिणा
भुजविजितविमानरत्नाधिरूढः प्रतस्थे पुरीम् ॥
R. 12. 104.

(5) शार्दूलललित.

Def. मः सो जः सतसा दिनेशऋतुभिः शार्दूलललितम् ।
Sch. G. म, स, ज, स, त, स (12 6.)
Ex. कृत्वा कंसमृगे पराक्रमविधिं शार्दूलललितं
यश्चक्रे क्षिति भारकारिषु हरं चैद्यप्रभृतिषु ।
संतोषं परमं तु देवनिवहे त्रैलोक्यशरणं
श्रेयो नः स तनोत्वपारमहिमा लक्ष्मीप्रियतमः ॥

Metres with 19 Syllables in a quarter.

(अतिधृति.)

(1) मेघविस्फूर्जिता.

Def. रसर्त्वश्वैर्य्मौ न्सौ ररगुरुयुतौ मेघविस्फूर्जिता स्यात् ।
Sch. G. य, म, न, स, र, र, ग (6. 6. 7.)
Ex. कदंबामोदाढ्या विपिनपवनः केकिनः कांतकेकाः
विनिद्राः कंदल्यो दिशि दिशि मुदा दर्दुरा दृप्तनादाः ।
निशा नृत्यद्विद्युद्विलसितलसन्मेघविस्फूर्जिता चेत्
प्रियः स्वाधीनोऽसौ दनुजदलनो राज्यमस्मात्किमन्यत् ॥

(2) शार्दूलविक्रीडित.

Def. सूर्याश्वैर्यदि मः सजौ सततगाः शार्दूलविक्रीडितम् ।
Sch. G. म, स, ज, स, त, त, ग (12. 7.)
Ex. वेदांतेषु यमाहुरेकपुरुषं व्याप्य स्थितं रोदसी
यस्मिन्नीश्वर इत्यनन्यविषयः शब्दो यथार्थाक्षरः ।
अंतर्यश्च मुमुक्षुभिर्नियमितप्राणादिभिर्मृग्यते
स स्थाणुः स्थिरभक्तियोगसुलभो निःश्रेयसायास्तु वः ॥
V. 1. 1.

(3) सुमधुरा.

Def. म्रौ भ्नौ मो नो गुरुश्चेद् हयऋतुरसैरुक्ता सुमधुरा ।
Sch. G. म, र, भ, न, म, न, ग (7. 6. 6.)
Ex. वेदार्थान् प्राकृतस्त्वं वदसि न च ते जिह्वा निपतिता
मध्याह्ने वीक्षसेऽर्कं न तव सहसा दृष्टिर्विचालिता ।
दीप्ताग्नौ पाणिमंतः क्षिपसि स च ते दग्धो भवति नो
चारित्र्याच्चारुदत्तं चलयसि न ते देहं हरति भूः ॥
Mk. 9. 21.

(4) सुरसा.

Def. म्रौ भ्नौ यो नो गुरुश्चेत् स्वरमुनिकरणैराह सुरसाम् ।
Sch. G. म, र, भ, न, य, न, ग (7. 7. 5.)
Ex. कामक्रीडासतृष्णो मधुसमयसमारंभरभसात्
कालिंदीकूलकुंजे विहरणकुतुकाकृष्टहृदया ।
गोविंदो बल्लवीनामधररससुधां प्राप्य सुरसां
शंके पीयूषपानैः प्रचयकृतसुखं व्यस्मरदसौ ॥

Metres with 20 Syllables in a quarter.

(कृति.)

(1) गीतिका.

Def. सजसा भरौ सलगा यदा कथिता तदा खलु गीतिका ।
Sch. G. स, ज, स, भ, र, स, ल, ग (5. 7. 8.)
Ex. करतालचंचलकंकणस्वनमिश्रणेन मनोरमा
रमणीयवेणुनिनादरंगिमसंगमेन सुखावहा ।
बहलानुरागनिवासरासमुद्भवा तव रागिणं
विदधौ हरिं खलु बल्लवीजनचारुचामरगीतिका ॥

(2) सुवदना.

Def. ज्ञेया सप्ताश्वषड्भिर्मरभनययुता म्लौ गः सुवदना ।
Sch. G. म, र, भ, न, य, म, ल, ग (7. 7. 6.)

Ex. उत्तुंगास्तुंगकूलं स्रुतमदसलिलाः प्रस्यंदि सलिलं
श्यामाः श्यामोपकंठद्रुममतिमुखराः कल्लोलमुखरम् ।
स्रोतःखातावसीदत्तटमुरुदशनैरुत्सादिततटाः
शोणं सिंदूरशोणा मम गजपतयः पास्यंति शतशः ॥
Mu. 4. 16.

Metres with 21 Syllables in a quarter.

(प्रकृति.)

(1) पंचकावली.

(Also called सरसी, धृतश्री.)

Def. नजभजजा जरौ नरपते कथिता भुवि पंचकावली ।
Sch. G. न, ज, भ, ज, ज, ज, र (7. 7. 7.)
Ex. तुरगशताकुलस्य परितः परमेकतुरंगजन्मनः
प्रमथितभूभृतः प्रतिपथं मथितस्य भृशं महीभृता ।
परिचलतो बलानुजबलस्य पुरः सततं धृतश्रिय-
श्चिरगलितश्रियो जलनिधेश्च तदाऽभवदंतरं महत् ॥
Si. 3. 82.

(2) स्रग्धरा.

Def. म्रभ्नैर्यानां त्रयेण त्रिमुनियुता स्रग्धरा कीर्तितेयम् ।
Sch. G. म, र, भ, न, य, य, य (7. 7. 7.)
Ex. या सृष्टिः स्रष्टुराद्या वहति विधिहुतं या हविर्या च होत्री
ये द्वे कालं विधत्तः श्रुतिविषयगुणा या स्थिता व्याप्य विश्वम् ।
यामाहुः सर्वभूतप्रकृतिरिति यया प्राणिनः प्राणवंतः
प्रत्यक्षाभिः प्रपन्नस्तनुभिरवतु वस्ताभिरष्टाभिरीशः ॥
S. 1. 1.

Metres with 22 Syllables in a quarter.

(आकृति.)

हंसी.

Def. मौ गौ नाश्चत्वारो गो गो वसुभुवनयतिरिति भवति हंसी
Sch. G. म, म, त, न, न, न, न, त, ग (8. 14.)
Ex. सार्धं कांतेनैकांतेऽसौ विकचकमलमधु सुरभि पिबंती
कामक्रीडाकूतस्फीतप्रमदसरसतरमलघु रसंती ।
कालिंदीये पद्मारण्ये पवनपतनपरितरलपरागे
कंसाराते पश्य स्वेच्छं सरमसगतिरिह विलसति हंसी ॥

Metres with 23 Syllables in a quarter.

(विकृति.)

अद्रितनया.

Def. नजभजभा जभौ लघुगुरू बुधैस्तु गदितेयमद्रितनया ।
Sch. G. न, ज, भ, ज, भ, ज, भ, ल, ग (11. 12.)
Ex. खरनरशौर्यपावकशिखापतंगनिभमप्रदृप्तदनुजो
जलधिसुतविलासवसतिः सतां गतिरशेषमान्य महिमा ।
भुवनहितावतारचतुरश्चराचरधरोऽवतीर्ण इह हि
क्षितिवलयेऽस्ति कंसशमनस्त्ववेति तमवोचदद्रितनया ।

Metres with 24 Syllables in a quarter.

(संस्कृति.)

तन्वी.

Def. भूतमुनीनैर्यतिरिह भतनाः स्भौ भनयाश्च यपि भवति तन्वी
Sch. G. भ, त, न, स, भ, भ, न, य (5. 7. 11.)

Metres with 25 Syllables in a quarter.

(अतिकृति.)

क्रौंचपदा.

Def. क्रौंचपदा भ्मौ स्भौ ननना न्गाविषुशरवसुमुनिविरतिरिह भवेत्
Sch. G. भ, म, स, भ, न, न, न, ग (5. 5. 8. 7.)

Metres with 26 Syllables in a quarter.

(उत्कृति.)

भुजंगविजृंभित.

Def. वस्वीशाश्वैश्छेदोपेतं ममतनयुगनरसलगैर्भुजंगविजृंभितम्
Sch. G. म, म, त, न, न, न, र, स, ल, ग (8. 11. 7.)

दंडक.

Metres with 27 or more letters in each quarter are designated by the geaeral name दंडक. The highest number of syllables in a quarter of this species of metre is said to be 999. In each quarter there must be first two *naganas* or six short syllables, and the remaining may be either *raganas* or *yaganas*, or all the feet may be *saganas*. The Classes of दंडक usually menrioned are चंडवृष्टिप्रयात, प्रचितक मत्तमातंगलीलाकर, सिंहविक्रांत, कुसुमस्तवक, अनंगशेखर, संग्राम &c. Mâl 5. 23 is an instance of the last species of Daṇḍaka.

SECTION B.

अर्धसमवृत्त. (Half-equal Metres.)

(1) अपरवक्त्र.

(Sometimes called वैतालीय.)

Def. अयुजि ननरला गुरुः समे
तदपरवक्त्रमिदं नजौ जरौ ।
Sch. G. न, न, र, ल, ग (odd quarter)
न, ज, ज, र (even quarter)
Ex. स्फुटसुमधुरवेणुगीतिभि-
स्तमपरवक्त्रमवेत्य माधवम् ।
मृगयुवतिगणैः समं स्थिता
व्रजवनिता धृतचित्तविभ्रमा ॥

(2) उपचित्र.

Def. विषमे यदि सौ सलगा दले
भौ युजि भाद्गुरुकावुपचित्रम् ।
Sch. G. स, स, स, ल, ग (odd quarter)
भ, भ, भ, ग, ग (even quarter)
Ex. मुरवैरिवपुस्तनुतां मुदं
हेमनिभांशुकचंदनलिप्तम् ।

गगनं चपलामिलितं यथा
शारदनीरधरैरुपचित्रम् ॥

(3) पुष्पिताग्रा.

(Also called औपच्छंदसिक.)

Def. अयुजि नयुगरेफतो यकारो
युजि तु नजौ जरगाश्च पुष्पिताग्रा ।

Sch. G. न, न, र, य (odd quarter)
न, ज, ज, र, ग (even quarter)

Ex. अथ मदनवधूरुपप्लवांतं
व्यसनकृशा परिपालयांबभूव ।
शशिन इव दिवातनस्य लेखा
किरणपरिक्षयधूसरा प्रदोषम् ॥ Ku. 4. 46.

(4) वियोगिनी.

(Also called वैतालीय or सुंदरी.)

Def. विषमे ससजा गुरुः समे
सभरा लोऽथ गुरुर्वियोगिनी ।

Sch. G. स, स, ज, ग (odd quarter)
स, भ, र, ल, ग (even quarter)

Ex. सहसा विदधीत न क्रिया-
मविवेकः परमापदां पदम् ।
वृणते हि विमृश्यकारिणं
गुणलुब्धाः स्वयमेव संपदः ॥ Ki. 2. 30.
See R. 8, or Ku. 4.

(5) वेगवती.

Def. सयुगात्सगुरू विषमे चेद् ।
भाविह वेगवती युजि भाद्गौ ।

Sch. G. स, स, स, ग (odd quarter)
भ, भ, भ, ग (even quarter)

Ex. स्मरवेगवती व्रजरामा
केशववंशरवैरतिमुग्धा ।
रभसान्न गुरून् गणयंती
केलिनिकुंजगृहाय जगाम ॥

(6) हरिणप्लुता.

Def. सयुगात्सलघू विषमे गुरु-
र्युजि नभौ भरकौ हरिणप्लुता ।

Sch. G. स, स, स, ल, ग (odd quarter)
न, भ, भ, र (even quarter)

Ex. स्फुटफेनचया हरिणप्लुणता
बलिमनोज्ञतटा तरणेः सुता ।
कलहंसकुलारवशालिनी
विहरतो हरति स्म हरेर्मनः ॥

N. B.—Metres like अपरवक्त्र or औपच्छंदसिक and वैतालीय or वियोगिनी are usually treated as *jâtis*; (see Section D). But they are sometimes defined in the Gaṇa scheme, and are, therefore, given under the class of Vṛittas.

SECTION C.

विषमवृत्त. (Unequal Metres.)

The most common metre of this class is called उद्गता.

Def. प्रथमे सजौ यदि सलौ च
नसजगुरुकाण्यनंतरम् ।
यद्यथ भनजलगाः स्युरथो
सजसा जगौ च भवतीयमुद्गता ॥

Sch. G. स, ज, स, ल (first quarter)
न, स, ज, ग (second ,,)
भ, न, ज, ल, ग (third ,,)
स, ज, स, ज, ग (fourth ,,)

Ex. अथ वासवस्य वचनेन
रुचिरवदनस्त्रिलोचनम् ।
क्लांतिरहितमभिराधयितुं
विधिवत्तपांसि विदधे धनंजयः ॥ Ki. 12. 1.
See *Si.* 15 also.

Another variety of उद्गता is mentioned wherein the third quarter has भ, न, भ, ग instead of भ, न, ज, ल and ग.

Other kinds of metre in which every quarter of the stanza differs in the number of syllables, are included under the general name 'Gâthâ'. The same name is applicable to stanzas consisting of any number of quarters other than four. As in the case of उपजाति, any two or more quarters of a regular metre may be combined to form अर्धसमवृत्त or विषमवृत्त.

SECTION D.

जाति. (Metres regulated by the number of syllabic instants.)

(*a*) The most common variety of such metres is आर्या. It is said to have nine sub-divisions:—

पथ्या विपुला चपला मुखचपला जघनचपला च ।
गीत्युपगीत्युद्गीतय आर्यागीतिर्नवैव वार्तायाः ॥

Of these nine kinds the last four are generally used and deserve mention.

(1) आर्या.

Def. यस्याः पादे प्रथमे द्वादशमात्रास्तथा तृतीयेपि ।
अष्टादश द्वितीये चतुर्थके पंचदश सार्या ॥ *Srut.* 4.

The first and third quarters must each contain 12 Mâtrâs or syllabic instants (one being allotted to a short vowel, and two to a long one), the second 18, and the fourth 15.

Ex. प्रतिपक्षेणापि पतिं सेवंते भर्तृवत्सलाः साध्व्यः ।
अन्यसरितां शतानि हि समुद्रगाः प्रापयंत्यब्धिम् ॥
M. 5. 19.

The whole of Govardhana's आर्यासप्तशती is written in this metre.

(2) गीति.

Def. आर्यापूर्वार्धसमं द्वितीयमपि भवति यत्र हंसगते ।
छंदोविदस्तदानीं गीतिं तामृतवाणि भाषंते ॥
Srut. 5.

The first and third quarters of this metre must contain 12 syllabic instants each, and the second and fourth 18 each.

Ex. पाटीर तव पटीयान्कः परिपाटीमिमामुरीकर्तुम् ।
यत्पिंषतामपि नृणां पिष्टोऽपि तनोषि परिमलैः पुष्टिम् ॥
Bv. 1. 12.

(3) उपगीति.

Def. आर्योत्तरार्धतुल्यं प्रथमार्धमपि प्रयुक्तं चेत् ।
कामिनि तामुपगीतिं प्रतिभाषंते महाकवयः ॥
*S*rut. 6.

The first and third quarters of this metre must contain 12 syllabic instants each, and the second and fourth 15 each.

Ex. नतगोपसुंदरीणां रासोल्लासे मुरारातिम् ।
अस्मारयदुपगीतिः स्वर्गकुरंगदृशां गीतिः ॥

(4) उद्गीति.

Def. आर्याशकलद्वितये विपरीते पुनरिहोद्गीतिः ।

The first and third quarters of this metre must contain 12 syllabic instants each, the second 15, and the fourth 18.

Ex. नारायणस्य संततमुद्गीतिः संस्मृतिर्भक्त्या ।
अर्चायामासक्तिर्दुस्तरसंसारसागरे तरणिः ॥

(5) आर्यागीति.

Def. आर्याप्राग्दलमंतेऽधिकगुरु तादृक्परार्धमार्यागीतिः ।

The first and third quarters of this metre must contain 12 syllabic instants each, and the third and fourth 20 each.

Ex. सवधूकाः सुखिनोऽस्मि-
न्नवरतममंदरागतामरसदृशः ।
नासेवंते रसव-
न्नवरतममंदरागतामरसदृशः ॥ *S*i. 4. 51.

Note. All these five sorts are sometimes defined in the Gaṇa scheme.

(*b*) वैतालीय.

Def. षड्विषमेऽष्टौ समे कलास्ताश्च समे स्युर्निरंतराः ॥
न समात्र पराश्रिता कला वैतालीयेऽंते रलौ गुरुः ।

This is a stanza of four quarters, the first and third of which contain the time of fourteen short syllables, and the second and fourth sixteen. Again, the first and third quarters of this metre must contain 6 syllabic instants, and the second and fourth 8 each, followed by a रगण (◡ — ◡) and a short and a long vowel (◡ —). The rules further require that the syllabic instants in the even quarter should not be all composed of short syllables or long syllables, and that the even syllabic instant in each quarter (*i. e.* the 2nd, 4th, and 6th) should not be formed conjointly with the next (*i. e.* 3rd, 5th, and 7th).

Ex. कुशलं खलु तुभ्यमेव तद्-
वचनं कृष्ण यदभ्यधामहम् ।
उपदेशपराः परेष्वपि
स्वविनाशाभिमुखेषु साधवः ॥ *S*i. 16. 41.

(*c*) औपच्छंदसिक.

Def. पर्यंते र्यौ तथैव शेषमौपच्छंदसिकं सुधीभिरुक्तम् ॥

This is the same as वैतालीय except that at the end of each quarter there must be a रगण and यगण instead of रगण and ल, ग only ; in other words, it is the same as वैतालीय with only a long syllable added at the end of each quarter.

Ex. वपुषा परमेण भूधराणा-
मथ संभाव्य पराक्रमं बिभेदे ।
मृगमाशु विलोकयांचकार
स्थिरदंष्ट्रोग्रमुखं महेंद्रसूनुः ॥ Ki. 13. 1.

So in the next 52 verses of the same canto. See *S*i. 20 also.

It will be noticed that वियोगिनी or सुंदरी and अपरवक्त्र are only particular cases of वैतालीय, and पुष्पिताग्रा and मालभारिणी, of औपच्छंदसिक. Prosodists treat both these classes of metres in the Gaṇa scheme as well as in the Mâtrâ scheme ; hence they have been noticed here as well as in Section C.

(*d*) मात्रासमक.

The metre called मात्रासमक consists of four quarters each of which contains 16 syllabic instants. The most general variety is that in which the ninth syllabic instant is composed of a short syllable, and the last is a long syllable. It is defined as मात्रासमकं नवमो ल्गांत्यः ।

But there are several varieties of this metre arising from particular syllabic instants being short or long. For example, if the 9th and 12th moments are formed by short syllables, and the 15th and 16th by a long one, and the rest are optional, it is called वानवासिका. If the 5th, 8th, and 9th are formed by short syllables, and the 15th and 16th by a long one, it is called **चित्रा**. If the 5th and 8th are short, as also the 9th and 10th, and 15th and 16th are long, it is called उपचित्रा. And if the 5th, 8th, and 12th are short, 15th and 16th long, and the rest indeterminate, it is called विश्लोक. Sometimes two or more of these varieties are combined in the same stanza, and in that case the measure is called पादाकुलक, In which there is no other restriction than that each quarter should have sixteen syllabic instants.

Ex. मूढ जहीहि धनागमतृष्णां
कुरु तनुबुद्धे मनसि वितृष्णाम् ।
यल्लभसे निजकर्मोपात्तं
वित्तं तेन विनोदय चित्तम् ॥ Moha M. 1.

APPENDIX II.

Giving the dates &c. of important Sanskrit Writers.

आर्यभट्ट A well-known astronomer. Born A. D. 476.

उद्भट One of the earliest writers on Alankâra. He was the chief Pandit or Sabhâpati of king Jayâpîda of Kâshmir (779-813 A. D.).

कय्यट Author of the भाष्यप्रदीप, being a commentary on Patanjali's महाभाष्य. He is considered by Dr. Buhler to be not older than the 13th century.

कल्हण The author of the well-known राजतरंगिणी 'the chronicle of kings'. He was a contemporary of Jayasimha of Kâshmir who reigned from 1129-1150 A. D.

कालिदास The celebrated author of the अभिज्ञान-शकुंतल, विक्रमोर्वशीय, मालविकाग्निमित्र, रघुवंश, कुमारसंभव, मेघदूत, ऋतुसंहार ; also of the poems नलोदय and of some other minor works. The earliest known authentic reference to Kâlidâsa is in an inscription dated 556 Sake or 634 A. D. in which he and Bhâravi are spoken of as being renowned poets. The verse is as follows :—

येनायोजि नवेश्म
स्थिरमर्थविधौ विवेकिना जिनवेश्म।
स विजयतां रविकीर्तिः
कविताश्रितकालिदासभारविकीर्तिः ॥

Bâṇa's reference to him in the beginning of his Harsha-charita also shows that he must have flourished before the time of Bâṇa *i. e.* before the first half of the seventh century. But how long before the seventh century the poet flourished is not yet known : According to Mallinatha's explanation on Me. 14 निचुल and दिङ्नाग were contemporaries of Kâlidâsa. If Mallinatha's suggestion be correct—and it is very doubtful if it be really so—then our poet must have lived in the middle of the sixth century which is the date usually assigned to दिङ्नाग.

There is one point which, if definitely settled, would give the poet's precise date. It is the mention by Kâlidâsa of his patron Vikrama. Who this Vikrama is it has not yet been definitely settled. Popular tradition indentifies him with the founder of the Samvat Era which is said to have commenced 56 B. C. If this view be correct, Kâlidâsa must be considered as belonging to the first century before Christ. But some scholars have recently come to the conclusion that what is called the era of Vikramâditya 56. B. C. was a date arrived at by taking the date of the great battle of Korur in which Vikrama finally defeated the Mlechchas, *i. e.* 544 A. D. and then by throwing back the beginning of the new era 600 years before that date, *i. e.* 56 B. C. If this conclusion be accepted as correct—and scholars do not seem to have yet agreed on the point—Kâlidâsa must have flourished in the sixth century A. D. The question is still an open one.

क्षेमेन्द्र A well-known poet of Kashmir, author of समयमातृका and several other works. He flourished during the second and the third quarter of the 11th century.

जगद्धर N. of a celebrated commentator, who has written commentaries on the Mâlatî-Mâdhava and Veni-Samhâra. He lived after the 14th century.

जगन्नाथपंडित N. of a celebrated modern author. His most celebrated work is the रसगंगाधर a treatise on Rhetoric or Poetics ; his other works are भामिनीविलास, the five *laharies* (गंगा, पीयूष, सुधा, अमृत, करुणा), and a few minor works. He is supposed to have flourished during the time of the Emperor Shah Jahan of Delhi. He must have also seen the latter end of Jehangir's reign, and the temporary accession of Dârâ to the throne in 1658. His date,—at least, his active career—lay, therefore between 1620 and 1660 A. D.

जयदेव Author of that charming lyric poem the Gîtagovinda. He was an inhabitant of the village Kinduwilva in the Vîrabhûmi district of Bengal. He is said to have lived in the time of a king called Lakshmaṇsena who is indentified by Dr. Buhler with the Vaidya king of Bengal whose inscription is dated Vikrama Samvat 1173 or 1116 A. D. The poet must have, therefore, flourished in the 12th century.

दंडिन् Author of the Dasakumârcharita and Kâvyâdarsa. He flourished in the latter half of the sixth century, and was a contemporary of Bâṇa, according to Mâdhavâchârya.

पतंजलि The celebrated author of the Mahâbhâshya. He is said to have lived about 150 B. C.

नारायण (भट्टनारायण) Author of the Venî-Samhâra. He must have flourished before the 9th century as his work is frequently quoted by the poet Anandavardhana in his work called ध्वन्यालोक. This poet flourished under the reign of Avantivarman 855-884 A. D. (Râj. T. 5. 34).

बाण The well-known author of the Harshachrita, Kâdâmbarî and Chaṇḍikâsataka. Pârvatîpariṇaya and Ratnâvali are also ascribed to him. His date has been indisputably fixed by that of his patron Harsha-vardhana of Kânyakubja who was reigning during the whole of Hiouen Thsang's travels in India which lasted from 629 to 645 A. D. Bâṇa must, therefore, have lived in the latter half of the sixth or the first half of the seventh century. The date of Bâṇa is useful in ascertaining the dates—at least the *termini ad quem*—of several writers mentioned by him in his introduction to the Harsha-charita.

बिल्हण Author of the Mahâkâvya Vikramânkadeva-charita and of Chaurapanchâsikâ. He flourished in the latter half of the 11th century.

भट्टि A son of Sri Svâmin, who lived in Vallabhi during the reign of king Srîdharasena or of Narendra, the son of Srîdhara, who is supposed by Lassen to have reigned from 530 to 545 A. D.

भर्तृहरि Author of the three Satakas and of the Vâkyapadîya. Mr. Telang gives it as his opinion that he must have flourished about the close of the first and the beginning of the second century of the Christian era. Tradition makes him brother of king Vikrama, and if this Vikrama be accepted as the same who defeated the Mlechchas in 544 A. D., we must suppose Bhartrihari to have flourished in the latter half of the sixth century.

भवभूति The well-known author of the Mahâvîr-charita, Mâlatî-Mâdhava, and Uttararâmacharita. He was a native of Vidarbha and lived at the court of king Yasovarman of Kânyakubja, who was subdued by Lalitâditya of Kashmir (693-729 A. D.) Bhavabhûti flourished therefore at the end of the 7th century, and this date is consistent with Bâṇa's omission of his name. All anecdotes about the contemporaneity of Kâlidâsa and Bhavabhûti must be rejected as absolute myths.

भारवि Author of the Kirâtârjunîya. mentioned along with Kâlidâsa in an inscription dated 634. See कालिदास.

भास Mentioned by Bâṇa and Kâlidâsa as their predecessor. Flourished before the 7th century.

मयूर Father in-law of Bâṇa and author of the Sûrya-Sataka composed by him to be freed from leprosy. A contemporary of Bâṇa q v.

मम्मट N of the author of the Kâvyaprakâsa. He must have flourished before 1294 A. D., in which year a commentary on that work by name Jayantî was written by one Jayanta.

मुरारि Author of the Anargha-râghava mentioned by the poet Ratnâkara (who flourished in the 9th century) in Haravijaya 38. 67. He must therefore be placed before the 9th century.

रत्नाकर Author of the Mahâkâvya called Haravijaya and patronized by Avantivarman (855-884 A. D.).

राजशेखर Author of Bâla-Râmâyaṇa, Bâla-Bhârata and Vidhasâlabhanjikâ. He lived after Bhavabhûti and before the end of the tenth century, that is, he flourished between the end of the 7th and the middle of the 10th century.

वराहमिहिर A celebrated astronomer, author of the Brihat-Samhitâ. He died in 587 A. D.

विक्रम See कालिदास.

विशाखदत्त Author of the Mudrârâkshasa. The 7th or 8th century is regarded by Mr. Telang as the probable date of the production of the drama.

शंकर The celebrated teacher of the Vedânta philosophy and author of the शारीरकभाष्य and of a large number of original works, especially on Vendânta. He is said to have been born in 788 A. D. and to have died in 820 at the early age of 32. But some scholars (Mr. Telang, Dr. Bhandarkar &c.) have tried to show that Sankara's date must be the 6th or 7th century at the latest. See Introduction to Mudrârâkshasa.

सुबंधु The author of Vâsavadattâ mentioned by Bâṇa, and so not later than the 7th century. He mentions a work of Dharma-kîrti by name बौद्धसंगति which is supposed to belong to the sixth century.

श्रीहर्ष The reputed author of the Naishadha-charita and of 7 or 8 other works. He is generally placed in the latter half of the 12th century. Wilson says that Srîharsha succeeded his father Kalasa in 1113, and that the Ratnâvali, a play ascribed to the king, must have been written by him between 1113 and 1125 the close of his reign. But the Ratnâvali must be regarded as a work of an earlier date as it is largely quoted in the Dasarûpa, a work of the last part of the 10th century.

हर्ष The patron of Bâṇa, see बाण. The Ratnâvali is supposed to have been written by Bâṇa and published under his patron's name.

APPENDIX III.

On important Geographical names in ancient India.

अंग N. of an important kingdom situated on the right bank of the Ganges. Its capital was Champâ, also called Angapurî. This town stood on the Ganges about 24 miles west of a rocky island, and is, therefore, considered to be the same as, or situated very near, the modern Bhâgalpur.

अंध्र N. of a people and their country. It is said to be the same as the modern Telangaṇa, and the mouths of the Godâvarî were in the possession of the Andhras. But the limits were probably confined to the Ghâts on the west, and the rivers Godâvarî and Kṛishnâ on the north and south. It bordered on Kalinga ; (see Dk. 7th Ullâsa,) and its capital अंध्रनगर is probably the old town of Vengi or Vegi.

अवंति N. of a country, north of the Narmadâ ; its capital was Ujjayinî, also called Avantipurî or Avantî and Visâlâ, (cf. Me. 30) situated on the Siprâ. It is the western part of Mâlva. In the time of the Mahâbhârata the county extended on the south to the banks of the Narmadâ and on the west probably to the banks of the Mahi or Myhe. On the north of Avantî lay another principality with its capital Dasapura on the Charmaṇvati river, which appears to be the modern town of Dholpur, and was the capital of Rantideva.

अश्मक An old name of Travancore.

आनर्त See सोराष्ट्र.

इंद्रप्रस्थ (also called हरिप्रस्थ, शक्रप्रस्थ &c.) identified with the modern Delhi, though it stood on the left bank of the Yamunâ, while Delhi stands on the right.

उत्कल or ओड्र N. of a county, the modern Orissa, which lay to the south of Tâmralipta, and extended to the river Kapisâ ; cf. R. 4. 38. The chief towns of this province are Cuttak and Purî where the celebrated temple of Jagannâth is situated.

कनखल N. of a village near Hardvâra which is situated on the Ganges at the southern base of the Sewalika mountains. कनखल was also the name of the surrounding mountains.

कपिशा See under सुह्म.

कालिंग N. of a country lying to the south of Odra or orissa and extending to the mouths of the Godâvarî. It is indentified with the Northern Circars. Its capital कलिंगनगर was in ancient times at some distance from the sea-coast (cf. Dk. 7th Ullâsa,) and was probably at Râjamahendri ; See अंध्र also.

कांची See under द्रविड.

कामरूप An important kingdom said to have extended from the banks of the Karatoyâ or Sadânîrâ to the extremities of Assâm. It must have extended upto the Himâlaya on the north and the borders of China on the east, as its king is said to have assisted Duryodhaṇa with an army of Kirâtas and Chînas. The ancient capital of this kingdom was प्राग्ज्योतिष on the other side of the Lauhitya or the river Brahmaputra ; cf. R. 4. 81.

कांबोज N. of a people and their country. They must have inhabited the Hindoo Koosh mountain which separates the Giljit valley from Balkh, and probably extended up to little Thibet and Lâdak. Their country was famous for handsome horses and shawls made of goats', rats', and dogs' wool, and abounded in walnut trees ; cf. R. 4. 69.

कुंतल N. of the country to the north of Chola. Kalyâṇa or Kollian Doorg south of Kurugade appears to have been its capital. The country represents the south-western portion of Hyderabad.

कुरुक्षेत्र N. of an extensive region or plain near Delhi, the scene of the great war between the Pâṇdvas and Kauravas. It is the tract near the holy lake called by the same name lying to the south of Thâneshvar, and extended from the south of the Sarasvatî to the north of the Drishadvatî. It is sometimes called समंतपंचक the tract of the 'five pools' of blood of the Kshatriyas slain by Parasurâma.

कुलूत N. of a country (modern Kulu) lying to the north-east of the Jalandar Doab and on the right bank of the Satadru. (Sutlej.)

कुशावती or कुशस्थली The capital of Dakshiṇa-Kosala and situated in the defiles of the Vindhya; it must have been to the north of the Narmadâ but south of the Vindhya, and is probably the same as Ramnagar in Bundelkhand. Râjasekhara calls the lord of Kusasthali मध्यदेशनरेंद्र, the lord of the middle-land or Bundelkhand.

केकय The country of the Kekayas bordering on Sindhu-Desa q. v.

केरल The strip of land between the Western Ghats and the sea north of the Kâverî. The principal rivers in this tract are the Netravati, the Sarâvati and the Kâli-Nadî, which is considered to be the same as the Muralâ referred to in R. 4. 55, and in U. 3, and forms the principal river of Kerala. Kerala corresponds to modern Kânarâ, and probably included Malabâr also and extended beyond the Kâveri.

कोशल N. of a country situated, according to the Râmâyaṇa, along the banks of Sarayû (or Gogra). It was divided into 'Uttara-Kosala' and 'Dakshiṇa Kosala'. The former is also called 'Ganda' and it must have therefore signified the country north of Ayodhyâ comprising Ganda and Baraitch. Aja, Dasaratha &c. are said to have ruled over this province. At the time of Râma's death his two sons Kusa and Lava reigned respectively at Kusâvatî in southern Kosala in the defiles of the Vindhyas, and at Srâvastî in northern Kosala.

कौशांबी N. of the capital of the Vatsa country. It was near the modern Kosam about 30 miles above Allahabad.

कौशिकी N. of a river (Kusi) which flowed on the east of Durbhanga through northern Bhâgalpur and western Poornea. Near the banks of this river stood the hermitage of the sage ऋष्यशृंग.

गौड or पुंड्र Northern Bengal. (Puṇḍra originally signifying the land of the ' Pooree ' cane.)

चेदि N. of a country and their people. The Chedis were also called Dâhalas and Traipuras; they occupied the banks of the Narmadâ and were the same as the people of दशार्ण q. v. Their capital was at one time त्रिपुरी q. v. The Chedis are considered by some to have inhabited the modern Bundelkhand in Central India, while by others their country is identified with the modern Chandail. The Haihayas or Kalachuris ruled at Mâhishmatî situated on the Narmadâ between the Vindhya and Riksha mountains, about Bhera ghar below Jabbalpur.

चोल N. of a country, situated on the banks of the Kâverî and said to cover the southern portion of Mysore. It was beyond the Kâverî, as Pulekasi II invaded it after crossing the river. The country latterly came to be called Karnâṭaka.

जनस्थान ' Human habitation ', a part of the great Daṇḍakâ forest which stood in the vicinity of the mountain called Prasravaṇa. The celebrated Panchavaṭî (identified by local tradition with the place of the same name situated about 2 miles from the present Nassik) stands in this tract.

जालंधर The modern Jalandar Doab, watered by the rivers Satadru and Vipâsâ. (Satlej and Beas.)

ताम्रपर्णी N. of a river rising in the Malaya Mountain. It appears to be the same as the Tâmbaravâri of the present day which rises in the eastern declivity of the western Ghats, runs through the district of Tinnevelly, and falls into the gulf of Manar ; cf. R. 4. 49–50 and B. R. 10. 56.

ताम्रलिप्त See under सुह्म.

त्रिगर्त A most arid country in ancient times. It stood for the desert on the east of the Satadru, and included the tract between the Sutlej and the Sarasvatî containing Loodiana and Pattiala on the north and some portion of the desert on the South.

त्रिपुर-री N. of the capital of the Chedis, ' made noisy by the waves of the Moon's daughter ', *i. e.* the Narmadâ, and therefore, situated on that river. It is identified with the modern Tevur 6 miles from Jabbalpur.

ब्रह्मपुर See under अवंति

दशार्ण N. of a Country, through which flows the Dasârṇâ (Dasan). It was the eastern part of Mâlava or Mâlvâ, its capital being Vidisâ–the modern Bhilsâ–situated on the Vetravati or Betva, cf. Me. 24, 25 and Kâdambarî. Kâlidâsa also makes Vidisâ a river which is probably the sâme as the Bees that joins the Betva.

द्रविड N. of a country to the south of the wild tract between the Krishṇâ and the Polar. In its larger sense it included the whole of the Coromandel coast to the south of the Godâvarî. But in its strict sense it must not have extended beyond the Kâverî. Its capital was Kânchî, the same as Conjeveram situated on the Vegavatî river 42 Miles south-west of Madras.

द्वारका See under सौराष्ट्र.

निषध N. of a country ruled over by Nala ; its capital is said to have been Alakâ, situated on the river Alakanandâ. It appears to have formed part of the modern Kumaon in northern India. This is also the name of one of the Varsha mountain.

पंचवटी See undr जनस्थान.

पंचाल N. of a celebrated region which lay, according to Râja–Sekhara (B. R. 10. 86), between the streams of the Yamunâ and the Ganges, and is, therefore, the Gangetic Doab. In the time of Drupada it extended from the banks of the Charmanvati (Chambal) upto Gangâdvâra on the north. The northern portion from Bhâgîrathî was called Uttara-Panchâla ', and its capital was Ahichhatra. The southern portion was called ' Dakshiṇa–Panchâla ', which was merged in the kingdom of Hastinâpura after the death of Drupada.

पद्मपुर The native place of the poet Bhavabhûti, situated somewhere near Chandrapura or Chândâ in the Nâgpur districts.

पद्मावती Identified with the modern Narwâr in Mâlva as being situated on the river *Sind* or Sindhu. The other rivers, that are in its vicinity, are Pârâ or Pârvatî, Lun, and Madhuvar which correspond to the Pârâ, Lavaṇâ and Madhumatî, mentioned by Bhavabhûti, as flowing in the vicinity of the town. This town was the scene of Bhavabhûti's Mâlati–Mâdhava.

पंपा N. of a celebrated lake, which is considered to be the same as the river Pennair, near which stands the *R*ishyamûka mountain. The river is known to rise from tanks ; the northern part especially from a stone tank in the centre of Chanderdoorg. This was probably the original Pampâ, and Chanderdoorg the *R*ishyamûka mountain. Subsequently the name was transferred from the tank to the river which rose from it.

पाटलिपुत्र N. of an important town in Magadha or south Behar situated at the confluence of the Ganges and the Sona (or Son). It was also called ' Kusumpura ' or ' Palibothra ' referred to in the classical accounts of India. It is said to have been destroyed by a river inundation about the middle of the eightth centuy A. D.

पांड्य N. of a country in the extreme south of India, and lying to the south-west of Choladesa. The mountain Malaya and the river Tâmraparṇî fix its position indisputably ; cf. B. R. 3. 31. It may be identified with the modern Tinnevelly. The holy island of Râmeshvara belonged to this kingdom. Kâlidâsa calls the capital of Pândya-desa the 'serpent-town' which is probably the same as Nagapattan 160 miles south of Madras ; cf. R. 6. 59-64.

पारसीक The people inhabiting Persia-perhaps applicable also to the tribes inhabiting the outlying districts on the north-western frontier. Horses from their country are mentioned under the name वनायुदेश्य.

पारियात्र One of the principal mountain chains in India. It is probably the same as the Sewalik mountains which run parallel to the Himâlaya and guard the Gangetic Doab on the north-east.

प्रतिष्ठान The capital of Purûravas, one of the earliest kings of the lunar dynasty ; situated opposite Prayâga or Allahabad. It is said in Harivamsa to have been situated on the north bank of the Ganges, in the district of Prayâga. Kâlidâsa places it at the junction of the Ganges and Yamunâ ; cf. V. 2.

मगध The country of the Magadhas or south Behar. Its old capital was गिरिव्रज (or राजगृह) which consisted of five hills विपुलगिरि, रत्नगिरि, उदयगिरि, शोणगिरि and वैभार (or व्याहार) गिरि. Its next capital was Pâtaliputra q. v. Magadha was also called कीकट in later literature.

मत्स्य or विराट N. of a country lying to the west of Dholpur ; the Pândavas are said to have entered it from the banks of the Yamunâ through the land of the Rohitakas and Sûrasenas towards the north of Dasârṇa. Vairâṭa, the capital of Viraṭa, is probably the same as Bairat 40 miles north of Jeypore.

मलय One of the seven principal chains of mountains in India. It is most probably to be identified with the southern portion of the Ghâts running from the south of Mysore, and forming the eastern boundary of Travancore. It is said by Bhavabhûti to be encircled by the river Kâverî (Mv. 5. 3, also R. 4. 46), and is said to teem in cardamoms, pepper, sandal and betel-nut trees. In R. 4. 51 Kâlidâsa calls the mountains Malaya and Dardura 'the two breasts of the southern region.' *Dardura* is, therefore, that portion of the Ghâts which forms the south-eastern boundary of Mysore.

महेंद्र One of the seven principal chains of mountains in India identified with Mahendra Mâle which divides Ganjam from the valley of the Mahânadî, and probably it included the whole of the eastern Ghats between the Mahânadî and Godâvarî.

महोदय (also called कान्यकुब्ज or गाधिनगर) is the same as the modern Kânyakubja or Kanoja, on the Ganges. In the seventh century it was the most celebrated place in India. Cf. B. R. 10. 88-89.

मानस A lake said to be situated in Hâṭaka which appears to be the same as Lâdak. On the north of Hâṭaka is Harivarsha, the country of the northern Kurus. The lake was celebrated in former times as the abode of Kinnaras, and is said by poets to be the annual resort of swans at the approach of the rains.

माहिष्मती See under चेदि.

मिथिला See under विदेह.

मुरल See under केरल.

मेकल The mount Amarkantaka, the source of the Narmadâ.

लाट N. of a country said to lie to the west of the Narmadâ ; it probably included Broach, Baroda, and Ahmadabad, and Khaira also according to some.

वंग (also called समतट or the 'Plains') A name for eastern Bengal (to be clearly distinguished from गौड or northern Bengal), including also the sea-coast of Bengal. It seems to have included at one time Tippera and the Garo hills.

वलभी See under सौराष्ट्र.

वाह्लीक, वाहीक A general name for the tribes inhabiting the Punjaub. Their country is the modern Bactria or Balkh. In the Bhârata they are said to have inhabited the country watered by the Indus and the five rivers of the Punjaub outside 'holy' India. The country was noted for its breed of horses and asa-fœtida.

विदर्भ The modern Berâr, a great kingdom in ancient times lying to the north of Kuntala and extending from the banks of the Krishṇâ to about the banks of the Narmadâ. On account of its great size, the country was also called 'Mahârâshtra'; cf. B. R. 10. 74. Kuṇḍinapura, also called Vidarbhâ, was its ancient capital, which robably stands for the modern Beder. The river Varadâ (Warda) divided Vidarbha into two parts, Amarâvati being he capital of the northern, and Pratishṭhâna of the southern part.

विदिशा See under दशार्ण.

विदेह N. of a country lying to the north-east of Magadha. Its capital Mithilâ is the same as Janakapur in Nepal north of Madhuvâṇî. Videha must have covered, in ancient times, besides a portion of Nepal, all such places as sîtâmâri, Sîtâkunda, or the northern part of the old district of Trihut and the north-western portion of Champaran.

विराट See मत्स्य.

वृंदावन 'Râdhâ's wood', now forming an important town a few miles north-west of Mathurâ, and standing on the left bank of the Yamunâ.

शक N. of a tribe inhabiting the countries on the north-western frontier of India, the Sacæ of the classical writers, and generally identified with the Scythians.

शुक्तिमत् One of the seven principal chains of mountains in India. Its position is not clearly ascertained, but it appears to be the Sub-Himâlayan range in the south of Nepal.

श्रावस्ती N. of a town in northern Kosala where Lava is said to have reigned; (it is called शरावती in R. 15. 97). It is identified with Sahet Mahet north of Ayodhyâ. It was also called धर्मपत्तन or धर्मपुरी.

सह्य One of the seven principal chains of mountains in India. It is still known as Sahyâdri, and is the same as the Western Ghâts as far as their junction with the Neilgherries north of the Malaya.

सिंधु See under पद्मावती.

सिंधुदेश: The country of the upper Indus.

सुह्म N. of a country which lay to the west of Vanga. Its capital ताम्रलिप्त (also called तामलिप्त, दामलिप्त, ताम्रलिप्ती and तमालिनी) is identified with the modern Tumlook on the right bank of the Cossye, which is the same as the कपिशा of Kâlidâsa. In ancient times the town was situated nearer to the sea, and was a place of considerable maritime trade. The Suhmas are sometimes called Râḍhas, the people of Western Bengal.

सौराष्ट्र (Also called आनर्त) The modern peninsula of Kattywâr. Dwârkâ is called आनर्तनगरी or अब्धिनगरी. The old Dwrâkâ stood near Madhupura 95 miles south-east of Dwrâkâ, and also near mount Raivataka, which appears to be the same as the Girinar hill near Junagad. Valabhi appears to have been the next capital of the country, the ruins of which were discovered at Bilbi 10 miles north-west of Bhownuggar. The celebrated lake Prabhâsa was situated in the same country and stood on the sea-coast.

स्रुघ्न N. of a town and district at some distance from Pâtaliputra. It is identified with the modern Sug on the old bed of the Yamunâ.

हस्तिनापुर N. of a celebrated town said to have been founded by king Hastin, one of the descendants of Bharata; said to be situated about 56 miles north-east of the modern Delhi on the banks of an old channel of the Ganges.

हेमकूट The 'golden-peaked' mountain, one of the ranges of mountains which divide the known continent into nine *Varshas* (वर्षपर्वत); it is generally supposed to be situated north of the Himâlaya—or between the Meru and the Himâlaya—forming with it the boundaries of the *Kimpurusha-varsha* or abode of *Kinnaras*; cf. K. 136. Kâlidâsa speaks of it as 'having plunged into the eastern and western oceans and emitting golden fluid'; see *S.* 7.
